THE COMPLETE WORKS OF
O. HENRY

O Henry

THE COMPLETE WORKS
OF
O. HENRY

GARDEN CITY   NEW YORK

DOUBLEDAY, DORAN & COMPANY, INC.

1936

ACKNOWLEDGMENT

FOR permission to use material in "Waifs and Strays" acknowledgment is due the Press Publishing Company, *Everybody's Magazine, Ainslee's Magazine, Hampton's Magazine,* the *Cosmopolitan,* the Macmillan Company, the John Lane Company, *Success,* the *Bookman,* the George Doran Company, Dodd, Mead and Company, *Current Literature,* and the *North American Review.*

CONTENTS

THE FOUR MILLION

HEART OF THE WEST

viii

CONTENTS

WHIRLIGIGS

THE VOICE OF THE CITY

CONTENTS

THE TRIMMED LAMP

STRICTLY BUSINESS

WAIFS AND STRAYS

PART I

TWELVE STORIES

PART II

CRITICAL AND BIOGRAPHICAL COMMENT

THE FOUR MILLION

THE FOUR MILLION

TOBIN'S PALM

TOBIN and me, the two of us, went down to Coney one day, for there was four dollars between us, and Tobin had need of distractions. For there was Katie Mahorner, his sweetheart, of County Sligo, lost since she started for America three months before with two hundred dollars, her own savings, and one hundred dollars from the sale of Tobin's inherited estate, a fine cottage and pig on the Bog Shannaugh. And since the letter that Tobin got saying that she had started to come to him not a bit of news had he heard or seen of Katie Mahorner. Tobin advertised in the papers, but nothing could be found of the colleen.

So, to Coney me and Tobin went, thinking that a turn at the chutes and the smell of the popcorn might raise the heart in his bosom. But Tobin was a hard-headed man, and the sadness stuck in his skin. He ground his teeth at the crying balloons; he cursed the moving pictures; and, though he would drink whenever asked, he scorned Punch and Judy, and was for licking the tintype men as they came.

So I gets him down a side way on a board walk where the attractions were some less violent. At a little six by eight stall Tobin halts, with a more human look in his eye.

"'Tis here," says he, "I will be diverted. I'll have the palm of me hand investigated by the wonderful palmist of the Nile, and see if what is to be will be."

Tobin was a believer in signs and the unnatural in nature. He possessed illegal convictions in his mind along the subjects of black cats, lucky numbers, and the weather predictions in the papers.

We went into the enchanted chicken coop, which was fixed mysterious with red cloth and pictures of hands with lines crossing 'em like a railroad centre. The sign over the door says it is Madame Zozo the Egyptian Palmist. There was a fat woman inside in a red jumper with pothooks and beasties embroidered upon it. Tobin gives her ten cents and extends one of his hands. She lifts Tobin's hand, which is own brother to the hoof of a drayhorse, and examines it to see whether 'tis a stone in the frog or a cast shoe he has come for.

"Man," says this Madame Zozo, "the line of your fate shows——"

"'Tis not me foot at all," says Tobin, interrupting. "Sure, 'tis no beauty, but ye hold the palm of me hand."

"The line shows," says the Madame, "that ye've not arrived at your time of life without bad luck. And there's more to come. The mount of Venus—or is that a stone bruise?—shows that ye've been in love. There's been trouble in your life on account of your sweetheart."

"'Tis Katie Mahorner she has references with," whispers Tobin to me in a loud voice to one side.

"I see," says the palmist, "a great deal of sorrow and tribulation with one

3

whom ye cannot forget. I see the lines of designation point to the letter K and the letter M in her name."

"Whist!" says Tobin to me; "do ye hear that?"

"Look out," goes on the palmist, "for a dark man and a light woman; for they'll both bring ye trouble. Ye'll make a voyage upon the water very soon, and have a financial loss. I see one line that brings good luck. There's a man coming into your life who will fetch ye good fortune. Ye'll know him when ye see him by his crooked nose."

"Is his name set down?" asks Tobin. "'Twill be convenient in the way of greeting when he backs up to dump off the good luck."

"His name," says the palmist, thoughtful looking, "is not spelled out by the lines, but they indicate 'tis a long one, and the letter 'o' should be in it. There's no more to tell. Good-evening. Don't block up the door."

"'Tis wonderful how she knows," says Tobin as we walk to the pier.

As we squeezed through the gates a nigger man sticks his lighted segar against Tobin's ear, and there is trouble. Tobin hammers his neck, and the women squeal, and by presence of mind I drag the little man out of the way before the police comes. Tobin is always in an ugly mood when enjoying himself.

On the boat going back, when the man calls "Who wants the good-looking waiter?" Tobin tried to plead guilty, feeling the desire to blow the foam off a crock of suds, but when he felt in his pocket he found himself discharged for lack of evidence. Somebody had disturbed his change during the commotion. So we sat, dry, upon the stools, listening to the Dagoes fiddling on deck. If anything, Tobin was lower in spirits and less congenial with his misfortunes than when we started

On a seat against the railing was a young woman dressed suitable for red automobiles, with hair the colour of an unsmoked meerschaum. In passing by Tobin kicks her foot without intentions, and, being polite to ladies when in drink, he tries to give his hat a twist while apologizing. But he knocks it off, and the wind carries it overboard.

Tobin came back and sat down, and I began to look out for him, for the man's adversities were becoming frequent. He was apt, when pushed so close by hard luck, to kick the best dressed man he could see, and try to take command of the boat.

Presently Tobin grabs my arm and says, excited: "Jawn," says he, "do ye know what we're doing? We're taking a voyage upon the water."

"There now," says I; "subdue yeself. The boat'll land in ten minutes more."

"Look," says he, "at the light lady upon the bench. And have ye forgotten the nigger man that burned me ear? And isn't the money I had gone—a dollar sixty-five it was?"

I thought he was no more than summing up his catastrophes so as to get violent with good excuse, as men will do, and I tried to make him understand such things was trifles.

"Listen," says Tobin. "Ye've no ear for the gift of prophecy or the miracles of the inspired. What did the palmist lady tell ye out of me hand? 'Tis coming true before your eyes. 'Look out,' says she, 'for a dark man and a light woman; they'll bring ye trouble.' Have ye forgot the nigger man, though he got some of it back from me fist? Can ye show me a lighter woman than the blonde lady that was the cause of me hat falling in the water? And where's the dollar sixty-five I had in me vest when we left the shooting gallery?"

The way Tobin put it, it did seem to corroborate the art of prediction, though it looked to me that these accidents could happen to any one at Coney without the implication of palmistry.

Tobin got up and walked around on deck, looking close at the passengers

out of his little red eyes. I asked him the interpretation of his movements. Ye never know what Tobin has in his mind until he begins to carry it
out.

"Ye should know," says he, "I'm working out the salvation promised by the
lines in me palm. I'm looking for the crooked-nose man that's to bring the
good luck. 'Tis all that will save us. Jawn, did ye ever see a straighter-
nosed gang of hellions in the days of your life?"

'Twas the nine-thirty boat, and we landed and walked up-town through
Twenty-second Street, Tobin being without his hat.

On a street corner, standing under a gas-light and looking over the elevated
road at the moon, was a man. A long man he was, dressed decent, with a segar
between his teeth, and I saw that his nose made two twists from bridge to
end, like the wriggle of a snake. Tobin saw it at the same time, and I heard
him breathe hard like a horse when you take the saddle off. He went straight
up to the man, and I went with him.

"Good-night to ye," Tobin says to the man. The man takes out a segar and
passes the compliments, sociable.

"Would ye hand us your name," asks Tobin, "and let us look at the size
of it? It may be our duty to become acquainted with ye."

"My name," says the man, polite, "is Friedenhausman—Maximus G. Friedenhausman."

"'Tis the right length," says Tobin. "Do you spell it with an 'o' anywhere
down the stretch of it?"

"I do not," says the man.

"*Can* ye spell it with an 'o'?" inquires Tobin, turning anxious.

"If your conscience," says the man with the nose, "is indisposed toward
foreign idioms ye might, to please yourself, smuggle the letter into the pen-
ultimate syllable."

"'Tis well," says Tobin. "Ye're in the presence of Jawn Malone and Daniel
Tobin."

"'Tis highly appreciated," says the man, with a bow. "And now since I
cannot conceive that ye would hold a spelling bee upon the street corner, will
ye name some reasonable excuse for being at large?"

"By the two signs," answers Tobin, trying to explain, "which ye display
according to the reading of the Egyptian palmist from the sole of me hand,
ye've been nominated to offset with good luck the lines of trouble leading to the
nigger man and the blonde lady with her feet crossed in the boat, besides the
financial loss of a dollar sixty-five, all so far fulfilled according to Hoyle."

The man stopped smoking and looked at me.

"Have ye any amendments," he asks, "to offer to that statement, or are ye
one too? I thought by the looks of ye ye might have him in charge."

"None," says I to him, "except that as one horseshoe resembles another so
are ye the picture of good luck as predicted by the hand of me friend. If
not, then the lines of Danny's hand may have been crossed, I don't know."

"There's two of ye," says the man with the nose, looking up and down for
the sight of a policeman. "I've enjoyed your company immense. Good-night."

With that he shoves his segar in his mouth and moves across the street,
stepping fast. But Tobin sticks close to one side of him and me at the other.

"What!" says he, stopping on the opposite sidewalk and pushing back his
hat; "do ye follow me? I tell ye," he says, very loud, "I'm proud to have met
ye. But it is my desire to be rid of ye. I am off to me home."

"Do," says Tobin, leaning against his sleeve. "Do be off to your home.
And I will sit at the door of it till ye come out in the morning. For the
dependence is upon ye to obviate the curse of the nigger man and the blonde
lady and the financial loss of the one-sixty-five."

"'Tis a strange hallucination," says the man, turning to me as a more reasonable lunatic. "Hadn't ye better get him home?"

"Listen, man," says I to him. "Daniel Tobin is as sensible as he ever was. Maybe he is a bit deranged on account of having drink enough to disturb but not enough to settle his wits, but he is no more than following out the legitimate path of his superstitions and predicaments, which I will explain to you." With that I relates the facts about the palmist lady and how the finger of suspicion points to him as an instrument of good fortune. "Now, understand, I concludes, "my position in this riot. I am the friend of me friend Tobin, according to me interpretations. 'Tis easy to be a friend to the prosperous, for it pays; 'tis not hard to be a friend to the poor, for ye get puffed up by gratitude and have your picture printed standing in front of a tenement with a scuttle of coal and an orphan in each hand. But it strains the art of friendship to be true friend to a born fool. And that's what I'm doing," says I, "for, in my opinion, there's no fortune to be read from the palm of me hand that wasn't printed there with the handle of a pick. And, though ye've got the crookedest nose in New York City, I misdoubt that all the fortune-tellers doing business could milk good luck from ye. But the lines of Danny's hand pointed to ye fair, and I'll assist him to experiment with ye until he's convinced ye're dry."

After that the man turns, sudden, to laughing. He leans against a corner and laughs considerable. Then he claps me and Tobin on the backs of us and takes us by an arm apiece.

"'Tis my mistake," says he. "How could I be expecting anything so fine and wonderful to be turning the corner upon me? I came near being found unworthy. Hard by," says he, "is a café, snug and suitable for the entertainment of idiosyncrasies. Let us go there and have a drink while we discuss the unavailability of the categorical."

So saying, he marched me and Tobin to the back room of a saloon, and ordered the drinks, and laid the money on the table. He looks at me and Tobin like brothers of his, and we have the segars.

"Ye must know," says the man of destiny, "that me walk in life is one that is called the literary. I wander abroad be night seeking idiosyncrasies in the masses and truth in the heavens above. When ye came upon me I was in contemplation of the elevated road in conjunction with the chief luminary of night. The rapid transit is poetry and art: the moon but a tedious, dry body, moving by rote. But these are private opinions, for, in the business of literature, the conditions are reversed. 'Tis me hope to be writing a book to explain the strange things I have discovered in life."

"Ye will put me in a book," says Tobin, disgusted; "will ye put me in a book?"

"I will not," says the man, "for the covers will not hold ye. Not yet. The best I can do is to enjoy ye meself, for the time is not ripe for destroying the limitations of print. Ye would look fantastic in type. All alone by meself must I drink this cup of joy. But, I thank ye, boys; I am truly grateful."

"The talk of ye," says Tobin, blowing through his moustache and pounding the table with his fist, "is an eyesore to me patience. There was good luck promised out of the crook of your nose, but ye bear fruit like the bang of a drum. Ye resemble, with your noise of books, the wind blowing through a crack. Sure, now, I would be thinking the palm of me hand lied but for the coming true of the nigger man and the blonde lady and——"

"Whist!" says the long man; "would ye be led astray by physiognomy? Me nose will do what it can within bounds. Let us have these glasses filled again, for 'tis good to keep idiosyncrasies well moistened, they being subject to deterioration in a dry moral atmosphere."

So, the man of literature makes good, to my notion, for he pays, cheerful, for everything, the capital of me and Tobin being exhausted by prediction. But Tobin is sore, and drinks quiet, with the red showing in his eye.

By and by we moved out, for 'twas eleven o'clock, and stands a bit upon the sidewalk. And then the man says he must be going home, and invites me and Tobin to walk that way. We arrives on a side street two blocks away where there is a stretch of brick houses with high stoops and iron fences. The man stops at one of them and looks up at the top windows which he finds dark.

"'Tis me humble dwelling," says he, "and I begin to perceive by the signs that me wife has retired to slumber. Therefore I will venture a bit in the way of hospitality. 'Tis me wish that ye enter the basement room, where we dine, and partake of a reasonable refreshment. There will be some fine cold fowl and cheese and a bottle or two of ale. Ye will be welcome to enter and eat, for I am indebted to ye for diversions."

The appetite and conscience of me and Tobin was congenial to the proposition, though 'twas sticking hard in Danny's superstitions to think that a few drinks and a cold lunch should represent the good fortune promised by the palm of his hand.

"Step down the steps," says the man with the crooked nose, "and I will enter by the door above and let ye in. I will ask the new girl we have in the kitchen," says he, "to make ye a pot of coffee to drink before ye go. 'Tis fine coffee Katie Mahorner makes for a green girl just landed three months. Step in," says the man, "and I'll send her down to ye."

THE GIFT OF THE MAGI

ONE dollar and eighty-seven cents. That was all. And sixty cents of it was in pennies. Pennies saved one and two at a time by bulldozing the grocer and the vegetable man and the butcher until one's cheeks burned with the silent imputation of parsimony that such close dealing implied. Three times Della counted it. One dollar and eighty-seven cents. And the next day would be Christmas.

There was clearly nothing to do but flop down on the shabby little couch and howl. So Della did it. Which instigates the moral reflection that life is made up of sobs, sniffles, and smiles, with sniffles predominating.

While the mistress of the home is gradually subsiding from the first stage to the second, take a look at the home. A furnished flat at $8 per week. It did not exactly beggar description, but it certainly had that word on the lookout for the mendicancy squad.

In the vestibule below was a letter-box into which no letter would go, and an electric button from which no mortal finger could coax a ring. Also appertaining thereunto was a card bearing the name "Mr. James Dillingham Young."

The "Dillingham" had been flung to the breeze during a former period of prosperity when its possessor was being paid $30 per week. Now, when the income was shrunk to $20, the letters of "Dillingham" looked blurred, as though they were thinking seriously of contracting to a modest and unassuming D. But whenever Mr. James Dillingham Young came home and reached his flat above he was called "Jim" and greatly hugged by Mrs. James Dillingham Young, already introduced to you as Della. Which is all very good.

Della finished her cry and attended to her cheeks with the powder rag. She stood by the window and looked out dully at a gray cat walking a gray fence in a gray backyard. Tomorrow would be Christmas Day, and she had only $1.87 with which to buy Jim a present. She had been saving every penny she could for months, with this result. Twenty dollars a week doesn't go far. Expenses had been greater than she had calculated. They always are. Only $1.87 to buy a present for Jim. Her Jim. Many a happy hour she had spent planning for something nice for him. Something fine and rare and sterling— something just a little bit near to being worthy of the honor of being owned by Jim.

There was a pier-glass between the windows of the room. Perhaps you have seen a pier-glass in an $8 flat. A very thin and very agile person may, by observing his reflection in a rapid sequence of longitudinal strips, obtain a fairly accurate conception of his looks. Della, being slender, had mastered the art.

Suddenly she whirled from the window and stood before the glass. Her eyes were shining brilliantly, but her face had lost its color within twenty seconds. Rapidly she pulled down her hair and let it fall to its full length.

Now, there were two possessions of the James Dillingham Youngs in which they both took a mighty pride. One was Jim's gold watch that had been his father's and his grandfather's. The other was Della's hair. Had the Queen of Sheba lived in the flat across the airshaft, Della would have let her hair hang out the window some day to dry just to depreciate Her Majesty's jewels and gifts. Had King Solomon been the janitor, with all his treasures piled up in the basement, Jim would have pulled out his watch every time he passed, just to see him pluck at his beard from envy.

So now Della's beautiful hair fell about her rippling and shining like a cascade of brown waters. It reached below her knee and made itself almost a garment for her. And then she did it up again nervously and quickly. Once she faltered for a minute and stood still while a tear or two splashed on the worn red carpet.

On went her old brown jacket; on went her old brown hat. With a whirl of skirts and with the brilliant sparkle still in her eyes, she fluttered out the door and down the stairs to the street.

Where she stopped the sign read: "Mme. Sofronie. Hair Goods of All Kinds." One flight up Della ran, and collected herself, panting. Madame, large, too white, chilly, hardly looked the "Sofronie."

"Will you buy my hair?" asked Della.

"I buy hair," said Madame. "Take yer hat off and let's have a sight at the looks of it."

Down rippled the brown cascade.

"Twenty dollars," said Madame, lifting the mass with a practised hand.

"Give it to me quick," said Della.

Oh, and the next two hours tripped by on rosy wings. Forget the hashed metaphor. She was ransacking the stores for Jim's present.

She found it at last. It surely had been made for Jim and no one else. There was no other like it in any of the stores, and she had turned all of them inside out. It was a platinum fob chain simple and chaste in design, properly proclaiming its value by substance alone and not by meretricious ornamentation —as all good things should do. It was even worthy of The Watch. As soon as she saw it she knew that it must be Jim's. It was like him. Quietness and value—the description applied to both. Twenty-one dollars they took from her for it, and she hurried home with the 87 cents. With that chain on his watch Jim might be properly anxious about the time in any company. Grand as the watch was, he sometimes looked at it on the sly on account of the old leather strap that he used in place of a chain.

When Della reached home her intoxication gave way a little to prudence and reason. She got out her curling irons and lighted the gas and went to work repairing the ravages made by generosity added to love. Which is always a tremendous task, dear friends—a mammoth task.

Within forty minutes her head was covered with tiny, close-lying curls that made her look wonderfully like a truant schoolboy. She looked at her reflection in the mirror long, carefully, and critically.

"If Jim doesn't kill me," she said to herself, "before he takes a second look at me, he'll say I look like a Coney Island chorus girl. But what could I do—oh! what could I do with a dollar and eighty-seven cents?"

At 7 o'clock the coffee was made and the frying-pan was on the back of the stove hot and ready to cook the chops.

Jim was never late. Della doubled the fob chain in her hand and sat on the corner of the table near the door that he always entered. Then she heard his step on the stair away down on the first flight, and she turned white for just a moment. She had a habit of saying little silent prayers about the simplest everyday things, and now she whispered: "Please God, make him think I am still pretty."

The door opened and Jim stepped in and closed it. He looked thin and very serious. Poor fellow, he was only twenty-two—and to be burdened with a family! He needed a new overcoat and he was without gloves.

Jim stopped inside the door, as immovable as a setter at the scent of quail. His eyes were fixed upon Della, and there was an expression in them that she could not read, and it terrified her. It was not anger, nor surprise, nor disapproval, nor horror, nor any of the sentiments that she had been prepared for. He simply stared at her fixedly with that peculiar expression on his face.

Della wriggled off the table and went for him.

"Jim, darling," she cried, "don't look at me that way. I had my hair cut off and sold it because I couldn't have lived through Christmas without giving you a present. It'll grow out again—you won't mind, will you? I just had to do it. My hair grows awfully fast. Say 'Merry Christmas!' Jim, and let's be happy. You don't know what a nice—what a beautiful, nice gift I've got for you."

"You've cut off your hair?" asked Jim, laboriously, as if he had not arrived at that patent fact yet even after the hardest mental labor.

"Cut it off and sold it," said Della. "Don't you like me just as well, anyhow? I'm me without my hair, ain't I?"

Jim looked about the room curiously.

"You say your hair is gone?" he said, with an air almost of idiocy.

"You needn't look for it," said Della. "It's sold, I tell you—sold and gone, too. It's Christmas Eve, boy. Be good to me, for it went for you. Maybe the hairs of my head were numbered," she went on with a sudden serious sweetness, "but nobody could ever count my love for you. Shall I put the chops on, Jim?"

Out of his trance Jim seemed quickly to wake. He enfolded his Della. For ten seconds let us regard with discreet scrutiny some inconsequential object in the other direction. Eight dollars a week or a million a year—what is the difference? A mathematician or a wit would give you the wrong answer. The magi brought valuable gifts, but that was not among them. This dark assertion will be illuminated later on.

Jim drew a package from his overcoat pocket and threw it upon the table.

"Don't make any mistake, Dell," he said, "about me. I don't think there's anything in the way of a haircut or a shave or a shampoo that could make me like my girl any less. But if you'll unwrap that package you may see why you had me going a while at first."

White fingers and nimble tore at the string and paper. And then an ecstatic scream of joy; and then, alas! a quick feminine change to hysterical tears and wails, necessitating the immediate employment of all the comforting powers of the lord of the flat.

For there lay The Combs—the set of combs, side and back, that Della had worshipped for long in a Broadway window. Beautiful combs, pure tortoise shell, with jewelled rims—just the shade to wear in the beautiful vanished hair. They were expensive combs, she knew, and her heart had simply craved and yearned over them without the least hope of possession. And now, they were hers, but the tresses that should have adorned the coveted adornments were gone.

But she hugged them to her bosom, and at length she was able to look up with dim eyes and a smile and say: "My hair grows so fast, Jim!"

And then Della leaped up like a little singed cat and cried, "Oh, oh!"

Jim had not yet seen his beautiful present. She held it out to him eagerly upon her open palm. The dull precious metal seemed to flash with a reflection of her bright and ardent spirit.

"Isn't it a dandy, Jim? I hunted all over town to find it. You'll have to look at the time a hundred times a day now. Give me your watch. I want to see how it looks on it."

Instead of obeying, Jim tumbled down on the couch and put his hands under the back of his head and smiled.

"Dell," said he, "let's put our Christmas presents away and keep 'em a while. They're too nice to use just at present. I sold the watch to get the money to buy your combs. And now suppose you put the chops on."

The magi, as you know, were wise men—wonderfully wise men—who brought gifts to the Babe in the manger. They invented the art of giving Christmas presents. Being wise, their gifts were no doubt wise ones, possibly bearing the privilege of exchange in case of duplication. And here I have lamely related to you the uneventful chronicle of two foolish children in a flat who most unwisely sacrificed for each other the greatest treasures of their house. But in a last word to the wise of these days let it be said that of all who give gifts these two were the wisest. Of all who give and receive gifts, such as they are wisest. Everywhere they are wisest. They are the magi.

A COSMOPOLITE IN A CAFÉ

At midnight the café was crowded. By some chance the little table at which I sat had escaped the eye of incomers, and two vacant chairs at it extended their arms with venal hospitality to the influx of patrons.

And then a cosmopolite sat in one of them, and I was glad, for I held a theory that since Adam no true citizen of the world has existed. We hear of them, and we see foreign labels on much luggage, but we find travellers instead of cosmopolites.

I invoke your consideration of the scene—the marble-topped tables, the range of leather-upholstered wall seats, the gay company, the ladies dressed in demi-state toilets, speaking in an exquisite visible chorus of taste, economy,

opulence or art; the sedulous and largess-loving *garçons*, the music wisely
catering to all with its raids upon the composers; the *mélange* of talk and
laughter—and, if you will, the Würzburger in the tall glass cones that bend
to your lips as a ripe cherry sways on its branch to the beak of a robber jay.
I was told by a sculptor from Mauch Chunk that the scene was truly Parisian.

My cosmopolite was named E. Rushmore Coglan, and he will be heard from
next summer at Coney Island. He is to establish a new "attraction" there,
he informed me, offering kingly diversion. And then his conversation rang
along parallels of latitude and longitude. He took the great, round world
in his hand, so to speak, familiarly, contemptuously, and it seemed no larger
than the seed of a Maraschino cherry in a *table d'hôte* grape fruit. He spoke
disrespectfully of the equator, he skipped from continent to continent, he derided the zones, he mopped up the high seas with his napkin. With a wave of
his hand he would speak of a certain bazaar in Hyderabad. Whiff! He would
have you on skis in Lapland. Zip! Now you rode the breakers with the
Kanakas at Kealaikahiki. Presto! He dragged you through an Arkansas
post-oak swamp, let you dry for a moment on the alkali plains of his Idaho
ranch, then whirled you into the society of Viennese archdukes. Anon he would
be telling you of a cold he acquired in a Chicago lake breeze and how old
Escamila cured it in Buenos Ayres with a hot infusion of the *chuchula* weed.
You would have addressed a letter to "E. Rushmore Coglan, Esq., the Earth,
Solar System, the Universe," and mailed it, feeling confident that it would
be delivered to him.

I was sure that I had found at last the one true cosmopolite since Adam,
and I listened to his world-wide discourse fearful lest I should discover in it
the local note of the mere globe-trotter. But his opinions never fluttered or
drooped; he was as impartial to cities, countries, and continents as the winds
or gravitation.

And as E. Rushmore Coglan prattled of this little planet I thought with
glee of a great almost-cosmopolite who wrote for the whole world and dedicated
himself to Bombay. In a poem he has to say that there is pride and rivalry
between the cities of the earth, and that "the men that breed from them, they
traffic up and down, but cling to their cities' hem as a child to the mother's
gown." And whenever they walk "by roaring streets unknown" they remember
their native city "most faithful, foolish, fond; making her mere-breathed name
their bond upon their bond." And my glee was roused because I had caught
Mr. Kipling napping. Here I had found a man not made from dust; one who
had no narrow boasts of birthplace or country, one who, if he bragged at all,
would brag of his whole round globe against the Martians and the inhabitants
of the Moon.

Expression on these subjects was precipitated from E. Rushmore Coglan by
the third corner to our table. While Coglan was describing to me the topography along the Siberian Railway the orchestra glided into a medley. The
concluding air was "Dixie," and as the exhilarating notes tumbled forth they
were almost overpowered by a great clapping of hands from almost every table.

It is worth a paragraph to say that this remarkable scene can be witnessed
every evening in numerous cafés in the City of New York. Tons of brew have
been consumed over theories to account for it. Some have conjectured hastily
that all Southerners in town hie themselves to cafés at nightfall. This applause of the "rebel" air in a Northern city does puzzle a little; but it is not
insolvable. The war with Spain, many years' generous mint and watermelon
crops, a few long-shot winners at the New Orleans race track, and the brilliant
banquets given by the Indiana and Kansas citizens who compose the North
Carolina Society have made the South rather a "fad" in Manhattan. Your
manicure will lisp softly that your left forefinger reminds her so much of a

gentleman's in Richmond, Va. Oh, certainly; but many a lady has to work now—the war, you know.

When "Dixie" was being played a dark-haired young man sprang up from somewhere with a Mosby guerrilla yell and waved frantically his soft-brimmed hat. Then he strayed through the smoke, dropped into the vacant chair at our table and pulled out cigarettes.

The evening was at the period when reserve is thawed. One of us mentioned three Würzburgers to the waiter; the dark-haired young man acknowledged his inclusion in the order by a smile and a nod. I hastened to ask him a question because I wanted to try out a theory I had.

"Would you mind telling me," I began, "whether you are from——"

The fist of E. Rushmore Coglan banged the table and I was jarred into silence.

"Excuse me," said he, "but that's a question I never like to hear asked. What does it matter where a man is from? Is it fair to judge a man by his post-office address? Why, I've seen Kentuckians who hated whiskey, Virginians who weren't descended from Pocahontas, Indianians who hadn't written a novel, Mexicans who didn't wear velvet trousers with silver dollars sewed along the seams, funny Englishmen, spendthrift Yankees, cold-blooded Southerners, narrow-minded Westerners, and New Yorkers who were too busy to stop for an hour on the street to watch a one-armed grocer's clerk do up cranberries in paper bags. Let a man be a man and don't handicap him with the label of any section."

"Pardon me," I said, "but my curiosity was not altogether an idle one. I know the South, and when the band plays 'Dixie' I like to observe. I have formed the belief that the man who applauds that air with special violence and ostensible sectional loyalty is invariably a native of either Secaucus, N. J., or the district between Murray Hill Lyceum and the Harlem River, this city. I was about to put my opinion to the test by inquiring of this gentleman when you interrupted with your own—larger theory, I must confess."

And now the dark-haired young man spoke to me, and it became evident that his mind also moved along its own set of grooves.

"I should like to be a periwinkle," said he, mysteriously, "on the top of a valley, and sing too-ralloo-ralloo."

This was clearly too obscure, so I turned again to Coglan.

"I've been around the world twelve times," said he. "I know an Esquimau in Upernavik who sends to Cincinnati for his neckties, and I saw a goat-herder in Uruguay who won a prize in a Battle Creek breakfast food puzzle competition. I pay rent on a room in Cairo, Egypt, and another in Yokohama all the year around. I've got slippers waiting for me in a tea-house in Shanghai, and I don't have to tell 'em how to cook my eggs in Rio Janeiro or Seattle. It's a mighty little old world. What's the use of bragging about being from the North, or the South, or the old manor house in the dale, or Euclid Avenue, Cleveland, or Pike's Peak, or Fairfax County, Va., or Hooligan's Flats or any place? It'll be a better world when we quit being fools about some mildewed town or ten acres of swampland just because we happened to be born there."

"You seem to be a genuine cosmopolite," I said, admiringly. "But it also seems that you would decry patriotism."

"A relic of the stone age," declared Coglan, warmly. "We are all brothers—Chinamen, Englishmen, Zulus, Patagonians and the people in the bend of the Kaw River. Some day all this petty pride in one's city or state or section or country will be wiped out, and we'll all be citizens of the world, as we ought to be."

"But while you are wandering in foreign lands," I persisted, "do not your thoughts revert to some spot—some dear and——"

"Nary a spot," interrupted E. R. Coglan, flippantly. "The terrestrial, globular, planetary hunk of matter, slightly flattened at the poles, and known as the Earth, is my abode. I've met a good many object-bound citizens of this country abroad. I've seen men from Chicago sit in a gondola in Venice on a moonlight night and brag about their drainage canal. I've seen a Southerner on being introduced to the King of England hand that monarch, without batting his eyes, the information that his grand-aunt on his mother's side was related by marriage to the Perkinses, of Charleston. I knew a New Yorker who was kidnapped for ransom by some Afghanistan bandits. His people sent over the money and he came back to Kabul with the agent. 'Afghanistan?' the natives said to him through an interpreter. 'Well, not so slow, do you think?' 'Oh, I don't know,' says he, and he begins to tell them about a cab driver at Sixth Avenue and Broadway. Those ideas don't suit me. I'm not tied down to anything that isn't 8,000 miles in diameter. Just put me down as E. Rushmore Coglan, citizen of the terrestrial sphere."

My cosmopolite made a large adieu and left me, for he thought he saw some one through the chatter and smoke whom he knew. So I was left with the would-be periwinkle, who was reduced to Würzburger without further ability to voice his aspirations to perch, melodious, upon the summit of a valley.

I sat reflecting upon my evident cosmopolite and wondering how the poet had managed to miss him. He was my discovery and I believed in him. How was it? "The men that breed from them they traffic up and down, but cling to their cities' hem as a child to the mother's gown."

Not so E. Rushmore Coglan. With the whole world for his——

My meditations were interrupted by a tremendous noise and conflict in another part of the café. I saw above the heads of the seated patrons E. Rushmore Coglan and a stranger to me engaged in terrific battle. They fought between the tables like Titans, and glasses crashed, and men caught their hats up and were knocked down, and a brunette screamed, and a blonde began to sing "Teasing."

My cosmopolite was sustaining the pride and reputation of the Earth when the waiters closed in on both combatants with their famous flying wedge formation and bore them outside, still resisting.

I called McCarthy, one of the French garçons, and asked him the cause of the conflict.

"The man with the red tie" (that was my cosmopolite), said he, "got hot on account of things said about the bum sidewalks and water supply of the place he come from by the other guy."

"Why," said I, bewildered, "that man is a citizen of the world—a cosmopolite. He——"

"Originally from Mattawamkeag, Maine, he said," continued McCarthy, "and he wouldn't stand for no knockin' the place."

BETWEEN ROUNDS

THE May moon shone bright upon the private boarding-house of Mrs. Murphy. By reference to the almanac a large amount of territory will be discovered upon which its rays also fell. Spring was in its heydey, with hay fever soon to follow. The parks were green with new leaves and buyers for the Western and Southern trade. Flowers and summer-resort agents were blowing; the air and answers to

Lawson were growing milder; hand-organs, fountains and pinochle were playing everywhere.

The windows of Mrs. Murphy's boarding-house were open. A group of boarders were seated on the high stoop upon round, flat mats like German pancakes.

In one of the second-floor front windows Mrs. McCaskey awaited her husband. Supper was cooling on the table. Its heat went into Mrs. McCaskey.

At nine McCaskey came. He carried his coat on his arm and his pipe in his teeth; and he apologized for disturbing the boarders on the steps as he selected spots of stone between them on which to set his size 9, width Ds.

As he opened the door of his room he received a surprise. Instead of the usual stove-lid or potato-masher for him to dodge, came only words.

Mr. McCaskey reckoned that the benign May moon had softened the breast of his spouse.

"I heard ye," came the oral substitutes for kitchenware. "Ye can apollygize to riff-raff of the streets for settin' yer unhandy feet on the tails of their frocks, but ye'd walk on the neck of yer wife the length of a clothes-line without so much as a 'Kiss me fut,' and I'm sure it's that long from rubberin' out the windy for ye and the victuals cold such as there's money to buy after drinkin' up yer wages at Gallegher's every Saturday evenin', and the gas man here twice to-day for his."

"Woman!" said Mr. McCaskey, dashing his coat and hat upon a chair, "the noise of ye is an insult to me appetite. When ye run down politeness ye take the mortar from between the bricks of the foundations of society. 'Tis no more than exercisin' the acrimony of a gentleman when ye ask the dissent of ladies blockin' the way for steppin' between them. Will ye bring the pig's face of ye out of the windy and see to the food?"

Mrs. McCaskey arose heavily and went to the stove. There was something in her manner that warned Mr. McCaskey. When the corners of her mouth went down suddenly like a barometer it usually foretold a fall of crockery and tinware.

"Pig's face, is it?" said Mrs. McCaskey, and hurled a stewpan full of bacon and turnips at her lord.

Mr. McCaskey was no novice at repartee. He knew what should follow the entrée. On the table was a roast sirloin of pork, garnished with shamrocks. He retorted with this, and drew the appropriate return of a bread pudding in an earthen dish. A hunk of Swiss cheese accurately thrown by her husband struck Mrs. McCaskey below one eye. When she replied with a well-aimed coffee-pot full of a hot, black, semi-fragrant liquid the battle, according to courses, should have ended.

But Mr. McCaskey was no 50-cent *table d'hôte*. Let cheap Bohemians consider coffee the end, if they would. Let them make that *faux pas*. He was foxier still. Finger-bowls were not beyond the compass of his experience. They were not to be had in the Pension Murphy; but their equivalent was at hand. Triumphantly he sent the granite-ware wash-basin at the head of his matrimonial adversary. Mrs. McCaskey dodged in time. She reached for a flatiron, with which, as a sort of cordial, she hoped to bring the gastronomical duel to a close. But a loud, wailing scream downstairs caused both her and Mr. McCaskey to pause in a sort of involuntary armistice.

On the sidewalk at the corner of the house Policeman Cleary was standing with one ear upturned, listening to the crash of household utensils.

" 'Tis Jawn McCaskey and his missis at it again," meditated the policeman. "I wonder shall I go up and stop the row. I will not. Married folks they are: and few pleasures they have. 'Twill not last long. Sure, they'll have to borrow more dishes to keep it up with."

And just then came the loud scream belowstairs, betokening fear or dire extremity. "'Tis probably the cat," said Policeman Cleary, and walked hastily in the other direction.

The boarders on the steps were fluttered. Mr. Toomey, an insurance solicitor by birth and an investigator by profession, went inside to analyze the scream. He returned with the news that Mrs. Murphy's little boy, Mike, was lost. Following the messenger, out bounced Mrs. Murphy—two hundred pounds in tears and hysterics, clutching the air and howling to the sky for the loss of thirty pounds of freckles and mischief. Bathos, truly; but Mr. Toomey sat down at the side of Miss Purdy, millinery, and their hands came together in sympathy. The two old maids, Misses Walsh, who complained every day about the noise in the halls, inquired immediately if anybody had looked behind the clock.

Major Grigg, who sat by his fat wife on the top step, arose and buttoned his coat. "The little one lost?" he exclaimed. "I will scour the city." His wife never allowed him out after dark. But now she said: "Go, Ludovic!" in a baritone voice. "Whoever can look upon that mother's grief without springing to her relief has a heart of stone." "Give me some thirty or—sixty cents, my love," said the Major. "Lost children sometimes stray far. I may need car-fares."

Old man Denny, hall room, fourth floor back, who sat on the lowest step, trying to read a paper by the street lamp, turned over a page to follow up the article about the carpenter's strike. Mrs. Murphy shrieked to the moon: "Oh, ar-r-Mike, f'r Gawd's sake, where is me little bit av a boy?"

"When'd ye see him last?" asked old man Denny, with one eye on the report of the Building Trades League.

"Oh," wailed Mrs. Murphy, "'twas yisterday, or maybe four hours ago! I dunno. But it's lost he is, me little boy Mike. He was playin' on the sidewalk only this mornin'—or was it Wednesday? I'm that busy with work, 'tis hard to keep up with dates. But I've looked the house over from top to cellar, and it's gone he is. Oh, for the love av Hiven——"

Silent, grim, colossal, the big city has ever stood against its revilers. They call it hard as iron; they say that no pulse of pity beats in its bosom; they compare its streets with lonely forests and deserts of lava. But beneath the hard crust of the lobster is found a delectable and luscious food. Perhaps a different simile would have been wiser. Still, nobody should take offence. We would call no one a lobster without good and sufficient claws.

No calamity so touches the common heart of humanity as does the straying of a little child. Their feet are so uncertain and feeble; the ways are so steep and strange.

Major Griggs hurried down to the corner, and up the avenue into Billy's place. "Gimme a rye-high," he said to the servitor. "Haven't seen a bow-legged, dirty-faced little devil of a six-year-old lost kid around here anywhere, have you?"

Mr. Toomey retained Miss Purdy's hand on the steps. "Think of that dear dear little babe," said Miss Purdy, "lost from his mother's side—perhaps already fallen beneath the iron hoofs of galloping steeds—oh, isn't it dreadful?"

"Ain't that right?" agreed Mr. Toomey, squeezing her hand. "Say I start out and help look for um!"

"Perhaps," said Miss Purdy, "you should. But, oh, Mr. Toomey, you are so dashing—so reckless—suppose in your enthusiasm some accident should befall you, then what——"

Old man Denny read on about the arbitration agreement, with one finger on the lines.

In the second floor front Mr. and Mrs. McCaskey came to the window to recover their second wind. Mr. McCaskey was scooping turnips out of his vest with a crooked forefinger, and his lady was wiping an eye that the salt of the roast pork had not benefited. They heard the outcry below, and thrust their heads out of the window.

" 'Tis little Mike is lost," said Mrs. McCaskey, in a hushed voice, "the beautiful, little, trouble-making angel of a gossoon!"

"The bit of a boy mislaid?" said Mr. McCaskey, leaning out of the window. "Why, now, that's bad enough, entirely. The childer, they be different. If 'twas a woman I'd be willin', for they leave peace behind 'em when they go."

Disregarding the thrust, Mrs. McCaskey caught her husband's arm.

"Jawn," she said, sentimentally, "Missis Murphy's little bye is lost. 'Tis a great city for losing little boys. Six years old he was. Jawn, 'tis the same age our little bye would have been if we had had one six years ago."

"We never did," said Mr. McCaskey, lingering with the fact.

"But if we had, Jawn, think what sorrow would be in our hearts this night, with our little Phelan run away and stolen in the city nowheres at all."

"Ye talk foolishness," said Mr. McCaskey. " 'Tis Pat he would be named, after me old father in Cantrim."

"Ye lie!" said Mrs. McCaskey, without anger. "Me brother was worth tin dozen bog-trotting McCaskeys. After him would the bye be named." She leaned over the window-sill and looked down at the hurrying and bustle below.

"Jawn," said Mrs. McCaskey, softly, "I'm sorry I was hasty wid ye."

" 'Twas hasty puddin', as ye say," said her husband, "and hurry-up turnips and get-a-move-on-ye coffee. 'Twas what ye could call a quick lunch, all right, and tell no lie."

Mrs. McCaskey slipped her arm inside her husband's and took his rough hand in hers.

"Listen at the cryin' of poor Mrs. Murphy," she said. " 'Tis an awful thing for a bit of a bye to be lost in this great big city. If 'twas our little Phelan, Jawn, I'd be breakin' me heart."

Awkwardly Mr. McCaskey withdrew his hand. But he laid it around the nearing shoulder of his wife.

" 'Tis foolishness, of course," said he, roughly, "but I'd be cut up some meself if our little—Pat was kidnapped or anything. But there never was any childer for us. Sometimes I've been ugly and hard with ye, Judy. Forget it."

They leaned together, and looked down at the heart-drama being acted below.

Long they sat thus. People surged along the sidewalk, crowding, questioning, filling the air with rumors, and inconsequent surmises. Mrs. Murphy plowed back and forth in their midst, like a soft mountain down which plunged an audible cataract of tears. Couriers came and went.

Loud voices and a renewed uproar were raised in front of the boarding-house.

"What's up now, Judy?" asked Mr. McCaskey.

" 'Tis Missis Murphy's voice," said Mrs. McCaskey, harking. "She says she's after finding little Mike asleep behind the roll of linoleum under the bed in her room."

Mr. McCaskey laughed loudly.

"That's yer Phelan," he shouted, sardonically. "Divil a bit would a Pat have done that trick. If the bye we never had is strayed and stole, by the powers, call him Phelan, and see him hide out under the bed like a mangy pup."

Mrs. McCaskey arose heavily, and went toward the dish closet, with the corners of her mouth drawn down.

Policeman Cleary came back around the corner as the crowd dispersed. Surprised, he upturned an ear toward the McCaskey apartment, where the crash of irons and chinaware and the ring of hurled kitchen utensils seemed as loud as before. Policeman Cleary took out his timepiece.

"By the deported snakes!" he exclaimed. "Jawn McCaskey and his lady have been fightin' for an hour and a quarter by the watch. The missis could give him forty pounds weight. Strength to his arm."

Policeman Cleary strolled back around the corner.

Old man Denny folded his paper and hurried up the steps just as Mrs. Murphy was about to lock the door for the night.

THE SKYLIGHT ROOM

First Mrs. Parker would show you the double parlors. You would not dare to interrupt her description of their advantages and of the merits of the gentleman who had occupied them for eight years. Then you would manage to stammer forth the confession that you were neither a doctor nor a dentist. Mrs. Parker's manner of receiving the admission was such that you could never afterward entertain the same feeling toward your parents, who had neglected to train you up in one of the professions that fitted Mrs. Parker's parlors.

Next you ascended one flight of stairs and looked at the second-floor-back at $8. Convinced by her second-floor manner that it was worth the $12 that Mr. Toosenberry always paid for it until he left to take charge of his brother's orange plantation in Florida near Palm Beach, where Mrs. McIntyre always spent the winters that had the double front room with private bath, you managed to babble that you wanted something still cheaper.

If you survived Mrs. Parker's scorn, you were taken to look at Mr. Skidder's large hall room on the third floor. Mr. Skidder's room was not vacant. He wrote plays and smoked cigarettes in it all day long. But every room-hunter was made to visit his room to admire the lambrequins. After each visit, Mr. Skidder, from the fright caused by possible eviction, would pay something on his rent.

Then—oh, then—if you still stood on one foot, with your hot hand clutching the three moist dollars in your pocket, and hoarsely proclaimed your hideous and culpable poverty, nevermore would Mrs. Parker be cicerone of yours. She would honk loudly the word "Clara," she would show you her back, and march downstairs. Then Clara, the colored maid, would escort you up the carpeted ladder that served for the fourth flight, and show you the Skylight Room. It occupied 7 x 8 feet of floor space in the middle of the hall. On each side of it was a dark lumber closet or storeroom.

In it was an iron cot, a washstand and a chair. A shelf was the dresser. Its four bare walls seemed to close in upon you like the sides of a coffin. Your hand crept to your throat, you gasped, you looked up as from a well—and breathed once more. Through the glass of the little skylight you saw a square of blue infinity.

"Two dollars, suh," Clara would say in her half-contemptuous, half-Tuskegeenial tones.

One day Miss Leeson came hunting for a room. She carried a typewriter made to be lugged around by a much larger lady. She was a very little girl, with eyes and hair that had kept on growing after she had stopped and that always looked as if they were saying: "Goodness me! Why didn't you keep up with us?"

Mrs. Parker showed her the double parlors. "In this closet," she said, "one could keep a skeleton or anæsthetic or coal——"

"But I am neither a doctor nor a dentist," said Miss Leeson, with a shiver.

Mrs. Parker gave her the incredulous, pitying, sneering, icy stare that she kept for those who failed to qualify as doctors or dentists, and led the way to the second-floor-back.

"Eight dollars?" said Miss Leeson. "Dear me! I'm not Hetty if I do look green. I'm just a poor little working girl. Show me something higher and lower."

Mr. Skidder jumped and strewed the floor with cigarette stubs at the rap on his door.

"Excuse me, Mr. Skidder," said Mrs. Parker, with her demon's smile at his pale looks. "I didn't know you were in. I asked the lady to have a look at your lambrequins."

"They're too lovely for anything," said Miss Leeson, smiling in exactly the way the angels do.

After they had gone Mr. Skidder got very busy erasing the tall, black-haired heroine from his latest (unproduced) play and inserted a small, roguish one with heavy, bright hair and vivacious features.

"Anna Held'll jump at it," said Mr. Skidder to himself, putting his feet up against the lambrequins and disappearing in a cloud of smoke like an aërial cuttlefish.

Presently the tocsin call of "Clara!" sounded to the world the state of Miss Leeson's purse. A dark goblin seized her, mounted a Stygian stairway, thrust her into a vault with a glimmer of light in its top and muttered the menacing and cabalistic words "Two dollars!"

"I'll take it!" sighed Miss Leeson, sinking down upon the squeaky iron bed.

Every day Miss Leeson went out to work. At night she brought home papers with handwriting on them and made copies with her typewriter. Sometimes she had no work at night, and then she would sit on the steps of the high stoop with the other roomers. Miss Leeson was not intended for a skylight room when the plans were drawn for her creation. She was gay-hearted and full of tender, whimsical fancies. Once she let Mr. Skidder read to her three acts of his great (unpublished) comedy, "It's No Kid; or, The Heir of the Subway."

There was rejoicing among the gentlemen roomers whenever Miss Leeson had time to sit on the steps for an hour or two. But Miss Longnecker, the tall blonde who taught in a public school and said, "Well, really!" to everything you said, sat on the top step and sniffed. And Miss Dorn, who shot at the moving ducks at Coney every Sunday and worked in a department store, sat on the bottom step and sniffed. Miss Leeson sat on the middle step and the men would quickly group around her.

Especially Mr. Skidder, who had cast her in his mind for the star part in a private, romantic (unspoken) drama in real life. And especially Mr. Hoover, who was forty-five, fat, flush and foolish. And especially very young Mr. Evans, who set up a hollow cough to induce her to ask him to leave off cigarettes. The men voted her "the funniest and jolliest ever," but the sniffs on the top step and the lower step were implacable.

.   .   .   .

I pray you let the drama halt while Chorus stalks to the footlights and drops an epicedian tear upon the fatness of Mr. Hoover. Tune the pipes to the tragedy of tallow, the bane of bulk, the calamity of corpulence. Tried out, Falstaff might have rendered more romance to the ton than would have Romeo's rickety ribs to the ounce. A lover may sigh, but he must not puff. To the train of Momus are the fat men remanded. In vain beats the faithfullest heart above a 52-inch belt. Avaunt, Hoover! Hoover, forty-five, flush and foolish, might carry off Helen herself; Hoover, forty-five, flush, foolish and fat is meat for perdition. There was never a chance for you, Hoover.

As Mrs. Parker's roomers sat thus one summer's evening, Miss Leeson looked up into the firmament and cried with her little gay laugh:

"Why, there's Billy Jackson! I can see him from down here, too."

All looked up—some at the windows of skyscrapers, some casting about for an airship, Jackson-guided.

"It's that star," explained Miss Leeson, pointing with a tiny finger. "Not the big one that twinkles—the steady blue one near it. I can see it every night through my skylight. I named it Billy Jackson."

"Well, really!" said Miss Longnecker. "I didn't know you were an astronomer, Miss Leeson."

"Oh, yes," said the small star gazer, "I know as much as any of them about the style of sleeves they're going to wear next fall in Mars."

"Well, really!" said Miss Longnecker. "The star you refer to is Gamma, of the constellation Cassiopeia. It is nearly of the second magnitude, and its meridian passage is——"

"Oh," said the very young Mr. Evans, "I think Billy Jackson is a much better name for it."

"Same here," said Mr. Hoover, loudly breathing defiance to Miss Longnecker. "I think Miss Leeson has just as much right to name stars as any of those old astrologers had."

"Well, really!" said Miss Longnecker.

"I wonder whether it's a shooting star," remarked Miss Dorn. "I hit nine ducks and a rabbit out of ten in the gallery at Coney Sunday."

"He doesn't show up very well from down here," said Miss Leeson. "You ought to see him from my room. You know you can see stars even in the daytime from the bottom of a well. At night my room is like the shaft of a coal mine, and it makes Billy Jackson look like the big diamond pin that Night fastens her kimono with."

There came a time after that when Miss Leeson brought no formidable papers home to copy. And when she went out in the morning, instead of working, she went from office to office and let her heart melt away in the drip of cold refusals transmitted through insolent office boys. This went on.

There came an evening when she wearily climbed Mrs. Parker's stoop at the hour when she always returned from her dinner at the restaurant. But she had had no dinner.

As she stepped into the hall Mr. Hoover met her and seized his chance. He asked her to marry him, and his fatness hovered above her like an avalanche. She dodged, and caught the balustrade. He tried for her hand, and she raised it and smote him weakly in the face. Step by step she went up, dragging herself by the railing. She passed Mr. Skidder's door as he was red-inking a stage direction for Myrtle Delorme (Miss Leeson) in his (unaccepted) comedy, to "pirouette across stage from L to the side of the Count." Up the carpeted ladder she crawled at last and opened the door of the skylight room.

She was too weak to light the lamp or to undress. She fell upon the iron cot, her fragile body scarcely hollowing the worn springs. And in that Erebus of a room she slowly raised her heavy eyelids, and smiled.

For Billy Jackson was shining down on her, calm and bright and constant through the skylight. There was no world about her. She was sunk in a pit of blackness, with but that small square of pallid light framing the star that she had so whimsically and oh, so ineffectually, named. Miss Longnecker must be right: it was Gamma, of the constellation Cassiopeia, and not Billy Jackson. And yet she could not let it be Gamma.

As she lay on her back, she tried twice to raise her arm. The third time she got two thin fingers to her lips and blew a kiss out of the black pit to Billy Jackson. Her arm fell back limply.

"Good-bye, Billy," she murmured, faintly. "You're millions of miles away and you won't even twinkle once. But you kept where I could see you most of the time up there when there wasn't anything else but darkness to look at, didn't you? . . . Millions of miles. . . . Good-bye, Billy Jackson."

Clara, the colored maid, found the door locked at 10 the next day, and they forced it open. Vinegar, and the slapping of wrists and burnt feathers proving of no avail, some one ran to 'phone for an ambulance.

In due time it backed up to the door with much gong-clanging, and the capable young medico, in his white linen coat, ready, active, confident, with his smooth face half debonair, half grim, danced up the steps.

"Ambulance call to 49," he said, briefly. "What's the trouble?"

"Oh, yes, doctor," sniffed Mrs. Parker, as though her trouble that there should be trouble in the house was the greater. "I can't think what can be the matter with her. Nothing we could do would bring her to. It's a young woman, a Miss Elsie—yes, a Miss Elsie Leeson. Never before in my house——"

"What room?" cried the doctor in a terrible voice, to which Mrs. Parker was a stranger.

"The skylight room. It——"

Evidently the ambulance doctor was familiar with the location of skylight rooms. He was gone up the stairs, four at a time. Mrs. Parker followed slowly, as her dignity demanded.

On the first landing she met him coming back bearing the astronomer in his arms. He stopped and let loose the practised scalpel of his tongue, not loudly. Gradually Mrs. Parker crumpled as a stiff garment that slips down from a nail. Ever afterward there remained crumples in her mind and body. Sometimes her curious roomers would ask her what the doctor said to her.

"Let that be," she would answer. "If I can get forgiveness for having heard it I will be satisfied."

The ambulance physician strode with his burden through the pack of hounds that follow the curiosity chase, and even they fell back along the sidewalk abashed, for his face was that of one who bears his own dead.

They noticed that he did not lay down upon the bed prepared for it in the ambulance the form that he carried, and all that he said was: "Drive like h—l, Wilson," to the driver.

That is all. Is it a story? In the next morning's paper I saw a little news item, and the last sentence of it may help you (as it helped me) to weld the incidents together.

It recounted the reception into Bellevue Hospital of a young woman who had been removed from No. 49 East —— Street, suffering from debility induced by starvation. It concluded with these words:

"Dr. William Jackson, the ambulance physician who attended the case, says the patient will recover."

A SERVICE OF LOVE

WHEN one loves one's Art no service seems too hard.

That is our premise. This story shall draw a conclusion from it, and show at the same time that the premise is incorrect. That will be a new thing in logic, and a feat in story-telling somewhat older than the great wall of China.

Joe Larrabee came out of the post-oak flats of the Middle West pulsing with

a genius for pictorial art. At six he drew a picture of the town pump with a prominent citizen passing it hastily. This effort was framed and hung in the drug-store window by the side of the ear of corn with an uneven number of rows. At twenty he left for New York with a flowing necktie and a capital tied up somewhat closer.

Delia Caruthers did things in six octaves so promisingly in a pine-tree village in the South that her relatives chipped in enough in her chip hat for her to go "North" and "finish." They could not see her f——, but that is our story.

Joe and Delia met in an atelier where a number of art and music students had gathered to discuss chiaroscuro, Wagner, music, Rembrandt's works, pictures, Waldteufel, wall paper, Chopin and Oolong.

Joe and Delia became enamored one of the other, or each of the other, as you please, and in a short time were married—for (see above), when one loves one's Art no service seems too hard.

Mr. and Mrs. Larrabee began housekeeping in a flat. It was a lonesome flat—something like the A sharp way down at the left-hand end of the keyboard. And they were happy; for they had their Art, and they had each other. And my advice to the rich young man would be—sell all thou hast, and give it to the poor —janitor for the privilege of living in a flat with your Art and your Delia.

Flat-dwellers shall indorse my dictum that theirs is the only true happiness. If a home is happy it cannot fit too close—let the dresser collapse and become a billiard table; let the mantel turn to a rowing machine, the escritoire to a spare bedchamber, the washstand to an upright piano; let the four walls come together, if they will, so you and your Delia are between. But if home be the other kind, let it be wide and long—enter you at the Golden Gate, hang your hat on Hatteras, your cape on Cape Horn and go out by the Labrador.

Joe was painting in the class of the great Magister—you know his fame. His fees are high; his lessons are light—his high-lights have brought him renown. Delia was studying under Rosenstock—you know his repute as a disturber of the piano keys.

They were mighty happy as long as their money lasted. So is every—but I will not be cynical. Their aims were very clear and defined. Joe was to become capable very soon of turning out pictures that old gentlemen with thin side-whiskers and thick pocketbooks would sandbag one another in his studio for the privilege of buying. Delia was to become familiar and then contemptuous with Music, so that when she saw the orchestra seats and boxes unsold she could have sore throat and lobster in a private dining-room and refuse to go on the stage.

But the best, in my opinion, was the home life in the little flat—the ardent, voluble chats after the day's study; the cozy dinners and fresh, light breakfasts; the interchange of ambitions—ambitions interwoven each with the other's or else inconsiderable—the mutual help and inspiration; and—overlook my artlessness—stuffed olives and cheese sandwiches at 11 P. M.

But after a while Art flagged. It sometimes does, even if some switch' doesn't flag it. Everything going out and nothing coming in, as the vulg' say. Money was lacking to pay Mr. Magister and Herr Rosenstock their When one loves one's Art no service seems too hard. So, Delia said she ' music lessons to keep the chafing dish bubbling.

For two or three days she went out canvassing for pupils. One came home elated.

"Joe, dear," she said, gleefully, "I've a pupil. And, oh, the l' General—General A. B. Pinkney's daughter—on Seventy-first splendid house, Joe—you ought to see the front door! Byza' would call it. And inside! Oh, Joe, I never saw anything li'

"My pupil is his daughter Clementina. I dearly love '

delicate thing—dresses always in white; and the sweetest, simplest manners!
Only eighteen years old. I'm to give three lessons a week; and, just think, Joe!
$5 a lesson. I don't mind it a bit; for when I get two or three more pupils I
can resume my lessons with Herr Rosenstock. Now, smooth out that wrinkle
between your brows, dear, and let's have a nice supper."

"That's all right for you, Dele," said Joe, attacking a can of peas with a
carving knife and a hatchet, "but how about me? Do you think I'm going to let
you hustle for wages while I philander in the regions of high art? Not by the
bones of Benvenuto Cellini! I guess I can sell papers or lay cobblestones, and
bring in a dollar or two."

Delia came and hung about his neck.

"Joe, dear, you are silly. You must keep on at your studies. It is not as if
I had quit my music and gone to work at something else. While I teach I learn.
I am always with my music. And we can live as happily as millionaires on $15
a week. You mustn't think of leaving Mr. Magister."

"All right," said Joe, reaching for the blue scalloped vegetable dish. "But I
hate for you to be giving lessons. It isn't Art. But you're a trump and a dear
to do it."

"When one loves one's Art no service seems too hard," said Delia.

"Magister praised the sky in that sketch I made in the park," said Joe. "And
Tinkle gave me permission to hang two of them in his window. I may sell one
if the right kind of a moneyed idiot sees them."

"I'm sure you will," said Delia, sweetly. "And now let's be thankful for
Gen. Pinkney and this veal roast."

During all of the next week the Larrabees had an early breakfast. Joe was
enthusiastic about some morning-effect sketches he was doing in Central Park,
and Delia packed him off breakfasted, coddled, praised and kissed at 7 o'clock.
Art is an engaging mistress. It was most times 7 o'clock when he returned in
the evening.

At the end of the week Delia, sweetly proud but languid, triumphantly tossed
three five-dollar bills on the 8 x 10 (inches) centre table of the 8 x 10 (feet)
flat parlor.

"Sometimes," she said, a little wearily, "Clementina tries me. I'm afraid she
doesn't practise enough, and I have to tell her the same things so often. And
then she always dresses entirely in white, and that does get monotonous. But
Gen. Pinkney is the dearest old man! I wish you could know him, Joe. He comes
in sometimes when I am with Clementina at the piano—he is a widower, you
know—and stands there pulling his white goatee. 'And how are the semiquavers
and the demisemiquavers progressing?' he always asks.

"I wish you could see the wainscoting in that drawing room, Joe! And those
Astrakhan rug portières. And Clementina has such a funny little cough. I hope
she is stronger than she looks. Oh, I really am getting attached to her, she is
so gentle and high bred. Gen. Pinkney's brother was once Minister to Bolivia."

And then Joe, with the air of a Monte Cristo, drew forth a ten, a five, a two
and a one—all legal tender notes—and laid them beside Delia's earnings.

"Sold that watercolor of the obelisk to a man from Peoria," he announced,
overwhelmingly.

"Don't joke with me," said Delia—"not from Peoria!"

"All the way. I wish you could see him, Dele. Fat man with a woolen muffler
and a quill toothpick. He saw the sketch in Tinkle's window and thought it was
a windmill at first. He was game, though, and bought it anyhow. He ordered
another—an oil sketch of the Lackawanna freight depot—to take back with him.
My lessons! Oh, I guess Art is still in it."

"I'm so glad you're kept on," said Delia, heartily. "You're bound to win, dear.

Thirty-three dollars! We never had so much to spend before. We'll have oysters to-night."

"And filet mignon with champignons," said Joe. "Where is the olive fork?"

On the next Saturday evening Joe reached home first. He spread his $18 on the parlor table and washed what seemed to be a great deal of dark paint from his hands.

Half an hour later Delia arrived, her right hand tied up in a shapeless bundle of wraps and bandages.

"How is this?" asked Joe after the usual greetings. Delia laughed, but not very joyously.

"Clementina," she explained, "insisted upon a Welsh rabbit after her lesson. She is such a queer girl. Welsh rabbits at 5 in the afternoon. The General was there. You should have seen him run for the chafing dish, Joe, just as if there wasn't a servant in the house. I know Clementina isn't in good health; she is so nervous. In serving the rabbit she spilled a great lot of it, boiling hot, over my hand and wrist. It hurt awfully, Joe. And the dear girl was so sorry! But Gen. Pinkney!—Joe, that old man nearly went distracted. He rushed downstairs and sent somebody—they said the furnace man or somebody in the basement—out to a drug store for some oil and things to bind it up with. It doesn't hurt so much now."

"What's this?" asked Joe, taking the hand tenderly and pulling at some white strands beneath the bandages.

"It's something soft," said Delia, "that had oil on it. Oh, Joe, did you sell another sketch?" she had seen the money on the table.

"Did I?" said Joe; "just ask the man from Peoria. He got his depot to-day, and he isn't sure but he thinks he wants another parkscape and a view on the Hudson. What time this afternoon did you burn your hand, Dele?"

"Five o'clock, I think," said Dele, plaintively. "The iron—I mean the rabbit came off the fire about that time. You ought to have seen Gen. Pinkney, Joe, when——"

"Sit down here a moment, Dele," said Joe. He drew her to the couch, sat beside her and put his arm across her shoulders.

"What have you been doing for the last two weeks, Dele?" he asked.

She braved it for a moment or two with an eye full of love and stubbornness, and murmured a phrase or two vaguely of Gen. Pinkney; but at length down went her head and out came the truth and tears.

"I couldn't get any pupils," she confessed. "And I couldn't bear to have you give up your lessons; and I got a place ironing shirts in that big Twenty-fourth Street laundry. And I think I did very well to make up both General Pinkney and Clementina, don't you, Joe? And when a girl in the laundry set down a hot iron on my hand this afternoon I was all the way home making up that story about the Welsh rabbit. You're not angry, are you, Joe? And if I hadn't got the work you mightn't have sold your sketches to that man from Peoria."

"He wasn't from Peoria," said Joe, slowly.

"Well, it doesn't matter where he was from. How clever you are, Joe—and—kiss me, Joe—and what made you ever suspect that I wasn't giving music lessons to Clementina?"

"I didn't," said Joe, "until to-night. And I wouldn't have then, only I sent up this cotton waste and oil from the engine-room this afternoon for a girl upstairs who had her hand burned with a smoothing-iron. I've been firing the engine in that laundry for the last two weeks."

"And then you didn't——"

"My purchaser from Peoria," said Joe, "and Gen. Pinkney are both creations of the same art—but you wouldn't call it either painting or music."

And then they both laughed, and Joe began:

"When one loves one's Art no service seems——"

But Delia stopped him with her hand on his lips. "No," she said—"just 'When one loves.'"

THE COMING-OUT OF MAGGIE

EVERY Saturday night the Clover Leaf Social Club gave a hop in the hall of the Give and Take Athletic Association on the East Side. In order to attend one of these dances you must be a member of the Give and Take—or, if you belong to the division that starts off with the right foot in waltzing, you must work in Rhinegold's paper-box factory. Still, any Clover Leaf was privileged to escort or be escorted by an outsider to a single dance. But mostly each Give and Take brought the paper-box girl that he affected; and few strangers could boast of having shaken a foot at the regular hops.

Maggie Toole, on account of her dull eyes, broad mouth and left-handed style of footwork in the two-step, went to the dances with Anna McCarty and her "fellow." Anna and Maggie worked side by side in the factory, and were the greatest chums ever. So Anna always made Jimmy Burns take her by Maggie's house every Saturday night so that her friend could go to the dance with them.

The Give and Take Athletic Association lived up to its name. The hall of the association in Orchard Street was fitted out with muscle-making inventions. With the fibres thus builded up the members were wont to engage the police and rival social and athletic organizations in joyous combat. Between these more serious occupations the Saturday night hops with the paper-box factory girls came as a refining influence and as an efficient screen. For sometimes the tip went 'round, and if you were among the elect that tiptoed up the dark back stairway you might see as neat and satisfying a little welter-weight affair to a finish as ever happened inside the ropes.

On Saturdays Rhinegold's paper-box factory closed at 3 P. M. On one such afternoon Anna and Maggie walked homeward together. At Maggie's door Anna said, as usual: "Be ready at seven sharp, Mag, and Jimmy and me'll come by for you."

But what was this? Instead of the customary humble and grateful thanks from the non-escorted one there was to be perceived a high poised head, a prideful dimpling at the corners of a broad mouth, and almost a sparkle in a dull brown eye.

"Thanks, Anna," said Maggie; "but you and Jimmy needn't bother to-night. I've a gentleman friend that's coming round to escort me to the hop."

The comely Anna pounced upon her friend, shook her, chided and beseeched her. Maggie Toole catch a fellow! Plain, dear, loyal, unattractive Maggie, so sweet as a chum, so unsought for a two-step or a moonlit bench in the little park. How was it? When did it happen? Who was it?

"You'll see to-night," said Maggie, flushed with the wine of the first grapes she had gathered in Cupid's vineyard. "He's swell all right. He's two inches taller than Jimmy, and an up-to-date dresser. I'll introduce him, Anna, just as soon as we get to the hall."

Anna and Jimmy were among the first Clover Leafs to arrive that evening. Anna's eyes were brightly fixed upon the door of the hall to catch the first glimpse of her friend's "catch."

At 8:30 Miss Toole swept into the hall with her escort. Quickly her triumphant eye discovered her chum under the wing of her faithful Jimmy.

"Oh, gee!" cried Anna, "Mag ain't made a hit—oh, no! Swell fellow? well, I guess! Style? Look at 'um."

"Go as far as you like," said Jimmy, with sandpaper in his voice. "Cop him out if you want him. These new guys always win out with the push. Don't mind me. He don't squeeze all the lines, I guess. Huh!"

"Shut up, Jimmy. You know what I mean. I'm glad for Mag. First fellow she ever had. Oh, here they come."

Across the floor Maggie sailed like a coquettish yacht convoyed by a stately cruiser. And truly, her companion justified the encomiums of the faithful chum. He stood two inches taller than the average Give and Take athlete; his dark hair curled; his eyes and his teeth flashed whenever he bestowed his frequent smiles. The young men of the Clover Leaf Club pinned not their faith to the graces of person as much as they did to its prowess, its achievements in hand-to-hand conflicts, and its preservation from the legal duress that constantly menaced it. The member of the association who would bind a paper-box maiden to his conquering chariot scorned to employ Beau Brummel airs. They were not considered honorable methods of warfare. The swelling biceps, the coat straining at its buttons over the chest, the air of conscious conviction of the supereminence of the male in the cosmogony of creation, even a calm display of bow legs as subduing and enchanting agents in the gentle tourneys of Cupid—these were the approved arms and ammunition of the Clover Leaf gallants. They viewed, then, the genuflexions and alluring poses of this visitor with their chins at a new angle.

"A friend of mine, Mr. Terry O'Sullivan," was Maggie's formula of introduction. She led him around the room, presenting him to each new-arriving Clover Leaf. Almost was she pretty now, with the unique luminosity in her eyes that comes to a girl with her first suitor and a kitten with its first mouse.

"Maggie Toole's got a fellow at last," was the word that went round among the paper-box girls. "Pipe Mag's floor-walker"—thus the Give and Takes expressed their indifferent contempt.

Usually at the weekly hops Maggie kept a spot on the wall warm with her back. She felt and showed so much gratitude whenever a self-sacrificing partner invited her to dance that his pleasure was cheapened and diminished. She had even grown used to noticing Anna joggle the reluctant Jimmy with her elbow as a signal for him to invite her chum to walk over his feet through a two-step.

But to-night the pumpkin had turned to a coach and six. Terry O'Sullivan was a victorious Prince Charming, and Maggie Toole winged her first butterfly flight. And though our tropes of fairyland be mixed with those of entomology they shall not spill one drop of ambrosia from the rose-crowned melody of Maggie's one perfect night.

The girls besieged her for introduction to her "fellow." The Clover Leaf young men, after two years of blindness, suddenly perceived charms in Miss Toole. They flexed their compelling muscles before her and bespoke her for the dance.

Thus she scored; but to Terry O'Sullivan the honors of the evening fell thick and fast. He shook his curls; he smiled and went easily through the seven motions for acquiring grace in your own room before an open window ten minutes each day. He danced like a faun; he introduced manner and style and atmosphere; his words came trippingly upon his tongue, and—he waltzed twice in succession with the paper-box girl that Dempsey Donovan brought.

Dempsey was the leader of the association. He wore a dress suit, and could chin the bar twice with one hand. He was one of "Big Mike" O'Sullivan's lieutenants, and was never troubled by trouble. No cop dared to arrest him.

Whenever he broke a pushcart man's head or shot a member of the Heinrick B. Sweeney Outing and Literary Association in the kneecap, an officer would drop around and say:

"The Cap'n'd like to see ye a few minutes round to the office whin ye have time, Dempsey, me boy."

But there would be sundry gentlemen there with large gold fob chains and black cigars; and somebody would tell a funny story, and then Dempsey would go back and work half an hour with the six-pound dumbbells. So, doing a tight-rope act on a wire stretched across Niagara was a safe terpsichorean performance compared with waltzing twice with Dempsey Donovan's paper-box girl. At 10 o'clock the jolly round face of "Big Mike" O'Sullivan shone at the door for five minutes upon the scene. He always looked in for five minutes, smiled at the girls and handed out real perfectos to the delighted boys.

Dempsey Donovan was at his elbow instantly, talking rapidly. "Big Mike" looked carefully at the dancers, smiled, shook his head and departed.

The music stopped. The dancers scattered to the chairs along the walls. Terry O'Sullivan, with his entrancing bow, relinquished a pretty girl in blue, to her partner and started back to find Maggie. Dempsey intercepted him in the middle of the floor.

Some fine instinct that Rome must have bequeathed to us caused nearly every one to turn and look at them—there was a subtle feeling that two gladiators had met in the arena. Two or three Give and Takes with tight coat sleeves drew nearer.

"One moment, Mr. O'Sullivan," said Dempsey. "I hope you're enjoying yourself. Where did you say you lived?"

The two gladiators were well matched. Dempsey had, perhaps, ten pounds of weight to give away. The O'Sullivan had breadth with quickness. Dempsey had a glacial eye, a dominating slit of a mouth, an indestructible jaw, a complexion like a belle's and the coolness of a champion. The visitor showed more fire in his contempt and less control over his conspicuous sneer. They were enemies by the law written when the rocks were molten. They were each too splendid, too mighty, too incomparable to divide pre-eminence. One only must survive.

"I live on Grand," said O'Sullivan, insolently; "and no trouble to find me at home. Where do you live?"

Dempsey ignored the question.

"You say your name's O'Sullivan," he went on. "Well, 'Big Mike' says he never saw you before."

"Lots of things he never saw," said the favorite of the hop.

"As a rule," went on Dempsey, huskily sweet, "O'Sullivans in this district know one another. You escorted one of our lady members here, and we want a chance to make good. If you've got a family tree let's see a few historical O'Sullivan buds come out on it. Or do you want us to dig it out of you by the roots?"

"Suppose you mind your own business," suggested O'Sullivan, blandly.

Dempsey's eye brightened. He held up an inspired forefinger as though a brilliant idea had struck him.

"I've got it now," he said, cordially. "It was just a little mistake. You ain't no O'Sullivan. You are a ring-tailed monkey. Excuse us for not recognizing you at first."

O'Sullivan's eye flashed. He made a quick movement, but Andy Geoghan was ready and caught his arm.

Dempsey nodded at Andy and William McMahan, the secretary of the club, and walked rapidly toward a door at the rear of the hall. Two other members of the Give and Take Association swiftly joined the little group. Terry O'Sullivan was now in the hands of the Board of Rules and Social Referees. They spoke to him briefly and softly, and conducted him out through the same door at the rear.

This movement on the part of the Clover Leaf members requires a word of elucidation. Back of the association hall was a smaller room rented by the club. In this room personal difficulties that arose on the ballroom floor were settled, man to man, with the weapons of nature, under the supervision of the Board. No lady could say that she had witnessed a fight at a Clover Leaf hop in several years. Its gentlemen members guaranteed that.

So easily and smoothly had Dempsey and the Board done their preliminary work that many in the hall had not noticed the checking of the fascinating O'Sullivan's social triumph. Among these was Maggie. She looked about for her escort.

"Smoke up!" said Rose Cassidy. "Wasn't you on? Demps Donovan picked a scrap with your Lizzie-boy, and they've waltzed out to the slaughter room with him. How's my hair look done up this way, Mag?"

Maggie laid a hand on the bosom of her cheese-cloth waist.

"Gone to fight with Dempsey!" she said, breathlessly. "They've got to be stopped. Dempsey Donovan can't fight him. Why, he'll—he'll kill him!"

"Ah, what do you care?" said Rosa. "Don't some of 'em fight every hop?"

But Maggie was off, darting her zig-zag way through the maze of dancers. She burst through the rear door into the dark hall and then threw her solid shoulder against the door of the room of single combat. It gave way, and in the instant that she entered her eye caught the scene—the Board standing about with open watches; Dempsey Donovan in his shirt sleeves dancing light-footed, with the wary grace of the modern pugilist, within easy reach of his adversary; Terry O'Sullivan standing with arms folded and a murderous look in his dark eyes. And without slacking the speed of her entrance she leaped forward with a scream —leaped in time to catch and hang upon the arm of O'Sullivan that was suddenly uplifted, and to whisk from it the long, bright stiletto that he had drawn from his bosom.

The knife fell and rang upon the floor. Cold steel drawn in the rooms of the Give and Take Association! Such a thing had never happened before. Every one stood motionless for a minute. Andy Geoghan kicked the stiletto with the toe of his shoe curiously, like an antiquarian who has come upon some ancient weapon unknown to his learning.

And then O'Sullivan hissed something unintelligible between his teeth. Dempsey and the Board exchanged looks. And then Dempsey looked at O'Sullivan without anger, as one looks at a stray dog, and nodded his head in the direction of the door. "The back stairs, Giuseppi," he said, briefly. "Somebody'll pitch your hat down after you."

Maggie walked up to Dempsey Donovan. There was a brilliant spot of red in her cheeks, down which slow tears were running. But she looked him bravely in the eye.

"I knew it, Dempsey," she said, as her eyes grew dull even in their tears. "I knew he was a Guinea. His name's Tony Spinelli. I hurried in when they told me you and him was scrappin'. Them Guineas always carries knives. But you don't understand, Dempsey. I never had a fellow in my life. I got tired of comin' with Anna and Jimmy every night, so I fixed it with him to call himself O'Sullivan, and brought him along. I knew there'd be nothin' doin' for him if he came as a Dago. I guess I'll resign from the club now."

Dempsey turned to Andy Geoghan.

"Chuck that cheese slicer out of the window," he said, "and tell 'em inside that Mr. O'Sullivan has had a telephone message to go down to Tammany Hall."

And then he turned back to Maggie.

"Say, Mag," he said, "I'll see you home. And how about next Saturday night? Will you come to the hop with me if I call around for you?"

It was remarkable how quickly Maggie's eyes could change from dull to a shining brown.

"With you, Dempsey?" she stammered. "Say—will a duck swim?"

MAN ABOUT TOWN

THERE were two or three things that I wanted to know. I do not care about a mystery. So I began to inquire.

It took me two weeks to find out what women carry in dress suit cases. And then I began to ask why a mattress is made in two pieces. This serious query was at first received with suspicion because it sounded like a conundrum. I was at last assured that its double form of construction was designed to make lighter the burden of woman, who makes up beds. I was so foolish as to persist, begging to know why, then, they were not made in two equal pieces; whereupon I was shunned.

The third draught that I craved from the fount of knowledge was enlightenment concerning the character known as A Man About Town. He was more vague in my mind than a type should be. We must have a concrete idea of anything, even if it be an imaginary idea, before we can comprehend it. Now, I have a mental picture of John Doe that is as clear as a steel engraving. His eyes are weak blue; he wears a brown vest and a shiny black serge coat. He stands always in the sunshine chewing something; and he keeps half-shutting his pocket knife and opening it again with his thumb. And, if the Man Higher Up is ever found, take my assurance for it, he will be a large, pale man with blue wristlets showing under his cuffs, and he will be sitting to have his shoes polished within sound of a bowling alley, and there will be somewhere about him turquoises.

But the canvas of my imagination, when it came to limning the Man About Town, was blank. I fancied that he had a detachable sneer (like the smile of the Cheshire cat) and attached cuffs; and that was all. Whereupon I asked a newspaper reporter about him.

"Why," said he, "a 'Man About Town' is something between a 'rounder' and a 'clubman.' He isn't exactly—well, he fits in between Mrs. Fish's receptions and private boxing bouts. He doesn't—well, he doesn't belong either to the Lotos Club or to the Jerry McGeogheghan Galvanized Iron Workers' Apprentices' Left Hook Chowder Association. I don't exactly know how to describe him to you. You'll see him everywhere there's anything doing. Yes, I suppose he's a type. Dress clothes every evening; knows the ropes; calls every policeman and waiter in town by their first names. No; he never travels with the hydrogen derivatives. You generally see him alone or with another man."

My friend the reporter left me, and I wandered further afield. By this time the 3126 electric lights on the Rialto were alight. People passed, but they held me not. Paphian eyes rayed upon me, and left me unscathed. Diners, heimgangers, shop-girls, confidence men, panhandlers, actors, highwaymen, millionaires, and outlanders hurried, skipped, strolled, sneaked, swaggered, and scurried by me; but I took no note of them. I knew them all; I had read their hearts; they had served. I wanted my Man About Town. He was a type, and to drop him would be an error—a typograph—but no! let us continue.

Let us continue with a moral digression. To see a family reading the Sunday paper gratifies. The sections have been separated. Papa is earnestly scanning the page that pictures the young lady exercising before an open window, and bending—but there, there! Mamma is interested in trying to guess the missing letters in the word N—w Yo—k. The oldest girls are eagerly perusing the financial reports, for a certain young man remarked last Sunday night that he had taken a flyer in Q., X. & Z. Willie, the eighteen-year-old son, who attends the New York public school, is absorbed in the weekly article describing how to make over an old shirt, for he hopes to take a prize in sewing on graduation day.

Grandma is holding to the comic supplement with a two-hours' grip; and little Tottie, the baby, is rocking along the best she can with the real estate transfers. This view is intended to be reassuring, for it is desirable that a few lines of this story be skipped. For it introduces strong drink.

I went into a café to—and while it was being mixed I asked the man who grabs up your hot Scotch spoon as soon as you lay it down what he understood by the term, epithet, description, designation, characterization or appellation, viz.: a "Man About Town."

"Why," said he, carefully, "it means a fly guy that's wise to the all-night push —see? It's a hot sport that you can't bump to the rail anywhere between the Flatirons—see? I guess that's about what it means."

I thanked him and departed.

On the sidewalk a Salvation lassie shook her contribution receptacle gently against my waistcoat pocket.

"Would you mind telling me," I asked her, "if you ever meet with the character commonly denominated as 'A Man About Town' during your daily wanderings?"

"I think I know whom you mean," she answered, with a gentle smile. "We see them in the same places night after night. They are the devil's body guard, and if the soldiers of any army are as faithful as they are, their commanders are well served. We go among them, diverting a few pennies from their wickedness to the Lord's service."

She shook the box again and I dropped a dime into it.

In front of a glittering hotel a friend of mine, a critic, was climbing from a cab. He seemed at leisure; and I put my question to him. He answered me conscientiously, as I was sure he would.

"There is a type of 'Man About Town' in New York," he answered. "The term is quite familiar to me, but I don't think I was ever called upon to define the character before. It would be difficult to point you out an exact specimen. I would say, offhand, that it is a man who had a hopeless case of the peculiar New York disease of wanting to see and know. At 6 o'clock each day life begins with him. He follows rigidly the conventions of dress and manners; but in the business of poking his nose into places where he does not belong he could give pointers to a civet cat or a jackdaw. He is the man who has chased Bohemia about the town from rathskeller to roof garden and from Hester Street to Harlem until you can't find a place in the city where they don't cut their spaghetti with a knife. Your 'Man About Town' has done that. He is always on the scent of something new. He is curiosity, impudence, and omnipresence. Hansoms were made for him, and gold-banded cigars; and the curse of music at dinner. There are not so many of him; but his minority report is adopted everywhere.

"I'm glad you brought up the subject; I've felt the influence of this nocturnal blight upon our city, but I never thought to analyze it before. I can see now that your 'Man About Town' should have been classified long ago. In his wake spring up wine agents and cloak models; and the orchestra plays 'Let's All Go Up to Maud's' for him, by request, instead of Händel. He makes his rounds every evening; while you and I see the elephant once a week. When the cigar store is raided, he winks at the officer, familiar with his ground, and walks away immune, while you and I search among the Presidents for names, and among the stars for addresses to give the desk sergeant."

My friend, the critic, paused to acquire breath for fresh eloquence. I seized my advantage.

"You have classified him," I cried with joy. "You have painted his portrait in the gallery of city types. But I must meet one face to face. I must study the Man About Town at first hand. Where shall I find him? How shall I know him?"

Without seeming to hear me, the critic went on. And his cab-driver was waiting for his fare, too.

"He is the sublimated essence of Butt-in; the refined, intrinsic extract of Rubber; the concentrated, purified, irrefutable, unavoidable spirit of Curiosity and Inquisitiveness. A new sensation is the breath in his nostrils; when his experience is exhausted he explores new fields with the indefatigability of a——"

"Excuse me," I interrupted, "but can you produce one of this type? It is a new thing to me. I must study it. I will search the town over until I find one. Its habitat must be here on Broadway."

"I am about to dine here," said my friend. "Come inside, and if there is a Man About Town present I will point him out to you. I know most of the regular patrons here."

"I am not dining yet," I said to him. "You will excuse me. I am going to find my Man About Town this night if I have to rake New York from the Battery to Little Coney Island."

I left the hotel and walked down Broadway. The pursuit of my type gave a pleasant savor of life and interest to the air I breathed. I was glad to be in a city so great, so complex and diversified. Leisurely and with something of an air I strolled along with my heart expanding at the thought that I was a citizen of great Gotham, a sharer in its magnificence and pleasures, a partaker in its glory and prestige.

I turned to cross the street. I heard something buzz like a bee, and then I took a long, pleasant ride with Santos-Dumont.

When I opened my eyes I remembered a smell of gasoline, and I said aloud: "Hasn't it passed yet?"

A hospital nurse laid a hand that was not particularly soft upon my brow that was not at all fevered. A young doctor came along, grinned, and handed me a morning newspaper.

"Want to see how it happened?" he asked, cheerily. I read the article. Its headlines began where I heard the buzzing leave off the night before. It closed with these lines:

"——Bellevue Hospital, where it was said that his injuries were not serious. He appeared to be a typical Man About Town."

THE COP AND THE ANTHEM

On his bench in Madison Square Soapy moved uneasily. When wild geese honk high of nights, and when women without sealskin coats grow kind to their husbands, and when Soapy moves uneasily on his bench in the park, you may know that winter is near at hand.

A dead leaf fell in Soapy's lap. That was Jack Frost's card. Jack is kind to the regular denizens of Madison Square, and gives fair warning of his annual call. At the corners of four streets he hands his pasteboard to the North Wind, footman of the mansion of All Outdoors, so that the inhabitants thereof may make ready.

Soapy's mind became cognizant of the fact that the time had come for him to resolve himself into a singular Committee of Ways and Means to provide against the coming rigor. And therefore he moved uneasily on his bench.

The hibernatorial ambitions of Soapy were not of the highest. In them were no considerations of Mediterranean cruises, of soporific Southern skies or drifting in the Vesuvian Bay. Three months on the Island was what his soul craved. Three months of assured board and bed and congenial company, safe from Boreas and bluecoats, seemed to Soapy the essence of things desirable.

For years the hospitable Blackwell's had been his winter quarters. Just as his more fortunate fellow New Yorkers had bought their tickets to Palm Beach and the Riviera each winter, so Soapy had made his humble arrangements for his annual hegira to the Island. And now the time was come. On the previous night three Sabbath newspapers, distributed beneath his coat, about his ankles and over his lap, had failed to repulse the cold as he slept on his bench near the spurting fountain in the ancient square. So the Island loomed big and timely in Soapy's mind. He scorned the provisions made in the name of charity for the city's dependents. In Soapy's opinion the Law was more benign than Philanthropy. There was an endless round of institutions, municipal and eleemosynary, on which he might set out and receive lodging and food accordant with the simple life. But to one of Soapy's proud spirit the gifts of charity are encumbered. If not in coin you must pay in humiliation of spirit for every benefit received at the hands of philanthropy. As Cæsar had his Brutus, every bed of charity must have its toll of a bath, every loaf of bread its compensation of a private and personal inquisition. Wherefore it is better to be a guest of the law, which, though conducted by rules, does not meddle unduly with a gentleman's private affairs.

Soapy, having decided to go to the Island, at once set about accomplishing his desire. There were many easy ways of doing this. The pleasantest was to dine luxuriously at some expensive restaurant; and then, after declaring insolvency, be handed over quietly and without uproar to a policeman. An accommodating magistrate would do the rest.

Soapy left his bench and strolled out of the square and across the level sea of asphalt, where Broadway and Fifth Avenue flow together. Up Broadway he turned, and halted at a glittering café, where are gathered together nightly the choicest products of the grape, the silkworm, and the protoplasm.

Soapy had confidence in himself from the lowest button of his vest upward. He was shaven, and his coat was decent and his neat black, ready-tied four-in-hand had been presented to him by a lady missionary on Thanksgiving Day. If he could reach a table in the restaurant unsuspected success would be his. The portion of him that would show above the table would raise no doubt in the waiter's mind. A roasted mallard duck, thought Soapy, would be about the thing —with a bottle of Chablis, and then Camembert, a demi-tasse and a cigar. One dollar for the cigar would be enough. The total would not be so high as to call forth any supreme manifestation of revenge from the café management; and yet the meat would leave him filled and happy for the journey to his winter refuge.

But as Soapy set foot inside the restaurant door the head waiter's eye fell upon his frayed trousers and decadent shoes. Strong and ready hands turned him about and conveyed him in silence and haste to the sidewalk and averted the ignoble fate of the menaced mallard.

Soapy turned off Broadway. It seemed that his route to the coveted Island was not to be an epicurean one. Some other way of entering limbo must be thought of.

At a corner of Sixth Avenue electric lights and cunningly displayed wares behind plate-glass made a shop window conspicuous. Soapy took a cobblestone and dashed it through the glass. People came running around the corner, a policeman in the lead. Soapy stood still, with his hands in his pockets, and smiled at the sight of brass buttons.

"Where's the man that done that?" inquired the officer, excitedly.

"Don't you figure out that I might have had something to do with it?" said Soapy, not without sarcasm, but friendly, as one greets good fortune.

The policeman's mind refused to accept Soapy even as a clue. Men who smash windows do not remain to parley with the law's minions. They take to their heels. The policeman saw a man halfway down the block running to catch a car. With drawn club he joined in the pursuit. Soapy, with disgust in his heart, loafed along, twice unsuccessful.

On the opposite side of the street was a restaurant of no great pretensions. It catered to large appetites and modest purses. Its crockery and atmosphere were thick; its soup and napery thin. Into this place Soapy took his accusive shoes and telltale trousers without challenge. At a table he sat and consumed beefsteak, flapjacks, doughnuts and pie. And then to the waiter he betrayed the fact that the minutest coin and himself were strangers.

"Now, get busy and call a cop," said Soapy. "And don't keep a gentleman waiting."

"No cop for youse," said the waiter, with a voice like butter cakes and an eye like the cherry in a Manhattan cocktail. "Hey, Con!"

Neatly upon his left ear on the callous pavement two waiters pitched Soapy. He arose joint by joint, as a carpenter's rule opens, and beat the dust from his clothes. Arrest seemed but a rosy dream. The Island seemed very far away. A policeman who stood before a drug store two doors away laughed and walked down the street.

Five blocks Soapy travelled before his courage permitted him to woo capture again. This time the opportunity presented what he fatuously termed to himself a "cinch." A young woman of a modest and pleasing guise was standing before a show window gazing with sprightly interest at its display of shaving mugs and inkstands, and two yards from the window a large policeman of severe demeanor leaned against a water plug.

It was Soapy's design to assume the rôle of the despicable and execrated "masher." The refined and elegant appearance of his victim and the contiguity of the conscientious cop encouraged him to believe that he would soon feel the pleasant official clutch upon his arm that would insure his winter quarters on the right little, tight little isle.

Soapy straightened the lady missionary's ready-made tie, dragged his shrinking cuffs into the open, set his hat at a killing cant and sidled toward the young woman. He made eyes at her, was taken with sudden coughs and "hems," smiled, smirked and went brazenly through the impudent and contemptible litany of the "masher." With half an eye Soapy saw that the policeman was watching him fixedly. The young woman moved away a few steps, and again bestowed her absorbed attention upon the shaving mugs. Soapy followed, boldly stepping to her side, raised his hat and said:

"Ah there, Bedelia! Don't you want to come and play in my yard?"

The policeman was still looking. The persecuted young woman had but to beckon a finger and Soapy would be practically en route for his insular haven. Already he imagined he could feel the cozy warmth of the station-house. The young woman faced him and, stretching out a hand, caught Soapy's coat sleeve.

"Sure, Mike," she said, joyfully, "if you'll blow me to a pail of suds. I'd have spoke to you sooner, but the cop was watching."

With the young woman playing the clinging ivy to his oak Soapy walked past the policeman overcome with gloom. He seemed doomed to liberty.

At the next corner he shook off his companion and ran. He halted in the district where by night are found the lightest streets, hearts, vows and librettos. Women in furs and men in greatcoats moved gaily in the wintry air. A sudden fear seized Soapy that some dreadful enchantment had rendered him immune to arrest. The thought brought a little of panic upon it, and when he came upon another policeman lounging grandly in front of a transplendent theatre he caught at the immediate straw of "disorderly conduct."

On the sidewalk Soapy began to yell drunken gibberish at the top of his harsh voice. He danced, howled, raved, and otherwise disturbed the welkin.

The policeman twirled his club, turned his back to Soapy and remarked to a citizen.

" 'Tis one of them Yale lads celebratin' the goose egg they give to the Hartford College. Noisy; but no harm. We've instructions to lave them be."

Disconsolate, Soapy ceased his unavailing racket. Would never a policeman lay hands on him? In his fancy the Island seemed an unattainable Arcadia. He buttoned his thin coat against the chilling wind.

In a cigar store he saw a well-dressed man lighting a cigar at a swinging light. His silk umbrella he had set by the door on entering. Soapy stepped inside, secured the umbrella and sauntered off with it slowly. The man at the cigar light followed hastily.

"My umbrella," he said, sternly.

"Oh, is it?" sneered Soapy, adding insult to petit larceny. "Well, why don't you call a policeman? I took it. Your umbrella! Why don't you call a cop? There stands one on the corner."

The umbrella owner slowed his steps. Soapy did likewise, with a presentiment that luck would again run against him. The policeman looked at the two curiously.

"Of course," said the umbrella man—"that is—well, you know how these mistakes occur—I—if it's your umbrella I hope you'll excuse me—I picked it up this morning in a restaurant—If you recognize it as yours, why—I hope you'll——"

"Of course it's mine," said Soapy, viciously.

The ex-umbrella man retreated. The policeman hurried to assist a tall blonde in an opera cloak across the street in front of a street car that was approaching two blocks away.

Soapy walked eastward through a street damaged by improvements. He hurled the umbrella wrathfully into an excavation. He muttered against the men who wear helmets and carry clubs. Because he wanted to fall into their clutches, they seemed to regard him as a king who could do no wrong.

At length Soapy reached one of the avenues to the east where the glitter and turmoil was but faint. He set his face down this toward Madison Square, for the homing instinct survives even when the home is a park bench.

But on an unusually quiet corner Soapy came to a standstill. Here was an old church, quaint and rambling and gabled. Through one violet-stained window a soft light glowed, where, no doubt, the organist loitered over the keys, making sure of his mastery of the coming Sabbath anthem. For there drifted out to Soapy's ears sweet music that caught and held him transfixed against the convolutions of the iron fence.

The moon was above, lustrous and serene; vehicles and pedestrians were few; sparrows twittered sleepily in the eaves—for a little while the scene might have been a country churchyard. And the anthem that the organist played cemented Soapy to the iron fence, for he had known it well in the days when his life contained such things as mothers and roses and ambitions and friends and immaculate thoughts and collars.

The conjunction of Soapy's receptive state of mind and the influences about the old church wrought a sudden and wonderful change in his soul. He viewed with swift horror the pit into which he had tumbled, the degraded days, unworthy desires, dead hopes, wrecked faculties and base motives that made up his existence.

And also in a moment his heart responded thrillingly to this novel mood. An instantaneous and strong impulse moved him to battle with his desperate fate. He would pull himself out of the mire; he would make a man of himself again; he would conquer the evil that had taken possession of him. There was time; he was comparatively young yet: he would resurrect his old eager ambitions and pursue them without faltering. Those solemn but sweet organ notes had set up a revolution in him. To-morrow he would go into the roaring downtown district and find work. A fur importer had once offered him a place as driver. He would find him to-morrow and ask for the position. He would be somebody in the world. He would——

Soapy felt a hand laid on his arm. He looked quickly around into the broad face of a policeman.

"What are you doin' here?" asked the officer.

"Nothin'," said Soapy.

"Then come along," said the policeman.

"Three months on the Island," said the Magistrate in the Police Court the next morning.

AN ADJUSTMENT OF NATURE

In an art exhibition the other day I saw a painting that had been sold for $5,000. The painter was a young scrub out of the West named Kraft, who had a favorite food and a pet theory. His pabulum was an unquenchable belief in the Unerring Artistic Adjustment of Nature. His theory was fixed around corned-beef hash with poached egg. There was a story behind the picture, so I went home and let it drip out of a fountain-pen. The idea of Kraft—but that is not the beginning of the story.

Three years ago Kraft, Bill Judkins (a poet), and I took our meals at Cypher's, on Eighth Avenue. I say "took." When we had money, Cypher got it "off of" us, as he expressed it. We had no credit; we went in, called for food and ate it. We paid or we did not pay. We had confidence in Cypher's sullenness and smouldering ferocity. Deep down in his sunless soul he was either a prince, a fool, or an artist. He sat at a worm-eaten desk, covered with files of waiter's checks so old that I was sure the bottomest one was for clams that Hendrik Hudson had eaten and paid for. Cypher had the power, in common with Napoleon III and the goggle-eyed perch, of throwing a film over his eyes, rendering opaque the windows of his soul. Once when we left him unpaid, with egregious excuses, I looked back and saw him shaking with inaudible laughter behind his film. Now and then we paid up back scores.

But the chief thing at Cypher's was Milly. Milly was a waitress. She was a grand example of Kraft's theory of the artistic adjustment of nature. She belonged, largely, to waiting, as Minerva did to the art of scrapping, or Venus to the science of serious flirtation. Pedestalled and in bronze she might have stood with the noblest of her heroic sisters as "Liver-and-Bacon Enlivening the World." She belonged to Cypher's. You expected to see her colossal figure loom through that reeking blue cloud of smoke from frying fat just as you expect the Palisades to appear through a drifting Hudson River fog. There amid the steam of vegetables and the vapors of acres of "ham and," the crash of crockery, the clatter of steel, the screaming of "short orders," the cries of the hungering and all the horrid tumult of feeding man, surrounded by swarms of the buzzing winged beasts bequeathed us by Pharaoh, Milly steered her magnificent way like some great liner cleaving among the canoes of howling savages.

Our Goddess of Grub was built on lines so majestic that they could be followed only with awe. Her sleeves were always rolled above her elbows. She could have taken us three musketeers in her two hands and dropped us out of the window. She had seen fewer years than any of us, but she was of such superb Evehood and simplicity that she mothered us from the beginning. Cypher's store of eatables she poured out upon us with royal indifference to price and quantity, as from a cornucopia that knew no exhaustion. Her voice rang like a great silver bell; her smile was many-toothed and frequent; she seemed like a yellow sunrise on mountain tops. I never saw her but I thought of the Yosemite. And yet, somehow, I could never think of her as existing outside of Cypher's. There nature had placed her and she had taken root and grown mightily. She seemed happy, and took her few poor dollars on Saturday nights with the flushed pleasure of a child that receives an unexpected donation.

It was Kraft who first voiced the fear that each of us must have held latently. It came up apropos, of course, of certain questions of art at which we were hammering. One of us compared the harmony existing between a Haydn symphony and pistache ice cream to the exquisite congruity between Milly and Cypher's.

"There is a certain fate hanging over Milly," said Kraft, "and if it overtakes her she is lost to Cypher's and to us."

"She will grow fat?" asked Judkins, fearsomely.

"She will go to night school and become refined?" I ventured, anxiously.

"It is this," said Kraft, punctuating in a puddle of spilled coffee with a stiff forefinger. "Cæsar had his Brutus—the cotton has its bollworm, the chorus girl has her Pittsburger, the summer boarder has his poison ivy, the hero has his Carnegie medal, art has its Morgan, the rose has its——"

"Speak," I interrupted, much perturbed. "You do not think that Milly will begin to lace?"

"One day," concluded Kraft, solemnly, "there will come to Cypher's for a plate of beans a millionaire lumberman from Wisconsin, and he will marry Milly."

"Never!" exclaimed Judkins and I, in horror.

"A lumberman," repeated Kraft, hoarsely.

"And a millionaire lumberman!" I sighed, despairingly.

"From Wisconsin!" groaned Judkins.

We agreed that the awful fate seemed to menace her. Few things were less improbable. Milly, like some vast virgin stretch of pine woods, was made to catch the lumberman's eye. And well we knew the habits of the Badgers, once fortune smiled upon them. Straight to New York they hie, and lay their goods at the feet of the girl who serves them beans in a beanery. Why, the alphabet itself connives. The Sunday newspaper's headliner's work is cut for him.

"Winsome Waitress Wins Wealthy Wisconsin Woodsman."

For a while we felt that Milly was on the verge of being lost to us.

It was our love of the Unerring Artistic Adjustment of Nature that inspired us. We could not give her over to a lumberman, doubly accursed by wealth and provincialism. We shuddered to think of Milly, with her voice modulated

and her elbows covered, pouring tea in the marble teepee of a tree murderer.
No! In Cypher's she belonged—in the bacon smoke, the cabbage perfume, the
grand, Wagnerian chorus of hurled ironstone china and rattling casters.

Our fears must have been prophetic, for on that same evening the wildwood
discharged upon us Milly's preordained confiscator—our fee to adjustment and
order. But Alaska and not Wisconsin bore the burden of the visitation.

We were at our supper of beef stew and dried apples when he trotted in as
if on the heels of a dog team, and made one of the mess at our table. With
the freedom of the camps he assaulted our ears and claimed the fellowship of
men lost in the wilds of a hash house. We embraced him as a specimen, and
in three minutes we had all but died for one another as friends.

He was rugged and bearded and wind-dried. He had just come off the "trail,"
he said, at one of the North River ferries. I fancied I could see the snow dust
of Chilcoot yet powdering his shoulders. And then he strewed the table with
the nuggets, stuffed ptarmigans, bead work and seal pelts of the returned Klondiker, and began to prate to us of his millions.

"Bank drafts for two millions," was his summing up, "and a thousand a day
piling up from my claims. And now I want some beef stew and canned peaches.
I never got off the train since I mushed out of Seattle, and I'm hungry. The
stuff the niggers feed you on pullmans don't count. You gentlemen order what
you want."

And then Milly loomed up with a thousand dishes on her bare arm—loomed
up big and white and pink and awful as Mount Saint Elias—with a smile like
day breaking in a gulch. And the Klondiker threw down his pelts and nuggets
as dross, and let his jaw fall halfway, and stared at her. You could almost
see the diamond tiaras on Milly's brow and the hand-embroidered silk Paris
gowns that he meant to buy for her.

At last the bollworm had attacked the cotton—the poison ivy was reaching
out its tendrils to entwine the summer boarder—the millionaire lumberman,
thinly disguised as the Alaskan miner, was about to engulf our Milly and upset Nature's adjustment.

Kraft was the first to act. He leaped up and pounded the Klondiker's back.
"Come out and drink," he shouted. "Drink first and eat afterward." Judkins
seized one arm and I the other. Gaily, roaringly, irresistibly, in jolly-good-
fellow style, we dragged him from the restaurant to a café, stuffing his pockets
with his embalmed birds and indigestible nuggets.

There he rumbled a roughly good-humored protest. "That's the girl for my
money," he declared. "She can eat out of my skillet the rest of her life. Why,
I never see such a fine girl. I'm going back there and ask her to marry me.
I guess she won't want to sling hash any more when she sees the pile of dust
I've got."

"You'll take another whiskey and milk now," Kraft persuaded, with Satan's
smile. "I thought you up-country fellows were better sports."

Kraft spent his puny store of coin at the bar and then gave Judkins and me
such an appealing look that we went down to the last dime we had in toasting
our guest.

Then, when our ammunition was gone and the Klondiker, still somewhat
sober, began to babble again of Milly, Kraft whispered into his ear such a
polite, barked insult relating to people who were miserly with their funds, that
the miner crashed down handful after handful of silver and notes, calling for
all the fluids in the world to drown the imputation.

Thus the work was accomplished. With his own guns we drove him from the
field. And then we had him carted to a distant small hotel and put to bed with
his nuggets and baby seal-skins stuffed around him.

"He will never find Cypher's again," said Kraft. "He will propose to the first white apron he sees in a dairy restaurant to-morrow. And Milly—I mean the Natural Adjustment—is saved!"

And back to Cypher's went we three, and finding customers scarce, we joined hands and did an Indian dance with Milly in the centre.

This, I say, happened three years ago. And about that time a little luck descended upon us three, and we were enabled to buy costlier and less wholesome food than Cypher's. Our paths separated, and I saw Kraft no more and Judkins seldom.

But, as I said, I saw a painting the other day that was sold for $5,000. The title was "Boadicea," and the figures seemed to fill all out-of-doors. But of all the picture's admirers who stood before it, I believe I was the only one who longed for Boadicea to stalk from her frame bringing me corned-beef hash with poached egg.

I hurried away to see Kraft. His satanic eyes were the same, his hair was worse tangled, but his clothes had been made by a tailor.

"I didn't know," I said to him.

"We've bought a cottage in the Bronx with the money," said he. "Any evening at 7."

"Then," said I, "when you led us against the lumberman—the—Klondiker— it wasn't altogether on account of the Unerring Artistic Adjustment of Nature?"

"Well, not altogether," said Kraft, with a grin.

MEMOIRS OF A YELLOW DOG

I DON'T suppose it will knock any of you people off your perch to read a contribution from an animal. Mr. Kipling and a good many others have demonstrated the fact that animals can express themselves in remunerative English, and no magazine goes to press nowadays without an animal story in it, except the old-style monthlies that are still running pictures of Bryan and the Mont Pelée horror.

But you needn't look for any stuck-up literature in my piece, such as Bearoo, the bear, and Snakoo, the snake, and Tammanoo, the tiger, talk in the jungle books. A yellow dog that's spent most of his life in a cheap New York flat, sleeping in a corner on an old sateen underskirt (the one she spilled port wine on at the Lady 'Longshoremen's banquet), mustn't be expected to perform any tricks with the art of speech.

I was born a yellow pup; date, locality, pedigree and weight unknown. The first thing I can recollect, an old woman had me in a basket at Broadway and Twenty-third trying to sell me to a fat lady. Old Mother Hubbard was boosting me to beat the band as a genuine Pomeranian-Hambletonian-Red-Irish-Cochin-China-Stoke-Pogis fox terrier. The fat lady chased a V around among the samples of gros grain flannelette in her shopping bag till she cornered it, and gave up. From that moment I was a pet—a mamma's own wootsey squidlums. Say, gentle reader, did you ever have a 200-pound woman breathing a flavor of Camembert cheese and Peau d'Espagne pick you up and wallop her nose all over you, remarking all the time in an Emma Eames tone of voice: "Oh, oo's um oodlum, doodlum, woodlum, toodlum, bitsy-witsy skoodlums?"

From pedigreed yellow pup I grew up to be an anonymous yellow cur looking like a cross between an Angora cat and a box of lemons. But my mistress never tumbled. She thought that the two primeval pups that Noah chased into the ark were but a collateral branch of my ancestors. It took two policemen to keep her from entering me at the Madison Square Garden for the Siberian blood-hound prize.

I'll tell you about that flat. The house was the ordinary thing in New York, paved with Parian marble in the entrance hall and cobble-stones above the first floor. Our flat was three—well, not flights—climbs up. My mistress rented it unfurnished, and put in the regular things—1903 antique upholstered parlor set, oil chromo of geishas in a Harlem tea house, rubber plant and husband.

By Sirius! there was a biped I felt sorry for. He was a little man with sandy hair and whiskers a good deal like mine. Henpecked?—well, toucans and flamingoes and pelicans all had their bills in him. He wiped the dishes and listened to my mistress tell about the cheap, ragged things the lady with the squirrel-skin coat on the second floor hung out on her line to dry. And every evening while she was getting supper she made him take me out on the end of a string for a walk.

If men knew how women pass the time when they are alone they'd never marry. Laura Lean Jibbey, peanut brittle, a little almond cream on the neck muscles, dishes unwashed, half an hour's talk with the iceman, reading a package of old letters, a couple of pickles and two bottles of malt extract, one hour peeking through a hole in the window shade into the flat across the air-shaft—that's about all there is to it. Twenty minutes before time for him to come home from work she straightens up the house, fixes her rat so it won't show, and gets out a lot of sewing for a ten-minute bluff.

I led a dog's life in that flat. 'Most all day I lay there in my corner watching that fat woman kill time. I slept sometimes and had pipe dreams about being out chasing cats into basements and growling at old ladies with black mittens, as a dog was intended to do. Then she would pounce upon me with a lot of that drivelling poodle palaver and kiss me on the nose—but what could I do? A dog can't chew cloves.

I began to feel sorry for Hubby, dog my cats if I didn't. We looked so much alike that people noticed it when we went out; so we shook the streets that Morgan's cab drives down, and took to climbing the piles of last December's snow on the streets where cheap people live.

One evening when we were thus promenading, and I was trying to look like a prize St. Bernard, and the old man was trying to look like he wouldn't have murdered the first organ-grinder he heard play Mendelssohn's wedding-march, I looked up at him and said, in my way:

"What are you looking so sour about, you oakum trimmed lobster? She don't kiss you. You don't have to sit on her lap and listen to talk that would make the book of a musical comedy sound like the maxims of Epictetus. You ought to be thankful you're not a dog. Brace up, Benedick, and bid the blues begone."

The matrimonial mishap looked down at me with almost canine intelligence in his face.

"Why, doggie," says he, "good doggie. You almost look like you could speak. What is it, doggie—Cats."

Cats! Could speak!

But, of course, he couldn't understand. Humans were denied the speech of animals. The only common ground of communication upon which dogs and men can get together is in fiction.

In the flat across the hall from us lived a lady with a black-and-tan terrier. Her husband strung it and took it out every evening, but he always came home cheerful and whistling. One day I touched noses with the black-and-tan in the hall, and I struck him for an elucidation.

"See here, Wiggle-and-Skip," I says, "you know that it ain't the nature of a real man to play dry nurse to a dog in public. I never saw one leashed to a bow-wow yet that didn't look like he'd like to lick every other man that looked at him. But your boss comes in every day as perky and set up as an amateur prestidigitator doing the egg trick. How does he do it? Don't tell me he likes it."

"Him?" says the black-and-tan. "Why, he uses Nature's Own Remedy. He gets spifflicated. At first when we go out he's as shy as the man on the steamer who would rather play pedro when they make 'em all jackpots. By the time we've been in eight saloons he don't care whether the thing on the end of his line is a dog or a catfish. I've lost two inches of my tail trying to sidestep those swinging doors."

The pointer I got from that terrior—vaudeville please copy—set me to thinking.

One evening about 6 o'clock my mistress ordered him to get busy and do the ozone act for Lovey. I have concealed it until now, but that is what she called me. The black-and-tan was called "Tweetness." I consider that I have the bulge on him as far as you could chase a rabbit. Still "Lovey" is something of a nomenclatural tin can on the tail of one's self-respect.

At a quiet place on a safe street I tightened the line of my custodian in front of an attractive, refined saloon. I made a dead-ahead scramble for the doors, whining like a dog in the press despatches that lets the family know that little Alice is bogged while gathering lilies in the brook.

"Why, darn my eyes," says the old man, with a grin; "darn my eyes if the saffron-colored son of a seltzer lemonade ain't asking me in to take a drink. Lemme see—how long's it been since I saved shoe leather by keeping one foot on the foot-rest? I believe I'll——"

I knew I had him. Hot Scotches he took, sitting at a table. For an hour he kept the Campbells coming. I sat by his side rapping for the waiter with my tail, and eating free lunch such as mamma in her flat never equalled with her homemade truck bought at a delicatessen store eight minutes before papa comes home.

When the products of Scotland were all exhausted except the rye bread the old man unwound me from the table leg and played me outside like a fisherman plays a salmon. Out there he took off my collar and threw it into the street.

"Poor doggie," says he; "good doggie. She shan't kiss you any more. 'S a darned shame. Good doggie, go away and get run over by a street car and be happy."

I refused to leave. I leaped and frisked around the old man's legs happy as a pug on a rug.

"You old flea-headed woodchuck-chaser," I said to him—"you moon-baying, rabbit-pointing, egg-stealing old beagle, can't you see that I don't want to leave you? Can't you see that we're both Pups in the Wood and the missis is the cruel uncle after you with the dish towel and me with the flea liniment and a pink bow to tie on my tail. Why not cut that all out and be pards forever more?"

Maybe you'll say he didn't understand—maybe he didn't. But he kind of got a grip on the Hot Scotches, and stood still for a minute, thinking.

"Doggie," says he, finally, "we don't live more than a dozen lives on this earth, and very few of us live to be more than 300. If I ever see that flat any more I'm a flat, and if you do you're flatter; and that's no flattery. I'm offering 60 to 1 that Westward Ho wins out by the length of a dachshund."

There was no string, but I frolicked along with my master to the Twenty-third Street ferry. And the cats on the route saw reason to give thanks that prehensile claws had been given to them.

On the Jersey side my master said to a stranger who stood eating a currant bun:

"Me and my doggie, we are bound for the Rocky Mountains."

But what pleased me most was when my old man pulled both of my ears until I howled, and said:

"You common, monkey-headed, rat-tailed, sulphur-colored son of a door mat, do you know what I'm going to call you?"

I thought of "Lovey," and I whined dolefully.

"I'm going to call you 'Pete,'" says my master; and if I'd had five tails I couldn't have done enough wagging to do justice to the occasion.

THE LOVE-PHILTRE OF IKEY SCHOENSTEIN

THE Blue Light Drug Store is downtown, between the Bowery and First Avenue, where the distance between the two streets is the shortest. The Blue Light does not consider that pharmacy is a thing of bric-à-brac, scent and ice-cream soda. If you ask it for pain-killer it will not give you a bonbon.

The Blue Light scorns the labor-saving arts of modern pharmacy. It macerates its opium and percolates its own laudanum and paregoric. To this day pills are made behind its tall prescription desk—pills rolled out on its own pill-tile, divided with a spatula, rolled with the finger and thumb, dusted with calcined magnesia and delivered in little round pasteboard pill-boxes. The store is on a corner about which coveys of ragged-plumed, hilarious children play and become candidates for the cough drops and soothing syrups that wait for them inside.

Ikey Schoenstein was the night clerk of the Blue Light and the friend of his customers. Thus it is on the East Side, where the heart of pharmacy is not glacé. There, as it should be, the druggist is a counsellor, a confessor, an adviser, an able and willing missionary and mentor whose learning is respected, whose occult wisdom is venerated and whose medicine is often poured, untasted, into the gutter. Therefore Ikey's corniform, be-spectacled nose and narrow, knowledge-bowed figure was well known in the vicinity of the Blue Light, and his advice and notice were much desired.

Ikey roomed and breakfasted at Mrs. Riddle's two squares away. Mrs. Riddle had a daughter named Rosy. The circumlocution has been in vain—you must have guessed it—Ikey adored Rosy. She tinctured all his thoughts; she was the compound extract of all that was chemically pure and officinal—the dispensatory contained nothing equal to her. But Ikey was timid, and his hopes remained insoluble in the menstruum of his backwardness and fears. Behind his counter he was a superior being, calmly conscious of special knowledge and worth; outside he was a weak-kneed, purblind, motorman-cursed rambler, with ill-fitting clothes stained with chemicals and smelling of socotrine aloes and valerianate of ammonia.

The fly in Ikey's ointment (thrice welcome, pat trope!) was Chunk McGowan.

Mr. McGowan was also striving to catch the bright smiles tossed about by Rosy. But he was no out-fielder as Ikey was; he picked them off the bat. At the same time he was Ikey's friend and customer, and often dropped in a-the Blue Light Drug Store to have a bruise painted with iodine or get a cut rubber-plastered after a pleasant evening spent along the Bowery.

One afternoon McGowan drifted in in his silent, easy way, and sat, comely, smooth-faced, hard, indomitable, good-natured, upon a stool.

"Ikey," said he, when his friend had fetched his mortar and sat opposite, grinding gum benzoin to a powder, "get busy with your ear. It's drugs for me if you've got the line I need."

Ikey scanned the countenance of Mr. McGowan for the usual evidence of conflict, but found none.

"Take your coat off," he ordered. "I guess already that you have been stuck in the ribs with a knife. I have many times told you those Dagoes would do you up."

Mr. McGowan smiled. "Not them," he said. "Not any Dagoes. But you've located the diagnosis all right enough—it's under my coat, near the ribs. Say! Ikey—Rosy and me are goin' to run away and get married to-night."

Ikey's left forefinger was doubled over the edge of the mortar, holding it steady. He gave it a wild rap with the pestle, but felt it not. Meanwhile Mr. McGowan's smile faded to a look of perplexed gloom.

"That is," he continued, "if she keeps in the notion until the time comes. We've been layin' pipes for the getaway for two weeks. One day she says she will; the same evenin' she says nixy. We've agreed on to-night, and Rosy's stuck to the affirmative this time for two whole days. But it's five hours yet till the time, and I'm afraid she'll stand me up when it comes to the scratch."

"You said you wanted drugs," remarked Ikey.

Mr. McGowan looked ill at ease and harassed—a condition opposed to his usual line of demeanor. He made a patent-medicine almanac into a roll and fitted it with unprofitable carefulness about his finger.

"I wouldn't have this double handicap make a false start to-night for a million," he said. "I've got a little flat up in Harlem all ready, with chrysanthemums on the table and a kettle ready to boil. And I've engaged a pulpit pounder to be ready at his house for us at 9:30. It's got to come off. And if Rosy don't change her mind again!"—Mr. McGowan ceased, a prey to his doubts.

"I don't see then yet," said Ikey, shortly, "what makes it that you talk of drugs, or what I can be doing about it."

"Old man Riddle don't like me a little bit," went on the uneasy suitor, bent upon marshalling his arguments. "For a week he hasn't let Rosy step outside the door with me. If it wasn't for losin' a boarder they'd have bounced me long ago. I'm makin' $20 a week and she'll never regret flyin' the coop with Chunk McGowan."

"You will excuse me, Chunk," said Ikey. "I must make a prescription that is to be called for soon."

"Say," said McGowan, looking up suddenly, "say, Ikey, ain't there a drug of some kind—some kind of powders that'll make a girl like you better if you give 'em to her?"

Ikey's lip beneath his nose curled with the scorn of superior enlightenment; but before he could answer, McGowan continued:

"Tim Lacy told me he got some once from a croaker uptown and fed 'em to his girl in soda water. From the very first dose he was ace-high and everybody else looked like thirty cents to her. They was married in less than two weeks."

Strong and simple was Chunk McGowan. A better reader of men than Ikey was could have seen that his tough frame was strung upon fine wires. Like a good general who was about to invade the enemy's territory he was seeking to guard every point against possible failure.

"I thought," went on Chunk, hopefully, "that if I had one of them powders to

give Rosy when I see her at supper to-night it might brace her up and keep her
from reneging on the proposition to skip. I guess she don't need a mule team to
drag her away, but women are better at coaching than they are at running bases.
If the stuff'll work just for a couple of hours it'll do the trick."

"When is this foolishness of running away to be happening?" asked Ikey.

"Nine o'clock," said Mr. McGowan. "Supper's at seven. At eight Rosy goes
to bed with a headache, at nine old Parvenzano lets me through to his backyard,
where there's a board off Riddle's fence, next door. I go under her window and
help her down the fire-escape. We've got to make it early on the preacher's account. It's all dead easy if Rosy don't balk when the flag drops. Can you fix
me one of them powders, Ikey?"

Ikey Schoenstein rubbed his nose slowly.

"Chunk," said he, "it is of drugs of that nature that pharmaceutists must have
much carefulness. To you alone of my acquaintance would I intrust a powder
like that. But for you I shall make it, and you shall see how it makes Rosy to
think of you."

Ikey went behind the prescription desk. There he crushed to a powder two
soluble tablets, each containing a quarter of a grain of morphia. To them he
added a little sugar of milk to increase the bulk, and folded the mixture neatly
in a white paper. Taken by an adult this powder would insure several hours of
heavy slumber without danger to the sleeper. This he handed to Chunk Mc-
Gowan, telling him to administer it in a liquid if possible, and received the hearty
thanks of the backyard Lochinvar.

The subtlety of Ikey's action becomes apparent upon recital of his subsequent
move. He sent a messenger for Mr. Riddle and disclosed the plans of Mr. Mc-
Gowan for eloping with Rosy. Mr. Riddle was a stout man, brick-dusty of complexion and sudden in action.

"Much obliged," he said, briefly, to Ikey. "The lazy Irish loafer! My own
room's just above Rosy's. I'll just go up there myself after supper and load the
shot-gun and wait. If he comes in my backyard he'll go away in a ambulance
instead of a bridal chaise."

With Rosy held in the clutches of Morpheus for a many-hours deep slumber,
and the blood-thirsty parent waiting, armed and forewarned, Ikey felt that his
rival was close, indeed, upon discomfiture.

All night in the Blue Light Drug Store he waited at his duties for chance news
of the tragedy, but none came.

At eight o'clock in the morning the day clerk arrived and Ikey started hurriedly for Mrs. Riddle's to learn the outcome. And, lo! as he stepped out of the
store who but Chunk McGowan sprang from a passing street car and grasped his
hand—Chunk McGowan with a victor's smile and flushed with joy.

"Pulled it off," said Chunk with Elysium in his grin. "Rosy hit the fire-
escape on time to a second, and we was under the wire at the Reverend's at
9.30¼. She's up at the flat—she cooked eggs this mornin' in a blue kimono—
Lord! how lucky I am! You must pace up some day, Ikey, and feed with us.
I've got a job down near the bridge, and that's where I'm heading for now."

"The—the—powder?" stammered Ikey.

"Oh, that stuff you gave me!" said Chunk, broadening his grin; "well, it was
this way. I sat down at the supper table last night at Riddle's, and I looked
at Rosy, and I says to myself, 'Chunk, if you get the girl get her on the square
—don't try any hocus-pocus with a thoroughbred like her.' And I keeps the
paper you give me in my pocket. And then my lamps fall on another party
present, who, I says to myself, is failin' in a proper affection toward his comin'
son-in-law, so I watches my chance and dumps that powder in old man Riddle's
coffee—see?"

MAMMON AND THE ARCHER

OLD Anthony Rockwall, retired manufacturer and proprietor of Rockwall's Eureka Soap, looked out the library window of his Fifth Avenue mansion and grinned. His neighbour to the right—the aristocratic clubman, G. Van Schuylight Suffolk-Jones—came out to his waiting motor-car, wrinkling a contumelious nostril, as usual, at the Italian renaissance sculpture of the soap palace's front elevation.

"Stuck-up old statuette of nothing doing!" commented the ex-Soap King. "The Eden Musée'll get that old frozen Nesselrode yet if he don't watch out. I'll have this house painted red, white, and blue next summer and see if that'll make his Dutch nose turn up any higher."

And then Anthony Rockwall, who never cared for bells, went to the door of his library and shouted "Mike!" in the same voice that had once chipped off pieces of the welkin on the Kansas prairies.

"Tell my son," said Anthony to the answering menial, "to come in here before he leaves the house."

When young Rockwall entered the library the old man laid aside his newspaper, looked at him with a kindly grimness on his big, smooth, ruddy countenance, rumpled his mop of white hair with one hand and rattled the keys in his pocket with the other.

"Richard," said Anthony Rockwall, "what do you pay for the soap that you use?"

Richard, only six months home from college, was startled a little. He had not yet taken the measure of this sire of his, who was as full of unexpectednesses as a girl at her first party.

"Six dollars a dozen, I think, dad."

"And your clothes?"

"I suppose about sixty dollars, as a rule."

"You're a gentleman," said Anthony, decidedly. "I've heard of these young bloods spending $24 a dozen for soap, and going over the hundred mark for clothes. You've got as much money to waste as any of 'em, and yet you stick to what's decent and moderate. Now I use the old Eureka—not only for sentiment, but it's the purest soap made. Whenever you pay more than 10 cents a cake for soap you buy bad perfumes and labels. But 50 cents is doing very well for a young man in your generation, position and condition. As I said, you're a gentleman. They say it takes three generations to make one. They're off. Money'll do it as slick as soap grease. It's made you one. By hokey! it's almost made one of me. I'm nearly as impolite and disagreeable and ill-mannered as these two old knickerbocker gents on each side of me that can't sleep of nights because I bought in between 'em."

"There are some things that money can't accomplish," remarked young Rockwall, rather gloomily.

"Now, don't say that," said old Anthony, shocked. "I bet my money on money every time. I've been through the encyclopædia down to Y looking for something you can't buy with it; and I expect to have to take up the appendix next week. I'm for money against the field. Tell me something money won't buy."

"For one thing," answered Richard, rankling a little, "it won't buy one into the exclusive circles of society."

"Oho! won't it?" thundered the champion of the root of evil. "You tell me where your exclusive circles would be if the first Astor hadn't had the money to pay for his steerage passage over?"

Richard sighed.

"And that's what I was coming to," said the old man, less boisterously. "That's why I asked you to come in. There's something going wrong with you, boy. I've been noticing it for two weeks. Out with it. I guess I could lay my hands on eleven millions within twenty-four hours, besides the real estate. If it's your liver, there's the *Rambler* down in the bay, coaled, and ready to steam down to the Bahamas in two days."

"Not a bad guess, dad; you haven't missed it far."

"Ah," said Anthony, keenly; "what's her name?"

Richard began to walk up and down the library floor. There was enough comradeship and sympathy in this crude old father of his to draw his confidence.

"Why don't you ask her?" demanded old Anthony. "She'll jump at you. You've got the money and the looks, and you're a decent boy. Your hands are clean. You've got no Eureka soap on 'em. You've been to college, but she'll overlook that."

"I haven't had a chance," said Richard.

"Make one," said Anthony. "Take her for a walk in the park, or a straw ride, or walk home with her from church. Chance! Pshaw!"

"You don't know the social mill, dad. She's part of the stream that turns it. Every hour and minute of her time is arranged for days in advance. I must have that girl, dad, or this town is a blackjack swamp forevermore. And I can't write it—I can't do that."

"Tut!" said the old man. "Do you mean to tell me that with all the money I've got you can't get an hour or two of a girl's time for yourself?"

"I've put it off too late. She's going to sail for Europe at noon day after to-morrow for a two years' stay. I'm to see her alone to-morrow evening for a few minutes. She's at Larchmont now at her aunt's. I can't go there. But I'm allowed to meet her with a cab at the Grand Central Station to-morrow evening at the 8.30 train. We drive down Broadway to Wallack's at a gallop, where her mother and a box party will be waiting for us in the lobby. Do you think she would listen to a declaration from me during that six or eight minutes under those circumstances? No. And what chance would I have in the theatre or afterward? None. No, dad, this is one tangle that your money can't unravel. We can't buy one minute of time with cash; if we could, rich people would live longer. There's no hope of getting a talk with Miss Lantry before she sails."

"All right, Richard, my boy," said old Anthony, cheerfully. "You may run along down to your club now. I'm glad it ain't your liver. But don't forget to burn a few punk sticks in the joss house to the great god Mazuma from time to time. You say money won't buy time? Well, of course, you can't order eternity wrapped up and delivered at your residence for a price, but I've seen Father Time get pretty bad stone bruises on his heels when he walked through the gold diggings."

That night came Aunt Ellen, gentle, sentimental, wrinkled, sighing, oppressed by wealth, in to Brother Anthony at his evening paper, and began discourse on the subject of lovers' woes.

"He told me all about it," said Brother Anthony, yawning. "I told him my bank account was at his service. And then he began to knock money. Said money couldn't help. Said the rules of society couldn't be bucked for a yard by a team of ten-millionaires."

"Oh, Anthony," sighed Aunt Ellen, "I wish you would not think so much of money. Wealth is nothing where a true affection is concerned. Love is all-powerful. If he only had spoken earlier! She could not have refused our Richard. But now I fear it is too late. He will have no opportunity to address her. All your gold cannot bring happiness to your son."

At eight o'clock the next evening Aunt Ellen took a quaint old gold ring from a moth-eaten case and gave it to Richard.

"Wear it to-night, nephew," she begged. "Your mother gave it to me. Good luck in love she said it brought. She asked me to give it to you when you had found the one you loved."

Young Rockwall took the ring reverently and tried it on his smallest finger. It slipped as far as the second joint and stopped. He took it off and stuffed it into his vest pocket, after the manner of man. And then he 'phoned for his cab.

At the station he captured Miss Lantry out of the gabbing mob at eight thirty-two.

"We mustn't keep mamma and the others waiting," said she.

"To Wallack's Theatre as fast as you can drive!" said Richard, loyally.

They whirled up Forty-second to Broadway, and then down the white-starred lane that leads from the soft meadows of sunset to the rocky hills of morning.

At Thirty-fourth Street young Richard quickly thrust up the trap and ordered the cabman to stop.

"I've dropped a ring," he apologized, as he climbed out. "It was my mother's, and I'd hate to lose it. I won't detain you a minute—I saw where it fell."

In less than a minute he was back in the cab with the ring.

But within that minute a crosstown car had stopped directly in front of the cab. The cab-man tried to pass to the left, but a heavy express wagon cut him off. He tried the right and had to back away from a furniture van that had no business to be there. He tried to back out, but dropped his reins and swore dutifully. He was blockaded in a tangled mess of vehicles and horses.

One of those street blockades had occurred that sometimes tie up commerce and movement quite suddenly in the big city.

"Why don't you drive on?" said Miss Lantry, impatiently. "We'll be late."

Richard stood up in the cab and looked around. He saw a congested flood of wagons, trucks, cabs, vans and street cars filling the vast space where Broadway, Sixth Avenue, and Thirty-fourth Street cross one another as a twenty-six inch maiden fills her twenty-two inch girdle. And still from all the cross streets they were hurrying and rattling toward the converging point at full speed, and hurling themselves into the straggling mass, locking wheels and adding their drivers' imprecations to the clamor. The entire traffic of Manhattan seemed to have jammed itself around them. The oldest New Yorker among the thousands of spectators that lined the sidewalks had not witnessed a street blockade of the proportions of this one.

"I'm very sorry," said Richard, as he resumed his seat, "but it looks as if we are stuck. They won't get this jumble loosened up in an hour. It was my fault. If I hadn't dropped the ring we——"

"Let me see the ring," said Miss Lantry. "Now that it can't be helped, I don't care. I think theatres are stupid, anyway."

At 11 o'clock that night somebody tapped lightly on Anthony Rockwall's door.

"Come in," shouted Anthony, who was in a red dressing-down, reading a book of piratical adventures.

Somebody was Aunt Ellen, looking like a gray-haired angel that had been left on earth by mistake.

"They're engaged, Anthony," she said, softly. "She has promised to marry our Richard. On their way to the theatre there was a street blockade, and it was two hours before their cab could get out of it.

"And oh, Brother Anthony, don't ever boast of the power of money again. A little emblem of true love—a little ring that symbolized unending and unmercenary affection—was the cause of our Richard finding his happiness. He dropped it in the street, and got out to recover it. And before they could continue the blockade occurred. He spoke to his love and won her there while the cab was hemmed in. Money is dross compared with true love, Anthony."

"All right," said old Anthony. "I'm glad the boy has got what he wanted. I told him I wouldn't spare any expense in the matter if——"

"But, Brother Anthony, what good could your money have done?"

"Sister," said Anthony Rockwall. "I've got my pirate in a devil of a scrape. His ship has just been scuttled, and he's too good a judge of the value of money to let drown. I wish you would let me go on with this chapter."

The story should end here. I wish it would as heartily as you who read it wish it did. But we must go to the bottom of the well for truth.

The next day a person with red hands and a blue polka-dot necktie, who called himself Kelly, called at Anthony Rockwall's house, and was at once received in the library.

"Well," said Anthony, reaching for his check-book, "it was a good bilin' of soap. Let's see—you had $5,000 in cash."

"I paid out $300 more of my own," said Kelly. "I had to go a little above the estimate. I got the express wagons and cabs mostly for $5; but the trucks and two-horse teams mostly raised me to $10. The motormen wanted $10, and some of the loaded teams $20. The cops struck me hardest—$50 I paid two, and the rest $20 and $25. But didn't it work beautiful, Mr. Rockwall? I'm glad William A. Brady wasn't onto that little outdoor vehicle mob scene. I wouldn't want William to break his heart with jealousy. And never a rehearsal, either! The boys was on time to the fraction of a second. It was two hours before a snake could get below Greeley's statue."

"Thirteen hundred—there you are, Kelly," said Anthony, tearing off a check. "Your thousand, and the $300 you were out. You don't despise money, do you, Kelly?"

"Me?" said Kelly. "I can lick the man that invented poverty."

Anthony called Kelly when he was at the door.

"You didn't notice," said he, "anywhere in the tie-up, a kind of a fat boy without any clothes on shooting arrows around with a bow did you?"

"Why, no," said Kelly, mystified. "I didn't. If he was like you say, maybe the cops pinched him before I got there."

"I thought the little rascal wouldn't be on hand," chuckled Anthony. "Good-by, Kelly."

SPRINGTIME À LA CARTE

IT was a day in March.

Never, never begin a story this way when you write one. No opening could possibly be worse. It is unimaginative, flat, dry, and likely to consist of mere wind. But in this instance it is allowable. For the following paragraph, which should have inaugurated the narrative, is too wildly extravagant and preposterous to be flaunted in the face of the reader without preparation.

Sarah was crying over her bill of fare.

Think of a New York girl shedding tears on the menu card!

To account for this you will be allowed to guess that the lobsters were all out, or that she had sworn ice-cream off during Lent, or that she had ordered onions, or that she had just come from a Hackett matinée. And then, all these theories being wrong, you will please let the story proceed.

The gentleman who announced that the world was an oyster which he with his sword would open made a larger hit than he deserved. It is not difficult to open an oyster with a sword. But did you ever notice any one try to open the terrestrial bivalve with a typewriter? Like to wait for a dozen raw opened that way?

Sarah had managed to pry apart the shells with her unhandy weapon far enough to nibble a wee bit at the cold and clammy world within. She knew no more shorthand than if she had been a graduate in stenography just let slip upon the world by a business college. So, not being able to stenog, she could not enter that bright galaxy of office talent. She was a free-lance typewriter and canvassed for odd jobs of copying.

The most brilliant and crowning feat of Sarah's battle with the world was the deal she made with Schulenberg's Home Restaurant. The restaurant was next door to the old red brick in which she hall-roomed. One evening after dining at Schulenberg's 40-cent, five-course *table d'hôte* (served as fast as you throw the five baseballs at the colored gentleman's head) Sarah took away with her the bill of fare. It was written in an almost unreadable script neither English nor German, and so arranged that if you were not careful you began with a toothpick and rice pudding and ended with soup and the day of the week.

The next day Sarah showed Schulenberg a neat card on which the menu was beautifully typewritten with the viands temptingly marshalled under their right and proper heads from "hors d'œuvre" to "not responsible for over-coats and umbrellas."

Schulenberg became a naturalized citizen on the spot. Before Sarah left him she had him willingly committed to an agreement. She was to furnish typewritten bills of fare for the twenty-one tables in the restaurant—a new bill for each day's dinner, and new ones for breakfast and lunch as often as changes occurred in the food or as neatness required.

In return for this Schulenberg was to send three meals per diem to Sarah's hall room by a waiter—an obsequious one if possible—and furnish her each afternoon with a pencil draft of what Fate had in store for Schulenberg's customers on the morrow.

Mutual satisfaction resulted from the agreement. Schulenberg's patrons now knew what the food they ate was called even if its nature sometimes puzzled them. And Sarah had food during a cold, dull winter, which was the main thing with her.

And then the almanac lied, and said that spring had come. Spring comes when it comes. The frozen snows of January still lay like adamant in the cross-town streets. The hand-organs still played "In the Good Old Summertime," with their December vivacity and expression. Men began to make thirty-day notes to buy Easter dresses. Janitors shut off steam. And when these things happen one may know that the city is still in the clutches of winter.

One afternoon Sarah shivered in her elegant hall bedroom; "house heated; scrupulously clean; conveniences; seen to be appreciated." She had no work to do except Schulenberg's menu cards. Sarah sat in her squeaky willow rocker, and looked out the window. The calendar on the wall kept crying to her: "Springtime is here, Sarah—springtime is here, I tell you. Look at me, Sarah, my figures show it. You've got a neat figure yourself, Sarah—a—nice springtime figure—why do you look out the window so sadly?"

Sarah's room was at the back of the house. Looking out the window she could see the windowless rear brick wall of the box factory on the next street. But the wall was clearest crystal; and Sarah was looking down a grassy lane shaded with cherry trees and elms and bordered with raspberry bushes and Cherokee roses.

Spring's real harbingers are too subtle for the eye and ear. Some must have the flowering crocus, the wood-starring dogwood, the voice of bluebird—even so gross a reminder as the farewell handshake of the retiring buckwheat and oyster before they can welcome the Lady in Green to their dull bosoms. But to old earth's choicest kind there come straight, sweet messages from his newest bride, telling them they shall be no stepchildren unless they choose to be.

On the previous summer Sarah had gone into the country and loved a farmer. (In writing your story never hark back thus. It is bad art, and cripples interest. Let it march, march.)

Sarah stayed two weeks at Sunnybrook Farm. There she learned to love old Farmer Franklin's son Walter. Farmers have been loved and wedded and turned out to grass in less time. But young Walter Franklin was a modern agriculturist. He had a telephone in his cow house, and he could figure up exactly what effect next year's Canada wheat crop would have on potatoes planted in the dark of the moon.

It was in this shaded and raspberried lane that Walter had wooed and won her. And together they had sat and woven a crown of dandelions for her hair. He had immoderately praised the effect of the yellow blossoms against her brown tresses; and she had left the chaplet there, and walked back to the house swinging her straw sailor in her hands.

They were to marry in the spring—at the very first signs of spring, Walter said. And Sarah came back to the city to pound her typewriter.

A knock at the door dispelled Sarah's visions of that happy day. A waiter had brought the rough pencil draft of the Home Restaurant's next day fare in old Schulenberg's angular hand.

Sarah sat down to her typewriter and slipped a card between the rollers. She was a nimble worker. Generally in an hour and a half the twenty-one menu cards were written and ready.

To-day there were more changes on the bill of fare than usual. The soups were lighter; pork was eliminated from the entrées, figuring only with Russian turnips among the roasts. The gracious spirit of spring pervaded the entire menu. Lamb, that lately capered on the greening hillsides, was becoming exploited with the sauce that commemorated its gambols. The song of the oyster, though not silenced, was *dimuendo con amore*. The frying-pan seemed to be held, inactive, behind the beneficent bars of the broiler. The pie list swelled; the richer puddings had vanished; the sausage, with his drapery wrapped about him, barely lingered in a pleasant thanatopsis with the buckwheats and the sweet but doomed maple.

Sarah's fingers danced like midgets above a summer stream. Down through the courses she worked, giving each item its position according to its length with an accurate eye.

Just above the desserts came the list of vegetables. Carrots and peas, asparagus on toast, the perennial tomatoes and corn and succotash, lima beans, cabbage—and then——

Sarah was crying over her bill of fare. Tears from the depths of some divine despair rose in her heart and gathered to her eyes. Down went her head on the little typewriter stand; and the keyboard rattled a dry accompaniment to her moist sobs.

For she had received no letter from Walter in two weeks, and the next item on the bill of fare was dandelions—dandelions with some kind of egg—but bother the egg!—dandelions, with whose golden blooms Walter had crowned her his queen of love and future bride—dandelions, the harbingers of spring, her sorrow's crown of sorrow—reminder of her happiest days.

Madam, I dare you to smile until you suffer this test: Let the Marechal Niel roses that Percy brought you on the night you gave him your heart be served as a salad with French dressing before your eyes at a Schulenberg *table d'hôte.* Had Juliet so seen her love tokens dishonored the sooner would she have sought the lethean herbs of the good apothecary.

But what witch is Spring! Into the great cold city of stone and iron a message had to be sent. There was none to convey it but the little hardy courier of the fields with his rough green coat and modest air. He is a true soldier of fortune, this *dent-de-lion*—this lion's tooth, as the French chefs call him. Flowered, he will assist at love-making, wreathed in my lady's nut-brown hair; young and callow and unblossomed, he goes into the boiling pot and delivers the word of his sovereign mistress.

By and by Sarah forced back her tears. The cards must be written. But, still in a faint, golden glow from her dandelion dream, she fingered the typewriter keys absently for a little while, with her mind and heart in the meadow lane with her young farmer. But soon she came swiftly back to the rock-bound lanes of Manhattan, and the typewriter began to rattle and jump like a strike-breaker's motor car.

At 6 o'clock the waiter brought her dinner and carried away the typewritten bill of fare. When Sarah ate she set aside, with a sigh, the dish of dandelions with its crowning ovarious accompaniment. As this dark mass had been transformed from a bright and love-indorsed flower to be an ignominious vegetable, so had her summer hopes wilted and perished. Love may, as Shakespeare said, feed on itself: but Sarah could not bring herself to eat the dandelions that had graced, as ornaments, the first spiritual banquet of her heart's true affection.

At 7.30 the couple in the next room began to quarrel: the man in the room above sought for A on his flute; the gas went a little lower; three coal wagons started to unload—the only sound of which the phonograph is jealous; cats on the back fences slowly retreated toward Mukden. By these signs Sarah knew that it was time for her to read. She got out "The Cloister and the Hearth," the best non-selling book of the month, settled her feet on her trunk, and began to wander with Gerard.

The front door bell rang. The landlady answered it. Sarah left Gerard and Denys treed by a bear and listened. Oh, yes; you would, just as she did!

And then a strong voice was heard in the hall below, and Sarah jumped for her door, leaving the book on the floor and the first round easily the bear's.

You have guessed it. She reached the top of the stairs just as her farmer came up, three at a jump, and reaped and garnered her, with nothing left for the gleaners.

"Why haven't you written—oh, why?" cried Sarah.

"New York is a pretty large town," said Walter Franklin. "I came in a week ago to your old address. I found that you went away on a Thursday. That consoled some; it eliminated the possible Friday bad luck. But it didn't prevent my hunting for you with police and otherwise ever since!"

"I wrote!" said Sarah, vehemently.

"Never got it!"

"Then how did you find me?"

The young farmer smiled a springtime smile.

"I dropped into that Home Restaurant next door this evening," said he. "I don't care who knows it; I like a dish of some kind of greens at this time of the year. I ran my eye down that nice typewritten bill of fare looking for something in that line. When I got below cabbage I turned my chair over and hollered for the proprietor. He told me where you lived."

"I remember," sighed Sarah, happily. "That was dandelions below cabbage."

"I'd know that cranky capital W 'way above the line that your typewriter makes anywhere in the world," said Franklin.

"Why, there's no W in dandelions," said Sarah in surprise.

The young man drew the bill of fare from his pocket and pointed to a line.

Sarah recognized the first card she had typewritten that afternoon. There was still the rayed splotch in the upper right-hand corner where a tear had fallen. But over the spot where one should have read the name of the meadow plant, the clinging memory of their golden blossoms had allowed her fingers to strike strange keys.

Between the red cabbage and the stuffed green peppers was the item: "DEAREST WALTER, WITH HARD-BOILED EGG."

THE GREEN DOOR

Suppose you should be walking down Broadway after dinner, with ten minutes allotted to the consummation of your cigar while you are choosing between a diverting tragedy and something serious in the way of vaudeville. Suddenly a hand is laid upon your arm. You turn to look into the thrilling eyes of a beautiful woman, wonderful in diamonds and Russian sables. She thrusts hurriedly into your hand an extremely hot buttered roll, flashes out a tiny pair of scissors, snips off the second button of your overcoat, meaningly ejaculates the one word, "parallelogram!" and swiftly flies down a cross street, looking back fearfully over her shoulder.

That would be pure adventure. Would you accept it? Not you. You would flush with embarrassment; you would sheepishly drop the roll and continue down Broadway, fumbling feebly for the missing button. This you would do unless you are one of the blessed few in whom the pure spirit of adventure is not dead.

True adventurers have never been plentiful. They who are set down in print as such have been mostly business men with newly invented methods. They have been out after the things they wanted—golden fleeces, holy grails, lady loves, treasure, crowns and fame. The true adventurer goes forth aimless and uncalculating to meet and greet unknown fate. A fine example was the Prodigal Son —when he started back home.

Half-adventurers—brave and splendid figures—have been numerous. From the Crusades to the Palisades they have enriched the arts of history and fiction and the trade of historical fiction. But each of them had a prize to win, a goal to kick, an axe to grind, a race to run, a new thrust in tierce to deliver, a name to carve, a crow to pick—so they were not followers of true adventure.

In the big city the twin spirits Romance and Adventure are always abroad seeking worthy wooers. As we roam the streets they slyly peep at us and challenge us in twenty different guises. Without knowing why, we look up suddenly to see in a window a face that seems to belong to our gallery of intimate portraits; in a sleeping thoroughfare we hear a cry of agony and fear coming from an empty and shuttered house; instead of at our familiar curb a cab-driver deposits us before a strange door, which one, with a smile, opens for us and bids us enter; a slip of paper, written upon, flutters down to our feet from the high lattices of Chance; we exchange glances of instantaneous hate, affection, and fear with hurrying strangers in the passing crowds; a sudden souse of rain—and our umbrella may be sheltering the daughter of the Full Moon and first cousin of the Sidereal System; at every corner handkerchiefs drop, fingers beckon, eyes besiege, and the lost, the lonely, the rapturous, the mysterious, the perilous changing clues of adventure are slipped into our fingers. But few of us are willing to hold and follow them. We are grown stiff with the ramrod of convention down our backs. We pass on; and some day we come, at the end of a very dull ᴸife, to reflect that our romance has been a pallid thing of a marriage or two, a satin rosette kept in a safe-deposit drawer, and a lifelong feud with a steam radiator.

Rudolf Steiner was a true adventurer. Few were the evenings on which he did not go forth from his hall bedchamber in search of the unexpected and the egregious. The most interesting thing in life seemed to him to be what might lie just around the next corner. Sometimes his willingness to tempt fate led him into strange paths. Twice he had spent the night in a station-house; again and again he had found himself the dupe of ingenious and mercenary tricksters; his watch and money had been the price of one flattering allurement. But with undiminished ardor he picked up every glove cast before him into the merry lists of adventure.

One evening Rudolf was strolling along a cross-town street in the older central part of the city. Two streams of people filled the side-walks—the home-hurrying, and that restless contingent that abandons home for the specious welcome of the thousand-candle-power *table d'hôte*.

The young adventurer was of pleasing presence, and moved serenely and watchfully. By daylight he was a salesman in a piano store. He wore his tie drawn through a topaz ring instead of fastened with a stick pin; and once he had written to the editor of a magazine that "Junie's Love Test," by Miss Libbey, had been the book that had most influenced his life.

During his walk a violent chattering of teeth in a glass case on the sidewalk seemed at first to draw his attention (with a qualm) to a restaurant before which it was set; but a second glance revealed the electric letters of a dentist's sign high above the next door. A giant negro, fantastically dressed in a red embroidered coat, yellow trousers and a military cap, discreetly distributed cards to those of the passing crowd who consented to take them.

This mode of dentistic advertising was a common sight to Rudolf. Usually he passed the dispenser of the dentist's cards without reducing his store; but to-night the African slipped one into his hand so deftly that he retained it there smiling a little at the successful feat.

When he had travelled a few yards further he glanced at the card indifferently. Surprised, he turned it over and looked again with interest. One side of the card was blank; on the other was written in ink three words, "The Green Door." And then Rudolf saw, three steps in front of him, a man throw down the card the negro had given him as he passed. Rudolf picked it up. It was printed with the dentist's name and address and the usual schedule of "plate work" and "bridge work" and "crowns," and specious promises of "painless" operations.

The adventurous piano salesman halted at the corner and considered. Then he crossed the street walked down a block, recrossed and joined the upward current of people again. Without seeming to notice the negro as he passed the second time, he carelessly took the card that was handed him. Ten steps away he inspected it. In the same handwriting that appeared on the first card "The Green Door" was inscribed upon it. Three or four cards were tossed to the pavement by pedestrians both following and leading him. These fell blank side up. Rudolf turned them over. Every one bore the printed legend of the dental "parlors."

Rarely did the arch sprite Adventure need to beckon twice to Rudolf Steiner, his true follower. But twice it had been done, and the quest was on.

Rudolf walked slowly back to where the giant negro stood by the case of rattling teeth. This time as he passed he recived no card. In spite of his gaudy and ridiculous garb, the Ethiopian displayed a natural barbaric dignity as he stood, offering the cards suavely to some, allowing others to pass unmolested. Every half minute he chanted a harsh, unintelligible phrase akin to the jabber of car conductors and grand opera. And not only did he withhold a card this time but it seemed to Rudolf that he received from the shining and massive black countenance a look of cold, almost contemptuous disdain.

The look stung the adventurer. He read in it a silent accusation that he had been found wanting. Whatever the mysterious written words on the cards might mean, the black had selected him twice from the throng for their recipient; and now seemed to have condemned him as deficient in the wit and spirit to engage the enigma.

Standing aside from the rush, the young man made a rapid estimate of the building in which he conceived that his adventure must lie. Five stories high it rose. A small restaurant occupied the basement.

The first floor, now closed, seemed to house millinery or furs. The second floor, by the winking electric letters, was the dentist's. Above this a polyglot babel of signs struggled to indicate the abodes of palmists, dressmakers, musicians, and doctors. Still higher up draped curtains and milk bottles white on the window sills proclaimed the regions of domesticity.

After concluding his survey Rudolf walked briskly up the high flight of stone steps into the house. Up two flights of the carpeted stairway he continued; and at its top paused. The hallway there was dimly lighted by two pale jets of gas —one far to his right, the other nearer, to his left. He looked toward the nearer light and saw, within its wan halo, a green door. For one moment he hesitated; then he seemed to see the contumelious sneer of the African juggler of cards; and then he walked straight to the green door and knocked against it.

Moments like those that passed before his knock was answered measure the quick breath of true adventure. What might not be behind those green panels! Gamesters at play; cunning rogues baiting their traps with subtle skill; beauty in love with courage, and thus planning to be sought by it; danger, death, love disappointment, ridicule—any of these might respond to that temerarious rap.

A faint rustle was heard inside, and the door slowly opened. A girl not yet twenty stood there white-faced and tottering. She loosed the knob and swayed weakly, groping with one hand. Rudolf caught her and laid her on a faded couch that stood against the wall. He closed the door and took a swift glance around the room by the light of a flickering gas jet. Neat, but extreme poverty was the story that he read.

The girl lay still, as if in a faint. Rudolf looked around the room excitedly for a barrel. People must be rolled upon a barrel who—no, no; that was for drowned persons. He began to fan her with his hat. That was successful, for he struck her nose with the brim of his derby and she opened her eyes. And then the young man saw that hers, indeed, was the one missing face from his heart's gallery of intimate portraits. The frank, gray eyes, the little nose, turning pertly outward; the chestnut hair, curling like the tendrils of a pea vine, seemed the right end and reward of all his wonderful adventures. But the face was woefully thin and pale.

The girl looked at him calmly, and then smiled.

"Fainted, didn't I?" she asked, weakly. "Well, who wouldn't? You try going without anything to eat for three days and see!"

"Himmel!" exclaimed Rudolf, jumping up. "Wait till I come back."

He dashed out the green door and down the stairs. In twenty minutes he was back again kicking at the door with his toe for her to open it. With both arms he hugged an array of wares from the grocery and the restaurant. On the table he laid them—bread and butter, cold meats, cakes, pies, pickles, oysters, a roasted chicken, a bottle of milk and one of red-hot tea.

"This is ridiculous," said Rudolf, blusteringly, "to go without eating. You must quit making election bets of this kind. Supper is ready." He helped her to a chair at the table and asked: "Is there a cup for the tea?" "On the shelf by the window," she answered. When he turned again with the cup he saw her, with eyes shining rapturously, beginning upon a huge Dill pickle that she had rooted out from the paper bags with a woman's unerring instinct. He took it from her, laughingly, and poured the cup full of milk. "Drink that first," he ordered, "and then you shall have some tea, and then a chicken wing. If you are very good you shall have a pickle to-morrow. And now, if you'll allow me to be your guest we'll have supper."

He drew up the other chair. The tea brightened the girl's eyes and brought back some of her color. She began to eat with a sort of dainty ferocity like some starved wild animal. She seemed to regard the young man's presence and the aid he had rendered her as a natural thing—not as though she undervalued the conventions; but as one whose great stress gave her the right to put aside the artificial for the human. But gradually, with the return of strength and comfort, came also a sense of the little conventions that belong; and she began to tell him her little story. It was one of a thousand such as the city yawns at every day—the shop girl's story of insufficient wages, further reduced by "fines" that go to swell the store's profits; of time lost through illness; and then of lost positions, lost hope, and—the knock of the adventurer upon the green door.

But to Rudolf the history sounded as big as the Iliad or the crisis in "Junie's Love Test."

"To think of you going through all that," he exclaimed.

"It was something fierce," said the girl, solemnly.

"And you have no relatives or friends in the city?"

"None whatever."

"I am all alone in the world, too," said Rudolf, after a pause.

"I am glad of that," said the girl, promptly; and somehow it pleased the young man to hear that she approved of his bereft condition.

Very suddenly her eyelids dropped and she sighed deeply.

"I'm awfully sleepy," she said, "and I feel so good."

Rudolf rose and took his hat.

"Then I'll say good-night. A long night's sleep will be fine for you."

He held out his hand, and she took it and said "good-night." But her eyes asked a question so eloquently, so frankly and pathetically that he answered it with words.

"Oh, I'm coming back to-morrow to see how you are getting along. You can't get rid of me so easily."

Then, at the door, as though the way of his coming had been so much less important than the fact that he had come, she asked: "How did you come to knock at my door?"

He looked at her for a moment, remembering the cards, and felt a sudden jealous pain. What if they had fallen into other hands as adventurous as his? Quickly he decided that she must never know the truth. He would never let her know that he was aware of the strange expedient to which she had been driven by her great distress.

"One of our piano tuners lives in this house," he said. "I knocked at your door by mistake."

The last thing he saw in the room before the green door closed was her smile.

At the head of the stairway he paused and looked curiously about him. And then he went along the hallway to its other end; and, coming back, ascended to the floor above and continued his puzzled explorations. Every door that he found in the house was painted green.

Wondering, he descended to the sidewalk. The fantastic African was still there. Rudolf confronted him with his two cards in his hand.

"Will you tell me why you gave me these cards and what they mean?" he asked.

In a broad, good-natured grin the negro exhibited a splendid advertisement of his master's profession.

"Dar it is, boss," he said, pointing down the street. "But I 'spect you is a little late for de fust act."

Looking the way he pointed Rudolf saw above the entrance to a theatre the blazing electric sign of its new play, "The Green Door."

"I'm informed dat it's a fust-rate show, sah," said the negro. "De agent what represents it pussented me with a dollar, sah, to distribute a few of his cards along with de doctah's. May I offer you one of de doctah's cards, suh?"

At the corner of the block in which he lived Rudolf stopped for a glass of beer and a cigar. When he had come out with his lighted weed he buttoned his coat, pushed back his hat and said, stoutly, to the lamp post on the corner:

"All the same, I believe it was the hand of Fate that doped out the way for me to find her."

Which conclusion, under the circumstances, certainly admits Rudolf Steiner to the ranks of the true followers of Romance and Adventure.

FROM THE CABBY'S SEAT

THE cabby has his point of view. It is more single-minded, perhaps, than that of a follower of any other calling. From the high, swaying seat of his hansom he looks upon his fellow-men as nomadic particles, of no account except when possessed of migratory desires. He is Jehu, and you are goods in transit. Be you President or vagabond, to cabby you are only a Fare. He takes you up, cracks his whip, joggles your vertebræ and sets you down.

When time for payment arrives, if you exhibit a familiarity with legal rates you come to know what contempt is; if you find that you have left your pocket-book behind you are made to realize the mildness of Dante's imagination.

It is not an extravagant theory that the cabby's singleness of purpose and concentrated view of life are the results of the hansom's peculiar construction. The cock-of-the-roost sits aloft like Jupiter on an unsharable seat, holding your fate between two thongs of inconstant leather. Helpless, ridiculous, confined, bobbing like a toy mandarin, you sit like a rat in a trap—you, before whom butlers cringe on solid land—and must squeak upward through a slit in your peripatetic sarcophagus to make your feeble wishes known.

Then, in a cab, you are not even an occupant; you are contents. You are a cargo at sea, and the "cherub that sits up aloft" has Davy Jones's street and number by heart.

One night there were sounds of revelry in the big brick tenement house next door but one to McGary's Family Café. The sounds seemed to emanate from the apartments of the Walsh family. The sidewalk was obstructed by a assortment of interested neighbors, who opened a lane from time to time for a hurrying messenger bearing from McGary's goods pertinent to festivity and diversion. The sidewalk contingent was engaged in comment and discussion from which it made no effort to eliminate the news that Norah Walsh was being married.

In the fulness of time there was an eruption of the merry-makers to the sidewalk. The uninvited guests enveloped and permeated them, and upon the night air rose joyous cries, congratulations, laughter, and unclassified noises born of McGary's oblations to the hymeneal scene.

Close to the curb stood Jerry O'Donovan's cab. Night-hawk was Jerry called; but no more lustrous or cleaner hansom than his ever closed its doors upon point lace and November violets. And Jerry's horse! I am within bounds when I tell you that he was stuffed with oats until one of those old ladies who leave their dishes unwashed at home and go about having expressmen arrested, would have smiled—yes, smiled—to have seen him.

Among the shifting, sonorous, pulsing crowd glimpses could be had of Jerry's high hat, battered by the winds and rains of many years; of his nose like a carrot, battered by the frolicsome, athletic progeny of millionaires and by contumacious fares; of his brass-buttoned green coat, admired in the vicinity of McGary's. It was plain that Jerry had usurped the functions of his cab, and was carrying a "load." Indeed, the figure may be extended and he be likened to a bread-wagon if we admit the testimony of a youthful spectator, who was heard to remark "Jerry has got a bun."

From somewhere among the throng in the street or else out of the thin stream of pedestrians a young woman tripped and stood by the cab. The professional hawk's eye of Jerry caught the movement. He made a lurch for the cab, overturning three or four onlookers and himself—no! he caught the cap of a water-plug and kept his feet. Like a sailor shinning up the ratlins during a squall Jerry mounted to his professional seat. Once he was there McGary's liquids were baffled. He seesawed on the mizzenmast of his craft as safe as a Steeple Jack rigged to the flagpole of a skyscraper.

"Step in, lady," said Jerry, gathering his lines.

The young woman stepped into the cab; the doors shut with a bang; Jerry's whip cracked in the air; the crowd in the gutter scattered, and the fine hansom dashed away 'crosstown.

When the oat-spry horse had hedged a little his first spurt of speed Jerry broke the lid of his cab and called down through the aperture in the voice of a cracked megaphone, trying to please:

"Where, now, will ye be drivin' to?"

"Anywhere you please," came up the answer, musical and contented.

"'Tis drivin' for pleasure she is," thought Jerry. And then he suggested as a matter of course:

"Take a thrip around in the park, lady. 'Twill be ilegant cool and fine."

"Just as you like," answered the fare, pleasantly.

The cab headed for Fifth Avenue and sped up that perfect street. Jerry bounced and swayed in his seat. The potent fluids of McGary were disquieted and they sent new fumes to his head. He sang an ancient song of Killisnook and brandished his whip like a baton.

Inside the cab the fare sat up straight on the cushions, looking to right and left at the lights and houses. Even in the shadowed hansom her eyes shone like stars at twilight.

When they reached Fifty-ninth Street Jerry's head was bobbing and his reins were slack. But his horse turned in through the park gate and began the old familiar nocturnal round. And then the fare leaned back, entranced, and breathed deep the clean, wholesome odors of grass and leaf and bloom. And the wise beast in the shafts, knowing his ground, struck into his by-the-hour gait and kept to the right of the road.

Habit also struggled successfully against Jerry's increasing torpor. He raised the hatch of his storm-tossed vessel and made the inquiry that cabbies do make in the park.

"Like shtop at the Cas-sino, lady? Gezzer r'freshm's, 'n lish'n the music. Ev'body shtops."

"I think that would be nice," said the fare.

They reined up with a plunge at the Casino entrance. The cab doors flew open. The fare stepped directly upon the floor. At once she was caught in a web of ravishing music and dazzled by a panorama of lights and colors. Some one slipped a little square card into her hand on which was printed a number—34.

She looked around and saw her cab twenty yards away already lining up in its place among the waiting mass of carriages, cabs, and motor cars. And then a man who seemed to be all shirt-front danced backward before her; and next she was seated at a little table by a railing over which climbed a jessamine vine.

There seemed to be a wordless invitation to purchase; she consulted a collection of small coins in a thin purse, and received from them license to order a glass of beer. There she sat, inhaling and absorbing it all—the new-colored, new-shaped life in a fairy palace in an enchanted wood.

At fifty tables sat princes and queens clad in all the silks and gems of the world. And now and then one of them would look curiously at Jerry's fare. They saw a plain figure dressed in a pink silk of the kind that is tempered by the word "foulard," and a plain face that wore a look of love of life that the queens envied.

Twice the long hands of the clocks went round. Royalties thinned from their *al fresco* thrones, and buzzed or clattered away in their vehicles of state. The music retired into cases of wood and bags of leather and baize. Waiters removed cloths pointedly near the plain figure sitting almost alone.

Jerry's fare rose, and held out her numbered card simply:

"Is there anything coming on the ticket?" she asked.

A waiter told her it was her cab check, and that she should give it to the man at the entrance. This man took it, and called the number. Only three hansoms stood in line. The driver of one of them went and routed out Jerry asleep in his cab. He swore deeply, climbed to the captain's bridge and steered his craft to the pier. His fare entered, and the cab whirled into the cool fastnesses of the park along the shortest homeward cuts.

At the gate a glimmer of reason in the form of sudden suspicion seized upon Jerry's beclouded mind. One or two things occurred to him. He stopped his horse, raised the trap and dropped his phonographic voice, like a lead plummet, through the aperture:

"I want to see four dollars before goin' any further on th' thrip. Have ye got th' dough?"

"Four dollars!" laughed the fare, softly, "dear me, no. I've only got a few pennies and a dime or two."

Jerry shut down the trap and slashed his oat-fed horse. The clatter of hoofs strangled but could not drown the sound of his profanity. He shouted choking and gurgling curses at the starry heavens; he cut viciously with his whip at passing vehicles; he scattered fierce and everchanging oaths and imprecations along the streets, so that a late truck driver, crawling homeward, heard and was abashed. But he knew his recourse, and made for it at a gallop.

At the house with the green lights beside the steps he pulled up. He flung wide the cab doors and tumbled heavily to the ground.

"Come on, you," he said, roughly.

His fare came forth with the Casino dreamy smile still on her plain face. Jerry took her by the arm and led her into the police station. A gray-moustached sergeant looked keenly across the desk. He and the cabby were no strangers.

"Sargeant," began Jerry in his old raucous, martyred, thunderous tones of complaint. "I've got a fare here that——"

Jerry paused. He drew a knotted, red hand across his brow. The fog set up by McGary was beginning to clear away.

"A fare, sargeant," he continued, with a grin, "that I want to introduce to ye. It's me wife that I married at ould man Walsh's this evening. And a divil of a time we had, tis thrue. Shake hands wit th' sargeant, Norah, and we'll be off to home."

Before stepping into the cab Norah sighed profoundly.

"I've had such a nice time, Jerry," said she.

AN UNFINISHED STORY

WE no longer groan and heap ashes upon our heads when the flames of Tophet are mentioned. For, even the preachers have begun to tell us that God is radium, or ether or some scientific compound, and that the worst we wicked ones may expect is a chemical reaction. This is a pleasing hypothesis; but there lingers yet some of the old, goodly terror of orthodoxy.

There are but two subjects upon which one may discourse with a free imagination, and without the possibility of being controverted. You may talk of your dreams; and you may tell what you heard a parrot say. Both Morpheus and the bird are incompetent witnesses; and your listener dare not attack your recital. The baseless fabric of a vision, then, shall furnish my theme—chosen with apologies and regrets instead of the more limited field of pretty Polly's small talk.

I had a dream that was so far removed from the higher criticism that it had to do with the ancient, respectable, and lamented bar-of-judgment theory.

Gabriel had played his trump; and those of us who could not follow suit were arraigned for examination. I noticed at one side a gathering of professional bondsmen in solemn black and collars that buttoned behind; but it seemed there was some trouble about their real estate titles; and they did not appear to be getting any of us out.

A fly cop—an angel policeman—flew over to me and took me by the left wing. Near at hand was a group of very prosperous-looking spirits arraigned for judgment.

"Do you belong with that bunch?" the policeman asked.

"Who are they?" was my answer.

"Why," said he, "they are——"

But this irrelevant stuff is taking up space that the story should occupy.

Dulcie worked in a department store. She sold Hamburg edging, or stuffed peppers, or automobiles, or other little trinkets such as they keep in department stores. Of what she earned, Dulcie received six dollars per week. The remainder was credited to her and debited to somebody else's account in the ledger kept by G—— Oh, primal energy, you say, Reverend Doctor—— Well, then, in the Ledger of Primal Energy.

During her first year in the store, Dulcie was paid five dollars per week. It would be instructive to know how she lived on that amount. Don't care? Very well; probably you are interested in larger amounts. Six dollars is a larger amount. I will tell you how she lived on six dollars per week.

One afternoon at six, when Dulcie was sticking her hat pin within an eighth of an inch of her *medulla oblongata*, she said to her chum, Sadie—the girl that waits on you with her left side:

"Say, Sade, I made a date for dinner this evening with Piggy."

"You never did!" exclaimed Sadie, admiringly. "Well, ain't you the lucky one? Piggy's an awful swell; and he always takes a girl to swell places. He took Blanche up to the Hoffman House one evening, where they have swell music, and you see a lot of swells. You'll have a swell time, Dulce."

Dulcie hurried homeward. Her eyes were shining, and her cheeks showed the delicate pink of life's—real life's—approaching dawn. It was Friday; and she had fifty cents left of her last week's wages.

The streets were filled with the rush-hour floods of people. The electric lights of Broadway were glowing—calling moths from miles, from leagues, from hundreds of leagues out of darkness around to come in and attend the singeing school. Men in accurate clothes, with faces like those carved on cherry stones by the old salts in sailors' homes, turned and stared at Dulcie as she sped, unheeding, past them. Manhattan, the night-blooming cereus, was beginning to unfold its dead-white, heavy-odored petals.

Dulcie stopped in a store where goods were cheap and bought an imitation lace collar with her fifty cents. That money was to have been spent otherwise—fifteen cents for supper, ten cents for breakfast, ten cents for lunch. Another dime was to be added to her small store of savings; and five cents was to be squandered for licorice drops—the kind that made your cheek look like the toothache, and last as long. The licorice was an extravagance—almost a carouse—but what is life without pleasures?

Dulcie lived in a furnished room. There is this difference between a furnished room and a boarding-house. In a furnished room, other people do not know it when you go hungry.

Dulcie went up to her room—the third-floor-back in a West Side brownstone-front. She lit the gas. Scientists tell us that the diamond is the hardest substance known. Their mistake. Landladies know of a compound beside which the diamond is as putty. They pack it in the tips of gas-burners; and one may stand on a chair and dig at it in vain until one's fingers are pink and bruised. A hairpin will not remove it; therefore let us call it immovable.

So Dulcie lit the gas. In its one-fourth-candle-power glow we will observe the room.

Couch-bed, dresser, table, washstand, chair—of this much the landlady was guilty. The rest was Dulcie's. On the dresser were her treasures—a gilt china vase presented to her by Sadie, a calendar issued by a pickle works, a book on the divination of dreams, some rice powder in a glass dish, and a cluster of artificial cherries tied with a pink ribbon.

Against the wrinkly mirror stood pictures of General Kitchener, William Muldoon, the Duchess of Marlborough, and Benvenuto Cellini. Against one wall was a plaster of Paris plaque of an O'Callahan in a Roman helmet. Near it was a violent oleograph of a lemon-colored child assaulting an inflammatory butterfly. This was Dulcie's final judgment in art; but it had never been upset. Her rest had never been disturbed by whispers of stolen copes; no critic had elevated his eyebrows at her infantile entomologist.

Piggy was to call for her at seven. While she swiftly makes ready, let us discreetly face the other way and gossip.

For the room, Dulcie paid two dollars per week. On week-days her breakfast cost ten cents; she made coffee and cooked an egg over the gaslight while she was dressing. On Sunday mornings she feasted royally on veal chops and pineapple fritters at "Billy's" restaurant, at a cost of twenty-five cents—and tipped the waitress ten cents. New York presents so many temptations for one to run into extravagance. She had her lunches in the department-store restaurant at a cost of sixty cents for the week; dinners were $1.05. The evening papers—show me a New Yorker going without his daily paper!—came to six cents; and two Sunday papers—one for the personal column and the other to read—were ten cents. The total amounts to $4.76. Now, one has to buy clothes, and——

I give it up. I hear of wonderful bargains in fabrics, and of miracles performed with needle and thread; but I am in doubt. I hold my pen poised in vain when I would add to Dulcie's life some of those joys that belong to woman by virtue of all the unwritten, sacred, natural, inactive ordinances of the equity of heaven. Twice she had been to Coney Island and had ridden the hobby-horses. 'Tis a weary thing to count your pleasures by summers instead of by hours.

Piggy needs but a word. When the girls named him, an undeserving stigma was cast upon the noble family of swine. The words-of-three-letters lesson in the old blue spelling book begins with Piggy's biography. He was fat; he had the soul of a rat, the habits of a bat, and the magnanimity of a cat. . . . He wore expensive clothes; and was a connoisseur in starvation. He could look at a shop-girl and tell you to an hour how long it had been since she had eaten anything more nourishing than marshmallows and tea. He hung about the shopping districts, and prowled around in department stores with his invitations to dinner. Men who escort dogs upon the streets at the end of a string look down upon him. He is a type; I can dwell upon him no longer; my pen is not the kind intended for him; I am no carpenter.

At ten minutes to seven Dulcie was ready. She looked at herself in the wrinkly mirror. The reflection was satisfactory. The dark blue dress, fitting without a wrinkle, the hat with its jaunty black feather, the but-slightly-soiled gloves—all representing self-denial, even of food itself—were vastly becoming.

Dulcie forgot everything else for a moment except that she was beautiful, and that life was about to lift a corner of its mysterious veil for her to observe its wonders. No gentleman had ever asked her out before. Now she was going for a brief moment into the glitter and exalted show.

The girls said that Piggy was a "spender." There would be a grand dinner, and music, and splendidly dressed ladies to look at and things to eat that strangely twisted the girls' jaws when they tried to tell about them. No doubt she would be asked out again.

There was a blue pongee suit in a window that she knew—by saving twenty cents a week instead of ten in—let's see——Oh, it would run into years! But there was a second-hand store in Seventh Avenue where——

Somebody knocked at the door. Dulcie opened it. The landlady stood there with a spurious smile, sniffing for cooking by stolen gas.

"A gentleman's downstairs to see you," she said. "Name is Mr. Wiggins."

By such epithet was Piggy known to unfortunate ones who had to take him seriously.

Dulcie turned to the dresser to get her handkerchief; and then she stopped still, and bit her underlip hard. While looking in her mirror she had seen fairyland and herself, a princess, just awakening from a long slumber. She had forgotten one that was watching her with sad beautiful, stern eyes—the only one there was to approve or condemn what she did. Straight and slender and tall, with a look of sorrowful reproach on his handsome, melancholy face, General Kitchener fixed his wonderful eyes on her out of his gilt photograph frame on the dresser.

Dulcie turned like an automatic doll to the landlady.

"Tell him I can't go," she said, dully. "Tell him I'm sick, or something. Tell him I'm not going out."

After the door was closed and locked, Dulcie fell upon her bed, crushing her black tip, and cried for ten minutes. General Kitchener was her only friend. He was Dulcie's ideal of a gallant knight. He looked as if he might have a secret sorrow, and his wonderful moustache was a dream, and she was a little afraid of that stern yet tender look in his eyes. She used to have little fancies that he would call at the house sometime, and ask for her, with his sword clanking against his high boots. Once, when a boy was rattling a piece of chain against a lamp post she had opened the window and looked out. But there was no use. She knew that General Kitchener was away over in Japan, leading his army against the savage Turks; and he would never step out of his gilt frame for her. Yet one look from him had vanquished Piggy that night. Yes, for that night.

When her cry was over Dulcie got up and took off her best dress, and put on her old blue kimono. She wanted no dinner. She sang two verses of "Sammy." Then she became intensely interested in a little red speck on the side of her nose. And after that was attended to, she drew up a chair to the rickety table, and told her fortune with an old deck of cards.

"The horrid, impudent thing!" she said aloud. "And I never gave him a word or a look to make him think it!"

At nine o'clock Dulcie took a tin box of crackers and a little pot of raspberry jam out of her trunk and had a feast. She offered General Kitchener some jam on a cracker; but he only looked at her as the sphinx would have looked at a butterfly—if there are butterflies in the desert.

"Don't eat it if you don't want to," said Dulcie. "And don't put on so many airs and scold so with your eyes. I wonder if you'd be so superior and snippy if you had to live on six dollars a week."

It was not a good sign for Dulcie to be rude to General Kitchener. And then she turned Benvenuto Cellini face downward with a severe gesture. But that was not inexcusable; for she had always thought he was Henry VIII, and she did not approve of him.

At half-past nine Dulcie took a last look at the pictures on the dresser, turned out the light and skipped into bed. It's an awful thing to go to bed with a good-night look at General Kitchener, William Muldoon, the Duchess of Marlborough, and Benvenuto Cellini.

This story doesn't really get anywhere at all. The rest of it comes later—sometime when Piggy asks Dulcie again to dine with him, and she is feeling lonelier than usual, and General Kitchener happens to be looking the other way; and then——

As I said before, I dreamed that I was standing near a crowd of prosperous-looking angels, and a policeman took me by the wing and asked if I belonged with them.

"Who are they?" I asked.

"Why," said he, "they are the men who hired working-girls, and paid 'em five or six dollars a week to live on. Are you one of the bunch?"

"Not on your immortality," said I. "I'm only a fellow that set fire to an orphan asylum, and murdered a blind man for his pennies."

THE CALIPH, CUPID AND THE CLOCK

PRINCE MICHAEL, of the Electorate of Valleluna, sat on his favorite bench in the park. The coolness of the September night quickened the life in him like a rare, tonic wine. The benches were not filled; for park loungers, with their stagnant blood, are prompt to detect and fly home from the crispness of early autumn. The moon was just clearing the roofs of the range of dwellings that bounded the quadrangle on the east. Children laughed and played about the fine-sprayed fountain. In the shadowed spots fauns and hamadryads wooed, unconscious of the gaze of mortal eyes. A hand-organ—Philomel by the grace of our stage carpenter, Fancy—fluted and droned in a side street. Around the enchanted boundaries of the little park street cars spat and mewed and the stilted trains roared like tigers and lions prowling for a place to enter. And above the trees shone the great, round, shining face of an illuminated clock in the tower of an antique public building.

Prince Michael's shoes were wrecked far beyond the skill of the carefullest cobbler. The ragman would have declined any negotiations concerning his clothes. The two weeks' stubble on his face was gray and brown and red and greenish yellow—as if it had been made up from individual contributions from the chorus of a musical comedy. No man existed who had money enough to wear so bad a hat as his.

Prince Michael sat on his favorite bench and smiled. It was a diverting thought to him that he was wealthy enough to buy every one of those close-ranged, bulky, window-lit mansions that faced him, if he chose. He could have matched gold, equipages, jewels, art treasures, estates and acres with any Crœsus in this proud city of Manhattan, and scarcely have entered upon the bulk of his holdings. He could have sat at table with reigning sovereigns. The social world, the world of art, the fellowship of the elect, adulation, imitation, the homage of the fairest, honors from the highest, praise from the wisest, flattery, esteem, credit, pleasure, fame—all the honey of life was waiting in the comb in the hive of the world for Prince Michael, of the Electorate of Valleluna, whenever he might choose to take it. But his choice was to sit in rags and dinginess on a bench in a park. For he had tasted of the fruit of the tree of life, and, finding it bitter in his mouth, had stepped out of Eden for a time to seek distraction close to the unarmored, beating heart of the world.

These thoughts strayed dreamily through the mind of Prince Michael, as he smiled under the stubble of his polychromatic beard. Lounging thus, clad as the poorest of mendicants in the parks, he loved to study humanity. He found in altruism more pleasure than his riches, his station and all the grosser sweets of life had given him. It was his chief solace and satisfaction to alleviate individual distress, to confer favors upon worthy ones who had need of succor, to dazzle unfortunates by unexpected and bewildering gifts of truly royal magnificence, bestowed, however, with wisdom and judiciousness.

And as Prince Michael's eye rested upon the glowing face of the great clock in the tower, his smile, altruistic as it was, became slightly tinged with contempt. Big thoughts were the Prince's; and it was always with a shake of his head that he considered the subjugation of the world to the arbitrary measures of Time. The comings and goings of people in hurry and dread, controlled by the little metal moving hands of a clock, always made him sad.

By and by came a young man in evening clothes and sat upon the third bench from the Prince. For half an hour he smoked cigars with nervous haste, and then he fell to watching the face of the illuminated clock above the trees. His perturbation was evident, and the Prince noted, in sorrow, that its cause was connected, in some manner, with the slowly moving hands of the timepiece.

His Highness arose and went to the young man's bench.

"I beg your pardon for addressing you," he said, "but I perceive that you are disturbed in mind. If it may serve to mitigate the liberty I have taken I will add that I am Prince Michael, heir to the throne of the Electorate of Valleluna. I appear incognito, of course, as you may gather from my appearance. It is a fancy of mine to render aid to others whom I think worthy of it. Perhaps the matter that seems to distress you is one that would more readily yield to our mutual efforts."

The young man looked up brightly at the Prince. Brightly, but the perpendicular line of perplexity between his brows was not smoothed away. He laughed, and even then it did not. But he accepted the momentary diversion.

"Glad to meet you, Prince," he said, good humoredly. "Yes, I'd say you were incog. all right. Thanks for your offer of assistance—but I don't see where your butting-in would help things any. It's a kind of private affair, you know—but thanks all the same."

Prince Michael sat at the young man's side. He was often rebuffed but never offensively. His courteous manner and words forbade that.

"Clocks," said the Prince, "are shackles on the feet of mankind. I have observed you looking persistently at that clock. Its face is that of a tyrant, its numbers are false as those on a lottery ticket; its hands are those of a bunco steerer, who makes an appointment with you to your ruin. Let me entreat you to throw off its humiliating bonds and cease to order your affairs by that insensate monitor of brass and steel."

"I don't usually," said the young man. "I carry a watch except when I've got my radiant rags on."

"I know human nature as I do the trees and grass," said the Prince, with earnest dignity. "I am a master of philosophy, a graduate in art, and I hold the purse of a Fortunatus. There are few mortal misfortunes that I cannot alleviate or overcome. I have read your countenance, and found in it honesty and nobility as well as distress. I beg of you to accept my advice or aid. Do not belie the intelligence I see in your face by judging from my appearance of my ability to defeat your troubles."

The young man glanced at the clock again and frowned darkly. When his gaze strayed from the glowing horologue of time it rested intently upon a four-story red brick house in the row of dwellings opposite to where he sat. The shades were drawn, and the lights in many rooms shone dimly through them.

"Ten minutes to nine!" exclaimed the young man, with an impatient gesture of despair. He turned his back upon the house and took a rapid step or two in a contrary direction.

"Remain!" commanded Prince Michael, in so potent a voice that the disturbed one wheeled around with a somewhat chagrined laugh.

"I'll give her the ten minutes and then I'm off," he muttered, and then aloud to the Prince: "I'll join you in confounding all clocks, my friend, and throw in women, too."

"Sit down," said the Prince, calmly. "I do not accept your addition. Women are the natural enemies of clocks, and, therefore, the allies of those who would seek liberation from these monsters that measure our follies and limit our pleasures. If you will so far confide in me I would ask you to relate to me your story."

The young man threw himself upon the bench with a reckless laugh.

"Your Royal Highness, I will," he said, in tones of mock deference. "Do you see yonder house—the one with the three upper windows lighted? Well, at 6 o'clock I stood in that house with the young lady I am—that is, I was—engaged to. I had been doing wrong, my dear Prince—I had been a naughty boy, and she had heard of it. I wanted to be forgiven, of course—we are always wanting women to forgive us, aren't we, Prince?

"'I want time to think it over,' said she. 'There is one thing certain; I will either fully forgive you, or I will never see your face again. There will be no half-way business. At half-past eight,' she said, 'at exactly half-past eight you may be watching the middle upper window of the top floor. If I decide to forgive I will hang out of that window a white silk scarf. You will know by that that all is as was before, and you may come to me. If you see no scarf you may consider that everything between us is ended forever.' That," concluded the young man, bitterly, "is why I have been watching that clock. The time for the signal to appear has passed twenty-three minutes ago. Do you wonder that I am a little disturbed, my Prince of Rags and Whiskers?"

"Let me repeat to you," said Prince Michael, in his even, well-modulated tones, "that women are the natural enemies of clocks. Clocks are an evil, women a blessing. The signal may yet appear."

"Never, on your principality!" exclaimed the young man, hopelessly. "You don't know Marian—of course. She's always on time, to the minute. That was the first thing about her that attracted me. I've got the mitten instead of the scarf. I ought to have known at 8.31 that my goose was cooked. I'll go West on the 11.45 to-night with Jack Milburn. The jig's up. I'll try Jack's ranch awhile and top off with the Klondike and whiskey. Good-night—er—er—Prince."

Prince Michael smiled his enigmatic, gentle, comprehending smile and caught the coat sleeve of the other. The brilliant light in the Prince's eyes was softening to a dreamier, cloudy translucence.

"Wait," he said solemnly, "till the clock strikes. I have wealth and power and knowledge above most men, but when the clock strikes I am afraid. Stay by me until then. This woman shall be yours. You have the word of the hereditary Prince of Valleluna. On the day of your marriage I will give you $100,000 and a palace on the Hudson. But there must be no clocks in that palace—they measure our follies and limit our pleasures. Do you agree to that?"

"Of course," said the young man, cheerfully, "they're a nuisance, anyway—always ticking and striking and getting you late for dinner."

He glanced again at the clock in the tower. The hands stood at three minutes to nine.

"I think," said Prince Michael, "that I will sleep a little. The day has been fatiguing."

He stretched himself upon a bench with the manner of one who had slept thus before.

"You will find me in this park on any evening when the weather is suitable," said the Prince, sleepily. "Come to me when your marriage day is set and I will give you a check for the money."

"Thanks, Your Highness," said the young man, seriously. "It doesn't look as if I would need that palace on the Hudson, but I appreciate your offer, just the same."

Prince Michael sank into deep slumber. His battered hat rolled from the bench to the ground. The young man lifted it, placed it over the frowsy face and moved one of the grotesquely relaxed limbs into a more comfortable position. "Poor devil!" he said, as he drew the tattered clothes closer about the Prince's breast.

Sonorous and startling came the stroke of 9 from the clock tower. The young man sighed again, turned his face for one last look at the house of his relinquished hopes—and cried aloud profane words of holy rapture.

From the middle upper window blossomed in the dusk a waving, snowy, fluttering, wonderful, divine emblem of forgiveness and promised joy.

By came a citizen, rotund, comfortable, home-hurrying, unknowing of the delights of waving silken scarfs on the borders of dimly-lit parks.

"Will you oblige me with the time, sir?" asked the young man; and the citizen, shrewdly conjecturing his watch to be safe, dragged it out and announced:

"Twenty-nine and a half minutes past eight, sir."

And then, from habit, he glanced at the clock in the tower, and made further oration.

"By George! that clock's half an hour fast! First time in ten years I've known it to be off. This watch of mine never varies a——"

But the citizen was talking to vacancy. He turned and saw his hearer, a fast receding black shadow flying in the direction of a house with three lighted upper windows.

And in the morning came along two policemen on their way to the beats they owned. The park was deserted save for one dilapidated figure that sprawled, asleep, on a bench. They stopped and gazed upon it.

"It's Dopy Mike," said one. "He hits the pipe every night. Park bum for twenty years. On his last legs, I guess."

The other policeman stooped and looked at something crumpled and crisp in the hand of the sleeper.

"Gee!" he remarked. "He's doped out a fifty-dollar bill, anyway. Wish I knew the brand of hop that he smokes."

And then "Rap, rap, rap!" went the club of realism against the shoe soles of Prince Michael, of the Electorate of Valleluna.

SISTERS OF THE GOLDEN CIRCLE

THE Rubberneck Auto was about ready to start. The merry top-riders had been assigned to their seats by the gentlemanly conductor. The sidewalk was blockaded with sightseers who had gathered to stare at sightseers, justifying the natural law that every creature on earth is preyed upon by some other creature.

The megaphone man raised his instrument of torture; the inside of the great automobile began to thump and throb like the heart of a coffee drinker. The top-riders nervously clung to the seats; the old lady from Valparaiso, Indiana, shrieked to be put ashore. But, before a wheel turns, listen to a brief preamble through the cardiaphone, which shall point out to you an object of interest on life's sightseeing tour.

Swift and comprehensive is the recognition of white man for white man in African wilds; instant and sure is the spiritual greeting between mother and babe; unhesitatingly do master and dog commune across the slight gulf between animal and man; immeasurably quick and sapient are the brief messages between one and one's beloved. But all these instances set forth only slow and groping interchange of sympathy and thought beside one other instance which the Rubberneck coach shall disclose. You shall learn (if you have not learned already) what two beings of all earth's living inhabitants most quickly look into each other's hearts and souls when they meet face to face.

The gong whirred, and the Glaring-at-Gotham car moved majestically upon its instructive tour.

On the highest, rear seat was James Williams, of Cloverdale, Missouri, and his Bride.

Capitalize it, friend typo—that last word—word of words in the epiphany of life and love. The scent of the flowers, the booty of the bee, the primal drip of spring waters, the overture of the lark, the twist of lemon peel on the cocktail of creation—such is the bride. Holy is the wife; revered the mother; galliptious is the summer girl—but the bride is the certified check among the wedding presents that the gods send in when man is married to mortality.

The car glided up the Golden Way. On the bridge of the great cruiser the captain stood, trumpeting the sights of the big city to his passengers. Wide-mouthed and open-eared they heard the sights of the metropolis thundered forth to their eyes. Confused, delirious with excitement and provincial longings, they tried to make ocular responses to the megaphonic ritual. In the solemn spires of spreading cathedrals they saw the home of the Vanderbilts; in the busy bulk of the Grand Central depot they viewed, wonderingly, the frugal cot of Russel Sage. Bidden to observe the highlands of the Hudson, they gaped, unsuspecting, at the upturned mountains of a new-laid sewer.

To many the elevated railroad was the Rialto, on the stations of which uniformed men sat and made chop suey of your tickets. And to this day in the outlying districts many have it that Chuck Connors, with his hand on his heart, leads reform; and that but for the noble municipal efforts of one Parkhurst, a district attorney, the notorious "Bishop" Potter gang would have destroyed law and order from the Bowery to the Harlem River.

But I beg you to observe Mrs. James Williams—Hattie Chalmers that was— once the belle of Cloverdale. Pale-blue is the bride's, if she will; and this color she had honored. Willingly had the moss rosebud loaned to her cheeks of its pink—and as for the violet!—her eyes will do very well as they are, thank you. A useless strip of white chaf—oh, no, he was guiding the auto car—of white chiffon—or perhaps it was grenadine or tulle—was tied beneath her chin, pretending to hold her bonnet in place. But you know as well as I do that the hat pins did the work.

And on Mrs. James Williams's face was recorded a little library of the world's best thoughts in three volumes. Volume No. 1 contained the belief that James Williams was about the right sort of thing. Volume No. 2 was an essay on the world, declaring it to be a very excellent place. Volume No. 3 disclosed the belief that in occupying the highest seat in a Rubberneck auto they were travelling the pace that passes all understanding.

James Williams, you would have guessed, was about twenty-four. It will gratify you to know that your estimate was so accurate. He was exactly twenty-three years, eleven months and twenty-nine days old. He was well built, active, strong-jawed, good-natured, and rising. He was on his wedding trip.

Dear kind fairy, please cut out those orders for money and 40 H. P. touring cars and fame and a new growth of hair and the presidency of the boat club. Instead of any of them turn backward—oh, turn backward and give us just a teeny-weeny bit of our wedding trip over again. Just an hour, dear fairy, so we can remember how the grass and poplar trees looked, and the bow of those bonnet strings tied beneath her chin—even if it was the hat pins that did the work. Can't do it? Very well; hurry up with that touring car and the oil stock, then.

Just in front of Mrs. James Williams sat a girl in a loose tan jacket and a straw hat adorned with grapes and roses. Only in dreams and milliners' shops do we, alas! gather grapes and roses at one swipe. This girl gazed with large blue eyes, credulous, when the megaphone man roared his doctrine that millionaires were things about which we should be concerned. Between blasts she resorted to Epictetian philosophy in the form of pepsin chewing gum.

At this girl's right hand sat a young man about twenty-four. He was well built, active, strong-jawed, and good-natured. But if his description seems to follow that of James Williams, divest it of anything Cloverdalian. This man belonged to hard streets and sharp corners. He looked keenly about him, seeming to begrudge the asphalt under the feet of those upon whom he looked down from his perch.

While the megaphone barks at a famous hostelry, let me whisper you through the low-tuned cardiaphone to sit tight; for now things are about to happen, and the great city will close over them again as over a scrap of ticker tape floating down from the den of a Broad Street bear.

The girl in the tan jacket twisted around to view the pilgrims on the last seat. The other passengers she had absorbed; the seat behind her was her Bluebeard's chamber.

Her eyes met those of Mrs. James Williams. Between two ticks of a watch they exchanged their life's experiences, histories, hopes and fancies. And all, mind you, with the eye, before two men could have decided whether to draw steel or borrow a match.

The bride leaned forward low. She and the girl spoke rapidly together, their tongues moving quickly like those of two serpents—a comparison that is not meant to go further. Two smiles and a dozen nods closed the conference.

And now in the broad, quiet avenue in front of the Rubberneck car a man in dark clothes stood with uplifted hand. From the sidewalk another hurried to join him.

The girl in the fruitful hat quickly seized her companion by the arm and whispered in his ear. That young man exhibited proof of ability to act promptly. Crouching low, he slid over the edge of the car, hung lightly for an instant, and then disappeared. Half a dozen of the top-riders observed his feat wonderingly, but made no comment, deeming it prudent not to express surprise at what might be the conventional manner of alighting in this bewildering city. The truant passenger dodged a hansom and then floated past, like a leaf on a stream between a furniture van and a florist's delivery wagon.

The girl in the tan jacket turned again, and looked into the eyes of Mrs. James Williams. Then she faced about and sat still while the Rubberneck auto stopped at the flash of the badge under the coat of the plainclothes man.

"What's eating you?" demanded the megaphonist, abandoning his professional discourse for pure English.

"Keep her at anchor for a minute," ordered the officer. "There's a man on board we want—a Philadelphia burglar called 'Pinky' McGuire. There he is on the back seat. Look out for the side, Donovan."

Donovan went to the hind wheel and looked up at James Williams.

"Come down, old sport," he said pleasantly. "We've got you. Back to Sleepy-town for yours. It ain't a bad idea, hidin' on a Rubberneck, though. I'll remember that."

Softly through the megaphone came the advice of the conductor:

"Better step off, sir, and explain. The car must proceed on its tour."

James Williams belonged among the level heads. With necessary slowness he picked his way through the passengers down to the steps at the front of the car. His wife followed, but she first turned her eyes and saw the escaped tourist glide from behind the furniture van and slip behind a tree on the edge of the little park, not fifty feet away.

Descended to the ground, James Williams faced his captors with a smile. He was thinking what a good story he would have to tell in Cloverdale about having been mistaken for a burglar. The Rubberneck coach lingered, out of respect for its patrons. What could be a more interesting sight than this?

"My name is James Williams, of Cloverdale, Missouri," he said, kindly, so that they would not be too greatly mortified. "I have letters here that will show——"

"You'll come with us, please," announced the plainclothes man. "'Pinky' McGuire's description fits you like flannel washed in hot suds. A detective saw you on the Rubberneck up at Central Park and 'phoned down to take you in. Do your explaining at the station-house."

James Williams's wife—his bride of two weeks—looked him in the face with a strange, soft radiance in her eyes and a flush on her cheeks, looked him in the face and said:

"Go with 'em quietly, 'Pinky,' and maybe it'll be in your favor."

And then as the Glaring-at-Gotham car rolled away she turned and threw a kiss—his wife threw a kiss—at some one high up on the seats of the Rubberneck.

"Your girl gives you good advice, McGuire," said Donovan. "Come on now."

And then madness descended upon and occupied James Williams. He pushed his hat far upon the back of his head.

"My wife seems to think I am a burglar," he said, recklessly. "I never heard of her being crazy; therefore I must be. And if I'm crazy, they can't do anything to me for killing you two fools in my madness."

Whereupon he resisted arrest so cheerfully and industriously that cops had to be whistled for, and afterwards the reserves, to disperse a few thousand delighted spectators.

At the station-house the desk sergeant asked for his name.

"McDoodle, the Pink, or Pinky the Brute, I forget which," was James Williams's answer. "But you can bet I'm a burglar; don't leave that out. And you might add that it took five of 'em to pluck the Pink. I'd especially like to have that in the records."

In an hour came Mrs. James Williams, with Uncle Thomas, of Madison Avenue, in a respect-compelling motor car and proofs of the hero's innocence—for all the world like the third act of a drama backed by an automobile mfg. co.

After the police had sternly reprimanded James Williams for imitating a copyrighted burglar and given him as honorable a discharge as the department was capable of, Mrs. Williams rearrested him and swept him into an angle of the station-house. James Williams regarded her with one eye. He always said that Donovan closed the other while somebody was holding his good right hand. Never before had he given her a word of reproach or of reproof.

"If you can explain," he began rather stiffly, "why you——"

"Dear," she interrupted, "listen. It was an hour's pain and trial to you. I did it for her—I mean the girl who spoke to me on the coach. I was so happy, Jim—so happy with you that I didn't dare to refuse that happiness to another. Jim, they were married only this morning—those two; and I wanted him to get away. While they were struggling with you I saw him slip from behind his tree and hurry across the park. That's all of it, dear—I had to do it."

Thus does one sister of the plain gold band know another who stands in the enchanted light that shines but once and briefly for each one. By rice and satin bows does mere man become aware of weddings. But bride knoweth bride at the glance of an eye. And between them swiftly passes comfort and meaning in a language that man and widows wot not of.

THE ROMANCE OF A BUSY BROKER

PITCHER, confidential clerk in the office of Harvey Maxwell, broker, allowed a look of mild interest and surprise to visit his usually expressionless countenance when his employer briskly entered at half-past nine in company with his young lady stenographer. With a snappy "Good-morning, Pitcher," Maxwell dashed at his desk as though he were intending to leap over it, and then plunged into the great heap of letters and telegrams waiting there for him.

The young lady had been Maxwell's stenographer for a year. She was beautiful in a way that was decidedly unstenographic. She forewent the pomp of the alluring pompadour. She wore no chains, bracelets, or lockets. She had not the air of being about to accept an invitation to luncheon. Her dress was gray and plain, but it fitted her figure with fidelity and discretion. In her neat black turban hat was the gold-green wing of a macaw. On this morning she was softly and shyly radiant. Her eyes were dreamily bright, her cheeks genuine peach-blow, her expression a happy one, tinged with reminiscence.

Pitcher, still mildly curious, noticed a difference in her ways this morning. Instead of going straight into the adjoining room, where her desk was, she lingered, slightly irresolute, in the outer office. Once she moved over by Maxwell's desk, near enough for him to be aware of her presence.

The machine sitting at that desk was no longer a man; it was a busy New York broker, moved by buzzing wheels and uncoiling springs.

"Well—what is it? Anything?" asked Maxwell, sharply. His opened mail lay like a bank of stage snow on his crowded desk. His keen gray eye, impersonal and brusque, flashed upon her half impatiently.

"Nothing," answered the stenographer, moving away with a little smile.

"Mr. Pitcher," she said to the confidential clerk, "did Mr. Maxwell say anything yesterday about engaging another stenographer?"

"He did," answered Pitcher. "He told me to get another one. I notified the agency yesterday afternoon to send over a few samples this morning. It's 9.45 o'clock, and not a single picture hat or piece of pineapple chewing gum has showed up yet."

"I will do the work as usual, then," said the young lady, "until some one comes to fill the place." And she went to her desk at once and hung the black turban hat with the gold-green macaw wing in its accustomed place.

He who has been denied the spectacle of a busy Manhattan broker during a rush of business is handicapped for the profession of anthropology. The poet sings of the "crowded hour of glorious life." The broker's hour is not only crowded, but the minutes and seconds are hanging to all the straps and packing both front and rear platforms.

And this day was Harvey Maxwell's busy day. The ticker began to reel out jerkily its fitful coils of tape, the desk telephone had a chronic attack of buzzing. Men began to throng into the office and call at him over the railing, jovially, sharply, viciously, excitedly. Messenger boys ran in and out with messages and telegrams. The clerks in the office jumped about like sailors during a storm. Even Pitcher's face relaxed into something resembling animation.

On the Exchange there were hurricanes and landslides and snowstorms and glaciers and volcanoes, and those elemental disturbances were reproduced in miniature in the broker's offices. Maxwell shoved his chair against the wall and transacted business after the manner of a toe dancer. He jumped from ticker to 'phone, from desk to door with the trained agility of a harlequin.

In the midst of this growing and important stress the broker became suddenly aware of a high-rolled fringe of golden hair under a nodding canopy of velvet and ostrich tips, an imitation sealskin sacque and a string of beads as large as hickory nuts, ending near the floor with a silver heart. There was a self-possessed young lady connected with these accessories; and Pitcher was there to construe her.

"Lady from the Stenographer's Agency to see about the position," said Pitcher.

Maxwell turned half around, with his hands full of papers and ticker tape. "What position?" he asked, with a frown.

"Position of stenographer," said Pitcher. "You told me yesterday to call them up and have one sent over this morning."

"You are losing your mind, Pitcher," said Maxwell. "Why should I have given you any such instructions? Miss Leslie has given perfect satisfaction during the year she has been here. The place is hers as long as she chooses to retain it. There's no place open here, madam. Countermand that order with the agency, Pitcher, and don't bring any more of 'em in here."

The silver heart left the office, swinging and banging itself independently against the office furniture as it indignantly departed. Pitcher seized a moment to remark to the bookkeeper that the "old man" seemed to get more absent-minded and forgetful every day of the world.

The rush and pace of business grew fiercer and faster. On the floor they were pounding half a dozen stocks in which Maxwell's customers were heavy investors. Orders to buy and sell were coming and going as swift as the flight of swallows. Some of his own holdings were imperilled, and the man was working like some high-geared, delicate, strong machine—strung to full tension, going at full speed, accurate, never hesitating, with the proper word and decision and act ready and prompt as clockwork. Stocks and bonds, loans and mortgages, margins and securities—here was a world of finance, and there was no room in it for the human world or the world of nature.

When the luncheon hour drew near there came a slight lull in the uproar.

Maxwell stood by his desk with his hands full of telegrams and memoranda, with a fountain pen over his right ear and his hair hanging in disorderly strings over his forehead. His window was open, for the beloved janitress Spring had turned on a little warmth through the waking registers of the earth.

And through the window came a wandering—perhaps a lost—odor—a delicate, sweet odor of lilac that fixed the broker for a moment immovable. For this odor belonged to Miss Leslie; it was her own, and hers only.

The odor brought her vividly, almost tangibly before him. The world of finance dwindled suddenly to a speck. And she was in the next room—twenty steps away.

"By George, I'll do it now," said Maxwell, half aloud. "I'll ask her now. I wonder I didn't do it long ago."

He dashed into the inner office with the haste of a short trying to cover. He charged upon the desk of the stenographer.

She looked up at him with a smile. A soft pink crept over her cheek, and her eyes were kind and frank. Maxwell leaned one elbow on her desk. He still clutched fluttering papers with both hands and the pen was above his ear.

"Miss Leslie," he began, hurriedly, "I have but a moment to spare. I want to say something in that moment. Will you be my wife? I haven't had time to make love to you in the ordinary way, but I really do love you. Talk quick, please—those fellows are clubbing the stuffing out of Union Pacific."

"Oh, what are you talking about?" exclaimed the young lady. She rose to her feet and gazed upon him, round-eyed.

"Don't you understand?" said Maxwell, restively. "I want you to marry me. I love you, Miss Leslie. I wanted to tell you, and I snatched a minute when things had slackened up a bit. They're calling me for the 'phone now. Tell 'em to wait a minute, Pitcher. Won't you, Miss Leslie?"

The stenographer acted very queerly. At first she seemed overcome with amazement; then tears flowed from her wondering eyes; and then she smiled sunnily through them, and one of her arms slid tenderly about the broker's neck.

"I know now," she said, softly. "It's this old business that has driven everything else out of your head for the time. I was frightened at first. Don't you remember, Harvey? We were married last evening at 8 o'clock in the Little Church around the Corner."

AFTER TWENTY YEARS

THE policeman on the beat moved up the avenue impressively. The impressiveness was habitual and not for show, for spectators were few. The time was barely 10 o'clock at night, but chilly gusts of wind with a taste of rain in them had well nigh depeopled the streets.

Trying doors as he went, twirling his club with many intricate and artful movements, turning now and then to cast his watchful eye adown the pacific thoroughfare, the officer, with his stalwart form and slight swagger, made a fine picture of a guardian of the peace. The vicinity was one that kept early hours. Now and then you might see the lights of a cigar store or of an all-night lunch counter; but the majority of the doors belonged to business places that had long since been closed.

When about midway of a certain block the policeman suddenly slowed his walk. In the doorway of a darkened hardware store a man leaned, with an un-lighted cigar in his mouth. As the policeman walked up to him the man spoke up quickly.

"It's all right, officer," he said, reassuringly. "I'm just waiting for a friend. It's an appointment made twenty years ago. Sounds a little funny to you, doesn't it? Well, I'll explain if you'd like to make certain it's all straight. About that long ago there used to be a restaurant where this store stands—'Big Joe' Brady's restaurant."

"Until five years ago," said the policeman. "It was torn down then."

The man in the doorway struck a match and lit his cigar. The light showed a pale, square-jawed face with keen eyes, and a little white scar near his right eyebrow. His scarfpin was a large diamond, oddly set.

"Twenty years ago to-night," said the man, "I dined here at 'Big Joe' Brady's with Jimmy Wells, my best chum, and the finest chap in the world. He and I were raised here in New York, just like two brothers, together. I was eighteen and Jimmy was twenty. The next morning I was to start for the West to make my fortune. You couldn't have dragged Jimmy out of New York; he thought it was the only place on earth. Well, we agreed that night that we would meet here again exactly twenty years from that date and time, no matter what our conditions might be or from what distance we might have to come. We figured that in twenty years each of us ought to have our destiny worked out and our fortunes made, whatever they were going to be."

"It sounds pretty interesting," said the policeman. "Rather a long time be-tween meets, though, it seems to me. Haven't you heard from your friend since you left?"

"Well, yes, for a time we corresponded," said the other. "But after a year or two we lost track of each other. You see, the West is a pretty big proposition, and I kept hustling around over it pretty lively. But I know Jimmy will meet me here if he's alive, for he always was the truest, stanchest old chap in the world. He'll never forget. I came a thousand miles to stand in this door to-night, and it's worth it if my old partner turns up."

The waiting man pulled out a handsome watch, the lids of it set with small diamonds.

"Three minutes to ten," he announced. "It was exactly ten o'clock when we parted here at the restaurant door."

"Did pretty well out West, didn't you?" asked the policeman.

"You bet! I hope Jimmy has done half as well. He was a kind of plodder, though, good fellow as he was. I've had to compete with some of the sharpest wits going to get my pile. A man gets in a groove in New York. It takes the West to put a razor-edge on him."

The policeman twirled his club and took a step or two.

"I'll be on my way. Hope your friend comes around all right. Going to call time on him sharp?"

"I should say not!" said the other. "I'll give him half an hour at least. If Jimmy is alive on earth he'll be here by that time. So long, officer."

"Good-night, sir," said the policeman, passing on along his beat, trying doors as he went.

There was now a fine, cold drizzle falling, and the wind had risen from its uncertain puffs into a steady blow. The few foot passengers astir in that quarter hurried dismally and silently along with coat collars turned high and pocketed hands. And in the door of the hardware store the man who had come a thousand miles to fill an appointment, uncertain almost to absurdity, with the friend of his youth, smoked his cigar and waited.

About twenty minutes he waited, and then a tall man in a long overcoat, with collar turned up to his ears, hurried across from the opposite side of the street. He went directly to the waiting man.

"Is that you, Bob?" he asked, doubtfully.

"Is that you, Jimmy Wells?" cried the man in the door.

"Bless my heart!" exclaimed the new arrival, grasping both the other's hands with his own. "It's Bob, sure as fate. I was certain I'd find you here if you were still in existence. Well, well, well!—twenty years is a long time. The old restaurant's gone, Bob; I wish it had lasted, so we could have had another dinner there. How has the West treated you, old man?"

"Bully; it has given me everything I asked it for. You've changed lots, Jimmy. I never thought you were so tall by two or three inches."

"Oh, I grew a bit after I was twenty."

"Doing well in New York, Jimmy?"

"Moderately. I have a position in one of the city departments. Come on, Bob; we'll go around to a place I know of, and have a good long talk about old times."

The two men started up the street, arm in arm. The man from the West, his egotism enlarged by success, was beginning to outline the history of his career. The other, submerged in his overcoat, listened with interest.

At the corner stood a drug store, brilliant with electric lights. When they came into this glare each of them turned simultaneously to gaze upon the other's face.

The man from the West stopped suddenly and released his arm.

"You're not Jimmy Wells," he snapped. "Twenty years is a long time, but not long enough to change a man's nose from a Roman to a pug."

"It sometimes changes a good man into a bad one," said the tall man. "You've been under arrest for ten minutes, 'Silky' Bob. Chicago thinks you may have dropped over our way and wires us she wants to have a chat with you. Going quietly, are you? That's sensible. Now, before we go to the station here's a note I was asked to hand you. You may read it here at the window. It's from Patrolman Wells."

The man from the West unfolded the little piece of paper handed him. His hand was steady when he began to read, but it trembled a little by the time he had finished. The note was rather short.

Bob: I was at the appointed place on time. When you struck the match to light your cigar I saw it was the face of the man wanted in Chicago. Somehow I couldn't do it myself, so I went around and got a plain clothes man to do the job.

JIMMY.

LOST ON DRESS PARADE

Mr. Towers Chandler was pressing his evening suit in his hall bedroom. One iron was heating on a small gas stove; the other was being pushed vigorously back and forth to make the desirable crease that would be seen later on extending in straight lines from Mr. Chandler's patent leather shoes to the edge of his low-cut vest. So much of the hero's toilet may be intrusted to our confidence. The remainder may be guessed by those whom genteel poverty has driven to ignoble expedient. Our next view of him shall be as he descends the steps of his lodging-house immaculately and correctly clothed; calm, assured, handsome—in appearance the typical New York young clubman setting out, slightly bored, to inaugurate the pleasures of the evening.

Chandler's honorarium was $18 per week. He was employed in the office of an architect. He was twenty-two years old; he considered architecture to be truly an art; and he honestly believed—though he would not have dared to admit it in New York—that the Flatiron Building was inferior in design to the great cathedral in Milan.

Out of each week's earnings Chandler set aside $1. At the end of each ten weeks with the extra capital thus accumulated, he purchased one gentleman's evening from the bargain counter of stingy old Father Time. He arrayed himself in the regalia of millionaires and presidents; he took himself to the quarter where life is brightest and showiest, and there dined with taste and luxury. With ten dollars a man may, for a few hours, play the wealthy idler to perfection. The sum is ample for a well-considered meal, a bottle bearing a respectable label, commensurate tips, a smoke, cab fare, and the ordinary etceteras.

This one delectable evening culled from each dull seventy was to Chandler a source of renascent bliss. To the society bud comes but one début; it stands alone sweet in her memory when her hair was whitened; but to Chandler each ten weeks brought a joy as keen, as thrilling, as new as the first had been. To sit among *bon vivants* under palms in the swirl of concealed music, to look upon the *habitués* of such a paradise and to be looked upon by them—what is a girl's first dance and short-sleeved tulle compared with this?

Up Broadway Chandler moved with the vespertine dress parade. For this evening he was an exhibit as well as a gazer. For the next sixty-nine evenings he would be dining in cheviot and worsted at dubious *table d'hôtes*, at whirlwind lunch counters, on sandwiches and beer in his hall bedroom. He was willing to do that, for he was a true son of the great city of razzle-dazzle, and to him one evening in the limelight made up for many dark ones.

Chandler protracted his walk until the Forties began to intersect the great and glittering primrose way, for the evening was yet young, and when one is of the *beau monde* only one day in seventy, one loves to protract the pleasure. Eyes bright, sinister, curious, admiring, provocative, alluring were bent upon him, for his garb and air proclaimed him a devotee to the hour of solace and pleasure.

At a certain corner he came to a standstill, proposing to himself the question of turning back toward the showy and fashionable restaurant in which he usually dined on the evenings of his especial luxury. Just then a girl scuddled lightly around the corner, slipped on a patch of icy snow and fell plump upon the sidewalk.

Chandler assisted her to her feet with instant and solicitous courtesy. The girl hobbled to the wall of the building, leaned against it, and thanked him demurely.

"I think my ankle is strained," she said. "It twisted when I fell."

"Does it pain you much?" inquired Chandler.

"Only when I rest my weight upon it. I think I will be able to walk in a minute or two."

"If I can be of any further service," suggested the young man, "I will call a cab, or——"

"Thank you," said the girl, softly but heartily. "I am sure you need not trouble yourself any further. It was so awkward of me. And my shoe heels are horridly commonsense; I can't blame them at all."

Chandler looked at the girl and found her swiftly drawing his interest. She was pretty in a refined way; and her eye was both merry and kind. She was inexpensively clothed in a plain black dress that suggested a sort of uniform such as shop-girls wear. Her glossy dark-brown hair showed its coils beneath a cheap hat of black straw whose only ornament was a velvet ribbon and bow. She could have posed as a model for the self-respecting working girl of the best type.

A sudden idea came into the head of the young architect. He would ask this girl to dine with him. Here was the element that his splendid but solitary periodic feats had lacked. His brief season of elegant luxury would be doubly enjoyable if he could add to it a lady's society. This girl was a lady, he was sure—her manner and speech settled that. And in spite of her extremely plain attire he felt that he would be pleased to sit at table with her.

These thoughts passed swiftly through his mind, and he decided to ask her. It was a breach of etiquette, of course, but oftentimes wage-earning girls waived formalities in matters of this kind. They were generally shrewd judges of men; and thought better of their own judgment than they did of useless conventions. His ten dollars, discreetly expended, would enable the two to dine very well indeed. The dinner would no doubt be a wonderful experience thrown into the dull routine of the girl's life; and her lively appreciation of it would add to his own triumph and pleasure.

"I think," he said to her, with frank gravity, "that your foot needs a longer rest than you suppose. Now, I am going to suggest a way in which you can give it that and at the same time do me a favor. I was on my way to dine all by my lonely self when you came tumbling around the corner. You come with me and we'll have a cozy dinner and a pleasant talk together, and by that time your game ankle will carry you home very nicely, I am sure."

The girl looked quickly up into Chandler's clear, pleasant countenance. Her eyes twinkled once very brightly, and then she smiled ingenuously.

"But we don't know each other—it wouldn't be right, would it?" she said, doubtfully.

"There is nothing wrong about it," said the young man, candidly. "I'll introduce myself—permit me—Mr. Towers Chandler. After our dinner, which I will try to make as pleasant as possible, I will bid you good-evening, or attend you safely to your door, whichever you prefer."

"But, dear me!" said the girl, with a glance at Chandler's faultless attire. "In this old dress and hat!"

"Never mind that," said Chandler, cheerfully. "I'm sure you look more charming in them than any one we shall see in the most elaborate dinner toilette."

"My ankle does hurt yet," admitted the girl, attempting a limping step. "I think I will accept your invitation, Mr. Chandler. You may call me—Miss Marian."

"Come then, Miss Marian," said the young architect, gaily, but with perfect courtesy; "you will not have far to walk. There is a very respectable and good restaurant in the next block. You will have to lean on my arm—so—and walk slowly. It is lonely dining all by one's self. I'm just a little bit glad that you slipped on the ice."

When the two were established at a well-appointed table, with a promising waiter hovering in attendance, Chandler began to experience the real joy that his regular outing always brought to him.

The restaurant was not so showy or pretentious as the one further down Broadway, which he always preferred, but it was nearly so. The tables were well filled with prosperous-looking diners, there was a good orchestra, playing softly enough to make conversation a possible pleasure, and the cuisine and service were beyond criticism. His companion, even in her cheap hat and dress, held herself with an air that added distinction to the natural beauty of her face and figure.

And it is certain that she looked at Chandler, with his animated but self-possessed manner and his kindling and frank blue eyes, with something not far from admiration in her own charming face.

Then it was that the Madness of Manhattan, the Frenzy of Fuss and Feathers, the Bacillus of Brag, the Provincial Plague of Pose seized upon Towers Chandler. He was on Broadway, surrounded by pomp and style, and there were eyes to look at him. On the stage of that comedy he had assumed to play the one-night part of a butterfly of fashion and an idler of means and taste. He was dressed for the part, and all his good angels had not the power to prevent him from acting it.

So he began to prate to Miss Marian of clubs, of teas, of golf and riding and kennels and cotillions and tours abroad and threw out hints of a yacht lying at Larchmont. He could see that she was vastly impressed by this vague talk, so he endorsed his pose by random insinuations concerning great wealth, and mentioned familiarly a few names that are handled reverently by the proletariat. It was Chandler's short little day, and he was wringing from it the best that could be had, as he saw it. And yet once or twice he saw the pure gold of this girl shine through the mist that his egotism had raised between him and all objects.

"This way of living that you speak of," she said, "sounds so futile and purposeless. Haven't you any work to do in the world that might interest you more?"

"My dear Miss Marian," he exclaimed—"work! Think of dressing every day for dinner, of making half a dozen calls in an afternoon—with a policeman at every corner ready to jump into your auto and take you to the station, if you get up any greater speed than a donkey cart's gait. We do-nothings are the hardest workers in the land."

The dinner was concluded, the waiter generously fed, and the two walked out to the corner where they had met. Miss Marian walked very well now; her limp was scarcely noticeable.

"Thank you for a nice time," she said, frankly. "I must run home now. I liked the dinner very much, Mr. Chandler."

He shook hands with her, smiling cordially, and said something about a game of bridge at his club. He watched her for a moment, walking rather rapidly eastward, and then he found a cab to drive him slowly homeward.

In his chilly bedroom Chandler laid away his evening clothes for a sixty-nine days' rest. He went about it thoughtfully.

"That was a stunning girl," he said to himself. "She's all right, too, I'd be sworn, even if she does have to work. Perhaps if I'd told her the truth instead of all that razzle-dazzle we might—but, confound it! I had to play up to my clothes."

Thus spoke the brave who was born and reared in the wigwams of the tribe of the Manhattans.

The girl, after leaving her entertainer, sped swiftly cross-town until she arrived at a handsome and sedate mansion two squares to the east, facing on that avenue which is the highway of Mammon and the auxiliary gods. Here she entered hurriedly and ascended to a room where a handsome young lady in an elaborate house dress was looking anxiously out the window.

"Oh, you madcap!" exclaimed the elder girl, when the other entered. "When will you quit frightening us this way? It's two hours since you ran out in that rag of an old dress and Marie's hat. Mamma has been so alarmed. She sent Louis in the auto to try to find you. You are a bad, thoughtless Puss."

The elder girl touched a button, and a maid came in a moment.

"Marie, tell mamma that Miss Marian has returned."

"Don't scold, Sister. I only ran down to Mme. Theo's to tell her to use mauve insertion instead of pink. My costume and Marie's hat were just what I needed. Every one thought I was a shop-girl, I am sure."

"Dinner is over, dear; you stayed so late."

"I know. I slipped on the sidewalk and turned my ankle. I could not walk, so I hobbled into a restaurant and sat there until I was better. That is why I was so long."

The two girls sat in the window seat, looking out at the lights and the stream of hurrying vehicles in the avenue. The younger one cuddled down with her head in her sister's lap.

"We will have to marry some day," she said, dreamily—"both of us. We have so much money that we will not be allowed to disappoint the public. Do you want me to tell you the kind of a man I could love, Sis?"

"Go on, you scatterbrain," smiled the other.

"I could love a man with dark and kind blue eyes, who is gentle and respectful to poor girls, who is handsome and good and does not try to flirt. But I could love him only if he had an ambition, an object, some work to do in the world. I would not care how poor he was if I could help him build his way up. But, Sister dear, the kind of man we always meet—the man who lives an idle life between society and his clubs—I could not love a man like that, even if his eyes were blue and he were so kind to poor girls whom he met in the street."

BY COURIER

It was neither the season nor the hour when the Park had frequenters; and it is likely that the young lady, who was seated on one of the benches at the side of the walk, had merely obeyed a sudden impulse to sit for a while and enjoy a foretaste of coming Spring.

She rested there, pensive and still. A certain melancholy that touched her countenance must have been of recent birth, for it had not yet altered the fine and youthful contours of her cheek, nor subdued the arch though resolute curve of her lips.

A tall young man came striding through the park along the path near which she sat. Behind him tagged a boy carrying a suit-case. At sight of the young lady, the man's face changed to red and back to pale again. He watched her countenance as he drew nearer, with hope and anxiety mingled on his own. He passed within a few yards of her, but he saw no evidence that she was aware of his presence or existence.

Some fifty yards further on he suddenly stopped and sat on a bench at one side. The boy dropped the suit-case and stared at him with wondering, shrewd eyes. The young man took out his handkerchief and wiped his brow. It was a good handkerchief, a good brow, and the young man was good to look at. He said to the boy:

"I want you to take a message to that young lady on that bench. Tell her I am on my way to the station, to leave for San Francisco, where I shall join that Alaska moose-hunting expedition. Tell her that, since she has commanded me neither to speak nor to write to her, I take this means of making one last appeal to her sense of justice, for the sake of what has been. Tell her that to condemn and discard one who has not deserved such treatment, without giving him her reasons or a chance to explain is contrary to her nature as I believe it to be. Tell her that I have thus, to a certain degree, disobeyed her injunctions, in the hope that she may yet be inclined to see justice done. Go, and tell her that."

The young man dropped a half-dollar into the boy's hand. The boy looked at him for a moment with bright, canny eyes out of a dirty, intelligent face, and then set off at a run. He approached the lady on the bench a little doubtfully, but unembarrassed. He touched the brim of an old plaid bicycle cap perched on the back of his head. The lady looked at him coolly, without prejudice or favor.

"Lady," he said, "dat gent on de oder bench sent yer a song and dance by me. If yer don't know de guy, and he's tryin' to do de Johnny act, say de word, and I'll call a cop in t'ree minutes. If yer does know him, and he's on de square, w'y I'll spiel yer de bunch of hot air he sent yer."

The young lady betrayed a faint interest.

"A song and dance!" she said, in a deliberate, sweet voice that seemed to clothe her words in a diaphanous garment of impalpable irony. "A new idea—in the troubadour line, I suppose. I—used to know the gentleman who sent you so I think it will hardly be necessary to call the police. You may execute your song and dance, but do not sing too loudly. It is a little early yet for open-air vaudeville, and we might attract attention."

"Awe," said the boy, with a shrug down the length of him, "yer know what I mean, lady. 'Tain't a turn, it's wind. He told me to tell yer he's got his collars and cuffs in dat grip for a scoot clean out to 'Frisco. Den he's goin' to shoot snow-birds in de Klondike. He says yer told him not to send 'round no more pink notes nor come hangin' over de garden gate, and he takes dis means of puttin' yer wise. He says yer refereed him out like a has-been, and never give him no chance to kick at de decision. He says yer swiped him, and never said why."

The slightly awakened interest in the young lady's eyes did not abate. Perhaps it was caused by either the originality or the audacity of the snow-bird hunter, in thus circumventing her express commands against the ordinary modes of communication. She fixed her eye on a statue standing disconsolate in the dishevelled park, and spoke into the transmitter:

"Tell the gentleman that I need not repeat to him a description of my ideals. He knows what they have been and what they still are. So far as they touch on this case, absolute loyalty and truth are the ones paramount. Tell him that I have studied my own heart as well as one can, and I know its weakness as well as I do its needs. That is why I decline to hear his pleas, whatever they may be. I did not condemn him through hearsay or doubtful evidence, and that is why I made no charge. But, since he persists in hearing what he already well knows, you may convey the matter.

"Tell him that I entered the conservatory that evening from the rear, to cut a rose for my mother. Tell him I saw him and Miss Ashburton beneath the pink oleander. The tableau was pretty, but the pose and juxtaposition were too eloquent and evident to require explanation. I left the conservatory, and, at the same time, the rose and my ideal. You may carry that song and dance to your impresario."

"I'm shy on one word, lady. Jux—jux—put me wise on dat, will yer?"

"Juxtaposition—or you may call it propinquity—or, if you like, being rather too near for one maintaining the position of an ideal."

The gravel spun from beneath the boy's feet. He stood by the other bench. The man's eyes interrogated him, hungrily. The boy's were shining with the impersonal zeal of the translator.

"De lady says dat she's on to de fact dat gals is dead easy when a feller come spielin' ghost stories and tryin' to make up, and dat's why she won't listen to no soft-soap. She says she caught yer dead to rights, huggin' a bunch o' calico in de hot-house. She side-stepped in to pull some posies and yer was squeezin' der oder gal to beat de band. She says it looked cute, all right all right, but it made her sick. She says yer better git busy, and make a sneak for de train."

The young man gave a low whistle and his eyes flashed with a sudden thought. His hand flew to the inside pocket of his coat, and drew out a handful of letters. Selecting one, he handed it to the boy, following it with a silver dollar from his vest-pocket.

"Give that letter to the lady," he said, "and ask her to read it. Tell her that it should explain the situation. Tell her that, if she had mingled a little trust with her conception of the ideal, much heartache might have been avoided. Tell her that loyalty she prizes so much has never wavered. Tell her I am waiting for an answer."

The messenger stood before the lady.

"De gent says he's had de ski-bunk put on him widout no cause. He says he's no bum guy; and, lady, yer read dat letter, and I'll bet yer he's a white sport, all right."

The young lady unfolded the letter, somewhat doubtfully, and read it.

DEAR DR. ARNOLD: I want to thank you for your most kind and opportune aid to my daughter last Friday evening, when she was overcome by an attack of her old heart-trouble in the conservatory at Mrs. Waldron's reception. Had you not been near to catch her as she fell and to render proper attention, we might have lost her. I would be glad if you would call and undertake the treatment of her case.

Gratefully yours,
ROBERT ASHBURTON.

The young lady refolded the letter, and handed it to the boy.

"De gent wants an answer," said the messenger. "What's de word?"

The lady's eyes suddenly flashed on him, bright, smiling, and wet.

"Tell that guy on the other bench," she said, with a happy, tremulous laugh, "that his girl wants him."

THE FURNISHED ROOM

RESTLESS, shifting, fugacious as time itself is a certain vast bulk of the population of the red brick district of the lower West Side. Homeless, they have a hundred homes. They flit from furnished room to furnished room, transients forever—transients in abode, transients in heart and mind. They sing "Home, Sweet Home" in ragtime; they carry their *lares et penates* in a bandbox; their vine is entwined about a picture hat; a rubber plant is their fig tree.

Hence the houses of this district, having had a thousand dwellers, should have a thousand tales to tell, mostly dull ones, no doubt; but it would be strange if there could not be found a ghost or two in the wake of all these vagrant guests.

One evening after dark a young man prowled among these crumbling red mansions, ringing their bells. At the twelfth he rested his lean hand-baggage upon the step and wiped the dust from his hatband and forehead. The bell sounded faint and far away in some remote, hollow depths.

To the door of this, the twelfth house whose bell he had rung, came a housekeeper who made him think of an unwholesome, surfeited worm that had eaten its nut to a hollow shell and now sought to fill the vacancy with edible lodgers.

He asked if there was a room to let.

"Come in," said the housekeeper. Her voice came from her throat; her throat seemed lined with fur. "I have the third-floor back, vacant since a week back. Should you wish to look at it?"

The young man followed her up the stairs. A faint light from no particular source mitigated the shadows of the halls. They trod noiselessly upon a stair carpet that its own loom would have forsworn. It seemed to have become vegetable; to have degenerated in that rank, sunless air to lush lichen or spreading moss that grew in patches to the stair-case and was viscid under the foot like organic matter. At each turn of the stairs were vacant niches in the wall. Perhaps plants had once been set within them. If so they had died in that foul and tainted air. It may be that statues of the saints had stood there, but it was not difficult to conceive that imps and devils had dragged them forth in the darkness and down to the unholy depths of some furnished pit below.

"This is the room," said the housekeeper, from her furry throat. "It's a nice room. It ain't often vacant. I had some most elegant people in it last summer—no trouble at all, and paid in advance to the minute. The water's at the end of the hall. Sprowls and Mooney kept it three months. They done a vaudeville sketch. Miss B'retta Sprowls—you may have heard of her—Oh, that was just the stage names—right there over the dresser is where the marriage certificate hung, framed. The gas is here, and you see there is plenty of closet room. It's a room everybody likes. It never stays idle long."

"Do you have many theatrical people rooming here?" asked the young man.

"They comes and goes. A good proportion of my lodgers is connected with the theatres. Yes, sir, this is the theatrical district. Actor people never stays long anywhere. I get my share. Yes, they comes and they goes."

He engaged the room, paying for a week in advance. He was tired, he said, and would take possession at once. He counted out the money. The room had been made ready, she said, even to towels and water. As the housekeeper moved away he put, for the thousandth time, the question that he carried at the end of his tongue.

"A young girl—Miss Vashner—Miss Eloise Vashner—do you remember such a one among your lodgers? She would be singing on the stage, most likely. A fair girl, of medium height and slender, with reddish, gold hair and dark mole near her left eyebrow."

"No, I don't remember the name. Them stage people has names they change as often as their rooms. They comes and they goes. No, I don't call that one to mind."

No. Always no. Five months of ceaseless interrogation and the inevitable negative. So much time spent by days in questioning managers, agents, schools and choruses; by night among the audiences of theatres from all-star casts down to music halls so low that he dreaded to find what he most hoped for. He who had loved her best had tried to find her. He was sure that since her disappearance from home this great, water-girt city held her somewhere, but it was like a monstrous quicksand, shifting its particles constantly, with no foundation, its upper granules of to-day buried to-morrow in ooze and slime.

The furnished room received its latest guest with a first glow of pseudo-hospitality, a hectic, haggard, perfunctory welcome like the specious smile of a demirep. The sophistical comfort came in reflected gleams from the decayed furniture, the ragged brocade upholstery of a couch and two chairs, a foot-wide cheap pier glass between the two windows, from one or two gilt picture frames and a brass bedstead in a corner.

The guest reclined, inert, upon a chair, while the room, confused in speech as though it were an apartment in Babel, tried to discourse to him of its divers tenantry.

A polychromatic rug like some brilliant-flowered rectangular, tropical islet lay surrounded by a billowy sea of soiled matting. Upon the gay-papered wall were those pictures that pursue the homeless one from house to house—The Huguenot Lovers, The First Quarrel, The Wedding Breakfast, Psyche at the Fountain. The mantel's chastely severe outline was ingloriously veiled behind some pert drapery drawn rakishly askew like the sashes of the Amazonian ballet. Upon it was some desolate flotsam cast aside by the room's marooned when a lucky sail had borne them to a fresh port—a trifling vase or two, pictures of actresses, a medicine bottle, some stray cards out of a deck.

One by one, as the characters of a cryptograph became explicit, the little signs left by the furnished room's procession of guests developed a significance. The threadbare space in the rug in front of the dresser told that lovely woman had marched in the throng. The tiny fingerprints on the wall spoke of little prisoners trying to feel their way to sun and air. A splattered stain, raying like the shadow of a bursting bomb, witnessed where a hurled glass or bottle had splintered with its contents against the wall. Across the pier glass had been scrawled with a diamond in staggering letters the name "Marie." It seemed that the succession of dwellers in the furnished room had turned in fury—perhaps tempted beyond forebearance by its garish coldness—and wreaked upon it their passions. The furniture was chipped and bruised; the couch, distorted by bursting springs, seemed a horrible monster that had been slain during the stress of some grotesque convulsion. Some more potent upheaval had cloven a great slice from the marble mantel. Each plank in the floor owned its particular cant and shriek as from a separate and individual agony. It seemed incredible that all this malice and injury had been wrought upon the room by those who had called it for a time their home; and yet it may have been the cheated home instinct surviving blindly, the resentful rage at false household gods that had kindled their wrath. A hut that is our own we can sweep and adorn and cherish.

The young tenant in the chair allowed these thoughts to file, soft-shod, through his mind, while there drifted into the room furnished sounds and furnished scents. He heard in one room a tittering and incontinent, slack laughter; in others the monologue of a scold, the rattling of dice, a lullaby, and one crying dully; above him a banjo tinkled with spirit. Doors banged somewhere; the elevated trains roared intermittently; a cat yowled miserably upon a back fence. And he breathed the breath of the house—a dank savor rather than a smell—a cold, musty effluvium as from underground vaults mingled with the reeking exhalations of linoleum and mildewed and rotten woodwork.

Then suddenly, as he rested there, the room was filled with the strong, sweet odor of mignonette. It came as upon a single buffet of wind with such sureness and fragrance and emphasis that it almost seemed a living visitant. And the man cried aloud: "What, dear?" as if he had been called, and sprang up and faced about. The rich odor clung to him and wrapped him around. He reached out his arms for it, all his senses for the time confused and commingled. How could one be peremptorily called by an odor? Surely it must have been a sound. But, was it not the sound that had touched, that had caressed him?

"She has been in this room," he cried, and he sprang to wrest from it a token, for he knew he would recognize the smallest thing that had belonged to her or that she had touched. This enveloping scent of mignonette, the odor that she had loved and made her own—whence came it?

The room had been but carelessly set in order. Scattered upon the flimsy dresser scarf were half a dozen hairpins—those discreet, indistinguishable friends of womankind, feminine of gender, infinite mood and uncommunicative of tense. These he ignored, conscious of their triumphant lack of identity. Ransacking the drawers of the dresser he came upon a discarded, tiny, ragged handkerchief. He pressed it to his face. It was racy and insolent with heliotrope; he hurled it to the floor. In another drawer he found odd buttons, a theatre programme, a pawnbroker's card, two lost marshmallows, a book on the divination of dreams. In the last was a woman's black satin hair bow, which halted him, poised between ice and fire. But the black satin hair bow also is femininity's demure, impersonal common ornament and tells no tales.

And then he traversed the room like a hound on the scent, skimming the walls, considering the corners of the bulging matting on his hands and knees, rummaging mantel and tables, the curtains and hangings, the drunken cabinet in the corner, for a visible sign, unable to perceive that she was there beside, around, against, within, above him, clinging to him, wooing him, calling him so poignantly through the finer senses that even his grosser ones became cognizant of the call. Once again he answered loudly: Yes, dear!" and turned, wild-eyed, to gaze on vacancy, for he could not yet discern form and color and love and outstretched arms in the odor of mignonette. Oh, God! whence that odor, and since when have odors had a voice to call? Thus he groped.

He burrowed in crevices and corners, and found corks and cigarettes. These he passed in passive contempt. But once he found in a fold of the matting a half-smoked cigar, and this he ground beneath his heel with a green and trenchant oath. He sifted the room from end to end. He found dreary and ignoble small records of many a peripatetic tenant; but of her whom he sought, and who may have lodged there, and whose spirit seemed to hover there, he found no trace.

And then he thought of the housekeeper.

He ran from the haunted room downstairs and to a door that showed a crack of light. She came out to his knock. He smothered his excitement as best he could.

"Will you tell me, madam," he besought her, "who occupied the room I have before I came?"

"Yes, sir. I can tell you again. 'Twas Sprowls and Mooney, as I said. Miss B'retta Sprowls it was in the theatres, but Missis Mooney she was. My house is well known for respectability. The marriage certificate hung, framed, on a nail over——"

"What kind of a lady was Miss Sprowls—in looks, I mean?"

"Why, black-haired, sir, short, and stout, with a comical face. They left a week ago Tuesday."

"And before they occupied it?"

"Why, there was a single gentleman connected with the draying business. He left owing me a week. Before him was Missis Crowder and her two children, that stayed four months; and back of them was old Mr. Doyle, whose sons paid for him. He kept the room six months. That goes back a year, sir, and further I do not remember."

He thanked her and crept back to his room. The room was dead. The essence that had vivified it was gone. The perfume of mignonette had departed. In its place was the old, stale odor of mouldy house furniture, of atmosphere in storage.

The ebbing of his hope drained his faith. He sat staring at the yellow, singing gaslight. Soon he walked to the bed and began to tear the sheets into strips. With the blade of his knife he drove them tightly into every crevice around windows and door. When all was snug and taut he turned out the light, turned the gas full on again and laid himself gratefully upon the bed.

.   .   .   .

It was Mrs. McCool's night to go with the can for beer. So she fetched it and sat with Mrs. Purdy in one of those subterranean retreats where housekeepers foregather and the worm dieth seldom.

"I rented out my third-floor-back this evening," said Mrs. Purdy, across a fine circle of foam. "A young man took it. He went up to bed two hours ago."

"Now, did ye, Mrs. Purdy, ma'am?" said Mrs. McCool, with intense admiration. "You do be a wonder for rentin' rooms of that kind. And did ye tell him, then?" she concluded in a husky whisper laden with mystery.

"Rooms," said Mrs. Purdy, in her furriest tones, "are furnished for to rent. I did not tell him, Mrs. McCool."

"'Tis right ye are, ma'am; 'tis by renting rooms we kape alive. Ye have the rale sense for business, ma'am. There be many people will rayjict the rentin' of a room if they be tould a suicide has been after dyin' in the bed of it."

"As you say, we has our living to be making," remarked Mrs. Purdy.

"Yis, ma'am; 'tis true. 'Tis just one wake ago this day I helped ye lay out the third-floor-back. A pretty slip of a colleen she was to be killin' herself wid the gas—a swate little face she had, Mrs. Purdy, ma'am."

"She'd a-been called handsome, as you say," said Mrs. Purdy, assenting but critical, "but for that mole she had a-growin' by her left eyebrow. Do fill up your glass again, Mrs. McCool."

THE BRIEF DÉBUT OF TILDY

IF you do not know Bogle's Chop House and Family Restaurant it is your loss. For if you are one of the fortunate ones who dine expensively you should be interested to know how the other half consumes provisions. And if you belong to the half to whom waiters' checks are things of moment, you should know Bogle's, for there you get your money's worth—in quantity, at least.

Bogle's is situated in that highway of *bourgeoisie*, that boulevard of Brown-Jones-and-Robinson, Eighth Avenue. There are two rows of tables in the room, six in each row. On each table is a caster-stand, containing cruets of condiments and seasons. From the pepper cruet you may shake a cloud of something tasteless and melancholy, like volcanic dust. From the salt cruet you may expect nothing. Though a man should extract a sanguinary stream from the pallid turnip, yet will his prowess be balked when he comes to wrest salt from Bogle's cruets. Also upon each table stands the counterfeit of that benign sauce made "from the recipe of a nobleman in India."

At the cashier's desk sits Bogle, cold, sordid, slow, smouldering, and takes your money. Behind a mountain of toothpicks he makes your change, files your check, and ejects at you, like a toad, a word about the weather. Beyond a corroboration of his meteorological statement you would better not venture. You are not Bogle's friend; you are a fed, transient customer, and you and he may not meet again until the blowing of Gabriel's dinner horn. So take your change and go—to the devil if you like. There you have Bogle's sentiments.

The needs of Bogle's customers were supplied by two waitresses and a Voice. One of the waitresses was named Aileen. She was tall, beautiful, lively, gracious and learned in persiflage. Her other name? There was no more necessity for another name at Bogle's than there was for finger-bowls.

The name of the other waitress was Tildy. Why do you suggest Matilda? Please listen this time—Tildy—Tildy. Tildy was dumpy, plain-faced, and too anxious to please to please. Repeat the last clause to yourself once or twice, and make the acquaintance of the duplicate infinite.

The Voice at Bogle's was invisible. It came from the kitchen, and did not shine in the way of originality. It was a heathen Voice, and contented itself, with vain repetitions of exclamations emitted by the waitresses concerning food.

Will it tire you to be told again that Aileen was beautiful? Had she donned a few hundred dollars' worth of clothes and joined the Easter parade, and had you seen her, you would have hastened to say so yourself.

The customers at Bogle's were her slaves. Six tables full she could wait upon at once. They who were in a hurry restrained their impatience for the joy of merely gazing upon her swiftly moving, graceful figure. They who had finished eating ate more that they might continue in the light of her smiles. Every man there—and they were mostly men—tried to make his impression upon her.

Aileen could successfully exchange repartee against a dozen at once. And every smile that she sent forth lodged, like pellets from a scatter-gun, in as many hearts. And all this while she would be performing astounding feats with orders of pork and beans, pot roasts, ham-and, sausage-and-the-wheats, and any quantity of things on the iron and in the pan and straight up and on the side. With all this feasting and flirting and merry exchange of wit Bogle's came mighty near being a salon, with Aileen for its Madame Recamier.

If the transients were entranced by the fascinating Aileen, the regulars were her adorers. There was much rivalry among many of the steady customers. Aileen could have had an engagement every evening. At least twice a week some one took her to a theatre or to a dance. One stout gentleman whom she and Tildy had privately christened "The Hog" presented her with a turquoise ring. Another one known as "Freshy," who rode on the Traction Company's repair wagon, was going to give her a poodle as soon as his brother got the hauling contract in the Ninth. And the man who always ate spareribs and spinach and said he was a stock broker asked her to go to "Parsifal" with him.

"I don't know where this place is," said Aileen while talking it over with Tildy, "but the wedding-ring's got to be on before I put a stitch into a travelling dress—ain't that right? Well, I guess!"

But, Tildy!

In steaming, chattering, cabbage-scented Bogle's there was almost a heart tragedy. Tildy with the blunt nose, the hay-colored hair, the freckled skin, the bag-o'-meal figure, had never had an admirer. Not a man followed her with his eyes when she went to and fro in the restaurant save now and then when they glared with the beast-hunger for food. None of them bantered her gaily to coquettish interchanges of wit. None of them loudly "jollied" her of mornings as they did Aileen, accusing her, when the eggs were slow in coming, of late hours in the company of envied swains. No one had ever given her a turquoise ring or invited her upon a voyage to mysterious, distant "Parsifal."

Tildy was a good waitress, and the men tolerated her. They who sat at her tables spoke to her briefly with quotations from the bill of fare; and then raised their voices in honeyed and otherwise-flavored accents, eloquently addressed to the fair Aileen. They writhed in their chairs to gaze around and over the impending form of Tildy, that Aileen's pulchritude might season and make ambrosia of their bacon and eggs.

And Tildy was content to be the unwooed drudge if Aileen could receive the flattery and the homage. The blunt nose was loyal to the short Grecian. She was Aileen's friend; and she was glad to see her rule hearts and wean the attention of men from smoking pot-pie and lemon meringue. But deep below our freckles and hay-colored hair the unhandsomest of us dream of a prince or a princess, not vicarious, but coming to us alone.

There was a morning when Aileen tripped in to work with a slightly bruised eye; and Tildy's solicitude was almost enough to heal any optic.

"Fresh guy," explained Aileen, "last night as I was going home at Twenty-third and Sixth. Sashayed up, so he did, and made a break. I turned him down, cold, and he made a sneak; but followed me down to Eighteenth, and tried his hot air again. Gee! but I slapped him a good one, side of the face. Then he give me that eye. Does it look real awful, Til? I should hate that Mr. Nicholson should see it when he comes in for his tea and toast at ten."

Tildy listened to the adventure with breathless admiration. No man had ever tried to follow her. She was safe abroad at any hour of the twenty-four. What bliss it must have been to have had a man follow one and black one's eye for love!

Among the customers at Bogle's was a young man named Seeders, who worked in a laundry office. Mr. Seeders was thin and had light hair, and appeared to have been recently rough-dried and starched. He was too diffident to aspire to Aileen's notice; so he usually sat at one of Tildy's tables, where he devoted himself to silence and boiled weakfish.

One day when Mr. Seeders came in to dinner he had been drinking beer. There were only two or three customers in the restaurant. When Mr. Seeders had finished his weakfish he got up, put his arm around Tildy's waist, kissed her loudly and impudently, walked out upon the street, snapped his fingers in the direction of the laundry, and hied himself to play pennies in the slot machines at the Amusement Arcade.

For a few moments Tildy stood petrified. Then she was aware of Aileen shaking at her an arch forefinger, and saying:

"Why, Til, you naughty girl! Ain't you getting to be awful, Miss Slyboots! First thing I know you'll be stealing some of my fellows. I must keep an eye on you, my lady."

Another thing dawned upon Tildy's recovering wits. In a moment she had advanced from a hopeless, lowly admirer to be an Eve-sister of the potent Aileen. She herself was now a man-charmer, a mark for Cupid, a Sabine who must be coy when the Romans were at their banquet boards. Man had found her waist achievable and her lips desirable. The sudden and amatory Seeders had, as it were, performed for her a miraculous piece of one-day laundry work. He had taken the sackcloth of her uncomeliness, had washed, dried, starched and ironed it, and returned it to her sheer embroidered lawn—the robe of Venus herself.

The freckles on Tildy's cheeks merged into a rosy flush. Now both Circe and Psyche peeped from her brightened eyes. Not even Aileen herself had been publicly embraced and kissed in the restaurant.

Tildy could not keep the delightful secret. When trade was slack she went and stood at Bogle's desk. Her eyes were shining; she tried not to let her words sound proud and boastful.

"A gentleman insulted me to-day," she said. "He hugged me around the waist and kissed me."

"That so?" said Bogle, cracking open his business armor. "After this week you get a dollar a week more."

At the next regular meal when Tildy set food before customers with whom she had acquaintance she said to each of them modestly, as one whose merit needed no bolstering:

"A gentleman insulted me to-day in the restaurant. He put his arms around my waist and kissed me."

The diners accepted the revelation in various ways—some incredulously, some with congratulations: others turned upon her the stream of badinage that had hitherto been directed at Aileen alone. And Tildy's heart swelled in her bosom, for she saw at last the towers of Romance rise above the horizon of the gray plain in which she had for so long travelled.

For two days Mr. Seeders came not again. During that time Tildy established herself firmly as a woman to be wooed. She bought ribbons, and arranged her hair like Aileen's, and tightened her waist two inches. She had a thrilling but delightful fear that Mr. Seeders would rush in suddenly and shoot her with a pistol. He must have loved her desperately; and impulsive lovers are always blindly jealous.

Even Aileen had not been shot at with a pistol. And then Tildy rather hoped that he would not shoot at her, for she was always loyal to Aileen; and she did not want to over-shadow her friend.

At 4 o'clock on the afternoon of the third day Mr. Seeders came in. There were no customers at the tables. At the back end of the restaurant Tildy was refilling the mustard pots and Aileen was quartering pies. Mr. Seeders walked back to where they stood.

Tildy looked up and saw him, gasped, and pressed the mustard spoon against her heart. A red hair-bow was in her hair; she wore Venus's Eighth Avenue badge, the blue bead necklace with the swinging silver symbolic heart.

Mr. Seeders was flushed and embarrassed. He plunged one hand into his hip pocket and the other into a fresh pumpkin pie.

"Miss Tildy," said he, "I want to apologize for what I done the other evenin'. Tell you the truth, I was pretty well tanked up or I wouldn't of done it. I wouldn't do no lady that a-way when I was sober. So I hope, Miss Tildy, you'll accept my 'pology, and believe that I wouldn't of done it if I'd known what I was doin' and hadn't of been drunk."

With this handsome plea Mr. Seeders backed away, and departed, feeling that reparation had been made.

But behind the convenient screen Tildy had thrown herself flat upon a table among the butter chips and the coffee cups, and was sobbing her heart out—out and back again to the gray plain wherein travel they with blunt noses and hay-colored hair. From her knot she had torn the red hair-bow and cast it upon the floor. Seeders she despised utterly; she had but taken his kiss as that of a pioneer and prophetic prince who might have set the clocks going and the pages to running in fairyland. But the kiss had been maudlin and unmeant; the court had not stirred at the false alarm; she must forevermore remain the Sleeping Beauty.

Yet not all was lost. Aileen's arm was around her; and Tildy's red hand groped among the butter chips till it found the warm clasp of her friend's.

"Don't you fret, Til," said Aileen, who did not understand entirely. "That turnip-faced little clothespin of a Seeders ain't worth it. He ain't anything of a gentleman or he wouldn't ever of apologized."

HEART OF THE WEST

HEART OF THE WEST

HEARTS AND CROSSES

BALDY WOODS reached for the bottle, and got it. Whenever Baldy went for anything he usually—but this is not Baldy's story. He poured out a third drink that was larger by a finger than the first and second. Baldy was in consultation; and the consultee is worthy of his hire.

"I'd be king if I was you," said Baldy, so positively that his holster creaked and his spurs rattled.

Webb Yeager pushed back his flat-brimmed Stetson, and made further disorder in his straw-colored hair. The tonsorial recourse being without avail, he followed the liquid example of the more resourceful Baldy.

"If a man marries a queen, it oughtn't to make him a two-spot," declared Webb, epitomizing his grievances.

"Sure not," said Baldy, sympathetic, still thirsty, and genuinely solicitous concerning the relative value of the cards. "By rights you're a king. If I was you, I'd call for a new deal. The cards have been stacked on you—I'll tell you what you are, Webb Yeager."

"What?" asked Webb, with a hopeful look in his pale-blue eyes.

"You're a prince-consort."

"Go easy," said Webb. "I never black-guarded you none."

"It's a title," explained Baldy, "up among the picture-cards; but it don't take no tricks. I'll tell you, Webb. It's a brand they've got for certain animals in Europe. Say that you or me or one of them Dutch dukes marries in a royal family. Well, by and by our wife gets to be queen. Are we king? Not in a million years. At the coronation ceremonies we march between little casino and the Ninth Grand Custodian of the Royal Hall Bedchamber. The only use we are is to appear in photographs, and accept the responsibility for the heir-apparent. That ain't any square deal. Yes, sir, Webb, you're a prince-consort; and if I was you, I'd start a interregnum or a habeas corpus or somethin'; and I'd be king if I had to turn from the bottom of the deck."

Baldy emptied his glass to the ratification of his Warwick pose.

"Baldy," said Webb, solemnly, "me and you punched cows in the same outfit for years. We been runnin' on the same range, and ridin' the same trails since we was boys. I wouldn't talk about my family affairs to nobody but you. You was line-rider on the Nopalito Ranch when I married Santa McAllister. I was foreman then; but what am I now? I don't amount to a knot in a stake rope."

"When old McAllister was the cattle king of West Texas," continued Baldy with Satanic sweetness, "you was some tallow. You had as much to say on the ranch as he did."

"I did," admitted Webb, "up to the time he found out I was tryin' to get my rope over Santa's head. Then he kept me out on the range as far from the ranch-house as he could. When the old man died they commenced to call

87

Santa the 'cattle queen.' I'm boss of the cattle—that's all. She 'tends to all the business; she handles all the money; I can't sell even a beef-steer to a party of campers, myself. Santa's the 'queen'; and I'm Mr. Nobody."

"I'd be king if I was you," repeated Baldy Woods, the royalist. "When a man marries a queen he ought to grade up with her—on the hoof—dressed—dried—corned—any old way from the chaparral to the packing-house. Lots of folks thinks it's funny, Webb, that you don't have the say-so on the Nopalito. I ain't reflectin' none on Miz Yeager—she's the finest little lady between the Rio Grande and next Christmas—but a man ought to be boss of his own camp."

The smooth, brown face of Yeager lengthened to a mask of wounded melancholy. With that expression, and his rumpled yellow hair and guileless blue eyes, he might have been likened to a schoolboy whose leadership had been usurped by a youngster of superior strength. But his active and sinewy seventy-two inches and his girded revolvers forbade the comparison.

"What was that you called me, Baldy?" he asked. "What kind of a concert was it?"

"A 'consort,'" corrected Baldy—"'a prince-consort.' It's a kind of short-card pseudonym. You come in sort of between Jack-high and a four-card flush."

Webb Yeager sighed, and gathered the strap of his Winchester scabbard from the floor.

"I'm ridin' back to the ranch to-day," he said, half-heartedly. "I've got to start a bunch of beeves for San Antone in the morning."

"I'm your company as far as Dry Lake," announced Baldy. "I've got a round-up camp on the San Marcos cuttin' out two-year-olds."

The two *compañeros* mounted their ponies and trotted away from the little railroad settlement, where they had foregathered in the thirsty morning.

At Dry Lake, where their routes diverged, they reined up for a party cigarette. For miles they had ridden in silence save for the soft drum of the ponies' hoofs on the matted mesquite grass, and the rattle of the chaparral against their wooden stirrups. But in Texas discourse is seldom continuous. You may fill in a mile, a meal, and a murder between your paragraphs without detriment to your thesis. So, without apology, Webb offered an addendum to the conversation that had begun ten miles away.

"You remember, yourself, Baldy, that there was a time when Santa wasn't quite so independent. You remember the days when old McAllister was keepin' us apart, and how she used to send me the sign that she wanted to see me? Old man Mac promised to make me look like a colander if I ever come in gun-shot of the ranch. You remember the sign she used to send, Baldy—the heart with a cross inside of it?"

"Me?" cried Baldy, with intoxicated archness. "You old sugar-stealing coyote! Don't I remember! Why, you dad-blamed old long-horned turtle-dove, the boys in camp was all cognoscious about them hieroglyphs. The 'gizzard-and-crossbones' we used to call it. We used to see 'em on truck that was sent out from the ranch. They was marked in charcoal on the sacks of flour and in lead-pencil on the newspapers. I see one of 'em once chalked on the back of a new cook that old man McAllister sent out from the ranch—danged if I didn't."

"Santa's father," exclaimed Webb gently, "got her to promise that she wouldn't write to me or send me any word. That heart-and-cross sign was her scheme. Whenever she wanted to see me in particular she managed to put that mark on somethin' at the ranch that she knew I'd see. And I never laid eyes on it but what I burnt the wind for the ranch the same night. I used to see her in that coma mott back of the little horse-corral."

"We knowed it," chanted Baldy; "but we never let on. We was all for you. We knowed why you always kept that fast paint in camp. And when we see that gizzard-and-crossbones figured out on the truck from the ranch we knowed old Pinto was goin' to eat up miles that night instead of grass. You remember Scurry—that educated horse-wrangler we had—the college fellow that tangle-foot drove to the range? Whenever Scurry saw that come-meet-your-honey brand on anything from the ranch, he'd wave his hand like that, and say, 'Our friend Lee Andrews will again swim the Hell's point to-night.'"

"The last time Santa sent me the sign," said Webb, "was once when she was sick. I noticed it as soon as I hit camp, and I galloped Pinto forty mile that night. She wasn't at the coma mott. I went to the house; and old McAllister met me at the door. 'Did you come here to get killed?' says he; 'I'll disoblige you for once. I just started a Mexican to bring you. Santa wants you. Go in that room and see her. And then come out here and see me.'

"Santa was lyin' in bed pretty sick. But she gives out a kind of a smile, and her hand and mine lock horns, and I sets down by the bed—mud and spurs and chaps and all. 'I've heard you ridin' across the grass for hours, Webb,' she says. 'I was sure you'd come. You saw the sign?' she whispers. 'The minute I hit camp,' says I. ' 'Twas marked on the bag of potatoes and onions.' 'They're always together,' says she, soft like—'always together in life.' 'They go well together,' I says, 'in a stew.' 'I mean hearts and crosses,' says Santa. 'Our sign—to love and to suffer—that's what they mean.'

"And there was old Doc Musgrove amusin' himself with whisky and a palm-leaf fan. And by and by Santa goes to sleep; and Doc feels her forehead; and he says to me: 'You're not such a bad febrifuge. But you'd better slide out now, for the diagnosis don't call for you in regular doses. The little lady'll be all right when she wakes up.'

"I seen old McAllister outside. 'She's asleep,' says I. 'And now you can start in with your colander-work. Take your time; for I left my gun on my saddle-horn.'

"Old Mac laughs, and he says to me: 'Pumpin' lead into the best ranch-boss in West Texas don't seem to me good business policy. I don't know where I could get as good a one. It's the son-in-law idea, Webb, that makes me admire for to use you as a target. You ain't my idea for a member of the family. But I can use you on the Nopalito if you'll keep outside of a radius with the ranch-house in the middle of it. You go upstairs and lay down on a cot, and when you get some sleep we'll talk it over.'"

Baldy Woods pulled down his hat, and uncurled his leg from his saddle-horn. Webb shortened his rein, and his pony danced, anxious to be off. The two men shook hands with Western ceremony.

"*Adios*, Baldy," said Webb. "I'm glad I seen you and had this talk."

With a pounding rush that sounded like the rise of a covey of quail, the riders sped away toward different points of the compass. A hundred yards on his route Baldy reined in on the top of a bare knoll, and emitted a yell. He swayed on his horse; had he been on foot, the earth would have risen and conquered him; but in the saddle he was a master of equilibrium, and laughed at whisky, and despised the centre of gravity.

Webb turned in his saddle at the signal.

"If I was you," came Baldy's strident and perverting tones, "I'd be king!"

At eight o'clock on the following morning Bud Turner rolled from his saddle in front of the Nopalito ranch-house, and stumbled with whizzing rowels toward the gallery. Bud was in charge of the bunch of beef-cattle that was to strike the trail that morning for San Antonio. Mrs. Yeager was on the gallery watering a cluster of hyacinths growing in a red earthenware jar.

"King" McAllister had bequeathed to his daughter many of his strong characteristics—his resolution, his gay courage, his contumacious self-reliance, his pride as a reigning monarch of hoofs and horns. *Allegro* and *fortissimo* had been

McAllister's tempo and tone. In Santa they survived, transposed to the feminine key. Substantially, she preserved the image of the mother who had been summoned to wander in other and less finite green pastures long before the waxing herds of kine had conferred royalty upon the house. She had her mother's slim, strong figure and grave, soft prettiness that relieved in her the severity of the imperious McAllister eye and the McAllister air of royal independence.

Webb stood on one end of the gallery giving orders to two or three sub-bosses of various camps and outfits who had ridden in for instructions.

"'Morning," said Bud, briefly. "Where do you want them beeves to go in town—to Barber's, as usual?"

Now, to answer that had been the prerogative of the queen. All the reins of business—buying, selling, and banking—had been held by her capable fingers. The handling of the cattle had been entrusted fully to her husband. In the days of "King" McAllister, Santa had been his secretary and helper; and she had continued her work with wisdom and profit. But before she could reply, the prince-consort spake up with calm decision:

"You drive that bunch to Zimmerman and Nesbit's pens. I spoke to Zimmerman about it some time ago."

Bud turned on his high boot-heels.

"Wait!" called Santa quickly. She looked at her husband with surprise in her steady gray eyes.

"Why, what do you mean, Webb?" she asked, with a small wrinkle gathering between her brows. "I never deal with Zimmerman and Nesbit. Barber has handled every head of stock from this ranch in that market for five years. I'm not going to take the business out of his hands." She faced Bud Turner. "Deliver those cattle to Barber," she concluded positively.

Bud gazed impartially at the water-jar hanging on the gallery, stood on his other leg, and chewed a mesquite-leaf.

"I want this bunch of beeves to go to Zimmerman and Nesbit," said Webb, with a frosty light in his blue eyes.

"Nonsense," said Santa impatiently. "You'd better start on, Bud, so as to noon at the Little Elm waterhole. Tell Barber we'll have another lot of culls ready in about a month."

Bud allowed a hesitating eye to steal upward and meet Webb's. Webb saw apology in his look, and fancied he saw commiseration.

"You deliver them cattle," he said grimly, "to——"

"Barber," finished Santa sharply. "Let that settle it. Is there anything else you are waiting for, Bud?"

"No, m'm," said Bud. But before going he lingered while a cow's tail could have switched thrice; for man is man's ally; and even the Philistines must have blushed when they took Samson in the way they did.

"You hear your boss!" cried Webb, sardonically. He took off his hat, and bowed until it touched the floor before his wife.

"Webb," said Santa rebukingly, "you're acting mighty foolish to-day."

"Court fool, your Majesty," said Webb, in his slow tones, which had changed their quality. "What else can you expect? Let me tell you. I was a man before I married a cattle-queen. What am I now? The laughing-stock of the camps. I'll be a man again."

Santa looked at him closely.

"Don't be unreasonable, Webb," she said calmly. "You haven't been slighted in any way. Do I ever interfere in your management of the cattle? I know the business side of the ranch much better than you do. I learned it from Dad. Be sensible."

"Kingdoms and queendoms," said Webb, "don't suit me unless I am in the pictures, too. I punch the cattle and you wear the crown. All right. I'd rather be High Lord Chancellor of a cow-camp than the eight-spot in a queen-high flush. It's your ranch; and Barber gets the beeves."

Webb's horse was tied to the rack. He walked into the house and brought out his roll of blankets that he never took with him except on long rides, and his "slicker," and his longest stake-rope of plaited raw-hide. These he began to tie deliberately upon his saddle. Santa, a little pale, followed him.

Webb swung up into the saddle. His serious, smooth face was without expression except for a stubborn light that smouldered in his eyes.

"There's a herd of cows and calves," said he, "near the Hondo Water-hole on the Frio that ought to be moved away from timber. Lobos have killed three of the calves. I forgot to leave orders. You'd better tell Simms to attend to it."

Santa laid a hand on the horse's bridle, and looked her husband in the eye.

"Are you going to leave me, Webb?" she asked quietly.

"I am going to be a man again," he answered.

"I wish you success in a praiseworthy attempt," she said, with a sudden coldness. She turned and walked directly into the house.

Webb Yeager rode to the southeast as straight as the topography of West Texas permitted. And when he reached the horizon he might have ridden on into blue space as far as knowledge of him on the Nopalito went. And the days, with Sundays at their head, formed into hebdomadal squads; and the weeks, captained by the full moon, closed ranks into menstrual companies carrying "Tempus fugit" on their banners; and the months marched on toward the vast camp-ground of the years; but Webb Yeager came no more to the dominions of his queen.

One day a being named Bartholomew, a sheep-man—and therefore of little account—from the lower Rio Grande country, rode in sight of the Nopalito ranch-house, and felt hunger assail him. *Ex consuetudine* he was soon seated at the mid-day dinner-table of that hospitable kingdom. Talk like water gushed from him: he might have been smitten with Aaron's rod—that is your gentle shepherd when an audience is vouchsafed him whose ears are not overgrown with wool.

"Missis Yeager," he babbled, "I see a man the other day on the Rancho Seco down in Hidalgo County by your name—Webb Yeager was his. He'd just been engaged as manager. He was a tall, light-haired man, not saying much. Maybe he was some kin of yours, do you think?"

"A husband," said Santa cordially. "The Seco has done well. Mr. Yeager is one of the best stockmen in the West."

The dropping out of a prince-consort rarely disorganizes a monarchy. Queen Santa had appointed as *mayordomo* of the ranch, a trusty subject, named Ramsay, who had been one of her father's faithful vassals. And there was scarcely a ripple on the Nopalito ranch save when the gulf-breeze created undulations in the grass of its wide acres.

For several years the Nopalito had been making experiments with an English breed of cattle that looked down with aristocratic contempt upon the Texas long-horns. The experiments were found satisfactory; and a pasture had been set apart for the blue-bloods. The fame of them had gone forth into the chaparral and pear as far as men ride in saddles. Other ranches woke up, rubbed their eyes, and looked with new dissatisfaction upon the long-horns.

As a consequence, one day a sunburned, capable, silk-kerchiefed nonchalant youth, garnished with revolvers, and attended by three Mexican *vaqueros*, alighted at the Nopalito ranch and presented the following business-like epistle to the queen thereof.

Mrs. Yeager—The Nopalito Ranch:
DEAR MADAM:
  I am instructed by the owners of the Rancho Seco to purchase 100 head of
two and three-year-old cows of the Sussex breed owned by you. If you can fill
the order please deliver the cattle to the bearer; and a check will be forwarded
to you at once.

Respectfully,
WEBSTER YEAGER,
Manager of the Rancho Seco.

  Business is business, even—very scantily did it escape being written "especially"—in a kingdom.
  That night the 100 herd of cattle were driven up from the pasture and penned
in a corral near the ranch-house for delivery in the morning.
  When night closed down and the house was still, did Santa Yeager throw
herself down, clasping that formal note to her bosom, weeping, and calling out
a name that pride (either in one or the other) had kept from her lips many
a day? Or did she file the letter, in her business way, retaining her royal
balance and strength?
  Wonder, if you will; but royalty is sacred; and there is a veil. But this
much you shall learn.
  At midnight Santa slipped softly out of the ranch-house, clothed in something dark and plain. She paused for a moment under the live-oak trees. The
prairies were somewhat dim, and the moonlight was pale orange, diluted with
particles of an impalpable, flying mist. But the mock-bird whistled on every
bough of vantage; leagues of flowers scented the air; and a kindergarten of
little shadowy rabbits leaped and played in an open space near by. Santa
turned her face to the southeast and threw kisses thitherward; for there was
none to see.
  Then she sped silently to the blacksmith-shop, fifty yards away; and what she
did there can only be surmised. But the forge glowed red; and there was
a faint hammering such as Cupid might make when he sharpens his arrow-
points.
  Later she came forth with a queer-shaped, handled thing in one hand, and
a portable furnace, such as are seen in branding-camps, in the other. To the
corral where the Sussex cattle were penned she sped with these things swiftly in
the moonlight.
  She opened the gate and slipped inside the corral. The Sussex cattle were
mostly a dark red. But among this bunch was one that was milky white—
notable among the others.
  And now Santa shook from her shoulder something that we had not seen
before—a rope lasso. She freed the loop of it, coiling the length in her left
hand, and plunged into the thick of the cattle.
  The white cow was her object. She swung the lasso, which caught one horn
and slipped off. The next throw encircled the forefeet and the animal fell
heavily. Santa made for it like a panther; but it scrambled up and dashed
against her, knocking her over like a blade of grass.
  Again she made the cast, while the aroused cattle milled round the four sides
of the corral in a plunging mass. This throw was fair; the white cow came
to earth again; and before it could rise Santa had made the lasso fast around
a post of the corral with a swift and simple knot, and had leaped upon the cow
again with the rawhide hobbles.
  In one minute the feet of the animal were tied (no record-breaking deed) and
Santa leaned against the corral for the same space of time, panting and lax.

And then she ran swiftly to her furnace at the gate and brought the branding-iron, queerly shaped and white-hot.

The bellow of the outraged white cow, as the iron was applied, should have stirred the slumbering auricular nerves and consciences of the near-by subjects of the Nopalito, but it did not. And it was amid the deepest nocturnal silence that Santa ran like a lapwing back to the ranch-house and there fell upon a cot and sobbed—sobbed as though queens had hearts as simple ranchmen's wives have, and as though she would gladly make kings of prince-consorts, should they ride back again from over the hills and far away.

In the morning the capable, revolvered youth and his *vaqueros* set forth, driving the bunch of Sussex cattle across the prairies to the Rancho Seco. Ninety miles it was; a six days' journey, grazing and watering the animals on the way.

The beasts arrived at Rancho Seco one evening at dusk; and were received and counted by the foreman of the ranch.

The next morning at eight o'clock a horseman loped out of the brush to the Nopalito ranch-house. He dismounted stiffly, and strode, with whizzing spurs, to the house. His horse gave a great sigh and swayed foam-streaked, with down-drooping head and closed eyes.

But waste not your pity upon Belshazzar, the flea-bitten sorrel. To-day, in Nopalito horse-pasture he survives, pampered, beloved, unridden, cherished record-holder of long-distance rides.

The horseman stumbled into the house. Two arms fell around his neck and someone cried out in the voice of woman and queen alike: "Webb—oh, Webb!"

"I was a skunk," said Webb Yeager.

"Hush," said Santa, "did you see it?"

"I saw it," said Webb.

What they meant God knows; and you shall know, if you rightly read the primer of events.

"Be the cattle-queen," said Webb; "and overlook it if you can. I was a mangy, sheep-stealing coyote."

"Hush!" said Santa again, laying her fingers upon his mouth. "There's no queen here. Do you know who I am? I am Santa Yeager, First Lady of the Bedchamber. Come here."

She dragged him from the gallery into the room to the right. There stood a cradle with an infant in it—a red, ribald, unintelligible, babbling, beautiful infant, sputtering at life in an unseemly manner.

"There's no queen on this ranch," said Santa again. "Look at the king. He's got your eyes, Webb. Down on your knees and look at his Highness."

But jingling rowels sounded on the gallery and Bud Turner stumbled there again with the same query that he had brought, lacking a few days, a year ago.

"'Morning. Them beeves is just turned out on the trail. Shall I drive 'em to Barber's, or——"

He saw Webb and stopped, open-mouthed.

"Ba-ba-ba-ba-ba-ba!" shrieked the king in his cradle, beating the air with his fists.

"You hear your boss, Bud," said Webb Yeager, with a broad grin—just as he had said a year ago.

And that is all, except that when old man Quinn, owner of the Rancho Seco, went out to look over the herd of Sussex cattle that he had bought from the Nopalito ranch, he asked his new manager:

"What's the Nopalito ranch brand, Wilson?"

"X Bar Y," said Wilson.

"I thought so," said Quinn. "But look at that white heifer there; she's got another brand—a heart with a cross inside of it. What brand is that?"

THE RANSOM OF MACK

Me and old Mack Lonsbury, we got out of that Little Hide-and-Seek gold mine affair with about $40,000 apiece. I say "old" Mack; but he wasn't old. Forty-one, I should say; but he always seemed old.

"Andy," he says to me, "I'm tired of hustling. You and me have been working hard together for three years. Say we knock off for a while, and spend some of this idle money we've coaxed our way."

"The proposition hits me just right," says I. "Let's be nabobs a while and see how it feels. What'll we do—take in the Niagara Falls, or buck at faro?"

"For a good many years," says Mack, "I've thought that if I ever had extravagant money I'd rent a two-room cabin somewhere, hire a Chinaman to cook, and sit in my stocking feet and read Buckle's History of Civilization."

"That sounds self-indulgent and gratifying without vulgar ostentation," says I; "and I don't see how money could be better invested. Give me a cuckoo clock and a Sep Winner's Self-Instructor for the Banjo, and I'll join you."

A week afterward me and Mack hits this small town of Piña, about thirty miles out from Denver, and finds an elegant two-room house that just suits us. We deposited half-a-peck of money in the Piña bank and shook hands with every one of the 340 citizens in the town. We brought along the Chinaman and the cuckoo clock and Buckle and the Instructor with us from Denver; and they made the cabin seem like home at once.

Never believe it when they tell you riches don't bring happiness. If you could have seen old Mack sitting in his rocking-chair with his blue-yarn sock feet up in the window and absorbing in that Buckle stuff through his specs you'd have seen a picture of content that would have made Rockefeller jealous. And I was learning to pick out "Old Zip Coon" on the banjo, and the cuckoo was on time with his remarks, and Ah Sing was messing up the atmosphere with the handsomest smell of ham and eggs that ever laid the honeysuckle in the shade. When it got too dark to make out Buckle's nonsense and the notes in the Instructor, me and Mack would light our pipes and talk about science and pearl diving and sciatica and Egypt and spelling and fish and trade-winds and leather and gratitude and eagles, and a lot of subjects that we'd never had time to explain our sentiments about before.

One evening Mack spoke up and asked me if I was much apprised in the habits and policies of women folks.

"Why, yes," says I, in a tone of voice; "I know 'em from Alfred to Omaha. The feminine nature and similitude," says I, "is as plain to my sight as the Rocky Mountains is to a blue-eyed burro. I'm onto all their little sidesteps and punctual discrepancies."

"I tell you, Andy," says Mack, with a kind of sigh. "I never had the least amount of intersection with their predispositions. Maybe I might have had a proneness in respect to their vicinity, but I never took the time. I made my own living since I was fourteen; and I never seemed to get my ratiocinations equipped with the sentiments usually depicted toward the sect. I sometimes wish I had," says old Mack.

"They're an adverse study," says I, "and adapted to points of view. Although they vary in rationale, I have found 'em quite often obviously differing from each other in divergences of contrast."

"It seems to me," goes on Mack, "that a man had better take 'em in and secure his inspirations of the sect when he's young and so preordained. I let my chance go by; and I guess I'm too old now to go hopping into the curriculum."

"Oh, I don't know," I tells him. "Maybe you better credit yourself with a barrel of money and a lot of emancipation from a quantity of uncontent. Still, I don't regret my knowledge of 'em," I says. "It takes a man who understands the symptoms and by-plays of women-folks to take care of himself in this world."

We stayed on in Piña because we liked the place. Some folks might enjoy their money with noise and rapture and locomotion; but me and Mack we had had plenty of turmoils and hotel towels. The people were friendly; Ah Sing got the swing of the grub we liked; Mack and Buckle were as thick as two body-snatchers, and I was hitting out a cordial resemblance to "Buffalo Gals, Can't You Come Out To-night," on the banjo.

One day I got a telegram from Speight, the man that was working a mine I had an interest in out in New Mexico. I had to go out there; and I was gone two months. I was anxious to get back to Piña and enjoy life once more.

When I struck the cabin I nearly fainted. Mack was standing in the door; and if angels ever wept, I saw no reason why they should be smiling then.

That man was a spectacle. Yes; he was worse; he was a spyglass; he was the great telescope in the Lick Observatory. He had on a coat and shiny shoes and a white vest and a high silk hat; and a geranium as big as an order of spinach was spiked onto his front. And he was smirking and warping his face like an infernal storekeeper or a kid with colic.

"Hello, Andy," says Mack, out of his face. "Glad to see you back. Things have happened since you went away."

"I know it," says I, "and a sacrilegious sight it is. God never made you that way, Mack Lonsbury. Why do you scarify His works with this presumptious kind of ribaldry?"

"Why, Andy," said he, "they've elected me justice of the peace since you left."

I looked at Mack close. He was restless and inspired. A justice of the peace ought to be disconsolate and assuaged.

Just then a young woman passed on the sidewalk; and I saw Mack kind of half snicker and blush, and then he raised up his hat and smiled and bowed, and she smiled and bowed, and went on by.

"No hope for you," says I, "if you've got the Mary-Jane infirmity at your age. I thought it wasn't going to take on you. And patent leather shoes! All this in two little short months!"

"I'm going to marry the young lady who just passed to-night," says Mack, in a kind of a flutter.

"I forgot something at the post-office," says I, and walked away quick.

I overtook that young woman a hundred yards away. I raised my hat and told her my name. She was about nineteen; and young for her age. She blushed, and then looked at me cool, like I was the snow scene from the "Two Orphans."

"I understand you are to be married to-night," I said.

"Correct," says she. "You got any objections?"

"Listen, sissy," I begins.

"My name is Miss Rebosa Redd," says she in a pained way.

"I know it," says I. "Now, Rebosa, I'm old enough to have owed money to your father. And that old, specious, dressed-up, garbled, sea-sick ptomaine prancing around avidiously like an irremediable turkey gobbler with patent leather shoes on is my best friend. Why did you go and get him invested in this marriage business?"

"Why, he was the only chance there was," answered Miss Rebosa.

"Nay," says I, giving a sickening look of admiration at her complexion and style of features; "with your beauty you might pick any kind of a man. Listen, Rebosa. Old Mack ain't the man you want. He was twenty-two when you was *née* Reed, as the papers say. This bursting into bloom won't last with him. He's all ventilated with oldness and rectitude and decay. Old Mack's down with a case of Indian summer. He overlooked his bet when he was young; and now he's suing Nature for the interest on the promissory note he took from Cupid instead of the cash. Rebosa, are you bent on having this marriage occur?"

"Why, sure I am," says she, oscillating the pansies on her hat, "and so is somebody else, I reckon."

"What time is it to take place?" I asks.

"At six o'clock," says she.

I made up my mind right away what to do. I'd save old Mack if I could. To have a good, seasoned, ineligible man like that turn chicken for a girl that hadn't quit eating slate pencils and buttoning in the back was more than I could look on with easiness.

"Rebosa," says I, earnest, drawing upon my display of knowledge concerning the feminine intuitions of reason—"ain't there a young man in Piña—a nice young man that you think a heap of?"

"Yep," says Rebosa, nodding her pansies—"Sure there is! What do you think! Gracious!"

"Does he like you?" I asks. "How does he stand in the matter?"

"Crazy," says Rebosa. "Ma has to wet down the front steps to keep him from sitting there all the time. But I guess that'll be all over after to-night," she winds up with a sigh.

"Rebosa," says I, "you don't really experience any of this adoration called love for old Mack, do you?"

"Lord! no," says the girl, shaking her head. "I think he's as dry as a lava bed. The idea!"

"Who is this young man that you like, Rebosa?" I inquires.

"It's Eddie Bayles," says she. "He clerks in Crosby's grocery. But he don't make but thirty-five a month. Ella Noakes was wild about him once."

"Old Mack tells me," I says, "that he's going to marry you at six o'clock this evening."

"That's the time," says she. "It's to be at our house."

"Rebosa," says I, "listen to me. If Eddie Bayles had a thousand dollars cash—a thousand dollars, mind you, would buy him a store of his own—if you and Eddie had that much to excuse matrimony on, would you consent to marry him this evening at five o'clock?"

The girl looks at me a minute; and I can see these inaudible cogitations going on inside of her, as women will.

"A thousand dollars?" says she. "Of course I would."

"Come on," says I. "We'll go and see Eddie."

We went up to Crosby's store and called Eddie outside. He looked to be estimable and freckled; and he had chills and fever when I made my proposition.

"At five o'clock?" says he, "for a thousand dollars? Please don't wake me up! Well, you *are* the rich uncle retired from the spice business in India. I'll buy out old Crosby and run the store myself."

We went inside and got old man Crosby apart and explained it. I wrote my check for a thousand dollars and handed it to him. If Eddie and Rebosa married each other at five he was to turn the money over to them.

And then I gave 'em my blessing, and went to wander in the wildwood for a season. I sat on a log and made cogitations on life and old age and the zodiac and the ways of women and all the disorder that goes with a lifetime. I passed myself congratulations that I had probably saved my old friend Mack from his attack of Indian summer. I knew when he got well of it and shed his infatuation and his patent leather shoes, he would feel grateful. "To keep old Mack disinvolved," thinks I, "from relapses like this, is worth more than a thousand dollars." And most of all I was glad that I'd made a study of women, and wasn't to be deceived any by their means of conceit and evolution.

It must have been half-past five when I got back home. I stepped in; and there sat old Mack on the back of his neck in his old clothes with his blue socks on the window and the History of Civilization propped up on his knees.

"This don't look like getting ready for a wedding at six," I says, to seem innocent.

"Oh," says Mack, reaching for his tobacco, "that was postponed back to five o'clock. They sent me a note saying the hour had been changed. It's all over now. What made you stay away so long, Andy?"

"You heard about the wedding?" I asks.

"I operated it," says he. "I told you I was justice of the peace. The preacher is off East to visit his folks, and I'm the only one in town that can perform the dispensations of marriage. I promised Eddie and Rebosa a month ago I'd marry 'em. He's a busy lad; and he'll have a grocery of his own some day."

"He will," says I.

"There was lots of women at the wedding," says Mack, smoking up. "But I didn't seem to get any ideas from 'em. I wish I was informed in the structure of their attainments like you said you was."

"That was two months ago," says I, reaching up for the banjo.

TELEMACHUS, FRIEND

RETURNING from a hunting trip, I waited at the little town of Los Piños, in New Mexico, for the south-bound train, which was one hour late. I sat on the porch of the Summit House and discussed the functions of life with Telemachus Hicks, the hotel proprietor.

Perceiving that personalities were not out of order, I asked him what species of beast had long ago twisted and mutilated his left ear. Being a hunter, I was concerned in the evils that may befall one in the pursuit of game.

"That ear," says Hicks, "is the relic of true friendship."

"An accident?" I persisted.

"No friendship is an accident," said Telemachus; and I was silent.

"The only perfect case of true friendship I ever knew," went on my host, "was a cordial intent between a Connecticut man and a monkey. The monkey climbed palms in Barranquilla and threw down cocoanuts to the man. The man sawed them in two and made dippers, which he sold for two *reales* each and bought rum. The monkey drank the milk of the nuts. Through each being satisfied with his own share of the graft, they lived like brothers.

"But in the case of human beings, friendship is a transitory act, subject to discontinuance without further notice.

"I had a friend once, of the entitlement of Paisley Fish, that I imagined was sealed to me for an endless space of time. Side by side for seven years we had mined, ranched, sold patent churns, herded sheep, took photographs and other things, built wire fences, and picked prunes. Thinks I, neither homicide nor flattery nor riches nor sophistry nor drink can make trouble between me and Paisley Fish. We was friends an amount you could hardly guess at. We was friends in business, and we let our amicable qualities lap over and season our hours of recreation and folly. We certainly had days of Damon and nights of Pythias.

"One summer me and Paisley gallops down into these San Andrés mountains for the purpose of a month's surcease and levity, dressed in the natural store habiliments of man. We hit this town of Los Piños, which certainly was a roof-garden spot of the world, and flowing with condensed milk and honey. It had a street or two, and air, and hens, and a eating-house; and that was enough for us.

"We strikes the town after supper-time, and we concludes to sample whatever efficacy there is in this eating-house down by the railroad tracks. By the time we had set down and pried up our plates with a knife from the red oil-cloth, along intrudes Widow Jessup with the hot biscuit and fried liver.

"Now, there was a woman that would have tempted an anchovy to forget his vows. She was not so small as she was large; and a kind of welcome air seemed to mitigate her vicinity. The pink of her face was the *in hoc signo* of a culinary temper and a warm disposition, and her smile would have brought out the dogwood blossoms in December.

"Widow Jessup talks to us a lot of garrulousness about the climate and history and Tennyson and prunes and the scarcity of mutton, and finally wants to know where we came from.

"'Spring Valley,' says I.

"'Big Spring Valley,' chips in Paisley, out of a lot of potatoes and knuckle-bone of ham in his mouth.

"That was the first sign I noticed that the old *fidus Diogenes* business between me and Paisley Fish was ended forever. He knew how I hated a talkative person, and yet he stampedes into the conversation with his amendments and addendums of syntax. On the map it was Big Spring Valley; but I had heard Paisley himself call it Spring Valley a thousand times.

"Without saying any more, we went out after supper and set on the railroad track. We had been pardners too long not to know what was going on in each other's mind.

"'I reckon you understand,' says Paisley, 'that I've made up my mind to accrue that widow woman as part and parcel in and to my hereditaments forever, both domestic, sociable, legal, and otherwise, until death us do part.'

"'Why, yes,' says I, 'I read it between the lines, though you only spoke one. And I suppose you are aware,' says I, 'that I have a movement on foot that leads up to the widow's changing her name to Hicks, and leaves you writing to the society column to inquire whether the best man wears a japonica or seamless socks at the wedding!'

"'There'll be some hiatuses in your program,' says Paisley, chewing up a piece of a railroad tie. 'I'd give in to you,' says he, 'in 'most any respect if it was secular affairs, but this is not so. The smiles of woman,' goes on Paisley, 'is the whirlpool of Squills and Chalybeates, into which vortex the good ship Friendship is often drawn and dismembered. I'd assault a bear that was annoying you,' says Paisley, 'or I'd indorse your note, or rub the place between your shoulder-blades with opodeldoc the same as ever; but there my sense of etiquette ceases. In this fracas with Mrs. Jessup we play it alone. I've notified you fair.'

"And then I collaborates with myself, and offers the following resolutions and by-laws:

"'Friendship between man and man,' says I, 'is an ancient historical virtue enacted in the days when men had to protect each other against lizards with eighty-foot tails and flying turtles. And they've kept up the habit to this day, and stand by each other till the bellboy comes up and tells them the animals are not really there. I've often heard,' I says, 'about ladies stepping in and breaking up a friendship between men. Why should that be? I'll tell you, Paisley, the first sight and hot biscuit of Mrs. Jessup appears to have inserted a oscillation into each of our bosoms. Let the best man of us have her. I'll play you a square game, and won't do any underhanded work. I'll do all of my courting of her in your presence, so you will have an equal opportunity. With that arrangement I don't see why our steamboat of friendship should fall overboard in the medicinal whirlpools you speak of, whichever of us wins out.'

" 'Good old hoss!' says Paisley, shaking my hand. 'And I'll do the same,' says he. 'We'll court the lady synonymously, and without any of the prudery and bloodshed usual to such occasions. And we'll be friends still, win or lose.'

"At one side of Mrs. Jessup's eating-house was a bench under some trees where she used to sit in the breeze after the south-bound had been fed and gone. And there me and Paisley used to congregate after supper and make partial payments on our respects to the lady of our choice. And we was so honorable and circuitous in our calls that if one of us got there first we waited for the other before beginning any gallivantery.

"The first evening that Mrs. Jessup knew about our arrangement I got to the bench before Paisley did. Supper was just over, and Mrs. Jessup was out there with a fresh pink dress on, and almost cool enough to handle.

"I sat down by her and made a few specifications about the moral surface of nature as set forth by the landscape and the contiguous perspective. That evening was surely a case in point. The moon was attending to business in the section of sky where it belonged, and the trees was making shadows on the ground according to science and nature, and there was a kind of conspicuous hullabaloo going on in the bushes between the bullbats and the orioles and the jack-rabbits and other feathered insects of the forest. And the wind out of the mountains was singing like a jew's-harp in the pile of old tomato-cans by the railroad track.

"I felt a kind of sensation in my left side—something like dough rising in a crock by the fire. Mrs. Jessup had moved up closer.

" 'Oh, Mr. Hicks,' says she, 'when one is alone in the world, don't they feel it more aggravated on a beautiful night like this?'

"I rose up off of the bench at once.

" 'Excuse me, ma'am,' says I, 'but I'll have to wait till Paisley comes before I can give a audible hearing to leading questions like that.'

"And then I explained to her how we was friends cinctured by years of embarrassment and travel and complicity, and how we had agreed to take no advantage of each other in any of the more mushy walks of life, such as might be fomented by sentiment and proximity. Mrs. Jessup appears to think serious about the matter for a minute, and then she breaks into a species of laughter that makes the wildwood resound.

"In a few minutes Paisley drops around, with oil of bergamot on his hair, and sits on the other side of Mrs. Jessup, and inaugurates a sad tale of adventure in which him and Pieface Lumley has a skinning-match of dead cows in '95 for a silver-mounted saddle in the Santa Rita valley during the nine month's drought.

"Now, from the start of that courtship I had Paisley Fish hobbled and tied to a post. Each one of us had a different system of reaching out for the easy places in the female heart. Paisley's scheme was to petrify 'em with wonderful relations of events that he had either come across personally or in large print. I think he must have got his idea of subjugation from one of Shakespeare's shows I see once called 'Othello.' There is a colored man in it who acquires a duke's daughter by disbursing to her a mixture of the talk turned out by Rider Haggard, Lew Dockstader, and Dr. Parkhurst. But that style of courting don't work well off the stage.

"Now, I give you my own recipe for inveigling a woman into that state of affairs when she can be referred to as 'née Jones.' Learn how to pick up her hand and hold it, and she's yours. It ain't so easy. Some men grab at it so much like they was going to set a dislocation of the shoulder that you can smell the arnica and hear 'em tearing off bandages. Some take it up like a hot horseshoe, and hold it off at arm's length like a druggist pouring tincture of asafoetida in a bottle. And most of 'em catch hold of it and drag it right out before the lady's eyes like a boy finding a baseball in the grass, without giving her a chance to forget that the hand is growing on the end of her arm. Them ways are all wrong.

"I'll tell you the right way. Did you ever see a man sneak out in the backyard and pick up a rock to throw at a tomcat that was sitting on a fence looking at him? He pretends he hasn't got a thing in his hand, and that the cat don't see him, and that he don't see the cat. That's the idea. Never drag her hand out where she'll have to take notice of it. Don't let her know that you think she knows you have the least idea she is aware you are holding her hand. That was my rule of tactics; and as far as Paisley's serenade about hostilities and misadventure went, he might as well have been reading to her a time-table of the Sunday trains that stop at Ocean Grove, New Jersey.

"One night when I beat Paisley to the bench by one pipeful, my friendship gets subsidized for a minute, and I asks Mrs. Jessup if she didn't think a 'H' was easier to write than a 'J.' In a second her head was mashing the oleander flower in my button-hole, and I leaned over and—but I didn't.

"'If you don't mind,' says I, standing up, 'we'll wait for Paisley to come before finishing this. I've never done anything dishonorable yet to our friendship, and this won't be quite fair.'

"'Mr. Hicks,' says Mrs. Jessup, looking at me peculiar in the dark, 'if it wasn't for but one thing, I'd ask you to hike yourself down the gulch and never disresume your visits to my house.'

"'And what is that, ma'am?' I asks.

"'You are too good a friend not to make a good husband,' says she.

"In five minutes Paisley was on his side of Mrs. Jessup.

"'In Silver City, in the summer of '98,' he begins, 'I see Jim Bartholomew chew off a Chinaman's ear in the Blue Light Saloon on account of a crossbarred muslin shirt that—what was that noise?'

"I had resumed matters again with Mrs. Jessup right where we had left off.

"'Mrs. Jessup,' says I, 'has promised to make it Hicks. And this is another of the same sort.'

"Paisley winds his feet around a leg of the bench and kind of groans.

"'Lem,' says he, 'we been friends for seven years. Would you mind not kissing Mrs. Jessup quite so loud? I'd do the same for you.'

"'All right,' says I. 'The other kind will do as well.'

"'This Chinaman,' goes on Paisley, 'was the one that shot a man named Mullins in the spring of '97, and that was——'

"Paisley interrupted himself again.

"'Lem,' says he, 'if you was a true friend you wouldn't hug Mrs. Jessup quite so hard. I felt the bench shake all over just then. You know you told me you would give me an even chance as long as there was any.'

"'Mr. Man,' says Mrs. Jessup, turning around to Paisley, 'if you was to drop in to the celebration of mine and Mr. Hick's silver wedding, twenty-five years from now, do you think you could get it into that Hubbard squash you call your head that you are *nix cum rous* in this business? I've put up with you a long time because you was Mr. Hicks's friend; but it seems to me it's time for you to wear the willow and trot off down the hill.'

"'Mrs. Jessup,' says I, without losing my grasp on the situation as fiancé, 'Mr. Paisley is my friend, and I offered him a square deal and a equal opportunity as long as there was a chance.'

"'A chance!' says she. 'Well, he may think he has a chance; but I hope he won't think he's got a cinch, after what he's been next to all the evening.'

"Well, a month afterwards me and Mrs. Jessup was married in the Los Piños Methodist Church; and the whole town closed up to see the performance.

"When we lined up in front and the preacher was beginning to sing out his rituals and observances, I looks around and misses Paisley. I calls time on the preacher. 'Paisley ain't here,' says I. 'We've got to wait for Paisley. A friend once, a friend always—that's Telemachus Hicks,' says I. Mrs. Jessup's eyes snapped some; but the preacher holds up the incantations according to instructions.

"In a few minutes Paisley gallops up the aisle, putting on a cuff as he comes. He explains that the only dry-goods store in town was closed for the wedding, and he couldn't get the kind of a boiled shirt that his taste called for until he had broke open the back window of the store and helped himself. Then he ranges up on the other side of the bride, and the wedding goes on. I always imagined that Paisley calculated as a last chance that the preacher might marry him to the widow by mistake.

"After the proceedings was over we had tea and jerked antelope and canned apricots, and then the populace hiked itself away. Last of all Paisley shook me by the hand and told me I'd acted square and on the level with him and he was proud to call me a friend.

"The preacher had a small house on the side of the street that he'd fixed up to rent; and he allowed me and Mrs. Hicks to occupy it till the ten-forty train the next morning, when we was going on a bridal tour to El Paso. His wife had decorated it all up with hollyhocks and poison ivy, and it looked real festal and bowery.

"About ten o'clock that night I sets down in the front door and pulls off my boots a while in the cool breeze, while Mrs. Hicks was fixing around in the room. Right soon the light went out inside; and I sat there a while reverberating over old times and scenes. And then I heard Mrs. Hicks call out, 'Ain't you coming in soon, Lem?'

"'Well, well!' says I, kind of rousing up. 'Durn me if I wasn't waiting for old Paisley to——'

"But when I got that far," concluded Telemachus Hicks, "I thought somebody had shot this left ear of mine off with a forty-five. But it turned out to be only a lick from a broomhandle in the hands of Mrs. Hicks."

THE HANDBOOK OF HYMEN

'Tis the opinion of myself, Sanderson Pratt, who sets this down, that the educational system of the United States should be in the hands of the weather bureau. I can give you good reasons for it; and you can't tell me why our college professors shouldn't be transferred to the meteorological department. They have been learned to read; and they could very easily glance at the morning papers and then wire in to the main office what kind of weather to expect. But there's the other side of the proposition. I am going on to tell you how the weather furnished me and Idaho Green with an elegant education.

We was up in the Bitter Root Mountains over the Montana line prospecting for gold. A chin-whiskered man in Walla-Walla, carrying a line of hope as excess baggage, had grubstaked us; and there we was in the foothills pecking away, with enough grub on hand to last an army through a peace conference.

Along one day comes a mail-rider over the mountains from Carlos, and stops to eat three cans of green-gages, and leave us a newspaper of modern date. This paper prints a system of premonitions of the weather, and the card it dealt Bitter Root Mountains from the bottom of the deck was "warmer and fair, with light westerly breezes."

That evening it began to snow, with the wind strong in the east. Me and Idaho moved camp into an old empty cabin higher up the mountain, thinking it was only a November flurry. But after falling three foot on a level it went to work in earnest; and we knew we was snowed in. We got in plenty of firewood before it got deep, and we had grub enough for two months, so we let the elements rage and cut up all they thought proper.

If you want to instigate the art of manslaughter just shut two men up in a eighteen by twenty-foot cabin for a month. Human nature won't stand it.

When the first snowflakes fell me and Idaho Green laughed at each other's jokes and praised the stuff we turned out of a skillet and called bread. At the end of three weeks Idaho makes this kind of a edict to me. Says he:

"I never exactly heard sour milk dropping out of a balloon on the bottom of a tin pan, but I have an idea it would be music of the spears compared to this attenuated stream of asphyxiated thought that emanates out of your organs of conversation. The kind of half-masticated noises that you emit every day puts me in mind of a cow's cud, only she's lady enough to keep hers to herself, and you ain't."

"Mr. Green," says I, "you having been a friend of mine once, I have some hesitations in confessing to you that if I had my choice for society between you and a common yellow three-legged cur pup, one of the inmates of this here cabin would be wagging a tail just at present."

This way we goes on for two or three days, and then we quits speaking to one another. We divides up the cooking implements, and Idaho cooks his grub on one side of the fireplace, and me on the other. The snow is up to the windows, and we have to keep a fire all day.

You see me and Idaho never had any education beyond reading and doing "if John had three apples and James five" on a slate. We never felt any special need for a university degree, though we had acquired a species of intrinsic intelligence in knocking around the world that we could use in emergencies. But snowbound in that cabin in the Bitter Roots, we felt for the first time that if we had studied Homer or Greek and fractions and the higher branches of information, we'd have had some resources in the line of meditation and private thought. I've seen them Eastern college fellows working in camps all through the West, and I never noticed but what education was less of a drawback to 'em than you would think. Why, once over on Snake River, when Andrew McWilliams' saddle horse got the botts, he sent a buckboard ten miles for one of these strangers that claimed to be a botanist. But that horse died.

One morning Idaho was poking around with a stick on top of a little shelf that was too high to reach. Two books fell down to the floor. I started toward 'em but caught Idaho's eye. He speaks for the first time in a week.

"Don't burn your fingers," says he. "In spite of the fact that you're only fit to be the companion of a sleeping mud-turtle, I'll give you a square deal. And that's more than your parents did when they turned you loose in the world with the sociability of a rattlesnake and the bedside manner of a frozen turnip. I'll play you a game of seven-up, the winner to pick up his choice of the book, the loser to take the other."

We played; and Idaho won. He picked up his book; and I took mine. Then each of us got on his side of the house and went to reading.

I never was as glad to see a ten-ounce nugget as I was that book. And Idaho looked at his like a kid looks at a stick of candy.

Mine was a little book about five by six inches called "Herkimer's Handbook of Indispensable Information." I may be wrong, but I think that was the greatest book that ever was written. I've got it to-day; and I can stump you or any man fifty times in five minutes with the information in it. Talk about Solomon or the New York *Tribune!* Herkimer had cases on both of 'em. That man must have put in fifty years and travelled a million miles to find out all that stuff. There was the population of all cities in it, and the way to tell a girl's age, and the number of teeth a camel has. It told you the longest tunnel in the world, the number of the stars, how long it takes for chicken pox to break out, what a lady's neck ought to measure, the veto powers of Governors, the dates of the Roman aqueducts, how many pounds of rice going without three beers a day would buy, the average annual temperature of Augusta, Maine, the quantity of seed required to plant an acre of carrots in drills, antidotes for poisons, the number of hairs on a blond lady's head, how to preserve eggs, the height of all the mountains in the world, and the dates of all wars and battles, and how to restore drowned persons, and sunstroke, and the number of tacks in a pound, and how to make dynamite and flowers and beds, and what to do before the doctor comes—and a hundred times as many things besides. If there was anything Herkimer didn't know I didn't miss it out of the book.

I sat and read that book for four hours. All the wonders of education was compressed in it. I forgot the snow, and I forgot that me and old Idaho was on the outs. He was sitting still on a stool reading away with a kind of partly soft and partly mysterious look shining through his tan-bark whiskers.

"Idaho," says I, "what kind of a book is yours?"

Idaho must have forgot, too, for he answered moderate, without any slander or malignity.

"Why," says he, "this here seems to be a volume by Homer K. M."

"Homer K. M. what?" I asked.

"Why, just Homer K. M.," says he.

"You're a liar," says I, a little riled that Idaho should try to put me up a tree. "No man is going 'round signing books with his initials. If it's Homer K. M. Spoopendyke, or Homer K. M. McSweeney, or Homer K. M. Jones, why don't you say so like a man instead of biting off the end of it like a calf chewing off the tail of a shirt on a clothes-line?"

"I put it to you straight, Sandy," says Idaho, quiet. "It's a poem book," says he, "by Homer K. M. I couldn't get color out of it at first, but there's a vein if you follow it up. I wouldn't have missed this book for a pair of red blankets."

"You're welcome to it," says I. "What I want is a disinterested statement of facts for the mind to work on, and that's what I seem to find in the book I've drawn."

"What you've got," says Idaho, "is statistics, the lowest grade of information that exists. They'll poison your mind. Give me old K. M.'s system of surmises. He seems to be a kind of a wine agent. His regular toast is 'nothing doing,' and he seems to have a grouch, but he keeps it so well lubricated with booze that his worst kicks sound like an invitation to split a quart. But it's poetry," says Idaho, "and I have sensations of scorn for that truck of yours that tries to convey sense in feet and inches. When it comes to explaining the instinct of philosophy through the art of nature, old K. M. has got your man beat by drills, rows, paragraphs, chest measurement, and average annual rainfall."

So that's the way me and Idaho had it. Day and night all the excitement we got was studying our books. That snowstorm sure fixed us with a fine lot of attainments apiece. By the time the snow melted, if you had stepped up to me suddenly and said: "Sanderson Pratt, what would it cost per square foot to lay a roof with twenty by twenty-eight tin at nine dollars and fifty cents per box?" I'd have told you as quick as light could travel the length of a spade handle at the rate of one hundred and ninety-two thousand miles per second. How many can do it? You wake up 'most any man you know in the middle of the night, and ask him quick to tell you the number of bones in the human skeleton exclusive of the teeth, or what percentage of the vote of the Nebraska Legislature overrules a veto. Will he tell you? Try him and see.

About what benefit Idaho got out of his poetry book I didn't exactly know. Idaho boosted the wine-agent every time he opened his mouth; but I wasn't so sure.

This Homer K. M., from what leaked out of his libretto through Idaho, seemed to me to be a kind of a dog who looked at life like it was a tin can tied to his tail. After running himself half to death, he sits down, hangs his tongue out, and looks at the can and says:

"Oh, well, since we can't shake the growler, let's get it filled at the corner, and all have a drink on me."

Besides that, it seems he was a Persian; and I never hear of Persia producing anything worth mentioning unless it was Turkish rugs and Maltese cats.

That spring me and Idaho struck pay ore. It was a habit of ours to sell out quick and keep moving. We unloaded on our grubstaker for eight thousand dollars apiece; and then we drifted down to this little town of Rosa, on the Salmon River, to rest up, and get some human grub, and have our whiskers harvested.

Rosa was no mining-camp. It laid in the valley, and was as free of uproar and pestilence as one of them rural towns in the country. There was a three-mile trolley line champing its bit in the environs; and me and Idaho spent a week riding on one of the cars, dropping off of nights at the Sunset View Hotel. Being now well read as well as travelled, we was soon *pro re nata* with the best society in Rosa, and was invited out to the most dressed-up and high-toned entertainments. It was at a piano recital and quail-eating contest in the city hall, for the benefit of the fire company, that me and Idaho first met Mrs. D. Ormond Sampson, the queen of Rosa society.

Mrs. Sampson was a widow, and owned the only two-story house in town. It was painted yellow, and whichever way you looked from you could see it as plain as egg on the chin of an O'Grady on a Friday. Twenty-two men in Rosa besides me and Idaho was trying to stake a claim on that yellow house.

There was a dance after the song books and quail bones had been raked out of the Hall. Twenty-three of the bunch galloped over to Mrs. Sampson and asked for a dance. I side-stepped the two-step, and asked permission to escort her home. That's where I made a hit.

On the way home says she:

"Ain't the stars lovely and bright to-night, Mr. Pratt?"

"For the chance they've got," says I, "they're humping themselves in a mighty creditable way. That big one you see is sixty-six billions of miles distant. It took thirty-six years for light to reach us. With an eighteen-foot telescope you can see forty-three millions of 'em, including them of the thirteenth magnitude, which, if one was to go out now, you would keep on seeing it for twenty-seven hundred years."

"My!" says Mrs. Sampson. "I never knew that before. How warm it is! I'm as damp as I can be from dancing so much."

"That's easy to account for," says I, "when you happen to know that you've got two million sweat-glands working all at once. If every one of your perspiratory ducts, which are a quarter of an inch long, was placed end to end, they would reach a distance of seven miles."

"Lawsy!" says Mrs. Sampson. "It sounds like an irrigation ditch you was describing, Mr. Pratt. How do you get all this knowledge of information?"

"From observation, Mrs. Sampson," I tells her. "I keep my eyes open when I go about the world."

"Mr. Pratt," says she, "I always did admire a man of education. There are so few scholars among the sap-headed plug-uglies of this town that it is a real pleasure to converse with a gentleman of culture. I'd be gratified to have you call at my house whenever you feel so inclined."

And that was the way I got the goodwill of the lady in the yellow house. Every Tuesday and Friday evenings I used to go there and tell her about the wonders of the universe as discovered, tabulated, and complied from nature by Herkimer. Idaho and the other gay Lutherans of the town got every minute of the rest of the week that they could.

I never imagined that Idaho was trying to work on Mrs. Sampson with old K. M.'s rules of courtship till one afternoon when I was on my way over to take her a basket of wild hog-plums. I met the lady coming down the lane that led to her house. Her eyes was snapping, and her hat made a dangerous dip over one eye.

"Mr. Pratt," she opens up, "this Mr. Green is a friend of yours, I believe."

"For nine years," says I.

"Cut him out," says she. "He's no gentleman!"

"Why, ma'am," says I, "he's a plain incumbent of the mountain, with asperities and the usual failings of a spendthrift and a liar, but I never on the most momentous occasion had the heart to deny that he was a gentleman. It may be that in haberdashery and the sense of arrogance and display Idaho offends the eye, but inside, ma'am, I've found him impervious to the lower grades of crime and obesity. After nine years of Idaho's society, Mrs. Sampson," I winds up, "I should hate to impute him, and I should hate to see him imputed."

"It's right plausible of you, Mr. Pratt," says Mrs. Sampson, "to take up the curmudgeons in your friend's behalf; but it don't alter the fact that he has made proposals to me sufficiently obnoxious to ruffle the ignominy of any lady."

"Why, now, now, now!" says I. "Old Idaho do that! I could believe it of myself sooner. I never knew but one thing to deride in him; and a blizzard was responsible for that. Once while we was snowbound in the mountains he became a prey to a kind of spurious and uneven poetry, which may have corrupted his demeanor."

"It has," says Mrs. Sampson. "Ever since I knew him he has been reciting to me a lot of irreligious rhymes by some person he calls Ruby Ott, and who is no better than she should be, if you judge by her poetry."

"Then Idaho has struck a new book," says I, "for the one he had was by a man who writes under the *nom de plume* of K. M."

"He'd better have stuck to it," says Mrs. Sampson, "whatever it was. And to-day he caps the vortex. I get a bunch of flowers from him, and on 'em is pinned a note. Now, Mr. Pratt, you know a lady when you see her; and you know how I stand in Rosa society. Do you think for a moment that I'd skip out to the woods with a man along with a jug of wine and a loaf of bread, and go singing and cavorting up and down under the trees with him? I take a little claret with my meals, but I'm not in the habit of packing a jug of it into the brush and raising Cain in any such style as that. And of course he'd bring his book of verses along, too. He said so. Let him go on his scandalous picnics alone! Or let him take his Ruby Ott with him. I reckon she wouldn't kick unless it was on account of there being too much bread along. And what do you think of your gentleman friend now, Mr. Pratt?"

"Well, 'm," says I, "it may be that Idaho's invitation was a kind of poetry,

and meant no harm. Maybe it belonged to the class of rhymes they call figurative. They offend law and order, but they get sent through the mails on the
grounds that they mean something that they don't say. I'd be glad on Idaho's
account if you'd overlook it," says I, "and let us extricate our minds from the
low regions of poetry to the higher planes of fact and fancy. On a beautiful
afternoon like this, Mrs. Sampson," I goes on, "we should let our thoughts dwell
accordingly. Though it is warm here, we should remember that at the equator
the line of perpetual frost is at an altitude of fifteen thousand feet. Between
the latitudes of forty degrees and forty-nine degrees it is from four thousand to
nine thousand feet."

"Oh, Mr. Pratt," says Mrs. Sampson, "it's such a comfort to hear you say
them beautiful facts after getting such a jar from that minx of a Ruby's poetry!"

"Let us sit on this log at the roadside," says I, "and forget the inhumanity and
ribaldry of the poets. It is in the glorious columns of ascertained facts and legal-
ized measures that beauty is to be found. In this very log we sit upon, Mrs.
Sampson," says I, "is statistics more wonderful than any poem. The rings show
it was sixty years old. At the depth of two thousand feet it would become coal
in three thousand years. The deepest coal mine in the world is at Killingworth,
near Newcastle. A box four feet long, three feet wide, and two feet eight inches
deep will hold one ton of coal. If an artery is cut, compress it above the wound.
A man's leg contains thirty bones. The Tower of London was burned in 1841."

"Go on, Mr. Pratt," says Mrs. Sampson. "Them ideas is so original and soothing. I think statistics are just as lovely as they can be."

But it wasn't till two weeks later that I got all that was coming to me out of
Herkimer.

One night I was waked up by folks hollering "Fire!" all around. I jumped
up and dressed and went out of the hotel to enjoy the scene. When I seen it was
Mrs. Sampson's house, I gave forth a kind of yell, and I was there in two minutes.

The whole lower story of the yellow house was in flames, and every masculine,
feminine, and canine in Rosa was there, screeching and barking and getting in the
way of the firemen. I saw Idaho trying to get away from six firemen who were
holding him. They was telling him the whole place was on fire downstairs, and
no man could go in it and come out alive.

"Where's Mrs. Sampson?" I asks.

"She hasn't been seen," says one of the firemen. "She sleeps upstairs. We've
tried to get in, but we can't, and our company hasn't got any ladders yet."

I runs around to the light of the big blaze, and pulls the Handbook out of
my inside pocket. I kind of laughed when I felt it in my hands—I reckon I was
some daffy with the sensation of excitement.

"Herky, old boy," I says to it, as I flipped over the pages, "you ain't ever
lied to me yet, and you ain't ever throwed me down at a scratch yet. Tell me
what, old boy, tell me what!" says I.

I turned to "What to do in Case of Accidents," on page 117. I run my finger
down the page, and struck it. Good old Herkimer, he never overlooked anything!
It said:

SUFFOCATION FROM INHALING SMOKE OR GAS.—There is nothing better than
flaxseed. Place a few seed in the outer corner of the eye.

I shoved the Handbook back in my pocket, and grabbed a boy that was running by.

"Here," says I, giving him some money, "run to the drug store and bring
a dollars' worth of flaxseed. Hurry, and you'll get another one for yourself.
Now," I sings out to the crowd, "we'll have Mrs. Sampson!" And I throws
away my coat and hat.

Four of the firemen and citizens grabs hold of me. It's sure death, they say, to go in the house, for the floors was beginning to fall through.

"How in blazes," I sings out, kind of laughing yet, but not feeling like it, "do you expect me to put flaxseed in a eye without the eye?"

I jabbed each elbow in a fireman's face, kicked the bark off of one citizen's shin, and tripped the other one with a side hold. And then I busted into the house. If I die first I'll write you a letter and tell you if it's any worse down there than the inside of that yellow house was; but don't believe it yet. I was a heap more cooked than the hurry-up orders of broiled chicken that you get in restaurants. The fire and smoke had me down on the floor twice, and was about to shame Herkimer, but the firemen helped me with their little stream of water, and I got to Mrs. Sampson's room. She'd lost conscientiousness from the smoke, so I wrapped her in the bed clothes and got her on my shoulder. Well, the floors wasn't as bad as they said, or I never could have done it—not by no means.

I carried her out fifty yards from the house and laid her on the grass. Then, of course, every one of them other twenty-two plaintiffs to the lady's hand crowded around with tin dippers of water ready to save her. And up runs the boy with the flaxseed.

I unwrapped the covers from Mrs. Sampson's head. She opened her eyes and says:

"Is that you, Mr. Pratt?"

"S-s-sh," says I. "Don't talk till you've had the remedy."

I runs my arm around her neck and raises her head, gentle, and breaks the bag of flaxseed with the other hand; and as easy as I could I bends over and slips three or four of the seeds in the outer corner of her eye.

Up gallops the village doc by this time, and snorts around, and grabs at Mrs. Sampson's pulse, and wants to know what I mean by any such sandblasted nonsense.

"Well, old Jalap and Jerusalem oak seed," says I, "I'm no regular practitioner, but I'll show you my authority, anyway."

They fetched my coat, and I gets out the Handbook.

"Look on page 117," says I "at the remedy for suffocation by smoke or gas. Flaxseed in the outer corner of the eye, it says. I don't know whether it works as a smoke consumer or whether it hikes the compound gastro-hippopotamus nerve into action, but Herkimer says it, and he was called to the case first. If you want to make it a consultation, there's no objection."

Old doc takes the book and looks at it by means of his specs and a fireman's lantern.

"Well, Mr. Pratt," says he, "you evidently got on the wrong line in reading your diagnosis. The recipe for suffocation says: 'Get the patient into fresh air as quickly as possible, and place in a reclining position.' The flaxseed remedy is for 'Dust and Cinders in the Eye,' on the line above. But, after all——"

"See here," interrupts Mrs. Sampson, "I reckon I've got something to say in this consultation. That flaxseed done me more good than anything I ever tried." And then she raises up her head and lays it back on my arm again, and says: "Put some in the other eye, Sandy dear."

And so if you was to stop off at Rosa to-morrow, or any other day, you'd see a fine new yellow house with Mrs. Pratt, that was Mrs. Sampson, embellishing and adorning it. And if you was to step inside you'd see on the marble-top centre table in the parlor, "Herkimer's Handbook of Indispensable Information," all rebound in red morocco, and ready to be consulted on any subject pertaining to human happiness and wisdom.

THE PIMIENTA PANCAKES

WHILE we were rounding up a bunch of the Triangle-O cattle in the Frio bottoms a projecting branch of a dead mesquite caught my wooden stirrup and gave my ankle a wrench that laid me up in camp for a week.

On the third day of my compulsory idleness I crawled out near the grub wagon, and reclined helpless under the conversational fire of Judson Odom, the camp cook. Jud was a monologist by nature, whom Destiny, with customary blundering, had set in a profession wherein he was bereaved, for the greater portion of his time, of an audience.

Therefore, I was manna in the desert of Jud's obmutescence.

Betimes I was stirred by invalid longings for something to eat that did not come under the caption of "grub." I had visions of the maternal pantry "deep as first love, and wild with all regret," and then I asked:

"Jud, can you make pancakes?"

Jud laid down his sixshooter, with which he was preparing to pound an antelope steak, and stood over me in what I felt to be a menacing attitude. He further indorsed my impression that his pose was resentful by fixing upon me with his light blue eyes a look of cold suspicion.

"Say, you," he said, with candid, though not excessive, choler, "did you mean that straight, or was you trying to throw the gaff into me? Some of the boys been telling you about me and that pancake racket?"

"No, Jud," I said, sincerely, "I meant it. It seems to me I'd swap my pony and saddle for a stack of buttered brown pancakes with some first crop, open kettle, New Orleans sweetening. Was there a story about pancakes?"

Jud was mollified at once when he saw that I had not been dealing in allusions. He brought some mysterious bags and tin boxes from the grub wagon and set them in the shade of the hackberry where I lay reclined. I watched him as he began to arrange them leisurely and untie their many strings.

"No, not a story," said Jud, as he worked, "but just the logical disclosures in the case of me and that pink-eyed snoozer from Mired Mule Cañada and Miss Willella Learight. I don't mind telling you.

"I was punching then for old Bill Toomey, on the San Miguel. One day I gets all ensnared up in aspirations for to eat some canned grub that hasn't ever mooed or baaed or grunted or been in peck measures. So, I gets on my bronc and pushes the wind for Uncle Emsley Telfair's store at the Pimienta Crossing on the Neuces.

"About three in the afternoon I throwed my bridle over a mesquite limb and walked the last twenty yards into Uncle Emsley's store. I got up on the counter and told Uncle Emsley that the signs pointed to the devastation of the fruit crop of the world. In a minute I had a bag of crackers and a long-handled spoon, with an open can each of apricots and pineapples and cherries and green-gages beside of me with Uncle Emsley busy chopping away with the hatchet at the yellow clings. I was feeling like Adam before the apple stampede, and was digging my spurs into the side of the counter and working with my twenty-four-inch spoon when I happened to look out of the window into the yard of Uncle Emsley's house, which was next to the store.

"There was a girl standing there—an imported girl with fixings on—philandering with a croquet maul and amusing herself by watching my style of encouraging the fruit canning industry.

"I slid off the counter and delivered up my shovel to Uncle Emsley.

"'That's my niece,' says he; 'Miss Willella Learight, down from Palestine on a visit. Do you want that I should make you acquainted?'

" 'The Holy Land,' I says to myself, my thought milling some as I tried to run 'em into the corral. 'Why not? There was sure angels in Pales—— Why yes, Uncle Emsley,' I says out loud, 'I'd be awful edified to meet Miss Learight.'

"So Uncle Emsley took me out in the yard and gave us each other's entitlements.

"I never was shy about women. I never could understand why some men who can break a mustang before breakfast and shave in the dark, get all left-handed and full of perspiration and excuses when they see a bolt of calico draped around what belongs in it. Inside of eight minutes me and Miss Willella was aggravating the croquet balls around as amiable as second cousins. She gave me a dig about the quantity of canned fruit I had eaten, and I got back at her, flat-footed, about how a certain lady named Eve started the fruit trouble in the first free-grass pasture—'Over in Palestine, wasn't it?' says I, as easy and pat as roping a one-year-old.

"That was how I acquired cordiality for the proximities of Miss Willella Learight; and the disposition grew larger as time passed. She was stopping at Pimienta Crossing for her health, which was very good, and for the climate, which was forty per cent. hotter than Palestine. I rode over to see her once every week for a while; and then I figured it out that if I doubled the number of trips I would see her twice as often.

"One week I slipped in a third trip; and that's where the pancakes and the pink-eyed snoozer busted into the game.

"That evening, while I set on the counter with a peach and two damsons in my mouth, I asked Uncle Emsley how Miss Willella was.

" 'Why,' says Uncle Emsley, 'she's gone riding with Jackson Bird, the sheep man from over at Mired Mule Cañada.'

"I swallowed the peach seed and the two damson seeds. I guess somebody held the counter by the bridle while I got off; and then I walked out straight ahead till I butted against the mesquite where my roan was tied.

" 'She's gone riding,' I whispered in my bronc's ear, 'with Birdstone Jack, the hired mule from Sheep Man's Cañada. Did you get that, old Leather-and-Gallops?'

"That bronc of mine wept, in his way. He'd been raised a cow pony and he didn't care for snoozers.

"I went back and said to Uncle Emsley: 'Did you say a sheep man?'

" 'I said a sheep man,' says Uncle again. 'You must have heard tell of Jackson Bird. He's got eight sections of grazing and four thousand head of the finest Merinos south of the Arctic Circle.'

"I went out and sat on the ground in the shade of the store and leaned against a prickly pear. I sifted sand into my boots with unthinking hands while I soliloquized a quantity about this bird with the Jackson plumage to his name.

"I never had believed in harming sheep men. I see one, one day, reading a Latin grammar on hossback, and I never touched him! They never irritated me like they do most cowmen. You wouldn't go to work now, and impair and disfigure snoozers, would you, that eat on tables and wear little shoes and speak to you on subjects? I had always let 'em pass, just as you would a jack-rabbit; with a polite word and a guess about the weather, but no stopping to swap canteens. I never thought it was worth while to be hostile with a snoozer. And because I'd been lenient, and let 'em live, here was one going around riding with Miss Willella Learight!

"An hour by sun they come loping back, and stopped at Uncle Emsley's gate. The sheep person helped her off; and they stood throwing each other sentences all sprightful and sagacious for a while. And then this feathered Jackson flies up in his saddle and raises his little stewpot of a hat, and trots off in the direction of his mutton ranch. By this time I had turned the sand out of my boots and unpinned myself from the prickly pear; and by the time he gets half a mile out of Pimienta, I singlefoots up beside him on my bronc.

"I said that snoozer was pink-eyed, but he wasn't. His seeing arrangement was gray enough, but his eye-lashes was pink and his hair was sandy, and that gave you the idea. Sheep man——he wasn't more than a lamb man, anyhow—— a little thing with his neck involved in a yellow silk handkerchief, and shoes tied up in bowknots.

"'Afternoon!' says I to him. 'You now ride with a equestrian who is commonly called Dead-Moral-Certainty Judson, on account of the way I shoot. When I want a stranger to know me I always introduce myself before the draw, for I never did like to shake hands with ghosts.'

"'Ah,' says he, just like that—'Ah, I'm glad to know you, Mr. Judson. I'm Jackson Bird, from over at Mired Mule Ranch.'

"Just then one of my eyes saw a roadrunner skipping down the hill with a young tarantula in his bill, and the other eye noticed a rabbit-hawk sitting on a dead limb in a water-elm. I popped over one after the other with my forty-five, just to show him. 'Two out of three,' says I, 'Birds just naturally seem to draw my fire wherever I go.'

"'Nice shooting,' says the sheep man, without a flutter. 'But don't you sometimes ever miss the third shot? Elegant fine rain that was last week for the young grass, Mr. Judson?' says he.

"'Willie,' says I, riding over close to his palfrey, 'your infatuated parents may have denounced you by the name of Jackson, but you sure moulted into a twittering Willie—let us slough off this here analysis of rain and the elements, and get down to talk that is outside the vocabulary of parrots. That is a bad habit you have got of riding with young ladies over at Pimienta. I've known birds,' says I, 'to be served on toast for less than that. Miss Willella,' says I, 'don't ever want any nest made out of sheep's wool by a tomtit of the Jacksonian branch of ornithology. Now, are you going to quit, or do you wish for to gallop up against this Dead-Moral-Certainty attachment to my name, which is good for two hyphens and at least one set of funeral obsequies?'

"Jackson Bird flushed up some, and then he laughed.

"'Why, Mr. Judson,' says he, 'you've got the wrong idea. I've called on Miss Learight a few times; but not for the purpose you imagine. My object is purely a gastronomical one.'

"I reached for my gun.

"'Any coyote,' says I, 'that would boast of dishonorable——'

"'Wait a minute,' says this Bird, 'till I explain. What would I do with a wife? If you ever saw that ranch of mine! I do my own cooking and mending. Eating—that's all the pleasure I get out of sheep raising. Mr. Judson, did you ever taste the pancakes that Miss Learight makes?'

"'Me? No,' I told him. 'I never was advised that she was up to any culinary maneuvers.'

"'They're golden sunshine,' says he, 'honey-browned by the ambrosial fires of Epicurus. I'd give two years of my life to get the recipe for making them pancakes. That's what I went to see Miss Learight for,' says Jackson Bird, 'but I haven't been able to get it from her. It's an old recipe that's been in the family for seventy-five years. They hand it down from one generation to another, but they don't give it away to outsiders. If I could get that recipe, so I could make them pancakes for myself on my ranch, I'd be a happy man,' says Bird.

"'Are you sure,' I says to him, 'that it ain't the hand that mixes the pancakes that you're after?'

"'Sure,' says Jackson. 'Miss Learight is a mighty nice girl, but I can assure you my intentions go no further than the gastro—' but he seen my hand going down to my holster and he changed his similitude—'than the desire to procure a copy of the pancake recipe,' he finishes.

"'You ain't such a bad little man,' says I, trying to be fair. 'I was thinking some of making orphans of your sheep, but I'll let you fly away this time. But you stick to pancakes,' says I, 'as close as the middle one of a stack; and don't go and mistake sentiments for syrup, or there'll be singing at your ranch, and you won't hear it.'

"'To convince you that I am sincere,' says the sheep man, 'I'll ask you to help me. Miss Learight and you being closer friends, maybe she would do for you what she wouldn't for me. If you will get me a copy of that pancake recipe, I give you my word that I'll never call upon her again.'

"'That's fair,' I says, and I shook hands with Jackson Bird. 'I'll get it for you if I can, and glad to oblige.' And he turned off down the big pear flat on the Piedra, in the direction of Mired Mule; and I steered northwest for old Bill Toomey's ranch.

"It was five days afterward when I got another chance to ride over to Pimienta. Miss Willella and me passed a gratifying evening at Uncle Emsley's. She sang some, and exasperated the piano quite a lot with quotations from the operas. I gave imitations of a rattlesnake, and told her about Snaky McFee's new way of skinning cows, and described the trip I made to Saint Louis once. We was getting along in one another's estimations fine. Thinks I, if Jackson can now be persuaded to migrate, I win. I recollect his promise about the pancake receipt, and I thinks I will persuade it from Miss Willella and give it to him; and then if I catches Birdie off of Mired Mule again, I'll make him hop the twig.

"So, along about ten o'clock, I put on a wheedling smile and says to Miss Willella: 'Now, if there's anything I do like better than the sight of a red steer on green grass it's the taste of a nice hot pancake smothered in sugarhouse molasses.'

"Miss Willella gives a little jump on the piano stool, and looked at me curious.

"'Yes,' says she, 'they're real nice. What did you say was the name of that street in Saint Louis, Mr. Odom, where you lost your hat?'

"'Pancake Avenue,' says I, with a wink, to show her that I was on about the family receipt, and couldn't be side-corralled off of the subject. 'Come, now, Miss Willella,' I says; 'let's hear how you make 'em. Pancakes is just whirling in my head like wagon wheels. Start her off, now—pound of flour, eight dozen eggs, and so on. How does the catalogue of constituents run?'

"'Excuse me for a moment, please,' says Miss Willella, and she gives me a quick kind of sideways look, and slides off the stool. She ambled out into the other room, and directly Uncle Emsley comes in in his shirt sleeves, with a pitcher of water. He turns around to get a glass on the table, and I see a forty-five in his hip pocket. 'Great post-holes!' thinks I, 'but here's a family thinks a heap of cooking receipts, protecting it with firearms. I've known outfits that wouldn't do that much by a family feud.'

"'Drink this here down,' says Uncle Emsley, handing me the glass of water. 'You've rid too far to-day, Jud, and got yourself over-excited. Try to think about something else now.'

"'Do you know how to make them pancakes, Uncle Emsley?' I asked.

"'Well, I'm not as apprised in the anatomy of them as some,' says Uncle Emsley, 'but I reckon you take a sifter of plaster of paris and a little dough and saleratus and corn meal, and mix 'em with eggs and buttermilk as usual. Is old Bill going to ship beeves to Kansas City again this spring, Jud?'

"That was all the pancake specifications I could get that night. I didn't wonder that Jackson Bird found it uphill work. So I dropped the subject and talked with Uncle Emsley a while about hollow-horn and cyclones. And then Miss Willella came and said 'Good-night,' and I hit the breeze for the ranch.

"About a week afterward I met Jackson Bird riding out of Pimienta as I rode in, and we stopped in the road for a few frivolous remarks.

" 'Got the bill of particulars for them flap-jacks yet?' I asked him.

" 'Well, no,' says Jackson. 'I don't seem to have any success in getting hold of it. Did you try?'

" 'I did,' says I, 'and 'twas like trying to dig a prairie dog out of his hole with a peanut hull. That pancake receipt must be a jooka-lorum, the way they hold on to it.'

" 'I'm 'most ready to give it up,' says Jackson, so discouraged in his pronunciations that I felt sorry for him; 'but I did want to know how to make them pancakes to eat on my lonely ranch,' says he. 'I lie awake at nights thinking how good they are.'

" 'You keep on trying for it,' I tells him, 'and I'll do the same. One of us is bound to get a rope over its horns before long. Well, so-long, Jacksy.'

"You see, by this time we was on the peacefullest of terms. When I saw that he wasn't after Miss Willella I had more endurable contemplations of that sandy-haired snoozer. In order to help out the ambitions of his appetite I kept on trying to get that receipt from Miss Willella. But every time I would say 'pancakes' she would get sort of remote and fidgety about the eye, and try to change the subject. If I held her to it she would slide out and round up Uncle Emsley with his pitcher of water and hip-pocket howitzer.

"One day I galloped over to the store with a fine bunch of blue verbenas that I cut out of a herd of wild flowers over on Poisoned Dog Prairie. Uncle Emsley looked at 'em with one eye shut and says:

" 'Haven't ye heard the news?'

" 'Cattle up?' I asks.

" 'Willella and Jackson Bird was married in Palestine yesterday,' says he. 'Just got a letter this morning.'

"I dropped them flowers in a cracker-barrel, and let the news trickle in my ears and down toward my upper left-hand shirt pocket until it got to my feet.

" 'Would you mind saying that over again once more, Uncle Emsley?' says I. 'Maybe my hearing has got wrong, and you only said that prime heifers was 4.80 on the hoof, or something like that.'

" 'Married yesterday,' says Uncle Emsley, 'and gone to Waco and Niagara Falls on a wedding tour. Why, didn't you see none of the signs all along? Jackson Bird has been courting Willella ever since that day he took her out riding.'

" 'Then,' says I, in a kind of a yell, 'what was all this zizzaparoola he gives me about pancakes? Tell me *that*.'

"When I said 'pancakes' Uncle Emsley sort of dodged and stepped back.

" 'Somebody's been dealing me pancakes from the bottom of the deck,' I says, 'and I'll find out. I believe you know. Talk up,' says I, 'or we'll mix a panful of batter right here.'

"I slid over the counter after Uncle Emsley. He grabbed at his gun, but it was in a drawer, and he missed it two inches. I got him by the front of his shirt and shoved him in a corner.

" 'Talk pancakes,' says I, 'or be made into one. Does Miss Willella make 'em?'

" 'She never made one in her life and I never saw one,' says Uncle Emsley, soothing. 'Calm down now, Jud—calm down. You've got excited, and that wound in your head is contaminating your sense of intelligence. Try not to think about pancakes.'

" 'Uncle Emsley,' says I, 'I'm not wounded in the head except so far as my natural cogitative instincts run to runts. Jackson Bird told me he was calling on Miss Willella for the purpose of finding out her system of producing pancakes, and he asked me to help him get the bill of lading of the ingredients. I done so, with the results as you see. Have I been sodded down with Johnson grass by a pink-eyed snoozer, or what?'

"'Slack up your grip on my dress shirt,' says Uncle Emsley, 'and I'll tell you. Yes, it looks like Jackson Bird has gone and humbugged you some. The day after he went riding with Willella he came back and told me and her to watch out for you whenever you got to talking about pancakes. He said you was in camp once where they was cooking flapjacks, and one of the fellows cut you over the head with a frying pan. Jackson said that whenever you got over-hot or excited that wound hurt you and made you kind of crazy, and you went raving about pancakes. He told us to just get you worked off of the subject and soothed down, and you wouldn't be dangerous. So, me and Willella done the best by you we knew how. Well, well,' says Uncle Emsley, 'that Jackson Bird is sure a seldóm kind of a snoozer.'"

During the progress of Jud's story he had been slowly but deftly combining certain portions of the contents of his sacks and cans. Toward the close of it he set before me the finished product—a pair of red-hot, rich-hued pancakes on a tin plate. From some secret hoarding place he also brought a lump of excellent butter and a bottle of golden syrup.

"How long ago did these things happen?" I asked him.

"Three years," said Jud. They're living on the Mired Mule Ranch now. But I haven't seen either of 'em since. They say Jackson Bird was fixing his ranch up fine with rocking chairs and window curtains all the time he was putting me up the pancake tree. Oh, I got over it after a while. But the boys kept the racket up."

"Did you make these cakes by the famous recipe?" I asked.

"Didn't I tell you there wasn't no receipt?" said Jud. "The boys hollered pancakes till they got pancake hungry, and I cut this receipt out of a newspaper. How does the truck taste?"

"They're delicious," I answered. "Why don't you have some, too, Jud?"

I was sure I heard a sigh.

"Me?" said Jud. "I don't never eat 'em.'

SEATS OF THE HAUGHTY

GOLDEN by day and silver by night, a new trail now leads to us across the Indian Ocean. Dusky kings and princes have found out our Bombay of the West; and few be their trails that do not lead down Broadway on their journey for to admire and for to see.

If chance should ever lead you near a hotel that transiently shelters some one of these splendid touring grandees, I counsel you to seek Lucullus Polk among the republican tuft-hunters that besiege its entrances. He will be there. You will know him by his red, alert, Wellington-nosed face, by his manner of nervous caution mingled with determination, by his assumed promoter's or broker's air of busy impatience, and by his bright-red necktie, gallantly redressing the wrongs of his maltreated blue serge suit, like a battle standard, still waving above a lost cause. I found him profitable; and so may you. When you do look for him, look among the light-horse troop of Bedouins that besiege the picket-line of the travel-ling potentate's guards and secretaries—among the wild-eyed genii of Arabian Afternoons that gather to make astounding and egregious demands upon the prince's coffers.

I first saw Mr. Polk coming down the steps of the hotel at which sojourned His

Highness the Gaekwar of Baroda, most enlightened of the Mahratta princes, who, of late, ate bread and salt in our Metropolis of the Occident.

Lucullus moved rapidly, as though propelled by some potent moral force that imminently threatened to become physical. Behind him closely followed the impetus—a hotel detective, if ever white Alpine hat, hawk's nose, implacable watch chain, and loud refinement of manner spoke the truth. A brace of uniformed porters at his heels preserved the smooth decorum of the hotel, repudiating by their air of disengagement any suspicion that they formed a reserve squad of ejectment.

Safe on the sidewalk, Lucullus Polk turned and shook a freckled fist at the caravansary. And, to my joy, he began to breathe deep invective in strange words.

"Rides in howdahs, does he?" he cried loudly and sneeringly. "Rides on elephants in howdahs and calls himself a prince! Kings—yah! Comes over here and talks horse till you would think he was a president; and then goes home and rides in a private dining-room strapped onto an elephant. Well, well, well!"

The ejecting committee quietly retired. The scorner of princes turned to me and snapped his fingers.

"What do you think of that?" he shouted derisively. "The Gaekwar of Baroda rides on an elephant in a howdah! And there's old Bikram Shamsher Jang scorching up and down the pig-paths of Khatmandu on a motor-cycle. Wouldn't that maharajah you? And the Shah of Persia, that ought to have been Muley-on-the-spot for at least three, he's got the palanquin habit. And that funny-hat prince from Korea—wouldn't you think he could afford to amble around on a milk-white palfrey once in a dynasty or two? Nothing doing! His idea of a Balaklava charge is to tuck his skirts under him and do his mile in six days over the hog-wallows of Seoul on a bull-cart. That's the kind of visiting potentates that come to this country now. It's a hard deal, friend."

I murmured a few words of sympathy. But it was uncomprehending, for I did not know his grievance against the rulers who flash, meteor-like, now and then upon our shores.

"The last one I sold," continued the displeased one, "was to that three-horse-tailed Turkish pasha that came over a year ago. Five hundred dollars he paid for it, easy. I says to his executioner or secretary—he was a kind of a Jew or a Chinaman—'His Turkey Giblets is fond of horses, then?'

"'Him?' says the secretary. 'Well, no. He's got a big, fat wife in the harem named Bad Dora that he don't like. I believe he intends to saddle her up and ride her up and down the board-walk in the Bulbul Gardens a few times every day. You haven't got a pair of extra long spurs you could throw in on the deal, have you?' Yes, sir, there's mighty few real rough-riders among the royal sports these days."

As soon as Lucullus Polk got cool enough I picked him up, and with no greater effort than you would employ in persuading a drowning man to clutch a straw, I inveigled him into accompanying me to a cool corner in a dim café.

And it came to pass that men-servants set before us brewage; and Lucullus Polk spake unto me, relating the wherefores of his beleaguering the antechambers of the princes of the earth.

"Did you ever hear of the S. A. & A. P. Railroad in Texas? Well, that don't stand for Samaritan Actor's Aid Philanthropy. I was down that way managing a summer bunch of the gum and syntax-chewers that play the Idlewild Parks in the Western hamlets. Of course, we went to pieces when the soubrette ran away with a prominent barber of Beeville. I don't know what became of the rest of the company. I believe there were some salaries due; and the last I saw of the troupe was when I told them that forty-three cents was all the treasury contained. I say I never saw any of them after that; but I heard them for about twenty minutes. I didn't have time to look back. But after dark I came out of the woods and struck the S. A. & A. P. agent for means of transportation. He at once extended to me the courtesies of the entire railroad, kindly warning me, however, not to get aboard any of the rolling stock.

"About ten the next morning I steps off the ties into a village that calls itself Atascosa City. I bought a thirty-cent breakfast and a ten-cent cigar, and stood on Main Street jingling the three pennies in my pocket—dead broke. A man in Texas with only three cents in his pocket is no better off than a man that has no money and owes two cents.

"One of luck's favorite tricks is to soak a man for his last dollar so quick that he don't have time to look at it. There I was in a swell St. Louis tailor-made, blue-and-green plaid suit, and an eighteen-carat sulphate-of-copper scarf pin, with no hope in sight except the two great Texas industries, the cotton fields, and grading new railroads. I never picked cotton, and I never cottoned to a pick, so the outlook had ultramarine edges.

"All of a sudden, while I was standing on the edge of the wooden sidewalk, down out of the sky falls two fine gold watches into the middle of the street. One hits a chunk of mud and sticks. The other falls hard and flies open, making a fine drizzle of little springs and screws and wheels. I looks up for a balloon or an airship; but not seeing any, I steps off the sidewalk to investigate.

"But I hear a couple of yells and see two men running up the street in leather overalls and high-heeled boots and cartwheel hats. One man is six or eight feet high, with open-plumbed joints and a heartbroken cast of countenance. He picks up the watch that has stuck in the mud. The other man, who is little, with pink hair and white eyes, goes for the empty case, and says, 'I win.' Then the elevated pessimist goes down under his leather leg-holsters and hands a handful of twenty-dollar gold pieces to his albino friend. I don't know how much money it was; it looked as big as an earthquake-relief fund to me.

"'I'll have this here case filled up with works,' says Shorty, 'and throw you again for five hundred.'

"'I'm your company,' says the high man. 'I'll meet you at the Smoked Dog Saloon an hour from now.'

"The little man hustles away with a kind of Swiss movement toward a jewelry store. The heartbroken person stoops over and takes a telescopic view of my haberdashery.

"'Them's a mighty slick outfit of habiliments you have got on, Mr. Man,' says he. 'I'll bet a hoss you never acquired the right, title, and interest in and to them clothes in Atascosa City.'

"'Why no,' says I, being ready enough to exchange personalities with this moneyed monument of melancholy. 'I had this suit tailored from a special line of coatericks, vestures, and paintings in St. Louis. Would you mind putting me sane,' says I, 'on this watch-throwing contest? I've been used to seeing timepieces treated with more politeness and esteem—except women's watches, of course, which by nature they abuse by cracking walnuts with 'em and having 'em taken showing in tintype pictures.'

"'Me and George,' he explains, 'are up from the ranch, having a spell of fun. Up to last month we owned four sections of watered grazing down on the San Miguel. But along comes one of these oil prospectors and begins to bore. He strikes a gusher that flows out twenty thousand—or maybe it was twenty million—barrels of oil a day. And me and George gets one hundred and fifty thousand dollars—seventy-five thousand dollars apiece—for the land. So now and then we saddles up and hits the breeze for Atascosa City for a few days of excitement and damage. Here's a little bunch of the *dinero* that I drawed out of the bank this morning,' says he, and shows a roll of twenties and fifties as big around as a sleeping-car pillow. The yellowbacks glowed like a sun set on the gable end of John D's barn. My knees got weak, and I sa? down on the edge of the board sidewalk.

"'You must have knocked around a right smart,' goes on this oil Grease-us. 'I shouldn't be surprised if you have saw towns more livelier than what Atascosa City is. Sometimes it seems to me that there ought to be some more ways of having a good time than there is here, 'specially when you've got plenty of money and don't mind spending it.'

"Then this Mother Cary's chick of the desert sits down by me and we hold a conversationfest. It seems that he was money-poor. He'd lived in ranch camps all his life; and he confessed to me that his supreme idea of luxury was to ride into camp, tired out from a round-up, eat a peck of Mexican beans, hobble his brains with a pint of raw whisky, and go to sleep with his boots for a pillow. When this barge-load of unexpected money came to him and his pink but perky partner, George, and they hied themselves to this clump of outhouses called Atascosa City, you know what happened to them. They had money to buy anything they wanted; but they didn't know what to want. Their ideas of spendthriftiness were limited to three—whisky, saddles, and gold watches. If there was anything else in the world to throw away fortunes on, they had never heard about it. So, when they wanted to have a hot time, they'd ride into town and get a city directory and stand in front of the principal saloon and call up the population alphabetically for free drinks. Then they would order three or four new California saddles from the storekeeper, and play crack-loo on the sidewalk with twenty-dollar gold pieces. Betting who could throw his gold watch the farthest was an inspiration of George's; but even that was getting to be monotonous.

"Was I on to the opportunity? Listen.

"In thirty minutes I had dashed off a word picture of metropolitan joys that made life in Atascosa City look as dull as a trip to Coney Island with your own wife. In ten minutes more we shook hands on an agreement that I was to act as his guide, interpreter and friend in and to the aforesaid wassail and amenity. And Solomon Mills, which was his name, was to pay all expenses for a month. At the end of that time, if I had made good as director-general of the rowdy life, he was to pay me one thousand dollars. And then, to clinch the bargain, we called the roll of Atascosa City and put all of its citizens except the ladies and minors under the table, except one man named Horace Westervelt St. Claire. Just for that we bought a couple hatfuls of cheap silver watches and egged him out of town with 'em. We wound up by dragging the harness-maker out of bed and setting him to work on three new saddles; and then we went to sleep across the railroad track at the depot, just to annoy the S. A. &. A. P. Think of having seventy-five thousand dollars and trying to avoid the disgrace of dying rich in a town like that!

"The next day George, who was married or something, started back to the ranch. Me and Solly, as I now called him, prepared to shake off our moth balls and wing our way against the arc-lights of the joyous and tuneful East.

"'No way-stops,' says I to Solly, 'except long enough to get you barbered and haberdashed. This is no Texas feet shampetter,' says I, 'where you eat chili-con-carne-con-huevos and then holler "Whoopee!" across the plaza. We're now going against the real high life. We're going to mingle with the set that carries a Spitz, wears spats, and hits the ground in high spots.'

"Solly puts six thousand dollars in century bills in one pocket of his brown ducks, and bills of lading for ten thousand dollars on Eastern banks in another. Then I resume diplomatic relations with the S. A. &. A. P., and we hike in a northwesterly direction on our circuitous route to the spice gardens of the Yankee Orient.

"We stopped in San Antonio long enough for Solly to buy some clothes, and eight rounds of drinks for the guests and employees of the Menger Hotel, and order four Mexican saddles with silver trimmings and white Angora *suaderos* to be shipped down to the ranch. From there we made a big jump to St. Louis. We got there in time for dinner: and I put our thumb-prints on the register of the most expensive hotel in the city.

" 'Now,' says I to Solly, with a wink at myself, 'here's the first dinner-station we've struck where we can get a real good plate of beans.' And while he was up in his room trying to draw water out of the gas-pipe, I got one finger in the buttonhole of the head waiter's Tuxedo, drew him apart, inserted a two-dollar bill, and closed him up again.

" 'Frankoyse,' says I, 'I have a pal here for dinner that's been subsisting for years on cereals and short stogies. You see the chef and order a dinner for us such as you serve to Dave Francis and the general passenger agent of the Iron Mountain when they eat here. We've got more than Bernhardt's tent full of money; and we want the nose-bags crammed with all the Chief Deveries *de cuisine*. Object is no expense. Now, show us.'

"At six o'clock me and Solly sat down to dinner. Spread! There's nothing been seen like it since the Cambon snack. It was all served at once. The chef called it *dinnay à la poker*. It's a famous thing among the gormands of the West. The dinner comes in threes of a kind. There was guinea-fowls, guinea-pigs, and Guinness's stout; roast veal, mock turtle soup, and chicken pâté; shad-roe, caviar, and tapioca; canvas-back duck, canvas-back ham, and cottontail rabbit; Philadelphia capon, fried snails, and sloe-gin—and so on, in threes. The idea was that you eat nearly all you can of them, and then the waiter takes away the discard and gives you pears to fill on.

"I was sure Solly would be tickled to death with these hands, after the bob-tail flushes he'd been eating on the ranch; and I was a little anxious that he should, for I didn't remember his having honored my efforts with a smile since we left Atascosa City.

"We were in the main dining room, and there was a fine-dressed crowd there, all talking loud and enjoyable about the two St. Louis topics, the water supply and the color line. They mix the two subjects so fast that strangers often think they are discussing water-colors; and that has given the old town something of a rep as an art centre. And over in the corner was a fine brass band playing; and now, thinks I, Solly will become conscious of the spiritual oats of life nourishing and exhilarating his system. But *nong, mong frang*.

"He gazed across the table at me. There was four square yards of it, looking like the path of a cyclone that has wandered through a stock-yard, a poultry-farm, a vegetable-garden, and an Irish linen mill. Solly gets up and comes around to me.

" 'Luke,' says he, 'I'm pretty hungry after our ride. I thought you said they had some beans here. I'm going out and get something I can eat. You can stay and monkey with this artificial layout of grub if you want to.'

" 'Wait a minute,' says I.

"I called the waiter, and slapped 'S. Mills' on the back of the check for thirteen dollars and fifty cents.

" 'What do you mean,' says I, 'by serving gentlemen with a lot of truck only suitable for deck hands on a Mississippi steamboat? We're going out to get something decent to eat.'

"I walked up the street with the unhappy plainsman. He saw a saddle-shop open, and some of the sadness faded from his eyes. We went in, and he ordered and paid for two more saddles—one with a solid silver horn and nails and ornaments and a six-inch border of rhinestones and imitation rubies around the flaps. The other one had to have a gold-mounted horn, quadruple-plated stirrups, and the leather inlaid with silver beadwork wherever it would stand it. Eleven hundred dollars the two cost him.

"Then he goes out and heads toward the river, following his nose. In a little side street, where there was no street and no sidewalks and no houses, he finds what he is looking for. We go into a shanty and sit on high stools among stevedores and boatmen, and eat beans with tin spoons. Yes, sir, beans—beans boiled with salt pork.

"'I kind of thought we'd strike some over this way,' says Solly.

"'Delightful,' says I. 'That stylish hotel grub may appeal to some: but for me, give me the husky *table d'goat*.'

"When we had succumbed to the beans I leads him out of the tarpaulin-steam under a lamp post and pulls out a daily paper with the amusement column folded out.

"'But now, what ho for a merry round of pleasure,' says I. 'Here's one of Hall Caine's shows, and a stock-yard company in "Hamlet," and skating at the Hollowhorn Rink, and Sara Bernhardt, and the Shapely Syrens Burlesque Company. I should think, now, that the Shapely——'

"But what does this healthy, wealthy, and wise man do but reach his arms up to the second-story windows and gape noisily.

"'Reckon I'll be going to bed,' says he, 'it's about my time. St. Louis is a kind of quiet place, ain't it?'

"'Oh, yes,' says I; 'ever since the railroads ran in here the town's been practically ruined. And the building-and-loan associations and the fair have about killed it. Guess we might as well go to bed. Wait till you see Chicago though. Shall we get tickets for the Big Breeze to-morrow?'

"'Mought as well,' says Solly. 'I reckon all these towns are about alike.'

"Well, maybe the wise cicerone and personal conductor didn't fall hard in Chicago! Loolooville-on-the-Lake is supposed to have one or two things in it calculated to keep the rural visitor awake after the curfew rings. But not for the grass-fed man of the pampas! I tried him with theatres, rides in automobiles, sails on the lake, champagne suppers, and all those little inventions that hold the simple life in check; but in vain. Solly grew sadder day by day. And I got fearful about my salary, and knew I must play my trump card. So I mentioned New York to him, and informed him that these Western towns were no more than gateways to the great walled city of the whirling dervishes.

"After I bought the tickets I missed Soll. I knew his habits by then; so in a couple of hours I found him in a saddle-shop. They had some new ideas there in the way of trees and girths that had strayed down from the Canadian mounted police; and Solly was so interested that he almost looked reconciled to live. He invested about nine hundred dollars in there.

"At the depot I telegraphed a cigar-store man I knew in New York to meet me at the Twenty-third Street ferry with a list of all the saddle-stores in the city. I wanted to know where to look for Solly when he got lost.

"Now I'll tell you what happened in New York. I says to myself: 'Friend Heherezade, you want to get busy and make Bagdad look pretty to the sad sultan of the sour countenance, or it'll be the bowstring for yours.' But I never had any doubt I could do it.

"I began with him like you'd feed a starving man. I showed him the horse-cars on Broadway and the Staten Island ferry-boats. And then I piled up the sensations on him, but always keeping a lot of warmer ones up my sleeve.

"At the end of the third day he looked like a composite picture of five thousand orphans too late to catch a picnic steamboat, and I was wilting down a collar every two hours wondering how I could please him and whether I was going to get my thou. He went to sleep looking at the Brooklyn Bridge; he disregarded the sky-scrapers above the third story; it took three ushers to wake him up at the liveliest vaudeville in town.

"Once I thought I had him. I nailed a pair of cuffs on him one morning before he was awake; and I dragged him that evening to the palm-cage of one of the biggest hotels in the city—to see the Johnnies and the Alice-sit-by-the-hours. They were out in numerous quantities, with the fat of the land showing in their clothes. While we were looking them over, Solly divested himself of a fearful, rusty kind of laugh—like moving a folding bed with one roller broken. It was his first in two weeks, and it gave me hope.

"'Right you are,' says I. 'They're a funny lot of post-cards, aren't they?'

"'Oh, I wasn't thinking of them dudes and culls on the hoof,' says he. 'I was thinking of the time me and George put sheep-dip in Horsehead Johnson's whisky. I wish I was back in Atascosa City,' says he.

"I felt a cold chill run down my back. 'Me to play and mate in one move,' says I to myself.

"I made Solly promise to stay in the café for half an hour and I hiked out in a cab to Lolabelle Delatour's flat on Forty-third Street. I knew her well. She was a chorus-girl in a Broadway musical comedy.

"'Jane,' says I when I found her, 'I've got a friend from Texas here. He's all right, but—well, he carries weight. I'd like to give him a little whirl after the show this evening—bubbles, you know, and a buzz out to a casino for the whitebait and pickled walnuts. Is it a go?'

"'Can he sing?' asks Lolabelle.

"'You know,' says I, 'I wouldn't take him away from home unless his notes were good. He's got pots of money—bean-pots full of it.'

"'Bring him around after the second act,' says Lolabelle, 'and I'll examine his credentials and securities.'

"So about ten o'clock that evening I led Solly to Miss Delatour's dressing-room, and her maid let us in. In ten minutes in comes Lolabelle, fresh from the stage, looking stunning in the costume she wears when she steps from the ranks of the lady grenadiers and says to the king, 'Welcome to our May-day revels.' And you can bet it wasn't the way she spoke the lines that got her the part.

"As soon as Solly saw her he got up and walked straight out through the stage entrance into the street. I followed him. Lolabelle wasn't paying my salary. I wondered whether anybody was.

"'Luke,' says Solly, outside, 'that was an awful mistake. We must have got into the lady's private room. I hope I'm gentleman enough to do anything possible in the way of apologies. Do you reckon she'd ever forgive us?'

"'She may forget it,' says I. 'Of course it was a mistake. Let's go find some beans.'

"That's the way it went. But pretty soon afterward Solly failed to show up at dinner time for several days. I cornered him. He confessed that he had found a restaurant on Third Avenue where they cooked beans in Texas style. I made him take me there. The minute I set foot inside the door I threw up my hands.

"There was a young woman at the desk, and Solly introduced me to her. And then we sat down and had beans.

"Yes, sir, sitting at the desk was the kind of a young woman that can catch any man in the world as easy as lifting a finger. There's a way of doing it. She knew. I saw her working it. She was healthy-looking and plain dressed. She had her hair drawn back from her forehead and face—no curls or frizzes; that's the way she looked. Now I'll tell you the way they work the game; it's simple. When she wants a man, she manages it so that every time he looks at her he finds her looking at him. That's all.

"The next evening Solly was to go to Coney Island with me at seven. At eight o'clock he hadn't showed up. I went out and found a cab. I felt sure there was something wrong.

"'Drive to the Back Home Restaurant on Third Avenue,' says I. 'And if I don't find what I want there, take in these saddle-shops.' I handed him the list.

"'Boss,' says the cabby, 'I et a steak in that restaurant once. If you're real hungry, I advise you to try the saddle-shops first.'

"'I'm a detective,' says I, 'and I don't eat. Hurry up!'

"As soon as I got to the restaurant I felt in the lines of my palms that I should beware of a tall, red, damfool man, and I was going to lose a sum of money.

"Solly wasn't there. Neither was the smooth-haired lady.

"I waited; and in an hour they came in a cab and got out, hand in hand. I asked Solly to step around the corner for a few words. He was grinning clear across his face; but I had not administered the grin.

"'She's the greatest that ever sniffed the breeze,' says he.

"'Congrats,' says I. 'I'd like to have my thousand now, if you please.'

"'Well, Luke,' says he, 'I don't know that I've had such a skyhoodlin' fine time under your tutelage and dispensation. But I'll do the best I can for you—I'll do the best I can,' he repeats. 'Me and Miss Skinner was married an hour ago. We're leaving for Texas in the morning.'

"'Great!' says I. 'Consider yourself covered with rice and Congress gaiters. But don't let's tie so many satin bows on our business relations that we lose sight of 'em. How about my honorarium?'

"'Missis Mills,' says he, 'has taken possession of my money and papers except six bits. I told her what I'd agreed to give you; but she says it's an irreligious and illegal contract, and she won't pay a cent of it. But I ain't going to see you treated unfair,' says he. 'I've got eighty-seven saddles on the ranch what I've bought on this trip; and when I get back I'm going to pick out the best six in the lot and send 'em to you.'"

"And did he?" I asked, when Lucullus ceased talking.

"He did. And they are fit for kings to ride on. The six he sent me must have cost him three thousand dollars. But where is the market for 'em? Who would buy one except one of these rajahs and princes of Asia and Africa? I've got 'em all on the list. I know every tan royal dub and smoked princerino from Mindanao to the Caspian Sea."

"It's a long time between customers," I ventured.

"They're coming faster," said Polk. "Nowadays, when one of the murdering mutts gets civilized enough to abolish suttee and quit using his whiskers for a napkin, he calls himself the Roosevelt of the East, and comes over to investigate our Chautauquas and cocktails. I'll place 'em all yet. Now look here."

From an inside pocket he drew a tightly folded newspaper with much-worn edges, and indicated a paragraph.

"Read that," said the saddler to royalty. The paragraph ran thus:

His Highness Seyyid Feysal bin Turkee, Imam of Muskat, is one of the most progressive and enlightened rulers of the Old World. His stables contain more than a thousand horses of the purest Persian breeds. It is said that this powerful prince contemplates a visit to the United States at an early date.

"There!" said Mr. Polk triumphantly. "My best saddle is as good as sold—the one with turquoises set in the rim of the cantle. Have you three dollars that you could loan me for a short time?"

It happened that I had; and I did.

If this should meet the eye of the Imam of Muskat, may it quicken his whim to visit the land of the free! Otherwise I fear that I shall be longer than a short time separated from my dollars three.

HYGEIA AT THE SOLITO

IF you are knowing in the chronicles of the ring you will recall to mind an event in the early 'nineties when, for a minute and sundry odd seconds, a champion and a "would-be" faced each other on the alien side of an international river. So brief a conflict had rarely imposed upon the fair promise of true sport. The reporters made what they could of it, but, divested of padding, the action was sadly fugacious. The champion merely smote his victim, turned his back upon him, remarking, "I know what I done to dat stiff," and extended an arm like a ship's mast for his glove to be removed.

Which accounts for a trainload of extremely disgusted gentlemen in an uproar of fancy vests and neckwear being spilled from their Pullman in San Antonio in the early morning following the fight. Which also partly accounts for the unhappy predicament in which "Cricket" McGuire found himself as he tumbled from his car and sat upon the depot platform, torn by a spasm of that hollow, racking cough so familiar to San Antonian ears. At that time, in the uncertain light of dawn, that way passed Curtis Raidler, the Nueces County cattleman— may his shadow never measure under six feet two.

The cattleman, out this early to catch the south-bound for his ranch station, stopped at the side of the distressed patron of sport and spoke in the kindly drawl of his ilk and region, "Got it pretty bad, bud?"

"Cricket" McGuire, ex-feather-weight prize-fighter, tout, jockey, follower of the "ponies," all-around sport, and manipulator of the gum balls and walnut shells, looked up pugnaciously at the imputation cast by "bud."

"G'wan," he rasped "telegraph pole. I didn't ring for yer."

Another paroxysm wrung him, and he leaned limply against a convenient baggage truck. Raidler waited patiently, glancing around at the white hats, short overcoats, and big cigars thronging the platform. "You're from the No'th, ain't you, bud?" he asked when the other was partially recovered. "Come down to see the fight?"

"Fight!" snapped McGuire. "Puss-in-the-corner! 'Twas a hypodermic injection. Handed him just one like a squirt of dope, and he's asleep, and no tanbark needed in front of his residence. Fight!" He rattled a bit, coughed, and went on, hardly addressing the cattleman, but rather for the relief of voicing his troubles. "No more dead sure t'ings for me. But Rus Sage himself would have snatched at it. Five to one dat de boy from Cork wouldn't stay t'ree rounds is what I invested in. Put my last cent on, and could already smell the sawdust in dat all-night joint of Jimmy Delaney's on T'irty-seventh Street I was goin' to buy. And den—say, telegraph pole, what a gazaboo a guy is to put his whole roll on one turn of the gaboozlum!"

"You're plenty right," said the big cattleman; "more 'specially when you lose. Son, you get up and light out for a hotel. You got a mighty bad cough. Had it long?"

"Lungs," said McGuire comprehensively. "I got it. The croaks says I'll come to time for six months longer—maybe a year if I hold my gait. I wanted to settle down and take care of myself. Dat's why I speculated on dat five to one perhaps. I had a t'ousand iron dollars saved up. If I winned I was goin' to buy Delaney's café. Who'd a t'ought dat stiff would take a nap in de foist round —say?"

"It's a hard deal," commented Raidler, looking down at the diminutive form of McGuire crumpled against the truck. "But you go to a hotel and rest. There's the Menger and the Maverick, and——"

"And the Fi'th Av'noo, and the Waldorf-Astoria," mimicked McGuire. "Told you I went broke. I'm on de bum proper. I've got one dime left. Maybe a trip to Europe or a sail in me private yacht would fix me up—pa'per!"

He flung his dime at a newsboy, got his *Express*, propped his back against the truck, and was at once rapt in the account of his Waterloo, as expanded by the ingenious press.

Curtis Raidler interrogated an enormous gold watch, and laid his hand on McGuire's shoulder.

"Come on, bud," he said. "We got three minutes to catch the train."

Sarcasm seemed to be McGuire's vein.

"You ain't seen me cash in any chips or call a turn since I told you I was broke, a minute ago, have you? Friend, chase yourself away."

"You're going down to my ranch," said the cattleman, "and stay till you get well. Six months'll fix you good as new." He lifted McGuire with one hand, and half-dragged him in the direction of the train.

"What about the money?" said McGuire, struggling weakly to escape.

"Money for what?" asked Raidler, puzzled. They eyed each other, not understanding, for they touched only as at the gear of bevelled cog-wheels—at right angles, and moving upon different axes.

Passengers on the south-bound saw them seated together, and wondered at the conflux of two such antipodes. McGuire was five feet one, with a countenance belonging to either Yokohama or Dublin. Bright-beady of eye, bony of cheek and jaw, scarred, toughened, broken and reknit, indestructible, grisly, gladiatorial as a hornet, he was a type neither new nor unfamiliar. Raidler was the product of a different soil. Six feet two in height, miles broad, and no deeper than a crystal brook, he represented the union of the West and South. Few accurate pictures of his kind have been made, for art galleries are so small and the mutoscope is as yet unknown in Texas. After all, the only possible medium of portrayal of Raidler's kind would be the fresco—something high and simple and cool and unframed.

They were rolling southward on the International. The timber was huddling into little, dense green motts at rare distances before the inundation of the downright, vert prairies. This was the land of the ranches; the domain of the kings of the kine.

McGuire sat, collapsed into his corner of the seat, receiving with acid suspicion the conversation of the cattleman. What was the "game" of this big "geezer" who was carrying him off? Altruism would have been McGuire's last guess. "He ain't no farmer," thought the captive, "and he ain't no con man, for sure. W'at's his lay? You trail in, Cricket, and see how many cards he draws. You're up against it, anyhow. You got a nickel and gallopin' consumption, and you better lay low. Lay low and see w'at's his game."

At Rincon, a hundred miles from San Antonio, they left the train for a buckboard which was waiting there for Raidler. In this they travelled the thirty miles between the station and their destination. If anything could, this drive should have stirred the acrimonious McGuire to a sense of his ransom. They sped upon velvet wheels across an exhilarant savanna. The pair of Spanish ponies struck a nimble, tireless trot, which gait they occasionally relieved by a wild, untrammelled gallop. The air was wine and seltzer, perfumed, as they absorbed it, with the delicate redolence of prairie flowers. The road perished, and the buckboard swam the uncharted billows of the grass itself, steered by the practised hand of Raidler, to whom each tiny distant mott of trees was a signboard, each convolution of the low hills a voucher of course and distance. But McGuire reclined upon his spine, seeing nothing but a desert, and receiving the cattleman's advances with sullen distrust. "W'at's he up to?" was the burden of his thoughts; "w'at kind of a gold brick has the big guy got to sell?" McGuire was only applying the measure of the streets he had walked to a range bounded by the horizon and the fourth dimension.

A week before, while riding the prairies, Raidler had come upon a sick and weakling calf deserted and bawling. Without dismounting he had reached and slung the distressed bossy across his saddle, and dropped it at the ranch for the boys to attend to. It was impossible for McGuire to know or comprehend that, in the eyes of the cattleman, his case and that of the calf were identical in interest and demand upon his assistance. A creature was ill and helpless; he had the power to render aid—these were the only postulates required for the cattleman to act. They formed his system of logic and the most of his creed. McGuire was the seventh invalid whom Raidler had picked up thus casually in San Antonio, where so many thousand go for the ozone that is said to linger about its contracted streets. Five of them had been guests of Solito Ranch until they had been able to leave, cured or better, and exhausting the vocabulary of tearful gratitude. One came too late, but rested very comfortably, at last, under a ratama tree in the garden.

So, then, it was no surprise to the ranchhold when the buckboard spun to the door, and Raidler took up his debile *protégé* like a handful of rags and set him down upon the gallery.

McGuire looked upon things strange to him. The ranch-house was the best in the country. It was built of brick hauled one hundred miles by wagon, but it was of but one story, and its four rooms were completely encircled by a mud floor "gallery." The miscellaneous setting of horses, dogs, saddles, wagons, guns, and cow-punchers' paraphernalia oppressed the metropolitan eye of the wrecked sportsman.

"Well, here we are at home," said Raidler, cheeringly.

"It's a h—l of a looking place," said McGuire promptly, as he rolled upon the gallery floor, in a fit of coughing.

"We'll try to make it comfortable for you, buddy," said the cattleman, gently. "It ain't fine inside; but it's the outdoors, anyway, that'll do you the most good. This'll be your room, in here. Anything we got, you ask for it."

He led McGuire into the east room. The floor was bare and clean. White curtains waved in the gulf breeze through the open windows. A big willow rocker, two straight chairs, a long table covered with newspapers, pipes, tobacco, spurs, and cartridges stood in the centre. Some well-mounted heads of deer and one of an enormous black javeli projected from the walls. A wide, cool cot-bed stood in a corner. Nueces County people regarded this guest chamber as fit for a prince. McGuire showed his eye teeth at it. He took out his nickel and spun it up to the ceiling.

"T'ought I was lyin' about the money, did ye? Well, you can frisk me if you wanter. Dat's the last simoleon in the treasury. Who's goin' to pay?"

The cattleman's clear gray eyes looked steadily from under his grizzly brows into the huckleberry optics of his guest. After a little he said simply, and not ungraciously, "I'll be much obliged to you, son, if you won't mention money any more. Once was quite a plenty. Folks I ask to my ranch don't have to pay anything, and they very scarcely ever offers it. Supper'll be ready in half an hour. There's water in the pitcher, and some, cooler, to drink in that red jar hanging on the gallery."

"Where's the bell?" asked McGuire, looking about.

"Bell for what?"

"Bell to ring for things. I can't—see here," he exploded in a sudden weak fury, "I never asked you to bring me here. I never held you up for a cent. I never gave you a hard-luck story till you asked me. Here I am fifty mile from a bellboy or a cocktail. I'm sick. I can't hustle. Gee! but I'm up against it!" McGuire fell upon the cot and sobbed shiveringly.

Raidler went to the door and called. A slender, bright-complexioned Mexican youth about twenty came quickly. Raidler spoke to him in Spanish.

"Ylario, it is in my mind that I promised you the position of *vaquero* on the San Carlos range at the fall *rodeo*."

"*Si, señor*, such was your goodness."

"Listen. This *señorito* is my friend. He is very sick. Place yourself at his side. Attend to his wants at all times. Have much patience and care with him. And when he is well, or—and when he is well, instead of *vaquero* I will make you *mayordomo* of the Rancho de las Piedras. *Está bueno?*"

"*Si, si—mil gracias, señor.*" Ylario tried to kneel upon the floor in his gratitude, but the cattleman kicked at him benevolently, growling, "None of your opery-house antics, now."

Ten minutes later Ylario came from McGuire's room and stood before Raidler.

"The little *señor*," he announced, "presents his compliments" (Raidler credited Ylario with the preliminary) "and desires some pounded ice, one hot bath, one gin feez-z, that the windows be all closed, toast, one shave, one Newyorkheral', cigarettes, and to send one telegram."

Raidler took a quart bottle of whisky from his medicine cabinet. "Here, take him this," he said.

Thus was instituted the reign of terror at the Solito Ranch. For a few weeks McGuire blustered and boasted and swaggered before the cow-punchers who rode in for miles around to see this latest importation of Raidler's. He was an absolutely new experience to them. He explained to them all the intricate points of sparring and the tricks of training and defence. He opened to their minds' view all the indecorous life of a tagger after professional sports. His jargon of slang was a continuous joy and surprise to them. His gestures, his strange poses, his frank ribaldry of tongue and principle fascinated them. He was like a being from a new world.

Strange to say, this new world he had entered did not exist to him. He was an utter egoist of bricks and mortar. He had dropped out, he felt, into open space for a time, and all it contained was an audience for his reminiscences. Neither the limitless freedom of the prairie days nor the grand hush of the close-drawn, spangled nights touched him. All the hues of Aurora could not win him from the pink pages of a sporting journal. "Get something for nothing," was his mission in life; "T'irty-seventh" Street was his goal.

Nearly two months after his arrival he began to complain that he felt worse. It was then that he became the ranch's incubus, its harpy, its Old Man of the Sea. He shut himself in his room like some venomous kobold or flibbertigibbet, whining, complaining, cursing, accusing. The keynote of his plaint was that he had been inveigled into a gehenna against his will; that he was dying of neglect and lack of comforts. With all his dire protestations of increasing illness, to the eye of others he remained unchanged. His currant-like eyes were as bright and diabolic as ever; his voice was as rasping; his callous face, with the skin drawn tense as a drum-head, had no flesh to lose. A flush on his prominent cheek bones each afternoon hinted that a clinical thermometer might have revealed a symptom, and percussion might have established the fact that McGuire was breathing with only one lung, but his appearance remained the same.

In constant attendance upon him was Ylario, whom the coming reward of the *mayordomoship* must have greatly stimulated, for McGuire chained him to a bitter existence. The air—the man's only chance for life—he commanded to be kept out by closed windows and drawn curtains. The room was always blue and foul with cigarette smoke; whosoever entered it must sit, suffocating, and listen to the imp's interminable gasconade concerning his scandalous career.

The oddest thing of all was the relation existing between McGuire and his benefactor. The attitude of the invalid toward the cattleman was something like that of a peevish, perverse child toward an indulgent parent. When Raidler would leave the ranch McGuire would fall into a fit of malevolent, silent sullenness. When he returned, he would be met by a string of violent and stinging reproaches. Raidler's attitude toward his charge was quite inexplicable in its way. The cattleman seemed actually to assume and feel the character assigned him by McGuire's intemperate accusations—the character of tyrant and guilty oppressor. He seemed to have adopted the responsibility of the fellow's condition, and he always met his tirades with a pacific, patient, and even remorseful kindness that never altered.

One day Raidler said to him, "Try more air, son. You can have the buckboard and a driver every day if you'll go. Try a week or two in one of the cow camps. I'll fix you up plum comfortable. The ground, and the air next to it—them's the things to cure you. I knowed a man from Philadelphy, sicker than you are, got lost on the Guadalupe, and slept on the bare grass in sheep camps for two weeks. Well, sir, it started him getting well, which he done. Close to the ground— that's where the medicine in the air stays. Try a little hossback riding now. There's a gentle pony——"

"What've I done to yer?" screamed McGuire. "Did I ever doub'ecross yer? Did I ask you to bring me here? Drive me out to your camps if you wanter; or stick a knife in me and save trouble. Ride! I can't lift my feet. I couldn't sidestep a jab from a five-year-old kid. That's what your d—d ranch has done for me. There's nothing to eat, nothing to see, and nobody to talk to but a lot of Reubens who don't know a punching bag from a lobster salad."

"It's a lonesome place, for certain," apologized Raidler abashedly. "We got plenty, but it's rough enough. Anything you think of you want, the boys'll ride up and fetch it down for you."

It was Chad Murchison, a cow-puncher from the Circle Bar outfit, who first suggested that McGuire's illness was fraudulent. Chad had brought a basket of grapes for him thirty miles, and four out of his way, tied to his saddle-horn. After remaining in the smoke-tainted room for a while, he emerged and bluntly confided his suspicions to Raidler.

"His arm," said Chad, "is harder'n a diamond. He interduced me to what he called a shore-perplexus punch, and 'twas like being kicked twice by a mustang. He's playin' it low down on you, Curt. He ain't no sicker'n I am. I hate to say it, but the runt's workin' you for range and shelter."

The cattleman's ingenuous mind refused to entertain Chad's view of the case, and when, later, he came to apply the test, doubt entered not into his motives.

One day, about noon, two men drove up to the ranch, alighted, hitched, and came in to dinner; standing and general invitations being the custom of the country. One of them was a great San Antonio doctor, whose costly services had been engaged by a wealthy cowman who had been laid low by an accidental bullet. He was now being driven to the station to take the train back to town. After dinner Raidler took him aside, pushed a twenty-dollar bill against his hand, and said:

"Doc, there's a young chap in that room I guess has got a bad case of consumption. I'd like for you to look him over and see just how bad he is, and if we can do anything for him."

"How much was that dinner I just ate, Mr. Raidler?" said the doctor bluffly, looking over his spectacles. Raidler returned the money to his pocket. The doc-

tor immediately entered McGuire's room, and the cattleman seated himself upon
a heap of saddles on the gallery, ready to reproach himself in the event the verdict
should be unfavorable.

In ten minutes the doctor came briskly out. "Your man," he said promptly,
"is as sound as a new dollar. His lungs are better than mine. Respiration,
temperature, and pulse normal. Chest expansion four inches. Not a sign of
weakness anywhere. Of course I didn't examine for the bacillus, but it isn't there.
You can put my name to the diagnosis. Even cigarettes and a vilely close room
haven't hurt him. Coughs, does he? Well, you tell him it isn't necessary. You
asked if there is anything we could do for him. Well, I advise you to set him
digging post-holes or breaking mustangs. There's our team ready. Good-day,
sir." And like a puff of wholesome, blustery wind the doctor was off.

Raidler reached out and plucked a leaf from a mesquite bush by the railing, and
began chewing it thoughtfully.

The branding season was at hand, and the next morning Ross Hargis, foreman of the outfit, was mustering his force of some twenty-five men at the
ranch, ready to start for the San Carlos range, where the work was to begin.
By six o'clock the horses were all saddled, the grub wagon ready, and the cow-
punchers were swinging themselves upon their mounts, when Raidler bade them
wait. A boy was bringing up an extra pony, bridled and saddled, to the gate.
Raidler walked to McGuire's room and threw open the door. McGuire was lying
on his cot, not yet dressed, smoking.

"Get up," said the cattleman, and his voice was clear and brassy, like a bugle.

"How's that?" asked McGuire, a little startled.

"Get up and dress. I can stand a rattlesnake, but I hate a liar. Do I have to
tell you again?" He caught McGuire by the neck and stood him on the floor.

"Say, friend," cried McGuire wildly, "are you bug-house? I'm sick—see? I'll
croak if I got to hustle. What've I done to yer?"—he began his chronic whine—
"I never asked yer to——"

"Put on your clothes," called Raidler, in a rising tone.

Swearing, stumbling, shivering, keeping his amazed, shiny eyes upon the now
menacing form of the aroused cattleman, McGuire managed to tumble into his
clothes. Then Raidler took him by the collar and shoved him out and across the
yard to the extra pony hitched at the gate. The cow-punchers lolled in their
saddles, open-mouthed.

"Take this man," said Raidler to Ross Hargis, "and put him to work. Make
him work hard, sleep hard, and eat hard. You boys know I done what I could
for him, and he was welcome. Yesterday the best doctor in San Antone examined
him, and says he's got the lungs of a burro and the constitution of a steer. You
know what to do with him, Ross."

Ross Hargis only smiled grimly.

"Aw," said McGuire, looking intently at Raidler, with a peculiar expression
upon his face, "the croaker said I was all right, did he? Said I was fakin', did
he? You put him onto me. You t'ought I wasn't sick. You said I was a liar.
Say, friend, I talked rough, I know, but I didn't mean most of it. If you felt
like I did—aw! I forgot—I ain't sick, the croaker says. Well, friend, now
I'll go work for yer. Here's where you play even."

He sprang into the saddle easily as a bird, got the quirt from the horn, and
gave his pony a slash with it. "Cricket," who once brought in Good Boy by a
neck at Hawthorne—and a 10 to 1 shot—had his foot in the stirrups again.

McGuire led the cavalcade as they dashed away from San Carlos, and the cow-
punchers gave a yell of applause as they closed in behind his dust.

But in less than a mile he had lagged to the rear, and was last man when they
struck the patch of high chaparral below the horse pens. Behind a clump of this

he drew rein, and held a handkerchief to his mouth. He took it away drenched with bright, arterial blood, and threw it carefully into a clump of prickly pear. Then he slashed with his quirt again, gasped "G'wan" to his astonished pony, and galloped after the gang.

That night Raidler received a message from his old home in Alabama. There had been a death in the family; an estate was to divide, and they called for him to come. Daylight found him in the buckboard, skimming the prairies for the station. It was two months before he returned. When he arrived at the ranch-house he found it well-nigh deserted save for Ylario, who acted as a kind of steward during his absence. Little by little the youth made him acquainted with the work done while he was away. The branding camp, he was informed, was still doing business. On account of many severe storms the cattle had been badly scattered, and the branding had been accomplished but slowly. The camp was now in the valley of the Guadalupe, twenty miles away.

"By the way," said Raidler, suddenly remembering, "that fellow I sent along with them—McGuire—is he working yet?"

"I do not know," said Ylario. "Man's from the camp come verree few times to the ranch. So plentee work with the leetle calves. They no say. Oh, I think that fellow McGuire he dead much time ago."

"Dead!" said Raidler. "What you talking about?"

"Verree sick fellow, McGuire," replied Ylario, with a shrug of his shoulder. "I theenk he no live one, two month when he go away."

"Shucks!" said Raidler. "He humbugged you, too, did he? The doctor examined him and said he was sound as a mesquite knot."

"That doctor," said Ylario, smiling, "he tell you so? That doctor no see McGuire."

"Talk up," ordered Raidler. "What the devil do you mean?"

"McGuire," continued the boy tranquilly, "he getting drink water outside when that doctor come in room. That doctor take me and pound me all over here with his fingers"—putting his hand to his chest—"I not know for what. He put his ear here and here and here, and listen—I not know for what. He put his little glass stick in my mouth. He feel my arm here. He make me count like whisper—so—twenty, *treinta, cuarenta.* Who knows," concluded Ylario, with a deprecating spread of his hands, "for what that doctor do those verree droll and such-like things?"

"What horses are up?" asked Raidler, shortly.

"Paisano is grazing out behind the little corral, *señor.*"

"Saddle him for me at once."

Within a very few minutes the cattleman was mounted and away. Paisano, well named after that ungainly but swift-running bird, struck into his long lope that ate up the road like a strip of macaroni. In two hours and a quarter Raidler, from a gentle swell, saw the branding camp by a water hole in the Guadalupe. Sick with expectancy of the news he feared, he rode up, dismounted, and dropped Paisano's reins. So gentle was his heart that at that moment he would have pleaded guilty to the murder of McGuire.

The only being in the camp was the cook, who was just arranging the hunks of barbecued beef, and distributing the tin coffee cups for supper. Raidler evaded a direct question concerning the one subject in his mind.

"Everything all right in camp, Pete?" he managed to inquire.

"So, so," said Pete, conservatively. "Grub give out twice. Wind scattered the cattle, and we've had to rake the brush for forty mile. I need a new coffee-pot. And the mosquitos is some more hellish than common."

"The boys—all well?"

Pete was no optimist. Besides, inquiries concerning the health of cow-punchers were not only superfluous, but bordered on flaccidity. It was not like the boss to make them.

"What's left of 'em don't miss no calls to grub," the cook conceded.

"What's left of 'em?" repeated Raidler in a husky voice. Mechanically he began to look around for McGuire's grave. He had in his mind a white slab such as he had seen in the Alabama church-yard. But immediately he knew that was foolish.

"Sure," said Pete; "what's left. Cow camps change in two months. Some's gone."

Raidler nerved himself.

"That—chap—I sent along—McGuire—did—he——"

"Say," interrupted Pete, rising with a chunk of corn bread in each hand, "that was a dirty shame, sending that poor, sick kid to a cow camp. A doctor that couldn't tell he was graveyard meat ought to be skinned with a cinch buckle. Game as he was, too—it's a scandal among snakes—lemme tell you what he done. First night in camp the boys started to initiate him in the leather breeches degree. Ross Hargis busted him one swipe with his chaparreras, and what do you reckon the poor child did? Got up, the little skeeter, and licked Ross. Licked Ross Hargis. Licked him good. Hit him plenty and everywhere and hard. Ross'd just get up and pick out a fresh place to lay down on agin.

"Then that McGuire goes off there and lays down with his head in the grass and bleeds. A hem'ridge they calls it. He lays there eighteen hours by the watch, and they can't budge him. Then Ross Hargis, who loves any man who can lick him, goes to work and damns the doctors from Greenland to Poland Chiny; and him and Green Branch Johnson they gets McGuire in a tent, and spells each other feedin' him chopped raw meat and whisky.

"But it looks like the kid ain't got no appetite to git well, for they misses him from the tent in the night and finds him rootin' in the grass, and likewise a drizzle fallin'. 'Gwan,' he says, 'lemme go and die like I wanter. He said I was a liar and a fake and I was playin' sick. Lemme alone.'

"Two weeks," went on the cook, "he laid around, not noticin' nobody, and then——"

A sudden thunder filled the air, and a score of galloping centaurs crashed through the brush into camp.

"Illustrious rattlesnakes!" exclaimed Pete, springing all ways at once: "here's the boys come, and I'm an assassinated man if supper ain't ready in three minutes."

But Raidler saw only one thing. A little brown-faced, grinning chap, springing from his saddle in the full light of the fire. McGuire was not like that, and yet——

In another instant the cattleman was holding him by the hand and shoulder.

"Son, son, how goes it?" was all he found to say.

"Close to the ground, says you," shouted McGuire, crunching Raidler's fingers in a grip of steel; "and dat's where I found it—healt' and strengt', and tumbled to what a cheap skate I been actin'. T'anks fer kickin' me out, old man. And— say! de joke's on dat croaker, ain't it? I looked t'rough the window and see him playin' tag on dat Dago kid's solar plexus."

"You son of a tinker," growled the cattleman, "whyn't you talk up and say the doctor never examined you?"

"Aw—g'wan!" said McGuire, with a flash of his old asperity, "nobody can't bluff me. You never ast me. You made your spiel, and you t'rowed me out, and I let it go at dat. And, say, friend, dis chasin' cows is outer sight. Dis is de whitest bunch of sports I ever travelled with. You'll let me stay, won't yer, old man?"

Raidler looked wonderingly toward Ross Hargis.
"That cussed little runt," remarked Ross tenderly, "is the Jo-dartin'est hustler
—and the hardest hitter in anybody's cow camp."

AN AFTERNOON MIRACLE

At the United States end of an international river bridge, four armed rangers
sweltered in a little 'dobe hut, keeping a fairly faithful espionage upon the lagging trail of passengers from the Mexican side.

Bud Dawson, proprietor of the Top Notch Saloon, had, on the evening previous,
violently ejected from his premises one Leandro Garcia, for alleged violation of
the Top Notch code of behavior. Garcia had mentioned twenty-four hours as a
limit, by which time he would call and collect plentiful indemnity for personal
satisfaction.

This Mexican, although a tremendous braggart, was thoroughly courageous, and
each side of the river respected him for one of these attributes. He and a following of similar bravoes were addicted to the pastime of retrieving towns from
stagnation.

The day designated by Garcia for retribution was to be further signalized on
the American side by a cattlemen's convention, a bull fight, and an old settlers'
barbecue and picnic. Knowing the avenger to be a man of his word, and believing it prudent to court peace while three such gently social relaxations were in
progress, Captain McNulty, of the ranger company stationed there, detailed his
lieutenant and three men for duty at the end of the bridge. Their instructions
were to prevent the invasion of Garcia, either alone or attended by his gang.

Travel was slight that sultry afternoon, and rangers swore gently, and mopped
their brows in their convenient but close quarters. For an hour no one had
crossed save an old woman enveloped in a brown wrapper and a black mantilla,
driving before her a burro loaded with kindling wood tied in small bundles for
peddling. Then three shots were fired down the street, the sound coming clear
and snappy through the still air.

The four rangers quickened from sprawling, symbolic figures of indolence to
alert life, but only one rose to his feet. Three turned their eyes beseechingly but
hopelessly upon the fourth, who had gotten nimbly up and was buckling his
cartridge-belt around him. The three knew that Lieutenant Bob Buckley, in
command, would allow no man of them the privilege of investigating a row
when he himself might go.

The agile, broad-chested lieutenant, without a change of expression in his
smooth, yellow-brown, melancholy face, shot the belt strap through the guard of
the buckle, hefted his sixes in their holsters as a belle gives the finishing touches
to her toilette, caught up his Winchester, and dived for the door. There he
paused long enough to caution his comrades to maintain their watch upon the
bridge, and then plunged into the broiling highway.

The three relapsed into resigned inertia and plaintive comment.

"I've heard of fellows," grumbled Broncho Leathers, "what was wedded to
danger, but if Bob Buckley ain't committed bigamy with trouble, I'm a son of
a gun."

"Peculiarness of Bob is," inserted the Nueces Kid, "he ain't had proper trainin'.
He never learned how to git skeered. Now, a man ought to be skeered enough

when he tackles a fuss to hanker after readin' his name on the list of survivors, anyway."

"Buckley," commented Ranger No. 3, who was a misguided Eastern man, burdened with an education, "scraps in such a solemn manner that I have been led to doubt its spontaneity. I'm not quite onto his system, but he fights, like Tybalt, by the book of arithmetic."

"I never heard," mentioned Broncho, "about any of Dibble's ways of mixin' scrappin' and cipherin'."

"Triggernometry?" suggested the Nueces infant.

"That's rather better than I hoped from you," nodded the Easterner, approvingly. "The other meaning is that Buckley never goes into a fight without giving away weight. He seems to dread taking the slightest advantage. That's quite close to foolhardiness when you are dealing with horse-thieves and fence-cutters who would ambush you any night, and shoot you in the back if they could. Buckley's too full of sand. He'll play Horatius, and hold the bridge once too often some day."

"I'm on there," drawled the Kid; "I mind that bridge gang in the reader. Me, I go instructed for the other chap—Spurious Somebody—the one that fought and pulled his freight, to fight 'em on some other date."

"Anyway," summed up Broncho, "Bob's about the gamest man I ever see along the Rio Bravo. Great Sam Houston! If she gets any hotter she'll sizzle!" Broncho whacked at a scorpion with his four-pound Stetson felt, and the three watchers relapsed into comfortless silence.

How well Bob Buckley had kept his secret, since these men, for two years his side comrades in countless border raids and dangers, thus spake of him, not knowing that he was the most arrant physical coward in all that Rio Bravo country! Neither his friends nor his enemies had suspected him of aught else than the finest courage. It was purely a physical cowardice, and only by an extreme, grim effort of will had he forced his craven body to do the bravest deeds. Scourging himself always, as a monk whips his besetting sin, Buckley threw himself with apparent recklessness into every danger, with the hope of some day ridding himself of the despised affliction. But each successive test brought no relief, and the ranger's face by nature adapted to cheerfulness and good humor, became set to the guise of gloomy melancholy. Thus, while the frontier admired his deeds, and his prowess was celebrated in print and by word of mouth in many camp-fires in the valley of the Bravo, his heart was sick within him. Only himself knew of the horrible tightening of the chest, the dry mouth, the weakening of the spine, the agony of the strung nerves—the never-failing symptoms of his shameful malady.

One mere boy in his company was wont to enter a fray with a leg perched flippantly about the horn of his saddle, a cigarette hanging from his lips, which emitted smoke and original slogans of clever invention. Buckley would have given a year's pay to attain that devil-may-care method. Once the debonair youth said to him: "Buck, you go into a scrap like it was a funeral. Not," he added, with a complimentary wave of his tin cup, "but what it generally is."

Buckley's conscience was of the New England order with Western adjustments, and he continued to get his rebellious body into as many difficulties as possible; wherefore, on that sultry afternoon he chose to drive his own protesting limbs to investigation of that sudden alarm that had startled the peace and dignity of the State.

Two squares down the street stood the Top Notch Saloon. Here Buckley came upon signs of recent upheaval. A few curious spectators pressed about its front entrance, grinding beneath their heels the fragments of a plate-glass window. Inside, Buckley found Bud Dawson utterly ignoring a bullet wound in his shoulder, while he feelingly wept at having to explain why he failed to drop the "blamed masquerooter," who shot him. At the entrance of the ranger Bud turned appealingly to him for confirmation of the devastation he might have dealt.

"You know, Buck, I'd 'a' plum got him, first rattle, if I'd thought a minute. Come in amasquerootin', playin' female till he got the drop, and turned loose. I never reached for a gun, thinkin' it was sure Chihuahua Betty, or Mrs. Atwater, or anyhow one of the Mayfield girls comin' a-gunning', which they might, liable as not. I never thought of that blamed Garcia until——"

"Garcia!" snapped Buckley. "How did he get over here?"

Bud's bartender took the ranger by the arm and led him to the side door. There stood a patient gray burro cropping the grass along the gutter, with a load of kindling wood tied across its back. On the ground lay a black shawl and a voluminous brown dress.

"Masquerootin' in them things," called Bud, still resisting attempted ministrations to his wounds. "Thought he was a lady till he give a yell and winged me."

"He went down this side street," said the bartender. "He was alone, and he'll hide out till night when his gang comes over. You ought to find him in that Mexican lay-out below the depot. He's got a girl down there—Pancha Sales."

"How was he armed?" asked Buckley.

"Two pearl-handled sixes, and a knife."

"Keep this for me, Billy," said the ranger, handing over his Winchester. Quixotic, perhaps, but it was Bob Buckley's way. Another man—and a braver one—might have raised a posse to accompany him. It was Buckley's rule to discard all preliminary advantage.

The Mexican had left behind him a wake of closed doors and an empty street, but now people were beginning to emerge from their places of refuge with assumed unconsciousness of anything having happened. Many citizens who knew the ranger pointed out to him with alacrity the course of Garcia's retreat.

As Buckley swung along upon the trail he felt the beginning of the suffocating constriction about his throat, the cold sweat under the brim of his hat, the old, shameful, dreaded sinking of his heart as it went down, down, down in his bosom.

The morning train of the Mexican Central had that day been three hours late, thus failing to connect with the I. & G. N. on the other side of the river. Passengers for *Los Estados Unidos* grumblingly sought entertainment in the little swaggering mongrel town of two nations, for until the morrow, no other train would come to rescue them. Grumblingly, because two days later would begin the great fair and races in San Antone. Consider that at that time San Antone was the hub of the wheel of Fortune, and the names of its spokes were Cattle, Wool, Faro, Running Horses, and Ozone. In those times cattlemen played at crack-loo on the side-walks with double-eagles, and gentlemen backed their conception of the fortuitous card with stacks limited in height only by the interference of gravity. Wherefore, thither journeyed the sowers and the reapers—they who stampeded the dollars, and they who rounded them up. Especially did the caterers to the amusement of the people haste to San Antone. Two greatest shows on earth were already there, and dozens of smallest ones were on the way.

On a side track near the mean little 'dobe depot stood a private car, left there by the Mexican train that morning and doomed by an ineffectual schedule to ignobly await, amid squalid surroundings, connection with the next day's regular.

The car had been once a common day-coach, but those who had sat in it and cringed to the conductor's hatband slips would never have recognized it in its transformation. Paint and gilding and certain domestic touches had liberated it from any suspicion of public servitude. The whitest of lace curtains judiciously screened its windows. From its fore end drooped in the torrid air the flag of Mexico. From its rear projected the Stars and Stripes and a busy stove-pipe, the latter reinforcing in its suggestion of culinary comforts the general suggestion of privacy and ease. The beholder's eye, regarding its gorgeous sides, found interest to culminate in a single name in gold and blue letters extending almost its entire length—a single name, the audacious privilege of royalty and genius. Doubly, then, was this arrogant nomenclature here justified; for the name was that of "Alvarita, Queen of the Serpent Tribe." This, her car, was back from a triumphant tour of the principal Mexican cities, and now headed for San Antonio, where, according to promissory advertisement, she would exhibit her "Marvellous Dominion and Fearless Control over Deadly and Venomous Serpents, Handling them with Ease as they Coil and Hiss to the Terror of Thousands of Tongue-tied Tremblers!"

One hundred in the shade kept the vicinity somewhat depeopled. This quarter of the town was a ragged edge; its denizens the bubbling froth of five nations; its architecture tent, *jacal*, and 'dobe; its distractions the hurdy-gurdy and the informal contribution to the sudden stranger's store of experience. Beyond this dishonorable fringe upon the old town's jowl rose a dense mass of trees, surmounting and filling a little hollow. Through this bickered a small stream that perished down the sheer and disconcerting side of the great cañon of the Rio Bravo del Norte.

In this sordid spot was condemned to remain for certain hours the impotent transport of the Queen of the Serpent Tribe.

The front door of the car was open. Its forward end was curtained off into a small reception room. Here the admiring and propitiatory reporters were wont to sit and transpose the music of Señorita Alvarita's talk into the more florid key of the press. A picture of Abraham Lincoln hung against a wall; one of a cluster of school-girls grouped upon stone steps was in another place; a third was Easter lilies in a blood-red frame. A neat carpet was under foot. A pitcher, sweating cold drops, and a glass stood upon a fragile stand. In a willow rocker, reading a newspaper, sat Alvarita.

Spanish, you would say; Andalusian, or, better still, Basque; that compound, like a diamond, of darkness and fire. Hair, the shade of purple grapes viewed at midnight. Eyes, long, dusky, and disquieting with their untroubled directness of gaze. Face, haughty and bold, touched with a pretty insolence that gave it life. To hasten conviction of her charm, but glance at the stacks of handbills in the corner, green, and yellow, and white. Upon them you see an incompetent presentment of the señorita in her professional garb and pose. Irresistible, in black lace and yellow ribbons, she faces you; a blue racer is spiralled upon each bare arm; coiled twice about her waist and once about her neck, his horrid head close to hers, you perceive Kuku, the great eleven-foot Asian python.

A hand drew aside the curtain that partitioned the car, and a middle-aged, faded woman holding a knife and a half-peeled potato looked in and said:

"Alviry, are you right busy?"

"I'm reading the home paper, ma. What do you think! that pale, tow-headed Matilda Price got the most votes in the *News* for the prettiest girl in Gallipo —*lees*."

"Shuh! She wouldn't of done it if *you'd* been home, Alviry. Lord knows, I hope we'll be there before fall's over. I'm tired gallopin' round the world playin' we are dagoes, and givin' snake shows. But that ain't what I wanted to say. That there biggest snake's gone again. I've looked all over the car and can't find him. He must have been gone an hour. I remember hearin' somethin' rustlin' along the floor, but I thought it was you."

"Oh, blame that old rascal!" exclaimed the Queen, throwing down her paper. "This is the third time he's got away. George never *will* fasten down the lid to his box properly. I do believe he's *afraid* of Kuku. Now I've got to go hunt him."

"Better hurry; somebody might hurt him."

The Queen's teeth showed in a gleaming, contemptuous smile. "No danger. When they see Kuku outside they simply scoot away and buy bromides. There's a crick over between here and the river. That old scamp'd swap his skin any time for a drink of running water. I guess I'll find him there, all right."

A few minutes later Alvarita stepped upon the forward platform, ready for her quest. Her handsome black skirt was shaped to the most recent proclamation of fashion. Her spotless shirt-waist gladdened the eye in that desert of sunshine, a swelling oasis, cool and fresh. A man's split-straw hat sat firmly upon her coiled abundant hair. Beneath her serene, round, impudent chin a man's four-in-hand tie was jauntily knotted about a man's high, stiff collar. A parasol she carried, of white silk, and its fringe was lace, yellowly genuine.

I will grant Gallipolis as to her costume, but firmly to Seville or Valladolid I am held by her eyes; castanets, balconies, mantillas, serenades, ambuscades, escapades—all these their dark depths guaranteed.

"Ain't you afraid to go out alone, Alviry?" queried the Queen-mother anxiously. "There's so many rough people about. Mebbe you'd better——"

"I never saw anything I was afraid of yet, ma. 'Specially people. And men in particular. Don't you fret. I'll trot along back as soon as I find that runaway scamp."

The dust lay thick upon the bare ground near the tracks. Alvarita's eye soon discovered the serrated trail of the escaped python. It led across the depot grounds and away down a smaller street in the direction of the little cañon, as predicted by her. A stillness and lack of excitement in the neighborhood encouraged the hope that, as yet, the inhabitants were unaware that so formidable a guest traversed their highways. The heat had driven them indoors, whence outdrifted occasional shrill laughs, or the depressing whine of a maltreated concertina. In the shade a few Mexican children, like vivified stolid idols in clay, stared from their play, vision-struck and silent, as Alvarita came and went. Here and there a woman peeped from a door and stood dumb, reduced to silence by the aspect of the white silk parasol.

A hundred yards and the limits of the town were passed, scattered chaparral succeeding, and then a noble grove, overflowing the bijou cañon. Through this a small bright stream meandered. Park-like it was, with a kind of cockney ruralness further indorsed by the waste papers and rifled tins of picnickers. Up this stream, and down it, among its pseudo-sylvan glades and depressions, wandered the bright and unruffled Alvarita. Once she saw evidence of the recreant reptile's progress in his distinctive trail across a spread of fine sand in the arroyo. The living water was bound to lure him; he could not be far away.

So sure was she of his immediate proximity that she perched herself to idle for a time in the curve of a great creeper that looped down from a giant water-elm. To reach this she climbed from the pathway a little distance up the side of a steep and rugged incline. Around her chaparral grew thick and high. A late-blooming ratama tree dispensed from its yellow petals a sweet and persistent odor. Adown the ravine rustled a sedative wind, melancholy with the taste of sodden, fallen leaves.

Alvarita removed her hat, and undoing the oppressive convolutions of her hair, began to slowly arrange it in two long, dusky plaits.

From the obscure depths of a thick clump of evergreen shrubs five feet away, two small jewel-bright eyes were steadfastly regarding her. Coiled there lay Kuku, the great python; Kuku, the magnificent, he of the plated muzzle, the grooved lips, the eleven-foot stretch of elegantly and brilliantly mottled skin. The great python was viewing his mistress without a sound or motion to disclose his presence. Perhaps the splendid truant forefelt his capture, but, screened by the foliage, thought to prolong the delight of his escapade. What pleasure it was, after the hot and dusty car, to lie thus, smelling the running water, and feeling the agreeable roughness of the earth and stones against his body! Soon, very soon the Queen would find him, and he, powerless as a worm in her audacious hands, would be returned to the dark chest in the narrow house that ran on wheels.

Alvarita heard a sudden crunching of the gravel below her. Turning her head she saw a big, swarthy Mexican, with a daring and evil expression, contemplating her with an ominous, dull eye.

"What do you want?" she asked as sharply as five hairpins between her lips would permit, continuing to plait her hair, and looking him over with placid contempt. The Mexican continued to gaze at her, and showed his teeth in a white, jagged smile.

"I no hurt-y you, Señorita," he said.

"You bet you won't," answered the Queen, shaking back one finished, massive plait. "But don't you think you'd better move on?"

"Not hurt-y you—no. But maybeso take one *beso*—one li'l kees, you call him."

The man smiled again, and set his foot to ascend the slope. Alvarita leaned swiftly and picked up a stone the size of a cocoanut.

"Vamoose, quick," she ordered peremptorily, "you *coon!*"

The red of insult burned through the Mexican's dark skin.

"*Hidalgo, Yo!*" he shot between his fangs. "I am not neg-r-ro! *Diabla bonita,* for that you shall pay me."

He made two quick upward steps this time, but the stone, hurled by no weak arm, struck him square in the chest. He staggered back to the footway, swerved half around, and met another sight that drove all thoughts of the girl from his head. She turned her eyes to see what had diverted his interest. A man with red-brown, curling hair and a melancholy, sunburned, smooth-shaven face was coming up the path, twenty yards away. Around the Mexican's waist was buckled a pistol belt with two empty holsters. He had laid aside his sixes—possibly in the *jacal* of the fair Pancha—and had forgotten them when the passing of the fairer Alvarita had enticed him to her trail. His hands now flew instinctively to the holsters, but finding the weapons gone, he spread his fingers outward with the eloquent, abjuring, deprecating Latin gesture, and stood like a rock. Seeing his plight, the newcomer unbuckled his own belt containing two revolvers, threw it upon the ground, and continued to advance.

"Splendid!" murmured Alvarita, with flashing eyes.

As Bob Buckley, according to the mad code of bravery that his sensitive conscience imposed upon his cowardly nerves, abandoned his guns and closed in upon his enemy, the old, inevitable nausea of abject fear wrung him. His breath whistled through his constricted air passages. His feet seemed like lumps of lead. His mouth was dry as dust. His heart, congested with blood, hurt his ribs as it thumped against them. The hot June day turned to moist November. And still he advanced, spurred by a mandatory pride that strained its uttermost against his weakling flesh.

The distance between the two men slowly lessened. The Mexican stood, immovable, waiting. When scarce five yards separated them a little shower of loosened gravel rattled down from above to the ranger's feet. He glanced upward with instinctive caution. A pair of dark eyes, brilliantly soft, and fierily tender, encountered and held his own. The most fearful heart and the boldest one in all the Rio Bravo country exchanged a silent and inscrutable communication. Alvarita, still seated within her vine, leaned forward above the breast-high chaparral. One hand was laid across her bosom. One great dark braid curved forward over her shoulder. Her lips were parted; her face was lit with what seemed but wonder—great and absolute wonder. Her eyes lingered upon Buckley's. Let no one ask or presume to tell through what subtle medium the miracle was performed. As by a lightning flash two clouds will accomplish counterpoise and compensation of electric surcharge, so on that eye glance the man received his complement of manhood, and the maid conceded what enriched her womanly grace by its loss.

The Mexican, suddenly stirring, ventilated his attitude of apathetic waiting by conjuring swiftly from his bootleg a long knife. Buckley cast aside his hat, and laughed once aloud, like a happy school-boy at a frolic. Then, empty-handed, he sprang nimbly, and Garcia met him without default.

So soon was the engagement ended that disappointment imposed upon the ranger's war-like ecstasy. Instead of dealing the traditional downward stroke, the Mexican lunged straight with his knife. Buckley took the precarious chance, and caught his wrist, fair and firm. Then he delivered the good Saxon knock-out blow—always so pathetically disastrous to the fistless Latin races—and Garcia was down and out, with his head under a clump of prickly pears. The ranger looked up again to the Queen of the Serpents.

Alvarita scrambled down to the path.

"I'm mighty glad I happened along when I did," said the ranger.

"He—he frightened me so!" cooed Alvarita.

They did not hear the long, low hiss of the python under the shubs. Wiliest of the beasts, no doubt he was expressing the humiliation he felt at having so long dwelt in subjection to this trembling and coloring mistress of his whom he had deemed so strong and potent and fearsome.

Then came galloping to the spot the civic authorities; and to them the ranger awarded the prostrate disturber of the peace, whom they bore away limply across the saddle of one of their mounts. But Buckley and Alvarita lingered.

Slowly, slowly they walked. The ranger regained his belt of weapons. With a fine timidity she begged the indulgence of fingering the great .045's, with little "Ohs" and "Ahs" of new-born, delicious shyness.

The cañoncito was growing dusky. Beyond its terminus in the river bluff they could see the outer world yet suffused with the waning glory of sunset.

A scream—a piercing scream of fright from Alvarita. Back she cowered, and the ready, protecting arm of Buckley formed her refuge. What terror so dire as to thus beset the close of the reign of the never-before-daunted Queen?

Across the path there crawled a *caterpillar*—a horrid, fuzzy, two-inch cater-pillar! Truly, Kuku, thou wert avenged. Thus abdicated the Queen of the Serpent Tribe—*viva la reina!*

THE HIGHER ABDICATION

Curly the tramp sidled toward the free-lunch counter. He caught a fleeting glance from the bartender's eye, and stood still, trying to look like a business man who had just dined at the Menger and was waiting for a friend who had promised to pick him up in his motor car. Curly's histrionic powers were equal to the impersonation; but his make-up was wanting.

The bartender rounded the bar in a casual way, looking up at the ceiling as though he was pondering some intricate problem of kalsomining, and then fell upon Curly so suddenly that the roadster had no excuses ready. Irresistibly, but so composedly that it seemed almost absentmindedness on his part, the dispenser of drinks pushed Curly to the swinging doors and kicked him out, with a nonchalance that almost amounted to sadness. That was the way of the Southwest.

Curly arose from the gutter leisurely. He felt no anger or resentment toward his ejector. Fifteen years of tramphood spent out of the twenty-two years of his life had hardened the fibres of his spirit. The slings and arrows of outrageous fortune fell blunted from the buckler of his armored pride. With especial resignation did he suffer contumely and injury at the hands of bartenders. Naturally, they were his enemies; and unnaturally, they were often his friends. He had to take his chances with them. But he had not yet learned to estimate these cool, languid, Southwestern knights of the bung-starter, who had the manners of an Earl of Pawtucket, and who, when they disapproved of your presence, moved you with the silence and despatch of a chess automaton advancing a pawn.

Curly stood a few moments in the narrow, mesquite-paved street. San Antonio puzzled and disturbed him. Three days he had been a non-paying guest of the town, having dropped off there from a box car of an I. & G. N. freight, because Greaser Johnny had told him in Des Moines that the Alamo City was manna fallen, gathered, cooked, and served free with cream and sugar. Curly had found the tip partly a good one. There was hospitality in plenty of a careless, liberal, irregular sort. But the town itself was a weight upon his spirits after his experience with the rushing, business-like, systematized cities of the North and East. Here he was often flung a dollar, but too frequently a good-natured kick would follow it. Once a band of hilarious cowboys had roped him on Military Plaza and dragged him across the black soil until no respectable rag-bag would have stood sponsor for his clothes. The winding, doubling streets, leading nowhere, bewildered him. And then there was a little river, crooked as a pot-hook, that crawled through the middle of the town, crossed by a hundred little bridges so nearly alike that they got on Curly's nerves. And the last bartender wore a number nine shoe.

The saloon stood on a corner. The hour was eight o'clock. Homefarers and outgoers jostled Curly on the narrow stone sidewalk. Between the buildings to his left he looked down a cleft that proclaimed itself another thoroughfare. The alley was dark except for one patch of light. Where there was a light there were sure to be human beings. Where there were human beings after nightfall in San Antonio there might be food, and there was sure to be drink. So Curly headed for the light.

The illumination came from Schwegel's Café. On the sidewalk in front of it Curly picked up an old envelope. It might have contained a check for a million. It was empty; but the wanderer read the address, "Mr. Otto Schwegel," and the name of the town and State. The postmark was Detroit.

Curly entered the saloon. And now in the light it could be perceived that he bore the stamp of many years of vagabondage. He had none of the tidiness of the calculating and shrewd professional tramp. His wardrobe represented the cast-off specimens of half a dozen fashions and eras. Two factories had combined their efforts in providing shoes for his feet. As you gazed at him there passed through your mind vague impressions of mummies, wax figures, Russian exiles, and men lost on desert islands. His face was covered almost to his eyes with a curly brown beard that he kept trimmed short with a pocket-knife, and that had furnished him with his *nom de route*. Light-blue eyes, full of sullenness, fear, cunning, impudence, and fawning, witnessed the stress that had been laid upon his soul.

The saloon was small, and in its atmosphere the odors of meat and drink struggled for the ascendency. The pig and the cabbage wrestled with hydrogen and oxygen. Behind the bar Schwegel labored with an assistant whose epidermal pores showed no signs of being obstructed. Hot wienerwurst and sauerkraut were being served to purchasers of beer. Curly shuffled to the end of the bar, coughed hollowly, and told Schwegel that he was a Detroit cabinet-maker out of a job.

It followed as the night the day that he got his schooner and lunch.

"Was you acquainted maybe mit Heinrich Strauss in Detroit?" asked Schwegel.

"Did I know Heinrich Strauss?" repeated Curly, affectionately. "Why, say, 'Bo, I wish I had a dollar for every game of pinochle me and Heine has played on Sunday afternoons."

More beer and a second plate of steaming food was set before the diplomat. And then Curly, knowing to a fluid-drachm how far a "con" game would go, shuffled out into the unpromising street.

And now he began to perceive the inconveniences of this stony Southern town. There was none of the outdoor gaiety and brilliancy and music that provided distraction even to the poorest in the cities of the North. Here, even so early, the gloomy, rock-walled houses were closed and barred against the murky dampness of the night. The streets were mere fissures through which flowed gray wreaths of river mist. As he walked he heard laughter and the chink of coin and chips behind darkened windows, and music coming from every chink of wood and stone. But the diversions were selfish; the day of popular pastimes had not yet come to San Antonio.

But at length Curly, as he strayed, turned the sharp angle of another lost street and came upon a rollicking band of stockmen from the outlying ranches celebrating in the open in front of an ancient wooden hotel. One great roisterer from the sheep country who had just instigated a movement toward the bar, swept Curly in like a stray goat with the rest of his flock. The princes of kine and wool hailed him as a new zoölogical discovery, and uproariously strove to preserve him in the diluted alcohol of their compliments and regards.

An hour afterward Curly staggered from the hotel barroom dismissed by his fickle friends, whose interest in him had subsided as quickly as it had risen. Full—stoked with alcoholic fuel and cargoed with food, the only question remaining to disturb him was that of shelter and bed.

A drizzling, cold Texas rain had begun to fall—an endless, lazy, unintermittent downfall that lowered the spirits of men and raised a reluctant steam from the warm stones of the streets and houses. Thus comes the "norther" dousing gentle spring and amiable autumn with the chilling salutes and adieux of coming and departing winter.

Curly followed his nose down the first tortuous street into which his irresponsible feet conducted him. At the lower end of it, on the bank of the serpentine stream, he perceived an open gate in a cemented rock wall. Inside he saw camp fires and a row of low wooden sheds built against three sides of the enclosing wall. He entered the enclosure. Under the sheds many horses were champing at their oats and corn. Many wagons and buckboards stood about with their teams' harness thrown carelessly upon the shafts and doubletrees. Curly recognized the place as a wagon-yard, such as is provided by merchants for their out-of-town friends and customers. No one was in sight. No doubt the drivers of those wagons were scattered about the town "seeing the elephant and hearing the owl." In their haste to become patrons of the town's dispensaries of mirth and good cheer the last ones to depart must have left the great wooden gate swinging open.

Curly had satisfied the hunger of an anaconda and the thirst of a camel, so he was neither in the mood nor the condition of an explorer. He zigzagged his way to the first wagon that his eyesight distinguished in the semi-darkness under the shed. It was a two-horse wagon with a top of white canvas. The wagon was half filled with loose piles of wool sacks, two or three great bundles of gray blankets, and a number of bales, bundles, and boxes. A reasoning eye would have estimated the load at once as ranch supplies, bound on the morrow for some outlying hacienda. But to the drowsy intelligence of Curly they represented only warmth and softness and protection against the cold humidity of the night. After several unlucky efforts, at last he conquered gravity so far as to climb over a wheel and pitch forward upon the best and warmest bed he had fallen upon in many a day. Then he became instinctively a burrowing animal, and dug his way like a prairie-dog down among the sacks and blankets, hiding himself from the cold air as snug and safe as a bear in his den. For three nights sleep had visited Curly only in broken and shivering doses. So now, when Morpheus condescended to pay him a call, Curly got such a strangle hold on the mythological old gentleman that it was a wonder that any one else in the whole world got a wink of sleep that night.

Six cow-punchers of the Cibolo Ranch were waiting around the door of the ranch store. Their ponies cropped grass near by, tied in the Texas fashion—which is not tied at all. Their bridle reins had been dropped to the earth, which is a more effectual way of securing them (such is the power of habit and imagination) than you could devise out of a half-inch rope and a live-oak tree.

These guardians of the cow lounged about, each with a brown cigarette paper in his hand, and gently but unceasingly cursed San Revell, the storekeeper. Sam stood in the door, snapping the red elastic bands on his pink madras shirt-sleeves and looking down affectionately at the only pair of tan shoes within a forty-mile radius. His offence had been serious, and he was divided between humble apology and admiration for the beauty of his raiment. He had allowed the ranch stock of "smoking" to become exhausted.

"I thought sure there was another case of it under the counter, boys," he explained. "But it happened to be catterdges."

"You've sure got a case of happenedicitis," said Poky Rodgers, fence rider of the Largo Verde *potrero*. "Somebody ought to happen to give you a knock on the head with the butt end of a quirt. I've rode in nine miles for some tobacco; and it don't appear natural and seemly that you ought to be allowed to live."

"The boys was smokin' cut plug and dried mesquite leaves mixed when I left," sighed Mustang Taylor, horse wrangler of the Three Elm camp. "They'll be lookin' for me back by nine. They'll be settin' up, with their papers ready to roll a whiff of the real thing before bedtime. And I've got to tell 'em that this pink-eyed, sheep-headed, sulphur-footed, shirt-waisted son of a calico broncho, Sam Revell, hasn't got no tobacco on hand."

Gregorio Falcon, Mexican vaquero and best thrower of the rope on the Cibolo, pushed his heavy, silver-embroidered straw sombrero back upon his thicket of jet-black curls, and scraped the bottoms of his pockets for a few crumbs of the precious weed.

"Ah, Don Samuel," he said, reproachfully, but with his touch of Castilian manners, "escuse me. Dthey say dthe jackrabbeet and dthe sheep have dthe most leetle *sesos*—how you call dthem—brain-es? Ah, don't believe dthat, Don Samuel—escuse me. Ah dthink people w'at don't keep esmokin' tobacco, dthey—bot you weel escuse me, Don Samuel."

"Now, what's the use of chewin' the rag, boys," said the untroubled Sam, stooping over to rub the toes of his shoes with a red-and-yellow handkerchief. "Ranse took the order for some more smokin' to San Antone with him Tuesday. Pancho rode Ranse's hoss back yesterday; and Ranse is goin' to drive the wagon back himself. There wa'n't much of a load—just some woolsacks and blankets and nails and canned peaches and a few things we was out of. I look for Ranse to roll in to-day sure. He's an early starter and a hell-to-split driver, and he ought to be here not far from sundown."

"What plugs is he drivin'?" asked Mustang Taylor, with a smack of hope in his tones.

"The buckboard grays," said Sam.

"I'll wait a spell, then," said the wrangler. "Them plugs eat up a trail like a road-runner swallowin' a whip snake. And you may bust me open a can of green-gage plums, Sam, while I'm waitin' for somethin' better."

"Open me some yellow clings," ordered Poky Rodgers. "I'll wait, too."

The tobaccoless punchers arranged themselves comfortably on the steps of the store. Inside Sam chopped open with a hatchet the tops of the cans of fruit.

The store, a big, white wooden building like a barn, stood fifty yards from the ranch-house. Beyond it were the horse corrals; and still farther the wool sheds and the brush-topped shearing pens—for the Rancho Cibolo raised both cattle and sheep. Behind the store, at a little distance, were the grass-thatched *jacals* of the Mexicans who bestowed their allegiance upon the Cibolo.

The ranch-house was composed of four large rooms, with plastered adobe walls, and a two-room wooden ell. A twenty-feet-wide "gallery" circumvented the structure. It was set in a grove of immense live-oaks and water-elms near a lake—a long, not very wide, and tremendously deep lake in which, at nightfall, great gars leaped to the surface and plunged with the noise of hippopotamuses frolicking at their bath. From the trees hung garlands and massive pendants of the melancholy gray moss of the South. Indeed, the Cibolo ranch-house seemed more of the South than of the West. It looked as if old "Kiowa" Truesdell might have brought it with him from the lowlands of Mississippi when he came to Texas with his rifle in the hollow of his arm in '55.

But, though he did not bring the family mansion, Truesdell did bring something in the way of a family inheritance that was more lasting than brick or stone. He brought one end of the Truesdell-Curtis family feud. And when a Curtis bought the Rancho de los Olmos, sixteen miles from the Cibolo, there were lively times on the pear flats and in the chaparral thickets off the Southwest. In those days Truesdell cleaned the brush of many a wolf and tiger cat and Mexican lion; and one or two Curtises fell heirs to notches on his rifle stock. Also he buried a brother with a Curtis bullet in him on the bank of the lake at Cibolo. And then the Kiowa Indians made their last raid upon the ranches between the Frio and the Rio Grande, and Truesdell at the head of his rangers rid the earth of them to the last brave, earning his sobriquet. Then came prosperity in the form of waxing herds and broadening lands. And then old age and bitterness, when he sat, with his great mane of hair as white as the Spanish-dagger blossoms and his fierce, pale-blue eyes, on the shaded gallery at Cibolo, growling like the pumas that he had slain. He snapped his fingers at old age; the bitter taste to life did not come from that. The cup that stuck at his lips was that his only son Ransom wanted to marry a Curtis, the last youthful survivor of the other end of the feud.

For a while the only sounds to be heard at the store were the rattling of the tin spoons and the gurgling intake of the juicy fruits by the cow-punchers, the stamping of the grazing ponies, and the singing of a doleful song by Sam as he contentedly brushed his stiff auburn hair for the twentieth time that day before a crinkly mirror.

From the door of the store could be seen the irregular, sloping stretch of prairie to the south, with its reaches of light-green, billowing mesquite flats in the lower places, and its rises crowned with nearly black masses of short chaparral.   Through the mesquite flat wound the ranch road that, five miles away, flowed into the old government trail to San Antonio.   The sun was so low that the gentlest elevation cast its gray shadow miles into the green-gold of sunshine.

That evening ears were quicker than eyes.

The Mexican held up a tawny finger to still the scraping of tin against tin.

"One waggeen," said he, "cross dthe Arroyo Hondo.   Ah hear dthe wheel. Verree rockee place, dthe Hondo."

"You've got good ears, Gregorio," said Mustang Taylor.   "I never heard nothin' but the song-bird in the bush and the zephyr skally-hootin' across the peaceful dell."

In ten minutes Taylor remarked: "I see the dust of a wagon risin' right above the fur end of the flat."

"You have verree good eyes, señor," said Gregorio, smiling.

Two miles away they saw a faint cloud dimming the green ripples of the mesquites.   In twenty minutes they heard the clatter of the horses' hoofs: in five minutes more the gray plugs dashed out of the thicket, whickering for oats and drawing the light wagon behind them like a toy.

From the *jacals* came a cry of: "*El Amo!   El Amo!*"   Four Mexican youths raced to unharness the grays.   The cow-punchers gave a yell of greeting and delight.

Ranse Truesdell, driving, threw the reins to the ground and laughed.

"It's under the wagon sheet, boys," he said.   I know what you're waiting for. If Sam lets it run out again we'll use them yellow shoes of his for a target. There's two cases.   Pull 'em out and light up.   I know you all want a smoke."

After striking dry country Ranse had removed the wagon sheet from the bows and thrown it over the goods in the wagon.   Six pairs of hasty hands dragged it off and grabbled beneath the sacks and blankets for the cases of tobacco.

Long Collins, tobacco messenger from the San Gabriel outfit, who rode with the longest stirrups west of the Mississippi, delved with an arm like the tongue of a wagon.   He caught something harder than a blanket and pulled out a fearful thing—a shapeless, muddy bunch of leather tied together with wire and twine.   From its ragged end, like the head and claws of a disturbed turtle, protruded human toes.

"Who-ee!" yelled Long Collins.   "Ranse, are you a-packin' around of corpuses? Here's a—howlin' grasshoppers!"

Up from his long slumber popped Curly, like some vile worm from its burrow. He clawed his way out and sat blinking like a disreputable, drunken owl.   His face was as bluish-red and puffed and seamed and crosslined as the cheapest round steak of the butcher.   His eyes were swollen slits; his nose a pickled beet; his hair would have made the wildest thatch of a Jack-in-the-box look like the satin poll of a Cléo de Mérode.   The rest of him was scarecrow done to the life.

Ranse jumped down from his seat and looked at his strange cargo with wide-open eyes.

"Here, you maverick, what are you doing in my wagon?   How did you get in there?"

The punchers gathered around in delight.   For the time they had forgotten tobacco.

Curly looked around him slowly in every direction.   He snarled like a Scotch terrier through his ragged beard.

"Where is this?" he rasped through his parched throat.   "It's a damn farm in an old field.   What'd you bring me here for—say?   Did I say I wanted to come here?   What are you Reubs rubberin' at—hey?   G'wan or I'll punch some of yer faces."

"Drag him out, Collins," said Ranse.

Curly took a slide and felt the ground rise up and collide with his shoulder blades. He got up and sat on the steps of the store shivering from outraged nerves, hugging his knees and sneering. Taylor lifted out a case of tobacco and wrenched off its top. Six cigarettes began to glow, bringing peace and forgiveness to Sam.

"How'd you come in my wagon?" repeated Ranse, this time in a voice that drew a reply.

Curly recognized the tone. He had heard it used by freight brakemen and large persons in blue carrying clubs.

"Me?" he growled. "Oh, was you talkin' to me? Why, I was on my way to the Menger, but my valet had forgot to pack my pajamas. So I crawled into that wagon in the wagon-yard—see? I never told you to bring me out to this bloomin' farm—see?"

"What is it, Mustang?" asked Poky Rodgers, almost forgetting to smoke in his ecstasy. "What do it live on?"

"It's a galliwampus, Poky," said Mustang. "It's the thing that hollers 'williwallo' up in ellum trees in the low grounds of nights. I don't know if it bites."

"No, it ain't, Mustang," volunteered Long Collins. "Them galliwampuses has fins on their backs, and eighteen toes. This here is a hicklesnifter. It lives under the ground and eats cherries. Don't stand so close to it. It wipes out villages with one stroke of its prehensile tail.'"

Sam, the cosmopolite, who called bartenders in San Antone by their first name, stood in the door. He was a better zoölogist.

"Well, ain't that a Willie for your whiskers?" he commented. "Where'd you dig up the hobo, Ranse? Goin' to make an auditorium for inbreviates out of the ranch?"

"Say," said Curly, from whose panoplied breast all shafts of wit fell blunted. "Any of you kiddin' guys got a drink on you? Have your fun. Say, I've been hittin' the stuff till I don't know straight up."

He turned to Ranse. "Say, you shanghaied me on your d—d old prairie schooner—did I tell you to drive me to a farm? I want a drink. I'm goin' all to little pieces. What's doin'?"

Ranse saw that the tramp's nerves were racking him. He despatched one of the Mexican boys to the ranch-house for a glass of whisky. Curly gulped it down; and into his eyes came a brief, grateful glow—as human as the expression in the eye of a faithful setter dog.

"Thanky, boss," he said, quietly.

"You're thirty miles from a railroad, and forty miles from a saloon," said Ranse.

Curly fell back weakly against the steps.

"Since you are here," continued the ranchman, "come along with me. We can't turn you out on the prairie. A rabbit might tear you to pieces."

He conducted Curly to a large shed where the ranch vehicles were kept. There he spread out a canvas cot and brought blankets.

"I don't suppose you can sleep," said Ranse, "since you've been pounding your ear for twenty-four hours. But you can camp here till morning. I'll have Pedro fetch you up some grub."

"Sleep!" said Curly. "I can sleep a week. Say, sport, have you got a coffin nail on you?"

Fifty miles had Ransom Truesdell driven that day. And yet this is what he did.

Old "Kiowa" Truesdell sat in his great wicker chair reading by the light of an immense oil lamp. Ranse laid a bundle of newspapers fresh from town at his elbow.

"Back, Ranse?" said the old man, looking up.

"Son," old "Kiowa" continued, "I've been thinking all day about a certain
matter that we have talked about. I want you to tell me again. I've lived for
you. I've fought wolves and Indians and worse white men to protect you. You
never had any mother that you can remember. I've taught you to shoot straight,
ride hard, and live clean. Later on I've worked to pile up dollars that'll be
yours. You'll be a rich man, Ranse, when my chunk goes out. I've made you.
I've licked you into shape like a leopard cat licks its cubs. You don't belong
to yourself—you've got to be a Truesdell first. Now, is there to be any more
nonsense about this Curtis girl?"

"I'll tell you once more," said Ranse, slowly. "As I am a Truesdell and as
you are my father, I'll never marry a Curtis."

"Good boy," said old "Kiowa." "You'd better go get some supper."

Ranse went to the kitchen at the rear of the house. Pedro, the Mexican cook,
sprang up to bring the food he was keeping warm in the stove.

"Just a cup of coffee, Pedro," he said, and drank it standing. And then:

"There's a tramp on a cot in the wagon-shed. Take him something to eat.
Better make it enough for two."

Ranse walked out toward the *jacals*. A boy came running.

"Manuel, can you catch Vaminos, in the little pasture, for me?"

"Why not, señor? I saw him near the *puerta* but two hours past. He bears
a drag-rope."

"Get him and saddle him as quick as you can."

"*Prontito, señor.*"

Soon mounted, on Vaminos, Ranse leaned in the saddle, pressed with his knees,
and galloped eastward past the store, where sat Sam trying his guitar in the
moonlight.

Vaminos shall have a word—Vaminos the good dun horse. The Mexicans, who
have a hundred names for the colors of a horse, called him *gruyo*. He was a
mouse-colored, slate-colored, flea-bitten roan-dun, if you can conceive it. Down
his back from his mane to his tail went a line of black. He would live forever; and surveyors have not laid off as many miles in the world as he could
travel in a day.

Eight miles east of the Cibolo ranch-house Ranse loosened the pressure of his
knees, and Vaminos stopped under a big ratama tree. The yellow ratama blossoms showered fragrance that would have undone the roses of France. The
moon made the earth a great concave bowl with a crystal sky for a lid. In a
glade five jack-rabbits leaped and played together like kittens. Eight miles
farther east shone a faint star that appeared to have dropped below the horizon.
Night riders, who often steered their course by it, knew it to be the light in the
Rancho de los Olmos.

In ten minutes Yenna Curtis galloped to the tree on her sorrel pony Dancer.
The two leaned and clasped hands heartily.

"I ought to have ridden nearer your home," said Ranse. "But you never will
let me."

Yenna laughed. And in the soft light you could see her strong white teeth and
fearless eyes. No sentimentality there, in spite of the moonlight, the odor of the
ratamas, and the admirable figure of Ranse Truesdell, the lover. But she was
there, eight miles from her home, to meet him.

"How often have I told you, Ranse," she said, "that I am your half-way girl?
Always half-way."

"Well?" said Ranse, with a question in his tones.

"I did," said Yenna, with almost a sigh. "I told him after dinner when I
thought he would be in a good humor. Did you ever wake up a lion, Ranse, with
the mistaken idea that he would be a kitten? He almost tore the ranch to
pieces. It's all up. I love my daddy, Ranse, and I'm afraid—I'm afraid of him,

too. He ordered me to promise that I'd never marry a Truesdell. I promised. That's all. What luck did you have?"

"The same," said Ranse, slowly. "I promised him that his son would never marry a Curtis. Somehow I couldn't go against him. He's mighty old. I'm sorry, Yenna."

The girl leaned in her saddle and laid one hand on Ranse's, on the horn of his saddle.

"I never thought I'd like you better for giving me up," she said ardently, "but I do. I must ride back now, Ranse. I slipped out of the house and saddled Dancer myself. Good-night, neighbor."

"Good-night," said Ranse. "Ride carefully over them badger holes."

They wheeled and rode away in opposite directions. Yenna turned in her saddle and called clearly:

"Don't forget I'm your half-way girl, Ranse."

"Damn all family feuds and inherited scraps," muttered Ranse vindictively to the breeze as he rode back to the Cibolo.

Ranse turned his horse into the small pasture and went to his own room. He opened the lowest drawer of an old bureau to get out the packet of letters that Yenna had written him one summer when she had gone to Mississippi for a visit. The drawer stuck, and he yanked at it savagely—as a man will. It came out of the bureau, and bruised both his shins—as a drawer will. An old, folded yellow letter without an envelope fell from somewhere—probably from where it had lodged in one of the upper drawers. Ranse took it to the lamp and read it curiously.

Then he took his hat and walked to one of the Mexican *jacals*.

"Tía Juana," he said, "I would like to talk with you awhile."

An old, old Mexican woman, white-haired and wonderfully wrinkled, rose from a stool.

"Sit down," said Ranse, removing his hat and taking the one chair in the *jacal*. "Who am I, Tía Juana?" he asked, speaking Spanish.

"Don Ransom, our good friend and employer. Why do you ask?" answered the old woman wonderingly.

"Tía Juana, who am I?" he repeated, with his stern eyes looking into hers.

A frightened look came in the old woman's face. She fumbled with her black shawl.

"Who am I, Tía Juana?" said Ranse once more.

"Thirty-two years I have lived on the Rancho Cibolo," said Tía Juana. "I thought to be buried under the coma mott beyond the garden before these things should be known. Close the door, Don Ransom, and I will speak. I see in your face that you know."

An hour Ranse spent behind Tía Juana's closed door. As he was on his way back to the house Curly called to him from the wagon-shed.

The tramp sat on his cot, swinging his feet and smoking.

"Say, sport," he grumbled. "This is no way to treat a man after kidnappin' him. I went up to the store and borrowed a razor from that fresh guy and had a shave. But that ain't all a man needs. Say—can't you loosen up for about three fingers more of that booze? I never asked you to bring me to your d—d farm."

"Stand up out here in the light," said Ranse, looking at him closely.

Curly got up sullenly and took a step or two.

His face, now shaven smooth, seemed transformed. His hair had been combed, and it fell back from the right side of his forehead with a peculiar wave. The moonlight charitably softened the ravages of drink; and his aquiline, well-shaped nose and small, square-cleft chin almost gave distinction to his looks.

Ranse sat on the foot of the cot and looked at him curiously.

"Where did you come from—have you got any home or folks anywhere?"

"Me? Why, I'm a dook," said Curly. "I'm Sir Reginald—oh, cheese it. No; I don't know anything about my ancestors. I've been a tramp ever since I can remember. Say, old pal, are you going to set 'em up again to-night or not?"

"You answer my questions and maybe I will. How did you come to be a tramp?"

"Me?" answered Curly. "Why, I adopted that profession when I was an infant. Case of had to. First thing I can remember, I belonged to a big, lazy hobo called Beefsteak Charley. He sent me around to houses to beg. I wasn't hardly big enough to reach the latch of a gate."

"Did he ever tell you how he got you?" asked Ranse.

"Once when he was sober he said he bought me for an old six-shooter and six bits from a band of drunken Mexican sheep-shearers. But what's the diff? That's all I know."

"All right," said Ranse. "I reckon you're a maverick for certain. I'm going to put the Rancho Cibolo brand on you. I'll start you to work in one of the camps to-morrow."

"Work!" sniffed Curly, disdainfully. "What do you take me for? Do you think I'd chase cows, and hop-skip-and-jump around after crazy sheep like that pink-and-yellow guy at the store says these Reubs do? Forget it."

"Oh, you'll like it when you get used to it," said Ranse. "Yes, I'll send you up one more drink by Pedro. I think you'll make a first-class cow-puncher before I get through with you."

"Me?" said Curly. "I pity the cows you set me to chaperon. They can go chase themselves. Don't forget my nightcap, please, boss."

Ranse paid a visit to the store before going to the house. Sam Revell was taking off his tan shoes regretfully and preparing for bed.

"Any of the boys from the San Gabriel camp riding in early in the morning?" asked Ranse.

"Long Collins," said Sam, briefly. "For the mail."

"Tell him," said Ranse, "to take that tramp out to camp with him and keep him till I get there."

Curly was sitting on his blankets in the San Gabriel camp cursing talentedly when Ranse Truesdell rode up and dismounted on the next afternoon. The cow-punchers were ignoring the stray. He was grimy with dust and black dirt. His clothes were making their last stand in favor of the conventions.

Ranse went up to Buck Rabb, the camp boss, and spoke briefly.

"He's a plumb buzzard," said Buck. "He won't work, and he's the low-downest passel of inhumanity I ever see. I didn't know what you wanted done with him, Ranse, so I just let him set. That seems to suit him. He's been condemned to death by the boys a dozen times, but I told 'em maybe you was savin' him for torture."

Ranse took off his coat.

"I've got a hard job before me, Buck, I reckon, but it has to be done. I've got to make a man out of that thing. That's what I've come to camp for."

He went up to Curly.

"Brother," he said, "don't you think if you had a bath it would allow you to take a seat in the company of your fellow-man with less injustice to the atmosphere?"

"Run away, farmer," said Curly, sardonically. "Willie will send for nursey when he feels like having his tub."

The *charco*, or water hole, was twelve yards away. Ranse took one of Curly's ankles and dragged him like a sack of potatoes to the brink. Then with the strength and sleight of a hammer-thrower he hurled the offending member of society far into the lake.

Curly crawled out and up the bank spluttering like a porpoise.

Ranse met him with a piece of soap and a coarse towel in his hands.

"Go to the other end of the lake and use this," he said. "Buck will give you some dry clothes at the wagon."

The tramp obeyed without protest. By the time supper was ready he had returned to camp. He was hardly to be recognized in his new blue shirt and brown duck clothes. Ranse observed him out of the corner of his eye.

"Lordy, I hope he ain't a coward," he was saying to himself. "I hope he won't turn out to be a coward."

His doubts were soon allayed. Curly walked straight to where he stood. His light-blue eyes were blazing.

"Now I'm clean," he said, meaningly, "maybe you'll talk to me. Think you've got a picnic here, do you? You clodhoppers think you can run over a man because you know he can't get away. All right. Now, what do you think of that?"

Curly planted a stinging slap against Ranse's left cheek. The print of his hand stood out a dull red against the tan.

Ranse smiled happily.

The cow-punchers talk to this day of the battle that followed.

Somewhere in his restless tour of the cities Curly had acquired the art of self-defence. The ranchman was equipped only with the splendid strength and equilibrium of perfect health and the endurance conferred by decent living. The two attributes nearly matched. There were no formal rounds. At last the fibre of the clean liver prevailed. The last time Curly went down from one of the ranchman's awkward but powerful blows he remained on the grass, but looking up with an unquenched eye.

Ranse went to the water barrel and washed the red from a cut on his chin in the stream from the faucet.

On his face was a grin of satisfaction.

Much benefit might accrue to educators and moralists if they could know the details of the curriculum of reclamation through which Ranse put his waif during the month that he spent in the San Gabriel camp. The ranchman had no fine theories to work out—perhaps his whole stock of pedagogy embraced only a knowledge of horse-breaking and a belief in heredity.

The cow-punchers saw that their boss was trying to make a man out of the strange animal that he had sent among them; and they tacitly organized themselves into a faculty of assistants. But their system was their own.

Curly's first lesson stuck. He became on friendly and then on intimate terms with soap and water. And the thing that pleased Ranse most was that his "subject" held his ground at each successive higher step. But the steps were sometimes far apart.

Once he got at the quart bottle of whisky kept sacredly in the grub tent for rattlesnake bites, and spent sixteen hours on the grass, magnificently drunk. But when he staggered to his feet his first move was to find his soap and towel and start for the *charco*. And once, when a treat came from the ranch in the form of a basket of fresh tomatoes and young onions, Curly devoured the entire consignment before the punchers reached the camp at supper time.

And then the punchers punished him in their own way. For three days they did not speak to him, except to reply to his own questions or remarks. And they spoke with absolute and unfailing politeness. They played tricks on one another; they pounded one another hurtfully and affectionately; they heaped upon one another's heads friendly curses and obloquy; but they were polite to Curly. He saw it, and it stung him as much as Ranse hoped it would.

Then came a night that brought a cold, wet norther. Wilson, the youngest of the outfit, had lain in camp two days, ill with a fever. When Joe got up at daylight to begin breakfast he found Curly sitting asleep against a wheel of the grub wagon with only a saddle blanket around him, while Curly's blankets were stretched over Wilson to protect him from the rain and wind.

Three nights after that Curly rolled himself in his blanket and went to sleep. Then the other punchers rose up softly and began to make preparations. Ranse saw Long Collins tie a rope to the horn of a saddle. Others were getting out their six-shooters.

"Boys," said Ranse, "I'm much obliged. I was hoping you would. But I didn't like to ask."

Half a dozen six-shooters began to pop—awful yells rent the air—Long Collins galloped wildly across Curly's bed, dragging the saddle after him. That was merely their way of gently awaking their victim. Then they hazed him for an hour, carefully and ridiculously, after the code of cow camps. Whenever he uttered protest they held him stretched over a roll of blankets and thrashed him woefully with a pair of leather leggins.

And all this meant that Curly had won his spurs, that he was receiving the punchers' accolade. Nevermore would they be polite to him. But he would be their "pardner" and stirrup-brother, foot to foot.

When the fooling was ended all hands made a raid on Joe's big coffee-pot by the fire for a Java nightcap. Ranse watched the new knight carefully to see if he understood and was worthy. Curly limped with his cup of coffee to a log and sat upon it. Long Collins followed and sat by his side. Buck Rabb went and sat at the other. Curly—grinned.

And then Ranse furnished Curly with mounts and saddle and equipment, and turned him over to Buck Rabb, instructing him to finish the job.

Three weeks later Ranse rode from the ranch into Rabb's camp, which was then in Snake Valley. The boys were saddling for the day's ride. He sought out Long Collins among them.

"How about that bronco?" he asked.

Long Collins grinned.

"Reach out your hand, Ranse Truesdell," he said, "and you'll touch him. And you can shake his'n, too, if you like, for he's plumb white and there's none better in no camp."

Ranse looked again at the clear-faced, bronzed, smiling cow-puncher who stood at Collins's side. Could that be Curly? He held out his hand, and Curly grasped it with the muscles of a bronco-buster.

"I want you at the ranch," said Ranse.

"All right, sport," said Curly, heartily. "But I want to come back again. Say, pal, this is a dandy farm. And I don't want any better fun than hustlin' cows with this bunch of guys. They're all to the merry merry."

At the Cibolo ranch-house they dismounted. Ranse bade Curly wait at the door of the living room. He walked inside. Old "Kiowa" Truesdell was reading at a table.

"Good-morning, Mr. Truesdell," said Ranse.

The old man turned his white head quickly.

"How is this?" he began. "Why do you call me 'Mr.——'?"

When he looked at Ranse's face he stopped, and the hand that held his newspaper shook slightly.

"Boy," he said slowly, "how did you find it out?"

"It's all right," said Ranse, with a smile. "I made Tía Juana tell me. It was kind of by accident, but it's all right."

"You've been like a son to me," said old "Kiowa," trembling.

"Tía Juana told me all about it," said Ranse. "She told me how you adopted me when I was knee-high to a puddle duck out of a wagon train of prospectors that was bound West. And she told me how the kid—your own kid, you know—got lost or was run away with. And she said it was the same day that the sheep-shearers got on a bender and left the ranch."

"Our boy strayed from the house when he was two years old," said the old man. "And then along came these emigrant wagons with a youngster they didn't want; and we took you. I never intended you to know, Ranse. We never heard of our boy again."

"He's right outside, unless I'm mighty mistaken," said Ranse, opening the door and beckoning.

Curly walked in.

No one could have doubted. The old man and the young had the same sweep of hair, the same nose, chin, line of face, and prominent light-blue eyes.

Old "Kiowa" rose eagerly.

Curly looked about the room curiously. A puzzled expression came over his face. He pointed to the wall opposite.

"Where's the tick-tock?" he asked, absentmindedly.

"The clock," cried old "Kiowa" loudly. "The eight-day clock used to stand there. Why——"

He turned to Ranse, but Ranse was not there.

Already a hundred yards away, Vaminos, the good flea-bitten dun, was bearing him eastward like a racer through dust and chaparral towards the Rancho de los Olmos.

CUPID À LA CARTE

"THE dispositions of woman," said Jeff Peters, after various opinions on the subject had been advanced, "run, regular, to diversions. What a woman wants is what you're out of. She wants more of a thing when it's scarce. She likes to have souvenirs of things she never heard of. A one-sided view of objects is disjointing to the female composition.

" 'Tis a misfortune of mine, begotten by nature and travel," continued Jeff, looking thoughtfully between his elevated feet at the grocery stove, "to look deeper into some subjects than most people do. I've breathed gasoline smoke talking to street crowds in nearly every town in the United States. I've held 'em spellbound with music, oratory, sleight of hand, and prevarications, while I've sold 'em jewelry, medicine, soap, hair tonic, and junk of other nomina-tions. And during my travels, as a matter of recreation and expiation, I've taken cognizance some of women. It takes a man a lifetime to find out about one particular woman; but if he puts in, say, ten years, industrious and curious, he can acquire the general rudiments of the sex. One lesson I picked up was when I was working the West with a line of Brazilian diamonds and a patent fire kindler just after my trip from Savannah down through the cotton belt with Dalby's Anti-explosive Lamp Oil Powder. 'Twas when the Oklahoma country was in first bloom. Guthrie was rising in the middle of it like a lump of self-raising dough. It was a boom town of the regular kind—you stood in line to get a chance to wash your face; if you ate over ten minutes you had a lodging bill added on; if you slept on a plank at night they charged it to you as board the next morning.

"By nature and doctrines I am addicted to the habit of discovering choice places wherein to feed. So I looked around and found a proposition that exactly cut the mustard. I found a restaurant tent just opened up by an outfit that had drifted in on the tail of the boom. They had knocked together a box house, where they lived and did the cooking, and served the meals in a tent pitched against the side. That tent was joyful with placards on it calculated to redeem the world-worn pilgrim from the sinfulness of boarding houses and pick-me-up hotels. 'Try Mother's Home-Made Biscuits,' 'What's the Matter with Our Apple Dumplings and Hard Sauce?' 'Hot Cakes and Maple Syrup Like You Ate When a Boy,' 'Our Fried Chicken Never Was Heard to Crow'—there was literature doomed to please the digestions of man! I said to myself that mother's wandering boy should munch there that night. And so it came to pass. And there is where I contracted my case of Mame Dugan.

"Old Man Dugan was six feet by one of Indiana loafer, and he spent his time sitting on his shoulder blades in a rocking-chair in the shanty memoralizing the great corn-crop failure of '86. Ma Dugan did the cooking, and Mame waited on table.

"As soon as I saw Mame I knew there was a mistake in the census reports. There wasn't but one girl in the United States. When you come to specifications it isn't easy. She was about the size of an angel, and she had eyes, and ways about her. When you come to the kind of a girl she was, you'll find a belt of 'em reaching from the Brooklyn Bridge west as far as the courthouse in Council Bluffs, Ia. They earn their own living in stores, restaurants, factories, and offices. They're descended straight from Eve, and they're the crowd that's got woman's rights, and if a man wants to dispute it he's in line to get one of them against his jaw. They're chummy and honest and free and tender and sassy, and they look life straight in the eye. They've met man face to face, and discovered that he's a poor creature. They've dropped to it that the reports in the Seaside Library about his being a fairy prince lack confirmation.

"Mame was that sort. She was full of life and fun, and breezy; she passed the repartee with the boarders quick as a wink; you'd have smothered laughing. I am disinclined to make excavations into the insides of a personal affection. I am glued to the theory that the diversions and discrepancies of the indisposition known as love should be as private a sentiment as a toothbrush. 'Tis my opinion that the biographies of the heart should be confined with the historical romances of the liver to the advertising pages of the magazines. So, you'll excuse the lack of an itemized bill of my feelings toward Mame.

"Pretty soon I got a regular habit of dropping into the tent to eat at irregular times when there wasn't so many around. Mame would sail in with a smile, in a black dress and white apron, and say: 'Hello, Jeff—why don't you come at mealtime, Want to see how much trouble you can be, of course. Fried-chickenbeefsteakporkchopshamandeggspotpie'—and so on. She called me Jeff, but there was no significations attached. Designations was all she meant. The front names of any of us she used as they came to hand. I'd eat about two meals before I left, and string 'em out like a society spread where they changed plates and wives, and josh one another festively between bites. Mame stood for it, pleasant, for it wasn't up to her to take any canvas off the tent by declining dollars just because they were chipped in after meal times.

"It wasn't long until there was another fellow named Ed Collier got the between-meals affliction, and him and me put in bridges between breakfast and dinner, and dinner and supper, that made a three-ringed circus of that tent, and Mame's turn as waiter a continuous performance. That Collier man was saturated with designs and contrivings. He was in well-boring or insurance or claim-jumping or something—I've forgotten which. He was a man well lubricated with gentility and his words were such as recommended you to his point of view. So Collier and me infested the grub tent with care and activity. Mame was level full of impartiality. 'Twas like a casino hand the way she dealt out her favors—one to Collier and one to me and one to the board and not a card up her sleeve.

"Me and Collier naturally got acquainted, and gravitated together some on the outside. Divested of his stratagems, he seemed to be a pleasant chap, full of an amiable sort of hostility.

"'I notice you have an affinity for grubbing in the banquet hall after the guests have fled,' says I to him one day, to draw his conclusions.

"'Well, yes,' says Collier, reflecting; 'the tumult of a crowded board seems to harass my sensitive nerves.'

"'It exasperates mine some, too,' says I. 'Nice little girl, don't you think?'

"'I see,' says Collier, laughing. 'Well, now that you mention it, I have noticed that she doesn't seem to displease the optic nerve.'

"'She's a joy to mine,' says I, 'and I'm going after her. Notice is hereby served.'

"'I'll be as candid as you,' admits Collier, 'and if the drug stores don't run out of pepsin I'll give you a run for your money that'll leave you a dyspeptic at the wind-up.'

"So Collier and me begins the race; the grub department lays in new supplies; Mame waits on us, jolly and kind and agreeable, and it looks like an even break, with Cupid and the cook working overtime in Dugan's restaurant.

"'Twas one night in September when I got Mame to take a walk after supper when the things were all cleared away. We strolled out a distance and sat on a pile of lumber at the edge of town. Such opportunities was seldom, so I spoke my piece, explaining how the Brazilian diamonds and the fire kindler were laying up sufficient treasure to guarantee the happiness of two, and that both of 'm together couldn't equal the light from somebody's eyes, and that the name of Dugan should be changed to Peters, or reasons why not would be in order.

"Mame didn't say anything right away. Directly she gave a kind of shudder, and I began to learn something.

"'Jeff,' she says. 'I'm sorry you spoke. I like you as well as any of them, but there isn't the man in the world I'd ever marry, and there never will be. Do you know what a man is in my eye? He's a tomb. He's a sarcophagus for the interment of Beeksteakporkchopsliver'nbaconhamandeggs. He's that and nothing more. For two years I've watched men eat, eat, eat, until they represent nothing on earth to me but ruminant bipeds. They're absolutely nothing but something that goes in front of a knife and fork and plate at the table. They're fixed that way in my mind and memory. I've tried to overcome it, but I can't. I've heard girls rave about their sweethearts, but I never could understand it. A man and a sausage grinder and a pantry awake in me exactly the same sentiments. I went to a matinée once to see an actor the girls were crazy about. I got interested enough to wonder whether he liked his steak rare, medium, or well done, and his eggs over or straight up. That was all. No, Jeff; I'll marry no man and see him sit at the breakfast table and eat and come back to dinner and eat, and happen in again at supper to eat, eat, eat.'

"'But, Mame,' says I, 'it'll wear off. You've had too much of it. You'll marry some time, of course. Men don't eat always.'

"'As far as my observation goes, they do. No, I'll tell you what I'm going to do.' Mame turns, suddenly to animation and bright eyes. 'There's a girl named Susie Foster in Terre Haute, a chum of mine. She waits in the railroad eating house there. I worked two years in a restaurant in that town. Susie has it worse than I do, because the men who eat at railroad stations gobble. They try to flirt and gobble at the same time. Whew! Susie and I have it all planned out. We're saving our money, and when we get enough we're going to buy a little cottage and five acres we know of, and live together, and grow violets for the Eastern market. A man better not bring his appetite within a mile of that ranch.'

" 'Don't girls ever——' I commenced, but Mame heads me off, sharp.

" 'No, they don't. They nibble a little bit sometimes; that's all.'

" 'I thought the confect——'

" 'For goodness' sake, change the subject,' says Mame.

"As I said before, that experience put me wise that the feminine arrangement ever struggles after deceptions and illusions. Take England—beef made her; wieners elevated Germany; Uncle Sam owes his greatness to fried chicken and pie, but the young ladies of the Shetalkyou schools, they'll never believe it. Shakespeare, they allow, and Rubinstein, and the Rough Riders is what did the trick.

" 'Twas a situation calculated to disturb. I couldn't bear to give up Mame; and yet it pained me to think of abandoning the practice of eating. I had acquired the habit too early. For twenty-seven years I had been blindly rushing upon my fate, yielding to the insidious lures of that deadly monster, food. It was too late. I was a ruminant biped for keeps. It was lobster salad to a doughnut that my life was going to be blighted by it.

"I continued to board at the Dugan tent, hoping that Mame would relent. I had sufficient faith in true love to believe that since it has often outlived the absence of a square meal it might, in time, overcome the presence of one. I went on ministering to my fatal vice, although I felt that each time I shoved a potato into my mouth in Mame's presence I might be burying my fondest hopes.

"I think Collier must have spoken to Mame and got the same answer, for one day he orders a cup of coffee and a cracker, and sits nibbling the corner of it like a girl in the parlor, that's filled up in the kitchen, previous, on cold roast and fried cabbage. I caught on and did the same, and maybe we thought we'd made a hit! The next day we tried it again, and out comes Old Man Dugan fetching in his hands the fairy viands.

" 'Kinder off yer feed, ain't ye, gents?' he asks, fatherly and some sardonic. 'Thought I'd spell Mame a bit, seein' the work was light, and my rheumatiz can stand the strain.'

"So back me and Collier had to drop to the heavy grub again. I noticed about that time that I was seized by a most uncommon and devastating appetite. I ate until Mame must have hated to see me darken the door. Afterward I found out that I had been made the victim of the first dark and irreligious trick played on me by Ed Collier. Him and me had been taking drinks together uptown regular, trying to drown our thirst for food. That man had bribed about ten bartenders to always put a big slug of Appletree's Anaconda Appetite Bitters in every one of my drinks. But the last trick he played me was hardest to forget.

"One day Collier failed to show up at the tent. A man told me he left town that morning. My only rival now was the bill of fare. A few days before he left Collier had presented me with a two-gallon jug of fine whisky which he said a cousin had sent him from Kentucky. I now have reason to believe that it contained Appletree's Anaconda Appetite Bitters almost exclusively. I continued to devour tons of provisions. In Mame's eyes I remained a mere biped, more ruminant than ever.

"About a week after Collier pulled his freight there came a kind of side-show to town, and hoisted a tent near the railroad. I judged it was a sort of fake museum and curiosity business. I called to see Mame one night, and Ma Dugan said she and Thomas, her younger brother, had gone to the show. That same thing happened for three nights that week. Saturday night I caught her on the way coming back, and got to sit on the steps a while and talk to her. I noticed she looked different. Her eyes were softer, and shiny like. Instead of a Mame

Dugan to fly from the voracity of man and raise violets, she seemed to be a Mame more in line as God intended her, approachable, and suited to bask in the light of the Brazilians and the Kindler.

"'You seem to be right smart inveigled,' says I, 'with the Unparalleled Exhibition of the World's Living Curiosities and Wonders.'

"'It's a change,' says Mame.

"'You'll need another,' says I, 'if you keep on going every night.'

"'Don't be cross, Jeff,' says she; 'it takes my mind off business.'

"'Don't the curiosities eat?' I ask.

"'Not all of them. Some of them are wax.'

"'Look out, then, that you don't get stuck,' says I, kind of flip and foolish.

"Mame blushed. I didn't know what to think about her. My hopes raised some that perhaps my attentions had palliated man's awful crime of visibly introducing nourishment into his system. She talked some about the stars, referring to them with respect and politeness, and I drivelled a quantity about united hearts, homes made bright by true affection, and the Kindler. Mame listened without scorn and I says to myself, 'Jeff, old man, you're removing the hoodoo that has clung to the consumer of victuals; you're setting your heel upon the serpent that lurks in the gravy bowl.'

"Monday night I drop around. Mame is at the Unparalleled Exhibition with Thomas.

"'Now, may the curse of the forty-one seven-sided sea cooks,' says I, 'and the bad luck of the nine impenitent grasshoppers rest upon this self-same sideshow at once and forever. Amen. I'll go to see it myself to-morrow night and investigate its baleful charm. Shall man that was made to inherit the earth be bereft of his sweetheart first by a knife and fork and then by a ten-cent circus?'

"The next night before starting out for the exhibition tent I inquire and find out that Mame is not at home. She is not at the circus with Thomas this time, for Thomas waylays me in the grass outside of the grub tent with a scheme of his own before I had time to eat supper.

"'What'll you give me, Jeff,' says he, 'if I tell you something?'

"'The value of it, son,' I says.

"'Sis is stuck on a freak,' says Thomas, 'one of the side-show freaks. I don't like him. She does. I overheard 'em talking. Thought maybe you'd like to know. Say, Jeff, does it put you wise two dollars' worth? There's a target rifle up town that——'

"I frisked my pockets and commenced to dribble a stream of halves and quarters into Thomas's hat. The information was of the pile-driver system of news, and it telescoped my intellects for a while. While I was leaking small change and smiling foolish on the outside, and suffering disturbances internally, I was saying, idiotically and pleasantly:

"'Thank you, Thomas—thank you—er—a freak, you said, Thomas. Now, could you make out the monstrosity's entitlements a little clearer if you please, Thomas?'

"'This is the fellow,' says Thomas, pulling out a yellow handbill from his pocket and shoving it under my nose. 'He's the Champion Faster of the Universe. I guess that's why Sis got soft on him. He don't eat nothing. He's going to fast forty-nine days. This is the sixth. That's him.'

"I looked at the name Thomas pointed out—'Professor Eduardo Collieri.' 'Ah!' says I, in admiration, 'that's not so bad, Ed Collier. I give you credit for the trick. But I don't give you the girl until she's Mrs. Freak.'

"I hit the sod in the direction of the show. I came up to the rear of the tent, and, as I did so, a man wiggled out like a snake from under the bottom of the canvas, scrambled to his feet, and ran into me like a locoed bronco. I gathered him by the neck and investigated him by the light of the stars. It is Professor Eduardo Collieri, in human habiliments, with a desperate look in one eye and impatience in the other.

" 'Hello, Curiosity,' says I. 'Get still a minute and let's have a look at your freakship. How do you like being the willopus-wallopus or the bim-bam from Borneo, or whatever name you are denounced by in the side-show business?'

" 'Jeff Peters,' says Collier, in a weak voice. 'Turn me loose, or I'll slug you one. I'm in the extremest kind of a large hurry. Hands off!'

" 'Tut, tut, Eddie,' I answers, holding him hard; 'let an old friend gaze on the exhibition of your curiousness. It's an eminent graft you fell onto, my son. But don't speak of assaults and battery, because you're not fit. The best you've got is a lot of nerve and a mighty empty stomach.' And so it was. The man was as weak as a vegetarian cat.

" 'I'd argue this case with you, Jeff,' says he, regretful in his style, 'for an unlimited number of rounds if I had half an hour to train in and a slab of beef-steak two feet square to train with. Curse the man, I say, that invented the art of going foodless. May his soul in eternity be chained up within two feet of a bottomless pit of red-hot hash. I'm abandoning the conflict, Jeff; I'm deserting to the enemy. You'll find Miss Dugan inside contemplating the only living mummy and the informed hog. She's a fine girl, Jeff. I'd have beat you out if I could have kept up the grubless habit a little while longer. You'll have to admit that the fasting dodge was aces-up for a while. I figured it out that way. But, say, Jeff, it's said that love makes the world go around. Let me tell you, the announcement lacks verification. It's the wind from the dinner horn that does it. I love that Mame Dugan. I've gone six days without food in order to coincide with her sentiments. Only one bite did I have. That was when I knocked the tattooed man down with a war club and got a sandwich he was gobbling. The manager fined me all my salary; but salary wasn't what I was after. 'Twas that girl. I'd give my life for her, but I'd endanger my immortal soul for a beef stew. Hunger is a horrible thing, Jeff. Love and business and family and religion and art and patriotism are nothing but shadows of words when a man's starving!'

"In such language Ed Collier discoursed to me, pathetic. I gathered the diagnosis that his affections and his digestions had been implicated in a scramble and the commissary had won out. I never disliked Ed Collier. I searched my internal admonitions of suitable etiquette to see if I could find a remark of a consoling nature, but there was none convenient.

" 'I'd be glad, now,' says Ed, 'if you'll let me go. I've been hard hit, but I'll hit the ration supply harder. I'm going to clean out every restaurant in town. I'm going to wade waist deep in sirloins and swim in ham and eggs. It's an awful thing, Jeff Peters, for a man to come to this pass—to give up his girl for something to eat—it's worse than that man Esau, that swapped his copyright for a partridge—but then, hunger's a fierce thing. You'll excuse me, now, Jeff, for I smell a pervasion of ham frying in the distance, and my legs are crying out to stampede in that direction.'

" 'A hearty meal to you, Ed Collier,' I says to him, 'and no hard feelings. For myself, I am projected to be an unseldom eater, and I have condolence for your predicaments.'

"There was a sudden big whiff of frying ham smell on the breeze; and the Champion Faster gives a snort and gallops off in the dark toward fodder.

"I wish some of the cultured outfit that are always advertising the extenuating circumstances of love and romance had been there to see. There was Ed Collier, a fine man full of contrivances and flirtations, abandoning the girl of his heart and ripping out into the contiguous territory in the pursuit of sordid gruu. 'Twas a rebuke to the poets and a slap at the best-paying element of fiction. An empty stomach is a sure antidote to an overfull heart.

"I was naturally anxious to know how far Mame was infatuated with Collier and his stratagems. I went inside the Unparalleled Exhibition, and there she was. She looked surprised to see me, but unguilty.

"'It's an elegant evening outside,' says I. 'The coolness is quite nice and gratifying, and the stars are lined out, first class, up where they belong. Wouldn't you shake these by-products of the animal kingdom long enough to take a walk with a common human who never was on a programme in his life?'

"Mame gave a sort of sly glance around, and I knew what that meant.

"'Oh,' says I, 'I hate to tell you; but the curiosity that lives on wind has flew the coop. He just crawled out under the tent. By this time he has amalgamated himself with half the delicatessen truck in town.'

"'You mean Ed Collier?' says Mame.

"'I do,' I answers; 'and a pity it is that he has gone back to crime again. I met him outside the tent, and he exposed his intentions of devastating the food crop of the world. 'Tis enormously sad when one's ideal descends from his pedestal to make a seventeen-year locust of himself.'

"Mame locked me straight in the eye until she had corkscrewed my reflections.

"'Jeff,' says she, 'it isn't quite like you to talk that way. I don't care to hear Ed Collier ridiculed. A man may do ridiculous things, but they don't look ridiculous to the girl he does 'em for. That was the man in a hundred. He stopped eating just to please me. I'd be hardhearted and ungrateful if I didn't feel kindly toward him. Could you do what he did?'

"'I know,' says I, seeing the point, 'I'm condemned. I can't help it. The brand of the consumer is upon my brow. Mrs. Eve settled that business for me when she made the dicker with the snake. I fell from the fire into the frying-pan. I guess I'm the Champion Feaster of the Universe.' I spoke humble, and Mame mollified herself a little.

"'Ed Collier and I are good friends,' she said, 'the same as me and you. I gave him the same answer I did you—no marrying for me. I liked to be with Ed and talk to him. There was something mighty pleasant to me in the thought that here was a man who never used a knife and fork, and all for my sake.'

"'Wasn't you in love with him?' I asks, all injudicious. 'Wasn't there a deal on for you to become Mrs. Curiosity?'

"All of us do it sometimes. All of us get jostled out of the line of profitable talk now and then. Mame put on that little lemon *glacé* smile that runs between ice and sugar, and says, much too pleasant: 'You're short on credentials for asking that question, Mr. Peters. Suppose you do a forty-nine-day fast, just to give you ground to stand on, and then maybe I'll answer it.'

"So, even after Collier was kidnapped out of the way by the revolt of his appetite, my own prospects with Mame didn't seem to be improved. And then business played out in Guthrie.

"I had stayed too long there. The Brazilians I had sold commenced to show signs of wear, and the Kindler refused to light up right frequent on wet mornings. There is always a time, in my business, when the star of success says, 'Move on to the next town.' I was traveling by wagon at that time so as not to miss any of the small towns; so I hitched up a few days later and went down to tell Mame good-bye. I wasn't abandoning the game; I intended running over to Oklahoma City and work it for a week or two. Then I was coming back to institute fresh proceedings against Mame.

"What do I find at the Dugans' but Mame all conspicuous in a blue traveling dress, with her little trunk at the door. It seems that sister Lottie Bell, who is a typewriter in Terre Haute, is going to be married next Thursday, and Mame is off for a week's visit to be an accomplice at the ceremony. Mame is waiting for a freight wagon that is going to take her to Oklahoma, but I condemns the freight wagon with promptness and scorn, and offers to deliver the goods myself. Ma Dugan sees no reason why not, as Mr. Freighter wants pay for the job; so, thirty minutes later Mame and I pull out in my light spring wagon with white canvas cover, and head due south.

"That morning was of a praiseworthy sort. The breeze was lively, and smelled excellent of flowers and grass, and the little cottontail rabbits entertained themselves with skylarking across the road. My two Kentucky bays went for the horizon until it come sailing in so fast you wanted to dodge it like a clothesline. Mame was full of talk and rattled on like a kid about her old home and her school pranks and the things she liked and the hateful ways of those Johnson girls just across the street, 'way up in Indiana. Not a word was said about Ed Collier or victuals or such solemn subjects. About noon Mame looks and finds that the lunch she had put up in a basket had been left behind. I could have managed quite a collation, but Mame didn't seem to be grieving over nothing to eat, so I made no lamentations. It was a sore subject with me, and I ruled provender in all its branches out of my conversation.

"I am minded to touch light on explanations how I came to lose the way. The road was dim and well grown with grass; and there was Mame by my side confiscating my intellects and attention. The excuses are good or they are not, as they may appear to you. But I lost it, and at dusk that afternoon, when we should have been in Oklahoma City, we were seesawing along the edge of nowhere in some undiscovered river bottom, and the rain was falling in large, wet bunches. Down there in the swamps we saw a little log house on a small knoll of high ground. The bottom grass and the chaparral and the lonesome timber crowded all around it. It seemed to be a melancholy little house, and you felt sorry for it. 'Twas that house for the night, the way I reasoned it. I explained to Mame, and she leaves it to me to decide. She doesn't become galvanic and prosecuting, as most women would, but she says it's all right; she knows I didn't mean to do it.

"We found the house was deserted. It had two empty rooms. There was a little shed in the yard where beasts had once been kept. In a loft of it was a lot of old hay. I put my horses in there and gave them some of it, for which they looked at me sorrowful, expecting apologies. The rest of the hay I carried into the house by armfuls, with a view to accommodations. I also brought in the patent kindler and the Brazilians, neither of which are guaranteed against the action of water.

"Mame and I sat on the wagon seats on the floor, and I lit a lot of the Kindler on the hearth, for the night was chilly. If I was any judge, that girl enjoyed it. It was a change for her. It gave her a different point of view. She laughed and talked, and the Kindler made a dim light compared to her eyes. I had a pocketful of cigars, and as far as I was concerned there had never been any fall of man. We were at the same old stand in the Garden of Eden. Out there somewhere in the rain and the dark was the river of Zion, and the angel with the flaming sword had not yet put up the keep-off-the-grass sign. I opened up a gross or two of the Brazilians and made Mame put them on—rings, brooches, necklaces, eardrops, bracelets, girdles, and lockets. She flashed and sparkled like a million-dollar princess until she had pink spots in her cheeks and almost cried for a looking-glass.

"When it got late I made a fine bunk on the floor for Mame with the hay and my lap robes and blankets out of the wagon and persuaded her to lie down. I sat in the other room burning tobacco and listening to the pouring rain and meditating on the many vicissitudes that come to a man during the seventy years or so immediately preceding his funeral.

"I must have dozed a little before morning, for my eyes were shut, and when I opened them it was daylight, and there stood Mame with her hair all done up neat and correct, and her eyes bright with admiration of existence.

" 'Gee whiz, Jeff!' she exclaims, 'but I'm hungry. I could eat a——'

"I looked up and caught her eye. Her smile went back in and she gave me a cold look of suspicion. Then I laughed, and laid down on the floor to laugh easier. It seemed funny to me. By nature and geniality I am a hearty laugher, and I went the limit. When I came to, Mame was sitting with her back to me, all contaminated with dignity.

" 'Don't be angry, Mame,' I says, 'for I couldn't help it. It's the funny way you've done up your hair. If you could only see it!'

" 'You needn't tell stories, sir,' said Mame, cool and advised. 'My hair is all right. I know what you were laughing about. Why, Jeff, look outside,' she winds up, peeping through a chink between the logs. I opened the little wooden window and looked out. The entire river bottom was flooded, and the knob of land on which the house stood was an island in the middle of a rushing stream of yellow water a hundred yards wide. And it was still raining hard. All we could do was to stay there till the dove brought in the olive branch.

"I am bound to admit that conversations and amusements languished during the day. I was aware that Mame was getting a too prolonged onesided view of things again, but I had no way to change it. Personally, I was wrapped up in the desire to eat. I had hallucinations of hash and visions of ham, and I kept saying to myself all the time, 'What'll you have to eat, Jeff?—what'll you order, now, old man, when the waiter comes?' I picks out to myself all sorts of favorites from the bill of fare, and imagines them coming. I guess it's that way with all very hungry men. They can't get their cogitations trained on anything but something to eat. It shows that the little table with the broken-legged caster and the imitation Worcester sauce and the napkin covering up the coffee stains is the paramount issue, after all, instead of the question of immortality or peace between nations.

"I sat there, musing along, arguing with myself quite heated as to how I'd have my steak—with mushrooms or à la créole. Mame was on the other seat, pensive, her head leaning on her hand. 'Let the potatoes come home-fried,' I states in my mind, 'and brown the hash in the pan, with nine poached eggs on the side.' I felt, careful, in my own pockets to see if I could find a peanut or a grain or two of popcorn.

"Night came on again with the river still rising and the rain still falling. I looked at Mame and I noticed that desperate look on her face that a girl always wears when she passes an ice-cream lair. I knew that poor girl was hungry—maybe for the first time in her life. There was that anxious look in her eye that a woman has only when she has missed a meal or feels her skirt coming unfastened in the back.

"It was about eleven o'clock or so on the second night when we sat, gloomy, in our ship-wrecked cabin. I kept jerking my mind away from the subject of food, but it kept flopping back again before I could fasten it. I thought of everything good to eat I had ever heard of. I went away back to my kidhood and remembered the hot biscuit sopped in sorghum and bacon gravy with partiality and respect. Then I trailed along up the years, pausing at green apples and salt, flapjacks and maple, lye hominy, fried chicken Old Virginia style, corn on the cob, spareribs and sweet potato pie, and wound up with Georgia Brunswick stew, which is the top notch of good things to eat, because it comprises 'em all.

"They say a drowning man sees a panorama of his whole life pass before him. Well, when a man's starving he sees the ghost of every meal he ever ate set out before him, and he invents new dishes that would make the fortune of a chef.

If somebody would collect the last words of men who starved to death they'd have to sift 'em mighty fine to discover the sentiment, but they'd compile into a cook book that would sell into the millions.

"I guess I must have had my conscience pretty well inflicted with culinary mediations, for, without intending to do so, I says, out loud, to the imaginary waiter, 'Cut it thick and have it rare, with the French fried, and six, soft-scrambled, on toast.'

"Mame turned her head quick as a wink. Her eyes were sparkling and she smiled sudden.

"'Medium for me,' she rattles on, 'with the Juliennes, and three, straight up. Draw one, and brown the wheats, double order to come. Oh, Jeff, wouldn't it be glorious! And then I'd like to have a half fry, and a little chicken curried with rice, and a cup custard with ice cream, and——'

"'Go easy,' I interrupts; 'where's the chicken liver pie, and the kidney *sauté* on toast, and the roast lamb, and——'

"'Oh,' cuts in Mame, all excited, 'with mint sauce, and the turkey salad, and stuffed olives, and raspberry tarts, and——'

"'Keep it going,' says I. 'Hurry up with the fried squash, and the hot corn pone with sweet milk, and don't forget the apple dumpling with hard sauce, and the cross-barred dewberry pie——'

"Yes, for ten minutes we kept up that kind of restaurant repartee. We ranges up and down and backward and forward over the main trunk lines and the branches of the victual subject, and Mame leads the game, for she is apprised in the ramifications of grub, and the dishes she nominates aggravates my yearnings. It seems that there is set up a feeling that Mame will line up friendly again with food. It seems that she looks upon the obnoxious science of eating with less contempt than before.

"The next morning we find that the flood has subsided. I geared up the bays, and we splashed out through the mud, some precarious, until we found the road again. We were only a few miles wrong, and in two hours we were in Oklahoma City. The first thing we saw was a big restaurant sign, and we piled into there in a hurry. Here I finds myself sitting with Mame at table, with knives and forks and plates between us, and she not scornful, but smiling with starvation and sweetness.

"'Twas a new restaurant and well stocked. I designated a list of quotations from the bill of fare that made the waiter look out toward the wagon to see how many more might be coming.

"There we were, and there was the order being served. 'Twas a banquet for a dozen, but we felt like a dozen. I looked across the table at Mame and smiled, for I had recollections. Mame was looking at the table like a boy looks at his first stem-winder. Then she looked at me, straight in the face, and two big tears came in her eyes. The waiter was gone after more grub.

"'Jeff,' she says, soft like, 'I've been a foolish girl. I've looked at things from the wrong side. I never felt this way before. Men get hungry every day like this, don't they? They're big and strong, and they do the hard work of the world, and they don't eat just to spite silly waiter girls in restaurants, do they, Jeff? You said once—that is, you asked me—you wanted me to—well, Jeff, if you still care—I'd be glad and willing to have you always sitting across the table from me. Now give me something to eat, quick, please.'

"So, as I've said, a woman needs to change her point of view now and then. They get tired of the same old sights—the same old dinner table, washtub, and sewing machine. Give 'em a touch of the various—a little travel and a little rest, a little tomfoolery along with the tragedies of keeping house, a little petting after the blowing-up, a little upsetting and jostling around—and everybody in the game will have chips added to their stack by the play."

THE CABALLERO'S WAY

THE Cisco Kid had killed six men in more or less fair scrimmages, had murdered twice as many (mostly Mexicans), and had winged a larger number whom he modestly forbore to count. Therefore a woman loved him.

The Kid was twenty-five, looked twenty; and a careful insurance company would have estimated the probable time of his demise at, say, twenty-six. His habitat was anywhere between the Frio and the Rio Grande. He killed for the love of it—because he was quick-tempered—to avoid arrest—for his own amusement—any reason that came to his mind would suffice. He had escaped capture because he could shoot five-sixths of a second sooner than any sheriff or ranger in the service, and because he rode a speckled roan horse that knew every cowpath in the mesquite and pear thickets from San Antonio to Matamoras.

Tonia Perez, the girl who loved the Cisco Kid, was half Carmen, half Madonna, and the rest—oh, yes, a woman who is half Carmen and half Madonna can always be something more—the rest, let us say, was humming-bird. She lived in a grass-roofed *jacal* near a little Mexican settlement at the Lone Wolf Crossing of the Frio. With her lived a father or grandfather, a lineal Aztec, somewhat less than a thousand years old, who herded a hundred goats and lived in a continuous drunken dream from drinking *mescal*. Back of the *jacal* a tremendous forest of bristling pear, twenty feet high at its worst, crowded almost to its door. It was along the bewildering maze of this spinous thicket that the speckled roan would bring the Kid to see his girl. And once, clinging like a lizard to the ridge-pole, high up under the peaked grass roof, he had heard Tonia, with her Madonna face and Carmen beauty and humming-bird soul, parley with the sheriff's posse, denying knowledge of her man in her soft *mélange* of Spanish and English.

One day the adjutant-general of the State, who is, *ex officio*, commander of the ranger forces, wrote some sarcastic lines to Captain Duval of Company X, stationed at Laredo, relative to the serene and undisturbed existence led by murderers and desperadoes in the said captain's territory.

The captain turned the color of brick dust under his tan, and forwarded the letter, after adding a few comments, per ranger Private Bill Adamson, to ranger Lieutenant Sandridge, camped at a water hole on the Nueces with a squad of five men in preservation of law and order.

Lieutenant Sandridge turned a beautiful *couleur de rose* through his ordinary strawberry complexion, tucked the letter in his hip pocket, and chewed off the end of his gamboge moustache.

The next morning he saddled his horse and rode alone to the Mexican settlement at the Lone Wolf Crossing of the Frio, twenty miles away.

Six feet two, blond as a Viking, quiet as a deacon, dangerous as a machine gun, Sandridge moved among the *Jacales*, patiently seeking news of the Cisco Kid.

Far more than the law, the Mexicans dreaded the cold and certain vengeance of the lone rider that the ranger sought. It had been one of the Kid's pastimes to shoot Mexicans "to see them kick": if he demanded from them moribund Terpsichorean feats, simply that he might be entertained, what terrible and extreme penalties would be certain to follow should they anger him! One and all they lounged with upturned palms and shrugging shoulders, filling the air with *"quién sabes"* and denials of the Kid's acquaintance.

But there was a man named Fink who kept a store at the Crossing—a man of many nationalities, tongues, interests, and ways of thinking.

"No use to ask them Mexicans," he said to Sandridge. "They're afraid to tell. This *hombre* they call the Kid—Goodall is his name, ain't it?—he's been in my store once or twice. I have an idea you might run across him at—but I guess I don't keer to say, myself. I'm two seconds later in pulling a gun than I used to be and the difference is worth thinking about. But this Kid's got a half-Mexican girl at the Crossing that he comes to see. She lives in that *jacal* a hundred yards down the arroyo at the edge of the pear. Maybe she—no, I don't suppose she would, but that *jacal* would be a good place to watch, anyway."

Sandridge rode down to the *jacal* of Perez. The sun was low, and the broad shade of the great pear thicket already covered the grass-thatched hut. The goats were enclosed for the night in a brush corral near by. A few kids walked the top of it, nibbling the chaparral leaves. The old Mexican lay upon a blanket on the grass, already in a stupor from his mescal, and dreaming, perhaps, of the nights when he and Pizarro touched glasses to their New World fortunes—so old his wrinkled face seemed to proclaim him to be. And in the door of the *jacal* stood Tonia. And Lieutenant Sandridge sat in his saddle staring at her like a gannet agape at a sailorman.

The Cisco Kid was a vain person, as all eminent and successful assassins are, and his bosom would have been ruffled had he known that at a simple exchange of glances two persons, in whose minds he had been looming large, suddenly abandoned (at least for the time) all thought of him.

Never before had Tonia seen such a man as this. He seemed to be made of sunshine and blood-red tissue and clear weather. He seemed to illuminate the shadow of the pear when he smiled, as though the sun were rising again. The men she had known had been small and dark. Even the Kid, in spite of his achievements, was a stripling no larger than herself, with black straight hair and a cold marble face that chilled the noonday.

As for Tonia, though she sends description to the poorhouse, let her make a millionaire of your fancy. Her blue-black hair, smoothly divided in the middle and bound close to her head, and her large eyes full of the Latin melancholy, gave her the Madonna touch. Her motions and air spoke of the concealed fire and the desire to charm that she had inherited from the *gitanas* of the Basque province. As for the humming-bird part of her, that dwelt in her heart; you could not perceive it unless her bright red skirt and dark blue blouse gave you a symbolic hint of the vagarious bird.

The newly lighted sun-god asked for a drink of water. Tonia brought it from the red jar hanging under the brush shelter. Sandridge considered it necessary to dismount so as to lessen the trouble of her ministrations.

I play no spy; nor do I assume to master the thoughts of any human heart; but I assert, by the chronicler's right, that before a quarter of an hour had sped, Sandridge was teaching her how to plait a six-strand rawhide stake-rope, and Tonia had explained to him that were it not for her little English book that the peripatetic *padre* had given her and the little crippled *chivo*, that she fed from a bottle, she would be very, very lonely indeed.

Which leads to a suspicion that the Kid's fences needed repairing, and that the adjutant-general's sarcasm had fallen upon unproductive soil.

In his camp by the water hole Lieutenant Sandridge announced and reiterated his intention of either causing the Cisco Kid to nibble the black loam of the Frio country prairies or of haling him before a judge and jury. That sounded business-like. Twice a week he rode over to the Lone Wolf Crossing of the Frio, and directed Tonia's slim, slightly lemon-tinted fingers among the intricacies of the slowly growing lariata. A six-strand plait is hard to learn and easy to teach.

The ranger knew that he might find the Kid there at any visit. He kept his armament ready, and had a frequent eye for the pear thicket at the rear of the *jacal*. Thus he might bring down the kite and the humming-bird with one stone.

While the sunny-haired ornithologist was pursuing his studies the Cisco Kid was also attending to his professional duties. He moodily shot up a saloon in a small cow village on Quintana Creek, killed the town marshal (plugging him neatly in the centre of his tin badge), and then rode away, morose and unsatisfied. No true artist is uplifted by shooting an aged man carrying an old-style .38 bulldog.

On his way the Kid suddenly experienced the yearning that all men feel when wrong-doing loses its keen edge of delight. He yearned for the woman he loved to reassure him that she was his in spite of it. He wanted her to call his bloodthirstiness bravery and his cruelty devotion. He wanted Tonia to bring him water from the red jug under the brush shelter, and tell him how the *chivo* was thriving on the bottle.

The Kid turned the speckled roan's head up the ten-mile pear flat that stretches along the Arroyo Hondo until it ends at the Lone Wolf Crossing of the Frio. The roan whickered; for he had a sense of locality and direction equal to that of a belt-line street-car horse; and he knew he would soon be nibbling the rich mesquite grass at the end of a forty-foot stake rope while Ulysses rested his head in Circe's straw-roofed hut.

More weird and lonesome than the journey of an Amazonian explorer is the ride of one through a Texas pear flat. With dismal monotony and startling variety the uncanny and multiform shapes of the cacti lift their twisted trunks and fat, bristly hands to encumber the way. The demon plant, appearing to live without soil or rain, seems to taunt the parched traveler with its lush gray greenness. It warps itself a thousand times about what look to be open and inviting paths, only to lure the rider into blind and impassable spine-defended "bottoms of the bag," leaving him to retreat, if he can, with the points of the compass whirling in his head.

To be lost in the pear is to die almost the death of the thief on the cross, pierced by nails and with grotesque shapes of all the fiends hovering about.

But it was not so with the Kid and his mount. Winding, twisting, circling, tracing the most fantastic and bewildering trail ever picked out, the good roan lessened the distance to the Lone Wolf Crossing with every coil and turn that he made.

While they fared the Kid sang. He knew but one tune and he sang it, as he knew but one code and lived it, and but one girl and loved her. He was a single-minded man of conventional ideas. He had a voice like a coyote with bronchitis, but whenever he chose to sing his song he sang it. It was a conventional song of the camps and trail, running at its beginning as near as may be to these words:

> Don't you monkey with my Lulu girl
> Or I'll tell you what I'll do——

and so on. The roan was inured to it, and did not mind.

But even the poorest singer will, after a certain time, gain his own consent to refrain from contributing to the world's noises. So the Kid, by the time he was within a mile or two of Tonia's *jacal*, had reluctantly allowed his song to die away—not because his vocal performance had become less charming to his own ears, but because his laryngeal muscles were aweary.

As though he were in a circus ring the speckled roan wheeled and danced through the labyrinth of pear until at length his rider knew by certain landmarks that the Lone Wolf Crossing was close at hand. Then, where the pear was thinner, he caught sight of the grass roof of the *jacal* and the hackberry tree on the edge of the arroyo. A few yards farther the Kid stopped the roan and gazed intently through the prickly openings. Then he dismounted, dropped the roan's reins, and proceeded on foot, stooping and silent, like an Indian. The roan, knowing his part, stood still, making no sound.

The Kid crept noiselessly to the very edge of the pear thicket and reconnoitered between the leaves of a clump of cactus.

Ten yards from his hiding-place, in the shade of the *jacal*, sat his Tonia calmly plaiting a raw-hide lariat. So far she might surely escape condemnation; women have been known, from time to time, to engage in more mischievous occupations. But if all must be told, there is to be added that her head reposed against the broad and comfortable chest of a tall red-and-yellow man, and that his arm was about her, guiding her nimble small fingers that required so many lessons at the intricate six-strand plait.

Sandridge glanced quickly at the dark mass of pear when he heard a slight squeaking sound that was not altogether unfamiliar. A gun-scabbard will make that sound when one grasps the handle of a six-shooter suddenly. But the sound was not repeated; and Tonia's fingers needed close attention.

And then, in the shadow of death, they began to talk of their love; and in the still July afternoon every word they uttered reached the ears of the Kid.

"Remember, then," said Tonia, "you must not come again until I send for you. Soon he will be here. A *vaquero* at the *tienda* said to-day he saw him on the Guadalupe three days ago. When he is that near he always comes. If he comes and finds you here he will kill you. So, for my sake, you must come no more until I send you the word."

"All right," said the ranger. "And then what?"

"And then," said the girl, "you must bring your men here and kill him. If not, he will kill you."

"He ain't a man to surrender, that's sure," said Sandridge. "It's kill or be killed for the officer that goes up against Mr. Cisco Kid."

"He must die," said the girl. "Otherwise there will not be any peace in the world for thee and me. He has killed many. Let him so die. Bring your men, and give him no chance to escape."

"You used to think right much of him," said Sandridge.

Tonia dropped the lariat, twisted herself around, and curved a lemon-tinted arm over the ranger's shoulder.

"But then," she murmured in liquid Spanish, "I had not beheld thee, thou great, red mountain of a man! And thou art kind and good, as well as strong. Could one choose him, knowing thee? Let him die; for then I will not be filled with fear by day and night lest he hurt thee or me."

"How can I know when he comes?" asked Sandridge.

"When he comes," said Tonia, "he remains two days, sometimes three. Gregorio, the small son of old Luisa, the *lavandera*, has a swift pony. I will write a letter to thee and send it by him, saying how it will be best to come upon him. By Gregorio will the letter come. And bring many men with thee, and have much care, oh, dear red one, for the rattlesnake is not quicker to strike than is '*El Chivato*,' as they call him, to send a ball from his *pistola*."

"The Kid's handy with his gun, sure enough," admitted Sandridge, "but when I come for him I shall come alone. I'll get him by myself or not at all. The Cap wrote one or two things to me that make me want to do the trick without any help. You let me know when Mr. Kid arrives, and I'll do the rest."

"I will send you the message by the boy Gregorio," said the girl. "I knew you were braver than that small slayer of men who never smiles. How could I ever have thought I cared for him?"

It was time for the ranger to ride back to his camp on the water hole. Before he mounted his horse he raised the slight form of Tonia with one arm high from the earth for a parting salute. The drowsy stillness of the torpid summer air still lay thick upon the dreaming afternoon. The smoke from the fire in the *jacal*, where the *frijoles* blubbered in the iron pot, rose straight as a plumb-line above the clay-daubed chimney. No sound or movement disturbed the serenity of the dense pear thicket ten yards away.

When the form of Sandridge had disappeared, loping his big dun down the steep banks of the Frio crossing, the Kid crept back to his own horse, mounted him, and rode back along the tortuous trail he had come.

But not far. He stopped and waited in the silent depths of the pear until half an hour had passed. And then Tonia heard the high, untrue notes of his unmusical singing coming nearer and nearer; and she ran to the edge of the pear to meet him.

The Kid seldom smiled; but he smiled and waved his hat when he saw her. He dismounted, and his girl sprang into his arms. The Kid looked at her fondly. His thick black hair clung to his head like a wrinkled mat. The meeting brought a slight ripple of some undercurrent of feeling to his smooth, dark face that was usually as motionless as a clay mask.

'How's my girl?" he asked, holding her close.

"Sick of waiting so long for you, dear one," she answered. "My eyes are dim with always gazing into that devil's pincushion through which you come. And I can see into it such a little way, too. But you are here, beloved one, and I will not scold. *Qué mal muchacho!* not to come to see your *alma* more often. Go in and rest, and let me water your horse and stake him with the long rope. There is cool water in the jar for you."

The Kid kissed her affectionately.

"Not if the court knows itself do I let a lady stake my horse for me," said he. "But if you'll run in, *chica*, and throw a pot of coffee together while I attend to the *caballo*, I'll be a good deal obliged."

Besides his marksmanship the Kid had another attribute for which he admired himself greatly. He was *muy caballero*, as the Mexicans express it, where the ladies were concerned. For them he had always gentle words and consideration. He could not have spoken a harsh word to a woman. He might ruthlessly slay their husbands and brothers, but he could not have laid the weight of a finger in anger upon a woman. Wherefore many of that interesting division of humanity who had come under the spell of his politeness declared their disbelief in the stories circulated about Mr. Kid. One shouldn't believe everything one heard, they said. When confronted by their indignant men folk with proof of the *caballero's* deeds of infamy, they said maybe he had been driven to it, and that he knew how to treat a lady, anyhow.

Considering this extremely courteous idiosyncrasy of the Kid and the pride that he took in it, one can perceive that the solution of the problem that was presented to him by what he saw and heard from his hiding-place in the pear that afternoon (at least as to one of the actors) must have been obscured by difficulties. And yet one could not think of the Kid overlooking little matters of that kind.

At the end of the short twilight they gathered around a supper of *frijoles*, goat steaks, canned peaches, and coffee, by the light of a lantern in the *jacal*. Afterward, the ancestor, his flock corralled, smoked a cigarette and became a mummy in a gray blanket. Tonia washed the few dishes while the Kid dried them with the flour-sacking towel. Her eyes shone; she chatted volubly of the inconsequent happenings of her small world since the Kid's last visit; it was as all his other home-comings had been.

Then outside Tonia swung in a grass hammock with her guitar and sang sad *canciones de amor*.

"Do you love me just the same, old girl?" asked the Kid, hunting for his cigarette papers.

"Always the same, little one," said Tonia, her dark eyes lingering upon him.

"I must go over to Fink's," said the Kid, rising, "for some tobacco. I thought I had another sack in my coat. I'll be back in a quarter of an hour."

"Hasten," said Tonia, "and tell me—how long shall I call you my own this time? Will you be gone again to-morrow, leaving me to grieve, or will you be longer with your Tonia?"

"Oh, I might stay two or three days this trip," said the Kid, yawning. "I've been on the dodge for a month, and I'd like to rest up."

He was gone half an hour for his tobacco. When he returned Tonia was still lying in the hammock.

"It's funny," said the Kid, "how I feel. I feel like there was somebody lying behind every bush and tree waiting to shoot me. I never had mullygrubs like them before. Maybe it's one of them presumptions. I've got half a notion to light out in the morning before day. The Guadalupe country is burning up about that old Dutchman I plugged down there."

"You are not afraid—no one could make my brave little one fear."

"Well, I haven't been usually regarded as a jack-rabbit when it comes to scrapping; but I don't want a posse smoking me out when I'm in your *jacal*. Somebody might get hurt that oughtn't to."

"Remain with your Tonia; no one will find you here."

The Kid looked keenly into the shadows up and down the arroyo and toward the dim lights of the Mexican village.

"I'll see how it looks later on," was his decision.

At midnight a horseman rode into the rangers' camp, blazing his way by noisy "halloes" to indicate a pacific mission. Sandridge and one or two others turned out to investigate the row. The rider announced himself to be Domingo Sales, from the Lone Wolf Crossing. He bore a letter for Señor Sandridge. Old Luisa, the *lavandera*, had persuaded him to bring it, he said, her son Gregorio being too ill of a fever to ride.

Sandridge lighted the camp lantern and read the letter. These were its words:

DEAR ONE: He has come. Hardly had you ridden away when he came out of the pear. When he first talked he said he would stay three days or more. Then as it grew later he was like a wolf or a fox, and walked about without rest, looking and listening. Soon he said he must leave before daylight when it is dark and stillest. And then he seemed to suspect that I be not true to him. He looked at me so strange that I am frightened. I swear to him that I love him, his own Tonia. Last of all he said I must prove to him I am true. He thinks that even now men are waiting to kill him as he rides from my house. To escape he says he will dress in my clothes, my red skirt and the blue waist I wear and the brown mantilla over the head, and thus ride away. But before that he says that I must put on his clothes, his *pantalones* and *camisa* and hat, and ride away on his horse from the *jacal* as far as the big road beyond the crossing and back again. This before he goes, so he can tell if I am true and if men are hidden to shoot him. It is a terrible thing. An hour before daybreak this is to be. Come, my dear one, and kill this man and take me for your Tonia. Do not try to take hold of him alive, but kill him quickly. Knowing all, you should do that. You must come long before the time and hide yourself in the little shed near the *jacal* where the wagon and saddles are kept. It is dark in there. He will wear my red skirt and blue waist and brown mantilla. I send you a hundred kisses. Come surely and shoot quickly and straight.

THINE OWN TONIA.

Sandridge quickly explained to his men the official part of the missive. The rangers protested against his going alone.

"I'll get him easy enough," said the lieutenant. "The girl's got him trapped. And don't even think he'll get the drop on me."

Sandridge saddled his horse and rode to the Lone Wolf Crossing. He tied his big dun in a clump of brush on the arroyo, took his Winchester from its scabbard, and carefully approached the Perez *jacal*. There was only the half of a high moon drifted over by ragged, milk-white gulf clouds.

The wagon-shed was an excellent place for ambush; and the ranger got inside it safely. In the black shadow of the brush shelter in front of the *jacal* he could see a horse tied and hear him impatiently pawing the hard-trodden earth.

He waited almost an hour before two figures came out of the *jacal*. One, in man's clothes, quickly mounted the horse and galloped past the wagon-shed toward the crossing and village. And then the other figure, in skirt, waist, and mantilla over its head, stepped out into the faint moonlight, gazing after the rider. Sandridge thought he would take his chance then before Tonia rode back. He fancied she might not care to see it.

"Throw up your hands," he ordered, loudly, stepping out of the wagon-shed with his Winchester at his shoulder.

There was a quick turn of the figure, but no movement to obey, so the ranger pumped in the bullets—one—two—three—and then twice more; for you never could be too sure of bringing down the Cisco Kid. There was no danger of missing at ten paces, even in that half moonlight.

The old ancestor, asleep on his blanket, was awakened by the shots. Listening further, he heard a great cry from some man in mortal distress or anguish, and rose up grumbling at the disturbing ways of moderns.

The tall, red ghost of a man burst into the *jacal*, reaching one hand, shaking like a *tule* reed, for the lantern hanging on its nail. The other spread a letter on the table.

"Look at this letter, Perez," cried the man. "Who wrote it?"

"*Ah, Dios!* it is Señor Sandridge," mumbled the old man, approaching. "*Pues, señor*, that letter was written by 'El Chivato,' as he is called—by the man of Tonia. They say he is a bad man; I do not know. While Tonia slept he wrote the letter and sent it by this old hand of mine to Domingo Sales to be brought to you. Is there anything wrong in the letter? I am very old; and I did not know. *Valgame Dios!* it is a very foolish world; and there is nothing in the house to drink—nothing to drink."

Just then all that Sandridge could think of to do was to go outside and throw himself face downward in the dust by the side of his humming-bird, of whom not a feather fluttered. He was not a *caballero* by instinct, and he could not understand the niceties of revenge.

A mile away the rider who had ridden past the wagon-shed struck up a harsh, untuneful song, the words of which began:

> Don't you monkey with my Lulu girl
> Or I'll tell you what I'll do——

THE SPHINX APPLE

TWENTY miles out from Paradise, and fifteen miles short of Sunrise City, Bildad Rose, the stage-driver, stopped his team. A furious snow had been falling all day. Eight inches it measured now, on a level. The remainder of the road was not without peril in daylight, creeping along the ribs of a bijou range of ragged mountains. Now, when both snow and night masked its dangers, further travel was not to be thought of, said Bildad Rose. So he pulled up his four stout horses, and delivered to his five passengers oral deductions of his wisdom.

Judge Menefee, to whom men granted leadership and the initiatory as upon a silver salver, sprang from the coach at once. Four of his fellow-passengers followed, inspired by his example, ready to explore, to objurgate, to resist, to submit, to proceed, according as their prime factor might be inclined to sway them. The fifth passenger, a young woman, remained in the coach.

Bildad had halted upon the shoulder of the first mountain spur. Two rail-fences, ragged-black, hemmed the road. Fifty yards above the upper fence, showing a dark blot in the white drifts, stood a small house. Upon this house descended—or rather ascended—Judge Menefee and his cohorts with boyish whoops born of the snow and stress. They called; they pounded at window and door. At the inhospitable silence they waxed restive; they assaulted and forced the pregnable barriers, and invaded the premises.

The watchers from the coach heard stumblings and shoutings from the interior of the ravaged house. Before long a light within flickered, glowed, flamed high and bright and cheerful. Then came running back through the driving flakes the exuberant explorers. More deeply pitched than the clarion—even orchestral in volume—the voice of Judge Menefee proclaimed the succor that lay in apposition with their state of travail. The one room of the house was uninhabited, he said, and bare of furniture; but it contained a great fireplace; and they had discovered an ample store of chopped wood in a lean-to at the rear. Housing and warmth against the shivering night were thus assured. For the placation of Bildad Rose there was news of a stable, not ruined beyond service, with hay in a loft, near the house.

"Gentlemen," cried Bildad Rose from his seat, swathed in coats and robes, "tear me down two panels of that fence, so I can drive in. That is old man Redruth's shanty. I thought we must be nigh it. They took him to the foolish house in August."

Cheerfully the four passengers sprang at the snow-capped rails. The exhorted team tugged the coach up the slant to the door of the edifice from which a midsummer madness had ravished its proprietor. The driver and two of the passengers began to unhitch. Judge Menefee opened the door of the coach, and removed his hat.

"I have to announce, Miss Garland," said he, "the enforced suspension of our journey. The driver asserts that the risk in traveling the mountain road by night is too great even to consider. It will be necessary to remain in the shelter of this house until morning. I beg that you will feel that there is nothing to fear beyond a temporary inconvenience. I have personally inspected the house, and find that there are means to provide against the rigor of the weather, at least. You shall be made as comfortable as possible. Permit me to assist you to alight."

To the Judge's side came the passenger whose pursuit in life was the placing of the Little Goliath windmill. His name was Dunwoody; but that matters not much. In traveling merely from Paradise to Sunrise City one needs little or no name. Still, one who would seek to divide honors with Judge Madison L. Menefee deserves a cognomenal peg upon which Fame may hang a wreath. Thus spake, loudly and buoyantly, the aërial miller:

"Guess you'll have to climb out of the ark, Mrs. McFarland. This wigwam ain't exactly the Palmer House, but it turns snow, and they won't search your grip for souvenir spoons when you leave. We've got a fire going; and we'll fix you up with dry Trilbys and keep the mice away, anyhow, all right, all right."

One of the two passengers who were struggling in a *mêlée* of horses, harness, snow, and the sarcastic injunctions of Bildad Rose, called loudly from the whirl of his volunteer duties: "Say! some of you fellows get Miss Solomon into the house, will you? Whoa, there! you confounded brute!"

Again must it be gently urged that in traveling from Paradise to Sunrise City an accurate name is prodigality. When Judge Menefee—sanctioned to the act by his grey hair and widespread repute—had introduced himself to the lady passenger, she had, herself, sweetly breathed a name, in response, that the hearing of the male passengers had variously interpreted. In the not unjealous spirit of rivalry that eventuated, each clung stubbornly to his own theory. For the lady passenger to have reasseverated or corrected would have seemed didactic if not unduly solicitous of a specific acquaintance. Therefore the lady passenger permitted herself to be Garlanded and McFarlanded and Solomoned with equal and discreet complacency. It is thirty-five miles from Paradise to Sunrise City. *Compagnon de voyage* is name enough, by the gripsack of the Wandering Jew! for so brief a journey.

Soon the little party of wayfarers were happily seated in a cheerful arc before the roaring fire. The robes, cushions, and removable portions of the coach had been brought in and put to service. The lady passenger chose a place near the hearth at one end of the arc. There she graced almost a throne that her subjects had prepared. She sat upon cushions and leaned against an empty box and barrel, robe bespread, which formed a defence from the invading draughts. She extended her feet, delectably shod, to the cordial heat. She ungloved her hands, but retained about her neck her long fur boa. The unstable flames half revealed, while the warding boa half submerged, her face—a youthful face, altogether feminine, clearly moulded and calm with beauty's unchallenged confidence. Chivalry and manhood were here vying to please and comfort her. She seemed to accept their devoirs—not piquantly, as one courted and attended; not preeningly, as many of her sex unworthily reap their honors; nor yet stolidly, as the ox receives his hay; but concordantly with nature's own plan—as the lily ingests the drop of dew foreordained to its refreshment.

Outside the wind roared mightily, the fine snow whizzed through the cracks, the cold besieged the backs of the immolated six; but the elements did not lack a champion that night. Judge Menefee was attorney for the storm. The weather was his client, and he strove by special pleading to convince his companions in that frigid jury-box that they sojourned in a bower of roses, beset only by benignant zephyrs. He drew upon a fund of gaiety, wit, and anecdote, sophistical, but crowned with success. His cheerfulness communicated itself irresistibly. Each one hastened to contribute his quota toward the general optimism. Even the lady passenger was moved to expression.

"I think it is quite charming," she said, in her slow, crystal tones.

At intervals some one of the passengers would rise and humorously explore the room. There was little evidence to be collected of its habitation by old man Redruth.

Bildad Rose was called upon vivaciously for the ex-hermit's history. Now, since the stage-driver's horses were fairly comfortable and his passengers appeared to be so, peace and comity returned to him.

"The old didapper," began Bildad, somewhat irreverently, "infested this here house about twenty year. He never allowed nobody to come nigh him. He'd duck his head inside and slam the door whenever a team drove along. There was spinning-wheels up in his loft, all right. He used to buy his groceries and tobacco at Sam Tilly's store, on the Little Muddy. Last August he went up there dressed in a red bedquilt, and told Sam he was King Solomon, and that the Queen of Sheba was coming to visit him. He fetched along all the money he had—a little bag full of silver—and dropped it in Sam's well. 'She won't come,' says old man Redruth to Sam, 'if she knows I've got any money.'

"As soon as folks heard he had that sort of a theory about women and money they knowed he was crazy; so they sent down and packed him to the foolish asylum."

"Was there a romance in his life that drove him to a solitary existence?" asked one of the passengers, a young man who had an Agency.

"No," said Bildad, "not that I ever heard spoke of. Just ordinary trouble. They say he had had unfortunateness in the way of love derangements with a young lady when he was young; before he contracted red bedquilts and had his financial conclusions disqualified, I never heard of no romance."

"Ah!" exclaimed Judge Menefee, impressively; "a case of unrequited affection, no doubt."

"No, sir," returned Bildad, "not at all. She never married him. Marmaduke Mulligan, down at Paradise, seen a man once that come from old Redruth's town. He said Redruth was a fine young man, but when you kicked him on the pocket all you could hear jingle was a cuff-fastener and a bunch of keys. He was engaged to this young lady—Miss Alice—something was her name; I've forgot. This man said she was the kind of a girl you like to have reach across you in a car to pay the fare. Well, there come to the town a young chap all affluent and easy, and fixed up with buggies and mining stock and leisure time. Although she was a staked claim, Miss Alice and the new entry seemed to strike a mutual kind of a clip. They had calls and coincidences of going to the post office and such things as sometimes make a girl send back the engagement ring and other presents—'a rift within the loot,' the poetry man calls it.

"One day folks seen Redruth and Miss Alice standing talking at the gate. Then he lifts his hat and walks away, and that was the last anybody in that town seen of him, as far as this man knew."

"What about the young lady?" asked the young man who had an Agency.

"Never heard," answered Bildad. "Right there is where my lode of information turns to an old spavined crowbait, and folds its wings, for I've pumped it dry."

"A very sad——" began Judge Menefee, but his remark was curtailed by a higher authority.

"What a charming story!" said the lady passenger, in flute-like tones.

A little silence followed, except for the wind and the crackling of the fire.

The men were seated upon the floor, having slightly mitigated its inhospitable surface with wraps and stray pieces of boards. The man who was placing Little Goliath windmills arose and walked about to ease his cramped muscles.

Suddenly a triumphant shout came from him. He hurried back from a dusky corner of the room, bearing aloft something in his hand. It was an apple—a large, red-mottled, firm pippin, pleasing to behold. In a paper bag on a high shelf in that corner he had found it. It could have been no relic of the love-wrecked Redruth, for its glorious soundness repudiated the theory that it had laid on that musty shelf since August. No doubt some recent bivouackers, lunching in the deserted house, had left it there.

Dunwoody—again his exploits demand for him the honors of nomenclature—flaunted his apple in the faces of his fellow-marooners. "See what I found, Mrs. McFarland!" he cried, vaingloriously. He held the apple high up in the light of the fire, where it glowed a still richer red. The lady passenger smiled calmly—always calmly.

"What a charming apple!" she murmured, clearly.

For a brief space Judge Menefee felt crushed, humiliated, relegated. Second place galled him. Why had this blatant, obtrusive, unpolished man of wind-mills been selected by Fate instead of himself to discover the sensational apple? He could have made of the act a scene, a function, a' setting for some impromptu fanciful discourse or piece of comedy—and have retained the rôle of cynosure

Actually, the lady passenger was regarding this ridiculous Dunboddy or Woodbundy with an admiring smile, as if the fellow had performed a feat! And the windmill man swelled and gyrated like a sample of his own goods, puffed up with the wind that ever blows from the chorus land toward the domain of the star.

While the transported Dunwoody, with his Aladdin's apple, was receiving the fickle attentions of all, the resourceful jurist formed a plan to recover his own laurels.

With his courtliest smile upon his heavy but classic features, Judge Menefee advanced, and took the apple, as if to examine it, from the hand of Dunwoody. In his hand it became Exhibit A.

"A fine apple," he said, approvingly. "Really, my dear Mr. Dunwindy, you have eclipsed all of us as a forager. But I have an idea. This apple shall become an emblem, a token, a symbol, a prize bestowed by the mind and heart of beauty upon the most deserving."

The audience, except one, applauded. "Good on the stump, ain't he?" commented the passenger who was nobody in particular to the young man who had an Agency.

The unresponsive one was the windmill man. He saw himself reduced to the ranks. Never would the thought have occurred to him to declare his apple an emblem. He had intended after it had been divided and eaten, to create diversion by sticking the seeds against his forehead and naming them for young ladies of his acquaintance. One he was going to name Mrs. McFarland. The seed that fell off first would be—but 'twas too late now.

"The apple," continued Judge Menefee, charging his jury, "in modern days occupies, though undeservedly, a lowly place in our esteem. Indeed, it is so constantly associated with the culinary and the commercial that it is hardly to be classed among the polite fruits. But in ancient times this was not so. Biblical, historical, and mythological lore abounds with evidences that the apple was the aristocrat of fruits. We still say 'the apple of the eye' when we wish to describe something superlatively precious. We find in Proverbs the comparison to 'apples of silver.' No other product of tree or vine has been so utilized in figurative speech. Who has not heard of and longed for the 'apples of the Hesperides'? I need not call your attention to the most tremendous and significant instance of the apple's ancient prestige when its consumption by our first parents occasioned the fall of man from his state of goodness and perfection."

"Apples like them," said the windmill man, lingering with the objective article, "are worth $3.50 a barrel in the Chicago market."

"Now, what I have to propose," said Judge Menefee, conceding an indulgent smile to his interrupter, "is this: We must remain here, perforce, until morning. We have wood in plenty to keep us warm. Our next need is to entertain ourselves as best we can, in order that the time shall not pass too slowly. I propose that we place this apple in the hands of Miss Garland. It is no longer a fruit, but, as I said, a prize, in award, representing a great human idea. Miss Garland, herself, shall cease to be an individual—but only temporarily, I am happy to add"—(a low bow, full of the old-time grace). "She shall represent her sex; she shall be the embodiment, the epitome of womankind—the heart and brain, I may say, of God's masterpiece of creation. In this guise she shall judge and decide the question which follows:

"But a few minutes ago our friend, Mr. Rose, favored us with an entertaining but fragmentary sketch of the romance in the life of the former possessor of this habitation. The few facts that we have learned seem to me to open up a fascinating field for conjecture, for the study of human hearts, for the exercise of the imagination—in short, for story-telling. Let us make use of the opportunity. Let each one of us relate his own version of the story of Redruth, the hermit, and his lady-love, beginning where Mr. Rose's narrative ends—at the parting of the lovers at the gate. This much should be assumed and conceded —that the young lady was not necessarily to blame for Redruth's becoming a crazed and world-hating hermit. When we have done, Miss Garland shall render the JUDGMENT OF WOMAN. As the Spirit of her Sex she shall decide which version of the story best and most truly depicts human and love interest, and most faithfully estimates the character and acts of Redruth's betrothed according to the feminine view. The apple shall be bestowed upon him who is awarded the decision. If you are all agreed, we shall be pleased to hear the first story from Mr. Dinwiddie."

The last sentence captured the windmill man. He was not one to linger in the dumps.

"That's a first-rate scheme, Judge," he said, heartily. "Be a regular short-story vaudeville, won't it? I used to be correspondent for a paper in Springfield, and when there wasn't any news I faked it. Guess I can do my turn all right."

"I think the idea is charming," said the lady passenger, brightly. "It will be almost like a game."

Judge Menefee stepped forward and placed the apple in her hand impressively.

"In olden days," he said, profoundly, "Paris awarded the golden apple to the most beautiful."

"I was at the Exposition," remarked the windmill man, now cheerful again, "but I never heard of it. And I was on the Midway, too, all the time I wasn't at the machinery exhibit."

"But now," continued the Judge, "the fruit shall translate to us the mystery and wisdom of the feminine heart. Take the apple, Miss Garland. Hear our modest tales of romance, and then award the prize as you may deem it just."

The lady passenger smiled sweetly. The apple lay in her lap beneath her robes and wraps. She reclined against her protecting bulwark, brightly and cosily at ease. But for the voices and the wind one might have listened hopefully to hear her purr. Someone cast fresh logs upon the fire. Judge Menefee nodded suavely. "Will you oblige us with the initial story?" he asked.

The windmill man sat as sits a Turk, with his hat well back on his head on account of the draughts.

"Well," he began, without any embarrassment, "this is about the way I size up the difficulty: Of course Redruth was jostled a good deal by this duck who had money to play ball with who tried to cut him out of his girl. So he goes around, naturally, and asks her if the game is still square. Well, nobody wants a guy cutting in with buggies and gold bonds when he's got an option on a girl. Well, he goes around to see her. Well, maybe he's hot, and talks like the proprietor, and forgets that an engagement ain't always a lead-pipe cinch. Well, I guess that makes Alice warm under the lace yoke. Well, she answers back sharp. Well, he——"

"Say!" interrupted the passenger who was nobody in particular, "if you could put up a windmill on every one of them 'wells' you're using, you'd be able to retire from business, wouldn't you?"

The windmill man grinned good-naturedly.

"Oh, I ain't no *Guy de Mopassong*," he said, cheerfully. "I'm giving it to you in straight American. Well, she says something like this: 'Mr. Gold Bonds is only a friend,' says she; 'but he takes me riding and buys me theatre tickets, and that's what you never do. Ain't I to never have any pleasure in life while I can?' 'Pass this chatfield-chatfield thing along,' says Redruth:—'hand out the mitt to the Willie with creases in it or you don't put your slippers under my wardrobe.'

"Now that kind of train orders don't go with a girl that's got any spirit. I bet that girl loved her honey all the time. Maybe she only wanted, as girls do, to work the good thing for a little fun and caramels before she settled down to patch George's other pair, and be a good wife. But he is glued to the high horse, and won't come down. Well, she hands him back the ring, proper enough; and George goes away and hits the booze. Yep. That's what done it. I bet that girl fired the cornucopia with the fancy vest two days after her steady left. George boards a freight and checks his bag of crackers for parts unknown. He sticks to Old Booze for a number of years; and then the aniline and aquafortis gets the decision. 'Me for the hermit's hut,' says George, 'and the long whiskers, and the buried can of money that isn't there.'

"But that Alice, in my mind, was on the level. She never married, but took up typewriting as soon as the wrinkles began to show, and kept a cat that came when you said 'weeny—weeny—weeny!' I got too much faith in good women to believe they throw down the fellow they're stuck on every time for the dough." The windmill man ceased.

"I think," said the lady passenger, slightly moving upon her lowly throne, "that that is a char——"

"Oh, Miss Garland!" interposed Judge Menefee, with uplifted hand, "I beg of you, no comments! It would not be fair to the other contestants. Mr.— er—will you take the next turn?" The Judge addressed the young man who had the Agency.

"My version of the romance," began the young man, diffidently clasping his hands, "would be this: They did not quarrel when they parted. Mr. Redruth bade her good-bye and went out into the world to seek his fortune. He knew his love would remain true to him. He scorned the thought that his rival could make an impression upon a heart so fond and faithful. I would say that Mr. Redruth went out to the Rocky Mountains in Wyoming to seek for gold. One day a crew of pirates landed and captured him while at work, and——"

"Hey! what's that?" sharply called the passenger who was nobody in particular—"a crew of pirates landed in the Rocky Mountains! Will you tell us how they sailed——"

"Landed from a train," said the narrator, quietly and not without some readiness. "They kept him prisoner in a cave for months, and then they took him hundreds of miles away to the forests of Alaska. There a beautiful Indian girl fell in love with him, but he remained true to Alice. After another year of wandering in the woods, he set out with the diamonds——"

"What diamonds?" asked the unimportant passenger, almost with acerbity.

"The ones the saddlemaker showed him in the Peruvian temple," said the other, somewhat obscurely. "When he reached home, Alice's mother led him, weeping, to a green mound under a willow tree. 'Her heart was broken when you left,' said her mother. 'And what of my rival—of Chester McIntosh?' asked Mr. Redruth, as he knelt sadly by Alice's grave. 'When he found out,' she answered, 'that her heart was yours, he pined away day by day until, at length, he started a furniture store in Grand Rapids. We heard lately that he was bitten to death by an infuriated moose near South Bend, Ind., where he had gone to try to forget scenes of civilization.' With which, Mr. Redruth forsook the face of mankind and became a hermit, as we have seen.

"My story," concluded the young man with an Agency, "may lack the literary quality; but what I want it to show is that the young lady remained true. She cared nothing for wealth in comparison with true affection. I admire and believe in the fair sex too much to think otherwise."

The narrator ceased, with a sidelong glance at the corner where reclined the lady passenger.

Bildad Rose was next invited by Judge Menefee to contribute his story in the contest for the apple of judgment. The stage-driver's essay was brief.

"I'm not one of them lobo wolves," he said, "who are always blaming on women the calamities of life. My testimony in regards to the fiction story you ask for, Judge, will be about as follows: What ailed Redruth was pure laziness. If he had up and slugged this Percival De Lacey that tried to give him the outside of the road, and had kept Alice in the grape-vine swing with the blind-bridle on, all would have been well. The woman you want is sure worth taking pains for.

"'Send for me if you want me again,' says Redruth, and hoists his Stetson, and walks off. He'd have called it pride, but the nixycomlogical name for it is laziness. No woman don't like to run after a man. 'Let him come back, hisself,' says the girl; and I'll be bound she tells the boy with the pay ore to trot; and then spends her time watching out the window for the man with the empty pocket-book and the tickly moustache.

"I reckon Redruth waits about nine year expecting her to send him a note by a nigger asking him to forgive her. But she don't. 'This game won't work,' says Redruth; 'then so won't I.' And he goes in the hermit business and raises whiskers. Yes; laziness and whiskers was what done the trick. They travel together. You ever hear of a man with long whiskers and hair striking a bonanza? No. Look at the Duke of Marlborough and this Standard Oil snoozer. Have they got 'em?

"Now, this Alice didn't never marry, I'll bet a hoss. If Redruth had married somebody else she might have done so, too. But he never turns up. She has these here things they call fond memories, and maybe a lock of hair and a corset steel that he broke, treasured up. Them sort of articles is as good as a husband to some women. I'd say she played out a lone hand. I don't blame no woman for old man Redruth's abandonment of barber shops and clean shirts."

Next in order came the passenger who was nobody in particular. Nameless to us, he travels the road from Paradise to Sunrise City.

But him you shall see, if the firelight be not too dim, as he responds to the Judge's call.

A lean form, in rusty-brown clothing, sitting like a frog, his arms wrapped about his legs, his chin resting upon his knees. Smooth, oakum-colored hair; long nose; mouth like a satyr's, with upturned, tobacco-stained corners. An eye like a fish's; a red necktie with a horseshoe pin. He began with a rasping chuckle that gradually formed itself into words.

"Everybody wrong so far. What! a romance without any orange blossoms! Ho, ho! My money on the lad with the butterfly tie and the certified checks in his trouserings.

"Take 'em as they parted at the gate? All right. 'You never loved me,' says Redruth, wildly, 'or you wouldn't speak to a man who can buy you the ice cream.' 'I hate him,' says she. 'I loathe his side-bar buggy; I despise the elegant cream bonbons he sends me in gilt boxes covered with real lace; I feel that I could stab him to the heart when he presents me with a solid medallion locket with turquoises and pearls running in a vine around the border. Away with him! 'Tis only you I love.' 'Back to the cosy corner!' says Redruth. 'Was I bound and lettered in East Aurora? Get platonic, if you please. No jack-pots for mine. Go and hate your friend some more. For me the Nickerson girl on Avenue B, and gum, and a trolley ride.'

"Around that night comes John W. Crœsus. 'What! tears?' says he, arranging his pearl pin. 'You have driven my lover away,' says little Alice sobbing: 'I hate the sight of you.' 'Marry me, then,' says John W., lighting a Henry Clay. 'What!' she cries, indignantly, 'marry you! Never,' she says, 'until this blows over, and I can do some shopping, and you see about the license. There's a telephone next door if you want to call up the county clerk.'"

The narrator paused to give vent to his cynical chuckle.

"Did they marry?" he continued. "Did the duck swallow the June-bug? And then I take up the case of Old Boy Redruth. There's where you are all wrong again, according to my theory. What turned him into a hermit? One says laziness; one says remorse; one says booze. I say women did it. How old is the old man now?" asked the speaker, turning to Bildad Rose.

"I should say about sixty-five."

"All right. He conducted his hermit shop here for twenty years. Say he was twenty-five when he took off his hat at the gate. That leaves twenty years for him to account for, or else be docked. Where did he spend that ten and two fives? I'll give you my idea. Up for bigamy. Say there was the fat blonde in Saint Jo, and the panatela brunette at Skillet Ridge, and the gold tooth down in the Kaw valley. Redruth gets his cases mixed, and they send him up the road. He gets out after they are through with him, and says: 'Any line for me except the crinoline. The hermit trade is not overdone, and the stenographers never apply to 'em for work. The jolly hermit's life for me. No more long hairs in the comb or dill pickles lying around in the cigar tray.' You tell me they pinched old Redruth for the noodle villa just because he said he was King Solomon? Figs! He *was* Solomon. That's all of mine. I guess it don't call for any apples. Enclosed find stamps. It don't sound much like a prize winner."

Respecting the stricture laid by Judge Menefee against comments upon the stories, all were silent when the passenger who was nobody in particular had concluded. And then the ingenious originator of the contest cleared his throat to begin the ultimate entry for the prize. Though seated with small comfort upon the floor, you might search in vain for any abatement of dignity in Judge Menefee. The now diminishing firelight played softly upon his face, as clearly chiselled as a Roman emperor's on some old coin, and upon the thick waves of his honorable gray hair.

"A woman's heart!" he began, in even but thrilling tones—"who can hope to fathom it? The ways and desires of men are various. I think that the hearts of all women beat with the same rhythm, and to the same old tune of love. Love, to a woman, means sacrifice. If she be worthy of the name, no gold or rank will outweigh with her a genuine devotion.

"Gentlemen of the—er—I should say, my friends, the case of Redruth *versus* love and affection has been called. Yet, who is on trial? Not Redruth, for he has been punished. Not those immortal passions that clothe our lives with the joy of the angels. Then who? Each man of us here to-night stands at the bar to answer if chivalry or darkness inhabits his bosom. To judge us sits womankind in the form of one of its fairest flowers. In her hand she holds the prize, intrinsically insignificant, but worthy of our noblest efforts to win as a guerdon of approval from so worthy a representative of feminine judgment and taste.

"In taking up the imaginary history of Redruth and the fair being to whom he gave his heart, I must, in the beginning, raise my voice against the unworthy insinuation that the selfishness or perfidy or love of luxury of any woman drove him to renounce the world. I have not found woman to be so unspiritual or venal. We must seek elsewhere, among man's baser nature and lower motives for the cause.

"There was, in all probability, a lovers' quarrel as they stood at the gate on that memorable day. Tormented by jealousy, young Redruth vanished from his native haunts. But had he just cause to do so? There is no evidence for or against. But there is something higher than evidence: there is the grand, eternal belief in woman's goodness, in her steadfastness against temptation, in her loyalty even in the face of proffered riches.

"I picture to myself the rash lover, wandering, self-tortured, about the world. I picture his gradual descent, and, finally, his complete despair when he realizes that he has lost the most precious gift life had to offer him. Then his withdrawal from the world of sorrow and the subsequent derangement of his faculties becomes intelligible.

"But what do I see on the other hand? A lonely woman fading away as the years roll by; still faithful, still waiting, still watching for a form and listening for a step that will come no more. She is old now. Her hair is white and smoothly banded. Each day she sits at the door and gazes longingly down the dusty road. In spirit she is waiting there at the gate, just as he left her—his forever, but not here below. Yes; my belief in woman paints that picture in my mind. Parted forever on earth, but waiting! She in anticipation of a meeting in Elysium; he in the Slough of Despond."

"I thought he was in the bughouse," said the passenger who was nobody in particular.

Judge Menefee stirred, a little impatiently. The men sat, drooping, in grotesque attitudes. The wind had abated its violence; coming now in fitful, virulent puffs. The fire had burned to a mass of red coals which shed but a dim light within the room. The lady passenger in her cosy nook looked to be but a formless dark bulk, crowned by a mass of coiled, sleek hair and showing but a small space of snowy forehead above her clinging boa.

Judge Menefee got stiffly to his feet.

"And now, Miss Garland," he announced, "we have concluded. It is for you to award the prize to the one of us whose argument—especially, I may say, in regard to his estimate of true womanhood—approaches nearest to your own conception."

No answer came from the lady passenger. Judge Menefee bent over solicitously. The passenger who was nobody in particular laughed low and harshly. The lady was sleeping sweetly. The Judge essayed to take her hand to awaken her. In doing so he touched a small, cold, round, irregular something in her lap.

"She has eaten the apple," announced Judge Menefee, in awed tones, as he held up the core for them to see.

THE MISSING CHORD

I STOPPED overnight at the sheep ranch of Rush Kinney, on the Sandy Fork of the Nueces. Mr. Kinney, and I had been strangers up to the time when I called "Hallo!" at his hitching-rack; but from that moment until my departure on the next morning we were, according to the Texas code, undeniable friends.

After supper the ranchman and I lugged our chairs outside the two-room house, to its floorless gallery roofed with chaparral and sacuista grass. With the rear legs of our chairs sinking deep into the hard-packed loam, each of us reposed against an elm pillar of the structure and smoked El Toro tobacco, while we wrangled amicably concerning the affairs of the rest of the world.

As for conveying adequate conception of the engaging charm of that prairie evening, despair waits upon it. It is a bold chronicler who will undertake the description of a Texas night in the early spring. An inventory must suffice.

The ranch rested upon the summit of a lenient slope. The ambient prairie, diversified by arroyos and murky patches of brush and pear, lay around us like a darkened bowl at the bottom of which we reposed as dregs. Like a turquoise cover the sky pinned us there. The miraculous air, heady with ozone and made memorably sweet by leagues of wild flowerets, gave tang and savor to the breath. In the sky was a great, round, mellow searchlight which we knew to be no moon, but the dark lantern of summer, who came to hunt northward the cowering spring. In the nearest corral a flock of sheep lay silent until a groundless panic would send a squad of them huddling together with a drumming rush. For other sounds a shrill family of coyotes yapped beyond the shearing-pen, and whippoorwills twittered in the long grass. But even these dissonances hardly rippled the clear torrent of the mocking-birds' notes that fell from a dozen neighboring shrubs and trees. It would not have been preposterous for one to tiptoe and essay to touch the stars, they hung so bright and imminent.

Mr. Kinney's wife, a young and capable woman, we had left in the house. She remained to busy herself with the domestic round of duties in which I had observed that she seemed to take a buoyant and contented pride. In one room we had supped. Presently, from the other, as Kinney and I sat without, there burst a volume of sudden and brilliant music. If I could justly estimate the art of piano-playing, the construer of that rollicking fantasia had creditably mastered the secrets of the keyboard. A piano, and one so well played, seemed to me to be an unusual thing to find in that small and unpromising ranch-house. I must have looked my surprise at Rush Kinney, for he laughed in his soft Southern way, and nodded at me through the moonlit haze of our cigarettes.

"You don't often hear as agreeable a noise as that on a sheep-ranch," he remarked; "but I never see any reason for not playing up to the arts and graces just because we happen to live out in the brush. It's a lonesome life for a woman; and if a little music can make it any better, why not have it? That's the way I look at it."

"A wise and generous theory," I assented. "And Mrs. Kinney plays well. I am not learned in the science of music, but I should call her an uncommonly good performer. She has technic and more than ordinary power."

The moon was very bright, you will understand, and I saw upon Kinney's face a sort of amused and pregnant expression, as though there were things behind it that might be expounded.

"You came up the trail from the Double-Elm Fork," he said, promisingly. "As you crossed it you must have seen an old deserted *jacal* to your left under a coma mott."

"I did," said I. "There was a drove of *invalis* rooting around it. I could see by the broken corrals that no one lived there."

"That's where this music proposition started," said Kinney. "I don't mind telling you about it while we smoke. That's where old Cal Adams lived. He had about eight hundred graded merinos and a daughter that was solid silk and as handsome as a new stake-rope on a thirty-dollar pony. And I don't mind telling you that I was guilty in the second degree of hanging around old Cal's ranch all the time I could spare away from lambing and shearing. Miss Marilla was her name; and I had figured it out by the rule of two that she was destined to become the chatelaine and lady superior of Rancho Lomito, belonging to R. Kinney, Esq., where you are now a welcome and honored guest.

"I will say that old Cal wasn't distinguished as a sheepman. He was a little, old stoop-shouldered *hombre* about as big as a gun scabbard, with scraggy white whiskers, and condemned to the continuous use of language. Old Cal was so obscure in his chosen profession that he wasn't even hated by the cowmen. And when a sheepman don't get eminent enough to acquire the hostility of the cattlemen, he is mighty apt to die unwept and considerably unsung.

"But that Marilla girl was a benefit to the eye. And she was the most elegant kind of a housekeeper. I was the nearest neighbor, and I used to ride over to

the Double-Elm anywhere from nine to sixteen times a week with fresh butter
or a quarter of venison or a sample of new sheep-dip just as a frivolous excuse
to see Marilla. Marilla and me got to be extensively inveigled with each other,
and I was pretty sure I was going to get my rope around her neck and lead her
over to the Lomito. Only she was so everlastingly permeated with filial sentiments toward old Cal that I never could get her to talk about serious matters.

"You never saw anybody in your life that was as full of knowledge and had
less sense than old Cal. He was advised about all the branches of information
contained in learning, and he was up to all the rudiments of doctrines and enlightenment. You couldn't advance him any ideas on any of the parts of speech
or lines of thought. You would have thought he was a professor of the weather
and politics and chemistry and natural history and the origin of derivations.
Any subject you brought up old Cal could give you an abundant synopsis of it
from the Greek root up to the time it was sacked and on the market.

"One day just after the fall shearing I rides over to the Double-Elm with a
lady's magazine about fashions for Marilla and a scientific paper for old Cal.

"While I was tying my pony to a mesquite, out run Marilla, 'tickled to death'
with some news that couldn't wait.

"'Oh, Rush,' she says, all flushed up with esteem and gratification, 'what do you
think! Dad's going to buy me a piano. Ain't it grand? I never dreamed I'd
ever have one.'

"'It's sure joyful,' says I. 'I always admired the agreeable uproar of a piano.
It'll be lots of company for you. That's mighty good of Uncle Cal to do that.'

"'I'm all undecided,' says Marilla, 'between a piano and a organ. A parlor
organ is nice.'

"'Either of 'em,' says I, 'is first-class for mitigating the lack of noise around
a sheep-ranch. For my part,' I says, 'I shouldn't like anything better than to ride
home of an evening and listen to a few waltzes and jigs, with somebody about
your size sitting on the piano-stool and rounding up the notes.'

"'Oh, hush about that,' says Marilla, 'and go on in the house. Dad hasn't
rode out to-day. He's not feeling well.'

"Old Cal was inside, lying on a cot. He had a pretty bad cold and cough. I
stayed to supper.

"'Going to get Marilla a piano, I hear,' says I to him.

"'Why, yes, something of the kind, Rush,' says he. 'She's been hankering
for music for a long spell; and I allow to fix her up with something in that line
right away. The sheep sheared six pounds all around this fall; and I'm going
to get Marilla an instrument if it takes the price of the whole clip to do it.'

"'*Star wayno*,' says I. 'The little girl deserves it.'

"'I'm going to San Antone on the last load of wool,' says Uncle Cal, 'and
select an instrument for her myself.'

"'Wouldn't it be better,' I suggest, 'to take Marilla along and let her pick out
one that she likes?'

"I might have known that would set Uncle Cal going. Of course, a man like
him, that knew everything about everything, would look at that as a reflection on
his attainments.

"'No, sir, it wouldn't,' says he, pulling at his white whiskers. 'There ain't a
better judge of musical instruments in the whole world than what I am. I
had an uncle,' says he, 'that was a partner in a piano-factory, and I've seen
thousands of 'em put together. I know all about musical instruments from a
pipe-organ to a corn-stalk fiddle. There ain't a man lives, sir, that can tell me
any news about any instrument that has to be pounded, blowed, scraped, grinded,
picked, or wound with a key.'

"'You get me what you like, dad,' says Marilla, who couldn't keep her feet on the floor from joy. 'Of course you know what to select. I'd just as lief it was a piano or a organ or what.'

"'I see in St. Louis once what they call a orchestrion,' says Uncle Cal, 'that I judged was about the finest thing in the way of music ever invented. But there ain't room in this house for one. Anyway, I imagine they'd cost a thousand dollars. I reckon something in the piano line would suit Marilla the best. She took lessons in that respect for two years over at Birdstail. I wouldn't trust the buying of an instrument to anybody else but myself. I reckon if I hadn't took up sheep-raising I'd have been one of the finest composers or piano-and-organ manufacturers in the world.'

"That was Uncle Cal's style. But I never lost any patience with him, on account of his thinking so much of Marilla. And she thought just as much of him. He sent her to the academy over at Birdstail for two years when it took nearly every pound of wool to pay the expenses.

"Along about Tuesday Uncle Cal put out for San Antone on the last wagon-load of wool. Marilla's Uncle Ben, who lived in Birdstail, come over and stayed at the ranch while Uncle Cal was gone.

"It was ninety miles to San Antone, and forty to the nearest railroad-station, so Uncle Cal was gone about four days. I was over at the Double-Elm when he came rolling back one evening about sundown. And up there in the wagon, sure enough, was a piano or a organ—we couldn't tell which—all wrapped up in wool-sacks, with a wagon-sheet tied over it in case of rain. And out skips Marilla, hollering, 'Oh, oh!' with her eyes shining and her hair a-flying. 'Dad —dad,' she sings out, 'have you brought it—have you brought it?'—and it right there before her eyes, as women will do.

"'Finest piano in San Antone,' says Uncle Cal, waving his hand, proud. 'Genuine rosewood, and the finest, loudest tone you ever listened to. I heard the storekeeper play it, and I took it on the spot and paid cash down.'

"Me and Ben and Uncle Cal and a Mexican lifted it out of the wagon and carried it in the house and set it in a corner. It was one of them upright instruments, and not very heavy or very big.

"And then all of a sudden Uncle Cal flops over and says he's mighty sick. He's got a high fever, and he complains of his lungs. He gets into bed, while me and Ben goes out to unhitch and put the horses in the pasture, and Marilla flies around to get Uncle Cal something hot to drink. But first she puts both arms on that piano and hugs it with a soft kind of a smile, like you see kids doing with their Christmas toys.

"When I came in from the pasture, Marilla was in the room where the piano was. I could see by the strings and woolsacks on the floor that she had had it unwrapped. But now she was tying the wagon-sheet over it again, and there was a kind of solemn, whitish look on her face.

"'Ain't wrapping up the music again, are you, Marilla?' I asks. 'What's the matter with just a couple of tunes for to see how she goes under the saddle?'

"'Not to-night, Rush,' says she. 'I don't want to play any to-night. Dad's too sick. Just think, Rush, he paid three hundred dollars for it—nearly a third of what the wool-clip brought!'

"'Well, it ain't anyways in the neighborhood of a third of what you are worth,' I told her. 'And I don't think Uncle Cal is too sick to hear a little agitation of the piano-keys just to christen the machine.'

"'Not to-night, Rush,' says Marilla, in a way that she had when she wanted to settle things.

"But it seems that Uncle Cal was plenty sick, after all. He got so bad that Ben saddled up and rode over to Birdstail for Doc Simpson. I stayed around to see if I'd be needed for anything.

"When Uncle Cal's pain let up on him a little he called Marilla and says to her: 'Did you look at your instrument, honey? And do you like it?'

" 'It's lovely, dad,' says she, leaning down by his pillow; 'I never saw one so pretty. How dear and good it was of you to buy it for me!'

" 'I haven't heard you play on it any yet,' says Uncle Cal; 'and I've been listening. My side don't hurt quite so bad now—won't you play a piece, Marilla?'

"But no; she puts Uncle Cal off and soothes him down like you've seen women do with a kid. It seems she's made up her mind not to touch that piano at present.

"When Doc Simpson comes over he tells us that Uncle Cal has pneumonia the worst kind; and as the old man was past sixty and nearly on the lift anyhow, the odds was against his walking on grass any more.

"On the fourth day of his sickness he calls for Marilla again and wants to talk piano. Doc Simpson was there, and so was Ben and Mrs. Ben, trying to do all they could.

" 'I'd have made a wonderful success in anything connected with music,' says Uncle Cal. 'I got the finest instrument for the money in San Antone. Ain't that piano all right in every respect, Marilla?'

" 'It's just perfect, dad,' says she. 'It's got the finest tone I ever heard. But don't you think you could sleep a little now, dad?'

" 'No, I don't,' says Uncle Cal. 'I want to hear that piano. I don't believe you've even tried it yet. I went all the way to San Antone and picked it out for you myself. It took a third of the fall clip to buy it; but I don't mind that if it makes my good girl happier. Won't you play a little bit for dad, Marilla?'

"Doc Simpson beckoned Marilla to one side and recommended her to do what Uncle Cal wanted, so it would get him quieted. And her Uncle Ben and his wife asked her, too.

" 'Why not hit out a tune or two with the soft pedal on?' I asks Marilla. 'Uncle Cal has begged you so often. It would please him a good deal to hear you touch up the piano he's bought for you. Don't you think you might?'

"But Marilla stands there with big tears rolling down from her eyes and says nothing. And then she runs over and slips her arm under Uncle Cal's neck and hugs him tight.

" 'Why, last night, dad,' we heard her say, 'I played ever so much. Honest —I have been playing it. And it's such a splendid instrument, you don't know how I love it. Last night I played "Bonnie Dundee" and the "Anvil Polka" and the "Blue Danube"—and lots of pieces. You must surely have heard me playing a little, didn't you, dad? I didn't like to play loud when you was so sick.'

" 'Well, well,' says Uncle Cal, 'maybe I did. Maybe I did and forgot about it. My head is a little cranky at times. I heard the man in the store play it fine. I'm mighty glad you like it, Marilla. Yes, I believe I could go to sleep a while if you'll stay right beside me till I do.'

"There was where Marilla had me guessing. Much as she thought of that old man, she wouldn't strike a note on that piano that he'd bought her. I couldn't imagine why she told him she'd been playing it, for the wagon-sheet hadn't even been off of it since she put it back on the same day it come. I knew she could play a little anyhow, for I'd once heard her snatch some pretty fair dance-music out of an old piano at the Charco Largo Ranch.

"Well, in about a week the pneumonia got the best of Uncle Cal. They had the funeral over at Birdstail, and all of us went over. I brought Marilla back home in my buckboard. Her uncle Ben and his wife were going to stay there a few days with her.

"That night Marilla takes me in the room where the piano was, while the others were out on the gallery.

" 'Come here, Rush,' says she; 'I want you to see this now.'

"She unties the rope, and drags off the wagon-sheet.

"If you ever rode a saddle without a horse, or fired off a gun that wasn't loaded, or took a drink out of an empty bottle, why, then you might have been able to scare an opera or two out of the instrument Uncle Cal had bought.

'Instead of a piano, it was one of them machines they've invented to play the piano with. By itself it was about as musical as the holes of a flute without the flute.

"And that was the piano that Uncle Cal had selected; and standing by it was the good, fine, all-wool girl that never let him know it.

"And what you heard playing a while ago," concluded Mr. Kinney, "was that same deputy-piano machine; only just at present it's shoved up against a six-hundred-dollar piano that I bought for Marilla as soon as we was married."

A CALL LOAN

In those days the cattlemen were the anointed. They were the grandees of the grass, kings of the kine, lords of the lea, barons of beef and bone. They might have ridden in golden chariots had their tastes so inclined. The cattleman was caught in a stampede of dollars. It seemed to him that he had more money than was decent. But when he had bought a watch with precious stones set in the case so large that they hurt his ribs, and a California saddle with silver nails and Angora skin *suaderos*, and ordered everybody up to the bar for whisky—what else was there for him to spend money for?

Not so circumscribed in expedient for the reduction of surplus wealth were those lairds of the lariat who had womenfolk to their name. In the breast of the rib-sprung sex the genius of purse lightening may slumber through years of inopportunity, but never, my brothers, does it become extinct.

So, out of the chaparral came Long Bill Longley from the Bar Circle Branch on the Frio—a wife-driven man—to taste the urban joys of success. Something like half a million dollars he had, with an income steadily increasing.

Long Bill was a graduate of the camp and trail. Luck and thrift, a cool head, and a telescopic eye for mavericks had raised him from cowboy to be a cowman. Then came the boom in cattle, and Fortune, stepping gingerly among the cactus thorns, came and emptied her cornucopia at the doorstep of the ranch.

In the little frontier city of Chaparosa, Longley built a costly residence. Here he became a captive, bound to the chariot of social existence. He was doomed to become a leading citizen. He struggled for a time like a mustang in his first corral, and then he hung up his quirt and spurs. Time hung heavily on his hands. He organized the First National Bank of Chaparosa, and was elected its president.

One day a dyspeptic man, wearing double-magnifying glasses, inserted an official-looking card between the bars of the cashier's window of the First National Bank. Five minutes later the bank force was dancing at the beck and call of a national bank examiner.

This examiner, Mr. J. Edgar Todd, proved to be a thorough one.

At the end of it all the examiner put on his hat, and called the president, Mr. William R. Longley, into the private office.

"Well, how do you find things?" asked Longley, in his slow, deep tones. "Any brands in the round-up you didn't like the looks of?"

"The bank checks up all right, Mr. Longley," said Todd; "and I find your loans in very good shape—with one exception. You are carrying one very bad bit of paper—one that is so bad that I have been thinking that you surely do not realize the serious position it places you in. I refer to a call loan of $10,000 made to Thomas Merwin. Not only is the amount in excess of the maximum sum the bank can loan any individual legally, but it is absolutely without indorsement or security. Thus you have doubly violated the national banking laws, and have laid yourself open to criminal prosecution by the Government. A report of the matter to the Comptroller of the Currency—which I am bound to make—would, I am sure, result in the matter being turned over to the Department of Justice for action. You see what a serious thing it is."

Bill Longley was leaning his lengthy, slowly moving frame back in his swivel chair. His hands were clasped behind his head, and he turned a little to look the examiner in the face. The examiner was surprised to see a smile creep about the rugged mouth of the banker, and a kindly twinkle in his light-blue eyes. If he saw the seriousness of the affair, it did not show in his countenance.

"Of course, you don't know Tom Merwin," said Longley, almost genially. "Yes, I know about that loan. It hasn't any security except Tom Merwin's word. Somehow, I've always found that when a man's word is good, it's the best security there is. Oh, yes, I know the Government doesn't think so. I guess I'll see Tom about that note."

Mr. Todd's dyspepsia seemed to grow suddenly worse. He looked at the chaparral banker through his double-magnifying glasses in amazement.

"You see," said Longley, easily explaining the thing away, "Tom heard of 2000 head of two-year-olds down near Rocky Ford on the Rio Grande that could be had for $8 a head. I reckon 'twas one of old Laendro Garcia's outfits that he had smuggled over, and he wanted to make a quick turn on 'em. Those cattle are worth $15 on the hoof in Kansas City. Tom knew it and I knew it. He had $6,000, and I let him have the $10,000 to make the deal with. His brother Ed took 'em on to market three weeks ago. He ought to be back 'most any day now with the money. When he comes Tom'll pay that note."

The bank examiner was shocked. It was, perhaps, his duty to step out to the telegraph office and wire the situation to the Comptroller. But he did not. He talked pointedly and effectively to Longley for three minutes. He succeded in making the banker understand that he stood upon the border of a catastrophe. And then he offered a tiny loophole of escape.

"I am going to Hilldale's to-night," he told Longley, "to examine a bank there. I will pass through Chaparosa on my way back. At twelve o'clock to-morrow I shall call at this bank. If this loan has been cleared out of the way by that time it will not be mentioned in my report. If not—I will have to do my duty."

With that the examiner bowed and departed.

The President of the First National lounged in his chair half an hour longer, and then he lit a mild cigar, and went over to Tom Merwin's house. Merwin, a ranchman in brown duck, with a contemplative eye, sat with his feet upon a table, plaiting a rawhide quirt.

"Tom," said Longley, leaning against the table, "you heard anything from Ed yet?"

"Not yet," said Merwin, continuing his plaiting. "I guess Ed'll be along back now in a few days."

"There was a bank examiner," said Longley, "nosing around our place to-day, and he bucked a sight about that note of yours. You know I know it's all right, but the thing is against the banking laws. I was pretty sure you'd have paid it off before the bank was examined again, but the son-of-a-gun slipped in on us, Tom. Now, I'm short of cash myself just now, or I'd let you have the money to take it up with. I've got till twelve o'clock to-morrow, and then I've got to show the cash in place of that note or——"

"Or what, Bill?" asked Merwin, as Longley hesitated.

"Well, I suppose it means be jumped on with both of Uncle Sam's feet."

"I'll try to raise the money for you on time," said Merwin, interested in his plaiting.

"All right, Tom," concluded Longley, as he turned toward the door; "I knew you would if you could."

Merwin threw down his whip and went to the only other bank in town, a private one, run by Cooper & Craig.

"Cooper," he said, to the partner by that name, "I've got to have $10,000 to-day or to-morrow. I've got a house and lot here that's worth about $6000 and that's all the actual collateral. But I've got a cattle deal on that's sure to bring me in more than that much profit within a few days."

Cooper began to cough.

"Now, for God's sake don't say no," said Merwin. "I owe that much money on a call loan. It's been called, and the man that called it is a man I've laid on the same blanket with in cow-camps and ranger-camps for ten years. He can call anything I've got. He can call the blood out of my veins and it'll come. He's got to have the money. He's in a devil of a—— Well, he needs the money, and I've got to get it for him. You know my word's good, Cooper."

"No doubt of it," assented Cooper, urbanely, "but I've a partner, you know. I'm not free in making loans. And even if you had the best security in your hands, Merwin, we couldn't accommodate you in less than a week. We're just making a shipment of $15,000 to Myer Brothers in Rockdell, to buy cotton with. It goes down on the narrow gauge to-night. That leaves our cash quite short at present. Sorry we can't arrange it for you."

Merwin went back to his little bar office and plaited at his quirt again. About four o'clock in the afternoon he went to the First National and leaned over the railing of Longley's desk.

"I'll try to get that money for you to-night—I mean to-morrow, Bill."

"All right, Tom," said Longley, quietly.

At nine o'clock that night Tom Merwin stepped cautiously out of the small frame house in which he lived. It was near the edge of the little town, and few citizens were in the neighborhood at that hour. Merwin wore two six-shooters in a belt and a slouch hat. He moved swiftly down a lonely street, and then followed the sandy road that ran parallel to the narrow-gauge track until he reached the water-tank, two miles below the town. There Tom Merwin stopped, tied a black silk handkerchief about the lower part of his face, and pulled his hat down low.

In ten minutes the night train for Rockdell pulled up at the tank, having come from Chaparosa.

With a gun in each hand Merwin raised himself from behind a clump of chaparral and started for the engine. But before he had taken three steps, two long, strong arms clasped him from behind, and he was lifted from his feet and thrown, face downward, upon the grass. There was a heavy knee pressing against his back, and an iron hand grasping each of his wrists. He was held thus, like a child, until the engine had taken water, and until the train had moved, with accelerating speed, out of sight. Then he was released, and rose to his feet to face Bill Longley.

"The case never needed to be fixed up this way, Tom," said Longley. "I saw Cooper this evening, and he told me what you and him talked about. Then I went down to your house to-night and saw you come out with your guns on, and I followed you. Let's go back, Tom."

They walked away together, side by side.

" 'Twas the only chance I saw," said Merwin, presently. "You called your loan, and I tried to answer you. Now, what'll you do, Bill, if they sock it to you?"

"What would you have done if they'd socked it to you?" was the answer Longley made.

"I never thought I'd lay in a bush to stick up a train," remarked Merwin; "but a call loan's different. A call's a call with me. We've got twelve hours yet, Bill, before this spy jumps onto you. We've got to raise them spondulicks somehow. Maybe we can—Great Sam Houston! do you hear that?"

Merwin broke into a run, and Longley kept with him, hearing only a rather pleasing whistle somewhere in the night rendering the lugubrious air of "The Cowboy's Lament."

"It's the only tune he knows," shouted Merwin, as he ran. "I'll bet——"

They were at the door of Merwin's house. He kicked it open and fell over an old valise lying in the middle of the floor. A sunburned, firm-jawed youth, stained by travel, lay upon the bed puffing at a brown cigarette.

"What's the word, Ed?" gasped Merwin.

"So, so," drawled that capable youngster. "Just got in on the 9:30. Sold the bunch for fifteen, straight. Now, buddy, you want to quit kickin' a valise around that's got $29,000 in greenbacks in its in'ards."

THE PRINCESS AND THE PUMA

THERE had to be a king and queen, of course. The king was a terrible old man who wore sixshooters and spurs, and shouted in such a tremendous voice that the rattlers on the prairie would run into their holes under the prickly pear. Before there was a royal family they called the man "Whispering Ben." When he came to own 50,000 acres of land and more cattle than he could count, they called him O'Donnell "the Cattle King."

The queen had been a Mexican girl from Laredo. She made a good, mild, Coloradoclaro wife, and even succeeded in teaching Ben to modify his voice sufficiently while in the house to keep the dishes from being broken. When Ben got to be king she would sit on the gallery of Espinosa Ranch and weave rush mats. When wealth became so irresistible and oppressive that upholstered chairs and a centre table were brought down from San Antone in the wagons, she bowed her smooth, dark head, and shared the fate of the Danaë.

To avoid *lèse-majesté* you have been presented first to the king and queen. They do not enter the story, which might be called "The Chronicle of the Princess, the Happy Thought, and the Lion that Bungled his Job."

Josefa O'Donnell was the surviving daughter, the princess. From her mother she inherited warmth of nature and a dusky, semi-tropic beauty. From Ben O'Donnell the royal she acquired a store of intrepidity, common sense, and the faculty of ruling. The combination was worth going miles to see. Josefa while riding her pony at a gallop could put five out of six bullets through a tomato-can swinging at the end of a string. She could play for hours with a white kitten she owned, dressing it in all manner of absurd clothes. Scorning a pencil, she could tell you out of her head what 1545 two-year-olds would bring on the hoof, at $8.50 per head. Roughly speaking, the Espinosa Ranch is forty miles long and thirty broad—but mostly leased land. Josefa, on her pony, had prospected over every mile of it. Every cow-puncher on the range knew her by sight and was a loyal vassal. Ripley Givens, foreman of one of the Espinosa outfits, saw her one day, and made up his mind to form a royal matrimonial alliance. Presumptuous? No. In those days in the Nueces country a man was a man. And, after all, the title of cattle king does not presuppose blood royal. Often it only signifies that its owner wears the crown in token of his magnificent qualities in the art of cattle stealing.

One day Ripley Givens rode over to the Double Elm Ranch to inquire about a bunch of strayed yearlings. He was late in setting out on his return trip, and it was sundown when he struck the White Horse Crossing of the Nueces. From there to his own camp it was sixteen miles. To the Espinosa ranch-house it was twelve. Givens was tired. He decided to pass the night at the Crossing.

There was a fine water hole in the river-bed. The banks were thickly covered with great trees, undergrown with brush. Back from the water hole fifty yards was a stretch of curly mesquite grass—supper for his horse and bed for himself. Givens staked his horse, and spread out his saddle blankets to dry. He sat down with his back against a tree and rolled a cigarette. From somewhere in the dense timber along the river came a sudden, rageful, shivering wail. The pony danced at the end of his rope and blew a whistling snort of comprehending fear. Givens puffed at his cigarette, but he reached leisurely for his pistol-belt, which lay on the grass, and twirled the cylinder of his weapon tentatively. A great gar plunged with a loud splash into the water hole. A little brown rabbit skipped around a bunch of catclaw and sat twitching his whiskers and looking humorously at Givens. The pony went on eating grass.

It is well to be reasonably watchful when a Mexican lion sings soprano along the arroyos at sundown. The burden of his song may be that young calves and fat lambs are scarce, and that he has a carnivorous desire for your acquaintance.

In the grass lay an empty fruit can, cast there by some former sojourner. Givens caught sight of it with a grunt of satisfaction. In his coat pocket tied behind his saddle was a handful or two of ground coffee. Black coffee and cigarettes! What ranchero could desire more?

In two minutes he had a little fire going clearly. He started, with his can, for the water hole. When within fifteen yards of its edge he saw, between the bushes, a side-saddled pony with down-dropped reins cropping grass a little distance to his left. Just rising from her hands and knees on the brink of the water hole was Josefa O'Donnell. She had been drinking water, and she brushed the sand from the palms of her hands. Ten yards away, to her right, half concealed by a clump of sacuista, Givens saw the crouching form of the Mexican lion. His amber eyeballs glared hungrily; six feet from them was the tip of the tail stretched straight, like a pointer's. His hind-quarters rocked with the motion of the cat tribe preliminary to leaping.

Givens did what he could. His six-shooter was thirty-five yards away lying on the grass. He gave a loud yell, and dashed between the lion and the princess. The "rucus," as Givens called it afterward, was brief and somewhat confused. When he arrived on the line of attack he saw a dim streak in the air, and heard a couple of faint cracks. Then a hundred pounds of Mexican lion plumped down upon his head and flattened him, with a heavy jar, to the ground. He remembered calling out: "Let up, now—no fair gouging!" and then he crawled from under the lion like a worm, with his mouth full of grass and dirt, and a big lump on the back of his head where it had struck the root of a water-elm. The lion lay motionless. Givens, feeling aggrieved, and suspicious of fouls, shook his fist at the lion, and shouted: "I'll rastle you again for twenty——" and then he got back to himself.

Josefa was standing in her tracks, quietly reloading her silver-mounted .38. It had not been a difficult shot. The lion's head made an easier mark than a tomato-can swinging at the end of a string. There was a provoking, teasing, maddening smile upon her mouth and in her dark eyes. The would-be-rescuing knight felt the fire of his fiasco burn down to his soul. Here had been his chance, the chance that he had dreamed of; and Momus, and not Cupid, had presided over it. The satyrs in the wood were, no doubt, holding their sides in hilarious, silent laughter. There had been something like vaudeville—say Signor Givens and his funny knockabout act with the stuffed lion.

"Is that you, Mr. Givens?" said Josefa, in her deliberate, saccharine contralto. "You nearly spoiled my shot when you yelled. Did you hurt your head when you fell?"

"Oh, no," said Givens, quietly; "that didn't hurt." He stooped ignominiously and dragged his best Stetson hat from under the beast. It was crushed and wrinkled to a fine comedy effect. Then he knelt down and softly stroked the fierce, open-jawed head of the dead lion.

"Poor old Bill!" he exclaimed, mournfully.

"What's that?" asked Josefa, sharply.

"Of course you didn't know, Miss Josefa," said Givens, with an air of one allowing magnanimity to triumph over grief. "Nobody can blame you. I tried to save him, but I couldn't let you know in time."

"Save who?"

"Why, Bill. I've been looking for him all day. You see, he's been our camp pet for two years. Poor old fellow, he wouldn't have hurt a cottontail rabbit. It'll break the boys all up when they hear about it. But you couldn't tell, of course, that Bill was just trying to play with you."

Josefa's black eyes burned steadily upon him. Ripley Givens met the test successfully. He stood rumpling the yellow-brown curls on his head pensively. In his eyes was regret, not unmingled with a gentle reproach. His smooth features were set to a pattern of indisputable sorrow. Josefa wavered.

"What was your pet doing here?" she asked, making a last stand. "There's no camp near the White Horse Crossing."

"The old rascal ran away from camp yesterday," answered Givens, readily. "It's a wonder the coyotes didn't scare him to death. You see, Jim Webster, our horse wrangler, brought a little terrier pup into camp last week. The pup made life miserable for Bill—he used to chase him around and chew his hind legs for hours at a time. Every night when bedtime came Bill would sneak under one of the boy's blankets and sleep to keep the pup from finding him. I reckon he must have been worried pretty desperate or he wouldn't have run away. He was always afraid to get out of sight of camp."

Josefa looked at the body of the fierce animal. Givens gently patted one of the formidable paws that could have killed a yearling calf with one blow. Slowly a red flush widened upon the dark olive face of the girl. Was it the signal of shame of the true sportsman who has brought down ignoble quarry? Her eyes grew softer, and the lowered lids drove away all their bright mockery.

"I'm very sorry," she said, humbly; "but he looked so big, and jumped so high that——"

"Poor old Bill was hungry," interrupted Givens, in quick defence of the deceased. "We always made him jump for his supper in camp. He would lie down and roll over for a piece of meat. When he saw you he thought he was going to get something to eat from you."

Suddenly Josefa's eyes opened wide.

"I might have shot you!" she exclaimed. "You ran right in between. You risked your life to save your pet! That was fine, Mr. Givens. I like a man who is kind to animals."

Yes; there was even admiration in her gaze now. After all, there was a hero rising out of the ruins of the anti-climax. The look on Givens's face would have secured him a high position in the S. P. C. A.

"I always loved 'em," said he; "horses, dogs, Mexican lions, cows, alligators——"

"I hate alligators," instantly demurred Josefa; "crawly, muddy things!"

"Did I say alligators?" said Givens. "I meant antelopes, of course."

Josefa's conscience drove her to make further amends. She held out her hand penitently. There was a bright, unshed drop in each of her eyes.

"Please forgive me, Mr. Givens, won't you? I'm only a girl, you know, and I was frightened at first. I'm very, very sorry I shot Bill. You don't know how ashamed I feel. I wouldn't have done it for anything."

Givens took the proffered hand. He held it for a time while he allowed the generosity of his nature to overcome his grief at the loss of Bill. At last it was clear that he had forgiven her.

"Please don't speak of it any more, Miss Josefa. 'Twas enough to frighten any young lady the way Bill looked. I'll explain it all right to the boys."

"Are you really sure you don't hate me?" Josefa came closer to him impulsively. Her eyes were sweet—oh, sweet and pleading with gracious penitence. "I would hate any one who would kill my kitten. And how daring and kind of you to risk being shot when you tried to save him! How very few men would have done that!" Victory wrested from defeat! Vaudeville turned into drama! Bravo, Ripley Givens!

It was now twilight. Of course Miss Josefa could not be allowed to ride on to the ranch-house alone. Givens resaddled his pony in spite of that animal's reproachful glances, and rode with her. Side by side they galloped across the smooth grass, the princess and the man who was kind to animals. The prairie odors of fruitful earth and delicate bloom were thick and sweet around them. Coyotes yelping over there on the hill! No fear. And yet——

Josefa rode closer. A little hand seemed to grope. Givens found it with his own. The ponies kept an even gait. The hands lingered together, and the owner of one explained.

"I never was frightened before, but just think! How terrible it would be to meet a really wild lion! Poor Bill! I'm so glad you came with me!"

O'Donnell was sitting on the ranch gallery.

"Hello, Rip!" he shouted—"that you?"

"He rode in with me," said Josefa. "I lost my way and was late."

"Much obliged," called the cattle king. "Stop over, Rip, and ride to camp in the morning."

But Givens would not. He would push on to camp. There was a bunch of steers to start off on the trail at daybreak. He said good-night, and trotted away.

An hour later, when the lights were out, Josefa, in her night-robe, came to her door and called to the king in his own room across the brick-paved hallway:

"Say, pop, you know that old Mexican lion they call the 'Gotch-eared Devil' —the one that killed Gonzales, Mr. Martin's sheep herder, and about fifty calves on the Salada range? Well, I settled his hash this afternoon over at the White Horse Crossing. Put two balls in his head with my .38 while he was on the jump. I knew him by the slice gone from his left ear that old Gonzales cut off with his machete. You couldn't have made a better shot yourself, daddy."

"Bully for you!" thundered Whispering Ben from the darkness of the royal chamber.

THE INDIAN SUMMER OF DRY VALLEY JOHNSON

DRY VALLEY JOHNSON shook the bottle. You have to shake the bottle before using; for sulphur will not dissolve. Then Dry Valley saturated a small sponge with the liquid and rubbed it carefully into the roots of his hair. Besides sulphur there was sugar of lead in it and tincture of nux vomica and bay rum. Dry Valley found the recipe in a Sunday newspaper. You must next be told why a strong man came to fall a victim to a Beauty Hint.

Dry Valley had been a sheepman. His real name was Hector, but he had been rechristened after his range to distinguish him from "Elm Creek" Johnson, who ran sheep further down the Frio.

Many years of living face to face with sheep on their own terms wearied Dry Valley Johnson. So, he sold his ranch for eighteen thousand dollars and moved to Santa Rosa to live a life of gentlemanly ease. Being a silent and melancholy person of thirty-five—or perhaps thirty-eight—he soon became that cursed and earthcumbering thing—an elderlyish bachelor with a hobby. Some one gave him his first strawberry to eat, and he was done for.

Dry Valley bought a four-room cottage in the village, and a library on strawberry culture. Behind the cottage was a garden of which he made a strawberry patch. In his old gray woolen shirt, his brown duck trousers and high-heeled boots he sprawled all day on a canvas cot under a live-oak tree at his back door studying the history of the seductive scarlet berry.

The school teacher, Miss De Witt, spoke of him as "a fine, presentable man, for all his middle age." But the focus of Dry Valley's eyes embraced no women. They were merely beings who flew skirts as a signal for him to lift awkwardly his heavy, round-crowned, broad-brimmed felt Stetson whenever he met them, and then hurry past to get back to his beloved berries.

And all this recitative by the chorus is only to bring us to the point where you may be told why Dry Valley shook up the insoluble sulphur in the bottle. So long-drawn and inconsequential a thing is history—the anamorphous shadow of a milestone reaching down the road between us and the setting sun.

When his strawberries were beginning to ripen Dry Valley bought the heaviest buggy whip in the Santa Rosa store. He sat for many hours under the live-oak tree plaiting and weaving in an extension to its lash. When it was done he could snip a leaf from a bush twenty feet away with the cracker. For the bright, predatory eyes of Santa Rosa youth were watching the ripening berries, and Dry Valley was arming himself against their expected raids. No greater care had he taken of his tender lambs during his ranching days than he did of his cherished fruit, warding it from the hungry wolves that whistled and howled and shot their marbles and peered through the fence that surrounded his property.

In the house next to Dry Valley's lived a widow with a pack of children that gave the husbandman frequent anxious misgivings. In the woman there was a strain of the Spanish. She had wedded one of the name of O'Brien. Dry Valley was a connoisseur in cross strains; and he foresaw trouble in the offspring of this union.

Between the two homesteads ran a crazy picket fence overgrown with morning glory and wild gourd vines. Often he could see little heads with mops of black hair and flashing dark eyes dodging in and out between the pickets, keeping tabs on the reddening berries.

Late one afternoon Dry Valley went to the post office. When he came back, like Mother Hubbard he found the deuce to pay. The descendants of Iberian bandits and Hibernian cattle raiders had swooped down upon his strawberry patch. To the outraged vision of Dry Valley there seemed to be a sheep corral full of them; perhaps they numbered five or six. Between the rows of green plants they were stooped, hopping about like toads, gobbling silently and voraciously his finest fruit.

Dry Valley slipped into the house, got his whip, and charged the marauders. The lash curled about the legs of the nearest—a greedy ten-year-old—before they knew they were discovered. His screech gave warning; and the flock scampered for the fence like a drove of *javelis* flushed in the chaparral. Dry Valley's whip drew a toll of two more elfin shrieks before they dived through the vine-clad fence and disappeared.

Dry Valley, less fleet, followed them nearly to the pickets. Checking his useless pursuit, he rounded a bush, dropped his whip and stood, voiceless, motionless, the capacity of his powers consumed by the act of breathing and preserving the perpendicular.

Behind the bush stood Panchita O'Brien, scorning to fly. She was nineteen, the oldest of the raiders. Her night-black hair was gathered back in a wild mass and tied with a scarlet ribbon. She stood, with reluctant feet, yet nearer the brook than to the river; for childhood had environed and detained her.

She looked at Dry Valley Johnson for a moment with magnificent insolence, and before his eyes slowly crunched a luscious berry between her white teeth. Then she turned and walked slowly to the fence with a swaying, conscious motion, such as a duchess might make use of in leading a promenade. There she turned again and grilled Dry Valley Johnson once more in the dark flame of her audacious eyes, laughed a trifle school-girlishly, and twisted herself with pantherish quickness between the pickets to the O'Brien side of the wild gourd vine.

Dry Valley picked up his whip and went into his house. He stumbled as he went up the two wooden steps. The old Mexican woman who cooked his meals and swept his house called him to supper as he went through the rooms. Dry Valley went on, stumbled down the front steps, out the gate and down the road into a mesquite thicket at the edge of town. He sat down in the grass and laboriously plucked the spines from a prickly pear, one by one. This was his attitude of thought, acquired in the days when his problems were only those of wind and wool and water.

A thing had happened to the man—a thing that, if you are eligible, you must pray may pass you by. He had become enveloped in the Indian Summer of the Soul.

Dry Valley had had no youth. Even his childhood had been one of dignity and seriousness. At six he had viewed the frivolous gambols of the lambs on his father's ranch with silent disapproval. His life as a young man had been wasted. The divine fires and impulses, the glorious exaltations and despairs, the glow and enchantment of youth had passed above his head. Never a thrill of Romeo had he known; he was but a melancholy Jaques of the forest with a ruder philosophy, lacking the bitter-sweet flavor of experience that tempered the veteran years of the rugged ranger of Arden. And now in his sere and yellow leaf one scornful look from the eyes of Panchita O'Brien had flooded the autumnal landscape with a tardy and delusive summer heat.

But a sheepman is a hardy animal. Dry Valley Johnson had weathered too many northers to turn his back on a late summer, spiritual or real. Old? He would show them.

By the next mail went an order to San Antonio for an outfit of the latest clothes, colors and styles and prices no object. The next day went the recipe for the hair restorer clipped from a newspaper; for Dry Valley's sunburned auburn hair was beginning to turn silvery above his ears.

Dry Valley kept indoors closely for a week except for frequent sallies after youthful strawberry snatchers. Then, a few days later, he suddenly emerged brilliantly radiant in the hectic glow of his belated midsummer madness.

A jay-bird-blue tennis suit covered him outwardly, almost as far as his wrists and ankles. His shirt was ox-blood; his collar winged and tall; his necktie a floating oriflamme; his shoes a venomous bright tan, pointed and shaped on penitential lasts. A little flat straw hat with a striped band desecrated his weather-beaten head. Lemon-colored kid gloves protected his oak tough hands from the benignant May sunshine. This sad and optic-smiting creature teetered out of its den, smiling foolishly and smoothing its gloves for men and angels to see. To such a pass had Dry Valley Johnson been brought by Cupid, who always shoots game that is out of season with an arrow from the quiver of Momus. Reconstructing mythology, he had risen, a prismatic macaw, from the ashes of the gray-brown phœnix that had folded its tired wings to roost under the tree of Santa Rosa.

Dry Valley paused in the street to allow Santa Rosans within sight of him to be stunned; and then deliberately and slowly, as his shoes required, entered Mrs. O'Brien's gate.

Not until the eleven months' drought did Santa Rosa cease talking about Dry Valley Johnson's courtship of Panchita O'Brien. It was an unclassifiable procedure; something like a combination of cake-walking, deaf-and-dumb oratory, postage stamp flirtation, and parlor charades. It lasted two weeks and then came to a sudden end.

Of course Mrs. O'Brien favored the match as soon as Dry Valley's intentions were disclosed. Being the mother of a woman child, and therefore a charter member of the Ancient Order of the Rat-trap, she joyfully decked out Panchita for the sacrifice. The girl was temporarily dazzled by having her dresses lengthened and her hair piled up on her head, and came near forgetting that she was only a slice of cheese. It was nice, too, to have as good a match as Mr. Johnson paying you attentions and to see the other girls fluttering the curtains at their windows to see you go by with him.

Dry Valley bought a buggy with yellow wheels and a fine trotter in San Antonio. Every day he drove out with Panchita. He was never seen to speak to her when they were walking or driving. The consciousness of his clothes kept his mind busy; the knowledge that he could say nothing of interest kept him dumb; the feeling that Panchita was there kept him happy.

He took her to parties and dances, and to church. He tried—oh, no man ever tried so hard to be young as Dry Valley did. He could not dance; but he invented a smile which he wore on these joyous occasions, a smile that, in him, was as great a concession to mirth and gaiety as turning hand-springs would be in another. He began to seek the company of the young men in the town—even of the boys. They accepted him as a decided damper, for his attempts at sportiveness were so forced that they might as well have essayed their games in a cathedral. Neither he nor any other could estimate what progress he had made with Panchita.

The end came suddenly in one day, as often disappears the false afterglow before a November sky and wind.

Dry Valley was to call for the girl one afternoon at six for a walk. An afternoon walk in Santa Rosa was a feature of social life that called for the pink of one's wardrobe. So Dry Valley began gorgeously to array himself; and so early that he finished early, and went over to the O'Brien cottage. As he neared the porch on the crooked walk from the gate he heard sounds of revelry within. He stopped and looked through the honeysuckle vines in the open door.

Panchita was amusing her younger brothers and sisters. She wore a man's clothes—no doubt those of the late Mr. O'Brien. On her head was the smallest brother's straw hat decorated with an ink-striped paper band. On her hands were flapping yellow cloth gloves, roughly cut out and sewn for the masquerade. The same material covered her shoes, giving them the semblance of tan leather. High collar and flowing necktie were not omitted.

Panchita was an actress. Dry Valley saw his affectedly youthful gait, his limp where the right shoe hurt him, his forced smile, his awkward simulation of a gallant air, all reproduced with startling fidelity. For the first time a mirror had been held up to him. The corroboration of one of the youngsters calling, "Mamma, come and see Pancha do like Mr. Johnson," was not needed.

As softly as the caricatured tans would permit, Dry Valley tiptoed back to the gate and home again.

Twenty minutes after the time appointed for the walk Panchita tripped demurely out her gate in a thin, trim white lawn and sailor hat. She strolled up the sidewalk and slowed her steps at Dry Valley's gate, her manner expressing wonder at his unusual delinquency.

Then out of his door and down the walk strode—not the polychromatic victim of a lost summer time, but the sheepman, rehabilitated. He wore his old gray woolen shirt, open at the throat, his brown duck trousers stuffed into his runover boots, and his white felt sombrero on the back of his head. Twenty years or fifty he might look; Dry Valley cared not. His light blue eyes met Panchita's dark ones with a cold flash in them. He came as far as the gate. He pointed with his long arm to her house.

"Go home," said Dry Valley. "Go home to your mother. I wonder lightnin' don't strike a fool like me. Go home and play in the sand. What business have you got cavortin' around with grown men? I reckon I was locoed to be makin' a he poll-parrot out of myself for a kid like you. Go home and don't let me see you no more. Why I done it, will somebody tell me? Go home, and let me try and forget it."

Panchita obeyed and walked slowly toward her home, saying nothing. For some distance she kept her head turned and her large eyes fixed intrepidly upon Dry Valley's. At her gate she stood for a moment looking back at him, then ran suddenly and swiftly into the house.

Old Antonia was building a fire in the kitchen stove. Dry Valley stopped at the door and laughed harshly.

"I'm a pretty looking old rhinoceros to be gettin' stuck on a kid, ain't I, 'Tonia?" said he.

"Not verree good thing," agreed Antonia, sagely, "for too much old man to likee *muchacha*."

"You bet it ain't," said Dry Valley, grimly. "It's dum foolishness; and, besides, it hurts."

He brought at one armful the regalia of his aberration—the blue tennis suit, shoes, hat, gloves, and all, and threw them in a pile at Antonia's feet.

"Give them to your old man," said he, "to hunt antelope in."

Just as the first star presided palely over the twilight Dry Valley got his biggest strawberry book and sat on the back steps to catch the last of the reading light. He thought he saw the figure of someone in his strawberry patch. He laid aside the book, got his whip, and hurried forth to see.

It was Panchita. She had slipped through the picket fence and was halfway across the patch. She stopped when she saw him and looked at him without wavering.

A sudden rage—a humiliating flush of unreasoning wrath—came over Dry Valley. For this child he had made himself a motley to the view. He had tried to bribe Time to turn backward for himself; he had—been made a fool of. At last he had seen his folly. There was a gulf between him and youth over which he could not build a bridge even with yellow gloves to protect his hands. And the sight of his torment coming to pester him with her elfin pranks—

coming to plunder his strawberry vines like a mischievous school-boy—roused all his anger.

"I told you to keep away from here," said Dry Valley. "Go back to your home."

Panchita moved slowly toward him.

Dry Valley cracked his whip.

"Go back home," said Dry Valley, savagely, "and play theatricals some more. You'd make a fine man. You've made a fine one of me."

She came a step nearer, silent, and with that strange, defiant, steady shine in her eyes that had always puzzled him. Now it stirred his wrath.

His whiplash whistled through the air. He saw a red streak suddenly come out through her white dress above her knee where it had struck.

Without flinching and with the same unchanging dark glow in her eyes, Panchita came steadily toward him through the strawberry vines. Dry Valley's trembling hand released his whip handle. When within a yard of him Panchita stretched out her arms.

"God, kid!" stammered Dry Valley, "do you mean——?"

But the seasons are versatile; and it may have been Springtime, after all, instead of Indian Summer, that struck Dry Valley Johnson.

CHRISTMAS BY INJUNCTION

CHEROKEE was the civic father of Yellowhammer. Yellowhammer was a new mining town constructed mainly of canvas and undressed pine. Cherokee was a prospector. One day while his burro was eating quartz and pine burrs Cherokee turned up with his pick a nugget weighing thirty ounces. He staked his claim and then, being a man of breadth and hospitality, sent out invitations to his friends in three States to drop in and share his luck.

Not one of the invited guests sent regrets. They rolled in from the Gila country, from Salt River, from the Pecos, from Albuquerque and Phœnix and Santa Fé, and from the camps intervening.

When a thousand citizens had arrived and taken up claims they named the town Yellowhammer, appointed a vigilance committee, and presented Cherokee with a watch-chain made of nuggets.

Three hours after the presentation ceremonies Cherokee's claim played out. He had located a pocket instead of a vein. He abandoned it and staked others one by one. Luck had kissed her hand to him. Never afterward did he turn up enough dust in Yellowhammer to pay his bar bill. But his thousand invited guests were mostly prospering, and Cherokee smiled and congratulated them.

Yellowhammer was made up of men who took off their hats to a smiling loser; so they invited Cherokee to say what he wanted.

"Me?" said Cherokee, "oh, grubstakes will be about the thing. I reckon I'll prospect along up in the Mariposas. If I strike it up there I will most certainly let you all know about the facts. I never was any hand to hold out cards on my friends."

In May Cherokee packed his burro and turned its thoughtful, mouse-colored forehead to the north. Many citizens escorted him to the undefined limits of Yellowhammer and bestowed upon him shouts of commendation and farewells. Five pocket flasks without an air bubble between contents and cork were forced upon him; and he was bidden to consider Yellowhammer in perpetual commission for his bed, bacon and eggs, and hot water for shaving in the event that luck did not see fit to warm her hands by his campfire in the Mariposas.

The name of the father of Yellowhammer was given him by the gold hunters in accordance with their popular system of nomenclature. It was not necessary for a citizen to exhibit his baptismal certificate in order to acquire a cognomen. A man's name was his personal property. For convenience in calling him up to the bar and in designating him among other blue-shirted bipeds, a temporary appellation, title, or epithet was conferred upon him by the public. Personal peculiarities formed the source of the majority of such informal baptisms. Many were easily dubbed geographically from the regions from which they confessed to have hailed. Some announced themselves to be "Thompsons," and "Adamses," and the like, with a brazenness and loudness that cast a cloud upon their titles. A few vaingloriously and shamelessly uncovered their proper and indisputable names. This was held to be unduly arrogant, and did not win popularity. One man who said he was Chesterton L. C. Belmont, and proved it by letters, was given till sundown to leave the town. Such names as "Shorty," "Bow-legs," "Texas," "Lazy Bill," "Thirsty Rogers," "Limping Riley," "The Judge," and "California Ed" were in favor. Cherokee derived his title from the fact that he claimed to have lived for a time with that tribe in the Indian Nation.

On the twentieth day of December Baldy, the mail rider, brought Yellowhammer a piece of news.

"What do I see in Albuquerque," said Baldy, to the patrons of the bar, "but Cherokee all embellished and festooned up like the Czar of Turkey, and lavishin' money in bulk. Him and me seen the elephant and the owl, and we had specimens of this seidlitz powder wine; and Cherokee he audits all the bills, C. O. D. His pockets looked like a pool table's after a fifteen-ball run."

"Cherokee must have struck pay ore," remarked California Ed. "Well, he's white. I'm much obliged to him for his success."

"Seems like Cherokee would ramble down to Yellowhammer and see his friends," said another, slightly aggrieved. "But that's the way. Prosperity is the finest cure there is for lost forgetfulness."

"You wait," said Baldy; "I'm comin' to that. Cherokee strikes a three-foot vein up in the Mariposas that assays a trip to Europe to the ton, and he closes it out to a syndicate outfit for a hundred thousand hasty dollars in cash. Then he buys himself a baby sealskin overcoat and a red sleigh, and what do you think he takes it in his head to do next?"

"Chuck-a-luck," said Texas, whose ideas of recreation were the gamester's.

"Come and Kiss Me, Ma Honey," sang Shorty, who carried tintypes in his pocket and wore a red necktie while working on his claim.

"Bought a saloon?" suggested Thirsty Rogers.

"Cherokee took me to a room," continued Baldy, "and showed me. He's got that room full of drums and dolls and skates and bags of candy and jumping-jacks and toy lambs and whistles and such infantile truck. And what do you think he's goin' to do with them inefficacious knick-knacks? Don't surmise none— Cherokee told me. He's goin' to load 'em up in his red sleigh and—wait a minute, don't order no drinks yet—he's goin' to drive down here to Yellow-hammer and give the kids—the kids of this here town—the biggest Christmas tree and the biggest cryin' doll and Little Giant Boys' Tool Chest blowout that was ever seen west of Cape Hatteras."

Two minutes of absolute silence ticked away in the wake of Baldy's words. It was broken by the House, who, happily conceiving the moment to be ripe for extending hospitality, sent a dozen whisky glasses spinning down the bar, with the slower traveling bottle bringing up the rear.

"Didn't you tell him?" asked the miner called Trinidad.

"Well, no," answered Baldy, pensively; "I never exactly seen my way to.

"You see, Cherokee had this Christmas mess already bought and paid for; and he was all flattered up with self-esteem over his idea; and we had in a way flew the flume with that fizzy wine I speak of; so I never let on."

"I cannot refrain from a certain amount of surprise," said the Judge, as he hung his ivory-handled cane on the bar, "that our friend Cherokee should possess such an erroneous conception of—ah—his, as it were, own town."

"Oh, it ain't the eighth wonder of the terrestrial world," said Baldy. "Cherokee's been gone from Yellowhammer over seven months. Lots of things could happen in that time. How's he to know that there ain't a single kid in this town, and so far as emigration is concerned, none expected?"

"Come to think of it," remarked California Ed, "it's funny some ain't drifted in. Town ain't settled enough yet for to bring in the rubber-ring brigade, I reckon."

"To top off this Christmas-tree splurge of Cherokee's," went on Baldy, "he's goin' to give an imitation of Santa Claus. He's got a white wig and whiskers that disfigure him up exactly like the pictures of this William Cullen Longfellow in the books, and a red suit of fur-trimmed outside underwear, and eight-ounce gloves, and a stand-up, lay-down croshayed red cap. Ain't it a shame that a outfit like that can't get a chance to connect with a Annie and Willie prayer layout?"

"When does Cherokee allow to come over with his truck?" inquired Trinidad

"Mornin' before Christmas," said Baldy. "And he wants you folks to have a room fixed up and a tree hauled and ready. And such ladies to assist as can stop breathin' long enough to let it be a surprise for the kids."

The unblessed condition of Yellowhammer had been truly described. The voice of childhood had never gladdened its flimsy structures; the patter of restless little feet had never consecrated the one rugged highway between the two rows of tents and rough buildings. Later they would come. But now Yellowhammer was but a mountain camp, and nowhere in it were the roguish, expectant eyes, opening wide at dawn of the enchanting day; the eager, small hands to reach for Santa's bewildering hoard; the elated, childish voicings of the season's joy, such as the coming good things of the warmhearted Cherokee deserved.

Of women there were five in Yellowhammer. The assayer's wife, the proprietress of the Lucky Strike Hotel, and a laundress whose washtub panned out an ounce of dust a day. These were the permanent feminines; the remaining two were the Spangler Sisters, Misses Fanchon and Erma, of the Transcontinental Comedy Company, then playing in repertoire at the (improvised) Empire Theatre. But of children there were none. Sometimes Miss Fanchon enacted with spirit and address the part of robustious childhood; but between her delineation and the visions of adolescence that the fancy offered as eligible recipients of Cherokee's holiday stores there seemed to be fixed a gulf.

Christmas would come on Thursday. On Tuesday morning Trinidad, instead of going to work, sought the Judge at the Lucky Strike Hotel.

"It'll be a disgrace to Yellowhammer," said Trinidad, "if it throws Cherokee down on his Christmas-tree blowout. You might say that that man made this town. For one, I'm goin' to see what can be done to give Santa Claus a square deal."

"My coöperation," said the Judge, "would be gladly forthcoming. I am indebted to Cherokee for past favors. But, I do not see—I have heretofore regarded the absence of children rather as a luxury—but in this instance—still, I do not see——"

"Look at me," said Trinidad, "and you'll see old Ways and Means with the fur on. I'm goin' to hitch up a team and rustle a load of kids for Cherokee's Santa Claus act, if I have to rob an orphan asylum."

"Eureka!" cried the Judge, enthusiastically.

"No, you didn't," said Trinidad, decidedly. "I found it myself. I learned about that Latin word at school."

"I will accompany you," declared the Judge, waving his cane. "Perhaps such eloquence and gift of language as I may possess will be of benefit in persuading our young friends to lend themselves to our project."

Within an hour Yellowhammer was acquainted with the scheme of Trinidad and the Judge, and approved it. Citizens who knew of families with offspring within a forty-mile radius of Yellowhammer came forward and contributed their information. Trinidad made careful notes of all such, and then hastened to secure a vehicle and team.

The first stop scheduled was at a double loghouse fifteen miles out from Yellowhammer. A man opened the door at Trinidad's hail, and then came down and leaned upon the rickety gate. The doorway was filled with a close mass of youngsters, some ragged, all full of curiosity and health.

"It's this way," explained Trinidad. "We're from Yellowhammer, and we come kidnappin' in a gentle kind of a way. One of our leading citizens is stung with the Santa Claus affliction, and he's due in town to-morrow with half the folderols that's painted red and made in Germany. The youngest kid we got in Yellowhammer packs a forty-five and a safety razor. Consequently we're mighty shy on anybody to say 'Oh' and 'Ah' when we light the candles on the Christmas tree. Now, partner, if you'll loan us a few kids we guarantee to return 'em safe and sound on Christmas Day. And they'll come back loaded down with a good time and Swiss Family Robinsons and cornucopias and red drums and similar testimonials. What do you say?"

"In other words," said the Judge, "we have discovered for the first time in our embryonic but progressive little city the inconveniences of the absence of adolescence. The season of the year having approximately arrived during which it is a custom to bestow frivolous but often appreciated gifts upon the young and tender——"

"I understand," said the parent, packing his pipe with a forefinger. "I guess I needn't detain you gentlemen. Me and the old woman have got seven kids, so to speak; and, runnin' my mind over the bunch, I don't appear to hit upon none that we could spare for you to take over to your doin's. The old woman has got some popcorn candy and rag-dolls hid in the clothes chest, and we allow to give Christmas a little whirl of our own in a insignificant sort of style. No, I couldn't, with any degree of avidity, seem to fall in with the idea of lettin' none of 'em go. Thank you kindly, gentlemen."

Down the slope they drove and up another foothill to the ranch-house of Wiley Wilson. Trinidad recited his appeal and the Judge boomed out his ponderous antiphony. Mrs. Wiley gathered her two rosy-cheeked youngsters close to her skirts and did not smile until she had seen Wiley laugh and shake his head. Again a refusal.

Trinidad and the Judge vainly exhausted more than half their list before twilight set in among the hills. They spent the night at a stage road hostelry, and set out again early the next morning. The wagon had not acquired a single passenger.

"It's creepin' upon my faculties," remarked Trinidad, "that borrowin' kids at Christmas is somethin' like tryin' to steal butter from a man that's got hot pancakes a-comin'."

"It is undoubtedly an indisputable fact," said the Judge, "that the—ah—family ties seem to be more coherent and assertive at that period of the year."

On the day before Christmas they drove thirty miles, making four fruitless halts and appeals. Everywhere they found "kids" at a premium.

The sun was low when the wife of a section boss on a lonely railroad huddled her unavailable progeny behind her and said:

"There's a woman that's just took charge of the railroad eatin' house down at Granite Junction. I hear she's got a little boy. Maybe she might let him go."

Trinidad pulled up his mules at Granite Junction at five o'clock in the afternoon. The train had just departed with its load of fed and appeased passengers.

On the steps of the eating house they found a thin and glowering boy of ten smoking a cigarette. The dining-room had been left in chaos by the peripatetic appetites. A youngish woman reclined, exhausted, in a chair. Her face wore sharp lines of worry. She had once possessed a certain style of beauty that would never wholly leave her and would never wholly return. Trinidad set forth his mission.

"I'd count it a mercy if you'd take Bobby for a while," she said, wearily. "I'm on the go from morning till night, and I don't have time to 'tend to him. He's learning bad habits from the men. It'll be the only chance he'll have to get any Christmas."

The men went outside and conferred with Bobby. Trinidad pictured the glories of the Christmas tree and presents in lively colors.

"And, moreover, my young friend," added the Judge, "Santa Claus himself will personally distribute the offerings that will typify the gifts conveyed by the shepherds of Bethlehem to——"

"Aw, come off," said the boy, squinting his small eyes. "I ain't no kid. There ain't any Santa Claus. It's your folks that buys toys and sneaks 'em in when you're asleep. And they make marks in the soot in the chimney with the tongs to look like Santa's sleigh tracks."

"That might be so," argued Trinidad, "but Christmas trees ain't no fairy tale. This one's goin' to look like the ten-cent store in Albuquerque, all strung up in a redwood. There's tops and drums and Noah's arks and——"

"Oh, rats!" said Bobby, wearily. "I cut them out long ago. I'd like to have a rifle—not a target one—a real one, to shoot wildcats with; but I guess you won't have any of them on your old tree."

"Well, I can't say for sure," said Trinidad, diplomatically; "it might be. You go along with us and see."

The hope thus held out, though faint, won the boy's hesitating consent to go With this solitary beneficiary for Cherokee's holiday bounty, the canvassers spun along the homeward road.

In Yellowhammer the empty storeroom had been transformed into what might have passed as the bower of an Arizona fairy. The ladies had done their work well. At a Christmas tree, covered to the topmost branch with candles, spangles, and toys sufficient for more than a score of children, stood in the centre of the floor. Near sunset anxious eyes had begun to scan the street for the returning team of the child-providers. At noon that day Cherokee had dashed into town with his new sleigh piled high with bundles and boxes and bales of all sizes and shapes. So intent was he upon the arrangements for his altruistic plans that the dearth of childhood did not receive his notice. No one gave away the humiliating state of Yellowhammer, for the efforts of Trinidad and the Judge were expected to supply the deficiency.

When the sun went down Cherokee, with many winks and arch grins on his seasoned face, went into retirement with the bundle containing the Santa Claus raiment and a pack of containing special and undisclosed gifts.

"When the kids are rounded up," he instructed the volunteer arrangement committee, "light up the candles on the tree and set 'em to playin' 'Pussy Wants a Corner' and 'King William.' When they get good and at it, why—old Santa'll slide in the door. I reckon there'll be plenty of gifts to go 'round."

The ladies were flitting about the tree, giving it final touches that were never final. The Spangled Sisters were there in costume as Lady Violet de Vere and Marie, the maid, in their new drama, "The Miner's Bride." The theatre did not open until nine, and they were welcome assistants of the Christmas-tree committee. Every minute heads would pop out the door to look and listen for the approach of Trinidad's team. And now this became an anxious function, for night had fallen and it would soon be necessary to light the candles on the tree, and Cherokee was apt to make an irruption at any time in his Kriss Kringle garb.

At length the wagon of the child "rustlers" rattled down the street to the door. The ladies, with little screams of excitement, flew to the lighting of the candles. The men of Yellowhammer passed in and out restlessly or stood about the room in embarrassed groups.

Trinidad and the Judge, bearing the marks of protracted travel, entered, conducting between them a single impish boy, who stared with sullen, pessimistic eyes at the gaudy tree.

"Where are the other children?" asked the assayer's wife, the acknowledged leader of all social functions.

"Ma'am," said Trinidad with a sigh, "prospectin' for kids at Christmas time is like huntin' in limestone for silver. This parental business is one that I haven't no chance to comprehend. It seems that fathers and mothers are willin' for their offsprings to be drownded, stole, fed on poison oak, and et by catamounts 364 days in the year; but on Christmas Day they insists on enjoyin' the exclusive mortification of their company. This here young biped, ma'am, is all that washes out of our two days' manœuvres."

"Oh, the sweet little boy!" cooed Miss Erma, trailing her De Vere robes to centre of stage.

"Aw, shut up," said Bobby, with a scowl. "Who's a kid? You ain't, you bet."

"Fresh brat!" breathed Miss Erma, beneath her enamelled smile.

"We done the best we could," said Trinidad. "It's tough on Cherokee, but it can't be helped."

Then the door opened and Cherokee entered in the conventional dress of Saint Nick. A white rippling beard and flowing hair covered his face almost to his dark and shining eyes. Over his shoulder he carried a pack.

No one stirred as he came in. Even the Spangler Sisters ceased their coquettish poses and stared curiously at the tall figure. Bobby stood with his hands in his pockets gazing gloomily at the effeminate and childish tree. Cherokee put down his pack and looked wonderingly about the room. Perhaps he fancied that a bevy of eager children were being herded somewhere, to be loosed upon his entrance. He went up to Bobby and extended his red-mittened hand.

"Merry Christmas, little boy," said Cherokee. "Anything on the tree you want they'll get it down for you. Won't you shake hands with Santa Claus?"

"There ain't any Santa Claus," whined the boy. "You've got old false billy goat's whiskers on your face. I ain't no kid. What do I want with dolls and tin horses? The driver said you'd have a rifle, and you haven't. I want to go home."

Trinidad stepped into the breach. He shook Cherokee's hand in warm greeting.

"I'm sorry, Cherokee," he explained. "There never was a kid in Yellowhammer. We tried to rustle a bunch of 'em for your swaree, but this sardine was all we could catch. He's a atheist, and he don't believe in Santa Claus. It's a shame for you to be out all this truck. But me and the Judge was sure we could round up a wagonful of candidates for your gimcracks."

"That's all right," said Cherokee, gravely. "The expense don't amount to nothin' worth mentionin'. We can dump the stuff down a shaft or throw it away. I don't know what I was thinkin' about; but it never occurred to my cogitations that there wasn't any kids in Yellowhammer."

Meanwhile the company had relaxed into a hollow but praiseworthy imitation of a pleasure gathering.

Bobby had retreated to a distant chair, and was coldly regarding the scene with ennui plastered thick upon him. Cherokee, lingering with his original idea, went over and sat beside him.

"Where do you live, little boy?" he asked, respectfully.

"Granite Junction," said Bobby without emphasis.

The room was warm. Cherokee took off his cap, and then removed his beard and wig.

"Say!" exclaimed Bobby, with a show of interest, "I know your mug, all right."

"Did you ever see me before?" asked Cherokee.

"I don't know; but I've seen your picture lots of times."

"Where?"

The boy hesitated. "On the bureau at home," he answered.

"Let's have your name, if you please, buddy."

"Robert Lumsden. The picture belongs to my mother. She puts it under her pillow of nights. And once I saw her kiss it. I wouldn't. But women are that way."

Cherokee rose and beckoned to Trinidad.

"Keep this boy by you till I come back," he said. "I'm going to shed these Christmas duds, and hitch up my sleigh. I'm goin' to take this kid home."

"Well, infidel," said Trinidad, taking Cherokee's vacant chair, "and so you are too superannuated and effete to yearn for such mockeries as candy and toys, it seems."

"I don't like you," said Bobby, with acrimony. "You said there would be a rifle. A fellow can't even smoke. I wish I was at home."

Cherokee drove his sleigh to the door, and they lifted Bobby in beside him. The team of fine horses sprang away prancingly over the hard snow. Cherokee had on his $500 overcoat of baby sealskin. The laprobe that he drew about them was as warm as velvet.

Bobby slipped a cigarette from his pocket and was trying to snap a match.

"Throw that cigarette away," said Cherokee, in a quiet but new voice.

Bobby hesitated, and then dropped the cylinder overboard.

"Throw the box, too," commanded the new voice.

More reluctantly the boy obeyed.

"Say," said Bobby, presently, "I like you. I don't know why. Nobody never made me do anything I didn't want to do before."

"Tell me, kid," said Cherokee, not using his new voice, "are you sure your mother kissed that picture that looks like me?"

"Dead sure. I seen her do it."

"Didn't you remark somethin' a while ago about wanting a rifle?"

"You bet I did. Will you get me one?"

"To-morrow—silver-mounted."

Cherokee took out his watch.

"Half-past nine. We'll hit the Junction plumb on time with Christmas Day. Are you cold? Sit closer, son."

A CHAPARRAL PRINCE

NINE o'clock at last, and the drudging toil of the day was ended. Lena climbed to her room in the third half-story of the Quarrymen's Hotel. Since daylight she had slaved, doing the work of a full-grown woman, scrubbing the floors, washing the heavy ironstone plates and cups, making the beds, and supplying the insatiate demands for wood and water in that turbulent and depressing hostelry.

The din of the day's quarrying was over—the blasting and drilling, the creaking of the great cranes, the shouts of the foremen, the backing and shifting of the flat-cars hauling the heavy blocks of limestone. Down in the hotel office three or four of the laborers were growling and swearing over a belated game of checkers. Heavy odors of stewed meat, hot grease, and cheap coffee hung like a depressing fog about the house.

Lena lit the stump of a candle and sat limply upon her wooden chair. She was eleven years old, thin and ill-nourished. Her back and limbs were sore and aching. But the ache in her heart made the biggest trouble. The last straw had been added to the burden upon her small shoulders. They had taken away Grimm. Always at night, however tired she might be, she had turned to Grimm for comfort and hope. Each time had Grimm whispered to her that the prince or the fairy would come and deliver her out of the wicked enchantment. Every night she had taken fresh courage and strength from Grimm.

To whatever tale she read she found an analogy in her own condition. The woodcutter's lost child, the unhappy goose girl, the persecuted stepdaughter, the little maiden imprisoned in the witch's hut—all these were but transparent disguises for Lena, the overworked kitchenmaid in the Quarrymen's Hotel. And always when the extremity was direst came the good fairy or the gallant prince to the rescue.

So, here in the ogre's castle, enslaved by a wicked spell, Lena had leaned upon Grimm and waited, longing for the powers of goodness to prevail. But on the day before Mrs. Maloney had found the book in her room and had carried it away, declaring sharply that it would not do for servants to read at night; they lost sleep and did not work briskly the next day. Can one only eleven years old, living away from one's mamma, and never having any time to play, live entirely deprived of Grimm? Just try it once and you will see what a difficult thing it is.

Lena's home was in Texas, away up among the little mountains on the Pedernales River, in a little town called Fredericksburg. They are all German people who live in Fredericksburg. Of evenings they sit at little tables along the sidewalk and drink beer and play pinochle and scat. They are very thrifty people.

Thriftiest among them was Peter Hildesmuller, Lena's father. And that is why Lena was sent to work in the hotel at the quarries, thirty miles away. She earned three dollars every week there, and Peter added her wages to his well-guarded store. Peter had an ambition to become as rich as his neighbor, Hugo Heffelbauer, who smoked a meerschaum pipe three feet long and had wiener schnitzel and hassenpfeffer for dinner every day in the week. Asd now Lena was quite old enough to work and assist in the accumulation of riches. But conjecture, if you can, what it means to be sentenced at eleven years of age from a home in the pleasant little Rhine village to hard labor in the ogre's castle, where you must fly to serve the ogres, while they devour cattle and sheep, growling fiercely as they stamp white limestone dust from their great shoes for you to sweep and scour with your weak, aching fingers. And then —to have Grimm taken away from you!

Lena raised the lid of an old empty case that had once contained canned corn and got out a sheet of paper and a piece of pencil. She was going to write a letter to her mamma. Tommy Ryan was going to post it for her at Ballinger's. Tommy was seventeen, worked in the quarries, went home to Ballinger's every night, and was now waiting in the shadows under Lena's window for her to throw the letter out to him. That was the only way she could send a letter to Fredericksburg. Mrs. Maloney did not like for her to write letters.

The stump of candle was burning low, so Lena hastily bit the wood from around the lead of her pencil and began. This is the letter she wrote:

DEAREST MAMMA:—I want so much to see you. And Gretel and Claus and Heinrich and little Adolf. I am so tired. I want to see you. To-day I was slapped by Mrs. Maloney and had no supper. I could not bring in enough wood, for my hand hurt. She took my book yesterday. I mean "Grimms's Fairy Tales," which Uncle Leo gave me. It did not hurt any one for me to read the book. I try to work as well as I can, but there is so much to do. I read only a little bit every night. Dear mamma, I shall tell you what I am going to do. Unless you send for me to-morrow to bring me home I shall go to a deep place I know in the river and drown. It is wicked to drown, I suppose, but I wanted to see you, and there is no one else. I am very tired, and Tommy is waiting for the letter. You will excuse me, mamma, if I do it.

Your respectful and loving daughter,

LENA.

Tommy was still waiting faithfully when the letter was concluded, and when Lena dropped it out she saw him pick it up and start up the steep hillside. Without undressing she blew out the candle and curled herself upon the mattress on the floor.

At 10:30 o'clock old man Ballinger came out of his house in his stocking feet and leaned over the gate, smoking his pipe. He looked down the big road, white in the moonshine, and rubbed one ankle with the toe of his other foot. It was time for the Fredericksburg mail to come pattering up the road.

Old man Ballinger had waited only a few minutes when he heard the lively hoofbeats of Fritz's team of little black mules, and very soon afterward his covered spring wagon stood in front of the gate. Fritz's big spectacles flashed in the moonlight and his tremendous voice shouted a greeting to the postmaster of Ballinger's. The mail-carrier jumped out and took the bridles from the mules, for he always fed them oats at Ballinger's.

While the mules were eating from their feed bags old man Ballinger brought out the mail sack and threw it into the wagon.

Fritz Bergmann was a man of three sentiments—or to be more accurate—four, the pair of mules deserving to be reckoned individually. Those mules were the chief interest and joy of his existence. Next came the Emperor of Germany and Lena Hildesmuller.

"Tell me," said Fritz, when he was ready to start, "contains the sacks a letter to Frau Hildesmuller from the little Lena at the quarries? One came in the last mail to say that she is a little sick, already. Her mamma is very anxious to hear again."

"Yes," said old man Ballinger, "thar's a letter for Mrs. Helterskelter, or some sich name. Tommy Ryan brung it over when he come. Her little gal workin' over thar, you say?"

"In the hotel," shouted Fritz, as he gathered up the lines; "eleven years old and not bigger as a frankfurter. The close-fist of a Peter Hildesmuller!—some day shall I with a big club pound that man's dummkopf—all in and out the town. Perhaps in this letter Lena will say that she is yet feeling better. So, her mamma will be glad. Auf wiedersehen, Herr Ballinger—your feets will take cold out in the night air."

"So long, Fritzy," said old man Ballinger. "You got a nice cool night for your drive."

Up the road went the little black mules at their steady trot, while Fritz thundered at them occasional words of endearment and cheer.

These fancies occupied the mind of the mailcarrier until he reached the big

post-oak forest, eight miles from Ballinger's. Here his ruminations were scattered by the sudden flash and report of pistols and a whooping as if from a whole
tribe of Indians. A band of galloping centaurs closed in around the mail
wagon. One of them leaned over the front wheel, covered the driver with his
revolver, and ordered him to stop. Others caught at the bridles of Donder and
Blitzen.

"Donnerwetter!" shouted Fritz, with all his tremendous voice—"wass ist?
Release your hands from dose mules. Ve vas der United States mail!"

"Hurry up, Dutch!" drawled a melancholy voice. "Don't you know when
you're in a stick-up? Reverse your mules and climb out of the cart."

It is due to the breadth of Hondo Bill's demerit and the largeness of his
achievements to state that the holding up of the Fredericksburg mail was not
perpetrated by way of an exploit. As the lion while in the pursuit of prey
commensurate to his prowess might set a frivolous foot upon a casual rabbit in
his path, so Hondo Bill and his gang had swooped sportively upon the pacific
transport of Meinherr Fritz.

The real work of their sinister night ride was over. Fritz and his mail bag and
his mules came as a gentle relaxation, grateful after the arduous duties of their
profession. Twenty miles to the southeast stood a train with a killed engine,
hysterical passengers, and a looted express and mail car. That represented the
serious occupation of Hondo Bill and his gang. With a fairly rich prize of
currency and silver the robbers were making a wide detour to the west through
the less populous country, intending to seek safety in Mexico by means of some
fordable spot on the Rio Grande. The booty from the train had melted the
desperate bushrangers to jovial and happy skylarkers.

Trembling with outraged dignity and no little personal apprehension, Fritz
climbed out to the road after replacing his suddenly removed spectacles. The
band had dismounted and were singing, capering, and whooping, thus expressing
their satisfied delight in the life of a jolly outlaw. Rattlesnake Rogers, who
stood at the heads of the mules, jerked a little too vigorously at the rein of the
tender-mouthed Donder, who reared and emitted a loud, protesting snort of
pain. Instantly Fritz, with a scream of anger, flew at the bulky Rogers and
began assiduously to pommel that surprised free-booter with his fists.

"Villain!" shouted Fritz, "dog, bigstiff! Dot mule he has a soreness by his
mouth. I vill knock off your shoulders mit your head—robbermans!"

"Yi-yi!" howled Rattlesnake, roaring with laughter and ducking his head,
"somebody git this here sourkrout off'n me!"

One of the band jerked Fritz back by the coat-tail, and the woods rang with
Rattlesnake's vociferous comments.

"The dog-goned little wienerwurst," he yelled, amiably. "He's not so much
of a skunk, for a Dutchman. Took up for his animile plum quick, didn't he?
I like to see a man like his hoss, even if it is a mule. The dad-blamed little
Limburger he went for me, didn't he! Whoa, now, muley—I ain't a-goin' to hurt
your mouth agin any more."

Perhaps the mail would not have been tampered with had not Ben Moody, the
lieutenant, possessed certain wisdom that seemed to promise more spoils.

"Say, Cap," he said, addressing Hondo Bill, "there's liable to be good pickings
in these mail sacks. I've done some hoss tradin' with these Dutchmen around
Fredericksburg, and I know the style of the varmints. There's big money goes
through the mails to that town. Them Dutch risk a thousand dollars sent
wrapped in a piece of paper before they'd pay the banks to handle the money."

Hondo Bill, six feet two, gentle of voice and impulsive in action, was dragging
the sacks from the rear of the wagon before Moody had finished his speech. A
knife shone in his hand, and they heard the ripping sound as it bit through the
tough canvas. The outlaws crowded around and began tearing open letters and

packages, enlivening their labors by swearing affably at the writers, who seemed to have conspired to confute the prediction of Ben Moody. Not a dollar was found in the Fredericksburg mail.

"You ought to be ashamed of yourself," said Hondo Bill to the mail-carrier in solemn tones, "to be packing around such a lot of old, trashy paper as this. What d'you mean by it, anyhow? Where do you Dutchers keep your money at?"

The Ballinger mail sack opened like a cocoon under Hondo's knife. It contained but a handful of mail. Fritz had been fuming with terror and excitement until this sack was reached. He now remembered Lena's letter. He addressed the leader of the band, asking him that that particular missive be spared.

"Much obliged, Dutch," he said to the disturbed carrier. "I guess that's the letter we want. Got spondulicks in it, ain't it? Here she is. Make a light, boys."

Hondo found and tore open the letter to Mrs. Hildesmuller. The others stood about, lighting twisted-up letters one from another. Hondo gazed with mute disapproval at the single sheet of paper covered with the angular German script.

"Whatever is this you've humbugged us with, Dutchy? You call this here a valuable letter? That's a mighty low-down trick to play on your friends what come along to help you distribute your mail."

"That's Chiny writin'," said Sandy Grundy, peering over Hondo's shoulder.

"You're off your kazip," declared another of the gang, an effective youth, covered with silk handkerchiefs and nickel plating. "That's shorthand. I seen 'em do it once in court."

"Ach, no, no, no—dot is German," said Fritz. "It is no more as a little girl writing a letter to her mamma. One poor little girl, sick and vorking hard avay from home. Ach! it is a shame. Good Mr. Robberman, you vill please let me have dot letter?"

"What the devil do you take us for, old Pretzels?" said Hondo with sudden and surprising severity. "You ain't presumin' to insinuate that we gents ain't possessed of sufficient politeness for to take an interest in the miss's health, are you? Now, you go on, and you read that scratchin' out loud and in plain United States language to this here company of educated society."

Hondo twirled his six-shooter by its trigger guard and stood towering above the little German, who at once began to read the letter, translating the simple words into English. The gang of rovers stood in absolute silence, listening intently.

"How old is that kid?" asked Hondo when the letter was done.

"Eleven," said Fritz.

"And where is she at?"

"At dose rock quarries—working. Ach, mein Gott—little Lena, she speak of drowning. I do not know if she vill do it, but if she shall I schwear I vill dot Peter Hildesmuller shoot mit a gun."

"You Dutchers," said Hondo Bill, his voice swelling with fine contempt, "make me plenty tired. Hirin' out your kids to work when they ought to be playin' dolls in the sand. You're a hell of a sect of people. I reckon we'll fix your clock for a while just to show what we think of your old cheesy nation. Here, boys!"

Hondo Bill parleyed aside briefly with his band, and then they seized Fritz and conveyed him off the road to one side. Here they bound him fast to a tree with a couple of lariats. His team they tied to another tree near by.

"We ain't going to hurt you bad," said Hondo, reassuringly. "'Twon't hurt you to be tied up for a while. We will now pass you the time of day, as it is up to us to depart. Ausgespielt—nixcumrous, Dutchy. Don't get any more impatience."

Fritz heard a great squeaking of saddles as the men mounted their horses.

Then a loud yell and a great clatter of hoofs as they galloped pell-mell back along the Fredericksburg road.

For more than two hours Fritz sat against his tree, tightly but not painfully bound. Then from the reaction after his exciting adventure he sank into slumber. How long he slept he knew not, but he was at last awakened by a rough shake. Hands were untying his ropes. He was lifted to his feet, dazed, confused in mind, and weary of body. Rubbing his eyes, he looked and saw that he was again in the midst of the same band of terrible bandits. They shoved him up to the seat of his wagon and placed the lines in his hands.

"Hit it out for home, Dutch," said Hondo Bill's voice, commandingly. "You've given us lots of trouble and we're pleased to see the back of your neck. Spiel! Zwei bier! Vamoose!"

Hondo reached out and gave Blitzen a smart cut with his quirt.

The little mules sprang ahead, glad to be moving again. Fritz urged them along, himself dizzy and muddled over his fearful adventure.

According to schedule time, he should have reached Fredericksburg at day-light. As it was, he drove down the long street of the town at eleven o'clock A. M. He had to pass Peter Hildesmuller's house on his way to the post-office. He stopped his team at the gate and called. But Frau Hildesmuller was watching for him. Out rushed the whole family of Hildesmullers.

Frau Hildesmuller, fat and flushed, inquired if he had a letter from Lena, and then Fritz raised his voice and told the tale of his adventure. He told the contents of the letter that the robber had made him read, and then Frau Hildesmuller broke into wild weeping. Her little Lena drown herself! Why had they sent her from home? What could be done? Perhaps it would be too late by the time they could send for her now. Peter Hildesmuller dropped his meerschaum on the walk and it shivered into pieces.

"Woman!" he roared at his wife, "why did you let that child go away? It is your fault if she comes home to us no more."

Every one knew that it was Peter Hildesmuller's fault, so they paid no attention to his words.

A moment afterward a strange, faint voice was heard to call: "Mamma!" Frau Hildesmuller at first thought it was Lena's spirit calling, and then she rushed to the rear of Fritz's covered wagon, and, with a loud shriek of joy, caught up Lena herself, covering her pale little face with kisses and smothering her with hugs. Lena's eyes were heavy with the deep slumber of exhaustion, but she smiled and lay close to the one she had longed to see. There among the mail sacks, covered in a nest of strange blankets and comforters, she had lain asleep until wakened by the voices around her.

Fritz stared at her with eyes that bulged behind his spectacles.

"Gott in Himmel!" he shouted. "How did you get in that wagon? Am I going crazy as well as to be murdered and hanged by robbers this day?"

"You brought her to us, Fritz," cried Frau Hildesmuller. "How can we ever thank you enough?"

"Tell mamma how you came in Fritz's wagon," said Frau Hildesmuller.

"I don't know," said Lena. "But I know how I got away from the hotel. The Prince brought me."

"By the Emperor's crown!" shouted Fritz, "we are all going crazy."

"I always knew he would come," said Lena, sitting down on her bundle of bed-clothes on the sidewalk. "Last night he came with his armed knights and captured the ogre's castle. They broke the dishes and kicked down the doors. They pitched Mr. Maloney into a barrel of rain water and threw flour all over Mrs. Maloney. The workmen in the hotel jumped out of the windows and ran into the woods when the knights began firing their guns. They wakened me up and I peeped down the stair. And then the Prince came up and wrapped me in the bedclothes and carried me out. He was so tall and strong and fine. His face was as rough as a scrubbing brush, and he talked soft and kind and smelled of schnapps. He took me on his horse before him and we rode away among the knights. He held me close and I went to sleep that way, and didn't wake up till I got home."

"Rubbish!" cried Fritz Bergmann. "Fairy tales! How did you come from the quarries to my wagon?"

"The Prince brought me," said Lena, confidently.

And to this day the good people of Fredericksburg haven't been able to make her give any other explanation.

THE REFORMATION OF CALLIOPE

CALLIOPE CATESBY was in his humors again. Ennui was upon him. This goodly promontory, the earth—particularly that portion of it known as Quicksand—was to him no more than a pestilent congregation of vapors. Overtaken by the megrims, the philosopher may seek relief in soliloquy; my lady find solace in tears; the flaccid Easterner scold at the millinery bills of his women folk. Such recourse was insufficient to the denizens of Quicksand. Calliope, especially, was wont to express his ennui according to his lights.

Over night Calliope had hung out signals of approaching low spirits. He had kicked his own dog on the porch of the Occidental Hotel, and refused to apologize. He had become capricious and fault-finding in conversation. While strolling about he reached often for twigs of mesquite and chewed the leaves fiercely. That was always an ominous act. Another symptom alarming to those who were familiar with the different stages of his doldrums was his increasing politeness and a tendency to use formal phrases. A husky softness succeeded the usual penetrating drawl in his tones. A dangerous courtesy marked his manners. Later, his smile became crooked, the left side of his mouth slanting upward, and Quicksand got ready to stand from under.

At this stage Calliope generally began to drink. Finally, about midnight, he was seen going homeward, saluting those whom he met with exaggerated but inoffensive courtesy. Not yet was Calliope's melancholy at the danger point. He would seat himself at the window of the room he occupied over Silvester's tonsorial parlors and there chant lugubrious and tuneless ballads until morning, accompanying the noises by appropriate maltreatment of a jingling guitar. More magnanimous than Nero, he would thus give musical warning of the forthcoming municipal upheaval that Quicksand was scheduled to endure.

A quiet, amiable man was Calliope Catesby at other times—quiet to indolence, and amiable to worthlessness. At best he was a loafer and a nuisance; at worst he was the Terror of Quicksand. His ostensible occupation was something subordinate in the real estate line; he drove the beguiled Easterner in buckboards out to look over lots and ranch property. Originally he came from one of the Gulf States, his lank six feeet, slurring rhythm of speech, and sectional idioms giving evidence of his birthplace.

And yet, after taking on Western adjustments, this languid pine-box whittler, cracker barrel hugger, shady corner lounger of the cotton fields and sumac hills of the South became famed as a bad man among men who had made a life-long study of the art of truculence.

At nine the next morning Calliope was fit. Inspired by his own barbarous melodies and the contents of his jug, he was ready primed to gather fresh laurels from the diffident brow of Quicksand. Encircled and criss-crossed with cartridge belts, abundantly garnished with revolvers, and copiously drunk, he poured forth into Quicksand's main street. Too chivalrous to surprise and capture a town by silent sortie, he paused at the nearest corner and emitted his slogan—that fearful, brassy yell, so reminiscent of the steam piano, that had gained for him the classic appellation that had superseded his own baptismal name. Following close upon his vociferation came three shots from his forty-five by way of limbering up the guns and testing his aim. A yellow dog, the personal property of Colonel Swazey, the proprietor of the Occidental, fell feet upward in the dust with one farewell yelp. A Mexican who was crossing the street from the Blue Front grocery, carrying in his hand a bottle of kerosene, was stimulated to a sudden and admirable burst of speed, still grasping the neck of the shattered bottle. The new gilt weathercock on Judge Riley's lemon and ultramarine two-story residence shivered, flapped, and hung by a splinter, the sport of the wanton breezes.

The artillery was in trim. Calliope's hand was steady. The high, calm ecstasy of habitual battle was upon him, though slightly embittered by the sadness of Alexander in that his conquests were limited to the small world of Quicksand.

Down the street went Calliope, shooting right and left. Glass fell like hail; dogs vamosed; chickens flew, squawking; feminine voices shrieked concernedly to youngsters at large. The din was perforated at intervals by the *staccato* of the Terror's guns, and was drowned periodically by the brazen screech that Quicksand knew so well. The occasion of Calliope's low spirits were legal holidays in Quicksand. All along the main street in advance of his coming clerks were putting up shutters and closing doors. Business would languish for a space. The right of way was Calliope's, and as he advanced, observing the dearth of opposition and the few opportunities for distraction, his ennui perceptibly increased.

But some four squares farther down lively preparations were being made to minister to Mr. Catesby's love for interchange of compliments and repartee. On the previous night numerous messengers had hastened to advise Buck Patterson, the city marshal, of Calliope's impending eruption. The patience of that official, often strained in extending leniency toward the disturber's misdeeds, had been overtaxed. In Quicksand some indulgence was accorded the natural ebullition of human nature. Providing that the lives of the more useful citizens were not recklessly squandered, or too much property needlessly laid waste, the community sentiment was against a too strict enforcement of the law. But Calliope had raised the limit. His outbursts had been too frequent and too violent to come within the classification of a normal and sanitary relaxation of spirit.

Buck Patterson had been expecting and awaiting in his little ten-by-twelve frame office that preliminary yell announcing that Calliope was feeling blue. When the signal came the City Marshal rose to his feet and buckled on his guns. Two deputy sheriffs and three citizens who had proven the edible qualities of fire also stood up, ready to bandy with Calliope's leaden jocularities.

"Gather that fellow in," said Buck Patterson, setting for the lines of the campaign. Don't have no talk, but shoot as soon as you can get a show. Keep behind cover and bring him down. He's a nogood 'un. It's up to Calliope to turn up his toes this time, I reckon. Go to him all spraddled out, boys. And don't git too reckless, for what Calliope shoots at he hits."

Buck Patterson, tall, muscular, and solemn-faced, with his bright "City Marshal" badge shining on the breast of his blue flannel shirt, gave his posse directions for the onslaught upon Calliope. The plan was to accomplish the downfall of the Quicksand Terror without loss to the attaching party, if possible.

The splenetic Calliope, unconscious of retributive plots, was steaming down the channel, cannonading on either side, when he suddenly became aware of breakers ahead. The City Marshal and one of the deputies rose up behind some dry-goods boxes half a square to the front and opened fire. At the same time the rest of the posse, divided, shelled him from two side streets up which they were cautiously manœuvring from a well-executed detour.

The first volley broke the lock of one of Calliope's guns, cut a neat under-bit in his right ear, and exploded a cartridge in his crossbelt, scorching his ribs as it burst. Feeling braced up by this unexpected tonic to his spiritual depression, Calliope executed a fortissimo note from his upper registers, and returned the fire like an echo. The upholders of the law dodged at his flash, but a trifle too late to save one of the deputies a bullet just above the elbow, and the marshall a bleeding cheek from a splinter that a ball tore from a box he had ducked behind.

And now Calliope met the enemy's tactics in kind. Choosing with a rapid eye the street from which the weakest and least accurate fire had come, he invaded it at a double-quick, abandoning the unprotected middle of the street. With rare cunning the opposing force in that direction—one of the deputies and two of the valorous volunteers—waited, concealed by beer barrels, until Calliope had passed their retreat, and then peppered him from the rear. In another moment they were reinforced by the marshal and his other men, and then Calliope felt that in order to successfully prolong the delights of the controversy he must find some means of reducing the great odds against him. His eye fell upon a structure that seemed to hold out this promise, providing he could reach it.

Not far away was the little railroad station, its building a strong box house, ten by twenty feet, resting upon a platform four feet above ground. Windows were in each of its walls. Something like a fort it might become to a man thus sorely pressed by superior numbers.

Calliope made a bold and rapid spurt for it, the marshal's crowd "smoking" him as he ran. He reached the haven in safety, the station agent leaving the building by a window, like a flying squirrel, as the garrison entered the door.

Patterson and his supporters halted under protection of a pile of lumber and held consultations. In the station was an unterrified desperado who was an excellent shot and carried an abundance of ammunition. For thirty yards on each side of the besieged was a stretch of bare, open ground. It was a sure thing that the man who attempted to enter that unprotected area would be stopped by one of Calliope's bullets.

The City Marshall was resolved. He had decided that Calliope Catesby should no more wake the echoes of Quicksand with his strident whoop. He had so announced. Officially and personally he felt imperatively bound to put the soft pedal on that instrument of discord. It played bad tunes.

Standing near was a hand truck used in the manipulation of small freight. It stood by a shed full of sacked wool, a consignment from one of the sheep ranches. On this truck the marshal and his men piled three heavy sacks of wool. Stooping low, Buck Patterson started for Calliope's fort, slowly pushing this loaded truck before him for protection. The posse, scattering broadly, stood ready to nip the besieged in case he should show himself in an effort to repel the juggernaut of justice that was creeping upon him. Only once did Calliope make demonstration. He fired from a window and some tufts of wool spurted from the marshal's trustworthy bulwark. The return shots from the posse pattered against the window frame of the fort. No loss resulted on either side.

The marshal was too deeply engrossed in steering his protected battleship to be aware of the approach of the morning train until he was within a few feet of the platform. The train was coming up on the other side of it. It stopped only one minute at Quicksand. What an opportunity it would offer to Calliope! He had only to step out the other door, mount the train, and away.

Abandoning his breastworks, Buck, with his gun ready, dashed up the steps and into the room, driving open the closed door with one heave of his weighty shoulder. The members of the posse heard one shot fired inside, and then there was silence.

At length the wounded man opened his eyes. After a blank space he again could see and hear and feel and think. Turning his eyes about, he found himself lying on a wooden bench. A tall man with a perplexed countenance, wearing a big badge with "City Marshal" engraved upon it, stood over him. A little old woman in black, with a wrinkled face and sparkling black eyes was holding a wet handkerchief against one of his temples. He was trying to get these facts fixed in his mind and connected with past events, when the old woman began to talk.

"There now, great, big, strong man! That bullet never tetched ye! Jest skeeted along the side of your head and sort of paralyzed ye for a spell. I've heerd of sech things afore; con-cussion is what they names it. Abel Wadkins used to kill squirrels that way—barkin' em, Abe called it. You jest been barked, sir, and you'll be all right in a little bit. Feel lots better already, don't ye! You just lay still a while longer and let me bathe your head. You don't know me, I reckon, and 'tain't surprisin' that you shouldn't. I come in on that train from Alabama to see my son. Big son, ain't he? Lands! you wouldn't hardly think he'd ever been a baby, would ye? This is my son, sir."

Half turning, the old woman looked up at the standing man, her worn face lighting with a proud and wonderful smile. She reached out one veined and calloused hand and took one of her son's. Then smiling cheerily down at the prostrate man, she continued to dip the handkerchief in the waiting-room tin washbasin and gently apply it to his temple. She had the benevolent garrulity of old age.

"I ain't seen my son before," she continued, "in eight years. One of my nephews, Elkanah Price, he's a conductor on one of them railroads, and he got me a pass to come out here. I can stay a whole week on it, and then it'll take me back again. Jest think, now, that little boy of mine has got to be a officer—a city marshal of a whole town! That's something like a constable, ain't it? I never knowed he was a officer; he didn't say nothin' about it in his letters. I reckon he thought his old mother'd be skeered about the danger he was in. But, laws! I never was much of a hand to git skeered. 'Tain't no use. I heard them guns a-shootin' while I was gittin' off them cars, and I see smoke a-comin' out of the depot, but I jest walked right along. Then I see son's face lookin' out through the window. I knowed him at oncet. He met me at the door, and squeezed me 'most to death. And there you was, sir, a-lyin' there jest like you was dead, and I 'lowed we'd see what might be done to help sot you up."

"I think I'll sit up now," said the concussion patient. "I'm feeling pretty fair by this time."

He sat, somewhat weakly yet, leaning against the wall. He was a rugged man, big-boned and straight. His eyes, steady and keen, seemed to linger upon the face of the man standing so still above him. His look wandered often from the face he studied to the marshal's badge upon the other's breast.

"Yes, yes, you'll be all right," said the old woman, patting his arm, "if you don't get to cuttin' up agin, and havin' folks shootin' at you. Son told me about you, sir, while you was layin' senseless on the floor. Don't you take it as meddle-some fer an old woman with a son as big as you to talk about it. And you mustn't hold no grudge ag'in' my son for havin' to shoot at ye. A officer has got to take up for the law—it's his duty—and them that acts bad and lives wrong has to suffer. Don't blame my son any, sir—'tain't his fault. He's al-ways been a good boy—good when he was growin' up, and kind and 'bedient and well-behaved. Won't you let me advise you, sir, not to do so no more? Be a good man, and leave liquor alone and live peaceably and godly. Keep away from bad company and work honest and sleep sweet."

The black-mittened hand of the old pleader gently touched the breast of the man she addressed. Very earnest and candid her old, worn face looked. In her rusty black dress and antique bonnet she sat, near the close of a long life, and epitomized the experience of the world. Still the man to whom she spoke gazed above her head, contemplating the silent son of the old mother.

"What does the marshal say?" he asked. "Does he believe the advice is good? Suppose the marshal speaks up and says if the talk's all right?"

The tall man moved uneasily. He fingered the badge on his breast for a mo-ment, and then he put an arm around the old woman and drew her close to him. She smiled the unchanging mother smile of three-score years, and patted his big brown hand with her crooked, mittened fingers while her son spake.

"I say this," he said, looking squarely into the eyes of the other man, "that if I was in your place I'd follow it. If I was a drunken, desp'rate character, without shame or hope, I'd follow it. If I was in your place and you was in mine I'd say: 'Marshal, I'm willin' to swear if you'll give me the chance I'll quit the racket. I'll drop the tanglefoot and the gun play, and won't play hoss no more. I'll be a good citizen and go to work and quit my foolishness. So help me God!' That's what I'd say to you if you was marshal and I was in your place."

"Hear my son talkin'," said the old woman, softly. "Hear him, sir. You promise to be good and he won't do you no harm. Forty-one year ago his heart first beat ag'in' mine, and it's beat true ever since."

The other man rose to his feet, trying his limbs and stretching his muscles.

"Then," said he, "if you was in my place and said that, and I was marshal, I'd say: 'Go free, and do your best to keep your promise.'"

"Lawsy!" exclaimed the old woman, in a sudden flutter, "ef I didn't clear forget that trunk of mine! I see a man settin' it on the platform jest as I seen son's face in the window, and it went plum out of my head. There's eight jars of home-made quince jam in that trunk that I made myself. I wouldn't have nothin' happen to them jars for a red apple."

Away to the door she trotted, spry and anxious, and then Calliope Catesby spoke out to Buck Patterson:

"I just couldn't help it, Buck. I seen her through the window a-comin' in. She had never heard a word 'bout my tough ways. I didn't have the nerve to let her know I was a worthless cuss bein' hunted down by the community. There you was lyin' where my shot laid you, like you was dead. The idea struck me sudden, and I just took your badge off and fastened it onto myself, and I fastened my reputation onto you. I told her I was the marshal and you was a holy terror. You can take your badge back now, Buck."

With shaking fingers Calliope began to unfasten the disc of metal from his shirt.

"Easy there!" said Buck Patterson. "You keep that badge right where it is, Calliope Catesby. Don't you dare to take it off till the day your mother leaves this town. You'll be city marshal of Quicksand as long as she's here to know it. After I stir around town a bit and put 'em on I'll guarantee that nobody won't give the thing away to her. And say, you leather-headed, rip-roarin', low-down son of a locoed cyclone, you follow that advice she gave me! I'm goin' to take some of it myself, too."

"Buck," said Calliope, feelingly, "ef I don't I hope I may——"

"Shut up," said Buck. "She's a-comin' back."

THE GENTLE GRAFTER

THE GENTLE GRAFTER

THE OCTOPUS MAROONED

"A TRUST is its weakest point," said Jeff Peters.

"That," said I, "sounds like one of those unintelligible remarks such as, 'Why is a policeman?'"

"It is not," said Jeff. "There are no relations between a trust and a policeman. My remark was an epitogram—an axis—a kind of mulct'em in parvo. What it means is that a trust is like an egg, and it is not like an egg. If you want to break an egg you have to do it from the outside. The only way to break up a trust is from the inside. Keep sitting on it until it hatches. Look at the brood of young colleges and libraries that's chirping and peeping all over the country. Yes, sir, every trust bears in its own bosom the seeds of its destruction like a rooster that crows near a Georgia colored Methodist camp meeting, or a Republican announcing himself a candidate for governor of Texas."

I asked Jeff, jestingly, if he had ever, during his checkered, plaided, mottled, pied and dappled career, conducted an enterprise of the class to which the word "trust" had been applied. Somewhat to my surprise he acknowledged the corner.

"Once," said he. "And the state seal of New Jersey never bit into a charter that opened up a solider and safer piece of legitimate octopusing. We had everything in our favor—wind, water, police, nerve, and a clean monopoly of an article indispensable to the public. There wasn't a trust buster on the globe that could have found a weak spot in our scheme. It made Rockefeller's little kerosene speculation look like a bucket shop. But we lost out."

"Some unforeseen opposition came up, I suppose," I said.

"No, sir, it was just as I said. We were self-curbed. It was a case of auto-suppression. There was a rift within the loot, as Albert Tennyson says.

"You remember I told you that me and Andy Tucker was partners for some years. That man was the most talented conniver at stratagems I ever saw. Whenever he saw a dollar in another man's hand he took it as a personal grudge, if he couldn't take it any other way. Andy was educated, too, besides having a lot of useful information. He had acquired a big amount of experience out of books, and could talk for hours on any subject connected with ideas and discourse. He had been in every line of graft from lecturing on Palestine with a lot of magic lantern pictures of the annual Custom-made Clothiers' Association convention at Atlantic City to flooding Connecticut with bogus wood alcohol distilled from nutmegs.

"One Spring me and Andy had been over in Mexico on a flying trip during which a Philadelphia capitalist had paid us $2,500 for a half interest in a silver mine in Chihuahua. Oh, yes, the mine was all right. The other half interest must have been worth two or three hundred thousand. I often wondered who owned that mine.

"In coming back to the United States me and Andy stubbed our toes against

209

a little town in Texas on the bank of the Rio Grande. The name of it was Bird City; but it wasn't. The town had about 2,000 inhabitants, mostly men I figured out that their principal means of existence was in living close to tall chaparral. Some of 'em were stockmen and some gamblers and some horse peculators and plenty were in the smuggling line. Me and Andy put up at a hotel that was built like something between a roof-garden and a sectional book-case. It began to rain the day we got there. As the saying is, Juniper Aquarius was sure turning on the water plugs on Mount Amphibious.

"Now, there were three saloons in Bird City, though neither Andy nor me drank. But we could see the townspeople making a triangular procession from one to another all day and half the night. Everybody seemed to know what to do with as much money as they had.

"The third day of the rain it slacked up awhile in the afternoon, so me and Andy walked out to the edge of the town to view the mudscape. Bird City was built between the Rio Grande and a deep wide arroyo that used to be the old bed of the river. The bank between the stream and its old bed was cracking and giving away, when we saw it, on account of the high water caused by the rain. Andy looks at it a long time. That man's intellects was never idle. And then he unfolds to me a instantaneous idea that has occurred to him. Right there was organized a trust; and we walked back into town and put it on the market.

"First we went to the main saloon in Bird City, called the Blue Snake, and bought it. It cost us $1,200. And then we dropped in, casual, at Mexican Joe's place, referred to the rain, and bought him out for $500. The other one came easy at $400.

"The next morning Bird City woke up and found itself an island. The river had busted through its old channel, and the town was surrounded by roaring torrents. The rain was still raining, and there was heavy clouds in the northwest that presaged about six more mean annual rainfalls during the next two weeks. But the worst was yet to come.

"Bird City hopped out of its nest, waggled its pin feathers and strolled out for its matutinal toot. Lo! Mexican Joe's place was closed and likewise the other little 'dobe life saving station. So, naturally the body politic emits thirsty ejaculations of surprise and ports hellum for the Blue Snake. And what does it find there?

"Behind one end of the bar sits Jeffersonian Peters, octopus, with a six-shooter on each side of him, ready to make change or corpses as the case may be. There are three bartenders; and on the wall is a ten-foot sign reading: 'All Drinks One Dollar.' Andy sits on the safe in his neat blue suit and gold-banded cigar, on the lookout for emergencies. The town marshal is there with two deputies to keep order, having been promised free drinks by the trust.

"Well, sir, it took Bird City just ten minutes to realize that it was in a cage. We expected trouble; but there wasn't any. The citizens saw that we had 'em. The nearest railroad was thirty miles away; and it would be two weeks at least before the river would be fordable. So they began to cuss, amiable, and throw down dollars on the bar till it sounded like a selection on the xylophone.

"There was about 1,500 grown-up adults in Bird City that had arrived at years of indiscretion; and the majority of 'em required from three to twenty drinks a day to make life endurable. The Blue Snake was the only place where they could get 'em till the flood subsided. It was beautiful and simple as all truly great swindles are.

"About ten o'clock the silver dollars dropping on the bar slowed down to playing two-steps and marches instead of jigs. But I looked out the window and saw a hundred or two of our customers standing in line at Bird City Savings and Loan Co., and I knew they were borrowing more money to be sucked in by the clammy tendrils of the octopus.

"At the fashionable hour of noon everybody went home to dinner. We told the bartenders to take advantage of the lull, and do the same. Then me and Andy counted the receipts. We had taken in $1,300. We calculated that if Bird City would only remain an island for two weeks the trust would be able to endow the Chicago University with a new dormitory of padded cells for the faculty, and present every worthy poor man in Texas with a farm, provided he furnished the site for it.

"Andy was especial inroaded by self-esteem at our success, the rudiments of the scheme having originated in his own surmises and premonitions. He got off the safe and lit the biggest cigar in the house.

" 'Jeff,' says he, 'I don't suppose that anywhere in the world you could find three cormorants with brighter ideas about down-treading the proletariat than the firm of Peters, Satan and Tucker, incorporated. We have sure handed the small consumer a giant blow in the sole apoplectic region. No?'

" 'Well,' says I, 'it does look as if we would have to take up gastritis and golf or be measured for kilts in spite of ourselves. This little turn in bug juice is, verily, all to the Skibo. And I can stand it,' says I. 'I'd rather batten than bant any day.'

"Andy pours himself out four fingers of our best rye and does with it as was so intended. It was the first drink I had ever known him to take.

" 'By way of liberation,' says he, 'to the gods.'

"And then after thus doing umbrage to the heathen diabetes he drinks another to our success. And then he begins to toast the trade, beginning with Raisuli and the Northern Pacific, and on down the line to the little ones like the school book combine and the oleomargarine outrages and the Lehigh Valley and Great Scott Coal Federation.

" 'It's all right Andy,' says I, 'to drink the health of our brother monopolies, but don't overdo the wassail. You know our most eminent and loathed multi-corruptionists live on weak tea and dog biscuits.'

"Andy went in the back room awhile and came out dressed in his best clothes. There was a kind of murderous and soulful look of gentle riotousness in his eye that I didn't like. I watched him to see what turn the whiskey was going to take in him. There are two times when you never can tell what is going to happen. One is when a man takes his first drink; and the other is when a woman takes her latest.

"In less than an hour Andy's skate had turned to an ice yacht. He was outwardly decent and managed to preserve his aquarium, but inside he was impromptu and full of unexpectedness.

" 'Jeff,' says he, 'do you know that I'm a crater—a living crater?'

" 'That's a self-evident hypothesis,' says I. 'But you're not Irish. Why don't you say "creature," according to the rules and syntax of America?'

" 'I'm the crater of a volcano,' says he. 'I'm all aflame and crammed inside with an assortment of words and phrases that have got to have an exodus. I can feel millions of synonyms and parts of speech rising in me,' says he, 'and I've got to make a speech of some sort. Drink,' says Andy, 'always drives me to oratory.'

" 'It could do no worse,' says I.

" 'From my earliest recollections,' says he, 'alcohol seemed to stimulate my sense of recitation and rhetoric. Why, in Bryan's second campaign,' says Andy, 'they used to give me three gin rickeys and I'd speak for two hours longer than

Billy himself could on the silver question. Finally they persuaded me to take the gold cure.'

"'If you've got to get rid of your excess verbiage,' says I, 'why not go out on the river bank and speak a piece? It seems to me there was an old spellbinder named Cantharides that used to go out and disincorporate himself of his windy numbers along the seashore.'

"'No,' says Andy, 'I must have an audience. I feel like if I once turned loose people would begin to call Senator Beveridge the Grand Young Sphinx of the Wabash. I've got to get an audience together, Jeff, and get this oral distension assuaged or it may turn in on me and I'd go about feeling like a deckle-edge edition de luxe of Mrs. E. D. E. N. Southworth.'

"'On what special subject of the theorems and topics does your desire for vocality seem to be connected with?' I asks.

"'I ain't particular,' says Andy. 'I am equally good and varicose on all subjects. I can take up the matter of Russian immigration, or the poetry of John W. Keats, or the tariff, or Kabyle literature, or drainage, and make my audience weep, cry, sob and shed tears by turns.'

"'Well, Andy,' says I, 'if you are bound to get rid of this accumulation of vernacular suppose you go out in town and work it on some indulgent citizen. Me and the boys will take care of the business. Everybody will be through dinner pretty soon, and salt pork and beans makes a man pretty thirsty. We ought to take in $1,500 more by midnight.'

"So, Andy goes out of the Blue Snake, and I see him stopping men on the street and talking to 'em. By and by he has half a dozen in a bunch listening to him; and pretty soon I see him waving his arms and elocuting at a good-sized crowd on a corner. When he walks away they string out after him, talking all the time; and he leads 'em down the main street of Bird City with more men joining the procession as they go. It reminded me of the old legerdemain that I'd read in books about the Pied Piper of Heidsieck charming the children away from the town.

"One o'clock came; and then two, and three got under the wire for place; and not a Bird citizen came in for a drink. The streets were deserted except for some ducks and ladies going to the stores. There was only a light drizzle falling then.

"A lonesome man came along and stopped in front of the Blue Snake to scrape the mud off his boots.

"'Pardner,' says I, 'what has happened? This morning there was hectic gaiety afoot; and now it seems more like one of them ruined cities of Tyre and Siphon where the lone lizard crawls on the walls of the main port-cullis.'

"'The whole town,' says the muddy man, 'is up in Sperry's wool warehouse listening to your side-kicker make a speech. He is some gravy on delivering himself of audible sounds relating to matters and conclusions,' says the man.

"'Well, I hope he'll adjourn, sine qua non, pretty soon,' says I, 'for trade languishes.'

"Not a customer did we have that afternoon. At six o'clock two Mexicans brought Andy to the saloon lying across the back of a burro. We put him to bed while he still muttered and gesticulated with his hands and feet.

"Then I locked up the cash and went out to see what had happened. I met a man who told me all about it. Andy had made the finest two hour speech that had ever been heard in Texas, he said, or anywhere else in the world.

"'What was it about?' I asked.

"'Temperance,' says he. 'And when he got through, every man in Bird City signed the pledge for a year.'"

JEFF PETERS AS A PERSONAL MAGNET

JEFF PETERS has been engaged in as many schemes for making money as there are recipes for cooking rice in Charleston, S. C.

Best of all I like to hear him tell of his earlier days when he sold liniments and cough cures on street corners, living hand to mouth, heart to heart with the people, throwing heads or tails with fortune for his last coin.

"I struck Fisher Hill, Arkansaw," said he, "in buckskin suit, moccasins, long hair and a thirty-carat diamond ring that I got from an actor in Texarkana. I don't know what he ever did with the pocket knife I swapped him for it.

"I was Dr. Waugh-hoo, the celebrated Indian medicine man. I carried only one best bet just then, and that was Resurrection Bitters. It was made of life-giving plants and herbs accidentally discovered by Ta-qua-la, the beautiful wife of the chief of the Choctaw Nation, while gathering truck to garnish a platter of boiled dog for the annual corn dance.

"Business hadn't been good at the last town, so I only had five dollars. I went to the Fisher Hill druggist and he credited me for a half gross of eight ounce bottles and corks. I had the labels and ingredients in my valise, left over from the last town. Life began to look rosy again after I got in my hotel room with the water running from the tap, and the Resurrection Bitters lining up or the table by the dozen.

"Fake? No, sir. There was two dollars' worth of fluid extract of cinchona and a dime's worth of aniline in that half-gross of bitters. I've gone through towns years afterwards and had folks ask for 'em again.

"I hired a wagon that night and commenced selling the bitters on Main Street. Fisher Hill was a low, malarial town; and a compound hypothetical pneumo-cardiac anti-scorbutic tonic was just what I diagnosed the crowd as needing. The bitters started off like sweetbreads-on-toast at a vegetarian dinner. I had sold two dozen at fifty cents apiece when I felt somebody pull my coat tail. I knew what that meant; so I climbed down and sneaked a five-dollar bill into the hand of a man with a German silver star on his lapel.

"'Constable,' says I, 'it's a fine night.'

"'Have you got a city license,' he asks, 'to sell this illegitimate essence of spooju that you flatter by the name of medicine?'

"'I have not,' says I. 'I didn't know you had a city. If I can find it to-morrow I'll take one out if it's necessary.'

"'I'll have to close you up till you do,' says the constable.

"I quit selling and went back to the hotel. I was talking to the landlord about it.

"'Oh, you won't stand no show in Fisher Hill,' says he. 'Dr. Hoskins, the only doctor here, is a brother-in-law of the Mayor, and they won't allow no fake doctors to practice in town.'

"'I don't practice medicine,' says I, 'I've got a State peddler's license, and I take out a city one wherever they demand it.'

"I went to the Mayor's office the next morning and they told me he hadn't showed up yet. They didn't know when he'd be down. So Doc Waugh-hoo hunches down again in a hotel chair and lights a jimpson-weed regalia, and waits.

"By and by a young man in a blue necktie slips into the chair next to me and asks the time.

"'Half-past ten,' says I, 'and you are Andy Tucker. I've seen you work. Wasn't it you that put up the Great Cupid Combination package on the Southern States? Let's see, it was a Chilian diamond engagement ring, a wedding ring, a potato masher, a bottle of soothing syrup and Dorothy Vernon—all for fifty cents.'

"Andy was pleased to hear that I remembered him. He was a good street man; and he was more than that—he respected his profession, and he was satisfied with 300 per cent. profit. He had plenty of offers to go into the illegitimate drug and garden seed business; but he was never to be tempted off of the straight path.

"I wanted a partner, so Andy and me agreed to go out together. I told him about the situation on Fisher Hill and how finances was low on account of the local mixture of politics and jalap. Andy had just got in on the train that morning. He was pretty low himself, and was going to canvass the town for a few dollars to build a new battleship by popular subscription at Eureka Springs. So we went out and sat on the porch and talked it over.

"The next morning at eleven o'clock when I was sitting there alone, an Uncle Tom shuffles into the hotel and asked for the doctor to come and see Judge Banks, who, it seems, was the mayor and a mighty sick man.

"'I'm no doctor,' says I. 'Why don't you go and get the doctor?'

"'Boss,' says he. 'Doc Hoskin am done gone twenty miles in the country to see some sick persons. He's de only doctor in de town, and Massa Banks am powerful bad off. He sent me to ax you to please, suh, come.'

"'As man to man,' says I, 'I'll go and look him over.' So I put a bottle of Resurrection Bitters in my pocket and goes up on the hill to the mayor's mansion, the finest house in town, with a mansard roof and two cast-iron dogs on the lawn.

"This Mayor Banks was in bed all but his whiskers and feet. He was making internal noises that would have had everybody in San Francisco hiking for the parks. A young man was standing by the bed holding a cup of water.

"'Doc,' says the Mayor, 'I'm awful sick. I'm about to die. Can't you do nothing for me?'

"'Mr. Mayor,' says I, 'I'm not a regular preordained disciple of S. Q. Lapius. I never took a course in a medical college,' says I. 'I've just come as a fellow man to see if I could be of any assistance.'

"'I'm deeply obliged,' says he. 'Doc Waugh-hoo, this is my nephew, Mr. Biddle. He has tried to alleviate my distress, but without success. Oh, Lordy! Ow-ow-ow!!' he sings out.

"I nods at Mr. Biddle and sets down by the bed and feels the mayor's pulse. 'Let me see your liver—your tongue, I mean,' says I. Then I turns up the lids of his eyes and looks close at the pupils of 'em.

"'How long have you been sick?' I asked.

"'I was taken down—ow-ouch—last night,' says the Mayor. 'Gimme something for it, doc, won't you?'

"'Mr. Fiddle,' says I, 'raise the window shade a bit, will you?'

"'Biddle,' says the young man. 'Do you feel like you could eat some ham and eggs, Uncle James?'

"'Mr. Mayor,' says I, after laying my ear to his right shoulder blade and listening, 'you've got a bad attack of super-inflammation of the right clavicle of the harpsichord!'"

"'Good Lord!' says he, with a groan. 'Can't you rub something on it, or set it or anything?'

"I picks up my hat and starts for the door.

"'You ain't going, doc?' says the Mayor with a howl. 'You ain't going away and leave me to die with this—superfluity of the clapboards, are you?'

"'Common humanity, Dr. Whoa-ha,' says Mr. Biddle, 'ought to prevent your deserting a fellow-human in distress.'

"'Dr. Waugh-hoo, when you get through plowing,' says I. And then I walks back to the bed and throws back my long hair.

"'Mr. Mayor,' says I, 'there is only one hope for you. Drugs will do you no good. But there is another power higher yet, although drugs are high enough,' says I.

"'And what is that?' says he.

"'Scientific demonstrations,' says I. 'The triumph of mind over sarsaparilla. The belief that there is no pain and sickness except what is produced when we ain't feeling well. Declare yourself in arrears. Demonstrate.'

"'What is this paraphernalia you speak of, Doc?' says the Mayor. 'You ain't a Socialist, are you?'

"'I am speaking,' says I, 'of the great doctrine of psychic financiering—of the enlightened school of long-distance, sub-conscientious treatment of fallacies and meningitis—of that wonderful in-door sport known as personal magnetism.'

"'Can you work it, Doc?' asks the Mayor.

"'I'm one of the Sole Sanhedrims and Ostensible Hooplas of the Inner Pulpit,' says I. 'The lame talk and the blind rubber whenever I make a pass at 'em. I am a medium, a coloratura hypnotist and a spirituous control. It was only through me at the recent seances at Ann Arbor that the late president of the Vinegar Bitters Company could revisit the earth to communicate with his sister Jane. You see me peddling medicine on the streets,' says I, 'to the poor. I don't practice personal magnetism on them. I do not drag it in the dust,' says I, 'because they haven't got the dust.'

"'Will you treat my case?' asks the Mayor.

"'Listen,' says I. 'I've had a good deal of trouble with medical societies everywhere I've been. I don't practice medicine. But, to save your life, I'll give you the psychic treatment if you'll agree as mayor not to push the license question.'

"'Of course I will,' says he. 'And now get to work, Doc, for them pains are coming on again.'

"'My fee will be $250.00, cure guaranteed in two treatments,' says I.

"'All right,' says the Mayor. 'I'll pay it. I guess my life's worth that much.'

"I sat down by the bed and looked him straight in the eye.

"'Now,' says I, 'get your mind off the disease. You ain't sick. You haven't got a heart or a clavicle or a funny bone or brains or anything. You haven't got any pain. Declare error. Now you feel the pain that you didn't have leaving, don't you?'

"'I do feel some little better, Doc,' says the Mayor, 'darned if I don't. Now state a few lies about my not having this swelling in my left side, and I think I could be propped up and have some sausage and buckwheat cakes.'

"I made a few passes with my hands.

"'Now,' says I, 'the inflammation's gone. The right lobe of the perihelion has subsided. You're getting sleepy. You can't hold your eyes open any longer. For the present the disease is checked. Now, you are asleep.'

"The Mayor shut his eyes slowly and began to snore.

"'You observe, Mr. Tiddle,' says I, 'the wonders of modern science.'

"'Biddle,' says he. 'When will you give uncle the rest of the treatment, Dr. Pooh-pooh?'

"'Waugh-hoo,' says I. 'I'll come back at eleven to-morrow. When he wakes up give him eight drops of turpentine and three pounds of steak. Good morning.'

"The next morning I went back on time. 'Well, Mr. Riddle,' says I, when he opened the bedroom door, 'and how is uncle this morning?'

"'He seems much better,' says the young man.

"The Mayor's color and pulse was fine. I gave him another treatment, and he said the last of the pain left him.

"'Now,' says I, 'you'd better stay in bed for a day or two, and you'll be all right. It's a good thing I happened to be in Fisher Hill, Mr. Mayor,' says I, 'for all the remedies in the cornucopia that the regular schools of medicine use couldn't have saved you. And now that error has flew and pain proved a perjurer, let's allude to a cheerfuller subject—say the fee of $250. No checks, please, I hate to write my name on the back of a check almost as bad as I do on the front.'

"'I've got the cash here,' says the Mayor, pulling a pocket book from under his pillow.

"He counts out five fifty-dollar notes and holds 'em in his hand.

"'Bring the receipt,' he says to Biddle.

"I signed the receipt and the Mayor handed me the money. I put it in my inside pocket careful.

"'Now do your duty, officer,' says the Mayor, grinning much unlike a sick man.

"Mr. Biddle lays his hand on my arm.

"'You're under arrest, Dr. Waugh-hoo, alias Peters,' says he, 'for practising medicine without authority under the State law.'

"'Who are you?' I asks.

"'I'll tell you who he is,' says the Mayor, sitting up in bed. 'He's a detective employed by the State Medical Society. He's been following you over five counties. He came to me yesterday and we fixed up this scheme to catch you. I guess you won't do any more doctoring around these parts, Mr. Fakir. What was it you said I had, Doc?' the Mayor laughs, 'compound—well it wasn't softening of the brain, I guess, anyway.'

"'A detective,' says I.

"'Correct,' says Biddle. 'I'll have to turn you over to the sheriff.'

"'Let's see you do it,' says I, and I grabs Biddle by the throat and half throws him out the window, but he pulls a gun and sticks it under my chin, and I stand still. Then he puts handcuffs on me, and takes the money out of my pocket.

"'I witness,' says he, 'that they're the same bills that you and I marked, Judge Banks. I'll turn them over to the sheriff when we get to his office, and he'll send you a receipt. They'll have to be used as evidence in the case.'

"'All right, Mr. Biddle,' says the Mayor. 'And now, Doc Waugh-hoo,' he goes on, 'why don't you demonstrate? Can't you pull the cork out of your magnetism with your teeth and hocus-pocus them handcuffs off?'

"'Come on, officer,' says I, dignified. 'I may as well make the best of it.' And then I turns to old Banks and rattles my chains.

"'Mr. Mayor,' says I, 'the time will come soon when you'll believe that personal magnetism is a success. And you'll be sure that it succeeded in this case, too.'

"And I guess it did.

"When we got nearly to the gate, I says: 'We might meet somebody now, Andy. I reckon you better take 'em off, and——' Hey? Why, of course it was Andy Tucker. That was his scheme; and that's how we got the capital to go into business together."

MODERN RURAL SPORTS

JEFF PETERS must be reminded. Whenever he is called upon, pointedly, for a story, he will maintain that his life has been as devoid of incident as the longest of Trollope's novels. But lured, he will divulge. Therefore I cast many and divers flies upon the current of his thoughts before I feel a nibble.

"I notice," says I, "that the Western farmers, in spite of their prosperity, are running after their old populistic idols again."

"It's the running season," said Jeff, "for farmers, shad, maple trees and the Connemaugh River. I know something about farmers. I thought I struck one once that had got out of the rut; but Andy Tucker proved to me I was mistaken. 'Once a farmer, always a sucker,' said Andy. 'He's the man that's shoved into the front row among bullets, ballots and the ballet. He's the funny-bone and gristle of the country,' said Andy, 'and I don't know who we would do without him.'

"One morning me and Andy wakes up with sixty-eight cents between us in a yellow pine hotel on the edge of the predigested hoe-cake belt of Southern Indiana. How we got off the train there the night before I can't tell you; for she went through the village so fast that what looked like a saloon to us through the car window turned out to be a composite view of a drug store and a water tank two blocks apart. Why we got off at the first station we could, belongs to a little oroide gold watch and Alaska diamond deal we failed to pull off the day before, over the Kentucky line.

"When I woke up I heard roosters crowing, and smelt something like the fumes of nitro-muriatic acid and heard something heavy fall on the floor below us, and a man swearing.

"'Cheer up, Andy,' says I. 'We're in a rural community. Somebody has just tested a gold brick downstairs. We'll go out and get what's coming to us from a farmer; and then yoicks! and away.'

"Farmers was always a kind of reserve fund to me. Whenever I was in hard luck I'd go to the crossroads, hook a finger in a farmer's suspender, recite the prospectus of my swindle in a mechanical kind of a way, look over what he had, give him back his keys, whetstone, and papers that was of no value except to owner, and stroll away without asking any questions. Farmers are not fair game to me as high up in our business as me and Andy was; but there was times when we found 'em useful just as Wall Street does the Secretary of the Treasury now and then.

"When we went downstairs we saw we was in the midst of the finest farming section we ever see. About two miles away on a hill was a big white house in a grove surrounded by a widespread agricultural agglomeration of fields and barns and pastures and out-houses.

"'Whose house is that?' we asked the landlord.

"'That,' says he, 'is the domicile and the arboreal, terrestrial and horticultural accessories of Farmer Ezra Plunkett, one of our county's most progressive citizens.'

"After breakfast me and Andy, with eight cents capital left, casts the horoscope of the rural potentate.

"'Let me go alone,' says I. 'Two of us against one farmer would look as one-sided as Roosevelt using both hands to kill a grizzly.'

"'All right,' says Andy. 'I like to be a true sport even when I'm only collecting rebates from the rutabag raisers. What bait are you going to use for this Ezra thing?' Andy asks me.

"'Oh,' says I, 'the first thing that come to hand in the suit case. I reckon I'll take along some of the new income tax receipts; and the recipe for making clover honey out of clabber and apple peelings; and the order blanks for the McGuffey's readers, which afterwards turn out to be McCormick reapers; and the pearl necklace found on the train; and a pocket-size goldbrick; and a——"

"'That'll be enough,' says Andy. 'Any one of the lot ought to land on Ezra. And, say, Jeff, make that succotash fancier give you nice, clean, new bills. It's a disgrace to our Department of Agriculture, Civil Service and Pure Food Law the kind of stuff some of these farmers hand out to us. I've had to take rolls from 'em that looked like bundles of microbe cultures captured out of a Red Cross ambulance.'

"So, I goes to a livery stable and hires a buggy on my looks. I drove out to the Plunkett farm and hitched. There was a man sitting on the front steps of the house. He had on a white flannel suit, a diamond ring, golf cap and a pink ascot tie. 'Summer boarder,' says I to myself.

" 'I'd like to see Farmer Ezra Plunkett,' says I to him.

" 'You see him,' says he. 'What seems to be on your mind?'

"I never answered a word. I stood still, repeating to myself the rollicking lines of that merry jingle, 'The Man with the Hoe.' When I looked at this farmer, the little devices I had in my pocket for buncoing the pushed-back brows seemed as hopeless as trying to shake down the Beef Trust with a mittimus and a parlor rifle.

" 'Well,' says he, looking at me close, 'speak up. I see the left pocket of your coat sags a good deal. Out with the goldbrick first. I'm rather more interested in the bricks that I am in the trick sixty-day notes and the lost silver mine story.'

"I had a kind of cerebral sensation of foolishness in my ideas of ratiocination; but I pulled out the little brick and unwrapped my handkerchief off it.

" 'One dollar and eighty cents,' says the farmer, hefting it in his hand. 'Is it a trade?'

" 'The lead in it is worth more than that,' says I, dignified. I put it back in my pocket.

" 'All right,' says he. 'But I sort of wanted it for the collection I'm starting. I got a $5,000 one last week for $2.10.'

"Just then a telephone bell rings in the house.

" 'Come in, Bunk,' says the farmer, 'and look at my place. It's kind of lonesome here sometimes. I think that's New York calling.'

"We went inside. The room looked like a Broadway stockbroker's—light-oak desks, two 'phones, Spanish leather upholstered chairs and couches, oil paintings in gilt frames a foot deep and a ticker hitting off the news in one corner.

" 'Hello, hello!' says the funny farmer. 'Is that the Regent Theatre? Yes; this is Plunkett, of Woodbine Centre. Reserve four orchestra seats for Friday evening—my usual ones. Yes; Friday—good-bye.'

" 'I run over to New York every two weeks to see a show,' says the farmer, hanging up the receiver. 'I catch the eighteen-hour flyer at Indianapolis, spend ten hours in the heyday of night on the Yappian Way, and get home in time to see the chickens go to roost forty-eight hours later. Oh, the pristine Hubbard squasherino of the cave-dwelling period is getting geared up some for the annual meeting of the Don't-Blow-Out-the-Gas Association, don't you think, Mr. Bunk?'

" 'I seem to perceive,' says I, 'a kind of hiatus in the agrarian traditions in which, heretofore, I have reposed confidence.'

" 'Sure, Bunk,' says he. 'The yellow primrose on the river's brim is getting to look to us Reubs like a holiday edition de luxe of the Language of Flowers with deckle edges and frontispiece.'

"Just then the telephone calls him again.

" 'Hello, hello!' says he. 'Oh, that's Perkins, at Milldale. I told you $800 was too much for that horse. Have you got him there? Good. Let me see him. Get away from the transmitter. Now make him trot in a circle. Faster. Yes, I can hear him. Keep on—faster yet. . . . That'll do. Now lead him up to the phone. Closer. Get his nose nearer. There. Now wait. No; I don't want that horse. What? No; not at any price. He interferes; and he's windbroken. Good-bye.'

"Now, Bunk,' says the farmer, 'do you begin to realize that agriculture has had a hair cut? You belong in a bygone era. Why, Tom Lawson himself knows better than to try to catch an up-to-date agriculturist napping. It's Saturday, the Fourteenth, on the farm, you bet. Now, look here, and see how we keep up with the day's doings.'

"He shows me a machine on a table with two things for your ears like the penny-in-the-slot affairs. I puts it on and listens. A female voice starts up reading headlines of murders, accidents, and other political casualities.

"'What you hear,' says the farmer, 'is a synopsis of to-day's news in the New York, Chicago, St. Louis and San Francisco papers. It is wired in to our Rural News Bureau and served hot to subscribers. On this table you see the principal dailies and weeklies of the country. Also a special service of advance sheets of the monthly magazines.'

"I picks up one sheet and sees that it's headed: 'Special Advance Proofs. In July, 1909, the *Century* will say'—and so forth.

"The farmer rings up somebody—his manager, I reckon—and tells him to let that herd of 15 Jerseys go at $600 a head; and to sow the 900-acre field in wheat; and to have 200 extra cans ready at the station for the milk trolley car. Then he passes the Henry Clays and sets out a bottle of green chartreuse, and goes over and looks at the ticker tape.

"'Consolidated Gas up two points,' says he. 'Oh, very well.'

"'Ever monkey with copper?' I asks.

"'Stand back!' says he, raising his hand, 'or I'll call the dog. I told you not to waste your time.'

"After a while he says: 'Bunk, if you don't mind my telling you, your company begins to cloy slightly. I've got to write an article on the Chimera of Communism for a magazine, and attend a meeting of the Race Track Association this afternoon. Of course you understand by now that you can't get my proxy for your Remedy, whatever it may be.'

"Well, sir, all I could think of to do was to go out and get in the buggy. The horse turned round and took me back to the hotel. I hitched him and went in to see Andy. In his room I told him about this farmer, word for word; and I sat picking at the table cover like one bereft of sagaciousness.

"'I don't understand it,' says I, humming a sad and foolish little song to cover my humiliation.

"Andy walks up and down the room for a long time, biting the left end of his mustache as he does when in the act of thinking.

"'Jeff,' says he, finally, 'I believe your story of this expurgated rustic; but I am not convinced. It looks incredulous to me that he could not have inoculated himself against all the preordained systems of bucolic bunco. Now, you never regarded me as a man of special religious proclivities, did you, Jeff?' says Andy.

"'Well,' says I, 'No. But,' says I, not to wound his feelings, 'I have also observed many church members whose said proclivities were not so outwardly developed that they would show on a white handkerchief if you rubbed 'em with it.'

"'I have always been a deep student of nature from creation down,' says Andy, 'and I believe in an ultimatum design of Providence. Farmers was made for a purpose; and that was to furnish a livelihood to men like me and you. Else why was we given brains? It is my belief that the manna that the Israelites lived on for forty years in the wilderness was only a figurative word for farmers; and they kept up the practice to this day. And now,' says Andy, 'I am going to test my theory "Once a farmer, always a come-on," in spite of the veneering and the orifices that a spurious civilization has brought to him.'

"'You'll fail, same as I did,' says I. 'This one's shook off the shackles of the sheep-fold. He's entrenched behind the advantages of electricity, education, literature and intelligence.'

"'I'll try,' said Andy. 'There are certain Laws of Nature that Free Rural Delivery can't overcome.'

"Andy fumbles around awhile in the closet and comes out dressed in a suit with brown and yellow checks as big as your hand. His vest is red with blue dots, and he wears a high silk hat. I noticed he'd soaked his sandy mustache in a kind of blue ink.

"'Great Barnums?' says I. 'You're a ringer for a circus thimblerig man.'

"'Right,' says Andy. 'Is the buggy outside? Wait here till I come back. I won't be long.'

"Two hours afterwards Andy steps in the room and lays a wad of money on the table.

"'Eight hundred and sixty dollars,' says he. 'Let me tell you. He was in. He looked me over and began to guy me. I didn't say a word, but got out the walnut shells and began to roll the little ball on the table. I whistled a tune or two, and then I started up the old formula.

"'Step up lively, gentlemen,' says I, 'and watch the little ball. It costs you nothing to look. There you see it, and there you don't. Guess where the little joker is. The quickness of the hand deceives the eye.'

"'I steals a look at the farmer man. I see the sweat coming out on his forehead. He goes over and closes the front door and watches me some more. Directly he says: "I'll bet you twenty I can pick the shell the ball's under now."

"'After that,' goes on Andy, 'there is nothing new to relate. He only had $860 in cash in the house. When I left he followed me to the gate. There was tears in his eyes when he shook hands.

"'"Bunk,"' says he, '"thank you for the only real pleasure I've had in years. It brings up happy old days when I was only a farmer and not an agriculturist. God bless you."'"

Here Jeff Peters ceased, and I inferred that his story was done.

"Then you think——" I began.

"Yes," said Jeff. "Something like that. You let the farmers go ahead and amuse themselves with politics. Farming's a lonesome life; and they've been against the shell game before."

THE CHAIR OF PHILANTHROMATHEMATICS

"I SEE that the cause of Education has received the princely gift of more than fifty millions of dollars," said I.

I was gleaning the stray items from the evening papers while Jeff Peters packed his briar pipe with plug cut.

"Which same," said Jeff, "calls for a new deck, and a recitation by the entire class in philanthromathematics."

"Is that an allusion?" I asked.

"It is," said Jeff. "I never told you about the time when me and Andy Tucker was philanthropists, did I? It was eight years ago in Arizona. Andy and me was out in the Gila Mountains with a two-horse wagon prospecting for silver. We struck it, and sold out to parties in Tucson for $25,000. They paid our check at the bank in silver—a thousand dollars in a sack. We loaded it in our wagon and drove east a hundred miles before we recovered our presence of intellect. Twenty-five thousand dollars don't sound like so much when you're reading the annual report of the Pennsylvania Railroad or listening to an actor talking about his salary; but when you can raise up a wagon sheet and kick around your bootheel and hear every one of 'em ring against another it makes you feel like you was a night-and-day bank with the clock striking twelve.

"The third day we drove into one of the most specious and tidy little towns that Nature or Rand and McNally ever turned out. It was in the foothills, and mitigated with trees and flowers and about 2,000 head of cordial and dilatory inhabitants. The town seemed to be called Floresville, and Nature had not contaminated it with many railroads, fleas or Eastern tourists.

"Me and Andy deposited our money to the credit of Peters and Tucker in the Esperanza Savings Bank, and got rooms at the Skyview Hotel. After supper we lit up, and sat out on the gallery and smoked. Then was when the philanthropy idea struck me. I suppose every grafter gets it sometime.

"When a man swindles the public out of a certain amount he begins to get scared and wants to return part of it. And if you'll watch close and notice the way his charity runs you'll see that he tries to restore it to the same people he got it from. As a hydrostatical case, take, let's say, A. A made his millions selling oil to poor students who sit up nights studying political economy and methods for regulating the trusts. So back to the universities and colleges goes his conscience dollars.

"There's B got his from the common laboring man that works with his hands and tools. How's he to get some of the remorse fund back into their overalls?

" 'Aha!' says B, 'I'll do it in the name of Education. I've skinned the laboring man,' says he to himself, 'but, according to the old proverb, "Charity covers a multitude of skins." '

"So he puts up eighty million dollars' worth of libraries; and the boys with the dinner pail that builds 'em gets the benefit.

" 'Where's the books?' asks the reading public.

" 'I dinna ken,' says B. 'I offered ye libraries; and there they are. I suppose if I'd given ye preferred steel trust stock instead ye'd have wanted the water in it set out in cut glass decanters. Hoot, for ye!'

"But, as I said, the owning of so much money was beginning to give me philanthropitis. It was the first time me and Andy had ever made a pile big enough to make us stop and think how we got it.

" 'Andy,' says I, 'we're wealthy—not beyond the dreams of average; but in our humble way we are comparatively as rich as Greasers. I feel as if I'd like to do something for as well as to humanity.'

" 'I was thinking the same thing, Jeff,' says he. 'We've been gouging the public for a long time with all kinds of little schemes from selling self-igniting celluloid collars to flooding Georgia with Hoke Smith presidential campaign buttons. I'd like, myself, to hedge a bet or two in the graft game if I could do it without actually banging the cymbalines in the Salvation Army or teaching a bible class by the Bertillon system.'

" 'What'll we do?' says Andy. 'Give free grub to the poor or send a couple of thousand to George Cortelyou?'

" 'Neither,' says I. 'We've got too much money to be implicated in plain charity; and we haven't got enough to make restitution. So, we'll look about for something that's about half way between the two.'

"The next day in walking around Floresville we see on a hill a big red brick building that appears to be disinhabited. The citizens speak up and tell us that it was begun for a residence several years before by a mine owner. After running up the house he finds he only had $2.80 left to furnish it with, so he invests that in whiskey and jumps off the roof on a spot where he now requiescats in pieces.

"As soon as me and Andy saw that building the same idea struck both of us. We would fix it up with lights and pen wipers and professors, and put an iron dog and statues of Hercules and Father John on the lawn, and start one of the finest free educational institutions in the world right there.

"So we talks it over to the prominent citizens of Floresville, who falls in fine with the idea. They give a banquet in the engine house to us, and we make our bow for the first time as benefactors to the cause of progress and enlighten-ment. Andy makes an hour-and-a-half speech on the subject of irrigation in Lower Egypt, and we have a moral tune on the phonograph and pineapple sher-bet.

"Andy and me didn't lose any time in philanthropping. We put every man in town that could tell a hammer from a step ladder to work on the building, dividing it up into class rooms and lecture halls. We wire to Frisco for a car-load of desks, footballs, arithmetics, penholders, dictionaries, chairs for the pro-fessors, slates, skeletons, sponges, twenty-seven cravenetted gowns and caps for the senior class, and an open order for all the truck that goes with a first-class university. I took it on myself to put a campus and a curriculum on the list; but the telegraph operator must have got the words wrong, being an ignorant man, for when the goods come we found a can of peas and a curry-comb among 'em.

"While the weekly papers was having chalkplate cuts of me and Andy we wired an employment agency in Chicago to express us f. o. b., six professors im-mediately—one English literature, one up-to-date dead languages, one chemistry, one political economy—democrat preferred—one logic, and one wise to painting, Italian and music, with union card. The Esperanza bank guaranteed salaries, which was to run between $800 and $800.50.

"Well, sir, we finally got in shape. Over the front door was carved the words: 'The World's University; Peters & Tucker, Patrons and Proprietors.' And when September the first got a cross-mark on the calendar, the comeons begun to roll in. First the faculty got off the tri-weekly express from Tucson. They was mostly young, spectacled and red-headed, with sentiments divided between am-bition and food. Andy and me got 'em billeted on the Floresvillians and then laid for the students.

"They came in bunches. We had advertised the University in all the state papers, and it did us good to see how quick the country responded. Two hundred and nineteen husky lads aging along from 18 up to chin whiskers answered the clarion call of free education. They ripped open that town, sponged the seams, turned it, lined it with new mohair; and you couldn't have told it from Harvard or Goldfields at the March term of court.

"They marched up and down the streets waving flags with the World's Uni-versity colors—ultra-marine and blue—and they certainly made a lively place of Floresville. Andy made them a speech from the balcony of the Skyview Hotel, and the whole town was out celebrating.

"In about two weeks the professors got the students disarmed and herded into classes. I don't believe there's any pleasure equal to being a philanthropist. Me and Andy bought high silk hats and pretended to dodge the two reporters of the Floresville *Gazette*. The paper had a man to kodak us whenever we ap-peared on the street, and ran our pictures every week over the column headed 'Educational Notes.' Andy lectured twice a week at the University; and after-ward I would rise and tell a humorous story. Once the *Gazette* printed my pictures with Abe Lincoln on one side and Marshall P. Wilder on the other.

"Andy was as interested in philanthropy as I was. We used to wake up of nights and tell each other new ideas for booming the University.

"'Andy,' says I to him one day, 'there's something we overlooked. The boys ought to have dromedaries.'

"'What's that?' Andy asks.

" 'Why, something to sleep in, of course,' says I. 'All colleges have 'em.'

" 'Oh, you mean pajamas,' says Andy.

" 'I do not,' says I. 'I mean dromedaries.' But I never could make Andy understand; so we never ordered 'em. Of course, I meant them long bedrooms in colleges where the scholars sleep in a row.

"Well, sir, the World's University was a success. We had scholars from five States and territories, and Floresville had a boom. A new shooting gallery and a pawn shop and two more saloons started; and the boys got up a college yell that went this way:

" 'Raw, raw, raw,
Done, done, done,
Peters, Tucker,
Lots of fun.
Bow-wow-wow,
Haw-hee-haw,
World University,
Hip hurrah!"

"The scholars was a fine lot of young men, and me and Andy was as proud of 'em as if they belonged to our own family.

"But one day about the last of October Andy come to me and asks if I have any idea how much money we had left in the bank. I guesses about sixteen thousand. 'Our balance,' says Andy, 'is $821.62.'

" 'What!' says I, with a kind of a yell. 'Do you mean to tell me that them infernal clod-hopping, dough-headed, pup-faced, goose-brained, gate-stealing, rabbit-eared sons of horse thieves have soaked us for that much?'

" 'No less,' says Andy.

" 'Then, to Helvetia with philanthropy,' says I.

" 'Not necessarily,' says Andy. 'Philanthropy,' says he, 'when run on a good business basis is one of the best grafts going. I'll look into the matter and see if it can't be straightened out.'

"The next week I am looking over the payroll of our faculty when I run across a new name—Professor James Darnley McCorkle, chair of mathematics; salary $100 per week. I yells so loud that Andy runs in quick.

" 'What's this,' says I. 'A Professor of mathematics at more than $5,000 a year? How did this happen? Did he get in through the window and appoint himself?'

" 'I wired to Frisco for him a week ago,' says Andy. 'In ordering the faculty we seemed to have overlooked the chair of mathematics.'

" 'A good thing we did,' says I. 'We can pay his salary two weeks, and then our philanthropy will look like the ninth hole on the Skibo golf links.'

" 'Wait a while,' says Andy, 'and see how things turn out. We have taken up too noble a cause to draw out now. Besides, the further I gaze into the retail philanthropy business the better it looks to me. I never thought about investigating it before. Come to think of it now,' goes on Andy, 'all the philanthropists I ever knew had plenty of money. I ought to have looked into that matter long ago, and located which was the cause and which was the effect.'

"I had confidence in Andy's chicanery in financial affairs, so I left the whole thing in his hands. The University was flourishing fine, and me and Andy kept our silk hats shined up, and Floresville kept on heaping honors on us like we was millionaires instead of almost busted philanthropists.

"The students kept the town lively and prosperous. Some stranger came to town and started a faro bank over the Red Front livery stable, and began to amass money in quantities. Me and Andy strolled up one night and piked a dollar or two for sociability. There were about fifty of our students there drinking rum punches and shoving high stacks of blues and reds about the table as the dealer turned the cards up.

"'Why, dang it, Andy,' says I, 'these free-school-hunting, gander-headed, silk-socked little sons of sapsuckers have got more money than you and me ever had. Look at the rolls they're pulling out of their pistol pockets!'

"'Yes,' says Andy, 'a good many of them are sons of wealthy miners and stockmen. It's very sad to see 'em wasting their opportunities this way.'

"At Christmas all the students went home to spend the holidays. We had a farewell blowout at the University and Andy lectured on 'Modern Music and Prehistoric Literature of the Archipelagos.' Each one of the faculty answered to toasts, and compared me and Andy to Rockefeller and the Emperor Marcus Autolycus. I pounded on the table and yelled for Professor McCorkle; but it seems he wasn't present on the occasion. I wanted a look at the man that Andy thought could earn $100 a week in philanthropy that was on the point of making an assignment.

"The students all left on the night train; and the town sounded as quiet as the campus of a correspondence school at midnight. When I went to the hotel I saw a light in Andy's room and I opened the door and walked in.

"There sat Andy and the faro dealer at a table dividing a two-foot high stack of currency in thousand-dollar packages.

"'Correct,' says Andy. 'Thirty-one thousand apiece. Come in, Jeff,' says he. 'This is our share of the profits of the first half of the scholastic term of the World's University, incorporated and philanthropated. Are you convinced now,' says Andy, 'that philanthropy when practiced in a business way is an art that blesses him who gives as well as him who receives?'

"'Great!' says I, feeling fine. 'I'll admit you are the doctor this time.'

"'We'll be leaving on the morning train,' says Andy. 'You'd better get your collars and cuffs and press clippings together.'

"'Great!' says I. 'I'll be ready. But, Andy,' says I, 'I wish I could have met that Professor James Darnley McCorkle before he went. I had a curiosity to know that man.'

"'That'll be easy,' says Andy, turning around to the faro dealer.

"'Jim,' says Andy, 'shake hands with Mr. Peters.'"

THE HAND THAT RILES THE WORLD

"MANY of our great men," said I (apropos of many things), "have declared that they owe their success to the aid and encouragement of some brilliant woman."

"I know," said Jeff Peters. "I've read in history and mythology about Joan of Arc and Mme. Yale and Mrs. Caudle and Eve and other noted females of the past. But, in my opinion, the woman of to-day is of little use in politics or business. What's she best in, anyway?—men make the best cooks, milliners, nurses, housekeepers, stenographers, clerks, hair-dressers and launderers. About the only job left that a woman can beat a man in is female impersonator in vaudeville."

"I would have thought," said I, "that occasionally, anyhow, you would have found the wit and intuition of woman valuable to you in your lines of-er-business."

"Now, wouldn't you," said Jeff, with an emphatic nod—"wouldn't you have imagined that? But a woman is an absolutely unreliable partner in any straight swindle. She's liable to turn honest on you when you are depending upon her most. I tried 'em once."

"Bill Humble, an old friend of mine in the Territories, conceived the illusion that he wanted to be appointed United States Marshal. At that time me and Andy was doing a square, legitimate business of selling walking canes. If you unscrewed the head of one and turned it up to your mouth a half pint of good rye whiskey would go trickling down your throat to reward you for your act of intelligence. The deputies was annoying me and Andy some, and when Bill spoke to me about his officious aspirations, I saw how the appointment as Marshal might help along the firm of Peters & Tucker.

"'Jeff,' says Bill to me, 'you are a man of learning and education, besides having knowledge and information concerning not only rudiments but facts and attainments.'

"'I do,' says I, 'and I have never regretted it. I am not one,' says I, 'who would cheapen education by making it free. Tell me,' says I, 'which is of the most value to mankind, literature or horse racing?'

"'Why—er—, playing the po—I mean, of course, the poets and the great writers have got the call, of course,' says Bill.

"'Exactly,' says I. 'Then why do the master minds of finance and philanthropy,' says I, 'charge us $2 to get into a race-track and let us into a library free? Is that distilling into the masses,' says I, 'a correct estimate of the relative value of the two means of self-culture and disorder?'

"'You are arguing outside of my faculties of sense and rhetoric,' says Bill. 'What I wanted you to do is to go to Washington and dig out this appointment for me. I haven't no ideas of cultivation and intrigue. I'm a plain citizen and I need the job. I've killed seven men,' says Bill; 'I've got nine children; I've been a good Republican ever since the first of May; I can't read nor write, and I see no reason why I ain't illegible for the office. And I think your partner, Mr. Tucker,' goes on Bill, 'is also a man of sufficient ingratiation and connected system of mental delinquency to assist you in securing the appointment. I will give you preliminary,' says Bill, '$1,000 for drinks, bribes and carfare in Washington. If you land the job I will pay you $1,000 more, cash down, and guarantee you impunity in boot-legging whiskey for twelve months. Are you patriotic to the West enough to help me put this thing through the White-washed Wigwam of the Great Father of the most eastern flag station of the Pennsylvania Railroad?' says Bill.

"Well, I talked to Andy about it, and he liked the idea immense. Andy was a man of an involved nature. He was never content to plod along, as I was, selling to the peasantry some little tool like a combination steak beater, shoe horn, marcel waver, monkey wrench, nail file, potato masher and Multum in Parvo tuning fork. Andy had the artistic temper, which is not to be judged as a preacher's or a moral man's is by purely commercial deflections. So we accepted Bill's offer, and strikes out for Washington.

"Says I to Andy, when we get located at a hotel on South Dakota Avenue, G. S. S. W. 'Now Andy, for the first time in our lives we've got to do a real dishonest act. Lobbying is something we've never been used to; but we've got to scandalize ourselves for Bill Humble's sake. In a straight and legitimate business,' says I, 'we could afford to introduce a little foul play and chicanery, but in a disorderly and heinous piece of malpractice like this it seems to me that the straightforward and aboveboard way is the best. I propose,' says I, 'that we hand over $500 of this money to the chairman of the national campaign committee, get a receipt, lay the receipt on the President's desk and tell him about Bill.

The President is a man who would appreciate a candidate who went about getting office that way instead of pulling wires.

"Andy agreed with me, but after we talked the scheme over with the hotel clerk we give that plan up. He told us that there was only one way to get an appointment in Washington, and that was through a lady lobbyist. He gave us the address of one he recommended, a Mrs. Avery, who he said was high up in sociable and diplomatic rings and circles.

"The next morning at 10 o'clock me and Andy called at her hotel, and was shown up to her reception room.

"This Mrs. Avery was a solace and a balm to the eyesight. She had hair the color of the back of a twenty-dollar gold certificate, blue eyes and a system of beauty that would make the girl on the cover of a July magazine look like a cook on a Monongahela coal barge.

"She had on a low necked dress covered with silver spangles, and diamond rings and ear bobs. Her arms was bare; and she was using a desk telephone with one hand, and drinking tea with the other.

"'Well, boys,' says she after a bit, 'what is it?'

"I told her in as few words as possible what we wanted for Bill, and the price we could pay.

"'Those western appointments,' says she, 'are easy. Le'me see, now,' says she, 'who could put that through for us. No use fooling with Territorial delegates. I guess,' says she, 'that Senator Sniper would be about the man. He's from somewheres in the West. Let's see how he stands on my private menu card.' She takes some papers out of a pigeonhole with the letter 'S' over it.

"'Yes,' says she, 'he's marked with a star; that means "ready to serve." Now, let's see. "Age 55; married twice; Presbyterian, likes blondes, Tolstoi, poker and stewed terrapin; sentimental at third bottle of wine." Yes,' she goes on, 'I am sure I can have your friend, Mr. Bummer, appointed Minister to Brazil.'

"'Humble,' says I: 'And United States Marshal was the berth.'

"'Oh, yes,' says Mrs. Avery. 'I have so many deals of this sort I sometimes get them confused. Give me all the memoranda you have of the case, Mr. Peters, and come back in four days. I think it can be arranged by then.'

"So me and Andy goes back to our hotel and waits. Andy walks up and down and chews the left end of his mustache.

"'A woman of high intellect and perfect beauty is the rare thing, Jeff,' says he.

"'As rare,' says I, 'as an omelet made from the eggs of the fabulous bird known as the epidermis,' says I.

"'A woman like that,' says Andy, 'ought to lead a man to the highest positions of opulence and fame.'

"'I misdoubt,' says I, 'if any woman ever helped a man to secure a job any more than to have his meals ready promptly and spread a report that the other candidate's wife had once been a shoplifter. They are no more adapted for business and politics,' say I, 'than Algernon Charles Swinburne is to be floor manager at one of Chuck Connor's annual balls. I know,' says I to Andy, 'that sometimes a woman seems to step out into the kalsomine light as the charge d'affaires of her man's political job. But how does it come out? Say, they have a neat little berth somewhere as foreign consul of record to Afghanistan or lockkeeper on the Delaware and Raritan Canal. One day this man finds his wife putting on her overshoes and three months' supply of bird seed into the canary's cage. "Sioux Falls?" he asks with a kind of hopeful look in his eye. "No, Arthur" says she, "Washington. We're wasted here," says she. "You ought to be Toady Extraordinary to the Court of St. Bridget or Head Porter of the Island of Porto Rico. I'm going to see about it."

"'Then this lady,' I says to Andy, 'moves against the authorities at Washington with her baggage and munitions, consisting of five dozen indiscriminating letters written to her by a member of the Cabinet when she was 15; a letter of introduction from King Leopold to the Smithsonian Institution, and a pink silk costume with canary colored spats.

" 'Well, and then what?' I goes. 'She has the letters printed in the evening papers that match her costume, she lectures at an informal tea given in the palm room of the B. & O. Depot and then calls on the President. The ninth Assistant Secretary of Commerce and Labor, the first aide-de-camp of the Blue Room and an unidentified colored man are waiting there to grasp her by the hands—and feet. They carry her out to S. W. B. street and leave her on a cellar door. That ends it. The next time we hear of her she is writing postal cards to the Chinese Minister asking him to get Arthur a job in a tea store.'

" 'Then,' says Andy, 'you don't think Mrs. Avery will land the Marshalship for Bill?'

" 'I do not,' says I. 'I do not wish to be a septic, but I doubt if she can do as well as you and me could have done.'

" 'I don't agree with you,' says Andy. 'I'll bet you she does. I'm proud of having a higher opinion of the talent and the powers of negotiation of ladies.'

"We was back at Mrs. Avery's hotel at the time she appointed. She was looking pretty and fine enough, as far as that went, to make any man let her name every officer in the country. But I hadn't much faith in looks, so I was certainly surprised when she pulls out a document with the great seal of the United States on it, and 'William Henry Humble' in a fine, big hand on the back.

" 'You might have had it the next day, boys,' says Mrs. Avery, smiling. 'I hadn't the slightest trouble in getting it,' says she. 'I just asked for it, that's all. Now, I'd like to talk to you a while,' she goes on, 'but I'm awfully busy, and I know you'll excuse me. I've got an Ambassadorship, two Consulates and a dozen other minor applications to look after. I can hardly find time to sleep at all. You'll give my compliments to Mr. Humble when you get home, of course.'

"Well, I handed her the $500, which she pitched into her desk drawer without counting. I put Bill's appointment in my pocket and me and Andy made our adieus.

"We started back for the Territory the same day. We wired Bill: 'Job landed; get the tall glasses ready,' and we felt pretty good.

"Andy joshed me all the way about how little I knew about women.

" 'All right,' says I. 'I'll admit that she surprised me. But it's the first time I ever knew one of 'em to manipulate a piece of business on time without getting it bungled up in some way,' says I.

"Down about the edge of Arkansas I got out Bill's appointment and looked it over, and then I handed it to Andy to read. Andy read it, but didn't add any remarks to my silence.

"The paper was for Bill, all right, and a genuine document, but it appointed him post-master of Dade City, Fla.

"Me and Andy got off the train at Little Rock and sent Bill's appointment to him by mail. Then we struck northeast toward Lake Superior.

"I never saw Bill Humble after that."

THE EXACT SCIENCE OF MATRIMONY

"As I have told you before," said Jeff Peters, "I never had much confidence in the perfidiousness of woman. As partners or coeducators in the most innocent line of graft they are not trustworthy."

"They deserve the compliment," said I. "I think they are entitled to be called the honest sex."

"Why shouldn't they be?" said Jeff. "They've got the other sex either grafting or working overtime for 'em. They're all right in business until they get their emotions or tɦeir hair touched up too much. Then you want to have a flat-footed, heavy-breathing man with sandy whiskers, five kids and a building and loan mortgage ready as an understudy to take her desk. Now there was that widow lady that me and Andy Tucker engaged to help us in that little matrimonial agency scheme we floated out in Cairo.

"When you've got enough advertising capital—say a roll as big as the little end of a wagon tongue—there's money in matrimonial agencies. We had about $6,000 and we expected to double it in two months, which is about as long as a scheme like ours can be carried on without taking out a New Jersey charter.

"We fixed up an advertisement that read about like this:

"Charming widow, beautiful, home loving, 32 years, possessing $3,000 cash and owing valuable country property, would remarry. Would prefer a poor man with affectionate disposition to one with means, as she realizes that the solid virtues are oftenest to be found in the humble walks of life. No objection to elderly man or one of homely appearance if faithful and true and competent to manage property and invest money with judgment. Address, with particulars.

LONELY,
Care of Peters & Tucker, agents, Cairo, Ill.

" 'So far, so pernicious,' says I, when we had finished the literary concoction. 'And now,' says I, 'where is the lady?'

"Andy gives me one of his looks of calm irritation.

" 'Jeff,' says he 'I thought you had lost them ideas of realism in your art. Why should there be a lady? When they sell a lot of watered stock on Wall Street would you expect to find a mermaid in it? What has a matrimonial ad got to do with a lady?'

" 'Now listen,' says I. 'You know my rule, Andy, that in all my illegitimate inroads against the legal letter of the law the article sold must be existent, visible, producible. In that way and by a careful study of city ordinances and train schedules I have kept out of all trouble with the police that a five-dollar bill and a cigar could not square. Now, to work this scheme we've got to be able to produce bodily a charming widow or its equivalent with or without the beauty, hereditaments and appurtenances set forth in the catalogue and writ of errors, or hereafter be held by a justice of the peace.'

" 'Well,' says Andy, reconstructing his mind, 'maybe it would be safer in case the post office or the peace commission should try to investigate our agency. But where,' he says, 'could you hope to find a widow who would waste time on a matrimonal scheme that had no matrimony in it?'

"I told Andy that I thought I knew of the exact party. An old friend of mine, Zeke Trotter, who used to draw soda water and teeth in a tent show, had made his wife a widow a year before by drinking some dyspepsia cure of the old doctor's instead of the liniment that he always got boozed up on. I used to stop at their house often, and I thought we could get her to work with us.

" 'Twas only sixty miles to the little town where she lived, so I jumped out on the I. C. and finds her in the same cottage with the same sunflowers and roosters standing on the washtub. Mrs. Trotter fitted our ad first rate except, maybe, for beauty and age and property valuation. But she looked feasible and praiseworthy to the eye, and it was a kindness to Zeke's memory to give her the job.

" 'Is this an honest deal you are putting on, Mr. Peters?' she asks me when I tell her what we want.

"'Mrs. Trotter?' says I, 'Andy Tucker and me have computed the calculation that 3,000 men in this broad and fair country will endeavor to secure your fair hand and ostensible money and property through our advertisement. Out of that number something like thirty hundred will expect to give you in exchange, if they should win you, the carcass of a lazy and mercenary loafer, a failure in life, a swindler and contemptible fortune seeker.

"'Me and Andy,' says I, 'propose to teach these preyers upon society a lesson. It was with difficulty,' says I, 'that me and Andy could refrain from forming a corporation under the title of the Great Moral and Millennial Malevolent Matrimonial Agency. Does that satisfy you?'

"'It does, Mr. Peters,' says she. 'I might have known you wouldn't have gone into anything that wasn't opprobrious. But what will my duties be? Do I have to reject personally these 3,000 ramscallions you speak of, or can I throw them out in bunches?'

"'Your job, Mrs. Trotter,' says I, 'will be practically a cynosure. You will live at a quiet hotel and will have no work to do. Andy and I will attend to all the correspondence and business end of it.

"'Of course,' says I, 'some of the more ardent and impetuous suitors who can raise the railroad fare may come to Cairo to personally press their suit or whatever fraction of a suit they may be wearing. In that case you will be probably put to the inconvenience of kicking them out face to face. We will pay you $25 per week and hotel expenses.'

"'Give me five minutes,' says Mrs. Trotter, 'to get my powder rag and leave the front door key with a neighbor and you can let my salary begin.'

"So I conveys Mrs. Trotter to Cairo and establishes her in a family hotel far enough away from mine and Andy's quarters to be unsuspicious and available, and I tell Andy.

"'Great,' says Andy. 'And now that your conscience is appeased as to the tangibility and proximity of the bait, and leaving mutton aside, suppose we revenoo a noo fish.'

"So, we began to insert our advertisement in newspapers covering the country far and wide. One ad was all we used. We couldn't have used more without hiring so many clerks and marcelled paraphernalia that the sound of the gum chewing would have disturbed the Postmaster-General.

"We placed $2,000 in a bank to Mrs. Trotter's credit and gave her the book to show in case anybody might question the honesty and good faith of the agency. I knew Mrs. Trotter was square and reliable and it was safe to leave it in her name.

"With that one ad and me put in twelve hours a day answering letters.

"About one hundred a day was what came in. I never knew there was so many large hearted but indigent men in the country who were willing to acquire a charming widow and assume the burden of investing her money

"Most of them admitted that they ran principally to whiskers and lost jobs and were misunderstood by the world, but all of 'em were sure that they were so chock full of affection and manly qualities that the widow would be making the bargain of her life to get 'em.

"Every applicant got a reply from Peters & Tucker informing him that the widow had been deeply impressed by his straightforward and interesting letter and requesting them to write again stating more particulars; and enclosing photograph if convenient. Peters & Tucker also informed the applicant that their fee for handing over the second letter to their fair client would be $2, enclosed therewith.

"There you see the simple beauty of the scheme. About 90 per cent. of them domestic foreign noblemen raised the price somehow and sent it in. That was all there was to it. Except that me and Andy complained an amount about being put to the trouble of slicing open them envelopes, and taking the money out.

"Some few clients called in person. We sent 'em to Mrs. Trotter and she did the rest; except for three or four who came back to strike us for carfare. After the letters began to get in from the r. f d. districts Andy and me were taking in about $200 a day

"One afternoon when we were busiest and I was stuffing the two and ones into cigar boxes and Andy was whistling 'No Wedding Bells for Her' a small, slick man drops in and runs his eye over the walls like he was on the trail of a lost Gainesborough painting or two. As soon as I saw him I felt a glow of pride, be-cause we were running our business on the level.

"'I see you have quite a large mail to-day,' says the man.

"I reached and got my hat.

"'Come on,' says I. 'We've been expecting you. I'll show you the goods. How was Teddy when you left Washington?'

"I took him down to the Riverview Hotel and had him shake hands with Mrs. Trotter. Then I showed him her bank book with the $2,000 to her credit.

"'It seems to be all right,' says the Secret Service.

"'It is,' says I. 'And if you're not a married man I'll leave you to talk a while with the lady. We won't mention the two dollars.'

"'Thanks,' says he. 'If I wasn't, I might. Good day, Mr. Peters.'

"'Toward the end of three months we had taken in something over $5,000, and we saw it was time to quit. We had a good many complaints made to us; and Mrs. Trotter seemed to be tired of the job. A good many suitors had been calling to see her, and she didn't seem to like that.

"So we decides to pull out, and I goes down to Mrs. Trotter's hotel to pay her last week's salary and say farewell and get her check for $2,000.

"When I get there I found her crying like a kid that don't want to go to school.

"'Now, now,' says I, 'what's it all about? Somebody sassed you or you getting homesick?'

"'No, Mr. Peters,' says she. 'I'll tell you. You was always a friend of Zeke's, and I don't mind. Mr. Peters, I'm in love. I just love a man so hard I can't bear not to get him. He's just the ideal I've always had in mind.'

"'Then take him,' says I. 'That's is, if it's a mutual case. Does he return the sentiment according to the specifications and painfulness you have described?'

"'He does,' says she. 'But he's one of the gentlemen that's been coming to see me about the advertisement and he won't marry me unless I give him the $2,000. His name is William Wilkinson.' And then she goes off again in the agitations and hysterics of romance.

"'Mrs. Trotter,' says I, 'there's no man more sympathizing with a woman's affections than I am. Besides, you was once the life partner of one of my best friends. If it was left to me I'd say take this $2,000 and the man of your choice and be happy.

"'We could afford to do that, because we have cleaned up over $5,000 from these suckers that wanted to marry you. But,' says I, 'Andy Tucker is to be consulted.

"'He is a good man, but keen in business. He is my equal partner financially. I will talk to Andy,' says I, 'and see what can be done.'

"I goes back to our hotel and lays the case before Andy.

"'I was expecting something like this all the time,' says Andy. 'You can't trust a woman to stick by you in any scheme that involves her emotions and preferences.'

"'It's a sad thing, Andy,' says I, 'to think that we've been the cause of the breaking of a woman's heart.'

"'It is,' says Andy, 'and I tell you what I'm willing to do, Jeff. You've always been a man of a soft and generous disposition. Perhaps I've been too hard and worldly and suspicious. For once I'll meet you half way. Go to Mrs. Trotter and tell her to draw the $2,000 from the bank and give it to this man she's infatuated with and be happy.'

"I jumps and shakes Andy's hand for five minutes, and then I goes back to Mrs. Trotter and tells her, and she cries as hard for joy as she did for sorrow.

"Two days afterward me and Andy packed up to go.

"'Wouldn't you like to go down and meet Mrs. Trotter once before we leave?' I asks him. 'She'd like mightily to know you and express her encomiums and gratitude.'

"'Why, I guess not,' says Andy. 'I guess we'd better hurry and catch that train.'

"I was strapping our capital around me in a memory belt like we always carried it, when Andy pulls a roll of large bills out of his pocket and asks me to put 'em with the rest.

"'What's this?' says I.

"'It's Mrs. Trotter's two thousand,' says Andy.

"'How do you come to have it?' I asks.

"'She gave it to me,' says Andy. 'I've been calling on her three evenings a week for more than a month.'

"'Then you are William Wilkinson?' says I.

"'I was,' says Andy."

A MIDSUMMER MASQUERADE

"SATAN," said Jeff Peters, "is a hard boss to work for. When other people are having their vacation is when he keeps you the busiest. As old Dr. Watts or St. Paul or some other diagnostician says: 'He always finds somebody for idle hands to do.'

"I remember one summer when me and my partner, Andy Tucker, tried to take a layoff from our professional and business duties; but it seems that our work followed us wherever we went.

"Now, with a preacher it's different. He can throw off his responsibilities and enjoy himself. On the 31st of May he wraps mosquito netting and tin foil around the pulpit, grabs his niblick, breviary and fishing pole and hikes for Lake Como or Atlantic City according to the size of the loudness with which he has been called by his congregation. And, sir, for three months he don't have to think about business except to hunt around in Deuteronomy and Proverbs and Timothy to find texts to cover and exculpate such little midsummer penances as dropping a couple of looey door on rouge or teaching a Presbyterian widow to swim.

"But I was going to tell you about mine and Andy's summer vacation that wasn't one.

"We was tired of finance and all the branches of unsanctified ingenuity. Even Andy, whose brain rarely ever stopped working, began to make noises like a tennis cabinet.

"'Heigh ho!' says Andy. 'I'm tired. I've got that steam up the yacht Corsair and ho for the Riviera! feeling. I want to loaf and indict my soul, as Walt Whittier says. I want to play pinochle with Merry del Val or give a knouting to the tenants on my Tarrytown estates or do something summery and outside the line of routine and sand-bagging.'

"'Patience,' says I. 'You'll have to climb higher in the profession before you can taste the laurels that crown the footprints of the great captains of industry. Now, what I'd like, Andy,' says I, 'would be a summer sojourn in a mountain village far from scenes of larceny, labor and overcapitalization. I'm tired, too, and a month or so of sinlessness ought to leave us in good shape to begin again to take away the white man's burdens in the fall.'

"Andy fell in with the rest cure idea at once, so we struck the general passenger agents of all the railroads for summer resort literature, and took a week to study out where we should go. I reckon the first passenger agent in the world was that man Genesis. But there wasn't much competition in his day, and when he said: 'The Lord made the earth in six days, and all very good,' he hadn't any idea to what extent the press agents of the summer hotels would plagiarize from him later on.

"When we finished the booklets we perceived, easy, that the United States from Passadumkeg, Maine, to El Paso, and from Skagway to Key West was a paradise of glorious mountain peaks, crystal lakes, new laid-eggs, golf, girls, garages, cooling breezes, straw rides, open plumbing and tennis; and all within two hours' ride.

"So me and Andy dumps the books out the back window and packs our trunk and takes the 6 o'clock Tortoise Flyer for Crow Knob, a kind of a dernier resort in the mountains on the line of Tennessee and North Carolina.

"We was directed to a kind of private hotel called Woodchuck Inn, and thither me and Andy bent and almost broke our footsteps over the rocks and stumps. The Inn set back from the road in a big grove of trees, and it looked fine with its broad porches and a lot of women in white dresses rocking in the shade. The rest of Crow Knob was a post office and some scenery set at an angle of forty-five degrees and a welkin.

"Well, sir, when we got to the gate who do you suppose comes down the walk to greet us? Old Smoke-'em-out Smithers, who used to be the best open air painless dentist and electric liver pad faker in the Southwest.

"Old Smoke-'em-out is dressed clerico-rural, and has the mingled air of a landlord and a claim jumper. Which aspect he corroborates by telling us that he is the host and perpetrator of Woodchuck Inn. I introduces Andy, and we talk about a few volatile topics, such as will go around at meetings of boards of directors and old associates like us three were. Old Smoke-'em-out leads us into a kind of a summer house in the yard near the gate and took up the harp of life and smote on all the chords with his mighty right.

"'Gents,' says he, 'I'm glad to see you. Maybe you can help me out of a scrape. I'm getting a bit old for street work, so I leased this dogdays emporium so the good things would come to me. Two weeks before the season opened I gets a letter signed Lieut. Peary and one from the Duke of Marlborough, each wanting to engage board for part of the summer.

"'Well, sir, you gents know what a big thing for an obscure hustler it would be to have for guests two gentlemen whose names are famous from long association with icebergs and the Coburgs. So I prints a lot of handbills announcing that Woodchuck Inn would shelter these distinguished boarders during the summer, except in places where it leaked, and I sends 'em out to towns around as far as Knoxville and Charlotte and Fish Dam and Bowling Green.

"'And now look up there on the porch, gents,' says Smoke-'em-out, 'at them disconsolate specimens of their fair sex waiting for the arrival of the Duke and the Lieutenant. The house is packed from rafters to cellar with hero worshippers.

"'There's four normal school teachers and two abnormal; there's three high school graduates between 37 and 42; there's two literary old maids and one that can't write; there's a couple of society women and a lady from Haw River.

Two elocutionists are bunking in the corncrib, and I've put cots in the hayloft for the cook and the society editress of the Chattanooga *Opera Glass.* You see how names draw, gents.'

" 'Well,' says I, 'how is it that you don't seem to be biting your thumbs at good luck? You didn't use to be that way.'

" 'I ain't through,' says Smoke-'em-out. 'Yesterday was the day for the advent of the auspicious personages. I goes down to the depot to welcome 'em. Two apparently animate substances gets off the train, both carrying bags full of cro-quet mallets and these magic lanterns with pushbuttons.

" 'I compares these integers with the original signatures to the letters—and, well, gents, I reckon the mistake was due to my poor eyesight. Instead of be-ing the Lieutenant, the daisy chain and wild verbena explorer was none other than Levi T. Peevy, a soda water clerk from Asheville. And the Duke of Marl-borough turned out to be Theo. Drake of Murfreesborough, a bookkeeper in a grocery. What did I do? I kicked 'em both back on the train and watched 'em depart for the lowlands, the low. .

" 'Now you see the fix I'm in, gents,' goes on Smoke-'em-out Smithers. 'I told the ladies that the notorious visitors had been detained on the road by some unavoidable circumstances that made a noise like an ice jam and an heiress, but they would arrive a day or two later. When they find out that they've been deceived,' says Smoke-'em-out, 'every yard of cross-barred muslin and natural waved switch in the house will pack up and leave. It's a hard deal,' says old Smoke-'em-out.

" 'Friend,' says Andy, touching the old man on the æsophagus, 'why this jeremiad when the polar regions and the portals of Blenheim are conspiring to hand you prosperity on a hall-marked silver salver? We have arrived.'

" 'A light breaks out on Smoke-'em-out's face.

" 'Can you do it, gents?' he asks. 'Could ye do it? Could ye play the polar man and the little duke for the nice ladies? Will ye do it?'

"I see that Andy is superimposed with his old hankering for the oral and polyglot system of buncoing. That man had a vocabulary of about 10,000 words and synonyms, which arrayed themselves into contraband sophistries and parables when they came out.

" 'Listen,' says Andy to old Smoke-'em-out. 'Can we do it? You behold before you, Mr. Smithers, two of the finest equipped men on earth for inveigling the proletariat, whether by word of mouth, sleight-of-hand or swiftness of foot. Dukes come and go, explorers go and get lost, but me and Jeff Peters,' says Andy, 'go after the come-ons forever. If you say so, we're the two illustrious guests you were expecting. And you'll find,' says Andy, 'that we'll give you the true local color of the title rôles from the aurora borealis to the ducal portcullis.'

"Old Smoke-'em-out is delighted. He takes me and Andy up to the inn by an arm apiece, telling us on the way that the finest fruits of the can and luxuries of the fast freights should be ours without price as long as we would stay.

"On the porch Smoke-'em-out says: 'Ladies, I have the honor to introduce His Gracefulness the Duke of Marlborough and the famous inventor of the North Pole, Lieut. Peary.'

"The skirts all flutter and the rocking chairs squeak as me and Andy bows and then goes on in with old Smoke-'em-out to register. And then we washed up and turned our cuffs, and the landlord took us to the rooms he'd been saving for us and got out a demijohn of North Carolina real mountain dew.

"I expected trouble when Andy began to drink. He has the artistic metem-psychosis which is half drunk when sober and looks down on airships when stimulated.

"After lingering with the demijohn me and Andy goes out on the porch, where the ladies are to begin to earn our keep. We sit in two special chairs and then the schoolma'ams and literaterrers hunched their rockers close around us.

One lady says to me: 'How did that last venture of yours turn out, sir?'

"Now, I'd clean forgot to have an understanding with Andy which I was to be, the duke or the lieutenant. And I couldn't tell from her question whether she was referring to Arctic or matrimonial expeditions. So I gave an answer that would cover both cases.

"'Well, ma'am,' says I, 'it was a freeze out—right smart of a freeze out, ma'am.'

"And then the flood gates of Andy's perorations was opened and I knew which one of the renowned ostensible guests I was supposed to be. I wasn't either. Andy was both. And still furthermore it seemed that he was trying to be the mouthpiece of the entire British nobility and of Arctic exploration from Sir John Franklin down. It was the union of corn whiskey and the conscientious fictional form that Mr. W. D. Howletts admires so much.

"'Ladies,' says Andy, smiling semicircularly, 'I am truly glad to visit America. I do not consider the magna charta,' says he, 'or gas balloons or snow-shoes in any way a detriment to the beauty and charm of your American women, sky-scrapers or the architecture of your icebergs. The next time,' says Andy, 'that I go after the North Pole all the Vanderbilts in Greenland won't be able to turn me out in the cold—I mean make it hot for me.'

"'Tell us about one of your trips, Lieutenant,' says one of the normals.

"'Sure,' says Andy, getting the decision over a hiccup. 'It was in the spring of last year that I sailed the Castle of Blenheim up to latitude 87 degrees Fahrenheit and beat the record. Ladies,' says Andy, 'it was a sad sight to see a Duke allied by a civil and liturgical chattel mortgage to one of your first families lost in a region of semiannual days.' And then he goes on, 'At four bells we sighted Westminster Abbey, but there was not a drop to eat. At noon we threw out five sandbags, and the ship rose fifteen knots higher. At midnight,' continues Andy, 'the restaurants closed. Sitting on a cake of ice we ate seven hot dogs. All around us was snow and ice. Six times a night the boatswain rose up and tore a leaf off the calendar so we could keep time with the barometer. At 12,' says Andy, with a lot of anguish in his face, 'three huge polar bears sprang down the hatchway, into the cabin. And then——'

"'What then, Lieutenant?' says a schoolma'am, excitely.

"Andy gives a loud sob.

"'The Duchess shook me,' he cries out, and slides out of the chair and weeps on the porch.

"Well, of course, that fixed the scheme. The women boarders all left the next morning. The landlord wouldn't speak to us for two days, but when he found we had money to pay our way he loosened up.

"So me and Andy had a quiet, restful summer after all, coming away from Crow Knob with $1,100, that we enticed out of old Smoke-'em-out playing seven up."

SHEARING THE WOLF

JEFF PETERS was always eloquent when the ethics of his profession were under discussion.

"The only times," said he, "that me and Andy Tucker ever had any hiatuses in our cordial intents was when we differed on the moral aspects of grafting.

Andy had his standards and I had mine. I didn't approve of all of Andy's schemes for levying contributions from the public, and he thought I allowed my conscience to interfere too often for the financial good of the firm. We had high arguments sometimes. Once one word led on to another till he said I reminded him of Rockefeller.

"'I know how you mean that, Andy,' says I, 'but we have been friends too long for me to take offense, at a taunt that you will regret when you cool off. I have yet,' says I, 'to shake hands with a subpœna server.'

"One summer me and Andy decided to rest up a spell in a fine little town in the mountains of Kentucky called Grassdale. We was supposed to be horse drovers, and good decent citizens besides, taking a summer vacation. The Grassdale people liked us, and me and Andy declared a secession of hostilities, never so much as floating the fly leaf of a rubber concession prospectus or flashing a Brazilian diamond while we was there.

"One day the leading hardware merchant of Grassdale drops around to the hotel where me and Andy stopped, and smokes with us, sociable, on the side porch. We knew him pretty well from pitching quoits in the afternoons in the court house yard. He was a loud, red man, breathing hard, but fat and respectable beyond all reason.

"After we talk on all the notorious themes of the day, this Murkison—for such was his entitlements—takes a letter out of his coat pocket in a careful, careless way and hands it to us to read.

"'Now, what do you think of that?' says laughing—'a letter like that to ME!'

"Me and Andy sees at a glance what it is; but we pretend to read it through. It was one of them old-time typewritten green goods letters explaining how for $1,000 you could get $5,000 in bills that an expert couldn't tell from the genuine; and going on to tell how they were made from plates stolen by an employee of the Treasury at Washington.

"'Think of 'em sending a letter like that to ME!' says Murkison again.

"'Lots of good men get 'em,' says Andy. 'If you don't answer the first letter they let you drop. If you answer it they write again asking you to come on with your money and do business.'

"'But think of 'em writing to ME!' says Murkison.

"A few days later he drops around again.

"'Boys,' says he, 'I know you are all right or I wouldn't confide in you. I wrote to them rascals again just for fun. They answered and told me to come on to Chicago. They said telegraph to J. Smith when I would start. When I get there I'm to wait on a certain street corner till a man in a gray suit comes along and drops a newspaper in front of me. Then I am to ask how the water is, and he knows it's me and I know it's him.'

"'Ah, yes,' says Andy, gaping, 'it's the same old game. I've often read about it in the papers. Then he conducts you to the private abattoir in the hotel, where Mr. Jones is already waiting. They show you brand-new real money and sell you all you want at five for one. You see 'em put it in a satchel for you and know it's there. Of course it's brown paper when you come to look at it afterward.'

"'Oh, they couldn't switch it on me,' says Murkison. 'I haven't built up the best paying business in Grassdale without having witticisms about me. You say it's real money they show you, Mr. Tucker?'

"'I've always—I see by the papers that it always is,' says Andy.

"'Boys,' says Murkison, 'I've got it in my mind that them fellows can't fool me. I think I'll put a couple of thousand in my jeans and go up there and put it all over 'em. If Bill Murkison gets his eyes once on them bills they show him he'll never take 'em off of 'em. They offer $5 for $1, and they'll have to stick 'to the bargain if I tackle 'em. That's the kind of trader Bill Murkison is. Yes I jist believe I'll drop up Chicago way and take a 5 to 1 shot on J. Smith. I guess the water'll be fine enough.'

"Me and Andy tries to get this financial misquotation out of Murkison's head, but we might as well have tried to keep the man who rolls peanuts with a toothpick from betting on Bryan's election. No, sir; he was going to perform a public duty by catching these green goods swindlers at their own game. Maybe it would teach 'em a lesson.

"After Murkison left us me and Andy sat a while prepondering over our silent meditations and heresies of reason. In our idle hours we always improved our higher selves by ratiocination and mental thought.

"'Jeff,' says Andy after a long time, 'quite unseldom I have seen fit to impugn your molars when you have been chewing the rag with me about your conscientious way of doing business. I may have been often wrong. But here is a case where I think we can agree. I feel that it would be wrong for us to allow Mr. Murkison to go alone to meet those Chicago green goods men. There is but one way it can end. Don't you think we would both feel better if we was to intervene in some way and prevent the doing of this deed?'

"I got up and shook Andy Tucker's hand hard and long.

"'Andy,' says I, 'I may have had one or two hard thoughts about the heartlessness of your corporation, but I retract 'em now. You have a kind nucleus at the interior of your exterior after all. It does you credit. I was just thinking the same thing that you have expressed. It would not be honorable or praiseworthy,' says I, 'for us to let Murkison go on with this project he has taken up. If he is determined to go let us go with him and prevent this swindle from coming off.'

"Andy agreed with me; and I was glad to see that he was in earnest about breaking up this green goods scheme.

"'I don't call myself a religious man,' says I, 'or a fanatic in moral bigotry, but I can't stand still and see a man who has built up a business by his own efforts and brains and risk be robbed by an unscrupulous trickster who is a menace to the public good.'

"'Right, Jeff,' says Andy. 'We'll stick right along with Murkison if he insist on going and block this funny business. I'd hate to see any money dropped in it as bad as you would.'

"Well, we went to see Murkison.

"'No, boys,' says he. 'I can't consent to let the song of this Chicago siren waft by me on the summer breeze. I'll fry some fat out of this ignis fatuus or burn a hole in the skillet. But I'd be plumb diverted to death to have you all go along with me. Maybe you could help some when it comes to cashing in the ticket to that 5 to 1 shot. Yes, I'd really take it as a pastime and regalement if you boys would go along too.

"Murkison gives it out in Grassdale that he is going for a few days with Mr. Peters and Mr. Tucker to look over some iron ore property in West Virginia. He wires J. Smith that he will set foot in the spider web on a given date; and the three of us lights out for Chicago.

"On the way Murkison amuses himself with premonitions and advance pleasant recollections.

"'In a gray suit,' says he, 'on the southwest corner of Wabash Avenue and Lake Street. He drops the paper, and I ask how the water is. Oh, my, my, my!' And then he laughs all over for five minutes.

"Sometimes Murkison was serious and tried to talk himself out of his cogitations, whatever they was.

"'Boys,' says he, 'I wouldn't have this to get out in Grassdale for ten times a thousand dollars. It would ruin me there. But I know you all are all right. I think it's the duty of every citizen,' says he, 'to try to do up these robbers that prey upon the public. I'll show 'em whether the water's fine. Five dollars for one—that's what J. Smith offers, and he'll have to keep his contract if he does business with Bill Murkison.'

"We got into Chicago about 7 P. M. Murkison was to meet the gray man at half-past 9. We had dinner at a hotel and then went up to Murkison's room to wait for the time to come.

"'Now, boys,' says Murkison, 'let's get our gumption together and inoculate a plan for defeating the enemy. Suppose while I'm exchanging airy bandage with the gray capper you gents come along, by accident, you know, and holler: "Hello, Murk!" and shake hands with symptoms of surprise and familiarity. Then I take the capper aside and tell him you all are Jenkins and Brown of Grassdale, groceries and feed, good men and maybe willing to take a chance while away from home.'

"'"Bring 'em along," he'll say, of course, "if they care to invest." Now, how does that scheme strike you?'

"'What do you say, Jeff?' says Andy, looking at me.

"'Why, I'll tell you what I say,' says I. 'I say let's settle this thing right here now. I don't see any use of wasting any more time.' I took a nickel-plated .38 out of my pocket and clicked the cylinder around a few times.

"'You undevout, sinful, insidious hog,' says I to Murkison, 'get out that two thousand and lay it on the table. Obey with velocity,' says I, 'for otherwise alternatives are impending. I am preferably a man of mildness, but now and then I find myself in the middle of extremities. Such men as you,' I went on after he had laid the money out, 'is what keeps the jails and court houses going. You come up here to rob these men of their money. Does it excuse you?' I asks, 'that they were trying to skin you? No, sir; you was going to rob Peter to stand off Paul. You are ten times worse,' says I, 'than that green goods man. You go to church at home and pretend to be a decent citizen, but you'll come to Chicago and commit larceny from men that have built up a sound and profitable business by dealing with such contemptible scoundrels as you have tried to be to-day. How do you know,' says I, 'that that green goods man hasn't a large family dependent upon his extortions? It's you supposedly respectable citizens who are always on the lookout to get something for nothing,' says I, 'that support the lotteries and wild-cat mines and stock exchanges and wire tappers of this country. If it wasn't for you they'd go out of business. The green goods man you was going to rob,' says I, 'studied maybe for years to learn his trade. Every turn he makes he risks his money and liberty and maybe his life. You come up here all sanctified and vanoplied with respectability and a pleasing post office address to swindle him. If he gets the money you can squeal to the police. If you get it he hocks the gray suit to buy supper and says nothing. Mr. Tucker and me sized you up,' says I, 'and came along to see that you got what you deserved. Hand over the money,' says I, 'you grass-fed hypocrite.'

"I put the two thousand, which was all in $20 bills, in my inside pocket.

"'Now get out your watch,' says I to Murkison. 'No, I don't want it,' says I. 'Lay it on the table and you sit in that chair till it ticks off an hour. Then you can go. If you make any noise or leave any sooner we'll handbill you all over Grassdale. I guess your high position there is worth more than $2,000 to you.'

"Then me and Andy left.

"On the train Andy was a long time silent. Then he says: 'Jeff, do you mind my asking you a question?'

"'Two,' says I, 'or forty.'

"'Was that the idea you had,' says he, 'when we started out with Murkison?'

" 'Why certainly,' says I. 'What else could it have been? Wasn't it yours, too?'

"In about half an hour Andy spoke again. I think there are times when Andy don't exactly understand my system of ethics and moral hygiene.

" 'Jeff,' says he, 'some time when you have the leisure I wish you'd draw off a diagram and footnotes of that conscience of yours. I'd like to have it to refer to occasionally.' "

INNOCENTS OF BROADWAY

"I HOPE some day to retire from business," said Jeff Peters; "and when I do I don't want anybody to be able to say that I ever got a dollar of any man's money without giving him a quid pro rata for it. I've always managed to leave a customer some little gewgaw to paste in his scrapbook or stick between his Seth Thomas clock and the wall after we are through trading.

"There was one time I came near having to break this rule of mine and do a profligate and illaudable action, but I was saved from it by the laws and statutes of our great and profitable country.

"One summer me and Andy Tucker, my partner, went to New York to lay in our annual assortment of clothes and gents' furnishings. We was always pompous and regardless dressers, finding that looks went further than anything else in our business, except maybe our knowledge of railroad schedules and an autograph photo of the President that Loeb sent us, probably by mistake. Andy wrote a nature letter once and sent it in about animals that he had seen caught in a trap lots of times. Loeb must have read it 'triplets,' instead of 'trap lots,' and sent the photo. Anyhow, it was useful to us to show people as a guarantee of good faith.

"Me and Andy never cared much to do business in New York. It was too much like pothunting. Catching suckers in that town, is like dynamiting a Texas lake for bass. All you have to do anywhere between the North and East rivers is to stand in the street with an open bag marked, 'Drop packages of money here. No checks or loose bills taken.' You have a cop handy to club pikers who try to chip in post office orders and Canadian money, and that's all there is to New York for a hunter who loves his profession. So me and Andy used to just nature fake the town. We'd get out our spyglasses and watch the woodcocks along the Broadway swamps putting plaster casts on their broken legs, and then we'd sneak away without firing a shot.

"One day in the papier mâché palm room of a chloral hydrate and hops agency in a side street about eight inches off Broadway me and Andy had thrust upon us the acquaintance of a New Yorker. We had beer together until we discovered that each of us knew a man named Hellsmith, travelling for a stove factory in Duluth. This caused us to remark that the world was a very small place, and then this New Yorker busts his string and takes off his tin foil and excelsior packing and starts in giving us his Ellen Terris, beginning with the time he used to sell shoelaces to the Indians on the spot where Tammany Hall now stands.

"This New Yorker had made his money keeping a cigar store in Beekman Street, and he hadn't been above Fourteenth Street in ten years. Moreover, he had whiskers, and the time has gone by when a true sport will do anything to a man with whiskers. No grafter except a boy who is soliciting subscribers to an illustrated weekly to win the prize air rifle, or a widow, would have the heart to tamper with the man behind with the razor. He was a typical city Reub— I'd bet the man hadn't been out of sight of a skyscraper in twenty-five years.

"Well, presently this metropolitan backwoodsman pulls out a roll of bills with an old blue sleeve elastic fitting tight around it and opens it up.

" 'There's $5,000, Mr. Peters,' says he, shoving it over the table to me, 'saved during my fifteen years of business. Put that in your pocket and keep it for me, Mr. Peters. I'm glad to meet you gentlemen from the West, and I may take a drop too much. I want you to take care of my money for me. Now, let's have another beer.'

" 'You'd better keep this yourself,' says I. 'We are strangers to you, and you can't trust everybody you meet. Put your roll back in your pocket,' says I. 'And you'd better run along home before some farm-hand from the Kaw River bottoms strolls in here and sells you a copper mine.'

" 'O, I don't know,' says Whiskers, 'I guess Little Old New York can take care of herself. I guess I know a man that's on the square when I see him. I've always found the Western people all right. I ask you as a favor, Mr. Peters,' says he, 'to keep that roll in your pocket for me. I know a gentleman when I see him. And now let's have some more beer.'

"In about ten minutes this fall of manna leans back in his chair and snores. Andy looks at me and says: 'I reckon I'd better stay with him for five minutes or so, in case the waiter comes in.'

"I went out the side door and walked half a block up the street. And then I came back and sat down at the table.

" 'Andy,' says I, 'I can't do it. It's too much like swearing off taxes. I can't go off with this man's money without doing something to earn it like taking advantage of the Bankrupt act or leaving a bottle of eczema lotion in his pocket to make it look more like a square deal.'

" 'Well,' says Andy, 'it does seem kind of hard on one's professional pride to lope off with a bearded pard's competency, especially after he has nominated you custodian of his bundle in the sappy insouciance of his urban indiscrimination. Suppose we wake him up and see if we can formulate some commercial sophistry by which he will be enabled to give us both his money and a good excuse.'

"We wakes up Whiskers. He stretches himself and yawns out the hypothesis that he must have dropped off for a minute. And then he says he wouldn't mind sitting in at a little gentleman's game of poker. He used to play some when he attended high school in Brooklyn; and as he was out for a good time, why—and so forth.

"Andy brights up a little at that, for it looks like it might be a solution to our financial troubles. So we all three go to our hotel further down Broadway and have the cards and chips brought up to Andy's room. I tried once more to make this Babe in the Horticultural Gardens take his five thousand. But no.

" 'Keep that little roll for me, Mr. Peters,' says he, 'and oblige. I'll ask you fer it when I want it. I guess I know when I'm among friends. A man that's done business on Beekman Street for twenty years, right in the heart of the wisest little old village on earth, ought to know what he's about. I guess I can tell a gentleman from a con man or a flimflammer when I meet him. I've got some odd change, in my clothes—enough to start the game with, I guess.'

"He goes through his pockets and rains $20 gold certificates on the table till it looked like a $10,000 'Autumn Day in a Lemon Grove' picture by Turner in the salons. Andy almost smiled.

"The first round that was dealt, this boulevardier slaps down his hand, claims low and jack and big casino and rakes in the pot.

"Andy always took a pride in his poker playing. He got up from the table and looked sadly out of the window at the street cars.

" 'Well, gentlemen,' says the cigar man, 'I don't blame you for not wanting to play. I've forgotten the fine points of the game, I guess, it's been so long since I indulged. Now, how long are you gentlemen going to be in the city?'

"I told him about a week longer. He says that'll suit him fine. His cousin is coming over from Brooklyn that evening and they are going to see the sights of New York. His cousin, he says, is in the artificial limb and lead casket business, and hasn't crossed the bridge in eight years. They expect to have the time of their lives, and he winds up by asking me to keep his roll of money for him till next day. I tried to make him take it, but it only insulted him to mention it.

" 'I'll use what I've got in loose change,' says he. 'You keep the rest for me. I'll drop in on you and Mr. Tucker to-morrow afternoon about 6 or 7,' says he, 'and we'll have dinner together. Be good.'

"After Whiskers had gone Andy looked at me curious and doubtful.

" 'Well, Jeff,' says he, 'it looks like the ravens are trying to feed us two Elijahs so hard that if we turned 'em down again we ought to have the Audubon society after us. It won't do to put the crown aside too often. I know this is something like paternalism, but don't you think Opportunity has skinned its knuckles about enough knocking at our door?'

"I put my feet on the table and my hands in my pockets, which is an attitude unfavorable to frivolous thoughts.

" 'Andy,' says I, 'this man with the hirsute whiskers has got us in a predicament. We can't move hand or foot with his money. You and me have got a gentleman's agreement with Fortune that we can't break. We've done business in the West where it's more of a fair game. Out there the people we skin are trying to skin us, even the farmers and the remittance men that the magazines send out to write up Goldfields. But there's little sport in New York city for rod, reel or gun. They hunt here with either one of two things—a slungshot or a letter of introduction. The town has been stocked so full of carp that the game fish are all gone. If you spread a net here, do you catch legitimate suckers in it, such as the Lord intended to be caught—fresh guys who know it all, sports with a little coin and the nerve to play another man's game, street crowds out for the fun of dropping a dollar or two and village smarties who know just where the little pea is? No, sir,' says I. 'What the grafters live on here is widows and orphans, and foreigners who save up a bag of money and hand it over the first counter they see with an iron railing to it, and factory girls and little shopkeepers that never leave the block they do business on. That's what they call suckers here. They're nothing but canned sardines, and all the bait you need to catch 'em is a pocketknife and a soda cracker.

" 'Now, this cigar man,' I went on, 'is one of the types. He's lived twenty years on one street without learning as much as you would in getting a once-over shave from a lockjawed barber in a Kansas crossroads town. But he's a New Yorker, and he'll brag about that all the time when he isn't picking up live wires or getting in front of street cars or paying out money to wire-tappers or standing under a safe that's being hoisted into a sky-scraper. When a New Yorker does loosen up,' says I, 'it's like the spring decomposition of the ice jam in the Allegheny River. He'll swamp you with cracked ice and backwater if you don't get out of the way.

" 'It's mighty lucky for us, Andy,' says I, "that this cigar exponent with the parsley dressing saw fit to bedeck us with his childlike trust and altruism. For,' says I, 'this money of his is an eyesore to my sense of rectitude and ethics. We can't take it, Andy; you know we can't,' says I, 'for we haven't a shadow of a title to it—not a shadow. If there was the least bit of a way we could put in a claim to it I'd be willing to see him start in for another twenty years and make another $5,000 for himself, but we haven't sold him anything, we haven't been embroiled in a trade or anything commercial. He approached us friendly,' says

I, and with blind and beautiful idiocy laid the stuff in our hands. We'll have to give it back to him when he wants it.'

"'Your arguments,' says Andy, 'are past criticism or comprehension. No, we can't walk off with the money—as things now stand. I admire your conscious way of doing business, Jeff,' says Andy, 'and I wouldn't propose anything that wasn't square in line with your theories of morality and initiative.

"'But I'll be away to-night and most of to-morrow, Jeff,' says Andy, 'I've got some business affairs that I want to attend to. When this free greenbacks party comes in to-morrow afternoon hold him here till I arrive. We've all got an engagement for dinner, you know.'

"Well, sir, about 5 the next afternoon in trips the cigar man, with his eyes half open.

"Been having a glorious time, Mr. Peters,' says he. 'Took in all the sights. I tell you New York is the onliest only. Now if you don't mind,' say he 'I'll lie down on that couch and doze off for about nine minutes before Mr. Tucker comes. I'm not used to being up all night. And to-morrow, if you don't mind, Mr. Peters, I'll take that five thousand. I met a man last night that's got a sure winner at the race-track to-morrow. Excuse me for being so impolite as to go asleep, Mr. Peters.'

"And so this inhabitant of the second city in the world reposes himself and begins to snore, while I sit there musing over things and wishing I was back in the West, where you could always depend on a customer fighting to keep his money hard enough to let your conscience take it from him.

"At half-past 5 Andy comes in and sees the sleeping form.

"'I've been over to Trenton,' says Andy, pulling a document out of his pocket. 'I think I've got this matter fixed up all right, Jeff. Look at that.'

"I open the paper and see that it is a corporation charter issued by the State of New Jersey to 'The Peters & Tucker Consolidated and Amalgamated Aërial Franchise Development Company, Limited.'

"'It's to buy up rights of way for airship lines,' explained Andy. 'The Legislature wasn't in session, but I found a man at a postcard stand in the lobby that kept a stock of charters on hand. There are 100,000 shares,' says Andy, 'expected to reach a par value of $1. I had one blank certificate of stock printed.'

"Andy takes out the blank and begins to fill it in with a fountain pen.

"'The whole Bunch,' says he, 'goes to our friend in dreamland for $5,000. Did you learn his name?'

"'Make it out to bearer,' says I.

"We put the certificate of stock in the cigar man's hand and went out to pack our suit cases.

"On the ferryboat Andy says to me: "Is your conscience easy about taking the money now, Jeff?'

"Why shouldn't it be?' says I. 'Are we any better than any other Holding Corporation?' "

CONSCIENCE IN ART

"I NEVER could hold my partner, Andy Tucker, down to legitimate ethics of pure swindling," said Jeff Peters to me one day.

"Andy had too much imagination to be honest. He used to devise schemes of .

money-getting so fraudulent and high-financial that they wouldn't have been allowed in the bylaws of a railroad rebate system.

"Myself, I never believed in taking any man's dollars unless I gave him something for it—something in the way of rolled gold jewelry, garden seeds, lumbago lotion, stock certificates, stove polish or a crack on the head to show for his money. I guess I must have had New England ancestors away back and inherited some of their stanch and rugged fear of the police.

"But Andy's family tree was in different kind. I don't think he could have traced his descent any further back than a corporation.

"One summer while we was in the middle West, working down the Ohio valley with a line of family albums, headache powders and roach destroyer, Andy takes one of his notions of high and actionable financiering.

" 'Jeff,' says he, 'I've been thinking that we ought to drop these rutabaga fanciers and give our attention to something more nourishing and prolific. If we keep on snapshooting these hinds for their egg money we'll be classed as nature fakers. How about plunging into the fastnesses of the skyscraper country and biting some big bull caribous in the chest?'

" 'Well,' says I, 'you know my idiosyncrasies. I prefer a square, non-illegal style of business such as we are carrying on now. When I take money I want to leave some tangible object in the other fellow's hands for him to gaze at and to distract his attention from my spoor, even if it's only a Komical Kuss Trick Finger Ring for Squirting Perfume in a Friend's Eye. But if you've got a fresh idea, Andy,' says I, 'let's have a look at it. I'm not so wedded to petty graft that I would refuse something better in the way of a subsidy.'

" 'I was thinking,' says Andy, "of a little hunt without horn, hound or camera among the great herd of the Midas Americanus, commonly known as the Pittsburg millionaires.'

" 'In New York?' I asks.

" 'No, sir,' says Andy, 'in Pittsburg. That's their habitat. They don't like New York. They go there now and then just because it's expected of 'em.'

" 'A Pittsburg millionaire in New York is like a fly in a cup of hot coffee—he attracts attention and comment, but he don't enjoy it. New York ridicules him for "blowing" so much money in that town of sneaks and snobs, and sneers. The truth is, he don't spend anything while he is there. I saw a memorandum of expenses for a ten day's trip to Bunkum Town made by a Pittsburg man worth $15,000,000 once. Here's the way he set it down:

R. R. fare to and from	$ 21 00
Cab fare to and from hotel	2 00
Hotel bill @ $5 per day	50 00
Tips	5,750 00
Total	$5,823 00

" 'That's the voice of New York,' goes on Andy. 'The town's nothing but a head waiter. If you tip it too much it'll go and stand by the door and make fun of you to the hat check boy. When a Pittsburger wants to spend money and have a good time he stays at home. That's where we'll go to catch him.'

"Well, to make a dense story more condensed, me and Andy cached our paris green and antipyrine powders and albums in a friend's cellar, and took the trail to Pittsburg. Andy didn't have any especial prospectus of chicanery and violence drawn up, but he always had plenty of confidence that his immoral nature would rise to any occasion that presented itself.

"As a concession to my ideas of self-preservation and rectitude he promised that if I should take an active and incriminating part in any little business venture that we might work up, there should be something actual and cognizant to the senses of touch, sight, taste or smell to transfer to the victim for the money so my conscience might rest easy. After that I felt better and entered more cheerfully into the foul play.

"'Andy,' says I, as we strayed through the smoke along the cinderpath they call Smithfield Street, 'had you figured out how we are going to get acquainted with these coke kings and pig iron squeezers? Not that I would decry my own worth or system of drawing-room deportment, and work with the olive fork and pie knife,' says I, 'but isn't the entree nous into the salons of the stogie smokers going to be harder than you imagined?'

"'If there's any handicap at all,' says Andy, 'it's our own refinement and inherent culture. Pittsburg millionaires are a fine body of plain, wholehearted, unassuming, democratic men.

"'They are rough but uncivil in their manners, and though their ways are boisterous and unpolished, under it all they have a great deal of impoliteness and discourtesy. Nearly every one of 'em rose from obscurity,' says Andy, 'and they'll live in it till the town gets to using smoke consumers. If we act simple and unaffected and don't go too far from the saloons and keep making a noise like an import duty on steel rails we won't have any trouble in meeting some of 'em socially.'

"Well, Andy and me drifted about town three or four days getting our bearings. We got to knowing several millionaires by sight.

"One used to stop his automobile in front of our hotel and have a quart of champagne brought out to him. When the waiter opened it he'd turn it up to his mouth and drink it out of the bottle. That showed he used to be a glassblower before he made his money.

"One evening Andy failed to come to the hotel for dinner. About 11 o'clock he came into my room.

"'Landed one, Jeff,' says he. 'Twelve millions. Oil, rolling mills, real estate and natural gas. He's a fine man; no airs about him. Made all his money in the last five years. He's got professors posting him up now on education—art and literature and haberdashery and such things.

"'When I saw him he'd just won a bet of $10,000 with a Steel Corporation man that there'd be four suicides in the Allegheny rolling mills to-day. So everybody in sight had to walk up and have drinks on him. He took a fancy to me and asked me to dinner with him. We went to a restaurant in Diamond Alley and sat on stools and had sparkling Moselle and clam chowder and apple fritters.

"'Then he wanted to show me his bachelor apartment on Liberty Street. He's got ten rooms over a fish market with privilege of the bath on the next floor above. He told me it cost him $18,000 to furnish his apartment, and I believe it.

"'He's got $40,000 worth of pictures in one room, and $20,000 worth of curios and antiques in another. His name's Scudder, and he's 45, and taking lessons on the piano and 15,000 barrels of oil a day out of his wells.'

"'All right,' says I. 'Preliminary canter satisfactory. But, kay vooly, voo? What good is the art junk to us? And the oil?'

"'Now, that man,' says Andy, sitting thoughtfully on the bed, 'ain't what you would call an ordinary scutt. When he was showing me his cabinet of art curios his face lighted up like the door of a coke oven. He says that if some of his big deals go through he'll make J. P. Morgan's collection of sweatshop tapestry and Augusta, Me., beadwork look like the contents of an ostrich's craw thrown on a screen by a magic lantern.

"'And then he showed me a little carving,' went on Andy, 'that anybody could see was a wonderful thing. It was something like 2,000 years old, he said. It was a lotus flower with a woman's face in it carved out of a solid piece of ivory.

"Scudder looks it up in a catalogue and describes it. An Egyptian carver named Khafra made two of 'em for King Rameses II about the year B. C. The other one can't be found. The junkshops and antique bugs have rubbered all Europe for it, but it seems to be out of stock. Scudder paid $2,000 for the one he has.'

"'Oh, well,' says I, 'this sounds like the purling of a rill to me. I thought we came here to teach the millionaires business, instead of learning art from 'em?'

"'Be patient,' says Andy, kindly. 'Maybe we will see a rift in the smoke ere long.'

"All the next morning Andy was out. I didn't see him until about noon. He came to the hotel and called me into his room across the hall. He pulled a round-ish bundle about as big as a goose egg out of his pocket and unwrapped it. It was an ivory carving just as he had described the millionaire's to me.

"'I went in an old second-hand store and pawnshop a while ago,' says Andy, 'and I see this half hidden under a lot of old daggers and truck. The pawn-broker said he'd had it several years and thinks it was soaked by some Arabs or Turks or some foreign dubs that used to live down by the river.

"'I offered him $2 for it, and I must have looked like I wanted it, for he said it would be taking the pumpernickle out of his children's mouths to hold any conversation that did not lead up to a price of $335. I finally got it for $25.

"'Jeff,' goes on Andy, 'this is the exact counterpart of Scudder's carving. It's absolutely a dead ringer for it. He'll pay $2,000 for it as quick as he'd tuck a napkin under his chin. And why shouldn't it be the genuine other one, anyhow, that the old gypsy whittled out?'

"'Why not, indeed?' says I. 'And how shall we go about compelling him to make a voluntary purchase of it?'

"Andy had his plan all ready, and I'll tell you how we carried it out.

"I got a pair of blue spectacles, put on my black frock coat, rumpled my hair up and became Prof. Pickleman. I went to another hotel, registered, and sent a telegram to Scudder to come to see me at once on important art business. The elevator dumped him on me in less than an hour. He was a foggy man with a clarion voice, smelling of Connecticut wrappers and naphtha.

"'Hello, Profess!' he shouts. 'How's your conduct?'

"I rumpled my hair some more and gave him a blue glass stare.

"'Sir,' says I. 'Are you Cornelius T. Scudder? Of Pittsburg, Pennsylvania?'

"'I am,' says he. 'Come out and have a drink.'

"'I have neither the time nor the desire,' says I, 'for such harmful and deleterious amusements. I have come from New York,' says I, 'on a matter of busi—on a matter of art.

"'I learned there that you are the owner of an Egyptian ivory carving of the time of Rameses II., representing the head of Queen Isis in a lotus flower. There were only two of such carvings made. One has been lost for many years. I recently discovered and purchased the other in a pawn—in an obscure museum in Vienna. I wish to purchase yours. Name your price.'

"'Well, the great ice jams, Profess!' says Scudder. 'Have you found the other one? Me sell? No. I don't guess Cornelius Scudder needs to sell anything that he wants to keep. Have you got the carving with you, Profess?'

"I shows it to Scudder. He examines it careful all over.

"'It's the article,' says he. 'It's a duplicate of mine, every line and curve of it. Tell you what I'll do,' he says. 'I won't sell, but I'll buy. Give you $2,500 for yours.'

"'Since you won't sell, I will,' says I. 'Large bills, please. I'm a man of few words. I must return to New York to-night. I lecture to-morrow at the aquarium.'

"Scudder sends a check down and the hotel cashes it. He goes off with the piece of antiquity and I hurry back to Andy's hotel, according to arrangement.

"Andy is walking up and down the room looking at his watch.

"'Well?' he says.

"'Twenty-five hundred,' says I. 'Cash.'

"'We've got just eleven minutes,' says Andy, 'to catch the B. & O. westbound. Grab your baggage.'

"'What's the hurry?' says I. 'It was a square deal. And even if it was only an imitation of the original carving it'll take him some time to find it out. He seemed to be sure it was the genuine article.'

"'It was,' says Andy. 'It was his own. When I was looking at his curios yesterday he stepped out of the room for a moment and I pocketed it. Now, will you pick up your suit case and hurry?'

"'Then,' says I, 'why was that story about finding another one in the pawn——'

"'Oh,' says Andy, 'out of respect for that conscience of yours. Come on.'"

THE MAN HIGHER UP

ACROSS our two dishes of spaghetti, in a corner of Provenzano's restaurant, Jeff Peters was explaining to me the three kinds of graft.

Every winter Jeff comes to New York to eat spaghetti, to watch the shipping in East River from the depths of his chincilla overcoat, and to lay in a supply of Chicago-made clothing at one of the Fulton Street stores. During the other three seasons he may be found further west—his range is from Spokane to Tampa. In his profession he takes a pride which he supports and defends with a serious and unique philosophy of ethics. His profession is no new one. He is an incorporated, uncapitalized, unlimited asylum for the reception of the restless and unwise dollars of his fellow men.

In the wilderness of stone in which Jeff seeks his annual lonely holiday he is glad to palaver of his many adventures, as a boy will whistle after sundown in a wood. Wherefore, I mark on my calendar the time of his coming, and open a question of privilege at Provenzano's concerning the little wine-stained table in the corner between the rakish rubber plant and the framed palazzio della something on the wall.

"There are two kinds of grafts," said Jeff, "that ought to be wiped out by law. I mean Wall Street speculation, and burglary."

"Nearly everybody will agree with you as to one of them," said I, with a laugh.

"Well, burglary ought to be wiped out, too," said Jeff; and I wondered whether the laugh had been redundant.

"About three months ago," said Jeff, "it was my privilege to become familiar with a sample of each of the aforesaid branches of illegitimate art. I was *sine qua grata* with a member of the housebreakers' union and one of the John D. Napoleons of finance at the same time."

"Interesting combination," said I, with a yawn. "Did I tell you I bagged a duck and a ground squirrel at one shot last week over in the Ramapos?" I knew well how to draw Jeff's stories.

"Let me tell you first about these barnacles that clog the wheels of society by poisoning the springs of rectitude with their upas-like eye," said Jeff, with the pure gleam of the muck-raker in his own.

"As I said, three months ago I got into bad company. There are two times in a man's life when he does this—when he's dead broke, and when he's rich.

"Now and then the most legitimate business runs out of luck. It was out in Arkansas I made the wrong turn at a cross-road, and drives into this town of Peavine by mistake. It seems I had already assaulted and disfigured Peavine the spring of the year before. I had sold $600 worth of young fruit trees there —plums, cherries, peaches and pears. The Peaviners were keeping an eye on the country road and hoping I might pass that way again. I drove down Main Street as far as the Crystal Palace drug-store before I realized I had committed ambush upon myself and my white horse Bill.

"The Peaviners took me by surprise and Bill by the bridle and began a conversation that wasn't entirely disassociated with the subject of fruit trees. A committee of 'em ran some trace-chains through the armholes of my vest and escorted me through their gardens and orchards.

"Their fruit trees hadn't lived up to their labels. Most of 'em had turned out to be persimmons and dogwoods, with a grove or two of blackjacks and poplars. The only one that showed any signs of bearing anything was a fine young cottonwood that had put forth a hornet's nest and half of an old corset-cover.

"The Peaviners protracted our fruitless stroll to the edge of town. They took my watch and money on account; and they kept Bill and the wagon as hostages. They said the first time one of them dogwood trees put forth an Amsden's June peach I might come back and get my things. Then they took off the trace-chains and jerked their thumbs in the direction of the Rocky Mountains; and I struck a Lewis and Clark lope for the swollen rivers and impenetrable forests.

"When I regained intellectualness I found myself walking into an unidentified town on the A., T. & S. F. railroad. The Peaviners hadn't left anything in my pockets except a plug of chewing—they wasn't after my life—and that saved it. I bit off a chunk and sits down on a pile of ties by the track to recogitate my sensations of thought and perspicacity.

"And then along comes a fast freight which slows up a little at the town; and off of it drops a black bundle that rolls for twenty yards in a cloud of dust and then gets up and begins to spit soft coal and interjections. I see it is a young man broad across the face, dressed more for Pullmans than freights, and with a cheerful kind of smile in spite of it all that made Phœbe Snow's job look like a chimney-sweep's.

" 'Fall off?' says I.

" 'Nunk,' says he. 'Got off. Arrived at my destination. What town is this?'

" 'Haven't looked it up on the map yet,' says I. 'I got in about five minutes before you did. How does it strike you?'

" 'Hard,' says he, twisting one of his arms around. 'I believe that shoulder— no, it's all right.'

"He stoops over to brush the dust off his clothes, when out of his pocket drops a fine, nine-inch burglar's steel jimmy. He picks it up and looks at me sharp, and then grins and holds out his hand.

" 'Brother,' says he, 'greetings. Didn't I see you in Southern Missouri last summer selling colored sand at half-a-dollar a teaspoonful to put into lamps to keep the oil from exploding?'

" 'Oil,' says I, 'never explodes. It's the gas that forms that explodes.' But I shakes hands with him, anyway.

" 'My name's Bill Bassett,' says he to me, 'and if you'll call it professional pride instead of conceit, I'll inform you that you have the pleasure of meeting the best burglar that ever set a gum-shoe on ground drained by the Mississippi River.'

"Well, me and this Bill Bassett sits on the ties and exchanges brags as artists in kindred lines will do. It seems he didn't have a cent, either, and we went into close caucus. He explained why an able burglar sometimes had to travel on freights by telling me that a servant girl had played him false in Little Rock, and he was making a quick get-away.

" 'It's part of my business,' says Bill Bassett, 'to play up to the ruffles when I want to make a riffle as Raffles. 'Tis loves that makes the bit go 'round. Show me a house with the swag in it and a pretty parlor-maid, and you might as well call the silver melted down and sold, and me spilling truffles and that Château stuff on the napkin under my chin, while the police are calling it an inside job just because the old lady's nephew teaches a Bible class. I first make an impression on the girl,' says Bill, 'and when she lets me inside I make an impression on the locks. But this one in Little Rock done me,' says he. 'She saw me taking a trolley ride with another girl, and when I came 'round on the night she was to leave the door open for me it was fast. And I had keys made for the doors upstairs. But, no sir. She had sure cut off my locks. She was a Delilah,' says Bill Bassett.

"It seems that Bill tried to break in anyhow with his jimmy, but the girl emitted a succession of bravura noises like the top-riders of a tally-ho, and Bill had to take all the hurdles between there and the depot. As he had no baggage they tried hard to check his departure, but he made a train that was just pulling out.

" 'Well,' says Bill Bassett, when we had exchanged memoirs of our dead lives, 'I could eat. This town don't look like it was kept under a Yale lock. Suppose we commit some mild atrocity that will bring in temporary expense money. I don't suppose you've brought along any hair tonic or rolled gold watch-chains, or similar law-defying swindles that you could sell on the plaza to the pikers of the paretic populace, have you?'

" 'No,' says I, 'I left an elegant line of Patagonian diamonds earrings and rainy-day sunbursts in my valise at Peavine. But they're to stay there till some of them black-gum trees begin to glut the market with yellow clings and Japanese plums. I reckon we can't count on them unless we take Luther Burbank in for a partner.'

" 'Very well,' says Bassett, 'we'll do the best we can. Maybe after dark I'll borrow a hairpin from some lady, and open the Farmers and Drovers Marine Bank with it.'

"While we were talking, up pulls a passenger train to the depot near by. A person in a high hat gets off on the wrong side of the train and comes tripping down the track towards us. He was a little, fat man with a big nose and rat's eyes, but dressed expensive, and carrying a hand-satchel careful, as if it had eggs or railroad bonds in it. He passes by us and keeps on down the track, not appearing to notice the town.

" 'Come on,' says Bill Bassett to me, starting after him.

" 'Where?' I asks.

" 'Lordy!' says Bill, 'had you forgot you was in the desert? Didn't you see Colonel Manna drop down right before your eyes? Don't you hear the rustling of General Raven's wings? I'm surprised at you, Elijah.'

"We overtook the stranger in the edge of some woods, and, as it was after sun-down and in a quiet place, nobody saw us stop him. Bill takes the silk hat off the man's head and brushes it with his sleeve and put its back.

" 'What does this mean, sir?' says the man.

" 'When I wore one of these,' says Bill, 'and felt embarrassed, I always done that. Not having one now I had to use yours. I hardly know how to begin, sir, in explaining our business with you, but I guess we'll try your pockets first.'

"Bill Bassett felt in all of them, and looked disgusted.

" 'Not even a watch,' he says. 'Ain't you ashamed of yourself, you whited

sculpture? Going about dressed like a head-waiter, and financed like a Count.
You haven't even got carfare. What did you do with your transfer?'

"The man speaks up and says he has no assets or valuables of any sort.
But Bassett takes his hand-satchel and opens it. Out comes some collars and
socks and a half a page of a newspaper clipped out. Bill reads the clipping
careful, and holds out his hand to the held-up party.

"'Brother,' says he, 'greetings! Accept the apologies of friends. I am Bill
Bassett, the burglar. Mr. Peters, you must make the acquaintance of Mr.
Alfred E. Ricks. Shake hands. Mr. Peters,' says Bill, 'stands about halfway
between me and you, Mr. Ricks, in the line of havoc and corruption. He always
gives something for the money he gets. I'm glad to meet you, Mr. Ricks—you
and Mr. Peters. This is the first time I ever attended a full gathering of the
National Synod of Sharks—housebreaking, swindling, and financiering all represented. Please examine Mr. Rick's credentials, Mr. Peters.'

"The piece of newspaper that Bill Bassett handed me had a good picture of
this Ricks on it. It was a Chicago paper, and it had obloquies of Ricks in every
paragraph. By reading it over I harvested the intelligence that said alleged
Ricks had laid off all that portion of the State of Florida that lies under water
into town lots and sold 'em to alleged innocent investors from his magnificently
furnished offices in Chicago. After he had taken in a hundred thousand or so
dollars one of these fussy purchasers that are always making trouble (I've had
'em actually try gold watches I've sold 'em with acid) took a cheap excursion
down to the land where it is always just before supper to look at his lot and
see if it didn't need a new paling or two on the fence, and market a few lemons in
time for the Christmas present trade. He hires a surveyor to find his lot for him.
They run the line out and find the flourishing town of Paradise Hollow, so
advertised, to be about 40 rods and 16 poles S., 27° E. of the middle of Lake
Okeechobee. This man's lot was under thirty-six feet of water, and, besides,
had been preëmpted so long by the alligators and gars that his title looked
fishy.

"Naturally, the man goes back to Chicago and makes it as hot for Alfred E.
Ricks as the morning after a prediction of snow by the weather bureau. Ricks
defied the allegation, but he couldn't deny the alligators. One morning the papers
came out with a column about it, and Ricks come out by the fire-escape. It
seems the alleged authorities had beat him to the safe-deposit box where he kept
his winnings, and Ricks has to westward ho! with only feetwear and a dozen 15½
English pokes in his shopping bag. He happened to have some mileage left
in his book, and that took him as far as the town in the wilderness where he was
spilled out on me and Bill Bassett as Elijah III with not a raven in sight for any
of us.

"Then this Alfred E. Ricks lets out a squeak that he is hungry, too, and denies
the hypothesis that he is good for the value, let alone the price, of a meal. And
so, there was the three of us, representing, if we had a mind to draw syllogisms
and parabolas, labor and trade and capital. Now, when trade has no capital there
isn't a dicker to be made. And when capital has no money there's a stagnation
in steak and onions. That put it up to the man with the jimmy.

"'Brother bushrangers,' says Bill Bassett, 'never yet, in trouble, did I desert
a pal. Hard by, in yon wood, I seem to see unfurnished lodgings. Let us go
there and wait till dark.'

"There was an old, deserted cabin in the grove, and we three took possession of
it. After dark Bill Bassett tells us to wait, and goes out for half an hour. He
comes back with a armful of bread and spareribs and pies.

"'Panhandled 'em at a farmhouse on Washita Avenue,' says he. 'Eat, drink,
and be leary.'

"The full moon was coming up bright, so we sat on the floor of the cabin and ate in the light of it. And this Bill Bassett begins to brag.

"'Sometimes,' says he, with his mouth full of country produce, 'I lose all patience with you people that think you are higher up in the profession than I am. Now, what could either of you have done in the present emergency to set us on our feet again? Could you do it, Ricksy?'

"'I must confess, Mr. Bassett,' says Ricks, speaking nearly inaudible out of a slice of pie, 'that at this immediate juncture I could not, perhaps, promote an enterprise to relieve the situation. Large operations, such as I direct, naturally require careful preparation in advance. I——'

"'I know, Ricksy,' breaks in Bill Bassett. 'You needn't finish. You need $500 to make the first payment on a blond typewriter, and four roomsful of quartered oak furniture. And you need $500 more for advertising contracts. And you need two weeks' time for the fish to begin to bite. Your line of relief would be about as useful in an emergency as advocating municipal ownership to cure a man suffocated by eighty-cent gas. And your graft ain't much swifter, Brother Peters,' he winds up.

"'Oh,' says I, 'I haven't seen you turn anything into gold with your wand yet, Mr. Good Fairy. 'Most anybody could rub the magic ring for a little left-over victuals.'

"'That was only getting the pumpkin ready,' says Bassett, braggy and cheerful. 'The coach and six'll drive up to the door before you know it, Miss Cinderella. Maybe you've got some scheme under your sleeve-holders that will give us a start.'

"'Son,' says I, 'I'm fifteen years older than you are, and young enough yet to take out an endowment policy. I've been broke before. We can see the lights of that town not half a mile away. I learned under Montague Silver, the greatest street man that ever spoke from a wagon. There are hundreds of men walking those streets this moment with grease spots on their clothes. Give me a gasoline lamp, a dry-goods box, and a two-dollar bar of white castile soap, cut into little——'

"'Where's your two dollars?' snickered Bill Bassett into my discourse. There was no use arguing with that burglar.

"'No,' he goes on; 'you're both babes-in-the-wood. Finance has closed the mahogany desk, and trade has put the shutters up. Both of you look to labor to start the wheels going. All right. You admit it. To-night I'll show you what Bill Bassett can do.'

"Bassett tells me and Ricks not to leave the cabin till he comes back, even if it's daylight, and then he starts off toward town, whistling gay.

"This Alfred E. Ricks pulls off his shoes and his coat, lays a silk handkerchief over his hat, and lays down on the floor.

"'I think I will endeavor to secure a little slumber,' he squeaks. 'The day has been fatiguing. Good-night, my dear Mr. Peters.'

"'My regards to Morpheus,' says I. 'I think I'll sit up a while.'

"About two o'clock, as near as I could guess by my watch in Peavine, home comes our laboring man and kicks up Ricks, and calls us to the streak of bright moonlight shining in the cabin door. Then he spreads out five packages of one thousand dollars each on the floor, and begins to cackle over the nest-egg like a hen.

"'I'll tell you a few things about that town,' says he 'It's named Rocky Springs, and they're building a Masonic temple, and it looks like the Democratic candidate for mayor is going to get soaked by a Pop, and Judge Tucker's wife, who has been down with pleurisy, is some better. I had a talk on these liliputian thesises before I could get a siphon in the fountain of knowledge that I was after. And there's a bank there called the Lumberman's Fidelity and

Plowman's Savings Institution. It closed for business yesterday with $23,000 cash on hand. It will open this morning with $18,000—all silver—that's the reason I didn't bring more. There you are, trade and capital. Now, will you be bad?'

"'My young friend,' says Alfred E. Ricks, holding up his hands, 'have you robbed this bank? Dear me, dear me!'

"'You couldn't call it that,' says Bassett. '"Robbing" sounds harsh. All I had to do was to find out what street it was on. That town is so quiet that I could stand on the corner and hear the tumblers clicking in that safe lock—"right to 45; left twice to 80; right once to 60; left to 15"—as plain as the Yale captain giving orders in the football dialect. Now, boys,' says Bassett, 'this is an early rising town. They tell me the citizens are all up and stirring before daylight. I asked what for, and they said because breakfast was ready at that time. And what of merry Robin Hood? It must be Yoicks! and away with the tinkers' chorus. I'll stake you. How much do you want? Speak up. Capital.'

"'My dear young friend,' says this ground squirrel of a Ricks, standing on his hind legs and juggling nuts in his paws, 'I have friends in Denver who would assist me. If I had a hundred dollars I——'

"Bassett unpins a package of the currency and throws five twenties to Ricks.

"'Trade, how much?' he says to me.

"'Put your money up, Labor,' says I. 'I never yet drew upon honest toil for its hard-earned pittance. The dollars I get are surplus ones that are burning the pockets of damfools and greenhorns. When I stand on a street corner and sell a solid gold diamond ring to a yap for $3.00, I make just $2.60. And I know he's going to give it to a girl in return for all the benefits accruing from a $125.00 ring. His profits are $122.00. Which of us is the biggest fakir?'

"'And when you sell a poor woman a pinch of sand for fifty cents to keep her lamp from exploding,' says Bassett, 'what do you figure her gross earnings to be, with sand at forty cents a ton?'

"'Listen,' says I. 'I instruct her to keep her lamp clean and well filled. If she does that it can't burst. And with the sand in it she knows it can't and she don't worry. It's a kind of Industrial Christian Science. She pays fifty cents, and gets both Rockefeller and Mrs. Eddy on the job. It ain't everybody that can let the gold-dust twins do their work.'

"Alfred E. Ricks all but licks the dust off of Bill Bassett's shoes.

"'My dear young friend,' says he, 'I will never forget your generosity. Heaven will reward you. But let me implore you to turn from your ways of violence and crime.'

"'Mousie,' says Bill, 'the hole in the wainscoting for yours. Your dogmas and inculcations sound to me like the last words of a bicycle pump. What has your high moral, elevator-service system of pillage brought you to? Penurious-ness and want. Even Brother Peters, who insists upon contaminating the art of robbery with theories of commerce and trade, admitted he was on the lift. Both of you live by the gilded rule. Brother Peters,' says Bill, 'you'd better choose a slice of this embalmed currency. You're welcome.'

"I told Bill Bassett once more to put this money in his pocket. I never had the respect for burglary that some people have. I always gave something for the money I took, even if it was only some little trifle of a souvenir to remind 'em not to get caught again.

"And then Alfred E. Ricks grovels at Bill's feet again, and bids us adieu. He says he will have a team at a farmhouse, and drive to the station below, and take the train for Denver. It salubrified the atmosphere when that lamentable boll-worm took his departure. He was a disgrace to every non-industrial profession in the country. With all his big schemes and fine offices he had wound up unable even to get an honest meal except by the kindness of a strange and maybe unscrupulous burglar. I was glad to see him go, though I felt a little sorry for him, now that he was ruined forever. What could such a man do without a big capital to work with? Why, Alfred E. Ricks, as we left him, was as helpless as a turtle on its back. He couldn't have worked a scheme to beat a little girl out of a penny slate-pencil.

"When me and Bill Bassett was left alone I did a little sleight-of-mind turn in my head with a trade secret at the end of it. Thinks I, I'll show this Mr. Burglar Man the difference between business and labor. He had hurt some of my professional self-adulation by casting his Persians upon commerce and trade.

"'I won't take any of your money as a gift, Mr. Bassett,' says I to him, 'but if you'll pay my expenses as a travelling companion until we get out of the danger zone of the immoral deficit you have caused in this town's finances to-night I'll be obliged.'

"Bill Bassett agreed to that, and we hiked westward as soon as we could catch a safe train.

"When we got to a town in Arizona called Los Perros I suggested that we once more try our luck on terra-cotta. That was the home of Montague Silver, my old instructor, now retired from business. I knew Monty would stake me to web money if I could show him a fly buzzing 'round in the locality. Bill Bassett said all towns looked alike to him as he worked mainly in the dark. So we got off the train in Los Perros, a fine little town in the silver region.

"I had an elegant little sure thing in the way of a commercial slungshot that I intended to hit Bassett behind the ear with. I wasn't going to take his money while he was asleep, but I was going to leave him with a lottery ticket that would represent in experience to him $4,755—I think that was the amount he had when we got off the train. But the first time I hinted to him about an investment, he turns on me and disencumbers himself of the following terms and expressions.

"'Brother Peters,' says he, 'it ain't a bad idea to go into an enterprise of some kind, as you suggest. I think I will. But if I do it will be such a cold proposition that nobody but Robert E. Peary and Charlie Fairbanks will be able to sit on the board of directors.'

"'I thought you might want to turn your money over,' says I.

"'I do,' says he, 'frequently. I can't sleep on one side all night. I'll tell you, Brother Peters,' says he, 'I'm going to start a poker room. I don't seem to care for the humdrum in swindling, such as peddling egg-beaters and working off breakfast food on Barnum and Bailey for sawdust to strew in their circus rings. But the gambling business,' says he, 'from the profitable side of the table is a good compromise between swiping silver spoons and selling penwipers at a Waldorf-Astoria charity bazar.'

"'Then,' says I, 'Mr. Bassett, you don't care to talk over my little business proposition?'

"'Why,' says he, 'do you know, you can't get a Pasteur institute to start up within fifty miles of where I live. I bite so seldom.'

"So, Bassett rents a room over a saloon and looks around for some furniture and chromos. The same night I went to Monty Silver's house, and he let me have $200 on my prospects. Then I went to the only store in Los Perros that sold playing cards and bought every deck in the house. The next morning when the store opened I was there bringing all the cards back with me. I said that my partner that was going to back me in the game had changed his mind; and I wanted to sell the cards back again. The storekeeper took 'em at half price.

"Yes, I was seventy-five dollars loser up to that time. But while I had the cards that night I marked every one in every deck. That was labor. And then trade and commerce had their innings, and the bread I had cast upon the waters began to come back in the form of cottage pudding with wine sauce.

"Of course I was among the first to buy chips at Bill Bassett's game. He had bought the only cards there was to be had in town; and I knew the back of every one of them better than I know the back of my head when the barber shows me my haircut in the two mirrors.

"When the game closed I had the five thousand and a few odd dollars, and all Bill Bassett had was the wanderlust and a black cat he had bought for a mascot. Bill shook hands with me when I left.

"'Brother Peters,' says he, 'I have no business being in business. I was preordained to labor. When a No. 1 burglar tries to make a James out of his jimmy he perpetrates an improfundity. You have a well-oiled and efficacious system of luck at cards,' says he. 'Peace go with you.' And I never afterward sees Bill Bassett again."

"Well, Jeff," said I, when the Autolycan adventurer seemed to have divulged the gist of his tale, "I hope you took care of the money. That would be a respecta—that is a considerable working capital if you should choose some day to settle down to some sort of regular business."

"Me?" said Jeff, virtuously. "You can bet I've taken care of that five thousand."

He tapped his coat over the region of his chest exultantly.

"Gold mining stock," he explained, "every cent of it. Shares par value one dollar. Bound to go up 500 per cent. within a year. Nonassessable. The Blue Gopher Mine. Just discovered a month ago. Better get in yourself if you've any spare dollars on hand."

"Sometimes," said I, "these mines are not——"

"Oh, this one's solid as an old goose," said Jeff. "Fifty thousand dollars' worth of ore in sight, and 10 per cent. monthly earnings guaranteed."

He drew a long envelope from his pocket and cast it on the table.

"Always carry it with me," said he. "So the burglar can't corrupt or the capitalist break in and water it."

I looked at the beautifully engraved certificate of stock.

"In Colorado, I see," said I. "And, by the way, Jeff, what was the name of the little man who went to Denver—the one you and Bill met at the station?"

"Alfred E. Ricks," said Jeff, "was the toad's designation."

"I see," said I, "the president of this mining company signs himself A. L. Fredericks. I was wondering——"

"Let me see that stock," said Jeff quickly, almost snatching it from me.

To mitigate, even though slightly, the embarrassment I summoned the waiter and ordered another bottle of the Barbera. I thought it was the least I could do.

A TEMPERED WIND

THE first time my optical nerves was disturbed by the sight of Buckingham Skinner was in Kansas City. I was standing on a corner when I see Buck stick his straw-colored head out of a third-story window of a business block and holler, "Whoa, there! Whoa!" like you would in endeavoring to assuage a team of runaway mules.

I looked around; but all the animals I see in sight is a policeman, having his shoes shined, and a couple of delivery wagons hitched to posts. Then in a minute downstairs tumbles this Buckingham Skinner, and runs to the corner, and stands and gazes down the other street at the imaginary dust kicked up by the fabulous hoofs of the fictitious team of chimerical quadrupeds. And then B. Skinner goes back up to the third-story room again, and I see that the lettering on the window is "The Farmers' Friend Loan Company."

By and by Straw-top comes down again, and I crossed the street to meet him, for I had my ideas. Yes, sir, when I got close I could see where he overdone it. He was Reub all right as far as his blue jeans and cowhide boots went, but he had a matinée actor's hands, and the rye straw stuck over his ear looked like it belonged to the property man of the Old Homestead Co. Curiosity to know what his graft was got the best of me.

"Was that your team broke away and run just now?" I asks him, polite. "I tried to stop 'em," says I, "but I couldn't. I guess they're halfway back to the farm by now."

"Gosh blame them darned mules," says Straw-top, in a voice so good that I nearly apologized; "they're a'lus bustin' loose." And then he looks at me close, and then he takes off his hayseed hat, and says, in a different voice:

"I'd like to shake hands with Parley-voo Pickens, the greatest street man in the West, barring only Montague Silver, which you can no more than allow."

I let him shake hands with me.

"I learned under Silver," I said; "I don't begrudge him the lead. But what's your graft, son? I admit that the phantom flight of the non-existing animals at which you remarked 'Whoa!' has puzzled me somewhat. How do you win out on the trick?"

Buckingham Skinner blushed.

"Pocket money," says he; "that's all. I am temporarily unfinanced. This little coup de rye straw is good for forty dollars in a town of this size. How do I work it? Why, I involve myself, as you perceive, in the loathsome apparel of the rural dub. Thus embalmed I am Jonas Stubblefield—a name impossible to improve upon. I repair noisily to the office of some loan company conveniently located in the third-floor, front. There I lay my hat and yarn gloves on the floor and ask to mortgage my farm for $2,000 to pay for my sister's musical education in Europe. Loans like that always suit the loan companies. It's ten to one that when the note falls due the foreclosure will be leading the semiquavers by a couple of lengths.

"Well, sir, I reach in my pocket for the abstract of title; but I suddenly hear my team running away. I run to the window and emit the word—or exclamation, whichever it may be—viz, 'Whoa!' Then I hush downstairs and down the street, returning in a few minutes. 'Dang them mules,' I says; 'they done run away and busted the double tree and two traces. Now I got to hoof it home, for I never brought no money along. Reckon we'll talk about that loan some other time, gen'lemen.'

"Then I spreads out my tarpaulin, like the Israelites, and waits for the manna to drop.

"'Why, no, Mr. Stubblefield,' says the lobster-colored party in the specs and dotted piqué vest; 'oblige us by accepting this ten-dollar bill until to-morrow. Get your harness repaired and call in at ten. We'll be pleased to accommodate you in the matter of this loan.'

"It's a slight thing," says Buckingham Skinner, modest, "but, as I said, only for temporary loose change."

"It's nothing to be ashamed of," says I, in respect for his mortification; "in case of an emergency. Of course, it's small compared to organizing a trust or bridge whist, but even the Chicago University had to be started in a small way."

"What's your graft these days?" Buckingham Skinner asks me.

"The legitimate," says I. "I'm handling rhinestones and Dr. Oleum Sinapi's Electric Headache Battery and the Swiss Warbler's Bird Call, a small lot of the new queer ones and twos, and the Bonanza Budget, consisting of a rolled-gold wedding and engagement ring, six Egyptian lily bulbs, a combination pickle fork and nail-clipper, and fifty engraved visiting cards—no two names alike—all for the sum of 38 cents."

"Two months ago," says Buckingham Skinner, "I was doing well down in Texas with a patent instantaneous fire kindler, made of compressed wood ashes and benzine. I sold loads of 'em in towns where they like to burn niggers quick, without having to ask somebody for a light. And just when I was doing the best they strikes oil down there and puts me out of business. 'Your machine's too slow, now, pardner,' they tells me. 'We can have a coon in hell with this here petroleum before your old flint-and-tinder truck can get him warm enough to perfess religion.' And so I gives up the kindler and drifts up here to K. C. This little curtain-raiser you seen me doing, Mr. Pickens, with the simulated farm and the hypothetical team, ain't in my line at all, and I'm ashamed you found me working it."

"No man," says I, kindly, "need to be ashamed of putting the skibunk on a loan corporation for even so small a sum as ten dollars, when he is financially abashed. Still, it wasn't quite the proper thing. It's too much like borrowing money without paying it back."

I liked Buckingham Skinner from the start, for as good a man as ever stood over the axles and breathed gasoline smoke. And pretty soon we gets thick, and I let him in on a scheme I'd had in mind for some time, and offers to go partners.

"Anything," says Buck, "that is not actually dishonest will find me willing and ready. Let us perforate into the inwardness of your proposition. I feel degraded when I am forced to wear property straw in my hair and assume a bucolic air for the small sum of ten dollars. Actually, Mr. Pickens, it makes me feel like the Ophelia of the Great Occidental All-Star One-Night Consolidated Theatrical Aggregation."

This scheme of mine was one that suited my proclivities. By nature I am some sentimental, and have always felt gentle toward the mollifying elements of existence. I am disposed to be lenient with the arts and sciences; and I find time to instigate a cordiality for the more human works of nature, such as romance and the atmosphere and grass and poetry and the Seasons. I never skin a sucker without admiring the prismatic beauty of his scales. I never sell a little auriferous trifle to the man with the hoe without noticing the beautiful harmony there is between gold and green. And that's why I liked this scheme; it was so full of outdoor air and landscapes and easy money.

We had to have a young lady assistant to help us work this graft; and I asked Buck if he knew of one to fill the bill.

"One," says I, "that is cool and wise and strictly business from her pompadour to her Oxfords. No ex-toe-dancers or gum-chewers or crayon portrait canvassers for this."

Buck claimed he knew a suitable feminine and he takes me around to see Miss Sarah Malloy. The minute I see her I am pleased. She looked to be the goods as ordered. No sign of the three p's about her—no peroxide, patchouli, nor peau de soie; about twenty-two, brown hair, pleasant ways—the kind of a lady for the place.

"A description of the sandbag, if you please," she begins.

"Why, ma'am," says I, "this graft of ours is so nice and refined and romantic, it would make the balcony scene in 'Romeo and Juliet' look like second-story work."

We talked it over, and Miss Malloy agreed to come in as a business partner. She said she was glad to get a chance to give up her place as stenographer and secretary to a suburban lot company, and go into something respectable.

This is the way we worked our scheme. First, I figured it out by a kind of a proverb. The best grafts in the world are built up on copybook maxims and psalms and proverbs and Esau's fables. They seem to kind of hit off human nature. Our peaceful little swindle was constructed on the old· saying: "The whole push loves a lover."

One evening Buck and Miss Malloy drives up like blazes in a buggy to a farmer's door. She is pale but affectionate, clinging to his arm—always clinging to his arm. Any one can see that she is a peach and of the cling variety. They claim they are eloping for to be married on account of cruel parents. They ask where they can find a preacher. Farmer says, "B'gum there ain't any preacher nigher than Reverend Abels, four miles over on Caney Creek." Farmeress wipes her hand on her apron and rubbers through her specs.

Then, lo and look ye! Up the road from the other way joggs Parleyvoo Pickens in a gig, dressed in black, white necktie, long face, sniffing his nose, emitting a spurious kind of noise resembling the long-meter doxology.

"B'jinks!" says farmer, "if thar ain't a preacher now!"

It transpires that I am Rev. Abijah Green, travelling over to Little Bethel school-house for to preach next Sunday.

The young folks will have it they must be married, for pa is pursuing them with the plow mules and the buckboard. So the Reverend Green, after hesitation, marries 'em in farmer's parlor. And farmer grins and has in cider, and says "B'gum!" and farmeress sniffles a bit and pats the bride on the shoulder. And Parleyvoo Pickens, the wrong reverend, writes out a marriage certificate, and farmer and farmeress sign it as witnesses. And the parties of the first, second, and third part gets in their vehicles and rides away. Oh, that was an idyllic graft! True love and the lowing kine and the sun shining on the red barns—it certainly had all other impostures I know about beat to a batter.

I suppose I happened along in time to marry Buck and Miss Malloy at about twenty farm-houses. I hated to think how the romance was going to fade later on when all them marriage certificates turned up in banks where we'd discounted 'em, and the farmers had to pay them notes of hand they'd signed, running from $300 to $500.

On the 15th day of May us three divided about $6,000. Miss Malloy nearly cried with joy. You don't often see a tenderhearted girl or one that was so bent on doing right.

"Boys," says she, dabbing her eyes with a little handkerchief, "this stake comes in handier than a powder rag at a fat men's ball. It gives me a chance to reform. I was trying to get out of the real estate business when you fellows came along. But if you hadn't taken me in on this neat little proposition for removing the cuticle of the rutabaga propagators I'm afraid I'd have got into something worse. I was about to accept a place in one of these Women's Auxiliary Bazars, where they build a parsonage by selling a spoonful of chicken salad and a cream-puff for seventy-five cents and calling it a Business Men's Lunch.

"Now I can go into a square, honest business and give all them queer jobs the shake. I'm going to Cincinnati and start a palm reading and clairvoyant joint. As Madame Saramaloi, Egyptian Sorceress, I shall give everybody a dollar's worth of good honest prognostication. Good-by, boys. Take my advice and go into some decent fake. Get friendly with the police and newspapers and you'll be all right."

So then we all shook hands, and Miss Malloy left us. Me and Buck also rose up and sauntered off a few hundred miles; for we didn't care to be around when them marriage certificates fell due.

With about $4,000 between us we hit that bumptious little town off the New Jersey coast they call New York.

If there ever was an aviary overstocked with jays it is that Yaptown-on-the-Hudson. Cosmopolitan they call it. You bet. So's a piece of fly-paper. You listen close when they're buzzing and trying to pull their feet out of the sticky stuff. "Little old New York's good enough for us"—that's what they sing. There's enough Reubs walk down Broadway in one hour to buy up a week's output of the factory in Augusta, Maine, that makes Knaughty Knovelties and the little Phine Phun oroide gold finger ring that sticks a needle in your friend's hand.

You'd think New York people was all wise; but no. They don't get a chance to learn. Everything's too compressed. Even the hayseeds are baled hayseeds. But what else can you expect from a town that's shut off from the world by the ocean on one side and New Jersey on the other?

It's no place for an honest grafter with a small capital. There's too big a protective tariff on bunco. Even when Giovanni sells a quart of warm worms and chestnut hulls he has to hand out a pint to an insectivorous cop. And the hotel man charges double for everything in the bill that he sends by the patrol wagon to the altar where the duke is about to marry the heiress.

But old Badville-near-Coney is the ideal burg for a refined piece of piracy if you can pay the bunco duty. Imported grafts come pretty high. The custom-house officers that look after it carry clubs, and it's hard to smuggle in even a bib-and-tucker swindle to work Brooklyn with unless you can pay the toll. But now, me and Buck, having capital, descends upon New York to try and trade the metropolitan backwoodsmen a few glass beads for real estate just as the Vans did a hundred or two years ago.

At an East Side hotel we gets acquainted with Romulus G. Atterbury, a man with the finest head for financial operations I ever saw. It was all bald and glossy except for gray side whiskers. Seeing that head behind an office railing, and you'd deposit a million with it without a receipt. This Atterbury was well dressed, though he ate seldom; and the synopsis of his talk would make the conversation of a siren sound like a cab driver's kick. He said he used to be a member of the Stock Exchange, but some of the big capitalists got jealous and formed a ring that forced him to sell his seat.

Atterbury got to liking me and Buck and he begun to throw on the canvas for us some of the schemes that had caused his hair to evacuate. He had one scheme for starting a National Bank on $45 that made the Mississippi Bubble look as solid as a glass marble. He talked this to us for three days, and when his throat was good and sore we told him about the roll we had. Atterbury borrowed a quarter from us and went out and got a box of throat lozenges and started all over again. This time he talked bigger things, and he got us to see 'em as he did. The scheme he laid out looked like a sure winner, and he talked me and Buck into putting our capital against his burnished dome of thought. It looked all right for a kid-gloved graft. It seemed to be just about an inch and a half outside of the reach of the police, and as money-making as a mint. It was just what me and Buck wanted—a regular business at a permanent stand, with an open air spieling with tonsillitis on the street corners every evening.

So, in six weeks you see a handsome furnished set of offices down in the Wall Street neighborhood, with "The Golconda Gold Bond and Investment Company" in gilt letters on the door. And you see in his private room, with the door open, the secretary and treasurer, Mr. Buckingham Skinner, costumed like the lilies of the conservatory, with his high silk hat close to his hand. Nobody yet ever saw Buck outside of an instantaneous reach for his hat.

And you might perceive the president and general manager, Mr. R. G. Atterbury, with his priceless polished poll, busy in the main office room dictating letters to a shorthand countess, who has got pomp and a pompadour that is no less than a guarantee to investors.

There is a bookkeeper and an assistant, and a general atmosphere of varnish and culpability.

At another desk the eye is relieved by the sight of an ordinary man, attired with unscrupulous plainness, sitting with his feet up, eating apples, with his obnoxious hat on the back of his head. That man is no other than Colonel Tecumseh (once "Parleyvoo") Pickens, the vice-president of the company.

"No recherché rags for me," I says to Atterbury when we was organizing the stage properties of the robbery. "I'm a plain man," says I, "and I do not use pajamas, French, or military hair-brushes. Cast me for the rôle of the rhinestone-in-the-rough or I don't go on exhibition. If you can use me in my natural, though displeasing form, do so."

"Dress you up?" says Atterbury; "I should say not! Just as you are you're worth more to the business than a whole roomful of the things they pin chrysanthemums on. You're to play the part of the solid but disheveled capitalist from the Far West. You despise the conventions. You've got so many stocks you can afford to shake socks. Conservative, homely, rough, shrewd, saving—that's your pose. It's a winner in New York. Keep your feet on the desk and eat apples. Whenever anybody comes in eat an apple. Let 'em see you stuff the peelings in a drawer of your desk. Look as economical and rich and rugged as you can."

I followed out Atterbury's instructions. I played the Rocky Mountain capitalist without ruching or frills. The way I deposited apples peelings to my credit in a drawer when any customers came in made Hetty Green look like a spendthrift. I could hear Atterbury saying to victims, as he smiled at me, indulgent and venerating, "That's our vice-president, Colonel Pickens . . . fortune in Western investments . . . delightfully plain manners, but . . . could sign his check for half a million . . . simple as a child . . . wonderful head . . . conservative and careful almost to a fault."

Atterbury managed the business. Me and Buck never quite understood all of it, though he explained it to us in full. It seems the company was a kind of coöperative one, and everybody that bought stock shared in the profits. First, we officers bought up a controlling interest—we had to have that—of the shares at 50 cents a hundred—just what the printer charged us—and the rest went to the public at a dollar each. The company guaranteed the stockholders a profit of ten per cent. each month, payable on the last day thereof.

When any stockholder had paid in as much as $100, the company issued him a Gold Bond and he became a bondholder. I asked Atterbury one day what benefits and appurtenances these Gold Bonds was to an investor more so than the immunities and privileges enjoyed by the common sucker who only owned stock. Atterbury picked up one of them Gold Bonds, all gilt and lettered up with flourishes and a big red seal tied with a blue ribbon in a bowknot, and he looked at me like his feelings was hurt.

"My dear Colonel Pickens," says he, "you have no soul for Art. Think of a thousand homes made happy by possessing one of these beautiful gems of the lithographer's skill! Think of the joy in the household where one of these Gold Bonds hangs by a pink cord to the what-not, or is chewed by the baby, caroling gleefully upon the floor! Ah, I see your eye growing moist, Colonel— I have touched you, have I not?"

"You have not," says I, "for I've been watching you. The moisture you see is apple juice. You can't expect one man to act as a human cider-press and an art connoisseur too."

Atterbury attended to the details of the concern. As I understand it, they was simple. The investors in stock paid in their money, and—well, I guess that's all they had to do. The company received it, and—I don't call to mind anything else. Me and Buck knew more about selling corn salve than we did about Wall

Street, but even we could see how the Golconda Gold Bond Investment Company was making money. You take in money and pay back ten per cent. of it; it's plain enough that you make a clean, legitimate profit of 90 per cent., less expenses, as long as the fish bite.

Atterbury wanted to be president and treasurer too, but Buck winks an eye at him and says: "You was to furnish the brains. Do you call it good brain work when you propose to take in money at the door, too? Think again. I hereby nominate myself treasurer ad valorem, sine die, and by acclamation. I chip in that much brain work free. Me and Pickens, we furnished the capital, and we'll handle the unearned increment as it incremates."

It costs us $500 for office rent and first payment on furniture; $1,500 more went for printing and advertising. Atterbury knew his business. "Three months to a minute we'll last," says he. "A day longer than that and we'll have to either go under or go under an alias. By that time we ought to clean up $60,000. And then a money belt and a lower berth for me, and the yellow journals and the furniture men can pick the bones."

Our ads. done the work. "Country weeklies and Washington hand-press dailies of course," says I when we was ready to make contracts.

"Man," says Atterbury, "as its advertising manager you would cause a Limburger cheese factory to remain undiscovered during a hot summer. "The game we're after is right here in New York and Brooklyn and the Harlem reading-rooms. They're the people that the street-car fenders and the Answers to Correspondents columns and the pickpocket notices are made for. We want our ads. in the biggest city dailies, top of column, next to editorials on radium and pictures of the girl doing health exercises."

Pretty soon the money begins to roll in. Buck didn't have to pretend to be busy; his desk was piled high up with money orders and checks and greenbacks. People began to drop in the office and buy stock every day.

Most of the shares went in small amounts—$10 and $25 and $50, and a good many $2 and $3 lots. And the bald and inviolate cranium of President Atterbury shines with enthusiasm and demerit, while Colonel Tecumseh Pickens, the rude but reputable Crœsus of the West, consumes so many apples that the peelings hang to the floor from the mahogany garbage chest that he calls his desk.

Just as Atterbury said, we ran along about three months without being troubled. Buck cashed the paper as fast as it came in and kept the money in a safe deposit vault a block or so away. Buck never thought much of banks for such purposes. We paid the interest regular on the stock we'd sold, so there was nothing for anybody to squeal about. We had nearly $50,000 on hand and all three of us had been living as high as prize fighters out of training.

One morning, as me and Buck sauntered into the office, fat and flippant, from our noon grub, we met an easy-looking fellow, with a bright eye and a pipe in his mouth, coming out. We found Atterbury looking like he'd been caught a mile from home in a wet shower.

"Know that man?" he asked us.

We said we didn't.

"I don't either," says Atterbury, wiping off his head; "but I'll bet enough Gold Bonds to paper a cell in the Tombs that he's a newspaper reporter."

"What did he want?" asks Buck.

"Information," says our president. "Said he was thinking of buying some stock. He asked me about nine hundred questions, and every one of 'em hit some sore place in the business. I know he's on a paper. You can't fool me. You see a man about half shabby, with an eye like a gimlet, smoking cut plug, with dandruff on his coat collar, and knowing more than J. P. Morgan and Shakespeare put together—if that ain't a reporter I never saw one. I was afraid of this. I don't mind detectives and post-office inspectors—I talk to 'em eight minutes and then sell 'em stock—but them reporters take the starch out of my collar. Boys, J recommend that we declare a dividend and fade away. The signs point that way."

Me and Buck talked to Atterbury and got him to stop swearing and stand still. That fellow didn't look like a reporter to us. Reporters always pull out a pencil and tablet on you, and tell you a story you've heard, and strikes you for the drinks. But Atterbury was shaky and nervous all day.

The next day me and Buck comes down from the hotel about ten-thirty. On the way we buys the papers, and the first thing we see is a column on the front page about our little imposition. It was a shame the way that reporter intimated that we were no blood relatives of the late George W. Childs. He tells all about the scheme as he sees it, in a rich, racy kind of guying style that might amuse most anybody except a stockholder. Yes, Atterbury was right; it behooveth the gaily clad treasurer and the pearly pated president and the rugged vice-president of the Golconda Gold Bond and Investment Company to go away real sudden and quick that their days might be longer upon the land.

Me and Buck hurries down to the office. We finds on the stairs and in the hall a crowd of people trying to squeeze into our office, which is already jammed full inside to the railing. They've nearly all got Golconda stock and Gold Bonds in their hands. Me and Buck judged they'd been reading the papers, too.

We stopped and looked at our stockholders, some surprised. It wasn't quite the kind of a gang we supposed had been investing. They all looked like poor people; there was plenty of old women and lots of young girls that you'd say worked in factories and mills. Some was old men that looked like war veterans, and some was crippled, and a good many was just kids—bootblacks and newsboys and messengers. Some was working-men in overalls, with their sleeves rolled up. No one of the gang looked like a stockholder in anything unless it was a peanut stand. But they all had Golconda stock and looked as sick as you please.

I saw a queer kind of pale look come on Buck's face when he sized up the crowd. He stepped up to a sickly looking woman and says: "Madam, do you own any of this stock?"

"I put in a hundred dollars," says the woman, faint like. "It was all I had saved in a year. One of my children is dying at home now and I haven't a cent in the house. I came to see if I could draw out some. The circulars said you could draw it at any time. But they say now I will lose it all."

There was a smart kind of a kid in the gang—I guess he was a newsboy. "I got in twenty-fi' mister," he says, looking hopeful at Buck's silk hat and clothes. "Dey paid me two-fifty a mont' on it. Say, a man tells me dey can't do dat and be on the square? Is dat straight? Do you guess I can get out my twent-fi'?"

Some of the old women was crying. The factory girls was plumb distracted. They'd lost all their savings and they'd be docked for the time they lost coming to see about it.

There was one girl—a pretty one—in a red shawl, crying in the corner like her heart would dissolve. Buck goes over and asks her about it.

"It ain't so much losing the money, mister," says she, shaking all over, "though I've been two years saving it up; but Jakey won't marry me now. He'll take Rosa Steinfeld. I know J—J—Jakey. She's got $400 in the savings bank. Ai, ai, ai——" she sings out.

Buck looks all around with that same funny look on his face. And then we see leaning against the wall, puffing at his pipe, with his eye shining at us, this newspaper reporter. Buck and me walks over to him.

"You're a real interesting writer," says Buck. "How far do you mean to carry it? Anything more up your sleeve?"

"Oh, I'm just waiting around," says the reporter, smoking away, "in case any news turns up. It's up to your stockholders now. Some of them might complain, you know. Isn't that the patrol wagon now?" he says, listening to a sound outside. "No," he goes on, "that's Doc Whittleford's old cadaver coupé from the Roosevelt. I ought to know that gong. Yes, I suppose I've written some interesting stuff at times."

"You wait," says Buck; "I'm going to throw an item of news in your way."

Buck reaches in his pocket and hands me a key. I knew what he meant before he spoke. Confounded old buccaneer—I knew what he meant. They don't make them any better than Buck.

"Pick," says he, looking at me hard, "ain't this graft a little out of our line? Do we want Jakey to marry Rosa Steinfeld?"

"You've got my vote," says I. "I'll have it here in ten minutes." And I starts for the safe deposit vaults.

I comes back with the money done up in a big bundle, and then Buck and me takes the journalist reporter around to another door and we let ourselves into one of the office rooms.

"Now, my literary friend," says Buck, "take a chair, and keep still, and I'll give you an interview. You see before you two grafters from Graftersville, Grafter County, Arkansas. Me and Pick have sold brass jewelry, hair tonic, song books, marked cards, patent medicines, Connecticut Smyrna rugs, furniture polish, and albums in every town from Old Point Comfort to the Golden Gate. We've grafted a dollar whenever we saw one that had a surplus look to it. But we never went after the simoleon in the toe of the sock under the loose brick in the corner of the kitchen hearth. There's an old saying you may have heard—'fussily decency averni'—which means it's an easy slide from the street faker's dry goods box to a desk in Wall Street. We've took that slide, but we didn't know exactly what was at the bottom of it. Now, you ought to be wise, but you ain't. You've got New York wiseness, which means that you judge a man by the outside of his clothes. That ain't right. You ought to look at the lining and seams and the button-holes. While we are waiting for the patrol wagon you might get out your little stub pencil and take notes for another funny piece in the paper."

And then Buck turns to me and says: "I don't care what Atterbury thinks. He only put in brains, and if he gets his capital out he's lucky. But what do you say, Pick?"

"Me?" says I. "You ought to know me, Buck. I didn't know who was buying the stock."

"All right," says Buck. And then he goes through the inside door into the main office and looks at the gang trying to squeeze through the railing. Atterbury and his hat was gone. And Buck makes 'em a short speech.

"All you lambs get in line. You're going to get your wool back. Don't shove so. Get in a line—a *line*—not a pile. Lady, will you please stop bleating? Your money's waiting for you. Here, sonny, don't climb over that railing; your dimes are safe. Don't cry, sis; you ain't out a cent. Get in *line*, I say. Here, Pick, come and straighten 'em out and let 'em through and out by the other door."

Buck takes off his coat, pushes his silk hat on the back of his head, and lights up a reina victoria. He sits at the table with the boodle before him, all done up in neat packages. I gets the stockholders strung out and marches 'em, single file, through from the main room; and the reporter passes 'em out of the side door into the hall again. As they go by, Buck takes up the stock and the Gold Bonds, paying 'em cash, dollar for dollar, the same as they paid in. The shareholders of the Golconda Gold Bond and Investment Company can't hardly believe it. They almost grabs the money out of Buck's hands. Some of the women keep on crying, for it's a custom of the sex to cry when they have sorrow, to weep when they have joy, and to shed tears whenever they find themselves without either.

The old women's fingers shake when they stuff the skads in the bosoms of their rusty dresses. The factory girls just stoop over and flap their dry goods a second, and you hear the elastic go "pop" as the currency goes down in the ladies' department of the "Old Domestic Lisle-Thread Bank."

Some of the stockholders that had been doing the Jeremiah act the loudest outside had spasms of restored confidence and wanted to leave the money invested. "Salt away that chicken feed in your duds and skip along," says Buck. "What business have you got investing in bonds? The tea-pot or the crack in the wall behind the clock for your hoard of pennies."

When the pretty girl in the red shawl cashes in Buck hands her an extra twenty. "A wedding present," says our treasurer, "from the Golconda Company. And say—if Jakey ever follows his nose, even at a respectful distance, around the corner where Rosa Steinfeld lives, you are hereby authorized to knock a couple inches of it off."

When they was all paid off and gone, Buck calls the newspaper reporter and shoves the rest of the money over to him.

"You begun this," says Buck; "now finish it. Over there are the books, showing every share and bond issued. Here's the money to cover, except what we've spent to live on. You'll have to act as receiver. I guess you'll do the square thing on account of your paper. This is the best way we know how to settle it. Me and our substantial but apple-weary vice-president are going to follow the example of our revered president, and skip. Now, have you got enough news for to-day, or do you want to interview us on etiquette and the best way to make over an old taffeta skirt?"

"News!" says the newspaper man, taking his pipe out; "do you think I could use this? I don't want to lose my job. Suppose I go around to the office and tell 'em this happened. What'll the managing editor say? He'll just hand me a pass to Bellévue and tell me to come back when I get cured. I might turn in a story about a sea serpent wiggling up Broadway, but I haven't got the nerve to try 'em with a pipe like this. A get-rich-quick—excuse me—gang giving back the boodle! Oh, no. I'm not on the comic supplement."

"You can't understand it, of course," says Buck, with his hand on the door knob. "Me and Pick ain't Wall Streeters like you know 'em. We never allowed to swindle sick old women and working girls and take nickels off of kids. In the lines of graft we've worked we took money from the people the Lord made to be buncoed—sports and rounders and smart Alecks and street crowds, that always have a few dollars to throw away, and farmers that wouldn't ever be happy if the grafters didn't come around and play with 'em when they sold their crops. We never cared to fish for the kind of suckers that bite here. No, sir. We got too much respect for the profession and for ourselves. Good-by to you, Mr. Receiver."

"Here!" says the journalist reporter; "wait a minute. There's a broker I know on the next floor. Wait till I put this truck in his safe. I want you fellows to take a drink on me before you go."

"On you?" says Buck, winking solemn. "Don't you go and try to make 'em believe at the office you said that. Thanks. We can't spare the time, I reckon. So long."

And me and Buck slides out the door; and that's the way the Golconda Company went into involuntary liquefaction.

If you had seen me and Buck the next night you'd have had to go to a little bum hotel over near the West Side ferry landings. We was in a little back room, and I was filling up a gross of six-ounce bottles with hydrant water

colored red with aniline and flavored with cinnamon. Buck was smoking, contented, and he wore a decent brown derby in place of his silk hat.

"It's a good thing, Pick," says he, as he drove in the corks, "that we got Brady
to loan us his horse and wagon for a week. We'll rustle up a stake by then.
This hair tonic'll sell right along over in Jersey. Bald heads ain't popular over
there on account of the mosquitoes."

Directly I dragged out my valise and went down in it for labels.

"Hair tonic labels are out," says I. "Only about a dozen on hand."

"Buy some more," says Buck.

We investigated our pockets and found we had just enough money to settle our
hotel bill in the morning and pay our passage over the ferry.

"Plenty of the 'Shake-the-Shakes Chill Cure' labels," says I, after looking.

"What more do you want?" says Buck. "Slap 'em on. The chill season is just
opening up in the Hackensack low grounds. What's hair, anyway, if you have
to shake it off?"

We posted on the Chill Cure labels about half an hour and Buck says:

"Making an honest livin's better than that Wall Street, anyhow; ain't it,
Pick?"

"You bet," says I.

HOSTAGES TO MOMUS

I

I never got inside of the legitimate line of graft but once. But, one time, as I
say, I reversed the decision of the revised statutes and undertook a thing that
I'd have to apologize for even under the New Jersey trust laws.

Me and Caligula Polk, of Muskogee in the Creek Nation, was down in the Mexican State of Tamaulipas running a peripatetic lottery and monte game. Now,
selling lottery tickets is a government graft in Mexico, just like selling forty-
eight cents' worth of postage-stamps for forty-nine cents is over here. So Uncle
Porfirio he instructs the *rurales* to attend to our case.

Rurales? They're a sort of country police; but don't draw any mental crayon
portraits of the worthy constable with a tin star and a gray goatee. The *rurales*
—well, if we'd mount our Supreme Court on broncos, arm 'em with Winchesters,
and start 'em out after John Doe *et al.* we'd have about the same thing.

When the *rurales* started for us we started for the States. They chased us as
far as Matamoras. We hid in a brickyard; and that night we swum the Rio
Grande, Caligula with a brick in each hand, absent-minded, which he drops upon
the soil of Texas, forgetting he had 'em.

From there we migrated to San Antone, and then over to New Orleans, where
we took a rest. And in that town of cotton bales and other adjuncts to female
beauty we made the acquaintance of drinks invented by the Creoles during the
period of Louey Cans, in which they are still served at the side doors. The most
I can remember of this town is that me and Caligula and a Frenchman named
McCarty—wait a minute; Adolph McCarty—was trying to make the French
Quarter pay up the back trading-stamps due on the Louisiana Purchase, when
somebody hollers that the johndarms are coming. I have an insufficient recollection of buying two yellow tickets through a window; and I seemed to see a man
swing a lantern and say "All aboard!" I remembered no more, except that the

train butcher was covering me and Caligula up with Augusta J. Evans's works and figs.

When we become revised, we find that we have collided up against the State of Georgia at a spot hitherto unaccounted for in time tables except by an asterisk, which means that trains stop every other Thursday on signal by tearing up a rail. We was waked up in a yellow pine hotel by the noise of flowers and the smell of birds. Yes, sir, for the wind was banging sunflowers as big as buggy wheels against the weatherboarding and the chicken coop was right under the window. Me and Caligula dressed and went downstairs. The landlord was shelling peas on the front porch. He was six feet of chills and fever, and Hongkong in complexion though in other respects he seemed amenable in the exercise of his sentiments and features.

Caligula, who is a spokesman by birth, and a small man, though red-haired and impatient of painfulness of any kind, speaks up.

"Pardner," says he, "good-morning, and be darned to you. Would you mind telling us why we are at? We know the reason we are where, but can't exactly figure out on account of at what place."

"Well, gentlemen," says the landlord, "I reckoned you-all would be inquiring this morning. You all dropped off of the nine-thirty train here last night; and you was right tight. Yes, you was right smart in liquor. I can inform you that you are now in the town of Mountain Valley, in the State of Georgia."

"On top of that," says Caligula, "don't say that we can't have anything to eat."

"Sit down, gentlemen," says the landlord, "and in twenty minutes I'll call you to the best breakfast you can get anywhere in town."

That breakfast turned out to be composed of fried bacon and a yellowish edifice that proved up something between pound cake and flexible sandstone. The landlord calls it corn pone; and then he sets out a dish of the exaggerated breakfast food known as hominy; and so me and Caligula makes the acquaintance of the celebrated food that enabled every Johnny Reb to lick one and two-thirds Yankees for nearly four years at a stretch.

"The wonder to me is," says Caligula, "that Uncle Robert Lee's boys didn't chase the Grant and Sherman outfit clear up into Hudson's Bay. It would have made me that mad to eat this truck they call mahogany!"

"Hog and hominy," I explains, "is the staple food of this section."

"Then," says Caligula, "they ought to keep it where it belongs. I thought this was a hotel and not a stable. Now, if we was in Muskogee at the St. Lucifer House, I'd show you some breakfast grub. Antelope steaks and fried liver to begin on, and venison cutlets with *chili con carne* and pineapple fritters, and then some sardines and mixed pickles; and top it off with a can of yellow clings and a bottle of beer. You won't find a layout like that on the bill of affairs of any of your Eastern restauraws."

"Too lavish," says I. "I've travelled, and I'm unprejudiced. There'll never be a perfect breakfast eaten until some man grows arms long enough to stretch down to New Orleans for his coffee and over to Norfolk for his rolls, and reaches up to Vermont and digs a slice of butter out of a spring-house, and then turns over a beehive close to a white clover patch out in Indiana for the rest. Then he'd come pretty close to making a meal on the amber that the gods eat on Mount Olympia."

"Too ephemeral," says Caligula. "I'd want ham and eggs, or rabbit stew, anyhow, for a chaser. What do you consider the most edifying and casual in the way of a dinner?"

"I've been infatuated from time to time," I answers, "with fancy ramifications of grub such as terrapins, lobsters, reed birds, jambolaya, and canvas-covered ducks; but after all there's nothing less displeasing to me than a beefsteak smothered in mushrooms on a balcony in sound of the Broadway street cars, with a hand-organ playing down below, and the boys hollering extras about the latest suicide. For the wine, give me a reasonable Ponty Cany. And that's all, except a *demi-tasse*."

"Well," says Caligula, "I reckon in New York you get to be a conniseer; and when you go around with a *demi-tasse* you are naturally bound to buy 'em stylish grub."

"It's a great town for epicures," says I. "You'd soon fall into their ways if you was there."

"I've heard it was," says Caligula. "But I reckon I wouldn't. I can polish my fingernails all they need myself."

II

After breakfast we went out on the front porch, lighted up two of the landlord's *flor de upas* perfectos, and took a look at Georgia.

The installment of scenery visible to the eye looked mighty poor. As far as we could see was red hills all washed down with gullies and scattered over with patches of piny woods. Blackberry bushes was all that kept the rail fences from falling down. About fifteen miles over to the north was a little range of well-timbered mountains.

That town of Mountain Valley wasn't going. About a dozen people permeated along the sidewalks; but what you saw mostly was rain-barrels and roosters, and boys poking around with sticks in piles of ashes made by burning the scenery of Uncle Tom shows.

And just then there passes down on the other side of the street a high man in a long black coat and a beaver hat. All the people in sight bowed, and some crossed the street to shake hands with him; folks came out of stores and houses to holler at him; women leaned out of windows and smiled; and all the kids stopped playing to look at him. Our landlord stepped out on the porch and bent himself double like a carpenter's rule, and sung out, "Good-morning, Colonel," when he was a dozen yards gone by.

"And is that Alexander, pa?" says Caligula to the landlord; "and why is he called great?"

"That, gentlemen," says the landlord, "is no less than Colonel Jackson T. Rockingham, the president of the Sunrise & Edenville Tap Railroad, mayor of Mountain Valley, and chairman of the Perry County board of immigration and public improvements."

"Been away a good many years, hasn't he?" I asked.

"No, sir; Colonel Rockingham is going down to the post-office for his mail. His fellow-citizens take pleasure in greeting him thus every morning. The colonel is our most prominent citizen. Besides the height of the stock of the Sunrise & Edenville Tap Railroad, he owns a thousand acres of that land across the creek. Mountain Valley, delights, sir, to honor a citizen of such wealth and public spirit."

For an hour that afternoon Caligula sat on the back of his neck on the porch and studied a newspaper, which was unusual in a man who despised print. When he was through he took me to the end of the porch among the sunlight and drying dishtowels. I knew that Caligula had invented a new graft. For he chewed the ends of his mustache and ran the left catch of his suspenders up and down, which was his way.

"What is it now?" I asks. "Just so it ain't floating mining stocks or raising Pennsylvania pinks, we'll talk it over."

"Pennsylvania pinks? Oh, that refers to a coin-raising scheme of the Key-stoners. They burn the soles of old women's feet to make them tell where their money's hid."

Caligula's words in business was always few and bitter.

"You see them mountains," said he, pointing. "And you seen that colonel man that owns railroads and cuts more ice when he goes to the post-office than Roose-velt does when he cleans 'em out. What we're going to do is to kidnap the latter into the former, and inflict a ransom of ten thousand dollars."

"Illegality," says I, shaking my head.

"I knew you'd say that," says Caligula. "At first sight it does seem to jar peace and dignity. But it don't. I got the idea out of that newspaper. Would you commit aspersions on a equitable graft that the United States itself has con-doned and indorsed and ratified?"

"Kidnapping," says I, "is an immoral function in the derogatory list of the statutes. If the United States upholds it, it must be a recent enactment of ethics, along with race suicide and rural delivery."

"Listen," says Caligula, "and I'll explain the case set down in the papers. Here was a Greek citizen named Burdick Harris," says he, "captured for a graft by Africans; and the United States sends two gunboats to the State of Tangiers and makes the King of Morocco give up seventy thousand dollars to Raisuli."

"Go slow," says I. "That sounds too international to take in all at once. It's like 'thimble, thimble, who's got the naturalization papers?'"

"'Twas press despatches from Constantinople," says Caligula. "You'll see, six months from now. They'll be confirmed by the monthly magazines; and then it won't be long till you'll notice 'em alongside of photos of the Mount Pelee erup-tion photos in the while-you-get-your-hair-cut weeklies. It's all right, Pick. This African man Raisuli hides Burdick Harris up in the mountains, and adver-tises his price to the governments of different nations. Now, you wouldn't think for a minute," goes on Caligula, "that John Hay would have chipped in and helped this graft along if it wasn't a square game, would you?"

"Why, no," says I. "I've always stood right in with Bryan's policies, and I couldn't consciously say a word against the Republican administration just now. But if Harris was a Greek, on what system of international protocols did Hay interfere?"

"It ain't exactly set forth in the papers," says Caligula. "I suppose it's a matter of sentiment. You know he wrote this poem, 'Little Breeches'; and them Greeks wear little or none. But anyhow, John Hay sends the *Brooklyn* and the *Olympia* over, and they cover Africa with thirty-inch guns. And then Hay cables after the health of the *persona grata*. 'And how are they this morning?' he wires. 'Is Burdick Harris alive yet, or Mr. Raisuli dead?' And the King of Morocco sends up the seventy thousand dollars, and they turn Burdick Harris loose. And there's not half the hard feelings among the nations about this little kidnapping matter as there was about the peace congress. And Burdick Harris says to the reporters, in the Greek language, that he's often heard about the United States, and he admires Roosevelt next to Raisuli, who is one of the whitest and most gentlemanly kidnappers that he ever worked alongside of. So you see, Pick,' winds up Caligula, 'we've got the law of nations on our side. We'll cut this colonel man out of the herd, and corral him in them little mountains, and stick up his heirs and assigns for ten thousand dollars."

"Well, you seldom little red-headed territorial terror," I answers, "you can't bluff your uncle Tecumseh Pickens! I'll be your company in this graft. But I misdoubt if you've absorbed the inwardness of this Burdick Harris case, Calig; and if on any morning we get a telegram from the Secretary of State asking about the health of the scheme, I propose to acquire the most propinquitous and celeritous mule in this section and gallop diplomatically over into the neighboring and peaceful nation of Alabama."

III

Me and Caligula spent the next three days investigating the bunch of mountains into which we proposed to kidnap Colonel Jackson T. Rockingham. We finally selected an upright slice of topography covered with bushes and trees that you could only reach by a secret path that we cut up the side of it. And the only way to reach the mountain was to follow up the bend of a branch that wound among the elevations.

Then I took in hand an important subdivision of the proceedings. I went up to Atlanta on the train and laid in a two-hundred-and-fifty-dollar supply of the most gratifying and efficient lines of grub that money could buy. I always was an admirer of viands in their more palliative and revised stages. Hog and hominy are not only inartistic to my stomach, but they give indigestion to my moral sentiments. And I thought of Colonel Jackson T. Rockingham, president of the Sunrise & Edenville Tap Railroad, and how he would miss the luxury of his home fare as is so famous among wealthy Southerners. So I sunk half of mine and Caligula's capital in as elegant a layout of fresh and canned provisions as Burdick Harris or any other professional kidnappee ever saw in a camp.

I put another hundred in a couple of cases of Bordeaux, two quarts of cognac, two hundred Havana regalias with gold bands, and a camp stove and stools and folding cots. I wanted Colonel Rockingham to be comfortable; and I hoped after he gave up the ten thousand dollars he would give me and Caligula as good a name for gentlemen and entertainers as the Greek man did the friend of his that made the United States his bill collector against Africa. When the goods came down from Atlanta, we hired a wagon, moved them up on the little mountain, and established camp. And then we laid for the colonel.

We caught him one morning about two miles out from Mountain Valley, on his way to look after some of his burnt umber farm land. He was an elegant old gentleman, as thin and tall as a trout rod, with frazzled shirt-cuffs and specs on a black string. We explained to him, brief and easy, what we wanted; and Caligula showed him, careless, the handle of his forty-five under his coat.

"What?" says Colonel Rockingham. "Bandits in Perry County, Georgia! I shall see that the board of immigration and public improvements hears of this!"

"Be so unfoolhardy as to climb into that buggy," says Caligula, "by order of the board of perforation and public depravity. This is a business meeting, and we're anxious to adjourn *sine qua non.*"

We drove Colonel Rockingham over the mountain and up the side of it as far as the buggy could go. Then we tied the horse, and took our prisoner on foot up to the camp.

"Now, colonel," I says to him, "we're after the ransom, me and my partner; and no harm will come to you if the King of Mor—if your friends send up the dust. In the meantime, we are gentlemen the same as you. And if you give us your word not to try to escape, the freedom of the camp is yours."

"I give you my word," says the colonel.

"All right," says I; "and now it's eleven o'clock and me and Mr. Polk will proceed to inoculate the occasion with a few well-timed trivialities in the line of grub."

"Thank you," says the colonel; "I believe I could relish a slice of bacon and a plate of hominy."

"But you won't," says I, emphatic. "Not in this camp. We soar in higher regions than them occupied by your celebrated but repulsive dish."

While the colonel read his paper, me and Caligula took off our coats and went in for a little luncheon *de luxe* just to show him. Caligula was a fine cook of the Western brand. He could toast a buffalo or fricasse a couple of steers as easy as a woman could make a cup of tea. He was gifted in the way of knocking together edibles when haste and muscle and quantity was to be considered. He held the record west of the Arkansas River for frying pancakes with his left hand, broiling venison cutlets with his right and skinning a rabbit with his teeth at the same time. But I could do things *en casserole* and *à la creole,* and handle the oil and tabasco as gently and nicely as a French *chef.*

So at twelve o'clock we had a hot lunch ready that looked like a banquet on a Mississippi River steamboat. We spread it on the tops of two or three big boxes, opened two quarts of the red wine, set the olives and a canned oyster cocktail and a ready-made Martini by the colonel's plate, and called him to grub.

Colonel Rockingham drew up his campstool, wiped off his specs, and looked at the things on the table. Then I thought he was swearing; and I felt mean because I hadn't taken more pains with the victuals. But he wasn't; he was asking a blessing; and me and Caligula hung our heads and I saw a tear drop from the colonel's eye into his cocktail.

I never saw a man eat with so much earnestness and application—not hastily like a grammarian or one of the canal, but slow and appreciative, like a anaconda, or a real *vive bonjour.*

In an hour and a half the colonel leaned back. I brought him a pony of brandy and his black coffee, and set the box of Havana regalias on the table.

"Gentlemen," says he, blowing out the smoke and trying to breathe it back again, "when we view the eternal hills and the smiling and beneficent landscape, and reflect upon the goodness of the Creator who——"

"Excuse me, colonel," says I, "but there's some business to attention to now"; and I brought out paper and pen and ink and laid 'em before him. "Who do you want to send to for the money?" I asks.

"I reckon," says he, after thinking a bit, "to the vice-president of our rail-road, at the general offices of the Company in Edenville."

"How far is it to Edenville from here?" I asked.

"About ten miles," says he.

Then I dictated these lines, and Colonel Rockingham wrote them out:

I am kidnapped and held a prisoner by two desperate outlaws in a place which is useless to attempt to find. They demand ten thousand dollars at once for my release. The amount must be raised immediately, and these directions followed. Come alone with the money to Stony Creek, which runs out of Blacktop Mountains. Follow the bed of the creek till you come to a big flat rock on the left bank, on which is marked a cross in red chalk. Stand on the rock and wave a white flag. A guide will come to you and conduct you to where I am held. Lose no time.

After the colonel had finished this, he asked permission to tack on a postscript about how white he was being treated, so the railroad wouldn't feel uneasy in its bosom about him. We agreed to that. He wrote down that he had just had lunch with the two desperate ruffians; and then he set down the whole bill of fare, from cocktails to coffee. He wound up with the remark that dinner would be ready about six, and would probably be a more licentious and intemperate affair than lunch.

Me and Caligula read it, and decided to let it go; for we, being cooks, were amenable to praise, though it sounded out of place on a sight draft for ten thousand dollars.

I took the letter over to the Mountain Valley road and watched for a messenger. By and by a colored equestrian came along on horseback, riding toward Edenville.

I gave him a dollar to take the letter to the railroad offices; and then I went back to camp.

IV

About four o'clock in the afternoon, Caligula, who was acting as lookout, calls to me:

"I have to report a white shirt signaling on the starboard bow, sir."

I went down the mountain and brought back a fat, red man in an alpaca coat and no collar.

"Gentlemen," says Colonel Rockingham, "allow me to introduce my brother, Captain Duval C. Rockingham, vice-president of the Sunrise & Edenville Tap Railroad."

"Otherwise the King of Morocco," says I. "I reckon you don't mind my counting the ransom, just as a business formality."

"Well, no, not exactly," says the fat man, "not when it comes. I turned that matter over to our second vice-president. I was anxious after Brother Jackson's safetiness. I reckon he'll be along right soon. What does that lobster salad you mentioned taste like, Brother Jackson?"

"Mr. Vice-President," says I, "you'll oblige us by remaining here till the second V. P. arrives. This is a private rehearsal, and we don't want any road-side speculators selling tickets."

In half an hour Caligula sings out again:

"Sail ho! Looks like an apron on a broomstick."

I perambulated down the cliff again, and escorted up a man six foot three, with a sandy beard and no other dimensions that you could notice. Thinks I to myself, if he's got ten thousand dollars on his person it's in one bill and folded lengthwise.

"Mr. Patterson G. Coble, our second vice-president," announces the colonel.

"Glad to know you, gentlemen," says this Coble. "I came up to disseminate the tidings that Major Tallahassee Tucker, our general passenger agent, is now negotiating a peach-crate full of our railroad bonds with the Perry County Bank for a loan. My dear Colonel Rockingham, was that chicken gumbo or cracked goobers on the bill of fare in your note? Me and the conductor of fifty-six was having a dispute about it."

"Another white wings on the rocks!" hollers Caligula. "If I see any more I'll fire on 'em and swear they was torpedo-boats!"

The guide goes down again, and convoys into the lair a person in blue overalls carrying an amount of inebriety and a lantern. I am so sure that this is Major Tucker that I don't even ask him until we are up above; and then I discover that it is Uncle Timothy, the yard switchman at Edenville, who is sent ahead to flag our understandings with the gossip that Judge Prendergast, the railroad's attorney, is in the process of mortgaging Colonel Rockingham's farming lands to make up the ransom.

While he is talking, two men crawl from under the bushes into camp, and Caligula, with no white flag to disinter him from his plain duty, draws his gun. But again Colonel Rockingham intervenes and introduces Mr. Jones and Mr. Batts, engineer and fireman of train number forty-two.

"Excuse us," says Batts, "but me and Jim have hunted squirrels all over this mounting, and we don't need no white flag. Was that straight, colonel, about the plum pudding and pineapples and real store cigars?"

"Towel on a fishing-pole in the offing!" howls Caligula. "Suppose it's the firing line of the freight conductors and brakeman."

"My last trip down," says I, wiping off my face. "If the S. & E. T. wants to run an excursion up here just because we kidnapped their president, let 'em. We'll put out our sign. 'The Kidnapper's Cafe and Trainmen's Home.' "

This time I caught Major Tallahassee Tucker by his own confession, and I felt easier. I asked him into the creek, so I could drown him if he happened to be a track-walker or caboose porter. All the way up the mountain he driveled to me about asparagus on toast, a thing that his intelligence in life had skipped.

Up above I got his mind segregated from food and asked if he had raised the ransom.

"My dear sir," says he, "I succeeded in negotiating a loan on thirty thousand dollars' worth of the bonds of our railroad, and——"

"Never mind just now, major," says I. "It's all right, then. Wait till after dinner, and we'll settle the business. All of you gentlemen," I continues to the crowd, "are invited to stay to dinner. We have mutually trusted one another, and the white flag is supposed to wave over the proceedings."

"The correct idea," says Caligula, who was standing by me. "Two baggage-masters and a ticket agent dropped out of a tree while you was below the last time. Did the major man bring the money?"

"He says," I answered, "that he succeeded in negotiating the loan."

If any cooks ever earned ten thousand dollars in twelve hours me and Caligula did that day. At six o'clock we spread the top of the mountain with as fine a dinner as the personnel of any railroad ever engulfed. We opened all the wine, and we concocted entrées and *pièces de résistance*, and stirred up little savory *chef de cuisines* and organized a mass of grub such as has seldom instigated out of canned and bottled goods. The railroad gathered around it, and the wassail and diversions was intense.

After the feast me and Caligula, in the line of business, takes Major Tucker to one side and talks ransom. The major pulls out an agglomeration of currency about the size of the price of a town lot in the suburbs of Rabbitville, Arizona, and makes this outcry.

"Gentlemen," says he, "the stock of the Sunrise & Edenville railroad has depreciated some. The best I could do with thirty thousand dollars' worth of the bonds was to secure a loan of eighty-seven dollars and fifty cents. On the farming lands of Colonel Rockingham, Judge Prendergast was able to obtain, on a ninth mortgage, the sum of fifty dollars. You will find the amount, one hundred and thirty-seven fifty, correct."

"A railroad president," said I, looking this Tucker in the eye, "and the owner of a thousand acres of land; and yet——"

"Gentlemen," says Tucker, "The railroad is ten miles long. There don't any train run on it except when the crew goes out in the pines and gathers enough lightwood knots to get up steam. A long time ago, when times was good, the net earnings used to run as high as eighteen dollars a week. Colonel Rockingham's land has been sold for taxes thirteen times. There hasn't been a peach crop in this part of Georgia for two years. The wet spring killed the watermelons. Nobody around here has money enough to buy fertilizer; and land is so poor the corn crop failed, and there wasn't enough grass to support the rabbits. All the people have had to eat in this section for over a year is hog and hominy, and——"

"Pick," interrupts Caligula, mussing up his red hair, "what are you going to do with that chicken-feed?"

I hands the money back to Major Tucker; and then I goes over to Colonel Rockingham and slaps him on the back.

"Colonel," says I, "I hope you've enjoyed our little joke. We don't want to carry it too far. Kidnappers! Well, wouldn't it tickle your uncle? My name's Rhinegelder, and I'm a nephew of Chauncey Depew. My friend's a second cousin of the editor of *Puck*. So you can see. We are down South enjoying ourselves in our humorous way. Now, there's two quarts of cognac to open yet, and then the joke's over."

What's the use to go into details? One or two will be enough. I remember Major Tallahassee Tucker playing on a jew's-harp, and Caligula waltzing with his head on the watch pocket of a tall baggage-master. I hesitate to refer to the cake-walk done by me and Mr. Patterson G. Coble with Colonel Jackson T. Rockingham between us.

And even on the next morning, when you wouldn't think it possible, there was a consolation for me and Caligula. We knew that Raisuli himself never made half the hit with Burdick Harris that we did with the Sunrise & Edenville Tap Railroad.

THE ETHICS OF PIG

On an east-bound train I went into the smoker and found Jefferson Peters, the only man with a brain west of the Wabash River who can use his cerebrum and cerebellum, and medulla oblongata at the same time.

Jeff is in the line of unillegal graft. He is not to be dreaded by widows and orphans; he is a reducer of surplusage. His favorite disguise is that of the target-bird at which the spendthrift or the reckless investor may shy a few inconsequentional dollars. He is readily vocalized by tobacco; so, with the aid of two thick and easy-burning brevas, I got the story of his latest Autolycan adventure.

"In my line of business," said Jeff, "the hardest thing is to find an upright, trustworthy, strictly honorable partner to work a graft with. Some of the best men I ever worked with in a swindle would resort to trickery at times.

So, last summer, I thinks I will go over into this section of country where I hear the serpent has not yet entered, and see if I can find a partner naturally gifted with a talent for crime, but not yet contaminated by success.

"I found a village that seemed to show the right kind of a layout. The inhabitants hadn't found out that Adam had been dispossessed, and were going right along naming the animals and killing snakes just as if they were in the Garden of Eden. They call this town Mount Nebo, and it's up near the spot where Kentucky and West Virginia and North Carolina corner together. Them States don't meet? Well, it was in that neighborhood, anyway.

"After putting in a week proving I wasn't a revenue officer, I went over to the store where the rude fourflushers of the hamlet lied, to see if I could get a line on the kind of man I wanted.

"'Gentlemen,' says I, after we had rubbed noses and gathered 'round the dried-apple barrel. 'I don't suppose there's another community in the whole world into which sin and chicanery has less extensively permeated than this. Life here, where all the women are brave and propitious and all the men honest and expedient, must, indeed, be an idol. It reminds me,' says I, 'of Goldstein's beautiful ballad entitled "The Deserted Village," which says:

'Ill fares the land, to hastening ills a prey;
What art can drive its charms away?
The judge rode slowly down the lane, mother;
For I'm to be Queen of the May.'

"'Why, yes, Mr. Peters,' says the storekeeper. 'I reckon we air about as moral and torpid a community as there be on the mounting, according to censuses of opinion; but I reckon you ain't ever met Rufe Tatum.'

"'Why, no,' says the town constable, 'he can't hardly have ever. That air Rufe is shore the monstrousest scalawag that has escaped hangin' on the galluses. And that puts me in mind that I ought to have turned Rufe out of the lockup day before yesterday. The thirty days he got for killin' Yance Goodloe was up then. A day or two more won't hurt Rufe any, though.'

"'Shucks, now,' says I, in the mountain idiom, 'don't tell me there's a man in Mount Nebo as bad as that.'

"'Worse,' says the storekeeper. 'He steals hogs.'

"I think I will look up this Mr. Tatum; so a day or two after the constable turned him out I got acquainted with him and invited him out on the edge of town to sit on a log and talk business.

"What I wanted was a partner with a natural rural make-up to play a part in some little one-act outrages that I was going to book with the Pitfall & Gin circuit in some of the Western towns; and this R. Tatum was born for the rôle as sure as nature cast Fairbanks for the stuff that kept *Eliza* from sinking into the river.

"He was about the size of a first baseman; and he had ambiguous blue eyes like the china dog on the mantelpiece that Aunt Harriet used to play with when she was a child. His hair waved a little bit like the statue of the dinkus-thrower in the vacation at Rome, but the color of it reminded you of the 'Sunset in the Grand Cañon, by an American Artist,' that they hang over the stove-pipe holes in the salongs. He was the Reub, without needing a touch. You'd have known him for one, even if you'd seen him on the vaudeville stage with one cotton suspender and a straw over his ear.

"I told him what I wanted, and found him ready to jump at the job.

"'Overlooking such a trivial little peccadillo as the habit of manslaughter,' says I, 'what have you accomplished in the way of indirect brigandage or non-actionable thriftiness that you could point to, with or without pride, as an evidence of our qualifications for the position?'

"'Why,' says he, in his kind of Southern system of procrastinated accents, 'hain't you heard tell? There ain't any man, black or white, in the Blue Ridge that can tote off a shoat as easy as I can without bein' heard, seen, or cotched. I can lift a shoat,' he goes on, 'out of a pen, from under a porch, at the trough, in the woods, day or night, anywhere or anyhow, and I guarantee nobody won't hear a squeal. It's all in the way you grab hold of 'em and carry 'em afterwards. Some day,' goes on this gentle despoiler of pig-pens, 'I hope to become reckernized as the champion shoat-stealer of the world.'

"'It's proper to be ambitious,' says I; 'and hog-stealing will do very well for Mount Nebo; but in the outside world, M. Tatum, it would be considered as crude a piece of business as a bear raid on Bay State Gas. However, it will do as a guarantee of good faith. We'll go into partnership. I've got a thousand dollars cash capital; and with that homeward-plods atmosphere of yours we ought to be able to win out a few shares of Soon Parted, preferred, in the money market.'

"So I attaches Rufe, and we go away from Mount Nebo down into the lowlands. And all the way I coach him for his part in the grafts I had in mind. I had idled away two months on the Florida coast, and was feeling all to the Ponce de Leon, besides having so many new schemes up my sleeve that I had to wear kimonos to hold 'em.

"I intended to assume a funnel shape and mow a path nine miles wide through the farming belt of the Middle West; so we headed in that direction. But when we got as far as Lexington we found Binkley Brothers' circus there, and the blue-grass peasantry romping into town and pounding the Belgian blocks with their hand-pegged sabots as artless and arbitrary as an extra session of a Datto Bryan duma. I never pass a circus without pulling the valve-cord and coming down for a little Key West money; so I engaged a couple of rooms and board for Rufe and me at a house near the circus grounds run by a widow lady named Peevy. Then I took Rufe to a clothing store and gent's-outfitted him. He showed up strong, as I knew he would, after he was rigged up in the ready-made ruta-baga regalia. Me and old Misfitzky stuffed him into a bright blue suit with a Nile-green visible plaid effect, and riveted on a fancy vest of a light Tuskegee Normal tan color, a red necktie, and the yellowest pair of shoes in town.

They were the first clothes Rufe had ever worn except the gingham layette and the butternut top-dressing of his native kraal, and he looked as self-conscious as an Igorrote with a new nose-ring.

"That night I went down to the circus tents and opened a small shell game. Rufe was to be the capper. I gave him a roll of phony currency to bet with and kept a bunch of it in a special pocket to pay his winnings out of. No; I didn't mistrust him; but I simply can't manipulate the ball to lose when I see real money bet. My fingers go on a strike every time I try it.

"I set up my little table and began to show them how easy it was to guess which shell the little pea was under. The unlettered hinds gathered in a thick semicircle and began to nudge elbows and banter one another to bet. Then was when Rufe ought to have single-footed up and called the turn on the little joker for a few tens and fives to get them started. But, no Rufe. I'd seen him two or three times walking about and looking at the side-show pictures with his mouth full of peanut candy; but he never came nigh.

"The crowd piked a little; but trying to work the shells without a capper is like fishing without bait. I closed the game with only forty-two dollars of the unearned increment, while I had been counting on yanking the yeomen for two hundred at least. I went home at eleven and went to bed. I supposed that the circus had proved too alluring for Rufe, and that he had succumbed to it, concert and all; but I meant to give him a lecture on general business principles in the morning.

"Just after Morpheus had got both my shoulders to the shuck mattress I hears a houseful of unbecoming and ribald noises like a youngster screeching with green-apple colic. I opens my door and calls out in the hall for the widow lady, and when she sticks her head out, I says: 'Mrs. Peevy, ma'am, would you mind choking off that kid of yours so that honest people can get their rest?'

"'Sir,' says she, 'it's no child of mine. It's the pig squealing that your friend Mr. Tatum brought home to his room a couple of hours ago. And if you are uncle or second cousin or brother to it, I'd appreciate your stopping its mouth, sir, yourself, if you please.'

"I put on some of the polite outside habiliments of external society and went into Rufe's room. He had gotten up and lit his lamp, and was pouring some milk into a tin pan on the floor for a dingy-white, half-grown, squealing pig.

"'How is this, Rufe?' says I. 'You flimflammed in your part of the work to-night and put the game on crutches. And how do you explain the pig? It looks like back-sliding to me.'

"'Now, don't be too hard on me Jeff,' says he. 'You know how long I've been used to stealing shoats. It's got to be a habit with me. And to-night, when I see such a fine chance, I couldn't help takin' it.'

"'Well,' says I, 'maybe you've really got kleptopigia. And maybe when we get out of the pig belt you'll turn your mind to higher and more remunerative mis-conduct. Why you should want to stain your soul with such a distasteful, feeble-minded, perverted, roaring beast as that I can't understand.'

"'Why, Jeff,' says he, 'you ain't in sympathy with shoats. You don't under-stand 'em like I do. This here seems to me to be an animal of more than com-mon powers of ration and intelligence. He walked half across the room on his hind legs a while ago.'

"'Well, I'm going back to bed,' says I. 'See if you can impress it upon your friend's ideas of intelligence that he's not to make so much noise.'

" 'He was hungry,' says Rufe. 'He'll go to sleep and keep quiet now.'

"I always get up before breakfast and read the morning paper whenever I happen to be within the radius of a Hoe cylinder or a Washington hand-press. The next morning I got up early, and found a Lexington daily on the front porch where the carrier had thrown it. The first thing I saw in it was a double-column ad. on the front page that read like this:

FIVE THOUSAND DOLLARS REWARD

The above amount will be paid, and no questions asked, for the return, alive and uninjured, of Beppo, the famous European educated pig, that strayed or was stolen from the side-show tents of Binkley Bros.' circus last night.

GEO. B. TAPLEY, Business Manager.

At the circus grounds.

"I folded up the paper flat, put it into my inside pocket, and went to Rufe's room. He was nearly dressed, and was feeding the pig the rest of the milk and some apple-peelings.

" 'Well, well, well, good-morning all,' I says, hearty and amiable. 'So we are up? And piggy is having his breakfast. What had you intended doing with that pig, Rufe?'

" 'I'm going to crate him up,' says Rufe, 'and express him to ma in Mount Nebo. He'll be company for her while I am away.'

" 'He's a mighty fine pig,' says I, scratching him on the back.

" 'You called him a lot of names last night,' says Rufe.

" 'Oh, well,' says I, 'he looks better to me this morning. I was raised on a farm, and I'm very fond of pigs. I used to go to bed at sundown, so I never saw one by lamplight before. Tell you what I'll do, Rufe,' I says. 'I'll give you ten dollars for that pig.'

" 'I reckon I wouldn't sell this shoat,' says he. 'If it was any other one I might.'

" 'Why not this one?' I asked, fearful that he might know something.

" 'Why, because,' says he, 'it was the grandest achievement of my life. There ain't airy other man that could have done it. If I ever have a fireside and children, I'll sit beside it and tell 'em how their daddy toted off a shoat from a whole circus full of people. And maybe my grandchildren, too. They'll certainly be proud a whole passel. Why,' says he, 'there was two tents, one openin' into the other. This shoat was on a platform, tied with a little chain. I seen a giant and a lady with a fine chance of bushy white hair in the other tent. I got the shoat and crawled out from under the canvas again without him squeakin' as loud as a mouse. I put him under my coat, and I must have passed a hundred folks before I got out where the streets was dark. I reckon I wouldn't sell that shoat, Jeff. I'd want ma to keep it, so there'd be a witness to what I done.'

" 'The pig won't live long enough,' I says, 'to use as an exhibit in your senile fireside mendacity. Your grandchildren will have to take your word for it. I'll give you one hundred dollars for the animal.'

"Rufe looked at me astonished.

" 'The shoat can't be worth anything like that to you,' he says. 'What do you want him for?'

" 'Viewing me casuistically,' says I, with a rare smile, 'you wouldn't think that I've got an artistic side to my temper. But I have. I'm a collector of pigs. I've scoured the world for unusual pigs. Over in the Wabash Valley I've got a hog ranch with most every specimen on it, from a Merino to a Poland China.

This looks like a blooded pig to me, Rufe,' says I. 'I believe it's a genuine Berkshire. That's why I'd like to have it.'

"'I'd shore like to accommodate you,' says he, 'but I've got the artistic tencment, too. I don't see why it ain't art when you can steal a shoat better than anybody else can. Shoats is a kind of inspiration and genius with me. Specially this one. I wouldn't take two hundred and fifty for that animal.'

"'Now, listen,' says I, wiping off my forehead. 'It's not so much a matter of business with me as it is art; and not so much art as it is philanthropy. Being a connoisseur and disseminator of pigs, I wouldn't feel like I'd done my duty to the world unless I added that Berkshire to my collection. Not intrinsically, but according to the ethics of pigs as friends and coadjutors of mankind, I offer you five hundred dollars for the animal.'

"'Jeff,' says this pork esthete, 'it ain't money; it's sentiment with me.'

"'Seven hundred,' says I.

"'Make it eight hundred,' says Rufe, 'and I'll crush the sentiment out of my heart.'

"I went under my clothes for my money-belt, and counted him out forty twenty-dollar gold certificates.

"'I'll just take him into my own room,' says I, 'and lock him up till after breakfast.'

"I took the pig by the hind leg. He turned on a squeal like the steam calliope at the circus.

"'Let me tote him in for you,' says Rufe; and he picks up the beast under one arm, holding his snout with the other hand, and packs him into my room like a sleeping baby.

"After breakfast Rufe, who had a chronic case of haberdashery ever since I got his trousseau, says he believes he will amble down to Misfitzky's and look over some royal-purple socks. And then I got as busy as a one-armed man with the nettle-rash pasting on wall-paper. I found an old negro man with an express wagon to hire; and we tied the pig in a sack and drove down to the circus grounds.

"I found George B. Tapley in a little tent with a window flap open. He was a fattish man with an immediate eye, in a black skull-cap with a four-ounce diamond screwed into the bosom of his red sweater.

"'Are you George B. Tapley?' I asks.

"'I swear it,' says he.

"'Well, I've got it,' says I.

"'Designate,' says he. 'Are you the guinea pigs for the Asiatic python or the alfalfa for the sacred buffalo?'

"'Neither,' says I. 'I've got Beppo, the educated hog, in a sack in that wagon. I found him rooting up the flowers in my front yard this morning. I'll take the five thousand dollars in large bills, if it's handy.'

"George B. hustles out of his tent, and asks me to follow. We went into one of the side-shows. In there was a jet black pig with a pink ribbon around his neck lying on some hay and eating carrots that a man was feeding to him.

"'Hey, Mac,' calls G. B. 'Nothing wrong with the world-wide this morning, is there?'

"'Him? No,' says the man. 'He's got an appetite like a chorus girl at 1 A. M.'

"'How'd you get this pipe?' says Tapley to me. 'Eating too many pork chops last night?'

"I pulls out the paper and shows him the ad.

"'Fake,' says he. 'Don't know anything about it. You've beheld with your own eyes the marvelous, world-wide porcine wonder of the four-footed kingdom eating with preternatural sagacity his matutinal meal, unstrayed and unstole. Good-morning.'

"I was beginning to see. I got in the wagon and told Uncle Ned to drive to the most adjacent orifice of the nearest alley. There I took out my pig, got the range carefully for the other opening, set his sights, and gave him such a kick that he went out the other end of the alley twenty feet ahead of his squeal.

"Then I paid Uncle Ned his fifty cents, and walked down to the newspaper office. I wanted to hear it in cold syllables. I got the advertising man to his window.

"'To decide a bet,' says I, 'wasn't the man who had this ad. put in last night short and fat, with long black whiskers and a club-foot?'

"'He was not,' says the man. 'He would measure about six feet by four and a half inches, with corn-silk hair, and dressed like the pansies of the conservatory.'

"At dinner time I went back to Mrs. Peevy's.

"'Shall I keep some soup hot for Mr. Tatum till he comes back?' she asks.

"'If you do, ma'am,' says I, 'you'll more than exhaust for firewood all the coal in the bosom of the earth and all the forests on the outside of it.'

"So there, you see," said Jefferson Peters, in conclusion, "how hard it is ever to find a fair-minded and honest business-partner."

"But," I began, with the freedom of long acquaintance, "the rule should work both ways. If you had offered to divide the reward you would not have lost——"

Jeff's look of dignified reproach stopped me.

"That don't involve the same principles at all," said he. "Mine was a legitimate and moral attempt at speculation. Buy low and sell high—don't Wall Street indorse it? Bulls and bears and pigs—what's the difference? Why not bristles as well as horns and fur?"

ROADS OF DESTINY

ROADS OF DESTINY

ROADS OF DESTINY

> I go to seek on many roads
> What is to be.
> True heart and strong, with love to light—
> Will they not bear me in the fight
> To order, shun or wield or mould
> My Destiny?
>
> *Unpublished Poems of David Mignot.*

THE song was over. The words were David's; the air, one of the country-side. The company about the inn table applauded heartily, for the young poet paid for the wine. Only the notary, M. Papineau, shook his head a little at the lines, for he was a man of books, and he had not drunk with the rest.

David went out into the village street, where the night air drove the wine vapor from his head. And then he remembered that he and Yvonne had quarrelled that day, and that he had resolved to leave his home that night to seek fame and honor in the great world outside.

"When my poems are on every man's tongue," he told himself, in a fine exhilaration, "she will, perhaps, think of the hard words she spoke this day."

Except the roysterers in the tavern, the village folk were abed. David crept softly into his room in the shed of his father's cottage and made a bundle of his small store of clothing. With this upon a staff, he set his face outward upon the road that ran from Vernoy.

He passed his father's herd of sheep huddled in their nightly pen—the sheep he herded daily, leaving them to scatter while he wrote verses on scraps of paper. He saw a light yet shining in Yvonne's window, and a weakness shook his purpose of a sudden. Perhaps that light meant that she rued, sleepless, her anger, and that morning might—— But, no! His decision was made. Vernoy was no place for him. Not one soul there could share his thoughts. Out along that road lay his fate and his future.

Three leagues across the dim, moonlit champaign ran the road, straight as a plowman's furrow. It was believed in the village that the road ran to Paris, at least; and this name the poet whispered often to himself as he walked. Never so far from Vernoy had David travelled before.

THE LEFT BRANCH

Three leagues, then, the road ran, and turned into a puzzle. It joined with another and a larger road at right angles. David stood, uncertain, for a while, and then took the road to the left.

Upon this more important highway were, imprinted in the dust, wheel tracks left by the recent passage of some vehicle. Some half an hour later these traces were verified by the sight of a ponderous carriage mired in a little brook at the bottom of a steep hill. The driver and postilions were shouting and tugging at the horses' bridles. On the road at one side stood a huge, black-clothed man and a slender lady wrapped in a long, light cloak.

David saw the lack of skill in the efforts of the servants. He quietly assumed control of the work. He directed the outriders to cease their clamor at the horses and to exercise their strength upon the wheels. The driver alone urged the animals with his familiar voice; David himself heaved a powerful shoulder at the rear of the carriage, and with one harmonious tug the great vehicle rolled up on solid ground. The outriders climbed to their places.

David stood for a moment upon one foot. The huge gentleman waved a hand. "You will enter the carriage," he said, in a voice large, like himself, but smoothed by art and habit. Obedience belonged in the path of such a voice. Brief as was the young poet's hesitation, it was cut shorter still by a renewal of the command. David's foot went to the step. In the darkness he perceived dimly the form of the lady upon the rear seat. He was about to seat himself opposite, when the voice again swayed him to its will. "You will sit at the lady's side."

The gentleman swung his great weight to the forward seat. The carriage proceeded up the hill. The lady was shrunk, silent, into her corner. David could not estimate whether she was old or young, but a delicate, mild perfume from her clothes stirred his poet's fancy to the belief that there was loveliness beneath the mystery. Here was an adventure such as he had often imagined. But as yet he held no key to it, for no word was spoken while he sat with his impenetrable companions.

In an hour's time David perceived through the window that the vehicle traversed the street of some town. Then it stopped in front of a closed and darkened house, and a postilion alighted to hammer impatiently upon the door. A latticed window above flew wide and a night-capped head popped out.

"Who are ye that disturb honest folk at this time of night? My house is closed. 'Tis too late for profitable travellers to be abroad. Cease knocking at my door, and be off."

"Open!" spluttered the postilion, loudly; "open for Monseigneur the Marquis de Beaupertuys."

"Ah!" cried the voice above. "Ten thousand pardons, my lord. I did not know—the hour is so late—at once shall the door be opened, and the house placed at my lord's disposal."

Inside was heard the clink of chain and bar, and the door was flung open. Shivering with chill and apprehension, the landlord of the Silver Flagon stood, half clad, candle in hand, upon the threshold.

David followed the marquis out of the carriage. "Assist the lady," he was ordered. The poet obeyed. He felt her small hand tremble as he guided her descent. "Into the house," was the next command.

The room was the long dining-hall of the tavern. A great oak table ran down its length. The huge gentleman seated himself in a chair at the nearer end. The lady sank into another against the wall, with an air of great weariness. David stood, considering how best he might now take his leave and continue upon his way.

"My lord," said the landlord, bowing to the floor, "h-had I ex-expected this honor, entertainment would have been ready. T-t-there is wine and cold fowl and m-m-maybe——"

"Candles," said the marquis, spreading the fingers of one plump white hand in a gesture he had.

"Y-yes, my lord." He fetched half a dozen candles, lighted them, and set them upon the table.

"If monsieur would, perhaps, deign to taste a certain Burgundy—there is a cask——"

"Candles," said monsieur, spreading his fingers.

"Assuredly—quickly—I fly, my lord."

A dozen more lighted candles shone in the hall. The great bulk of the marquis overflowed his chair. He was dressed in fine black from head to foot save for the snowy ruffles at his wrist and throat. Even the hilt and scabbard of his sword were black. His expression was one of sneering pride. The ends of an upturned moustache reached nearly to his mocking eyes.

The lady sat motionless, and now David perceived that she was young, and possessed of pathetic and appealing beauty. He was startled from the contemplation of her forlorn loveliness by the booming voice of the marquis.

"What is your name and pursuit?"

"David Mignot. I am a poet."

The moustache of the marquis curled nearer to his eyes.

"How do you live?"

"I am also a shepherd; I guarded my father's flock," David answered, with his head high, but a flush upon his cheek.

"Then listen, master shepherd and poet, to the fortune you have blundered upon to-night. This lady is my niece, Mademoiselle Lucie de Varennes. She is of noble descent and is possessed of ten thousand francs a year in her own right. As to her charms, you have but to observe for yourself. If the inventory pleases your shepherd's heart, she becomes your wife at a word. Do not interrupt me. To-night I conveyed her to the château of the Comte de Villemaur, to whom her hand had been promised. Guests were present; the priest was waiting; her marriage to one eligible in rank and fortune was ready to be accomplished. At the altar this demoiselle, so meek and dutiful, turned upon me like a leopardess, charged me with cruelty and crimes, and broke, before the gaping priest, the troth I had plighted for her. I swore there and then, by ten thousand devils, that she should marry the first man we met after leaving the château, be he prince, charcoal-burner, or thief. You, Shepherd, are the first. Mademoiselle must be wed this night. If not you, then another. You have ten minutes in which to make your decision. Do not vex me with words or questions. Ten minutes, shepherd; and they are speeding."

The marquis drummed loudly with his white fingers upon the table. He sank into a veiled attitude of waiting. It was as if some great house had shut its doors and windows against approach. David would have spoken, but the huge man's bearing stopped his tongue. Instead, he stood by the lady's chair and bowed.

"Mademoiselle," he said, and he marvelled to find his words flowing easily before so much elegance and beauty. "You have heard me say I was a shepherd. I have also had the fancy, at times, that I am a poet. If it be the test of a poet to adore and cherish the beautiful, that fancy is now strengthened. Can I serve you in any way, mademoiselle?"

The young woman looked up at him with eyes dry and mournful. His frank, glowing face, made serious by the gravity of the adventure, his strong, straight figure and the liquid sympathy in his blue eyes, perhaps, also, her imminent need of long-denied help and kindness, thawed her to sudden tears.

"Monsieur," she said, in low tones, "you look to be true and kind. He is my uncle, the brother of my father, and my only relative. He loved my mother, and he hates me because I am like her. He has made my life one long terror. I am afraid of his very looks, and never before dared to disobey him. But to-night he would have married me to a man three times my age. You will forgive me for bringing this vexation upon you, monsieur. You will, of course, decline this mad act he tries to force upon you. But let me thank you for your generous words, at least. I have had none spoken to me in so long."

There was now something more than generosity in the poet's eyes. Poet he must have been, for Yvonne was forgotten; this fine, new loveliness held him with its freshness and grace. The subtle perfume from her filled him with strange emotions. His tender look fell warmly upon her. She leaned to it, thirstily.

"Ten minutes," said David, "is given me in which to do what I would devote years to achieve. I will not say I pity you, mademoiselle; it would not be true—I love you. I cannot ask love from you yet, but let me rescue you from this cruel man, and, in time, love may come. I think I have a future, I will not always be a shepherd. For the present I will cherish you with all my heart and make your life less sad. Will you trust your fate to me, mademoiselle?"

"Ah, you would sacrifice yourself from pity!"

"From love. The time is almost up, mademoiselle."

"You will regret it, and despise me."

"I will live only to make you happy, and myself worthy of you."

Her fine small hand crept into his from beneath her cloak.

"I will trust you," she breathed, "with my life. And—and love—may not be so far off as you think. Tell him. Once away from the power of his eyes I may forget."

David went and stood before the marquis. The black figure stirred, and the mocking eyes glanced at the great hall clock.

"Two minutes to spare. A shepherd requires eight minutes to decide whether he will accept a bride of beauty and income! Speak up, shepherd, do you consent to become mademoiselle's husband?"

"Mademoiselle," said David, standing proudly, "has done me the honor to yield to my request that she become my wife."

"Well said!" said the marquis. "You have yet the making of a courtier in you, master shepherd. Mademoiselle could have drawn a worse prize, after all. And now to be done with the affair as quick as the Church and the devil will allow!"

He struck the table soundly with his sword hilt. The landlord came, knee-shaking, bringing more candles in the hope of anticipating the great lord's whims. "Fetch a priest," said the marquis, "a priest; do you understand? In ten minutes have a priest here, or——"

The landlord dropped his candles and flew.

The priest came, heavy-eyed and ruffled. He made David Mignot and Lucie de Varennes man and wife, pocketed a gold piece that the marquis tossed him, and shuffled out again into the night.

"Wine," ordered the marquis, spreading his ominous fingers at the host.

"Fill glasses," he said, when it was brought. He stood up at the head of the table in the candlelight, a black mountain of venom and conceit, with something like the memory of an old love turned to poison in his eye, as it fell upon his niece.

"Monsieur Mignot," he said, raising his wine-glass, "drink after I say this to you: You have taken to be your wife one who will make your life a foul and wretched thing. The blood in her is an inheritance running black lies and red ruin. She will bring you shame and anxiety. The devil that descended to her is there in her eyes and skin and mouth that stoop even to beguile a peasant. There is your promise, monsieur poet, for a happy life. Drink your wine. At last, mademoiselle, I am rid of you."

The marquis drank. A little grievous cry, as if from a sudden wound, came from the girl's lips. David, with his glass in his hand, stepped forward three paces and faced the marquis. There was little of a shepherd in his bearing.

"Just now," he said calmly, "you did me the honor to call me 'monsieur.' May I hope, therefore, that my marriage to mademoiselle has placed me somewhat nearer to you in—let us say, reflected rank—has given me the right to stand more as an equal to monseigneur in a certain little piece of business I have in my mind?"

"You may hope, shepherd," sneered the marquis.

"Then," said David, dashing his glass of wine into the contemptuous eyes that mocked him, "perhaps you will condescend to fight me."

The fury of the great lord outbroke in one sudden curse like a blast from a horn. He tore his sword from its black sheath; he called to the hovering landlord: "A sword there, for this lout!" He turned to the lady, with a laugh that chilled her heart, and said: "You put much labor upon me, madame. It seems I must find you a husband and make you a widow in the same night."

"I know not sword-play," said David. He flushed to make the confession before his lady.

"'I know not sword-play,'" mimicked the marquis. "Shall we fight like peasants with oaken cudgels? *Hola!* François, my pistols!"

A postilion brought two shining great pistols ornamented with carven silver from the carriage holsters. The marquis tossed one upon the table near David's hand. "To the other end of the table," he cried; "even a shepherd may pull a trigger. Few of them attain the honor to die by the weapon of a De Beaupertuys."

The shepherd and the marquis faced each other from the ends of the long table. The landlord, in an ague of terror, clutched the air and stammered: "M-M-Monseigneur, for the love of Christ! not in my house!—do not spill blood —it will ruin my custom——" The look of the marquis, threatening him, paralyzed his tongue.

"Coward," cried the lord of Beaupertuys, "cease chattering your teeth long enough to give the word for us, if you can."

Mine host's knees smote the floor. He was without a vocabulary. Even sounds were beyond him. Still, by gestures he seemed to beseech peace in the name of his house and custom.

"I will give the word," said the lady, in a clear voice. She went up to David and kissed him sweetly. Her eyes were sparkling bright, and color had come to her cheek. She stood against the wall, and the two men levelled their pistols for her count.

"*Un—deux—trois!*"

The two reports came so nearly together that the candles flickered but once. The marquis stood, smiling, the fingers of his left hand resting, outspread, upon the end of the table. David remained erect, and turned his head very slowly, searching for his wife with his eyes. Then, as a garment falls from where it is hung, he sank, crumpled, upon the floor.

With a little cry of terror and despair, the widowed maid ran and stooped above him. She found his wound, and then looked up with her old look of pale melancholy. "Through his heart," she whispered. "Oh, his heart!"

"Come," boomed the great voice of the marquis, "out with you to the carriage! Daybreak shall not find you on my hands. Wed you shall be again, and to a living husband, this night. The next we come upon, my lady, highwayman or peasant. If the road yields no other, then the churl that opens my gates. Out with you to the carriage!"

The marquis, implacable and huge, the lady wrapped again in the mystery of her cloak, the postilion bearing the weapons—all moved out to the waiting carriage. The sound of its ponderous wheels rolling away echoed through the slumbering village. In the hall of the Silver Flagon the distracted landlord wrung his hands above the slain poet's body, while the flames of the four and twenty candles danced and flickered on the table.

THE RIGHT BRANCH

Three leagues, then, the road ran, and turned into a puzzle. It joined with another and a larger road at right angles. David stood, uncertain, for a while, and then took the road to the right.

Whither it led he knew not, but he was resolved to leave Vernoy far behind that night. He travelled a league and then passed a large château which showed testimony of recent entertainment. Lights shone from every window; from the great stone gateway ran a tracery of wheel tracks drawn in the dust by the vehicles of the guests.

Three leagues farther and David was weary. He rested and slept for a while on a bed of pine boughs at the roadside. Then up and on again along the unknown way.

Thus for five days he travelled the great road, sleeping upon Nature's balsamic beds or in peasants' ricks, eating of their black, hospitable bread, drinking from streams or the willing cup of the goatherd.

At length he crossed a great bridge and set his foot within the smiling city that has crushed or crowned more poets than all the rest of the world. His breath came quickly as Paris sang to him in a little undertone her vital chant of greeting—the hum of voice and foot and wheel.

High up under the eaves of an old house in the Rue Conti, David paid for lodging, and set himself, in a wooden chair, to his poems. The street, once sheltering citizens of import and consequence, was now given over to those who ever follow in the wake of decline.

The houses were tall and still possessed of a ruined dignity, but many of them were empty save for dust and the spider. By night there was the clash of steel and the cries of brawlers straying restlessly from inn to inn. Where once gentility abode was now but a rancid and rude incontinence. But here David found housing commensurate to his scant purse. Daylight and candlelight found him at pen and paper.

One afternoon he was returning from a foraging trip to the lower world, with bread and curds and a bottle of thin wine. Halfway up his dark stairway he met—or rather came upon, for she rested on the stair—a young woman of a beauty that should balk even the justice of a poet's imagination. A loose, dark cloak, flung open, showed a rich gown beneath. Her eyes changed swiftly with every little shade of thought. Within one moment they would be round and artless like a child's, and long and cozening like a gypsy's. One hand raised her gown, undraping a little shoe, high-heeled, with its ribbons dangling, untied. So heavenly she was, so unfitted to stoop, so qualified to charm and command! Perhaps she had seen David coming, and had waited for his help there.

Ah, would monsieur pardon that she occupied the stairway, but the shoe!—the naughty shoe! Alas! it would not remain tied. Ah! if monsieur *would* be so gracious!

The poet's fingers trembled as he tied the contrary ribbons. Then he would have fled from the danger of her presence, but the eyes grew long and cozening, like a gypsy's, and held him. He leaned against the balustrade, clutching his bottle of sour wine.

"You have been so good," she said, smiling. "Does monsieur, perhaps, live in the house?"

"Yes, madame. I—I think so, madame."

"Perhaps in the third story, then?"

"No, madame; higher up."

The lady fluttered her fingers with the least possible gesture of impatience.

"Pardon. Certainly I am not discreet in asking. Monsieur will forgive me? It is surely not becoming that I should inquire where he lodges."

"Madame, do not say so. I live in the——"

"No, no, no; do not tell me. Now I see that I erred. But I cannot lose the interest I feel in this house and all that is in it. Once it was my home. Often I come here but to dream of those happy days again. Will you let that be my excuse?"

"Let me tell you, then, for you need no excuse," stammered the poet. "I live in the top floor—the small room where the stairs turn."

"In the front room?" asked the lady, turning her head sidewise.

"The rear, madame."

The lady sighed, as if with relief.

"I will detain you no longer, then, monsieur," she said, employing the round and artless eye. "Take good care of my house. Alas! only the memories of it are mine now. Adieu, and accept my thanks for your courtesy."

She was gone, leaving but a smile and a trace of sweet perfume. David climbed the stairs as one in slumber. But he awoke from it, and the smile and the perfume lingered with him and never afterward did either seem quite to leave him. This lady of whom he knew nothing drove him to lyrics of eyes, chansons of swiftly conceived love, odes to curling hair, and sonnets to slippers on slender feet.

Poet he must have been, for Yvonne was forgotten; this fine, new loveliness held him with its freshness and grace. The subtle perfume about her filled him with strange emotions.

On a certain night three persons were gathered about a table in a room on the third floor of the same house. Three chairs and the table and a lighted candle upon it was all the furniture. One of the persons was a huge man, dressed in black. His expression was one of sneering pride. The ends of his upturned moustache reached nearly to his mocking eyes. Another was a lady, young and beautiful, with eyes that could be round and artless, like a child's, or long and cozening, like a gypsy's, but were now keen and ambitious, like any other conspirator's. The third was a man of action, a combatant, a bold and impatient executive, breathing fire and steel. He was addressed by the others as Captain Desrolles.

This man struck the table with his fist, and said, with controlled violence:

"To-night. To-night as he goes to midnight mass. I am tired of the plotting that gets nowhere. I am sick of signals and ciphers and secret meetings and such *baragouin*. Let us be honest traitors. If France is to be rid of him, let us kill in the open, and not hunt with snares and traps. To-night, I say. I back my words. My hand will do the deed. To-night, as he goes to mass."

The lady turned upon him a cordial look. Woman, however wedded to plots, must ever thus bow to rash courage. The big man stroked his upturned moustache.

"Dear captain," he said, in a great voice, softened by habit, "this time I agree with you. Nothing is to be gained by waiting. Enough of the palace guards belong to us to make the endeavor a safe one."

"To-night," repeated Captain Desrolles, again striking the table. "You have heard me, marquis; my hand will do the deed."

"But now," said the huge man, softly, "comes a question. Word must be sent to our partisans in the palace, and a signal agreed upon. Our stanchest men must accompany the royal carriage. At this hour what messenger can penetrate so far as the south doorway? Ribout is stationed there; once a message is placed in his hands, all will go well."

"I will send the message," said the lady.

"You, countess?" said the marquis, raising his eyebrows. "Your devotion is great, we know, but——"

"Listen!" exclaimed the lady, rising and resting her hands upon the table; "in a garret of this house lives a youth from the provinces as guileless and tender as the lambs he tended there. I have met him twice or thrice upon the stairs. I questioned him, fearing that he might dwell too near the room in which we are accustomed to meet. He is mine, if I will. He writes poems in his garret, and I think he dreams of me. He will do what I say. He shall take the message to the palace."

The marquis rose from his chair and bowed. "You did not permit me to finish my sentence, countess," he said. "I would have said: 'Your devotion is great, but your wit and charm are infinitely greater.'"

While the conspirators were thus engaged, David was polishing some lines addressed to his *amorette d'escalier*. He heard a timorous knock at his door, and opened it, with a great throb, to behold her there, panting as one in straits, with eyes wide open and artless, like a child's.

"Monsieur," she breathed, "I come to you in distress. I believe you to be good and true, and I know of no other help. How I flew through the streets among the swaggering men! Monsieur, my mother is dying. My uncle is a captain of guards in the palace of the king. Some one must fly to bring him. May I hope——"

"Mademoiselle," interrupted David, his eyes shining with the desire to do her service, "your hopes shall be my wings. Tell me how I may reach him."

The lady thrust a sealed paper into his hand.

"Go to the south gate—the south gate, mind—and say to the guards there, 'The falcon has left his nest.' They will pass you, and you will go to the south entrance to the palace. Repeat the words, and give this letter to the man who will reply 'Let him strike when he will.' This is the password, monsieur, entrusted to me by my uncle, for now when the country is disturbed and men plot against the king's life, no one without it can gain entrance to the palace grounds after nightfall. If you will, monsieur, take him this letter so that my mother may see him before she closes her eyes."

"Give it me," said David, eagerly. "But shall I let you return home through the streets alone so late? I——"

"No, no—fly. Each moment is like a precious jewel. Some time," said the lady, with eyes long and cozening, like a gypsy's, "I will try to thank you for your goodness."

The poet thrust the letter into his breast, and bounded down the stairway. The lady, when he was gone, returned to the room below.

The eloquent eyebrows of the marquis interrogated her.

"He is gone," she said, "as fleet and stupid as one of his own sheep, to deliver it."

The table shook again from the batter of Captain Desrolles's fist.

"Sacred name!" he cried; "I have left my pistols behind! I can trust no others."

"Take this," said the marquis, drawing from beneath his cloak a shining, great weapon, ornamented with carven silver. "There are none truer. But guard it closely, for it bears my arms and crest, and already I am suspected. Me, I must put many leagues between myself and Paris this night. To-morrow must find me in my château. After you, dear countess."

The marquis puffed out the candle. The lady, well cloaked, and the two gentlemen softly descended the stairway and flowed into the crowd that roamed along the narrow pavements of the Rue Conti.

David sped. At the south gate of the king's residence a halberd was laid to his breast, but he turned its point with the words: "The falcon has left his nest."

"Pass, brother," said the guard, "and go quickly."

On the south steps of the palace they moved to seize him, but again the *mot de passe* charmed the watchers. One among them stepped forward and began: "Let him strike——" But a flurry among the guards told of a surprise. A man of keen look and soldierly stride suddenly pressed through them and seized the letter which David held in his hand. "Come with me," he said, and led him inside the great hall. Then he tore open the letter and read it. He beckoned to a man uniformed as an officer of musketeers, who was passing. "Captain Tetreau, you will have the guards at the south entrance and the south gate arrested and confined. Place men known to be loyal in their places." To David he said: "Come with me."

He conducted him through a corridor and an anteroom into a spacious chamber, where a melancholy man, sombrely dressed, sat brooding in a great leather-covered chair. To that man he said:

"Sire, I have told you that the palace is as full of traitors and spies as a sewer is of rats. You have thought, sire, that it was my fancy. This man penetrated to your very door by their connivance. He bore a letter which I have intercepted. I have brought him here that your majesty may no longer think my zeal excessive."

"I will question him," said the king, stirring in his chair. He looked at David with heavy eyes dulled by an opaque film. The poet bent his knee.

"From where do you come?" asked the king.

"From the village of Vernoy, in the province of Eure-et-Loir, sire."

"What do you follow in Paris?"

"I—I would be a poet, sire."

"What did you in Vernoy?"

"I minded my father's flock of sheep."

The king stirred again, and the film lifted from his eyes.

"Ah! in the fields?"

"Yes, sire."

"You lived in the fields; you went out in the cool of the morning and lay among the hedges in the grass. The flock distributed itself upon the hillside; you drank of the living stream; you ate your sweet brown bread in the shade; and you listened, doubtless, to blackbirds piping in the grove. Is not that so, shepherd?"

"It is, sire," answered David, with a sigh; "and to the bees at the flowers, and, maybe, to the grape gatherers singing on the hill."

"Yes, yes," said the king, impatiently; "maybe to them; but surely to the blackbirds. They whistled often, in the grove, did they not?"

"Nowhere, sire, so sweetly as in Eure-et-Loir. I have endeavored to express their song in some verses that I have written."

"Can you repeat those verses?" asked the king, eagerly. "A long time ago I listened to the blackbirds. It would be something better than a kingdom if one could rightly construe their song. And at night you drove the sheep to the fold and then sat, in peace and tranquillity, to your pleasant bread. Can you repeat those verses, shepherd?"

"They run this way, sire," said David, with respectful ardor:

> "Lazy shepherd, see your lambkins
> Skip, ecstatic, on the mead;

> See the firs dance in the breezes,
> Hear Pan blowing at his reed.

> "Hear us calling from the tree-tops,
>   See us swoop upon your flock;
> Yield us wool to make our nests warm
>   In the branches of the——"

"If it please your majesty," interrupted a harsh voice, "I will ask a question or two of this rhymester. There is little time to spare. I crave pardon, sire, if my anxiety for your safety offends."

"The loyalty," said the king, "of the Duke d'Aumale is too well proven to give offence." He sank into his chair, and the film came again over his eyes.

"First," said the duke, "I will read you the letter he brought:

"To-night is the anniversary of the dauphin's death. If he goes, as is his custom, to midnight mass to pray for the soul of his son, the falcon will strike, at the corner of the Rue Esplanade. If this be his intention, set a red light in the upper room at the southwest corner of the palace, that the falcon may take heed.

"Peasant," said the duke, sternly, "you have heard these words. Who gave you this message to bring?"

"My lord duke," said David, sincerely, "I will tell you. A lady gave it me. She said her mother was ill, and that this writing would fetch her uncle to her bedside. I do not know the meaning of the letter, but I will swear that she is beautiful and good."

"Describe the woman," commanded the duke, "and how you came to be her dupe."

"Describe her!" said David with a tender smile. "You would command words to perform miracles. Well, she is made of sunshine and deep shade. She is slender, like the alders, and moves with their grace. Her eyes change while you gaze into them; now round, and then half shut as the sun peeps between two clouds. When she comes, heaven is all about her; when she leaves, there is chaos and a scent of hawthorn blossoms. She came to me in the Rue Conti, number twenty-nine."

"It is the house," said the duke, turning to the king, "that we have been watching. Thanks to the poet's tongue, we have a picture of the infamous Countess Quebedaux."

"Sire and my lord duke," said David, earnestly, "I hope my poor words have done no injustice. I have looked into that lady's eyes. I will stake my life that she is an angel, letter or no letter."

The duke looked at him steadily. "I will put you to the proof," he said, slowly. "Dressed as the king, you shall, yourself, attend mass in his carriage at midnight. Do you accept the test?"

David smiled. "I have looked into her eyes," he said. "I had my proof there. Take yours how you will."

Half an hour before twelve the Duke d'Aumale, with his own hands, set a red lamp in a southwest window of the palace. At ten minutes to the hour, David, leaning on his arm, dressed as the king, from top to toe, with his head bowed in his cloak, walked slowly from the royal apartments to the waiting carriage. The duke assisted him inside and closed the door. The carriage whirled away along its route to the cathedral.

On the *qui vive* in a house at the corner of the Rue Esplanade was Captain

Tetreau with twenty men, ready to pounce upon the conspirators when they should appear.

But it seemed that, for some reason, the plotters had slightly altered their plans. When the royal carriage had reached the Rue Christopher, one square nearer than the Rue Esplanade, forth from it burst Captain Desrolles, with his band of would-be regicides, and assailed the equipage. The guards upon the carriage, though surprised at the premature attack, descended and fought valiantly. The noise of conflict attracted the force of Captain Tetreau, and they came pelting down the street to the rescue. But, in the meantime, the desperate Desrolles had torn open the door of the king's carriage, thrust his weapon against the body of the dark figure inside, and fired.

Now, with loyal reinforcements at hand, the street rang with cries and the rasp of steel, but the frightened horses had dashed away. Upon the cushions lay the dead body of the poor mock king and poet, slain by a ball from the pistol of Monseigneur, the Marquis de Beaupertuys.

THE MAIN ROAD

Three leagues, then, the road ran, and turned into a puzzle. It joined with another and a larger road at right angles. David stood, uncertain, for a while, and then sat himself to rest upon its side.

Whither those roads led he knew not. Either way there seemed to lie a great world full of chance and peril. And then, sitting there, his eye fell upon a bright star, one that he and Yvonne had named for theirs. That set him thinking of Yvonne, and he wondered if he had not been too hasty. Why should he leave her and his home because a few hot words had come between them? Was love so brittle a thing that jealousy, the very proof of it, could break it? Mornings always brought a cure for the little heartaches of evening. There was yet time for him to return home without any one in the sweetly sleeping village of Vernoy being the wiser. His heart was Yvonne's; there where he had lived always he could write his poems and find his happiness.

David rose, and shook off his unrest and the wild mood that had tempted him. He set his face steadfastly back along the road he had come. By the time he had retravelled the road to Vernoy, his desire to rove was gone. He passed the sheepfold, and the sheep scurried, with a drumming flutter, at his late footsteps, warming his heart by the homely sound. He crept without noise into his little room and lay there, thankful that his feet had escaped the distress of new roads that night.

How well he knew woman's heart! The next evening Yvonne was at the well in the road where the young congregated in order that the *curé* might have business. The corner of her eye was engaged in a search for David, albeit her set mouth seemed unrelenting. He saw the look; braved the mouth, drew from it a recantation and, later, a kiss as they walked homeward together.

Three months afterward they were married. David's father was shrewd and prosperous. He gave them a wedding that was heard of three leagues away. Both the young people were favorites in the village. There was a procession in the streets, a dance on the green; they had the marionettes and a tumbler out from Dreux to delight the guests.

Then a year, and David's father died. The sheep and the cottage descended to him. He already had the seemliest wife in the village. Yvonne's milk pails and her brass kettles were bright—*ouf!* they blinded you in the sun when you passed that way. But you must keep your eyes upon her yard, for her flower beds were so neat and gay they restored to you your sight. And you might hear her sing, aye, as far as the double chestnut tree above Père Gruneau's blacksmith forge.

But a day came when David drew out paper from a long-shut drawer, and began to bite the end of a pencil. Spring had come again and touched his heart. Poet he must have been, for now Yvonne was well-nigh forgotten. This fine new loveliness of earth held him with its witchery and grace. The perfume from her woods and meadows stirred him strangely. Daily had he gone forth with his flock, and brought it safe at night. But now he stretched himself under the hedge and pieced words together on his bits of paper. The sheep strayed, and the wolves, perceiving that difficult poems make easy mutton, ventured from the woods and stole his lambs.

David's stock of poems grew larger and his flock smaller. Yvonne's nose and temper waxed sharp and her talk blunt. Her pans and kettles grew dull, but her eyes had caught their flash. She pointed out to the poet that his neglect was reducing the flock and bringing woe upon the household. David hired a boy to guard the sheep, locked himself in the little room in the top of the cottage, and wrote more poems. The boy, being a poet by nature, but not furnished with an outlet in the way of writing, spent his time in slumber. The wolves lost no time in discovering that poetry and sleep are practically the same; so the flock steadily grew smaller. Yvonne's ill temper increased at an equal rate. Sometimes she would stand in the yard and rail at David through his high window. Then you could hear her as far as the double chestnut tree above Père Gruneau's blacksmith forge.

M. Papineau, the kind, wise, meddling old notary, saw this, as he saw everything at which his nose pointed. He went to David, fortified himself with a great pinch of snuff, and said:

"Friend Mignot, I affixed the seal upon the marriage certificate of your father. It would distress me to be obliged to attest a paper signifying the bankruptcy of his son. But that is what you are coming to. I speak as an old friend. Now, listen to what I have to say. You have your heart set, I perceive, upon poetry. At Dreux, I have a friend, one Monsieur Bril—Georges Bril. He lives in a little cleared space in a houseful of books. He is a learned man; he visits Paris each year; he himself has written books. He will tell you when the catacombs were made, how they found out the names of the stars, and why the plover has a long bill. The meaning and the form of poetry is to him as intelligent as the baa of a sheep is to you. I will give you a letter to him, and you shall take him your poems and let him read them. Then you will know if you shall write more, or give your attention to your wife and business."

"Write the letter," said David. "I am sorry you did not speak of this sooner."

At sunrise the next morning he was on the road to Dreux with the precious roll of poems under his arm. At noon he wiped the dust from his feet at the door of Monsieur Bril. That learned man broke the seal of M. Papineau's letter, and sucked up its contents through his gleaming spectacles as the sun draws water. He took David inside to his study and sat him down upon a little island beat upon by a sea of books.

Monsieur Bril had a conscience. He flinched not even at a mass of manuscript the thickness of a finger length and rolled to an incorrigible curve. He broke the back of the roll against his knee and began to read. He slighted nothing; he bored into the lump as a worm into a nut, seeking for a kernel.

Meanwhile, David sat, marooned, trembling in the spray of so much literature. It roared in his ears. He held no chart or compass for voyaging in that sea. Half the world, he thought, must be writing books.

Monsieur Bril bored to the last page of the poems. Then he took off his spectacles and wiped them with his handkerchief.

"My old friend, Papineau, is well?" he asked.

"In the best of health," said David.

"How many sheep have you, Monsieur Mignot?"

"Three hundred and nine, when I counted them yesterday. The flock has had ill fortune. To that number it has decreased from eight hundred and fifty."

"You have a wife and a home, and lived in comfort. The sheep brought you plenty. You went into the fields with them and lived in the keen air and ate the sweet bread of contentment. You had but to be vigilant and recline there upon nature's breast, listening to the whistle of the blackbirds in the grove. Am I right thus far?"

"It was so," said David.

"I have read all your verses," continued Monsieur Bril, his eyes wandering about his sea of books as if he conned the horizon for a sale. "Look yonder, through that window, Monsieur Mignot; tell me what you see in that tree."

"I see a crow," said David, looking.

"There is a bird," said Monsieur Bril, "that shall assist me where I am disposed to shirk a duty. You know that bird, Monsieur Mignot; he is the philosopher of the air. He is happy through submission to his lot. None so merry or full-crawed as he with his whimsical eye and rollicking step. The fields yield him what he desires. He never grieves that his plumage is not gay, like the oriole's. And you have heard, Monsieur Mignot, the notes that nature has given him? Is the nightingale any happier, do you think?"

David rose to his feet. The crow cawed harshly from his tree.

"I thank you, Monsieur Bril," he said, slowly. "There was not, then, one nightingale note among all those croaks?"

"I could not have missed it," said Monsieur Bril, with a sigh. "I read every word. Live your poetry, man; do not try to write it any more."

"I thank you," said David, again. "And now I will be going back to my sheep."

"If you would dine with me," said the man of books, "and overlook the smart of it, I will give you reasons at length."

"No," said the poet, "I must be back in the fields cawing at my sheep."

Back along the road to Vernoy he trudged with his poems under his arm. When he reached his village he turned into the shop of one Zeigler, a Jew out of Armenia, who sold anything that came to his hand.

"Friend," said David, "wolves from the forest harass my sheep on the hills. I must purchase firearms to protect them. What have you?"

"A bad day, this, for me, friend Mignot," said Zeigler, spreading his hands, "for I perceive that I must sell you a weapon that will not fetch a tenth of its value. Only last week I bought from a peddler a wagon full of goods that he procured at a sale by a *commissionaire* of the crown. The sale was of the château and belongings of a great lord—I know not his title—who has been banished for conspiracy against the king. There are some choice firearms in the lot. This pistol—oh, a weapon fit for a prince!—it shall be only forty francs to you, friend Mignot—if I lost ten by the sale. But perhaps an arquebuse——"

"This will do," said David, throwing the money on the counter. "Is it charged?"

"I will charge it," said Zeigler. "And, for ten francs more, add a store of powder and ball."

David laid his pistol under his coat and walked to his cottage. Yvonne was not there. Of late she had taken to gadding much among the neighbors. But a fire was glowing in the kitchen stove. David opened the door of it and thrust his poems in upon the coals. As they blazed up they made a singing, harsh sound in the flue.

"The song of the crow!" said the poet.

He went up to his attic room and closed the door. So quiet was the village that a score of people heard the roar of the great pistol. They flocked thither, and up the stairs where the smoke, issuing, drew their notice.

The man laid the body of the poet upon his bed, awkwardly arranging it to conceal the torn plumage of the poor black crow. The women chattered in a luxury of zealous pity. Some of them ran to tell Yvonne.

M. Papineau, whose nose had brought him there among the first, picked up the weapon and ran his eye over its silver mountings with a mingled air of connoisseurship and grief.

"The arms," he explained, aside, to the *curé*, "and crest of Monseigneur, the Marquis de Beaupertuys."

THE GUARDIAN OF THE ACCOLADE

NOT the least important of the force of the Weymouth Bank was Uncle Bushrod. Sixty years had Uncle Bushrod given of faithful service to the house of Weymouth as chattel, servitor, and friend. Of the color of the mahogany bank furniture was Uncle Bushrod—thus dark was he externally; white as the uninked pages of the bank ledgers was his soul. Eminently pleasing to Uncle Bushrod would the comparison have been; for to him the only institution in existence worth considering was the Weymouth Bank, of which he was something between porter and generalissimo-in-charge.

Weymouth lay, dreamy and umbrageous, among the low foothills along the brow of a Southern valley. Three banks there were in Weymouthville. Two were hopeless, misguided enterprises, lacking the presence and prestige of a Weymouth to give them glory. The third was The Bank, managed by the Weymouths—and Uncle Bushrod. In the old Weymouth homestead—the red brick, white-porticoed mansion, the first to your right as you crossed Elder Creek, coming into town—lived Mr. Robert Weymouth (the president of the bank), his widowed daughter, Mrs. Vesey—called "Miss Letty" by every one—and her two children, Nan and Guy. There, also in a cottage on the grounds, resided Uncle Bushrod and Aunt Malindy, his wife. Mr. William Weymouth (the cashier of the bank) lived in a modern, fine house on the principal avenue.

Mr. Robert was a large, stout man, sixty-two years of age, with a smooth, plump face, long iron-gray hair and fiery blue eyes. He was high-tempered, kind, and generous, with a youthful smile and a formidable, stern voice that did not always mean what it sounded like. Mr. William was a milder man, correct in deportment and absorbed in business. The Weymouths formed The Family of Weymouthville, and were looked up to, as was their right of heritage.

Uncle Bushrod was the bank's trusted porter, messenger, vassal, and guardian. He carried a key to the vault, just as Mr. Robert and Mr. William did. Sometimes there was ten, fifteen, or twenty thousand dollars in sacked silver stacked on the vault floor. It was safe with Uncle Bushrod. He was a Weymouth in heart, honesty, and pride.

Of late Uncle Bushrod had not been without worry. It was on account of Marse Robert. For nearly a year Mr. Robert had been known to indulge in too much drink. Not enough, understand, to become tipsy, but the habit was getting a hold upon him, and every one was beginning to notice it. Half a dozen times a day he would leave the bank and step around to the Merchants' and Planters' Hotel to take a drink. Mr. Robert's usual keen judgment and business capacity became a little impaired. Mr. William, a Weymouth, but not so rich in experience, tried to dam the inevitable backflow of the tide, but with incomplete success. The deposits in the Weymouth Bank dropped from six figures to five. Past-due paper began to accumulate, owing to injudicious loans. No one cared to address Mr. Robert on the subject of temperance. Many of his friends said that the cause of it had been the death of his wife some two years before. Others hesitated on account of Mr. Robert's quick temper, which was extremely apt to resent personal interference of such a nature. Miss Letty and the children noticed the change and grieved about it. Uncle Bushrod also worried, but he was one of those who would not have dared to remonstrate, although he and Marse Robert had been raised almost as companions. But there was a heavier shock coming to Uncle Bushrod than that caused by the bank president's toddies and juleps.

Mr. Robert had a passion for fishing, which he usually indulged whenever the season and business permitted. One day, when reports had been coming in relating to the bass and perch, he announced his intention of making a two- or three-days' visit to the lakes. He was going down, he said, to Reedy Lake with Judge Archinard, an old friend.

Now, Uncle Bushrod was treasurer of the Sons and Daughters of the Burning Bush. Every association he belonged to made him treasurer without hesitation. He stood AA1 in colored circles. He was understood among them to be Mr. Bushrod Weymouth, of the Weymouth Bank.

The night following the day on which Mr. Robert mentioned his intended fishing-trip the old man woke up and rose from his bed at twelve o'clock, declaring he must go down to the bank and fetch the pass-book of the Sons and Daughters, which he had forgotten to bring home. The bookkeeper had balanced it for him that day, put the cancelled checks in it, and snapped two elastic bands around it. He put but one band around other pass-books.

Aunt Malindy objected to the mission at so late an hour, denouncing it as foolish and unnecessary, but Uncle Bushrod was not to be deflected from duty. "I done told Sister Adaline Hoskins," he said, "to come by here for dat book to-morrow mawnin' at sebin o'clock, for to kyar' it to de meetin' of de bo'd of 'rangements, and dat book gwine to be here when she come."

So, Uncle Bushrod put on his old brown suit, got his thick hickory stick, and meandered through the almost deserted streets of Weymouthville. He entered the bank, unlocking the side door, and found the pass-book where he had left it in the little back room used for private consultations, where he always hung his coat. Looking about casually, he saw that everything was as he had left it, and was about to start for home when he was brought to a standstill by the sudden rattle of a key in the front door. Some one came quickly in, closed the door softly, and entered the counting-room through the door in the iron railing.

That division of the bank's space was connected with the back room by a narrow passage-way, now in deep darkness. Uncle Bushrod, firmly gripping his hickory stick, tiptoed gently up this passage until he could see the midnight intruder into the sacred precincts of the Weymouth Bank. One dim gas-jet burned there, but even in its nebulous light he perceived at once that the prowler was the bank's president.

Wondering, fearful, undecided what to do, the old colored man stood motionless in the gloomy strip of hallway, and waited developments.

The vault, with its big iron door, was opposite him. Inside that was the safe, holding the papers of value, the gold and currency of the bank. On the floor of the vault was, perhaps, eighteen thousand dollars in silver.

The president took his key from his pocket, opened the vault and went inside, nearly closing the door behind him. Uncle Bushrod saw, through the narrow aperture, the flicker of a candle. In a minute or two—it seemed an hour to the watcher—Mr. Robert came out, bringing with him a large hand-satchel, handling it in a careful but hurried manner, as if fearful that he might be observed. With one hand he closed and locked the vault door.

With a reluctant theory forming itself beneath his wool, Uncle Bushrod waited and watched, shaking in his concealing shadow.

Mr. Robert set the satchel softly upon a desk, and turned his coat collar up about his neck and ears. He was dressed in a rough suit of gray, as if for travelling. He glanced with frowning intentness at the big office clock above the burning gas-jet, and then looked lingeringly about the bank—lingeringly and fondly, Uncle Bushrod thought, as one who bids farewell to dear and familiar scenes.

Now he caught up his burden again and moved promptly and softly out of the bank by the way he had come locking the front door behind him.

For a minute or longer Uncle Bushrod was as stone in his tracks. Had that midnight rifler of safes and vaults been any other on earth than the man he was, the old retainer would have rushed upon him and struck to save the Weymouth property. But now the watcher's soul was tortured by the poignant dread of something worse than mere robbery. He was seized by an accusing terror that said the Weymouth name and the Weymouth honor was about to be lost. Marse Robert robbing the bank! What else could it mean? The hour of the night, the stealthy visit to the vault, the satchel brought forth full and with expedition and silence, the prowler's rough dress, his solicitous reading of the clock, and noiseless departure—what else could it mean?

And then to the turmoil of Uncle Bushrod's thoughts came the corroborating recollection of preceding events—Mr. Robert's increasing intemperance and consequent many moods of royal high spirits and stern tempers; the casual talk he had heard in the bank of the decrease in business and difficulty in collecting loans. What else could it all mean but that Mr. Robert Weymouth was an absconder—was about to fly with the bank's remaining funds, leaving Mr. William, Miss Letty, little Nan, Guy, and Uncle Bushrod to bear the disgrace?

During one minute Uncle Bushrod considered these things, and then he awoke to sudden determination and action.

"Lawd! Lawd!" he moaned aloud, as he hobbled hastily toward the side door. "Sech a come-off after all dese here years of big doin's and fine doin's. Scan'lous sights upon de yearth when de Weymouth fambly done turn out robbers and 'bezzlers! Time for Uncle Bushrod to clean out somebody's chicken-coop and eben matters up. Oh, Lawd! Marse Robert, you ain't gwine do dat. 'N Miss Letty an' dem chillum so proud and talkin' 'Weymouth, Weymouth,' all de time! I'm gwine to stop you ef I can. 'Spec you shoot Mr. Nigger's head off ef he fool wid you, but I'm gwine stop you ef I can."

Uncle Bushrod, aided by his hickory stick, impeded by his rheumatism, hurried down the street toward the railroad station, where the two lines touching Weymouthville met. As he had expected and feared, he saw there Mr. Robert, standing in the shadow of the building, waiting for the train. He held the satchel in his hand.

When Uncle Bushrod came within twenty yards of the bank president, standing like a huge, gray ghost by the station wall, sudden perturbation seized him. The rashness and audacity of the thing he had come to do struck him fully. He would have been happy could he have turned and fled from the possibilities of the famous Weymouth wrath. But again he saw, in his fancy, the white, reproachful face of Miss Letty, and the distressed looks of Nan and Guy, should he fail in his duty and they questioned him as to his stewardship.

Braced by the thought, he approached in a straight line, clearing his throat and pounding with his stick so that he might be early recognized. Thus he might avoid the likely danger of too suddenly surprising the sometimes hasty Mr. Robert.

"Is that you, Bushrod?" called the clamant, clear voice of the gray ghost.

"Yes, suh, Marse Robert."

"What the devil are you doing out at this time of night?"

For the first time in his life, Uncle Bushrod told Marse Robert a falsehood. He could not repress it. He would have to circumlocute a little. His nerve was not equal to a direct attack.

"I done been down, suh, to see ol' Aunt M'ria Patterson. She taken sick in de night, and I kyar'ed her a bottle of M'lindy's medercine. Yes, suh."

"Humph!" said Robert. "You better get home out of the night air. It's damp. You'll hardly be worth killing to-morrow on account of your rheumatism. Think it'll be a clear day, Bushrod?"

"I 'low it will, suh. De sun sot red las' night."

Mr. Robert lit a cigar in the shadow, and the smoke looked like his gray ghost expanding and escaping into the night air. Somehow, Uncle Bushrod could barely force his reluctant tongue to the dreadful subject. He stood, awkward, shambling, with his feet upon the gravel and fumbling with his stick. But then, afar off—three miles away, at the Jimtown switch—he heard the faint whistle of the coming train, the one that was to transport the Weymouth name into the regions of dishonor and shame. All fear left him. He took off his hat and faced the chief of the clan he served, the great, royal, kind, lofty, terrible Weymouth,—he bearded him there at the brink of the awful thing that was about to happen.

"Marse Robert," he began, his voice quavering a little with the stress of his feelings, "you 'member de day dey-all rode de tunnament at Oak Lawn? De day, suh, dat you win in de ridin', and you crown Miss Lucy de queen?"

"Tournament?" said Mr. Robert, taking his cigar from his mouth, "Yes, I remember very well the—but what the deuce are you talking about tournaments here at midnight for? Go 'long home, Bushrod. I believe you're sleep-walking."

"Miss Lucy tetch you on de shoulder," continued the old man, never heeding, "wid a s'ord, and say: 'I mek you a knight, Suh Robert—rise up, pure and fearless and widout reproach.' Dat what Miss Lucy say. Dat's been a long time ago, but me nor you ain't forgot it. And den dar's another time we ain't forgot—de time when Miss Lucy lay on her las' bed. She sent for Uncle Bushrod, and she say: 'Uncle Bushrod, when I die, I want you to take good care of Mr. Robert. Seem like'—so Miss Lucy say—'he listen to you mo' dan to anybody else. He apt to be mighty fractious sometimes, and maybe he cuss you when you try to 'suade him but he need somebody what understand him to be 'round wid him. He am like a little child sometimes'—so Miss Lucy say, wid her eyes shinin' in her po', thin face—'but he always been'—dem was her words—'my knight, pure and fearless and widout reproach.'"

Mr. Robert began to mask, as was his habit, a tendency to soft-heartedness with a spurious anger.

"You—you old windbag!" he growled through a cloud of swirling cigar smoke. "I believe you are crazy. I told you to go home, Bushrod. Miss Lucy said that, did she? Well, we haven't kept the scutcheon very clear. Two years ago last week, wasn't it, Bushrod, when she died? Confound it! Are you going to stand there all night gabbing like a coffee-colored gander?"

The train whistled again. Now it was at the water tank, a mile away.

"Marse Robert," said Uncle Bushrod, laying his hand on the satchel that the banker held. "For Gawd's sake, don' take dis wid you. I knows what's in it. I knows where you got it in de bank. Don' kyar' it wid you. Dey's big trouble in dat valise for Miss Lucy and Miss Lucy's child's chillun. Hit's bound to destroy de name of Weymouth and bow down dem dat own it wid shame and triberlation. Marse Robert, you can kill dis ole nigger ef you will, but don't take away dis 'er' valise. If I ever crosses over de Jordan, what I gwine to say to Miss Lucy when she ax me: 'Uncle Bushrod, wharfo' didn' you take good care of Mr. Robert?' "

Mr. Robert Weymouth threw away his cigar and shook free one arm with that peculiar gesture that always preceded his outbursts of irascibility. Uncle Bushrod bowed his head to the expected storm, but he did not flinch. If the house of Weymouth was to fall, he would fall with it. The banker spoke, and Uncle Bushrod blinked with surprise. The storm was there, but it was suppressed to the quietness of a summer breeze.

"Bushrod," said Mr. Robert, in a lower voice than he usually employed, "you have overstepped all bounds. You have presumed upon the leniency with which you have been treated to meddle unpardonably. So you know what is in this satchel! Your long and faithful service is some excuse, but—go home, Bushrod —not another word!"

But Bushrod grasped the satchel with a firmer hand. The headlight of the train was now lightening the shadows about the station. The roar was increasing, and folks were stirring about at the track side.

"Marse Robert, gimme dis 'er' valise. I got a right, suh, to talk to you dis 'er' way. I slaved for you and 'tended to you from a child up. I went th'ough de war as yo' body-servant tell we whipped de Yankees and sent 'em back to de No'th. I was at yo' weddin', and I was n' fur away when yo' Miss Letty was bawn. And Miss Letty's chillun, dey watches to-day for Uncle Bushrod when he come home ever' evenin'. I been a' Weymouth, all 'cept in color and entitlements. Both of us is old, Marse Robert. 'Tain't goin' to be long tell we gwine to see Miss Lucy and has to give an account of our doin's. De ole nigger man won't be 'spected to say much mo' dan he done all he could by de fambly dat owned him. But de Weymouths, dey must say dey been livin' pure and fearless and widout reproach. Gimme dis valise, Marse Robert—I'm gwine to hab it. I'm gwine to take it back to de bank and lock it up in de vault. I'm gwine to do Miss Lucy's biddin'. Turn 'er loose, Marse Robert."

The train was standing at the station. Some men were pushing trucks along the side. Two or three sleepy passengers got off and wandered away into the night. The conductor stepped to the gravel, swung his lantern and called: "Hello, Frank!" at some one invisible. The bell clanged, the brakes hissed, the conductor drawled: "All aboard!"

Mr. Robert released his hold on the satchel. Uncle Bushrod hugged it to his breast with both arms, as a lover clasps his first beloved.

"Take it back with you, Bushrod," said Mr. Robert, thrusting his hands into his pockets. "And let the subject drop—now mind! You've said quite enough. I'm going to take this train. Tell Mr. William I will be back on Saturday. Good-night."

The banker climbed the steps of the moving train and disappeared in a coach. Uncle Bushrod stood motionless, still embracing the precious satchel. His eyes were closed and his lips were moving in thanks to the Master above for the salvation of the Weymouth honor. He knew Mr. Robert would return when he said he would. The Weymouths never lied. Nor now, thank the Lord! could it be said that they embezzled the money in banks.

Then awake to the necessity for further guardianship of Weymouth trust funds, the old man started for the bank with the redeemed satchel.

Three hours from Weymouthville, in the gray dawn, Mr. Robert alighted from the train at a lonely flag-station. Dimly he could see the figure of a man waiting on the platform and the shape of a spring-waggon, team and driver. Half a dozen lengthy bamboo fishing-poles projected from the wagon's rear.

"You're here, Bob," said Judge Archinard, Mr. Robert's old friend and school-mate. "It's going to be a royal day for fishing. I thought you said—why, didn't you bring along the stuff?"

The president of the Weymouth Bank took off his hat and rumpled his gray locks.

"Well, Ben, to tell you the truth, there's an infernally presumptuous old nigger belonging in my family that broke up the arrangement. He came down to the depot and vetoed the whole proceeding. He means all right, and—well, I reckon he is right. Somehow, he had found out what I had along—though I hid it in the bank vault and sneaked it out at midnight. I reckon he has noticed that I've been indulging a little more than a gentleman should, and he laid for me with some reaching arguments.

"I'm going to quit drinking," Mr. Robert concluded. "I've come to the con-clusion that a man can't keep it up and be quite what he'd like to be—'pure and fearless and without reproach'—that's the way old Bushrod quoted it."

"Well, I'll have to admit," said the judge, thoughtfully, as they climbed into the wagon, "that the old darkey's argument can't conscientiously be overruled."

"Still," said Mr. Robert, with a ghost of a sigh, "there was two quarts of the finest old silk-velvet Bourbon in that satchel you ever wet your lips with."

THE DISCOUNTERS OF MONEY

THE spectacle of the money-caliphs of the present day going about Bagdad-on-the-Subway trying to relieve the wants of the people is enough to make the great Al Raschid turn Haroun in his grave. If not so, then the assertion should do so, the real caliph having been a wit and a scholar and therefore a hater of puns.

How properly to alleviate the troubles of the poor is one of the greatest troubles of the rich. But one thing agreed upon by all professional philan-thropists is that you must never hand over any cash to your subject. The poor are notoriously temperamental; and when they get money they exhibit a strong tendency to spend it for stuffed olives and enlarged crayon portraits instead of giving it to the instalment man.

And still, old Haroun had some advantages as an eleemosynarian. He took around with him on his rambles his vizier, Giafar (a vizier is a composite of a chauffeur, a secretary of state, and a night-and-day bank), and old Uncle Mesrour, his executioner, who toted a snicker-snee. With this entourage a caliphing tour could hardly fail to be successful. Have you noticed lately any newspaper articles headed, "What Shall We Do With Our Ex-Presidents?" Well, now, suppose that Mr. Carnegie should engage *him* and Joe Gans to go about assisting in the distribution of free libraries? Do you suppose any town would have the hardihood to refuse one? That caliphalous combination would cause two libraries to grow where there had been only one set of E. P. Roe's works before.

But, as I said, the money-caliphs are handicapped. They have the idea that earth has no sorrow that dough cannot heal; and they rely upon it solely. Al Raschid administered justice, rewarded the deserving, and punished whom-soever he disliked on the spot. He was the originator of the short-story con-

test. Whenever he succored any chance pick-up in the bazaars he always made
the succoree tell the sad story of his life. If the narrative lacked construction, style, and *esprit* he commanded his vizier to dole him out a couple of
thousand ten-dollar notes of the First National Bank of the Bosphorus, or
else gave him a soft job as Keeper of the Bird Seed for the Bulbuls in the
Imperial Gardens. If the story was a cracker-jack, he had Mesrour, the executioner, whack off his head. The report that Haroun Al Raschid is yet alive
and is editing the magazine that your grandmother used to subscribe for lacks
confirmation.

And now follows the Story of the Millionaire, the Inefficacious Increment, and
the Babes Drawn from the Wood.

Young Howard Pilkins, the millionaire, got his money ornithologically. He
was a shrewd judge of storks, and got in on the ground floor at the residence
of his immediate ancestors, the Pilkins Brewing Company. For his mother
was a partner in the business. Finally old man Pilkins died from a torpid
liver, and then Mrs. Pilkins died from worry on account of torpid delivery-
wagons—and there you have young Howard Pilkins with 4,000,000, and a good
fellow at that. He was an agreeable, modestly arrogant young man, who implicitly believed that money could buy anything that the world had to offer.
And Bagdad-on-the-Subway for a long time did everything possible to encourage his belief.

But the Rat-trap caught him at last; he heard the spring snap, and found
his heart in a wire cage regarding a piece of cheese whose other name was Alice
von der Ruysling.

The Von der Ruyslings still live in that little square about which so much
has been said, and in which so little has been done. To-day you hear of Mr.
Tilden's underground passage, and you hear Mr. Gould's elevated passage, and
that about ends the noise in the world made by Gramercy Square. But once it
was different. The Von der Ruyslings live there yet, and they received *the first
key ever made to Gramercy Park*.

You shall have no description of Alice v. d. R. Just call up in your mind
the picture of your own Maggie or Vera or Beatrice, straighten her nose, soften
her voice, tone her down and then tone her up, make her beautiful and unattainable—and you have a faint dry-point etching of Alice. The family owned
a crumbly brick house and a coachman named Joseph in a coat of many colors,
and a horse so old that he claimed to belong to the order of the Perissodactyla,
and had toes instead of hoofs. In the year 1898 the family had to buy a new
set of harness for the Perissodactyl. Before using it they made Joseph smear
it over with a mixture of ashes and soot. It was the Von der Ruysling family
that bought the territory between the Bowery and East River and Rivington
Street and the Statue of Liberty, in the year 1649, from an Indian chief for a
quart of passementerie and a pair of Turkey-red portières designed for a Harlem
flat. I have always admired that Indian's perspicacity and good taste. All
this is merely to convince you that the Von der Ruyslings were exactly the kind
of poor aristocrats that turn down their noses at people who have money. Oh,
well, I don't mean that; I mean people who have *just* money.

One evening Pilkins went down to the red brick house in Gramercy Square,
and made what he thought was a proposal to Alice v. d. R. Alice, with her
nose turned down, and thinking of his money, considered it a proposition, and
refused it and him. Pilkins, summoning all his resources as any good general
would have done, made an indiscreet reference to the advantages that his money
would provide. That settled it. The lady turned so cold that Walter Well-
man himself would have waited until spring to make a dash for her in a dog-
sled.

But Pilkins was something of a sport himself. You can't fool all the millionaires every time the ball drops on the Western Union Building.

"If, at any time," he said to A. v. d. R., "you feel that you would like to reconsider your answer, send me a rose like that."

Pilkins audaciously touched a Jacque rose that she wore loosely in her hair.

"Very well," said she. "And when I do, you will understand by it that either you or I have learned something new about the purchasing power of money. You've been spoiled, my friend. No, I don't think I could marry you. To-morrow I will send you back the presents you have given me."

"Presents!" said Pilkins in surprise. "I never gave you a present in my life. I would like to see a full-length portrait of the man that you would take a present from. Why, you never would let me send you flowers or candy or even art calendars."

"You've forgotten," said Alice v. d. R., with a little smile. "It was a long time ago when our families were neighbors. You were seven, and I was trundling my doll on the sidewalk. You gave me a little gray, hairy kitten, with shoe-buttony eyes. Its head came off and it was full of candy. You paid five cents for it—you told me so. I haven't the candy to return to you—I hadn't developed a conscience at three, so I ate it. But I have the kitten yet, and I will wrap it up neatly to-night and send it to you to-morrow."

Beneath the lightness of Alice v. d. R.'s talk the steadfastness of her rejection showed firm and plain. So there was nothing left for him but to leave the crumbly red brick house, and be off with his abhorred millions.

On his way back, Pilkins walked through Madison Square. The hour hand of the clock hung about eight; the air was stingingly cool, but not at the freezing point. The dim little square seemed like a great, cold, unroofed room, with its four walls of houses, spangled with thousands of insufficient lights. Only a few loiterers were huddled here and there on the benches.

But suddenly Pilkins came upon a youth brave and, as if conflicting with summer sultriness, coatless, his white shirt-sleeves conspicuous in the light from the globe of an electric. Close at his side was a girl, smiling, dreamy, happy. Around her shoulders was, palpably, the missing coat of the cold-defying youth. It appeared to be a modern panorama of the Babes in the Wood, revised and brought up to date, with the exception that the robins hadn't turned up yet with the protecting leaves.

With delight the money-caliphs view a situation that they think is relievable while you wait.

Pilkins sat on the bench, one seat removed from the youth. He glanced cautiously and saw (as men do see; and women—oh! never can) that they were of the same order.

Pilkins leaned over after a short time and spoke to the youth, who answered smilingly, and courteously. From general topics the conversation concentrated to the bed-rock of grim personalities. But Pilkins did it as delicately and heartily as any caliph could have done. And when it came to the point, the youth turned to him, soft-voiced and with his undiminished smile.

"I don't want to seem unappreciative, old man," he said, with a youth's somewhat too-early spontaneity of address, "but, you see, I can't accept anything from a stranger. I know you're all right, and I'm tremendously obliged, but I couldn't think of borrowing from anybody. You see, I'm Marcus Clayton—the Claytons of Roanoke County, Virginia, you know. The young lady is Miss Eva Bedford—I reckon you've heard of the Bedfords. She's seventeen and one of the Bedfords of Bedford County. We've eloped from home to get married, and we wanted to see New York. We got in this afternoon. Somebody got my pocketbook on the ferry-boat, and I had only three cents in change outside of it. I'll get some work somewhere to-morrow, and we'll get married."

"But, I say, old man," said Pilkins, in confidential low tones, "you can't keep the lady out here in the cold all night. Now, as for hotels——"

"I told you," said the youth, with a broader smile, "that I didn't have but three cents. Besides, if I had a thousand, we'd have to wait here until morning. You can understand that, of course. I'm much obliged, but I can't take any of your money. Miss Bedford and I have lived an outdoor life, and we don't mind a little cold. I'll get work of some kind to-morrow. We've got a paper bag of cakes and chocolates, and we'll get along all right."

"Listen," said the millionaire, impressively. "My name is Pilkins, and I'm worth several million dollars. I happen to have in my pockets about $800 or $900 in cash. Don't you think you are drawing it rather fine when you decline to accept as much of it as will make you and the young lady comfortable at least for the night?"

"I can't say, sir, that I do think so," said Clayton of Roanoke County. "I've been raised to look at such things differently. But I'm mightily obliged to you, just the same."

"Then you force me to say good-night," said the millionaire.

Twice that day had his money been scorned by simple ones to whom his dollars had appeared as but tin tobacco-tags. He was no worshipper of the actual minted coin or stamped paper, but he had always believed in its almost unlimited power to purchase.

Pilkins walked away rapidly, and then turned abruptly and returned to the bench where the young couple sat. He took off his hat and began to speak. The girl looked at him with the same sprightly, glowing interest that she had been giving to the lights and statuary and sky-reaching buildings that made the old square seem so far away from Bedford County.

"Mr——er——Roanoke," said Pilkins, "I admire your——your indepen——your idiocy so much that I'm going to appeal to your chivalry. I believe that's what you Southerners call it when you keep a lady sitting outdoors on a bench on a cold night just to keep your old, out-of-date pride going. Now, I've a friend—— a lady——whom I have known all my life——who lives a few blocks from here—— with her parents and sisters and aunts, and all that kind of endorsement, of course. I am sure this lady would be happy and pleased to put up——that is, to have Miss——er——Bedford give her the pleasure of having her as a guest for the night. Don't you think, Mr. Roanoke, of——er——Virginia, that you could unbend your prejudices that far?"

Clayton of Roanoke rose and held out his hand.

"Old man," he said, "Miss Bedford will be much pleased to accept the hospitality of the lady you refer to."

He formally introduced Mr. Pilkins to Miss Bedford. The girl looked at him sweetly and comfortably. "It's a lovely evening, Mr. Pilkins——don't you think so?" she said slowly.

Pilkins conducted them to the crumbly red brick house of the Von der Ruyslings. His card brought Alice downstairs wondering. The runaways were sent into the drawing-room, while Pilkins told Alice all about it in the hall.

"Of course, I will take her in," said Alice. "Haven't those Southern girls a thoroughbred air? Of course, she will stay here. You will look after Mr. Clayton, of course."

"Will I?" said Pilkins, delightedly. "Oh, yes, I'll look after him! As a citizen of New York, and therefore a part owner of its public parks, I'm going to extend to him the hospitality of Madison Square to-night. He's going to sit there on a bench till morning. There's no use arguing with him. Isn't he wonderful? I'm glad you'll look after the little lady, Alice. I tell you those

Babes in the Wood made my—that is, er—made Wall Street and the Bank of England look like penny arcades."

Miss von der Ruysling whisked Miss Bedford of Bedford County up to restful regions upstairs. When she came down, she put an oblong small pasteboard box into Pilkins' hands.

"Your present," she said, "that I am returning to you."

"Oh, yes, I remember," said Pilkins, with a sigh, "the woolly kitten."

He left Clayton on a park bench, and shook hands with him heartily.

"After I get work," said the youth, "I'll look you up. Your address is on your card, isn't it? Thanks. Well, good-night. I'm awfully obliged to you for your kindness. No, thanks, I don't smoke. Good-night."

In his room, Pilkins opened the box and took out the staring, funny kitten, long ago ravaged of his candy and minus one shoe-button eye. Pilkins looked at it sorrowfully.

"After all," he said, "I don't believe that just money alone will——"

And then he gave a shout and dug into the bottom of the box for something else that had been the kitten's resting-place—a crushed but red, red, fragrant, glorious, promising Jacqueminot rose.

THE ENCHANTED PROFILE

THERE are few Caliphesses. Women are Scheherazades by birth, predilection, instinct, and arrangement of the vocal cords. The thousand and one stories are being told every day by hundreds of thousands of viziers' daughters to their respective sultans. But the bow-string will get some of 'em yet if they don't watch out.

I heard a story, though, of one Lady Caliph. It isn't precisely an Arabian Nights story, because it brings in Cinderella, who flourished her dishrag in another epoch and country. So, if you don't mind the mixed dates (which seem to give it an Eastern flavor, after all), we'll get along.

In New York there is an old, old hotel. You have seen woodcuts of it in the magazines. It was built—let's see—at a time when there was nothing above Fourteenth Street except the old Indian trail to Boston and Hammerstein's office. Soon the old hostelry will be torn down. And, as the stout walls are riven apart and the bricks go roaring down the chutes, crowds of citizens will gather at the nearest corners and weep over the destruction of a dear old landmark. Civic pride is strong in New Bagdad; and the wettest weeper and the loudest howler against the iconoclasts will be the man (originally from Terre Haute) whose fond memories of the old hotel are limited to his having been kicked out from its free-lunch counter in 1873.

At this hotel always stopped Mrs. Maggie Brown. Mrs. Brown was a bony woman of sixty, dressed in the rustiest black, and carrying a handbag made, apparently, from the hide of the original animal that Adam decided to call an alligator. She always occupied a small parlor and bedroom at the top of the hotel at a rental of two dollars per day. And always, while she was there each day came hurrying to see her many men, sharp-faced, anxious-looking, with only seconds to spare. For Maggie Brown was said to be the third richest woman in the world; and these solicitous gentlemen were only the city's wealthiest brokers and business men seeking trifling loans of half a dozen millions or so from the dingy old lady with the prehistoric handbag.

The stenographer and typewriter of the Acropolis Hotel (there! I've let the name of it out!) was Miss Ida Bates. She was a holdover from the Greek classics. There wasn't a flaw in her looks. Some old-timer in paying his regards to a lady said: "To have loved her was a liberal education." Well, even to have looked over the black hair and neat white shirtwaist of Miss Bates was equal to a full course in any correspondence school in the country. She sometimes did a little typewriting for me and, as she refused to take the money in advance, she came to look upon me as something of a friend and protégé. She had unfailing kindliness and good nature; and not even a white-lead drummer or a fur importer had ever dared to cross the dead line of good behavior in her presence. The entire force of the Acropolis, from the owner, who lived in Vienna, down to the head porter, who had been bedridden for sixteen years, would have sprung to her defence in a moment.

One day I walked past Miss Bates's little sanctum Remingtorium, and saw in her place a black-haired unit—unmistakably a person—pounding with each of her forefingers upon the keys. Musing on the mutability of temporal affairs, I passed on. The next day I went on a two weeks' vacation. Returning, I strolled through the lobby of the Acropolis, and saw, with a little warm glow of auld lang syne, Miss Bates, as Grecian and kind and flawless as ever, just putting the cover on her machine. The hour for closing had come; but she asked me in to sit for a few minutes in the dictation chair. Miss Bates explained her absence and return to the Acropolis Hotel in words identical with or similar to these following:

"Well, Man, how are the stories coming?"

"Pretty regularly," said I. "About equal to their going."

"I'm sorry," said she. "Good typewriting is the main thing in a story. You've missed me, haven't you?"

"No one," said I, "whom I have ever known knows as well as you do how to space properly belt buckles, semicolons, hotel guests, and hairpins. But you've been away, too. I saw a package of peppermint-pepsin in your place the other day."

"I was going to tell you about it," said Miss Bates, "if you hadn't interrupted me.

"Of course, you know about Maggie Brown, who stops here. Well, she's worth $40,000,000. She lives in Jersey in a ten-dollar flat. She's always got more cash on hand than half a dozen business candidates for vice-president. I don't know whether she carries it in her stocking or not, but I know she's mighty popular down in the part of the town where they worship the golden calf.

"Well, about two weeks ago, Mrs. Brown stops at the door and rubbers at me for ten minutes. I'm sitting with my side to her, striking off some manifold copies of a copper-mine proposition for a nice old man from Tonopah. But I always see everything all around me. When I'm hard at work I can see things through my side-combs; and I can leave one button unbuttoned in the back of my shirtwaist and see who's behind me. I didn't look around, because I make from eighteen to twenty dollars a week, and I didn't have to.

"That evening at knocking-off time she sends for me to come up to her apartment. I expected to have to typewrite about two thousand words of notes-of-hand, liens, and contracts, with a ten-cent tip in sight; but I went. Well, Man, I was certainly surprised. Old Maggie Brown had turned human.

"'Child,' says she, 'you're the most beautiful creature I ever saw in my life. I want you to quit your work and come and live with me. I've no kith or kin,' says she, 'except a husband and a son or two, and I hold no communication with any of 'em. They're extravagant burdens on a hard-working woman.

I want you to be a daughter to me. They say I'm stingy and mean, and the papers print lies about my doing my own cooking and washing. It's a lie,' she goes on. 'I put my washing out, except the handkerchiefs and stockings and petticoats and collars, and light stuff like that. I've got forty million dollars in cash and stocks and bonds that are as negotiable as Standard Oil, preferred, at a church fair. I'm a lonely old woman and I need companionship. You're the most beautiful human being I ever saw,' says she. 'Will you come and live with me? I'll show 'em whether I can spend money or not,' she says.

"Well, Man, what would you have done? Of course, I fell to it. And, to tell you the truth, I began to like old Maggie. It wasn't all on account of the forty millions and what she could do for me. I was kind of lonesome in the world, too. Everybody's got to have somebody they can explain to about the pain in their left shoulder and how fast patent-leather shoes wear out when they begin to crack. And you can't talk about such things to men you meet in hotels—they're looking for just such openings.

"So I gave up my job in the hotel and went with Mrs. Brown. I certainly seemed to have a mash on her. She'd look at me for half an hour at a time when I was sitting, reading, or looking at the magazines.

"One time I says to her: 'Do I remind you of some deceased relative or friend of your childhood, Mrs. Brown? I've noticed you give me a pretty good optical inspection from time to time.'

" 'You have a face,' she says, 'exactly like a dear friend of mine—the best friend I ever had. But I like you for yourself, child, too,' she says.

"And say, Man, what do you suppose she did? Loosened up like a Marcel wave in the surf at Coney. She took me to a swell dressmaker and gave her à la carte to fit me out—money no object. They were rush orders, and madame locked the front door and put the whole force to work.

"Then we moved to—where do you think?—no; guess again—that's right— the Hotel Bonton. We had a six-room apartment; and it cost $100 a day. I saw the bill. I began to love that old lady.

"And then, Man, when my dresses began to come in—oh, I won't tell you about 'em! you couldn't understand. And I began to call her Aunt Maggie. You've read about Cinderella, of course. Well, what Cinderella said when the prince fitted that 3½ A on her foot was a hard-luck story compared to the things I told myself.

"Then Aunt Maggie says she is going to give me a coming-out banquet in the Bonton that'll make moving Vans of all the old Dutch families on Fifth Avenue.

" 'I've been out before, Aunt Maggie,' says I. 'But I'll come out again. But you know,' says I, 'that this is one of the swellest hotels in the city. And you know—pardon me—that it's hard to get a bunch of notables together unless you've trained for it.'

" 'Don't fret about that, child,' says Aunt Maggie. 'I don't send out invitations—I issue orders. I'll have fifty guests here that couldn't be brought together again at any reception unless it were given by King Edward or William Travers Jerome. They are men, of course, and all of 'em either owe me money or intend to. Some of their wives won't come, but a good many will.'

"Well, I wish you could have been at that banquet. The dinner service was all gold and cut glass. There were about forty men and eight ladies present besides Aunt Maggie and I. You'd never have known the third richest woman in the world. She had on a new black silk dress with so much passementerie on it that it sounded exactly like a hailstorm I heard once when I was staying all night with a girl that lived on a top-floor studio.

"And my dress!—say, Man, I can't waste the words on you. It was all hand-made lace—where there was any of it at all—and it cost $300. I saw the bill. The men were all baldheaded or white-side-whiskered, and they kept up a running fire of light repartee about 3-per cents, and Bryan and the cotton crop.

"On the left of me was something that talked like a banker, and on my right was a young fellow who said he was a newspaper artist. He was the only —well, I was going to tell you.

"After the dinner was over Mrs. Brown and I went up to the apartment. We had to squeeze our way through a mob of reporters all the way through the halls. That's one of the things money does for you. Say, do you happen to know a newspaper artist named Lathrop—a tall man with nice eyes and an easy way of talking? No, I don't remember what paper he works on. Well, all right.

"When we got upstairs Mrs. Brown telephones for the bill right away. It came, and it was $600. I saw the bill. Aunt Maggie fainted. I got her on a lounge and opened the bead-work.

"'Child,' says she, when she got back to the world, 'what was it? A raise of rent or an income-tax?'

"'Just a little dinner,' says I. 'Nothing to worry about—hardly a drop in the bucket-shop. Sit up and take notice—a dispossess notice, if there's no other kind.'

"But, say, Man, do you know what Aunt Maggie did? She got cold feet! She hustled me out of that Hotel Bonton at nine the next morning. We went to a rooming-house on the lower West Side. She rented one room that had water on the floor below and light on the floor above. After we got moved all you could see in the room was about $1,500 worth of new swell dresses and a one-burner gas-stove.

"Aunt Maggie had had a sudden attack of the hedges. I guess everybody has got to go on a spree once in their life. A man spends his on highballs, and a woman gets woozy on clothes. But with forty million dollars—say! I'd like to have a picture of—but, speaking of pictures, did you ever run across a newspaper artist named Lathrop—a tall—oh, I asked you that before, didn't I? He was mighty nice to me at the dinner. His voice just suited me. I guess he must have thought I was to inherit some of Aunt Maggie's money.

"Well, Mr. Man, three days of that light-housekeeping was plenty for me. Aunt Maggie was affectionate as ever. She'd hardly let me get out of her sight. But let me tell you. She was a hedger from Hedgersville, Hedger County. Seventy-five cents a day was the limit she set. We cooked our own meals in the room. There I was, with a thousand dollars' worth of the latest things in clothes, doing stunts over a one-burner gas-stove.

"As I say, on the third day I flew the coop. I couldn't stand for throwing together a fifteen-cent kidney stew while wearing, at the same time, a $150 house-dress, with Valenciennes lace insertion. So I goes into the closet and puts on the cheapest dress Mrs. Brown had bought for me—it's the one I've got on now—not so bad for $75, is it? I'd left all my own clothes in my sister's flat in Brooklyn.

"'Mrs. Brown, formerly "Aunt Maggie,"' says I to her, 'I am going to extend my feet alternately, one after the other, in such a manner and direction that this tenement will recede from me in the quickest possible time. I am no worshipper of money,' says I, 'but there are some things I can't stand. I can stand the fabulous monster that I've read about that blows hot birds and cold bottles with the same breath. But I can't stand a quitter,' says I. 'They say you've got forty million dollars—well, you'll never have any less. And I was beginning to like you, too,' says I.

"Well, the late Aunt Maggie kicks till the tears flow. She offers to move into a swell room with a two-burner stove and running water.

"'I've spent an awful lot of money, child,' says she. 'We'll have to economize for a while. You're the most beautiful creature I ever laid eyes on,' she says, 'and I don't want you to leave me.'

"Well, you see me, don't you? I walked straight to the Acropolis and asked for my job back, and I got it. How did you say your writings were getting along? I know you've lost out some by not having me to typewrite 'em. Do you ever have 'em illustrated? And, by the way, did you ever happen to know a newspaper artist—oh, shut up! I know I asked you before. I wonder what paper he works on? It's funny, but I couldn't help thinking that he wasn't thinking about the money he might have been thinking I was thinking I'd get from old Maggie Brown. If I only knew some of the newspaper editors I'd——"

The sound of an easy footstep came from the doorway. Ida Bates saw who it was with her back-hair comb. I saw her turn pink, perfect statue that she was—a miracle that I share with Pygmalion only.

"Am I excusable?" she said to me—adorable petitioner that she became. "It's —it's Mr. Lathrop. I wonder if it really wasn't the money—I wonder, if after all, he——"

Of course, I was invited to the wedding. After the ceremony I dragged Lathrop aside.

"You an artist," said I, "and haven't figured out why Maggie Brown conceived such a strong liking for Miss Bates—that was? Let me show you."

The bride wore a simple white dress as beautifully draped as the costumes of the ancient Greeks. I took some leaves from one of the decorative wreaths in the little parlor, and made a chaplet of them, and placed them on née Bates' shining chestnut hair, and made her turn her profile to her husband.

"By jingo!" said he. "Isn't Ida's head a dead ringer for the lady's head on the silver dollar?"

"NEXT TO READING MATTER"

HE compelled my interest as he stepped from the ferry at Desbrosses Street. He had the air of being familiar with hemispheres and worlds, and of entering New York as the lord of a demesne who revisited it in after years of absence. But I thought that, with all his air, he had never before set foot on the slippery cobblestones of the City of Too Many Caliphs.

He wore loose clothes of a strange bluish drab color, and a conservative, round Panama hat without the cock-a-loop indentations and cants with which Northern fanciers disfigure the tropic head-gear. Moreover, he was the homeliest man I have ever seen. His ugliness was less repellent than startling—arising from a sort of Lincolnian ruggedness and irregularity ·of feature that spellbound you with wonder and dismay. So may have looked afrites or the shapes metamorphosed from the vapor of the fisherman's vase. As he afterward told me, his name was Judson Tate; and he may as well be called so at once. He wore his green silk tie through a topaz ring; and he carried a cane made of the vertebræ of a shark.

Judson Tate accosted me with some large and casual inquiries about the city's streets and hotels, in the manner of one who had but for the moment forgotten the trifling details. I could think of no reason for dispraising my own quiet hotel in the downtown district; so the mid-morning of the night found us already victualed and drinked (at my expense), and ready to be chaired and tobaccoed in a quiet corner of the lobby.

There was something on Judson Tate's mind, and, such as it was, he tried to convey it to me. Already he had accepted me as his friend; and when I looked at his great, snuff-brown first-mate's hand, with which he brought emphasis to his periods, within six inches of my nose, I wondered if, by any chance, he was as sudden in conceiving enmity against strangers.

When this man began to talk I perceived in him a certain power. His voice was a persuasive instrument, upon which he played with a somewhat specious but effective art. He did not try to make you forget his ugliness; he flaunted it in your face and made it part of the charm of his speech. Shutting your eyes, you would have trailed after this rat-catcher's pipes at least to the walls of Hamelin. Beyond that you would have had to be more childish to follow. But let him play his own tune to the words set down, so that if all is too dull, the art of music may bear the blame.

"Women," said Judson Tate, "are mysterious creatures."

My spirits sank. I was not there to listen to such a world-old hypothesis— to such a time-worn, long-ago-refuted, bald, feeble, illogical, vicious, patent sophistry—to an ancient, baseless, wearisome, ragged, unfounded, insidious falsehood originated by women themselves, and by them insinuated, foisted, thrust, spread, and ingeniously promulgated into the ears of mankind by under-handed, secret, and deceptive methods, for the purpose of argumenting, further-ing, and reinforcing their own charms and designs.

"Oh, I don't know!" said I, vernacularly.

"Have you ever heard of Oratama?" he asked.

"Possibly," I answered. "I seem to recall a toe dancer—or a suburban addition—or was it a perfume?—of some such name."

"It is a town," said Judson Tate, "on the coast of a foreign country of which you know nothing and could understand less. It is a country governed by a dictator and controlled by revolutions and insubordination. It was there that a great life-drama was played, with Judson Tate, the homeliest man in America, and Fergus McMahan, the handsomest adventurer in history or fiction, and Señorita Anabela Zamora, the beautiful daughter of the alcalde of Oratama, as chief actors. And, another thing—nowhere else on the globe except in the department of Trienta y tres in Uruguay does the *chuchula* plant grow. The products of the country I speak of are valuable woods, dye-stuffs, gold, rubber, ivory, and cocoa."

"I was not aware," said I, "that South America produced any ivory."

"There you are twice mistaken," said Judson Tate, distributing the words over at least an octave of his wonderful voice. "I did not say that the country I spoke of was in South America—I must be careful, my dear man; I have been in politics there, you know. But, even so—I have played chess against its president with a set carved from the nasal bones of the tapir—one of our native specimens of the order of *perissodactyle ungulates* inhabiting the Cordilleras— which was as pretty ivory as you would care to see.

"But it was of romance and adventure and the ways of women that I was going to tell you, and not of zoölogical animals.

"For fifteen years I was the ruling power behind old Sancho Benavides, the Royal High Thumbscrew of the republic. You've seen his picture in the papers —a mushy black man with whiskers like the notes on a Swiss music-box cyl-inder, and a scroll in his right hand like the ones they write births on in the family Bible. Well, that chocolate potentate used to be the biggest item of in-terest anywhere between the color line and the parallels of latitude. It was three throws, horses, whether he was to wind up in the Hall of Fame or the Bureau of Combustibles. He'd have been sure called the Roosevelt of the Southern Continent if it hadn't been that Grover Cleveland was President at the time. He'd hold office a couple of terms, then he'd sit out for a hand—always after appointing his own successor for the interims.

"But it was not Benavides, the Liberator, who was making all this fame for himself. Not him. It was Judson Tate. Benavides was only the chip over the bug. I gave him the tip when to declare war and increase import duties and wear his state trousers. But that wasn't what I wanted to tell you. How did I get to be It? I'll tell you. Because I'm the most gifted talker that ever made vocal sounds since Adam first opened his eyes, pushed aside the smelling-salts, and asked: 'Where am I?'

"As you observe, I am about the ugliest man you ever saw outside the gallery of photographs of the New England early Christian Scientists. So, at an early age, I perceived that what I lacked in looks I must make up in eloquence. That I've done. I get what I go after. As the back-stop and still small voice of old Benavides I made all the great historical powers-behind-the-throne, such as Talleyrand, Mrs. de Pompadour, and Loeb, look as small as the minority report of a Duma. I could talk nations into or out of debt, harangue armies to sleep in the battlefield, reduce insurrections, inflammations, taxes, appropriations or surpluses with a few words, and call up the dogs of war or the dove of peace with the same bird-like whistle. Beauty and epaulettes and curly moustaches and Grecian profiles in other men were never in my way. When people first look at me they shudder. Unless they are in the last stages of *angina pectoris* they are mine in ten minutes after I begin to talk. Women and men—I win 'em as they come. Now, you wouldn't think women would fancy a man with a face like mine, would you?"

"Oh, yes, Mr. Tate," said I. "History is bright and fiction dull with homely men who have charmed women. There seems——"

"Pardon me," interrupted Judson Tate, "but you don't quite understand. You have yet to hear my story.

"Fergus McMahan was a friend of mine in the capital. For a handsome man I'll admit he was the duty-free merchandise. He had blond curls and laughing blue eyes and was featured regular. They said he was a ringer for the statue they call Heer Mees, the god of speech and eloquence resting in some museum in Rome. Some German anarchist, I suppose. They are always resting and talking.

"But Fergus was no talker. He was brought up with the idea that to be beautiful was to make good. His conversation was about as edifying as listening to a leak dropping in a tin dish-pan at the head of the bed when you want to go to sleep. But he and me got to be friends—maybe because we was so opposite, don't you think? Looking at the Hallowe'en mask that I call my face when I'm shaving seemed to give Fergus pleasure; and I'm sure that whenever I heard the feeble output of throat noises that he called conversation I felt contented to be a gargoyle with a silver tongue.

"One time I found it necessary to go down to this coast town of Oratama to straighten out a lot of political unrest and chop off a few heads in the customs and military departments. Fergus, who owned the ice and sulphur-match concessions of the republic, says he'll keep me company.

"So, in a jangle of mule-train bells, we gallops into Oratama, and the town belonged to us as much as Long Island Sound doesn't belong to Japan when T. R. is at Oyster Bay. I say us; but I mean me. Everybody for four nations, two oceans, one bay and isthmus, and five archipelagoes around had heard of Judson Tate. Gentleman adventurer, they called me. I had been written up in five columns of the yellow journals, 40,000 words (with marginal decorations) in a monthly magazine, and a stickful on the twelfth page of the New York *Times*. If the beauty of Fergus McMahan gained any part of our reception in Oratama,

I'll eat the price-tag in my Panama. It was me that they hung out paper flowers and palm branches for. I am not a jealous man; I am stating facts. The people were Nebuchadnezzars; they bit the grass before me; there was no dust in the town for them to bite. They bowed down to Judson Tate. They knew that I was the power behind Sancho Benavides. A word from me was more to them than a whole deckle-edged library from East Aurora in sectional bookcases was from anybody else. And yet there are people who spend hours fixing their faces —rubbing in cold cream and massaging the muscles (always toward the eyes) and taking in the slack with tincture of benzoin and electrolyzing moles—to what end? Looking handsome. Oh, what a mistake! It's the larynx that the beauty doctors ought to work on. It's words more than warts, talk more than talcum, palaver more than power, blarney more than bloom that counts—the phonograph instead of the photograph. But I was going to tell you.

"The local Astors put me and Fergus up at the Centipede Club, a frame building built on posts sunk in the surf. The tide's only nine inches. The Little Big High Low Jack-in-the-game of the town came around and kowtowed. Oh, it wasn't to Herr Mees. They had heard about Judson Tate.

"One afternoon me and Fergus McMahan was sitting on the seaward gallery of the Centipede, drinking iced rum and talking.

"'Judson,' says Fergus, 'there's an angel in Oratama.'

"'So long,' says I, 'as it ain't Gabriel, why talk as if you had heard a trump blow?'

"'It's the Señorita Anabela Zamora,' says Fergus. 'She's—she's—she's as lovely as—as hell!'

"'Bravo!' says I, laughing heartily. 'You have a true lover's eloquence to paint the beauties of your inamorata. You remind me,' says I, 'of Faust's wooing of Marguerite—that is, if he wooed her after he went down the trap-door of the stage.'

"'Judson,' says Fergus, 'you know you are as beautiless as a rhinoceros. You can't have any interest in women. I'm awfully gone on Miss Anabela. And that's why I'm telling you.'

"'Oh, seguramente,' says I. 'I know I have a front elevation like an Aztec god that guards a buried treasure that never did exist in Jefferson County, Yucatan. But there are compensations. For instance, I am It in this country as far as the eye can reach, and then a few perches and poles. And again,' says I, 'when I engage people in a set-to of oral, vocal, and laryngeal utterances, I do not usually confine my side of the argument to what may be likened to a cheap phonographic reproduction of the ravings of a jellyfish.'

"'Oh, I know,' says Fergus, amiable, 'that I'm not handy at small talk. Or large, either. That's why I'm telling you. I want you to help me.'

"'How can I do it?' I asked.

"'I have subsidized,' says Fergus, 'the services of Señorita Anabela's duenna, whose name is Francesca. You have a reputation in this country, Judson,' says Fergus, 'of being a great man and a hero.'

"'I have,' says I. 'And I deserve it.'

"'And I,' says Fergus, 'am the best-looking man between the arctic circle and antarctic ice pack.'

"'With limitations,' says I, 'as to physiognomy and geography, I freely concede you to be.'

"'Between the two of us,' says Fergus, 'we ought to land the Señorita Anabela Zamora. The lady, as you know, is of an old Spanish family, and further than looking at her driving in the family carruaje of afternoons around the piaza, or catching a glimpse of her through a barred window of evenings, she is as unapproachable as a star.'

"'Land her for which one of us?' says I.

" 'For me, of course,' says Fergus. 'You've never seen her. Now, I've had Francesca point me out to her as being you on several occasions. When she sees me on the plaza, she thinks she's looking at Don Judson Tate, the greatest hero, statesman, and romantic figure in the country. With your reputation and my looks combined in one man, how can she resist him? She's heard all about your thrilling history, of course. And she's seen me. Can any woman want more?' asks Fergus McMahan.

" 'Can she do with less?' I ask. 'How can we separate our mutual attractions, and how shall we apportion the proceeds?'

"Then Fergus tells me his scheme.

"The house of the alcalde, Don Luis Zamora, he says, has a *patio*, of course— a kind of inner courtyard opening from the street. In an angle of it is his daughter's window—as dark a place as you could find. And what do you think he wants me to do? Why, knowing my freedom, charm, and skilfulness of tongue, he proposes that I go into the *patio* at midnight, when the hobgoblin face of me cannot be seen, and make love to her for him—for the pretty man that she has just seen on the plaza, thinking him to be Don Judson Tate.

"Why shouldn't I do it for him—for my friend, Fergus McMahan? For him to ask me was a compliment—an acknowledgment of his own shortcomings.

" 'You little, lily-white, fine-haired, highly polished piece of dumb sculpture,' says I, 'I'll help you. Make your arrangements and get me in the dark outside her window and my stream of conversation opened up with the moonlight tremolo stop turned on, and she's yours.'

" 'Keep your face hid, Jud,' says Fergus. 'For heaven's sake, keep your face hid. I'm a friend of yours in all kinds of sentiment, but this is a business deal. If I could talk I wouldn't ask you. But seeing me and listening to you I don't see why she can't be landed.'

" 'By you?' says I.

" 'By me,' says Fergus.

"Well, Fergus and the duenna, Francesca, attended to the details. And one night they fetched me a long black cloak with a high collar, and led me to the house at midnight. I stood by the window in the *patio* until I heard a voice as soft and sweet as an angel's whisper on the other side of the bars. I could see only a faint, white-clad shape inside; and, true to Fergus, I pulled the collar of my cloak high up, for it was July in the wet season, and the nights were chilly. And, smothering a laugh as I thought of the tongue-tied Fergus, I began to talk.

"Well, sir, I talked an hour at the Señorita Anabela. I say 'at' because it was not 'with.' Now and then she would say: 'Oh, Señor,' or 'Now, ain't you foolin'?' or 'I know you don't mean that,' and such things as women will when they are being rightly courted. Both of us knew English and Spanish; so in two languages I tried to win the heart of the lady for my friend Fergus. But for the bars to the window I could have done it in one. At the end of the hour she dismissed me and gave me a big, red rose. I handed it over to Fergus when I got home.

"For three weeks every third or fourth night I impersonated my friend in the *patio* at the window of Señorita Anabela. At last she admitted that her heart was mine, and spoke of having seen me every afternoon when she drove in the plaza. It was Fergus she had seen, of course. But it was my talk that won her. Suppose Fergus had gone there and tried to make a hit in the dark with his beauty all invisible, and not a word to say for himself!

"On the last night she promised to be mine—that is, Fergus's. And she put her hand between the bars for me to kiss. I bestowed the kiss and took the news to Fergus.

" 'You might have left that for me to do,' says he.

" 'That'll be your job hereafter,' says I. 'Keep on doing that and don't try to talk. Maybe after she thinks she's in love she won't notice the difference between real conversation and the inarticulate sort of droning that you give forth.'

"Now, I had never seen Señorita Anabela. So, the next day Fergus asks me to walk with him through the plaza and view the daily promenade and exhibition of Oratama society, a sight that had no interest for me. But I went; and children and dogs took to the banana groves and mangrove swamps as soon as they had a look at my face.

" 'Here she comes,' said Fergus, twirling his moustache—'the one in white, in the open carriage with the black horse.'

"I looked and felt the ground rock under my feet. For Señorita Anabela Zamora was the most beautiful woman in the world, and the only one from that moment on, so far as Judson Tate was concerned. I saw at a glance that I must be hers and she mine forever. I thought of my face and nearly fainted; and then I thought of my other talents and stood upright again. And I had been wooing her for three weeks for another man!

"As Señorita Anabela's carriage rolled slowly past, she gave Fergus a long, soft glance from the corners of her night-black eyes, a glance that would have sent Judson Tate up into heaven in a rubber-tired chariot. But she never looked at me. And that handsome man only ruffles his curls and smirks and prances like a lady-killer at my side.

" 'What do you think of her, Judson?' asks Fergus, with an air.

" 'This much,' says I. 'She is to be Mrs. Judson Tate. I am no man to play tricks on a friend. So take your warning.'

"I thought Fergus would die laughing.

" 'Well, well, well,' said he, 'you old dough-face! Struck too, are you? That's great! But you're too late. Francesca tells me that Anabela talks of nothing but me, day and night. Of course, I'm awfully obliged to you for making that chin-music to her of evenings. But, do you know, I've an idea that I could have done it as well myself.'

" 'Mrs. Judson Tate,' says I. 'Don't forget the name. You've had the use of my tongue to go with your good looks, my boy. You can't lend me your looks; but hereafter my tongue is my own. Keep your mind on the name that's to be on the visiting cards two inches by three and a half—"Mrs. Judson Tate." That's all.'

" 'All right,' says Fergus, laughing again. 'I've talked with her father, the alcalde, and he's willing. He's to give a *baile* to-morrow evening in his new warehouse. If you were a dancing man, Jud, I'd expect you around to meet the future Mrs. McMahan.'

"But on the next evening, when the music was playing loudest at the Alcalde Zamora's *baile*, into the room steps Judson Tate in new white linen clothes as if he were the biggest man in the whole nation, which he was.

"Some of the musicians jumped off the key when they saw my face, and one or two of the timidest señoritas let out a screech or two. But up prances the alcalde and almost wipes the dust off my shoes with his forehead. No mere good looks could have won me that sensational entrance.

" 'I hear much, Señor Zamora,' says I, 'of the charm of your daughter. It would give me great pleasure to be presented to her.'

"There were about six dozen willow rocking-chairs, with pink tidies tied on to them, arranged against the walls. In one of them sat Señorita Anabela in white Swiss and red slippers, with pearls and fireflies in her hair. Fergus was at the other end of the room trying to break away from two maroons and a claybank girl.

"The alcalde leads me up to Anabela and presents me. When she took the first look at my face she dropped her fan and nearly turned her chair over from the shock. But I'm used to that.

"I sat down by her and began to talk. When she heard me speak she jumped, and her eyes got as big as alligator pears. She couldn't strike a balance between the tones of my voice and the face I carried. But I kept on talking in the key of C, which is the ladies' key; and presently she sat still in her chair and a dreamy look came into her eyes. She was coming my way. She knew of Judson Tate, and what a big man he was, and the big things he had done; and that was in my favor. But, of course, it was some shock to her to find out that I was not the pretty man that had been pointed out to her as the great Judson. And then I took the Spanish language, which is better than English for certain purposes, and played on it like a harp of a thousand strings. I ranged from the second G below the staff up to F-sharp above it. I set my voice to poetry, art, romance, flowers, and moonlight. I repeated some of the verses that I had murmured to her in the dark at her window; and I knew from a sudden soft sparkle in her eye that she recognized in my voice the tones of her midnight mysterious wooer.

"Anyhow, I had Fergus McMahan going. Oh, the vocal is the true art—no doubt about that. Handsome is as handsome palavers. That's the renovated proverb.

"I took Señorita Anabela for a walk in the lemon grove while Fergus, disfiguring himself with an ugly frown, was waltzing with the claybank girl. Before we returned I had permission to come to her window in the *patio* the next evening at midnight and talk some more.

"Oh, it was easy enough. In two weeks Anabela was engaged to me, and Fergus was out. He took it calm, for a handsome man, and told me he wasn't going to give in.

"'Talk may be all right in its place, Judson,' he says to me, 'although I've never thought it worth cultivating. But,' says he, 'to expect mere words to back up successfully a face like yours in a lady's good graces is like expecting a man to make a square meal on the ringing of a dinner-bell.'

"But I haven't begun on the story I was going to tell you yet.

"One day I took a long ride in the hot sunshine, and then took a bath in the cold waters of a lagoon on the edge of the town before I'd cooled off.

"That evening after dark I called at the alcalde's to see Anabela. I was calling regular every evening then, and we were to be married in a month. She was looking like a bulbul, a gazelle, and a tea-rose, and her eyes were as soft and bright as two quarts of cream skimmed off from the Milky Way. She looked at my rugged features without any expression of fear or repugnance. Indeed, I fancied that I saw a look of deep admiration and affection, such as she had cast at Fergus on the plaza.

"I sat down, and opened my mouth to tell Anabela what she loved to hear—that she was a trust, monopolizing all the loveliness of earth. I opened my mouth, and instead of the usual vibrating words of love and compliment, there came forth a faint wheeze such as a baby with croup might emit. Not a word—not a syllable—not an intelligible sound. I had caught cold in my laryngeal regions when I took my injudicious bath.

"For two hours I sat trying to entertain Anabela. She talked a certain amount, but it was perfunctory and diluted. The nearest approach I made to speech was to formulate a sound like a clam trying to sing 'A Life on the Ocean Wave' at low tide. It seemed that Anabela's eyes did not rest upon me as often as usual. I had nothing with which to charm her ears. We looked at pictures and she played the guitar occasionally, very badly. When I left, her parting manner seemed cool—or at least thoughtful.

"This happened for five evenings consecutively.

"On the sixth day she ran away with Fergus McMahan.

"It was known that they fled in a sailing yacht bound for Belize. I was only eight hours behind them in a small steam launch belonging to the Revenue Department.

"Before I sailed, I rushed into the *botica* of old Manuel Iquito, a half-breed Indian druggist. I could not speak, but I pointed.to my throat and made a sound like escaping steam. He began to yawn. In an hour, according to the customs of the country, I would have been waited on. I reached across the counter, seized him by the throat, and pointed again to my own. He yawned once more, and thrust into my hand a small bottle containing a black liquid.

"'Take one small spoonful every two hours,' says he.

"I threw him a dollar and skinned for the steamer.

"I steamed into the harbor at Belize thirteen seconds behind the yacht that Anabela and Fergus were on. They started for the shore in a dory just as my skiff was lowered over the side. I tried to order my sailormen to row faster, but the sounds died in my larynx before they came to the light. Then I thought of old Iquito's medicine, and I got out his bottle and took a swallow of it.

"The two boats landed at the same moment. I walked straight up to Anabela and Fergus. Her eyes rested upon me for an instant; then she turned them, full of feeling and confidence, upon Fergus. I knew I could not speak, but I was desperate. In speech lay my only hope. I could not stand beside Fergus and challenge comparison in the way of beauty. Purely involuntarily, my larynx and epiglottis attempted to reproduce the sounds that my mind was calling upon my vocal organs to send forth.

"To my intense surprise and delight the words rolled forth beautifully clear, resonant, exquisitely modulated, full of power, expression, and long-repressed emotion.

"'Señorita Anabela,' says I, 'may I speak with you aside for a moment?'

"You don't want details about that, do you? Thanks. The old eloquence had come back all right. I led her under a cocoanut palm and put my old verbal spell on her again.

"'Judson,' says she, 'when you are talking to me I can hear nothing else— I can see nothing else—there is nothing and nobody else in the world for me.'

"Well, that's about all of the story. Anabela went back to Oratama in the steamer with me. I never heard what became of Fergus. I never saw him any more. Anabela is now Mrs. Judson Tate. Has my story bored you much?"

"No," said I. "I am always interested in psychological studies. A human heart—and especially a woman's—is a wonderful thing to contemplate."

"It is," said Judson Tate. "And so are the trachea and the bronchial tubes of man. And the larynx, too. Did you ever make a study of the windpipe?"

"Never," said I. "But I have taken much pleasure in your story. May I ask after Mrs. Tate, and inquire of her present health and whereabouts?"

"Oh, sure," said Judson Tate. "We are living in Bergen Avenue, Jersey City. The climate down in Oratama didn't suit Mrs. T. I don't suppose you ever dissected the arytenoid cartilages of the epiglottis, did you?"

"Why, no," said I, "I am no surgeon."

"Pardon me," said Judson Tate, "but every man should know enough of anatomy and therapeutics to safeguard his own health. A sudden cold may set up capillary bronchitis or inflammation of the pulmonary vesicles, which may result in a serious affection of the vocal organs."

"Perhaps so," said I, with some impatience; "but that is neither here nor there. Speaking of the strange manifestations of the affection of women, I——"

"Yes, yes," interrupted Judson Tate, "they have peculiar ways. But, as I was going to tell you: when I went back to Oratama I found out from Manuel Iquito what was in that mixture he gave me for my lost voice. I told you how quick it cured me. He made that stuff from the *chuchula* plant. Now, look here."

Judson Tate drew an oblong white pasteboard box from his pocket.

"For any cough," he said, "or cold, or hoarseness, or bronchial affection whatsoever, I have here the greatest remedy in the world. You see the formula printed on the box. Each tablet contains licorice, 2 grains; balsam tolu, $\frac{1}{10}$ grain; oil of anise, $\frac{1}{20}$ minim; oil of tar, $\frac{1}{60}$ minim; oleo-resin of cubebs, $\frac{1}{60}$ minim; fluid extract of *chuchula*, $\frac{1}{10}$ minim.

"I am in New York," went on Judson Tate, "for the purpose of organizing a company to market the greatest remedy for throat affections ever discovered. At present I am introducing the lozenges in a small way. I have here a box containing four dozen, which I am selling for the small sum of fifty cents. If you are suffering——"

I got up and went away without a word. I walked slowly up to the little park near my hotel, leaving Judson Tate alone with his conscience. My feelings were lacerated. He had poured gently upon me a story that I might have used. There was a little of the breath of life in it, and some of the synthetic atmosphere that passes, when cunningly tinkered, in the marts. And, at the last it had proven to be a commercial pill, deftly coated with the sugar of fiction. The worst of it was that I could not offer it for sale. Advertising departments and countingrooms look down upon me. And it would never do for the literary. Therefore I sat upon a bench with other disappointed ones until my eyelids drooped.

I went to my room, and, as my custom is, read for an hour stories in my favorite magazines. This was to get my mind back to art again.

And as I read each story, I threw the magazines sadly and hopelessly, one by one, upon the floor. Each author, without one exception to bring balm to my heart, wrote liltingly and sprightly a story of some particular make of motorcar that seemed to control the sparking plug of his genius.

And when the last one was hurled from me I took heart.

"If readers can swallow so many proprietary automobiles," I said to myself, "they ought not to strain at one of Tate's Compound Magic Chuchula Bronchial Lozenges."

And so if you see this story in print you will understand that business is business, and that if Arts gets very far ahead of Commerce, she will have to get up and hustle.

I may as well add, to make a clean job of it, that you can't buy the *chuchula* plant in the drug stores.

ART AND THE BRONCO

OUT of the wilderness had come a painter. Genius, whose coronations alone are democratic, had woven a chaplet of chaparral for the brow of Lonny Briscoe. Art, whose divine expression flows impartially from the fingertips of a cowboy or a dilettante emperor, had chosen for a medium the Boy Artist of the San Saba. The outcome, seven feet by twelve of besmeared canvas, stood, gilt-framed, in the lobby of the Capitol.

The legislature was in session; the capital city of that great Western state was enjoying the season of activity and profit that the congregation of the solons bestowed. The boarding houses were corralling the easy dollars of the gamesome lawmakers. The greatest state in the West, an empire in area and resources, had arisen and repudiated the old libel or barbarism, lawbreaking, and bloodshed. Order reigned within her borders. Life and property were as safe there, sir, as anywhere among the corrupt cities of the effete East. Pillow-shams, churches, strawberry feasts and *habeas corpus* flourished. With impunity might the tender-foot ventilate his "stovepipe." or his theories of culture. The arts and sciences receive nurture and subsidy. And, therefore, it behooved the legislature of this great state to make appropriation for the purchase of Lonny Briscoe's immortal painting.

Rarely has the San Saba country contributed to the spread of the fine arts. Its sons have excelled in the soldier graces, in the throw of the lariat, the manipulation of the esteemed .45, the intrepidity of the one-card draw, and the nocturnal stimulation of towns from undue lethargy; but, hitherto, it had not been famed as a stronghold of æsthetics. Lonny Briscoe's brush had removed that disability. Here, among the limestone rocks, the succulent cactus, and the drought-parched grass of that arid valley, had been born the Boy Artist. Why he came to woo art is beyond postulation. Beyond doubt, some spore of the afflatus must have sprung up within him in spite of the desert soil of San Saba. The tricksy spirit of creation must have incited him to attempted expression and then have sat hilarious among the white-hot sands of the valley, watching its mischievous work. For Lonny's picture, viewed as a thing of art, was something to have driven away dull care from the bosoms of the critics.

The painting—one might almost say panorama—was designed to portray a typical Western scene, interest culminating in a central animal figure, that of a stampeding steer, life-size, wild-eyed, fiery, breaking away in a mad rush from the herd that, close-ridden by a typical cowpuncher, occupied a position somewhat in the right background of the picture. The landscape presented fitting and faithful accessories. Chaparral, mesquite, and pear were distributed in just proportions. A Spanish dagger-plant, with its waxen blossoms in a creamy aggregation as large as a water-bucket, contributed floral beauty and variety. The distance was undulating prairie, bisected by stretches of the intermittent streams peculiar to the region lined with the rich green of live-oak and water-elm. A richly mottled rattlesnake lay coiled beneath a pale green clump of prickly pear in the foreground. A third of the canvas was ultramarine and lake white —the typical Western sky and the flying clouds, rainless and feathery.

Between two plastered pillars in the commodious hallway near the door of the chamber of representatives stood the painting. Citizens and lawmakers passed there by twos and groups and sometimes crowds to gaze upon it. Many—perhaps a majority of them—had lived the prairie life and recalled easily the familiar scene. Old cattlemen stood, reminiscent and candidly pleased, chatting with brothers of former camps and trails of the days it brought back to mind. Art critics were few in the town, and there was heard none of that jargon of color, perspective, and feeling such as the East loves to use as a curb and a rod to the pretensions of the artist. 'Twas a great picture, most of them agreed, admiring the gilt frame—larger than any they had ever seen.

Senator Kinney was the picture's champion and sponsor. It was he who so often stepped forward and asserted, with the voice of a bronchobuster, that it would be a lasting blot, sir, upon the name of this great state if it should decline to recognize in a proper manner the genius that had so brilliantly transferred to imperishable canvas a scene so typical of the great sources of our state's wealth and prosperity, land—and—er—live-stock.

Senator Kinney represented a section of the state in the extreme West—400 miles from the San Saba country—but the true lover of art is not limited by metes and bounds. Nor was Senator Mullens, representing the San Saba country, lukewarm in his belief that the state should purchase the painting of his constituent. He was advised that the San Saba country was unanimous in its

.dmiration of the great painting by one of its own denizens. Hundreds of con-
.oisseurs had straddled their broncos and ridden miles to view it before its
.emoval to the capital. Senator Mullens desired reëlection, and he knew the
importance of the San Saba vote. He also knew that with the help of Senator
Kinney—who was a power in the legislature—the thing could be put through.
Now, Senator Kinney had an irrigation bill that he wanted passed for the benefit
of his own section, and he knew Senator Mullens could render him valuable aid
and information, the San Saba country already enjoying the benefits of similar
legislation. With these interests happily dovetailed, wonder at the sudden interest in art at the state capital must, necessarily, be small. Few artists have
uncovered their first picture to the world under happier auspices than did Lonny
Briscoe.

Senators Kinney and Mullens came to an understanding in the matter of irrigation and art while partaking of long drinks in the café of the Empire Hotel.

"H'm!" said Senator Kinney, "I don't know. I'm no art critic, but it seems
to me the thing won't work. It looks like the worst kind of a chromo to me.
I don't want to cast any reflections upon the artistic talent of your constituent,
Senator, but I, myself, wouldn't give six bits for the picture—without the frame.
How are you going to cram a thing like that down the throat of a legislature that
kicks about a little item in the expense bill of six hundred and eighty-one dollars for rubber erasers for only one term? It's wasting time. I'd like to help
you, Mullens, but they'd laugh us out of the Senate chamber if we were to try it."

"But you don't get the point," said Senator Mullens, in his deliberate tones,
tapping Kinney's glass with his long forefinger. "I have my own doubts as to
what the picture is intended to represent, a bullfight or a Japanese allegory,
but I want this legislature to make an appropriation to purchase. Of course, the
subject of the picture should have been in the state historical line, but it's too
late to have the paint scraped off and changed. The state won't miss the money
and the picture can be stowed away in a lumber-room where it won't annoy any
one. Now, here's the point to work on, leaving art to look after itself—the
chap that painted the picture is the grandson of Lucien Briscoe."

"Say it again," said Kinney, leaning his head thoughtfully. "Of the old,
original Lucien Briscoe?"

"Of him. 'The man who,' you know. The man who carved the state out of
the wilderness. The man who settled the Indians. The man who cleaned out
the horse thieves. The man who refused the crown. The state's favorite son.
Do you see the point now?"

"Wrap up the picture," said Kinney. "It's as good as sold. Why didn't you
say that at first, instead of philandering along about art. I'll resign my seat in
the Senate and go back to chain-carrying for the county surveyor the day I
can't make this state buy a picture calcimined by a grandson of Lucien Briscoe.
Did you ever hear of a special appropriation for the purchase of a home for the
daughter of One-Eyed Smothers? Well, that went through like a motion to adjourn, and old One-Eyed never killed half as many Indians as Briscoe did. About
what figure had you and the calceminer agreed upon to sandbag the treasury for?"

"I thought," said Mullens, "that maybe five hundred——"

"Five hundred!" interrupted Kinney, as he hammered on his glass for a lead
pencil and looked around for a waiter. "Only five hundred for a red steer on the
hoof delivered by a grandson of Lucien Briscoe! Where's your state pride, man?
Two thousand is what it'll be. You'll introduce the bill and I'll get up on the
floor of the Senate and wave the scalp of every Indian old Lucien ever murdered.
Let's see, there was something else proud and foolish he did, wasn't there? Oh,
yes; he declined all emoluments and benefits he was entitled to. Refused his
head-right and veteran donation certificates. Could have been governor, but
wouldn't. Declined a pension. Now's the state's chance to pay up. It'll have to

take the picture, but then it deserves some punishment for keeping the Briscoe family waiting so long. We'll bring this thing up about the middle of the month, after the tax bill is settled. Now, Mullens, you send over, as soon as you can, and get me the figures on the cost of those irrigation ditches and the statistics about the increased production per acre. I'm going to need you when that bill of mine comes up. I reckon we'll be able to pull along pretty well together this session and maybe others to come, eh, Senator?"

Thus did fortune elect to smile upon the Boy Artist of the San Saba. Fate had already done her share when she arranged his atoms in the cosmogony of ceration as the grandson of Lucien Briscoe.

The original Briscoe had been a pioneer both as to territorial occupation and in certain acts prompted by a great and simple heart. He had been one of the first settlers and crusaders against the wild forces of nature, the savage and the shallow politician. His name and memory were revered equally with any upon the list comprising Houston, Boone, Crockett, Clark, and Green. He had lived simply, independently, and unvexed by ambition. Even a less shrewd man that Senator Kinney could have prophesied that his state would hasten to honor and reward his grandson, come out of the chaparral at even so late a day.

And so, before the great picture by the door of the chamber of representatives at frequent times for many days could be found the breezy, robust form of Senator Kinney and be heard his clarion voice reciting the past deeds of Lucien Briscoe in connection with the handiwork of his grandson. Senator Mullens's work was more subdued in sight and sound, but directed along identical lines.

Then, as the day for the introduction of the bill for appropriation draws nigh, up from the San Saba country rides Lonny Briscoe and a loyal lobby of cowpunchers, bronco-back, to boost the cause of art and glorify the name of friendship, for Lonny is one of them, a knight of stirrup and chaparreras, as handy with the lariat and .45 as he is with brush and palette.

On a March afternoon the lobby dashed, with a whoop, into town. The cowpunchers had adjusted their garb suitable from that prescribed for the range to the more conventional requirements of town. They had conceded their leather chaparreras and transferred their six-shooters and belts from their persons to the horns of their saddles. Among them rode Lonny, a youth of twenty-three, brown, solemn-faced, ingenuous, bowlegged, reticent, bestriding Hot Tamales, the most sagacious cow pony west of the Mississippi. Senator Mullens had informed him of the bright prospects of the situation; had even mentioned—so great was his confidence in the capable Kinney—the price that the state would, in all likelihood, pay. It seemed to Lonny that fame and fortune were in his hands. Certainly, a spark of the divine fire was in the little brown centaur's breast, for he was counting the two thousand dollars as but a means to future development of his talent. Some day he would paint a picture even greater than this— one, say, twelve feet by twenty, full of scope and atmosphere and action.

During the three days that yet intervened before the coming of the date fixed for the introduction of the bill, the centaur lobby did valiant service. Coatless, spurred, weather-tanned, full of enthusiasm expressed in bizarre terms, they loafed in front of the painting with tireless zeal. Reasoning not unshrewdly, they estimated that their comments upon its fidelity to nature would be received as expert evidence. Loudly they praised the skill of the painter whenever there were ears near to which such evidence might be profitably addressed. Lem Perry, the leader of the claque, had a somewhat set speech, being uninventive in the construction of new phrases.

"Look at the two-year-old, now," he would say, waving a cinnamon-brown hand toward the salient point of the picture. "Why, dang my hide, the critter's alive. I can jest hear him 'lumpety-lump,' a-cuttin' away from the herd, pretendin' he's skeered. He's a mean scamp, that there steer. Look at his eyes a-wallin' and his tail a-wavin'. He's true and nat'ral to life. He's jest hankerin' fur a cow pony to round him up and send him scootin' back to the bunch. Dang my hide! jest look at that tail of his'n a-wavin'. Never knowed a steer to wave his tail any other way, dang my hide ef I did."

Jud Shelby, while admitting the excellence of the steer, resolutely confined himself to open admiration of the landscape, to the end that the entire picture receive its meed of praise.

"That piece of range," he declared, "is a dead ringer for Dead Hoss Valley. Same grass, same lay of the land, same old Whipper-will Creek skallyhootin' in and out of them motts of timber. Them buzzards on the left is circlin' 'round over Sam Kildrake's old paint hoss that killed hisself over-drinkin' on a hot day. You can't see the hoss for that mott of ellums on the creek, but he's thar. Anybody that was goin' to look for Dead Hoss Valley and come across this picture, why, he'd jest light off'n his bronco and hunt a place to camp."

Skinny Rogers, wedded to comedy, conceived a complimentary little piece of acting that never failed to make an impression. Edging quite near to the picture, he would suddenly, at favorable moments, emit a piercing and awful "Yi-yi!" leap high and away, coming down with a great stamp of heels and whirring of rowels upon the stone-flagged floor.

"Jeeming Christopher!"—so ran his lines—"thought that rattler was a gin-u-ine one. Ding baste my skin if I didn't. Seemed to me I heard him rattle. Look at the blamed, unconverted insect a-layin' under that pear. Little more, and somebody would a-been snake-bit."

With these artful dodges, contributed by Lonny's faithful coterie, with the sonorous Kinney perpetually sounding the picture's merits, and with the solvent prestige of the pioneer Briscoe covering it like a precious varnish, it seemed that the San Saba country could not fail to add a reputation as an art centre to its well-known superiority in steer-roping contests and achievements with the precarious busted flush. This was created for the picture an atmosphere, due rather to externals than to the artist's brush, but through it the people seemed to gaze with more of admiration. There was a magic in the name of Briscoe that counted high against faulty technique and crude coloring. The old Indian fighter and wolf slayer would have smiled grimly in his happy hunting grounds had he known that his dilettante ghost was thus figuring as an art patron two generations after his uninspired existence.

Came the day when the Senate was expected to pass the bill of Senator Mullens appropriating two thousand dollars for the purchase of the picture. The gallery of the Senate chamber was early preëmpted by Lonny and the San Saba lobby. In the front row of chairs they sat, wild-haired, self-conscious, jingling, creaking, and rattling, subdued by the majesty of the council hall.

The bill was introduced, went to the second reading, and then Senator Mullens spoke for it dryly, tediously, and at length. Senator Kinney then arose, and the welkin seized the bell-rope preparatory to ringing. Oratory was at that time a living thing; the world had not quite come to measure its questions by geometry and the multiplication table. It was the day of the silver tongue, the sweeping gesture, the decorative apostrophe, the moving peroration.

The Senator spoke. The San Saba contingent sat, breathing hard, in the gallery, its disordered hair hanging down to its eyes, its sixteen-ounce hats shifted restlessly from knee to knee. Below, the distinguished Senators either lounged at their desks with the abandon of proven statesmanship or maintained correct attitudes indicative of a first term.

Senator Kinney spoke for an hour. History was his theme—history mitigated by patriotism and sentiment. He referred casually to the picture in the outer hall—it was unnecessary, he said, to dilate upon its merits—the Senators had seen for themselves. The painter of the picture was the grandson of Lucien Briscoe. Then came the word-pictures of Briscoe's life set forth in thrilling colors. His rude and venturesome life, his simple-minded love for the commonwealth he helped to upbuild, his contempt for rewards and praise, his extreme and sturdy independence, and the great services he had rendered the state. The subject of the oration was Lucien Briscoe; the painting stood in the background serving simply as a means, now happily brought forward, through which the state might bestow a tardy recompense upon the descendant of its favorite son. Frequent enthusiastic applause from the Senators testified to the well reception of the sentiment.

The bill passed without an opposing vote. To-morrow it would be taken up by the House. Already was it fixed to glide through that body on rubber tires, Blandford, Grayson, and Plummer, all wheel-horses and orators, and provided with plentiful memoranda concerning the deeds of pioneer Briscoe, had agreed to furnish the motive power.

The San Saba lobby and its protégé stumbled awkwardly down the stairs and out into the Capitol yard. Then they herded closely and gave one yell of triumph. But one of them—Buck-Kneed Summers it was—hit the key with the thoughtful remark:

"She cut the mustard," he said, "all right. I reckon they're goin' to buy Lon's steer. I ain't right much on the parlyment'ry but I gather that's what the signs added up. But she seems to me, Lonny, the argyment ran principal to grandfather, instead of paint. It's reasonable calculatin' that you want to be glad you got the Briscoe brand on you, my son."

That remark clinched in Lonny's mind an unpleasant, vague suspicion to the same effect. His reticence increased, and he gathered grass from the ground, chewing it pensively. The picture as a picture had been humiliatingly absent from the Senator's arguments. The painter had been held up as a grandson, pure and simple. While this was gratifying on certain lines, it made art look little and slab-sided. The Boy Artist was thinking.

The hotel Lonny stopped at was near the Capitol. It was near to the one o'clock dinner hour when the appropriation had been passed by the Senate. The hotel clerk told Lonny that a famous artist from New York had arrived in town that day and was in the hotel. He was on his way westward to New Mexico to study the effect of sunlight upon the ancient walls of the Zuñis. Modern stone reflects light. Those ancient building materials absorb it. The artist wanted this effect in a picture he was painting and was travelling two thousand miles to get it.

Lonny sought this man out after dinner and told his story. The artist was an unhealthy man, kept alive by genius and indifference to life. He went with Lonny to the Capitol and stood there before the picture. The artist pulled his beard and looked unhappy.

"Should like to have your sentiments," said Lonny, "just as they run out of the pen."

"It's the way they'll come," said the painter man. "I took three different kinds of medicine before dinner—by the tablespoonful. The taste still lingers. I am primed for telling the truth. You want to know if the picture is, or if it isn't?"

"Right," said Lonny. "Is it wool or cotton? Should I paint some more or cut it out and ride herd a-plenty?"

"I heard a rumor during pie," said the artist, "that the state is about to pay you two thousand dollars for this picture."

"It's passed the Senate," said Lonny, "and the House rounds it up to-morrow."

"That's lucky," said the pale man. "Do you carry a rabbit's foot?"

"No," said Lonny, "but it seems I had a grandfather. He's considerable mixed up in the color scheme. It took me a year to paint that picture. Is she entirely awful or not? Some says, now, that that steer's tail ain't badly drawed. They think it's proportioned nice. Tell me."

The artist glanced at Lonny's wiry figure and nut-brown skin. Something stirred him to a passing irritation.

"For Art's sake, son," he said, fractiously, "don't spend any more money for paint. It isn't a picture at all. It's a gun. You hold up the state with it, if you like, and get your two thousand, but don't get in front of any more canvas. Live under it. Buy a couple of hundred ponies with the money—I'm told they're that cheap—and ride, ride, ride. Fill your lungs and eat and sleep and be happy. No more pictures. You look healthy. That's genius. Cultivate it." He looked at his watch. "Twenty minutes to three. Four capsules and one tablet at three. That's all you wanted to know, isn't it?"

At three o'clock the cowpunchers rode up for Lonny, bringing Hot Tamales, saddled. Traditions must be observed. To celebrate the passage of the bill by the Senate the gang must ride wildly through the town, creating uproar and excitement. Liquor must be partaken of, the suburbs shot up, and the glory of the San Saba country vociferously proclaimed. A part of the programme had been carried out in the saloons on the way up.

Lonny mounted Hot Tamales, the accomplished little beast prancing with fire and intelligence. He was glad to feel Lonny's bow-legged grip against his ribs again. Lonny was his friend, and he was willing to do things for him.

"Come on, boys," said Lonny, urging Hot Tamales into a gallop with his knees. With a whoop, the inspired lobby tore after him through the dust. Lonny led his cohorts straight for the Capitol. With a wild yell, the gang indorsed his now evident intention of riding into it. Hooray for San Saba!

Up the six broad, limestone steps clattered the broncos of the cowpunchers. Into the resounding hallway they pattered, scattering in dismay those passing on foot. Lonny, in the lead, shoved Hot Tamales direct for the great picture. At that hour a downpouring, soft light from the second-story windows bathed the big canvas. Against the darker background of the hall the painting stood out with valuable effect. In spite of the defects of the art you could almost fancy that you gazed out upon a landscape. You might well flinch a step from the convincing figure of the life-sized steer stampeding across the grass. Perhaps it thus seemed to Hot Tamales. The scene was in his line. Perhaps he only obeyed the will of his rider. His ears pricked up; he snorted. Lonny leaned forward in the saddle and elevated his elbows, wing-like. Thus signals the cowpuncher to his steed to launch himself full speed ahead. Did Hot Tamales fancy he saw a steer, red and cavorting, that should be headed off and driven back to herd? There was a fierce clatter of hoofs, a rush, a gathering of steely flank muscles, a leap to the jerk of the bridle rein, and Hot Tamales, with Lonny bending low in the saddle to dodge the top of the frame, ripped through the great canvas like a shell from a mortar, leaving the cloth hanging in ragged shreds about a monstrous hole.

Quickly Lonny pulled up his pony, and rounded the pillars. Spectators came running, too astounded to add speech to the commotion. The sergeant-at-arms of the House came forth, frowned, looked ominous, and then grinned. Many of the legislators crowded out to asberve the tumult. Lonny's cowpunchers were stricken to silent horror by his mad deed.

Senator Kinney happened to be among the earliest to emerge. Before he could speak Lonny leaned in his saddle as Hot Tamales pranced, pointed his quirt at the Senator, and said, calmly:

"That was a fine speech you made to-day, mister, but you might as well let up on that 'propriation business. I ain't askin' the state to give me nothin'.

I thought I had a picture to sell to it, but it wasn't one. You said a heap of things about Grandfather Briscoe that makes me kind of proud I'm his grandson. Well, the Briscoes ain't takin' presents from the state yet. Anybody can have the frame that wants it. Hit her up, boys."

Away scuttled the San Saba delegation out of the hall, down the steps, along the dusty street.

Halfway to the San Saba country they camped that night. At bedtime Lonny stole away from the campfire and sought Hot Tamales, placidly eating grass at the end of his stake rope. Lonny hung upon his neck, and his art aspirations went forth forever in one long, regretful sigh. But as he thus made renunciation his breath formed a word or two.

"You was the only one, Tamales, what seen anything in it. It *did* look like a steer, didn't it, old hoss?"

PHŒBE

"You are a man of many novel adventures and varied enterprises," I said to Captain Patricio Maloné. "Do you believe that the possible element of good luck or bad luck—if there is such a thing as luck—has influenced your career or persisted for or against you to such an extent that you were forced to attribute results to the operation of the aforesaid good luck or bad luck?"

This question (of almost the dull insolence of legal phraseology) was put while we sat in Rousselin's little red-tiled café near Congo Square in New Orleans.

Brown-faced, white-hatted, finger-ringed captains of adventure came often to Rousselin's for the cognac. They came from sea and land, and were chary of relating the things they had seen—not because they were more wonderful than the fantasies of the Ananiases of print, but because they were so different. And I was a perpetual wedding-guest, always striving to cast my buttonhole over the finger of one of these mariners of fortune. This Captain Maloné was a Hibero-Iberian creole who had gone to and fro in the earth and walked up and down in it. He looked like any other well-dressed man of thirty-five whom you might meet, except that he was hopelessly weather-tanned, and wore on his chain an ancient ivory-and-gold Peruvian charm against evil, which has nothing at all to do with his story.

"My answer to your question," said the captain, smiling, "will be to tell you the story of Bad-Luck Kearney. That is, if you don't mind hearing it."

My reply was to pound on the table for Rousselin.

"Strolling along Tchoupitoulas Street one night," began Captain Maloné, "I noticed, without especially taxing my interest, a small man walking rapidly toward me. He stepped upon a wooden cellar door, crashed through it, and disappeared. I rescued him from a heap of soft coal below. He dusted himself briskly, swearing fluently in a mechanical tone, as an underpaid actor recites the gipsy's curse. Gratitude and the dust in his throat seemed to call for fluids to clear them away. His desire for liquidation was expressed so heartily that I went with him to a café down the street where we had some vile vermouth and bitters.

"Looking across that little table I had my first clear sight of Francis Kearny. He was about five feet seven, but as tough as a cypress knee. His hair was darkest red, his mouth such a mere slit that you wondered how the flood of

his words came rushing from it. His eyes were the brightest and lightest blue
and the hopefulest that I ever saw. He gave the double impression that he was
at bay and that you had better not crowd him further.

"'Just in from a gold-hunting expedition on the coast of Costa Rica,' he
explained. 'Second mate of a banana steamer told me the natives were panning
out enough from the beach sands to buy all the rum, red calico, and parlor
melodeons in the world. The day I got there a syndicate named Incorporated
Jones gets a government concession to all minerals from a given point. For
a next choice I take coast fever and count green and blue lizards for six
weeks in a grass hut. I had to be notified when I was well, for the reptiles
were actually there. Then I shipped back as third cook on a Norwegian tramp
that blew up her boiler two miles below Quarantine. I was due to bust through
that cellar door here to-night, so I hurried the rest of the way up the river,
roustabouting on a lower coast packet that made a landing for every fisherman
that wanted a plug of tobacco. And now I'm here for what comes next. And
it'll be along, it'll be along,' said this queer Mr. Kearny; 'it'll be along on the
beams of my bright but not very particular star.'

"From the first the personality of Kearny charmed me. I saw in him the bold
heart, the restless nature, and the valiant front against the buffets of fate
that make his countrymen such valuable comrades in risk and adventure. And
just then I was wanting such men. Moored at a fruit company's pier I had
a 500-ton steamer ready to sail the next day with a cargo of sugar, lumber,
and corrugated iron for a port in—well, let us call the country Esperando—it
has not been long ago, and the name of Patricio Maloné is still spoken there
when its unsettled politics are discussed. Beneath the sugar and iron were packed
a thousand Winchester rifles. In Aguas Frias, the capital, Don Rafael Valdevia,
Minister of War, Esperando's greatest-hearted and most able patriot, awaited
my coming. No doubt you have heard, with a smile, of the insignificant wars
and uprisings in those little tropic republics. They make but a faint clamor
against the din of great nations' battles; but down there, under all the
ridiculous uniforms and petty diplomacy and senseless countermarching and
intrigue, are to be found statesmen and patriots. Don Rafael Valdevia was one.
His great ambition was to raise Esperando into peace and honest prosperity and
the respect of the serious nations. So he waited for my rifles in Aguas Frias.
But one would think I am trying to win a recruit in you! No: it was Francis
Kearny I wanted. And so I told him, speaking long over our execrable vermouth,
breathing the stifling odor from garlic and tarpaulins, which, as you know, is
the distinctive flavor of cafés in the lower slant of our city. I spoke of the
tyrant President Cruz and the burdens that his greed and insolent cruelty laid
upon the people. And at that Kearny's tears flowed. And then I dried them
with a picture of the fat rewards that would be ours when the oppressor
should be overthrown and the wise and generous Valdevia in his seat. Then
Kearny leaped to his feet and wrung my hand with the strength of a roustabout.
He was mine, he said, till the last minion of the hated despot was hurled from
the highest peaks of the Cordilleras into the sea.

"I paid the score and we went out. Near the door Kearny's elbow overturned an upright glass showcase, smashing it into little bits. I paid the
storekeeper the price he asked.

"'Come to my hotel for the night,' I said to Kearny. 'We sail to-morrow at
noon.'

"He agreed; but on the sidewalk he fell to cursing again in the dull,
monotonous, glib way that he had done when I pulled him out of the coal
cellar.

"'Captain,' said he, 'before we go any further, it's no more than fair to tell
you that I'm known from Baffin's Bay to Tierra del Fuego as "Bad-Luck"

Kearny. And I'm It. Everything I get into goes up in the air except a balloon. Every bet I ever made I lost except when I coppered it. Every boat I ever sailed on sank except the submarines. Everything I was ever interested in went to pieces except a patent bombshell that I invented. Everything I ever took hold of and tried to run I ran into the ground except when I tried to plough. And that's why they call me Bad-Luck Kearny. I thought I'd tell you.'

"'Bad-luck,' said I, 'or what goes by the name, may now and then tangle the affairs of any man. But if it persist beyond the estimate of what we may call the "averages" there must be a cause for it.'

"'There is,' said Kearny, emphatically, 'and when we walk another square I will show it to you.'

"Surprised, I kept by his side until we came to Canal Street and out into the middle of its great width.

"Kearny seized me by an arm and painted a tragic fore-finger at a rather brilliant star that shone steadily about thirty degrees above the horizon.

"'That's Saturn,' said he, 'the star that presides over bad luck and evil and disappointment and nothing doing and trouble. I was born under that star. Every move I make, up bobs Saturn and blocks it. He's the hoodoo planet of the heavens. They say he's 73,000 miles in diameter and no solider of body than split-pea soup, and he's got as many disreputable and malignant rings as Chicago. Now, what kind of a star is that to be born under?'

"I asked Kearny where he had obtained all this astonishing knowledge.

"'From Azrath, the great astrologer of Cleveland, Ohio,' said he. 'That man looked at a glass ball and told me my name before I'd taken a chair. He prophesied the date of my birth and death before I'd said a word. And then he cast my horoscope, and the sidereal system socked me in the solar plexus. It was bad luck for Francis Kearny from A to Izard and for his friends that were implicated with him. For that I gave up ten dollars. This Azrath was sorry, but he respected his profession too much to read the heavens wrong for any man. It was night time, and he took me out on a balcony and gave me a free view of the sky. And he showed me which Saturn was, and how to find it in different balconies and longitudes.

"'But Saturn wasn't all. He was only the man higher up. He furnishes so much bad luck that they allow him a gang of deputy sparklers to help hand it out. They're circulating and revolving and hanging around the main supply all the time, each one throwing the hoodoo on his own particular district.

"'You see that ugly little red star about eight inches above and to the right of Saturn?' Kearny asked me. 'Well, that's her. That's Phœbe. She's got me in charge. "By the day of your birth," says Azrath to me, "your life is subjected to the influence of Saturn. By the hour and minute of it you must dwell under the sway and direct authority of Phœbe, the ninth satellite." So said this Azarth.' Kearny shook his fist viciously skyward. 'Curse her, she's done her work well,' said he. 'Ever since I was astrologized, bad luck has followed me like my shadow, as I told you. And for many years before. Now, Captain, I've told you my handicap as a man should. If you're afraid this evil star of mine might cripple your scheme, leave me out of it.'

"I reassured Kearny as well as I could. I told him that for the time we would banish both astrology and astronomy from our heads. The manifest valor and enthusiasm of the man drew me. 'Let us see what a little courage and diligence will do against bad luck, I said. 'We will sail to-morrow for Esperando.'

"Fifty miles down the Mississippi our steamer broke her rudder. We sent for a tug to tow us back and lost three days. When we struck the blue waters of the Gulf, all the storm clouds of the Atlantic seemed to have concentrated above us. We thought surely to sweeten those leaping waves with our sugar, and to stack our arms and lumber on the floor of the Mexican Gulf.

"Kearny did not seek to cast off one iota of the burden of our danger from the shoulders of his fatal horoscope. He weathered every storm on deck, smoking a black pipe, to keep which alight rain and sea-water seemed but as oil. And he shook his fist at the black clouds behind which his baleful star winked its unseen eye. When the skies cleared one evening, he reviled his malignant guardian with grim humor.

" 'On watch, aren't you, you red-headed vixen? Out making it hot for little Francis Kearny and his friends, according to Hoyle. Twinkle, twinkle, little devil! You're a lady, aren't you?—dogging a man with bad luck just because he happened to be born while your boss was floorwalker. Get busy and sink the ship, you one-eyed banshee. Phœbe! H'm! Sounds as mild as a milkmaid. You can't judge a woman by her name. Why couldn't I have had a man star? I can't make the remarks to Phœbe that I could to a man. Oh, Phœbe, you be— blasted!'

"For eight days gales and squalls and water-spouts beat us from our course. Five days only should have landed us in Esperando. Our Jonah swallowed the bad credit of it with appealing frankness; but that scarcely lessened the hardships our cause was made to suffer.

"At last one afternoon we steamed into the calm estuary of the little Rio Escondido. Three miles up this we crept, feeling for the shallow channel between the low banks that were crowded to the edge with gigantic trees and riotous vegetation. Then our whistle gave a little toot, and in five minutes we heard a shout and Carlos—my brave Carlos Quintana—crashed through the tangled vines waving his cap madly for joy.

"A hundred yards away was his camp, where three hundred chosen patriots of Esperando were awaiting our coming. For a month Carlos had been drilling them there in the tactics of war, and filling them with the spirit of revolution and liberty.

" 'My Captain—*compadre mío!*' shouted Carlos, while yet my boat was being lowered. 'You should see them in the drill by *companies*—in the column wheel—in the march by fours—they are superb! Also in the manual of arms— but, alas! performed only with sticks of bamboo. The guns, *captain*—say that you have brought the guns!'

" 'A thousand Winchesters, Carlos,' I called to him. 'And two Gatlings.'

" '*Válgame Dios!*' he cried, throwing his cap in the air. 'We shall sweep the world!'

"At that moment Kearny tumbled from the steamer's side into the river. He could not swim, so the crew threw him a rope and drew him back aboard. I caught his eye and his look of pathetic but still bright and undaunted consciousness of his guilty luck. I told myself that although he might be a man to shun, he was also one to be admired.

"I gave orders to the sailing-master that the arms, ammunition, and provisions were to be landed at once. That was easy in the steamer's boats, except for the two Gatling guns. For their transportation ashore we carried a stout flatboat, brought for the purpose in the steamer's hold.

"In the meantime I walked with Carlos to the camp and made the soldiers a little speech in Spanish, which they received with enthusiasm; and then I had some wine and a cigarette in Carlos's tent. Later we walked back to the river to see how the unloading was being conducted.

"The small arms and provisions were already ashore, and the petty officers had squads of men conveying them to camp. One Gatling had been safely landed; the other was just being hoisted over the side of the vessel as we arrived. I noticed Kearny darting about on board, seeming to have the ambition of ten men, and to be doing the work of five. I think his zeal bubbled over when he saw Carlos and me. A rope's end was swinging loose from some part of the tackle. Kearny leaped impetuously and caught it. There was a crackle and a hiss and a smoke of scorching hemp, and the Gatling dropped straight as a plummet through the bottom of the flatboat and buried itself in twenty feet of water and five feet of river mud.

"I turned my back on the scene. I heard Carlo's loud cries as if from some extreme grief too poignant for words. I heard the complaining murmur of the crew and the maledictions of Torres, the sailing-master—I could not bear to look.

"By night some degree of order had been restored in camp. Military rules were not drawn strictly, and the men were grouped about the fires of their several messes, playing games of chance, singing their native songs, or discussing with voluble animation the contingencies of our march upon the capital.

"To my tent, which had been pitched for me close to that of my chief lieutenant, came Kearny, indomitable, smiling, bright-eyed, bearing no traces of the buffets of his evil star. Rather was his aspect that of a heroic martyr whose tribulations were so high-sourced and glorious that he even took a splendor and a prestige from them.

"'Well, Captain,' said he, 'I guess you realize that Bad-Luck Kearny is still on deck. It was a shame, now, about that gun. She only needed to be slewed two inches to cle r the rail; and that's why I grabbed that rope's end. Who'd have thought that a sailor—even a Sicilian lubber on a banana coaster—would have fastened a line in a bow-knot? Don't think I'm trying to dodge the responsibility, Captain. It's my luck.'

"'There are men, Kearny,' said I, gravely, 'who pass through life blaming upon luck and chance the mistakes that result from their own faults and incompetency. I do not say that you are such a man. But if all your mishaps are traceable to that tiny star, the sooner we endow our colleges with chairs of moral astronomy, the better.'

"'It isn't the size of the star that counts,' said Kearny; 'it's the quality. Just the way it is with women. That's why they gave the biggest planets masculine names, and the little stars feminine ones—to even things up when it comes to getting their work in. Suppose they had called my star Agamemnon or Bill McCarty or something like that instead of Phœbe. Every time one of those old boys touched their calamity button and sent me down one of their wireless pieces of bad luck, I could talk back and tell 'em what I thought of 'em in suitable terms. But you can't address such remarks to a Phœbe.'

"'It pleases you to make a joke of it, Kearny,' said I, without smiling. 'But it is no joke to me to think of my Gatling mired in the river ooze.'

"'As to that,' said Kearny, abandoning his light mood at once, 'I have already done what I could. I have had some experience in hoisting stone in quarries. Torres and I have already spliced three hawsers and stretched them from the steamer's stern to a tree on shore. We will rig a tackle and have the gun on terra firma before noon to-morrow.'

"One could not remain long at outs with Bad-Luck Kearny.

"'Once more,' said I to him, 'we will waive this question of luck. Have you ever had experience in drilling raw troops?'

"'I was first sergeant and drill-master,' said Kearny, 'in the Chilean army for one year. And captain of artillery for another.'

"'What became of your command?' I asked.

"'Shot down to a man,' said Kearny, 'during the revolutions against Balmaceda.'

"Somehow the misfortunes of the evil-starred one seemed to turn to me their comedy side. I lay back upon my goat's-hide cot and laughed until the woods echoed. Kearny grinned. 'I told you how it was,' he said.

" 'To-morrow,' I said, 'I shall detail one hundred men under your command for manual-of-arms drill and company evolutions. You will rank as lieutenant. Now, for God's sake, Kearny,' I urged him, 'try to combat this superstition if it is one. Bad luck may be like any other visitor—preferring to stop where it is expected. Get your mind off stars. Look upon Esperando as your planet of good fortune.'

" 'I thank you, Captain,' said Kearny quietly. 'I will try to make it the best handicap I ever ran.'

"By noon the next day the submerged Gatling was rescued, as Kearny had promised. Then Carlos and Manuel Ortiz and Kearny (my lieutenants) distributed Winchesters among the troops and put them through an incessant rifle drill. We fired no shots, blank or solid, for of all coasts Esperando is the stillest; and we had no desire to sound any warnings in the ear of that corrupt government until they should carry with them the message of Liberty and the downfall of Oppression.

"In the afternoon came a mule-rider bearing a written message to me from Don Rafael Valdevia in the capital, Aguas Frias.

"Whenever that man's name comes to my lips, words of tribute to his greatness, his noble simplicity, and his conspicuous genius follow irrepressibly. He was a traveller, a student of peoples and governments, a master of sciences, a poet, an orator, a leader, a soldier, a critic of the world's campaigns and the idol of the people of Esperando. I had been honored by his friendship for years. It was I who first turned his mind to the thought that he should leave for his monument a new Esperando—a country freed from the rule of unscrupulous tyrants, and a people made happy and prosperous by wise and impartial legislation. When he had consented he threw himself into the cause with the undivided zeal with which he endowed all of his acts. The coffers of his fortune were opened to those of us to whom were entrusted the secret moves of the game. His popularity was already so great that he had practically forced President Cruz to offer him the portfolio of Minister of War.

"The time, Don Rafael said in his letter, was ripe. Success, he prophesied, was certain. The people were beginning to clamor publicly against Cruz's misrule. Bands of citizens in the capital were even going about of nights hurling stones at public buildings and expressing their dissatisfaction. A bronze statue of President Cruz in the Botanical Gardens had been lassoed about the neck and overthrown. It only remained for me to arrive with my force and my thousand rifles, and for himself to come forward and proclaim himself the people's savior, to overthrow Cruz in a single day. There would be but a half-hearted resistance from the six hundred government troops stationed in the capital. The country was ours. He presumed that by this time my steamer had arrived at Quintana's camp. He proposed the eighteenth of July for the attack. That would give us six days in which to strike camp and march to Aguas Frias. In the meantime Don Rafael remained my good friend and *compadre en la causa de la libertad*.

"On the morning of the 14th we began our march toward the sea-following range of mountains, over the sixty-mile trail to the capital. Our small arms and provisions were laden on pack mules. Twenty men harnessed to each Gatling gun rolled them smoothly along the flat, alluvial lowlands. Our troops, well shod and well fed, moved with alacrity and heartiness. I and my three lieutenants were mounted on the tough mountain ponies of the country.

"A mile out of camp one of the pack mules, becoming stubborn, broke away from the train and plunged from the path into the thicket. The alert Kearny spurred quickly after it and intercepted its flight. Rising in his stirrups, he released one foot and bestowed upon the mutinous animal a hearty kick. The mule tottered and fell with a crash broadside upon the ground. As we gathered around it, it walled its great eyes almost humanly toward Kearny and ex-

pired. That was bad; but worse, to our minds, was the concomitant disaster.
Part of the mule's burden had been one hundred pounds of the finest coffee to
be had in the tropics. The bag burst and spilled the priceless brown mass of the
ground berries among the dense vines and weeds of the swampy land. *Mala
suerte!* When you take away from an Esperandan his coffee, you abstract his
patriotism and 50 per cent. of his value as a soldier. The men began to rake up
the precious stuff; but I beckoned Kearny back along the trail where they would
not hear. The limit had been reached.

"I took from my pocket a wallet of money and drew out some bills.

" 'Mr. Kearny,' said I, 'here are some funds belonging to Don Rafael Valdevia,
which I am expending in his cause. I know of no better service it can buy for
him than this. Here is one hundred dollars. Luck or no luck, we part company
here. Star or no star, calamity seems to travel by your side. You will return
to the steamer. She touches at Amotapa to discharge her lumber and iron, and
then puts back to New Orleans. Hand this note to the sailing-master, who will
give you passage.' I wrote on a leaf torn from my book, and placed it and the
money in Kearny's hand.

" 'Good-bye,' I said, extending my own. 'It is not that I am displeased with
you; but there is no place in this expedition for—let us say, the Señorita Phœbe.'
I said this with a smile, trying to smooth the thing for him. 'May you have
better luck, *compañero.*'

"Kearny took the money and the paper.

" 'It was just a little touch,' said he, 'just a little lift with the toe of my
boot—but what's the odds?—that blamed mule would have died if I had only
dusted his ribs with a powder puff. It was my luck. Well, Captain, I would
have liked to be in that little fight with you over in Aguas Frias. Success to the
cause. *Adiós!*'

"He turned around and set off down the trail without looking back. The unfortunate mule's pack-saddle was transferred to Kearny's pony, and we again
took up the march.

"Four days we journeyed over the foot-hills and mountains, fording icy torrents, winding around the crumbling brows of ragged peaks, creeping along the
rocky flanges that overlooked awful precipices, crawling breathlessly over tottering bridges that crossed bottomless chasms.

"On the evening of the seventeenth we camped by a little stream on the bare
hills five miles from Aguas Frias. At daybreak we were to take up the march
again.

"At midnight I was standing outside my tent inhaling the fresh cold air. The
stars were shining bright in the cloudless sky, giving the heavens their proper
aspect of illimitable depth and distance when viewed from the vague darkness of
the blotted earth. Almost at its zenith was the planet Saturn; and with a half-
smile I observed the sinister red sparkle of his malignant attendant—the demon
star of Kearny's ill luck. And then my thoughts strayed across the hills to the
scene of our coming triumph where the heroic and noble Don Rafael awaited our
coming to set a new and shining star in the firmament of nations.

"I heard a slight rustling in the deep grass to my right. I turned and saw
Kearny coming toward me. He was ragged and dew-drenched and limping. His
hat and one boot were gone. About one foot he had tied some makeshift of cloth
and grass. But his manner as he approached was that of a man who knows his
own virtues well enough to be superior to rebuffs.

" 'Well, sir,' I said, staring at him coldly, 'if there is anything in persistence, I
see no reason why you should not succeed in wrecking and ruining us yet.'

" 'I kept half a day's journey behind,' said Kearny, fishing out a stone from
the covering of his lame foot, 'so the bad luck wouldn't touch you. I couldn't
help it, Captain; I wanted to be in on this game. It was a pretty tough trip,

especially in the department of the commissary. In the low grounds there were always bananas and oranges. Higher up it was worse; but your men left a good deal of goat meat hanging on the bushes in the camps. Here's your hundred dollars. You're nearly there now, Captain. Let me in on the scrapping to-morrow.'

"'Not for a hundred times a hundred would I have the tiniest thing go wrong with my plans now,' I said, 'whether caused by evil planets or the blunders of mere man. But yonder is Aguas Frias, five miles away, and a clear road. I am of the mind to defy Saturn and all his satellites to spoil our success now. At any rate, I will not turn away to-night as weary a traveller and as good a soldier as you are, Lieutenant Kearny. Manuel Ortiz's tent is there by the brightest fire. Rout him out and tell him to supply you with food and blankets and clothes. We march again at daybreak.'

"Kearny thanked me briefly but feelingly and moved away.

"He had gone scarcely a dozen steps when a sudden flash of bright light illumined the surrounding hills; a sinister, growing, hissing sound like escaping steam filled my ears. Then followed a roar as of distant thunder, which grew louder every instant. This terrifying noise culminated in a tremendous explosion, which seemed to rock the hills as an earthquake would; the illumination waxed to a glare so fierce that I clapped my hands to my eyes to save them. I thought the end of the world had come. I could think of no natural phenomenon that would explain it. My wits were staggering. The deafening explosion trailed off into the rumbling roar that had preceded it; and through this I heard the frightened shouts of my troops as they stumbled from their resting-places and rushed wildly about. Also I heard the harsh tones of Kearny's voice crying: 'They'll blame it on me, of course, and what the devil it is, it's not Francis Kearny that can give you an answer.'

"I opened my eyes. The hills were still there, dark and solid. It had not been, then, a volcano or an earthquake. I looked up at the sky and saw a comet-like trail crossing the zenith and extending westward—a fiery trail waning fainter and narrower each moment.

"'A meteor!' I called aloud. 'A meteor has fallen. There is no danger.'

"And then all other sounds were drowned by a great shout from Kearny's throat. He had raised both hands above his head and was standing tiptoe.

"'PHŒBE'S GONE!' he cried, with all his lungs. 'She's busted and gone to hell. Look, Captain, the little red-headed hoodoo has blown herself to smithereens. She found Kearny too tough to handle, and she puffed up with spite and meanness till her boiler blew up. It'll be Bad-Luck Kearny no more. Oh, let us be joyful!

"'Humpty Dumpty sat on a wall;
Humpty busted, and that'll be all!'

"I looked up, wondering, and picked out Saturn in his place. But the small red twinkling luminary in his vicinity, which Kearny had pointed out to me as his evil star, had vanished. I had seen it there but half an hour before; there was no doubt that one of those awful and mysterious spasms of nature had hurled it from the heavens.

"I clapped Kearny on the shoulder.

"'Little man,' said I, 'let this clear the way for you. It appears that astrology has failed to subdue you. Your horoscope must be cast anew with pluck and loyalty for controlling stars. I play you to win. Now, get to your tent, and sleep. Daybreak is the word.'

"At nine o'clock on the morning of the eighteenth of July I rode into Aguas Frias with Kearny at my side. In his clean linen suit and with his military poise and keen eye he was a model of a fighting adventurer. I had visions of him riding as commander of President Valdevias body-guard when the plums of the new republic should begin to fall.

"Carlos followed with the troops and supplies. He was to halt in a wood outside the town and remain concealed there until he received the word to advance.

"Kearny and I rode down the Calle Ancha toward the *residencia* of Don Rafael at the other side of the town. As we passed the superb white buildings of the University of Esperando, I saw at an open window the gleaming spectacles and bald head of Herr Bergowitz, professor of the natural sciences and friend of Don Rafael and of me and of the cause. He waved his hand to me, with his broad, bland smile.

"There was no excitement apparent in Aguas Frias. The people went about leisurely as at all times; the market was thronged with bareheaded women buying fruit and *carne;* we heard the twang and tinkle of string bands in the patios of the *cantinas.* We could see that it was a waiting game that Don Rafael was playing.

"His *residencia* was a large but low building around a great courtyard in grounds crowded with ornamental trees and tropic shrubs. At his door an old woman who came informed us that Don Rafael had not yet risen.

"'Tell him,' said I, 'that Captain Maloné and a friend wish to see him at once. Perhaps he has overslept.'

"She came back looking frightened.

"'I have called,' she said, 'and rung his bell many times, but he does not answer.'

"I knew where his sleeping-room was. Kearny and I pushed by her and went to it. I put my shoulder against the thin door and forced it open.

"In an armchair by a great table covered with maps and books sat Don Rafael with his eyes closed. I touched his hand. He had been dead many hours. On his head above one ear was a wound caused by a heavy blow. It had ceased to bleed long before.

"I made the old woman call a *mozo,* and dispatched him in haste to fetch Herr Bergowitz.

"He came, and we stood about as if we were half stunned by the awful shock. Thus can the letting of a few drops of blood from one man's veins drain the life of a nation.

"Presently Herr Bergowitz stooped and picked up a darkish stone the size of an orange which he saw under the table. He examined it closely through his great glasses with the eye of science.

"'A fragment,' said he, 'of detonating meteor. The most remarkable one in twenty years exploded above this city a little after midnight this morning.'

"The professor looked quickly up at the ceiling. We saw the blue sky through a hole the size of an orange nearly above Don Rafael's chair.

"I heard a familiar sound, and turned. Kearny had thrown himself on the floor and was babbling his compendium of bitter, blood-freezing curses against the star of his evil luck.

"Undoubtedly Phœbe had been feminine. Even when hurtling on her way to fiery dissolution and everlasting doom, the last word had been hers."

Captain Maloné was not unskilled in narrative. He knew the point where a story should end. I sat reveling in his effective conclusion when he aroused me by continuing:

"Of course," said he, "our schemes were at an end. There was no one to take Don Rafael's place. Our little army melted away like dew before the sun.

"One day after I had returned to New Orleans I related this story to a friend who holds a professorship in Tulane University.

"When I had finished he laughed and asked whether I had any knowledge of

Kearny's luck afterward. I told him no, that I had seen him no more; but that when he left me, he had expressed confidence that his future would be successful now that his unlucky star had been overthrown.

"'No doubt,' said the professor, 'he is happier not to know one fact. If he derives his bad luck from Phœbe, the ninth satellite of Saturn, that malicious lady is still engaged in overlooking his career. The star close to Saturn that he imagined to be her was near that planet simply by the chance of its orbit—probably at different times he has regarded many other stars that happened to be in Saturn's neighborhood as his evil one. The real Phœbe is visible only through a very good telescope.'

"About a year afterward," continued Captain Maloné, "I was walking down a street that crossed the Poydras Market. An immensely stout, pink-faced lady in black satin crowded me from the narrow sidewalk with a frown. Behind her trailed a little man laden to the gunwales with bundles and bags of goods and vegetables.

"It was Kearny—but changed. I stopped and shook one of his hands, which still clung to a bag of garlic and red peppers.

"'How is the luck, old *compañero?*' I asked him. I had not the heart to tell him the truth about his star.

"'Well,' said he, 'I am married, as you may guess.'

"'Francis!' called the big lady, in deep tones, 'are you going to stop in the street talking all day?'

"'I am coming, Phœbe dear,' said Kearny hastening after her."

Captain Maloné ceased again.

"After all, do you believe in luck?" I asked.

"Do you?" answered the captain, with his ambiguous smile shaded by the brim of his soft straw hat.

A DOUBLE-DYED DECEIVER

THE trouble began in Laredo. It was the Llano Kid's fault, for he should have confined his habit of manslaughter to Mexicans. But the Kid was past twenty; and to have only Mexicans to one's credit at twenty is to blush unseen on the Rio Grande border.

It happened in old Justo Valdo's gambling house. There was a poker game at which sat players who were not all friends, as happens often where men ride in from afar to shoot Folly as she gallops. There was a row over so small a matter as a pair of queens; and when the smoke had cleared away it was found that the Kid had committed an indiscretion, and his adversary had been guilty of a blunder. For, the unfortunate combatant, instead of being a Greaser, was a high-blooded youth from the cow ranches, of about the Kid's own age and possessed of friends and champions. His blunder in missing the Kid's right ear only a sixteenth of an inch when he pulled his gun did not lessen the indiscretion of the better marksman.

The Kid, not being equipped with a retinue, nor bountifully supplied with personal admirers and supporters—on account of a rather umbrageous reputation, even for the border—considered it not incompatible with his indisputable gameness to perform that judicious tractional act known as "pulling his freight."

Quickly the avengers gathered and sought him. Three of them overtook him within a rod of the station. The Kid turned and showed his teeth in that brilliant but mirthless smile that usually preceded his deeds of insolence and violence, and his pursuers fell back without making it necessary for him even to reach for his weapon.

But in this affair the Kid had not felt the grim thirst for encounter that usually urged him on to battle. It had been a purely chance row, born of the cards and certain epithets impossible for a gentleman to brook that had passed between the two. The Kid had rather liked the slim, haughty, brown-faced young chap whom his bullet had cut off in the first pride of manhood. And now he wanted no more blood. He wanted to get away and have a good long sleep somewhere in the sun on the mesquite grass with his handkerchief over his face. Even a Mexican might have crossed his path in safety while he was in this mood.

The Kid openly boarded the north-bound passenger train that departed five minutes later. But at Webb, a few miles out, where it was flagged to take on a traveller, he abandoned that manner of escape. There were telegraph stations ahead; and the Kid looked askance at electricity and steam. Saddle and spur were his rocks of safety.

The man whom he had shot was a stranger to him. But the Kid knew that he was of the Coralitos outfit from Hidalgo; and that the punchers from that ranch were more relentless and vengeful than Kentucky feudists when wrong or harm was done to one of them. So, with the wisdom that has characterized many great fighters, the Kid decided to pile up as many leagues as possible of chaparral and pear between himself and the retaliation of the Coralitos bunch.

Near the station was a store; and near the store, scattered among the mesquits and elms, stood the saddled horses of the customers. Most of them waited, half asleep, with sagging limbs and drooping heads. But one, a long-legged roan with a curved neck, snorted and pawed the turf. Him the Kid mounted, gripped with his knees, and slapped gently with the owner's own quirt.

If the slaying of the temerarious card-player had cast a cloud over the Kid's standing as a good and true citizen, this last act of his veiled his figure in the darkest shadows of disrepute. On the Rio Grande border if you take a man's life you sometimes take trash; but if you take his horse, you take a thing the loss of which renders him poor, indeed, and which enriches you not—if you are caught. For the Kid there was no turning back now.

With the springing roan under him he felt little care or uneasiness. After a five-mile gallop he drew in to the plainsman's jogging trot, and rode north-eastward toward the Nueces River bottoms. He knew the country well—it's most tortuous and obscure trails through the great wilderness of brush and pear, and its camps and lonesome ranches where one might find safe entertainment. Always he bore to the east; for the Kid had never seen the ocean, and he had a fancy to lay his hand upon the mane of the great Gulf, the gamesome colt of the greater waters.

So after three days he stood on the shore at Corpus Christi, and looked out across the gentle ripples of a quiet sea.

Captain Boone, of the schooner *Flyaway*, stood near his skiff, which one of his crew was guarding in the surf. When ready to sail he had discovered that one of the necessaries of life, in the parallelogrammatic shape of plug tobacco, had been forgotten. A sailor had been dispatched for the missing cargo. Meanwhile the captain paced the sands, chewing profanely at his pocket store.

A slim, wiry youth in high-heeled boots came down to the water's edge. His face was boyish, but with a premature severity that hinted at a man's experience. His complexion was naturally dark; and the sun and wind of an outdoor life had burned it to a coffee-brown. His hair was as black and straight as an Indian's; his face had not yet been upturned to the humiliation of a razor; his eyes were a cold and steady blue. He carried his left arm somewhat away from his body, for pearl-handled .45s are frowned upon by town marshals, and are a little bulky when packed in the left armhole of one's vest. He looked beyond Captain Boone at the gulf with the impersonal and expressionless dignity of a Chinese emperor.

"Thinkin' of buyin' that 'ar gulf, buddy?" asked the captain, made sarcastic by his narrow escape from the tobaccoless voyage.

"Why, no," said the Kid gently, "I reckon not. I never saw it before. I was just looking at it. Not thinking of selling it, are you?"

"Not this trip," said the captain. "I'll send it to you C. O. D. when I get back to Buenas Tierras. Here comes that capstan-footed lubber with the chewin'. I ought to've weighed anchor an hour ago."

"Is that your ship out there?" asked the Kid.

"Why, yes," answered the captain, "if you want to call a schooner a ship, and I don't mind lyin'. But you better say Miller and Gonzales, owners, and ordinary plain, Billy-de-damned old Samuel K. Boone, skipper."

"Where are you going to?" asked the refugee.

"Buenas Tierras, coast of South America—I forget what they called the country the last time I was there. Cargo—lumber, corrugated iron, and machetes."

"What kind of a country is it?" asked the Kid—"hot or cold?"

"Warmish, buddy," said the captain. "But a regular Paradise Lost for elegance of scenery and be-yooty of geography. Ye're wakened every morning by the sweet singin' of red birds with seven purple tails, and the sighin' of breezes in the posies and roses. And the inhabitants never work, for they can reach out and pick steamer baskets of the choicest hothouse fruit without gettin' out of bed. And there's no Sunday and no ice and no rent and no troubles and no use and no nothin'. It's a great country for a man to go to sleep with, and wait for somethin' to turn up. The bananys and oranges and hurricanes and pineapples that ye eat comes from there."

"That sounds to me!" said the Kid, at last betraying interest. "What'll the expressage be to take me out there with you?"

"Twenty-four dollars," said Captain Boone; "grub and transportation. Second cabin. I haven't got a first cabin."

"You've got my company," said the Kid, pulling out a buckskin bag.

With three hundred dollars he had gone to Laredo for his regular "blowout." The duel in Valdos's had cut short his season of hilarity, but it had left him with nearly $200 for aid in the flight that it had made necessary.

"All right, buddy," said the captain. "I hope your ma won't blame me for this little childish escapade of yours." He beckoned to one of the boat's crew. "Let Sanchez lift you out to the skiff so you won't get your feet wet."

Thacker, the United States consul at Buenas Tierras, was not yet drunk. It was only eleven o'clock; and he never arrived at his desired state of beatitude —a state where he sang ancient maudlin vaudeville songs and pelted his screaming parrot with banana peels—until the middle of the afternoon. So, when he looked up from his hammock at the sound of a slight cough, and saw the Kid standing in the door of the consulate, he was still in a condition to extend the hospitality and courtesy due from the representative of a great nation. "Don't disturb yourself," said the Kid easily. "I just dropped in. They told me it was customary to light at your camp before starting in to round up the town. I just came in on a ship from Texas."

"Glad to see you, Mr.——." said the consul.

The Kid laughed.

"Sprague Dalton," he said. "It sounds funny to me to hear it. I'm called the Llano Kid in the Rio Grande country."

"I'm Thacker," said the consul. "Take that cane-bottom chair. Now if you've come to invest, you want somebody to advise you. These dingies will cheat you out of the gold in your teeth if you don't understand their ways. Try a cigar?"

"Much obliged," said the Kid, "but if it wasn't for my corn shucks and the little bag in my back pocket I couldn't live a minute." He took out his "makings," and rolled a cigarette.

"They speak Spanish here," said the consul. "You'll need an interpreter. If there's anything I can do, why, I'd be delighted. If you're buying fruit lands or looking for a concession of any sort, you'll want somebody who knows the ropes to look out for you."

"I speak Spanish," said the Kid, "about nine times better than I do English. Everybody speaks it on the range where I come from. And I'm not in the market for anything."

"You speak Spanish?" said Thacker, thoughtfully. He regarded the Kid absorbedly.

"You look like a Spaniard, too," he continued. "And you're from Texas. And you can't be more than twenty or twenty-one. I wonder if you've got any nerve."

"You got a deal of some kind to put through?" asked the Texan, with unexpected shrewdness.

"Are you open to a proposition?" said Thacker.

"What's the use to deny it?" said the Kid. "I got into a little gun frolic down in Laredo, and plugged a white man. There wasn't any Mexican handy. And I come down to your parrot-and-monkey range just for to smell the morning-glories and marigolds. Now, do you *sabe?*"

Thacker got up and closed the door.

"Let me see your hand," he said.

He took the Kid's left hand, and examined the back of it closely.

"I can do it," he said, excitely. "Your flesh is as hard as wood and as healthy as a baby's. It will heal in a week."

"If it's a fist fight you want to back me for," said the Kid, "don't put your money up yet. Make it gun work, and I'll keep you company. But no bare-handed scrapping, like ladies at a tea-party, for me."

"It's easier than that," said Thacker. "Just step here, will you?"

Through the window he pointed to a two-story white-stuccoed house with wide galleries rising amid the deep-green tropical foliage on a wooded hill that sloped gently from the sea.

"In that house," said Thacker, "a fine old Castilian gentleman and his wife are yearning to gather you into their arms and fill your pockets with money. Old Santos Urique lives there. He owns half the gold-mines in the country."

"You haven't been eating loco weed, have you?" asked the Kid.

"Sit down again," said Thacker, "and I'll tell you. Twelve years ago they lost a kid. No, he didn't die—although most of 'em here do from drinking the surface water. He was a wild little devil, even if he wasn't but eight years old. Everybody knows about it. Some Americans who were through here prospecting for gold had letters to Señor Urique, and the boy was a favorite with them. They filled his head with big stories about the States; and about a month after they left, the kid disappeared, too. He was supposed to have stowed himself away among the banana bunches on a fruit steamer, and gone to New Orleans. He was seen once afterward in Texas, it was thought, but they never heard anything more of him. Old Urique has spent thousands of dollars having him looked for. The madam was broken up worst of all. The kid was her life. She wears mourning yet. But they say she believes he'll come back to her some day, and never gives up hope. On the back of the boy's left hand was tattooed a flying eagle carrying a spear in his claws. That's old Urique's coat of arms or something that he inherited in Spain."

The Kid raised his left hand slowly and gazed at it curiously.

"That's it," said Thacker, reaching behind the official desk for his bottle of smuggled brandy. "You're not so slow. I can do it. What was I consul at Sandakan for? I never knew till now. In a week I'll have the eagle bird with the frog-sticker blended in so you'd think you were born with it. I brought a set of the needles and ink just because I was sure you'd drop in some day, Mr. Dalton."

"Oh, hell," said the Kid. "I thought I told you my name!"

"All right, 'Kid,' then. It won't be that long. How does 'Señorito Urique' sound, for a change?"

"I never played son any that I remember of," said the Kid. "If I had any parents to mention they went over the divide about the time I gave my first bleat. What is the plan of your round-up?"

Thacker leaned back against the wall and held his glass up to the light.

"We've come now," said he, "to the question of how far you're willing to go in a little matter of the sort."

"I told you why I came down here," said the Kid simply.

"A good answer," said the consul. "But you won't have to go that far. Here's the scheme. After I get the trade-mark tattooed on your hand I'll notify old Urique. In the meantime I'll furnish you with all of the family history I can find out, so you can be studying up points to talk about. You've got the looks, you speak the Spanish, you know the facts, you can tell about Texas, you've got the tattoo mark. When I notify them that the rightful heir has returned and is waiting to know whether he will be received and pardoned, what will happen? They'll simply rush down here and fall on your neck, and the curtain goes down for refreshments and a stroll in the lobby."

"I'm waiting," said the Kid. "I haven't had my saddle off in your camp long, pardner, and I never met you before; but if you intend to let it go at a parental blessing, why, I'm mistaken in my man, that's all."

"Thanks," said the consul. "I haven't met anybody in a long time that keeps up with an argument as well as you do. The rest of it is simple. If they take you in only for a while it's long enough. Don't give 'em time to hunt up the strawberry mark on your left shoulder. Old Urique keeps anywhere from $50,000 to $100,000 in his house all the time in a little safe that you could open with a shoe buttoner. Get it. My skill as a tattooer is worth half the boodle. We go halves and catch a tramp steamer for Rio Janeiro. Let the United States go to pieces if it can't get along without my services. Qué dice, señor?"

"It sounds to me!" said the Kid, nodding his head. "I'm out for the dust."

"All right, then," said Thacker. "You'll have to keep close until we get the bird on you. You can live in the back room here. I do my own cooking, and I'll make you as comfortable as a parsimonious government will allow me."

Thacker had set the time at a week, but it was two weeks before the design that he patiently tattooed upon the Kid's hand was to his notion. And then Thacker called a *muchacho*, and dispatched this note to the intended victim:

EL SEÑOR DON SANTOS URIQUE,
     La Casa Blanca,

MY DEAR SIR:

I beg permission to inform you that there is in my house as a temporary guest a young man who arrived in Buenas Tierras from the United States some days ago. Without wishing to excite any hopes that may not be realized, I think there is a possibility of his being your long-absent son. It might be well for you to call and see him. If he is, it is my opinion that his intention was to return to his home, but upon arriving here, his courage failed him from doubts as to how he would be received. Your true servant,

THOMPSON THACKER.

Half an hour afterward—quick time for Buenas Tierras—Señor Urique's ancient landau drove to the consul's door, with the barefooted coachman beating and shouting at the team of fat, awkward horses.

A tall man with a white moustache alighted, and assisted to the ground a lady who was dressed and veiled in unrelieved black.

The two hastened inside, and were met by Thacker with his best diplomatic bow. By his desk stood a slender young man with clear-cut, sunbrowned features and smoothly brushed black hair.

Señora Urique threw back her heavy veil with a quick gesture. She was past middle age, and her hair was beginning to silver, but her full, proud figure and clear olive skin retained traces of the beauty peculiar to the Basque province. But, once you had seen her eyes, and comprehended the great sadness that was revealed in their deep shadows and hopeless expression, you saw that the woman lived only in some memory.

She bent upon the young man a long look of the most agonized questioning. Then her great black eyes turned, and her gaze rested upon his left hand. And then with a sob, not loud, but seeming to shake the room, she cried *"Hijo mío!"* and caught the Llano Kid to her heart.

A month afterward the Kid came to the consulate in response to a message sent by Thacker.

He looked the young Spanish caballero. His clothes were imported, and the wiles of the jewellers had not been spent upon him in vain. A more than respectable diamond shone on his finger as he rolled a shuck cigarette.

"What's doing?" asked Thacker.

"Nothing much," said the Kid calmly. "I eat my first iguana steak to-day. They're them big lizards, you *sabe?* I reckon, though, that frijoles and side bacon would do me about as well. Do you care for iguanas, Thacker?"

"No, nor for some other kinds of reptiles," said Thacker.

It was three in the afternoon, and in another hour he would be in his state of beatitude.

"It's time you were making good, sonny," he went on, with an ugly look on his reddened face. "You're not playing up to me square. You've been the prodigal son for four weeks now, and you could have had veal for every meal on a gold dish if you'd wanted it. Now, Mr. Kid, do you think it's right to leave me out so long on a husk diet? What's the trouble? Don't you get your filial eyes on anything that looks like cash in the Casa Blanca? Don't tell me you don't. Everybody knows where old Urique keeps his stuff. It's U. S. currency, too; he don't accept anything else. What's doing? Don't say 'nothing' this time."

"Why, sure," said the Kid, admiring his diamond, "there's plenty of money up there. I'm no judge of collateral in bunches, but I will undertake for to say that I've seen the rise of $50,000 at a time in that tin grub box that my adopted father calls his safe. And he lets me carry the key sometimes just to show me that he knows I'm the real little Francisco that strayed from the herd a long time ago."

"Well, what are you waiting for?" asked Thacker angrily. "Don't you forget that I can upset your apple-cart any day I want to. If old Urique knew you were an impostor, what sort of things would happen to you? Oh, you don't know this country, Mr. Texas Kid. The laws here have got mustard spread between 'em. These people here'd stretch you out like a frog that had been stepped on, and give you about fifty sticks at every corner of the plaza. And they'd wear every stick out, too. What was left of you they'd feed to alligators."

"I might as well tell you now, pardner," said the Kid, sliding down low on his steamer chair, "that things are going to stay just as they are. They're about right now."

"What do you mean?" asked Thacker, rattling the bottom of his glass on his desk.

"The scheme's off," said the Kid. "And whenever you have the pleasure of speaking to me address me as Don Francisco Urique. I'll guarantee I'll answer to it. We'll let Colonel Urique keep his money. His little tin safe is as good as the time-locker in the First National Bank of Laredo as far as you and me are concerned."

"You're going to throw me down, then, are you?" said the consul.

"Sure," said the Kid, cheerfully. "Throw you down. That's it. And now I'll tell you why. The first night I was up at the colonel's house they introduced me to a bedroom. No blankets on the floor—a real room, with a bed and things in it. And before I was asleep, in comes this artificial mother of mine and tucks in the covers. 'Panchito,' she says, 'my little lost one, God has brought you back to me. I bless His name forever.' It was that, or some truck like that, she said. And down comes a drop or two of rain and hits me on the nose. And all that stuck by me, Mr. Thacker. And it's been that way ever since. And it's got to stay that way. Don't you think that it's for what's in it for me, either, that I say so. If you have any such ideas keep 'em to yourself. I haven't had much truck with women in my life, and no mothers to speak of, but here's a lady that we've got to keep fooled. Once she stood it; twice she won't. I'm a low-down wolf, and the devil may have sent me on this trail instead of God, but I'll travel it to the end. And now, don't forget that I'm Don Francisco Urique whenever you happen to mention my name."

"I'll expose you to-day, you—you double-dyed traitor," stammered Thacker.

The Kid arose and, without violence, took Thacker by the throat with a hand of steel, and shoved him slowly into a corner. Then he drew from under his left arm his pearl-handled .45 and poked the cold muzzle of it against the consul's mouth.

"I told you why I come here," he said, with his old freezing smile. "If I leave here, you'll be the reason. Never forget it, pardner. Now, what is my name?"

"Er—Don Francisco Urique," gasped Thacker.

From outside came a sound of wheels, and the shouting of someone, and the sharp thwacks of a wooden whipstock upon the backs of fat horses.

The Kid put up his gun, and walked toward the door. But he turned again and came back to the trembling Thacker, and held up his left hand with its back toward the consul.

"There's one more reason," he said, slowly, "why things have got to stand as they are. The fellow I killed in Laredo had one of them same pictures on his left hand."

Outside, the ancient landau of Don Santos Urique rattled to the door. The coachman ceased his bellowing. Señora Urique, in a voluminous gay gown of white lace and flying ribbons, leaned forward with a happy look in her great soft eyes.

"Are you within, dear son?" she called, in the rippling Castilian.

"Madre mía, yo vengo [mother, I come]," answered the young Don Francisco Urique.

THE PASSING OF BLACK EAGLE

For some months of a certain year a grim bandit infested the Texas border along the Rio Grande. Peculiarly striking to the optic nerve was this notorious marauder. His personality secured him the title of "Black Eagle, the Terror of the Border." Many fearsome tales are on record concerning the doings of him and his followers. Suddenly, in the space of a single minute, Black Eagle vanished from earth. He was never heard of again. His own band never even guessed the mystery of his disappearance. The border ranches and settlements feared he would come again to ride and ravage the mesquite flats. He never will. It is to disclose the fate of Black Eagle that this narrative is written.

The initial movement of the story is furnished by the foot of a bartender in St. Louis. His discerning eye fell upon the form of Chicken Ruggles as he pecked with avidity at the free lunch. Chicken was a "hobo." He had a long nose like the bill of a fowl, an inordinate appetite for poultry, and a habit of gratifying it without expense, which accounts for the name given him by his fellow vagrants.

Physicians agree that the partaking of liquids at meal times is not a healthy practice. The hygiene of the saloon promulgates the opposite. Chicken had neglected to purchase a drink to accompany his meal. The bartender rounded the counter, caught the injudicious diner by the ear with a lemon squeezer, led him to the door and kicked him into the street.

Thus the mind of Chicken was brought to realize the signs of coming winter. The night was cold; the stars shone with unkindly brilliancy; people were hurrying along the streets in two egotistic, jostling streams. Men had donned their overcoats, and Chicken knew to an exact percentage the increased difficulty of coaxing dimes from those buttoned-in vest pockets. The time had come for his annual exodus to the South.

A little boy, five or six years old, stood looking with covetous eyes in a confectioner's window. In one small hand he held an empty two-ounce vial; in the other he grasped tightly something flat and round, with a shining milled edge. The scene presented a field of operations commensurate to Chicken's talents and daring. After sweeping the horizon to make sure that no official tug was cruising near, he insidiously accosted his prey. The boy, having been early taught by his household to regard altruistic advances with extreme suspicion, received the overtures coldly.

Then Chicken knew that he must make one of those desperate, nerve-shattering plunges into speculation that fortune sometimes requires of those who would win her favor. Five cents was his capital, and this he must risk against the chance of winning what lay within the close grasp of the youngster's chubby hand. It was a fearful lottery, Chicken knew. But he must accomplish his end by strategy, since he had a wholesome terror of plundering infants by force. Once, in a park, driven by hunger, he had committed an onslaught upon a bottle of peptonized infant's food in the possession of an occupant of a baby carriage. The outraged infant had so promptly opened its mouth and pressed the button that communicated with the welkin that help arrived, and Chicken did his thirty days in a snug coop. Wherefore he was, as he said, "leary of kids."

Beginning artfully to question the boy concerning his choice of sweets, he gradually drew out the information he wanted. Mamma said he was to ask the drug-store man for ten cents' worth of paregoric in the bottle; he was to keep his hand shut tight over the dollar; he must not stop to talk to any one

in the street; he must ask the drug-store man to wrap up the change and put
it in the pocket of his trousers. Indeed, they had pockets—two of them! And
he liked chocolate creams best.

Chicken went into the store and turned plunger. He invested his entire capital
in C. A. N. D. Y. stocks, simply to pave the way to the greater risk following.

He gave the sweets to the youngster, and had the satisfaction of perceiving that
confidence was established. After that it was easy to obtain leadership of the
expedition, to take the investment by the hand and lead it to a nice drug store
he knew of in the same block. There Chicken, with a parental air, passed over
the dollar and called for the medicine, while the boy crunched his candy, glad
to be relieved of the responsibility of the purchase. And then the successful
investor searching his pockets, found an overcoat button—the extent of his
winter trousseau—and, wrapping it carefully, placed the ostensible change in
the pocket of confiding juvenility. Setting the youngster's face homeward, and
patting him benevolently on the back—for Chicken's heart was as soft as those
of his feathered namesakes—the speculator quit the market with a profit of
1,700 per cent. on his invested capital.

Two hours later an Iron Mountain freight engine pulled out of the railroad
yards, Texas bound, with a string of empties. In one of the cattle cars, half
buried in excelsior, Chicken lay at ease. Beside him in his nest was a quart
bottle of very poor whisky and a paper bag of bread and cheese. Mr. Ruggles,
in his private car, was on his trip south for the winter season.

For a week that car was trundled southward, shifted, laid over, and manipulated after the manner of rolling stock, but Chicken stuck to it, leaving it only
at necessary times to satisfy his hunger and thirst. He knew it must go down
to the cattle country, and San Antonio, in the heart of it, was his goal. There
the air was salubrious and mild; the people indulgent and long-suffering. The
bartenders there would not kick him. If he should eat too long or too often at
one place they would swear at him as if by rote and without heat. They swore
so drawlingly, and they rarely paused short of their full vocabulary, which was
copious, so that Chicken had often gulped a good meal during the process of the
vituperative prohibition. The season there was always spring-like; the plazas
were pleasant at night, with music and gayety: except during the slight and
infrequent cold snaps one could sleep comfortably out of doors in case the interiors should develop inhospitality.

At Texarkana his car was switched to the I. and G. N. Then still southward
it trailed until, at length, it crawled across the Colorado bridge at Austin, and
lined out, straight as an arrow, for the run to San Antonio.

When the freight halted at that town Chicken was fast asleep. In ten minutes
the train was off again for Laredo, the end of the road. Those empty cattle
cars were for distribution along the line at points from which the ranches
shipped their stock.

When Chicken awoke his car was stationary. Looking out between the slats
he saw it was a bright, moonlit night. Scrambling out, he saw his car with
three others abandoned on a little siding in a wild and lonesome country. A
cattle pen and chute stood on one side of the track. The railroad bisected a
vast, dim ocean of prairie, in the midst of which Chicken, with his futile rolling
stock, was as completely stranded as was Robinson with his land-locked boat.

A white post stood near the rails. Going up to it, Chicken read the letters
at the top, S. A. 90. Laredo was nearly as far to the south. He was almost a
hundred miles from any town. Coyotes began to yelp in the mysterious sea
around him. Chicken felt lonesome. He had lived in Boston without an education, in Chicago without nerve, in Philadelphia without a sleeping place, in
New York without a pull, and in Pittsburg sober, and yet he had never felt
so lonely as now.

Suddenly through the intense silence, he heard the whicker of a horse. The sound came from the side of the track toward the east, and Chicken began to explore timorously in that direction. He stepped high along the mat of curly mesquite grass, for he was afraid of everything there might be in this wilderness—snakes, rats, brigands, centipedes, mirages, cowboys, fandangoes, tarantulas, tamales—he had read of them in the story papers. Rounding a clump of prickly pear that reared high its fantastic and menacing array of rounded heads, he was struck to shivering terror by a snort and a thunderous plunge, as the horse, himself startled, bounded away some fifty yards, and then resumed his grazing. But here was the one thing in the desert that Chicken did not fear. He had been reared on a farm; he had handled horses, understood them, and could ride.

Approaching slowly and speaking soothingly, he followed the animal, which, after its first flight, seemed gentle enough, and secured the end of the twenty-foot lariat that dragged after him in the grass. It required him but a few moments to contrive the rope into an ingenious nose-bridle, after the style of the Mexican *borsal*. In another he was upon the horse's back and off at a splendid lope, giving the animal free choice of direction. "He will take me somewhere," said Chicken to himself.

It would have been a thing of joy, that untrammelled gallop over the moonlit prairie, even to Chicken, who loathed exertion, but that his mood was not for it. His head ached; a growing thirst was upon him; the "somewhere" whither his lucky mount might convey him was full of dismal peradventure.

And now he noted that the horse moved to a definite goal. Where the prairie lay smooth he kept his course straight as an arrow toward the east. Deflected by hill or arroyo or impracticable spinous brakes, he quickly flowed again into the current, charted by his unerring instinct. At last, upon the side of a gentle rise, he suddenly subsided to a complacent walk. A stone's cast away stood a little mott of coma trees; beneath it a *jacal* such as the Mexicans erect—a one-room house of upright poles daubed with clay and roofed with grass or tule reeds. An experienced eye would have estimated the spot as the headquarters of a small sheep ranch. In the moonlight the ground in the nearby corral showed pulverized to a level smoothness by the hoofs of the sheep. Everywhere was carelessly distributed the paraphernalia of the place—ropes, bridles, saddles, sheep pelts, wool sacks, feed troughs, and camp litter. The barrel of drinking water stood in the end of the two-horse wagon near the door. The harness was piled, promiscuous, upon the wagon tongue, soaking up the dew.

Chicken slipped to earth, and tied the horse to a tree. He halloed again and again, but the house remained quiet. The door stood open, and he entered cautiously. The light was sufficient for him to see that no one was at home. He struck a match and lighted a lamp that stood on a table. The room was that of a bachelor ranchman who was content with the necessaries of life. Chicken rummaged intelligently until he found what he had hardly dared hope for—a small brown jug that still contained something near a quart of his desire.

Half an hour later, Chicken—now a gamecock of hostile aspect—emerged from the house with unsteady steps. He had drawn upon the absent ranchman's equipment to replace his own ragged attire. He wore a suit of coarse brown ducking, the coat being a sort of rakish bolero, jaunty to a degree. Boots he had donned, and spurs that whirred with every lurching step. Buckled around him was a belt full of cartridges with a big six-shooter in each of its two holsters.

Prowling about, he found blankets, a saddle and bridle with which he caparisoned his steed. Again mounting, he rode swiftly away, singing a loud and tuneless song.

Bud King's band of desperadoes, outlaws and horse and cattle thieves were in camp at a secluded spot on the bank of the Frio. Their depredations in the Rio Grande country, while no bolder than usual, had been advertised more extensively, and Captain Kinney's company of rangers had been ordered down to look after them. Consequently, Bud King, who was a wise general, instead of cutting out a hot trail for the upholders of the law, as his men wished to do, retired for the time to the prickly fastnesses of the Frio valley.

Though the move was a prudent one, and not incompatible with Bud's well-known courage, it raised dissension among the members of the band. In fact, while they thus lay ingloriously *perdu* in the brush, the question of Bud King's fitness for the leadership was argued, with closed doors, as it were, by his followers. Never before had Bud's skill or efficiency been brought to criticism; but his glory was waning (and such is glory's fate) in the light of a newer star. The sentiment of the band was crystallizing into the opinion that Black Eagle could lead them with more luster, profit, and distinction.

This Black Eagle—sub-titled the "Terror of the Border"—had been a member of the gang about three months.

One night while they were in camp on the San Miguel water-hole a solitary horseman on the regulation fiery steed dashed in among them. The newcomer was of a portentous and devastating aspect. A beak-like nose with a predatory curve projected above a mass of bristling, blue-black whiskers. His eye was cavernous and fierce. He was spurred, sombreroed, booted, garnished with revolvers, abundantly drunk, and very much unafraid. Few people in the country drained by the Rio Bravo would have cared thus to invade alone the camp of Bud King. But this fell bird swooped fearlessly upon them and demanded to be fed.

Hospitality in the prairie country is not limited. Even if your enemy pass your way you must feed him before you shoot him. You must empty your larder into him before you empty your lead. So the stranger of undeclared intentions was set down to a mighty feast.

A talkative bird he was, full of most marvellous loud tales and exploits, and speaking a language at times obscure but never colorless. He was a new sensation to Bud King's men, who rarely encountered new types. They hung, delighted, upon his vainglorious boasting, the spicy strangeness of his lingo, his contemptuous familiarity with life, the world, and remote places, and the extravagant frankness with which he conveyed his sentiments.

To their guest the band of outlaws seemed to be nothing more than a congregation of country bumpkins whom he was "stringing for grub" just as he would have told his stories at the back door of a farmhouse to wheedle a meal. And, indeed, his ignorance was not without excuse, for the "bad man" of the Southwest does not run to extremes. Those brigands might justly have been taken for a little party of peaceable rustics assembled for a fish-fry or pecan gathering. Gentle of manner, slouching of gait, soft-voiced, unpicturesquely clothed; not one of them presented to the eye any witness of the desperate records they had earned.

For two days the glittering stranger within the camp was feasted. Then, by common consent, he was invited to become a member of the band. He consented, presenting for enrollment the prodigious name of "Captain Montressor." This name was immediately overruled by the band, and "Piggy" substituted as a compliment to the awful and insatiate appetite of its owner.

Thus did the Texas border receive the most spectacular brigand that ever rode its chaparral.

For the next three months Bud King conducted business as usual, escaping encounters with law officers and being content with reasonable profits. The band ran off some very good companies of horses from the ranges, and a few bunches of fine cattle which they got safely across the Rio Grande and disposed of to fair advantage. Often the band would ride into the little villages and Mexican settlements, terrorizing the inhabitants and plundering for the provisions and ammunition they needed. It was during these bloodless raids that Piggy's ferocious aspect and frightful voice gained him a renown more widespread and glorious than those other gentle-voiced and sad-faced desperadoes could have acquired in a lifetime.

The Mexicans, most apt in nomenclature, first called him The Black Eagle, and used to frighten the babes by threatening them with tales of the dreadful robber who carried off little children in his great beak. Soon the name extended, and Black Eagle, the Terror of the Border, became a recognized factor in exaggerated newspaper reports and ranch gossip.

The country from the Nueces to the Rio Grande was a wild but fertile stretch, given over to the sheep and cattle ranches. Range was free; the inhabitants were few; the law was mainly a letter, and the pirates met with little opposition until the flaunting and garish Piggy gave the band undue advertisement. Then McKinney's ranger company headed for those precincts, and Bud King knew that it meant grim and sudden war or else temporary retirement. Regarding the risk to be unnecessary, he drew off his band to an almost inaccessible spot on the bank of the Frio. Wherefore, as has been said, dissatisfaction arose among the members, and impeachment proceedings against Bud were premeditated, with Black Eagle in high favor for the succession. Bud King was not unaware of the sentiment, and he called aside Cactus Taylor, his trusted lieutenant, to discuss it.

"If the boys," said Bud, "ain't satisfied with me, I'm willin' to step out. They're buckin' against my way of handlin' 'em. And 'specially because I concludes to hit the brush while Sam Kinney is ridin' the line. I saves 'em from bein' shot or sent up on a state contract, and they up and says I'm no good."

"It ain't so much that," explained Cactus, "as it is they're plum locoed about Piggy. They want them whiskers and that nose of his to split the wind at the head of the column."

"There's somethin' mighty seldom about Piggy," declared Bud, musingly. "I never yet see anything on the hoof that he exactly grades up with. He can shore holler a plenty, and he straddles a hoss from where you laid the chunk. But he ain't never been smoked yet. You know, Cactus, we ain't had a row since he's been with us. Piggy's all right for skearin' the greaser kids and layin' waste a cross-roads store. I reckon he's the finest canned oyster buccaneer and cheese pirate that ever was, but how's his appetite for fightin'? I've knowed some citizens you'd think was starvin' for trouble get a bad case of dyspepsy the first dose of lead they had to take."

"He talks all spraddled out," said Cactus, "'bout the rookuses he's been in. He claims to have saw the elephant and hearn the owl."

"I know," replied Bud, using the cow-puncher's expressive phrase of skepticism, "but it sounds to me!"

This conversation was held one night in camp while the other members of the band—eight in number—were sprawling around the fire, lingering over their supper. When Bud and Cactus ceased talking they heard Piggy's formidable voice holding forth to the others as usual while he was engaged in checking, though never satisfying, his ravening appetite.

"Wat's de use," he was saying, "of chasin' little red cowses and hosses 'round for t'ousands of miles? Dere ain't nuttin' in it. Gallopin' t'rough dese bushes and briers, and gettin' a t'irst dat a brewery couldn't put out, and missin' meals! Say! You know what I'd do if I was main finger of dis bunch? I'd stick up a train. I'd blow de express car and make hard dollars where you guys gets wind. Youse makes me tired. Dis sook-cow kind of cheap sport gives me a pain."

Later on, a deputation waited on Bud. They stood on one leg, chewed mesquite twigs and circumlocuted, for they hated to hurt his feelings. Bud foresaw their business, and made it easy for them. Bigger risks and larger profits was what they wanted.

The suggestion of Piggy's about holding up a train had fired their imagination and increased their admiration for the dash and boldness of the instigator. They were such simple, artless, and custom-bound bush-rangers that they had never before thought of extending their habits beyond the running off of live-stock and the shooting of such of their acquaintances as ventured to interfere.

Bud acted "on the level," agreeing to take a subordinate place in the gang until Black Eagle should have been given a trial as leader.

After a great deal of consultation, studying of time-tables and discussion of the country's topography, the time and place for carrying out their new enterprise was decided upon. At that time there was a feedstuff famine in Mexico and a cattle famine in certain parts of the United States, and there was a brisk international trade. Much money was being shipped along the railroads that connected the two republics. It was agreed that the most promising place for the contemplated robbery was at Espina, a little station on the I. and G. N., about forty miles north of Laredo. The train stopped there one minute; the country around was wild and unsettled; the station consisted of but one house in which the agent lived.

Black Eagle's band set out, riding by night. Arriving in the vicinity of Espina they rested their horses all day in a thicket a few miles distant.

The train was due at Espina at 10:30 P. M. They could rob the train and be well over the Mexican border with their booty by daylight the next morning.

To do Black Eagle justice, he exhibited no signs of flinching from the responsible honors that had been conferred upon him.

He assigned his men to their respective posts with discretion, and coached them carefully as to their duties. On each side of the track four of the band were to lie concealed in the chaparral. Gotch-Ear Rodgers was to stick up the station agent. Bronco Charlie was to remain with the horses, holding them in readiness. At a spot where it was calculated the engine would be when the train stopped, Bud King was to lie hidden on one side, and Black Eagle himself on the other. The two would get the drop on the engineer and fireman, force them to descend and proceed to the rear. Then the express car would be looted, and the escape made. No one was to move until Black Eagle gave the signal by firing his revolver. The plan was perfect.

At ten minutes to train time every man was at his post, effectually concealed by the thick chaparral that grew almost to the rails. The night was dark and lowering, with a fine drizzle falling from the flying gulf clouds. Black Eagle crouched behind a bush within five yards of the track. Two sixshooters were belted around him. Occasionally he drew a large black bottle from his pocket and raised it to his mouth.

A star appeared far down the track which soon waxed into the headlight of the approaching train. It came on with an increasing roar; the engine bore down upon the ambushing desperadoes with a glare and a shriek like some avenging monster come to deliver them to justice. Black Eagle flattened himself upon the ground. The engine, contrary to their calculations, instead of stopping between him and Bud King's place of concealment, passed fully forty yards farther before it came to a stand.

The bandit leader rose to his feet and peered around the bush. His men all lay quiet, awaiting the signal. Immediately opposite Black Eagle was a thing that drew his attention. Instead of being a regular passenger train it was a mixed one. Before him stood a box car, the door of which, by some means, had been left slightly open. Black Eagle went up to it and pushed the door farther open. An odor came forth—a damp, rancid, familiar, musty, intoxicating, beloved odor stirring strongly at old memories of happy days and travels. Black Eagle sniffed at the witching smell as the returned wanderer smells of the rose that twines his boyhood's cottage home. Nostalgia seized him. He put his hand inside. Excelsior—dry, springy, curly, soft, enticing, covered the floor. Outside the drizzle had turned to a chilling rain.

The train bell clanged. The bandit chief unbuckled his belt and cast it, with its revolvers, upon the ground. His spurs followed quickly, and his broad sombrero. Black Eagle was moulting. The train started with a rattling jerk. The ex-Terror of the Border scrambled into the box car and closed the door. Stretched luxuriously upon the excelsior, with the black bottle clasped closely to his breast, his eyes closed, and a foolish, happy smile upon his terrible features Chicken Ruggles started upon his return trip.

Undisturbed, with the band of desperate bandits lying motionless, awaiting the signal to attack, the train pulled out from Espina. As its speed increased, and the black masses of chaparral went whizzing past on either side, the express messenger, lighting his pipe, looked through his window and remarked, feelingly:

"What a jim-dandy place for a hold-up!"

A RETRIEVED REFORMATION

A GUARD came to the prison shoe-shop, where Jimmy Valentine was assiduously stitching uppers, and escorted him to the front office. There the warden handed Jimmy his pardon, which had been signed that morning by the governor. Jimmy took it in a tired kind of way. He had served nearly ten months of a four-year sentence. He had expected to stay only about three months, at the longest. When a man with as many friends on the outside as Jimmy Valentine had is received in the "stir" it is hardly worth while to cut his hair.

"Now, Valentine," said the warden, "you'll go out in the morning. Brace up, and make a man of yourself. You're not a bad fellow at heart. Stop cracking safes, and live straight."

"Me?" said Jimmy, in surprise. "Why, I never cracked a safe in my life."

"Oh, no," laughed the warden. "Of course not. Let's see, now. How was it you happened to get sent up on that Springfield job? Was it because you wouldn't prove an alibi for fear of compromising somebody in extremely high-toned society? Or was it simply a case of a mean old jury that had it in for you? It's always one or the other with you innocent victims."

"Me?" said Jimmy, still blankly virtuous. "Why, warden, I never was in Springfield in my life!"

"Take him back, Cronin," smiled the warden, "and fix him up with outgoing clothes. Unlock him at seven in the morning, and let him come to the bull-pen. Better think over my advice, Valentine."

At a quarter past seven on the next morning Jimmy stood in the warden's outer office. He had on a suit of the villainously fitting, ready-made clothes and a pair of the stiff, squeaky shoes that the state furnishes to its discharged compulsory guests.

The clerk handed him a railroad ticket and the five-dollar bill with which the law expected him to rehabilitate himself into good citizenship and prosperity.

The warden gave him a cigar, and shook hands. Valentine, 9762, was chronicled on the books "Pardoned by Governor," and Mr. James Valentine walked out into the sunshine.

Disregarding the song of the birds, the waving green trees, and the smell of the flowers, Jimmy headed straight for a restaurant. There he tasted the first sweet joys of liberty in the shape of a broiled chicken and a bottle of white wine —followed by a cigar a grade better than the one the warden had given him. From there he proceeded leisurely to the depot. He tossed a quarter into the hat of a blind man sitting by the door, and boarded his train. Three hours set him down in a little town near the state line. He went to the café of one Mike Dolan and shook hands with Mike, who was alone behind the bar.

"Sorry we couldn't make it sooner, Jimmy, me boy," said Mike. "But we had that protest from Springfield to buck against, and the governor nearly balked. Feeling all right?"

"Fine," said Jimmy. "Got my key?"

He got his key and went upstairs, unlocking the door of a room at the rear. Everything was just as he had left it. There on the floor was still Ben Price's collar-button that had been torn from that eminent detective's shirt-band when they had overpowered Jimmy to arrest him.

Pulling out from the wall a folding-bed, Jimmy slid back a panel in the wall and dragged out a dust-covered suit-case. He opened this and gazed fondly at the finest set of burglar's tools in the East. It was a complete set, made of specially tempered steel, the latest designs in drills, punches, braces and bits, jimmies, clamps, and augers, with two or three novelties invented by Jimmy himself, in which he took pride. Over nine hundred dollars they had cost him to have made at ——, a place where they make such things for the profession.

In half an hour Jimmy went downstairs and through the café. He was now dressed in tasteful and well-fitting clothes, and carried his dusted and cleaned suit-case in his hand.

"Got anything on?" asked Mike Dolan, genially.

"Me?" said Jimmy, in a puzzled tone. "I don't understand. I'm representing the New York Amalgamated Short Snap Biscuit Cracker and Frazzled Wheat Company."

This statement delighted Mike to such an extent that Jimmy had to take a seltzer-and-milk on the spot. He never touched "hard" drinks.

A week after the release of Valentine, 9762, there was a neat job of safe-burglary done in Richmond, Indiana, with no clue to the author. A scant eight hundred dollars was all that was secured. Two weeks after that a patented, improved, burglar-proof safe in Logansport was opened like a cheese to the tune of fifteen hundred dollars, currency; securities and silver untouched. That began to interest the rogue-catchers. Then an old-fashioned bank-safe in Jefferson City became active and threw out of its crater an eruption of bank-notes amounting to five thousand dollars. The losses were now high enough to bring the matter up into Ben Price's class of work. By comparing notes, a remarkable similarity in the methods of the burglaries was noticed. Ben Price investigated the scenes of the robberies, and was heard to remark:

"That's Dandy Jim Valentine's autograph. He's resumed business. Look at that combination knob—jerked out as easy as pulling up a radish in wet weather. He's got the only clamps that can do it. And look how clean those tumblers were punched out! Jimmy never has to drill but one hole. Yes, I guess I want Mr. Valentine. He'll do his bit next time without any short-time or clemency foolishness."

Ben Price knew Jimmy's habits. He had learned them while working up the Springfield case. Long jumps, quick get-aways, no confederates, and a taste for good society—these ways had helped Mr. Valentine to become noted as a successful dodger of retribution. It was given out that Ben Price had taken up the trail of the elusive cracksman, and other people with burglar-proof safes felt more at ease.

One afternoon Jimmy Valentine and his suit-case climbed out of the mail-hack in Elmore, a little town five miles off the railroad down in the black-jack country of Arkansas. Jimmy, looking like an athletic young senior just home from college, went down the board sidewalk toward the hotel.

A young lady crossed the street, passed him at the corner and entered a door over which was the sign "The Elmore Bank." Jimmy Valentine looked into her eyes, forgot what he was, and became another man. She lowered her eyes and colored slightly. Young men of Jimmy's style and looks were scarce in Elmore.

Jimmy collared a boy that was loafing on the steps of the bank as if he were one of the stock-holders, and began to ask him questions about the town, feeding him dimes at intervals. By and by the young lady came out, looking royally unconscious of the young man with the suitcase, and went her way.

"Isn't that young lady Miss Polly Simpson?" asked Jimmy, with specious guile.

"Naw," said the boy. "She's Annabel Adams. Her pa owns this bank. What'd you come to Elmore for? Is that a gold watch-chain? I'm going to get a bulldog. Got any more dimes?"

Jimmy went to the Planters' Hotel, registered as Ralph D. Spencer, and engaged a room. He leaned on the desk and declared his platform to the clerk. He said he had come to Elmore to look for a location to go into business. How was the shoe business, now, in the town? He had thought of the shoe business. Was there an opening?

The clerk was impressed by the clothes and manner of Jimmy. He, himself, was something of a pattern of fashion to the thinly gilded youth of Elmore, but he now perceived his shortcomings. While trying to figure out Jimmy's manner of tying his four-in-hand he cordially gave information.

Yes, there ought to be a good opening in the shoe line. There wasn't an exclusive shoe-store in the place. The dry-goods and general stores handled them. Business in all lines was fairly good. Hoped Mr. Spencer would decide to locate in Elmore. He would find it a pleasant town to live in, and the people very sociable.

Mr. Spencer thought he would stop over in the town a few days and look over the situation. No, the clerk needn't call the boy. He would carry up his suit-case, himself; it was rather heavy.

Mr. Ralph Spencer, the phœnix that arose from Jimmy Valentine's ashes—ashes left by the flame of a sudden and alterative attack of love—remained in Elmore, and prospered. He opened a shoe-store and secured a good run of trade.

Socially he was also a success, and made many friends. And he accomplished the wish of his heart. He met Miss Annabel Adams, and became more and more captivated by her charms.

At the end of a year the situation of Mr. Ralph Spencer was this: he had won the respect of the community, his shoe-store was flourishing, and he and Annabel were engaged to be married in two weeks. Mr. Adams, the typical, plodding, country banker, approved of Spencer. Annabel's pride in him almost equalled her affection. He was as much at home in the family of Mr. Adams and that of Annabel's married sister as if he were already a member.

One day Jimmy sat down in his room and wrote this letter, which he mailed to the safe address of one of his old friends in St. Louis:

DEAR OLD PAL:

I want you to be at Sullivan's place, in Little Rock, next Wednesday night, at nine o'clock. I want you to wind up some little matters for me. And, also, I want to make you a present of my kit of tools. I know you'll be glad to get them—you couldn't duplicate the lot for a thousand dollars. Say, Billy, I've quit the old business—a year ago. I've got a nice store. I'm making an honest living, and I'm going to marry the finest girl on earth two weeks from now. It's the only life, Billy—the straight one. I wouldn't touch a dollar of another man's money now for a million. After I get married I'm going to sell out and go West, where there won't be so much danger of having old scores brought up against me. I tell you, Billy, she's an angel. She believes in me; and I wouldn't do another crooked thing for the whole world. Be sure to be at Sully's, for I must see you. I'll bring along the tools with me.

Your old friend,
JIMMY.

On the Monday night after Jimmy wrote this letter, Ben Price jogged unobtrusively into Elmore in a livery buggy. He lounged about town in his quiet way until he found out what he wanted to know. From the drug-store across the street from Spencer's shoe-store he got a good look at Ralph D. Spencer.

"Going to marry the banker's daughter are you, Jimmy?" said Ben to himself, softly. "Well, I don't know!"

The next morning Jimmy took breakfast at the Adamses. He was going to Little Rock that day to order his wedding-suit and buy something nice for Annabel. That would be the first time he had left town since he came to Elmore. It had been more than a year now since those last professional "jobs," and he thought he could safely venture out.

After breakfast quite a family party went down town together—Mr. Adams, Annabel, Jimmy, and Annabel's married sister with her two little girls, aged five and nine. They came by the hotel where Jimmy still boarded, and he ran up to his room and brought along his suitcase. Then they went on to the bank. There stood Jimmy's horse and buggy and Dolph Gibson, who was going to drive him over to the railroad station.

All went inside the high, carved oak railings into the banking-room—Jimmy included, for Mr. Adams's future son-in-law was welcome anywhere. The clerks were pleased to be greeted by the good-looking, agreeable young man who was going to marry Miss Annabel. Jimmy set his suit-case down. Annabel, whose heart was bubbling with happiness and lively youth, put on Jimmy's hat and picked up the suit-case. "Wouldn't I make a nice drummer?" said Annabel. "My! Ralph, how heavy it is. Feels like it was full of gold bricks."

"Lot of nickel-plated shoe-horns in there," said Jimmy, coolly, "that I'm going to return. Thought I'd save express charges by taking them up. I'm getting awfully economical."

The Elmore Bank had just put in a new safe and vault. Mr. Adams was very proud of it, and insisted on an inspection by every one. The vault was a small one, but it had a new patented door. It fastened with three solid steel bolts thrown simultaneously with a single handle, and had a time-lock. Mr. Adams beamingly explained its workings to Mr. Spencer, who showed a courteous but not too intelligent interest. The two children, May and Agatha, were delighted by the shining metal and funny clock and knobs.

While they were thus engaged Ben Price sauntered in and leaned on his elbow, looking casually inside between the railings. He told the teller that he didn't want anything; he was just waiting for a man he knew.

Suddenly there was a scream or two from the women, and a commotion. Unperceived by the elders, May, the nine-year-old girl, in a spirit of play, had shut Agatha in the vault. She had then shot the bolts and turned the knob of the combination as she had seen Mr. Adams do.

The old banker sprang to the handle and tugged at it for a moment. "The door can't be opened," he groaned. "The clock hasn't been wound nor the combination set."

Agatha's mother screamed again, hysterically.

"Hush!" said Mr. Adams, raising his trembling hand. "All be quite for a moment. Agatha!" he called as loudly as he could. "Listen to me." During the following silence they could just hear the faint sound of the child wildly shrieking in the dark vault in a panic of terror.

"My precious darling!" wailed the mother. "She will die of fright! Open the door! Oh, break it open! Can't you men do something?"

"There isn't a man nearer than Little Rock who can open that door," said Mr. Adams, in a shaky voice. "My God! Spencer, what shall we do? That child—she can't stand it long in there. There isn't enough air, and, besides, she'll go into convulsions from fright."

Agatha's mother, frantic now, beat the door of the vault with her hands. Somebody wildly suggested dynamite. Annabel turned to Jimmy, her large eyes full of anguish, but not yet despairing. To a woman nothing seems quite impossible to the powers of the man she worships.

"Can't you do something, Ralph—*try*, won't you?"

He looked at her with a queer, soft smile on his lips and in his keen eyes.

"Annabel," he said, "give me that rose you are wearing, will you?"

Hardly believing that she heard him aright, she unpinned the bud from the bosom of her dress, and placed it in his hand. Jimmy stuffed it into his vest-pocket, threw off his coat and pulled up his shirt-sleeves. With that act Ralph D. Spencer passed away and Jimmy Valentine took his place.

"Get way from the door, all of you," he commanded, shortly.

He set his suit-case on the table, and opened it out flat. From that time on he seemed to be unconscious of the presence of any one else. He laid out the shining, queer implements swiftly and orderly, whistling softly to himself as he always did when at work. In a deep silence and immovable, the others watched him as if under a spell.

In a minute Jimmy's pet drill was biting smoothly into the steel door. In ten minutes—breaking his own burglarious record—he threw back the bolts and opened the door.

Agatha, almost collapsed, but safe, was gathered into her mother's arms.

Jimmy Valentine put on his coat, and walked outside the railings toward the front door. As he went he thought he heard a far-away voice that he once knew call "Ralph!" But he never hesitated.

At the door a big man stood somewhat in his way.

"Hello, Ben!" said Jimmy, still with his strange smile. "Got around at last, have you? Well, let's go. I don't know that it makes much difference, now."

And then Ben Price acted rather strangely.

"Guess you're mistaken, Mr. Spencer," he said. "Don't believe I recognize you. Your buggy's waiting for you, ain't it?"

And Ben Price turned and strolled down the street.

CHERCHEZ LA FEMME

ROBBINS, reporter for the *Picayune*, and Dumars, of *L'Abeille*—the old French newspaper that has buzzed for nearly a century—were good friends, well proven by years of ups and downs together. They were seated where they had a habit of meeting—in the little, Creole-haunted café of Madame Tibault, in Dumaine Street. If you know the place, you will experience a thrill of pleasure in re-calling it to mind. It is small and dark, with six little polished tables, at which you may sit and drink the best coffee in New Orleans, and concoctions of absinthe equal to Sazerac's best. Madame Tibault, fat and indulgent, presides at the desk, and takes your money. Nicolette and Mémé, Madame's nieces, in charming bib aprons, bring the desirable beverages.

Dumars, with true Creole luxury, was sipping his absinthe, with half-closed eyes, in a swirl of cigarette smoke. Robbins was looking over the morning *Pic.*, detecting, as young reporters will, the gross blunders in the make-up, and the envious blue-pencilling his own stuff had received. This item, in the advertising columns, caught his eye, and with an exclamation of sudden interest he read it aloud to his friend.

PUBLIC AUCTION.—At three o'clock this afternoon there will be sold to the highest bidder all the common property of the Little Sisters of Samaria, at the home of the Sisterhood, in Bonhomme Street. The sale will dispose of the build-ing, ground, and the complete furnishings of the house and chapel, without reserve.

This notice stirred the two friends to a reminiscent talk concerning an episode in their journalistic career that had occurred about two years before. They recalled the incidents, went over the old theories, and discussed it anew from the different perspective time had brought.

There were no other customers in the café. Madame's fine ear had caught the line of their talk, and she came over to their table—for had it not been her lost money—her vanished twenty thousand dollars—that had set the whole matter going?

The three took up the long-abandoned mystery, threshing over the old, dry chaff of it. It was in the chapel of this house of the Little Sisters of Samaria that Robbins and Dumars had stood during that eager, fruitless news search of theirs, and looked upon the gilded statue of the Virgin.

"Thass so, boys," said Madame, summing up. "Thass ver' wicked man, M'sieur Morin. Everybody shall be cert' he steal those money I plaze in his hand to keep safe. Yes. He's boun' spend that money, somehow." Madame turned a broad and comprehensive smile upon Dumars. "I ond'stand you, M'sieur Dumars, those day you come ask me fo' tell ev'ything I know 'bout M'sieur Morin. Ah! yes, I know most time when those men lose money you say 'Cherchez la femme'—there is somewhere the woman. But not for M'sieur Morin. No, boys. Before he shall die, he is like one saint. You might's well, M'sieur Dumars, go try find those money in those statue of Virgin Mary that M'sieur Morin present at those p'tite sœurs, as try find one femme."

At Madame Tibault's last words, Robbins started slightly and cast a keen, sidelong glance at Dumars. The Creole sat, unmoved, dreamily watching the spirals of his cigarette smoke.

It was then nine o'clock in the morning and, a few minutes later, the two friends separated, going different ways to their day's duties. And now follows the brief story of Madame Tibault's vanished thousands:

New Orleans will readily recall to mind the circumstances attendant upon the death of Mr. Gaspard Morin, in that city. Mr. Morin was an artistic goldsmith and jeweller in the old French Quarter, and a man held in the highest esteem. He belonged to one of the oldest French families, and was of some distinction as an antiquary and historian. He was a bachelor, about fifty years of age. He lived in quiet comfort, at one of those rare old hostelries in Royal Street. He was found in his rooms, one morning, dead from unknown causes.

When his affairs came to be looked into, it was found that he was practically insolvent, his stock of goods and personal property barely—but nearly enough to free him from censure—covering his liabilities. Following came the disclosure that he had been intrusted with the sum of twenty thousand dollars by a former upper servant in the Morin family, one Madame Tibault, which she had received as a legacy from relatives in France.

The most searching scrutiny by friends and the legal authorities failed to reveal the disposition of the money. It had vanished, and left no trace. Some weeks before his death, Mr. Morin had drawn the entire amount, in gold coin, from the bank where it had been placed while he looked about (he told Madame Tibault) for a safe investment. Therefore, Mr. Morin's memory seemed doomed to bear the cloud of dishonesty, while Madame was, of course, disconsolate.

Then it was that Robbins and Dumars, representing their respective journals, began one of those pertinacious private investigations which, of late years, the press has adopted as a means to glory and the satisfaction of public curiosity.

"*Cherchez la femme*," said Dumars.

"That's the ticket!" agreed Robbins. "All roads lead to the eternal feminine. We will find the woman."

They exhausted the knowledge of the staff of Mr. Morin's hotel, from the bell-boy down to the proprietor. They gently, but inflexibly, pumped the family of the deceased as far as his cousins twice removed. They artfully sounded the employees of the late jeweller, and dogged his customers for information concerning his habits. Like bloodhounds they traced every step of the supposed defaulter, as nearly as might be, for years along the limited and monotonous paths he had trodden.

At the end of their labors, Mr. Morin stood, an immaculate man. Not one weakness that might be served up as a criminal tendency, not one deviation from the path of rectitude, not even a hint of a predilection for the opposite sex, was found to be placed to his debit. His life had been as regular and austere as a monk's; his habits, simple and unconcealed. Generous, charitable, and a model in propriety, was the verdict of all who knew him.

"What, now?" asked Robbins, fingering his empty notebook.

"*Cherchez la femme*," said Dumars, lighting a cigarette. "Try Lady Bellairs."

This piece of femininity was the race-track favorite of the season. Being feminine, she was erratic in her gaits, and there were a few heavy losers about town who had believed she could be true. The reporters applied for information.

Mr. Morin? Certainly not. He was never even a spectator at the races. Not that kind of a man. Surprised the gentlemen should ask.

"Shall we throw it up?" suggested Robbins, "and let the puzzle department have a try?"

"*Cherchez la femme*," hummed Dumars, reaching for a match. "Try the Little Sisters of What-d'-you-call-'em."

It had developed, during the investigation, that Mr. Morin had held this benevolent order in particular favor. He had contributed liberally toward its support and had chosen its chapel as his favorite place of private worship. It was said that he went there daily to make his devotions at the altar. Indeed, toward the last of his life his whole mind seemed to have fixed itself upon religious matters, perhaps to the detriment of his worldly affairs.

Thither went Robbins and Dumars, and were admitted through the narrow doorway in the blank stone wall that frowned upon Bonhomme Street. An old woman was sweeping the chapel. She told them that Sister Félicité, the head of the order, was then at prayer at the altar in the alcove. In a few moments she would emerge. Heavy, black curtains screened the alcove. They waited.

Soon the curtains were disturbed, and Sister Félicité came forth. She was tall, tragic, bony, and plain-featured, dressed in the black gown and severe bonnet of the sisterhood.

Robbins, a good rough-and-tumble reporter, but lacking the delicate touch, began to speak.

They represented the press. The lady had, no doubt, heard of the Morin affair. It was necessary, in justice to that gentleman's memory, to probe the mystery of the lost money. It was known that he had come often to this chapel. Any information, now, concerning Mr. Morin's habits, tastes, the friends he had, and so on, would be of value in doing him posthumous justice.

Sister Félicité had heard. Whatever she knew would be willingly told, but it was very little. Monsieur Morin had been a good friend to the order, sometimes contributing as much as a hundred dollars. The sisterhood was an independent one, depending entirely upon private contributions for the means to carry on its charitable work. Mr. Morin had presented the chapel with silver candlesticks and an altar cloth. He came every day to worship in the chapel, sometimes remaining for an hour. He was a devout Catholic, consecrated to holiness. Yes, and also in the alcove was a statue of the Virgin that he had himself modeled, cast, and presented to the order. Oh, it was cruel to cast a doubt upon so good a man!

Robbins was also profoundly grieved at the imputation. But, until it was found what Mr. Morin had done with Madame Tibault's money, he feared the tongue of slander would not be stilled. Sometimes—in fact, very often—in affairs of the kind there was—er—as the saying goes—er—a lady in the case. In absolute confidence, now—if—perhaps——

Sister Félicité's large eyes regarded him solemnly.

"There was one woman," she said, slowly, "to whom he bowed—to whom he gave his heart."

Robbins fumbled rapturously for his pencil.

"Behold the woman!" said Sister Félicité, suddenly, in deep tones.

She reached a long arm and swept aside the curtain of the alcove. In there was a shrine, lit to a glow of soft color by the light pouring through a stained-glass window. Within a deep niche in the bare stone wall stood an image of the Virgin Mary, the color of pure gold.

Dumars, a conventional Catholic, succumbed to the dramatic in the act. He bowed his head for an instant and made the sign of the cross. The somewhat abashed Robbins, murmuring an indistinct apology, backed awkwardly away. Sister Félicité drew back the curtain, and the reporters departed.

On the narrow stone sidewalk of Bonhomme Street, Robbins turned to Dumars, with unworthy sarcasm.

"Well, what next? Churchy law fem?"

"Absinthe," said Dumars.

With the history of the missing money thus partially related, some conjecture may be formed of the sudden idea that Madame Tibault's words seemed to have suggested to Robbins's brain.

Was it so wild a surmise—that the religious fanatic had offered up his wealth —or, rather, Madame Tibault's—in the shape of a material symbol of his consuming devotion? Stranger things have been done in the name of worship. Was it not possible that the lost thousands were molded into that lustrous image? That the goldsmith had formed it of the pure and precious metal, and set it there, through some hope of a perhaps disordered brain to propitiate the saints and pave the way to his own selfish glory?

That afternoon, at five minutes to three, Robbins entered the chapel door of the Little Sisters of Samaria. He saw, in the dim light, a crowd of perhaps a hundred people gathered to attend the sale. Most of them were members of various religious orders, priests and churchmen, come to purchase the paraphernalia of the chapel, lest they fall into desecrating hands. Others were business men and agents come to bid upon the realty. A clerical-looking brother had volunteered to wield the hammer, bringing to the office of auctioneer the anomaly of choice diction and dignity of manner.

A few of the minor articles were sold, and then two assistants brought forward the image of the Virgin.

Robbins started the bidding at ten dollars. A stout man, in an ecclesiastical garb, went to fifteen. A voice from another part of the crowd raised to twenty. The three bid alternately, raising by bids of five, until the offer was fifty dollars. Then the stout man dropped out, and Robbins, as a sort of *coup de main*, went to a hundred.

"One hundred and fifty," said the other voice.

"Two hundred," bid Robbins, boldly.

"Two-fifty," called his competitor, promptly.

The reporter hesitated for the space of a lightning flash, estimating how much he could borrow from the boys in the office, and screw from the business manager from his next month's salary.

"Three hundred," he offered.

"Three-fifty," spoke up the other, in a louder voice—a voice that sent Robbins diving suddenly through the crowd in its direction, to catch Dumars, its owner, ferociously by the collar.

"You unconverted idiot!" hissed Robbins, close to his ear—"pool!"

"Agreed!" said Dumars, coolly. "I couldn't raise three hundred and fifty dollars with a search-warrant, but I can stand half. What you come bidding against me for?"

"I thought I was the only fool in the crowd," explained Robbins.

No one else bidding, the statue was knocked down to the syndicate at their last offer. Dumars remained with the prize, while Robbins hurried forth to wring from the resources and credit of both the price. He soon returned with the money, and the two musketeers loaded their precious package into a carriage and drove with it to Dumar's room, in old Chartres Street, near by. They lugged it, covered with a cloth, up the stairs, and deposited it on a table. A hundred pounds it weighed, if an ounce, and at that estimate, according to their calculation, if their daring theory were correct, it stood there, worth twenty thousand golden dollars.

Robbins removed the covering, and opened his pocket-knife.

"*Sacré!*" muttered Dumars, shuddering. "It is the Mother of Christ. What would you do?"

"Shut up, Judas!" said Robbins, coldly. "It's too late for you to be saved now."

With a firm hand, he clipped a slice from the shoulder of the image. The cut showed a dull, grayish metal, with a thin coating of gold leaf.

"Lead!" announced Robbins, hurling his knife to the floor—"gilded!"

"To the devil with it!" said Dumars, forgetting his scruples. "I must have a drink."

Together they walked moodily to the café of Madame Tibault, two squares away.

It seemed that Madame's mind had been stirred that day to fresh recollections of the past services of the two young men in her behalf.

"You mustn't sit by those table," she interposed, as they were about to drop into their accustomed seats. "Thass so, boys. But no. I mek you come at this room, like my *trés bons amis*. Yes. I goin' mek for you myself one *anisette* and one *café royale* ver' fine. Ah! I lak treat my fren' nize. Yes. Plis come in this way."

Madame led them into the little back room, into which she sometimes invited the especially favored of her customers. In two comfortable armchairs, by a big window that opened upon the courtyard, she placed them, with a low table between. Bustling hospitably about, she began to prepare the promised refreshments.

It was the first time the reporters had been honored with admission to the sacred precincts. The room was in dusky twilight, flecked with gleams of the polished fine woods and burnished glass and metal that the Creoles love. From the little courtyard a tiny fountain sent in an insinuating sound of trickling waters, to which a banana plant by the window kept time with its tremulous leaves.

Robbins, an investigator by nature, sent a curious glance roving about the room. From some barbaric ancestor, Madame had inherited a *penchant* for the crude in decoration.

The walls were adorned with cheap lithographs—florid libels upon nature, addressed to the taste of the *bourgeoisie*—birthday cards, garish newspaper supplements, and specimens of art-advertising calculated to reduce the optic nerve to stunned submission. A patch of something unintelligible in the midst of the more candid display puzzled Robbins, and he rose and took a step nearer, to interrogate it at closer range. Then he leaned weakly against the wall, and called out:

"Madame Tibault! Oh, madame! Since when—oh! since when have you been in the habit of papering your walls with five thousand dollar United States four per cent. gold bonds? Tell me—is this a Grimm's fairy tale, or should I consult an oculist?"

At his words, Madame Tibault and Dumars approached.

"H'what you say?" said Madame, cheerily. "H'what you say, M'sieur Robbin'? *Bon!* Ah those nize li'l peezes papier! One tam I think those w'at you call calendair, wiz ze li'l day of mont' below. But, no. Those wall is broke in those plaze, M'sieur Robbin', and I plaze those li'l peezes papier to conceal ze crack. I did think the couleur harm'nize so well with the wall papier. Where I get them from? Ah, yes, I remem' ver' well. One day M'sieur Morin, he come at my house—thass 'bout one mont' before he shall die—thass 'long 'bout tam he promise fo' inves' those money fo' me. M'sieur Morin, he leave thoze li'l peezes papier in those table, and say ver' much 'bout money thass hard for me to ond'stan. *Mais* I never see those money again. Thass ver' wicked man, M'sieur Morin. H'what you call those peezes papier, M'sieur Robbin'—*oon!*"

Robbins explained.

"There's your twenty thousand dollars, with coupons attached," he said, running his thumb around the edge of the four bonds. "Better get an expert to peel them off for you. Mister Morin was all right. I'm going out to get my ears trimmed."

He dragged Dumars by the arm into the outer room. Madame was screaming for Nicolette and Mémé to come and observe the fortune returned to her by M'sieur Morin, that best of men, that saint in glory.

"Marsy," said Robbins. "I'm going on a jamboree. For three days the esteemed *Pic.* will have to get along without my valuable services. I advise you to join me. Now, that green stuff you drink is no good. It stimulates thought. What we want to do is to forget to remember. I'll introduce you to the only lady in this case that is guaranteed to produce the desired results. Her name is Belle of Kentucky, twelve-year-old Bourbon. In quarts. How does the idea strike you?"

"*Allons!*" said Dumars. "*Cherchez la femme.*"

FRIENDS IN SAN ROSARIO

THE west-bound stopped at San Rosario on time at 8:20 A. M. A man with a thick black-leather wallet under his arm left the train and walked rapidly up the main street of the town. There were other passengers who also got off at San Rosario, but they either slouched limberly over to the railroad eating-house or the Silver Dollar saloon, or joined the groups of idlers about the station.

Indecision had no part in the movements of the man with the wallet. He was short in stature, but strongly built, with very light, closely trimmed hair, smooth, determined face, and aggressive, gold-rimmed nose glasses. He was well dressed in the prevailing Eastern style. His air denoted a quiet but conscious reserve force, if not actual authority.

After walking a distance of three squares he came to the center of the town's business area. Here another street of importance crossed the main one, forming the hub of San Rosario's life and commerce. Upon one corner stood the post-office. Upon another Rubensky's Clothing Emporium. The other two diagonally opposing corners were occupied by the town's two banks, the First National and the Stockmen's National. Into the First National Bank of San Rosario the new-comer walked, never slowing his brisk step until he stood at the cashier's window. The bank opened for business at nine, and the working force was already assembled, each member preparing his department for the day's business. The cashier was examining the mail when he noticed the stranger standing at his window.

"Bank doesn't open 'til nine," he remarked, curtly, but without feeling. He had had to make that statement so often to early birds since San Rosario adopted city banking hours.

"I am well aware of that," said the other man, in cool, brittle tones. "Will you kindly receive my card?"

The cashier drew the small, spotless parallelogram inside the bars of his wicket, and read:

> J. F. C. NETTLEWICK
>
> National Bank Examiner

"Oh—er—will you walk around inside, Mr.—er—Nettlewick. Your first visit —didn't know your business, of course. Walk right around, please."

The examiner was quickly inside the sacred precincts of the bank, where he was ponderously introduced to each employee in turn by Mr. Edlinger, the cashier—a middle-aged gentleman of deliberation, discretion, and method.

"I was kind of expecting Sam Turner round again, pretty soon," said Mr. Edlinger. "Sam's been examining us now for about four years. I guess you'll find us all right, though, considering the tightness in business. Not overly much money on hand, but able to stand the storms, sir, stand the storms."

"Mr. Turner and I have been ordered by the Comptroller to exchange districts," said the examiner, in his decisive, formal tones. "He is covering my old territory in southern Illinois and Indiana. I will take the cash first, please."

Perry Dorsey, the teller, was already arranging his cash on the counter for the examiner's inspection. He knew it was right to a cent, and he had nothing to fear, but he was nervous and flustered. So was every man in the bank. There was something so icy and swift, so impersonal and uncompromising about this man that his very presence seemed an accusation. He looked to be a man who would never make nor overlook an error.

Mr. Nettlewick first seized the currency, and with a rapid, almost juggling motion, counted it by packages. Then he spun the sponge cup toward him and verified the count by bills. His thin, white fingers flew like some expert musician's upon the keys of a piano. He dumped the gold upon the counter with a crash, and the coins whined and sang as they skimmed across the marble slab from the tips of his nimble digits. The air was full of fractional currency when he came to the halves and quarters. He counted the last nickel and dime. He had the scales brought, and he weighed every sack of silver in the vault. He questioned Dorsey concerning each of the cash memoranda—certain checks, charge slips, etc., carried over from the previous day's work—with unimpeachable courtesy, yet with something so mysteriously momentous in his frigid manner, that the teller was reduced to pink cheeks and a stammering tongue.

This newly imported examiner was so different from Sam Turner. It had been Sam's way to enter the bank with a shout, pass the cigars, and tell the latest stories he had picked up on his rounds. His customary greeting to Dorsey had been, "Hello, Perry! Haven't skipped out with the boodle yet, I see." Turner's way of counting the cash had been different, too. He would finger the packages of bills in a tired kind of way, and then go into the vault and kick over a few sacks of silver, and the thing was done. Halves and quarters and dimes? Not for Sam Turner. "No chicken feed for me," he would say when they were set before him. "I'm not in the agricultural department." But, then, Turner was a Texan, an old friend of the bank's president, and had known Dorsey since he was a baby.

While the examiner was counting the cash, Major Thomas B. Kingman—known to every one as "Major Tom"—the president of the First National, drove up to the side door with his old dun horse and buggy, and came inside. He saw the examiner busy with the money, and, going into the little "pony corral," as he called it, in which his desk was railed off, he began to look over his letters.

Earlier, a little incident had occurred that even the sharp eyes of the examiner had failed to notice. When he had begun his work at the cash counter, Mr. Edlinger had winked significantly at Roy Wilson, the youthful bank messenger, and nodded his head slightly toward the front door. Roy understood, got his hat and walked leisurely out, with his collector's book under his arm. Once outside, he made a beeline for the Stockmen's National. That bank was also getting ready to open. No customers had, as yet, presented themselves.

"Say, you people!" cried Roy, with the familiarity of youth and long acquaintance, "you want to get a move on you. There's a new bank examiner over at the First, and he's a stem-winder. He's counting nickels on Perry, and he's got the whole outfit bluffed. Mr. Edlinger gave me the tip to let you know."

Mr. Buckley, president of the Stockmen's National—a stout, elderly man, looking like a farmer dressed for Sunday—heard Roy from his private office at the rear and called him.

"Has Major Kingman come down to the bank yet?" he asked of the boy.

"Yes, sir, he was just driving up as I left," said Roy.

"I want you to take him a note. Put it into his own hands as soon as you get back."

Mr. Buckley sat down and began to write.

Roy returned and handed to Major Kingman the envelope containing the note. The major read it, folded it, and slipped it into his vest pocket. He leaned back in his chair for a few moments as if he were meditating deeply, and then rose and went into the vault. He came out with the bulky, old-fashioned leather note case stamped on the back in gilt letters, "Bills Discounted." In this were the notes due the bank with their attached securities, and the major, in his rough way, dumped the lot upon his desk and began to sort them over.

By this time Nettlewick had finished his count of the cash. His pencil fluttered like a swallow over the sheet of paper on which he had set his figures. He opened his black wallet, which seemed to be also a kind of secret memorandum book, made a few rapid figures in it, wheeled and transfixed Dorsey with the glare of his spectacles. That look seemed to say: "You're safe this time, but——"

"Cash all correct," snapped the examiner. He made a dash for the individual bookkeeper, and, for a few minutes there was a fluttering of ledger leaves and a sailing of balance sheets through the air.

"How often do you balance your pass-books?" he demanded, suddenly.

"Er—once a month," faltered the individual bookkeeper, wondering how many years they would give him.

"All right," said the examiner, turning and charging upon the general bookkeeper, who had the statements of his foreign banks and their reconcilement memoranda ready. Everything there was found to be all right. Then the stub book of the certificates of deposit. Flutter—flutter—zip—zip—check! All right. List of over-drafts, please. Thanks. H'm-m. Unsigned bills of the bank, next. All right

Then came the cashier's turn, and easy-going Mr. Edlinger rubbed his nose and polished his glasses nervously under the quick fire of questions concerning the circulation, undivided profits, bank real estate, and stock ownership.

Presently Nettlewick was aware of a big man towering above him at his elbow—a man sixty years of age, rugged and hale, with a rough, grizzled beard, a mass of gray hair, and a pair of penetrating blue eyes that confronted the formidable glasses of the examiner without a flicker.

"Er—Major Kingman, our president—er—Mr. Nettlewick," said the cashier.

Two men of very different types shook hands. One was a finished product of the world of straight lines, conventional methods, and formal affairs. The other was something freer, wider, and nearer to nature. Tom Kingman had not been cut to any pattern. He had been mule-driver, cowboy, ranger, soldier, sheriff, prospector and cattleman. Now, when he was bank president, his old comrades from the prairies, of the saddle, tent, and trail, found no change in him. He had made his fortune when Texas cattle were at the high tide of value, and had organized the First National Bank of San Rosario. In spite of his largeness of heart and sometimes unwise generosity toward his old friends, the bank had prospered, for Major Tom Kingman knew men as well as he knew cattle. Of late years the cattle business had known a depression, and the major's bank was one of the few whose losses had not been great.

"And now," said the examiner, briskly, pulling out his watch, "the last thing is the loans. We will take them up now, if you please."

He had gone through the First National at almost record-breaking speed —but thoroughly, as he did everything. The running order of the bank was smooth and clean, and that had facilitated his work. There was but one other bank in the town. He received from the Government a fee of twenty-five dollars for each bank that he examined. He should be able to go over those loans and discounts in half an hour. If so, he could examine the other bank immediately afterward, and catch the 11:45, the only other train that day in the direction he was working. Otherwise, he would have to spend the night and Sunday in this uninteresting Western town. That was why Mr. Nettlewick was rushing matters.

"Come with me, sir," said Major Kingman, in his deep voice, that united the Southern drawl with the rhythmic twang of the West; "We will go over them together. Nobody in the bank knows those notes as I do. Some of 'em are a little wobbly on their legs, and some are mavericks without extra many brands on their backs, but they'll 'most all pay out at the round-up."

The two sat down at the president's desk. First, the examiner went through the notes at lightning speed, and added up their total, finding it to agree with the amount of loans carried on the book of daily balances. Next, he took up the larger loans, inquiring scrupulously into the condition of their endorsers or securities. The new examiner's mind seemed to course and turn and make unexpected dashes hither and thither like a bloodhound seeking a trail. Finally he pushed aside all the notes except a few, which he arranged in a neat pile before him, and began a dry, formal little speech.

"I find, sir, the condition of your bank to be very good, considering the poor crops and the depression in the cattle interests of your state. The clerical work seems to be done accurately and punctually. Your past-due paper is moderate in amount, and promises only a small loss. I would recommend the calling in of your large loans, and the making of only sixty and ninety day or call loans until general business revives. And now, there is one thing more, and I will have finished with the bank. Here are six notes aggregating something like $40,000. They are secured, according to their faces, by various stocks, bonds, shares, etc., to the value of $70,000. Those securities are missing from the notes to which they should be attached. I suppose you have them in the safe or vault. You will permit me to examine them."

Major Tom's light-blue eyes turned unflinchingly toward the examiner.

"No, sir," he said, in a low but steady tone; "those securities are neither in the safe nor the vault. I have taken them. You may hold me personally responsible for their absence."

Nettlewick felt a slight thrill. He had not expected this. He had struck a momentous trail when the hunt was drawing to a close.

"Ah!" said the examiner. He waited a moment, and then continued: "May I ask you to explain more definitely?"

"The securities were taken by me," repeated the major. "It was not for my own use, but to save an old friend in trouble. Come in here, sir, and we'll talk it over."

He led the examiner into the bank's private office at the rear, and closed the door. There was a desk, and a table, and half-a-dozen leather-covered chairs. On the wall was the mounted head of a Texas steer with horns five feet from tip to tip. Opposite hung the major's old cavalry saber that he had carried at Shiloh and Fort Pillow.

Placing a chair for Nettlewick, the major seated himself by the window, from which he could see the post-office and the carved limestone front of the Stockman's National. He did not speak at once, and Nettlewick felt, perhaps, that the ice should be broken by something so near its own temperature as the voice of official warning.

"Your statement," he began, "since you have failed to modify it, amounts, as you must know, to a very serious thing. You are aware, also, of what my duty must compel me to do. I shall have to go before the United States Commissioner and make——"

"I know, I know," said Major Tom, with a wave of his hand. "You don't suppose I'd run a bank without being posted on national banking laws and the revised statutes! Do your duty. I'm not asking any favors. But I spoke of my friend. I did want you to hear me tell you about Bob."

Nettlewick settled himself in his chair. There would be no leaving San Rosario for him that day. He would have to telegraph to the Comptroller of the Currency; he would have to swear out a warrant before the United States Commissioner for the arrest of Major Kingman; perhaps he would be ordered to close the bank on account of the loss of the securities. It was not the first crime the examiner had unearthed. Once or twice the terrible upheaval of human emotions that his investigations had loosed had almost caused a ripple in his official calm. He had seen bank men kneel and plead and cry like women for a chance—an hour's time—the overlooking of a single error. One cashier had shot himself at his desk before him. None of them had taken it with the dignity and coolness of this stern old Westerner. Nettlewick felt that he owed it to him at least to listen if he wished to talk. With his elbow on the arm of his chair, and his square chin resting upon the fingers of his right hand, the bank examiner waited to hear the confession of the president of the First National Bank of San Rosario.

"When a man's your friend," began Major Tom, somewhat didactically, "for forty years, and tried by water, fire, earth, and cyclones, when you can do him a little favor you feel like doing it."

("Embezzle for him $70,000 worth of securities," thought the examiner.)

"We were cowboys together, Bob and I," continued the major, speaking slowly, and deliberately, and musingly, as if his thoughts were rather with the past than the critical present, "and we prospected together for gold and silver over Arizona, New Mexico, and a good part of California. We were both in the war of 'sixty-one, but in different commands. We've fought Indians and horse thieves side by side; we've starved for weeks in a cabin in the Arizona mountains, buried twenty feet deep in snow; we've ridden herd together when the wind blew so hard the lightning couldn't strike—well, Bob and I have been through some rough spells since the first time we met in the branding camp of the old Anchor-Bar ranch. And during that time we've found it necessary more than once to help each other out of tight places. In those days it was expected of a man to stick to his friend, and he didn't ask any credit for it. Probably next day you'd need him to get at your back and help stand off a band of Apaches, or put a tourniquet on your leg above a rattlesnake bite and ride for whisky. So, after all, it was give and take, and if you didn't stand square with your pardner, why, you might be shy one when you needed him. But Bob was a man who was willing to go further than that. He never played a limit.

"Twenty years ago I was sheriff of this county and I made Bob my chief deputy. That was before the boom in cattle when we both made our stake. I was sheriff and collector, and it was a big thing for me then. I was married, and we had a boy and a girl—a four and a six year old. There was a comfortable house next to the courthouse, furnished by the county, rent free, and I was saving some money. Bob did most of the office work. Both of us had seen rough times and plenty of rustling and danger, and I tell you it was great to hear the rain and the sleet dashing against the windows of nights, and be warm and safe and comfortable, and know you could get up in the morning and be shaved and have folks call you 'mister.' And then, I had the finest wife and kids that ever struck the range, and my old friend with me enjoying the first fruits of prosperity and white shirts, and I guess I was happy. Yes, I was happy about that time."

The major sighed and glanced casually out of the window. The bank examiner changed his position, and leaned his chin upon his other hand.

"One winter," continued the major, "the money for the county taxes came pouring in so fast that I didn't have time to take the stuff to the bank for a week. I just shoved the checks into a cigar box and the money into a sack, and locked them in the big safe that belonged in the sheriff's office.

"I had been overworked that week, and was about sick, anyway. My nerves were out of order, and my sleep at night didn't seem to rest me. The doctor had some scientific name for it, and I was taking medicine. And so, added to the rest, I went to bed at night with that money on my mind. Not that there was much need of being worried, for the safe was a good one, and nobody but Bob and I knew the combination. On Friday night there was about $6,500 in cash in the bag. On Saturday morning I went to the office as usual. The safe was locked, and Bob was writing at his desk. I opened the safe, and the money was gone. I called Bob, and roused everybody in the courthouse to announce the robbery. It struck me that Bob took it pretty quiet, considering how much it reflected upon both him and me.

"Two days went by and we never got a clew. It couldn't have been burglars, for the safe had been opened by the combination in the proper way. People must have begun to talk, for one afternoon in comes Alice—that's my wife—and the boy and girl, and Alice stamps her foot, and her eyes flash, and she cries out, 'The lying wretches—Tom, Tom!' and I catch her in a faint, and bring her 'round little by little, and she lays her head down and cries and cries for the first time since she took Tom Kingman's name and fortunes. And Jack and Zilla—the youngsters—they were always wild as tigers cubs to rush at Bob and climb all over him whenever they were allowed to come to the courthouse—they stood and kicked their little shoes, and herded together like scared partridges. They were having their first trip down into the shadows of life. Bob was working at his desk, and he got up and went out without a word. The grand jury was in session then, and the next morning Bob went before them and confessed that he stole the money. He said he lost it in a poker game. In fifteen minutes they had found a true bill and sent me the warrant to arrest the man with whom I'd been closer than a thousand brothers for many a year.

"I did it, and then I said to Bob, pointing: 'There's my house, and here's my office, and up there's Maine, and out that way is California, and over there is Florida—and that's your range 'til court meets. You're in my charge, and I take the responsibility. You be here when you're wanted.'

"'Thanks, Tom,' he said, kind of carelessly; 'I was sort of hoping you wouldn't lock me up. Court meets next Monday, so, if you don't object, I'll just loaf around the office until then. I've got one favor to ask, if it isn't too much. If you'd let the kids come out in the yard once in a while and have a romp I'd like it.'

"'Why not?' I answered him. 'They're welcome, and so are you. And come to my house the same as ever.' You see, Mr. Nettlewick, you can't make a friend of a thief, but neither can you make a thief of a friend, all at once."

The examiner made no answer. At that moment was heard the shrill whistle of a locomotive pulling into the depot. That was the train on the little, narrow-gauge road that struck into San Rosario from the south. The major cocked his ear and listened for a moment, and looked at his watch. The narrow-gauge was in on time—10:35. The major continued:

"So Bob hung around the office, reading the papers and smoking. I put another deputy to work in his place, and, after a while, the first excitement of the case wore off.

"One day when we were alone in the office Bob came over to where I was sitting. He was looking sort of grim and blue—the same look he used to get when he'd been up watching for Indians all night or herd-riding.

"'Tom,' says he, 'it's harder than standing off redskins; it's harder than lying in the lava desert forty miles from water; but I'm going to stick it out to the end. You know that's been my style. But if you'd tip me the smallest kind of a sign—if you'd just say, "Bob I understand," why, it would make it lots easier.'

"I was surprised. 'I don't know what you mean, Bob,' I said. 'Of course, you know that I'd do anything under the sun to help you that I could. But you've got me guessing.'

"'All right, Tom,' was all he said, and he went back to his newspaper and lit another cigar.

"It was the night before the court met when I found out what he meant. I went to bed that night with the same old, light-headed, nervous feeling come back upon me. I dropped off to sleep about midnight. When I woke I was standing half dressed in one of the courthouse corridors. Bob was holding one of my arms, our family doctor the other, and Alice was shaking me and half crying. She had sent for the doctor without my knowing it, and when he came they had found me out of bed and missing, and had begun a search.

"'Sleep-walking,' said the doctor.

"All of us went back to the house, and the doctor told us some remarkable stories about the strange things people had done while in that condition. I was feeling rather chilly after my trip out, and, as my wife was out of the room at the time, I pulled open the door of an old wardrobe that stood in the room and dragged out a big quilt I had seen in there. With it tumbled out the bag of money for stealing which Bob was to be tried—and convicted—in the morning.

"'How the jumping rattlesnakes did that get there?' I yelled, and all hands must have seen how surprised I was. Bob knew in a flash.

"'You darned old snoozer,' he said, with the old-time look on his face, 'I saw you put it there. I watched you open the safe and take it out, and I followed you. I looked through the window and saw you hide it in that wardrobe.'

"'Then, you blankety-blank, flop-eared, sheep-headed coyote, what did you say you took it for?'

"'Because,' said Bob, simply, 'I didn't know you were asleep.'

"I saw him glance toward the door of the room where Jack and Zilla were, and I knew then what it meant to be a man's friend from Bob's point of view."

Major Tom paused, and again directed his glance out of the window. He saw someone in the Stockmen's National Bank reach and draw a yellow shade down the whole length of its plate-glass, big front window, although the position of the sun did not seem to warrant such a defensive movement against its rays.

Nettlewick sat up straight in his chair. He had listened patiently, but without consuming interest, to the major's story. It had impressed him as irrelevant to the situation, and it could certainly have no effect upon the consequences. Those Western people, he thought, had an exaggerated sentimentality. They were not business-like. They needed to be protected from their friends. Evidently the major had concluded. And what he had said amounted to nothing.

"May I ask," said the examiner, "if you have anything further to say that bears directly upon the question of those abstracted securities?"

"Abstracted securities, sir!" Major Tom turned suddenly in his chair, his blue eyes flashing upon the examiner. "What do you mean, sir?"

He drew from his coat pocket a batch of folded papers held together by a rubber band, tossed them into Nettlewick's hands, and rose to his feet.

"You'll find those securities there, sir, every stock, bond, and share of 'em. I took them from the notes while you were counting the cash. Examine and compare them for yourself."

The major led the way back into the banking room. The examiner, astounded, perplexed, nettled, at sea, followed. He felt that he had been made the victim of something that was not exactly a hoax, but that left him in the shoes of one who had been played upon, used, and then discarded, without even an inkling of the game. Perhaps, also, his official position had been irreverently juggled with. But there was nothing he could take hold of. An official report of the matter would be an absurdity. And, somehow, he felt that he would never know anything more about the matter than he did then.

Frigidly, mechanically, Nettlewick examined the securities, found them to tally with the notes, gathered his black wallet, and rose to depart.

"I will say," he protested, turning the indignant glare of his glasses upon Major Kingman, "that your statements—your misleading statements, which you have not condescended to explain—do not appear to be quite the thing, regarded either as business or humor. I do not understand such motives or actions."

Major Tom looked down at him serenely and not unkindly.

"Son," he said, "there are plenty of things in the chaparral, and on the prairies, and up the cañons that you don't understand. But I want to thank you for listening to a garrulous old man's prosy story. We old Texans love to talk about our adventures and our old comrades, and the home folks have long ago learned to run when we begin with 'Once upon a time,' so we have to spin our yarns to the stranger within our gates."

The major smiled, but the examiner only bowed coldly, and abruptly quitted the bank. They saw him travel diagonally across the street in a straight line and enter the Stockmen's National Bank.

Major Tom sat down at his desk and drew from his vest pocket the note Roy had given him. He had read it once, but hurriedly, and now, with something like a twinkle in his eyes, he read it again. These were the words he read:

DEAR TOM:

I hear there's one of Uncle Sam's greyhound's going through you, and that means that we'll catch him inside of a couple of hours, maybe. Now, I want you to do something for me. We've got just $2,200 in the bank, and the law requires that we have $20,000. I let Ross and Fisher have $18,000 late yesterday afternoon to buy up that Gibson bunch of cattle. They'll realize $40,000 in less than thirty days on the transaction, but that won't make my cash on hand look any prettier to that bank examiner. Now, I can't show him those notes, for they're just plain notes of hand without any security in sight, but you know very well that Pink Ross and Jim Fisher are two of the finest white men God ever made, and they'll do the square thing. You remember Jim Fisher—he was the one who shot that faro dealer in El Paso. I wired Sam Bradshaw's bank to send me $20,000, and it will get in on the narrow-gauge at 10:35. You can't let a bank examiner in to count $2,200 and close your doors. Tom, you hold that examiner. Hold him. Hold him if you have to rope him and sit on his head. Watch our front window after the narrow-gauge gets in, and when we've got the cash inside we'll pull down the shade for a signal. Don't turn him loose till then. I'm counting on you, Tom.

Your Old Pard,
BOB BUCKLEY,
Prest. Stockmen's National.

The major began to tear the note into small pieces and throw them into his waste basket. He gave a satisfied little chuckle as he did so.

"Confounded old reckless cowpuncher!" he growled, contentedly, "that pays him some on account for what he tried to do for me in the sheriff's office twenty years ago."

THE FOURTH IN SALVADOR

On a summer's day, while the city was rocking with the din and red uproar of patriotism, Billy Casparis told me this story.

In his way, Billy is Ulysses, Jr. Like Satan, he comes from going to and fro upon the earth and walking up and down in it. To-morrow morning while you are cracking your breakfast egg he may be off with his little alligator grip to boom a town site in the middle of Lake Okeechobee or to trade horses with the Patagonians.

We sat at a little, round table, and between us were glasses holding big lumps of ice, and above us leaned an artificial palm. And because our scene was set with the properties of the one they recalled to his mind, Billy was stirred to narrative.

"It reminds me," said he, "of a Fourth I helped to celebrate down in Salvador. 'Twas while I was running an ice factory down there, after I unloaded that silver mine I had in Colorado. I had what they called a 'conditional concession.' They made me put up a thousand dollars cash forfeit that I would make ice continuously for six months. If I did that I could draw down my ante. If I failed to do so the government took the pot. So the inspectors kept dropping in, trying to catch me without the goods.

"One day when the thermometer was at 110, the clock at half-past one, and the calendar at July third, two of the little, brown, oily nosers in red trousers slid in to make an inspection. Now, the factory hadn't turned out a pound of ice in three weeks, for a couple of reasons. The Salvador heathen wouldn't buy it; they said it made things cold they put it in. And I couldn't make any more, because I was broke. All I was holding on for was to get down my thousand so I could leave the country. The six months would be up on the sixth of July.

"Well, I showed 'em all the ice I had. I raised the lid of a darkish vat, and there was an elegant 100-pound block of ice, beautiful and convincing to the eye. I was about to close down the lid again when one of those brunette sleuths flops down on his red knees and lays a slanderous and violent hand on my guarantee of good faith. And in two minutes more they had dragged out on the floor that fine chunk of molded glass that had cost me fifty dollars to have shipped down from Frisco.

"'Ice-y?' says the fellow that played me the dishonorable trick; 'verree warm ice-y. Yes. The day is that hot, señor. Yes. Maybeso it is of desirableness to leave him out to get the cool. Yes.'

"'Yes,' says I, 'yes,' for I knew they had me. 'Touching's believing, ain't it, boys? Yes. Now there's some might say the seats of your trousers are sky blue, but 'tis my opinion they are red. Let's apply the tests of the laying on of hands and feet.' And so I hoisted both those inspectors out of the door on the toe of my shoe, and sat down to cool off on my block of disreputable glass.

"And, as I live without oats, while I sat there, homesick for money and without a cent to my ambition, there came on the breeze the most beautiful smell my nose had entered for a year. God knows where it came from in that backyard of a country—it was a bouquet of soaked lemon peel, cigar stumps, and stale beer—exactly the smell of Goldbrick Charley's place on Fourteenth Street where I used to play pinochle of afternoons with the third-rate actors. And that smell drove my troubles through me and clinched 'em at the back. I began to long for my country and feel sentiments about it; and I said words about

Salvador that you wouldn't think could come legitimate out of an ice factory.

"And while I was sitting there, down through the blazing sunshine in his clean, white clothes comes Maximilian Jones, an American interested in rubber and rosewood.

"'Great carrambos!' says I, when he stepped in, for I was in a bad temper, 'didn't I have catastrophes enough? I know what you want. You want to tell me that story again about Johnny Ammiger and the widow on the train. You've told it nine times already this month.'

"'It must be the heat,' says Jones, stopping in the door, amazed. 'Poor Billy. He's got bugs. Sitting on ice, and calling his best friends pseudonyms. Hi!—*muchacho!*' Jones called my force of employees, who was sitting in the sun, playing with his toes, and told him to put on his trousers and run for the doctor.

"'Come back,' says I. 'Sit down, Maxy, and forget it. 'Tis not ice you see, nor a lunatic upon it. 'Tis only an exile full of homesickness sitting on a lump of glass that's just cost him a thousand dollars. Now, what was it Johnny said to the widow first? I'd like to hear it again, Maxy—honest. Don't mind what I said.'

"Maximilian Jones and I sat down and talked. He was about as sick of the country as I was, for the grafters were squeezing him for half the profits of his rosewood and rubber. Down in the bottom of a tank of water I had a dozen bottles of sticky Frisco beer; and I fished these up, and we fell to talking about home and the flag and Hail Columbia and home-fried potatoes; and the drivel we contributed would have sickened any man enjoying those blessings. But at that time we were out of 'em. You can't appreciate home till you've left it, money till it's spent, your wife till she's joined a woman's club, nor Old Glory till you see it hanging on a broomstick on the shanty of a consul in a foreign town.

"And sitting there me and Maximilian Jones, scratching at our prickly heat and kicking at the lizards on the floor, became afflicted with a dose of patriotism and affection for our country. There was me, Billy Casparis, reduced from a capitalist to a pauper by over-addiction to my glass (in the lump), declares my troubles off for the present and myself to be an uncrowned sovereign of the greatest country on earth. And Maximilian Jones pours out whole drug stores of his wrath on oligarchies and potentates in red trousers and calico shoes. And we issues a declaration of interference in which we guarantee that the fourth day of July shall be celebrated in Salvador with all the kinds of salutes, explosions, honors of war, oratory, and liquids known to tradition. Yes, neither me nor Jones breathed with soul so dead. There shall be rucuses in Salvador, we say, and the monkeys had better climb the tallest cocoanut trees and the fire department get out its red sashes and two tin buckets.

"About this time into the factory steps a native man incriminated by the name of General Mary Esperanza Dingo. He was some pumpkin both in politics and color, and the friend of me and Jones. He was full of politeness and a kind of intelligence, having picked up the latter and managed to preserve the former during a two years' residence in Philadelphia studying medicine. For a Salvadorian he was not such a calamitous little man, though he always would play jack, queen, king, ace, deuce for a straight.

"General Mary sits with us and has a bottle. While he was in the States he had acquired a synopsis of the English language and the art of admiring our institutions. By and by the General gets up and tiptoes to the doors and windows and other stage entrances, remarking 'Hist!' at each one. They all do that in Salvador before they ask for a drink of water or the time of day, being conspirators from the cradle and matinée idols by proclamation.

"'Hit!' says General Dingo again, and then he lays his chest on the table quite like Gaspard the Miser. 'Good friends, señores, to-morrow will be the great day of Liberty and Independence. The hearts of Americans and Salvadorians should beat together. Of your history and your great Washington I know. Is it not so?'

"Now, me and Jones thought that nice of the General to remember when the Fourth came. It made us feel good. He must have heard the news going round in Philadelphia about that disturbance we had with England.

"'Yes,' says me and Maxy together, 'we knew it. We were talking about it when you came in. And you can bet your bottom concession that there'll be fuss and feathers in the air to-morrow. We are few in numbers, but the welkin may as well reach out to push the button, for it's got to ring.'

"'I, too, shall assist,' says the General, thumping his collar-bone. 'I, too, am on the side of Liberty. Noble Americans, we will make the day one to be never forgotten.'

"'For us American whisky,' says Jones—'none of your Scotch smoke or anisada or Three Star Hennessey to-morrow. We'll borrow the consul's flag; old man Billfinger shall make orations, and we'll have a barbecue on the plaza.'

"'Fireworks,' says I, 'will be scarce; but we'll have all the cartridges in the shops for our guns. I've got two navy sixes I brought from Denver.'

"'There is one cannon,' said the General; 'one big cannon that will go "BOOM!" And three hundred men with rifles to shoot.'

"'Oh, say!' says Jones, 'Generalissimo, you're the real silk elastic. We'll make it a joint international celebration. Please, General, get a white horse and a blue sash and be grand marshal.'

"'With my sword,' says the General, rolling his eyes, 'I shall ride at the head of the brave men who gather in the name of Liberty.'

"'And you might,' we suggest, "see the comandante and advise him that we are going to prize things up a bit. We Americans, you know, are accustomed to using municipal regulations for gun wadding when we line up to help the eagle scream. He might suspend the rules for one day. We don't want to get in the calaboose for spanking his soldiers if they get in our way, do you see?'

"'Hist!' says General Mary. 'The comandante is with us, heart and soul. He will aid us. He is one of us.'

"We made all the arrangements that afternoon. There was a buck coon from Georgia in Salvador who had drifted down there from a busted-up colored colony that had been started on some possumless land in Mexico. As soon as he heard us say 'barbecue' he wept for joy and groveled on the ground. He dug his trench on the plaza, and got half a beef on the coals for an all-night roast. Me and Maxy went to see the rest of the Americans in the town and they all sizzled like a seidlitz with joy at the idea of solemnizing an old-time Fourth.

"There were six of us all together—Martin Dillard, a coffee planter; Henry Barnes, a railroad man; old man Billfinger, an educated tintype taker; me and Jonesy, and Jerry, the boss of the barbecue. There was also an Englishman in town named Sterrett, who was there to write a book on Domestic Architecture of the Insect World. We felt some bashfulness about inviting a Britisher to help crow over his own country, but we decided to risk it, out of our personal regard for him.

"We found Sterrett in pajamas working at his manuscript with a bottle of brandy for a paper weight.

"'Englishman,' says Jones, 'let us interrupt your disquisition on bug houses for a moment. To-morrow is the Fourth of July. We don't want to hurt your feelings, but we're going to commemorate the day when we licked you by a little refined debauchery and nonsense—something that can be heard about five miles off. If you are broad-gauged enough to taste whisky at your own wake, we'd be pleased to have you join us.'

"'Do you know,' says Sterrett, setting his glasses on his nose, 'I like your cheek in asking me if I'll join you; blast me if I don't. You might have known I would, without asking. Not as a traitor to my own country, but for the intrinsic joy of a blooming row.'

"On the morning of the Fourth I woke up in that old shanty of an ice factory feeling sore. I looked around at the wreck of all I possessed, and my heart was full of bile. From where I lay on my cot I could look through the window and see the consul's old ragged Stars and Stripes hanging over his shack. 'You're all kinds of a fool, Billy Casparis,' I says to myself; 'and of all your crimes against sense it does look like this idea of celebrating the Fourth should receive the award of demerit. Your business is busted up, your thousand dollars is gone into the kitty of this corrupt country on that last bluff you made, you've got just fifteen Chili dollars left, worth forty-six cents each at bedtime last night and steadily going down. To-day you'll blow in your last cent hurrahing for that flag, and to-morrow you'll be living on bananas from the stalk and screwing your drinks out of your friends. What's the flag done for you? While you were under it you worked for what you got. You wore your finger nails down skinning suckers, and salting mines, and driving bears and alligators off your town lot additions. How much does patriotism count for on deposit when the little man with the green eye-shade in the savings-bank adds up your book? Suppose you were to get pinched over here in this irreligious country for some little crime or other, and appealed to your country for protection— what would it do for you? Turn your appeal over to a committee of one railroad man, an army officer, a member of each labour union, and a colored man to investigate whether any of your ancestors were ever related to a cousin of Mark Hanna, and then file the papers in the Smithsonian Institution until after the next election. That's the kind of a sidetrack the Stars and Stripes would switch you on to.'

"You can see that I was feeling like an indigo plant; but after I washed my face in some cool water, and got out my navys and ammunition, and started up to the Saloon of the Immaculate Saints where we were to meet, I felt better. And when I saw those other American boys come swaggering into the trysting place—cool, easy, conspicuous fellows, ready to risk any kind of a one-card draw, or to fight grizzlies, fire, or extradition, I began to feel glad I was one of 'em. So, I says to myself again: 'Billy, you've got fifteen dollars and a country left this morning—blow in the dollars and blow up the town as an American gentleman should on Independence Day.'

"It is my recollection that we began the day along conventional lines. The six of us—for Sterrett was along—made progress among the cantinas divesting the bars as we went of all strong drink bearing American labels. We kept informing the atmosphere as to the glory and preëminence of the United States and its ability to subdue, outjump, and eradicate the other nations of the earth. And, as the findings of American labels grew more plentiful, we became more contaminated with patriotism. Maximilian Jones hopes that our late foe, Mr. Sterrett, will not take offense at our enthusiasm. He sets down his bottle and shakes Sterrett's hand. 'As white man to white man,' says he, 'denude our uproar of the slightest taint of personality. Excuse us for Bunker Hill, Patrick Henry, and Waldorf Astor, and such grievances as might lie between us as nations.'

"'Fellow hoodlums,' says Sterrett, 'on behalf of the Queen I ask you to cheese it. It is an honor to be a guest at disturbing the peace under the American flag. Let us chant the passionate strains of "Yankee Doodle" while the señor behind the bar mitigates the occasion with another round of cochineal and aqua fortis.'

"Old Man Billfinger, being charged with a kind of rhetoric, makes speeches

every time we stop. We explained to such citizens as we happened to step
on that we were celebrating the dawn of our private brand of liberty, and to
please enter such inhumanities as we might commit on the list of unavoidable
casualties.

"About eleven o'clock our bulletins read: 'A considerable rise in temperature,
accompanied by thirst and other alarming symptoms.' We hooked arms and
stretched our line across the narrow streets, all of us armed with Winchesters
and navys for purposes of noise and without malice. We stopped on a street
corner and fired a dozen or so rounds, and began a serial assortment of United
States whoops and yells, probably the first ever heard in that town.

"When we made that noise things began to liven up. We heard a pattering
up a side street, and here came General Mary Esperanza Dingo on a white horse
with a couple of hundred brown boys following him in red undershirts and bare
feet, dragging guns ten feet long. Jones and me had forgot all about General
Mary and his promise to help us celebrate. We fired another salute and gave
another yell, while the General shook hands with us and waved his sword.

"'Oh, General,' shouts Jones, 'this is great. This will be a real pleasure to the
eagle. Get down and have a drink.'

"'Drink?' says the general. 'No. There is no time to drink. Viva la
Libertad!'

"'Don't forget E Pluribus Unum!' says Henry Barnes.

"'Viva it good and strong,' says I. 'Likewise viva George Washington. God
save the Union, and,' I says, bowing to Sterrett, 'don't discard the Queen.'

"'Thanks, says Sterret. 'The next round's mine. All in to the bar Army,
too.'

"But we were deprived of Sterrett's treat by a lot of gunshots several squares
away, which General Dingo seemed to think he ought to look after He spurred
his old white plug up that way, and the soldiers scuttled along after him.

"'Mary is a real tropical bird,' says Jones. 'He's turned out the infantry to
help us do honor to the Fourth. We'll get that cannon he spoke of after a
while and fire some window-breakers with it. But just now I want some of
that barbecued beef. Let us on to the plaza.'

"There we found the meat gloriously done, and Jerry waiting, anxious. We
sat around on the grass, and got hunks of it on our tin plates. Maximilian
Jones, always made tender-hearted by drink, cried some because George Washington couldn't be there to enjoy the day. 'There was a man I love, Billy,'
he says, weeping on my shoulder. 'Poor George! To think he's gone, and missed
the fireworks. A little more salt, please, Jerry.'

"From what we could hear, General Dingo seemed to be kindly contributing
some noise while we feasted. There were guns going off around town, and pretty
soon we heard that cannon go 'BOOM!' just as he said it would. And then men
began to skim along the edge of the plaza, dodging in among the orange trees
and houses. We certainly had things stirred up in Salvador. We felt proud of
the occasion and grateful to General Dingo. Sterrett was about to take a bite
off a juicy piece of rib when a bullet took it away from his mouth.

"'Somebody's celebrating with ball cartridges,' says he, reaching for another
piece. 'Little over-zealous for a non-resident patriot, isn't it?'

"'Don't mind it,' I says to him. ''Twas an accident. They happen, you
know, on the Fourth. After one reading of the Declaration of Independence in
New York I've known the S. R. O. sign to be hung out at all the hospitals and
police stations.'

"But then Jerry gives a howl and jumps up with one hand clapped to the
back of his leg where another bullet has acted over-zealous. And then comes a
quantity of yells, and round a corner and across the plaza gallops General
Mary Esperanza Dingo embracing the neck of his horse, with his men running

behind him, mostly dropping their guns by way of discharging ballast. And chasing 'em all is a company of feverish little warriors wearing blue trousers and caps.

"'Assistance, *amigos*,' the General shouts, trying to stop his horse. 'Assistance, in the name of Liberty!'

"'That's the Compañía Azul, the President's bodyguard,' says Jones. 'What a shame! They've jumped on poor old Mary just because he was helping us to celebrate. Come on, boys, it's our Fourth;—do we let that little squad of A. D. T.'s break it up?'

"'I vote No,' says Martin Dillard, gathering his Winchester. "It's the privilege of an American citizen to drink, drill, dress up, and be dreadful on the Fourth of July, no matter whose country he's in.'

"'Fellow citizens!' says old man Billfinger, 'In the darkest hour of Freedom's birth, when our brave forefathers promulgated the principles of undying liberty, they never expected that a bunch of blue jays like that should be allowed to bust up an anniversary. Let us preserve and protect the Constitution.'

"We made it unanimous, and then we gathered our guns and assaulted the blue troops in force. We fired over their heads, and then charged 'em with a yell, and they broke and ran. We were irritated at having our barbecue disturbed, and we chased 'em a quarter of a mile. Some of 'em we caught and kicked hard. The General rallied his troops and joined in the chase. Finally they scattered in a thick banana grove, and we couldn't flush a single one. So we sat down and rested.

"If I were to be put, severe, through the third degree, I wouldn't be able to tell much about the rest of the day. I mind that we pervaded the town considerable, calling upon the people to bring out more armies for us to destroy. I remember seeing a crowd somewhere, and a tall man that wasn't Billfinger making a Fourth of July speech from a balcony. And that was about all.

"Somebody must have hauled the old ice factory up to where I was, and put it around me, for there's where I was when I woke up the next morning. As soon as I could recollect my name and address I got up and held an inquest. My last cent was gone. I was all in.

"And then a neat black carriage drives to the door, and out steps General Dingo and a bay man in a silk hat and tan shoes.

"'Yes,' says I to myself, 'I see it now. You're the Chief de Policeos and High Lord Chamberlain of the Calaboosum; and you want Billy Casparis for excess of patriotism and assault with intent. All right. Might as well be in jail, anyhow.'

"But it seems that General Mary is smiling, and the bay man shakes my hand, and speaks in the American dialect.

"'General Dingo has informed me, Señor Casparis, of your gallant service in our cause. I desire to thank you with my person. The bravery of you and the other *señores Americanos* turned the struggle for liberty in our favor. Our party triumphed. The terrible battle will live forever in history.'

"'Battle?' says I; 'what battle?' and I ran my mind back along history, trying to think.

"'Señor Casparis is modest,' says General Dingo. 'He led his brave *compadres* into the thickest of the fearful conflict. Yes. Without their aid the revolution would have failed.'

"'Why, now,' says I, 'don't tell me there was a revolution yesterday. That was only a Fourth of——'

"But right there I abbreviated. It seemed to me it might be best.

"'After the terrible struggle,' says the bay man, 'President Bolano was forced to fly. To-day Caballo is President by proclamation. Ah, yes. Beneath the new administration I am the head of the Department of Mercantile Concessions.

On my file I find one report, Señor Casparis, that you have not made ice in accord with your contract.' And here the bay man smiles at me, 'cute.

"'Oh, well,' says I, 'I guess the report's straight. I know they caught me. That's all there is to it.'

"'Do not say so,' says the bay man. He pulls off a glove and goes over and lays his hand on that chunk of glass.

"'Ice,' says he, nodding his head, solemn.

"General Dingo also steps over and feels of it.

"'Ice,' says the General; 'I'll swear to it.'

"'If Señor Casparis,' says the bay man, 'will present himself to the treasury on the sixth day of this month he will receive back the thousand dollars he did deposit as a forfeit. *Adiós, señor.*'

"The General and the bay man bowed themselves out, and I bowed as often as they did.

"And when the carriage rolls away through the sand I bows once more, deeper than ever, till my hat touches the ground. But this time 'twas not intended for them. For, over their heads, I saw the old flag fluttering in the breeze above the consul's roof; and 'twas to it I made my profoundest salute."

THE EMANCIPATION OF BILLY

In the old, old, square-porticoed mansion, with the wry window-shutters and the paint peeling off in discolored flakes, lived one of the last of the war governors.

The South has forgotten the enmity of the great conflict, but it refuses to abandon its old traditions and idols. In "Governor" Pemberton, as he was still fondly called, the inhabitants of Elmville saw the relic of their state's ancient greatness and glory. In his day he had been a man large in the eye of his country. His state had pressed upon him every honor within its gift. And now when he was old, and enjoying a richly merited repose outside the swift current of public affairs, his townsmen loved to do him reverence for the sake of the past.

The Governor's decaying "mansion" stood upon the main street of Elmville within a few feet of its rickety paling-fence. Every morning the Governor would descend the steps with extreme care and deliberation—on account of his rheumatism—and then the click of his gold-headed cane would be heard as he slowly proceeded up the rugged brick sidewalk. He was now nearly seventy-eight, but he had grown old gracefully and beautifully. His rather long, smooth hair and flowing, parted whiskers were snow-white. His full-skirted frock-coat was always buttoned snugly about his tall, spare figure. He wore a high, well-kept silk hat—known as a "plug" in Elmville—and nearly always gloves. His manners were punctilious, and somewhat overcharged with courtesy.

The Governor's walks up Lee Avenue, the principal street, developed in their course into a sort of memorial, triumphant procession. Everyone he met saluted him with profound respect. Many would remove their hats. Those who were honored with his personal friendship would pause to shake hands, and then you would see exemplified the genuine *beau idéal* Southern courtesy.

Upon reaching the corner of the second square from the mansion, the Governor would pause. Another street crossed the avenue there, and traffic, to the extent of several farmers' wagons and a peddler's cart or two, would rage about the junction. Then the falcon eye of General Deffenbaugh would perceive the situation, and the General would hasten, with ponderous solicitude, from his office in the First National Bank building to the assistance of his old friend.

When the two exchanged greetings the decay of modern manners would become accusingly apparent. The General's bulky and commanding figure would bend lissomely at a point where you would have regarded its ability to do so with incredulity. The Governor's cherished rheumatism would be compelled, for the moment, to give way before a genuflexion brought down from the days of the cavaliers. The Governor would take the General's arm and be piloted safely between the hay-wagons and the sprinkling-cart to the other side of the street. Proceeding to the post-office in the care of his friend, the esteemed statesman would there hold an informal levée among the citizens who were come for their morning mail. Here, gathering two or three prominent in law, politics, or family, the pageant would make a stately progress along the Avenue, stopping at the Palace Hotel, where, perhaps, would be found upon the register the name of some guest deemed worthy of an introduction to the state's venerable and illustrious son. If any such were found, an hour or two would be spent in recalling the faded glories of the Governor's long-vanished administration.

On the return march the General would invariably suggest that, His Excellency being no doubt fatigued, it would be wise to recuperate for a few minutes at the Drug Emporium of Mr. Appleby R. Fentress (an elegant gentleman, sir— one of the Chatham County Fentresses—so many of our best-blooded families have had to go into trade, sir, since the war).

Mr. Appleby R. Fentress was a connoisseur in fatigue. Indeed, if he had not been, his memory alone should have enabled him to prescribe, for the majestic invasion of his pharmacy was a casual happening that had surprised him almost daily for years. Mr. Fentress knew the formula of, and possessed the skill to compound, a certain potion antagonistic to fatigue, the salient ingredient of which he described (no doubt in pharmaceutical terms) as "genuine old handmade Clover Leaf '59, Private Stock."

Nor did the ceremony of administering the potion ever vary. Mr. Fentress would first compound two of the celebrated mixtures—one for the Governor, and the other for the General to "sample." Then the Governor would make this little speech in his high, piping, quavering voice:

"No, sir—not one drop until you have prepared one for yourself and joined us, Mr. Fentress. Your father, sir, was one of my most valued supporters and friends during My Administration, and any mark of esteem I can confer upon his son is not only a pleasure but a duty, sir."

Blushing with delight at the royal condescension, the druggist would obey, and all would drink to the General's toast: "The prosperity of our grand old state, gentlemen—the memory of her glorious past—the health of her Favorite Son."

Some one of the Old Guard was always at hand to escort the Governor home. Sometimes the General's business duties denied him the privilege, and then Judge Broomfield or Colonel Titus, or one of the Ashford County Slaughters would be on hand to perform the rite.

Such were the observances attendant upon the Governor's morning stroll to the post-office. How much more magnificent, impressive, and spectacular, then, was the scene at public functions when the General would lead forth the silver-haired relic of former greatness, like some rare and fragile waxwork figure, and trumpet his pristine eminence to his fellow citizens!

General Deffenbaugh was the Voice of Elmville. Some said he was Elmville. At any rate, he had no competitor as the Mouthpiece. He owned enough stock in the *Daily Banner* to dictate its utterance, enough shares in the First National Bank to be the referee of its loans, and a war record that left him without a rival for first place at barbecues, school commencements, and Decoration Days. Besides these acquirements he was possessed with endowments. His personality was inspiring and triumphant. Undisputed sway had molded him to the likeness of a fatted Roman emperor. The tones of his voice were not otherwise than clarion. To say that the General was public-spirited would fall short of doing him justice. He had spirit enough for a dozen publics. And as a sure foundation for it all, he had a heart that was big and stanch. Yes; General Deffenbaugh was Elmville.

One little incident that usually occurred during the Governor's morning walk has had its chronicling delayed by more important matters. The procession was accustomed to halt before a small brick office on the Avenue, fronted by a short flight of steep wooden steps. A modest tin sign over the door bore the words: "Wm. B. Pemberton: Attorney-at-Law."

Looking inside, the General would roar: "Hello, Billy, my boy." The less-distinguished members of the escort would call: "Morning, Billy." The Governor would pipe: "Good-morning, William."

Then a patient-looking little man with hair turning gray along the temples would come down the steps and shake hands with each one of the party. All Elmville shook hands when it met.

The formalities concluded, the little man would go back to his table, heaped with law books and papers, while the procession would proceed.

Billy Pemberton was, as his sign declared, a lawyer, by profession. By occupation and common consent he was the Son of his Father. This was the shadow in which Billy lived, the pit out of which he had unsuccessfully striven for years to climb and, he had come to believe, the grave in which his ambitions were destined to be buried. Filial respect and duty he paid beyond the habit of most sons, but he aspired to be known and appraised by his own deeds and worth.

After many years of tireless labor he had become known in certain quarters far from Elmville as a master of the principles of the law. Twice he had gone to Washington and argued cases before the highest tribunal with such acute logic and learning that the silken gowns on the bench had rustled from the force of it. His income from his practice had grown until he was able to support his father, in the old family mansion (which neither of them would have thought of abandoning, rickety as it was) in the comfort and almost the luxury of the old extravagant days. Yet, he remained to Elmville as only "Billy" Pemberton, the son of our distinguished and honored fellow-townsman, "ex-Governor Pemberton." Thus was he introduced at public gatherings where he sometimes spoke, haltingly and prosily, for his talents were too serious and deep for extempore brilliancy; thus was he presented to strangers and to the lawyers who made the circuit of the courts; and so the *Daily Banner* referred to him in print. To be "the son of" was his doom. Whatever he should accomplish would have to be sacrificed upon the altar of this magnificent but fatal parental precedence.

The peculiarity and the saddest thing about Billy's ambition was that the only world he thirsted to conquer was Elmville. His nature was diffident and unassuming. National or State honors might have oppressed him. But, above all things, he hungered for the appreciation of the friends among whom he had been born and raised. He would not have plucked one leaf from the garlands that were so lavishly bestowed upon his father, he merely rebelled against having his own wreaths woven from those dried and self-same branches. But Elmville "Billied" and "sonned" him to his concealed but lasting chagrin, until at length he grew more reserved and formal and studious than ever.

There came a morning when Billy found among his mail a letter from a very high source, tendering him the appointment to an important judicial position in the new island possessions of our country. The honor was a distinguished one, for the entire nation had discussed the probable recipients of these positions, and had agreed that the situation demanded only men of the highest character, ripe learning, and evenly balanced mind.

Billy could not subdue a certain exultation at this token of the success of his long and arduous labors, but, at the same time, a whimsical smile lingered around his mouth, for he foresaw in which Elmville would place the credit. "We congratulate Governor Pemberton upon the mark of appreciation conferred upon his son"—"Elmville rejoices with our honored citizen, Governor Pemberton, at his son's success"—"Put her there, Billy!"—"Judge Billy Pemberton, sir; son of our State's war hero and the people's pride!"—these were the phrases, printed and oral, conjured up by Billy's prophetic fancy. Grandson of his State, and step-child of Elmville—thus had fate fixed his kinship to the body politic.

Billy lived with his father in the old mansion. The two and an elderly lady—a distant relative—comprised the family. Perhaps, though, old Jeff, the Governor's ancient colored body-servant, should be included. Without doubt, he would have claimed the honor. There were other servants, but Thomas Jefferson Pemberton, sah, was a member of "de fambly."

Jeff was the one Elmvillian who gave to Billy the gold of approval unmixed with the alloy of paternalism. To him "Mars William" was the greatest man in Talbot County. Beaten upon though he was by the shining light that emanates from an ex-war governor, and loyal as he remained to the old *régime*, his faith and admiration were Billy's. As valet to a hero, and a member of the family, he may have had superior opportunities for judging.

Jeff was the first one to whom Billy revealed the news. When he reached home for supper Jeff took his "plug" hat and smoothed it before hanging it upon the hall-rack.

"Dar now!" said the old man: "I knowed it was er comin', I knowed it was gwine ter happen. Er Judge, you says, Mars William? Dem Yankees done made you er judge? It's high time, sah, dey was doin' somep'n to make up for dey rescality endurin' de war. I boun' dey holds a confab and says: 'Le's make Mars William Pemberton er judge, and dat'll settle it.' Does you have to go away down to dem Fillypines, Mars William, or kin you judge 'em from here?"

"I'd have to live there most of the time, of course," said Billy.

"I wonder what de Gubnor gwine say 'bout dat," speculated Jeff.

Billy wondered too.

After supper, when the two sat in the library, according to their habit, the Governor smoking his clay pipe and Billy his cigar, the son dutifully confessed to having been tendered the appointment.

For a long time the Governor sat, smoking, without making any comment. Billy reclined in his favorite rocker, waiting, perhaps still flushed with satisfaction over the tender that had come to him, unsolicited, in his dingy little office, above the heads of the intriguing, time-serving, clamorous multitude.

At last the Governor spoke; and, though his words were seemingly irrelevant, they were to the point. His voice had a note of martyrdom running through its senile quaver.

"My rheumatism has been growing steadily worse these past months, William."

"I am sorry, Father," said Billy, gently.

"And I am nearly seventy-eight. I am getting to be an old man. I can recall the names of but two or three who were in public life during My Administration. What did you say is the nature of this position that is offered you, William?"

"A Federal judgeship, Father. I believe it is considered to be a somewhat flattering tender. It is outside of politics and wire-pulling, you know."

"No doubt, no doubt. Few of the Pembertons have engaged in professional life for nearly a century. None of them have ever held Federal positions.

They have been landholders, slave-owners, and planters on a large scale. One or two of the Derwents—your mother's family—were in the law. Have you decided to accept this appointment, William?"

"I am thinking it over," said Billy, slowly, regarding the ash of his cigar.

"You have been a good son to me," continued the Governor, stirring his pipe with the handle of a penholder.

"I've been your son all my life," said Billy, darkly.

"I am often gratified," piped the Governor, betraying a touch of complacency, "by being congratulated upon having a son with such sound and sterling qualities. Especially in this, our native town, is your name linked with mine in the talk of our citizens."

"I never knew anyone to forget the vinculum," murmured Billy, unintelligibly.

"Whatever prestige," pursued the parent, "I may be possessed of, by virtue of my name and services to the state, has been yours to draw upon freely. I have not hesitated to exert it in your behalf whenever opportunity offered. And you have deserved it, William. You've been the best of sons. And now this appointment comes to take you away from me. I have but a few years left to live. I am almost dependent upon others now, even in walking and dressing. What would I do without you, my son?"

The Governor's pipe dropped to the floor. A tear trickled from his eye. His voice had risen, and crumbled to a weakling falsetto, and ceased. He was an old, old man about to be bereft of the son that cherished him.

Billy rose, and laid his hand upon the Governor's shoulder.

"Don't worry, father," he said, cheerfully. "I'm not going to accept. Elmville is good enough for me. I'll write to-night and decline it."

At the next interchange of devoirs between the Governor and General Deffenbaugh on Lee Avenue, His Excellency, with a comfortable air of self-satisfaction, spoke of the appointment that had been tendered to Billy.

The General whistled.

"That's a plum for Billy," he shouted. "Who'd have thought that Billy—but, confound it, it's been in him all the time. It's a boost for Elmville. It'll send real estate up. It's an honor to our state. It's a compliment to the South. We've all been blind about Billy. When does he leave? We must have a reception. Great Gatlings! that job's eight thousand a year! There's been a car-load of lead-pencils worn to stubs figuring on those appointments. Think of it! Our little, wood-sawing, mealy-mouthed Billy! Angel unawares doesn't begin to express it. Elmville is disgraced forever unless she lines up in a hurry for ratification and apology."

The venerable Moloch smiled fatuously. He carried the fire with which to consume all these tributes to Billy, the smoke of which would ascend as an incense to himself.

"William," said the Governor, with modest pride, "has declined the appointment. He refuses to leave me in my old age. He is a good son."

The General swung around and laid a large forefinger upon the bosom of his friend. Much of the General's success had been due to his dexterity in establishing swift lines of communication between cause and effect.

"Governor," he said, with a keen look in his big, ox-like eyes, "you've been complaining to Billy about your rheumatism."

"My dear General," replied the Governor, stiffly, "my son is forty-two. He is quite capable of deciding such questions for himself. And I, as his parent, feel it my duty to state that your remark about—er—rheumatism is a mighty poor shot from a very small bore, sir, aimed at a purely personal and private affliction."

"If you will allow me," retorted the General, "you've afflicted the public with it for some time; and 'twas no small bore, at that."

This first tiff between the two old comrades might have grown into something more serious but for the fortunate interruption caused by the ostentatious approach of Colonel Titus and another one of the court retinue from the right county, to whom the General confided the coddled statesman and went his way.

After Billy had so effectually entombed his ambitions, and taken the veil, so to speak, in a sonnery, he was surprised to discover how much lighter of heart and happier he felt. He realized what a long, restless struggle he had maintained, and how much he had lost by failing to cull the simple but wholesome pleasures by the way. His heart warmed now to Elmville and the friends who had refused to set him upon a pedestal. It was better, he began to think, to be "Billy" and his father's son, and to be hailed familiarly by cheery neighbors and grown-up playmates, than to be "Your Honor," and sit among strangers, hearing, maybe, through the arguments of learned counsel, that old man's feeble voice crying: "What would I do without you, my son?"

Billy began to surprise his acquaintances by whistling as he walked up the street; others he astounded by slapping them disrespectfully upon their backs and raking up old anecdotes he had not had the time to recollect for years. Though he hammered away at his law cases as thoroughly as ever, he found more time for relaxation and the company of his friends. Some of the younger set were actually after him to join the golf club. A striking proof of his abandonment to obscurity was his adoption of a most undignified, rakish little soft hat, reserving the "plug" for Sundays and state occasions. Billy was beginning to enjoy Elmville, though that irreverent burgh had neglected to crown him with bay and myrtle.

All the while uneventful peace pervaded Elmville. The Governor continued to make his triumphal parades to the post-office with the General as chief marshal, for the slight squall that had rippled their friendship had, to all indications, been forgotten by both.

But one day Elmville woke to sudden excitement. The news had come that a touring presidential party would honor Elmville by a twenty-minute stop. The Executive had promised a five-minute address from the balcony of the Palace Hotel.

Elmville arose as one man—that man being, of course, General Deffenbaugh—to receive becomingly the chieftain of all the clans. The train with the tiny Stars and Stripes fluttering from the engine pilot arrived. Elmville had done her best. There were bands, flowers, carriages, uniforms, banners, and committees without end. High-school girls in white frocks impeded the steps of the party with roses strewn nervously in bunches. The chieftain had seen it all before—scores of times. He could have pictured it exactly in advance, from the Blue-and-Gray speech down to the smallest rosebud. Yet his kindly smile of interest greeted Elmville's display as if it had been the only and original.

In the upper rotunda of the Palace Hotel the town's most illustrious were assembled for the honor of being presented to the distinguished guests previous to the expected address. Outside, Elmville's inglorious but patriotic masses filled the streets.

Here, in the hotel General Deffenbaugh was holding in reserve Elmville's trump card. Elmville knew; for the trump was a fixed one, and its lead consecrated by archaic custom.

At the proper moment Governor Pemberton, beautifully venerable, magnificently antique, tall, paramount, stepped forward upon the arm of the General.

Elmville watched and harked with bated breath. Never until now—when a Northern President of the United States should clasp hands with ex-war-Governor Pemberton—would the breach be entirely closed—would the country be made one and indivisible—no North not much South, very little East, and no West to speak of. So Elmville excitedly scraped kalsomine from the walls of the Palace Hotel with its Sunday best, and waited for the Voice to speak.

And Billy! We had nearly forgotten Billy. He was cast for Son, and he waited patiently for his cue. He carried his "plug" in his hand, and felt serene. He admired his father's striking air and pose. After all, it was a great deal to be son of a man who could so gallantly hold the position of a cynosure for three generations.

General Deffenbaugh cleared his throat. Elmville opened its mouth, and squirmed. The chieftain with the kindly, fateful face was holding out his hand, smiling. Ex-war-Governor Pemberton extended his own across the chasm. But what was this the General was saying?

"Mr. President, allow me to present to you one who has the honor to be the father of our foremost distinguished citizen, learned and honored jurist, beloved townsman, and model Southern gentleman—the Honorable William B. Pemberton."

THE ENCHANTED KISS

BUT a clerk in the Cut-rate Drug Store was Samuel Tansey, yet his slender frame was a pad that enfolded the passion of Romeo, the gloom of Lara, the romance of D'Artagnan, and the desperate inspiration of Melnotte. Pity, then, that he had been denied expression, that he was doomed to the burden of utter timidity and diffidence, that Fate had set him tongue-tied and scarlet before the muslin-clad angels whom he adored and vainly longed to rescue, clasp, comfort, and subdue.

The clock's hands were pointing close upon the hour of ten while Tansey was playing billiards with a number of his friends. On alternate evenings he was released from duty at the store after seven o'clock. Even among his fellow men Tansey was timorous and constrained. In his imagination he had done valiant deeds and performed acts of distinguished gallantry; but in fact he was a shallow youth of twenty-three, with an over-modest demeanor and scant vocabulary.

When the clock struck ten, Tansey hastily laid down his cue and struck sharply upon the show-case with a coin for the attendant to come and receive the pay for his score.

"What's your hurry, Tansey?" called one. "Got another engagement?"

"Tansey got an engagement!" echoed another. "Not on your life. Tansey's got to get home at ten by Mother Peek's orders."

"It's no such thing," chimed in a pale youth, taking a large cigar from his mouth; "Tansey's afraid to be late because Miss Katie might come downstairs to unlock the door, and kiss him in the hall."

This delicate piece of raillery sent a fiery tingle into Tansey's blood, for the indictment was true—barring the kiss. That was a thing to dream of; to wildly hope for; but too remote and sacred a thing to think of lightly.

Casting a cold and contemptuous look at the speaker—a punishment commensurate with his own diffident spirit—Tansey left the room, descending the stairs into the street.

For two years he had silently adored Miss Peek, worshipping her from a spiritual distance through which her attractions took on stellar brightness and mystery. Mis. Peek kept a few choice boarders, among whom was Tansey. The other young men romped with Katie, chased her with crickets in their fingers, and "jollied" her with an irreverent freedom that turned Tansey's heart into cold lead in his bosom. The signs of his adoration were few—a tremulous "Good morning," stealthy glances at her during meals, and occasionally (Oh, rapture!) a blushing, delirious game of cribbage with her in the parlor on some rare evening when a miraculous lack of engagement kept her at home. Kiss him in the hall! Aye, he feared it, but it was an ecstatic fear such as Elijah must have felt when the chariot lifted him into the unknown.

But to-night the gibes of his associates had stung him to a feeling of forward, lawless mutiny; a defiant, challenging, atavistic recklessness. Spirit of corsair, adventurer, lover, poet, Bohemian, possessed him. The stars he saw above him seemed no more unattainable, no less high, than the favor of Miss Peek or the fearsome sweetness of her delectable lips. His fate seemed to him strangely dramatic and pathetic, and to call for a solace consonant with its extremity. A saloon was near by, and to this he flitted. calling for absinthe—beyond doubt the drink most adequate to his mood—the tipple of the roué, the abandoned, the vainly sighing lover.

Once he drank of it, and again, and then again until he felt a strange, exalted sense of non-participation in worldly affairs pervade him. Tansey was no drinker; his consumption of three absinthe anisettes within almost as few minutes proclaimed his unproficiency in the art; Tansey was merely flooding with unproven liquor his sorrows; which record and tradition alleged to be drownable.

Coming out upon the sidewalk, he snapped his fingers defiantly in the direction of the Peek homestead, turned the other way, and voyaged, Columbus-like, into the wilds of an enchanted street. Nor is the figure exorbitant, for, beyond his store the foot of Tansey had scarcely been set for years—store and boarding-house; between these ports he was chartered to run, and contrary currents had rarely deflected his prow.

Tansey aimlessly protracted his walk, and, whether it was his unfamiliarity with the district, his recent accession of audacious errantry, or the sophistical whisper of a certain green-eyed fairy, he came at last to tread a shuttered, blank, and echoing, thoroughfare, dark and unpeopled. And, suddenly, this way came to an end (as many streets do in the Spanish-built, archaic town of San Antone), butting its head against an imminent, high, brick wall. No—the street still lived! To the right and to the left it breathed through slender tubes of exit —narrow, somnolent ravines, cobble paved and unlighted. Accommodating a rise in the street to the right was reared a phantom flight of five luminous steps of limestone, flanked by a wall of the same height and of the same material.

Upon one of these steps Tansey seated himself and bethought him of his love, and how she might never know she was his love. And of Mother Peek, fat, vigilant and kind; not unpleased, Tansey thought, that he and Katie should play cribbage in the parlor together. For the Cut-rate had not cut his salary, which, sordidly speaking. ranked him star boarder at the Peeks'. And he thought of Captain Peek, Katie's father, a man he dreaded and abhorred; a genteel loafer and spendthrift, battening upon the labor of his women-folk; a very queer fish, and, according to repute, not of the freshest.

The night had turned chill and foggy. The heart of the town, with its noises, was left behind. Reflected from the high vapors, its distant lights were manifest in quivering, cone-shaped streamers, in questionable blushes of unnamed colors, in unstable, ghostly waves of far, electric flashes. Now that the darkness was become more friendly, the wall against which the street splintered developed a stone coping topped with an armature of spikes. Beyond it loomed what ap-

peared to be the acute angles of mountain peaks, pierced here and there by little
lambent parallelograms. Considering this vista, Tansey at length persuaded himself that the seeming mountains were, in fact, the convent of Santa Mercedes,
with which ancient and bulky pile he was better familiar from different coigns
of view. A pleasant noise of singing in his ears reënforced his opinion. High,
sweet, holy carolling, far and harmonious and uprising, as of sanctified nuns at
their responses. At what hour did the Sisters sing? He tried to think—was it
six, eight, twelve? Tansey leaned his back against the limestone wall and wondered. Strange things followed. The air was full of white, fluttering pigeons
that circled about, and settled upon the convent wall. The wall blossomed with
a quantity of shining green eyes that blinked and peered at him from the solid
masonry. A pink, classic nymph came from an excavation in the cavernous road
and danced, barefoot and airy, upon the ragged flints. The sky was traversed
by a company of beribboned cats, marching in stupendous, aërial procession. The
noise of singing grew louder; an illumination of unseasonable fireflies danced past,
and strange whispers came out of the dark without meaning or excuse.

Without amazement Tansey took note of these phenomena. He was on some
new plane of understanding, though his mind seemed to him clear and, indeed,
happily tranquil.

A desire for movement and exploration seized him: he rose and turned into the
black gash of street to his right. For a time the high wall formed one of its
boundaries, but farther on, two rows of black-windowed houses closed it in.

Here was the city's quarter once given over to the Spaniard. Here were still
his forbidding abodes of concrete and adobe, standing cold and indomitable
against the century. From the murky fissure, the eye saw, flung against the
sky, the tangled filigree of his Moorish balconies. Through stone archways
breaths of dead, vault-chilled air coughed upon him; his feet struck jingling iron
rings in staples stone-buried for half a cycle. Along these paltry avenues had
swaggered the arrogant Don, had caracoled and serenaded and blustered while the
tomahawk and the pioneer's rifle were already uplifted to expel him from a
continent. And Tansey, stumbling through this old-world dust, looked up, dark
as it was, and saw Andalusian beauties glimmering on the balconies. Some of
them were laughing and listening to the goblin music that still followed; others
harked fearfully through the night, trying to catch the hoof beats of caballeros
whose last echoes from those stones had died away a century ago. Those women
were silent, but Tansey heard the jangle of horseless bridle-bits, the whirr of
riderless rowels, and, now and then, a muttered malediction in a foreign tongue.
But he was not frightened. Shadows, nor shadows of sounds could daunt him.
Afraid? No. Afraid of Mother Peek? Afraid to face the girl of his heart?
Afraid of tipsy Captain Peek? Nay! nor of these apparitions, nor of that spectral
singing that always pursued him. Singing! He would show them! He lifted
up a strong and untuneful voice:

"When you hear them bells go tingalingling,"

serving notice upon those mysterious agencies that if it should come to a face-to-
face encounter

"There'll be a hot time
In the old town
To-night!"

How long Tansey consumed in treading this haunted byway was not clear to
him, but in time he emerged into a more commodious avenue. When within a

few yards of the corner he perceived, through a window, that a small confectionery of mean appearance was set in the angle. His same glance that estimated its meagre equipment, its cheap soda-water fountain and stock of tobacco and sweets, took cognizance of Captain Peek within lighting a cigar at a swinging gaslight.

As Tansey rounded the corner Captain Peek came out, and they met *vis-à-vis*. An exultant joy filled Tansey when he found himself sustaining the encounter with implicit courage. Peek, indeed! He raised his hand, and snapped his fingers loudly.

It was Peek himself who quailed guiltily before the valiant mien of the drug clerk. Sharp surprise and a palpable fear bourgeoned upon the Captain's face. And, verily, that face was one to rather call up such expressions upon the faces of others. The face of a libidinous heathen idol, small eyed, with carven folds in the heavy jowls, and a consuming, pagan license in its expression. In the gutter just beyond the store Tansey saw a closed carriage standing with its back toward him and a motionless driver perched in his place.

"Why, it's Tansey!" exclaimed Captain Peek. "How are you, Tansey? H-have a cigar, Tansey?"

"Why, it's Peek!" cried Tansey, jubilant at his own temerity. "What deviltry are you up to now, Peek? Back streets and a closed carriage! Fie! Peek!"

"There's no one in the carriage," said the Captain, smoothly.

"Everybody out of it is in luck," continued Tansey, aggressively. "I'd love for you to know, Peek, that I'm not stuck on you. You're a bottle-nosed scoundrel."

"Why, the little rat's drunk!" cried the Captain, joyfully; "only drunk, and I thought he was on! Go home, Tansey, and quit bothering grown persons on the street."

But just then a white-clad figure sprang out of the carriage, and a shrill voice—Katie's voice—sliced the air: "Sam! Sam!—help me, Sam!"

Tansey sprang toward her, but Captain Peek interposed his bulky form. Wonder of wonders! the whilom spiritless youth struck out with his right, and the hulking Captain went over in a swearing heap. Tansey flew to Katie, and took her in his arms like a conquering knight. She raised her face, and he kissed her—violets! electricity! caramels! champagne! Here was the attainment of a dream that brought no disenchantment.

"Oh, Sam," cried Katie, when she could, "I knew you would come to rescue me. What do you suppose the mean things were going to do with me?"

"Have your picture taken," said Tansey, wondering at the foolishness of his remark.

"No, they were going to eat me. I heard them talking about it."

"Eat you!" said Tansey, after pondering a moment. "That can't be; there's no plates."

But a sudden noise warned him to turn. Down upon him were bearing the Captain and a monstrous long-bearded dwarf in a spangled cloak and red trunkhose. The dwarf leaped twenty feet and clutched him. The Captain seized Katie and hurled her, shrieking, back into the carriage, himself followed, and the vehicle dashed away. The dwarf lifted Tansey high above his head and ran with him into the store. Holding him with one hand, he raised the lid of an enormous chest half filled with cakes of ice, flung Tansey inside, and closed down the cover.

The force of the fall must have been great, for Tansey lost consciousness. When his faculties revived his first sensation was one of severe cold along his back and limbs. Opening his eyes, he found himself to be seated upon the limestone steps still facing the wall and convent of Santa Mercedes. His first thought was of the ecstatic kiss from Katie. The outrageous villainy of Captain Peek.

the unnatural mystery of the situation, his preposterous conflict with the improbable dwarf—these things roused and angered him, but left no impression of the unreal.

"I'll go back there to-morrow," he grumbled aloud, "and knock the head off that comic-opera squab. Running out and picking up perfect strangers, and shoving them into cold storage!"

But the kiss remained uppermost in his mind. "I might have done that long ago," he mused. "She liked it, too. She called me 'Sam' four times. I'll not go up that street again. Too much scrapping. Guess I'll move down the other way. Wonder what she meant by saying they were going to eat her!"

Tansey began to feel sleepy, but after a while he decided to move along again. This time he ventured into the street to his left. It ran level for a distance, and then dipped gently downward, opening into a vast, dim, barren space—the old Military Plaza. To his left, some hundred yards distant, he saw a cluster of flickering lights along the Plaza's border. He knew the locality at once.

Huddled within narrow confines were the remnants of the once-famous purveyors of the celebrated Mexican national cookery. A few years before, their nightly encampments upon the historic Alamo Plaza, in the heart of the city, had been a carnival, a saturnalia that was renowned throughout the land. Then the caterers numbered hundreds; the patrons thousands. Drawn by the coquettish *señoritas*, the music of the weird Spanish minstrels, and the strange piquant Mexican dishes served at a hundred competing tables, crowds thronged the Alamo Plaza all night. Travellers, rancheros, family parties, gay gasconading rounders, sight-seers and prowlers of polygot, owlish San Antone mingled there at the centre of the city's fun and frolic. The popping of corks, pistols, and questions; the glitter of eyes, jewels, and daggers; the ring of laughter and coin —these were the order of the night.

But now no longer. To some half-dozen tents, fires, and tables had dwindled the picturesque festival, and these had been relegated to an ancient disused plaza.

Often had Tansey strolled down to these stands at night to partake of the delectable *chili-con-carne*, a dish evolved by the genius of Mexico, composed of delicate meats minced with aromatic herbs and the poignant *chili colorado*—a compound full of singular savour and a fiery zest delightful to the Southron's palate.

The titillating odor of this concoction came now, on the breeze, to the nostrils of Tansey, awakening in him hunger for it. As he turned in that direction he saw a carriage dash up to the Mexicans' tents out of the gloom of the Plaza. Some figures moved back and forward in the uncertain light of the lanterns, and then the carriage was driven swiftly away.

Tansey approached, and sat at one of the tables covered with gaudy oil-cloth. Traffic was dull at the moment. A few half-grown boys noisily fared at another table; the Mexicans hung listless and phlegmatic about their wares. And it was still. The night hum of the city crowded to the wall of dark buildings surrounding the Plaza, and subsided to an indefinite buzz through which sharply perforated the crackle of the languid fires and the rattle of fork and spoon. A sedative wind blew from the southeast. The starless firmament pressed down upon the earth like a leaden cover.

In all that quiet Tansey turned his head suddenly, and saw, without disquietude, a troop of spectral horsemen deploy into the Plaza and charge a luminous line of infantry that advanced to sustain the shock. He saw the fierce flame of cannon and small arms, but heard no sound. The careless victuallers lounged vacantly, not deigning to view the conflict. Tansey mildly wondered to what nations these mute combatants might belong; turned his back to them and ordered his *chili* and coffee from the Mexican woman who advanced to serve him. This woman was old and careworn; her face was lined like the rind of a cantaloupe. She fetched the viands from a vessel set by the smouldering fire, and then retired to a tent, dark within, that stood near by.

Presently Tansey heard a turmoil in the tent; a wailing, broken-hearted plead‑ ing in the harmonious Spanish tongue, and then two figures tumbled out into the light of the lanterns. One was the old woman; the other was a man clothed with a sumptuous and flashing splendor. The woman seemed to clutch and beseech from him something against his will. The man broke from her and struck her brutally back into the tent, where she lay, whimpering and invisible. Observ‑ ing Tansey, he walked rapidly to the table where he sat. Tansey recognized him to be Ramon Torres, a Mexican, the proprietor of the stand he was patron‑ izing.

Torres was a handsome, nearly full‑blooded descendant of the Spanish, seem‑ ingly about thirty years of age, and of a haughty, but extremely courteous de‑ meanor. To‑night he was dressed with signal magnificence. His costume was that of a triumphant *matador*, made of purple velvet almost hidden by jeweled embroidery. Diamonds of enormous size flashed upon his garb and his hands. He reached for a chair, and, seating himself at the opposite side of the table, began to roll a finical cigarette.

"Ah, Meester Tansee," he said, with a sultry fire in his silky, black eye, "I give myself pleasure to see you this evening. Meester Tansee, you have many times come to eat at my table. I theenk you a safe man—a verree good friend. How much would it please you to leeve forever?"

"Not come back any more?" inquired Tansey.

"No; not leave—*leeve;* the not‑to‑die."

"I would call that," said Tansey, "a snap."

Torres leaned his elbows upon the table, swallowed a mouthful of smoke, and spake—each word being projected in a little puff of gray.

"How old do you theenk I am, Meester Tansee?"

"Oh, twenty‑eight or thirty."

"Thees day," said the Mexican, "ees my birthday. I am four hundred and three years of old to‑day."

"Another proof," said Tansey, airily, "of the healthfulness of our climate."

"Eet is not the air. I am to relate to you a secret of verree fine value. Listen me, Meester Tansee. At the age of twenty‑three I arrive in Mexico from Spain. When? In the year fifteen hundred nineteen, with the *soldados* of Hernando Cortez. I come to thees country seventeen fifteen. I saw your Alamo reduced. It was like yesterday to me. Three hundred ninety‑six year ago I learn the secret always to leeve. Look at these clothes I wear—at these *diamantes*. Do you theenk I buy them with the money I make with selling the *chili‑con‑carne,* Meester Tansee?"

"I should think not," said Tansey, promptly. Torres laughed loudly.

"*Válgame Dios!* but I do. But it not the kind you eating now. I make a deeferent kind, the eating of wnich makes men to always leeve. What do you think! One thousand people I supply—*diez pesos* each one pays me the month. You see! ten thousand *pesos* everee month! *Qué diablos!* how not I wear the fine *ropo!* You see that old woman try to hold me back a little while ago? That ees my wife. When I marry her she is young—seventeen year—*bonita*—. Like the rest she ees become old and—what you say!—tough? I am the same— young all the time. To‑night I resolve to dress myself and find another wife befitting my age. This old woman try to scr‑r‑ratch my face. Ha! Ha! Meester Tansee—same way they do *entre los Americanos.*"

"And this health‑food you spoke of?" said Tansey.

"Hear me," said Torres, leaning over the table until he lay flat upon it; "eet is the *chili‑con‑carne* made not from the beef or the chicken, but from the flesh of the *señorita*—young and tender. That ees the secret. Everee month you must eat it, having care to do so before the moon is full, and you will not die any times. See how I trust you, friend Tansee! To-night I have bought one young ladee—veree pretty—so *fina, gorda, blandita!* To-morrow the *chili* will be ready. *Ahora si!* One thousand dollars I pay for thees young ladee. From an *Americano* I have bought—a verree tip-top man—*el Capitan Peek—Qué es, Señor?*"

For Tansey had sprung to his feet, upsetting the chair. The words of Katie reverberated in his ears: "They're going to eat me, Sam." This, then, was the monstrous fate to which she had been delivered by her unnatural parent. The carriage he had seen drive up from the Plaza was Captain Peek's. Where was Katie? Perhaps already——

Before he could decide what to do a loud scream came from the tent. The old Mexican woman ran out, a flashing knife in her hand. "I have released her," she cried. "You shall kill no more. They will hang you—*ingrato—encantador!*"

Torres, with a hissing exclamation, sprang at her.

"Ramoncito!" she shrieked; "once you loved me."

The Mexican's arm raised and descended. "You are old," he cried; and she fell and lay motionless.

Another scream; the flaps of the tent were flung aside, and there stood Katie, white with fear, her wrists still bound with a cruel cord.

"Sam!" she cried, "save me again!"

Tansey rounded the table, and flung himself, with superb nerve, upon the Mexican. Just then a clangor began; the clocks of the city were tolling the midnight hour. Tansey clutched at Torres, and, for a moment, felt in his grasp the crunch of velvet and the cold facets of the glittering gems. The next instant, the bedecked caballero turned in his hands to a shrunken, leather-visaged, white-bearded, old, old screaming mummy, sandalled, ragged, four hundred and three. The Mexican woman was crawling to her feet, and laughing. She shook her brown hand in the face of the whining *viejo.*

"Go, now," she cried, "and seek your señorita. It was I, Ramoncito, who brought you to this. Within each moon you eat of the life-giving *chili.* It was I that kept the wrong time for you. You should have eaten *yesterday* instead of *to-morrow.* It is too late. Off with you, *hombre!* You are too old for me!"

"This," decided Tansey, releasing his hold of the graybeard, "is a private family matter concerning age, and no business of mine."

With one of the table knives he hastened to saw asunder the fetters of the fair captive; and then, for the second time that night he kissed Katie Peek—tasted again the sweetness, the wonder, the thrill of it, attained once more the maximum of his incessant dreams.

The next instant an icy blade was driven deep between his shoulders; he felt his blood slowly congeal; heard the senile cackle of the perennial Spaniard; saw the Plaza rise and reel till the zenith crashed into the horizon—and knew no more.

When Tansey opened his eyes again he was sitting upon those self-same steps gazing upon the dark bulk of the sleeping convent. In the middle of his back was still the acute, chilling pain. How had he been conveyed back there again? He got stiffly to his feet and stretched his cramped limbs. Supporting himself against the stonework he revolved in his mind the extravagant adventures that had befallen him each time he had strayed from the steps that night. In reviewing them certain features strained his credulity. Had he really met Captain Peek or Katie or the unparalleled Mexican in his wanderings—had he really encountered them under commonplace conditions and his over-stimulated brain had supplied the incongruities? However that might be, a sudden, elating thought caused him an intense joy. Nearly all of us have, at some point in our lives—either to excuse our own stupidity or placate our consciences—promulgated some theory of fatalism. We have set up an intelligent Fate that works by codes and signals. Tansey had done likewise; and now he read, through the night's incidents, the finger-prints of destiny. Each excursion that he had made had led to the one paramount finale—to Katie and that kiss, which survived and grew strong and intoxicating in his memory. Clearly, Fate was holding up to him the mirror that night, calling him to observe what awaited him at the end of whichever road he might take. He immediately turned, and hurried homeward.

Clothed in an elaborate, pale blue wrapper, cut to fit, Miss Katie Peek reclined in an arm-chair before a waning fire in her room. Her little, bare feet were thrust into house-shoes rimmed with swan's down. By the light of a small lamp she was attacking the society news of the latest Sunday paper. Some happy substance, seemingly indestructible, was being rhythmically crushed between her small white teeth. Miss Katie read of functions and furbelows, but she kept a vigilant ear for outside sounds and a frequent eye upon the clock over the mantel. At every footstep upon the asphalt sidewalk her smooth, round chin would cease for a moment its regular rise and fall, and a frown of listening would pucker her pretty brows.

At last she heard the latch of the iron gate click. She sprang up, tripped swiftly to the mirror, where she made a few of those feminine, flickering passes at her front hair and throat which are warranted to hypnotize the approaching guest.

The door-bell rang. Miss Katie, in her haste, turned the blaze of the lamp lower instead of higher, and hastened noiselessly downstairs into the hall. She turned the key, the door opened, and Mr. Tansey side-stepped in.

"Why, the i-de-a!" exclaimed Miss Katie, "is this you, Mr. Tansey? It's after midnight. Aren't you ashamed to wake me up at such an hour to let you in? You're just *awful!*"

"I was late," said Tansey, brilliantly.

"I should think you were! Ma was awfully worried about you. When you weren't in by ten, that hateful Tom McGill said you were out calling on another—said you were out calling on some young lady. I just despise Mr. McGill. Well, I'm not going to scold you any more, Mr. Tansey, if it *is* a little late—Oh! I turned it the wrong way!"

Miss Katie gave a little scream. Absent-mindedly she had turned the blaze of the lamp entirely out instead of higher. It was very dark.

Tansey heard a musical, soft giggle, and breathed an entrancing odor of heliotrope. A groping light hand touched his arm.

"How awkward I was! Can you find your way—Sam?"

"I—I think I have a match, Miss K-Katie."

A scratching sound; a flame; a glow of light held at arm's length by the recreant follower of Destiny illuminating a tableau which shall end the ignominious chronicle—a maid with unkissed, curling, contemptuous lips slowly lifting the lamp chimney and allowing the wick to ignite; then waving a scornful and abjuring hand toward the staircase—the unhappy Tansey erstwhile champion in the prophetic lists of fortune, ingloriously ascending to his just and certain doom, while (let us imagine) half within the wings stands the imminent figure of Fate jerking wildly at the wrong strings, and mixing things up in her usual able manner.

A DEPARTMENTAL CASE

In Texas you may travel a thousand miles in a straight line. If your course is a crooked one, it is likely that both the distance and your rate of speed may be

vastly increased. Clouds there sail serenely against the wind. The whippoor-
will delivers its disconsolate cry with the notes exactly reversed from those of his
Northern brother. Given a drought and a subsequently lively rain, and lo! from
a glazed and stony soil will spring in a single night blossomed lilies, miraculously
fair. Tom Green County was once the standard of measurement. I have forgotten how many New Jerseys and Rhode Islands it was that could have been stowed
away and lost in its chaparral. But the legislative axe has slashed Tom Green
into a handful of counties hardly larger than European kingdoms. The legislature convenes at Austin, near the centre of the state; and, while the representative from Rio Grande country is gathering his palm leaf fan and his linen duster
to set out for the capital, the Pan-handle solon winds his muffler above his well-
buttoned overcoat and kicks the snow from his well-greased boots ready for the
same journey. All this merely to hint that the big ex-republic of the Southwest
forms a sizable star on the flag, and to prepare for the corollary that things
sometimes happen there uncut to pattern and unfettered by metes and bounds.

The Commissioner of Insurance, Statistics, and History of the State of Texas
was an official of no very great or very small importance. The past tense is
used, for now he is Commissioner of Insurance alone. Statistics and history are
no longer proper nouns in the government records.

In the year 188–, the governor appointed Luke Coonrod Standifer to be the
head of this department. Standifer was then fifty-five years of age, and a
Texan to the core. His father had been one of the state's earliest settlers and
pioneers. Standifer himself had served the commonwealth as Indian fighter,
soldier, ranger, and legislator. Much learning he did not claim, but he had drunk
pretty deep of the spring of experience.

If other grounds were less abundant, Texas should be well up in the lists of
glory as the grateful republic. For both as republic and state, it has busily
heaped honors and solid rewards upon its sons who rescued it from the wilderness.

Wherefore and therefore, Luke Coonrod Standifer, son of Ezra Standifer, ex-
Terry ranger, simon-pure democrat, and lucky dweller in an unrepresented por-
tion of the politico-geographical map, was appointed Commissioner of Insurance,
Statistics, and History.

Standifer accepted the honor with some doubt as to the nature of the office he
was to fill and his capacity for filling it—but he accepted, and by wire. He
immediately set out from the little country town where he maintained (and was
scarcely maintained by) a somnolent and unfruitful office of surveying and map-
drawing. Before departing, he had looked up under the I's, S's, and H's in the
"Encyclopædia Britannica" what information and preparation toward his official
duties that those weighty volumes afforded.

A few weeks of incumbency diminished the new commissioner's awe of the
great and important office he had been called upon to conduct. An increasing
familiarity with its workings soon restored him to his accustomed placid course
of life. In his office was an old spectacled clerk—a consecrated, informed, able
machine, who held his desk regardless of changes of administrative heads. Old
Kauffman instructed his new chief gradually in the knowledge of the department without seeming to do so, and kept the wheels revolving without the slip of
a cog.

Indeed, the Department of Insurance, Statistics, and History carried no great
heft of the burden of state. Its main work was the regulating of the business
done in the state by foreign insurance companies, and the letter of the law was
its guide. As for statistics—well, you wrote letters to county officers, and scis-
sored other people's reports, and each year you got out a report of your own
about the corn crop and the cotton crop and pecans and pigs and black and white
population, and a great many columns of figures headed "bushels" and "acres"

and "square miles," etc.—and there you were. History? The branch was purely a receptive one. Old ladies interested in the science bothered you some with long reports of proceedings of their historical societies. Some twenty or thirty people would write you each year that they had secured Sam Houston's pocket-knife or Santa Ana's whisky-flask or Davy Crockett's rifle—all absolutely authenticated —and demanded legislative appropriation to purchase. Most of the work in the history branch went into pigeonholes.

One sizzling August afternoon the commissioner reclined in his office chair, with his feet upon the long, official table covered with green billiard cloth. The commissioner was smoking a cigar, and dreamily regarding the quivering landscape framed by the window that looked upon the treeless capitol grounds. Perhaps he was thinking of the rough and ready life he had led, of the old days of breathless adventure and movement, of the comrades who now trod other paths or had ceased to tread any, of the changes civilization and peace had brought, and, maybe, complacently, of the snug and comfortable camp pitched for him under the dome of the capitol of the state that had not forgotten his services.

The business of the department was lax. Insurance was easy. Statistics were not in demand. History was dead. Old Kauffman, the efficient and perpetual clerk, had requested an infrequent half-holiday, incited to the unusual dissipation by the joy of having successfully twisted the tail of a Connecticut insurance company that was trying to do business contrary to the edicts of the great Lone Star State.

The office was very still. A few subdued noises trickled in through the open door from the other departments—a dull tinkling crash from the treasurer's office adjoining, as a clerk tossed a bag of silver to the floor of the vault—the vague, intermittent clatter of a dilatory typewriter—a dull tapping from the state geologist's quarters as if some woodpecker had flown in to bore for his prey in the cool of the massive building—and then a faint rustle, and the light shuffling of the well-worn shoes along the hall, the sounds ceasing at the door toward which the commissioner's lethargic back was presented. Following this, the sound of a gentle voice speaking words unintelligible to the commissioner's somewhat dormant comprehension, but giving evidence of bewilderment and hesitation.

The voice was feminine; the commissioner was of the race of cavaliers who make salaam before the trail of a skirt without considering the quality of its cloth.

There stood in the door a faded woman, one of the numerous sisterhood of the unhappy. She was dressed all in black—poverty's perpetual mourning for lost joys. Her face had the contours of twenty and the lines of forty. She may have lived that intervening score of years in a twelve-month. There was about her yet an aurum of indignant, unappeased, protesting youth that shone faintly through the premature veil of unearned decline.

"I beg your pardon, ma'am," said the commissioner, gaining his feet to the accompaniment of a great creaking and sliding of his chair.

"Are you the governor, sir?" asked the vision of melancholy.

The commissioner hesitated at the end of his best bow, with his hand in the bosom of his double-breasted "frock." Truth at last conquered.

"Well, no, ma'am. I am not the governor. I have the honor to be Commissioner of Insurance, Statistics, and History. Is there anything, ma'am, I can do for you? Won't you have a chair, ma'am?"

The lady subsided into the chair handed her, probably from purely physical reasons. She wielded a cheap fan—last token of gentility to be abandoned. Her clothing seemed to indicate a reduction almost to extreme poverty. She looked at the man who was not the governor, and saw kindliness and simplicity and a rugged, unadorned courtliness emanating from a countenance tanned, and toughened by forty years of outdoor life. Also, she saw that his eyes were clear and strong and blue. Just as they had been when he used them to skim the horizon for raiding Kiowas and Sioux. His mouth was as set and firm as it had been on that day when he bearded the old Lion Sam Houston himself, and defied him during that season when secession was the theme. Now, in bearing and dress, Luke Coonrod Standifer endeavored to do credit to the important arts and sciences of Insurance, Statistics, and History. He had abandoned the careless dress of his country home. Now, his broad-brimmed black slouch hat, and his long-tailed "frock" made him not the least imposing of the official family, even if his office was reckoned to stand at the tail of the list.

"You wanted to see the governor, ma'am?" asked the commissioner, with a deferential manner he always used toward the fair sex.

"I hardly know," said the lady, hesitatingly. "I suppose so." And then, suddenly drawn by the sympathetic look of the other, she poured forth the story of her need.

It was a story so common that the public has come to look at its monotony instead of its pity. The old tale of an unhappy married life—made so by a brutal, conscienceless husband, a robber, a spendthrift, a moral coward, and a bully, who failed to provide even the means of the barest existence. Yes, he had come down in the scale so low as to strike her. It happened only the day before—there was the bruise on one temple—she had offended his highness by asking for a little money to live on. And yet she must needs, womanlike, append a plea for her tyrant—he was drinking; he had rarely abused her thus when sober.

"I thought," mourned this pale sister of sorrow, "that maybe the state might be willing to give me some relief. I've heard of such things being done for the families of old settlers. I've heard tell that the state used to give land to the men who fought for it against Mexico, and settled up the country, and helped drive out the Indians. My father did all of that, and he never received anything. He never would take it. I thought the governor would be the one to see, and that's why I came. If Father was entitled to anything, they might let it come to me."

"It's possible, ma'am," said Standifer, "that such might be the case. But 'most all the veterans and settlers got their land certificates issued and located long ago. Still, we can look that up in the land office and be sure. Your father's name, now, was——"

"Amos Colvin, sir."

"Good Lord!" exclaimed Standifer, rising and unbuttoning his tight coat, excitedly. "Are you Amos Colvin's daughter? Why, ma'am, Amos Colvin and me were thicker than two hoss thieves for more than ten years! We fought Kiowas, drove cattle, and rangered side by side nearly all over Texas. I remember seeing you once before, now. You were a kid, about seven, a-riding a little yellow pony up and down. Amos and me stopped at your home for a little grub when we were trailing that band of Mexican cattle thieves down through Karnes and Bee. Great tarantulas! and you're Amos Colvin's little girl! Did you ever hear your father mention Luke Standifer—just kind of casually—as if he'd met me once or twice?"

A little pale smile flitted across the lady's white face.

"It seems to me," she said, "that I don't remember hearing him talk about much else. Every day there was some story he had to tell about what he and you had done. Mighty near the last thing I heard him tell was about the time when the Indians wounded him, and you crawled out to him through the grass, with a canteen of water, while they——"

"Yes, yes—well—oh, that wasn't anything," said Standifer, "hemming" loudly and buttoning his coat again briskly. "And now, ma'am, who was the infernal skunk—I beg your pardon, ma'am—who was the gentleman you married?"

"Benton Sharp."

The commissioner plumped down again into his chair with a groan. This gentle, sad little woman in the rusty black gown the daughter of his oldest friend, the wife of Benton Sharp! Benton Sharp, one of the most noted "bad" men in that part of the state—a man who had been a cattle thief, an outlaw, a desperado, and was now a gambler, a swaggering bully, who plied his trade in the larger frontier towns, relying upon his record and the quickness of his gun play to maintain his supremacy. Seldom did anyone take the risk of going "up against" Benton Sharp. Even the law officers were content to let him make his own terms of peace. Sharp was a ready and an accurate shot, and as lucky as a brand-new penny at coming clear from his scrapes. Standifer wondered how this pillaging eagle ever came to be mated with Amos Colvin's little dove, and expressed his wonder.

Mrs. Sharp sighed.

"You see, Mr. Standifer, we didn't know anything about him, and he can be very pleasant and kind when he wants to. We lived down in the little town of Goliad. Benton came riding down that way and stopped there a while. I reckon I was some better looking then than I am now. He was good to me for a whole year after we were married. He insured his life for me for five thousand dollars. But for the last six months he has done everything but kill me. I often wish he had done that, too. He got out of money for a while, and abused me shamefully for not having anything he could spend. Then Father died and left me the little home in Goliad. My husband made me sell that and turned me out into the world. I've barely been able to live, for I'm not strong enough to work. Lately, I heard he was making money in San Antonio, so I went there, and found him, and asked for a little help. This," touching the livid bruise on her temple, "is what he gave me. So I came on to Austin to see the governor. I once heard Father say that there was some land or a pension coming to him from the state that he never would ask for."

Luke Standifer rose to his feet, and pushed his chair back. He looked rather perplexedly around the big office with its handsome furniture.

"It's a long trail to follow," he said, slowly, "trying to get back dues from the government. There's red tape and lawyers and rulings and evidences and courts to keep you waiting. I'm not certain," continued the commissioner, with a profoundly meditative frown, "whether this department that I'm the boss of has any jurisdiction or not. It's only Insurance, Statistics, and History, ma'am, and it don't sound as if it would cover the case. But sometimes a saddle blanket can be made to stretch. You keep your seat, just for a few minutes, ma'am, till I step into the next room and see about it."

The state treasurer was seated within his massive, complicated railings, reading a newspaper. Business for the day was about over. The clerks lolled at their desks, awaiting the closing hour. The Commissioner of Insurance, Statistics, and History entered, and leaned in at the window.

The treasurer, a little, brisk old man, with snow-white moustache and beard, jumped up youthfully and came forward to greet Standifer. They were friends of old.

"Uncle Frank," said the commissioner, using the familiar name by which the historic treasurer was addressed by every Texan, "how much money have you got on hand?"

The treasurer named the sum of the last balance down to the odd cents—something more than a million dollars.

The commissioner whistled lowly, and his eyes grew hopefully bright.

"You know, or else you've heard of, Amos Colvin, Uncle Frank?"

"Knew him well," said the treasurer, promptly. "A good man. A valuable citizen. One of the first settlers in the Southwest."

"His daughter," said Standifer, "is sitting in my office. She's penniless. She's married to Benton Sharp, a coyote and a murderer. He's reduced her to want and broken her heart. Her father helped build up this state, and it's the state's turn to help his child. A couple of thousand dollars will buy back her home and let her live in peace. The State of Texas can't afford to refuse it. Give me the money, Uncle Frank, and I'll give it to her right away. We'll fix up the red-tape business afterward."

The treasurer looked a little bewildered.

"Why, Standifer," he said, "you know I can't pay a cent out of the treasury without a warrant from the comptroller. I can't disburse a dollar without a voucher to show for it."

The commissioner betrayed a slight impatience.

"I'll give you a voucher," he declared. "What's this job they've given me for? Am I just a knot on a mesquite stump? Can't my office stand for it? Charge it up to Insurance and the other two sideshows. Don't Statistics show that Amos Colvin came to this state when it was in the hands of Greasers and rattlesnakes and Comanches, and fought day and night to make a white man's country of it? Don't they show that Amos Colvin's daughter is brought to ruin by a villain who's trying to pull down what you and I and old Texans shed our blood to build up? Don't History show that the Lone Star State never yet failed to grant relief to the suffering and oppressed children of the men who made her the grandest commonwealth in the Union? If Statistics and History don't bear out the claim of Amos Colvin's child I'll ask the next legislature to abolish my office. Come, now, Uncle Frank, let her have the money. I'll sign the papers officially, if you say so; and then if the governor or the comptroller or the janitor or anybody else makes a kick, by the Lord I'll refer the matter to the people, and see if they won't indorse the act."

The treasurer looked sympathetic but shocked. The commissioner's voice had grown louder as he rounded off the sentences that, however praiseworthy they might be in sentiment, reflected somewhat upon the capacity of the head of a more or less important department of state. The clerks were beginning to listen.

"Now, Standifer," said the treasurer, soothingly, "you know I'd like to help in this matter, but stop and think a moment, please. Every cent in the treasury is expended only by appropriation made by the legislature, and drawn out by checks issued by the comptroller. I can't control the use of a cent of it. Neither can you. Your department isn't disbursive—it isn't even administrative—it's purely clerical. The only way for the lady to obtain relief is to petition the legislature, and——"

"To the devil with the legislature," said Standifer, turning away.

The treasurer called him back.

"I'd be glad, Standifer, to contribute a hundred dollars personally toward the immediate expenses of Colvin's daughter." He reached for his pocketbook.

"Never mind, Uncle Frank," said the commissioner, in a softer tone. "There's no need of that. She hasn't asked for anything of that sort yet. Besides, her case is in my hands. I see now what a little rag-tag, bob-tail, gotch-eared department I've been put in charge of. It seems to be about as important as an almanac or a hotel register. But while I'm running it, it won't turn away any daughters of Amos Colvin without stretching its jurisdiction to cover, if possible. You want to keep your eye on the Department of Insurance, Statistics, and History."

The commissioner returned to his office, looking thoughtful. He opened and closed an inkstand on his desk many times with extreme and undue attention before he spoke. "Why don't you get a divorce?" he asked, suddenly.

"I haven't the money to pay for it," answered the lady.

"Just at present," announced the commissioner, in a formal tone, "the powers of my department appear to be considerably stringhalted. Statistics seem to be overdrawn at the bank, and History isn't good for a square meal. But you've come to the right place, ma'am. The department will see you through. Where did you say your husband is, ma'am?"

"He was in San Antonio yesterday. He is living there now."

Suddenly the commissioner abandoned his official air. He took the faded little woman's hands in his, and spoke in the old voice he used on the trail and around campfires.

"Your name's Amanda, isn't it?"

"Yes, sir."

"I thought so. I've heard your dad say it often enough. Well, Amanda, here's your father's best friend, the head of a big office in the state government, that's going to help you out of your troubles. And here's the old bush-whacker and cowpuncher that your father has helped out of scrapes time and time again wants to ask you a question. Amanda, have you got enough money to run you for the next two or three days?"

Mrs. Sharp's white face flushed the least bit.

"Plenty, sir—for a few days."

"All right, then, ma'am. Now you go back where you are stopping here, and you come to the office again the day after to-morrow at four o'clock in the afternoon. Very likely by that time there will be something definite to report to you." The commissioner hesitated, and looked a trifle embarrassed. "You said your husband had insured his life for $5,000. Do you know whether the premiums have been kept paid upon it or not?"

"He paid for a whole year in advance about five months ago," said Mrs. Sharp. "I have the policy and receipts in my trunk."

"Oh, that's all right, then," said Standifer. "It's best to look after things of that sort. Some day they may come in handy."

Mrs. Sharp departed, and soon afterward Luke Standifer went down to the little hotel where he boarded and looked up the railroad time-table in the daily paper. Half an hour later he removed his coat and vest, and strapped a peculiarly constructed pistol holster across his shoulders, leaving the receptacle close under his left armpit. Into the holster he shoved a short-barreled .44-calibre revolver. Putting on his clothes again, he strolled down to the station and caught the five-twenty afternoon train for San Antonio.

The San Antonio *Express* of the following morning contained this sensational piece of news:

BENTON SHARP MEETS HIS MATCH

The Most Noted Desperado in Southwest Texas Shot to Death in the Gold Front Restaurant—Prominent State Official Successfully Defends Himself Against the Noted Bully—Magnificent Exhibition of Quick Gun Play.

Last night about eleven o'clock Benton Sharp, with two other men, entered the Gold Front Restaurant and seated themselves at a table. Sharp had been drinking, and was loud and boisterous, as he always was when under the influence of liquor. Five minutes after the party was seated a tall, well-dressed, elderly gentleman entered the restaurant. Few present recognized the Honorable Luke Standifer, the recently appointed Commissioner of Insurance, Statistics, and History.

Going over to the same side where Sharp was, Mr. Standifer prepared to take a seat at the next table. In hanging his hat upon one of the hooks along the wall he let it fall upon Sharp's head. Sharp turned, being in an especially ugly humor, and cursed the other roundly. Mr. Standifer apologized calmly for the accident, but Sharp continued his vituperations. Mr. Standifer was observed to draw near and speak a few sentences to the desperado in so low a tone that no one else caught the words. Sharp sprang up, wild with rage. In the meantime Mr. Standifer had stepped some yards away, and was standing quietly with his arms folded across the breast of his loosely hanging coat.

With that impetuous and deadly rapidity that made Sharp so dreaded, he reached for the gun he always carried in his hip pocket—a movement that has preceded the death of at least a dozen men at his hands. Quick as the motion was, the bystanders assert that it was met by the most beautiful exhibition of lightning gun-pulling ever witnessed in the Southwest. As Sharp's pistol was being raised—and the act was really quicker than the eye could follow—a glittering .44 appeared as if by some conjuring trick in the right hand of Mr. Standifer, who, without a perceptible movement of his arm, shot Benton Sharp through the heart. It seems that the new Commissioner of Insurance, Statistics, and History has been an old-time Indian fighter and ranger for many years, which accounts for the happy knack he has of handling a .44.

It is not believed that Mr. Standifer will be put to any inconvenience beyond a necessary formal hearing to-day, as all the witnesses who were present unite in declaring that the deed was done in self-defense.

When Mrs. Sharp appeared at the office of the commissioner, according to appointment, she found that gentleman calmly eating a golden russet apple. He greeted her without embarrassment and without hesitation at approaching the subject that was the topic of the day.

"I had to do it, ma'am," he said, simply, "or get it myself. Mr. Kauffman," he added, turning to the old clerk, "please look up the records of the Security Life Insurance Company and see if they are all right."

"No need to look," grunted Kauffman, who had everything in his head. "It's all O. K. They pay all losses within ten days."

Mrs. Sharp soon rose to depart. She had arranged to remain in town until the policy was paid. The commissioner did not detain her. She was a woman, and he did not know just what to say to her at present. Rest and time would bring her what she needed.

But, as she was leaving, Luke Standifer indulged himself in an official remark:

"The Department of Insurance, Statistics, and History, ma'am, has done the best it could with your case. 'Twas a case hard to cover according to red tape. Statistics failed, and History missed fire, but, if I may be permitted to say it, we came out particularly strong on Insurance."

THE RENAISSANCE AT CHARLEROI

GRANDEMONT CHARLES was a little Creole gentleman, aged thirty-four, with a bald spot on the top of his head and the manners of a prince. By day he was a clerk in a cotton broker's office in one of those cold, rancid mountains of oozy brick, down near the levee in New Orleans. By night, in his three-story-high *chambre garnie* in the old French Quarter he was again the last male descendant of the Charles family, that noble house that had lorded it in France, and had pushed its way smiling, rapiered, and courtly into Louisiana's early and brilliant days. Of late years the Charleses had subsided into the more republican but scarcely less royally carried magnificence and ease of plantation life along the Mississippi. Perhaps Grandemont was even Marquis de Brassé. There was that title in the family. But a marquis on seventy-five dollars per month! *Vraiment!* Still, it has been done on less.

Grandemont had saved out of his salary the sum of six hundred dollars. Enough, you would say, for any man to marry on. So, after a silence of two years on that subject, he reopened that most hazardous question to Mlle. Adèle Fauquier, riding down to Meade d'Or, her father's plantation. Her answer was the same that it had been any time during the last ten years: "First find my brother, Monsieur Charles."

This time he had stood before her, perhaps discouraged by a love so long and hopeless, being dependent upon a contingency so unreasonable, and demanded to be told in simple words whether she loved him or no.

Adèle looked at him steadily out of her gray eyes that betrayed no secrets and answered, a little more softly:

"Grandemont, you have no right to ask that question unless you can do what I ask of you. Either bring back brother Victor to us or the proof that he died."

Somehow, though five times thus rejected, his heart was not so heavy when he left. She had not denied that she loved. Upon what shallow waters can the bark of passion remain afloat! Or, shall we play the doctrinaire, and hint that at thirty-four the tides of life are calmer and cognizant of many sources instead of but one—as at four-and-twenty?

Victor Fauquier would never be found. In those early days of his disappearance there was money to the Charles name, and Grandemont had spent the dollars as if they were picayunes in trying to find the lost youth. Even then he had had small hope of success, for the Mississippi gives up a victim from its oily tangles only at the whim of its malign will.

A thousand times had Grandemont conned in his mind the scene of Victor's disappearance. And, at each time that Adèle had set her stubborn but pitiful alternative against his suit, still clearer it repeated itself in his brain.

The boy had been the family favorite: daring, winning, reckless. His unwise fancy had been captured by a girl on the plantation—the daughter of an overseer. Victor's family was in ignorance of the intrigue, as far as it had gone. To save them the inevitable pain that his course promised, Grandemont strove to prevent it. Omnipotent money smoothed the way. The overseer and his daughter left, between a sunset and dawn, for an undesignated bourne. Grandemont was confident that this stroke would bring the boy to reason. He rode over to Meade d'Or to talk with him. The two strolled out of the house and grounds, crossed the road, and, mounting the levee, walked its broad path while they conversed. A thundercloud was hanging, imminent, above, but, as yet, no rain fell. At Grandemont's disclosure of his interference in the clandestine romance, Victor attacked him, in a wild and sudden fury. Grandemont, though of slight frame, possessed muscles of iron. He caught the wrists amid a shower of blows descending upon him, bent the lad backward and stretched him upon the levee path. In a little while the gust of passion was spent, and he was allowed to rise. Calm now, but a powder mine where he had been but a whiff of the tantrums, Victor extended his hand toward the dwelling house of Meade d'Or.

"You and they," he cried, "have conspired to destroy my happiness. None of you shall ever look upon my face again."

Turning, he ran swiftly down the levee, disappearing in the darkness, Grandemont followed as well as he could, calling to him, but in vain. For longer than an hour he pursued the search. Descending the side of the levee, he penetrated the rank density of weeds and willows that undergrew the trees until the river's edge, shouting Victor's name. There was never an answer, though once he thought he heard a bubbling scream from the dun waters sliding past. Then the storm broke, and he returned to the house drenched and dejected.

There he explained the boy's absence sufficiently, he thought, not speaking of the tangle that had led to it, for he hoped that Victor would return as soon as his anger had cooled. Afterward, when the threat was made good and they saw his face no more, he found it difficult to alter his explanations of that night, and there clung a certain mystery to the boy's reasons for vanishing as well as to the manner of it.

It was on that night that Grandemont first perceived a new and singular expression in Adèle's eyes whenever she looked at him. And through the years following that expression was always there. He could not read it, for it was born of a thought she would never otherwise reveal.

Perhaps, if he had known that Adèle had stood at the gate on that unlucky night, where she had followed, lingering to await the return of her brother and lover, wondering why they had chosen so tempestuous an hour and so black a spot to hold converse—if he had known that a sudden flash of lightning had revealed to her sight that short, sharp struggle as Victor was sinking under his hands, he might have explained everything, and she——

I know not what she would have done. But one thing is clear—there was something besides her brother's disappearance between Grandemont's pleadings for her hand and Adèle's "yes." Ten years had passed, and what she had seen during the space of that lightning flash remained an indelible picture. She had loved her brother, but was she holding out for the solution of that mystery or for the "Truth"! Women have been known to reverence it, even as an abstract principle. It is said there have been a few who, in the matter of their affections, have considered a life to be a small thing as compared with a lie. That I do not know. But, I wonder, had Grandemont cast himself at her feet crying that his hand had sent Victor to the bottom of that inscrutable river, and that he could no longer sully his love with a lie, I wonder if—I wonder what she would have done!

But, Grandemont Charles, Arcadian little gentleman, never guessed the meaning of that look in Adèle's eyes; and from this last bootless payment of his devoirs he rode away as rich as ever in honor and love, but poor in hope.

That was in September. It was during the first winter month that Grandemont conceived his idea of the *renaissance*. Since Adèle would never be his, and wealth without her were useless trumpery, why need he add to that hoard of slowly harvested dollars? Why should he even retain that hoard?

Hundreds were the cigarettes he consumed over his claret, sitting at the little polished tables in the Royal street cafés while thinking over his plan. By and by he had it perfect. It would cost, beyond doubt, all the money he had, but— *le jeu vaut la chandelle*—for some hours he would be once more a Charles of Charleroi. Once again should the nineteenth of January, that most significant day in the fortunes of the house of Charles, be fittingly observed. On that date the French king had seated a Charles by his side at table; on that date Armand Charles, Marquis de Brassé, landed, like a brilliant meteor, in New Orleans; it was the date of his mother's wedding; of Grandemont's birth. Since Grandemont could remember until the breaking up of the family that anniversary had been the synonym for feasting, hospitality, and proud commemoration.

Charleroi was the old family plantation, lying some twenty miles down the river. Years ago the estate had been sold to discharge the debts of its too-bountiful owners. Once again it had changed hands, and now the must and mildew of litigation had settled upon it. A question of heirship was in the courts, and the dwelling house of Charleroi, unless the tales told of ghostly powdered and laced Charleses haunting its unechoing chambers were true, stood uninhabited.

Grandemont found the solicitor in chancery who held the keys pending the decision. He proved to be an old friend of the family. Grandemont explained briefly that he desired to rent the house for two or three days. He wanted to give a dinner at his old home to a few friends. That was all.

"Take it for a week—a month, if you will," said the solicitor; "but do not speak to me of rental." With a sigh he concluded: "The dinners I have eaten under that roof, *mon fils!*"

There came to many of the old-established dealers in furniture, china, silverware, decorations, and household fittings at their stores on Canal, Chartres, St. Charles and Royal streets, a quiet young man with a little bald spot on the top of his head, distinguished manners, and the eye of a *connoisseur*, who explained what he wanted. To hire the complete and elegant equipment of a dining-room, hall, reception-room, and cloak-rooms. The goods were to be packed and sent, by boat, to the Charleroi landing, and would be returned within three or four days. All damage or loss to be promptly paid for.

Many of those old merchants knew Grandemont by sight, and the Charleses of old by association. Some of them were of Creole stock and felt a thrill of responsive sympathy with the magnificently indiscreet design of this impoverished clerk who would revive but for a moment the ancient flame of glory with the fuel of his savings.

"Choose what you want," they said to him. "Handle everything carefully. See that the damage bill is kept low, and the charges for the loan will not oppress you."

To the wine merchants next; and here a doleful slice was lopped from the six hundred. It was an exquisite pleasure to Grandemont once more to pick among the precious vintages. The champagne bins lured him like the abodes of sirens, but these he was forced to pass. With his six hundred he stood before them as a child with a penny stands before a French doll. But he bought with taste and discretion of other wines—Chablis, Moselle, Crâteau d'Or, Hochheimer, and port of right age and pedigree.

The matter of the cuisine gave him some studious hours until he suddenly recollected André—André, their old *chef*—the most sublime master of French Creole cookery in the Mississippi Valley. Perhaps he was yet somewhere about the plantation. The solicitor had told him that the place was still being cultivated, in accordance with a compromise agreement between the litigants.

On the next Sunday after the thought Grandemont rode, horseback, down to Charleroi. The big, square house with its two long ells looked blank and cheerless with its closed shutters and doors.

The shrubbery in the yard was ragged and riotous. Fallen leaves from the grove littered the walks and porches. Turning down the lane at the side of the house, Grandemont rode on to the quarters of the plantation hands. He found the workers streaming back from church, careless, happy, and bedecked in gay yellows, reds, and blues.

Yes, André was still there; his wool a little grayer; his mouth as wide; his laughter as ready as ever. Grandemont told him of his plan, and the old *chef* swayed with pride and delight. With a sigh of relief, knowing that he need have no further concern until the serving of that dinner was announced, he placed in André's hands a liberal sum for the cost of it, giving *carte blanche* for its creation.

Among the blacks were also a number of the old house servants. Absalom, the former major domo, and a half-dozen of the younger men, once waiters and attachés of the kitchen, pantry, and other domestic departments, crowded around to meet "*M'shi Grande.*" Absalom guaranteed to marshal, of these, a corps of assistants that would perform with credit the serving of the dinner.

After distributing a liberal largesse among the faithful, Grandemont rode back to town well pleased. There were many other smaller details to think of and provide for, but eventually the scheme was complete, and now there remained only the issuance of the invitations to his guests.

Along the river within the scope of a score of miles dwelt some half-dozen families with whose princely hospitality that of the Charleses had been contemporaneous. They were the proudest and most august of the old régime. Their small circle had been a brilliant one; their social relations close and warm; their houses full of rare welcome and discriminating bounty. Those friends, said Grandemont, should once more, if never again, sit at Charleroi on a nineteenth of January to celebrate the festal day of his house.

Grandemont had his cards of invitation engraved. They were expensive, but beautiful. In one particular their good taste might have been disputed; but the Creole allowed himself that one feather in the cap of his fugacious splendor. Might he not be allowed, for the one day of the *renaissance*, to be "Grandemont du Puy Charles, of Charleroi"? He sent the invitations out early in January so that the guests might not fail to receive due notice.

At eight o'clock in the morning of the nineteenth, the lower coast steamboat *River Belle* gingerly approached the long unused landing at Charleroi. The bridge was lowered, and a swarm of the plantation hands streamed along the rotting pier, bearing ashore a strange assortment of freight. Great shapeless bundles and bales and packets swathed in cloths and bound with ropes; tubs and urns of palms, evergreens, and tropical flowers; tables, mirrors, chairs, couches, carpets, and pictures—all carefully bound and padded against the dangers of transit.

Grandemont was among them, the busiest there. To the safe conveyance of certain large hampers eloquent with printed cautions to delicate handling he gave his superintendence, for they contained the fragile china and glassware. The dropping of one of those hampers would have cost him more than he could have saved in a year.

The last article unloaded, the *River Belle* backed off and continued her course down stream. In less than an hour everything had been conveyed to the house. And came then Absalom's task, directing the placing of the furniture and wares. There was plenty of help, for that day was always a holiday in Charleroi, and the Negroes did not suffer the old traditions to lapse. Almost the entire population of the quarters volunteered their aid. A score of piccaninnies were sweeping at the leaves in the yard. In the big kitchen at the rear André was lording it with his old-time magnificence over his numerous sub-cooks and scullions. Shutters were flung wide; dust spun in clouds; the house echoed to voices and the tread of busy feet. The prince had come again, and Charleroi woke from its long sleep.

The full moon, as she rose across the river that night and peeped above the levee, saw a sight that had been long missing from her orbit. The old plantation house shed a soft and alluring radiance from every window. Of its two-score rooms only four had been refurnished—the large reception chamber, the dining hall, and two smaller rooms for the convenience of the expected guests. But lighted wax candles were set in the windows of every room.

The dining hall was the *chef-d'œuvre*. The long table, set with twenty-five covers, sparkled like a winter landscape with its snowy napery and china and the icy gleam of crystal. The chaste beauty of the room had required small adornment. The polished floor burned to a glowing ruby with the reflection of candle light. The rich wainscoting reached halfway to the ceiling. Along and above this had been set the relieving lightness of a few water-color sketches of fruit and flower.

The reception chamber was fitted in a simple but elegant style. Its arrangement suggested nothing of the fact that on the morrow the rooms would again be cleared and abandoned to the dust and the spider. The entrance hall was imposing with palms and ferns and the light of an immense candelabrum.

At seven o'clock Grandemont, in evening dress, with pearls—a family passion—in his spotless linen, emerged from somewhere. The invitations had specified eight as the dining hour. He drew an armchair upon the porch, and sat there, smoking cigarettes and half dreaming.

The moon was an hour high. Fifty yards back from the gate stood the house, under its noble grove. The road ran in front, and then came the grass-grown levee and the insatiate river beyond. Just above the levee top a tiny red light was creeping down and a tiny green one was creeping up. Then the passing steamers saluted, and the hoarse din startled the drowsy silence of the melancholy lowlands. The stillness returned, save for the little voices of the night—the owl's recitative, the capriccio of the crickets, the concerto of the frogs in the grass. The piccaninnies and the dawdlers from the quarters had been dismissed to their confines, and the mêlée of the day was reduced to an orderly and intelligent silence. The six colored waiters, in their white jackets, paced, cat-footed, about the table, pretending to arrange where all was beyond betterment. Absalom, in black and shining pumps, posed, superior, here and there where the lights set off his grandeur. And Grandemont rested in his chair, waiting for his guests.

He must have drifted into a dream—and an extravagant one—for he was master of Charleroi and Adèle was his wife. She was coming out to him now; he could hear her steps; he could feel her hand upon his shoulder——

"*Pardon moi, M'shi Grande*"—it was Absalom's hand touching him, it was Absalom's voice, speaking the *patois* of the blacks—"but it is eight o'clock."

Eight o'clock. Grandemont sprang up. In the moonlight he could see the row of hitching-posts outside the gate. Long ago the horses of the guests should have stood there. They were vacant.

A chanted roar of indignation, a just, waxing bellow of affront and dishonored genius came from André's kitchen, filling the house with rhythmic protest. The beautiful dinner, the pearl of a dinner, the little excellent superb jewel of a dinner! But one moment more of waiting and not even the thousand thunders of black pigs of the quarters would touch it!

"They are a little late," said Grandemont, calmly. "They will come soon. Tell André to hold back dinner. And ask him if, by some chance, a bull from the pastures has broken, roaring, into the house."

He seated himself again to his cigarettes. Though he had said it, he scarcely believed Charleroi would entertain company that night. For the first time in history the invitation of a Charles had been ignored. So simple in courtesy and honor was Grandemont and, perhaps, so serenely confident in the prestige of his name, that the most likely reasons for his vacant board did not occur to him.

Charleroi stood by a road traveled daily by people from those plantations whither his invitations had gone. No doubt even on the day before the sudden reanimation of the old house they had driven past and observed the evidences of long desertion and decay. They had looked at the corpse of Charleroi and then at Grandemont's invitations, and, though the puzzle or tasteless hoax or whatever the thing meant left them perplexed, they would not seek its solution by the folly of a visit to that deserted house.

The moon was now above the grove, and the yard was pied with deep shadows save where they lightened in the tender glow of outpouring candlelight. A crisp breeze from the river hinted at the possibility of frost when the night should have become older. The grass at one side of the steps were specked with the white stubs of Grandemont's cigarettes. The cotton-broker's clerk sat in his chair with the smoke spiralling above him. I doubt that he once thought of the little fortune he had so impotently squandered. Perhaps it was compensation enough for him to sit thus at Charleroi for a few retrieved hours. Idly his mind wandered in and out many fanciful paths of memory. He smiled to himself as a paraphrased line of Scripture strayed into his mind: "A certain *poor* man made a feast."

He heard the sound of Absalom coughing a note of summons. Grandemont stirred. This time he had not been asleep—only drowsing.

"Nine o'clock, *M'shi Grande*," said Absalom in the uninflected voice of a good servant who states a fact unqualified by personal opinion.

Grandemont rose to his feet. In their time all the Charleses had been proven, and they were gallant losers.

"Serve dinner," he said, calmly. And then he checked Absalom's movement to obey, for something clicked the gate latch and was coming down the walk towards the house. Something that shuffled its feet and muttered to itself as it came. It stopped in the current of light at the foot of the steps and spake, in the universal whine of the gadding mendicant.

"Kind sir, could you spare a poor, hungry man, out of luck, a little to eat? And to sleep in the corner of a shed? For"—the thing concluded, irrelevantly— "I can sleep now. There are no mountains to dance reels in the night; and the copper kettles are all scoured bright. The iron band is still around my ankle, and a link, if it is your desire I should be chained."

It set a foot upon the step and drew up the rags that hung upon the limb. Above the distorted shoe, caked with the dust of a hundred leagues, they saw the link and the iron band. The clothes of the tramp were wrecked to piebald tatters by sun and rain and wear. A mat of brown, tangled hair and beard covered his head and face, out of which his eyes stared distractedly. Grandemont noticed that he carried in one hand a white, square card.

"What is that?" he asked.

"I picked it up, sir, at the side of the road." The vagabond handed the card to Grandemont. "Just a little to eat, sir. A little parched corn, a *tortilla*, or a handful of beans. Goat's meat I cannot eat. When I cut their throats they cry like children."

Grandemont held up the card. It was one of his own invitations to dinner. No doubt someone had cast it away from a passing carriage after comparing it with the tenantless house at Charleroi.

"From the hedges and highways bid them come," he said to himself, softly smiling. And then to Absalom: "Send Louis to me."

Louis, once his own body-servant, came promptly, in his white jacket.

"This gentleman," said Grandemont, "will dine with me. Furnish him with bath and clothes. In twenty minutes have him ready and dinner served."

Louis approached the disreputable guest with the suavity due to a visitor to Charleroi, and spirited him away to inner regions.

Promptly, in twenty minutes, Absalom announced dinner, and, a moment later, the guest was ushered into the dining hall where Grandemont waited, standing, at the head of the table. The attentions of Louis had transformed the stranger into something resembling the polite animal. Clean linen and an old evening suit that had been sent down from town to clothe a waiter had worked a miracle with his exterior. Brush and comb had partially subdued the wild disorder of his hair. Now he might have passed for no more extravagant a thing than one of those *poseurs* in art and music who affect such oddity of guise. The man's countenance and demeanor, as he approached the table, exhibited nothing of the awkwardness or confusion to be expected from his Arabian Nights change. He allowed Absalom to seat him at Grandemont's right hand with the manner of one thus accustomed to be waited upon.

"It grieves me," said Grandemont, "to be obliged to exchange names with a guest. My own name is Charles."

"In the mountains," said the wayfarer, "they call me Gringo. Along the roads they call me Jack."

"I prefer the latter," said Grandemont. "A glass of wine with you, Mr. Jack."

Course after course was served by the supernumerous waiters. Grandemont, inspired by the results of André's exquisite skill in cookery and his own in the selection of wines, became the model host, talkative, witty, and genial. The guest was fitful in conversation. His mind seemed to be sustaining a succession of waves of dementia followed by intervals of comparative lucidity. There was the glassy brightness of recent fever in his eyes. A long course of it must have been the cause of his emaciation and weakness, his distracted mind, and the dull pallor that showed even through the tan of wind and sun.

"Charles," he said to Grandemont—for thus he seemed to interpret his name— "you never saw the mountains dance, did you?"

"No, Mr. Jack," answered Grandemont, gravely, "the spectacle has been denied me. But, I assure you, I can understand it must be a diverting sight. The big ones, you know, white with snow on the tops, waltzing—décolleté, we may say."

"You first scour the kettles," said Mr. Jack, leaning toward him excitedly, "to cook the beans in the morning, and you lie down on a blanket and keep quite still. Then they come out and dance for you. You would go out and dance with them but you are chained every night to the centre pole of the hut. You believe the mountains dance, don't you, Charlie?"

"I contradict no traveler's tales," said Grandemont, with a smile.

Mr. Jack laughed loudly. He dropped his voice to a confidential whisper.

"You are a fool to believe it," he went on. "They don't really dance. It's the fever in your head. It's the hard work and the bad water that does it. You are sick for weeks and there is no medicine. The fever comes on every evening, and then you are as strong as two men. One night the *compañia* are lying drunk with *mescal*. They have brought back sacks of silver dollars from a ride, and they drink to celebrate. In the night you file the chain in two and go down the mountain. You walk for miles—hundreds of them. By and by the mountains are all gone, and you come to the prairies. They do not dance at night; they are merciful, and you sleep. Then you come to the river, and it says things to you. You follow it down, down, but you can't find what you are looking for."

Mr. Jack leaned back in his chair, and his eyes slowly closed. The food and wine had steeped him in a deep calm. The tense strain had been smoothed from his face. The languor of repletion was claiming him. Drowsily he spoke again.

"It's bad manners—I know—to go to sleep—at table—but—that was—such a good dinner—Grande, old fellow."

Grande! The owner of the name started and set down his glass. How should this wretched tatterdemalion whom he had invited, Caliph-like, to sit at his feast know his name?

Not at first, but soon, little by little, the suspicion, wild and unreasonable as it was, stole into his brain. He drew out his watch with hands that almost balked him by their trembling, and opened the back case. There was a picture there—a photograph fixed to the inner side.

Rising, Grandemont shook Mr. Jack by the shoulder. The weary guest opened his eyes. Grandemont held the watch.

"Look at this picture, Mr. Jack. Have you ever——"

"My sister Adèle!"

The vagrant's voice rang loud and sudden through the room. He started to his feet, but Grandemont's arms were about him, and Grandemont was calling him "Victor!—Victor Fauquier! *Merci, merci, mon Dieu!*"

Too far overcome by sleep and fatigue was the lost one to talk that night. Days afterward, when the tropic *calentura* had cooled in his veins, the disordered fragments he had spoken were completed in shape and sequence. He told the story of his angry flight, of toils and calamities on sea and shore, of his ebbing and flowing fortune in southern lands, and of his latest peril when, held a captive, he served menially in a stronghold of bandits in the Sonora Mountains of Mexico. And of the fever that seized him there and his escape and delirium, during which he strayed, perhaps led by some marvelous instinct, back to the river on whose bank he had been born. And of the proud and stubborn thing in his blood that had kept him silent through all those years, clouding the honor of one, though he knew it not, and keeping apart two loving hearts. "What a thing is love!" you may say. And if I grant it, you shall say, with me: "What a thing is pride!"

On a couch in the reception chamber Victor lay, with a dawning understanding in his heavy eyes and peace in his softened countenance. Absalom was preparing a lounge for the transient master of Charleroi, who, to-morrow, would be again the clerk of a cotton broker, but also——

"To-morrow," Grandemont was saying, as he stood by the couch of his guest, speaking the words with his face shining as must have shone the face of Elijah's charioteer when he announced the glories of that heavenly journey— "To-morrow I will take you to Her."

ON BEHALF OF THE MANAGEMENT

THIS is the story of the man manager, and how he held his own until the very last paragraph.

I had it from Sully Magoon, viva voce. The words are indeed his; and if they do not constitute truthful fiction my memory should be taxed with the blame.

It is not deemed amiss to point out, in the beginning, the stress that is laid upon the masculinity of the manager. For, according to Sully, the term when applied to the feminine division of mankind has precisely an opposite meaning. The woman manager (he says) economizes, saves, oppresses her household with bargains and contrivances, and looks sourly upon any pence that are cast to the fiddler for even a single jig-step on life's arid march. Wherefore her men-folk call her blessed and praise her; and then sneak out the back door to see the Gilhooly Sisters do a buck-and-wing dance.

Now, the man manager (I still quote Sully) is a Cæsar without a Brutus. He is an autocrat without responsibility, a player who imperils no stake of his own. His office is to enact, to reverberate, to boom, to expand, to out-coruscate— profitably, if he can. Bill-paying and growing gray hairs over results belong to his principals. It is his to guide the risk, to be the Apotheosis of Front, the three-tailed Bashaw of Bluff, the Essential Oil of Razzle-Dazzle.

We sat at luncheon, and Sully Magoon told me. I asked for particulars.

"My old friend Denver Galloway was a born manager," said Sully. "He first saw the light of day in New York at three years of age. He was born in Pittsburgh, but his parents moved East the third summer afterward.

"When Denver grew up, he went into the managing business. At the age of eight he managed a news-stand for the Dago that owned it. After that he was manager at different times of a skating-rink, a livery-stable, a policy game, a restaurant, a dancing academy, a walking match, a burlesque company, a dry-goods store, a dozen hotels and summer resorts, an insurance company, and a district leader's campaign. That campaign, when Coughlin was elected on the East Side, gave Denver a boost. It got him a job as manager of a Broad-way hotel, and for a while he managed Senator O'Grady's campaign in the nine-teenth.

"Denver was a New Yorker all over. I think he was out of the city just twice before the time I'm going to tell you about. Once he went rabbit-shooting in Yonkers. The other time I met him just landing from a North River ferry. 'Been out West on a big trip, Sully, old boy,' said he. 'Gad! Sully, I had no idea we had such a big country. It's immense. Never conceived of the mag-nificence of the West before. It's gorgeous and glorious and infinite. Makes the East seem cramped and little. It's a grand thing to travel and get an idea of the extent and resources of our country.'

"I'd made several little runs out to California and down to Mexico and up through Alaska, so I sits down with Denver for a chat about the things he saw.

" 'Took in the Yosemite, out there, of course?' I asks.

" 'Well—no,' says Denver, 'I don't think so. At least, I don't recollect it. You see, I only had three days, and I didn't get any farther west than Youngstown, Ohio.'

"About two years ago I dropped into New York with a little flypaper proposi-tion about a Tennessee mica mine that I wanted to spread out in a nice, sunny window, in the hopes of catching a few. I was coming out of a printing-shop one afternoon with a batch of fine, sticky prospectuses when I ran against Denver coming around a corner. I never saw him looking so much like a tiger-lily. He was as beautiful and new as a trellis of sweet peas, and as rollicking as a clarinet solo. We shook hands, and he asked me what I was doing, and I gave him the outlines of the scandal I was trying to create in mica.

" 'Pooh, pooh! for your mica,' says Denver. 'Don't you know better, Sully, than to bump up against the coffers of little old New York with anything as transparent as mica? Now, you come with me over to the Hotel Brunswick. You're just the man I was hoping for. I've got something there in sepia and curled hair that I want you to look at.'

" 'You putting up at the Brunswick?' I asks.

" 'Not a cent,' says Denver, cheerful. 'The syndicate that owns the hotel puts up. I'm manager.'

"The Brunswick wasn't one of them Broadway pot-houses all full of palms and hyphens and flowers and costumes—kind of a mixture of lawns and laun-dries. It was on one of the East Side avenues; but it was a solid, old-time caravansary such as the Mayor of Skaneateles or the Governor of Missouri might stop at. Eight stories high it stalked up, with new striped awnings, and the electrics had it as light as day.

" 'I've been manager here for a year,' says Denver, as we drew nigh. 'When I took charge,' says he, 'nobody nor nothing ever stopped at the Brunswick. The clock over the clerk's desk used to run for weeks without winding. A man feel dead with heart-disease on the sidewalk in front of it one day, and when they went to pick him up he was two blocks away. I figured out a scheme to catch the West Indies and South American trade. I persuaded the owners to invest a few more thousands, and I put every cent of it in electric lights, cayenne pepper, gold-leaf, and garlic. I got a Spanish-speaking force of employees and a string band; and there was talk going around of a cockfight in the basement every Sunday. Maybe I didn't catch the nut-brown gang! From Havana to Patagonia the Don Señors knew about the Brunswick. We get the high-fliers from Cuba and Mexico and the couple of Americas farther south;

and they've simply got the boodle to bombard every bullfinch in the bush with.'

"When we get to the hotel, Denver stops me at the door.

" 'There's a little liver-colored man,' says he, 'sitting in a big leather chair to your right, inside. You sit down and watch him for a few minutes, and then tell me what you think.'

"I took a chair, while Denver circulates around in the big rotunda. The room was about full of curly-headed Cubans and South American brunettes of different shades; and the atmosphere was international with cigarette smoke, lit up by diamond rings and edged off with a whisper of garlic.

"That Denver Galloway was sure a relief to the eye. Six feet two he was, red-headed, and pink-gilled as a sun-perch. And the air he had! Court of Saint James, Chauncey Olcott, Kentucky colonels, Count of Monte Cristo, grand opera—all these things he reminded you of when he was doing the honors. When he raised his finger the hotel porters and bell-boys skated across the floor like cockroaches, and even the clerk behind the desk looked as meek and unimportant as Andy Carnegie.

"Denver passed around, shaking hands with his guests, and saying over the two or three Spanish words he knew until it was like a coronation rehearsal or a Bryan barbecue in Texas.

"I watched the little man he told me to. 'Twas a little foreign person in a double-breasted frock-coat, trying to touch the floor with his toes. He was the color of vici kid, and his whiskers was like excelsior made out of mahogany wood. He breathed hard, and he never once took his eyes off of Denver. There was a look of admiration and respect on his face like you see on a boy that's following a champion baseball team, or the Kaiser William looking at himself in a glass.

"After Denver goes his rounds he takes me into his private office.

" 'What's your report on the dingy I told you to watch?' he asks.

" 'Well,' says I, 'if you was as big a man as he takes you to be, nine rooms and bath in the Hall of Fame, rent free till October 1st, would be about your size.'

" 'You've caught the idea,' says Denver. 'I've given him the wizard grip and the cabalistic eye. The glamor that emanates from yours truly has enveloped him like a North River fog. He seems to think that Señor Galloway is the man who. I guess they don't raise 74-inch sorrel-tops with romping ways down in his precinct. Now, Sully,' goes on Denver, 'if you was asked, what would you take the little man to be?'

" 'Why,' says I, 'the barber around the corner or, if he's royal, the king of the boot-blacks.'

" 'Never judge by looks,' says Denver; 'he's the dark-horse candidate for president of a South American republic.'

" 'Well,' says I, 'he didn't look quite that bad to me.'

"Then Denver draws his chair up close and gives out his scheme.

" 'Sully,' says he, with seriousness and levity, 'I've been a manager of one thing and another for over twenty years. That's what I was cut out for—to have somebody else to put up the money and look after the repairs and the police and taxes while I run the business. I never had a dollar of my own invested in my life. I wouldn't know how it felt to have the dealer rake in a coin of mine. But I can handle other people's stuff and manage other people's enterprises. I've had an ambition to get hold of something big—something higher than hotels and lumber-yards and local politics. I want to be manager of something way up—like a railroad or a diamond trust or an automobile factory. Now here comes this little man from the tropics with just what I want, and he's offered me the job.'

"'What job?' I asks. 'Is he going to revive the Georgia Minstrels or open a cigar store?'

"'He's no 'coon,' says Denver, severe. 'He's General Rompiro—General Josey Alfonso Sapolio Jew-Ann Rompiro—he has his cards printed by a news-ticker. He's the real thing, Sully, and he wants me to manage his campaign—he wants Denver C. Galloway for a president-maker. Think of that, Sully! Old Denver romping down to the tropics, plucking lotos-flowers and pineapples with one hand and making presidents with the other! Won't it make Uncle Mark Hanna mad? And I want you to go too, Sully. You can help me more than any man I know. I've been herding that brown man for a month in the hotel so he wouldn't stray down around Fourteenth Street and get roped in by that crowd of refugee tamale-eaters down there. And he's landed, and D. C. G. is manager of General J. A. S. J. Rompiro's presidental campaign in the great republic of—what's its name?'

"Denver gets down an atlas from a shelf, and we have a look at the afflicted country. 'Twas a dark blue one, on the west coast, about the size of a special delivery stamp.

"'From what the General tells me,' says Denver, 'and from what I can gather from the encyclopædia and by conversing with the janitor of the Astor Library, it'll be as easy to handle the vote of that country as it would be for Tammany to get a man named Geoghan appointed on the White Wings force.'

"'Why don't General Rumptyro stay at home,' says I, 'and manage his own canvass?'

"'You don't understand South American politics,' says Denver, getting out the cigars. 'It's this way. General Rompiro had the misfortune of becoming a popular idol. He distinguished himself by leading the army in pursuit of a couple of sailors who had stolen the plaza—or the carramba, or something belonging to the government. The people called him a hero and the government got jealous. The president sends for the chief of the Department of Public Edifices. "Find me a nice, clean adobe wall," says he, "and stand Señor Rompiro up against it. Then call out a file of soldiers and—then let him be up against it." Something,' goes on Denver, 'like the way they've treated Hobson and Carrie Nation in our country. So the General had to flee. But he was thoughtful enough to bring along his roll. He's got sinews of war enough to buy a battleship and float her off in the christening fluid.'

"'What chance has he got to be president?'

"'Wasn't I just giving you his rating?' says Denver. 'His country is one of the few in South America where the presidents are elected by popular ballot. The General can't go there just now. It hurts to be shot against a wall. He needs a campaign manager to go down and whoop things up for him—to get the boys in line and the new two-dollar bills afloat and the babies kissed and the machine in running order. Sully, I don't want to brag, but you remember how I brought Coughlin under the wire for leader of the nineteenth? Ours was the banner district. Don't you suppose I know how to manage a little monkey-cage of a country like that? Why, with the dough the General's willing to turn loose I could put two more coats of Japan varnish on him and have him elected Governor of Georgia. New York has got the finest lot of campaign managers in the world, Sully, and you give me a feeling of hauteur when you cast doubts on my ability to handle the political situation in a country so small that they have to print the names of the towns in the appendix and footnotes.'

"I argued with Denver some. I told him that politics down in that tropical atmosphere was bound to be different from the nineteenth district; but I might just as well have been a Congressman from North Dakota trying to get an appropriation for a lighthouse and a coast survey. Denver Galloway had ambitions in the manager line, and what I said didn't amount to as much as a fig-leaf at the National Dressmakers' Convention. 'I'll give you three days to cogitate about going,' says Denver; 'and I'll introduce you to General Rompiro to-morrow, so you can get his ideas drawn right from the rose wood.'

"I put on my best reception-to-Booker-Washington manner the next day and tapped the distinguished rubber-plant for what he knew.

"General Rompiro wasn't so gloomy inside as he appeared on the surface. He was polite enough; and he exuded a number of sounds that made a fair stagger at arranging themselves into language. It was English he aimed at, and when his system of syntax reached your mind it wasn't past you to understand it. If you took a college professor's magazine essay and a Chinese laundryman's explanation of a lost shirt and jumbled 'em together, you'd have about what the General handed you out for conversation. He told me all about his bleeding country, and what they were trying to do for it before the doctor came. But he mostly talked of Denver C. Galloway.

"'Ah, señor,' says he, 'that is the most fine of mans. Never I have seen one man so magnifico, so gr-r-rand, so conformable to make done things so swiftly by other mans. He shall make other mans do the acts and himself to order and regulate, until we arrive at seeing accomplishments of a suddenly. Oh, yes, señor. In my countree there is not such mans of so beegness, so good talk, so compliments, so strongness of sense and such. Ah, that Señor Galloway!'

"'Yes,' says I, 'old Denver is the boy you want. , He's managed every kind of business here except filibustering, and he might as well complete the list.'

"Before the three days was up I decided to join Denver in his campaign. Denver got three months' vacation from his hotel owners. For a week we lived in a room with the General, and got all the pointers about his country that we could interpret from the noises he made. When we got ready to start, Denver had a pocket full of memorandums, and letters from the General to his friends, and a list of names and addresses of loyal politicians who would help along the boom of the exiled popular idol. Besides these liabilities we carried assets to the amount of $20,000 in assorted United States currency. General Rompiro looked like a burnt effigy, but he was Br'er Fox himself when it came to the real science of politics.

"'Here is moneys,' says the General, 'of a small amount. There is more with me—moocho more. Plentee moneys shall you be supplied, Señor Galloway. More I shall send you at all times that you need. I shall desire to pay feefty —one hundred thousand pesos, if necessario, to be elect. How no? Sacramento! If that I am president and do not make one meelion dolla in the one year you shall keek me on that side!—válgame Dios!'

"Denver got a Cuban cigar-maker to fix up a little cipher code with English and Spanish words, and gave the General a copy, so we could cable him bulletins about the election, or for more money, and then we were ready to start. General Rompiro escorted us to the steamer. On the pier he hugged Denver around the waist and sobbed. 'Noble mans,' says he, 'General Rompiro propels into you his confidence and trust. Go, in the hands of the saints to do the work for your friend. Viva la libertad!'

"'Sure,' says Denver. 'And viva la liberality an' la soaperino and hoch der land of the lotus and the vote us. Don't worry, General. We'll have you elected as sure as bananas grow upside down.'

"'Make pictures on me,' pleads the General—'make pictures on me for money as it is needful.'

"'Does he want to be tattooed, would you think?' asks Denver, wrinkling up his eyes.

"'Stupid!' says I. 'He wants you to draw on him for election expenses. It'll be worse than tattooing. More like an autopsy.'

"Me and Denver steamed down to Panama, and then hiked across the Isthmus, and then by steamer again down to the town of Espiritu on the coast of the General's country.

"That was a town to send J. Howard Payne to the growler. I'll tell you how you could make one like it. Take a lot of Filipino huts and a couple of hundred brick-kilns and arrange 'em in squares in a cemetery. Cart down all the conservatory plants in the Astor and Vanderbilt greenhouses, and stick 'em about wherever there's room. Turn all the Bellevue patients and the barbers' convention and the Tuskegee school loose in the streets, and run the thermometer up to 120 in the shade. Set a fringe of the Rocky Mountains around the rear, let it rain, and set the whole business on Rockaway Beach in the middle of January—and you'd have a good imitation of Espiritu.

"It took me and Denver about a week to get acclimated. Denver sent out the letters the General had given him, and notified the rest of the gang that there was something doing at the captain's office. We set up headquarters in an old 'dobe house on a side street where the grass was waist high. The election was only four weeks off; but there wasn't any excitement. The home candidate for president was named Roadrickeys. This town of Espiritu wasn't the capital any more than Cleveland, Ohio, is the capital of the United States, but it was the political centre where they cooked up revolutions, and made up the slates.

"At the end of the week Denver says the machine is started running.

"'Sully,' says he, 'we've got a walkover. Just because General Rompiro ain't Don Juan-on-the-spot the other crowd ain't at work. They're as full of apathy as a territorial delegate during the chaplain's prayer. Now, we want to introduce a little hot stuff in the way of campaigning, and we'll surprise 'em at the polls.'

"'How are you going to go about it?' I asks.

"'Why, the usual way,' says Denver, surprised. 'We'll get the orators on our side out every night to make speeches in the native lingo, and have torch-light parades under the shade of the palms, and free drinks, and buy up all the brass bands, of course, and—well, I'll turn the baby-kissing over to you, Sully—I've seen a lot of 'em.'

"'What else?' says I.

"'Why, you know,' says Denver. 'We get the heelers out with the crackly two-spots, and coal-tickets, and orders for groceries, and have a couple of picnics out under the banyan trees, and dances in the Firemen's Hall—and the usual things. But first of all, Sully, I'm going to have the biggest clam-bake down on the beach that was ever seen south of the tropic of Capricorn. I figured that out from the start. We'll stuff the whole town and the jungle folk for miles around with clams. That's the first thing on the programme. Suppose you go out now, and make the arrangements for that. I want to look over the estimates the General made of the vote in the coast districts.'

"I had learned some Spanish in Mexico, so I goes out, as Denver says, and in fifteen minutes I come back to headquarters.

"'If there ever was a clam in this country nobody ever saw it,' I says.

"'Great sky-rockets!' says Denver, with his mouth and eyes open. 'No clams? How in the—who ever saw a country without clams? What kind of a—how's an election to be pulled off without a clam-bake, I'd like to know? Are you sure there's no clams, Sully?'

"'Not even a can,' says I.

"'Then for God's sake go out and try to find out what the people here do eat. We've got to fill 'em up with grub of some kind.'

"I went out again. Sully was manager. In half an hour I gets back.

"'They eat,' says I, 'tortillas, cassava, carne de chivo, arroz con pello, aquacates, zapates, yucca, and huevos fritos.'

"'A man that would eat them things," says Denver, getting a little mad, 'ought to have his vote challenged.'

"In a few more days the campaign managers from the other towns came sliding into Espiritu. Our headquarters was a busy place. We had an interpreter, and ice-water, and drinks, and cigars, and Denver flashed the General's roll so often that it got so small you couldn't have bought a Republican vote in Ohio with it.

"And then Denver cabled to General Rompiro for ten thousand dollars more and got it.

"There were a number of Americâns in Espiritu, but they were all in business or grafts of some kind, and wouldn't take any hand in politics, which was sensible enough. But they showed me and Denver a fine time, and fixed us up so we could get decent things to eat and drink. There was one American, named Hicks, used to come and loaf at the headquarters. Hicks had had fourteen years of Espiritu. He was six feet four and weighed in at 135. Cocoa was his line; and coast fever and the climate had taken all the life out of him. They said he hadn't smiled in eight years. His face was three feet long, and it never moved except when he opened it to take quinine. He used to sit in our headquarters and kill fleas and talk sarcastic.

"'I don't take much interest in politics,' says Hicks, one day, 'but I'd like you to tell me what you're trying to do down here, Galloway?'

"'We're boosting General Rompiro, of course,' says Denver. 'We're going to put him in the presidential chair. I'm his manager.'

"'Well,' says Hicks, 'if I was you I'd be a little slower about it. You've got a long time ahead of you, you know.'

"'Not any longer than I need,' says Denver

"Denver went ahead and worked things smooth. He dealt out money on the quiet to his lieutenants, and they were always coming after it. There was free drinks for everybody in town, and bands playing every night, and fireworks, and there was a lot of heelers going around buying up votes day and night for the new style of politics in Espiritu, and everybody liked it.

"The day set for the election was November 4th. On the night before Denver and me were smoking our pipes in headquarters, and in comes Hicks and unjoints himself, and sits in a chair, mournful. Denver is cheerful and confident. 'Rompiro will win in a romp,' says he. 'We'll carry the country by 10,000. It's all over but the vivas. To-morrow will tell the tale.'

"'What's going to happen to-morrow?' asks Hicks.

"'Why, the presidential election, of course,' says Denver.

"'Say,' says Hicks, looking kind of funny, 'didn't anybody tell you fellows that the election was held a week before you came? Congress changed the date to July 27th. Roadrickeys was elected by 17,000. I thought you was booming old Rompiro for next term, two years from now. Wondered if you was going to keep up such a hot lick that long.'

"I dropped my pipe on the floor. Denver bit the stem off of his. Neither of us said anything.

"And then I heard a sound like somebody ripping a clapboard off of a barn-roof. 'Twas Hicks laughing for the first time in eight years."

Sully Magoon paused while the waiter poured us black coffee.

"Your friend was, indeed, something of a manager," I said.

"Wait a minute," said Sully, "I haven't given you any idea of what he could do yet. That's all to come.

"When we got back to New York there was General Rompiro waiting for us on the pier. He was dancing like a cinnamon bear, all impatient for the news, for Denver had just cabled him when we would arrive and nothing more.

"'Am I elect?' he shouts. 'Am I elect, friend of mine? Is it that mine country have demand General Rompiro for the president? The last dollar of mine have I sent you that last time. It is necessario that I am elect. I have no more money. Am I elect, Señor Galloway?'

"Denver turns to me.

" 'Leave me with old Rompey, Sully,' he says. 'I've got to break it to him gently. 'Twould be indecent for other eyes to witness the operation. This is the time, Sully,' says he, 'when old Denver has got to make good as a jollier and a silver-tongued sorcerer, or else give up all the medals he's earned.'

"A couple of days later I went around to the hotel. There was Denver in his old place, looking like the hero of two historical novels, and telling 'em what a fine time he'd had down on his orange plantation in Florida.

" 'Did you fix things up with the General?' I ask him.

" 'Did I?' says Denver. 'Come and see.'

"He takes me by the arm and walks me to the dining-room door. There was a little chocolate-brown fat man in a dress suit, with his face shining with joy as he swelled himself and skipped about the floor. Danged if Denver hadn't made General Rompiro head waiter of the Hotel Brunswick!"

"Is Mr. Galloway still in the managing business?" I asked, as Mr. Magoon ceased.

Sully shook his head.

"Denver married an auburn-haired widow that owns a big hotel in Harlem. He just helps around the place."

WHISTLING DICK'S CHRISTMAS STOCKING

IT was with much caution that Whistling Dick slid back the door of the box-car, for Article 5716, City Ordinances, authorized (perhaps unconstitutionally) arrest on suspicion, and he was familiar of old with this ordinance. So, before climbing out, he surveyed the field with all the care of a good general.

He saw no change since his last visit to this big, almsgiving, long-suffering city of the South, the cold weather paradise of the tramps. The levee where his freight-car stood was pimpled with dark bulks of merchandise. The breeze reeked with the well-remembered, sickening smell of the old tarpaulins that covered bales and barrels. The dun river slipped along among the shipping with an oily gurgle. Far down toward Chalmette he could see the great bend in the stream, outlined by the row of electric lights. Across the river Algiers lay, a long, irregular blot, made darker by the dawn which lightened the sky beyond. An industrious tug or two, coming for some early sailing ship, gave a few appalling toots, that seemed to be the signal for breaking day. The Italian luggers were creeping nearer their landing, laden with early vegetables and shellfish. A vague roar, subterranean in quality, from dray wheels and street cars, began to make itself heard and felt; and the ferryboats, the Mary Anns of water craft, stirred sullenly to their menial morning tasks.

Whistling Dick's red head popped suddenly back into the car. A sight too imposing and magnificent for his gaze had been added to the scene. A vast, in-comparable policeman rounded a pile of rice sacks and stood within twenty yards of the car. The daily miracle of the dawn, now being performed above Algiers, received the flattering attention of this specimen of municipal official splendor. He gazed with unbiased dignity at the faintly glowing colors until, at last, he turned to them his broad back, as if convinced that legal interference was not needed, and the sunrise might proceed unchecked. So he turned his face to the

rice bags, and, drawing a flat flask from an inside pocket, he placed it to his lips
and regarded the firmament.

Whistling Dick, professional tramp, possessed a half-friendly acquaintance with
this officer. They had met several times before on the levee at night, for the
officer, himself a lover of music, had been attracted by the exquisite whistling of
the shiftless vagabond. Still, he did not care, under the present circumstances,
to renew the acquaintance. There is a difference between meeting a policeman
upon a lonely wharf and whistling a few operatic airs with him, and being
caught by him crawling out of a freight-car. So Dick waited, as even a New
Orleans policeman must move on some time—perhaps it is a retributive law of
nature—and before long "Big Fritz" majestically disappeared between the trains
of cars.

Whistling Dick waited as long as his judgment advised, and then slid swiftly
to the ground. Assuming as far as possible the air of an honest laborer who
seeks his daily toil, he moved across the network of railway lines, with the
intention of making his way by quiet Girod Street to a certain bench in Lafayette
Square, where, according to appointment, he hoped to rejoin a pal known as
"Slick," this adventurous pilgrim having preceded him by one day in a cattle-
car into which a loose slat had enticed him.

As Whistling Dick picked his way where night still lingered among the big,
reeking, musty warehouses, he gave way to the habit that had won for him
his title. Subdued, yet clear, with each note as true and liquid as a bobolink's,
his whistle tinkled about the dim, cold mountains of brick like drops of rain
falling into a hidden pool. He followed an air, but it swam mistily into a
swirling current of improvisation. You could cull out the trill of mountain
brooks, the staccato of green rushes shivering above chilly lagoons, the pipe
of sleepy birds.

Rounding a corner, the whistler collided with a mountain of blue and brass.

"So," observed the mountain calmly, "you are already pack. Und dere vill
not pe frost before two veeks yet! Und you haf forgotten how to vistle. Dere
was a valse note in dot last bar."

"Watcher know about it?" said Whistling Dick, with tentative familiarity;
"you wit yer little Gherman-band nixcumrous chunes. Watcher know about
music? Pick yer ears, and listen agin. Here's de way I whistled it—see?"

He puckered his lips, but the big policeman held up his hand.

"Shtop," he said, "und learn der right way. Und learn also dot a rolling
shtone can't vistle for a cent."

Big Fritz's heavy moustache rounded into a circle, and from its depths came
a sound deep and mellow as that from a flute. He repeated a few bars of the air
the tramp had been whistling. The rendition was cold, but correct, and he
emphasized the note he had taken exception to.

"Dot p is p natural, and not p vlat. Py der vay, you petter pe glad I meet you.
Von hour later, und I vould haf to put you in a gage to vistle mit der chail
pirds. Der orders are to bull all der pums after sunrise."

"To which?"

"To bull der pums—eferybody mitout fisible means. Dirty days is der price, or
fifteen tollars."

"Is dat straight, or a game you givin' me?"

"It's der pest tip you efer had. I gif it to you pecause I pelief you are not
so bad as der rest. Und pecause you gan vistle 'Der Freischütz' bezzer dan I
myself gan. Don't run against any more bolicemans aroundt der corners, but go
away from town a few tays. Goot-pye."

So Madame Orleans had at last grown weary of the strange and ruffled brood
that came yearly to nestle beneath her charitable pinions.

After the big policeman had departed, Whistling Dick stood for an irresolute

minute, feeling all the outraged indignation of a deliquent tenant who is ordered
to vacate his premises. He had pictured to himself a day of dreamful ease when
he should have joined his pal; a day of lounging on the wharf, munching the
bananas and cocoanuts scattered in unloading the fruit steamers; and then a feast
along the free-lunch counters from which the easy-going owners were too good-
natured or too generous to drive him away, and afterward a pipe in one of the
little flowery parks and a snooze in some shady corner of the wharf. But here
was a stern order to exile, and one that he knew must be obeyed. So, with a
wary eye open for the gleam of brass buttons, he began his retreat toward a
rural refuge. A few days in the country need not necessarily prove disastrous.
Beyond the possibility of a slight nip of frost, there was no formidable evil to
be looked for.

However, it was with a depressed spirit that Whistling Dick passed the old
French market on his chosen route down the river. For safety's sake he still
presented to the world his portrayal of the part of the worthy artisan on his
way to labor. A stall-keeper in the market, undeceived, hailed him by the
generic name of his ilk, and "Jack" halted, taken by surprise. The vendor,
melted by this proof of his own acuteness, bestowed a foot of Frankfurter and
half a loaf, and thus the problem of breakfast was solved.

When the streets, from topographical reasons, began to shun the river bank
the exile mounted to the top of the levee, and on its well-trodden path pursued
his way. The suburban eye regarded him with cold suspicion, individuals reflected the stern spirit of the city's heartless edict. He missed the seclusion of
the crowded town and the safety he could always find in the multitude.

At Chalmette, six miles upon his desultory way, there suddenly menaced him
a vast and bewildering industry. A new port was being established; the dock
was being built, compresses were going up; picks and shovels and barrows struck
at him like serpents from every side. An arrogant foreman bore down upon
him, estimating his muscles with the eye of a recruiting-sergeant. Brown men
and black men all about him were toiling away. He fled in terror.

By noon he had reached the country of the plantations, the great, sad, silent
levels bordering the mighty river. He overlooked fields of sugar-cane so vast
that their farthest limits melted into the sky. The sugar-making season was well
advanced, and the cutters were at work; the wagons creaked drearily after them;
the Negro teamsters inspired the mules to greater speed with mellow and sonorous imprecations. Dark-green groves, blurred by the blue of distance, showed
where the plantation-houses stood. The tall chimneys of the sugar-mills caught
the eye miles distant, like lighthouses at sea.

At a certain point Whistling Dick's unerring nose caught the scent of frying
fish. Like a pointer to a quail, he made his way down the levee side straight
to the camp of a credulous and ancient fisherman, whom he charmed with song
and story, so that he dined like an admiral, and then like a philosopher an-
nihilated the worst three hours of the day by a nap under the trees.

When he awoke and again continued his hegira, a frosty sparkle in the air
succeeded the drowsy warmth of the day, and as this portent of a chilly night
translated itself to the brain of Sir Peregrine, he lengthened his stride and
bethought him of shelter. He traveled a road that faithfully followed the convolutions of the levee, running along its base, but whither he knew not. Bushes
and rank grass crowded it to the wheel ruts, and out of this ambuscade the
pests of the lowlands swarmed after him, humming a keen vicious soprano.
And as the night grew nearer, although colder, the whine of the mosquitoes became a greedy, petulant snarl that shut out all other sounds. To his right,
against the heavens, he saw a green light moving, and, accompanying it, the
masts and funnels of a big incoming steamer, moving as upon a screen at a
magic-lantern show. And there were mysterious marshes at his left, out of which

came queer gurgling cries and a choked croaking. The whistling vagrant struck up a merry warble to offset these melancholy influences, and it is likely that never before, since Pan himself jigged it on his reeds, had such sounds been heard in those depressing solitudes.

A distant clatter in the rear quickly developed into the swift beat of horses' hoofs, and Whistling Dick stepped aside into the dew-wet grass to clear the track. Turning his head, he saw approaching a fine team of stylish grays drawing a double surrey. A stout man with a white moustache occupied the front seat, giving all his attention to the rigid lines in his hands. Behind him sat a placid, middle-aged lady and a brilliant-looking girl hardly arrived at young ladyhood. The lap-robe had slipped partly from the knees of the gentleman driving, and Whistling Dick saw two stout canvas bags between his feet—bags such as, while loafing in cities, he had seen warily transferred between express waggons and bank doors. The remaining space in the vehicle was filled with parcels of various sizes and shapes.

As the surrey swept even with the sidetracked tramp, the bright-eyed girl, seized by some merry, madcap impulse, leaned out toward him with a sweet, dazzling smile, and cried, "Mer-ry Christ-mas!" in a shrill, plaintive treble.

Such a thing had not often happened to Whistling Dick, and he felt handicapped in devising the correct response. But lacking time for reflection, he let his instinct decide, and snatching off his battered derby, he rapidly extended it at arm's length, and drew it back with a continuous motion, and shouted a loud, but ceremonious, "Ah, there!" after the flying surrey.

The sudden movement of the girl had caused one of the parcels to become unwrapped, and something limp and black fell from it into the road. The tramp picked it up and found it to be a new black silk stocking, long and fine and slender. It crunched crisply, and yet with a luxurious softness, between his fingers.

"Ther bloomin' little skeezicks!" said Whistling Dick, with a broad grin bisecting his freckled face. "W'ot d' yer think of dat, now! Mer-ry Chris-mus! Sounded like a cuckoo clock, dat's what she did. Dem guys is swells, too, bet yer life, an' der old 'un stacks dem sacks of dough down under his trotters like dey was common as dried apples. Been shoppin' fer Chrismus, and de kid's lost one of her new socks w'ot she was goin' to hold up Santy wid. De bloomin' little skeezicks! Wit' her 'Mer-ry Chris-mus!' W'ot 'd yer t'ink! Same as to say, 'Hello, Jack, how goes it?' and as swell as Fift' Av'noo, and as easy as a blow-out in Cincinnat'."

Whistling Dick folded the stocking carefully and stuffed it into his pocket.

It was nearly two hours later when he came upon signs of habitation. The buildings of an extensive plantation were brought into view by a turn in the road. He easily selected the planter's residence in a large square building with two wings, with numerous good-sized, well-lighted windows, and broad verandas running around its full extent. It was set upon a smooth lawn, which was faintly lit by the far-reaching rays of the lamps within. A noble grove surrounded it, and old-fashioned shrubbery grew thickly about the walls and fences. The quarters of the hands and the mill buildings were situated at a distance in the rear.

The road was now enclosed on each side by a fence, and presently, as Whistling Dick drew nearer the houses, he suddenly stopped and sniffed the air.

"If dere ain't a hobo stew cookin' somewhere in dis immediate precinct," he said to himself, "me nose has quit tellin' de trut'."

Without hesitation he climbed the fence to windward. He found himself in an apparently disused lot, where piles of old bricks were stacked, and rejected, decaying lumber. In a corner he saw the faint glow of a fire that had become little more than a bed of living coals, and he thought he could see some dim human forms sitting or lying about it. He drew nearer, and by the light of a little blaze that suddenly flared up he saw plainly the fat figure of a ragged man in an old brown sweater and cap.

"Dat man," said Whistling Dick to himself softly, "is a dead ringer for Boston Harry. I'll try him wit' de high sign."

He whistled one or two bars of a rag-time melody, and the air was immediately taken up, and then quickly ended with a peculiar run. The first whistler walked confidently up to the fire. The fat man looked up and spake in a loud, asthmatic wheeze:

"Gents, the unexpected but welcome addition to our circle is Mr. Whistling Dick, an old friend of mine for whom I fully vouches. The waiter will lay another cover at once. Mr. W. D. will join us at supper, during which function he will enlighten us in regard to the circumstances that give us the pleasure of his company."

"Chewin' de stuffin' out'n de dictionary, as usual, Boston," said Whistling Dick; "but t'anks all de same for de invitashun. I guess I finds meeself here about de same way as yous guys. A cop gimme de tip dis mornin'. Yous workin' on dis farm?"

"A guest," said Boston sternly, "shouldn't never insult his entertainers until he's filled up wid grub. 'Tain't good business sense. Workin'!—but I will restrain myself. We five—me, Deaf Pete, Blinky, Goggles, and Indiana Tom—got put on to this scheme of Noo Orleans to work visiting gentlemen upon her dirty streets, and we hit the road last evening just as the tender hues of twilight had flopped down upon the daisies and things. Blinky, pass the empty oyster-can at your left to the empty gentleman at your right."

For the next ten minutes the gang of roadsters paid their undivided attention to the supper. In an old five-gallon kerosene can they had cooked a stew of potatoes, meat, and onions, which they partook of from smaller cans they had found scattered about the vacant lot.

Whistling Dick had known Boston Harry of old, and knew him to be one of the shrewdest and most successful of his brotherhood. He looked like a prosperous stock-drover or a solid merchant from some country village. He was stout and hale, with a ruddy, always smoothly shaven face. His clothes were strong and neat, and he gave special attention to his decent-appearing shoes. During the past ten years he had acquired a reputation for working a larger number of successfully managed confidence games than any of his acquaintances, and he had not a day's work to be counted against him. It was rumored among his associates that he had saved a considerable amount of money. The four other men were fair specimens of the slinking, ill-clad, noisome genus who carried their labels of "suspicious" in plain view.

After the bottom of the large can had been scraped, and pipes lit at the coals, two of the men called Boston aside and spake with him lowly and mysteriously. He nodded decisively, and then said aloud to Whistling Dick:

"Listen, sonny, to some plain talky-talk. We five are on a lay. I've guaranteed you to be square, and you're to come in on the profits equal with the boys, and you've got to help. Two hundred hands on this plantation are expecting to be paid a week's wages to-morrow morning. To-morrow's Christmas, and they want to lay off. Says the boss: 'Work from five to nine in the morning to get a train load of sugar off, and I'll pay every man cash down for the week and a day extra.' They say: 'Hooray for the boss! It goes.' He drives to Noo Orleans to-day, and fetches back the cold dollars. Two thousand and seventy-four fifty is the amount. I got the figures from a man who talks too much, who got 'em from the bookkeeper. The boss of this plantation thinks he's going to pay this wealth to the hands. He's got it down wrong; he's going to pay it to us. It's going to stay in the leisure class, where it belongs. Now half of this haul goes to me, and the other half the rest of you may divide. Why the difference? I represent the brains. It's my scheme. Here's the way we're going to get it. There's some company at supper in the house, but they'll leave about nine. They've just happened in for an hour or so. If they don't go pretty soon, we'll work the scheme anyhow. We want all night to get away good with the dollars. They're heavy. About nine o'clock Deaf Pete and Blinky'll go down the road about a quarter beyond the house, and set fire to a big cane-field there that the cutters haven't touched yet. The wind's just right to have it roaring in two minutes. The alarm'll be given, and every man Jack about the place will be down there in ten minutes, fighting fire. That'll leave the money sacks and the women alone in the house for us to handle. You've heard cane burn? Well, there's mighty few women can screech loud enough to be heard above its crackling. The thing's dead safe. The only danger is in being caught before we can get far enough away with the money. Now, if you——"

"Boston," interrupted Whistling Dick, rising to his feet, "t'anks for de grub yous fellers has given me, but I'll be movin' on now."

"What do you mean?" asked Boston, also rising.

"W'y, you can count me outer dis deal. You oughter know that. I'm on de bum all right enough, but dat other t'ing don't go wit' me. Burglary is no good. I'll say good night and many t'anks fer——"

Whistling Dick had moved away a few steps as he spoke, but he stopped very suddenly. Boston had covered him with a short revolver of roomy calibre.

"Take your seat," said the tramp leader. "I'd feel mighty proud of myself if I let you go and spoil the game. You'll stick right in this camp until we finish the job. The end of that brick pile is your limit. You go two inches beyond that, and I'll have to shoot. Better take it easy, now."

"It's my way of doin'," said Whistling Dick. "Easy goes. You can depress de muzzle of dat twelve-incher, and run 'em back on de trucks. I remains, as de newspapers says, 'in yer midst.'"

*All right," said Boston, lowering his piece, as the other returned and took his seat again on a projecting plank in a pile of timber. "Don't try to leave; that's all. I wouldn't miss this chance even if I had to shoot an old acquaintance to make it go. I don't want to hurt anybody specially, but this thousand dollars I'm going to get will fix me for fair. I'm going to drop the road, and start a saloon in a little town I know about. I'm tired of being kicked around."

Boston Harry took from his pocket a cheap silver watch and held it near the fire.

"It's a quarter to nine," he said. "Pete, you and Blinky start. Go down the road past the house and fire the cane in a dozen places. Then strike for the levee, and come back on it, instead of the road, so you won't meet anybody. By the time you get back the men will all be striking out for the fire, and we'll break for the house and collar the dollars. Everybody cough up what matches he's got."

The two surly tramps made a collection of all the matches in the party, Whistling Dick contributing his quota with propitiatory alacrity, and then they departed in the dim starlight in the direction of the road.

Of the three remaining vagrants, two, Goggles and Indiana Tom, reclined lazily upon convenient lumber and regarded Whistling Dick with undisguised disfavor. Boston, observing that the dissenting recruit was disposed to remain peaceably, relaxed a little of his vigilance. Whistling Dick arose presently and strolled leisurely up and down keeping carefully within the territory assigned him.

"Dis planter chap," he said, pausing before Boston Harry, "w'ot makes yer t'ink he's got de tin in de house wit' 'im?"

"I'm advised of the facts in the case," said Boston. "He drove to Noo Orleans and got it, I say, to-day. Want to change your mind now and come in?'

"Naw, I was just askin'. Wot kind o' team did de boss drive?"

"Pair of grays."

"Double surrey?"

"Yep."

"Women folks along?"

"Wife and kid. Say, what morning paper are you trying to pump news for?"

"I was just conversin' to pass de time away. I guess dat team passed me in de road dis evenin'. Dat's all."

As Whistling Dick put his hands into his pockets and continued his curtailed beat up and down by the fire, he felt the silk stocking he had picked up in the road.

"Ther bloomin' little skeezicks," he muttered, with a grin.

As he walked up and down he could see, through a sort of natural opening or lane among the trees, the planter's residence some seventy-five yards distant. The side of the house toward him exhibited spacious, well-lighted windows through which a soft radiance streamed, illuminating the broad veranda and some extent of the lawn beneath.

"What's that you said?" asked Boston, sharply.

"Oh, nuttin' 't all," said Whistling Dick, lounging carelessly, and kicking meditatively at a little stone on the ground.

"Just as easy," continued the warbling vagrant softly to himself, "an' sociable an' swell, an' sassy, wit' her 'Mer-ry Chris-mus.' Wot d'yer t'ink, now!"

Dinner, two hours late, was being served in the Bellemeade plantation dining-room.

The dining-room and all its appurtenances spoke of an old régime that was here continued rather than suggested to the memory. The plate was rich to the extent that its age and quaintness alone saved it from being showy; there were interesting names signed in the corners of the pictures on the walls; the viands were of the kind that bring a shine into the eyes of gourmets. The service was swift, silent, lavish, as in the days when the waiters were assets like the plate. The names by which the planter's family and their visitors addressed one another were historic in the annals of two nations. Their manners and conversation had that most difficult kind of ease—the kind that still preserves punctilio. The planter himself seemed to be the dynamo that generated the larger portion of the gaiety and wit. The younger ones at the board found it more than difficult to turn back on him his guns of raillery and banter. It is true, the young men attempted to storm his works repeatedly, incited by the hope of gaining the approbation of their fair companions; but even when they sped a well-aimed shaft, the planter forced them to feel defeat by the tremendous discomfiting thunder of the laughter with which he accompanied his retorts. At the head of the table, serene, matronly, benevolent, reigned the mistress of the house, placing here and there the right smile, the right word, the encouraging glance.

The talk of the party was too desultory, too evanescent to follow, but at last they came to the subject of the tramp nuisance, one that had of late vexed the plantations for many miles around. The planter seized the occasion to direct his good-natured fire of raillery at the mistress, accusing her of encouraging the plague. "They swarm up and down the river every winter," he said. "They overrun New Orleans, and we catch the surplus, which is generally the worst part. And, a day or two ago, Madame New Orleans, suddenly discovering that she can't go shopping without brushing her skirts against great rows of the vagabonds sunning themselves on the banquettes, says to the police: 'Catch 'em all,' and the police catch a dozen or two, and the remaining three or four thousand overflow up and down the levees, and madame there"—pointing tragically with the carving-knife at her—"feeds them. They won't work, they defy my overseers, and they make friends with my dogs; and you, madame, feed them before my eyes, and intimidate me when I would interfere. Tell us, please, how many to-day did you thus incite to future laziness and depredation?"

"Six, I think," said madame, with a reflective smile; "but you know two of them offered to work, for you heard them yourself."

The planter's disconcerting laugh rang out again.

"Yes, at their own trades. And one was an artificial-flower maker, and the other a glass-blower. Oh, they were looking for work! Not a hand would they consent to lift to labor of any other kind."

"And another one," continued the soft-hearted mistress, "used quite good language. It was really extraordinary for one of his class. And he carried a watch. And had lived in Boston. I don't believe they are all bad. They have always seemed to me to rather lack development. I always look upon them as children with whom wisdom has remained at a standstill while whiskers have continued to grow. We passed one this evening as we were driving home who had a face as good as it was incompetent. He was whistling the intermezzo from 'Cavalleria' and blowing the spirit of Mascagni himself into it."

A bright-eyed young girl who sat at the left of the mistress leaned over and said in a confidential undertone:

"I wonder, Mamma, if that tramp we passed on the road found my stocking, and do you think he will hang it up to-night? Now I can hang up but one. Do you know why I wanted a new pair of silk stockings when I have plenty? Well, old Aunt Judy says, if you hang up two that have never been worn, Santa Claus will fill one with good things, and Monsieur Pambe will place in the other payment for all the words you have spoken—good or bad—on the day before Christmas. That's why I've been unusually nice and polite to everyone to-day. Monsieur Pambe, you know, is a witch gentleman; he——"

The words of the young girl were interrupted by a startling thing.

Like the wraith of some burned-out shooting star, a black streak came crashing through the window-pane and upon the table, where it shivered into fragments a dozen pieces of crystal and china ware, and then glanced between the heads of the guests to the wall, imprinting therein a deep, round indentation, at which, to-day, the visitor to Bellemeade marvels as he gazes upon it and listens to this tale as it is told.

The women screamed in many keys, and the men sprang to their feet, and would have laid their hands upon their swords had not the verities of chronology forbidden.

The planter was the first to act; he sprang to the intruding missile and held it up to view.

"By Jupiter!" he cried. "A meteoric shower of hosiery! Has communication at last been established with Mars?"

"I should say—ahem!—Venus," ventured a young gentleman visitor, looking hopefully for approbation toward the unresponsive young-lady visitors.

The planter held at arm's length the unceremonious visitor—a long dangling black stocking. "It's loaded," he announced.

As he spoke he reversed the stocking, holding it by the toe, and down from it dropped a roundish stone, wrapped about by a piece of yellowish paper. "Now for the first interstellar message of the century!" he cried; and nodding to the company, who had crowded about him, he adjusted his glasses with provoking deliberation, and examined it closely. When he finished he had changed from the jolly host to the practical, decisive man of business. He immediately struck a bell, and said to the silent-footed mulatto man who responded: "Go and tell

Mr. Wesley to get Reeves and Maurice and about ten stout hands they can rely upon, and come to the hall door at once. Tell him to have the men arm themselves, and bring plenty of ropes and plough lines. Tell him to hurry." And then he read aloud from the paper these words:

To the Gent of de Hous:
Dere is five tuff hoboes xcept meself in the vaken lot near de road war de old brick piles is. Dey got me stuck up wid a gun see and I taken dis means of comunikaten. 2 of der lads is gone down to set fire to de cain field below de hous and when yous fellers goes to turn de hoes on it de hole gang is goin to rob de house of de money yoo gotto pay off wit say git a move on ye say de kid dropt dis sock in der rode tel her mery crismus de same as she told me. Ketch de bums down de rode first and den sen a relefe core to get me out of soke youres truly,   Whistlen Dick.

There was some quiet, but rapid, maneuvering at Bellemeade during the ensuing half hour, which ended in five disgusted and sullen tramps being captured and locked securely in an out-house pending the coming of the morning and retribution. For another result, the visiting young gentleman had secured the unqualified worship of the visiting young ladies by their distinguished and heroic conduct. For still another, behold Whistling Dick, the hero, seated at the planter's table, feasting upon viands his experience had never before included, and waited upon by admiring feminity in shapes of such beauty and "swellness" that even his ever-full mouth could scarcely prevent him from whistling. He was made to disclose in detail his adventure with the evil gang of Boston Harry, and how he cunningly wrote the note and wrapped it around the stone and placed it in the toe of the stocking, and, watching his chance, sent it silently, with a wonderful centrifugal momentum, like a comet, at one of the big lighted windows of the dining-room.

The planter vowed that the wanderer should wander no more; that his was a goodness and an honesty that should be rewarded, and that a debt of gratitude had been made that must be paid; for had he not saved them from a doubtless imminent loss, and maybe a greater calamity? He assured Whistling Dick that he might consider himself a charge upon the honor of Bellemeade; that a position suited to his powers would be found for him at once, and hinted that the way would be heartily smoothed for him to rise to as high places of emolument and trust as the plantation afforded.

But now, they said, he must be weary, and the immediate thing to consider was rest and sleep. So the mistress spoke to a servant, and Whistling Dick was conducted to a room in the wing of the house occupied by the servants. To this room, in a few minutes, was brought a portable tin bathtub filled with water, which was placed on a piece of oiled cloth upon the floor. There the vagrant was left to pass the night.

By the light of a candle he examined the room. A bed, with the covers neatly turned back, revealed snowy pillows and sheets. A worn, but clean, red carpet covered the floor. There was a dresser with a beveled mirror, a washstand with a flowered bowl and pitcher; the two or three chairs were softly upholstered. A little table held books, papers, and a day-old cluster of roses in a jar. There were towels on a rack and soap in a white dish.

Whistling Dick set his candle on a chair and placed his hat carefully under the table. After satisfying what we must suppose to have been his curiosity by a sober scrutiny, he removed his coat, folded it, and laid it upon the floor, near the wall, as far as possible from the unused bathtub. Taking his coat for a pillow, he stretched himself luxuriously upon the carpet.

When, on Christmas morning, the first streaks of dawn broke above the marshes, Whistling Dick awoke and reached instinctively for his hat. Then he remembered that the skirts of Fortune had swept him into their folds on the night previous, and he went to the window and raised it, to let the fresh breath of the morning cool his brow and fix the yet dream-like memory of his good luck within his brain.

As he stood there, certain dread and ominous sounds pierced the fearful hollow of his ear.

The force of plantation workers, eager to complete the shortened task allotted to them, were all astir. The mighty din of the ogre Labor shook the earth, and the poor tattered and forever disguised Prince in search of his fortune held tight to the window-sill even in the enchanted castle, and trembled.

Already from the bosom of the mill came the thunder of rolling barrels of sugar, and (prison-like sounds) there was a great rattling of chains as the mules were harried with stimulant imprecations to their places by the wagon-tongues. A little vicious "dummy" engine, with a train of flat cars in tow, stewed and fumed on the plantation tap of the narrow-gauge railroad, and a toiling, hurrying, hallooing stream of workers were dimly seen in the half darkness loading the train with the weekly output of sugar. Here was a poem, an epic—nay, a tragedy—with work, the curse of the world, for its theme.

The December air was frosty, but the sweat broke out upon Whistling Dick's face. He thrust his head out of the window and looked down. Fifteen feet below him, against the wall of the house, he could make out that a border of flowers grew, and by that token he overhung a bed of soft earth.

Softly as a burglar goes, he clambered out upon the sill, lowered himself until he hung by his hands alone, and then dropped safely. No one seemed to be about upon this side of the house. He dodged low and skimmed swiftly across the yard to the low fence. It was an easy matter to vault this, for a terror urged him such as lifts the gazelle over the thorn bush when the lion pursues. A crash through the dew-drenched weeds on the roadside, a clutching, slippery rush up the grassy side of the levee to the footpath at the summit, and—he was free!

The east was blushing and brightening. The wind, himself a vagrant rover, saluted his brother upon the cheek. Some wild geese, high above, gave cry. A rabbit skipped along the path before him, free to turn to the right or to the left as his mood should send him. The river slid past, and certainly no one could tell the ultimate abiding place of its waters.

A small, ruffled, brown-breasted bird, sitting upon a dogwood sapling, began a soft, throaty, tender little piping in praise of the dew which entices foolish worms from their holes; but suddenly he stopped, and sat with his head turned sidewise, listening.

From the path along the levee there burst forth a jubilant, stirring, buoyant, thrilling whistle, loud and keen and clear as the cleanest notes of the piccolo. The soaring sound rippled and trilled and arpeggioed as the songs of wild birds do not; but it had a wild free grace that, in a way, reminded the small brown bird of something familiar, but exactly what he could not tell. There was in it the bird call, or reveille, that all birds know; but a great waste of lavish, unmeaning things that art had added and arranged, besides, and that were quite puzzling and strange; and the little brown bird sat with his head on one side until the sound died away in the distance.

The little bird did not know that the part of that strange warbling that he understood was just what kept the warbler without his breakfast; but he knew very well that the part he did not understand did not concern him, so he gave a little flutter of his wings and swooped down like a brown bullet upon a big fat worm that was wriggling along the levee path.

THE HALBERDIER OF THE LITTLE RHEINSCHLOSS

Go sometimes into the *Bierhalle* and restaurant called Old Munich. Not long ago it was a resort of interesting Bohemians, but now only artists and musicians and literary folk frequent it. But the Pilsener is yet good, and I take some diversion from the conversation of Waiter No. 18.

For many years the customers of Old Munich have accepted the place as a faithful copy from the ancient German town. The big hall with its smoky rafters, rows of imported steins, portrait of Goethe, and verses painted on the walls—translated into German from the original of the Cincinnati poets—seems atmospherically correct when viewed through the bottom of a glass.

But not long ago the proprietors added the room above, called it the Little Rheinschloss, and built in a stairway. Up there was an imitation stone parapet, ivy-covered, and the walls were painted to represent depth and distance, with the Rhine winding at the base of the vineyarded slopes, and the castle of Ehrenbreitstein looming directly opposite the entrance. Of course there were tables and chairs; and you could have beer and food brought you, as you naturally would on the top of a castle on the Rhine.

I went into Old Munich one afternoon when there were few customers, and sat at my usual table near the stairway. I was shocked and almost displeased to perceive that the glass cigar-case by the orchestra stand had been smashed to smithereens. I did not like things to happen in Old Munich. Nothing had ever happened there before.

Waiter No. 18 came and breathed on my neck. I was his by right of discovery. Eighteen's brain was built like a corral. It was full of ideas which, when he opened the gate, came huddling out like a flock of sheep that might get together afterward or might not. I did not shine as a shepherd. As a type Eighteen fitted nowhere. I did not find out if he had a nationality, family, creed, grievance, hobby, soul, preference, home, or vote. He only came always to my table and, as long as his leisure would permit, let words flutter from him like swallows leaving a barn at daylight.

"How did the cigar-case come to be broken, Eighteen?" I asked, with a certain feeling of personal grievance.

"I can tell you about that, sir," said he, resting his foot on the chair next to mine. "Did you ever have anybody hand you a double handful of good luck while both your hands was full of bad luck, and stop to notice how your fingers behaved?"

"No riddles, Eighteen," said I. "Leave out palmistry and manicuring."

"You remember," said Eighteen, "the guy in the hammered brass Prince Albert and the oroide gold pants and the amalgamated copper hat, that carried the combination meat-axe, ice-pick, and liberty-pole, and used to stand on the first landing as you go up to the Little Rindslosh?"

"Why, yes," said I. "The halberdier. I never noticed him particularly. I remember I thought he was only a suit of armour. He had a perfect poise."

"He had more than that," said Eighteen. "He was me friend. He was an advertisement. The boss hired him to stand on the stairs for a kind of scenery to show there was something doing in the has-been line upstairs. What did you call him—a what kind of beer?"

"A halberdier," said I. "That was an ancient man-at-arms of many hundred years ago."

"Some mistake," said Eighteen. "This one wasn't that old. He wasn't over twenty-three or four."

"It was the boss's idea, rigging a man up in an ante-bellum suit of tinware and standing him on the landing of the slosh. He bought the goods at a Fourth Avenue antique store, and hung a sign out: 'Able-bodied hal—halberdier wanted. Costume furnished.'

"The same morning a young man with wrecked good clothes and a hungry look comes in, bringing the sign with him. I was filling the mustard-pots at my station.

"'I'm it,' says he, 'whatever it is. But I never halberdiered in a restaurant. Put me on. Is it a masquerade?'

"'I hear talk in the kitchen of a fishball,' says I.

"'Bully for you, Eighteen,' says he. 'You and I'll get on. Show me the boss's desk.'

"Well, the boss tries the Harveyized pajamas on him, and they fitted him like the scales on a baked redsnapper, and he gets the job. You've seen what it is—he stood straight up in the corner of the first landing with his halberd to his shoulder, looking right ahead and guarding the Portugals of the castle. The boss is nutty about having the true Old-World flavor to his joint. 'Halberdiers goes with Rindsloshes,' says he, 'just as rats goes with rathskellers and white cotton stockings with Tyrolean villages.' The boss is a kind of a antiologist, and is all posted úpon data and such information.

"From 8 P. M. to two in the morning was the Halberdier's hours. He got two meals with us help and a dollar a night. I eat with him at the table. He liked me. He never told his name. He was traveling impromptu, like kings, I guess. The first time at supper I says to him. 'Have some more of the spuds, Mr. Frelinghuysen.' 'Oh, don't be so formal, and offish, Eighteen,' says he. 'Call me Hal—that's short for halberdier.' 'Oh, don't think I wanted to pry for names,' says I. 'I know all about the dizzy fall from wealth and greatness. We've got a count washing dishes in the kitchen; and the third bartender used to be a Pullman conductor. And they *work*, Sir Percival,' says I, sarcastic.

"'Eighteen,' says he, 'as a friendly devil in a cabbage-scented hell, would you mind cutting up this piece of steak for me? I don't say that it's got more muscle than I have, but—— And then he shows me the insides of his hands. They were blistered and cut and corned and swelled up till they looked like a couple of flank steaks criss-crossed with a knife—the kind the butchers hide and take home, knowing what is the best.

"'Shoveling coal,' says he, 'and piling bricks and loading drays. But they gave out, and I had to resign. I was born for a halberdier, and I've been educated for twenty-four years to fill the position. Now, quit knocking my profession, and pass along a lot more of that ham. I'm holding the closing exercises,' says he, 'of a forty-eight-hour fast.'

"The second night he was on the job he walks down from his corner to the cigar-case and calls for cigarettes. The customers at the tables all snicker out loud to show their acquaintance with history. The boss is on.

"'An'—let's see—oh, yes—'An anarchism,' says the boss. 'Cigarettes was not made at the time when halberdiers was invented.'

"'The ones you sell was,' says Sir Percival. 'Caporal wins from chronology by the length of a cork tip.' So he gets 'em and lights one, and puts the box in his brass helmet and goes back to patrolling the Rindslosh.

"He made a big hit, 'specially with the ladies. Some of 'em would poke him with their fingers to see if he was real or only a kind of a stuffed figure they burn in elegy. And when he'd move they'd squeak, and make eyes at him as they went up to the slosh. He looked fine in his halberdashery. He slept at $2 a week in a hall-room on Third Avenue. He invited me up there one night. He had a little book on the washstand that he read instead of shopping in the saloons after hours. 'I'm on to that,' says I, 'from reading about it in novels. All the heroes on the bum carry the little book. It's either Tantalus or Liver or Horace, and it's printed in Latin, and you're a college man. And I wouldn't be surprised,' says I, 'if you wasn't educated, too.' But it was only the batting averages of the League for the last ten years.

"One night, about half-past eleven, there comes in a party of these high-rollers that are always hunting up new places to eat in and poke fun at. There was a swell girl in a 40 H.-P. auto tan coat and veil, and a fat old man with white side-whiskers, and a young chap that couldn't keep his feet off the tail of the girl's coat, and an oldish lady that looked upon life as immoral and unnecessary. 'How perfectly delightful,' they says, 'to sup in a slosh.' Up the stairs they go; and in half a minute back down comes the girl, her skirts swishing like the waves on the beach. She stops on the landing and looks our halberdier in the eye.

"'You!' she says, with a smile that reminded me of lemon sherbet. I was waiting upstairs in the slosh, then, and I was right down here by the door, putting some vinegar and cayenne into an empty bottle of tabasco, and I heard all they said.

"'It,' says Sir Percival, without moving. 'I'm only local color. Are my hauberk, helmet, and halberd on straight?'

"'Is there an explanation to this?' says she. 'Is it a practical joke such as men play in those Griddle-cake and Lamb Clubs? I'm afraid I don't see the point. I heard, vaguely, that you were away. For three months I—we have not seen you or heard from you.'

"'I'm halberdiering for my living,' says the statue. 'I'm working,' says he. 'I don't suppose you know what work means.'

"'Have you—have you lost your money?' she asks.

"Sir Percival studies a minute.

"'I am poorer,' says he, 'than the poorest sandwich man on the streets—if I don't earn my living.'

"'You call this work?' says she. 'I thought a man worked with his hands or his head instead of becoming a mountebank.'

"'The calling of a halberdier,' says he, 'is an ancient and honorable one. Sometimes,' says he, 'the man-at-arms at the door has saved the castle while the plumed knights were cake-walking in the banquet-halls above.'

"'I see you're not ashamed,' says she, 'of your peculiar tastes. I wonder, though, that the manhood I used to think I saw in you didn't prompt you to draw water or hew wood instead of publicly flaunting your ignominy in this disgraceful masquerade.'

"Sir Percival kind of rattles his armor and says: 'Helen, will you suspend sentence in this matter for just a little while? You don't understand,' says he. 'I've got to hold this job down a bit longer.'

"'You like being a harlequin—or halberdier, as you call it?' says she.

"'I wouldn't get thrown out of the job just now,' says he, with a grin, 'to be appointed Minister to the Court of St. James's.'

"And then the 40 H.-P. girl's eyes sparkled as hard as diamonds.

"'Very well,' says she. 'You shall have full run of your serving-man's tastes this night.' And she swims over to the boss's desk and gives him a smile that knocks the specks off his nose.

"'I think your Rindslosh,' says she, 'is as beautiful as a dream. It is a little slice of the Old World set down in New York. We shall have a nice supper up there; but if you will grant us one favor the illusion will be perfect—give us your halberdier to wait on our table.'

"That hit the boss's antiology hobby just right. 'Sure,' says he, 'dot vill be fine. Und der orchestra shall blay "Die Wacht am Rhein" all der time.' And he goes over and tells the halberdier to go upstairs and hustle the grub at the swells' table.

"'I'm on the job,' says Sir Percival, taking off his helmet and hanging it on his halberd and leaning 'em in the corner. The girl goes up and takes her seat and I see her jaw squared tight under her smile. 'We're going to be waited on by a real halberdier,' says she, 'one who is proud of his profession. Isn't it sweet?'

"'Ripping,' says the swell young man. 'Much prefer a waiter,' says the fat old gent. 'I hope he doesn't come from a cheap museum,' says the old lady; 'he might have microbes in his costume.'

"Before he goes to the table, Sir Percival takes me by the arm. 'Eighteen,' says he, 'I've got to pull off this job without a blunder. You coach me straight or I'll take that halberd and make hash out of you.' And then he goes up to the table with his coat of mail on and a napkin over his arm and waits for the order.

"'Why, it's Deering!' says the young swell. 'Hello, old man. What the——'

"'Beg pardon, sir,' interrupts the halberdier, 'Im waiting on the table.'

"The old man looks at him grim, like a Boston bull. 'So, Deering,' he says, 'you're at work yet.'

"'Yes, sir,' says Sir Percival, quiet and gentlemanly as I could have been myself, 'for almost three months, now.' 'You haven't been discharged during the time?' asks the old man. 'Not once, sir,' says he, 'though I've had to change my work several times.'

"'Waiter,' orders the girl, short and sharp, 'another napkin.' He brings her one, respectful.

"I never saw more devil, if I may say it, stirred up in a lady. There was two bright red spots on her cheeks, and her eyes looked exactly like a wildcat's I'd seen in the zoo. Her foot kept slapping the floor all the time.

"'Waiter,' she orders, 'bring me filtered water without ice. Bring me a footstool. Take away this empty salt-cellar.' She kept him on the jump. She was sure giving the halberdier his.

"'There wasn't but a few customers up in the slosh at that time, so I hung out near the door so I could help Sir Percival serve.

"He got along fine with the olives and celery and the bluepoints. That was easy. And then the consommé came up the dumb-waiter all in one big silver tureen. Instead of serving it from the side-table he picks it up between his hands and starts to the dining-table with it. When nearly there he drops the tureen smash on the floor, and the soup soaks all the lower part of that girl's swell silk dress.

"'Stupid—incompetent,' says she, giving him a look. 'Standing in a corner with a halberd seems to be your mission in life.'

"'Pardon me, lady,' says he. 'It was just a little bit hotter than blazes. I couldn't help it.'

"The old man pulls out a memorandum book and hunts in it. 'The 25th of April, Deering,' says he. 'I know it,' says Sir Percival. 'And ten minutes to twelve o'clock,' says the old man. 'By Jupiter! you haven't won yet.' And he pounds the table with his fist and yells to me: 'Waiter, call the manager at once—tell him to hurry here as fast as he can.' I go after the boss, and old Brockman hikes up to the slosh on the jump.

"'I want this man discharged at once,' roars the old guy. 'Look what he's done. Ruined my daughter's dress. It cost at least $600. Discharge this awkward lout at once or I'll sue you for the price of it.'

"'Dis is bad pizness,' says the boss. 'Six hundred dollars is much. I reckon I vill haf to——'

"'Wait a minute, Herr Brockmann,' says Sir Percival, easy and smiling. But he was worked up under his tin suitings; I could see that. And then he made the finest, neatest little speech I ever listened to. I can't give you the words, of course. He give the millionaires a lovely roast in a sarcastic way, describing their automobiles and opera-boxes and diamonds; and then he got around to the working-classes and the kind of grub they eat and the long hours they work—and all that sort of stuff—bunkum, of course. 'The restless rich,' says he, 'never content with their luxuries, always prowling among the haunts of the poor and humble, amusing themselves with the imperfections and misfortunes of their fellow men and women. And even here, Herr Brockmann,' he says, 'in this beautiful Rindslosh, a grand and enlightening reproduction of Old-World history and architecture, they come to disturb its symmetry and picturesqueness by demanding in their arrogance that the halberdier of the castle wait upon their table! I have faithfully and conscientiously,' says he, 'performed my duties as a halberdier. I know nothing of a waiter's duties. It was the insolent whim of these transient, pampered aristocrats that I should be detailed to serve them food. Must I be blamed—must I be deprived of the means of a livelihood,' he goes on, 'on account of an accident that was the result of their own presumption and haughtiness? But what hurts me more than all,' says Sir Percival, 'is the desecration that has been done to this splendid Rindslosh—the confiscation of its halberdier to serve menially at the banquet board.'

"Even I could see that this stuff was piffle; but it caught the boss.

"'Mein Gott,' says he, 'you vas right. Ein halberdier have not got der right to dish up soup. Him I vill not discharge. Have anoder waiter if you like, and let mein halberdier go back and stand mit his halberd. But, gentlemen,' he says, pointing to the old man, 'you go ahead and sue mit der dress. Sue me for $600 or $6,000. I stand der suit.' And the boss puffs off downstairs. Old Brockmann was an all-right Dutchman.

"Just then the clock strikes twelve, and the old guy laughs loud. 'You win, Deering,' says he. 'Let me explain to all,' he goes on. 'Some time ago Mr. Deering asked me for something that I did not want to give him.' (I looks at the girl, and she turns as red as a pickled beet.) 'I told him,' says the old guy, 'if he would earn his own living for three months without once being discharged for incompetence, I would give him what he wanted. It seems that the time was up at twelve o'clock to-night. I came near fetching you, though, Deering, on that soup question,' says the old boy, standing up and grabbing Sir Percival's hand.

"The halberdier lets out a yell and jumps three feet high.

"'Look out for those hands,' says he, and he holds 'em up. You never saw such hands except on a laborer in a limestone quarry.

"'Heavens, boy!' says old side-whiskers, 'what have you been doing to 'em?'

"'Oh,' says Sir Percival, 'little chores like hauling coal and excavating rock till they went back on me. And when I couldn't hold a pick or a whip I took up halberdiering to give 'em a rest. Tureens full of hot soup don't seem to be a particularly soothing treatment.'

"I would have bet on that girl. That high-tempered kind always go as far the other way, according to my experience. She whizzes round the table like a cyclone and catches both his hands in hers. 'Poor hands—dear hands,' she sings out, and sheds tears on 'em and holds 'em close to her bosom. Well, sir, with all that Rindslosh scenery it was just like a play. And the halberdier sits down at the table at the girl's side, and I served the rest of the supper. And that was about all, except that when they left he shed his hardware store and went with 'em."

I dislike to be side-tracked from an original proposition.

"But you haven't told me, Eighteen," said I, "how the cigar-case came to be broken."

"Oh, that was last night," said Eighteen. "Sir Percival and the girl drove up in a cream-colored motor-car, and had dinner in the Rindslosh. 'The same table, Billy,' I heard her say as they went up. I waited on 'em. We've got a new halberdier now, a bow-legged guy with a face like a sheep. As they came downstairs Sir Percival passes him a ten-case note. The new halberdier drops his halberd, and it falls on the cigar-case. That's how that happened."

TWO RENEGADES

In the Gate City of the South the Confederate Veterans were reuniting; and I stood to see them march, beneath the tangled flags of the great conflict, to the hall of their oratory and commemoration.

While the irregular and halting line was passing I made onslaught upon it and dragged forth from the ranks my friend Barnard O'Keefe, who had no right to be there. For he was a Northerner born and bred; and what should he be doing hallooing for the Stars and Bars among those gray and moribund veterans? And why should he be trudging, with his shining, martial, humorous, broad face, among those warriors of a previous and alien generation?

I say I dragged him forth, and held him till the last hickory leg and waving goatee had stumbled past. And then I hustled him out of the crowd into a cool interior; for the Gate City was stirred that day, and the hand-organs wisely eliminated "Marching Through Georgia" from their repertories.

"Now, what deviltry are you up to?" I asked of O'Keefe when there were a table and things in glasses between us.

O'Keefe wiped his heated face and instigated a commotion among the floating ice in his glass before he chose to answer.

"I am assisting at the wake," said he, "of the only nation on earth that ever did me a good turn. As one gentleman to another, I am ratifying and celebrating the foreign policy of the late Jefferson Davis, as fine a statesman as ever settled the financial question of a country. Equal ratio—that was his platform—a barrel of money for a barrel of flour—a pair of $20 bills for a pair of boots—a hatful of currency for a new hat—say, ain't that simple compared with W. J. B.'s little old oxidized plank?"

"What talk is this?" I asked. "Your financial digression is merely a subterfuge. Why were you marching in the ranks of the Confederate Veterans?"

"Because, my lad," answered O'Keefe, "the Confederate Government in its might and power interposed to protect and defend Barnard O'Keefe against immediate and dangerous assassination at the hands of a bloodthirsty foreign country after the United States of America had overruled his appeal for protection, and had instructed Private Secretary Cortelyou to reduce his estimate of the Republican majority for 1905 by one vote."

"Come, Barney," said I, "the Confederate States of America has been out of existence nearly forty years. You do not look older yourself. When was it that the deceased government exerted its foreign policy in your behalf?"

"Four months ago," said O'Keefe, promptly. "The infamous foreign power I alluded to is still staggering from the official blow dealt it by Mr. Davis's contraband aggregation of states. That's why you see me cake-walking with the ex-rebs to the illegitimate tune about 'simmón-seeds and cotton. I vote for the Great Father in Washington, but I am not going back on Mars' Jeff. You say the

Confederacy has been dead forty years? Well, if it hadn't been for it, I'd have been breathing to-day with soul so dead I couldn't have whispered a single cuss-word about my native land. The O'Keefes are not overburdened with ingratitude."

I must have looked bewildered. "The war was over," I said vacantly, "in——" O'Keefe laughed loudly, scattering my thoughts.

"Ask old Doc Millikin if the war is over!" he shouted, hugely diverted. "Oh, no! Doc hasn't surrendered yet. And the Confederate States! Well, I just told you they bucked officially and solidly and nationally against a foreign government four months ago and kept me from being shot. Old Jeff's country stepped in and brought me off under its wing while Roosevelt was having a gunboat painted and waiting for the National Campaign Committee to look up whether I had ever scratched the ticket."

"Isn't there a story in this, Barney?" I asked.

"No," said O'Keefe; "but I'll give you the facts. You know I went down to Panama when this irritation about a canal began. I thought I'd get in on the ground floor. I did, and had to sleep on it, and drink water with little zoos in it; so, of course, I got the Chagres fever. That was in a little town called San Juan on the coast.

"After I got the fever hard enough to kill a Port-au-Prince nigger, I had a relapse in the shape of Doc Millikin.

"There was a doctor to attend a sick man! If Doc Millikin had your case, he made the terrors of death seem like an invitation to a donkey-party. He had the bedside manners of a Piute medicine-man and the soothing presence of a dray loaded with iron bridge-girders. When he laid his hand on your fevered brow you felt like Cap John Smith just before Pocahontas went his bail.

"Well, this old medical outrage floated down to my shack when I sent for him. He was built like a shad, and his eyebrows was black, and his white whiskers trickled down from his chin like milk coming out of a sprinkling-pot. He had a nigger boy along carrying an old tomato-can full of calomel, and a saw.

"Doc felt my pulse, and then he began to mess up some calomel with an agricultural implement that belonged to the trowel class.

"'I don't want any death-mask made yet, Doc,' I says, 'nor my liver put in a plaster-of-paris cast. I'm sick; and it's medicine I need, not frescoing.'

"'You're a blame Yankee, ain't you?' asked Doc, going on mixing up his Portland cement.

"'I'm from the North,' says I, 'but I'm a plain man, and don't care for mural decorations. When you get the Isthmus all asphalted over with that boll-weevil prescription, would you mind giving me a dose of pain-killer, or a little strychnine on toast to ease up this feeling of unhealthiness that I have got?'

"'They was all sassy, just like you,' says old Doc, 'but we lowered their temperature considerable. Yes, sir, I reckon we sent a good many of ye over to old *mortuis nisi bonum*. Look at Antietam and Bull Run and Seven Pines and around Nashville! There never was a battle where we didn't lick ye unless you was ten to our one. I knew you were a blame Yankee the minute I laid eyes on you.'

"'Don't reopen the chasm, Doc,' I begs him. 'Any Yankeeness I may have is geographical; and, as far as I am concerned, a Southerner is as good as a Filipino any day. I'm feeling too bad to argue. Let's have secession without misrepresentation, if you say so; but what I need is more laudanum and less Lundy's Lane. If you're mixing that compound gefloxide of gefloxicum for me, please fill my ears with it before you get around to the battle of Gettysburg, for there is a subject full of talk.'

"By this time Doc Millikin had thrown up a line of fortifications on square pieces of paper; and he says to me: 'Yank, take one of these powders every two hours. They won't kill you. I'll be around again about sundown to see if you're alive.'

"Old Doc's powders knocked the chagres. I stayed in San Juan, and got to knowing him better. He was from Mississippi, and the red-hottest Southerner that ever smelled mint. He made Stonewall Jackson and R. E. Lee look like Abolitionists. He had a family somewhere down near Yazoo City; but he stayed away from the States on account of an uncontrollable liking he had for the absence of a Yankee government. Him and me got as thick personally as the Emperor of Russia and the dove of peace, but sectionally we didn't amalgamate.

"'Twas a beautiful system of medical practice introduced by old Doc into that isthmus of land. He'd take that bracket-saw and the mild chloride and his hypodermic, and treat anything from yellow fever to a personal friend.

"Besides his other liabilities Doc could play a flute for a minute or two. He was guilty of two tunes—'Dixie' and another one that was mighty close to the 'Suwanee River'—you might say one of its tributaries. He used to come down and sit with me while I was getting well, and aggrieve his flute and say unreconstructed things about the North. You'd have thought the smoke from the first gun at Fort Sumter was still floating around in the air.

"You know that was about the time they staged them property revolutions down there, that wound up in the fifth act with the thrilling canal scene where Uncle Sam has nine curtain-calls holding Miss Panama by the hand, while the bloodhounds keep Senator Morgan treed up in a cocoanut-palm.

"That's the way it wound up; but at first it seemed as if Colombia was going to make Panama look like one of the $3.98 kind, with dents made in it in the factory, like they wear at North Beach fish fries. For mine, I played the straw-hat crowd to win; and they gave me a colonel's commission over a brigade of twenty-seven men in the left wing and second joint of the insurgent army.

"The Colombian troops were awfully rude to us. One day when I had my brigade in a sandy spot, with its shoes off doing a battalion drill by squads, the Government army rushed from behind a bush at us, acting as noisy and disagreeable as they could.

"My troops enfiladed, left-faced, and left the spot. After enticing the enemy for three miles or so we struck a brier-patch and had to sit down. When we were ordered to throw up our toes and surrender we obeyed. Five of my best staff-officers fell, suffering extremely with stone-bruised heels.

"Then and there those Colombians took your friend Barney, sir, stripped him of the insignia of his rank, consisting of a pair of brass knuckles and a canteen of rum, and dragged him before a military court. The presiding general went through the usual legal formalities that sometimes cause a case to hang on the calendar of a South American military court as long as ten minutes. He asked me my age, and then sentenced me to be shot.

"They woke up the court interpreter, an American named Jenks, who was in the rum business and vice versa, and told him to translate the verdict.

"Jenks stretched himself and took a morphine tablet.

"'You've got to back up against th' 'dobe, old man,' says he to me. 'Three weeks, I believe, you get. Haven't got a chew of fine-cut on you, have you?'

"'Translate that again, with footnotes and a glossary,' says I. 'I don't know whether I'm discharged, condemned, or handed over to the Gerry Society.'

"'Oh,' says Jenks, 'don't you understand? You're to be stood up against a 'dobe wall and shot in two or three weeks—three, I think, they said.'

"'Would you mind asking 'em which?' says I. 'A week don't amount to much after you are dead, but it seems a real nice long spell while you are alive.'

"'It's two weeks,' says the interpreter, after inquiring in Spanish of the court. 'Shall I ask 'em again?'

"'Let be,' says I. 'Let's have a stationary verdict. If I keep on appealing this way they'll have me shot about ten days before I was captured. No, I haven't got any fine-cut.'

"They sends me over to the *calaboza* with a detachment of colored postal-telegraph boys carrying Enfield rifles, and I am locked up in a kind of brick bakery. The temperature in there was just about the kind mentioned in the cooking recipes that call for a quick oven.

"Then I gives a silver dollar to one of the guards to send for the United States consul. He comes around in pajamas with a pair of glasses on his nose and a dozen or two inside of him.

"'I'm to be shot in two weeks,' says I. 'And although I've made a memorandum of it, I don't seem to get it off my mind. You want to call up Uncle Sam on the cable as quick as you can and get him all worked up about it. Have 'em send the *Kentucky* and the *Kearsarge* and the *Oregon* down right away. That'll be about enough battleships; but it wouldn't hurt to have a couple of cruisers and a torpedo-boat destroyer, too. And—say, if Dewey isn't busy, better have him come along on the fastest one of the fleet.'

"'Now, see here, O'Keefe,' says the consul, getting the best of a hiccup, 'what do you want to bother the State Department about this matter for?'

"'Didn't you hear me?' says I; 'I'm to be shot in two weeks. Did you think I said I was going to a lawn-party? And it wouldn't hurt if Roosevelt could get the Japs to send down the *Yellowyamtiskookum* or the *Ogotosingsing* or some other first-class cruiser to help. It would make me feel safer.'

"'Now, what you want,' says the consul, 'is not to get excited. I'll send you over some chewing tobacco and some banana fritters when I go back. The United States can't interfere in this. You know you were caught insurging against the government, and you're subject to the laws of this country. Tell you the truth, I've had an intimation from the State Department—unofficially, of course—that whenever a soldier of fortune demands a fleet of gunboats in a case of revolutionary *katzenjammer*, I should cut the cable, give him all the tobacco he wants, and after he's shot take his clothes, if they fit me, for part payment of my salary.'

"'Consul,' says I to him, 'this is a serious question. You are representing Uncle Sam. This ain't any little international tomfoolery, like a universal peace congress or the christening of the *Shamrock IV*. I'm an American citizen and I demand protection. I demand the Mosquito fleet, and Schley, and the Atlantic squadron, and Bob Evans, and General E. Byrd Grubb, and two or three protocols. What are you going to do about it?'

"'Nothing doing,' says the consul.

"'Be off with you, then,' says I, out of patience with him, 'and send me Doc Millikin. Ask Doc to come and see me.'

"Doc comes and looks through the bars at me, surrounded by dirty soldiers, with even my shoes and canteen confiscated, and he looks mightily pleased.

"'Hello, Yank,' says he, 'getting a little taste of Johnson's Island, now, ain't ye?'

"'Doc,' says I, 'I've just had an interview with the U. S. consul. I gather from his remarks that I might just as well have been caught selling suspenders in Kishineff under the name of Rosenstein as to be in my present condition. It seems that the only maritime aid I am to receive from the United States is some navy-plug to chew. Doc,' says I, 'can't you suspend hostilities on the slavery question long enough to do something for me?'

"'It ain't been my habit,' Doc Millikin answers, 'to do any painless dentistry when I find a Yank cutting an eyetooth. So the Stars and Stripes ain't landing any marines to shell the huts of the Colombian cannibals, hey? Oh, say, can you see by the dawn's early light the star-spangled banner has fluked in the fight? What's the matter with the War Department, hey? It's a great thing to be a citizen of a gold-standard nation, ain't it?'

"'Rub it in, Doc, all you want,' says I. 'I guess we're weak on foreign policy.'

"'For a Yank,' says Doc, putting on his specs and talking more mild, 'you ain't so bad. If you had come from below the line I reckon I would have liked you right smart. Now since your country has gone back on you, you have to come to the old doctor whose cotton you burned and whose mules you stole and whose niggers you freed to help you. Ain't that so, Yank?'

"'It is,' says I heartily, 'and let's have a diagonsis of the case right away, for in two weeks' time all you can do is to hold an autoposy and I don't want to be amputated if I can help it.'

"'Now,' says Doc, business-like, 'it's easy enough for you to get out of this scrape. Money'll do it. You've got to pay a long string of 'em from General Pomposo down to this anthropoid ape guarding your door. About $10,000 will do the trick. Have you got the money?'

"'Me?' says I. 'I've got one Chili dollar, two *real* pieces, and a *medio*.'

"'Then if you've any last words, utter 'em,' says that old reb. 'The roster of your financial budget sounds quite much to me like the noise of a requiem.'

"'Change the treatment,' says I. 'I admit that I'm short. Call a consultation or use radium or smuggle me in some saws or something.'

"'Yank,' says Doc Millikin, 'I've a good notion to help you. There's only one government in the world that can get you out of this difficulty; and that's the Confederate States of America, the grandest nation that ever existed.'

"Just as you said to me I says to Doc; 'Why, the Confederacy ain't a nation. It's been absolved forty years ago.'

"'That's a campaign lie,' says Doc. 'She's running along as solid as the Roman Empire. She's the only hope you've got. Now, you, being a Yank, have got to go through with some preliminary obsequies before you can get official aid. You've got to take the oath of allegiance to the Confederate Government. Then I'll guarantee she does all she can for you. What do you say, Yank?—it's your last chance.'

"'If you're fooling with me, Doc,' I answers, 'you're no better than the United States. But as you say it's the last chance, hurry up and swear me. I always did like corn whisky and 'possum anyhow. I believe I'm half Southerner by nature. I'm willing to try the Ku Klux in place of the khaki. Get brisk.'

"Doc Millikin thinks awhile, and then he offers me this oath of allegiance to take without any kind of a chaser:

"'I, Barnard O'Keefe, Yank, being of sound body but a Republican mind, hereby swear to transfer my fealty, respect, and allegiance to the Confederate States of America, and the Government thereof, in consideration of said government, through its official acts and powers, obtaining my freedom and release from confinement and sentence of death brought about by the exuberance of my Irish proclivities and my general pizenness as a Yank.'

"I repeated these words after Doc, but they seemed to me a kind of hocus-pocus; and I don't believe any life-insurance company in the country would have issued me a policy on the strength of 'em.

"Doc went away saying he would communicate with his government immediately.

"Say—you can imagine how I felt—me to be shot in two weeks and my only hope for help being a government that's been dead so long that it isn't even remembered except on Decoration Day and when Joe Wheeler signs the voucher for his pay-check. But it was all there was in sight; and somehow I thought Doc Millikin had something up his old alpaca sleeve that wasn't all foolishness.

"Around to the jail comes old Doc again in about a week. I was flea-bitten, a mite sarcastic, and fundamentally hungry.

" 'Any Confederate ironclads in the offing?' I asks. 'Do you notice any sounds resembling the approach of Jeb Stewart's cavalry overland or Stonewall Jackson sneaking up in the rear? If you do, I wish you'd say so.'

" 'It's too soon yet for help to come,' says Doc.

" 'The sooner the better,' says I. 'I don't care if it gets in fully fifteen minutes before I am shot; and if you happen to lay eyes on Beauregard or Albert Sidney Johnson or any of the relief corps, wig-wag 'em to hike along.'

" 'There's been no answer received yet,' says Doc.

" 'Don't forget,' says I, 'that there's only four days more. I don't know how you propose to work this thing, Doc,' I says to him; 'but it seems to me I'd sleep better if you had got a government that was alive and on the map—like Afghanistan or Great Britain, or old man Kruger's kingdom,' to take this matter up. I don't mean any disrespect to your Confederate States, but I can't help feeling that my chances of being pulled out of this scrape was decidedly weakened when General Lee surrendered.'

" 'It's your only chance,' said Doc; 'don't quarrel with it. What did your own country do for you?'

"It was only two days before the morning I was to be shot when Doc Millikin came around again.

" 'All right, Yank,' says he. 'Help's come. The Confederate States of America is going to apply for your release. The representatives of the government arrived on a fruit-steamer last night.'

" 'Bully!' says I—'bully for you, Doc! I suppose it's marines with a Gatling. I'm going to love your country all I can for this.'

" 'Negotiations,' says old Doc, 'will be opened between the two governments at once. You will know later on to-day if they are successful.'

"About four in the afternoon a soldier in red trousers brings a paper round to the jail, and they unlocks the door and I walks out. The guard at the door bows and I bows, and I steps into the grass and wades around to Doc Millikin's shack.

"Doc was sitting in his hammock playing 'Dixie,' soft and low and out of tune, on his flute. I interrupted him at 'Look away! look away!' and shook his hand for five minutes.

" 'I never thought,' says Doc, taking a chew fretfully, 'that I'd ever try to save any blame Yank's life. But, Mr. O'Keefe, I don't see but what you are entitled to be considered part human, anyhow. I never thought Yanks had any of the rudiments of decorum and laudability about them. I reckon I might have been too aggregative in my tabulation. But it ain't me you want to thank—it's the Confederate States of America.'

" 'And I'm much obliged to 'em,' says I. 'It's a poor man that wouldn't be patriotic with a country that's saved his life. I'll drink to the Stars and Bars whenever there's a flag-staff and a glass convenient. But where,' says I, 'are the rescuing troops? If there was a gun fired or a shell burst, I didn't hear it.'

"Doc Millikin raises up and points out the window with his flute at the banana-steamer loading with fruit.

" 'Yank,' says he, 'there's a steamer that's going to sail in the morning. If I was you, I'd sail on it. The Confederate Government's done all it can for you. There wasn't a gun fired. The negotiations was carried on secretly between the two nations by the purser of that steamer. I got him to do it because I didn't want to appear in it. Twelve thousand dollars was paid to the officials in bribes to let you go.'

" 'Man!' says I, sitting down hard—'twelve thousand—how will I ever—who could have—where did the money come from?'

" 'Yazoo City,' says Doc Millikin; 'I've got a little saved up there. Two barrels full. It looks good to these Colombians. 'Twas Confederate money, every dollar of it. Now do you see why you'd better leave before they try to pass some of it on an expert?'

"'I do,' says I.

"'Now, let's hear you give the password,' says Doc Millikin.

"'Hurrah for Jeff Davis!' says I.

"'Correct,' says Doc. 'And let me tell you something. The next tune I learn on my flute is going to be "Yankee Doodle." I reckon there's some Yanks that are not so pizen. Or, if you was me, would you try "The Red, White, and Blue"?'"

THE LONESOME ROAD

BROWN as a coffee-berry, rugged, pistoled, spurred, wary, indefeasible, I saw my old friend, Deputy-Marshal Buck Caperton, stumble, with jingling rowels, into a chair in the marshal's outer office.

And because the courthouse was almost deserted at that hour, and because Buck would sometimes relate to me things that were out of print, I followed him in and tricked him into talk through knowledge of a weakness he had. For, cigarettes rolled with sweet corn husk were as honey to Buck's palate; and though he could finger the trigger of a forty-five with skill and suddenness, he never could learn to roll a cigarette.

It was through no fault of mine (for I rolled the cigarettes tight and smooth), but the upshot of some whim of his own, that instead of to an Odyssey of the chaparral, I listened to—a dissertation upon matrimony! This from Buck Caperton! But I maintain that the cigarettes were impeccable, and crave absolution for myself.

"We just brought in Jim and Bud Granberry," said Buck. "Train robbing, you know. Held up the Aransas Pass last month. We caught 'em in the Twenty-Mile pear flat, south of the Nueces."

"Have much trouble corralling them?" I asked, for here was the meat that my hunger for epics craved.

"Some," said Buck; and then, during a little pause, his thoughts stampeded off the trail. "It's kind of queer about women," he went on, "and the place they're supposed to occupy in botany. If I was asked to classify them I'd say they was a human loco weed. Ever see a bronc that had been chewing loco? Ride him up to a puddle of water two feet wide, and he'll give a snort and fall back on you. It looks as big as the Mississippi River to him. Next trip he'd walk into a cañon a thousand feet deep thinking it was a prairie-dog hole. Same way with a married man.

"I was thinking of Perry Rountree, that used to be my sidekicker before he committed matrimony. In them days me and Perry hated indisturbances of any kind. We roamed around considerable, stirring up the echoes and making 'em attend to business. Why, when me and Perry wanted to have some fun in a town it was a picnic for the census takers. They just counted the marshal's posse that it took to subdue us, and there was your population. But then there came along this Mariana Good-night girl and looked at Perry sideways, and he was all bridle-wise and saddle-broke before you could skin a yearling.

"I wasn't even asked to the wedding. I reckon the bride had my pedigree and the front elevation of my habits all mapped out, and she decided that Perry would trot better in double harness without any unconverted mustang like Buck Caperton whickering around on the matrimonial range. So it was six months before I saw Perry again.

"One day I was passing on the edge of town, and I see something like a man in a little yard by a little house with a sprinkling-pot squirting water on a rose-bush. Seemed to me, I'd seen something like it before, and I stopped at the gate, trying to figure out its brands. 'Twas not Perry Rountree, but 'twas the kind of a curdled jellyfish matrimony had made out of him.

"Homicide was what that Mariana had perpetrated. He was looking well enough, but he had on a white collar and shoes, and you could tell in a minute that he'd speak polite and pay taxes and stick his little finger out while drinking, just like a sheep man or a citizen. Great skyrockets! but I hated to see Perry all corrupted and Willie-ized like that.

"He came out to the gate and shook hands; and I says, with scorn, and speaking like a paroquet with the pip: 'Beg pardon—Mr. Rountree, I believe. Seems to me I sagatiated in your associations once, if I am not mistaken.'

"'Oh, go to the devil, Buck,' says Perry, polite, as I was afraid he'd be.

"'Well, then,' says I, 'you poor, contaminated adjunct of a sprinkling-pot and degraded household pet, what did you go and do it for? Look at you, all decent and unriotous, and only fit to sit on juries and mend the wood-house door. You was a man once. I have hostility for all such acts. Why don't you go in the house and count the tidies or set the clock, and not stand out here in the atmosphere? A jack-rabbit might come along and bite you.'

"'Now, Buck,' says Perry, speaking mild, and some sorrowful, 'you don't understand. A married man has got to be different. He feels different from a tough old cloudburst like you. It's sinful to waste time pulling up towns just to look at their roots, and playing faro and looking upon red liquor, and such restless policies as them.'

"'There was a time,' I says, and I expect I sighed when I mentioned it, 'when a certain domesticated little Mary's lamb I could name was some instructed himself in the line of pernicious sprightliness. I never expected, Perry, to see you reduced down from a full-grown pestilence to such a frivolous fraction of a man. Why,' says I, 'you've got a necktie on; and you speak a senseless kind of indoor drivel, that reminds me of a storekeeper or a lady. You look to me like you might tote an umbrella and wear suspenders, and go home of nights.'

"'The little woman,' says Perry, 'has made some improvements, I believe. You can't understand, Buck. I haven't been away from the house at night since we was married.'

"We talked on a while, me and Perry, and, as sure as I live, that man interrupted me in the middle of my talk to tell me about six tomato plants he had growing in his garden. Shoved his agricultural degradation right up under my nose while I was telling him about the fun we had tarring and feathering that faro dealer at California Pete's layout! But by and by Perry shows a flicker of sense.

"'Buck,' says he, "I'll have to admit that it is a little dull at times. Not that I'm not perfectly happy with the little woman, but a man seems to require some excitement now and then. Now, I'll tell you: Mariana's gone visiting this afternoon, and she won't be home till seven o'clock. That's the limit for both of us—seven o'clock. Neither of us ever stays out a minute after that time unless we are together. Now, I'm glad you came along, Buck,' says Perry, 'for I'm feeling just like having one more rip-roaring razoo with you for the sake of old times. What you say to us putting in the afternoon having fun?—I'd like it fine,' says Perry.

"I slapped that old captive range-rider half across his little garden.

"'Get your hat, you old dried-up alligator,' I shouts, 'you ain't dead yet. You're part human, anyhow, if you did get all bogged up in matrimony. We'll take this town to pieces and see what makes it tick. We'll make all kinds of profligate demands upon the science of cork pulling. You'll grow horns yet, old muley cow,' says I, punching Perry in the ribs, 'if you trot around on the trail of vice with your Uncle Buck.'

"'I'll have to be home by seven, you know,' says Perry again.

"Oh, yes,' says I, winking to myself, for I knew the kind of seven o'clocks Perry Rountree got back by after he once got to passing repartee with the bartenders.

"We goes down to the Gray Mule saloon—that old 'dobe building by the depot.

"'Give it a name,' says I, as soon as we got one hoof on the foot-rest.

"'Sarsaparilla,' says Perry.

"You could have knocked me down with a lemon peeling.

"'Insult me as much as you want to,' I says to Perry, "but don't startle the bartender. He may have heart-disease. Come on, now; your tongue got twisted. The tall glasses,' I orders, 'and the bottle in the left hand corner of the ice-chest.'

"'Sarsaparilla,' repeats Perry, and then his eyes get animated, and I see he's got some great scheme in his mind he wants to emit.

"'Buck,' he says, all interested, 'I'll tell you what! I want to make this a red-letter day. I've been keeping close at home, and I want to turn myself a-loose. We'll have the highest old time you ever saw. We'll go in the back room here and play checkers till half-past six.'

"I leaned against the bar, and I says to Gotch-eared Mike, who was on watch:

"'For God's sake don't mention this. You know what Perry used to be. He's had the fever, and the doctor says we must humor him.'

"'Give us the checker-board and the men, Mike,' says Perry. 'Come on, Buck, I'm just wild to have some excitement.'

"I went in the back room with Perry. Before we closed the door, I says to Mike:

"'Don't ever let it straggle out from under your hat that you seen Buck Caperton fraternal with sarsaparilla or *persona grata* with a checker-board, or I'll make a swallow-fork in your other ear.'

"I locked the door and me and Perry played checkers. To see that poor old humiliated piece of household bric-à-brac sitting there and sniggering out loud whenever he jumped a man, and all obnoxious with animation when he got into my king row, would have made a sheep-dog sick with mortification. Him that was once satisfied only when he was pegging six boards at keno or giving the faro dealers nervous prostration—to see him pushing them checkers about like Sally Louisa at a school-children's party—why, I was all smothered up with mortification.

"And I sits there playing the black men, all sweating for fear somebody I knew would find it out. And I thinks to myself some about this marrying business, and how it seems to be the same kind of a game as that Mrs. Delilah played. She give her old man a hair cut, and everybody knows what a man's head looks like after a woman cuts his hair. And then when the Pharisees came around to guy him he was so 'shamed he went to work and kicked the whole house down on top of the whole outfit. 'Them married men,' thinks I, 'lose all their spirit and instinct for riot and foolishness. They won't drink, they won't buck the tiger, they won't even fight. What do they want to go and stay married for?' I asks myself.

"But Perry seems to be having hilarity in considerable quantities.

"'Buck old hoss,' says he, 'isn't this just the hell-roaringest time we ever had in our lives? I don't know when I've been stirred up so. You see, I've been sticking pretty close to home since I married, and I haven't been on a spree in a long time.'

"'Spree!' Yes, that's what he called it. Playing checkers in the back room of the Gray Mule! I suppose it did seem to him a little immoral and nearer to a prolonged debauch than standing over six tomato plants with a sprinkling-pot.

"Every little bit Perry looks at his watch and says:

" 'I got to be home, you know, Buck, at seven.'

" 'All right,' I'd say. 'Romp along and move. This here excitement's killing me. If I don't reform some, and loosen up the strain of this checkered dissipation I won't have a nerve left.'

"It might have been half-past six when commotions began to go on outside in the street. We heard a yelling and a six-shootering, and a lot of galloping and maneuvers.

" 'What's that?' I wonders.

" 'Oh, some nonsense outside,' says Perry. 'It's your move. We just got time to play this game.'

" 'I'll just take a peep through the window,' says I, 'and see. You can't expect a mere mortal to stand the excitement of having a king jumped and listen to an unidentified conflict going on at the same time.'

" 'The Gray Mule saloon was one of them old Spanish 'dobe buildings, and the back room only had two little windows a foot wide, with iron bars in 'em. I looked out one, and I see the cause of the rucus.

"There was the Trimble gang—ten of 'em—the worst outfit of desperadoes and horse-thieves in Texas, coming up the street shooting right and left. They was coming right straight for the Gray Mule. Then they got past the range of my sight, but we heard 'em ride up to the front door, and then they socked the place full of lead. We heard the big looking-glass behind the bar knocked all to pieces and the bottles crashing. We could see Gotch-eared Mike in his apron running across the plaza like a coyote, with the bullets puffing up the dust all around him. Then the gang went to work in the saloon, drinking what they wanted and smashing what they didn't.

"Me and Perry both knew that gang, and they knew us. The year before Perry married, him and me was in the same ranger company—and we fought that outfit down on the San Miguel, and brought back Ben Trimble and two others for murder.

" 'We can't get out,' says I. 'We'll have to stay in here till they leave.'

"Perry looked at his watch.

" 'Twenty-five to seven,' says he. 'We can finish that game. I got two men on you. It's your move, Buck. I got to be home at seven, you know.'

"We sat down and went on playing. The Trimble gang had a roughhouse for sure. They were getting good and drunk. They'd drink a while and holler a while, and then they'd shoot up a few bottles and glasses. Two or three times they came and tried to open our door. Then there was some more shooting outside, and I looked out the window again. Ham Gossett, the town marshal, had a posse in the houses and stores across the street, and was trying to bag a Trimble or two through the windows.

"I lost that game of checkers. I'm free in saying that I lost three kings that I might have saved if I had been corralled in a more peaceful pasture. But that drivelling married man sat there and cackled when he won a man like an unintelligent hen picking up a grain of corn.

"When the game was over Perry gets up and looks at his watch.

" 'I've had a glorious time, Buck,' says he, 'but I'll have to be going now. It's a quarter to seven, and I got to be home by seven, you know.'

"I thought he was joking.

" 'They'll clear out or be dead drunk in half an hour or an hour,' says I. 'You ain't that tired of being married that you want to commit any more sudden suicide, are you?' says I, giving him the laugh.

" 'One time,' says Perry, 'I was half an hour late getting home. I met Mariana on the street looking for me. If you could have seen her, Buck—but you don't understand. She knows what a wild kind of a snoozer I've been, and she's afraid something will happen. I'll never be late getting home again. I'll say good-bye to you now, Buck.'

"I got between him and the door.

"'Married man,' says I, 'I know you was christened a fool the minute the preacher tangled you up, but don't you never sometimes think one little think on a human basis? There's ten of that gang in there, and they're pizen with whisky and desire for murder. They'll drink you up like a bottle of booze before you get halfway to the door. Be intelligent, now, and use at least wild-hog sense. Sit down and wait till we have some chance to get out with being carried in baskets.'

"'I got to be home by seven, Buck,' repeats this hen-pecked thing of little wisdom, like an unthinking poll parrot. 'Mariana,' says he, ''ll be looking out for me.' And he reaches down and pulls a leg out of the checker table. 'I'll go through this Trimble outfit,' says he, 'like a cottontail through a brush corral. I'm not pestered any more with a desire to engage in rucuses, but I got to be home by seven. You lock the door after me, Buck. And don't you forget—I won three out of them five games. I'd play longer, but Mariana——'

"'Hush up, you old locoed road runner,' I interrupts. 'Did you ever notice your Uncle Buck locking doors against trouble? I'm not married,' says I, 'but I'm as big a d—n fool as any Mormon. One from four leaves three,' says I, and I gathers out another leg of the table. "We'll get home by seven,' says I, 'whether it's the heavenly one or the other. May I see you home?' says I, 'you sarsaparilla-drinking, checker-playing glutton for death and destruction.'

"We opened the door easy, and then stampeded for the front. Part of the gang was lined up at the bar; part of 'em was passing over the drinks, and two or three was peeping out the door and window taking shots at the marshal's crowd. The room was so full of smoke we got halfway to the front door before they noticed us. Then I heard Berry Trimble's voice somewhere yell out:

"'How'd that Buck Caperton get in here?' and he skinned the side of my neck with a bullet. I reckon he felt bad over that miss, for Berry's the best shot south of the Southern Pacific Railroad. But the smoke in the saloon was some too thick for good shooting.

"Me and Perry smashed over two of the gang with our table legs, which didn't miss like the guns did, and as we run out the door I grabbed a Winchester from a fellow who was watching the outside, and I turned and regulated the account of Mr. Berry.

"Me and Perry got out and around the corner all right. I never much expected to get out, but I wasn't going to be intimidated by that married man. According to Perry's idea, checkers was the event of the day, but if I am any judge of gentle recreations that little table-leg parade through the Gray Mule saloon deserved the head-lines in the bill of particulars.

"'Walk fast,' says Perry, 'it's two minutes to seven, and I got to be home by——'

"'Oh, shut up,' says I. 'I had an appointment as chief performer at an inquest at seven, and I'm not kicking about not keeping it.'

"I had to pass by Perry's little house. His Mariana was standing at the gate. We got there at five minutes past seven. She had on a blue wrapper, and her hair was pulled back smooth like little girls do when they want to look grown-folksy. She didn't see us till we got close, for she was gazing up the other way. Then she backed around, and saw Perry, and a kind of look scooted around over her face—danged if I can describe it. I heard her breathe long, just like a cow when you turn her calf in the lot, and she says: 'You're late, Perry.'

"'Five minutes,' says Perry, cheerful. 'Me and old Buck was having a game of checkers.'

"Perry introduces me to Mariana, and they ask me to come in. No, sir-ee. I'd had enough truck with married folks for that day. I says I'll be going along, and that I've spent a very pleasant afternoon with my old partner—'especially,' says I, just to jostle Perry, 'during that game when the table legs came all loose.' But I'd promised him not to let her know anything.

"I've been worrying over that business ever since it happened," continued Buck. "There's one thing about it that's got me all twisted up, and I can't figure it out."

"What was that?" I asked, as I rolled and handed Buck the last cigarette.

"Why, I'll tell you: When I saw the look that little woman give Perry when she turned round and saw him coming back to the ranch safe—why was it I got the idea all in a minute that that look of hers was worth more than the whole caboodle of us—sarsaparilla, checkers, and all, and that the d—n fool in the game wasn't named Perry Rountree at all?"

CABBAGES AND KINGS

CABBAGES AND KINGS

THE PROEM

BY THE CARPENTER

THEY will tell you in Anchuria, that President Miraflores, of that volatile republic, died by his own hand in the coast town of Coralio; that he had reached thus far in flight from the inconveniences of an imminent revolution; and that one hundred thousand dollars, government funds, which he carried with him in an American leather valise as a souvenir of his tempestuous administration, was never afterward recovered.

For a *real*, a boy will show you his grave. It is back of the town near a little bridge that spans a mangrove swamp. A plain slab of wood stands at its head. Some one has burned upon the headstone with a hot iron this inscription:

RAMON ANGEL DE LAS CRUZES
Y MIRAFLORES
PRESIDENTE DE LA REPUBLICA
DE ANCHURIA
QUE SEA SU JUEZ DIOS

It is characteristic of this buoyant people that they pursue no man beyond the grave. "Let God be his judge!"—Even with the hundred thousand unfound, though they greatly coveted, the hue and cry went no further than that.

To the stranger or the guest the people of Coralio will relate the story of the tragic end of their former president; how he strove to escape from the country with the public funds and also with Doña Isabel Guilbert, the young American opera singer; and how, being apprehended by members of the opposing political party in Coralio, he shot himself through the head rather than give up the funds, and, in consequence, the Señorita Guilbert. They will relate further that Doña Isabel, her adventurous bark of fortune shoaled by the simultaneous loss of her distinguished admirer and the souvenir hundred thousand, dropped anchor on this stagnant coast, awaiting a rising tide.

They say, in Coralio, that she found a prompt and prosperous tide in the form of Frank Goodwin, an American resident of the town, an investor who had grown wealthy by dealing in the products of the country—a banana king, a rubber prince, a sarsaparilla, indigo, and mahogany baron. The Señorita Guilbert, you will be told, married Señor Goodwin one month after the president's death, thus, in the very moment when Fortune had ceased to smile, wresting from her a gift greater than the prize withdrawn.

Of the American, Don Frank Goodwin, and of his wife the natives have nothing but good to say. Don Frank has lived among them for years, and has compelled their respect. His lady is easily queen of what social life the sober coast affords. The wife of the governor of the district, herself, who was of the proud Castilian family of Monteleon y Dolorosa de los Santos y Mendez, feels honored to unfold

431

her napkin with olive-hued, ringed hands at the table of Señora Goodwin. Were you to refer (with your northern prejudices) to the vivacious past of Mrs. Goodwin when her audacious and gleeful abandon in light opera captured the mature president's fancy, or to her share in that statesman's downfall and malfeasance, the Latin shrug of the shoulder would be your only answer and rebuttal. What prejudices there were in Coralio concerning Señora Goodwin seemed now to be in her favor, whatever they had been in the past.

It would seem that the story is ended, instead of begun; that the close of tragedy and the climax of a romance have covered the ground of interest; but, to the more curious reader it shall be some slight instruction to trace the close threads that underlie the ingenuous web of circumstances.

The headpiece bearing the name of President Miraflores is daily scrubbed with soap-bark and sand. An old half-breed Indian tends the grave with fidelity and the dawdling minuteness of inherited sloth. He chops down the weeds and ever-springing grass with his machete, he plucks ants and scorpions and beetles from it with his horny fingers, and sprinkles its turf with water from the plaza fountain. There is no grave anywhere so well kept and ordered.

Only by following out the underlying threads will it be made clear why the old Indian, Galvez, is secretly paid to keep green the grave of President Miraflores by one who never saw that unfortunate statesman in life or in death, and why that one was wont to walk in the twilight, casting from a distance looks of gentle sadness upon that unhonored mound.

Elsewhere than at Coralio one learns of the impetuous career of Isabel Guilbert. New Orleans gave her birth and the mingled French and Spanish creole nature that tinctured her life with such turbulence and warmth. She had little education, but a knowledge of men and motives that seemed to have come by instinct. Far beyond the common woman was she endowed with intrepid rashness, with a love for the pursuit of adventure to the brink of danger, and with desire for the pleasures of life. Her spirit was one to chafe under any curb; she was Eve after the fall, but before the bitterness of it was felt. She wore life as a rose in her bosom.

Of the legion of men who had been at her feet it was said that but one was so fortunate as to engage her fancy. To President Miraflores, the brilliant but unstable ruler of Anchuria, she yielded the key to her resolute heart. How, then, do we find her (as the Coralians would have told you) the wife of Frank Goodwin, and happily living a life of dull and dreamy inaction?

The underlying threads reach far, stretching across the sea. Following them out it will be made plain why "Shorty" O'Day, of the Columbia Detective Agency, resigned his position. And, for a lighter pastime, it shall be a duty and a pleasing sport to wander with Momus beneath the tropic stars where Melpomene once stalked austere. Now to cause laughter to echo from those lavish junglos and frowning crags where formerly rang the cries of pirates' victims; to lay aside pike and cutlass and attack with quip and jollity; to draw one saving titter of mirth from the rusty casque of Romance—this were pleasant to do in the shade of the lemon-trees on that coast that is curved like lips set for smiling.

For there are yet tales of the Spanish Main. That segment of continent washed by the tempestuous Caribbean, and presenting to the sea a formidable border of tropical jungle topped by the overweening Cordilleras, is still begirt by mystery and romance. In past times buccaneers and revolutionists roused the echoes of its cliffs, and the condor wheeled perpetually above where, in the green groves, they made food for him with their matchlocks and toledos. Taken and retaken by sea rovers, by adverse powers and by sudden uprising of rebellious factions, the historic 300 miles of adventurous coast has scarcely known for hundreds of years whom rightly to call its master. Pizarro, Balboa, Sir Francis Drake, and Bolivar did what they could to make it a part of Christendom. Sir

John Morgan, Lafitte, and other eminent swashbucklers bombarded and pounded it in the name of Abaddon.

The game still goes on. The guns of the rovers are silenced; but the tintype man, the enlarged photograph brigand, the kodaking tourist and the scouts of the gentle brigade of fakirs have found it out, and carry on the work. The hucksters of Germany, France, and Sicily now bag its small change across their counters. Gentleman adventurers throng the waiting-rooms of its rulers with proposals for railways and concessions. The little *opéra-bouffe* nations play at government and intrigue until some day a big, silent gunboat glides into the offing and warns them not to break their toys. And with these changes comes also the small adventurer, with empty pockets to fill, light of heart, busy-brained—the modern fairy prince, bearing an alarm clock with which, more surely than by the sentimental kiss, to awaken the beautiful tropics from their centuries' sleep. Generally he wears a shamrock, which he matches pridefully against the extravagant palms; and it is he who has driven Melpomene to the wings, and set Comedy to dancing before the footlights of the Southern Cross.

So, there is a little tale to tell of many things. Perhaps to the promiscuous ear of the Walrus it shall come with most avail; for in it there are indeed shoes and ships and sealing-wax and cabbage-palms and presidents instead of kings.

Add to these a little love and counterplotting, and scatter everywhere throughout the maze a trail of tropical dolars—dollars warmed no more by the torrid sun than by the hot palms of the scouts of Fortune—and, after all, here seems to be Life, itself, with talk enough to weary the most garrulous of Walruses.

"FOX-IN-THE-MORNING"

CORALIO reclined, in the mid-day heat, like some vacuous beauty lounging in a guarded harem. The town lay at the sea's edge on a strip of alluvial coast. It was set like a little pearl in an emerald band. Behind it, and seeming almost to topple, imminent, above it, rose the sea-following range of the Cordilleras. In front the sea was spread, a smiling band, but even more incorruptible than the frowning mountains. The waves swished along the smooth beach; the parrots screamed in the orange and ceiba-trees; the palms waved their limber fronds foolishly like an awkward chorus at the prima donna's cue to enter.

Suddenly the town was full of excitement. A native boy dashed down a grass-grown street, shrieking: *"Busca el Señor Goodwin. Ha venido un telegrama por él!"*

The word passed quickly. Telegrams do not often come to anyone in Coralio. The cry for Señor Goodwin was taken up by a dozen officious voices. The main street running parallel to the beach became populated with those who desired to expedite the delivery of the despatch. Knots of women with complexions varing from palest olive to deepest brown gathered at street corners and plaintively carolled: *"Un telegrama por Señor Goodwin!"* The *comandante*, Don Señor el Coronel Encarnación Rios, who was loyal to the Ins and suspected Goodwin's devotion to the Outs, hissed: "Aha!" and wrote in his secret memorandum book the accusive fact that Señor Goodwin had on that momentous date received a telegram.

In the midst of the hullabaloo a man stepped to the door of a small wooden building and looked out. Above the door was a sign that read "Keogh and Clancy"—a nomenclature that seemed not to be indigenous to that tropical soil.

The man in the door was Billy Keogh, scout of fortune and progress and latter-day rover of the Spanish Main. Tintypes and photographs were the weapons with which Keogh and Clancy were at that time assailing the hopeless shores. Outside the shop were set two large frames filled with specimens of their art and skill.

Keogh leaned in the doorway, his bold and humorous countenance wearing a look of interest at the unusual influx of life and sound into the street. When the meaning of the disturbance became clear to him he placed a hand beside his mouth and shouted: "Hey! Frank!" in such a robustious voice that the feeble clamor of the natives was drowned and silenced.

Fifty yards away, on the seaward side of the street, stood the abode of the consul for the United States. Out from the door of this building tumbled Goodwin at the call. He had been smoking with Willard Geddie, the consul, on the back porch of the consulate, which was conceded to be the coolest spot in Coralio.

"Hurry up," shouted Keogh. "There's a riot in town on account of a telegram that's come for you. You want to be careful about these things, my boy. It won't do to trifle with the feelings of the public this way. You'll be getting a pink note some day with violet scent on it; and then the country'll be steeped in the throes of a revolution."

Goodwin had strolled up the street and met the boy with the message. The ox-eyed women gazed at him with shy admiration, for his type drew them. He was big, blond, and jauntily dressed in white linen, with buckskin *zapatos*. His manner was courtly, with a sort of kindly truculence in it tempered by a merciful eye. When the telegram had been delivered, and the bearer of it dismissed with a gratuity, the relieved populace returned to the contiguities of shade from which curiosity had drawn it—the women to their baking in the mud ovens under the orange-trees, or to the interminable combing of their long, straight hair; the men to their cigarettes and gossip in the cantinas.

Goodwin sat on Keogh's doorstep and read his telegram. It was from Bob Englehart, an American, who lived in San Mateo, the capital city of Anchuria, eighty miles in the interior. Englehart was a gold miner, an ardent revolutionist and "good people." That he was a man of resource and imagination was proven by the telegram he had sent. It had been his task to send a confidential message to his friend in Coralio. This could not have been accomplished in either Spanish or English, for the eye politic in Anchuria was an active one. The Ins and the Outs were perpetually on their guard. But Englehart was a diplomatist. There existed but one code upon which he might make requisition with promise of safety—the great and potent code of Slang. So, here is the message that slipped, unconstrued, through the fingers of curious officials, and came to the eye of Goodwin:

His Nibs skedalled yesterday per jack-rabbit line with all the coin in the kitty and the bundle of muslin he's spoony about. The boodle is six figures short. Our crowd in good shape, but we need the spondulicks. You collar it. The main guy and the dry goods are headed for the briny. You know what to do.
                                                                                BOB.

This screed, remarkable as it was, had no mystery for Goodwin. He was the most successful of the small advance-guard of speculative Americans that had invaded Anchuria, and he had not reached that enviable pinnacle without having well exercised the arts of foresight and deduction. He had taken up political intrigue as a matter of business. He was acute enough to wield a certain influence among the leading schemers, and he was prosperous enough to be able to purchase the respect of the petty office-holders. There was always a revolu-

tionary party; and to it he had always allied himself; for the adherents of a
new administration received the rewards of their labors. There was now a
Liberal party seeking to overturn President Miraflores. If the wheel successfully
revolved, Goodwin stood to win a concession to 30,000 manzanas of the finest
coffee lands in the interior. Certain incidents in the recent career of President
Miraflores had excited a shrewd suspicion in Goodwin's mind that the government was near a dissolution from another cause than that of a revolution, and
now Englehart's telegram had come as a corroboration of his wisdom.

The telegram, which had remained unintelligible to the Anchurian linguists
who had applied to it in vain their knowledge of Spanish and elemental English,
conveyed a stimulating piece of news to Goodwin's understanding. It informed
him that the president of the republic had decamped from the capital city with
the contents of the treasury. Furthermore, that he was accompanied in his
flight by that winning adventuress Isabel Guilbert, the opera singer, whose troupe
of performers had been entertained by the president at San Mateo during the past
month on a scale less modest than that with which royal visitors are often
content. The reference to the "jack-rabbit line" could mean nothing else than
the mule-back system of transport that prevailed between Coralio and the capital. The hint that the "boodle" was "six figures short" made the condition of
the national treasury lamentably clear. Also it was convincingly true that the
ingoing party—its way now made a pacific one—would need the "spondulicks."
Unless its pledges should be fulfilled, and the spoils held for the delectation of
the victors, precarious indeed would be the position of the new government.
Therefore it was exceeding necessary to "collar the main guy," and recapture the
sinews of war and government.

Goodwin handed the message to Keogh.

"Read that, Billy," he said. "It's from Bob Englehart. Can you manage
the cipher?"

Keogh sat in the other half of the doorway, and carefully perused the telegram.

" 'Tis not a cipher," he said, finally. " 'Tis what they call literature, and
that's a system of language put in the mouths of people that they've never
been introduced to by writers of imagination. The magazines invented it, but I
never knew before that President Norvin Green had stamped it with the seal
of his approval. 'Tis now no longer literature, but language. The dictionaries
tried, but they couldn't make it go for anything but dialect. Sure, now that the
Western Union indorses it, it won't be long till a race of people will spring up
that speaks it."

"You're running too much to philology, Billy," said Goodwin. "Do you make
out the meaning of it?"

"Sure," replied the philosopher of Fortune. "All languages come easy to the
man who must know 'em. I've even failed to misunderstand an order to evacuate
in classical Chinese when it was backed up by the muzzle of a breech-loader. This
little literary essay I hold in my hands means a game of Fox-in-the-Morning.
Ever play that, Frank, when you was a kid?"

"I think so," said Goodwin, laughing. "You join hands all 'round, and——"

"You do not," interrupted Keogh. "You've got a fine sporting game mixed
up in your head with 'All Around the Rosebush.' The spirit of 'Fox-in-the-
Morning' is opposed to the holding of hands. I'll tell you how it's played.
This president man and his companion in play, they stand up over in San
Mateo, ready for the run, and shout: 'Fox-in-the-Morning!' Me and you,
standing here, we say: 'Goose and the Gander!' They say: 'How many miles
is it to London town?' We say: 'Only a few, if your legs are long enough.
How many comes out?' They say: 'More than you're able to catch.' And then
the game commences."

"I catch the idea," said Goodwin. "It won't do to let the goose and gander slip through our fingers, Billy; their feathers are too valuable. Our crowd is prepared and able to step into the shoes of the government at once; but with the treasury empty we'd stay in power about as long as a tenderfoot would stick on an untamed bronco. We must play the fox on every foot of the coast to prevent their getting out of the country."

"By the mule-back schedule," said Keogh, "it's five days down from San Mateo. We've got plenty of time to set our outposts. There's only three places on the coast where they can hope to sail from—here and Solitas and Alazán. They're the only points we'll have to guard. It's as easy as a chess problem— fox to play, and mate in three moves. Oh, goosey, goosey, gander, whither do you wander? By the blessing of the literary telegraph the boodle of this be-nighted fatherland shall be preserved to the honest political party that is seeking to overthrow it."

The situation had been justly outlined by Keogh. The down trail from the capital was at all times a weary road to travel. A jiggety-joggety journey it was; ice-cold and hot, wet and dry. The trail climbed appalling mountains, wound like a rotten string about the brows of breathless precipices, plunged through chilling snow-fed streams, and wriggled like a snake through sunless forests teeming with menacing insect and animal life. After descending to the foothills it turned to a trident, the central prong ending at Alazan. Another branched off to Coralio; the third penetrated to Solitas. Between the sea and the foothills stretched the five miles breadth of alluvial coast. Here was the flora of the tropics in its rankest and most prodigal growth. Spaces here and there had been wrested from the jungle and planted with bananas and cane and orange groves. The rest was a riot of wild vegetation, the home of monkeys, tapirs, jaguars, alligators and prodigious reptiles and insects. Where no road was cut a serpent could scarcely make its way through the tangle of vines and creepers. Across the treacherous mangrove swamps few things without wings could safely pass. Therefore the fugitives could hope to reach the coast only by one of the routes named.

"Keep the matter quiet, Billy," advised Goodwin. "We don't want the Ins to know that the president is in flight. I suppose Bob's information is something of a scoop in the capital as yet. Otherwise he would not have tried to make his message a confidential one; and besides, everybody would have heard the news. I'm going around now to see Dr. Zavalla, and start a man up the trail to cut the telegraph wire."

As Goodwin rose, Keogh threw his hat upon the grass by the door and expelled a tremendous sigh.

"What's the trouble, Billy?" asked Goodwin, pausing. "That's the first time I ever heard you sigh."

"'Tis the last," said Keogh. "With that sorrowful puff of wind I resign myself to a life of praiseworthy but harassing honesty. What are tintypes, if you please, to the opportunities of the great and hilarious class of ganders and geese? Not that I would be a president, Frank—and the boodle he's got is too big for me to handle—but in some ways I feel my conscience hurting me for addicting myself to photographing a nation instead of running away with it. Frank, did you ever see the 'bundle of muslin' that His Excellency has wrapped up and carried off?"

"Isabel Guilbert?" said Goodwin, laughing. "No, I never did. From what I've heard of her, though, I imagine that she wouldn't stick at anything to carry her point. Don't get romantic, Billy. Sometimes I begin to fear that there's Irish blood in your ancestry."

"I never saw her either," went on Keogh; "but they say she's got all the ladies of mythology, sculpture, and fiction reduced to chromos. They say she can look at a man once, and he'll turn monkey and climb trees to pick cocoanuts for her. Think of that president man with Lord knows how many hundreds of thousands of dollars in one hand, and this muslin siren in the other, galloping down hill on a sympathetic mule amid songbirds and flowers! And here is Billy Keogh, because he is virtuous, condemned to the unprofitable swindle of slandering the faces of missing links on tin for an honest living! 'Tis an injustice of nature."

"Cheer up," said Goodwin. "You are a pretty poor fox to be envying a gander. Maybe the enchanting Guilbert will take a fancy to you and your tintypes after we impoverish her royal escort."

"She could do worse," reflected Keogh; "but she won't. 'Tis not a tintype gallery, but the gallery of the gods that she's fitted to adorn. She's a very wicked lady, and the president man is in luck. But I hear Clancy swearing in the back room for having to do all the work." And Keogh plunged for the rear of the "gallery," whistling gaily in a spontaneous way that belied his recent sigh over the questionable good luck of the flying president.

Goodwin turned from the main street into a much narrower one that intersected it at a right angle.

These side streets were covered by a growth of thick, rank grass, which was kept to a navigable shortness by the machetes of the police. Stone sidewalks, little more than a ledge in width, ran along the base of the mean and monotonous adobe houses. At the outskirts of the village these streets dwindled to nothing; and here were set the palm-thatched huts of the Caribs and the poorer natives, and the shabby cabins of negroes from Jamaica and the West India islands. A few structures raised their heads above the red-tiled roofs of the one-story houses—the bell tower of the *Calaboza*, the Hotel de los Estranjeros, the residence of the Vesuvius Fruit Company's agent, the store and residence of Bernard Brannigan, a ruined cathedral in which Columbus had once set foot, and, most imposing of all, the Casa Morena—the summer "White House" of the President of Anchuria. On the principal street running along the beach—the Broadway of Coralio—were the larger stores, the government *bodega* and post-office, the *cuartel*, the rum-shops and the market place.

On his way Goodwin passed the house of Bernard Brannigan. It was a modern wooden building, two stories in height. The ground floor was occupied by Brannigan's store, the upper one contained the living apartments. A wide cool porch ran around the house half way up its outer walls. A handsome, vivacious girl neatly dressed in flowing white leaned over the railing and smiled down upon Goodwin. She was no darker than many an Andalusian of high descent, and she sparkled and glowed like a tropical moonlight.

"Good evening, Miss Paula," said Goodwin, taking off his hat, with his ready smile. There was little difference in his manner whether he addressed women or men. Everybody in Coralio liked to receive the salutation of the big American.

"Is there any news, Mr. Goodwin? Please don't say no. Isn't it warm? I feel just like Mariana in her moated grange—or was it a range?—it's hot enough."

"No, there's no news to tell, I believe," said Goodwin, with a mischievous look in his eye, "except that old Geddie is getting grumpier and crosser every day. If something doesn't happen to relieve his mind I'll have to quit smoking on his back porch—and there's no other place available that is cool enough."

"He isn't grumpy," said Paula Brannigan, impulsively, "when he——"

But she ceased suddenly, and drew back with a deepening color; for her mother had been a *mestizo* lady, and the Spanish blood had brought to Paula a certain shyness that was an adornment to the other half of her demonstrative nature.

THE LOTUS AND THE BOTTLE

WILLARD GEDDIE, consul for the United States in Coralio, was working leisurely on his yearly report. Goodwin, who had strolled in as he did daily for a smoke on the much coveted porch, had found him so absorbed in his work that he departed after roundly abusing the consul for his lack of hospitality.

"I shall complain to the civil service department," said Goodwin;—"or is it a department?—perhaps it's only a theory. One gets neither civility nor service from you. You won't talk; and you won't set out anything to drink. What kind of a way is that of representing your government?"

Goodwin strolled out and across to the hotel to see if he could bully the quarantine doctor into a game on Coralio's solitary billiard table. His plans were completed for the interception of the fugitives from the capital; and now it was but a waiting game that he had to play.

The consul was interested in his report. He was only twenty-four; and he had not been in Coralio long enough for his enthusiasm to cool in the heat of the tropics—a paradox that may be allowed between Cancer and Capricorn.

So many thousand bunches of bananas, so many thousand oranges and cocoanuts, so many ounces of gold dust, pounds of rubber, coffee, indigo and sarsaparilla—actually, exports were twenty per cent. greater than for the previous year!

A little thrill of satisfaction ran through the consul. Perhaps, he thought, the State Department, upon reading his introduction, would notice—and then he leaned back in his chair and laughed. He was getting as bad as the others. For the moment he had forgotten that Coralio was an insignificant town in an insignificant republic lying along the by-ways of a second-rate sea. He thought of Gregg, the quarantine doctor, who subscribed for the London *Lancet*, expecting to find it quoting his reports to the home Board of Health concerning the yellow fever germ. The consul knew that not one in fifty of his acquaintances in the States had ever heard of Coralio. He knew that two men, at any rate, would have to read his report—some underling in the State Department and a compositor in the Public Printing Office. Perhaps the typesticker would note the increase of commerce in Coralia, and speak of it, over the cheese and beer, to a friend.

He had just written: "Most unaccountable is the supineness of the large exporters in the United States in permitting the French and German houses to practically control the trade interests of this rich and productive country"—when he heard the hoarse notes of a steamer's siren.

Geddie laid down his pen and gathered his Panama hat and umbrella. By the sound he knew it to be the *Valhalla*, one of the line of fruit vessels plying for the Vesuvius Company. Down to *niños* of five years, everyone in Coralio could name you each incoming steamer by the note of her siren.

The consul sauntered by a roundabout, shaded way to the beach. By reason of long practice he gauged his stroll so accurately that by the time he arrived on the sandy shore the boat of the customs officials was rowing back from the steamer, which had been boarded and inspected according to the laws of Anchuria.

There is no harbor at Coralio. Vessels of the draught of the *Valhalla* must ride at anchor a mile from shore. When they take on fruit it is conveyed on lighters and freighter sloops. At Solitas, where there was a fine harbour, ships of many kinds were to be seen, but in the roadstead off Coralio scarcely any save the fruiters paused. Now and then a tramp coaster, or a mysterious brig from Spain, or a saucy French barque would hang innocently for a few days in the offing. Then the custom-house crew would become doubly vigilant and wary. At night a sloop or two would be making strange trips in and out along the shore; and in the morning the stock of Three-Star Hennessey, wines and drygoods in Coralio would be found vastly increased. It has also been said that the customs officials jingled more silver in the pockets of their red-striped trousers, and that the record books showed no increase in import duties received.

The customs boat and the *Valhalla* gig reached the shore at the same time. When they grounded in the shallow water there was still five yards of rolling surf between them and dry sand. Then half-clothed Caribs dashed into the water, and brought in on their backs the *Valhalla's* purser and the little native officials in their cotton undershirts, blue trousers with red stripes, and flapping straw hats.

At college Geddie had been a treasure as a first-baseman. He now closed his umbrella, stuck it upright in the sand, and stooped, with his hands resting upon his knees. The purser, burlesquing the pitcher's contortions, hurled at the consul the heavy roll of newspapers, tied with a string, that the steamer always brought for him. Geddie leaped high and caught the roll with a sounding "thwack." The loungers on the beach—about a third of the population of the town—laughed and applauded delightedly. Every week they expected to see that roll of papers delivered and received in that same manner, and they were never disappointed. Innovations did not flourish in Coralio.

The consul re-hoisted his umbrella and walked back to the consulate.

This home of a great nation's representative was a wooden structure of two rooms, with a native-built gallery of poles, bamboo and nipa palm running on three sides of it. One room was the official apartment, furnished chastely with a flat-top desk, a hammock, and three uncomfortable cane-seated chairs. Engravings of the first and latest president of the country represented hung against the wall. The other room was the consul's living apartment.

It was eleven o'clock when he returned from the beach, and therefore breakfast time. Chanca, the Carib woman who cooked for him, was just serving the meal on the side of the gallery facing the sea—a spot famous as the coolest in Coralio. The breakfast consisted of shark's fin soup, stew of land crabs, breadfruit, a boiled iguana steak, aguacates, a freshly cut pineapple, claret and coffee.

Geddie took his seat, and unrolled with luxurious laziness his bundle of newspapers. Here in Coralio for two days or longer he would read of goings-on in the world very much as we of the world read those whimsical contributions to inexact science that assume to portray the doings of the Martians. After he had finished with the papers they would be sent on the rounds of the other English-speaking residents of the town.

The paper that came first to his hand was one of those bulky mattresses of printed stuff upon which the readers of certain New York journals are supposed to take their Sabbath literary nap. Opening this the consul rested it upon the table, supporting its weight with the aid of the back of a chair. Then he partook of his meal deliberately, turning the leaves from time to time and glancing half idly at the contents.

Presently he was struck by something familiar to him in a picture—a half-page, badly printed reproduction of a photograph of a vessel. Languidly interested, he leaned for a nearer scrutiny and a view of the florid headlines of the column next to the picture.

Yes; he was not mistaken. The engraving was of the eight-hundred-ton yacht *Idalia*, belonging to "that prince of good fellows, Midas of the money market, and society's pink of perfection, J. Ward Tolliver."

Slowly sipping his black coffee, Geddie read the column of print. Following a listed statement of Mr. Tolliver's real estate and bonds, came a description of the yacht's furnishings, and then the grain of news no bigger than a mustard seed. Mr. Tolliver, with a party of favored guests, would sail the next day on a six weeks' cruise along the Central American and South American coasts and among the Bahama Islands. Among the guests were Mrs. Cumberland Payne and Miss Ida Payne, of Norfolk.

The writer, with the fatuous presumption that was demanded of him by his readers, had concocted a romance suited to their palates. He bracketed the names of Miss Payne and Mr. Tolliver until he had well-nigh read the marriage ceremony over them. He played coyly and insinuatingly upon the strings of "*on dit*" and "Madame Rumor" and "a little bird" and "no one would be surprised," and ended with congratulations.

Geddie, having finished his breakfast, took his papers to the edge of the gallery, and sat there in his favorite steamer chair with his feet on the bamboo railing. He lighted a cigar, and looked out upon the sea. He felt a glow of satisfaction at finding he was so little disturbed by what he had read. He told himself that he had conquered the distress that had sent him, a voluntary exile, to this far land of the lotus. He could never forget Ida, of course; but there was no longer any pain in thinking about her. When they had had that misunderstanding and quarrel he had impulsively sought his consulship with the desire to retaliate upon her by detaching himself from her world and presence. He had succeeded thoroughly in that. During the twelve months of his life in Coralio no word had passed between them, though he had sometimes heard of her through the dilatory correspondence with the few friends to whom he still wrote. Still he could not repress a little thrill of satisfaction at knowing that she had not yet married Tolliver or any one else. But evidently Tolliver had not yet abandoned hope.

Well, it made no difference to him now. He had eaten of the lotus. He was happy and content in this land of perpetual afternoon. Those old days of life in the States seemed like an irritating dream. He hoped Ida would be as happy as he was. The climate as balmy as that of distant Avalon; the fetterless, idyllic round of enchanted days; the life among this indolent, romantic people—a life full of music, flowers, and low laughter; the influence of the imminent sea and mountains, and the many shapes of love and magic and beauty that bloomed in the white tropic nights—with all he was more than content. Also, there was Paula Brannigan.

Geddie intended to marry Paula—if, of course, she would consent; but he felt rather sure that she would do that. Somehow, he kept postponing his proposal. Several times he had been quite near to it; but a mysterious something always held him back. Perhaps it was only the unconscious, instinctive conviction that the act would sever the last tie that bound him to his old world.

He could be very happy with Paula. Few of the native girls could be compared with her. She had attended a convent school in New Orleans for two years; and when she chose to display her accomplishments no one could detect any difference between her and the girls of Norfolk and Manhattan. But it was delicious to see her at home dressed, as she sometimes was, in the native costume, with bare shoulders and flowing sleeves.

Bernard Brannigan was the great merchant of Coralio. Besides his store, he maintained a train of pack mules, and carried on a lively trade with the interior towns and villages. He had married a native lady of high Castilian descent, but with a tinge of Indian brown showing through her olive cheek. The union of the Irish and the Spanish had produced, as it so often has, an offshoot of rare beauty and variety. They were very excellent people indeed, and the upper story of their house was ready to be placed at the service of Geddie and Paula as soon as he should make up his mind to speak about it.

By the time two hours were whiled away the consul tired of reading. The papers lay scattered about him on the gallery. Reclining there, he gazed dreamily out upon an Eden. A clump of banana plants interposed their broad shields between him and the sun. The gentle slope from the consulate to the sea was covered with the dark-green foliage of lemon-trees and orange-trees just bursting into bloom. A lagoon pierced the land like a dark, jagged crystal, and above it a pale ceiba-tree rose almost to the clouds. The waving cocoanut palms on the beach flared their decorative green leaves against the slate of an almost quiescent sea. His senses were cognizant of brilliant scarlet and ochres amid the vert of the coppice, of odors of fruit and bloom and the smoke from Chanca's clay oven under the calabash-tree; of the treble laughter of the native women in their huts, the song of the robin, the salt taste of the breeze, the diminuendo of the faint surf running along the shore—and, gradually, of a white speck, growing to a blur, that intruded itself upon the drab prospect of the sea.

Lazily interested, he watched this blur increase until it became the *Idalia* steaming at full speed, coming down the coast. Without changing his position he kept his eyes upon the beautiful white yacht as she drew swiftly near and came opposite to Coralio. Then, sitting upright, he saw her float steadily past and on. Scarcely a mile of sea had separated her from the shore. He had seen the frequent flash of her polished brass work and the stripes of her deck-awnings—so much, and no more. Like a ship on a magic lantern slide the *Idalia* had crossed the illuminated circle of the consul's little world, and was gone. Save for the tiny cloud of smoke that was left hanging over the brim of the sea, she might have been an immaterial thing, a chimera of his idle brain.

Geddie went into his office and sat down to dawdle over his report. If the reading of the article in the paper had left him unshaken, this silent passing of the *Idalia* had done for him still more. It had brought the calm and peace of a situation from which all uncertainty had been erased. He knew that men sometimes hope without being aware of it. Now, since she had come two thousand miles and had passed without a sign, not even his unconscious self need cling to the past any longer.

After dinner, when the sun was low behind the mountains, Geddie walked on the little strip of beach under the cocoanuts. The wind was blowing mildly landward, and the surface of the sea was rippled by tiny wavelets.

A miniature breaker, spreading with a soft "swish" upon the sand, brought with it something round and shiny that rolled back again as the wave receded. The next influx beached it clear, and Geddie picked it up. The thing was a long-necked wine bottle of colorless glass. The cork had been driven in tightly to the level of the mouth, and the end covered with dark-red sealing-wax. The bottle contained only what seemed to be a sheet of paper, much curled from the manipulation it had undergone while being inserted. In the sealing-wax was the impression of a seal—probably of a signet-ring, bearing the initials of a monogram; but the impression had been hastily made, and the letters were past anything more certain than a shrewd conjecture. Ida Payne had always worn a signet-ring in preference to any other finger decoration. Geddie thought he could make out the familiar "I P"; and a queer sensation of disquietude went over him. More personal and intimate was this reminder of her than had been the sight of the vessel she was doubtless on. He walked back to his house, and set the bottle on his desk.

Throwing off his hat and coat, and lighting a lamp—for the night had crowded precipitately upon the brief twilight—he began to examine his piece of sea salvage.

By holding the bottle near the light and turning it judiciously, he made out that it contained a double sheet of note-paper filled with close writing; further, that the paper was of the same size and shade as that always used by Ida; and that, to the best of his belief, the handwriting was hers. The imperfect glass of the bottle so distorted the rays of light that he could read no word of the writing; but certain capital letters, of which he caught comprehensive glimpses, were Ida's, he felt sure.

There was a little smile both of perplexity and amusement in Geddie's eyes as he set the bottle down, and laid three cigars side by side on his desk. He fetched his steamer chair from the gallery, and stretched himself comfortably. He would smoke those three cigars while considering the problem.

For it amounted to a problem. He almost wished that he had not found the bottle; but the bottle was there. Why should it have drifted in from the sea, whence come so many disquieting things, to disturb his peace?

In this dreamy land, where time seemed so redundant, he had fallen into the habit of bestowing much thought upon even trifling matters.

He began to speculate upon many fanciful theories concerning the story of the bottle, rejecting each in turn.

Ships in danger of wreck or disablement sometimes cast forth such precarious messengers calling for aid. But he had seen the *Idalia* not three hours before, safe and speeding. Suppose the crew had mutinied and imprisoned the passengers below, and the message was one begging for succor! But, premising such an improbable outrage, would the agitated captives have taken the pains to fill four pages of note-paper with carefully penned arguments to their rescue?

Thus by elimination he soon rid the matter of the more unlikely theories, and was reduced—though aversely—to the less assailable one that the bottle contained a message to himself. Ida knew he was in Coralio; she must have launched the bottle while the yacht was passing and the wind blowing fairly toward the shore.

As soon as Geddie reached this conclusion a wrinkle came between his brows and a stubborn look settled around his mouth. He sat looking out through the doorway at the gigantic fire-flies traversing the quiet streets.

If this was a message to him from Ida, what could it mean save an overture toward a reconciliation? And if that, why had she not used the safe methods of the post instead of this uncertain and even flippant means of communication? A note in an empty bottle, cast into the sea! There was something light and frivolous about it, if not actually contemptuous.

The thought stirred his pride and subdued whatever emotions had been resurrected by the finding of the bottle.

Geddie put on his coat and hat and walked out. He followed a street that led him along the border of the little plaza where a band was playing and people were rambling, care-free and indolent. Some timorous *señoritas* scurrying past with fire-flies tangled in the jetty braids of their hair glanced at him with shy, flattering eyes. The air was languorous with the scent of jasmin and orange-blossoms.

The consul stayed his steps at the house of Bernard Brannigan. Paula was swinging in a hammock on the gallery. She rose from it like a bird from its nest. The color came to her cheek at the sound of Geddie's voice.

He was charmed at the sight of her costume—a flounced muslin dress, with a little jacket of white flannel, all made with neatness and style. He suggested a stroll, and they walked out to the old Indian well on the hill road. They sat on the curb, and there Geddie made the expected but long-deferred speech. Certain though he had been that she would not say him nay, he was thrilled with joy at the completeness and sweetness of her surrender. Here was surely a heart made for love and steadfastness. Here was no caprice or questionings or captious standards of convention.

When Geddie kissed Paula at her door that night he was happier than he had ever been before. "Here in this hollow lotus land, ever to live and lie reclined" seemed to him, as it has seemed to many mariners, the best as well as the easiest. His future would be an ideal one. He had attained a Paradise without a serpent. His Eve would be indeed a part of him, unbeguiled, and therefore more beguiling. He had made his decision to-night, and his heart was full of serene, assured content.

Geddie went back to his house whistling that finest and saddest love song, "La Golondrina." At the door his tame monkey leaped down from his shelf, chattering briskly. The consul turned to his desk to get him some nuts he usually kept there. Reaching for them in the half-darkness, his hand struck against the bottle. He started as if he had touched the cold rotundity of a serpent. He had forgotten that the bottle was there.

He lighted the lamp and fed the monkey. Then, very deliberately, he lighted a cigar, and took the bottle in his hand, and walked down the path to the beach. There was a moon, and the sea was glorious. The breeze had shifted, as it did each evening, and was now rushing steadily seaward.

Stepping to the water's edge, Geddie hurled the unopened bottle far out into the sea. It disappeared for a moment, and then shot upward twice its length. Geddie stood still, watching it. The moonlight was so bright that he could see it bobbing up and down with the little waves. Slowly it receded from the shore, flashing and turning as it went. The wind was carrying it out to sea. Soon it became a mere speck, doubtfully discerned at irregular intervals; and then the mystery of it was swallowed up by the greater mystery of the ocean. Geddie stood still upon the beach, smoking and looking out upon the water.

"Simon!—Oh, Simon!—wake up there, Simon!" bawled a sonorous voice at the edge of the water.

Old Simon Cruz was a half-breed fisherman and smuggler who lived in a hut on the beach. Out of his earliest nap Simon was thus awakened.

He slipped on his shoes and went outside. Just landing from one of the *Valhalla's* boats was the third mate of that vessel, who was an acquaintance of Simon's, and three sailors from the fruiter.

"Go up, Simon," called the mate, "and find Dr. Gregg or Mr. Goodwin or anybody that's a friend to Mr. Geddie, and bring 'em here at once."

"Saints of the skies!" said Simon, sleepily, "nothing has happened to Mr. Geddie?"

"He's under that tarpauling," said the mate, pointing to the boat, "and he's rather more than half drowned. We seen him from the steamer nearly a mile out from shore, swimmin' like mad after a bottle that was floatin' in the water, outward bound. We lowered the gig and started for him. He nearly had his hand on the bottle, when he gave out and went under. We pulled him out in time to save him, maybe; but the doctor is the one to decide that."

"A bottle?" said the old man, rubbing his eyes. He was not yet fully awake. "Where is the bottle?"

"Driftin' along out there some'eres," said the mate, jerking his thumb toward the sea. "Get on with you, Simon."

SMITH

GOODWIN and the ardent patriot, Zavalla, took all the precautions that their foresight could contrive to prevent the escape of President Miraflores and his companion. They sent trusted messengers up the coast to Solitas and Alazan to warn the local leaders of the flight, and to instruct them to patrol the water line and arrest the fugitives at all hazards should they reveal themselves in that territory. After this was done there remained only to cover the district about Coralio and await the coming of the quarry. The nets were well spread. The roads were so few, the opportunities for embarkation so limited, and the two or three probable points of exit so well guarded that it would be strange indeed if there should slip through the meshes so much of the country's dignity, romance, and collateral. The president would, without doubt, move as secretly as possible, and endeavor to board a vessel by stealth from some secluded point along the shore.

On the fourth day after the receipt of Englehart's telegram the *Karlsefin*, a Norwegian steamer chartered by the New Orleans fruit trade, anchored off Coralio with three hoarse toots of her siren. The *Karlsefin* was not one of the line operated by the Vesuvius Fruit Company. She was something of a dilettante, doing odd jobs for a company that was scarcely important enough to figure as a rival to the Vesuvius. The movements of the *Karlsefin* were dependent upon the state of the market. Sometimes she would ply steadily between the Spanish Main and New Orleans in the regular transport of fruit; next she would be making erratic trips to Mobile or Charleston, or even as far north as New York, according to the distribution of the fruit supply.

Goodwin lounged upon the beach with the usual crowd of idlers that had gathered to view the steamer. Now that President Miraflores might be expected to reach the borders of his adjured country at any time, the orders were to keep a strict and unrelenting watch. Every vessel that approached the shores might now be considered a possible means of escape for the fugitives; and an eye was kept even on the sloops and dories that belonged to the seagoing contingent of Coralio. Goodwin and Zavalla moved everywhere, but without ostentation, watching the loopholes of escape.

The customs officials crowded importantly into their boat and rowed out to the *Karlsefin*. A boat from the steamer landed her purser with his papers, and took out the quarantine doctor with his green umbrella and clinical thermometer. Next a swarm of Caribs began to load upon lighters the thousands of bunches of bananas heaped upon the shore and row them out to the steamer. The *Karlsefin* had no passenger list, and was soon done with the attention of the authorities. The purser declared that the steamer would remain at anchor until morning, taking on her fruit during the night. The *Karlsefin* had come, he said, from New York, to which port her latest load of oranges and cocoanuts had been conveyed. Two or three of the freighter sloops were engaged to assist in the work, for the captain was anxious to make a quick return in order to reap the advantage offered by a certain dearth of fruit in the States.

About four o'clock in the afternoon another of those marine monsters, not very familiar in those waters, hove in sight, following the fateful *Idalia*—a graceful steam yacht, painted a light buff, clean-cut as a steel engraving. The beautiful vessel hovered off shore, see-sawing the waves as lightly as a duck in a rain barrel. A swift boat manned by a crew in uniform came ashore, and a stocky-built man leaped to the sands.

The new-comer seemed to turn a disapproving eye upon the rather motley congregation of native Anchurians, and made his way at once toward Goodwin, who was the most conspicuously Anglo-Saxon figure present. Goodwin greeted him with courtesy.

Conversation developed that the newly landed one was named Smith, and that he had come in a yacht. A meagre biography, truly; for the yacht was most apparent; and the "Smith" not beyond a reasonable guess before the revelation. Yet to the eye of Goodwin, who had seen several things, there was a discrepancy between Smith and his yacht. A bullet-headed man Smith was, with an oblique, dead eye and the moustache of a cocktail-mixer. And unless he had shifted costumes before putting off for shore he had affronted the deck of his correct vessel clad in a pearl-gray derby, a gay plaid suit and vaudeville neckwear. Men owning pleasure yachts generally harmonize better with them.

Smith looked business, but he was no advertiser. He commented upon the scenery, remarking upon its fidelity to the pictures in the geography; and then inquired for the United States consul. Goodwin pointed out the starred-and-striped bunting hanging above the little consulate, which was concealed behind the orange-trees.

"Mr. Geddie, the consul, will be sure to be there," said Goodwin. "He was very nearly drowned a few days ago while taking a swim in the sea, and the doctor has ordered him to remain indoors for some time."

Smith plowed his way through the sand to the consulate, his haberdashery creating violent discord against the smooth tropical blues and greens.

Geddie was lounging in his hammock, somewhat pale of face and languid in pose. On that night when the *Valhalla's* boat had brought him ashore apparently drenched to death by the sea, Dr. Gregg and his other friends had toiled for hours to preserve the little spark of life that remained to him. The bottle, with its impotent message, was gone out to sea, and the problem that it had provoked was reduced to a simple sum in addition—one and one make two, by the rule of arithmetic; one by the rule of romance.

There is a quaint old theory that man may have two souls—a peripheral one which serves ordinarily, and a central one which is stirred only at certain times, but then with activity and vigor. While under the domination of the former a man will shave, vote, pay taxes, give money to his family, buy subscription books and comport himself on the average plan. But let the central soul suddenly become dominant, and he may, in the twinkling of an eye, turn upon the partner of his joys with furious execration; he may change his politics while you could snap your fingers; he may deal out deadly insult to his dearest friend; he may get him, instanter, to a monastery or a dance hall; he may elope, or hang himself—or he may write a song or poem, or kiss his wife unasked, or give his funds to the search of a microbe. Then the peripheral soul will return; and we have our safe, sane citizen again. It is but the revolt of the Ego against Order; and its effect is to shake up the atoms only that they may settle where they belong.

Geddie's revulsion had been a mild one—no more than a swim in a summer sea after so inglorious an object as a drifting bottle. And now he was himself again. Upon his desk, ready for the post, was a letter to his government tendering his resignation as consul, to be effective as soon as another could be appointed in his place. For Bernard Brannigan, who never did things in a half-way manner, was to take Geddie at once for a partner in his very profitable and various enterprises; and Paula was happily engaged in plans for refurnishing and decorating the upper story of the Brannigan house.

The consul rose from his hammock when he saw the conspicuous stranger in his door.

"Keep your seat, old man," said the visitor, with an airy wave of his large hand. "My name's Smith; and I've come in a yacht. You are the consul—is that right? A big, cool guy on the beach directed me here. Thought I'd pay my respects to the flag."

"Sit down," said Geddie. "I've been admiring your craft ever since it came in sight. Looks like a fast sailer. What's her tonnage?"

"Search me!" said Smith. "I don't know what she weighs in at. But she's got a tidy gait. The *Rambler*—that's her name—don't take the dust of anything afloat. This is my first trip on her. I'm taking a squint along this coast just to get an idea of the countries where the rubber and red pepper and revolutions come from. I had no idea there was so much scenery down here. Why, Central Park ain't in it with this neck of the woods. I'm from

New York. They get monkeys, and cocoanuts, and parrots down here—is that right?"

"We have them all," said Geddie. "I'm quite sure that our fauna and flora would take a prize over Central Park."

"Maybe they would," admitted Smith, cheerfully. "I haven't seen them yet. But I guess you've got us skinned on the animal and vegetation question. You don't have much travel here, do you?"

"Travel?" queried the consul. "I suppose you mean passengers on the steamers. No; very few people land in Coralio. An investor now and then—tourists and sight-seers generally go further down the coast to one of the larger towns where there is a harbor."

"I see a ship out there loading up with bananas," said Smith. "Any passengers come on her?"

"That's the *Karlsefin*," said the consul. "She's a tramp fruiter—made her last trip to New York, I believe. No; she brought no passengers. I saw her boat come ashore, and there was no one. About the only exciting recreation we have here is watching steamers when they arrive; and a passenger on one of them generally causes the whole town to turn out. If you are going to remain in Coralio a while, Mr. Smith, I'll be glad to take you around to meet some people. There are four or five American chaps that are good to know, besides the native high-fliers."

"Thanks," said the yachtsman, "but I wouldn't put you to the trouble. I'd like to meet the guys you speak of, but I won't be here long enough to do much knocking around. That cool gent on the beach spoke of a doctor; can you tell me where I could find him? The *Rambler* ain't quite as steady on her feet as a Broadway hotel; and a fellow gets a touch of seasickness now and then. Thought I'd strike the croaker for a handful of the little sugar pills, in case I need 'em."

"You will be apt to find Dr. Gregg at the hotel," said the consul. "You can see it from the door—it's that two-story building with the balcony, where the orange-trees are."

The Hotel de los Estranjeros was a dreary hostelry, in great disuse both by strangers and friends. It stood at a corner of the Street of the Holy Sepulchre. A grove of small orange-trees crowded against one side of it, enclosed by a low, rock wall over which a tall man might easily step. The house was of plastered adobe, stained a hundred shades of color by the salt breeze and the sun. Upon its upper balcony opened a central door and two windows containing broad jalousies instead of sashes.

The lower floor communicated by two doorways with the narrow, rock-paved sidewalk. The *pulperia*—or drinking shop—of the proprietress, Madama Timotea Ortiz, occupied the ground floor. On the bottles of brandy, *anisada*, Scotch "smoke" and inexpensive wines behind the little counter the dust lay thick save where the fingers of infrequent customers had left irregular prints. The upper story contained four or five guest-rooms which were rarely put to their destined use. Sometimes a fruit-grower, riding in from his plantation to confer with his agent, would pass a melancholy night in the dismal upper story; sometimes a minor native official on some trifling government quest would have his pomp and majesty awed by Madama's sepulchral hospitality. But Madama sat behind her bar content, nor desiring to quarrel with Fate. If any one required meat, drink, or lodging at the Hotel de los Estranjeros they had but to come, and be served. *Está bueno.* If they came not, why, then, they came not. *Está bueno.*

As the exceptional yachtsman was making his way down the precarious sidewalk of the Street of the Holy Sepulchre, the solitary permanent guest of that decaying hotel sat at its door, enjoying the breeze from the sea.

Dr. Gregg, the quarantine physician, was a man of fifty or sixty, with a florid face and the longest beard between Topeka and Terra del Fuego. He held his position by virtue of an appointment by the Board of Health of a seaport city in one of the Southern states. That city feared the ancient enemy of every Southern seaport—the yellow fever—and it was the duty of Dr. Gregg to examine crew and passengers of every vessel leaving Coralio for preliminary symptoms. The duties were light, and the salary, for one who lived in Coralio, ample. Surplus time there was in plenty; and the good doctor added to his gains by a large private practice among the residents of the coast. The fact that he did not know ten words of Spanish was no obstacle; a pulse could be felt and a fee collected without one being a linguist. Add to the description the facts that the doctor had a story to tell concerning the operation of trepanning which no listener had ever allowed him to conclude, and that he believed in brandy as a prophylactic; and the special points of interest possessed by Dr. Gregg will have become exhausted.

The doctor had dragged a chair to the sidewalk. He was coatless, and he leaned back against the wall and smoked, while he stroked his beard. Surprise came into his pale blue eyes when he caught sight of Smith in his unusual and prismatic clothes.

"You're Dr. Gregg—is that right?" said Smith, feeling the dog's head pin in his tie. "The constable—I mean the consul, told me you hung out at this caravansary. My name's Smith; and I came in a yacht. Taking a cruise around, looking at the monkeys and pineapple-trees. Come inside and have a drink, Doc. This café looks on the blink, but I guess it can set out something wet."

"I will join you, sir, in just a taste of brandy," said Dr. Gregg, rising quickly. "I find that as a prophylactic a little brandy is almost a necessity in this climate."

As they turned to enter the *pulperia* a native man, barefoot, glided noiselessly up and addressed the doctor in Spanish. He was yellowish-brown, like an over-ripe lemon; he wore a cotton shirt and ragged linen trousers girded by a leather belt. His face was like an animal's, live and wary, but without promise of much intelligence. This man jabbered with animation and so much seriousness that it seemed a pity that his words were to be wasted.

Dr. Gregg felt his pulse.

"You sick?" he inquired.

"*Mi mujer está enferma en la casa,*" said the man, thus endeavoring to convey the news, in the only language open to him, that his wife lay ill in her palm-thatched hut.

The doctor drew a handful of capsules filled with a white powder from his trousers pocket. He counted out ten of them into the native's hand, and held up his forefinger impressively.

"Take one," said the doctor, "every two hours." He then held up two fingers, shaking them emphatically before the native's face. Next he pulled out his watch and ran his finger round its dial twice. Again the two fingers confronted the patient's nose. "Two—two—two hours," repeated the doctor.

"*Si Señor,*" said the native, sadly.

He pulled a cheap silver watch from his own pocket and laid it in the doctor's hand. "Me bring," said he, struggling painfully with his scant English, "other watchy to-morrow." Then he departed down-heartedly with his capsules.

"A very ignorant race of people, sir," said the doctor, as he slipped the watch into his pocket. "He seems to have mistaken my directions for taking the physic for the fee. However, it is all right. He owes me an account, anyway. The chances are that he won't bring the other watch. You can't depend on anything they promise you. About that drink, now? How did you come to

Coralio, Mr. Smith? I was not aware that any boats except the *Karlsefin* had arrived for some days."

The two leaned against the deserted bar; and Madama set out a bottle without waiting for the doctor's order. There was no dust on it.

After they had drank twice Smith said:

"You say there were no passengers on the *Karlsefin*, Doc? Are you sure about that? It seems to me I heard somebody down on the beach say that there was one or two aboard."

"They were mistaken, sir. I myself went out and put all hands through a medical examination, as usual. The *Karlsefin* sails as soon as she gets her bananas loaded, which will be about daylight in the morning, and she got everything ready this afternoon. No, sir, there was no passenger list. Like that Three-Star? A French schooner landed two slooploads of it a month ago. If any customs duties on it went to the distinguished republic of Anchuria you may have my hat. If you won't have another, come out and let's sit in the cool a while. It isn't often we exiles get a chance to talk with somebody from the outside world."

The doctor brought out another chair to the sidewalk for his new acquaintance. The two seated themselves.

"You are a man of the world," said Dr. Gregg; "a man of travel and experience. Your decision in a matter of ethics and, no doubt, on the points of equity, ability, and professional probity should be of value. I would be glad if you will listen to the history of a case that I think stands unique in medical annals.

"About nine years ago, while I was engaged in the practice of medicine in my native city, I was called to treat a case of contusion of the skull. I made the diagnosis that a splinter of bone was pressing upon the brain, and that the surgical operation known as trepanning was required. However, as the patient was a gentleman of wealth and position, I called in for consultation, Dr.——"

Smith rose from his chair, and laid a hand, soft with apology, upon the doctor's shirt sleeve.

"Say, Doc," he said, solemnly, "I want to hear that story. You've got me interested; and I don't want to miss the rest of it. I know it's a loola by the way it begins; and I want to tell it at the next meeting of the Barney O'Flynn Association, if you don't mind. But I've got one or two matters to attend to first. If I get 'em attended to in time I'll come right back and hear you spiel the rest before bedtime—is that right?"

"By all means," said the doctor, "get your business attended to, and then return. I shall wait up for you. You see, one of the most prominent physicians at the consultation diagnosed the trouble as a blood clot; another said it was an abscess, but I——"

"Don't tell me now, Doc. Don't spoil the story. Wait till I come back. I want to hear it as it runs off the reel—is that right?"

The mountains reached up their bulky shoulders to receive the level gallop of Apollo's homing steeds, the day died in the lagoons and in the shadowed banana groves and in the mangrove swamps, where the great blue crabs were beginning to crawl to land for their nightly ramble. And it died, at last, upon the highest peaks. Then the brief twilight, ephemeral as the flight of a moth, came and went; the Southern Cross peeped with its topmost eye above a row of palms, and the fire-flies heralded with their torches the approach of soft-footed night.

In the offing the *Karlsefin* swayed at anchor, her lights seeming to penetrate the water to countless fathoms with their shimmering, lanceolate reflections. The Caribs were busy loading her by means of the great lighters heaped full from the piles of fruit ranged upon the shore.

On the sandy beach, with his back against a cocoanut-tree and the stubs of many cigars lying around him, Smith sat waiting, never relaxing his sharp gaze in the direction of the steamer.

The incongruous yachtsman had concentrated his interest upon the innocent fruiter. Twice had he been assured that no passengers had come to Coralio on board of her. And yet, with a persistence not to be attributed to an idling voyager, he had appealed the case to the higher court of his own eye-sight. Surprisingly like some gay-coated lizard, he crouched at the foot of tne cocoanut palm, and with the beady, shifting eyes of the selfsame reptile, sustained his espionage on the *Karlsefin*.

On the white sands a whiter gig belonging to the yacht was drawn up, guarded by one of the white-ducked crew. Not far away in a *pulperia* on the shore-following Calle Grande three other sailors swaggered with their cues around Coralio's solitary billiard-table. The boat lay there as if under orders to be ready for use at any moment. There was in the atmosphere a hint of expectation, of waiting for something to occur, which was foreign to the air of Coralio.

Like some passing bird of brilliant plumage, Smith alights on this palmy shore but to preen his wings for an instant and then to fly away upon silent pinions. When morning dawned there was no Smith, no waiting gig, no yacht in the offing. Smith left no intimation of his mission there, no footprints to show where he had followed the trail of his mystery on the sands of Coralio that night. He came; he spake his strange jargon of the asphalt and the cafés; he sat under the cocoanut-tree, and vanished. The next morning Coralio, Smithless, ate its fried plantain and said: "The man of pictured clothing went himself away." With the *siesta* the incident passed, yawning, into history.

So, for a time, must Smith pass behind the scenes of the play. He comes no more to Coralio nor to Dr. Gregg, who sits in vain, wagging his redundant beard, waiting to enrich his derelict audience with his moving tale of trepanning and jealousy.

But prosperously to the lucidity of these loose pages, Smith shall flutter among them again. In the nick of time he shall come to tell us why he strewed so many anxious cigar stumps around the cocoanut palm that night. This he must do; for, when he sailed away before the dawn in his yacht *Rambler,* he carried with him the answer to a riddle so big and preposterous that few in Anchuria had ventured even to propound it.

CAUGHT

THE plans for the detention of the flying President Miraflores and his companion at the coast line seemed hardly likely to fail. Dr. Zavalla himself had gone to the port of Alazan to establish a guard at that point. At Coralio the Liberal patriot Varras could be depended upon to keep close watch. Goodwin held himself responsible for the district about Coralio.

The news of the president's flight had been disclosed to no one in the coast towns save trusted members of the ambitious political party that was desirous of succeeding to power. The telegraph wire running from San Mateo to the coast had been cut far up on the mountain trail by an emissary of Zavalla's. Long before this could be repaired and word received along it from the capital the fugitives would have reached the coast and the question of escape or capture been solved.

Goodwin had stationed armed sentinels at frequent intervals along the shore for a mile in each direction from Coralio. They were instructed to keep a vigilant lookout during the night to prevent Miraflores from attempting to embark stealthily by means of some boat or sloop found by chance at the water's edge. A dozen patrols walked the streets of Coralio unsuspected, ready to intercept the truant official should he show himself there.

Goodwin was very well convinced that no precautions had been overlooked. He strolled about the streets that bore such high-sounding names and were but narrow, grass-covered lanes, lending his own aid to the vigil that had been intrusted to him by Bob Englehart.

The town had begun the tepid round of its nightly diversions. A few leisurely dandies, clad in white duck, with flowing neckties, and swinging slim bamboo canes, threaded the grassy by-ways toward the houses of their favored señoritas. Those who wooed the art of music dragged tirelessly at whining concertinas, or fingered lugubrious guitars at doors and windows. An occasional soldier from the *cuartel*, with flapping straw hat, without coat or shoes, hurried by, balancing his long gun like a lance in one hand. From every density of the foliage the giant tree frogs sounded their loud and irritating clatter. Further out, where the by-ways perished at the brink of the jungle, the guttural cries of marauding baboons and the coughing of the alligators in the black estuaries fractured the vain silence of the wood.

By ten o'clock the streets were deserted. The oil lamps that had burned, a sickly yellow, at random corners, had been extinguished by some economical civic agent. Coralio lay sleeping calmly between toppling mountains and encroaching sea like a stolen babe in the arms of its abductors. Somewhere over in that tropical darkness—perhaps already threading the profundities of the alluvial lowlands—the high adventurer and his mate were moving toward land's end. The game of Fox-in-the-Morning should be coming soon to its close.

Goodwin, at his deliberate gait, passed the long, low *cuartel* where Coralio's contingent of Anchuria's military force slumbered, with its bare toes pointed heavenward. There was a law that no civilian might come so near the headquarters of that citadel of war after nine o'clock, but Goodwin was always forgetting the minor statutes.

"*Quién vive?*" shrieked the sentinel, wrestling prodigiously with his lengthy musket.

"*Americano,*" growled Goodwin, without turning his head, and passed on, unhalted.

To the right he turned, and to the left up the street that ultimately reached the Plaza Nacional. When within the toss of a cigar stump from the intersecting Street of the Holy Sepulchre, he stopped suddenly in the pathway.

He saw the form of a tall man, clothed in black and carrying a large valise, hurry down the cross-street in the direction of the beach. And Goodwin's second glance made him aware of a woman at the man's elbow on the farther side, who seemed to urge forward, if not even to assist, her companion in their swift but silent progress. They were no Coralians, those two.

Goodwin followed at increased speed, but without any of the artful tactics that are so dear to the heart of the sleuth. The American was too broad to feel the instinct of the detective. He stood as an agent for the people of Anchuria, and but for political reasons he would have demanded then and there the money. It was the design of his party to secure the imperilled fund, to restore it to the treasury of the country, and to declare itself in power without bloodshed or resistance.

The couple halted at the door of the Hotel de los Estranjeros, and the man struck upon the wood with the impatience of one unused to his entry being stayed. Madama was long in response; but after a time her light showed, the door was opened, and the guests housed.

Goodwin stood in the quiet street, lighting another cigar. In two minutes a faint gleam began to show between the slats of the jalousies in the upper story of the hotel. "They have engaged rooms," said Goodwin to himself. "So, then, their arrangements for sailing have yet to be made."

At that moment there came along one Estebán Delgado, a barber, an enemy to existing government, a jovial plotter against stagnation in any form. This barber was one of Coralio's saddest dogs, often remaining out of doors as late as eleven, post meridian. He was a partisan Liberal; and he greeted Goodwin with flatulent importance as a brother in the cause. But he had something important to tell.

"What think you, Don Frank!" he cried, in the universal tone of the conspirator. "I have to-night shaved la barba—what you call the 'weeskers' of the Presidente himself, of this countree! Consider! He sent for me to come. In the poor casita of an old woman he awaited me—in a verree leetle house in a dark place. Carramba!—el Señor Presidente to make himself thus secret and obscured! I think he desired not to be known—but, carajo! can you shave a man and not see his face? This gold piece he gave me, and said it was to be all quite still. I think, Don Frank, there is what you call a chip over the bug."

"Have you ever seen President Miraflores before?" asked Goodwin.

"But once," answered Estebán. "He is tall; and he had weeskers, verree black and sufficient."

"Was any one else present when you shaved him?"

"An old Indian woman, Señor, that belonged with the casa, and one señorita—a ladee of so much beautee!—ah, Dios!"

"All right, Estebán," said Goodwin. "It's very lucky that you happened along with your tonsorial information. The new administration will be likely to remember you for this."

Then in a few words he made the barber acquainted with the crisis into which the affairs of the nation had culminated, and instructed him to remain outside, keeping watch upon the two sides of the hotel that looked upon the street, and observing whether any one should attempt to leave the house by any door or window. Goodwin himself went to the door through which the guests had entered, opened it and stepped inside.

Madama had returned downstairs from her journey above to see after the comfort of her lodgers. Her candle stood upon the bar. She was about to take a thimbleful of rum as a solace for having her rest disturbed. She looked up without surprise or alarm as her third caller entered.

"Ah! it is the Señor Goodwin. Not often does he honor my poor house by his presence."

"I must come oftener," said Goodwin, with the Goodwin smile. "I hear that your cognac is the best between Belize to the north and Rio to the south. Set out the bottle, Madama, and let us have the proof in un vasito for each of us."

"My aguardiente," said Madama, with pride, "is the best. It grows, in beautiful bottles, in the dark places among the banana-trees. Si, Señor. Only at midnight can they be picked by sailor-men who bring them, before daylight comes, to your back door. Good aguardiente is a verree difficult fruit to handle, Señor Goodwin."

Smuggling, in Coralio, was much nearer than competition to being the life of trade. One spoke of it slyly, yet with a certain conceit, when it had been well accomplished.

"You have guests in the house to-night," said Goodwin, laying a silver dollar upon the counter.

"Why not?" said Madama, counting the change. "Two; but the smallest while finished to arrive. One señor, not quite old, and one señorita of sufficient handsomeness. To their rooms they have ascended, not desiring the to-eat nor the to-drink. Two rooms—*Número* 9 and *Número* 10."

"I was expecting that gentleman and that lady," said Goodwin. "I have important *negocios* that must be transacted. Will you allow me to see them?"

"Why not?" sighed Madama, placidly. "Why should not Señor Goodwin ascend and speak to his friends? *Está bueno*. Room *Número* 9 and room *Número* 10."

Goodwin loosened in his coat pocket the American revolver that he carried, and ascended the steep, dark stairway.

In the hallway above, the saffron light from a hanging lamp allowed him to select the gaudy numbers on the doors. He turned the knob of Number 9, entered and closed the door behind him.

If that was Isabel Guilbert seated by the table in that poorly furnished room, report had failed to do her charms justice. She rested her head upon one hand. Extreme fatigue was signified in every line of her figure; and upon her countenance a deep perplexity was written. Her eyes were gray-irised, and of that mould that seems to have belonged to the orbs of all the famous queens of hearts. Their whites were singularly clear and brilliant, concealed above the irises by heavy horizontal lids, and showing a snowy line below them. Such eyes denote great nobility, vigor, and, if you can conceive of it, a most generous selfishness. She looked up when the American entered with an expression of surprised inquiry, but without alarm.

Goodwin took off his hat and seated himself, with his characteristic deliberate ease, upon a corner of the table. He held a lighted cigar between his fingers. He took this familiar course because he was sure that preliminaries would be wasted upon Miss Guilbert. He knew her history, and the small part that the conventions had played in it.

"Good evening," he said. "Now, madame, let us come to business at once. You will observe that I mention no names, but I know who is in the next room, and what he carries in that valise. That is the point which brings me here. I have come to dictate terms of surrender."

The lady neither moved nor replied, but steadily regarded the cigar in Goodwin's hand.

"We," continued the dictator, thoughtfully regarding the neat buckskin shoe on his gently swinging foot—"I speak for a considerable majority of the people—demand the return of the stolen funds belonging to them. Our terms go very little further than that. They are very simple. As an accredited spokesman, I promise that our interference will cease if they are accepted. Give up the money, and you and your companion will be permitted to proceed wherever you will. In fact, assistance will be given you in the matter of securing a passage by any outgoing vessel you may choose. It is on my personal responsibility that I add congratulations to the gentleman in Number 10 upon his taste in feminine charms."

Returning his cigar to his mouth, Goodwin observed her, and saw that her eyes followed it and rested upon it with icy and significant concentration. Apparently she had not heard a word he had said. He understood, tossed the cigar out the window, and, with an amused laugh, slid from the table to his feet.

"That is better," said the lady. "It makes it possible for me to listen to you. For a second lesson in good manners, you might now tell me by whom I am being insulted."

"I am sorry," said Goodwin, leaning one hand on the table, "that my time is too brief for devoting much of it to a course of etiquette. Come, now; I appeal to your good sense. You have shown yourself, in more than one instance, to be well aware of what is to your advantage. This is an occasion that demands the exercise of your undoubted intelligence. There is no mystery here. I am Frank Goodwin; and I have come for the money. I entered this room at a venture. Had I entered the other I would have had it before now. Do you want it in words? The gentleman in Number 10 has betrayed a great trust. He has robbed his people of a large sum, and it is I who will prevent their losing it. I do not say who that gentleman is; but if I should be forced to see him •and he should prove to be a certain high official of the republic, it will be my duty to arrest him. The house is guarded. I am offering you liberal terms. It is not absolutely necessary that I confer personally with the gentleman in the next room. Bring me the valise containing the money, and we will call the affair ended."

The lady arose from her chair and stood for a moment, thinking deeply. "Do you live here, Mr. Goodwin?" she asked, presently.

"Yes."

"What is your authority for this intrusion?"

"I am an instrument of the republic. I was advised by wire of the movements of the—gentleman in Number 10."

"May I ask you two or three questions? I believe you to be a man more apt to be truthful than—timid. What sort of a town is this—Coralio, I think they call it?"

"Not much of a town," said Goodwin, smiling. "A banana town, as they run. Grass huts, 'dobes, five or six two-story houses, accommodations limited, population half-breed Spanish and Indian, Caribs and blackamoors. No sidewalks to speak or, no amusements. Rather unmoral. That's an offhand sketch, of course."

"Are there any inducements, say in a social or in a business way, for people to reside here?"

"Oh, yes," answered Goodwin, smiling broadly. "There are no afternoon teas, no hand-organs, no department stores—and there is no extradition treaty."

"He told me," went on the lady, speaking as if to herself, and with a slight frown, "that there were towns on this coast of beauty and importance; that there was a pleasing social order—especially an American colony of cultured residents."

"There is an American colony," said Goodwin, gazing at her in some wonder. "Some of the members are all right. Some are fugitives from justice from the States. I recall two exiled bank presidents, one army paymaster under a cloud, a couple of manslayers, and a widow—arsenic, I believe, was the suspicion in her case. I myself complete the colony, but, as yet, I have not distinguished myself by any particular crime."

"Do not lose hope," said the lady, dryly; "I see nothing in your actions to-night to guarantee your further obscurity. Some mistake has been made; I do not know just where. But *him* you shall not disturb to-night. The journey has fatigued him so that he has fallen asleep, I think, in his clothes. You talk of stolen money! I do not understand you. Some mistake has been made. I will convince you. Remain where you are and I will bring you the valise that you seem to covet so, and show it to you."

She moved toward the closed door that connected the two rooms, but stopped, and half turned and bestowed upon Goodwin a grave, searching look that ended in a quizzical smile.

"You force my door," she said, "and you follow your ruffianly behavior with the basest accusations; and yet"—she hesitated, as if to reconsider what she was about to say—"and yet—it is a puzzling thing—I am sure there has been some mistake."

She took a step toward the door, but Goodwin stayed her by a light touch upon her arm. I have said before that women turned to look at him in the streets. He was the viking sort of man, big, good-looking, and with an air of kindly truculence. She was dark and proud, glowing or pale as her mood moved her. I do not know if Eve were light or dark, but if such a woman had stood in the garden I know that the apple would have been eaten. This woman was to be Goodwin's fate, and he did not know it; but he must have felt the first throes of destiny, for, as he faced her, the knowledge of what report named her turned bitter in his throat."

"If there has been any mistake," he said, hotly, "it was yours. I do not blame the man who has lost his country, his honor, and is about to lose the poor consolation of his stolen riches as much as I blame you, for, by Heaven! I can very well see how he was brought to it. I can understand, and pity him. It is such women as you that strew this degraded coast with wretched exiles, that make men forget their trusts, that drag——"

The lady interrupted him with a weary gesture.

"There is no need to continue your insults," she said, coldly. "I do not understand what you are saying, nor do I know what mad blunder you are making; but if the inspection of the contents of a gentleman's portmanteau will rid me of you, let us delay it no longer."

She passed quickly and noiselessly into the other room, and returned with the heavy leather valise, which she handed to the American with an air of patient contempt.

Goodwin set the valise quickly upon the table and began to unfasten the straps. The lady stood by, with an expression of infinite scorn and weariness upon her face.

The valise opened wide to a powerful, sidelong wrench. Goodwin dragged out two or three articles of clothing, exposing the bulk of its contents—package after package of tightly packed United States bank and treasury notes of large denomination. Reckoning from the high figures written upon the paper bands that bound them, the total must have come closely upon the hundred thousand mark.

Goodwin glanced swiftly at the woman, and saw, with surprise and a thrill of pleasure that he wondered at, that she had experienced an unmistakable shock. Her eyes grew wide, she gasped, and leaned heavily against the table. She had been ignorant, then, he inferred, that her companion had looted the government treasury. But why, he angrily asked himself, should he be so well pleased to think this wandering and unscrupulous singer not so black as report had painted her?

A noise in the other room startled them both. The door swung open, and a tall, elderly, dark complexioned man, recently shaven, hurried into the room.

All the pictures of President Miraflores represent him as the possessor of a luxuriant supply of dark and carefully tended whiskers; but the story of the barber, Estebán, had prepared Goodwin for the change.

The man stumbled in from the dark room, his eyes blinking at the lamplight, and heavy from sleep.

"What does this mean?" he demanded in excellent English, with a keen and perturbed look at the American—"robbery?"

"Very near it," answered Goodwin. "But I rather think I'm in time to prevent it. I represent the people to whom this money belongs, and I have come to convey it back to them." He thrust his hand into a pocket of his loose linen coat.

The other man's hand went quickly behind him.

"Don't draw," called Goodwin, sharply; "I've got you covered from my pocket."

The lady stepped forward, and laid one hand upon the shoulder of her hesitating companion. She pointed to the table. "Tell me the truth—the truth," she said, in a low voice. "Whose money is that?"

The man did not answer. He gave a deep, long-drawn sigh, leaned and kissed her on the forehead, stepped back into the other room and closed the door.

Goodwin foresaw his purpose, and jumped for the door, but the report of the pistol echoed as his hand touched the knob. A heavy fall followed, and some one swept him aside and struggled into the room of the fallen man.

A desolation, thought Goodwin, greater than that derived from the loss of cavalier and gold must have been in the heart of the enchantress to have wrung from her, in that moment, the cry of one turning to the all-forgiving, all-comforting earthly consoler—to have made her call out from that bloody and dishonored room—"Oh, mother, mother, mother!"

But there was an alarm outside. The barber, Esteban, at the sound of the shot, had raised his voice; and the shot itself had aroused half the town. A pattering of feet came up the street, and official orders rang out on the still air. Goodwin had a duty to perform. Circumstances had made him the custodian of his adopted country's treasure. Swiftly cramming the money into the valise, he closed it, leaned far out of the window and dropped it into a thick orange-tree in the little inclosure below.

They will tell you in Coralio, as they delight in telling the stranger, of the conclusion of that tragic flight. They will tell you how the upholders of the law came apace when the alarm was sounded—the *Comandante* in red slippers and a jacket like a head waiter's and girded sword, the soldiers with their interminable guns, followed by outnumbering officers struggling into their gold lace and epaulettes; the bare-footed policemen (the only capables in the lot), and ruffled citizens of every hue and description.

They say that the countenance of the dead man was marred sadly by the effects of the shot; but he was identified as the fallen president by both Goodwin and the barber Esteban. On the next morning messages began to come over the mended telegraph wire; and the story of the flight from the capital was given out to the public. In San Mateo the revolutionary party had seized the sceptre of government, without opposition, and the *vivas* of the mercurial populace quickly effaced the interest belonging to the unfortunate Miraflores.

They will relate to you how the new government sifted the towns and raked the roads to find the valise containing Anchuria's surplus capital, which the president was known to have carried with him, but all in vain. In Coralio Señor Goodwin himself led the searching party which combed that town as carefully as a woman combs her hair; but the money was not found.

So they buried the dead man, without honors, back of the town near the little bridge that spans the mangrove swamp; and for a *real* a boy will show you his grave. They say that the old woman in whose hut the barber shaved the president placed the wooden slab at his head, and burned the inscription upon it with a hot iron.

You will hear also that Señor Goodwin, like a tower of strength, shielded Doña Isabel Guilbert through those subsequent distressful days; and that his scruples as to her past career (if he had any) vanished; and her adventuresome waywardness (if she had any) left her, and they were wedded and were happy.

The American built a home on a little foot hill near the town. It is a conglomerate structure of native woods that, exported, would be worth a fortune, and of brick, palm, glass, bamboo and adobe. There is a paradise of nature about it; and something of the same sort within. The natives speak of its interior with hands uplifted in admiration. There are floors polished like mirrors and covered with hand-woven Indian rugs of silk fibre, tall ornaments and pictures, musical instruments and papered walls—"figure-it-to-yourself!" they exclaim.

But they cannot tell you in Coralio (as you shall learn) what became of the money that Frank Goodwin dropped into the orange-tree. But that shall come later; for the palms are fluttering in the breeze, bidding us to sport and gaiety.

CUPID'S EXILE NUMBER TWO

THE United States of America, after looking over its stock of consular timber, selected Mr. John De Graffanreid Atwood, of Dalesburg, Alabama, for a successor to Willard Geddie, resigned.

Without prejudice to Mr. Atwood, it will have to be acknowledged that, in this instance, it was the man who sought the office. As with the self-banished Geddie, it was nothing less than the artful smiles of lovely women that had driven Johnny Atwood to the desperate expedient of accepting office under a despised Federal Government so that he might go far, far away and never see again the false, fair face that had wrecked his young life. The consulship at Coralio seemed to offer a retreat sufficiently removed and romantic enough to inject the necessary drama into the pastoral scenes of Dalesburg life.

It was while playing the part of Cupid's exile that Johnny added his handiwork to the long list of casualties along the Spanish Main by his famous manipulation of the shoe market, and his unparalleled feat of elevating the most despised and useless weed in his own country from obscurity to be a valuable product in international commerce.

The trouble began, as trouble often begins instead of ending with a romance. In Dalesburg there was a man named Elijah Hemstetter, who kept a general store. His family consisted of one daughter called Rosine, a name that atoned much for "Hemstetter." This young woman was possessed of plentiful attractions, so that the young men of the community were agitated in their bosoms. Among the more agitated was Johnny, the son of Judge Atwood, who lived in the big colonial mansion on the edge of Dalesburg.

It would seem that the desirable Rosine should have been pleased to return the affection of an Atwood, a name honored all over the state long before and since the war. It does seem that she should have gladly consented to have been led into that stately but rather empty colonial mansion. But not so. There was a cloud on the horizon, a threatening, cumulus cloud, in the shape of a lively and shrewd young farmer in the neighborhood who dared to enter the lists as a rival to the high-born Atwood,

One night Johnny propounded to Rosine a question that is considered of much importance by the young of the human species. The accessories were all there—moonlight, oleanders, magnolias, the mock-bird's song. Whether or no the shadow of Pinkney Dawson, the prosperous young farmer, came between them on that occasion is not known; but Rosine's answer was unfavorable. Mr. John De Graffenreid Atwood bowed till his hat touched the lawn grass, and went away with his head high, but with a sore wound in his pedigree and heart. A Hemstetter refuse an Atwood! Zounds!

Among other accidents of that year was a Democratic president. Judge Atwood was a warhorse of Democracy. Johnny persuaded him to set the wheels moving for some foreign appointment. He would go away—away. Perhaps in years to come Rosine would think how true, how faithful his love had been, and would drop a tear—maybe in the cream she would be skimming for Pink Dawson's breakfast.

The wheels of politics revolved; and Johnny was appointed consul to Coralio. Just before leaving he dropped in at Hemstetter's to say good-bye. There was a queer, pinkish look about Rosine's eyes; and had the two been alone, the United States might have had to cast about for another consul. But Pink Dawson was there, of course, talking about his 400-acre orchard, and the three-mile alfalfa tract, and the 200-acre pasture. So Johnny shook hands with Rosine as coolly as if he were only going to run up to Montgomery for a couple of days. They had the royal manner when they chose, those Atwoods.

"If you happen to strike anything in the way of a good investment down there, Johnny," said Pink Dawson, "just let me know, will you? I reckon I could lay my hands on a few extra thousands 'most any time for a profitable deal."

"Certainly, Pink," said Johnny, pleasantly. "If I strike anything of the sort I'll let you in with pleasure."

So Johnny went down to Mobile and took a fruit steamer for the coast of Anchuria.

When the new consul arrived in Coralio the strangeness of the scenes diverted him much. He was only twenty-two; and the grief of youth is not worn like a garment as it is by older men. It has its seasons when it reigns; and then it is unseated for a time by the assertion of the keen senses.

Billy Keogh and Johnny seemed to conceive a mutual friendship at once. Keogh took the new consul about town and presented him to the handful of Americans and the smaller number of French and Germans who made up the "foreign" contingent. And then, of course, he had to be more formally introduced to the native officials, and have his credentials transmitted through an interpreter.

There was something about the young Southerner that the sophisticated Keogh liked. His manner was simple almost to boyishness; but he possessed the cool carelessness of a man of far greater age and experience. Neither uniforms nor titles, red tape nor foreign languages, mountains nor sea weighed upon his spirits. He was heir to all the ages, an Atwood, of Dalesburg; and you might know every thought conceived in his bosom.

Geddie came down to the consulate to explain the duties and workings of the office. He and Keogh tried to interest the new consul in their description of the work that his government expected him to perform.

"It's all right," said Johnny from the hammock that he had set up as the official reclining place. "If anything turns up that has to be done I'll let you fellows do it. You can't expect a Democrat to work during his first term of holding office."

"You might look over these headings," suggested Geddie, "of the different lines of exports you will have to keep account of. The fruit is classified; and there are the valuable woods, coffee, rubber——"

"That last account sounds all right," interrupted Mr. Atwood. "Sounds as if it could be stretched. I want to buy a new flag, a monkey, a guitar and a barrel of pineapples. Will that rubber account stretch over 'em?"

"That's merely statistics," and Geddie, smiling. "The expense account is what you want. It is supposed to have a slight elasticity. The 'stationery' items are sometimes carelessly audited by the State Department."

"We're wasting our time," said Keogh. "This man was born to hold office. He penetrates to the root of the art at one step of his eagle eye. The true genius of government shows its hand in every word of his speech."

"I didn't take this job with any intention of working," explained Johnny, lazily. "I wanted to go somewhere in the world where they didn't talk about farms. There are none here, are there?"

"Not the kind you are acquainted with," answered the ex-consul. "There is no such art here as agriculture. There never was a plow or a reaper within the boundaries of Anchuria."

"This is the country for me," murmured the consul and immediately he fell asleep.

The cheerful tintypist pursued his intimacy with Johnny in spite of open charges that he did so to obtain a preëmption on a seat in the coveted spot, the rear gallery of the consulate. But whether his designs were selfish or purely friendly, Keogh achieved that desirable privilege. Few were the nights on which the two could not be found reposing there in the sea breeze, with their heels on the railing, and the cigars and brandy conveniently near.

One evening they had sat thus, mainly silent, for their talk had dwindled before the stilling influence of an unusual night.

There was a great, full moon; and the sea was mother-of-pearl. Almost every sound was hushed, for the air was but faintly stirring; and the town lay panting, waiting for the night to cool. Off-shore lay the fruit steamer *Andador*, of the Vesuvius line, full-laden and scheduled to sail at six in the morning. There were no loiterers on the beach. So bright was the moonlight that the two men could see the small pebbles shining on the beach where the gentle surf wetted them.

Then down the coast, tacking close to shore, slowly swam a little sloop, white-winged like some snowy sea fowl. Its course lay within twenty points of the wind's eye; so it veered in and out again in long slow strokes like the movements of a graceful skater.

Again the tactics of its crew brought it close in shore, this time nearly opposite the consulate; and then there blew from the sloop clear and surprising notes as if from a horn of elfland. A fairy bugle it might have been, sweet and silvery and unexpected, playing with spirit the familiar air of "Home, Sweet Home."

It was a scene set for the land of the lotus. The authority of the sea and the tropics, the mystery that attends unknown sails, and the prestige of drifting music on moonlit waters gave it an anodynous charm. Johnny Atwood felt it, and thought of Dalesburg; but as soon as Keogh's mind had arrived at a theory concerning the peripatetic solo he sprang to the railing, and his ear-rending yawp fractured the silence of Coralio like a cannon shot.

"Mel-lin-ger a-hoy!"

The sloop was now on its outward tack; but from it came a clear, answering hail:

"Good-bye, Billy . . . go-ing home—bye!"

The *Andador* was the sloop's destination. No doubt some passenger with a saling permit from some up-the-coast point had come down in this sloop to catch the regular fruit steamer on its return trip. Like a coquettish pigeon the little boat tacked on its eccentric way until at last its white sail was lost to sight against the larger bulk of the fruiter's side.

"That's old H. P. Mellinger," explained Keogh, dropping back into his chair. "He's going back to New York. He was private secretary of the late hot-foot president of this grocery and fruit stand that they call a country. His job's over now; and I guess old Mellinger is glad."

"Why does he disappear to music, like Zo-zo, the magic queen?" asked Johnny. "Just to show 'em that he doesn't care?"

"That noise you heard is a phonograph," said Keogh. "I sold him that. Mellinger had a graft in this country that was the only thing of its kind in the world. The tooting machine saved it for him once, and he always carried it around with him afterward."

"Tell me about it," demanded Johnny, betraying interest.

"I'm no disseminator of narratives," said Keogh. "I can use language for purposes of speech; but when I attempt a discourse the words come out as they will, and they may make sense when they strike the atmosphere, or they may not."

"I want to hear about that graft," persisted Johnny. "You've got no right to refuse. I've told you all about every man, woman and hitching post in Dalesburg."

"You shall hear it," said Keogh. "I said my instincts of narrative were perplexed. Don't you believe it. It's an art I've acquired along with many other of the graces and sciences."

THE PHONOGRAPH AND THE GRAFT

"WHAT was this graft?" asked Johnny, with the impatience of the great public to whom tales are told.

"'Tis contrary to art and philosophy to give you the information," said Keogh, calmly. "The art of narrative consists in concealing from your audience everything it wants to know until after you expose your favorite opinions on topics foreign to the subject. A good story is like a bitter pill with the sugar coating inside of it. I will begin, if you please, with a horoscope located in the Cherokee Nation; and end with a moral tune on the phonograph.

"Me and Henry Horsecollar brought the first phonograph to this country. Henry was a quarter-breed, quarter-back Cherokee, educated East in the idioms of football, and West in contraband whisky, and a gentleman, the same as you and me. He was easy and romping in his ways; a man about six foot, with a kind of rubber-tire movement. Yes, he was a little man about five foot five, or five foot eleven. He was what you would call a medium tall man of average smallness. Henry had quit college once, and the Muscogee jail three times—the last-named institution on account of introducing and selling whisky in the territories. Henry Horsecollar never let any cigar stores come up and stand behind him. He didn't belong to that tribe of Indians.

"Henry and me met at Texarkana, and figured out this phonograph scheme. He had $360 which came to him out of a land allotment in the reservation. I had run down from Little Rock on account of a distressful scene I had witnessed on the street there. A man stood on a box and passed around some gold watches, screw case, stem-winders, Elgin movement, very elegant. Twenty bucks they cost you over the counter. At three dollars the crowd fought for the tickets. The man happened to find a valise full of them handy, and he passed them out like putting hot biscuits on a plate. The backs were hard to unscrew, but the crowd put its ear to the case, and they ticked mollifying and agreeable. Three of these watches were genuine tickers; the rest were only kickers. Hey? Why, empty cases with one of them horny black bugs that fly around electric lights in 'em. Them bugs kick off minutes and seconds industrious and beautiful. So, this man I was speaking of cleaned up $288; and then he went away, because he knew that when it came time to wind watches in Little Rock an entomologist would be needed, and he wasn't one.

"So, as I say, Henry had $360, and I had $288. The idea of introducing the phonograph to South America was Henry's; but I took to it freely, being fond of machinery of all kinds.

" 'The Latin races,' says Henry, explaining easily in the idioms he learned at college, 'are peculiarly adapted to be victims of the phonograph. They have the artistic temperament. They yearn for music and color and gaiety. They give wampum to the hand-organ man and the four-legged chicken in the tent when they're months behind with the grocery and the bread-fruit tree.'

" 'Then,' says I, 'we'll export canned music to the Latins; but I'm mindful of Mr. Julius Cæsar's account of 'em where he says: *"Omnia Gallia in tres partes divisa est"*; which is the same as to say, "We will need all of our gall in devising means to tree them parties." '

"I hated to make a show of education; but I was disinclined to be overdone in syntax by a mere Indian, a member of a race to which we owe nothing except the land on which the United States is situated.

"We bought a fine phonograph in Texarkana—one of the best make—and half a trunkful of records. We packed up, and took the T. and P. for New Orleans. From that celebrated centre of molasses and disfranchised coon songs we took a steamer for South America.

"We landed at Solitas, forty miles up the coast from here. 'Twas a palatable enough place to look at. The houses were clean and white; and to look at 'em stuck around among the scenery they reminded you of hard-boiled eggs served with lettuce. There was a block of skyscraper mountains in the suburbs; and they kept pretty quiet, like they had crept up there and were watching the town. And the sea was remarking 'Sh-sh-sh' on the beach; and now and then a ripe cocoanut would drop kerblip in the sand; and that was all there was doing. Yes, I judge that town was considerably on the quiet. I judge that after Gabriel quits blowing his horn, and the car starts, with Philadelphia swinging to the last strap, and Pine Gully, Arkansas, hanging onto the rear step, this town of Solitas will wake up and ask if anybody spoke.

"The captain went ashore with us, and offered to conduct what he seemed to like to call the obsequies. He introduced Henry and me to the United States Consul, and a roan man, the head of the Department of Mercenary and Licentious Dispositions, the way it read upon his sign.

" 'I touch here a week again from to-day,' says the captain.

" 'By that time,' we told him, 'we'll be amassing wealth in the interior towns with our galvanized prima donna and correct imitations of Sousa's band excavating a march from a tin mine.'

" 'Ye'll not,' says the captain. 'Ye'll be hypnotized. Any gentleman in the audience who kindly steps upon the stage and looks this country in the eye will be converted to the hypothesis that he's but a fly in the Elgin creamery. Ye'll be standing knee deep in the surf waiting for me, and your machine for making Hamburger steak out of the hitherto respected art of music will be playing "There's no place like home." '

"Henry skinned a twenty off his roll, and received from the Bureau of Mercenary Dispositions a paper bearing a red seal and a dialect story, and no change.

"Then we got the consul full of red wine, and struck him for a horoscope. He was a thin, youngish kind of a man, I should say past fifty, sort of French-Irish in his affections, and puffed up with disconsolation. Yes, he was a flattened kind of a man, in whom drink lay stagnant, inclined to corpulence and misery. Yes, I think he was a kind of a Dutchman, being very sad and genial in his ways.

"'The marvellous invention,' he says, 'entitled the phonograph, has never invaded these shores. The people have never heard it. They would not believe it if they should. Simple-hearted children of nature, progress has never condemned them to accept the work of a can-opener as an overture, and rag-time might incite them to a bloody revolution. But you can try the experiment. The best chance you have is that the populace may not wake up when you play. There's two ways,' says the consul, 'they may take it. They may become inebriated with attention, like an Atlanta colonel listening to "Marching Through Georgia," or they will get excited and transpose the key of the music with an axe and yourselves into a dungeon. In the latter case,' says the consul, 'I'll do my duty by cabling to the State Department, and I'll wrap the Stars and Stripes around you when you come to be shot, and threaten them with the vengeance of the greatest gold export and financial reserve nation on earth. The flag is full of bullet holes now,' says the consul, 'made in that way. Twice before,' says the consul, 'I have cabled our government for a couple of gunboats to protect American citizens. The first time the Department sent me a pair of gum boots. The other time was when a man named Pease was going to be executed here. They referred that appeal to the Secretary of Agriculture. Let us now disturb the señor behind the bar for a subsequence of the red wine.'

"Thus soliloquized the consul of Solitas to me and Henry Horsecollar.

"But, notwithstanding, we hired a room that afternoon in the Calle de los Angeles, the main street that runs along the shore, and put our trunks there. 'Twas a good-sized room, dark and cheerful, but small. 'Twas on a various street, diversified by houses and conservatory plants. The peasantry of the city passed to and fro on the fine pasturage between the sidewalks. 'Twas, for the world, like an opera chorus when the Royal Kafoozlum is about to enter.

"We were rubbing the dust off the machine and getting fixed to start business the next day, when a big, fine-looking white man in white clothes stopped at the door and looked in. We extended the invitations, and he walked inside and sized us up. He was chewing a long cigar, and wrinkling his eyes, meditative, like a girl trying to decide which dress to wear to the party.

"'New York?' he says to me finally.

"'Originally, and from time to time,' I says. 'Hasn't it rubbed off yet?'

"'It's simple,' says he, 'when you know how. It's the fit of the vest. They don't cut vests right anywhere else. Coats, maybe, but not vests.'

"The white man looks at Henry Horsecollar and hesitates.

"'Injun,' says Henry! 'tame Injun.'

"'Mellinger,' says the man—'Homer P. Mellinger. Boys, you're confiscated. You're babies in the wood without a chaperon or referee, and it's my duty to start you going. I'll knock out the props and launch you proper in the pellucid waters of this tropical mud puddle. You'll have to be christened, and if you'll come with me I'll break a bottle of wine across your bows, according to Hoyle.'

"Well, for two days Homer P. Mellinger did the honors. That man cut ice in Anchuria. He was It. He was the Royal Kafoozlum. If me and Henry was babes in the wood, he was a Robin Redbreast from the topmost bough. Him and me and Henry Horsecollar locked arms, and toted that phonograph around, and had wassail and diversions. Everywhere we found doors open we went inside and set the machine going, and Mellinger called upon the people to observe the artful music and his two lifelong friends, the Señores Americanos. The opera chorus was agitated with esteem, and followed us from house to house. There was a different kind of drink to be had with every tune. The natives had acquirements of a pleasant thing in the way of a drink that gums itself to the recollection. They chop off the end of a green cocoanut, and pour in on the juice of it French brandy and other adjuvants. We had them and other things.

"Mine and Henry's money was counterfeit. Everything was on Homer P.

Mellinger. That man could find rolls of bills concealed in places on his person where Hermann the Wizard couldn't have conjured out a rabbit or an omelette. He could have founded universities, and made orchid collections, and then had enough left to purchase the colored vote of his country. Henry and me wondered what his graft was. One evening he told us.

"'Boys,' said he, 'I've deceived you. You think I'm a painted butterfly; but in fact I'm the hardest worked man in this country. Ten years ago I landed on its shores; and two years ago on the point of its jaw. Yes, I guess I can get the decision over this ginger cake commonwealth at the end of any round I choose. I'll confide in you because you are my countrymen and guests, even if you have assaulted my adopted shores with the worst system of noises ever set to music.

"'My job is private secretary to the president of this republic; and my duties are running it. I'm not headlined in the bills, but I'm the mustard in the salad dressing just the same. There isn't a law goes before Congress, there isn't a concession granted, there isn't an import duty levied but what H. P. Mellinger he cooks and seasons it. In the front office I fill the president's inkstand and search visiting statesmen for dirks and dynamite; but in the back room I dictate the policy of the government. You'd never guess in the world how I got my pull. It's the only graft of its kind on earth. I'll put you wise. You remember the old top-liner in the copy book—"Honesty is the Best Policy"? That's it. I'm working honesty for a graft. I'm the only honest man in the republic. The government knows it; the people know it; the boodlers know it; the foreign investors know it. I make the government keep its faith. If a man is promised a job he gets it. If outside capital buys a concession it gets the goods. I run a monopoly of square dealing here. There's no competition. If Colonel Diogenes were to flash his lantern in this precinct he'd have my address inside of two minutes. There isn't big money in it, but it's a sure thing, and lets a man sleep of nights.'

"Thus Homer P. Mellinger made oration to me and Henry Horsecollar. And, later, he divested himself of this remark:

"'Boys, I'm to hold a *soirée* this evening with a gang of leading citizens, and I want your assistance. You bring the musical corn sheller and give the affair the outside appearance of a function. There's important business on hand, but it mustn't show. I can talk to you people. I've been pained for years on account of not having anybody to blow off and brag to. I get homesick sometimes, and I'd swap the entire perquisites of office for just one hour to have a stein and a caviare sandwich somewhere on Thirty-fourth Street, and stand and watch the street cars go by, and smell the peanut roaster at old Giuseppe's fruit stand.'

"'Yes,' said I, 'there's fine caviare at Billy Renfrow's café, corner of Thirty-fourth and——'

"'God knows it,' interrupts Mellinger, 'and if you'd told me you knew Billy Renfrow I'd have invented tons of ways of making you happy. Billy was my side-kicker in New York. There is a man who never knew what crooked was. Here I am working Honesty for a graft, but that man loses money on it. Carrambos! I get sick at times of this country. Everything's rotten. From the executive down to the coffee pickers, they're plotting to down each other and skin their friends. If a mule driver takes off his hat to an official, that man figures it out that he's a popular idol, and sets his pegs to stir up a revolution and upset the administration. It's one of my little chores as private secretary to smell out these revolutions and affix the kibosh before they break out and scratch the paint off the government property. That's why I'm down here now in this mildewed coast town. The governor of the district and his crew are plotting to uprise. I've got every one of their names, and they're invited to listen to the phonograph to-night, compliments of H. P. M. That's the way I'll get them in a bunch, and things are on the programme to happen to them."

"We three were sitting at table in the cantina of the Purified Saints. Mellinger poured out wine, and was looking some worried; I was thinking.

"'They're a sharp crowd,' he says, kind of fretful. 'They're capitalized by a foreign syndicate after rubber, and they're loaded to the muzzle for bribing. I'm sick,' goes on Mellinger, 'of comic opera. I want to smell East River and wear suspenders again. At times I feel like throwing up my job, but I'm d—n fool enough to be sort of proud of it. "There's Mellinger," they say here. "*Por Dios!* you can't touch him with a million." I'd like to take that record back and show it to Billy Renfrow some day; and that tightens my grip whenever I see a fat thing that I could corral just by winking one eye—and losing my graft. By —, they can't monkey with me. They know it. What money I get I make honest and spend it. Some day I'll make a pile and go back and eat caviare with Billy. To-night I'll show you how to handle a bunch of corruptionists. I'll show them what Mellinger, private secretary, means when you spell it with the cotton and tissue paper off.'

"Mellinger appears shaky, and breaks his glass against the neck of the bottle.

"I says to myself, 'White man, if I'm not mistaken there's been a bait laid out where the tail of your eye could see it.'

"That night, according to arrangements, me and Henry took the phonograph to a room in a 'dobe house in a dirty side street, where the grass was knee high. 'Twas a long room, lit with smoky oil lamps. There was plenty of chairs, and a table at the back end. We set the phonograph on the table. Mellinger was there, walking up and down, disturbed in his predicaments. He chewed cigars and spat 'em out, and he bit the thumb nail of his left hand.

"By and by the invitations to the musicale came sliding in by pairs and threes and spade flushes. Their color was of a diversity, running from a three-days' smoked meerschaum to a patent-leather polish. They were as polite as wax, being devastated with enjoyments to give Señor Mellinger the good evenings. I understood their Spanish talk—I ran a pumping engine two years in a Mexican silver mine, and had it pat—but I never let on.

"Maybe fifty of 'em had come, and was seated, when in slid the king bee, the governor of the district. Mellinger met him at the door, and escorted him to the grand stand. When I saw that Latin man I knew that Mellinger, private secretary, had all the dances on his card taken. That was a big, squashy man, the color of a rubber overshoe, and he had an eye like a head waiter's.

"Mellinger explained, fluent, in the Castilian idioms, that his soul was disconcerted with joy at introducing to his respected friends America's greatest invention, the wonder of the age. Henry got the cue and run on an elegant brass-band record and the festivities became initiated. The governor man had a bit of English under his hat, and when the music was choked off he says:

"'Ver-r-ree fine. *Gr-r-r-r-racias*, the American gentleemen, the so esplendeed moosic as to playee.'

"The table was a long one, and Henry and me sat at the end of it next the wall. The governor sat at the other end. Homer P. Mellinger stood at the side of it. I was just wondering how Mellinger was going to handle his crowd, when the home talent suddenly opened the services.

"That governor man was suitable for uprisings and policies. I judge he was a ready kind of man, who took his own time. Yes, he was full of attention and immediateness. He leaned his hands on the table and imposed his face toward the secretary man.

"'Do the American señores understand Spanish?' he asks in his native accents.

"'They do not,' says Mellinger.

"'Then listen,' goes on the Latin man, prompt. 'The musics are of sufficient prettiness, but not of necessity. Let us speak of business. I well know why we are here, since I observe my compatriots. You had a whisper yesterday Señor Mellinger, of our proposals. To-night we will speak out. We know that you stand in the president's favor, and we know your influence. The government will be changed. We know the worth of your services. We esteem your friendship and aid so much that'—Mellinger raises his hand, but the governor man bottles him up. 'Do not speak until I have done.'

"The governor man then draws a package wrapped in paper from his pocket, and lays it on the table by Mellinger's hand.

"'In that you will find fifty thousand dollars in money of your country. You can do nothing against us, but you can be worth that for us. Go back to the capital and obey our instructions. Take that money now. We trust you. You will find with it a paper giving in detail the work you will be expected to do for us. Do not have the unwiseness of refuse.'

"The governor man paused, with his eyes fixed on Mellinger, full of expressions and observances. I looked at Mellinger, and was glad Billy Renfrow couldn't see him then. The sweat was popping out on his forehead, and he stood dumb, tapping the little package with the ends of his fingers. The colorado-maduro gang was after his graft. He had only to change his politics, and stuff five fingers in his inside pocket.

"Henry whispers to me and wants the pause in the programme interpreted. I whisper back: 'H. P. is up against a bribe, senator's size, and the coons have got him going.' I saw Mellinger's hand moving closer to the package. 'He's weakening,' I whispered to Henry. 'We'll remind him,' says Henry, 'of the peanut-roaster on Thirty-fourth Street, New York.'

"Henry stooped down and got a record from the basketful we'd brought, slid it in the phonograph, and started her off. It was a cornet solo, very neat and beautiful, and the name of it was 'Home, Sweet Home.' Not one of them fifty-odd men in the room moved while it was playing, and the governor man kept his eyes steady on Mellinger. I saw Mellinger's head go up little by little, and his hand came creeping away from the package. Not until the last note sounded did anybody stir. And then Homer P. Mellinger takes up the bundle of boodle and slams it in the governor man's face.

"'That's my answer,' says Mellinger, private secretary, 'and there'll be another in the morning. I have proofs of conspiracy against every man of you. The show is over, gentlemen.'

"'There's one more act,' puts in the governor man. 'You are a servant, I believe, employed by the president to copy letters and answer raps at the door. I am governor here. Señores, I call upon you in the name of the cause to seize this man.'

"That brindled gang of conspirators shoved back their chairs and advanced in force. I could see where Mellinger had made a mistake in massing his enemy so as to make a grand-stand play. I think he made another one, too; but we can pass that, Mellinger's idea of a graft and mine being different, according to estimations and points of view.

"There was only one window and door in that room, and they were in the front end. Here was fifty odd Latin men coming in a bunch to obstruct the legislation of Mellinger. You may say there were three of us, for me and Henry, simultaneous, declared New York City and the Cherokee Nation in sympathy with the weaker party.

"Then it was that Henry Horsecollar rose to a point of disorder and intervened, showing, admirable, the advantages of education as applied to the American Indian's natural intellect and native refinement. He stood up and smoothed back his hair on each side with his hands as you have seen little girls do when they play.

"'Get behind me, both of you,' says Henry.

"'What's it to be, chief?' I asked.

"'I'm going to buck centre,' says Henry, in his football idioms. 'There isn't a tackle in the lot of them. Follow me close, and rush the game.'

"Then that cultured Red Man exhaled an arrangement of sounds with his mouth that made the Latin aggregation pause, with thoughtfulness and hesitations. The matter of his proclamation seemed to be a co-operation of the Carlisle war-whoop with the Cherokee college yell. He went at the chocolate team like a bean out of a little boy's nigger shooter. His right elbow laid out the governor man on the gridiron, and he made a lane the length of the crowd so wide that a woman could have carried a step-ladder through it without striking against anything. All Mellinger and me had to do was to follow.

"It took us just three minutes to get out of that street around to military headquarters, where Mellinger had things his own way. A colonel and a battalion of bare-toed infantry turned out and went back to the scene of the musicale with us, but the conspirator gang was gone. But we recaptured the phonograph with honors of war, and marched back to the *cuartel* with it playing All Coons Look Alike to Me.'

"The next day Mellinger takes me and Henry to one side, and begins to shed tens and twenties.

"'I want to buy that phonograph,' says he. 'I liked that last tune it played at the *soirée*.'

"'This is more money than the machine is worth,' says I.

"''Tis government expense money,' says Mellinger. 'The government pays for it, and it's getting the tune-grinder cheap.'

"Me and Henry knew that pretty well. We knew that it had saved Homer P. Mellinger's graft when he was on the point of losing it; but we never let him know we knew it.

"'Now you boys better slide off further down the coast for a while,' says Mellinger, 'till I get the screws put on these fellows here. If you don't they'll give you trouble. And if you ever happen to see Billy Renfrow again before I do, tell him I'm coming back to New York as soon as I can make a stake—honest.'

"Me and Henry laid low until the day the steamer came back. When we saw the captain's boat on the beach we went down and stood in the edge of the water. The captain grinned when he saw us.

"'I told you you'd be waiting,' he says. 'Where's the Hamburger machine?'

"'It stays behind,' I says, 'to play "Home, Sweet Home."'

"'I told you so,' says the captain again. 'Climb in the boat.'

"And that," said Keogh, "is the way me and Henry Horsecollar introduced the phonograph into this country. Henry went back to the States, but I've been rummaging around in the tropics ever since. They say Mellinger never travelled a mile after that without his phonograph. I guess it kept him reminded about his graft whenever he saw the siren voice of the boodler tip him the wink with a bribe in its hand."

"I suppose he's taking it home with him as a souvenir," remarked the consul.

"Not as a souvenir," said Keogh. "He'll need two of 'em in New York, running day and night."

MONEY MAZE

THE new administration of Anchuria entered upon its duties and privileges with enthusiasm. Its first act was to send an agent to Coralio with imperative orders to recover, if possible, the sum of money ravished from the treasury by the ill-fated Miraflores.

Colonel Emilio Falcon, the private secretary of Losada, the new president, was despatched from the capital upon this important mission.

The position of private secretary to a tropical president is a responsible one. He must be a diplomat, a spy, a ruler of men, a body-guard to his chief, and a smeller-out of plots and nascent revolutions. Often he is the power behind the throne, the dictator of policy; and a president chooses him with a dozen times the care with which he selects a matrimonial mate.

Colonel Falcon, a handsome and urbane gentleman of Castilian courtesy and débonnaire manners, came to Coralio with the task before him of striking upon the cold trail of the lost money. There he conferred with the military authorities, who had received instructions to co-operate with him in the search.

Colonel Falcon established his headquarters in one of the rooms of the Casa Morena. Here for a week he held informal sittings—must as if he were a kind of unified grand jury—and summoned before him all those whose testimony might illumine the financial tragedy that had accompanied the less momentous one of the late president's death.

Two or three who were thus examined, among whom was the barber Estebán, declared that they had identified the body of the president before its burial.

"Of a truth," testified Estebán before the mighty secretary, "it was he, the president. Consider!—how could I shave a man and not see his face? He sent for me to shave him in a small house. He had a beard very black and thick. Had I ever seen the president before? Why not? I saw him once ride forth in a carriage from the *vapor* in Solitas. When I shaved him he gave me a gold piece, and said there was to be no talk. But I am a Liberal—I am devoted to my country—and I spake of these things to Señor Goodwin."

"It is known," said Colonel Falcon, smoothly, "that the late President took with him an American leather valise, containing a large amount of money. Did you see that?"

"*De veras*—no," Estebán answered. "The light in the little house was but a small lamp by which I could scarcely see to shave the President. Such a thing there may have been, but I did not see it. No. Also in the room was a young lady—a señorita of much beauty—that I could see even in so small a light. But the money, señor, or the thing in which it was carried—that I did not see."

The *comandante* and other officers gave testimony that they had been awakened and alarmed by the noise of a pistol-shot in the Hotel de los Estranjeros. Hurrying thither to protect the peace and dignity of the republic, they found a man lying dead, with a pistol clutched in his hand. Beside him was a young woman, weeping sorely. Señor Goodwin was also in the room when they entered it. But of the valise of money they saw nothing.

Madame Timotea Ortiz, the proprietress of the hotel in which the game of Fox-in-the-Morning had been played out, told of the coming of the two guests to her house.

"To my house they came," said she—"one *señor*, not quite old, and one *señorita* of sufficient handsomeness. They desired not to eat or to drink—not even of my *aguardiente*, which is the best. To their rooms they ascended—*Número Nueve* and *Número Diez.* Later came Señor Goodwin, who ascended to speak with them. Then I heard a great noise like that of a *canon,* and they said that the *pobre Presidente* had shot himself. *Está bueno.* I saw nothing of money or of the thing you call *veliz* that you say he carried it in."

Colonel Falcon soon came to the reasonable conclusion that if any one in Coralio could furnish a clue to the vanished money, Frank Goodwin must be the man. But the wise secretary pursued a different course in seeking information from the American. Goodwin was a powerful friend to the new administration, and one who was not to be carelessly dealt with in respect to either his honesty or his courage. Even the private secretary of His Excellency hesitated to have this rubber prince and mahogany baron haled before him as a common citizen of Anchuria. So he sent Goodwin a flowery 'epistle, each word-petal dripping with honey, requesting the favor of an interview. Goodwin replied with an invitation to dinner at his own house.

Before the hour named the American walked over to the Casa Morena, and greeted his guest frankly and friendly. Then the two strolled, in the cool of the afternoon, to Goodwin's home in the environs.

The American left Colonel Falcon in a big, cool, shadowed room with a floor of inlaid and polished woods that any millionaire in the States would have envied, excusing himself for a few minutes. He crossed a *patio,* shaded with deftly arranged awnings and plants, and entered a long room looking upon the sea in the opposite wing of the house. The broad jalousies were opened wide, and the ocean breeze flowed in through the room, an invisible current of coolness and health. Goodwin's wife sat near one of the windows, making a water-color sketch of the afternoon seascape.

Here was a woman who looked to be happy. And more—she looked to be content. Had a poet been inspired to pen just similes concerning her favor, he would have likened her full, clear eyes, with their white-encircled, gray irises, to moonflowers. With none of the goddesses whose traditional charms have become coldly classic would the discerning rhymester have compared her. She was purely Paradisaic, not Olympian. If you can imagine Eve, after the eviction, beguiling the flaming warriors and serenely re-entering the Garden, you will have her. Just so human, and still so harmonious with Eden seemed Mrs. Goodwin.

When her husband entered she looked up, and her lips curved and parted; her eyelids fluttered twice or thrice—a movement remindful (Poesy forgive us!) of the tail-wagging of a faithful dog—and a little ripple went through her like the commotion set up in a weeping willow by a puff of wind. Thus she ever acknowledged his coming, were it twenty times a day. If they who sometimes sat over their wine in Coralio, reshaping old, diverting stories of the madcap career of Isabel Guilbert, could have seen the wife of Frank Goodwin that afternoon in the estimable aura of her happy wifehood, they might have disbelieved, or have agreed to forget, those graphic annals of the life of the one for whom their president gave up his country and his honor.

"I have brought a guest to dinner," said Goodwin. "One Colonel Falcon, from San Mateo. He is come on government business. I do not think you will care to see him, so I prescribe for you one of those convenient and indisputable feminine headaches."

"He has come to inquire about the lost money, has he not?" asked Mrs. Goodwin, going on with her sketch.

"A good guess!" acknowledged Goodwin. "He has been holding an inquisition among the natives for three days. I am next on his list of witnesses, but as he feels shy about dragging one of Uncle Sam's subjects before him, he consents to give it the outward appearance of a social function. He will apply the torture over my own wine and provender."

"Has he found any one who saw the valise of money?"

"Not a soul. Even Madame Ortiz, whose eyes are so sharp for the sight of a revenue official, does not remember that there was any baggage."

Mrs. Goodwin laid down her brush and sighed.

"I am so sorry, Frank," she said, "that they are giving you so much trouble about the money. But we can't let them know about it, can we?"

"Not without doing our intelligence a great injustice," said Goodwin, with a smile and a shrug that he had picked up from the natives. "*Americano*, though I am, they would have me in the *calaboza* in half an hour if they knew we had appropriated that valise. No; we must appear as ignorant about the money as the other ignoramuses in Coralio."

"Do you think that this man they have sent suspects you?" she asked, with a little pucker of her brows.

"He'd better not," said the American, carelessly. "It's lucky that no one caught a sight of the valise except myself. As I was in the rooms when the shot was fired, it is not surprising that they should want to investigate my part in the affair rather closely. But there's no cause for alarm. This colonel is down on the list of events for a good dinner, with a dessert of American 'bluff' that will end the matter, I think."

Mrs. Goodwin rose and walked to the window. Goodwin followed and stood by her side. She leaned to him, and rested in the protection of his strength, as she had always rested since that dark night on which he had first made himself her tower of refuge. Thus they stood for a little while.

Straight through the lavish growth of tropical branch and leaf and vine that confronted them had been cunningly trimmed a vista, that ended at the cleared environs of Coralio, on the banks of the mangrove swamp. At the other end of the aërial tunnel they could see the grave and wooden headpiece that bore the name of the unhappy President Miraflores. From this window when the rains forbade the open, and from the green and shady slopes of Goodwin's fruitful lands when the skies were smiling, his wife was wont to look upon that grave with a gentle sadness that was now scarcely a mar to her happiness.

"I loved him so, Frank!" she said, "even after that terrible flight and its awful ending. And you have been so good to me, and have made me so happy. It has all grown into such a strange puzzle. If they were to find out that we got the money do you think they would force you to make the amount good to the government?"

"They would undoubtedly try," answered Goodwin. "You are right about its being a puzzle. And it must remain a puzzle to Falcon and all his countrymen until it solves itself. You and I, who know more than any one else, only know half of the solution. We must not let even a hint about this money get abroad. Let them come to the theory that the president concealed it in the mountains during his journey, or that he found means to ship it out of the country before he reached Coralio. I don't think that Falcon suspects me. He is making a close investigation, according to his orders, but he will find out nothing."

Thus they spake together. Had any one overheard or overseen them as they discussed the lost funds of Anchuria there would have been a second puzzle presented. For upon the faces and in the bearing of each of them was visible (if countenances are to be believed) Saxon honesty and pride and honorable thoughts. In Goodwin's steady eyes and firm lineaments, moulded into material shape by the inward spirit of kindness and generosity and courage, there was nothing reconcilable with his words.

As for his wife, physiognomy championed her even in the face of their accusive talk. Nobility was in her guise; purity was in her glance. The devotion that she manifested had not even the appearance of that feeling that now and then inspires a woman to share the guilt of her partner out of the pathetic greatness of her love. No, there was a discrepancy here between what the eye would have seen and the ear have heard.

Dinner was served to Goodwin and his guest in the *patio*, under cool foliage and flowers. The American begged the illustrious secretary to excuse the absence of Mrs. Goodwin, who was suffering, he said, from a headache brought on by a slight *calentura*.

After the meal they lingered, according to the custom, over their coffee and cigars. Colonel Falcon, with true Castilian delicacy, waited for his host to open the question that they had met to discuss. He had not long to wait. As soon as the cigars were lighted, the American cleared the way by inquiring whether the secretary's investigations in the town had furnished him with any clue to the lost funds.

"I have found no one yet," admitted Colonel Falcon, "who even had sight of the valise or the money. Yet I have persisted. It has been proven in the capital that President Miraflores set out from San Mateo with one hundred thousand dollars belonging to the government, accompanied by *Señorita* Isabel Guilbert, the opera singer. The Government, officially and personally, is loath to believe," concluded Colonel Falcon, with a smile, "that our last president's tastes would have permitted him to abandon on the route, as excess baggage, either of the desirable articles with which his flight was burdened."

"I suppose you would like to hear what I have to say about the affair," said Goodwin, coming directly to the point. "It will not require many words.

"On that night, with others of our friends here, I was keeping a lookout for the President, having been notified of his flight by a telegram in our national cipher from Englehart, one of our leaders in the capital. About ten o'clock that night I saw a man and a woman hurrying along the streets. They went to the Hotel de los Estranjeros, and engaged rooms. I followed them upstairs, leaving Estebán, who had come up, to watch outside. The barber had told me that he had shaved the beard from the President's face that night; therefore I was prepared, when I entered the rooms, to find him with a smooth face. When I apprehended him in the name of the people he drew a pistol and shot himself instantly. In a few minutes many officers and citizens were on the spot. I suppose you have been informed of the subsequent facts."

Goodwin paused. Losada's agent maintained an attitude of waiting, as if he expected a continuance.

"And now," went on the American, looking steadily into the eyes of the other man, and giving each word a deliberate emphasis, "you will oblige me by attending carefully to what I have to add. I saw no valise or receptacle of any kind, or any money belonging to the Republic of Anchuria. If President Miraflores decamped with any funds belonging to the treasury of this country, or to himself, or to any one else, I saw no trace of it in the house or elsewhere, at that time or at any other. Does that statement cover the ground of the inquiry you wished to make of me?"

Colonel Falcon bowed, and described a fluent curve with his cigar. His duty was performed. Goodwin was not to be disputed. He was a loyal supporter of the government, and enjoyed the full confidence of the new president. His rectitude had been the capital that had brought him fortune in Anchuria, just as it had formed the lucrative "graft" of Mellinger, the secretary of Miraflores.

"I thank you, *Señor* Goodwin," said Falcon, "for speaking plainly. Your word will be sufficient for the President. But, *Señor* Goodwin, I am instructed to pursue every clue that presents itself in this matter. There is one that I have not yet touched upon. Our friends in France, *señor*, have a saying, '*Cherchez la femme*,' when there is a mystery without a clue. But here we do not have to search. The woman who accompanied the late president in his flight must surely——"

"I must interrupt you there," interposed Goodwin. "It is true that when I entered the hotel for the purpose of intercepting President Miraflores I found a lady there. I must beg of you to remember that that lady is now my wife. I speak for her as I do for myself. She knows nothing of the fate of the valise or of the money that you are seeking. You will say to his excellency that I guarantee her innocence. I do not need to add to you, Colonel Falcon, that I do not care to have her questioned or disturbed."

Colonel Falcon bowed again.

"*Por supuesto*, no!" he cried. And to indicate that the inquiry was ended he added: "And now, *señor*, let me beg of you to show me that sea view from your *galería* of which you spoke. I am a lover of the sea."

In the early evening Goodwin walked back to the town with his guest, leaving him at the corner of the Calle Grande. As he was returning homeward one "Beelzebub" Blythe, with the air of a courtier and the outward aspect of a scarecrow, pounced upon him hopefully from the door of a *pulpería*.

Blythe had been re-christened "Beelzebub" as an acknowledgment of the greatness of his fall. Once in some distant Paradise Lost, he had foregathered with the angels of the earth. But Fate had hurled him headlong down to the tropics, where flamed in his bosom a fire that was seldom quenched. In Coralio they called him a beachcomber; but he was, in reality, a categorical idealist who strove to anamorphosize the dull verities of life by the means of brandy and rum. As Beelzebub, himself, might have held in his clutch with unwitting tenacity his harp or crown during his tremendous fall, so his namesake had clung to his gold-rimmed eyeglasses as the only souvenir of his lost estate. These he wore with impressiveness and distinction while he combed beaches and extracted toll from his friends. By some mysterious means he kept his drink-reddened face always smoothly shaven. For the rest he sponged gracefully upon whomsoever he could for enough to keep him pretty drunk, and sheltered from the rains and night dews.

"Hallo, Goodwin!" called the derelict, airily. "I was hoping I'd strike you. I wanted to see you particularly. Suppose we go where we can talk. Of course you know there's a chap down here looking up the money old Miraflores lost."

"Yes," said Goodwin, "I've been talking with him. Let's go into Espada's place. I can spare you ten minutes."

They went into the *pulpería* and sat at a little table upon stools with rawhide tops.

"Have a drink?" said Goodwin.

"They can't bring it too quickly," said Blythe. "I've been in a drought ever since morning. Hi—*muchacho!—el aguardiente por acá.*"

"Now, what do you want to see me about?" asked Goodwin, when the drinks were before them.

"Confound it, old man," drawled Blythe, "why do you spoil a golden moment like this with business? I wanted to see you—well, this has the preference." He gulped down his brandy, and gazed longingly into the empty glass.

"Have another?" suggested Goodwin.

"Between gentlemen," said the fallen angel, "I don't quite like your use of that word 'another.' It isn't quite delicate. But the concrete idea that the word represents is not displeasing."

The glasses were refilled. Blythe sipped blissfully from his, as he began to enter the state of a true idealist.

"I must trot along in a minute or two," hinted Goodwin. "Was there anything in particular?"

Blythe did not reply at once.

"Old Losada would make it a hot country," he remarked at length, "for the man who swiped that gripsack of treasury boodle, don't you think?"

"Undoubtedly, he would," agreed Goodwin calmly, as he rose leisurely to his feet. "I'll be running over to the house now, old man. Mrs. Goodwin is alone. There was nothing important you had to say, was there?"

"That's all," said Blythe. "Unless you wouldn't mind sending in another drink from the bar as you go out. Old Espada has closed my account to profit and loss. And pay for the lot, will you, like a good fellow?"

"All right," said Goodwin. "*Buenas noches.*"

"Beelzebub" Blythe lingered over his cups, polishing his eyeglasses with a disreputable handkerchief.

"I thought I could do it, but I couldn't," he muttered to himself after a time. "A gentleman can't blackmail the man that he drinks with."

THE ADMIRAL

SPILLED milk draws few tears from an Anchurian administration. Many are its lacteal sources; and the clocks' hands point forever to milking time. Even the rich cream skimmed from the treasury by the bewitched Miraflores did not cause the newly-installed patriots to waste time in unprofitable regrets. The government philosophically set about supplying the deficiency by increasing the import duties and by "suggesting" to wealthy private citizens that contributions according to their means would be considered patriotic and in order. Prosperity was expected to attend the reign of Losada, the new president. The ousted office-holders and military favorites organized a new "Liberal" party, and began to lay their plans for a resuccession. Thus the game of Anchurian politics began, like a Chinese comedy, to unwind slowly its serial length. Here and there Mirth peeps for an instant from the wings and illumines the florid lines.

A dozen quarts of champagne in conjunction with an informal sitting of the president and his cabinet led to the establishment of the navy and the appointment of Felipe Carrera as its admiral.

Next to the champagne the credit of the appointment belongs to Don Sabas Placido, the newly confirmed Minister of War.

The President had requested a convention of his cabinet for the discussion of questions politic and for the transaction of certain routine matters of state. The session had been signally tedious; the business and the wine prodigiously dry. A sudden, prankish humor of Don Sabas, impelling him to the deed, spiced the grave affairs of state with a whiff of agreeable playfulness.

In the dilatory order of business had come a bulletin from the coast department of Orilla del Mar reporting the seizure by the custom-house officers at the town of Coralio of the sloop *Estrella del Noche* and her cargo of drygoods, patent medicines, granulated sugar and three-star brandy. Also six Martini rifles and a barrel of American whisky. Caught in the act of smuggling, the sloop with its cargo was now, according to law, the property of the republic.

The Collector of Customs, in making his report, departed from the conventional forms so far as to suggest that the confiscated vessel be converted to the use of the government. The prize was the first capture to the credit of the department in ten years. The collector took opportunity to pat his department on the back. It often happened that government officers required transportation from point to point along the coast, and means were usually lacking. Furthermore, the sloop could be manned by a loyal crew and employed as a coast guard to discourage the pernicious art of smuggling. The collector also ventured to nominate one to whom the charge of the boat could be safely intrusted—a young man of Coralio, Felipe Carrera—not, be it understood, one of extreme wisdom, but loyal and the best sailor along the coast.

It was upon this hint that the Minister of War acted, executing a rare piece of drollery that so enlivened the tedium of executive session.

In the constitution of this small, maritime banana republic was a forgotten section that provided for the maintenance of a navy. This provision—with many other wiser ones—had lain inert since the establishment of the republic. Anchuria had no navy and had no use for one. It was characteristic of Don Sabas—a man at once merry, learned, whimsical and audacious—that he should have disturbed the dust of this musty and sleeping statute to increase the humor of the world by so much as a smile from his indulgent colleagues.

With delightful mock seriousness the Minister of War proposed the creation of a navy. He argued its need and the glories it might achieve with such gay and witty zeal that the travesty overcame with its humor even the swart dignity of President Losada himself.

The champagne was bubbling trickily in the veins of the mercurial statesmen. It was not the custom of the grave governors of Anchuria to enliven their sessions with a beverage so apt to cast a veil of disparagement over sober affairs. The wine had been a thoughtful compliment tendered by the agent of the Vesuvius Fruit Company as a token of amicable relations—and certain consummated deals —between that company and the republic of Anchuria.

The jest was carried to its end. A formidable, official document was prepared, encrusted with chromatic seals and jaunty with fluttering ribbons, bearing the florid signatures of state. This commission conferred up el Señor Don Felipe Carrera the title of Flag Admiral of the Republic of Anchuria. Thus within the space of a few minutes and the dominion of a dozen "extra dry," the country took its place among the naval powers of the world, and Felipe Carrera became entitled to a salute of nineteen guns whenever he might enter port.

The southern races are lacking in that particular kind of humor that finds entertainment in the defects and misfortunes bestowed by Nature. Owing to this defect in their constitution they are not moved to laughter (as are their northern brothers) by the spectacle of the deformed, the feeble-minded or the insane.

Felipe Carrera was sent upon earth with but half his wits. Therefore, the people of Coralio called him "*El pobrecito loco*"—"the poor little crazed one"— saying that God had sent but half of him to earth, retaining the other half.

A sombre youth, glowering, and speaking only at the rarest times, Felipe was but negatively "loco." On shore he generally refused all conversation. He seemed to know that he was badly handicapped on land, where so many kinds of understanding are needed; but on the water his only talent set him equal with most men. Few sailors whom God had carefully and completely made could handle a sailboat as well. Five points nearer the wind than even the best of them he could sail his sloop. When the elements raged and set other men to cowering, the deficiencies of Felipe seemed of little importance. He was a perfect sailor, if an imperfect man. He owned no boat, but worked among the crews of the schooners and sloops that skimmed the coast, trading and freighting fruit out to the steamers where there was no harbor. It was through his famous skill and boldness on the sea, as well as for the pity felt for his mental imperfections, that he was recommended by the collector as a suitable custodian of the captured sloop.

When the outcome of Don Sabas' little pleasantry arrived in the form of the imposing and preposterous commission, the collector smiled. He had not expected such prompt and overwhelming response to his recommendation. He despatched a *muchacho* at once to fetch the future admiral.

The collector waited in his official quarters. His office was in the Calle Grande, and the sea breezes hummed through its windows all day. The collector, in white linen and canvas shoes, philandered with papers on an antique desk. A parrot, perched on a pen rack, seasoned the official tedium with a fire of choice Castilian imprecations. Two rooms opened into the collector's. In one the clerical force of young men of variegated complexions transacted with glitter and parade their several duties. Through the open door of the other room could be seen a bronze babe, guiltless of clothing, that rollicked upon the floor. In a grass hammock a thin woman, tinted a pale lemon, played a guitar and swung contentedly in the breeze. Thus surrounded by the routine of his high duties and the visible tokens of agreeable domesticity, the collector's heart was further made happy by the power placed in his hands to brighten the fortunes of the "innocent" Felipe.

Felipe came and stood before the collector. He was a lad of twenty, not ill-favored in looks, but with an expression of distant and pondering vacuity. He wore white cotton trousers, down the seams of which he had sewed red stripes with some vague aim at military decoration. A flimsy blue shirt fell open at his throat; his feet were bare; he held in his hand the cheapest of straw hats from the States.

"Señor Carrera," said the collector, gravely, producing the showy commission, "I have sent for you at the President's bidding. This document that I present to you confers upon you the title of Admiral of this great republic, and gives you absolute command of the naval forces and fleet of our country. You may think, friend Felipe, that we have no navy—but yes! The sloop the *Estrella del Noche*, that my brave men captured from the coast smugglers, is to be placed under your command. The boat is to be devoted to the services of your country. You will be ready at all times to convey officials of the government to points along the coast where they may be obliged to visit. You will also act as a coast-guard to prevent, as far as you may be able, the crime of smuggling. You will uphold the honor and prestige of your country at sea, and endeavor to place Anchuria among the proudest naval powers of the world. These are your instructions as the Minister of War desires me to convey them to you. *Por Dios!* I do not know how all this is to be accomplished, for not one word did his letter contain in respect to a crew or to the expenses of this navy. Perhaps you are to provide a crew yourself, Señor Admiral—I do not know—but it is a very high honor that has descended upon you. I now hand you your commission. When you are ready for the boat I will give orders that she shall be made over into your charge. That is as far as my instructions go."

Felipe took the commission that the collector handed to him. He gazed through the open window at the sea for a moment, with his customary expression of deep but vain pondering. Then he turned without having spoken a word, and walked swiftly away through the hot sand of the street.

"*Pobrecito loco!*" sighed the collector; and the parrot on the pen racks screeched "Loco!—loco!—loco!"

The next morning a strange procession filed through the streets to the collector's office. At its head was the admiral of the navy. Somewhere Felipe had raked together a pitiful semblance of a military uniform—a pair of red trousers, a dingy blue short jacket heavily ornamented with gold braid, and an old fatigue cap that must have been cast away by one of the British soldiers in Belize and brought away by Felipe on one of his coasting voyages. Buckled around his waist was an ancient ship's cutlass contributed to his equipment by Pedro Lafitte, the baker, who proudly asserted its inheritance from his ancestor, the illustrious buccaneer. At the admiral's heels tagged his newly shipped crew—three grinning, glossy, black Caribs, bare to the waist, the sand spurting in showers from the spring of their naked feet.

Briefly and with dignity Felipe demanded his vessel of the collector. And now a fresh honor awaited him. The collector's wife, who played the guitar and read novels in the hammock all day, had more than a little romance in her placid yellow bosom. She had found in an old book an engraving of a flag that purported to be the naval flag of Anchuria. Perhaps it had so been designed by the founders of the nation; but, as no navy had ever been established, oblivion had claimed the flag. Laboriously with her own hands she had made a flag after the pattern—a red cross upon a blue-and-white ground. She presented it to Felipe with these words: "Brave sailor, this flag is of your country. Be true, and defend it with your life. Go you with God."

For the first time since his appointment the admiral showed a flicker of emotion. He took the silken emblem, and passed his hand reverently over its surface. "I am the admiral," he said to the collector's lady. Being on land he could bring himself to no more exuberant expression of sentiment. At sea with the flag at the masthead of his navy, some more eloquent exposition of feelings might be forthcoming.

Abruptly the admiral departed with his crew. For the next three days they were busy giving the *Estrella del Noche* a new coat of white paint trimmed with blue. And then Felipe further adorned himself by fastening a handful of brilliant parrot's plumes in his cap. Again he tramped with his faithful crew to the collector's office and formally notified him that the sloop's name had been changed to *El Nacional*.

During the next few months the navy had its troubles. Even an admiral is perplexed to know what to do without any orders. But none came. Neither did any salaries. *El Nacional* swung idly at anchor.

When Felipe's little store of money was exhausted he went to the collector and raised the question of finances.

"Salaries!" exclaimed the collector, with hands raised; "*Valgame Dios!* not one *centavo* of my own pay have I received for the last seven months. The pay of an admiral, do you ask? *Quién sabe?* Should it be less than three thousand *pesos? Mira!* you will see a revolution in this country very soon. A good sign of it is when the government calls all the time for *pesos, pesos, pesos,* and pays none out."

Felipe left the collector's office with a look almost of content on his sombre face. A revolution would mean fighting, and then the government would need his services. It was rather humiliating to be an admiral without anything to do, and have a hungry crew at your heels begging for *reales* to buy plantains and tobacco with.

When he returned to where his happy-go-lucky Caribs were waiting they sprang up and saluted, as he had drilled them to do.

"Come, *muchachos*," said the admiral; "it seems that the government is poor. It had no money to give us. We will earn what we need to live upon. Thus will we serve our country. Soon"—his heavy eyes almost lighted up—"it may gladly call upon us for help."

Thereafter *El Nacional* turned out with the other coast craft and became a wage-earner. She worked with the lighters freighting bananas and oranges out to the fruit steamers that could not approach nearer than a mile from the shore. Surely a self-supporting navy deserves red letters in the budget of any nation.

After earning enough at freighting to keep himself and his crew in provisions for a week Felipe would anchor the navy and hang about the little telegraph office, looking like one of the chorus of an insolvent comic opera troupe besieging the manager's den. A hope for orders from the capital was always in his heart. That his services as admiral had never been called into requirement hurt his pride and patriotism. At every call he would inquire, gravely and expectantly,

for despatches. The operator would pretend to make a search, and then reply:
"Not yet, it seems, *Señor el Almirante—poco tiempo!*"

Outside in the shade of the lime-trees the crew chewed sugar cane or slumbered,
well content to serve a country that was contented with so little service.

One day in the early summer the revolution predicted by the collector flamed
out suddenly. It had long been smoldering. At the first note of alarm the admiral of the navy force and fleet made all sail for a larger port on the coast
of a neighboring republic, where he traded a hastily collected cargo of fruit for
its value in cartridges for the five Martini rifles, the only guns that the navy
could boast. Then to the telegraph office sped the admiral. Sprawling in his
favorite corner, in his fast-decaying uniform, with his prodigious sabre distributed
between his red legs, he waited for the long-delayed, but now soon expected, orders.

"Not yet, *Señor el Almirante,*" the telegraph clerk would call to him—"*poco
tiempo!*"

At the answer the admiral would plump himself down with a great rattling of
scabbard to await the infrequent tick of the little instrument on the table.

"They will come," would be his unshaken reply; "I am the admiral."

THE FLAG PARAMOUNT

AT the head of the insurgent party appeared that Hector and learned Theban
of the southern republic, Don Sabás Placido. A traveller, a soldier, a poet, a
scientist, a statesman, and a connoisseur—the wonder was that he could content
himself with the petty, remote life of his native country.

"It is a whim of Placido's," said a friend who knew him well, "to take up
political intrigue. It is not otherwise than as if he had come upon a new *tempo*
in music, a new bacillus in the air, a new scent, or rhyme, or explosive. He
will squeeze this revolution dry of sensations, and a week afterward will forget
it, skimming the seas of the world in his brigantine to add to his already world-
famous collections. Collections of what? *Por Dios!* of everything from postage
stamps to prehistoric stone idols."

But, for a mere dilettante, the æsthetic Placido seemed to be creating a
lively row. The people admired him; they were fascinated by his brilliancy
and flattered by his taking an interest in so small a thing as his native country.
They rallied to the call of his lieutenants in the capital, where (somewhat contrary to arrangements) the army remained faithful to the government. There
was also lively skirmishing in the coast towns. It was rumored that the revolution was aided by the Vesuvius Fruit Company, the power that forever stood
with chiding smile and uplifted finger to keep Anchuria in the class of good
children. Two of its steamers, the *Traveler* and the *Salvador,* were known to
have conveyed insurgent troops from point to point along the coast.

As yet there had been no actual uprising in Coralio. Military law prevailed,
and the ferment was bottled for the time. And then came the word that everywhere the revolutionists were encountering defeat. In the capital the president's
forces triumphed; and there was a rumor that the leaders of the revolt had been
forced to fly, hotly pursued.

In the little telegraph office at Coralio there was always a gathering of officials
and loyal citizens, awaiting news from the seat of government. One morning

the telegraph key began clicking, and presently the operator called, loudly: "One telegram for *el Almirante*, Don Señor Felipe Carrera!"

There was a shuffling sound, a great rattling of tin scabbard, and the admiral, prompt at his spot of waiting, leaped across the room to receive it.

The message was handed to him. Slowly spelling it out, he found it to be his first official order—thus running:

Proceed immediately with your vessel to mouth of Rio Ruiz; transport beef and provisions to barracks at Alforan.

Martinez, General.

Small glory, to be sure, in this, his country's first call. But it had called, and joy surged in the admiral's breast. He drew his cutlass belt to another buckle hole, roused his dozing crew, and in a quarter of an hour *El Nacional* was tacking swiftly down coast in a stiff landward breeze.

The Rio Ruiz is a small river, emptying into the sea ten miles below Coralio. That portion of the coast is wild and solitary. Through a gorge in the Cordilleras rushes the Rio Ruiz, cold and bubbling, to glide, at last, with breadth and leisure, through an alluvial morass into the sea.

In two hours *El Nacional* entered the river's mouth. The banks were crowded with a disposition of formidable trees. The sumptuous undergrowth of the tropics overflowed the land, and drowned itself in the fallow waters. Silently the sloop entered there, and met a deeper silence. Brilliant with greens and ochres and floral scarlets, the umbrageous mouth of the Rio Ruiz furnished no sound or movement save of the sea-going water as it purled against the prow of the vessel. Small chance there seemed of wresting beef or provisions from that empty solitude.

The admiral decided to cast anchor, and, at the chain's rattle, the forest was stimulated to instant and resounding uproar. The mouth of the Rio Ruiz had only been taking a morning nap. Parrots and baboons screeched and barked in the trees; a whirring and a hissing and a booming marked the awakening of animal life; a dark blue bulk was visible for an instant, as a startled tapir fought his way through the vines.

The navy, under orders, hung in the mouth of the little river for hours. The crew served the dinner of shark's fin soup, plantains, crab gumbo and sour wine. The admiral, with a three-foot telescope, closely scanned the impervious foliage fifty yards away.

It was nearly sunset when a reverberating "hallo-o-o!" came from the forest to their left. It was answered; and three men, mounted upon mules, crashed through the tropic tangle to within a dozen yards of the river's bank. There they dismounted; and one, unbuckling his belt, struck each mule a violent blow with his sword scabbard, so that they, with a fling of heels, dashed back again into the forest.

Those were strange-looking men to be conveying beef and provisions. One was a large and exceedingly active man, of striking presence. He was of the purest Spanish type, with curling, gray-besprinkled, dark hair, blue, sparkling eyes, and the pronounced air of a *caballero grande*. The other two were small, brown-faced men, wearing white military uniforms, high riding boots and swords. The clothes of all were drenched, bespattered and rent by the thicket. Some stress of circumstance must have driven them, *diable à quatre*, through flood, mire and jungle.

"*O-hé! Señor Almirante*," called the large man. "Send to us your boat."

The dory was lowered, and Felipe, with one of the Caribs, rowed toward the left bank.

The large man stood near the water's brink, waist deep in the curling vines.

As he gazed upon the scarecrow figure in the stern of the dory a sprightly interest beamed upon his mobile face.

Months of wageless and thankless service had dimmed the admiral's splendor. His red trousers were patched and ragged. Most of the bright buttons and yellow braid were gone from his jacket. The visor of his cap was torn, and depended almost to his eyes. The admiral's feet were bare.

"Dear admiral," cried the large man, and his voice was like a blast from a horn, "I kiss your hands. I knew we could build upon your fidelity. You had our despatch—from General Martinez. A little nearer with your boat, dear Admiral. Upon these devils of shifting vines we stand with the smallest security."

Felipe regarded him with a stolid face.

"Provisions and beef for the barracks at Alforan," he quoted.

"No fault of the butchers, *Almirante mio*, that the beef awaits you not. But you are come in time to save the cattle. Get us aboard your vessel, señor, at once. You first, *caballeros—á priesa!* Come back for me. The boat is too small."

The dory conveyed the two officers to the sloop, and returned for the large man.

"Have you so gross a thing as food, good admiral?" he cried, when aboard. "And, perhaps, coffee? Beef and provisions! *Nombre de Dios!* a little longer and we could have eaten one of those mules that you, Colonel Rafael, saluted so feelingly with your sword scabbard at parting. Let us have food; and then we will sail—for the barracks at Alforan—no?"

The Caribs prepared a meal, to which the three passengers of *El Nacional* set themselves with famished delight. About sunset, as was its custom, the breeze veered and swept back from the mountains, cool and steady, bringing a taste of the stagnant lagoons and mangrove swamps that guttered the lowlands. The mainsail of the sloop was hoisted and swelled to it, and at that moment they heard shouts and a waxing clamor from the bosky profoundities of the shore.

"The butchers, my dear admiral," said the large man, smiling, "too late for the slaughter."

Further than his orders to his crew, the admiral was saying nothing. The topsail and jib were spread, and the sloop glided out of the estuary. The large man and his companions had bestowed themselves with what comfort they could about the bare deck. Belike, the thing big in their minds had been their departure from that critical shore; and now that the hazard was so far reduced their thoughts were loosed to the consideration of further deliverance. But when they saw the sloop turn and fly up coast again they relaxed, satisfied with the course the admiral had taken.

The large man sat at ease, his spirited blue eye engaged in the contemplation of the navy's commander. He was trying to estimate this sombre and fantastic lad, whose impenetrable stolidity puzzled him. Himself a fugitive, his life sought, and chafing under the smart of defeat and failure, it was characteristic of him to transfer instantly his interest to the study of a thing new to him. It was like him, too, to have conceived and risked all upon this last desperate and madcap scheme—this message to a poor, crazed *fanático* cruising about with his grotesque uniform and his farcical title. But his companions had been at their wits' end; escape had seemed incredible; and now he was pleased with the success of the plan they had called crack-brained and precarious.

The brief tropic twilight seemed to slide swiftly into the pearly splendor of a moonlight night. And now the lights of Coralio appeared, distributed against the darkening shore to their right. The admiral stood, silent, at the tiller; the Caribs, like black panthers, held the sheets, leaping noiselessly at his short commands. The three passengers were watching intently the sea before them, and when at length they came in sight of the bulk of a steamer lying a mile out from the town, with her lights radiating deep into the water, they held a sudden

voluble and close-headed converse. The sloop was speeding as if to strike midway between ship and shore.

The large man suddenly separated from his companions and approached the
scarecrow at the helm.

"My dear admiral," he said, "the government has been exceedingly remiss. I
feel all the shame for it that only its ignorance of your devoted service has prevented it from sustaining. An inexcusable oversight has been made. A vessel,
a uniform and a crew worthy of your fidelity shall be furnished you. But just
now, dear admiral, there is business of moment afoot. The steamer lying there
is the *Salvador.* I and my friends desire to be conveyed to her, where we are
sent on the government's business. Do us the favor to shape your course accordingly."

Without replying, the admiral gave a sharp command, and put the tiller hard
to port. *El Nacional* swerved, and headed straight as an arrow's course for the
shore.

"Do me the favor," said the large man, a trifle restively, "to acknowledge, at
least, that you catch the sound of my words." It was possible that the fellow
might be lacking in senses as well as intellect.

The admiral emitted a croaking, harsh laugh, and spake.

"They will stand you," he said, "with your face to a wall and shoot you dead.
That is the way they kill traitors. I knew you when you stepped into my boat.
I have seen your picture in a book. You are Sabas Placido, traitor to your
country. With your face to a wall. So, you will die. I am the admiral, and
I will take you to them. With your face to a wall. Yes."

Don Sabas half turned and waved his hand, with a ringing laugh, toward his
fellow fugitives. "To you, *caballeros,* I have related the history of that session
when we issued that O! so ridiculous commission. Of a truth our jest has been
turned against us. Behold the Frankenstein's monster we have created!"

Don Sabas glanced toward the shore. The lights of Coralio were drawing near.
He could see the beach, the warehouse of the *Bodega Nacional,* the long, low
cuartel occupied by the soldiers, and, behind that, gleaming in the moonlight, a
stretch of high adobe wall. He had seen men stood with their faces to that wall
and shot dead.

Again he addressed the extravagant figure at the helm.

"It is true," he said, "that I am fleeing the country. But, receive the assurance that I care very little for that. Courts and camps everywhere are open to
Sabas Placido. *Vaya!* what is this molehill of a republic—this pig's head of a
country—to a man like me? I am a *paisano* of everywhere. In Rome, in London, in Paris, in Vienna, you will hear them say: 'Welcome back, Don Sabas.'
Come!—*tonto*—baboon of a boy—admiral, whatever you call yourself, turn your
boat. Put us on board the *Salvador,* and here is your pay—five hundred *pesos*
in money of the *Estados Unidos*—more than your lying government will pay you
in twenty years."

Don Sabas pressed a plump purse against the youth's hand. The admiral
gave no heed to the words or the movement. Braced against the helm, he was
holding the sloop dead on her shoreward course. His dull face was lit almost
to intelligence by some inward conceit that seemed to afford him joy, and found
utterance in another parrot-like cackle.

"That is why they do it," he said—"so that you will not see the guns. They
fire—boom!—and you fall dead. With your face to the wall. Yes."

The admiral called a sudden order to his crew. The lithe, silent Caribs made
fast the sheets they held, and slipped down the hatchway into the hold of the
sloop. When the last one had disappeared, Don Sabas, like a big, brown leopard,
leaped forward, closed and fastened the hatch and stood, smiling.

"No rifles, if you please, dear admiral," he said. "It was a whimsey of mine once to compile a dictionary of the Carib *lengua*. So, I understood your order. Perhaps now you will——"

He cut short his words, for he heard the dull "swish" of iron scraping along tin. The admiral had drawn the cutlass of Pedro Lafitte, and was darting upon him. The blade descended, and it was only by a display of surprising agility that the large man escaped, with only a bruised shoulder, the glancing weapon. He was drawing his pistol as he sprang, and the next instant he shot the admiral down.

Don Sabas stooped over him, and rose again.

"In the heart," he said briefly. "*Señores*, the navy is abolished."

Colonel Rafael sprang to the helm, and the other officer hastened to loose the mainsail sheets. The boom swung round; *El Nacional* veered and began to tack industriously for the *Salvador*.

"Strike that flag, señor," called Colonel Rafael. "Our friends on the steamer will wonder why we are sailing under it."

"Well said," cried Don Sabas. Advancing to the mast he lowered the flag to the deck, where lay its too loyal supporter. Thus ended the Minister of War's little piece of after-dinner drollery, and by the same hand that began it.

Suddenly Don Sabas gave a great cry of joy, and ran down the slanting deck to the side of Colonel Rafael. Across his arm he carried the flag of the extinguished navy.

"*Mire! mire! señor*. Ah, *Dios!* Already can I hear that great bear of an *Oestreicher* shout, '*Du hast mein herz gebrochen!*' *Mire!* Of my friend, Herr Grunitz, of Vienna, you have heard me relate. That man has travelled to Ceylon for an orchid—to Patagonia for a headdress—to Benares for a slipper—to Mozambique for a spearhead to add to his famous collections. Thou knowest, also, *amigo* Rafael, that I have been a gatherer of curios. My collection of battle flags of the world's navies was the most complete in existence until last year. Then Herr Grunitz secured two, O! such rare specimens. One of a Barbary state, and one of the Makarooroos, a tribe on the west coast of Africa. I have not those, but they can be procured. But this flag, señor—do you know what it is? Name of God! do you know? See that red cross upon the blue-and-white ground! You never saw it before? *Seguarmente no*. It is the naval flag of your country. *Mire!* This rotten tub we stand upon is its navy—that dead cockatoo lying there was its commander—that stroke of cutlass and single pistol shot a sea battle. All a piece of absurd foolery, I grant you—but authentic. There has never been another flag like this, and there never will be another. No. It is unique in the whole world. Yes. Think of what that means to a collector of flags! Do you know, *Coronel mío*, how many golden crowns Herr Grunitz would give for this flag? Ten thousand, likely. Well, a hundred thousand would not buy it. Beautiful flag! Only flag! Little devil of a most heaven-born flag! *O-hé!* old grumbler beyond the ocean. Wait till Don Sabas comes again to the Königin Strasse. He will let you kneel and touch the folds of it with one finger. *O-hé!* old spectacled ransacker of the world!"

Forgotten was the impotent revolution, the danger, the loss, the gall of defeat. Possessed solely by the inordinate and unparalleled passion of the collector, he strode up and down the little deck, clasping to his breast with one hand the paragon of a flag. He snapped his fingers triumphantly toward the east. He shouted the paean to his prize in trumpet tones, as though he would make old Grunitz hear in his musty den beyond the sea.

They were waiting, on the *Salvador*, to welcome them. The sloop came close alongside the steamer where her sides were sliced almost to the lower deck for the loading of fruit. The sailors of the *Salvador* grappled and held her there.

Captain McLeod leaned over the side.

"Well, *señor*, the jig is up, I'm told."

"The jig is up?" Don Sabas looked perplexed for a moment. "That revolution—ah, yes!" With a shrug of his shoulders he dismissed the matter.

The captain learned of the escape and the imprisoned crew.

"Caribs?" he said; "no harm in them." He slipped down into the sloop and kicked loose the hasp of the hatch. The black fellows came tumbling up, sweating but grinning.

"Hey! black boys!" said the captain, in a dialect of his own; "you sabe, catchy boat and vamos back same place quick."

They saw him point to themselves, the sloop and Coralio. "Yas, yas!" they cried, with broader grins and many nods.

The four—Don Sabas, the two officers and the captain—moved to quit the sloop. Don Sabas lagged a little behind, looking at the still form of the late admiral, sprawled in his paltry trappings.

"*Pobrecito loco*," he said softly.

He was a brilliant cosmopolite and a *cognoscente* of high rank; but, after all, he was of the same race and blood and instinct as this people. Even as the simple *paisanos* of Coralio had said it, so said Don Sabas. Without a smile, he looked, and said, "The poor little crazed one!"

Stooping he raised the limp shoulders, drew the priceless and induplicable flag under them and over the breast, pinning it there with the diamond star of the Order of San Carlos that he took from the collar of his own coat.

He followed after the others, and stood with them upon the deck of the *Salvador*. The sailors that steadied *El Nacional* shoved her off. The jabbering Caribs hauled away at the rigging; the sloop headed for the shore.

And Herr Grunitz's collection of naval flags was still the finest in the world.

THE SHAMROCK AND THE PALM

ONE night when there was no breeze, and Coralio seemed closer than ever to the gratings of Avernus, five men were grouped about the door of the photograph establishment of Keogh and Clancy. Thus, in all the scorched and exotic places of the earth, Caucasians meet when the day's work is done to preserve the fulness of their heritage by the aspersion of alien things.

Johnny Atwood lay stretched upon the grass in the undress uniform of a Carib, and prated feebly of the cool water to be had in the cucumber-wood pumps of Dalesburg. Dr. Gregg, through the prestige of his whiskers and as a bribe against the relation of his imminent professional tales, was conceded the hammock that was swung between the door jamb and a calabash-tree. Keogh had moved out upon the grass a little table that held the instrument for burnishing completed photographs. He was the only busy one of the group. Industriously from between the cylinders of the burnisher rolled the finished depictments of Coralio's citizens. Blanchard, the French mining engineer, in his cool linen viewed the smoke of his cigarette through his calm glasses, impervious to the heat. Clancy sat on the steps, smoking his short pipe. His mood was the gossip's; the others were reduced, by the humidity, to the state of disability desirable in an audience.

Clancy was an American with an Irish diathesis and cosmopolitan proclivities. Many businesses had claimed him, but not for long. The roadster's blood was in his veins. The voice of the tintype was but one of the many callings that had wooed him upon so many roads. Sometimes he could be persuaded to oral

construction of his voyages into the informal and egregious. To-night there
were symptoms of divulgement in him.

"'Tis elegant weather for filibusterin'," he volunteered. "It reminds me of
the time I struggled to liberate a nation from the poisonous breath of a tyrant's
clutch. 'Twas hard work. 'Tis strainin' to the back and makes corns on the
hands."

"I didn't know you had ever lent your sword to an oppressed people," murmured Atwood, from the grass.

"I did," said Clancy; "and they turned it into a plowshare."

"What country was so fortunate as to secure your aid?" airily inquired
Blanchard.

"Where's Kamchatka?" asked Clancy, with seeming irrelevance.

"Why, off Siberia somewhere in the Arctic regions," somebody answered,
doubtfully.

"I thought that was the cold one," said Clancy, with a satisfied nod. "I'm
always gettin' the two names mixed. 'Twas Guatemala, then—the hot one—I've
been filibusterin' with. Ye'll find that country on the map. 'Tis in the district
known as the tropics. By the foresight of Providence, it lies on the coast so
the geography man could run the names of the towns off into the water. They're
an inch long, small type, composed of Spanish dialects, and, 'tis my opinion, of
the same system of syntax that blew up the *Maine*. Yes, 'twas that country I
sailed against, single-handed, and endeavored to liberate it from a tyrannical
government with a single-barreled pickaxe, unloaded at that. Ye don't understand, of course. 'Tis a statement demandin' elucidation and apologies.

"'Twas in New Orleans one morning about the first of June; I was standin'
down on the wharf, lookin' about at the ships in the river. There was a little
steamer moored right opposite me that seemed about ready to sail. The funnels
of it were throwin' out smoke, and a gang of roustabouts were carryin' aboard
a pile of boxes that was stacked up on the wharf. The boxes were about two
feet square, and somethin' like four feet long, and they seemed to be pretty heavy.

"I walked over, careless, to the stack of boxes. I saw one of them had been
broken in handlin'. 'Twas curiosity made me pull up the loose top and look
inside. The box was packed full of Winchester rifles. 'So, so,' says I to myself;
'somebody's gettin' a twist on the neutrality laws. Somebody's aidin' with munitions of war. I wonder where the popguns are goin'?'

"I heard somebody cough, and I turned around. There stood a little, round,
fat man with a brown face and white clothes, a first-class-looking little man,
with a four-karat diamond on his finger and his eye full of interrogations and
respects. I judged he was a kind of foreigner—may be from Russia or Japan
or the archipelagoes.

"'Hist!' says the round man, full of concealments and confidences. 'Will the
señor respect the discoveryments he has made, that the mans on the ship shall
not be acquaint? The señor will be a gentleman that shall not expose one
thing that by accident occur.'

"'Monseer,' says I—for I judged him to be a kind of Frenchman—'receive my
most exasperated assurances that your secret is safe with James Clancy. Furthermore, I will go so far as to remark, Veev la Liberty—veev it good and strong.
Whenever you hear of a Clancy obstructin' the abolishment of existin' governments you may notify me by return mail.'

"'The señor is good,' says the dark, fat man, smilin' under his black mustache.
'Wish you to come aboard my ship and drink of wine a glass.'

"Bein' a Clancy, in two minutes me and the foreigner man were seated at a
table in the cabin of the steamer, with a bottle between us. I could hear the
heavy boxes bein' dumped into the hold. I judged that cargo must consist of at
least 2,000 Winchesters. Me and the brown man drank the bottle of stuff, and

he called the steward to bring another. When you amalgamate a Clancy with the contents of a bottle you practically instigate secession. I had heard a good deal about these revolutions in them tropical localities, and I begun to want a hand in it.

"'You goin' to stir things up in your country ain't you, monseer?' says I, with a wink to let him know I was on.

"'Yes, yes,' said the little man, pounding his fist on the table. 'A change of the greatest will occur. Too long have the people been oppressed with the promises and the never-to-happen things to become. The great work it shall be carry on. Yes. Our forces shall in the capital city strike of the soonest. *Carrambos!*'

"'*Carrambos* is the word,' says I, beginning to invest myself with enthusiasm and more wine, 'likewise veeva, as I said before. May the shamrock of old—I mean the banana-vine or the pie-plant, or whatever the imperial emblem may be of your down-trodden country, wave forever.'

"'A thousand thank-yous,' says the round man, 'for your emission of amicable utterances. What our cause needs of the very most is mans who will work do, to lift it along. Oh, for one thousands strong, good mans to aid the General De Vega that he shall to his country bring those success and glory! It is hard—oh, so hard to find good mans to help in the work.'

"'Monseer,' says I, leanin' over the table and graspin' his hand, 'I don't know where your country is, but me heart bleeds for it. The heart of a Clancy was never deaf to the sight of an oppressed people. The family is filibusterers by birth, and foreigners by trade. If you can use James Clancy's arms and his blood in denudin' your shores of the tyrant's yoke they're yours to command.'

"General De Vega was overcome with joy to confiscate my condolence of his conspiracies and predicaments. He tried to embrace me across the table, but his fatness, and the wine that had been in the bottles, prevented. Thus was I welcomed into the ranks of filibustery. Then the general man told me his country had the name of Guatemala, and was the greatest nation laved by any ocean whatever anywhere. He looked at me with tears in his eyes, and from time to time he would emit the remark, 'Ah! big, strong, brave mans! That is what my country need.'

"General De Vega, as was the name by which he denounced himself, brought out a document for me to sign, which I did, makin' a fine flourish and curlycue with the tail of the 'y.'

"'Your passage-money,' says the general, business-like, 'shall from your pay be deduct.'

"''Twill not,' says I, haughty. 'I'll pay my own passage.' A hundred and eighty dollars I had in my inside pocket, and 'twas no common filibuster I was goin' to be, filibusterin' for me board and clothes.

"The steamer was to sail in two hours, and I went ashore to get some things together I'd need. When I came aboard I showed the general with pride the outfit. 'Twas a fine Chinchilla overcoat, Arctic overshoes, fur cap and earmuffs, with elegant fleece-lined gloves and woolen muffler.

"'*Carrambos!*' says the little general. 'What clothes are these that shall go to the tropic?' And then the little spalpeen laughs, and he calls the captain, and the captain calls the purser, and they pipe up the chief engineer, and the whole gang leans against the cabin and laughs at Clancy's wardrobe for Guatemala.

"I reflects a bit, serious, and asks the general again to denominate the terms by which his country is called. He tells me, and I see then that 'twas the t'other one, Kamchatka, I had in mind. Since then I've had difficulty in separatin' the two nations in name, climate and geographic disposition.

"I paid my passage—twenty-four dollars, first cabin—and ate at table with the officer crowd. Down on the lower deck was a gang of second-class passengers, about forty of them, seemin' to be Dagoes and the like. I wondered what so many of them were goin' along for.

"Well, then, in three days we sailed alongside that Guatemala. 'Twas a blue country, and not yellow as 'tis miscolored on the map. We landed at a town on the coast, where a train of cars was waitin' for us on a dinky little railroad. The boxes on the steamer were brought ashore and loaded on the cars. The gang of Dagoes got aboard, too, the general and me in the front car. Yes, me and General De Vega headed the revolution, as it pulled out of the seaport town. That train travelled about as fast as a policeman goin' to a riot. It penetrated the most conspicuous lot of fuzzy scenery ever seen outside a geography. We run some forty miles in seven hours, and the train stopped. There was no more railroad. 'Twas a sort of camp in a damp gorge full of wildness and melancholies. They was gradin' and choppin' out the forests ahead to continue the road. 'Here,' says I to myself, 'is the romantic haunt of the revolutionists. Here will Clancy, by the virtue that is in a superior race and the inculcation of Fenian tactics, strike a tremendous blow for liberty.'

"They unloaded the boxes from the train and begun to knock the tops off. From the first one that was open I saw General De Vega take the Winchester rifles and pass them around to a squad of morbid soldiery. The other boxes was opened next, and, believe me or not, divil another gun was to be seen. Every other box in the load was full of pickaxes and spades.

"And then—sorrow be upon them tropics—the proud Clancy and the dishonored Dagoes, each one of them, had to shoulder a pick or a spade, and march away to work on that dirty little railroad. Yes; 'twas that the Dagoes shipped for, and 'twas that the filibusterin' Clancy signed for, though unbeknownst to himself at the time. In after days I found out about it. It seems 'twas hard to get hands to work on that road. The intelligent natives of the country was too lazy to work. Indeed the saints know, 'twas unnecessary. By stretchin' out one hand, they could seize the most delicate and costly fruits of the earth, and, by stretchin' out the other, they could sleep for days at a time without hearin' a seven-o'clock whistle or the footsteps of the rent man upon the stairs. So, regular, the steamers travelled to the United States to seduce labor. Usually the imported spade-slingers died in two or three months from eatin' the over-ripe water and breathin' the violent tropical scenery. Wherefore they made them sign contracts for a year, when they hired them, and put an armed guard over the poor divils to keep them from runnin' away.

"'Twas thus I was double-crossed by the tropics through a family failin' of goin' out of the way to hunt disturbances.

"They gave me a pick, and I took it, meditatin' an insurrection on the spot; but there was the guards handlin' the Winchesters careless, and I come to the conclusion that discretion was the best part of filibusterin'. There was about a hundred of us in the gang startin' out to work, and the word was given to move. I steps out of the ranks and goes up to that General De Vega man, who was smokin' a cigar and gazin' upon the scene with satisfactions and glory. He smiles at me polite and devilish. 'Plenty work,' says he, 'for big, strong mans in Guatemala. Yes. T'irty dollars in the month. Good pay. Ah, yes. You strong, brave man. Bimeby we push those railroad in the capital very quick. They want you go work now. *Adios,* strong mans.'

"'Monseer,' says I, lingerin', 'will you tell a poor little Irishman this: When I set foot on your cockroachy steamer, and breathed liberal and revolutionary sentiments into your sour wine, did you think I was conspirin' to sling a pick on your contemptuous little railroad? And when you answered me with patriotic recitations, humping up the star-spangled cause of liberty, did you have meditations of reducin' me to the ranks of the stump-grubbin' Dagoes in the chain-gangs of your vile and grovelin' country?'

"The general man expanded his rotundity and laughed considerable. Yes, he laughed very long and loud, and I, Clancy, stood and waited.

"'Comical mans!' he shouts, at last. 'So you will kill me from the laughing. Yes; it is hard to find the brave, strong mans to aid my country. Revolutions? Did I speak of r-r-revolutions? Not one word. I say, big, strong mans is need in Guatemala. So. The mistake is of you. You have looked in those one box containing those gun for the guard. You think all boxes is contain gun? No. 'There is not war in Guatemala. But work? Yes. Good. T'irty dollar in the month. You shall shoulder one pickaxe, señor, and dig for the liberty and prosperity of Guatemala. Off to your work. The guard waits for you.'

"'Little, fat poodle dog of a brown man,' says I, quiet, but full of indignations and discomforts, 'things shall happen to you. Maybe not right away, but as soon as J. Clancy can formulate somethin' in the way of repartee.'

"The boss of the gang orders us to work. I tramps off with the Dagoes, and I hears the distinguished patriot and kidnapper laughin' hearty as we go.

"'Tis a sorrowful fact, for eight weeks I built railroads for that misbehavin' country. I filibustered twelve hours a day with a heavy pick and a spade, choppin' away the luxurious landscape that grew upon the right of way. We worked in swamps that smelled like there was a leak in the gas mains, trampin' down a fine assortment of the most expensive hot-house plants and vegetables. The scene was tropical beyond the wildest imagination of the geography man. The trees was all sky-scrapers; the under-brush was full of needles and pins; there was monkeys jumpin' around and crocodiles and pink-tailed mockin'-birds, and ye stood knee-deep in the rotten water and grabbed roots for the liberation of Guatemala. Of nights we would build smudges in camp to discourage the mosquitoes, and sit in the smoke, with the guards pacin' all around us. There was two hundred men workin' on the road—mostly Dagoes, nigger-men, Spanish-men and Swedes. Three or four were Irish.

"One old man named Halloran—a man of Hibernian entitlements and discretions, explained it to me. He had been workin' on the road a year. Most of them died in less than six months. He was dried up to gristle and bone and shook with chills every third night.

"'When you first come,' says he, 'ye think ye'll leave right away. But they hold out your first month's pay for your passage over, and by that time the tropics has its grip on ye. Ye're surrounded by a ragin' forest full of disreputable beasts—lions and baboons and anacondas—waitin' to devour ye. The sun strikes ye hard, and melts the marrow in your bones. Ye get similar to the lettuce-eaters the poetry-book speaks about. Ye forget the elevated sintiments of life, such as patriotism, revenge, disturbances of the peace and the dacint love of a clane shirt. Ye do your work, and ye swallow the kerosene ile and rubber pipestems dished up to ye by the Dago cook for food. Ye light your pipeful, and say to yourilf, "Nixt week I'll break away," and ye go to sleep and call yersilf a liar, for ye know ye'll never do it.'

"'Who is this general man,' asks I, 'that calls himself De Vega?'

"''Tis the man,' says Halloran, 'who is tryin' to complete the finishin' of the railroad. 'Twas the project of a private corporation, but it was busted, and then the government took it up. De Vegy is a big politician, and wants to be president. The people want the railroad completed, as they're taxed mighty on account of it. The De Vegy man is pushin' it along as a campaign move.'

"''Tis not my way,' says I, 'to make threats against any man, but there's an account to be settled between the railroad man and James O'Dowd Clancy.'

"''Twas that way I thought, mesilf, at first,' Halloran says, with a big sigh, 'until I got to be a lettuce-eater. The fault's wid these tropics. They rejuices a man's system. 'Tis a land, as the poet says, "Where it always seems to be after dinner." I does me work and smokes me pipe and sleeps. There's little else in life, anyway. Ye'll get that way yersilf, mighty soon. Don't be harborin' any sintiments at all, Clancy.'

"'I can't help it,' says I; 'I'm full of 'em. I enlisted in the revolutionary army of this dark country in good faith to fight for its liberty, honors and silver candlesticks; instead of which I am set to amputatin' its scenery and grubbin' its roots. 'Tis the general man will have to pay for it.'

"Two months I worked on that railroad before I found a chance to get away. One day a gang of us was sent back to the end of the completed line to fetch some picks that had been sent down to Port Barrios to be sharpened. They were brought on a hand-car, and I noticed, when I started away, that the car was left there on the track.

"That night, about twelve, I woke up Halloran and told him my scheme.

"'Run away?' says Halloran. 'Good Lord, Clancy, do ye mean it? Why, I ain't got the nerve. It's too chilly, and I ain't slept enough. Run away? I told you, Clancy, I've eat the lettuce. I've lost my grip. 'Tis the tropics that's done it. 'Tis like the poet says: "Forgotten are our friends that we have left behind; in the hollow lettuce-land we will live and lay reclined." You better go on, Clancy, I'll stay, I guess. It's too early and cold, and I'm sleepy.'

"So I had to leave Halloran. I dressed quiet, and slipped out of the tent we were in. When the guard came along I knocked him over, like a ninepin, with a green cocoanut I had, and made for the railroad. I got on that hand-car and made it fly. 'Twas yet a while before daybreak when I saw the lights of Port Barrios about a mile away. I stopped the hand-car there and walked to the town. I stepped inside the corporations of that town with care and hesitations. I was not afraid of the army of Guatemala, but me soul quaked at the prospect of a hand-to-hand struggle with its employment bureau. 'Tis a country that hires its help easy and keeps 'em long. Sure I can fancy Missis America and Missis Guatemala passin' a bit of gossip some fine, still night across the mountains. 'Oh, dear,' says Missis America, 'and it's a lot of trouble I'm havin' ag'in with the help, señora, ma'am.' 'Laws, now!' says Missis Guatemala, 'you don't say so, ma'am! Now, mine never think of leavin' me—te-he! ma'am,' snickers Missis Guatemala.

"I was wonderin' how I was goin' to move away from them tropics without bein' hired again. Dark as it was, I could see a steamer ridin' in the harbor, with smoke emergin' from her stacks. I turned down a little grass street that run down to the water. On the beach I found a little brown nigger-man just about to shove off in a skiff.

"'Hold on, Sambo,' says I, 'savve English?'

"'Heap plenty, yes,' says he, with a pleasant grin.

"'What steamer is that?' I asks him, 'and where is it going? And what's the news, and the good word and the time of day?'

"'That steamer the *Conchita*,' said the brown man, affable and easy, rollin' a cigarette. 'Him come from New Orleans for load banana. Him got load last night. I think him sail in one, two hour. Verree nice day we shall be goin' to have. You hear some talkee 'bout big battle, maybe so? You think catchee General De Vega, señor? Yes? No?'

"'How's that, Sambo?' says I. 'Big battle? What battle? Who wants catchee General De Vega? I've been up at my old gold mines in the interior for a couple of months, and haven't heard any news.'

"'Oh,' says the nigger-man, proud to speak the English, 'verree great revolution in Guatemala one week ago. General De Vega, him try be president. Him raise armee—one—five—ten thousand mans for fight at the government. Those one government send five—forty—hundred thousand soldier to suppress revolution. They fight big battle yesterday at Lomagrande—that about nineteen or fifty mile in the mountain. That government soldier wheep General De Vega—

oh, most bad. Five hundred—nine hundred—two thousand of his mans is kill. That revolution is smash suppress—bust—very quick. General De Vega, him r-r-run away fast on one big mule. Yes, *carrambos!* The general, him r-r-run away, and his armee is kill. That government soldier, they try to find General De Vega verree much. They want catchee him for shoot. You think they catchee that general, señor?'

" 'Saints grant it!' says I. ' 'Twould be the judgment of Providence for settin' the warlike talent of a Clancy to gradin' the tropics with a pick and shovel. But 'tis not so much a question of insurrections now, me little man, as 'tis of the hired-man problem. 'Tis anxious I am to resign a situation of responsibility and trust with the white wings department of your great and degraded country. Row me in your little boat out to that steamer, and I'll give ye five dollars— sinker pacers—sinker pacers,' says I, reducin' the offer to the language and denomination of the tropic dialects.

" '*Cinco pesos*,' repeats the little man. 'Five dollee, you give?'

" 'Twas not such a bad little man. He had hesitations at first, sayin' that passengers leavin' the country had to have papers and passports, but at last he took me out alongside the steamer.

"Day was just breakin' as we struck her, and there wasn't a soul to be seen on board. The water was very still, and the nigger-man gave me a lift from the boat, and I climbed onto the steamer where her side was sliced to the deck for loadin' fruit. The hatches was open, and I looked down and saw the cargo of bananas that filled the hold to within six feet of the top. I thinks to myself, 'Clancy, you better go as a stowaway. It's safer. The steamer men might hand you back to the employment bureau. The tropic'll get you, Clancy, if you don't watch out.'

"So I jumps down easy among the bananas and digs out a hole to hide in among the bunches. In an hour or so I could hear the engines goin', and feel the steamer rockin', and I knew we were off to sea. They left the hatches open for ventilation, and pretty soon it was light enough in the hold to see fairly well. I got to feelin' a bit hungry, and thought I'd have a light fruit lunch, by way of refreshment. I creeped out of the hole I'd made and stood up straight. Just then I saw another man crawl up about ten feet away and reach out and skin a banana and stuff it into his mouth. 'Twas a dirty man, black-faced and ragged and disgraceful of aspect. Yes, the man was a ringer for the pictures of the fat Weary Willie in the funny papers. I looked again, and saw it was my general man—De Vega, the great revolutionist, mule-rider and pick-axe importer. When he saw me the general hesitated with his mouth filled with banana and his eyes the size of cocoanuts.

" 'Hist!' I says. 'Not a word, or they'll put us off and make us walk. "Veev la Liberty!" ' I adds, copperin' the sentiment by shovin' a banana into the source of it. I was certain the general wouldn't recognize me. The nefarious work of the tropics had left me lookin' different. There was half an inch of roan whiskers coverin' me face, and me costume was a pair of blue overalls and a red shirt.

" 'How you come in the ship, señor?' asked the general as soon as he could speak.

" 'By the back door—whist!' says I. ' 'Twas a glorious blow for liberty we struck,' I continues; 'but we was overpowered by numbers. Let us accept our defeat like brave men and eat another banana.'

" 'Were you in the cause of liberty fightin', señor?' says the general, sheddin' tears on the cargo.

" 'To the last,' says I. ' 'Twas I led the last desperate charge against the minions of the tyrant. But it made them mad, and we was forced to retreat. 'Twas I, general, procured the mule upon which you escaped. Could you give that ripe bunch a little boost this way, general? It's a bit out of my reach. Thanks.'

"'Say you so, brave patriot?' said the general, again weepin'. 'Ah, *Dios!* And I have not the means to reward your devotion. Barely did I my life bring away. *Carrambos!* what a devil's animal was that mule, señor! Like ships in one storm was I dashed about. The skin on myself was ripped away with the thorns and vines. Upon the bark of a hundred trees did that beast of the infernal bump, and cause outrage to the legs of mine. In the night to Port Barrios I came. I dispossess myself of that mountain of mule and hasten along the water shore. I find a little boat to be tied. I launch myself and row to the steamer. I cannot see any mans on board, so I climbed one rope which hang at the side. I then myself hide in the bananas. Surely, I say, if the ship captains view me, they shall throw me again to those Guatemala. Those things are not good. Guatemala will shoot General De Vega. Therefore, I am hide and remain silent. Life itself is glorious. Liberty, it is pretty good; but so good as life I do not think.'

"Three days, as I said, was the trip to New Orleans. The general man and me got to be cronies of the deepest dye. Bananas we ate until they were distasteful to the sight and an eyesore to the palate, but to bananas alone was the bill of fare reduced. At night I crawls out, careful, on the lower deck, and gets a bucket of fresh water.

"That General De Vega was a man inhabited by an engorgement of words and sentences. He added to the monotony of the voyage by divestin' himself of conversation. He believed I was a revolutionist of his own party, there bein', as he told me, a good many Americans and other foreigners in its ranks. 'Twas a braggart and a conceited little gabbler it was, though he considered himself a hero. 'Twas on himself he wasted all his regrets at the failin' of his plot. Not a word did the little balloon have to say about the other misbehavin' idiots that had been shot, or run themselves to death in his revolution.

"The second day out he was feelin' pretty braggy and uppish for a stowed-away conspirator that owed his existence to a mule and stolen bananas. He was tellin' me about the great railroad he had been buildin', and he relates what he calls a comic incident about a fool Irishman he inveigled from New Orleans to sling a pick on his little morgue of a narrow-gauge line. 'Twas sorrowful to hear the little, dirty general tell the opprobrious story of how he put salt upon the tail of that reckless and silly bird, Clancy. Laugh, he did, hearty and long. He shook with laughin', the black-faced rebel and outcast, standin' neck-deep in bananas, without friends or country.

"'Ah, señor,' he snickers, 'to the death you would have laughed at that drollest Irish. I say to him: "Strong, big mans is need very much in Guatemala." "I will blows strike for your down-pressed country," he say. "That shall you do," I tell him. Ah! it was an Irish so comic. He sees one box break upon the wharf that contain for the guard a few gun. He think there is gun in all the box. But that is all pick-axe. Yes. Ah! señor, could you the face of that Irish have seen when they set him to the work!'

"'Twas thus the ex-boss of the employment bureau contributed to the tedium of the trip with merry jests and anecdote. But now and then he would weep upon the bananas and make oration about the lost cause of liberty and the mule.

"'Twas a pleasant sound when the steamer bumped against the pier in New Orleans. Pretty soon we heard the pat-a-pat of hundreds of bare feet, and the Dago gang that unloads the fruit jumped on the deck and down into the hold. Me and the general worked a while at passin' up the bunches, and they thought we were part of the gang. After about an hour we managed to slip off the steamer onto the wharf.

"'Twas a great honor on the hands of an obscure Clancy, havin' the entertainment of the representative of a great foreign filibusterin' power. I first bought for the general and myself many long drinks and things to eat that were not bananas. The general man trotted along at my side, leavin' all the arrange- ments to me. I led him up to Lafayette Square and set him on a bench in the little park. Cigarettes I had bought for him, and he humped himself down on the seat like a little fat, contented hobo. I look him over as he sets there, and what I see pleases me. Brown by nature and instinct, he is now brindled with dirt and dust. Praise to the mule, his clothes is mostly strings and flaps. Yes, the looks of the general man is agreeable to Clancy.

"I ask him, delicate, if, by any chance, he brought away anybody's money with him from Guatemala. He sighs and bumps his shoulders against the bench. Not a cent. All right. Maybe, he tells me, some of his friends in the tropic outfit will send him funds later. The general was as clear a case of no visible means as I ever saw.

"I told him not to move from the bench, and then I went up to the corner of Poydras and Carondelet. Along there is O'Hara's beat. In five minutes along comes O'Hara, a big, fine man, red-faced, with shinin' buttons, swingin' his club. 'Twould be a fine thing for Guatemala to move into O'Hara's precinct. 'Twould be a fine bit of recreation for Danny to suppress revolutions and uprisin's once or twice a week with his club.

"'Is 5046 workin' yet, Danny?' says I, walkin' up to him.

"'Overtime,' says O'Hara, lookin' over me suspicious. 'Want some of it?'

"Fifty-forty-six is the celebrated city ordinance authorizin' arrest, conviction, and imprisonment of persons that succeed in concealin' their crimes from the police.

"'Don't ye know Jimmy Clancy?' says I. 'Ye pink-gilled monster.' So, when O'Hara recognized me beneath the scandalous exterior bestowed upon me by the tropics, I backed him into a doorway and told him what I wanted, and why I wanted it. 'All right, Jimmy,' says O'Hara. 'Go back and hold the bench. I'll be along in ten minutes.'

"In that time O'Hara strolled through Lafayette Square and spied two Weary Willies disgracin' one of the benches. In ten minutes more J. Clancy and General De Vega, late candidate for the presidency of Guatemala, was in the station house. The general is badly frightened, and calls upon me to proclaim his dis- tinguishments and rank.

"'The man,' says I to the police, 'used to be a railroad man. He's on the bum now. 'Tis a little bughouse he is, on account of losin' his job.'

"'*Carrambos!*' says the general, fizzin' like a little soda-water fountain, 'you fought, señor, with my forces in my native country. Why do you say the lies? You shall say I am the General De Vega, one soldier, one *caballero*——'

"'Railroader,' says I again. 'On the hog. No good. Been livin' for three days on stolen bananas. Look at him. Ain't that enough?'

"Twenty-five dollars or sixty days, was what the recorder gave the general. He didn't have a cent, so he took the time. They let me go, as I knew they would, for I had money to show, and O'Hara spoke for me. Yes; sixty days he got. 'Twas just so long that I slung a pick for the great country of Kam— Guatemala."

Clancy paused. The bright starlight showed a reminiscent look of happy con- tent on his seasoned features. Keogh leaned in his chair and gave his partner a slap on his thinly-clad back that sounded like the crack of the surf on the sands.

"Tell 'em, you divil," he chuckled, "how you got even with the tropical general in the way of agricultural maneuvrings."

"Havin' no money," concluded Clancy, with unction, "they set him to work his fine out with a gang from the parish prison clearing Ursulines Street. Around the corner was a saloon decorated genially with electric fans and cool merchandise. I made that me headquarters, and every fifteen minutes I'd walk around and take a look at the little man filibusterin' with a rake and shovel. 'Twas just such a hot broth of a day as this has been. And I'd call at him 'Hey, monseer!' and he'd look at me black, with the damp showin' through his shirt in places.

" 'Fat, strong mans,' says I to General De Vega, 'is needed in New Orleans. Yes. To carry on the good work. Carrambos! Erin go bragh!' "

THE REMNANTS OF THE CODE

BREAKFAST in Coralio was at eleven. Therefore the people did not go to market early. The little wooden market-house stood on a patch of short-trimmed grass, under the vivid green foliage of a bread-fruit tree.

Thither one morning the venders leisurely convened, bringing their wares with them. A porch or platform six feet wide encircled the building, shaded from the mid-morning sun by the projecting, grass-thatched roof. Upon this platform the venders were wont to display their goods—newly-killed beef, fish, crabs, fruit of the country, cassava, eggs, *dulces* and high, tottering stacks of native tortillas as large around as the sombrero of a Spanish grandee.

But on this morning they whose stations lay on the seaward side of the market-house, instead of spreading their merchandise formed themselves into a softly jabbering and gesticulating group. For there upon their space of the platform was sprawled, asleep, the unbeautiful figure of "Beelzebub" Blythe. He lay upon a ragged strip of cocoa matting, more than ever a fallen angel in appearance. His suit of coarse flax, soiled, bursting at the seams, crumpled into a thousand diversified wrinkles and creases, inclosed him absurdly, like the garb of some effigy that had been stuffed in sport and thrown there after indignity had been wrought upon it. But firmly upon the high bridge of his nose reposed his gold-rimmed glasses, the surviving badge of his ancient glory.

The sun's rays, reflecting quiveringly from the rippling sea upon his face, and the voices of the marketmen woke "Beelzebub" Blythe. He sat up, blinking, and leaned his back against the wall of the market. Drawing a blighted silk handkerchief from his pocket, he assiduously rubbed and burnished his glasses. And while doing this he became aware that his bedroom had been invaded, and that polite brown and yellow men were beseeching him to vacate in favor of their market stuff.

If the señor would have the goodness—a thousand pardons for bringing to him molestation—but soon would come the *compradores* for the day's provisions—surely they had ten thousand regrets at disturbing him!

In this manner they expanded to him the intimation that he must clear out and cease to clog the wheels of trade.

Blythe stepped from the platform with the air of a prince leaving his canopied couch. He never quite lost that air, even at the lowest point of his fall. It is clear that the college of good breeding does not necessarily maintain a chair of morals within its walls.

Blythe shook out his wry clothing, and moved slowly up the Calle Grande through the hot sand. He moved without a destination in his mind. The little town was languidly stirring to its daily life. Golden-skinned babies tumbled over one another in the grass. The sea breeze brought him appetite, but nothing to satisfy it. Throughout Coralio were its morning odors—those from the

heavily fragrant tropical flowers and from the bread baking in the outdoor ovens
of clay and the pervading smoke of their fires. Where the smoke cleared, the
crystal air, with some of the efficacy of faith, seemed to remove the mountains
almost to the sea, bringing them so near that one might count the scarred glades
on their wooded sides. The light-footed Caribs were swiftly gliding to their
tasks at the waterside. Already along the bosky trails from the banana groves
files of horses were slowly moving, concealed, except for their nodding heads and
plodding legs, by the bunches of green-golden fruit heaped upon their backs. On
doorsills sat women combing their long, black hair and calling, one to another,
across the narrow thoroughfares. Peace reigned in Coralio—arid and bald peace;
but still peace.

On that bright morning when Nature seemed to be offering the lotus on the
Dawn's golden platter "Beelzebub" Blythe had reached rock bottom. Further
descent seemed impossible. That last night's slumber in a public place had done
for him. As long as he had had a roof to cover him there had remained, un-
bridged, the space that separates a gentleman from the beasts of the jungle and
the fowls of the air. But now he was little more than a whimpering oyster led
to be devoured on the sands of a Southern sea by the artful walrus, Circumstance,
and the implacable carpenter, Fate.

To Blythe money was now but a memory. He had drained his friends of all
that their good-fellowship had to offer; then he had squeezed them to the last
drop of their generosity; and at the last, Aaron-like, he had smitten the rock
of their hardening bosoms for the scattering, ignoble drops of Charity itself.

He had exhausted his credit to the last *real*. With the minute keenness of the
shameless sponger he was aware of every source in Coralio from which a glass
of rum, a meal, or a piece of silver could be wheedled. Marshalling each such
source in his mind, he considered it with all the thoroughness and penetration
that hunger and thirst lent him for the task. All his optimism failed to thresh
a grain of hope from the chaff of his postulations. He had played out the
game. That one night in the open had shaken his nerves. Until then there
had been left to him at least a few grounds upon which he could base his un-
blushing demands upon his neighbors' stores. Now he must beg instead of
borrowing. The most brazen sophistry could not dignify by the name of "loan"
the coin contemptuously flung to a beach-comber who slept on the bare boards of
the public market.

But on this morning no beggar would have more thankfully received a charitable coin, for the demon thirst had him by the throat—the drunkard's matutinal
thirst that requires to be slaked at each morning station on the road to Tophet.

Blythe walked slowly up the street, keeping a watchful eye for any miracle
that might drop manna upon him in his wilderness. As he passed the popular
eating house of Madama Vasquez, Madama's boarders were just sitting down to
freshly-baked bread, *aguacates*, pines and delicious coffee that sent forth odorous
guarantee of its quality upon the breeze. Madama was serving; she turned her
shy, stolid, melancholy gaze for a moment out the window; she saw Blythe, and
her expression turned more shy and embarrassed. "Beelzebub" owed her twenty
pesos. He bowed as he had once bowed to less embarrassed dames to whom he
owed nothing, and passed on.

Merchants and their clerks were throwing open the solid wooden doors of their
shops. Polite but cool were the glances they cast upon Blythe as he lounged
tentatively by with the remains of his old jaunty air; for they were his creditors
almost without exception.

At the little fountain in the *plaza* he made an apology for a toilet with his
wetted handkerchief. Across the open square filed the dolorous line of friends
of the prisoners in the *calaboza*, bearing the morning meal of the immured. The

food in their hands aroused small longing in Blythe. It was drink that his soul craved, or money to buy it.

In the streets he met many with whom he had been friends and equals, and whose patience and liberality he had gradually exhausted. Willard Geddie and Paula cantered past him with the coolest of nods, returning from their daily horseback ride along the old Indian road. Keogh passed him at another corner, whistling cheerfully and bearing a prize of newly-laid eggs for the breakfast of himself and Clancy. The jovial scout of Fortune was one of Blythe's victims who had plunged his hand oftenest into his pocket to aid him. But now it seemed that Keogh, too, had fortified himself against further invasions. His curt greeting and the ominous light in his full gray eye quickened the steps of "Beelzebub," whom desperation had almost incited to attempt an additional "loan."

Three drinking shops the forlorn one next visited in succession. In all of these his money, his credit, and his welcome had long since been spent; but Blythe felt that he would have fawned in the dust at the feet of an enemy that morning for one draught of *aguardiente*. In two of the *pulperías* his courageous petition for drink was met with a refusal so polite that it stung worse than abuse. The third establishment had acquired something of American methods; and here he was seized bodily and cast out upon his hands and knees.

This physical indignity caused a singular change in the man. As he picked himself up and walked away, an expression of absolute relief came upon his features. The specious and conciliatory smile that had been graven there was succeeded by a look of calm and sinister resolve. "Beelzebub" had been floundering in the sea of improbity, holding by a slender life-line to the respectable world that had cast him overboard. He must have felt that with this ultimate shock the line had snapped, and have experienced the welcome ease of the drowning swimmer who has ceased to struggle.

Blythe walked to the next corner and stood there while he brushed the sand from his garments and repolished his glasses.

"I've got to do it—oh, I've got to do it," he told himself, aloud. "If I had a quart of rum I believe I could stave it off yet—for a little while. But there's no more rum for—'Beelzebub,' as they call me. By the flames of Tartarus! if I'm to sit at the right hand of Satan somebody has got to pay the court expenses. You'll have to pony up, Mr. Frank Goodwin. You're a good fellow; but a gentleman must draw the line at being kicked into the gutter. Blackmail isn't a pretty word, but it's the next station on the road I'm travelling."

With purpose in his steps Blythe now moved rapidly through the town by way of its landward environs. He passed through the squalid quarters of the improvident negroes and on beyond the picturesque shacks of the poorer *mestizos*. From many points along his course he could see, through the umbrageous glades, the house of Frank Goodwin on its wooded hill. And as he crossed the little bridge over the lagoon he saw the old Indian, Galvez, scrubbing at the wooden slab that bore the name of Miraflores. Beyond the lagoon the lands of Goodwin began to slope gently upward. A grassy road, shaded by a munificent and diverse array of tropical flora, wound from the edge of an outlying banana grove to the dwelling. Blythe took this road with long and purposeful strides.

Goodwin was seated on his coolest gallery, dictating letters to his secretary, a sallow and capable native youth. The household adhered to the American plan of breakfast; and that meal had been a thing of the past for the better part of an hour.

The castaway walked to the steps, and flourished a hand.

"Good morning, Blythe," said Goodwin, looking up. "Come in and have a chair. Anything I can do for you?"

"I want to speak to you in private."

Goodwin nodded at his secretary, who strolled out under a mango tree and lit a cigarette. Blythe took the chair that he had left vacant.

"I want some money," he began, doggedly.

"I'm sorry," said Goodwin, with equal directness, "but you can't have any. You're drinking yourself to death, Blythe. Your friends have done all they could to help you to brace up. You won't help yourself. There's no use furnishing you with money to ruin yourself with any longer."

"Dear man," said Blythe, tilting back his chair, "it isn't a question of social economy now. It's past that. I like you, Goodwin; and I've come to stick a knife between your ribs. I was kicked out of Espada's saloon this morning; and Society owes me reparation for my wounded feelings."

"I didn't kick you out."

"No; but in a general way you represent Society; and in a particular way you represent my last chance. I've had to come down to it, old man—I tried to do it a month ago when Losada's man was here turning things over; but I couldn't do it then. Now it's different. I want a thousand dollars, Goodwin; and you have to give it to me."

"Only last week," said Goodwin, with a smile, "a silver dollar was all you were asking for."

"An evidence," said Blythe, flippantly, "that I was still virtuous—though under heavy pressure. The wages of sin should be something higher than a *peso* worth forty-eight cents. Let's talk business. I am the villain in the third act; and I must have my merited, if only temporary, triumph. I saw you collar the late president's valiseful of boodle. Oh, I know it's blackmail; but I'm liberal about the price. I know I'm a cheap villain—one of the regular sawmill-drama kind—but you're one of my particular friends, and I don't want to stick you hard."

"Suppose you go into the details," suggested Goodwin, calmly arranging his letters on the table.

"All right," said "Beelzebub." "I like the way you take it. I despise histrionics; so you will please prepare yourself for the facts without any red fire, calcium or grace notes on the saxophone.

"On the night that His Fly-by-night Excellency arrived in town I was very drunk. You will excuse the pride with which I state that fact; but it was quite a feat for me to attain that desirable state. Somebody had left a cot out under the orange trees in the yard of Mádama Ortiz's hotel. I stepped over the wall, laid down upon it, and fell asleep. I was awakened by an orange that dropped from the tree upon my nose; and I laid there for awhile cursing Sir Isaac Newton, or whoever it was that invented gravitation, for not confining his theory to apples.

"And then along came Mr. Miraflores and his true-love with the treasury in a valise, and went into the hotel. Next you hove in sight, and held a pow-wow with the tonsorial artist who insisted upon talking shop after hours. I tried to slumber again; but once more my rest was disturbed—this time by the noise of the popgun that went off upstairs. Then that valise came crashing down into an orange tree just above my head; and I arose from my couch, not knowing when it might begin to rain Saratoga trunks. When the army and the constabulary began to arrive, with their medals and decorations hastily pinned to their pajamas, and their snickersnees drawn, I crawled into the welcome shadow of a banana plant. I remained there for an hour, by which time the excitement and the people had cleared away. And then, my dear Goodwin—excuse me—I saw you sneak back and pluck that ripe and juicy valise from the orange tree. I followed you, and saw you take it to your own house. A hundred-thousand-dollar crop from one orange tree in a season about breaks the record of the fruit-growing industry.

"Being a gentleman at that time, of course I never mentioned the incident to any one. But this morning I was kicked out of a saloon, my code of honor is all out at the elbows, and I'd sell my mother's prayer-book for three fingers of *aguardiente*. I'm not putting on the screws hard. It ought to be worth a thousand to you for me to have slept on that cot through the whole business without waking up and seeing anything."

Goodwin opened two more letters, and made memoranda in pencil on them. Then he called "Manuel!" to his secretary, who came, spryly.

"The *Ariel*—when does she sail?" asked Goodwin.

"Señor," answered the youth, "at three this afternoon. She drops down-coast to Punta Soledad to complete her cargo of fruit. From there she sails for New Orleans without delay."

"*Bueno!*" said Goodwin. "These letters may wait yet awhile."

The secretary returned to his cigarette under the mango tree.

"In round numbers," said Goodwin, facing Blythe squarely, "how much money do you owe in this town, not including the sums you have 'borrowed' from me?"

"Five hundred—at a rough guess," answered Blythe, lightly.

"Go somewhere in the town and draw up a schedule of your debts," said Goodwin. "Come back here in two hours, and I will send Manuel with the money to pay them. I will also have a decent outfit of clothing ready for you. You will sail on the *Ariel* at three. Manuel will accompany you as far as the deck of the steamer. There he will hand you one thousand dollars in cash. I suppose that we needn't discuss what you will be expected to do in return."

"Oh, I understand," piped Blythe, cheerily. "I was asleep all the time on the cot under Madama Ortiz's orange trees; and I shake off the dust of Coralio forever. I'll play fair. No more of the lotus for me. Your proposition is O. K. You're a good fellow, Goodwin; and I let you off light. I'll agree to everything. But in the meantime—I've a devil of a thirst on, old man——"

"Not a *centavo*," said Goodwin, firmly, "until you are on board the *Ariel*. You would be drunk in thirty minutes if you had money now."

But he noticed the blood-streaked eyeballs, the relaxed form, and the shaking hands of "Beelzebub"; and he stepped into the dining room through the low window, and brought out a glass and a decanter of brandy.

"Take a bracer, anyway, before you go," he proposed, even as a man to the friend whom he entertains.

"Beelzebub" Blythe's eyes glistened at the sight of the solace for which his soul burned. To-day for the first time his poisoned nerves had been denied their steadying dose; and their retort was a mounting torment. He grasped the decanter and rattled its crystal mouth against the glass in his trembling hand. He flushed the glass, and then stood erect, holding it aloft for an instant. For one fleeting moment he held his head above the drowning waves of his abyss. He nodded easily at Goodwin, raised his brimming glass and murmured a "health" that men had used in his ancient Paradise Lost. And then so suddenly that he spilled the brandy over his hand, he set down his glass, untasted.

"In two hours," his dry lips muttered to Goodwin, as he marched down the steps and turned his face toward the town.

In the edge of the cool banana grove "Beelzebub" halted, and snapped the tongue of his belt buckle into another hole.

"I couldn't do it," he explained, feverishly, to the waving banana fronds. "I wanted to, but I couldn't. A gentleman can't drink with the man that he blackmails."

SHOES

JOHN DE GRAFFENREID ATWOOD ate of the lotus, root, stem, and flower. The tropics gobbled him up. He plunged enthusiastically into his work, which was to try to forget Rosine.

Now, they who dine on the lotus rarely consume it plain. There is a sauce *au diable* that goes with it; and the distillers are the chefs who prepare it. And on Johnny's menu card it read "brandy." With a bottle between them, he and Billy Keogh would sit on the porch of the little consulate at night and roar out great, indecorous songs, until the natives, slipping hastily past, would shrug a shoulder and mutter things to themselves about the "*Americanos diablos.*"

One day Johnny's *mozo* brought the mail and dumped it on the table. Johnny leaned from his hammock, and fingered the four or five letters dejectedly. Keogh was sitting on the edge of the table chopping lazily with a paper knife at the legs of a centipede that was crawling among the stationery. Johnny was in that phase of lotus-eating when all the world tastes bitter in one's mouth.

"Same old thing!" he complained. "Fool people writing for information about the country. They want to know all about raising fruit, and how to make a fortune without work. Half of 'em don't even send stamps for a reply. They think a consul hasn't anything to do but write letters. Slit those envelopes for me, old man, and see what they want. I'm feeling too rocky to move."

Keogh, acclimated beyond all possibility of ill-humor, drew his chair to the table with smiling compliance on his rose-pink countenance, and began to slit open the letters. Four of them were from citizens in various parts of the United States who seemed to regard the consul at Coralio as a cyclopædia of information. They asked long lists of questions, numerically arranged, about the climate, products, possibilities, laws, business chances, and statistics of the country in which the consul had the honor of representing his own government.

"Write 'em, please, Billy," said that inert official, "just a line, referring them to the latest consular report. Tell 'em the State Department will be delighted to furnish the literary gems. Sign my name. Don't let your pen scratch, Billy; it'll keep me awake."

"Don't snore," said Keogh, amiably, "and I'll do your work for you. You need a corps of assistants, anyhow. Don't see how you ever get out a report. Wake up a minute!—here's one more letter—it's from your own town, too—Dalesburg."

"That so?" murmured Johnny, showing a mild obligatory interest. "What's it about?"

"Postmaster writes," explained Keogh. "Says a citizen of the town wants some facts and advice from you. Says the citizen has an idea in his head of coming down where you are and opening a shoe store. Wants to know if you think the business would pay. Says he's heard of the boom along this coast, and wants to get in on the ground floor."

In spite of the heat and his bad temper, Johnny's hammock swayed with his laughter. Keogh laughed too; and the pet monkey on the top shelf of the bookcase chattered in shrill sympathy with the ironical reception of the letter from Dalesburg.

"Great bunions!" exclaimed the consul. "Shoe store! What'll they ask about next, I wonder? Overcoat factory, I reckon. Say, Billy—of our 3,000 citizens, how many do you suppose ever had on a pair of shoes?"

Keogh reflected judicially.

"Let's see—there's you and me and——"

"Not me," said Johnny, promptly and incorrectly, holding up a foot encased in a disreputable deerskin *zapato.* "I haven't been a victim to shoes in months."

"But you've got 'em, though," went on Keogh. "And there's Goodwin and Blanchard and Geddie and old Lutz and Doc Gregg and that Italian that's agent for the banana company, and there's old Delgado—no; he wears sandals. And, oh, yes; there's Madama Ortiz, 'what kapes the hotel'—she had on a pair of red slippers at the *baile* the other night. And Miss Pasa, her daughter, that went to school in the States—she brought back some civilized notions in the way of footgear. And there's the *comandante's* sister that dresses up her feet on feast-days—and Mrs. Geddie, who wears a two with a Castilian instep—and that's about all the ladies. Let's see—don't some of the soldiers at the *cuartel*—no: that's so; they're allowed shoes only when on the march. In barracks they turn their little toeses out to grass."

" 'Bout right," agreed the consul. "Not over twenty out of the three thousand ever felt leather on their walking arrangements. Oh, yes; Coralio is just the town for an enterprising shoe store—that doesn't want to part with its goods. Wonder if old Patterson is trying to jolly me! He always was full of things he called jokes. Write him a letter, Billy. I'll dictate it. We'll jolly him back a few."

Keogh dipped his pen, and wrote at Johnny's dictation. With many pauses, filled in with smoke and sundry travellings of the bottle and glasses, the following reply to the Dalesburg communication was perpetrated:

Mr. Obadiah Patterson,
    Dalesburg, Ala.
Dear Sir: In reply to your favor of July 2d, I have the honor to inform you that, according to my opinion, there is no place on the habitable globe that presents to the eye stronger evidence of the need of a first-class shoe store than does the town of Coralio. There are 3,000 inhabitants in the place, and not a single shoe store! The situation speaks for itself. This coast is rapidly becoming the goal of enterprising business men, but the shoe business is one that has been sadly overlooked or neglected. In fact, there are a considerable number of our citizens actually without shoes at present.

Besides the want above mentioned, there is also a crying need for a brewery, a college of higher mathematics, a coal yard, and a clean and intellectual Punch and Judy show. I have the honor to be, sir,

> Your Obt. Servant,
> John de Graffenreid Atwood,
>   *U. S. Consul at Coralio.*

P. S.—Hello! Uncle Obadiah. How's the old burg racking along? What would the government do without you and me? Look out for a green-headed parrot and a bunch of bananas soon, from your old friend

> Johnny.

"I throw in that postscript," explained the consul, "so Uncle Obadiah won't take offence at the official tone of the letter! Now, Billy, you get that correspondence fixed up, and send Pancho to the post-office with it. The *Ariadne* takes the mail out to-morrow if they make up that load of fruit to-day."

The night programme in Coralio never varied. The recreations of the people were soporific and flat. • They wandered about, barefoot and aimless, speaking lowly and smoking cigar or cigarette. Looking down on the dimly lighted ways one seemed to see a threading maze of brunette ghosts tangled with a procession of insane fire-flies. In some houses the thrumming of lugubrious guitars added to the depression of the *triste* night. Giant tree-frogs rattled in the foliage as loudly as the end man's "bones" in a minstrel troupe. By nine o'clock the streets were almost deserted.

Not at the consulate was there often a change of bill. Keogh would come there nightly, for Coralio's one cool place with the little seaward porch of that official residence.

The brandy would be kept moving; and before midnight sentiment would begin to stir in the heart of the self-exiled consul. Then he would relate to Keogh the story of his ended romance. Each night Keogh would listen patiently to the tale, and be ready with untiring sympathy.

"But don't you think for a minute"—thus Johnny would always conclude his woeful narrative—"that I'm grieving about that girl, Billy. I've forgotten her. She never enters my mind. If she were to enter that door right now, my pulse wouldn't gain a beat. That's all over long ago."

"Don't I know it?" Keogh would answer. "Of course you've forgotten her. Proper thing to do. Wasn't quite O. K. of her to listen to the knocks that—er—Dink Pawson kept giving you."

"Pink Dawson!"—a world of contempt would be in Johnny's tones—"Poor white trash! That's what he was. Had five hundred acres of farming land, though; and that counted. Maybe I'll have a chance to get back at him some day. The Dawsons weren't anybody. Everybody in Alabama knows the Atwoods. Say, Billy—did you know my mother was a De Graffenreid?"

"Why, no," Keogh would say; "is that so?" He had heard it some three hundred times.

"Fact. The De Graffenreids of Hancock County. But I never think of that girl any more, do I, Billy?"

"Not for a minute, my boy," would be the last sounds heard by the conqueror of Cupid.

At this point Johnny would fall into a gentle slumber, and Keogh would saunter out to his own shack under the calabash tree at the edge of the plaza.

In a day or two the letter from the Dalesburg postmaster and its answer had been forgotten by the Coralio exiles. But on the 26th day of July the fruit of the reply appeared upon the tree of events.

The *Andador*, a fruit steamer that visited Coralio regularly, drew into the offing and anchored. The beach was lined with spectators while the quarantine doctor and the custom-house crew rowed out to attend to their duties.

An hour later Billy Keogh lounged into the consulate, clean and cool in his linen clothes, and grinning like a pleased shark.

"Guess what?" he said to Johnny, lounging in his hammock.

"Too hot to guess," said Johnny, lazily.

"Your shoe-store man's come," said Keogh, rolling the sweet morsel on his tongue, "with a stock of goods big enough to supply the continent as far down as Terra del Fuego. They're carting his cases over to the custom-house now. Six barges full they brought ashore and have paddled back for the rest. Oh, ye saints in glory! won't there be regalements in the air when he gets onto the joke and has an interview with Mr. Consul? It'll be worth nine years in the tropics just to witness that one joyful moment."

Keogh loved to take his mirth easily. He selected a clean place on the matting and lay upon the floor. The walls shook with his enjoyment. Johnny turned half over and blinked.

"Don't tell me," he said, "that anybody was fool enough to take that letter seriously."

"Four-thousand-dollar stock of goods!" gasped Keogh, in ecstasy. "Talk about coals to Newcastle! Why didn't he take a ship-load of palm-leaf fans to Spitzbergen while he was about it? Saw the old codger on the beach. You ought to have been there when he put on his specs and squinted at the five hundred or so barefooted citizens standing around."

"Are you telling the truth, Billy?" asked the consul, weakly.

"Am I? You ought to see the buncoed gentleman's daughter he brought along. Looks! She makes the brick-dust señoritas here look like tar-babies."

"Go on," said Johnny, "if you can stop that asinine giggling. I hate to see a grown man make a laughing hyena of himself."

"Name is Hemstetter," went on Keogh. "He's a—— Hello! what's the matter now?"

Johnny's moccasined feet struck the floor with a thud as he wriggled out of his hammock.

"Get up, you idiot," he said, sternly, "or I'll brain you with this inkstand. That's Rosine and her father. Gad! what a drivelling idiot old Patterson is! Get up, here, Billy Keogh, and help me. What the devil are we going to do? Has all the world gone crazy?"

Keogh rose and dusted himself. He managed to regain a decorous demeanor.

"Situation has got to be met, Johnny," he said, with some success at seriousness. "I didn't think about its being your girl until you spoke. First thing to do is to get them comfortable quarters. You go down and face the music, and I'll trot out to Goodwin's and see if Mrs. Goodwin won't take them in. They've got the decentest house in town."

"Bless you, Billy!" said the consul. "I knew you wouldn't desert me. The world's bound to come to an end, but maybe we can stave it off for a day or two."

Keogh hoisted his umbrella and set out for Goodwin's house. Johnny put on his coat and hat. He picked up the brandy bottle, but set it down again without drinking, and marched bravely down to the beach.

In the shade of the custom-house walls he found Mr. Hemstetter and Rosine surrounded by a mass of gaping citizens. The customs officers were ducking and scraping, while the captain of the *Andador* interpreted the business of the new arrivals. Rosine looked healthy and very much alive. She was gazing at the strange scenes around her with amused interest. There was a faint blush upon her round cheek as she greeted her old admirer. Mr. Hemstetter shook hands with Johnny in a very friendly way. He was an oldish, impractical man— one of that numerous class of erratic business men who are forever dissatisfied, and seeking a change.

"I am very glad to see you, John—may I call you John?" he said. "Let me thank you for your prompt answer to our postmaster's letter of inquiry. He volunteered to write to you on my behalf. I was looking about for something different in the way of a business in which the profits would be greater. I had noticed in the papers that this coast was receiving much attention from investors. I am extremely grateful for your advice to come. I sold out everything that I possess, and invested the proceeds in as fine a stock of shoes as could be bought in the North. You have a picturesque town here, John. I hope business will be as good as your letter justifies me in expecting."

Johnny's agony was abbreviated by the arrival of Keogh, who hurried up with the news that Mrs. Goodwin would be much pleased to place rooms at the disposal of Mr. Hemstetter and his daughter. So there Mr. Hemstetter and Rosine were at once conducted and left to recuperate from the fatigue of the voyage, while Johnny went down to see that the cases of shoes were safely stored in the customs warehouse pending their examination by the officials. Keogh, grinning like a shark, skirmished about to find Goodwin, to instruct him not to expose to Mr. Hemstetter the true state of Coralio as a shoe market until Johnny had been given a chance to redeem the situation, if such a thing were possible.

That night the consul and Keogh held a desperate consultation on the breezy porch of the consulate.

"Send 'em back home," began Keogh, reading Johnny's thoughts.

"I would," said Johnny, after a little silence; "but I've been lying to you, Billy."

"All right about that," said Keogh, affably.

"I've told you hundreds of times," said Johnny, slowly, "that I had forgotten that girl, haven't I?"

"About three hundred and seventy-five," admitted the monument of patience.

"I lied," repeated the consul, "every time. I never forgot her for one minute. I was an obstinate ass for running away just because she said 'No' once. And I was too proud a fool to go back. I talked with Rosine a few minutes this evening up at Goodwin's. I found out one thing. You remember that farmer fellow who was always after her?"

"Dink Pawson?" asked Keogh.

"Pink Dawson. Well, he wasn't a hill of beans to her. She says she didn't believe a word of the things he told her about me. But I'm sewed up now, Billy. That tomfool letter we sent ruined whatever chance I had left. She'll despise me when she finds out that her old father has been made the victim of a joke that a decent school boy wouldn't have been guilty of. Shoes! Why he couldn't sell twenty pairs of shoes in Coralio if he kept store here for twenty years. You put a pair of shoes on one of these Caribs or Spanish brown boys and what'd he do? Stand on his head and squeal until he'd kicked 'em off. None of 'em ever wore shoes and they never will. If I send 'em back home I'll have to tell the whole story, and what'll she think of me? I want that girl worse than ever, Billy, and now when she's in reach I've lost her forever because I tried to be funny when the thermometer was at 102."

"Keep cheerful," said the optimistic Keogh. "And let 'em open the store. I've been busy myself this afternoon. We can stir up a temporary boom in foot-gear anyhow. I'll buy six pairs when the doors open. I've been around and seen all the fellows and explained the catastrophe. They'll all buy shoes like they was centipedes. Frank Goodwin will take cases of 'em. The Geddies want about eleven pairs between 'em. Clancy is going to invest the savings of weeks, and even old Doc Gregg wants three pairs of alligator-hide slippers if they've got any tens. Blanchard got a look at Miss Hemstetter; and as he's a Frenchman, no less than a dozen pairs will do for him."

"A dozen customers," said Johnny, "for a $4,000 stock of shoes! It won't work. There's a big problem here to figure out. You go home, Billy, and leave me alone. I've got to work at it all by myself. Take that bottle of Three-star along with you—no, sir; not another ounce of booze for the United States consul. I'll sit here to-night and pull out the think stop. If there's a soft place on this proposition anywhere I'll land on it. If there isn't there'll be another wreck to the credit of the gorgeous tropics."

Keogh left, feeling that he could be of no use. Johnny laid a handful of cigars on a table and stretched himself in a steamer chair. When the sudden daylight broke, silvering the harbor ripples, he was still sitting there. Then he got up, whistling a little tune, and took his bath.

At nine o'clock he walked down to the dingy little cable office and hung for half an hour over a blank. The result of his application was the following message, which he signed and had transmitted at a cost of $33:

To PINKNEY DAWSON,
   Dalesburg, Ala.
Draft for $100 comes to you next mail. Ship me immediately 500 pounds stiff, dry cockleburrs. New use here in arts. Market price twenty cents pound. Further orders likely. Rush.

SHIPS

WITHIN a week a suitable building had been secured in the Calle Grande, and Mr. Hemstetter's stock of shoes arranged upon their shelves. The rent of the store was moderate; and the stock made a fine showing of neat white boxes, attractively displayed.

Johnny's friends stood by him loyally. On the first day Keogh strolled into the store in a casual kind of way about once every hour, and bought shoes. After he had purchased a pair each of extension soles, congress gaiters, button kids, low-quartered calfs, dancing pumps, rubber boots, tans of various hues, tennis shoes and flowered slippers, he sought out Johnny to be prompted as to names of other kinds that he might inquire for. The other English-speaking residents also played their parts nobly by buying often and liberally. Keogh was grand marshal, and made them distribute their patronage, thus keeping up a fair run of custom for several days.

Mr. Hemstetter was gratified by the amount of business done thus far; but expressed surprise that the natives were so backward with their custom.

"Oh, they're awfully shy," explained Johnny, as he wiped his forehead nervously. "They'll get the habit pretty soon. They'll come with a rush when they do come."

One afternoon Keogh dropped into the consul's office, chewing an unlighted cigar thoughtfully.

"Got anything up your sleeve?" he inquired of Johnny. "If you have it's about time to show it. If you can borrow some gent's hat in the audience, and make a lot of customers for an idle stock of shoes come out of it, you'd better spiel. The boys have all laid in enough foot-wear to last 'em ten years; and there's nothing doing in the shoe store but dolcy far nienty. I just came by there. Your venerable victim was standing in the door, gazing through his specs at the bare toes passing by his emporium. The natives here have got the true artistic temperament. Me and Clancy took eighteen tin-types this morning in two hours. There's been but one pair of shoes sold all day. Blanchard went in and bought a pair of fur-lined house-slippers because he thought he saw Miss Hemstetter go into the store. I saw him throw the slippers into the lagoon afterwards."

"There's a Mobile fruit steamer coming in to-morrow or next day," said Johnny. "We can't do anything until then."

"What are you going to do—try to create a demand?"

"Political economy isn't your strong point," said the consul, impudently. "You can't create a demand. But you can create a necessity for a demand. That's what I am going to do."

Two weeks after the consul sent his cable, a fruit steamer brought him a huge, mysterious brown bale of some unknown commodity. Johnny's influence with the custom-house people was sufficiently strong for him to get the goods turned over to him without the usual inspection. He had the bale taken to the consulate and snugly stowed in the back room.

That night he ripped open a corner of it and took out a handful of the cockleburrs. He examined them with the care with which a warrior examines his arms before he goes forth to battle for his lady-love and life. The burrs were the ripe August product, as hard as filberts, and bristling with spines as tough and sharp as needles. Johnny whistled softly a little tune, and went out to find Billy Keogh.

Later in the night, when Coralio was steeped in slumber, he and Billy went forth into the deserted streets with their coats bulging like balloons. All up and down the Calle Grande they went, sowing the sharp burrs carefully in the sand, along the narrow sidewalks, in every foot of grass between the silent houses. And then they took the side streets and byways, missing none. No place where the foot of man, woman or child might fall was slighted. Many trips they made to and from the prickly hoard. And then, nearly at the dawn, they laid themselves down to rest calmly, as great generals do after planning a victory according to the revised tactics, and slept, knowing that they had sowed with the accuracy of Satan sowing tares and the perseverance of Paul planting.

With the rising sun came the purveyors of fruits and meats, and arranged their wares in and around the little market-house. At one end of the town near the seashore the market-house stood; and the sowing of the burrs had not been carried that far. The dealers waited long past the hour when their sales usually began. None came to buy. "*Qué hay?*" they began to exclaim, one to another.

At their accustomed time, from every 'dobe and palm hut and grass-thatched shack and dim *patio* glided women—black women, brown women, lemon-colored women, women dun and yellow and tawny. They were the marketers starting to purchase the family supply of cassava, plantains, meat, fowls, and tortillas. Décolleté they were and bare-armed and bare-footed, with a single skirt reaching below the knee. Stolid and ox-eyed, they stepped from their doorways into the narrow paths or upon the soft grass of the streets.

The first to emerge uttered ambiguous squeals, and raised one foot quickly. Another step and they sat down, with shrill cries of alarm, to pick at the new and painful insects that had stung them upon the feet. "*Qué picadores diablos!*" they screeched to one another across the narrow ways. Some tried the grass instead of the paths, but there they were also stung and bitten by the strange little prickly balls. They plumped down in the grass, and added their lamentations to those of their sisters in the sandy paths. All through the town was heard the plaint of the feminine jabber. The venders in the market still wondered why no customers came.

Then men, lords of the earth, came forth. They, too, began to hop, to dance, to limp, and to curse. They stood stranded and foolish, or stooped to pluck at the scourge that attacked their feet and ankles. Some loudly proclaimed the pest to be poisonous spiders of an unknown species.

And then the children ran out for their morning romp. And now to the uproar was added the howls of limping infants and cockleburred childhood. Every minute the advancing day brought forth fresh victims.

Doña Maria Castillas y Buenventura de las Casas stepped from her honored doorway, as was her daily custom, to procure fresh bread from the *panadería* across the street. She was clad in a skirt of flowered yellow satin, a chemise of ruffled linen, and wore a purple mantilla from the looms of Spain. Her lemon-tinted feet, alas! were bare. Her progress was majestic, for were not her ancestors hidalgos of Aragon? Three steps she made across the velvety grass, and set her aristocratic sole upon a bunch of Johnny's burrs. Doña Maria Castillas y Buenventura de las Casas emitted a yowl even as a wild-cat. Turning about, she fell upon hands and knees, and crawled—ay, like a beast of the field she crawled back to her honorable door-sill.

Don Señor Ildefonso Federico Valdazar, *Juez de la Paz*, weighing twenty stone, attempted to convey his bulk to the *pulpería* at the corner of the plaza in order to assuage his matutinal thirst. The first plunge of his unshod foot into the cool grass struck a concealed mine. Don Ildefonso fell like a crumpled cathedral, crying out that he had been fatally bitten by a deadly scorpion. Everywhere were the shoeless citizens hopping, stumbling, limping, and picking from their feet the venomous insects that had come in a single night to harass them.

The first to perceive the remedy was Estebán Delgado, the barber, a man of travel and education. Sitting upon a stone, he plucked burrs from his toes, and made oration:

"Behold, my friend, these bugs of the devil! I know them well. They soar through the skies in swarms like pigeons. These are the dead ones that fell during the night. In Yucatan I have seen them as large as oranges. Yes! There they hiss like serpents, and have wings like bats. It is the shoes—the shoes that one needs! *Zapatos—zapatos para mi!*"

Estebán hobbled to Mr. Hemstetter's store, and bought shoes. Coming out, he swaggered down the street with impunity, reviling loudly the bugs of the devil. The suffering ones sat up or stood upon one foot and beheld the immune barber. Men, women, and children took up the cry: *"Zapatos! zapatos!"*

The necessity for the demand had been created. The demand followed. That day Mr. Hemstetter sold three hundred pairs of shoes.

"It is really surprising," he said to Johnny, who came up in the evening to help him straighten out the stock, "how trade is picking up. Yesterday I made but three sales."

"I told you they'd whoop things up when they got started," said the consul.

"I think I shall order a dozen more cases of goods, to keep the stock up," said Mr. Hemstetter, beaming through his spectacles.

"I wouldn't send in any orders yet," advised Johnny. "Wait till you see how the trade holds up."

Each night Johnny and Keogh sowed the crop that grew dollars by day. At the end of ten days two-thirds of the stock of shoes had been sold; and the stock of cockleburrs was exhausted. Johnny cabled to Pink Dawson for another 500 pounds, paying twenty cents per pound as before. Mr. Hemstetter carefully made up an order for $1,500 worth of shoes from Northern firms. Johnny hung about the store until this order was ready for the mail, and succeeded in destroying it before it reached the postoffice.

That night he took Rosine under the mango tree by Goodwin's porch, and confessed everything. She looked him in the eye, and said: "You are a very wicked man. Father and I will go back home. You say it was a joke? I think it is a very serious matter."

But at the end of half an hour's argument the conversation had been turned upon a different subject. The two were considering the respective merits of pale blue and pink wall paper with which the old colonial mansion of the Atwoods in Dalesburg was to be decorated after the wedding.

On the next morning Johnny confessed to Mr. Hemstetter. The shoe merchant put on his spectacles, and said through them: "You strike me as being a most extraordinary young scamp. If I had not managed this enterprise with good business judgment my entire stock of goods might have been a complete loss. Now, how do you propose to dispose of the rest of it?"

When the second invoice of cockleburrs arrived Johnny loaded them and the remainder of the shoes into a schooner, and sailed down the coast to Alazan.

There, in the same dark and diabolical manner, he repeated his success; and came back with a bag of money and not so much as a shoestring.

And then he besought his great Uncle of the waving goatee and starred vest to accept his resignation, for the lotus no longer lured him. He hankered for the spinach and cress of Dalesburg.

The services of Mr. William Terence Keogh as acting consul, *pro tem.*, were suggested and accepted, and Johnny sailed with the Hemstetters back to his native shores.

Keogh slipped into the sinecure of the American consulship with the ease that never left him even in such high places. The tintype establishment was soon to become a thing of the past, although its deadly work along the peaceful and helpless Spanish Main was never effaced. The restless partners were about to be off again, scouting ahead of the slow ranks of Fortune. But now they would take different ways. There were rumors of a promising uprising in Peru; and thither the martial Clancy would turn his adventurous steps. As for Keogh, he was figuring in his mind and on quires of Government letter-heads a scheme that dwarfed the art of misrepresenting the human countenance upon tin.

"What suits me," Keogh used to say, "in the way of a business proposition is something diversified that looks like a longer shot than it is—something in the way of a genteel graft that isn't worked enough for the correspondence schools to be teaching it by mail. I take the long end; but I like to have at least as good a chance to win as a man learning to play poker on an ocean steamer, or running for governor of Texas on the Republican ticket. And when I cash in my winnings, I don't want to find any widows' and orphans' chips in my stack."

The grass-grown globe was the green table on which Keogh gambled. The games he played were of his own invention. He was no grubber after the diffident dollar. Nor did he care to follow it with horn and hounds. Rather he loved to coax it with egregious and brilliant flies from its habitat in the waters of strange streams. Yet Keogh was a business man; and his schemes, in spite of their singularity, were as solidly set as the plans of a building contractor. In Arthur's time Sir William Keogh would have been a Knight of the Round Table. In these modern days he rides abroad, seeking the Graft instead of the Grail.

Three days after Johnny's departure, two small schooners appeared off Coralio. After some delay a boat put off from one of them, and brought a sunburned young man ashore. This young man had a shrewd and calculating eye; and he gazed with amazement at the strange things that he saw. He found on the beach some one who directed him to the consul's office; and thither he made his way at a nervous gait.

Keogh was sprawled in the official chair, drawing caricatures of his uncle's head on an official pad of paper. He looked up at his visitor.

"Where's Johnny Atwood?" inquired the sunburned young man, in a business tone.

"Gone," said Keogh, working carefully at Uncle Sam's necktie.

"That's just like him," remarked the nut-brown one, leaning against the table. "He always was a fellow to gallivant around instead of 'tending to business. Will he be in soon?"

"Don't think so," said Keogh, after a fair amount of deliberation.

"I s'pose he's out at some of his tomfoolery," conjectured the visitor, in a tone of virtuous conviction. "Johnny never would stick to anything long enough to succeed. I wonder how he manages to run his business here, and never be 'round to look after it."

"I'm looking after the business just now," admitted the *pro tem.* consul.

"Are you—then, say!—where's the factory?"

"What factory?" asked Keogh, with a mildly polite interest.

"Why, the factory where they use them cockleburrs. Lord knows what they use 'em for, anyway! I've got the basements of both them ships out there loaded with 'em. I'll give you a bargain in this lot. I've had every man, woman, and child around Dalesburg that wasn't busy pickin' 'em for a month. I hired these ships to bring 'em over. Everybody thought I was crazy. Now, you can have this lot for fifteen cents a pound, delivered on land. And if you want more I guess old Alabam' can come up to the demand. Johnny told me when he left home that if he struck anything down here that there was any money in he'd let me in on it. Shall I drive the ships in and hitch?"

A look of supreme, almost incredulous, delight dawned in Keogh's ruddy countenance. He dropped his pencil. His eyes turned upon the sunburned young man with joy in them mingled with fear lest his ecstasy should prove a dream.

"For God's sake, tell me," said Keogh, earnestly, "are you Dink Pawson?"

"My name is Pinkney Dawson," said the cornerer of the cockleburr market.

Billy Keogh slid rapturously and gently from his chair to his favorite strip of matting on the floor.

There were not many sounds in Coralio on that sultry afternoon. Among those that were may be mentioned a noise of enraptured and unrighteous laughter from a prostrate Irish-American, while a sunburned young man, with a shrewd eye, looked on him with wonder and amazement. Also the "tramp, tramp, tramp" of many well-shod feet in the streets outside. Also the lonesome wash of the waves that beat along the historic shores of the Spanish Main.

MASTERS OF ARTS

A TWO-INCH stub of a blue pencil was the wand with which Keogh performed the preliminary acts of his magic. So, with this he covered paper with diagrams and figures while he waited for the United States of America to send down to Coralio a successor to Atwood, resigned.

The new scheme that his mind had conceived, his stout heart indorsed, and his blue pencil corroborated, was laid around the characteristics and human frailties of the new president of Anchuria. These characteristics, and the situation out of which Keogh hoped to wrest a golden tribute, deserve chronicling contributive to the clear order of events.

President Losada—many called him Dictator—was a man whose genius would have made him conspicuous even among Anglo-Saxons, had not that genius been intermixed with other traits that were petty and subversive. He had some of the lofty patriotism of Washington (the man he most admired), the force of Napoleon, and much of the wisdom of the sages. These characteristics might have justified him in the assumption of the title of "The Illustrious Liberator," had they not been accompanied by a stupendous and amazing vanity that kept him in the less worthy ranks of the dictators.

Yet he did his country great service. With a mighty grasp he shook it nearly free from the shackles of ignorance and sloth and the vermin that fed upon it, and all but made it a power in the council of nations. He established schools and hospitals, built roads, bridges, railroads and palaces, and bestowed generous subsidies upon the arts and sciences. He was the absolute despot and the idol of his people. The wealth of the country poured into his hands. Other presidents had been rapacious without reason. Losada amassed enormous wealth, but his people had their share of the benefits.

The joint in his armor was his insatiate passion for monuments and tokens commemorating his glory. In every town he caused to be erected statues of himself bearing legends in praise of his greatness. In the walls of every public edifice, tablets were fixed reciting his splendor and the gratitude of his subjects. His statuettes and portraits were scattered throughout the land in every house and hut. One of the sycophants in his court painted him as St. John, with a halo and a train of attendants in full uniform. Losada saw nothing incongruous in this picture, and had it hung in a church in the capital. He ordered from a French sculptor a marble group including himself with Napoleon, Alexander the Great, and one or two others whom he deemed worthy of the honor.

He ransacked Europe for decorations, employing policy, money and intrigue to cajole the orders he coveted from kings and rulers. On state occasions his breast was covered from shoulder to shoulder with crosses, stars, golden roses, medals and ribbons. It was said that the man who could contrive for him a new decoration, or invent some new method of extolling his greatness, might plunge a hand deep into the treasury.

This was the man upon whom Billy Keogh had his eye. The gentle buccaneer had observed the rain of favors that fell upon those who ministered to the president's vanities, and he did not deem it his duty to hoist his umbrella against the scattering drops of liquid fortune.

In a few weeks the new consul arrived, releasing Keogh from his temporary duties. He was a young man fresh from college, who lived for botany alone. The consulate at Coralio gave him the opportunity to study tropical flora. He wore smoked glasses, and carried a green umbrella. He filled the cool, back porch of the consulate with plants and specimens so that space for a bottle and chair was not to be found. Keogh gazed on him sadly, but without rancour, and began to pack his gripsack. For his new plot against stagnation along the Spanish Main required of him a voyage overseas.

Soon came the *Karlsefin* again—she of the trampish habits—gleaning a cargo of cocoanuts for a speculative descent upon the New York market. Keogh was booked for a passage on the return trip.

"Yes, I'm going to New York," he explained to the group of his countrymen that had gathered on the beach to see him off. "But I'll be back before you miss me. I've undertaken the art education of this piebald country, and I'm not the man to desert it while it's in the early throes of tintypes."

With this mysterious declaration of his intentions Keogh boarded the *Karlsefin*.

Ten days later, shivering, with the collar of his thin coat turned high, he burst into the studio of Carolus White at the top of a tall building in Tenth Street, New York City.

Carolus White was smoking a cigarette and frying sausages over an oil stove. He was only twenty-three, and had noble theories about art.

"Billy Keogh!" exclaimed White, extending the hand that was not busy with the frying pan. "From what part of the uncivilized world, I wonder!"

"Hello, Carry," said Keogh, dragging forward a stool, and holding his fingers close to the stove. "I'm glad I found you so soon. I've been looking for you all day in the directories and art galleries. The free-lunch man on the corner told me where you were, quick. I was sure you'd be painting pictures yet."

Keogh glanced about the studio with the shrewd eye of a connoisseur in business.

"Yes, you can do it," he declared, with many gentle nods of his head. "That big one in the corner with the angels and green clouds and band-wagon is just the sort of thing we want. What would you call that, Carry—scene from Coney Island, ain't it?"

"That," said White, "I had intended to call 'The Translation of Elijah,' but you may be nearer right than I am."

"Name doesn't matter," said Keogh, largely; "it's the frame and the varieties of paint that does the trick. Now, I can tell you in a minute what I want. I've come on a little voyage of two thousand miles to take you in with me on a scheme. I thought of you as soon as the scheme showed itself to me. How would you like to go back with me and paint a picture? Ninety days for the trip, and five thousand dollars for the job."

"Cereal food or hair-tonic posters?" asked White.

"It isn't an ad."

"What kind of a picture is it to be?"

"It's a long story," said Keogh.

"Go ahead with it. If you don't mind, while you talk I'll just keep my eye on these sausages. Let 'em get one shade deeper than a Vandyke brown and you spoil 'em."

Keogh explained his project. They were to return to Coralio, where White was to pose as a distinguished American portrait painter who was touring in the tropics as a relaxation from his arduous and remunerative professional labors. It was not an unreasonable hope, even to those who had trod in the beaten paths of business, that an artist with so much prestige might secure a commission to perpetuate upon canvas the lineaments of the president, and secure a share of the *pesos* that were raining upon the caterers to his weaknesses.

Keogh had set his price at ten thousand dollars. Artists had been paid more for portraits. He and White were to share the expenses of the trip, and divide the possible profits. Thus he laid the scheme before White, whom he had known in the West before one declared for Art and the other became a Bedouin.

Before long the two machinators abandoned the rigor of the bare studio for a snug corner of a café. There they sat far into the night, with old envelopes and Keogh's stub of blue pencil between them.

At twelve o'clock White doubled up in his chair, with his chin on his fist, and shut his eyes at the unbeautiful wall-paper.

"I'll go you, Billy," he said, in the quiet tones of decision. "I've got two or three hundred saved up for sausages and rent; and I'll take the chance with you. Five thousand! It will give me two years in Paris and one in Italy. I'll begin to pack to-morrow."

"You'll begin in ten minutes," said Keogh. "It's to-morrow now. The *Karlsefin* starts back at four P. M. Come on to your painting shop, and I'll help you."

For five months in the year Coralio is the Newport of Anchuria. Then only does the town possess life. From November to March it is practically the seat of government. The president with his official family sojourns there; and society follows him. The pleasure-loving people make the season one long holiday of amusement and rejoicing. *Fiestas*, balls, games, sea bathing, processions and small theatres contribute to their enjoyment. The famous Swiss band from the capital plays in the little plaza every evening, while the fourteen carriages and vehicles in the town circle in funereal but complacent procession. Indians from the interior mountains, looking like prehistoric stone idols, come down to peddle their handiwork in the streets. The people throng the narrow ways, a chattering, happy, careless stream of buoyant humanity. Preposterous children rigged out with the shortest of ballet skirts and gilt wings, howl, underfoot, among the effervescent crowds. Especially is the arrival of the presidential party, at the opening of the season, attended with pomp, show and patriotic demonstrations of enthusiasm and delight.

When Keogh and White reached their destination, on the return trip of the *Karlsefin*, the gay winter season was well begun. As they stepped upon the beach they could hear the band playing in the plaza. The village maidens, with fireflies already fixed in their dark locks, were gliding, barefoot and coy-eyed, along the paths. Dandies in white linen, swinging their canes, were beginning their seductive strolls. The air was full of human essence, of artificial enticement, of coquetry, indolence, pleasure—the man-made sense of existence.

The first two or three days after their arrival were spent in preliminaries. Keogh escorted the artist about town, introducing him to the little circle of English-speaking residents and pulling whatever wires he could to effect the spreading of White's fame as a painter. And then Keogh planned a more spectacular demonstration of the idea he wished to keep before the public.

He and White engaged rooms in the Hotel de los Estranjeros. The two were clad in new suits of immaculate duck, with American straw hats, and carried canes of remarkable uniqueness and inutility. Few caballeros in Coralia—even the gorgeously uniformed officers of the Anchurian army—were as conspicuous for ease and elegance of demeanor as Keogh and his friend, the great American painter, Señor White.

White set up his easel on the beach and made striking sketches of the mountain and sea views. The native population formed at his rear in a vast, chattering semicircle to watch his work. Keogh, with his care for details, had arranged for himself a pose which he carried out with fidelity. His rôle was that of friend to the great artist, a man of affairs and leisure. The visible emblem of his position was a pocket camera.

"For branding the man who owns it," said he, "a genteel dilettante with a bank account and an easy conscience, a steam-yacht ain't in it with a camera. You see a man doing nothing but loafing around making snap-shots, and you know right away he reads up well in 'Bradstreet.' You notice these old million-aire boys—soon as they get through taking everything else in sight they go to taking photographs. People are more impressed by a kodak than they are by a title or a four-carat scarf-pin." So Keogh strolled blandly about Coralio, snap-ping the scenery and the shrinking señoritas, while White posed conspicuously in the higher regions of art.

Two weeks after their arrival, the scheme began to bear fruit. An aide-de-camp of the president drove to the hotel in a dashing victoria. The president desired that Señor White come to the Casa Morena for an informal interview.

Keogh gripped his pipe tightly between his teeth. "Not a cent less than ten thousand," he said to the artist—"remember the price. And in gold or its equivalent—don't let him stick you with this bargain-counter stuff they call money here."

"Perhaps it isn't that he wants," said White.

"Get out!" said Keogh, with splendid confidence. "I know what he wants. He wants his picture painted by the celebrated young American painter and filibuster now sojourning in this down-trodden country. Off you go."

The victoria sped away with the artist. Keogh walked up and down, puffing great clouds of smoke from his pipe, and waited. In an hour the victoria swept again to the door of the hotel, deposited White, and vanished. The artist dashed up the stairs, three at a step. Keogh stopped smoking, and became a silent interrogation point.

"Landed," exclaimed White, with his boyish face flushed with elation. "Billy, you are a wonder. He wants a picture. I'll tell you all about it. By Heavens! that dictator chap is a corker! He's a dictator clear down to his finger-ends. He's a kind of combination of Julius Cæsar, Lucifer and Chauncey Depew done in sepia. Polite and grim—that's his way. The room I saw him in was about ten acres big, and looked like a Mississippi steamboat with its gilding and mirrors and white paint. He talks English better than I can ever hope to. The matter of the price came up. I mentioned ten thousand. I expected him to call the guard and have me taken out and shot. He didn't move an eyelash. He just waved one of his chestnut hands in a careless way, and said, 'Whatever you say.' I am to go back to-morrow and discuss with him the details of the picture."

Keogh hung his head. Self-abasement was easy to read in his downcast countenance.

"I'm failing, Carry," he said, sorrowfully. "I'm not fit to handle these man's-size schemes any longer. Peddling oranges in a push-cart is about the suitable graft for me. When I said ten thousand, I swear I thought I had sized up that brown man's limit to within two cents. He'd have melted down for fifteen thousand just as easy. Say—Carry—you'll see the old man Keogh safe in some nice, quiet idiot asylum, won't you, if he makes a break like that again?"

The Casa Morena, although only one story in height, was a building of brown stone, luxurious as a palace in its interior. It stood on a low hill in a walled garden of splendid tropical flora at the upper edge of Coralio. The next day the president's carriage came again for the artist. Keogh went out for a walk along the beach, where he and his "picture box" were now familiar sights. When he returned to the hotel White was sitting in a steamer-chair on the balcony.

"Well," said Keogh, "did you and His Nibs decide on the kind of chromo he wants?"

White got up and walked back and forth on the balcony a few times. Then he stopped and laughed strangely. His face was flushed, and his eyes were bright with a kind of angry amusement.

"Look here, Billy," he said, somewhat roughly, "when you first came to me in my studio and mentioned a picture, I thought you wanted a Smashed Oats or a Hair Tonic poster painted on a range of mountains or the side of a continent. Well, either of those jobs would have been Art in its highest form compared to the one you've steered me against. I can't paint that picture, Billy. You've got to let me out. Let me try to tell you what that barbarian wants. He had it all planned out and even a sketch made of his idea. The old boy doesn't draw badly at all. But, ye goddesses of Art! listen to the monstrosity he expects me to paint. He wants himself in the centre of the canvas, of course. He is to be painted as Jupiter sitting on Olympus, with the clouds at his feet. At one side of him stands George Washington, in full regimentals, with his hand on the president's shoulder. An angel with outstretched wings hovers overhead, and is placing a laurel wreath on the president's head, crowning him—Queen of the May, I suppose. In the background is to be cannon, more angels and soldiers. The man who would paint that picture would have to have the soul of a dog, and would deserve to go down into oblivion without even a tin can tied to his tail to sound his memory."

Little beads of moisture crept out all over Billy Keogh's brow. The stub of his blue pencil had not figured out a contingency like this. The machinery of his plan had run with flattering smoothness until now. He dragged another chair upon the balcony, and got White back to his seat. He lit his pipe with apparent calm.

"Now, sonny," he said, with gentle grimness, "you and me will have an Art to Art talk. You've got your art and I've got mine. Yours is the real Pierian stuff that turns up its nose at bock-beer signs and oleographs of the Old Mill. Mine's the art of Business. This was my scheme, and it worked out like two-and-two. Paint that president man as Old King Cole, or Venus, or a landscape, or a fresco, or a bunch of lilies, or anything he thinks he looks like. But get the paint on the canvas and collect the spoils. You wouldn't throw me down, Carry, at this stage of the game. Think of that ten thousand."

"I can't help thinking of it," said White, "and that's what hurts. I'm tempted to throw every ideal I ever had down in the mire, and steep my soul in infamy by painting that picture. That five thousand meant three years of foreign study to me, and I'd almost sell my soul for that."

"Now it ain't as bad as that," said Keogh, soothingly. "It's a business proposition. It's so much paint and time against money. I don't fall in with your idea that that picture would so everlastingly jolt the art side of the question. George Washington was all right, you know, and nobody could say a word against the angel. I don't think so bad of that group. If you was to give Jupiter a pair of epaulets and a sword, and kind of work the clouds around to look like a blackberry patch, it wouldn't make such a bad battle scene. Why, if we hadn't already settled on the price, he ought to pay an extra thousand for Washington, and the angel ought to raise it five hundred."

"You don't understand, Billy," said White, with an uneasy laugh. "Some of us fellows who try to paint have big notions about Art. I wanted to paint a picture some day that people would stand before and forget that it was made of paint. I wanted it to creep into them like a bar of music and mushroom there like a soft bullet. And I wanted 'em to go away and ask, 'What else has he done?' And I didn't want 'em to find a thing; not a portrait nor a magazine cover nor an illustration nor a drawing of a girl—nothing but *the* picture. That's why I've lived on fried sausages, and tried to keep true to myself. I persuaded myself to do this portrait for the chance it might give to me to study abroad. But this howling, screaming caricature! Good Lord! can't you see how it is?"

"Sure," said Keogh, as tenderly as he would have spoken to a child, and he laid a long fore-finger on White's knee. "I see. It's bad to have your art all slugged up like that. I know. You wanted to paint a big thing like the panorama of the battle of Gettysburg. But let me kalsomine you a little mental sketch to consider. Up to date we're out $385.50 on this scheme. Our capital took every cent both of us could raise. We've got about enough left to get back to New York on. I need my share of that ten thousand. I want to work a copper deal in Idaho, and make a hundred thousand. That's the business end of the thing. Come down off your art perch, Carry, and let's land that hatful of dollars."

"Billy," said White, with an effort, "I'll try. I won't say I'll do it, but I'll try. I'll go at it, and put it through if I can."

"That's business," said Keogh heartily. "Good boy! Now, here's another thing—rush that picture—crowd it through as quick as you can. Get a couple of boys to help you mix the paint if necessary. I've picked up some pointers around town. The people here are beginning to get sick of Mr. President. They say he's been too free with concessions; and they accuse him of trying to make a dicker with England to sell out the country. We want that picture done and paid for before there's any row."

In the great *patio* of Casa Morena, the president caused to be stretched a huge canvas. Under this White set up his temporary studio. For two hours each day the great man sat to him.

White worked faithfully. But, as the work progressed, he had seasons of bitter scorn, of infinite self-contempt, of sullen gloom and sardonic gaiety. Keogh, with the patience of a great general, soothed, coaxed, argued—kept him at the picture.

At the end of a month White announced that the picture was completed—Jupiter, Washington, angels, clouds, cannon and all. His face was pale and his mouth drawn straight when he told Keogh. He said the president was much pleased with it. It was to be hung in the National Gallery of Statesmen and Heroes. The artist had been requested to return to Casa Morena on the following day to receive payment. At the appointed time he left the hotel, silent under his friend's joyful talk of their success.

An hour later he walked into the room where Keogh was waiting, threw his hat on the floor, and sat upon the table.

"Billy," he said, in strained and laboring tones, "I've a little money out West in a small business that my brother is running. It's what I've been living on while I've been studying art. I'll draw out my share and pay you back what you've lost on this scheme."

"Lost!" exclaimed Keogh, jumping up. "Didn't you get paid for the picture?"

"Yes, I got paid," said White. "But just now there isn't any picture, and there isn't any pay. If you care to hear about it, here are the edifying details. The president and I were looking at the painting. His secretary brought a bank draft on New York for ten thousand dollars and handed it to me. The moment I touched it I went wild. I tore it into little pieces and threw them on the floor. A workman was repainting the pillars inside the *patio*. A bucket of his paint happened to be convenient. I picked up his brush and slapped a quart of blue paint all over that ten-thousand-dollar nightmare. I bowed, and walked out. The president didn't move or speak. That was one time he was taken by surprise. It's tough on you, Billy, but I couldn't help it."

There seemed to be excitement in Coralio. Outside there was a confused, rising murmur pierced by high-pitched cries. *"Abajo el traidor—Muerte al traidor!"* were the words they seemed to form.

"Listen to that!" exclaimed White, bitterly: "I know that much Spanish. They're shouting, 'Down with the traitor!' I heard them before. I felt that they meant me. I was a traitor to Art. The picture had to go."

" 'Down with the blank fool' would have suited your case better," said Keogh, with fiery emphasis. "You tear up ten thousand dollars like an old rag because the way you've spread on five dollars' worth of paint hurts your conscience. Next time I pick a side-partner in a scheme the man has got to go before a notary and swear he never even heard the word 'ideal' mentioned."

Keogh strode from the room, white-hot. White paid little attention to his resentment. The scorn of Billy Keogh seemed a trifling thing beside the greater self-scorn he had escaped.

In Coralio the excitement waxed. An outburst was imminent. The cause of this demonstration of displeasure was the presence in the town of a big, pink-cheeked Englishman, who, it was said, was an agent of his government come to clinch the bargain by which the president placed his people in the hands of a foreign power. It was charged that not only had he given away priceless concessions, but that the public debt was to be transferred into the hands of the English, and the custom-houses turned over to them as a guarantee. The long-enduring people had determined to make their protest felt.

On that night, in Coralio and in other towns, their ire found vent. Yelling mobs, mercurial but dangerous, roamed the streets. They overthrew the great bronze statue of the president that stood in the centre of the plaza, and hacked it to shapeless pieces. They tore from public buildings the tablets set there proclaiming the glory of the "Illustrious Liberator." His pictures in the government office were demolished. The mobs even attacked the Casa Morena, but were driven away by the military, which remained faithful to the executive. All the night terror reigned.

The greatness of Losada was shown by the fact that by noon the next day order was restored, and he was still absolute. He issued proclamations denying positively that any negotiations of any kind had been entered into with England. Sir Stafford Vaughn, the pink-cheeked Englishman, also declared in placards and in public print that his presence there had no international significance. He was a traveller without guile. In fact (so he stated), he had not even spoken with the president or been in his presence since his arrival.

During this disturbance, White was preparing for his homeward voyage in the steamship that was to sail within two or three days. About noon, Keogh, the restless, took his camera out with the hope of speeding the lagging hours. The town was now as quiet as if peace had never departed from her perch on the red-tiled roofs.

About the middle of the afternoon, Keogh hurried back to the hotel with something decidedly special in his air. He retired to the little room where he developed his pictures.

Later on he came out to White on the balcony, with a luminous, grim, predatory smile on his face.

"Do you know what that is?" he asked, holding up a 4 x 5 photograph mounted on cardboard.

"Snap-shot of a señorita sitting in the sand—alliteration unintentional," guessed White, lazily.

"Wrong," said Keogh with shining eyes. "It's a slung-shot. It's a can of dynamite. It's a gold mine. It's a sight-draft on your president man for twenty thousand dollars—yes, sir—twenty thousand this time, and no spoiling the picture. No ethics of art in the way. Art! You with your smelly little tubes! I've got you skinned to death with a kodak. Take a look at that."

White took the picture in his hand, and gave a long whistle.

"Jove," he exclaimed, "but wouldn't that stir up a row in town if you let it be seen. How in the world did you get it, Billy?"

"You know that high wall around the president man's back garden? I was up there trying to get a bird's-eye of the town. I happened to notice a chink in the wall where a stone and a lot of plaster had slid out. Thinks I, I'll take a peep through to see how Mr. President's cabbages are growing. The first thing I saw was him and this Sir Englishman sitting at a little table about twenty feet away. They had the table all spread over with documents, and they were hobnobbing over them as thick as two pirates. 'Twas a nice corner of the garden, all private and shady with palms and orange trees, and they had a pail of champagne set by handy in the grass. I knew then was the time for me to make my big hit in Art. So I raised the machine up to the crack, and pressed the button. Just as I did so them old boys shook hands on the deal—you see they took that way in the picture."

Keogh put on his coat and hat.

"What are you going to do with it?" asked White.

"Me," said Keogh in a hurt tone, "why, I'm going to tie a pink ribbon to it and hang it on the what-not, of course. I'm surprised at you. But while I'm out you just try to figure out what gingercake potentate would be most likely to want to buy this work of art for his private collection—just to keep it out of circulation."

The sunset was reddening the tops of the cocoanut palms when Billy Keogh came back from Casa Morena. He nodded to the artist's questioning gaze; and lay down on a cot with his hands under the back of his head.

"I saw him. He paid the money like a little man. They didn't want to let me in at first. I told 'em it was important. Yes, that president man is on the plenty-able list. He's got a beautiful business system about the way he uses his brains. All I had to do was to hold up the photograph so he could see it, and name the price. He just smiled, and walked over to a safe and got the cash. Twenty one-thousand-dollar brand-new United States Treasury notes he laid on the table, like I'd pay out a dollar and a quarter. Fine notes, too—they crackled with a sound like burning the brush off a ten-acre lot."

"Let's try the feel of one," said White, curiously. "I never saw a thousand-dollar bill." Keogh did not immediately respond.

"Carry," he said, in an absent-minded way, "you think a heap of your art, don't you?"

"More," said White, frankly, "than has been for the financial good of myself and my friends."

"I thought you were a fool the other day," went on Keogh, quietly, "and I'm not sure now that you wasn't. But if you was, so am I. I've been in some funny deals, Carry, but I've always managed to scramble fair, and match my brains and capital against the other fellow's. But when it comes to—well, when you've got the other fellow cinched, and the screws on him, and he's got to put up—why, it don't strike me as being a man's game. They've got a name for it, you know; it's—confound you, don't you understand? A fellow feels—it's something like that blamed art of yours—he—well, I tore that photograph up and laid the pieces on that stack of money and shoved the whole business back across the table. 'Excuse me, Mr. Losada,' I said, 'but I guess I've made a mistake in the price. You get the photo for nothing.' Now, Carry, you get out the pencil, and we'll do some more figuring. I'd like to save enough out of our capital for you to have some fried sausages in your joint when you get back to New York."

DICKY

THERE is little consecutiveness along the Spanish Main. Things happen there intermittently. Even Time seems to hang his scythe daily on the branch of an orange tree while he takes a siesta and a cigarette.

After the ineffectual revolt against the administration of President Losada, the country settled again into quiet toleration of the abuses with which he had been charged. In Coralio old political enemies went arm-in-arm, lightly eschewing for the time all differences of opinion.

The failure of the art expedition did not stretch the cat-footed Keogh upon his back. The ups and downs of Fortune made smooth travelling for his nimble steps. His blue pencil stub was at work again before the smoke of the steamer on which White sailed had cleared away from the horizon. He had but to speak a word to Geddie to find his credit negotiable for whatever goods he wanted from the store of Brannigan & Company. On the same day on which White arrived in New York, Keogh, at the rear of a train of five pack mules loaded with hard-ware and cutlery, set his face toward the grim, interior mountains. There the Indian tribes wash gold dust from the auriferous streams; and when a market is brought to them trading is brisk and *muy bueno* in the Cordilleras.

In Coralio Time folded his wings and paced wearily along his drowsy path. They who had most cheered the torpid hours were gone. Clancy had sailed on a Spanish barque for Colon, contemplating a cut across the isthmus and then a further voyage to end at Calao, where the fighting was said to be on. Geddie, whose quiet and genial nature had once served to mitigate the frequent dull reaction of lotus eating, was now a home-man, happy with his bright orchid, Paula, and never even dreaming of or regretting the unsolved, sealed and monogramed Bottle whose contents, now inconsiderable, were held safely in the keeping of the sea.

Well may the Walrus, most discerning and eclectic of beasts, place sealing-wax midway on his programme of topics that fall pertinent and diverting upon the ear.

Atwood was gone—he of the hospitable back porch and ingenuous cunning. Dr. Gregg, with his trepanning story smouldering within him, was a whiskered volcano, always showing signs of imminent eruption, and was not to be con-sidered in the ranks of those who might contribute to the amelioration of ennui. The new consul's note chimed with the sad sea waves and the violent tropical greens—he had not a bar of Scheherezade or of the Round Table in his lute. Goodwin was employed with large projects: what time he was loosed from them found him at his home, where he loved to be. Therefore it will be seen that there was a dearth of fellowship and entertainment among the foreign con-tingent of Coralio.

And then Dicky Maloney dropped down from the clouds upon the town, and amused it.

Nobody knew where Dicky Maloney hailed from or how he reached Coralio. He appeared there one day; and that was all. He afterward said that he came on the fruit steamer *Thor;* but an inspection of the *Thor's* passenger list of that date was found to be Maloneyless. Curiosity, however, soon perished; and Dicky took his place among the odd fish cast up by the Caribbean.

He was an active, devil-may-care, rollicking fellow with an engaging gray eye, the most irresistible grin, a rather dark or much sunburned complexion, and a head of the fieriest red hair ever seen in that country. Speaking the Spanish language as well as he spoke English, and seeming always to have plenty of silver in his pockets, it was not long before he was a welcome companion withersoever he went. He had an extreme fondness for *vino blanco*, and gained the reputation of being able to drink more of it than any three men in town. Everybody called him "Dicky"; everybody cheered up at the sight of him—especially the natives, to whom his marvellous red hair and his free-and-easy style were a constant delight and envy. Wherever you went in the town you would soon see Dicky or hear his genial laugh, and find around him a group of admirers who appreciated him both for his good nature and the white wine he was always so ready to buy.

A considerable amount of speculation was had concerning the object of his sojourn there, until one day he silenced this by opening a small shop for the sale of tobacco, *dulces* and the handiwork of the interior Indians—fibre-and-silk-woven goods, deerskin *zapatos* and basketwork of *tule* reeds. Even then he did not change his habits; for he was drinking and playing cards half the day and night with the *comandante*, the collector of customs, the *Jefe Político* and other gay dogs among the native officials.

One day Dicky saw Pasa, the daughter of Madama Ortiz, sitting in the side-door of the Hotel des los Estranjeros. He stopped in his tracks, still, for the first time in Coralio; and then he sped, swift as a deer, to find Vasquez, a gilded native youth, to present him.

The young men had named Pasa "*La Santita Naranjadita.*" *Naranjadita* is a Spanish word for a certain color that you must go to more trouble to describe in English. By saying "The little saint, tinted the most beautiful delicate-slightly-orange-golden," you will approximate the description of Madama Ortiz's daughter.

La Madama Ortiz sold rum in addition to other liquors. Now, you must know that the rum expiates whatever opprobrium attends upon the other commodities. For rum-making, mind you, is a government monopoly; and to keep a government dispensary assures respectability if not preëminence. Moreover, the saddest of precisions could find no fault with the conduct of the shop. Customers drank there in the lowest of spirits and fearsomely, as in the shadow of the dead; for Madama's ancient and vaunted lineage counteracted even the rum's behest to be merry. For, was she not of the Iglesias, who landed with Pizarro? And had not her deceased husband been *comisionado de caminos y puentes* for the district?

In the evenings Pasa sat by the window in the room next to the one where they drank, and strummed dreamily upon her guitar. And then, by twos and threes, would come visiting young caballeros and occupy the prim line of chairs set against the wall of this room. They were there to beseige the heart of "*La Santita.*" Their method (which is not proof against intelligent competition) consisted of expanding the chest, looking valorous, and consuming a gross or two of cigarettes. Even saints delicately oranged prefer to be wooed differently.

Doña Pasa would tide over the vast chasms of nicotinized silence with music from her guitar, while she wondered if the romances she had read about gallant and more—more contiguous cavaliers were all lies. At somewhat regular intervals Madama would glide in from the dispensary with a sort of drought-suggesting gleam in her eye, and there would be a rustling of stiffly-starched white trousers as one of the caballeros would propose an adjournment to the bar.

That Dicky Maloney would, sooner or later, explore this field was a thing to be foreseen. There were few doors in Coralio into which his red head had not been poked.

In an incredibly short space of time after his first sight of her he was there, seated close beside her rocking chair. There were no back-against-the-wall poses in Dicky's theory of wooing. His plan of subjection was an attack at close range. To carry the fortress with one concentrated, ardent, eloquent, irresistible *escalade*—that was Dicky's way.

Pasa was descended from the proudest Spanish families in the country. Moreover, she had had unusual advantages. Two years in a New Orleans school had elevated her ambitions and fitted her for a fate above the ordinary maidens of her native land. And yet here she succumbed to the first red-haired scamp with a glib tongue and a charming smile that came along and courted her properly.

Very soon Dicky took her to the little church in the corner of the plaza, and "Mrs. Maloney" was added to her string of distinguished names.

And it was her fate to sit, with her patient, saintly eyes and figure like a bisque Psyche, behind the sequestered counter of the little shop, while Dicky drank and philandered with his frivolous acquaintances.

The women, with their naturally fine instinct, saw a chance for vivisection, and delicately taunted her with his habits. She turned upon them in a beautiful, steady blaze of sorrowful contempt.

"You meat-cows," she said, in her level, crystal-clear tones; "you know nothing of a man. Your men are *maromeros*. They are fit only to roll cigarettes in the shade until the sun strikes and shrivels them up. They drone in your hammocks and you comb their hair and feed them with fresh fruit. My man is no such blood. Let him drink of the wine. When he has taken sufficient of it to drown one of your *flaccitos* he will come home to me more of a man than one thousand of your *pobrecitos*. *My* hair he smooths and braids; to me he sings; he himself removes my *zapatos*, and there, there, upon each instep leaves a kiss. He holds—Oh, you will never understand! Blind ones who have never known a *man*."

Sometimes mysterious things happened at night about Dicky's shop. While the front of it was dark, in the little room back of it Dicky and a few of his friends would sit about a table carrying on some kind of very quiet *negocios* until quite late. Finally he would let them out the front door very carefully, and go upstairs to his little saint. These visitors were generally conspirator-like men with dark clothes and hats. Of course, these dark doings were noticed after a while, and talked about.

Dicky seemed to care nothing at all for the society of the alien residents of the town. He avoided Goodwin, and his skilful escape from the trepanning story of Dr. Gregg is still referred to, in Coralio, as a masterpiece of lightning diplomacy.

Many letters arrived, addressed to "Mr. Dicky Maloney," or "Señor Dickee Maloney," to the considerable pride of Pasa. That so many people should desire to write to him only confirmed her own suspicion that the light from his red head shone around the world. As to their contents she never felt curiosity. There was a wife for you!

The one mistake Dicky made in Coralio was to run out of money at the wrong time. Where his money came from was a puzzle, for the sales of his shop were next to nothing, but that source failed, and at a peculiarly unfortunate time. It was when the *comandante*, Don Señor el Coronel Encarnatión Rios, looked upon the little saint seated in the shop and felt his heart go pitapat.

The *comandante*, who was versed in all the intricate arts of gallantry, first delicately hinted at his sentiments by donning his dress uniform and strutting up and down fiercely before her window. Pasa, glancing demurely with her saintly eyes, instantly perceived his resemblance to her parrot, Chichi, and was diverted to the extent of a smile. The *comandante* saw the smile, which was not intended for him. Convinced of an impression made, he entered the shop, confidently, and advanced to open compliment. Pasa froze; he pranced; she flamed royally; he was charmed to injudicious persistence; she commanded him to leave the shop; he tried to capture her hand,—and Dicky entered, smiling broadly, full of white wine and the devil.

He spent five minutes in punishing the *comandante* scientifically and carefully, so that the pain might be prolonged as far as possible. At the end of that time he pitched the rash wooer out the door upon the stones of the street, senseless.

A barefooted policeman who had been watching the affair from across the street blew a whistle. A squad of four soldiers came running from the *cuartel* around the corner. When they saw that the offender was Dicky, they stopped, and blew more whistles, which brought out reënforcements of eight. Deeming the odds against them sufficiently reduced, the military advanced upon the disturber.

Dicky, being thoroughly imbued with the martial spirit, stooped and drew the *comandante's* sword, which was girded about him, and charged his foe. He chased the standing army four squares, playfully prodding its squealing rear and hacking at its ginger-colored heels.

But he was not so successful with the civic authorities. Six muscular, nimble policemen overpowered him and conveyed him, triumphantly but warily, to jail. "*El Diablo Colorado*" they dubbed him, and derided the military for its defeat.

Dicky, with the rest of the prisoners, could look out through the barred door at the grass of the little plaza, at a row of orange trees and the red tile roofs and 'dobe walls of a line of insignificant stores.

At sunset along a path across this plaza came a melancholy procession of sad-faced women bearing plantains, cassaba, bread and fruit—each coming with food to some wretch behind those bars to whom she still clung and furnished the means of life. Twice a day—morning and evening—they were permitted to come. Water was furnished to her compulsory guests by the republic, but no food.

That evening Dicky's name was called by the sentry, and he stepped before the bars of the door. There stood his little saint, a black mantilla draped about her head and shoulders, her face like glorified melancholy, her clear eyes gazing longingly at him as if they might draw him between the bars to her. She brought a chicken, some oranges, *dulces* and a loaf of white bread. A soldier inspected the food, and passed it in to Dicky. Pasa spoke calmly as she always did, briefly, in her thrilling, flute-like tones. "Angel of my life," she said, "let it not be long that thou art away from me. Thou knowest that life is not a thing to be endured with thou not at my side. Tell me if I can do aught in this matter. If not, I will wait—a little while. I come again in the morning."

Dicky, with his shoes removed so as not to disturb his fellow prisoners, tramped the floor of the jail half the night condemning his lack of money and the cause of it—whatever that might have been. He knew very well that money would have brought his release at once.

For two days succeeding Pasa came at the appointed times and brought him food. He eagerly inquired each time if a letter or package had come for him, and she mournfully shook her head.

On the morning of the third day she brought only a small loaf of bread. There were dark circles under her eyes. She seemed as calm as ever.

"By jingo," said Dicky, who seemed to speak in English or Spanish as the whim seized him, "this is dry provender, *muchachita*. Is this the best you can dig up for a fellow?"

Pasa looked at him as a mother looks at a beloved but capricious babe.

"Think better of it," she said, in a low voice; "since for the next meal there will be nothing. The last *centavo* is spent." She pressed close against the grating.

"Sell the goods in the shop—take anything for them."

"Have I not tried? Did I not offer them for one-tenth their cost? Not even one *peso* would any one give. There is not one *real* in this town to assist Dickee Malonee."

Dick clenched his teeth grimly. "That's the *comandante*," he growled.

"He's responsible for that sentiment. Wait, oh, wait till the cards are all out."

Pasa lowered her voice to almost a whisper. "And, listen, heart of my heart," she said, "I have endeavored to be brave, but I cannot live without thee. Three days now——"

Dicky caught a faint gleam of steel from the folds of her mantilla. For once she looked in his face and saw it without a smile, stern, menacing and purposeful. Then he suddenly raised his hand and his smile came back like a gleam of sunshine. The hoarse signal of an incoming steamer's siren sounded in the harbor. Dicky called to the sentry who was pacing before the door: "What steamer comes?"

"The *Catarina*."

"Of the Vesuvius line?"

"Without doubt, of that line."

"Go you, *picarilla*," said Dicky joyously to Pasa, "to the American consul. Tell him I wish to speak with him. See that he comes at once. And look you! let me see a different look in those eyes, for I promise your head shall rest upon this arm to-night."

It was an hour before the consul came. He held his green umbrella under his arm, and mopped his forehead impatiently.

"Now, see here, Maloney," he began, captiously, "you fellows seem to think you can cut up any kind of row, and expect me to pull you out of it. I'm neither the War Department nor a gold mine. This country has its laws, you know, and there's one against pounding the senses out of the regular army. You Irish are forever getting into trouble. I don't see what I can do. Anything like tobacco, now, to make you comfortable—or newspapers——"

"Son of Eli," interrupted Dicky, gravely, "you haven't changed an iota. That is almost a duplicate of the speech you made when old Koen's donkeys and geese got into the chapel loft, and the culprits wanted to hide in your room."

"Oh, heavens!" exclaimed the consul, hurriedly adjusting his spectacles. "Are you a Yale man, too? Were you in that crowd? I don't seem to remember any one with red—any one named Maloney. Such a lot of collegemen seem to have misused their advantages. One of the best mathematicians of the class of '91 is selling lottery tickets in Belize. A Cornell man dropped off here last month. He was second steward on a guano boat. I'll write to the department if you like, Maloney. Or if there's any tobacco, or newspa——"

"There's nothing," interrupted Dicky, shortly, "but this. You go tell the captain of the *Catarina* that Dicky Maloney wants to see him as soon as he can conveniently come. Tell him where I am. Hurry. That's all."

The consul, glad to be let off so easily, hurried away. The captain of the *Catarina*, a stout man, Sicilian born, soon appeared, shoving, with little ceremony, through the guards to the jail door. The Vesuvius Fruit Company had a habit of doing things that way in Anchuria.

"I am exceedingly sorry—exceedingly sorry," said the captain, "to see this occur. I place myself at your service, Mr. Maloney. What you need shall be furnished. Whatever you say shall be done."

Dickey looked at him unsmilingly. His red hair could not detract from his attitude of severe dignity as he stood, tall and calm, with his now grim mouth forming a horizontal line.

"Captain De Lucco, I believe I still have funds in the hands of your company —ample and personal funds. I ordered a remittance last week. The money has not arrived. You know what is needed in this game. Money and money and more money. Why has it not been sent?"

"By the *Cristóbal*," replied De Lucco, gesticulating, "it was despatched. Where is the *Cristóbal*? Off Cape Antonio I spoke her with a broken shaft. A tramp coaster was towing her back to New Orleans. I brought money ashore thinking your need for it might not withstand delay. In this envelope is one thousand dollars. There is more if you need it, Mr. Maloney."

"For the present it will suffice," said Dicky, softening as he crinkled the envelope and looked down at the half-inch thickness of smooth, dingy bills.

"The long green!" he said, gently, with a new reverence in his gaze. "Is there anything it will not buy, Captain?"

"I had three friends," replied De Lucco, who was a bit of a philosopher, "who had money. One of them speculated in stocks and made ten million; another is in heaven, and the third married a poor girl whom he loved."

"The answer, then," said Dicky, "is held by the Almighty, Wall Street and Cupid. So, the question remains."

"This," queried the captain, including Dicky's surroundings in a significant gesture of his hand, "is it—it is not—it is not connected with the business of your little shop? There is no failure in your plans?"

"No, no," said Dicky. "This is merely the result of a little private affair of mine, a digression from the regular line of business. They say for a complete life a man must know poverty, love, and war. But they don't go well together, *capitán mío.* No; there is no failure in my business. The little shop is doing very well."

When the captain had departed Dicky called the sergeant of the jail and asked:

"Am I *preso* by the military or the civil authority?"

"Surely there is no martial law in effect now, señor."

"*Bueno.* Now go or send to the alcalde, the *Juez de la Paz* and the *Jefe de los Policios.* Tell them I am prepared at once to satisfy the demands of justice." A folded bill of the "long green" slid into the sergeant's hands.

Then Dicky's smile came back again, for he knew that the hours of his captivity were numbered; and he hummed, in time with the sentry's tread:

> "*They're hanging men and women now,*
> *For lacking of the green.*"

So, that night Dicky sat by the window of the room over his shop and his little saint sat close by, working at something silken and dainty. Dicky was thoughtful and grave. His red hair was in an unusual state of disorder. Pasa's fingers often ached to smooth and arrange it, but Dicky would never allow it. He was poring, to-night, over a great litter of maps and books and papers on his table until that perpendicular line came between his brows that always distressed Pasa. Presently she went and brought his hat, and stood with it until he looked up, inquiringly.

"It is sad for you here," she explained. "Go out and drink *vino blanco.* Come back when you get that smile you used to wear. That is what I wish to see."

Dicky laughed and threw down his papers. "The *vino blanco* stage is past. It has served its turn. Perhaps, after all, there was less entered my mouth and more my ears than people thought. But, there will be no more maps or frowns to-night. I promise you that. Come."

They sat upon a reed *silleta* at the window and watched the quivering gleams from the lights of the *Catarina* reflected in the harbor.

Presently Pasa rippled out one of her infrequent chirrups of audible laughter.

"I was thinking," she began, anticipating Dicky's question, "of the foolish things girls have in their minds. Because I went to school in the States I used to have ambitions. Nothing less than to be the president's wife would satisfy me. And, look, thou red picaroon, to what obscure fate thou hast stolen me!"

"Don't give up hope," said Dicky, smiling. "More than one Irishman has been the ruler of a South American country. There was a dictator of Chili named O'Higgins. Why not a President Maloney, of Anchuria? Say the word, *santita mía*, and we'll make the race."

"No, no, no, thou red-haired, reckless one!" sighed Pasa; "I am content"— she laid her head against his arm—"here."

ROUGE ET NOIR

It has been indicated that disaffection followed the elevation of Losada to the presidency. This feeling continued to grow. Throughout the entire republic there seemed to be a spirit of silent, sullen discontent. Even the old Liberal party to which Goodwin, Zavalla and other patriots had lent their aid was disappointed. Losada had failed to become a popular idol. Fresh taxes, fresh import duties and, more than all, his tolerance of the outrageous oppression of citizens by the military had rendered him the most obnoxious president since the despicable Alforan. The majority of his own cabinet were out of sympathy with him. The army, which he had courted by giving it license to tyrannize, had been his main, and thus far adequate support.

But the most impolitic of the administration's moves had been when it antagonized the Vesuvius Fruit Company, an organization plying twelve steamers and with cash and capital somewhat larger than Anchuria's surplus and debt combined.

Reasonably an established concern like the Vesuvius would become irritated at having a small, retail republic with no rating at all attempt to squeeze it. So when the government proxies applied for a subsidy they encountered a polite refusal. The president at once retaliated by clapping an export duty of one *real* per bunch on bananas—a thing unprecedented in fruit-growing countries. The Vesuvius Company had invested large sums in wharves and plantations along the Anchuria coast, their agents had erected fine homes in the towns where they had their headquarters, and heretofore had worked with the republic in good-will and with advantage to both. It would lose an immense sum if compelled to move out. The selling price of bananas from Vera Cruz to Trinidad was three *reals* per bunch. This new duty of one-*real* would have ruined the fruit growers in Anchuria and have seriously discommoded the Vesuvius Company had it declined to pay it. But for some reason, the Vesuvius continued to buy Anchuria fruit, paying four *reals* for it; and not suffering the growers to bear the loss.

This apparent victory deceived His Excellency; and he began to hunger for more of it. He sent an emissary to request a conference with a representative of the fruit company. The Vesuvius sent Mr. Franzoni, a little, stout, cheerful man, always cool, and whistling airs from Verdi's operas. Señor Espirición, of the office of the Minister of Finance, attempted the sandbagging in behalf of Anchuria. The meeting took place in the cabin of the *Salvador*, of the Vesuvius line.

Señor Espirición opened negotiations by announcing that the government contemplated the building of a railroad to skirt the alluvial coast lands. After touching upon the benefits such a road would confer upon the interests of the Vesuvius, he reached the definite suggestion that a contribution to the road's expenses of, say, fifty thousand *pesos* would not be more than an equivalent to benefits received.

Mr. Franzoni denied that his company would receive any benefits from a contemplated road. As its representative he must decline to contribute fifty thousand *pesos*. But he would assume the responsibility of offering twenty-five.

Did Señor Espiritión understand Señor Franzoni to mean twenty-five thousand *pesos?*

By no means. Twenty-five *pesos*. And in silver; not in gold.

"Your offer insults my government," cried Señor Espiritión, rising with indignation.

"Then," said Mr. Franzoni, in warning tone, *"we will change it."*

The offer was never changed. Could Mr. Franzoni have meant the government?

This was the state of affairs in Anchuria when the winter season opened at Coralio at the end of the second year of Losada's administration. So, when the government and society made its annual exodus to the seashore it was evident that the presidential advent would not be celebrated by unlimited rejoicing. The tenth of November was the day set for the entrance into Coralio of the gay company from the capital. A narrow-gauge railroad runs twenty miles into the interior from Solitas. The government party travels by carriage from San Mateo to this road's terminal point, and proceeds by train to Solitas. From here they march in grand procession to Coralio where, on the day of their coming, festivities and ceremonies abound. But this season saw an ominous dawning of the tenth of November.

Although the rainy season was over, the day seemed to hark back to reeking June. A fine drizzle of rain fell all during the forenoon. The procession entered Coralio amid a strange silence.

President Losada was an elderly man, grizzly bearded, with a considerable ratio of Indian blood revealed in his cinnamon complexion. His carriage headed the procession, surrounded and guarded by Captain Cruz and his famous troop of one hundred light horse *"El Ciento Huilando."* Colonel Rocas followed, with a regiment of the regular army.

The president's sharp, beady eyes glanced about him for the expected demonstration of welcome; but he faced a stolid, indifferent array of citizens. Sightseers the Anchurians are by birth and habit, and they turned out to their last able-bodied unit to witness the scene; but they maintained an accusive silence. They crowded the streets to the very wheel ruts; they covered the red tile roofs to the eaves, but there was never a *"viva"* from them. No wreaths of palm and lemon branches or gorgeous strings of paper roses hung from the windows and balconies as was the custom. There was an apathy, a dull, dissenting disapprobation, that was the more ominous because it puzzled. No one feared an outburst, a revolt of the discontents, for they had no leader. The president and those loyal to him had never even heard whispered a name among them capable of crystallizing the dissatisfaction into opposition. No, there could be no danger. The people always procured a new idol before they destroyed an old one.

At length, after a prodigious galloping and curvetting of red-sashed majors, gold-laced colonels and epauletted generals, the procession formed for its annual progress down the Calle Grande to the Casa Morena, where the ceremony of welcome to the visiting president always took place.

The Swiss band led the line of march. After it pranced the local *comandante*, mounted, and a detachment of his troops. Next came a carriage with four members of the cabinet, conspicuous among them the Minister of War, old General Pilar, with his white moustache and his soldierly bearing. Then the president's vehicle, containing also the Ministers of Finance and State; and surrounded by Captain Cruz's light horse formed in a close double file of fours. Following them, the rest of the officials of state, the judges and distinguished military and social ornaments of public and private life.

As the band struck up, and the movement began, like a bird of ill-omen the

Valhalla, the swiftest steamship of the Vesuvius line, glided into the harbor in plain view of the president and his train. Of course, there was nothing menacing about its arrival—a business firm does not go to war with a nation—but it reminded Señor Espiritión and others in those carriages that the Vesuvius Fruit Company was undoubtedly carrying something up its sleeve for them.

By the time the van of the procession had reached the government building, Captain Cronin, of the *Valhalla*, and Mr. Vincenti, member of the Vesuvius Company, had landed and were pushing their way, bluff, hearty, and nonchalant, through the crowd on the narrow sidewalk. Clad in white linen, big, debonair, with an air of good-humored authority, they made conspicuous figures among the dark mass of unimposing Anchurians, as they penetrated to within a few yards of the steps of the Casa Morena. Looking easily above the heads of the crowd, they perceived another that towered above the undersized natives. It was the fiery poll of Dicky Maloney against the wall close by the lower step; and his broad, seductive grin showed that he recognized their presence.

Dicky had attired himself becomingly for the festive occasion in a well-fitting black suit. Pasa was close by his side, her head covered with the ubiquitous black mantilla.

Mr. Vincenti looked at her attentively.

"Botticelli's Madonna," he remarked, gravely. "I wonder when she got into the game. I don't like his getting tangled with the women. I hoped he would keep away from them."

Captain Cronin's laugh almost drew attention from the parade.

"With that head of hair! Keep away from the women! And a Maloney! Hasn't he got a license? But, nonsense aside, what do you think of the prospects? It's a species of filibustering out of my line."

Vincenti glanced again at Dicky's head and smiled.

"*Rouge et noir*," he said. "There you have it. Make your play, gentlemen. Our money is on the red."

"The lad's game," said Cronin, with a commending look at the tall, easy figure by the steps. "But 'tis all like fly-by-night theatricals to me. The talk's bigger than the stage; there's a smell of gasoline in the air, and they're their own audience and scene-shifters."

They ceased talking, for General Pilar had descended from the first carriage and had taken his stand upon the top step of Casa Morena. As the oldest member of the cabinet, custom had decreed that he should make the address of welcome, presenting the keys of the official residence to the president at its close.

General Pilar was one of the most distinguished citizens of the republic. Hero of three wars and innumerable revolutions, he was an honored guest at European courts and camps. An eloquent speaker and a friend to the people, he represented the highest type of the Anchurians.

Holding in his hand the gilt keys of Casa Morena, he began his address in a historical form, touching upon each administration and the advance of civilization and prosperity from the first striving after liberty down to present times. Arriving at the régime of President Losada, at which point, according to precedent, he should have delivered a eulogy upon its wise conduct and the happiness of the people, General Pilar paused. Then he silently held up the bunch of keys high above his head, with his eyes closely regarding it. The ribbon with which they were bound fluttered in the breeze.

"It still blows," cried the speaker, exultantly. "Citizens of Anchuria, give thanks to the saints this night that our air is still free."

Thus disposing of Losada's administration, he abruptly reverted to that of Olivarra, Anchuria's most popular ruler. Olivarra had been assassinated nine years before while in the prime of life and usefulness. A faction of the Liberal party led by Losada himself had been accused of the deed. Whether guilty or not, it was eight years before the ambitious and scheming Losada had gained his goal.

Upon this theme General Pilar's eloquence was loosed. He drew the picture of the beneficent Olivarra with a loving hand. He reminded the people of the peace, the security, and the happiness they had enjoyed during that period. He recalled in vivid detail and with significant contrast the last winter sojourn of President Olivarra in Coralio, when his appearance at their fiestas was the signal for thundering *vivas* of love and approbation.

The first public expression of sentiment from the people that day followed. A low, sustained murmur went among them like the surf rolling along the shore.

"Ten dollars to a dinner at the Saint Charles," remarked Mr. Vincenti, "that *rouge* wins."

"I never bet against my own interests," said Captain Cronin, lighting a cigar. "Long-winded old boy, for his age. What's he talking about?"

"My Spanish," replied Vincenti, "runs about ten words to the minute; his is something around two hundred. Whatever he's saying, he's getting them warmed up."

"Friends and brothers," General Pilar was saying, "could I reach out my hand this day across the lamentable silence of the grave to Olivarra 'the Good,' to the ruler who was one of you, whose tears fell when you sorrowed, and whose smile followed your joy—I would bring him back to you, but—Olivarra is dead—dead at the hands of a craven assassin!"

The speaker turned and gazed boldly into the carriage of the president. His arm remained extended aloft as if to sustain his peroration. The president was listening, aghast, at this remarkable address of welcome. He was sunk back upon his seat, trembling with rage and dumb surprise, his dark hands tightly gripping the carriage cushions.

Half rising, he extended one arm toward the speaker, and shouted a harsh command at Captain Cruz. The leader of the "Flying Hundred" sat his horse, immovable, with folded arms, giving no sign of having heard. Losada sank back again, his dark features distinctly paling.

"Who says that Olivarra is dead?" suddenly cried the speaker, his voice, old as he was, sounding like a battle trumpet. "His body lies in the grave, but to the people he loved he has bequeathed his spirit—yes, more—his learning, his courage, his kindness—yes, more—his youth, his image—people of Anchuria, have you forgotten Ramon, the son of Olivarra?"

Cronin and Vincenti, watching closely, saw Dicky Maloney suddenly raise his hat, tear off his shock of red hair, leap up the steps and stand at the side of General Pilar. The Minister of War laid his arm across the young man's shoulders. All who had known President Olivarra saw again his same lion-like pose, the same frank, undaunted expression, the same high forehead with the peculiar line of the clustering, crisp black hair.

General Pilar was an experienced orator. He seized the moment of breathless silence that preceded the storm.

"Citizens of Anchuria," he trumpeted, holding aloft the keys to Casa Morena, "I am here to deliver these keys—the keys to your homes and liberty—to your chosen president. Shall I deliver them to Enrico Olivarra's assassin, or to his son?"

"Olivarra! Olivarra!" the crowd shrieked and howled. All vociferated the magic name—men, women, children and the parrots.

And the enthusiasm was not confined to the blood of the plebs. Colonel Rocas ascended the steps and laid his sword theatrically at young Ramon Olivarra's feet. Four members of the cabinet embraced him. Captain Cruz gave a command, and twenty of *El Ciento Huilando* dismounted and arranged themselves in a cordon about the steps of Casa Morena.

But Ramon Olivarra seized that moment to prove himself a born genius and politician. He waved those soldiers aside, and descended the steps to the street. There, without losing his dignity or the distinguished elegance that the loss of his red hair brought him, he took the proletariat to his bosom—the barefooted, the dirty, Indians, Caribs, babies, beggars old, young, saints, soldiers and sinners—he missed none of them.

While this act of the drama was being presented, the scene shifters had been busy at the duties that had been assigned to them. Two of Cruz's dragoons had seized the bridle reins of Losada's horses; others formed a close guard around the carriage; and they galloped off with the tyrant and his two unpopular Ministers. No doubt a place had been prepared for them. There are a number of well-barred stone apartments in Coralio.

"*Rouge* wins," said Mr. Vincenti, calmly lighting another cigar.

Captain Cronin had been intently watching the vicinity of the stone steps for some time.

"Good boy!" he exclaimed suddenly, as if relieved. "I wondered if he was going to forget his Kathleen Mavourneen."

Young Olivarra had reascended the steps and spoken a few words to General Pilar. Then that distinguished veteran descended to the ground and approached Pasa, who still stood, wonder-eyed, where Dicky had left her. With his plumed hat in his hand, and his medals and decorations shining on his breast, the general spoke to her and gave her his arm, and they went up the stone steps of the Casa Morena together. And then Ramon Olivarra stepped forward and took both her hands before all the people.

And while the cheering was breaking out afresh everywhere, Captain Cronin and Mr. Vincenti turned and walked back toward the shore where the gig was waiting for them.

"There'll be another '*presidente proclamada*' in the morning," said Mr. Vincenti, musingly. "As a rule they are not as reliable as the elected ones, but this youngster seems to have some good stuff in him. He planned and manœuvred the entire campaign. Olivarra's widow, you know, was wealthy. After her husband was assassinated she went to the States, and educated her son at Yale. The Vesuvius Company hunted him up, and backed him in the little game."

"It's a glorious thing," said Cronin, half jestingly, "to be able to discharge a government, and insert one of your own choosing, in these days."

"Oh, it is only a matter of business," said Vincenti, stopping and offering the stump of his cigar to a monkey that swung down from a lime tree; "and that is what moves the world of to-day. That extra *real* on the price of bananas had to go. We took the shortest way of removing it."

TWO RECALLS

THERE remain three duties to be performed before the curtain falls upon the patched comedy. Two have been promised: the third is no less obligatory.

It was set forth in the programme of this tropic vaudeville that it would be made known why Shorty O'Day, of the Columbia Detective Agency, lost his position. Also that Smith should come again to tell us what mystery he followed that night on the shores of Anchuria when he strewed so many cigar stumps around the cocoanut palm during his lonely night vigil on the beach.

These things were promised; but a bigger thing yet remains to be accomplished —the clearing up of a seeming wrong that has been done according to the array of chronicled facts (truthfully set forth) that have been presented. And one voice, speaking, shall do these three things.

Two men sat on a stringer of a North River pier in the City of New York. A steamer from the tropics had begun to unload bananas and oranges on the pier. Now and then a banana or two would fall from an overripe bunch, and one of the two men would shamble forward, seize the fruit and return to share it with his companion.

One of the men was in the ultimate stage of deterioration. As far as rain and wind and sun could wreck the garments he wore, it had been done. In his person the ravages of drink were as plainly visible. And yet, upon his high-bridged, rubicund nose was jauntily perched a pair of shining and flawless gold-rimmed glasses.

The other man was not so far gone upon the descending Highway of the Incompetents. Truly, the flower of his manhood had gone to seed—seed that, perhaps, no soil might sprout. But there were still cross-cuts along where he travelled through which he might yet regain the pathway of usefulness without disturbing the slumbering Miracles. This man was short and compactly built. He had an oblique, dead eye, like that of a string-ray, and the moustache of a cocktail mixer. We know the eye and the moustache; we know that Smith of the luxurious yacht, the gorgeous raiment, the mysterious mission, the magic disappearance, has come again, though shorn of the accessories of his former state.

At his third banana, the man with the nose glasses spat it from him with a shudder.

"Deuce take all fruit!" he remarked, in a patrician tone of disgust. "I lived for two years where these things grow. The memory of their taste lingers with you. The oranges are not so bad. Just see if you can gather a couple of them, O'Day, when the next broken crate comes up."

"Did you live down with the monkeys?" asked the other, made tepidly garrulous by the sunshine and the alleviating meal of juicy fruit. "I was down there, once myself. But only for a few hours. That was when I was with the Columbia Detective Agency. The monkey people did me up. I'd have my job yet if it hadn't been for them. I'll tell you about it.

"One day the chief sent a note around to the office that read: 'Send O'Day here at once for a big piece of business.' I was the crack detective of the agency at that time. They always handed me the big jobs. The address the chief wrote from was down in the Wall Street district.

"When I got there I found him in a private office with a lot of directors who were looking pretty fuzzy. They stated the case. The president of the Republic Insurance Company had skipped with about a tenth of a million dollars in cash. The directors wanted him back pretty bad, but they wanted the money worse. They said they needed it. They had traced the old gent's movements to where he boarded a tramp fruit steamer bound for South America that same morning with his daughter and a big gripsack—all the family he had.

"One of the directors had his steam yacht coaled and with steam up, ready for the trip; and he turned her over to me, cart blongsh. In four hours I was on board of her, and hot on the trail of the fruit tub. I had a pretty good idea where old Wahrfield—that was his name, J. Churchill Wahrfield—would head for. At that time we had a treaty with about every foreign country except Belgium and that banana republic Anchuria. There wasn't a photo of old Wahrfield to be had in New York—he had been foxy there—but I had his description. And besides, the lady with him would be a dead-give-away anywhere. She was one of the high-flyers in Society—not the kind that have their pictures in the Sunday papers—but the real sort that open chrysanthemum shows and christen battleships.

"Well, sir, we never got a sight of that fruit tub on the road. The ocean is a pretty big place; and I guess we took different paths across it. But we kept going toward this Anchuria, where the fruiter was bound for.

"We struck the monkey coast one afternoon about four. There was a ratty-looking steamer off shore taking on bananas. The monkeys were loading her up with big barges. It might be the one the old man had taken, and it might not. I went ashore to look around. The scenery was pretty good. I never saw any finer on the New York stage. I struck an American on shore, a big, cool chap, standing around with the monkeys. He showed me the consul's office. The consul was a nice young fellow. He said the fruiter was the *Karlsefin*, running generally to New Orleans, but took her last cargo to New York. Then I was sure my people were on board, although everybody told me that no passengers had landed. I didn't think they would land until after dark, for they might have been shy about it on account of seeing that yacht of mine hanging around. So, all I had to do was to wait and nab 'em when they came ashore. I couldn't arrest old Wahrfield without extradition papers, but my play was to get the cash. They generally give up if you strike 'em when they're tired and rattled and short on nerve.

"After dark I sat under a cocoanut tree on the beach for a while, and then I walked around and investigated that town some, and it was enough to give you the lions. If a man could stay in New York and be honest, he'd better do it than to hit that monkey town with a million.

"Dinky little mud houses; grass over your shoe tops in the streets; ladies in low-neck-an-short-sleeves walking around smoking cigars; tree frogs rattling like a hose cart going to a ten blow; big mountains dropping gravel in the back yards; and the sea licking the paint off in front—no, sir—a man had better be in God's country living on free lunch than there.

"The main street ran along the beach, and I walked down it, and then turned up a kind of lane where the houses were made of poles and straw. I wanted to see what the monkeys did when they weren't climbing cocoanut trees. The very first shack I looked in I saw my people. They must have come ashore while I was promenading. A man about fifty, smooth face, heavy eyebrows, dressed in black broadcloth, looking like he was just about to say, 'Can any little boy in the Sunday School answer that?' He was freezing on to a grip that weighed like a dozen gold bricks, and a swell girl—a regular peach, with a Fifth Avenue cut—was sitting on a wooden chair. An old black woman was fixing some coffee and beans on a table. The light they had came from a lantern hung on a nail. I went and stood in the door, and they looked at me, and I said:

" 'Mr. Wahrfield, you are my prisoner. I hope, for the lady's sake, you will take the matter sensibly. You know why I want you.'

" 'Who are you?' says the old gent.

" 'O'Day,' says I, 'of the Columbia Detective Agency. And now, sir, let me give you a piece of good advice. You go back and take your medicine like a man. Hand 'em back the boodle; and maybe they'll let you off light. Go back easy, and I'll put in a word for you. I'll give you five minutes to decide.' I pulled out my watch and waited.

"Then the young lady chipped in. She was one of the genuine high-steppers. You could tell by the way her clothes fit and the style she had that Fifth Avenue was made for her.

" 'Come inside,' she says. 'Don't stand in the door and disturb the whole street with that suit of clothes. Now, what is it you want?'

" 'Three minutes gone,' I said. 'I'll tell you again while the other two tick off.

" 'You'll admit being the president of the Republic, won't you?'

"'I am,' says he.

"'Well, then,' says I, 'it ought to be plain to you. Wanted, in New York, J. Churchill Wahrfield, president of the Republic Insurance Company.

"'Also the funds belonging to said company, now in that grip, in the unlawful possession of said J. Churchill Wahrfield.'

"'Oh-h-h-h!' says the young lady, as if she was thinking, 'you want to take us back to New York?'

"'To take Mr. Wahrfield. There's no charge against you, miss. There'll be no objection, of course, to your returning with your father.'

"Of a sudden the girl gave a tiny scream and grabbed the old boy around the neck. 'Oh, father, father!' she says, kind of contralto, 'can this be true? Have you taken money that is not yours? Speak, father!' It made you shiver to hear the tremolo stop she put on her voice.

"The old boy looked pretty bughouse when she first grappled him, but she went on, whispering in his ear and patting his off shoulder till he stood still, but sweating a little.

"She got him to one side and they talked together a minute, and then he put on some gold eyeglasses and walked up and handed me the grip.

"'Mr. Detective,' he says, talking a little broken. 'I conclude to return with you. I have finished to discover that life on this desolate and displeased coast would be worse than to die, itself. I will go back and hurl myself upon the mercy of the Republic Company. Have you brought a sheep?'

"'Sheep!' says I; 'I haven't a single——'

"'Ship,' cut in the young lady. 'Don't get funny. Father is of German birth, and doesn't speak perfect English. How did you come?'

"The girl was all broke up. She had a handkerchief to her face, and kept saying every little bit, 'Oh, father, father!' She walked up to me and laid her lily-white hand on the clothes that had pained her at first. I told her I came in a private yacht.

"'Mr. O'Day,' she says. 'Oh, take us away from this horrid country at once. Can you! Will you! Say you will.'

"'I'll try,' I said, concealing the fact that I was dying to get them on salt water before they could change their mind.

"One thing they both kicked against was going through the town to the boat landing. Said they dreaded publicity, and now that they were going to return, they had a hope that the thing might yet be kept out of the papers. They swore they wouldn't go unless I got them out to the yacht without any one knowing it, so I agreed to humor them.

"The sailors who rowed me ashore were playing billiards in a bar-room near the water, waiting for orders, and I proposed to have them take the boat down the beach half a mile or so, and take us up there. How to get them word was the question, for I couldn't leave the grip with the prisoner, and I couldn't take it with me, not knowing but what the monkeys might stick me up.

"The young lady says the old colored woman would take them a note. I sat down and wrote it, and gave it to the dame with plain directions what to do, and she grins like a baboon and shakes her head.

"Then Mr. Wahrfield handed her a string of foreign dialect, and she nods her head and says, 'See, señor,' maybe fifty times, and lights out with the note.

"'Old Augusta only understands German,' said Miss Wahrfield, smiling at me. 'We stopped in her house to ask where we could find lodging, and she insisted upon our having coffee. She tells us she was raised in a German family in San Domingo.'

"'Very likely,' I said. 'But you can search me for German words, except *nix verstay* and *noch einst*. I would have called that "See, señor" French, though, on a gamble.'

"Well, we three make a sneak around the edge of town so as not to be seen. We got tangled in vines and ferns and the banana bushes and tropical scenery a good deal. The monkey suburbs was as wild as places in Central Park. We came out on the beach a good half mile below. A brown chap was lying asleep under a cocoanut tree, with a ten-foot musket beside him. Mr. Wahrfield takes up the gun and pitches it into the sea. 'The coast is guarded,' he says. 'Rebellion and plots ripen like fruit.' He pointed to the sleeping man, who never stirred. 'Thus,' he says, 'they perform trusts. Children!'

"I saw our boat coming, and I struck a match and lit a piece of newspaper to show them where we were. In thirty minutes we were on board the yacht.

"The first thing, Mr. Wahrfield and his daughter and I took the grip into the owner's cabin, opened it up and took an inventory. There was one hundred and five thousand dollars, United States treasury notes, in it, beside a lot of diamond jewelry and a couple of hundred Havana cigars. I gave the old man the cigars and a receipt for the rest of the lot, as agent for the company, and locked the stuff up in my private quarters.

"I never had a pleasanter trip than that one. After we got to sea the young lady turned out to be the jolliest ever. The very first time we sat down to dinner, and the steward filled her glass with champagne—that director's yacht was a regular floating Waldorf-Astoria—she winks at me and says, 'What's the use to borrow trouble, Mr. Fly Cop? Here's hoping you may live to eat the hen that scratches on your grave.' There was a piano on board, and she sat down to it and sung better than you give up two cases to hear plenty times. She knew about nine operas clear through. She was sure enough *bon ton* and swell. She wasn't one of the 'among others present' kind; she belonged on the special mention list!

"The old man, too, perked up amazingly on the way. He passed the cigars, and says to me once, quite chipper, out of a cloud of smoke, 'Mr. O'Day, somehow I think the Republic Company will not give me the much trouble. Guard well the gripvalise of the money, Mr. O'Day, for that it must be returned to them that it belongs when we finish to arrive.'

"When we landed in New York I 'phoned to the chief to meet us in that director's office. We got in a cab and went there. I carried the grip, and we walked in, and I was pleased to see that the chief had got together that same old crowd of moneybugs with pink faces and white vests to see us march in. I set the grip on the table. 'There's the money,' I said.

" 'And your prisoner?' said the chief.

"I pointed to Mr. Wahrfield, and he stepped forward and says:

" 'The honor of a word with you, sir, to explain.'

"He and the chief went into another room and stayed ten minutes. When they came back the chief looked as black as a ton of coal.

" 'Did this gentleman,' he says to me, 'have this valise in his possession when you first saw him?'

" 'He did,' said I.

"The chief took up the grip and handed it to the prisoner with a bow, and says to the director crowd: 'Do any of you recognize this gentleman?'

"They all shook their pink faces.

" 'Allow me to present,' he goes on, 'Señor Miraflores, president of the Republic of Anchuria. The señor has generously consented to overlook this outrageous blunder, on condition that we undertake to secure him against the annoyance of public comment. It is a concession on his part to overlook an insult for which he might claim international redress. I think we can gratefully promise him secrecy in the matter.'

"They gave him a pink nod all round.

" 'O'Day,' he says to me. 'As a private detective you're wasted. In a war, where kidnapping governments is in the rules, you'd be invaluable. Come down to the office at eleven.'

"I knew what that meant.

"'So that's the president of the monkeys,' says I. 'Well, why couldn't he have said so?'

"Wouldn't it jar you?"

THE VITAGRAPHOSCOPE

VAUDEVILLE is intrinsically episodic and discontinuous. Its audiences do not demand dénouements. Sufficient unto each "turn" is the evil thereof. No one cares how many romances the singing comédienne may have had if she can capably sustain the limelight and a high note or two. The audiences reck not if the performing dogs get to the pound the moment they have jumped through their last hoop. They do not desire bulletins about the possible injuries received by the comic bicyclist who retires head-first from the stage in a crash of (property) china-ware. Neither do they consider that their seat coupons entitle them to be instructed whether or no there is a sentiment between the lady solo banjoist and the Irish monologist.

Therefore let us have no lifting of the curtain upon a tableau of the united lovers, backgrounded by defeated villainy and derogated by the comic, osculating maid and butler, thrown in as a sop to the Cerberi of the fifty-cent seats.

But our programme ends with a brief "turn" or two; and then to the exits. Whoever sits the show out may find, if he will, the slender thread that binds together, though ever so slightly, the story that, perhaps, only the Walrus will understand.

Extracts from a letter from the first vice-president of the Republic Insurance Company, of New York City, to Frank Goodwin, of Coralio, Republic of Anchuria.

My Dear Mr. Goodwin:—Your communication per Messrs. Howland and Fourchet, of New Orleans, has reached us. Also their draft on N. Y. for $100,000, the amount abstracted from the funds of this company by the late J. Churchill Wahrfield, its former president. . . . The officers and directors unite in requesting me to express to you their sincere esteem and thanks for your prompt, and much appreciated return of the entire missing sum within two weeks from the time of its disappearance. . . . Can assure you that the matter will not be allowed to receive the least publicity. . . . Regret exceedingly the distressing death of Mr. Wahrfield by his own hand, but. . . . Congratulations on your marriage to Miss Wahrfield . . . many charms, winning manners, noble and womanly nature and envied position in the best metropolitan society. . . .

Cordially yours,

LUCIUS E. APPLEGATE.

First Vice-President the Republic Insurance Company.

The Vitagraphoscope
(Moving Pictures)

The Last Sausage

SCENE—*An Artist's Studio.* The artist, a young man of prepossessing appearance, sits in a dejected attitude, amid a litter of sketches, with his head resting upon his hand. An oil stove stands on a pine box in the centre of the studio. The artist rises, tightens his waist belt to another hole, and lights the stove. He goes to a tin bread box, half-hidden by a screen, takes out a solitary link of sausage, turns the box up-side-down to show that there is no more, and chucks the sausage into a frying-pan, which he sets upon the stove. The flame of the stove goes out, showing that there is no more oil. The artist, in evident despair, seizes the sausage, in a sudden access of rage, and hurls it violently from him. At the same time a door opens, and a man who enters receives the sausage forcibly against his nose. He seems to cry out; and is observed to make a dance step or two, vigorously. The newcomer is a ruddy-faced, active, keen-looking man, apparently of Irish ancestry. Next he is observed to laugh immoderately; he kicks over the stove; he claps the artist (who is vainly striving to grasp his hand) vehemently upon the back. Then he goes through a pantomime which to the sufficiently intelligent spectator reveals that he has acquired large sums of money by trading pot-metal hatchets and razors to the Indians of the Cordillera Mountains for gold dust. He draws a roll of money as large as a small loaf of bread from his pocket, and waves it above his head, while at the same time he makes pantomime of drinking from a glass. The artist hurriedly secures his hat, and the two leave the studio together.

The Writing on the Sands

SCENE—*The Beach at Nice.* A woman, beautiful, still young, exquisitely clothed, complacent, poised, reclines near the water, idly scrawling letters in the sand with the staff of her silken parasol. The beauty of her face is audacious; her languid pose is one that you feel to be impermanent—you wait, expectant, for her to spring or glide or crawl, like a panther that has unaccountably become stock-still. She idly scrawls in the sand; and the word that she always writes is "Isabel." A man sits a few yards away. You can see that they are companions, even if no longer comrades. His face is dark and smooth, and almost inscrutable—but not quite. The two speak little together. The man also scratches on the sand with his cane. And the word that he writes is "Anchuria." And then he looks out where the Mediterranean and the sky intermingle, with death in his gaze.

The Wilderness and Thou

SCENE—*The Borders of a Gentleman's Estate in a Tropical Land.* An old Indian, with a mahogany-colored face, is trimming the grass on a grave by a mangrove swamp. Presently he rises to his feet and walks slowly toward a grove that is shaded by the gathering, brief twilight. In the edge of the grove stands a man who is stalwart, with a kind and courteous air, and a woman of a serene and clear-cut loveliness. When the old Indian comes up to them the man drops money in his hand. The grave-tender, with the stolid pride of his race, takes it as his due, and goes his way. The two in the edge of the grove turn back along the dim pathway, and walk close, close—for, after all, what is the world at its best but a little round field of the moving pictures with two walking together in it?

CURTAIN

OPTIONS

OPTIONS

"THE ROSE OF DIXIE"

WHEN *The Rose of Dixie* magazine was started by a stock company in Toombs City, Georgia, there was never but one candidate for its chief editorial position in the minds of its owners. Col. Aquila Telfair was the man for the place. By all the rights of learning, family, reputation, and Southern traditions, he was its foreordained, fit, and logical editor. So, a committee of the patriotic Georgia citizens who had subscribed the founding fund of $100,000 called upon Colonel Telfair at his residence, Cedar Heights, fearful lest the enterprise and the South should suffer by his possible refusal.

The colonel received them in his great library, where he spent most of his days. The library had descended to him from his father. It contained ten thousand volumes, some of which had been published as late as the year 1861. When the deputation arrived, Colonel Telfair was seated at his massive white-pine centre-table, reading Burton's "Anatomy of Melancholy." He arose and shook hands punctiliously with each member of the committee. If you were familiar with *The Rose of Dixie* you will remember the colonel's portrait, which appeared in it from time to time. You could not forget the long, carefully brushed white hair, the hooked, high-bridged nose, slightly twisted to the left; the keen eyes under the still black eyebrows; the classic mouth beneath the drooping white mustache, slightly frazzled at the ends.

The committee solicitously offered him the position of managing editor, humbly presenting an outline of the field that the publication was designed to cover and mentioning a comfortable salary. The colonel's lands were growing poorer each year and were much cut up by red gullies. Besides, the honor was not one to be refused.

In a forty-minute speech of acceptance, Colonel Telfair gave an outline of English literature from Chaucer to Macaulay, re-fought the battle of Chancellorsville, and said that, God helping him, he would so conduct *The Rose of Dixie* that its fragrance and beauty would permeate the entire world, hurling back into the teeth of the Northern minions their belief that no genius or good could exist in the brains and hearts of the people whose property they had destroyed and whose rights they had curtailed.

Offices for the magazine were partitioned off and furnished in the second floor of the First National Bank building; and it was for the colonel to cause *The Rose of Dixie* to blossom and flourish or to wilt in the balmy air of the land of flowers.

The staff of assistants and contributors that Editor-Colonel Telfair drew about him was a peach. It was a whole crate of Georgia peaches. The first assistant editor, Tolliver Lee Fairfax, had had a father killed during Pickett's charge. The second assistant, Keats Unthank, was the nephew of one of Morgan's Raiders. The book reviewer, Jackson Rockingham, had been the youngest soldier in the Confederate army, having appeared on the field of battle with a sword in one hand and a milk-bottle in the other. The art editor, Roncesvalles Sykes, was a third cousin to a nephew of Jefferson Davis. Miss Lavinia Terhune, the colonel's stenographer and typewriter, had an aunt who had once been kissed by Stonewall Jackson. Tommy Webster, the head office boy, got his job by having recited Father Ryan's poems, complete, at the commencement exercises of the Toombs City High School. The girls who wrapped and addressed the magazines were members of old Southern families in Reduced Circumstances. The cashier was a scrub named Hawkins, from Ann Arbor, Michigan, who had recommendations and a bond from a guarantee company filed with the owners. Even Georgia stock companies sometimes realize that it takes live ones to bury the dead.

Well, sir, if you believe me, *The Rose of Dixie* blossomed five times before anybody heard of it except the people who buy their hooks and eyes in Toombs City. Then Hawkins climbed off his stool and told on 'em to the stock company. Even in Ann Arbor he had been used to having his business propositions heard of at least as far away as Detroit. So an advertising manager was engaged—Beauregard Fitzhugh Banks—a young man in a lavender necktie, whose grandfather had been the Exalted High Pillow-slip of the Kuklux Klan.

In spite of which *The Rose of Dixie* kept coming out every month. Although in every issue it ran photos of either the Taj Mahal or the Luxembourg Gardens, or Carmencita or La Follette, a certain number of people bought it and subscribed for it. As a boom for it, Editor-Colonel Telfair ran three different views of Andrew Jackson's old home, "The Hermitage," a full-page engraving of the second battle of Manassas, entitled "Lee to the Rear!" and a five-thousand-word biography of Belle Boyd in the same number. The subscription list that month advanced 118. Also there were poems in the same issue by Leonina Vashti Haricot (pen-name), related to the Haricots of Charleston, South Carolina, and Bill Thompson, nephew of one of the stockholders. And an article from a special society correspondent describing a tea-party given by the swell Boston and English set, where a lot of tea was spilled overboard by some of the guests masquerading as Indians.

One day a person whose breath would easily cloud a mirror, he was so much alive, entered the office of *The Rose of Dixie*. He was a man about the size of a real-estate agent, with a self-tied tie and a manner that he must have borrowed conjointly from W. J. Bryan, Hackenschmidt, and Hetty Green. He was shown into the editor-colonel's *pons asinorum*. Colonel Telfair rose and began a Prince Albert bow.

"I'm Thacker," said the intruder, taking the editor's chair—"T. T. Thacker, of New York."

He dribbled hastily upon the colonel's desk some cards, a bulk manila envelope, and a letter from the owners of *The Rose of Dixie*. This letter introduced Mr. Thacker, and politely requested Colonel Telfair to give him a conference and whatever information about the magazine he might desire.

"I've been corresponding with the secretary of the magazine owners for some time," said Thacker, briskly. "I'm a practical magazine man myself, and a circulation booster as good as any, if I do say it. I'll guarantee an increase of anywhere from ten thousand to a hundred thousand a year for any publication that isn't printed in a dead language. I've had my eye on *The Rose of Dixie* ever since it started. I know every end of the business from editing to setting up the classified ads. Now, I've come down here to put a good bunch of money in the magazine, if I can see my way clear. It ought to be made to pay. The secretary tells me it's losing money. I don't see why a magazine in the South, if it's properly handled, shouldn't get a good circulation in the North, too."

Colonel Telfair leaned back in his chair and polished his gold-rimmed glasses.

"Mr. Thacker," said he, courteously but firmly, "*The Rose of Dixie* is a publication devoted to the fostering and the voicing of Southern genius. Its watch-word, which you may have seen on the cover, is 'Of, For, and By the South.'"

"But you wouldn't object to a Northern circulation, would you?" asked Thacker.

"I suppose," said the editor-colonel, "that it is customary to open the circulation lists to all. I do not know. I have nothing to do with the business affairs of the magazine. I was called upon to assume editorial control of it, and I have devoted to its conduct such poor literary talents as I may possess and whatever store of erudition I may have acquired."

"Sure," said Thacker. "But a dollar is a dollar anywhere, North, South, or West—whether you're buying codfish, goober peas, or Rocky Ford cantaloupes. Now, I've been looking over your November number. I see one here on your desk. You don't mind running over it with me?

"Well, your leading article is all right. A good write-up of the cotton-belt with plenty of photographs is a winner any time. New York is always interested in the cotton crop. And this sensational account of the Hatfield-McCoy feud, by a schoolmate of a niece of the Governor of Kentucky, isn't such a bad idea. It happened so long ago that most people have forgotten it. Now, here's a poem three pages long called 'The Tyrant's Foot,' by Lorella Lascelles. I've pawed around a good deal over manuscripts, but I never saw her name on a rejection slip."

"Miss Lascelles," said the editor, "is one of our most widely recognized Southern poetesses. She is closely related to the Alabama Lascelles family, and made with her own hands the silken Confederate banner that was presented to the governor of that state at his inauguration."

"But why," persisted Thacker, "is the poem illustrated with a view of the M. & O. Railroad depot at Tuscaloosa?"

"The illustration," said the colonel, with dignity, "shows a corner of the fence surrounding the old homestead where Miss Lascelles was born."

"All right," said Thacker. "I read the poem, but I couldn't tell whether it was about the depot or the battle of Bull Run. Now, here's a short story called 'Rosie's Temptation,' by Fosdyke Piggott. It's rotten. What is a Piggott, anyway?"

"Mr. Piggott," said the editor, "is a brother of the principal stockholder of the magazine."

"All's right with the world—Piggott passes," said Thacker. "Well, this article on Arctic exploration and the one on tarpon fishing might go. But how about this write-up of the Atlanta, New Orleans, Nashville, and Savannah breweries? It seems to consist mainly of statistics about their output and the quality of their beer. What's the chip over the bug?"

"If I understand your figurative language," answered Colonel Telfair, "it is this: the article you refer to was handed to me by the owners of the magazine with instructions to publish it. The literary quality of it did not appeal to me. But, in a measure, I feel impelled to conform, in certain matters, to the wishes of the gentlemen who are interested in the financial side of *The Rose*."

"I see," said Thacker. "Next we have two pages of selections from 'Lalla Rookh,' by Thomas Moore. Now, what Federal prison did Moore escape from, or what's the name of the F. F. V. family that he carries as a handicap?"

"Moore was an Irish poet who died in 1852," said Colonel Telfair, pityingly. "He is a classic. I have been thinking of reprinting his translation of Anacreon serially in the magazine."

"Look out for the copyright laws," said Thacker, flippantly. "Who's Bessie Belleclair, who contributes the essay on the newly completed water-works plant in Milledgeville?"

"The name, sir," said Colonel Telfair, "is the *nom de guerre* of Miss Elvira Simpkins. I have not the honor of knowing the lady; but her contribution was sent us by Congressman Brower, of her native state. Congressman Brower's mother was related to the Polks of Tennessee."

"Now, see here, Colonel," said Thacker, throwing down the magazine, "this won't do. You can't successfully run a magazine for one particular section of the country. You've got to make a universal appeal. Look how the Northern publications have catered to the South and encouraged the Southern writers. And you've got to go far and wide for your contributors. You've got to buy stuff according to its quality, without any regard to the pedigree of the author. Now, I'll bet a quart of ink that this Southern parlor organ you've been running has never played a note that originated above Mason & Hamlin's line. Am I right?"

"I have carefully and conscientiously rejected all contributions from that section of the country—if I understand your figurative language aright," replied the colonel.

"All right. Now, I'll show you something."

Thacker reached for his thick manila envelope and dumped a mass of type-written manuscript on the editor's desk.

"Here's some truck," said he, "that I paid cash for, and brought along with me."

One by one he folded back the manuscripts and showed their first pages to the colonel.

"Here are four short stories by four of the highest priced authors in the United States—three of 'em living in New York, and one commuting. There's a special article on Vienna-bred society by Tom Vampson. Here's an Italian serial by Captain Jack—no—it's the other Crawford. Here are three separate exposés of city governments by Sniffings, and here's a dandy entitled 'What Women Carry in Dress-Suit Cases'—a Chicago newspaper woman hired herself out for five years as a lady's maid to get that information. And here's a Synopsis of Preceding Chapters of Hall Caine's new serial to appear next June. And here's a couple of pounds of *vers de société* that I got at a rate from the clever magazines. That's the stuff that people everywhere want. And now here's a write-up with photographs at the ages of four, twelve, twenty-two, and thirty of George B. McClellan. It's a prognostication. He's bound to be elected Mayor of New York. It'll make a big hit all over the country. He——"

"I beg your pardon," said Colonel Telfair, stiffening in his chair. "What was the name?"

"Oh, I see," said Thacker, with half a grin. "Yes, he's a son of the General. We'll pass that manuscript up. But, if you'll excuse me, Colonel, it's a magazine we're trying to make go off—not the first gun at Fort Sumter. Now, here's a thing that's bound to get next to you. It's an original poem by James Whit-comb Riley. J. W. himself. You know what that means to a magazine. I won't tell you what I had to pay for that poem; but I'll tell you this—Riley can make more money writing with a fountain-pen than you or I can with one that lets the ink run. I'll read you the last two stanzas:

> "Pa lays around 'n' loafs all day,
>   'N' reads and makes us leave him be.
> He lets me do just like I please,
>   'N' when I'm bad he laughs at me,
> 'N' when I holler loud 'n' say
>   Bad words 'n' then begin to tease
> The cat, 'n' pa just smiles, ma's mad
>   'N' gives me Jesse crost her knees.
> I always wondered why that wuz—
>   I guess it's cause
>   Pa never does.

" 'N' after all the lights are out
I'm sorry 'bout it; so I creep
Out of my trundle bed to ma's
'N' say I love her a whole heap,
'N' kiss her, 'n' I hug her tight.
'N' it's too dark to see her eyes,
But every time I do I know
She cries 'n' cries 'n' cries 'n' cries.
I always wondered why that wuz—
I guess it's cause
Pa never does.

"That's the stuff," continued Thacker. "What do you think of that?"

"I am not unfamiliar with the works of Mr. Riley," said the colonel, deliberately. "I believe he lives in Indiana. For the last ten years I have been somewhat of a literary recluse, and am familiar with nearly all the books in the Cedar Heights library. I am also of the opinion that a magazine should contain a certain amount of poetry. Many of the sweetest singers of the South have already contributed to the pages of *The Rose of Dixie.* I, myself, have thought of translating from the original for publication in its pages the works of the great Italian poet Tasso. Have you ever drunk from the fountain of this immortal poet's lines, Mr. Thacker?"

"Not even a demi-Tasso," said Thacker. "Now, let's come to the point, Colonel Telfair. I've already invested some money in this as a flyer. That bunch of manuscripts cost me $4,000. My object was to try a number of them in the next issue—I believe you make up less than a month ahead—and see what effect it has on the circulation. I believe that by printing the best stuff we can get in the North, South, East, or West we can make the magazine go. You have there the letter from the owning company asking you to coöperate with me in the plan. Let's chuck out some of this slush that you've been publishing just because the writers are related to the Skoopdoodles of Skoopdoodle County. Are you with me?"

"As long as I continue to be the editor of *The Rose,*" said Colonel Telfair, with dignity, "I shall be its editor. But I desire also to conform to the wishes of its owners if I can do so conscientiously."

"That's the talk," said Thacker, briskly. "Now, how much of this stuff I've brought can we get into the January number? We want to begin right away."

"There is yet space in the January number," said the editor, "for about eight thousand words, roughly estimated."

"Great!" said Thacker. "It isn't much, but it'll give the readers some change from goobers, governors, and Gettysburg. I'll leave the selection of the stuff I brought to fill the space to you, as it's all good. I've got to run back to New York, and I'll be down again in a couple of weeks."

Colonel Telfair slowly swung his eye-glasses by their broad, black ribbon.

"The space in the January number that I referred to," said he, measuredly, "has been held open purposely, pending a decision that I have not yet made. A short time ago a contribution was submitted to *The Rose of Dixie* that is one of the most remarkable literary efforts that has ever come under my observation. None but a master mind and talent could have produced it. It would about fill the space that I have reserved for its possible use."

Thacker looked anxious.

"What kind of stuff is it?" he asked. "Eight thousand words sounds suspicious. The oldest families must have been collaborating. Is there going to be another secession?"

"The author of the article," continued the colonel, ignoring Thacker's allusions, "is a writer of some reputation. He has also distinguished himself in other ways. I do not feel at liberty to reveal to you his name—at least not until I have decided whether or not to accept his contribution."

"Well," said Thacker, nervously, "is it a continued story, or an account of the unveiling of the new town pump in Whitmire, South Carolina, or a revised list of General Lee's body-servants, or what?"

"You are disposed to be facetious," said Colonel Telfair, calmly. "The article is from the pen of a thinker, a philosopher, a lover of mankind, a student, and a rhetorician of high degree."

"It must have been written by a syndicate," said Thacker. "But, honestly, Colonel, you want to go slow. I don't know of any eight-thousand-word single doses of written matter that are read by anybody these days, except Supreme Court briefs and reports of murder trials. You haven't by any accident gotten hold of a copy of one of Daniel Webster's speeches, have you?"

Colonel Telfair swung a little in his chair and looked steadily from under his bushy eyebrows at the magazine promoter.

"Mr. Thacker," he said, gravely, "I am willing to segregate the somewhat crude expression of your sense of humor from the solicitude that your business investments undoubtedly have conferred upon you. But I must ask you to cease your jibes and derogatory comments upon the South and the Southern people. They, sir, will not be tolerated in the office of *The Rose of Dixie* for one moment. And before you proceed with more of your covert insinuations that I, the editor of this magazine, am not a competent judge of the merits of the matter submitted to its consideration, I beg that you will first present some evidence or proof that you are my superior in any way, shape, or form relative to the question in hand."

"Oh, come, Colonel," said Thacker, good-naturedly. "I didn't do anything like that to you. It sounds like an indictment by the fourth assistant attorney-general. Let's get back to business. What's this 8,000 to 1 shot about?"

"The article," said Colonel Telfair, acknowledging the apology by a slight bow, "covers a wide area of knowledge. It takes up theories and questions that have puzzled the world for centuries, and disposes of them logically and concisely. One by one it holds up to view the evils of the world, points out the way of eradicating them, and then conscientiously and in detail commends the good. There is hardly a phase of human life that it does not discuss wisely, calmly, and equitably. The great policies of governments, the duties of private citizens, the obligations of home life, law, ethics, morality—all these important subjects are handled with a calm wisdom and confidence that I must confess has captured my admiration."

"It must be a crackerjack," said Thacker, impressed.

"It is a great contribution to the world's wisdom," said the colonel. "The only doubt remaining in my mind as to the tremendous advantage it would be to us to give it publication in *The Rose of Dixie* is that I have not yet sufficient information about the author to give his work publicity in our magazine."

"I thought you said he is a distinguished man," said Thacker.

"He is," replied the colonel, "both in literary and in other more diversified and extraneous fields. But I am extremely careful about the matter that I accept for publication. My contributors are people of unquestionable repute and connections, which fact can be verified at any time. As I said, I am holding this article until I can acquire more information about its author. I do not know whether I will publish it or not. If I decide against it, I shall be much pleased, Mr. Thacker, to substitute the matter that you are leaving with me in its place."

Thacker was somewhat at sea.

"I don't seem to gather," said he, "much about the gist of this inspired piece of literature. It sounds more like a dark horse than Pegasus to me."

"It is a human document," said the colonel-editor, confidently, "from a man of great accomplishments who, in my opinion, has obtained a stronger grasp on the world and its outcomes than that of any man living to-day."

Thacker rose to his feet excitedly.

"Say!" he said. "It isn't possible that you've cornered John D. Rockefeller's memoirs, is it? Don't tell me that all at once."

"No, sir," said Colonel Telfair. "I am speaking of mentality and literature, not of the less worthy intricacies of trade."

"Well, what's the trouble about running the article," asked Thacker, a little impatiently, "if the man's well known and has got the stuff?"

Colonel Telfair sighed.

"Mr. Thacker," said he, "for once I have been tempted. Nothing has yet appeared in *The Rose of Dixie* that has not been from the pen of one of its sons or daughters. I know little about the author of this article except that he has acquired prominence in a section of the country that has always been inimical to my heart and mind. But I recognize his genius; and, as I have told you, I have instituted an investigation of his personality. Perhaps it will be futile. But I shall pursue the inquiry. Until that is finished, I must leave open the question of filling the vacant space in our January number."

Thacker arose to leave.

"All right, Colonel," he said, as cordially as he could. "You use your own judgment. If you've really got a scoop or something that will make 'em sit up, run it instead of my stuff. I'll drop in again in about two weeks. Good luck!"

Colonel Telfair and the magazine promoter shook hands.

Returning a fortnight later, Thacker dropped off a very rocky Pullman at Toombs City. He found the January number of the magazine made up and the forms closed.

The vacant space that had been yawning for type was filled by an article that was headed thus:

SECOND MESSAGE TO CONGRESS

Written for

THE ROSE OF DIXIE

BY

A Member of the Well-Known

BULLOCH FAMILY, OF GEORGIA

T. ROOSEVELT

THE THIRD INGREDIENT

THE (so-called) Vallambrosa Apartment House is not an apartment house. It is composed of two old-fashioned, brownstone-front residences welded into one. The parlor floor of one side is gay with the wraps and headgear of a modiste; the other is lugubrious with the sophistical promises and grisly display of a painless dentist. You may have a room there for two dollars a week or you may have one for twenty dollars. Among the Vallambrosa's roomers are stenographers, musicians, brokers, shopgirls, space-rate writers, art students, wire-tappers, and other people who lean far over the banister-rail when the door-bell rings.

This treatise shall have to do with but two of the Vallambrosians—though meaning no disrespect to the others.

At six o'clock one afternoon Hetty Pepper came back to her third-floor rear $3.50 room in the Vallambrosa with her nose and chin more sharply pointed than usual. To be discharged from the department store where you have been working four years, and with only fifteen cents in your purse, does have a tendency to make your features appear more finely chiselled.

And now for Hetty's thumb-nail biography while she climbs the two flights of stairs.

She walked into the Biggest Store one morning four years before, with seventy-five other girls, applying for a job behind the waist department counter. The phalanx of wage-earners formed a bewildering scene of beauty, carrying a total mass of blond hair sufficient to have justified the horseback gallops of a hundred Lady Godivas.

The capable, cool-eyed, impersonal, young, bald-headed man, whose task it was to engage six of the contestants, was aware of a feeling of suffocation as if he were drowning in a sea of frangipanni, while white clouds, hand-embroidered, floated about him. And then a sail hove in sight. Hetty Pepper, homely of countenance, with small, contemptuous green eyes and chocolate-colored hair, dressed in a suit of plain burlap and a common-sense hat, stood before him with every one of her twenty-nine years of life unmistakably in sight.

"You're on!" shouted the bald-headed young man, and was saved. And that is how Hetty came to be employed in the Biggest Store. The story of her rise to an eight-dollar-a-week salary is the combined stories of Hercules, Joan of Arc, Una, Job, and Little-Red-Riding-Hood. You shall not learn from me the salary that was paid her as a beginner. There is a sentiment growing about such things, and I want no millionaire store-proprietors climbing the fire-escape of my tenement-house to throw dynamite bombs into my skylight boudoir.

The story of Hetty's discharge from the Biggest Store is so nearly a repetition of her engagement as to be monotonous.

In each department of the store there is an omniscient, omnipresent, and omnivorous person carrying always a mileage book and a red necktie, and referred to as a "buyer." The destinies of the girls in his department who live on (see Bureau of Victual Statistics)—so much per week are in his hands.

This particular buyer was a capable, cool-eyed, impersonal, young, bald-headed man. As he walked along the aisles of his department he seemed to be sailing on a sea of frangipanni, while white clouds, machine-embroidered, floated around him. Too many sweets bring surfeit. He looked upon Hetty Pepper's homely countenance, emerald eyes, and chocolate-colored hair as a welcome oasis of green in a desert of cloying beauty. In a quiet angle of a counter he pinched her arm kindly, three inches above the elbow. She slapped him three feet away with one good blow of her muscular and not especially lily-white right. So, now you know why Hetty Pepper came to leave the Biggest Store at thirty minutes' notice, with one good dime and a nickel in her purse.

This morning's quotations list the price of rib beef at six cents per (butcher's) pound. But on the day that Hetty was "released" by the B. S. the price was seven and one half cents. That fact is what makes this story possible. Otherwise, the extra four cents would have——

But the plot of nearly all the good stories in the world is concerned with shorts who were unable to cover; so, you can find no fault with this one.

Hetty mounted with her rib beef to her $3.50 third-floor-back. One hot, savory beef-stew for supper, a night's good sleep, and she would be fit in the morning to apply again for the tasks of Hercules, Joan of Arc, Una, Job, and Little-Red-Riding-Hood.

In her room she got the graniteware stew-pan out of the 2 x 4 foot china—er —I mean earthenware closet, and began to dig down in a rat's-nest of paper bags for the potatoes and onions. She came out with her nose and chin just a little sharper pointed.

There was neither a potato nor an onion. Now, what kind of a beef-stew can you make out of simply beef? You can make oyster-soup without oysters, turtle-soup without turtles, coffee-cake without coffee, but you can't make beef-stew without potatoes and onions.

But rib beef alone, in an emergency, can make an ordinary pine door look like a wrought-iron.gambling-house portal to the wolf. With salt and pepper and a tablespoonful of flour (first well stirred in a little cold water) 'twill serve—'tis not so deep as a lobster à la Newburgh, nor so wide as a church festival dough-nut; but 'twill serve.

Hetty took her stew-pan to the rear of the third-floor hall. According to the advertisements of the Vallambrosa there was running water to be found there. Between you and me and the water-meter, it only ambled or walked through the faucets; but technicalities have no place here. There was also a sink where housekeeping roomers often met to dump their coffee grounds and glare at one another's kimonos.

At this sink Hetty found a girl with heavy, gold-brown, artistic hair and plaintive eyes washing two large "Irish" potatoes. Hetty knew the Vallambrosa as well as any one not owning "double hextra-magnifying eyes" could compass its mysteries. The kimonos were her encyclopædia, her "Who's What?" her clearing-house of news, of goers and comers. From a rose-pink kimono edged with Nile green she had learned that the girl with the potatoes was a miniature-painter living in a kind of attic—or "studio," as they prefer to call it—on the top floor. Hetty was not certain in her mind what a miniature was; but it certainly wasn't a house; because house-painters, although they wear splashy overalls and poke ladders in your face on the street, are known to indulge in a riotous profusion of food at home.

The potato girl was quite slim and small, and handled her potatoes as an old bachelor uncle handles a baby who is cutting teeth. She had a dull shoemaker's knife in her right hand, and she had begun to peel one of the potatoes with it.

Hetty addressed her in the punctiliously formal tone of one who intends to be cheerfully familiar with you in the second round.

"Beg pardon," she said, "for butting into what's not my business, but if you peel them potatoes you lose out. They're new Bermudas. You want to scrape 'em. Lemme show you."

She took a potato and the knife, and began to demonstrate.

"Oh, thank you," breathed the artist. "I didn't know. And I *did* hate to see the thick peeling go; it seemed such a waste. But I thought they always had to be peeled. When you've got only potatoes to eat, the peelings count, you know."

"Say, kid," said Hetty, staying her knife, "you ain't up against it, too, are you?"

The miniature artist smiled starvedly.

"I suppose I am. Art—or, at least, the way I interpret it—doesn't seem to be much in demand. I have only these potatoes for my dinner. But they aren't so bad boiled and hot, with a little butter and salt."

"Child," said Hetty, letting a brief smile soften her rigid features, "Fate has sent me and you together. I've had it handed to me in the neck, too; but I've got a chunk of meat in my room as big as a lap-dog. And I've done everything to get potatoes except pray for 'em. Let's me and you bunch our commissary departments and make a stew of 'em. We'll cook it in my room. If we only had an onion to go in it! Say, kid, you haven't got a couple of pennies that've slipped down into the lining of your last winter's sealskin, have you? I could step down to the corner and get one at old Giuseppe's stand. A stew without an onion in worse'n a matinée without candy."

"You may call me Cecilia," said the artist. "No; I spent my last penny three days ago."

"Then we'll have to cut the onion out instead of slicing it in," said Hetty. "I'd ask the janitress for one, but I don't want 'em hep just yet to the fact that I'm pounding the asphalt for another job. But I wish we did have an onion."

In the shop-girl's room the two began to prepare their supper. Cecilia's part was to sit on the couch helplessly and beg to be allowed to do something, in the voice of a cooing ring-dove. Hetty prepared the rib beef, putting it in cold salted water in the stew-pan and setting it on the one-burner gas-stove.

"I wish we had an onion," said Hetty, as she scraped the two potatoes.

On the wall opposite the couch was pinned a flaming, gorgeous advertising picture of one of the new ferryboats of the P. U. F. F. Railroad that had been built to cut down the time between Los Angeles and New York City one eighth of a minute.

Hetty, turning her head during her continuous monologue, saw tears running from her guest's eyes as she gazed on the idealized presentment of the speeding, foam-girdled transport.

"Why, say, Cecilia, kid," said Hetty, poising her knife, "is it as bad art as that? I ain't a critic, but I thought it kind of brightened up the room. Of course, a manicure-painter could tell it was a bum picture in a minute. I'll take it down if you say so. I wish to the holy Saint Potluck we had an onion."

But the miniature miniature-painter had tumbled down, sobbing, with her nose indenting the hard-woven drapery of the couch. Something was here deeper than the artistic temperament offended at crude lithography.

Hetty knew. She had accepted her rôle long ago. How scant the words with which we try to describe a single quality of a human being! When we reach the abstract we are lost. The nearer to Nature that the babbling of our lips comes, the better do we understand. Figuratively (let us say), some people are Bosoms, some are Hands, some are Heads, some are Muscles, some are Feet, some are Backs for burdens.

Hetty was a Shoulder. Hers was a sharp, sinewy shoulder; but all her life people had laid their heads upon it, metaphorically or actually, and had left there all or half their troubles. Looking at Life anatomically, which is as good a way as any, she was preordained to be a Shoulder. There were few truer collar-bones anywhere than hers.

Hetty was only thirty-three, and she had not yet outlived the little pang that visited her whenever the head of youth and beauty leaned upon her for consolation. But one glance in her mirror always served as an instantaneous pain-killer. So she gave one pale look into the crinkly old looking-glass on the wall above the gas-stove, turned down the flame a little lower from the bubbling beef and potatoes, went over to the couch, and lifted Cecilia's head to its confessional.

"Go on and tell me, honey," she said. "I know now that it ain't art that's worrying you. You met him on a ferry-boat, didn't you? Go on, Cecilia, kid, and tell your—your Aunt Hetty about it."

But youth and melancholy must first spend the surplus of sighs and tears that waft and float the barque of romance to its harbor in the delectable isles. Presently, through the stringy tendons that formed the bars of the confessional, the penitent—or was it the glorified communicant of the sacred flame?—told her story without art or illumination.

"It was only three days ago. I was coming back on the ferry from Jersey City. Old Mr. Schrum, an art dealer, told me of a rich man in Newark who wanted a miniature of his daughter painted. I went to see him and showed him some of my work. When I told him the price would be fifty dollars he laughed at me like a hyena. He said an enlarged crayon twenty times the size would cost him only eight dollars.

"I had just enough money to buy my ferry ticket back to New York. I felt as if I didn't want to live another day. I must have looked as I felt, for I saw *him* on the row of seats opposite me, looking at me as if he understood. He was nice-looking, but, oh, above everything else, he looked kind. When one is tired or unhappy or hopeless, kindness counts more than anything else.

"When I got so miserable that I couldn't fight against it any longer, I got up and walked slowly out the rear door of the ferry-boat cabin. No one was there, and I slipped quickly over the rail, and dropped into the water. Oh, friend Hetty, it was cold, cold!

"For just one moment I wished I was back in the old Vallambrosa, starving and hoping. And then I got numb, and didn't care. And then I felt that somebody else was in the water close by me, holding me up. He had followed me, and jumped in to save me.

"Somebody threw a thing like a big, white doughnut at us, and he made me put my arms through the hole. Then the ferry-boat backed, and they pulled us on board. Oh, Hetty, I was so ashamed of my wickedness in trying to drown myself; and, besides, my hair had all tumbled down and was sopping wet, and I was such a sight.

"And then some men in blue clothes came around; and *he* gave them his card, and I heard him tell them he had seen me drop my purse on the edge of the boat outside the rail, and in leaning over to get it I had fallen overboard. And then I remembered having read in the papers that people who try to kill themselves are locked up in cells with people who try to kill other people, and I was afraid.

"But some ladies on the boat took me downstairs to the furnace-room and got me nearly dry and did up my hair. When the boat landed, *he* came and put me in a cab. He was all dripping himself, but laughed as if he thought it was all a joke. He begged me, but I wouldn't tell him my name nor where I lived, I was so ashamed."

"You were a fool, child," said Hetty, kindly. "Wait till I turn the light up a bit. I wish to Heaven we had an onion."

"Then he raised his hat," went on Cecilia, "and said: 'Very well. But I'll find you, anyhow. I'm going to claim my rights of salvage.' Then he gave money to the cab-driver and told him to take me where I wanted to go, and walked away. What is 'salvage,' Hetty?"

"The edge of a piece of goods that ain't hemmed," said the shop-girl. "You must have looked pretty well frazzled out to the little hero boy."

"It's been three days," moaned the miniature-painter, "and he hasn't found me yet."

"Extend the time," said Hetty. "This is a big town. Think of how many girls he might have to see soaked in water with their hair down before he would recognize you. The stew's getting on fine—but, oh, for an onion! I'd even use a piece of garlic if I had it."

The beef and potatoes bubbled merrily, exhaling a mouth-watering savor that yet lacked something, leaving a hunger on the palate, a haunting, wistful desire for some lost and needful ingredient.

"I came near drowning in that awful river," said Cecilia, shuddering.

"It ought to have more water in it," said Hetty; "the stew, I mean. I'll go get some at the sink."

"It smells good," said the artist.

"That nasty old North River?" objected Hetty. "It smells to me like soap factories and wet setter-dogs—oh, you mean the stew. Well, I wish we had an onion for it. Did he look like he had money?"

"First he looked kind," said Cecilia. "I'm sure he was rich; but that matters so little. When he drew out his bill-folder to pay the cabman you couldn't help seeing hundreds and thousands of dollars in it. And I looked over the cab doors and saw him leave the ferry station in a motor-car; and the chauffeur gave him his bearskin to put on, for he was sopping wet. And it was only three days ago."

"What a fool!" said Hetty, shortly.

"Oh, the chauffeur wasn't wet," breathed Cecilia. "And he drove the car away very nicely."

"I mean *you*," said Hetty. "For not giving him your address."

"I never give my address to chauffeurs," said Cecilia, haughtily.

"I wish we had one," said Hetty, disconsolately.

"What for?"

"For the stew, of course— Oh, I mean an onion."

Hetty took a pitcher and started to the sink at the end of the hall.

A young man came down the stairs from above just as she was opposite the lower step. He was decently dressed, but pale and haggard. His eyes were dull with the stress of some burden of physical or mental woe. In his hand he bore an onion—a pink, smooth, solid, shining onion, as large around as a ninety-eight-cent alarm clock.

Hetty stopped. So did the young man. There was something Joan of Arc-ish, Herculean and Una-ish in the look and pose of the shoplady—she had cast off the rôles of Job and Little-Red-Riding-Hood. The young man stopped at the foot of the stairs and coughed distractedly. He felt marooned, held up, attacked, assailed, levied upon, sacked, assessed, panhandled, brow-beaten, though he knew not why. It was the look in Hetty's eyes that did it. In them he saw the Jolly Roger fly to the masthead and an able seaman with a dirk between his teeth scurry up the ratlines and nail it there. But as yet he did not know that the cargo he carried was the thing that had caused him to be so nearly blown out of the water without even a parley.

"*Beg* your pardon," said Hetty, as sweetly as her dilute acetic acid tones permitted, "but did you find that onion on the stairs? There was a hole in the paper bag; and I've just come out to look for it."

The young man coughed for half a minute. The interval may have given him the courage to defend his own property. Also, he clutched his pungent prize greedily, and, with a show of spirit, faced his grim waylayer.

"No," he said, huskily, "I didn't find it on the stairs. It was given to me by Jack Bevens, on the top floor. If you don't believe it, ask him. I'll wait until you do."

"I know about Bevens," said Hetty, sourly. "He writes books and things up there for the paper-and-rags man. We can hear the postman guy him all over the house when he brings them thick envelopes back. Say—do you live in the Vallambrosa?"

"I do not," said the young man. "I come to see Bevens sometimes. He's my friend. I live two blocks west."

"What are you going to do with the onion?—*begging* your pardon," said Hetty.

"I'm going to eat it."

"Raw?"

"Yes: as soon as I get home."

"Haven't you got anything else to eat with it?"

The young man considered briefly.

"No," he confessed; "there's not another scrap of anything in my diggings to eat. I think old Jack is pretty hard up for grub in his shack, too. He hated to give up the onion, but I worried him into parting with it."

"Man," said Hetty, fixing him with her world-sapient eyes, and laying a bony but impressive finger on his sleeve, "you've known trouble, too, haven't you?"

"Lots," said the onion owner, promptly. "But this onion is my own property, honestly come by. If you will excuse me, I must be going."

"Listen," said Hetty, paling a little with anxiety. "Raw onion is a mighty poor diet. And so is a beef-stew without one. Now, if your Jack Bevens' friend, I guess you're nearly right. There's a little lady—a friend of mine—in my room there at the end of the hall. Both of us are out of luck; and we had just potatoes and meat between us. They're stewing now. But it ain't got any soul. There's something lacking to it. There's certain things in life that are naturally intended to fit and belong together. One is pink cheese-cloth and green roses, and one is ham and eggs, and one is Irish and trouble. And the other one is beef and potatoes *with* onions. And still another one is people who are up against it and other people in the same fix."

The young man went into a protracted paroxysm of coughing. With one hand he hugged his onion to his bosom.

"No doubt; no doubt," said he, at length. "But, as I said, I must be going because——"

Hetty clutched his sleeve firmly.

"Don't be a Dago, Little Brother. Don't eat raw onions. Chip in toward the dinner and line yourself inside with the best stew you ever licked a spoon over. Must two ladies knock a young gentleman down and drag him inside for the honor of dining with 'em? No harm shall befall you, Little Brother. Loosen up and fall into line."

The young man's pale face relaxed into a grin.

"Believe I'll go you," he said, brightening. "If my onion is as good as a credential, I'll accept the invitation gladly."

"It's as good as that, but better as seasoning," said Hetty. You come and stand outside the door till I ask my lady friend if she has any objections. And don't run away with that letter of recommendation before I come out."

Hetty went into her room and closed the door. The young man waited outside.

"Cecilia, kid," said the shop-girl, oiling the sharp saw of her voice as well as she could, "there's an onion outside. With a young man attached. I've asked him in to dinner. You ain't going to kick, are you?"

"Oh, dear!" said Cecilia, sitting up and patting her artistic hair. She cast a mournful glance at the ferry-boat poster on the wall.

"Nit," said Hetty. "It ain't him. You're up against real life now. I believe you said your hero friend had money and automobiles. This is a poor skeezicks that's got nothing to eat but an onion. But he's easy-spoken and not a freshy. I imagine he's been a gentleman, he's so low down now. And we need the onion. Shall I bring him in? I'll guarantee his behavior."

"Hetty, dear," sighed Cecilia, "I'm so hungry. What difference does it make whether he's a prince or a burglar? I don't care. Bring him in if he's got anything to eat with him."

Hetty went back into the hall. The onion man was gone. Her heart missed a beat, and a gray look settled over her face except on her nose and cheek-bones. And then the tides of life flowed in again, for she saw him leaning out of the front window at the other end of the hall. She hurried there. He was shouting to someone below. The noise of the street overpowered the sound of her foot-steps. She looked down over his shoulder, saw whom he was speaking to, and heard his words. He pulled himself in from the window-sill and saw her standing over him.

Hetty's eyes bored into him like two steel gimlets.

"Don't lie to me," she said, calmly. "What were you going to do with that onion?"

The young man suppressed a cough and faced her resolutely. His manner was that of one who had been bearded sufficiently.

"I was going to eat it," said he, with emphatic slowness; "just as I told you before."

"And you have nothing else to eat at home?"

"Not a thing."

"What kind of work do you do?"

"I am not working at anything just now."

"Then why," said Hetty, with her voice set on its sharpest edge, "do you lean out of a window and give orders to chauffeurs in green automobiles in the street below?"

The young man flushed, and his dull eyes began to sparkle.

"Because, madam," said he, in *accelerando* tones, "I pay the chauffeur's wages and I own the automobile—and also this onion—this onion, madam."

He flourished the onion within an inch of Hetty's nose. The shop-lady did not retreat a hair's-breadth.

"Then why do you eat onions," she said, with biting contempt, "and nothing else?"

"I never said I did," retorted the young man, heatedly. "I said I had nothing else to eat where I live. I am not a delicatessen storekeeper."

"Then why," pursued Hetty, inflexibly, "were you going to eat a raw onion?"

"My mother," said the young man, "always made me eat one for a cold. Pardon my referring to a physical infirmity; but you may have noticed that I have a very, very severe cold. I was going to eat the onion and go to bed. I wonder why I am standing here and apologizing to you for it."

"How did you catch this cold?" went on Hetty, suspiciously.

The young man seemed to have arrived at some extreme height of feeling. There were two modes of descent open to him—a burst of rage or a surrender to the ridiculous. He chose wisely; and the empty hall echoed his hoarse laughter.

"You're a dandy," said he. "And I don't blame you for being careful. I don't mind telling you. I got wet. I was on a North River ferry a few days ago when a girl jumped overboard. Of course, I——"

Hetty extended her hand, interrupting his story.

"Give me the onion," she said.

The young man set his jaw a trifle harder.

"Give me the onion," she repeated.

He grinned, and laid it in her hand.

Then Hetty's infrequent, grim, melancholy smile showed itself. She took the young man's arm and pointed with her other hand to the door of her room.

"Little Brother," she said, "go in there. The little fool you fished out of the river is there waiting for you. Go on in. I'll give you three minutes before I come. Potatoes is in there, waiting. Go on in, Onions."

After he had tapped at the door and entered, Hetty began to peel and wash the onion at the sink. She gave a gray look at the gray roofs outside and the smile on her face vanished by little jerks and twitches.

"But it's us," she said, grimly, to herself, "it's *us* that furnished the beef."

THE HIDING OF BLACK BILL

A LANK, strong, red-faced man with a Wellington beak and small, fiery eyes tempered by flaxen lashes, sat on the station platform at Los Pinos swinging his legs to and fro. At his side sat another man, fat, melancholy, and seedy, who seemed to be his friend. They had the appearance of men to whom life had appeared as a reversible coat—seamy on both sides.

"Ain't seen you in about four years, Ham," said the seedy man. "Which way you been travelling?"

"Texas," said the red-faced man. "It was too cold in Alaska for me. And I found it warm in Texas. I'll tell you about one hot spell I went through there.

"One morning I steps off the International at a water-tank and lets it go on without me. 'Twas a ranch country, and fuller of spitehouses than New York City. Only out there they build 'em twenty miles away so you can't smell what they've got for dinner, instead of running 'em up two inches from their neighbors' windows.

"There wasn't any roads in sight, so I footed it 'cross country. The grass was shoe-top deep, and the mesquite timber looked just like a peach orchard. It was so much like a gentleman's private estate that every minute you expected a kennelful of bulldogs to run out and bite you. But I must have walked twenty miles before I came in sight of a ranch-house. It was a little one, about as big as an elevated railroad station.

"There was a little man in a white shirt and brown overalls and pink handkerchief around his neck rolling cigarettes under a tree in front of the door.

"'Greetings,' says I. 'Any refreshments, welcome, emoluments, or even work for a comparative stranger?'

"'Oh, come in,' says he, in a refined tone. 'Sit down on that stool, please. I didn't hear your horse coming.'

"'He isn't near enough yet,' says I. 'I walked. I don't want to be a burden, but I wonder if you have three or four gallons of water handy.'

"'You do look pretty dusty,' says he; 'but our bathing arrangements——'

"'It's a drink I want,' says I. 'Never mind the dust that's on the outside.'

"He gets me a dipper of water out of a red jar hanging up, and then goes on:

"'Do you want work?'

"'For a time,' says I. 'This is a rather quiet section of the country, isn't it?'

"'It is,' says he. 'Sometimes—so I have been told—one sees no human being pass for weeks at a time. I've been here only a month. I bought the ranch from an old settler who wanted to move farther west.'

"'It suits me,' says I. 'Quiet and retirement are good for a man sometimes. And I need a job. I can tend bar, salt mines, lecture, float stock, do a little middle-weight slugging, and play the piano.'

"'Can you herd sheep?' asks the little ranchman.

"'Do you mean have I heard sheep?' says I.

"'Can you herd 'em—take charge of a flock of 'em?' says he.

"'Oh,' says I, 'now I understand. You mean chase 'em around and bark at 'em like collie dogs. Well, I might,' says I. 'I've never exactly done any sheep-herding, but I've often seen 'em from car windows masticating daisies, and they don't look dangerous.'

"'I'm short a herder,' says the ranchman. 'You never can depend on the Mexicans. I've only got two flocks. You may take out my bunch of muttons—there are only eight hundred of 'em—in the morning, if you like. The pay is twelve dollars a month and your rations furnished. You camp in a tent on the prairie with your sheep. You do your own cooking, but wood and water are brought to your camp. It's an easy job.'

" 'I'm on,' says I. 'I'll take the job even if I have to garland my brow and hold on to a crook and wear a loose effect and play on a pipe like the shepherds do in pictures.'

"So the next morning the little ranchman helps me drive the flock of muttons from the corral to about two miles out and let 'em graze on a little hillside on the prairie. He gives me a lot of instructions about not letting bunches of them stray off from the herd, and driving 'em down to a water-hole to drink at noon.

" 'I'll bring out your tent and camping outfit and rations in the buckboard before night,' says he.

" 'Fine,' says I. 'And don't forget the rations. Nor the camping outfit. And be sure to bring the tent. Your name's Zollicoffer, ain't it?'

" 'My name,' said he, 'is Henry Ogden.'

" 'All right, Mr. Ogden,' says I. 'Mine is Mr. Percival Saint Clair.'

"I herded sheep for five days on the Rancho Chiquito; and then the wool entered my soul. That getting next to Nature certainly got next to me. I was lonesomer than Crusoe's goat. I've seen a lot of persons more entertaining as companions than those sheep were. I'd drive 'em to the corral and pen 'em every evening, and then cook my corn-bread and mutton and coffee, and lie down in a tent the size of a tablecloth, and listen to the coyotes and whip-poor-wills singing around the camp.

"The fifth evening, after I had corralled my costly but uncongenial muttons, I walked over to the ranch-house and stepped in the door.

" 'Mr. Ogden,' says I, 'you and me have got to get sociable. Sheep are all very well to dot the landscape and furnish eight-dollar cotton suitings for man, but for table-talk and fireside companions they rank along with five-o'clock teazers. If you've got a deck of cards, or a parcheesi outfit, or a game of authors, get 'em out, and let's get on a mental basis. I've got to do something in an intellectual line, if it's only to knock somebody's brains out.'

"This Henry Ogden was a peculiar kind of ranchman. He wore finger-rings and a big gold watch and careful neckties. And his face was calm, and his nose-spectacles was kept very shiny. I saw once, in Muscogee, an outlaw hung for murdering six men, who was a dead ringer for him. But I knew a preacher in Arkansas that you would have taken to be his brother. I didn't care much for him either way; what I wanted was some fellowship and communion with holy saints or lost sinners—anything sheepless would do.

" 'Well, Saint Clair,' says he, laying down the book he was reading, 'I guess it must be pretty lonesome for you at first. And I don't deny that it's monotonous for me. Are you sure you corralled your sheep so they won't stray out?'

" 'They're shut up as tight as the jury of a millionaire murderer,' says I. 'And I'll be back with them long before they'll need their trained nurse.'

"So Ogden digs up a deck of cards, and we play casino. After five days and nights of my sheep-camp it was like a toot on Broadway. When I caught big casino I felt as excited as if I had made a million in Trinity. And when H. O. loosened up a little and told the story about the lady in the Pullman car I laughed for five minutes.

"That showed what a comparative thing life is. A man may see so much that he'd be bored to turn his head to look at a $3,000,000 fire for Joe Weber or the Adriatic Sea. But let him herd sheep for a spell, and you'll see him splitting his ribs laughing at 'Curfew Shall Not Ring To-night,' or really enjoying himself playing cards with ladies.

"By-and-by Ogden gets out a decanter of Bourbon, and there is a total eclipse of sheep.

" 'Do you remember reading in the papers about a month ago,' says he, 'about a train hold-up on the M. K. & T.? The express agent was shot through the shoulder and about $15,000 in currency taken. And it's said that only one man did the job.'

"'Seems to me I do,' says I. 'But such things happen so often they don't linger long in the human Texas mind. Did they overtake, overhaul, seize, or lay hands upon the despoiler?'

"'He escaped,' says Ogden. 'And I was just reading in a paper to-day that the officers have tracked him down into this part of the country. It seems the bills the robbers got were all the first issue of currency to the Second National Bank of Espinosa City. And so they've followed the trail where they've been spent, and it leads this way.'

"Ogden pours out some more Bourbon, and shoves me the bottle.

"'I imagine,' says I, after ingurgitating another modicum of the royal booze, 'that it wouldn't be at all a disingenuous idea for a train-robber to run down into this part of the country to hide for a spell. A sheep-ranch, now,' says I, 'would be the finest kind of a place. Who'd ever expect to find such a desperate character among these song-birds and muttons and wild flowers? And, by the way,' says I, kind of looking H. Ogden over, 'was there any description mentioned to this single-handed terror? Was his lineaments or height and thickness or teeth fillings or style of habiliments set forth in print?'

"'Why, no,' says Ogden; 'because they say nobody got a good sight of him because he wore a mask. But they know it was a train-robber called Black Bill, because he always works alone and because he dropped a handkerchief in the express-car that had his name on it.'

"'All right,' says I. 'I approve of Black Bill's retreat to the sheep-ranges. I guess they won't find him.'

"'There's one thousand dollars reward for his capture,' says Ogden.

"'I don't need that kind of money,' says I, looking Mr. Sheepman straight in the eye. 'The twelve dollars a month you pay me is enough. I need a rest, and I can save up until I get enough to pay my fare to Texarkana, where my widowed mother lives. If Black Bill,' I goes on, looking significantly at Ogden, 'was to have come down this way—say, a month ago—and bought a little sheep-ranch and——'

"'Stop,' says Ogden, getting out of his chair and looking pretty vicious. 'Do you mean to insinuate——'

"'Nothing,' says I; 'no insinuations. I'm stating a hypodermical case. I say, if Black Bill had come down here and bought a sheep-ranch and hired me to Little-Boy-Blue 'em and treated me square and friendly, as you've done, he'd never have anything to fear from me. A man is a man, regardless of any complications he may have with sheep or railroad trains. Now you know where I stand.'

"Ogden looks black as camp-coffee for nine seconds, and then he laughs, amused.

"'You'll do, Saint Clair,' says he. 'If I *was* Black Bill I wouldn't be afraid to trust you. Let's have a game or two of seven-up to-night. That is, if you don't mind playing with a train-robber.'

"'I've told you,' says I, 'my oral sentiments, and there's no strings to 'em.'

"While I was shuffling after the first hand, I asks Ogden, as if the idea was a kind of a casualty, where he was from.

"'Oh,' says he, 'from the Mississippi Valley.'

"'That's a nice little place,' says I. 'I've often stopped over there. But didn't you find the sheets a little damp and the food poor? Now, I hail,' says I, 'from the Pacific Slope. Ever put up there?'

"'Too draughty,' says Ogden. 'But if you're ever in the Middle West just mention my name, and you'll get foot-warmers and dripped coffee.'

"'Well,' says I, 'I wasn't exactly fishing for your private telephone number and the middle name of your aunt that carried off that Cumberland Presbyterian minister. It don't matter. I just want you to know you are safe in the hands of your shepherd. Now, don't play hearts on spades, and don't get nervous.'

"'Still harping,' says Ogden, laughing again. 'Don't you suppose that if I was Black Bill and thought you suspected me, I'd put a Winchester bullet into you and stop my nervousness if I had any?'

"'Not any,' says I. 'A man who's got the nerve to hold up a train single-handed wouldn't do a trick like that. I've knocked about enough to know that them are the kind of men who put a value on a friend. Not that I can claim being a friend of yours, Mr. Ogden,' says I, 'being only your sheep-herder; but under more expeditious circumstances we might have been.'

"'Forget the sheep temporarily, I beg,' says Ogden, 'and cut for deal.'

"About four days afterwards, while my muttons was nooning on the water-hole and I deep in the interstices of making a pot of coffee, up rides softly on the grass a mysterious person in the garb of the being he wished to represent. He was dressed somewhere between a Kansas City detective, Buffalo Bill, and the town dog-catcher of Baton Rouge. His chin and eye wasn't moulded on fighting lines, so I knew he was only a scout.

"'Herdin' sheep?' he asks me.

"'Well,' says I, 'to a man of your evident gumptional endowments, I wouldn't have the nerve to state that I am engaged in decorating old bronzes or oiling bicycle sprockets.'

"'You don't talk or look like a sheep-herder to me,' says he.

"'But you talk like what you look like to me,' says I.

"And then he asks me who I was working for, and I shows him Rancho Chiquito, two miles away, in the shadow of a low hill, and he tells me he's a deputy sheriff.

"'There's a train-robber called Black Bill supposed to be somewhere in these parts,' says the scout. 'He's been traced as far as San Antonio, and may be farther. Have you seen or heard of any strangers around here during the past month?'

"'I have not,' says I, 'except a report of one over at the Mexican quarters of Loomis' ranch, on the Frio.'

"'What do you know about him?' asks the deputy.

"'He's three days old,' says I.

"'What kind of a looking man is the man you work for?' he asks. 'Does old George Ramey own this place yet? He's run sheep here for the last ten years, but never had no success.'

"'The old man had sold out and gone West,' I tells him. 'Another sheep-fancier bought him out about a month ago.'

"'What kind of a looking man is he?' asks the deputy again.

"'Oh,' says I, 'a big, fat kind of a Dutchman with long whiskers and blue specs. I don't think he knows a sheep from a ground-squirrel. I guess old George soaked him pretty well on the deal,' says I.

"After indulging himself in a lot more non-communicative information and two thirds of my dinner, the deputy rides away.

"That night I mentions the matter to Ogden.

"'They're drawing the tendrils of the octopus around Black Bill,' says I. And then I told him about the deputy sheriff, and how I'd described him to the deputy, and what the deputy said about the matter.

"'Oh, well,' says Ogden, 'let's don't borrow any of Black Bill's troubles. We've a few of our own. Get the Bourbon out of the cupboard and we'll drink to his health—unless,' says he, with his little cackling laugh, 'you're prejudiced against train-robbers.'

"'I'll drink,' says I, 'to any man who's a friend to a friend. And I believe that Black Bill,' I goes on, 'would be that. So here's to Black Bill, and may he have good luck.'

"And both of us drank.

"About two weeks later comes shearing-time. The sheep had to be driven up to the ranch, and a lot of frowzy-headed Mexicans would snip the fur off them with back-action scissors. So the afternoon before the barbers were to come I hustled my underdone muttons over the hill, across the dell, down by the winding brook, and up to the ranch-house, where I penned 'em in a corral and bade 'em my nightly adieus.

"I went from there to the ranch-house. I find H. Ogden, Esquire, lying asleep on his little cot bed. I guess he had been overcome by anti-insomnia or dis-wakefulness or some of the diseases peculiar to the sheep business. His mouth and vest were open, and he breathed like a second-hand bicycle pump. I looked at him and gave vent to just a few musings. 'Imperial Cæsar,' says I, 'asleep in such a way, might shut his mouth and keep the wind away.'

"A man asleep is certainly a sight to make angels weep. What good is all his brain, muscle, backing, nerve, influence, and family connections? He's at the mercy of his enemies, and more so of his friends. And he's about as beautiful as a cab-horse leaning against the Metropolitan Opera House at 12:30 A. M. dreaming of the plains of Arabia. Now, a woman asleep you regard as different. No matter how she looks, you know it's better for all hands for her to be that way.

"Well, I took a drink of Bourbon and one for Ogden, and started in to be comfortable while he was taking his nap. He had some books on his table on indigenous subjects, such as Japan and drainage and physical culture—and some tobacco, which seemed more to the point.

"After I'd smoked a few, and listened to the sartorial breathing of H. O., I happened to look out the window toward the shearing-pens, where there was a kind of a road coming up from a kind of a road across a kind of a creek farther away.

"I saw five men riding up to the house. All of 'em carried guns across their saddles, and among 'em was the deputy that had talked to me at my camp.

"They rode up careful, in open formation, with their guns ready. I set apart with my eye the one I opinionated to be the boss muckraker of this law-and-order cavalry.

"'Good-evening, gents,' says I. 'Won't you 'light and tie your horses?'

"The boss rides up close, and swings his gun over till the opening in it seems to cover my whole front elevation.

"'Don't you move your hands none,' says he, 'till you and me indulge in a adequate amount of necessary conversation.'

"'I will not,' says I. 'I am no deaf-mute, and therefore will not have to disobey your injunctions in replying.'

"'We are on the lookout,' says he, 'for Black Bill, the man that held up the Katy for $15,000 in May. We are searching the ranches and everybody on 'em. What is your name, and what do you do on this ranch?'

"'Captain,' says I, 'Percival Saint Clair is my occupation, and my name is sheep-herder. I've got my flock of veals—no, muttons—penned here to-night. The searchers are coming to-morrow to give them a haircut—with baa-a-rum, I suppose.'

"'Where's the boss of this ranch?' the captain of the gang asks me.

"'Wait just a minute, cap'n,' says I. 'Wasn't there a kind of a reward offered for the capture of this desperate character you have referred to in your preamble?'

"'There's a thousand dollars reward offered,' says the captain, 'but it's for his capture and conviction. There don't seem to be no provision made for an informer.'

"'It looks like it might rain in a day or so,' says I, in a tired way, looking up at the cerulean blue sky.

"'If you know anything about the locality, disposition, or secretiveness of this here Black Bill,' says he, in a severe dialect, 'you are amiable to the law in not reporting it.'

"'I heard a fence-rider say,' says I, in a desultory kind of voice, 'that a Mexican told a cowboy named Jake over at Pidgin's store on the Nueces that he heard that Black Bill had been seen in Matamoras by a sheepman's cousin two weeks ago.'

"'Tell you what I'll do, Tight Mouth,' says the captain, after looking me over for bargains. 'If you put us on so we can scoop Black Bill, I'll pay you a hundred dollars out of my own—out of our own—pockets. That's liberal,' says he. 'You ain't entitled to anything. Now, what do you say?'

"'Cash down now?' I ask.

"The captain has a sort of discussion with his helpmates, and they all produce the contents of their pockets for analysis. Out of the general results they figured up $102.30 in cash and $31 worth of plug tobacco.

"'Come nearer, capitan meeo,' says I, 'and listen.' He so did.

"'I am mighty poor and low down in the world,' says I. 'I am working for twelve dollars a month trying to keep a lot of animals together whose only thought seems to be to get asunder. Although,' says I, 'I regard myself as some better than the State of South Dakota, it's a come-down to a man who has heretofore regarded sheep only in the form of chops. I'm pretty far reduced in the world on account of foiled ambitions and rum and a kind of cocktail they make along the P. R. R. all the way from Scranton to Cincinnati—dry gin, French vermouth, one squeeze of a lime, and a good dash of orange bitters. If you're ever up that way, don't fail to let one try you. And, again,' says I, 'I have never yet went back on a friend. I've stayed by 'em when they had plenty, and when adversity's overtaken me I've never forsook 'em.

"'But,' I goes on, 'this is not exactly the case of a friend. Twelve dollars a month is only bowing-acquaintance money. And I do not consider brown beans and cornbread the food of friendship. I am a poor man,' says I, 'and I have a widowed mother in Texarkana. You will find Black Bill,' says I, 'lying asleep in this house on a cot in the room to your right. He's the man you want, as I know from his words and conversation. He was in a way a friend,' I explains, 'and if I was the man I once was the entire product of the mines of Gondola would not have tempted me to betray him. But,' says I, 'every week half of the beans was wormy, and not nigh enough wood in camp.

"'Better go in careful, gentlemen,' says I. 'He seems impatient at times, and when you think of his late professional pursuits one would look for abrupt actions if he was come upon sudden.'

"So the whole posse unmounts and ties their horses, and unlimbers their ammunition and equipments, and tiptoes into the house. And I follows, like Delilah when she set the Philip Steins on to Samson.

"The leader of the posse shakes Ogden and wakes him up. And then he jumps up and two more of the reward-hunters grab him. Ogden was mighty tough with all his slimness, and gives 'em as neat a single-footed tussle against odds as I ever see.

"'What does this mean?' he says, after they had him down.

"'You're scooped in, Mr. Black Bill,' says the captain. 'That's all.'

"'It's an outrage,' says H. Ogden, madder yet.

"'It was,' says the peace-and-good-will man. 'The Katy wasn't bothering you, and there's a law against monkeying with express packages.'

"And he sits on H. Ogden's stomach and goes through his pockets symptomatically and careful.

"'I'll make you perspire for this,' says Ogden, perspiring some himself. 'I can prove who I am.'

"'So can I,' says the captain, as he draws from H. Ogden's inside coat-pocket a handful of new bills of the Second National Bank of Espinosa City. 'Your regular engraved Tuesdays-and-Fridays visiting-card wouldn't have a louder voice in proclaiming your indemnity than this here currency. You can get up now and prepare to go with us and expatriate your sins.'

"H. Ogden gets up and fixes his necktie. He says no more after they have taken the money off of him.

"'A well-greased idea,' says the sheriff captain, admiring, 'to slip off down here and buy a little sheep-ranch where the hand of man is seldom heard. It was the slickest hide-out I ever see,' says the captain.

"So one of the men goes to the shearing-pen and hunts up the other herder, a Mexican they call John Sallies, and he saddles Ogden's horse, and the sheriffs all ride up close around him with their guns in hand, ready to take their prisoner to town.

"Before starting, Ogden puts the ranch in John Sallies' hands and gives him orders about the shearing and where to graze the sheep, just as if he intended to be back in a few days. And a couple of hours afterward one Percival Saint Clair, an ex-sheep-herder of the Rancho Chiquito, might have been seen, with a hundred and nine dollars——wages and blood money—in his pocket, riding south on another horse belonging to said ranch."

The red-faced man paused and listened. The whistle of a coming freight-train sounded far away among the low hills.

The fat, seedy man at his side sniffed, and shook his frowzy head slowly and disparagingly.

"What is it, Snipy?" asked the other. "Got the blues again?"

"No, I ain't," said the seedy one, sniffing again. "But I don't like your talk. You and me have been friends, off and on, for fifteen year; and I never yet knew or heard of you giving anybody up to the law—not no one. And here was a man whose saleratus you had et and at whose table you had played games of cards—if casino can be so called. And yet you inform him to the law and take money for it. It never was like you, I say."

"This H. Ogden," resumed the red-faced man, "through a lawyer, proved himself free by alibis and other legal terminalities, as I so heard afterward. He never suffered no harm. He did me favors, and I hated to hand him over."

"How about the bills they found in his pocket?" asked the seedy man.

"I put 'em there," said the red-faced man, "while he was asleep, when I saw the posse riding up. I was Black Bill. Look out, Snipy, here she comes! We'll board her on the bumpers when she takes water."

SCHOOLS AND SCHOOLS

I

OLD Jerome Warren lived in a hundred-thousand-dollar house at 35 East Fifty-Soforth Street. He was a downtown broker, so rich that he could afford to walk—for his health—a few blocks in the direction of his office every morning and then call a cab.

He had an adopted son, the son of an old friend named Gilbert—Cyril Scott could play him nicely—who was becoming a successful painter as fast as he could squeeze the paint out of his tubes. Another member of the household was Barbara Ross, a step-niece. Man is born to trouble; so, as old Jerome had no family of his own, he took up the burdens of others.

Gilbert and Barbara got along swimmingly. There was a tacit and tactical understanding all round that the two would stand up under a floral bell some high noon, and promise the minister to keep old Jerome's money in a state of high commotion. But at this point complications must be introduced.

Thirty years before, when old Jerome was young Jerome, there was a brother of his named Dick. Dick went West to seek his or somebody else's fortune. Nothing was heard of him until one day old Jerome had a letter from his brother. It was badly written on ruled paper that smelled of salt bacon and coffee-grounds. The writing was asthmatic and the spelling St. Vitusy.

It appeared that instead of Dick having forced Fortune to stand and deliver, he had been held up himself, and made to give hostages to the enemy. That is, as his letter disclosed, he was on the point of pegging out with a complication of disorders that even whiskey had failed to check. All that his thirty years of prospecting had netted him was one daughter, nineteen years old, as per invoice, whom he was shipping East, charges prepaid, for Jerome to clothe, feed, educate, comfort, and cherish for the rest of her natural life or until matrimony should them part.

Old Jerome was a board-walk. Everybody knows that the world is supported by the shoulders of Atlas; and that Atlas stands on a rail-fence; and that the rail-fence is built on a turtle's back. Now, the turtle has to stand on something; and that is a board-walk made of men like old Jerome.

I do not know whether immortality shall accrue to man; but if not so, I would like to know when men like old Jerome get what is due them?

They met Nevada Warren at the station. She was a little girl, deeply sunburned and wholesomely good-looking, with a manner that was frankly unsophisticated, yet one that not even a cigar-drummer would intrude upon without thinking twice. Looking at her, somehow you would expect to see her in a short skirt and leather leggings, shooting glass balls or taming mustangs. But in her plain white waist and black skirt she sent you guessing again. With an easy exhibition of strength she swung along a heavy valise, which the uniformed porters tried in vain to wrest from her.

"I am sure we shall be the best of friends," said Barbara, pecking at the firm, sunburned cheek.

"I hope so," said Nevada.

"Dear little niece," said old Jerome, "you are as welcome to my house as if it were your father's own."

"Thanks," said Nevada.

"And I am going to call you 'cousin,'" said Gilbert, with his charming smile.

"Take the valise, please," said Nevada. "It weighs a million pounds. It's got samples from six of dad's old mines in it," she explained to Barbara. "I calculate they'd assay about nine cents to the thousand tons, but I promised him to bring them along."

II

It is a common custom to refer to the usual complications between one man and two ladies, or one lady and two men, or a lady and a man and a nobleman, or—well, any of these problems—as the triangle. But they are never unqualified triangles. They are always isosceles—never equilateral. So, upon the coming of Nevada Warren, she and Gilbert and Barbara Ross lined up into such a figurative triangle; and of that triangle Barbara formed the hypotenuse.

One morning old Jerome was lingering long after breakfast over the dullest morning paper in the city before setting forth to his downtown fly-trap. He had become quite fond of Nevada, finding in her much of his dead brother's quiet independence and unsuspicious frankness.

A maid brought in a note for Miss Nevada Warren.

"A messenger-boy delivered it at the door, please," she said. "He's waiting for an answer."

Nevada, who was whistling a Spanish waltz between her teeth, and watching the carriages and autos roll by in the street, took the envelope. She knew it was from Gilbert, before she opened it, by the little gold palette in the upper left-hand corner.

After tearing it open she pored over the contents for a while, absorbedly. Then, with a serious face, she went and stood at her uncle's elbow.

"Uncle Jerome, Gilbert is a nice boy, isn't he?"

"Why, bless the child!" said old Jerome, crackling his paper loudly; "of course he is. I raised him myself."

"He wouldn't write anything to anybody that wasn't exactly—I mean that everybody couldn't know and read, would he?"

"I'd just like to see him try it," said uncle, tearing a handful from his newspaper. "Why, what——"

"Read this note he just sent me, uncle, and see if you think it's all right and proper. You see, I don't know much about city people and their ways."

Old Jerome threw his paper down and set both his feet upon it. He took Gilbert's note and fiercely perused it twice, and then a third time.

"Why, child," said he, "you had me almost excited, although I was sure of that boy. He's a duplicate of his father, and he was a gilt-edged diamond. He only asks if you and Barbara will be ready at four o'clock this afternoon for an automobile drive over to Long Island. I don't see anything to criticize in it except the stationery. I always did hate that shade of blue."

"Would it be all right to go?" asked Nevada, eagerly.

"Yes, yes, yes, child, of course. Why not? Still, it pleases me to see you so careful and candid. Go, by all means."

"I didn't know," said Nevada, demurely. "I thought I'd ask you. Couldn't you go with us, uncle?"

"I? No, no, no, no! I've ridden once in a car that boy was driving. Never again! But it's entirely proper for you and Barbara to go. Yes, yes. But I will not. No, no, no, no!"

Nevada flew to the door, and said to the maid:

"You bet we'll go. I'll answer for Miss Barbara. Tell the boy to say to Mr. Warren, 'You bet we'll go.'"

"Nevada," called old Jerome, "pardon me, my dear, but wouldn't it be as well to send him a note in reply? Just a line would do."

"No, I won't bother about that," said Nevada, gayly. "Gilbert will understand—he always does. I never rode in an automobile in my life; but I've paddled a canoe down Little Devil River through the Lost Horse Cañon, and if it's any livelier than that I'd like to know!"

III

Two months are supposed to have elapsed.

Barbara sat in the study of the hundred-thousand-dollar house. It was a good place for her. Many places are provided in the world where men and women may repair for the purpose of extricating themselves from divers difficulties. There are cloisters, wailing-places, watering-places, confessionals, hermitages, lawyers' offices, beauty-parlors, air-ships, and studies; and the greatest of these are studies.

It usually takes a hypotenuse a long time to discover that it is the longest side of a triangle. But it's a long line that has no turning.

Barbara was alone. Uncle Jerome and Nevada had gone to the theatre. Barbara had not cared to go. She wanted to stay at home and study in the study. If you, miss, were a stunning New York girl, and saw every day that a brown, ingenuous Western witch was getting hobbles and a lasso on the young man you wanted for yourself, you, too, would lose taste for the oxidized silver setting of a musical comedy.

Barbara sat by the quartered-oak library table. Her right arm rested upon the table, and her dextral fingers nervously manipulated a sealed letter. The letter was addressed to Nevada Warren; and in the upper left-hand corner of the envelope was Gilbert's little gold palette. It had been delivered at nine o'clock, after Nevada had left.

Barbara would have given her pearl necklace to know what that letter contained; but she could not open and read it by the aid of steam, or a pen-handle, or a hair-pin, or any of the generally approved methods, because her position in society forbade such an act. She had tried to read some of the lines of the letter by holding the envelope up to a strong light and pressing it hard against the paper, but Gilbert had too good a taste in stationery to make that possible.

At eleven-thirty the theatre-goers returned. It was a delicious winter night. Even so far as from the cab to the door they were powdered thickly with the big flakes downpouring diagonally from the east. Old Jerome growled good-naturedly about villainous cab service and blockaded streets. Nevada, colored like a rose, with sapphire eyes, babbled of the stormy nights in the mountains around dad's cabin. During all these wintry apostrophes, Barbara, cold at heart, sawed wood—the only appropriate thing she could think of to do.

Old Jerome went immediately upstairs to hot-water-bottles and quinine. Nevada fluttered into the study, the only cheerfully lighted room, subsided into an armchair, and, while at the interminable task of unbuttoning her elbow gloves, gave oral testimony as to the demerits of the "show."

"Yes, I think Mr. Fields is really amusing—sometimes," said Barbara. "Here is a letter for you, dear, that came by special delivery just after you had gone."

"Who is it from?" asked Nevada, tugging at a button.

"Well, really," said Barbara, with a smile, "I can only guess. The envelope has that queer little thing in one corner that Gilbert calls a palette, but which looks to me rather like a gilt heart on a schoolgirl's valentine."

"I wonder what he's writing to me about," remarked Nevada, listlessly.

"We're all alike," said Barbara; "all women. We try to find out what is in a letter by studying the postmark. As a last resort we use scissors, and read it from the bottom upward. Here it is."

She made a motion as if to toss the letter across the table to Nevada.

"Great catamounts!" exclaimed Nevada. "These centre-fire buttons are a nuisance. I'd rather wear buckskins. Oh, Barbara, please shuck the hide off that letter and read it. It'll be midnight before I get these gloves off!"

"Why, dear, you don't want me to open Gilbert's letter to you? It's for you, and you wouldn't wish any one else to read it, of course!"

Nevada raised her steady, calm, sapphire eyes from her gloves.

"Nobody writes me anything that everybody mightn't read," she said. "Go on, Barbara. Maybe Gilbert wants us to go out in his car again to-morrow."

Curiosity can do more things than kill a cat; and if emotions, well recognized as feminine, are inimical to feline life, then jealousy would soon leave the whole world catless. Barbara opened the letter, with an indulgent, slightly bored air.

"Well, dear," she said, "I'll read it if you want me to."

She slit the envelope, and read the missive with swift-travelling eyes; read it again, and cast a quick, shrewd glance at Nevada, who, for the time, seemed to consider gloves as the world of her interest, and letters from rising artists as no more than messages from Mars.

For a quarter of a minute Barbara looked at Nevada with a strange steadfastness; and then a smile so small that it widened her mouth only the sixteenth part of an inch, and narrowed her eyes no more than a twentieth flashed like an inspired thought across her face.

Since the beginning no woman has been a mystery to another woman. Swift as light travels, each penetrates the heart and mind of another, sifts her sister's words of their cunningest disguises, reads her most hidden desires, and plucks the sophistry from her wiliest talk like hairs from a comb, twiddling them sardonically between her thumb and fingers before letting them float away on the breezes of fundamental doubt. Long ago Eve's son rang the door-bell of the family residence in Paradise Park, bearing a strange lady on his arm, whom he introduced. Eve took her daughter-in-law aside and lifted a class-c eyebrow.

"The Land of Nod," said the bride, languidly flirting the leaf of a palm. "I suppose you've been there, of course?"

"Not lately," said Eve, absolutely unstaggered. "Don't you think the apple-sauce they serve over there is execrable? I rather like that mulberry-leaf tunic effect, dear; but, of course, the real fig goods are not to be had over there. Come over behind this lilac-bush while the gentlemen split a celery tonic. I think the caterpillar-holes have made your dress open a little in the back."

So, then and there—according to the records—was the alliance formed by the only two who's-who ladies in the world. Then it was agreed that women should forever remain as clear as a pane of glass—though glass was yet to be discovered—to other women, and that she should palm herself off on a man as a mystery.

Barbara seemed to hesitate.

"Really, Nevada," she said, with a little show of embarrassment, "you shouldn't have insisted on my opening this. I—I'm sure it wasn't meant for any one else to know."

Nevada forgot her gloves for a moment.

"Then read it aloud," she said. "Since you've already read it, what's the difference? If Mr. Warren has written to me something that any one else oughtn't to know, that is all the more reason why everybody should know it."

"Well," said Barbara, "this is what it says: 'Dearest Nevada—Come to my studio at twelve o'clock to-night. Do not fail.'" Barbara rose and dropped the note in Nevada's lap. "I'm awfully sorry," she said, "that I knew. It isn't like Gilbert. There must be some mistake. Just consider that I am ignorant of it, will you, dear? I must go upstairs now, I have such a headache. I'm sure I don't understand the note. Perhaps Gilbert has been dining too well, and will explain. Good night!"

IV

Nevada tiptoed to the hall, and heard Barbara's door close upstairs. The bronze clock in the study told the hour of twelve was fifteen minutes away. She ran swiftly to the front door, and let herself out into the snowstorm. Gilbert Warren's studio was six squares away.

By aërial ferry the white, silent forces of the storm attacked the city from beyond the sullen East River. Already the snow lay a foot deep on the pavements, the drifts heaping themselves like scaling-ladders against the walls of the besieged town. The Avenue was as quiet as a street in Pompeii. Cabs now and then skimmed past like white-winged gulls over a moonlit ocean; and less frequent motor-cars—sustaining the comparison—hissed through the foaming waves like submarine boats on their jocund, perilous journeys.

Nevada plunged like a wind-driven storm-petrel on her way. She looked up at the ragged sierras of cloud-capped buildings that rose above the streets, shaded by the night lights and the congealed vapors to gray, drab, ashen, lavender, dun, and cerulean tints. They were so like the wintry mountains of her Western home that she felt a satisfaction such as the hundred-thousand-dollar house had seldom brought her.

A policeman caused her to waver on a corner, just by his eye and weight.

"Hello, Mabel!" said he. "Kind of late for you to be out, ain't it?"

"I—I am just going to the drug store," said Nevada, hurrying past him.

The excuse serves as a passport for the most sophisticated. Does it prove that woman never progresses, or that she sprang from Adam's rib, full-fledged in intellect and wiles?

Turning eastward, the direct blast cut down Nevada's speed one half. She made zigzag tracks in the snow; but she was as tough as a piñon sapling, and bowed to it as gracefully. Suddenly the studio-building loomed before her, a familiar landmark, like a cliff above some well-remembered cañon. The haunt of business and its hostile neighbor, art, was darkened and silent. The elevator stopped at ten.

Up eight flights of Stygian stairs Nevada climbed, and rapped firmly at the door numbered "89." She had been there many times before, with Barbara and Uncle Jerome.

Gilbert opened the door. He had a crayon pencil in one hand, a green shade over his eyes, and a pipe in his mouth. The pipe dropped to the floor.

"Am I late?" asked Nevada. "I came as quick as I could. Uncle and me were at the theatre this evening. Here I am, Gilbert!"

Gilbert did a Pygmalion-and-Galatea act. He changed from a statue of stupefaction to a young man with a problem to tackle. He admitted Nevada, got a whiskbroom, and began to brush the snow from her clothes. A great lamp, with a green shade, hung over an easel, where the artist had been sketching in crayon.

"You wanted me," said Nevada, simply, "and I came. You said so in your letter. What did you send for me for?"

"You read my letter?" inquired Gilbert, sparring for wind.

"Barbara read it to me. I saw it afterward. It said: 'Come to my studio at twelve to-night, and do not fail.' I thought you were sick, of course, but you don't seem to be."

"Aha!" said Gilbert, irrelevantly. "I'll tell you why I asked you to come, Nevada. I want you to marry me immediately—to-night. What's a little snowstorm? Will you do it?"

"You might have noticed that I would, long ago," said Nevada. "And I'm rather stuck on the snowstorm idea, myself. I surely would hate one of those flowery church noon-weddings. Gilbert, I didn't know you had grit enough to propose in this way. Let's shock 'em—it's our funeral, ain't it?"

"You bet!" said Gilbert. "Where did I hear that expression?" he added to himself. "Wait a minute, Nevada; I want to do a little 'phoning."

He shut himself up in a little dressing-room, and called upon the lightnings of the heavens—condensed into unromantic numbers and districts.

"That you, Jack? You confounded sleepy-head! Yes, wake up; this is me—or I—oh, bother the difference in grammar! I'm going to be married right away. Yes! Wake up your sister—don't answer me back; bring her along, too—you *must*. Remind Agnes of the time I saved her from drowning in Lake Ronkonkoma—I know it's caddish to refer to it, but she *must* come with you. Yes! Nevada is here, waiting. We've been engaged quite a while. Some opposition among the relatives, you know, and we have to pull it off this way. We're waiting here for you. Don't let Agnes out-talk you—bring her! You will? Good old boy! I'll order a carriage to call for you, double-quick time. Confound you, Jack, you're all right!"

Gilbert returned to the room where Nevada waited.

"My old friend, Jack Peyton, and his sister were to have been here at a quarter to twelve," he explained; "but Jack is so confoundedly slow. I've just 'phoned them to hurry. They'll be here in a few minutes. I'm the happiest man in the world, Nevada! What did you do with the letter I sent you to-day?"

"I've got it cinched here," said Nevada, pulling it out from beneath her opera-cloak.

Gilbert drew the letter from the envelope and looked it over carefully. Then he looked at Nevada thoughtfully.

"Didn't you think it rather queer that I should ask you to come to my studio at midnight?" he asked.

"Why, no," said Nevada, rounding her eyes. "Not if you needed me. Out West, when a pal sends you a hurry call—ain't that what you say here?—we get there first and talk about it after the row is over. And it's usually snowing there, too, when things happen. So I didn't mind."

Gilbert rushed into another room, and came back burdened with overcoats warranted to turn wind, rain, or snow.

"Put this raincoat on," he said, holding it for her. "We have a quarter of a mile to go. Old Jack and his sister will be here in a few minutes." He began to struggle into a heavy coat. "Oh, Nevada," he said, "just look at the headlines on the front page of that evening paper on the table, will you? It's about your section of the West, and I know it will interest you."

He waited a full minute, pretending to find trouble in the getting on of his overcoat, and then turned. Nevada had not moved. She was looking at him with strange and pensive directness. Her cheeks had a flush on them beyond the color that had been contributed by the wind and snow; but her eyes were steady.

"I was going to tell you," she said, "anyhow, before you—before we—before—well, before anything. Dad never gave me a day of schooling. I never learned to read or write a darned word. Now if——"

Pounding their uncertain way upstairs, the feet of Jack, the somnolent, and Agnes, the grateful, were heard.

V

When Mr. and Mrs. Gilbert Warren were spinning softly homeward in a closed carriage, after the ceremony, Gilbert said:

"Nevada, would you really like to know what I wrote you in the letter that you received to-night?"

"Fire away!" said his bride.

"Word for word," said Gilbert, "it was this: 'My dear Miss Warren—You were right about the flower. It was a hydrangea, and not a lilac.'"

"All right," said Nevada. "But let's forget it. The joke's on Barbara, anyway!"

THIMBLE, THIMBLE

THESE are the directions for finding the office of Carteret & Carteret, Mill Supplies and Leather Belting:

You follow the Broadway trail down until you pass the Crosstown Line, the Bread Line, and the Dead Line, and come to the Big Cañons of the Moneygrubber Tribe. Then you turn to the left, to the right, dodge a push-cart and the tongue of a two-ton four-horse dray, and hop, skip, and jump to a granite ledge on the side of a twenty-one-story synthetic mountain of stone and iron. In the twelfth story is the office of Carteret & Carteret. The factory where they make the mill supplies and leather belting is in Brooklyn. Those commodities—to say nothing of Brooklyn—not being of interest to you, let us hold the incidents within the confines of a one-act, one-scene play, thereby lessening the toil of the reader and the expenditure of the publisher. So, if you have the courage to face four pages of type and Carteret & Carteret's office boy, Percival, you shall sit on a varnished chair in the inner office and peep at the little comedy of the Old Nigger Man, the Hunting-Case Watch, and the Open-Faced Question—mostly borrowed from the late Mr. Frank Stockton, as you will conclude.

First, biography (but pared to the quick) must intervene. I am for the inverted sugar-coated quinine pill—the bitter on the outside.

The Carterets were, or was (Columbia College professors please rule), an old Virginia family. Long time ago the gentlemen of the family had worn lace ruffles and carried tinless foils and owned plantations and had slaves to burn. But the war had greatly reduced their holdings. (Of course you can perceive at once that this flavor has been shoplifted from Mr. F. Hopkinson Smith, in spite of the "et" after "Carter.") Well, anyhow:

In digging up the Carteret history I shall not take you farther back than the year 1620. The two original American Carterets came over in that year, but by different means of transportation. One brother, named John, came in the *Mayflower* and became a Pilgrim Father. You've seen his pictures on the covers of the Thanksgiving magazines, hunting turkeys in the deep snow with a blunderbuss. Blandford Carteret, the other brother, crossed the pond in his own brigantine, landed on the Virginia coast, and became an F. F. V. John became distinguished for piety and shrewdness in business; Blandford for his pride, juleps, marksmanship, and vast slave-cultivated plantations.

Then came the Civil War. (I must condense this historical interpolation.) Stonewall Jackson was shot; Lee surrendered; Grant toured the world; cotton went to nine cents; Old Crow whiskey and Jim Crow cars were invented; the Seventy-ninth Massachusetts Volunteers returned to the Ninety-seventh Alabama Zouaves the battle flag of Lundy's Lane which they bought at a second-hand store in Chelsea, kept by a man named Skzchnzski; Georgia sent the President a sixty-pound watermelon—and that brings us up to the time when the story begins. My! but that was sparring for an opening! I really must brush up on my Aristotle.

The Yankee Carterets went into business in New York long before the war. Their house, as far as Leather Belting and Mill Supplies was concerned, was as musty and arrogant and solid as one of those old East India tea-importing concerns that you read about in Dickens. There were some rumors of a war behind its counters, but not enough to affect the business.

During and after the war, Blandford Carteret, F. F. V., lost his plantations, juleps, marksmanship, and life. He bequeathed little more than his pride to his surviving family. So it came to pass that Blandford Carteret, the Fifth, aged fifteen, was invited by the leather-and-mill-supplies branch of that name to come North and learn business instead of hunting foxes and boasting of the glory of his fathers on the reduced acres of his impoverished family. The boy jumped at the chance; and at the age of twenty-five, sat in the office of the firm equal partner with John, the Fifth, of the blunderbuss-and-turkey branch. Here the story begins again.

The young men were about the same age, smooth of face, alert, easy of manner, and with an air that promised mental and physical quickness. They were razored, blue-serged, straw-hatted, and pearl stick-pinned like other young New Yorkers who might be millionaires or bill clerks.

One afternoon at four o'clock, in the private office of the firm, Blandford Carteret opened a letter that a clerk had just brought to his desk. After reading it, he chuckled audibly for nearly a minute. John looked around from his desk inquiringly.

"It's from mother," said Blandford. "I'll read you the funny part of it. She tells me all the neighborhood news first, of course, and then cautions me against getting my feet wet and musical comedies. After that come vital statistics about calves and pigs and an estimate of the wheat crop. And now I'll quote some:

"'And what do you think! Old Uncle Jake, who was seventy-six last Wednesday, must go travelling. Nothing would do but he must go to New York and see his "young Marster Blandford." Old as he is, he has a deal of common sense, so I've let him go. I couldn't refuse him—he seemed to have concentrated all his hopes and desires into this one adventure into the wide world. You know he was born on the plantation, and has never been ten miles away from it in his life. And he was your father's body servant during the war, and has been always a faithful vassal and servant of the family. He has often seen the gold watch—the watch that was your father's and your father's father's. I told him it was to be yours, and he begged me to allow him to take it to you and to put it into your hands himself.

"'So he has it, carefully enclosed in a buckskin case, and is bringing it to you with all the pride and importance of a king's messenger. I gave him money for the round trip and for a two weeks' stay in the city. I wish you would see to it that he gets comfortable quarters—Jake won't need much looking after—he's able to take care of himself. But I have read in the papers that African bishops and colored potentates generally have much trouble in obtaining food and lodging in the Yankee metropolis. That may be all right; but I don't see why the best hotel there shouldn't take Jake in. Still, I suppose it's a rule.

"'I gave him full directions about finding you, and packed his valise myself. You won't have to bother with him; but I do hope you'll see that he is made comfortable. Take the watch that he brings you—it's almost a decoration. It has been worn by true Carterets, and there isn't a stain upon it nor a false movement of the wheels. Bringing it to you is the crowning joy of old Jake's life. I wanted him to have that little outing and that happiness before it is too late. You have often heard us talk about how Jake, pretty badly wounded himself, crawled through the reddened grass at Chancellorsville to where your father lay with the bullet in his dear heart, and took the watch from his pocket to keep it from the "Yanks."

"'So, my son, when the old man comes consider him as a frail but worthy messenger from the old-time life and home.

"'You have been so long away from home and so long among the people that we have always regarded as aliens that I'm not sure that Jake will know you when he sees you. But Jake has a keen perception, and I rather believe that he will know a Virginia Carteret at sight. I can't conceive that even ten years in Yankeeland could change a boy of mine. Anyhow, I'm sure you will know

Jake. I put eighteen collars in his valise. If he should have to buy others, he wears a number 15½. Please see that he gets the right ones. He will be no trouble to you at all.

" 'If you are not too busy, I'd like for you to find him a place to board where they have white-meal corn-bread, and try to keep him from taking his shoes off in your office or on the street. His right foot swells a little, and he likes to be comfortable.

" 'If you can spare the time, count his handkerchiefs when they come back from the wash. I bought him a dozen new ones before he left. He should be there about the time this letter reaches you. I told him to go straight to your office when he arrives.' "

As soon as Blandford had finished the reading of this, something happened (as there should happen in stories and must happen on the stage).

Percival, the office boy, with his air of despising the world's output of mill supplies and leather belting, came in to announce that a colored gentleman was outside to see Mr. Blandford Carteret.

"Bring him in," said Blandford, rising.

John Carteret swung around in his chair and said to Percival: "Ask him to wait a few minutes outside. We'll let you know when to bring him in."

Then he turned to his cousin with one of those broad, slow smiles that was an inheritance of all the Carterets, and said:

"Bland, I've always had a consuming curiosity to understand the differences that you haughty Southerners believe to exist between 'you all' and the people of the North. Of course, I know that you consider yourselves made out of finer clay and look upon Adam as only a collateral branch of your ancestry; but I don't know why. I never could understand the differences between us."

"Well, John," said Blandford, laughing, "what you don't understand about it is just the difference, of course. I suppose it was the feudal way in which we live that gave us our lordly baronial airs and feeling of superiority."

"But you are not feudal now," went on John. "Since we licked you and stole your cotton and mules you've had to go to work just as we 'damyankees,' as you call us, have always been doing. And you're just as proud and exclusive and upper-classy as you were before the war. So it wasn't your money that caused it."

"Maybe it was the climate," said Blandford lightly, "or maybe our negroes spoiled us. I'll call old Jake in, now. I'll be glad to see the old villain again."

"Wait just a moment," said John. "I've got a little theory I want to test. You and I are pretty much alike in our general appearance. Old Jake hasn't seen you since you were fifteen. Let's have him in and play fair and see which of us gets the watch. The old darky surely ought to be able to pick out his 'young marster' without any trouble. The alleged aristocratic superiority of a 'reb' ought to be visible to him at once. He couldn't make the mistake of handing over the timepiece to a Yankee, of course. The loser buys the dinner this evening and two dozen 15½ collars for Jake. Is it a go?"

Blandford agreed heartily. Percival was summoned, and told to usher the "colored gentleman" in.

Uncle Jake stepped inside the private office cautiously. He was a little old man, as black as soot, wrinkled and bald except for a fringe of white wool, cut decorously short, that ran over his ears and around his head. There was nothing of the stage "uncle" about him: his black suit nearly fitted him; his shoes shone, and his straw hat was banded with a gaudy ribbon. In his right hand he carried something carefully concealed by his closed fingers.

Uncle Jake stopped a few steps from the door. Two young men sat in their revolving desk-chairs ten feet apart and looked at him in friendly silence. His gaze slowly shifted many times from one to the other. He felt sure that he was in the presence of one, at least, of the revered family among whose fortunes his life had begun and was to end.

One had the pleasing but haughty Carteret air; the other had the unmistakable straight, long family nose. Both had the keen black eyes, horizontal brows, and thin, smiling lips that had distinguished both the Carteret of the *Mayflower* and him of the brigantine. Old Jake had thought that he could have picked out his young master instantly from a thousand Northerners; but he found himself in difficulties. The best he could do was to use strategy.

"Howdy, Marse Blandford—howdy, suh?" he said, looking midway between the young men.

"Howdy, Uncle Jake?" they both answered pleasantly and in unison. "Sit down. Have you brought the watch?"

Uncle Jake chose a hard-bottom chair at a respectful distance, sat on the edge of it, and laid his hat carefully on the floor. The watch in its buckskin case he gripped tightly. He had not risked his life on the battlefield to rescue that watch from his "old marster's" foes to hand it over again to the enemy without a struggle.

"Yes, suh; I got it in my hand, suh. I'm gwine give it to you right away in jus' a minute. Old Missus told me to put it in young Marse Blandford's hand and tell him to wear it for the family pride and honor. It was a mighty lonesome trip for an old nigger man to make—ten thousand miles, it must be, back to old Vi'ginia, suh. You've growed mightily, young marster. I wouldn't have reconnized you but for yo' powerful resemblance to the old marster."

With admirable diplomacy the old man kept his eyes roaming in the space between the two men. His words might have been addressed to either. Though neither wicked nor perverse, he was seeking for a sign.

Blandford and John exchanged winks.

"I reckon you done got you ma's letter," went on Uncle Jake. "She said she was gwine to write to you about my comin' along up this er-way."

"Yes, yes, Uncle Jake," said John, briskly. "My cousin and I have just been notified to expect you. We are both Carterets, you know."

"Although one of us," said Blandford, "was born and raised in the North."

"So if you will hand over the watch——" said John.

"My cousin and I——" said Blandford.

"Will then see to it——" said John.

"That comfortable quarters are found for you," said Blandford.

With creditable ingenuity, old Jake set up a cackling, high-pitched, protracted laugh. He beat his knee, picked up his hat and bent the brim in an apparent paroxysm of humorous appreciation. The seizure afforded him a mask behind which he could roll his eye impartially between, above, and beyond his two tormentors.

"I sees what!" he chuckled, after a while. "You gen'lemen is tryin' to have fun with the po' old nigger. But you can't fool old Jake. I knowed you, Marse Blandford, the minute I sot eyes on you. You was a po' skimpy little boy no mo' than about fo'teen when you lef' home to come No'th; but I knowed you the minute I sot eyes on you. You is the mawtal image of old marster. The other gen'leman resembles you mightily, suh; but you can't fool old Jake on a member of the old Vi'ginia family. No, suh."

At exactly the same time both Carterets smiled and extended a hand for the watch.

Uncle Jake's wrinkled black face lost the expression of amusement into which he had vainly twisted it. He knew that he was being teased, and that it made little real difference, as far as its safety went, into which of those outstretched hands he placed the family treasure. But it seemed to him that not only his own pride and loyalty but much of the Virginia Carterets' was at stake. He had heard down South during the war about that other branch of the family that lived in the North and fought on "the yuther side," and it had always grieved him. He had followed his "old marster's" fortunes from stately luxury through war to almost poverty. And now, with the last relic and reminder of him, blessed by "old missus," and entrusted implicitly to his care, he had come ten thousand miles (as it seemed) to deliver it into the hands of the one who was to wear it and wind it and cherish it and listen to it tick off the unsullied (hours that marked the lives of the Carterets—of Virginia.

His experience and conception of the Yankees had been an impression of tyrants —"low-down, common trash"—in blue, laying waste with fire and sword. He had seen the smoke of many burning homesteads almost as grand as Carteret Hall ascending to the drowsy Southern skies. And now he was face to face with one of them—and he could not distinguish him from his "young marster" whom he had come to find and bestow upon him the emblem of his kingship—even as the arm "clothed in white samite, mystic, wonderful" laid Excalibur in the right hand of Arthur. He saw before him two young men, easy, kind, courteous, welcoming, either of whom might have been the one he sought. Troubled, bewildered, sorely grieved at his weakness of judgment, old Jake abandoned his loyal subterfuges. His right hand sweated against the buckskin cover of the watch. He was deeply humiliated and chastened. Seriously, now, his prominent, yellow-white eyes closed scanned the two young men. At the end of his scrutiny he was conscious of but one difference between them. One wore a narrow black tie with a white pearl stickpin. The other's "four-in-hand" was a narrow blue one pinned with a black pearl.

And then, to old Jake's relief, there came a sudden distraction. Drama knocked at the door with imperious knuckles, and forced Comedy to the wings, and Drama peeped with a smiling but set face over the footlights.

Percival, the hater of mill supplies, brought in a card, which he handed, with the manner of one bearing a cartel, to Blue-Tie.

"Olivia De Ormond," read Blue-Tie from the card. He looked inquiringly at his cousin.

"Why not have her in," said Black-Tie, "and bring matters to a conclusion?"

"Uncle Jake," said one of the young men, "would you mind taking that chair over there in the corner for a while? A lady is coming in—on some business. We'll take up your case afterward."

The lady whom Percival ushered in was young and petulantly, decidedly, freshly, consciously, and intentionally pretty. She was dressed with such expensive plainness that she made you consider lace and ruffles as mere tatters and rags. But one great ostrich plume that she wore would have marked her anywhere in the army of beauty as the wearer of the merry helmet of Navarre.

Miss De Ormond accepted the swivel chair at Blue-Tie's desk. Then the gentlemen drew leather-upholstered seats conveniently near, and spoke of the weather.

"Yes," said she, "I noticed it was warmer. But I mustn't take up too much of your time during business hours. That is," she continued, "unless we talk business."

She addressed her words to Blue-Tie with a charming smile.

"Very well," said he. "You don't mind my cousin being present, do you? We are generally rather confidential with each other—especially in business matters."

"Oh, no," carolled Miss De Ormond. "I'd rather he did hear. He knows all about it, anyhow. In fact, he's quite a material witness because he was present when you—when it happened. I thought you might want to talk things over before—well, before any action is taken, as I believe the lawyers say."

"Have you anything in the way of a proposition to make?" asked Black-Tie.

Miss De Ormond looked reflectively at the neat toe of one of her dull kid pumps

"I had a proposal made to me," she said. "If the proposal sticks it cuts out the proposition. Let's have that settled first."

"Well, as far as——" began Blue-Tie.

"Excuse me, cousin," interrupted Black-Tie, "if you don't mind my cutting in." And then he turned, with a good-natured air, toward the lady.

"Now, let's recapitulate a bit," he said, cheerfully. "All three of us, besides other mutual acquaintances, have been out on a good many larks together."

"I'm afraid I'll have to call the birds by another name," said Miss De Ormond.

"All right," responded Black-Tie, with unimpaired cheerfulness; "suppose we say 'squabs' when we talk about the 'proposal' and 'larks' when we discuss the 'proposition.' You have a quick mind, Miss De Ormond. Two months ago some half-dozen of us went in a motor-car for a day's run into the country. We stopped at a road-house for dinner. My cousin proposed marriage to you then and there. He was influenced to do so, of course, by the beauty and charm which no one can deny that you possess."

"I wish I had you for a press agent, Mr. Carteret," said the beauty, with a dazzling smile.

"You are on the stage, Miss De Ormond," went on Black-Tie. "You have had, doubtless, many admirers, and perhaps other proposals. You must remember, too, that we were a party of merrymakers on that occasion. There were a good many corks pulled. That the proposal of marriage was made to you by my cousin we cannot deny. But hasn't it been your experience that, by common consent, such things lose their seriousness when viewed in the next day's sunlight? Isn't there something of a 'code' among good 'sports'—I use the word in its best sense—that wipes out each day the follies of the evening previous?"

"Oh, yes," said Miss De Ormond. "I know that very well. And I've always played up to it. But as you seem to be conducting the case—with the silent consent of the defendant—I'll tell you something more. I've got letters from him repeating the proposal. And they're signed too."

"I understand," said Black-Tie, gravely. "What's your price for the letters?"

"I'm not a cheap one," said Miss De Ormond. "But I had decided to make you a rate. You both belong to a swell family. Well, if I *am* on the stage nobody can say a word against me truthfully. And the money is only a secondary consideration. It isn't the money I was after. I—I believed him—and—and I liked him."

She cast a soft, entrancing glance at Blue-Tie from under her long eyelashes.

"And the price?" went on Black-Tie, inexorably.

"Ten thousand dollars," said the lady, sweetly.

"Or——"

"Or the fulfilment of the engagement to marry."

"I think it is time," interrupted Blue-Tie, "for me to be allowed to say a word or two. You and I, cousin, belong to a family that has held its head pretty high. You have been brought up in a section of the country very different from the one where our branch of the family lived. Yet both of us are Carterets, even if some of our ways and theories differ. You remember, it is a tradition of the family, that no Carteret ever failed in chivalry to a lady or failed to keep his word when it was given."

Then Blue-Tie, with frank decision showing on his countenance, turned to Miss De Ormond.

"Olivia," said he, "on what date will you marry me?"

Before she could answer, Black-Tie again interposed.

"It is a long journey," said he, "from Plymouth Rock to Norfolk Bay. Between the two points we find the changes that nearly three centuries have brought. In that time the old order has changed. We no longer burn witches or torture slaves. And to-day we neither spread our cloaks on the mud for ladies to walk over nor treat them to the ducking-stool. It is the age of common sense, adjustment, and proportion. All of us—ladies, gentlemen, women, men, Northerners, Southerners, lords, caitiffs, actors, hardware-drummers, senators, hod-carriers, and politicians—are coming to a better understanding. Chivalry is one of our words that changes its meaning every day. Family pride is a thing of many constructions—it may show itself by maintaining a moth-eaten arrogance in a cob-webbed Colonial mansion or by the prompt paying of one's debts.

"Now, I suppose you've had enough of my monologue. I've learned something of business and a little of life; and I somehow believe, cousin, that our great-great-grandfathers, the original Carterets, would endorse my view of this matter."

Black-Tie wheeled around to his desk, wrote in a checkbook and tore out the check, the sharp rasp of the perforated leaf making the only sound in the room. He laid the check within easy reach of Miss De Ormond's hand.

"Business is business," said he. "We live in a business age. There is my personal check for $10,000. What do you say, Miss De Ormond—will it be orange blossoms or cash?"

Miss De Ormond picked up the check carelessly, folded it indifferently, and stuffed it into her glove.

"Oh, this'll do," she said, calmly. "I just thought I'd call and put it up to you. I guess you people are all right. But a girl has feelings, you know. I've heard one of you was a Southerner—I wonder which one of you it is?"

She arose, smiled sweetly, and walked to the door. There, with a flash of white teeth and a dip of the heavy plume, she disappeared.

Both of the cousins had forgotten Uncle Jake for the time. But now they heard the shuffling of his shoes as he came across the rug toward them from his seat in the corner.

"Young marster," he said, "take yo' watch."

And without hesitation he laid the ancient timepiece in the hand of its rightful owner.

SUPPLY AND DEMAND

FINCH keeps a hats-cleaned-by-electricity-while-you-wait establishment, nine feet by twelve, in Third Avenue. Once a customer, you are always his. I do not know his secret process, but every four days your hat needs to be cleaned again.

Finch is a leathern, sallow, slow-footed man, between twenty and forty. You would say he had been brought up a bushelman in Essex Street. When business is slack he likes to talk, so I had my hat cleaned even oftener than it deserved, hoping Finch might let me into some of the secrets of the sweatshops.

One afternoon I dropped in and found Finch alone. He began to anoint my headpiece de Panama with his mysterious fluid that attracted dust and dirt like a magnet.

"They say the Indians weave 'em under water," said I, for a leader.

"Don't you believe it," said Finch. "No Indian or white man could stay under water that long. Say, do you pay much attention to politics? I see in the paper something about a law they've passed called 'the law of supply and demand.'"

I explained to him as well as I could that the reference was to a politico-economical law, and not to a legal statute.

"I didn't know," said Finch. "I heard a good deal about it a year or so ago, but in a one-sided way."

"Yes," said I, "political orators use it a great deal. In fact, they never give it a rest. I suppose you heard some of those cart-tail fellows spouting on the subject over here on the east side."

"I heard it from a king," said Finch—"the white king of a tribe of Indians in South America."

I was interested but not surprised. The big city is like a mother's knee to many who have strayed far and found the roads rough beneath their uncertain feet. At dusk they come home and sit upon the door-step. I know a piano player in a cheap café who has shot lions in Africa, a bell-boy who fought in the British army against the Zulus, an express-driver whose left arm had been cracked like a lobster's claw for a stew-pot of Patagonian cannibals when the boat of his rescuers hove in sight. So a hat-cleaner who has been a friend of a king did not oppress me.

"A new band?" asked Finch, with his dry, barren smile.

"Yes," said I, "and half an inch wider." I had had a new band five days before.

"I meets a man one night," said Finch, beginning his story—"a man brown as snuff, with money in every pocket, eating schweiner-knuckel in Schlagel's. That was two years ago, when I was a hose-cart driver for No. 98. His discourse runs to the subject of gold. He says that certain mountains in a country down South that he calls Guadymala is full of it. He says the Indians wash it out of the streams in plural quantities.

"'Oh, Geronimo!' says I. 'Indians! There's no Indians in the South,' I tell him, 'except Elks, Maccabees, and the buyers for the fall dry-goods trade. The Indians are all on the reservations,' says I.

"'I'm telling you this with reservations,' says he. 'They ain't Buffalo Bill Indians; they're squattier and more pedigreed. They call 'em Inkers and Aspics, and they was old inhabitants when Mazuma was king of Mexico. They wash the gold out of the mountain streams,' says the brown man, 'and fills quills with it; and then they empty 'em into red jars till they are full; and then they pack it in buckskin sacks of one arroba each—an arroba is twenty-five pounds—and store it in a stone house, with an engraving of a idol with marcelled hair, playing a flute, over the door.'

"'How do they work off this unearth increment?' I asks.

"'They don't,' says the man. 'It's a case of "Ill fares the land with the great deal of velocity where wealth accumulates and there ain't any reciprocity."'

"After this man and me got through our conversation, which left him dry of information, I shook hands with him and told him I was sorry I couldn't believe him. And a month afterward I landed on the coast of this Guadymala with $1,300 that I had been saving up for five years. I thought I knew what Indians liked, and I fixed myself accordingly. I loaded down four pack-mules with red woollen blankets, wrought-iron pails, jewelled side-combs for the ladies, glass necklaces, and safety-razors. I hired a black mozo, who was supposed to be a mule-driver and an interpreter too. It turned out that he could interpret mules all right, but he drove the English language much too hard. His name sounded like a Yale-key when you push it in wrong side up, but I called him McClintock, which was close to the noise.

"Well, this gold village was forty miles up in the mountains, and it took us nine days to find it. But one afternoon McClintock led the other mules and myself over a rawhide bridge stretched across a precipice five thousand feet deep, it seemed to me. The hoofs of the beasts drummed on it just like before George M. Cohan makes his first entrance on the stage.

"This village was built of mud and stone, and had no streets. Some few yellow-

and-brown persons popped their heads out-of-doors, looking about like Welsh rabbits with Worcester sauce on 'em. Out of the biggest house, that had a kind of a porch around it, steps a big white man, red as a beet in color, dressed in fine tanned deerskin clothes, with a gold chain around his neck, smoking a cigar. I've seen United States Senators of his style of features and build, also head-waiters and cops.

"He walks up and takes a look at us, while McClintock disembarks and begins to interpret to the lead mule while he smokes a cigarette.

" 'Hello, Buttinsky,' says the fine man to me. 'How did you get in the game? I didn't see you buy any chips. Who gave you the keys of the city?'

" 'I'm a poor traveller,' says I. 'Especially muleback. You'll excuse me. Do you run a hack line or only a bluff?'

" 'Segregate yourself from your pseudo-equine quadruped,' says he, 'and come inside.'

"He raises a finger, and a villager runs up.

" 'This man will take care of your outfit,' says he, 'and I'll take care of you.'

"He leads me into the biggest house, and sets out the chairs and a kind of a drink the color of milk. It was the finest room I ever saw. The stone walls was hung all over with silk shawls, and there was red and yellow rugs on the floor, and jars of red pottery and Angora goat skins, and enough bamboo furniture to misfurnish half a dozen seaside cottages.

" 'In the first place,' says the man, 'you want to know who I am. I'm sole lessee and proprietor of this tribe of Indians. They call me the Grand Yacuma, which is to say King or Main Finger of the bunch. I've got more power here than a chargé d'affaires, a charge of dynamite, and a charge account at Tiffany's combined. In fact, I'm the Big Stick, with as many extra knots on it as there is on the record run of the *Lusitania*. Oh, I read the papers now and then,' says he. 'Now, let's hear your entitlements,' he goes on, 'and the meeting will be open.'

" 'Well,' says I, 'I am known as one W. D. Finch. Occupation, capitalist. Address, 541 East Thirty-second——'

" 'New York,' chips in the Noble Grand. 'I know,' says he, grinning. 'It ain't the first time you've seen it go down on the blotter. I can tell by the way you hand it out. Well, explain "capitalist." '

"I tells this boss plain what I come for and how I come to came.

" 'Gold-dust?' says he, looked as puzzled as a baby that got a feather stuck on its molasses finger. 'That's funny. This ain't a gold-mining country. And you invested all your capital on a stranger's story? Well, well! These Indians of mine—they are the last of the tribe of Peches—are simple as children. They know nothing of the purchasing power of gold. I'm afraid you've been imposed on,' says he.

" 'Maybe so,' says I, 'but it sounded pretty straight to me.'

" 'W. D.,' says the King, all of a sudden, 'I'll give you a square deal. It ain't often I get to talk to a white man, and I'll give you a show for your money. It may be these constituents of mine have a few grains of gold-dust hid away in their clothes. To-morrow you may get out these goods you've brought up and see if you can make any sales. Now, I'm going to introduce myself unofficially. My name is Shane—Patrick Shane. I own this tribe of Peche Indians by right of conquest—single handed and unafraid. I drifted up here four years ago, and won 'em by my size and complexion and nerve. I learned their language in six weeks—it's easy: you simply emit a string of consonants as long as your breath holds out and then point at what you're asking for.

" 'I conquered 'em, spectacularly,' goes on King Shane, 'and then I went at 'em with economical politics, law, sleight-of-hand, and a kind of New England ethics and parsimony. Every Sunday, or as near as I can guess at it, I preach to 'em

in the council-house (I'm the council) on the law of supply and demand. I praise
supply and knock demand. I use the same text every time. You wouldn't think,
W. D.,' says Shane, 'that I had poetry in me, would you?'

" 'Well,' says I, 'I wouldn't know whether to call it poetry or not.'

" 'Tennyson,' says Shane, 'furnishes the poetic gospel I preach. I always considered him the boss poet. Here's the way the text goes:

> For, not to admire, if a man could learn it, were more
> Than to walk all day like a Sultan of old in a garden of spice.

" 'You see, I teach 'em to cut out demand—that supply is the main thing. I
teach 'em not to des're anything beyond their simplest needs. A little mutton, a
little cocoa, and a little fruit brought up from the coast—that's all they want to
make 'em happy. I've got 'em well trained. They make their own clothes and
hats out of a vegetable fibre and straw, and they're a contented lot. It's a great
thing,' winds up Shane, 'to have made a people happy by the incultivation of
such simple institutions.'

"Well, the next day, with the King's permission, I has the McClintock open up
a couple of sacks of my goods in the little plaza of the village. The Indians
swarmed around by the hundred and looked the bargain-counter over. I shook
red blankets at 'em, flashed finger-rings and ear-bobs, tried pearl necklaces and
side-combs on the women, and a line of red hosiery on the men. 'Twas no use.
They looked on like hungry graven images, but I never made a sale. I asked
McClintock what was the trouble. Mac yawned three or four times, rolled a
cigarette, made one or two confidential side remarks to a mule, and then condescended to inform me that the people had no money.

"Just then up strolls King Patrick, big and red and royal as usual, with the
gold chain over his chest and his cigar in front of him.

" 'How's business, W. D.?' he asks.

" 'Fine,' says I. 'It's a bargain-day rush. I've got one more line of goods
to offer before I shut up shop. I'll try 'em with safety-razors. I've got two
gross that I bought at a fire sale.'

"Shane laughs till some kind of mameluke or private secretary he carries with
him has to hold him up.

" 'O my sainted Aunt Jerusha!' says he 'ain't you one of the Babes in the
Goods, W. D.? Don't you know that no Indians ever shave? They pull out
their whiskers instead.'

" 'Well,' says I, 'that's just what these razors would do for 'em—they wouldn't
have any kick coming if they used 'em once.'

"Shane went away, and I could hear him laughing a block, if there had been
any block.

" 'Tell 'em,' says I to McClintock, 'it ain't money I want—tell 'em I'll take
gold-dust. Tell 'em I'll allow 'em sixteen dollars an ounce for it in trade. That's
what I'm out for—the dust.'

"Mac interprets, and you'd have thought a squadron of cops had charged the
crowd to disperse it. Every uncle's nephew and aunt's niece of 'em faded away
inside of two minutes.

"At the royal palace that night me and the King talked it over.

" 'They've got the dust hid out somewhere,' says I, 'or they wouldn't have been
so sensitive about it.'

" 'They haven't,' says Shane. 'What's this gag you've got about gold? You
been reading Edward Allan Poe? They ain't got any gold.'

" 'They put it in quills,' says I, 'and then they empty it in jars, and then into
sacks of twenty-five pounds each. I got it straight.'

" 'W. D.,' says Shane, laughing and chewing his cigar, 'I don't often see a white man, and I feel like putting you on. I don't think you'll get away from here alive, anyhow, so I'm going to tell you. Come over here.'

"He draws aside a silk fibre curtain in a corner of the room and shows me a pile of buckskin sacks.

"'Forty of 'em,' says Shane. 'One arroba in each one. In round numbers, $220,000 worth of gold-dust you see there. It's all mine. It belongs to the Grand Yacuma. They bring it all to me. Two hundred and twenty thousand dollars—think of that, you glass-bead peddler,' says Shane—'and all mine.'

"'Little good it does you,' says I, contemptuously and hatefully. 'And so you are the government depository of this gang of moneyless money-makers? Don't you pay enough interest on it to enable one of your depositors to buy an Augusta (Maine) Pullman carbon diamond worth $200 for $4.85?'

"'Listen,' says Patrick Shane, with the sweat coming out on his brow. 'I'm confidant with you, as you have, somehow, enlisted my regards. Did you ever,' he says, 'feel the avoirdupois power of gold—not the troy weight of it, but the sixteen-ounces-to-the-pound force of it?'

"'Never,' says I. 'I never take in any bad money.'

"Shane drops down on the floor and throws his arms over the sacks of gold-dust.

"'I love it,' says he. 'I want to feel the touch of it day and night. It's my pleasure in life. I come in this room, and I'm a king and a rich man. I'll be a millionaire in another year. The pile's getting bigger every month. I've got the whole tribe washing out the sands in the creeks. I'm the happiest man in the world, W. D. I just want to be near this gold, and know it's mine and it's increasing every day. Now, you know,' says he, 'why my Indians wouldn't buy your goods. They can't. They bring all the dust to me. I'm their king. I've taught 'em not to desire or admire. You might as well shut up shop.'

"'I'll tell you what you are,' says I. 'You're a plain, contemptible miser. You preach supply and you forget demand. Now, supply,' I goes on, 'is never anything but supply. On the contrary,' says I, 'demand is a much broader syllogism and assertion. Demand includes the rights of our women and children, and charity and friendship, and even a little begging on the street corners. They've both got to harmonize equally. And I've got a few things up my commercial sleeve yet,' says I, 'that may jostle your preconceived ideas of politics and economy.'

"The next morning I had McClintock bring up another mule-load of goods to the plaza and open it up. The people gathered around the same as before.

"I got out the finest line of necklaces, bracelets, hair-combs, and earrings that I carried, and had the women put 'em on. And then I played trumps.

"Out of my last pack I opened up a half gross of hand-mirrors, with solid tin-foil backs, and passed 'em around among the ladies. That was the first introduction of looking-glasses among the Peche Indians.

"Shane walks by with his big laugh.

"'Business looking up any?' he asks.

"'It's looking at itself right now,' says I.

"By-and-by a kind of murmur goes through the crowd. The women had looked into the magic crystal and seen that they were beautiful, and was confiding the secret to the men. The men seemed to be urging the lack of money and hard times just before the election, but their excuses didn't go.

"Then was my time.

"I called McClintock away from an animated conversation with his mules and told him to do some interpreting.

"'Tell 'em,' says I, 'that gold-dust will buy for them these befitting ornaments for kings and queens of the earth. Tell 'em the yellow sand they wash out of the waters for the High Sanctified Yacomay and Chop Suey of the tribe will buy the precious jewels and charms that will make them beautiful and preserve and pickle them from evil spirits. Tell 'em the Pittsburgh banks are paying four per cent. interest on deposits by mail, while this get-rich-frequently custodian of the public funds ain't even paying attention. Keep telling 'em, Mac,' says I, 'to let the gold-dust family do their work. Talk to 'em like a born anti-Bryanite,' says I. 'Remind 'em that Tom Watson's gone back to Georgia,' say I.

"McClintock waves his hand affectionately at one of his mules, and then hurls a few stickfuls of minion type at the mob of shoppers.

"A gutta-percha Indian man, with a lady hanging on his arm, with three strings of my fish-scale jewelry and imitation marble beads around her neck, stands up on a block of stone and makes a talk that sounds like a man shaking dice in a box to fill aces and sixes.

"'He says,' says McClintock, 'that the people not know that gold-dust will buy their things. The women very mad. The Grand Yacuma tell them it no good but for keep to make bad spirits keep away.'

"'You can't keep bad spirits away from money,' says I.

"'They say,' goes on McClintock, 'the Yacuma fool them. They raise plenty row.'

"'Going! Going!' says I. 'Gold-dust or cash takes the entire stock. The dust weighed before you, and taken at sixteen dollars the ounce—the highest price on the Guadymala coast.'

"Then the crowd disperses all of a sudden, and I don't know what's up. Mac and me packs away the hand-mirrors and jewelry they had handed back to us, and we had the mules back to the corral they had set apart for our garage.

"While we was there we heard great noises of shouting, and down across the plaza runs Patrick Shane, hotfoot, with his clothes ripped half off, and scratches on his face like a cat had fought him hard for every one of its lives.

"'They're looting the treasury, W. D.,' he sings out. 'They're going to kill me and you, too. Unlimber a couple of mules at once. We'll have to make a get-away in a couple of minutes.'

"'They've found out,' says I, 'the truth about the law of supply and demand.'

"'It's the women, mostly,' says the King. 'And they used to admire me so!'

"'They hadn't seen looking-glasses then,' says I.

"'They've got knives and hatchets,' says Shane; 'hurry!'

"'Take that roan mule,' says I. 'You and your law of supply! I'll ride the dun, for he's two knots per hour the faster. The roan has a stiff knee, but he may make it,' says I. 'If you'd included reciprocity in your political platform I might have given you the dun,' says I.

"Shane and McClintock and me mounted our mules and rode across the rawhide bridge just as the Peches reached the other side and began firing stones and long knives at us. We cut the thongs that held up our end of the bridge and headed for the coast."

A tall, bulky policeman came into Finch's shop at that moment and leaned an elbow on the showcase. Finch nodded at him friendly.

"I heard down at Casey's," said the cop, in rumbling, husky tones, "that there was going to be a picnic of the Hat-Cleaners' Union over at Bergen Beach, Sunday. Is that right?"

"Sure," said Finch. "There'll be a dandy time."

"Gimme five tickets," said the cop, throwing a five-dollar bill on the showcase.

"Why," said Finch, "ain't you going it a little too——"

"Go to h——!" said the cop. "You got 'em to sell, ain't you? Somebody's got to buy 'em. Wish I could go along."

I was glad to see Finch so well thought of in his neighborhood.

And then in came a wee girl of seven, with dirty face and pure blue eyes and a smutched and insufficient dress.

"Mamma says," she recited, shrilly, "that you must give me eighty cents for the grocer and nineteen for the milkman and five cents for me to buy hokey-pokey with—but she didn't say that," the elf concluded, with a hopeful but honest grin.

Finch shelled out the money, counting it twice, but I noticed that the total sum that the small girl received was one dollar and four cents.

"That's the right kind of a law," remarked Finch as he carefully broke some of the stitches of my hatband so that it would assuredly come off within a few days—"the law of supply and demand. But they've both got to work together. I'll bet," he went on, with his dry smile, "she'll get jelly beans with that nickel—she likes 'em. What's supply if there's no demand for it?"

"What ever became of the King?" I asked, curiously.

"Oh, I might have told you," said Finch. "That was Shane came in and bought the tickets. He came back with me, and he's on the force now."

BURIED TREASURE

THERE are many kinds of fools. Now, will everybody please sit still until they are called upon specifically to rise?

I had been every kind of fool except one. I had expended my patrimony, pretended my matrimony, played poker, lawn-tennis, and bucket-shops—parted soon with my money in many ways. But there remained one rôle of the wearer of cap and bells that I had not played. That was the Seeker after Buried Treasure. To few does the delectable furor come. But of all the would-be followers in the hoof-prints of King Midas none has found a pursuit so rich in pleasurable promise.

But, going back from my theme a while—as lame pens must do—I was a fool of the sentimental sort. I saw May Martha Mangum, and was hers. She was eighteen, the color of the white ivory keys of a new piano, beautiful, and possessed by the exquisite solemnity and pathetic witchery of an unsophisticated angel doomed to live in a small, dull, Texas prairie town. She had a spirit and charm that could have enabled her to pluck rubies like raspberries from the crown of Belgium or any other sporty kingdom, but she did not know it, and I did not paint the picture for her.

You see, I wanted May Martha Mangum for to have and to hold. I wanted her to abide with me, and put my slippers and pipe away every day in places where they cannot be found of evenings.

May Martha's father was a man hidden behind whiskers and spectacles. He lived for bugs and butterflies and all insects that fly or crawl or buzz or get down your back or in the butter. He was an etymologist, or words to that effect. He spent his life seining the air for flying fish of the June-bug order, and then sticking pins through 'em and calling 'em names.

He and May Martha were the whole family. He prized her highly as a fine specimen of the *racibus humanus* because she saw that he had food at times, and put his clothes on right side before, and kept his alcohol-bottles filled. Scientists, they say, are apt to be absent-minded.

There was another besides myself who thought May Martha Mangum one to be desired. That was Goodloe Banks, a young man just home from college. He had all the attainments to be found in books—Latin, Greek, philosophy, and especially the higher branches of mathematics and logic.

If it hadn't been for his habit of pouring out this information and learning on every one that he addressed, I'd have liked him pretty well. But, even as it was, he and I were, you would have thought, great pals.

We got together every time we could because each of us wanted to pump the other for whatever straws we could find which way the wind blew from the heart of May Martha Mangum—rather a mixed metaphor; Goodloe Banks would never have been guilty of that. That is the way of rivals.

You might say that Goodloe ran to books, manners, culture, rowing intellect, and clothes. I would have put you in mind more of a baseball and Friday-night debating societies—by way of culture—and maybe of a good horseback rider.

But in our talks together, and in our visits and conversation with May Martha, neither Goodloe Banks nor I could find out which one of us she preferred. May Martha was a natural-born non-committal, and knew in her cradle how to keep people guessing.

As I said, old man Mangum was absent-minded. After a long time he found out one day—a little butterfly must have told him—that two young men were trying to throw a net over the head of the young person, a daughter, or some such technical appendage, who looked after his comforts.

I never knew scientists could rise to such occasions. Old Mangum orally labelled and classified Goodloe and myself easily among the lowest orders of the vertebrates; and in English, too, without going any further into Latin than simple references to *Orgetorix*, *Rex Helvetii*—which is as far as I ever went, myself. And he told us that if he ever caught us around his house again he would add us to his collection.

Goodloe Banks and I remained away five days, expecting the storm to subside. When we dared to call at the house again May Martha Mangum and her father were gone. Gone! The house they had rented was closed. Their little store of goods and chattels was gone also.

And not a word of farewell to either of us from May Martha—not a white, fluttering note pinned to the hawthorn-bush; not a chalk-mark on the gate-post nor a postcard in the post-office to give us a clue.

For two months Goodloe Banks and I—separately—tried every scheme we could think of to track the runaways. We used our friendship and influence with the ticket-agent, with livery-stable men, railroad conductors, and our one lone, lorn constable, but without results.

Then we became better friends and worse enemies than ever. We forgathered in the back room of Snyder's saloon every afternoon after work, and played dominoes, and laid conversational traps to find out from each other if anything had been discovered. That is the way of rivals.

Now, Goodloe Banks had a sarcastic way of displaying his own learning and putting me in the class that was reading "Poor Jane Ray, her bird is dead, she cannot play." Well, I rather liked Goodloe, and I had a contempt for his college learning, and I was always regarded as good-natured, so I kept my temper. And I was trying to find out if he knew anything about May Martha, so I endured his society.

In talking things over one afternoon he said to me:

"Suppose you do find her, Ed, whereby would you profit? Miss Mangum has a mind. Perhaps it is yet uncultured, but she is destined for higher things than you could give her. I have talked with no one who seemed to appreciate more the enchantment of the ancient poets and writers and the modern cults that have assimilated and expended their philosophy of life. Don't you think you are wasting your time looking for her?"

"My idea," said I, "of a happy home is an eight-room house in a grove of live-oaks by the side of a *charco* on a Texas prairie. A piano," I went on, "with an automatic player in the sitting-room, three thousand head of cattle under fence for a starter, a buckboard and ponies always hitched at a post for 'the missus'— and May Martha Mangum to spend the profits of the ranch as she pleases, and to abide with me, and put my slippers and pipe away every day in places where they cannot be found of evenings. That," said I, "is what is to be; and a fig— a dried, Smyrna, Dago-stand fig—for your curriculums, cults, and philosophy."

"She is meant for higher things," repeated Goodloe Banks.

"Whatever she is meant for," I answered, "just now she is out of pocket. And I shall find her as soon as I can without aid of the colleges."

"The game is blocked," said Goodloe, putting down a domino; and we had the beer.

Shortly after that a young farmer whom I knew came into town and brought me a folded blue paper. He said his grandfather had just died. I concealed a tear, and he went on to say that the old man had jealously guarded this paper for twenty years. He left it to his family as part of his estate, the rest of which consisted of two mules and a hypotenuse of non-arable land.

The sheet of paper was of the old, blue kind used during the rebellion of the abolitionists against the secessionists. It was dated June 14, 1863, and it described the hiding-place of ten burro-loads of gold and silver coin valued at three hundred thousand dollars. Old Rundle—grandfather of his grandson, Sam— was given the information by a Spanish priest who was in on the treasure-burying, and who died many years before—no, afterward—in old Rundle's house. Old Rundle wrote it down from dictation.

"Why didn't your father look this up?" I asked young Rundle.

"He went blind before he could do so," he replied.

"Why didn't you hunt for it yourself?" I asked.

"Well," said he, "I've only known about the paper for ten years. First there was the spring ploughin' to do, and then choppin' the weeds out of the corn; and then come takin' fodder; and mighty soon winter was on us. It seemed to run along that way year after year."

That sounded perfectly reasonable to me, so I took it up with young Lee Rundle at once.

The directions on the paper were simple. The whole burro cavalcade laden with the treasure started from an old Spanish mission in Dolores County. They travelled due south by the compass until they reached the Alamito River. They forded this, and buried the treasure on the top of a little mountain shaped like a pack-saddle standing in a row between two higher ones. A heap of stones marked the place of the buried treasure. All the party except the Spanish priest were killed by Indians a few days later. The secret was a monopoly. It looked good to me.

Lee Rundle suggested that we rig out a camping outfit, hire a surveyor to run out the line from the Spanish mission, and then spend the three hundred thousand dollars seeing the sights in Fort Worth. But, without being highly educated, I knew a way to save time and expense.

We went to the State land-office and had a practical, what they call a "working," sketch made of all the surveys of land from the old mission to the Alamito River. On this map I drew a line due southward to the river. The length of lines of each survey and section of land was accurately given on the sketch. By these we found the point on the river and had a "connection" made with it and an important, well-identified corner of the Los Animos five-league survey—a grant made by King Philip of Spain.

By doing this we did not need to have the line run out by a surveyor. It was a great saving of expense and time.

So, Lee Rundle and I fitted out a two-horse wagon team with all the accessories, and drove a hundred and forty-nine miles to Chico, the nearest town to the point we wished to reach. There we picked up a deputy county surveyor. He found the corner of the Los Animos survey for us, ran out the five thousand seven hundred and twenty varas west that our sketch called for, laid a stone on the spot, had coffee and bacon, and caught the mail-stage back to Chico.

I was pretty sure we would get that three hundred thousand dollars. Lee Rundle's was to be only one third, because I was paying all the expenses. With that two hundred thousand dollars I knew I could find May Martha Mangum if she was on earth. And with it I could flutter the butterflies in old man Mangum's dovecot, too. If I could find that treasure!

But Lee and I established camp. Across the river were a dozen l'ttle mountains densely covered by cedar-brakes, but not one shaped like a pack-saddle. That did not deter us. Appearances are deceptive. A pack-saddle, like beauty, may exist only in the eye of the beholder.

I and the grandson of the treasure examined those cedar-covered hills with the care of a lady hunting for the wicked flea. We explored every side, top, circumference, mean elevation, angle, slope and concavity of every one for two miles up and down the river. We spent four days doing so. Then we hitched up the roan and the dun, and hauled the remains of the coffee and bacon the one hundred and forty-nine miles back to Concho City.

Lee Rundle chewed much tobacco on the return trip. I was busy driving, because I was in a hurry.

As shortly as could be after our empty return, Goodloe Banks and I forgathered in the back room of Synder's saloon to play dominoes and fish for information. I told Goodloe about my expedition after the buried treasure.

"If I could have found that three hundred thousand dollars," I said to him, "I could have scoured and sifted the surface of the earth to find May Martha Mangum."

"She is meant for higher things," said Goodloe. "I shall find her myself. But, tell me how you went about discovering the spot where this unearthed increment was imprudently buried."

I told him in the smallest detail. I showed him the draughtsman's sketch with the distances marked plainly upon it.

After glancing over it in a masterly way, he leaned back in his chair and bestowed upon me an explosion of sardonic, superior, collegiate laughter.

"Well, you *are* a fool, Jim," he said, when he could speak.

"It's your play," said I, patiently, fingering my double six.

"Twenty," said Goodloe, making two crosses on the table with his chalk.

"Why am I a fool?" I asked. "Buried treasure has been found before in many places."

"Because," said he, "in calculating the point on the river where your line would strike you neglected to allow for the variation. The variation there would be nine degrees west. Let me have your pencil."

Goodloe Banks figured rapidly on the back of an envelope.

"The distance, from north to south, of the line run from the Spanish mission," said he, "is exactly twenty-two miles. It was run by a pocket-compass, according to your story. Allowing for the variation, the point on the Alamito River where you should have searched for your treasure is exactly six miles and nine hundred and forty-five varas farther west than the place you hit upon. Oh, what a fool you are, Jim!"

"What is this variation that you speak of?" I asked. "I thought figures never lied."

"The variation of the magnetic compass," said Goodloe, "from the true meridian."

He smiled in his superior way; and then I saw come out in his face the singular, eager, consuming cupidity of the seeker after buried treasure.

"Sometimes," he said with the air of the oracle, "these old traditions of hidden money are not without foundation. Suppose you let me look over that paper describing the location. Perhaps together we might——"

The result was that Goodloe Banks and I, rivals in love, became companions in adventure. We went to Chico by stage from Huntersburg, the nearest railroad town. In Chico we hired a team drawing a covered spring-wagon and camping paraphernalia. We had the same surveyor run out our distance, as revised by Goodloe and his variations, and then dismissed him and sent him on his homeward road.

It was night when we arrived. I fed the horses and made a fire near the bank of the river and cooked supper. Goodloe would have helped, but his education had not fitted him for practical things.

But while I worked he cheered me with the expression of great thoughts handed down from the dead ones of old. He quoted some translations from the Greek at much length.

"Anacreon," he explained. "That was a favorite passage with Miss Mangum—as I recited it."

"She is meant for higher things," said I, repeating his phrase.

"Can there be anything higher," asked Goodloe, "than to dwell in the society of the classics, to live in the atmosphere of learning and culture? You have often decried education. What of your wasted efforts through your ignorance of simple mathematics? How soon would you have found your treasure if my knowledge had not shown you your error?"

"We'll take a look at those hills across the river first," said I, "and see what we find. I am still doubtful about variations. I have been brought up to believe that the needle is true to the pole."

The next morning was a bright June one. We were up early and had breakfast. Goodloe was charmed. He recited—Keats, I think it was, and Kelly or Shelley—while I broiled the bacon. We were getting ready to cross the river, which was little more than a shallow creek there, and explore the many sharp-peaked, cedar-covered hills on the other side.

"My good Ulysses," said Goodloe, slapping me on the shoulder while I was washing the tin breakfast plates, "let me see the enchanted document once more. I believe it gives directions for climbing the hill shaped like a pack-saddle. I never saw a pack-saddle. What is it like, Jim?"

"Score one against culture," said I. "I'll know it when I see it."

Goodloe was looking at old Rundle's document when he ripped out a most uncollegiate swear-word.

"Come here," he said, holding the paper up against the sunlight. "Look at that," he said, laying his finger against it.

On the blue paper—a thing I had never noticed before—I saw stand out in white letters the word and figures: "Malvern, 1898."

"What about it?" I asked.

"It's the water-mark," said Goodloe. "The paper was manufactured in 1898. The writing on the paper is dated 1863. This is a palpable fraud."

"Oh, I don't know," said I. "The Rundles are pretty reliable, plain, uneducated country people. Maybe the paper manufacturers tried to perpetrate a swindle."

And then Goodloe Banks went as wild as his education permitted. He dropped the glasses off his nose and glared at me.

"I've often told you you were a fool," he said. "You have let yourself be imposed upon by a clodhopper. And you have imposed upon me."

"How," I asked, "have I imposed upon you?"

"By your ignorance," said he. "Twice I have discovered serious flaws in your plans that a common-school education should have enabled you to avoid. And," he continued, "I have been put to expense that I could ill afford in pursuing this swindling quest. I am done with it."

I rose and pointed a large pewter spoon at him, fresh from the dish-water.

"Goodloe Banks," I said, "I care not one parboiled navy bean for your education. I always barely tolerated it in any one, and I despised it in you. What has your learning done for you? It is a curse to yourself and a bore to your friends. Away," I said—"away with your water-marks and variations. They are nothing to me. They shall not deflect me from the quest."

I pointed with my spoon across the river to a small mountain shaped like a pack-saddle.

"I am going to search that mountain," I went on, "for the treasure. Decide now whether you are in it or not. If you wish to let a water-mark or a variation shake your soul, you are no true adventurer. Decide."

A white cloud of dust began to rise far down the river road. It was the mail-wagon from Hesperus to Chico. Goodloe flagged it.

"I am done with the swindle," said he, sourly. "No one but a fool would pay any attention to that paper now. Well, you always were a fool, Jim. I leave you to your fate."

He gathered his personal traps, climbed into the mail-wagon, adjusted his glasses nervously, and flew away in a cloud of dust.

After I had washed the dishes and staked the horses on new grass, I crossed the shallow river and made my way slowly through the cedar-brakes up to the top of the hill shaped like a pack-saddle.

It was a wonderful June day. Never in my life had I seen so many birds, so many butterflies, dragon-flies, grasshoppers, and such winged and stinged beasts of the air and fields.

I investigated the hill shaped like a pack-saddle from base to summit. I found an absolute absence of signs relating to buried treasure. There was no pile of stones, no ancient blazes on the trees, none of the evidences of the three hundred thousand dollars, as set forth in the document of old man Rundle.

I came down the hill in the cool of the afternoon. Suddenly, out of the cedar-brake I stepped into a beautiful green valley where a tributary small stream ran into the Alamito River.

And there I was startled to see what I took to be a wild man, with unkempt beard and ragged hair, pursuing a giant butterfly with brilliant wings.

"Perhaps he is an escaped madman," I thought; and wondered how he had strayed so far from seats of education and learning.

And then I took a few more steps and saw a vine-covered cottage near the small stream. And in a little grassy glade I saw May Martha Mangum plucking wild flowers.

She straightened up and looked at me. For the first time since I knew her I saw her face—which was the color of the white keys of a new piano—turn pink. I walked toward her without a word. She let the gathered flowers trickle slowly from her hand to the grass.

"I knew you would come, Jim," she said, clearly. "Father wouldn't let me write, but I knew you would come."

What followed, you may guess—there was my wagon and team just across the river.

I've often wondered what good too much education is to a man if he can't use it for himself. If all the benefits of it are to go to others, where does it come in?

For May Martha Mangum abides with me. There is an eight-room house in a live-oak grove, and a piano with an automatic player, and a good start toward the three thousand head of cattle is under fence.

And when I ride home at night my pipe and slippers are put away in places where they cannot be found.

But who cares for that? Who cares—who cares?

TO HIM WHO WAITS

THE Hermit of the Hudson was hustling about his cave with unusual animation.

The cave was on or in the top of a little spur of the Catskills that had strayed down to the river's edge, and, not having a ferry ticket, had to stop there. The bijou mountains were densely wooded and were infested by ferocious squirrels and woodpeckers that forever menaced the summer transients. Like a badly sewn strip of white braid, a macadamized road ran between the green skirt of the hills and the foamy lace of the river's edge. A dim path wound from the comfortable road up a rocky height to the hermit's cave. One mile upstream was the Viewpoint Inn, to which summer folk from the city came; leaving cool, electric-fanned apartments that they might be driven about in burning sunshine, shrieking, in gasoline launches, by spindle-legged Modreds bearing the blankest of shields.

Train your lorgnette upon the hermit and let your eye receive the personal touch that shall endear you to the hero.

A man of forty, judging him fairly, with long hair curling at the ends, dramatic eyes, and a forked brown beard like those that were imposed upon the West some years ago by self-appointed "divine healers" who succeeded the grasshopper crop. His outward vesture appeared to be a kind of gunny-sacking, cut and made into a garment that would have made the fortune of a London tailor. His long, well-shaped fingers, delicate nose, and poise of manner raised him high above the class of hermits who fear water and bury money in oyster-cans in their caves in spots indicated by rude crosses chipped in the stone wall above.

The hermit's home was not altogether a cave. The cave was an addition to the hermitage, which was a rude hut made of poles daubed with clay and covered with the best quality of rust-proof zinc roofing.

In the house proper there were stone slabs for seats, a rustic bookcase made of unplaned poplar planks, and a table formed of a wooden slab laid across two upright pieces of granite—something between the furniture of a Druid temple and that of a Broadway beefsteak dungeon. Hung against the walls were skins of wild animals purchased in the vicinity of Eighth Street and University Place, New York.

The rear of the cabin merged into the cave. There the hermit cooked his meals on a rude stone hearth. With infinite patience and an old axe he had chopped natural shelves in the rocky walls. On them stood his stores of flour, bacon, lard, talcum-powder, kerosene, baking-powder, soda-mint tablets, pepper, salt, and Olivo-Cremo Emulsion for chaps and roughness of the hands and face.

The hermit had hermited there for ten years. He was an asset of the Viewpoint Inn. To its guests he was second in interest only to the Mysterious Echo in the Haunted Glen. And the Lover's Leap beat him only a few inches, flat-footed. He was known far (but not very wide, on account of the topography) as a scholar of brilliant intellect who had forsworn the world because he had been jilted in a love affair. Every Saturday night the Viewpoint Inn sent to him surreptitiously a basket of provisions. He never left the immediate outskirts of his hermitage. Guests of the inn who visited him said his store of knowledge, wit, and scintillating philosophy was simply wonderful, you know. That summer the Viewpoint Inn was crowded with guests. So, on Saturday nights, there were extra cans of tomatoes, and sirloin steak, instead of "rounds," in the hermit's basket.

Now you have the material allegations in the case. So, make way for Romance.

Evidently the hermit expected a visitor. He carefully combed his long hair and parted his apostolic beard. When the ninety-eight-cent alarm-clock on a stone shelf announced the hour of five he picked up his gunny-sacking skirts, brushed them carefully, gathered an oaken staff, and strolled slowly into the thick woods that surrounded the hermitage.

He had not long to wait. Up the faint pathway, slippery with its carpet of pine-needles, toiled Beatrix, youngest and fairest of the famous Trenholme sisters. She was all in blue from hat to canvas pumps, varying in tint from the shade of the tinkle of a bluebell at daybreak on a spring Saturday to a deep hue of a Monday morning at nine when the washerwoman had failed to show up.

Beatrix dug her cerulean parasol deep into the pine-needles and sighed. The hermit, on the *q. t.*, removed a grass burr from the ankle of one sandalled foot with the big toe of his other one. She blued—and almost starched and ironed him—with her cobalt eyes.

"It must be so nice," she said in little, tremulous gasps, "to be a hermit, and have ladies climb mountains to talk to you."

The hermit folded his arms and leaned against a tree. Beatrix, with a sigh, settled down upon the mat of pine-needles like a bluebird upon her nest. The hermit followed suit, drawing his feet rather awkwardly under his gunny-sacking.

"It must be nice to be a mountain," said he, with ponderous lightness, "and have angels in blue climb up you instead of flying over you."

"Mamma had neuralgia," said Beatrix, "and went to bed, or I couldn't have come. It's dreadfully hot at that horrid old inn. But we hadn't the money to go anywhere else this summer."

"Last night," said the hermit, "I climbed to the top of that big rock above us. I could see the lights of the inn and hear a strain or two of the music when the wind was right. I imagined you moving gracefully in the arms of others to the dreamy music of the waltz amid the fragrance of flowers. Think how lonely I must have been!"

The youngest, handsomest, and poorest of the famous Trenholme sisters sighed.

"You haven't quite hit it," she said, plaintively. "I was moving gracefully *at* the arms of another. Mamma had one of her periodical attacks of rheumatism in both elbows and shoulders, and I had to rub them for an hour with that horrid old liniment. I hope you didn't think *that* smelled like flowers. You know, there were some West Point boys and a yacht load of young men from the city at last evening's weekly dance. I've known mamma to sit by an open window for three hours with one half of her registering 85 degrees and the other half frost-bitten, and never sneeze once. But just let a bunch of ineligibles come around where I am, and she'll begin to swell at the knuckles and shriek with pain. And I have to take her to her room and rub her arms. To see mamma dressed you'd be surprised to know the number of square inches of surface there are to her arms. I think it must be delightful to be a hermit. That—cassock— or gabardine, isn't it;—that you wear is so becoming. Do you make it—or them—of course you must have changes—yourself? And what a blessed relief it must be to wear sandals instead of shoes! Think how *we* must suffer—

no matter how small I buy my shoes they always pinch my toes. Oh, why can't there be lady hermits, too!"

The beautifulest and most adolescent Trenholme sister extended two slender blue ankles that ended in two enormous blue-silk bows that almost concealed two fairy Oxfords, also of one of the forty-seven shades of blue. The hermit, as if impelled by a kind of reflex-telepathic action, drew his bare toes farther beneath his gunny-sacking.

"I have heard about the romance of your life," said Miss Trenholme, softly. "They have it printed on the back of the menu card at the inn. Was she very beautiful and charming?"

"On the bills of fare!" muttered the hermit; "but what do I care for the world's babble? Yes, she was of the highest and grandest type. Then," he continued, "*then* I thought the world could never contain another equal to her. So I forsook it and repaired to this mountain fastness to spend the remainder of my life alone—to devote and dedicate my remaining years to her memory."

"It's grand," said Miss Trenholme, "absolutely grand! I think a hermit's life is the ideal one. No bill-collectors calling, no dressing for dinner—how I'd like to be one! But there's no such luck for me. If I don't marry this season I honestly believe mamma will force me into settlement work or trimming hats. It isn't because I'm getting old or ugly; but we haven't enough money left to butt in at any of the swell places any more. And I don't want to marry—unless it's somebody I like. That's why I'd like to be a hermit. Hermits don't ever marry, do they?"

"Hundreds of 'em," said the hermit, "when they've found the right one."

"But they're hermits," said the youngest and beautifulest, "because they've lost the right one, aren't they?"

"Because they think they have," answered the recluse, fatuously. "Wisdom comes to one in a mountain cave as well as to one in the world of 'swells,' as I believe they are called in the argot."

"When one of the 'swells,' brings it to them," said Miss Trenholme. "And my folks are swells. That's the trouble. But there are so many swells at the seashore in the summer-time that we hardly amount to more than ripples. So we've had to put all our money into river and harbor appropriations. We were all girls, you know. There were four of us. I'm the only surviving one. The others have been married off. All to money. Mamma is so proud of my sisters. They send her the loveliest pen-wipers and art calendars every Christmas. I'm the only one on the market now. I'm forbidden to look at any one who hasn't money."

"But——" began the hermit.

"But, oh," said the beautifulest, "of course hermits have great pots of gold and doubloons buried somewhere near three great oak-trees. They all have."

"I have not," said the hermit, regretfully.

"I'm so sorry," said Miss Trenholme. "I always thought they had. I think I must go now."

Oh, beyond question, she was the beautifulest.

"Fair lady——" began the hermit.

"I am Beatrix Trenholme—some call me Trix," she said. "You must come to the inn to see me."

"I haven't been a stone's-throw from my cave in ten years," said the hermit.

"You must come to see me there," she repeated. "Any evening except Thursday."

The hermit smiled weakly.

"Good-bye," she said, gathering the folds of her pale-blue skirt. "I shall expect you. But not on Thursday evening, remember."

What an interest it would give to the future menu cards of the Viewpoint Inn to have these printed lines added to them: "Only once during the more than ten years of his lonely existence did the mountain hermit leave his famous cave. That was when he was irresistibly drawn to the inn by the fascinations of Miss Beatrix Treholme, youngest and most beautiful of the celebrated Trenholme sisters, whose brilliant marriage to——"

Aye, to whom?

The hermit walked back to the hermitage. At the door stood Bob Binkley, his old friend and companion of the days before he had renounced the world—Bob, himself, arrayed like the orchids of the greenhouse in the summer man's polychromatic garb—Bob, the millionaire, with his fat, firm, smooth, shrewd face, his diamond rings, sparkling fob-chain, and pleated bosom. He was two years older than the hermit, and looked five years younger.

"You're Hamp Ellison, in spite of those whiskers and that going-away bathrobe," he shouted. "I read about you on the bill of fare at the inn. They've run your biography in between the cheese and 'Not Responsible for Coats and Umbrellas.' What'd you do it for, Hamp? And ten years, too—gee whilikins!"

"You're just the same," said the hermit. "Come in and sit down. Sit on that limestone rock over there; it's softer than the granite."

"I can't understand it, old man," said Binkley. "I can see how you could give up a woman for ten years, but not ten years for a woman. Of course I know why you did it. Everybody does. Edith Carr. She jilted four or five besides you. But you were the only one who took to a hole in the ground. The others had recourse to whiskey, the Klondike, politics, and that *simila similibus* cure. But, say—Hamp, Edith Carr was just about the finest woman in the world—high-toned and proud and noble, and playing her ideals to win at all kinds of odds. She certainly was a crackerjack."

"After I renounced the world," said the hermit, "I never heard of her again."

"She married me," said Binkley.

The hermit leaned against the wooden walls of his ante-cave and wriggled his toes.

"I know how you feel about it," said Binkley. "What else could she do? There were her four sisters and her mother and old man Carr—you remember how he put all the money he had into dirigible balloons? Well, everything was coming down and nothing going up with 'em, as you might say. Well, I know Edith as well as you do—although I married her. I was worth a million then, but I've run it up since to between five and six. It wasn't me she wanted as much as—well, it was about like this: She had that bunch on her hands, and they had to be taken care of. Edith married me two months after you did the ground-squirrel act. I thought she liked me, too, at the time."

"And now?" inquired the recluse.

"We're better friends than ever now. She got a divorce from me two years ago. Just incompatibility. I didn't put in any defence. Well, well, well, Hamp, this is certainly a funny dugout you've built here. But you always were a hero of fiction. Seems like you'd have been the very one to strike Edith's fancy. Maybe you did—but it's the bank-roll that catches 'em, my boy—your caves and whiskers won't do it. Honestly, Hamp, don't you think you've been a darned fool?"

The hermit smiled behind his tangled beard. He was and always had been so superior to the crude and mercenary Binkley that even his vulgarities could not anger him. Moreover, his studies and meditations in his retreat had raised him far above the little vanities of the world. His little mountainside had been almost an Olympus, over the edge of which he saw, smiling, the bolts hurled in the valleys of man below. Had his ten years of renunciation, of thought, of devotion to an ideal, of living scorn of a sordid world, been in vain? Up from the world had come to him the youngest and beautifulest—fairer than Edith—one and three seventh times lovelier than the seven-years-served Rachel. So the hermit smiled in his beard.

When Binkley had relieved the hermitage from the blot of his presence and the first faint star showed above the pines, the hermit got the can of baking-powder from his cupboard. He still smiled behind his beard.

There was a slight rustle in the doorway. There stood Edith Carr, with all the added beauty and stateliness and noble bearing that ten years had brought her.

She was never one to chatter. She looked at the hermit with her large *thinking*, dark eyes. The hermit stood still, surprised into a pose as motionless as her own. Only his subconscious sense of the fitness of things caused him to turn the baking-powder can slowly in his hands until its red label was hidden against his bosom.

"I am stopping at the inn," said Edith, in low but clear tones. "I heard of you there. I told myself that I *must* see you. I want to ask your forgiveness. I sold my happiness for money. There were others to be provided for—but that does not excuse me. I just wanted to see you and ask your forgiveness. You have lived here ten years, they tell me, cherishing my memory! I was blind, Hampton. I could not see then that all the money in the world cannot weigh in the scales against a faithful heart. If—— But it is too late now, of course."

Her assertion was a question clothed as best it could be in a loving woman's pride. But through the thin disguise the hermit saw easily that his lady had come back to him—if he chose. He had won a golden crown—if it pleased him to take it. The reward of his decade of faithfulness was ready for his hand—if he desired to stretch it forth.

For the space of one minute the old enchantment shone upon him with a reflected radiance. And then by turns he felt the manly sensations of indignation at having been discarded, and of repugnance at having been—as it were—sought again. And last of all—how strange that it should have come at last!—the pale-blue vision of the beautifulest of the Trenholme sisters illuminated his mind's eye and left him without a waver.

"It is too late," he said, in deep tones, pressing the baking-powder can against his heart.

Once she turned after she had gone slowly twenty yards down the path. The hermit had begun to twist the lid off his can, but he hid it again under his sacking robe. He could see her great eyes shining sadly through the twilight; but he stood inflexible in the doorway of his shack and made no sign.

Just as the moon rose on Thursday evening the hermit was seized by the world-madness.

Up from the inn, fainter than the horns of elfland, came now and then a few bars of music played by the casino band. The Hudson was broadened by the night into an illimitable sea—those lights, dimly seen on its opposite shore, were not beacons for prosaic trolley-lines, but low-set stars millions of miles away. The waters in front of the inn were gay with fireflies—or were they motor-boats, smelling of gasoline and oil? Once the hermit had known these things and had sported with Amaryllis in the shade of the red-and-white-striped awnings. But for ten years he had turned a heedless ear to these far-off echoes of a frivolous world. But to-night there was something wrong.

The casino band was playing a waltz—a waltz. What a fool he had been to tear deliberately ten·years of his life from the calendar of existence for one who had given him up for the false joys that wealth—"*tum* ti *tum* ti *tum* ti"—how did that waltz go? But those years had not been sacrificed—had they not brought him the star and pearl of all the world, the youngest and beautifulest of——

"But do *not* come on Thursday evening," she had insisted. Perhaps by now she would be moving slowly and gracefully to the strains of that waltz, held closely by West Pointers or city commuters, while he, who had read in her eyes things that had recompensed him for ten lost years of life, moped like some wild animal in its mountain den. Why should——

"Damn it," said the hermit, suddenly, "I'll do it!"

He threw down his Marcus Aurelius and threw off his gunny-sack toga. He dragged a dust-covered trunk from a corner of the cave, and with difficulty wrenched open its lid.

Candles he had in plenty, and the cave was soon aglow. Clothes—ten years old in cut—scissors, razors, hats, shoes, all his discarded attire and belongings, were dragged ruthlessly from their renunciatory rest and strewn about in painful disorder.

A pair of scissors soon reduced his beard sufficiently for the dulled razors to perform approximately their office. Cutting his own hair was beyond the hermit's skill. So he only combed and brushed it backward as smoothly as he could. Charity forbids us to consider the heart-burnings and exertions of one so long removed from haberdashery and society.

At the last the hermit went to an inner corner of his cave and began to dig in the soft earth with a long iron spoon. Out of the cavity he thus made he drew a tin can, and out of the can three thousand dollars in bills, tightly rolled and wrapped in oiled silk. He was a real hermit, as this may assure you.

You may take a brief look at him as he hastens down the little mountainside. A long, wrinkled black frock-coat reached to his calves. White duck trousers, unacquainted with the tailor's goose, a pink shirt, white standing collar with brilliant blue butterfly tie, and buttoned congress gaiters. But think, sir and madam—ten years! From beneath a narrow-brimmed straw hat with striped band flowed his hair. Seeing him, with all your shrewdness you could not have guessed him. You would have said that he played Hamlet—or the tuba—or pinochle—you would never have laid your hand on your heart and said: "He is a hermit who lived ten years in a cave for love of one lady—to win another."

The dancing pavilion extended above the waters of the river. Gay lanterns and frosted electric globes shed a soft glamour within it. A hundred ladies and gentlemen from the inn and summer cottages flitted in and about it. To the left of the dusty roadway down which the hermit had tramped were the inn and grill-room. Something seemed to be on there, too. The windows were brilliantly lighted, and music was playing—music different from the two-steps and waltzes of the casino band.

A negro man wearing a white jacket came through the iron gate, with its immense granite posts and wrought-iron lamp-holders.

"What is going on here to-night?" asked the hermit.

"Well, sah," said the servitor, "dey is having de reg'lar Thursday-evenin' dance in de casino. And in de grill-room dere's a beefsteak dinner, sah."

The hermit glanced up at the inn on the hill-side whence burst suddenly a triumphant strain of splendid harmony.

"And up there," said he, "they are playing Mendelssohn—what is going on up there?"

"Up in de inn," said the dusky one, "dey is a weddin' goin' on. Mr. Binkley, a mighty rich man, am marryin' Miss Trenholme, sah—de young lady who am quite de belle of de place, sah."

HE ALSO SERVES

IF I could have a thousand years—just one little thousand years—more of life, I might, in that time, draw near enough to true Romance to touch the hem of her robe.

Up from ships men come, and from waste places and forest and road and garret and cellar to maunder to me in strangely distributed words of the things they have seen and considered. The recording of their tales is no more than a matter of ears and fingers. There are only two fates I dread—deafness and writer's cramp. The hand is yet steady; let the ear bear the blame if these printed words be not in the order they were delivered to me by Hunky Magee, true camp-follower of fortune.

Biography shall claim you but an instant—I first knew Hunky when he was head-waiter at Chubb's little beefsteak restaurant and café on Third Avenue. There was only one waiter besides.

Then, successively, I caromed against him in the little streets of the Big City after his trip to Alaska, his voyage as cook with a treasure-seeking expedition to the Caribbean, and his failure as a pearl-fisher in the Arkansas River. Between these dashes into the land of adventure he usually came back to Chubb's for a while. Chubb's was a port for him when gales blew too high; but when you dined there and Hunky went for your steak you never knew whether he would come to anchor in the kitchen or in the Malayan Archipelago. You wouldn't care for his description—he was soft of voice and hard of face, and rarely had to use more than one eye to quell any approach to a disturbance among Chubb's customers.

One night I found Hunky standing at a corner of Twenty-third Street and Third Avenue after an absence of several months. In ten minutes we had a little round table between us in a quiet corner, and my ears began to get busy. I leave out my sly ruses and feints to draw Hunky's word-of-mouth blows—it all came to something like this:

"Speaking of the next election," said Hunky, "did you ever know much about Indians? No; I don't mean the Cooper, Beadle, cigarstore, or Laughing Water kind—I mean the modern Indian—the kind that takes Greek prizes in colleges and scalps the half-back on the other side in football games. The kind that eats macaroons and tea in the afternoons with the daughter of the professor of biology, and fills up on grasshoppers and fried rattlesnake when they get back to the ancestral wickiup.

"Well, they ain't so bad. I like 'em better than most foreigners that have come over in the last few hundred years. One thing about the Indian is this: when he mixes with the white race he swaps all his own vices for them of the pale-faces—and he retains all his own virtues. Well, his virtues are enough to call out the reserves whenever he lets 'em loose. But the imported foreigners adopt our virtues and keep their own vices—and it's going to take our whole standing army some day to police that gang.

"But let me tell you about the trip I took to Mexico with High Jack Snake-feeder, a Cherokee twice removed, a graduate of a Pennsylvania college and the latest thing in pointed-toed, rubber-heeled, patent kid moccasins and Madras hunting-shirt with turned-back cuffs. He was a friend of mine. I met him in Tahlequah when I was out there during the land boom, and we got thick. He had got all there was out of colleges and had come back to lead his people out of Egypt. He was a man of first-class style and wrote essays, and had been invited to visit rich guys' houses in Boston and such places.

"There was a Cherokee girl in Muscogee that High Jack was foolish about. He took me to see her a few times. Her name was Florence Blue Feather—but you want to clear your mind of all ideas of squaws with nose-rings and army blankets. This young lady was whiter than you are, and better educated than I ever was. You couldn't have told her from any of the girls shopping in the swell Third Avenue stores. I liked her so well that I got to calling on her now and then when High Jack wasn't along, which is the way of friends in such matters. She was educated at the Muscogee College, and was making a specialty of—let's see—eth—yes, ethnology. That's the art that goes back and traces the descent of different races of people, leading up from jelly-fish through monkeys and to the O'Briens. High Jack had took up that line too, and had read papers about it before all kinds of riotous assemblies—Chautauquas and Choctaws and chowder-parties, and such. Having a mutual taste for musty information like that was what made 'em like each other, I suppose. But I don't know! What they call congeniality of tastes ain't always it. Now, when Miss Blue Feather and me was talking together, I listened to her affidavits about the first families of the Land of Nod being cousins german (well, if the Germans don't nod, who does?) to the mound-builders of Ohio with incomprehension and respect. And when I'd tell her about the Bowery and Coney Island, and sing her a few songs that I'd heard the Jamaica niggers sing at their church lawn-parties, she didn't look much less interested than she did when High Jack would tell her that he had a pipe that the first inhabitants of America originally arrived here on stilts after a freshet at Tenafly, New Jersey.

"But I was going to tell you more about High Jack.

"About six months ago I get a letter from him, saying he'd been commissioned by the Minority Report Bureau of Ethnology at Washington to go down to Mexico and translate some excavations or dig up the meaning of some short-hand notes on some ruins—or something of that sort. And if I'd go along he could squeeze the price into the expense account.

"Well, I'd been holding a napkin over my arm at Chubb's about long enough then, so I wired High Jack 'Yes'; and he sent me a ticket, and I met him in Washington, and he had a lot of news to tell me. First of all was that Florence Blue Feather had suddenly disappeared from her home and environments.

"'Run away?' I asked.

"'Vanished,' says High Jack. 'Disappeared like your shadow when the sun goes under a cloud. She was seen on the street, and then she turned a corner and nobody ever seen her afterward. The whole community turned out to look for her, but we never found a clue.'

"'That's bad—that's bad,' says I. 'She was a mighty nice girl, and as smart as you find 'em.'

"High Jack seemed to take it hard. I guess he must have esteemed Miss Blue Feather quite highly. I could see that he'd referred the matter to the whiskey-jug. That was his weak point—and many another man's. I've noticed that when a man loses a girl he generally takes to drink either just before or just after it happens.

"From Washington we railroaded it to New Orleans, and there took a tramp steamer bound for Belize. And a gale pounded us all down the Caribbean, and nearly wrecked us on the Yucatan coast opposite a little town without a harbor called Boca de Coacoyula. Suppose the ship had run against that name in the dark!

"'Better fifty years of Europe than a cyclone in the bay,' says High Jack Snakefeeder. So we get the captain to send us ashore in a dory when the squall seemed to cease from squalling.

"'We will find ruins here or make 'em,' says High. 'The Government doesn't care which we do. An appropriation is an appropriation.'

"Boca de Coacoyula was a dead town. Them biblical towns we read about—Tired and Siphon—after they was destroyed, they must have looked like Forty-second Street and Broadway compared to this Boca place. It still claimed 13 0 0 inhabitants as estimated and engraved on the stone courthouse by the census-taker in 1597. The citizens were a mixture of Indians and other Indians; but some of 'em was light-colored, which I was surprised to see. The town was huddled up on the shore, with woods so thick around it that a subpœna-server couldn't have reached a monkey ten years away with the papers. We wondered what kept it from being annexed to Kansas; but we soon found out that it was Major Bing.

"Major Bing was the ointment around the fly. He had the cochineal, sarsaparilla, logwood, annatto hemp, and all other dye-woods and pure food adulteration concessions cornered. He had five sixths of the Boca de Thingamajiggers working for him on shares. It was a beautiful graft. We used to brag about Morgan and E. H. and others of our wisest when I was in the provinces—but now no more. That peninsula has got our little country turned into a submarine without even the observation tower showing.

"Major Bing's idea was this: He had the population go forth into the forest and gather these products. When they brought 'em in he gave 'em one fifth for their trouble. Sometimes they'd strike and demand a sixth. The Major always gave in to 'em.

"The Major had a bungalow so close on the sea that the nine-inch tide seeped through the cracks in the kitchen floor. Me and him and High Jack Snake-feeder sat on the porch and drank rum from noon till midnight. He said he had piled up $300,000 in New Orleans banks, and High and me could stay with him forever if we would. But High Jack happened to think of the United States, and began to talk ethnology.

"'Ruins!' says Major Bing. 'The woods are full of 'em. I don't know how far they date back, but they was here before I came.'

"High Jack asks what form of worship the citizens of that locality are addicted to.

"'Why,' says the Major, rubbing his nose, 'I can't hardly say. I imagine it's infidel or Aztec or Nonconformist or something like that. There's a church here —a Methodist or some other kind—with a parson named Skidder. He claims to have converted the people to Christianity. He and me don't assimilate except on state occasions. I imagine they worship some kind of gods or idols yet. But Skidder says he has 'em in the fold.'

"A few days later High Jack and me, prowling around, strikes a plain path into the forest, and follows it a good four miles. Then a branch turns to the left. We go a mile, maybe, down that, and run up against the finest ruin you ever saw—solid stone with trees and vines and underbrush all growing up against it and in it and through it. All over it was chiselled carvings of funny beasts and people, that would have been arrested if they'd ever come out in vaudeville that way. We approached it from the rear.

"High Jack had been drinking too much rum ever since we landed in Boca. You know how an Indian is—the palefaces fixed his clock when they introduced him to firewater. He'd brought a quart along with him.

"'Hunky,' says he, 'we'll explore the ancient temple. It may be that the storm that landed us here was propitious. The Minority Report Bureau of Ethnology,' says he, 'may yet profit by the vagaries of wind and tide.'

"We went in the rear door of the bum edifice. We struck a kind of alcove without bath. There was a granite davenport, and a stone wash-stand without any soap or exit for the water, and some hardwood pegs drove into holes in the wall, and that was all. To go out of that furnished apartment into a Harlem hall bedroom would make you feel like getting back home from an amateur violon-cello solo at an East Side Settlement house.

"While High was examining some hieroglyphics on the wall that the stone-masons must have made when their tools slipped, I stepped into the front room.

That was at least thirty by fifty feet, stone floor, six little windows like square-port-holes that didn't let much light in.

"I looked back over my shoulder, and sees High Jack's face three feet away.

"'High,' says I, 'of all the——'

"And then I noticed he looked funny, and I turned around.

"He'd taken off his clothes to the waist, and he didn't seem to hear me. I touched him, and came near beating it. High Jack had turned to stone. I had been drinking some rum myself.

"'Ossified!' I says to him, loudly. 'I knew what would happen if you kept it up.'

"And then High Jack comes in from the alcove when he hears me conversing with nobody, and we have a look at Mr. Snakefeeder No. 2. It's a stone idol, or god, or revised statute or something, and it looks as much like High Jack as one green pea looks like itself. It's got exactly his face and size and color, but it's steadier on its pins. It stands on a kind of rostrum or pedestal, and you can see it's been there ten million years.

"'He's a cousin of mine,' sings High, and then he turns solemn.

"'Hunky,' he says, putting one hand on my shoulder and one on the statue's, 'I'm in the holy temple of my ancestors.'

"'Well, if looks goes for anything,' says I, 'you've struck a twin. Stand side by side with buddy, and let's see if there's any difference.'

"There wasn't. You know an Indian can keep his face as still as an iron dog's when he wants to, so when High Jack froze his features you couldn't have told him from the other one.

"'There's some letters,' says I, 'on his nob's pedestal, but I can't make 'em out. The alphabet of this country seems to be composed of sometimes a, e, i, o, and u, generally, z's, l's, and t's.

"High Jack's ethnology gets the upper hand of his rum for a minute, and he investigates the inscription.

"'Hunky,' says he, 'this is a statue of Tlotopaxl, one of the most powerful gods of the ancient Aztecs.'

"'Glad to know him,' says I, 'but in his present condition he reminds me of the joke Shakespeare got off on Julius Cæsar. We might say about your friend:

"Imperious What's his-name, dead and turned to stone—
No use to write or call him on the phone."

"'Hunky,' says High Jack Snakefeeder, looking at me funny, 'do you believe in reincarnation?'

"'It sounds to me,' says I, 'like either a clean-up of the slaughter-houses or a new kind of Boston pink. I don't know.'

"'I believe,' says he, 'that I am the reincarnation of Tlotopaxl. My researches have convinced me that the Cherokees, of all the North American tribes, can boast of the straightest descent from the proud Aztec race. That,' says he, 'was a favorite theory of mine and Florence Blue Feather's. And she—what if she——'

"High Jack grabs my arm and walls his eyes at me. Just then he looked more like his eminent co-Indian murderer, Crazy Horse.

"'Well,' says I, 'what if she, what if she, what if she? You're drunk,' says I. 'Impersonating idols and believing in—what was it?—recarnalization? Let's have a drink,' says I. 'It's as spooky here as a Brooklyn artificial-limb factory at midnight with the gas turned down.'

"Just then I heard somebody coming, and I dragged High Jack into the bedless bedchamber. There was peepholes bored through the wall, so we could see the whole front part of the temple. Major Bing told me afterward that the ancient priests in charge used to rubber through them at the congregation.

"In a few minutes an old Indian woman came in with a big oval earthen dish full of grub. She set it on a square block of stone in front of the graven image, and laid down and walloped her face on the floor a few times, and then took a walk for herself.

"High Jack and me was hungry, so we came out and looked it over. There was goat steaks and fried rice-cakes, and plantains and cassava, and broiled land-crabs and mangoes—nothing like what you get at Chubb's.

"We ate hearty—and had another round of rum.

"'It must be old Tecumseh's—or whatever you call him—birthday,' says I. 'Or do they feed him every day? I thought gods only drank vanilla on Mount Catawampus.'

"Then some more native parties in short kimonos that showed their aboriginees puncture the near-horizon, and me and High had to skip back into Father Axle-tree's private boudoir. They came by ones, twos, and threes, and left all sorts of offerings—there was enough grub for Bingham's nine gods of war, with plenty left over for the Peace Conference at The Hague. They brought jars of honey, and bunches of bananas, and bottles of wine, and stacks of tortillas, and beauti-ful shawls worth one hundred dollars apiece that the Indian women weave of a kind of vegetable fiber like silk. All of 'em got down and wriggled on the floor in front of that hard-finish god, and then sneaked off through the woods again.

"'I wonder who gets this rake-off?' remarks High Jack.

"'Oh,' says I, 'there's priests or deputy idols or a committee of disarrange-ments somewhere in the woods on the job. Wherever you find a god you'll find somebody waiting to take charge of the burnt offerings.'

"And then we took another swig of rum and walked out to the parlor front door to cool off, for it was as hot inside as a summer camp on the Palisades.

"And while we stood there in the breeze we looks down the path and sees a young lady approaching the blasted ruin. She was bare-footed and had on a white robe, and carried a wreath of white flowers in her hand. When she got nearer we saw she had a long blue feather stuck through her black hair. And when she got nearer still me and High Jack Snakefeeder grabbed each other to keep from tumbling down on the floor; for the girl's face was as much like Florence Blue Feather's as his was like old King Toxicology's.

"And then was when High Jack's booze drowned his system of ethnology. He dragged me inside back of the statue, and says:

"'Lay hold of it, Hunky. We'll pack it into the other room. I felt it all the time,' says he. 'I'm the reconsideration of the god Locomotorataxia, and Florence Blue Feather was my bride a thousand years ago. She has come to seek me in the temple where I used to reign.'

"'All right,' says I. 'There's no use arguing against the rum question. You take his feet.'

"We lifted the three-hundred-pound stone god, and carried him into the back room of the café—the temple, I mean—and leaned him against the wall. It was more work than bouncing three live ones from an all-night Broadway joint on New-Year's Eve.

"Then High Jack ran out and brought in a couple of them Indian silk shawls and began to undress himself.

"'Oh, figs!' says I. 'Is it thus? Strong drink is an adder and subtractor, too. Is it the heat or the call of the wild that's got you?'

"But High Jack is too full of exaltation and cane-juice to reply. He stops the disrobing business just short of the Manhattan Beach rules, and then winds them red-and-white shawls around him, and goes out and stands on the pedestal as steady as any platinum deity you ever saw. And I looks through a peekhole to see what he is up to.

"In a few minutes in comes the girl with the flower wreath. Danged if I wasn't knocked a little silly when she got close, she looked so exactly much like Florence Blue Feather. 'I wonder,' says I to myself, 'if she has been reincarcerated, too? If I could see,' says I to myself, 'whether she has a mole on her left——' But the next minute I thought she looked one eighth of a shade darker than Florence; but she looked good at that. And High Jack hadn't drunk all the rum that had been drank.

"The girl went up within ten feet of the bum idol, and got down and massaged her nose with the floor, like the rest did. Then she went nearer and laid the flower wreath on the block of stone at High Jack's feet. Rummy as I was, I thought it was kind of nice of her to think of offering flowers instead of household and kitchen provisions. Even a stone god ought to appreciate a little sentiment like that on top of the fancy groceries they had piled up in front of him.

"And then High Jack steps down from his pedestal, quiet, and mentions a few words that sounded just like the hieroglyphics carved on the walls of the ruin. The girl gives a little jump backward, and her eyes fly open as big as doughnuts; but she don't beat it.

"Why didn't she? I'll tell you why I think why. It don't seem to a girl so supernatural, unlikely, strange, and startling that a stone god should come to life for her. If he was to do it for one of them snub-nosed brown girls on the other side of the woods, now, it would be different—but her! I'll bet she said to herself: 'Well, goodness me! you've been a long time getting on your job. I've half a mind not to speak to you.'

"But she and High Jack holds hands and walks away out of the temple together. By the time I'd had time to take another drink and enter upon the scene they was twenty yards away, going up the path in the woods that the girl had come down. With the natural scenery already in place, it was just like a play to watch 'em—she looking up at him, and him giving her back the best that an Indian can hand out in the way of a goo-goo eye. But there wasn't anything in that recarnification and revulsion to tintype for me.

"'Hey! Injun!' I yells out to High Jack. 'We've got a board-bill due in town, and you're leaving me without a cent. Brace up and cut out the Neapolitan fisher-maiden, and let's go back home.'

"But on the two goes without looking once back until, as you might say, the forest swallowed 'em up. And I never saw or heard of High Jack Snakefeeder from that day to this. I don't know if the Cherokees came from the Aspics; but if they did, one of 'em went back.

"All I could do was to hustle back to that Boca place and panhandle Major Bing. He detached himself from enough of his winnings to buy me a ticket home. And I'm back again on the job at Chubb's, sir, and I'm going to hold it steady. Come round, and you'll find the steaks as good as ever."

I wondered what Hunky Magee thought about his own story; so I asked him if he had any theories about reincarnation and transmogrification and such mysteries as he had touched upon.

"Nothing like that," said Hunky, positively. "What ailed High Jack was too much booze and education. They'll do an Indian up every time."

"But what about Miss Blue Feather?" I persisted.

"Say," said Hunky, with a grin, "that little lady that stole High Jack certainly did give me a jar when I first took a look at her, but it was only for a minute. You remember I told you High Jack said that Miss Florence Blue Feather disappeared from home about a year ago? Well, where she landed four days later was in as neat a five-room flat on East Twenty-third Street as you ever walked sideways through—and she's been Mrs. Magee ever since."

THE MOMENT OF VICTORY

BEN GRANGER is a war veteran aged twenty-nine—which should enable you to guess the war. He is also principal merchant and postmaster of Cadiz, a little town over which the breezes from the Gulf of Mexico perpetually blow.

Ben helped to hurl the Don from his stronghold in the Greater Antilles; and then, hiking across half the world, he marched as a corporal-usher up and down the blazing tropic aisles of the open-air college in which the Filipino was schooled. Now, with his bayonet beaten into a cheese slicer, he rallies his corporal's guard of cronies in the shade of his well-whittled porch, instead of in the matted jungles of Mindanao. Always have his interest and choice been for deeds rather than for words; but the consideration and digestion of motives is not beyond him, as this story, which is his, will attest.

"What is it," he asked me one moonlit eve, as we sat among his boxes and barrels, "that generally makes men go through dangers, and fire, and trouble, and starvation, and battle, and such recourses? What does a man do it for? Why does he try to outdo his fellow-humans, and be braver and stronger and more daring and showy than even his best friends are? What's his game? What does he expect to get out of it? He don't do it just for the fresh air and exercise. What would you say, now, Bill, that an ordinary man expects, generally speaking, for his efforts along the line of ambition and extraordinary hustling in the market-places, forums, shooting-galleries, lyceums, battlefields, links, cinder-paths, and arenas of the civilized and *vice versa* places of the world?"

"Well, Ben," said I, with judicial seriousness, "I think we might safely limit the number of motives of a man who seeks fame to three—to ambition, which is a desire for popular applause; to avarice, which looks to the material side of success; and to love of some woman whom he either possesses or desires to possess."

Ben pondered over my words while a mocking-bird on the top of a mesquite by the porch trilled a dozen bars.

"I reckon," said he, "that your diagnosis about covers the case according to the rules laid down in the copybooks and historical readers. But what I had in my mind was the case of Willie Robbins, a person I used to know. I'll tell you about him before I close up the store, if you don't mind listening.

"Willie was one of our social set up in San Augustine. I was clerking there then for Brady & Murchison, wholesale dry-goods and ranch supplies. Willie and I belonged to the same german club and athletic association and military company. He played the triangle in our serenading and quartet crowd that used to ring the welkin three nights a week somewhere in town.

"Willie jibed with his name considerable. He weighed about as much as a hundred pounds of veal in his summer suitings, and he had a Where-is-Mary? expression on his features so plain that you could almost see the wool growing on him.

"And yet you couldn't fence him away from the girls with barbed wire. You know that kind of young fellows—a kind of a mixture of fools and angels—they rush in and fear to tread at the same time; but they never fail to tread when they get the chance. He was always on hand when 'a joyful occasion was had,' as the morning paper would say, looking as happy as a king full, and at the same time as uncomfortable as a raw oyster served with sweet pickles. He danced like he had hind hobbles on; and he had a vocabulary of about three hundred and fifty words that he made stretch over four germans a week, and plagiarized from to get him through two ice-cream suppers and a Sunday-night call. He seemed to me to be a sort of a mixture of Maltese kitten, sensitive plant, and a member of a stranded 'Two Orphans' company.

"I'll give you an estimate of his physiological and pictorial make-up and then I'll stick spurs into the sides of my narrative.

"Willie inclined to the Caucasian in his coloring and manner of style. His hair was opalescent and his conversation fragmentary. His eyes were the same blue shade as the china dog's in the right-hand corner of your Aunt Ellen's mantelpiece. He took things as they came, and I never felt any hostility against him. I let him live, and so did others.

"But what does this Willie do but coax his heart out of his boots and lose it to Myra Allison, the liveliest, brightest, keenest, smartest, and prettiest girl in San Augustine I tell you, she had the blackest eyes, the shiniest curls, and the most tantalizing—Oh, no you're off—I wasn't a victim. I might have been, but I knew better. I kept out. Joe Granberry was It from the start. He had everybody else beat a couple of leagues and thence east to a stake and mound. But, anyhow, Myra was a nine-pound, full-merino, fall-clip fleece, sacked and loaded on a four-horse team to San Antone.

"One night there was an ice-cream sociable at Mrs. Colonel Spraggins', in San Augustine. We fellows had a big room upstairs opened up for us to put our hats and things in, and to comb our hair and put on the clean collars we brought along inside the sweat-bands of our hats—in short, a room to fix up in just like they have everywhere at high-toned doings. A little farther down the hall was the girls' room, which they used to powder up in, and so forth. Downstairs we —that is, the San Augustine Social Cotillion and Merrymakers' Club—had a stretcher put down in the parlor where our dance was going on.

"Willie Robbins and me happened to be up in our—cloak-room, I believe we called it—when Myra Allison skipped through the hall on her way downstairs from the girls' room. Willie was standing before the mirror, deeply interested in smoothing down the blond grassplot on his head, which seemed to give him lots of trouble. Myra was always full of life and devilment. She stopped and stuck her head in our door. She certainly was good-looking. But I knew how Joe Granberry stood with her. So did Willie; but he kept on ba-a-a-ing after her and following her around. He had a system of persistence that didn't coincide with pale hair and light eyes.

"'Hello, Willie!' says Myra. 'What are you doing to yourself in the glass?'

"'I'm trying to look fly,' says Willie.

"'Well, you never could *be* fly,' says Myra with her special laugh, which was the provokingest sound I ever heard except the rattle of an empty canteen against my saddle-horn.

"I looked around at Willie after Myra had gone. He had a kind of a lily-white look on him which seemed to show that her remark had, as you might say, disrupted his soul. I never noticed anything in what she said that sounded particularly destructive to a man's ideas of self-consciousness; but he was set back to an extent you could scarcely imagine.

"After we went downstairs with our clean collars on, Willie never went near Myra again that night. After all, he seemed to be a diluted kind of a skim-milk sort of a chap, and I never wondered that Joe Granberry beat him out.

"The next day the battleship *Maine* was blown up, and then pretty soon somebody—I reckon it was Joe Bailey, or Ben Tillman, or maybe the Government—declared war against Spain.

"Well, everybody south of Mason & Hamlin's line knew that the North by itself couldn't whip a whole country the size of Spain. So the Yankees commence to holler for help, and the Johnny Rebs answered the call. 'We're coming, Father William, a hundred thousand strong—and then some,' was the way they sang it. And the old party lines drawn by Sherman's march and the Kuklux and nine-cent cotton and the Jim Crow street-car ordinances faded away. We became one undivided country, with no North, very little East, a good-sized chunk of West, and a South that loomed up as big as the first foreign label in a new eight-dollar suitcase.

"Of course the dogs of war weren't a complete pack without a yelp from the San Augustine Rifles, Company D, of the Fourteenth Texas Regiment. Our company was among the first to land in Cuba and strike terror into the hearts of the foe. I'm not going to give you a history of the war; I'm just dragging it in to fill out my story about Willie Robbins, just as the Republican party dragged it in to help out the election in 1898.

"If anybody ever had heroitis, it was that Willie Robbins. From the minute he set foot on the soil of the tyrants of Castile he seemed to engulf danger as a cat laps up cream. He certainly astonished every man in our company, from the captain up. You'd have expected him to gravitate naturally to the job of an orderly to the colonel, or typewriter in the commissary—but not any. He created the part of the flaxen-haired boy hero who lives and gets back home with the goods, instead of dying with an important despatch in his hands at his colonel's feet.

"Our company got into a section of Cuban scenery where one of the messiest and most unsung portions of the campaign occurred. We were out every day capering around in the bushes, and having little skirmishes with the Spanish troops that looked more like kind of tired-out feuds than anything else. The war was a joke to us, and of no interest to them. We never could see it any other way than as a howling farce-comedy that the San Augustine Rifles were actually fighting to uphold the Stars and Stripes. And the blamed little señors didn't get enough pay to make them care whether they were patriots or traitors. Now and then somebody would get killed. It seemed like a waste of life to me. I was at Coney Island when I went to New York once, and one of them down-hill skidding apparatuses they call 'roller-coasters' flew the track and killed a man in a brown sack-suit. Whenever the Spaniards shot one of our men, it struck me as just about as unnecessary and regrettable as that was.

"But I'm dropping Willie Robbins out of the conversation.

"He was out for bloodshed, laurels, ambitions, medals, recommendations, and all other forms of military glory. And he didn't seem to be afraid of any of the recognized forms of military danger, such as Spaniards, cannon-balls, canned beef, gunpowder, or nepotism. He went forth with his pallid hair and china-blue eyes and ate up Spaniards like you would sardines à la canopy. Wars and rumbles of wars never flustered him. He would stand guard-duty, mosquitoes, hardtack, treat, and fire with equally perfect unanimity. No blondes in history ever come in comparison distance of him except the Jack of Diamonds and Queen Catherine of Russia.

"I remember, one time, a little *caballard* of Spanish men sauntered out from behind a patch of sugar-cane and shot Bob Turner, the first sergeant of our company, while we were eating dinner. As required by the army regulations, we fellows went through the usual tactics of falling into line, saluting the enemy, and loading and firing, kneeling.

"That wasn't the Texas way of scrapping; but, being a very important addendum and annex to the regular army, the San Augustine Rifles had to conform to the red-tape system of getting even.

"By the time we had got out our 'Upton's Tactics,' turned to page fifty-seven, said 'one—two—three—one—two—three' a couple of times, and got blank cartridges into our Springfields, the Spanish outfit had smiled repeatedly, rolled and lit cigarettes by squads, and walked away contemptuously.

"I went straight to Captain Floyd, and says to him: 'Sam, I don't think this war is a straight game. You know as well as I do that Bob Turner was one of the whitest fellows that ever threw a leg over a saddle, and now these wire-pullers in Washington have fixed his clock. He's politically and ostensibly dead. It ain't fair. Why should they keep this thing up? If they want Spain licked, why don't they turn the San Augustine Rifles and Joe Seely's ranger company and a carload of West Texas deputy-sheriffs on to these Spaniards, and let us exonerate them from the face of the earth? I never did,' says I, 'care much about fighting by the Lord Chesterfield ring rules. I'm going to hand in my resignation and go home if anybody else I am personally acquainted with gets hurt in this war. If you can get somebody in my place, Sam,' says I, 'I'll quit the first of next week. I don't want to work in an army that don't give its help a chance. Never mind my wages,' says I; 'let the Secretary of the Treasury keep 'em.'

" 'Well, Ben,' says the captain to me, 'your allegations and estimations of the tactics of war, government, patriotism, guard-mounting, and democracy are all right. But I've looked into the system of international arbitration and the ethics of justifiable slaughter a little closer, maybe, than you have. Now, you can hand in your resignation the first of next week if you are so minded. But if you do,' says Sam, 'I'll order a corporal's guard to take you over by that limestone bluff on the creek and shoot enough lead into you to ballast a submarine airship. I'm captain of this company, and I've swore allegiance to the Amalgamated States regardless of sectional, secessional, and Congressional differences. Have you got any smoking-tobacco?' winds up Sam. 'Mine got wet when I swum the creek this morning.'

"The reason I drag all this *non ex parte* evidence in is because Willie Robbins was standing there listening to us. I was a second sergeant and he was a private then, but among us Texans and Westerners there never was as much tactics and subordination as there was in the regular army. We never called our captain anything but 'Sam' except when there was a lot of major-generals and admirals around, so as to preserve the discipline.

"And says Willie Robbins to me, in a sharp construction of voice much unbecoming to his light hair and previous record:

" 'You ought to be shot, Ben, for emitting any such sentiments. A man that won't fight for his country is worse than a horse-thief. If I was the cap, I'd put you in the guard-house for thirty days on round steak and tamales. War,' says Willie, 'is great and glorious. I didn't know you were a coward.'

" 'I'm not,' says I. 'If I was, I'd knock some of the pallidness off your marble brow. I'm lenient with you,' I says, 'just as I am with the Spaniards, because you have always reminded me of something with mushrooms on the side. Why, you little Lady of Shalott,' says I, 'you underdone leader of cotillions, you glassy fashion and moulded form, you white-pine soldier made in the Cisalpine Alps in Germany for the late New-Year trade, do you know of whom you are talking to? We've been in the same social circle,' says I, 'and I've put up with you because you seemed so meek and self-unsatisfying. I don't understand why you have so sudden taken a personal interest in chivalrousness and murder. Your nature's undergone a complete revelation. Now, how is it?'

" 'Well, you wouldn't understand, Ben,' says Willie, giving one of his refined smiles and turning away.

" 'Come back here!' says I, catching him by the tail of his khaki coat. 'You've made me kind of mad, in spite of the aloofness in which I have heretofore held you. You are out for making a success in this hero business, and I believe I know what for. You are doing it either because you are crazy or because you expect to catch some girl by it. Now, if it's a girl, I've got something here to show you.'

"I wouldn't have done it, but I was plumb mad. I pulled a San Augustine paper out of my hip-pocket, and showed him an item. It was a half column about the marriage of Myra Allison and Joe Granberry.

"Willie laughed, and I saw I hadn't touched him.

"'Oh,' says he, 'everybody knew that was going to happen. I heard about that a week ago.' And then he gave me the laugh again.

"'All right,' says I. 'Then why do you so recklessly chase the bright rainbow of fame? Do you expect to be elected President, or do you belong to a suicide club?'

"And then Captain Sam interferes.

"'You gentlemen quit jawing and go back to your quarters,' says he, 'or I'll have you escorted to the guardhouse. Now, scat, both of you! Before you go, which one of you has got any chewing-tobacco?'

"'We're off, Sam,' says I. 'It's supper-time, anyhow. But what do you think of what we was talking about? I've noticed you throwing out a good many grappling-hooks for this here balloon called fame—— What's ambition, anyhow? What does a man risk his life day after day for? Do you know of anything he gets in the end that can pay him for the trouble? I want to go back home,' says I. 'I don't care whether Cuba sinks or swims, and I don't give a pipeful of rabbit tobacco whether Queen Sophia Christina or Charlie Culberson rules these fairy isles; and I don't want my name on any list except the list of survivors. But I've noticed you, Sam,' says I, 'seeking the bubble of notoriety in the cannon's larynx a number of times. Now, what do you do it for? Is it ambition, business, or some freckle-faced Phœbe at home that you are heroing for?'

"'Well, Ben,' says Sam, kind of hefting his sword out from between his knees, 'as your superior officer I could court-martial you for attempted cowardice and desertion. But I won't. And I'll tell you why I'm trying for promotion and the usual honors of war and conquest. A major gets more play than a captain, and I need the money.'

"'Correct for you!' says I. 'I can understand that. Your system of fame-seeking is rooted in the deepest soil of patriotism. But I can't comprehend,' says I, 'why Willie Robbins, whose folks at home are well off, and who used to be as meek and undesirous of notice as a cat with cream on his whiskers, should all at once develop into a warrior bold with the most fire-eating kind of proclivities. And the girl in his case seems to have been eliminated by marriage to another fellow. I reckon,' says I, 'it's a plain case of just common ambition. He wants his name, maybe, to go thundering down the corners of time. It must be that.'

"Well, without itemizing his deeds, Willie sure made good as a hero. He simply spent most of his time on his knees begging our captain to send him on forlorn hopes and dangerous scouting expeditions. In every fight he was the first man to mix it at close quarters with the Don Alfonsos. He got three or four bullets planted in various parts of his autonomy. Once he went off with a detail of eight men and captured a whole company of Spanish. He kept Captain Floyd busy writing out recommendations of his bravery to send in to head-quarters; and he began to accumulate medals for all kinds of things—heroism and target-shooting and valor and tactics and uninsubordination, and all the little accomplishments that look good to the third assistant secretaries of the War Department.

"Finally, Cap Floyd got promoted to be a major general, or a knight commander of the main herd, or something like that. He pounded around on a white horse, all desecrated up with gold-leaf and hen-feathers and a Good Templar's hat, and wasn't allowed by the regulations to speak to us. And Willie Robbins was made captain of our company.

"And maybe he didn't go after the wreath of fame then! As far as I could see it was him that ended the war. He got eighteen of us boys—friends of his, too—killed in battles that he stirred up himself and that didn't seem to me necessary at all. One night he took twelve of us and waded through a little rill about a hundred and ninety yards wide, and climbed a couple of mountains, and sneaked through a mile of neglected shrubbery and a couple of rock-quarries and into a rye-straw village, and captured a Spanish general named, as they said, Benny Veedus. Benny seemed to me hardly worth the trouble, being a blackish man without shoes or cuffs, and anxious to surrender and throw himself on the commissary of his foe.

"But that job gave Willie the big boost he wanted. The San Augustine *News* and the Galveston, St. Louis, New York, and Kansas City papers printed his picture and columns of stuff about him. Old San Augustine simply went crazy over its 'gallant son.' The *News* had an editorial tearfully begging the government to call off the regular army and the national guard, and let Willie carry on the rest of the war single-handed. It said that a refusal to do so would be regarded as a proof that the Northern jealousy of the South was still as rampant as ever.

"If the war hadn't ended pretty soon, I don't know to what heights of gold braid and encomiums Willie would have climbed; but it did. There was a secession of hostilities just three days after he was appointed a colonel, and got in three more medals by registered mail and shot two Spaniards while they were drinking lemonade in an ambuscade.

"Our company went back to San Augustine when the war was over. There wasn't anywhere else for it to go. And what do you think? The old town notified us in print, by wire cable, special delivery, and a nigger named Saul sent on a gray mule to San Antone, that they was going to give us the biggest blow-out, complimentary, alimentary, and elementary, that ever disturbed the kildees on the sand-flats outside of the immediate contiguity of the city.

"I say 'we,' but it was all meant for ex-Private, Captain *de facto*, and Colonel-elect Willie Robbins. The town was crazy about him. They notified us that the reception they were going to put up would make the Mardi Gras in New Orleans look like an afternoon tea in Bury St. Edmonds with a curate's aunt.

"Well, the San Augustine Rifles got back home on schedule time. Everybody was at the depot giving forth Roosevelt-Democrat—they used to be called Rebel —yells. There was two brass-bands, and the mayor, and schoolgirls in white frightening the street-car horses by throwing Cherokee roses in the streets, and —well, maybe you've seen a celebration by a town that was inland and out of water.

"They wanted Brevet Colonel Willie to get into a carriage and be drawn by prominent citizens and some of the city aldermen to the armory, but he stuck to his company and marched at the head of it up Sam Houston Avenue. The buildings on both sides was covered with flags and audiences, and everybody hollered 'Robbins!' or 'Hello, Willie!' as we marched up in files of fours. I never saw a illustriouser-looking human in my life than Willie was. He had at least seven or eight medals and diplomas and decorations on the breast of his khaki coat; he was sunburnt the color of a saddle, and he certainly done himself proud.

"They told us at the depot that the court-house was to be illuminated at half-past seven, and there would be speeches and chili-con-carne at the Palace Hotel. Miss Delphine Thompson was to read an original poem by James Whitcomb Ryan, and Constable Hooker had promised us a salute of nine guns from Chicago that he had arrested that day.

"After we had disbanded in the armory, Willie says to me:

"'Want to walk out a piece with me?'

"'Why, yes,' says I, 'if it ain't so far that we can't hear the tumult and the shouting die away. I'm hungry myself,' says I, 'and I'm pining for some home grub, but I'll go with you.'

"Willie steered me down some side streets till we came to a little white cottage in a new lot with a twenty-by-thirty-foot lawn decorated with brickbats and old barrel-staves.

" 'Halt and give the countersign,' says I to Willie. 'Don't you know this dugout? It's the bird's-nest that Joe Granberry built before he married Myra Allison. What you going there for?'

"But Willie already had the gate open. He walked up the brick walk to the steps, and I went with him. Myra was sitting in a rocking chair on the porch, sewing. Her hair was smoothed back kind of hasty and tied in a knot. I never noticed till then that she had freckles. Joe was at one side of the porch, in his shirt-sleeves, with no collar on, and no signs of a shave, trying to scrape out a hole among the brickbats and tin cans to plant a little fruit-tree in. He looked up but never said a word, and neither did Myra.

"Willie was sure dandy-looking in his uniform, with medals strung on his breast and his new gold-handled sword. You'd never have taken him for the little white-headed snipe that the girls used to order about and make fun of. He just stood there for a minute, looking at Myra with a peculiar little smile on his face; and then he says to her, slow, and kind of holding on to his words with his teeth:

" '*Oh, I don't know! Maybe I could if I tried!*'

"That was all that was said. Willie raised his hat, and we walked away.

"And, somehow, when he said that, I remembered, all of a sudden, the night of that dance and Willie brushing his hair before the looking-glass, and Myra sticking her head in the door to guy him.

"When we got back to Sam Houston Avenue, Willie says:

" 'Well, so long, Ben. I'm going down home and get off my shoes and take a rest.'

" 'You?' says I. 'What's the matter with you? Ain't the courthouse jammed with everybody in town waiting to honor the hero? And two brass-bands, and recitations and flags and jags, and grub to follow waiting for you?'

"Willie sighs.

" 'All right, Ben,' says he. 'Darned if I didn't forget all about that.'

"And that's why I say," concluded Ben Granger, "that you can't tell where ambition begins any more than you can where it is going to wind up."

THE HEAD-HUNTER

WHEN the war between Spain and George Dewey was over, I went to the Philippine Islands. There I remained as bush-whacker correspondent for my paper until its managing editor notified me that an eight-hundred-word cablegram describing the grief of a pet carabao over the death of an infant Moro was not considered by the office to be war news. So I resigned, and came home.

On board the trading-vessel that brought me back I pondered much upon the strange things I had sensed in the weird archipelago of the yellow-brown people. The manœuvres and skirmishings of the petty war interested me not: I was spellbound by the outlandish and unreadable countenance of that race that had turned its expressionless gaze upon us out of an unguessable past.

Particularly during my stay in Mindanao had I been fascinated and attracted by that delightfully original tribe of heathen known as the head-hunters. Those grim, flinty, relentless little men, never seen, but chilling the warmest noonday by the subtle terror of their concealed presence, paralleling the trail of their prey through unmapped forests, across perilous mountain-tops, adown bottomless chasms, into uninhabitable jungles, always near with the invisible hand of death uplifted, betraying their pursuit only by such signs as a beast or a bird or a gliding serpent might make—a twig crackling in the awful sweat-soaked night, a drench of dew showering from the screening foliage of a giant tree, a whisper at even from the rushes of a water-level—a hint of death for every mile and every hour—they amused me greatly, those little fellows of one idea.

When you think of it, their method is beautifully and almost hilariously effective and simple.

You have your hut in which you live and carry out the destiny that was decreed for you. Spiked to the jamb of your bamboo doorway is a basket made of green withes, plaited. From time to time as vanity or ennui or love or jealousy or ambition may move you, you creep forth with your snickersnee and take up the silent trail. Back from it you come, triumphant, bearing the severed, gory head of your victim, which you deposit with pardonable pride in the basket at the side of your door. It may be the head of your enemy, your friend, or a stranger, according as competition, jealousy, or simple sportiveness has been your incentive to labor.

In any case, your reward is certain. The village men, in passing, stop to congratulate you, as your neighbor on weaker planes of life stops to admire and praise the begonias in your front yard. Your particular brown maid lingers with fluttering bosom, casting soft tiger's eyes at the evidence of your love for her. You chew betel-nut and listen, content, to the intermittent soft drip from the ends of the severed neck arteries. And you show your teeth and grunt like a water-buffalo—which is as near as you can come to laughing—at the thought that the cold, acephalous body of your door ornament is being spotted by wheeling vultures in the Mindanaoan wilds.

Truly, the life of the merry head-hunter captivated me. He had reduced art and philosophy to a simple code. To take your adversary's head, to basket it at the portal of your castle, to see it lying there, a dead thing, with its cunning and stratagems and power gone—— Is there a better way to foil his plots, to refute his arguments, to establish your superiority over his skill and wisdom?

The ship that brought me home was captained by an erratic Swede, who changed his course and deposited me, with genuine compassion, in a small town on the Pacific coast of one of the Central American republics a few hundred miles south of the port to which he had engaged to convey me. But I was wearied of movement and exotic fancies; so I leaped contentedly upon the firm sands of the village of Mojada, telling myself I should be sure to find there the rest that I craved. After all, far better to linger there (I thought), lulled by the sedative plash of the waves and the rustling of palm-fronds, than to sit upon the horsehair sofa of my parental home in the East, and there, cast down by currant wine and cake, and scourged by fatuous relatives, drivel into the ears of gaping neighbors sad stories of the death of colonial governors.

When first I saw Chloe Greene she was standing, all in white, in the doorway of her father's tile-roofed 'dobe house. She was polishing a silver cup with a cloth, and she looked like a pearl laid against black velvet. She turned on me a flatteringly protracted but a wiltingly disapproving gaze, and then went inside, humming a light song to indicate the value she placed upon my existence.

Small wonder: for Dr. Stamford (the most disreputable professional man between Juneau and Valparaiso) and I were zigzagging along the turfy street, tunelessly singing the words of "Auld Lang Syne" to the air of "Muzzer's Little Coal-Black Coon." We had come from the ice factory, which was Mojada's palace of wickedness, where we had been playing billiards and opening black bottles, white with frost, that we dragged with strings out of old Sandoval's ice-cold vats.

I turned in sudden rage to Dr. Stamford, as sober as the verger of a cathedral. In a moment I had become aware that we were swine cast before a pearl.

"You beast," I said, "this is half your doing. And the other half is the fault of this cursed country. I'd better have gone back to Sleepytown and died in a wild orgy of currant wine and buns than to have had this happen."

Stamford filled the empty street with his roaring laughter.

"You, too!" he cried. "And all as quick as the popping of a cork. Well, she does seem to strike agreeably upon the retina. But don't burn your fingers. All Mojada will tell you that Louis Devoe is the man."

"We will see about that," said I. "And, perhaps, whether he is *a* man as well as *the* man."

I lost no time in meeting Louis Devoe. That was easily accomplished, for the foreign colony in Mojada numbered scarce a dozen; and they gathered daily at a half-decent hotel kept by a Turk, where they managed to patch together the fluttering rags of country and civilization that were left them. I sought Devoe before I did my pearl of the doorway, because I had learned a little of the game of war, and knew better than to strike for a prize before testing the strength of the enemy.

A sort of cold dismay—something akin to fear—filled me when I had estimated him. I found a man so perfectly poised, so charming, so deeply learned in the world's rituals, so full of tact, courtesy, and hospitality, so endowed with grace and ease and a kind of careless, haughty power that I almost over-stepped the bounds in probing him, in turning him on the spit to find the weak point that I so craved for him to have. But I left him whole—I had to make bitter acknowledgment to myself that Louis Devoe was a gentleman worthy of my best blows; and I swore to give him them. He was a great merchant of the country, a wealthy importer and exporter. All day he sat in a fastidiously appointed office, surrounded by works of art and evidences of his high culture, directing through glass doors and windows the affairs of his house.

In person he was slender and hardly tall. His small, well-shaped head was covered with thick brown hair, trimmed short, and he wore a thick brown beard also cut close and to a fine point. His manners were a pattern.

Before long I had become a regular and a welcome visitor at the Greene home. I shook my wild habits from me like a worn-out cloak. I trained for the conflict with the care of a prize-fighter and the self-denial of a Brahmin.

As for Chloe Greene, I shall weary you with no sonnets to her eyebrow. She was a splendidly feminine girl, as wholesome as a November pippin, and no more mysterious than a window-pane. She had whimsical little theories that she had deduced from life, and that fitted the maxims of Epictetus like princess gowns. I wonder, after all, if that old duffer wasn't rather wise!

Chloe had a father, the Reverend Homer Greene, and an intermittent mother, who sometimes palely presided over a twilight teapot. The Reverend Homer was a burr-like man with a life-work. He was writing a concordance to the Scriptures, and had arrived as far as Kings. Being, presumably, a suitor for his daughter's hand, I was timber for his literary outpourings. I had the family tree of Israel drilled into my head until I used to cry aloud in my sleep. "And Aminadab begat Jay Eye See," and so forth, until he had tackled another book. I once made a calculation that the Reverend Homer's concordance would be worked up as far as the Seven Vials mentioned in Revelations about the third day after they were opened.

Louis Devoe, as well as I, was a visitor and an intimate friend of the Greenes. It was there I met him the oftenest, and a more agreeable man or a more accomplished I have never hated in my life.

Luckily or unfortunately, I came to be accepted as a Boy. My appearance was youthful, and I suppose I had that pleading and homeless air that always draws the motherliness that is in women and the cursed theories and hobbies of paterfamilias.

Chloe called me "Tommy," and made sisterly fun of my attempts to woo her. With Devoe she was vastly more reserved. He was the man of romance, one to stir her imagination and deepest feelings had her fancy leaned toward him. I was closer to her, but standing in no glamour; I had the task before me of winning her in what seems to me the American way of fighting—with cleanness and pluck and everyday devotion to break away the barriers of friendship that divided us, and to take her, if I could, between sunrise and dark, abetted by neither moonlight nor music nor foreign wiles.

Chloe gave no sign of bestowing her blithe affections upon either of us. But one day she let out to me an inkling of what she preferred in a man. It was tremendously interesting to me, but not illuminating as to its application. I had been tormenting her for the dozenth time with the statement and catalogue of my sentiments toward her.

"Tommy," said she, "I don't want a man to show his love for me by leading an army against another country and blowing people off the earth with cannons."

"If you mean that the opposite way," I answered, "as they say women do, I'll see what I can do. The papers are full of this diplomatic row in Russia. My people know some big people in Washington who are right next to the army people, and I could get an artillery commission and——"

"I'm not that way," interrupted Chloe. "I mean what I say. It isn't the big things that are done in the world, Tommy, that count with a woman. When the knights were riding abroad in their armor to slay dragons, many a stay-at-home page won a lonesome lady's hand by being on the spot to pick up her glove and be quick with her cloak when the wind blew. The man I am to like best, whoever he shall be, must show his love in little ways. He must never forget, after hearing it once, that I do not like to have any one walk at my left side; that I detest bright-colored neckties; that I prefer to sit with my back to a light; that I like candied violets; that I must not be talked to when I am looking at the moonlight shining on water, and that I very, very often long for dates stuffed with English walnuts."

"Frivolity," I said, with a frown. "Any well-trained servant would be equal to such details."

"And he must remember," went on Chloe, "to remind me of what I want when I do not know, myself, what I want."

"You're rising in the scale," I said. "What you seem to need is a first-class clairvoyant."

"And if I say that I am dying to hear a Beethoven sonata, and stamp my foot when I say it, he must know by that that what my soul craves is salted almonds; and he will have them ready in his pocket."

"Now," said I, "I am at a loss. I do not know whether your soul's affinity is to be an impresario or a fancy grocer."

Chloe turned her pearly smile upon me.

"Take less than half of what I said as a jest," she went on. "And don't think too lightly of the little things, Boy. Be a paladin if you must, but don't let it show on you. Most women are only very big children, and most men are only very little ones. Please us; don't try to over-power us. When we want a hero we can make one out of even a plain grocer the third time he catches our handkerchief before it falls to the ground."

That evening I was taken down with pernicious fever. That is a kind of coast fever with improvements and high-geared attachments. Your temperature goes up among the threes and fours and remains there, laughing scornfully and feverishly at the cinchona trees and the coaltar derivatives. Pernicious fever is a case for a simple mathematician instead of a doctor. It is merely this formula: Vitality + the desire to live — the duration of the fever = the result.

I took to my bed in the two-roomed thatched hut where I had been comfortably established, and sent for a gallon of rum. That was not for myself. Drunk, Stamford was the best doctor between the Andes and the Pacific. He came, sat at my bedside, and drank himself into condition.

"My boy," said he, "my lily-white and reformed Romeo, medicine will do you no good. But I will give you quinine, which, being bitter, will arouse in you hatred and anger—two stimulants that will add ten per cent. to your chances. You are as strong as a caribou calf, and you will get well if the fever doesn't get in a knockout blow when you're off your guard."

For two weeks I lay on my back feeling like a Hindoo widow on a burning ghat. Old Atasca, an untrained Indian nurse, sat near the door like a petrified statue of What's-the-Use, attending to her duties, which were, mainly, to see that time went by without slipping a cog. Sometimes I would fancy myself back in the Philippines, or, at worse times, sliding off the horse-hair sofa in Sleepytown.

One afternoon I ordered Atasca to vamose, and got up and dressed carefully. I took my temperature, which I was pleased to find 104. I paid almost dainty attention to my dress, choosing solicitously a necktie of a dull and subdued hue. The mirror showed that I was looking little the worse from my illness. The fever gave brightness to my eyes and color to my face. And while I looked at my reflection my color went and came again as I thought of Chloe Greene and the millions of eons that had passed since I'd seen her, and of Louis Devoe and the time he had gained on me.

I went straight to her house. I seemed to float rather than walk; I hardly felt the ground under my feet; I thought pernicious fever must be a great boon to make one feel so strong.

I found Chloe and Louis Devoe sitting under the awning in front of the house. She jumped up and met me with a double handshake.

"I'm glad, glad, glad to see you out again!" she cried, every word a pearl strung on the string of her sentence. "You are well, Tommy—or better, of course. I wanted to come to see you, but they wouldn't let me."

"Oh, yes," said I, carelessly, "it was nothing. Merely a little fever. I am out again, as you see."

We three sat there and talked for half an hour or so. Then Chloe looked out yearningly and almost piteously across the ocean. I could see in her sea-blue eyes some deep and intense desire. Devoe, curse him! saw it too.

"What is it?" we asked, in unison.

"Cocoanut-pudding," said Chloe, pathetically. "I've wanted some—oh, so badly, for two days. It's got beyond a wish; it's an obsession."

"The cocoanut season is over," said Devoe, in that voice of his that gave thrilling interest to his most commonplace words. "I hardly think one could be found in Mojada. The natives never use them except when they are green and the milk is fresh. They sell all the ripe ones to the fruiterers."

"Wouldn't a broiled lobster or a Welsh rabbit do as well?" I remarked, with the engaging idiocy of a pernicious-fever convalescent.

Chloe came as near pouting as a sweet disposition and a perfect profile would allow her to come.

The Reverend Homer poked his ermine-lined face through the doorway and added a concordance to the conversation.

"Sometimes," said he, "old Campos keeps the dried nuts in his little store on the hill. But it would be far better, my daughter, to restrain unusual desires, and partake thankfully of the daily dishes that the Lord has set before us."

"Stuff!" said I.

"How was that?" asked the Reverend Homer, sharply.

"I say it's tough," said I, "to drop into the vernacular, that Miss Greene should be deprived of the food she desires—a simple thing like kalsomine-pudding. Perhaps," I continued, solicitously, "some pickled walnuts or a fricassee of Hungarian butternuts would do as well."

Every one looked at me with a slight exhibition of curiosity.

Louis Devoe arose and made his adieus. I watched him until he had sauntered slowly and grandiosely to the corner, around which he turned to reach his great warehouse and store. Chloe made her excuses, and went inside for a few minutes to attend to some detail affecting the seven-o'clock dinner. She was a passed mistress in housekeeping. I had tasted her puddings and bread with beatitude.

When all had gone, I turned casually and saw a basket made of plaited green withes hanging by a nail outside the door-jamb. With a rush that made my hot temples throb there came vividly to my mind recollections of the head-hunters—*those grim, flinty, relentless little men, never seen but chilling the warmest noonday by the subtle terror of their concealed presence. . . . From time to time, as vanity or ennui or love or jealousy or ambition may move him, one creeps forth with his snickersnee and takes up the silent trail. . . . Back he comes triumphant, bearing the severed, gory head of his victim. . . . His particular brown or white maid lingers, with fluttering bosom, casting soft tiger's eyes at the evidence of his love for her.*

I stole softly from the house and returned to my hut. From its supporting nails in the wall I took a machete as heavy as a butcher's cleaver and sharper than a safety-razor. And then I chuckled softly to myself, and set out to the fastidiously appointed private office of Monsieur Louis Devoe, usurper to the hand of the Pearl of the Pacific.

He was never slow at thinking; he gave one look at my face and another at the weapon in my hand as I entered his door, and then he seemed to fade from my sight. I ran to the back door, kicked it open, and saw him running like a deer up the road toward the wood that began two hundred yards away. I was after him, with a shout. I remember hearing children and women screaming, and seeing them flying from the road.

He was fleet, but I was stronger. A mile, and I had almost come up with him. He doubled cunningly and dashed into a brake that extended into a small cañon. I crashed through this after him, and in five minutes had him cornered in an angle of insurmountable cliffs. There his instinct of self-preservation steadied him, as it will steady even animals at bay. He turned to me, quite calm, with a ghastly smile.

"Oh, Rayburn!" he said, with such an awful effort at ease that I was impolite enough to laugh rudely in his face. "Oh, Rayburn!" said he, "come, let's have done with this nonsense! Of course, I know it's the fever and you're not yourself; but collect yourself, man—give me that ridiculous weapon, now, and let's go back and talk it over."

"I will go back," said I, "carrying your head with me. We will see how charmingly it can discourse when it lies in the basket at her door."

"Come," said he, persuasively, "I think better of you than to suppose that you try this sort of thing as a joke. But even the vagaries of a fever-crazed lunatic come some time to a limit. What is this talk about heads and baskets? Get yourself together and throw away that absurd cane-chopper. What would Miss Greene think of you?" he ended, with the silky cajolery that one would use toward a fretful child.

"Listen," said I. "At last you have struck upon the right note. What would she think of me? Listen," I repeated.

"There are women," I said, "who look upon horsehair sofas and currant wine as dross. To them even the calculated modulation of your well-trimmed talk sounds like the dropping of rotten plums from a tree in the night. They are the maidens who walk back and forth in the villages, scorning the emptiness of the baskets at the doors of the young men who would win them. One, such as they," I said, "is waiting. Only a fool would try to win a woman by drooling like a braggart in her doorway or by waiting upon her whims like a footman. They are all daughters of Herodias, and to gain their hearts one must lay the heads of his enemies before them with his own hands. Now, bend your neck, Louis Devoe. Do not be a coward as well as 'a chatterer at a lady's tea-table."

"There, there!" said Devoe, falteringly. "You know me, don't you, Rayburn?"

"Oh, yes," I said, "I know you. I know you. I know you. But the basket is empty. The old men of the village and the young men and both the dark maidens and the ones who are as fair as pearls, walk back and forth and see its emptiness. Will you kneel now, or must we have a scuffle? It is not like you to make things go roughly and with bad form. But the basket is waiting for your head."

With that he went to pieces. I had to catch him as he tried to scamper past me like a scared rabbit. I stretched him out and got a foot on his chest, but he squirmed like a worm, although I appealed repeatedly to his sense of propriety and the duty he owed to himself as a gentleman not to make a row. But at last he gave me the chance, and I swung the machete.

It was not hard work. He flopped like a chicken during the six or seven blows that it took to sever his head; but finally he lay still, and I tied his head in my handkerchief. The eyes opened and shut thrice while I walked a hundred yards. I was red to my feet with the drip, but what did that matter? With delight I felt under my hands the crisp touch of his short, thick brown hair and close-trimmed beard.

I reached the house of the Greenes and dumped the head of Louis Devoe into the basket that still hung by the nail in the door-jamb. I sat in a chair under the awning and waited. The sun was within two hours of setting. Chloe came out and looked surprised.

"Where have you been, Tommy?" she asked. "You were gone when I came out."

"Look in the basket," I said, rising to my feet. She looked, and gave a little scream—of delight, I was pleased to note.

"Oh, Tommy!" she said. "It was just what I wanted you to do. It's leaking a little, but that doesn't matter. Wasn't I telling you? It's the little things that count. And you remembered."

Little things! She held the ensanguined head of Louis Devoe in her white apron. Tiny streams of red widened on her apron and dripped upon the floor. Her face was bright and tender.

"Little things, indeed!" I thought again. "The head-hunters are right. These are the things that women like you to do for them."

Chloe came close to me. There was no one in sight. She looked up at me with sea-blue eyes that said things they had never said before.

"You think of me," she said. "You are the man I was describing. You think of little things, and they are what make the world worth living in. The man for me must consider my little wishes, and make me happy in small ways. He must bring me little red peaches in December if I wish for them, and then I will love him till June. I will have no knight in armor slaying his rival or killing dragons for me. You please me very well, Tommy."

I stooped and kissed her. Then a moisture broke out on my forehead, and I began to feel weak. I saw the red stains vanish from Chloe's apron, and the head of Louis Devoe turn to a brown, dried cocoanut.

"There will be cocoanut-pudding for dinner, Tommy, boy," said Chloe, gayly, "and you must come. I must go in for a little while."

She vanished in a delightful flutter.

Dr. Stamford tramped up hurriedly. He seized my pulse as though it were his own property that I had escaped with.

"You are the biggest fool outside of any asylum!" he said, angrily. "Why did you leave your bed? And the idiotic things you've been doing!—and no wonder, with your pulse going like a sledge-hammer."

"Name some of them," said I.

"Devoe sent for me," said Stamford. "He saw you from his window go to old Campos' store, chase him up the hill with his own yard-stick, and then come back and make off with his biggest cocoanut."

"It's the little things that count, after all," said I.

"It's your little bed that counts with you just now," said the doctor. "You come with me at once, or I'll throw up the case. You're as loony as a loon."

So I got no cocoanut-pudding that evening, but I conceived a distrust as to the value of the method of the head-hunters. Perhaps for many centuries the maidens of the villages may have been looking wistfully at the heads in the baskets at the doorways, longing for other and lesser trophies.

NO STORY

To avoid having this book hurled into a corner of the room by the suspicious reader, I will assert in time that this is not a newspaper story. You will encounter no shirt-sleeved, omniscient city editor, no prodigy "cub" reporter just off the farm, no scoop, no story—no anything.

But if you will concede me the setting of the first scene in the reporters' room of the *Morning Beacon*, I will repay the favor by keeping strictly my promises set forth above.

I was doing space-work on the *Beacon*, hoping to be put on a salary. Some one had cleared with a rake or a shovel a small space for me at the end of a long table piled high with exchanges, *Congressional Records*, and old files. There I did my work. I wrote whatever the city whispered or roared or chuckled to me on my diligent wanderings about its streets. My income was not regular.

One day Tripp came in and leaned on my table. Tripp was something in the mechanical department—I think he had something to do with the pictures, for he smelled of photographers' supplies, and his hands were always stained and cut up with acids. He was about twenty-five and looked forty. Half of his face was covered with short, curly red whiskers that looked like a door-mat with the "welcome" left off. He was pale and unhealthy and miserable and fawning, and an assiduous borrower of sums ranging from twenty-five cents to a dollar. One dollar was his limit. He knew the extent of his credit as well as the Chemical National Bank knows the amount of H_2O that collateral will show on analysis. When he sat on my table he held one hand with the other to keep both from shaking. Whiskey. He had a spurious air of lightness and bravado about him that deceived no one, but was useful in his borrowing because it was so pitifully and perceptibly assumed.

This day I had coaxed from the cashier five shining silver dollars as a grumbling advance on a story that the Sunday editor had reluctantly accepted. So if I was not feeling at peace with the world, at least an armistice had been declared; and I was beginning with ardor to write a description of the Brooklyn Bridge by moonlight.

"Well, Tripp," said I, looking up at him rather impatiently, "how goes it?" He was looking to-day more miserable, more cringing and haggard and downtrodden than I had ever seen him. He was at that stage of misery where he drew your pity so fully that you longed to kick him.

"Have you got a dollar?" asked Tripp, with his most fawning look and his dog-like eyes that blinked in the narrow space between his high-growing matted beard and his low-growing matted hair.

"I have," said I; and again I said, "I have," more loudly and inhospitably, "and four besides. And I had hard work corkscrewing them out of old Atkinson, I can tell you. And I drew them," I continued, "to meet a want—a hiatus—a demand—a need—an exigency—a requirement of exactly five dollars."

I was driven to emphasis by the promonition that I was to lose one of the dollars on the spot.

"I don't want to borrow any," said Tripp, and I breathed again. "I thought you'd like to get put onto a good story," he went on. "I've got a rattling fine one for you. You ought to make it run a column at least. It'll make a dandy if you work it up right. It'll probably cost you a dollar or two to get the stuff. I don't want anything out of it myself."

I became placated. The proposition showed that Tripp appreciated past favors, although he did not return them. If he had been wise enough to strike me for a quarter then he would have got it.

"What is the story?" I asked, poising my pencil with a finely calculated editorial air.

"I'll tell you," said Tripp. "It's a girl. A beauty. One of the howlingest Amsden's Junes you ever saw. Rosebuds covered with dew—violets in their mossy bed—and truck like that. She's lived on Long Island twenty years and never saw New York City before. I ran against her on Thirty-fourth Street. She'd just got in on the East River ferry. I tell you, she's a beauty that would take the hydrogen out of all the peroxides in the world. She stopped me on the street and asked me where she could find George Brown. Asked me where she could find *George Brown in New York City!* What do you think of that?

"I talked to her, and found that she was going to marry a young farmer named Dodd—Hiram Dodd—next week. But it seems that George Brown still holds the championship in her youthful fancy. George had greased his cowhide boots some years ago, and came to the city to make his fortune. But he forgot to remember to show up again at Greenburg, and Hiram got in as second-best choice. But when it comes to the scratch Ada—her name's Ada Lowery— saddles a nag and rides eight miles to the railroad station- and catches the 6:45 A. M. train for the city. Looking for George, you know—you understand about women—George wasn't there, so she wanted him.

"Well, you know, I couldn't leave her loose in Wolftown-on-the-Hudson. I suppose she thought the first person she inquired of would say: 'George Brown? —why, yes—lemme see—he's a short man with light-blue eyes, ain't he? Oh, yes—you'll find George on One Hundred and Twenty-fifth Street, right next to the grocery. He's bill-clerk in a saddle-and-harness store.' That's about how innocent and beautiful she is. You know those little Long Island water-front villages like Greenburg—a couple of duck-farms for sport, and clams and about nine summer visitors for industries. That's the kind of a place she comes from. But, say—you ought to see her!

"What could I do? I don't know what money looks like in the morning. And she'd paid her last cent of pocket-money for her railroad ticket except a quarter, which she had squandered on gum-drops. She was eating them out of a paper-bag. I took her to a boarding-house on Thirty-second Street where I used to live, and hocked her. She's in soak for a dollar. That's old Mother McGinnis' price per day. I'll show you the house."

"What words are these, Tripp?" said I. "I thought you said you had a story. Every ferryboat that crosses the East River brings or takes away girls from Long Island."

The premature lines on Tripp's face grew deeper. He frowned seriously from his tangle of hair. He separated his hands and emphasized his answer with one shaking forefinger.

"Can't you see," he said, "what a rattling fine story it would make? You could do it fine. All about the romance, you know, and describe the girl, and put a lot of stuff in it about true love, and sling in a few stickfuls of funny business—joshing the Long Islanders about being green, and, well—you know how to do it. You ought to get fifteen dollars out of it, anyhow. And it'll cost you only about four dollars. You'll make a clear profit of eleven."

"How will it cost me four dollars?" I asked, suspiciously.

"One dollar to Mrs. McGinnis," Tripp answered, promptly, "and two dollars to pay the girl's fare back home."

"And the fourth dimension?" I inquired, making a rapid mental calculation.

"One dollar to me," said Tripp, "for whiskey. Are you on?"

I smiled enigmatically and spread my elbows as if to begin writing again. But this grim, abject, specious, subservient, burr-like wreck of a man would not be shaken off. His forehead suddenly became shiningly moist.

"Don't you see," he said, with a sort of desperate calmness, "that this girl has got to be sent home to-day—not to-night nor to-morrow, but to-day? I can't do anything for her. You know, I'm the janitor and corresponding secretary of the Down-and-Out Club. I thought you could make a newspaper story out of it and win out a piece of money on general results. But, anyhow, don't you see that she's got to get back home before night?"

And then I began to feel that dull, leaden, soul-depressing sensation known as the sense of duty. Why should that sense fall upon one as a weight and a burden? I knew that I was doomed that day to give up the bulk of my store of hard-wrung coin to the relief of this Ada Lowery. But I swore to myself that Tripp's whiskey dollar would not be forthcoming. He might play knight-errant at my expense, but he would indulge in no wassail afterward, commemorating my weakness and gullibility. In a kind of chilly anger I put on my coat and hat.

Tripp, submissive, cringing, vainly endeavoring to please, conducted me *via* the street-cars to the human pawn-shop of Mother McGinnis. I paid the fares. It seemed that the collodion-scented Don Quixote and the smallest minted coin were strangers.

Tripp pulled the bell at the door of the mouldy red-brick boarding-house. At its faint tinkle he paled, and crouched as a rabbit makes ready to spring away at the sound of a hunting-dog. I guessed what a life he had led, terror-haunted by the coming footsteps of landladies.

"Give me one of the dollars—quick!" he said.

The door opened six inches. Mother McGinnis stood there with white eyes—they were white, I say—and a yellow face, holding together at her throat with one hand a dingy pink flannel dressing-sack. Tripp thrust the dollar through the space without a word, and it bought us entry.

"She's in the parlor," said the McGinnis, turning the back of her sack upon us.

In the dim parlor a girl sat at the cracked marble centre-table weeping comfortably and eating gum-drops. She was a flawless beauty. Crying had only made her brilliant eyes brighter. When she crunched a gum-drop you thought only of the poetry of motion and envied the senseless confection. Eve at the age of five minutes must have been a ringer for Miss Ada Lowery at nineteen or twenty. I was introduced, and a gum-drop suffered neglect while she conveyed to me a naïve interest, such as a puppy dog (a prize winner) might bestow upon a crawling beetle or a frog.

Tripp took his stand by the table, with the fingers of one hand spread upon it, as an attorney or a master of ceremonies might have stood. But he looked the master of nothing. His faded coat was buttoned high, as if it sought to be charitable to deficiencies of tie and linen. I thought of a Scotch terrier at the sight of his shifty eyes in the glade between his tangled hair and beard. For one ignoble moment I felt ashamed of having been introduced as his friend in the presence of so much beauty in distress. But evidently Tripp meant to conduct the ceremonies, whatever they might be. I thought I detected in his actions and pose an intention of foisting the situation upon me as material for a newspaper story, in a lingering hope of extracting from me his whiskey dollar.

"My friend" (I shuddered), "Mr. Chalmers," said Tripp, "will tell you, Miss Lowery, the same that I did. He's a reporter, and he can hand out the talk better than I can. That's why I brought him with me." (O Tripp, wasn't it the *silver*-tongued orator you wanted?) "He's wise to a lot of things, and he'll tell you now what's best to do."

I stood on one foot, as it were, as I sat in my rickety chair.

"Why—er—Miss Lowery," I began, secretly enraged at Tripp's awkward opening, "I am at your service, of course, but—er—as I haven't been apprized of the circumstances of the case, I—er——"

"Oh," said Miss Lowery, beaming for a moment, "it ain't as bad as that—there ain't any circumstances. It's the first time I've ever been in New York except once when I was five years old, and I had no idea it was such a big town. And I met Mr.—Mr. Snip on the street and asked him about a friend of mine, and he brought me here and asked me to wait."

"I advise you, Miss Lowery," said Tripp, "to tell Mr. Chalmers all. He's a friend of mine" (I was getting used to it by this time), "and he'll give you the right tip."

"Why, certainly," said Miss Ada, chewing a gum-drop toward me. "There ain't anything to tell except that—well, everything's fixed for me to marry Hiram Dodd next Thursday evening. Hi has got two hundred acres of land with a lot of shore-front, and one of the best truck-farms on the Island. But this morning I had my horse saddled up—he's a white horse named Dancer—and I rode over to the station. I told 'em at home I was going to spend the day with Susie Adams. It was a story, I guess, but I don't care. And I came to New York on the train, and I met Mr.—Mr. Flip on the street and asked him if he knew where I could find G—G——"

"Now, Miss Lowery," broke in Tripp, loudly, and with much bad taste, I thought, as she hesitated with her word, "you like this young man, Hiram Dodd, don't you? He's all right, and good to you, ain't he?"

"Of course I like him," said Miss Lowery, emphatically. "Hi's all right. And of course he's good to me. So is everybody."

I could have sworn it myself. Throughout Miss Ada Lowery's life all men would be good to her. They would strive, contrive, struggle, and compete to hold umbrellas over her hat, check her trunk, pick up her handkerchief, and buy for her soda at the fountain.

"But," went on Miss Lowery, "last night I got to thinking about G—George and I——"

Down went the bright gold head upon her dimpled, clasped hands on the table. Such a beautiful April storm! Unrestrainedly she sobbed. I wished I could have comforted her. But I was not George. And I was glad I was not Hiram—and yet I was sorry, too.

By-and-by the shower passed. She straightened up, brave and halfway smiling. She would have made a splendid wife, for crying only made her eyes more bright and tender. She took a gum-drop and began her story.

"I guess I'm a terrible hayseed," she said, between her little gulps and sighs, "but I can't help it. G—George Brown and I were sweethearts since he was eight and I was five. When he was nineteen—that was four years ago—he left Greenburg and went to the city. He said he was going to be a policeman or a railroad president or something. And then he was coming back for me. But I never heard from him any more. And I—I—liked him."

Another flow of tears seemed imminent, but Tripp hurled himself into the crevasse and dammed it. Confound him, I could see his game. He was trying to make a story of it for his sordid ends and profit.

"Go on, Mr. Chalmers," said he, "and tell the lady what's the proper caper. That's what I told her—you'd hand it to her straight. Spiel up."

I coughed, and tried to feel less wrathful toward Tripp. I saw my duty. Cunningly I had been inveigled, but I was securely trapped. Tripp's first dictum to me had been just and correct. The young lady must be sent back to Greenburg that day. She must be argued with, convinced, assured, instructed, ticketed, and returned without delay. I hated Hiram and despised George; but duty must be done. *Noblesse oblige* and only five silver dollars are not strictly romantic compatibles, but sometimes they can be made to jibe. It was mine to be Sir Oracle, and then pay the freight. So I assumed an air that mingled Solomon's with that of the general passenger agent of the Long Island Railroad.

"Miss Lowery," said I, as impressively as I could, "life is rather a queer proposition, after all." There was a familiar sound to these words after I had spoken them, and I hoped Miss Lowery had never heard Mr. Cohan's song. "Those whom we first love we seldom wed. Our earlier romances, tinged with the magic radiance of youth, often fail to materialize." The last three words sounded somewhat trite when they struck the air. "But those fondly cherished dreams," I went on, "may cast a pleasant afterglow on our future lives, however impracticable and vague they may have been. But life is full of realities as well as visions and dreams. One cannot live on memories. May I ask, Miss Lowery, if you think you could pass a happy—that is, a contented and harmonious life with Mr.—er—Dodd—if in other ways than romantic recollections he seems to—er—fill the bill, as I might say?"

"Oh, Hi's all right," answered Miss Lowery. "Yes, I could get along with him fine. He's promised me an automobile and a motor-boat. But somehow, when it got so close to the time I was to marry him, I couldn't help wishing—well, just thinking about George. Something must have happened to him or he'd have written. On the day he left, he and me got a hammer and a chisel and cut a dime into two pieces. I took one piece and he took the other, and we promised to be true to each other and always keep the pieces till we saw each other again. I've got mine at home now in a ring-box in the top drawer of my dresser. I guess I was silly to come up here looking for him. I never realized what a big place it is."

And then Tripp joined in with a little grating laugh that he had, still trying to drag in a little story or drama to earn the miserable dollar that he craved.

"Oh, the boys from the country forget a lot when they come to the city and learn something. I guess George, maybe, is on the bum, or got roped in by some other girl, or maybe gone to the dogs on account of whiskey or the races. You listen to Mr. Chalmers and go back home, and you'll be all right."

But now the time was come for action, for the hands of the clock were moving close to noon. Frowning upon Tripp, I argued gently and philosophically with Miss Lowery, delicately convincing her of the importance of returning home at once. And I impressed upon her the truth that it would not be absolutely necessary to her future happiness that she mention to Hi the wonders or the fact of her visit to the city that had swallowed up the unlucky George.

She said she had left her horse (unfortunate Rosinante) tied to a tree near the railroad station. Tripp and I gave her instructions to mount the patient steed as soon as she arrived and ride home as fast as possible. There she was to recount the exciting adventure of a day spent with Susie Adams. She could "fix" Susie—I was sure of that—and all would be well.

And then, being susceptible to the barbed arrows of beauty, I warmed to the adventure. The three of us hurried to the ferry, and there I found the price of a ticket to Greenburg to be but a dollar and eighty cents. I bought one, and a red, red rose with the twenty cents for Miss Lowery. We saw her aboard her ferry-boat, and stood watching her wave her handkerchief at us until it was the tiniest white patch imaginable. And then Tripp and I faced each other, brought back to earth, left dry and desolate in the shade of the sombre verities of life.

The spell wrought by beauty and romance was dwindling. I looked at Tripp and almost sneered. He looked more careworn, contemptible, and disreputable than ever. I fingered the two silver dollars remaining in my pocket and looked at him with the half-closed eyelids of contempt. He mustered up an imitation of resistance.

"Can't you get a story out of it?" he asked, huskily. "Some sort of a story, even if you have to fake part of it?"

"Not a line," said I. "I can fancy the look on Grimes' face if I should try to put over any slush like this. But we've helped the little lady out, and that'll have to be our only reward."

"I'm sorry," said Tripp, almost inaudibly. "I'm sorry you're out your money. Now, it seemed to me like a find of a big story, you know—that is, a sort of thing that would write up pretty well."

"Let's try to forget it," said I, with a praiseworthy attempt at gayety, "and take the next car 'cross town."

I steeled myself against his unexpressed but palpable desire. He should not coax, cajole, or wring from me the dollar he craved. I had had enough of that wild-goose chase.

Tripp feebly unbuttoned his coat of the faded pattern and glossy seams to reach for something that had once been a handkerchief deep down in some obscure and cavernous pocket. As he did so I caught the shine of a cheap silver-plated watch-chain across his vest, and something dangling from it caused me to stretch forth my hand and seize it curiously. It was the half of a silver dime that had been cut in halves with a chisel.

"What?" I said, looking at him keenly.

"Oh, yes," he responded, dully. "George Brown, alias Tripp. What's the use?"

Barring the W. C. T. U., I'd like to know if anybody disapproves of my having produced promptly from my pocket Tripp's whiskey dollar and unhesitatingly laying it in his hand.

THE HIGHER PRAGMATISM

WHERE to go for wisdom has become a question of serious import. The ancients are discredited; Plato is boiler-plate; Aristotle is tottering; Marcus Aurelius is reeling; Æsop has been copyrighted by Indiana; Solomon is too solemn; you couldn't get anything out of Epictetus with a pick.

The ant, which for many years served as a model of intelligence and industry in the school-readers, has been proven to be a doddering idiot and a waster of time and effort. The owl to-day is hooted at. Chautauqua conventions have abandoned culture and adopted diabolo. Graybeards give glowing testimonials to the venders of patent hair-restorers. There are typographical errors in the almanacs published by the daily newspapers. College professors have become——

But there shall be no personalities.

To sit in classes, to delve into the encyclopedia or the past-performances page, will not make us wise. As the poet says, "Knowledge comes, but wisdom lingers." Wisdom is dew, which, while we know it not, soaks into us, refreshes us, and makes us grow. Knowledge is a strong stream of water turned on us through a hose. It disturbs our roots.

Then, let us rather gather wisdom. But how to do so requires knowledge. If we know a thing, we know it; but very often we are not wise to it that we are wise, and——

But let's go on with the story.

II

Once upon a time I found a ten-cent magazine lying on a bench in a little city park. Anyhow, that was the amount he asked me for when I sat on the bench next to him. He was a musty, dingy, and tattered magazine, with some queer stories bound in him, I was sure. He turned out to be a scrap-book.

"I am a newspaper reporter," I said to him, to try him. "I have been detailed to write up some of the experiences of the unfortunate ones who spend their evenings in this park. May I ask you to what you attribute your downfall in——"

I was interrupted by a laugh from my purchase—a laugh so rusty and unpractised that I was sure it had been his first for many a day.

"Oh, no, no," said he. "You ain't a reporter. Reporters don't talk that way. They pretend to be one of us, and say they've just got on the blind baggage from St. Louis. I can tell a reporter on sight. Us park bums get to be fine judges of human nature. We sit here all day and watch the people go by. I can size up anybody who walks past my bench in a way that would surprise you."

"Well," I said, "go on and tell me. How do you size me up?"

"I should say," said the student of human nature with unpardonable hesitation, "that you was, say, in the contracting business—or maybe worked in a store—or was a sign-painter. You stopped in the park to finish your cigar, and thought you'd get a little free monologue out of me. Still, you might be a plasterer or a lawyer—it's getting kind of dark, you see. And your wife won't let you smoke at home."

I frowned gloomily.

"But, judging again," went on the reader of men, "I'd say you ain't got a wife."

"No," said I, rising restlessly. "No, no, no, I ain't. But I will have, by the arrows of Cupid. That is if——"

My voice must have trailed away and muffled itself in uncertainty and despair.

"I see you have a story yourself," said the dusty vagrant—imprudently, it seemed to me. "Suppose you take your dime back and spin your yarn for me. I'm interested myself in the ups and downs of unfortunate ones who spend their evenings in the park."

Somehow, that amused me. I looked at the frowsy derelict with more interest. I did have a story. Why not tell it to him? I had told none of my friends. I had always been a reserved and bottled-up man. It was psychical timidity or sensitiveness—perhaps both. And I smiled to myself in wonder when I felt an impulse to confide in this stranger and vagabond.

"Jack," said I.

"Mack," said he.

"Mack," said I, "I'll tell you."

"Do you want the dime back in advance?" said he. I handed him a dollar.

"The dime," said I, "was the price of listening to *your* story."

"Right on the point of the jaw," said he. "Go on."

And then, incredible as it may seem to the lovers in the world who confide their sorrows only to the night wind and the gibbous moon, I laid bare my secret to that wreck of all things that you would have supposed to be in sympathy with love.

I told him of the days and weeks and months that I had spent in adoring Mildred Telfair. I spoke of my despair, my grievous days and wakeful nights, my dwindling hopes and distress of mind. I even pictured to this night-prowler her beauty and dignity, the great sway she had in society, and the magnificence of her life as the elder daughter of an ancient race whose pride overbalanced the dollars of the city's millionaires.

"Why don't you cop the lady out?" asked Mack, bringing me down to earth and dialect again.

I explained to him that my worth was so small, my income so minute, and my fears so large that I hadn't the courage to speak to her of my worship. I told him that in her presence I could only blush and stammer, and that she looked upon me with a wonderful, maddening smile of amusement.

"She kind of moves in the professional class, don't she?" asked Mack.

"The Telfair family——" I began, haughtily.

"I mean professional beauty," said my hearer.

"She is greatly and widely admired," I answered, cautiously.

"Any sisters?"

"One."

"You know any more girls?"

"Why, several," I answered. "And a few others."

"Say," said Mack, "tell me one thing—can you hand out the dope to other girls? Can you chin 'em and make matinée eyes at 'em and squeeze 'm? You know what I mean. You're just shy when it comes to this particular dame— the professional beauty—ain't that right?"

"In a way you have outlined the situation with approximate truth," I admitted.

"I thought so," said Mack, grimly. "Now, that reminds me of my own case. I'll tell you about it."

I was indignant, but concealed it. What was this loafer's case or anybody's case compared with mine? Besides, I had given him a dollar and ten cents.

"Feel my muscle," said my companion, suddenly flexing his biceps. I did so mechanically. The fellows in gyms are always asking you to do that. His arm was as hard as cast-iron.

"Four years ago," said Mack, "I could lick any man in New York outside of the professional ring. Your case and mine is just the same. I come from the West Side—between Thirtieth and Fourteenth—and I won't give the number on the door. I was a scrapper when I was ten, and when I was twenty no amateur in the city could stand up four rounds with me. 'S a fact. You know Bill McCarty? No? He managed the smokers for some of them swell clubs. Well, I knocked out everything Bill brought up before me. I was a middle-weight, but could train down to a welter when necessary. I boxed all over the West Side at bouts and benefits and private entertainments, and was never put out once.

"But, say, the first time I put my foot in the ring with a professional I was no more than a canned lobster. I dunno how it was—I seemed to lose heart. I guess I got too much imagination. There was a formality and publicness about it that kind of weakened my nerve. I never won a fight in the ring. Light-weights and all kinds of scrubs used to sign up with my manager and then walk up and tap me on the wrist and see me fall. The minute I seen the crowd and a lot of gents in evening clothes down in front, and seen a professional come inside the ropes, I got as weak as ginger-ale.

"Of course, it wasn't long till I couldn't get no backers, and I didn't have any more chances to fight a professional—or many amateurs, either. But lemme tell you—I was as good as most men inside the ring or out. It was just that dumb, dead feeling I had when I was up against a regular that always done me up.

"Well, sir, after I had got out of the business, I got a mighty grouch on. I used to go round town licking private citizens and all kinds of unprofessionals just to please myself. I'd lick cops in dark streets and car-conductors and cab-drivers and draymen whenever I could start a row with 'em. It didn't make any difference how big they were, or how much science they had, I got away with 'em. If I'd only just have had the confidence in the ring that I had beating up the best men outside of it, I'd be wearing black pearls and heliotrope silk socks to-day.

"One evening I was walking along near the Bowery, thinking about things, when along comes a slumming-party. About six or seven they was, all in swallowtails, and these silk hats that don't shine. One of the gang kind of shoves me off the sidewalk. I hadn't had a scrap in three days, and I just says, 'De-light-ed' and hits him back of the ear.

"Well, we had it. That Johnnie put up as decent a little fight as you'd want to see in the moving pictures. It was on a side street, and no cops around. The other guy had a lot of science, but it only took me about six minutes to lay him out.

"Some of the swallowtails dragged him up against some steps and began to fan him. Another one of 'em comes over to me and says:

"'Young man, do you know what you've done?'

"'Oh, beat it,' says I. 'I've done nothing but a little punching-bag work. Take Freddy back to Yale and tell him to quit studying sociology on the wrong side of the sidewalk.'

"'My good fellow,' says he, 'I don't know who you are, but I'd like to. You've knocked out Reddy Burns, the champion middle-weight of the world! He came to New York yesterday, to try to get a match on with Jim Jeffries. If you——'

"But when I come out of my faint I was laying on the floor in a drug-store saturated with aromatic spirits of ammonia. If I'd known that was Reddy Burns, I'd have got down in the gutter and crawled past him instead of handing him one like I did. Why, if I'd ever been in a ring and seen him climbing over the ropes, I'd have been all to the sal-volatile.

"So that's what imagination does," concluded Mack. "And as I said, your case and mine is simultaneous. You'll never win out. You can't go up against the professionals. I tell you, it's a park bench for yours in this romance business."

Mack, the pessimist, laughed harshly.

"I'm afraid I don't see the parallel," I said, coldly. "I have only a very slight acquaintance with the prize ring."

The derelict touched my sleeve with his fore-finger, for emphasis, as he explained his parable.

"Every man," said he, with some dignity, "has got his lamps on something that looks good to him. With you, it's this dame that you're afraid to say your say to. With me, it was to win out in the ring. Well, you'll lose just like I did."

"Why do you think I shall lose?" I asked, warmly.

"'Cause," said he, "you're afraid to go in the ring. You dassen't stand up before a professional. Your case and mine is just the same. You're a amateur; and that means that you'd better keep outside of the ropes."

"Well, I must be going," I said, rising and looking with elaborate care at my watch.

When I was twenty feet away the park-bencher called to me.

"Much obliged for the dollar," he said. "And for the dime. But you'll never get 'er. You're in the amateur class."

"Serves you right," I said to myself, "for hobnobbing with a tramp. His impudence!"

But, as I walked, his words seemed to repeat themselves over and over again in my brain. I think I even grew angry at the man.

"I'll show him!" I finally said, aloud. "I'll show him that I can fight Reddy Burns, too—even knowing who he is."

I hurried to a telephone-booth and rang up the Telfair residence.

A soft, sweet voice answered. Didn't I know that voice? My hand holding the receiver shook.

"Is that *you?*" said I, employing the foolish words that form the vocabulary of every talker through the telephone.

"Yes, this is I," came back the answer in the low, clear-cut tones that are an inheritance of Telfairs. "Who is it, please?"

"It's me," said I, less ungrammatically than egotistically. "It's me, and I've got a few things that I want to say to you right now and immediately and straight to the point."

"*Dear* me," said the voice. "Oh, it's you, Mr. Arden!"

I wondered if any accent on the first word was intended. Mildred was fine at saying things that you had to study out afterward.

"Yes," said I, "I hope so. And now to come down to brass tacks." I thought that rather a vernacularism, if there is such a word, as soon as I had said it; but I didn't stop to apologize. "You know, of course, that I love you, and that I have been in that idiotic state for a long time. I don't want any more foolishness about it—that is, I mean I want an answer from you right now. Will you marry me or not? Hold the wire, please. Keep out, Central. Hello, hello! Will you, or will you *not?*"

That was just the uppercut for Reddy Burns' chin. The answer came back:

"Why, Phil, dear, of course I will! I didn't know that you—that is, you never said—oh, come up to the house, please—I can't say what I want to over the 'phone. You are so importunate. But please come up to the house, won't you?"

Would I?

I rang the bell of the Telfair house violently. Some sort of a human came to the door and shooed me into the drawing-room.

"Oh, well," said I to myself, looking at the ceiling, "any one can learn from any one. That was a pretty good philosophy of Mack's, anyhow. He didn't take advantage of his experience, but I get the benefit of it. If you want to get into the professional class, you've got to——"

I stopped thinking then. Someone was coming down the stairs. My knees began to shake. I knew then how Mack had felt when a professional began to climb over the ropes. I looked around foolishly for a door or a window by which I might escape. If it had been any other girl approaching, I mightn't have——

But just then the door opened, and Bess, Mildred's younger sister, came in. I'd never seen her look so much like a glorified angel. She walked straight up to me, and—and——

I'd never noticed before what perfectly wonderful eyes and hair Elizabeth Telfair had.

"Phil," she said, in the Telfair sweet, thrilling tones, "why didn't you tell me about it before? I thought it was sister you wanted all the time, until you telephoned to me a few minutes ago!"

I suppose Mack and I always will be hopeless amateurs. But, as the thing has turned out in my case, I'm mighty glad of it.

BEST-SELLER

I

ONE day last summer I went to Pittsburgh—well, I had to go there on business.

My chair-car was profitably well filled with people of the kind one usually sees on chair-cars. Most of them were ladies in brown-silk dresses cut with square yokes, with lace insertion and dotted veils, who refused to have the windows raised. Then there was the usual number of men who looked as if they might be in almost any business and going almost anywhere. Some students of human nature can look at a man in a Pullman and tell you where he is from, his occupation and his stations in life, both flag and social; but I never could. The only way I can correctly judge a fellow-traveller is when the train is held up by robbers, or when he reaches at the same time I do for the last towel in the dressing-room of the sleeper.

The porter came and brushed the collection of soot on the window-sill off to the left knee of my trousers. I removed it with an air of apology. The temperature was eighty-eight. One of the dotted-veiled ladies demanded the closing of two more ventilators, and spoke loudly of Interlaken. I leaned back idly in chair No. 7, and looked with the tepidest curiosity at the small, black, bald-spotted head just visible above the back of No. 9.

Suddenly No. 9 hurled a book to the floor between his chair and the window, and, looking, I saw that it was "The Rose Lady and Trevelyan" one of the best-selling novels of the present day. And then the critic or Philistine, which-ever he was, veered his chair toward the window, and I knew him at once for John A. Pescud of Pittsburgh, travelling salesman for a plate-glass company—an old acquaintance whom I had not seen in two years.

In two minutes we were faced, had shaken hands, and had finished with such topics as rain, prosperity, health, residence, and destination. Politics might have followed next; but I was not so ill-fated.

I wish you might know John A. Pescud. He is of the stuff that heroes are not often lucky enough to be made of. He is a small man with a wide smile, and an eye that seems to be fixed upon that little red spot on the end of your nose. I never saw him wear but one kind of necktie, and he believes in cuff-holders and button-shoes. He is as hard and true as anything ever turned out by the Cambria Steel Works; and he believes that as soon as Pittsburgh makes smoke-consumers compulsory, St. Peter will come down and sit at the foot of Smithfield Street, and let somebody else attend to the gate up in the branch heaven. He believes that "our" plate-glass is the most important commodity in the world, and that when a man is in his home town he ought to be decent and law-abiding.

During my acquaintance with him in the City of Diurnal Night I had never known his views on life, romance, literature, and ethics. We had browsed, during our meetings, on local topics and then parted, after Château Margaux, Irish stew, flannel-cakes, cottage-pudding, and coffee (hey, there!—with milk separate). Now I was to get more of his ideas. By way of facts, he told me that business had picked up since the party conventions, and that he was going to get off at Coketown.

II

"Say," said Pescud, stirring his discarded book with the toe of his right shoe; "did you ever read one of these best-sellers? I mean the kind where the hero is an American swell—sometimes even from Chicago—who falls in love with a royal princess from Europe who is travelling under an alias, and follows her to her father's kingdom or principality? I guess you have. They're all alike. Sometimes this going-away masher is a Washington newspaper correspondent, and sometimes he is a Van Something from New York, or a Chicago wheat-broker worth fifty millions. But he's always ready to break into the king row of any foreign country that sends over their queens and princesses to try the new plush seats on the Big Four or the B. and O. There doesn't seem to be any other reason in the book for their being here.

"Well, this fellow chases the royal chair-warmer home as I said, and finds out who she is. He meets her on the *corso* or the *strasse* one evening and gives us ten pages of conversation. She reminds him of the difference in their stations, and that gives him a chance to ring in three solid pages about America's uncrowned sovereigns. If you'd take his remarks and set 'em to music, and then take the music away from 'em, they'd sound exactly like one of George Cohan's songs.

"Well, you know how it runs on, if you've read any of 'em—he slaps the king's Swiss bodyguards around like everything whenever they get in his way. He's a great fencer, too. Now, I've known of some Chicago men who were pretty notorious fences, but I never heard of any fencers coming from there. He stands on the first landing of the royal staircase in Castle Schutzen-festenstein with a gleaming rapier in his hand, and makes a Baltimore broil of six platoons of traitors who come to massacre the said king. And then he has to fight duels with a couple of chancellors, and foil a plot by four Austrian archdukes to seize the kingdom for a gasoline-station.

"But the great scene is when his rival for the princess' hand, Count Feodor, attacks him between the portcullis and the ruined chapel, armed with a mitrailleuse, a yataghan, and a couple of Siberian bloodhounds. This scene is what runs the best-seller into the twenty-ninth edition before the publisher has had time to draw a check for the advance royalties.

"The American hero shucks his coat and throws it over the heads of the bloodhounds, give the mitrailleuse a slap with his mitt, says 'Yah!' to the yataghan, and lands in Kid McCoy's best style on the count's left eye. Of course, we have a neat little prize-fight right then and there. The count—in order to make the go possible—seems to be an expert at the art of self-defence, himself; and here we have the Corbett-Sullivan fight done over into literature. The book ends with the broker and the princess doing a John Cecil Clay cover under the linden-trees on the Gorgonzola Walk. That winds up the love-story plenty good enough. But I notice that the book dodges the final issue. Even a best-seller has sense enough to shy at either leaving a Chicago grain-broker on the throne of Lobsterpotsdam or bringing over a real princess to eat fish and potato salad in an Italian chalet on Michigan Avenue What do you think about 'em?"

"Why," said I, "I hardly know, John. There's a saying: 'Love levels all ranks,' you know."

"Yes," said Pescud, "but these kind of love-stories are rank—on the level. I know something about literature, even if I am in plate-glass. These kind of books are wrong, and yet I never go into a train but what they pile 'em up on me. No good can come out of an international clinch between the Old World aristocracy and one of us fresh Americans. When people in real life marry, they generally hunt up somebody in their own station. A fellow usually picks out a girl that went to the same high-school and belonged to the same singing-society that he did. When young millionaires fall in love, they always select the chorus-girl that likes the same kind of sauce on the lobster that he does. Washington newspaper correspondents always marry widow ladies ten years older than themselves who keep boarding-houses. No, sir, you can't make a novel sound right to me when it makes one of C. D. Gibson's bright young men go abroad and turn kingdoms upside down just because he's a Taft American and took a course at a gymnasium. And listen how they talk, too!"

Pescud picked up the best-seller and hunted his page.

"Listen at this," said he. "Trevelyan is chinning with the Princess Alwyna at the back end of the tulip-garden. This is how it goes:

"Say not so, dearest and sweetest of earth's fairest flowers. Would I aspire? You are a star set high above me in a royal heaven; I am only—myself. Yet I am a man, and I have a heart to do and dare. I have no title save that of an uncrowned sovereign; but I have an arm and a sword that yet might free Schutzenfestenstein from the plots of traitors.

"Think of a Chicago man packing a sword, and talking about freeing anything that sounded as much like canned pork as that! He'd be much more likely to fight to have an import duty put on it."

"I think I understand you, John," said I. "You want fiction-writers to be consistent wtih their scenes and characters. They shouldn't mix Turkish pashas with Vermont farmers, or English dukes with Long Island clam-diggers, or Italian countesses with Montana cowboys, or Cincinnati brewery agents with the rajahs of India."

"Or plain business men with aristocracy high above 'em," added Pescud. "It don't jibe. People are divided into classes, whether we admit it or not, and it's everybody's impulse to stick to their own class. They do it, too. I don't see why people go to work and buy hundreds of thousands of books like that. You don't see or hear of any such didoes and capers in real life."

III

"Well, John," said I, "I haven't read a best-seller in a long time. Maybe I've had notions about them somewhat like yours. But tell me more about yourself. Getting along all right with the company?"

"Bully," said Pescud, brightening at once. "I've had my salary raised twice since I saw you, and I get a commission, too. I've bought a neat slice of real estate out in the East End, and have run up a house on it. Next year the firm is going to sell me some shares of stock. Oh, I'm in on the line of General Prosperity, no matter who's elected!"

"Met your affinity yet, John?" I asked.

"Oh, I didn't tell you about that, did I?" said Pescud with a broader grin.

"O-ho!" I said. "So you've taken time enough off from your plate-glass to have a romance?"

"No, no," said John. "No romance—nothing like that! But I'll tell you about it.

"I was on the south-bound, going to Cincinnati, about eighteen months ago, when I saw, across the aisle, the finest looking girl I'd ever laid eyes on. Nothing spectacular, you know, but just the sort you want for keeps. Well, I never was up to the flirtation business, either handkerchief, automobile, postage-stamp, or door-step, and she wasn't the kind to start anything. She read a book and minded her business, which was to make the world prettier and better just by residing in it. I kept on looking out of the side doors of my eyes, and finally the proposition got out of the Pullman class into a case of a cottage with a lawn and vines running over the porch. I never thought of speaking to her, but I let the plate-glass business go to smash for a while.

"She changed cars at Cincinnati and took a sleeper to Louisville over the L. and N. There she bought another ticket, and went on through Shelbyville, Frankford, and Lexington. Along there I began to have a hard time keeping up with her. The trains came along when they pleased, and didn't seem to be going anywhere in particular, except to keep on the track and the right of way as much as possible. Then they began to stop at junctions instead of towns, and at last they stopped altogether. I'll bet Pinkerton would outbid the plate-glass people for my services any time if they knew how I managed to shadow that young lady. I contrived to keep out of her sight as much as I could, but I never lost track of her.

"The last station she got off at was away down in Virginia, about six in the afternoon. There were about fifty houses and four hundred niggers in sight. The rest was red mud, mules, and speckled hounds.

"A tall old man, with a smooth face and white hair, looking as proud as Julius Cæsar and Roscoe Conkling on the same post-card, was there to meet her. His clothes were frazzled, but I didn't notice that till later. He took her little satchel, and they started over the plank walks and went up a road along the hill. I kept along a piece behind 'em, trying to look like I was hunting a garnet ring in the sand that my sister had lost at a picnic the previous Saturday.

"They went in a gate on top of the hill. It nearly took my breath away when I looked up. Up there in the biggest grove I ever saw was a tremendous house with round white pillars about a thousand feet high, and the yard was so full of rose-bushes and box-bushes and lilacs that you couldn't have seen the house if it hadn't been as big as the Capitol at Washington.

"'Here's where I have to trail,' says I to myself. I thought before that she seemed to be in moderate circumstances, at least. This must be the Governor's mansion, or the Agricultural Building of a new World's Fair, anyhow. I'd better go back to the village and get posted by the postmaster, or drug the druggist for some information.

"In the village I found a pine hotel called the Bay View House. The only excuse for the name was a bay horse grazing in the front yard. I set my sample-case down, and tried to be ostensible. I told the landlord I was taking orders for plate-glass.

"'I don't want no plates,' says he, 'but I do need another glass molasses-pitcher.'

"By-and-by I got him down to local gossip and answering questions.

"'Why,' says he, 'I thought everybody knowed who lived in the big white house on the hill. It's Colonel Allyn, the biggest man and finest quality in Virginia, or anywhere else. They're the oldest family in the State. That was his daughter that got off the train. She's been up to Illinois to see her aunt, who is sick.'

"I registered at the hotel, and on the third day I caught the young lady walking in the front yard, down next to the paling fence. I stopped and raised my hat—there wasn't any other way.

"'Excuse me,' says I, 'can you tell me where Mr. Hinkle lives?'

"She looks at me as cool as if I was the man come to see about the weeding of the garden, but I thought I saw just a slight twinkle of fun in her eyes.

"'No one of that name lives in Birchton,' says she. 'That is,' she goes on, 'as far as I know. Is the gentleman you are seeking white?'

"'Well, that tickled me. 'No kidding,' says I. 'I'm not looking for smoke, even if I do come from Pittsburgh.'

"'You are quite a distance from home,' says she.

"'I'd have gone a thousand miles farther,' says I.

"'Not if you hadn't waked up when the train started in Shelbyville,' says she; and then she turned almost as red as one of the roses on the bushes in the yard. I remembered I had dropped off to sleep on a bench in the Shelbyville station, waiting to see which train she took, and only just managed to wake up in time.

"And then I told her why I had come, as respectful and earnest as I could. And I told her everything about myself, and what I was making, and how that all I asked was just to get acquainted with her and try to get her to like me.

"She smiles a little, and blushes some, but her eyes never get mixed up. They look straight at whatever she's talking to.

"'I never had any one talk like this to me before, Mr. Pescud,' says she. 'What did you say your name is—John?'

"'John A.,' says I.

"'And you came mighty near missing the train at Powhatan Junction, too,' says she, with a laugh that sounded as good as a mileage-book to me.

"'How did you know?' I asked.

"'Men are very clumsy,' said she. 'I knew you were on every train. I thought you were going to speak to me, and I'm glad you didn't.'

"Then we had more talk; and at last a kind of proud, serious look came on her face, and she turned and pointed a finger at the big house.

"'The Allyns,' says she, 'have lived in Elmcroft for a hundred years. We are a proud family. Look at that mansion. It has fifty rooms. See the pillars and porches and balconies. The ceilings in the reception-rooms and the ball-room are twenty-eight feet high. My father is a lineal descendant of belted earls.'

"'I belted one of 'em once in the Duquesne Hotel, in Pittsburgh,' says I, 'and he didn't offer to resent it. He was there dividing his attentions between Monongahela whiskey and heiresses, and he got fresh.'

"'Of course,' she goes on, 'my father wouldn't allow a drummer to set his foot in Elmcroft. If he knew that I was talking to one over the fence he would lock me in my room.'

"'Would you let me come there?' says I. 'Would you talk to me if I was to call? For,' I goes on, 'if you said I might come and see you, the earls might be belted or suspendered, or pinned up with safety-pins, as far as I am concerned.'

" 'I must not talk to you,' she says, 'because we have not been introduced. It is not exactly proper. So I will say good-bye, Mr.——'

" 'Say the name,' says I. 'You haven't forgotten it.'

" 'Pescud,' says she, a little mad.

" 'The rest of the name!' I demands, cool as could be.

" 'John,' says she.

" 'John—what?' I says.

" 'John A.,' says she, with her head high. 'Are you through, now?'

" 'I'm coming to see the belted earl to-morrow,' I says.

" 'He'll feed you to his fox-hounds,' says she, laughing.

" 'If he does, it'll improve their running,' says I. 'I'm something of a hunter myself.'

" 'I must be going in now,' says she. 'I oughtn't to have spoken to you at all. I hope you'll have a pleasant trip back to Minneapolis—or Pittsburgh, was it? Good-bye!'

" 'Good-night,' says I, 'and it wasn't Minneapolis. What's your name, first, please?'

"She hesitated. Then she pulled a leaf off a bush, and said:

" 'My name is Jessie,' says she.

" 'Good-night, Miss Allyn,' says I.

"The next morning at eleven, sharp, I rang the doorbell of that World's Fair main building. After about three quarters of an hour an old nigger man about eighty showed up and asked what I wanted. I gave him my business card, and said I wanted to see the colonel. He showed me in.

"Say, did you ever crack open a wormy English walnut? That's what that house was like. There wasn't enough furniture in it to fill an eight-dollar flat. Some old horsehair lounges and three-legged chairs and some framed ancestors on the walls were all that met the eye. But when Colonel Allyn comes in, the place seemed to light up. You could almost hear a band playing, and see a bunch of old-timers in wigs and white stockings dancing a quadrille. It was the style of him, although he had on the same shabby clothes I saw him wear at the station.

"For about nine seconds he had me rattled, and I came mighty near getting cold feet and trying to sell him some plate-glass. But I got my nerve back pretty quick. He asked me to sit down, and I told him everything. I told him how I followed his daughter from Cincinnati, and what I did it for, and all about my salary and prospects, and explained to him my little code of living— to be always decent and right in your home town; and when you're on the road never take more than four glasses of beer a day or play higher than a twenty-five-cent limit. At first I thought he was going to throw me out of the window, but I kept on talking. Pretty soon I got a chance to tell him that story about the Western Congressman who had lost his pocketbook and the grass widow— you remember that story. Well, that got him to laughing, and I'll bet that was the first laugh those ancestors and horsehair sofas had heard in many a day.

"We talked two hours. I told him everything I knew; and then he began to ask questions and I told him the rest. All I asked of him was to give me a chance. If I couldn't make a hit with the little lady, I'd clear out, and not bother any more. At last he says:

" 'There was a Sir Courtenay Pescud in the time of Charles I, if I remember rightly.'

" 'If there was,' says I, 'he can't claim kin with our bunch. We've always lived in and around Pittsburgh. I've got an uncle in the real-estate business, and one in trouble somewhere out in Kansas. You can inquire about any of the rest of us from anybody in old Smoky Town, and get satisfactory replies. Did you ever run across that story about the captain of the whaler who tried to make a sailor say his prayers?' says I.

" 'It occurs to me that I have never been so fortunate,' says the colonel.

"So I told it to him. Laugh! I was wishing to myself that he was a customer. What a bill of glass I'll sell him! And then he says:

" 'The relating of anecdotes and humorous occurrences has always seemed to me, Mr. Pescud, to be a particularly agreeable way of promoting and perpetuating amenities between friends. With your permission, I will relate to you a fox-hunting story with which I was personally connected, and which may furnish you some amusement.'

"So he tells it. It takes forty minutes by the watch. Did I laugh? Well, say! When I got my face straight he calls in old Pete, the superannuated darky, and sends him down to the hotel to bring up my valise. It was Elmcroft for me while I was in the town.

"Two evenings later I got a chance to speak a word with Miss Jessie alone on the porch while the colonel was thinking up another story.

" 'It's going to be a fine evening,' says I.

" 'He's coming,' says she. 'He's going to tell you, this time, the story about the old negro and the green watermelons. It always comes after the one about the Yankees and the game rooster. There was another time,' she goes on, 'that you nearly got left—it was at Pulaski City.'

" 'Yes,' says I, 'I remember. My foot slipped as I was jumping on the step, and I nearly tumbled off.'

" 'I know,' says she. 'And—and I—*I was afraid you had, John A. I was afraid you had.*'

"And then she skips into the house through one of the big windows."

IV

"Coketown!" droned the porter, making his way through the slowing car.

Pescud gathered his hat and baggage with the leisurely promptness of an old traveller.

"I married her a year ago," said John. "I told you I built a house in the East End. The belted—I mean the colonel—is there, too. I find him waiting at the gate whenever I get back from a trip to hear any new story I might have picked up on the road."

I glanced out of the window. Coketown was nothing more than a ragged hillside dotted with a score of black dismal huts propped up against dreary mounts of slag and clinkers. It rained in slanting torrents, too, and the rills foamed and splashed down through the black mud to the railroad-tracks.

"You won't sell much plate-glass here, John," said I. "Why do you get off at this end-o'-the-world?"

"Why," said Pescud, "the other day I took Jessie for a little trip to Philadelphia, and coming back she thought she saw some petunias in a pot in one of those windows over there just like some she used to raise down in the old Virginia home. So I thought I'd drop off here for the night, and see if I could dig up some of the cuttings or blossoms for her. Here we are. Goodnight, old man. I gave you the address. Come out and see us when you have time."

The train moved forward. One of the dotted brown ladies insisted on having windows raised, now that the rain beat against them. The porter came along with his mysterious wand and began to light the car.

I glanced downward and saw the best-seller. I picked it up and set it carefully farther along on the floor of the car. where the raindrops would not fall upon it. And then, suddenly, I smiled, and seemed to see that life has no geographical metes and bounds.

"Good-luck to you, Trevelyan," I said. "And may you get the petunias for your princess!"

RUS IN URBE

CONSIDERING men in relation to money, there are three kinds whom I dislike: men who have more money than they can spend; men who have more money than they do spend; and men who spend more money than they have. Of the three varieties, I believe I have the least liking for the first. But, as a man, I liked Spencer Grenville North pretty well, although he had something like two or ten or thirty millions—I've forgotten exactly how many.

I did not leave town that summer. I usually went down to a village on the south shore of Long Island. The place was surrounded by duck-farms, and the ducks and dogs and whip-poor-wills and rusty windmills made so much noise that I could sleep as peacefully as if I were in my own flat six doors from the elevated railroad in New York. But that summer I did not go. Remember that. One of my friends asked me why I did not. I replied: "Because, old man, New York is the finest summer resort in the world." You have heard that phrase before. But that is what I told him.

I was press-agent that year for Binkley & Bing, the theatrical managers and producers. Of course you know what a press-agent is. Well, he is not. That is the secret of being one.

Binkley was touring France in his new C. & N. Williamson car, and Bing had gone to Scotland to learn curling, which he seemed to associate in his mind with hot tongs rather than with ice. Before they left they gave me June and July, on salary, for my vacation, which act was in accord with their large spirit of liberality. But I remained in New York, which I had decided was the finest summer resort in——

But I said that before.

On July the 10th, North came to town from his camp in the Adirondacks. Try to imagine a camp with sixteen rooms, plumbing, eiderdown quilts, a butler, a garage, solid silver plate, and a long-distance telephone. Of course it was in the woods—if Mr. Pinchot wants to preserve the forests let him give every citizen two or ten or thirty million dollars, and the trees will all gather around the summer camps, as the Birnam woods came to Dunsinane, and be preserved.

North came to see me in my three rooms and bath, extra charge for light when used extravagantly or all night. He slapped me on the back (I would rather have my shins kicked any day), and greeted me with outdoor obstreperousness and revolting good spirits. He was insolently brown and healthy-looking, and offensively well dressed.

"Just ran down for a few days," said he, "to sign some papers and stuff like that. My lawyer wired me to come. Well, you indolent cockney, what are you doing in town? I took a chance and telephoned, and they said you were here. What's the matter with that Utopia on Long Island where you used to take your typewriter and your villainous temper every summer? Anything wrong with the—er—swans, weren't they, that used to sing on the farms at night?"

"Ducks," said I. "The songs of swans are for luckier ears. They swim and curve their necks in artificial lakes on the estates of the wealthy to delight the eyes of the favorites of Fortune."

"Also in Central Park," said North, "to delight the eyes of immigrants and bummers. I've seen 'em there lots of times. But why are you in the city so late in the summer?"

"New York City," I began to recite, "is the finest sum——"

"No, you don't," said North, emphatically. "You don't spring that old one on me. I know you know better. Man, you ought to have gone up with us this summer. The Prestons are there, and Tom Volney and the Monroes and Lulu Stanford and the Miss Kennedy and her aunt that you liked so well."

"I never liked Miss Kennedy's aunt," I said.

"I didn't say you did," said North. "We are having the greatest time we've ever had. The pickerel and trout are so ravenous that I believe they would swallow your hook with a Montana copper-mine prospectus fastened on it. And we've a couple of electric launches; and I'll tell you what we do every night or two—we tow a rowboat behind each one with a big phonograph and a boy to change the discs in 'em. On the water, and twenty yards behind you, they are not so bad. And there are passably good roads through the woods where we go motoring. I shipped two cars up there. And the Pinecliff Inn is only three miles away. You know the Pinecliff. Some good people are there this season, and we run over to the dances twice a week. Can't you go back with me for a week, old man?"

I laughed. "Northy," said I—"if I may be so familiar with a millionaire, because I hate both the names Spencer and Grenville—your invitation is meant kindly, but—the city in the summer-time for me. Here, while the *bourgeoisie* is away, I can live as Nero lived—barring, thank Heaven, the fiddling—while the city burns at ninety in the shade. The tropics and the zones wait upon me like handmaidens. I sit under Florida palms and eat pomegranates while Boreas himself, electrically conjured up, blows upon me his Arctic breath. As for trout, you know, yourself, that Jean, at Maurice's, cooks them better than any one else in the world."

"Be advised," said North. "My chef has pinched the blue ribbon from the lot. He lays some slices of bacon inside the trout, wraps it all in corn-husks—the husks of green corn, you know—buries them in hot ashes and covers them with live coals. We build fires on the bank of the lake and have fish suppers."

"I know," said I. "And the servants bring down tables and chairs and damask cloths, and you eat with silver forks. I know the kind of camps that you millionaires have. And there are champagne pails set about, disgracing the wild flowers, and, no doubt, Madame Tetrazzini to sing in the boat pavilion after the trout."

"Oh, no," said North, concernedly, "we were never as bad as that. We did have a variety troupe up from the city three or four nights, but they weren't stars by as far as light can travel in the same length of time. I always like a few home comforts even when I'm roughing it. But don't tell me you prefer to stay in the city during summer. I don't believe it. If you do, why did you spend your summers there for the last four years, even sneaking away from town on a night train, and refusing to tell your friends where this Arcadian village was?"

"Because," said I, "they might have followed me and discovered it. But since then I have learned that Amaryllis has come to town. The coolest things, the freshest, the brightest, the choicest, are to be found in the city. If you've nothing on hand this evening I will show you."

"I'm free," said North, "and I have my light car outside. I suppose, since you've been converted to the town, that your idea of rural sport is to have a little whirl between bicycle cops in Central Park and then a mug of sticky ale in some stuffy rathskeller under a fan that can't stir up as many revolutions in a week as Nicaragua can in a day."

"We'll begin with the spin through the Park, anyhow," I said. I was chok-

ing with the hot, stale air of my little apartment, and I wanted that breath of
the cool to brace me for the task of proving to my friend that New York was
the greatest—and so forth.

"Where can you find air any fresher or purer than this?" I asked, as we sped
into Central's boskiest dell.

"Air!" said North, contemptuously. "Do you call this air?—this muggy
vapor, smelling of garbage and gasoline smoke. Man, I wish you could get
one sniff of the real Adirondack article in the pine woods at daylight."

"I have heard of it," said I. "But for fragrance and tang and a joy in the
nostrils I would not give one puff of sea breeze across the bay, down on my little
boat dock on Long Island, for ten of your turpentine-scented tornadoes."

"Then why," asked North, a little curiously, "don't you go there instead of
staying cooped up in this Greater Bakery?"

"Because," said I, doggedly, "I have discovered that New York is the greatest
summer——"

"Don't say that again," interrupted North, "unless you've actually got a job
as General Passenger Agent of the Subway. You can't really believe it."

I went to some trouble to try to prove my theory to my friend. The Weather
Bureau and the season had conspired to make the argument worthy of an able
advocate.

The city seemed stretched on a broiler directly above the furnaces of Avernus.
There was a kind of tepid gayety afoot and awheel in the boulevards, mainly
evinced by languid men strolling about in straw hats and evening clothes, and
rows of idle taxicabs with their flags up, looking like a blockaded Fourth of July
procession. The hotels kept up a specious brilliancy and hospitable outlook, but
inside one saw vast empty caverns, and the footrails at the bars gleamed brightly
from long disaquaintance with the sole-leather of customers. In the cross-town
streets the steps of the old brown-stone houses were swarming with "stoopers,"
that motley race hailing from skylight room and basement, bringing out their
straw door-step mats to sit and fill the air with strange noises and opinions.

North and I dined on the top of a hotel; and here, for a few minutes, I
thought I had made a score. An east wind, almost cool, blew across the roofless
roof. A capable orchestra concealed in a bower of wistaria played with sufficient
judgment to make the art of music probable and the art of conversation possible.

Some ladies in reproachless summer gowns at other tables gave animation and
color to the scene. And an excellent dinner, mainly from the refrigerator,
seemed to successfully back my judgment as to summer resorts. But North
grumbled all during the meal, and cursed his lawyers and prated so of his confounded camp in the woods that I began to wish he would go back there and
leave me in my peaceful city retreat.

After dining we went to a roof-garden vaudeville that was being much praised.
There we found a good bill, an artificially cooled atmosphere, cold drinks, prompt
service, and a gay, well-dressed audience. North was bored.

"If this isn't comfortable enough for you on the hottest August night for five
years," I said, a little sarcastically, "you might think about the kids down in
Delancey and Hester streets lying out on the fire-escapes with their tongues
hanging out, trying to get a breath of air that hasn't been fried on both sides.
The contrast might increase your enjoyment."

"Don't talk Socialism," said North. "I gave five hundred dollars to the free
ice fund on the first of May. I'm contrasting these stale, artificial, hollow,
wearisome 'amusements' with the enjoyment a man can get in the woods. You
should see the firs and pines do skirt-dances during a storm; and lie down
flat and drink out of a mountain branch at the end of a day's tramp after the
deer. That's the only way to spend a summer. Get out and live with Nature."

"I agree with you absolutely," said I, with emphasis.

For one moment I had relaxed my vigilance, and had spoken my true sentiments. North looked at me long and curiously.

"Then why, in the name of Pan and Apollo," he asked, "have you been singing this deceitful pæan to summer in town?"

I suppose I looked my guilt.

"Ha," said North, "I see. May I ask her name?"

"Annie Ashton," said I, simply. "She played Nannette in Binkley & Bing's production of 'The Silver Cord.' She is to have a better part next season."

"Take me to see her," said North.

Miss Ashton lived with her mother in a small hotel. They were out of the West, and had a little money that bridged the seasons. As press-agent of Binkley & Bing I had tried to keep her before the public. As Robert James Vandiver, I had hoped to withdraw her; for if ever one was made to keep company with said Vandiver and smell the salt breeze on the south shore of Long Island and listen to the ducks quack in the watches of the night, it was the Ashton set forth above.

But she had a soul above ducks—above nightingales; aye, even above the birds of paradise. She was very beautiful, with quiet ways, and seemed genuine. She had both taste and talent for the stage, and she liked to stay at home and read and make caps for her mother. She was unvaryingly kind and friendly with Binkley & Bing's press-agent. Since the theatre had closed she had allowed Mr. Vandiver to call in an unofficial rôle. I had often spoken to her of my friend, Spencer Grenville North; and so, as it was early, the first turn of the vaudeville being not yet over, we left to find a telephone.

Miss Ashton would be very glad to see Mr. Vandiver and Mr. North.

We found her fitting a new cap on her mother. I never saw her look more charming.

North made himself disagreeably entertaining. He was a good talker, and had a way with him. Besides, he had two, ten, or thirty millions, I've forgotten which. I incautiously admired the mother's cap, whereupon she brought out her store of a dozen or two, and I took a course in edgings and frills. Even though Annie's fingers had pinked, or ruched, or hemmed, or whatever you do to 'em, they palled upon me. And I could hear North drivelling to Annie about his odious Adirondack camp.

Two days after that I saw North in his motor-car with Miss Ashton and her mother. On the next afternoon he dropped in on me.

"Bobby," said he, "this old burg isn't such a bad proposition in the summertime, after all. Since I've been knocking around it looks better to me. There are some first-rate musical comedies and light operas on the roofs and in the outdoor gardens. And if you hunt up the first places and stick to soft drinks, you can keep about as cool here as you can in the country. Hang it! when you come to think of it, there's nothing much to the country, anyhow. You get tired and sunburned and lonesome, and you have to eat any old thing that the cook dishes up to you."

"It makes a difference, doesn't it?" said I.

"It certainly does. Now, I found some whitebait yesterday, at Maurice's, with a new sauce that beats anything in the trout line I ever tasted."

"It makes a difference, doesn't it?" I said.

"Immense. The sauce is the main thing with whitebait."

"It makes a difference, doesn't it?" I asked, looking him straight in the eye. He understood.

"Look here, Bob," he said, "I was going to tell you. I couldn't help it. I'll play fair with you, but I'm going in to win. She is the 'one particular' for me."

"All right," said I. "It's a fair field. There are no rights for you to encroach upon."

On Thursday afternoon Miss Ashton invited North and myself to have tea in her apartment. He was devoted, and she was more charming than usual. By avoiding the subject of caps I managed to get a word or two into and out of the talk. Miss Ashton asked me in a make-conversational tone something about the next season's tour.

"Oh," said I, "I don't know about that. I'm not going to be with Binkley & Bing next season."

"Why, I thought," said she, "that they were going to put Number One road company under your charge. I thought you told me so."

"They were," said I, "but they won't. I'll tell you what I'm going to do. I'm going to the south shore of Long Island and buy a small cottage I know there on the edge of the bay. And I'll buy a catboat and a rowboat and a shotgun and a yellow dog. I've got money enough to do it. And I'll smell the salt wind all day when it blows from the sea and the pine odor when it blows from the land. And, of course, I'll write plays until I have a trunk full of 'em on hand.

"And the next thing and the biggest thing I'll do will be to buy that duck-farm next door. Few people understand ducks. I can watch 'em for hours. They can march better than any company in the National Guard, and they can play 'follow my leader' better than the entire Democratic party. Their voices don't amount to much, but I like to hear 'em. They wake you up a dozen times 'a night, but there's a homely sound about their quacking that is more musical to me than the cry of 'Fresh strawber-rees!' under your window in the morning when you want to sleep.

"And," I went on, enthusiastically, "do you know the value of ducks besides their beauty and intelligence and order and sweetness of voice? Picking their feathers gives an unfailing and never-ceasing income. On a farm that I know the feathers were sold for $400 in one year. Think of that! And the ones shipped to the market will bring in more money than that. Yes, I am for the ducks and the salt breeze coming over the bay. I think I shall get a Chinaman cook, and with him and the dog and the sunsets for company I shall do well. No more of this dull, baking, senseless, roaring city for me."

Miss Ashton looked surprised. North laughed.

"I am going to begin one of my plays tonight," I said, "so I must be going." And with that I took my departure.

A few days later Miss Ashton telephoned to me, asking me to call at four in the afternoon. I did.

"You have been very good to me," she said, hesitatingly, "and I thought I would tell you. I am going to leave the stage."

"Yes," said I, "I suppose you will. They usually do when there's so much money."

"There is no money," she said, "or very little. Our money is almost gone."

"But I am told," said I, "that he has something like two or ten or thirty millions—I have forgotten which."

"I know what you mean," she said. "I will not pretend that I do not. I am not going to marry Mr. North."

"Then why are you leaving the stage?" I asked, severely. "What else can you do to earn a living?"

She came closer to me, and I can see the look in her eyes yet as she spoke.

"I can pick ducks," she said.

We sold the first year's feathers for $350.

A POOR RULE

I HAVE always maintained, and asserted from time to time, that woman is no mystery; that man can foretell, construe, subdue, comprehend, and interpret her. That she is a mystery has been foisted by herself upon credulous mankind. Whether I am right or wrong we shall see. As "Harper's Drawer" used to say in bygone years: "The following good story is told of Miss——, Mr.—— Mr.——, and Mr.——."

We shall have to omit "Bishop X" and "the Rev.——," for they do not belong.

In those days Paloma was a new town on the line of the Southern Pacific. A reporter would have called it a "mushroom" town; but it was not. Paloma was first, and last, of the toadstool variety.

The train stopped there at noon for the engine to drink and for the passengers both to drink and to dine. There was a new yellow-pine hotel, also a wool ware-house, and perhaps three dozen box residences. The rest was composed of tents, cow ponies, "black-waxy" mud, and mesquite-trees, all bound round by a horizon. Paloma was an about-to-be city. The houses represented faith; the tents hope; the twice-a-day train, by which you might leave, creditably sustained the rôle of charity.

The Parisian Restaurant occupied the muddiest spot in the town while it rained, and the warmest when it shone. It was operated, owned, and perpe-trated by a citizen known as Old Man Hinkle, who had come out of Indiana to make his fortune in this land of condensed milk and sorghum.

There was a four-room, unpainted, weather-boarded box house in which the family lived. From the kitchen extended a "shelter" made of poles covered with chaparral brush. Under this was a table and two benches, each twenty feet long, the product of Paloma home carpentry. Here was set forth the roast mutton, the stewed apples, boiled beans, soda-biscuits, puddińorpie, and hot coffee of the Parisian menu.

Ma Hinkle and a subordinate known to the ears as "Betty," but denied to the eyesight, presided at the range. Pa Hinkle himself, with salamandrous thumbs, served the scalding viands. During rush hours a Mexican youth, who rolled and smoked cigarettes between courses, aided him in waiting on the guests. As is customary at Parisian banquets I placed the sweets at the end of my wordy menu.

Ileen Hinkle!

The spelling is correct, for I have seen her write it. No doubt she had been named by ear; but she so splendidly bore the orthography that Tom Moore him-self (had he seen her) would have endorsed the phonography.

Ileen was the daughter of the house, and the first Lady Cashier to invade the territory south of an east-and-west line drawn through Galveston and Del Rio. She sat on a high stool in a rough pine grand-stand—or was it a temple?—under the shelter at the door of the kitchen. There was a barbed-wire protection in front of her, with a little arch under which you passed your money. Heaven knows why the barbed wire; for every man who dined Parisianly there would have died in her service. Her duties were light; each meal was a dollar; you put it under the arch, and she took it.

I set out with the intent to describe Ileen Hinkle to you. Instead, I must refer you to the volume of Edmund Burke entitled: *A Philosophical Inquiry into the Origin of Our Ideas of the Sublime and Beautiful*. It is an exhaustive treatise, dealing first with the primitive conceptions of beauty—roundness and smoothness, I think they are, according to Burke. It is well said. Rotundity is a patent charm; as for smoothness—the more new wrinkles a woman acquires, the smoother she becomes.

Ileen was a strictly vegetable compound, guaranteed under the Pure Ambrosia and Balm-of-Gilead Act of the year of the fall of Adam. She was a fruit-stand blonde—strawberries, peaches, cherries, etc. Her eyes were wide apart, and she possessed the calm that precedes a storm that never comes. But it seems to me 'that words (at any rate per) are wasted in an effort to describe the beautiful. Like fancy, "It is engendered in the eyes." There are three kinds of beauties—I was foreordained to be homiletic; I can never stick to a story.

The first is the freckle-faced, snub-nosed girl whom you like. The second is Maud Adams. The third is, or are, the ladies in Bouguereau's paintings. Ileen Hinkle was the fourth. She was the mayoress of Spotless Town. There were a thousand golden apples coming to her as Helen of the Troy laundries.

The Parisian Restaurant was within a radius. Even from beyond its circumference men rode in to Paloma to win her smiles. They got them. One meal—one smile—one dollar. But, with all her impartiality, Ileen seemed to favor three of her admirers above the rest. According to the rules of politeness, I will mention myself last.

The first was an artificial product known as Bryan Jacks—a name that had obviously met with reverses. Jacks was the outcome of paved cities. He was a small man made of some material resembling flexible sandstone. His hair was the color of a brick Quaker meeting-house; his eyes were twin cranberries; his mouth was like the aperture under a drop-letters-here sign.

He knew every city from Bangor to San Francisco, thence north to Portland, thence S. 45 E. to a given point in Florida. He had mastered every art, trade, game, business, profession, and sport in the world, had been present at, or hurrying on his way to, every headline event that had occurred between oceans since he was five years old. You might open the atlas, place your finger at random upon the name of a town, and Jacks would tell you the front names of three prominent citizens before you could close it again. He spoke patronizingly and even disrespectfully of Broadway, Beacon Hill, Michigan, Euclid, and Fifth avenues, and the St. Louis Four Courts. Compared with him as a cosmopolite, the Wandering Jew would have seemed a mere hermit. He had learned everything the world could teach him, and he would tell you about it.

I hate to be reminded of Pollok's "Course of Time," and so do you; but every time I saw Jacks I would think of the poet's description of another poet by the name of G. G. Byron who "Drank early; deeply drank—drank draughts that common millions might have quenched; then died of thirst because there was no more to drink."

That fitted Jacks, except that, instead of dying, he came to Paloma, which was about the same thing. He was a telegrapher and station-and-express agent at seventy-five dollars a month. Why a young man who knew everything and could do everything was content to serve in such an obscure capacity i never could understand, although he let out a hint once that it was as a personal favor to the president and stockholders of the S. P. Ry. Co.

One more line of description, and I turn Jacks over to you. He wore bright blue clothes, yellow shoes, and a bow tie made of the same cloth as his shirt.

My rival No. 2 was Bud Cunningham, whose services had been engaged by a ranch near Paloma to assist in compelling refractory cattle to keep within the bounds of decorum and order. Bud was the only cowboy off the stage that I ever saw who looked like one on it. He wore the sombrero, the chaps, and the handkerchief tied at the back of his neck.

Twice a week Bud rode in from the Val Verde Ranch to sup at the Parisian Restaurant. He rode a many-high-handed Kentucky horse at a tremendously fast lope, which animal he would rein up so suddenly under the big mesquite at the corner of the brush shelter that his hoofs would plough canals yards long in the loam.

Jacks and I were regular boarders at the restaurant, of course.

The front room of the Hinkle House was as neat a little parlor as there was in the black-waxy country. It was all willow rocking-chairs, and home-knit tidies, and albums, and conch shells in a row. And a little upright piano in one corner.

Here Jacks and Bud and I—or sometimes one or two of us, according to our good-luck—used to sit of evenings when the tide of trade was over, and "visit" Miss Hinkle.

Ileen was a girl of ideas. She was destined for higher things (if there can be anything higher) than taking in dollars all day through a barbed-wire wicket. She had read and listened and thought. Her looks would have formed a career for a less ambitious girl; but, rising superior to mere beauty, she must establish something in the nature of a *salon*—the only one in Paloma.

"Don't you think that Shakespeare was a great writer?" she would ask, with such a pretty little knit of her arched brows that the late Ignatius Donnelly, himself, had he seen it, could scarcely have saved his Bacon.

Ileen was of the opinion, also, that Boston is more cultured than Chicago; that Rosa Bonheur was one of the greatest of women painters; that Westerners are more spontaneous and open-hearted than Easterners; that London must be a very foggy city, and that California must be quite lovely in the springtime. And of many other opinions indicating a keeping up with the world's best thought.

These, however, were but gleaned from hearsay and evidence: Ileen had theories of her own. One, in particular, she disseminated to us untiringly. Flattery she detested. Frankness and honesty of speech and action, she declared, were the chief mental ornaments of man and woman. If ever she could like any one, it would be for those qualities.

"I'm awfully weary," she said, one evening, when we three musketeers of the mesquite were in the little parlor, "of having compliments on my looks paid to me. I know I'm not beautiful."

(Bud Cunningham told me afterward that it was all he could do to keep from calling her a liar when she said that.)

"I'm only a little Middle-Western girl," went on Ileen, "who just wants to be simple and neat, and tries to help her father make a humble living."

(Old Man Hinkle was shipping a thousand silver dollars a month, clear profit, to a bank in San Antonio.)

Bud twisted around in his chair and bent the rim of his hat, from which he could never be persuaded to separate. He did not know whether she wanted what she said she wanted or what she knew she deserved. Many a wiser man has hesitated at deciding. Bud decided.

"Why—ah, Miss Ileen, beauty, as you might say, ain't everything. Not sayin' that you haven't your share of good looks, I always admired more than anything else about you the nice, kind way you treat your ma and pa. Any one what's good to their parents and is a kind of home-body don't specially need to be too pretty."

Ileen gave him one of her sweetest smiles. "Thank you, Mr. Cunningham," she said. "I consider that one of the finest compliments I've had in a long time. I'd so much rather hear you say that than to hear you talk about my eyes and hair. I'm glad you believe me when I say I don't like flattery."

Our cue was there for us. Bud had made a good guess. You couldn't lose Jacks. He chimed in next.

"Sure thing, Miss Ileen," he said; "the good-lookers don't always win out. Now, you ain't bad looking, of course—but that's nix-cum-rous. I knew a girl once in Dubuque with a face like a cocoanut, who could skin the cat twice on a horizontal bar without changing hands. Now, a girl might have the California peach crop mashed to a marmalade and not be able to do that. I've seen—er—worse lookers than *you*, Miss Ileen; but what I like about you is the business way you've got of doings things. Cool and wise—that's the winning way for a girl. Mr. Hinkle told me the other day you'd never taken in a lead silver dollar or a plugged one since you've been on the job. Now, that's the stuff for a girl—that's what catches me."

Jacks got his smile, too.

"Thank you, Mr. Jacks," said Ileen. "If you only knew how I appreciate any one's being candid and not a flatterer! I get so tired of people telling me I'm pretty. I think it is the loveliest thing to have friends who tell you the truth."

Then I thought I saw an expectant look on Ileen's face as she glanced toward me. I had a wild, sudden impulse to dare fate, and tell her of all the beautiful handiwork of the Great Artificer she was the most exquisite—that she was a flawless pearl gleaming pure and serene in a setting of black mud and emerald prairies—that she was—a—a corker; and that as for mine, I cared not if she were as cruel as a serpent's tooth to her fond parents, or if she couldn't tell a plugged dollar from a bridle buckle, if I might sing, chant, praise, glorify, and worship her peerless and wonderful beauty.

But I refrained. I feared the fate of a flatterer. I had witnessed her delight at the crafty and discreet words of Bud and Jacks. No! Miss Hinkle was not one to be beguiled by the plated-silver tongue of a flatterer. So I joined the ranks of the candid and honest. At once I became mendacious and didactic.

"In all ages, Miss Hinkle," said I, "in spite of the poetry and romance of each, intellect in woman has been admired more than beauty. Even in Cleopatra, herself, men found more a charm in her queenly mind than in her looks."

"Well, I should think so!" said Ileen. "I've seen pictures of her that weren't so much. She had an awfully long nose."

"If I may say so," I went on, "you remind me of Cleopatra, Miss Ileen."

"Why, my nose isn't so long!" said she, opening her eyes wide and touching that comely feature with a dimpled forefinger.

"Why—er—I mean," said I—"I mean as to mental endowments."

"Oh!" said she; and then I got my smile just as Bud and Jacks got theirs.

"Thank every one of you," she said, very, very sweetly, "for being so frank and honest with me. That's the way I want you to be always. Just tell me plainly and truthfully what you think, and we'll all be the best friends in the world. And now, because you've been so good to me, and understand so well how I dislike people who do nothing but pay me exaggerated compliments, I'll sing and play a little for you."

Of course, we expressed our thanks and joy; would have been better pleased if Ileen had remained in her low rocking-chair face to face with us and let us gaze upon her. For she was no Adelina Patti—not even on the farewellest of the diva's farewell tours. She had a cooing little voice like that of a turtle-dove that could almost fill the parlor when the windows and doors were closed, and Betty was not rattling the lids of the stove in the kitchen. She had a gamut that I estimate at about eight inches on the piano; and her runs and trills sounded like the clothes bubbling in your grandmother's iron washpot. Believe that she must have been beautiful when I tell you that it sounded like music to us.

Ileen's musical taste was catholic. She would sing through a pile of sheet music on the left-hand top of the piano, laying each slaughtered composition on the right-hand top. The next evening she would sing from right to left. Her favorites were Mendelssohn, and Moody and Sankey. By request she always wound up with "Sweet Violets" and "When the Leaves Begin to Turn."

When we left at ten o'clock the three of us would go down to Jack's little wooden station and sit on the platform, swinging our feet and trying to pump one another for clues as to which way Miss Ileen's inclinations seemed to lean. That is the way of rivals—they do not avoid and glower at one another; they convene and converse and construe—striving by the art politic to estimate the strength of the enemy.

One day there came a dark horse to Paloma, a young lawyer who at once flaunted his shingle and himself spectacularly upon the town. His name was C. Vincent Vesey. You could see at a glance that he was a recent graduate of a Southwestern law school. His Prince Albert coat, light striped trousers, broad-brimmed soft black hat, and narrow white muslin bow tie proclaimed that more loudly than any diploma could. Vesey was a compound of Daniel Webster, Lord Chesterfield, Beau Brummel, and Little Jack Horner. His coming boomed Paloma. The next day after he arrived an addition to the town was surveyed and laid off in lots.

Of course, Vesey, to further his professional fortunes, must mingle with the citizenry and outliers of Paloma. And, as well as with the soldier men, he was bound to seek popularity with the gay dogs of the place. So Jacks and Bud Cunningham and I came to be honored by his acquaintance.

The doctrine of predestination would have been discredited had not Vesey seen Ileen Hinkle and become fourth in the tourney. Magnificently, he boarded at the yellow-pine hotel instead of at the Parisian Restaurant; but he came to be a formidable visitor in the Hinkle parlor. His competition reduced Bud to an inspired increase of profanity, drove Jacks to an outburst of slang so weird that it sounded more horrible than the most trenchant of Bud's imprecations, and made me dumb with gloom.

For Vesey had the rhetoric. Words flowed from him like oil from a gusher. Hyperbole, compliment, praise, appreciation, honeyed gallantry, golden opinions, eulogy, and unveiled panegyric vied with one another for preeminence in his speech. We had small hopes that Ileen could resist his oratory and Prince Albert.

But a day came that gave us courage.

About dusk one evening I was sitting on the little gallery in front of the Hinkle parlor, waiting for Ileen to come, when I heard voices inside. She had come into the room with her father, and Old Man Hinkle began to talk to her. I had observed before that he was a shrewd man, and not unphilosophic.

"Ily," said he, "I notice there's three or four young fellers that have been callin' to see you regular for quite a while. Is there any one of 'em you like better than another?"

"Why, pa," she answered, "I like all of 'em very well. I think Mr. Cunningham and Mr. Jacks and Mr. Harris are very nice young men. They are so frank and honest in everything they say to me. I haven't known Mr. Vesey very long, but I think he's a very nice young man, he's so frank and honest in everything he says to me."

"Now, that's what I'm gittin' at," says old Hinkle. "You've always been sayin' you like people what tell the truth and don't go humbuggin' you with compliments and bogus talk. Now, suppose you make a test of these fellers, and see which one of 'em will talk the straightest to you."

"But how'll I do it, pa?"

"I'll tell you how. You know you sing a little bit, Ily; you took music lessons nearly two years in Logansport. It wasn't long, but it was all we could afford then. And your teacher said you didn't have any voice, and it was a waste of money to keep on. Now, suppose you ask the fellers what they think of your singin', and see what each one of 'em tells you. The man that'll tell you the truth about it'll have a mighty lot of nerve, and 'll do to tie to. What do you think of the plan?"

"All right, pa," said Ileen. "I think it's a good idea. I'll try it."

Ileen and Mr. Hinkle went out of the room through the inside door. Unobserved, I hurried down to the station. Jacks was at his telegraph table waiting for eight o'clock to come. It was Bud's night in town, and when he rode in I repeated the conversation to them both. I was loyal to my rivals, as all true admirers of all Ileens should be.

Simultaneously the three of us were smitten by an uplifting thought. Surely this test would eliminate Vesey from the contest. He, with his unctuous flattery, would be driven from the lists. Well we remembered Ileen's love of frankness and honesty—how she treasured truth and candor above vain compliment and blandishment.

Linking arms, we did a grotesque dance of joy up and down the platform, singing "Muldoon Was a Solid Man" at the top of our voices.

That evening four of the willow rocking-chairs were filled besides the lucky one that sustained the trim figure of Miss Hinkle. Three of us waited with suppressed excitement the application of the test. It was tried on Bud first.

"Mr. Cunningham," said Ileen, with her dazzling smile, after she had sung "When the Leaves Begin to Turn," "what do you really think of my voice? Frankly and honestly, now, as you know I want you to always be toward me."

Bud squirmed in his chair at his chance to show the sincerity that he knew was required of him.

"Tell you the truth, Miss Ileen," he said, earnestly, "you ain't got much more voice than a weasel—just a little squeak, you know. Of course, we all like to hear you sing, for it's kind of sweet and soothin' after all, and you look most mighty well sittin' on the piano-stool as you do faced around. But as for real singin'—I reckon you couldn't call it that."

I looked closely at Ileen to see if Bud had overdone his frankness, but her pleased smile and sweetly spoken thanks assured me that we were on the right track.

"And what do you think, Mr. Jacks?" she asked next.

"Take it from me," said Jacks, "you ain't in the prima donna class. I've heard 'em warble in every city in the United States; and I tell you your vocal output don't go. Otherwise, you've got the grand opera bunch sent to the soap factory—in looks, I mean; for the high screeches generally look like Mary Ann on her Thursday out. But nix for the gargle work. Your epiglottis ain't a real side-stepper—its footwork ain't good."

With a merry laugh at Jack's criticism, Ileen looked inquiringly at me.

I admit that I faltered a little. Was there not such a thing as being too frank? Perhaps I even hedged a little in my verdict; but I stayed with the critics.

"I am not skilled in scientific music, Miss Ileen," I said, "but frankly I cannot praise very highly the singing voice that Nature has given you. It has long been a favorite comparison that a great singer sings like a bird. Well, there are birds and birds. I would say that your voice reminds me of the thrush's—throaty and not strong, nor of much compass or variety—but still—er—sweet—in—er—its—way, and—er——"

"Thank you, Mr. Harris," interrupted Miss Hinkle. "I knew I could depend upon your frankness and honesty."

And then C. Vincent Vesey drew back one sleeve from his snowy cuff, and the water came down at Lodore.

My memory cannot do justice to his masterly tribute to that priceless, God-given treasure—Miss Hinkle's voice. He raved over it in terms that, if they had been addressed to the morning stars when they sang together, would have made that stellar choir explode in a meteoric shower of flaming self-satisfaction.

He marshalled on his white finger-tips the grand opera stars of all the continents, from Jenny Lind to Emma Abbott, only to depreciate their endowments.

He spoke of larynxes, of chest notes, of phrasing, arpeggios, and other strange paraphernalia of the throaty art. He admitted, as though driven to a corner, that Jenny Lind had a note or two in the high register that Miss Hinkle had not yet acquired—but—"!!!"—that was a mere matter of practice and training.

And, as a peroration, he predicted—solemnly predicted—a career in vocal art for the "coming star of the Southwest—and one of which grand old Texas may well be proud," hitherto unsurpassed in the annals of musical history.

When we left at ten, Ileen gave each of us her usual warm, cordial handshake, entrancing smile, and invitation to call again. I could not see that one was favored above or below another—but three of us knew—we knew.

We knew that frankness and honesty had won, and that the rivals now numbered three instead of four.

Down at the station Jacks brought out a pint bottle of the proper stuff, and we celebrated the downfall of a blatant interloper.

Four days went by without anything happening worthy of recount.

On the fifth, Jacks and I, entering the brush arbor for our supper, saw the Mexican youth, instead of a divinity in a spotless waist and a navy-blue skirt, taking in the dollars through the barbed-wire wicket.

We rushed into the kitchen, meeting Pa Hinkle coming out with two cups of hot coffee in his hands.

"Where's Ileen?" we asked, in recitative.

Pa Hinkle was a kindly man. "Well, gents," said he, "it was a sudden notion she took; but I've got the money, and I let her have her way. She's gone to a corn—a conservatory in Boston for four years for to have her voice cultivated. Now, excuse me to pass, gents, for this coffee's hot, and my thumbs is tender."

That night there were four instead of three of us sitting on the station platform and swinging our feet. C. Vincent Vesey was one of us. We discussed things while dogs barked at the moon that rose, as big as a five-cent piece or a flour-barrel, over the chaparral.

And what we discussed was whether it is better to lie to a woman or to tell her the truth.

And as all of us were young then, we did not come to a decision.

SIXES AND SEVENS

SIXES AND SEVENS

THE LAST OF THE TROUBADOURS

INEXORABLY Sam Galloway saddled his pony. He was going away from the Rancho Altito at the end of a three months' visit. It is not to be expected that a guest should put up with wheat coffee and biscuits yellow-streaked with saleratus for longer than that. Nick Napoleon, the big Negro man cook, had never been able to make good biscuits. Once before, when Nick was cooking at the Willow Ranch, Sam had been forced to fly from his *cuisine*, after only a six weeks' sojourn.

On Sam's face was an expression of sorrow, deepened with regret and slightly tempered by the patient forgiveness of a connoisseur who cannot be understood. But very firmly and inexorably he buckled his saddle-cinches, looped his stake-rope and hung it to his saddle-horn, tied his slicker and coat on the cantle, and looped his quirt on his right wrist. The Merrydews (householders of the Rancho Altito), men, women, children, and servants, vassals, visitors, employés, dogs, and casual callers were grouped in the "gallery" of the ranch house, all with face set to the tune of melancholy and grief. For, as the coming of Sam Galloway to any ranch, camp, or cabin between the rivers Frio or Bravo del Norte aroused joy, so his departure caused mourning and distress.

And then, during absolute silence, except for the bumping of a hind elbow of a hound dog as he pursued a wicked flea, Sam tenderly and carefully tied his guitar across his saddle on top of his slicker and coat. The guitar was in a green duck bag; and if you catch the significance of it, it explains Sam.

Sam Galloway was the Last of the Troubadours. Of course you know about the troubadours. The encyclopædia says they flourished between the eleventh and the thirteenth centuries. What they flourished doesn't seem clear—you may be pretty sure it wasn't a sword: maybe it was a fiddlebow, or a forkful of spaghetti, or a lady's scarf. Anyhow, Sam Galloway was one of 'em.

Sam put on a martyred expression as he mounted his pony. But the expression on his face was hilarious compared with the one on his pony's. You see, a pony gets to know his rider mighty well, and it is not unlikely that cow ponies in pastures and at hitching racks had often guyed Sam's pony for being ridden by a guitar player instead of by a rollicking, cussing, all-wool cowboy. No man is a hero to his saddle-horse. And even an escalator in a department store might be excused for tripping up a troubadour.

Oh, I know I'm one; and so are you. You remember the stories you memorize and the card tricks you study and that little piece on the piano—how does it go——ti-tum-te-tum-ti-tum——those little Arabian Ten-Minute Entertainments that you furnish when you go up to call on your rich Aunt Jane. You should know that *omnæ personæ in tres partes divisæ sunt.* Namely: Barons, Troubadours, and Workers. Barons have no inclination to read such folderol as this; and Workers have no time: so I know you must be a Troubadour, and that you will understand Sam Galloway. Whether we sing, act, dance, write, lecture, or paint, we are only troubadours; so let us make the worst of it.

The pony with the Dante Alighieri face, guided by the pressure of Sam's knees, bore that wandering minstrel sixteen miles southeastward. Nature was in her most benignant mood. League after league of delicate, sweet flowerets made fragrant the gently undulating prairie. The east wind tempered the spring warmth; wool-white clouds flying in from the Mexican Gulf hindered the direct rays of the April sun. Sam sang songs as he rode. Under his pony's bridle he had tucked some sprigs of chaparral to keep away the deer flies. Thus crowned, the long-faced quadruped looked more Dantesque than before, and, judging by his countenance, seemed to think of Beatrice.

Straight as topography permitted, Sam rode to the sheep ranch of old man Ellison. A visit to a sheep ranch seemed to him desirable just then. There had been too many people, too much noise, argument, competition, confusion, at Rancho Altito. He had never conferred upon old man Ellison the favour of sojourning at his ranch; but he knew he would be welcome. The troubadour is his own passport everywhere. The Workers in the castle let down the draw-bridge to him, and the Baron sets him at his left hand at table in the banquet hall. There ladies smile upon him and applaud his songs and stories, while the Workers bring boars' heads and flagons. If the Baron nods once or twice in his carved oaken chair, he does not do it maliciously.

Old man Ellison welcomed the troubadour flatteringly. He had often heard praises of Sam Galloway from other ranchmen who had been complimented by his visits, but had never aspired to such an honor for his own humble barony. I say barony because old man Ellison was the Last of the Barons. Of course, Mr. Bulwer-Lytton lived too early to know him or he wouldn't have conferred that sobriquet upon Warwick. In life it is the duty and the function of the Baron to provide work for the Workers and lodging and shelter for the Troubadours.

Old man Ellison was a shrunken old man, with a short, yellow-white beard and a face lined and seamed by past-and-gone trouble. His ranch was a little two-room box house in a grove of hackberry trees in the lonesomest part of the sheep country. His household consisted of a Kiowa Indian man cook, four hounds, a pet sheep, and a half-tamed coyote chained to a fence-post. He owned 3,000 sheep, which he ran on two sections of leased land and many thousands of acres neither leased nor owned. Three or four times a year some one who spoke his language would ride up to his gate and exchange a few bald ideas with him. Those were red-letter days to old man Ellison. Then in what illuminated, embossed, and gorgeously decorated capitals must have been written the day on which a troubadour—a troubadour who, according to the encyclopædia, should have flourished between the eleventh and the thirteenth centuries—drew rein at the gates of his baronial castle!

Old man Ellison's smiles came back and filled his wrinkles when he saw Sam. He hurried out of the house in his shuffling, limping way to greet him.

"Hello, Mr. Ellison," called Sam, cheerfully. "Thought I'd drop over and see you a while. Notice you've had fine rains on your range. They ought to make good grazing for your spring lambs."

"Well, well, well," said old man Ellison. "I'm mighty glad to see you, Sam. I never thought you'd take the trouble to ride over to as out-of-the-way an old ranch as this. But you're mighty welcome. 'Light. I've got a sack of new oats in the kitchen—shall I bring out a feed for your hoss?"

"Oats for him?" said Sam, derisively. "No, sir-ee. He's as fat as a pig now on grass. He don't get rode enough to keep him in condition. I'll just turn him in the horse pasture with a drag rope on if you don't mind."

I am positive that never during the eleventh and thirteenth centuries did Baron, Troubadour, and Worker amalgamate as harmoniously as their parallels did that evening at old man Ellison's sheep ranch. The Kiowa's biscuits were light and tasty and his coffee strong. Ineradicable hospitality and appreciation glowed on old man Ellison's weather-tanned face. As for the troubadour, he said to himself that he had stumbled upon pleasant places indeed. A well-cooked, abundant meal, a host whom his lightest attempt to entertain seemed to delight far beyond the merits of the exertion, and the reposeful atmosphere that his sensitive soul at that time craved united to confer upon him a satisfaction and luxurious ease that he had seldom found on his tours of the ranches.

After the delectable supper, Sam untied the green duck bag and took out his guitar. Not by way of payment, mind you—neither Sam Galloway nor any other of the true troubadours are lineal descendants of the late Tommy Tucker. You have read of Tommy Tucker in the works of the esteemed but often obscure Mother Goose. Tommy Tucker sang for his supper. No true troubadour would do that. He would have his supper, and then sing for Art's sake.

Sam Galloway's repertoire comprised about fifty funny stories and between thirty and forty songs. He by no means stopped there. He could talk through twenty cigarettes on any topic that you brought up. And he never sat up when he could lie down; and never stood when he could sit. I am strongly disposed to linger with him, for I am drawing a portrait as well as a blunt pencil and a tattered thesaurus will allow.

I wish you could have seen him: he was small and tough and inactive beyond the power of imagination to conceive. He wore an ultramarine-blue woollen shirt laced down the front with a pearl-gray, exaggerated sort of shoestring, indestructible brown duck clothes, inevitable high-heeled boots with Mexican spurs, and a Mexican straw sombrero.

That evening Sam and old man Ellison dragged their chairs out under the hackberry trees. They lighted cigarettes; and the troubadour gaily touched his guitar. Many of the songs he sang were the weird, melancholy, minor-keyed *canciones* that he had learned from the Mexican sheep herders and *vaqueros*. One, in particular, charmed and soothed the soul of the lonely baron. It was a favourite song of the sheep herders, beginning: "*Huile, huile, palomita,*" which being translated means, "Fly, fly, little dove." Sam sang it for old man Ellison many times that evening.

The troubadour stayed on at the old man's ranch. There was peace and quiet and appreciation there, such as he had not found in the noisy camps of the cattle kings. No audience in the world could have crowned the work of poet, musician, or artist with more worshipful and unflagging approval than that bestowed upon his efforts by old man Ellison. No visit by a royal personage to a humble woodchopper or peasant could have been received with more flattering thankfulness and joy.

On a cool, canvas-covered cot in the shade of the hackberry trees Sam Galloway passed the greater part of his time. There he rolled his brown paper cigarettes, read such tedious literature as the ranch afforded, and added to his repertoire of improvisations that he played so expertly on his guitar. To him, as a slave ministering to a great lord, the Kiowa brought cool water from the red jar hanging under the brush shelter, and food when he called for it. The prairie zephyrs fanned him mildly; mocking-birds at morn and eve competed with but scarce equalled the sweet melodies of his lyre; a perfumed stillness seemed to fill all his world. While old man Ellison was pottering among his flocks of sheep on his mile-an-hour pony, and while the Kiowa took his siesta in the burning sunshine at the end of the kitchen, Sam would lie on his cot thinking what a happy world he lived in, and how kind it is to the ones whose mission in life it is to give entertainment and pleasure. Here he had food and lodging as good as he had ever longed for; absolute immunity from care or exertion or strife; an endless welcome, and a host whose delight at the sixteenth repetition of a song or a story was as keen as at its initial giving. Was there ever a troubadour of old who struck upon as royal a castle in his wanderings? While he lay thus, meditating upon his blessings, little brown cottontails would shyly frolic through the yard; a covey of white-topknotted blue quail would run past, in single file, twenty yards away; a *paisano* bird, out hunting for tarantulas, would hop upon the fence and salute him with sweeping flourishes of its long tail. In the eighty-acre horse pasture the pony with the Dantesque face grew fat and almost smiling. The troubadour was at the end of his wanderings.

Old man Ellison was his own *vaciero*. That means that he supplied his sheep camps with wood, water, and rations by his own labors instead of hiring a *vaciero*. On small ranches it is often done.

One morning he started for the camp of Encarnación Felipe de la Cruz y Monto Piedras (one of his sheep herders) with the week's usual rations of brown beans, coffee, meal, and sugar. Two miles away on the trail from old Fort Ewing he met, face to face, a terrible being called King James, mounted on a fiery, prancing, Kentucky-bred horse.

King James's real name was James King; but people reversed it because it seemed to fit him better, and also because it seemed to please his majesty. King James was the biggest cattleman between the Alamo plaza in San Antone and Bill Hopper's saloon in Brownsville. Also he was the loudest and most offensive bully and braggart and bad man in southwest Texas. And he always made good whenever he bragged; and the more noise he made the more dangerous he was. In the story papers it is always the quiet, mild-mannered man with light blue eyes and a low voice who turns out to be really dangerous; but in real life and in this story such is not the case. Give me my choice between assaulting a large, loud-mouthed rough-houser and an inoffensive stranger with blue eyes sitting quietly in a corner, and you will see something doing in the corner every time.

King James, as I intended to say earlier, was a fierce, two-hundred-pound, sun-burned, blond man, as pink as an October strawberry, and with two horizontal slits under shaggy red eyebrows for eyes. On that day he wore a flannel shirt that was tan-colored, with the exception of certain large areas which were darkened by transudations due to the summer sun. There seemed to be other clothing and garnishings about him, such as brown duck trousers stuffed into immense boots, and red handkerchiefs and revolvers; and a shotgun laid across his saddle and a leather belt with millions of cartridges shining in it—but your mind skidded off such accessories; what held your gaze was just the two little horizontal slits that he used for eyes.

This was the man that old man Ellison met on the trail; and when you count up in the baron's favor that he was sixty-five and weighed ninety-eight pounds and had heard of King James's record and that he (the baron) had a hankering for the *vita simplex* and had no gun with him and wouldn't have used it if he had, you can't censure him if I tell you that the smiles with which the troubadour had filled his wrinkles went out of them and left them plain wrinkles again. But he was not the kind of baron that flies from danger. He reined in the mile-an-hour pony (no difficult feat), and saluted the formidable monarch.

King James expressed himself with royal directness.

"You're that old snoozer that's running sheep on this range, ain't you?" said he. "What right have you got to do it? Do you own the land, or lease any?"

"I have two sections leased from the state," said old man Ellison, mildly.

"Not by no means, you haven't," said King James. "Your lease expired yesterday; and I had a man at the land office on the minute to take it up. You don't control a foot of grass in Texas. You sheep men have got to git. Your time's up. It's a cattle country, and there ain't any room in it for snoozers. This range you've got your sheep on is mine. I'm putting up a wire fence, forty by sixty miles; and if there's a sheep inside of it when it's done it'll be a dead one. I'll give you a week to move yours away. If they ain't gone by then, I'll send six men over here with Winchesters to make mutton out of the whole lot. And if I find you here at the same time this is what you'll get."

King James patted the breech of his shotgun warningly.

Old man Ellison rode on to the camp of Encarnación. He sighed many times, and the wrinkles in his face grew deeper. Rumors that the old order was about to change had reached him before. The end of Free Grass was in sight. Other troubles, too, had been accumulating upon his shoulders. His flocks were decreasing instead of growing; the price of wool was declining at every clip; even Bradshaw, the storekeeper at Frio City, at whose store he bought his ranch supplies, was dunning him for his last six months' bill and threatening to cut him off. And so this last greatest calamity suddenly dealt out to him by the terrible King James was a crusher.

When the old man got back to the ranch at sunset he found Sam Galloway lying on his cot, propped against a roll of blankets and wool sacks, fingering his guitar.

"Hello, Uncle Ben," the troubadour called, cheerfully. "You rolled in early this evening. I been trying a new twist on the Spanish Fandango to-day. I just about got it. Here's how she goes—listen."

"That's fine, that's mighty fine," said old man Ellison, sitting on the kitchen step and rubbing his white, Scotch-terrier whiskers. "I reckon you've got all the musicians beat east and west, Sam, as far as the roads are cut out."

"Oh, I don't know," said Sam reflectively. "But I certainly do get there on variations. I guess I can handle anything in five flats about as well as any of 'em. But you look kind of fagged out, Uncle Ben—ain't you feeling right well this evening?"

"Little tired; that's all, Sam. If you ain't played yourself out, let's have that Mexican piece that starts off with: '*Huile, huile, palomita.*' It seems that that song always kind of soothes and comforts me after I've been riding far or anything bothers me."

"Why, *seguramente, señor*," said Sam. "I'll hit her up for you as often as you like. And before I forget about it, Uncle Ben, you want to jerk Bradshaw up about them last hams he sent us. They're just a little bit strong."

A man sixty-five years old, living on a sheep ranch and beset by a complication of disasters, cannot successfully and continuously dissemble. Moreover, a troubadour has eyes quick to see unhappiness in others around him—because it disturbs his own ease. So, on the next day, Sam again questioned the old man about his air of sadness and abstraction. Then old man Ellison told him the story of King James's threats and orders and that pale melancholy and red ruin appeared to have marked him for their own. The troubadour took the news thoughtfully. He had heard much about King James.

On the third day of the seven days of grace allowed him by the autocrat of the range, old man Ellison drove his buckboard to Frio City to fetch some necessary supplies for the ranch. Bradshaw was hard but not implacable. He divided the old man's order by two, and let him have a little more time. One article secured was a new, fine ham for the pleasure of the troubadour.

Five miles out of Frio City on his way home the old man met King James riding into town. His majesty could never look anything but fierce and menacing, but to-day his slits of eyes appeared to be a little wider than they usually were.

"Good day," said the king, gruffly. "I've been wanting to see you. I hear it said by a cowman from Sandy yesterday that you was from Jackson County, Mississippi, originally. I want to know if that's a fact."

"Born there," said old man Ellison, "and raised there till I was twenty-one."

"This man says," went on King James, "that he thinks you was related to the Jackson County Reeveses. Was he right?"

"Aunt Caroline Reeves," said the old man, "was my half-sister."

"She was my aunt," said King James. "I run away from home when I was sixteen. Now, let's re-talk over some things that we discussed a few days ago. They call me a bad man; and they're only half right. There's plenty of room in my pasture for your bunch of sheep and their increase for a long time to come. Aunt Caroline used to cut out sheep in cake dough and bake 'em for me. You keep your sheep where they are, and use all the range you want. How's your finances?"

The old man related his woes in detail, dignifiedly, with restraint and candor.

"She used to smuggle extra grub into my school basket—I'm speaking of Aunt Caroline," said King James. "I'm going over to Frio City to-day, and I'll ride back by your ranch to-morrow. I'll draw $2,000 out of the bank there and bring it over to you; and I'll tell Bradshaw to let you have anything you want on credit. You are bound to have heard the old saying at home, that the Jackson County Reeveses and Kings would stick closer by each other than chestnut burrs. Well, I'm a King yet whenever I run across a Reeves. So you look out for me along about sundown to-morrow, and don't you worry about nothing. Shouldn't wonder if the dry spell don't kill out the young grass."

Old man Ellison drove happily ranchward. Once more the smiles filled out his wrinkles. Very suddenly, by the magic of kinship and the good that lies somewhere in all hearts, his troubles had been removed.

On reaching the ranch he found that Sam Galloway was not there. His guitar hung by its buckskin string to a hackberry limb, moaning as the gulf breeze blew across its masterless strings.

The Kiowa endeavored to explain.

"Sam, he catch pony," said he, "and say he ride to Frio City. What for no can damn sabe. Say he come back to-night. Maybe so. That all."

As the first stars came out the troubadour rode back to his haven. He pastured his pony and went into the house, his spurs jingling martially.

Old man Ellison sat at the kitchen table, having a tin cup of before-supper coffee. He looked contented and pleased.

"Hello, Sam," said he, "I'm darned glad to see ye back. I don't know how I managed to get along on this ranch, anyhow, before ye dropped in to cheer things up. I'll bet ye've been skylarking around with some of them Frio City gals, now, that's kept ye so late."

And then old man Ellison took another look at Sam's face and saw that the minstrel had changed to the man of action.

And while Sam is unbuckling from his waist old man Ellison's six-shooter, that the latter had left behind when he drove to town, we may well pause to remark that anywhere and whenever a troubadour lays down the guitar and takes up the sword trouble is sure to follow. It is not the expert thrust of Athos nor the cold skill of Aramis nor the iron wrist of Porthos that we have to fear—it is the Gascon's fury—the wild and unacademic attack of the troubadour—the sword of D'Artagnan.

"I done it," said Sam. "I went over to Frio City to do it. I couldn't let him put the skibunk on you, Uncle Ben. I met him in Summer's saloon. I knowed what to do. I said a few things to him that nobody else heard. He reached for his gun first—half a dozen fellows saw him do it—but I got mine unlimbered first. Three doses I gave him—right around the lungs, and a saucer could have covered up all of 'em. He won't bother you no more."

"This—is—King—James—you speak—of?" asked old man Ellison, while he sipped his coffee.

"You bet it was. And they took me before the county judge; and the witnesses what saw him draw his gun first was all there. Well, of course, they put me under $300 bond to appear before the court, but there was four or five boys on the spot ready to sign the bail. He won't bother you no more, Uncle Ben. You ought to have seen how close them bullet holes was together. I reckon playing a guitar as much as I do must kind of limber a fellow's trigger finger a little, don't you think, Uncle Ben?"

Then there was a little silence in the castle except for the spluttering of a venison steak that the Kiowa was cooking.

"Sam," said old man Ellison, stroking his white whiskers with a tremulous hand, "would you mind getting the guitar and playing that '*Huile, huile, palomita*' piece once or twice? It always seems to be kind of soothing and comforting when a man's tired and fagged out."

There is no more to be said, except that the title of the story is wrong. It should have been called "The Last of the Barons." There never will be an end to the troubadours; and now and then it does seem that the jingle of their guitars will drown the sound of the muffled blows of the pickaxes and trip hammers of all the Workers in the world.

THE SLEUTHS

In the Big City a man will disappear with the suddenness and completeness of the flame of a candle that is blown out. All the agencies of inquisition—the hounds of the trail, the sleuths of the city's labyrinths, the closet detectives of theory and induction—will be invoked to the search. Most often the man's face will be seen no more. Sometimes he will reappear in Sheboygan or in the wilds of Terre Haute, calling himself one of the synonyms of "Smith," and without memory of events up to a certain time, including his grocer's bill. Sometimes it will be found, after dragging the rivers, and polling the restaurants to see if he may be waiting for a well-done sirloin, that he has moved next door.

This snuffing out of a human being like the erasure of a chalk man from a blackboard is one of the most impressive themes in dramaturgy.

The case of Mary Snyder, in point, should not be without interest.

A man of middle age, of the name of Meeks, came from the West to New York to find his sister, Mrs. Mary Snyder, a widow, aged fifty-two, who had been living for a year in a tenement house in a crowded neighborhood.

At her address he was told that Mary Snyder had moved away longer than a month before. No one could tell him her new address.

On coming out Mr. Meeks addressed a policeman who was standing on the corner, and explained his dilemma.

"My sister is very poor," he said, "and I am anxious to find her. I have recently made quite a lot of money in a lead mine, and I want her to share my prosperity. There is no use in advertising her, because she cannot read."

The policeman pulled his mustache and looked so thoughtful and mighty that Meeks could almost feel the joyful tears of his sister Mary dropping upon his bright blue tie.

"You go down in the Canal Street neighborhood," said the policeman, "and get a job drivin' the biggest dray you can find. There's old women always gettin' knocked over by drays down there. You might see 'er among 'em. If you don't want to do that you better go 'round to headquarters and get 'em to put a fly cop onto the dame."

At police headquarters, Meek received ready assistance. A general alarm was sent out and copies of a photograph of Mary Snyder that her brother had were distributed among the stations. In Mulberry Street the chief assigned Detective Mullins to the case.

The detective took Meeks aside and said:

"This is not a very difficult case to unravel. Shave off your whiskers, fill your pockets with good cigars, and meet me in the café of the Waldorf at three o'clock this afternoon."

Meeks obeyed. He found Mullins there. They had a bottle of wine, while the detective asked questions concerning the missing woman.

"Now," said Mullins, "New York is a big city, but we've got the detective business systematized. There are two ways we can go about finding your sister. We will try one of 'em first. You say she's fifty-two?"

"A little past," said Meeks.

The detective conducted the Westerner to a branch advertising office of one of the largest dailies. There he wrote the following "ad" and submitted it to Meeks.

"Wanted, at once—one hundred attractive chorus girls for a new musical comedy. Apply all day at No.—— Broadway."

Meeks was indignant.

"My sister," said he, "is a poor, hard-working, elderly woman. I do not see what aid an advertisement of this kind would be toward finding her."

"All right," said the detective. "I guess you don't know New York. But if you've got a grouch against this scheme we'll try the other one. It's a sure thing. But it'll cost you more."

"Never mind the expense," said Meeks; "we'll try it."

The sleuth led him back to the Waldorf. "Engage a couple of bedrooms and a parlor," he advised, "and let's go up."

This was done, and the two were shown to a superb suite on the fourth floor. Meeks looked puzzled. The detective sank into a velvet armchair, and pulled out his cigar case.

"I forgot to suggest, old man," he said, "that you should have taken the rooms by the month. They wouldn't have stuck you so much for 'em."

"By the month!" exclaimed Meeks. "What do you mean?"

"Oh, it'll take time to work the game this way. I told you it would cost you more. We'll have to wait till spring. There'll be a new city directory out then. Very likely your sister's name and address will be in it."

Meeks rid himself of the city detective at once. On the next day some one advised him to consult Shamrock Jolnes, New York's famous private detective, who demanded fabulous fees, but performed miracles in the way of solving mysteries and crimes.

After waiting for two hours in the anteroom of the great detective's apartment, Meeks was shown into his presence. Jolnes sat in a purple dressing-gown at an inlaid ivory chess table, with a magazine before him, trying to solve the mystery of "They." The famous sleuth's thin, intellectual face, piercing eyes, and rate per word are too well known to need description.

Meeks set forth his errand. "My fee, if successful, will be $500," said Shamrock Jolnes.

Meeks bowed his agreement to the price.

"I will undertake your case, Mr. Meeks," said Jolnes, finally. "The disappearance of people in this city has always been an interesting problem to me. I remember a case that I brought to a successful outcome a year ago. A family bearing the name of Clark disappeared suddenly from a small flat in which they were living. I watched the flat building for two months for a clue. One day it struck me that a certain milkman and a grocer's boy always walked backward when they carried their wares upstairs. Following out by induction the idea that this observation gave me, I at once located the missing family. They had moved into the flat across the hall and changed their name to Kralc."

Shamrock Jolnes and his client went to the tenement house where Mary Snyder had lived, and the detective demanded to be shown the room in which she had lived. It had been occupied by no tenant since her disappearance.

The room was small, dingy, and poorly furnished. Meeks seated himself dejectedly on a broken chair, while the great detective searched the walls and floors and the few sticks of old, rickety furniture for a clue.

At the end of half an hour Jolnes had collected a few seemingly unintelligible articles—a cheap black hatpin, a piece torn off a theatre programme, and the end of a small torn card on which was the word "Left" and the characters "C 12."

Shamrock Jolnes leaned against the mantel for ten minutes, with his head resting upon his hand, and an absorbed look upon his intellectual face. At the end of that time he exclaimed, with animation:

"Come, Mr. Meeks; the problem is solved. I can take you directly to the house where your sister is living. And you may have no fears concerning her welfare, for she is amply provided with funds—for the present at least."

Meeks felt joy and wonder in equal proportions.

"How did you manage it?" he asked, with admiration in his tones.

Perhaps Jolnes's only weakness was a professional pride in his wonderful achievements in induction. He was ever ready to astound and charm his listeners by describing his methods.

"By elimination," said Jolnes, spreading his clues upon a little table, "I got rid of certain parts of the city to which Mrs. Snyder might have removed. You see this hatpin? That eliminates Brooklyn. No woman attempts to board a car at the Brooklyn Bridge without being sure that she carries a hatpin with which to fight her way into a seat. And now I will demonstrate to you that she could not have gone to Harlem. Behind this door are two hooks in the wall. Upon one of these Mrs. Snyder has hung her bonnet, and upon the other her shawl. You will observe that the bottom of the hanging shawl has gradually made a soiled streak against the plastered wall. The mark is clean-cut, proving that there is no fringe on the shawl. Now, was there ever a case where a middle-aged woman, wearing a shawl, boarded a Harlem train without there being a fringe on the shawl to catch in the gate and delay the passengers behind her? So we eliminate Harlem.

"Therefore I conclude that Mrs. Snyder has not moved very far away. On this torn piece of card you see the word 'Left,' the letter 'C,' and the number '12.' Now, I happen to know that No. 12 Avenue C is a first-class boarding house, far beyond your sister's means—as we suppose. But then I find this piece of a theatre programme, crumpled into an odd shape. What meaning does it convey? None to you, very likely, Mr. Meeks; but it is eloquent to one whose habits and training take cognizance of the smallest things.

"You have told me that your sister was a scrub woman. She scrubbed the floors of offices and hallways. Let us assume that she procured such work to perform in a theatre. Where is valuable jewellery lost the oftenest, Mr. Meeks? In the theatres, of course. Look at that piece of programme, Mr. Meeks. Observe the round impression in it. It has been wrapped around a ring—perhaps a ring of great value. Mrs. Snyder found the ring while at work in the theatre. She hastily tore off a piece of a programme, wrapped the ring carefully, and thrust it into her bosom. The next day she disposed of it, and with her increased means, looked about her for a more comfortable place in which to live. When I reach thus far in the chain I see nothing impossible about No. 12 Avenue C. It is there we will find your sister, Mr. Meeks."

Shamrock Jolnes concluded his convincing speech with the smile of a successful artist. Meeks's admiration was too great for words. Together they went to No. 12 Avenue C. It was an old-fashioned brown-stone house in a prosperous and respectable neighborhood.

They rang the bell, and on inquiring were told that no Mrs. Snyder was known there, and that not within six months had a new occupant come to the house.

When they reached the sidewalk again, Meeks examined the clues which he had brought away from his sister's old room.

"I am no detective," he remarked to Jolnes as he raised the piece of theatre programme to his nose, "but it seems to me that instead of a ring having been wrapped in this paper it was one of those round peppermint drops. And this piece with the address on it looks to me like the end of a seat coupon—No. 12, row C, left aisle."

Shamrock Jolnes had a far-away look in his eyes.

"I think you would do well to consult Juggins," said he.

"Who is Juggins?" asked Meeks.

"He is the leader," said Jolnes, "of a new modern school of detectives. Their methods are different from ours, but it is said that Juggins has solved some extremely puzzling cases. I will take you to him."

They found the greater Juggins in his office. He was a small man with light hair, deeply absorbed in reading one of the bourgeois works of Nathaniel Hawthorne.

The two great detectives of different schools shook hands with ceremony, and Meeks was introduced.

"State the facts," said Juggins, going on with his reading.

When Meeks ceased, the greater one closed his book and said:

"Do I understand that your sister is fifty-two years of age, with a large mole on the side of her nose, and that she is a very poor widow, making a scanty living by scrubbing, and with a very homely face and figure?"

"That describes her exactly," admitted Meeks. Juggins rose and put on his hat.

"In fifteen minutes," he said, "I will return, bringing you her present address."

Shamrock Jolnes turned pale, but forced a smile.

Within the specified time Juggins returned and consulted a little slip of paper held in his hand.

"Your sister, Mary Snyder," he announced calmly, "will be found at No. 162 Chilton Street. She is living in the back hall bedroom, five flights up. The house is only four blocks from here," he continued, addressing Meeks. "Suppose you go and verify the statement and then return here. Mr. Jolnes will await you, I dare say."

Meeks hurried away. In twenty minutes he was back again, with a beaming face.

"She is there and well!" he cried. "Name your fee!"

"Two dollars," said Juggins.

When Meeks had settled his bill and departed, Shamrock Jolnes stood with his hat in his hand before Juggins.

"If it would not be asking too much," he stammered—"if you would favor me so far—would you object to——"

"Certainly not," said Juggins, pleasantly. "I will tell you how I did it. You remember the description of Mrs. Snyder? Did you ever know a woman like that who wasn't paying weekly instalments on an enlarged crayon portrait of herself? The biggest factory of that kind in the country is just around the corner. I went there and got her address off the books. That's all."

WITCHES' LOAVES

MISS MARTHA MEACHAM kept the little bakery on the corner (the one where you go up three steps, and the bell tinkles when you open the door).

Miss Martha was forty, her bank-book showed a credit of two thousand dollars, and she possessed two false teeth and a sympathetic heart. Many people have married whose chances to do so were much inferior to Miss Martha's.

Two or three times a week a customer came in in whom she began to take an interest. He was a middle-aged man, wearing spectacles and a brown beard trimmed to a careful point.

He spoke English with a strong German accent. His clothes were worn and darned in places, and wrinkled and baggy in others. But he looked neat, and had very good manners.

He always bought two loaves of stale bread. Fresh bread was five cents a loaf. Stale ones were two for five. Never did he call for anything but stale bread.

Once Miss Martha saw a red and brown stain on his fingers. She was sure then that he was an artist and very poor. No doubt he lived in a garret, where he painted pictures and ate stale bread and thought of the good things to eat in Miss Martha's bakery.

Often when Miss Martha sat down to her chops and light rolls and jam and tea she would sigh, and wish that the gentle-mannered artist might share her tasty meal instead of eating his dry crust in that draughty attic. Miss Martha's heart, as you have been told, was a sympathetic one.

In order to test her theory as to his occupation, she brought from her room one day a painting that she had bought at a sale, and set it against the shelves behind the bread counter.

It was a Venetian scene. A splendid marble palazzo (so it said on the picture) stood in the foreground—or rather forewater. For the rest there were gondolas (with the lady trailing her hand in the water), clouds, sky, and chiaroscuro in plenty. No artist could fail to notice it.

Two days afterward the customer came in.

"Two loafs of stale bread, if you blease.

"You haf here a fine bicture, madame," he said while she was wrapping up the bread.

, "Yes?" says Miss Martha, revelling in her own cunning. "I do so admire art and" (no, it would not do to say "artists" thus early) "and paintings," she substituted. "You think it is a good picture?"

"Der balace," said the customer, "is not in good drawing. Der bairspective of it is not true. Goot morning, madame."

He took his bread, bowed, and hurried out.

Yes, he must be an artist. Miss Martha took the picture back to her room.

How gentle and kindly his eyes shone behind his spectacles! What a broad brow he had! To be able to judge perspective at a glance—and to live on stale bread! But genius often has to struggle before it is recognized.

What a thing it would be for art and perspective if genius were backed by two thousand dollars in bank, a bakery, and a sympathetic heart to—— But these were day-dreams, Miss Martha.

Often now when he came he would chat for a while across the showcase. He seemed to crave Miss Martha's cheerful words.

He kept on buying stale bread. Never a cake, never a pie, never one of her delicious Sally Lunns.

She thought he began to look thinner and discouraged. Her heart ached to add something good to eat to his meagre purchase, but her courage failed at the act. She did not dare affront him. She knew the pride of artists.

Miss Martha took to wearing her blue-dotted silk waist behind the counter. In the back room she cooked a mysterious compound of quince seeds and borax. Ever so many people use it for the complexion.

One day the customer came in as usual, laid his nickel on the showcase, and called for his stale loaves. While Miss Martha was reaching for them there was a great tooting and clanging, and a fire-engine came lumbering past.

The customer hurried to the door to look, as any one will. Suddenly inspired, Miss Martha seized the opportunity.

On the bottom shelf behind the counter was a pound of fresh butter that the dairyman had left ten minutes before. With bread knife Miss Martha made a deep slash in each of the stale loaves, inserted a generous quantity of butter, and pressed the loaves tight again.

When the customer turned once more she was tying the paper around them.

When he had gone, after an unusually pleasant little chat, Miss Martha smiled to herself, but not without a slight fluttering of the heart.

Had she been too bold? Would he take offense? But surely not. There was no language of edibles. Butter was no emblem of unmaidenly forwardness.

For a long time that day her mind dwelt on the subject. She imagined the scene when he should discover her little deception.

He would lay down his brushes and palette. There would stand his easel with the picture he was painting in which the perspective was beyond criticism.

He would prepare for his luncheon of dry bread and water. He would slice into a loaf—ah!

Miss Martha blushed. Would he think of the hand that placed it there as he ate? Would he——

The front door bell jangled viciously. Somebody was coming in, making a great deal of noise.

Miss Martha hurried to the front. Two men were there. One was a young man smoking a pipe—a man she had never seen before. The other was her artist.

His face was very red, his hat was on the back of his head, his hair was wildly rumpled. He clinched his two fists and shook them ferociously at Miss Martha. *At Miss Martha.*

"*Dummkopf!*" he shouted with extreme loudness; and then "*Tausendonfer!*" or something like it in German.

The young man tried to draw him away.

"I vill not go," he said angrily, "else I shall told her."

He made a bass drum of Miss Martha's counter.

"You haf shpoilt me," he cried, his blue eyes blazing behind his spectacles. "I vill tell you. You vas von *meddlingsome old cat!*"

Miss Martha leaned weakly against the shelves and laid one hand on her blue-dotted silk waist. The young man took the other by the collar.

"Come on," he said, "you've said enough." He dragged the angry one out at the door to the sidewalk, and then came back.

"Guess you ought to be told, ma'am," he said, "what the row is about. That's Blumberger. He's an architectural draftsman. I work in the same office with him.

"He's been working hard for three months drawing a plan for a new city hall. It was a prize competition. He finished inking the lines yesterday. You know, a draftsman always makes his drawing in pencil first. When it's done he rubs out the pencil lines with handfuls of stale bread crumbs. That's better than India rubber.

"Blumberger's been buying the bread here. Well, to-day—well, you know, ma'am, that butter isn't—well, Blumberger's plan isn't good for anything now except to cut up into railroad sandwiches."

Miss Martha went into the back room. She took off the blue-dotted silk waist and put on the old brown serge she used to wear. Then she poured the quince seed and borax mixture out of the window into the ash can.

THE PRIDE OF THE CITIES

SAID Mr. Kipling, "The cities are full of pride, challenging each to each." Even so.

New York was empty. Two hundred thousand of its people were away for the summer. Three million eight hundred thousand remained as caretakers and to pay the bills of the absentees. But the two hundred thousand are an expensive lot.

The New Yorker sat at a roof-garden table, ingesting solace through a straw. His panama lay upon a chair. The July audience was scattered among vacant seats as widely as out-fielders when the champion batter steps to the plate. Vaudeville happened at intervals. The breeze was cool from the bay; around and above—everywhere except on the stage—were stars. Glimpses were to be had of waiters, always disappearing, like startled chamois. Prudent visitors who had ordered refreshments by 'phone in the morning were now being served. The New Yorker was aware of certain drawbacks to his comfort, but content beamed softly from his rimless eye-glasses. His family was out of town. The drinks were warm; the ballet was suffering from lack of both tune and talcum—but his family would not return until September.

Then up into the garden stumbled the man from Topaz City, Nevada. The gloom of the solitary sight-seer enwrapped him. Bereft of joy through loneliness, he stalked with a widower's face through the halls of pleasure. Thirst for human companionship possessed him as he panted in the metropolitan draught. Straight to the New Yorker's table he steered.

The New Yorker, disarmed and made reckless by the lawless atmosphere of a roof garden, decided upon utter abandonment of his life's traditions. He resolved to shatter with one rash, dare-devil, impulsive, hair-brained act the conventions that had hitherto been woven into his existence. Carrying out this radical and precipitous inspiration he nodded slightly to the stranger as he drew nearer the table.

The next moment found the man from Topaz City in the list of the New Yorker's closest friends. He took a chair at the table, he gathered two others for his feet, he tossed his broad-brimmed hat upon a fourth, and told his life's history to his new-found pard.

The New Yorker warmed a little, as an apartment-house furnace warms when the strawberry season begins. A waiter who came within hail in an unguarded moment was captured and paroled on an errand to the Doctor Wily experimental station. The ballet was now in the midst of a musical vagary, and danced upon the stage programmed as Bolivian peasants, clothed in some portions of its anatomy as Norwegian fisher maidens, in others as ladies-in-waiting of Marie Antoinette, historically denuded in other portions so as to represent sea nymphs, and presenting the *tout ensemble* of a social club of Central Park West housemaids at a fish fry.

"Been in the city long?" inquired the New Yorker, getting ready the exact tip against the waiter's coming with large change from the bill.

"Me?" said the man from Topaz City. "Four days. Never in Topaz City, was you?"

"I!" said the New Yorker. "I was never farther west than Eighth Avenue. I had a brother who died on Ninth, but I met the cortège at Eighth. There was a bunch of violets on the hearse, and the undertaker mentioned the incident to avoid mistake. I cannot say that I am familiar with the West."

"Topaz City," said the man who occupied four chairs, "is one of the finest towns in the world."

"I presume that you have seen the sights of the metropolis," said the New Yorker. "Four days is not a sufficient length of time in which to view even our most salient points of interest, but one can possibly form a general impression. Our architectural supremacy is what generally strikes visitors to our city most forcibly. Of course you have seen our Flatiron Building. It is considered——"

"Saw it," said the man from Topaz City. "But you ought to come out our way. It's mountainous, you know, and the ladies all wear short skirts for climbing and——"

"Excuse me," said the New Yorker, "but that isn't exactly the point. New York must be a wonderful revelation to a visitor from the West. Now, as to our hotels——"

"Say," said the man from Topaz City, "that reminds me—there were sixteen stage robbers shot last year within twenty miles of——"

"I was speaking of hotels," said the New Yorker. "We lead Europe in that respect. And as far as our leisure class is concerned we are far——"

"Oh, I don't know," interrupted the man from Topaz City. "There were twelve tramps in our jail when I left home. I guess New York isn't so——"

"Beg pardon, you seem to misapprehend the idea. Of course, you visited the Stock Exchange and Wall Street, where the——"

"Oh, yes," said the man from Topaz City, as he lighted a Pennsylvania stogie, "and I want to tell you that we've got the finest town marshal west of the Rockies. Bill Rainer he took in five pickpockets out of the crowd when Red Nose Thompson laid the corner-stone of his new saloon. Topaz City don't allow——"

"Have another Rhine wine and seltzer," suggested the New Yorker. "I've never been West, as I said; but there can't be any place out there to compare with New York. As to the claims of Chicago I——"

"One man," said the Topazite—"one man only has been murdered and robbed in Topaz City in the last three——"

"Oh, I know what Chicago is," interposed the New Yorker. "Have you been up Fifth Avenue to see the magnificent residences of our mil——"

"Seen 'em all. You ought to know Reub Stegall, the assessor of Topaz. When old man Tilbury, that owns the only two-story house in town, tried to swear his taxes from $6,000 down to $450.75, Reub buckled on his forty-five and went down to see——"

"Yes, yes, but speaking of our great city—one of its greatest features is our superb police department. There is no body of men in the world that can equal it for——"

"That waiter gets around like a Langley flying machine," remarked the man from Topaz City, thirstily. "We've got men in our town, too, worth $400,000. There's old Bill Withers and Colonel Metcalf and——"

"Have you seen Broadway at night?" asked the New Yorker, courteously. "There are few streets in the world that can compare with it. When the electrics are shining and the pavements are alive with two hurrying streams of elegantly clothed men and beautiful women attired in the costliest costumes that wind in and out in a close maze of expensively——"

"Never knew but one case in Topaz City," said the man from the West. "Jim Bailey, our mayor, had his watch and chain and $235 in cash taken from his pocket while——"

"That's another matter," said the New Yorker. "While you are in our city you should avail yourself of every opportunity to see its wonders. Our rapid transit system——"

"If you was out in Topaz," broke in the man from there, "I could show you a whole cemetery full of people that got killed accidentally. Talking about mangling folks up! why, when Berry Rogers turned loose that old double-barrelled shot-gun of his loaded with slugs at anybody——"

"Here, waiter!" called the New Yorker. "Two more of the same. It is acknowledged by every one that our city is the centre of art, and literature, and learning. Take, for instance, our after-dinner speakers. Where else in the country would you find such wit and eloquence as emanate from Depew and Ford, and——"

"If you take the papers," interrupted the Westerner, "you must have read of Pete Webster's daughter. The Websters live two blocks north of the courthouse in Topaz City. Miss Tillie Webster, she slept forty days and nights without waking up. The doctors said that——"

"Pass the matches, please," said the New Yorker. "Have you observed the expedition with which new buildings are being run up in New York? Improved inventions in steel framework and——"

"I noticed," said the Nevadian, "that the statistics of Topaz City showed only one carpenter crushed by falling timbers last year and he was caught in a cyclone."

"They abuse our sky line," continued the New Yorker, "and it is likely that we are not yet artistic in the construction of our buildings. But I can safely assert that we lead in pictorial and decorative art. In some of our houses can be found masterpieces in the way of paintings and sculpture. One who has the entrée to our best galleries will find——"

"Back up," exclaimed the man from Topaz City. "There was a game last month in our town in which $90,000 changed hands on a pair of——"

"Ta-romt-tara!" went the orchestra. The stage curtain, blushing pink at the name "Asbestos" inscribed upon it, came down with a slow midsummer movement. The audience trickled leisurely down the elevator and stairs.

On the sidewalk below, the New Yorker and the man from Topaz City shook hands with alcoholic gravity. The elevated crashed raucously, surface cars hummed and clanged, cabmen swore, newsboys shrieked, wheels clattered ear-piercingly. The New Yorker conceived a happy thought, with which he aspired to clinch the pre-eminence of his city.

"You must admit," said he, "that in the way of noise New York is far ahead of any other——"

"Back to the everglades!" said the man from Topaz City. "In 1900, when Sousa's band and the repeating candidate were in our town you couldn't——"

The rattle of an express wagon drowned the rest of the words.

•

HOLDING UP A TRAIN

NOTE. The man who told me these things was for several years an outlaw in the Southwest and a follower of the pursuit he so frankly describes. His description of the *modus operandi* should prove interesting, his counsel of value to the potential passenger in some future "hold-up," while his estimate of the pleasures of train robbing will hardly induce any one to adopt it as a profession. I give the story in almost exactly his own words.

O. H.

MOST people would say, if their opinion was asked for, that holding up a train would be a hard job. Well, it isn't; it's easy. I have contributed some to the uneasiness of railroads and the insomnia of express companies, and the most trouble I ever had about a hold-up was in being swindled by unscrupulous people while spending the money I got. The danger wasn't anything to speak of, and we didn't mind the trouble.

One man has come pretty near robbing a train by himself; two have succeeded a few times; three can do it if they are hustlers, but five is about the right number. The time to do it and the place depend upon several things.

The first "stick-up" I was ever in happened in 1890. Maybe the way I got into it will explain how most train robbers start in the business. Five out of six Western outlaws are just cowboys out of a job and gone wrong. The sixth is a tough from the East who dresses up like a bad man and plays some low-down trick that gives the boys a bad name. Wire fences and "nesters" made five of them; a bad heart made the sixth.

Jim S—— and I were working on the 101 Ranch in Colorado. The nesters had the cowman on the go. They had taken up the land and elected officers who were hard to get along with. Jim and I rode into La Junta one day, going south from a round-up. We were having a little fun without malice toward anybody when a farmer administration cut in and tried to harvest us. Jim shot a deputy marshal, and I kind of corroborated his side of the argument. We skirmished up and down the main street, the boomers having bad luck all the time. After a while we leaned forward and shoved for the ranch down on the Ceriso. We were riding a couple of horses that couldn't fly, but they could catch birds.

A few days after that, a gang of the La Junta boomers came to the ranch and wanted us to go back with them. Naturally, we declined. We had the house on them, and before we were done refusing, that old 'dobe was plumb full of lead. When dark came we fagged 'em a batch of bullets and shoved out the back door for the rocks. They sure smoked us as we went. We had to drift, which we did, and rounded up down in Oklahoma.

Well, there wasn't anything we could get there, and, being mighty hard up, we decided to transact a little business with the railroads. Jim and I joined forces with Tom and Ike Moore—two brothers who had plenty of sand they were willing to convert into dust. I can call their names, for both of them are dead. Tom was shot while robbing a bank in Arkansas; Ike was killed during the more dangerous pastime of attending a dance in the Creek Nation.

We selected a place on the Santa Fé where there was a bridge across a deep creek surrounded by heavy timber. All passenger trains took water at the tank close to one end of the bridge. It was a quiet place, the nearest house being five miles away. The day before it happened, we rested our horses and "made medicine" as to how we should get about it. Our plans were not at all elaborate, as none of us had ever engaged in a hold-up before.

The Santa Fé flyer was due at the tank at 11:15 P. M. At eleven, Tom and I lay down on one side of the track, and Jim and Ike took the other. As the train rolled up, the headlight flashing far down the track and the steam hissing from the engine, I turned weak all over. I would have worked a whole year on the ranch for nothing to have been out of that affair right then. Some of the nerviest men in the business have told me that they felt the same way the first time.

The engine had hardly stopped when I jumped on the running-board on one side, while Jim mounted the other. As soon as the engineer and fireman saw our guns they threw up their hands without being told, and begged us not to shoot, saying they would do anything we wanted them to.

"Hit the ground," I ordered, and they both jumped off. We drove them before us down the side of the train. While this was happening, Tom and Ike had been blazing away, one on each side of the train, yelling like Apaches, so as to keep the passengers herded in the cars. Some fellow stuck a little twenty-two calibre out one of the coach windows and fired it straight up in the air. I let drive and smashed the glass just over his head. That settled everything like resistance from that direction.

By this time all my nervousness was gone. I felt a kind of pleasant excitement as if I were at a dance or a frolic of some sort. The lights were all out in the coaches, and, as Tom and Ike gradually quit firing and yelling, it got to be almost as still as a graveyard. I remember hearing a little bird chirping in a bush at the side of the track, as if it were complaining at being waked up.

I made the fireman get a lantern, and then I went to the express car and yelled to the messenger to open up or get perforated. He slid the door open and stood in it with his hands up. "Jump overboard, son," I said, and he hit the dirt like a lump of lead. There were two safes in the car—a big one and a little one. By the way, I first located the messenger's arsenal—a double-barrelled shot-gun with buckshot cartridges and a thirty-eight in a drawer. I drew the cartridges from the shot-gun, pocketed the pistol, and called the messenger inside. I shoved my gun against his nose and put him to work. He couldn't open the big one, but he did the little one. There was only nine hundred dollars in it. That was mighty small winnings for our trouble, so we decided to go through the passengers. We took our prisoners to the smoking-car, and from there sent the engineer through the train to light up the coaches. Beginning with the first one, we placed a man at each door and ordered the passengers to stand between the seats with their hands up.

If you want to find out what cowards the majority of men are, all you have to do is rob a passenger train. I don't mean because they don't resist—I'll tell you later on why they can't do that—but it makes a man feel sorry for them the way they lose their heads. Big, burly drummers and farmers and ex-soldiers and high-collared dudes and sports that, a few moments before, were filling the car with noise and bragging, get so scared that their ears flop.

There were very few people in the day coaches at that time of night, so we made a slim haul until we got to the sleeper. The Pullman conductor met me at one door while Jim was going round to the other one. He very politely informed me that I could not go into that car, as it did not belong to the railroad company, and, besides, the passengers had already been greatly disturbed by the shouting and firing. Never in all my life have I met with a finer instance of official dignity and reliance upon the power of Mr. Pullman's great name. I jabbed my six-shooter so hard against Mr. Conductor's front that I afterward found one of his vest buttons so firmly wedged in the end of the barrel that I had to shoot it out. He just shut up like a weak-springed knife and rolled down the car steps.

I opened the door of the sleeper and stepped inside. A big, fat old man came wabbling up to me, puffing and blowing. He had one coat-sleeve on and was trying to put his vest on over that. I don't know who he thought I was.

"Young man, young man," says he, "you must keep cool and not get excited. Above everything, keep cool."

"I can't," says I. "Excitement's just eating me up." And then I let out a yell and turned loose my forty-five through the skylight.

That old man tried to dive into one of the lower berths, but a screech came out of it, and a bare foot that took him in the bread-basket and landed him on the floor. I saw Jim coming in the other door, and I hollered for everybody to climb out and line up.

They commenced to scramble down, and for a while we had a three-ringed circus. The men looked as frightened and tame as a lot of rabbits in a deep snow. They had on, on an average, about a quarter of a suit of clothes and one shoe apiece. One chap was sitting on the floor of the aisle, looking as if he were working a hard sum in arithmetic. He was trying, very solemn, to pull a lady's number two shoe on a number nine foot.

The ladies didn't stop to dress. They were so curious to see a real, live train robber, bless 'em, that they just wrapped blankets and sheets around themselves and came out, squeaky and fidgety looking. They always show more curiosity and sand than the men do.

We got them all lined up and pretty quiet, and I went through the bunch. I found very little on them—I mean in the way of valuables. One man in the line was a sight. He was one of those big, overgrown, solemn snoozers that sit on the platform at lectures and look wise. Before crawling out he had managed to put on his long, frocktailed coat and his high silk hat. The rest of him was nothing but pajamas and bunions. When I dug into that Prince Albert, I expected to drag out at least a block of gold mine stock or an armful of Government bonds, but all I found was a little boy's French harp about four inches long. What it was there for, I don't know. I felt a little mad because he had fooled me so. I stuck the harp up against his mouth.

"If you can't pay—play," I says.

"I can't play," says he.

"Then learn right off quick," says I, letting him smell the end of my gun-barrel.

He caught hold of the harp, turned red as a beet, and commenced to blow. He blew a dinky little tune I remembered hearing when I was a kid:

> Prettiest little gal in the country—oh!
> Mammy and Daddy told me so.

I made him keep on playing it all the time we were in the car. Now and then he'd get weak and off the key, and I'd turn my gun on him and ask what was the matter with that little gal, and whether he had any intention of going back on her, which would make him start up again like sixty. I think that old boy standing there in his silk hat and bare feet, playing his little French harp, was the funniest sight I ever saw. One little red-headed woman in the line broke out laughing at him. You could have heard her in the next car.

Then Jim held them steady while I searched the berths. I grappled around in those beds and filled a pillow-case with the strangest assortment of stuff you ever saw. Now and then I'd come across a little pop-gun pistol, just about right for plugging teeth with, which I'd throw out the window. When I finished with the collection, I dumped the pillow-case load in the middle of the aisle. There were a good many watches, bracelets, rings and pocket-books, with a sprinkling of false teeth, whiskey flasks, face-powder boxes, chocolate caramels, and heads of hair of various colors and lengths. There were also about a dozen ladies stockings into which jewelry, watches, and rolls of bills had been stuffed and then wadded up tight and stuck under the mattresses. I offered to return what I called the "scalps," saying that we were not Indians on the warpath, but none of the ladies seemed to know to whom the hair belonged.

One of the women—and a good-looker she was—wrapped in a striped blanket saw me pick up one of the stockings that was pretty chunky and heavy about the toe, and she snapped out:

"That's mine, sir. You're not in the business of robbing women, are you?"

Now, as this was our first hold-up, we hadn't agreed upon any code of ethics, so I hardly knew what to answer. But, anyway, I replied: "Well, not as a specialty. If this contains your personal property you can have it back."

"It just does," she declared eagerly, and reached out her hand for it.

"You'll excuse my taking a look at the contents," I said, holding the stocking up by the toe. Out dumped a big gent's gold watch, worth two hundred, a gent's leather pocket-book, that we afterward found to contain six hundred dollars, a 32-calibre revolver and the only thing of the lot that could have been a lady's personal property was a silver bracelet worth about fifty cents.

"I said: "Madame, here's your property," and handed her the bracelet. "Now," I went on, "how can you expect us to act square with you when you try to deceive us in this manner? I'm surprised at such conduct."

The young woman flushed up as if she had been caught doing something dishonest. Some other woman down the line called out: "The mean thing!" I never knew whether she meant the other lady or me.

When we finished our job we ordered everybody back to bed, told 'em goodnight very politely at the door, and left. We rode forty miles before daylight and then divided the stuff. Each one of us got $1,752.85 in money. We lumped the jewelry around. Then we scattered, each man for himself.

That was my first train robbery, and it was about as easily done as any of the ones that followed. But that was the last and only time I ever went through the passengers. I don't like that part of the business. Afterward I stuck strictly to the express car. During the next eight years I handled a good deal of money.

The best haul I made was just seven years after the first one. We found out about a train that was going to bring out a lot of money to pay off the soldiers at a government post. We stuck that train up in broad daylight. Five of us lay in the sandhills near a little station. Ten soldiers were guarding the money on the train, but they might just as well have been at home in a furlough. We didn't even allow them to stick their heads out the windows to see the fun. We had no trouble at all in getting the money, which was all in gold. Of course, a big howl was raised at the time about the robbery. It was government stuff, and the Government got sarcastic and wanted to know what the convoy of soldiers went along for. The only excuse given was that nobody was expecting an attack among those bare sandhills in daytime. I don't know what the Government thought about the excuse, but I know that it was a good one. The surprise—that is the keynote of the train-robbing business. The papers published all kinds of stories about the loss, finally agreeing that it was between nine thousand and ten thousand dollars. The Government sawed wood. Here are the correct figures, printed for the first time—forty-eight thousand dollars. If anybody will take the trouble to look over Uncle Sam's private accounts for that little debit to profit and loss, he will find that I am right to a cent.

But that time we were expert enough to know what to do. We rode due west twenty miles, making a trail that a Broadway policeman could have followed, and then we doubled back, hiding our tracks. On the second night after the hold-up, while posses were scouring the country in every direction, Jim and I were eating supper in the second story of a friend's house in the town where the alarm started from. Our friend pointed out to us, in an office across the street, a printing press at work striking off handbills offering a reward for our capture.

I have been asked what we do with the money we get. Well, I never could account for a tenth part of it after it was spent. It goes fast and freely. An outlaw has to have a good many friends. A highly respected citizen may, and often does, get along with very few, but a man on the dodge has got to have "sidekickers." With angry posses and reward-hungry officers cutting out a hot trail for him, he must have a few places scattered about the country where he can stop and feed himself and his horse and get a few hours' sleep without having to keep both eyes open. When he makes a haul he feels like dropping some of the coin with these friends, and he does it liberally. Sometimes I have, at the end of a hasty visit at one of these havens of refuge, flung a handful of gold and bills into the laps of the kids playing on the floor, without knowing whether my contribution was a hundred dollars or a thousand.

When old-timers make a big haul they generally go far away to one of the big cities to spend their money. Green hands, however successful a hold-up they make, nearly always give themselves away by showing too much money near the place where they got it.

I was in a job in '94 where we got twenty thousand dollars. We followed our favorite plan for a get-away—that is, doubled on our trail—and laid low for a time near the scene of the train's bad luck. One morning I picked up a newspaper and read an article with big headlines stating that the marshal, with eight deputies and a posse of thirty armed citizens, had the train robbers surrounded in a mesquite thicket on the Cimarron, and that it was a question of only a few hours when they would be dead men or prisoners. While I was reading that article I was sitting at breakfast in one of the most elegant private residences in Washington City, with a flunky in knee pants standing behind my chair. Jim was sitting across the table talking to his half-uncle, a retired naval officer, whose name you have often seen in the accounts of doings in the capital. We had gone there and bought rattling outfits of good clothes, and were resting from our labors among the nabobs. We must have been killed in that mesquite thicket, for I can make an affidavit that we didn't surrender.

Now I propose to tell why it is easy to hold up a train, and, then, why no one should ever do it.

In the first place, the attacking party has all the advantage. That is, of course, supposing that they are old-timers with the necessary experience and courage. They have the outside and are protected by the darkness, while the others are in the light, hemmed into a small space, and exposed, the moment they show a head at a window or door, to the aim of a man who is a dead shot and who won't hesitate to shoot..

But, in my opinion, the main condition that makes train robbing easy is the element of *surprise* in connection with the imagination of the passengers. If you have ever seen a horse that has eaten loco weed you will understand what I mean when I say that the passengers get locoed. That horse gets the awfullest imagination on him in the world. You can't coax him to cross a little branch stream two feet wide. It looks as big to him as the Mississippi River. That's just the way with the passenger. He thinks there are a hundred men yelling and shooting outside, when maybe there are only two or three. And the muzzle of a forty-five looks like the entrance to a tunnel. The passenger is all right, although he may do mean little tricks, like hiding a wad of money in his shoe and forgetting to dig-up until you jostle his ribs some with the end of your six-shooter; but there's no harm in him.

As to the train crew, we never had any more trouble with them than if they had been so many sheep. I don't mean that they are cowards; I mean that they have got sense. They know they're not up against a bluff. It's the same way with the officers. I've seen secret service men, marshals, and railroad detectives fork over their change as meek as Moses. I saw one of the bravest marshals I ever knew hide his gun under his seat and dig up along with the rest while I was taking toll. He wasn't afraid; he simply knew that we had the drop on the whole outfit. Besides, many of those officers have families and they feel that they oughtn't to take chances; whereas death has no terrors for the man who holds up a train. He expects to get killed some day, and he generally does. My advice to you, if you should ever be in a hold-up, is to line up with the cowards and save your bravery for an occasion when it may be of some benefit to you. Another reason why officers are backward about mixing things with a train robber is a financial one. Every time there is a scrimmage and somebody gets killed, the officers lose money. If the train robber gets away they swear out a warrant against John Doe *et al.* and travel hundreds of miles and sign vouchers for thousands on the trail of the fugitives, and the Government foots the bills. So, with them, it is a question of mileage rather than courage.

I will give one instance to support my statement that the surprise is the best card in playing for a hold-up.

Along in '92 the Daltons were cutting out a hot trail for the officers down in the Cherokee Nation. Those were their lucky days, and they got so reckless and sandy, that they used to announce beforehand what job they were going to undertake. Once they gave it out that they were going to hold up the M. K. & T. flyer on a certain night at the station of Pryor Creek, in Indian Territory.

That night the railroad company got fifteen deputy marshals in Muscogee and put them on the train. Beside them they had fifty armed men hid in the depot at Pryor Creek.

When the Katy Flyer pulled in not a Dalton showed up. The next station was Adair, six miles away. When the train reached there, and the deputies were having a good time explaining what they would have done to the Dalton gang if they had turned up, all at once it sounded like an army firing outside. The conductor and brakeman came running into the car yelling, "Train robbers!"

Some of those deputies lit out of the door, hit the ground, and kept on running. Some of them hid their Winchesters under the seats. Two of them made a fight and were both killed.

It took the Daltons just ten minutes to capture the train and whip the escort. In twenty minutes more they robbed the express car of twenty-seven thousand dollars and made a clean get-away.

My opinion is that those deputies would have put up a stiff fight at Pryor Creek, where they were expecting trouble, but they were taken by surprise and "locoed" at Adair, just as the Daltons, who knew their business, expected they would.

I don't think I ought to close without giving some deductions from my experience of eight years "on the dodge." It doesn't pay to rob trains. Leaving out the question of right and morals, which I don't think I ought to tackle, there is very little envy in the life of an outlaw. After a while money ceases to have any value in his eyes. He gets to looking upon the railroads and express companies as his bankers, and his six-shooters as a cheque book good for any amount. He throws away money right and left. Most of the time he is on the jump, riding day and night, and he lives so hard between times that he doesn't enjoy the taste of high life when he gets it. He knows that his time is bound to come to lose his life or liberty, and that the accuracy of his aim, the speed of his horse, and the fidelity of his "sider," are all that postpone the inevitable.

It isn't that he loses any sleep over danger from the officers of the law. In all my experience I never knew officers to attack a band of outlaws unless they out-numbered them at least three to one.

But the outlaw carries one thought constantly in his mind—and that is what makes him so sore against life, more than anything else—he knows where the marshals get their recruits of deputies. He knows that the majority of these upholders of the law were once lawbreakers, horse thieves, rustlers, highwaymen, and outlaws like himself, and that they gained their positions, and immunity by turning state's evidence, by turning traitor and delivering up their comrades to imprisonment and death. He knows that some day—unless he is shot first—his Judas will set to work, the trap will be laid, and he will be the surprised instead of a surpriser at a stick-up.

That is why the man who holds up trains picks his company with a thousand times the care with which a careful girl chooses a sweetheart. That is why he raises himself from his blankets of nights and listens to the tread of every horse's hoofs on the distant road. That is why he broods suspiciously for days upon a jesting remark or an unusual movement of a tired comrade, or the broken mutterings of his closest friend, sleeping by his side.

And it is one of the reasons why the train-robbing profession is not so pleasant a one as either of its collateral branches—politics or cornering the market.

ULYSSES AND THE DOGMAN

Do you know the time of the dogmen?

When the forefinger of twilight begins to smudge the clear-drawn lines of the Big City there is inaugurated an hour devoted to one of the most melancholy sights of urban life.

Out from the towering flat crags and apartment peaks of the cliff dwellers of New York steals an army of beings that were once men. Even yet they go upright upon two limbs and retain human form and speech; but you will observe that they are behind animals in progress. Each of these beings follows a dog, to which he is fastened by an artificial ligament.

These men are all victims to Circe. Not willingly do they become flunkeys to Fido, bell boys to bull terriers, and toddlers after Towzer. Modern Circe, instead of turning them into animals, has kindly left the difference of a six-foot leash between them. Every one of those dogmen has been either cajoled, bribed, or commanded by his own particular Circe to take the dear Household pet out for an airing.

By their faces and manner you can tell that the dogmen are bound in a hopeless enchantment. Never will there come even a dog-catcher Ulysses to remove the spell.

The faces of some are stonily set. They are past the commiseration, the curiosity, or the jeers of their fellow-beings. Years of matrimony, of continuous compulsory canine constitutionals, have made them callous. They unwind their beasts from lamp posts, or the ensnared legs of profane pedestrians, with the stolidity of mandarins manipulating the strings of their kites.

Others, more recently reduced to the ranks of Rover's retinue, take their medicine sulkily and fiercely. They play the dog on the end of their line with the pleasure felt by the girl out fishing when she catches a sea-robin on her hook. They glare at you threateningly if you look at them, as if it would be their delight to let slip the dogs of war. These are half-mutinous dogmen, not quite Circe-ized, and you will do well not to kick their charges, should they sniff around your ankles.

Others of the tribe do not seem to feel so keenly. They are mostly unfresh youths, with gold caps and drooping cigarettes, who do not harmonize with their dogs. The animals they attend wear satin bows in their collars; and the young men steer them so assiduously that you are tempted to the theory that some personal advantage, contingent upon satisfactory service, waits upon the execution of their duties.

The dogs thus personally conducted are of many varieties; but they are one in fatness, in pampered, diseased vileness of temper, in insolent, snarling capriciousness of behavior. They tug at the leash fractiously, they make leisurely nasal inventory of every door step, railing, and post. They sit down to rest when they choose; they wheeze like the winner of a Third Avenue beefsteak-eating contest;

they blunder clumsily into open cellars and coal holes; they lead the dogmen a merry dance.

These unfortunate dry nurses of dogdom, the cur cuddlers, mongrel managers, Spitz stalkers, poodle pullers, Skye scrapers, dachshund dandlers, terrier trailers, and Pomeranian pushers of the cliff-dwelling Circes follow their charges meekly. The doggies neither fear nor respect them. Masters of the house these men whom they hold in leash may be, but they are not masters of them. From cosy corner to fire escape, from divan to dumbwaiter, doggy's snarl easily drives this two-legged being who is commissioned to walk at the other end of his string during his outing.

One twilight the dogmen came forth as usual at their Circes' pleading, guerdon, or crack of the whip. One among them was a strong man, apparently of too solid virtues for this airy vocation. His expression was melancholic, his manner depressed. He was leashed to a vile white dog, loathsomely fat, fiendishly ill-natured, gloatingly intractable toward his despised conductor.

At a corner nearest to his apartment house the dogman turned down a side street, hoping for fewer witnesses to his ignominy. The surfeited beast waddled before him, panting with spleen and the labor of motion.

Suddenly the dog stopped. A tall, brown, long-coated, wide-brimmed man stood like a Colossus blocking the sidewalk and declaring:

"Well, I'm a son of a gun!"

"Jim Berry!" breathed the dogman, with exclamation points in his voice.

"Sam Telfair," cried Wide-Brim again, "you ding-basted old willy walloo, give us your hoof!"

Their hands clasped in the brief, tight greeting of the West that is death to the handshake microbe.

"You old fat rascal!" continued Wide-Brim, with a wrinkled brown smile; "it's been five years since I seen you. I been in this town a week, but you can't find nobody in such a place. Well, you dinged old married man, how are they coming?"

Something mushy and heavily soft like raised dough leaned against Jim's leg and chewed his trousers with a yeasty growl.

"Get to work," said Jim, "and explain this yard-wide hydrophobia yearling you've throwed your lasso over. Are you the pound-master of this burg? Do you call that a dog or what?"

"I need a drink," said the dogman, dejected at the reminder of his old dog of the sea. "Come on."

Hard by was a café. 'Tis ever so in the big city.

They sat at a table, and the bloated monster yelped and scrambled at the end of his leash to get at the café cat.

"Whiskey," said Jim to the waiter.

"Make it two," said the dogman.

"You're fatter," said Jim, "and you look subjugated. I don't know about the East agreeing with you. All the boys asked me to hunt you up when I started. Sandy King, he went to the Klondike. Watson Burrel, he married the oldest Peters girl. I made some money buying beeves, and I bought a lot of wild land up on the Little Powder. Going to fence next fall. Bill Rawlins, he's gone to farming. You remember Bill, of course—he was courting Marcella—excuse me, Sam—I mean the lady you married, while she was teaching school at Prairie View. But you was the lucky man. How is Missis Telfair?"

"S-h-h-h!" said the dogman, signalling the waiter; "give it a name."

"Whiskey," said Jim.

"Make it two," said the dogman.

"She's well," he continued, after his chaser. "She refused to live anywhere but in New York, where she came from. We live in a flat. Every evening at six I take that dog out for a walk. It's Marcella's pet. There never were two animals on earth, Jim, that hated one another like me and that dog does. His name's Lovekins. Marcella dresses for dinner while we're out. We eat tabble dote. Ever try one of them, Jim?"

"No, I never," said Jim. "I seen the signs, but I thought the said 'table de hole.' I thought it was French for pool tables. How does it taste?"

"If you're going to be in the city for awhile we will——"

"No, sir-ee. I'm starting for home this evening on the 7:25. Like to stay longer, but I can't."

"I'll walk down to the ferry with you," said the dogman.

The dog had bound a leg each of Jim and the chair together, and had sunk into a comatose slumber. Jim stumbled, and the leash was slightly wrenched. The shrieks of the awakened beast rang for a block around.

"If that's your dog," said Jim, when they were on the street again, "what's to hinder you from running that habeas corpus you've got around his neck over a limb and walking off and forgetting him?"

"I'd never dare to," said the dogman, awed at the bold proposition. "He sleeps in the bed. I sleep on a lounge. He runs howling to Marcella if I look at him. Some night, Jim, I'm going to get even with that dog. I've made up my mind to do it. I'm going to creep over with a knife and cut a hole in his mosquito bar so they can get in to him. See if I don't do it!"

"You ain't yourself, Sam Telfair. You ain't what you was once. I don't know about these cities and flats over here. With my own eyes I seen you stand off both the Tillotson boys in Prairie View with the brass faucet out of a molasses barrel. And I seen you rope and tie the wildest steer on Little Powder in 39 1-2."

"I did, didn't I?" said the other, with a temporary gleam in his eye. "But that was before I was dogmatized."

"Does Missis Telfair——" began Jim.

"Hush!" said the dogman. "Here's another café."

They lined up at the bar. The dog fell asleep at their feet.

"Whiskey," said Jim.

"Make it two," said the dogman.

"I thought about you," said Jim, "when I bought that wild land. I wished you was out there to help me with the stock."

"Last Tuesday," said the dogman, "he bit me on the ankle because I asked for cream in my coffee. He always gets the cream."

"You'd like Prairie View now," said Jim. "The boys from the round-ups for fifty miles around ride in there. One corner of my pasture is in sixteen miles of the town. There's a straight forty miles of wire on one side of it."

"You pass through the kitchen to get to the bedroom," said the dogman, "and you pass through the parlor to get to the bathroom, and you back out through the dining room to get into the bedroom so you can turn around and leave by the kitchen. And he snores and barks in his sleep, and I have to smoke in the park on account of his asthma."

"Don't Missis Telfair——" began Jim.

"Oh, shut up!" said the dogman. "What is it this time?"

"Whiskey," said Jim.

"Make it two," said the dogman.

"Well, I'll be racking along down toward the ferry," said the other.

"Come on, there, you mangy, turtle-backed, snake-headed, bench-legged ton-and-a-half of soap grease!" shouted the dogman, with a new note in his voice and a new hand on the leash. The dog scrambled after them, with an angry whine at such unusual language from his guardian.

At the foot of Twenty-third Street the dogman led the way through swinging doors.

"Last chance," said he. "Speak up."

"Whiskey," said Jim.

"Make it two," said the dogman.

"I don't know," said the ranchman, "where I'll find the man I want to take charge of the Little Powder outfit. I want somebody I know something about. Finest stretch of prairie and timber you ever squinted your eye over, Sam. Now if you was——"

"Speaking of hydrophobia," said the dogman, "the other night he chewed a piece out of my leg because I knocked a fly off of Marcella's arm. 'It ought to be cauterized,' says Marcella, and I was thinking so myself. I telephones for the doctor, and when he comes Marcella says to me: 'Help me hold the poor dear while the doctor fixes his mouth. Oh, I hope he got no virus on any of his toofies when he bit you.' Now what do you think of that?"

"Does Missis Telfair——" began Jim.

"Oh, drop it," said the dogman. "Come again!"

"Whiskey," said Jim.

"Make it two," said the dogman.

They walked on to the ferry. The ranchman stepped to the ticket window.

Suddenly the swift landing of three or four heavy kicks was heard, the air was rent by piercing canine shrieks, and a pained, outraged, lubberly, bow-legged pudding of a dog ran frenziedly up the street alone.

"Ticket to Denver," said Jim.

"Make it two," shouted the ex-dogman, reaching for his inside pocket.

THE CHAMPION OF THE WEATHER

If you should speak of the Kiowa Reservation to the average New Yorker he probably wouldn't know whether you were referring to a new political dodge at Albany or a leitmotif from "Parsifal." But out in the Kiowa Reservation advices have been received concerning the existence of New York.

A party of us were on a hunting trip in the Reservation. Bud Kingsbury, our guide, philosopher, and friend, was broiling antelope steaks in camp one night. One of the party, a pinkish-haired young man in a correct hunting costume, sauntered over to the fire to light a cigarette, and remarked carelessly to Bud:

"Nice night!"

"Why, yes," said Bud, "as nice as any night could be that ain't received the Broadway stamp of approval."

Now, the young man was from New York, but the rest of us wondered how Bud guessed it. So, when the steaks were done, we besought him to lay bare his system of ratiocination. And as Bud was something of a Territorial talking machine he made oration as follows:

"How did I know he was from New York? Well, I figured it out as soon as he sprung them two words on me. I was in New York myself a couple of years ago, and I noticed some of the earmarks and hoof tracks of the Rancho Manhattan."

"Found New York rather different from the Panhandle, didn't you, Bud?" asked one of the hunters.

"Can't say that I did," answered Bud; "anyways, not more than some. The main trail in that town which they call Broadway is plenty traveled, but they're about the same brand of bipeds that tramp around in Cheyenne and Amarillo. At first I was sort of rattled by the crowds, but I soon says to myself, 'Here, now, Bud; they're just plain folks like you and Geronimo and Grover Cleveland and the Watson boys, so don't get all flustered up with consternation under your saddle blanket,' and then I feels calm and peaceful, like I was back in the Nation again at a ghost dance or a green corn pow-pow.

"I'd been saving up for a year to give this New York a whirl. I knew a man named Summers that lived there, but I couldn't find him; so I played a lone hand at enjoying the intoxicating pleasures of the corn-fed metropolis.

"For a while I was so frivolous and locoed by the electric lights and the noises of the phonographs and the second-story railroads that I forgot one of the crying needs of my Western system of natural requirements. I never was no hand to deny myself the pleasures of social vocal intercourse with friends and strangers. Out in the Territories when I meet a man I never saw before, inside of nine minutes I know his income, religion, size of collar, and his wife's temper, and how much he pays for clothes, alimony, and chewing tobacco. It's a gift with me not to be penurious with my conversation.

"But this here New York was inaugurated on the idea of abstemiousness in regard to the parts of speech. At the end of three weeks nobody in the city had fired even a blank syllable in my direction except the waiter in the grub emporium where I fed. And as his outpourings of syntax wasn't nothing but plagiarisms from the bill of fare, he never satisfied my yearnings, which was to have somebody hit. If I stood next to a man at a bar he'd edge off and give a Baldwin-Ziegler look as if he suspected me of having the North Pole concealed on my person. I began to wish that I'd gone to Abilene or Waco for my *paseado;* for the mayor of them places will drink with you, and the first citizen you meet will tell you his middle name and ask you to take a chance in a raffle for a music box.

"Well, one day when I was particular hankering for to be gregarious with something more loquacious than a lamp post, a fellow in a caffy says to me, says he:

"'Nice day!'

"He was a kind of a manager of the place, and I reckon he'd seen me in there a good many times. He had a face like a fish and an eye like Judas, but I got up and put one arm around his neck.

"'Pardner,' I says, 'sure it's a nice day. You're the first gentleman in all New York to observe that the intricacies of human speech might not be altogether wasted on William Kingsbury. But don't you think,' says I, 'that 'twas a little cool early in the morning; and ain't there a feeling of rain in the air tonight? But along about noon it sure was gallupsious weather. How's all up to the house? You doing right well with the caffy, now?'

"Well, sir, that galoot just turns his back and walks off stiff, without a word, after all my trying to be agreeable! I didn't know what to make of it. That night I finds a note from Summers, who'd been away from town, giving the address of his camp. I goes up to his house and has a good, old-time talk with his folks. And I tells Summers about the actions of this coyote in the caffy, and desires interpretation.

"'Oh,' says Summers, 'he wasn't intending to strike up a conversation with you. That's just the New York style. He'd seen you was a regular customer and he spoke a word or two just to show you he appreciated your custom. You oughtn't to have followed it up. That's about as far as we care to go with a stranger. A word or so about the weather may be ventured, but we don't generally make it the basis of an acquaintance.'

"'Billy,' says I, 'the weather and its ramifications is a solemn subject with me. Meteorology is one of my sore points. No man can open up the question of temperature or humidity or the glad sunshine with me, and then turn tail on it without its leading to a falling barometer. I'm going down to see that man again and give him a lesson in the art of continuous conversation. You say New York etiquette allows him two words and no answer. Well, he's going to turn himself into a weather bureau and finish what he begun with me, besides indulging in neighborly remarks on other subjects.'

"Summers talked agin it, but I was irritated some and I went on the street car back to that caffy.

"The same fellow was there yet, walking round in a sort of black corral where there was tables and chairs. A few people was sitting around having drinks and sneering at one another.

"I called that man to one side and herded him into a corner. I unbuttoned enough to show him a thirty-eight I carried stuck under my vest.

"'Pardner,' I says, 'a brief space ago I was in here and you seized the opportunity to say it was a nice day. When I attempted to coroborate your weather signal, you turned your back and walked off. Now,' says I, 'you frog-hearted, language-shy, stiff-necked cross between a Spitzbergen sea cook and a muzzled oyster, you resume where you left off in your discourse on the weather.'

"The fellow looks at me and tries to grin, but he sees I don't and he comes around serious.

"'Well,' says he, eyeing the handle of my gun, 'it was rather a nice day; some warmish, though.'

"'Particulars, you mealy-mouthed snoozer,' I says—'let's have the specifica-tions—expatiate—fill in the outlines. When you start anything with me in shorthand it's bound to turn out a storm signal.'

"'Looked like rain yesterday,' says the man, 'but it cleared off fine in the forenoon. I hear the farmers are needing rain right badly up-State.'

"'That's the kind of a canter,' says I. 'Shake the New York dust off your hoofs and be a real agreeable kind of a centaur. You broke the ice, you know, and we're getting better acquainted every minute. Seems to me I asked you about your family?'

"'They're all well, thanks,' says he. 'We—we have a new piano.'

"'Now you're coming it,' I says. 'This cold reserve is breaking up at last. That little touch about the piano almost makes us brothers. What's the youngest kid's name?' I asks him.

"'Thomas,' says he. 'He's just getting well from the measles.'

"'I feel like I'd known you always,' says I. 'Now there was just one more —are you doing right well with the caffy, now?'

"'Pretty well,' he says. 'I'm putting away a little money.'

"'Glad to hear it,' says I. 'Now go back to your work and get civilized. Keep your hands off the weather unless you're ready to follow it up in a personal manner. It's a subject that naturally belongs to sociability and the forming of new ties, and I hate to see it handed out in small change in a town like this.'

"So the next day I rolls up my blankets and hits the trail away from New York City."

For many minutes after Bud ceased talking we lingered around the fire, and then all hands began to disperse for bed.

As I was unrolling my bedding I heard the pinkish-haired young man saying to Bud, with something like anxiety in his voice:

"As I say, Mr. Kingsbury, there is something really beautiful about this night. The delightful breeze and the bright stars and the clear air unite in making it wonderfully attractive."

"Yes," said Bud, "it's a nice night."

MAKES THE WHOLE WORLD KIN

THE burglar stepped inside the window quickly, and then he took his time. A burglar who respects his art always takes his time before taking anything else.

The house was a private residence. By its boarded front door and untrimmed Boston ivy the burglar knew that the mistress of it was sitting on some ocean-side piazza telling a sympathetic man in a yachting cap that no one had ever understood her sensitive, lonely heart. He knew by the light in the third-story front windows, and by the lateness of the season, that the master of the house had come home, and would soon extinguish his light and retire. For it was September of the year and of the soul, in which season the house's good man comes to consider roof gardens and stenographers as vanities, and to desire the return of his mate and the more durable blessings of decorum and the moral excellencies.

The burglar lighted a cigarette. The guarded glow of the match illuminated his salient points for a moment. He belonged to the third type of burglars.

This third type has not yet been recognized and accepted. The police have made us familiar with the first and second. Their classification is simple. The collar is the distinguishing mark.

When a burglar is caught who does not wear a collar he is decribed as a degenerate of the lowest type, singularly vicious and depraved, and is suspected of being the desperate criminal who stole the handcuffs out of Patrolman Hennessy's pocket in 1878 and walked away to escape arrest.

The other well-known type is the burglar who wears a collar. He is always referred to as a Raffles in real life. He is invariably a gentleman by daylight, breakfasting in a dress suit, and posing as a paper-hanger, while after dark he plies his nefarious occupation of burglary. His mother is an extremely wealthy and respected resident of Ocean Grove, and when he is conducted to his cell he asks at once for a nail file and the *Police Gazette*. He always has a wife in every State in the Union and fiancées in all the Territories, and the newspapers print his matrimonial gallery out of their stock of cuts of the ladies who were cured by only one bottle after having been given up by five doctors, experiencing great relief after the first dose.

The burglar wore a blue sweater. He was neither a Raffles nor one of the chefs from Hell's Kitchen. The police would have been baffled had they attempted to classify him. They have not yet heard of the respectable, unassuming burglar who is neither above nor below his station.

This burglar of the third class began to prowl. He wore no masks, dark lanterns, or gum shoes. He carried a 38-calibre revolver in his pocket, and he chewed peppermint gum thoughtfully.

The furniture of the house was swathed in its summer dust protectors. The silver was far away in safe-deposit vaults. The burglar expected no remarkable "haul." His objective point was that dimly lighted room where the master of the house should be sleeping heavily after whatever solace he had sought to lighten the burden of his loneliness. A "touch" might be made there to the extent of legitimate, fair professional profits—loose money, a watch, a jeweled stick-pin —nothing exorbitant or beyond reason. He had seen the window left open and had taken the chance.

The burglar softly opened the door of the lighted room. The gas was turned low. A man lay in the bed asleep. On the dresser lay many things in confusion —a crumpled roll of bills, a watch, keys, three poker chips, crushed cigars, a pink silk hair bow, and an unopened bottle of bromo-seltzer for a bulwark in the morning.

The burglar took three steps toward the dresser. The man in the bed suddenly uttered a squeaky groan and opened his eyes. His right hand slid under his pillow, but remained there.

"Lay still," said the burglar in conversational tone. Burglars of the third type do not hiss. The citizen in the bed looked at the round end of the burglar's pistol and lay still.

"Now hold up both your hands," commanded the burglar.

The citizen had a little, pointed, brown-and-gray beard, like that of a painless dentist. He looked solid, esteemed, irritable, and disgusted. He sat up in bed and raised his right hand above his head.

"Up with the other one," ordered the burglar. "You might be amphibious and shoot with your left. You can count two, can't you? Hurry up, now."

"Can't raise the other one," said the citizen with a contortion of his lineaments.

"What's the matter with it?"

"Rheumatism in the shoulder."

"Inflammatory?"

"Was. The inflammation has gone down."

The burglar stood for a moment or two, holding his gun on the afflicted one. He glanced at the plunder on the dresser and then, with a half-embarrassed air back at the man in the bed. Then he, too, made a sudden grimace.

"Don't stand there making faces," snapped the citizen, bad-humoredly. "If you've come to burgle why don't you do it? There's some stuff lying around."

"'Scuse me," said the burglar, with a grin; "but it just socked me one, too. It's good for you that rheumatism and me happens to be old pals. I got it in my left arm, too. Most anybody but me would have popped you when you wouldn't hoist that left claw of yours."

"How long have you had it?" inquired the citizen.

"Four years. I guess that ain't all. Once you've got it, it's you for a rheumatic life—that's my judgment."

"Ever try rattlesnake oil?" asked the citizen interestedly.

"Gallons," said the burglar. "If all the snakes I've used the oil of was strung out in a row they'd reach eight times as far as Saturn, and the rattles could be heard at Valparaiso, Indiana, and back."

"Some use Chiselum's Pills," remarked the citizen.

"Fudge!" said the burglar. "Took 'em five months. No good. I had some relief the year I tried Finkelham's Extract, Balm of Gilead poultices, and Pott's Pain Pulverizer; but I think it was the buckeye I carried in my pocket what done the trick."

"Is yours worse in the morning or at night?" asked the citizen.

"Night," said the burglar; "just when I'm busiest. Say, take down that arm of yours—I guess you won't— Say! did you ever try Blickerstaff's Blood Builder?"

"I never did. Does yours come in paroxysms or is it a steady pain?"

The burglar sat down on the foot of the bed and rested his gun on his crossed knee.

"It jumps," said he. "It strikes me when I ain't looking for it. I had to give up second-story work because I got stuck sometimes half-way up. Tell you what—I don't believe the bloomin' doctors know what is good for it."

"Same here. I've spent a thousand dollars without getting any relief. Yours swell any?"

"Of mornings. And when it's goin' to rain—great Christopher!"

"Me, too," said the citizen. "I can tell when a streak of humidity the size of a tablecloth starts from Florida on its way to New York. And if I pass a theatre where there's an 'East Lynne' matinée going on, the moisture starts my left arm jumping like a toothache."

"It's undiluted—hades!" said the burglar.

"You're dead right," said the citizen.

The burglar looked down at his pistol and thrust it into his pocket with an awkward attempt at ease.

"Say, old man," he said, constrainedly, "ever try opodeldoc?"

"Slop!" said the citizen, angrily. "Might as well rub on restaurant butter."

"Sure," concurred the burglar. "It's a salve suitable for little Minnie when the kitty scratches her finger. I'll tell you what! We're up against it. I only find one thing that eases her up. Hey? Little old sanitary, ameliorating, lest-we-forgot Booze. Say—this job's off—'scuse me—get on your clothes and let's go out and have some. 'Scuse the liberty, but—ouch! There she goes again!"

"For a week," said the citizen, "I haven't been able to dress myself without help. I'm afraid Thomas is in bed, and——"

"Climb out," said the burglar, "I'll help you get into your duds."

The conventional returned as a tidal wave and flooded the citizen. He stroked his brown-and-gray beard.

"It's very unusual——" he began.

"Here's your shirt," said the burglar, "fall out. I know a man who said Omberry's Ointment fixed him in two weeks so he could use both hands in tying his four-in-hand."

As they were going out the door the citizen turned and started back.

"'Liked to forgot my money," he explained; "laid it on the dresser last night."

The burglar caught him by the right sleeve.

"Come on," he said, bluffly. "I ask you. Leave it alone. I've got the price. Ever try witch hazel and oil of wintergreen?"

AT ARMS WITH MORPHEUS

I NEVER could quite understand how Tom Hopkins came to make that blunder, for he had been through a whole term at a medical college—before he inherited his aunt's fortune—and had been considered strong in therapeutics.

We had been making a call together that evening, and afterward Tom ran up to my rooms for a pipe and a chat before going on to his own luxurious apartments. I had stepped into the other room for a moment when I heard Tom sing out:

"Oh, Billy, I'm going to take about four grains of quinine, if you don't mind —I'm feeling all blue and shivery. Guess I'm taking cold."

"All right," I called back. "The bottle is on the second shelf. Take it in a spoonful of that elixir of eucalyptus. It knocks the bitter out."

After I came back we sat by the fire and got our briars going. In about eight minutes Tom sank back into a gentle collapse.

I went straight to the medicine cabinet and looked.

"You unimitigated hayseed!" I growled. "See what money will do for a man's brains!"

There stood the morphine bottle with the stopple out, just as Tom had left it.

I routed out another young M.D. who roomed on the floor above, and sent him for old Doctor Gales, two squares away. Tom Hopkins has too much money to be attended by rising young practitioners alone.

When Gales came we put Tom through as expensive a course of treatment as the resources of the profession permit. After the more drastic remedies we gave him citrate of caffeine in frequent doses and strong coffee, and walked him up and down the floor between two of us. Old Gales pinched him and slapped his face and worked hard for the big check he could see in the distance. The young M.D. from the next floor gave Tom a most hearty, rousing kick, and then apologized to me.

"Couldn't help it," he said. "I never kicked a millionaire before in my life. I may never have another opportunity."

"Now," said Doctor Gales, after a couple of hours, "he'll do. But keep him awake for another hour. You can do that by talking to him and shaking him up occasionally. When his pulse and respiration are normal then let him sleep. I'll leave him with you now."

I was left alone with Tom, whom we had laid on a couch. He lay very still, and his eyes were half closed. I began my work of keeping him awake.

"Well, old man," I said, "you've had a narrow squeak, but we've pulled you through. When you were attending lectures, Tom, didn't any of the professors ever casually remark that m-o-r-p-h-i-a never spells 'quinia,' especially in four-grain doses? But I won't pile it up on you until you get on your feet. But you ought to have been a druggist, Tom; you're splendidly qualified to fill prescriptions."

Tom looked at me with a faint and foolish smile.

"B'ly," he murmured, "I feel jus' like a hum'n bird flyin' around a jolly lot of most 'shpensive roses. Don' bozzer me. Goin' sleep now.'

And he went to sleep in two seconds. I shook him by the shoulder.

"Now, Tom," I said, severely, "this won't do. The big doctor said you must stay awake for at least an hour. Open your eyes. You're not entirely safe yet, you know. Wake up."

Tom Hopkins weighs one hundred and ninety-eight. He gave me another somnolent grin, and fell into deeper slumber. I would have made him move about, but I might as well have tried to make Cleopatra's needle waltz around the room with me. Tom's breathing became stertorous, and that, in connection with morphia poisoning, means danger.

Then I began to think. I could not rouse his body; I must strive to excite his mind. "Make him angry," was an idea that suggested itself. "Good!" I thought; but how? There was not a joint in Tom's armor. Dear old fellow! He was good nature itself, and a gallant gentleman, fine and true and clean as sunlight. He came from somewhere down South, where they still have ideals and a code. New York had charmed but had not spoiled him. He had that old-fashioned, chivalrous reverence for women, that—Eureka!—there was my idea! I worked the thing up for a minute or two in my imagination. I chuckled to myself at the thought of springing a thing like that on old Tom Hopkins. Then I took him by the shoulder and shook him till his ears flopped. He opened his eyes lazily. I assumed an expression of scorn and contempt, and pointed my finger within two inches of his nose.

"Listen to me, Hopkins," I said, in cutting and distinct tones, "you and I have been good friends, but I want you to understand that in the future my doors are closed against any man who acts as much like a scoundrel as you have."

Tom looked the least bit interested.

"What's the matter, Billy?" he muttered, composedly. "Don't your clothes fit you?"

"If I were in your place," I went on, "which, thank God, I am not, I think I would be afraid to close my eyes. How about that girl you left waiting for you down among those lonesome Southern pines—the girl that you've forgotten since you came into your confounded money? Oh, I know what I'm talking about. While you were a poor medical student she was good enough for you.

But now, since you are a millionaire, it's different. I wonder what she thinks of the performances of that peculiar class of people which she has been taught to worship—the Southern gentlemen? I'm sorry, Hopkins, that I was forced to speak about these matters, but you've covered it up so well and played your part so nicely that I would have sworn you were above such unmanly tricks."

Poor Tom. I could scarcely keep from laughing outright to see him struggling against the effects of the opiate. He was distinctly angry, and I didn't blame him. Tom had a Southern temper. His eyes were open now, and they showed a gleam or two of fire. But the drug still clouded his mind and bound his tongue.

"C-c-confound you," he stammered, "I'll s-smash you."

He tried to rise from the couch. With all his size he was very weak now. I thrust him back with one arm. He lay there glaring like a lion in a trap.

"That will hold you for a while, you old loony," I said to myself. I got up and lit my pipe, for I was needing a smoke. I walked around a bit, congratulating myself on my brilliant idea.

I heard a snore. I looked around. Tom was asleep again. I walked over and punched him on the jaw. He looked at me as pleasant and ungrudging as an idiot. I chewed my pipe and gave it to him hard.

"I want you to recover yourself and get out of my rooms as soon as you can," I said, insultingly. "I've told you what I think of you. If you have any honor or honesty left you will think twice before you attempt again to associate with gentlemen. She's a poor girl, isn't she?" I sneered. "Somewhat too plain and unfashionable for us since we got our money. Be ashamed to walk on Fifth Avenue with her, wouldn't you? Hopkins, you're forty-seven times worse than a cad. Who cares for your money? I don't. I'll bet that girl don't. Perhaps if you didn't have it you'd be more of a man. As it is you've made a cur of yourself, and"—I thought that quite dramatic—"perhaps broken a faithful heart." (Old Tom Hopkins breaking a faithful heart!) "Let me be rid of you as soon as possible."

I turned my back on Tom, and winked at myself in a mirror. I heard him moving, and I turned again quickly. I didn't want a hundred and ninety-eight pounds falling on me from the rear. But Tom had only turned partly over, and laid one arm across his face. He spoke a few words rather more distinctly than before.

"I couldn't have—talked this way—to you, Billy, even if I'd heard people—lyin' 'bout you. But jus' soon's I can s-stand up—I'll break your neck—don't f'get it."

I did feel a little ashamed then. But it was to save Tom. In the morning, when I explained it, we would have a good laugh over it together.

In about twenty minutes Tom dropped into a sound, easy slumber. I felt his pulse, listened to his respiration, and let him sleep. Everything was normal, and Tom was safe. I went into the other room and tumbled into bed.

I found Tom up and dressed when I awoke the next morning. He was entirely himself again with the exception of shaky nerves and a tongue like a white-oak chip.

"What an idiot I was," he said, thoughtfully. "I remember thinking that quinine bottle looked queer while I was taking the dose. Have much trouble in bringing me 'round?"

I told him no. His memory seemed bad about the entire affair. I concluded that he had no recollection of my efforts to keep him awake, and decided not to enlighten him. Some other time, I thought, when he was feeling better, we would have some fun over it.

When Tom was ready to go he stopped, with the door open, and shook my hand.

"Much obliged, old fellow," he said, quietly, "for taking so much trouble with me—and for what you said. I'm going down to telegraph to the little girl."

A GHOST OF A CHANCE

"ACTUALLY, a *hod!*" repeated Mrs. Kinsolving, pathetically.

Mrs. Bellamy Bellmore arched a sympathetic eyebrow. Thus she expressed condolence and a generous amount of apparent surprise.

"Fancy her telling everywhere," recapitulated Mrs. Kinsolving, "that she saw a ghost in the apartment she occupied here—our choicest guest-room—a ghost, carrying a hod on its shoulder—the ghost of an old man in overalls, smoking a pipe and carrying a hod! The very absurdity of the thing shows her malicious intent. There never was a Kinsolving that carried a hod. Every one knows that Mr. Kinsolving's father accumulated his money by large building contracts, but he never worked a day with his own hands. He had this house built from his own plans; but—oh, a hod! Why need she have been so cruel and malicious?"

"It is really too bad," murmured Mrs. Bellmore, with an approving glance of her fine eyes about the vast chamber done in lilac and old gold. "And it was in this room she saw it. Oh, no, I'm not afraid of ghosts. Don't have the least fear on my account. I'm glad you put me in here. I think family ghosts so interesting. But, really, the story does sound a little inconsistent. I should have expected something better from Mrs. Fischer-Suympkins. Don't they carry bricks in hods? Why should a ghost bring bricks into a villa built of marble and stone? I'm so sorry, but it makes me think that age is beginning to tell upon Mrs. Fischer-Suympkins."

"This house," continued Mrs. Kinsolving, "was built upon the site of an old one used by the family during the Revolution. There wouldn't be anything strange in its having a ghost. And there was a Captain Kinsolving who fought in General Greene's army, though we've never been able to secure any papers to vouch for it. If there is to be a family ghost, why couldn't it have been his, instead of a bricklayer's?"

"The ghost of a Revolutionary ancestor wouldn't be a bad idea," agreed Mrs. Bellmore; "but you know how arbitrary and inconsiderate ghosts can be. Maybe, like love, they are 'engendered in the eye.' One advantage of those who see ghosts is that their stories can't be disproved. By a spiteful eye, a Revolutionary knapsack might easily be construed to be a hod. Dear Mrs. Kinsolving, think no more of it. I am sure it was a knapsack."

"But she told everybody!" mourned Mrs. Kinsolving inconsolable. "She insisted upon the details. There is the pipe. And how are you going to get out of the overalls?"

"Sha'n't get into them," said Mrs. Bellmore, with a prettily suppressed yawn; "too stiff and wrinkly. Is that you, Felice? Prepare my bath, please. Do you dine at seven at Clifftop, Mrs. Kinsolving? So kind of you to run in for a chat before dinner! I love those little touches of informality with a guest. They give such a home flavor to a visit. So sorry; I must be dressing. I am so indolent I always postpone it until the last moment."

Mrs. Fischer-Suympkins had been the first large plum that the Kinsolvings had drawn from the social pie. For a long time, the pie itself had been out of reach on a top shelf. But the purse and the pursuit had at last lowered it. Mrs. Fischer-Suympkins was the heliograph of the smart society parading corps. The glitter of her wit and actions passed along the line, transmitting whatever was latest and most daring in the game of peep-show. Formerly, her fame and leadership had been secure enough not to need the support of such artifices as handing around live frogs for favors at a cotillion. But, now, these things were necessary to the holding of her throne. Besides, middle age had come to preside, incongruous, at her capers. The sensational papers had cut her space from a page to two columns. Her wit developed a sting; her manners became more rough and inconsiderate, as if she felt the royal necessity of establishing her autocracy by scorning the conventionalities that bound lesser potentates.

To some pressure at the command of the Kinsolvings, she had yielded so far as to honor their house by her presence, for an evening and night. She had her revenge upon her hostess by relating, with grim enjoyment and sarcastic humor, her story of the vision carrying the hod. To that lady, in raptures at having penetrated thus far toward the coveted inner circle, the result came as a crushing disappointment. Everybody either sympathized or laughed, and there was little to choose between the two modes of expression.

But, later on, Mrs. Kinsolving's hopes and spirits were revived by the capture of a second and greater prize.

Mrs. Bellamy Bellmore had accepted an invitation to visit at Clifftop, and would remain for three days. Mrs. Bellmore was one of the younger matrons, whose beauty, descent, and wealth gave her a reserved seat in the holy of holies that required no strenuous bolstering. She was generous enough thus to give Mrs. Kinsolving the accolade that was so poignantly desired; and, at the same time, she thought how much it would please Terence. Perhaps it would end by solving him.

Terence was Mrs. Kinsolving's son, aged twenty-nine, quite good-looking enough, and with two or three attractive and mysterious traits. For one, he was very devoted to his mother, and that was sufficiently odd to deserve notice. For others, he talked so little that it was irritating, and he seemed either very shy or very deep. Terence interested Mrs. Bellmore, because she was not sure which it was. She intended to study him a little longer unless she forgot the matter. If he was only shy, she would abandon him, for shyness is a bore. If he was deep, she would also abandon him, for depth is precarious.

On the afternoon of the third day of her visit, Terence hunted up Mrs. Bellmore, and found her in a nook actually looking at an album.

"It's so good of you," said he, "to come down here and retrieve the day for us. I suppose you have heard that Mrs. Fischer-Suympkins scuttled the ship before she left. She knocked a whole plank out of the bottom with a hod. My mother is grieving herself ill about it. Can't you manage to see a ghost for us while you are here, Mrs. Bellmore—a bang-up, swell ghost, with a coronet on his head and a cheque book under his arm?"

"That was a naughty old lady, Terence," said Mrs. Bellmore, "to tell such stories. Perhaps you gave her too much supper. Your mother doesn't really take it seriously, does she?"

"I think she does," answered Terence. "One would think every brick in the hod had dropped on her. It's a good mammy, and I don't like to see her worried. It's to be hoped that the ghost belongs to the hod-carriers' union, and will go out on a strike. If he doesn't there will be no peace in this family."

"I'm sleeping in the ghost-chamber," said Mrs. Bellmore, pensively. "But it's so nice I wouldn't change it, even if I were afraid, which I'm not. It wouldn't do for me to submit a counter story of a desirable, aristocratic shade, would it? I would do so, with pleasure, but it seems to me that it would be too obviously an antidote for the other narrative to be effective."

"True," said Terence, running two fingers thoughtfully into his crisp brown hair; "that would never do. How would it work to see the same ghost again, minus the overalls, and have gold bricks in the hod? That would elevate the spectre from degrading toil to a financial plane. Don't you think that would be respectable enough?"

"There was an ancestor who fought against the Britishers, wasn't there? Your mother said something to that effect."

"I believe so; one of those old chaps in raglan vests and golf trousers. I don't care a continental for a Continental, myself. But the mother has set her heart on pomp and heraldry and pyrotechnics, and I want her to be happy."

"You are a good boy, Terence," said Mrs. Bellmore, sweeping her silks close to one side of her; "not to beat your mother. Sit here by me, and let's look at the album, just as people used to do twenty years ago. Now, tell me about every one of them. Who is this tall, dignified gentleman leaning against the horizon, with one arm on the Corinthian column?"

"That old chap with the big feet?" inquired Terence, craning his neck. "That's great-uncle O'Brannigan. He used to keep a rathskeller on the Bowery."

"I asked you to sit down, Terence. If you are not going to amuse, or obey me, I shall report in the morning that I saw a ghost wearing an apron and carrying schooners of beer. Now, that is better. To be shy, at your age, Terence, is a thing that you should blush to acknowledge."

At breakfast on the last morning of her visit, Mrs. Bellmore startled and entranced every one present by announcing positively that she had seen the ghost.

"Did it have a—a—a——?" Mrs. Kinsolving, in her suspense and agitation, could not bring out the word.

"No, indeed—far from it."

There was a chorus of questions from others at the table. "Weren't you frightened?" "What did it do?" "How did it look?" "How was it dressed?" "Did it say anything?" "Didn't you scream?"

"I'll try to answer everything at once," said Mrs. Bellmore, heroically, "although I'm frightfully hungry. Something awakened me—I'm not sure whether it was a noise or a touch—and there stood the phantom. I never burn a light at night, so the room was quite dark, but I saw it plainly. I wasn't dreaming. It was a tall man, all misty white from head to foot. It wore the full dress of the old Colonial days—powdered hair, baggy coat skirts, lace ruffles, and a sword. It looked intangible and luminous in the dark, and moved without a sound. Yes, I was a little frightened at first—or startled, I should say. It was the first ghost I had ever seen. No, it didn't say anything. I didn't scream. I raised up on my elbow, and then it glided silently away, and disappeared when it reached the door."

Mrs. Kinsolving was in the seventh heaven. "The description is that of Captain Kinsolving, of General Greene's army, one of our ancestors," she said, in a voice that trembled with pride and relief. "I really think I must apologize for our ghostly relative, Mrs. Bellmore. I am afraid he must have badly disturbed your rest."

Terence sent a smile of pleased congratulation toward his mother. Attainment was Mrs. Kinsolving's, at last, and he loved to see her happy.

"I suppose I ought to be ashamed to confess," said Mrs. Bellmore, who was now enjoying her breakfast, "that I wasn't very much disturbed. I presume it would have been the customary thing to scream and faint, and have all of you running about in picturesque costumes. But, after the first alarm was over, I really couldn't work myself up to a panic. The ghost retired from the stage quietly and peacefully, after doing its little turn, and I went to sleep again."

Nearly all listened, politely accepted Mrs. Bellmore's story as a made-up affair, charitably offered as an offset to the unkind vision seen by Mrs. Fischer-Suympkins. But one or two present perceived that her assertions bore the genuine stamp of her own convictions. Truth and candor seemed to attend upon every word. Even a scoffer at ghosts—if he were very observant—would have been forced to admit that she had, at least in a very vivid dream, been honestly aware of the weird visitor.

Soon Mrs. Bellmore's maid was packing. In two hours the auto would come to convey her to the station. As Terence was strolling upon the east piazza, Mrs. Bellmore came up to him, with a confidential sparkle in her eye.

"I didn't wish to tell the others all of it," she said, "but I will tell you. In a way, I think you should be held responsible. Can you guess in what manner that ghost awakened me last night?"

"Rattled chains," suggested Terence, after some thought, "or groaned? They usually do one or the other."

"Do you happen to know," continued Mrs. Bellmore, with sudden irrelevancy, "if I resemble any one of the female relatives of your restless ancestor, Captain Kinsolving?"

"Don't think so," said Terence, with an extremely puzzled air. "Never heard of any of them being noted beauties."

"Then, why," said Mrs. Bellmore, looking the young man gravely in the eye, "should that ghost have kissed me, as I'm sure it did?"

"Heavens!" exclaimed Terence, in wide-eyed amazement; "you don't mean that, Mrs. Bellmore! Did he actually kiss you?"

"I said *it*," corrected Mrs. Bellmore. "I hope the impersonal pronoun is correctly used."

"But why did you say I was responsible?"

"Because you are the only living male relative of the ghost."

"I see. 'Unto the third and fourth generation.' But, seriously, did he—did it —how do you——?"

"Know? How does any one know? I was asleep, and that is what awakened me, I'm almost certain."

"Almost?"

"Well, I awoke just as—oh, can't you understand what I mean? When anything arouses you suddenly you are not positive whether you dreamed, or— and yet you know that—— Dear me. Terence, must I dissect the most elementary sensations in order to accommodate your extremely practical intelligence?"

"But, about kissing ghosts, you know," said Terence, humbly, "I require the most primary instruction. I never kissed a ghost. Is it—is it——?"

"The sensation," said Mrs. Bellmore, with deliberate, but slightly smiling, emphasis, "since you are seeking instruction, is a mingling of the material and the spiritual."

"Of course," said Terence, suddenly growing serious, "it was a dream or some kind of an hallucination. Nobody believes in spirits, these days. If you told the tale out of kindness of heart, Mrs. Bellmore, I can't express how grateful I am to you. It has made my mother supremely happy. That Revolutionary ancestor was a stunning idea."

Mrs. Bellmore sighed. "The usual fate of ghost-seers is mine," she said, resignedly. "My privileged encounter with a spirit is attributed to lobster salad or mendacity. Well, I have, at least, one memory left from the wreck—a kiss from the unseen world. Was Captain Kinsolving a very brave man, do you know, Terence?"

"He was licked at Yorktown, I believe," said Terence, reflecting. "They say he skedaddled with his company, after the first battle there."

"I thought he must have been timid," said Mrs. Bellmore, absently. "He might have had another."

"Another battle?" asked Terence, dully.

"What else could I mean? I must go and get ready now; the auto will be here in an hour. I've enjoyed Clifftop immensely. Such a lovely morning, isn't it, Terence?"

On her way to the station, Mrs. Bellmore took from her bag a silk handkerchief, and looked at it with a little peculiar smile. Then she tied it in several very hard knots, and threw it, at a convenient moment, over the edge of the cliff along which the road ran.

In his room, Terence was giving some directions to his man, Brooks. "Have this stuff done up in a parcel," he said, "and ship it to the address on that card."

The card was that of a New York costumer. The "stuff" was a gentleman's costume of the days of '76, made of white satin, with silver buckles, white silk stockings, and white kid shoes. A powdered wig and a sword completed the dress.

"And look about, Brooks," added Terence, a little anxiously, "for a silk handkerchief with my initials in one corner. I must have dropped it somewhere."

It was a month later when Mrs. Bellmore and one or two others of the smart crowd were making up a list of names for a coaching trip through the Catskills. Mrs. Bellmore looked over the list for a final censoring. The name of Terence Kinsolving was there. Mrs. Bellmore ran her prohibitive pencil lightly through the name.

"Too shy!" she murmured, sweetly, in explanation.

JIMMY HAYES AND MURIEL

I

SUPPER was over, and there had fallen upon the camp the silence that accompanies the rolling of corn-husk cigarettes. The water hole shone from the dark earth like a patch of fallen sky. Coyotes yelped. Dull thumps indicated the rocking-horse movements of the hobbled ponies as they moved to fresh grass. A half-troop of the Frontier Battalion of Texas Rangers were distributed about the fire.

A well-known sound—the fluttering and scraping of chaparral against wooden stirrups—came from the thick brush above the camp. The rangers listened cautiously. They heard a loud and cheerful voice call out reassuringly:

"Brace up, Muriel, old girl, we're 'most there now! Been a long ride for ye, ain't it, ye old antediluvian handful of animated carpet-tacks? Hey, now, quit a tryin' to kiss me! Don't hold on to my neck so tight—this here paint hoss ain't any too shore-footed, let me tell ye. He's liable to dump us both off, if we don't watch out."

Two minutes of waiting brought a tired "paint" pony single-footing into camp. A gangling youth of twenty lolled in the saddle. Of the "Muriel" whom he had been addressing, nothing was to be seen.

"Hi, fellows!" shouted the rider, cheerfully. "This here's a letter fer Lieutenant Manning."

He dismounted, unsaddled, dropped the coils of his stake-rope, and got his hobbles from the saddle-horn. While Lieutenant Manning, in command, was reading the letter, the newcomer rubbed solicitously at some dried mud in the loops of the hobbles, showing a consideration for the forelegs of his mount.

"Boys," said the lieutenant, waving his hand to the rangers, "this is Mr. James Hayes. He's a new member of the company. Captain McLean sends him down from El Paso. The boys will see that you have some supper, Hayes, as soon as you get your pony hobbled."

The recruit was received cordially by the rangers. Still, they observed him shrewdly and with suspended judgment. Picking a comrade on the border is done with ten times the care and discretion with which a girl chooses a sweetheart. On your "side-kicker's" nerve, loyalty, aim, and coolness your own life may depend many times.

After a hearty supper Hayes joined the smokers about the fire. His appearance did not settle all the questions in the minds of his brother rangers. They saw simply a loose, lank youth with tow-colored sun-burned hair and a berry-brown, ingenuous face that wore a quizzical, good-natured smile.

"Fellows," said the new ranger, "I'm goin' to interduce to you a lady friend of mine. Ain't ever heard anybody call her a beauty, but you'll all admit she's got some fine points about her. Come along, Muriel!"

He held open the front of his blue flannel shirt. Out of it crawled a horned frog. A bright red ribbon was tied jauntily around its spiky neck. It crawled to its owner's knee and sat there motionless.

"This here Muriel," said Hayes, with an oratorical wave of his hand, "has got qualities. She never talks back, she always stays at home, and she's satisfied with one red dress for every day and Sunday, too."

"Look at that blame insect!" said one of the rangers with a grin. "I've seen plenty of them horny frogs, but I never knew anybody to have one for a side-partner. Does the blame thing know you from anybody else?"

"Take it over there and see," said Hayes.

The stumpy little lizard known as the horned frog is harmless. He has the hideousness of the prehistoric monsters whose reduced descendant he is, but he is gentler than the dove.

The ranger took Muriel from Hayes's knee and went back to his seat on a roll of blankets. The captive twisted and clawed and struggled vigorously in his hand. After holding it for a moment or two, the ranger set it upon the ground. Awkwardly, but swiftly, the frog worked its four oddly moving legs until it stopped close by Hayes's foot.

"Well, dang my hide!" said the other ranger. "The little cuss knows you. Never thought them insects had that much sense!"

II

JIMMY HAYES became a favorite in the ranger camp. He had an endless store of good nature, and a mild, perennial quality of humor that is well adapted to camp life. He was never without his horned frog. In the bosom of his shirt during rides, on his knee or shoulder in camp, under his blankets at night, the ugly little beast never left him.

Jimmy was a humorist of a type that prevails in the rural South and West. Unskilled in originating methods of amusing or in witty conceptions, he had hit upon a comical idea and clung to it reverently. It had seemed to Jimmy a very funny thing to have about his person, with which to amuse his friends, a tame horned frog with a red ribbon around its neck. As it was a happy idea, why not perpetuate it?

The sentiments existing between Jimmy and the frog cannot be exactly determined. The capability of the horned frog for lasting affection is a subject upon which we have no symposiums. It is easier to guess Jimmy's feelings. Muriel was his *chef d'œuvre* of wit, and as such he cherished her. He caught flies for her, and shielded her from sudden northers. Yet his care was half selfish, and when the time came she repaid him a thousand fold. Other Muriels have thus overbalanced the light attentions of other Jimmies.

Not at once did Jimmy Hayes attain full brotherhood with his comrades. They loved him for his simplicity and drollness, but there hung above him a great sword of suspended judgment. To make merry in camp is not all of a ranger's life. There are horse-thieves to trail, desperate criminals to run down, bravos to battle with, bandits to rout out of the chaparral, peace and order to be compelled at the muzzle of a six-shooter. Jimmy had been "'most generally a cow-puncher," he said; he was inexperienced in ranger methods of warfare. Therefore the rangers speculated apart and solemnly as to how he would stand fire. For, let it be known, the honor and pride of each ranger company is the individual bravery of its members.

For two months the border was quiet. The rangers lolled, listless, in camp. And then—bringing joy to the rusting guardians of the frontier—Sebastiano Saldar, an eminent Mexican desperado and cattle-thief, crossed the Rio Grande with his gang and began to lay waste the Texas side. There were indications that Jimmy Hayes would soon have the opportunity to show his mettle. The rangers patrolled with alacrity, but Saldar's men were mounted like Lochinvar, and were hard to catch.

One evening, about sundown, the rangers halted for supper after a long ride. Their horses stood panting, with their saddles on. The men were frying bacon and boiling coffee. Suddenly, out of the brush, Sebastiano Saldar and his gang dashed upon them with blazing six-shooters and high-voiced yells. It was a neat surprise. The rangers swore in annoyed tones, and got their Winchesters busy; but the attack was only a spectacular dash of the purest Mexican type. After the florid demonstration the raiders galloped away, yelling, down the river. The rangers mounted and pursued; but in less than two miles the fagged ponies labored so that Lieutenant Manning gave the word to abandon the chase and return to the camp.

Then it was discovered that Jimmy Hayes was missing. Some one remembered having seen him run for his pony when the attack began, but no one had set eyes on him since. Morning came, but no Jimmy. They searched the country around, on the theory that he had been killed or wounded, but without success. Then they followed after Saldar's gang, but it seemed to have disappeared. Manning concluded that the wily Mexican had recrossed the river after his theatric farewell. And, indeed, no further depredations from him were reported.

This gave the rangers time to nurse a soreness they had. As has been said, the pride and honor of the company is the individual bravery of its members. And now they believed that Jimmy Hayes had turned coward at the whiz of Mexican bullets. There was no other deduction. Buck Davis pointed out that not a shot was fired by Saldar's gang after Jimmy was seen running for his horse. There was no way for him to have been shot. No, he had fled from his first fight, and afterward he would not return, aware that the scorn of his comrades would be a worse thing to face than the muzzles of many rifles.

So Manning's detachment of McLean's company, Frontier Battalion, was gloomy. It was the first blot on its escutcheon. Never before in the history of the service had a ranger shown the white feather. All of them had liked Jimmy Hayes, and that made it worse.

Days, weeks, and months went by, and still that little cloud of unforgotten cowardice hung above the camp.

III

NEARLY a year afterward—after many camping grounds and many hundreds of miles guarded and defended—Lieutenant Manning, with almost the same detachment of men, was sent to a point only a few miles below their old camp on the river to look after some smuggling there. One afternoon, while they were riding through a dense mesquite flat, they came upon a patch of open hog-wallow prairie. There they rode upon the scene of an unwritten tragedy.

In a big hog-wallow lay the skeletons of three Mexicans. Their clothing alone served to identify them. The largest of the figures had once been Sebastiano Saldar. His great, costly sombrero, heavy with gold ornamentation—a hat famous all along the Rio Grande—lay there pierced by three bullets. Along the ridge of the hog-wallow rested the rusting Winchesters of the Mexicans—all pointing in the same direction.

The rangers rode in that direction for fifty yards. There, in a little depression of the ground, with his rifle still bearing upon the three, lay another skeleton. It had been a battle of extermination. There was nothing to identify the solitary defender. His clothing—such as the elements had left distinguishable—seemed to be of the kind that any ranchman or cowboy might have worn.

"Some cow-puncher," said Manning, "that they caught out alone. Good boy! He put up a dandy scrap before they got him. So that's why we didn't hear from Don Sebastiano any more!"

And then, from beneath the weather-beaten rags of the dead man, there wriggled out a horned frog with a faded red ribbon around its neck, and sat upon the shoulder of its long quiet master. Mutely it told the story of the untried youth and the swift "paint" pony—how they had outstripped all their comrades that day in the pursuit of the Mexican raiders, and how the boy had gone down upholding the honor of the company.

The ranger troop herded close, and a simultaneous wild yell arose from their lips. The outburst was at once a dirge, an apology, an epitaph, and a pæan of triumph. A strange requiem, you may say, over the body of a fallen comrade; but if Jimmy Hayes could have heard it he would have understood.

THE DOOR OF UNREST

I SAT an hour by sun, in the editor's room of the Montopolis *Weekly Bugle*. I was the editor.

The saffron rays of the declining sunlight filtered through the cornstalks in Micajah Widdup's garden-patch, and cast an amber glory upon my paste-pot. I sat at the editorial desk in my non-rotary revolving chair, and prepared my editorial against the oligarchies. The room, with its one window, was already a prey to the twilight. One by one, with my trenchant sentences, I lopped off the heads of the political hydra, while I listened, full of kindly peace, to the home-coming cowbells and wondered what Mrs. Flanagan was going to have for supper.

Then in from the dusky, quiet street there drifted and perched himself upon a corner of my desk old Father Time's younger brother. His face was beardless and as gnarled as an English walnut. I never saw clothes such as he wore. They would have reduced Joseph's coat to a monochrome. But the colors were not the dyer's. Stains and patches and the work of sun and rust were responsible for the diversity. On his coarse shoes was the dust, conceivably, of a thousand leagues. I can describe him no further, except to say that he was little and weird and old—old I began to estimate in centuries when I saw him. Yes, and I remember that there was an odor, a faint odor like aloes, or possibly like myrrh or leather; and I thought of museums.

And then I reached for a pad and pencil, for business is business, and visits of the oldest inhabitants are sacred and honorable, requiring to be chronicled.

"I am glad to see you, sir," I said. "I would offer you a chair, but—you see, sir," I went on, "I have lived in Montopolis only three weeks, and I have not met many of our citizens." I turned a doubtful eye upon his dust-stained shoes, and concluded with a newspaper phrase, "I suppose that you reside in our midst?"

My visitor fumbled in his raiment, drew forth a soiled card, and handed it to me. Upon it was written, in plain but unsteadily formed characters, the name "Michob Ader."

"I am glad you called, Mr. Ader," I said. "As one of our older citizens, you must view with pride the recent growth and enterprise of Montopolis. Among other improvements, I think I can promise that the town will now be provided with a live, enterprising newspa——"

"Do ye know the name on that card?" asked my caller, interrupting me.

"It is not a familiar one to me," I said.

Again he visited the depths of his ancient vestments. This time he brought out a torn leaf of some book or journal, brown and flimsy with age. The heading of the page was the *Turkish Spy* in old-style type; the printing upon it was this:

"There is a man come to Paris in this year 1643 who pretends to have lived these sixteen hundred years. He says of himself that he was a shoemaker in Jerusalem at the time of the Crucifixion; that his name is Michob Ader; and that when Jesus, the Christian Messias, was condemned by Pontius Pilate, the Roman president, he paused to rest while bearing his cross to the place of crucifixion before the door of Michob Ader. The shoemaker struck Jesus with his fist, saying: 'Go; why tarrist thou?' The Messias answered him: 'I indeed am going; but thou shalt tarry until I come'; thereby condemning him to live until the day of judgment. He lives for ever, but at the end of every hundred years he falls into a fit or trance, on recovering from which he finds himself in the same state of youth in which he was when Jesus suffered, being then about thirty years of age.

"Such is the story of the Wandering Jew, as told by Michob Ader, who relates——" Here the printing ended.

I must have muttered aloud something to myself about the Wandering Jew, for the old man spake up, bitterly and loudly.

" 'Tis a lie," said he, "like nine tenths of what ye call history. 'Tis a Gentile I am, and no Jew. I am after footing it out of Jerusalem, my son; but if that makes me a Jew, then everything that comes out of a bottle is babies' milk. Ye have my name on the card ye hold; and ye have read the bit of paper they call the *Turkish Spy* that printed the news when I stepped into their office on the 12th day of June, in the year 1643, just as I have called upon ye to-day."

I laid down my pencil and pad. Clearly it would not do. Here was an item for the local column of the *Bugle* that—but it would not do. Still, fragments of the impossible "personal" began to flit through my conventionalized brain. "Uncle Michob is as spry on his legs as a young chap of only a thousand or so." "Our venerable caller relates with pride that George Wash—— no, Ptolemy the Great—once dandled him on his knee at his father's house." "Uncle Michob says that our wet spring was nothing in comparison with the dampness that ruined the crops around Mount Ararat when he was a boy——" But no, no—it would not do.

I was trying to think of some conversational subject with which to interest my visitor, and was hesitating between walking matches and the Pliocene Age, when the old man suddenly began to weep poignantly and distressfully.

"Cheer up, Mr. Ader," I said, a little awkwardly; "this matter may blow over in a few hundred years more. There has already been a decided reaction in favor of Judas Iscariot and Colonel Burr and the celebrated violinist, Signor Nero. This is the age of whitewash. You must not allow yourself to become down-hearted."

Unknowingly, I had struck a chord. The old man blinked belligerently through his senile tears.

"'Tis time," he said, "that the liars be doin' justice to somebody. Yer historians are no more than a pack of old women gabblin' at a wake. A finer man than the Imperor Nero niver wore sandals. Man, I was at the burnin' of Rome. I knowed the Imperor well, for in them days I was a well-known char-acter. In thim days they had rayspect for a man that lived for ever.

"But 'twas of the Imperor Nero I was goin' to tell ye. I struck into Rome, up the Appian Way, on the night of July the 16th, the year 64. I had just stepped down by way of Siberia and Afghanistan; and one foot of me had a frost-bite, and the other a blister burned by the sand of the desert; and I was feelin' a bit blue from doin' patrol duty from the North Pole down to the Last Chance corner in Patagonia, and bein' miscalled a Jew in the bargain. Well, I'm tellin' ye I was passin' the Circus Maximus, and it was dark as pitch over the way, and then I heard somebody sing out, 'Is that you, Michob?'

"Over ag'inst the wall, hid out amongst a pile of barrels and old dry-goods boxes, was the Imperor Nero wid his togy wrapped around his toes, smokin' a long, black segar.

"'Have one, Michob?' says he.

"'None of the weeds for me,' says I—'nayther pipe nor segar. What's the use,' says I, 'of smokin' when ye've got not the ghost of a chance of killin' yeself by doin' it?'

"'True for ye, Michob Ader, my perpetual Jew,' says the Imperor; 'ye're not always wandering. Sure, 'tis danger gives the spice of our pleasures—next to their bein' forbidden.'

"'And for what,' says I, 'do ye smoke be night in dark places widout even a cinturion in plain clothes to attend ye?'

"'Have ye ever heard, Michob,' says the Imperor, 'of predestinarianism?'

"'I've had the cousin of it,' says I. 'I've been on the trot with pedestrianism for many a year, and more to come, as ye well know.'

"'The longer word,' says me friend Nero, 'is the tachin' of this new sect of people they call the Christians. 'Tis them that's raysponsible for me smokin' be night in holes and corners of the dark.'

"And then I sets down and takes off a shoe and rubs me foot that is frosted, and the Imperor tells me about it. It seems that since I passed that way before, the Imperor had mandamused the Impress wid a divorce suit, and Misses Poppæa, a cilibrated lady, was ingaged, widout riferences, as housekeeper at the palace. 'All in one day,' says the Imperor, 'she puts up new lace windy-curtains in the palace and joins the anti-tobacco society, and whin I feels the need of a smoke I must be after sneakin' out to these piles of lumber in the dark.' So there in the dark me and the Imperor sat, and I told him of me travels. And when they say tne Imperor was an incindiary, they lie. 'Twas that night the fire started that burnt the city. 'Tis my opinion that it began from a stump of segar that he threw down among the boxes. And 'tis a lie that he fiddled. He did all he could for six days to stop it, sir."

And now I detected a new flavor to Mr. Michob Ader. It had not been myrrh or balm or hyssop that I had smelled. The emanation was the odor of bad whiskey—and, worse still, of low comedy—the sort that small humorists manufacture by clothing the grave and reverend things of legend and history in the vulgar, topical frippery that passes for a certain kind of wit. Michob Ader as an impostor, claiming nineteen hundred years, and playing his part with the decency of respectable lunacy, I could endure; but as a tedious wag, cheapening his egregious story with song-book levity, his importance as an entertainer grew less.

And then, as if he suspected my thoughts, he suddenly shifted his key.

"You'll excuse me, sir," he whined, "but sometimes I get a little mixed in my head. I am a very old man; and it is hard to remember everything."

I knew that he was right, and that I should not try to reconcile him with Roman history; so I asked for news concerning other ancients with whom he had walked familiar.

Above my desk hung an engraving of Raphael's cherubs. You could yet make out their forms, though the dust blurred their outlines strangely.

"Ye calls them 'cher-rubs,'" cackled the old man. "Babes, ye fancy they are, with wings. And there's one wid legs and a bow and arrow that ye call Cupid—I know where they was found. The great-great-great-grandfather of thim all was a billy-goat. Bein' an editor, sir, do ye happen to know where Solomon's Temple stood?"

I fancied that it was in—in Persia? Well, I did not know.

"'Tis not in history nor in the Bible where it was. But I saw it, meself. The first pictures of cher-rubs and cupids was sculptured upon thim walls and pillars. Two of the biggest, sir, stood in the adytum to form the baldachin over the Ark. But the wings of thim sculptures was intindid for horns. And the faces was the faces of goats. Ten thousand goats there was in and about the temple. And your cher-rubs was billy-goats in the days of King Solomon, but the painters misconstrued the horns into wings.

"And I knew Tamerlane, the lame Timour, sir, very well. I saw him at Keghut and at Zaranj. He was a little man no larger than yerself, with hair the color of an amber pipe stem. They buried him at Samarkand. I was at the wake, sir. Oh, he was a fine-built man in his coffin, six feet long, with black whiskers to his face. And I see 'em throw turnips at the Imperor Vispacian in Africa. All over the world I have tramped, sir, without the body of me findin' any rest. 'Twas so commanded. I saw Jerusalem destroyed, and Pompeii go up in the fireworks; and I was at the coronation of Charlemagne and the lynchin' of Joan of Arc. And everywhere I go there comes storms and revolutions and plagues and fires. 'Twas so commanded. Ye have heard of the Wandering Jew. 'Tis all so, except that divil a bit am I Jew. But history lies, as I have told ye. Are ye quite sure, sir, that ye haven't a drop of whiskey convenient? Ye well know that I have many miles of walking before me."

"I have none," said I, "and, if you please, I am about to leave for my supper."

I pushed my chair back creakingly. This ancient landlubber was becoming as great an affliction as any cross-bowed mariner. He shook a musty effluvium from his piebald clothes, overturned my inkstand, and went on with his insufferable nonsense.

"I wouldn't mind it so much," he complained, "if it wasn't for the work I must do on Good Fridays. Ye know about Pontius Pilate, sir, of course. His body, whin he killed himself, was pitched into a lake on the Alps mountains. Now, listen to the job that 'tis mine to perform on the night of every Good Friday. The ould divil goes down in the pool and drags up Pontius, and the water is bilin' and spewin' like a wash pot. And the ould divil sets the body on top of a throne on the rocks, and thin comes me share of the job. Oh, sir, ye would pity me thin—ye would pray for the poor Wandering Jew that niver was a Jew if ye could see the horror of the thing that I must do. 'Tis I that must fetch a bowl of water and kneel down before it till it washes its hands. I declare to ye that Pontius Pilate, a man dead two hundred years, dragged up with the lake slime coverin' him and fishes wrigglin' inside of him widout eyes, and in the discomposition of the body, sits there, sir, and washes his hands in the bowl I hold for him on Good Fridays. 'Twas so commanded."

Clearly, the matter had progressed far beyond the scope of the *Bugle's* local column. There might have been employment here for the alienist or for those who circulate the pledge; but I had had enough of it. I got up, and repeated that I must go.

At this he seized my coat, grovelled upon my desk, and burst again into distressful weeping. Whatever it was about, I said to myself that his grief was genuine.

"Come now, Mr. Ader," I said, soothingly; "what is the matter?"

The answer came brokenly through his racking sobs: "Because I would not . . . let the poor Christ . . . rest . . . upon the step."

His hallucination seemed beyond all reasonable answer; yet the effect of it upon him scarcely merited disrespect. But I knew nothing that might assuage it; and I told him once more that both of us should be leaving the office at once.

Obedient at last, he raised himself from my dishevelled desk, and permitted me to half lift him to the floor. The gale of his grief had blown away his words; his freshet of tears had soaked away the crust of his grief. Reminiscence died in him—at least, the coherent part of it.

" 'Twas me that did it," he muttered, as I led him toward the door—"me, the shoemaker of Jerusalem."

I got him to the sidewalk, and in the augmented light I saw that his face was seared and lined and warped by a sadness almost incredibly the product of a single lifetime.

And then high up in the firmamental darkness we heard the clamant cries of some great passing birds. My Wandering Jew lifted his hand, with side-tilted head.

"The Seven Whistlers!" he said, as one introduces well-known friends.

"Wild geese," said I; "but I confess that their number is beyond me."

"They follow me everywhere," he said. " 'Twas so commanded. What ye hear is the souls of the seven Jews that helped with the Crucifixion. Sometimes they're plovers and sometimes geese, but ye'll find them always flyin' where I go."

I stood, uncertain how to take my leave. I looked down the street, shuffled my feet, looked back again—and felt my hair rise. The old man had disappeared.

And then my capillaries relaxed, for I dimly saw him footing it away through the darkness. But he walked so swiftly and silently and contrary to the gait promised by his age that my composure was not all restored, though I knew not why.

That night I was foolish enough to take down some dust-covered volumes from my modest shelves. I searched "Hermippus Redivvus' and "Salathiel" and the "Pepys Collection" in vain. And then in a book called "The Citizen of the World," and in one two centuries old, I came upon what I desired. Michob Ader had indeed come to Paris in the year 1643, and related to the *Turkish Spy* an extraordinary story. He claimed to be the Wandering Jew, and that——

But here I fell asleep, for my editorial duties had not been light that day.

Judge Hoover was the *Bugle's* candidate for congress. Having to confer with him, I sought his home early the next morning; and we walked together down town through a little street with which I was unfamiliar.

"Did you ever heard of Michob Ader?" I asked him, smiling.

"Why, yes," said the judge. "And that reminds me of my shoes he has for mending. Here is his shop now."

Judge Hoover stepped into a dingy, small shop. I looked up at the sign, and saw "Mike O'Bader, Boot and Shoe Maker," on it. Some wild geese passed above, honking clearly. I scratched my ear and frowned, and then trailed into the shop.

There sat my Wandering Jew on his shoemaker's bench, trimming a half sole. He was drabbled with dew, grass-stained, unkempt, and miserable; and on his face was still the unexplained wretchedness; the problematic sorrow, the esoteric woe, that had been written there by nothing less, it seemed, than the stylus of the centuries.

Judge Hoover inquired kindly concerning his shoes. The old shoemaker looked up, and spoke sanely enough. He had been ill, he said, for a few days. The next day the shoes would be ready. He looked at me, and I could see that I had no place in his memory. So out we went, and on our way.

"Old Mike," remarked the candidate, "has been on one of his sprees. He gets crazy drunk regularly once a month. But he's a good shoemaker."

"What is his history?" I inquired.

"Whiskey," epitomized Judge Hoover. "That explains him."

I was silent, but I did not accept the explanation. And so, when I had the chance, I asked old man Sellers, who browsed daily on my exchanges.

"Mike O'Bader," said he, "was makin' shoes in Montopolis when I come here goin' on fifteen year ago. I guess whiskey's his trouble. Once a month he gets off the track, and stays so a week. He's got a rigmarole somethin' about his bein' a Jew peddler that he tells ev'rybody. Nobody won't listen to him any more. When he's sober he ain't sich a fool—he's got a sight of books in the back room of his shop that he reads. I guess you can lay all his trouble to whiskey."

But again I would not. Not yet was my Wandering Jew rightly construed for me. I trust that women may not be allowed a title to all the curiosity in the world. So when Montopolis's oldest inhabitant (some ninety score years younger than Michob Ader) dropped in to acquire promulgation in print, I siphoned his perpetual trickle of reminiscence in the direction of the uninterpreted maker of shoes.

Uncle Abner was the Complete History of Montopolis, bound in butternut.

"O'Bader," he quavered, "come here in '69. He was the first shoemaker in the place. Folks generally considers him crazy at times now. But he don't harm nobody. I s'pose drinkin' upset his mind—yes, drinkin' very likely done it. It's a powerful bad thing, drinkin'. I'm an old, old man, sir, and I never see no good in drinkin'."

I felt disappointment. I was willing to admit drink in the case of my shoemaker, but I preferred it as a recourse instead of a cause. Why had he pitched upon his perpetual, strange note of the Wandering Jew? Why his unutterable grief during his aberration? I could not yet accept whiskey as an explanation.

"Did Mike O'Bader ever have a great loss or trouble of any kind?" I asked.

"Lemme see! About thirty year ago there was somethin' of the kind, I recollect. Montopolis, sir, in them days used to be a mighty strict place.

"Well, Mike O'Bader had a daughter then—a right pretty girl. She was too gay a sort for Montopolis, so one day she slips off to another town and runs away with a circus. It was two years before she comes back, all fixed up in fine clothes and rings and jewelry, to see Mike. He wouldn't have nothin' to do with her, so she stays around town awhile, anyway. I reckon the men folks wouldn't have raised no objections, but the women egged 'em on to order her to leave town. But she had plenty of spunk, and told 'em to mind their own business.

"So one night they decided to run her away. A crowd of men and women drove her out of her house, and chased her with sticks and stones. She run to her father's door, callin' for help. Mike opens it, and when he sees who it is he hits her with his fist and knocks her down and shuts the door.

"And then the crowd kept on chunkin' her till she run clear out of town. And the next day they finds her drowned dead in Hunter's mill pond. I mind it all now. That was thirty year ago."

I leaned back in my non-rotary revolving chair and nodded gently, like a mandarin, at my paste-pot.

"When old Mike has a spell," went on Uncle Abner, tepidly garrulous, "he thinks he's the Wanderin' Jew."

"He is," said I, nodding away.

And Uncle Abner cackled insinuatingly at the editor's remark, for he was expecting at least a "stickful" in the "Personal Notes" of the *Bugle*.

THE DUPLICITY OF HARGRAVES

WHEN Major Pendleton Talbot, of Mobile, sir, and his daughter, Miss Lydia Talbot, came to Washington to reside, they selected for a boarding place a house that stood fifty yards back from one of the quietest avenues. It was an old-fashioned brick building, with a portico upheld by tall white pillars. The yard was shaded by stately locusts and elms, and a catalpa tree in season rained its pink and white blossoms upon the grass. Rows of high box bushes lined the fence and walks. It was the Southern style and aspect of the place that pleased the eyes of the Talbots.

In this pleasant, private boarding house they engaged rooms, including a study for Major Talbot, who was adding the finishing chapters to his book, "Anecdotes and Reminiscences of the Alabama Army, Bench, and Bar."

Major Talbot was of the old, old South. The present day had little interest or excellence in his eyes. His mind lived in that period before the Civil War, when the Talbots owned thousands of acres of fine cotton land and the slaves to till them; when the family mansion was the scene of princely hospitality, and drew its guests from the aristocracy of the South. Out of that period he had brought all of its old pride and scruples of honor, and antiquated and punctilious politeness, and (you would think) its wardrobe.

Such clothes were surely never made within fifty years. The major was tall, but whenever he made that wonderful, archaic genuflexion he called a bow, the corners of his frock coat swept the floor. That garment was a surprise even to Washington, which has long ago ceased to shy at the frocks and broad-brimmed hats of Southern congressmen. One of the boarders christened it a "Father Hubbard," and it certainly was high in the waist and full in the skirt.

But the major, with all his queer clothes, his immense area of plaited, ravelling shirt bosom, and the little black string tie with the bow always slipping on one side, both was smiled at and liked in Mrs. Vardeman's select boarding house. Some of the young department clerks would often "string him," as they called it, getting him started upon the subject dearest to him—the traditions and history of his beloved Southland. During his talks he would quote freely from the "Anecdotes and Reminiscences." But they were very careful not to let him see their designs, for in spite of his sixty-eight years, he could make the boldest of them uncomfortable under the steady regard of his piercing gray eyes.

Miss Lydia was a plump, little old maid of thirty-five, with smoothly drawn, tightly twisted hair that made her look still older. Old fashioned, too, she was; but ante-bellum glory did not radiate from her as it did from the major. She possessed a thrifty common sense; and it was she who handled the finances of the family, and met all comers when there were bills to pay. The major regarded board bills and wash bills as contemptible nuisances. They kept coming in so persistently and so often. Why, the major wanted to know, could they not be filed and paid in a lump sum at some convenient period—say when the "Anecdotes and Reminiscences" had been published and paid for? Miss Lydia would calmly go on with her sewing and say, "We'll pay as we go as long as the money lasts, and then perhaps they'll have to lump it."

Most of Mrs. Vardeman's boarders were away during the day, being nearly all department clerks and business men; but there was one of them who was about the house a great deal from morning to night. This was a young man named Henry Hopkins Hargraves—every one in the house addressed him by his full name—who was engaged at one of the popular vaudeville theatres. Vaudeville has risen to such a respectable plane in the last few years, and Mr. Hargraves was such a modest and well-mannered person, that Mrs. Vardeman could find no objection to enrolling him upon her list of boarders.

At the theatre Hargraves was known as an all-round dialect comedian, having a large repertoire of German, Irish, Swede, and black-face specialties. But Mr. Hargraves was ambitious, and often spoke of his great desire to succeed in legitimate comedy.

This young man appeared to conceive a strong fancy for Major Talbot. Whenever that gentleman would begin his Southern reminiscences, or repeat some of the liveliest of the anecdotes, Hargraves could always be found, the most attentive among his listeners.

For a time the major showed an inclination to discourage the advances of the "play actor," as he privately termed him; but soon the young man's agreeable manner and indubitable appreciation of the old gentleman's stories completely won him over.

It was not long before the two were like old chums. The major set apart each afternoon to read to him the manuscript of his book. During the anecdotes Hargraves never failed to laugh at exactly the right point. The major was moved to declare to Miss Lydia one day that young Hargraves possessed remarkable perception and a gratifying respect for the old régime. And when it came to talking of those old days—if Major Talbot liked to talk, Mr. Hargraves was entranced to listen.

Like almost all old people who talk of the past, the major loved to linger over details. In describing the splendid, almost royal, days of the old planters, he would hesitate until he had recalled the name of the Negro who held his horse, or the exact date of certain minor happenings, or the number of bales of cotton raised in such a year; but Hargraves never grew impatient or lost interest. On the contrary, he would advance questions on a variety of subjects connected with the life of that time, and he never failed to extract ready replies.

The fox hunts, the 'possum suppers, the hoe downs and jubilees in the Negro quarters, the banquets in the plantation-house hall, when invitations went for fifty miles around; the occasional feuds with the neighboring gentry; the major's duel with Rathbone Culbertson about Kitty Chalmers, who afterward married a Thwaite of South Carolina; and private yacht races for fabulous sums on Mobile Bay; the quaint beliefs, improvident habits, and loyal virtues of the old slaves—all these were subjects that held both the major and Hargraves absorbed for hours at a time.

Sometimes, at night, when the young man would be coming upstairs to his room after his turn at the theatre was over, the major would appear at the door of his study and beckon archly to him. Going in, Hargraves would find a little table set with a decanter, sugar bowl, fruit, and a big bunch of fresh green mint.

"It occurred to me," the major would begin—he was always ceremonious—"that perhaps you might have found your duties at the—at your place of occupation—sufficiently arduous to enable you, Mr. Hargraves, to appreciate what the poet might well have had in his mind when he wrote, 'tired Nature's sweet restorer,'—one of our Southern juleps."

It was a fascination to Hargraves to watch him make it. He took rank among artists when he began, and he never varied the process. With what delicacy he bruised the mint; with what exquisite nicety he estimated the ingredients; with what solicitous care he capped the compound with the scarlet fruit glowing against the dark green fringe! And then the hospitality and grace with which he offered it, after the selected oat straws had been plunged into its tinkling depths!

After about four months in Washington, Miss Lydia discovered one morning that they were almost without money. The "Anecdotes and Reminiscences" was completed, but·publishers had not jumped at the collected gems of Alabama sense and wit. The rental of a small house which they still owned in Mobile was two months in arrears. Their board money for the month would be due in three days. Miss Lydia called her father to a consultation.

"No money?" said he with a surprised look. "It is quite annoying to be called on so frequently for these petty sums. Really, I——"

The major searched his pockets. He found only a two-dollar bill, which he returned to his vest pocket.

"I must attend to this at once, Lydia," he said. "Kindly get me my umbrella and I will go down town immediately. The congressman from our district, General Fulghum, assured me some days ago that he would use his influence to get my book published at an early date. I will go to his hotel at once and see what arrangement has been made."

With a sad little smile Miss Lydia watched him button his "Father Hubbard" and depart, pausing at the door, as he always did, to bow profoundly.

That evening, at dark, he returned. It seemed that Congressman Fulghum had seen the publisher who had the major's manuscript for reading. That person had said that if the anecdotes, etc., were carefully pruned down about one half, in order to eliminate the sectional and class prejudice with which the book was dyed from end to end, he might consider its publication.

The major was in a white heat of anger, but regained his equanimity, according to his code of manners, as soon as he was in Miss Lydia's presence.

"We must have money," said Miss Lydia, with a little wrinkle above her nose. "Give me the two dollars, and I will telegraph to Uncle Ralph for some to-night."

The major drew a small envelope from his upper vest pocket and tossed it on the table.

"Perhaps it was injudicious," he said mildly, "but the sum was so merely nominal that I bought tickets to the theatre to-night. It's a new war drama, Lydia. I thought you would be pleased to witness its first production in Washington. I am told that the South has very fair treatment in the play. I confess I should like to see the performance myself."

Miss Lydia threw up her hands in silent despair.

Still, as the tickets were bought, they might as well be used. So that evening, as they sat in the theatre listening to the lively overture, even Miss Lydia was minded to relegate their troubles, for the hour, to second place. The major, in spotless linen, with his extraordinary coat showing only where it was closely buttoned, and his white hair smoothly roached, looked really fine and distinguished. The curtain went up on the first act of "A Magnolia Flower," revealing a typical Southern plantation scene. Major Talbot betrayed some interest.

"Oh, see!" exclaimed Miss Lydia, nudging his arm, and pointing to her programme.

The major put on his glasses and read the line in the cast of characters that her finger indicated.

Col. Webster Calhoun. . . . H. Hopkins Hargraves.

"It's our Mr. Hargraves," said Miss Lydia. "It must be his first appearance in what he calls 'the legitimate.' I'm so glad for him."

Not until the second act did Col. Webster Calhoun appear upon the stage. When he made his entry Major Talbot gave an audible sniff, glared at him, and seemed to freeze solid. Miss Lydia uttered a little ambiguous squeak and crumpled her programme in her hand. For Colonel Calhoun was made up as nearly resembling Major Talbot as one pea does another. The long, thin, white hair, curly at the ends, the aristocratic beak of a nose, the crumpled, wide, ravelling shirt front, the string tie, with the bow nearly under one ear, were almost exactly duplicated. And then, to clinch the imitation, he wore the twin to the major's supposed to be one unparalleled coat. High-collared, baggy, empire-waisted, ample-skirted, hanging a foot lower in front than behind, the garment could have been designed from no other pattern. From then on, the major and Miss Lydia sat bewitched, and saw the counterfeit presentment of a haughty Talbot "dragged," as the major afterward expressed it, "through the slanderous mire of a corrupt stage."

Mr. Hargraves had used his opportunities well. He had caught the major's little idiosyncrasies of speech, accent, and intonation and his pompous court-liness to perfection—exaggerating all to the purpose of the stage. When he performed that marvelous bow that the major fondly imagined to be the pink of all salutations, the audience sent forth a sudden round of hearty applause.

Miss Lydia sat immovable, not daring to glance toward her father. Some-times her hand next to him would be laid against her cheek, as if to conceal the smile which, in spite of her disapproval, she could not entirely suppress.

The culmination of Hargraves's audacious imitation took place in the third act. The scene is where Colonel Calhoun entertains a few of the neighboring planters in his "den."

Standing at a table in the centre of the stage, with his friends grouped about him, he delivers that inimitable, rambling, character monologue so famous in "A Magnolia Flower," at the same time that he deftly makes juleps for the party.

Major Talbot, sitting quietly, but white with indignation, heard his best stories retold, his pet theories and hobbies advanced and expanded, and the dream of the "Anecdotes and Reminiscences" served, exaggerated and garbled. His fav-orite narrative—that of his duel with Rathbone Culbertson—was not omitted, and it was delivered with more fire, egotism, and gusto than the major himself put into it.

The monologue concluded with a quaint, delicious, witty little lecture on the art of concocting a julep, illustrated by the act. Here Major Talbot's delicate but showy science was reproduced to a hair's breadth—from his dainty handling of the fragrant weed—"the one-thousandth part of a grain too much pressure, gentlemen, and you extract the bitterness, instead of the aroma, of this heaven-bestowed plant"—to his solicitous selection of the oaten straws.

At the close of the scene the audience raised a tumultuous roar of appreciation. The portrayal of the type was so exact, so sure and thorough, that the leading characters in the play were forgotten. After repeated calls, Hargraves came before the curtain and bowed, his rather boyish face bright and flushed with the knowledge of success.

At last Miss Lydia turned and looked at the major. His thin nostrils were working like the gills of a fish. He laid both shaking hands upon the arms of his chair to rise.

"We will go, Lydia," he said, chokingly. "This is an abominable—desecration."

Before he could rise, she pulled him back into his seat.

"We will stay it out," she declared. "Do you want to advertise the copy by exhibiting the original coat?" So they remained to the end.

Hargraves's success must have kept him up late that night, for neither at the breakfast nor at the dinner table did he appear.

About three in the afternoon he tapped at the door of Major Talbot's study. The major opened it, and Hargraves walked in with his hands full of the morning papers—too full of his triumph to notice anything unusual in the major's demeanor.

"I put it all over 'em last night, major," he began, exultantly. "I had my inning, and, I think, scored. Here's what the *Post* says:

"His conception and portrayal of the old-time Southern colonel, with his absurd grandiloquence, his eccentric garb, his quaint idioms and phrases, his moth-eaten pride of family, and his really kind heart, fastidious sense of honor, and lovable simplicity, is the best delineation of a character rôle on the boards to-day. The coat worn by Colonel Calhoun is itself nothing less than an evolution of genius. Mr. Hargraves has captured his public.

"How does that sound, major, for a first nighter?"

"I had the honor"—the major's voice sounded ominously frigid—"of witnessing your very remarkable performance, sir, last night."

Hargraves looked disconcerted.

"You were there? I didn't know you ever—I didn't know you cared for the theatre. Oh, I say, Major Talbot," he exclaimed, frankly, "don't you be offended. I admit I did get a lot of pointers from you that helped me out wonderfully in the part. But it's a type, you know—not individual. The way the audience caught on shows that. Half the patrons of that theatre are Southerners. They recognized it."

"Mr. Hargraves," said the major, who had remained standing, "you have put upon me an unpardonable insult. You have burlesqued my person, grossly betrayed my confidence, and misused my hospitality. If I thought you possessed the faintest conception of what is the sign manual of a gentleman, or what is due one, I would call you out, sir, old as I am. I will ask you to leave the room, sir."

The actor appeared to be slightly bewildered, and seemed hardly to take in the full meaning of the old gentleman's words.

"I am truly sorry you took offence," he said, regretfully. "Up here we don't look at things just as you people do. I know men who would buy out half the house to have their personality put on the stage so the public would recognize it."

"They are not from Alabama, sir," said the major, haughtily.

"Perhaps not. I have a pretty good memory, major; let me quote a few lines from your book. In response to a toast at a banquet given in—Milledgeville, I believe—you uttered, and intend to have printed these words:

"The Northern man is utterly without sentiment or warmth except in so far as the feelings may be turned to his own commercial profit. He will suffer without resentment any imputation cast upon the honor of himself or his loved ones that does not bear with it the consequence of pecuniary loss. In his charity, he gives with a liberal hand; but it must be heralded with the trumpet and chronicled in brass.

"Do you think that picture is fairer than the one you saw of Colonel Calhoun last night?"

"The description," said the major, frowning, "is—not without grounds. Some exag—latitude must be allowed in public speaking."

"And in public acting," replied Hargraves.

"That is not the point," persisted the major, unrelenting. "It was a personal caricature. I positively decline to overlook it, sir."

"Major Talbot," said Hargraves, with a winning smile, "I wish you would understand me. I want you to know that I never dreamed of insulting you. In my profession, all life belongs to me. I take what I want, and what I can, and return it over the footlights. Now, if you will, let's let it go at that. I came in to see you about something else. We've been pretty good friends for some months, and I'm going to take the risk of offending you again. I know you are hard up for money—never mind how I found out; a boarding house is no place to keep such matters secret—and I want you to let me help you out of the pinch. I've been there often enough myself. I've been getting a fair salary all the season, and I've saved some money. You're welcome to a couple hundred—or even more—until you get——"

"Stop!" commanded the major, with his arm outstretched. "It seems that my book didn't lie, after all. You think your money salve will heal all the hurts of honor. Under no circumstances would I accept a loan from a casual acquaintance; and as to you, sir, I would starve before I would consider your insulting offer of a financial adjustment of the circumstances we have discussed. I beg to repeat my request relative to your quitting the apartment."

Hargraves took his departure without another word. He also left the house the same day, moving, as Mrs. Vardeman explained at the supper table, nearer the vicinity of the down-town theatre, where "A Magnolia Flower" was booked for a week's run.

Critical was the situation with Major Talbot and Miss Lydia. There was no one in Washington to whom the major's scruples allowed him to apply for a loan. Miss Lydia wrote a letter to Uncle Ralph, but it was doubtful whether that relative's constricted affairs would permit him to furnish help. The major was forced to make an apologetic address to Mrs. Vardeman regarding the delayed payment for board, referring to "delinquent rentals" and "delayed remittances" in a rather confused strain.

Deliverance came from an entirely unexpected source.

Late one afternoon the door maid came up and announced an old colored man who wanted to see Major Talbot. The major asked that he be sent up to his study. Soon an old darkey appeared in the doorway, with his hat in hand, bowing, and scraping with one clumsy foot. He was quite decently dressed in a baggy suit of black. His big, coarse shoes shone with a metallic lustre suggestive of stove polish. His bushy wool was gray—almost white. After middle life, it is difficult to estimate the age of a Negro. This one might have seen as many years as had Major Talbot.

"I be bound you don't know me, Mars' Pendleton," were his first words.

The major rose and came forward at the old, familiar style of address. It was one of the old plantation darkeys without a doubt; but they had been widely scattered, and he could not recall the voice or face.

"I don't believe I do," he said, kindly—"unless you will assist my memory."

"Don't you 'member Cindy's Mose, Mars' Pendleton, what 'migrated 'mediately after de war?"

"Wait a moment," said the major, rubbing his forehead with the tips of his fingers. He loved to recall everything connected with those beloved days. "Cindy's Mose," he reflected. "You worked among the horses—breaking the colts. Yes, I remember now. After the surrender, you took the name of—don't prompt me—Mitchell, and went to the West—to Nebraska."

"Yassir, yassir,"—the old man's face stretched with a delighted grin—"dat's him, dat's it. Newbraska. Dat's me—Mose Mitchell. Old Uncle Mose Mitchell, dey calls me now. Old mars', your pa, gimme a pah of dem mule colts when I lef' fur to staht me goin' with. You 'member dem colts, Mars' Pendleton?'

"I don't seem to recall the colts," said the major. "You know I was married the first year of the war and living at the old Follinsbee place. But sit down, sit down, Uncle Mose. I'm glad to see you. I hope you have prospered."

Uncle Mose took a chair and laid his hat carefully on the floor beside it.

"Yassir; of late I done mouty famous. When I first got to Newbraska, dey folks come all roun' me to see dem mule colts. Dey ain't see no mules like dem in Newbraska. I sold dem mules for three hundred dollars. Yassir—three hundred.

"Den I open a blacksmith shop, suh, and made some money and bought some lan'. Me and my old 'oman done raised up seb'm chillun, and all doin' well 'cept two of 'em what died. Fo' year ago a railroad come along and staht a town slam ag'inst my lan', and, suh, Mars' Pendleton, Uncle Mose am worth lem'm thousand dollars in money, property, and lan'."

"I'm glad to hear it," said the major, heartily. "Glad to hear it."

"And dat little baby of yo'n, Mars' Pendleton—one what you name Miss Lyddy—I be bound dat little tad done growed up tell nobody wouldn't know her."

The major stepped to the door and called: "Lydia, dear, will you come?"

Miss Lydia, looking quite grown up and a little worried, came in from her room.

"Dar, now! What'd I tell you? I knowed dat baby done be plum growed up. You don't 'member Uncle Mose, child?"

"This is Aunt Cindy's Mose, Lydia," explained the major. "He left Sunnymead for the West when you were two years old."

"Well," said Miss Lydia, "I can hardly be expected to remember you, Uncle Mose, at that age. And, as you say, I'm 'plum growed up,' and was a blessed long time ago. But I'm glad to see you, even if I can't remember you."

And she was. And so was the major. Something alive and tangible had come to link them with the happy past. The three sat and talked over the olden times, the major and Uncle Mose, correcting or prompting each other as they reviewed the plantation scenes and days.

The major inquired what the old man was doing so far from his home.

"Uncle Mose am a delicate," he explained, "to de grand Baptis' convention in dis city. I never preached none, but bein' a residin' elder in de church, and able fur to pay my own expenses, dey sent me along."

"And how did you know we were in Washington?" inquired Miss Lydia.

"Dey's a cullud man works in de hotel whar I stops, what comes from Mobile. He told me he seen Mars' Pendleton comin' outen dish here house one mawnin'.

"What I come fur," continued Uncle Mose, reaching into his pocket—"besides de sight of home folks—was to pay Mars' Pendleton what I owes him."

"Owe me?" said the major, in surprise.

"Yassir—three hundred dollars." He handed the major a roll of bills. "When I lef' old mars' says: 'Take dem mule colts, Mose, and, if it be so you gits able, pay fur 'em.' Yas sir—dem was his words. De war had done lef' old mars' po' hisself. Old mars' bein' 'long ago dead, de debt descends to Mars' Pendleton. Three hundred dollars. Uncle Mose is plenty able to pay now. When dat railroad buy my lan' I laid off to pay for dem mules. Count de money, Mars' Pendleton. Dat's what I sold dem mules fur. Yassir."

Tears were in Major Talbot's eyes. He took Uncle Mose's hand and laid his other upon his shoulder.

"Dear, faithful old servitor," he said in an unsteady voice, "I don't mind saying to you that 'Mars' Pendleton' spent his last dollar in the world a week ago. We will accept this money, Uncle Mose, since, in a way, it is a sort of payment, as well as a token of the loyalty and devotion of the old régime. Lydia, my dear, take the money. You are better fitted than I to manage its expenditure."

"Take it, honey," said Uncle Mose. "Hit belongs to you. Hit's Talbot money."

After Uncle Mose had gone, Miss Lydia had a good cry—for joy; and the major turned his face to a corner, and smoked his clay pipe volcanically.

The succeeding days saw the Talbots restored to peace and ease. Miss Lydia's face lost its worried look. The major appeared in a new frock coat, in which he looked like a wax figure personifying the memory of his golden age. Another publisher who read the manuscript of the "Anecdotes and Reminiscences" thought that, with a little retouching and toning down of the high lights, he could make a really bright and salable volume of it. Altogether, the situation was comfortable, and not without the touch of hope that is often sweeter than arrived blessings.

One day, about a week after their piece of good luck, a maid brought a letter for Miss Lydia to her room. The postmark showed that it was from New York. Not knowing any one there, Miss Lydia, in a mild flutter of wonder, sat down by her table and opened the letter with her scissors. This was what she read:

DEAR MISS TALBOT:

I thought you might be glad to learn of my good fortune. I have received and accepted an offer of two hundred dollars per week by a New York stock company to play Colonel Calhoun in "A Magnolia Flower."

There is something else I wanted you to know. I guess you'd better not tell Major Talbot. I was anxious to make him some amends for the great help he was to me in studying the part, and for the bad humor he was in about it. He refused to let me, so I did it anyhow. I could easily spare the three hundred.

Sincerely yours,
H. HOPKINS HARGRAVES.

P. S. How did I play Uncle Mose?

Major Talbot, passing through the hall, saw Miss Lydia's door open and stopped.

"Any mail for us this morning, Lydia dear?" he asked.

Miss Lydia slid the letter beneath a fold of her dress.

"The *Mobile Chronicle* came," she said, promptly. "It's on the table in your study."

LET ME FEEL YOUR PULSE

So I went to a doctor.

"How long has it been since you took any alcohol into your system?" he asked. Turning my head sidewise, I answered, "Oh, quite awhile."

He was a young doctor, somewhere between twenty and forty. He wore heliotrope socks, but he looked like Napoleon. I liked him immensely.

"Now," said he, "I am going to show you the effect of alcohol upon your circulation." I think it was "circulation" he said; though it may have been "advertising."

He bared my left arm to the elbow, brought out a bottle of whiskey, and gave me a drink. He began to look more like Napoleon. I began to like him better.

Then he put a tight compress on my upper arm, stopped my pulse with his fingers, and squeezed a rubber bulb connected with an apparatus on a stand that looked like a thermometer. The mercury jumped up and down without seeming to stop anywhere; but the doctor said it registered two hundred and thirty-seven or one hundred and sixty-five or some such number.

"Now," said he, "you see what alcohol does to the blood-pressure."

"It's marvelous," said I, "but do you think it a sufficient test? Have one on me, and let's try the other arm." But, no!

Then he grasped my hand. I thought I was doomed and he was saying good-bye. But all he wanted to do was to jab a needle into the end of a finger and compare the red drop with a lot of fifty-cent poker chips that he had fastened to a card.

"It's the hæmoglobin test," he explained. "The color of your blood is wrong."

"Well," said I, "I know it should be blue; but this is a country of mix-ups. Some of my ancestors were cavaliers; but they got thick with some people on Nantucket Island, so——"

"I mean," said the doctor, "that the shade of red is too light."

"Oh," said I, "it's a case of matching instead of matches."

The doctor then pounded me severely in the region of the chest. When he did that I don't know whether he reminded me most of Napoleon or Battling or Lord Nelson. Then he looked grave and mentioned a string of grievances that the flesh is heir to—mostly ending in "itis." I immediately paid him fifteen dollars on account.

"Is or are it or some or any of them necessarily fatal?" I asked. I thought my connection with the matter justified my manifesting a certain amount of interest.

"All of them," he answered, cheerfully. "But their progress may be arrested. With care and proper continuous treatment you may live to be eighty-five or ninety."

I began to think of the doctor's bill. "Eighty-five would be sufficient, I am sure," was my comment. I paid him ten dollars more on account.

"The first thing to do," he said, with renewed animation, "is to find a sanitarium where you will get a complete rest for a while, and allow your nerves to get into a better condition. I myself will go with you and select a suitable one."

So he took me to a mad-house in the Catskills. It was on a bare mountain frequented only by infrequent frequenters. You could see nothing but stones and boulders, some patches of snow, and scattered pine trees. The young physician in charge was most agreeable. He gave me a stimulant without applying a compress to the arm. It was luncheon time, and we were invited to partake. There were about twenty inmates at little tables in the dining room. The young physician in charge came to our table and said: "It is a custom with our guests not to regard themselves as patients, but merely as tired ladies and gentlemen taking a rest. Whatever slight maladies they may have are never alluded to in conversation."

My doctor called loudly to a waitress to bring some phosphoglycerate of lime hash, dog-bread, bromo-seltzer pancakes, and nux vomica tea for my repast. Then a sound arose like a sudden wind storm among pine trees. It was produced by every guest in the room whispering loudly, "Neurasthenia!"—except one man with a nose, whom I distinctly heard say, "Chronic alcoholism." I hope to meet him again. The physician in charge turned and walked away.

An hour or so after luncheon he conducted us to the workshop—say fifty yards from the house. Thither the guests had been conducted by the physican in charge's understudy and sponge-holder—a man with feet and a blue sweater. He was so tall that I was not sure he had a face; but the Armour Packing Company would have been delighted with his hands.

"Here," said the physician in charge, "our guests find relaxation from past mental worries by devoting themselves to physical labor—recreation, in reality."

There were turning-lathes, carpenters' outfits, clay-modelling tools, spinning-wheels, weaving-frames, treadmills, bass drums, enlarged-crayon-portrait apparatuses, blacksmith forges, and everything, seemingly, that could interest the paying lunatic guests of a first-rate sanitarium.

"The lady making mud pies in the corner," whispered the physician in charge, "is no other than—Lulu Lulington, the authoress of the novel entitled 'Why Love Loves.' What she is doing now is simply to rest her mind after performing that piece of work."

I had seen the book. "Why doesn't she do it by writing another one instead?" I asked.

As you see, I wasn't as far gone as they thought I was.

"The gentleman pouring water through the funnel," continued the physician in charge, "is a Wall Street broker broken down from overwork."

I buttoned my coat.

Others he pointed out were architects playing with Noah's arks, ministers reading Darwin's "Theory of Evolution," lawyers sawing wood, tired-out society ladies talking Ibsen to the blue-sweatered sponge-holder, a neurotic millionaire lying asleep on the floor, and a prominent artist drawing a little red wagon around the room.

"You look pretty strong," said the physician in charge of me. "I think the best mental relaxation for you would be throwing small boulders over the mountainside and then bringing them up again."

I was a hundred yards away before my doctor overtook me.

"What's the matter?" he asked.

"The matter is," said I, "that there are no aeroplanes handy. So I am going to merrily and hastily jog the foot-pathway to yon station and catch the first unlimited-soft-coal express back to town."

"Well," said the doctor, "perhaps you are right. This seems hardly the suitable place for you. But what you need is rest—absolute rest and exercise."

That night I went to a hotel in the city, and said to the clerk: "What I need is absolute rest and exercise. Can you give me a room with one of those tall folding beds in it, and a relay of bellboys to work it up and down while I rest?"

The clerk rubbed a speck off one of his finger nails and glanced sidewise at a tall man in a white hat sitting in the lobby. That man came over and asked me politely if I had seen the shrubbery at the west entrance. I had not, so he showed it to me and then looked me over.

"I thought you had 'em," he said, not unkindly, "but I guess you're all right. You'd better go see a doctor, old man."

A week afterward my doctor tested my blood pressure again without the preliminary stimulant. He looked to me a little less like Napoleon. And his socks were of a shade of tan that did not appeal to me.

"What you need," he decided, "is sea air and companionship."

"Would a mermaid——" I began; but he slipped on his professional manner.

"I myself," he said, "will take you to the Hotel Bonair off the coast of Long Island and see that you get in good shape. It is a quiet, comfortable resort where you will soon recuperate."

The Hotel Bonair proved to be a nine-hundred-room fashionable hostelry on an island off the main shore. Everybody who did not dress for dinner was shoved into a side dining room and given only a terrapin and champagne table d'hôte. The bay was a great stamping ground for wealthy yachtsmen. The *Corsair* anchored there the day we arrived. I saw Mr. Morgan standing on deck eating a cheese sandwich and gazing longingly at the hotel. Still, it was a very inexpensive place. Nobody could afford to pay their prices. When you went away you simply left your baggage, stole a skiff, and beat it for the mainland in the night.

When I had been there one day I got a pad of monogrammed telegraph blanks at the clerk's desk and began to wire to all my friends for get-away money. My doctor and I played one game of croquet on the golf links and went to sleep on the lawn.

When we got back to town a thought seemed to occur to him suddenly. "By the way," he asked, "how do you feel?"

"Relieved of very much," I replied.

Now a consulting physician is different. He isn't exactly sure whether he is to be paid or not, and this uncertainty insures you either the most careful or the most careless attention. My doctor took me to see a consulting physician. He made a poor guess and gave me careful attention. I liked him immensely. He put me through some coördination exercises.

"Have you a pain in the back of your head?" he asked. I told him I had not. "Shut your eyes," he ordered, "put your feet close together, and jump backward as far as you can."

I always was a good backward jumper with my eyes shut, so I obeyed. My head struck the edge of the bathroom door, which had been left open and was only three feet away. The doctor was very sorry. He had overlooked the fact that the door was open. He closed it.

"Now touch your nose with your right forefinger," he said.

"Where is it?" I asked.

"On your face" said he.

"I mean my right forefinger," I explained.

"Oh, excuse me," said he. He reopened the bathroom door, and I took my finger out of the crack of it. After I had performed the marvelous digito-nasal feat I said:

"I do not wish to deceive you as to symptoms, Doctor; I really have something like a pain in the back of my head." He ignored the symptom and examined my heart carefully with a latest-popular-air-penny-in-the-slot ear-trumpet. I felt like a ballad. "Now," he said, "gallop like a horse for about five minutes around the room."

I gave the best imitation I could of a disqualified Percheron being led out of Madison Square Garden. Then, without dropping in a penny, he listened to my chest again.

"No glanders in our family, Doc," I said.

The consulting physician held up his forefinger within three inches of my nose. "Look at my finger," he commanded.

"Did you ever try Pears'——" I began; but he went on with his test rapidly.

"Now look across the bay. At my finger. Across the bay. At my finger. At my finger. Across the bay. Across the bay. At my finger. Across the bay." This for about three minutes.

He explained that this was a test of the action of the brain. It seemed easy to me. I never once mistook his finger for the bay. I'll bet that if he had used the phrases: "Gaze, as it were, unpreoccupied, outward—or rather laterally—in the direction of the horizon, underlaid, so to speak, with the adjacent fluid inlet," and "Now, returning—or rather, in a manner, withdrawing your attention, bestow it upon my upraised digit"—I'll bet, I say, that Henry James himself could have passed the examination.

After asking me if I had ever had a grand uncle with curvature of the spine or a cousin with swelled ankles, the two doctors retired to the bathroom and sat on the edge of the bath tub for their consultation. I ate an apple, and gazed first at my finger and then across the bay.

The doctors came out looking grave. More: they looked tombstones and Tennessee-papers-please-copy. They wrote out a diet list to which I was to be restricted. It had everything that I had ever heard of to eat on it, except snails. And I never eat a snail unless it overtakes me and bits me first.

"You must follow this diet strictly," said the doctors.

"I'd follow it a mile if I could get one-tenth of what's on it," I answered.

"Of next importance," they went on, "is outdoor air and exercise. And here is a prescription that will be of great benefit to you."

Then all of us took something. They took their hats, and I took my departure.

I went to a druggist and showed him the prescription.

"It will be $2.87 for an ounce bottle," he said.

"Will you give me a piece of your wrapping cord?" said I.

I made a hole in the prescription, ran the cord through it, tied it around my neck, and tucked it inside. All of us have a little superstition, and mine runs to a confidence in amulets.

Of course there was nothing the matter with me, but I was very ill. I couldn't work, sleep, eat, or bowl. The only way I could get any sympathy was to go without shaving for four days. Even then somebody would say: "Old man, you look as hardy as a pine knot. Been up for a jaunt in the Maine woods, eh?"

Then, suddenly, I remembered that I must have outdoor air and exercise. So I went down South to John's. John is an approximate relative by verdict of a preacher standing with a little book in his hands in a bower of chrysanthemums while a hundred thousand people looked on. John has a country house seven miles from Pineville. It is at an altitude and on the Blue Ridge Mountains in a state too dignified to be dragged into this controversy. John is mica, which is more valuable and clearer than gold.

He met me at Pineville, and we took the trolley car to his home. It is a big, neighborless cottage on a hill surrounded by a hundred mountains. We got off at his little private station, where John's family and Amaryllis met and greeted us. Amaryllis looked at me a trifle anxiously.

A rabbit came bounding across the hill between us and the house. I threw down my suit-case and pursued it hotfoot. After I had run twenty yards and seen it disappear, I sat down on the grass and wept disconsolately.

"I can't catch a rabbit any more," I sobbed. "I'm of no further use in the world. I may as well be dead."

"Oh, what is it—what is it, Brother John?" I heard Amaryllis say.

"Nerves a little unstrung," said John, in his calm way. "Don't worry. Get up, you rabbit-chaser, and come on to the house before the biscuits get cold." It was about twilight, and the mountains came up nobly to Miss Murfree's descriptions of them.

Soon after dinner I announced that I believed I could sleep for a year or two, including legal holidays. So I was shown to a room as big and cool as a flower garden, where there was a bed as broad as a lawn. Soon afterward the remainder of the household retired, and then there fell upon the land a silence.

I had not heard a silence before in years. It was absolute. I raised myself on my elbow and listened to it. Sleep! I thought that if I only could hear a star twinkle or a blade of grass sharpen itself I could compose myself to rest. I thought once that I heard a sound like the sail of a catboat flapping as it veered about in a breeze, but I decided that it was probably only a tack in the carpet. Still I listened.

Suddenly some belated little bird alighted upon the window-sill, and, in what he no doubt considered sleepy tones, enunciated the noise generally translated as "cheep!"

I leaped into the air.

"Hey! what's the matter down there?" called John from his room above mine.

"Oh, nothing," I answered, "except that I accidentally bumped my head against the ceiling."

The next morning I went out on the porch and looked at the mountains. There were forty-seven of them in sight. I shuddered, went into the big hall sitting room of the house, selected "Pancoast's Family Practice of Medicine" from a bookcase, and began to read. John came in, took the book away from me, and led me outside. He has a farm of three hundred acres furnished with the usual complement of barns, mules, peasantry, and harrows with three front teeth broken off. I had seen such things in my childhood, and my heart began to sink.

Then John spoke of alfalfa, and I brightened at once. "Oh, yes," said I, "wasn't she in the chorus of—let's see——"

"Green, you know," said John, "and tender, and you plow it under after the first season."

"I know," said I, "and the grass grows over her."

"Right," said John. "You know something about farming, after all."

"I know something of some farmers," said I, "and a sure scythe will mow them down some day."

On the way back to the house a beautiful and inexplicable creature walked across our path. I stopped irresistibly fascinated, gazing at it. John waited patiently, smoking his cigarette. He is a modern farmer. After ten minutes he said: "Are you going to stand there looking at that chicken all day? Breakfast is nearly ready."

"A chicken?" said I.

"A white Orpington hen, if you want to particularize."

"A white Orpington hen?" I repeated, with intense interest. The fowl walked slowly away with graceful dignity, and I followed like a child after the Pied Piper. Five minutes more were allowed me by John, and then he took me by the sleeve and conducted me to breakfast.

After I had been there a week I began to grow alarmed. I was sleeping and eating well and actually beginning to enjoy life. For a man in my desperate condition that would never do. So I sneaked down to the trolley-car station, took the car for Pineville, and went to see one of the best physicians in town. By this time I knew exactly what to do when I needed medical treatment. I hung my hat on the back of a chair, and said rapidly:

"Doctor, I have cirrhosis of the heart, indurated arteries, neurasthenia, neuritis, acute indigestion, and convalescence. I am going to live on a strict diet. I shall also take a tepid bath at night and a cold one in the morning. I shall endeavor to be cheerful, and fix my mind on pleasant subjects. In the way of drugs I intend to take a phosphorus pill three times a day, preferably after meals, and a tonic composed of the tinctures of gentian, cinchona, calisaya, and cardamon compound. Into each teaspoonful of this I shall mix tincture of nux vomica, beginning with one drop and increasing it a drop each day until the maximum dose is reached. I shall drop this with a medicine-dropper, which can be procured at a trifling cost at any pharmacy. Good-morning."

I took my hat and walked out. After I had closed the door I remembered something that I had forgotten to say. I opened it again. The doctor had not moved from where he had been sitting, but he gave a slightly nervous start when he saw me again.

"I forgot to mention," said I, "that I shall also take absolute rest and exercise."

After this consultation I felt much better. The reëstablishing in my mind of the fact that I was hopelessly ill gave me so much satisfaction that I almost became gloomy again. There is nothing more alarming to a neurasthenic than to feel himself growing well and cheerful.

John looked after me carefully. After I had evinced so much interest in his White Orpington chicken he tried his best to divert my mind, and was particular to lock his hen house of nights. Gradually the tonic mountain air, the wholesome food, and the daily walks among the hills so alleviated my malady that I became utterly wretched and despondent. I heard of a country doctor who lived in the mountains near-by. I went to see him and told him the whole story. He was a gray-bearded man with clear, blue, wrinkled eyes, in a home-made suit of gray jeans.

In order to save time I diagnosed my case, touched my nose with my right fore-finger, struck myself below the knee to make my foot kick, sounded my chest, stuck out my tongue, and asked him the price of cemetery lots in Pineville.

He lit his pipe and looked at me for about three minutes. "Brother," he said, after a while, "you are in a mighty bad way. There's a chance for you to pull through, but it's a mighty slim one."

"What can it be?" I asked, eagerly. "I have taken arsenic and gold, phosphorus, exercise, nux vomica, hydrotherapeutic baths, rest, excitement, codein, and aromatic spirits of ammonia. Is there anything left in the pharmacopœia?"

"Somewhere in these mountains," said the doctor, "there's a plant growing—a flowering plant that'll cure you, and it's about the only thing that will. It's of a kind that's as old as the world; but of late it's powerful scarce and hard to find. You and I will have to hunt it up. I'm not engaged in active practice now: I'm getting along in years; but I'll take your case. You'll have to come every day in the afternoon and help me hunt for this plant till we find it. The city doctors may know a lot about new scientific things, but they don't know much about the cures that nature carries around in her saddle bags."

So every day the old doctor and I hunted the cure-all plant among the mountains and valleys of the Blue Ridge. Together we toiled up steep heights so slippery with fallen autumn leaves that we had to catch every sapling and branch within our reach to save us from falling. We waded through gorges and chasms, breast-deep with laurel and ferns; we followed the banks of mountain streams for miles, we wound our way like Indians through brakes of pine—road side, hill side, river side, mountain side we explored in our search for the miraculous plant.

As the old doctor said, it must have grown scarce and hard to find. But we followed our quest. Day by day we plumbed the valleys, scaled the heights, and tramped the plateaus in search of the miraculous plant. Mountain-bred, he never seemed to tire. I often reached home too fatigued to do anything except fall into bed and sleep until morning. This we kept up for a month.

One evening after I had returned from a six-mile tramp with the old doctor, Amaryllis and I took a little walk under the trees near the road. We looked at the mountains drawing their royal-purple robes around them for their night's repose.

"I'm glad you're well again," she said. "When you first came you frightened me. I thought you were really ill."

"Well again!" I almost shrieked. "Do you know that I have only one chance in a thousand to live?"

Amaryllis looked at me in surprise. "Why," said she, "you are as strong as one of the plow-mules, and sleep ten or twelve hours every night, and you are eating us out of house and home. What more do you want?"

"I tell you," said I, "that unless we find the magic—that is, the plant we are looking for—in time, nothing can save me. The doctor tells me so."

"What doctor?"

"Doctor Tatum—the old doctor who lives halfway up Black Oak Mountain. Do you know him?"

"I have known him since I was able to talk. And is that where you go every day—is it he who takes you on these long walks and climbs that have brought back your health and strength? God bless the old doctor."

Just then the old doctor himself drove slowly down the road in his rickety old buggy. I waved my hand at him and shouted that I would be on hand the next day at the usual time. He stopped his horse and called to Amaryllis to come out to him. They talked for five minutes while I waited. Then the old doctor drove on.

When we got to the house Amaryllis lugged out an encyclopædia and sought a word in it. "The doctor said," she told me, "that you needn't call any more as a patient, but he'd be glad to see you any time as a friend. And then he told me to look up my name in the encyclopædia and tell you what it means. It seems to be the name of a genus of flowering plants, and also the name of a country girl in Theocritus and Virgil. What do you suppose the doctor meant by that?"

"I know what he meant," said I. "I know now."

A word to a brother who may have come under the spell of the unquiet Lady Neurasthenia.

The formula was true. Even though gropingly at times, the physicians of the walled cities had put their fingers upon the specific medicament.

And so for the exercise one is referred to good Doctor Tatum on Black Oak Mountain—take the road to your right at the Methodist meeting house in the pine-grove.

Absolute rest and exercise!

What rest more remedial than to sit with Amaryllis in the shade, and, with a sixth sense, read the wordless Theocritan idyl of the gold-bannered blue mountains marching orderly into the dormitories of the night?

OCTOBER AND JUNE

The Captain gazed gloomily at his sword that hung upon the wall. In the closet near by was stored his faded uniform, stained and worn by weather and service. What a long, long time it seemed since those old days of war's alarms!

And now, veteran that he was of his country's strenuous times, he had been reduced to abject surrender by a woman's soft eyes and smiling lips. As he sat in his quiet room he held in his hand the letter he had just received from her—the letter that had caused him to wear that look of gloom. He re-read the fatal paragraph that had destroyed his hope.

In declining the honor you have done me in asking me to be your wife, I feel that I ought to speak frankly. The reason I have for so doing is the great difference between our ages. I like you very, very much, but I am sure that our marriage would not be a happy one. I am sorry to have to refer to this, but I believe that you will appreciate my honesty in giving you the true reason.

The Captain sighed, and leaned his head upon his hand. Yes, there were many years between their ages. But he was strong and rugged, he had position and wealth. Would not his love, his tender care, and the advantages he could bestow upon her make her forget the question of age? Besides, he was almost sure that she cared for him.

The Captain was a man of prompt action. In the field he had been distinguished for his decisiveness and energy. He would see her and plead his cause again in person. Age!—what was it to come between him and the one he loved?

In two hours he stood ready, in light marching order, for his greatest battle. He took the train for the old Southern town in Tennessee where she lived.

Theodora Deming was on the steps of the handsome, porticoed old mansion, enjoying the summer twilight, when the Captain entered the gate and came up the gravelled walk. She met him with a smile that was free from embarrassment. As the Captain stood on the step below her, the difference in their ages did not appear so great. He was tall and straight and clear-eyed and browned. She was in the bloom of lovely womanhood.

"I wasn't expecting you," said Theodora; "but now that you've come you may sit on the step. Didn't you get my letter?"

"I did," said the Captain, "and that's why I came. I say, now, Theo, reconsider your answer, won't you."

Theodora smiled softly upon him. He carried his years well. She was really fond of his strength, his wholesome looks, his manliness—perhaps, if——

"No, no," she said, shaking her head, positively; "it's out of the question. I like you a whole lot, but marrying won't do. My age and yours are—but don't make me say it again—I told you in my letter."

The Captain flushed a little through the bronze on his face. He was silent for a while, gazing sadly into the twilight. Beyond a line of woods that he could see was a field where the boys in blue had once bivouacked on their march toward the sea. How long ago it seemed now! Truly, Fate and Father Time had tricked him sorely. Just a few years interposed between himself and happiness!

Theodora's hand crept down and rested in the clasp of his firm brown one. She felt, at least, that sentiment that is akin to love.

"Don't take it so hard, please," she said, gently. "It's all for the best. I've reasoned it out very wisely all by myself. Some day you'll be glad I didn't marry you. It would be very nice and lovely for a while—but, just think! In only a few short years what different tastes we would have. One of us would want to sit by the fireside and read, and maybe nurse neuralgia or rheumatism of evenings, while the other would be crazy for balls and theatres and late suppers. No, my dear friend. While it isn't exactly January and May, it's a clear case of October and pretty early in June."

"I'd always do what you wanted me to do, Theo. If you wanted to——"

"No, you wouldn't. You think now that you would, but you wouldn't. Please don't ask me any more."

The Captain had lost his battle. But he was a gallant warrior, and when he rose to make his final adieu his mouth was grimly set and his shoulders were squared.

He took the train for the North that night. On the next evening he was back in his room, where his sword was hanging against the wall. He was dressing for dinner, tying his white tie into a very careful bow. And at the same time he was indulging in a pensive soliloquy.

" 'Pon my honor, I believe Theo was right, after all. Nobody can deny that she's a peach, but she must be twenty-eight, at the very kindest calculation."

For you see, the Captain was only nineteen, and his sword had never been drawn except on the parade ground at Chattanooga, which was as near as he ever got to the Spanish-American War.

THE CHURCH WITH AN OVERSHOT-WHEEL

LAKELANDS is not to be found in the catalogues of fashionable summer resorts. It lies on a low spur of the Cumberland range of mountains on a little tributary of the Clinch River. Lakelands proper is a contented village of two dozen houses situated on a forlorn, narrow-gauge railroad line. You wonder whether the railroad lost itself in the pine woods and ran into Lakelands from fright and loneliness, or whether Lakelands got lost and huddled itself along the railroad to wait for the cars to carry it home.

You wonder again why it was named Lakelands. There are no lakes, and the lands about are too poor to be worth mentioning.

Half a mile from the village stands the Eagle House, a big, roomy old mansion run by Josiah Rankin for the accommodation of visitors who desire the mountain air at inexpensive rates. The Eagle House is delightfully mismanaged. It is full of ancient instead of modern improvements, and it is altogether as comfortably neglected and pleasingly disarranged as your own home. But you are furnished with clean rooms and good and abundant fare: yourself and the piny woods must do the rest. Nature has provided a mineral spring, grape-vine swings, and croquet—even the wickets are wooden. You have Art to thank only for the fiddle-and-guitar music twice a week at the hop in the rustic pavilion.

The patrons of the Eagle House are those who seek recreation as a necessity, as well as a pleasure. They are busy people, who may be likened to clocks that need a fortnight's winding to insure a year's running of their wheels. You will find students there from the lower towns, now and then an artist, or a geologist absorbed in construing the ancient strata of the hills. A few quiet families spend the summers there; and often one or two tired members of that patient sisterhood known to Lakelands as "schoolmarms."

A quarter of a mile from the Eagle House was what would have been described to its guests as "an object of interest" in a catalogue, had the Eagle House issued a catalogue. This was an old, old mill that was no longer a mill. In the words of Josiah Rankin, it was "the only church in the United States, sah, with a overshot-wheel; and the only mill in the world, sah, with pews and a pipe-organ." The guests of the Eagle House attended the old mill church each Sabbath, and heard the preacher liken the purified Christian to bolted flour ground to usefulness between the millstones of experience and suffering.

Every year about the beginning of autumn there came to the Eagle House one Abram Strong, who remained for a time an honored and beloved guest. In Lakelands he was called "Father Abram," because his hair was so white, his face so strong and kind and florid, his laugh so merry, and his black clothes and broad hat so priestly in appearance. Even new guests after three or four days' acquaintance gave him this familiar title.

Father Abram came a long way to Lakelands. He lived in a big, roaring town in the Northwest where he owned mills, not little mills with pews and an organ in them, but great, ugly, mountain-like mills that the freight trains crawled around all day like ants round an ant-heap. And now you must be told about Father Abram and the mill that was a church, for their stories run together.

In days when the church was a mill, Mr. Strong was the miller. There was no jollier, dustier, busier, happier miller in all the land than he. He lived in a little cottage across the road from the mill. His hand was heavy, but his toll was light, and the mountaineers brought their grain to him across many weary miles of rocky roads.

The delight of the miller's life was his little daughter, Aglaia. That was a brave name, truly, for a flaxen-haired toddler; but the mountaineers love sonorous and stately names. The mother had encountered it somewhere in a book, and the deed was done. In her babyhood Aglaia herself repudiated the name, as far as common use went, and persisted in calling herself "Dums." The miller and his wife often tried to coax from Aglaia the source of this mysterious name, but without results. At last they arrived at a theory. In the little garden behind the cottage was a bed of rhododendrons in which the child took a peculiar delight and interest. It may have been that she perceived in "Dums" a kinship to the formidable name of her favorite flowers.

When Aglaia was four years old she and her father used to go through a little performance in the mill every afternoon, that never failed to come off, the weather permitting. When supper was ready her mother would brush her hair and put on a clean apron and send her across to the mill to bring her father home. When the miller saw her coming in the mill door he would come forward, all white with the flour dust, and wave his hand and sing an old miller's song that was familiar in those parts and ran something like this:

> "The wheel goes round,
>   The grist is ground,
>   The dusty miller's merry.
> He sings all day,
> His work is play,
>   While thinking of his dearie."

Then Aglaia would run to him laughing, and call: "Da-da, come take Dums home"; and the miller would swing her to his shoulder and march over to supper, singing the miller's song. Every evening this would take place.

One day, only a week after her fourth birthday, Aglaia disappeared. When last seen she was plucking wild flowers by the side of the road in front of the cottage. A little while later her mother went out to see that she did not stray too far away, and she was already gone.

Of course every effort was made to find her. The neighbors gathered and searched the woods and the mountains for mile around. They dragged every foot of the mill race and the creek for a long distance below the dam. Never a trace of her did they find. A night or two before there had been a family of wanderers camped in a grove near by. It was conjectured that they might have stolen the child; but when their wagon was overtaken and searched she could not be found.

The miller remained at the mill for nearly two years; and then his hope of finding her died out. He and his wife moved to the Northwest. In a few years he was the owner of a modern mill in one of the important milling cities in that region. Mrs. Strong never recovered from the shock caused by the loss of Aglaia, and two years after they moved away the miller was left to bear his sorrow alone.

When Abram Strong became prosperous he paid a visit to Lakelands and the old mill. The scene was a sad one for him, but he was a strong man, and always appeared cheery and kindly. It was then that he was inspired to convert the old mill into a church. Lakelands was too poor to build one; and the still poorer mountaineers could not assist. There was no place of worship nearer than twenty miles.

The miller altered the appearance of the mill as little as possible. The big overshot-wheel was left in its place. The young people who came to the church used to cut their initials in its soft and slowly decaying wood. The dam was partly destroyed, and the clear mountain stream rippled unchecked down its rocky bed. Inside the mill the changes were greater. The shafts and millstones and belts and pulleys were, of course, all removed. There were two rows of benches with aisles between, and a little raised platform and pulpit at one end. On three sides overhead was a gallery containing seats, and reached by a stairway inside. There was also an organ—a real pipe organ—in the gallery, that was the pride of the congregation of the Old Mill Church. Miss Phœbe Summers was the organist. The Lakelands boys proudly took turns at pumping it for her at each Sunday's service. The Rev. Mr. Bainbridge was the preacher, and rode down from Squirrel Gap on his old white horse without ever missing a service. And Abram Strong paid for everything. He paid the preacher five hundred dollars a year; and Miss Phœbe two hundred dollars.

Thus, in memory of Aglaia, the old mill was converted into a blessing for the community in which she had once lived. It seemed that the brief life of the child had brought about more good than the three score years and ten of many. But Abram Strong set up yet another monument to her memory.

Out from his mills in the Northwest came the "Aglaia" flour, made from the hardest and finest wheat that could be raised. The country soon found out that the "Aglaia" flour had two prices. One was the highest market price, and the other was—nothing.

Wherever there happened a calamity that left people destitute—a fire, a flood, a tornado, a strike, or a famine, there would go hurrying a generous consignment of the "Aglaia" at its "nothing" price. It was given away cautiously and judiciously, but it was freely given, and not a penny could the hungry ones pay for it. There got to be a saying that whenever there was a disastrous fire in the poor districts of a city the fire chief's buggy reached the scene first, next the "Aglaia" flour wagon, and then the fire engines.

So this was Abram Strong's other monument to Aglaia. Perhaps to a poet the theme may seem too utilitarian for beauty; but to some the fancy will seem sweet and fine that the pure, white, virgin flour, flying on its mission of love and charity, might be likened to the spirit of the lost child whose memory it signalized.

There came a year that brought hard times to the Cumberlands. Grain crops everywhere were light, and there were no local crops at all. Mountain floods had done much damage to property. Even game in the woods was so scarce that the hunters brought hardly enough home to keep their folks alive. Especially about Lakelands was the rigor felt.

As soon as Abram Strong heard of this his messages flew; and the little narrow-gauge cars began to unload "Aglaia" flour there. The miller's orders were to store the flour in the gallery of the Old Mill Church; and that every one who attended the church was to carry home a sack of it.

Two weeks after that Abram Strong came for his yearly visit to the Eagle House, and became "Father Abram" again.

That season the Eagle House had fewer guests than usual. Among them was Rose Chester. Miss Chester came to Lakelands from Atlanta, where she worked in a department store. This was the first vacation outing of her life. The wife of the store manager had once spent a summer at the Eagle House. She had taken a fancy to Rose, and had persuaded her to go there for her three weeks' holiday. The manager's wife gave her a letter to Mrs. Rankin, who gladly received her in her own charge and care.

Miss Chester was not very strong. She was about twenty, and pale and delicate from an indoor life. But one week of Lakelands gave her a brightness and spirit that changed her wonderfully. The time was early September when the Cumberlands are at their greatest beauty. The mountain foliage was growing brilliant with autumnal colors; one breathed aerial champagne, the nights were deliciously cool, causing one to snuggle cosily under the warm blankets of the Eagle House.

Father Abram and Miss Chester became great friends. The old miller learned her story from Mrs. Rankin, and his interest went out quickly to the slender, lonely girl who was making her own way in the world.

The mountain country was new to Miss Chester. She had lived many years in the warm, flat town of Atlanta; and the grandeur and variety of the Cumberlands delighted her. She was determined to enjoy every moment of her stay. Her little hoard of savings had been estimated so carefully in connection with her expenses that she knew almost to a penny what her very small surplus would be when she returned to work.

Miss Chester was fortunate in gaining Father Abram for a friend and companion. He knew every road and peak and slope of the mountains near Lakelands. Through him she became acquainted with the solemn delight of the shadowy, tilted aisles of the pine forests, the dignity of the bare crags, the crystal, tonic mornings, the dreamy, golden afternoons full of mysterious sadness. So her health improved and her spirits grew light. She had a laugh as genial and hearty in its feminine way as the famous laugh of Father Abram. Both of them were natural optimists; and both knew how to present a serene and cheerful face to the world.

One day Miss Chester learned from one of the guests the history of Father Abram's lost child. Quickly she hurried away and found the miller seated on his favorite rustic bench near the chalybeate spring. He was surprised when his little friend slipped her hand into his, and looked at him with tears in her eyes.

"Oh, Father Abram," she said. "I'm so sorry! I didn't know until to-day about your little daughter. You will find her yet some day— Oh, I hope you will."

The miller looked down at her with his strong, ready smile.

"Thank you, Miss Rose," he said, in his usual cheery tones. "But I do not expect to find Aglaia. For a few years I hoped that she had been stolen by vagrants, and that she still lived; but I have lost that hope. I believe that she was drowned."

"I can understand," said Miss Chester, "how the doubt must have made it so hard to bear. And yet you are so cheerful and so ready to make other people's burdens light. Good Father Abram!"

"Good Miss Rose!" mimicked the miller, smiling. "Who thinks of others more than you do?"

A whimsical mood seemed to strike Miss Chester.

"Oh, Father Abram," she cried, "wouldn't it be grand if I should prove to be your daughter? Wouldn't it be romantic? And wouldn't you like to have me for a daughter?"

"Indeed, I would," said the miller, heartily. "If Aglaia had lived I could wish for nothing better than for her to have grown up to be just such a little woman as you are. Maybe you are Aglaia," he continued, falling in with her playful mood; "can't you remember when we lived at the mill?"

Miss Chester fell swiftly into serious meditation. Her large eyes were fixed vaguely upon something in the distance. Father Abram was amused at her quick return to seriousness. She sat thus for a long time before she spoke.

"No," she said at length, with a long sigh, "I can't remember anything at all about a mill. I don't think that I ever saw a flour mill in my life until I saw your funny little church. And if I were your little girl I would remember it, wouldn't I? I'm so sorry, Father Abram."

"So am I," said Father Abram, humoring her. "But if you cannot remember that you are my little girl, Miss Rose, surely you can recollect being some one else's. You remember your own parents, of course."

"Oh, yes; I remember them very well—especially my father. He wasn't a bit like you, Father Abram. Oh, I was only making believe. Come, now, you've rested long enough. You promised to show me the pool where you can see the trout playing, this afternoon. I never saw a trout."

Late one afternoon Father Abram set out for the old mill alone. He often went to sit and think of the old days when he lived in the cottage across the road. Time had smoothed away the sharpness of his grief until he no longer found the memory of those times painful. But whenever Abram Strong sat in the melancholy September afternoons on the spot where "Dums" used to run in every day with her yellow curls flying, the smile that Lakelands always saw upon his face was not there.

The miller made his way slowly up the winding, steep road. The trees crowded so close to the edge of it that he walked in their shade, with his hat in his hand. Squirrels ran playfully upon the old rail fence at his right. Quails were calling to their young broods in the wheat stubble. The low sun sent a torrent of pale gold up the ravine that opened to the west. Early September!— it was within a few days only of the anniversary of Aglaia's disappearance.

The old overshot-wheel, half covered with mountain ivy, caught patches of the warm sunlight filtering through the trees. The cottage across the road was still standing, but it would doubtless go down before the next winter's mountain blasts. It was overrun with morning glory and wild gourd vines, and the door hung by one hinge.

Father Abram pushed open the mill door, and entered softly. And then he stood still, wondering. He heard the sound of some one within, weeping inconsolably. He looked, and saw Miss Chester sitting in a dim pew, with her head bowed upon an open letter that her hands held.

Father Abram went to her, and laid one of his strong hands firmly upon hers. She looked up, breathed his name, and tried to speak further.

"Not yet, Miss Rose," said the miller, kindly. "Don't try to talk yet. There's nothing as good for you as a nice, quiet little cry when you are feeling blue."

It seemed that the old miller, who had known so much sorrow himself, was a magician in driving it away from others. Miss Chester's sobs grew easier. Presently she took her little plain-bordered handkerchief and wiped away a drop or two that had fallen from her eyes upon Father Abram's big hand. Then she looked up and smiled through her tears. Miss Chester could always smile before her tears had dried, just as Father Abram could smile through his own grief. In that way the two were very much alike.

The miller asked her no questions; but by and by Miss Chester began to tell him.

It was the old story that always seems so big and important to the young, and that brings reminiscent smiles to their elders. Love was the theme, as may be supposed. There was a young man in Atlanta, full of all goodness and the graces, who had discovered that Miss Chester also possessed these qualities above all other people in Atlanta or anywhere else from Greenland to Patagonia. She showed Father Abram the letter over which she had been weeping. It was a manly, tender letter, a little superlative and urgent, after the style of love letters written by young men full of goodness and the graces. He proposed for Miss Chester's hand in marriage at once. Life, he said, since her departure for a three weeks visit, was not to be endured. He begged for an immediate answer; and if it were favorable he promised to fly, ignoring the narrow-gauge railroad, at once to Lakelands.

"And now where does the trouble come in?" asked the miller when he had read the letter.

"I cannot marry him," said Miss Chester.

"Do you want to marry him?" asked Father Abram.

"Oh, I love him," she answered, "but——" Down went her head and she sobbed again.

"Come, Miss Rose," said the miller; "you can give me your confidence. I do not question you, but I think you can trust me."

"I do trust you," said the girl. "I will tell you why I must refuse Ralph. I am nobody; I haven't even a name; the name I call myself is a lie. Ralph is a noble man. I love him with all my heart, but I can never be his."

"What talk is this?" said Father Abram. "You said that you remember your parents. Why do you say that you have no name? I do not understand."

"I do remember them," said Miss Chester. "I remember them too well. My first recollections are of our life somewhere in the far South. We moved many times to different towns and states. I have picked cotton, and worked in factories, and have often gone without enough food and clothes. My mother was sometimes good to me; my father was always cruel, and beat me. I think they were both idle and unsettled.

"One night when we were living in a little town on a river near Atlanta they had a great quarrel. It was while they were abusing and taunting each other that I learned—oh, Father Abram, I learned that I didn't even have the right to be—don't you understand? I had no right even to a name; I was nobody.

"I ran away that night. I walked to Atlanta and found work. I gave myself the name of Rose Chester, and have earned my own living ever since. Now you know why I cannot marry Ralph—and, oh, I can never tell him why."

Better than any sympathy, more helpful than pity, was Father Abram's depreciation of her woes.

"Why, dear! is that all?" he said. "Fie, fie! I thought something was in the way. If this perfect young man is a man at all he will not care a pinch of bran for your family tree. Dear Miss Rose, take my word for it, it is yourself he cares for. Tell him frankly, just as you have told me, and I'll warrant that he will laugh at your story, and think all the more of you for it."

"I shall never tell him," said Miss Chester, sadly. "And I shall never marry him nor any one else. I have not the right."

But they saw a long shadow come bobbing up the sunlit road. And then came a shorter one bobbing by its side; and presently two strange figures approached the church. The long shadow was made by Miss Phœbe Summers, the organist, come to practice. Tommy Teague, aged twelve, was responsible for the shorter shadow. It was Tommy's day to pump the organ for Miss Phœbe, and his bare toes proudly spurned the dust of the road.

Miss Phœbe, in her lilac-spray chintz dress, with her accurate little curls hanging over each ear, courtesied low to Father Abram, and shook her curls ceremoniously at Miss Chester. Then she and her assistant climbed the steep stairway to the organ loft.

In the gathering shadows below, Father Abram and Miss Chester lingered. They were silent; and it is likely that they were busy with their memories. Miss Chester sat, leaning her head on her hand, with her eyes fixed far away. Father Abram stood in the next pew, looking thoughtfully out of the door at the road and the ruined cottage.

Suddenly the scene was transformed for him back almost a score of years into the past. For, as Tommy pumped away, Miss Phœbe struck a low bass note on the organ and held it to test the volume of air that it contained. The church ceased to exist, so far as Father Abram was concerned. The deep, booming vibration that shook the little frame building was no note from an organ, but the humming of the mill machinery. He felt sure that the old overshot-wheel was turning; that he was back again, a dusty, merry miller in the old mountain mill. And now evening was come, and soon would come Aglaia with flying colors, toddling across the road to take him home to supper. Father Abram's eyes were fixed upon the broken door of the cottage.

And then came another wonder. In the gallery overhead the sacks of flour were stacked in long rows. Perhaps a mouse had been at one of them; anyway, the jar of the deep organ note shook down between the cracks of the gallery floor a stream of flour, covering Father Abram from head to foot with the white dust. And then the old miller stepped into the aisle, and waved his arms and began to sing the miller's song:

> "The wheel goes round,
> The grist is ground,
> The dusty miller's merry."

—and then the rest of the miracle happened. Miss Chester was leaning forward from her pew, as pale as the flour itself, her wide-open eyes staring at Father Abram like one in a waking dream. When he began the song she stretched out her arms to him; her lips moved; she called to him in dreamy tones: "Da-da, come take Dums home!"

Miss Phœbe released the low key of the organ. But her work had been well done. The note that she struck had beaten down the doors of a closed memory; and Father Abram held his lost Aglaia close in his arms.

When you visit Lakelands they will tell you more of this story. They will tell you how the lines of it were afterward traced, and the history of the miller's daughter revealed after the gipsy wanderers had stolen her on that September day, attracted by her childish beauty. But you should wait until you sit comfortably on the shaded porch of the Eagle House, and then you can have the story at your ease. It seems best that our part of it should close while Miss Phœbe's deep bass note was yet reverberating softly.

And yet, to my mind, the finest thing of it all happened while Father Abram and his daughter were walking back to the Eagle House in the long twilight, almost too glad to speak.

"Father," she said, somewhat timidly and doubtfully, "have you a great deal of money?"

"A great deal?" said the miller. "Well, that depends. There is plenty unless you want to buy the moon or something equally expensive."

"Would it cost very, very much," asked Aglaia, who had always counted her dimes so carefully, "to send a telegram to Atlanta?"

"Ah," said Father Abram, with a little sigh, "I see. You want to ask Ralph to come."

Aglaia looked up at him with a tender smile.

"I want to ask him to wait," she said, "I have just found my father, and I want it to be just we two for a while. I want to tell him he will have to wait."

NEW YORK BY CAMP FIRE LIGHT

AWAY out in the Creek Nation we learned things about New York.

We were on a hunting trip, and were camped one night on the bank of a little stream. Bud Kingsbury was our skilled hunter and guide, and it was from his lips that we had explanations of Manhattan and the queer folks that inhabit it. Bud had once spent a month in the metropolis, and a week or two at other times, and he was pleased to discourse to us of what he had seen.

Fifty yards away from our camp was pitched the teepee of a wandering family of Indians that had come up and settled there for the night. An old, old

Indian woman was trying to build a fire under an iron pot hung upon three sticks.

Bud went over to her assistance, and soon had her fire going. When he came back we complimented him playfully upon his gallantry.

"Oh," said Bud, "don't mention it. It's a way I have. Whenever I see a lady trying to cook things in a pot and having trouble I always go to the rescue. I done the same thing once in a high-toned house in New York City. Heap big society teepee on Fifth Avenue. That Injun lady kind of recalled it to my mind. Yes, I endeavors to be polite and help the ladies out."

The camp demanded the particulars.

"I was manager of the Triangle B Ranch in the Panhandle," said Bud. "It was owned at that time by old man Sterling, of New York. He wanted to sell out, and he wrote for me to come on to New York and explain the ranch to the syndicate that wanted to buy. So I sends to Fort Worth and has a forty-dollar suit of clothes made, and hits the trail for the big village.

"Well, when I got there, old man Sterling and his outfit certainly laid themselves out to be agreeable. We had business and pleasure so mixed up that you couldn't tell whether it was a treat or a trade half the time. We had trolley rides, and cigars, and theatre round-ups, and rubber parties."

"Rubber parties?" said a listener, inquiringly.

"Sure," said Bud. "Didn't you never attend 'em? You walk around and try to look at the tops of the skyscrapers. Well, we sold the ranch, and old man Sterling asks me 'round to his house to take grub on the night before I started back. It wasn't any high-collared affair—just me and the old man and his wife and daughter. But they was a fine-haired outfit all right, and the lilies of the field wasn't in it. They made my Fort Worth clothes carpenter look like a dealer in horse blankets and gee strings. And then the table was all pompous with flowers, and there was a whole kit of tools laid out beside everybody's plate. You'd have thought you was fixed out to burglarize a restaurant before you could get your grub. But I'd been in New York over a week then, and I was getting on to stylish ways. I kind of trailed behind and watched others use the hardware supplies, and then I tackled the chuck with the same weapons. It ain't much trouble to travel with the high-flyers after you find out their gait. I got along fine. I was feeling cool and agreeable, and pretty soon I was talking away fluent as you please, all about the ranch and the West, and telling 'em how the Indians eat grasshopper stew and snakes, and you never saw people so interested.

"But the real joy of that feast was that Miss Sterling. Just a little trick she was, not bigger than two bits' worth of chewing plug; but she had a way about her that seemed to say she was the people, and you believed it. And yet, she never put on any airs, and she smiled at me the same as if I was a millionaire while I was telling about a Creek dog feast and listened like it was news from home.

"By and by, after we had eat oysters and some watery soup and truck that never was in my repertory, a Methodist preacher brings in a kind of camp stove arrangement, all silver, on long legs, with a lamp under it.

"Miss Sterling lights up and begins to do some cooking right on the supper table. I wondered why old man Sterling didn't hire a cook with all the money he had. Pretty soon she dished out some cheesy tasting truck that she said was rabbit, but I swear there had never been a Molly cotton tail in a mile of it.

"The last thing on the programme was lemonade. It was brought around in little flat glass bowls and set by your plate. I was pretty thirsty, and I picked up mine and took a big swig of it. Right there was where the little lady had made a mistake. She had put in the lemon all right, but she'd forgot the sugar. The best housekeepers slip up sometimes. I thought maybe Miss Sterling was just learning to keep house and cook—that rabbit would surely make you think so—

and I says to myself, 'Little lady, sugar or no sugar I'll stand by you,' and I raises up my bowl again and drinks the last drop of the lemonade. And then all the balance of 'em picks up their bowls and does the same. And then I gives Miss Sterling the laugh proper, just to carry it off like a joke, so she wouldn't feel bad about the mistake.

"After we all went into the sitting room she sat down and talked to me quite awhile.

"'It was so kind of you, Mr. Kingsbury,' says she, 'to bring my blunder off so nicely. It was so stupid of me to forget the sugar.'

"'Never you mind,' says I, 'some lucky man will throw his rope over a mighty elegant little housekeeper some day, not far from here.'

"'If you mean me, Mr. Kingsbury,' says she laughing out loud, 'I hope he will be as lenient with my poor housekeeping as you have been.'

"'Don't mention it,' says I. 'Anything to oblige the ladies.'"

Bud ceased his reminiscences. And then some one asked him what he considered the most striking and prominent trait of New Yorkers.

"The most visible and peculiar trait of New York folks," answered Bud, "is New York. Most of 'em has New York on the brain. They have heard of other places, such as Waco, and Paris, and Hot Springs, and London; but they don't believe in 'em. They think that town is all Merino. Now to show you how much they care for their village I'll tell you about one of 'em that strayed out as far as the Triangle B while I was working there.

"This New Yorker come out there looking for a job on the ranch. He said he was a good horseback rider, and there were pieces of tanbark hanging on his clothes yet from his riding school.

"Well, for a while they put him to keeping books in the ranch store, for he was a devil at figures. But he got tired of that, and asked for something more in the line of activity. The boys on the ranch liked him all right, but he made us tired shouting New York all the time. Every night he'd tell us about East River and J. P. Morgan and the Eden Musee and Hetty Green and Central Park till we used to throw tin plates and branding irons at him.

"One day this chap gets on a pitching pony, and the pony kind of sidled up his back and went to eating grass while the New Yorker was coming down.

"He come down on his head on a chunk of mesquit wood, and he didn't show any designs toward getting up again. We laid him out in a tent, and he begun to look pretty dead. So Gideon Pease saddles up and burns the wind for old Doc Sleeper's residence in Dogtown, thirty miles away.

"The doctor comes over and he investigates the patient.

"'Boys,' says he, 'you might as well go to playing seven-up for his saddle and clothes, for his head's fractured and if he lives ten minutes it will be a remarkable case of longevity.'

"Of course we didn't gamble for the poor rooster's saddle—that was one of Doc's jokes. But we stood around feeling solemn, and all of us forgive him for having talked us to death about New York.

"I never saw anybody about to hand in his checks act more peaceful than this fellow. His eyes were fixed 'way up in the air, and he was using rambling words to himself all about sweet music and beautiful streets and white-robed forms, and he was smiling like dying was a pleasure.

"'He's about gone now,' said Doc. 'Whenever they begin to think they see heaven it's all off.'

"Blamed if that New York man didn't sit right up when he heard the Doc say that.

"'Say,' says he, kind of disappointed, 'was that heaven? Confound it all, I thought it was Broadway. Some of you fellows get my clothes. I'm going to get up.'

"And I'll be blamed," concluded Bud, "if he wasn't on the train with a ticket for New York in his pocket four days afterward!"

THE ADVENTURES OF SHAMROCK JOLNES

I AM so fortunate as to count Shamrock Jolnes, the great New York detective, among my muster of friends. Jolnes is what is called the "inside man" of the city detective force. He is an expert in the use of the typewriter, and it is his duty, whenever there is a "murder mystery" to be solved, to sit at a desk telephone at headquarters and take down the message of "cranks" who 'phone in their confessions to having committed the crime.

But on certain "off" days when confessions are coming in slowly and three or four new papers have run to earth as many different guilty persons, Jolnes will knock about the town with me, exhibiting, to my great delight and instruction, his marvellous powers of observation and deduction.

The other day I dropped in at Headquarters and found the great detective gazing thoughtfully at a string that was tied tightly around his little finger.

"Good morning, Whatsup," he said, without turning his head. "I'm glad to notice that you've had your house fitted up with electric lights at last."

"Will you please tell me," I said, in surprise, "how you knew that? I am sure that I never mentioned the fact to any one, and the wiring was a rush order not completed until this morning."

"Nothing easier," said Jolnes, genially. "As you came in I caught the odor of the cigar you are smoking. I know an expensive cigar; and I know that not more than three men in New York can afford to smoke cigars and pay gas bills too at the present time. That was an easy one. But I am working just now on a little problem of my own."

"Why have you that string on your finger?" I asked.

"That's the problem," said Jolnes. "My wife tied that on this morning to remind me of something I was to send up to the house. Sit down, Whatsup, and excuse me for a few moments."

The distinguished detective went to a wall telephone, and stood with the receiver to his ear for probably ten minutes.

"Were you listening to a confession?" I asked, when he had returned to his chair.

"Perhaps," said Jolnes, with a smile, "it might be called something of the sort. To be frank with you, Whatsup, I've cut out the dope. I've been increasing the quantity for so long that morphine doesn't have much effect on me any more. I've got to have something more powerful. That telephone I just went to is connected with a room in the Waldorf where there's an author's reading in progress. Now, to get at the solution of this string."

After five minutes of silent pondering, Jolnes looked at me, with a smile, and nodded his head.

"Wonderful man!" I exclaimed; "already?"

"It is quite simple," he said, holding up his finger. "You see that knot? That is to prevent my forgetting. It is, therefore, a forget-me-knot. A forget-me-not is a flower. It was a sack of flour that I was to send home!"

"Beautiful!" I could not help crying out in admiration.

"Suppose we go out for a ramble," suggested Jolnes.

"There is only one case of importance on hand now. Old man McCarty, one hundred and four years old, died from eating too many bananas. The evidence points so strongly to the Mafia that the police have surrounded the Second Avenue Katzenjammer Gambrinus Club No. 2, and the capture of the assassin in only the matter of a few hours. The detective force has not yet been called on for assistance."

Jolnes and I went out and up the street toward the corner, where we were to catch a surface car.

Halfway up the block we met Rheingelder, an acquaintance of ours, who held a City Hall position.

"Good morning, Rheingelder," said Jolnes, halting.

"Nice breakfast that was you had this morning."

Always on the lookout for the detective's remarkable feats of deduction, I saw Jolnes's eyes flash for an instant upon a long yellow splash on the shirt bosom and a smaller one upon the chin of Rheingelder—both undoubtedly made by the yolk of an egg.

"Oh, dot is some of your detectiveness," said Rheingelder, shaking all over with a smile. "Vell, I bet you trinks and cigars all around dot you cannot tell vot I haf eaten for breakfast."

"Done," said Jolnes. "Sausage, pumpernickel, and coffee."

Rheingelder admitted the correctness of the surmise and paid the bet. When we had proceeded on our way I said to Jolnes:

"I thought you looked at the egg spilled on his chin and shirt front."

"I did," said Jolnes. "That is where I began my deduction. Rheingelder is a very economical, saving man. Yesterday eggs dropped in the market to twenty-eight cents per dozen. To-day they are quoted at forty-two. Rheingelder ate eggs yesterday, and to-day he went back to his usual fare. A little thing like this isn't anything, Whatsup; it belongs to the primary arithmetic class."

When we boarded the street car we found the seats all occupied—principally by ladies. Jolnes and I stood on the rear platform.

About the middle of the car there sat an elderly man with a short, gray beard, who looked to be the typical, well-dressed New Yorker. At successive corners other ladies climbed aboard, and soon three or four of them were standing over the man, clinging to straps and glaring meaningly at the man who occupied the coveted seat. But he resolutely retained his place.

"We New Yorkers," I remarked to Jolnes, "have about lost our manners, as far as the exercise of them in public goes."

"Perhaps so," said Jolnes, lightly; "but the man you evidently refer to happens to be a very chivalrous and courteous gentleman from Old Virginia. He is spending a few days in New York with his wife and two daughters, and he leaves for the South to-night."

"You know him, then?" I said, in amazement.

"I never saw him before we stepped on the car," declared the detective, smilingly.

"By the gold tooth of the Witch of Endor!" I cried, "if you can construe all that from his appearance you are dealing in nothing else than black art."

"The habit of observation—nothing more," said Jolnes. "If the old gentleman gets off the car before we do, I think I can demonstrate to you the accuracy of my deduction."

Three blocks farther along the gentleman rose to leave the car. Jolnes addressed him at the door:

"Pardon me, sir, but are you not Colonel Hunter, of Norfolk, Virginia?"

"No, suh," was the extremely courteous answer. "My name, suh, is Ellison— Major Winfield R. Ellison, from Fairfax County, in the same state. I know a good many people, suh, in Norfolk—the Goodriches, the Tollivers, and the Crabtrees, suh, but I never had the pleasure of meeting yo' friend, Colonel

Hunter. I am happy to say, suh, that I am going back to Virginia to-night, after having spent a week in yo' city with my wife and three daughters. I shall be in Norfolk in about ten days, and if you will give me yo' name, suh, I will take pleasure in looking up Colonel Hunter and telling him that you inquired after him, suh."

"Thank you," said Jolnes; "tell him that Reynolds sent his regards, if you will be so kind."

I glanced at the great New York detective and saw that a look of intense chagrin had come upon his clear-cut features. Failure in the slightest point always galled Shamrock Jolnes.

"Did you say your *three* daughters?" he asked of the Virginia gentleman.

"Yes, suh, my three daughters, all as fine girls as there are in Fairfax County," was the answer.

With that Major Ellison stopped the car and began to descend the step. Shamrock Jolnes clutched his arm.

"One moment, sir," he begged, in an urbane voice in which I alone detected the anxiety—"am I not right in believing that one of the young ladies is an *adopted* daughter?"

"You are, suh," admitted the major, from the ground, "but how 'the devil you knew it, suh, is mo' than I can tell."

"And mo' than I can tell, too," I said, as the car went on.

Jolnes was restored to his calm, observant serenity by having wrested victory from his apparent failure; so after we got off the car he invited me into a café promising to reveal the process of his latest wonderful feat.

"In the first place," he began after we were comfortably seated, "I knew the gentleman was no New Yorker because he was flushed and uneasy and restless on account of the ladies that were standing, although he did not rise and give them his seat. I decided from his appearance that he was a Southerner rather than a Westerner.

"Next I began to figure out his reason for not relinquishing his seat to a lady when he evidently felt strongly, but not overpoweringly, impelled to do so. I very quickly decided upon that. I noticed that one of his eyes had received a severe jab in one corner, which was red and inflamed, and that all over his face were tiny round marks about the size of the end of an uncut lead pencil. Also upon both of his patent-leather shoes were a number of deep imprints shaped like ovals cut off square at one end.

"Now, there is only one district in New York City where a man is bound to receive scars and wounds and indentations of that sort—and that is along the sidewalks of Twenty-third Street and a portion of Sixth Avenue south of there. I knew from the imprints of trampling French heels on his feet and the marks of countless jabs in the face from umbrellas and parasols carried by women in the shopping district that he had been in conflict with the amazonian troops. And as he was a man of intelligent appearance, I knew he would not have braved such dangers unless he had been dragged thither by his own women folk. Therefore, when he got on the car his anger at the treatment he had received was sufficient to make him keep his seat in spite of his traditions of Southern chivalry."

"That is all very well," I said, "but why did you insist upon daughters—and especially two daughters? Why couldn't a wife alone have taken him shopping?"

"There had to be daughters," said Jolnes, calmly. "If he had only a wife, and she near his own age, he could have bluffed her into going alone. If he had a young wife she would prefer to go alone. So there you are."

"I'll admit that," I said; "but, now, why two daughters? And how, in the name of all the prophets, did you guess that one was adopted when he told you he had three?"

"Don't say guess," said Jolnes, with a touch of pride in his air; "there is no such word in the lexicon of ratiocination. In Major Ellison's buttonhole there was a carnation and a rosebud backed by a geranium leaf. No woman ever combined a carnation and a rosebud into a boutonnière. Close your eyes, Whatsup, and give the logic of your imagination a chance. Cannot you see the lovely Adele fastening the carnation to the lapel so that papa may be gay upon the street? And then the romping Edith May dancing up with sisterly jealousy to add her rosebud to the adornment?"

"And then," I cried, beginning to feel enthusiasm, "when he declared that he had three daughters——"

"I could see," said Jolnes, "one in the background who added no flower; and I knew that she must be——"

"Adopted!" I broke in. "I give you every credit; but how did you know he was leaving for the South to-night?"

"In his breast pocket," said the great detective, "something large and oval made a protuberance. Good liquor is scarce on trains, and it is a long journey from New York to Fairfax County."

"Again, I must bow to you," I said. "And tell me this, so that my last shred of doubt will be cleared away; why did you decide that he was from Virginia?"

"It was very faint, I admit," answered Shamrock Jolnes, "but no trained observer could have failed to detect the odor of mint in the car."

THE LADY HIGHER UP

NEW YORK CITY, they said, was deserted; and that accounted, doubtless, for the sounds carrying so far in the tranquil summer air. The breeze was south-by-southwest; the hour was midnight; the theme was a bit of feminine gossip by wireless mythology. Three hundred and sixty-five feet above the heated asphalt the tiptoeing symbolic deity on Manhattan pointed her vacillating arrow straight, for the time, in the direction of her exalted sister on Liberty Island. The lights of the great Garden were out; the benches in the Square were filled with sleepers in postures so strange that beside them the writhing figures in Doré's illustrations of the Inferno would have straightened into tailor's dummies. The statue of Diana on the tower of the Garden—its constancy shown by its weathercock ways, its innocence by the coating of gold that it has acquired, its devotion to style by its single, graceful flying scarf, its candor and artlessness by its habit of ever drawing the long bow, its metropolitanism by its posture of swift flight to catch a Harlem train—remained poised with its arrow pointed across the upper bay. Had that arrow sped truly and horizontally it would have passed fifty feet above the head of the heroic matron whose duty it is to offer a cast-ironical welcome to the oppressed of other lands.

Seaward this lady gazed, and the furrows between steamship lines began to cut steerage rates. The translators, too, have put an extra burden upon her. "Liberty Lighting the World" (as her creator christened her) would have had a no more responsible duty, except for the size of it, than that of an electrician or a Standard Oil magnate. But to "enlighten" the world (as our learned civic guardians "Englished" it) requires abler qualities. And so poor Liberty, instead of having a sinecure as a mere illuminator, must be converted into a Chautauqua schoolma'am, with the oceans for her field instead of the placid, classic lake. With a fireless torch and an empty head must she dispel the shadows of the world, and teach it its A, B, C's.

"Ah, there, Mrs. Liberty!" called a clear, rollicking soprano voice through the still, midnight air.

"Is that you, Miss Diana? Excuse my not turning my head. I'm not as flighty and whirly-whirly as some. And 'tis so hoarse I am I can hardly talk on account of the peanut-hulls left on the stairs in me throat by that last boatload of tourists from Marietta, Ohio. 'Tis after being a fine evening, miss."

"If you don't mind my asking," came the bell-like tones of the golden statue, "I'd like to know where you got that City Hall brogue. I didn't know that Liberty was necessarily Irish."

"If ye'd studied the history of art in its foreign complications ye'd not need to ask," replied the offshore statue. "If ye wasn't so light-headed and giddy ye'd know that I was made by a Dago and presented to the American people on behalf of the French Government for the purpose of welcomin' Irish immigrants into the Dutch city of New York. 'Tis that I've been doing night and day since I was erected. Ye must know, Miss Diana, that 'tis with statues the same as with people—'tis not their makers nor the purposes for which they were created that influence the operations of their tongues at all—it's the associations with which they become associated, I'm telling ye."

"You're dead right," agreed Diana. "I notice it on myself. If any of the old guys from Olympus were to come along and hand me any hot air in the ancient Greek I couldn't tell it from a conversation between a Coney Island car conductor and a five-cent fare."

"I'm right glad ye've made up your mind to be sociable, Miss Diana," said Mrs. Liberty. "'Tis a lonesome life I have down here. Is there anything doin' up in the city, Miss Diana, dear?"

"Oh, la, la, la!—no," said Diana. "Notice that 'la, la, la,' Aunt Liberty? Got that from 'Paris by Night' on the roof garden under me. You'll hear that 'la, la, la' at the Café McCann now, along with 'garsong.' The bohemian crowd there have become tired of 'garsong' since O'Rafferty, the head waiter, punched three of them for calling him it. Oh, no; the town's strictly on the bum these nights. Everybody's away. Saw a downtown merchant on the roof garden this evening with his stenographer. Show was so dull he went to sleep. A waiter biting on a dime tip to see if it was good half woke him up. He looks around and sees his little pothooks perpetrator. 'H'm!' says he, 'will you take a letter, Miss De St. Montmorency?' 'Sure, in a minute,' says she, 'if you make it an X.' That was the best thing happened on the roof. So you see how dull it is. La, la, la!"

"'Tis fine ye have it up there in society, Miss Diana. Ye have the cat show and the horse show and the military tournaments where the privates look grand as generals and the generals try to look grand as floor-walkers. And ye have the Sportsmen's Show, where the girl that measures 36, 19, 45 cooks breakfast food in a birch-bark wigwam on the banks of the Grand Canal of Venice conducted by one of the Vanderbilts, Bernard McFadden, and the Reverends Dowie and Duss. And ye have the French ball, where the original Cohens and the Robert Emmet-Sangerbund Society dance the Highland fling one with another. And ye have the grand O'Ryan ball, which is the most beautiful pageant in the world, where the French students vie with the Tyrolean warblers in doin' the cake walk. Ye have the best job for a statue in the whole town, Miss Diana."

"'Tis weary work," sighed the island statue, "disseminatin' the science of liberty in New York Bay. Sometimes when I take a peep down at Ellis Island and see the gang of immigrants I'm supposed to light up, 'tis tempted I am to blow out the gas and let the coroner write out their naturalization papers."

"Say, it's a shame, ain't it, to give you the worst end of it?" came the sympathetic antiphony of the steeplechase goddess. "It must be awfully lonesome down there with so much water around you. I don't see how you ever keep your hair in curl. And that Mother Hubbard you are wearing went out ten years ago. I think those sculptor guys ought to be held for damages for putting iron or marble clothes on a lady. That's where Mr. St. Gaudens was wise. I'm always a little ahead of the styles; but they're coming my way pretty fast. Excuse my back a moment—I caught a puff of wind from the north—shouldn't wonder if things had loosened up in Esopus. There, now! It's in the West—I should think that gold plank would have calmed the air out in that direction. What were you saying, Mrs. Liberty?"

"A fine chat I've had with ye, Miss Diana, ma'am, but I see one of them European steamers a-sailin' up the Narrows, and I must be attendin' to me duties. 'Tis me job to extend aloft the torch of Liberty to welcome all them that survive the kicks that the steerage stewards give 'em while landin'. Sure 'tis a great country ye can come to for $8.50, and the doctor waitin' to send ye back home free if he sees yer eyes red from cryin' for it."

The golden statue veered in the changing breeze, menacing many points on the horizon with its aureate arrow.

"So long, Aunt Liberty," sweetly called Diana of the Tower. "Some night, when the wind's right, I'll call you up again. But—say! you haven't got such a fierce kick coming about your job. I've kept pretty good watch on the island of Manhattan since I've been up here. That's a pretty sick-looking bunch of liberty chasers they dump down at your end of it; but they don't all stay that way. Every little while up here I see guys signing checks and voting the right ticket, and encouraging the arts and taking a bath every morning, that was shoved ashore by a dock laborer born in the United States who never earned over forty dollars a month. Don't run down your job, Aunt Liberty; you're all right, all right."

THE GREATER CONEY

"NEXT Sunday," said Dennis Carnahan, "I'll be after going down to see the new Coney Island that's risen like a phœnix bird from the ashes of the old resort. I'm going with Norah Flynn, and we'll fall victims to all the dry goods deceptions, from the red-flannel eruption of Mount Vesuvius to the pink silk ribbons on the race-suicide problems in the incubator kiosk.

"Was I there before? I was. I was there last Tuesday. Did I see the sights? I did not.

"Last Monday I amalgamated myself with the Bricklayers' Union, and in accordance with the rules I was ordered to quit work the same day on account of a sympathy strike with the Lady Salmon Canners' Lodge No. 2, of Tacoma, Washington.

" 'Twas disturbed I was in mind and proclivities by losing me job, bein' already harassed in me soul on account of havin' quarrelled with Norah Flynn a week before by reason of hard words spoken at the Dairymen and Street-Sprinkler Drivers' semi-annual ball, caused by jealousy and prickly heat and that divil, Andy Coghlin.

"So, I says, it will be Coney for Tuesday; and if the chutes and the short change and the green-corn silk between the teeth don't create diversions and get me feeling better, then I don't know at all.

"Ye will have heard that Coney has received moral reconstruction. The old Bowery, where they used to take your tintype by force and give ye knockout drops before having your palm read, is now called the Wall Street of the island.

The wienerwurst stands are required by law to keep a news ticker in 'em; and the doughnuts are examined every four years by a retired steamboat inspector. The nigger man's head that was used by the old patrons to throw baseballs at is now illegal; and, by order of the Police Commissioner the image of a man drivin' an automobile has been substituted. I hear that the old immoral amusements have been suppressed. People who used to go down from New York to sit in the sand and dabble in the surf. now give up their quarters to squeeze through turnstiles and see imitations of city fires and floods painted on canvas. The reprehensible and degradin' resorts that disgraced old Coney are said to be wiped out. The wipin'-out process consists of raisin' the price from 10 cents to 25 cents, and hirin' a blonde named Maudie to sell tickets instead of Mickey, the Bowery Bite. That's what they say—I don't know.

"But to Coney I goes a-Tuesday. I gets off the 'L' and starts for the glitterin' show. 'Twas a fine sight. The Babylonian towers and the Hindoo roof gardens was blazin' with thousands of electric lights, and the streets was thick with people. 'Tis a true thing they say that Coney levels all rank. I see millionaires eatin' popcorn and trampin' along with the crowd; and I see eight-dollar-a-week clothin'-store clerks in red automobiles fightin' one another for who'd squeeze the horn when they come to a corner.

"'I made a mistake,' I says to myself. 'Twas not Coney I needed. When a man's sad 'tis not scenes of hilarity he wants. 'Twould be far better for him to meditate in a graveyard or to attend services at the Paradise Roof Gardens. 'Tis no consolation when a man's lost his sweetheart to order hot corn and have the waiter bring him the powdered sugar cruet instead of salt and then conceal himself, or to have Zozookum, the gipsy palmist, tell him that he has three children and to look out for another serious calamity; price twenty-five cents.

"I walked far away down on the beach, to the ruins of an old pavilion near one corner of this new private park, Dreamland. A year ago that old pavilion was standin' up straight and the old-style waiters was slammin' a week's supply of clam chowder down in front of you for a nickel and callin' you 'cully' friendly, and vice was rampant, and you got back to New York with enough change to take a car at the bridge. Now they tell me that they serve Welsh rabbits on Surf Avenue, and you get the right change back in the movin'-picture joints.

"I sat down at one side of the old pavilion and looked at the surf spreadin' itself on the beach, and thought about the time me and Norah Flynn sat on that spot last summer. 'Twas before reform struck the island; and we was happy. We had tintypes and chowder in the ribald dives, and the Egyptian Sorceress of the Nile told Norah out of her hand, while I was waitin' in the door, that 'twould be the luck of her to marry a red-headed gossoon with two crooked legs, and I was overrunnin' with joy on account of the illusion. And 'twas there that Norah Flynn put her two hands in mine a year before and we talked of flats and the things she could cook and the love business that goes with such episodes. And that was Coney as we loved it, and as the hand of Satan was upon it, friendly and noisy and your money's worth, with no fence around the ocean and not too many electric lights to show the sleeve of a black serge coat against a white shirtwaist.

"I sat with my back to the parks where they had the moon and the dreams and the steeples corralled, and longed for the old Coney. There wasn't many people on the beach. Lots of them was feedin' pennies to the slot machines to see the 'Interrupted Courtship' in the movin' pictures; and a good many was takin' the air in the Canals of Venice and some was breathin' the smoke of the sea battle by actual warships in a tank filled with real water. A few was down on the sands enjoyin' the moonlight and the water. And the heart of me was heavy for the new morals of the old island, while the bands behind me played and the sea pounded on the bass drum in front.

"And directly I got up and walked along the old pavilion, and there on the other side of, half in the dark, was a slip of a girl sittin' on the tumble-down timbers, and unless I'm a liar she was cryin' by herself there, all alone.

"'Is it trouble you are in, now, Miss,' says I; 'and what's to be done about it?'

"''Tis none of your business at all, Denny Carnahan,' says she, sittin' up straight. And it was the voice of no other than Norah Flynn.

"'Then it's not,' says I, 'and we're after having a pleasant evening, Miss Flynn. Have ye seen the sights of this new Coney Island, then? I presume ye have come here for that purpose,' says I.

"'I have,' says she. 'Me mother and Uncle Tim they are waiting beyond. 'Tis an elegant evening I've had. I've seen all the attractions that be.'

"'Right ye are,' says I to Norah; and I don't know when I've been that amused. After disportin' meself among the most laughable moral improvements of the revised shell games I took meself to the shore for the benefit of the cool air. 'And did ye observe the Durbar, Miss Flynn?'

"'I did,' says she, reflectin'; 'but 'tis not safe, I'm thinkin', to ride down them slantin' things into the water.'

"'How did ye fancy the shoot the chutes?' I asks.

"'True, then, I'm afraid of guns,' says Norah. 'They make such noise in my ears. But Uncle Tim, he shot them, he did, and won cigars. 'Tis a fine time we had this day, Mr. Carnahan.'

"'I'm glad you've enjoyed yourself,' I says. 'I suppose you've had a roarin' fine time seein' the sights. And how did the incubators and the helter-skelter and the midgets suit the taste of ye?'

"'I—I wasn't hungry,' says Norah, faint. 'But mother ate a quantity of all of 'em. I'm that pleased with the fine things in the new Coney Island,' says she, 'that it's the happiest day I've seen in a long time, at all.'

"'Did you see Venice?' says I.

"'We did,' says she. 'She was a beauty. She was all dressed in red, she was, with——'

"I listened no more to Norah Flynn. I stepped up and gathered her in my arms.

"''Tis a story-teller ye are, Norah Flynn,' says I. 'Ye've seen no more of the greater Coney Island that I have meself. Come, now, tell the truth—ye came to sit by the old pavilion by the waves where you sat last summer and made Dennis Carnahan a happy man. Speak up, and tell the truth.'

"Norah stuck her nose against me vest.

"'I despise it, Denny,' she says, half cryin'. 'Mother and Uncle Tim went to see the shows, but I came down here to think of you. I couldn't bear the lights and the crowd. Are you forgivin' me, Denny, for the words we had?'

"''Twas me fault,' says I. 'I came here for the same reason meself. Look at the lights, Norah,' I says, turning my back to the sea—'ain't they pretty?'

"'They are,' says Norah, with her eyes shinin'; 'and do ye hear the bands playin'? Oh, Denny, I think I'd like to see it all.'

"'The old Coney is gone, darlin',' I says to her. 'Everything moves. When a man's glad it's not scenes of sadness he wants. 'Tis a great Coney we have here, but we couldn't see it till we got in the humor for it. Next Sunday, Norah darlin', we'll see the new place from end to end.'"

LAW AND ORDER

I FOUND myself in Texas recently, revisiting old places and vistas. At a sheep ranch where I had sojourned many years ago, I stopped for a week. And, as all visitors do, I heartily plunged into the business at hand, which happened to be that of dipping the sheep.

Now, this process is so different from ordinary human baptism that it deserves a word of itself. A vast iron cauldron with half the fires of Avernus beneath it is partly filled with water that soon boils furiously. Into that is cast concentrated lye, lime, and sulphur, which is allowed to stew and fume until the witches' broth is strong enough to scorce the third arm of Palladino herself.

Then this concentrated brew is mixed in a long, deep vat with cubic gallons of hot water, and the sheep are caught by their hind legs and flung into the compound. After being thoroughly ducked by means of a forked pole in the hands of a gentleman detailed for that purpose, they are allowed to clamber up an incline into a corral and dry or die, as the state of their constitutions may decree. If you ever caught an able-bodied, two-year-old mutton by the hind legs and felt the 750 volts of kicking that he can send through your arm seventeen times before you can hurl him into the vat, you will, of course, hope that he may die instead of dry.

But this is merely to explain why Bud Oakley and I gladly stretched ourselves on the bank of the near-by *charco* after the dipping, glad for the welcome inanition and pure contact with the earth after our muscle-racking labors. The flock was a small one, and we finished at three in the afternoon; so Bud brought from the *morral* on his saddle horn, coffee and a coffee pot and a big hunk of bread and some side bacon. Mr. Mills, the ranch owner and my old friend, rode away to the ranch with his force of Mexican *trabajadores*.

While the bacon was frizzling nicely, there was the sound of horses' hoofs behind us. Bud's six-shooter lay in its scabbard ten feet away from his hand. He paid not the slightest heed to the approaching horseman. This attitude of a Texas ranchman was so different from the old-time custom that I marvelled. Instinctively I turned to inspect the possible foe that menaced us in the rear. I saw a horseman dressed in black, who might have been a lawyer or a parson or an undertaker, trotting peaceably along the road by the *arroyo*.

Bud noticed my precautionary movement and smiled sarcastically and sorrowfully.

"You've been away too long," said he. "You don't need to look around any more when anybody gallops up behind you in this state, unless something hits you in the back; and even then it's liable to be only a bunch of tracts or a petition to sign against the trusts. I never looked at that *hombre* that rode by; but I'll bet a quart of sheep dip that he's some double-dyed son of a popgun out rounding up prohibition votes."

"Times have changed, Bud," said I, oracularly. "Law and order is the rule now in the South and the Southwest."

I caught a cold gleam from Bud's pale blue eyes.

"Not that I——" I began, hastily.

"Of course you don't," said Bud, warmly. "You know better. You've lived here before. Law and order, you say? Twenty years ago we had 'em here. We only had two or three laws, such as against murder before witnesses, and being caught stealing horses, and voting the Republican ticket. But how is it now? All we get is orders; and the laws go out of the state. Them legislators set up there at Austin and don't do nothing but make laws against kerosene oil and schoolbooks being brought into the state. I reckon they was afraid some man would go home some evening after work and light up and get an education and go to work and make laws to repeal aforesaid laws. Me, I'm for the old days when law and order meant what they said. A law was a law, and a order was a order."

"But——" I began.

"I was going on," continued Bud, "while this coffee is boiling, to describe to you a case of genuine law and order that I knew of once in the times when cases was decided in the chambers of a six-shooter instead of a supreme court.

"You've heard of old Ben Kirkman, the cattle king? His ranch run from the Nueces to the Rio Grande. In them days, as you know, there was cattle barons and cattle kings. The difference was this: when a cattleman went to San Antone and bought beer for the newspaper reporters and only give them the number of cattle he actually owned, they wrote him up for a baron. When he bought 'em champagne wine and added in the amount of cattle he had stole, they called him a king.

"Luke Summers was one of his range bosses. And down to the king's ranch comes one day a bunch of these Oriental people from New York or Kansas City or thereabouts. Luke was detailed with a squad to ride about with 'em, and see that the rattlesnakes got fair warning when they was coming, and drive the deer out of their way. Among the bunch was a black-eyed girl that wore a number two shoe. That's all I noticed about her. But Luke must have seen more, for he married her one day before the *caballard* started back, and went over on Canada Verde and set up a ranch of his own. I'm skipping over the sentimental stuff on purpose, because I never saw or wanted to see any of it. And Luke takes me along with him because we was old friends and I handles cattle to suit him.

"I'm skipping over much what followed, because I never saw or wanted to see any of it—but three years afterward there was a boy kid stumbling and blubbering around the galleries and floors of Luke's ranch. I never had no use for kids; but it seems they did. And I'm skipping over much what followed until one day out to the ranch drives in hacks and buck-boards a lot of Mrs. Summers's friends from the East—a sister or so and two or three men. One looked like an uncle to somebody; and one looked like nothing; and the other one had on corkscrew pants and spoke in a tone of voice. I never liked a man who spoke in a tone of voice.

"I'm skipping over much what followed; but one afternoon when I rides up to the ranch house to get some orders about a drove of beeves that was to be shipped, I hears something like a popgun go off. I waits at the hitching rack, not wishing to intrude on private affairs. In a little while Luke comes out and gives some orders to some of his Mexican hands, and they go and hitch up sundry and divers vehicles; and mighty soon out comes one of the sisters or so and some of the two or three men. But two of the two or three men carries between 'em the cork-screw man who spoke in a tone of voice, and lays him flat down in one of the wagons. And they all might have been seen wending their way away.

"'Bud,' says Luke to me, 'I want you to fix up a little and go up to San Antone with me.'

"'Let me get on my Mexican spurs,' says I, 'and I'm your company.'

"One of the sisters or so seems to have stayed at the ranch with Mrs. Summers and the kid. We rides to Encinal and catches the International, and hits San Antone in the morning. After breakfast Luke steers me straight to the office of a lawyer. They go in a room and talk and then come out.

"'Oh, there won't be any trouble, Mr. Summers,' says the lawyer. 'I'll acquaint Judge Simmons with the facts to-day; and the matter will be put through as promptly as possible. Law and order reigns in this state as swift and sure as any in the country.'

"'I'll wait for the decree if it won't take over half an hour,' says Luke.

"'Tut, tut,' says the lawyer man. 'Law must take its course. Come back day after to-morrow at half-past nine.'

"At that time me and Luke shows up, and the lawyer hands him a folded document. And Luke writes him out a check.

"On the sidewalk Luke holds up the paper to me and puts a finger the size of a kitchen door latch on it and says:

" 'Decree of ab-so-lute divorce with cus-to-dy of the child.'

" 'Skipping over much what has happened of which I know nothing,' says I, 'it looks to me like a split. Couldn't the lawyer man have made it a strike for you?'

" 'But,' says he, in a pained style, 'that child is the one thing I have to live for. *She* may go; but the boy is mine!—think of it—I have the cus-to-dy of the child.'

" 'All right,' says I. 'If it's the law, let's abide by it. But I think,' says I, 'that Judge Simmons might have used exemplary clemency, or whatever is the legal term, in our case.'

"You see, I wasn't inveigled much into the desirableness of having infants around a ranch, except the kind that feed themselves and sell for so much on the hoof when they grow up. But Luke was struck with that sort of parental foolishness that I never could understand. All the way riding from the station back to the ranch, he kept pulling that decree out of his pocket and laying his finger on the back of it and reading off to me the sum and substance of it. 'Cus-to-dy of the child, Bud,' says he. 'Don't forget it—cus-to-dy of the child.'

"But when we hits the ranch we finds our decree of court obviated, *nolle prossed*, and remanded for trial. Mrs. Summers and the kid was gone. They tell us that an hour after me and Luke had started for San Antone she had a team hitched and lit out for the nearest station with her trunks and the youngster.

"Luke takes out his decree once more and reads off its emoluments.

" 'It ain't possible, Bud,' says he, 'for this to be. It's contrary to law and order. It's wrote as plain as day here—"Cus-to-dy of the child." '

" 'There is what you might call a human leaning,' says I, 'toward smashing 'em both—not to mention the child.'

" 'Judge Simmons,' goes on Luke, 'is a incorporated officer of the law. She can't take the boy away. He belongs to me by statutes passed and approved by the state of Texas.'

" 'And he's removed from the jurisdiction of mundane mandamuses,' says I, 'by the unearthly statutes of female partiality. Let us praise the Lord and be thankful for whatever small mercies——' I begins; but I see Luke don't listen to me. Tired as he was, he calls for a fresh horse and starts back again for the station.

"He come back two weeks afterward, not saying much.

" 'We can't get the trail,' says he; 'but we've done all the telegraphing that the wires'll stand, and we've got these city rangers they call detectives on the lookout. In the meantime, Bud,' says he, 'we'll round up them cows on Brush Creek, and wait for the law to take its course.' "

And after that we never alluded to allusions, as you might say.

"Skipping over much what happened in the next twelve years, Luke was made sheriff of Mojada County. He made me his office deputy. Now, don't get in your mind no wrong apparitions of a office deputy doing sums in a book or mashing letters in a cider press. In them days his job was to watch the back windows so nobody didn't plug the sheriff in the rear while he was adding up mileage at his desk in front. And in them days I had qualifications for the job. And there was law and order in Mojada County, and schoolbooks, and all the whiskey you wanted, and the Government built its own battleships instead of collecting nickels from the school children to do it with. And, as I say, there was law and order instead of enactments and restrictions such as disfigure our umpire state to-day. We had our office at Bildad, the county seat, from which we emerged forth on necessary occasions to soothe whatever fracases and unrest that might occur in our jurisdiction.

"Skipping over much what happened while me and Luke was sheriff, I want to give you an idea of how the law was respected in them days. Luke was what you would call one of the most conscious men in the world. He never knew much book law, but he had the inner emoluments of justice and mercy inculcated into his system. If a respectable citizen shot a Mexican or held up a train and cleaned out the safe in the express car, and Luke ever got hold of him, he'd give the guilty party such a reprimand and a cussin' out that he'd probable never do it again. But once let somebody steal a horse (unless it was a Spanish pony), or cut a wire fence, or otherwise impair the peace and indignity of Mojada County, Luke and me would be on 'em with habeas corpuses and smokeless powder and all the modern inventions of equity and etiquette.

"We certainly had our county on a basis of lawfulness. I've know persons of Eastern classification with little spotted caps and buttoned-up shoes to get off the train at Bildad and eat sandwiches at the railroad station without being shot at or even roped and drug about by the citizens of the town.

"Luke had his own ideas of legality and justice. He was kind of training me to succeed him when he went out of office. He was always looking ahead to the time when he'd quit sheriffing. What he wanted to do was to build a yellow house with lattice-work under the porch and have hens scratching in the yard. The one main thing in his mind seemed to be the yard.

" 'Bud,' he says to me, 'by instinct and sentiment I'm a contractor. I want to be a contractor. That's what I'll be when I get out of office.'

" 'What kind of a contractor?' says I. 'It sounds like a kind of business to me. You ain't going to haul cement or establish branches or work on a railroad, are you?'

" 'You don't understand,' says Luke. 'I'm tired of space and horizons and territory and distances and things like that. What I want is reasonable contraction. I want a yard with a fence around it that you can go out and set on after supper and listen to whip-poor-wills,' says Luke.

"That's the kind of a man he was. He was homelike, although he'd had bad luck in such investments. But he never talked about them times on the ranch. It seemed like he'd forgotten about it. I wondered how, with his ideas of yards and chickens and notions of lattice-work, he'd seemed to have got out of his mind that kid of his that had been taken away from him, unlawful, in spite of his decree of court. But he wasn't a man you could ask about such things as he didn't refer to in his own conversation.

"I reckon he'd put all his emotions and ideas into being sheriff. I've read in books about men that was disappointed in these poetic and fine-haired and high-collared affairs with ladies renouncing truck of that kind and wrapping themselves up into some occupation like painting pictures, or herding sheep, or science, or teaching school—something to make 'em forget. Well, I guess that was the way with Luke. But, as he couldn't paint pictures, he took it out in rounding up horse thieves and in making Mojada County a safe place to sleep in if you was well armed and not afraid of requisitions or tarantulas.

"One day there passes through Bildad a bunch of these money investors from the East, and they stopped off there, Bildad being the dinner station on the I. & G. N. They was just coming back from Mexico looking after mines and such. There was five of 'em—four solid parties, with gold watch chains, that would grade up over two hundred pounds on the hoof, and one kid about seventeen or eighteen.

"This youngster had on one of them cowboy suits such as tenderfoots bring West with 'em; and you could see he was aching to wing a couple of Indians or bag a grizzly or two with the little pearl-handled gun he had buckled around his waist.

"I walked down to the depot to keep an eye on the outfit and see that they didn't locate any land or scare the cow ponies hitched in front of Murchison's store or act otherwise unseemly. Luke was away after a gang of cattle thieves down on the Frio, and I always looked after the law and order when he wasn't there.

"After dinner this boy comes out of the dining room while the train was waiting, and prances up and down the platform ready to shoot all antelope, lions, or private citizens that might endeavor to molest or come too near him. He was a good-looking kid; only he was like all them tenderfoots—he didn't know a law-and-order town when he saw it.

"By and by along comes Pedro Johnson, the proprietor of the Crystal Palace *chili-concarne* stand in Bildad. Pedro was a man who liked to amuse himself; so he kind of herd rides this youngster, laughing at him, tickled to death. I was too far away to hear, but the kid seems to mention some remarks to Pedro, and Pedro goes up and slaps him about nine feet away, and laughs harder than ever. And then the boy gets up quicker than he fell and jerks out his little pearl-handle, and—bing! bing! bing! Pedro gets it three times in special and treasured portions of his carcass. I saw the dust fly off his clothes every time the bullets hit. Sometimes them little thirty-twos cause worry at close range.

"The engine bell was ringing, and the train starting off slow. I goes up to the kid and places him under arrest, and takes away his gun. But the first thing I knew that *caballard* of capitalists makes a break for the train. One of 'em hesitates in front of me for a second, and kind of smiles and shoves his hand up against my chin, and I sort of laid down on the platform and took a nap. I never was afraid of guns; but I don't want any person except a barber to take liberties like that with my face again. When I woke up, the whole outfit—train, boy, and all—was gone. I asked about Pedro, and they told me the doctor said he would recover provided his wounds didn't turn out to be fatal.

"When Luke got back three days later, and I told him about it, he was mad all over.

"'Why'n't you telegraph to San Antone,' he asks, 'and have the bunch arrested there?'

"'Oh, well,' says I, 'I always did admire telegraphy; but astronomy was what I had took up just then.' That capitalist sure knew how to gesticulate with his hands.

"Luke got madder and madder. He investigates and finds in the depot a card one of the men had dropped that gives the address of some *hombre* called Scudder in New York City.

"'Bud,' says Luke, 'I'm going after that bunch. I'm going there and get the man or boy, as you say he was, and bring him back. I'm sheriff of Mojada County, and I shall keep law and order in its precincts while I'm able to draw a gun. And I want you to go with me. No Eastern Yankee can shoot up a respectable and well-known citizen of Bildad, 'specially with a thirty-two calibre, and escape the law. Pedro Johnson,' says Luke, 'is one of our most prominent citizens and business men. I'll appoint Sam Bell acting sheriff with penitentiary powers while I'm away, and you and me will take a six forty-five northbound to-morrow evening and follow up this trail.'

"'I'm your company,' says I. 'I never see this New York, but I'd like to. But, Luke,' says I, 'don't you have to have a dispensation or a habeas corpus or something from the state, when you reach out that far for rich men and malefactors?'

"'Did I have a requisition,' says Luke, 'when I went over into the Brazos bottoms and brought back Bill Grimes and two more for holding up the International? Did me and you have a search warrant or a posse comitatus when we rounded up them six Mexican cow thieves down in Hidalgo? It's my business to keep order in Mojada County.'

"'And it's my business as office deputy,' says I, 'to see that business is carried on according to law. Between us both we ought to keep things pretty well cleaned up.'

"So, the next day, Luke packs a blanket and some collars and his mileage book

in a haversack, and him and me hits the breeze for New York. It was a powerful long ride. The seats in the cars was too short for six-footers like us to
sleep comfortable on; and the conductor had to keep us from getting off at every
town that had five-story houses in it. But we got there finally; and we seemed
to see right away that he was right about it.

"'Luke,' says I, 'as office deputy and from a law standpoint, it don't look to
me like this place is properly and legally in the jurisdiction of Mojada County,
Texas."

"'From the standpoint of order,' says he, 'it's amenable to answer for its sins
to the properly appointed authorities from Bildad to Jerusalem.'

"'Amen,' says I. 'But let's turn our trick sudden, and ride. I don't like the
looks of this place.'

"'Think of Pedro Johnson,' says Luke, 'a friend of mine and yours shot down
by one of these gilded abolitionists at his very door!'

"'It was at the door of the freight depot,' says I. 'But the law will not be
balked at a quibble like that.'

"We put up at one of them big hotels on Broadway. The next morning I goes
down about two miles of stairsteps to the bottom and hunts for Luke. It ain't
no use. It looks like San Jacinto day in San Antone. There's a thousand
folks milling around in a kind of a roofed-over plaza with marble pavements and
trees growing right out of 'em, and I see no more chance of finding Luke than
if we was hunting each other in the big pear flat down below Old Fort Ewell.
But soon Luke and me runs together in one of the turns of them marble alleys.

"'It ain't no use, Bud,' says he. 'I can't find no place to eat at. I've been
looking for restaurant signs and smelling for ham all over the camp. But I'm
used to going hungry when I have to. Now,' says he, 'I'm going out and get
a hack and ride down to the address on this Scudder card. You stay here and
try to hustle some grub. But I doubt if you'll find it. I wish we'd brought along
some cornmeal and bacon and beans. I'll be back when I see this Scudder, if
the trail ain't wiped out.'

"So I starts foraging for breakfast. For the honor of old Mojada County I
didn't want to seem green to them abolitionists, so every time I turned a corner
in them marble halls I went up to the first desk or counter I see and looks
around for grub. If I didn't see what I wanted I asked for something else. In
about half an hour I had a dozen cigars, five story magazines, and seven or eight
railroad time-tables in my pockets, and never a smell of coffee or bacon to point
out the trail.

"Once a kind lady sitting at a table and playing a game kind of like pushpin
told me to go into a closet that she called No. 3. I went in and shut the door,
and the blamed thing lit itself up. I set down on a stool before a shelf and
waited. Thinks I, 'This is a private dining room.' But no waiter never came.
When I got to sweating good and hard, I goes out again.

"'Did you get what you wanted?' says she.

"'No, ma'am,' says I. 'Not a bite.'

"'Then there's no charge,' says she.

"'Thanky, ma'am,' says I, and I takes up the trail again.

"By and by I thinks I'll shed etiquette; and I picks up one of them boys with
blue clothes and yellow buttons in front, and he leads me to what he calls the
caffay breakfast room. And the first thing I lays my eyes on when I go in is that
boy that had shot Pedro Johnson. He was setting all alone at a little table,
hitting a egg with a spoon like he was afraid he'd break it.

"I takes the chair across the table from him; and he looks insulted and makes
a move like he was going to get up.

"'Keep still, son,' says I. 'You're apprehended, arrested, and in charge of the Texas authorities. Go on and hammer that egg some more if it's the inside of it you want. Now, what did you shoot Mr. Johnson, of Bildad, for?'

"'And may I ask who you are?' says he.

"'You may,' says I. 'Go ahead.'

"'I suppose you're on,' says this kid, without batting his eyes. 'But what are you eating? Here, waiter!' he calls out, raising his finger. 'Take this gentleman's order.'

"'A beefsteak,' says I, 'and some fried eggs and a can of peaches and a quart of coffee will about suffice.'

"We talk awhile about the sundries of life and then he says:

"'What are you going to do about that shooting? I had a right to shoot that man,' says he. 'He called me names that I couldn't overlook, and then he struck me. He carried a gun, too. What else could I do?'

"'We'll have to take you back to Texas,' says I.

"'I'd like to go back,' says the boy, with a kind of a grin—'if it wasn't on an occasion of this kind. It's the life I like. I've always wanted to ride and shoot and live in the open air ever since I can remember.'

"'Who was this gang of stout parties you took this trip with?' I asks.

"'My stepfather,' says he, 'and some business partners of his in some Mexican mining and land schemes.'

"'I saw you shoot Pedro Johnson,' says I, 'and I took that little popgun away from you that you did it with. And when I did so I noticed three or four little scars in a row over your right eyebrow. You've been in rookus before, haven't you?'

"'I've had these scars ever since I can remember,' says he. 'I don't know how they came there.'

"'Was you ever in Texas before?' says I.

"'Not that I remember of,' says he. 'But I thought I had when we struck the prairie country. But I guess I hadn't.'

"'Have you got a mother?' I asks.

"'She died five years ago,' says he.

"Skipping over the most of what followed—when Luke came back I turned the kid over to him. He had seen Scudder and told him what he wanted; and it seems that Scudder got active with one of these telephones as soon as he left. For in about an hour afterward there comes to our hotel some of these city rangers in everyday clothes that they call detectives, and marches the whole outfit of us to what they call a magistrate's court. They accuse Luke of attempted kidnapping, and ask him what he has to say.

"'This snipe,' says Luke to the judge, 'shot and wilfully punctured with malice and forethought one of the most respected and prominent citizens of the town of Bildad, Texas, Your Honor. And in so doing laid himself liable to the penitence of law and order. And I hereby make claim and demand restitution of the State of New York City for the said alleged criminal; and I know he done it.'

"'Have you the usual and necessary requisition papers from the governor of your state?' asks the judge.

"'My usual papers,' says Luke, 'was taken away from me at the hotel by these gentlemen who represent law and order in your city. They was two Colt's .45's that I've packed for nine years; and if I don't get 'em back, there'll be more trouble. You can ask anybody in Mojada County about Luke Summers. I don't usually need any other kind of papers for what I do.'

"I see the judge looks mad, so I steps up and says:

"'Your Honor, the aforesaid defendant, Mr. Luke Summers, sheriff of Mojada County, Texas, is as fine a man as ever threw a rope or upheld the statutes and codicils of the greatest state in the Union. But he——'

"The judge hits his table with a wooden hammer and asks who I am.

"'Bud Oakley,' says I. 'Office deputy of the sheriff's office of Mojada County, Texas. Representing,' says I, 'the Law. Luke Summers,' I goes on, 'represents Order. And if Your Honor will give me about ten minutes in private talk, I'll explain the whole thing to you, and show you the equitable and legal requisition papers which I carry in my pocket.'

"The judge kind of half smiles and says he will talk with me in his private room. In there I put the whole thing up to him in such language as I had, and when we goes outside, he announces the verdict that the young man is delivered into the hands of the Texas authorities; and calls the next case.

"Skipping over much of what happened on the way back, I'll tell you how the thing wound up in Bildad.

"When we got the prisoner in the sheriff's office, I says to Luke:

"'You remember that kid of yours—that two-year-old that they stole away from you when the bust-up come?'

"Luke looks black and angry. He'd never let anybody talk to him about that business, and he never mentioned it himself.

"'Toe the mark,' says I. 'Do you remember when he was toddling around on the porch and fell down on a pair of Mexican spurs and cut four little holes over his right eye? Look at the prisoner,' says I, 'look at his nose and the shape of his head and—why, you old fool, don't you know your own son?—I knew him,' says I, 'when he perforated Mr. Johnson at the depot.'

"Luke comes over to me shaking all over. I never saw him lose his nerve before.

"'Bud,' says he, 'I've never had that boy out of my mind one day or one night since he was took away. But I never let on. But can we hold him?—Can we make him stay?—I'll make the best man of him that ever put his foot in a stirrup. Wait a minute,' says he, all excited and out of his mind—'I've got something here in my desk—I reckon it'll hold legal yet—I've looked at it a thousand times—"Cus-to-dy of the child," says Luke—"Cus-to-dy of the child." We can hold him on that, can't we? Le'me see if I can find that decree.'

"Luke begins to tear his desk to pieces.

"'Hold on,' says I. 'You are Order and I'm Law. You needn't look for that paper, Luke. It ain't a decree any more. It's requisition papers. It's on file in that Magistrate's office in New York. I took it along when we went, because I was office deputy and knew the law.'

"'I've got him back,' says Luke. 'He's mine again. I never thought——'

"'Wait a minute,' says I. 'We've got to have law and order. You and me have got to preserve 'em both in Mojada County according to our oath and conscience. The kid shot Pedro Johnson, one of Bildad's most prominent and——'

"'Oh, hell!' says Luke. 'That don't amount to anything. That fellow was half Mexican, anyhow.'"

TRANSFORMATION OF MARTIN BURNEY

IN behalf of Sir Walter's soothing plant let us look into the case of Martin Burney.

They were constructing the Speedway along the west bank of the Harlem River. The grub-boat of Dennis Corrigan, sub-contractor, was moored to a tree on the bank. Twenty-two men belonging to the little green island toiled there at the sinew-cracking labor. One among them, who wrought in the kitchen of the grub-boat, was of the race of the Goths. Over them all stood the exorbitant Corrigan, harrying them like the captain of a galley crew. He paid them so little that most of the gang, work as they might, earned little more than food and tobacco; many of them were in debt to him. Corrigan boarded them all in the grub-boat, and gave them good grub, for he got it back in work.

Martin Burney was furthest behind of all. He was a little man, all muscles and hands and feet, with a gray-red, stubby beard. He was too light for the work, which would have glutted the capacity of a steam shovel.

The work was hard. Besides that, the banks of the river were humming with mosquitoes. As a child in a dark room fixes his regard on the pale light of a comforting window, these toilers watched the sun that brought around the one hour of the day that tasted less bitter. After the sundown supper they would huddle together on the river bank, and send the mosquitoes whining and eddying back from the malignant puffs of twenty-three reeking pipes. Thus socially banded against the foe, they wrenched out of the hour a few well-smoked drops from the cup of joy.

Each week Burney grew deeper in debt. Corrigan kept a small stock of goods on the boat, which he sold to the men at prices that brought him no loss. Burney was a good customer at the tobacco counter. One sack when he went to work in the morning and one when he came in at night, so much was his account swelled daily. Burney was something of a smoker. Yet it was not true that he ate his meals with a pipe in his mouth, which had been said of him. The little man was not discontented. He had plenty to eat, plenty of tobacco, and a tyrant to curse; so why should not he, an Irishman, be well satisfied?

One morning as he was starting with the others for work he stopped at the pine counter for his usual sack of tobacco.

"There's no more for ye," said Corrigan. "Your account's closed. Ye are a losing investment. No, not even tobaccy, my son. No more tobaccy on account. If ye want to work and eat, do so, but the smoke of ye has all ascended. 'Tis my advice that ye hunt a new job."

"I have no tobaccy to smoke in my pipe this day, Mr. Corrigan," said Burney, not quite understanding that such a thing could happen to him.

"Earn it," said Corrigan, "and then buy it."

Burney stayed on. He knew of no other job. At first he did not realize that tobacco had got to be his father and mother, his confessor and sweetheart, and wife and child.

For three days he managed to fill his pipe from the other men's sacks, and then they shut him off, one and all. They told him, rough but friendly, that of all things in the world tobacco must be quickest forthcoming to a fellow-man desiring it, but that beyond the immediate temporary need requisition upon the store of a comrade is pressed with great danger to friendship.

Then the blackness of the pit arose and filled the heart of Burney. Sucking the corpse of his deceased dudheen, he staggered through his duties with his barrowful of stones and dirt, feeling for the first time that the curse of Adam was upon him. Other men bereft of a pleasure might have recourse to other delights, but Burney had only two comforts in life. One was his pipe, the other was an ecstatic hope that there would be no Speedways to build on the other side of Jordan.

At meal times he would let the other men go first into the grub-boat, and then he would go down on his hands and knees, grovelling fiercely upon the ground where they had been sitting, trying to find some stray crumbs of tobacco. Once he sneaked down the river bank and filled his pipe with dead willow leaves. At the first whiff of the smoke he spat in the direction of the boat and put the finest curse he ever knew on Corrigan—one that began with the first Corrigans born on earth and ended with the Corrigans that shall hear the trumpet of Gabriel blow. He began to hate Corrigan with all his shaking nerves and soul. Even murder occurred to him in a vague sort of way. Five days he went without the taste of tobacco—he who had smoked all day and thought the night misspent in which he had not awakened for a pipeful or two under the bedclothes.

One day a man stopped at the boat to say that there was work to be had in the Bronx Park, where a large number of laborers were required in making some improvements.

After dinner Burney walked thirty yards down the river bank away from the maddening smell of the others' pipes. He sat down upon a stone. He was thinking he would set out for the Bronx. At least he could earn tobacco there. What if the books did say he owed Corrigan? Any man's work was worth his keep. But then he hated to go without getting even with the hard-hearted screw who had put his pipe out. Was there any way to do it?

Softly stepping among the clods came Tony, he of the race of Goths, who worked in the kitchen. He grinned at Burney's elbow, and that unhappy man, full of race animosity and holding urbanity in contempt, growled at him: "What d'ye want, ye——Dago?"

Tony also contained a grievance—and a plot. He, too, was a Corrigan hater, and had been primed to see it in others.

"How you like-a Mr. Corrigan?" he asked. "You think-a him a nice-a man?"

"To hell with 'm," he said. "May his liver turn to water, and the bones of him crack in the cold of his heart. May dog fennel grow upon his ancestors' graves, and the grandsons of his children be born without eyes. May whiskey turn to clabber in his mouth, and every time he sneezes may he blister the soles of his feet. And the smoke of his pipe—may it make his eyes water, and the drops fall on the grass that his cows eat and poison the butter that he spreads on his bread."

Though Tony remained a stranger to the beauties of this imagery, he gathered from it the conviction that it was sufficiently anti-Corrigan in its tendency. So, with the confidence of a fellow-conspirator, he sat by Burney upon the stone and unfolded his plot.

It was very simple in design. Every day after dinner it was Corrigan's habit to sleep for an hour in his bunk. At such times it was the duty of the cook and his helper, Tony, to leave the boat so that no noise might disturb the autocrat. The cook always spent this hour in walking exercise. Tony's plan was this. After Corrigan should be asleep he (Tony) and Burney would cut the mooring ropes that held the boat to the shore. Tony lacked the nerve to do the deed alone. Then the awkward boat would swing out into a swift current and surely overturn against a rock there was below.

"Come on and do it," said Burney. "If the back of ye aches from the lick he gave ye as the pit of me stomach does for the taste of a bite of smoke, we can't cut the ropes too quick."

"All a-right," said Tony. "But better wait 'bout-a ten minute more. Give-a Corrigan plenty time get good-a sleep."

They waited, sitting upon the stone. The rest of the men were at work out of sight around a bend in the road. Everything would have gone well—except, perhaps, with Corrigan, had not Tony been moved to decorate the plot with its conventional accompaniment. He was of dramatic blood, and perhaps he intuitively divined the appendage to villainous machinations as prescribed by the stage. He pulled from his shirt bosom a long, black, beautiful, venomous cigar, and handed it to Burney.

"You like-a smoke while we wait?" he asked.

Burney clutched it and snapped off the end as a terrier bites at a rat. He laid it to his lips like a long-lost sweetheart. When the smoke began to draw he gave a long, deep sigh, and the bristles of his gray-red mustache curled down over the cigar like the talons of an eagle. Slowly the red faded from the whites of his eyes. He fixed his gaze dreamily upon the hills across the river. The minutes came and went.

" 'Bout time to go now," said Tony. "That damn-a Corrigan he be in the reever very quick."

Burney started out of his trance with a grunt. He turned his head and gazed with a surprised and pained severity at his accomplice. He took the cigar partly from his mouth, but sucked it back again immediately, chewed it lovingly once or twice, and spoke in virulent puffs, from the corner of his mouth:

"What is it, ye yaller haythen? Would ye lay contrivances against the enlightened races of the earth, ye instigator of illegal crimes? Would ye seek to persuade Martin Burney into the dirty tricks of an indecent Dago? Would ye be for murderin' your benefactor, the good man that gives ye food and work? Take that, ye punkin-colored assassin!"

The torrent of Burney's indignation carried with it bodily assault. The toe of his shoe sent the would-be cutter of ropes tumbling from his seat.

Tony arose and fled. His vendetta he again relegated to the files of things that might have been. Beyond the boat he fled and away—away; he was afraid to remain.

Burney, with expanded chest, watched his late co-plotter disappear. Then he, too, departed, setting his face in the direction of the Bronx.

In his wake was a rank and pernicious trail of noisome smoke that brought peace to his heart and drove the birds from the roadside into the deepest thickets.

THE CALIPH AND THE CAD

SURELY there is no pastime more diverting than that of mingling, incognito, with persons of wealth and station. Where else but in those circles can one see life in its primitive, crude state unhampered by the conventions that bind the dwellers in a lower sphere?

There was a certain Caliph of Bagdad who was accustomed to go down among the poor and lowly for the solace obtained from the relation of their tales and histories. Is it not strange that the humble and poverty-stricken have not availed themselves of the pleasure they might glean by donning diamonds and silks and playing Caliph among the haunts of the upper world?

There was one who saw the possibilities of thus turning the tables on Haroun al Raschid. His name was Corny Brannigan, and he was a truck driver for a Canal Street importing firm. And if you read further you will learn how he turned upper Broadway into Bagdad and learned something about himself that he did not know before.

Many people would have called Corny a snob—preferably by means of a telephone. His chief interest in life, his chosen amusement, and his sole diversion after working hours, was to place himself in juxtaposition—since he could not hope to mingle—with people of fashion and means.

Every evening after Corny had put up his team and dined at a lunch-counter that made immediateness a specialty, he would clothe himself in evening raiment as correct as any you will see in the palm rooms. Then he would betake himself to that ravishing, radiant roadway devoted to Thespis, Thais, and Bacchus.

For a time he would stroll about the lobbies of the best hotels, his soul steeped in blissful content. Beautiful women, cooing like doves, but feathered like birds of Paradise, flicked him with their robes as they passed. Courtly gentlemen attended them, gallant and assiduous. And Corny's heart within him swelled like Sir Lancelot's, for the mirror spoke to him as he passed and said: "Corny, lad, there's not a guy among 'em that looks a bit the sweller than yerself. And you drivin' of a truck and them swearin' off their taxes and playin' the red in art galleries with the best in the land!"

And the mirrors spake the truth. Mr. Corny Brannigan had acquired the outward polish, if nothing more. Long and keen observation of polite society had gained for him its manner, its genteel air, and—most difficult of acquirement —its repose and ease.

Now and then in the hotels Corny had managed conversation and temporary acquaintance with substantial, if not distinguished, guests. With many of these he had exchanged cards, and the ones he received he carefully treasured for his own use later. Leaving the hotel lobbies, Corny would stroll leisurely about, lingering at the theatre entrance, dropping into the fashionable restaurants as if seeking some friend. He rarely patronized any of these places; he was no bee come to suck honey, but a butterfly flashing his wings among the flowers whose calyces held no sweets for him. His wages were not large enough to furnish him with more than the outside garb of the gentleman. To have been one of the beings he so cunningly imitated, Corny Brannigan would have given his right hand.

One night Corny had an adventure. After absorbing the delights of an hour's lounging in the principal hotels along Broadway, he passed up into the stronghold of Thespis. Cab drivers hailed him as a likely fare, to his prideful content. Languishing eyes were turned upon him as a hopeful source of lobsters and the delectable, ascendant globules of effervescence. These overtures and unconscious compliments Corny swallowed as manna, and hoped Bill, the off horse, would be less lame in the left forefoot in the morning.

Beneath a cluster of milky globes of electric light Corny paused to admire the sheen of his low-cut patent leather shoes. The building occupying the angle was a pretentious café. Out of this came a couple, a lady in a white, cobwebby evening gown, with a lace wrap like a wreath of mist thrown over it, and a man, tall, faultless, assured—too assured. They moved to the edge of the sidewalk and halted. Corny's eye, ever alert for "pointers" in "swell" behavior, took them in with a sidelong glance.

"The carriage is not here," said the lady. "You ordered it to wait?"

"I ordered it for nine-thirty," said the man. "It should be here now."

A familiar note in the lady's voice drew a more especial attention from Corny. It was pitched in a key well known to him. The soft electric shone upon her face. Sisters of sorrow have no quarters fixed for them. In the index to the book of breaking hearts you will find that Broadway follows very soon after the Bowery. This lady's face was sad, and her voice was attuned with it. They waited, as if for the carriage. Corny waited too, for it was out of doors, and he was never tired of accumulating and profiting by knowledge of gentlemanly conduct.

"Jack," said the lady, "don't be angry. I've done everything I could to please you this evening. Why do you act so?"

"Oh, you're an angel," said the man. "Depend upon woman to throw the blame upon a man."

"I'm not blaming you. I'm only trying to make you happy."

"You go about it in a very peculiar way."

"You have been cross with me all the evening without any cause."

"Oh, there isn't any cause except—you make me tired."

Corny took out his card case and looked over his collection. He selected one that read: "Mr. R. Lionel Whyte-Melville, Bloomsbury Square, London." This card he had inveigled from a tourist at the King Edward Hotel. Corny stepped up to the man and presented it with a correctly formal air.

"May I ask why I am selected for the honor?" asked the lady's escort.

Now, Mr. Corny Brannigan had a very wise habit of saying little during his imitations of the Caliph of Bagdad. The advice of Lord Chesterfield: "Wear a black coat and hold your tongue," he believed in without having heard. But now speech was demanded and required of him.

"No gent," said Corny, "would talk to a lady like you done. Fie upon you, Willie! Even if she happens to be your wife you ought to have more respect for your clothes than to chin her back that way. Maybe it ain't my butt-in, but it goes, anyhow—you strike me as bein' a whole lot to the wrong."

The lady's escort indulged in more elegantly expressed but fetching repartee. Corny, eschewing his truck driver's vocabulary, retorted as nearly as he could in polite phrases. Then diplomatic relations were severed; there was a brief but lively set-to with other than oral weapons, from which Corny came forth easily victor.

A carriage dashed up, driven by a tardy and solicitous coachman.

"Will you kindly open the door for me?" asked the lady. Corny assisted her to enter, and took off his hat. The escort was beginning to scramble up from the sidewalk.

"I beg your pardon, ma'am," said Corny, "if he's your man."

"He's no man of mine," said the lady. "Perhaps he—but there's no chance of his being now. Drive home, Michael. If you care to take this—with my thanks."

Three red roses were thrust out through the carriage window into Corny's hand. He took them, and the hand for an instant; and then the carriage sped away.

Corny gathered his foe's hat and began to brush the dust from his clothes.

"Come along," said Corny, taking the other man by the arm.

His late opponent was yet a little dazed by the hard knocks he had received. Corny led him carefully into a saloon three doors away.

"The drinks for us," said Corny, "me and my friend."

"You're a queer feller," said the lady's late escort—"lick a man and then want to set 'em up."

"You're my best friend," said Corny, exultantly. "You don't understand? Well, listen. You just put me wise to somethin'. I been playin' gent a long time, thinkin' it was just the glad rags I had and nothin' else. Say—you're a swell, ain't you? Well, you trot in that class, I guess. I don't; but I found out one thing— I'm a gentleman, by —— and I know, it now. What'll you have to drink?"

THE DIAMOND OF KALI

THE original news item concerning the diamond of the goddess Kali was handed in to the city editor. He smiled and held it for a moment above the waste-basket. Then he laid it back on his desk and said: "Try the Sunday people; they might work something out of it."

The Sunday editor glanced the item over and said: "H'm!" Afterward he sent for a reporter and expanded his comment.

"You might see General Ludlow," he said, "and make a story out of this if you can. Diamond stories are a drug; but this one is big enough to be found by a scrubwoman wrapped up in a piece of newspaper and tucked under the corner of the hall linoleum. Find out first if the General has a daughter who intends to go on the stage. If not, you can go ahead with the story. Run cuts of the Kohinoor and J. P. Morgan's collection, and work in pictures of the Kimberley mines and Barney Barnato. Fill in with a tabulated comparison of the values of diamonds, radium, and veal cutlets since the meat strike; and let it run to a half page."

On the following day the reporter turned in his story. The Sunday editor let his eye sprint along its lines. "H'm!" he said again. This time the copy went into the waste-basket with scarcely a flutter.

The reporter stiffened a little around the lips; but he was whistling softly and contentedly between his teeth when I went over to talk with him about an hour later.

"I don't blame the 'old man,'" said he, magnanimously, "for cutting it out. It did sound like funny business; but it happened exactly as I wrote it. Say, why don't you fish that story out of the w.-b., and use it? Seems to me it's as good as the tommyrot you write."

I accepted the tip, and if you read further you will learn the facts about the diamond of the goddess Kali as vouched for by one of the most reliable reporters on the staff.

Gen. Marcellus B. Ludlow lives in one of those decaying but venerated old red-brick mansions in the West Twenties. The General is a member of an old New York family that does not advertise. He is a globe-trotter by birth, a gentleman by predilection, a millionaire by the mercy of Heaven, and a connoisseur of precious stones by occupation.

The reporter was admitted promptly when he made himself known at the General's residence at about eight thirty on the evening that he received the assignment. In the magnificent library he was greeted by the distinguished traveller and connoisseur, a tall, erect gentleman in the early fifties, with a nearly white mustache, and a bearing so soldierly that one perceived in him scarcely a trace of the national Guardsman. His weather-beaten countenance lit up with a charming smile of interest when the reporter made known his errand.

"Ah, you have heard of my latest find. I shall be glad to show you what I conceive to be one of the six most valuable blue diamonds in existence."

The General opened a small safe in a corner of the library and brought forth a plush-covered box. Opening this, he exposed to the reporter's bewildered gaze a huge and brilliant diamond—nearly as large as a hailstone.

"This stone," said the General, "is something more than a mere jewel. It once formed the central eye of the three-eyed goddess Kali, who is worshipped by one of the fiercest and most fanatical tribes of India. If you will arrange yourself comfortably I will give you a brief history of it for your paper."

General Ludlow brought a decanter of whisky and glasses from a cabinet, and set a comfortable armchair for the lucky scribe.

"The Phansigars, or Thugs, of India," began the General, "are the most dangerous and dreaded of the tribes of North India. They are extremists in religion, and worship the horrid goddess Kali in the form of images. Their rites are interesting and bloody. The robbing and murdering of travellers are taught as a worthy and obligatory deed by their strange religious code. Their worship of the three-eyed goddess Kali is conducted so secretly that no traveller has ever heretofore had the honor of witnessing the ceremonies. That distinction was reserved for myself.

"While at Sakaranpur, between Delhi and Khelat, I used to explore the jungle in every direction in hope of learning something new about these mysterious Phansigars.

"One evening at twilight I was making my way through a teakwood forest, when I came upon a deep circular depression in an open space, in the centre of which was a rude stone temple. I was sure that this was one of the temples of the Thugs, so I concealed myself in the undergrowth to watch.

"When the moon rose the depression in the clearing was suddenly filled with hundreds of shadowy, swiftly gliding forms. Then a door opened in the temple, exposing a brightly illuminated image of the goddess Kali, before which a white-robed priest began a barbarous incantation, while the tribe of worshippers prostrated themselves upon the earth.

"But what interested me most was the central eye of the huge wooden idol. I could see by its flashing brilliancy that it was an immense diamond of the purest water.

"After the rites were concluded the Thugs slipped away into the forest as silently as they had come. The priest stood for a few minutes in the door of the temple enjoying the cool of the night before closing his rather warm quarters. Suddenly a dark, lithe shadow slipped down into the hollow, leaped upon the priest, and struck him down with a glittering knife. Then the murderer sprang a the image of the goddess like a cat and pried out the glowing central eye of Kali with his weapon. Straight toward me he ran with his royal prize. When he was within two paces I rose to my feet and struck him with all my force between the eyes. He rolled over senseless and the magnificent jewel fell from his hand. That is the splendid blue diamond you have just seen—a stone worthy of a monarch's crown."

"That's a corking story," said the reporter. "That decanter is exactly like the one that John W. Gates always sets out during an interview."

"Pardon me," said General Ludlow, "for forgetting hospitality in the excitement of my narrative. Help yourself."

"Here's looking at you," said the reporter.

"What I am afraid of now," said the General, lowering his voice, "is that I may be robbed of the diamond. The jewel that formed an eye of their goddess is their most sacred symbol. Somehow the tribe suspected me of having it; and members of the band have followed me half around the earth. They are the most cunning and cruel fanatics in the world, and their religious vows would compel them to assassinate the unbeliever who has desecrated their sacred treasure.

"Once in Lucknow three of their agents, disguised as servants in a hotel, endeavored to strangle me with a twisted cloth. Again, in London, two Thugs, made up as street musicians, climbed into my window at night and attacked me. They have even tracked me to this country. My life is never safe. A month ago, while I was at a hotel in the Berkshires, three of them sprang upon me from the roadside weeds. I saved myself then by my knowledge of their customs."

"How was that, General?" asked the reporter.

"There was a cow grazing near by," said General Ludlow, "a gentle Jersey cow. I ran to her side and stood. The three Thugs ceased their attack, knelt and struck the ground thrice with their foreheads. Then, after many respectful salaams, they departed."

"Afraid the cow would hook?" asked the reporter.

"No; the cow is a sacred animal to the Phansigars. Next to their goddess they worship the cow. They have never been known to commit any deed of violence in the presence of the animal they reverence."

"It's a mighty interesting story," said the reporter. "If you don't mind I'll take another drink, and then a few notes."

"I will join you," said General Ludlow, with a courteous wave of his hand.

"If I were you," advised the reporter, "I'd take that sparkler to Texas. Get on a cow ranch there, and the Pharisees——"

"Phansigars," corrected the General.

"Oh, yes; the fancy guys would run up against a long horn every time they made a break."

General Ludlow closed the diamond case and thrust it into his bosom.

"The spies of the tribe have found me out in New York," he said, straightening his tall figure. "I'm familiar with the East Indian cast of countenance, and I know that my every movement is watched. They will undoubtedly attempt to rob and murder me here."

"Here?" exclaimed the reporter, seizing the decanter and pouring out a liberal amount of its contents.

"At any moment," said the General. "But as a soldier and a connoisseur I shall sell my life and my diamond as dearly as I can."

At this point of the reporter's story there is a certain vagueness, but it can be gathered that there was a loud crashing at the rear of the house they were in. General Ludlow buttoned his coat closely and sprang for the door. But the reporter clutched him firmly with one hand, while he held the decanter with the other.

"Tell me before we fly," he urged, in a voice thick with some inward turmoil, "do any of your daughters contemplate going on the stage?"

"I have no daughters—fly for your life—the Phansigars are upon us!" cried the General.

The two men dashed out of the front door of the house.

The hour was late. As their feet struck the sidewalk strange men of dark and forbidding appearance seemed to rise up out of the earth and encompass them. One with Asiatic features pressed close to the General and droned in a terrible voice:

"Buy cast clo'!"

Another, dark-whiskered and sinister, sped lithely to his side and began in a whining voice:

"Say, mister, have yer got a dime fer a poor feller what——"

They hurried on, but only into the arms of a black-eyed, dusky-browed being, who held out his hat under their noses, while a confederate of Oriental hue turned the handle of a street organ near by.

Twenty steps farther on General Ludlow and the reporter found themselves in the midst of half a dozen villainous-looking men with high-turned coat collars and faces bristling with unshaven beards.

"Run for it!" hissed the General. "They have discovered the possessor of the diamond of the goddess Kali."

The two men took to their heels. The avengers of the goddess pursued.

"Oh, Lordy!" groaned the reporter, "there isn't a cow this side of Brooklyn. We're lost!"

When near the corner they both fell over an iron object that rose from the sidewalk close to the gutter. Clinging to it desperately, they awaited their fate.

"If I only had a cow!" moaned the reporter—"or another nip from that decanter, General!"

As soon as the pursuers observed where their victims had found refuge they suddenly fell back and retreated to a considerable distance.

"They are waiting for reinforcements in order to attack us," said General Ludlow.

But the reporter emitted a ringing laugh, and hurled his hat triumphantly into the air.

"Guess again," he shouted, and leaned heavily upon the iron object. "Your old fancy guys or thugs, whatever you call 'em, are up to date. Dear General, this is a pump we've stranded upon—same as a cow in New York (hic!) see?

Thas'h why the 'nfuriated smoked guys don't attack us—see? Sacred an'mal, the pump in N' York, my dear General!"

But further down in the shadows of Twenty-eighth Street the marauders were holding a parley.

"Come on, Reddy," said one. "Let's go frisk the old 'un. He's been showin' a sparkler as big as a hen egg all around Eighth Avenue for two weeks past."

"Not on your silhouette," decided Reddy. "You see 'em rallyin' round The Pump? They're friends of Bill's. Bill won't stand for nothin' of this kind in his district since he got that bid to Esopus."

This exhausts the facts concerning the Kali diamond. But it is deemed not inconsequent to close with the following brief (paid) item that appeared two days later in a morning paper.

"It is rumored that a niece of Gen. Marcellus B. Ludlow, of New York City, will appear on the stage next season.

"Her diamonds are said to be extremely valuable and of much historic interest."

THE DAY WE CELEBRATE

"IN the tropics" ("Hop-along" Bibb, the bird fancier, was saying to me) "the seasons, months, fortnights, week-ends, holidays, dog-days, Sundays, and yesterdays get so jumbled together in the shuffle that you never know when a year has gone by until you're in the middle of the next one."

"Hop-along" Bibb kept his bird store on lower Fourth Avenue. He was an ex-seaman and beachcomber who made regular voyages to southern ports and imported personally conducted invoices of talking parrots and dialectic paroquets. He had a stiff knee, neck, and nerve. I had gone to him to buy a parrot to present, at Christmas, to my Aunt Joanna.

"This one," said I, disregarding his homily on the subdivisions of time— "this one that seems all red, white and blue—to what genus of beasts does he belong? He appeals at once to my patriotism and to my love of discord in color schemes."

"That's a cockatoo from Ecuador," said Bibb. "All he has been taught to say is 'Merry Christmas.' A seasonable bird. He's only seven dollars; and I'll bet many a human has stuck you for money by making the same speech to you."

And then Bibb laughed suddenly and loudly.

"That bird," he exclaimed, "reminds me. He's got his dates mixed. He ought to be saying '*E pluribus unum*,' to match his feathers, instead of trying to work the Santa Claus graft. It reminds me of the time me and Liverpool Sam got our ideas of things tangled up on the coast of Costa Rica on account of the weather and other phenomena to be met with in the tropics.

"We were, as it were, stranded on that section of the Spanish Main with no money to speak of and no friends that should be talked about either. We had stoked and second-cooked ourselves down there on a fruit steamer from New Orleans to try our luck, which was discharged, after we got there, for lack of evidence. There was no work suitable to our instincts; so me and Liverpool began to subsist cn the red rum of the country and such fruit as we could reap where we had not sown. It was an alluvial town, called Soledad, where there was no harbor or future or recourse. Between steamers the town slept and drank rum.

It only woke up when there were bananas to ship. It was like a man sleeping through dinner until the dessert.

"When me and Liverpool got so low down that the American consul wouldn't speak to us we knew we'd struck bed rock.

"We boarded with a snuff-brown lady named Chica, who kept a rum-shop and a ladies' and gents' restaurant in a street called the *calle de los* Forty-seven Inconsolable Saints. When our credit played out there, Liverpool, whose stomach overshadowed his sensations of *noblesse oblige*, married Chica. This kept us in rice and fried plantain for a month; and then Chica pounded Liverpool one morning sadly and earnestly for fifteen minutes with a casserole handed down from the stone age, and we knew that we had out-welcomed our liver. That night we signed an engagement with Don Jaime McSpinosa, a hybrid banana fancier of the place, to work on his fruit preserves nine miles out of town. We had to do it or be reduced to sea water and broken doses of feed and slumber.

"Now, speaking of Liverpool Sam, I don't malign or inexculpate him to you any more than I would to his face. But in my opinion, when an Englishman gets as low as he can he's got to dodge so that the dregs of other nations don't drop ballast on him out of their balloons. And if he's a Liverpool Englishman, why, fire-damp is what he's got to look out for. Being a natural American, that's my personal view. But Liverpool and me had much in common. We were without decorous clothes or ways and means of existence; and, as the saying goes, misery certainly does enjoy the society of accomplices.

"Our job on old McSpinosa's plantation was chopping down banana stalks and loading the bunches of fruit on the backs of horses. Then a native dressed up in an alligator-hide belt, a machete, and a pair of AA sheeting pajamas, drives 'em over to the coast and piles 'em up on the beach.

"You ever been in a banana grove? It's as solemn as a rathskeller at seven A. M. It's like being lost behind the scenes at one of these mushroom musical shows. You can't see the sky for the foliage above you; and the ground is knee deep in rotten leaves; and it's so still that you can hear the stalks growing again after you chop 'em down.

"At night me and Liverpool herded in a lot of grass huts on the edge of a lagoon, with the red, yellow, and black employés of Don Jaime. There we lay fighting mosquitoes and listening to the monkeys squalling and the alligators grunting and splashing in the lagoon until daylight with only snatches of sleep between times.

"We soon lost all idea of what time of the year it was. It's just about eighty degrees there in December and June and on Fridays and at midnight and ele·tion day and any other old time. Sometimes it rains more than at others, and that's all the difference you notice. A man is liable to live along there without noticing any fugiting of tempus until some day the undertaker calls in for him just when he's beginning to think about cutting out the gang and saving up a little to invest in real estate.

"I don't know how long we worked for Don Jaime; but it was through two or three rainy spells, eight or ten hair cuts, and the life of three pairs of sail-cloth trousers. All the money we earned went for rum and tobacco; but we ate, and that was something.

"All of a sudden one day me and Liverpool find the trade of committing surgical operations on banana stalks turning to aloes and quinine in our mouths. It's a seizure that often comes upon white men in Latin and geographical countries. We wanted to be addressed again in language and see the smoke of a steamer and read the real estate transfers and gents' outfitting ads in an old newspaper. Even Soledad seemed like a center of civilization to us, so that evening we put our thumbs on our nose at Don Jaime's fruit stand and shook his grass burrs off our feet.

"It was only twelve miles to Soledad, but it took me and Liverpool two days to get there. It was banana grove nearly all the way; and we got twisted time and again. It was like paging the palm room of a New York hotel for a man named Smith.

"When we saw the houses of Soledad between the trees all my disinclination toward this Liverpool Sam rose up in me. I stood him while we were two white men against the banana brindles; but now, when there were prospects of my exchanging even cuss words with an American citizen, I put him back in his proper place. And he was a sight, too, with his rum-painted nose and his red whiskers and elephant feet with leather sandals strapped to them. I suppose I looked about the same.

" 'It looks to me,' says I, 'like Great Britain ought to be made to keep such gin-swilling, scurvy, unbecoming mud larks as you at home instead of sending 'em over here to degrade and taint foreign lands. We kicked you out of America once and we ought to put on rubber boots and do it again.'

" 'Oh, you go to 'ell,' says Liverpool, which was about all the repartee he ever had.

"Well, Soledad, looked fine to me after Don Jaime's plantation. Liverpool and me walked into it side by side, from force of habit, past the calabosa and the Hotel Grande, down across the plaza toward Chica's hut, where we hoped that Liverpool, being a husband of hers, might work his luck for a meal.

"As we passed the two-story little frame house occupied by the American Club, we noticed that the balcony had been decorated all around with wreaths of evergreens and flowers, and the flag was flying from the pole on the roof. Stanzey, the consul, and Arkright, a gold-mine owner, were smoking on the balcony. Me and Liverpool waved our dirty hands toward 'em and smiled real society smiles; but they turned their backs to us and went on talking. And we had played whist once with the two of 'em up to the time when Liverpool held all thirteen trumps for four hands in succession. It was some holiday, we knew; but we didn't know the day nor the year.

"A little further along we saw a reverend man named Pendergast, who had come to Soledad to build a church, standing under a cocoanut palm with his little black alpaca coat and green umbrella.

" 'Boys, boys!' says he, through his blue spectacles, 'is it as bad as this? Are you so far reduced?'

" 'We're reduced,' says I, 'to very vulgar fractions.'

" 'It is indeed sad,' says Pendergast, 'to see my countrymen in such circumstances.'

" 'Cut 'arf of that out, old party,' says Liverpool. 'Cawn't you tell a member of the British upper classes when you see one?'

" 'Shut up,' I told Liverpool. 'You're on foreign soil now, or that portion of it that's not on you.'

" 'And on this day, too!' goes on Pendergast, grievous—'on this most glorious day of the year when we should all be celebrating the dawn of Christian civilization and the downfall of the wicked.'

" 'I did notice bunting and bouquets decorating the town, reverend,' says I, 'but I didn't know what taint it was for. We've been so long out of touch with calendars that we didn't know whether it was summer time or Saturday afternoon.

" 'Here is two dollars,' says Pendergast, digging up two Chili silver wheels and handing 'em to me. 'Go, men, and observe the rest of the day in a befitting manner.'

"Me and Liverpool thanked him kindly, and walked away.

" 'Shall we eat?' I asks.

" 'Oh 'ell!' says Liverpool. 'What's money for?'

"'Very well, then,' I says, 'since you insist upon it, we'll drink.'

"So we pull up in a rum shop and get a quart of it and go down on the beach under a cocoanut tree and celebrate.

"Not having eaten anything but oranges in two days, the rum has immediate effect; and once more I conjure up great repugnance toward the British nation.

"'Stand up here,' I says to Liverpool, 'you scum of a despot limited monarchy, and have another dose of Bunker Hill. That good man, Mr. Pendergast,' says I, 'said we were to observe the day in a befitting manner, and I'm not going to see his money misapplied.'

"'Oh, you go to 'ell!'" says Liverpool, and I started in with a fine left-hander on his right eye.

"Liverpool had been a fighter once, but dissipation and bad company had taken the nerve out of him. In ten minutes I had him lying on the sand waving the white flag.

"'Get up,' says I, kicking him in the ribs, 'and come along with me.'

"Liverpool got up and followed behind me because it was his habit, wiping the red off his face and nose. I led him to Reverend Pendergast's shack and called him out.

"'Look at this, sir,' says I—'look at this thing that was once a proud Britisher. You gave us two dollars and told us to celebrate the day. The star-spangled banner still waves. Hurrah for the stars and eagles!'

"'Dear me,' says Pendergast, holding up his hands. 'Fighting on this day of all days! On Christmas day, when peace on——'

"'Christmas, hell!' says I. "'I thought it was the Fourth of July.'"

"Merry Christmas!" said the red, white, and blue cockatoo.

"Take him for six dollars," said Hop-along Bibb. "He's got his dates and colors mixed."

ROLLING STONES

ROLLING STONES

THE DREAM

[This was the last work of O. Henry. The *Cosmopolitan Magazine* had ordered it from him and, after his death, the unfinished manuscript was found in his room, on his dusty desk. The story as it here appears was published in the *Cosmopolitan* for September, 1910.]

MURRAY dreamed a dream.

Both psychology and science grope when they would explain to us the strange adventures of our immaterial selves when wandering in the realm of "Death's twin brother, Sleep." This story will not attempt to be illuminative; it is no more than record of Murray's dream. One of the most puzzling phases of that strange waking sleep is that dreams which seem to cover months or even years may take place within a few seconds or minutes.

Murray was waiting in his cell in the ward of the condemned. An electric arc light in the ceiling of the corridor shone brightly upon his table. On a sheet of white paper an ant crawled wildly here and there as Murray blocked its way with an envelope. The electrocution was set for eight o'clock in the evening. Murray smiled at the antics of the wisest of insects.

There were seven other condemned men in the chamber. Since he had been there Murray had seen three taken out to their fate; one gone mad and fighting like a wolf caught in a trap; one, no less mad, offering up a sanctimonious lip-service to Heaven; the third, a weakling, collapsed and strapped to a board. He wondered with what credit to himself his own heart, foot, and face would meet his punishment; for this was his evening. He thought it must be nearly eight o'clock.

Opposite his own in the two rows of cells was the cage of Bonifacio, the Sicilian slayer of his betrothed and of two officers who came to arrest him. With him Murray had played checkers many a long hour, each calling his move to his unseen opponent across the corridor.

Bonifacio's great booming voice with its indestructible singing quality called out:

"Eh, Meestro Murray; how you feel—all-a right—yes?"

"All right, Bonifacio," said Murray steadily, as he allowed the ant to crawl upon the envelope and then dumped it gently on the stone floor.

"Dat's good-a, Meestro Murray. Men like us, we must-a die like-a men. My time come nex'-a week. All-a right. Remember, Meestro Murray, I beat-a you dat las' game of de check. Maybe we play again some-a time. I don'-a know. Maybe we have to call-a de move damn-a loud to play de check where dey goin' send us."

Bonifacio's hardened philosophy, followed closely by his deafening, musical peal of laughter, warmed rather than chilled Murray's numbed heart. Yet, Bonifacio had until next week to live.

The cell-dwellers heard the familiar, loud click of the steel bolts as the door at the end of the corridor was opened. Three men came to Murray's cell and unlocked it. Two were prison guards; the other was "Len"—no; that was in the old days; now the Reverend Leonard Winston, a friend and neighbor from their barefoot days.

"I got them to let me take the prison chaplain's place," he said, as he gave Murray's hand one short, strong grip. In his left hand he held a small Bible, with his forefinger marking a page.

Murray smiled slightly and arranged two or three books and some penholders orderly on his small table. He would have spoken, but no appropriate words seemed to present themselves to his mind.

The prisoners had christened this cellhouse, eighty feet long, twenty-eight feet wide, Limbo Lane. The regular guard of Limbo Lane, an immense, rough, kindly man, drew a pint bottle of whiskey from his pocket and offered it to Murray, saying:

"It's the regular thing, you know. All has it who feel like they need a bracer. No danger of it becoming a habit with 'em, you see."

Murray drank deep into the bottle.

"That's the boy!" said the guard. "Just a little nerve tonic, and everything goes smooth as silk."

They stepped into the corridor, and each one of the doomed seven knew. Limbo Lane is a world on the outside of the world; but it had learned, when deprived of one or more of the five senses, to make another sense supply the deficiency. Each one knew that it was nearly eight, and that Murray was to go to the chair at eight. There is also in the many Limbo Lanes an aristocracy of crime. The man who kills in the open, who beats his enemy or pursuer down, flushed by the primitive emotions and the ardor of combat, holds in contempt the human rat, the spider, and the snake.

So, of the seven condemned only three called their farewells to Murray as he marched down the corridor between the two guards—Bonifacio, Marvin, who had killed a guard while trying to escape from the prison, and Bassett, the train-robber, who was driven to it because the express-messenger wouldn't raise his hands when ordered to do so. The remaining four smoldered, silent, in their cells, no doubt feeling their social ostracism in Limbo Lane society more keenly than they did the memory of their less picturesque offences against the law.

Murray wondered at his own calmness and nearly indifference. In the execution room were about twenty men, a congregation made up of prison officers, newspaper reporters, and lookers-on who had succeeded.

Here, in the very middle of a sentence, the hand of Death interrupted the telling of O. Henry's last story. He had planned to make this story different from his others, the beginning of a new series in a style he had not previously attempted. "I want to show the public," he said, "that I can write something new—new for me, I mean—a story without slang, a straightforward dramatic plot treated in a way that will come nearer my idea of real story-writing." Before starting to write the present story, he outlined briefly how he intended to develop it: Murray, the criminal accused and convicted of the brutal murder of his sweetheart—a murder prompted by jealous rage—at first faces the death penalty, calm, and, to all outward appearances, indifferent to his fate. As he nears the electric chair he is overcome by a revulsion of feeling. He is left dazed, stupefied, stunned. The entire scene in the death-chamber—the witnesses, the spectators, the preparations for execution—become unreal to him. The thought flashes through his brain that a terrible mistake is being made. Why is he being strapped to the chair? What has he done? What crime has he committed? In the few moments while the straps are being adjusted a vision comes to him. He dreams a dream. He sees a little country cottage, bright, sun-lit, nestling in a bower of flowers. A woman is there, and a little child. He speaks with them and finds that they are his wife, his child—and the cottage their home. So, after all, it is a mistake. Some one has frightfully, irretrievably blundered. The accusation, the trial, the conviction, the sentence to death in the electric chair—all a dream. He takes his wife in his arms and kisses the child. Yes, here is happiness. It was a dream. Then—at a sign from the prison warden the fatal current is turned on.

Murray had dreamed the wrong dream.

A RULER OF MEN

[Written at the prime of his popularity and power, this characteristic and amusing story was published in *Everybody's Magazine*, August, 1906.]

I WALKED the streets of the City of Insolence, thirsting for the sight of a stranger face. For the City is a desert of familiar types as thick and alike as the grains in a sand-storm; and you grow to hate them as you do a friend who is always by you, or one of your kin.

And my desire was granted, for I saw near a corner of Broadway and Twenty-ninth Street, a little flaxen-haired man with a face like a scaly-bark hickory-nut, selling to a fast-gathering crowd a tool that omnigeneously proclaimed itself a can-opener, a screw-driver, a button-hook, a nail-file, a shoe-horn, a watch-guard, a potato-peeler, and an ornament to any gentleman's key-ring.

And then a stall-fed cop shoved himself through the congregation of customers. The vender, plainly used to having his seasons of trade thus abruptly curtailed, closed his satchel and slipped like a weasel through the opposite segment of the circle. The crowd scurried aimlessly away like ants from a disturbed crumb. The cop, suddenly becoming oblivious of the earth and its inhabitants, stood still, swelling his bulk and putting his club through an intricate drill of twirls. I hurried after Kansas Bill Bowers, and caught him by an arm.

Without his looking at me or slowing his pace, I found a five-dollar bill crumpled neatly into my hand.

"I wouldn't have thought, Kansas Bill," I said, "that you'd hold an old friend that cheap."

Then he turned his head, and the hickory-nut cracked into a wide smile.

"Give back the money," said he, "or I'll have the cop after you for false pretenses. I thought you was the cop."

"I want to talk to you, Bill," I said. "When did you leave Oklahoma? Where is Reddy McGill now? Why are you selling those impossible contraptions on the street? How did your Big Horn gold-mine pan out? How did you get so badly sunburned? What will you drink?"

"A year ago," answered Kansas Bill, systematically. "Putting up windmills in Arizona. For pin money to buy etceteras with. Salted. Been down in the tropics. Beer."

We foregathered in a propitious place and became Elijahs, while a waiter of dark plumage played the raven to perfection. Reminiscence needs must be had before I could steer Bill into his epic mood.

"Yes," said he, "I mind the time Timoteo's rope broke on that cow's horns while the calf was chasing you. You and that cow! I'd never forget it."

"The tropics," said I, "are a broad territory. What part of Cancer or Capricorn have you been honoring with a visit?"

"Down along China or Peru—or maybe the Argentine Confederacy," said Kansas Bill. "Anyway 'twas among a great race of people, off-colored but progressive. I was there three months."

"No doubt you are glad to be back among the truly great race," I surmised. "Especially among New Yorkers, the most progressive and independent citizens of any country in the world," I continued, with the fatuity of the provincial who has eaten the Broadway lotus.

"Do you want to start an argument?" asked Bill.

"Can there be one?" I answered.

"Has an Irishman humor, do you think?" asked he.

"I have an hour or two to spare," said I, looking at the café clock.

"Not that the Americans aren't a great commercial nation," conceded Bill. "But the fault laid with the people who wrote lies for fiction."

"What was this Irishman's name?" I asked.

"Was that last beer cold enough?" said he.

"I see there is talk of further outbreaks among the Russian peasants," I remarked.

"His name was Barney O'Connor," said Bill.

Thus, because of our ancient prescience of each other's trail of thought, we travelled ambiguously to the point where Kansas Bill's story began:

"I met O'Connor in a boarding-house on the West Side. He invited me to his hall-room to have a drink, and we became like a dog and a cat that had been raised together. There he sat, a tall, fine, handsome man, with his feet against one wall and his back against the other, looking over a map. On the bed and sticking three feet out of it was a beautiful gold sword with tassels on it and rhinestones in the handle.

"'What's this?' says I (for by that time we were well acquainted). 'The annual parade in vilification of the ex-snakes of Ireland? And what's the line of march? Up Broadway to Forty-second; thence east to McCarty's café; thence——'

"'Sit down on the wash-stand,' says O'Connor, 'and listen. And cast no perversions on the sword. 'Twas my father's in old Munster. And this map, Bowers, is no diagram of a holiday procession. If ye look again ye'll see that it's the continent known as South America, comprising fourteen green, blue, red, and yellow countries, all crying out from time to time to be liberated from the yoke of the oppressor.'

"'I know,' says I to O'Connor. 'The idea is a literary one. The ten-cent magazine stole it from "Ridpath's History of the World from the Sand-stone Period to the Equator." You'll find it in every one of 'em. It's a continued story of a soldier of fortune, generally named O'Keefe, who gets to be dictator while the Spanish-American populace cries "Cospetto!" and other Italian maledictions. I misdoubt if it's ever been done. You're not thinking of trying that, are you, Barney?' I asks.

"'Bowers,' says he, 'you're a man of education and courage.'

"'How can I deny it?' says I. 'Education runs in my family; and I have acquired courage by a hard struggle with life.'

"'The O'Connors,' says he, 'are a warlike race. There is me father's sword; and here is the map. A life of inaction is not for me. The O'Connors were born to rule. 'Tis a ruler of men I must be.'

"'Barney,' I says to him, 'why don't you get on the force and settle down to a quiet life of carnage and corruption instead of roaming off to foreign parts? In what better way can you indulge your desire to subdue and maltreat the oppressed?'

"'Look again at the map,' says he, 'at the country I have the point on me knife on. 'Tis that one I have selected to aid and overthrow with me father's sword.'

"'I see,' says I. 'It's the green one; and that does credit to your patriotism, and it's the smallest one; and that does credit to your judgment.'

"'Do ye accuse me of cowardice?' says Barney, turning pink.

"'No man,' says I, 'who attacks and confiscates a country single-handed could be called a coward. The worst you can be charged with is plagiarism or imitation. If Anthony Hope and Roosevelt let you get away with it, nobody else will have any right to kick.'

"'I'm not joking,' says O'Connor. 'And I've got $1,500 cash to work the scheme with. I've taken a liking to you. Do you want it, or not?'

"'I'm not working,' I told him; 'but how is it to be? Do I eat during the fomentation of the insurrection, or am I only to be Secretary of War after the country is conquered? Is it to be a pay envelope or only a portfolio?'

"'I'll pay all expenses,' says O'Connor. 'I want a man I can trust. If we succeed you may pick out any appointment you want in the gift of the government.'

"'All right, then,' says I. 'You can get me a bunch of draying contracts and then a quick-action consignment to a seat on the Supreme Court bench so I won't be in line for the presidency. The kind of cannon they chasten their presidents with in that country hurt too much. You can consider me on the pay-roll.'

"Two weeks afterward O'Connor and me took a steamer for the small, green, doomed country. We were three weeks on the trip. O'Connor said he had his plans all figured out in advance; but being the commanding general, it consorted with his dignity to keep the details concealed from his army and cabinet, commonly known as William T. Bowers. Three dollars a day was the price for which I joined the cause of liberating an undiscovered country from the ills that threatened or sustained it. Every Saturday night on the steamer I stood in line at parade rest, and O'Connor handed over the twenty-one dollars.

"The town we landed at was named Guayaquerita, so they told me. 'Not for me,' says I. 'It'll be little old Hilldale or Tompkinsville or Cherry Tree Corners when I speak of it. It's a clear case where Spelling Reform ought to butt in and disenvowel it.'

"But the town looked fine from the bay when we sailed in. It was white, with green ruching, and lace ruffles on the skirt when the surf slashed up on the sand. It looked as tropical and dolce far ultra as the pictures of Lake Ronkonkoma in the brochure of the passenger department of the Long Island Railroad.

"We went through the quarantine and custom house indignities; and then O'Connor leads me to a 'dobe house on a street called 'The Avenue of the Dolorous Butterflies of the Individual and Collective Saints.' Ten feet wide it was, and knee-deep in alfalfa and cigar stumps.

"'Hooligan Alley,' says I, rechristening it.

"''Twill be our headquarters,' says O'Connor. 'My agent here, Don Fernando Pacheco, secured it for us.'

"So in that house O'Connor and me established the revolutionary centre. In the front room we had ostensible things such as fruit, a guitar, and a table with a conch shell on it. In the back room O'Connor had his desk and a large looking-glass and his sword hid in a roll of straw matting. We slept on hammocks that we hung to hooks in the wall; and took our meals at the Hotel Inglés, a beanery run on the American plan by a German proprietor with Chinese cooking served à la Kansas City lunch counter.

"It seems that O'Connor really did have some sort of system planned out beforehand. He wrote plenty of letters; and every day or two some native gent would stroll round to headquarters and be shut up in the back room for half an hour with O'Connor and the interpreter. I noticed that when they went in they were always smoking eight-inch cigars and at peace with the world; but when they came out they would be folding up a ten- or twenty-dollar bill and cursing the government horribly.

"One evening after we had been in Guaya—in this town of Smellville-by-the-Sea—about a month, and me and O'Connor were sitting outside the door helping along old tempus fugit with rum and ice and limes, I says to him:

" 'If you'll excuse a patriot that don't exactly know what he's patronizing, for the question—what is your scheme for subjugating this country? Do you intend to plunge it into bloodshed, or do you mean to buy its votes peacefully and honorably at the polls?'

" 'Bowers,' says he, 'ye're a fine little man and I intend to make great use of ye after the conflict. But ye do not understand statecraft. Already by now we have a network of strategy clutching with invisible fingers at the throat of the tyrant Calderas. We have agents at work in every town in the republic. The Liberal party is bound to win. On our secret lists we have the names of enough sympathizers to crush the administration forces at a single blow.'

" 'A straw vote,' says I, 'only shows which way the hot air blows.'

" 'Who has accomplished this?' goes on O'Connor. 'I have. I have directed everything. The time was ripe when we came, so my agents inform me. The people are groaning under burdens of taxes and levies. Who will be their natural leader when they rise? Could it be any one but meself? 'Twas only yesterday that Zaldas, our representative in the province of Durasnas, tells me that the people, in secret, already call me "El Library Door," which is the Spanish manner of saying "The Liberator." '

" 'Was Zaldas that maroon-colored old Aztec with a paper collar on and unbleached domestic shoes?' I asked.

" 'He was,' says O'Connor.

" 'I saw him tucking a yellow-back into his vest pocket as he came out,' says I. 'It may be,' says I, 'that they call you a library door, but they treat you more like the side door of a bank. But let us hope for the worst.'

" 'It has cost money, of course,' says O'Connor; 'but we'll have the country in our hands inside of a month.'

"In the evenings we walked about in the plaza and listened to the band playing and mingled with the populace at its distressing and obnoxious pleasures. There were thirteen vehicles belonging to the upper classes, mostly rock-aways and old-style barouches, such as the mayor rides in at the unveiling of the new poor-house at Milledgeville, Alabama. Round and round the desiccated fountain in the middle of the plaza they drove, and lifted their high silk hats to their friends. The common people walked around in barefooted bunches, puffing stogies that a Pittsburg millionaire wouldn't have chewed for a dry smoke on Ladies' Day at his club. And the grandest figure in the whole turnout was Barney O'Connor. Six foot two he stood in his Fifth Avenue clothes, with his eagle eye and his black moustache that tickled his ears. He was a born dictator and czar and hero and harrier of the human race. It looked to me that all eyes were turned upon O'Connor, and that every woman there loved him, and every man feared him. Once or twice I looked at him and thought of funnier things that had happened than his winning out in his game; and I began to feel like a Hidalgo de Officio de Grafto de South America myself. And then I would come down again to solid bottom and let my imagination gloat, as usual, upon the twenty-one American dollars due me on Saturday night.

" 'Take note,' says O'Connor to me as thus we walked, 'of the mass of the peo-

ple. Observe their oppressed and melancholy air. Can ye not see that they are
ripe for revolt? Do ye not perceive that they are disaffected?'

"'I do not,' says I. 'Nor disinfected either. I'm beginning to understand
these people. When they look unhappy they're enjoying themselves. When they
feel unhappy they go to sleep. They're not the kind of people to take an interest
in revolutions.'

"'They'll flock to our standard,' says O'Connor. 'Three thousand men in this
town alone will spring to arms when the signal is given. I am assured of that.
But everything is in secret. There is no chance for us to fail.'

"On Hooligan Alley, as I prefer to call the street our headquarters was on,
there was a row of flat 'dobe houses with red tile roofs, some straw shacks full of
Indians and dogs, and one two-story wooden house with balconies a little farther
down. That was where General Tumbalo, the comandante and commander of the
military forces, lived. Right across the street was a private residence built like
a combination bake-oven and folding-bed. One day, O'Connor and me were passing it, single file, on the flange they called a sidewalk, when out of the window
flies a big red rose. O'Connor, who is ahead, picks it up, presses it to his fifth
rib, and bows to the ground. By Carrambos! that man certainly had the Irish
drama chaunceyized. I looked around expecting to see the little boy and girl in
white sateen ready to jump on his shoulder while he jolted their spinal columns
and ribs together through a breakdown, and sang: 'Sleep, Little One, Sleep.'

"As I passed the window I glanced inside and caught a glimpse of a white
dress and a pair of big, flashing black eyes and gleaming teeth under a dark
lace mantilla.

"When we got back to our house O'Connor began to walk up and down the
floor and twist his moustaches.

"'Did ye see her eyes, Bowers?' he asks me.

"'I did,' says I, 'and I can see more than that. It's all coming out according to the story-books. I knew there was something missing. 'Twas the love
interest. What is it that comes in Chapter VII to cheer the gallant Irish adventurer? Why, Love, of course—Love that makes the hat go around. At last
we have the eyes of midnight hue and the rose flung from the barred window.
Now, what comes next? The underground passage—the intercepted letter—the
traitor in camp—the hero thrown into a dungeon—the mysterious message from
the señorita—then the outburst—the fighting on the plaza—the——'

"'Don't be a fool,' says O'Connor, interrupting. 'But that's the only woman
in the world for me, Bowers. The O'Connors are as quick to love as they are to
fight. I shall wear that rose over me heart when I lead me men into action.
For a good battle to be fought there must be some woman to give it power.'

"'Every time,' I agreed, 'if you want to have a good lively scrap. There's
only one thing bothering me. In the novels the light-haired friend of the hero
always gets killed. Think 'em all over that you've read, and you'll see that I'm
right. I think I'll step down to the Botica Española and lay in a bottle of walnut stain before war is declared.'

"'How will I find out her name?' says O'Connor, laying his chin in his hand.

"'Why don't you go across the street and ask her?' says I.

"'Will ye never regard anything in life seriously?' says O'Connor, looking
down at me like a school-master.

"'Maybe she meant the rose for me,' I said, whistling the Spanish Fandango.

"For the first time since I'd known O'Connor, he laughed. He got up and
roared and clapped his knees, and leaned against the wall till the tiles on the
roof clattered to the noise of his lungs. He went into the back room and looked
at himself in the glass and began and laughed all over from the beginning
again. Then he looked at me and repeated himself. That's why I asked you if
you thought an Irishman had any humor. He'd been doing farce comedy from

the day I saw him without knowing it; and the first time he had an idea advanced to him with any intelligence in it he acted like two twelfths of the sextet in a 'Floradora' road company.

"The next afternoon he comes in with a triumphant smile and begins to pull something like ticker tape out of his pocket.

" 'Great!' says I. 'This is something like home. How is Amalgamated Copper to-day?'

" 'I've got her name,' says O'Connor, and he reads off something like this: 'Doña Isabel Antonia Inez Lolita Carreras y Buencaminos y Monteleon. She lives with her mother,' explains O'Connor. 'Her father was killed in the last revolution. She is sure to be in sympathy with our cause.'

"And sure enough the next day she flung a little bunch of roses clear across the street into our door. O'Connor dived for it and found a piece of paper curled around a stem with a line in Spanish on it. He dragged the interpreter out of his corner and got him busy. The interpreter scratched his head, and gave us as a translation three best bets: 'Fortune had got a face like the man fighting'; 'Fortune looks like a brave man'; and 'Fortune favors the brave.' We put our money on the last one.

" 'Do ye see?' says O'Connor. 'She intends to encourage me sword to save her country.'

" 'It looks to me like an invitation to supper,' says I.

"So every day this señorita sits behind the barred windows and exhausts a conservatory or two, one posy at a time. And O'Connor walks like a Dominecker rooster and swells his chest and swears to me he will win her by feats of arms and big deeds on the gory field of battle.

"By and by the revolution began to get ripe. One day O'Connor takes me into the back room and tells me all.

" 'Bowers,' says he, 'at twelve o'clock one week from to-day the struggle will take place. It has pleased ye to find amusement and diversion in this project because ye have not sense enough to perceive that it is easily accomplished by a man of courage, intelligence, and historical superiority, such as meself. The whole world over,' says he, 'the O'Connors have ruled men, women, and nations. To subdue a small and indifferent country like this is a trifle. Ye see what little bare footed manikins the men of it are. I could lick four of 'em single-handed.'

" 'No doubt,' says I. 'But could you lick six? And suppose they hurled an army of seventeen against you?'

" 'Listen,' says O'Connor, 'to what will occur. At noon next Tuesday 25,000 patriots will rise up in the towns of the republic. The government will be absolutely unprepared. The public buildings will be taken, the regular army made prisoners, and the new administration set up. In the capital it will not be so easy on account of most of the army being stationed there. They will occupy the president's palace and the strongly fortified government buildings and stand a siege. But on the very day of the outbreak a body of our troops will begin a march to the capital from every town as soon as the local victory has been won. The thing is so well planned that it is an impossibility for us to fail. I meself will lead the troops from here. The new president will be Señor Espadas, now Minister of Finance in the present cabinet.'

" 'What do you get?' I asked.

" ' 'Twill be strange,' said O'Connor, smiling, 'if I don't have all the jobs handed to me on a silver salver to pick what I choose. I've been the brains of the scheme, and when the fighting opens I guess I won't be in the rear rank. Who managed it so our troops could get arms smuggled into this country? Didn't I arrange it with a New York firm before I left there? Our financial agents inform me that 20,000 stands of Winchester rifles have been delivered a month ago at a secret place up coast and distributed among the towns. I tell you, Bowers, the game is already won.'

"Well, that kind of talk kind of shook my disbelief in the infallibility of the serious Irish gentleman soldier of fortune. It certainly seemed that the patriotic grafters had gone about the thing in a business way. I looked upon O'Connor with more respect, and began to figure on what kind of uniform I might wear as Secretary of War.

"Tuesday, the day set for the revolution, came around according to schedule. O'Connor said that a signal had been agreed upon for the uprising. There was an old cannon on the beach near the national warehouse. That had been secretly loaded and promptly at twelve o'clock was to be fired off. Immediately the revolutionists would seize their concealed arms, attack the comandante's troops in the cuartel, and capture the custom-house and all government property and supplies.

"I was nervous all the morning. And about eleven o'clock O'Connor became infused with the excitement and martial spirit of murder. He geared his father's sword around him, and walked up and down in the back room like a lion in the Zoo suffering from corns. I smoked a couple of dozen cigars, and decided on yellow stripes down the trouser legs of my uniform.

"At half-past eleven O'Connor asks me to take a short stroll through the streets to see if I could notice any signs of the uprising. I was back in fifteen minutes.

"'Did you hear anything?' he asks.

"'I did,' says I. 'At first I thought it was drums. But it wasn't; it was snoring. Everybody in town's asleep.'

"O'Connor tears out his watch.

"'Fools!' says he. 'They've set the time right at the siesta hour when everybody takes a nap. But the cannon will wake 'em up. Everything will be all right, depend upon it.'

"Just at twelve o'clock we heard the sound of a cannon—BOOM!—shaking the whole town.

"O'Connor loosens his sword in its scabbard and jumps for the door. I went as far as the door and stood in it.

"People were sticking their heads out of doors and windows. But there was one grand sight that made the landscape look tame.

"General Tumbalo, the comandante, was rolling down the steps of his residential dugout, waving a five-foot sabre in his hand. He wore his cocked and plumed hat and his dress-parade coat covered with gold braid and buttons. Sky-blue pajamas, one rubber boot, and one red-plush slipper completed his make-up.

"The general had heard the cannon, and he puffed down the sidewalk toward the soldiers' barracks as fast as his rudely awakened two hundred pounds could travel.

"O'Connor sees him and lets out a battle-cry and draws his father's sword and rushes across the street and tackles the enemy.

"Right there in the street he and the general gave an exhibition of blacksmithing and butchery. Sparks flew from their blades, the general roared, and O'Connor gave the slogan of his race and proclivities.

"Then the general's sabre broke in two; and he took to his ginger-colored heels crying out, 'Policios,' at every jump. O'Connor chased him a block, imbued with the sentiment of man-slaughter, and slicing buttons off the general's coat tails with the paternal weapon. At the corner five barefooted policemen in cotton undershirts and straw hats climbed over O'Connor and subjugated him according to the municipal statutes.

"They brought him past the late revolutionary head-quarters on the way to jail. I stood in the door. A policeman had him by each hand and foot, and they dragged him on his back through the grass like a turtle. Twice they stopped, and the odd policeman took another's place while he rolled a cigarette. The great soldier of fortune turned his head and looked at me as they passed. I blushed, and lit another cigar. The procession passed on, and at ten minutes past twelve everybody had gone back to sleep again.

"In the afternoon the interpreter came around and smiled as he laid his hand on the big red jar we usually kept ice-water in.

" 'The ice-man didn't call to-day,' says I. 'What's the matter with everything, Sancho?'

" 'Ah, yes,' says the liver-colored linguist. 'They just tell me in the town. Verree bad act that Señor O'Connor make fight with General Tumbalo. Yes. General Tumbalo great soldier and big mans.'

" 'What'll they do to Mr. O'Connor?' I asks.

" 'I talk little while presently with the Juez de la Paz—what you call Justice-with-the-peace,' says Sancho. 'He tell me it verree bad crime that one Señor Americano try kill General Tumbalo. He say they keep Señor O'Connor in jail six months; then have trial and shoot him with guns. Verree sorree.'

" 'How about this revolution that was to be pulled off?' I asks.

" 'Oh,' says this Sancho, 'I think too hot weather for revolution. Revolution better in winter-time. Maybe so next winter. *Quién sabe?*'

" 'But the cannon went off,' says I. 'The signal was given.'

" 'That big sound?' says Sancho, grinning. 'The boiler in ice factory he blow up—BOOM! Wake everybody up from siesta. Verree sorree. No ice. Mucho hot day.'

"About sunset I went over to the jail, and they let me talk to O'Connor through the bars.

" 'What's the news, Bowers?' says he. 'Have we taken the town? I've been expecting a rescue party all the afternoon. I haven't heard any firing. Has any word been received from the capital?'

" 'Take it easy, Barney,' says I. 'I think there's been a change of plans. There's something more important to talk about. Have you any money?'

" 'I have not,' says O'Connor. 'The last dollar went to pay our hotel bill yesterday. Did our troops capture the custom-house? There ought to be plenty of government money there.'

" 'Segregate your mind from battles,' says I. 'I've been making inquiries. You're to be shot six months from date for assault and battery. I'm expecting to receive fifty years at hard labor for vagrancy. All they furnish you while you're a prisoner is water. You depend on your friends for food. I'll see what I can do.'

"I went away and found a silver Chile dollar in an old vest of O'Connor's. I took him some fried fish and rice for his supper. In the morning I went down to a lagoon and had a drink of water, and then went back to the jail. O'Connor had a porterhouse steak look in his eye.

" 'Barney,' says I, 'I've found a pond full of the finest kind of water. It's the grandest, sweetest, purest water in the world. Say the word and I'll go fetch you a bucket of it and you can throw this vile government stuff out the window. I'll do anything I can for a friend.'

" 'Has it come to this?' says O'Connor, raging up and down his cell. 'Am I to be starved to death and then shot? I'll make those traitors feel the weight of an O'Connor's hand when I get out of this.' And then he comes to the bars and speaks softer. 'Has nothing been heard from Doña Isabel?' he asks. 'Though every one else in the world fail,' says he, 'I trust those eyes of hers. She will find a way to effect my release. Do ye think ye could communicate with her? One word from her—even a rose would make me sorrow light. But don't let her know except with the utmost delicacy, Bowers. These high-bred Castilians are sensitive and proud.'

"'Well said, Barney,' says I. 'You've given me an idea. I'll report later. Something's got to be pulled off quick, or we'll both starve.'

"I walked out and down to Hooligan Alley, and then on the other side of the street. As I went past the window of Doña Isabel Antonia Concha Regalia, out flies the rose as usual and hits me on the ear.

"The door was open, and I took off my hat and walked in. It wasn't very light inside, but there she sat in a rocking-chair by the window smoking a black cheroot. And when I got closer I saw that she was about thirty-nine, and had never seen a straight front in her life. I sat down on the arm of her chair, and took the cheroot out of her mouth and stole a kiss.

"'Hullo, Izzy,' I says. 'Excuse my unconventionality, but I feel like I have known you for a month. Whose Izzy is oo?'"

"The lady ducked her head under her mantilla, and drew in a long breath. I thought she was going to scream, but with all that intake of air she only came out with: 'Me likee Americanos.'

"As soon as she said that, I knew that O'Connor and me would be doing things with a knife and fork before the day was over. I drew a chair beside her, and inside of half an hour we were engaged. Then I took my hat and said I must go out for a while.

"'You come back?' says Izzy, in alarm.

"'Me go bring preacher,' says I. 'Come back twenty minutes. We marry now. How you likee?'

"'Marry to-day?' says Izzy. 'Good!'

"I went down on the beach to the United States consul's shack. He was a grizzly man, eighty-two pounds, smoked glasses, five foot eleven, pickled. He was playing chess with an india-rubber man in white clothes.

"'Excuse me for interrupting,' says I, 'but can you tell me how a man could get married quick?'

"The consul gets up and fingers in a pigeonhole.

"'I believe I had a license to perform the ceremony myself, a year or two ago,' he said. 'I'll look, and——'

"I caught hold of his arm.

"'Don't look it up,' says I. 'Marriage is a lottery anyway. I'm willing to take the risk about the license if you are.'

"The consul went back to Hooligan Alley with me. Izzy called her ma to come in, but the old lady was picking a chicken in the patio and begged to be excused. So we stood up and the consul performed the ceremony.

"That evening Mrs. Bowers cooked a great supper of stewed goat, tamales, baked bananas, fricasseed red peppers and coffee. Afterward I sat in the rocking-chair by the front window, and she sat on the floor plunking at a guitar and happy, as she should be, as Mrs. William T. B.

"All at once I sprang up in a hurry. I'd forgotten all about O'Connor. I asked Izzy to fix up a lot of truck for him to eat.

"'That big, oogly man,' said Izzy. 'But all right—he your friend.'

"I pulled a rose out a bunch in a jar, and took the grub-basket around to the jail. O'Connor ate like a wolf. Then he wiped his face with a banana peel and said: 'Have you heard nothing from Doña Isabel yet?'

"'Hist!' says I, slipping the rose between the bars. 'She sends you this. She bids you take courage. At nightfall two masked men brought it to the ruined château in the orange grove. How did you like that goat hash, Barney?'

"O'Connor pressed the rose to his lips.

" 'This is more to me than all the food in the world,' says he. 'But the supper was fine. Where did you raise it?'

" 'I've negotiated a stand-off at a delicatessen hut downtown,' I tells him. 'Rest easy. If there's anything to be done I'll do it.'

"So things went along that way for some weeks. Izzy was a great cook; and if she had had a little more poise of character and smoked a little better brand of tobacco we might have drifted into some sense of responsibility for the honor I had conferred on her. But as time went on I began to hunger for the sight of a real lady standing before me in a street-car. All I was staying in that land of bilk and money for was because I couldn't get away, and I thought it no more than decent to stay and see O'Connor shot.

"One day our old interpreter drops around and after smoking an hour says that the judge of the peace sent him to request me to call on him. I went to his office in a lemon grove on a hill at the edge of the town; and there I had a surprise. I expected to see one of the usual cinnamon-colored natives in congress gaiters and one of Pizzaro's cast-off hats. What I saw was an elegant gentleman of a slightly claybank complexion sitting in an upholstered leather chair, sipping a highball and reading Mrs. Humphry Ward. I had smuggled into my brain a few words of Spanish by the help of Izzy, and I began to remark in a rich Andalusian brogue:

" 'Beunas dias, señor. Yo tengo—yo tengo——'

" 'Oh, sit down, Mr. Bowers,' says he. 'I spent eight years in your country in colleges and law schools. Let me mix you a highball. Lemon peel, or not?'

"Thus we got along. In about half an hour I was beginning to tell him about the scandal in our family when Aunt Elvira ran away with a Cumberland Presbyterian preacher. Then he says to me:

" 'I sent for you, Mr. Bowers, to let you know that you can have your friend Mr. O'Connor now. Of course we had to make a show of punishing him on account of his attack on General Tumbalo. It is arranged that he shall be released to-morrow night. You and he will be conveyed on board the fruit steamer Voyager, bound for New York, which lies in the harbor. Your passage will be arranged for.'

" 'One moment, judge,' says I; 'that revolution——'

"The judge lays back in his chair and howls.

" 'Why,' says he presently, 'that was all a little joke fixed up by the boys around the court-room, and one or two of our cut-ups, and a few clerks in the stores. The town is bursting its sides with laughing. The boys made themselves up to be conspirators, and they—what you call it?—stick Señor O'Connor for his money. It is very funny.'

" 'It was,' says I. 'I saw the joke all along. I'll take another highball, if your Honor don't mind.'

"The next evening just at dark a couple of soldiers brought O'Connor down to the beach, where I was waiting under a cocoanut-tree.

" 'Hist!' says I in his ear. 'Doña Isabel has arranged our escape. Not a word!'

"They rowed us in a boat out to a little steamer that smelled of table d'hôte salad oil and bone phosphate.

"The great, mellow, tropical moon was rising as we steamed away. O'Connor leaned on the taffrail or rear balcony of the ship and gazed silently at Guaya—at Buncoville-on-the-Beach. He had the red rose in his hand.

" 'She will wait,' I heard him say. 'Eyes like hers never deceive. But I shall see her again. Traitors cannot keep an O'Connor down forever.'

" 'You talk like a sequel,' says I. 'But in Volume II please omit the light-haired friend who totes the grub to the hero in his dungeon cell.'

"And thus reminiscing, we came back to New York."

There was a little silence broken only by the familiar roar of the streets after Kansas Bill Bowers ceased talking.

"Did O'Connor ever go back?" I asked.

"He attained his heart's desire," said Bill. "Can you walk two blocks? I'll show you."

He led me eastward and down a flight of stairs that was covered by a curious-shaped glowing, pagoda-like structure. Signs and figures on the tiled walls and supporting columns attested that we were in the Grand Central station of the subway. Hundreds of people were on the midway platform.

An uptown express dashed up and halted. It was crowded. There was a rush for it by a still larger crowd.

Towering above every one there a magnificent, broad-shouldered, athletic man leaped into the centre of the struggle. Men and women he seized in either hand and hurled them like manikins toward the open gates of the train.

Now and then some passenger with a shred of soul and self-respect left to him turned to offer remonstrance; but the blue uniform on the towering figure, the fierce and conquering glare of his eye and the ready impact of his ham-like hands glued together the lips that would have spoken complaint.

When the train was full, then he exhibited to all who might observe and admire his irresistible genius as a ruler of men. With his knees, with his elbows, with his shoulders, with his resistless feet he shoved, crushed, slammed, heaved, kicked, flung, pounded the overplus of passengers aboard. Then with the sounds of its wheels drowned by the moans, shrieks, prayers, and curses of its unfortunate crew, the express dashed away.

"That's him. Ain't he a wonder?" said Kansas Bill, admiringly. "That tropical country wasn't the place for him. I wish the distinguished traveler, writer, war correspondent, and playright, Richmond Hobson Davis, could see him now. O'Connor ought to be dramatized."

THE ATAVISM OF JOHN TOM LITTLE BEAR

[O. Henry thought this the best of the Jeff Peters stories, all the rest of which are included in "The Gentle Grafter," except "Cupid à la Carte" in the "Heart of the West." "The Atavism of John Tom Little Bear" appeared in *Everybody's Magazine* for July, 1903.]

I SAW a light in Jeff Peters's room over the Red Front Drug Store. I hastened toward it, for I had not known that Jeff was in town. He is a man of the Hadji breed, of a hundred occupations, with a story to tell (when he will) of each one.

I found Jeff repacking his grip for a run down to Florida to look at an orange grove for which he had traded, a month before, his mining claim on the Yukon. He kicked me a chair, with the same old humorous, profound smile on his seasoned countenance. It had been eight months since we had met, but his greeting was such as men pass from day to day. Time is Jeff's servant, and the continent is a big lot across which he cuts to his many roads.

For a while we skirmished along the edges of unprofitable talk which culminated in that unquiet problem of the Philippines.

"All them tropical races," said Jeff, "could be run out better with their own jockeys up. The tropical man knows what he wants. All he wants is a season ticket to the cock-fights and a pair of Western Union climbers to go up the bread-fruit tree. The Anglo-Saxon man wants him to learn to conjugate and wear suspenders. He'll be happiest in his own way."

I was shocked.

"Education, man," I said, "is the watchword. In time they will rise to our standard of civilization. Look at what education has done for the Indian."

"O-ho!" sang Jeff, lighting his pipe (which was a good sign). "Yes, the Indian! I'm looking. I hasten to contemplate the redman as a standard bearer of progress. He's the same as the other brown boys. You can't make an Anglo-Saxon of him. Did I ever tell you about the time my friend John Tom Little Bear bit off the right ear of the arts of culture and education and spun the teetotum back round to where it was when Columbus was a little boy? I did not?

"John Tom Little Bear was an educated Cherokee Indian and an old friend of mine when I was in the Territories. He was a graduate of one of them Eastern football colleges that have been so successful in teaching the Indian to use the gridiron instead of burning his victims at the stake. As an Anglo-Saxon, John Tom was copper-colored in spots. As an Indian, he was one of the whitest men I ever knew. As a Cherokee, he was a gentleman on the first ballot. As a ward of the nation, he was mighty hard to carry at the primaries.

"John Tom and me got together and began to make medicine—how to get up some lawful, genteel swindle which we might work in a quiet way so as not to excite the stupidity of the police or the cupidity of the larger corporations. We had close upon $500 between us, and we pined to make it grow, as all respectable capitalists do.

"So we figured out a proposition which seems to be as honorable as a gold mine prospectus and as profitable as a church raffle. And inside of thirty days you find us swarming into Kansas with a pair of fluent horses and a red camping wagon on the European plan. John Tom is Chief Wish-Heap-Dough, the famous Indian medicine man and Samaritan Sachem of the Seven Tribes. Mr. Peters is business manager and half owner. We needed a third man, so we looked around and found J. Conyngham Binkly leaning against the want column of a newspaper. This Binkly has a disease for Shakespearian rôles, and an hallucination about a 200 nights' run on the New York stage. But he confesses that he never could earn the butter to spread on his William S. rôles, so he is willing to drop to the ordinary baker's kind, and be satisfied with a 200-mile run behind the medicine ponies. Besides Richard III, he could do twenty-seven coon songs and banjo specialties, and was willing to cook, and curry the horses. We carried a fine line of excuses for taking money. One was a magic soap for removing grease spots and quarters from clothes. One was a Sum-wah-tah, the great Indian Remedy made from a prairie herb revealed by the Great Spirit in a dream to his favorite medicine men, the great chiefs McGarrity and Siberstein, bottlers, Chicago. And the other was a frivolous system of pick-pocketing the Kansasters that had the department stores reduced to a decimal fraction. Look ye! A pair of silk garters, a dream book, one dozen clothespins, a gold tooth, and 'When Knighthood Was in Flower' all wrapped up in a genuine Japanese silkarina handkerchief and handed to the handsome lady by Mr. Peters for the trivial sum of fifty cents, while Professor Binkly entertains us in a three-minute round with the banjo.

"'Twas an eminent graft we had. We ravaged peacefully through the State, determined to remove all doubt as to why 'twas called bleeding Kansas. John Tom Little Bear, in full Indian chief's costume, drew crowds away from the parchesi sociables and government ownership conversaziones. While at the football college in the East he had acquired quantities of rhetoric and the art of calisthenics and sophistry in his classes, and when he stood up in the red wagon and explained to the farmers, eloquent, about chilblains and hyperæsthesia of the cranium, Jeff couldn't hand out the Indian Remedy fast enough for 'em.

"One night we was camped on the edge of a little town out west of Salina. We always camped near a stream, and put up a little tent. Sometimes we sold out of the Remedy unexpected, and then Chief Wish-Heap-Dough would have a dream in which the Manitou commanded him to fill up a few bottles of Sum-wah-tah at the most convenient place. 'Twas about ten o'clock, and we'd just got in from a street performance. I was in the tent with a lantern, figuring up the day's profits. John Tom hadn't taken off his Indian make-up, and was sitting by the campfire minding a fine sirloin steak in the pan for the Professor till he finished his hair-raising scene with the trained horses.

"All at once out of dark bushes comes a pop like a fire-cracker, and John Tom gives a grunt and digs out of his bosom a little bullet that has dented itself against his collar-bone. John Tom makes a dive in the direction of the fire-works, and comes back dragging by the collar a kid about nine or ten years young, in a velveteen suit, with a little nickel-mounted rifle in his hand about as big as a fountain-pen.

" 'Here, you papoose,' says John Tom, 'what are you gunning for with that howitzer? You might hit somebody in the eye. Come out, Jeff, and mind the steak. Don't let it burn, while I investigate this demon with the pea shooter.'

" 'Cowardly redskin,' says the kid like he was quoting from a favorite author. 'Dare to burn me at the stake and the paleface will sweep you from the prairies like—like everything. Now, you lemme go, or I'll tell mamma.'

"John Tom plants the kid on a camp-stool, and sits down by him. 'Now, tell the big chief,' he says, 'why you try to shoot pellets into your Uncle John's system. Didn't you know it was loaded?'

" 'Are you a Indian?' asks the kid, looking up cute as you please at John Tom's buckskin and eagle feathers. 'I am,' says John Tom. 'Well, then, that's why,' answered the boy, swinging his feet. I nearly let the steak burn watching the nerve of the youngster.

" 'O-ho!' says John Tom, 'I see. You're the Boy Avenger. And you've sworn to rid the continent of the savage redman. Is that about the way of it, son?'

"The kid halfway nodded his head. And then he looked glum. 'Twas indecent to wring his secret from his bosom before a single brave had fallen before his parlor-rifle.

" 'Now, tell us where your wigwam is, papoose,' says John Tom—'where you live? Your mamma will be worrying about your being out so late. Tell me, and I'll take you home.'

"The kid grins. 'I guess not,' he says. 'I live thousands and thousands of miles over there.' He gyrated his hand toward the horizon. 'I come on the train,' he says, 'by myself. I got off here because the conductor said my ticket had ex-pirated.' He looks at John Tom with sudden suspicion. 'I bet you ain't a Indian,' he says. 'You don't talk like a Indian. You look like one, but all a Indian can say is "heap good" and "paleface die." Say, I bet you are one of them make-believe Indians that sell medicine on the streets. I saw one once in Quincy.'

" 'You never mind,' says John Tom, 'whether I'm a cigar-sign or a Tammany cartoon. The question before the council is what's to be done with you. You've run away from home. You've been reading Howells. You've disgraced the profession of boy avengers by trying to shoot a tame Indian, and never saying: "Die, dog of a redskin! You have crossed the path of the Boy Avenger nineteen times too often." What do you mean by it?'

"The kid thought for a minute. 'I guess I made a mistake,' he says. 'I ought to have gone farther west. They find 'em wild out there in the cañons.'

He holds out his hand to John Tom, the little rascal. 'Please excuse me, sir,' says he, 'for shooting at you. I hope it didn't hurt you. But you ought to be more careful. When a scout sees a Indian in his war-dress, his rifle must speak.' Little Bear gave a big laugh with a whoop at the end of it, and swings the kid ten feet high and sets him on his shoulder, and the runaway fingers the fringe and the eagle feathers and is full of the joy the white man knows when he dangles his heels against an inferior race. It is plain that Little Bear and that kid are chums from that on. The little renegade has already smoked the pipe of peace with the savage; and you can see in his eye that he is figuring on a tomahawk and a pair of moccasins, children's size.

"We have supper in the tent. The youngster looks upon me and the Professor as ordinary braves, only intended as a background to the camp scene. When he is seated on a box of Sum-wah-tah, with the edge of the table sawing his neck, and his mouth full of beefsteak, Little Bear calls for his name. 'Roy,' says the kid, with a sirloiny sound to it. But when the rest of it and his post-office address is referred to, he shakes his head. 'I guess not,' he says. 'You'll send me back. I want to stay with you. I like this camping out. At home, we fellows had a camp in our back yard. They called me Roy, the Red Wolf! I guess that'll do for a name. Gimme another piece of beefsteak, please.'

"We had to keep that kid. We knew there was a hullabaloo about him some-wheres, and that Mamma, and Uncle Harry, and Aunt Jane, and the Chief of Police were hot after finding his trail, but not another word would he tell us. In two days he was the mascot of the Big Medicine outfit, and all of us had a sneaking hope that his owners wouldn't turn up. When the red wagon was doing business he was in it, and passed up the bottles to Mr. Peters as proud and satisfied as a prince that's abjured a two-hundred-dollar crown for a million-dollar parvenuess. Once John Tom asked him something about his papa. 'I ain't got any papa,' he says. 'He runned away and left us. He made my mamma cry. Aunt Lucy says he's a shape.' 'A what?' somebody asks him. 'A shape,' says the kid; 'some kind of a shape—lemme see—oh, yes, a feendenuman shape. I don't know what it means.' John Tom was for putting our brand on him, and dressing him up like a little chief, with wampum and beads, but I vetoes it. 'Somebody's lost that kid, is my view of it, and they may want him. You let me try him with a few stratagems, and see if I can't get a look at his visiting-card.'

"So that night I goes up to Mr. Roy Blank by the camp-fire, and looks at him contemptuous and scornful. 'Snickenwitzel!' says I, like the word made me sick; 'Snickenwitzel! Bah! Before I'd be named Snickenwitzel!'

"'What's the matter with you, Jeff?' says the kid, opening his eyes wide.

"'Snickenwitzel!' I repeats, and I spat the word out. 'I saw a man to-day from your town and he told me your name. I'm not surprised you was ashamed to tell it. Snickenwitzel! Whew!'

"Ah, here, now,' says the boy, indignant and wriggling all over, 'what's the matter with you? That ain't my name. It's Conyers. What's the matter with you?'

"'And that's not the worst of it,' I went on quick, keeping him hot and not giving him time to think. 'We thought you was from a nice, well-to-do family. Here's Mr. Little Bear, a chief of the Cherokees, entitled to wear nine otter tails on his Sunday blanket, and Professor Binkly, who plays Shakespeare and the banjo, and me, that's got hundreds of dollars in that black tin box in the wagon, and we've got to be careful about the company we keep. That man tells me your folks live 'way down in little old Hencoop Alley, where there are no side-walks, and the goats eat off the table with you.'

"That kid was almost crying now. ' 'Tain't so,' he splutters. 'He—he don't know what he's talking about. We live on Poplar Av'noo. I don't 'sociate with goats. What's the matter with you?'

"'Poplar Avenue,' says I, sarcastic. 'Poplar Avenue! That's a street to live on! It only runs two blocks and then falls off a bluff. You can throw a keg of nails the whole length of it. Don't talk to me about Poplar Avenue.'

"'It's—it's miles long,' says the kid. "Our number's 862 and there are lots of houses after that. What's the matter with—aw, you make me tired, Jeff.'

"'Well, well, now,' says I. 'I guess that man made a mistake. Maybe it was some other boy he was talking about. If I catch him I'll teach him to go around slandering people.' And after supper I goes up town and telegraphs to Mrs. Conyers, 862 Poplar Avenue, Quincy, Ill., that the kid is safe and sassy with us, and will be held for further orders. In two hours an answer comes to hold him tight, and she'll start for him by next train.

"The next train was due at 6 P. M. the next day, and me and John Tom was at the depot with the kid. You might scour the plains in vain for the big Chief Wish-Heap-Dough. In his place is Mr. Little Bear, in the human habiliments of the Anglo-Saxon sect; and the leather of his shoes is patented and the loop of his necktie is copyrighted. For these things John Tom had grafted on him at college along with metaphysics and the knockout guard for the low tackle. But for his complexion, which is some yellowish, and the black mop of his straight hair, you might have thought here was an ordinary man out of the city directory that subscribes for magazines and pushes the lawn-mower in his shirt-sleeves of evenings.

"Then the train rolled in, and a little woman in a gray dress, with sort of illuminating hair, slides off and looks around quick. And the Boy Avenger sees her, and yells 'Mamma,' and she cries 'O!' and they meet in a clinch, and now the pesky redskin can come forth from their caves on the plains without fear any more of the rifle of Roy, the Red Wolf. Mrs. Conyers comes up and thanks me an' John Tom without the usual extremities you always look for in a woman. She says just enough, in a way to convince, and there is no incidental music by the orchestra. I made a few illiterate requisitions upon the art of conversation, at which the lady smiles friendly, as if she had known me a week. And then Mr. Little Bear adorns the atmosphere with the various idioms into which education can fracture the wind of speech. I could see the kid's mother didn't quite place John Tom; but it seemed she was apprised in his dialects, and she played up to his lead in the science of making three words do the work of one.

"That kid introduced us, with some footnotes and explanations that made things plainer than a week of rhetoric. He danced around, and punched us in the back, and tried to climb John Tom's leg. 'This is John Tom, mamma,' says he. 'He's an Indian. He sells medicine in a red wagon. I shot him, but he wasn't wild. The other one's Jeff. He's a fakir, too. Come on and see the camp where we live, won't you, mamma?'

"It is plain to see that the life of the woman is in that boy. She has got him again where her arms can gather him, and that's enough. She's ready to do anything to please him. She hesitates the eighth of a second and takes another look at these men. I imagine she says to herself about John Tom, 'Seems to be a gentleman, if his hair don't curl.' And Mr. Peters she disposes of as follows: 'No ladies' man, but a man who knows a lady.'

"So we all rambled down to the camp as neighborly as coming from a wake. And there she inspects the wagon and pats the place with her hand where the kid used to sleep, and dabs around her eyewinkers with her handkerchief. And Professor Binkly gives us 'Trovatore' on one string of the banjo, and is about to slide off into Hamlet's monologue when one of the horses gets tangled in his rope and he must go look after him, and says something about 'foiled again.'

"When it got dark me and John Tom walked back to the Corn Exchange Hotel, and the four of us had supper there. I think the trouble started at that supper, for then was when Mr. Little Bear made an intellectual balloon ascension. I held on to the tablecloth, and listened to him soar. That redman, if I could judge, had the gift of information. He took languages, and did with it all a Roman can do with macaroni. His vocal remarks was all embroidered over with the most scholarly verbs and prefixes. And his syllables was smooth, and fitted nicely to the joints of his idea. I thought I'd heard him talk before, but I hadn't. And it wasn't the size of his words, but the way they come; and 'twasn't his subjects, for he spoke of common things like cathedrals and football and poems and catarrh and souls and freight rates and sculpture. Mrs. Conyers understood his accents, and the elegant sounds went back and forth between 'em. And now and then Jefferson D. Peters would intervene a few shopworn, senseless words to have the butter passed or another leg of the chicken.

"Yes, John Tom Little Bear appeared to be inveigled some in his bosom about that Mrs. Conyers. She was of the kind that pleases. She had the good looks and more, I'll tell you. You take one of those cloak models in a big store. They strike you as being on the impersonal system. They are adapted for the eye. What they run to is inches around and complexion, and the art of fanning the delusion that the sealskin would look just as well on the lady with the warts and the pocket-book. Now, if one of them models was off duty, and you took it, and it would say 'Charlie' when you pressed it, and sit up at the table, why, then you would have something similar to Mrs. Conyers. I could see how John Tom could resist any inclination to hate that white squaw.

"The lady and the kid stayed at the hotel. In the morning, they say, they will start for home. Me and Little Bear left at eight o'clock, and sold Indian Remedy on the courthouse square till nine. He leaves me and the Professor to drive down to camp, while he stays up town. I am not enamored with that plan, for it shows John Tom is uneasy in his composures, and that leads to firewater, and sometimes to the green-corn dance and costs. Not often does Chief Wish-Heap-Dough get busy with the firewater, but whenever he does there is heap much doing in the lodges of the palefaces who wear blue and carry the club.

"At half-past nine Professor Binkly is rolled in his quilt snoring in blank verse, and I am sitting by the fire listening to the frogs. Mr. Little Bear slides into camp and sits down against a tree. There is no symptoms of firewater.

"'Jeff,' says he, after a long time, 'a little boy came West to hunt Indians.'

"'Well, then?' says I, for I wasn't thinking as he was.

"'And he bagged one,' says John Tom, 'and 'twas not with a gun, and he never had on a velveteen suit of clothes in his life.' And then I began to catch his smoke.

"'I know it,' says I. 'And I'll bet you his pictures are on valentines, and fool men are his game, red and white.'

"'You win on the red,' says John Tom, calm. 'Jeff, for how many ponies do you think I could buy Mrs. Conyers?'

"'Scandalous talk!' I replies. ''Tis not a paleface custom.' John Tom laughs loud and bites into his cigar. 'No,' he answers; ''tis the savage equivalent for the dollars of the white man's marriage settlement. Oh, I know. There's an eternal wall between the races. If I could do it, Jeff, I'd put a torch to every white college that a redman has ever set foot inside. Why don't you leave us alone,' he says, 'to our own ghost-dances and dog-feasts and our dingy squaws to cook our grass-hopper soup and darn our moccasins?'

"'Now, you don't mean disrespect to the perennial blossom entitled education?' says I, scandalized, 'because I wear it in the bosom of my own intellectual shirt-waist. I've had education,' says I, 'and never took any harm from it.'

"'You lasso us,' goes on Little Bear, not noticing my prose insertions, 'and teach us what is beautiful in literature and life, and how to appreciate what is fine in men and women. What have you done to me?' says he. 'You've made me a Cherokee Moses. You've taught me to hate the wigwams and love the white man's ways. I can look over into the promised land and see Mrs. Con-yers, but my place is—on the reservation.'

"Little Bear stands up in his chief's dress, and laughs again. 'But, white man Jeff,' he goes on, 'the paleface provides a recourse. 'Tis a temporary one, but it gives a respite and the name of it is whiskey.' And straight off he walks up the path to town again. 'Now,' says I in my mind, 'may the Manitou moves him to do only bailable things this night!' For I perceive that John Tom is about to avail himself of the white man's solace.

"Maybe it was 10:30, as I sat smoking, when I hear pit-a-pats on the path, and here comes Mrs. Conyers running, her hair twisted up any way, and a look on her face that says burglars and mice and the flour's-all-out rolled in one. 'Oh, Mr. Peters,' she calls out, as they will, 'oh, oh!' I made a quick think, and I spoke the gist of it out loud. 'Now,' says I, 'we've been brothers, me and that Indian, but I'll make a good one of him in two minutes if——'

"'No, no,' she says, wild and cracking her knuckles, 'I haven't seen Mr. Little Bear. 'Tis my—husband. He's stolen my boy. Oh,' she says, 'just when I had him back in my arms again! That heartless villain! Every bitterness life knows,' she says, 'he's made me drink. My poor little lamb, that ought to be warm in his bed, carried off by that fiend!'

"'How did all this happen?' I ask. 'Let's have the facts.'

"'I was fixing his bed,' she explains, 'and Roy was playing on the hotel porch and he drives up to the steps. I heard Roy scream, and ran out. My hus-band had him in the buggy then. I begged him for my child. This is what he gave me.' She turns her face to the light. There is a crimson streak running across her cheek and mouth. 'He did that with his whip,' she says.

"'Come back to the hotel,' says I, 'and we'll see what can be done.'

"On the way she tells me some of the wherefores. When he slashed her with the whip he told her he found out she was coming for the kid, and he was on the same train. Mrs. Conyers had been living with her brother, and they'd watched the boy always, as her husband had tried to steal him before. I judge that man was worse that a street railway promoter. It seems he had spent her money and slugged her and killed her canary bird, and told it around that she had cold feet.

"At the hotel we found a mass meeting of five infuriated citizens chewing tobacco and denouncing the outrage. Most of the town was asleep by ten o'clock. I talks to the lady some quiet, and tells her I will take the one o'clock train for the next town, forty miles east, for it is likely that the esteemed Mr. Con-yers will drive there to take the cars. 'I don't know,' I tells her, 'but what he has legal rights; but if I find him I can give him an illegal left in the eye, and tie him up for a day or two, anyhow, on a disturbal of the peace proposi-tion.'

"Mrs. Conyers goes inside and cries with the landlord's wife, who is fixing some catnip tea that will make everything all right for the poor dear. The landlord comes out on the porch, thumbing his one suspender, and says to me:

"'Ain't had so much excitement in town since Bedford Steegall's wife swal-lered a spring lizard. I seen him through the winder hit her with the buggy whip, and everything. What's that suit of clothes cost you you got on? 'Pears like we'd have some rain, don't it? Say, doc, that Indian of yorn's on a kind of a whizz to-night, ain't he? He comes along just before you did, and I told him about this here occurrence. He gives a cur'us kind of a hoot, and trotted off. I guess our constable'll have him in the lock-up 'fore morning.'

"I thought I'd sit on the porch and wait for the one o'clock train. I wasn't feeling saturated with mirth. Here was John Tom on one of his sprees, and this kidnapping business losing sleep for me. But then, I'm always having trouble with other people's troubles. Every few minutes Mrs. Conyers would come out on the porch and look down the road the way the buggy went, like she expected to see that kid coming back on a white pony with a red apple in his hand. Now, wasn't that like a woman? And that brings up cats. 'I saw a mouse go in this hole,' says Mrs. Cat; 'you can go prize up a plank over there if you like; I'll watch this hole.'

"About a quarter to one o'clock the lady comes out again, restless, crying easy, as females do for their own amusement, and she looks down that road again and listens. 'Now, ma'am,' says I, 'there's no use watching cold wheel-tracks. By this time they're halfway to——' 'Hush,' she says, holding up her hand. And I do here something coming 'flip-flap' in the dark; and then there is the awfulest war-whoop ever heard outside of Madison Square Garden at a Buffalo Bill matinée. And up the steps and on to the porch jumps the disrespectable Indian. The lamp in the hall shines on him, and I fail to recognize Mr. J. T. Little Bear, alumnus of the class of '91. What I see is a Cherokee brave, and the warpath is what he has been traveling. Firewater and other things have got him going. His buckskin is hanging in strings, and his feathers are mixed up like a frizzly hen's. The dust of miles is on his moccasins, and the light in his eye is the kind the aborigines wear. But in his arms he brings that kid, his eyes half closed, with his little shoes dangling and one hand fast around the Indian's collar.

"'Papoose!' says John Tom, and I notice that the flowers of the white man's syntax have left his tongue. He is the original proposition in bear's claws and copper color. 'Me bring,' says he, and he lays the kid in his mother's arms. 'Run fifteen mile,' says John Tom—'Ugh! Catch white man. Bring papoose.'

"The little woman is in extremities of gladness. She must wake up that stir-up trouble youngster and hug him and make proclamation that he is his mamma's own precious treasure. I was about to ask questions, but I looked at Mr. Little Bear, and my eye caught the sight of something in his belt. 'Now go to bed, ma'am,' says I, 'and this gadabout youngster likewise, for there's no more danger, and the kidnapping business is not what it was earlier in the night.'

"I inveigled John Tom down to camp quick, and when he tumbled over asleep I got that thing out of his belt and disposed of it where the eye of education can't see it. For even the football colleges disapprove of the art of scalp-taking in their curriculums.

"It is ten o'clock next day when John Tom wakes up and looks around. I am glad to see the nineteenth century in his eyes again.

"'What was it, Jeff?' he asks.

"'Heap firewater,' says I.

"John Tom frowns, and thinks a little. 'Combined,' says he directly, 'with the interesting little physiological shake-up known as reversion to type. I remember now. Have they gone yet?'

"'On the 7:30 train,' I answers.

"'Ugh!' says John Tom; 'better so. Paleface, bring big Chief Wish-Heap-Dough a little bromo-seltzer, and then he'll take up the red man's burden again.'"

HELPING THE OTHER FELLOW

[Originally published in *Munsey's Magazine*, December, 1908.]

"But can thim that helps others help thimselves!"
—*Mulvaney.*

THIS is the story that William Trotter told me on the beach at Aguas Frescas while I waited for the gig of the captain of the fruit steamer *Andador* which was to take me abroad. Reluctantly I was leaving the Land of Always Afternoon. William was remaining, and he favored me with a condensed oral autobiography as we sat on the sands in the shade cast by the Bodega Nacional.

As usual, I became aware that the Man from Bombay had already written the story; but as he had compressed it to an eight-word sentence, I have become an expansionist, and have quoted his phrase above, with apologies to him and best regards to *Terence*.

II

"Don't you ever have a desire to go back to the land of derby hats and starched collars?" I asked him. "You seem to be a handy man and a man of action," I continued, "and I am sure I could find you a comfortable job somewhere in the States."

Ragged, shiftless, barefooted, a confirmed eater of the lotos, William Trotter had pleased me much, and I hated to see him gobbled up by the tropics.

"I've no doubt you could," he said, idly splitting the bark from a section of sugar-cane. "I've no doubt you could do much for me. If every man could do as much for himself as he can for others, every country in the world would be holding millenniums instead of centennials."

There seemed to be a pabulum in W. T.'s words. And then another idea came to me.

I had a brother in Chicopee Falls who owned manufactories—cotton, or sugar, or A. A. sheetings, or something in the commercial line. He was vulgarly rich, and therefore reverenced art. The artistic temperament of the family was monopolized at my birth. I knew that Brother James would honor my slightest wish. I would demand from him a position in cotton, sugar, or sheeting for William Trotter—something say, at two hundred a month or thereabouts. I confided my beliefs and made my large proposition to William. He had pleased me much, and he was ragged.

While we were talking, there was a sound of firing guns—four or five, rattlingly, as if by a squad. The cheerful noise came from the direction of the cuartel, which is a kind of make-shift barracks for the soldiers of the republic.

"Hear that?" said William Trotter. "Let me tell you about it.

"A year ago I landed on this coast with one solitary dollar. I have the same sum in my pocket to-day. I was second cook on a tramp fruiter; and they marooned me here early one morning, without benefit of clergy, just because I poulticed the face of the first mate with cheese omelette at dinner. The fellow had kicked because I'd put horseradish in it instead of cheese.

"When they threw me out of the yawl into three feet of surf, I waded ashore and sat down under a palm-tree. By and by a fine-looking white man with a red face and white clothes, genteel as possible, but somewhat under the influence, came and sat down beside me.

"I had noticed there was a kind of a village back of the beach, and enough scenery to outfit a dozen moving-picture shows. But I thought, of course, it was a cannibal suburb, and I was wondering whether I was to be served with carrots or mushrooms. And, as I say, this dressed-up man sits beside me, and we become friends in the space of a minute or two. For an hour we talked, and he told me all about it.

"It seems that he was a man of parts, conscientiousness, and plausibility, besides being educated and a wreck to his appetites. He told me all about it. Colleges had turned him out, and distilleries had taken him in. Did I tell you his name? It was Clifford Wainwright. I didn't exactly catch the cause of his being cast away on that particular stretch of South America; but I reckon it was his own business. I asked him if he'd ever been second cook on a tramp fruiter, and he said no: so that concluded my line of surmises. But he talked like the encyclopedia from 'A—Berlin' to 'Trilo—Zyria.' And he carried a watch—a silver arrangement with works, and up to date within twenty-four hours, anyhow.

"'I'm pleased to have met you,' says Wainwright. 'I'm a devotee to the great joss Booze; but my ruminating facilities are unrepaired,' says he—or words to that effect. 'And I hate,' says he, 'to see fools trying to run the world.'

"'I never touch a drop,' says I, 'and there are many kinds of fools; and the world runs on its own apex, according to science, with no meddling from me.'

"'I was referring,' says he, 'to the president of this republic. His country is in a desperate condition. Its treasury is empty, it's on the verge of war with Nicamala, and if it wasn't for the hot weather the people would be starting revolutions in every town. Here is a nation,' goes on Wainwright, 'on the brink of destruction. A man of intelligence could rescue it from its impending doom in one day by issuing the necessary edicts and orders. President Gomez knows nothing of statesmanship or policy. Do you know Adam Smith?'

"'Lemme see,' says I. 'There was a one-eared man named Smith in Fort Worth, Texas, but I think his first name was——'

"'I am referring to the political economist,' says Wainwright.

"'S'mother Smith, then,' says I. 'The one I speak of never was arrested.'

"So Wainwright boils some more with indignation at the insensibility of people who are not corpulent to fill public positions; and then he tells me he is going out to the president's summer palace, which is four miles from Aguas Frescas, to instruct him in the art of running steam-heated republics.

"'Come along with me, Trotter,' says he, 'and I'll show you what brains can do.'

"'Anything in it?' I asks.

"'The satisfaction,' says he, 'of redeeming a country of two hundred thousand population from ruin back to prosperity and peace.'

"'Great,' says I. 'I'll go with you. I'd prefer to eat a live broiled lobster just now; but give me liberty as second choice if I can't be in at the death.'

"Wainwright and me permeates through the town, and he halts at a rum-dispensary.

"'Have you any money?' he asks.

"'I have,' says I, fishing out my silver dollar. 'I always go about with adequate sums of money.'

"'Then we'll drink,' says Wainwright.

"'Not me,' says I. 'Not any demon rum or any of its ramifications for mine. It's one of my non-weaknesses.'

"'It's my failing,' says he. 'What's your particular soft point?'

"'Industry,' says I, promptly. 'I'm hard-working, diligent, industrious, and energetic.'

"'My dear Mr. Trotter,' says he, 'surely I've known you long enough to tell you you are a liar. Every man must have his own particular weakness, and his own particular strength in other things. Now, you will buy me a drink of rum, and we will call on President Gomez.'

III

"Well, sir," Trotter went on, "we walks the four miles out, through a virgin conservatory of palms and ferns and other roof-garden products, to the president's summer White House. It was blue, and reminded you of what you see on the stage in the third act, which they describe as 'same as the first' on the programs.

"There was more than fifty people waiting outside the iron fence that surrounded the house and grounds. There was generals and agitators and épergnes in gold-laced uniforms, and citizens in diamonds and Panama hats—all waiting to get an audience with the Royal Five-Card Draw. And in a kind of summer-house in front of the mansion we could see a burnt-sienna man eating breakfast out of gold dishes and taking his time. I judged that the crowd outside had come out for their morning orders and requests, and was afraid to intrude.

"But C. Wainwright wasn't. The gate was open, and he walked inside and up to the president's table as confident as a man who knows the head waiter in a fifteen-cent restaurant. And I went with him, because I had only seventy-five cents, and there was nothing else to do.

"The Gomez man rises from his chair, and looks, colored man as he was, like he was about to call out for corporal of the guard, post number one. But Wainwright says some phrases to him in a peculiarly lubricating manner; and the first thing you know we was all three of us seated at the table, with coffee and rolls and iguana cutlets coming as fast as about ninety peons could rustle 'em.

"And then Wainwright begins to talk; but the president interrupts him.

"'You Yankees,' says he, polite, 'assuredly take the cake for assurance, I assure you'—or words to that effect. He spoke English better than you or me. 'You've had a long walk,' says he, 'but it's nicer in the cool morning to walk than to ride. May I suggest some refreshments?' says he.

"'Rum,' says Wainwright.

"'Gimme a cigar,' says I.

"Well, sir, the two talked an hour, keeping the generals and equities all in their good uniforms waiting outside the fence. And while I smoked, silent, I listened to Clifford Wainwright making a solid republic out of the wreck of one. I didn't follow his arguments with any special collocation of international intelligibility; but he had Mr. Gomez's attention glued and riveted. He takes out a pencil and marks the white linen tablecloth all over with figures and estimates and deductions. He speaks more or less disrespectfully of import and export duties and custom-house receipts and taxes and treaties and budgets and concessions and such truck that politics and government require; and when he gets through the Gomez man hops up and shakes his hand and says he's saved the country and the people.

"'You shall be rewarded,' says the President.

"'Might I suggest another—rum?' says Wainwright.

"'Cigar for me—darker brand,' says I.

"Well, sir, the president sent me and Wainwright back to the town in a victoria hitched to two flea-bitten selling-platers—but the best the country afforded.

"I found out afterwards that Wainwright was a regular beachcomber—the smartest man on the whole coast, but kept down by rum. I liked him.

"One day I inveigled him into a walk out a couple of miles from the village, where there was an old grass hut on the bank of a little river. While he was sitting on the grass, talking beautiful of the wisdom of the world that he had learned in books, I took hold of him easy and tied his hands and feet together with leather thongs that I had in my pocket.

" 'Lie still,' says I, 'and meditate on the exigencies and irregularities of life till I get back.'

"I went to a shack in Aguas Frescas where a mighty wise girl named Timotea Carrizo lived with her mother. The girl was just about as nice as you ever saw. In the States she would have been called a brunette; but she was better than a brunette—I should say she was what you might term an écru shade. I knew her pretty well. I told her about my friend Wainwright. She gave me a double handful of bark—calisaya, I think it was—and some more herbs that I was to mix with it, and told me what to do. I was to make tea of it and give it to him, and keep him from rum for a certain time. And for two weeks I did it. You know, I liked Wainwright. Both of us was broke; but Timotea sent us goat-meat and plantains and tortillas every day; and at last I got the curse of drink lifted from Clifford Wainwright. He lost his taste for it. And in the cool of the evening him and me would sit on the roof of Timotea's mother's hut, eating harmless truck like coffee and rice and stewed crabs, and playing the accordion.

"About that time President Gomez found out that the advice of C. Wainwright was the stuff he had been looking for. The country was pulling out of debt, and the treasury had enough boodle in it for him to amuse himself occasionally with the night-latch. The people were beginning to take their two-hour siestas again every day—which was the surest sign of prosperity.

"So down from the regular capital he sends for Clifford Wainwright and makes him his private secretary at twenty thousand Peru dollars a year. Yes, sir—so much. Wainwright was on the water-wagon—thanks to me and Timotea—and he was soon in clover with the government gang. Don't forget what done it—calisaya bark with them other herbs mixed—make a tea of it, and give a cupful every two hours. Try it yourself. It takes away the desire.

"As I said, a man can do a lot more for another party than he can for himself. Wainwright, with his brains, got a whole country out of trouble and on its feet; but what could he do for himself? And without any special brains, but with some nerve and common sense, I put him on his feet because I never had the weakness that he did—nothing but a cigar for mine, thanks. And——"

Trotter paused. I looked at his tattered clothes and at his deeply sunburnt, hard, thoughtful face.

"Didn't Cartright ever offer to do anything for you?" I asked.

"Wainwright," corrected Trotter. "Yes, he offered me some pretty good jobs. But I'd have had to leave Aguas Frescas; so I didn't take any of 'em up. Say, I didn't tell you much about that girl—Timotea. We rather hit it off together. She was as good as you find 'em anywhere—Spanish, mostly, with just a twist of lemon-peel on top. What if they did live in a grass hut and went bare-armed?

"A month ago," went on Trotter, "she went away. I don't know where to. But——"

"You'd better come back to the States," I insisted. "I can promise you positively that my brother will give you a position in cotton, sugar, or sheetings—I am not certain which."

"I think she went back with her mother," said Trotter, "to the village in the mountains that they come from. Tell me, what would this job you speak of pay?"

"Why," said I, hesitating over commerce, "I should say fifty or a hundred dollars a month—maybe two hundred."

"Ain't it funny," said Trotter, digging his toes in the sand, "what a chump a man is when it comes to paddling his own canoe? I don't know. Of course,

I'm not making a living here. I'm on the bum. But—well, I wish you could have seen that Timotea. Every man has his own weak spot."

The gig from the *Andador* was coming ashore to take out the captain, purser, and myself, the lone passenger.

"I'll guarantee," said I, confidently, "that my brother will pay you seventy-five dollars a month."

"All right, then," said William Trotter. "I'll——"

But a soft voice called across the blazing sands. A girl, faintly lemon-tinted, stood in the Calle Real and called. She was bare-armed—but what of that?

"It's her!" said William Trotter, looking. "She's come back! I'm obliged; but I can't take the job. Thanks, just the same. Ain't it funny how we can't do nothing for ourselves, but we can do wonders for the other fellow? You was about to get me with your financial proposition; but we've all got our weak points. Timotea's mine. And, say!" Trotter had turned to leave, but he retraced the step or two that he had taken. "I like to have left you without saying goodbye," said he. "It kind of rattles you when they go away unexpected for a month and come back the same way. Shake hands. So long! Say, do you remember them gunshots we heard a while ago up at the cuartel? Well, I knew what they was, but I didn't mention it. It was Clifford Wainwright being shot by a squad of soldiers against a stone wall for giving away secrets of state to that Nicamala republic. Oh, yes, it was rum that did it. He backslided and got his. I guess we all have our weak points, and can't do much toward helping ourselves. Mine's waiting for me. I'd have liked to have that job with your brother, but—we've all got our weak points. So long!"

IV

A big black Carib carried me on his back through the surf to the ship's boat. On the way the purser handed me a letter that he had brought for me at the last moment from the post-office in Aguas Frescas. It was from my brother. He requested me to meet him at the St. Charles Hotel in New Orleans and accept a position with his house—in either cotton, sugar, or sheetings, and with five thousand dollars a year as my salary.

When I arrived at the Crescent City I hurried away—far away from the St. Charles to a dim *chambre garnie* in Bienville Street. And there, looking down from my attic window from time to time at the old, yellow, absinthe house across the street, I wrote this story to buy my bread and butter.

"Can thim that helps others help thimselves?"

THE MARIONETTES

[Originally published in *The Black Cat* for April, 1902, The Short Story Publishing Co.]

THE policeman was standing at the corner of Twenty-fourth Street and a prodigiously dark alley near where the elevated railroad crosses the street. The time was two o'clock in the morning; the outlook a stretch of cold, drizzling, unsociable blackness until the dawn.

A man, wearing a long overcoat, with his hat tilted down in front, and carrying something in one hand, walked softly but rapidly out of the black alley. The policeman accosted him civilly, but with the assured air that is linked with conscious authority. The hour, the alley's musty reputation, the pedestrian's haste, the burden he carried—these easily combined into the "suspicious circumstances" that required illumination at the officer's hands.

The "suspect" halted readily and tilted back his hat, exposing, in the flicker of the electric lights, an emotionless, smooth countenance with a rather long nose and steady dark eyes. Thrusting his gloved hand into a side pocket of his overcoat, he drew out a card and handed it to the policeman. Holding it to catch the uncertain light, the officer read the name "Charles Spencer James, M.D." The street and number of the address were of a neighborhood so solid and respectable as to subdue even curiosity. The policeman's downward glance at the article carried in the doctor's hand—a handsome medicine case of black leather, with small silver mountings—further endorsed the guarantee of the card.

"All right, doctor," said the officer, stepping aside, with an air of bulky affability. "Orders are to be extra careful. Good many burglars and hold-ups lately. Bad night to be out. Not so cold, but—clammy."

With a formal inclination of his head, and a word or two corroborative of the officer's estimate of the weather, Doctor James continued his somewhat rapid progress. Three times that night had a patrolman accepted his professional card and the sight of his paragon of a medicine case as vouchers for his honesty of person and purpose. Had any one of those officers seen fit, on the morrow, to test the evidence of that card he would have found it borne out by the doctor's name on a handsome doorplate, his presence, calm and well dressed, in his well-equipped office—provided it were not too early, Doctor James being a late riser—and the testimony of the neighborhood to his good citizenship, his devotion to his family, and his success as a practitioner the two years he had lived among them.

Therefore, it would have much surprised any one of those zealous guardians of the peace could they have taken a peep into that immaculate medicine case. Upon opening it, the first article to be seen would have been an elegant set of the latest conceived tools used by the "box man," as the ingenious safe burglar now denominates himself. Specially designed and constructed were the implements—the short but powerful "jimmy," the collection of curiously fashioned keys, the blued drills and punches of the finest temper—capable of eating their way into chilled steel as a mouse eats into a cheese, and the clamps that fasten like a leech to the polished door of a safe and pull out the combination knob as a dentist extracts a tooth. In a little pouch in the inner side of the "medicine" case was a four-ounce vial of nitroglycerine, now half empty. Underneath the tools was a mass of crumpled banknotes and a few handfuls of gold coin, the money, altogether, amounting to eight hundred and thirty dollars.

To a very limited circle of friends Doctor James was known as "The Swell 'Greek.'" Half of the mysterious term was a tribute to his cool and gentlemanlike manners; the other half denoted, in the argot of the brotherhood, the leader, the planner, the one who, by the power and prestige of his address and position, secured the information upon which they based their plans and desperate enterprises.

Of this elect circle the other members were Skitsie Morgan and Gum Decker, expert "box men," and Leopold Pretzfelder, a jeweller down town, who manipulated the "sparklers" and other ornaments collected by the working trio. All good and loyal men, as loose-tongued as Memnon and as fickle as the North Star.

That night's work had not been considered by the firm to have yielded more than a moderate repayal for their pains. An old-style two-story side-bolt safe in the dingy office of a very wealthy old-style dry-goods firm on a Saturday night should have excreted more than twenty-five hundred dollars. But that was all they found, and they had divided it, the three of them, into equal shares upon the spot, as was their custom. Ten or twelve thousand was what they expected. But one of the proprietors had proved to be just a trifle too old style. Just after dark he had carried home in a shirt box most of the funds on hand.

Doctor James proceeded up Twenty-fourth Street, which was, to all appearance, depopulated. Even the theatrical folk, who affect this district as a place of residence, were long since abed. The drizzle had accumulated upon the street; puddles of it among the stones received the fire of the arc lights, and returned it, shattered into a myriad liquid spangles. A captious wind, shower-soaked and chilling, coughed from the laryngeal flues between the houses.

As the practitioner's foot struck even with the corner of a tall brick residence of more pretension than its fellows the front door popped open, and a bawling negress clattered down the steps to the pavement. Some medley of words came forth from her mouth, addressed, like as not, to herself—the recourse of her race when alone and beset by evil. She looked to be one of that old vassal class of the South—voluble, familiar, loyal, irrepressible; her person pictured it—fat, neat, aproned, kerchiefed.

This sudden apparition, spewed from the silent house, reached the bottom of the steps as Doctor James came opposite. Her brain transferring its energies from sound to sight, she ceased her clamor and fixed her pop-eyes upon the case the doctor carried.

"Bress de Lawd!" was the benison the sight drew from her. "Is you a doctor, suh?"

"Yes, I am a physician," said Doctor James, pausing.

"Den fo' God's sake come and see Mister Chandler, suh. He done had a fit or sump'n. He layin' jist like he wuz dead. Miss Amy sont me to git a doctor. Lawd knows whar old Cindy'd a skeared one up from, if you, suh, hadn't come along. Ef old Mar's knowed one ten-hundredth part of dese doin's dey'd be shootin' gwine on, suh—pistol shootin'—leb'm feet marked off on de ground, and ev'ybody a-duellin'. And dat po' lamb, Miss Amy——"

"Lead the way," said Doctor James, setting his foot upon the step, "if you want me as a doctor. As an auditor I'm not open to engagements."

The negress preceded him into the house and up a flight of thickly carpeted stairs. Twice they came to dimly lighted branching hallways. At the second one the now panting conductress turned down a hall, stopping at a door and opening it.

"I done brought de doctor, Miss Amy."

Doctor James entered the room, and bowed slightly to a young lady standing by the side of a bed. He set his medicine case upon a chair, removed his overcoat, throwing it over the case and the back of the chair, and advanced with quiet self-possession to the bedside.

There lay a man, sprawling as he had fallen—a man dressed richly in the prevailing mode, with only his shoes removed; lying relaxed, and as still as the dead.

There emanated from Doctor James an aura of calm force and reserve strength that was as manna in the desert to the weak and desolate among his patrons. Always had women, especially, been attracted by something in his sick-room manner. It was not the indulgent suavity of the fashionable healer, but a manner of poise, of sureness, of ability to overcome fate, of deference and protection and devotion. There was an exploring magnetism in his steadfast, luminous brown eyes; a latent authority in the impassive, even priestly, tranquillity of his smooth countenance that outwardly fitted him for the part of confidant and consoler. Sometimes, at his first professional visit, women would tell him where they hid their diamonds at night from the burglars.

With the ease of much practice, Doctor James's unroving eyes estimated the order and quality of the room's furnishings. The appointments were rich and costly. The same glance had secured cognizance of the lady's appearance. She was small and scarcely past twenty. Her face possessed the title to a winsome prettiness, now obscured by (you would say) rather a fixed melancholy than the more violent imprint of a sudden sorrow. Upon her forehead, above one eyebrow, was a livid bruise, suffered, the physician's eye told him, within the past six hours.

Doctor James's fingers went to the man's wrist. His almost vocal eyes questioned the lady.

"I am Mrs. Chandler," she responded, speaking with the plaintive Southern slur and intonation. "My husband was taken suddenly ill about ten minutes before you came. He has had attacks of heart trouble before—some of them were very bad." His clothed state and the late hour seemed to prompt her to further explanation. "He had been out late; to—a supper, I believe."

Doctor James now turned his attention to his patient. In whichever of his "professions" he happened to be engaged he was wont to honor the "case" or the "job" with his whole interest.

The sick man appeared to be about thirty. His countenance bore a look of boldness and dissipation, but was not without a symmetry of feature and the fine lines drawn by a taste and indulgence in humor that gave the redeeming touch. There was an odor of spilled wine about his clothes.

The physician laid back his outer garments, and then, with a penknife, slit the shirt-front from collar to waist. The obstacles cleared, he laid his ear to the heart and listened intently.

"Mitral regurgitation?" he said, softly, when he rose. The words ended with the rising inflection of uncertainty. Again he listened long; and this time he said, "Mitral insufficiency," with the accent of an assured diagnosis.

"Madam," he began, in the reassuring tones that had so often allayed anxiety, "there is a probability——" As he slowly turned his head to face the lady, he saw her fall, white and swooning, into the arms of the old negress.

"Po' lamb! po' lamb! Has dey done killed Aunt Cindy's own blessed child? May de Lawd 'stroy wid his wrath dem what stole her away; what break dat angel heart; what left——"

"Lift her feet," said Doctor James, assisting to support the drooping form. "Where is her room? She must be put to bed."

"In here, suh." The woman nodded her kerchiefed head toward a door. "Dat's Miss Amy's room."

They carried her in there, and laid her on the bed. Her pulse was faint, but regular. She passed from the swoon, without recovering consciousness, into a profound slumber.

"She is quite exhausted," said the physician. "Sleep is a good remedy. When she wakes, give her a toddy—with an egg in it, if she can take it. How did she get that bruise upon her forehead?"

"She done got a lick there, suh. De po' lamb fell—— No, suh"—the old woman's racial mutability swept her in a sudden flare of indignation—"old Cindy ain't gwineter lie for dat debble. He done it, suh. May de Lawd wither de hand what—dar now! Cindy promise her sweet lamb she ain't gwine tell. Miss Amy got hurt, suh, on de head."

Doctor James stepped to a stand where a handsome lamp burned, and turned the flame low.

"Stay here with your mistress," he ordered, "and keep quiet so she will sleep. If she wakes, give her the toddy. If she grows any weaker, let me know. There is something strange about it."

"Dar's mo' strange t'ings dan dat 'round here," began the negress, but the physician hushed her in a seldom-employed peremptory, concentrated voice with which he had often allayed hysteria itself. He returned to the other room, closing the door softly behind him. The man on the bed had not moved, but his eyes were open. His lips seemed to form words. Doctor James bent his head to listen. "The money! the money!" was what they were whispering.

"Can you understand what I say?" asked the doctor, speaking low, but distinctly.

The head nodded slightly.

"I am a physician, sent for by your wife. You are Mr. Chandler, I am told. You are quite ill. You must not excite or distress yourself at all."

The patient's eyes seemed to beckon to him. The doctor stooped to catch the same faint words.

"The money—the twenty thousand dollars."

"Where is this money?—in the bank?"

The eyes expressed a negative. "Tell her"—the whisper was growing fainter—"the twenty thousand dollars—her money"—his eyes wandered about the room.

"You have placed this money somewhere?"—Doctor James's voice was toiling like a siren's to conjure the secret from the man's failing intelligence—"Is it in this room?"

He thought he saw a fluttering assent in the dimming eyes. The pulse under his fingers was as fine and small as a silk thread.

There arose in Doctor James's brain and heart the instincts of his other profession. Promptly, as he acted in everything, he decided to learn the whereabouts of this money, and at the calculated and certain cost of a human life.

Drawing from his pocket a little pad of prescription blanks, he scribbled upon one of them a formula suited, according to the best practice, to the needs of the sufferer. Going to the door of the inner room, he softly called the old woman, gave her the prescription, and bade her take it to some drug store and fetch the medicine.

When she had gone, muttering to herself, the doctor stepped to the bedside of the lady. She still slept soundly; her pulse was a little stronger; her forehead was cool, save where the inflammation of the bruise extended, and a slight moisture covered it. Unless disturbed, she would yet sleep for hours. He found the key in the door, and locked it after him when he returned.

Doctor James looked at his watch. He could call half an hour his own, since before that time the old woman could scarcely return from her mission. Then he sought and found water in a pitcher and a glass tumbler. Opening his medicine case he took out the vial containing the nitroglycerine—"the oil," as his brethren of the brace-and-bit, term it.

One drop of the faint yellow, thickish liquid he let fall in the tumbler. He took out his silver hypodermic syringe case, and screwed the needle into its place. Carefully measuring each modicum of water in the graduated glass barrel of the syringe, he diluted the one drop with nearly half a tumbler of water.

Two hours earlier that night Doctor James had, with that syringe, injected the undiluted liquid into a hole drilled in the lock of a safe, and had destroyed, with one dull explosion, the machinery that controlled the movement of the bolts. He now purposed, with the same means, to shiver the prime machinery of a human being—to rend its heart—and each shock was for the sake of the money to follow.

The same means, but in a different guise. Whereas, that was the giant in its rude, primary dynamic strength, this was the courtier, whose no less deadly arms were concealed by velvet and lace. For the liquid in the tumbler and in the syringe that the physician carefully filled was now a solution of glonoin, the most powerful heart stimulant known to medical science. Two ounces had riven the solid door of the iron safe; with one fiftieth part of a minim he was now about to still forever the intricate mechanism of a human life.

But not immediately. It was not so intended. First there would be a quick increase of vitality; a powerful impetus given to every organ and faculty. The heart would respond bravely to the fatal spur; the blood in the veins return more rapidly to its source.

But, as Doctor James well knew, over-stimulation in this form of heart disease means death, as sure as by a rifle shot. When the clogged arteries should suffer congestion from the increased flow of blood pumped into them by the power of the burglar's "oil," they would rapidly become "no thoroughfare," and the fountain of life would cease to flow.

The physician bared the chest of the unconscious Chandler. Easily and skilfully he injected, subcutaneously, the contents of the syringe into the muscles of the region over the heart. True to his neat habits in both professions, he next carefully dried his needle and re-inserted the fine wire that threaded it when not in use.

In three minutes Chandler opened his eyes, and spoke, in a voice faint but audible, inquiring who attended upon him. Doctor James again explained his presence there.

"Where is my wife?" asked the patient.

"She is asleep—from exhaustion and worry," said the doctor. "I would not awaken her, unless——"

"It isn't—necessary." Chandler spoke with spaces between his words caused by his short breath that some demon was driving too fast. "She wouldn't—thank you to disturb her—on my—account."

Doctor James drew a chair to the bedside. Conversation must not be squandered.

"A few minutes ago," he began, in the grave, candid tones of his other profession, "you were trying to tell me something regarding some money. I do not seek your confidence, but it is my duty to advise you that anxiety and worry will work against your recovery. If you have any communication to make about this—to relieve your mind about this—twenty thousand dollars, I think was the amount you mentioned—you would better do so."

Chandler could not turn his head, but he rolled his eyes in the direction of the speaker.

"Did I—say where this—money is?"

"No," answered the physician. "I only inferred, from your scarcely intelligible words, that you felt a solicitude concerning its safety. If it is in this room——"

Doctor James paused. Did he only seem to perceive a flicker of understanding, a gleam of suspicion upon the ironical features of his patient? Had he seemed too eager? Had he said too much? Chandler's next words restored his confidence.

"Where—should it be," he gasped, "but in—the safe—there?"

With his eyes he indicated a corner of the room, where now, for the first time, the doctor perceived a small iron safe, half-concealed by the trailing end of a window curtain.

Rising, he took the sick man's wrist. His pulse was beating in great throbs, with ominous intervals between.

"Lift your arm," said Doctor James.

"You know—I can't move, Doctor."

The physician stepped swiftly to the hall door, opened it, and listened. All was still. Without further circumvention he went to the safe, and examined it. Of a primitive make and simple design, it afforded a little more security than protection against light-fingered servants. To his skill it was a mere toy, a thing of straw and pasteboard. The money was as good as in his hands. With his clamps he could draw the knob, punch the tumblers, and open the door in two minutes. Perhaps, in another way, he might open it in one.

Kneeling upon the floor, he laid his ear to the combination plate, and slowly turned the knob. As he had surmised, it was locked at only a "day com."—upon one number. His keen ear caught the faint warning click as the tumbler was disturbed; he used the clue—the handle turned. He swung the door wide open.

The interior of the safe was bare—not even a scrap of paper rested within the hollow iron cube.

Doctor James rose to his feet and walked back to the bed.

A thick dew had formed upon the dying man's brow, but there was a mocking, grim smile on his lips and in his eyes.

"I never—saw it before," he said, painfully, "medicine and—burglary wedded! Do you—make the—combination pay—dear Doctor?"

Than that situation afforded, there was never a more rigorous test of Doctor James's greatness. Trapped by the diabolic humor of his victim into a position both ridiculous and unsafe, he maintained his dignity as well as his presence of mind. Taking out his watch, he waited for the man to die.

"You were—just a shade—too—anxious—about that money. But it never was—in any danger—from you, dear Doctor. It's safe. Perfectly safe. It's all—in the hands—of the bookmakers. Twenty—thousand—Amy's money. I played it at the races—lost every—cent of it. I've been a pretty bad boy, Burglar—excuse me—Doctor, but I've been a square sport. I don't think—I ever met—such an—eighteen-carat rascal as you are, Doctor—excuse me—Burglar, in all my rounds. Is it contrary—to the ethics—of your—gang, Burglar, to give a victim—excuse me—patient, a drink of water?"

Doctor James brought him a drink. He could scarcely swallow it. The reaction from the powerful drug was coming in regular, intensifying waves. But his moribund fancy must have one more grating fling.

"Gambler—drunkard—spendthrift—I've been those, but—a doctor-burglar!"

The physician indulged himself to but one reply to the other's caustic taunts. Bending low to catch Chandler's fast crystallizing gaze, he pointed to the sleeping lady's door with a gesture so stern and significant that the prostrate man half-lifted his head, with his remaining strength, to see. He saw nothing; but he caught the cold words of the doctor—the last sounds he was to hear:

"I never yet—struck a woman."

It were vain to attempt to con such men. There is no curriculum that can reckon with them in its ken. They are offshoots from the types whereof men say, "He will do this," or "He will do that." We only know that they exist; and that we can observe them, and tell one another of their bare performances, as children watch and speak of the marionettes.

Yet it were a droll study in egoism to consider these two—one an assassin and a robber, standing above his victim; the other baser in his offences, if a lesser law-breaker, lying, abhorred, in the house of the wife he had persecuted, spoiled, and smitten, one a tiger, the other a dog-wolf—to consider each of them sickening at the foulness of the other; and each flourishing out of the mire of his manifest guilt his own immaculate standard—of conduct, if not of honor.

The one retort of Doctor James must have struck home to the other's remaining shreds of shame and manhood, for it proved the *coup de grâce*. A deep blush suffused his face—an ignominious *rosa mortis;* the respiration ceased, and, with scarcely a tremor, Chandler expired.

Close following upon his last breath came the negress, bringing the medicine. With a hand gently pressing upon the closed eyelids, Doctor James told her of the end. Not grief, but a hereditary *rapprochement* with death in the abstract, moved her to a dismal, watery sniffling, accompanied by her usual jeremiad.

"Dar now! It's in de Lawd's hands. He am de jedge ob de transgressor, and de suppo't of dem in distress. He gwine hab suppo't us now. Cindy done paid out de last quarter fer dis bottle of physic, and it nebber come to no use."

"Do I understand," asked Doctor James, "that Mrs. Chandler has no money?"

"Money, suh? You know what make Miss Amy fall down and so weak? Stahvation, suh. Nothin' to eat in dis house but some crumbly crackers in three days. Dat angel sell her finger rings and watch mont's ago. Dis fine house, suh, wid de red cyarpets and shiny bureaus, it's all hired; and de man talkin' scan'lous about de rent. Dat debble—'scuse me, Lawd—he done in Yo' hands fer jedgment, now—he made way wid everything."

The physician's silence encouraged her to continue. The history that he gleaned from Cindy's disordered monologue was an old one, of illusion, wilfulness, disaster, cruelty, and pride. Standing out from the blurred panorama of her gabble were little clear pictures—an ideal home in the far South; a quickly repented marriage; an unhappy season, full of wrongs and abuse, and, of late, an inheritance of money that promised deliverance; its seizure and waste by the dog-wolf during a two months' absence, and his return in the midst of a scandalous carouse. Unobtruded, but visible between every line, ran a pure white thread through the smudged warp of the story—the simple, all-enduring, sublime love of the old negress, following her mistress unswervingly through everything to the end.

When at last she paused, the physician spoke, asking if the house contained whiskey or liquor of any sort. There was, the old woman informed him, half a bottle of brandy left in the sideboard by the dog-wolf.

"Prepare a toddy as I told you," said Doctor James. "Wake your mistress; have her drink it, and tell her what has happened."

Some ten minutes afterward, Mrs. Chandler entered, supported by old Cindy's arm. She appeared to be a little stronger since her sleep and the stimulant she had taken. Doctor James had covered, with a sheet, the form upon the bed.

The lady turned her mournful eyes once, with a half-frightened look, toward it, and pressed closer to her protector. Her eyes were dry and bright. Sorrow seemed to have done its utmost with her. The fount of tears was dried; feeling itself paralyzed.

Doctor James was standing near the table, his overcoat donned, his hat and medicine case in his hand. His face was calm and impassive—practice had inured him to the sight of human suffering. His lambent brown eyes alone expressed a discreet professional sympathy.

He spoke kindly and briefly, stating that, as the hour was late, and assistance, no doubt, difficult to procure, he would himself send the proper persons to attend to the necessary finalities.

"One matter, in conclusion," said the doctor, pointing to the safe with its still wide-open door. "Your husband, Mrs. Chandler, toward the end, felt that he could not live; and directed me to open that safe, giving me the number upon which the combination is set. In case you may need to use it, you will remember that the number is forty-one. Turn several times to the right; then to the left once; stop at forty-one. He would not permit me to waken you, though he knew the end was near.

"In that safe he said he had placed a sum of money not large—but enough to enable you to carry out his last request. That was that you should return to your old home, and, in after days, when time shall have made it easier, forgive his many sins against you."

He pointed to the table, where lay an orderly pile of banknotes, surmounted by two stacks of gold coins.

"The money is there—as he described it—eight hundred and thirty dollars. I beg to leave my card with you, in case I can be of any service later on."

So, he had thought of her—and kindly—at the last! So late! And yet the lie fanned into life one last spark of tenderness where she had thought all was turned to ashes and dust. She cried aloud "Rob! Rob!" She turned, and, upon the ready bosom of her true servitor, diluted her grief in relieving tears. It is well to think, also, that in the years to follow, the murderer's falsehood shone like a little star above the grave of love, comforting her, and gaining the forgiveness that is good in itself, whether asked for or no.

Hushed and soothed upon the dark bosom, like a child, by a crooning, babbling sympathy, at last she raised her head—but the doctor was gone.

THE MARQUIS AND MISS SALLY

[Originally published in *Everybody's Magazine*, June, 1903.]

WITHOUT knowing it, Old Bill Bascom had the honor of being overtaken by fate the same day with the Marquis of Borodale.

The Marquis lived in Regent Square, London. Old Bill lived on Limping Doe Creek, Hardeman County, Texas. The cataclysm that engulfed the Marquis took the form of a bursting bubble known as the Central and South American Mahogany and Caoutchouc Monopoly. Old Bill's Nemesis was in the no less perilous shape of a band of civilized Indian cattle thieves from the Territory who ran off his entire herd of four hundred head, and shot old Bill dead as he trailed after them. To even up the consequences of the two catastrophes, the Marquis, as soon as he found that all he possessed would pay only fifteen shillings on the pound of his indebtedness, shot himself.

Old Bill left a family of six motherless sons and daughters, who found themselves without even a red steer left to eat or a red cent to buy one with.

The Marquis left one son, a young man, who had come to the States and established a large and well-stocked ranch in the Panhandle of Texas. When this young man learned the news he mounted his pony and rode to town. There he placed everything he owned except his horse, saddle, Winchester, and fifteen dollars in his pockets, in the hands of his lawyers, with instructions to sell and forward the proceeds to London to be applied upon the payment of his father's debts. Then he mounted his pony and rode southward.

One day, arriving about the same time, but by different trails, two young chaps rode up to the Diamond-Cross ranch, on the Little Piedra, and asked for work. Both were dressed neatly and sprucely in cowboy costume. One was a straight-set fellow, with delicate, handsome features, short brown hair, and smooth face, sunburned to a golden brown. The other applicant was stouter and broad-shouldered, with fresh red complexion, somewhat freckled, reddish, curling hair, and a rather plain face, made attractive by laughing eyes and a pleasant mouth.

The superintendent of the Diamond-Cross was of the opinion that he could give them work. In fact, word had reached him that morning that the camp cook—a most important member of the outfit—had straddled his broncho and departed, being unable to withstand the fire of fun and practical jokes of which he was, ex officio, the legitimate target.

"Can either of you cook?" asked the superintendent.

"I can," said the reddish-haired fellow, promptly. "I've cooked in camp quite a lot. I'm willing to take the job until you've got something else to offer."

"Now, that's the way I like to hear a man talk," said the superintendent, approvingly. "I'll give you a note to Saunders, and he'll put you to work."

Thus the names of John Bascom and Charles Norwood were added to the payroll of the Diamond-Cross. The two left for the round-up camp immediately after dinner. Their directions were simple, but sufficient: "Keep down the arroyo for fifteen miles till you get there." Both being strangers from afar, young, spirited, and thus thrown together by chance for a long ride, it is likely that the comradeship that afterward existed so strongly between them began that afternoon as they meandered along the little valley of the Candad Verda.

They reached their destination just after sunset. The main camp of the round-up was comfortably located on the bank of a long water-hole, under a fine mott of timber. A number of small A tents pitched upon grassy spots and the big wall tent for provisions showed that the camp was intended to be occupied for a considerable length of time.

The round-up had ridden in but a few moments before, hungry and tired, to a supperless camp. The boys were engaged in an emulous display of anathemas supposed to fit the case of the absconding cook. While they were unsaddling and hobbling their ponies, the newcomers rode in and inquired for Pink Saunders. The boss of the round-up came forth and was given the superintendent's note.

Pink Saunders, though a boss during working hours, was a humorist in camp, where everybody, from cook to superintendent, is equal. After reading the note he waved his hand toward the camp and shouted, ceremoniously, at the top of his voice, "Gentlemen, allow me to present to you the Marquis and Miss Sally."

At the words both the new arrivals betrayed confusion. The newly employed cook started, with a surprised look on his face, but, immediately recollecting that "Miss Sally" is the generic name for the male cook in every west Texas cow camp, he recovered his composure with a grin at his own expense.

His companion showed little less discomposure, even turning angrily, with a bitten lip, and reaching for his saddle pommel, as if to remount his pony; but "Miss Sally" touched his arm and said, laughingly, "Come now, Marquis; that was quite a compliment from Saunders. It's that distinguished air of yours and aristocratic nose that made him call you that."

He began to unsaddle, and the Marquis, restored to equanimity, followed his example. Rolling up his sleeves, Miss Sally sprang for the grub wagon, shouting:

"I'm the new cook b'thunder! Some of you chaps rustle a little wood for a fire, and I'll guarantee you a hot square meal inside of thirty minutes." Miss Sally's energy and good-humor as he ransacked the grub wagon for coffee, flour, and bacon, won the good opinion of the camp instantly.

And also, in days following, the Marquis, after becoming better acquainted, proved to be a cheerful, pleasant fellow, always a little reserved, and taking no part in the rough camp frolics; but the boys gradually came to respect this reserve—which fitted the title Saunders had given him—and even to like him for it. Saunders had assigned him to a place holding the herd during the cuttings. He proved to be a skilful rider and as good with the lariat or in the branding pen as most of them.

The Marquis and Miss Sally grew to be quite close comrades. After supper was over, and everything cleaned up, you would generally find them together, Miss Sally smoking his brier-root pipe, and the Marquis plaiting a quirt or scraping rawhide for a new pair of hobbles.

The superintendent did not forget his promise to keep an eye on the cook. Several times, when visiting the camp, he held long talks with him. He seemed to have taken a fancy to Miss Sally. One afternoon he rode up, on his way back to the ranch from a tour of the camps, and said to him:

"There'll be a man here in the morning to take your place. As soon as he shows up you come to the ranch. I want you to take charge of the ranch accounts and correspondence. I want somebody that I can depend upon to keep things straight when I'm away. The wages'll be all right. The Diamond-Cross 'll hold its end up with a man who'll look after its interests."

"All right," said Miss Sally, as quietly as if he had expected the notice all along. "Any objections to my bringing my wife down to the ranch?"

"You married?" said the superintendent, frowning a little. "You didn't mention it when we were talking."

"Because I'm not," said the cook. "But I'd like to be. Thought I'd wait till I got a job under roof. I couldn't ask her to live in a cow camp."

"Right," agreed the superintendent. "A camp isn't quite the place for a married man—but—well, there's plenty of room at the house, and if you suit us as well as I think you will you can afford it. You write to her to come on."

"All right," said Miss Sally again, "I'll ride in as soon as I am relieved to-morrow."

It was a rather chilly night, and after supper the cow-punchers were lounging about a big fire of dried mesquite chunks.

Their usual exchange of jokes and repartee had dwindled almost to silence, but silence in a cow camp generally betokens the brewing of mischief.

Miss Sally and the Marquis were seated upon a log, discussing the relative merits of the lengthened or shortened stirrup in long-distance riding. The Marquis arose presently and went to a tree near by to examine some strips of rawhide he was seasoning for making a lariat. Just as he left a little puff of wind blew some scraps of tobacco from a cigarette that Dry-Creek Smithers was rolling, into Miss Sally's eyes. While the cook was rubbing at them, with tears flowing. "Phonograph" Davis—so called on account of his strident voice—arose and began a speech.

"Fellers and citizens! I desire to perpound a interrogatory. What is the most grievous spectacle what the human mind can contemplate?"

A volley of answers responded to his question.

"A busted flush!"

"A Maverick when you ain't got your branding iron!"

"Yourself!"

"The hole in the end of some other feller's gun!"

"Shet up, you ignoramuses," said old Taller, the fat cow-puncher. "Phony knows what it is. He's waitin' for to tell us."

"No, fellers and citizens," continued Phonograph. "Them spectacles you've e-numerated air shore grievous, and way up yonder close to the so-lution, but they ain't it. The most grievous spectacle air that"—he pointed to Miss Sally, who was still rubbing his streaming eyes—"a trustin' and a in-veegled female a-weepin' tears on account of her heart bein' busted by a false deceiver. Air we men or air we catamounts to gaze upon the blightin' of our Miss Sally's affections by a a-risto-crat, which has come among us with his superior beauty and his glitterin' title to give the weeps to the lovely critter we air bound to pertect? Air we goin' to act like men, or air we goin' to keep on eatin' soggy chuck from her cryin' so plentiful over the bread-pan?"

"It's a gallopin' shame," said Dry-Creek, with a sniffle. "It ain't human. I've noticed the varmint a-palaverin' round her frequent. And him a Marquis! Ain't that a title, Phony?"

"It's somethin' like a king," the Brushy Creek Kid hastened to explain, "only lower in the deck. Guess it comes in between the Jack and the ten-spot."

"Don't misconstruct me," went on Phonograph, "as undervaluatin' the a-risto-crats. Some of 'em air proper people and can travel right along with the Watson boys. I've herded some with 'em myself. I've viewed the elephant with the Mayor of Fort Worth, and I've listened to the owl with the gen'ral passenger agent of the Katy, and they can keep up with the percession from where you laid the chunk. But when a Marquis monkeys with the innocent affections of a cook-lady, may I inquire what the case seems to call for?"

"The leathers," shouted Dry-Creek Smithers.

"You hear 'er, Charity!" was the Kid's form of corroboration.

"We've got your company," assented the cowpunchers, in chorus.

Before the Marquis realized their intention, two of them seized him by each arm and led him up to the log. Phonograph Davis, self-appointed to carry out the sentence, stood ready, with a pair of stout leather leggings in his hands.

It was the first time they had ever laid hands on the Marquis during their somewhat rude sports.

"What are you up to?" he asked, indignantly, with flashing eyes.

"Go easy, Marquis," whispered Rube Fellows, one of the boys that held him. "It's all in fun. Take it good-natured and they'll let you off light. They're only goin' to stretch you over the log and tan you eight or ten times with the leg-gin's. 'Twon't hurt much."

The Marquis, with an exclamation of anger, his white teeth gleaming, suddenly exhibited a surprising strength. He wrenched with his arms so violently that the four men were swayed and dragged many yards from the log. A cry of anger escaped him, and then Miss Sally, his eyes cleared of the tobacco, saw, and he immediately mixed with the struggling group.

But at that moment a loud "Hallo!" rang in their ears, and a buckboard drawn by a team of galloping mustangs spun into the campfire's circle of light. Every man turned to look, and what they saw drove from their minds all thoughts of carrying out Phonograph Davis's rather time-worn contribution to the evening's amusement. Bigger game than the Marquis was at hand, and his captors released him and stood staring at the approaching victim.

The buckboard and team belonged to Sam Holly, a cattleman from the Big Muddy. Sam was driving, and with him was a stout, smooth-faced man, wear-ing a frock coat and a high silk hat. That was the county judge, Mr. Dave Hackett, candidate for reëlection. Sam was escorting him about the country, among the camps, to shake up the sovereign voters.

The men got out, hitched the team to a mesquite, and walked toward the fire.

Instantly every man in camp, except the Marquis, Miss Sally, and Pink Saun-ders, who had to play host, uttered a frightful yell of assumed terror and fled on all sides into the darkness.

"Heavens alive!" exclaimed Hackett, "are we as ugly as that? How do you do, Mr. Saunders? Glad to see you again. What are you doing to my hat, Holly?"

"I was afraid of this hat," said Sam Holly, meditatively. He had taken the hat from Hackett's head and was holding it in his hand, looking dubiously around at the shadows beyond the firelight where now absolute stillness reigned. "What do you think, Saunders?"

Pink grinned.

"Better elevate it some," he said, in the tone of one giving disinterested advice. "The light ain't none too good. I wouldn't want it on my head."

Holly stepped upon the hub of a hind wheel of the grub wagon and hung the hat upon a limb of a live-oak. Scarcely had his foot touched the ground when the crash of a dozen six-shooters split the air, and the hat fell to the ground riddled with bullets.

A hissing noise was heard as if from a score of rattlesnakes, and the cow-punchers emerged on all sides from the darkness, stepping high, with ludicrously exaggerated caution, and "hist"-ing to one another to observe the utmost prudence in approaching. They formed a solemn, wide circle about the hat, gazing at it in manifest alarm, and seized every few moments by little stampedes of panicky flight.

"It's the varmint," said one in awed tones, "that flits up and down in the low grounds at night, saying, 'Willie-wallo!'"

"It's the venomous Kypootum," proclaimed another. "It stings after it's dead, and hollers after it's buried."

"It's the chief of the hairy tribe," said Phonograph Davis. "But it's stone dead, now, boys."

"Don't you believe it," demurred Dry-Creek. "It's only 'possumin'.' It's the dreaded Highgollacum fantod from the forest. There's only one way to destroy its life."

He led forward Old Taller, the 240-pound cow-puncher. Old Taller placed the hat upright on the ground and solemnly sat upon it, crushing it as flat as a pancake.

Hackett had viewed these proceedings with wide-open eyes. Sam Holly saw that his anger was rising and said to him:

"Here's where you win or lose, Judge. There are sixty votes on the Diamond Cross. The boys are trying your mettle. Take it as a joke, and I don't think you'll regret it." And Hackett saw the point and rose to the occasion.

Advancing to where the slayers of the wild beast were standing above its remains and declaring it to be at last defunct, he said, with deep earnestness:

"Boys, I must thank you for this gallant rescue. While driving through the arroyo that cruel monster that you have so fearlessly and repeatedly slaughtered sprang upon us from the tree tops. To you I shall consider that I owe my life, and also, I hope, reëlection to the office for which I am again candidate. Allow me to hand you my card."

The cow-punchers, always so sober-faced while engaged in their monkey-shines, relaxed into a grin of approval.

But Phonograph Davis, his appetite for fun not yet appeased, had something more up his sleeve.

"Pardner," he said, addressing Hackett with grave severity, "many a camp would be down on you for turnin' loose a pernicious varmint like that in it; but, bein' as we all escaped without loss of life, we'll overlook it. You can play square with us if you'll do it."

"How's that?" asked Hackett, suspiciously.

"You're authorized to perform the sacred rights and lefts of mattermony, air you not?"

"Well, yes," replied Hackett. "A marriage ceremony conducted by me would be legal."

"A wrong air to be righted in this here camp," said Phonograph, virtuously. "A a-ristocrat have slighted a 'umble but beautchoos female wat's pinin' for his affections. It's the jooty of the camp to drag forth the haughty descendant of a hundred—or maybe a hundred and twenty-five—earls, even so at the p'int of a lariat, and jine him to the weepin' lady. Fellows! round up Miss Sally and the Marquis, there's goin' to be a weddin'."

This whim of Phonograph's was received with whoops of appreciation. The cow-punchers started to apprehend the principals of the proposed ceremony.

"Kindly prompt me," said Hackett, wiping his forehead, though the night was cool, "how far this thing is to be carried. And might I expect any further portions of my raiment to be mistaken for wild animals and killed?"

"The boys are livelier than usual to-night," said Saunders. "The ones they are talking about marrying are two of the boys—a herd rider and the cook. It's another joke. You and Sam will have to sleep here to-night anyway; p'rhaps you'd better see 'em through with it. Maybe they'll quiet down after that."

The matchmakers found Miss Sally seated on the tongue of the grub wagon, calmly smoking his pipe. The Marquis was leaning idly against one of the trees under which the supply tent was pitched.

Into this tent they were both hustled, and Phonograph, as master of ceremonies, gave orders for the preparations.

"You, Dry-Creek and Jimmy, and Ben and Taller—hump yourselves to the wildwood and rustle flowers for the blow-out—mesquite'll do—and get the Spanish dagger blossom at the corner of the horse corral for the bride to pack. You, Limpy, get out that red and yaller blanket of your'n for Miss Sally's skyirt. Marquis, you'll do 'thout fixin'; nobody don't ever look at the groom."

During their absurd preparation, the two principals were left alone for a few minutes in the tent. The Marquis suddenly showed wild perturbation.

"This foolishness must not go on," he said, turning to Miss Sally a face white in the light of the lantern, hanging to the ridge-pole.

"Why not?" said the cook, with an amused smile. "It's fun for the boys; and they've always let you off pretty light in their frolics. I don't mind it."

"But you don't understand," persisted the Marquis, pleadingly. "That man is county judge, and his acts are binding. I can't—oh, you don't know——"

The cook stepped forward and took the Marquis's hands.

"Sally Bascom," he said, "I KNOW!"

"You know!" faltered the Marquis, trembling. "And you—want to——"

"More than I ever wanted anything. Will you—here come the boys!"

The cow-punchers crowded in, laden with armfuls of decorations.

"Perfidious coyote!" said Phonograph, sternly, addressing the Marquis. "Air you willing to patch up the damage you've did this ere slab-sided but trustin' bunch o' calico by single-footin' easy to the altar, or will we have to rope ye, and drag you thar?"

The Marquis pushed back his hat, and leaned jauntily against some high-piled sacks of beans. His cheeks were flushed, and his eyes were shining.

"Go on with the rat killin'," said he.

A little while after a procession approached the tree under which Hackett, Holly, and Saunders were sitting smoking.

Limpy Walker was in the lead, extracting a doleful tune on his concertina. Next came the bride and groom. The cook wore the gorgeous Navajo blanket tied around his waist and carried in one hand the waxen-white Spanish dagger blossom as large as a peck-measure and weighing fifteen pounds. His hat was ornamented with mesquite branches and yellow ratama blooms. A resurrected mosquito bar served as a veil. After them stumbled Phonograph Davis, in the character of the bride's father, weeping into a saddle blanket with sobs that could be heard a mile away. The cow-punchers followed by twos, loudly commenting upon the bride's appearance, in a supposed imitation of the audiences at fashionable weddings.

Hackett rose as the procession halted before him, and after a little lecture upon matrimony, asked:

"What are your names?"

"Sally and Charles," answered the cook.

"Join hands, Charles and Sally."

Perhaps there never was a stranger wedding. For, wedding it was, though only two of those present knew it.

When the ceremony was over, the cow-punchers gave one yell of congratulation and immediately abandoned their foolery for the night. Blankets were unrolled and sleep became the paramount question.

The cook (divested of his decorations) and the Marquis lingered for a moment in the shadow of the grub wagon. The Marquis leaned her head against his shoulder.

"I didn't know what else to do," she was saying. "Father was gone, and we kids had to rustle. I had helped him so much with the cattle that I thought

I'd turn cowboy. There wasn't anything else I could make a living at. I wasn't much stuck on it though, after I got here, and I'd have left only——"

"Only what?"

"You know. Tell me something. When did you first—what made you——"

"Oh, it was as soon as we struck the camp, when Saunders bawled out 'The Marquis and Miss Sally!' I saw how rattled you got at the name, and I had my sus——"

"Cheeky!" whispered the Marquis. "And why should you think that I thought he was calling me 'Miss Sally'?"

"Because," answered the cook, calmly, "I was the Marquis. My father was the Marquis of Borodale. But you'll excuse that, won't you, Sally? It really isn't my fault, you know."

A FOG IN SANTONE

[Published in *The Cosmopolitan*, October, 1912. Probably written in 1904, or shortly after O. Henry's first successes in New York.]

THE drug clerk looked sharply at the white face half concealed by the high-turned overcoat collar.

"I would rather not supply you," he said, doubtfully. "I sold you a dozen morphine tablets less than an hour ago."

The customer smiles wanly. "The fault is in your crooked streets. I didn't intend to call upon you twice, but I guess I got tangled up. Excuse me."

He draws his collar higher, and moves out slowly. He stops under an electric light at the corner, and juggles absorbedly with three or four little pasteboard boxes. "Thirty-six," he announces to himself. "More than plenty." For a gray mist had swept upon Santone that night, an opaque terror that laid a hand to the throat of each of the city's guests. It was computed that three thousand invalids were hibernating in the town. They had come from far and wide, for here, among these contracted river-side streets, the goddess Ozone has elected to linger.

Purest atmosphere, sir, on earth! You might think from the river winding through our town that we are malarial, but, no, sir! Repeated experiments made both by the Government and local experts show that our air contains nothing deleterious—nothing but ozone, sir, pure ozone. Litmus paper tests made all along the river show—but you can read it all in the prospectuses; or the Santonian will recite it for you, word by word.

We may achieve climate, but weather is thrust upon us. Santone, then, cannot be blamed for this cold gray fog that came and kissed the lips of the three thousand, and then delivered them to the cross. That night the tubercles, whose ravages hope holds in check, multiplied. The writhing fingers of the pale mist did not go thence bloodless. Many of the wooers of ozone capitulated with the enemy that night, turning their faces to the wall in that dumb, isolated apathy that so terrifies their watchers. On the red streams of Hemorrhagia a few souls drifted away, leaving behind pathetic heaps, white and chill as the fog itself. Two or three came to view this atmospheric wraith as the ghost of impossible joys, sent to whisper to them of the egregious folly it is to inhale breath into the lungs, only to exhale it again, and these used whatever came handy to their relief, pistols, gas, or the beneficent muriate.

The purchaser of the morphine wanders into the fog, and at length finds himself upon a little iron bridge, one of the score or more in the heart of the city, under which the small tortuous river flows. He leans on the rail and gasps, for here the mist has concentrated, lying like a footpad to garrote such of the Three Thousand as creep that way. The iron bridge guys rattle to the strain of his cough, a mocking phthisical rattle, seeming to say to him: "Clickety-clack! just a little rusty cold, sir—but not from our river. Litmus paper all along the banks and nothing but ozone. Clacket-y-clack!"

The Memphis man at last recovers sufficiently to be aware of another over-coated man ten feet away, leaning on the rail, and just coming out of a paroxysm. There is a freemasonry among the Three Thousand that does away with formalities and introductions. A cough is your card; a hemorrhage a letter of credit. The Memphis man, being nearer recovered, speaks first.

"Goodall. Memphis—pulmonary tuberculosis—guess last stages." The Three Thousand economize on words. Words are breath and they need breath to write checks for the doctors.

"Hurd," gasps the other. "Hurd; of T'leder. T'leder, Ah-hia. Catarrhal bronkeetis. Name's Dennis, too—doctor says. Says I'll live four weeks if I—take care of myself. Got your walking papers yet?"

"My doctor," says Goodall of Memphis, a little boastingly, "gives me three months."

"Oh," remarks the man from Toledo, filling up great gaps in his conversation with wheezes, "damn the difference. What's months! Expect to—cut mine down to one week—and die in a hack—a four wheeler, not a cough. Be considerable moanin' of the bars when I put out to sea. I've patronized 'em pretty freely since I struck my—present gait. Say, Goodall of Memphis—if your doctor has set your pegs so close—why don't you—get on a big spree and go—to the devil quick and easy—like I'm doing?"

"A spree," says Goodall, as one who entertains a new idea, "I never did such a thing. I was thinking of another way, but——"

"Come on," invites the Ohioan, "and have some drinks. I've been at it—for two days, but the inf—ernal stuff won't bite like it used to. Goodall of Memphis, what's your respiration?"

"Twenty-four."

"Daily—temperature?"

"Hundred and four."

"You can do it in two days. It'll take me a—week. Tank up, friend Goodall—have all the fun you can; then—off you go, in the middle of a jag, and s-s-save trouble and expense. I'm a s-son of a gun if this ain't a health resort—for your whiskers! A Lake Erie fog'd get lost here in two minutes."

"You said something about a drink," says Goodall.

A few minutes later they line up at a glittering bar, and hang upon the arm rest. The bartender, blond, heavy, well-groomed, sets out their drinks, instantly perceiving that he serves two of the Three Thousand. He observes that one is a middle-aged man, well-dressed, with a lined and sunken face; the other a mere boy who is chiefly eyes and overcoat. Disguising well the tedium begotten by many repetitions, the server of drinks begins to chant the sanitary saga of Santone. "Rather a moist night, gentlemen, for our town. A little fog from our river, but nothing to hurt. Repeated Tests."

"Damn your litmus papers," gasps Toledo—"without any—personal offense intended."

"We've heard of 'em before. Let 'em turn red, white, and blue. What we want is a repeated test of that—whiskey. Come again. I paid for the last round, Goodall of Memphis."

The bottle oscillates from one to the other, continues to do so, and is not removed from the counter. The bartender sees two emaciated invalids dispose of enough Kentucky Belle to floor a dozen cowboys, without displaying any emotion save a sad and contemplative interest in the peregrinations of the bottle. So he is moved to manifest a solicitude as to the consequences.

"Not on your Uncle Mark Hanna," responds Toledo, "will we get drunk. We've been—vaccinated with whiskey—and—cod liver oil. What would send you to the police station—only gives us a thirst. S-s-set out another bottle."

It is slow work trying to meet death by that route. Some quicker way must be found. They leave the saloon and plunge again into the mist. The sidewalks are mere flanges at the base of the houses; the streets a cold ravine, the fog filling it like a freshet. Not far away is the Mexican quarter. Conducted as if by wires along the heavy air comes a guitar's tinkle, and the demoralizing voice of some señorita singing:

> "En las tardes sombrillos del invierro
> En el prado a Marar me reclino
> Y maldigo mi fausto destino—
> Una vida la mas infeliz."

The words of it they do not understand—neither Toledo nor Memphis, but words are the least important things in life. The music tears the breasts of the seekers after Nepenthe, inciting Toledo to remark:

"Those kids of mine—I wonder—by God, Mr. Goodall of Memphis, we had too little of that whiskey! No slow music in mine, if you please. It makes you disremember to forget."

Hurd of Toledo, here pulls out his watch, and says:

"I'm a son of a gun! Got an engagement for a hack ride out to San Pedro Springs at eleven. Forgot it. A fellow from Noo York, and me, and the Castillo sisters at Rhinegelder's Garden. That Noo York chap's a lucky dog—got one whole lung—good for a year yet. Plenty of money, too. He pays for everything. I can't afford—to miss the jamboree. Sorry you ain't going along. Good-bye, Goodall of Memphis."

He rounds the corner and shuffles away, casting off thus easily the ties of acquaintanceship as the moribund do, the season of dissolution being man's supreme hour of egoism and selfishness. But he turns and calls back through the fog to the other: "I say, Goodall of Memphis! If you get there before I do, tell 'em Hurd's a-comin' too. Hurd, of T'leder, Ah-hia."

Thus Goodall's tempter deserts him. That youth, uncomplaining and uncaring, takes a spell at coughing, and, recovered, wanders desultorily on down the street, the name of which he neither knows nor recks. At a certain point he perceives swinging doors, and hears, filtering between them, a noise of wind and string instruments. Two men enter from the street as he arrives, and he follows them in. There is a kind of ante-chamber, plentifully set with palms and cactuses and oleanders. At little marble-topped tables some people sit, while softshod attendants bring the beer. All is orderly, clean, melancholy, gay, of the German method of pleasure. At his right is the foot of a stairway. A man there holds out his hand. Goodall extends his, full of silver, the man selects therefrom a coin. Goodall goes upstairs and sees there two galleries extending along the sides of a concert hall which he now perceives to lie below and beyond the anteroom he first entered. These galleries are divided into boxes or stalls, which bestow with the aid of hanging lace curtains a certain privacy upon their occupants.

Passing with aimless feet down the aisle contiguous to these saucy and discreet compartments, he is half checked by the sight in one of them of a young woman, alone and seated in an attitude of reflection. This young woman becomes aware of his approach. A smile from her brings him to a standstill, and her subsequent invitation draws him, though hesitating, to the other chair in the box, a little table between them.

Goodall is only nineteen. There are some whom, when the terrible god Phthisis wishes to destroy he first makes beautiful; and the boy is one of these. His face is wax, and an awful pulchritude is born of the menacing flame in his cheeks. His eyes reflect an unearthly vista engendered by the certainty of his doom. As it is forbidden man to guess accurately concerning his fate, it is inevitable that he shall tremble at the slightest lifting of the veil.

The young woman is well-dressed, and exhibits a beauty of distinctly feminine and tender sort; an Eve-like comeliness that scarcely seems predestined to fade.

It is immaterial, the steps by which the two mount to a certain plane of good understanding; they are short and few, as befits the occasion.

A button against the wall of the partition is frequently disturbed and a waiter comes and goes at a signal.

Pensive beauty would nothing of wine; two thick plaits of her blonde hair hang almost to the floor; she is a lineal descendant of the Lorelei. So the waiter brings the brew; effervescent, icy, greenish golden. The orchestra on the stage is playing "Oh, Rachel." The youngsters have exchanged a good bit of information. She calls him "Walter" and he calls her "Miss Rosa."

Goodall's tongue is loosened and he has told her everything about himself, about his home in Tennessee, the old pillared mansion under the oaks, the stables, the hunting; the friends he has; down to the chickens, and the box bushes bordering the walks. About his coming South for the climate, hoping to escape the hereditary foe of his family. All about his three months on a ranch; the deer hunts, the rattlers, and the rollicking in the cow camps. Then of his advent to Santone, where he had indirectly learned, from a great specialist, that his life's calendar probably contains but two more leaves. And then of this death-white, choking night which has come and strangled his fortitude and sent him out to seek a port amid its depressing billows.

"My weekly letter from home failed to come," he told her, "and I was pretty blue. I knew I had to go before long and I was tired of waiting. I went out and bought morphine at every drug store where they would sell me a few tablets. I got thirty-six quarter grains, and was going back to my room and take them, but I met a queer fellow on a bridge, who had a new idea."

Goodall fillips a little pasteboard box upon the table. "I put 'em all together in there."

Miss Rosa, being a woman, must raise the lid, and give a slight shiver at the innocent-looking triturates. "Horrid things! but those little, white bits—they could never kill one!"

Indeed they could. Walter knew better. Nine grains of morphia! Why, half the amount might.

Miss Rosa demands to know about Mr. Hurd, of Toledo, and is told. She laughs like a delighted child. "What a funny fellow! But tell me more about your home and your sisters, Walter. I know enough about Texas and tarantulas and cowboys."

The theme is dear, just now, to his mood, and he lays before her the simplest details of a true home; the little ties and endearments that so fill the exile's heart. Of his sisters, one, Alice, furnishes him a theme he loves to dwell upon.

"She is like you, Miss Rosa," he says. "Maybe not quite so pretty, but just as nice, and good, and——"

"There! Walter," says Miss Rosa, sharply, "now talk about something else."

But a shadow falls upon the wall outside, preceding a big, softly treading man, finely dressed, who pauses a second before the curtains and then passes on. Presently comes the waiter with a message: "Mr. Rolfe says——"

"Tell Rolfe I'm engaged."

"I don't know why it is," says Goodall, of Memphis, "but I don't feel as bad as I did. An hour ago I wanted to die, but since I've met you, Miss Rosa, I'd like so much to live."

The young woman whirls around the table, lays an arm behind his neck and kisses him on the cheek.

"You must, dear boy," she says. "I know what was the matter. It was the miserable foggy weather that has lowered your spirit and mine too—a little. But look, now."

With a little spring she has drawn back the curtains. A window is in the wall opposite, and lo! the mist is cleared away. The indulgent moon is out again, revoyaging the plumbless sky. Roof and parapet and spire are softly pearl enamelled. Twice, thrice the retrieved river flashes back, between the houses, the light of the firmament. A tonic day will dawn, sweet and prosperous.

"Talk of death when the world is so beautiful!" says Miss Rosa, laying her hand on his shoulder. "Do something to please me, Walter. Go home to your rest and say: 'I mean to get better,' and do it."

"If you ask it," says the boy, with a smile, "I will."

The waiter brings full glasses. Did they ring? No; but it is well. He may leave them. A farewell glass. Miss Rosa says: "To your better health, Walter." He says: "To our next meeting."

His eyes look no longer into the void, but gaze upon the antithesis of death. His foot is set in an undiscovered country to-night. He is obedient, ready to go. "Good-night," she says.

"I never kissed a girl before," he confesses, "except my sisters."

"You didn't this time," she laughs, "I kissed you—good-night."

"When shall I see you again?" he persists.

"You promised me to go home," she frowns, "and get well. Perhaps we shall meet again soon. Good-night." He hesitates, his hat in hand. She smiles broadly and kisses him once more upon the forehead. She watches him far down the aisle, then sits again at the table.

The shadow falls once more against the wall. This time the big, softly stepping man parts the curtains and looks in. Miss Rosa's eyes meet his and for half a minute they remain thus, silent, fighting a battle with that king of weapons. Presently the big man drops the curtains and passes on.

The orchestra ceases playing suddenly, and an important voice can be heard loudly talking in one of the boxes farther down the aisle. No doubt some citizen entertains there some visitor to the town, and Miss Rosa leans back in her chair and smiles at some of the words she catches:

"Purest atmosphere—in the world—litmus paper all long—nothing hurtful—our city—nothing but pure ozone."

The waiter returns for the tray and glasses. As he enters, the girl crushes a little empty pasteboard box in her hand and throws it in a corner. She is stirring something in her glass with her hatpin.

"Why, Miss Rosa," says the waiter with the civil familiarity he uses—"putting salt in your beer this early in the night!"

THE FRIENDLY CALL

[Published in "Monthly Magazine Section," July, 1910.]

WHEN I used to sell hardware in the West, I often "made" a little town called Saltillo, in Colorado. I was always certain of securing a small or a larger order from Simon Bell, who kept a general store there. Bell was one of those six-foot, low-voiced products, formed from a union of the West and the South. I liked him. To look at him you would think he should be robbing stage coaches or juggling gold mines with both hands; but he would sell you a paper of tacks or a spool of thread, with ten times more patience and courtesy than any sales-lady in a city department store.

I had a twofold object in my last visit to Saltillo. One was to sell a bill of goods; the other to advise Bell of a chance that I knew of by which I was certain he could make a small fortune.

In Mountain City, a town on the Union Pacific, five times larger than Saltillo, a mercantile firm was about to go to the wall. It had a lively and growing custom, but was on the edge of dissolution and ruin. Mismanagement and the gambling habits of one of the partners explained it. The condition of the firm was not yet public property. I had my knowledge of it from a private source. I knew that, if the ready cash were offered, the stock and good will could be bought for about one fourth their value.

On arriving in Saltillo I went to Bell's store. He nodded to me, smiled his broad, lingering smile, went on leisurely selling some candy to a little girl, then came around the counter and shook hands.

"Well," he said (his invariably preliminary jocosity at every call I made), "I suppose you are out here making kodak pictures of the mountains. It's the wrong time of the year to buy any hardware, of course."

I told Bell about the bargain in Mountain City. If he wanted to take advantage of it, I would rather have missed a sale than have him overstocked in Saltillo.

"It sounds good," he said, with enthusiasm. "I'd like to branch out and do a bigger business, and I'm obliged to you for mentioning it. But—well, you come and stay at my house to-night and I'll think about it."

It was then after sundown and time for the larger stores in Saltillo to close. The clerks in Bell's put away their books, whirled the combination of the safe, put on their coats and hats and left for their homes. Bell padlocked the big, double wooden front doors, and we stood, for a moment, breathing the keen, fresh mountain air coming across the foothills.

A big man walked down the street and stopped in front of the high porch of the store. His long, black moustache, black eyebrows, and curly black hair contrasted queerly with his light, pink complexion, which belonged, by rights, to a blonde. He was about forty, and wore a white vest, a white hat, a watch chain made of five-dollar gold pieces linked together, and a rather well-fitting two-piece gray suit of the cut that college boys of eighteen are wont to affect. He glanced at me distrustfully, and then at Bell with coldness and, I thought, something of enmity in his expression.

"Well," asked Bell, as if he were addressing a stranger, "did you fix up that matter?"

"Did I!" the man answered, in a resentful tone. "What do you suppose I've been here two weeks for? The business is to be settled to-night. Does that suit you, or have you got something to kick about?"

"It's all right," said Bell. "I knew you'd do it."

"Of course you did," said the magnificent stranger. "Haven't I done it before?"

"You have," admitted Bell. "And so have I. How do you find it at the hotel?"

"Rocky grub. But I ain't kicking. Say—can you give me any pointers about managing that—affair? It's my first deal in that line of business, you know."

"No, I can't," answered Bell, after some thought. "I've tried all kinds of ways. You'll have to try some of your own."

"Tried soft soap?"

"Barrels of it."

"Tried a saddle girth with a buckle on the end of it?"

"Never none. Started to once; and here's what I got."

Bell held out his right hand. Even in the deepening twilight I could see on the back of it a long, white scar, that might have been made by a claw or a knife or some sharp-edged tool.

"Oh, well," said the florid man, carelessly, "I'll know what to do later on."

He walked away without another word. When he had gone ten steps he turned and called to Bell:

"You keep well out of the way when the goods are delivered, so there won't be any hitch in the business."

"All right," answered Bell, "I'll attend to my end of the line."

This talk was scarcely clear in its meaning to me; but as it did not concern me, I did not let it weigh upon my mind. But the singularity of the other man's appearance lingered with me for a while; and as we walked toward Bell's house I remarked to him:

"Your customer seems to be a surly kind of fellow—not one that you'd like to be snowed in with in a camp on a hunting trip."

"He is that," assented Bell, heartily. "He reminds me of a rattlesnake that's been poisoned by the bite of a tarantula."

"He doesn't look like a citizen of Saltillo," I went on.

"No," said Bell, "he lives in Sacramento. He's down here on a little business trip. His name is George Ringo, and he's been my best friend—in fact, the only friend I ever had—for twenty years."

I was too surprised to make any further comment.

Bell lived in a comfortable, plain, square, two-story white house on the edge of the little town. I waited in the parlor—a room depressingly genteel—furnished with red plush, straw matting, looped-up lace curtains, and a glass case large enough to contain a mummy, full of mineral specimens.

While I waited I heard, upstairs, that unmistakable sound instantly recognized the world over—a bickering woman's voice, rising as her anger and fury grew. I could hear, between the gusts, the temperate rumble of Bell's tones, striving to oil the troubled waters.

The storm subsided soon; but not before I had heard the woman say, in a lower, concentrated tone, rather more carrying than her high-pitched railings: "This is the last time. I tell you—the last time. Oh, you *will* understand."

The household seemed to consist of only Bell and his wife and a servant or two. I was introduced to Mrs. Bell at supper.

At first sight she seemed to be a handsome woman, but I soon perceived that her charm had been spoiled. An uncontrolled petulance, I thought, and emotional egotism, an absence of poise and a habitual dissatisfaction had marred her womanhood. During the meal, she showed that false gayety, spurious kindliness and reactionary softness that mark the woman addicted to tantrums. Withal, she was a woman who might be attractive to many men.

After supper, Bell and I took our chairs outside, set them on the grass in the moonlight and smoked. The full moon is a witch. In her light, truthful men dig up for you nuggets of purer gold; while liars squeeze out brighter colors from the tubes of their invention. I saw Bell's broad, slow smile come out upon his face and linger there.

"I reckon you think George and me are a funny kind of friends," he said. "The fact is we never did take much interest in each other's company. But his idea and mine, of what a friend should be, was always synonymous and we lived up to it, strict, all these years. Now, I'll give you an idea of what our idea is.

"A man don't need but one friend. The fellow who drinks your liquor and hangs around you, slapping you on the back and taking up your time, telling you how much he likes you, ain't a friend, even if you did play marbles at school and fish in the same creek with him. As long as you don't need a friend one of that kind may answer. But a friend, to my mind, is one you can deal with on a strict reciprocity basis like me and George have always done.

"A good many years ago, him and me was connected in a number of ways. We put our capital together and run a line of freight wagons in New Mexico, and we mined some and gambled a few. And then, we got into trouble of one or two kinds; and I reckon that got us on a better understandable basis than anything else did, unless it was the fact that we never had much personal use for each other's ways. George is the vainest man I ever see, and the biggest brag. He could blow the biggest geyser in the Yosemite valley back into its hole with one whisper. I am a quiet man, and fond of studiousness and thought. The more we used to see each other, personally, the less we seemed to like to be together. If he ever had slapped me on the back and snivelled over me like I've seen men do to what they called their friends, I know I'd have had a rough-and-tumble with him on the spot. Same way with George. He hated my ways as bad as I did his. When we were mining, we lived in separate tents, so as not to intrude our obnoxiousness on each other.

"But after a long time, we begun to know each of us could depend on the other when we were in a pinch, up to his last dollar, word of honor or perjury, bullet, or drop of blood we had in the world. We never even spoke of it to each other, because that would have spoiled it. But we tried it out, time after time, until we came to know. I've grabbed my hat and jumped a freight and rode 200 miles to identify him when he was about to be hung by mistake, in Idaho, for a train robber. Once, I laid sick of typhoid in a tent in Texas, without a dollar or a change of clothes, and sent for George in Boise City. He came on the next train. The first thing he did before speaking to me, was to hang up a little looking glass on the side of the tent and curl his moustache and rub some hair dye on his head. His hair is naturally a light reddish. Then he gave me the most scientific cussing I ever had, and took off his coat.

" 'If you wasn't a Moses-meek little Mary's lamb, you wouldn't have been took down this way,' says he. 'Haven't you got gumption enough not to drink swamp water or fall down and scream whenever you have a little colic or feel a mosquito bite you?' He made me a little mad.

" 'You've got the bedside manners of a Piute medicine man,' says I. 'And I wish you'd go away and let me die a natural death. I'm sorry I sent for you.'

" 'I've a mind to,' says George, 'for nobody cares whether you live or die. But now I've been tricked into coming, I might as well stay until this little attack of indigestion or nettle rash or whatever it is, passes away.'

"Two weeks afterward, when I was beginning to get around again, the doctor laughed and said he was sure that my friend's keeping me mad all the time did more than his drugs to cure me.

"So that's the way George and me was friends. There wasn't any sentiment about it—it was just give and take, and each of us knew that the other was ready for the call at any time.

"I remember, once, I played a sort of joke on George, just to try him. I felt a little mean about it afterward, because I never ought to have doubted he'd do it.

"We was both living in a little town in the San Luis valley, running some flocks of sheep and a few cattle. We were partners, but, as usual, we didn't live together. I had an old aunt, out from the East, visiting for the summer, so I rented a little cottage. She soon had a couple of cows and some pigs and chickens to make the place look like home. George lived alone in a little cabin half a mile out of town.

"One day a calf that we had, died. That night I broke its bones, dumped it into a coarse sack and tied it up with wire. I put on an old shirt, tore a sleeve 'most out of it, and the collar half off, tangled up my hair, put some red ink on my hands and splashed some of it over my shirt and face. I must have looked like I'd been having the fight of my life. I put the sack in a wagon and drove out to George's cabin. When I hallooed, he came out in a yellow dressing-gown, a Turkish cap, and patent leather shoes. George always was a great dresser.

"I dumped the bundle to the ground.

" 'Sh-sh!' says I, kind of wild in my way. 'Take that and bury it, George, out somewhere behind your house—bury it just like it is. And don——'

" 'Don't get excited,' says George. 'And for the Lord's sake go and wash your hands and face and put on a clean shirt.'

"And he lights his pipe, while I drive away at a gallop. The next morning he drops around to our cottage, where my aunt was fiddling with her flowers and truck in the front yard. He bends himself and bows and makes compliments as he could do, when so disposed, and begs a rose bush from her, saying he had turned up a little land back of his cabin, and wanted to plant something on it by way of usefulness and ornament. So my aunt, flattered, pulls up one of her biggest by the roots and gives it to him. Afterward I see it growing where he planted it, in a place where the grass had been cleared off and the dirt levelled. But neither George nor me ever spoke of it to each other again."

The moon rose higher, possibly drawing water from the sea, pixies from their dells, and certainly more confidences from Simms Bell, the friend of a friend.

"There come a time, not long afterward," he went on, "when I was able to do a good turn for George Ringo. George had made a little pile of money in beeves and he was up in Denver, and he showed up when I saw him, wearing deer-skin vests, yellow shoes, clothes like the awnings in front of drug stores, and his hair dyed so blue that it looked black in the dark. He wrote me to come up there, quick—that he needed me, and to bring the best outfit of clothes I had. I had 'em on when I got the letter, so I left on the next train. George was——"

Bell stopped for half a minute, listening intently.

"I thought I heard a team coming down the road," he explained. "George was at a summer resort on a lake near Denver and was putting on as many airs as he knew how. He had rented a little two-room cottage, and had a Chihuahua dog and a hammock and eight different kinds of walking sticks.

" 'Simms,' he says to me, 'there's a widow woman here that's pestering the soul out of me with her intentions. I can't get out of her way. It ain't that she ain't handsome and agreeable, in a sort of style, but her attentions is serious, and I ain't ready for to marry nobody and settle down. I can't go to no festivity nor sit on the hotel piazza or mix in any of the society round-ups, but what she cuts me out of the herd and puts her daily brand on me. I like this here place,' goes on George, 'and I'm making a hit here in the most censorious circles, so I don't want to have to run away from it. So I sent for you.'

" 'What do you want me to do?' I asks George.

" 'Why,' says he, 'I want you to head her off. I want you to cut me out. I want you to come to the rescue. Suppose you seen a wildcat about for to eat me, what would you do;"

" 'Go for it,' says I.

" 'Correct,' says George. 'Then go for this Mrs. De Clinton the same.'

" 'How am I to do it?' I asks. 'By force and awfulness or in some gentler and less lurid manner?'

" 'Court her,' George says, 'get her off my trail. Feed her. Take her out in boats. Hang around her and stick to her. Get her mashed on you if you can. Some women are pretty big fools. Who knows but what she might take a fancy to you.'

"'Had you ever thought,' I asks, 'of repressing your fatal fascinations in her presence; of squeezing a harsh note in the melody of your siren voice, of veiling your beauty—in other words, of giving her the bounce yourself?'

"George sees no essence of sarcasm in my remark. He twists his moustache and looks at the points of his shoes.

"'Well, Simms,' he said, 'you know how I am about the ladies. I can't hurt none of their feelings. I'm by nature polite and esteemful of their intents and purposes. This Mrs. De Clinton don't appear to be the suitable sort for me. Besides, I ain't a marrying man by all means.'

"'All right,' said I, 'I'll do the best I can in the case.'

"So I bought a new outfit of clothes and a book on etiquette and made a dead set for Mrs. De Clinton. She was a fine-looking woman, cheerful and gay. At first, I almost had to hobble her to keep her from loping around at George's heels; but finally I got her so she seemed glad to go riding with me and sailing on the lake; and she seemed real hurt on the mornings when I forgot to send her a bunch of flowers. Still, I didn't like the way she looked at George, sometimes, out of the corner of her eye. George was having a fine time now, going with the whole bunch just as he pleased. Yes'm," continued Bell, "she certainly was a fine-looking woman at that time. She's changed some since, as you might have noticed at the supper table."

"What!" I exclaimed.

"I married Mrs. De Clinton," went on Bell. "One evening while were were up at the lake. When I told George about it, he opened his mouth and I thought he was going to break our traditions and say something grateful, but he swallowed it back.

"'All right,' says he, playing with his dog. 'I hope you won't have too much trouble. Myself, I'm not never going to marry.'

"That was three years ago," said Bell. "We came here to live. For a year we got along medium fine. And then everything changed. For two years I've been having something that rhymes first-class with my name. You heard the row upstairs this evening? That was a merry welcome compared to the usual average. She's tired of me and of this little town life and she rages all day, like a panther in a cage. I stood it until two weeks ago and then I had to send out The Call. I located George in Sacramento. He started the day he got my wire."

Mrs. Bell came out of the house swiftly toward us. Some strong excitement or anxiety seemed to possess her, but she smiled a faint hostess smile, and tried to keep her voice calm.

"The dew is falling," she said, "and it's growing rather late. Wouldn't you gentlemen rather come into the house?"

Bell took some cigars from his pocket and answered: "It's most too fine a night to turn in yet. I think Mr. Ames and I will walk out along the road a mile or so and have another smoke. I want to talk with him about some goods that I want to buy."

"Up the road or down the road?" asked Mrs. Bell.

"Down," said Bell.

I thought she breathed a sigh of relief.

When we had gone a hundred yards and the house became concealed by trees, Bell guided me into the thick grove that lined the road and back through them toward the house again. We stopped within twenty yards of the house, concealed by the dark shadows. I wondered at this maneuver. And then I heard in the distance coming down the road beyond the house, the regular hoofbeats of a team of horses. Bell held his watch in a ray of moonlight.

"On time, within a minute," he said. "That's George's way."

The team slowed up as it drew near the house and stopped in a patch of black shadows. We saw the figure of a woman carrying a heavy valise move swiftly from the other side of the house, and hurry to the waiting vehicle. Then it rolled away briskly in the direction from which it had come.

I looked at Bell inquiringly, I suppose. I certainly asked him no question.

"She's running away with George," said Bell, simply. "He's kept me posted about the progress of the scheme all along. She'll get a divorce in six months and then George will marry her. He never helps anybody halfway. It's all arranged between them."

I began to wonder what friendship was, after all.

When we went into the house, Bell began to talk easily on other subjects; and I took his cue. By and by the big chance to buy out the business in Mountain City came back to my mind and I began to urge it upon him. Now that he was free, it would be easier for him to make the move; and he was sure of a splendid bargain.

Bell was silent for some minutes, but when I looked at him I fancied that he was thinking of something else—that he was not considering the project.

"Why, no, Mr. Ames," he said, after a while, "I can't make that deal. I'm awful thankful to you, though, for telling me about it. But I've got to stay here. I can't go to Mountain City."

"Why?" I asked.

"Missis Bell," he replied, "won't live in Mountain City. She hates the place and wouldn't go there. I've got to keep right on here in Saltillo."

"Mrs. Bell!" I exclaimed, too puzzled to conjecture what he meant.

"I ought to explain," said Bell. "I know George and I know Mrs. Bell. He's impatient in his ways. He can't stand things that fret him, long, like I can. Six months, I give them—six months of married life, and there'll be another disunion. Mrs. Bell will come back to me. There's no other place for her to go. I've got to stay here and wait. At the end of six months, I'll have to grab a satchel and catch the first train. For George will be sending out The Call."

A DINNER AT ——[1]

[The story referred to in this skit appears in "The Trimmed Lamp" under the same title—"The Badge of Policeman O'Roon."]

THE ADVENTURES OF AN AUTHOR WITH HIS OWN HERO

ALL that day—in fact from the moment of his creation—Van Sweller had conducted himself fairly well in my eyes. Of course I had had to make many concessions; but in return he had been no less considerate. Once or twice we had had sharp, brief contentions over certain points of behavior; but, prevailingly, give and take had been our rule.

His morning toilet provoked our first tilt. Van Sweller went about it confidently.

"The usual thing, I suppose, old chap," he said, with a smile and a yawn. "I ring for a b. and s., and then I have my tub. I splash a good deal in the water,

1 See advertising column, "Where to Dine Well," in the daily newspapers.

of course. You are aware that there are two ways in which I can receive Tommy Carmichael when he looks in to have a chat about polo. I can talk to him through the bathroom door, or I can be picking at a grilled bone which my man has brought in. Which would you prefer?"

I smiled with diabolic satisfaction at his coming discomfiture.

"Neither," I said. "You will make your appearance on the scene when a gentleman should—after you are fully dressed, which indubitably private function shall take place behind closed doors. And I will feel indebted to you if, after you do appear, your deportment and manners are such that it will not be necessary to inform the public, in order to appease its apprehension, that you have taken a bath."

Van Sweller slightly elevated his brows.

"Oh, very well," he said, a trifle piqued. "I rather imagine it concerns you more than it does me. Cut the 'tub' by all means, if you think best. But it has been the usual thing, you know."

This was my victory; but after Van Sweller emerged from his apartments in the "Beaujolie" I was vanquished in a dozen small but well-contested skirmishes. I allowed him a cigar; but routed him on the question of naming its brand. But he worsted me when I objected to giving him a "coat unmistakably English in its cut." I allowed him to "stroll down Broadway," and even permitted "passers by" (God knows there's nowhere to pass but by) to "turn their heads and gaze with evident admiration at his erect figure." I demeaned myself, and, as a barber, gave him a "smooth, dark face with its keen, frank eye, and firm jaw."

Later on he looked in at the club and saw Freddy Vavasour, polo team captain, dawdling over grilled bone No. 1.

"Dear old boy," began Van Sweller; but in an instant I had seized him by the collar and dragged him aside with the scantiest courtesy.

"For heaven's sake talk like a man," I said, sternly. "Do you think it is manly to use those mushy and inane forms of address? That man is neither dear nor old nor a boy."

To my surprise Van Sweller turned upon me a look of frank pleasure.

"I am glad to hear you say that," he said, heartily. "I used those words because I have been forced to say them so often. They really are contemptible. Thanks for correcting me, dear old boy."

Still I must admit that Van Sweller's conduct in the park that morning was almost without flaw. The courage, the dash, the modesty, the skill, and fidelity that he displayed atoned for everything.

This is the way the story runs.

Van Sweller has been a gentleman member of the "Rugged Riders," the company that made a war with a foreign country famous. Among his comrades was Lawrence O'Roon, a man whom Van Sweller liked. A strange thing—and a hazardous one in fiction—was that Van Sweller and O'Roon resembled each other mightily in face, form, and general appearance. After the war Van Sweller pulled wires, and O'Roon was made a mounted policeman.

Now, one night in New York there are commemorations and libations by old comrades, and in the morning, Mounted Policeman O'Roon, unused to potent liquids—another premise hazardous in fiction—finds the earth bucking and bounding like a bronco, with no stirrup into which he may insert foot and save his honor and his badge.

Noblesse oblige? Surely. So out along the driveways and bridle paths trots Hudson Van Sweller in the uniform of his incapacitated comrade, as like unto him as one French pea is unto a *petit pois.*

It is, of course, jolly larks for Van Sweller, who has wealth and social position enough for him to masquerade safely even as a police commissioner doing his duty, if he wished to do so. But society, not given to scanning the countenances of mounted policemen, sees nothing unusual in the officer on the beat. And then comes the runaway.

That is a fine scene—the swaying victoria, the impetuous, daft horses plunging through the line of scattering vehicles, the driver stupidly holding his broken reins, and the ivory-white face of Amy Ffolliott, as she clings desperately with each slender hand. Fear has come and gone: it has left her expression pensive and just a little pleading, for life is not so bitter.

And then the clatter and swoop of Mounted Policeman Van Sweller! Oh, it was—but the story has not yet been printed. When it is you shall learn how he sent his bay like a bullet after the imperilled victoria. A Crichton, a Crœsus, and a Centaur in one, he hurls the invincible combination into the chase.

When the story is printed you will admire the breathless scene where Van Sweller checks the headlong team. And then he looks into Amy Ffolliott's eyes and sees two things—the possibilities of a happiness he has long sought, and a nascent promise of it. He is unknown to her; but he stands in her sight illuminated by the hero's potent glory, she his and he hers by all the golden, fond, unreasonable laws of love and light literature.

Ay, that is a rich moment. And it will stir you to find Van Sweller in that fruitful nick of time thinking of his comrade O'Roon, who is cursing his gyrating bed and incapable legs in an unsteady room in a West Side hotel while Van Sweller holds his badge and his honor.

Van Sweller hears Miss Ffolliott's voice thrillingly asking the name of her preserver. If Hudson Van Sweller, in policeman's uniform, has saved the life of palpitating beauty in the park—where is Mounted Policeman O'Roon, in whose territory the deed is done? How quickly by a word can the hero reveal himself, thus discarding his masquerade of ineligibility and doubling the romance! But there is his friend!

Van Sweller touches his cap. "It's nothing, Miss," he says, sturdily; "that's what we are paid for—to do our duty." And away he rides. But the story does not end there.

As I have said, Van Sweller carried off the park scene to my decided satisfaction. Even to me he was a hero when he foreswore, for the sake of his friend, the romantic promise of his adventure. It was later in the day, amongst the more exacting conventions that encompass the society hero, when we had our liveliest disagreement. At noon he went to O'Roon's room and found him far enough recovered to return to his post, which he at once did.

At about six o'clock in the afternoon Van Sweller fingered his watch, and flashed at me a brief look full of such shrewd cunning that I suspected him at once.

"Time to dress for dinner, old man," he said, with exaggerated carelessness.

"Very well," I answered, without giving him a clue to my suspicions; "I will go with you to your rooms and see that you do the thing properly. I suppose that every author must be a valet to his own hero."

He affected cheerful acceptance of my somewhat officious proposal to accompany him. I could see that he was annoyed by it, and that fact fastened deeper in my mind the conviction that he was meditating some act of treachery.

When he had reached his apartments he said to me, with a too patronizing air: "There are, as you perhaps know, quite a number of little distinguishing touches to be had out of the dressing process. Some writers rely almost wholly upon them. I suppose that I am to ring for my man, and that he is to enter noiselessly, with an expressionless countenance."

"He may enter," I said, with decision, "and only enter. Valets do not usually enter a room shouting college songs or with St. Vitus's dance in their faces;

---

[1] See advertising column, "Where to Dine Well," in the daily newspapers.

so the contrary may be assumed without fatuous or gratuitous asseveration."

"I must ask you to pardon me," continued Van Sweller, gracefully, "for annoying you with questions, but some of your methods are a little new to me. Shall I don a full-dress suit with an immaculate white tie—or is there another tradition to be upset?"

"You will wear," I replied, "evening dress, such as a gentleman wears. If it is full, your tailor should be responsible for its bagginess. And I will leave it to whatever erudition you are supposed to possess whether a white tie is rendered any whiter by being immaculate. And I will leave it to the consciences of you and your man whether a tie that is not white, and therefore not immaculate, could possibly form any part of a gentleman's evening dress. If not, then the perfect tie is included and understood in the term 'dress,' and its expressed addition predicates either a redundancy of speech or the spectacle of a man wearing two ties at once."

With this mild but deserved rebuke I left Van Sweller in his dressing-room, and waited for him in his library.

About an hour later his valet came out, and I heard him telephone for an electric cab. Then out came Van Sweller, smiling, but with that sly, secretive design in his eye that was puzzling me.

"I believe," he said, easily, as he smoothed a glove, "that I will drop in at ——[1] for dinner."

I sprang up, angrily, at his words. This, then, was the paltry trick he had been scheming to play upon me. I faced him with a look so grim that even his patrician poise was flustered.

"You will never do so," I exclaimed, "with my permission. What kind of a return is this," I continued, hotly, "for the favors I have granted you? I gave you a 'Van' to your name when I might have called you 'Perkins' or 'Simpson.' I have humbled myself so far as to brag of your polo ponies, your automobiles, and the iron muscles that you acquired when you were stroke-oar of your 'varsity eight,' or 'eleven,' whichever it is. I created you for the hero of this story; and I will not submit to having you queer it. I have tried to make you a typical young New York gentlemen of the highest social station and breeding. You have no reason to complain of my treatment to you. Amy Ffolliott, the girl you are to win, is a prize for any man to be thankful for, and cannot be equalled for beauty—provided the story is illustrated by the right artist. I do not understand why you should try to spoil everything. I had thought you were a gentleman."

"What is it you are objecting to, old man?" asked Van Sweller, in a surprised tone.

"To your dining at ——,[1]" I answered. "The pleasure would be yours, no doubt, but the responsibility would fall upon me. You intend deliberately to make me out a tout for a restaurant. Where you dine to-night has not the slightest connection with the thread of our story. You know very well that the plot requires that you be in front of the Alhambra Opera House at 11:30 where you are to rescue Miss Ffolliott a second time as the fire engine crashes into her cab. Until that time your movements are immaterial to the reader. Why can't you dine out of sight somewhere, as many a hero does, instead of insisting upon an inapposite and vulgar exhibition of yourself?"

"My dear fellow," said Van Sweller, politely, but with a stubborn tightening of his lips, "I'm sorry it doesn't please you, but there's no help for it. Even a character in a story has rights that an author cannot ignore. The hero of a story of New York social life must dine at ——[1] at least once during its action."

"'Must,'" I echoed, disdainfully; "why 'must'? Who demands it?"

"The magazine editors," answered Van Sweller, giving me a glance of significant warning.

"But why?" I persisted.

"To please subscribers around Kankakee, Ill.," said Van Sweller, without hesitation.

"How do you know these things?" I inquired, with sudden suspicion. "You never came into existence until this morning. You are only a character in fiction, anyway. I, myself, created you. How is it possible for you to know anything?"

"Pardon me for referring to it," said Van Sweller, with a sympathetic smile, "but I have been the hero of hundreds of stories of this kind."

I felt a slow flush creeping into my face.

"I thought . . ." I stammered; "I was hoping . . . that is . . . Oh, well, of course an absolutely original conception in fiction is impossible in these days."

"Metropolitan types," continued Van Sweller, kindly, "do not offer a hold for much originality. I've sauntered through every story in pretty much the same way. Now and then the women writers have made me cut some rather strange capers, for a gentleman; but the men generally pass me along from one to another without much change. But never yet, in any story, have I failed to dine at ——.[1]"

"You will fail this time," I said, emphatically.

"Perhaps so," admitted Van Sweller, looking out of the window into the street below, "but if so it will be for the first time. The authors all send me there. I fancy that many of them would have liked to accompany me, but for the little matter of the expense."

"I say I will be touting for no restaurant," I repeated, loudly. "You are subject to my will, and I declare that you shall not appear of record this evening until the time arrives for you to rescue Miss Ffolliott again. If the reading public cannot conceive that you have dined during that interval at some one of the thousands of establishments provided for that purpose that do not receive literary advertisement it may suppose, for aught I care, that you have gone fasting."

"Thank you," said Van Sweller, rather coolly, "you are hardly courteous. But take care! it is at your own risk that you attempt to disregard a fundamental principle in metropolitan fiction—one that is dear alike to author and reader. I shall, of course, attend to my duty when it comes time to rescue your heroine; but I warn you that it will be your loss if you fail to send me to-night to dine at ——.[1]"

"I will take the consequences if there are to be any," I replied. "I am not yet come to be sandwich man for an eating-house."

I walked over to a table where I had left my cane and gloves. I heard the whirr of the alarm in the cab below and I turned quickly. Van Sweller was gone.

I rushed down the stairs and out to the curb. An empty hansom was just passing. I hailed the driver excitedly.

"See that auto cab halfway down the block?" I shouted. "Follow it. Don't lose sight of it for an instant, and I will give you two dollars!"

If I only had been one of the characters in my story instead of myself I could easily have offered $10 or $25 or even $100. But $2 was all I felt justified in expending, with fiction at its present rates.

The cab driver, instead of lashing his animal into a foam, proceeded at a deliberate trot that suggested a by-the-hour arrangement.

But I suspected Van Sweller's design; and when we lost sight of his cab I ordered my driver to proceed at once to ——.[1]

I found Van Sweller at a table under a palm, just glancing over the menu, with a hopeful waiter hovering at his elbow.

[1] See advertising column, "Where to Dine Well," in the daily newspapers.

"Come with me," I said, inexorably. "You will not give me the slip again. Under my eye you shall remain until 11:30."

Van Sweller countermanded the order for his dinner, and arose to accompany me. He could scarcely do less. A fictitious character is but poorly equipped for resisting a hungry but live author who comes to drag him forth from a restaurant. All he said was: "You were just in time; but I think you are making a mistake. You cannot afford to ignore the wishes of the great reading public."

I took Van Sweller to my own rooms—to my room. He had never seen anything like it before.

"Sit on that trunk," I said to him, "while I observe whether the landlady is stalking us. If she is not, I will get things at a delicatessen store below, and cook something for you in a pan over the gas jet. It will not be so bad. Of course nothing of this will appear in the story."

"Jove! old man!" said Van Sweller, looking about him with interest, "this is a jolly little closet you live in! Where the devil do you sleep?—Oh, that pulls down! And I say—what is this under the corner of the carpet?—Oh, a frying pan! I see—clever idea! Fancy cooking over the gas! What larks it will be!"

"Think of anything you could eat?" I asked; "try a chop, or what?"

"Anything," said Van Sweller, enthusiastically, "except a grilled bone."

Two weeks afterward the postman brought me a large, fat envelope. I opened it, and took out something that I had seen before, and this typewritten letter from a magazine that encourages society fiction:

Your short story, "The Badge of Policeman O'Roon," is herewith returned. We are sorry that it has been unfavorably passed upon; but it seems to lack in some of the essential requirements of our publication.

The story is splendidly constructed; its style is strong and inimitable, and its action and character-drawing deserve the highest praise. As a story *per se* it has merit beyond anything that we have read for some time. But, as we have said, it fails to come up to some of the standards we have set.

Could you not re-write the story, and inject into it the social atmosphere, and return it to us for further consideration? It is suggested to you that you have the hero, Van Sweller, drop in for luncheon or dinner once or twice at ——[1] or at the ——[1] which will be in line with the changes desired.

Very truly yours,
THE EDITORS.

SOUND AND FURY

[O. Henry wrote this for *Ainslee's Magazine*, where it appeared in March, 1903.]

PERSONS OF THE DRAMA

MR. PENNE . . . . *An Author*
MISS LORE . . . . *An Amanuensis*

SCENE—*Workroom of* Mr. Penne's *popular novel factory.*

MR. PENNE—Good morning, Miss Lore. Glad to see you so prompt. We should finish that June installment for the *Epoch* to-day. Leverett is crowding

---

[1] See advertising column, "Where to Dine Well," in the daily newspapers.

me for it. Are you quite ready? We will resume where we left off yesterday. (*Dictates.*) "Kate, with a sigh, rose from his knees, and——"

MISS LORE—Excuse me; you mean "rose from *her* knees," instead of "his," don't you?

MR. PENNE—Er—no—"his," if you please. It is the love scene in the garden. (*Dictates.*) "Rose from his knees where, blushing with youth's bewitching coyness, she had rested for a moment after Courtland had declared his love. The hour was one of supreme and tender joy. When Kate—scene that Cortland never——"

MISS LORE—Excuse me; but wouldn't it be more grammatical to say "when Kate *saw*," instead of "seen"?

MR. PENNE—The context will explain. (*Dictates.*) "When Kate—scene that Cortland never forgot—came tripping across the lawn it seemed to him the fairest sight that earth had ever offered to his gaze."

MISS LORE—Oh!

MR. PENNE (*dictates*)—"Kate had abandoned herself to the joy of her new-found love so completely that no shadow of her former grief was cast upon it. Cortland, with his arm firmly entwined about her waist, knew nothing of her sighs——"

MISS LORE—Goodness! If he couldn't tell her size with his arm around——

MR. PENNE (*frowning*)—"Of her sighs and tears of the previous night."

MISS LORE—Oh!

MR. PENNE (*dictates*)—"To Cortland the chief charm of this girl was her look of innocence and unworldliness. Never had nun——"

MISS LORE—How about changing that to "never had any"?

MR. PENNE (*emphatically*)—"Never had nun in cloistered cell a face more sweet and pure."

MISS LORE—Oh!

MR. PENNE (*dictates*)—"But now Kate must hasten back to the house lest her absence be discovered. After a fond farewell she turned and sped lightly away. Cortland's gaze followed her. He watched her rise——"

MISS LORE—Excuse me, Mr. Penne; but how could he watch her eyes while her back was turned toward him?

MR. PENNE (*with extreme politeness*)—Possibly you would gather my meaning more intelligently if you would wait for the conclusion of the sentence. (*Dictates*). "Watched her rise as gracefully as a fawn as she mounted the eastern terrace."

MISS LORE—Oh!

MR. PENNE (*dictates*)—"And yet Cortland's position was so far above that of this rustic maiden that he dreaded to consider the social upheaval that would ensue should he marry her. In no uncertain tones the traditional voices of his caste and world cried out loudly to him to let her go. What should follow——"

MISS LORE (*looking up with a start*)—I'm sure I can't say, Mr. Penne. Unless (*with a giggle*) you would want to add "Gallegher."

MR. PENNE (*coldly*)—Pardon me. I was not seeking to impose upon you the task of a collaborator. Kindly consider the question of a part of the text.

MISS LORE—Oh!

MR. PENNE (*dictates*)—"On one side was love and Kate; on the other side his heritage of social position and family pride. Would love win? Love, that the poets tell us will last forever!" (*Perceives that Miss Lore looks fatigued, and looks at his watch.*) That's a good long stretch. Perhaps we'd better 'snock off a bit.

(Miss Lore *does not reply.*)

MR. PENNE—I said, Miss Lore, we've been at it quite a long time—wouldn't you like to knock off for a while?

MISS LORE—Oh! Were you addressing me before? I put what you said down. I thought it belonged in the story. It seemed to fit in all right. Oh, no; I'm not tired.

MR. PENNE—Very well, then, we will continue. (*Dictates*.) "In spite of these qualms and doubts, Cortland was a happy man. That night at the club he silently toasted Kate's bright eyes in a bumper of the rarest vintage. Afterward he set out for a stroll with, as Kate on——"

MISS LORE—Excuse me, Mr. Penne, for venturing a suggestion; but don't you think you might state that in a less coarse manner?

MR. PENNE (*astounded*)—Wh-wh—I'm afraid I fail to understand you.

MISS LORE—His condition. Why not say he was "full" or "intoxicated"? It would sound much more elegant than the way you express it.

MR. PENNE (*still darkly wandering*)—Will you kindly point out, Miss Lore, where I have intimated that Cortland was "full," if you prefer that word?

MISS LORE (*calmly consulting her stenographic notes*)—It is right here, word for word. (*Reads*.) "Afterward he set out for a stroll with a skate on."

MR. PENNE (*with peculiar emphasis*)—Ah! And now will you kindly take down the expurgated phrase? (*Dictates*.) "Afterward he set out for a stroll with, as Kate on one occasion had fancifully told him, her spirit leaning upon his arm."

MISS LORE—Oh!

MR. PENNE (*dictates*)—Chapter thirty-four. Heading—"What Kate Found in the Garden." "That fragrant summer morning brought gracious tasks to all. The bees were at the honeysuckle blossoms on the porch. Kate, singing a little song, was training the riotous branches of her favorite woodbine. The sun, himself, had rows——"

MISS LORE—Shall I say "had risen"?

MR. PENNE (*very slowly and with desperate deliberation*)—"The — sun — himself — had — rows — of — blushing — pinks — and — hollyhocks — and — hyacinths — waiting — that — he — might — dry — their — dew-drenched — cups."

MISS LORE—Oh!

MR. PENNE (*dictates*)—"The earliest trolley, scattering the birds from its pathway like some marauding cat, brought Cortland over from Oldport. He had forgotten his fair——"

MISS LORE—Hm! Wonder how he got the conductor to——

MR. PENNE (*very loudly*)—"Forgotten his fair and roseate visions of the night in the practical light of the sober morn."

MISS LORE—Oh!

MR. PENNE (*dictates*)—"He greeted her with his usual smile and manner. 'See the waves,' he cried, pointing to the heaving waters of the sea, 'ever wooing and returning to the rock-bound shore.' ' 'Ready to break,' Kate said, with——"

MISS LORE—My! One evening he has his arm around her, and the next morning he's ready to break her head! Just like a man!

MR. PENNE (*with suspicious calmness*)—There are times, Miss Lore, when a man becomes so far exasperated that even a woman—— But suppose we finish the sentence. (*Dictates*.) " 'Ready to break,' Kate said, with the thrilling look of a soul-awakened woman, 'into foam and spray, destroying themselves upon the shore they love so well.' "

MISS LORE—Oh!

MR. PENNE (*dictates*)—"Cortland, in Kate's presence heard faintly the voice of caution. Thirty years had not cooled his ardor. It was in his power to bestow great gifts upon this girl. He still retained the beliefs that he had at twenty." (*To Miss Lore, wearily*) I think that will be enough for the present.

MISS LORE (*wisely*)—Well, if he had the twenty that he believed he had, it might buy her a rather nice one.

MR. PENNE (*faintly*)—The last sentence was my own. We will discontinue for the day, Miss Lore.

MISS LORE—Shall I come again to-morrow?

MR. PENNE (*helpless under the spell*)—If you will be so good.

(*Exit* Miss Lore.)

ASBESTOS CURTAIN

TICTOCQ

[These two farcical stories about Tictocq appeared in the *Rolling Stone*. They are reprinted here with all of their local references because, written hurriedly and for neighborly reading, they nevertheless have an interest for the admirer of O. Henry. They were written in 1894.]

THE GREAT FRENCH DETECTIVE, IN AUSTIN

A Successful Political Intrigue

CHAPTER I

IT is not generally know that Tictocq, the famous French detective, was in Austin last week. He registered at the Avenue Hotel under an assumed name, and his quiet and reserved manners singled him out at once for one not to be singled out.

No one knows why he came to Austin, but to one or two he vouchsafed the information that his mission was an important one from the French Government.

One report is that the French Minister of State has discovered an old statute among the laws of the empire, resulting from a treaty between the Emperor Charlemagne and Governor Roberts which expressly provides for the north gate of the Capital grounds being kept open, but this is merely a conjecture.

Last Wednesday afternoon a well-dressed gentleman knocked at the door of Tictocq's room in the hotel.

The detective opened the door.

"Monsieur Tictocq, I believe," said the gentleman.

"You will see on the register that I sign my name Q. X. Jones," said Tictocq, "and gentlemen would understand that I wish to be known as such. If you do not like being referred to as no gentleman, I will give you satisfaction any time after July 1st, and fight Steve O'Donnell, John McDonald, and Ignatius Donnelly in the meantime if you desire."

"I do not mind it in the least," said the gentleman. "In fact, I am accustomed to it. I am Chairman of the Democratic Executive Committee, Platform No. 2, and I have a friend in trouble. I knew you were Tictocq from your resemblance to yourself."

"Entrez vous," said the detective.

The gentleman entered and was handed a chair.

"I am a man of few words," said Tictocq. "I will help your friend if possible. Our countries are great friends. We have given you Lafayette and French fried potatoes. You have given us California champagne and—taken back Ward McAllister. State your case."

"I will be very brief," said the visitor. "In room No. 76 in this hotel is stopping a prominent Populist Candidate. He is alone. Last night some one stole his socks. They cannot be found. If they are not recovered, his party will attribute their loss to the Democracy. They will make great capital of the burglary, although I am sure it was not a political move at all. The socks must be recovered. You are the only man that can do it."

Tictocq bowed.

"'Am I to have carte blanche to question every person connected with the hotel?"

"The proprietor has already been spoken to. Everything and everybody is at your service."

Tictocq consulted his watch.

"Come to this room to-morrow afternoon at 6 o'clock with the landlord, the Populist Candidate, and any other witnesses elected from both parties, and I will return the socks."

"Bien, Monsieur; schlafen sie wohl."

"Au revoir."

The Chairman of the Democratic Executive Committee, Platform No. 2, bowed courteously and withdrew.

. . . .

Tictocq sent for the bell boy.

"Did you go to room 76 last night?"

"Yes, sir."

"Who was there?"

"An old hayseed what come on the 7:25."

"What did he want?"

"The bouncer."

"What for?"

"To put the light out."

"Did you take anything while in the room?"

"No, he didn't ask me."

"What is your name?"

"Jim."

"You can go."

CHAPTER II

The drawing-rooms of one of the most magnificent private residences in Austin are a blaze of lights. Carriages line the streets in front, and from gate to doorway is spread a velvet carpet, on which the delicate feet of the guests may tread.

The occasion is the entrée into society of one of the fairest buds in the City of the Violet Crown. The rooms are filled with the culture, the beauty, the youth and fashion of society. Austin society is acknowledged to be the wittiest, the most select, and the highest bred to be found southwest of Kansas City.

Mrs. Rutabaga St. Vitus, the hostess, is accustomed to draw around her a circle of talent and beauty rarely equalled anywhere. Her evenings come nearer approaching the dignity of a salon than any occasion, except, perhaps, a Tony Faust and Marguerite reception at the Iron Front.

Miss St. Vitus, whose advent into society's maze was heralded by such an auspicious display of hospitality, is a slender brunette, with large, lustrous eyes, a winning smile, and a charming ingénue manner. She wears a china silk, cut princesse, with diamond ornaments, and a couple of towels inserted in the back to conceal prominence of shoulder blades. She is chatting easily and naturally on a plush-covered tête-à-tête with Harold St. Clair, the agent for a Minneapolis pants company. Her friend and schoolmate, Elsie Hicks, who married three drummers in one day, a week or two before, and won a wager of two dozen bottles of Budweiser from the handsome and talented young hack-driver, Bum Smithers, is promenading in and out the low French windows with Ethelbert Windup, the popular young candidate for hide inspector, whose name is familiar to every one who reads police court reports.

Somewhere, concealed by shrubbery, a band is playing, and during the pauses in conversation, onions can be smelt frying in the kitchen.

Happy laughter rings out from ruby lips, handsome faces grow tender as they bend over white necks and drooping heads; timid eyes convey things that lips dare not speak, and beneath silken bodice and broadcloth, hearts beat time to the sweet notes of "Love's Young Dream."

"And where have you been for some time past, you recreant cavalier?" says Miss St. Vitus to Harold St. Clair. "Have you been worshipping at another shrine? Are you recreant to your whilom friends? Speak, Sir Knight, and defend yourself."

"Oh, come off," says Harold, in his deep, musical baritone; "I've been having a devil of a time fitting pants on a lot of bow-legged jays from the cotton-patch. Got knobs on their legs, some of 'em big as gourds, and all expect a fit. Did you ever try to measure a bow-legged—I mean—can't you imagine what a jam-swizzled time I have getting pants to fit 'em? Business dull too, nobody wants 'em over three dollars."

"You witty boy," says Miss St. Vitus. "Just as full of bon mots and clever sayings as ever. What do you take now?"

"Oh, beer."

"Give me your arm and let's go into the drawing-room and draw a cork. I'm chewing a little cotton myself."

Arm in arm, the handsome couple pass across the room, the cynosure of all eyes. Luderic Hetherington, the rising and gifted night-watchman at the Lone Star slaughter house, and Mabel Grubb, the daughter of the millionaire owner of the Humped-backed Camel saloon, are standing under the oleanders as they go by.

"She is very beautiful," says Luderic.

"Rats," says Mabel.

A keen observer would have noted all this time the figure of a solitary man who seemed to avoid the company but by adroit changing of his position, and perfectly cool and self-possessed manner, avoided drawing any especial attention to himself.

The lion of the evening is Herr Professor Ludwig von Bum, the pianist.

He had been found drinking beer in a saloon on East Pecan Street by Colonel St. Vitus about a week before, and according to the Austin custom in such cases, was invited home by the colonel, and the next day accepted into society, with large music classes at his service.

Professor von Bum is playing the lovely symphony in G minor from Beethoven's "Songs Without Music." The grand chords fill the room with exquisite harmony. He plays the extremely difficult passages in the obligato home run in a masterly manner, and when he finishes with that grand te deum with arpeggios on the side, there is that complete hush in the room that is dearer to the artist's heart than the loudest applause.

The professor looks around.

The room is empty.

Empty with the exception of Tictocq, the great French detective, who springs from behind a mass of tropical plants to his side.

The professor rises in alarm.

"Hush," says Tictocq: "Make no noise at all. You have already made enough."

Footsteps are heard outside.

"Be quick," says Tictocq: "give me those socks. There is not a moment to spare."

"Vas sagst du?"

"Ah, he confesses," says Tictocq. "No socks will do but those you carried off from the Populist Candidate's room."

The company is returning, no longer hearing the music.

Tictocq hesitates not. He seizes the professor, throws him upon the floor, tears off his shoes and socks, and escapes with the latter through the open window into the garden.

CHAPTER III

Tictocq's room in the Avenue Hotel.

A knock is heard at the door.

Tictocq opens it and looks at his watch.

"Ah," he says, "it is just six. Entrez, Messieurs."

The messieurs entrez. There are seven of them; the Populist Candidate who is there by invitation, not knowing for what purpose; the chairman of the Democratic Executive Committee, Platform No. 2; the hotel proprietor, and three or four Democrats and Populists, as near as could be found out.

"I don't know," begins the Populist Candidate, "what in the h——"

"Excuse me," says Tictocq, firmly. "You will oblige me by keeping silent until I make my report. I have been employed in this case, and I have unravelled it. For the honor of France I request that I be heard with attention."

"Certainly," says the chairman; "we will be pleased to listen."

Tictocq stands in the centre of the room. The electric light burns brightly above him. He seems the incarnation of alertness, vigor, cleverness, and cunning.

The company seat themselves in chairs along the wall.

"When informed of the robbery," begins Tictocq, "I first questioned the bell boy. He knew nothing. I went to the police headquarters. They knew nothing. I invited one of them to the bar to drink. He said there used to be a little colored boy in the Tenth Ward who stole things and kept them for recovery by the police, but failed to be at the place agreed upon for arrest one time, and had been sent to jail.

"I then began to think. I reasoned. No man, said I, would carry a Populist's socks in his pocket without wrapping them up. He would not want to do so in the hotel. He would want a paper. Where would he get one? At the *Statesman* office, of course. I went there. A young man with his hair combed down on his forehead sat behind the desk. I knew he was writing society items, for a young lady's slipper, a piece of cake, a fan, a half emptied bottle of cocktail, a bunch of roses, and a police whistle lay on the desk before him.

"Can you tell me if a man purchased a paper here in the last three months?" I said.

"Yes," he replied; "we sold one last night."

"Can you describe the man?"

"Accurately. He had blue whiskers, a wart between his shoulder blades, a touch of colic, and an occupation tax on his breath."

"Which way did he go?"

"Out."

"I then went——"

"Wait a minute," said the Populist Candidate, rising: "I don't see why in the h——"

"Once more I must beg that you will be silent," said Tictocq, rather sharply. "You should not interrupt me in the midst of my report."

"I made one false arrest," continued Tictocq. "I was passing two finely dressed gentlemen on the street, when one of them remarked that he had 'stole his socks.' I handcuffed him and dragged him to a lighted store, when his companion explained to me that he was somewhat intoxicated and his tongue was not entirely manageable. He had been speaking of some business transaction, and what he intended to say was that he had 'sold his stocks.'

"I then released him.

"An hour afterward I passed a saloon, and saw this Professor von Bum drinking beer at a table. I knew him in Paris. I said 'here is my man.' He worshipped Wagner, lived on limburger cheese, beer, and credit, and would have stolen anybody's socks. I shadowed him to the reception at Colonel St. Vitus's, and in an opportune moment I seized him and tore the socks from his feet. There they are."

With a dramatic gesture, Tictocq threw a pair of dingy socks upon the table, folded his arms, and threw back his head.

With a loud cry of rage, the Populist Candidate sprang once more to his feet. "Gol darn it! I WILL say what I want to. I——"

The two other Populists in the room gazed at him coldly and sternly.

"Is this tale true?" they demanded of the Candidate.

"No, by gosh, it ain't!" he replied, pointing a trembling finger at the Democratic Chairman. "There stands the man who has concocted the whole scheme. It is an infernal, unfair political trick to lose votes for our party. How far has this thing gone?" he added, turning savagely to the detective.

"All the newspapers have my written report on the matter, and the *Statesman* will have it in plate matter next week," said Tictocq, complacently.

"All is lost!" said the Populists, turning toward the door.

"For God's sake, my friends," pleaded the Candidate, following them; "listen to me; I swear before high heaven that I never wore a pair of socks in my life. It is all a devilish campaign lie."

The Populists turn their backs.

"The damage is already done," they said. "The people have heard the story. You have yet time to withdraw decently before the race."

All left the room except Tictocq and the Democrats.

"Let's all go down and open a bottle of fizz on the Finance Committee," said the Chairman of the Executive Committee, Platform No. 2.

TRACKED TO DOOM

OR

THE MYSTERY OF THE RUE DE PEYCHAUD

'Tis midnight in Paris.

A myriad of lamps that line the Champs Élysées and the Rouge et Noir, cast their reflection in the dark waters of the Seine as it flows gloomily past the Place Vendôme and the black walls of the Convent Notadam.

The great French capital is astir.

It is the hour when crime and vice and wickedness reign.

Hundreds of fiacres drive madly through the streets conveying women, flashing with jewels and as beautiful as dreams, from opera and concert, and the little bijou supper rooms of the Café Tout le Temps are filled with laughing groups, while bon mots, persiflage, and repartee fly upon the air—the jewels of thought and conversation.

Luxury and poverty brush each other in the streets. The homeless gamin, begging a sou with which to purchase a bed, and the spendthrift roué, scattering golden louis d'or, tread the same pavement.

When other cities sleep, Paris has just begun her wild revelry.

The first scene of our story is a cellar beneath the Rue de Peychaud.

The room is filled with smoke of pipes, and is stifling with the reeking breath of its inmates. A single flaring gas jet dimly lights the scene, which is one Rembrandt or Moreland and Keisel would have loved to paint.

A garçon is selling absinthe to such of the motley crowd as have a few sous, dealing it out in niggardly portions in broken teacups.

Leaning against the bar is Carnaignole Cusheau—generally known as the Gray Wolf.

He is the worst man in Paris.

He is more than four feet ten in height, and his sharp, ferocious-looking face and the mass of long, tangled gray hair that covers his face and head, have earned for him the name he bears.

His striped blouse lies open at the neck and falls outside of his dingy leather trousers. The handle of a deadly looking knife protrudes from his belt. One stroke of its blade would open a box of the finest French sardines.

"Voilà, Gray Wolf," cries Couteau, the bartender. "How many victims to-day? There is no blood upon your hands. Has the Gray Wolf forgotten how to bite?"

"Sacré Bleu, Mille Tonnerre, by George," hisses the Gray Wolf. "Monsieur Couteau, you are bold indeed to speak to me thus.

"By Ventre St. Gris! I have not even dined to-day. Spoils indeed. There is no living in Paris now. But one rich American have I garroted in a fortnight.

"Bah! those Democrats. They have ruined the country. With their income tax and their free trade, they have destroyed the millionaire business. Carrambo! Diable! D—n it!"

"Hist!" suddenly says Chamounix the rag-picker, who is worth 20,000,000 francs, "some one comes!"

The cellar door opened and a man crept softly down the rickety steps. The crowd watches him with silent awe.

He went to the bar, laid his card on the counter, bought a drink of absinthe, and then drawing from his pocket a little mirror, set it up on the counter and proceeded to don a false beard and hair and paint his face into wrinkles, until he closely resembled an old man seventy-one years of age.

He then went into a dark corner and watched the crowd of people with sharp, ferret-like eyes.

Gray Wolf slipped cautiously to the bar and examined the card left by the newcomer.

"Holy Saint Bridget!" he exclaims. "It is Tictocq, the detective."

Ten minutes later a beautiful woman enters the cellar.

Tenderly nurtured, and accustomed to every luxury that money could procure, she had, when a young vivandière at the Convent of Saint Susan de la Moutarde, run away with the Gray Wolf, fascinated by his many crimes and the knowledge that his business never allowed him to scrape his feet in the hall or snore.

"Parbleu, Marie," snarls the Gray Wolf. "Que voulez vous? Avez-vous le beau cheval de mon frère, oule joli chien de votre père?"

"No, no, Gray Wolf," shouts the motley group of assassins, rogues, and pickpockets, even their hardened hearts appalled at his fearful words. "Mon Dieu! You cannot be so cruel!"

"Tiens!" shouts the Gray Wolf, now maddened to desperation, and drawing his gleaming knife. "Voilà! Canaille! Tout le monde, carte blanche embonpoint sauve que peut entre nous revenez nous a nous moutons!"

The horrified sans-culottes shrink back in terror as the Gray Wolf seizes Maria by the hair and cuts her into twenty-nine pieces, each exactly the same size.

As he stands with reeking hands above the corpse, amid a deep silence, the old, gray-bearded man who has been watching the scene springs forward, tears off his false beard and locks, and Tictocq, the famous French detective, stands before them.

Spellbound and immovable, the denizens of the cellar gaze at the greatest modern detective as he goes about the customary duties of his office.

He first measures the distance from the murdered woman to a point on the wall, then he takes down the name of the bartender and the day of the month and the year. Then drawing from his pocket a powerful microscope, he examines a little of the blood that stands upon the floor in little pools.

"Mon Dieu!" he mutters, "it is as I feared—human blood."

He then enters rapidly in a memorandum book the result of his investigations, and leaves the cellar.

Tictocq bends his rapid steps in the direction of the headquarters of the Paris gendarmerie, but suddenly pausing, he strikes his hand upon his brow with a gesture of impatience.

"Mille tonnerre," he mutters. "I should have asked the name of that man with the knife in his hand."

. . . .

It is reception night at the palace of the Duchess Valerie du Bellairs.

The apartments are flooded with a mellow light from paraffine candles in solid silver candelabra.

The company is the most aristocratic and wealthy in Paris.

Three or four brass bands are playing behind a portière between the coal shed, and also behind time. Footmen in gay-laced livery bring in beer noiselessly and carry out apple-peelings dropped by the guests.

Valerie, seventh Duchess du Bellairs, leans back on a solid gold ottoman on eiderdown cushions, surrounded by the wittiest, the bravest, and the handsomest courtiers in the capital.

"Ah, madame," said the Prince Champvilliers, of Palais Royale, corner of Seventy-third Street, "as Montesquiaux says, 'Rien de plus bon tutti frutti'— Youth seems your inheritance. You are to-night the most beautiful, the wittiest in your own salon. I can scarce believe my own senses, when I remember that thirty-one years ago you——"

"Saw it off!" says the Duchess, peremptorily.

The Prince bows low, and drawing a jewelled dagger, stabs himself to the heart.

"The displeasure of your grace is worse than death," he says, as he takes his overcoat and hat from a corner of the mantelpiece and leaves the room.

"Voilà," says Bèebè Françillon, fanning herself languidly. "That is the way with men. Flatter them, and they kiss your hand. Loose but a moment the silken leash that holds them captive through their vanity and self-opinionativeness, and the son-of-a-gun gets on his ear at once. The devil go with him, I say."

"Ah, mon Princesse," sighs the Count Pumpernickel, stooping and whispering with eloquent eyes into her ear. "You are too hard upon us. Balzac says, 'All women are not to themselves what no one else is to another.' Do you not agree with him?"

"Cheese it!" says the Princess. "Philosophy palls upon me. I'll shake you."

"Hosses?" says the Count.

Arm and arm they go out to the salon au Beurre.

Armande de Fleury, the young pianissimo danseuse from the Folies Bergère, is about to sing.

She slightly clears her throat and lays a voluptuous cud of chewing gum upon the piano as the first notes of the accompaniment ring through the salon.

As she prepares to sing, the Duchess du Bellairs grasps the arm of her ottoman in a vicelike grip, and she watches with an expression of almost anguished suspense.

She scarcely breathes.

Then, as Armande de Fleury, before uttering a note, reels, wavers, turns white as snow and falls dead upon the floor, the Duchess breathes a sigh of relief.

The Duchess had poisoned her.

Then the guests crowd about the piano, gazing with bated breath, and shuddering as they look upon the music rack and observe that the song that Armande came so near singing is "Sweet Marie."

Twenty minutes later a dark and muffled figure was seen to emerge from a recess in the mullioned wall of the Arc de Triomphe and pass rapidly northward.

It was no other than Tictocq, the detective.

The network of evidence was fast being drawn about the murderer of Marie Cusheau.

. . . .

It is midnight on the steeple of the Cathedral of Notadam.

It is also the same time at other given points in the vicinity.

The spire of the Cathedral is 20,000 feet above the pavement, and a casual observer, by making a rapid mathematical calculation, would have readily perceived that this Cathedral is, at least, double the height of others that measure only 10,000 feet.

At the summit of the spire there is a little wooden platform on which there is room for but one man to stand.

Crouching on this precarious footing, which swayed dizzily with every breeze that blew, was a man closely muffled, and disguised as a wholesale grocer.

Old François Beongfallong, the great astronomer, who is studying the sidereal spheres from his attic window in the Rue de Bologny, shudders as he turns his telescope upon the solitary figure upon the spire.

"Sacré Bleu!" he hisses between his new celluloid teeth. "It is Tictocq, the detective. I wonder whom he is following now?"

While Tictocq is watching with lynx-like eyes the hill of Montmartre, he suddenly hears a heavy breathing beside him, and turning gazes into the ferocious eyes of the Gray Wolf.

Carnaignole Cusheau had put on his W. U. Tel. Co climbers and climbed the steeple.

"Parbleu, monsieur," says Tictocq. "To whom am I indebted for the honor of this visit?"

The Gray Wolf smiled softly and depreciatingly.

"You are Tictocq, the detective?" he said.

"I am."

"Then listen. I am the murderer of Marie Cusheau. She was my wife and she had cold feet and ate onions. What was I to do? Yet life is sweet to me.

I so not wish to be guillotined. I have heard that you are on my track. Is it true that the case is in your hands?"

"It is."

"Thank le bon Dieu, then, I am saved."

The Gray Wolf carefully adjusts the climbers on his feet and descends the spire.

Tictocq takes out his notebook and writes in it.

"At last," he says, "I have a clue."

.   .   .   .

Monsieur le Compte Carnaignole Cusheau, once known as the Gray Wolf, stands in the magnificent drawing-room of his palace on East 47th Street.

Three days after his confession to Tictocq, he happened to look in the pockets of a discarded pair of pants and found twenty million francs in gold.

Suddenly the door opens and Tictocq, the detective, with a dozen gensd'arme enters the room.

"You are my prisoner," says the detective.

"On what charge?"

"The murder of Marie Cusheau on the night of August 17th."

"Your proofs?"

"I saw you do it, and your own confession on the spire of Notadam."

The Count laughed and took a paper from his pocket.

"Read this," he said, "here is proof that Marie Cusheau died of heart failure."

Tictocq looked at the paper.

It was a check for 100,000 francs.

Tictocq dismissed the gensd'arme with a wave of his hand.

"We have made a mistake, monsieurs," he said, but as he turns to leave the room, Count Carnaignole stops him.

"One moment, monsieur."

The Count Carnaignole tears from his own face a false beard and reveals the flashing eyes and well-known features of Tictocq, the detective.

Then, springing forward, he snatches a wig and false eyebrows from his visitor, and the Gray Wolf, grinding his teeth in rage, stands before him.

The murderer of Marie Cusheau was never discovered.

A SNAPSHOT AT THE PRESIDENT

[This is the kind of waggish editorial O. Henry was writing in 1894 for the readers of the *Rolling Stone*. The reader will do well to remember that the paper was for local consumption and that the allusions are to a very special place and time.]

(It will be remembered that about a month ago there were special rates offered to the public for a round trip to the City of Washington. The price of the ticket being exceedingly low, we secured a loan of twenty dollars from a public-spirited citizen of Austin, by mortgaging our press and cow, with the additional security of our brother's name and a slight draught on Major Hutchinson for $4,000.

We purchased a round trip ticket, two loaves of Vienna bread, and quite a large piece of cheese, which we handed to a member of our reportorial staff, with instructions to go to Washington, interview President Cleveland, and get a scoop, if possible, on all other Texas papers.

Our reporter came in yesterday morning, via the Manor dirt road, with a large piece of folded cotton bagging tied under each foot.

It seems that he lost his ticket in Washington, and having divided the Vienna bread and cheese with some disappointed office seekers who were coming home by the same route, he arrived home hungry, desiring food, and with quite an appetite.

Although somewhat late, we give his description of his interview with President Cleveland.)

I AM chief reporter on the staff of the *Rolling Stone*.

About a month ago the managing editor came into the room where we were both sitting engaged in conversation and said:

"Oh, by the way, go to Washington and interview President Cleveland."

"All right," said I. "Take care of yourself."

Five minutes later I was seated in a palatial drawing-room car bounding up and down quite a good deal on the elastic plush-covered seat.

I shall not linger upon the incidents of the journey. I was given carte blanche to provide myself with every comfort, and to spare no expense that I could meet. For the regalement of my inside the preparations had been lavish. Both Vienna and Germany had been called upon to furnish dainty viands suitable to my palate.

I changed cars and shirts once only on the journey. A stranger wanted me to also change a two-dollar bill, but I haughtily declined.

The scenery along the entire road to Washington is diversified. You find a portion of it on one hand by looking out of the window, and upon turning the gaze upon the other side the eye is surprised and delighted to discovering some more of it.

There were a great many Knights of Pythias on the train. One of them insisted upon my giving him the grip I had with me, but he was unsuccessful.

On arriving in Washington, which city I instantly recognized from reading the history of George, I left the car so hastily that I forgot to fee Mr. Pullman's representative.

I went immediately to the Capitol.

In a spirit of jew d'esprit I had had made a globular representation of a "rolling stone." It was of wood, painted a dark color, and about the size of a small cannon ball. I had attached to it a twisted pendant about three inches long to indicate moss. I had resolved to use this in place of a card, thinking people would readily recognize it as an emblem of my paper.

I had studied the arrangement of the Capitol, and walked directly to Mr. Cleveland's private office.

I met a servant in the hall, and held up my card to him smilingly.

I saw his hair rise on his head, and he ran like a deer to the door, and, lying down, rolled down the long flight of steps into the yard.

"Ah," said I to myself, "he is one of our delinquent subscribers."

A little farther along I met the President's private secretary, who had been writing a tariff letter and cleaning a duck gun for Mr. Cleveland.

When I showed him the emblem of my paper he sprang out of a high window into a hothouse filled with rare flowers.

This somewhat surprised me.

I examined myself. My hat was on straight, and there was nothing at all alarming about my appearance.

I went into the President's private office.

He was alone. He was conversing with Tom Ochiltree. Mr. Ochiltree saw my little sphere, and with a loud scream rushed out of the room.

President Cleveland slowly turned his eyes upon me.

He also saw what I had in my hand, and said in a husky voice:

"Wait a moment, please."

He searched his coat pocket, and presently found a piece of paper on which some words were written.

He laid this on his desk and rose to his feet, raised one hand above him, and said in deep tones:

"I die for Free Trade, my country, and—and—all that sort of thing."

I saw him jerk a string, and a camera snapped on another table, taking our picture as we stood.

"Don't die in the House, Mr. President," I said. "Go over into the Senate Chamber."

"Peace, murderer!" he said. "Let your bomb do its deadly work."

"I'm no bum," I said, with spirit. "I represent the *Rolling Stone* of Austin, Texas, and this I hold in my hand does the same thing, but, it seems, unsuccessfully."

The President sank back in his chair greatly relieved.

"I thought you were a dynamiter," he said. "Let me see; Texas! Texas!" He walked to a large wall map of the United States, and placing his finger thereon at about the location of Idaho, ran it down in a zigzag, doubtful way until he reached Texas.

"Oh, yes, here it is. I have so many things on my mind, I sometimes forget what I should know well.

"Let's see; Texas? Oh, yes, that's the State where Ida Wells and a lot of colored people lynched a socialist named Hogg for raising a riot at a camp-meeting. So you are from Texas. I know a man from Texas named Dave Culberson. How is Dave and his family? Has Dave got any children?"

"He has a boy in Austin," I said, "working around the Capitol."

"Who is President of Texas now?"

"I don't exactly——"

"Oh excuse me. I forgot again. I thought I heard some talk of its having been made a Republic again."

"Now, Mr. Cleveland," I said, "you answer some of my questions."

A curious film came over the President's eyes. He sat stiffly in his chair like an automaton.

"Proceed," he said.

"What do you think of the political future of this country?"

"I will state that political exigencies demand emergentistical promptitude, and while the United States is indissoluble in conception and invisible in intent, treason and internecine disagreement have ruptured the consanguinity of patriotism, and——"

"One moment, Mr. President," I interrupted; "would you mind changing that cylinder? I could have gotten all that from the American Press Association if I had wanted plate matter. Do you wear flannels? What is your favorite poet, brand of catsup, bird, flower, and what are you going to do when you are out of a job?"

"Young man," said Mr. Cleveland, sternly, "you are going a little too far. My private affairs do not concern the public."

I begged his pardon, and he recovered his good humor in a moment.

"You Texans have a great representative in Senator Mills," he said. "I think the greatest two speeches I ever heard were his address before the Senate advocating the removal of the tariff on salt and increasing it on chloride of sodium."

"Tom Ochiltree is also from our State," I said.

"Oh, no, he isn't. You must be mistaken," replied Mr. Cleveland, "for he says he is. I really must go down to Texas some time, and see the State. I want to go up into the Panhandle and see if it is really shaped like it is on the map."

"Well, I must be going," said I.

"When you get back to Texas," said the President, rising, "you must write to me. Your visit has awakened in me quite an interest in your State which I fear I have not given the attention it deserves. There are many historical and otherwise interesting places that you have revived in my recollection—the Alamo, where Davy Jones fell; Goliad, Sam Houston's surrender to Montezuma, the petrified boom found near Austin, five-cent cotton and the Siamese Democratic platform born in Dallas. I should so much like to see the gals in Galveston, and go to the wake in Waco. I am glad I met you. Turn to the left as you enter the hall and keep straight on out." I made a low bow to signify that the interview was at an end, and withdrew immediately. I had no difficulty in leaving the building as soon as I was outside.

I hurried downtown in order to obtain refreshments at some place where viands had been placed upon the free list.

I shall not describe my journey back to Austin. I lost my return ticket somewhere in the White House, and was forced to return home in a manner not especially beneficial to my shoes. Everybody was well in Washington when I left, and all send their love.

AN UNFINISHED CHRISTMAS STORY

[Probably begun several years before his death. Published, as it here appears, in *Short Stories*, January, 1911.]

Now, a Christmas story should be one. For a good many years the ingenious writers have been putting forth tales for the holiday numbers that employed every subtle, evasive, indirect, and strategic scheme they could invent to disguise the Christmas flavor. So far has this new practice been carried that nowadays when you read a story in a holiday magazine the only way you can tell it is a Christmas story is to look at the footnote which reads: ["The incidents in the above story happened on December 25th.—Ed."]

There is progress in this; but it is all very sad. There are just as many real Christmas stories as ever, if we would only dig 'em up. Me, I am for the Scrooge and Marley Christmas story, and the Annie and Willie's prayer poem, and the long lost son coming home on the stroke of twelve to the poorly thatched cottage with his arms full of talking dolls and popcorn balls and—Zip! you hear the second mortgage on the cottage go flying off it into the deep snow.

So, this is to warn you that there is no subterfuge about this story—and you might come upon stockings hung to the mantel and plum puddings and hark! the chimes! and wealthy misers loosening up and handing over penny whistles to lame newsboys if you read further.

Once I knocked at a door (I have so many things to tell you I keep on losing sight of the story). It was the front door of a furnished room house in West 'Teenth Street. I was looking for a young illustrator named Paley originally and irrevocably from Terre Haute. Paley doesn't enter even into the first serial rights of this Christmas story; I mention him simply in explaining why I came to knock at the door—some people have so much curiosity.

The door was opened by the landlady. I had seen hundreds like her. And I had smelled before that cold, dank, furnished draught of air that hurried by her to escape immurement in the furnished house.

She was stout, and her face and hands were as white as though she had been drowned in a barrel of vinegar. One hand held together at her throat a button-less flannel dressing sacque whose lines had been cut by no tape or butterick known to mortal woman. Beneath this a too long, flowered, black sateen skirt was draped about her, reaching the floor in stiff wrinkles and folds.

The rest of her was yellow. Her hair, in some bygone age, had been dipped in the fountain of folly presided over by the merry nymph Hydrogen; but now, except at the roots, it had returned to its natural grim and grizzled white.

Her eyes and teeth and finger nails were yellow. Her chops hung low and shook when she moved. The look on her face was exactly that smileless look of fatal melancholy that you may have seen on the countenance of a hound left sit-ting on the doorstep of a deserted cabin.

I inquired for Paley. After a long look of cold suspicion the landlady spoke, and her voice matched the dingy roughness of her flannel sacque.

Paley? Was I sure that was the name? And wasn't it, likely, Mr. Sander-son I meant, in the third floor rear? No; it was Paley I wanted. Again that frozen, shrewd, steady study of my soul from her pale-yellow, unwinking eyes, trying to penetrate my mask of deception and rout out my true motives from my lying lips. There was a Mr. Tompkins in the front hall bedroom two flights up. Perhaps it was he I was seeking. He worked of nights; he never came in till seven in the morning. Or if it was really Mr. Tucker (thinly dis-guised as Paley) that I was hunting I would have to call between five and——

But no; I held firmly to Paley. There was no such name among her lodgers. Click! the door closed swiftly in my face; and I heard through the panels the clanking of chains and bolts.

I went down the steps and stopped to consider. The number of this house was 43. I was sure Paley had said 43—or perhaps it was 45 or 47—I decided to try 47, the second house farther along.

I rang the bell. The door opened; and there stood the same woman. I wasn't confronted by just a resemblance—it was the *same* woman holding to-gether the same old sacque at her throat and looking at me with the same yellow eyes as if she had never seen me before on earth. I saw on the knuckle of her second finger the same red-and-black spot made, probably, by a recent burn against a hot stove.

I stood speechless and gaping while one with moderate haste might have told fifty. I couldn't have spoken Paley's name even if I had remembered it. I did the only thing that a brave man who believes there are mysterious forces in nature that we do not yet fully comprehend could have done in the circumstances. I backed down the steps to the sidewalk and then hurried away frontward, fully understanding how incidents like that must bother the psychical research people and the census takers.

Of course I heard an explanation of it afterward, as we always do about in-explicable things.

The landlady was Mrs. Kannon; and she leased three adjoining houses, which she made into one by cutting arched doorways through the walls. She sat in the middle house and answered the three bells.

I wonder why I have maundered so slowly through the prologue. I have it! it was simply to say to you, in the form of introduction rife through the Middle West: "Shake hands with Mrs. Kannon."

For, it was in her triple house that the Christmas story happened; and it was there where I picked up the incontrovertible facts from the gossip of many roomers and met Stickney—and saw the necktie.

Christmas came that year on Thursday, and snow came with it.

Stickney (Harry Clarence Fowler Stickney to whomsoever his full baptismal cognominal burdens may be of interest) reached his address at six-thirty Wednesday afternoon. "Address" is New Yorkese for "Home." Stickney roomed at 45 West 'Teenth Street, third floor rear hall room. He was twenty years and four months old, and he worked in a cameras-of-all-kinds, photographic supplies and films-developed store. I don't know what kind of work he did in the store; but you must have seen him. He is the young man who always comes behind the counter to wait on you and lets you talk for five minutes, telling him what you want. When you are done, he calls the proprietor at the top of his voice to wait on you, and walks away whistling between his teeth.

I don't want to bother about describing to you his appearance; but, if you are a man reader, I will say that Stickney looked precisely like the young chap that you always find sitting in your chair smoking a cigarette after you have missed a shot while playing pool—not billiards, but pool—when you want to sit down yourself.

There are some to whom Christmas gives no Christmassy essence. Of course, prosperous people and comfortable people who have homes or flats or rooms with meals, and even people who live in apartment houses with hotel service get something of the Christmas flavor. They give one another presents with the cost mark scratched off with a penknife; and they hang holly wreaths in the front windows, and when they are asked whether they prefer light or dark meat from the turkey they say: "Both, please," and giggle and have lots of fun. And the very poorest people have the best time of it. The Army gives 'em a dinner, and the 10 A. M. issue of the Night Final edition of the newspaper with the largest circulation in the city leaves a basket at their door full of an apple, a Lake Ronkonkoma squab, a scrambled eggplant, and a bunch of Kalamazoo bleached parsley. The poorer you are the more Christmas does for you.

But, I'll tell you what kind of a mortal Christmas seems to be only the day before the twenty-sixth day of December. It's the chap in the big city earning sixteen dollars a week, with no friends and few acquaintances, who finds himself with only fifty cents in his pocket on Christmas eve. He can't accept charity; he can't borrow; he knows no one who would invite him to dinner. I have a fancy that when the shepherds left their flocks to follow the star of Bethlehem there was a bandy-legged young fellow among them who was just learning the sheep business. So they said to him, "Bobby, we're going to investigate this star route and see what's in it. If it should turn out to be the first Christmas day we don't want to miss it. And, as you are not a wise man, and as you couldn't possibly purchase a present to take along, suppose you stay behind and mind the sheep." So as we may say, Harry Stickney was a direct descendant of the shepherd who was left behind to take care of the flocks.

Getting back to facts, Stickney rang the door-bell of 45. He had a habit of forgetting his latchkey.

Instantly the door opened and there stood Mrs. Kannon, clutching her sacque together at the throat and gorgonizing him with her opaque yellow eyes.

(To give you good measure, here is a story within a story. Once a roomer in 47 who had a Scotch habit, not kilts, but a habit of drinking Scotch—began to figure to himself what might happen if two persons should ring the doorbells of 43 and 47 at the same time. Visions of two halves of Mrs. Kannon appearing respectively and simultaneously at the two entrances, each clutching at a side of an open, flapping sacque that could never meet, overpowered him. Bellevue got him.)

"Evening," said Stickney cheerlessly, as he distributed little piles of muddy slush along the hall matting. "Think we'll have snow?"

"You left your key," said——

(Here the manuscript ends.)

THE UNPROFITABLE SERVANT

[Left unfinished and published as it here appears in *Everybody's Magazine*, December, 1911.]

I AM the richer by the acquaintance of four newspaper men. Singly, they are my encyclopedias, friends, mentors, and sometimes bankers. But now and then it happens that all of them will pitch upon the same print-worthy incident of the passing earthly panorama and will send in reportorial constructions thereof to their respective journals. It is then that, for me, it is to laugh. For it seems that to each of them, trained and skilled as he may be, the same occurrence presents a different facet of the cut diamond, life.

One will have it (let us say) that Mme. André Macarté's apartment was looted by six burglars, who descended via the fire-escape and bore away a ruby tiara valued at two thousand dollars and a five-hundred-dollar prize Spitz dog, which (in violation of the expectoration ordinance) was making free with the halls of the Wutta-pesituckquesunoowetunquah Apartments.

My second "chiel" will take notes to the effect that while a friendly game of pinochle was in progress in the tenement rooms of Mrs. Andy McCarty, a lady guest named Ruby O'Hara threw a burglar down six flights of stairs, where he was pinioned and held by a two-thousand-dollar English bulldog amid a crowd of five hundred excited spectators.

My third chronicler and friend will gather the news threads of the happening in his own happy way; setting forth on the page for you to read that the house of Antonio Macartini was blown up at 6 A. M., by the Black Hand Society, on his refusing to leave two thousand dollars at a certain street corner, killing a pet five-hundred-dollar Pomeranian belonging to Alderman Rubitara's little daughter (see photo and diagram opposite).

Number four of my history-makers will simply construe from the premises the story that while an audience of two thousand enthusiasts was listening to a Rubinstein concert on Sixth Street, a woman who said she was Mrs. Andrew M. Carter threw a brick through a plate-glass window valued at five hundred dollars. The Carter woman claimed that some one in the building had stolen her dog.

Now, the discrepancies in these registrations of the day's doings need do no one hurt. Surely, one newspaper is enough for any man to prop against his morning water-bottle to fend off the smiling hatred of his wife's glance. If he be foolish enough to read four he is no wiser than a Higher Critic.

I remember (probably as well as you do) having read the parable of the talents. A prominent citizen, about to journey into a far country, first hands over to his servants his goods. To one he gives five talents; to another two; to another one—to every man according to his several ability, as the text has it. There are two versions of this parable, as you well know. There may be more— I do not know.

When the p. c. returns he requires an accounting. Two servants have put their talents out at usury and gained one hundred per cent. Good. The unprofitable one simply digs up the talent deposited with him and hands it out on demand. A pattern of behavior for trust companies and banks, surely! In one version we read that he had wrapped it in a napkin and laid it away. But the commentator informs us that the talent mentioned was composed of 750 ounces of silver—about $900 worth. So the chronicler who mentioned the napkin had either to reduce the amount of the deposit or do a lot of explaining about the size of the napery used in those days. Therefore in his version we note that he uses the word "pound" instead of "talent."

A pound of silver may very well be laid away—and carried away—in a napkin, as any hotel or restaurant man will tell you.

But let us get away from our mutton.

When the returned nobleman finds that the one-talented servant has nothing to hand over except the original fund entrusted to him, he is as angry as a multimillionaire would be if some one should hide under his bed and make a noise like an assessment. He orders the unprofitable servant cast into outer darkness, after first taking away his talent and giving it to the one-hundred-per-cent. financier, and breathing strange saws, saying: "From him that hath not shall be taken away even that which he hath." Which is the same as to say: "Nothing from nothing leaves nothing."

And now closer draw the threads of parable, precept, allegory, and narrative, leading nowhere if you will, or else weaving themselves into the little fiction story about Cliff McGowan and his one talent. There is but a definition to follow; and then the homely actors trip on.

Talent: A gift, endowment, or faculty; some peculiar ability, power, or accomplishment, natural or acquired. (A metaphor borrowed from the parable in Matt. XXV, 14–30.)

In New York City to-day there are (estimated) 125,000 living creatures training for the stage. This does not include seals, pigs, dogs, elephants, prizefighters, Carmens, mind-readers, or Japanese wrestlers. The bulk of them are in the ranks of the Four Million. Out of this number will survive a thousand.

Nine hundred of these will have attained their fulness of fame when they shall dubiously indicate with the point of a hatpin a blurred figure in a flashlight photograph of a stage tout ensemble with the proud commentary: "That's me."

Eighty, in the pinkest of (male) Louis XIV court costumes, shall welcome the Queen of the (mythical) Pawpaw Isles in a few well-memorized words, turning a tip-tilted nose upon the nine hundred.

Ten, in tiny lace caps, shall dust Ibsen furniture for six minutes after the rising of the curtain.

Nine shall attain the circuits, besieging with muscle, skill, eye, hand, voice, wit, brain, heel, and toe the ultimate nigh walls of stardom.

One shall inherit Broadway. Sic venit gloria mundi.

Cliff McGowan and Mac McGowan were cousins. They lived on the West Side and were talented. Singing, dancing, imitations, trick bicycle riding, boxing, German and Irish dialect comedy, and a little sleight-of-hand and balancing of wheat straws and wheelbarrows on the ends of their chins came as easy to them as it is for you fix your rat so it won't show or to dodge a creditor through the swinging-doors of a well-lighted café—according as you may belong to the one or the other division of the greatest prestidigitators—the people. They were slim, pale, consummately self-possessed youths, whose fingernails were always irreproachably (and clothes seams reproachfully) shiny. Their conversation was in sentences so short that they made Kipling's seem as long as court citations.

Having the temperament they did no work. Any afternoon you could find them on Eighth Avenue either in front of Spinelli's barber shop, Mike Dugan's

place, or the Limerick Hotel, rubbing their forefinger nails with dingy silk handkerchiefs. At any time, if you had happened to be standing, undecisive, near a
pool-table, and Cliff and Mac had, casually, as it were, drawn near, mentioning
something, disinterestedly, about a game, well, indeed, would it have been for
you had you gone your way, unresponsive. Which assertion, carefully considered,
is a study in tense, punctuation, and advice to strangers.

Of all kinships it is likely that the closest is that of cousin. Between cousins
there exist the ties of race, name, and favor—ties thicker than water, and yet
not coagulated with the jealous precipitations of brotherhood or the enjoining
obligations of the matrimonial yoke. You can bestow upon a cousin almost the
interest and affection that you would give to a stranger; you need not feel
toward him the contempt and embarrassment that you have for one of your
father's sons—it is the closer clan-feeling that sometimes makes the branch of a
tree stronger than its trunk.

Thus were the two McGowans bonded. They enjoyed a quiet celebrity in their
district, which was a strip west of Eighth Avenue with the Pump for its pivot.
Their talents were praised in a hundred "joints"; their friendship was famed even
in a neighborhood where men had been known to fight off the wives of their
friends—when domestic onslaught was being made upon their friends by the
wives of their friends. (Thus do the limitations of English force us to
repetends.)

So, side by side, grim, sallow, lowering, inseparable, undefeated, the cousins
fought their way into the temple of Art—art with a big A, which causes to
intervene a lesson in geometry.

One night at about eleven o'clock Del Delano dropped into Mike's place on
Eighth Avenue. From that moment, instead of remaining a Place, the café became a Resort. It was as though King Edward had condescended to mingle
with ten-spots of a different suit; or Joe Gans had casually strolled in to look
over the Tuskegee School; or Mr. Shaw, of England, had accepted an invitation
to read selections from "Rena, the Snow-Bird" at an unveiling of the proposed
monument to James Owen O'Connor at Chinquapin Falls, Mississippi. In spite
of these comparisons, you will have to be told why the patronizing of a third-
rate saloon on the West Side by the said Del Delano conferred such a specific
honor upon the place.

Del Delano could not make his feet behave; and so the world paid him $300
a week to see them misconduct themselves on the vaudeville stage. To make
the matter plain to you (and to swell the number of words), he was the best
fancy dancer on any of the circuits between Ottawa and Corpus Christi. With
his eyes fixed on vacancy and his feet apparently fixed on nothing, he "nightly
charmed thousands," as his press-agent incorrectly stated. Even taking night
performance and matinée together, he scarcely could have charmed more than
eighteen hundred, including those who left after Zora, the Nautch girl, had
squeezed herself through a hoop twelve inches in diameter, and those who were
waiting for the moving pictures.

But Del Delano was the West Side's favorite; and nowhere is there a more
loyal Side. Five years before our story was submitted to the editors, Del had
crawled from some Tenth Avenue basement like a lean rat and had bitten his way
into the Big Cheese. Patched, half starved, cuffless, and as scornful of the
Hook as an interpreter of Ibsen, he had danced his way into health (as you and I
view it) and fame in sixteen minutes on Amateur Night at Creary's (Variety)
Theatre in Eighth Avenue. A bookmaker (one of the kind that talent wins
with instead of losing) sat in the audience, asleep, dreaming of an impossible
pick-up among the amateurs. After a snore, a glass of beer from the handsome
waiter, and a temporary blindness caused by the diamonds of a transmontane
blonde in Box E, the bookmaker woke up long enough to engage Del Delano for a

three-weeks' trial engagement fused with a trained-dog short-circuit covering the three Washingtons—Heights, Statue, and Square.

By the time this story was read and accepted, Del Delano was drawing his three hundred dollars a week, which, divided by seven (Sunday acts not in costume being permissible), dispels the delusion entertained by most of us that we have seen better days. You can easily imagine the worshipful agitation of Eighth Avenue whenever Del Delano honored it with a visit after his terpsichorean act in a historically great and vilely ventilated Broadway theatre. If the West Side could claim forty-two minutes out of his forty-two weeks' bookings every year, it was an occasion for bonfires and repainting of the Pump. And now you know why Mike's saloon is a Resort, and no longer a simple Place.

Del Delano entered Mike's alone. So nearly concealed in a fur-lined overcoat and a derby two sizes too large for him was Prince Lightfoot that you saw of his face only his pale, hatchet-edged features and a pair of unwinking, cold, light blue eyes. Nearly every man lounging at Mike's bar recognized the renowned product of the West Side. To those who did not, wisdom was conveyed by prodding elbows and growls of one-sided introduction.

Upon Charley, one of the bartenders, both fame and fortune descended simultaneously. He had once been honored by shaking hands with the great Delano at a Seventh Avenue boxing bout. So with lungs of brass he now cried: "Hello, Del, old man; what'll it be?"

Mike, the proprietor, who was cranking the cash register, heard. On the next day he raised Charley's wages five a week.

Del Delano drank a pony beer, paying for it carelessly out of his nightly earnings of $42.85⅞. He nodded amiably but coldly at the long line of Mike's patrons and strolled past them into the rear room of the café. For he heard in there sounds pertaining to his own art—the light, stirring staccato of a buck-and-wing dance.

In the back room Mac McGowan was giving a private exhibition of the genius of his feet. A few young men sat at tables looking on critically while they amused themselves seriously with beer. They nodded approval at some new fancy steps of Mac's own invention.

At the sight of the great Del Delano, the amateur's feet stuttered, blundered, clicked a few times, and ceased to move. The tongues of one's shoes become tied in the presence of the Master. Mac's sallow face took on a slight flush.

From the uncertain cavity between Del Delano's hat brim and the lapels of his high fur coat collar came a thin puff of cigarette smoke and then a voice:

"Do that last step over again, kid. And don't hold your arms quite so stiff. Now, then!"

Once more Mac went through his paces. According to the traditions of the man dancer, his entire being was transformed into mere feet and legs. His gaze and expression became cataleptic; his body, unbending above the waist, but as light as a cork, bobbed like the same cork dancing on the ripples of a running brook. The beat of his heels and toes pleased you like a snare-drum obligato. The performance ended with an amazing clatter of leather against wood that culminated in a sudden flat-footed stamp, leaving the dancer erect and as motionless as a pillar of the colonial portico of a mansion in a Kentucky prohibition town. Mac felt that he had done his best and that Del Delano would turn his back upon him in derisive scorn.

An approximate silence followed, broken only by the mewing of a café cat and the hubbub and uproar of a few million citizens and transportation facilities outside.

Mac turned a hopeless but nervy eye upon Del Delano's face. In it he read disgust, admiration, envy, indifference, approval, disappointment, praise, and contempt.

Thus, in the countenances of those we hate or love we find what we most desire or fear to see. Which is an assertion equalling in its wisdom and chiaroscuro the most famous sayings of the most foolish philosophers that the world has ever known.

Del Delano retired within his overcoat and hat. In two minutes he emerged and turned his left side to Mac. Then he spoke.

"You've got a foot movement, kid, like a baby hippopotamus trying to side-step a jab from a humming-bird. And you hold yourself like a truck driver having his picture taken in a Third Avenue photograph gallery. And you haven't got any method or style. And your knees are about as limber as a couple of Yale pass-keys. And you strike the eye as weighing, let us say, 450 pounds while you work. But, say, would you mind giving me your name?"

"McGowan," said the humbled amateur—"Mac McGowan."

Delano the Great slowly lighted a cigarette and continued, through its smoke:

"In other words, you're rotten. You can't dance. But I'll tell you one thing you've got."

"Throw it all off your system while you're at it," said Mac. "What've I got?"

"Genius," said Del Delano. "Except myself, it's up to you to be the best fancy dancer in the United States, Europe, Asia, and the colonial possessions of all three."

"Smoke up!" said Mac McGowan.

"Genius," repeated the Master—"you've got a talent for genius. Your brains are in your feet, where a dancer's ought to be. You've been self-taught until you're almost ruined, but not quite. What you need is a trainer. I'll take you in hand and put you at the top of the profession. There's room there for the two of us. You may beat me," said the Master, casting upon him a cold, savage look combining so much rivalry, affection, justice, and human hate that it stamped him at once as one of the little great ones of the earth—"you may beat me; but I doubt it. I've got the start and the pull. But at the top is where you belong. Your name, you say, is Robinson?"

"McGowan," repeated the amateur, "Mac McGowan."

"It don't matter," said Delano. "Suppose you walk up to my hotel with me. I'd like to talk to you. Your footwork is the worst I ever saw, Madigan—but —well, I'd like to talk to you. You may not think so, but I'm not so stuck up. I came off of the West Side myself. That overcoat cost me eight hundred dollars; but the collar ain't so high but what I can see over it. I taught myself to dance, and I put in most of nine years at it before I shook a foot in public. But I had genius. I didn't go too far wrong in teaching myself as you've done. You've got the rottenest method and style of anybody I ever saw."

"Oh, I don't think much of the few little steps I take," said Mac, with hypocritical lightness.

"Don't talk like a package of self-raising buckwheat flour," said Del Delano. "You've had a talent handed to you by the Proposition Higher Up; and it's up to you to do the proper thing with it. I'd like to have you go up to my hotel for a talk, if you will."

In his rooms in the King Clovis Hotel, Del Delano put on a scarlet house coat bordered with gold braid and set out Apollinaris and a box of sweet crackers.

Mac's eye wandered.

"Forget it," said Del. Drink and tobacco may be all right for a man who makes his living with his hands; but they won't do if you're depending on your head or your feet. If one end of you gets tangled, so does the other. That's why beer and cigarettes don't hurt piano players and picture painters. But you've got to cut 'em out if you want to do mental or pedal work. Now, have a cracker, and then we'll talk some."

"All right," said Mac. "I take it as an honor, of course, for you to notice my hopping around. Of course I'd like to do something in a professional line. Of course I can sing a little and do card tricks and Irish and German comedy stuff, and of course I'm not so bad on the trapeze and comic bicycle stunts and Hebrew monologues and——"

"One moment," interrupted Del Delano, "before we begin. I said you couldn't dance. Well, that wasn't quite right. You've only got two or three bad tricks in your method. You're handy with your feet, and you belong at the top, where I am. I'll put you there. I've got six weeks continuous in New York; and in four I can shape up your style till the booking agents will fight one another to get you. And I'll do it, too. I'm of, from, and for the West Side. 'Del Delano' looks good on bill-boards, but the family name's Crowley. Now, Mackintosh—McGowan, I mean—you've got your chance—fifty times a better one than I had."

"I'd be a shine to turn it down," said Mac. "And I hope you understand I appreciate it. Me and my cousin Cliff McGowan was thinking of getting a try-out at Creary's on amateur night a month from to-morrow."

"Good stuff!" said Delano. "I got mine there. Junius T. Rollins, the booker for Kuhn & Dooley, jumped on the stage and engaged me after my dance. And the boards were an inch deep in nickels and dimes and quarters. There wasn't but nine penny pieces found in the lot."

"I ought to tell you," said Mac, after two minutes of pensiveness, "that my cousin Cliff can beat me dancing. We've always been what you might call pals. If you'd take him up instead of me, now, it might be better. He's invented a lot of steps that I can't cut."

"Forget it," said Delano. "Mondays, Wednesdays, Fridays, and Saturdays of every week from now till amateur night, a month off, I'll coach you. I'll make you as good as I am; and nobody could do more for you. My act's over every night at 10:15. Half an hour later I'll take you up and drill you till twelve. I'll put you at the top of the bunch, right where I am. You've got talent. Your style's bum; but you've got the genius. You let me manage it. I'm from the West Side myself, and I'd rather see one of the same gang win out before I would an East-Sider, or any of the Flatbush or Hackensack Meadow kind of butt-iners. I'll see that Junius Rollins is present on your Friday night; and if he don't climb over the footlights and offer you fifty a week as a starter, I'll let you draw it down from my own salary every Monday night. Now, am I talking on the level or am I not?"

Amateur night at Creary's Eighth Avenue Theatre is cut by the same pattern as amateur nights elsewhere. After the regular performance the humblest talent may, by previous arrangement with the management, make its début upon the public stage. Ambitious non-professionals, mostly self-instructed, display their skill and powers of entertainment along the broadest lines. They may sing, dance, mimic, juggle, contort, recite, or disport themselves along any of the ragged boundary lines of Art. From the ranks of these anxious tyros are chosen the professionals that adorn or otherwise make conspicuous the full-blown stage. Press-agents delight in recounting to open-mouthed and close-eared reporters stories of the humble beginnings of the brilliant stars whose orbits they control.

Such and such a prima donna (they will tell you) made her initial bow to the public while turning handsprings on an amateur night. One great matinée favorite made his début on a generous Friday evening singing coon songs of his own composition. A tragedian famous on two continents and an island first attracted attention by an amateur impersonation of a newly landed Scandinavian peasant girl. One Broadway comedian that turns 'em away got a booking on a Friday night by reciting (seriously) the graveyard scene in "Hamlet."

Thus they get their chance. Amateur night is a kindly boon. It is charity divested of alms-giving. It is a brotherly hand reached down by members of the best united band of coworkers in the world to raise up less fortunate ones without labelling them beggars. It gives you the chance, if you can grasp it, to step for a few minutes before some badly painted scenery and during the playing by the orchestra of some ten or twelve bars of music, and while the soles of your shoes may be clearly holding to the uppers, to secure a salary equal to a Congressman's or any orthodox minister's. Could an ambitious student of literature or financial methods get a chance like that by spending twenty minutes in a Carnegie library? I do not trow so.

But shall we look in at Creary's? Let us say that the specific Friday night had arrived on which the fortunate Mac McGowan was to justify the flattering predictions of his distinguished patron and, incidentally, drop his silver talent into the slit of the slot-machine of fame and fortune that gives up reputation and dough. I offer, sure of your acquiescence, that we now forswear hypocritical philosophy and bigoted comment, permitting the story to finish itself in the dress of material allegations—a medium more worthy, when held to the line, than the most laborious creations of the word-milliners. . .

(Page of manuscript missing here.)

easily among the wings with his patron, the great Del Delano. For, whatever footlights shone in the City-That-Would-Be-Amused, the freedom of their unshaded side was Del's. And if he should take up an amateur—see? and bring him around—see? and, winking one of his cold blue eyes, say to the manager: "Take it from me—he's got the goods—see?" you wouldn't expect that amateur to sit on an unpainted bench sudorifically awaiting his turn, would you? So Mac strolled around largely with the nonpareil; and the seven waited, clammily, on the bench.

A giant in shirt-sleeves with a grim, kind face in which many stitches had been taken by surgeons from time to time, i. e., with a long stick, looped at the end. He was the man with the Hook. The manager, with his close-smoothed blond hair, his one-sided smile, and his abnormally easy manner, pored with patient condescension over the difficult program of the amateurs. The last of the professional turns—the Grand March of the Happy Huzzard—had been completed; the last wrinkle and darn of their blue silkolene cotton tights had vanished from the stage. The man in the orchestra who played the kettle-drum, cymbals, triangle, sandpaper, whangdoodle, hoofbeats, and catcalls, and fired the pistol shots, had wiped his brow. The illegal holiday of the Romans had arrived.

While the orchestra plays the famous waltz from "The Dismal Wife," let us bestow two hundred words upon the psychology of the audience.

The orchestra floor was filled by People. The boxes contained Persons. In the galleries was the Foreordained Verdict. The claque was there as it had originated in the Stone Age and was afterward adopted by the French. Every Micky and Maggie who sat upon Creary's amateur bench, wise beyond their talents, knew that their success or doom lay already meted out to them by that crowded, whistling, roaring mass of Romans in the three galleries. They knew that the winning or the losing of the game for each one lay in the strength of the "gang" aloft that could turn the applause to its favorite. On a Broadway first night a wooer of fame may win it from the ticket buyers over the heads of the cognoscenti. But not so at Creary's. The amateur's fate is arithmetical. The number of his supporting admirers present at his try-out decides it in advance. But how these outlying Friday nights put to a certain shame the Mondays, Tuesdays, Wednesdays, Thursdays, Saturdays, and matinées of the Broadway stage you should know. . . .

(Here the manuscript ends.)

ARISTOCRACY VERSUS HASH

[From the *Rolling Stone.*]

THE snake reporter of the *Rolling Stone* was wandering up the avenue last night on his way home from the Y. M. C. A. rooms when he was approached by a gaunt, hungry-looking man with wild eyes and dishevelled hair. He accosted the reporter in a hollow, weak voice.

" 'Can you tell me, Sir, where I can find in this town a family of scrubs?'

" 'I don't understand exactly.'

" 'Let me tell you how it is,' said the stranger, inserting his forefinger in the reporter's buttonhole and badly damaging his chrysanthemum. 'I am a representative from Soapstone County, and I and my family are houseless, homeless, and shelterless. We have not tasted food for over a week. I brought my family with me, as I have indigestion and could not get around much with the boys. Some days ago I started out to find a boarding house, as I cannot afford to put up at a hotel. I found a nice aristocratic-looking place, that suited me, and went in and asked for the proprietress. A very stately lady with a Roman nose came in the room. She had one hand laid across her stom—across her waist, and the other held a lace handkerchief. I told her I wanted board for myself and family, and she condescended to take us. I asked for her terms, and she said $300 per week.

" 'I had two dollars in my pocket and I gave her that for a fine teapot that I broke when I fell over the table when she spoke.'

" 'You appear surprised,' says she. 'You will please remembah that I am the widow of Governor Riddle of Georgiah; my family is very highly connected; I give you board as a favah; I nevah considah money any equivalent for the advantage of my society, I——'

" 'Well, I got out of there, and I went to some other places. The next lady was a cousin of General Mahone of Virginia, and wanted four dollars an hour for a back room with a pink motto and a Burnet granite bed in it. The next one was an aunt of Davy Crockett, and asked eight dollars a day for a room furnished in imitation of the Alamo, with prunes for breakfast and one hour's conversation with her for dinner. Another one said she was a descendant of Benedict Arnold on her father's side and Captain Kidd on the other.

" 'She took more after Captain Kidd.

" 'She only had one meal and prayers a day, and counted her society worth $100 a week.

" 'I found nine widows of Supreme Judges, twelve relicts of Governors and Generals, and twenty-two ruins left by various happy Colonels, Professors, and Majors, who valued their aristocratic worth from $90 to $900 per week, with weak-kneed hash and dried apples on the side. I admire people of fine descent, but my stomach yearns for pork and beans instead of culture. Am I not right?"

" 'Your words,' said the reporter, 'convince me that you have uttered what you have said.'

" 'Thanks. You see how it is. I am not wealthy; I have only my per diem and my per quisites, and I cannot afford to pay for high lineage and moldy ancestors. A little corned beef goes further with me than a coronet, and when I am cold a coat of arms does not warm me.'

" 'I greatly fear,' said the reporter, with a playful hiccough, 'that you have run against a high-toned town. Most all the first-class boarding houses here are run by ladies of the old Southern families, the very first in the land.'

" 'I am now desperate,' said the Representative, as he chewed a tack awhile, thinking it was a clove. 'I want to find a boarding house where the proprietress was an orphan found in a livery stable, whose father was a dago from East Austin, and whose grandfather was never placed on the map. I want a scrubby, ornery, low-down, snuff-dipping, back-woodsy, piebald gang, who never heard of finger bowls or Ward McAllister, but who can get up a mess of hot corn-bread and Irish stew at regular market quotations.'

" 'Is there such a place in Austin?'

"The snake reporter sadly shook his head. 'I do not know,' he said, 'but I will shake you for the beer.'

"Ten minutes later the slate in the Blue Ruin saloon bore two additional characters: 10."

THE PRISONER OF ZEMBLA

[From the *Rolling Stone.*]

So the king fell into a furious rage, so that none durst go near him for fear, and he gave out that since the Princess Ostla had disobeyed him there would be a great tourney, and to the knight who should prove himself of the greatest valor he would give the hand of the princess.

And he sent forth a herald to proclaim that he would do this.

And the herald went about the country making his desire known, blowing a great tin horn and riding a noble steed that pranced and gambolled; and the villagers gazed upon him and said: "Lo, that is one of them tin-horn gamblers concerning which the chroniclers have told us."

And when the day came, the king sat in the grandstand, holding the gage of battle in his hand, and by his side sat the Princess Ostla, looking very pale and beautiful, but with mournful eyes from which she scarce could keep the tears. And the knights which came to the tourney gazed upon the princess in wonder at her beauty, and each swore to win so that he could marry her and board with the king. Suddenly the heart of the princess gave a great bound, for she saw among the knights one of the poor students with whom she had been in love.

The knights mounted and rode in a line past the grandstand, and the king stopped the poor student, who had the worst horse and the poorest caparisons of any of the knights and said:

"Sir Knight, prithee tell me of what that marvellous shacky and rusty-looking armor of thine is made?"

"Oh, king," said the young knight, "seeing that we are about to engage in a big fight, I would call it scrap iron, wouldn't you?"

"Ods Bodkins!" said the king. "The youth hath a pretty wit."

About this time the Princess Ostla, who began to feel better at the sight of her lover, slipped a piece of gum into her mouth and closed her teeth upon it, and even smiled a little and showed the beautiful pearls with which her mouth was set. Whereupon, as soon as the knights perceived this, 217 of them went over to the king's treasurer and settled for their horse feed and went home.

"It seems very hard," said the princess, "that I cannot marry when I chews."

But two of the knights were left, one of them being the princess's lover.

"Here's enough for a fight, anyhow," said the king. "Come hither, O knights, will ye joust for the hand of this fair lady?"

"We joust will," said the knights.

The two knights fought for two hours, and at length the princess's lover prevailed and stretched the other upon the ground. The victorious knight made his horse caracole before the king and bowed low in his saddle.

On the Princess Ostla's cheeks was a rosy flush; in her eyes the light of excitement vied with the soft glow of love; her lips were parted, her lovely hair unbound, and she grasped the arms of her chair and leaned forward with heaving bosom and happy smile to hear the words of her lover.

"You have foughten well, sir knight," said the king. "And if there is any boon you crave you have but to name it."

"Then," said the knight, "I will ask you this: I have bought the patent rights in your kingdom for Schneider's celebrated monkey wrench, and I want a letter from you endorsing it."

"You shall have it," said the king, "but I must tell you that there is not a monkey in my kingdom."

With a yell of rage the victorious knight threw himself on his horse and rode away at a furious gallop.

The king was about to speak, when a horrible suspicion flashed upon him and he fell dead upon the grandstand.

"My God!" he cried. "He has forgotten to take the princess with him!"

A STRANGE STORY

[From the *Rolling Stone.*]

In the northern part of Austin there once dwelt an honest family by the name of Smothers. The family consisted of John Smothers, his wife, himself, their little daughter, five years of age and her parents, making six people toward the population of the city when counted for a special write-up, but only three by actual count.

One night after supper the little girl was seized with a severe colic, and John Smothers hurried downtown to get some medicine.

He never came back.

The little girl recovered and in time grew up to womanhood.

The mother grieved very much over her husband's disappearance, and it was nearly three months before she married again, and moved to San Antonio.

The little girl also married in time, and after a few years had rolled around, she also had a little girl five years of age.

She still lived in the same house where they dwelt when her father had left and never returned.

One night by a remarkable coincidence her little girl was taken with cramp colic on the anniversary of the disappearance of John Smothers, who would now have been her grandfather if he had been alive and had a steady job.

"I will go downtown and get some medicine for her," said John Smith (for it was none other than he whom she had married).

"No, no, dear John," cried his wife. "You, too, might disappear forever, and then forget to come back."

So John Smith did not go, and together they sat by the bedside of little Pansy for that was Pansy's name).

After a little Pansy seemed to grow worse, and John Smith again attempted to go for medicine, but his wife would not let him.

Suddenly the door opened, and an old man, stooped and bent, with long white hair, entered the room.

"Hello, here is grandpa," said Pansy. She had recognized him before any of the others.

The old man drew a bottle of medicine from his pocket and gave Pansy a spoonful.

She got well immediately.

"I was a little late," said John Smothers, "as I waited for a street car."

FICKLE FORTUNE OR HOW GLADYS HUSTLED

[From the *Rolling Stone*.]

"Press me no more, Mr. Snooper," said Gladys Vavasour-Smith. "I can never be yours."

"You have led me to believe different, Gladys," said Bertram D. Snooper.

The setting sun was flooding with golden light the oriel windows of a magnificent mansion situated in one of the most aristocratic streets west of the brick yard.

Bertram D. Snooper, a poor but ambitious and talented young lawyer, had just lost his first suit. He had dared to aspire to the hand of Gladys Vavasour-Smith, the beautiful and talented daughter of one of the oldest and proudest families in the county. The bluest blood flowed in her veins. Her grandfather had sawed wood for the Hornsbys and an aunt on her mother's side had married a man who had been kicked by General Lee's mule.

The lines about Bertram D. Snooper's hands and mouth were drawn tighter as he paced to and fro, waiting for a reply to the question he intended to ask Gladys as soon as he thought of one.

At last an idea occurred to him.

"Why will you not marry me?" he asked in an inaudible tone.

"Because," said Gladys, firmly, speaking easily with great difficulty, "the progression and enlightenment that the woman of to-day possesses demand that the man shall bring to the marriage altar a heart and body as free from the debasing and hereditary iniquities that now no longer exist except in the chimerical imagination of enslaved custom."

"It is as I expected," said Bertram, wiping his heated brow on the window curtain. "You have been reading books."

"Besides that," continued Gladys, ignoring the deadly charge, "you have no money."

The blood of the Snoopers rose hastily and mantled the cheek of Bertram D. He put on his coat and moved proudly to the door.

"Stay here till I return," he said, "I will be back in fifteen years."

When he had finished speaking he ceased and left the room.

When he had gone, Gladys felt an uncontrollable yearning take possession of her. She said slowly, rather to herself than for publication, "I wonder if there was any of that cold cabbage left from dinner."

She then left the room.

When she did so, a dark-complexioned man with black hair and gloomy, desperate-looking clothes, came out of the fireplace where he had been concealed and stated:

"Aha! I have you in my power at last, Bertram D. Snooper. Gladys Vavasour-Smith shall be mine. I am in the possession of secrets that not a soul in the world suspects. I have papers to prove that Bertram Snooper is the heir to the Tom Basset estate,[1] and I have discovered that Gladys' grandfather who sawed wood for the Hornsbys was also a cook in Major Rhoads Fisher's command during the war. Therefore, the family repudiate her, and she will marry me in order to drag their proud name down in the dust. Ha, ha, ha!"

As the reader has doubtless long ago discovered, this man was no other than Henry R. Grasty. Mr. Grasty then proceeded to gloat some more, and then with a sardonic laugh left for New York.

*   *   *   *   *   *   *   *   *   *

Fifteen years have elapsed.

Of course, our readers will understand that this is only supposed to be the case.

It really took less than a minute to make the little stars that represent an interval of time.

We could not afford to stop a piece in the middle and wait fifteen years before continuing it.

We hope this explanation will suffice. We are careful not to create any wrong impressions.

Gladys Vavasour-Smith and Henry R. Grasty stood at the marriage altar.

Mr. Grasty had evidently worked his rabbit's foot successfully, although he was quite a while in doing so.

Just as the preacher was about to pronounce the fatal words on which he would have realized ten dollars and had the laugh on Mr. Grasty, the steeple of the church fell off and Bertram D. Snooper entered.

The preacher fell to the ground with a dull thud. He could ill afford to lose ten dollars. He was hastily removed and a cheaper one secured.

Bertram D. Snooper held a *Statesman* in his hand.

"Aha!" he said, "I thought I would surprise you. I just got in this morning. Here is a paper noticing my arrival."

He handed it to Henry R. Grasty.

Mr. Grasty looked at the paper and turned deadly pale. It was dated three weeks after Mr. Snooper's arrival.

"Foiled again!" he hissed.

"Speak, Bertram D. Snooper," said Gladys, "why have you come between me and Henry?"

"I have just discovered that I am the sole heir to Tom Bean's estate and am worth two million dollars."

With a glad cry Gladys threw herself in Bertram's arms.

Henry R. Grasty drew from his breast pocket a large tin box and opened it, took therefrom 467 pages of closely written foolscap.

"What you say is true, Mr. Snooper, but I ask you to read that," he said, handing it to Bertram Slooper.

Mr. Snooper had no sooner read the document than he uttered a piercing shriek and bit off a large chew of tobacco.

"All is lost," he said.

"What is that document?" asked Gladys. Governor Hogg's message?"

"It is not as bad as that," said Bertram, "but it deprives me of my entire fortune. But I care not for that, Gladys, since I have won you."

"What is it? Speak, I implore you," said Gladys.

"Those papers," said Henry R. Grasty, "are the proofs of my appointment as administrator of the Tom Bean estate."

[1] An estate famous in Texas legal history. It took many, many years for adjustment and a large part of the property was, of course, consumed as expenses of litigation.

With a loving cry Gladys threw herself in Henry R. Grasty's arms.

*   *   *   *   *   *   *   *   *   *   *   *

Twenty minutes later Bertram D. Snooper was seen deliberately to enter a beer saloon on Seventeenth Street.

AN APOLOGY

[This appeared in the *Rolling Stone* shortly before it "suspended publication" never to resume.]

THE person who sweeps the office, translates letters from foreign countries, deciphers communications from graduates of business colleges, and does most of the writing for this paper, has been confined for the past two weeks to the under side of a large red quilt, with a joint caucus of la grippe and measles.

We have missed two issues of the *Rolling Stone,* and are now slightly convalescent, for which we desire to apologize and express our regrets.

Everybody's term of subscription will be extended long enough to cover all missed issues, and we hope soon to report that the goose remains suspended at a favorable altitude. People who have tried to run a funny paper and entertain a congregation of large piebald measles at the same time will understand something of the tact, finesse, and hot sassafras tea required to do so. We expect to get out the paper regularly from this time on, but are forced to be very careful, as improper treatment and deleterious after-effects of measles, combined with the high price of paper and presswork, have been known to cause a relapse. Any one not getting their paper regularly will please come down and see about it, bringing with them a ham or any little delicacy relished by invalids.

LORD OAKHURST'S CURSE

[This story was sent to Dr. Beall of Greensboro, N. C. in a letter in 1883, and so is one of O. Henry's earliest attempts at writing.

I

LORD OAKHURST lay dying in the oak chamber in the eastern wing of Oakhurst Castle. Through the open window in the calm of the summer evening, came the sweet fragrance of the early violets and budding trees, and to the dying man it seemed as if earth's loveliness and beauty were never so apparent as on this bright June day, his last day of life.

His young wife, whom he loved with a devotion and strength that the presence of the king of terrors himself could not alter, moved about the apartment, weeping and sorrowful, sometimes arranging the sick man's pillow and inquiring of him in low, mournful tones if anything could be done to give him comfort, and again, with stifled sobs, eating some chocolate caramels which she carried in the pocket of her apron. The servants went to and fro with that quiet and subdued tread. which prevails in a house where death is an expected guest, and even the crash of broken china and shivered glass, which announced their approach, seemed to fall upon the ear with less violence and sound than usual.

Lord Oakhurst was thinking of days gone by, when he wooed and won his beautiful young wife, who was then but a charming and innocent girl. How clearly and minutely those scenes rose up at the call of his memory. He seemed to be standing once more beneath the old chestnut grove where they had plighted their troth in the twilight under the stars; while the rare fragrance of the June roses and the smell of supper came gently by on the breeze. There he had told her his love; how that his whole happiness and future joy lay in the hope that he might win her for a bride; that if she would trust her future to his care the devotedness of his lifetime should be hers, and his only thought would be to make her life one long day of sunshine and peanut candy.

How plainly he remembered how she had, with girlish shyness and coyness, at first hesitated, and murmured something to herself about "an old bald-headed galoot," but when he told her that to him life without her would be a blasted mockery, and that his income was £50,000 a year, she threw herself on to him and froze there with the tenacity of a tick on a brindled cow, and said, with tears of joy, "Hen-ery, I am thine."

And now he was dying. In a few short hours his spirit would rise up at the call of the Destroyer and, quitting his poor, weak, earthly frame, would go forth into that dim and dreaded Unknown Land, and solve with certainty that Mystery which revealeth itself not to mortal man.

II

A carriage drove rapidly up the avenue and stopped at the door. Sir Everhard FitzArmond, the famous London physician, who had been telegraphed for, alighted and quickly ascended the marble steps. Lady Oakhurst met him at the door, her lovely face expressing great anxiety and grief. "Oh, Sir Everhard, I am so glad you have come. He seems to be sinking rapidly. Did you bring the cream almonds I mentioned in the telegram?"

Sir Everhard did not reply, but silently handed her a package, and, slipping a couple of cloves into his mouth, ascended the stairs that led to Lord Oakhurst's apartment. Lady Oakhurst followed.

Sir Everhard approached the bedside of his patient and laid his hand gently on this sick man's diagnosis. A shade of feeling passed over his professional countenance as he gravely and solemnly pronounced these words: "Madam, your husband has croaked."

Lady Oakhurst at first did not comprehend his technical language, and her lovely mouth let up for a moment on the cream almonds. But soon his meaning flashed upon her, and she seized an ax that her husband was accustomed to keep by his bedside to mangle his servants with, and struck open Lord Oakhurst's cabinet containing his private papers, and with eager hands opened the document which she took therefrom. Then, with a wild, unearthly shriek that would have made a steam piano go out behind a barn and kick itself in despair, she fell senseless to the floor.

Sir Everhard FitzArmond picked up the paper and read its contents. It was Lord Oakhurst's will, bequeathing all his property to a scientific institution which should have for its object the invention of a means for extracting peach brandy from sawdust.

Sir Everhard glanced quickly around the room. No one was in sight. Dropping the will, he rapidly transferred some valuable ornaments and rare specimens of gold and silver filigree work from the centre table to his pockets, and rang the bell for the servants.

III—THE CURSE

Sir Everhard FitzArmond descended the stairway of Oakhurst Castle and passed out into the avenue that led from the doorway to the great iron gates of the park. Lord Oakhurst had been a great sportsman during his life and always kept a well-stocked kennel of curs, which now rushed out from their hiding places and with loud yelps sprang upon the physician, burying their fangs in his lower limbs and seriously damaging his apparel.

Sir Everhard, startled out of his professional dignity and usual indifference to human suffering, by the personal application of feeling, gave vent to a most horrible and blighting CURSE and ran with great swiftness to his carriage and drove off toward the city.

BEXAR SCRIP NO. 2692

[From the *Rolling Stone*, Saturday, March 5, 1894.]

WHENEVER you visit Austin you should by all means go to see the General Land Office.

As you pass up the avenue you turn sharp round the corner of the court house, and on a steep hill before you you see a mediæval castle.

You think of the Rhine; the "castled crag of Drachenfels"; the Lorelei; and the vine-clad slopes of Germany. And German it is in every line of its architecture and design.

The plan was drawn by an old draftsman from the "Vaterland," whose heart still loved the scenes of his native land, and it is said he reproduced the design of a certain castle near his birthplace with remarkable fidelity.

Under the present administration a new coat of paint has vulgarized its ancient and venerable walls. Modern tiles have replaced the limestone slabs of its floors, worn in hollows by the tread of thousands of feet, and smart and gaudy fixtures have usurped the place of the time-worn furniture that has been consecrated by the touch of hands that Texas will never cease to honor.

But even now, when you enter the building, you lower your voice, and time turns backward for you, for the atmosphere which you breathe is cold with the exudations of buried generations.

The building is stone with a coating of concrete; the walls are immensely thick; it is cold in the summer and warm in the winter; it is isolated and sombre; standing apart from the other state buildings, sullen and decaying, brooding on the past.

Twenty years ago it was much the same as now; twenty years from now the garish newness will be worn off and it will return to its appearance of gloomy decadence.

People living in other states can form no conception of the vastness and importance of the work performed and the significance of the millions of records and papers composing the archives of this office.

The title deeds, patents, transfers, and legal documents connected with every foot of land owned in the state of Texas are filed here.

Volumes could be filled with accounts of the knavery, the double-dealing, the cross purposes, the perjury, the lies, the bribery, the alteration and erasing, the suppressing and destroying of papers, the various schemes and plots that for the sake of the almighty dollar have left their stains upon the records of the General Land Office.

No reference is made to the employees. No more faithful, competent, and efficient force of men exists in the clerical portions of any government, but there is—or was, for their day is now over—a class of land speculators commonly called land sharks, unscrupulous and greedy, who have left their trail in every department of this office, in the shape of titles destroyed, patents cancelled, homes demolished and torn away, forged transfers and lying affidavits.

Before the modern tiles were laid upon the floors, there were deep hollows in the limestone slabs, worn by the countless feet that daily trod uneasily through its echoing corridors, pressing from file room to business room, from commissioner's sanctum to record books and back again.

The honest but ignorant settler, bent on saving the little plot of land he called home, elbowed the wary land shark who was searching the records for evidence to oust him; the lordly cattle baron, relying on his influence and money, stood at the Commissioner's desk side by side with the preëmptor, whose little potato patch lay like a minute speck of island in the vast, billowy sea of his princely pastures, and played the old game of "freeze-out," which is as old as Cain and Abel.

The trail of the serpent is through it all.

Honest, earnest men have wrought for generations striving to disentangle the shameful coil that certain years of fraud and infamy have wound. Look at the files and see the countless endorsements of those in authority:

"Transfer doubtful—locked up."

"Certificate a forgery—locked up."

"Signature a forgery."

"Patent refused—duplicate patented elsewhere."

"Field notes forged."

"Certificates stolen from office"—and so on, ad infinitum.

The record books, spread upon long tables in the big room upstairs, are open to the examination of all.

Open them, and you will find the dark and greasy fingerprints of half a century's handling. The quick hand of the land grabber has fluttered the leaves a million times; the damp clutch of the perturbed tiller of the soil has left traces of his calling on the ragged leaves.

Interest centres in the file room.

This is a large room, built as a vault, fireproof, and entered by but a single door.

There is "No Admission" on the portal; and the precious files are handed out by a clerk in charge only on presentation of an order signed by the Commissioner or chief clerk.

In years past too much laxity prevailed in its management, and the files were handled by all comers, simply on their request, and returned at their will or not at all.

In those days most of the mischief was done. In the file room, there are about —— files, each in a paper wrapper, and comprising the title papers of a particular tract of land.

You ask the clerk in charge for the papers relating to any survey in Texas. They are arranged simply in districts and numbers.

He disappears from the door, you hear the sliding of a tin box, the lid snaps, and the file is in your hand.

Go up there some day and call for Bexar Scrip No. 2692.

The file clerk stares at you for a second, says shortly:

"Out of file."

It has been missing twenty years.

The history of that file has never been written before.

Twenty years ago there was a shrewd land agent living in Austin who devoted his undoubted talents and vast knowledge of land titles, and the laws governing them, to the locating of surveys made by illegal certificates, or improperly made, and otherwise of no value through non-compliance with the statutes, or whatever flaws his ingenious and unscrupulous mind could unearth.

He found a fatal defect in the title of the land as on file in Bexar Scrip No. 2692 and placed a new certificate upon the survey in his own name.

The law was on his side.

Every sentiment of justice, of right, and humanity was against him.

The certificate by virtue of which the original survey had been made was missing.

It was not to be found in the file, and no memorandum or date on the wrapper to show that it had ever been filed.

Under the law the land was vacant, unappropriated public domain, and open to location.

The land was occupied by a widow and her only son, and she supposed her title good.

The railroad had surveyed a new line through the property, and it had doubled in value.

Sharp, the land agent, did not communicate with her in any way until he had filed his papers, rushed his claim through the departments and into the patent room for patenting.

Then he wrote her a letter, offering her the choice of buying from him or vacating at once.

He received no reply.

One day he was looking through some files and came across the missing certificate. Some one, probably an employee of the office, had by mistake, after making some examination, placed it in the wrong file, and curiously enough another inadvertence, in there being no record of its filing on the wrapper, had completed the appearance of its having never been filed.

Sharp called for the file in which it belonged and scrutinized it carefully, fearing he might have overlooked some endorsement regarding its return to the office.

On the back of the certificate was plainly endorsed the date of filing, according to law, and signed by the chief clerk.

If this certificate should be seen by the examining clerk, his own claim, when it came up for patenting, would not be worth the paper on which it was written.

Sharp glanced furtively around. A young man, or rather a boy about eighteen years of age, stood a few feet away regarding him closely with keen black eyes.

Sharp, a little confused, thrust the certificate into the file where it properly belonged and began gathering up the other papers.

The boy came up and leaned on the desk beside him.

"A right interesting office, sir!" he said. "I have never been in here before. All those papers, now, they are about lands, are they not? The titles and deeds, and such things?"

"Yes," said Sharp. "They are supposed to contain all the title papers."

"This one, now," said the boy, taking up Bexar Scrip No. 2692, "what land does this represent the title of? Ah, I see 'Six hundred and forty acres in B—— county? Absalom Harris, original grantee.' Please tell me, I am so ignorant of these things, how can you tell a good survey from a bad one? I am told that there are a great many illegal and fraudulent surveys in this office. I suppose this one is all right?"

"No," said Sharp. "The certificate is missing. It is invalid."

"That paper I just saw you place in that file I suppose is something else—field notes, or a transfer probably?"

"Yes," said Sharp, hurriedly, "corrected field notes. Excuse me, I am a little pressed for time."

The boy was watching him with bright, alert eyes.

It would never do to leave the certificate in the file; but he could not take it out with that inquisitive boy watching him.

He turned to the file room, with a dozen or more files in his hands, and accidentally dropped part of them on the floor. As he stooped to pick them up he swiftly thrust Bexar Scrip No. 2692 in the inside breast pocket of his coat.

This happened at just half-past four o'clock, and when the file clerk took the files he threw them in a pile in his room, came out and locked the door.

The clerks were moving out of the doors in long, straggling lines.

It was closing time.

Sharp did not desire to take the file from the Land Office.

The boy might have seen him place the file in his pocket, and the penalty of the law for such an act was very severe.

Some distance back from the file room was the draftsman's room now entirely vacated by its occupants.

Sharp dropped behind the outgoing stream of men, and slipped slyly into this room.

The clerks trooped noisily down the iron stairway, singing, whistling, and talking.

Below, the night watchman awaited their exist, ready to close and bar the great doors to the south and east.

It is his duty to take careful note each day that no one remains in the building after the hour of closing.

Sharp waited until all sounds had ceased.

It was his intention to linger until everything was quiet, and then to remove the certificate from the file, and throw the latter carelessly on some draftsman's desk, as if it had been left there during the business of the day.

He knew also that he must remove the certificate from the office or destroy it, as the chance finding of it by a clerk would lead to its immediately being restored to its proper place, and the consequent discovery that his location over the old survey was absolutely worthless.

As he moved cautiously along the stone floor the loud barking of the little black dog, kept by the watchman, told that his sharp ears had heard the sounds of his steps.

The great, hollow rooms echoed loudly, move as lightly as he could.

Sharp sat down at a desk and laid the file before him.

In all his queer practices and cunning tricks he had not yet included any act that was down-right criminal.

He had always kept on the safe side of the law, but in the deed he was about to commit there was no compromise to be made with what little conscience he had left.

There is no well-defined boundary line between honesty and dishonesty.

The frontiers of one blend with the outside limits of the other, and he who attempts to tread this dangerous ground may be sometimes in the one domain and sometimes in the other; so the only safe road is the broad highway that leads straight through and has been well defined by line and compass.

Sharp was a man of what is called high standing in the community. That is, his word in a trade was as good as any man's; his check was as good as so much cash, and so regarded; he went to church regularly; went in good society and owed no man anything.

He was regarded as a sure winner in any land trade he chose to make, but that was his occupation.

The act he was about to commit now would place him forever in the ranks of those who chose evil for their portion—if it was found out.

More than that, it would rob a widow and her son of property soon to be of great value, which, if not legally theirs, was theirs certainly by every claim of justice.

But he had gone too far to hesitate.

His own survey was in the patent room for patenting. His own title was about to be perfected by the State's own hand.

The certificate must be destroyed.

He leaned his head on his hands for a moment, and as he did so a sound behind him caused his heart to leap with guilty fear, but before he could rise, a hand came over his shoulder and grasped the file.

He rose quickly, as white as paper, rattling his chair loudly on the stone floor.

The boy who had spoken to him earlier stood contemplating him with contemptuous and flashing eyes, and quietly placed the file in the left breast pocket of his coat.

"So, Mr. Sharp, by nature as well as by name," he said, "it seems that I was right in waiting behind the door in order to see you safely out. You will appreciate the pleasure I feel in having done so when I tell you my name is Harris. My mother owns the land on which you have filed, and if there is any justice in Texas she shall hold it. I am not certain, but I think I saw you place a paper in this file this afternoon, and it is barely possible that it may be of value to me. I was also impressed with the idea that you desired to remove it again, but had not the opportunity. Anyway, I shall keep it until to-morrow and let the Commissioner decide."

Far back among Mr. Sharp's ancestors there must have been some of the old berserker blood, for his caution, his presence of mind left him, and left him possessed of a blind, devilish, unreasoning rage that showed itself in a moment in the white glitter of his eye.

"Give me that file, boy," he said, thickly, holding out his hand.

"I am no such fool, Mr. Sharp," said the youth. "This file shall be laid before the Commissioner to-morrow for examination. If he finds—— Help! Help!"

Sharp was upon him like a tiger and bore him to the floor. The boy was strong and vigorous, but the suddenness of the attack gave him no chance to resist. He struggled up again to his feet, but it was an animal, with blazing eyes and cruel-looking teeth, that fought him, instead of a man.

Mr. Sharp, a man of high standing and good report, was battling for his reputation.

Presently there was a dull sound, and another, and still one more, and a blade flashing white and then red, and Edward Harris dropped down like some stuffed effigy of a man, that boys make for sport, with his limbs all crumpled and lax, on the stone floor of the Land Office.

The old watchman was deaf, and heard nothing.

The little dog barked at the foot of the stairs until his master made him come into his room.

Sharp stood there for several minutes holding in his hand his bloody clasp knife, listening to the cooing of the pigeons on the roof, and the loud ticking of the clock above the receiver's desk.

A map rustled on the wall and his blood turned to ice; a rat ran across some strewn papers, and his scalp prickled, and he could scarcely moisten his dry lips with his tongue.

Between the file room and the draftsman's room there is a door that opens on a small dark spiral stairway that winds from the lower floor to the ceiling at the top of the house.

This stairway was not used then, nor is it now.

It is unnecessary, inconvenient, dusty, and dark as night, and was a blunder of the architect who designed the building.

This stairway ends above at the tent-shaped space between the roof and the joists.

That space is dark and forbidding, and being useless is rarely visited.

Sharp opened this door and gazed for a moment up this narrow cobwebbed stairway.

·   ·   ·   ·   ·   ·   ·   ·   ·   ·   ·   ·   ·

After dark that night a man opened cautiously one of the lower windows of the Land Office, crept out with great circumspection and disappeared in the shadows.

·   ·   ·   ·   ·   ·   ·   ·   ·   ·   ·   ·   ·

One afternoon, a week after this time, Sharp lingered behind again after the clerks had left and the office closed.

The next morning the first comers noticed a broad mark in the dust on the upstairs floor, and the same mark was observed below stairs near a window.

It appeared as if some heavy and rather bulky object had been dragged along through the limestone dust. A memorandum book with "E. Harris" written on the flyleaf was picked up on the stairs, but nothing particular was thought of any of these signs.

Circulars and advertisements appeared for a long time in the papers asking for information concerning Edward Harris, who left his mother's home on a certain date and had never been heard of since.

After a while these things were succeeded by affairs of more recent interest, and faded from the public mind.

·   ·   ·   ·   ·   ·   ·   ·   ·   ·   ·   ·   ·

Sharp died two years ago, respected and regretted. The last two years of his life were clouded with a settled melancholy for which his friends could assign no reason.

The bulk of his comfortable fortune was made from the land he obtained by fraud and crime.

The disappearance of the file was a mystery that created some commotion in the Land Office, but he got his patent.

·   ·   ·   ·   ·   ·   ·   ·   ·   ·   ·   ·   ·

It is a well-known tradition in Austin and vicinity that there is a buried treasure of great value somewhere on the banks of Shoal Creek, about a mile west of the city.

Three young men living in Austin recently became possessed of what they thought was a clue of the whereabouts of the treasure, and Thursday night they repaired to the place after dark and plied the pickaxe and shovel with great diligence for about three hours.

At the end of that time their efforts were rewarded by the finding of a box buried about four feet below the surface, which they hastened to open.

The light of a lantern disclosed to their view the fleshless bones of a human skeleton with clothing still wrapping its uncanny limbs.

They immediately left the scene and notified the proper authorities of their ghastly find.

On closer examination, in the left breast pocket of the skeleton's coat, there was found a flat, oblong packet of papers, cut through and through in three places by a knife blade, and so completely soaked and clotted with blood that it had become an almost indistinguishable mass.

With the aid of a microscope and the exercise of a little imagination this much can be made out of the letters at the top of the papers:

B—x a— ——rip N—2—92.

QUERIES AND ANSWERS

[From the *Rolling Stone*, June 23, 1894.]

CAN you inform me where I can buy an interest in a newspaper of some kind? I have some money and would be glad to invest it in something of the sort, if some one would allow me to put in my capital against his experience.

COLLEGE GRADUATE.

Telegraph us your address at once, day message. Keep telegraphing every ten minutes at our expense until we see you. Will start on first train after receiving your wire.

Who was the author of the line, "Breathes there a man with soul so dead" ?

G. F.

This was written by a visitor to the State Saengerfest of 1892 while conversing with a member who had just eaten a large slice of limburger cheese.

Where can I get the "Testimony of the Rocks"?

GEOLOGIST.

See the reports of the campaign committees after the election in November.

Please state what the seven wonders of the world are. I know five of them, I think, but can't find out the other two.

SCHOLAR.

The Temple of Diana, at Lexington, Ky.; the Great Wall of China; Judge Von Rosenberg (the Colossus of Roads); the Hanging Gardens at Albany; a San Antonio Sunday school; Mrs. Frank Leslie, and the Populist party.

What day did Christmas come on in the year 1847?

CONSTANT READER.

The 25th of December.

What does an F. F. V. mean?

IGNORANT.

What does he mean by what? If he takes you by the arm and tells you how much you are like a brother of his in Richmond, he means Feel For Your Vest, for he wants to borrow a five. If he holds his head high and don't speak to you on the street he means that he already owes you ten and is Following a Fresh Victim.

Please decide a bet for us. My friend says that the sentence, "The negro bought the watermelon *of* the farmer" is correct, and I say it should be "The negro bought the watermelon from the farmer." Which is correct?

R.

Neither. It should read, "The negro stole the watermelon from the farmer."

When do the Texas game laws go into effect?

HUNTER.

When you sit down at the table.

Do you know where I can trade a section of fine Panhandle land for a pair of pants with a good title?

LAND AGENT.

We do not. You can't raise anything on land in that section. A man can always raise a dollar on a good pair of pants.

Name in order the three best newspapers in Texas.

ADVERTISER.

Well, the Galveston *News* runs about second, and the San Antonio *Express* third. Let us hear from you again.

Has a married woman any rights in Texas?

PROSPECTOR.

Hush, Mr. Prospector. Not quite so loud, if you please. . Come up to the office some afternoon, and if everything seems quiet, come inside, and look at our eye, and our suspenders hanging on to one button, and feel the lump on the top of our head. Yes, she has some rights of her own, and everybody else's she can scoop in.

Who was the author of the sayings, "A public office is a public trust," and "I would rather be right than President"?

Eli Perkins.

Is the Lakeside Improvement Company making anything out of their own town tract on the lake?

INQUISITIVE.

Yes, lots.

POEMS

[This and the other poems that follow have been found in files of the *Rolling Stone*, in the Houston *Post's* Postscripts and in manuscript. There are many others, but these few have been selected rather arbitrarily, to round out this collection.]

THE PEWEE

In the hush of the drowsy afternoon,
When the very wind on the breast of June
Lies settled, and hot white tracery
Of the shattered sunlight filters free
Through the unstinted leaves to the pied cool sward;
On a dead tree branch sings the saddest bard
  Of the birds that be;
  'Tis the lone Pewee.
Its note is a sob, and its note is pitched
In a single key, like a soul bewitched
  To a mournful minstrelsy.

"Pewee, Pewee," doth it ever cry;
A sad, sweet minor threnody
That threads the aisles of the dim hot grove
Like a tale of a wrong or a vanished love;
And the fancy comes that the wee dun bird
Perchance was a maid, and her heart was stirred
  By some lover's rhyme
  In a golden time,
And broke when the world turned false and cold;
And her dreams grew dark and her faith grew cold
  In some fairy far-off clime.

And her soul crept into the Pewee's breast;
And forever she cries with a strange unrest
For something lost, in the afternoon;
For something missed from the lavish June;
For the heart that died in the long ago;
For the livelong pain that pierceth so:
  Thus the Pewee cries,
  While the evening lies
Steeped in the languorous still sunshine,
Rapt, to the leaf and the bough and the vine
  Of some hopeless paradise.

NOTHING TO SAY

"You can tell your paper," the great man said,
 "I refused an interview.
I have nothing to say on the question, sir;
 Nothing to say to you."

And then he talked till the sun went down
 And the chickens went to roost;
And he seized the collar of the poor young man,
 And never his hold he loosed.

And the sun went down and the moon came up,
  And he talked till the dawn of day;
Though he said, "On this subject mentioned by you,
  I have nothing whatever to say."

And down the reporter dropped to sleep
  And flat on the floor he lay;
And the last he heard was the great man's words,
  "I have nothing at all to say."

THE MURDERER

"I push my boat among the reeds;
  I sit and stare about;
Queer slimy things crawl through the weeds,
  Put to a sullen rout.
I paddle under cypress trees;
  All fearfully I peer
Through oozy channels when the breeze
  Comes rustling at my ear.

"The long moss hangs perpetually;
  Gray scalps of buried years;
Blue crabs steal out and stare at me,
  And seem to gauge my fears;
I start to hear the eel swim by;
  I shudder when the crane
Strikes at his prey; I turn to fly
  At drops of sudden rain.

"In every little cry of bird
  I hear a tracking shout;
From every sodden leaf that's stirred
  I see a face frown out;
My soul shakes when the water rat
  Cowed by the blue snake flies;
Black knots from tree holes glimmer at
  Me with accusive eyes.

"Through all the murky silence rings
  A cry not born of earth;
An endless, deep, unechoing thing
  That owns not human birth.
I see no colors in the sky
  Save red, as blood is red;
I pray to God to still that cry
  From pallid lips and dead.

"One spot in all that stagnant waste
  I shun as moles shun light,
And turn my prow to make all haste
  To fly before the night.

A poisonous mound hid from the sun,
  Where crabs hold revelry;
Where eels and fishes feed upon
  The Thing that once was He.

"At night I steal along the shore;
  Within my hut I creep;
But awful stars blink through the door,
  To hold me from my sleep.
The river gurgles like his throat,
  In little choking coves,
And loudly dins that phantom note
  From out the awful groves.

"I shout with laughter through the night:
  I rage in greatest glee;
My fears all vanish with the light
  Oh! splendid nights they be!
I see her weep; she calls his name;
  He answers not, nor will;
My soul with joy is all aflame;
  I laugh, and laugh, and thrill.

"I count her teardrops as they fall;
  I flout my daytime fears;
I mumble thanks to God for all
  These gibes and happy jeers.
But, when the warning dawn awakes,
  Begins my wandering;
With stealthy strokes through tangled brakes,
  A wasted, frightened thing."

SOME POSTSCRIPTS

TWO PORTRAITS

Wild hair flying, in a matted maze,
Hand firm as iron, eyes all ablaze;
Bystanders timidly, breathlessly gaze,
As o'er the keno board boldly he plays.
                    —That's Texas Bill.

Wild hair flying, in a matted maze,
Hand firm as iron, eyes all ablaze;
Bystanders timidly, breathlessly gaze,
As o'er the keyboard boldly he plays.
                    —That's Paderewski.

A CONTRIBUTION

There came unto ye editor
  A poet, pale and wan,
And at the table sate him down,
  A roll within his hand.

Ye editor accepted it,
　And thanked his lucky fates;
Ye poet had to yield it up
　To a king full on eights.

THE OLD FARM

Just now when the whitening blossoms flare
　On the apple trees and the growing grass
Creeps forth, and a balm is in the air;
　With my lighted pipe and well-filled glass
　　Of the old farm I am dreaming,
　　And softly smiling, seeming
　　To see the bright sun beaming
　　Upon the old home farm.

And when I think how we milked the cows,
　And hauled the hay from the meadows low;
And walked the furrows behind the plows,
　And chopped the cotton to make it grow
　　I'd much rather be here dreaming
　　And smiling, only seeming
　　To see the hot sun gleaming
　　Upon the old home farm.

VANITY

A Poet sang so wondrous sweet
　That toiling thousands paused and listened long;
So lofty, strong and noble were his themes,
　It seemed that strength supernal swayed his song.

He, god-like, chided poor, weak, weeping man,
　And bade him dry his foolish, shameful tears;
Taught that each soul on its proud self should lean,
　And from that rampart scorn all earth-born fears.

The Poet grovelled on a fresh heaped mound,
　Raised o'er the clay of one he'd fondly loved;
And cursed the world, and drenched the sod with tears
　And all the flimsy mockery of his precepts proved.

THE LULLABY BOY

The lullaby boy to the same old tune
　Who abandons his drum and toys
For the purpose of dying in early June
　Is the kind the public enjoys.

But, just for a change, please sing us a song,
　Of the sore-toed boy that's fly,
And freckled and mean, and ugly and **bad,**
　And positively will not die.

CHANSON DE BOHÊME

Lives of great men all remind us
  Rose is red and violet's blue;
Johnny's got his gun behind us
  'Cause the lamb loved Mary too.
—Robert Burns' "Hocht Time in the **aud Town.**"

I'd rather write this, as bad as it is
  Than be Will Shakespeare's shade;
I'd rather be known as an F. F. V.
  Than in Mount Vernon laid.
I'd rather count ties from Denver to Troy
  Then to head Booth's old programme;
I'd rather be special for the New York *World*
  Than to lie with Abraham.

For there's stuff in the can, there's Dolly and Fan
  And a hundred things to choose;
There's a kiss in the ring, and every old thing
  That a real live man can use.

I'd rather fight flies in a boarding house
  Than fill Napoleon's grave,
And snuggle up warm in my three slat bed
  Than be André the brave.
I'd rather distribute a coat of red
  On the town with a wad of dough
Just now, than to have my cognomen
  Spelled "Michael Angelo."

For a small live man, if he's prompt on hand
  When the good things pass around,
While the world's on tap has a better snap
  Than a big man under ground.

HARD TO FORGET

I'm thinking to-night of the old farm, Ned,
  And my heart is heavy and sad
As I think of the days that by have fled
  Since I was a little lad.
There rises before me each spot I know
  Of the old home in the dell,
The fields, and woods, and meadows below
  That memory holds so well.

The city is pleasant and lively, Ned,
  But what to us is its charm?
To-night all my thoughts are fixed, instead,
  On our childhood's old home farm.
I know you are thinking the same, dear Ned,
  With your head bowed on your arm,
For to-morrow at four we'll be jerked out of bed
  To plow on that darned old farm.

DROP A TEAR IN THIS SLOT

He who, when torrid Summer's sickly glare
Beat down upon the city's parched walls,
Sat him within a room scarce 9 by 9,
And, with tongue hanging out and panting **breath,**
Perspiring, pierced by pangs of prickly heat,
Wrote variations of the seaside joke
We all do know and always loved so well,
And of cool breezes and sweet girls that lay
In shady nooks, and pleasant windy coves
Anon
Will in that self-same room, with tattered quilt
Wrapped round him, and blue stiffening hands,
All shivering, fireless, pinched by winter's blasts,
Will hale us forth upon the rounds once more,
So that we may expect it not in vain,
The joke of how with curses deep and coarse
Papa puts up the pipe of parlor stove.
So ye
Who greet with tears this olden favorite,
Drop one for him who, though he strives to **please**
Must write about the things he never sees.

TAMALES

This is the Mexican
Don José Calderon
One of God's countrymen.
Land of the buzzard.
Cheap silver dollar, and
Cacti and murderers.
Why has he left his land
Land of the lazy man,
Land of the pulque
Land of the bull fight,
Fleas and revolution.

This is the reason,
Hark to the wherefore;
Listen and tremble.
One of his ancestors,
Ancient and garlicky,
Probably grandfather,
Died with his boots on.
Killed by the Texans,
Texans with big guns,
At San Jacinto.
Died without benefit
Of priest or clergy;
Died full of minie balls,
Mescal and pepper.

Don José Calderon
Heard of the tragedy.

Heard of it, thought of it,
Vowed a deep vengeance;
Vowed retribution
On the Americans,
Murderous gringos,
Especially Texans.
"Válgame Dios! qué
Ladrones, diablos,
Matadores, mentidores,
Carracos y perros,
Voy a matarles,
Con sólo mis manos,
Toditas sin falta."
Thus swore the Hidalgo
Don José Calderon.

He hied him to Austin.
Bought him a basket,
A barrel of pepper,
And another of garlic;
Also a rope he bought.
That was his stock in trade;
Nothing else had he.
Nor was he rated in
Dun or in Bradstreet,
Though he meant business,
Don José Calderon,
Champion of Mexico,
Don José Calderon,
Seeker of vengeance.

With his stout lariat,
Then he caught swiftly
Tomcats and puppy dogs,
Caught them and cooked them,
Don José Calderon,
Vower of vengeance.
Now on the sidewalk
Sits the avenger
Selling Tamales to
Innocent purchasers.
Dire is thy vengeance,
Oh, José Calderon,
Pitiless Nemesis
Fearful Redresser
Of the wrongs done to thy
Sainted grandfather.

Now the doomed Texans,
Rashly hilarious,
Buy of the deadly wares,
Buy and devour.
Rounders at midnight,
Citizens solid,
Bankers and newsboys,

Bootblacks and preachers,
Rashly importunate,
Courting destruction,
Buy and devour.
Beautiful maidens
Buy and devour,
Gentle society youths
Buy and devour.

Buy and devour
This thing called Tamale;
Made of rat terrier,
Spitz dog and poodle,
Maltese cat, boarding house
Steak and red pepper,
Garlic and tallow,
Corn meal and shucks.
Buy without shame
Sit on store steps and eat,
Stand on the street and eat,
Ride on the cars and eat,
Strewing the shucks around
Over creation.

Dire is thy vengeance,
Don José Calderon,
For the slight thing we did
Killing thy grandfather.
What boots it if we killed
Only one greaser,
Don José Calderon?
This is your deep revenge,
You have greased all of us,
Greased a whole nation
With your Tamales,
Don José Calderon.
Santos Esperitos,
Vicente Camillo,
Quitana de Rios,
De Rosa y Ribera.

LETTERS

[Letter to Mr. Gilman Hall, O. Henry's friend and Associate Editor of *Everybody's Magazine.*]

"the Callie"—
Excavation Road—   Sundy.
my dear mr. hall:
    in your october E'bodys' i read a story in which i noticed some sentences as follows:

"Day in, day out, day in, day out, day in, day out, day in, day out, day in, day out, it had rained, rained, and rained and rained & rained & rained & rained & rained till the mountains loomed like a chunk of rooined velvet."

And the other one was: "i don't keer whether you are any good or not," she cried. "You're alive! You're alive! You're alive! You're alive! You're alive! You're alive! You're alive! You're alive! You're alive! You're alive! You're alive! You're alive! You're alive! You're alive! You're alive! You're alive!"

I thought she would never stop saying it, on and on and on and on and on and on and on and on and on and on and on and on. "You're alive! You're alive! You're alive! You're alive! You're alive! You're alive! You're alive! You're ALIVE!

"You're alive! You're alive! You're alive! You're alive! You're alive! You're alive! You're alive! You're ALIVE!

"YOU'RE ALIVE!"

Say, bill; do you get this at a rate, or does every word go?

i want to know, because if the latter is right i'm going to interduce in compositions some histerical personages that will loom up large as repeeters when the words are counted up at the polls.

Yours truly

O. henry

28 West 26th St.,

West of Broadway

Mr. hall,
part editor
of everybody's.

KYNTOEKNEEYOUGH RANCH, November 31, 1883.

[Letter to Mrs. Hall, a friend back in North Carolina. This is one of the earliest letters found.]

Dear Mrs. Hall:

As I have not heard from you since the shout you gave when you set out from the station on your way home I guess you have not received some seven or eight letters from me, and hence your silence. The mails are so unreliable that they may all have been lost. If you don't get this you had better send to Washington and get them to look over the dead letter office for the others. I have nothing to tell you of any interest, except that we all nearly froze to death last night, thermometer away below 32 degrees in the shade all night.

You ought by all means to come back to Texas this winter; you would love it more and more; that same little breeze that you looked for so anxiously last summer is with us now, as cold as Callum Bros. suppose their soda water to be.

My sheep are doing finely; they never were in better condition. They give me very little trouble, for I have never been able to see one of them yet. I will proceed to give you all the news about this ranch. Dick has got his new house well under way, the pet lamb is doing finely, and I take the cake for cooking mutton steak and fine gravy. The chickens are doing mighty well, the garden produces magnificent prickly pears and grass; onions are worth two for five cents, and Mr. Haynes has shot a Mexican.

Please send by express to this ranch 75 cooks and 200 washwomen, blind or wooden legged ones preferred. The climate has a tendency to make them walk off every two or three days, which must be overcome. Ed Brockman has quit the store and I think is going to work for Lee among the cows. Wears a red sash and swears so fluently that he has been mistaken often for a member of the Texas Legislature.

If you see Dr. Beall bow to him for me, politely but distantly; he refuses to waste a line upon me. I suppose he is too much engaged in courting to write any letters. Give Dr. Hall my profoundest regards. I think about him invariably whenever he is occupying my thoughts.

Influenced by the contents of the *Bugle*, there is an impression general at this ranch that you are president, secretary, and committee, &c., of the various associations of fruit fairs, sewing societies, church fairs, Presbytery, general assembly, conference, medical conventions, and baby shows that go to make up the glory and renown of North Carolina in general, and while I heartily congratulate the aforesaid institutions on their having such a zealous and efficient officer, I tremble lest their requirements leave you not time to favor me with a letter in reply to this, and assure you that if you would so honor me I would highly appreciate the effort. I would rather have a good long letter from you than many *Bugles*. In your letter be certain to refer as much as possible to the advantages of civilized life over the barbarous; you might mention the theatres you see there, the nice things you eat, warm fires, niggers to cook and bring in wood; a special reference to nice beefsteak would be advisable. You know our being reminded of these luxuries makes us contented and happy. When we hear of you people at home eating turkeys and mince pies and getting drunk Christmas and having a fine time generally we become more and more reconciled to this country and would not leave it for anything.

I must close now as I must go and dress for the opera. Write soon.

Yours very truly,

W. S. PORTER.

TO DR. W. P. BEALL

[Dr. Beall, of Greensboro, N. C., was one of young Porter's dearest friends. Between them there was an almost regular correspondence during Porter's first years in Texas.]

LA SALLE COUNTY, Texas, December 8, 1883.

Dear Doctor: I send you a play—a regular high art full orchestra, gilt-edged drama. I send it to you because of old acquaintance and as a revival of old associations. Was I not ever ready in times gone by to generously furnish a spatula and other assistance when you did buy the succulent watermelon? And was it not by my connivance and help that you did oft from the gentle Oscar Mayo skates entice? But I digress. I think that I have so concealed the identity of the characters introduced that no one will be able to place them, as they all appear under fictitious names, although I admit that many of the incidents and scenes were suggested by actual experiences of the author in your city.

You will, of course, introduce the play upon the stage if proper arrangements can be made. I have not yet had an opportunity of ascertaining whether Edwin Booth, John McCullough, or Henry Irving can be secured. However, I will leave all such matters to your judgment and taste. Some few suggestions I will make with regard to the mounting of the piece which may be of value to you.

Discrimination will be necessary in selecting a fit person to represent the character of Bill Slax, the tramp. The part is that of a youth of great beauty and noble manners, temporarily under a cloud, and is generally rather difficult to fill properly. The other minor characters, such as damfools, citizens, police, customers, countrymen, &c., can be very easily supplied, especially the first.

Let it be announced in the *Patriot* for several days that in front of Benbow Hall, at a certain hour, a man will walk a tight rope seventy feet from the ground who has never made the attempt before; that the exhibition will be FREE, and that the odds are 20 to 1 that the man will be killed. A large crowd will gather. Then let the Guilford Grays charge one side, the Reidsville Light Infantry the other, with fixed bayonets, and a man with a hat commence taking up a collection in the rear. By this means they can be readily driven into the hall and the door locked.

I have studied a long time about devising a plan for obtaining pay from the audience and have finally struck upon the only feasible one I think.

After the performance let some one come out on the stage and announce that James Forbis will speak two hours. The result, easily explainable by philosophical and psychological reasons, will be as follows: The minds of the audience, elated and inspired by the hope of immediate departure when confronted by such a terror-inspiring and dismal prospect, will collapse with the fearful reaction which will take place, and for a space of time they will remain in a kind of comatose, farewell-vain-world condition. Now, as this is the time when the interest of the evening is at its highest pitch, let the melodious strains of the orchestra steal forth as a committee appointed by the managers of lawyers, druggists, doctors, and revenue officers, go around and relieve the audience of the price of admission for each one. Where one person has no money let it be made up from another, but on no account let the whole sum taken be more than the just amount at usual rates.

As I said before, the characters in the play are purely imaginary, and therefore not to be confounded with real persons. But lest any one, feeling some of the idiosyncrasies and characteristics apply too forcibly to his own high moral and irreproachable self, should allow his warlike and combative spirits to arise, you might as you go, kind of casually like, produce the impression that I rarely miss my aim with a Colt's forty-five, but if that does not have the effect of quieting the splenetic individual, and he still thirsts for Bill Slax's gore, just inform him that if he comes out here he can't get any whiskey within two days' journey of my present abode, and water will have to be his only beverage while on the warpath. This, I am sure, will avert the bloody and direful conflict.

Accept my lasting regards and professions of respect.

Ever yours,

BILL SLAX.

TO DR. W. P. BEALL

My dear Doctor: I wish you a happy, &c., and all that sort of thing, don't you know, &c., &c. I send you a few little productions in the way of poetry, &c., which, of course, were struck off in an idle moment. Some of the pictures are not good likenesses, and so I have not labelled them, which you may do as fast [as] you discover whom they represent, as some of them resemble others more than themselves, but the poems are good without exception, and will compare favorably with Baron Alfred's latest on spring.

I have just come from a hunt, in which I mortally wounded a wild hog, and as my boots are full of thorns I can't write any longer than this paper will contain, for it's all I've got, because I'm too tired to write any more for the reason that I have no news to tell.

I see by the *Patriot* that you are Superintendent of Public Health, and assure you that all such upward rise as you make like that will ever be witnessed with interest and pleasure by me, &c., &c. Give my regards to Dr. and Mrs. Hall. It would be uncomplimentary to your powers of perception as well as superfluous to say that I will now close and remain, yours truly,

W. S. PORTER.

LETTER TO DR. W. P. BEALL

LA SALLE COUNTY, Texas, February 27, 1884.

My dear Doctor: Your appreciated epistle of the 18th received. I was very glad to hear from you. I hope to hear again if such irrelevant correspondence will not interfere with your duties as Public Health Eradicator, which I believe is the office you hold under county authority. I supposed the very dramatic Shakespearian comedy to be the last, as I heard nothing from you previous before your letter, and was about to write another of a more exciting character, introducing several bloody single combats, a dynamite explosion, a ladies' oyster supper for charitable purposes, &c., also comprising some mysterious sub rosa transactions known only to myself and a select few, new songs and dances, and the Greensboro Poker Club. Having picked up a few points myself relative to this latter amusement, I feel competent to give a lucid, glittering portrait of the scenes presented under its auspices. But if the former drama has reached you safely, I will refrain from burdening you any more with the labors of general stage manager, &c.

If long hair, part of a sombrero, Mexican spurs, &c., would make a fellow famous, I already occupy a topmost niche in the Temple Frame. If my wild, untamed aspect had not been counteracted by my well-known benevolent and amiable expression of countenance, I would have been arrested long ago by the Rangers on general suspicions of murder and horse stealing. In fact, I owe all my present means of lugubrious living to my desperate and bloodthirsty appearance, combined with the confident and easy way in which I tackle a Winchester rifle. There is a gentleman who lives about fifteen miles from the ranch, who for amusement and recreation, and not altogether without an eye to the profit, keeps a general merchandise store. This gent for the first few months has been trying very earnestly to sell me a little paper, which I would like much to have, but am not anxious to purchase. Said paper is my account, receipted. Occasionally he is absent, and the welcome news coming to my ear, I mount my fiery hoss and gallop wildly up to the store, enter with something of the sang froid, grace, abandon, and recherché nonchalance with which Charles Yates ushers ladies and gentlemen to their seats in the opera-house, and, nervously fingering my butcher knife, fiercely demand goods and chattels of the clerk. This plan always succeeds. This is by way of explanation of this vast and unnecessary stationery of which this letter is composed. I am always in too big a hurry to demur at kind and quality, but when I get to town I will write you on small gilt-edged paper that would suit even the fastidious and discriminating taste of a Logan.

When I get to the city, which will be shortly, I will send you some account of this country and its inmates.

You are right, I have almost forgotten what a regular old, gum-chewing, ice-cream-destroying, opera ticket vortex, ivory-clawing girl looks like. Last summer a very fair specimen of this kind ranged over about Fort Snell, and I used to ride over twice a week on mail days and chew the end of my riding whip while she "Stood on the Bridge" and "Gathered up Shells on the Sea Shore" and wore the "Golden Slippers." But she has vamoosed, and my ideas on the subject are again growing dim.

If you see anybody about to start to Texas to live, especially to this part, if you will take your scalpyouler and sever the jugular vein, cut the brachiopod artery and hamstring him, after he knows what you have done for him he will rise and call you blessed. This country is a silent but eloquent refutation of Bob Ingersoll's theory; a man here gets prematurely insane, melancholy and unreliable and finally dies of lead poisoning, in his boots, while in a good old land like Greensboro a man can die, as they do every day, with all the benefits of the clergy.

W. S. PORTER.

AUSTIN, Texas, April 21, 1885.

Dear Dave: I take my pen in hand to let you know that I am well, and hope these few lines will find you as well as can be expected.

I carried out your parting injunction of a floral nature with all the solemnity and sacredness that I would have bestowed upon a dying man's last request. Promptly at half-past three I repaired to the robbers' den, commonly known as Radams Horticultural and Vegetable Emporium, and secured the high-priced offerings according to promise. I asked if the bouquets were ready, and the polite but piratical gentleman in charge pointed proudly to two objects on the counter reposing in a couple of vases, and said they were.

I then told him I feared there was some mistake, as no buttonhole bouquets had been ordered, but he insisted on his former declaration, and so I brought them away and sent them to their respective destinations.

I thought it a pity to spoil a good deck of cards by taking out only one, so I bundled up the whole deck, and inserted them in the bouquet, but finally concluded it would not be right to *violet* (JOKE) my promise and I *rose* (JOKE) superior to such a mean trick and sent only one as directed.

I have a holiday to-day, as it is San Jacinto day. Thermopylae had its messenger of defeat, but the Alamo had none. Mr. President and fellow citizens, those glorious heroes who fell for their country on the bloody field of San Jacinto, etc.

There is a bazaar to-night in the representatives' hall. You people out in Colorado don't know anything. A bazaar is cedar and tacks and girls and raw-cake and step-ladders and Austin Grays and a bass solo by Bill Stacy, and net profits $2.65.

Albert has got his new uniform and Alf Menille is in town, and the store needs the "fine Italian hand" of the bookkeeper very much, besides some of his plain Anglo-Saxon conversation.

Was interviewed yesterday by Gen'l Smith, Clay's father. He wants Jim S. and me to represent a manufactory in Jeff. City: Convict labor. Says parties in Galveston and Houston are making good thing of it. Have taken him up. Hope to be at work soon. Glad, by jingo! Shake. What'll you have? Claret and sugar? Better come home. Colorado no good.

Strange thing happened in Episcopal Church Sunday. Big crowd. Choir had sung jolly tune and preacher come from behind scenes. Everything quiet. Suddenly fellow comes down aisle. Late. Everybody looks. Disappointment. It is a stranger. Jones and I didn't go. Service proceeds.

Jones talks about his mashes and Mirabeau B. Lamar, daily. Yet there is hope. Cholera infantum; Walsh's crutch; Harvey, or softening of the brain may carry him off yet.

Society notes are few. Bill Stacey is undecided where to spend the summer.

Henry Harrison will resort at Wayland and Crisers. Charlie Cook will not go near a watering place if he can help it.

If you don't strike a good thing out West, I hope we will see you soon.

Yours as ever,

W. S. P.

AUSTIN, Texas, April 28, 1885.

Dear Dave: I received your letter in answer to mine, which you never got till sometime after you had written.

I snatch a few moments from my arduous labors to reply. The Colorado has been on the biggest boom I have seen since '39. In the pyrotechnical and not strictly grammatical language of the *Statesman*—The cruel, devastating flood swept, on a dreadful holocaust of swollen, turbid waters, surging and dashing in mad fury which have never been equalled in human history. A pitiable sight was seen the morning after the flood. Six hundred men, out of employment, were seen standing on the banks of the river, gazing at the rushing stream, laden with débris of every description. A wealthy New York Banker, who was present, noticing the forlorn appearance of these men, at once began to collect a subscription for them, appealing in eloquent terms for help for these poor sufferers by the flood. He collected one dollar and five horn buttons. The dollar he had given himself. He learned on inquiry that these men had not been at any employment in six years, and all they had lost by the flood was a few fishing poles. The Banker put his dollar in his pocket and stepped up to the Pearl Saloon.

As you will see by this morning's paper, there is to be a minstrel show next Wednesday for benefit of Austin Grays.

I attended the rehearsal last night, but am better this morning, and the doctor thinks I will pull through with careful attention.

The jokes are mostly mildewed, rockribbed, and ancient as the sun. I can give you no better idea of the tout ensemble and sine die of the affair than to state that Scuddy is going to sing a song. . . .

Mrs. Harrell brought a lot of crystallized fruits from New Orleans for you. She wants to know if she shall send them around on Bois d'arc or keep them 'til you return. Answer.

Write to your father. He thinks you are leaving him out, writing to everybody else first. Write.

We have the boss trick here now. Have sold about ten boxes of cigars betting on it in the store.

Take four nickels, and solder them together so the solder will not appear. Then cut out of three of them a square hole like this: (Illustration.) Take about twelve other nickels, and on top of them you lay a small die with the six up, that will fit easily in the hole without being noticed. You lay the four nickels over this, and all presents the appearance of a stack of nickles. You do all this privately so everybody will suppose it is nothing but a stack of five-cent pieces. You then lay another small die on top of the stack with the ace up. You have a small tin cup shaped like this (Illustration) made for the purpose. You let everybody see the ace, and then say you propose to turn the ace into a six. You lay the tin cup carefully over the stack this way, and feel around in your pocket for a pencil and not finding one. . . .

[The rest of this letter is lost]

AUSTIN, Texas, May 10, 1885.

Dear Dave: I received your two letters and have commenced two or three in reply, but always failed to say what I wanted to, and destroyed them all. I heard from Joe that you would probably remain in Colorado. I hope you will

succeed in making a good thing out of it, if you conclude to do so, but would
like to see you back again in Austin. If there is anything I can do for you
here let me know.

Town is fearfully dull, except for the frequent raids of the Servant Girl Anni-
hilators, who make things lively during the dead hours of the night; if it were
not for them, items of interest would be very scarce, as you may see by the
Statesman.

Our serenading party has developed new and alarming modes of torture for our
helpless and sleeping victims. Last Thursday night we loaded up a small organ
on a hack and with our other usual instruments made an assault upon the quiet
air of midnight that made the atmosphere turn pale.

After going the rounds we were halted on the Avenue by Fritz Hartkopf and
ordered into his *salon.* We went in, carrying the organ, etc. A large crowd of
bums immediately gathered, prominent among which were to be seen Percy
James, Theodore Hillyer, Randolph Burmond, Charlie Hicks, and after partaking
freely of lemonade we wended our way down, and were duly halted and treated
in the same manner by other hospitable gentlemen.

We were called in at several places while wit and champagne, Rhine Wine,
etc., flowed in a most joyous and hilarious manner. It was one of the most
recherché and per diem affairs ever known in the city. Nothing occurred to mar
the pleasure of the hour, except a trifling incident that might be construed as
malapropos and post-meridian by the hypercritical. Mr. Charles Sims on attempting to introduce Mr. Charles Hicks and your humble servant to young
ladies, where we had been invited inside, forgot our names and required to be
informed on the subject before proceeding.

                                                        Yours
                                                        W. S. P.

AUSTIN, Texas, December 22, 1885.

Dear Dave: Everything wept at your departure. Especially the clouds. Last
night the clouds had a silver lining, three dollars and half's worth. I fulfilled
your engagement in grand, tout ensemble style, but there is a sad bonjour look
about the thirty-eight cents left in my vest pocket that would make a hired man
weep. All day long the heavens wept, and the heavy, somber clouds went drifting about overhead, and the north wind howled in maniacal derision, and the
hack drivers danced on the pavements in wild, fierce glee, for they knew too
well what the stormy day betokened. The hack was to call for me at eight. At
five minutes to eight I went upstairs and dressed in my usual bijou and operatic
style, and rolled away to the opera. Emma sang finely. I applauded at the
wrong times, and praised her rendering of the chromatic scale when she was
performing on "c" flat andante pianissimo, but otherwise the occasion passed
off without anything to mar the joyousness of the hour. Everybody was there.
Isidor Moses and John Ireland, and Fritz Hartkopf and Prof. Herzog and Bill
Stacy and all the bong ton elight. You will receive a draft to-day through the
First National Bank of Colorado for $3.65, which you will please honor.

There is no news, or there are no news, either you like to tell. Lavaca Street
is very happy and quiet and enjoys life, for Jones was sat on by his Uncle Wash
and feels humble and don't sing any more, and the spirit of peace and repose
broods over its halls. Martha rings the matin bell, it seems to me before cock
crow or ere the first faint streaks of dawn are limned in the eastern sky by the
rosy fingers of Aurora. At noon the foul ogre cribbage stalks rampant, and
seven-up for dim, distant oysters that only the eye of faith can see.

The hour grows late. The clock strikes! Another day has vanished. Gone
into the dim recesses of the past leaving its record of misspent hours, false
hopes, and disappointed expectations. May a morrow dawn that will bring

recompense and requital for the sorrows of the days gone by, and a new order of things when there will be more starch in cuff and collar, and less in handkerchiefs.

Come with me out into the starlight night. So calm, so serene, ye lights of heaven, so high above earth; so pure and majestic and mysterious; looking down on the mad struggle of life here below, is there no pity in your never-closing eyes for us mortals on which you shine?

Come with me on to the bridge. Ah, see there, far below, the dark, turbid stream. Rushing and whirling and eddying under the dark pillars with ghostly murmur and siren whisper. What shall we find in your depths? The stars do not reflect themselves in your waters, they are too dark and troubled and swift! What shall we find in your depths? Rest?—Peace?—catfish? Who knows? 'Tis but a moment. A leap! A plunge!—and—then oblivion or another world? Who can tell? A man once dived into your depths and brought up a horse collar and a hoop-skirt. Ah! what do we know of the beyond? We know that death comes, and we return no more to our world of trouble and care—but where do we go? Are there lands where no traveler has been? A chaos—perhaps where no human foot has trod—perhaps Bastrop—perhaps New Jersey! Who knows? Where do people go who are in McDade? Do they go where they have to fare worse? They cannot go where they have worse fare.

Let us leave the river. The night grows cold. We could pierce the future or pay the toll. Come, the ice factory is deserted! No one sees us. My partner, W. P. Anderson, will never destroy himself. Why? His credit is good. No one will sue a side-partner of mine!

You have heard of a brook murmuring, but you never knew a sewer sighed? But we digress! We will no longer pursue a side issue like this. Au revoir. I will see you later.

Yours truly,
WILLIAM SHAKESPEARE INGOMAR JUNIUS BRUTUS CALLIOPE SIX-HANDED EUCHRE GROVER CLEVELAND HILL CITY QUARTETTE JOHNSON.

AN EARLY PARABLE

In one of his early letters, written from Austin, O. Henry wrote a long parable that was evidently to tell his correspondent some of the local gossip. Here it is:

Once upon a time there was a maiden in a land not far away—a maiden of much beauty and rare accomplishments. She was beloved by all on account of her goodness of heart, and her many charms of disposition. Her father was a great lord, rich and powerful, and a mighty man, and he loved his daughter with exceeding great love, and he cared for her with jealous and loving watchfulness, lest any harm should befall her, or even the least discomfort should mar her happiness and cause any trouble in her smooth and peaceful life. The cunningest masters were engaged to teach her from her youngest days; she played upon the harpsichord the loveliest and sweetest music; she wrought fancy work in divers strange and wonderful forms that might puzzle all beholders as to what manner of things they might be; she sang, and all listeners hearkened thereunto, as to the voice of an angel; she danced stately minuets with the gay knights as graceful as a queen and as light as the thistledown borne above the clover blossoms by the wind; she could paint upon china, rare and unknown flowers the like unto which man never saw in colors, crimson and blue and yellow, glorious to behold; she conversed in unknown tongues whereof no man knew the meaning and sense; and created wild admiration in all, by the ease and grace with which she did play upon a new and strange instrument of wondrous sound and structure which she called a banjo.

She had gone into a strange land, far away beyond the rivers that flowed through her father's dominion—farther than one could see from the highest castle tower—up into the land of ice and snow, where wise men, famous for learning and ancient lore, had gathered together from many lands and countries the daughters of great men. Kings and powerful rulers, railroad men, bankers, mighty men who wished to bring up their children to be wise and versed in all things old and new. Here, the Princess abode for many seasons, and she sat at the feet of old wise men, who could tell of the world's birth, and the stars, and read the meaning of the forms of the rocks that make the high mountains and knew the history of all created things that are; and here she learned to speak strange tongues, and studied the deep mysteries of the past—the secrets of the ancients; Chaldic lore; Etruscan inscription; hidden and mystic sciences, and knew the names of all the flowers and things that grow in fields or wood; even unto the tiniest weed by the brook.

In due time the Princess came back to her father's castle. The big bell boomed from the high tower; the heavy iron gates were thrown open; banners floated all along the battlemented walls, and in the grand hall, servants and retainers hurried to and fro, bearing gold dishes, and great bowls of flaming smoking punch, while oxen were roasted whole and hogsheads of ale tapped on the common by the castle walls, and thither hied them the villagers one and all to make merry at the coming of the dear Princess again. "She will come back so wise and learned," they said, "so far above us that she will not notice us as she did once," but not so: the Princess with a red rose in her hair, and dressed so plain and neat that she looked more like a farmer's daughter than a great king's, came down among them from her father's side with nods of love and welcome on her lips, and a smile upon her face, and took them by the hands as in the old days, and none among them so lowly or so poor but what received a kind word from the gracious Princess, and carried away in their hearts glad feelings that she was still the same noble and gracious lady she always was. Then night came, and torches by thousands lit up the great forest, and musicians played and bonfires glowed, with sparks flying like myriads of stars among the gloomy trees.

In the great castle hall were gathered the brave knights and the fairest ladies in the kingdom. The jolly old King, surrounded by the wise men and officers of state, moved about among his guests, stately and courteous, ravishing music burst forth from all sides, and down the hall moved the fair Princess in the mazy dance, on the arm of a knight who gazed upon her face in rapt devotion and love. Who was he that dared to look thus upon the daughter of the King, sovereign prince of the kingdom, and the heiress of her father's wealth and lands?

He had no title, no proud name to place beside a royal one, beyond that of an honorable knight, but who says that that is not a title that, borne worthily, makes a man the peer of any that wears a crown?

He had loved her long. When a boy they had roamed together in the great forest about the castle, and played among the fountains of the court like brother and sister. The King saw them together often and smiled and went his way and said nothing. The years went on and they were together as much as they could be. The summer days when the court went forth into the forest mounted on prancing steeds to chase the stags with hounds; all clad in green and gold with waving plumes and shining silver and ribbons of gay colors, this knight was by the Princess' side to guide her through the pathless swamps where the hunt ranged, and saw that no harm came to her. And now that she had come back after years of absence, he went to her with fear lest she should have changed from her old self, and would not be to him as she was when they were boy and girl together. But no, there was the same old kindly welcome, the same smiling greeting, the warm pressure of the hand, the glad look in the eyes as of yore. The Knight's heart beat wildly and a dim new-awakened hope arose in him. Was she too far away, after all?

He felt worthy of her, and of any one in fact, but he was without riches, only a knight-errant with his sword for his fortune, and his great love his only title; and he had always refrained from ever telling her anything of his love, for his pride prevented him, and you know a poor girl even though she be a princess cannot say to a man, "I am rich, but, let that be no bar between us, I am yours and will let my wealth pass if you will give up your pride." No princess can say this, and the Knight's pride would not let him say anything of the kind and so you see there was small chance of their ever coming to an understanding.

Well, the feasting and dancing went on, and the Knight and the Princess danced and sang together, and walked out where the moon was making a white wonder of the great fountain, and wandered under the rows of great oaks, but spoke no word of love, though no mortal man knows what thoughts passed in their heads; and she gave long accounts of the wonders she had seen in the far, icy north, in the great school of wise men, and the Knight talked of the wild and savage men he had seen in the Far West, where he had been in battles with the heathen in a wild and dreary land; and she heard with pity his tales of suffering and trials in the desert among wild animals and fierce human kings; and inside the castle the music died away and the lights grew dim and the villagers had long since gone to their homes and the Knight and the Princess still talked of old times, and the moon climbed high in the eastern sky.

One day there came news from a country far to the west where lay the possessions of the Knight. The enemy had robbed him of his treasure, driven away his cattle, and he found it was best to hie him away and rescue his inheritance and goods. He buckled on his sword and mounted his good war-horse. He rode to the postern gate of the castle to make his adieus to the Princess.

When he told her he was going away to the wild western country to do battle with the heathen, she grew pale, and her eyes took on a look of such pain and fear that the Knight's heart leaped and then sank in his bosom, as his pride still kept him from speaking the words that might have made all well.

She bade him farewell in a low voice, and tears even stood in her eyes, but what could she say or do?

The Knight put spurs to his horse, and dashed away over the hills without ever looking back, and the Princess stood looking over the gate at him till the last sight of his plume below the brow of the hill. The Knight was gone. Many suitors flocked about the Princess. Mighty lords and barons of great wealth were at her feet and attended her every journey. They came and offered themselves and their fortunes again and again, but none of them found favor in her eyes. "Will the Princess listen to no one?" they began to say among themselves. "Has she given her heart to some one who is not among us?" No one could say.

A great and mighty physician, young and of wondrous power in his art, telephoned to her every night if he might come down. How his suit prospered no one could tell, but he persevered with great and astonishing diligence. A powerful baron who assisted in regulating the finances of the kingdom and who was a direct descendant of a great prince who was cast into a lion's den, knelt at her feet.

A gay and lively lord who lived in a castle hung with ribbons and streamers and gay devices of all kinds, with other nobles of like character, prostrated themselves before her, but would listen to none of them.

The Princess rode about in quiet ways in the cool evenings upon a gray palfrey, alone and very quiet, and she seemed to grow silent and thoughtful as time went on and no news came from the western wars, and the Knight came not back again.

[Written to his daughter Margaret.]

TOLEDO, Ohio, Oct. 1, 1900.

Dear Margaret: I got your very nice, long letter a good many days ago. It didn't come straight to me, but went to a wrong address first. I was very glad indeed to hear from you, and very, very sorry to learn of your getting your finger so badly hurt. I don't think you were to blame at all, as you couldn't know just how that villainous old "hoss" was going to bite. I do hope that it will heal up nicely and leave your finger strong. I am learning to play the mandolin, and we must get you a guitar, and we will learn a lot of duets together when I come home which will certainly not be later than next summer, and maybe earlier.

I suppose you have started to school again some time ago. I hope you like to go, and don't have to study too hard. When one grows up, a thing they never regret is that they went to school long enough to learn all they could. It makes everything easier for them, and if they like books and study they can always content and amuse themselves that way even if other people are cross and tiresome, and the world doesn't go to suit them.

You mustn't think that I've forgotten somebody's birthday. I couldn't find just the thing I wanted to send, but I know where it can be had, and it will reach you in a few days. So, when it comes you'll know it is for a birthday remembrance.

I think you write the prettiest hand of any little girl (or big one, either) I ever knew. The letters you make are as even and regular as printed ones. The next time you write, tell me how far you have to go to school and whether you go alone or not.

I am busy all the time writing for the papers and magazines all over the country, so I don't have a chance to come home, but I'm going to try to come this winter. If I don't I will by summer *sure*, and then you'll have somebody to boss and make trot around with you.

Write me a letter whenever you have some time to spare, for I am always glad and anxious to hear from you. Be careful when you are on the streets not to feed shucks to strange dogs, or pat snakes on the head or shake hands with cats you haven't been introduced to, or stroke the noses of electric car horses.

Hoping you are well and your finger is getting all right, I am, with much love, as ever,

PAPA.

My dear Margaret: Here it is summertime, and the bees are blooming and the flowers are singing and the birds making honey, and we haven't been fishing yet. Well, there's only one more month till July, and then we'll go, and no mistake. I thought you would write and tell me about the high water around Pittsburg some time ago, and whether it came up to where you live, or not. And I haven't heard a thing about Easter, and about the rabbit's eggs—but I suppose you have learned by this time that eggs grow on egg plants and are not laid by rabbits.

I would like very much to hear from you oftener, it has been more than a month now since you wrote. Write soon and tell me how you are, and when school will be out, for we want plenty of holidays in July so we can have a good time. I am going to send you something nice the last of this week. What do you guess it will be?

Lovingly,

PAPA.

The Caledonia

WEDNESDAY.

My dear Mr. Jack:

I owe Gilman Hall $175 (or mighty close to it) pussonally—so he tells me. I thought it was only about $30, but he has been keeping the account.

He's just got to have it to-day. *McClure's* will pay me some money on the 15th of June, but I can't get it until then. I was expecting it before this—anyhow before Gilman left, but they stick to the letter.

I wonder if you could give me a check for that much to pay him to-day. If you will I'll hold up my right hand—thus: that I'll have you a *first-class story on your desk before the last of this week*.

I reckon I'm pretty well overdrawn, but I've sure got to see that Hall gets his before he leaves. I don't want anything for myself.

Please, sir, let me know right away, by return boy if you'll do it.

If you can't, I'll have to make a quick dash at the three-ball magazines; and I do hate to tie up with them for a story.

The Same

SYDNEY PORTER.

MR. J. O. H. COSGRAVE,
    at this time editor of *Everybody's Magazine.*

A letter to Gilman Hall, written just before the writer's marriage to Miss Sara Lindsay Coleman of Asheville, N. C.

WEDNESDAY.

Dear Gilman:

Your two letters received this A. M. Mighty good letters, too, and cheering.

Mrs. Jas. Coleman is writing Mrs. Hall to-day. She is practically the hostess at Wynn Cottage where the hullabaloo will occur.

Say, won't you please do one or two little things for me before you leave, as you have so kindly offered?

(1) Please go to Tiffany's and get a wedding ring, size 5⅛. Sara says the bands worn now are quite narrow—and that's the kind she wants.

(2) And bring me a couple of dress collars, size 16½. I have ties.

(3) And go to a florist's—there is one named Mackintosh (or something like that) on Broadway, East side of street five or six doors nortn of 26th St., where I used to buy a good many times. He told me he could ship flowers in good shape to Asheville—you might remind him that I used to send flowers to 36 West 17th Street some time ago. I am told by the mistress of ceremonies that I am to furnish two bouquets—one of lilies of the valley and one of pale pink roses. Get plenty of each—say enough lilies to make a large bunch to be carried in the hand and say three or four dozen of the roses.

I note what you say about hard times and will take heed. I'm not going into any extravagances at all, and I'm going to pitch into hard work just as soon as I get the rice grains out of my ear.

I wired you to-day "MS. mailed to-day, please rush one century by wire."

That will exhaust the Reader check—if it isn't too exhausted itself to come. You, of course, will keep the check when it arrives—I don't think they will fall down on it surely. I wrote Howland a pretty sharp letter and ordered him to send it at once care of *Everybody's.*

When this story reaches you it will cut down the overdraft "right smart," but if the house is willing I'd mighty well like to run it up to the limit again, because cash is sure scarce, and I'll have to have something like $300 more to see me through. The story I am sending is a new one; I still have another partly written for you, which I shall finish and turn in before I get back to New York and then we'll begin to clean up all debts.

Just after the wedding we are going to Hot Spring, N. C., only thirty-five miles from Asheville, where there is a big winter resort hotel, and stay there about a week or ten days. Then back to New York.

Please look over the story and arrange for bringing me the $300 when you come—it will still keep me below the allowed limit and thereafter I will cut down instead of raising it.

Just had a 'phone message from S. L. C. saying how pleased she was with your letter to her.

I'm right with you on the question of the "home-like" system of having fun. I think we'll all agree beautifully on that. I've had all the cheap bohemia that I want. I can tell you, none of the "climbers" and the cocktail crowd are going to bring their *vaporings* into my house. It's for the clean, merry life, with your best friends in the game and a general concentration of energies and aims. I am having a cedarwood club cut from the mountains with knots on it, and I am going to stand in my hallway (when I have one) and edit with it the cards of all callers. You and Mrs. will have latchkeys, of course.

Yes, I think you'd better stay at the hotel—— Of course they'd want you out at Mrs. C's. But suppose we take Mrs. Hall out there, and you and I remain at the B. P. We'll be out at the Cottage every day anyhow, and it'll be scrumptious all round.

I'm simply tickled to death that "you all" are coming.

The protoplasm is in Heaven; all's right with the world. Pippa passes.

Yours as ever,

BILL.

FRIDAY.

My dear Col. Griffith:

Keep your shirt on. I found I had to re-write the story when it came in. I am sending you part of it so you will have something tangible to remind you that you can't measure the water from the Pierian Spring in spoonfuls.

I've got the story in much better form; and I'll have the rest of it ready this evening.

I'm sorry to have delayed it; but it's best for both of us to have it a little late and a good deal better.

I'll send over the rest before closing time this afternoon or the first thing in the morning.

In its revised form I'm much better pleased with it.

Yours truly,

SYDNEY PORTER.

[Mr. Al. Jennings, of Oklahoma City, was an early friend of O. Henry's. Now, in 1912, a prominent attorney, Mr. Jennings, in his youth, held up trains.]

N. Y. SUNDAY.

28 W. 26.

ALGIE JENNINGS, ESQ., THE WEST.

Dear Bill:

Glad you've been sick too. I'm well again. Are you?

Well, as I had nothing to do I thought I would write you a letter; and as I have nothing to say I will close.

How are ye, Bill? How's old Initiative and Referendum? When you coming back to Manhattan? You wouldn't know the old town now. Main Street is building up, and there is talk of an English firm putting up a new hotel. I saw Duffy a few days ago. He looks kind of thoughtful as if he were trying to calculate how much he'd have been ahead on Gerald's board and clothes by now if you had taken him with you. Mrs. Hale is up in Maine for a 3 weeks' vacation.

Say, Bill, I'm sending your MS. back by mail to-day. I kept it a little longer after you sent for it because one of the McClure & Phillips firm wanted to see it first. Everybody says it is full of good stuff, but thinks it should be put in a more connected shape by some skilful writer who has been trained to that sort of work.

It seems to me that you ought to do better with it out there than you could here. If you can get somebody out there to publish it it ought to sell all right. N. Y. is a pretty cold proposition and it can't see as far as the Oklahoma country when it is looking for sales. How about trying Indianapolis or Chicago? Duffy told me about the other MS. sent out by your friend Abbott. Kind of a bum friendly trick, wasn't it?

Why don't you get "Arizona's Hand" done and send it on? Seems to me you could handle a short story all right.

My regards to Mrs. Jennings and Bro. Frank. Write some more.

Still
BILL.

N. Y., May 23, '05.

Dear Jennings:

Got your letter all right. Hope you'll follow it soon.

I'd advise you not to build any high hopes on your book—just consider that you're on a little pleasure trip, and taking it along as a side line. Mighty few MSS. ever get to be books, and mighty few books pay.

I have to go to Pittsburg the first of next week to be gone about 3 or 4 days. If you decide to come here any time after the latter part of next week I will be ready to meet you. Let me know in advance a day or two.

Gallot is in Grand Rapids—maybe he will run over for a day or two.

In haste and truly yours,
W. S. P.

[It was hard to get O. Henry to take an interest in his books. He was always eager to be at the undone work, to be writing a new story instead of collecting old ones. This letter came from North Carolina. It shows how much thought he gave always to titles.]

LAND O' THE SKY, Monday, 1909.

My dear Colonel Steger: As I wired you to-day, I like "Man About Town" for a title.

But I am sending in a few others for you to look at; and if any other suits you better, I'm agreeable. Here they are, in preferred order:

The Venturers.

Transfers.

Merry-Go-Rounds.

Babylonica.

Brickdust from Babel.

Babes in the Jungle.

If none of these hit you right, let me know and I'll get busy again. But I think "Man About Town" is about the right thing. It gives the city idea without using the old hackneyed words.

I am going to write you a letter in a day or so "touchin' on and appertainin' to" other matters and topics. I am still improving and feeling pretty good. Colonel Bingham has put in a new ash-sifter and expects you to come down and see that it works all right.

All send regards to you. You seem to have made quite a hit down here for a Yankee.

Salutations and good wishes.

Yours,

S. P.

[This letter was found unfinished, among his papers after his death. His publishers had discussed many times his writing of a novel, but the following letter constitutes the only record of his own opinions in the matter. The date is surely 1909 or 1910.]

My dear Mr. Steger: My idea is to write the story of a man—an individual, not a type—but a man who, at the same time, I want to represent a "human nature type," if such a person could exist. The story will teach no lesson, inculcate no moral, advance no theory.

I want it to be something that it won't or can't be—but as near as I can make it—the *true* record of a man's thoughts, his description of his mischances and adventures, his *true* opinions of life as he has seen it and his *absolutely honest* deductions, comments, and views upon the different phases of life that he passes through.

I do not remember ever to have read an autobiography, a biography, or a piece of fiction that told the *truth*. Of course, I have read stuff such as Rousseau and Zola and George Moore; and various memoirs that were supposed to be window panes in their respective breasts; but, mostly, all of them were either liars, actors, or posers. (Of course, I'm not trying to belittle the greatness of their literary expression.)

All of us have to be prevaricators, hypocrites, and liars every day of our lives; otherwise the social structure would fall into pieces the first day. We must act in one another's presence just as we must wear clothes. It is for the best.

The trouble about writing the truth has been that the writers have kept in their minds one or another or all of three thoughts that made a handicap—they were trying either for to do a piece of immortal literature, or to shock the public or to please editors. Some of them succeeded in all three, but they did not write the *truth*. Most autobiographies are insincere from beginning to end. About the only chance for the truth to be told is in fiction.

It is well understood that "all the truth" cannot be told in print—but how about "nothing but the truth"? That's what I want to do.

I want the man who is telling the story to tell it—not as he would to a reading public or to a confessor—but something in this way: Suppose he were marooned on an island in mid-ocean with no hope of ever being rescued; and, in order to pass away some of the time he should tell a story *to himself* embodying his adventure and experiences and opinions. Having a certain respect for himself (let us hope) he would leave out the "realism" that he would have no chance of selling in the market; he would omit the lies and self-conscious poses, and would turn out to his one auditor something real and true.

So, as truth is not to be found in history, autobiography, press reports (nor at the bottom of an H. G. Wells), let us hope that fiction may be the means of bringing out a few grains of it.

The "hero" of the story will be a man born and "raised" in a somnolent little southern town. His education is about a common school one, but he learns afterward from reading and life. I'm going to try to give him a "style" in narrative and speech—the best I've got in the shop. I'm going to take him through all the main phases of life—wild adventure, city, society, something of the "under world," and among many characteristic planes of the phases. I want him to acquire all the sophistication that experience can give him, and always preserve his individual honest *human* view, and have him tell the *truth* about everything.

It is time to say now, that by the "truth" I don't mean the objectionable stuff that so often masquerades under the name. I mean true opinions, a true estimate of all things as they seem to the "hero." If you find a word or a suggestive line or sentence in any of my copy, you cut it out and deduct it from the royalties.

I want this man to be a man of natural intelligence, of individual character, absolutely open and broad minded; and show how the Creator of the earth has got him in a rat trap—put him here "willy nilly" (you know the Omar verse); and then I want to show what he does about it. There is always the eternal question from the Primal Source—"What are you going to do about it?"

Please don't think for the half of a moment that the story is going to be anything of an autobiography. I have a distinct character in my mind for the part, and he does not at all

[Here the letter ends. He never finished it.]

THE STORY OF "HOLDING UP A TRAIN"

In "Sixes and Sevens" there appears an article entitled "Holding Up a Train." Now the facts were given to O. Henry by an old and dear friend who, in his wild avenging youth, had actually held up trains. To-day he is Mr. Al Jennings, of Oklahoma City, Okla., a prominent attorney. He has permitted the publication of two letters O. Henry wrote him, the first outlining the story as he thought his friend Jennings ought to write it, and the second announcing that, with O. Henry's revision, the manuscript had been accepted.

From W. S. Porter to Al Jennings, September 21st (year not given but probably 1902).

DEAR PARD:

In regard to that article—I will give you my idea of what is wanted. Say we take for a title "The Art and Humor of the Hold-up"—or something like that. I would suggest that in writing you assume a character. We have got to respect the conventions and delusions of the public to a certain extent. An article written as you would naturally write it would be regarded as a fake and an imposition. Remember that the traditions must be preserved wherever they will not interfere with the truth. Write in as simple, plain, and unembellished a style as you know how. Make your sentences short. Put in as much realism and as many facts as possible. Where you want to express an opinion or comment on the matter do it as practically and plainly as you can. Give it *life* and the vitality of *facts*.

Now, I will give you a sort of general synopsis of my idea—of course, everything is subject to your own revision and change. The article, we will say, is written by a *typical* train hoister—one without your education and powers of expression (bouquet) but intelligent enough to convey his ideas from *his standpoint*—not from John Wanamaker's. Yet, in order to please John, we will have to assume a virtue that we do not possess. Comment on the moral side of the proposition as little as possible. Do not claim that holding up trains is the only business a gentleman would engage in, and, on the contrary, do not depreciate a profession that is really only financiering with spurs on. Describe the *facts* and *details*—all that part of the proceedings that the passenger sitting with his hands up in a Pullman looking into the end of a tunnel in the hands of one of the performers does not see. Here is a rough draft of my idea: Begin abruptly, without any philosophizing, with your idea of the best times, places, and conditions for the hold-up—compare your opinions of this with those of others—mention some poorly conceived attempts and failures of others, giving your opinion why—as far as possible refer to actual occurrences, and incidents—describe the manner of a hold-up, how many men is best, where they are stationed, how do they generally go into it, nervous? or joking? or solemnly. The details of stopping the train, the duties of each man of the gang—the behavior of the train crew and passengers (here give as many brief odd and humorous incidents as you can think of). Your opinions on going through the passengers, when is it done and when not done. How is the boodle gotten at? How does the express clerk generally take it? Anything done with the mail car? *Under what circumstances will a train robber shoot a passenger or a train man*—suppose a man refuses to throw up his hands? Queer articles found on passengers (a chance here for some imaginative work)—queer and laughable incidents of any kind. Refer whenever apropos to actual hold-ups and facts concerning them of interest. What could two or three brave and determined passengers do if they were to try? Why don't they try? How long does it take to do the business. Does the train man ever stand in with the hold-up? Best means of getting away—how and when is the money divided. How is it mostly spent. Best way to maneuver afterward. How to get caught and how not to. Comment on the methods of officials who try to capture. (Here's your chance to get even.)

These ideas are some that occur to me casually. You will, of course, have many far better. I suggest that you make the article anywhere from 4,000 to 6,000 words. Get as much meat in it as you can, and by the way—stuff it full of western *genuine* slang—(not the eastern story paper kind). Get all the quaint cowboy expressions and terms of speech you can think of.

Information is what we want, clothed in the peculiar western style of the character we want to present. The main idea is to be *natural, direct*, and *concise.*

I hope you will understand what I say. I don't. But try her a whack and send it along as soon as you can, and let's see what we can do. By the way, Mr. "Everybody" pays good prices. I thought I would, when I get your story, put it into the shape my judgment decides upon, and then send both your MS. and mine to the magazine. If he uses mine, we'll whack up shares on the proceeds. If he uses yours, you get the check direct. If he uses neither, we are out only a few stamps.

Sincerely your friend,
W. S. P.

And here is the letter telling his "pard" that the article had been bought by *Everybody's Magazine.* This is dated Pittsburg, October 24th, obviously the same year:

DEAR PARD.

You're It. I always told you you were a genius. All you need is to succeed in order to make a success.

I enclose pub^{rs} letter which explains itself. When you see your baby in print don't blame me if you find strange ear marks and brands on it. I slashed it and cut it and added lots of stuff that never happened, but I followed your facts and ideas, and that is what made it valuable. I'll think up some other idea for an article and we'll collaborate again some time—eh?

I have all the work I can do, and am selling it right along. Have averaged about $150 per month since August 1st. And yet I don't overwork—don't think

I ever will. I commence about 9 A. M. and generally knock off about 4 or 5 P. M.

As soon as check mentioned in letter comes I'll send you your "sheer" of the boodle.

By the way, please keep my *nom de plume* strictly to yourself. I don't want any one to know just yet.

Give my big regards to Billy. Reason with him and try to convince him that we believe him to be pure merino and of more than average width. With the kindest remembrances to yourself I remain,

Your friend,

W. S. P.

At this time O. Henry was unknown and thought himself lucky to sell a story at any price.

WHIRLIGIGS

WHIRLIGIGS

THE WORLD AND THE DOOR

A FAVORITE dodge to get your story read by the public is to assert that it is true, and then add that Truth is stranger than Fiction. I do not know if the yarn I am anxious for you to read is true; but the Spanish purser of the fruit steamer *El Carrero* swore to me by the shrine of Santa Guadalupe that he had the facts from the U. S. vice-consul at La Paz—a person who could not possibly have been cognizant of half of them.

As for the adage quoted above, I take pleasure in puncturing it by affirming that I read in a purely fictional story the other day the line: "'Be it so,' said the policeman." Nothing so strange has yet cropped out in Truth.

When H. Ferguson Hedges, millionaire promoter, investor, and man-about-New-York, turned his thoughts upon matters convivial, and word of it went "down the line," bouncers took a precautionary turn at the Indian clubs, waiters put ironstone china on his favorite tables, cab drivers crowded close to the curbstone in front of all-night cafés, and careful cashiers in his regular haunts charged up a few bottles to his account by way of preface and introduction.

As a money power a one-millionaire is of small account in a city where the man who cuts your slice of beef behind the free-lunch counter rides to work in his own automobile. But Hedges spent his money as lavishly, loudly, and showily as though he were only a clerk squandering a week's wages. And, after all, the bartender takes no interest in your reserve fund. He would rather look you up on his cash register than in Bradstreet.

On the evening that the material allegation of facts begins, Hedges was bidding dull care begone in the company of five or six good fellows—acquaintances and friends who had gathered in his wake.

Among them were two younger men—Ralph Merriam, a broker, and Wade, his friend.

Two deep-sea cabmen were chartered. At Columbus Circle they hove to long enough to revile the statue of the great navigator, unpatriotically rebuking him for having voyaged in search of land instead of liquids. Midnight overtook the party marooned in the rear of a cheap café far uptown.

Hedges was arrogant, overriding, and quarrelsome. He was burly and tough, iron-gray but vigorous, "good" for the rest of the night. There was a dispute—about nothing that matters—and the five-fingered words were passed—the words that represent the glove cast into the lists. Merriam played the rôle of the verbal Hotspur.

Hedges rose quickly, seized his chair, swung it once and smashed wildly down at Merriam's head. Merriam dodged, drew a small revolver and shot Hedges in the chest. The leading roysterer stumbled, fell in a wry heap, and lay still.

Wade, a commuter, had formed that habit of promptness. He juggled Mer-

853

riam out a side door, walked him to the corner, ran him a block and caught a hansom. They rode five minutes and then got out on a dark corner and dismissed the cab. Across the street the lights of a small saloon betrayed its hectic hospitality.

"Go in the back room of that saloon," said Wade, "and wait. I'll go find out what's doing and let you know. You may take two drinks while I am gone—no more."

At ten minutes to one o'clock Wade returned.

"Brace up, old chap," he said. "The ambulance got there just as I did. The doctor says he's dead. You may have one more drink. You let me run this thing for you. You've got to skip. I don't believe a chair is legally a deadly weapon. You've got to make tracks, that's all there is to it."

Merriam complained of the cold querulously, and asked for another drink. "Did you notice what big veins he had on the back of his hands?" he said. "I never could stand—I never could——"

"Take one more," said Wade, "and then come on. I'll see you through."

Wade kept his promise so well that at eleven o'clock the next morning Merriam, with a new suit case full of new clothes and hair-brushes, stepped quietly on board a little 500-ton fruit steamer at an East River pier. The vessel had brought the season's first cargo of limes from Port Limon, and was homeward bound. Merriam had his bank balance of $2,800 in his pocket in large bills, and brief instructions to pile up as much water as he could between himself and New York. There was no time for anything more.

From Port Limon Merriam worked down the coast by schooner and sloop to Colon, thence across the isthmus to Panama, where he caught a tramp bound for Callao and such intermediate ports as might tempt the discursive skipper from his course.

It was at La Paz that Merriam decided to land—La Paz the Beautiful, a little harborless town smothered in a living green ribbon that banded the foot of a cloud-piercing mountain. Here the little steamer stopped to tread water while the captain's dory took him ashore that he might feel the pulse of the cocoanut market. Merriam went too, with his suit case, and remained.

Kalb, the vice-consul, a Græco-Armenian citizen of the United States, born in Hesse-Darmstadt, and educated in Cincinnati ward primaries, considered all Americans his brothers and bankers. He attached himself to Merriam's elbow, introduced him to every one in La Paz who wore shoes, borrowed ten dollars and went back to his hammock.

There was a little wooden hotel in the edge of a banana grove, facing the sea, that catered to the tastes of the few foreigners that had dropped out of the world into the *triste* Peruvian town. At Kalb's introductory: "Shake hands with ——," he had obediently exchanged manual salutations with a German doctor, one French and two Italian merchants, and three or four Americans who were spoken of as gold men, rubber men, mahogany men— anything but men of living tissue.

After dinner Merriam sat in a corner of the broad front *galeria* with Bibb, a Vermonter interested in hydraulic mining, and smoked and drank Scotch "smoke." The moonlit sea, spreading infinitely before him, seemed to separate him beyond all apprehension from his old life. The horrid tragedy in which he had played such a disastrous part now began, for the first time since he stole on board the fruiter, a wretched fugitive, to lose its sharper outlines. Distance lent assuagement to his view. Bibb had opened the flood-gates of a stream of long-dammed discourse, overjoyed to have captured an audience that had not suffered under a hundred repetitions of his views and theories.

"One year more," said Bibb, "and I'll go back to God's country. Oh, I know it's pretty here, and you get *dolce far niente* handed to you in chunks, but this country wasn't made for a white man to live in. You've got to have to plug through snow now and then, and see a game of baseball and wear a stiff collar and have a policeman cuss you. Still, La Paz is a good sort of a pipe-dreamy old hole. And Mrs. Conant is here. When any of us feels particularly like jumping into the sea we rush around to her house and propose. It's nicer to be rejected by Mrs. Conant than it is to be drowned. And they say drowning is a delightful sensation."

"Many like her here?" asked Merriam.

"Not anywhere," said Bibb, with a comfortable sigh. "She's the only white woman in La Paz. The rest range from a dappled dun to the color of a b-flat piano key. She's been here a year. Comes from—well, you know how a woman can talk—ask 'em to say 'string' and they'll say 'crow's foot' or 'cat's cradle.' Sometimes you'd think she was from Oshkosh, and again from Jacksonville, Florida, and the next day from Cape Cod."

"Mystery?" ventured Merriam.

"M—well, she looks it; but her talk's translucent enough. But that's a woman. I suppose if the Sphinx were to begin talking she'd merely say: 'Goodness me! more visitors coming for dinner, and nothing to eat but the sand which is here.' But you won't think about that when you meet her, Merriam. You'll propose to her too."

To make a hard story soft, Merriam did meet her and propose to her. He found her to be a woman in black with hair the color of a bronze turkey's wings, and mysterious, *remembering* eyes that—well, that looked as if she might have been a trained nurse looking on when Eve was created. Her words and manner, though, were translucent, as Bibbs had said. She spoke, vaguely, of friends in California and some of the lower parishes in Louisiana. The tropical climate and indolent life suited her; she had thought of buying an orange grove later on; La Paz, all in all, charmed her.

Merriam's courtship of the Sphinx lasted three months, although he did not know that he was courting her. He was using her as an antidote for remorse, until he found, too late, that he had acquired the habit. During that time he had received no news from home. Wade did not know where he was; and he was not sure of Wade's exact address, and was afraid to write. He thought he had better let matters rest as they were for a while.

One afternoon he and Mrs. Conant hired two ponies and rode out along the mountain trail as far as the little cold river that came tumbling down the foothills. There they stopped for a drink, and Merriam spoke his piece—he proposed, as Bibb had prophesied.

Mrs. Conant gave him one glance of brilliant tenderness, and then her face took on such a strange, haggard look that Merriam was shaken out of his intoxication and back to his senses.

"I beg your pardon, Florence," he said, releasing her hand; "but I'll have to hedge on part of what I said. I can't ask you to marry me, of course. I killed a man in New York—a man who was my friend—shot him down—in quite a cowardly manner, I understand. Of course, the drinking didn't excuse it. Well, I couldn't resist having my say; and I'll always mean it. I'm here as a fugitive from justice, and—I suppose that ends our acquaintance."

Mrs. Conant plucked little leaves assiduously from the low-hanging branch of a lime tree.

"I suppose so," she said, in low and oddly uneven tones; "but that depends upon you. I'll be as honest as you were. I poisoned my husband. I am a self-made widow. A man cannot love a murderess. So I suppose that ends our acquaintance."

She looked up at him slowly. His face turned a little pale, and he stared at her blankly, like a deaf-and-dumb man who was wondering what it was all about.

She took a swift step toward him, with stiffened arms and eyes blazing.

"Don't look at me like that!" she cried, as though she were in acute pain. "Curse me, or turn your back on me, but don't look that way. Am I a woman to be beaten? If I could show you—here on my arms, and on my back are scars—and it has been more than a year—scars that he made in his brutal rages. A holy nun would have risen and struck the fiend down. Yes, I killed him. The foul and horrible words that he hurled at me that last day are repeated in my ears every night when I sleep. And then came his blows, and the end of my endurance. I got the poison that afternoon. It was his custom to drink every night in the library before going to bed a hot punch made of rum and wine. Only from my fair hands would he receive it—because he knew that the fumes of spirits always sickened me. That night when the maid brought it to me I sent her downstairs on an errand. Before taking him his drink I went to my little private cabinet and poured into it more than a teaspoonful of tincture of aconite—enough to kill three men, so I had learned. I had drawn $6,000 that I had in bank, and with that and a few things in a satchel I left the house without any one seeing me. As I passed the library I heard him stagger up and fall heavily on a couch. I took a night train for New Orleans, and from there I sailed to the Bermudas. I finally cast anchor in La Paz. And now what have you to say? Can you open your mouth?"

Merriam came back to life.

"Florence," he said, earnestly, "I want you. I don't care what you've done. If the world——"

"Ralph," she interrupted, almost with a scream, "be my world!"

Her eyes melted; she relaxed magnificently and swayed toward Merriam so suddenly that he had to jump to catch her.

Dear me! in such scenes how the talk runs into artificial prose. But it can't be helped. It's the subconscious smell of the footlights' smoke that's in all of us. Stir the depths of your cook's soul sufficiently and she will discourse in Bulwer-Lyttonese.

Merriam and Mrs. Conant were very happy. He announced their engagement at the Hotel Orilla del Mar. Eight foreigners and four native Astors pounded his back and shouted insincere congratulations at him. Pedrito, the Castilian-mannered barkeep, was goaded to extra duty until his agility would have turned a Boston cherry-phosphate clerk a pale lilac with envy.

They were both very happy. According to the strange mathematics of the god of mutual affinity, the shadows that clouded their pasts when united became only half as dense instead of darker. They shut the world out and bolted the doors. Each was the other's world. Mrs. Conant lived again. The remembering look left her eyes. Merriam was with her every moment that was possible. On a little plateau under a grove of palms and calabash trees they were going to build a fairy bungalow. They were to be married in two months. Many hours of the day they had their heads together over the house plans. Their joint capital would set up a business in fruit or woods that would yield a comfortable support. "Good-night, my world," would say Mrs. Conant every evening when Merriam left her for his hotel. They were very happy. Their love had, circumstantially, that element of melancholy in it that it seems to require to attain its supremest elevation. And it seemed that their mutual great misfortune or sin was a bond that nothing could sever.

One day a steamer hove in the offing. Bare-legged and bare-shouldered La

Paz scampered down to the beach, for the arrival of a steamer was their loop-the-loop, circus, Emancipation Day, and four-o'clock tea.

When the steamer was near enough, wise ones proclaimed that she was the *Pájaro*, bound up-coast from Callao to Panama.

The *Pájaro* put on brakes a mile off shore. Soon a boat came bobbing shoreward. Merriam strolled down on the beach to look on. In the shallow water the Carib sailors sprang out and dragged the boat with a mighty rush to the firm shingle. Out climbed the purser, the captain, and two passengers ploughing their way through the deep sand toward the hotel. Merriam glanced toward them with the mild interest due to strangers. There was something familiar to him in the walk of one of the passengers. He looked again, and his blood seemed to turn to strawberry ice cream in his veins. Burly, arrogant, debonair as ever, H. Ferguson Hedges, the man he had killed, was coming toward him ten feet away.

When Hedges saw Merriam his face flushed a dark red. Then he shouted in his old, bluff way: "Hello, Merriam. Glad to see you. Didn't expect to find you out here. Quinby, this is my old friend Merriam, of New York—Merriam, Mr. Quinby."

Merriam gave Hedges and then Quinby an ice-cold hand.

"Br-r-r-r!" said Hedges. "But you've got a frappéd flipper! Man, you're not well. You're as yellow as a Chinaman. Malarial here? Steer us to a bar if there is such a thing, and let's take a prophylactic."

Merriam, still half comatose, led them toward the Hotel Orilla del Mar.

"Quinby and I," explained Hedges, puffing through the slippery sand, "are looking out along the coast for some investments. We've just come up from Concepción and Valparaiso and Lima. The captain of this subsidized ferry boat told us there was some good picking around here in silver mines. So we got off. Now, where is that café, Merriam? Oh, in this portable soda-water pavilion?"

Leaving Quinby at the bar, Hedges drew Merriam aside.

"Now, what does this mean?" he said, with gruff kindness. "Are you sulking about that fool row we had?"

"I thought," stammered Merriam—"I heard—they told me you were—that I had——"

"Well, you didn't, and I'm not," said Hedges. "That fool young ambulance surgeon told Wade I was a candidate for a coffin just because I'd got tired and quit breathing. I laid up in a private hospital for a month; but here I am, kicking as hard as ever. Wade and I tried to find you, but couldn't. Now, Merriam, shake hands and forget it all. I was as much to blame as you were; and the shot really did me good—I came out of the hospital as healthy and fit as a cab horse. Come on; that drink's waiting."

"Old man," said Merriam, brokenly, "I don't know how to thank you—I—well, you know——"

"Oh, forget it," boomed Hedges. "Quinby'll die of thirst if we don't join him."

Bibb was sitting on the shady side of the gallery waiting for the eleven-o'clock breakfast. Presently Merriam came out and joined him. His eye was strangely bright.

"Bibb, my boy," said he, slowly waving his hand, "do you see those mountains and that sea and sky and sunshine?—they're mine, Bibbsy—all mine."

"You go in," said Bibb, "and take eight grains of quinine, right away. It won't do in this climate for a man to get to thinking he's Rockefeller, or James O'Neill either."

Inside, the purser was untying a great roll of newspapers, many of them weeks old, gathered in the lower ports by the *Pájaro* to be distributed at casual stopping-places. Thus do the beneficent voyagers scatter news and entertainment among the prisoners of sea and mountains.

Tío Pancho, the hotel proprietor, set his great silver-rimmed *anteojos* upon his nose and divided the papers into a number of smaller rolls. A barefooted *muchacho* dashed in, desiring the post of messenger.

"*Vien venido*," said Tío Pancho. "This to Señora Conant; that to el Doctor S-S-Schlegel—*Dios!* what a name to say!—that to Señor Davis—one for Don Alberto. These two for the *Casa de Huéspedes, Numero 6, en la calle de las Buenas Gracias.* And say to them all, *muchacho*, that the *Pájaro* sails for Panama at three this afternoon. If any have letters to send by the post, let them come quickly, that they may first pass through the *correo.*"

Mrs. Conant received her roll of newspapers at four o'clock. The boy was late in delivering them, because he had been deflected from his duty by an iguana that crossed his path and to which he immediately gave chase. But it made no hardship, for she had no letters to send.

She was idling in a hammock in the *patio* of the house that she occupied, half awake, half happily dreaming of the paradise that she and Merriam had created out of the wrecks of their pasts. She was content now for the horizon of that shimmering sea to be the horizon of her life. They had shut out the world and closed the door.

Merriam was coming to her house at seven, after his dinner at the hotel. She would put on a white dress and an apricot-colored lace mantilla, and they would walk an hour under the cocoanut palms by the lagoon. She smiled contentedly, and chose a paper at random from the roll the boy had brought.

At first the words of a certain headline of a Sunday newspaper meant nothing to her; they conveyed only a visualized sense of familiarity. The largest type ran thus: "Lloyd B. Conant secures divorce." And then the sub headings: "Well-known Saint Louis paint manufacturer wins suit, pleading one year's absence of wife." "Her mysterious disappearance recalled." "Nothing has been heard of her since."

Twisting herself quickly out of the hammock, Mrs. Conant's eye soon traversed the half-column of the *Recall.* It ended thus: "It will be remembered that Mrs. Conant disappeared one evening in March of last year. It was freely rumored that her marriage with Llody B. Conant resulted in much unhappiness. Stories were not wanting to the effect that his cruelty toward his wife had more than once taken the form of physical abuse. After her departure a full bottle of tincture of aconite, a deadly poison, was found in a small medicine cabinet in her bedroom. This might have been an indication that she meditated suicide. It is supposed that she abandoned such an intention if she possessed it, and left her home instead."

Mrs. Conant slowly dropped the paper, and sat on a chair, clasping her hands tightly.

"Let me think—O God!—let me think," she whispered. "I took the bottle with me . . . I threw it out of the window of the train . . . I—— . . . there was another bottle in the cabinet . . . there were two, side by side—the aconite —and the valerian that I took when I could not sleep . . . If they found the aconite bottle full, why—but, he is alive, of course—I gave him a harmless dose of valerian . . . I am not a murderess in fact . . . Ralph, I—O God, don't let this be a dream!"

She went into the part of the house that she rented from the old Peruvian man and his wife, shut the door, and walked up and down her room swiftly and feverishly for half an hour. Merriam's photograph stood in a frame on a table. She picked it up, looked at it with a smile of exquisite tenderness, and— dropped four tears on it. And Merriam only twenty rods away! Then she stood still for ten minutes, looking into space. She looked into space through a slowly opening door. On her side of the door was the building material for a castle of Romance—love, an Arcady of waving palms, a lullaby of waves on the shore of a haven of rest, respite, peace, a lotus land of dreamy ease and security—a life of poetry and heart's ease and refuge. Romanticist, will you tell me what Mrs. Conant saw on the other side of the door? You cannot?— that is, you will not? Very well; then listen.

She saw herself go into a department store and buy five spools of silk thread and three yards of gingham to make an apron for the cook. "Shall I charge it, ma'am?" asks the clerk. As she walked out a lady whom she met greeted her cordially. "Oh, where did you get the pattern for those sleeves, dear Mrs. Conant?" she said. At the corner a policeman helped her across the street and touched his helmet. "Any callers?" she asked the maid when she reached home. "Mrs. Waldron," answered the maid, "and the two Misses Jenkinson." "Very well," she said. "You may bring me a cup of tea, Maggie."

Mrs. Conant went to the door and called Angela, the old Peruvian woman. "If Mateo is there send him to me." Mateo, a half-breed, shuffling and old but efficient, came.

"Is there a steamer or a vessel of any kind leaving this coast to-night or to-morrow that I can get passage on?" she asked.

Mateo considered.

"At Punta Reina, thirty miles down the coast, señora," he answered, "there is a small steamer loading with cinchona and dyewoods. She sails for San Francisco to-morrow at sunrise. So says my brother, who arrived in his sloop to-day, passing by Punta Reina."

"You must take me in that sloop to the steamer to-night. Will you do that?"

"Perhaps——" Mateo shrugged a suggestive shoulder. Mrs. Conant took a handful of money from a drawer and gave it to him.

"Get the sloop ready behind the little point of land below the town," she ordered. "Get sailors, and be ready to sail at six o'clock. In half an hour bring a cart partly filled with straw into the *patio* here, and take my trunk to the sloop. There is more money yet. Now, hurry."

For one time Mateo walked away without shuffling his feet.

"Angela," cried Mrs. Conant, almost fiercely, "come and help me pack. I am going away. Out with this trunk. My clothes first. Stir yourself. Those dark dresses first. Hurry."

From the first she did not waver from her decision. Her view was clear and final. Her door had opened and let the world in. Her love for Merriam was not lessened; but it now appeared a hopeless and unrealizable thing. The visions of their future that had seemed so blissful and complete had vanished. She tried to assure herself that her renunciation was rather for his sake than for her own. Now that she was cleared of her burden—at least, technically— would not his own weigh too heavily upon him? If she should cling to him, would not the difference forever silently mar and corrode their happiness? Thus she reasoned; but there were a thousand little voices calling to her that she could feel rather than hear, like the hum of distant, powerful machinery— the little voices of the world, that, when raised in unison, can send their insistent call through the thickest door.

Once, while packing, a brief shadow of the lotus dream came back to her. She held Merriam's picture to her heart with one hand, while she threw a pair of shoes into the trunk with her other.

At six o'clock Mateo returned and reported the sloop ready. He and his brother lifted the trunk into the cart, covered it with straw, and conveyed it to the point of embarkation. From there they transferred it on board in the sloop's dory. Then Mateo returned for additional orders.

Mrs. Conant was ready. She had settled all business matters with Angela, and was impatiently waiting. She wore a long, loose black-silk duster that she often walked about in when the evenings were chilly. On her head was a small round hat, and over it the apricot-colored lace mantilla.

Dusk had quickly followed the short twilight. Mateo led her by dark and grass-grown streets toward the point behind which the sloop was anchored. On turning a corner they beheld the Hotel Orilla del Mar three streets away, nebulously aglow with its array of kerosene lamps.

Mrs. Conant paused, with streaming eyes. "I must, *I must* see him once before I go," she murmured in anguish. But even then she did not falter in her decision. Quickly she invented a plan by which she might speak to him, and yet make her departure without his knowing. She would walk past the hotel, ask some one to call him out, and talk a few moments on some trivial excuse, leaving him expecting to see her at her home at seven.

She unpinned her hat and gave it to Mateo. "Keep this, and wait here till I come," she ordered. Then she draped the mantilla over her head as she usually did when walking after sunset, and went straight to the Orilla del Mar.

She was glad to see the bulky, white-clad figure of Tío Pancho standing alone on the gallery.

"Tío Pancho," she said, with a charming smile, "may I trouble you to ask Mr. Merriam to come out for just a few moments that I may speak with him?"

Tío Pancho bowed as an elephant bows.

"*Buenas tardes,* Señora Conant," he said, as a cavalier talks. And then he went on, less at his ease:

"But does not the señora know that Señor Merriam sailed on the *Pájaro* for Panama at three o'clock of this afternoon?"

THE THEORY AND THE HOUND

Not many days ago my old friend from the tropics, J. P. Bridger, United States consul on the island of Ratona, was in the city. We had wassail and jubilee and saw the Flatiron building, and missed seeing the Bronxless menagerie by about a couple of nights. And then, at the ebb tide, we were walking up a street that parallels and parodies Broadway.

A woman with a comely and mundane countenance passed us, holding in leash a wheezing, vicious, waddling brute of a yellow pug. The dog entangled himself with Bridger's legs and mumbled his ankles in a snarling, peevish, sulky bite. Bridger, with a happy smile, kicked the breath out of the brute; the woman showered us with a quick rain of well-conceived adjectives that left us in no doubt as to our place in her opinion, and we passed on. Ten yards farther an old woman with disordered white hair and her bankbook tucked well hidden beneath her tattered shawl begged. Bridger stopped and disinterred for her a quarter from his holiday waistcoat.

On the next corner a quarter of a ton of well-clothed man with a rice-powdered, fat, white jowl, stood holding the chain of a devil-born bulldog whose forelegs were strangers by the length of a dachshund. A little woman in a last-season's hat confronted him and wept, which was plainly all she could do, while he cursed her in low, sweet, practised tones.

Bridger smiled again—strictly to himself—and this time he took out a little memorandum book and made a note of it. This he had no right to do without due explanation, and I said so.

"It's a new theory," said Bridger, "that I picked up down in Ratona. I've been gathering support for it as I knock about. The world isn't ripe for it yet, but—well, I'll tell you; and then you run your mind back along the people you've known and see what you make of it."

And so I cornered Bridger in a place where they have artificial palms and wine; and he told me the story which is here in my words and on his responsibility.

One afternoon at three o'clock, on the island at Ratona, a boy raced along the beach screaming, "*Pájaro*, ahoy!"

Thus he made known the keenness of his hearing and the justice of his discrimination in pitch.

He who first heard and made oral proclamation concerning the toot of an approaching steamer's whistle, and correctly named the steamer, was a small hero in Ratona—until the next steamer came. Wherefore, there was rivalry among the barefoot youth of Ratona, and many fell victims to the softly blown conch shells of sloops which, as they enter harbor, sound surprisingly like a distant steamer's signal. And some could name you the vessel when its call, in your duller ears, sounded no louder than the sigh of the wind through the branches of the cocoanut palms.

But to-day he who proclaimed the *Pájaro* gained his honors. Ratona bent its ear to listen; and soon the deep-tongued blast grew louder and nearer, and at length Ratona saw above the line of palms on the low "point" the two black funnels of the fruiter slowly creeping toward the mouth of the harbor.

You must know that Ratona is an island twenty miles off the south of a South American republic. It is a port of that republic; and it sleeps sweetly in a smiling sea, toiling not nor spinning; fed by the abundant tropics where all things "ripen, cease and fall toward the grave."

Eight hundred people dream life away in a green-embowered village that follows the horseshoe curve of its bijou harbor. They are mostly Spanish and Indian mestizos, with a shading of San Domingo Negroes, a lightening of pure-blood Spanish officials, and a slight leavening of the froth of three or four pioneering white races. No steamers touch at Ratona save the fruit steamers which take on their banana inspectors there on their way to the coast. They leave Sunday newspapers, ice, quinine, bacon, watermelons, and vaccine matter at the island and that is about all the touch Racona gets with the world.

The *Pájaro* paused at the mouth of the harbor, rolling heavily in the swell that sent the whitecaps racing beyond the smooth water inside. Already two dories from the village—one conveying fruit inspectors, the other going for what it could get—were halfway out to the steamer.

The inspector's dory was taken on board with them, and the *Pájaro* steamed away for the mainland for its load of fruit.

The other boat returned to Ratona bearing a contribution from the *Pájora's* store of ice, the usual roll of newspapers, and one passenger—Taylor Plunkett, sheriff of Chatham County, Kentucky.

Bridger, the United States consul at Ratona, was cleaning his rifle in the official shanty under a bread-fruit tree twenty yards from the water of the harbor. The consul occupied a place somewhat near the tail of his political party's procession. The music of the band wagon sounded very faintly to him in the distance. The plums of office went to others. Bridger's share of the spoils—the consulship at Ratona—was little more than a prune—a dried prune from the boarding-house department of the public crib. But $900 yearly was opulence in Ratona. Besides, Bridger had contracted a passion for shooting alligators in the lagoons near his consulate, and he was not unhappy.

He looked up from a careful inspection of his rifle lock and saw a broad man filling his doorway. A broad, noiseless, slow-moving man sunburned almost to the brown of Vandyke. A man of forty-five, neatly clothed in homespun, with scanty light hair, a close-clipped brown-and-gray beard and pale-blue eyes expressing mildness and simplicity.

"You are Mr. Bridger, the consul," said the broad man. "They directed me here. Can you tell me what those big bunches of things like gourds are in those trees that look like feather dusters along the edge of the water?"

"Take that chair," said the consul, reoiling his cleaning rag. "No, the other one—that bamboo thing won't hold you. Why, they're cocoanuts—green cocoanuts. The shell of 'em is always a light green before they're ripe."

"Much obliged," said the other man, sitting down carefully. "I didn't quite like to tell the folks at home they were olives unless I was sure about it. My name is Plunkett. I'm sheriff of Chatham County, Kentucky. I've got extradition papers in my pocket authorizing the arrest of a man on this island. They've been signed by the President of this country, and they're in correct shape. The man's name is Wade Williams. He's in the cocoanut raising business. What he's wanted for is the murder of his wife two years ago. Where can I find him?"

The consul squinted an eye and looked through his rifle barrel.

"There's nobody on the island who calls himself 'Williams,'" he remarked.

"Didn't suppose there was," said Plunkett mildly. "He'll do by any other name."

"Besides myself," said Bridger, "there are only two Americans on Ratona—Bob Reeves and Henry Morgan."

"The man I want sells cocoanuts," suggested Plunkett.

"You see that cocoanut walk extending up to the point?" said the consul, waving his hand toward the open door. "That belongs to Bob Reeves. Henry Morgan owns half the trees to loo'ard on the island."

"One month ago," said the sheriff, "Wade Williams wrote a confidential letter to a man in Chatham County, telling him where he was and how he was getting along. The letter was lost; and the person that found it gave it away. They sent me after him, and I've got the papers. I reckon he's one of your cocoanut men for certain."

"You've got his picture, of course," said Bridger. "It might be Reeves or Morgan, but I'd hate to think it. They're both as fine fellows as you'd meet in an all-day auto ride."

"No," doubtfully answered Plunkett; "there wasn't any picture of Williams to be had. And I never saw him myself. I've been sheriff only a year. But I've got a pretty accurate description of him. About 5 feet 11; dark hair and eyes; nose inclined to be Roman; heavy about the shoulders; strong, white teeth, with none missing; laughs a good deal, talkative; drinks considerably but never to intoxication; looks you square in the eye when talking; age thirty-five. Which one of your men does that description fit?"

The consul grinned broadly.

"I'll tell you what you do," he said, laying down his rifle and slipping on his dingy black alpaca coat. "You come along, Mr. Plunkett, and I'll take you up to see the boys. If you can tell which one of 'em your description fits better than it does the other you have the advantage of me."

Bridger conducted the sheriff out and along the hard beach close to which the tiny houses of the village were distributed. Immediately back of the town rose sudden, small, thickly wooded hills. Up one of these, by means of steps cut in the hard clay, the consul led Plunkett. On the very verge of an eminence was perched a two-room wooden cottage with a thatched roof. A Carib woman was washing clothes outside. The consul ushered the sheriff to the door of the room that overlooked the harbor.

Two men were in the room, about to sit down, in their shirt sleeves, to a table spread for dinner. They bore little resemblance one to the other in detail; but the general description given by Plunkett could have been justly applied to either. In height, color of hair, shape of nose, build, and manners each of them tallied with it. They were fair types of jovial, ready-witted, broad-gauged Americans who had gravitated together for companionship in an alien land.

"Hello, Bridger!" they called in unison at sight of the consul. "Come and have dinner with us!" And then they noticed Plunkett at his heels, and came forward with hospitable curiosity.

"Gentlemen," said the consul, his voice taking on unaccustomed formality, "this is Mr. Plunkett. Mr. Plunkett—Mr. Reeves and Mr. Morgan."

The cocoanut barons greeted the newcomer joyously. Reeves seemed about an inch taller than Morgan, but his laugh was not quite as loud. Morgan's eyes were deep brown; Reeves's were black. Reeves was the host and busied himself with fetching other chairs and calling to the Carib woman for supplemental table ware. It was explained that Morgan lived in a bamboo shack to "loo'ard," but that every day the two friends dined together. Plunkett stood still during the preparations, looking about mildly with his pale-blue eyes. Bridger looked apologetic and uneasy.

At length two other covers were laid and the company was assigned to places. Reeves and Morgan stood side by side across the table from the visitors. Reeves nooded genially as a signal for all to seat themselves. And then suddenly Plunkett raised his hand with a gesture of authority. He was looking straight between Reeves and Morgan.

"Wade Williams," he said quietly, "you are under arrest for murder."

Reeves and Morgan instantly exchanged a quick, bright glance, the quality of which was interrogation, with a seasoning of surprise. Then, simultaneously they turned to the speaker with a puzzled and frank deprecation in their gaze.

"Can't say that we understand you, Mr. Plunkett," said Morgan, cheerfully. "Did you say 'Williams'?"

"What's the joke, Bridgy?" asked Reeves, turning to the consul with a smile. Before Bridger could answer, Plunkett spoke again.

"I'll explain," he said, quietly. "One of you don't need any explanation, but this is for the other one. One of you is Wade Williams of Chatham County, Kentucky. You murdered your wife on May 5, two years ago, after ill-treating and abusing her continually for five years. I have the proper papers in my pocket for taking you back with me, and you are going. We will return on the fruit steamer that comes back by this island to-morrow to leave its inspectors. I acknowledge, gentlemen, that I'm not quite sure which one of you is Williams. But Wade Williams goes back to Chatham County to-morrow. I want you to understand that."

A great sound of merry laughter from Morgan and Reeves went out over the still harbor. Two or three fishermen in the fleet of sloops anchored there looked up at the house of the *diablos Americanos* on the hill and wondered.

"My dear Mr. Plunkett," cried Morgan, conquering his mirth, "the dinner is getting cold. Let us sit down and eat. I am anxious to get my spoon into that shark-fin soup. Business afterward."

"Sit down, gentlemen, if you please," added Reeves, pleasantly. "I am sure Mr. Plunkett will not object. Perhaps a little time may be of advantage to him in identifying—the gentleman he wishes to arrest."

"No objections, I'm sure," said Plunkett, dropping into his chair heavily. "I'm hungry myself. I didn't want to accept the hospitality of you folks without giving you notice; that's all."

Reeves set bottles and glasses on the table.

"There's cognac," he said, "and anisada, and Scotch 'smoke,' and rye. Take your choice."

Bridger chose rye, Reeves poured three fingers of Scotch for himself, Morgan took the same. The sheriff, against much protestation, filled his glass from the water bottle.

"Here's to the appetite," said Reeves, raising his glass, "of Mr. Williams!" Morgan's laugh and his drink encountering sent him into a choking-splutter. All began to pay attention to the dinner, which was well cooked and palatable.

"Williams!" called Plunkett, suddenly and sharply.

All looked up wonderingly. Reeves found the sheriff's mild eye resting upon him. He flushed a little.

"See here," he said, with some asperity, "my name's Reeves, and I don't want you to——" But the comedy of the thing came to his rescue and he ended with a laugh.

"I suppose, Mr. Plunkett," said Morgan, carefully seasoning an alligator pear, "that you are aware of the fact that you will import a good deal of trouble for yourself into Kentucky if you take back the wrong man—that is, of course, if you take anybody back?"

"Thank you for the salt," said the sheriff. "Oh, I'll take somebody back. It'll be one of you two gentlemen. Yes, I know I'll get stuck for damages if I make a mistake. But I'm going to try to get the right man."

"I'll tell you what you do," said Morgan, leaning forward with a jolly twinkle in his eyes. "You take me. I'll go without any trouble. The cocoanut business hasn't panned out well this year, and I'd like to make some extra money out of your bondsmen."

"That's not fair," chimed in Reeves. "I got only $16 a thousand for my last shipment. Take me, Mr. Plunkett."

"I'll take Wade Williams," said the sheriff, patiently, "or I'll come pretty close to it."

"It's like dining with a ghost," remarked Morgan, with a pretended shiver. "The ghost of a murderer, too! Will somebody pass the toothpicks to the shade of the naughty Mr. Williams?"

Plunkett seemed as unconcerned as if he were dining at his own table in Chatham County. He was a gallant trencherman, and the strange tropic viands tickled his palate. Heavy, commonplace, almost slothful in his movements, he appeared to be devoid of all the cunning and watchfulness of the sleuth. He even ceased to observe, with any sharpness or attempted discrimination, the two men, one of whom he had undertaken with surprising self-confidence to drag away upon the serious charge of wife-murder. Here, indeed, was a problem set before him that if wrongly solved would have amounted to his serious discomfiture, yet there he sat puzzling his soul (to all appearances) over the novel flavor of a broiled iguana cutlet.

The consul felt a decided discomfort. Reeves and Morgan were his friends and pals; yet the sheriff from Kentucky had a certain right to his official aid and moral support. So Bridger sat the silentest around the board and tried to estimate the peculiar situation. His conclusion was that both Reeves and Morgan, quickwitted, as he knew them to be, had conceived at the moment of Plunkett's disclosure of his mission—and in the brief space of a lightning flash— the idea that the other might be the guilty Williams; and that each of them had decided in that moment loyally to protect his comrade against the doom that threatened him. This was the consul's theory, and if he had been a bookmaker at a race of wits for life and liberty he would have offered heavy odds against the plodding sheriff from Chatham County, Kentucky.

When the meal was concluded the Carib woman came and removed the dishes and cloth. Reeves strewed the table with excellent cigars, and Plunkett, with the others, lighted one of these with evident gratification.

"I may be dull," said Morgan, with a grin and a wink at Bridger; "but I want to know if I am. Now, I say this is all a joke of Mr. Plunkett's concocted to frighten two babes-in-the-woods. Is this Williamson to be taken seriously or not?"

"'Williams,'" corrected Plunkett, gravely. "I never got off any jokes in my life. I know I wouldn't travel 2,000 miles to get off a poor one as this would be if I didn't take Wade Williams back with me. Gentlemen!" continued the sheriff, now letting his mild eyes travel impartially from one of the company to another, "see if you can find any joke in this case. Wade Williams is listening to the words I utter now; but out of politeness I will speak of him as a third person. For five years he made his wife lead the life of a dog—No; I'll take that back. No dog in Kentucky was ever treated as she was. He spent the money that she brought him—spent it at races, at the card table, and on horses and hunting. He was a good fellow to his friends, but a cold, sullen demon at home. He wound up the five years of neglect by striking her with his closed hand—a hand as hard as a stone—when she was ill and weak from suffering. She died the next day; and he skipped. That's all there is to it. It's enough. I never saw Williams; but I knew his wife. I'm not a man to tell half. She and I were keeping company when she met him. She went to Louisville on a visit and saw him there. I'll admit that he spoilt my chances in no time. I lived then on the edge of the Cumberland Mountains. I was elected sheriff of Chatham County a year after Wade Williams killed his wife. My official duty sends me out here after him; but I'll admit that there's personal feeling, too. And he's going back with me. Mr.—er—Reeves, will you pass me a match?"

"Awfully imprudent of Williams," said Morgan, putting his feet up against the wall, "to strike a Kentucky lady. Seems to me I've heard they were scrappers."

"Bad, bad Williams," said Reeves, pouring out more "Scotch."

The two men spoke lightly, but the consul saw and felt the tension and the carefulness in their actions and words. "Good old fellows," he said to himself; "they're both all right. Each of 'em is standing by the other like a little brick church."

And then a dog walked into the room where they sat—a black-and-tan hound, long-eared, lazy, confident of welcome.

Plunkett turned his head and looked at the animal, which halted, confidently, within a few feet of his chair.

Suddenly the sheriff, with a deep-mouthed oath, left his seat and bestowed upon the dog a vicious and heavy kick, with his ponderous shoe.

The hound, heart-broken, astonished, with flapping ears and incurved tail, uttered a piercing yelp of pain and surprise.

Reeves and the consul remained in their chairs, saying nothing, but astonished at the unexpected show of intolerance from the easy-going man from Chatham County.

But Morgan, with a suddenly purpling face, leaped to his feet and raised a threatening arm above the guest.

"You—brute!" he shouted, passionately; "why did you do that?"

Quickly the amenities returned, Plunkett muttered some indistinct apology and regained his seat. Morgan with a decided effort controlled his indignation and also returned to his chair.

And then Plunkett, with the spring of a tiger, leaped around the corner of the table and snapped handcuffs on the paralyzed Morgan's wrists.

"Hound-lover and woman-killer!" he cried; "get ready to meet your God."
When Bridger had finished I asked him:

"Did he get the right man?"

"He did," said the consul.

"And how did he know?" I inquired, being in a kind of bewilderment.

"When he put Morgan in the dory," answered Bridger, "the next day to take him aboard the *Pájaro*, this man Plunkett stopped to shake hands with me and I asked him the same question.

"'Mr. Bridger,' said he, 'I'm a Kentuckian, and I've seen a great deal of both men and animals. And I never yet saw a man that was overfond of horses and dogs but what was cruel to women.'"

THE HYPOTHESES OF FAILURE

LAWYER GOOCH bestowed his undivided attention upon the engrossing arts of his profession. But one flight of fancy did he allow his mind to entertain. He was fond of likening his suite of office room to the bottom of a ship. The rooms were three in number, with a door opening from one to another. These doors could also be closed.

"Ships," Lawyer Gooch would say, "are constructed for safety, with separate, water-tight compartments in their bottoms. If one compartment spring a leak it fills with water; but the good ship goes on unhurt. Were it not for the separating bulkheads one leak would sink the vessel. Now it often happens that while I am occupied with clients, other clients with conflicting interests call. With the assistance of Archibald—an office boy with a future—I cause the dangerous influx to be diverted into separate compartments, while I sound with my legal plummet the depth of each. If necessary, they may be baled into the hallway and permitted to escape by way of the stairs, which we may term the lee scuppers. Thus the good ship of business is kept afloat; whereas if the element that supports her were allowed to mingle freely in her hold we might be swamped—ha, ha, ha!"

The law is dry. Good jokes are few. Surely it might be permitted Lawyer Gooch to mitigate the bore of briefs, the tedium of torts and the prosiness of processes with even so light a levy upon the good property of humor.

Lawyer Gooch's practice leaned largely to the settlement of marital infelicities. Did matrimony languish through complications, he mediated, soothed, and arbitrated. Did it suffer from implications, he readjusted, defended, and championed. Did it arrive at the extremity of duplications, he always got light sentences for his clients.

But not always was Lawyer Gooch the keen, armed, wily belligerent, ready with his two-edged sword to lop off the shackles of Hymen. He had been known to build up instead of demolishing, to reunite instead of severing, to lead erring and foolish ones back into the fold instead of scattering the flock. Often had he by his eloquent and moving appeals sent husband and wife, weeping, back into each other's arms. Frequently he had coached childhood so successfully that, at the psychological moment (and at a given signal), the plaintive pipe of "Papa, won't you tum home adain to me and muvver?" had won the day and upheld the pillars of a tottering home.

Unprejudiced persons admitted that Lawyer Gooch received as big fees from these reyoked clients as would have been paid him had the cases been contested in court. Prejudiced ones intimated that his fees were doubled, because the penitent couples always came back later for the divorce, anyhow.

There came a season in June when the legal ship of Lawyer Gooch (to borrow his own figure) was nearly becalmed. The divorce mill grinds slowly in June. It is the month of Cupid and Hymen.

Lawyer Gooch, then, sat idle in the middle room of his clientless suite. A small anteroom connected—or rather separated—this apartment from the hallway. Here was stationed Archibald, who wrested from visitors their cards or oral nomenclature which he bore to his master while they waited.

Suddenly, on this day, there came a great knocking at the outermost door.

Archibald, opening it, was thrust aside as superfluous by the visitor, who without due reverence at once penetrated to the office of Lawyer Gooch and threw himself with good-natured insolence into a comfortable chair facing that gentleman.

"You are Phineas C. Gooch, attorney-at-law?" said the visitor, his tone of voice and inflection making his words at once a question, an assertion, and an accusation.

Before committing himself by a reply, the lawyer estimated his possible client in one of his brief but shrewd and calculating glances.

The man was of the emphatic type—large-sized, active, bold and debonair in demeanor, vain beyond a doubt, slightly swaggering, ready and at ease. He was well clothed, but with a shade too much ornateness. He was seeking a lawyer; but if that fact would seem to saddle him with troubles they were not patent in his beaming eye and courageous air.

"My name is Gooch," at length the lawyer admitted. Upon pressure he would also have confessed to the Phineas C. But he did not consider it good practice to volunteer information. "I did not receive your card," he continued, by way of rebuke, "so I——"

"I know you didn't," remarked the visitor, coolly; "and you won't just yet. Light up?" He threw a leg over an arm of his chair, and tossed a handful of rich-hued cigars upon the table. Lawyer Gooch knew the brand. He thawed just enough to accept the invitation to smoke.

"You are a divorce lawyer," said the cardless visitor. This time there was no interrogation in his voice. Nor did his words constitute a simple assertion. They formed a charge—a denunciation—as one would say to a dog: "You are a dog." Lawyer Gooch was silent under the imputation.

"You handle," continued the visitor, "all the various ramifications of busted-up connubiality. You are a surgeon, we might say, who extracts Cupid's darts when he shoots 'em into the wrong parties. You furnish patent, incandescent lights for premises where the torch of Hymen has burned so low you can't light a cigar at it. Am I right, Mr. Gooch?"

"I have undertaken cases," said the lawyer, guardedly, "in the line to which your figurative speech seems to refer. Do you wish to consult me professionally, Mr. ——" The lawyer paused, with significance.

"Not yet," said the other, with an arch wave of his cigar, "not just yet. Let us approach the subject with the caution that should have been used in the original act that makes this pow-wow necessary. There exists a matrimonial jumble to be straightened out. But before I give you names I want your honest —well, anyhow, your professional opinion on the merits of the mix-up. I want you to size up the catastrophe—abstractly—you understand? I'm Mr. Nobody; and I've got a story to tell you. Then you say what's what. Do you get my wireless?"

"You want to state a hypothetical case?" suggested Lawyer Gooch.

"That's the word I was after. 'Apothecary' was the best shot I could make at it in my mind. The hypothetical goes. I'll state the case. Suppose there's a woman—a deuced fine-looking woman—who has run away from her husband and home? She's badly mashed on another man who went to her town to work up some real estate business. Now, we may as well call this woman's husband Thomas R. Billings, for that's his name. I'm giving you straight tips on the cognomens. The Lothario chap is Henry K. Jessup. The Billingses lived in a little town called Susanville—a good many miles from here. Now, Jessup leaves Susanville two weeks ago. The next day Mrs. Billings follows him. She's dead gone on this man Jessup; you can bet your law library on that."

Lawyer Gooch's client said this with such unctuous satisfaction that even the callous lawyer experienced a slight ripple of repulsion. He now saw clearly in his fatuous visitor the conceit of the lady-killer, the egoistic complacency of the successful trifler.

"Now," continued the visitor, "suppose this Mrs. Billings wasn't happy at home? We'll say she and her husband didn't gee worth a cent. They've got in‚compatibility to burn. The things she likes, Billings wouldn't have as a gift with trading-stamps. It's Tabby and Rover with them all the time. She's an edu‚cated woman in science and culture, and she reads things out loud at meetings. Billings is not on. He don't appreciate progress and obelisks and ethics, and things of that sort. Old Billings is simply a blink when it comes to such things. The lady is out and out above his class. Now, lawyer, don't it look like a fair equalization of rights and wrongs that a woman like that should be allowed to throw down Billings and take the man that can appreciate her?"

"Incompatibility," said Lawyer Gooch, "is undoubtedly the source of much marital discord and unhappiness. Where it is positively proved, divorce would seem to be the equitable remedy. Are you—excuse me—is this man Jessup one to whom the lady may safely trust her future?"

"Oh, you can bet on Jessup," said the client, with a confident wag of his head. "Jessup's all right. He'll do the square thing. Why, he left Susanville just to keep people from talking about Mrs. Billings. But she followed him up, and now, of course, he'll stick to her. When she gets a divorce, all legal and proper, Jessup will do the proper thing."

"And now," said Lawyer Gooch, "continuing the hypothesis, if you prefer, and supposing that my services should be desired in the case, what——"

The client rose impulsively to his feet.

"Oh, dang the hypothetical business," he exclaimed, impatiently. "Let's let her drop, and get down to straight talk. You ought to know who I am by this time. I want that woman to have her divorce. I'll pay for it. The day you set Mrs. Billings free I'll pay you five hundred dollars.'"

Lawyer Gooch's client banged his fist upon the table to punctuate his gen‚erosity.

"If that is the case——" began the lawyer.

"Lady to see you, sir," bawled Archibald, bouncing in from his anteroom. He had orders to always announce immediately any client that might come. There was no sense in turning business away.

Lawyer Gooch took client number one by the arm and led him sauvely into one of the adjoining rooms. "Favor me by remaining here a few minutes, sir," said he. "I will return and resume our consultation with the least possible delay. I am rather expecting a visit from a very wealthy old lady in connection with a will. I will not keep you waiting long."

The breezy gentleman seated himself with obliging acquiescence, and took up a magazine. The lawyer returned to the middle office, carefully closing behind him the connecting door.

"Show the lady in, Archibald," he said to the office boy, who was awaiting the order.

A tall lady, of commanding presence and sternly handsome, entered the room. She wore robes—robes; not clothes—ample and fluent. In her eye could be perceived the lambent flame of genius and soul. In her hand was a green bag of the capacity of a bushel, and an umbrella that also seemed to wear a robe, ample and fluent. She accepted a chair.

"Are you Mr. Phineas C. Gooch, the lawyer?" she asked, in formal and unconciliatory tones.

"I am," answered Lawyer Gooch, without circumlocution. He never circumlocuted when dealing with a woman. Women circumlocute. Time is wasted when both sides in debate employ the same tactics.

"As a lawyer, sir," began the lady, "you may have acquired some knowledge of the human heart. Do you believe that the pusillanimous and petty conventions of our artificial social life should stand as an obstacle in the way of a noble and affectionate heart when it finds its true mate among the miserable and worthless wretches in the world that are called men?"

"Madam," said Lawyer Gooch, in the tone that he used in curbing his female clients, "this is an office for conducting the practice of law. I am a lawyer, not a philosopher, nor the editor of an 'Answers to the Lovelorn' column of a newspaper. I have other clients waiting. I will ask you kindly to come to the point."

"Well, you needn't get so stiff around the gills about it," said the lady, with a snap of her luminous eyes and a startling gyration of her umbrella. "Business is what I've come for. I want your opinion in the matter of a suit for divorce, as the vulgar would call it, but which is really only the readjustment of the false and ignoble conditions that the short-sighted laws of man have interposed between a loving——"

"I beg your pardon, madam," interrupted Lawyer Gooch, with some impatience, "for reminding you again that this is a law office. Perhaps Mrs. Wilcox——"

"Mrs. Wilcox is all right," cut in the lady, with a hint of asperity. "And so are Tolstoi, and Mrs. Gertrude Atherton, and Omar Khayyam, and Mr. Edward Bok. I've read 'em all. I would like to discuss with you the divine right of the soul as opposed to the freedom-destroying restrictions of a bigoted and narrow-minded society. But I will proceed to business. I would prefer to lay the matter before you in an impersonal way until you pass upon its merits. That is to describe it as a supposable instance, without——"

"You wish to state a hypothetical case?" said Lawyer Gooch.

"I was going to say that," said the lady, sharply. "Now, suppose there is a woman who is all soul and heart and aspirations for a complete existence. This woman has a husband who is far below her in intellect, in taste—in everything. Bah! he is a brute. He despises literature. He sneers at the lofty thoughts of the world's great thinkers. He thinks only of real estate and such sordid things. He is no mate for a woman with soul. We will say that this unfortunate wife one day meets with her ideal—a man with brain and heart and force. She loves him. Although this man feels the thrill of a new-found affinity he is too noble, too honorable to declare himself. He flies from the presence of his beloved. She flies after him, trampling, with superb indifference, upon the fetters with which an unenlightened social system would bind her. Now, what will a divorce cost? Eliza Ann Timmins, the poetess of Sycamore Gap, got one for three hundred and forty dollars. Can I—I mean can this lady I speak of get one that cheap?"

"Madam," said Lawyer Gooch, "your last two or three sentences delight me with their intelligence and clearness. Can we not now abandon the hypothetical and come down to names and business?"

"I should say so," exclaimed the lady, adopting the practical with admirable readiness. "Thomas R. Billings is the name of the low brute who stands between the happiness of his legal—his legal, but not his spiritual—wife and Henry K.

Jessup, the noble man whom nature intended for her mate. I," concluded the client, with an air of dramatic revelation, "am Mrs. Billings!'"

"Gentleman to see you, sir," shouted Archibald, invading the room almost at a handspring. Lawyer Gooch arose from his chair.

"Mrs. Billings," he said, courteously, "allow me to conduct you into the adjoining office apartment for a few minutes. I am expecting a very wealthy old gentleman on business connected with a will. In a very short while I will join you, and continue our consultation."

With his accustomed chivalrous manner, Lawyer Gooch ushered his soulful client into the remaining unoccupied room, and came out, closing the door with circumspection.

The next visitor introduced by Archibald was a thin, nervous, irritable-looking man of middle age, with a worried and apprehensive expression of countenance. He carried in one hand a small satchel, which he set down upon the floor beside the chair which the lawyer placed for him. His clothing was of good quality, but it was worn without regard to neatness or style, and appeared to be covered with the dust of travel.

"You make a specialty of divorce cases," he said, in an agitated but business-like tone.

"I may say," began Lawyer Gooch, "that my practice has not altogether avoided——"

"I know you do," interrupted client number three. "You needn't tell me. I've heard all about you. I have a case to lay before you without necessarily disclosing any connection that I might have with it—that is——"

"You wish," said Lawyer Gooch, "to state a hypothetical case."

"You may call it that. I am a plain man of business. I will be as brief as possible. We will first take up the hypothetical woman. We will say she is married uncongenially. In many ways she is a superior woman. Physically she is considered to be handsome. She is devoted to what she calls literature—poetry and prose, and such stuff. Her husband is a plain man in the business walks of life. Their home has not been happy, although the husband has tried to make it so. Some time ago a man—a stranger—came to the peaceful town in which they lived and engaged in some real estate operations. This woman met him, and became unaccountably infatuated with him. Her attentions became so open that the man felt the community to be no safe place for him, so he left it. She abandoned husband and home, and followed him. She forsook her home, where she was provided with every comfort, to follow this man who had inspired her with such a strange affection. Is there anything more to be deplored," concluded the client, in a trembling voice, "than the wrecking of a home by a woman's uncalculating folly?"

Lawyer Gooch delivered the cautious opinion that there was not.

"This man she has gone to join," resumed the visitor, "is not the man to make her happy. It is a wild and foolish self-deception that makes her think he will. Her husband, in spite of their many disagreements, is the only one capable of dealing with her sensitive and peculiar nature. But this she does not realize now."

"Would you consider a divorce the logical cure in the case you present?" asked Lawyer Gooch, who felt that the conversation was wandering too far from the field of business.

"A divorce!" exclaimed the client, feelingly—almost tearfully. "No, no—not that I have read, Mr. Gooch, of many instances where your sympathy and kindly interest led you to act as a mediator between estranged husband and wife, and brought them together again. Let us drop the hypothetical case—I need conceal no longer that it is I who am the sufferer in this sad affair—the names you shall have—Thomas R. Billings and Wife—and Henry K. Jessup, the man with whom she is infatuated."

Client number three laid his hand upon Mr. Gooch's arm. Deep emotion was written upon his careworn face. "For Heaven's sake," he said, fervently, "help me in this hour of trouble. Seek out Mrs. Billings, and persuade her to abandon this distressing pursuit of her lamentable folly. Tell her, Mr. Gooch, that her husband is willing to receive her back to his heart and home—promise her anything that will induce her to return. I have heard of your success in these matters. Mrs. Billings cannot be very far away. I am worn out with travel and weariness. Twice during the pursuit I saw her, but various circumstances prevented our having an interview. Will you undertake this mission for me, Mr. Gooch, and earn my everlasting gratitude?"

"It is true," said Lawyer Gooch, frowning slightly at the other's last words, but immediately calling up an expression of virtuous benevolence, "that on a number of occasions I have been successful in persuading couples who sought the severing of their matrimonial bonds to think better of their rash intentions and return to their homes reconciled. But I assure you that the work is often exceedingly difficult. The amount of argument, perseverance, and, if I may be allowed to say it, eloquence that it requires would astonish you. But this is a case in which my sympathies would be wholly enlisted. I feel deeply for you, sir, and I would be most happy to see husband and wife reunited. But my time," concluded the lawyer, looking at his watch as if suddenly reminded of the fact, "is valuable.'"

"I am aware of that," said the client, "and if you will take the case and persuade Mrs. Billings to return home and leave the man alone that she is following—on that day I will pay you the sum of one thousand dollars. I have made a little money in real estate during the recent boom in Susanville, and I will not begrudge that amount."

"Retain your seat for a few moments, please," said Lawyer Gooch, arising and again consulting his watch. "I have another client waiting in an adjoining room whom I had very nearly forgotten. I will return in the briefest possible space."

The situation was now one that fully satisfied Lawyer Gooch's love of intricacy and complication. He revelled in cases that presented such subtle problems and possibilities. It pleased him to think that he was master of the happiness and fate of the three individuals who sat, unconscious of one another's presence, within his reach. His old figure of the ship glided into his mind. But now the figure failed, for to have filled every compartment of an actual vessel would have been to endanger her safety; while here, with his compartments full, his ship of affairs could but sail on to the advantageous port of a fine, fat fee. The thing for him to do, of course, was to wring the best bargain he could from some one of his anxious cargo.

First he called to the office boy: "Lock the outer door, Archibald, and admit no one." Then he moved, with long, silent strides, into the room in which client number one waited. That gentleman sat, patiently scanning the pictures in the magazine, with a cigar in his mouth and his feet upon a table.

"Well," he remarked, cheerfully, as the lawyer entered, "have you made up your mind? Does five hundred dollars go for getting the fair lady a divorce?"

"You mean that as a retainer?" asked Lawyer Gooch, softly interrogative.

"Hey? No; for the whole job. It's enough, ain't it?"

"My fee," said Lawyer Gooch, "would be one thousand five hundred dollars. Five hundred dollars down, and the remainder upon issuance of the divorce."

A loud whistle came from client number one. His feet descended to the floor.

"Guess we can't close the deal," he said, arising. "I cleaned up five hundred dollars in a little real estate dicker down in Susanville. I'd do anything I could to free the lady, but it outsizes my pile."

"Could you stand one thousand two hundred dollars?" asked the lawyer, insinuatingly.

"Five hundred is my limit, I tell you. Guess I'll have to hunt up a cheaper lawyer." The client put on his hat.

"Out this way, please," said Lawyer Gooch, opening the door that led into the hallway.

As the gentleman flowed out of the compartment and down the stairs, Lawyer Gooch smiled to himself. "Exit Mr. Jessup," he murmured, as he fingered the Henry Clay tuft of hair at his ear. "And now for the forsaken husband." He returned to the middle office, and assumed a businesslike manner.

"I understand," he said to client number three, "that you agree to pay one thousand dollars if I bring about, or am instrumental in bringing about, the return of Mrs. Billings to her home, and her abandonment of her infatuated pursuit of the man for whom she has conceived such a violent fancy. Also that the case is now unreservedly in my hands on that basis. Is that correct?"

"Entirely," said the other, eagerly. "And I can produce the cash any time at two hours' notice."

Lawyer Gooch stood up at his full height. His thin figure seemed to expand. His thumbs sought the armholes of his vest. Upon his face was a look of sympathetic benignity that he always wore during such undertakings.

"Then, sir," he said, in kindly tones, "I think I can promise you an early relief from your troubles. I have that much confidence in my powers of argument and persuasion, in the natural impulses of the human heart toward good, and in the strong influence of a husband's unfaltering love. Mrs. Billings, sir, is here—in that room——" the lawyer's long arm pointed to the door. "I will call her in at once; and our united pleadings——"

Lawyer Gooch paused, for client number three had leaped from his chair as if propelled by steel springs, and clutched his satchel.

"What the devil," he exclaimed, harshly, "do you mean? That woman in there! I thought I shook her off forty miles back."

He ran to the open window, looked out below, and threw one leg over the sill.

"Stop!" cried Lawyer Gooch, in amazement. "What would you do? Come, Mr. Billings, and face your erring but innocent wife. Our combined entreaties cannot fail to——"

"Billings!" shouted the now thoroughly moved client; "I'll Billings you, you old idiot!"

Turning, he hurled his satchel with fury at the lawyer's head. It struck that astounded peacemaker between the eyes, causing him to stagger backward a pace or two. When Lawyer Gooch recovered his wits he saw that his client had disappeared. Rushing to the window, he leaned out, and saw the recreant gathering himself up from the top of a shed upon which he had dropped from the second-story window. Without stopping to collect his hat he then plunged downward the remaining ten feet to the alley, up which he flew with prodigious celerity until the surrounding building swallowed him up from view.

Lawyer Gooch passed his hand tremblingly across his brow. It was an habitual act with him, serving to clear his thoughts. Perhaps also it now seemed to soothe the spot where a very hard alligator-hide satchel had struck.

The satchel lay upon the floor, wide open, with its contents spilled about. Mechanically Lawyer Gooch stooped to gather up the articles. The first was a collar; and the omniscient eye of the man of law perceived, wonderingly, the initials H. K. J. marked upon it. Then came a comb, a brush, a folded map and a piece of soap. Lastly, a handful of old business letters, addressed—every one of them—to "Henry K. Jessup, Esq."

Lawyer Gooch closed the satchel, and set it upon the table. He hesitated for a moment, and then put on his hat and walked into the office boy's anteroom.

"Archibald," he said mildly, as he opened the hall door, "I am going to the Supreme Court rooms. In five minutes you may step into the inner office, and inform the lady who is waiting there that"—here Lawyer Gooch made use of the vernacular—"that there's nothing doing."

CALLOWAY'S CODE

THE New York *Enterprise* sent H. B. Calloway as special correspondent to the Russo-Japanese-Portsmouth war.

For two months Calloway hung about Yokohama and Tokio, shaking dice with the other correspondents for drinks of 'rickshaws—oh, no, that's something to ride in; anyhow, he wasn't earning the salary that his paper was paying him. But that was not Calloway's fault. The little brown men who held the strings of Fate between their fingers were not ready for the readers of the *Enterprise* to season their breakfast bacon and eggs with the battles of the descendants of the gods.

But soon the column of correspondents that were to go out with the First Army tightened their field-glass belts and went down to the Yalu with Kuroki. Calloway was one of these.

Now, this is no history of the battle of the Yalu River. That has been told in detail by the correspondents who gazed at the shrapnel smoke rings from a distance of three miles. But, for justice's sake, let it be understood that the Japanese commander prohibited a nearer view.

Calloway's feat was accomplished before the battle. What he did was to furnish the *Enterprise* with the biggest beat of the war. That paper published exclusively and in detail the news of the attack on the lines of the Russian General Zassulitch on the same day that it was made. No other paper printed a word about it for two days afterward, except a London paper, whose account was absolutely incorrect and untrue.

Calloway did this in face of the fact that General Kuroki was making his moves and laying his plans with the profoundest secrecy as far as the world outside his camps was concerned. The correspondents were forbidden to send out any news whatever of his plans; and every message that was allowed on the wires was censored with rigid severity.

The correspondent for the London paper handed in a cablegram describing Kuroki's plans; but as it was wrong from beginning to end the censor grinned and let it go through.

So, there they were—Kuroki on one side of the Yalu with forty-two thousand infantry, five thousand cavalry, and one hundred and twenty-four guns. On the other side Zassulitch waited for him with only twenty-three thousand men, and with a long stretch of river to guard. And Calloway had got hold of some important inside information that he knew would bring the *Enterprise* staff around a cablegram as thick as flies around a Park Row lemonade stand. If he could only get that message past the censor—the new censor who had arrived and taken his post that day!

Calloway did the obviously proper thing. He lit his pipe and sat down on a gun carriage to think it over. And there we must leave him; for the rest of the story belongs to Vesey, a sixteen-dollar-a-week reporter on the *Enterprise*.

Calloway's cablegram was handed to the managing editor at four o'clock in the afternoon. He read it three times; and then drew a pocket mirror from a pigeon-hole in his desk, and looked at his reflection carefully. Then he went over to the desk of Boyd, his assistant (he usually called Boyd when he wanted him), and laid the cablegram before him.

"It's from Calloway," he said. "See what you make of it."

The message was dated at Wi-ju, and these were the words of it:

Foregone preconcerted rash witching goes muffled rumor mine dark silent unfortunate richmond existing great hotly brute select mooted parlous beggars ye angel incontrovertible.

Boyd read it twice.

"It's either a cipher or a sunstroke," said he.

"Ever hear of anything like a code in the office—a secret code?" asked the m. e., who had held his desk for only two years. Managing editors come and go.

"None except the vernacular that the lady specials write in," said Boyd. "Couldn't be an acrostic, could it?"

"I thought of that," said the m. e., "but the beginning letters contain only four vowels. It must be a code of some sort."

"Try 'em in groups," suggested Boyd. "Let's see—'Rash witching goes'— not with me it doesn't. 'Muffled rumor mine'—must have an underground wire. 'Dark silent unfortunate richmond'—no reason why he should knock that town so hard. 'Existing great hotly'—no, it doesn't pan out. I'll call Scott."

The city editor came in a hurry, and tried his luck. A city editor must know something about everything; so Scott knew a little about cipher-writing.

"It may be what is called an inverted alphabet cipher," said he. "I'll try that. 'R' seems to be the oftenest used initial letter, with the exception of 'm.' Assuming 'r' to mean 'e,' the most frequently used vowel, we transpose the letters —so."

Scott worked rapidly with his pencil for two minutes; and then showed the first word according to his reading—the word "Scejtzez."

"Great!" cried Boyd. "It's a charade. My first is a Russian General. Go on, Scott."

"No, that won't work," said the city editor. "It's undoubtedly a code. It's impossible to read it without the key. Has the office ever used a cipher code?"

"Just what I was asking," said the m. e. "Hustle everybody up that ought to know. We must get at it some way. Calloway has evidently got hold of something big, and the censor has put the screws on, or he wouldn't have cabled in a lot of chop suey like this."

Throughout the office of the *Enterprise* a dragnet was sent, hauling in such members of the staff as would be likely to know of a code, past or present, by reason of their wisdom, information, natural intelligence, or length of servitude. They got together in a group in the city room, with the m. e. in the centre. No one had heard of a code. All began to explain to the head investigator that newspapers never use a code, anyhow—that is, a cipher code. Of course the Associated Press stuff is a sort of code—an abbreviation, rather—but—

The m. e. knew all that, and said so. He asked each man how long he had worked on the paper. Not one of them had drawn pay from an *Enterprise* envelope for longer than six years. Calloway had been on the paper twelve years.

"Try old Heffelbauer," said the m. e. "He was here when Park Row was a potato patch."

Heffelbauer was an institution. He was half janitor, half handy-man about the office, and half watchman—thus becoming the peer of thirteen and one-half tailors. Sent for, he came, radiating his nationality.

"Heffelbauer," said the m. e., "did you ever hear of a code belonging to the office a long time ago—a private code? You know what a code is, don't you?"

"Yah," said Heffelbauer. "Sure I know vat a code is. Yah, apout dwelf or fifteen year ago der office had a code. Der reborters in der city-room haf it here."

"Ah!" said the m. e. "We're getting on the trail now. Where was it kept, Heffelbauer? What do you know about it?"

"Somedimes," said the retainer, "dey keep it in der little room behind der library room."

"Can you find it?" asked the m. e., eagerly. "Do you know where it is?"

"Mein Gott!" said Heffelbauer. "How long you dink a code live? Der reborters call him a maskeet. But von day he but mit his head der editor, und——'"

"Oh, he's talking about a goat," said Boyd. "Get out, Heffelbauer."

Again discomfited, the concerted wit and resource of the *Enterprise* huddled around Calloway's puzzle, considering its mysterious words in vain.

Then Vesey came in.

Vesey was the youngest reporter. He had a thirty-two-inch chest and wore a number fourteen collar; but his bright Scotch plaid suit gave him presence and conferred no obscurity upon his whereabouts. He wore his hat in such a position that people followed him about to see him take it off, convinced that it must be hung upon a peg driven into the back of his head. He was never without an immense, knotted, hard-wood cane with a German-silver tip on its crooked handle. Vesey was the best photograph hustler in the office. Scott said it was because no living human being could resist the personal triumph it was to hand his picture over to Vesey. Vesey always wrote his own news stories, except the big ones, which were sent to the rewrite men. Add to this fact that among all the inhabitants, temples, and groves of the earth nothing existed that could abash Vesey, and his dim sketch is concluded.

Vesey butted into the circle of cipher readers very much as Heffelbauer's "code" would have done, and asked what was up. Some one explained, with the touch of half-familiar condescension that they always used toward him. Vesey reached out and took the cablegram from the m. e.'s hand. Under the protection of some special Providence, he was always doing appalling things like that, and coming off unscathed.

"It's a code," said Vesey. "Anybody got the key?"

"The office has no code," said Boyd, reaching for the message. Vesey held on to it.

"Then old Calloway expects us to read it, anyhow," said he. "He's up a tree, or something, and he's made this up so as to get it by the censor. It's up to us. Gee! I wish they had sent me, too. Say—we can't afford to fall down on our end of it. 'Foregone, preconcerted rash, witching'—h'm."

Vesey sat down on a table corner and began to whistle softly, frowning at the cablegram.

"Let's have it, please," said the m. e. "We've got to get to work on it."

"I believe I've got a line on it," said Vesey. "Give me ten minutes."

He walked to his desk, threw his hat into a waste-basket, spread out flat on his chest like a gorgeous lizard, and started his pencil going. The wit and wisdom of the *Enterprise* remained in a loose group, and smiled at one another, nodding their heads toward Vesey. Then they began to exchange their theories about the cipher.

It took Vesey exactly fifteen minutes. He brought to the m. e. a pad with the code-key written on it.

"I felt the swing of it as soon as I saw it," said Vesey. "Hurrah for old Calloway! He's done the Japs and every paper in town that prints literature instead of news. Take a look at that."

Thus had Vesey set forth the reading of the code:

> Foregone—conclusion
> Preconcerted—arrangement
> Rash—act
> Witching—hour of midnight
> Goes—without saying
> Muffled—report
> Rumor—hath it
> Mine—host
> Dark—horse
> Silent—majority
> Unfortunate—pedestrians [1]
> Richmond—in the field
> Existing—conditions
> Great—White Way
> Hotly—contested
> Brute—force
> Select—few
> Mooted—question
> Parlous—times
> Beggars—description
> Ye—correspondent
> Angel—unawares
> Incontrovertible—fact

"It's simply newspaper English," explained Vesey. "I've been reporting on the *Enterprise* long enough to know it by heart. Old Calloway gives us the cue word, and we use the word that naturally follows it just as we use 'em in the paper. Read it over, and you'll see how pat they drop into their places. Now, here's the message he intended us to get."

Vesey handed out another sheet of paper.

Concluded arrangement to act at hour of midnight without saying. Report hath it that a large body of cavalry and an overwhelming force of infantry will be thrown into the field. Conditions white. Way contested by only a small force. Question the *Times* description. Its correspondent is unaware of the facts.

"Great stuff!" cried Boyd, excitedly. "Kuroki crosses the Yalu to-night and attacks. Oh, we won't do a thing to the sheets that make up with Addison's essays, real estate transfers, and bowling scores!"

"Mr. Vesey," said the m. e., with his jollying-which-you-should-regard-as-a-favor manner, "you have cast a serious reflection upon the literary standards of the paper that employs you. You have also assisted materially in giving us the biggest 'beat' of the year. I will let you know in a day or two whether

[1] Mr. Vesey afterward explained that the logical journalistic complement of the word "unfortunate" was once the word "victim." But, since the automobile became so popular, the correct following word is now "pedestrians." Of course, in Calloway's code it meant infantry.

you are to be discharged or retained at larger salary. Somebody send Ames to me."

Ames was the king-pin, the snowy-petalled marguerite, the star-bright looloo of the rewrite men. He saw attempted murder in the pains of green-apple colic, cyclones in the summer zephyr, lost children in every top-spinning urchin, an uprising of the down-trodden masses in every hurling of a derelict potato at a passing automobile. When not rewriting, Ames sat on the porch of his Brooklyn villa playing checkers with his ten-year-old son.

Ames and the "war editor" shut themselves in a room. There was a map in there stuck full of little pins that represented armies and divisions. Their fingers had been itching for days to move those pins along the crooked line of the Yalu. They did so now; and in words of fire Ames translated Calloway's brief message into a front page masterpiece that set the world talking. He told of the secret councils of the Japanese officers; gave Kuroki's flaming speeches in full; counted the cavalry and infantry to a man and a horse; described the quick and silent building of the bridge at Suikauchen, across which the Mikado's legions were hurled upon the surprised Zassulitch, whose troops were widely scattered along the river. And the battle!—well, you know what Ames can do with a battle if you give him just one smell of smoke for a foundation. And in the same story, with seemingly supernatural knowledge, he gleefully scored the most profound and ponderous paper in England for the false and misleading account of the intended movements of the Japanese First Army printed in its issue of *the same date.*

Only one error was made; and that was the fault of the cable operator at Wi-ju. Calloway pointed it out after he came back. The word "great" in his code should have been "gage" and its complemental words "of battle." But it went to Ames "conditions white," and of course he took that to mean snow. His description of the Japanese army struggling through the snowstorm, blinded by the whirling flakes, was thrillingly vivid. The artists turned out some effective illustrations that made a hit as pictures of the artillery dragging their guns through the drifts. But, as the attack was made on the first day of May, the "conditions white" excited some amusement. But it made no difference to the *Enterprise,* anyway.

It was wonderful. And Calloway was wonderful in having made the new censor believe that his jargon of words meant no more than a complaint of the dearth of news and a petition for more expense money. And Vesey was wonderful. And most wonderful of all are words, and how they make friends one with another, being oft associated, until not even obituary notices them do part.

On the second day following, the city editor halted at Vesey's desk where the reporter was writing the story of a man who had broken his leg by falling into a coal-hole—Ames having failed to find a murder motive in it.

"The old man says your salary is to be raised to twenty a week," said Scott.

"All right," said Vesey. "Every little helps. Say—Mr. Scott, which would you say—'We can state without fear of successful contradiction,' or, 'On the whole it can be safely asserted'?"

A MATTER OF MEAN ELEVATION

ONE winter the Alcazar Opera Company of New Orleans made a speculative trip along the Mexican, Central American, and South American coasts. The venture proved a most successful one. The music-loving, impressionable Spanish-Americans deluged the company with dollars and "vivas." The manager waxed plump and amiable. But for the prohibitive climate he would have put forth the distinctive flower of his prosperity—the overcoat of fur, braided, frogged, and opulent. Almost was he persuaded to raise the salaries of his company. But with a mighty effort he conquered the impulse toward such an unprofitable effervescence of joy.

At Macuto, on the coast of Venezuela, the company scored its greatest success. Imagine Coney Island translated into Spanish and you will comprehend Macuto. The fashionable season is from November to March. Down from La Guayra and Caracas and Valencia and other interior towns flock the people for their holiday season. There are bathing and fiestas and bull fights and scandal. And then the people have a passion for music that the bands in the plaza and on the sea beach stir but do not satisfy. The coming of the Alcazar Opera Company aroused the utmost ardor and zeal among the pleasure seekers.

The illustrious Guzman Blanco, President and Dictator of Venezuela, sojourned in Macuto with his court for the season. That potent ruler—who himself paid a subsidy of 40,000 pesos each year to grand opera in Caracas—ordered one of the government warehouses to be cleared for a temporary theatre. A stage was quickly constructed and rough wooden benches made for the audience. Private boxes were added for the use of the President and the notables of the army and Government.

The company remained in Macuto for two weeks. Each performance filled the house as closely as it could be packed. Then the music-mad people fought for room in the open doors and windows, and crowded about, hundreds deep on the outside. Those audiences formed a brilliantly diversified patch of color. The hue of their faces ranged from the clear olive of the pure-blood Spaniards down through the yellow and brown shades of the mestizos to the coal-black Carib and the Jamaica Negro. Scattered among them were little groups of Indians with faces like stone idols, wrapped in gaudy fibre-woven blankets—Indians down from the mountain states of Zamora and Los Andes and Miranda to trade their gold dust in the coast towns.

The spell cast upon these denizens of the interior fastnesses was remarkable. They sat in petrified ecstasy, conspicuous among the excitable Macutians, who wildly strove with tongue and hand to give evidence of their delight. Only once did the sombre rapture of these aboriginals find expression. During the rendition of "Faust," Guzman Blanco, extravagantly pleased by the "Jewel Song," cast upon the stage a purse of gold pieces. Other distinguished citizens followed his lead to the extent of whatever loose coin they had convenient, while some of the fair and fashionable señoras were moved, in imitation, to fling a jewel or a ring or two at the feet of the Marguerite—who was, according to the bills, Mlle Nina Giraud. Then from different parts of the house rose sundry of the stolid hillmen and cast upon the stage little brown and dun bags that fell with soft "thumps" and did not rebound. It was, no doubt, pleasure at the tribute to her art that caused Mlle Giraud's eyes to shine so brightly when she opened these little deerskin bags in her dressing room and found them to contain pure gold dust. If so, the pleasure was rightly hers, for her voice in song, pure, strong, and thrilling with the feeling of the emotional artist, deserved the tribute that it earned.

But the triumph of the Alcazar Opera Company is not the theme: it but leans upon and colors it. There happened in Macuto a tragic thing, an unsolvable mystery, that sobered for a time the gaiety of the happy season.

One evening between the short twilight and the time when she should have whirled upon the stage in the red and black of the ardent Carmen, Mlle Nina Giraud disappeared from the sight and ken of 6,000 pairs of eyes and as many minds in Macuto. There was the usual turmoil and hurrying to seek her. Messengers flew to the little French-kept hotel where she stayed; others of the company hastened here or there where she might be lingering in some *tienda* or unduly prolonging her bath upon the beach. All search was fruitless. Mademoiselle had vanished.

Half an hour passed and she did not appear. The dictator, unused to the caprices of prime donne, became impatient. He sent an aide from his box to say to the manager that if the curtain did not at once rise he would immediately hale the entire company to the calabosa, though it would desolate his heart, indeed, to be compelled to such an act. Birds in Macuto could be made to sing.

The manager abandoned hope, for the time, of Mlle Giraud. A member of the chorus, who had dreamed hopelessly for years of the blessed opportunity, quickly Carmenized herself and the opera went on.

Afterward, when the lost cantatrice appeared not, the aid of the authorities was invoked. The President at once set the army, the police, and all citizens to the search. Not one clue to Mlle Giraud's disappearance was found. The Alcazar left to fill engagements farther down the coast.

On the way back the steamer stopped at Macuto and the manager made anxious inquiry. Not a trace of the lady had been discovered. The Alcazar could do no more. The personal belongings of the missing lady were stored in the hotel against her possible later reappearance and the opera company continued upon its homeward voyage to New Orleans.

. . . .

On the *camino real* along the beach the two saddle mules and the four pack mules of Señor Don Johnny Armstrong stood, patiently awaiting the crack of the whip of the *arriero*, Luis. That would be the signal for the start on another long journey into the mountains. The pack mules were loaded with a varied assortment of hardware and cutlery. These articles Don Johnny traded to the interior Indians for the gold dust that they washed from the Andean streams and stored in quills and bags against his coming. It was a profitable business, and Señor Armstrong expected soon to be able to purchase the coffee plantation that he coveted.

Armstrong stood on the narrow sidewalk, exchanging garbled Spanish with old Peralto, the rich native merchant who had just charged him four prices for half a gross of pot-metal hatchets, and abridged English with Rucker, the little German who was Consul for the United States.

"Take with you, señor," said Peralto, "the blessings of the saints upon your journey."

"Better try quinine," growled Rucker through his pipe. "Take two grains every night. And don't make your trip too long, Johnny, because we haf needs of you. It is ein villainous game dot Melville play of whist, and dere is no oder substitute. *Auf wiedersehen*, und keep your eyes dot mule's ear between when you on der edge of der brecipices ride."

The bells of Luis's mule jingled and the pack train filed after the warning note. Armstrong waved a good-bye and took his place at the trail of the procession. Up the narrow street they turned, and passed the two-story wooden Hotel Inglés, where Ives and Dawson and Richards and the rest of the chaps were dawdling on the broad piazza, reading week-old newspapers. They crowded to the railing and shouted many friendly and wise and foolish farewells after him. Across the plaza they trotted slowly past the bronze statue of Guzman Blanco, within its fence of bayoneted rifles captured from revolutionists, and out of the town between the rows of thatched huts swarming with the unclothed youth of Macuto. They plunged into the damp coolness of banana groves at length to emerge upon a bright stream, where brown women in scant raiment laundered clothes destructively upon the rocks. Then the pack train, fording the stream, attacked the sudden ascent, and bade adieu to such civilization as the coast afforded.

For weeks Armstrong, guided by Luis, followed his regular route among the mountains. After he had collected an arroba of the precious metal, winning a profit of nearly $5,000, the heads of the lightened mules were turned down-trail again. Where the head of the Guarico River springs from a great gash in the mountainside, Luis halted the train.

"Half a day's journey from here, Señor," said he, "is the village of Tacuzama, which we have never visited. I think many ounces of gold may be procured there. It is worth the trial."

Armstrong concurred, and they turned again upward toward Tacuzama. The trail was abrupt and precipitous, mounting through a dense forest. As night fell, dark and gloomy, Luis once more halted. Before them was a black chasm, bisecting the path as far as they could see.

Luis dismounted. "There should be a bridge," he called, and ran along the cleft a distance. "It is here," he cried, and remounting, led the way. In a few moments Armstrong heard a sound as though a thunderous drum were beating somewhere in the dark. It was the falling of the mules' hoofs upon the bridge made of strong hides lashed to poles and stretched across the chasm. Half a mile further was Tacuzama. The village was a congregation of rock and mud huts set in the profundity of an obscure wood. As they rode in a sound inconsistent with that brooding solitude met their ears. From a long, low mud hut that they were nearing rose the glorious voice of a woman in song. The words were English, the air familiar to Armstrong's memory, but not to his musical knowledge.

He slipped from his mule and stole to a narrow window in one end of the house. Peering cautiously inside, he saw, within three feet of him, a woman of marvellous, imposing beauty, clothed in a splendid loose robe of leopard skins. The hut was packed close to the small space in which she stood with the squatting figures of Indians.

The woman finished her song and seated herself close to the little window, as if grateful for the unpolluted air that entered it. When she had ceased several of the audience rose and cast little softly falling bags at her feet. A harsh murmur—no doubt a barbarous kind of applause and comment—went through the grim assembly.

Armstrong was used to seizing opportunities promptly. Taking advantage of the noise he called to the woman in a low but distinct voice: "Do not turn your head this way, but listen. I am an American. If you need assistance tell me how I can render it. Answer as briefly as you can."

The woman was worthy of his boldness. Only by a sudden flush of her pale cheek did she acknowledge understanding of his words. Then she spoke, scarcely moving her lips.

"I am held a prisoner by these Indians. God knows I need help. In two hours come to the little hut twenty yards toward the mountain-side. There will be a light and a red curtain in the window. There is always a guard at the door whom you will have to overcome. For the love of heaven, do not fail to come."

The story seems to shrink from adventure and rescue and mystery. The theme is one too gentle for those brave and quickening tones. And yet it reaches as far back as time itself. It has been named "environment," which is as weak a word as any to express the unnamable kinship of man to nature, that queer fraternity that causes stones and trees and salt water and clouds to play upon our emotions. Why are we made serious and solemn and sublime by mountain heights, grave and contemplative by an abundance of overhanging trees, reduced to inconstancy and monkey capers by the ripples on a sandy beach? Did the protoplasm—but enough. The chemists are looking into the matter, and before long they will have all life in the table of the symbols.

Briefly, then, in order to confine the story within scientific bounds, John Armstrong went to the hut, choked the Indian guard and carried away Mlle Giraud. With her was also conveyed a number of pounds of gold dust she had collected during her six months' forced engagement in Tacuzama. The Carabobo Indians are easily the most enthusiastic lovers of music between the equator and the French Opera House in New Orleans. They are also strong believers that the advice of Emerson was good when he said: "The thing thou wantest, O discontented man—take it, and pay the price." A number of them had attended the performance of the Alcazar Opera Company in Macuto, and found Mlle Giraud's style and technique satisfactory. They wanted her, so they took her one evening suddenly and without any fuss. They treated her with much consideration, exacting only one song recital each day. She was quite pleased at being rescued by Mr. Armstrong. So much for mystery and adventure. Now to resume the theory of the protoplasm.

John Armstrong and Mlle Giraud rode among the Andean peaks, enveloped in their greatness and sublimity. The mightiest cousins, furthest removed, in Nature's great family became conscious of the tie. Among those huge piles of primordial upheaval, amid those gigantic silences and elongated fields of distance the littlenesses of men are precipitated as one chemical throws down a sediment from another. They moved reverently, as in a temple. Their souls were uplifted in unison with the stately heights. They traveled in a zone of majesty and peace.

To Armstrong the woman seemed almost a holy thing. Yet bathed in the white, still dignity of her martyrdom that purified her earthly beauty and gave out, it seemed, an aura of transcendent loveliness, in those first hours of companionship she drew from him an adoration that was half human love, half the worship of a descended goddess.

Never yet since her rescue had she smiled. Over her dress she still wore the robe of leopard skins, for the mountain air was cold. She looked to be some splendid princess belonging to those wild and awesome altitudes. The spirit of the region chimed with hers. Her eyes were always turned upon the somber cliffs, the blue gorges, and the snow-clad turrets, looking a sublime melancholy equal to their own. At times on the journey she sang thrilling te deums and misereres that struck the true note of the hills, and made their route seem like a solemn march down a cathedral aisle. The rescued one spoke but seldom, her mood partaking of the hush of nature that surrounded them. Armstrong looked upon her as an angel. He could not bring himself to the sacrilege of attempting to woo her as other women may be wooed.

On the third day they had descended as far as the *tierra templada*, the zona of the table lands and foot hills. The mountains were receding in their rear, but still towered, exhibiting yet impressively their formidable heads. Here they met signs of man. They saw the white houses of coffee plantations gleam across the clearings. They struck into a road where they met travelers and pack-mules. Cattle were grazing on the slopes. They passed a little village where the round-eyed *niños* shrieked and called at sight of them.

Mlle Giraud laid aside her leopard-skin robe. It seemed to be a trifle incongruous now. In the mountains it had appeared fitting and natural. And if Armstrong was not mistaken she laid aside with it something of the high dignity of her demeanor. As the country became more populous and significant of comfortable life he saw, with a feeling of joy, that the exalted princess and priestess of the Andean peaks was changing to a woman—an earth woman, but no less enticing. A little color crept to the surface of her marble cheek. She arranged the conventional dress that the removal of the robe now disclosed with the solicitous touch of one who is conscious of the eyes of others. She smoothed the careless sweep of her hair. A mundane interest, long latent in the chilling atmosphere of the ascetic peaks, showed in her eyes.

This thaw in his divinity sent Armstrong's heart going faster. So might an Arctic explorer thrill at his first ken of green fields and liquescent waters. They were on a lower plane of earth and life and were succumbing to its peculiar, subtle influence. The austerity of the hills no longer thinned the air they breathed. About them was the breath of fruit and corn and builded homes, the comfortable smell of smoke and warm earth and the consolations man has placed between himself and the dust of his brother earth from which he sprung. While traversing those awful mountains, Mlle Giraud had seemed to be wrapped in their spirit of reverent reserve. Was this that same woman—now palpitating, warm, eager, throbbing with conscious life and charm, feminine to her fingertips? Pondering over this, Armstrong felt certain misgivings intrude upon his thoughts. He wished he could stop there with this changing creature, descending no farther. Here was the elevation and environment to which her nature seemed to respond with its best. He feared to go down upon the man-dominated levels. Would her spirit not yield still further in that artificial zone to which they were descending?

Now from a little plateau they saw the sea flash at the edge of the green lowlands. Mlle Giraud gave a little, catching sigh.

"Oh, look, Mr. Armstrong, there is the sea! Isn't it lovely? I'm so tired of mountains." She heaved a pretty shoulder in a gesture of repugnance. "Those horrid Indians! Just think of what I suffered! Although I suppose I attained my ambition of becoming a stellar attraction, I wouldn't care to repeat the engagement. It was very nice of you to bring me away. Tell me, Mr. Armstrong —honestly, now—do I look such an awful, awful fright? I haven't looked into a mirror, you know, for months."

Armstrong made answer according to his changed moods. Also he laid his hand upon hers as it rested upon the horn of her saddle. Luis was at the head of the pack train and could not see. She allowed it to remain there, and her eyes smiled frankly into his.

Then at sundown they dropped upon the coast level under the palms and lemons among the vivid greens and scarlets and ochres of the *tierra caliente*. They rode into Macuto, and saw the line of volatile bathers frolicking in the surf. The mountains were very far away.

Mlle Giraud's eyes were shining with a joy that could not have existed under the chaperonage of the mountain-tops. There were other spirits calling to her— nymphs of the orange groves, pixies from the chattering surfs, imps, born of the music, the perfumes, colors and the insinuating presence of humanity. She laughed aloud, musically, at a sudden thought.

"Won't there be a sensation?" she called to Armstrong. "Don't I wish I had an engagement just now, though! What a picnic the press agent would have! 'Held a prisoner by a band of savage Indians subdued by the spell of her wonderful voice'—wouldn't that make great stuff? But I guess I quit the game winner, anyhow—there ought to be a couple of thousand dollars in that sack of gold dust I collected as encores, don't you think?"

He left her at the door of the little Hotel de Buen Descansar, where she had stopped before. Two hours later he returned to the hotel. He glanced in at the open door of the little combined reception room and café.

Half a dozen of Macuto's representative social and official *caballeros* were distributed about the room. Señor Villablanca, the wealthy rubber concessionist, reposed his fat figure on two chairs, with an emollient smile beaming upon his chocolate-colored face. Guilbert, the French mining engineer, leered through his polished nose-glasses. Colonel Mendez, of the regular army, in gold-laced uniform and fatuous grin, was busily extracting corks from champagne bottles. Other patterns of Macutian gallantry and fashion pranced and posed. The air was hazy with cigarette smoke. Wine dripped upon the floor.

Perched upon a table in the centre of the room in an attitude of easy preeminence was Mlle Giraud. A chic costume of white lawn and cherry ribbons supplanted her traveling garb. There was a suggestion of lace, and a frill or two, with a discreet, small implication of hand-embroidered pink hosiery. Upon her lap rested a guitar. In her face was the light of resurrection, the peace of elysium attained through fire and suffering. She was singing to a lively accompaniment a little song:

> "When you see de big round moon
> Comin' up like a balloon,
> Dis nigger skips fur to kiss de lips
> Of his stylish, black-faced coon."

The singer caught sight of Armstrong.

"Hi! there, Johnny," she called; "I've been expecting you for an hour. What kept you? Gee! but these smoked guys are the slowest you ever saw. They ain't on, at all. Come along in, and I'll make this coffee-colored old sport with the gold epaulettes open one for you right off the ice."

"Thank you," said Armstrong; "not just now, I believe. I've several things to attend to."

He walked out and down the street, and met Rucker coming up from the Consulate.

"Play you a game of billiards," said Armstrong. "I want something to take the taste of the sea level out of my mouth."

"GIRL"

In gilt letters on the ground glass of the door of room No. 962 were the words: "Robbins & Hartley, Brokers." The clerks had gone. It was past five, and with the solid tramp of a drove of prize Percherons, scrub-women were invading the cloud-capped twenty-story office building. A puff of red-hot air flavored with lemon peelings, soft-coal smoke, and train oil came in through the half-open windows.

Robbins, fifty, something of an overweight beau, and addicted to first nights and hotel palm-rooms, pretended to be envious of his partner's commuter's joys.

"Going to be something doing in the humidity line to-night," he said. "You out-of-town chaps will be the people, with your katydids and moonlight and long drinks and things out on the front porch."

Hartley, twenty-nine, serious, thin, good-looking, nervous, sighed and frowned a little.

"Yes," said he, "we always have cool nights in Floralhurst, especially in the winter."

A man with an air of mystery came in the door and went up to Hartley.

"I've found where she lives," he announced in the portentous half-whisper that makes the detective at work a marked being to his fellow men.

Hartley scowled him into a state of dramatic silence and quietude. But by that time Robbins had got his cane and set his tie pin to his liking, and with a debonair nod went out to his metropolitan amusements.

"Here is the address," said the detective in a natural tone, being deprived of an audience to foil.

Hartley took the leaf torn out of the sleuth's dingy memorandum book. On it were pencilled the words "Vivienne Arlington, No. 341 East —th Street, care of Mrs. McComus."

"Moved there a week ago," said the detective. "Now, if you want any shadowing done, Mr. Hartley, I can do you as fine a job in that line as anybody in the city. It will be only $7 a day and expenses. Can send in a daily type-written report, covering——"

"You needn't go on," interrupted the broker. "It isn't a case of that kind. I merely wanted the address. How much shall I pay you?"

"One day's work," said the sleuth. "A terner will cover it."

Hartley paid the man and dismissed him. Then he left the office and boarded a Broadway car. At the first large crosstown artery of travel he took an eastbound car that deposited him in a decaying avenue, whose ancient structures once sheltered the pride and glory of the town.

Walking a few squares, he came to the building that he sought. It was a new flat-house, bearing carved upon its cheap stone portal its sonorous name, "The Vallambrosa." Fire-escapes zigzagged down its front—these laden with household goods, drying clothes, and squalling children evicted by the midsummer heat. Here and there a pale rubber plant peeped from the miscellaneous mass, as if wondering to what kingdom it belonged—vegetable, animal, or artificial.

Hartley pressed the "McComus" button. The door latch clicked spasmodically—now hospitably, now doubtfully, as though in anxiety whether it might be admitting friends or duns. Hartley entered and began to climb the stairs after the manner of those who seek their friends in city flat-houses—which is the manner of a boy who climbs an apple-tree, stopping when he comes upon what he wants.

On the fourth floor he saw Vivienne standing in an open door. She invited him inside, with a nod and a bright, genuine smile. She placed a chair for him near a window, and poised herself gracefully upon the edge of one of those Jekyll-and-Hyde pieces of furniture that are masked and mysteriously hooded, unguessable bulks by day and inquisitorial racks of torture by night.

Hartley cast a quick, critical, appreciative glance at her before speaking, and told himself that his taste in choosing had been flawless.

Vivienne was about twenty-one. She was of the purest Saxon type. Her hair was a ruddy golden, each filament of the neatly gathered mass shining with its own lustre and delicate graduation of color. In perfect harmony were her ivory-clear complexion and deep sea-blue eyes that looked upon the world with the ingenuous calmness of a mermaid or the pixie of an undiscovered mountain stream. Her frame was strong and yet possessed the grace of absolute naturalness. And yet with all her Northern clearness and frankness of line and coloring, there seemed to be something of the tropics in her—something of languor in the droop of her pose, of love of ease in her ingenious complacency of satisfaction and comfort in the mere act of breathing—something that seemed to claim for her a right as a perfect work of nature to exist and be admired equally with a rare flower or some beautiful, milk-white dove among its sober-hued companions.

She was dressed in a white waist and dark skirt—that discreet masquerade of goose-girl and duchess.

"Vivienne," said Hartley, looking at her pleadingly, "you did not answer my last letter. It was only by nearly a week's search that I found where you had moved to. Why have you kept me in suspense when you knew how anxiously I was waiting to see you and hear from you?"

The girl looked out the window dreamily.

"Mr. Hartley," she said hesitatingly, "I hardly know what to say to you. I realize all the advantages of your offer, and sometimes I feel sure that I could be contented with you. But, again, I am doubtful. I was born a city girl, and I am afraid to bind myself to a quiet suburban life."

"My dear girl," said Hartley, ardently, "have I not told you that you shall have everything that your heart can desire that is in my power to give you? You shall come to the city for the theatres, for shopping, and to visit your friends as often as you care to. You can trust me, can you not?"

"To the fullest," she said, turning her frank eyes upon him with a smile. "I know you are the kindest of men, and that the girl you get will be a lucky one. I learned all about you when I was at the Montgomerys'."

"Ah!" exclaimed Hartley, with a tender, reminiscent light in his eye; "I remember well the evening I first saw you at the Montgomerys'. Mrs. Montgomery was sounding your praises to me all the evening. And she hardly did you justice. I shall never forget that supper. Come, Vivienne, promise me. I want you. You'll never regret coming with me. No one else will ever give you as pleasant a home."

The girl sighed and looked down at her folded hands.

A sudden jealous suspicion seized Hartley.

"Tell me, Vivienne," he asked, regarding her keenly, "is there another—is there some one else?"

A rosy flush crept slowly over her fair cheeks and neck.

"You shouldn't ask that, Mr. Hartley," she said, in some confusion. "But I will tell you. There is one other—but he has no right—I have promised him nothing."

"His name?" demanded Hartley, sternly.

"Townsend."

"Rafford Townsend!" exclaimed Hartley, with a grim tightening of his jaw. "How did that man come to know you? After all I've done for him——"

"His auto has just stopped below," said Vivienne, bending over the window-sill. "He's coming for his answer. Oh, I don't know what to do!"

The bell in the flat kitchen whirred. Vivienne hurried to press the latch button.

"Stay here," said Hartley. "I will meet him in the hall."

Townsend, looking like a Spanish grandee in his light tweeds, Panama hat, and curling black mustache, came up the stairs three at a time. He stopped at sight of Hartley and looked foolish.

"Go back," said Hartley, firmly, pointing downstairs with his forefinger.

"Hullo!" said Townsend, feigning surprise. "What's up? What are you doing here, old man?"

"Go back," repeated Hartley, inflexibly. "The Law of the Jungle. Do you want the Pack to tear you to pieces? The kill is mine."

"I came here to see a plumber about the bathroom connections," said Townsend, bravely.

"All right," said Hartley. "You shall have that lying plaster to stick upon your traitorous soul. But, go back."

Townsend went downstairs, leaving a bitter word to be wafted up the draught of the stair-case. Hartley went back to his wooing.

"Vivienne," said he, masterfully. "I have got to have you. I will take no more refusals or dilly-dallying."

"When do you want me?" she asked.

"Now. As soon as you can get ready."

She stood calmly before him and looked him in the eye.

"Do you think for one moment," she said, "that I would enter your home while Héloïse is there?"

Hartley cringed as if from an unexpected blow. He folded his arms and paced the carpet once or twice.

"She shall go," he declared, grimly. Drops stood upon his brow. "Why should I let that woman make my life miserable? Never have I seen one day of freedom from trouble since I have known her. You are right, Vivienne. Héloïse must be sent away before I can take you home. But she shall go. I have decided. I will turn her from my doors."

"When will you do this?" asked the girl.

Hartley clinched his teeth and bent his brows together.

"To-night," he said, resolutely. "I will send her away to-night."

"Then," said Vivienne, "my answer is 'yes.' Come for me when you will."

She looked into his eyes with a sweet, sincere light in her own. Hartley could scarcely believe that her surrender was true, it was so swift and complete.

"Promise me," he said, feelingly, "on your word and honor."

"On my word and honor," repeated Vivienne, softly.

At the door he turned and gazed at her happily, but yet as one who scarcely trusts the foundations of his joy.

"To-morrow," he said, with a forefinger of reminder uplifted.

"To-morrow," she repeated with a smile of truth and candor.

In an hour and forty minutes Hartley stepped off the train at Floralhurst. A brisk walk of ten minutes brought him to the gate of a handsome two-story cottage set upon a wide and well-tended lawn. Halfway to the house he was met by a woman with jet-black braided hair and flowing white summer gown, who half strangled him without apparent cause.

When they stepped into the hall she said:

"Mamma's here. The auto is coming for her in half an hour. She came to dinner, but there's no dinner."

"I've something to tell you," said Hartley. "I thought to break it to you gently, but since your mother is here we may as well out with it."

He stooped and whispered something at her ear.

His wife screamed. Her mother came running into the hall. The dark-haired woman screamed again—the joyful scream of a well-beloved and petted woman.

"Oh, mamma!" she cried, ecstatically, "what do you think? Vivienne is coming to cook for us! She is the one that stayed with the Montgomerys a whole year. And now, Billy, dear," she concluded, "you must go right down into the kitchen and discharge Héloïse. She has been drunk again the whole day long."

SOCIOLOGY IN SERGE AND STRAW

THE season of irresponsibility is at hand. Come, let us twine round our brows wreaths of poison ivy (that is for idiocy), and wander hand in hand with sociology in the summer fields.

Likely as not the world is flat. The wise men have tried to prove that it is round, with indifferent success. They pointed out to us a ship going to sea, and bade us observe that, at length, the convexity of the earth hid from our view all but the vessel's topmast. But we picked up a telescope and looked, and saw the decks and hull again. Then the wise men said: "Oh, pshaw! anyhow, the variation of the intersection of the equator and the ecliptic proves it." We could not see this through our telescope, so we remained silent. But it stands to reason that, if the world were round, the queues of Chinamen would stand straight up from their heads instead of hanging down their backs, as travelers assure us they do.

Another hot-weather corroboration of the flat theory is the fact that all of life, as we know it, moves in little, unavailing circles. More justly than to anything else, it can be likened to the game of baseball. Crack! we hit the ball, and away we go. If we earn a run (in life we call it success) we get back to the home plate and sit upon a bench. If we are thrown out, we walk back to the home plate—and sit upon a bench.

The circumnavigators of the alleged globe may have sailed the rim of a watery circle back to the same port again. The truly great return at the high tide of their attainments to the simplicity of a child. The billionaire sits down at his mahogany to his bowl of bread and milk. When you reach the end of your career, just take down the sign "Goal" and look at the other side of it. You will find "Beginning Point" there. It has been reversed while you were going around the track.

But this is humor, and must be stopped. Let us get back to the serious questions that arise whenever sociology turns summer boarder. You are invited to consider the scene of the story—wild, Atlantic waves, thundering against a wooded and rock-bound shore—in the Greater City of New York.

The town of Fishampton, on the south shore of Long Island, is noted for its clam fritters and the summer residence of the Van Plushvelts.

The Van Plushvelts have a hundred million dollars, and their name is a household word with tradesmen and photographers.

On the fifteenth of June the Van Plushvelts boarded up the front door of their city house, carefully deposited their cat on the sidewalk, instructed the caretaker not to allow it to eat any of the ivy on the walls, and whizzed away in a 40-horse-power to Fishampton to stray alone in the shade—Amaryllis not being in their class. If you are a subscriber to the *Toadies' Magazine*, you have often—— You say you are not? Well, you buy it at a news-stand, thinking that the newsdealer is not wise to you. But he knows about it all. HE knows—HE knows! I say that you have often seen in the *Toadies' Magazine* pictures of the Van Plushvelts' summer home; so it will not be described here. Our business is with young Haywood Van Plushvelt, sixteen years old, heir to the century of millions, darling of the financial gods, and great grandson of Peter Van Plushvelt, former owner of a particularly fine cabbage patch that has been ruined by an intrusive lot of downtown skyscrapers.

One afternoon young Haywood Van Plushvelt strolled out between the granite gate posts of "Dolce far Niente"—that's what they called the place; and it was an improvement on dolce Far Rockaway, I can tell you.

Haywood walked down into the village. He was human, after all, and his prospective millions weighed upon him. Wealth had wreaked upon him its direfullest. He was the product of private tutors. Even under his first hobby-horse had tan bark been strewn. He had been born with a gold spoon, lobster fork, and fish-set in his mouth. For which I hope, later, to submit justification, I must ask your consideration of his haberdashery and tailoring.

Young Fortunatus was dressed in a neat suit of dark blue serge, a neat white straw hat, neat low-cut tan shoes, linen of the well-known "immaculate" trade mark, a neat, narrow four-in-hand tie, and carried a slender, neat, bamboo cane.

Down Persimmon Street (there's never tree north of Haggerstown, Md.) came from the village "Smoky" Dodson, fifteen and a half, worst boy in Fishampton. "Smoky" was dressed in a ragged red sweater, wrecked and weather-worn golf cap, run-over shoes, and trousers of the "serviceable" brand. Dust, clinging to the moisture induced by free exercise, darkened wide areas of his face. "Smoky" carried a baseball bat, and a league ball that advertised itself in the rotundity of his trousers pocket. Haywood stopped and passed the time of day.

"Going to play ball?" he asked.

"Smoky's" eyes and countenance confronted him with a frank blue-and-freckled scrutiny.

"Me?" he said, with deadly mildness; "sure not. Can't you see I've got a divin' suit on? I'm goin' up in a submarine balloon to catch butterflies with a two-inch auger."

"Excuse me," said Haywood, with the insulting politeness of his caste, "for mistaking you for a gentleman. I might have known better."

"How might you have known better if you thought I was one?" said "Smoky," unconsciously a logician.

"By your appearance," said Haywood. "No gentleman is dirty, ragged, and a liar."

"Smoky" hooted once like a ferry-boat, spat on his hand, got a firm grip on his baseball bat and then dropped it against the fence.

"Say," said he, "I knows you. You're the pup that belongs in that swell private summer sanitarium for city guys over there. I seen you come out of the gate. You can't bluff nobody because you're rich. And because you got on swell clothes. Arabella! Yah!"

"Ragamuffin!" said Haywood.

"Smoky" picked up a fence-rail splinter and laid it on his shoulder.

"Dare you to knock it off," he challenged.

"I wouldn't soil my hands with you," said the aristocrat.

"'Fraid," said "Smoky" concisely. "Youse city ducks ain't got the sand. I kin lick you with one hand."

"I don't wish to have any trouble with you," said Haywood. "I asked you a civil question; and you replied like a—like a—a cad."

"Wot's a cad?" asked "Smoky."

"A cad is a disagreeable person," answered Haywood, "who lacks manners and doesn't know his place. They sometimes play baseball."

"I can tell you what a mollycoddle is," said "Smoky." "It's a monkey dressed up by its mother and sent out to pick daisies on the lawn."

"When you have the honor to refer to the members of my family," said Haywood, with some dim ideas of a code in his mind, "you'd better leave the ladies out of your remarks."

"Ho! ladies!" mocked the rude one. "I say ladies! I know what them rich women in the city does. They drink cocktails and swear and give parties to gorillas. The papers say so."

Then Haywood knew that it must be. He took off his coat, folded it neatly and laid it on the roadside grass, placed his hat upon it and began to unknot his blue silk tie.

"Hadn't yer better ring fer your maid, Arabella?" taunted "Smoky." "Wot yer going to do—go to bed?"

"I'm going to give you a good trouncing," said the hero. He did not hesitate, although the enemy was far beneath him socially. He remembered that his father once thrashed a cabman, and the papers gave it two columns, first page. And the *Toadies' Magazine* had a special article on Upper Cuts by the Upper Classes, and ran new pictures of the Van Plushvelt country seat, at Fishampton.

"Wot's trouncing?" asked "Smoky," suspiciously. "I don't want your old clothes. I'm no—oh, you mean to scrap! My, my! I won't do a thing to mamma's pet. Criminy! I'd hate to be a hand-laundered thing like you."

"Smoky" waited with some awkwardness for his adversary to prepare for battle. His own decks were always clear for action. When he should spit upon the palm of his terrible right it was equivalent to "You may fire now, Gridley."

The hated patrician advanced, with his shirt sleeves neatly rolled up. "Smoky" waited, in an attitude of ease, expecting the affair to be conducted according to Fishampton's rules of war. These allowed combat to be prefaced by stigma, recrimination, epithet, abuse, and insult gradually increasing in emphasis and degree. After a round of these "you're anothers" would come the chip knocked from the shoulder, or the advance across the "dare" line drawn with a toe on the ground. Next light taps given and taken, these also increasing in force until finally the blood was up and fists going at their best.

But Haywood did not know Fishampton's rules. *Noblesse oblige* kept a faint smile on his face as he walked slowly up to "Smoky" and said:

"Going to play ball?"

"Smoky" quickly understood this to be a putting of the previous question, giving him the chance to make a practical apology by answering it with civility and relevance.

"Listen this time," said he. "I'm goin' skatin' on the river. Don't you see me automobile with Chinese lanterns on it standin' and waitin' for me?"

Haywood knocked him down.

"Smoky" felt wronged. To thus deprive him of preliminary wrangle and objurgation was to send an armored knight full tilt against a crashing lance without permitting him first to caracole around the list to the flourish of trumpets. But he scrambled up and fell upon his foe, head, feet, and fists.

The fight lasted one round of an hour and ten minutes. It was lengthened until it was more like a war or a family feud than a fight. Haywood had learned some of the science of boxing and wrestling from his tutors, but these he discarded for the more instinctive methods of battle handed down by the cave-dwelling Van Plushvelts.

So, when he found himself, during the mêlée, seated upon the kicking and roaring "Smoky's" chest, he improved the opportunity by vigorously kneading handfuls of sand and soil into his adversary's ears, eyes, and mouth, and when "Smoky" got the proper leg hold and "turned" him, he fastened both hands in the Plushvelt hair and pounded the Plushvelt head against the lap of mother earth. Of course, the strife was not incessantly active. There were seasons when one sat upon the other, holding him down, while each blew like a grampus, spat out the more inconveniently large sections of gravel and earth, and strove to subdue the spirit of his opponent with a frightful and soul-paralyzing glare.

At last, it seemed that in the language of the ring, their efforts lacked steam. They broke away, and each disappeared in a cloud as he brushed away the dust of the conflict. As soon as his breath permitted, Haywood walked close to "Smoky" and said:

"Going to play ball?"

"Smoky" looked pensively at the sky, at his bat lying on the ground, and at the "leaguer" rounding his pocket.

"Sure," he said off-handedly. "The 'Yellowjackets' play the 'Long Islands.' I'm cap'n of the 'Long Islands.'"

"I guess I didn't mean to say you were ragged," said Haywood. "But you are dirty, you know."

"Sure," said "Smoky." "Yer get that way knockin' around. Say, I don't

believe them New York papers about ladies drinkin' and havin' monkeys dinin'
at the table with 'em. I guess they're lies, like they print about people eatin'
out of silver plates, and ownin' dogs that cost $100."

"Certainly," said Haywood. "What do you play on your team?"

"Ketcher. Ever play any?"

"Never in my life," said Haywood. "I've never known any fellows except one
or two of my cousins."

"Jer like to learn? We're goin' to have a practice game before the match.
Wanter come along? I'll put yer in left-field, and yer won't be long ketchin' on."

"I'd like it bully," said Haywood. "I've always wanted to play baseball."

The ladies' maids of New York and the families of Western mine owners with
social ambitions will remember well the sensation that was created by the report that the young multi-millionaire, Haywood Van Plushvelt, was playing ball
with the village youths of Fishampton. It was conceded that the millennium of
democracy had come. Reporters and photographers swarmed to the island. The
papers printed half-page pictures of him as short-stop stopping a hot grounder.
The *Toadies' Magazine* got out a Bat and Ball number that covered the subject historically, beginning with the vampire bat and ending with the Patriarchs'
ball—illustrated with interior views of the Van Plushvelt country seat. Ministers, educators, and sociologists everywhere hailed the event as the tocsin call
that proclaimed the universal brotherhood of man.

One afternoon I was reclining under the trees near the shore at Fishampton
in the esteemed company of an eminent, bald-headed young sociologist. By way
of note it may be inserted that all sociologists are more or less bald, and exactly
thirty-two. Look 'em over.

The sociologist was citing the Van Plushvelt case as the most important "up-
lift" symptom of a generation and as an excuse for his own existence.

Immediately before us were the village baseball grounds. And now came the
sportive youth of Fishampton and distributed themselves, shouting, about the
diamond.

"There," said the sociologist, pointing, "there is young Plushvelt."

I raised myself (so far a cosycophant with Mary Ann) and gazed.

Young Van Plushvelt sat upon the ground. He was dressed in a ragged red
sweater, wrecked and weather-worn golf cap, run-over shoes, and trousers of
the "serviceable" brand. Dust clinging to the moisture induced by free exercise, darkened the wide areas of his face.

"That is he," repeated the sociologist. If he had said "him" I could have been
less vindictive.

On a bench, with an air, sat the young millionaire's chum.

He was dressed in a neat suit of dark blue serge, a neat white straw hat,
neat low-cut tan shoes, linen of the well-known "immaculate" trade mark, a
neat, narrow four-in-hand tie, and carried a slender, neat bamboo cane.

I laughed loudly and vulgarly.

"What you want to do," said I to the sociologist, "is to establish a reformatory
for the Logical Vicious Circle. Or else I've got wheels. It looks to me as if
things are running round and round in circles instead of getting anywhere."

"What do you mean?" asked the man of progress.

"Why, look what he has done to 'Smoky,'" I replied.

"You will always be a fool," said my friend, the sociologist, getting up and
walking away.

THE RANSOM OF RED CHIEF

It looked like a good thing: but wait till I tell you. We were down South, in Alabama—Bill Driscoll and myself—when this kidnapping idea struck us. It was, as Bill afterward expressed it, "during a moment of temporary mental apparition"; but we didn't find that out till later.

There was a town down there, as flat as a flannel-cake, and called Summit, of course. It contained inhabitants of as undeleterious and self-satisfied a class of peasantry as ever clustered around a Maypole.

Bill and me had a joint capital of about six hundred dollars, and we needed just two thousand dollars more to pull off a fraudulent town-lot scheme in Western Illinois with. We talked it over on the front steps of the hotel. Philoprogenitiveness, says we, is strong in semi-rural communities; therefore, and for other reasons, a kidnapping project ought to do better there than in the radius of newspapers that send reporters out in plain clothes to stir up talk about such things. We knew that Summit couldn't get after us with anything stronger than constables and, maybe, some lackadaisical bloodhounds and a diatribe or two in the *Weekly Farmers' Budget*. So, it looked good.

We selected for our victim the only child of a prominent citizen named Ebenezer Dorset. The father was respectable and tight, a mortgage fancier and a stern, upright collection-plate passer and forecloser. The kid was a boy of ten, with bas-relief freckles, and hair the color of the cover of the magazine you buy at the news-stand when you want to catch a train. Bill and me figured that Ebenezer would melt down for a ransom of two thousand dollars to a cent. But wait till I tell you.

About two miles from Summit was a little mountain, covered with a dense cedar brake. On the rear elevation of this mountain was a cave. There we stored provisions.

One evening after sundown, we drove in a buggy past old Dorset's house. The kid was in the street, throwing rocks at a kitten on the opposite fence.

"Hey, little boy!" says Bill, "would you like to have a bag of candy and a nice ride?"

The boy catches Bill neatly in the eye with a piece of brick.

"That will cost the old man an extra five hundred dollars," says Bill, climbing over the wheel.

That boy put up a fight like a welter-weight cinnamon bear; but, at last, we got him down in the bottom of the buggy and drove away. We took him up to the cave, and I hitched the horse in the cedar brake. After dark I drove the buggy to the little village, three miles away, where we had hired it, and walked back to the mountain.

Bill was pasting court-plaster over the scratches and bruises on his features. There was a fire burning behind the big rock at the entrance of the cave, and the boy was watching a pot of boiling coffee, with two buzzard tail-feathers stuck in his red hair. He points a stick at me when I come up, and says:

"Ha! cursed paleface, do you dare to enter the camp of Red Chief, the terror of the plains?"

"He's all right now," says Bill, rolling up his trousers and examining some bruises on his shins. "We're playing Indian. We're making Buffalo Bill's show look like magic-lantern views of Palestine in the town hall. I'm Old Hank, the Trapper, Red Chief's captive, and I'm to be scalped at daybreak. By Geronimo! that kid can kick hard."

Yes, sir, that boy seemed to be having the time of his life. The fun of camping out in a cave had made him forget that he was a captive himself. He immediately christened me Snake-eye, the Spy, and announced that, when his braves returned from the warpath, I was to be broiled at the stake at the rising of the sun.

Then we had supper; and he filled his mouth full of bacon and bread and gravy, and began to talk. He made a during-dinner speech something like this:

"I like this fine. I never camped out before; but I had a pet 'possum once, and I was nine last birthday. I hate to go to school. Rats ate up sixteen of Jimmy Talbot's aunt's speckled hen's eggs. Are there any real Indians in these woods? I want some more gravy. Does the trees moving make the wind blow? We had five puppies. What makes your nose so red, Hank? My father has lots of money. Are the stars hot? I whipped Ed Walker twice, Saturday. I don't like girls. You dassent catch toads unless with a string. Do oxen make any noise? Why are oranges round? Have you got beds to sleep on in this cave? Amos Murray has got six toes. A parrot can talk, but a monkey or a fish can't. How many does it take to make twelve?"

Every few minutes he would remember that he was a pesky redskin, and pick up his stick rifle and tiptoe to the mouth of the cave to rubber for the scouts of the hated paleface. Now and then he would let out a war-whoop that made Old Hank the Trapper shiver. That boy had Bill terrorized from the start.

"Red Chief," says I to the kid, "would you like to go home?"

"Aw, what for?" says he. "I don't have any fun at home. I hate to go to school. I like to camp out. You won't take me back home again, Snake-eye, will you?"

"Not right away," says I. "We'll stay here in the cave awhile."

"All right!" says he. "That'll be fine. I never had such fun in all my life."

We went to bed about eleven o'clock. We spread down some wide blankets and quilts and put Red Chief between us. We weren't afraid he'd run away. He kept us awake for three hours, jumping up and reaching for his rifle and screeching: "Hist! pard," in mine and Bill's ears, as the fancied crackle of a twig or the rustle of a leaf revealed to his young imagination the stealthy approach of the outlaw band. At last, I fell into a troubled sleep, and dreamed that I had been kidnapped and chained to a tree by a ferocious pirate with red hair.

Just at daybreak, I was awakened by a series of awful screams from Bill. They weren't yells, or howls, or shouts, or whoops, or yawps, such as you'd expect from a manly set of vocal organs—they were simply indecent, terrifying, humiliating screams, such as women emit when they see ghosts or caterpillars. It's an awful thing to hear a strong, desperate, fat man scream incontinently in a cave at daybreak.

I jumped up to see what the matter was. Red Chief was sitting on Bill's chest, with one hand twined in Bill's hair. In the other he had the sharp case-knife we used for slicing bacon; and he was industriously and realistically trying to take Bill's scalp, according to the sentence that had been pronounced upon him the evening before.

I got the knife away from the kid and made him lie down again. But, from that moment, Bill's spirit was broken. He laid down on his side of the bed, but he never closed an eye again in sleep as long as that boy was with us. I dozed off for a while, but along toward sun-up I remembered that Red Chief had said I was to be burned at the stake at the rising of the sun. I wasn't nervous or afraid; but I sat up and lit my pipe and leaned against a rock.

"What you getting up so soon for, Sam?" asked Bill.

"Me?" says I. "Oh, I got a kind of pain in my shoulder. I thought sitting up would rest it."

"You're a liar!" says Bill. "You're afraid. You was to be burned at sunrise, and you was afraid he'd do it. And he would, too, if he could find a match.

Ain't it awful, Sam? Do you think anybody will pay out money to get a little imp like that back home?"

"Sure," said I. "A rowdy kid like that is just the kind that parents dote on. Now, you and the Chief get up and cook breakfast, while I go up on the top of this mountain and reconnoitre."

I went up on the peak of the little mountain and ran my eye over the contiguous vicinity. Over towards Summit I expected to see the sturdy yeomanry of the village armed with scythes and pitchforks beating the countryside for the dastardly kidnappers. But what I saw was a peaceful landscape dotted with one man ploughing with a dun mule. Nobody was dragging the creek; no couriers dashed hither and yon, bringing tidings of no news to the distracted parents. There was a sylvan attitude of somnolent sleepiness pervading that section of the external outward surface of Alabama that lay exposed to my view. "Perhaps," says I to myself, "it has not yet been discovered that the wolves have borne away the tender lambkin from the fold. Heaven help the wolves!" says I, and I went down the mountain to breakfast.

When I got to the cave I found Bill backed up against the side of it, breathing hard, and the boy threatening to smash him with a rock half as big as a cocoanut.

"He put a red-hot boiled potato down my back," explained Bill, "and then mashed it with his foot; and I boxed his ears. Have you got a gun about you, Sam?"

I took the rock away from the boy and kind of patched up the argument. "I'll fix you," says the kid to Bill. "No man ever yet struck the Red Chief but he got paid for it. You better beware!"

After breakfast the kid takes a piece of leather with strings wrapped around it out of his pocket and goes outside the cave unwinding it.

"What's he up to now?" says Bill, anxiously. "You don't think he'll run away, do you, Sam?"

"No fear of it," says I. "He don't seem to be much of a home body. But we've got to fix up some plan about the ransom. There don't seem to be much excitement around Summit on account of his disappearance; but maybe they haven't realized yet that he's gone. His folks may think he's spending the night with Aunt Jane or one of the neighbors. Anyhow, he'll be missed to-day. To-night we must get a message to his father demanding the two thousand dollars for his return."

Just then we heard a kind of war-whoop, such as David might have emitted when he knocked out the champion Goliath. It was a sling that Red Chief had pulled out of his pocket, and he was whirling it around his head.

I dodged, and heard a heavy thud and a kind of a sigh from Bill, like a horse gives out when you take his saddle off. A niggerhead rock the size of an egg had caught Bill just behind his left ear. He loosened himself all over and fell in the fire across the frying pan of hot water for washing the dishes. I dragged him out and poured cold water on his head for half an hour.

By and by, Bill sits up and feels behind his ear and says: "Sam, do you know who my favorite Biblical character is?"

"Take it easy," says I. "You'll come to your senses presently."

"King Herod," says he. "You won't go away and leave me here alone, will you, Sam?"

I went out and caught that boy and shook him until his freckles rattled.

"If you don't behave," says I, "I'll take you straight home. Now, are you going to be good, or not?"

"I was only funning," says he, sullenly. "I didn't mean to hurt Old Hank. But what did he hit me for? I'll behave, Snake-eye, if you won't send me home, and if you'll let me play the Black Scout to-day."

"I don't know the game," says I. "That's for you and Mr. Bill to decide.

He's your playmate for the day. I'm going away for a while, on business. Now, you come in and make friends with him and say you are sorry for hurting him, or home you go, at once."

I made him and Bill shake hands, and then I took Bill aside and told him I was going to Poplar Cove, a little village three miles from the cave, and find out what I could about how the kidnapping had been regarded in Summit. Also, I thought it best to send a peremptory letter to old man Dorset that day, demanding the ransom and dictating how it should be paid.

"You know, Sam," says Bill, "I've stood by you without batting an eye in earthquakes, fire and flood—in poker games, dynamite outrages, police raids, train robberies, and cyclones. I never lost my nerve yet till we kidnapped that two-legged skyrocket of a kid. He's got me going. You won't leave me long with him, will you, Sam?"

"I'll be back some time this afternoon," says I. "You must keep the boy amused and quiet till I return. And now we'll write the letter to old Dorset."

Bill and I got paper and pencil and worked on the letter while Red Chief, with a blanket wrapped around him, strutted up and down, guarding the mouth of the cave. Bill begged me tearfully to make the ransom fifteen hundred dollars instead of two thousand. "I ain't attempting," says he, "to decry the celebrated moral aspect of parental affection, but we're dealing with humans, and it ain't human for anybody to give up two thousand dollars for that forty-pound chunk of freckled wildcat. I'm willing to take a chance at fifteen hundred dollars. You can charge the difference up to me."

So, to relieve Bill, I acceded, and we collaborated a letter that ran this way:

EBENEZER DORSET, ESQ.:

We have your boy concealed in a place far from Summit. It is useless for you or the most skilful detectives to attempt to find him. Absolutely, the only terms on which you can have him restored to you are these: We demand fifteen hundred dollars in large bills for his return; the money to be left at midnight to-night at the same spot and in the same box as your reply—as hereinafter described. If you agree to these terms, send your answer in writing by a solitary messenger to-night at half-past eight o'clock. After crossing Owl Creek on the road to Poplar Grove, there are three large trees about a hundred years apart, close to the fence of the wheat field on the right-hand side. At the bottom of the fence-post, opposite the third tree, will be found a small pasteboard box.

The messenger will place the answer in this box and return immediately to Summit.

If you attempt any treachery or fail to comply with our demand as stated, you will never see your boy again.

If you pay the money as demanded, he will be returned to you safe and well within three hours. These terms are final, and if you do not accede to them no further communication will be attempted.

TWO DESPERATE MEN.

I addressed this letter to Dorset, and put it in my pocket. As I was about to start, the kid comes up to me and says:

"Aw, Snake-eye, you said I could play the Black Scout while you was gone."

"Play it, of course," says I. "Mr. Bill will play with you. What kind of a game is it?"

"I'm the Black Scout," says Red Chief, "and I have to ride to the stockade to warn the settlers that the Indians are coming. I'm tired of playing Indian myself. I want to be the Black Scout."

"All right," says I. "It sounds harmless to me. I guess Mr. Bill will help you foil the pesky savages."

"What am I to do?" asks Bill, looking at the kid suspiciously.

"You are the hoss," says Black Scout. "Get down on your hands and knees. How can I ride to the stockade without a hoss?"

"You'd better keep him interested," said I, "till we get the scheme going. Loosen up."

Bill gets down on his all fours, and a look comes in his eye like a rabbit's when you catch it in a trap.

"How far is it to the stockade, kid?" he asks, in a husky manner of voice.

"Ninety miles," says the Black Scout. "And you have to hump yourself to get there on time. Whoa, now!"

The Black Scout jumps on Bill's back and digs his heels in his side.

"For Heaven's sake," says Bill, "hurry back, Sam, as soon as you can. I wish we hadn't made the ransom more than a thousand. Say, you quit kicking me or I'll get up and warm you good."

I walked over to Poplar Cove and sat around the post-office and store, talking with the chaw-bacons that came in to trade. One whiskerando says that he hears Summit is all upset on account of Elder Ebenezer Dorset's boy having been lost or stolen. That was all I wanted to know. I bought some smoking tobacco, referred casually to the price of black-eyed peas, posted my letter surreptitiously, and came away. The postmaster said the mail-carrier would come by in an hour to take the mail on to Summit.

When I got back to the cave Bill and the boy were not to be found. I explored the vicinity of the cave, and risked a yodel or two, but there was no response.

So I lighted my pipe and sat down on a mossy bank to await developments.

In about half an hour I heard the bushes rustle, and Bill wabbled out into the little glade in front of the cave. Behind him was the kid, stepping softly like a scout, with a broad grin on his face. Bill stopped, took off his hat, and wiped his face with a red handkerchief. The kid stopped about eight feet behind him.

"Sam," says Bill, "I suppose you'll think I'm a renegade, but I couldn't help it. I'm a grown person with masculine proclivities and habits of self-defense, but there is a time when all systems of egotism and predominance fail. The boy is gone. I sent him home. All is off. There was martyrs in old times," goes on Bill, "that suffered death rather than give up the particular graft they enjoyed. None of 'em ever was subjugated to such supernatural tortures as I have been. I tried to be faithful to our articles of depredation; but there came a limit."

"What's the trouble, Bill?" I asks him.

"I was rode," says Bill, "the ninety miles to the stockade, not barring an inch. Then, when the settlers was rescued, I was given oats. Sand ain't a palatable substitute. And then, for an hour I had to try to explain to him why there was nothin' in holes, how a road can run both ways, and what makes the grass green. I tell you, Sam, a human can only stand so much. I takes him by the neck of his clothes and drags him down the mountain. On the way he kicks my legs black and blue from the knees down; and I've got to have two or three bites on my thumb and hand cauterized.

"But he's gone"—continues Bill—"gone home. I showed him the road to Summit and kicked him about eight feet nearer there at one kick. I'm sorry we lose the ransom; but it was either that or Bill Driscoll to the madhouse."

Bill is puffing and blowing, but there is a look of ineffable peace and growing content on his rose-pink features.

"Bill," says I, "there isn't any heart disease in your family, is there?"

"No," says Bill, "nothing chronic except malaria and accidents. Why?"

"Then you might turn around," says I, "and have a look behind you."

Bill turns and sees the boy, and loses his complexion and sits down plump on the ground and begins to pluck aimlessly at grass and little sticks. For an hour I was afraid of his mind. And then I told him that my scheme was to put the whole job through immediately and that we would get the ransom and be off with it by midnight if old Dorset fell in which our proposition. So Bill braced up enough to give the kid a weak sort of a smile and a promise to play the Russian in a Japanese war with him as soon as he felt a little better.

I had a scheme for collecting that ransom without danger of being caught by counterplots that ought to commend itself to professional kidnappers. The tree under which the answer was to be left—and the money later on—was close to the road fence with big, bare fields on all sides. If a gang of constables should be watching for any one to come for the note they could see him a long way off crossing the fields or in the road. But no, sirree! At half-past eight I was up in that tree as well hidden as a tree toad, waiting for the messenger to arrive.

Exactly on time, a half-grown boy rides up the road on a bicycle, locates the pasteboard box at the foot of the fence-post, slips a folded piece of paper into it, and pedals away again back toward Summit.

I waited an hour and then concluded the thing was square. I slid down the tree, got the note, slipped along the fence till I struck the woods, and was back at the cave in another half an hour. I opened the note, got near the lantern, and read it to Bill. It was written with a pen in a crabbed hand, and the sum and substance of it was this:

TWO DESPERATE MEN.

Gentlemen: I received your letter to-day by post, in regard to the ranson you ask for the return of my son. I think you are a little high in your demands, and I hereby make you a counter-proposition, which I am inclined to believe you will accept. You bring Johnny home and pay me two hundred and fifty dollars in cash, and I agree to take him off your hands. You had better come at night, for the neighbors believe he is lost, and I couldn't be responsible for what they would do to anybody they saw bringing him back. Very respectfully,

                                        EBENEZER DORSET.

"Great pirates of Penzance," says I; "of all the impudent——"

But I glanced at Bill, and hesitated. He had the most appealing look in his eyes I ever saw on the face of a dumb or a talking brute.

"Sam," says he, "what's two hundred and fifty dollars, after all? We've got the money. One night of this kid will send me to a bed in Bedlam. Besides being a thorough gentleman, I think Mr. Dorset is a spendthrift for making us such a liberal offer. You ain't going to let the chance go, are you?"

"Tell you the truth, Bill," says I, "this little he ewe lamb has somewhat got on my nerves too. We'll take him home, pay the ransom, and make our get-away."

We took him home that night. We got him to go by telling him that his father had bought a silver-mounted rifle and a pair of moccasins for him, and we were to hunt bears the next day.

It was just twelve o'clock when we knocked at Ebenezer's front door. Just at the moment when I should have been abstracting the fifteen hundred dollars from the box under the tree, according to the original proposition, Bill was counting out two hundred and fifty dollars into Dorset's hand.

When the kid found out we were going to leave him at home he started up a howl like a calliope and fastened himself as tight as a leech to Bill's leg. His father peeled him away gradually, like a porous plaster.

"How long can you hold him?" asks Bill.

"I'm not as strong as I used to be," says old Dorset, "but I think I can promise you ten minutes."

"Enough," says Bill. "In ten minutes I shall cross the Central, Southern, and Middle Western States, and be legging it trippingly for the Canadian border."

And, as dark as it was, and as fat as Bill was, and as good a runner as I am, he was a good mile and a half out of Summit before I could catch up with him.

THE MARRY MONTH OF MAY

PRITHEE, smite the poet in the eye when he would sing to you praises of the month of May. It is a month presided over by the spirits of mischief and madness. Pixies and flibbertigibbets haunt the budding woods; Puck and his train of midgets are busy in town and country.

In May Nature holds up at us a chiding finger, bidding us remember that we are not gods, but overconceited members of her own great family. She reminds us that we are brothers to the chowder-doomed clam and the donkey; lineal scions of the pansy and the chimpanzee, and but cousins-german to the cooing doves, the quacking ducks, and the housemaids and policemen in the parks.

In May Cupid shoots blindfolded—millionaires marry stenographers; wise professors woo white-aproned gum-chewers behind quick-lunch counters; school-ma'ams make big bad boys remain after school; lads with ladders steal lightly over lawns where Juliet waits in her trellised window with her telescope packed; young couples out for a walk come home married; old chaps put on white spats and promenade near the Normal School; even married men, grown unwontedly tender and sentimental, whack their spouses on the back and growl: "How goes it, old girl?"

This May, who is no goddess, but Circe, masquerading at the dance given in honor of the fair débutante, Summer, puts the kibosh on us all.

Old Mr. Coulson groaned a little, and then sat up straight in his invalid's chair. He had the gout very bad in one foot, a house near Grammercy Park, half a million dollars, and a daughter. And he had a housekeeper. Mrs. Widdup. The fact and the name deserve a sentence each. They have it.

When May poked Mr. Coulson he became elder brother to the turtle-dove. In the window near which he sat were boxes of jonquils, of hyacinths, geraniums, and pansies. The breeze brought their odor into the room. Immediately there was a well-contested round between the breath of the flowers and the able and active effluvium from gout liniment. The liniment won easily; but not before the flowers got an uppercut to old Mr. Coulson's nose. The deadly work of the implacable, false enchantress May was done.

Across the park to the olfactories of Mr. Coulson came other unmistakable, characteristic, copyrighted smells of spring that belong to the-big-city-above-the-Subway, alone. The smells of hot asphalt, underground caverns, gasoline, patchouli, orange peel, sewer gas, Albany grabs, Egyptian cigarettes, mortar and the undried ink on newspapers. The inblowing air was sweet and mild. Sparrows wrangled happily everywhere outdoors. Never trust May.

Mr. Coulson twisted the ends of his white mustache, cursed his foot, and pounded a bell on the table by his side.

In came Mrs. Widdup. She was comely to the eye, fair, flustered, forty, and foxy.

"Higgins is out, sir," she said, with a smile suggestive of vibratory massage. "He went to post a letter. Can I do anything for you, sir?"

"It's time for my aconite," said old Mr. Coulson. "Drop it for me. The bottle's there. Three drops. In water. D— that is, confound Higgins! There's nobody in this house cares if I die here in this chair for want of attention."

Mrs. Widdup sighed deeply.

"Don't be saying that, sir," she said. "There's them that would care more than any one knows. Thirteen drops you said, sir?"

"Three," said old man Coulson.

He took his dose and then Mrs. Widdup's hand. She blushed. Oh, yes, it can be done. Just hold your breath and compress the diaphragm.

"Mrs. Widdup," said Mr. Coulson, "the springtime's full upon us."

"Ain't that right?" said Mrs. Widdup. "The air's real warm. And there's bock-beer signs on every corner. And the park's all yaller and pink and blue with flowers; and I have such shooting pains up my legs and body."

"'In the spring,'" quoted Mr. Coulson, curling his mustache, "'a y— that is, a man's—fancy lightly turns to thoughts of love.'"

"Lawsy, now!" exclaimed Mrs. Widdup; "ain't that right? Seems like it's in the air."

"'In the spring,'" continued old Mr. Coulson, "'a livelier iris shines upon the burnished dove.'"

"They do be lively, the Irish," sighed Mrs. Widdup, pensively.

"Mrs. Widdup," said Mr. Coulson, making a face at a twinge of his gouty foot, "this would be a lonesome house without you. I'm an—that is, I'm an elderly man—but I'm worth a comfortable lot of money. If half a million dollars' worth of Government bonds and the true affection of a heart that, though no longer beating with the first ardor of youth, can still throb with genuine——'

The loud noise of an overturned chair near the portières of the adjoining room interrupted the venerable and scarcely suspecting victim of May.

In stalked Miss Van Meeker Constantia Coulson, bony, durable, tall, high-nosed, frigid, well-bred, thirty-five, in-the-neighborhood-of-Gramercy-Parkish. She put up a lorgnette. Mrs. Widdup hastily stooped and arranged the bandages on Mr. Coulson's gouty foot.

"I thought Higgins was with you," said Miss Van Meeker Constantia.

"Higgins went out," explained her father, "and Mrs. Widdup answered the bell. That is better now, Mrs. Widdup, thank you. No; there is nothing else I require."

The housekeeper retired, pink under the cool, inquiring stare of Miss Coulson.

"This spring weather is lovely, isn't it, daughter?" said the old man, consciously conscious.

"That's just it," replied Miss Van Meeker Constantia Coulson, somewhat obscurely. "When does Mrs. Widdup start on her vacation, papa?"

"I believe she said a week from to-day," said Mr. Coulson.

Miss Van Meeker Constantia stood for a minute at the window gazing toward the little park, flooded with the mellow afternoon sunlight. With the eye of a botanist she viewed the flowers—most potent weapons of insidious May. With the cool pulses of a virgin of Cologne she withstood the attack of the ethereal mildness. The arrows of the pleasant sunshine fell back, frostbitten, from the cold panoply of her unthrilled bosom. The odor of the flowers waked no soft sentiments in the unexplored recesses of her dormant heart. The chirp of the sparrows gave her a pain. She mocked at May.

But although Miss Coulson was proof against the season, she was keen enough to estimate its power. She knew that elderly men and thick-waisted women jumped as educated fleas in the ridiculous train of May, the merry mocker of the months. She had heard of foolish old gentlemen marrying their housekeepers before. What a humiliating thing, afer all, was this feeling called love!

The next morning at 8 o'clock, when the iceman called, the cook told him that Miss Coulson wanted to see him in the basement.

"Well, ain't I the Olcott and Depew; not mentioning the first name at all?" said the iceman, admiringly, of himself.

As a concession he rolled his sleeves down, dropped his icehooks on a syringa and went back. When Miss Van Meeker Constantia Coulson addressed him he took off his hat.

"There is a rear entrance to this basement," said Miss Coulson, "which can be reached by driving into the vacant lot next door, where they are excavating for a building. I want you to bring in that way within two hours 1,000 pounds of ice. You may have to bring another man or two to help you. I will show you where I want it placed. I also want 1,000 pounds a day delivered the same way for the next four days. Your company may charge the ice on our regular bill. This is for your extra trouble."

Miss Coulson tendered a ten-dollar bill. The iceman bowed, and held his hat in his two hands behind him.

"Not if you'll excuse me, lady. It'll be a pleasure to fix things up for you any way you please."

Alas for May!

About noon Mr. Coulson knocked two glasses off his table, broke the spring of his bell, and yelled for Higgins at the same time.

"Bring an axe," commanded Mr. Coulson, sardonically, "or send out for a quart of prussic acid, or have a policeman come in and shoot me. I'd rather that than be frozen to death."

"It does seem to be getting cold, sir," said Higgins. "I hadn't noticed it before. I'll close the window, sir."

"Do," said Mr. Coulson. "They call this spring, do they? If it keeps up long I'll go back to Palm Beach. House feels like a morgue."

Later Miss Coulson dutifully came in to inquire how the gout was progressing.

"'Stantia," said the old man, "how is the weather outdoors?"

"Bright," answered Miss Coulson, "but chilly."

"Feels like the dead of winter to me," said Mr. Coulson.

"An instance," said Constantia, gazing abstractedly out of the window, "of 'winter lingering in the lap of spring,' though the metaphor is not in the most refined taste."

A little later she walked down by the side of the little park and on westward to Broadway to accomplish a little shopping.

A little later than that Mrs. Widdup entered the invalid's room.

"Did you ring, sir?" she asked, dimpling in many places. "I asked Higgins to go to the drug store, and I thought I heard your bell."

"I did not," said Mr. Coulson.

"I'm afraid," said Mrs. Widdup, "I interrupted you, sir, yesterday when you were about to say something."

"How comes it, Mrs. Widdup," said old man Coulson, sternly, "that I find it so cold in this house?"

"Cold, sir?" said the housekeeper, "why, now, since you speak of it it do seem cold in this room. But outdoors it's as warm and fine as June, sir. And how this weather do seem to make one's heart jump out of one's shirt waist, sir. And the ivy all leaved out on the side of the house, and the hand-organs playing, and the children dancing on the sidewalk—'tis a great time for speaking out what's in the heart. You were saying yesterday, sir——"

"Woman!" roared Mr. Coulson; "you are a fool. I pay you to take care of this house. I am freezing to death in my own room, and you come in and drivel to me about ivy and hand-organs. Get me an overcoat at once. See that all doors and windows are closed below. An old, fat, irresponsible, one-sided object like you prattling about springtime and flowers in the middle of winter! When Higgins comes back, tell him to bring me a hot rum punch. And now get out!"

But who shall shame the bright face of May? Rogue though she be and disturber of sane men's peace, no wise virgin's cunning nor cold storage shall make her bow her head in the bright galaxy of months.

Oh, yes, the story was not quite finished.

A night passed, and Higgins helped old man Coulson in the morning to his chair by the window. The cold of the room was gone. Heavenly odors and fragrant mildness entered.

In hurried Mrs. Widdup, and stood by his chair. Mr. Coulson reached his bony hand and grasped her plump one.

"Mrs. Widdup," he said, "this house would be no home without you. I have half a million dollars. If that and the true affection of a heart no longer in its youthful prime, but still not cold could——"

"I found out what made it cold," said Mrs. Widdup, leaning against his chair. " 'Twas ice—tons of it—in the basement and in the furnace room, everywhere. I shut off the registers that it was coming through into your room, Mr. Coulson, poor soul! And now it's May-time again."

"A true heart," went on old man Coulson, a little wanderingly, "that the springtime has brought to life again, and—but what will my daughter say, Mrs. Widdup?"

"Never fear, sir," said Mrs. Widdup, cheerfully, "Miss Coulson, she ran away with the iceman last night, sir!"

A TECHNICAL ERROR

I NEVER cared especially for feuds, believing them to be even more overrated products of our country than grapefruit, scrapple, or honeymoons. Nevertheless, if I may be allowed, I will tell you of an Indian Territory feud of which I was press-agent, camp-follower, and inaccessory during the fact.

I was on a visit to Sam Durkee's ranch, where I had a great time falling off unmanicured ponies and waving my bare hand at the lower jaws of wolves about two miles away. Sam was a hardened person of about twenty-five, with a reputation for going home in the dark with perfect equanimity, though often with reluctance.

Over in the Creek Nation was a family bearing the name of Tatum. I was told that the Durkees and Tatums had been feuding for years. Several of each family had bitten the grass, and it was expected that more Nebuchadnezzars would follow. A younger generation of each family was growing up, and the grass was keeping pace with them. But I gathered that they had fought fairly; that they had not lain in cornfields and aimed at the division of their enemies' suspenders in the back—partly, perhaps, because there were no cornfields, and nobody wore more than one suspender. Nor had any woman or child of either house ever been harmed. In those days—and you will find it so yet—their women were safe.

Sam Durkee had a girl. (If it were an all-fiction magazine that I expected to sell this story to, I should say, "Mr. Durkee rejoiced in a fiancée.") Her name was Ella Baynes. They appeared to be devoted to each other, and to have perfect confidence in each other, as all couples do who are and have or aren't and haven't. She was tolerably pretty, with a heavy mass of brown hair that helped her along. He introduced me to her, which seemed not to lessen her preference for 'him; so I reasoned that they were surely soul-mates.

Miss Baynes lived in Kingfisher, twenty miles from the ranch. Sam lived on a gallop between the two places.

One day there came to Kingfisher a courageous young man, rather small, with smooth face and regular features. He made many inquiries about the business of the town, and especially of the inhabitants cognominally. He said he was from Muscogee, and he looked it, with his yellow shoes and crocheted four-in-hand. I met him once when I rode in for the mail. He said his name was Beverly Travers, which seemed rather improbable.

There were active times on the ranch just then, and Sam was too busy to go to town often. As an incompetent and generally worthless guest, it devolved upon me to ride in for little things such as post cards, barrels of flours, baking-powder, smoking-tobacco, and—letters from Ella.

One day, when I was messenger for half a gross of cigarette papers and a couple of wagon tires, I saw the alleged Beverly Travers in a yellow-wheeled buggy with Ella Baynes, driving about town as ostentatiously as the black, waxy mud would permit. I knew that this information would bring no balm of Gilead to Sam's soul, so I refrained from including it in the news of the city that I retailed on my return. But on the next afternoon an elongated ex-cowboy of the name of Simmons, an old-time pal of Sam's, who kept a feed store in Kingfisher, rode out to the ranch and rolled and burned many cigarettes before he would talk. When he did make oration, his words were these:

"Say, Sam, there's been a description of a galoot miscallin' himself Bevel-edged Travels impairing the atmospheric air of Kingfisher for the past two weeks. You know who he was? He was not otherwise than Ben Tatum, from the Creek Nation, son of old Gopher Tatum that your Uncle Newt shot last February. You know what he done this morning? He killed your brother Lester—shot him in the co't-house yard."

I wondered if Sam had heard. He pulled a twig from a mesquite bush, chewed it gravely, and said:

"He did, did he? He killed Lester?"

"The same," said Simmons. "And he did more. He run away with your girl, the same as to say Miss Ella Baynes. I thought you might like to know, so I rode out to impart the information."

"I am much obliged, Jim," said Sam, taking the chewed twig from his mouth. "Yes, I'm glad you rode out. Yes, I'm right glad."

"Well, I'll be ridin' back, I reckon. That boy I left in the feed store don't know hay from oats. He shot Lester in the *back*."

"Shot him in the back?"

"Yes, while he was hitchin' his hoss."

"I'm much obliged, Jim."

"I kind of thought you'd like to know as soon as you could."

"Come in and have some coffee before you ride back, Jim?"

"Why, no, I reckon not; I must get back to the store."

"And you say——"

"Yes, Sam. Everybody seen 'em drive away together in a buckboard, with a big bundle, like clothes, tied up in the back of it. He was drivin' the team he brought over with him from Muscogee. They'll be hard to overtake right away."

"And which——"

"I was goin' on to tell you. They left on the Guthrie road; but there's no tellin' which forks they'll take—you know that."

"All right, Jim; much obliged."

"You're welcome, Sam."

Simmons rolled a cigarette and stabbed his pony with both heels. Twenty yards away he reined up and called back:

"You don't want no—assistance, as you might say?"

"Not any, thanks."

"I didn't think you would. Well, so long!"

Sam took out and opened a bone-handled pocket-knife and scraped a dried piece of mud from his left boot. I thought at first he was going to swear a vendetta on the blade of it, or recite "The Gipsy's Curse." The few feuds I had ever seen or read about usually opened that way. This one seemed to be presented with a new treatment. Thus offered on the stage, it would have been hissed off, and one of Belasco's thrilling melodramas demanded instead.

"I wonder," said Sam, with a profoundly thoughtful expression, "if the cook has any cold beans left over!"

He called Wash, the Negro cook, and finding that he had some, ordered him to heat up the pot and make some strong coffee. Then we went into Sam's private room, where he slept, and kept his armory, dogs, and the saddles of his favorite mounts. He took three or four six-shooters out of a bookcase and began to look them over, whistling "The Cowboy's Lament" abstractedly. Afterward he ordered the two best horses on the ranch saddled and tied to the hitching-post.

Now, in the feud business, in all sections of the country, I have observed that in one particular there is a delicate but strict etiquette belonging. You must not mention the word or refer to the subject in the presence of a feudist. It would be more reprehensible than commenting upon the mole on the chin of your rich aunt. I found, later on, that there is another unwritten rule, but I think that belongs solely to the West.

It yet lacked two hours to supper-time; but in twenty minutes Sam and I were plunging deep into the reheated beans, hot coffee, and cold beef.

"Nothing like a good meal before a long ride," said Sam. "Eat hearty."

I had a sudden suspicion.

"Why did you have two horses saddled?" I asked

"One, two—one, two," said Sam. "You can count, can't you?"

His mathematics carried with it a momentary qualm and a lesson. The thought had not occurred to him that the thought could possibly occur to me not to ride at his side on that red road to revenge and justice. It was the higher calculus. I was booked for the trail. I began to eat more beans.

In an hour we set forth at a steady gallop eastward. Our horses were Kentucky-bred, strengthened by the mesquite grass of the west. Ben Tatum's steeds may have been swifter, and he had a good lead; but if he had heard the punctual thuds of the hoofs of those trailers of ours, born in the heart of feud-land, he might have felt that retribution was creeping up on the hoof-prints of his dapper nags.

I knew that Ben Tatum's card to play was flight—flight until he came within the safer territory of his own henchmen and supporters. He knew that the man pursuing him would follow the trail to any end where it might lead.

During the ride Sam talked of the prospect for rain, of the price of beef, and of the musical glasses. You would have thought he had never had a brother or a sweetheart or an enemy on earth. There are some subjects too big even for the words in the "Unabridged." Knowing this phase of the feud code, but not having practised it sufficiently, I overdid the thing by telling some slightly funny anecdotes. Sam laughed at exactly the right place—laughed with his mouth. When I caught sight of his mouth, I wished I had been blessed with enough sense of humor to have suppressed those anecdotes.

Our first sight of them we had in Guthrie. Tired and hungry, we stumbled, unwashed, into a little yellow-pine hotel and sat at a table. In the opposite corner we saw the fugitives. They were bent upon their meal, but looked around at times uneasily.

The girl was dressed in brown—one of these smooth, half-shiny, silky-looking affairs with lace collar and cuffs, and what I believe they call an accordion-pleated skirt. She wore a thick brown veil down to her nose, and a broad-brimmed straw hat with some kind of feathers adorning it. The man wore plain, dark clothes, and his hair was trimmed very short. He was such a man as you might see anywhere.

There they were—the murderer and the woman he had stolen. There we were—the rightful avenger, according to the code, and the supernumerary who writes these words.

For one time, at least, in the heart of the supernumerary there rose the killing instinct. For one moment he joined the force of combatants—orally.

"What are you waiting for, Sam?" I said in a whisper. "Let him have it now!"

Sam gave a melancholy sigh.

"You don't understand; but *he* does," he said. "*He* knows. Mr. Tender-foot, there's a rule out here among white men in the Nation that you can't shoot a man when he's with a woman. I never knew it to be broke yet. You *can't* do it. You've got to get him in a gang of men or by himself. That's why. He knows it, too. We all know. So, that's Mr. Ben Tatum! One of the 'pretty men'! I'll cut him out of the herd before they leave the hotel, and regulate his account!"

After supper the flying pair disappeared quickly. Although Sam haunted lobby and stairway and halls half the night, in some mysterious way the fugitives eluded him; and in the morning the veiled lady in the brown dress with the accordion-pleated skirt and the dapper young man with the close-clipped hair, and the buckboard with the prancing nags, were gone.

It is a monotonous story, that of the ride; so it shall be curtailed. Once again we overtook them on a road. We were about fifty yards behind. They turned in the buckboard and looked at us; then drove on without whipping up their horses. Their safety no longer lay in speed. Ben Tatum knew. He knew that the only rock of safety left to him was the code. There is no doubt that, had he been alone, the matter would have been settled quickly with Sam Durkee in the usual way; but he had something at his side that kept still the trigger-finger of both. It seemed likely that he was no coward.

So, you may perceive that woman, on occasions, may postpone instead of precipitating conflict between man and man. But not willingly or consciously. She is oblivious of codes.

Five miles farther, we came upon the future great Western city of Chandler. The horses of pursuers and pursued were starved and weary. There was one hotel that offered danger to man and entertainment to beast; so the four of us met again in the dining room at the ringing of a bell so resonant and large that it had cracked the welkin long ago. The dining room was not as large as the one at Guthrie.

Just as we were eating apple pie—how Ben Davises and tragedy impinge upon each other!—I noticed Sam looking with keen intentness at our quarry where they were seated at a table across the room. The girl still wore the brown dress with lace collar and cuffs, and the veil drawn down to her nose. The man bent over his plate, with his close-cropped head held low.

"There's a code," I heard Sam say, either to me or to himself, "that won't let you shoot a man in the company of a woman; but, by thunder, there ain't one to keep you from killing a woman in the company of a man!"

And, quicker than my mind could follow his argument, he whipped a Colt's automatic from under his left arm and pumped six bullets into the body that the brown dress covered—the brown dress with the lace collar and cuffs and the accordion-pleated skirt.

The young person in the dark sack suit, from whose head and from whose life a woman's glory had been clipped, laid her head on her arms stretched upon the table; while people came running to raise Ben Tatum from the floor in his feminine masquerade that had given Sam the opportunity to set aside, technically, the obligations of the code.

SUITE HOMES AND THEIR ROMANCE

FEW young couples in the Big-City-of-Bluff began their married existence with greater promise of happiness than did Mr. and Mrs. Claude Turpin. They felt no especial animosity toward each other; they were comfortably established in a handsome apartment house that had a name and accommodations like those of a sleeping-car; they were living as expensively as the couple on the next floor above who had twice their income; and their marriage had occurred on a wager, a ferry-boat, and first acquaintance, thus securing a sensational newspaper notice of their names attached to pictures of the Queen of Roumania and M. Santos-Dumont.

Turpin's income was $200 per month. On pay day, after calculating the amounts due for rent, instalments on furniture and piano, gas, and bills owed to the florist, confectioner, milliner, tailor, wine merchant, and cab company, the Turpins would find that they still had $200 left to spend. How to do this is one of the secrets of metropolitan life.

The domestic life of the Turpins was a beautiful picture to see. But you couldn't gaze upon it as you could at an oleograph of "Don't Wake Grandma," or "Brooklyn by Moonlight."

You had to blink when you looked at it; and you heard a fizzing sound just like the machine with a "scope" at the end of it. Yes; there wasn't much repose about the picture of the Turpins' domestic life. It was something like "Spearing Salmon in the Columbia River," or "Japanese Artillery in Action."

Every day was just like another; as the days are in New York. In the morning Turpin would take bromo-seltzer, his pocket change from under the clock, his hat, no breakfast, and his departure for the office. At noon Mrs. Turpin would get out of bed and humor, put on a kimono, airs, and the water to boil for coffee.

Turpin lunched downtown. He came home at 6 to dress for dinner. They always dined out. They strayed from the chop-house to chop-sueydom, from terrace to table d'hôte, from rathskeller to roadhouse, from café to casino, from Maria's to the Martha Washington. Such is domestic life in the great city. Your vine is the mistletoe; your fig tree bears dates. Your household gods are Mercury and John Howard Payne. For the wedding march you now hear only "Come with the Gypsy Bride." You rarely dine at the same place twice in succession. You tire of the food; and, besides, you want to give them time for the question of that souvenir silver sugar bowl to blow over.

The Turpins were therefore happy. They made many warm and delightful friends, some of whom they remembered the next day. Their home life was an ideal one, according to the rules and regulations of the Book of Bluff.

There came a time when it dawned upon Turpin that his wife was getting away with too much money. If you belong to the near-swell class in the Big City, and your income is $200 per month, and you find at the end of the month, after looking over the bills for current expenses, that you, yourself, have spent $150, you very naturally wonder what has become of the other $50. So you suspect your wife. And perhaps you give her a hint that something needs explanation.

"I say, Vivien," said Turpin, one afternoon when they were enjoying in rapt silence the peace and quiet of their cozy apartment, "you've been creating a hiatus big enough for a dog to crawl through in this month's honorarium. You haven't been paying your dress-maker anything on account, have you?"

There was a moment's silence. No sounds could be heard except the breathing of the fox terrier, and the subdued, monotonous sizzling of Vivien's fulvous locks against the insensate curling irons. Claude Turpin, sitting upon a pillow that he had thoughtfully placed upon the convolutions of the apartment sofa, narrowly watched the riante, lovely face of his wife.

"Claudie, dear," said she, touching her finger to her ruby tongue and testing the unresponsive curling irons, "you do me an injustice. Mme. Toinette has not seen a cent of mine since the day you paid your tailor ten dollars on account."

Turpin's suspicions were allayed for the time. But one day soon there came an anonymous letter to him that read:

Watch your wife. She is blowing in your money secretly. I was a sufferer just as you are. The place is No. 345 Blank Street. A word to the wise, etc.
                                        A Man Who Knows.

Turpin took this letter to the captain of police of the precinct that he lived in.

"My precinct is as clean as a hound's tooth," said the captain. "The lid's shut down as close there as it is over the eye of a Williamsburg girl when she's kissed at a party. But if you think there's anything queer at the address, I'll go there with ye."

On the next afternoon at 3, Turpin and the captain crept softly up the stairs of No. 345 Blank Street. A dozen plain-clothes men, dressed in full police uniforms, so as to allay suspicion, waited in the hall below.

At the top of the stairs was a door, which was found to be locked. The captain took a key from his pocket and unlocked it. The two men entered.

They found themselves in a large room, occupied by twenty or twenty-five elegantly clothed ladies. Racing charts hung against the walls, a ticker clicked in one corner; with a telephone receiver to his ear a man was calling out the various positions of the horses in a very exciting race. The occupants of the room looked up at the intruders; but, as if reassured by the sight of the captain's uniform, they reverted their attention to the man at the telephone.

"You see," said the captain to Turpin, "the value of an anonymous letter! No high-minded and self-respecting gentleman should consider one worthy of notice. Is your wife among this assembly, Mr. Turpin?"

"She is not," said Turpin.

"And if she was," continued the captain, "would she be within the reach of the tongue of slander? These ladies constitute a Browning Society. They meet to discuss the meaning of the great poet. The telephone is connected with

Boston, whence the parent society transmits frequently its interpretations of
the poems. Be ashamed of yer suspicions, Mr. Turpin."

"Go soak your shield," said Turpin. "Vivien knows how to take care of
herself in a pool-room. She's not dropping anything on the ponies. There
must be something queer going on here."

"Nothing but Browning," said the captain. "Hear that?"

"Thanatopsis by a nose," drawled the man at the telephone.

"That's not Browning; that's Longfellow," said Turpin, who sometimes read
books.

"Back to the pasture!" exclaimed the captain. "Longfellow made the pacing-
to-wagon record of 7.53 'way back in 1868."

"I believe there's something queer about this joint," repeated Turpin.

"I don't see it," said the captain.

"I know it looks like a pool-room, all right," persisted Turpin, "but that's
all a blind. Vivien has been dropping a lot of coin somewhere. I believe
there's some underhanded work going on here."

A number of racing sheets were tacked close together, covering a large space
on one of the walls. Turpin, suspicious, tore several of them down. A door,
previously hidden, was revealed. Turpin placed an ear to the crack and listened
intently. He heard the soft hum of many voices, low and guarded laughter,
and a sharp, metallic clicking and scraping as if from a multitude of tiny but
busy objects.

"My God! It is as I feared!" whispered Turpin to himself. "Summon your
men at once!" he called to the captain. "She is in there, I know."

At the blowing of the captain's whistle the uniformed plain-clothes men
rushed up the stairs into the pool-room. When they saw the betting paraphernalia distributed around they halted, surprised and puzzled to know why
they had been summoned.

But the captain pointed to the locked door and bade them break it down.
In a few moments they demolished it with the axes they carried. Into the other
room sprang Claude Turpin, with the captain at his heels.

The scene was one that lingered long in Turpin's mind. Nearly a score of
women—women expensively and fashionably clothed, many beautiful and of refined appearance—had been seated at little marble-topped tables. When the
police burst open the door they shrieked and ran here and there like gayly
plumed birds that had been disturbed in a tropical grove. Some became
hysterical; one or two fainted; several knelt at the feet of the officers and
besought them for mercy on account of their families and social position.

A man who had been seated behind a desk had seized a roll of currency as
large as the ankle of a Paradise Roof Gardens chorus girl and jumped out
of the window. Half a dozen attendants huddled at one end of the room,
breathless from fear.

Upon the tables remained the damning and incontrovertible evidences of the
guilt of the habituées of that sinister room—dish after dish heaped high with
ice cream, and surrounded by stacks of empty ones, scraped to the last spoonful.

"Ladies," said the captain to his weeping circle of prisoners. "I'll not hold
any of yez. Some of yez I recognize as having fine houses and good standing
in the community, with hard-working husbands and childer at home. But I'll
read ye a bit of a lecture before ye go. In the next room there's a 20-to-1
shot just dropped in under the wire three lengths ahead of the field. Is this
the way we waste your husbands' money instead of helping earn it? Home
wid yez! The lid's on the ice-cream freezer in this precinct."

Claude Turpin's wife was among the patrons of the raided room. He led
her to their apartment in stern silence. There she wept so remorsefully and

besought his forgiveness so pleadingly that he forgot his just anger, and soon he gathered his penitent golden-haired Vivien in his arms and forgave her.

"Darling," she murmured, half sobbingly, as the moonlight drifted through the open window, glorifying her sweet, upturned face, "I know I done wrong. I will never touch ice cream again. I forgot you were not a millionaire. I used to go there every day. But to-day I felt some strange, sad presentiment of evil, and I was not myself. I ate only eleven saucers."

"Say no more," said Claude, gently, as he fondly caressed her waving curls.

"And you are sure that you fully forgive me?" asked Vivien, gazing at him entreatingly with dewy eyes of heavenly blue.

"Almost sure, little one," answered Claude, stooping and lightly touching her snowy forehead with his lips. "I'll let you know later on. I've got a month's salary down on Vanilla to win the three-year-old steeplechase to-morrow; and if the ice-cream hunch is to the good you are It again—see?"

THE WHIRLIGIG OF LIFE

JUSTICE-OF-THE PEACE Benaja Widdup sat in the door of his office smoking his elder-stem pipe. Halfway to the Zenith the Cumberland range rose blue-gray in the afternoon haze. A speckled hen swaggered down the main street of the "settlement," cackling foolishly.

Up the road came a sound of creaking axles, and then a slow cloud of dust, and then a bull-cart bearing Ransie Bilbro and his wife. The cart stopped at the Justice's door, and the two climbed down. Ransie was a narrow six feet of sallow brown skin and yellow hair. The imperturbability of the mountains hung upon him like a suit of armor. The woman was calicoed, angled, snuff-brushed, and weary with unknown desires. Through it all gleamed a faint protest of cheated youth unconscious of its loss.

The Justice of the Peace slipped his feet into his shoes, for the sake of dignity, and moved to let them enter.

"We-all," said the woman, in a voice like the wind blowing through pine boughs, "wants a divo'ce." She looked at Ransie to see if he noted any flaw or ambiguity or evasion or partiality or self-partisanship in her statement of their business.

"A divo'ce," repeated Ransie, with a solemn nod. "We-all can't git along together nohow. It's lonesome enough fur to live in the mount'ins when a man and a woman keers fur one another. But when she's a-spittin' like a wildcat or a-sullenin' like a hoot-owl in the cabin, a man ain't got no call to live with her."

"When he's a no-'count varmint," said the woman, without any especial warmth, "a-traipsin' along of scalawags and moonshiners and a-layin' on his back pizen 'ith co'n whiskey, and a-pesterin' folks with a pack o' hungry, triflin' houn's to feed!"

"When she keeps a-throwin' skillet lids," came Ransie's antiphony, "and slings b'ilin' water on the best coon-dog in the Cumberlands, and sets herself agin' cookin' a man's victuals, and keeps him awake o' nights accusin' him of a sight of doin's!"

"When he's al'ays a-fightin' the revenues, and gits a hard name in the mount'ins fur a mean man, who's gwine to be able fur to sleep o' nights?"

The Justice of the Peace stirred deliberately to his duties. He placed his one chair and a wooden stool for his petitioners. He opened his book of statutes on the table and scanned the index. Presently he wiped his spectacles and shifted his inkstand.

"The law and the statutes," said he, "air silent on the subjeck of divo'ce as fur as the jurisdiction of this co't air concerned. But, accordin' to equity and the Constitution and the golden rule, it's a bad barg'in that can't run both ways. If a justice of the peace can marry a couple, it's plain that he is bound to be able to divo'ce 'em. This here office will issue a decree of divo'ce and abide by the decision of the Supreme Co't to hold it good."

Ransie Bilbro drew a small tobacco-bag from his trousers pocket. Out of this he shook upon the table a five-dollar noté. "Sold a b'arskin and two foxes fur that," he remarked. "It's all the money we got."

"The regular price of a divo'ce in this co't," said the Justice, "air five dollars." He stuffed the bill into the pocket of his homespun vest with a deceptive air of indifference. With much bodily toil and mental travail he wrote the decree upon half a sheet of foolscap, and then copied it upon the other. Ransie Bilbro and his wife listened to his reading of the document that was to give them freedom:

Know all men by these presents that Ransie Bilbro and his wife, Ariela Bilbro, this day personally appeared before me and promises that hereinafter they will neither love, honor, nor obey each other, neither for better nor worse, being of sound mind and body, and accept summons for divorce according to the peace and dignity of the State. Herein fail not, so help you God. Benaja Widdup, justice of the peace in and for the county of Piedmont, State of Tennessee.

The Justice was about to hand one of the documents to Ransie. The voice of Ariela delayed the transfer. Both men looked at her. Their dull masculinity was confronted by something sudden and unexpected in the woman.

"Judge, don't you give him that air paper yit. 'Taint all settled, nohow. I got to have my rights first. I got to have my ali-money. 'Tain't no kind of a way to do fur a man to divo'ce his wife 'thout her havin' a cent fur to do with. I'm a-layin' off to be a-goin' up to brother Ed's up on Hogback Mount'in. I'm bound fur to hev a pa'r of shoes and some snuff and things besides. Ef Rance kin affo'd a divo'ce, let him pay me ali-money."

Ransie Bilbro was stricken to dumb perplexity. There had been no previous hint of alimony. Women were always bringing up startling and unlooked-for issues.

Justice Benaja Widdup felt that the point demanded judicial decision. The authorities were also silent on the subject of alimony. But the woman's feet were bare. The trail to Hogback Mountain was steep and flinty.

"Ariela Bilbro," he asked, in official tones, "how much did you 'low would be good and sufficient ali-money in the case befo' the co't?"

"I 'lowed," she answered, "fur the shoes and all, to say five dollars. That ain't much fur ali-money, but I reckon that'll git me up to brother Ed's."

"The amount," said the Justice, "air not onreasonable. Ransie Bilbro, you air ordered by the co't to pay the plaintiff the sum of five dollars befo' the decree of divo'ce air issued."

"I hain't no mo' money," breathed Ransie, heavily. "I done paid you all I had."

"Otherwise," said the Justice, looking severely over his spectacles, "you air in contempt of co't."

"I reckon if you gimme till to-morrow," pleaded the husband, "I mout be able to rake or scrape it up somewhars. I never looked for to be a-payin' no ali-money."

"The case air adjourned," said Benaja Widdup, "till to-morrow, when you-all will present yo'selves and obey the order of the co't. Followin' of which the decrees of divo'ce will be delivered." He sat down in the door and began to loosen a shoestring.

"We mout as well go down to Uncle Ziah's," decided Ransie, "and spend the night." He climbed into the cart on one side, and Ariela climbed in on the other. Obeying the flap of his rope, the little red bull slowly came around on a tack, and the cart crawled away in the nimbus arising from its wheels.

Justice-of-the-peace Benaja Widdup smoked his elder-stem pipe. Late in the afternoon he got his weekly paper, and read it until the twilight dimmed its lines. Then he lit the tallow candle on his table, and read until the moon rose, marking the time for supper. He lived in the double log cabin on the slope near the girdled poplar. Going home to supper he crossed a little branch darkened by a laurel thicket. The dark figure of a man stepped from the laurels and pointed a rifle at his breast. His hat was pulled down low, and something covered most of his face.

"I want yo' money," said the figure, " 'thout any talk. I'm gettin' nervous, and my finger's a-wabblin' on this here trigger."

"I've only got f-f-five dollars," said the Justice, producing it from his vest pocket.

"Roll it up," came the order, "and stick it in the end of this here gun-bar'l."

The bill was crisp and new. Even fingers that were clumsy and trembling found little difficulty in making a spill of it and inserting it (this with less ease) into the muzzle of the rifle.

"Now I reckon you kin be goin' along," said the robber.

The Justice lingered not on his way.

The next day came the little red bull, drawing the cart to the office door. Justice Benaja Widdup had his shoes on, for he was expecting the visit. In his presence Ransie Bilbro handed to his wife a five-dollar bill. The official's eye sharply viewed it. It seemed to curl up as though it had been rolled and inserted into the end of a gun-barrel. But the Justice refrained from comment. It is true that other bills might be inclined to curl. He handed each one a decree of divorce. Each stood awkwardly silent, slowly folding the guarantee of freedom. The woman cast a shy glance full of constraint at Ransie.

"I reckon you'll be goin' back up to the cabin," she said, "along 'ith the bull-cart. There's bread in the tin box settin' on the shelf. I put the bacon in the b'ilin'-pot to keep the hounds from gittin' it. Don't forget to wind the clock to-night."

"You air a-goin' to your brother Ed's?" asked Ransie, with fine unconcern.

"I was 'lowin' to get along up thar afore night. I ain't sayin' as they'll pester theyselves any to make me welcome, but I hain't nowhar else fur to go. It's a right smart ways, and I reckon I better be goin'. I'll be a-sayin' good-bye, Ranse—that is, if you keer fur to say so."

"I don't know as anybody's a hound dog," said Ransie, in a martyr's voice, "fur to not want to say good-bye—'less you air so anxious to git away that you don't want me to say it."

Ariela was silent. She folded the five-dollar bill and her decree carefully, and placed them in the bosom of her dress. Benaja Widdup watched the money disappear with mournful eyes behind his spectacles.

And then with his next words he achieved rank (as his thoughts ran) with either the great crowd of the world's sympathizers or the little crowd of its great financiers.

"Be kind o' lonesome in the old cabin to-night, Ranse," she said.

Ransie Bilbro stared out at the Cumberlands, clear blue now in the sunlight. He did not look at Ariela.

"I 'low it might be lonesome," he said; "but when folks gits mad and wants a divo'ce, you can't make folks stay."

"There's others wanted a divo'ce," said Ariela, speaking to the wooden stool. "Besides, nobody don't want nobody to stay."

"Nobody never said they didn't."

"Nobody never said they did. I reckon I better start on now to brother Ed's."

"Nobody can't wind that old clock."

"Want me to go back along 'ith you in the cart and wind it fur you, Ranse?"

The mountaineer's countenance was proof against emotion. But he reached out a big hand and enclosed Ariela's thin brown one. Her soul peeped out once through her impassive face, hallowing it.

"Them hounds sha'n't pester you no more," said Ransie. "I reckon I been mean and low down. You wind that clock, Ariela."

"My heart hit's in that cabin, Ranse," she whispered, "along 'ith you. I ain't a-goin' to git mad no more. Le's be startin', Ranse, so's we kin git home by sundown."

Justice-of-the-peace Benaja Widdup interposed as they started for the door, forgetting his presence.

"In the name of the State of Tennessee," he said, "I forbid you-all to be a-defyin' of its laws and statutes. This co't is mo' than willin' and full of joy to see the clouds of discord and misunderstandin' rollin' away from two lovin' hearts, but it air the duty of the co't to p'eserve the morals and integrity of the State. The co't reminds you that you air no longer man and wife, but air divo'ced by regular decree, and as such air not entitled to the benefits and 'purtenances of the mattermonal estate."

Ariela caught Ransie's arm. Did those words mean that she must lose him now when they had just learned the lesson of life?

"But the co't air prepared," went on the Justice, "fur to remove the disabilities set up by the decree of divo'ce. The co't air on hand to perform the solemn ceremony of marri'ge, thus fixin' things up and enablin' the parties in the case to resume the honor'ble and elevatin' state of mattermony which they desires. The fee fur performin' said ceremony will be, in this case, to wit, five dollars."

Ariela caught the gleam of promise in his words. Swiftly her hand went to her bosom. Freely as an alighting dove the bill fluttered to the Justice's table. Her sallow cheek colored as she stood hand in hand with Ransie and listened to the reuniting words.

Ransie helped her into the cart, and climbed in beside her. The little red bull turned once more, and they set out, hand-clasped, for the mountains.

Justice-of-the-peace Benaja Widdup sat in his door and took off his shoes. Once again he fingered the bill tucked down in his vest pocket. Once again he smoked his elder-stem pipe. Once again the speckled hen swaggered down the main street of the "settlement," cackling foolishly.

A SACRIFICE HIT

THE editor of the *Hearthstone Magazine* has his own ideas about the selection of manuscript for his publication. His theory is no secret; in fact, he will expound it to you willingly sitting at his mahogany desk, smiling benignantly and tapping his knee gently with his gold-rimmed eye-glasses.

"The *Hearthstone*," he will say, "does not employ a staff of readers. We obtain opinions of the manuscripts submitted to us directly from types of the various classes of our readers."

That is the editor's theory; and this is the way he carries it out:

When a batch of MSS. is received the editor stuffs every one of his pockets full of them and distributes them as he goes about during the day. The office employees, the hall porter, the janitor, the elevator man, messenger boys, the waiters at the café where the editor has luncheon, the man at the news-stand where he buys his evening paper, the grocer and the milkman, the guard on the 5:30 uptown elevated train, the ticket-chopper at Sixty—th street, the cook and maid at his home—these are the readers who pass upon MSS. sent in to the *Hearthstone Magazine*. If his pockets are not entirely emptied by the time he reaches the bosom of his family the remaining ones are handed over to his wife to read after the baby goes to sleep. A few days later the editor gathers in the MSS. during his regular rounds and considers the verdict of his assorted readers.

This system of making up a magazine has been very successful; and the circulation, paced by the advertising rates, is making a wonderful record of speed.

The *Hearthstone* Company also publishes books, and its imprint is to be found on several successful works—all recommended, says the editor, by the *Hearthstone's* army of volunteer readers. Now and then (according to talkative members of the editorial staff) the *Hearthstone* has allowed manuscripts to slip through its fingers on the advice of its heterogeneous readers, that afterward proved to be famous sellers when brought out by other houses.

For instance (the gossips say), "The Rise and Fall of Silas Latham" was unfavorably passed upon by the elevator-man; the office-boy unanimously rejected "The Boss"; "In the Bishop's Carriage" was contemptuously looked upon by the street-car conductor; "The Deliverance" was turned down by a clerk in the subscription department whose wife's mother had just begun a two months' visit at his home; "The Queen's Quair" came back from the janitor with the comment: "So is the book."

But nevertheless the *Hearthstone* adheres to its theory and system, and it will never lack volunteer readers; for each one of the widely scattered staff, from the young lady stenographer in the editorial office to the man who shovels in coal (whose adverse decision lost to the *Hearthstone* Company the manuscript of "The Under World"), has expectations of becoming editor of the magazine some day.

This method of the *Hearthstone* was well known to Allen Slayton when he wrote his novelette entitled "Love Is All." Slayton had hung about the editorial offices of all the magazines so persistently that he was acquainted with the inner workings of every one in Gotham.

He knew not only that the editor of the *Hearthstone* handed his MSS. around among different types of people for reading, but that the stories of sentimental love-interest went to Miss Puffkin, the editor's stenographer. Another of the editor's peculiar customs was to conceal invariably the name of the writer from his readers of MSS. so that a glittering name might not influence the sincerity of their reports.

Slayton made "Love Is All" the effort of his life. He gave it six months of the best work of his heart and brain. It was a pure love-story, fine, elevated, romantic, passionate—a prose poem that set the divine blessing of love (I am transposing from the manuscript) high above all earthly gifts and honors, and listed it in the catalogue of heaven's choicest rewards. Slayton's literary ambition was intense. He would have sacrificed all other worldly possessions to have gained fame in his chosen art. He would almost have cut off his right hand, or have offered himself to the knife of the appendicitis fancier to have realized his dream of seeing one of his efforts published in the *Hearthstone.*

Slayton finished "Love Is All," and took it to the *Hearthstone* in person. The office of the magazine was in a large, conglomerate building, presided under by a janitor.

As the writer stepped inside the door on his way to the elevator a potato masher flew through the hall, wrecking Slayton's hat, and smashing the glass of the door. Closely following in the wake of the utensil flew the janitor, a bulky, unwholesome man, suspenderless and sordid, panic-stricken and breathless. A frowsy, fat woman with flying hair followed the missile. The janitor's foot slipped on the tiled floor, he fell in a heap with an exclamation of despair. The woman pounced upon him and seized his hair. The man bellowed lustily.

Her vengeance wreaked, the virago rose and stalked, triumphant as Minerva, back to some cryptic domestic retreat at the rear. The janitor got to his feet, blown and humiliated.

"This is married life," he said to Slayton with a certain bruised humor. "That's the girl I used to lay awake of nights thinking about. Sorry about your hat, mister. Say, don't snitch to the tenants about this, will yer? I don't want to lose me job."

Slayton took the elevator at the end of the hall and went up to the offices of the *Hearthstone.* He left the MS. of "Love Is All" with the editor, who agreed to give him an answer as to its availability at the end of a week.

Slayton formulated his great winning scheme on his way down. It struck him with one brilliant flash, and he could not refrain from admiring his own genius in conceiving the idea. That very night he set about carrying it into execution.

Miss Puffkin, the *Hearthstone* stenographer, boarded in the same house with the author. She was an oldish, thin, exclusive, languishing, sentimental maid; and Slayton had been introduced to her some time before.

The writer's daring and self-sacrificing project was this: he knew that the editor of the *Hearthstone* relied strongly upon Miss Puffkin's judgment in the manuscript of romantic and sentimental fiction. Her taste represented the immense average of mediocre women who devour novels and stories of that type. The central idea and keynote of "Love Is All" was love at first sight—the enrapturing, irresistible, soul-thrilling feeling that compels a man or a woman to recognize his or her spirit-mate as soon as heart speaks to heart. Suppose he should impress this divine truth upon Miss Puffkin personally!—would she not surely indorse her new and rapturous sensations by recommending highly to the editor of the *Hearthstone* the novelette "Love Is All"?

Slayton thought so. And that night he took Miss Puffkin to the theatre. The next night he made vehement love to her in the dim parlor of the boarding-house. He quoted freely from "Love Is All"; and he wound up with Miss Puffkin's head on his shoulder, and visions of literary fame dancing in his head.

But Slayton did not stop at love-making. This, he said to himself, was the turning point of his life; and, like a true sportsman, he "went the limit." On Thursday night he and Miss Puffkin walked over to the Big Church in the Middle of the Block and were married.

Brave Slayton! Chateaubriand died in a garret, Byron courted a widow, Keats starved to death, Poe mixed his drinks, De Quincey hit the pipe, Ade lived in Chicago, James kept on doing it, Dickens wore white socks, De Maupassant wore a strait-jacket, Tom Watson became a Populist, Jeremiah wept, all these authors did these things, for the sake of literature, but thou didst cap them all; thou marriedst a wife for to carve for thyself a niche in the temple of fame!

On Friday morning Mrs. Slayton said she would go over to the *Hearthstone* office, hand in one or two manuscripts that the editor had given her to read, and resign her position as stenographer.

"Was there anything—er—that—er—you particularly fancied in the stories you are going to turn in?" asked Slayton with a thumping heart.

"There was one—a novelette, that I liked so much," said his wife. "I haven't read anything in years that I thought was half as nice and true to life."

That afternoon Slayton hurried down to the *Hearthstone* office. He felt that his reward was close at hand. With a novelette in the *Hearthstone*, literary reputation would soon be his.

The office boy met him at the railing in the outer office. It was not for unsuccessful authors to hold personal colloquy with the editor except at rare intervals.

Slayton hugging himself internally, was nursing in his heart the exquisite hope of being able to crush the office boy with his forthcoming success.

He inquired concerning his novelette. The office boy went into the sacred precincts and brought forth a large envelope, thick with more than the bulk of a thousand checks.

"The boss told me to tell you he's sorry," said the boy, "but your manuscript ain't available for the magazine."

Slayton stood dazed. "Can you tell me," he stammered, "whether or no Miss Puff—that is my—I mean Miss Puffkin—handed in a novelette this morning that she had been asked to read?"

"Sure she did," answered the office boy, wisely. "I heard the old man say that Miss Puffkin said it was a daisy. The name of it was, 'Married for the Mazuma, or a Working Girl's Triumph.'

"Say, you!" said the office boy, confidentially, "your name's Slayton, ain't it? I guess I mixed cases on you without meanin' to do it. The boss gave me some manuscript to hand around the other day and I got the ones for Miss Puffkin and the janitor mixed. I guess it's all right, though."

And then Slayton looked closer and saw on the cover of his manuscript, under the title "Love Is All," the janitor's comment scribbled with a piece of charcoal:

"The—you say!"

THE ROADS WE TAKE

Twenty miles west of Tucson the "Sunset Express" stopped at a tank to take on water. Besides the aqueous addition the engine of that famous flyer acquired some other things that were not good for it.

While the fireman was lowering the feeding hose, Bob Tidball, "Shark" Dodson, and a quarter-bred Creek Indian called John Big Dog climbed on the engine and showed the engineer three round orifices in pieces of ordnance that they carried. These orifices so impressed the engineer with their possibilities that he raised both hands in a gesture such as accompanies the ejaculation "Do tell!"

At the crisp command of Shark Dodson, who was leader of the attacking force, the engineer descended to the ground and uncoupled the engine and tender. Then John Big Dog, perched upon the coal, sportively held two guns upon the engine driver and the fireman, and suggested that they run the engine fifty yards away and there await further orders.

Shark Dodson and Bob Tidball, scorning to put such low-grade ore as the passengers through the mill, struck out for the rich pocket of the express car. They found the messenger serene in the belief that the "Sunset Express" was taking on nothing more stimulating and dangerous than aqua pura. While Bob was knocking this idea out of his head with the butt-end of his six-shooter Shark Dodson was already dosing the express-car safe with dynamite.

The safe exploded to the tune of $30,000, all gold and currency. The passengers thrust their heads casually out of the windows to look for the thunder-cloud. The conductor jerked at the bell rope, which sagged down loose and un-resisting, at his tug. Shark Dodson and Bob Tidball, with their booty in a stout canvas bag, tumbled out of the express car and ran awkwardly in their high-heeled boots to the engine.

The engineer, sullenly angry but wise, ran the engine, according to orders, rapidly away from the inert train. But before this was accomplished the ex-press messenger, recovered from Bob Tidball's persuader to neutrality, jumped out of his car with a Winchester rifle and took a trick in the game. Mr. John Big Dog, sitting on the coal tender, unwittingly made a wrong lead by giving an imitation of a target, and the messenger trumped him. With a ball exactly between his shoulder blades the Creek chevalier of industry rolled off to the ground, thus increasing the share of his comrades in the loot by one-sixth each.

Two miles from the tank the engineer was ordered to stop.

The robbers waved a defiant adieu and plunged down the steep slope into the thick woods that lined the track. Five minutes of crashing through a thicket of chaparral brought them to open woods, where the three horses were tied to low-hanging branches. One was waiting for John Big Dog, who would never ride by night or day again. This animal the robbers divested of saddle and bridle and set free. They mounted the other two with the bag across one pommel, and rode fast and with discretion through the forest and up a primeval, lonely gorge. Here the animal that bore Bob Tidball slipped on a mossy boulder and broke a foreleg. They shot him through the head at once and sat down to hold a council of flight. Made secure for the present by the tortuous trail they had traveled, the question of time was no longer so big. Many miles and hours lay between them and the spryest posse that could follow. Shark Dodson's horse, with trailing rope and dropped bridle, panted and cropped thankfully of the grass along the stream in the gorge. Bob Tidball opened the sack, and drew out double handfuls of the neat packages of currency and the one sack of gold and chuckled with the glee of a child.

"Say, you old double-decked pirate," he called joyfully to Dodson, "you said we could do it—you got a head for financing that knocks the horns off of anything in Arizona."

"What are we going to do about a hoss for you, Bob? We ain't got long to wait here. They'll be on our trail before daylight in the mornin'."

"Oh, I guess that cayuse of yourn'll carry double for a while," answered the sanguine Bob. "We'll annex the first animal we come across. By jingoes, we made a haul, didn't we? Accordin' to the marks on this money there's $30,000—$15,000 apiece!"

"It's short of what I expected," said Shark Dodson, kicking softly at the pack-ages with the toe of his boot. And then he looked pensively at the wet sides of his tired horse.

"Old Bolivar's mighty nigh played out," he said, slowly. "I wish that sorrel of yours hadn't got hurt."

"So do I," said Bob, heartily, "but it can't be helped. Bolivar's got plenty of bottom—he'll get us both far enough to get fresh mounts. Dang it, Shark, I can't help thinkin' how funny it is that an Easterner like you can come out here and give us Western fellows cards and spades in the desperado business. What part of the East was you from, anyway?"

"New York State," said Shark Dodson, sitting down on a boulder and chewing a twig. "I was born on a farm in Ulster County. I ran away from home when I was seventeen. It was an accident my comin' West. I was walkin' along the road with my clothes in a bundle, makin' for New York City. I had an idea of goin' there and makin' lots of money. I always felt like I could do it. I came to a place one evenin' where the road forked and I didn't know which fork to take. I studied about it for half an hour and then I took the left-hand. That night I run into the camp of a Wild West show that was travelin' among the little towns, and I went West with it. I've often wondered if I wouldn't have turned out different if I'd took the other road."

"Oh, I reckon you'd have ended up about the same," said Bob Tidball, cheerfully philosophical. "It ain't the roads we take; it's what's inside of us that makes us turn out the way we do."

Shark Dodson got up and leaned against a tree.

"I'd a good deal rather that sorrel of yourn hadn't hurt himself, Bob," he said again, almost pathetically.

"Same here," agreed Bob; "he sure was a first-rate kind of a crowbait. But Bolivar, he'll pull us through all right. Reckon we'd better be movin' on, hadn't we, Shark? I'll bag the boodle ag'in and we'll hit the trail for higher timber."

Bob Tidball replaced the spoil in the bag and tied the mouth of it tightly with a cord. When he looked up the most prominent object that he saw was the muzzle of Shark Dodson's .45 held upon him without a waver.

"Stop your funnin'," said Bob, with a grin. "We got to be hittin' the breeze."

"Set still," said Shark. "You ain't goin' to hit no breeze, Bob. I hate to tell you, but there ain't any chance for but one of us. Bolivar, he's plenty tired, and he can't carry double."

"We been pards, me and you, Shark Dodson, for three years," Bob said quietly. "We've risked our lives together time and again. I've always give you a square deal, and I thought you was a man. I've heard some queer stories about you shootin' one or two men in a peculiar way, but I never believed 'em. Now if you're just havin' a little fun with me, Shark, put your gun up, and we'll get on Bolivar and vamoose. If you mean to shoot—shoot, you blackhearted son of a tarantula!"

Shark Dodson's face bore a deeply sorrowful look.

"You don't know how bad I feel," he sighed, "about that sorrel of yourn breakin' his leg, Bob."

The expression on Dodson's face changed in an instant to one of cold ferocity mingled with inexorable cupidity. The soul of the man showed itself for a moment like an evil face in the window of a reputable house.

Truly Bob Tidball was never to "hit the breeze" again. The deadly .45 of the false friend cracked and filled the gorge with a roar that the walls hurled back with indignant echoes. And Bolivar, unconscious accomplice, swiftly bore away the last of the holders-up of the "Sunset Express," not put to the stress of "carrying double."

But as Shark Dodson galloped away the woods seemed to fade from his view; the revolver in his right hand turned to the curved arm of a mahogany chair; his saddle was strangely upholstered, and he opened his eyes and saw his feet, not in stirrups, but resting quietly on the edge of a quartered-oak desk.

I am telling you that Dodson, of the firm of Dodson & Decker, Wall Street brokers, opened his eyes. Peabody, the confidential clerk, was standing by his chair, hesitating to speak. There was a confused hum of wheels below, and the sedative buzz of an electric fan.

"Ahem! Peabody," said Dodson, blinking. "I must have fallen asleep. I had a most remarkable dream. What is it, Peabody?"

"Mr. Williams, sir, of Tracy & Williams, is outside. He has come to settle his deal in X. Y. Z. The market caught him short, sir, if you remember."

"Yes, I remember. What is X. Y. Z. quoted at to-day, Peabody?"

"One eighty-five, sir."

"Then that's his price."

"Excuse me," said Peabody, rather nervously, "for speaking of it, but I've been talking to Williams. He's an old friend of yours, Mr. Dodson, and you practically have a corner in X. Y. Z. I thought you might—that is, I thought you might not remember that he sold you the stock at 98. If he settles at the market price it will take every cent he has in the world and his home too to deliver the shares."

The expression on Dodson's face changed in an instant to one of cold ferocity mingled with inexorable cupidity. The soul of the man showed itself for a moment like an evil face in the window of a reputable house.

"He will settle at one eighty-five," said Dodson. "Bolivar cannot carry double."

A BLACKJACK BARGAINER

THE most disreputable thing in Yancey Goree's law office was Goree himself, sprawled in his creaky old armchair. The rickety little office, built of red brick, was set flush with the street—the main street of the town of Bethel.

Bethel rested upon the foot-hills of the Blue Ridge. Above it the mountains were piled to the sky. Far below it the turbid Catawba gleamed yellow along its disconsolate valley.

The June day was at its sultriest hour. Bethel dozed in the tepid shade. Trade was not. It was so still that Goree, reclining in his chair, distinctly heard the clicking of the chips in the grand-jury room, where the "court-house gang" was playing poker. From the open back door of the office a well-worn path meandered across the grassy lot to the court-house. The treading out of that path had cost Goree all he ever had—first inheritance of a few thousand dollars, next the old family home, and, latterly, the last shreds of his self-respect and manhood. The "gang" had cleaned him out. The broken gambler had turned drunkard and parasite; he had lived to see this day come when the men who had stripped him denied him a seat at the game. His word was no longer to be taken. The daily bout at cards had arranged itself accordingly, and to him was assigned the ignoble part of the onlooker. The sheriff, the county clerk, a sportive deputy, a gay attorney, and a chalk-faced man hailing "from the valley," sat at table, and the sheared one was thus tacitly advised to go and grow more wool.

Soon wearying of his ostracism, Goree had departed for his office, muttering to himself as he unsteadily traversed the unlucky pathway. After a drink of corn whiskey from a demijohn under the table, he had flung himself into the chair, staring, in a sort of maudlin apathy, out at the mountains immersed in the summer haze. The little white patch he saw away up on the side of Blackjack was Laurel, the village near which he had been born and bred. There, also, was the birthplace of the feud between the Gorees and the Coltranes. Now no direct heir of the Gorees survived except this plucked and singed bird of misfortune. To the Coltranes, also, but one male supporter was left—Colonel Abner Coltrane, a man of substance and standing, a member of the State Legislature, and a contemporary with Goree's father. The feud had been a typical one of the region; it had left a red record of hate, wrong, and slaughter.

But Yancey Goree was not thinking of feuds. His befuddled brain was hopelessly attacking the problem of the future maintenance of himself and his favorite follies. Of late, old friends of the family had seen to it that he had whereof to eat and a place to sleep, but whiskey they would not buy for him, and he must have whiskey. His law business was extinct; no case had been intrusted to him in two years. He had been a borrower and a sponge, and it seemed that if he fell no lower it would be from lack of opportunity. One more chance— he was saying to himself—if he had one more stake at the game, he thought he could win; but he had nothing left to sell, and his credit was more than exhausted.

He could not help smiling, even in his misery, as he thought of the man to whom, six months before, he had sold the old Goree homestead. There had come from "back yan'" in the mountains two of the strangest creatures, a man named Pike Garvey and his wife. "Back yan'," with a wave of the hand toward the hills, was understood among the mountaineers to designate the remotest fastnesses, the unplumbed gorges, the haunts of lawbreakers, the wolf's den, and the boudoir of the bear. In the cabin far up on Blackjack's shoulder, in the wildest part of these retreats, this odd couple had lived for twenty years. They had neither dog nor children to mitigate the heavy silence of the hills. Pike Garvey was little known in the settlements, but all who had dealt with him pronounced him "crazy as a loon." He acknowledged no occupation save that of a squirrel hunter, but he "moonshined" occasionally by way of diversion. Once the "revenues" had dragged him from his lair, fighting silently and desperately like a terrier, and he had been sent to state's prison for two years. Released, he popped back into his hole like an angry weasel.

Fortune, passing over many anxious wooers, made a freakish flight into Blackjack's bosky pockets to smile upon Pike and his faithful partner.

One day a party of spectacled, knickerbockered, and altogether absurd prospectors invaded the vicinity of the Garveys' cabin. Pike lifted his squirrel rifle off the hook and took a shot at them at long range on the chance of their being revenues. Happily he missed, and the unconscious agents of good luck drew nearer, disclosing their innocence of anything resembling law or justice. Later on, they offered the Garveys an enormous quantity of ready, green, crisp money for their thirty-acre patch of cleared land, mentioning, as an excuse for such a mad action, some irrelevant and inadequate nonsense about a bed of mica underlying the said property.

When the Garveys became possessed of so many dollars that they faltered in computing them, the deficiencies of life on Blackjack began to grow prominent. Pike began to talk of new shoes, a hogshead of tobacco to set in the corner, a new lock to his rifle; and, leading Martella to a certain spot on the mountainside, he pointed out to her how a small cannon—doubtless a thing not beyond the scope of their fortune in price—might be planted so as to command and defend the sole accessible trail to the cabin, to the confusion of revenues and meddling strangers forever.

But Adam reckoned without his Eve. These things represented to him the applied power of wealth, but there slumbered in his dingy cabin an ambition that soared far above his primitive wants. Somewhere in Mrs. Garvey's bosom still survived a spot of femininity unstarved by twenty years of Blackjack. For so long a time the sounds in her ears had been the scaly-barks dropping in the woods at noon, and the wolves singing among the rocks at night, and it was enough to have purged her vanities. She had grown fat and sad and yellow and dull. But when the means came, she felt a rekindled desire to assume the perquisites of her sex—to sit at tea tables; to buy inutile things; to whitewash the hideous veracity of life with a little form and ceremony. So she coldly vetoed Pike's proposed system of fortifications, and announced that they would descend upon the world, and gyrate socially.

And thus, at length, it was decided, and the thing done. The village of Laurel was their compromise between Mrs. Garvey's preference for one of the large valley towns and Pike's hankering for primeval solitudes. Laurel yielded a halting round of feeble social distractions comportable with Martella's ambitions, and was not entirely without recommendation to Pike, its contiguity to the mountains presenting advantages for sudden retreat in case fashionable society should make it advisable.

Their descent upon Laurel had been coincident with Yancey Goree's feverish desire to convert property into cash, and they bought the old Goree homestead, paying four thousand dollars ready money into the spendthrifts shaking hand.

Thus it happened that while the disreputable last of the Gorees sprawled in his disreputable office, at the end of his row, spurned by the cronies whom he had gorged, strangers dwelt in the halls of his fathers.

A cloud of dust was rolling slowly up the parched street, with something traveling in the midst of it. A little breeze wafted the cloud to one side, and a new, brightly painted carryall, drawn by a slothful gray horse, became visible. The vehicle deflected from the middle of the street as it neared Goree's office, and stopped in the gutter directly in front of his door.

On the front seat sat a gaunt, tall men, dressed in black broadcloth, his rigid hands incarcerated in yellow kid gloves. On the back seat was a lady who triumphed over the June heat. Her stout form was armored in a skin-tight silk dress of the description known as "changeable," being a gorgeous combination of shifting hues. She sat erect, waving a much-ornamented fan, with her eyes fixed stonily far down the street. However Martella's Garvey's heart might be rejoicing at the pleasures of her new life, Blackjack had done his work with her exterior. He had carved her countenance to the image of emptiness and inanity; had imbued her with the stolidity of his crags and the reserve of his hushed interiors. She always seemed to hear, whatever her surroundings were, the scaly-barks falling and pattering down the mountainside. She could always hear the awful silence of Blackjack sounding through the stillest of nights.

Goree watched this solemn equipage, as it drove to his door, with only faint interest; but when the lank driver wrapped the reins about his whip, and awkwardly descended, and stepped into the office, he rose unsteadily to receive him, recognizing Pike Garvey, the new, the transformed, the recently civilized.

The mountaineer took the chair Goree offered him. They who cast doubts upon Garvey's soundness of mind had a strong witness in the man's countenance. His face was too long, a dull saffron in hue, and immobile as a statue's. Pale-blue, unwinking round eyes without lashes added to the singularity of his gruesome visage. Goree was at a loss to account for the visit.

"Everything all right at Laurel, Mr. Garvey?" he inquired.

"Everything all right, sir, and mighty pleased is Missis Garvey and me with the property. Missis Garvey likes yo' old place, and she likes the neighborhood. Society is what she 'lows she wants, and she is gettin' of it. The Rogerses, the

Hapgoods, the Pratts, and the Troys hev been to see Missis Garvey, and she hev et meals to most of thar houses. The best folks hev axed her to differ'nt kinds of doin's. I cyan't say, Mr. Goree, that sech things suits me—fur me, give me them thar." Garvey's huge yellow-gloved hand flourished in the direction of the mountains. "That's whar I b'long, 'mongst the wild honey bees and the b'ars. But that ain't what I come fur to say, Mr. Goree. Thar's somethin' you got what me and Missis Garvey wants to buy."

"Buy!" echoed Goree. "From me?" Then he laughed harshly. "I reckon you are mistaken about that. I sold out to you, as you yourself expressed it, 'lock, stock, and barrel.' There isn't even a ramrod left to sell."

"You've got it; and we 'uns want it. Take the money,' says Missis Garvey, 'and buy it fa'r and squar'.'"

Goree shook his head. "The cupboard's bare," he said.

"We've riz," pursued the mountaineer, undeflected from his object, "a heap. We was pore as possums, and now we could hev folks to dinner every day. We been reco'nized, Missis Garvey says, by the best society. But there's somethin' we need we ain't got. She says it ought to been put in the 'ventory ov the sale, but it 'tain't thar. Take the money, then,' she says, 'and buy it fa'r and squar'.'"

"Out with it," said Goree, his racked nerves growing impatient.

Garvey threw his slouch hat upon the table, and leaned forward, fixing his unblinking eyes upon Goree's.

"There's a old feud," he said, distinctly and slowly, "'tween you 'uns and the Coltranes."

Goree frowned ominously. To speak of his feud to a feudist is a serious breach of the mountain etiquette. The man from "back yan'" knew it as well as the lawyer did.

"Na offense," he went on, "but purely in the way of business. Missis Garvey hev studied all about feuds. Most of the quality folks in the mountains hev 'em. The Settles and the Goforths, the Rankins and the Boyds, the Silers and the Galloways, hev all been cyarin' on feuds f'om twenty to a hundred year. The last man to drap was when yo' uncle, Jedge Paisley Goree, 'journed co't and shot Len Coltrane f'om the bench. Missis Garvey and me, we come f'om the po' white trash. Nobody wouldn't pick a feud with we'uns, no mo'n with a fam'ly of tree-toads. Quality people everywhar, says Missis Garvey, has feuds. We 'uns ain't quality, but we're buyin' into it as fur as we can. Take the money, then,' says Missis Garvey, 'and buy Mr. Goree's feud, fa'r and squar'.'"

The squirrel hunter straightened a leg half across the room, drew a roll of bills from his pocket, and threw them on the table.

"Thar's two hundred dollars, Mr. Goree; what you would call a fa'r price for a feud that's been 'lowed to run down like yourn hev. Thar's only you left to cyar' on yo' side of it, and you'd make mighty po' killin'. I'll take it off yo' hands, and it'll set me and Missis Garvey up among the quality. Thar's the money."

The little roll of currency on the table slowly untwisted itself, writhing and jumping as its folds relaxed. In the silence that followed Garvey's last speech the rattling of the poker chips in the court-house could be plainly heard. Goree knew that the sheriff had just won a pot, for the subdued whoop with which he always greeted a victory floated across the square upon the crinkly heat waves. Beads of moisture stood on Goree's brow. Stooping, he drew the wicker-covered demijohn from under the table, and filled a tumbler from it.

"A little corn liquor, Mr. Garvey? Of course you are joking about—what you spoke of? Opens quite a new market, doesn't it? Feuds, prime, two-fifty to three. Feuds, slightly damaged—two hundred, I believe you said, Mr. Garvey?"

Goree laughed self-consciously.

The mountaineer took the glass Goree handed him, and drank the whiskey without a tremor of the lids of his staring eyes. The lawyer applauded the feat by a look of envious admiration. He poured his own drink, and took it like a drunkard, by gulps, and with shudders at the smell and taste.

"Two hundred," repeated Garvey. "Thar's the money."

A sudden passion flared up in Goree's brain. He struck the table with his fist. One of the bills flipped over and touched his hand. He flinched as if something had stung him.

"Do you come to me," he shouted, "seriously with such a ridiculous, insulting, darned-fool proposition?"

"It's fa'r and squar'," said the squirrel hunter, but he reached out his hand as if to take back the money; and then Goree knew that his own flurry of rage had not been from pride or resentment, but from anger at himself, knowing that he would set foot in the deeper depths that were being opened to him. He turned in an instant from an outraged gentlemen to an anxious chafferer recommending his goods.

"Don't be in a hurry, Garvey," he said, his face crimson and his speech thick. "I accept your p-p-proposition, though it's dirt cheap at two hundred. A t-trade's all right when both p-purchaser and b-buyer are s-satisfied. Shall I w-wrap it up for you, Mr. Garvey?"

Garvey rose, and shook out his broadcloth. "Missis Garvey will be pleased. You air out of it, and it stands Coltrane and Garvey. Just a scrap ov writin', Mr. Goree, you bein' a lawyer, to show we traded."

Goree seized a sheet of paper and a pen. The money was clutched in his moist hand. Everything else suddenly seemed to grow trivial and light.

"Bill of sale, by all means. 'Right, title, and interest in and to' . . . 'forever warrant and——' No, Garvey, we'll have to leave out that 'defend,'" said Goree with a loud laugh. "You'll have to defnd this title yourself."

The mountaineer received the amazing screed that the lawyer handed him, folded it with immense labor, and placed it carefully in his pocket.

Goree was standing near the window. "Step here," he said, raising his finger, "and I'll show you your recently purchased enemy. There he goes, down the other side of the street."

The mountaineer crooked his long frame to look through the window in the direction indicated by the other. Colonel Abner Coltrane, an erect, portly gentleman of about fifty wearing the inevitable long, double-breasted frock coat of the Southern lawmaker, and an old high silk hat, was passing on the opposite sidewalk. As Garvey looked, Goree glanced at his face. If there be such a thing as a yellow wolf, here was its counterpart. Garvey snarled as his unhuman eyes followed the moving figure, disclosing long amber-colored fangs.

"Is that him? Why, that's the man who sent me to the pen'tentiary once!"

"He used to be district attorney," said Goree, carelessly. "And, by the way, he's a first-class shot."

"I kin hit a squirrel's eye at a hundred yard," said Garvey. "So that thar's Coltrane! I made a better trade than I was thinkin'. I'll take keer ov this feud, Mr. Goree, better'n you ever did!"

He moved toward the door, but lingered there, betraying a slight perplexity.

"Anything else to-day?" inquired Goree with frothy sarcasm. "Any family traditions, ancestral ghosts, or skeletons in the closet? Prices as low as the lowest."

"Thar was another thing," replied the unmoved squirrel hunter, "that Missis Garvey was thinkin' of. 'Tain't so much in my line as t'other, but she wanted partic'lar that I should inquire, and ef you was willin', 'pay fur it,' she says, 'fa'r and squar'.' Thar's a buryin' groun', as you know, Mr. Goree, in the yard of yo' old place, under the cedars. Them that lies thar is yo' folks what was killed by the Coltranes. The monyments has the names on 'em. Missis Garvey says a fam'ly buryin' groun' is a sho' sign of quality. She says ef we git the feud, thar's somethin' else ought to go with it. The names on them monyments is 'Goree,' but they can be changed to ourn by——"

"Go! Go!" screamed Goree, his face turning purple. He stretched out both hands toward the mountaineer, his fingers hooked and shaking. "Go, you ghoul! Even a Ch-Chinaman protects the g-graves of his ancestors—go!"

The squirrel hunter slouched out of the door to his carryall. While he was climbing over the wheel Goree was collecting, with feverish celerity, the money that had fallen from his hand to the floor. As the vehicle slowly turned about, the sheep, with a coat of newly grown wool, was hurrying, in indecent haste, along the path to the court-house.

At three o'clock in the morning they brought him back to his office, shorn and unconscious. The sheriff, the sportive deputy, the county clerk, and the gay attorney carried him, the chalk-faced man "from the valley" acting as escort.

"On the table," said one of them, and they deposited him there among the litter of his unprofitable books and papers.

"Yance thinks a lot of a pair of deuces when he's liquored up," sighed the sheriff, reflectively.

"Too much," said the gay attorney. "A man has no business to play poker who drinks as much as he does. I wonder how much he dropped to-night."

"Close to two hundred. What I wonder is whar he got it. Yance ain't had a cent fur over a month, I know."

"Struck a client, maybe. Well, let's get home before daylight. He'll be all right when he wakes up, except for a sort of beehive about the cranium."

The gang slipped away through the early morning twilight. The next eye to gaze upon the miserable Goree was the orb of day. He peered through the uncurtained window, first deluging the sleeper in a flood of faint gold, but soon pouring upon the mottled red of his flesh a searching, white, summer heat. Goree stirred, half unconsciously, among the table's débris, and turned his face from the window. His movement dislodged a heavy law book, which crashed upon the floor. Opening his eyes, he saw, bending over him, a man in a black frock coat. Looking higher, he discovered a well-worn silk hat, and beneath it the kindly, smooth face of Colonel Abner Coltrane.

A little uncertain of the outcome, the colonel waited for the other to make some sign of recognition. Not in twenty years had male members of these two families faced each other in peace. Goree's eyelids puckered as he strained his blurred sight toward this visitor, and then he smiled serenely.

"Have you brought Stella and Lucy over to play?" he said, calmly.

"Do you know me, Yancey?" asked Coltrane.

"Of course I do. You brought me a whip with a whistle in the end."

So he had—twenty-four years ago; when Yancey's father was his best friend.

Goree's eyes wandered about the room. The colonel understood. "Lie still, and I'll bring you some," said he. There was a pump in the yard at the rear, and Goree closed his eyes, listening with rapture to the click of its handle and the bubbling of the falling stream. Coltrane brought a pitcher of the cool water, and held it for him to drink. Presently Goree sat up—a most forlorn object, his summer suit of flax soiled and crumpled, his discreditable head tousled and unsteady. He tried to wave one of his hands toward the colonel.

"Ex-excuse—everything, will you?" he said. "I must have drunk too much whiskey last night, and gone to bed on the table." His brows knitted into a puzzled frown.

"Out with the boys a while?" asked Coltrane, kindly.

"No, I went nowhere. I haven't had a dollar to spend in the last two months. Struck the demijohn too often, I reckon, as usual."

Colonel Coltrane touched him on the shoulder.

"A little while ago, Yancey," he began, "you asked me if I had brought Stella
and Lucy over to play. You weren't quite awake then, and must have been dreaming you were a boy again. You are awake now, and I want you to listen to me.
I have come from Stella and Lucy to their old playmate, and to my old friend's
son. They know that I am going to bring you home with me, and you will find
them as ready with a welcome as they were in the old days. I want you to come
to my house and stay until you are yourself again, and as much longer as you
will. We heard of your being down in the world, and in the midst of temptation, and we agreed that you should come over and play at our house once more.
Will you come, my boy? Will you drop our old family trouble and come with
me?"

"Trouble!" said Goree, opening his eyes wide. "There was never any trouble
between us that I know of. I'm sure we've always been the best friends. But,
good Lord, Colonel, how could I go to your home as I am—a drunken wretch, a
miserable, degraded spendthrift and gambler——"

He lurched from the table to his armchair, and began to weep maudlin tears,
mingled with genuine drops of remorse and shame. Coltrane talked to him persistently and reasonably, reminding him of the simple mountain pleasures of
which he had once been so fond, and insisting upon the genuineness of the invitation.

Finally he landed Goree by telling him he was counting upon his help in the
engineering and transportation of a large amount of felled timber from a high
mountainside to a waterway. He knew that Goree had once invented a device for
this purpose—a series of slides and chutes—upon which he had justly prided
himself. In an instant the poor fellow, delighted at the idea of his being of use
to any one, had paper spread upon the table, and was drawing rapid but pitifully
shaky lines in demonstration of what he could and would do.

The man was sickened of the husks; his prodigal heart was turning again toward the mountains. His mind was yet strangely clogged, and his thoughts and
memories were returning to his brain one by one, like carrier pigeons over a
stormy sea. But Coltrane was satisfied with the progress he had made.

Bethel received the surprise of its existence that afternoon when a Coltrane
and a Goree rode amicably together through the town. Side by side they rode,
out from the dusty streets and gaping townspeople, down across the creek bridge,
and up toward the mountain. The prodigal had brushed and washed and combed
himself to a more decent figure, but he was unsteady in the saddle, and he seemed
to be deep in the contemplation of some vexing problem. Coltrane left him in
his mood, relying upon the influence of changed surroundings to restore his
equilibrium.

Once Goree was seized with a shaking fit, and almost came to a collapse. He
had to dismount and rest at the side of the road. The colonel, forseeing such a
condition, had provided a small flask of whiskey for the journey but when it
was offered to him Goree refused it almost with violence, declaring he would
never touch it again. By and by he was recovered, and went quietly enough for
a mile or two. Then he pulled up his horse suddenly, and said:

"I lost two hundred dollars last night, playing poker. Now, where did I get
that money?"

"Take it easy, Yancey. The mountain air will soon clear it up. We'll go fishing, first thing, at the Pinnacle Falls. The trout are jumping there like bull-
frogs. We'll take Stella and Lucy along, and have a picnic on Eagle Rock.
Have you forgotten how a hickory-cured-ham sandwich tastes, Yancey, to a hungry fisherman?"

Evidently the colonel did not believe the story of his lost wealth; so Goree retired again into brooding silence.

By late afternoon they had traveled ten of the twelve miles between Bethel and

Laurel. Half a mile this side of Laurel lay the old Goree place; a mile or two beyond the village lived the Coltranes. The road was now steep and laborious, but the compensations were many. The tilted aisles of the forest were opulent with leaf and bird and bloom. The tonic air put to shame the pharmacopœia. The glades were dark with mossy shade, and bright with shy rivulets winking from the ferns and laurels. On the lower side they viewed, framed in the near foliage, exquisite sketches of the far valley swooning in its opal haze.

Coltrane was pleased to see that his companion was yielding to the spell of the hills and woods. For now they had but to skirt the base of Painter's Cliff; to cross Elder Branch and mount the hill beyond, and Goree would have to face the squandered home of his fathers. Every rock he passed, every tree, every foot of the roadway, was familiar to him. Though he had forgotten the woods, they thrilled him like the music of "*Home, Sweet Home.*"

They rounded the cliff, descended into Elder Branch, and paused there to let the horses drink and splash in the swift water. On the right was a rail fence that cornered there, and followed the road and stream. Inclosed by it was the old apple orchard of the home place; the house was yet concealed by the brow of the steep hill. Inside and along the fence, pokeberries, elders, sassafras, and sumac grew high and dense. At a rustle of their branches, both Goree and Coltrane glanced up, and saw a long, yellow, wolfish face above the fence, staring at them with pale, unwinking eyes. The head quickly disappeared; there was a violent swaying of the bushes, and an ungainly figure ran up through the apple orchard in the direction of the house, zigzagging among the trees.

"That's Garvey," said Coltrane; "the man you sold out to. There's no doubt but he's considerably cracked. I had to send him up for moonshining once, several years ago, in spite of the fact that I believed him irresponsible. Why, what's the matter, Yancey?"

Goree was wiping his forehead, and his face had lost its color. "Do I look queer, too?" he asked, trying to smile. "I'm just remembering a few more things." Some of the alcohol had evaporated from his brain. "I recollect now where I got that two hundred dollars."

"Don't think of it," said Coltrane, cheerfully. "Later on we'll figure it all out together."

They rode out of the branch, and when they reached the foot of the hill Goree stopped again.

"Did you ever suspect I was a very vain kind of fellow, Colonel?" he asked. "Sort of foolish proud about appearances?"

The colonel's eyes refused to wander to the soiled, sagging suit of flax and the faded slouch hat.

"It seems to me," he replied, mystified, but humoring him, "I remember a young buck about twenty, with the tightest coat, the sleekest hair, and the prancingest saddle horse in the Blue Ridge."

"Right you are," said Goree, eagerly. "And it's in me yet, though it don't show. Oh, I'm as vain as a turkey gobbler, and as proud as Lucifer. I'm going to ask you to indulge this weakness of mine in a little matter."

"Speak out, Yancey. We'll create you Duke of Laurel and Baron of Blue Ridge, if you choose; and you shall have a feather out of Stella's peacock's tail to wear in your hat."

"I'm in earnest. In a few minutes we'll pass the house up there on the hill where I was born, and where my people have lived for nearly a century. Strangers live there now—and look at me! I am about to show myself to them ragged and poverty-stricken, a wastrel and a beggar. Colonel Coltrane, I'm ashamed to do it. I want you to let me wear your coat and hat until we are out of sight beyond. I know you think it a foolish pride, but I want to make as good a showing as I can when I pass the old place."

"Now, what does this mean?" said Coltrane to himself, as he compared his companion's sane looks and quiet demeanor with his strange request. But he was already unbuttoning the coat, assenting readily, as if the fancy were in no wise to be considered strange.

The coat and hat fitted Goree well. He buttoned the former about him with a look of satisfaction and dignity. He and Coltrane were nearly the same size—rather tall, portly, and erect. Twenty-five years were between them, but in appearance they might have been brothers. Goree looked older than his age; his face was puffy and lined; the colonel had the smooth, fresh complexion of a temperate liver. He put on Goree's disreputable old flax coat and faded slouch hat.

"Now," said Goree, taking up the reins, "I'm all right. I want you to ride about ten feet in the rear as we go by, Colonel, so that they can get a good look at me. They'll see I'm no back number yet, by any means. I guess I'll show up pretty well to them once more, anyhow. Let's ride on."

He set out up the hill at a smart trot, the colonel following, as he had been requested.

Goree sat straight in the saddle, with head erect, but his eyes were turned to the right, sharply scanning every shrub and fence and hiding-place in the old homestead yard. Once he muttered to himself, "Will the crazy fool try it, or did I dream half of it?"

It was when he came opposite the little family burying ground that he saw what he had been looking for—a puff of white smoke, coming from the thick cedars in one corner. He toppled so slowly to the left that Coltrane had time to urge his horse to that side, and catch him with one arm.

The squirrel hunter had not overpraised his aim. He had sent the bullet where he intended, and where Goree had expected that it would pass—through the breast of Colonel Abner Coltrane's black frock coat.

Goree leaned heavily against Coltrane, but he did not fall. The horses kept pace, side by side, and the colonel's arm kept him steady. The little white houses of Laurel shone through the trees, half a mile away. Goree reached out one hand and groped until it rested upon Coltrane's fingers, which held his bridle.

"Good friend," he said, and that was all.

Thus did Yancey Goree, as he rode past his old home, make, considering all things, the best showing that was in his power.

THE SONG AND THE SERGEANT

HALF a dozen people supping at a table in one of the upper-Broadway all-night restaurants were making too much noise. Three times the manager walked past them with a politely warning glance; but their argument had waxed too warm to be quelled by a manager's gaze. It was midnight, and the restaurant was filled with patrons from the theatres of that district. Some among the dispersed audiences must have recognized among the quarrelsome sextet the faces of the players belonging to the Carroll Comedy Company.

Four of the six made up the company. Another was the author of the comedietta, "A Gay Coquette," which the quartet of players had been presenting with fair success at several vaudeville houses in the city. The sixth at the table was a person inconsequent in the realm of art, but one at whose bidding many lobsters had perished.

Loudly the six maintained their clamorous debate. No one of the party was silent except when answers were stormed from him by the excited ones. That was the comedian of "A Gay Coquette." He was a young man with a face even too melancholy for his profession. The oral warfare of four immoderate tongues was directed at Miss Clarice Carroll, the twinkling star of the small aggregation. Excepting the downcast comedian, all members of the party united in casting upon her with vehemence the blame of some momentous misfortune. Fifty times they told her: "It is your fault, Clarice—it is you alone who spoilt the scene. It is only of late that you have acted this way. At this rate the sketch will have to be taken off."

Miss Carroll was a match for any four. Gallic ancestry gave her a variety that could easily mount to fury. Her large eyes flashed a scorching denial at her accusers. Her slender, eloquent arms constantly menaced the tableware. Her high, clear soprano voice rose to what would have been a scream had it not possessed so pure a musical quality. She hurled back at the attacking four their denunciations in tones sweet, but of too great carrying power for a Broadway restaurant.

Finally they exhausted her patience both as a woman and an artist. She sprang up like a panther, managed to smash half a dozen plates and glasses with one royal sweep of her arm, and defied her critics. They rose and wrangled more loudly. The comedian sighed and looked a trifle sadder and disinterested. The manager came tripping and suggested peace. He was told to go to the popular synonym for war so promptly that the affair might have happened at The Hague.

Thus was the manager angered. He made a sign with his hand and a waiter slipped out of the door. In twenty minutes the party of six was in a police station facing a grizzled and philosophical desk sergeant.

"Disorderly conduct in a restaurant," said the policeman who had brought the party in.

The author of "A Gay Coquette" stepped to the front. He wore nose-glasses and evening clothes, even if his shoes had been tans before they met the patent-leather-polish bottle.

"Mr. Sergeant," said he, out of his throat, like Actor Irving, "I would like to protest against this arrest. The company of actors who are performing in a little play that I have written, in company with a friend and myself, were having a little supper. We became deeply interested in the discussion as to which one of the cast is responsible for a scene in the sketch that lately has fallen so flat that the piece is about to become a failure. We may have been rather noisy and intolerant of interruption by the restaurant people; but the matter was of considerable importance to all of us. You see that we are sober and are not the kind of people who desire to raise disturbances. I hope that the case will not be pressed and that we may be allowed to go."

"Who makes the charge?" asked the sergeant.

"Me," said a white-aproned voice in the rear. "De restaurant sent me to. De gang was raisin' a rough-house and breakin' dishes."

"The dishes were paid for," said the playwright. "They were not broken purposely. In her anger, because we remonstrated with her for spoiling the scene, Miss——"

"It's not true, sergeant," cried the clear voice of Miss Clarice Carroll. In a long coat of tan silk and a red-plumed hat, she bounded before the desk.

"It's not my fault," she cried, indignantly. "How dare they say such a thing! I've played the title rôle ever since it was staged, and if you want to know who made it a success, ask the public—that's all."

"What Miss Carroll says is true in part," said the author. "For five months the comedietta was a drawing card in the best houses. But during the last two weeks it has lost favor. There is one scene in it in which Miss Carroll made a big hit. Now she hardly gets a hand out of it. She spoils it by acting it entirely different from her old way."

"It is not my fault," reiterated the actress.

"There are only two of you on in the scene," argued the playwright, hotly, "you and Delmars, here——"

"Then it's his fault," declared Miss Carroll, with a lightning glance of scorn from her dark eyes. The comedian caught it, and gazed with increased melancholy at the panels of the sergeant's desk.

The night was a dull one in that particular police station.

The sergeant's long-blunted curiosity awoke a little.

"I've heard you," he said to the author. And then he addressed the thin-faced and ascetic-looking lady of the company who played "Aunt Turnip-top" in the little comedy.

"Who do you think spoils the scene you are fussing about?" he asked.

"I'm no knocker," said that lady, "and everybody knows it. So, when I say that Clarice falls down every time in that scene I'm judging her art and not herself. She was great in it once. She does it something fierce now. It'll dope the show if she keeps it up."

The sergeant looked at the comedian.

"You and the lady have this scene together, I understand. I suppose there's no use asking you which one of you queers it?"

The comedian avoided the direct rays from the two fixed stars of Miss Carroll's eyes.

"I don't know," he said, looking down at his patent-leather toes.

"Are you one of the actors?" asked the sergeant of a dwarfish youth with a middle-aged face.

"Why, say!" replied the last Thespian witness, "you don't notice any tin spear in my hands, do you? You haven't heard me shout: 'See, the Emperor comes!' since I've been in here, have you? I guess I'm on the stage long enough for 'em not to start a panic by mistaking me for a thin curl of smoke rising above the footlights."

"In your opinion, if you've got one," said the sergeant, "is the frost that gathers on the scene in question the work of the lady or the gentleman who takes part in it?"

The middle-aged youth looked pained.

"I regret to say," he answered, "that Miss Carroll seems to have lost her grip on that scene. She's all right in the rest of the play, but—but I tell you, sergeant, she can do it—she has done it equal to any of 'em—and she can do it again."

Miss Carroll ran forward, glowing and palpitating.

"Thank you, Jimmy, for the first good word I've had in many a day," she cried. And then she turned her eager face toward the desk.

"I'll show you, sergeant, whether I am to blame. I'll show them whether I can do that scene. Come, Mr. Delmars, let us begin. You will let us, won't you, sergeant?"

"How long will it take?" asked the sergeant, dubiously.

"Eight minutes," said the playwright. "The entire play consumes but thirty."

"You may go ahead," said the sergeant. "Most of you seem to side against the little lady. Maybe she had a right to crack up a saucer or two in that restaurant. We'll see how she does the turn before we take that up."

The matron of the police station had been standing near, listening to the

singular argument. She came nigher and stood near the sergeant's chair. Two
or three of the reserves strolled in, big and yawning.

"Before begining the scene," said the playwright, "and assuming that you
have not seen a production of 'A Gay Coquette,' I will make a brief but necessary explanation. It is a musical-farce-comedy—burlesque-comedietta. As the
title implies, Miss Carroll's rôle is that of a gay, rollicking, mischievous, heartless coquette. She sustains that character throughout the entire comedy part of
the production. And I have designed the extravaganza features so that she may
preserve and present the same coquettish idea.

"Now, the scene in which we take exception to Miss Carroll's acting is called
the 'gorilla dance.' She is costumed to represent a wood nymph, and there is a
great song-and-dance scene with a gorilla—played by Mr. Delmars, the comedian.
A tropical-forest stage is set.

"That used to get four and five recalls. The main thing was the acting and
the dance—it was the funniest thing in New York for five months. Delmar's
song, 'I'll Woo Thee to My Sylvan Home,' while he and Miss Carroll were cutting
hide-and-seek capers among the tropical plants, was a winner."

"What's the trouble with the scene now?" asked the sergeant.

"Miss Carroll spoils it right in the middle of it," said the playwright, wrathfully.

With a wide gesture of her ever-moving arms the actress waved back the little
group of spectators, leaving a space in front of the desk for the scene of her
vindication or fall. Then she whipped off her long tan cloak and tossed it across
the arm of the policeman who still stood officially among them.

Miss Carroll had gone to supper well cloaked, but in the costume of the tropic
wood nymph. A skirt of fern leaves touched her knee; she was like a humming
bird—green and golden and purple.

And then she danced a fluttering, fantastic dance, so agile and light and mazy
in her steps that the other three members of the Carroll Comedy Company broke
into applause at the art of it.

And at the proper time Delmars leaped out at her side, mimicking the uncouth, hideous bounds of the gorilla so funnily that the grizzled sergeant himself
gave a short laugh like the closing of a padlock. They danced together the gorilla
dance, and won a hand from all.

Then began the most fantastic part of the scene—the wooing of the nymph
by the gorilla. It was a kind of dance itself—eccentric and prankish, with the
nymph in coquettish and seductive retreat, followed by the gorilla as he sang
"I'll Woo Thee to My Sylvan Home."

The song was a lyric of merit. The words were nonsense, as befitted the play,
but the music was worthy of something better. Delmars struck into it in a rich
tenor that owned a quality that shamed the flippant words.

During one verse of the song the wood nymph performed the grotesque evolutions designed for the scene. At the middle of the second verse she stood still,
with a strange look on her face, seeming to gaze dreamily into the depths of the
scenic forest. The gorilla's last leap had brought him to her feet, and there he
knelt, holding her hand, until he had finished the haunting lyric that was set in
the absurd comedy like a diamond in a piece of putty.

When Delmars ceased Miss Carroll started, and covered a sudden flow of tears
with both hands.

"There!" cried the playwright, gesticulating with violence; "there you have
it, sergeant. For two weeks she has spoiled that scene in just that manner at
every performance. I have begged her to consider that it is not Ophelia or Juliet
that she is playing. Do you wonder now at our impatience? Tears for the
gorilla song! The play is lost!"

Out of her bewitchment, whatever it was, the wood nymph flared suddenly, and pointed a desperate finger at Delmars.

"It is you—you have done this," she cried, wildly. "You never sang that song that way until lately. It is your doing."

"I give it up," said the sergeant.

And then the gray-haired matron of the police station came forward from behind the sergeant's chair.

"Must an old woman teach you all?" she said. She went up to Miss Carroll and took her hand.

"The man's wearing his heart out for you, my dear. Couldn't you tell it the first note you heard him sing? All of his monkey flip-flops wouldn't have kept it from me. Must you be deaf as well as blind? That's why you couldn't act your part, child. Do you love him or must he be a gorilla for the rest of his days?"

Miss Carroll whirled around and caught Delmars with a lightning glance of her eye. He came toward her, melancholy.

"Did you hear, Mr. Delmars?" she asked, with a catching breath.

"I did," said the comedian. "It is true. I didn't think there was any use. I tried to let you know with the song."

"Silly!" said the matron; "why didn't you speak?"

"No, no," cried the wood nymph, "his way was the best. I didn't know, but—it was just what I wanted, Bobby."

She sprang like a green grasshopper; and the comedian opened his arms, and —smiled.

"Get out of this," roared the desk sergeant to the waiting waiter from the restaurant. "There's nothing doing here for you."

ONE DOLLAR'S WORTH

THE judge of the United States court of the district lying along the Rio Grande border found the following letter one morning in his mail:

JUDGE:

When you sent me up for four years you made a talk. Among other hard things, you called me a rattlesnake. Maybe I am one—anyhow, you hear me rattling now. One year after I got to the pen, my daughter died of—well, they said it was poverty and the disgrace together. You've got a daughter, Judge, and I'm going to make you know how it feels to lose one. And I'm going to bite that district attorney that spoke against me. I'm free now, and I guess I've turned to rattlesnake all right. I feel like one. I don't say much, but this is my rattle. Look out what I strike.

Yours respectfully,
RATTLESNAKE.

Judge Derwent threw the letter carelessly aside. It was nothing new to receive such epistles from desperate men whom he had been called upon to judge. He felt no alarm. Later on he showed the letter to Littlefield, the young district attorney, for Littlefield's name was included in the threat, and the judge was punctilious in matters between himself and his fellow men.

Littlefield honored the rattle of the writer, as far as it concerned himself, with a smile of contempt; but he frowned a little over the reference to the Judge's daughter, for he and Nancy Derwent were to be married in the fall.

Littlefield went to the clerk of the court and looked over the records with him. They decided that the letter might have been sent by Mexico Sam, a half-breed border desperado who had been imprisoned for manslaughter four years before. Then official duties crowded the matter from his mind, and the rattle of the revengeful serpent was forgotten.

Court was in session at Brownsville. Most of the cases to be tried were charges of smuggling, counterfeiting, post-office robberies, and violations of Federal laws along the border. One case was that of a young Mexican, Rafael Ortiz, who had been rounded up by a clever deputy marshal in the act of passing a counterfeit silver dollar. He had been suspected of many such deviations from rectitude, but this was the first time that anything provable had been fixed upon him. Ortiz languished cozily in jail, smoking brown cigarettes and waiting for trial. Kilpatrick, the deputy, brought the counterfeit dollar and handed it to the district attorney in his office in the court-house. The deputy and a reputable druggist were prepared to swear that Ortiz paid for a bottle of medicine with it. The coin was a poor counterfeit, soft, dull-looking, and made principally of lead. It was the day before the morning on which the docket would reach the case of Ortiz, and the district attorney was preparing himself for the trial.

"Not much need of having in high-priced experts to prove the coin's queer, is there, Kil?" smiled Littlefield, as he thumped the dollar down upon the table, where it fell with no more ring than would have come from a lump of putty.

"I guess the Greaser's as good as behind the bars," said the deputy, easing up his holsters. "You've got him dead. If it had been just one time, these Mexicans can't tell good money from bad; but this little yaller rascal belongs to a gang of counterfeiters, I know. This is the first time I've been able to catch him doing the trick. He's got a girl down there in them Mexican jacals on the river bank. I seen her one day when I was watching him. She's as pretty as a red heifer in a flower bed."

Littlefield shoved the counterfeit dollar into his pocket, and slipped his memoranda of the case into an envelope. Just then a bright, winsome face, as frank and jolly as a boy's, appeared in the doorway, and in walked Nancy Derwent.

"Oh, Bob, didn't court adjourn at twelve to-day until to-morrow?" she asked of Littlefield.

"It did," said the district attorney, "and I'm very glad of it. I've got a lot of rulings to look up, and——"

"Now, that's just like you. I wonder you and Father don't turn to law books or rulings or something! I want you to take me out plover-shooting this afternoon. Long Prairie is just alive with them. Don't say no, please! I want to try my new twelve-bore hammerless. I've sent to the livery stable to engage Fly and Bess for the buckboard; they stand fire so nicely. I was sure you would go."

They were to be married in the fall. The glamour was at its height. The plovers won the day—or, rather, the afternoon—over the calf-bound authorities. Littlefield began to put his papers away.

There was a knock at the door. Kilpatrick answered it. A beautiful, dark-eyed girl with a skin tinged with the faintest lemon color walked into the room. A black shawl was thrown over her head and wound once around her neck.

She began to talk in Spanish, a voluble, mournful stream of melancholy music.

Littlefield did not understand Spanish. The deputy did, and he translated her talk by portions, at intervals holding up his hands to check the flow of her words.

"She came to see you, Mr. Littlefield. Her name's Joya Treviñas. She wants to see you about—well, she's mixed up with that Rafael Ortiz. She's his—she's his girl. She says he's innocent. She says she made the money and got him to pass it. Don't you believe her, Mr. Littlefield. That's the way with these Mexican girls; they'll lie, steal, or kill for a fellow when they get stuck on him. Never trust a woman that's in love!"

"Mr. Kilpatrick!"

Nancy Derwent's indignant exclamation caused the deputy to flounder for a moment in attempting to explain that he had misquoted his own sentiments, and then he went on with the translation:

"She says she's willing to take his place in the jail if you'll let him out. She says she was down sick with the fever, and the doctor said she'd die if she didn't have medicine. That's why he passed the lead dollar on the drug store. She says it saved her life. This Rafael seems to be her honey, all right; there's a lot of stuff in her talk about love and such things that you don't want to hear."

It was an old story to the district attorney.

"Tell her," said he, "that I can do nothing. The case comes up in the morning, and he will have to make his fight before the court."

Nancy Derwent was not so hardened. She was looking with sympathetic interest at Joya Treviñas and at Littlefield alternately. The deputy repeated the district attorney's words to the girl. She spoke a sentence or two in a low voice, pulled her shawl closely about her face, and left the room.

"What did she say then?" asked the district attorney.

"Nothing special," said the deputy. "She said: 'If the life of the one'—let's see how it went—'*Si la vida de ella a quien tu amas*—if the life of the girl you love is ever in danger, remember Rafael Ortiz.'"

Kilpatrick strolled out through the corridor in the direction of the marshal's office.

"Can't you do anything for them, Bob?" asked Nancy. "It's such a little thing—just one counterfeit dollar—to ruin the happiness of two lives! She was in danger of death, and he did it to save her. Doesn't the law know the feeling of pity?"

"It hasn't a place in jurisprudence, Nan," said Littlefield, "especially *in re* the district attorney's duty. I'll promise you that the prosecution will not be vindictive; but the man is as good as convicted when the case is called. Witnesses will swear to his passing the bad dollar which I have in my pocket at this moment as 'Exhibit A.' There are no Mexicans on the jury, and it will vote Mr. Greaser guilty without leaving the box."

The plover-shooting was fine that afternoon, and in the excitement of the sport the case of Rafael and the grief of Joya Treviñas was forgotten. The district attorney and Nancy Derwent drove out from the town three miles along a smooth, grassy road, and then struck across a rolling prairie toward a heavy line of timber on Piedra Creek. Beyond this creek lay Long Prairie, the favorite haunt of the plover. As they were nearing the creek they heard the galloping of a horse to their right, and saw a man with black hair and a swarthy face riding toward the woods at a tangent, as if he had come up behind them.

"I've seen that fellow somewhere," said Littlefield, who had a memory for faces, "but I can't exactly place him. Some ranchman, I suppose, taking a short cut home."

They spent an hour on Long Prairie, shooting from the buckboard. Nancy

Derwent, an active, outdoor Western girl, was pleased with her twelve-bore. She had bagged within two brace of her companion's score.

They started homeward at a gentle trot. When within a hundred yards of Piedra Creek a man rode out of the timber directly toward them.

"It looks like the man we saw coming over," remarked Miss Derwent.

As the distance between them lessened, the district attorney suddenly pulled up his team sharply, with his eyes fixed upon the advancing horseman. That individual had drawn a Winchester from its scabbard on his saddle and thrown it over his arm.

"Now I know you, Mexico Sam!" muttered Littlefield to himself. "It *was* you who shook your rattles in that gentle epistle."

Mexico Sam did not leave things long in doubt. He had a nice eye in all matters relating to firearms, so when he was within good rifle range, but outside of danger from No. 8 shot, he threw up his Winchester and opened fire upon the occupants of the buckboard.

The first shot cracked the back of the seat within the two-inch space between the shoulders of Littlefield and Miss Derwent. The next went through the dashboard and Littlefield's trouser leg.

The district attorney hustled Nancy out of the buckboard to the ground. She was a little pale, but asked no questions. She had the frontier instinct that accepts conditions in an emergency without superfluous argument. They kept their guns in hand, and Littlefield hastily gathered some handfuls of cartridges from the pasteboard box on the seat and crowded them into his pockets.

"Keep behind the horses, Nan," he commanded. "That fellow is a ruffian I sent to prison once. He's trying to get even. He knows our shot won't hurt him at that distance."

"All right, Bob," said Nancy, steadily. "I'm not afraid. But you come close, too. Whoa, Bess; stand still, now!"

She stroked Bess's mane. Littlefield stood with his gun ready, praying that the desperado would come within range.

But Mexico Sam was playing his vendetta along safe lines. He was a bird of different feather from the plover. His accurate eye drew an imaginary line of circumference around the area of danger from bird-shot, and upon this line he rode. His horse wheeled to the right, and as his victims rounded to the safe side of their equine breastwork he sent a ball through the district attorney's hat. Once he miscalculated in making a detour, and overstepped his margin. Littlefield's gun flashed, and Mexico Sam ducked his head to the harmless patter of the shot. A few of them stung his horse, which pranced promptly back to the safety line.

The desperado fired again. A little cry came from Nancy Derwent. Littlefield whirled, with blazing eyes, and saw the blood trickling down her cheek.

"I'm not hurt, Bob—only a splinter struck me. I think he hit one of the wheel-spokes."

"Lord!" groaned Littlefield. "If I only had a charge of buckshot!"

The ruffian got his horse still, and took careful aim. Fly gave a snort and fell in the harness, struck in the neck. Bess, now disabused of the idea that plover were being fired at, broke her traces and galloped wildly away. Mexican Sam sent a ball neatly through the fullness of Nancy Derwent's shooting jacket.

"Lie down—lie down!" snapped Littlefield. "Close to the horse—flat on the ground—so." He almost threw her upon the grass against the back of the recumbent Fly. Oddly enough, at that moment the words of the Mexican girl returned to his mind:

"If the life of the girl you love is ever in danger, remember Rafael Ortiz."

Littlefield uttered an exclamation.

"Open fire on him, Nan, across the horse's back! Fire as fast as you can! You can't hurt him, but keep him dodging shot for one minute while I try to work a little scheme."

Nancy gave a quick glance at Littlefield, and saw him take out his pocket-knife and open it. Then she turned her face to obey orders, keeping up a rapid fire at the enemy.

Mexico Sam waited patiently until this inocuous fusillade ceased. He had plenty of time, and he did not care to risk the chance of a bird-shot in his eye if it could be avoided by a little caution. He pulled his heavy Stetson low down over his face until the shots ceased. Then he drew a little nearer, and fired with careful aim at what he could see of his victims above the fallen horse.

Neither of them moved. He urged his horse a few steps nearer. He saw the district attorney rise to one knee, and deliberately level his shotgun. He pulled his hat down and awaited the harmless rattle of the tiny pellets.

The shotgun blazed with a heavy report. Mexico Sam sighed, turned limp all over, and slowly fell from his horse—a dead rattlesnake.

At ten o'clock the next morning court opened, and the case of the United States *versus* Rafael Ortiz was called. The district attorney, with his arm in a sling, rose and addressed the court.

"May it please your honor," he said, "I desire to enter a *nolle pros.* in this case. Even though the defendant should be guilty, there is not sufficient evidence in the hands of the government to secure a conviction. The piece of counterfeit coin upon the identity of which the case was built is not now available as evidence. I ask, therefore. that the case be stricken off."

At the noon recess, Kilpatrick strolled into the district attorney's office.

"I've just been down to take a squint at old Mexico Sam," said the deputy. "They've got him laid out. Old Mexico was a tough outfit, I reckon. The boys was wonderin' down there what you shot him with. Some said it must have been nails. I never see a gun carry anything to make holes like he had."

"I shot him," said the district attorney, "with Exhibit A of your counterfeiting case. Lucky thing for me—and somebody else—that it was as bad money as it was! It sliced up into slugs very nicely. Say, Kil, can't you go down to the jacals and find where that Mexican girl lives? Miss Derwent wants to know."

A NEWSPAPER STORY

AT 8 A. M. it lay on Giuseppi's news-stand, still damp from the presses. Giuseppi, with the cunning of his ilk, philandered on the opposite corner leaving his patrons to help themselves, no doubt on a theory related to the hypothesis of the watched pot.

This particular newspaper was, according to its custom and design, an educator, a guide, a monitor, a champion, and a household counsellor and *vade mecum*.

From its many excellencies might be selected three editorials. One was in simple and chaste but illuminating language directed to parents and teachers, deprecating corporal punishment for children.

Another was an accusive and significant warning addressed to a notorious labor leader who was on the point of instigating his clients to a troublesome strike.

The third was an eloquent demand that the police force be sustained and aided in everything that tended to increase its efficiency as public guardians and servants.

Besides these more important chidings and requisitions upon the store of good citizenship was a wise prescription or form of procedure laid out by the editor of the heart-to-heart column in the specific case of a young man who had complained of the obduracy of his lady love, teaching him how he might win her.

Again, there was, on the beauty page, a complete answer to a young lady inquirer who desired admonition toward the securing of bright eyes, rosy cheeks, and a beautiful countenance.

One other item requiring special cognizance was a brief "personal," running thus:

DEAR JACK:—Forgive me. You were right. Meet me at corner of Madison and —th at 8:30 this morning. We leave at noon.

PENITENT.

At 8 o'clock a young man with a haggard look and the feverish gleam of unrest in his eye dropped a penny and picked up the top paper as he passed Giuseppi's stand. A sleepless night had left him a late riser. There was an office to be reached by nine, and a shave and a hasty cup of coffee to be crowded into the interval.

He visited his barber shop and then hurried on his way. He pocketed his paper, meditating a belated perusal of it at the luncheon hour. At the next corner it fell from his pocket, carrying with it his pair of new gloves. Three blocks he walked, missed the gloves and turned back fuming.

Just on the half-hour he reached the corner where lay the gloves and paper. But he strangely ignored that which he had come to seek. He was holding two little hands as tightly as ever he could and looking into two penitent brown eyes, while joy rioted in his heart.

"Dear Jack," she said, "I knew you would be here on time."

"I wonder what she means by that," he was saying to himself; "but it's all right, it's all right."

A big wind puffed out of the west, picked up the paper from the sidewalk, opened it and sent it flying and whirling down a side street. Up that street was driving a skittish bay to a spider-wheel buggy the young man who had written to the heart-to-heart editor for a recipe that he might win her for whom he sighed.

The wind, with a prankish flurry, flapped the flying newspaper against the face of the skittish bay. There was a lengthened streak of bay mingled with the red of running gear that stretched itself out for four blocks. Then a water-hydrant played its part in the cosmogony, the buggy became match wood as foreordained, and the driver rested very quietly where he had been flung on the asphalt in front of a certain brownstone mansion.

They came out and had him inside very promptly. And there was one who made herself a pillow for his head, and cared for no curious eyes, bending over and saying, "Oh, it was you; it was you all the time, Bobby! Couldn't you see it? And if you die, why, so must I, and——"

But in all this wind we must hurry to keep in touch with our paper.

Policeman O'Brine arrested it as a character dangerous to traffic. Straightening its dishevelled leaves with his big, slow fingers, he stood a few feet from the family entrance of the Shandon Bells Café. One headline he spelled out ponderously. "The Papers to the Front in a Move to Help the Police."

But, whist! The voice of Danny, the head bartender, through the crack of the door: "Here's a nip for ye, Mike, ould man."

Behind the widespread, amicable columns of the press Policeman O'Brine receives swiftly his nip of the real stuff. He moves away, stalwart, refreshed, fortified, to his duties. Might not the editor man view with pride the early, the spiritual, the literal fruit that had blessed his labors.

Policeman O'Brine folded the paper and poked it playfully under the arm of a small boy that was passing. That boy was named Johnny, and he took the paper home with him. His sister was named Gladys, and she had written to the beauty editor of the paper asking for the practicable touchstone of beauty. That was weeks ago, and she had ceased to look for an answer. Gladys was a pale girl, with dull eyes and a discontented expression. She was dressing to go up to the avenue to get some braid. Beneath her skirt she pinned two leaves of the paper Johnny had brought. When she walked the rustling sound was an exact imitation of the real thing.

On the street she met the Brown girl from the flat below and stopped to talk. The Brown girl turned green. Only silk at $5 a yard could make the sound that she heard when Gladys moved. The Brown girl, consumed by jealousy, said something spiteful and went her way, with pinched lips.

Gladys proceeded toward the avenue. Her eyes now sparkled like jagerfonteins. A rosy bloom visited her cheeks; a triumphant, subtle, vivifying smile transfigured her face. She was beautiful. Could the beauty editor have seen her then! There was something in her answer in the paper, I believe, about cultivating a kind feeling toward others in order to make plain features attractive.

The labor leader against whom the paper's solemn and weighty editorial injunction was laid was the father of Gladys and Johnny. He picked up the remains of the journal from which Gladys had ravished a cosmetic of silken sounds. The editorial did not come under his eye, but instead it was greeted by one of those ingenious and specious puzzle problems that enthrall alike the simpleton and the sage.

The labor leader tore off half of the page, provided himself with table, pencil, and paper and glued himself to the puzzle.

Three hours later, after waiting vainly for him at the appointed place, other more conservative leaders declared and ruled in favor of arbitration, and the strike with its attendant dangers was averted. Subsequent editions of the paper referred, in colored inks, to the clarion tone of its successful denunciation of the labor leader's intended designs.

The remaining leaves of the active journal also went loyally to the proving of its potency.

When Johnny returned from school he sought a secluded spot and removed the missing columns from the inside of his clothing, where they had been artfully distributed so as to successfully defend such areas as are generally attacked during scholastic castigations. Johnny attended a private school and had had trouble with his teacher. As has been said, there was an excellent editorial against corporal punishment in that morning's issue, and no doubt it had its effect.

After this can any one doubt the power of the press?

TOMMY'S BURGLAR

At ten o'clock P. M. Felicia, the maid, left by the basement door with the policeman to get a raspberry phosphate around the corner. She detested the policeman and objected earnestly to the arrangement. She pointed out, not unreasonably, that she might have been allowed to fall asleep over one of St. George Rathbone's novels on the third floor, but she was overruled. Raspberries and cops were not created for nothing.

The burglar got into the house without much difficulty; because we must have action and not too much description in a 2,000-word story.

In the dining room he opened the slide of his dark lantern. With a brace and centrebit he began to bore into the lock of the silver-closet.

Suddenly a click was heard. The room was flooded with electric light. The dark velvet portières parted to admit a fair-haired boy of eight in pink pajamas, bearing a bottle of olive oil in his hand.

"Are you a burglar?" he asked, in a sweet, childish voice.

"Listen to that," exclaimed the man, in a hoarse voice. "Am I a burglar? Wot do you suppose I have a three days' growth of bristly beard on my face for, and a cap with flaps? Give me the oil, quick, and let me grease the bit, so I won't wake up your mamma, who is lying down with a headache, and left you in charge of Felicia who has been faithless to her trust."

"Oh, dear," said Tommy, with a sigh. "I thought you would be more up-to-date. This oil is for the salad when I bring lunch from the pantry for you. And mamma and papa have gone to the Metropolitan to hear De Reszke. But that isn't my fault. It only shows how long the story has been knocking around among the editors. If the author had been wise he'd have changed it to Caruso in the proofs."

"Be quiet," hissed the burglar, under his breath. "If you raise an alarm I'll wring your neck like a rabbit's."

"Like a chicken's," corrected Tommy. "You had that wrong. You don't wring rabbits' necks."

"Aren't you afraid of me?" asked the burglar.

"You know I'm not," answered Tommy. "Don't you suppose I know fact from fiction? If this wasn't a story I'd yell like an Indian when I saw you; and you'd probably tumble downstairs and get pinched on the sidewalk."

"I see," said the burglar, "that you're on to your job. Go on with the performance."

Tommy seated himself in an armchair and drew his toes up under him.

"Why do you go around robbing strangers, Mr. Burglar? Have you no friends?"

"I see what you're driving at," said the burglar, with a dark frown. "It's the same old story. Your innocence and childish insouciance is going to lead me back into an honest life. Every time I crack a crib where there's a kid around, it happens."

"Would you mind gazing with wolfish eyes at the plate of cold beef that the butler has left on the dining table?" said Tommy. "I'm afraid it's growing late."

The burglar accommodated.

"Poor man," said Tommy. "You must be hungry. If you will please stand in a listless attitude I will get you something to eat."

The boy brought a roast chicken, a jar of marmalade, and a bottle of wine from the pantry. The burglar seized a knife and fork sullenly.

"It's only been an hour," he grumbled, "since I had a lobster and a pint of musty ale up on Broadway. I wish these story writers would let a fellow have a pepsin tablet, anyhow, between feeds."

"My papa writes books," remarked Tommy.

The burglar jumped to his feet quickly.

"You said he had gone to the opera," he hissed, hoarsely and with immediate suspicion.

"I ought to have explained," said Tommy. "He didn't buy the tickets." The burglar sat again and toyed with the wishbone.

"Why do you burgle houses?" asked the boy, wonderingly.

"Because," replied the burglar, with a sudden flow of tears. "God bless my little brown-haired boy Bessie at home."

"Ah," said Tommy, wrinkling his nose, "you got that answer in the wrong place. You want to tell your hard-luck story before you pull out the child stop."

"Oh, yes," said the burglar, "I forgot. Well, once I lived up in Milwaukee, and——"

"Take the silver," said Tommy, rising from his chair.

"Hold on," said the burglar. "But I moved away. I could find no other employment. For a while I managed to support my wife and child by passing confederate money; but, alas! I was forced to give that up because it did not belong to the union. I became desperate and a burglar."

"Have you ever fallen into the hands of the police?" asked Tommy.

"I said 'burglar,' not 'beggar,' " answered the cracksman.

"After you finish your lunch," said Tommy, "and experience the usual change of heart, how shall we wind up the story?"

"Suppose," said the burglar, thoughtfully, "that Tony Pastor turns out earlier than usual to-night, and your father gets in from 'Parsifal' at 10:30. I am thoroughly repentant because you have made me think of my own little boy Bessie, and——"

"Say," said Tommy, "haven't you got that wrong?"

"Not on your colored crayon drawings by B. Cory Kilvert," said the burglar. "It's always a Bessie that I have at home, artlessly prattling to the pale-cheeked burglar's bride. As I was saying, your father opens the front door just as I am departing with admonitions and sandwiches that you have wrapped up for me. Upon recognizing me as an old Harvard classmate he starts back in——"

"Not in surprise?" interrupted Tommy, with wide-open eyes.

"He starts back in the doorway," continued the burglar. And then he rose to his feet and began to shout: "Rah, rah, rah! rah, rah, rah! rah, rah, rah!"

"Well," said Tommy, wonderingly, "that's the first time I ever knew a burglar to give a college yell when he was burglarizing a house, even in a story."

"That's one on you," said the burglar, with a laugh. "I was practising the dramatization. If this is put on the stage that college touch is about the only thing that will make it go."

Tommy looked his admiration.

"You're on, all right," he said.

"And there's another mistake you've made," said the burglar. "You should have gone some time ago and brought me the $9 gold piece your mother gave you on your birthday to take to Bessie."

"But she didn't give it to me to take to Bessie," said Tommy, pouting.

"Come, come!" said the burglar, sternly. "It's not nice of you to take advantage because the story contains an ambiguous sentence. You know what I mean. It's mighty little I get out of these fictional jobs, anyhow. I lose all the loot, and I have to reform every time; and all the swag I'm allowed is the blamed little fol-de-rols and luck-pieces that you kids hand over. Why, in one story, all I got was a kiss from a little girl who came in on me when I was opening a safe. And it tasted of molasses candy, too. I've a good notion to tie this table cover over your head and keep on into the silver-closet."

"Oh, no, you haven't," said Tommy, wrapping his arms around his knees. "Because if you did no editor would buy the story. You know you've got to preserve the unities."

"So've you," said the burglar, rather glumly. "Instead of sitting here talking impudence and taking the bread out of a poor man's mouth, what you'd like to be doing is hiding under the bed and screeching at the top of your voice."

"You're right, old man," said Tommy, heartily. "I wonder what they make us do it for? I think the S. P. C. C. ought to interfere. I'm sure it's neither agreeable nor usual for a kid of my age to butt in when a full-grown burglar is at work and offer him a red sled and a pair of skates not to awaken his sick mother. And look how they make the burglars act! You'd think editors would know—but what's the use?"

The burglar wiped his hands on the tablecloth and arose with a yawn.

"Well, let's get through with it," he said. "God bless you, my little boy! you have saved a man from committing a crime this night. Bessie shall pray for you as soon as I get home and give her her orders. I shall never burglarize another house—at least not until the June magazines are out. It'll be your little sister's turn then to run in on me while I am abstracting the U. S. 4 per cent. from the tea urn and buy me off with her coral necklace and a falsetto kiss."

"You haven't got all the kicks coming to you," sighed Tommy, crawling out of his chair. "Think of the sleep I'm losing. But it's tough on both of us, old man. I wish you could get out of the story and really rob somebody. Maybe you'll have the chance if they dramatize us."

"Never!" said the burglar, gloomily. "Between the box office and my better impulses that your leading juveniles are supposed to awaken and the magazines that pay on publication, I guess I'll always be broke."

"I'm sorry," said Tommy, sympathetically. "But I can't help myself any more than you can. It's one of the canons of household fiction that no burglar shall be successful. The burglar must be foiled by a kid like me, or by a young lady heroine, or at the last moment by his old pal, Red Mike, who recognizes the house as one in which he used to be the coachman. You have got the worst end of it in any kind of a story."

"Well, I suppose I must be clearing out now," said the burglar, taking up his lantern and bracebit.

"You have to take the rest of this chicken and the bottle of wine with you for Bessie and her mother," said Tommy, calmly.

"But confound it," exclaimed the burglar, in an annoyed tone, "they don't want it. I've got five cases of Château de Beychsvelle at home that was bottled in 1853. That claret of yours is corked. And you couldn't get either of them to look at a chicken unless it was stewed in champagne. You know, after I get out of the story I don't have so many limitations. I make a turn now and then."

"Yes, but you must take them," said Tommy, loading his arms with the bundles.

"Bless you, young master!" recited the burglar, obedient. "Second-Story Saul will never forget you. And now hurry and let me out, kid. Our 2,000 words must be nearly up."

Tommy led the way through the hall toward the front door. Suddenly the burglar stopped and called to him softly: "Ain't there a cop out there in front somewhere sparking the girl?"

"Yes," said Tommy, "but what——"

"I'm afraid he'll catch me," said the burglar. "You mustn't forget that this is fiction."

"Great head!" said Tommy, turning. "Come out by the back door."

A CHAPARRAL CHRISTMAS GIFT

The original cause of the trouble was about twenty years in growing.

At the end of that time it was worth it.

Had you lived anywhere within fifty miles of Sundown Ranch you would have heard of it. It possessed a quantity of jet-black hair, a pair of extremely frank, deep-brown eyes, and a laugh that rippled across the prairie like the sound of a hidden brook. The name of it was Rosita McMullen; and she was the daughter of old man McMullen of the Sundown Sheep Ranch.

There came riding on red roan steeds—or, to be more explicit, on a paint and flea-bitten sorrel—two wooers. One was Madison Lane, and the other was the Frio Kid. But at that time they did not call him the Frio Kid, for he had not earned the honors of special nomenclature. His name was simply Johnny McRoy.

It must not be supposed that these two were the sum of the agreeable Rosita's admirers. The bronchos of a dozen others champed their bits at the long hitching rack of the Sundown Ranch. Many were the sheeps'-eyes that were cast in those savannas that did not belong to the flocks of Dan McMullen. But of all the cavaliers, Madison Lane and Johnny McRoy galloped far ahead, wherefore they are to be chronicled.

Madison Lane, a young cattleman from the Nueces country, won the race. He and Rosita were married one Christmas day. Armed, hilarious, vociferous, magnanimous, the cowmen and the sheepmen, laying aside their hereditary hatred, joined forces to celebrate the occasion.

Sundown Ranch was sonorous with the cracking of jokes and sixshooters, the shine of buckles and bright eyes, the outspoken congratulations of the herders of kine.

But while the wedding feast was at its liveliest there descended upon it Johnny McRoy, bitten by jealousy, like one possessed.

"I'll give you a Christmas present," he yelled, shrilly, at the door, with his .45 in his hand. Even then he had some reputation as an offhand shot.

His first bullet cut a neat underbit in Madison Lane's right ear. The barrel of his gun moved an inch. The next shot would have been the bride's had not Carson, a sheepman, possessed a mind with triggers somewhat well oiled and in repair. The guns of the wedding party had been hung, in their belts, upon nails in the wall when they sat at table, as a concession to good taste. But Carson, with great promptness, hurled his plate of roast venison and frijoles at McRoy, spoiling his aim. The second bullet then, only shattered the white petals of a Spanish dagger flower suspended two feet above Rosita's head.

The guests spurned their chairs and jumped for their weapons. It was considered an improper act to shoot the bride and groom at a wedding. In about six seconds there were twenty or so bullets due to be whizzing in the direction of Mr. McRoy.

"I'll shoot better next time," yelled Johnny; "and there'll be a next time." He backed rapidly out of the door.

Carson, the sheepman, spurred on to attempt further exploits by the success of his plate throwing, was first to reach the door. McRoy's bullet from the darkness laid him low.

The cattlemen then swept out upon him, calling for vengeance, for, while the slaughter of a sheepman has not always lacked condonement, it was a decided misdemeanor in this instance. Carson was innocent; he was no accomplice at the matrimonial proceedings; nor had any one heard him quote the line "Christmas comes but once a year" to the guests.

But the sortie failed in its vengeance. McRoy was on his horse and away, shouting back curses and threats as he galloped into the concealing chaparral.

That night was the birthnight of the Frio Kid. He became the "bad man" of that portion of the State. The rejection of his suit by Miss McMullen turned him to a dangerous man. When officers went after him for the shooting of Carson, he killed two of them, and entered upon the life of an outlaw. He became a marvellous shot with either hand. He would turn up in towns and settlements, raise a quarrel at the slightest opportunity, pick off his man, and laugh at the officers of the law. He was so cool, so deadly, so rapid, so inhumanly bloodthirsty that none but faint attempts were ever made to capture him. When he was at last shot and killed by a little one-armed Mexican who was nearly dead himself from fright, the Frio Kid had the deaths of eighteen men on his head. About half of these were killed in fair duels depending upon the quickness of the draw. The other half were men whom he assassinated from absolute wantonness and cruelty.

Many tales are told along the border of his impudent courage and daring. But he was not one of the breed of desperadoes who have seasons of generosity and even of softness. They say he never had mercy on the object of his anger. Yet at this and every Christmastide it is well to give each one credit, if it can be done, for whatever speck of good he may have possessed. If the Frio Kid ever did a kindly act or felt a throb of generosity in his heart it was once at such a time and season, and this is the way it happened.

One who has been crossed in love should never breathe the odor of the blossoms of the ratama tree. It stirs the memory to a dangerous degree.

One December in the Frio country there was a ratama tree in full bloom, for the winter had been as warm as springtime. That way rode the Frio Kid and his satellite and co-murderer, Mexican Frank. The kid reined in his mustang, and sat in his saddle, thoughtful and grim, with dangerously narrowing eyes. The rich, sweet scent touched him somewhere beneath his ice and iron.

"I don't know what I've been thinking about, Mex," he remarked in his usual mild drawl, "to have forgot all about a Christmas present I got to give. I'm going to ride over to-morrow night and shoot Madison Lane in his own house. He got my girl—Rosita would have had me if he hadn't cut into the game. I wonder why I happened to overlook it up to now?"

"Ah, shucks, Kid," said Mexican, "don't talk foolishness. You know you can't get within a mile of Mad Lane's house to-morrow night. I see old man Allen day before yesterday, and he says Mad is going to have Christmas doings at his house. You remember how you shot up the festivities when Mad was married, and about the threats you made? Don't you suppose Mad Lane'll kind of keep his eye open for a certain Mr. Kid? You plumb make me tired, Kid, with such remarks."

"I'm going," repeated the Frio Kid, without heat, "to go to Madison Lane's Christmas doings, and kill him. I ought to have done it a long time ago. Why, Mex, just two weeks ago I dreamed me and Rosita was married instead of her and him; and we was living in a house, and I could see her smiling at me, and —oh! h—l, Mex, he got her; and I'll get him—yes, sir, on Christmas Eve he got her, and then's when I'll get him."

"There's other ways of committing suicide," advised Mexican. "Why don't you go and surrender to the sheriff?"

"I'll get him," said the Kid.

Christmas Eve fell as balmy as April. Perhaps there was a hint of far-away frostiness in the air, but it tingled like seltzer, perfumed faintly with late prairie blossoms and the mesquite grass.

When night came the five or six rooms of the ranch-house were brightly lit.

In one room was a Christmas tree, for the Lanes had a boy of three, and a dozen or more guests were expected from the nearer ranches.

At nightfall Madison Lane called aside Jim Belcher and three other cowboys employed on his ranch.

"Now, boys," said Lane, "keep your eyes open. Walk around the house and watch the road well. All of you know the 'Frio Kid,' as they call him now, and if you see him, open fire on him without asking any questions. I'm not afraid of his coming around, but Rosita is. She's been afraid he'd come in on us every Christmas since we were married."

The guests had arrived in buckboards and on horseback, and were making themselves comfortable inside.

The evening went along pleasantly. The guests enjoyed and praised Rosita's excellent supper, and afterward the men scattered in groups about the rooms or on the broad "gallery," smoking and chatting.

The Christmas tree, of course, delighted the youngsters, and above all were they pleased when Santa Claus himself in magnificent white beard and furs appeared and began to distribute the toys.

"It's my papa," announced Billy Sampson, aged six. "I've seen him wear 'em before."

Berkly, a sheepman, an old friend of Lane, stopped Rosita as she was passing by him on the gallery, where he was sitting smoking.

"Well, Mrs. Lane," said he, "I suppose by this Christmas you've gotten over being afraid of that fellow McRoy, haven't you? Madison and I have talked about it, you know."

"Very nearly," said Rosita, smiling, "but I am still nervous sometimes. I shall never forget that awful time when he came so near to killing us."

"He's the most cold-hearted villain in the world," said Berkly. "The citizens all along the border ought to turn out and hunt him down like a wolf."

"He has committed awful crimes," said Rosita, "but—I—don't—know. I think there is a spot of good somewhere in everybody. He was not always bad—that I know."

Rosita turned into the hallway between the rooms. Santa Claus, in muffling whiskers and furs, was just coming through.

"I heard what you said through the window, Mrs. Lane," he said. "I was just going down in my pocket for a Christmas present for your husband. But I've left one for you, instead. It's in the room to your right."

"Oh, thank you, kind Santa Claus," said Rosita, brightly.

Rosita went into the room, while Santa Claus stepped into the cooler air of the yard.

She found no one in the room but Madison.

"Where is my present that Santa said he left for me in here?" she asked.

"Haven't seen anything in the way of a present," said her husband, laughing, "unless he could have meant me."

The next day Gabriel Radd, the foreman of the XO Ranch, dropped into the post-office at Loma Alta.

"Well, the Frio Kid's got his dose of lead at last," he remarked to the postmaster.

"That so? How'd it happen?"

"One of old Sanchez's Mexican sheep herders did it!—think of it! the Frio Kid killed by a sheep herder! The Greaser saw him riding along past his camp about twelve o'clock last night, and was so skeered that he up with a Winchester and let him have it. Funniest part of it was that the Kid was dressed all up with white Angora-skin whiskers and a regular Santy Claus rig-out from head to foot. Think of the Frio Kid playing Santy!"

A LITTLE LOCAL COLOR

I MENTIONED to Rivington that I was in search of characteristic New York scenes and incidents—something typical, I told him, without necessarily having to spell the first syllable with an "i."

"Oh, for your writing business," said Rivington; "you couldn't have applied to a better shop. What I don't know about little old New York wouldn't make a sonnet to a sunbonnet. I'll put you right in the middle of so much local color that you won't know whether you are a magazine cover or in the erysipelas ward. When do you want to begin?"

Rivington is a young-man-about-town and a New Yorker by birth, preference, and incommutability.

I told him that I would be glad to accept his escort and guardianship so that I might take notes of Manhattan's grand, gloomy, and peculiar idiosyncrasies, and that the time of so doing would be at his own convenience.

"We'll begin this very evening," said Rivington, himself interested, like a good fellow. "Dine with me at seven, and then I'll steer you up against metropolitan phases so thick you'll have to have a kinetoscope to record 'em."

So I dined with Rivington pleasantly at his club, in Forty-eleventh Street, and then we set forth in pursuit of the elusive tincture of affairs.

As we came out of the club there stood two men on the sidewalk near the steps in earnest conversation.

"And by what process of ratiocination," said one of them, "do you arrive at the conclusion that the division of society into producing and non-possessing classes predicates failure when compared with competitive systems that are monopolizing in tendency and result inimically to industrial evolution?"

"Oh, come off your perch!" said the other man, who wore glasses. "Your premises won't come out in the wash. You wind-jammers who apply bandy-legged theories to concrete categorical syllogisms and logical conclusions skally-bootin' into the infinitesimal ragbag. You can't pull my leg with an old sophism with whiskers on it. You quote Marx and Hyndman and Kautsky—what are they?—shines! Tolstoi?—his garret is full of rats. I put it to you over the home-plate that the idea of a coöperative commonwealth and an abolishment of competitive systems simply takes the rag off the bush and gives me hyperesthesia of the roopteetoop! The skookum house for yours!"

I stopped a few yards away and took out my little notebook.

"Oh, come ahead," said Rivington, somewhat nervously; "you don't want to listen to that."

"Why, man," I whispered, "this is just what I do want to hear. These slang types are among your city's most distinguishing features. Is this the Bowery variety? I really must hear more of it."

"If I follow you," said the man who had spoken first, "you do not believe it possible to reorganize society on the basis of common interest?"

"Shinny on your own side!" said the man with glasses. "You never heard any such music from my foghorn. What I said was that I did not believe it practicable just now. The guys with wads are not in the frame of mind to slack upon the mazuma, and the man with the portable tin banqueting canister isn't exactly ready to join the Bible class. You can bet your variegated socks that the situation is all spiflicated up from the Battery to breakfast! What the country needs is for some bully old bloke like Cobden or some wise guy like old Ben Franklin to sashay up to the front and biff the nigger's head with the baseball. Do you catch my smoke? What?"

Rivington pulled me by the arm impatiently.

"Please come on," he said. "Let's go see something. This isn't what you want."

"Indeed, it is," I said resisting. "This tough talk is the very stuff that counts. There is a picturesqueness about the speech of the lower order of people that is quite unique. Did you say that this is the Bowery variety of slang?"

"Oh, well," said Rivington, giving it up, "I'll tell you straight. That's one of our college professors talking. He ran down for a day or two at the club. It's a sort of fad with him lately to use slang in his conversation. He thinks it improves language. The man he is talking to is one of New York's famous social economists. Now will you come on? You can't use that, you know."

"No," I agreed; "I can't use that. Would you call that typical of New York?"

"Of course not," said Rivington, with a sigh of relief. "I'm glad you see the difference. But if you want to hear the real old tough Bowery slang I'll take you down where you'll get your fill of it."

"I would like it," I said; "that is, if it's the real thing. I've often read it in books, but I never heard it. Do you think it will be dangerous to go unprotected among those characters?"

"Oh, no," said Rivington; "not at this time of night. To tell the truth, I haven't been along the Bowery in a long time, but I know it as well as I do Broadway. We'll look up some of the typical Bowery boys and get them to talk. It'll be worth your while. They talk a peculiar dialect that you won't hear anywhere else on earth."

Rivington and I went east in a Forty-second Street car and then south on the Third Avenue line.

At Houston Street we got off and walked.

"We are now on the famous Bowery," said Rivington; "the Bowery celebrated in song and story."

We passed block after block of "gents'" furnishing stores—the windows full of shirts with prices attached and cuffs inside. In other windows were neckties and no shirts. People walked up and down the sidewalks.

"In some ways," said I, "this reminds me of Kokomono, Ind., during the peach-crating season."

Rivington was nettled.

"Step into one of these saloons or vaudeville shows," said he, "with a large roll of money, and see how quickly the Bowery will sustain its reputation."

"You make impossible conditions," said I, coldly.

By and by Rivington stopped and said we were in the heart of the Bowery. There was a policeman on the corner whom Rivington knew.

"Hallo, Donahue!" said my guide. "How goes it? My friend and I are down this way looking up a bit of local color. He's anxious to meet one of the Bowery types. Can't you put us on to something genuine in that line—something that's got the color, you know?"

Policeman Donahue turned himself about ponderously, his florid face full of good-nature. He pointed with his club down the street.

"Sure!" he said, huskily. "Here comes a lad now that was born on the Bowery and knows every inch of it. If he's ever been above Bleecker Street he's kept it to himself."

A man about twenty-eight or twenty-nine, with a smooth face, was sauntering toward us with his hands in his coat pockets. Policeman Donahue stopped him with a courteous wave of his club.

"Evening, Kerry," he said. "Here's a couple of gents, friends of mine, that want to hear you spiel something about the Bowery. Can you reel 'em off a few yards?"

"Certainly, Donahue," said the young man, pleasantly. "Good evening, gentlemen," he said to us, with a pleasant smile. Donahue walked off on his beat.

"This is the goods," whispered Rivington, nudging me with his elbow. "Look at his jaw!"

"Say, cull," said Rivington, pushing back his hat, "wot's doin'? Me and my friend's taking a look down de old line—see? De copper tipped us off dat you was wise to de Bowery. Is dat right?"

I could not help admiring Rivington's power of adapting himself to his surroundings.

"Donahue was right," said the young man, frankly; "I was brought up on the Bowery. I have been newsboy, teamster, pugilist, member of an organized band of 'toughs,' bartender, and a 'sport' in various meanings of the word. The experience certainly warrants the supposition that I have at least a passing acquaintance with a few phases of Bowery life. I will be pleased to place whatever knowledge and experience I have at the service of my friend Donahue's friends."

Rivington seemed ill at ease.

"I say," he said—somewhat entreatingly, "I thought—you're not stringing us, are you? It isn't just the kind of talk we expected. You haven't even said 'Hully gee!' once. Do you really belong on the Bowery?"

"I am afraid," said the Bowery boy, smilingly, "that at some time you have been enticed into one of the dives of literature and had the counterfeit coin of the Bowery passed upon you. The 'argot' to which you doubtless refer was the invention of certain of your literary 'discoverers' who invaded the unknown wilds below Third Avenue and put strange sounds into the mouths of the inhabitants. Safe in their homes far to the north and west, the credulous readers who were beguiled by this new 'dialect' perused and believed. Like Marco Polo and Mungo Park—pioneers indeed, but ambitious souls who could not draw the line of demarcation between discovery and invention—the literary bones of these explorers are dotting the trackless wastes of the subway. While it is true that after the publication of the mythical language attributed to the dwellers along the Bowery certain of its pat phrases and apt metaphors were adopted and, to a limited extent, used in this locality, it was because our people are prompt in assimilating whatever is to their commercial advantage. To the tourists who visited our newly discovered clime, and who expressed a realization of their literary guide books, they supplied the demands of the market.

"But perhaps I am wandering from the question. In what way can I assist you, gentlemen? I beg you will believe that the hospitality of the streets is extended to all. There are, I regret to say, many catchpenny places of entertainment, but I cannot conceive that they would entice you."

I felt Rivington lean somewhat heavily against me.

"Say!" he remarked, with uncertain utterance; "come and have a drink with us."

"Thank you, but I never drink. I find that alcohol, even in the smallest quantities, alters the perspective. And I must preserve my perspective, for I am studying the Bowery. I have lived in it nearly thirty years, and I am just beginning to understand its heartbeats. It is like a great river fed by a hundred alien streams. Each influx brings strange seeds on its flood, strange silt and weeds, and now and then a flower of rare promise. To construe this river requires a man who can build dykes against the overflow, who is a naturalist, a geologist, a humanitarian, a diver, and a strong swimmer. I love my Bowery. It was my cradle and is my inspiration. I have published one book. The critics have been kind. I put my heart in it. I am writing another, into which I hope to put both heart and brain. Consider me your guide, gentlemen. Is there anything I can take you to see, any place to which I can conduct you?"

I was afraid to look at Rivington except with one eye.

"Thanks," said Rivington. "We were looking up . . . that is . . . my friend . . . confound it; it's against all precedent, you know . . . awfully obliged . . . just the same."

"In case," said our friend, "you would like to meet some of our Bowery young men I would be pleased to have you visit the quarters of our East Side Kappa Delta Phi Society, only two blocks east of here."

"Awfully sorry," said Rivington, "but my friend's got me on the jump to-night. He's a terror when he's out after local color. Now, there's nothing I would like better than to drop in at the Kappa Delta Phi, but—some other time!"

We said our farewells and boarded a home-bound car. We had a rabbit on upper Broadway, and then I parted with Rivington on a street corner.

"Well, anyhow," said he, braced and recovered, "it couldn't have happened anywhere but in little old New York."

Which, to say the least, was typical of Rivington.

GEORGIA'S RULING

IF you should chance to visit the General Land Office, step into the draughtsmen's room and ask to be shown the map of Salado County. A leisurely German—possibly old Kampfer himself—will bring it to you. It will be four feet square, on heavy drawing-cloth. The lettering and the figures will be beautifully clear and distinct. The title will be in splendid, undecipherable German text, ornamented with classic Teutonic designs—very likely Ceres or Pomona leaning against the initial letters with cornucopias venting grapes and weiners. You must tell him that this is not the map you wish to see; that he will kindly bring you its official predecessor. He will then say, "Ach, so!" and bring out a map half the size of the first, dim, old, tattered, and faded.

By looking carefully near its northwest corner you will presently come upon the worn contours of Chiquito River, and, maybe, if your eyes are good, discern the silent witness to this story.

The Commissioner of the Land Office was of the old style; his antique courtesy was too formal for his day. He dressed in fine black, and there was a suggestion of Roman drapery in his long coat-skirts. His collars were "undetached" (blame haberdashery for the word); his tie was a narrow, funereal strip, tied in the same knot as were his shoe-strings. His gray hair was a trifle too long behind, but he kept it smooth and orderly. His face was clean-shaven, like the old statesmen's. Most people thought it a stern face, but when its official expression was off, a few had seen altogether a different countenance. Especially tender and gentle it had appeared to those who were about him during the last illness to his only child.

The Commissioner had been a widower for years, and his life, outside his official duties, had been so devoted to little Georgia that people spoke of it as a touching and admirable thing. He was a reserved man, and dignified almost to austerity, but the child had come below it all and rested upon his very heart, so that she scarcely missed the mother's love that had been taken away. There was a wonderful companionship between them, for she had many of his own ways, being thoughtful and serious beyond her years.

One day, while she was lying with the fever burning brightly in her cheeks, she said suddenly:

"Papa, I wish I could do something good for a whole lot of children!"

"What would you like to do, dear?" asked the Commissioner. "Give them a party?"

"Oh, I don't mean those kind. I mean poor children who haven't homes, and aren't loved and cared for as I am. I tell you what, Papa!"

"What, my own child?"

"If I shouldn't get well, I'll leave them you—not *give* you, but just lend you, for you must come to mamma and me when you die too. If you can find time, wouldn't you do something to help them, if I ask you, Papa?"

"Hush, hush dear, dear child," said the Commissioner, holding her hot little hand against his cheek; "you'll get well real soon, and you and I will see what we can do for them together."

But in whatsoever paths of benevolence, thus vaguely premeditated, the Commissioner might tread, he was not to have the company of his beloved. That night the little frail body grew suddenly too tired to struggle further, and Georgia's exit was made from the great stage when she had scarcely begun to speak her little piece before the footlights. But there must be a stage manager who understands. She had given the cue to the one who was to speak after her.

A week after she was laid away, the Commissioner reappeared at the office, a little more courteous, a little paler and sterner, with the black frock-coat hanging a little more loosely from his tall figure.

His desk was piled with work that had accumulated during the four heart-breaking weeks of his absence. His chief clerk had done what he could, but there were questions of law, of fine judicial decisions to be made concerning the issue of patents, the marketing and leasing of school lands, the classification into grazing, agricultural, watered, and timbered, of new tracts to be opened to settlers.

The Commissioner went to work silently and obstinately, putting back his grief as far as possible, forcing his mind to attack the complicated and important business of his office. On the second day after his return he called the porter, pointed to a leather-covered chair that stood near his own, and ordered it removed to a lumber-room at the top of the building. In that chair Georgia would always sit when she came to the office for him of afternoons.

As time passed, the Commissioner seemed to grow more silent, solitary, and reserved. A new phase of mind developed in him. He could not endure the presence of a child. Often when a clattering youngster belonging to one of the clerks would come chattering into the big business-room adjoining his little apartment, the Commissioner would steal softly and close the door. He would always cross the street to avoid meeting the school-children when they came dancing along in happy groups upon the side-walk, and his firm mouth would close into a mere line.

It was nearly three months after the rains had washed the last dead flower-petals from the mound above little Georgia when the "land-shark" firm of Hamlin and Avery filed papers upon what they considered the "fattest" vacancy of the year.

It should not be supposed that all who were termed "land-sharks" deserved the name. Many of them were reputable men of good business character. Some of them could walk into the most august councils of the state and say: "Gentlemen, we would like to have this, and that, and matters go thus." But, next to a three years' drought and the boll-worm, the Actual Settler hated the land-shark. The land-shark haunted the Land Office, where all the land records were kept, and hunted "vacancies"—that is, tracts of unappropriated public domain, generally invisible upon the official maps, but actually existing "upon the

ground." The law entitled any one possessing certain State scrip to file by virtue of same upon any land not previously legally appropriated. Most of the
scrip was now in the hands of the land-sharks. Thus, at the cost of a few hundred dollars, they often secured lands worth as many thousands. Naturally, the
search for "vacancies" was lively.

But often—very often—the land they thus secured, though legally "unappropriated," would be occupied by happy and contented settlers, who had labored
for years to build up their homes, only to discover that their titles were worthless, and to receive peremptory notice to quit. Thus came about the bitter and
not unjustifiable hatred felt by the toiling settlers toward the shrewd and seldom
merciful speculators who so often turned them forth destitute and homeless from
their fruitless labors. The history of the state teems with their antagonism.
Mr. Land-shark seldom showed his face on "locations" from which he should
have to eject the unfortunate victims of a monstrously tangled land system,
but let his emissaries do the work. There was lead in every cabin, moulded into
balls for him; many of his brothers had enriched the grass with their blood.
The fault of it all lay far back.

When the state was young, she felt the need of attracting newcomers, and of
rewarding those pioneers already within her borders. Year after year she issued land scrip—Headrights, Bounties, Veteran Donations, Confederates; and
to railroads, irrigation companies, colonies, and tillers of the soil galore. All
required of the grantee was that he or it should have the scrip properly surveyed
upon the public domain by the county or district surveyor, and the land thus
appropriated became the property of him or it, or his or its heirs and assigns,
forever.   ·

In those days—and here is where the trouble began—the state's domain was
practically inexhaustible, and the old surveyors, with princely—yes, even Western American—liberality, gave good measure and overflowing. Often the jovial
man of metes and bounds would dispense altogether with the tripod and chain.
Mounted on a pony that could cover something near a "vara" at a step, with a
pocket compass to direct his course, he would trot out a survey by counting the
beat of his pony's hoofs, mark his corners, and write out his field notes with the
complacency produced by an act of duty well performed. Sometimes—and who
could blame the surveyor?—when the pony was "feeling his oats," he might step
a little higher and farther, and in that case the beneficiary of the scrip might
get a thousand or two more acres in his survey than the scrip called for. But
look at the boundless leagues the state had to spare! However, no one ever
had to complain of the pony under-stepping. Nearly every old survey in the
state contained an excess of land.

In later years, when the state became more populous, and land values increased,
this careless work entailed incalculable trouble, endless litigation, a period of
riotous land-grabbing, and no little bloodshed. The land-sharks voraciously attacked these excesses in the old surveys, and filed upon such portions with new
scrip as unappropriated public domain. Wherever the identifications of the
old tracts were vague, and the corners were not to be clearly established, the
Land Office would recognize the newer locations as valid, and issue title to the
locators. Here was the greatest hardship to be found. These old surveys, taken
from the pick of the land, were already nearly all occupied by unsuspecting and
peaceful settlers, and thus their titles were demolished, and the choice was placed
before them either to buy their land over at a double price or to vacate it, with
their families and personal belongings, immediately. Land locators sprang up
by hundreds. The country was held up and searched for "vacancies" at the
point of a compass. Hundreds of thousands of dollars' worth of splendid acres
were wrested from their innocent purchasers and holders. There began a vast
hegira of evicted settlers in tattered wagons; going nowhere cursing injustice,

stunned, purposeless, homeless, hopeless. Their children began to look up to them for bread, and cry.

It was in consequence of these conditions that Hamlin and Avery had filed upon a strip of land about a mile wide and three miles long, comprising about two thousand acres, it being the excess over complement of the Elias Denny three-league survey on Chiquito River, in one of the middle-western counties. This two-thousand-acre body of land was asserted by them to be vacant land, and improperly considered a part of the Denny survey. They based this assertion and their claim upon the land upon the demonstrated facts that the beginning corner of the Denny survey was plainly identified; that its field notes called to run west 5,760 varas, and then called for Chiquito River; thence it ran south, with the meanders—and so on—and that the Chiquito River was, on the ground, fully a mile farther west from the point reached by course and distance. To sum up: there were two thousand acres of vacant land between the Denny survey proper and Chiquito River.

One sweltering day in July the Commissioner called for the papers in connection with this new location. They were brought, and heaped, a foot deep, upon his desk—field notes, statements, sketches, affidavits, connecting lines—documents of every description that shrewdness and money could call to the aid of Hamlin and Avery.

The firm was pressing the Commissioner to issue a patent upon their location. They possessed inside information concerning a new railroad that would probably pass somewhere near this land.

The General Land Office was very still while the Commissioner was delving into the heart of the mass of evidence. The pigeons could be heard on the roof of the old, castle-like building, cooing and fretting. The clerks were droning everywhere, scarcely pretending to earn their salaries. Each little sound echoed hollow and loud from the bare, stone-flagged floors, the plastered walls, and the iron-joisted ceiling. The impalpable, perpetual limestone dust that never settled whitened a long streamer of sunlight that pierced the tattered window-awning.

It seemed that Hamlin and Avery had builded well. The Denny survey was carelessly made, even for a careless period. Its beginning corner was identical with that of a well-defined old Spanish grant, but its other calls were sinfully vague. The field notes contained no other object that survived—no tree, no natural object save Chiquito River, and it was a mile wrong there. According to precedent, the Office would be justified in giving in its complement by course and distance, and considering the remainder vacant instead of a mere excess.

The Actual Settler was besieging the office with wild protests *in re*. Having the nose of a pointer and the eye of a hawk for the land-shark, he had observed his myrmidons running the lines upon his ground. Making inquiries, he learned that the spoiler had attacked his home, and he left the plow in the furrow and took his pen in hand.

One of the protests the Commissioner read twice. It was from a woman, a widow, the granddaughter of Elias Denny himself. She told how her grandfather had sold most of the survey years before at a trivial price—land that was now a principality in extent and value. Her mother had also sold a part, and she herself had succeeded to this western portion, along Chiquito River. Much of it she had been forced to part with in order to live, and now she owned only about three hundred acres, on which she had her home. Her letter wound up rather pathetically:

"I've got eight children, the oldest fifteen years. I work all day and half the night to till what little land I can and keep us in clothes and books. I teach my children too. My neighbors is all poor and has big families. The drought kills the crops every two or three years and then we has hard times to get enough to eat. There is ten families on this land what the land-sharks is trying to rob us of, and all of them got titles from me. I sold to them cheap, and they ain't paid out yet, but part of them is, and if their land should be took from them I would die. My grandfather was an honest man, and he helped to build up this state, and he taught his children to be honest, and how could I make it up to them who bought from me? Mr. Commissioner, if you let them land-sharks take the roof from over my children and the little from them as they has to live on, whoever again calls this state great or its government just will have a lie in their mouths."

The Commissioner laid this letter aside with a sigh. Many, many such letters he had received. He had never been hurt by them, nor had he ever felt that they appealed to him personally. He was but the state's servant, and must follow its laws. And yet, somehow, this reflection did not always eliminate a certain responsible feeling that hung upon him. Of all the state's officers he was supremest in his department, not even excepting the Governor. Broad, general land laws he followed, it was true, but he had a wide latitude in particular ramifications. Rather than law, what he followed was Rulings: Office Rulings and precedents. In the complicated and new questions that were being engendered by the state's development the Commissioner's ruling was rarely appealed from. Even the courts sustained it when its equity was apparent.

The Commissioner stepped to the door and spoke to a clerk in the other room —spoke as he always did, as if he were addressing a prince of the blood:

"Mr. Weldon, will you be kind enough to ask Mr. Ashe, the state school-land appraiser, to please come to my office as soon as convenient?"

Ashe came quickly from the big table where he was arranging his reports.

"Mr. Ashe," said the Commissioner, "you worked along the Chiquito River, in Salado County, during your last trip, I believe. Do you remember anything of the Elias Denny three-league survey?"

"Yes, sir, I do," the blunt, breezy surveyor answered. "I crossed it on my way to Block H, on the north side of it. The road runs with the Chiquito River, along the valley. The Denny survey fronts three miles on the Chiquito."

"It is claimed," continued the Commissioner, "that it fails to reach the river by as much as a mile."

The appraiser shrugged his shoulder. He was by birth and instinct an Actual Settler, and the natural foe of the land-shark.

"It has always been considered to extend to the river," he said, dryly.

"But that is not the point I desired to discuss," said the Commissioner. "What kind of country is this valley portion of (let us say, then) the Denny tract?"

The spirit of the Actual Settler beamed in Ashe's face.

"Beautiful," he said, with enthusiasm. "Valley as level as this floor, with just a little swell on, like the sea, and rich as cream. Just enough brakes to shelter the cattle in winter. Black loamy soil for six feet, and then clay. Holds water. A dozen nice little houses on it, with windmills and gardens. People pretty poor, I guess—too far from market—but comfortable. Never saw so many kids in my life."

"They raise flocks?" inquired the Commissioner.

"Ho, ho! I mean two-legged kids," laughed the surveyor; "two-legged, and bare-legged, and tow-headed."

"Children! oh, children!" mused the Commissioner, as though a new view had opened to him; "they raise children!"

"It's a lonesome country, Commissioner," said the surveyor. "Can you blame 'em?"

"I suppose," continued the Commissioner, slowly, as one carefully pursues deductions from a new, stupendous theory, "not all of them are tow-headed. It would not be unreasonable, Mr. Ashe, I conjecture, to believe that a portion of them have brown, or even black, hair."

"Brown and black sure," said Ashe; "also red."

"No doubt," said the Commissioner. "Well, I thank you for your courtesy in informing me, Mr. Ashe. I will not detain you any longer from your duties."

Later, in the afternoon, came Hamlin and Avery, big, handsome, genial, sauntering men, clothed in white duck and low-cut shoes. They permeated the whole office with an aura of debonair prosperity. They passed among the clerks and left a wake of abbreviated given names and fat brown cigars.

These were the aristocracy of the land-sharks, who went in for big things. Full of serene confidence in themselves, there was no corporation, no syndicate, no railroad company or attorney general too big for them to tackle. The peculiar smoke of their rare, fat brown cigars was to be perceived in the sanctum of every department of state, in every committee-room of the Legislature, in every bank parlor and every private caucus-room in the state capital. Always pleasant, never in a hurry, in seeming to possess unlimited leisure, people wondered when they gave their attention to the many audacious enterprises in which they were known to be engaged.

By and by the two dropped carelessly into the Commissioner's room and reclined lazily in the big, leather-upholstered arm-chairs. They drawled a good-natured complaint of the weather, and Hamlin told the Commissioner an excellent story he had amassed that morning from the Secretary of State.

But the Commissioner knew why they were there. He had half promised to render a decision that day upon their location.

The chief clerk now brought in a batch of duplicate certificates for the Commissioner to sign. As he traced his sprawling signature, "Hollis Summerfield, Comr. Genl. Land Office," on each one, the chief clerk stood, deftly removing them and applying the blotter.

"I notice," said the chief clerk, "you've been going through that Salado County location. Kampfer is making a new map of Salado, and I believe is platting in that section of the county now."

"I will see it," said the Commissioner. A few moments later he went to the draughtsmen's room.

As he entered he saw five or six of the draughtsmen grouped about Kampfer's desk, gargling away at each other in pectoral German, and gazing at something thereupon. At the Commissioner's approach they scattered to their several places. Kampfer, a wizened little German, with long, frizzled ringlets and a watery eye, began to stammer forth some sort of an apology, the Commissioner thought, for the congregation of his fellows about his desk.

"Never mind," said the Commissioner, "I wish to see the map you are making"; and, passing around the old German, seated himself upon the high draughtsman's stool. Kampfer continued to break English in trying to explain.

"Herr Gommissioner, I assure you blenty sat I haf not it bremediated—sat it wass—sat it itself make. Look you! from se field notes wass it blatted—blease to observe se calls: South, 10 degrees west 1,050 varas; south, 10 degrees each 300 varas; south, 100; south, 9 west, 200; south, 40 degrees west, 400—and so on. Herr Gommissioner, nefer would I have——"

The Commissioner raised one white hand, silently. Kampfer dropped his pipe and fled.

With a hand at each side of his face, and his elbows resting upon the desk, the Commissioner sat staring at the map which was spread and fastened there—staring at the sweet and living profile of little Georgia drawn thereupon—at her face, pensive, delicate, and infantile, outlined in a perfect likeness.

When his mind at length came to inquire into the reason of it, he saw that it must have been, as Kampfer had said, unpremeditated. The old draughtsman had been platting in the Elias Denny survey, and Georgia's likeness, striking though it was, was formed by nothing more than the meanders of Chiquito River. Indeed, Kampfer's blotter, whereon his preliminary work was done, showed the laborious tracings of the calls and the countless pricks of the compasses. Then, over his faint penciling, Kampfer had drawn in India ink with a full, firm pen the similitude of Chiquito River, and forth had blossomed mysteriously the dainty, pathetic profile of the child.

The Commissioner sat for half an hour with his face in his hands, gazing downward, and none dared approach him. Then he arose and walked out. In the business office he paused long enough to ask that the Denny file be brought to his desk.

He found Hamlin and Avery still reclining in their chairs, apparently oblivious of business. They were lazily discussing summer opera, it being their habit—perhaps their pride also—to appear supernaturally indifferent whenever they stood with large interests imperilled. And they stood to win more on this stake than most people knew. They possessed inside information to the effect that a new railroad would, within a year, split this very Chiquito River valley and send land values, ballooning all along its route. A dollar under thirty thousand profit on this location, if it should hold good, would be a loss to their expectations. So, while they chatted lightly and waited for the Commissioner to open the subject, there was a quick, side-long sparkle in their eyes, evincing a desire to read their title clear to those fair acres on the Chiquito.

A clerk brought in the file. The Commissioner seated himself and wrote upon it in red ink. Then he rose to his feet and stood for a while looking straight out of the window. The Land Office capped the summit of a bold hill. The eyes of the Commissioner passed over the roofs of many houses set in a packing of deep green, the whole checkered by strips of blinding white streets. The horizon, where his gaze was focussed, swelled to a fair wooded eminence flecked with faint dots of shining white. There was a cemetery, where lay many who were forgotten, and a few who had not lived in vain. And one lay there occupying very small space, whose childish heart had been large enough to desire, while near its last beats, good to others. The Commissioner's lips moved slightly as he whispered to himself: "It was her last will and testament, and I have neglected it so long!"

The big brown cigars of Hamlin and Avery were fireless, but they still gripped them between their teeth and waited, while they marvelled at the absent expression upon the Commissioner's face.

By and by he spoke suddenly and promptly.

"Gentlemen, I have just indorsed the Elias Denny survey for patenting. This office will not regard your location upon a part of it as legal." He paused a moment, and then, extending his hand as those dear old-time ones used to do in debate, he enunciated the spirit of that Ruling that subsquently drove the land-sharks to the wall, and placed the seal of peace and security over the doors of ten thousand homes.

"And, furthermore," he continued, with a clear, soft light upon his face, "it may interest you to know that from this time on this office will consider that when a survey of land made by virtue of a certificate granted by this state to the men who wrested it from the wilderness and the savage—made in good faith, settled in good faith, and left in good faith to their children or innocent purchasers—when such a survey, although overrunning its complement, shall call for any natural object visible to the eye of man, to that object it shall hold, and be good and valid. And the children of this state shall lie down to sleep at night, and rumors of disturbers of title shall not disquiet them. For," concluded the Commissioner, "of such is the Kingdom of Heaven."

In the silence that followed, a laugh floated up from the patent-room below.

The man who carried down the Denny file was exhibiting it among the clerks. "Look here," he said, delightedly, "the old man has forgotten his name. He's written 'Patent to original grantee,' and signed it 'Georgia Summerfield, Comr.'"

The speech of the Commissioner rebounded lightly from the impregnable Hamlin and Avery. They smiled, rose gracefully, spoke of the baseball team, and argued feelingly that quite a perceptible breeze had arisen from the east. They lit fresh fat brown cigars, and drifted courteously away. But later they made another tiger-spring for their quarry in the courts. But the courts, according to reports in the papers, "coolly roasted them" (a remarkable performance, suggestive of liquid-air didoes), and sustained the Commissioner's Ruling.

And this Ruling itself grew to be a Precedent, and the Actual Settler framed it, and taught his children to spell from it, and there was sound sleep o' nights from the pines to the sage-brush, and from the chaparral to the great brown river of the north.

But I think, and I am sure the Commissioner never thought otherwise, that whether Kampfer was a snuffy old instrument of destiny, or whether the meanders of the Chiquito accidentally platted themselves into that memorable sweet profile or not, there was brought about "something good for a whole lot of children," and the result ought to be called "Georgia's Ruling."

BLIND MAN'S HOLIDAY

Alas for the man and for the artist with the shifting point of perspective! Life shall be a confusion of ways to the one; the landscape shall rise up and confound the other. Take the case of Lorison. At one time he appeared to himself to be the feeblest of fools; at another he conceived that he followed ideals so fine that the world was not yet ready to accept them. During one mood he cursed his folly; possessed by the other, he bore himself with a serene grandeur akin to greatness: in neither did he attain the perspective.

Generations before, the name had been "Larsen." His race had bequeathed him its fine-strung, melancholy temperament, its saving balance of thrift and industry.

From his point of perspective he saw himself an outcast from society, forever to be a shady skulker along the ragged edge of respectability; a denizen des trois-quarts de monde, that pathetic spheroid lying between the haut and the demi, whose inhabitants envy each of their neighbors, and are scorned by both. He was self-condemned to this opinion, as he was self-exiled, through it, to this quaint Southern city a thousand miles from his former home. Here he had dwelt for longer than a year, knowing but few, keeping in a subjective world of shadows which was invaded at times by the perplexing bulks of jarring realities. Then he fell in love with a girl whom he met in a cheap restaurant, and his story begins.

The Rue Chartres, in New Orleans, is a street of ghosts. It lies in the quarter where the Frenchman, in his prime, set up his translated pride and glory; where, also the arrogant don had swaggered, and dreamed of gold and grants and ladies' gloves. Every flagstone has its grooves worn by footsteps going royally to the wooing and the fighting. Every house has a princely heartbreak; each doorway its untold tale of gallant promise and slow decay.

By night the Rue Chartres is now but a murky fissure, from which the groping wayfarer sees, flung against the sky, the tangled filigree of Moorish iron balconies. The old houses of monsieur stand yet, indomitable against the century, but their essence is gone. The street is one of ghosts to whosoever can see them.

A faint heartbeat of the street's ancient glory still survives in a corner occupied by the Café Carabine d'Or. Once men gathered there to plot against kings, and to warn presidents. They do so yet, but they are not the same kind of men. A brass button will scatter these; those would have set their faces against an army. Above the door hangs the sign board, upon which has been depicted a vast animal of unfamiliar species. In the act of firing upon this monster is represented an unobtrusive human leveling an obtrusive gun, once the color of bright gold. Now the legend above the picture is faded beyond conjecture; the gun's relation to the title is a matter of faith; the menaced animal, wearied of the long aim of the hunter, has resolved itself into a shapeless blot.

The place is known as "Antonio's," as the name, white upon the red-lit transparency, and gilt upon the windows, attests. There is a promise in "Antonio"; a justifiable expectancy of savory things in oil and pepper and wine, and perhaps an angel's whisper of garlic. But the rest of the name is "O'Riley." Antonio O'Riley!

The Carabine d'Or is an ignominious ghost of the Rue Chartres. The café where Bienville and Conti dined, where a prince has broken bread, is become a "family ristaurant."

Its customers are working men and women, almost to a unit. Occasionally you will see chorus girls from the cheaper theatres, and men who follow avocations subject to quick vicissitudes; but at Antonio's—name rich in Bohemian promise, but tame in fulfillment—manners debonair and gay are toned down to the "family" standard. Should you light a cigarette, mine host will touch you on the "arrum" and remind you that the proprieties are menaced. "Antonio" entices and beguiles from fiery legend without, but "O'Riley" teaches decorum within.

It was at this restaurant that Lorison first saw the girl. A flashy fellow with a predatory eye had followed her in, and had advanced to take the other chair at the little table where she stopped, but Lorison slipped into the seat before him. Their acquaintance began, and grew, and now for two months they had sat at the same table each evening, not meeting by appointment, but as if by a series of fortuitous and happy accidents. After dining, they would take a walk together in one of the little city parks, or among the panoramic markets where exhibits a continuous vaudeville of sights and sounds. Always at eight o'clock their steps led them to a certain street corner, where she prettily but firmly bade him good-night and left him. "I do not live far from here," she frequently said, "and you must let me go the rest of the way alone."

But now Lorison had discovered that he wanted to go the rest of the way with her, or happiness would depart, leaving him on a very lonely corner of life. And at the same time that he made the discovery, the secret of his banishment from the society of the good laid its finger in his face and told him it must not be.

Man is too thoroughly an egoist not to be also an egotist; if he love, the object shall know it. During a lifetime he may conceal it through stress of expediency and honor, but it shall bubble from his dying lips, though it disrupt a neighborhood. It is known, however, that most men do not wait so long to disclose their passion. In the case of Lorison, his particular ethics positively forbade him to declare his sentiments, but he must needs dally with the subject, and woo by innuendo at least.

On this night, after the usual meal at the Carabine d'Or, he strolled with his companion down the dim old street toward the river.

The Rue Chartres perishes in the old Place d'Armes. The ancient Cabildo, where Spanish justice fell like hail, faces it, and the Cathedral, another provincial ghost, overlooks it. Its centre is a little, iron-railed park of flowers and immaculate gravelled walks, where citizens take the air of evenings. Pedestalled high above it, the General sits his cavorting steed, with his face turned stonily down the river toward English Turn, whence come no more Britons to bombard his cotton bales.

Often the two sat in this square, but to-night Lorison guided her past the stone-stepped gate, and still riverward. As they walked, he smiled to himself to think that all he knew of her—except that he loved her—was her name, Norah Greenway, and that she lived with her brother. They had talked about everything except themselves. Perhaps her reticence had been caused by his.

They came, at length, upon the levee, and sat upon a great, prostrate beam. The air was pungent with the dust of commerce. The great river slipped yellowly past. Across it Algiers lay, a longitudinous black bulk against a vibrant electric haze sprinkled with exact stars.

The girl was young and of the piquant order. A certain bright melancholy pervaded her; she possessed an untarnished, pale prettiness doomed to please. Her voice, when she spoke, dwarfed her theme. It was the voice capable of investing little subjects with a large interest. She sat at ease, bestowing her skirts with the little womanly touch, serene as if the begrimed pier were a summer garden. Lorison poked the rotting boards with his cane.

He began by telling her that he was in love with some one to whom he durst not speak of it. "And why not?" she asked, accepting swiftly his fatuous presentation of a third person of straw. "My place in the world," he answered, "is none to ask a woman to share. I am an outcast from honest people; I am wrongly accused of one crime, and am, I believe, guilty of another."

Thence he plunged into the story of his abdication from society. The story, pruned of his moral philosophy, deserves no more than the slightest touch. It is no new tale, that of the gambler's declension. During one night's sitting he lost, and then had imperilled a certain amount of his employer's money, which, by accident, he carried with him. He continued to lose, to the last wager, and then began to gain, leaving the game winner to a somewhat formidable sum. The same night his employer's safe was robbed. A search was had; the winnings of Lorison were found in his room, their total forming an accusative nearness to the sum purloined. He was taken, tried, and, through incomplete evidence, released, smutched with the sinister *devoirs* of a disagreeing jury.

"It is not in the unjust accusation," he said to the girl, "that my burden lies, but in the knowledge that from the moment I staked the first dollar of the firm's money I was a criminal—no matter whether I lost or won. You see why it is impossible for me to speak of love to her."

"It is a sad thing," said Norah, after a little pause, "to think what very good people there are in the world."

"Good?" said Lorison.

"I was thinking of this superior person whom you say you love. She must be a very poor sort of creature."

"I do not understand."

"Nearly," she continued, "as poor a sort of creature as yourself."

"You do not understand," said Lorison, removing his hat and sweeping back his fine, light hair. "Suppose she loved me in return, and were willing to marry me. Think, if you can, what would follow. Never a day would pass but she would be reminded of her sacrifice. I would read a condescension in her smile, a pity even in her affection, that would madden me. No. The thing would stand between us forever. Only equals should mate. I could never ask her to come down upon my lower plane."

An arc light faintly shone upon Lorison's face. An illumination from within also pervaded it. The girl saw the rapt, ascetic look; it was the face either of Sir Galahad or Sir Fool.

"Quite starlike," she said, "is this unapproachable angel. Really too high to be grasped."

"By me, yes."

She faced him suddenly. "My dear friend, would you prefer your star fallen?"

Lorison made a wide gesture. "You push me to the bald fact," he declared; "you are not in sympathy with my argument. But I will answer you so. If I could reach my particular star, to drag it down, I would not do it; but if it were fallen, I would pick it up, and thank Heaven for the privilege."

They were silent for some minutes. Norah shivered, and thrust her hands deep into the pockets of her jacket. Lorison uttered a remorseful exclamation.

"I'm not cold," she said. "I was just thinking. I ought to tell you something. You have selected a strange confidante. But you cannot expect a chance acquaintance, picked up in a doubtful restaurant, to be an angel."

"Norah!" cried Lorison.

"Let me go on. You have told me about yourself. We have been such good friends. I must tell you now what I never wanted you to know. I am—worse than you are. I was on the stage . . . I sang in the chorus . . . I was pretty bad, I guess . . . I stole diamonds from the prima donna . . . they arrested me . . . I gave most of them up, and they let me go . . . I drank wine every night . . . a great deal . . . I was very wicked, but——"

Lorison knelt quickly by her side and took her hands.

"Dear Norah!" he said, exultantly. "It is you, it is you I love! You never guessed it, did you? 'Tis you I meant all the time. Now I can speak. Let me make you forget the past. We have both suffered; let us shut out the world, and live for each other. Norah, do you hear me say I love you?"

"In spite of——"

"Rather say because of it. You have come out of your past noble and good. Your heart is an angel's. Give it to me."

"A little while ago you feared the future too much to even speak."

"But for you; not for myself. Can you love me?"

She cast herself, wildly sobbing, upon his breast.

"Better than life—than truth itself—than everything."

"And my own past," said Lorison, with a note of solicitude—"can you forgive and——"

"I answered you that," she whispered, "when I told you I loved you." She leaned away, and looked thoughtfully at him. "If I had not told you about myself, would you have—would you——"

"No," he interrupted; "I would never have let you know I loved you. I would never have asked you this—Norah, will you be my wife?"

She wept again.

"Oh, believe me; I am good now—I am no longer wicked! I will be the best wife in the world. Don't think I am—bad any more. If you do I shall die, I snall die!"

While he was consoling her, she brightened up eager and impetuous. "Will you marry me to-night?" she said. "Will you prove it that way? I have a reason for wishing it to be to-night. Will you?"

Of one of two things was this exceeding frankness the outcome: either of importunate brazenness or of utter innocence. The lover's perspective contained only the one.

"The sooner," said Lorison, "the happier I shall be."

"What is there to do?" she asked. "What do you have to get? Come! You should know."

Her energy stirred the dreamer to action.

"A city directory first," he cried, gayly, "to find where the man lives who gives licenses to happiness. We will go together and rout him out. Cabs, cars, policemen, telephones, and ministers shall aid us."

"Father Rogan shall marry us," said the girl, with ardor. "I will take you to him."

An hour later the two stood at the open doorway of an immense, gloomy brick building in a narrow and lonely street. The license was tight in Norah's hand.

"Wait here a moment," she said, "till I find Father Rogan."

She plunged into the black hallway, and the lover was left standing, as it were, on one leg outside. His impatience was not greatly taxed. Gazing curiously into what seemed the hallway to Erebus, he was presently reassured by a stream of light that bisected the darkness, far down the passage. Then he heard her call, and fluttered lampward, like the moth. She beckoned him through a doorway into the room whence emanated the light. The room was bare of nearly everything except books, which had subjugated all its space. Here and there little spots of territory had been reconquered. An elderly, bald man, with a superlatively calm, remote eye, stood by a table with a book in his hand, his finger still marking a page. His dress was sombre and appertained to a religious order. His eye denoted an acquaintance with the perspective.

"Father Rogan," said Norah, "this is *he*."

"The two of ye," said Father Rogan, "want to get married?"

They did not deny it. He married them. The ceremony was quickly done. One who could have witnessed it, and felt its scope, might have trembled at the terrible inadequacy of it to rise to the dignity of its endless chain of results.

Afterward the priest spake briefly, as if by rote, of certain other civil and legal addenda that either might or should, at a later time, cap the ceremony. Lorison tendered a fee, which was declined, and before the door closed after the departing couple Father Rogan's book popped open again where his finger marked it.

In the dark hall Norah whirled and clung to her companion, tearful.

"Will you never, never be sorry?"

At last she was reassured.

At the first light they reached upon the street, she asked the time, just as she had each night. Lorison looked at his watch. Half-past eight.

Lorison thought it was from habit that she guided their steps toward the corner where they always parted. But, arrived there, she hesitated, and then released his arm. A drug store stood on the corner; its bright, soft light shone upon them.

"Please leave me here as usual to-night," said Norah, sweetly. "I must—I would rather you would. You will not object? At six to-morrow evening I will meet you at Antonio's. I want to sit with you there once more. And then —I will go where you say." She gave him a bewildering, bright smile, and walked swiftly away.

Surely it needed all the strength of her charm to carry off this astounding behaviour. It was no discredit to Lorison's strength of mind that his head began to whirl. Pocketing his hands, he rambled vacuously over to the druggist's windows, and began assiduously to spell over the names of the patent medicines therein displayed.

As soon as he had recovered his wits, he proceeded along the street in an aimless fashion. After drifting for two or three squares, he flowed into a somewhat more pretentious throughfare, a way much frequented by him in his solitary ramblings. For here was a row of shops devoted to traffic in goods of the widest range of choice—handiworks of art, skill and fancy, products of nature and labor from every zone.

Here, for a time, he loitered among the conspicuous windows, where was set, emphasized by congested floods of light, the cunningest spoil of the interiors. There were few passers, and of this Lorison was glad. He was not of the world. For a long time he had touched his fellow man only at the gear of a levelled cog-wheel—at right angles, and upon a different axis. He had dropped into a distinctly new orbit. The stroke of ill fortune had acted upon him, in effect, as a blow delivered upon the apex of a certain ingenious toy, the musical top, which, when thus buffeted while spinning, gives forth, with scarcely retarded motion, a complete change of key and chord.

Strolling along the pacific avenue, he experienced a singular, supernatural calm, accompanied by an unusual activity of brain. Reflecting upon recent affairs, he assured himself of his happiness in having won for a bride the one he had so greatly desired, yet he wondered mildly at his dearth of active emotion. Her strange behavior in abandoning him without valid excuse on his bridal eve aroused in him only a vague and curious speculation. Again, he found himself contemplating, with complaisant serenity, the incidents of her somewhat lively career. His perspective seemed to have been queerly shifted.

As he stood before a window near a corner, his ears were assailed by a waxing clamor and commotion. He stood close to the window to allow passage to the cause of the hubbub—a procession of human beings, which rounded the corner and headed in his direction. He perceived a salient hue of blue and a glitter of brass about a central figure of dazzling white and silver, and a ragged wake of black, bobbing figures.

Two ponderous policemen were conducting between them a woman dressed as if for the stage, in a short, white, satiny skirt reaching to the knees, pink stockings, and a sort of sleeveless bodice bright with relucent, armor-like scales. Upon her curly light hair was perched, at a rollicking angle, a shining tin helmet. The costume was to be instantly recognized as one of those amazing conceptions to which competition has harried the inventors of the spectacular ballet. One of the officers bore a long cloak upon his arm, which, doubtless, had been intended to veil the candid attractions of their effulgent prisoner, but, for some reason, it had not been called into use, to the vociferous delight of the tail of the procession.

Compelled by a sudden and vigorous movement of the woman, the parade halted before the window by which Lorison stood. He saw that she was young, and, at the first glance, was deceived by a sophistical prettiness of her face, which waned before a more judicious scrutiny. Her look was bold and reckless, and upon her countenance, where yet the contours of youth survived, were the finger-marks of old age's credentialed courier, Late Hours.

The young woman fixed her unshrinking gaze upon Lorison, and called to him in the voice of the wronged heroine in straits:

"Say! You look like a good fellow; come and put up the bail, won't you? I've done nothing to get pinched for. It's all a mistake. See how they're treating me! You won't be sorry, if you'll help me out of this. Think of your sister or your girl being dragged along the streets this way! I say, come along now, like a good fellow."

It may be that Lorison, in spite of the unconvincing bathos of this appeal, showed a sympathetic face, for one of the officers left the woman's side, and went over to him.

"It's all right, sir," he said, in a husky, confidential tone; "she's the right party. We took her after the first act at the Green Light Theatre, on a wire from the chief of police of Chicago. It's only a square or two to the station. Her rig's pretty bad, but she refused to change clothes—or, rather," added the officer, with a smile, "to put on some. I thought I'd explain matters to you so you wouldn't think she was being imposed upon."

"What is the charge?" asked Lorison.

"Grand larceny. Diamonds. Her husband is a jeweler in Chicago. She cleaned his show case of the sparklers, and skipped with a comic opera troupe."

The policeman, perceiving that the interest of the entire group of spectators was centred upon himself and Lorison—their conference being regarded as a possible new complication—was fain to prolong the situation—which reflected his own importance—by a little afterpiece of philosophical comment.

"A gentleman like you, sir," he went on, affably, "would never notice it, but it comes in my line to observe what an immense amount of trouble is made by that combination—I mean the stage, diamonds, and light-headed women who aren't satisfied with good homes. I tell you, sir, a man these days and nights wants to know what his women folks are up to."

The policeman smiled a good-night, and returned to the side of his charge, who had been intently watching Lorison's face during the conversation, no doubt for some indication of his intention to render succor. Now, at the failure of the sign, and at the movement made to continue the ignominious progress, she abandoned hope, and addressed him thus, pointedly:

"You damn chalk-faced quitter! You were thinking of giving me a hand, but you let the cop talk you out of it the first word. You're a dandy to tie to. Say, if you ever get a girl, she'll have a picnic. Won't she work you to the queen's taste! Oh, my!" She concluded with a taunting, shrill laugh that rasped Lorison like a saw. The policemen urged her forward; the delighted train of gaping followers closed up the rear; and the captive Amazon, accepting her fate, extended the scope of her maledictions so that none in hearing might seem to be slighted.

Then there came upon Lorison an overwhelming revulsion of his perspective. It may be that he had been ripe for it, that the abnormal condition of mind in which he had for so long existed was already about to revert to its balance; howe-er, it is certain that the events of the last few minutes had furnished the channel, if not the impetus, for the change.

The initial determining influence had been so small a thing as the fact and manner of his having been approached by the officer. That agent had, by the style of his accost, restored the loiterer to his former place in society. In an instant he had been transformed from a somewhat rancid prowler along the fishy side streets of gentility into an honest gentleman, with whom even so lordly a guardian of the peace might agreeably exchange the compliments.

This, then, first broke the spell, and set thrilling in him a resurrected longing for the fellowship of his kind, and the rewards of the virtuous. To what end, he vehemently asked himself, was this fanciful self-accusation, this empty renunciation, this moral squeamishness through which he had been led to abandon what was his heritage in life, and not beyond his deserts? Technically, he was uncondemned; his sole guilty spot was in thought rather than deed, and cognizance of it unshared by others. For what good, moral or sentimental, did he slink, retreating like the hedgehog from his own shadow, to and fro in this musty Bohemia that lacked even the picturesque?

But the thing that struck home and set him raging was the part played by the Amazonian prisoner. To the counterpart of that astounding belligerent—identical, at least, in the way of experience—to one, by her own confession, thus far fallen, had he, not three hours since, been united in marriage. How desirable and natural it had seemed to him then, and how monstrous it seemed now! How the words of diamond thief number two yet burned in his ears: "If you ever get a girl, she'll have a picnic." What did that mean but that women in-

stinctively knew him for one they could hoodwink? Still again there reverberated the policeman's sapient contribution to his agony: "A man these
days and nights wants to know what his women folks are up to." Oh, yes, he
had been a fool; he had looked at things from the wrong standpoint.

But the wildest note in all the clamor was struck by pain's forefinger, jealousy.
Now, at least, he felt that keenest sting—a mounting love unworthily bestowed.
Whatever she might be, he loved her; he bore in his own breast his doom. A
grating, comic flavor to his predicament struck him suddenly, and he laughed
creakingly as he swung down the echoing pavement. An impetuous desire to act,
to battle with his fate, seized him. He stopped upon his heel, and smote his
palms together triumphantly. His wife was—where? But there was a tangible
link; an outlet more or less navigable, through which his derelict ship of
matrimony might yet be safely towed—the priest!

Like all imaginative men with pliable natures, Lorison was, when thoroughly
stirred, apt to become tempestuous. With a high and stubborn indignation upon
him, he retraced his steps to the intersecting street by which he had come.
Down this he hurried to the corner where he had parted with—an astringent
grimace tinctured the thought—his wife. Thence still back he harked, following
through an unfamiliar district his stimulated recollections of the way they had
come from that preposterous wedding. Many times he went abroad, and nosed
his way back to the trail, furious.

At last, when he reached the dark, calamitous building in which his madness
had culminated, and found the black hallway, he dashed down it, perceiving no
light or sound. But he raised his voice, hailing loudly; reckless of everything
but that he should find the old mischief-maker with the eyes that looked too far
away to see the disaster he had wrought. The door opened, and in the stream
of light Father Rogan stood, his book in hand, with his finger marking the
place.

"Ah!" cried Lorison. "You are the man I want. I had a wife of you a few
hours ago. I would not trouble you, but I neglected to note how it was done.
Will you oblige me with the information whether the business is beyond remedy?"

"Come inside," said the priest; "there are other lodgers in the house, who
might prefer sleep to even a gratified curiosity."

Lorison entered the room and took the chair offered him. The priest's eyes
looked a courteous interrogation.

"I must apologize again," said the young man, "for so soon intruding upon
you with my marital infelicities, but as my wife has neglected to furnish me
with her address, I am deprived of the legitimate recourse of a family row."

"I am quite a plain man," said Father Rogan, pleasantly; "but I do not see
how I am to ask you questions."

"Pardon my indirectness," said Lorison; "I will ask one. In this room to-
night you pronounced me to be a husband. You afterward spoke of additional
rites or performances that either should or could be effected. I paid little attention to your words then, but I am hungry to hear them repeated now. As
matters stand, am I married past all help?"

"You are as legally and as firmly bound," said the priest, "as though it had
been done in a cathedral, in the presence of thousands. The additional observances I referred to are not necessary to the strictest legality of the act, but
were advised as a precaution for the future—for convenience of proof in such
contingencies as wills, inheritances, and the like."

Lorison laughed harshly.

"Many thanks," he said. "Then there is no mistake, and I am the happy
benedict. I suppose I should go stand upon the bridal corner, and when my
wife gets through walking the streets she will look me up."

Father Rogan regarded him calmly.

"My son," he said, "when a man and woman come to me to be married I always marry them. I do this for the sake of other people whom they might go away and marry if they did not marry each other. As you see, I do not seek your confidence; but your case seems to me to be one not altogether devoid of interest. Very few marriages that have come to my notice have brought such well-expressed regret within so short a time. I will hazard one question: were you not under the impression that you loved the lady you married, at the time you did so?"

"Loved her!" cried Lorison, wildly. "Never so well as now, though she told me she deceived and sinned and stole. Never more than now, when, perhaps, she is laughing at the fool she cajoled and left, with scarcely a word, to return to God only knows what particular line of her former folly."

Father Rogan answered nothing. During the silence that succeeded, he sat with a quiet expectation beaming in his full, lambent eye.

"If you would listen——" began Lorison. The priest held up his hand.

"As I hoped," he said. "I thought you would trust me. Wait but a moment." He brought a long clay pipe, filled and lighted it.

"Now, my son," he said.

Lorison poured a twelvemonth's accumulated confidence into Father Rogan's ear. He told all; not sparing himself or omitting the facts of his past, the events of the night, or his disturbing conjectures and fears.

"The main point," said the priest, when he had concluded, "seems to me to be this—are you reasonably sure that you love this woman whom you have married?"

"Why," exclaimed Lorison, rising impulsively to his feet—"why should I deny it? But look at me—am I fish, flesh, or fowl? That is the main point to me, I assure you."

"I understand you," said the priest, also rising, and laying down his pipe. "The situation is one that has taxed the endurance of much older men than you —in fact, especially much older men than you. I will try to relieve you from it, and this night. You shall see for yourself into exactly what predicament you have fallen, and how you shall, possibly, he extricated. There is no evidence so credible as that of the eyesight."

Father Rogan moved about the room, and donned a soft black hat. Buttoning his coat to his throat, he laid his hand on the doorknob. "Let us walk," he said.

The two went out upon the street. The priest turned his face down it, and Lorison walked with him through a squalid district, where the houses loomed, awry and desolate-looking, high above them. Presently they turned into a less dismal side street, where the houses were smaller, and, though hinting of the most meagre comfort, lacked the concentrated wretchedness of the more populous byways.

At a segregated, two-story house Father Rogan halted, and mounted the steps with the confidence of a familiar visitor. He ushered Lorison into a narrow hallway, faintly lighted by a cobwebbed hanging lamp. Almost immediately a door to the right opened and a dingy Irishwoman protruded her head.

"Good evening to ye, Mistress Geehan," said the priest, unconsciously, it seemed, falling into a delicately flavored brogue. "And is it yourself can tell me if Norah has gone out again, the night, maybe?"

"Oh, it's yer blissid riverence! Sure and I can tell ye the same. The purty darlin' wint out, as usual, but a bit later. And she says: 'Mother Geehan,' says she, 'it's me last noight out, praise the saints, this noight is!' And oh, yer riverence, the swate, beautiful drame of a dress she had this toime! White satin and silk and ribbons, and lace about the neck and arrums—'twas a sin, yer riverence, the gold was spint upon it."

The priest heard Lorison catch his breath painfully and a faint smile flickered across his own clean-cut mouth.

"Well, then, Mistress Geehan," said he, "I'll just step upstairs and see the bit boy for a minute, and I'll take this gentleman up with me."

"He's awake, thin," said the woman. "I've just come down from sitting wid him the last hour, tilling him fine shtories of ould County Tyrone. 'Tis a greedy gossoon, it is, yer riverence, for me shtories."

"Small the doubt," said Father Rogan, "There's no rocking would put him to slape the quicker, I'm thinking."

Amid the woman's shrill protest against the retort, the two men ascended the steep stairway. The priest pushed open the door of a room near its top.

"Is that you already, sister?" drawled a sweet, childish voice from the darkness.

"It's only ould Father Denny come to see ye, darlin'; and a foine gintleman I've brought to make ye a gr-r-and call. And ye resaves us fast aslape in bed! Shame on yez manners!"

"Oh, Father Denny, is that you? I'm glad. And will you light the lamp, please? It's on the table by the door. And quit talking like Mother Geehan, Father Denny."

The priest lit the lamp, and Lorison saw a tiny, towsled-haired boy, with a thin, delicate face, sitting up in a small bed in a corner. Quickly, also, his rapid glance considered the room and its contents. It was furnished with more than comfort, and its adornments plainly indicated a woman's discerning taste. An open door beyond revealed the blackness of an adjoining room's interior.

The boy clutched both of Father Rogan's hands. "I'm so glad you came," he said; "but why did you come in the night? Did sister send you?"

"Off wid ye! Am I to be sint about, at me age, as was Terence McShane, of Ballymahone? I come on me own r-r-responsibility."

Lorison had also advanced to the boy's bedside. He was fond of children; and the wee fellow, laying himself down to sleep alone in that dark room, stirred his heart.

"Aren't you afraid, little man?" he asked, stooping down beside him.

"Sometimes," answered the boy, with a shy smile, "when the rats make too much noise. But nearly every night, when sister goes out, Mother Geehan stays a while with me, and tells me funny stories. I'm not often afraid, sir."

"This brave little gentleman," said Father Rogan, "is a scholar of mine. Every day from half-past six to half-past eight—when sister comes for him—he stops in my study, and we find out what's in the inside of books. He knows multiplication, division, and fractions; and he's throubling me to begin wid the chronicles of Ciaran of Clonmacnoise, Corurac McCullenan and Cuan O'Lochain, the gr-r-reat Irish hishtorians." The boy was evidently accustomed to the priest's Celtic pleasantries. A little, appreciative grin was all the attention the insinuation of pedantry received.

Lorison, to have saved his life, could not have put to the child one of those vital questions that were wildly beating about, unanswered, in his own brain. The little fellow was very like Norah; he had the same shining hair and candid eyes.

"Oh, Father Denny," cried the boy, suddenly, "I forgot to tell you! Sister is not going away at night any more! She told me so when she kissed me good-night as she was leaving. And she said she was so happy, and then she cried. Wasn't that queer? But I'm glad; aren't you?"

"Yes, lad. And now, ye omadhaun, go to sleep, and say good-night; we must be going."

"Which shall I do first, Father Denny?"

"Faith, he's caught me again! Wait till I get the sassenach into the annals of Tageruach, the hagiographer; I'll give him enough of the Irish idiom to make him more respectful."

The light was out, and the small, brave voice bidding them good-night from the dark room. They groped downstairs, and tore away from the garrulity of Mother Geehan.

Again the priest steered them through the dim ways, but this time in another direction. His conductor was serenely silent, and Lorison followed his example to the extent of seldom speaking. Serene he could not be. His heart beat suffocatingly in his breast. The following of this blind, meanacing trail was pregnant with he knew not what humiliating revelation to be delivered at its end.

They came into a more pretentious street, where trade, it could be surmised, flourished by day. And again the priest paused; this time before a lofty building, whose great doors and windows in the lowest floor were carefully shuttered and barred. Its higher apertures were dark, save in the third story, the windows of which were brilliantly lighted. Lorison's ear caught a distant, regular, pleasing thrumming, as of music above. They stood at an angle of the building. Up, along the side nearest them, mounted an iron stairway. At its top was an upright, illuminated parallelogram. Father Rogan had stopped, and stood, musing.

"I will say this much," he remarked, thoughtfully: "I believe you to be a better man than you think yourself to be, and a better man than I thought some hours ago. But do not take this," he added, with a smile, "as much praise. I promised you a possible deliverance from an unhappy perplexity. I will have to modify that promise. I can only remove the mystery that enhanced that perplexity. Your deliverance depends upon yourself. Come."

He led his companion up the stairway. Halfway up, Lorison caught him by the sleeve. "Remember," he gasped, "I love that woman."

"You desired to know."

"I—— Go on."

The priest reached the landing at the top of the stairway. Lorison, behind him, saw that the illuminated space was the glass upper half of a door opening into the lighted room. The rhythmic music increased as they neared it; the stairs shook with the mellow vibrations.

Lorison stopped breathing when he set foot upon the highest step, for the priest stood aside, and motioned him to look through the glass of the door.

His eye, accustomed to the darkness, met first a blinding glare, and then he made out the faces and forms of many people, amid an extravagant display of splendid robings—billowy laces, brilliant-hued finery, ribbons, silks, and misty drapery. And then he caught the meaning of that jarring hum, and he saw the tired, pale, happy face of his wife, bending, as were a score of others, over her sewing machine—toiling, toiling. Here was the folly she pursued, and the end of his quest.

But not his deliverance, though even then remorse struck him. His shamed soul fluttered once more before it retired to make room for the other and better one. For, to temper his thrill of joy, the shine of the satin and the glimmer of ornaments, recalled the disturbing figure of the bespangled Amazon, and the base duplicate histories lit by the glare of footlights and stolen diamonds. It is past the wisdom of him who only sets the scenes, either to praise or blame the man. But this time his love overcame his scruples. He took a quick step, and reached out his hand for the doorknob. Father Rogan was quicker to arrest it and draw him back.

"You use my trust in you queerly," said the priest, sternly. "What are you about to do?"

"I am going to my wife," said Lorison. "Let me pass."

"Listen," said the priest, holding him firmly by the arm. "I am about to put you in possession of a piece of knowledge of which, thus far, you have scarcely proved deserving. I do not think you ever will; but I will not dwell upon that. You see in that room the woman you married, working for a frugal living for herself, and a generous comfort for an idolized brother. This building belongs to the chief costumer of the city. For months the advance orders for the coming Mardi Gras festivals have kept the work going day and night. I myself secured employment here for Norah. She toils here each night from nine o'clock until daylight, and, besides, carries home with her some of the finer costumes, requiring more delicate needlework, and works there part of the day. Somehow, you two have remained strangely ignorant of each other's lives. Are you convinced now that your wife is not walking the streets?"

"Let me go to her," cried Lorison, again struggling, "and beg her forgiveness!"

"Sir," said the priest, "do you owe her nothing? Be quiet. It seems so often that Heaven lets fall its choicest gifts into hands that must be taught to hold them. Listen again. You forgot that repentant sin must not compromise, but look up, for redemption, to the purest and best. You went to her with the fine-spun sophistry that peace could be found in a mutual guilt; and she, fearful of losing what her heart so craved, thought it worth the price to buy it with a desperate, pure, beautiful lie. I have known her since the day she was born; she is as innocent and unsullied in life and deed as a holy saint. In that lowly street where she dwells she first saw the light, and she has lived there ever since, spending her days in generous self-sacrifice, for others. Och, ye spalpeen!" continued Father Rogan, raising his finger in kindly anger at Lorison. "What for, I wonder, could she be afther making a fool of hersuf, and shamin' her swate soul with lies, for the like of you!"

"Sir," said Lorison, trembling, "say what you please of me. Doubt it as you must, I will yet prove my gratitude to you, and my devotion to her. But let me speak to her once now, let me kneel for just one moment at her feet, and——"

"Tut, tut!" said the priest. "How many acts of a love drama do you think an old bookworm like me capable of witnessing? Besides, what kind of figures do we cut, spying upon the mysteries of midnight millinery! Go to meet your wife to-morrow, as she ordered you, and obey her thereafter, and maybe some time I shall get forgiveness for the part I have played in this night's work. Off wid yez down the shtairs, now! 'Tis late, and an ould man like me should be takin' his rest."

MADAME BO-PEEP, OF THE RANCHES

"AUNT ELLEN," said Octavia, cheerfully, as she threw her black kid gloves carefully at the dignified Persian cat on the window-seat, "I'm a pauper."

"You are so extreme in your statements, Octavia, dear," said Aunt Ellen, mildly, looking up from her paper. "If you find yourself temporarily in need of some small change for bonbons, you will find my purse in the drawer of the writing desk."

Octavia Beaupree removed her hat and seated herself on a footstool near her aunt's chair, clasping her hands about her knees. Her slim and flexible figure, clad in a modish mourning costume, accommodated itself easily and gracefully to the trying position. Her bright and youthful face, with its pair of sparkling, life-enamored eyes, tried to compose itself to the seriousness that the occasion seemed to demand.

"You good auntie, it isn't a case of bonbons; it is abject, staring, unpicturesque poverty, with ready-made clothes, gasolined gloves, and probably one-o'clock dinners all waiting with the traditional wolf at the door. I've just come from my lawyer, Auntie, and, 'Please, ma'am, I ain't got nothink 't all. Flowers, lady? Buttonhole, gentleman? Pencils, sir, three for five, to help a poor widow?' Do I do it nicely, Auntie, or, as a bread-winner accomplishment, were my lessons in elocution entirely wasted?"

"Do be serious, my dear," said Aunt Ellen, letting her paper fall to the floor, "long enough to tell me what you mean. Colonel Beaupree's estate——"

"Colonel Beaupree's estate," interrupted Octavia, emphasizing her words with appropriate dramatic gestures, "is of Spanish castellar architecture. Colonel Beaupree's resources are—wind. Colonel Beaupree's stocks are—water. Colonel Beaupree's income is—all in. The statement lacks the legal technicalities to which I have been listening for an hour, but that is what it means when translated."

"Octavia!" Aunt Ellen was now visibly possessed by consternation. "I can hardly believe it. And it was the impression that he was worth a million. And the De Peysters themselves introduced him!"

Octavia rippled out a laugh, and then became properly grave.

"*De mortuis nil*, Auntie—not even the rest of it. The dear old colonel—what a gold brick he was, after all! I paid for my bargain fairly—I'm all here, am I not?—items: eyes, fingers, toes, youth, old family, unquestionable position in society as called for in the contract—no wild-cat stock here." Octavia picked up the morning paper from the floor. "But I'm not going to 'squeal'—isn't that what they call it when you rail at Fortune because you've lost the game?" She turned the pages of the paper calmly. "'Stock market'—no use for that. 'Society's doings'—that's done. Here is my page—the wish column. A Van Dresser could not be said to 'want' for anything, of course. Chambermaids, cooks, canvassers, stenographers——"

"Dear," said Aunt Ellen, with a little tremor in her voice, "please do not talk in that way. Even if your affairs are in so unfortunate a condition, there is my three thousand——"

Octavia sprang up lithely, and deposited a smart kiss on the delicate cheek of the prim little elderly maid.

"Blessed auntie, your three thousand is just sufficient to insure your Hyson to be free from willow leaves and keep the Persian in sterilized cream. I know I'd be welcome, but I prefer to strike bottom like Beelzebub rather than hang around like the Peri listening to the music from the side entrance. I'm going to earn my own living. There's nothing else to do. I'm a—— Oh, oh, oh!—I had forgotten. There's one thing saved from the wreck. It's a corral—no, a ranch in—let me see—Texas; an asset, dear old Mr. Bannister called it. How pleased he was to show me something he could describe as unencumbered! I've a description of it among those stupid papers he made me bring away with me from his office. I'll try to find it."

Octavia found her shopping-bag, and drew from it a long envelope filled with typewritten documents.

"A ranch in Texas," sighed Aunt Ellen. "It sounds to me more like a liability than an asset. Those are the places where the centipedes are found, and cowboys, and fandangos."

"'The Rancho de las Sombras,'" read Octavia from a sheet of violently purple typewriting, "'is situated one hundred and ten miles southeast of San Antonio, and thirty-eight miles from its nearest railroad station, Nopal, on the I. and G. N. Ranch consists of 7,680 acres of well-watered land, with title conferred by State patents, and twenty-two sections, or 14,080 acres, partly under yearly running lease and partly bought under State's twenty-year-purchase act. Eight thousand graded merino sheep, with the necessary equipment of horses, vehicles, and general ranch paraphernalia. Ranch-house built of brick, with six rooms comfortably furnished according to the requirements of the climate. All within a strong barbed-wire fence.

" 'The present ranch manager seems to be competent and reliable, and is rapidly placing upon a paying basis a business that, in other hands, had been allowed to suffer from neglect and misconduct.

" 'This property was secured by Colonel Beaupree in a deal with a Western irrigation syndicate, and the title to it seems to be perfect. With careful management and the natural increase of land values, it ought to be made the foundation for a comfortable fortune for its owner.' "

When Octavia ceased reading, Aunt Ellen uttered something as near a sniff as her breeding permitted.

"The prospectus," she said, with uncompromising metropolitan suspicion, "doesn't mention the centipedes, or the Indians. And you never did like mutton, Octavia. I don't see what advantage you can derive from this—desert."

But Octavia was in a trance. Her eyes were steadily regarding something quite beyond their focus. Her lips were parted, and her face was lighted by the kindling furor of the explorer, the ardent, stirring disquiet of the adventurer. Suddenly she clasped her hands together exultantly.

"The problem solves itself, auntie," she cried. "I'm going to that ranch. I'm going to live on it. I'm going to learn to like mutton, and even concede the good qualities of centipedes—at a respectful distance. It's just what I need. It's a new life that comes when my old one is just ending. It's a release, auntie; it isn't a narrowing. Think of the gallops over those leagues of prairies, with the wind tugging at the roots of your hair, the coming close to the earth and learning over again the stories of the growing grass and the little wild flowers without names! Glorious is what it will be. Shall I be a shepherdess with a Watteau hat, and a crook to keep the bad wolves from the lambs, or a typical Western ranch girl, with short hair, like the pictures of her in the Sunday papers? I think the latter. And they'll have my picture, too, with the wild-cats I've slain, single-handed, hanging from my saddle horn. 'From the Four Hundred to the Flocks' is the way they'll headline it, and they'll print photographs of the old Van Dresser mansion and the church where I was married. They won't have my picture, but they'll get an artist to draw it. I'll be wild and woolly, and I'll grow my own wool."

"Octavia!" Aunt Ellen condensed into the one word all the protests she was unable to utter.

"Don't say a word, auntie. I'm going. I'll see the sky at night fit down on the world like a big butter-dish cover, and I'll make friends again with the stars that I haven't had a chat with since I was a wee child. I wish to go. I'm tired of all this. I'm glad I haven't any money. I could bless Colonel Beaupree for that ranch, and forgive him for all his bubbles. What if the life will be rough and lonely! I—I deserve it. I shut my heart to everything except that miserable ambition. I—oh, I wish to go away, and forget—forget!"

Octavia swerved suddenly to her knees, laid her flushed face in her aunt's lap, and shook with turbulent sobs.

Aunt Ellen bent over her, and smoothed the coppery-brown hair.

"I didn't know," she said, gently; "I didn't know—that. Who was it, dear?"

When Mrs. Octavia Beaupree, née Van Dresser, stepped from the train at Nopal, her manner lost, for the moment, some of that easy certitude which had always marked her movements. The town was of recent establishment, and seemed to have been hastily constructed of undressed lumber and flapping canvas. The element that had congregated about the station, though not offensively demonstrative, was clearly composed of citizens accustomed to and prepared for rude alarms.

Octavia stood on the platform, against the telegraph office, and attempted to choose by intuition from the swaggering, straggling string of loungers, the manager of the Rancho de las Sombras, who had been instructed by Mr. Bannister to meet her there. That tall, serious-looking, elderly man in the blue flannel shirt and white tie she thought must be he. But, no; he passed by, removing his gaze from the lady as hers rested on him, according to the Southern custom. The manager, she thought, with some impatience at being kept waiting, should have no difficulty in selecting her. Young women wearing the most recent thing in ash-colored traveling suits were not so plentiful in Nopal!

Thus keeping a speculative watch on all persons of possible managerial aspect, Octavia, with a catching breath and a start of surprise, suddenly became aware of Teddy Westlake hurring along the platform in the direction of the train— of Teddy Westlake or his sun-browned ghost in cheviot, boots and leather-girdled hat—Theodore Westlake, Jr., amateur polo (almost) champion, all-round butterfly and cumberer of the soil; but a broader, surer, more emphasized and determined Teddy than the one she had known a year ago when last she saw him.

He perceived Octavia at almost the same time, deflected his course, and steered for her in his old, straightforward way. Something like awe came upon her as the strangeness of his metamorphosis was brought into closer range; the rich, red-brown of his complexion brought out so vividly his straw-colored mustache and steel-gray eyes. He seemed more grown-up, and, somehow, farther away. But, when he spoke, the old, boyish Teddy came back again. They had been friends from childhood.

"Why, 'Tave!" he exclaimed, unable to reduce his perplexity to coherence. "How—what—when—where?"

"Train," said Octavia; "necessity; ten minutes ago; home. Your complexion's gone, Teddy. Now, how—what—when—where?"

"I'm working down here," said Teddy. He cast side glances about the station as one does who tries to combine politeness with duty.

"You didn't notice on the train," he asked, "an old lady with gray curls and a poodle, who occupied two seats with her bundles and quarrelled with the conductor, did you?"

"I think not," answered Octavia, reflecting. "And you haven't, by any chance, noticed a big, gray-mustached man in a blue shirt and six-shooters, with little flakes of merino wool sticking in his hair, have you?"

"Lots of 'em," said Teddy, with symptoms of mental delirium under the strain. "Do you happen to know any such individual?"

"No; the description is imaginary. Is your interest in the old lady whom you describe a personal one?"

"Never saw her in my life. She's painted entirely from fancy. She owns the little piece of property where I earn my bread and butter—the Rancho de las Sombras. I drove up to meet her according to arrangement with her lawyer."

Octavia leaned against the wall of the telegraph office. Was this possible? And didn't he know?

"Are you the manager of that ranch?" she asked, weakly.

"I am," said Teddy, with pride.

"I am Mrs. Beaupree," said Octavia, faintly; "but my hair never would curl, and I was polite to the conductor."

For a moment that strange, grown-up look came back, and removed Teddy miles away from her.

"I hope you'll excuse me," he said, rather awkwardly. "You see, I've been down here in the chaparral a year. I hadn't heard. Give me your checks, please, and I'll have your traps loaded into the wagon. José will follow with them. We travel ahead in the buckboard."

Seated by Teddy in a feather-weight buck-board, behind a pair of wild, cream-colored Spanish ponies, Octavia abandoned all thought for the exhilaration of the present. They swept out of the little town and down the level road toward the south. Soon the road dwindled and disappeared, and they struck across a world carpeted with an endless reach of curly mesquite grass. The wheels made no sound. The tireless ponies bounded ahead at an unbroken gallop. The temperate wind, made fragrant by thousands of acres of blue and yellow wild flowers, roared gloriously in their ears. The motion was aërial, ecstatic, with a thrilling sense of perpetuity in its effect. Octavia sat silent, possessed by a feeling of elemental, sensual bliss. Teddy seemed to be wrestling with some internal problem.

"I'm going to call you madama," he announced as the result of his labors. "That is what the Mexicans will call you—they're nearly all Mexicans on the ranch, you know. That seems to me about the proper thing."

"Very well, Mr. Westlake," said Octavia, primly.

"Oh, now," said Teddy, in some consternation, "that's carrying the thing too far, isn't it?"

"Don't worry me with your beastly etiquette. I'm just beginning to live. Don't remind me of anything artificial. If only this air could be bottled! This much alone is worth coming for. Oh, look! there goes a deer!"

"Jack-rabbit," said Teddy, without turning his head.

"Could I—might I drive?" suggested Octavia, panting, with rose-tinted cheeks and the eye of an eager child.

"On one condition. Could I—might I smoke?"

"Forever!" cried Octavia, taking the lines with solemn joy. "How shall I know which way to drive?"

"Keep her sou' by sou'east, and all sail set. You see that black speck on the horizon under that lowermost Gulf cloud? That's a group of live-oaks and a landmark. Steer halfway between that and the little hill to the left. I'll recite you the whole code of driving rules for the Texas prairies: keep the reins from under the horses' feet, and swear at 'em frequent."

"I'm too happy to swear, Ted. Oh, why do people buy yachts or travel in palace-cars, when a buckboard and a pair of plugs and a spring morning like this can satisfy all desire?"

"Now, I'll ask you," protested Teddy, who was futilely striking match after match on the dashboard, "not to call those denizens of the air plugs. They can kick out a hundred miles between daylight and dark." At last he succeeded in snatching a light for his cigar from the flame held in the hollow of his hands.

"Room!" said Octavia, intensely. "That's what produces the effect. I know now what I've wanted—scope—range—room!"

"Smoking-room," said Teddy, unsentimentally. "I love to smoke in a buck-board. The wind blows the smoke into you and out again. It saves exertion."

The two fell so naturally into their old-time goodfellowship that it was only by degrees that a sense of the strangeness of the new relations between them came to be felt.

"Madama," said Teddy, wonderingly, "however did you get it into your head to cut the crowd and come down here? Is it a fad now among the upper classes to trot off to sheep ranches instead of to Newport?"

"I was broke, Teddy," said Octavia, sweetly, with her interest centred upon steering safely between a Spanish dagger plant and a clump of chaparral; "I haven't a thing in the world but this ranch—not even any other home to go to."

"Come, now," said Teddy, anxiously but incredulously, "you don't mean it?"

"When my husband," said Octavia, with a shy slurring of the word, "died three months ago I thought I had a reasonable amount of the world's goods. His lawyer exploded that theory in a sixty-minute fully illustrated lecture. I took to the sheep as a last resort. Do you happen to know of any fashionable caprice among the gilded youth of Manhattan that induces them to abandon polo and club windows to become managers of sheep ranches?"

"It's easily explained in my case," responded Teddy, promptly. "I had to go to work. I couldn't have earned my board in New York, so I chummed a while with old Sandford, one of the syndicate that owned the ranch before Colonel Beaupree bought it, and got a place down here. I wasn't manager at first. I jogged around on ponies and studied the business in detail, until I got all the points in my head. I saw where it was losing and what the remedies were, and then Sandford put me in charge. I get a hundred dollars a month, and I earn it."

"Poor Teddy!" said Octavia, with a smile.

"You needn't. I like it. I save half my wages, and I'm as hard as a water plug. It beats polo."

"Will it furnish bread and tea and jam for another outcast from civilization?"

"The spring shearing," said the manager, "just cleaned up a deficit in last year's business. Wastefulness and inattention have been the rule heretofore. The autumn clip will leave a small profit over all expenses. Next year there will be jam."

When, about four o'clock in the afternoon, the ponies rounded a gentle, brush-covered hill, and then swooped, like a double cream-colored cyclone, upon the Rancho de las Sombras, Octavia gave a little cry of delight. A lordly grove of magnificent live-oaks cast an area of grateful, cool shade, whence the ranch had drawn its name, "de las Sombras'—of the shadows. The house, of red brick, one story, ran low and long beneath the trees. Through its middle, dividing its six rooms in half, extended a broad, arched passageway, picturesque with flowering cactus and hanging red earthen jars. A "gallery," low and broad, encircled the building. Vines climbed about it, and the adjacent ground was, for a space, covered with transplanted grass and shrubs. A little lake, long and narrow, glimmered in the sun at the rear. Farther away stood the shacks of the Mexican workers, the corrals, wool sheds and shearing pens. To the right lay the low hills, splattered with dark patches of chaparral; to the left the unbounded green prairie blending against the blue heavens.

"It's a home, Teddy," said Octavia, breathlessly; "that's what it is—it's a home."

"Not so bad for a sheep ranch," admitted Teddy, with excusable pride. "I've been tinkering on it at odd times."

A Mexican youth sprang from somewhere in the grass, and took charge of the creams. The mistress and the manager entered the house.

"Here's Mrs. MacIntyre," said Teddy, as a placid, neat, elderly lady came out upon the gallery to meet them. "Mrs. Mac, here's the boss. Very likely she will be wanting a hunk of bacon and a dish of beans after her drive."

Mrs. MacIntyre, the housekeeper, as much a fixture on the place as the lake or the live-oaks, received the imputation of the ranch's resources of refreshment with mild indignation, and was about to give it utterances when Octavia spoke.

"Oh, Mrs. MacIntyre, don't apologize for Teddy. Yes, I call him Teddy. So does every one whom he hasn't duped into taking him seriously. You see, we used to cut paper dolls and play jackstraws together ages ago. No one minds what he says."

"No," said Teddy, "no one minds what he says, just so he doesn't do it again."

Octavia cast one of those subtle, sidelong glances toward him from beneath her lowered eyelids—a glance that Teddy used to describe as an upper-cut. But

there was nothing in his ingenuous, weather-tanned face to warrant a suspicion
that he was making an allusion—nothing. Beyond a doubt, thought Octavia, he
had forgotten.

"Mr. Westlake likes his fun," said Mrs. MacIntyre, as she conducted Octavia
to her rooms. "But," she added, loyally, "people around here usually pay attention to what he says when he talks in earnest. I don't know what would
have become of this place without him."

Two rooms at the east end of the house had been arranged for the occupancy
of the ranch's mistress. When she entered them a slight dismay seized her at
their bare appearance and the scantiness of their furniture; but she quickly reflected that the climate was a semi-tropical one, and was moved to appreciation
of the well-conceived efforts to conform to it. The sashes had already been
removed from the big windows, and white curtains waved in the Gulf breeze
that streamed through the wide jalousies. The bare floor was amply strewn
with cool rugs; the chairs were inviting, deep, dreamy willows; the walls were
papered with a light, cheerful olive. One whole side of her sitting room was
covered with books on smooth, unpainted pine shelves. She flew to these at
once. Before her was a well-selected library. She caught glimpses of titles of
volumes of fiction and travel not yet seasoned from the dampness of the press.

Presently, recollecting that she was now in a wilderness given over to mutton,
centipedes, and privations, the incongruity of these luxuries struck her, and,
with intuitive feminine suspicion, she began turning to the fly-leaves of volume
after volume. Upon each one was inscribed in fluent characters the name of
Theodore Westlake, Jr.

Octavia, fatigued by her long journey, retired early that night. Lying upon
her white, cool bed, she rested deliciously, but sleep coquetted long with her.
She listened to faint noises whose strangeness kept her faculties on the alert
—the fractious yelping of the coyotes, the ceaseless, low symphony of the wind,
the distant booming of the frogs about the lake, the lamentation of a concertina
in the Mexicans' quarters. There were many conflicting feelings in her heart
—thankfulness and rebellion, peace and disquietude, loneliness and a sense of
protecting care, happiness and an old, haunting pain.

She did what any other woman would have done—sought relief in a wholesome tide of unreasonable tears, and her last words, murmured to herself before
slumber, capitulating, came softly to woo her, were, "He has forgotten."

The manager of the Rancho de las Sombras was no dilettante. He was a
"hustler." He was generally up, mounted, and away of mornings before the
rest of the household were awake, making the rounds of the flocks and camps.
This was the duty of the major-domo, a stately old Mexican with a princely air
and manner, but Teddy seemed to have a great deal of confidence in his own
eyesight. Except in the busy seasons, he nearly always returned to the ranch to
breakfast at eight o'clock, with Octavia and Mrs. MacIntyre, at the little table
set in the central hallway, bringing with him a tonic and breezy cheerfulness
full of the health and flavor of the prairies.

A few days after Octavia's arrival he made her get out one of her riding skirts,
and curtail it to a shortness demanded by the chaparral brakes.

With some misgivings she donned this and the pair of buckskin leggings he
prescribed in addition, and, mounted upon a dancing pony, rode with him to
view her possessions. He showed her everything—the flocks of ewes, muttons and
grazing lambs, the dipping vats, the shearing pens, the uncouth merino rams
in their little pasture, the water-tanks prepared against the summer drought—
giving account of his stewardship with a boyish enthusiasm that never flagged.

Where was the old Teddy that she knew so well? This side of him was
the same, and it was a side that pleased her; but this was all she ever saw of
him now. Where was his sentimentality—those old, varying moods of impetuous

love-making, of fanciful, quixotic devotion, of heart-breaking gloom, of alternating, absurd tenderness and haughty dignity? His nature had been a sensitive one, his temperament bordering closely on the artistic. She knew that, besides being a follower of fashion and its fads and sports, he had cultivated tastes of a finer nature. He had written things, he had tampered with colors, he was something of a student in certain branches of art, and once she had been admitted to all his aspirations and thoughts. But now—and she could not avoid the conclusion—Teddy had barricaded against her every side of himself except one —the side that showed the manager of the Rancho de las Sombras and a jolly chum who had forgiven and forgotten. Queerly enough the words of Mr. Bannister's description of her property came into her mind—"all inclosed within a strong barbed-wire fence."

"Teddy's fenced, too," said Octavia to herself.

It was not difficult for her to reason out the cause of his fortifications. It had originated one night at the Hammersmiths' ball. It occurred at a time soon after she had decided to accept Colonel Beaupree and his millions, which was no more than her looks and the entrée she held to the inner circles were worth. Teddy had proposed with all his impetuosity and fire, and she looked him straight in the eyes, and said, coldly and finally: "Never let me hear any such silly nonsense from you again." "You won't," said Teddy, with a new expression around his mouth, and—now Teddy was inclosed within a strong barbed-wire fence.

It was on this first ride of inspection that Teddy was seized by the inspiration that suggested the name of Mother Goose's heroine, and he at once bestowed it upon Octavia. The idea, supported by both a similarity of names and identity of occupations, seemed to strike him as a peculiarly happy one, and he never tired of using it. The Mexicans on the ranch also took up the name, adding another syllable to accommodate their lingual incapacity for the final "p," gravely referring to her as "La Madama Bo-Peepy." Eventually it spread, and "Madame Bo-Peep's ranch" was as often mentioned as the "Rancho de las Sombras."

Came the long, hot season from May to September, when work is scarce on the ranches. Octavia passed the days in a kind of lotus-eater's dream. Books, hammocks, correspondence with a few intimate friends, a renewed interest in her old water-color box and easel—these disposed of the sultry hours of daylight. The evenings were always sure to bring enjoyment. Best of all were the rapturous horseback rides with Teddy, when the moon gave light over the wind-swept leagues, chaperoned by the wheeling night-hawk and the startled owl. Often the Mexicans would come up from their shacks with their guitars and sing the weirdest of heart-breaking songs. There were long, cosy chats on the breezy gallery, and an interminable warfare of wits between Teddy and Mrs. MacIntyre, whose abundant Scotch shrewdness often more than overmatched the lighter humor in which she was lacking.

And the nights came, one after another, and were filed away by weeks and months—nights soft and languorous and fragrant, that should have driven Strephon to Chloe over wires however barbed, that might have drawn Cupid himself to hunt, lasso in hand, among those amorous pastures—but Teddy kept his fences up.

One July night Madame Bo-Peep and her ranch manager were sitting on the east gallery. Teddy had been exhausting the science of prognostication as to the probabilities of a price of twenty-four cents for the autumn clip, and had then subsided into an anæsthetic cloud of Havana smoke. Only as incompetent a judge as a woman would have failed to note long ago that at least a third of his salary must have gone up in the fumes of those imported Regalias.

"Teddy," said Octavia, suddenly, and rather sharply, "what are you working down here on a ranch for?"

"One hundred per," said Teddy, glibly, "and found."

"I've a good mind to discharge you."

"Can't do it," said Teddy, with a grin.

"Why not?" demanded Octavia, with argumentative heat.

"Under contract. Terms of sale respect all unexpired contracts. Mine runs until 12 P. M., December thirty-first. You might get up at midnight on that date and fire me. If you try it sooner I'll be in a position to bring legal proceedings."

Octavia seemed to be considering the prospects of litigation.

"But," continued Teddy, cheerfully, "I've been thinking of resigning anyway."

Octavia's rocking-chair ceased its motion. There were centipedes in this country, she felt sure; and Indians; and vast, lonely, desolate, empty wastes; all within strong barbed-wire fence. There was a Van Dresser pride, but there was also a Van Dresser heart. She must know for certain whether or not he had forgotten.

"Ah, well, Teddy," she said, with a fine assumption of polite interest, "it's lonely down here; you're longing to get back to the old life—to polo and lobsters and theatres and balls."

"Never cared much for balls," said Teddy, virtuously.

"You're getting old, Teddy. Your memory is failing. Nobody ever knew you to miss a dance, unless it occurred on the same night with another one which you attended. And you showed such shocking bad taste, too, in dancing too often with same partner. Let me see, what was that Forbes girl's name—the one with wall eyes—Mabel, wasn't it?"

"No; Adèle. Mabel was the one with the bony elbows. That wasn't wall in Adèle's eyes. It was soul. We used to talk sonnets together, and Verlaine. Just then I was trying to run a pipe from the Pierian spring."

"You were on the floor with her," said Octavia, undeflected, "five times at the Hammersmiths'."

"Hammersmiths' what?" questioned Teddy, vacuously.

"Ball—ball," said Octavia, viciously. "What were we talking of?"

"Eyes, I thought," said Teddy, after some reflection; "and elbows."

"Those Hammersmiths," went on Octavia, in her sweetest society prattle, after subduing an intense desire to yank a handful of sunburnt, sandy hair from the head lying back contentedly against the canvas of the steamer chair, "had too much money. Mines, wasn't it? It was something that paid something to the ton. You couldn't get a glass of plain water in their house. Everything at that ball was dreadfully overdone."

"It was," said Teddy.

"Such a crowd there was!" Octavia continued conscious that she was talking the rapid drivel of a school-girl describing her first dance. "The balconies were as warm as the rooms. I—lost—something at that ball." The last sentence was uttered in a tone calculated to remove the barbs from miles of wire.

"So did I," confessed Teddy, in a lower voice.

"A glove," said Octavia, falling back as the enemy approached her ditches.

"Caste," said Teddy, halting his firing line without loss. "I hobnobbed, half evening, with one of Hammersmith's miners, a fellow who kept his hands in his pockets, and talked like an archangel about reduction plants and drifts and levels and sluice-boxes."

"A pearl-gray glove, nearly new," sighed Octavia, mournfully.

"A bang-up chap, that McArdle," maintained Teddy, approvingly. "A man who hated olives and elevators; a man who handled mountains as croquettes, and built tunnels in the air; a man who never uttered a word of silly nonsense in his life. Did you sign those lease-renewal applications yet, madama? They've got to be on file in the land office by the thirty-first."

Teddy turned his head lazily. Octavia's chair was vacant.

A certain centipede, crawling along the lines marked out by fate, expounded the situation. It was early one morning while Octavia and Mrs. MacIntyre were trimming the honeysuckle on the west gallery. Teddy had risen and departed hastily before daylight in response to a word that a flock of ewes had been scattered from their bedding ground during the night by a thunder-storm.

The centipede, driven by destiny, showed himself on the floor of the gallery, and then, the screeches of the two women giving him his cue, he scuttled with all his yellow legs through the open door into the furthermost west room, which was Teddy's. Arming themselves with domestic utensils selected with regard to their length, Octavia and Mrs. MacIntyre, with much clutching of skirts and skirmishing for the position of rear guard in the attacking force, followed.

Once outside, the centipede seemed to have disappeared, and his prospective murderers began a thorough but cautious search for their victim.

Even in the midst of such a dangerous and absorbing adventure Octavia was conscious of an awed curiosity on finding herself in Teddy's sanctum. In that room he sat alone, silently communing with those secret thoughts that he now shared with no one, dreamed there whatever dreams he now called on no one to interpret.

It was the room of a Spartan or a soldier. In one corner stood a wide, canvas-covered cot; in another, a small bookcase; in another, a grim stand of Winchesters and shotguns. An immense table, strewn with letters, papers, and documents and surmounted by a set of pigeon-holes, occupied one side.

The centipede showed genius in concealing himself in such bare quarters. Mrs. MacIntyre was poking a broom-handle behind the bookcase. Octavia approached Teddy's cot. The room was just as the manager had left it in his hurry. The Mexican maid had not yet given it her attention. There was his big pillow with the imprint of his head still in the centre. She thought the horrid beast might have climbed the cot and hidden itself to bite Teddy. Centipedes were thus cruel and vindictive toward managers.

She cautiously overturned the pillow, and then parted her lips to give the signal for reinforcements at sight of a long, slender, dark object lying there. But, repressing it in time, she caught up a glove, a pearl-gray glove, flattened—it might be conceived—by many, many months of nightly pressure beneath the pillow of the man who had forgotten the Hammersmiths' ball. Teddy must have left so hurriedly that morning that he had, for once, forgotten to transfer it to its resting-place by day. Even managers, who are notoriously wily and cunning, are sometimes caught up with.

Octavia slid the gray glove into the bosom of her summery morning gown. It was hers. Men who put themselves within a strong barbed-wire fence, and remember Hammersmith balls only by the talk of miners about sluice-boxes, should not be allowed to possess such articles.

After all, what a paradise this prairie country was! How it blossomed like the rose when you found things that were thought to be lost! How delicious was that morning breeze coming in the windows, fresh and sweet with the breath of the yellow ratama blooms! Might one not stand, for a minute, with shining, far-gazing eyes, and dream that mistakes might be corrected?

Why was Mrs. MacIntyre poking about so absurdly with a broom?

"I've found it," said Mrs. MacIntyre, banging the door. "Here it is."

"Did you lose something?" asked Octavia, with sweetly polite non-interest.

"The little devil!" said Mrs. MacIntyre, driven to violence. "Ye've no forgotten him alretty?"

Between them they slew the centipede. Thus was he rewarded for his agency toward the recovery of things lost at the Hammersmiths' ball.

It seems that Teddy, in due course, remembered the glove, and when he returned to the house at sunset made a secret but exhaustive search for it. Not until evening, upon the moonlit eastern gallery, did he find it. It was upon the hand that he had thought lost to him forever, and so he was moved to repeat certain nonsense that he had been commanded never, never to utter again. Teddy's fences were down.

This time there was no ambition to stand in the way, and the wooing was as natural and successful as should be between ardent shepherd and gentle shepherdess.

The prairies changed to a garden. The Rancho de las Sombras became the Ranch of Light.

A few days later Octavia received a letter from Mr. Bannister, in reply to one she had written to him asking some questions about her business. A portion of the letter ran as follows:

I am at a loss to account for your references to the sheep ranch. Two months after your departure to take up your residence upon it, it was discovered that Colonel Beaupree's title was worthless. A deed came to light showing that he disposed of the property before his death. The matter was reported to your manager, Mr. Westlake, who at once repurchased the property. It is entirely beyond my powers of conjecture to imagine how you have remained in ignorance of this fact. I beg that you will at once confer with that gentleman, who will, at least, corroborate my statement.

Octavia sought Teddy, with battle in her eye.

"What are you working on this ranch for?" she asked once more.

"One hundred——" he began to repeat, but saw in her face that she knew. She held Mr. Bannister's letter in her hand. He knew that the game was up.

"It's my ranch," said Teddy, like a schoolboy detected in evil. "It's a mighty poor manager that isn't able to absorb the boss's business if you give him time."

"Why were you working down here?" pursued Octavia, still struggling after the key to the riddle of Teddy.

"To tell the truth, 'Tave," said Teddy, with quiet candor, "it wasn't for the salary. That about kept me in cigars and sunburn lotions. I was sent south by my doctor. 'Twas that right lung that was going to the bad on account of over-exercise and strain at polo and gymnastics. I needed climate and ozone and rest and things of that sort."

In an instant Octavia was close against the vicinity of the affected organ. Mr. Bannister's letter fluttered to the floor.

"It's—it's well now, isn't it, Teddy?"

"Sound as a mesquite chunk. I deceived you in one thing. I paid fifty thousand for your ranch as soon as I found you had no title. I had just about that much income accumulated at my banker's while I've been herding sheep down here, so it was almost like picking the thing up on a bargain-counter for a penny. There's another little surplus of unearned increment piling up there, 'Tave. I've been thinking of a wedding trip in a yacht with white ribbons tied to the mast, through the Mediterranean, and then up among the Hebrides and down Norway to the Zuyder Zee."

"And I was thinking," said Octavia, softly, "of a wedding gallop with my manager among the flocks of sheep and back to a wedding breakfast with Mrs. MacIntyre on the gallery, with, maybe, a sprig of orange blossom fastened to the red jar above the table."

Teddy laughed, and began to chant:

> "Little Bo-Peep has lost her sheep,
> And doesn't know where to find 'em.

Let 'em alone, and they'll come home,
And——"

Octavia drew his head down, and whispered in his ear.
But that is one of the tales they brought behind them.

THE VOICE OF THE CITY

THE VOICE OF THE CITY

THE VOICE OF THE CITY

THE VOICE OF THE CITY

TWENTY-FIVE years ago the school children used to chant their lessons. The manner of their delivery was a singsong recitative between the utterance of an Episcopal minister and the drone of a tired sawmill. I mean no disrespect. We must have lumber and sawdust.

I remember one beautiful and instructive little lyric that emanated frcm the physiology class. The most striking line of it was this:

"The shin-bone is the long-est bone in the human bod-y."

What an inestimable boon it would have been if all the corporeal and spiritual facts pertaining to man had thus been tunefully and logically inculcated in our youthful minds! But what we gained in anatomy, music, and philosophy was meagre.

The other day I became confused. I needed a ray of light. I turned back to those school days for aid. But in all the nasal harmonies we whined forth from those hard benches I could not recall one that treated of the voice of agglomerated mankind.

In other words, of the composite vocal message of massed humanity.

In other words, of the Voice of a Big City.

Now, the individual voice is not lacking. We can understand the song of the poet, the ripple of the brook, the meaning of the man who wants $5 until next Monday, the inscriptions on the tombs of the Pharoahs, the language of flowers, the "step lively" of the conductor, and the prelude of the milk cans at 4 A. M. Certain large-eared ones even assert that they are wise to the vibrations of the tympanum produced by concussion of the air emanating from Mr. H. James. But who can comprehend the meaning of the voice of the city?

I went out for to see.

First, I asked Aurelia. She wore white Swiss and a hat with flowers on it, and ribbons and ends of things fluttered here and there.

"Tell me," I said, stammeringly, for I have no voice of my own, "what does this big—er—enormous—er—whopping city say? It must have a voice of some kind. Does it ever speak to you? How do you interpret its meaning? It is a tremendous mass, but it must have a key."

"Like a Saratoga trunk?" asked Aurelia.

"No," said I. "Please do not refer to the lid. I have a fancy that every city has a voice. Each one has something to say to the one who can hear it. What does the big one say to you?"

"All cities," said Aurelia, judicially, "say the same thing. When they get ʾhrough saying it there is an echo from Philadelphia. So, they are unanimous."

"Here are 4,000,000 people," said I, scholastically, "compressed upon an island, which is mostly lamb surrounded by Wall Street water. The conjunction of so many units into so small a space must result in an identity—or, or rather a homogeneity—that finds its oral expression through a common channel. It is,

977

as you might say, a consensus of translation, concentrating in a crystallized, general idea which reveals itself in what may be termed the Voice of the City. Can you tell me what it is?"

Aurelia smiled wonderfully. She sat on the high stoop. A spray of insolent ivy bobbed against her right ear. A ray of impudent moonlight flickered upon her nose. But I was adamant, nickel-plated.

"I must go and find out," I said, "what is the Voice of this City. Other cities have voices. It is an assignment. I must have it. New York," I continued, in a rising tone, "had better not hand me a cigar and say: 'Old man, I can't talk for publication.' No other city acts in that way. Chicago says, unhesitatingly, 'I will'; Philadelphia says, 'I should'; New Orleans says, 'I used to'; Louisville says, 'Don't care if I do'; St. Louis says, 'Excuse me'; Pittsburg says, 'Smoke up.' Now, New York——"

Aurelia smiled.

"Very well," said I, "I must go elsewhere and find out."

I went into a palace, tile-floored, cherub-ceilinged, and square with the cop. I put my foot on the brass rail and said to Billy Magnus, the best bartender in the diocese:

"Billy, you've lived in New York a long time—what kind of a song-and-dance does this old town give you? What I mean is, doesn't the gab of it seem to kind of bunch up and slide over the bar to you in a sort of amalgamated tip that hits off the burg in a kind of an epigram with a dash of bitters and a slice of——"

"Excuse me a minute," said Billy, "somebody's punching the button at the side door."

He went away; came back with an empty tin bucket; again vanished with it full; returned and said to me:

"That was Mame. She rings twice. She likes a glass of beer for supper. Her and the kid. If you ever saw that little skeesicks of mine brace up in his high chair and take his beer and—— But, say, what was yours? I get kind of excited when I hear them two rings—was it the baseball score or gin fizz you asked for?"

"Ginger ale," I answered.

I walked up to Broadway. I saw a cop on the corner. The cops take kids up, women across, and men in. I went up to him.

"If I'm not exceeding the spiel limit," I said, "let me ask you. You see New York during its vocative hours. It is the function of you and your brother cops to preserve the acoustics of the city. There must be a civic voice that is intelligible to you. At night during your lonely rounds you must have heard it. What is the epitome of its turmoil and shouting? What does the city say to you?"

"Friend," said the policeman, spinning his club, "it don't say nothing. I get my orders from the man higher up. Say, I guess you're all right. Stand here for a few minutes and keep an eye open for the roundsman."

The cop melted into the darkness of the side street. In ten minutes he had returned.

"Married last Tuesday," he said, half gruffly. "You know how they are. She comes to that corner at nine every night for a—comes to say 'hello!' I generally manage to be there. Say, what was it you asked me a bit ago—what's doing in the city? Oh, there's a roof-garden or two just opened, twelve blocks up."

I crossed a crow's-foot of street-car tracks, and skirted the edge of an umbrageous park. An artificial Diana, gilded, heroic, poised, wind-ruled, on the tower, shimmered in the clear light of her namesake in the sky. Along came my poet, hurrying, hatted, haired, emitting dactyls, spondees and dactylis. I seized him.

"Bill," said I (in the mazagine he is Cleon), "give me a lift. I am on an assignment to find out the Voice of the City. You see, it's a special order. Ordinarily a symposium comprising the views of Henry Clews, John L. Sullivan, Edwin Markham, May Irwin and Charles Schwab would be about all. But this is a different matter. We want a broad, poetic, mystic vocalization of the city's soul and meaning. You are the very chap to give me a hint. Some years ago a man got at the Niagara Falls and gave us its pitch. The note was about two feet below the lowest G on the piano. Now, you can't put New York into a note unless it's better indorsed than that. But give me an idea of what it would say if it should speak. It is bound to be a mighty and far-reaching utterance. To arrive at it we must take the tremendous crash of the chords of the day's traffic, the laughter and music of the night, the solemn tones of Dr. Parkhurst, the rag-time, the weeping, the stealthy hum of cab-wheels, the shout of the press agent, the tinkle of fountains on the roof-gardens, the hullabaloo of the strawberry vender and the covers of *Everybody's Magazine*, the whispers of the lovers in the parks—all these sounds must go into your Voice—not combined, but mixed, and of the mixture an essence made; and of the essence an extract—an audible extract, of which one drop shall form the thing we seek."

"Do you remember," asked the poet, with a chuckle, "that California girl we met at Stiver's studio last week? Well, I'm on my way to see her. She repeated that poem of mine, 'The Tribute of Spring,' word for word. She's the smartest proposition in this town just at present. Say, how does this confounded tie look? I spoiled four before I got one to set right."

"And the Voice that I asked you about?" I inquired.

"Oh, she doesn't sing," said Cleon. "But you ought to hear her recite my 'Angel of the Inshore Wind.'"

I passed on. I cornered a newsboy and he flashed at me prophetic pink papers that outstripped the news by two revolutions of the clock's longest hand.

"Son," I said, while I pretended to chase coins in my penny pocket, "doesn't it sometimes seem to you as if the city ought to be able to talk? All these ups and downs and funny business and queer things happening every day—what would it say, do you think, if it could speak?"

"Quit yer kiddin'," said the boy. "Wot paper yer want? I got no time to waste. It's Mag's birthday, and I want thirty cents to git her a present."

Here was no interpreter of the city's mouth-piece. I bought a paper, and consigned its undeclared treaties, its premeditated murders and unfought battles to an ash can.

Again I repaired to the park and sat in the moon shade. I thought and thought, and wondered why none could tell me what I asked for.

And then, as swift as light from a fixed star, the answer came to me. I arose and hurried—hurried as so many reasoners must, back around my circle. I knew the answer and I hugged it in my breast as I flew, fearing lest some one would stop me and demand my secret.

Aurelia was still on the stoop. The moon was higher and the ivy shadows were deeper. I sat at her side and we watched a little cloud tilt at the drifting moon and go asunder quite pale and discomfited.

And then, wonder of wonders and delight of delights! our hands somehow touched, and our fingers closed together and did not part.

After half an hour Aurelia said, with that smile of hers:

"Do you know, you haven't spoken a word since you came back!"

"That," said I, nodding wisely, "is the Voice of the City."

THE COMPLETE LIFE OF JOHN HOPKINS

THERE is a saying that no man has tasted the full flavor of life until he has known poverty, love, and war. The justness of this reflection commends it to the lover of condensed philosophy. The three conditions embrace about all there is in life worth knowing. A surface thinker might deem that wealth should be added to the list. Not so. When a poor man finds a long-hidden quarter-dollar that has slipped through a rip into his vest lining, he sounds the pleasure of life with a deeper plummet than any millionaire can hope to cast.

It seems that the wise executive power that rules life has thought best to drill man in these three conditions; and none may escape all three. In rural places the terms do not mean so much. Poverty is less pinching; love is temperate; war shrinks to contests about boundary lines and the neighbors' hens. It is in the cities that our epigram gains in truth and vigor; and it has remained for one John Hopkins to crowd the experience into a rather small space of time.

The Hopkins flat was like a thousand others. There was a rubber plant in one window; a flea-bitten terrier sat in the other, wondering when he was to have his day.

John Hopkins was like a thousand others. He worked at $20 per week in a nine-story, red-brick building at either Insurance, Buckle's Hoisting Engines, Chiropody, Loans, Pulleys, Boas Renovated, Waltz Guaranteed in Five Lessons, or Artificial Limbs. It is not for us to wring Mr. Hopkins's avocation from these outward signs that be.

Mrs. Hopkins was like a thousand others. The auriferous tooth, the sedentary disposition, the Sunday afternoon wanderlust, the draught upon the delicatessen store for home-made comforts, the furor for department store marked-down sales, the feeling of superiority to the lady in the third-floor front who wore genuine ostrich tips and had two names over her bell, the mucilaginous hours during which she remained glued to the window sill, the vigilant avoidance of the in-stalment man, the tireless patronage of the acoustics of the dumb-waiter shaft —all the attributes of the Gotham flat-dweller were hers.

One moment yet of sententiousness and the story moves.

In the Big City large and sudden things happen. You round a corner and thrust the rib of your umbrella into the eye of your old friend from Kootenai Falls. You stroll out to pluck a Sweet William in the park—and lo! bandits attack you—you are ambulanced to the hospital—you marry your nurse; are divorced—get squeezed while short on U. P. S. and D. O. W. N. S.—stand in the bread line—marry an heiress, take out your laundry and pay your club dues— seemingly all in the wink of an eye. You travel the streets, and a finger beckons to you, a handkerchief is dropped for you, a brick is dropped upon you, the elevator cable or your bank breaks, a table d'hôte or your wife disagrees with you, and Fate tosses you about like cork crumbs in wine opened by an un-feed waiter. The City is a sprightly youngster, and you are red paint upon its toy, and you get licked off.

John Hopkins sat, after a compressed dinner, in his glove-fitting straight-front flat. He sat upon a hornblende couch and gazed, with satiated eyes, at Art Brought Home to the People in the shape of "The Storm" tacked against the wall. Mrs. Hopkins discoursed droningly of the dinner smells from the flat across the hall. The flea-bitten terrier gave Hopkins a look of disgust and showed a man-hating tooth.

Here was neither poverty, love, nor war; but upon such barren stems may be grafted those essentials of a complete life.

John Hopkins sought to inject a few raisins of conversation into the tasteless dough of existence. "Putting a new elevator in at the office," he said, discarding the nominative noun, "and the boss has turned out his whiskers."

"You don't mean it!" commented Mrs. Hopkins.

"Mr. Whipples," continued John, "wore his new spring suit down to-day. I liked it fine. It's a gray with——" He stopped, suddenly stricken by a need that made itself known to him. "I believe I'll walk down to the corner and get a five-cent cigar," he concluded.

John Hopkins took his hat and picked his way down the musty halls and stairs of the flat-house.

The evening air was mild, and the streets shrill with the careless cries of children playing games controlled by mysterious rhythms and phrases. Their elders held the doorways and steps with leisurely pipe and gossip. Paradoxically, the fire-escapes supported lovers in couples who made no attempt to fly the mounting conflagration they were there to fan.

The corner cigar store aimed at by John Hopkins was kept by a man named Freshmayer, who looked upon the earth as a sterile promontory.

Hopkins, unknown in the store, entered and called genially for his "bunch of spinach, carfare grade." This imputation deepened the pessimism of Freshmayer; but he set out a brand that came perilously near to filling the order. Hopkins bit off the roots of his purchase, and lighted up at the swinging gas jet. Feeling in his pockets to make payment, he found not a penny there.

"Say, my friend," he explained, frankly, "I've come out without any change. Hand you that nickel first time I pass."

Joy surged in Freshmayer's heart. Here was corroboration of his belief that the world was rotten and man a peripatetic evil. Without a word he rounded the end of his counter and made earnest onslaught upon his customer. Hopkins was no man to serve as a punching-bag for a pessimistic tobacconist. He quickly bestowed upon Freshmayer a colorado-maduro eye in return for the ardent kick that he received from the dealer in goods for cash only.

The impetus of the enemy's attack forced the Hopkins line back to the sidewalk. There the conflict raged; the pacific wooden Indian, with his carven smile, was overturned, and those of the street who delighted in carnage pressed round to view the zealous joust.

But then came the inevitable cop and imminent inconvenience for both the attacker and attacked. John Hopkins was a peaceful citizen, who worked at rebuses of nights in a flat, but he was not without the fundamental spirit of resistance that comes with the battle-rage. He knocked the policeman into a grocer's sidewalk display of goods and gave Freshmayer a punch that caused him temporarily to regret that he had not made it a rule to extend a five-cent line of credit to certain customers. Then Hopkins took spiritedly to his heels down the sidewalk, closely followed by the cigar-dealer and the policeman, whose uniform testified to the reason in the grocer's sign that read: "Eggs cheaper than anywhere else in the city."

As Hopkins ran he became aware of a big, low, red, racing automobile that kept abreast of him in the street. This auto steered in to the side of the sidewalk, and the man guiding it motioned to Hopkins to jump into it. He did so without slackening his speed, and fell into the turkey-red upholstered seat beside the chauffeur. The big machine, with a diminuendo cough, flew away like an albatross down the avenue into which the street emptied.

The driver of the auto sped his machine without a word. He was masked beyond guess in the goggles and diabolic garb of the chauffeur.

"Much obliged, old man," called Hopkins, gratefully. "I guess you've got sporting blood in you, all right, and don't admire the sight of two men trying to soak one. Little more and I'd have been pinched."

The chauffeur made no sign that he had heard. Hopkins shrugged a shoulder and chewed at his cigar, to which his teeth had clung grimly throughout the mêlée.

Ten minutes and the auto turned into the open carriage entrance of a noble mansion of brown stone, and stood still. The chauffeur leaped out, and said:

"Come quick. The lady, she will explain. It is the great honor you will have, monsieur. Ah, that milady could call upon Armand to do this thing! But, no, I am only one chauffeur."

With vehement gestures the chauffeur conducted Hopkins into the house. He was ushered into a small but luxurious reception chamber. A lady, young, and possessing the beauty of visions, rose from a chair. In her eyes smouldered a becoming anger. Her high-arched, thread-like brows were ruffled into a delicious frown.

"Milady," said the chauffeur, bowing low, "I have the honor to relate to you that I went to the house of Monsieur Long and found him to be not at home. As I came back I see this gentleman in combat against—how you say—greatest odds. He is fighting with five—ten—thirty men—gendarmes, *aussi*. Yes, milady, he what you call 'swat' one—three—eight policemans. If that Monsieur Long is out I say to myself this gentleman he will serve milady so well, and I bring him here.'

"Very well, Armand," said the lady, "you may go." She turned to Hopkins.

"I sent my chauffeur," she said, "to bring my cousin, Walter Long. There is a man in this house who has treated me with insult and abuse. I have complained to my aunt, and she laughs at me. Armand says you are brave. In these prosaic days men who are both brave and chivalrous are few. May I count upon your assistance?"

John Hopkins thrust the remains of his cigar into his coat pocket. He looked upon this winning creature and felt his first thrill of romance. It was a knightly love, and contained no disloyalty to the flat with the flea-bitten terrier and the lady of his choice. He had married her after a picnic of the Lady Label Stickers' Union, Lodge No. 2, on a dare and a bet of new hats and chowder all around with his friend, Billy McManus. This angel who was begging him to come to her rescue was something too heavenly for chowder, and as for hats—golden, jewelled crowns for her!

"Say," said John Hopkins, "just show me the guy that you've got the grouch at. I've neglected my talents as a scrapper heretofore, but this is my busy night."

"He is in there," said the lady, pointing to a closed door. "Come. Are you sure that you do not falter or fear?"

"Me?" said John Hopkins. "Just give me one of those roses in the bunch you are wearing, will you?"

The lady gave him a red, red rose. John Hopkins kissed it, stuffed it into his vest pocket, opened the door and walked into the room. It was a handsome library, softly but brightly lighted. A young man was there, reading.

"Books on etiquette is what you want to study," said John Hopkins, abruptly. "Get up here, and I'll give you some lessons. Be rude to a lady, will you?"

The young man looked mildly surprised. Then he arose languidly, dextrously caught the arms of John Hopkins and conducted him irresistibly to the front door of the house.

"Beware, Ralph Branscombe," cried the lady, who had followed, "what you do to the gallant man who has tried to protect me."

The young man shoved John Hopkins gently out the door and then closed it.

"Bess," he said calmly, "I wish you would quit reading historical novels. How in the world did that fellow get in here?"

"Armand brought him," said the young lady. "I think you are awfully mean

not to let me have that St. Bernard. I sent Armand for Walter. I was so
angry with you."

"Be sensible, Bess," said the young man, taking her arm. "That dog isn't
safe. He has bitten two or three people around the kennels. Come now, let's go
tell auntie we are in good humor again."

Arm in arm, they moved away.

John Hopkins walked to his flat. The janitor's five-year-old daughter was
playing on the steps. Hopkins gave her a nice, red rose and walked upstairs.
Mrs. Hopkins was philandering with curl-papers.

"Get your cigar?" she asked, disinterestedly.

"Sure," said Hopkins, "and I knocked around a while outside. It's a nice
night."

He sat upon the hornblende sofa, took out the stump of his cigar, lighted it,
and gazed at the graceful figures in "The Storm" on the opposite wall.

"I was telling you," said he, "about Mr. Whipple's suit. It's a gray, with an
invisible check, and it looks fine."

A LICKPENNY LOVER

THERE were 3,000 girls in the Biggest Store. Masie was one of them. She was
eighteen and a saleslady in the gents' gloves. Here she became versed in two
varieties of human beings—the kind of gents who buy their gloves in department
stores and the kind of women who buy gloves for unfortunate gents. Besides
this wide knowledge of the human species, Masie had acquired other information.
She had listened to the promulgated wisdom of the 2,999 other girls and had
stored it in a brain that was as secretive and wary as that of a Maltese cat.
Perhaps nature, foreseeing that she would lack wise counsellors, had mingled the
saving ingredient of shrewdness along with her beauty, as she has endowed the
silver fox of the priceless fur above the other animals with cunning.

For Masie was beautiful. She was a deep-tinted blonde, with the calm poise
of a lady who cooks butter cakes in a window. She stood behind her counter
in the Biggest Store; and as you closed your hand over the tape-line for your
glove measure you thought of Hebe; and as you looked again you wondered how
she had come by Minerva's eyes.

When the floorwalker was not looking Masie chewed tutti frutti; when he was
looking she gazed up as if at the clouds and smiled wistfully.

That is the shopgirl smile, and I enjoin you to shun it unless you are well
fortified with callosity of the heart, caramels, and a congeniality for the capers
of Cupid. This smile belonged to Masie's recreation hours and not to the store;
but the floorwalker must have his own. He is the Shylock of the stores. When
he comes nosing around the bridge of his nose is a toll-bridge. It is goo-goo eyes
or "git" when he looks toward a pretty girl. Of course not all floorwalkers are
thus. Only a few days ago the papers printed news of one over eighty years of
age.

One day Irving Carter, painter, millionaire, traveller, poet, automobilist, happened to enter the Biggest Store. It is due to him to add that his visit was not
voluntary. Filial duty took him by the collar and dragged him inside, while
his mother philandered among the bronze and terra-cotta statuettes.

Carter strolled across to the glove counter in order to shoot a few minutes on the wing. His need for gloves was genuine; he had forgotten to bring a pair with him. But his action hardly calls for apology, because he had never heard of glove-counter flirtations.

As he neared the vicinity of his fate he hesitated, suddenly conscious of this unknown phase of Cupid's less worthy profession.

Three or four cheap fellows, sonorously garbed, were leaning over the counters, wrestling with the mediatorial hand-coverings, while giggling girls played vivacious seconds to their lead upon the strident string of coquetry. Carter would have retreated, but he had gone too far. Masie confronted him behind her counter with a questioning look in eyes as coldly, beautifully, warmly blue as the glint of summer sunshine on an iceberg drifting in Southern seas.

And then Irving Carter, painter, millionaire, etc., felt a warm flush rise to his aristocratically pale face. But not from diffidence. The blush was intellectual in origin. He knew in a moment that he stood in the ranks of the ready-made youths who wooed the giggling girls at other counters. Himself leaned against the oaken trysting place of a cockney Cupid with a desire in his heart for the favor of a glove salesgirl. He was no more than Bill and Jack and Mickey. And then he felt a sudden tolerance for them, and an elating, courageous contempt for the conventions upon which he had fed, and an unhesitating determination to have this perfect creature for his own.

When the gloves were paid for and wrapped Carter lingered for a moment. The dimples at the corners of Masie's damask mouth deepened. All gentlemen who bought gloves lingered in just that way. She curved an arm, showing like Psyche's through her shirt-waist sleeve, and rested an elbow upon the show-case edge.

Carter had never before encountered a situation of which he had not been perfect master. But now he stood far more awkward than Bill or Jack or Mickey. He had no chance of meeting this beautiful girl socially. His mind struggled to recall the nature and habits of shopgirls as he had read or heard of them. Somehow he had received the idea that they sometimes did not insist too strictly upon the regular channels of introduction. His heart beat loudly at the thought of proposing an unconventional meeting with this lovely and virginal being. But the tumult in his heart gave him courage.

After a few friendly and well-received remarks on general subjects, he laid his card by her hand on the counter.

"Will you please pardon me," he said, "if I seem too bold; but I earnestly hope you will allow me the pleasure of seeing you again. There is my name; I assure you that it is with the greatest respect that I ask the favor of becoming one of your fr—— acquaintances. May I not hope for the privilege?"

Masie knew men—especially men who buy gloves. Without hesitation she looked him frankly and smilingly in the eyes, and said:

"Sure. I guess you're all right. I don't usually go out with strange gentlemen, though. It ain't quite ladylike. When should you want to see me again?"

"As soon as I may," said Carter. "If you would allow me to call at your home, I——"

Masie laughed musically. "Oh, gee, no!" she said, emphatically. "If you could see our flat once! There's five of us in three rooms. I'd just like to see ma's face if I was to bring a gentleman friend there!"

"Anywhere, then," said the enamored Carter, "that will be convenient to you."

"Say," suggested Masie, with a bright-idea look in her peach-blow face; "I guess Thursday night will about suit me. Suppose you come to the corner of Eighth Avenue and Forty-eighth Street at 7:30. I live right near the corner. But I've got to be back home by eleven. Ma never lets me stay out after eleven."

Carter promised gratefully to keep the tryst, and then hastened to his mother, who was looking about for him to ratify her purchase of a bronze Diana.

A salesgirl, with small eyes and an obtuse nose, strolled near Masie, with a friendly leer.

"Did you make a hit with his nobs, Masie?" she asked, familiarly.

"The gentleman asked permission to call," answered Masie, with the grand air, as she slipped Carter's card into the bosom of her waist.

"Permission to call!" echoed small eyes, with a snigger. "Did he say anything about dinner in the Waldorf and a spin in his auto afterward?"

"Oh, cheese it!" said Masie, wearily. "You've been used to swell things, I don't think. You've had a swelled head ever since that hose-cart driver took you out to a chop suey joint. No, he never mentioned the Waldorf; but there's a Fifth Avenue address on his card, and if he buys the supper you can bet your life there won't be no pigtail on the waiter what takes the order."

As Carter glided away from the Biggest Store with his mother in his electric runabout, he bit his lip with a dull pain at his heart. He knew that love had come to him for the first time in all the twenty-nine years of his life. And that the object of it should make so readily an appointment with him at a street corner, though it was a step toward his desires, tortured him with misgivings.

Carter did not know the shopgirl. He did not know that her home is often either a scarcely habitable tiny room or a domicile filled to overflowing with kith and kin. The street corner is her parlor, the park is her drawing room; the avenue is her garden walk; yet for the most part she is as inviolate mistress of herself in them as is my lady inside her tapestried chamber.

One evening at dusk, two weeks after their first meeting, Carter and Masie strolled arm-in-arm into a little, dimly-lit park. They found a bench, tree-shadowed and secluded, and sat there.

For the first time his arm stole gently around her. Her golden-bronze head slid restfully against his shoulder.

"Gee!" sighed Masie, thankfully. "Why didn't you ever think of that before?"

"Masie," said Carter, earnestly, "you surely know that I love you. I ask you sincerely to marry me. You know me well enough by this time to have no doubts of me. I want you, and I must have you. I care nothing for the difference in our stations."

"What is the difference?" asked Masie, curiously.

"Well, there isn't any," said Carter, quickly, "except in the minds of foolish people. It is in my power to give you a life of luxury. My social position is beyond dispute, and my means are ample."

"They all say that," remarked Masie. "It's the kid they all give you. I suppose you really work in a delicatessen or follow the races. I ain't as green as I look."

"I can furnish you all the proofs you want," said Carter, gently. "And I want you, Masie. I loved you the first day I saw you."

"They all do," said Masie, with an amused laugh, "to hear 'em talk. If I could meet a man that got stuck on me the third time he'd seen me I think I'd get mashed on him."

"Please don't say such things," pleaded Carter. "Listen to me, dear. Ever since I first looked into your eyes you have been the only woman in the world for me."

"Oh, ain't you the kidder!" smiled Masie. "How many other girls did you ever tell that?"

But Carter persisted. And at length he reached the flimsy, fluttering little soul of the shopgirl that existed somewhere deep down in her lovely bosom. His words penetrated the heart whose very lightness was its safest armor. She looked up at him with eyes that saw. And a warm glow visited her cool cheeks. Tremblingly, awfully, her moth wings closed, and she seemed about to settle upon the flower of love. Some faint glimmer of life and its possibilities on the other side of her glove counter dawned upon her. Carter felt the change and crowded the opportunity.

"Marry me, Masie," he whispered, softly, "and we will go away from this ugly city to beautiful ones. We will forget work and business, and life will be one long holiday. I know where I should take you—I have been there often. Just think of a shore where summer is eternal, where the waves are always rippling on the lovely beach and the people are happy and free as children. We will sail to those shores and remain there as long as you please. In one of those far-away cities there are grand and lovely palaces and towers full of beautiful pictures and statues. The streets of the city are water, and one travels about in——"

"I know," said Masie, sitting up suddenly. "Gondolas."

"Yes," smiled Carter.

"I thought so," said Masie.

"And then," continued Carter, "we will travel on and see whatever we wish in the world. After the European cities we will visit India and the ancient cities there, and ride on elephants and see the wonderful temples of the Hindoos and the Brahmins and the Japanese gardens and the camel trains and chariot races in Persia, and all the queer sights of foreign countries. Don't you think you would like it, Masie?"

Masie rose to her feet.

"I think we had better be going home," she said, coolly. "It's getting late."

Carter humored her. He had come to know her varying, thistle-down moods, and that it was useless to combat them. But he felt a certain happy triumph. He had held for a moment, though but by a silken thread, the soul of his wild Psyche, and hope was stronger within him. Once she had folded her wings and her cool hand had closed about his own.

At the Biggest Store the next day Masie's chum, Lulu, waylaid her in an angle of the counter.

"How are you and your swell friend making it?" she asked.

"Oh, him?" said Masie, patting her side curls. "He ain't in it any more. Say, Lu, what do you think that fellow wanted me to do?"

"Go on the stage?" guessed Lulu, breathlessly.

"Nit; he's too cheap a guy for that. He wanted me to marry him and go down to Coney Island for a wedding tour!"

DOUGHERTY'S EYE-OPENER

BIG JIM DOUGHERTY was a sport. He belonged to that race of men. In Manhattan it is a distinct race. They are the Caribs of the North—strong, artful, self-sufficient, clannish, honorable within the laws of their race, holding in lenient contempt neighboring tribes who bow to the measure of Society's tape-line. I refer, of course, to the titled nobility of sportdom. There is a class which bears as a qualifying adjective the substantive belonging to a wind instrument made of a cheap and base metal. But the tin mines of Cornwall never produced the material for manufacturing descriptive nomenclature for "Big Jim" Dougherty.

The habitat of the sport is the lobby or the outside corner of certain hotels and combination restaurants and cafés. They are mostly men of different sizes, running from small to large; but they are unanimous in the possession of a recently shaven, blue-black cheek and chin and dark overcoats (in season) with black velvet collars.

Of the domestic life of the sport little is known. It has been said that Cupid and Hymen sometimes take a hand in the game and copper the queen of hearts to lose. Daring theorists have averred—not content with simply saying —that a sport often contracts a spouse, and even incurs descendants. Sometimes he sits in the game of politics; and then at chowder picnics there is a revelation of a Mrs. Sport and little Sports in glazed hats with tin pails.

But mostly the sport is Oriental. He believes his women-folk should not be too patent. Somewhere behind grilles or flower-ornamented fire escapes they await him. There, no doubt, they tread on rugs from Teheran and are diverted by the bulbul and play upon the dulcimer and feed upon sweetmeats. But away from his home the sport is an integer. He does not, as men of other races in Manhattan do, become the convoy in his unoccupied hours of fluttering laces and high heels that tick off delectably the happy seconds of the evening parade. He herds with his own race at corners, and delivers a commentary in his Carib lingo upon the passing show.

"Big Jim" Dougherty had a wife, but he did not wear a button portrait of her upon his lapel. He had a home in one of those brown-stone, iron-railed streets on the west side that look like a recently excavated bowling alley of Pompeii.

To this home of his Mr. Dougherty repaired each night when the hour was so late as to promise no further diversion in the arch domains of sport. By that time the occupant of the monogamistic harem would be in dreamland, the bulbul silenced and the hour propitious for slumber.

"Big Jim" always arose at twelve, meridian, for breakfast, and soon afterward he would return to the rendezvous of his "crowd."

He was always vaguely conscious that there was a Mrs. Dougherty. He would have received without denial the charge that the quiet, neat, comfortable little woman across the table at home was his wife. In fact, he remembered pretty well that they had been married for nearly four years. She would often tell him about the cute tricks of Spot, the canary, and the light-haired lady that lived in the window of the flat across the street.

"Big Jim" Dougherty even listened to this conversation of hers sometimes. He knew that she would have a nice dinner ready for him every evening at seven when he came for it. She sometimes went to matinées, and she had a talking machine with six dozen records. Once when her Uncle Amos blew in on a wind from up-state she went with him to the Eden Musée. Surely these things were diversions enough for any woman.

One afternoon Mr. Dougherty finished his breakfast, put on his hat and got away fairly for the door. When his hand was on the knob he heard his wife's voice.

"Jim," she said, firmly, "I wish you would take me out to dinner this evening. It has been three years since you have been outside the door with me."

"Big Jim" was astounded. She had never asked anything like this before. It had the flavor of a totally new proposition. But he was a game sport.

"All right," he said. "You be ready when I come at seven. None of this 'wait two minutes till I primp an hour or two' kind of business, now, Dele."

"I'll be ready," said his wife, calmly.

At seven she descended the stone steps in the Pompeian bowling alley at the side of "Big Jim" Dougherty. She wore a dinner gown made of a stuff that the spiders must have woven, and of a color that a twilight sky must have contributed. A light coat with many admirably unnecessary capes and adorably inutile ribbons floated downward from her shoulders. Fine feathers do make fine birds; and the only reproach in the saying is for the man who refuses to give up his earnings for the ostrich-tip industry.

"Big Jim" Dougherty was troubled. There was a being at his side whom he did not know. He thought of the sober-hued plumage that this bird of paradise was accustomed to wear in her cage, and this winged revelation puzzled him. In some way she reminded him of the Delia Cullen that he had married four years before. Shyly and rather awkwardly he stalked at her right hand.

"After dinner I'll take you back home, Dele," said Mr. Dougherty, "and then I'll drop back up to Seltzer's with the boys. You can have swell chuck to-night if you want it. I made a winning on Anaconda yesterday; so you can go as far as you like."

Mr. Dougherty had intended to make the outing with his unwonted wife an inconspicuous one. Uxoriousness was a weakness that the precepts of the Caribs did not countenance. If any of his friends of the track, the billiard cloth or the square circle had wives they had never complained of the fact in public. There were a number of table d'hôte places on the cross streets near the broad and shining way; and to one of these he had proposed to escort her, so that the bushel might not be removed from the light of his domesticity.

But while on the way Mr. Dougherty altered those intentions. He had been casting stealthy glances at his attractive companion and he was seized with the conviction that she was no selling plater. He resolved to parade with his wife past Seltzer's café, where at this time a number of his tribe would be gathered to view the daily evening procession. Yes; and he would take her to dine at Hoogley's, the swellest slow-lunch warehouse on the line, he said to himself.

The congregation of smooth-faced tribal gentlemen were on watch at Seltzer's. As Mr. Dougherty and his reorganized Delia passed they stared, momentarily petrified, and then removed their hats—a performance as unusual to them as was the astonishing innovation presented to their gaze by "Big Jim." On the latter gentleman's impassive face there appeared a slight flicker of triumph—a faint flicker, no more to be observed than the expression called there by the draft of little casino to a four-card spade flush.

Hoogley's was animated. Electric lights shone—as, indeed, they were expected to do. And the napery, the glassware, and the flowers also meritoriously performed the spectacular duties required of them. The guests were numerous, well-dressed, and gay.

A waiter—not necessarily obsequious—conducted "Big Jim" Dougherty and his wife to a table.

"Play that menu straight across for what you like, Dele," said "Big Jim." "It's you for a trough of the gilded oats to-night. It strikes me that maybe we've been sticking too fast to home fodder."

"Big Jim's" wife gave her order. He looked at her with respect. She had mentioned truffles; and he had not known that she knew what truffles were. From the wine list she designated an appropriate and desirable brand. He looked at her with some admiration.

She was beaming with the innocent excitement that woman derives from the exercise of her gregariousness. She was talking to him about a hundred things with animation and delight. And as the meal progressed her cheeks, colorless from a life indoors, took on a delicate flush. "Big Jim" looked around the room and saw that none of the women there had her charm. And then he thought of the three years she had suffered immurement, uncomplaining, and a flush of shame warmed him, for he carried fair play as an item in his creed.

But when the Honorable Patrick Corrigan, leader in Dougherty's district and a friend of his, saw them and came over to the table, matters got to the three-quarter stretch. The Honorable Patrick was a gallant man, both in deeds and words. As for the Blarney stone, his previous actions toward it must have been pronounced. Heavy damages for breach of promise could surely have been obtained had the Blarney stone seen fit to sue the Honorable Patrick.

"Jimmy, old man!" he called; he clapped Dougherty on the back; he shone like a midday sun upon Delia.

"Honorable Mr. Corrigan—Mrs. Dougherty," said "Big Jim."

The Honorable Patrick became a fountain of entertainment and admiration. The waiter had to fetch a third chair for him; he made another at the table, and the wineglasses were refilled.

"You selfish old rascal!" he exclaimed, shaking an arch finger at "Big Jim," "to have kept Mrs. Dougherty a secret from us."

And then "Big Jim" Dougherty, who was no talker, sat dumb, and saw the wife who had dined every evening for three years at home, blossom like a fairy flower. Quick, witty, charming, full of light and ready talk, she received the experienced attack of the Honorable Patrick on the field of repartee and surprised, vanquished, delighted him. She unfolded her long-closed petals and around her the room became a garden. They tried to include "Big Jim" in the conversation, but he was without a vocabulary.

And then a stray bunch of politicians and good fellows who lived for sport came into the room. They saw "Big Jim" and the leader, and over they came and were made acquainted with Mrs. Dougherty. And in a few minutes she was holding a salon. Half a dozen men surrounded her, courtiers all, and six found her capable of charming. "Big Jim" sat, grim, and kept saying to himself: "Three years, three years!"

The dinner came to an end. The Honorable Patrick reached for Mrs. Dougherty's cloak; but that was a matter of action instead of words, and Dougherty's big hand got it first by two seconds.

While the farewells were being said at the door the Honorable Patrick smote Dougherty mightily between the shoulders.

"Jimmy, me boy," he declared, in a giant whisper, "the madam is a jewel of the first water. Ye're a lucky dog."

"Big Jim" walked homeward with his wife. She seemed quite as pleased with the lights and show windows in the streets as with the admiration of the men in Hoogley's. As they passed Seltzer's they heard the sound of many voices in the café. The boys would be starting the drinks around now and discussing past performances.

At the door of their home Delia paused. The pleasure of the outing radiated softly from her countenance. She could not hope for Jim of evenings, but the glory of this one would lighten her lonely hours for a long time.

"Thank you for taking me out, Jim," she said, gratefully. "You'll be going back to Seltzer's now, of course."

"To —— with Seltzer's," said "Big Jim," emphatically. "And d— Pat Corrigan! Does he think I haven't got any eyes?"

And the door closed behind both of them.

"LITTLE SPECK IN GARNERED FRUIT"

The honeymoon was at its full. There was a flat with the reddest of new carpets, tasselled portières and six steins with pewter lids arranged on a ledge above the wainscoting of the dining-room. The wonder of it was yet upon them. Neither of them had ever seen a yellow primrose by the river's brim; but if such a sight had met their eyes at that time it would have seemed like—well, whatever the poet expected the right kind of people to see in it besides a primrose.

The bride sat in the rocker with her feet resting upon the world. She was wrapt in rosy dreams and a kimono of the same hue. She wondered what the people in Greenland and Tasmania and Beloochistan were saying one to another about her marriage to Kid McGarry. Not that it made any difference. There was no welter-weight from London to the Southern Cross that could stand up four hours—no; four rounds—with her bridegroom. And he had been hers for three weeks; and the crook of her little finger could sway him more than the fist of any 142-pounder in the world.

Love, when it is ours, is the other name for self-abnegation and sacrifice. When it belongs to people across the airshaft it means arrogance and self-conceit.

The bride crossed her oxfords and looked thoughtfully at the distemper Cupids on the ceiling.

"Precious," said she, with the air of Cleopatra asking Antony for Rome done up in tissue paper and delivered at residence, "I think I would like a peach."

Kid McGarry arose and put on his coat and hat. He was serious, shaven, sentimental, and spry.

"All right," said he, as coolly as though he were only agreeing to sign articles to fight the champion of England. "I'll step down and cop one out for you— see?"

"Don't be long," said the bride. "I'll be lonesome without my naughty boy. Get a nice, ripe one."

After a series of farewells that would have befitted an imminent voyage to foreign parts, the Kid went down to the street.

Here he not unreasonably hesitated, for the season was yet early spring, and there seemed small chance of wresting anywhere from those chill streets and stores the coveted luscious guerdon of summer's golden prime.

At the Italian's fruit-stand on the corner he stopped and cast a contemptuous eye over the display of papered oranges, highly polished apples, and wan, sun-hungry bananas.

"Gotta da peach?" asked the Kid in the tongue of Dante, the lover of lovers.

"Ah, no," sighed the vender. "Not for one mont-com-a da peach. Too soon. Gotta da nice-a orange. Like-a da orange?"

Scornful, the Kid pursued his quest. He entered the all-night chop-house, café, and bowling-alley of his friend and admirer, Justus O'Callahan. The O'Callahan was about in his institution, looking for leaks.

"I want it straight," said the Kid to him. "The old woman has got a hunch that she wants a peach. Now, if you've got a peach, Cal, get it out quick. I want it and others like it if you've got 'em in plural quantities."

"The house is yours," said O'Callahan. "But there's no peach in it. It's too soon. I don't suppose you could even find 'em at one of the Broadway joints. That's too bad. When a lady fixes her mouth for a certain kind of fruit nothing else won't do. It's too late now to find any of the first-class fruiterers open. But if you think the missis would like some nice oranges I've just got a box of fine ones in that she might——"

"Much obliged, Cal. It's a peach proposition right from the ring of the gong. I'll try further."

The time was nearly midnight as the Kid walked down the West-Side avenue. Few stores were open, and such as were practically hooted at the idea of a peach.

But in her moated flat the bride confidently awaited her Persian fruit. A champion welter-weight not find a peach?—not stride triumphantly over the seasons and the zodiac and the almanac to fetch an Amsden's June or a Georgia cling to his owny-own?

The Kid's eye caught sight of a window that was lighted and gorgeous with nature's most entrancing colors. The light suddenly went out. The Kid sprinted and caught the fruiterer locking his door.

"Peaches?" said he, with extreme deliberation.

"Well, no, sir. Not for three or four weeks yet. I haven't any idea where you might find some. There may be a few in town from under the glass, but they'd be hard to locate. Maybe at one of the more expensive hotels—some place where there's plenty of money to waste. I've got some very fine oranges, though—from a shipload that came in to-day."

The Kid lingered on the corner for a moment, and then set out briskly toward a pair of green lights that flanked the steps of a building down a dark side street.

"Captain around anywhere?" he asked of the desk sergeant of the police station.

At that moment the captain came briskly forward from the rear. He was in plain clothes and had a busy air.

"Hello, Kid," he said to the pugilist. "Thought you were bridal-touring?"

"Got back yesterday. I'm a solid citizen now. Think I'll take an interest in municipal doings. How would it suit you to get into Denver Dick's place to-night, Cap?"

"Past performances," said the captain, twisting his moustache. "Denver was closed up two months ago."

"Correct," said the Kid. "Rafferty chased him out of the Forty-third. He's running in your precinct now, and his game's bigger than ever. I'm down on this gambling business. I can put you against his game."

"In my precinct?" growled the captain. "Are you sure, Kid? I'll take it as a favor. Have you got the entrée? How is it to be done?"

"Hammers," said the Kid. "They haven't got any steel on the doors yet. You'll need ten men. No; they won't let me in the place. Denver has been trying to do me. He thought I tipped him off for the other raid. I didn't, though. You want to hurry. I've got to get back home. The house is only three blocks from here."

Before ten minutes had sped the captain with a dozen men stole with their guide into the hall-way of a dark and virtuous-looking building in which many businesses were conducted by day.

"Third floor, rear," said the Kid, softly. "I'll lead the way."

Two axemen faced the door that he pointed out to them.

"It seems all quiet," said the captain, doubtfully. "Are you sure your tip is straight?"

"Cut away!" said the Kid. "It's on me if it ain't."

The axes crashed through the as yet unprotected door. A blaze of light from within poured through the smashed panels. The door fell, and the raiders sprang into the room with their guns handy.

The big room was furnished with the gaudy magnificence dear to Denver Dick's western ideas. Various well-patronized games were in progress. About fifty men who were in the room rushed upon the police in a grand break for personal liberty. The plain-clothes men had to do a little club-swinging. More than half the patrons escaped.

Denver Dick had graced his game with his own presence that night. He led the rush that was intended to sweep away the smaller body of raiders. But when he saw the Kid his manner became personal. Being in the heavy-weight class he cast himself joyfully upon his slighter enemy, and they rolled down a flight of stairs in each other's arms. On the landing they separated and arose, and then the Kid was able to use some of his professional tactics, which had been useless to him while in the excited clutch of a 200-pound sporting gentleman who was about to lose $20,000 worth of paraphernalia.

After vanquishing his adversary the Kid hurried upstairs and through the gambling-room into a smaller apartment connecting by an arched doorway.

Here was a long table set with choicest chinaware and silver, and lavishly furnished with food of that expensive and spectacular sort of which the devotees of sport are supposed to be fond. Here again was to be perceived the liberal and florid taste of the gentleman with the urban cognomenal prefix.

A No. 10 patent leather shoe protruded a few of its inches outside the table-cloth along the floor. The Kid seized this and plucked forth a black man in a white tie and the garb of a servitor.

"Get up!" commanded the Kid. "Are you in charge of this free lunch?"

"Yes, sah, I was. Has they done pinched us ag'in, boss?"

"Looks that way. Listen to me. Are there any peaches in this layout? If there ain't I'll have to throw up the sponge."

"There was three dozen, sah, when the game opened this evenin'; but I reckon the gentlemen done eat 'em all up. If you'd like to eat a fustrate orange, sah, I kin find you some."

"Get busy," ordered the Kid sternly, "and move whatever peach crop you've got quick or there'll be trouble. If anybody oranges me again to-night, I'll knock his face off."

The raid on Denver Dick's high-priced and prodigal luncheon revealed one lone, last peach that had escaped the epicurean jaws of the followers of chance. Into the Kid's pocket it went, and that indefatigable forager departed immediately with his prize. With scarcely a glance at the scene on the sidewalk below, where the officers were loading their prisoners into the patrol wagons, he moved homeward with long, swift strides.

His heart was light as he went. So rode the knights back to Camelot after perils and high deeds done for their ladies fair. The Kid's lady had commanded him and he had obeyed. True, it was but a peach that she had craved; but it had been no small deed to glean a peach at midnight from that wintry city where yet the February snows lay like iron. She had asked for a peach; she was his bride; in his pocket the peach was warming in his hand that held it for fear that it might fall out and be lost.

On the way the Kid turned in at an all-night drug store and said to the spectacled clerk:

"Say, sport, I wish you'd size up this rib of mine and see if it's broke. I was in a little scrap and bumped down a flight or two of stairs."

The druggist made an examination.

"It isn't broken," was his diagnosis; "but you have a bruise there that looks like you'd fallen off the Flatiron twice."

"That's all right," said the Kid. "Let's have your clothesbrush, please."

The bride waited in the rosy glow of the pink lamp shade. The miracles were not all passed away. By breathing a desire for some slight thing—a flower, a pomegranate, a—oh, yes, a peach—she could send forth her man into the night, into the world which could not withstand him, and he would do her bidding.

And now he stood by her chair and laid the peach in her hand.

"Naughty boy!" she said, fondly. "Did I say a peach? I think I would much rather have had an orange."

Blest be the bride.

THE HARBINGER

Long before the springtide is felt in the dull bosom of the yokel does the city man know that the grass-green goddess is upon her throne. He sits at his breakfast eggs and toast, begirt by stone walls, opens his morning paper and sees journalism leave vernalism at the post.

For, whereas, spring's couriers were once the evidence of our finer senses, now the Associated Press does the trick.

The warble of the first robin in Hackensack, the stirring of the maple sap in Bennington, the budding of the pussy willows along Main Street in Syracuse, the first chirp of the bluebird, the swan song of the Blue Point, the annual tornado in St. Louis, the plaint of the peach pessimist from Pompton, N. J., the regular visit of the tame wild goose with a broken leg to the pond near Bilgewater Junction, the base attempt of the Drug Trust to boost the price of quinine foiled in the House by Congressman Jinks, the first tall poplar struck by lightning and the usual stunned picnickers who had taken refuge, the first crack of the ice jam in the Allegheny River, the finding of a violet in its mossy bed by the Correspondent at Round Corners—these are the advance signs of the burgeoning season that are wired into the wise city, while the farmer sees nothing but winter upon his dreary fields.

But these be mere externals. The true harbinger is the heart. When Strephon seeks his Chloe and Mike his Maggie, then only is spring arrived and the newspaper report of the five-foot rattler killed in Squire Pettigrew's pasture confirmed.

Ere the first violet blew, Mr. Peters, Mr. Ragsdale and Mr. Kidd sat together on a bench in Union Square and conspired. Mr. Peters was the D'Artagnan of the loafers there. He was the dingiest, the laziest, the sorriest brown blot against the green background of any bench in the park. But just then he was the most important of the trio.

Mr. Peters had a wife. This had not heretofore affected his standing with Ragsy and Kidd. But to-day it invested him with a peculiar interest. His friends, having escaped matrimony, had shown a disposition to deride Mr. Peters for his venture on that troubled sea. But at last they had been forced to acknowledge that either he had been gifted with a large foresight or that he was one of Fortune's lucky sons.

For, Mrs. Peters had a dollar. A whole dollar bill, good and receivable by the Government for customs, taxes, and all public dues. How to get possession of that dollar was the question up for discussion by the three musty musketeers.

"How do you know it was a dollar?" asked Ragsy, the immensity of the sum inclining him to scepticism.

"The coalman seen her have it," said Mr. Peters. "She went out and done some washing yesterday. And look what she give me for breakfast—the heel of a loaf and a cup of coffee, and her with a dollar!"

"It's fierce," said Ragsy.

"Say we go up and punch 'er and stick a towel in 'er mouth and cop the coin," suggested Kidd, viciously. "Y' ain't afraid of a woman, are you?"

"She might holler and have us pinched," demurred Ragsy. "I don't believe in slugging no woman in a houseful of people."

"Gent'men," said Mr. Peters, severely, through his russet stubble, "remember that you are speaking of my wife. A man who would lift his hand to a lady except in the way of——"

"Maguire," said Ragsy, pointedly, "has got his bock beer sign out. If we had a dollar we could——"

"Hush up!" said Mr. Peters, licking his lips. "We got to get that case note somehow, boys. Ain't what's a man's wife's his? Leave it to me. I'll go over to the house and get it. Wait here for me."

"I've seen 'em give up quick, and tell you where it's hid if you kick 'em in the ribs," said Kidd.

"No man would kick a woman," said Peters, virtuously. "A little choking— just a touch on the wind-pipe—that gets away with 'em—and no marks left. Wait for me. I'll bring back that dollar, boys."

High up in a tenement-house between Second Avenue and the river lived the Peterses in a back room so gloomy that the landlord blushed to take the rent for it. Mrs. Peters worked at sundry times, doing odd jobs of scrubbing and washing. Mr. Peters had a pure, unbroken record of five years without having earned a penny. And yet they clung together, sharing each other's hatred and misery, being creatures of habit. Of habit, the power that keeps the earth from flying to pieces; though there is some silly theory of gravitation.

Mrs. Peters reposed her 200 pounds on the safer of the two chairs and gazed stolidly out the one window at the brick wall opposite. Her eyes were red and damp. The furniture could have been carried away on a pushcart, but no pushcart man would have removed it as a gift.

The door opened to admit Mr. Peters. His fox-terrier eyes expressed a wish. His wife's diagnosis located correctly the seat of it, but misread it hunger instead of thirst.

"You'll get nothing more to eat till night," she said, looking out of the window again. "Take your hound-dog's face out of the room."

Mr. Peter's eye calculated the distance between them. By taking her by surprise it might be possible to spring upon her, overthrow her, and apply the throttling tactics of which he had boasted to his waiting comrades. True, it had been only a boast; never yet had he dared to lay violent hands upon her; but with the thoughts of the delicious, cool bock or Culmbacher bracing his nerves, he was near to upsetting his own theories of the treatment due by a gentleman to a lady. But, with his loafer's love for the more artistic and less strenuous way, he chose diplomacy first, the high card in the game—the assumed attitude of success already attained.

"You have a dollar," he said, loftily, but significantly in the tone that goes with the lighting of a cigar—when the properties are at hand.

"I have," said Mrs. Peters, producing the bill from her bosom and crackling it, teasingly.

"I am offered a position in a—in a tea store," said Mr. Peters. "I am to begin work tomorrow. But it will be necessary for me to buy a pair of——"

"You are a liar," said Mrs. Peters, reinterring the note. "No tea store, nor no A B C store, nor no junk shop would have you. I rubbed the skin off both me hands washin' jumpers and overalls to make that dollar. Do you think it come out of them suds to buy the kind you put into you? Skiddoo! Get your mind off of money."

Evidently the poses of Talleyrand were not worth one hundred cents on that dollar. But diplomacy is dexterous. The artistic temperament of Mr. Peters lifted him by the straps of his congress gaiters and set him on new ground. He called up a look of desperate melancholy to his eyes.

"Clara," he said, hollowly, "to struggle further is useless. You have always misunderstood me. Heaven knows I have striven with all my might to keep my head above the waves of misfortune, but——"

"Cut out the rainbow of hope and that stuff about walkin' one by one through the narrow isles of Spain," said Mrs. Peters, with a sigh. "I've heard it so often. There's an ounce bottle of carbolic on the shelf behind the empty coffee can. Drink hearty."

Mr. Peters reflected. What next! The old expedients had failed. The two musty musketeers were awaiting him hard by the ruined château—that is to say, on a park bench with rickety cast-iron legs. His honor was at stake. He had engaged to storm the castle singlehanded and bring back the treasure that was to furnish them wassail and solace. And all that stood between him and the coveted dollar was his wife, once a little girl whom he could—aha!—why not again? Once with soft words he could, as they say, twist her around his little finger. Why not again? Not for years had he tried it. Grim poverty and mutual hatred had killed all that. But Ragsy and Kidd were waiting for him to bring that dollar!

Mr. Peters took a surreptitiously keen look at his wife. Her formless bulk overflowed the chair. She kept her eyes fixed out the window in a strange kind of trance. Her eyes showed that she had been recently weeping.

"I wonder," said Mr. Peters to himself, "if there'd be anything in it."

The window was open upon its outlook of brick walls and drab, barren back yards. Except for the mildness of the air that entered it might have been midwinter yet in the city that turns such a frowning face to besieging spring. But spring doesn't come with the thunder of cannon. She is a sapper and a miner, and you must capitulate.

"I'll try it," said Mr. Peters to himself, making a wry face.

He went up to his wife and put his arm across her shoulders.

"Clara, darling," he said in tones that shouldn't have fooled a baby seal, "why should we have hard words? Ain't you my own tootsum wootsum?"

A black mark against you, Mr. Peters, in the sacred ledger of Cupid. Charges of attempted graft are filed against you, and of forgery and utterance of two of Love's holiest of appellations.

But the miracle of spring was wrought. Into the back room over the back alley between the black walls had crept the Harbinger. It was ridiculous, and yet—— Well, it is a rat trap, and you, madam and sir and all of us, are in it.

Red and fat and crying like Niobe or Niagara, Mrs. Peters threw her arms around her lord and dissolved upon him. Mr. Peters would have striven to extricate the dollar bill from its deposit vault, but his arms were bound to his sides.

"Do you love me, James?" asked Mrs. Peters.

"Madly," said James, "but——"

"You are ill!" exclaimed Mrs. Peters. "Why are you so pale and tired looking?"

"I feel weak," said Mr. Peters. "I——"

"Oh, wait; I know what it is. Wait, James. I'll be back in a minute."

With a parting hug that revived in Mr. Peters recollections of the Terrible Turk, his wife hurried out of the room and down the stairs.

Mr. Peters hitched his thumbs under his suspenders.

"All right," he confided to the ceiling. "I've got her going. I hadn't any idea the old girl was soft any more under the foolish rib. Well, sir; ain't I the Claude Melnotte of the lower East Side? What? It's a 100 to 1 shot that I get the dollar. I wonder what she went out for. I guess she's gone to tell Mrs. Muldoon on the second floor, that we're reconciled. I'll remember this. Soft soap! And Ragsy was talking about slugging her!"

Mrs. Peters came back with a bottle of sarsaparilla.

"I'm glad I happened to have that dollar," she said. "You're all run down, honey."

Mr. Peters had a tablespoonful of the stuff inserted into him. Then Mrs. Peters sat on his lap and murmured:

"Call me tootsum wootsums again, James."

He sat still, held there by his materialized goddess of spring.

Spring had come.

On the bench in Union Square Mr. Ragsdale and Mr. Kidd squirmed, tongue-parched, awaiting D'Artagnan and his dollar.

"I wish I had choked her at first," said Mr. Peters to himself.

WHILE THE AUTO WAITS

PROMPTLY at the beginning of twilight, came again to that quiet corner of that quiet, small park the girl in gray. She sat upon a bench and read a book, for there was yet to come a half hour in which print could be accomplished.

To repeat: Her dress was gray, and plain enough to mask its impeccancy of style and fit. A large-meshed veil imprisoned her turban hat and a face that shone through it with a calm and unconscious beauty. She had come there at the same hour on the day previous, and on the day before that; and there was one who knew it.

The young man who knew it hovered near, relying upon burnt sacrifices to the great joss, Luck. His piety was rewarded, for, in turning a page, her book slipped from her fingers and bounded from the bench a full yard away.

The young man pounced upon it with instant avidity, returning it to its owner with that air that seems to flourish in parks and public places—a compound of gallantry and hope, tempered with respect for the policeman on the beat. In a pleasant voice, he risked an inconsequent remark upon the weather—that introductory topic responsible for so much of the world's unhappiness—and stood poised for a moment, awaiting his fate.

The girl looked him over leisurely; at his ordinary, neat dress and his features distinguished by nothing particular in the way of expression.

"You may sit down, if you like," she said, in a full, deliberate contralto. "Really, I would like to have you do so. The light is too bad for reading. I would prefer to talk."

The vassal of Luck slid upon the seat by her side with complaisance.

"Do you know," he said, speaking the formula with which park chairmen open their meetings, "that you are quite the stunningest girl I have seen in a long time? I had my eye on you yesterday. Didn't know somebody was bowled over by those pretty lamps of yours, did you, honeysuckle?"

"Whoever you are," said the girl, in icy tones, "you must remember that I am a lady. I will excuse the remark you have just made because the mistake was, doubtless, not an unnatural one—in your circle. I asked you to sit down; if the invitation must constitute me your honeysuckle, consider it withdrawn."

"I earnestly beg your pardon," pleaded the young man. His expression of satisfaction had changed to one of penitence and humility. "It was my fault, you know—I mean, there are girls in parks, you know—that is, of course, you don't know, but——"

"Abandon the subject, if you please. Of course I know. Now, tell me about these people passing and crowding, each way, along these paths. Where are they going? Why do they hurry so? Are they happy?"

The young man had promptly abandoned his air of coquetry. His cue was now for a waiting part; he could not guess the rôle he would be expected to play.

"It is interesting to watch them," he replied, postulating her mood. "It is the wonderful drama of life. Some are going to supper and some to—er—other places. One wonders what their histories are."

"I do not," said the girl; "I am not so inquisitive. I come here to sit because here, only, can I be near the great, common, throbbing heart of humanity. My part in life is cast where its beats are never felt. Can you surmise why I spoke to you, Mr.——?"

"Parkenstacker," supplied the young man. Then he looked eager and hopeful.

"No," said the girl, holding up a slender finger, and smiling slightly. "You would recognize it immediately. It is impossible to keep one's name out of print. Or even one's portrait. This veil and this hat of my maid furnish me with an *incog.* You should have seen the chauffeur stare at it when he thought I did not see. Candidly, there are five or six names that belong in the holy of holies, and mine, by the accident of birth, is one of them. I spoke to you, Mr. Stackenpot——"

"Parkenstacker," corrected the young man, modestly.

"——Mr. Parkenstacker, because I wanted to talk, for once, with a natural man —one unspoiled by the despicable gloss of wealth and supposed social superiority. Oh! you do not know how weary I am of it—money, money, money! And of the men who surround me, dancing like little marionettes all cut by the same pattern. I am sick of pleasure, of jewels, of travel, of society, of luxuries of all kinds."

"I always had an idea," ventured the young man, hesitatingly, "that money must be a pretty good thing."

"A competence is to be desired. But when you have so many millions that——!" She concluded the sentence with a gesture of despair. "It is the monotony of it," she continued, "that palls. Drives, dinners, theatres, balls, suppers, with the gilding of superfluous wealth over it all. Sometimes the very tinkle of the ice in my champagne glass nearly drives me mad."

Mr. Parkenstacker looked ingenuously interested.

"I have always liked," he said, "to read and hear about the ways of wealthy and fashionable folks. I suppose I am a bit of a snob. But I like to have my information accurate. Now, I had formed the opinion that champagne is cooled in the bottle and not by placing ice in the glass."

The girl gave a musical laugh of genuine amusement.

"You should know," she explained, in an indulgent tone, "that we of the non-useful class depend for our amusement upon departure from precedent. Just now it is a fad to put ice in champagne. The idea was originated by a visiting Prince of Tartary while dining at the Waldorf. It will soon give way to some other whim. Just as at a dinner party this week on Madison Avenue a green kid glove was laid by the plate of each guest to be put on and used while eating olives."

"I see," admitted the young man, humbly. "These special diversions of the inner circle do not become familiar to the common public."

"Sometimes," continued the girl, acknowledging his confession of error by a slight bow, "I have thought that if I ever should love a man it would be one of lowly station. One who is a worker and not a drone. But, doubtless, the claims of caste and wealth will prove stronger than my inclination. Just now I am besieged by two. One is a Grand Duke of a German principality. I think he has, or has had, a wife, somewhere, driven mad by his intemperance and cruelty. The other is an English Marquis, so cold and mercenary that I even prefer the diabolism of the Duke. What is it that impels me to tell you these things, Mr. Packenstacker?'

"Parkenstacker," breathed the young man. "Indeed, you cannot know how much I appreciate your confidences."

The girl contemplated him with a calm, impersonal regard that befitted the difference in their stations.

"What is your line of business, Mr. Parkenstacker?" she asked.

"A very humble one. But I hope to rise in the world. Were you really in earnest when you said that you could love a man of lowly position?"

"Indeed I was. But I said 'might.' There is the Grand Duke and the Marquis, you know. Yes; no calling could be too humble were the man what I would wish him to be."

"I work," declared Mr. Parkenstacker, "in a restaurant."

The girl shrank slightly.

"Not as a waiter?" she said, a little imploringly. "Labor is noble, but—personal attendance, you know—valets and——"

"I am not a waiter. I am cashier in"—on the street they faced that bounded the opposite side of the park was the brilliant electric sign "RESTAURANT"—"I am cashier in that restaurant you see there."

The girl consulted a tiny watch set in a bracelet of rich design upon her left wrist, and rose, hurriedly. She thrust her book into a glittering reticule suspended from her waist, for which, however, the book was too large.

"Why are you not at work?" she asked.

"I am on the night turn," said the young man; "it is yet an hour before my period begins. May I not hope to see you again?"

"I do not know. Perhaps—but the whim may not seize me again. I must go quickly now. There is a dinner, and a box at the play—and, oh! the same old round. Perhaps you noticed an automobile at the upper corner of the park as you came. One with a white body."

"And red running gear?" asked the young man, knitting his brows reflectively.

"Yes. I always come in that. Pierre waits for me there. He supposes me to be shopping in the department store across the square. Conceive of the bondage of the life wherein we must deceive even our chauffeurs. Good-night."

"But it is dark now," said Mr. Parkenstacker, "and the park is full of rude men. May I not walk——?"

"If you have the slightest regard for my wishes," said the girl, firmly, "you will remain at this bench for ten minutes after I have left. I do not mean to accuse you, but you are probably aware that autos generally bear the monogram of their owner. Again, good-night."

Swift and stately she moved away through the dusk. The young man watched her graceful form as she reached the pavement at the park's edge, and turned up along it toward the corner where stood the automobile. Then he treacherously and unhesitatingly began to dodge and skim among the park trees and shrubbery in a course parallel to her route, keeping her well in sight.

When she reached the corner she turned her head to glance at the motor car, and then passed it, continuing on across the street. Sheltered behind a convenient standing cab, the young man followed her movements closely with his eyes. Passing down the sidewalk of the street opposite the park, she entered the restaurant with the blazing sign. The place was one of those frankly glaring establishments, all white paint and glass, where one may dine cheaply and conspicuously. The girl penetrated the restaurant to some retreat at its rear, whence she quickly emerged without her hat and veil.

The cashier's desk was well to the front. A red-haired girl on the stool climbed down, glancing pointedly at the clock as she did so. The girl in gray mounted in her place.

The young man thrust his hands into his pockets and walked slowly back along the sidewalk. At the corner his foot struck a small, paper-covered volume lying there, sending it sliding to the edge of the turf. By its picturesque cover he recognized it as the book the girl had been reading. He picked it up carelessly, and saw that its title was "New Arabian Nights," the author being of the name of Stevenson. He dropped it again upon the grass, and lounged, irresolute, for a minute. Then he stepped into the automobile, reclined upon the cushions, and said two words to the chauffeur:

"Club, Henri."

A COMEDY IN RUBBER

ONE may hope, in spite of the metaphorists, to avoid the breath of the deadly upas tree; one may, by great good fortune, succeed in blacking the eye of the basilisk; one might even dodge the attentions of Cerberus and Argus, but no man, alive or dead, can escape the gaze of the Rubberer.

New York is the Caoutchouc City. There are many, of course, who go their ways, making money, without turning to the right or the left, but there is a tribe abroad wonderfully composed, like the Martians, solely of eyes and means of locomotion.

These devotees of curiosity swarm, like flies, in a moment in a struggling, breathless circle about the scene of an unusual occurrence. If a workman opens a manhole, if a street car runs over a man from North Tarrytown, if a little boy drops an egg on his way home from the grocery, if a casual house or two drops into the subway, if a lady loses a nickel through a hole in the lisle thread, if the police drag a telephone and a racing chart forth from an Ibsen Society reading-room, if Senator Depew or Mr. Chuck Connors walks out to take the air—if any of these incidents or accidents takes place, you will see the mad, irresistible rush of the "rubber" tribe to the spot.

The importance of the event does not count. They gaze with equal interest and absorption at a chorus girl or at a man painting a liver pill sign. They will form as deep a cordon around a man with a club-foot as they will around a balked automobile. They have the furor rubberendi. They are optical gluttons, feasting and fattening on the misfortunes of their fellow beings. They gloat and pore and glare and squint and stare with their fishy eyes like goggle-eyed perch at the hook baited with calamity.

It will seem that Cupid would find these ocular vampires too cold game for his calorific shafts, but have we not yet to discover an immune even among the Protozoa? Yes, beautiful Romance descended upon two of this tribe, and love came into their hearts as they crowded about the prostrate form of a man who had been run over by a brewery wagon.

William Pry was the first on the spot. He was an expert at such gatherings. With an expression of intense happiness on his features, he stood over the victim of the accident, listening to his groans as if to the sweetest music. When the crowd of spectators had swelled to a closely packed circle William saw a violent commotion in the crowd opposite him. Men were hurled aside like ninepins by the impact of some moving body that clove them like the rush of a tornado. With elbows, umbrella, hat-pin, tongue, and fingernails doing their duty, Violet Seymour forced her way through the mob of onlookers to the first row. Strong men who even had been able to secure a seat on the 5:30 Harlem express staggered back like children as she bucked centre. Two large lady spectators who had seen the Duke of Roxburgh married and had often blocked traffic on Twenty-third Street fell back into the second row with ripped shirt-waists when Violet had finished with them. William Pry loved her at first sight.

The ambulance removed the unconscious agent of Cupid. William and Violet remained after the crowd had dispersed. They were true Rubberers. People who leave the scene of an accident with the ambulance have not genuine caoutchouc in the cosmogony of their necks. The delicate, fine flavor of the affair is to be had only in the after-taste—in gloating over the spot, in gazing fixedly at the houses opposite, in hovering there in a dream more exquisite than the opium-eater's ecstasy. William Pry and Violet Seymour were connoisseurs in casualties. They knew how to extract full enjoyment from every incident.

Presently they looked at each other. Violet had a brown birthmark on her neck as large as a silver half-dollar. William fixed his eyes upon it. William Pry had inordinately bowed legs. Violet allowed her gaze to linger unswervingly upon them. Face to face they stood thus for moments, each staring at the other. Etiquette would not allow them to speak; but in the Caoutchouc City it is permitted to gaze without stint at the trees in the parks and at the physical blemishes of a fellow creature.

At length with a sigh they parted. But Cupid had been the driver of the brewery wagon, and the wheel that broke a leg united two fond hearts.

The next meeting of the hero and heroine was in front of a board fence near Broadway. The day had been a disappointing one. There had been no fights on the street, children had kept from under the wheels of the street cars, cripples and fat men in negligée shirts were scarce; nobody seemed to be inclined to slip on banana peels or fall down with heart disease. Even the sport from Kokomo, Ind., who claims to be a cousin of ex-Mayor Low and scatters nickels from a cab window, had not put in his appearance. There was nothing to stare at, and William Pry had premonitions of ennui.

But he saw a large crowd scrambling and pushing excitedly in front of a billboard. Sprinting for it, he knocked down an old woman and a child carrying a bottle of milk, and fought his way like a demon into the mass of spectators. Already in the inner line stood Violet Seymour with one sleeve and two gold fillings gone, a corset steel puncture and a sprained wrist, but happy. She was looking at what there was to see. A man was painting upon the fence: "Eat Bricklets—They Fill Your Face."

Violet blushed when she saw William Pry. William jabbed a lady in a black silk raglan in the ribs, kicked a boy in the shin, hit an old gentleman on the left ear and managed to crowd nearer to Violet. They stood for an hour looking at the man paint the letters. Then William's love could be repressed no longer. He touched her on the arm.

"Come with me," he said. "I know where there is a bootblack without an Adam's apple."

She looked up at him shyly, yet with unmistakable love transfiguring her countenance.

"And you have saved it for me?" she asked, trembling with the first dim ecstasy of a woman beloved.

Together they hurried to the bootblack's stand. An hour they spent there gazing at the malformed youth.

A window-cleaner fell from the fifth story to the sidewalk beside them. As the ambulance came clanging up William pressed her hand joyously. "Four ribs at least and a compound fracture," he whispered, swiftly. "You are not sorry that you met me, are you, dearest?"

"Me?" said Violet, returning the pressure. "Sure not. I could stand all day rubbering with you."

The climax of the romance occurred a few days later. Perhaps the reader will remember the intense excitement into which the city was thrown when Eliza Jane, a colored woman, was served with a subpoena. The Rubber Tribe encamped on the spot. With his own hands William Pry placed a board upon two beer kegs in the street opposite Eliza Jane's residence. He and Violet sat there for three days and nights. Then it occurred to a detective to open the door and serve the subpoena. He sent for a kinetoscope and did so.

Two souls with such congenial tastes could not long remain apart. As a policeman drove them away with his night stick that evening they plighted their troth. The seeds of love had been well sown, and had grown up, hardy and vigorous, into a—let us call it a rubber plant.

The wedding of William Pry and Violet Seymour was set for June 10. The Big Church in the Middle of the Block was banked high with flowers. The populous tribe of Rubberers the world over is rampant over weddings. They are the pessimists of the pews. They are the guyers of the groom and the banterers of the bride. They come to laugh at your marriage, and should you escape from Hymen's tower on the back of death's pale steed they will come to the funeral and sit in the same pew and cry over your luck. Rubber will stretch.

The church was lighted. A grosgrain carpet lay over the asphalt to the edge of the sidewalk. Bridesmaids were patting one another's sashes awry and speaking of the Bride's freckles. Coachmen tied white ribbons on their whips and bewailed the space of time between drinks. The minister was musing over his possible fee, essaying conjecture whether it would suffice to purchase a new broadcloth suit for himself and a photograph of Laura Jane Libbey for his wife. Yea, Cupid was in the air.

And outside the church, oh, my brothers, surged and heaved the rank and file of the tribe of Rubberers. In two bodies they were, with the grosgrain carpet and cops with clubs between. They crowded like cattle, they fought, they pressed and surged and swayed and trampled one another to see a bit of a girl in a white veil acquire license to go through a man's pockets while he sleeps.

But the hour for the wedding came and went, and the bride and bridegroom came not. And impatience gave way to alarm and alarm brought about search, and they were not found. And then two big policemen took a hand and dragged out of the furious mob of onlookers a crushed and trampled thing, with a wedding ring in its vest pocket and a shredded and hysterical woman beating her way to the carpet's edge, ragged, bruised and obstreperous.

William Pry and Violet Seymour, creatures of habit, had joined in the seething game of the spectators, unable to resist the overwhelming desire to gaze upon themselves entering, as bride and bridegroom, the rose-decked church.

Rubber will out.

ONE THOUSAND DOLLARS

"ONE thousand dollars," repeated Lawyer Tolman, solemnly and severely, "and here is the money."

Young Gillian gave a decidedly amused laugh as he fingered the thin package of new fifty-dollar notes.

"It's such a confoundedly awkward amount," he explained, genially, to the lawyer. "If it had been ten thousand a fellow might wind up with a lot of fireworks and do himself credit. Even fifty dollars would have been less trouble."

"You heard the reading of your uncle's will," continued Lawyer Tolman, professionally dry in his tones. "I do not know if you paid much attention to its details. I must remind you of one. You are required to render to us an account of the manner of expenditure of this $1,000 as soon as you have disposed of it. The will stipulates that. I trust that you will so far comply with the late Mr. Gillian's wishes."

"You may depend upon it," said the young man, politely, "in spite of the extra expense it will entail. I may have to engage a secretary. I was never good at accounts."

Gillian went to his club. There he hunted out one whom he called Old Bryson.

Old Bryson was calm and forty and sequestered. He was in a corner reading a book, and when he saw Gillian approaching he sighed, laid down his book and took off his glasses.

"Old Bryson, wake up," said Gillian. "I've a funny story to tell you."

"I wish you would tell it to someone in the billiard room," said Old Bryson. "You know how I hate your stories."

"This is a better one than usual," said Gillian, rolling a cigarette; "and I'm glad to tell it to you. It's too sad and funny to go with the rattling of billiard balls. I've just come from my late uncle's firm of legal corsairs. He leaves me an even thousand dollars. Now, what can a man possibly do with a thousand dollars?"

"I thought," said Old Bryson, showing as much interest as a bee shows in a vinegar cruet, "that the late Septimus Gillian was worth something like half a million."

"He was," assented Gillian, joyously, "and that's where the joke comes in. He's left his whole cargo of doubloons to a microbe. That is, part of it goes to the man who invents a new bacillus and the rest to establish a hospital for doing away with it again. There are one or two trifling bequests on the side. The butler and the housekeeper get a seal ring and $10 each. His nephew gets $1,000."

"You've always had plenty of money to spend," observed Old Bryson.

"Tons," said Gillian. "Uncle was the fairy godmother as far as an allowance was concerned."

"Any other heirs?" asked Old Bryson.

"None." Gillian frowned at his cigarette and kicked the upholstered leather of a divan uneasily. "There is a Miss Hayden, a ward of my uncle, who lived in his house. She's a quiet thing—musical—the daughter of somebody who was unlucky enough to be his friend. I forgot to say that she was in on the seal ring and $10 joke, too. I wish I had been. Then I could have had two bottles of brut, tipped the waiter with the ring, and had the whole business off my hands. Don't be superior and insulting, Old Bryson—tell me what a fellow can do with a thousand dollars."

Old Bryson rubbed his glasses and smiled. And when Old Bryson smiled, Gillian knew that he intended to be more offensive than ever.

"A thousand dollars," he said, "means much or little. One man may buy a happy home with it and laugh at Rockefeller. Another could send his wife South with it and save her life. A thousand dollars would buy pure milk for one hundred babies during June, July, and August and save fifty of their lives. You could count upon a half hour's diversion with it at faro in one of the fortified art galleries. It would furnish an education to an ambitious boy. I am told that a genuine Corot was secured for that amount in an auction room yesterday. You could move to a New Hampshire town and live respectably two years on it. You could rent Madison Square Garden for one evening with it, and lecture your audience, if you should have one, on the precariousness of the profession of heir presumptive."

"People might like you, Old Bryson," said Gillian, almost unruffled, "if you wouldn't moralize. I asked you to tell me what I could do with a thousand dollars."

"You?" said Bryson, with a gentle laugh. "Why, Bobby Gillian, there's only one logical thing you could do. You can go buy Miss Lotta Lauriere a diamond pendant with the money, and then take yourself off to Idaho and inflict your presence upon a ranch. I advise a sheep ranch, as I have a particular dislike for sheep."

"Thanks," said Gillian, rising. "I thought I could depend upon you, Old Bryson. You've hit on the very scheme. I wanted to chuck the money in a lump, for I've got to turn in an account for it, and I hate itemizing."

Gillian phoned for a cab and said to the driver:

"The stage entrance of the Columbine Theatre."

Miss Lotta Lauriere was assisting nature with a powder puff, almost ready for her call at a crowded matinée, when her dresser mentioned the name of Mr. Gillian.

"Let it in," said Miss Lauriere. "Now, what is it, Bobby? I'm going on in two minutes."

"Rabbit-foot your right ear a little," suggested Gillian, critically. "That's better. It won't take two minutes for me. What do you say to a little thing in the pendant line? I can stand three ciphers with a figure one in front of 'em."

"Oh, just as you say," carolled Miss Lauriere. "My right glove, Adams. Say, Bobby, did you see that necklace Della Stacey had on the other night? Twenty-two hundred dollars it cost at Tiffany's. But, of course—pull my sash a little to the left, Adams."

"Miss Lauriere for the opening chorus!" cried the call boy without.

Gillian strolled out to where his cab was waiting.

"What would you do with a thousand dollars if you had it?" he asked the driver.

"Open a s'loon," said the cabby promptly and huskily. "I know a place I could take money in with both hands. It's a four-story brick on a corner. I've got it figured out. Second story—Chinks and chop suey; third floor—manicures and foreign missions; fourth floor—poolroom. If you was thinking of putting up the cap——"

"Oh, no," said Gillian, "I merely asked from curiosity. I take you by the hour. Drive till I tell you to stop."

Eight blocks down Broadway Gillian poked up the trap with his cane and got out. A blind man sat upon a stool on the sidewalk selling pencils. Gillian went out and stood before him.

"Excuse me," he said, "but would you mind telling me what you would do if you had a thousand dollars?"

"You got out of that cab that just drove up, didn't you?" asked the blind man.

"I did," said Gillian.

"I guess you are all right," said the pencil dealer, "to ride in a cab by daylight. Take a look at that, if you like."

He drew a small book from his coat pocket and held it out. Gillian opened it and saw that it was a bank deposit book. It showed a balance of $1,785 to the blind man's credit.

Gillian returned the book and got into the cab.

"I forgot something," he said. "You may drive to the law offices of Tolman & Sharp, at —— Broadway."

Lawyer Tolman looked at him hostilely and inquiringly through his gold-rimmed glasses.

"I beg your pardon," said Gillian, cheerfully, "but may I ask you a question? It is not an impertinent one, I hope. Was Miss Hayden left anything by my uncle's will besides the ring and the $10?"

"Nothing," said Mr. Tolman.

"I thank you very much, sir," said Gillian, and out he went to his cab. He gave the driver the address of his late uncle's home.

Miss Hayden was writing letters in the library. She was small and slender and clothed in black. But you would have noticed her eyes. Gillian drifted in with his air of regarding the world as inconsequent.

"I've just come from old Tolman's," he explained. "They've been going over the papers down there. They found a"—Gillian searched his memory for a legal term—"they found an amendment or a postscript or something to the will. It seemed that the old boy loosened up on second thoughts and willed you a thousand dollars. I was driving up this way and Tolman asked me to bring you the money. Here it is. You'd better count it to see if it's right." Gillian laid the money beside her hand on the desk.

Miss Hayden turned white. "Oh!" she said, and again "Oh!"

Gillian half turned and looked out of the window.

"I suppose, of course," he said, in a low voice, "that you know I love you."

"I am sorry," said Miss Hayden, taking up her money.

"There is no use?" asked Gillian, almost light-heartedly.

"I am sorry," she said again.

"May I write a note?" asked Gillian, with a smile. He seated himself at the big library table. She supplied him with paper and pen, and then went back to her secrétaire.

Gillian made out his account of his expenditure of the thousand dollars in these words:

"Paid by the black sheep, Robert Gillian, $1,000 on account of the eternal happiness, owed by Heaven to the best and dearest woman on earth."

Gillian slipped his writing into an envelope, bowed and went his way.

His cab stopped again at the offices of Tolman & Sharp.

"I have expended the thousand dollars," he said, cheerily, to Tolman of the gold glasses, "and I have come to render account of it, as I agreed. There is quite a feeling of summer in the air—do you not think so, Mr. Tolman?" He tossed a white envelope on the lawyer's table. "You will find there a memorandum, sir, of the *modus operandi* of the vanishing of the dollars."

Without touching the envelope, Mr. Tolman went to a door and called his partner, Sharp. Together they explored the caverns of an immense safe. Forth they dragged as trophy of their search a big envelope sealed with wax. This they forcibly invaded, and wagged their venerable heads together over its contents. Then Tolman became spokesman.

"Mr. Gillian," he said, formally, "there was a codicil to your uncle's will. It was intrusted to us privately, with instructions that it be not opened until you had furnished us with a full account of your handling of the $1,000 bequest in the will. As you have fulfilled the conditions, my partner and I have read the codicil. I do not wish to encumber your understanding with its legal phraseology, but I will acquaint you with the spirit of its contents.

"In the event that your disposition of the $1,000 demonstrates that you possess any of the qualifications that deserve reward, much benefit will accrue to you. Mr. Sharp and I are named as the judges, and I assure you that we will do our duty strictly according to justice—with liberality. We are not at all unfavorably disposed toward you, Mr. Gillian. But let us return to the letter of the codicil. If your disposal of the money in question has been prudent, wise, or unselfish, it is in our power to hand you over bonds to the value of $50,000, which have been placed in our hands for that purpose. But if—as our client, the late Mr. Gillian, explicitly provides—you have used this money as you have used money in the past—I quote the late Mr. Gillian—in reprehensible dissipation among disreputable associates—the $50,000 is to be paid to Miriam Hayden, ward of the late Mr. Gillian, without delay. Now, Mr. Gillian, Mr.

Sharp and I will examine your account in regard to the $1,000. You submit it in writing, I believe. I hope you will repose confidence in our decision."

Mr. Tolman reached for the envelope. Gillian was a little the quicker in taking it up. He tore the account and its cover leisurely into strips and dropped them into his pocket.

"It's all right," he said, smilingly. "There isn't a bit of need to bother you with this. I don't suppose you'd understand these itemized bets, anyway. I lost the thousand dollars on the races. Good-day to you, gentlemen."

Tolman & Sharp shook their heads mournfully at each other when Gillian left, for they heard him whistling gayly in the hallway as he waited for the elevator.

THE DEFEAT OF THE CITY

ROBERT WALMSLEY'S descent upon the city resulted in a Kilkenny struggle. He came out of the fight victor by a fortune and a reputation. On the other hand, he was swallowed up by the city. The city gave him what he demanded and then branded him with its brand. It remodelled, cut, trimmed, and stamped him to the pattern it approves. It opened its social gates to him and shut him in on a close-cropped, formal lawn with the select herd of ruminants. In dress, habits, manners, provincialism, routine, and narrowness he acquired that charming insolence, that irritating completeness, that sophisticated crassness, that overbalanced poise that makes the Manhattan gentleman so delightfully small in his greatness.

One of the up-state rural counties pointed with pride to the successful young metropolitan lawyer as a product of its soil. Six years earlier this country had removed the wheat straw from between its huckleberry-stained teeth and emitted a derisive and bucolic laugh as old man Walmsley's freckle-faced "Bob" abandoned the certain three-per-diem meals of the one-horse farm for the discontinuous quick lunch counters of the three-ringed metropolis. At the end of the six years no murder trial, coaching party, automobile accident or cotillion was complete in which the name of Robert Walmsley did not figure. Tailors waylaid him in the street to get a new wrinkle from the cut of his unwrinkled trousers. Hyphenated fellows in the clubs and members of the oldest subpœnaed families were glad to clap him on the back and allow him three letters of his name.

But the Matterhorn of Robert Walmsley's success was not scaled until he married Alicia Van Der Pool. I cite the Matterhorn, for just so high and cool and white and inaccessible was this daughter of the old burghers. The social Alps that ranged about her—over whose bleak passes a thousand climbers struggled—reached only to her knees. She towered in her own atmosphere, serene, chaste, prideful, wading in no fountains, dining no monkeys, breeding no dogs for bench shows. She was a Van Der Pool. Fountains were made to play for her; monkeys were made for other people's ancestors; dogs, she understood, were created to be companions of blind persons and objectionable characters who smoked pipes.

This was the Matterhorn that Robert Walmsley accomplished. If he found, with the good poet with the game foot and artificially curled hair, that he who ascends to mountain tops will find the loftiest peaks most wrapped in clouds and snow, he concealed his chilblains beneath a brave and smiling exterior. He was a lucky man and knew it, even though he were imitating the Spartan boy with an ice-cream freezer beneath his doublet frappéeing the region of his heart.

After a brief wedding tour abroad, the couple returned to create a decided ripple in the calm cistern (so placid and cool and sunless it is) of the best society. They entertained at their red brick mausoleum of ancient greatness in an old square that is a cemetery of crumbled glory. And Robert Walmsley was proud of his wife; although while one of his hands shook his guests' the other held tightly to his alpenstock and thermometer.

One day Alicia found a letter written to Robert by his mother. It was an unerudite letter, full of crops and motherly love and farm notes. It chronicled the health of the pig and the recent red calf, and asked concerning Robert's in return. It was a letter direct from the soil, straight from home, full of biographies of bees, tales of turnips, pæans of new-laid eggs, neglected parents and the slump in dried apples.

"Why have I not been shown your mother's letters?" asked Alicia. There was always something in her voice that made you think of lorgnettes, of accounts at Tiffany's, of sledges smoothly gliding on the trail from Dawson to Forty Mile, of the tinkling of pendent prisms on your grandmothers' chandeliers, of snow lying on a convent roof; of a police sergeant refusing bail. "Your mother," continued Alicia, "invites us to make a visit to the farm. I have never seen a farm. We will go there for a week or two, Robert."

"We will," said Robert, with the grand air of an associate Supreme Justice concurring in an opinion. "I did not lay the invitation before you because I thought you would not care to go. I am much pleased at your decision."

"I will write to her myself," answered Alicia, with a faint foreshadowing of enthusiasm. "Félice shall pack my trunks at once. Seven, I think, will be enough. I do not suppose that your mother entertains a great deal. Does she give many house parties?"

Robert arose, and as attorney for rural places filed a demurrer against six of the seven trunks. He endeavored to define, picture, elucidate, set forth and describe a farm. His own words sounded strange in his ears. He had not realized how thoroughly urbsidized he had become.

A week passed and found them landed at the little country station five hours out from the city. A grinning, stentorian, sarcastic youth driving a mule to a spring wagon hailed Robert savagely.

"Hallo, Mr. Walmsley. Found your way back at last, have you? Sorry I couldn't bring in the automobile for you, but dad's bull-tonguing the ten-acre clover patch with it to-day. Guess you'll excuse my not wearing a dress suit over to meet you—it ain't six o'clock yet, you know."

"I'm glad to see you, Tom," said Robert, grasping his brother's hand. "Yes, I've found my way at last. You've a right to say 'at last.' It's been over two years since the last time. But it will be oftener after this, my boy."

Alicia, cool in the summer heat as an Arctic wraith, white as a Norse snow maiden in her flimsy muslin and fluttering lace parasol, came round the corner of the station; and Tom was stripped of his assurance. He became chiefly eyesight clothed in blue jeans, and on the homeward drive to the mule alone did he confide in language the inwardness of his thoughts.

They drove homeward. The low sun dropped a spendthrift flood of gold upon the fortunate fields of wheat. The cities were far away. The road lay curling around wood and dale and hill like a ribbon lost from the robe of careless summer. The wind followed like a whinnying colt in the track of Phœbus's steeds.

By and by the farmhouse peeped gray out of its faithful grove; they saw the long lane with its convoy of walnut trees running from the road to the house; they smelled the wild rose and the breath of cool, damp willows in the

creek's bed. And then in unison all the voices of the soil began a chant addressed
to the soul of Robert Walmsley. Out of the tilted aisles of the dim wood they
came hollowly; they chirped and buzzed from the parched grass; they trilled
from the ripples of the creek ford; they floated up in clear Pan's pipe notes from
the dimming meadows; the whippoorwills joined in as they pursued midges in
the upper air; slow-going cow-bells struck out a homely accompaniment—and
this was what each one said: "You've found your way back at last, have you?"

The old voices of the soil spoke to him. Leaf and bud and blossom conversed
with him in the old vocabulary of his careless youth—the inanimate things,
the familiar stones and rails, the gates and furrows and roofs and turns of road
had an eloquence, too, and a power in the transformation. The country had
smiled and he had felt the breath of it, and his heart was drawn as if in a moment
back to his old love. The city was far away.

This rural atavism, then, seized Robert Walmsley and possessed him. A
queer thing he noticed in connection with it was that Alicia, sitting at his side,
suddenly seemed to him a stranger. She did not belong to this recurrent phase.
Never before had she seemed so remote, so colorless and high—so intangible and
unreal. And yet he had never admired her more than when she sat there by
him in the rickety spring wagon, chiming no more with his mood and with her
environment than the Matterhorn chimes with a peasant's cabbage garden.

That night when the greetings and the supper were over, the entire family,
including Buff, the yellow dog, bestrewed itself upon the front porch. Alicia,
not haughty but silent, sat in the shadow dressed in an exquisite pale-gray tea
gown. Robert's mother discoursed to her happily concerning marmalade and
lumbago. Tom sat on the top step; Sisters Millie and Pam on the lowest step
to catch the lightning bugs. Mother had the willow rocker. Father sat in the
big armchair with one of its arms gone. Buff sprawled in the middle of the porch
in everybody's way. The twilight pixies and pucks stole forth unseen and plunged
other poignant shafts of memory into the heart of Robert. A rural madness
entered his soul. The city was far away.

Father sat without his pipe, writhing in his heavy boots, a sacrifice to rigid
courtesy. Robert shouted: "No, you don't!" He fetched the pipe and lit it; he
seized the old gentleman's boots and tore them off. The last one slipped suddenly, and Mr. Robert Walmsley, of Washington Square, tumbled off the porch
backward with Buff on top of him, howling fearfully. Tom laughed sarcastically.

Robert tore off his coat and vest and hurled them into a lilac bush.

"Come out here, you landlubber," he cried to Tom, "and I'll put grass seed
on your back. I think you called me a 'dude' a while ago. Come along and
cut your capers."

Tom understood the invitation and accepted it with delight. Three times they
wrestled on the grass, "side holds," even as the giants of the mat. And twice
was Tom forced to bite grass at the hands of the distinguished lawyer. Dishevelled, panting, each still boasting of his own prowess, they stumbled back to
the porch. Millie cast a pert reflection upon the qualities of a city brother.
In an instant Robert had secured a horrid katydid in his fingers and bore down
upon her. Screaming wildly, she fled up the lane pursued by the avenging glass
of form. A quarter of a mile and they returned, she full of apology to the victorious "dude." The rustic mania possessed him unabatedly.

"I can do up a cowpenful of you slow hayseeds," he proclaimed, vaingloriously.
"Bring on your bulldogs, your hired men, and your log-rollers."

He turned handsprings on the grass that prodded Tom to envious sarcasm.
And then, with a whoop, he clattered to the rear and brought back Uncle Ike,
a battered colored retainer of the family, with his banjo, and strewed sand on the
porch and danced "Chicken in the Bread Tray" and did buck-and-wing wonders
for half an hour longer. Incredibly wild and boisterous things he did. He sang,

he told stories that set all but one shrieking, he played the yokel, the humorous clodhopper; he was mad, mad with the revival of the old life in his blood.

He became so extravagant that once his mother sought gently to reprove him. Then Alicia moved as though she were about to speak, but she did not. Through it all she sat immovable, a slim, white spirit in the dusk that no man might question or read.

By and by she asked permission to ascend to her room, saying that she was tired. On her way she passed Robert. He was standing in the door, the figure of vulgar comedy, with ruffled hair, reddened face and unpardonable confusion of attire—no trace there of the immaculate Robert Walmsley, the courted clubman and ornament of select circles. He was doing a conjuring trick with some household utensils, and the family, now won over to him without exception, was beholding him with worshipful admiration.

As Alicia passed in Robert started suddenly. He had forgotten for the moment that she was present. Without a glance at him she went on upstairs.

After that the fun grew quiet. An hour passed in talk, and then Robert went up himself.

She was standing by the window when he entered their room. She was still clothed as when they were on the porch. Outside and crowding against the window was a giant apple tree, full blossomed.

Robert sighed and went near the window. He was ready to meet his fate. A confessed vulgarian, he foresaw the verdict of justice in the shape of that still, whiteclad form. He knew the rigid lines that a Van Der Pool would draw. He was a peasant gambolling indecorously in the valley, and the pure, cold, white, unthawed summit of the Matterhorn could not but frown on him. He had been unmasked by his own actions. All the polish, the poise, the form that the city had given him had fallen from him like an ill-fitting mantle at the first breath of a country breeze. Dully he awaited the approaching condemnation.

"Robert," said the calm, cool voice of his judge, "I thought I married a gentleman."

Yes, it was coming. And yet, in the face of it, Robert Walmsley was eagerly regarding a certain branch of the apple tree upon which he used to climb out of that very window. He believed he could do it now. He wondered how many blossoms there were on the tree—ten millions? But here was someone speaking again:

"I thought I married a gentleman," the voice went on, "but——"

Why had she come and was standing so close by his side?

"But I find that I have married"—was this Alicia talking?—"something better —a man— Bob, dear, kiss me, won't you?"

The city was far away.

THE SHOCKS OF DOOM

THERE is an aristocray of the public parks and even of the vagabonds who use them for their private apartments. Vallance felt rather than knew this, but when he stepped down out of his world into chaos his feet brought him directly to Madison Square.

Raw and astringent as a schoolgirl—of the old order—young May breathed austerely among the budding trees. Vallance buttoned his coat, lighted his last cigarette and took his seat upon a bench. For three minutes he mildly regretted the last hundred of his last thousand that it had cost him when the bicycle cop put an end to his last automobile ride. Then he felt in every pocket and found not a single penny. He had given up his apartment that morning. His furniture had gone toward certain debts. His clothes, save what were upon him, had descended to his man-servant for back wages. As he sat, there was not in the whole city for him a bed or a broiled lobster or a street-car fare or a carnation for his buttonhole unless he should obtain them by sponging on his friends or by false pretenses. Therefore he had chosen the park.

And all this was because an uncle had disinherited him, and cut down his allowance from liberality to nothing. And all that was because his nephew had disobeyed him concerning a certain girl, who comes not into the story—therefore, all readers who brush their hair towards its roots may be warned to read no further. There was another nephew, of a different branch, who had once been the prospective heir and favorite. Being without grace or hope, he had long ago disappeared in the mire. Now dragnets were out for him; he was to be rehabilitated and restored. And so Vallance fell grandly as Lucifer to the lowest pit, joining the tattered ghosts in the little park.

Sitting there he leaned far back on the hard bench and laughed a jet of cigarette smoke up to the lowest tree branches. The sudden severing of all his life's ties had brought him a free, thrilling, almost joyous elation. He felt precisely the sensation of the aëronaut when he cuts loose his parachute and lets his balloon drift away.

The hour was nearly ten. Not many loungers were on the benches. The park-dweller, though a stubborn fighter against autumnal coolness, is slow to attack the advance line of spring's chilly cohorts.

Then arose one from a seat near the leaping fountain, and came and sat himself at Vallance's side. He was either young or old; cheap lodging-houses had flavored him mustily; razors and combs had passed him by; in him drink had been bottled and sealed in the devil's bond. He begged a match, which is the form of introduction among park benchers, and then he began to talk.

"You're not one of the regulars," he said to Vallance. "I know tailored clothes when I see 'em. You just stopped for a moment on your way through the park. Don't mind my talking to you for a while? I've got to be with somebody. I'm afraid—I'm afraid. I've told two or three of those bummers over there about it. They think I'm crazy. Say—let me tell you—all I've had to eat to-day was a couple of bretzels and an apple. To-morrow I'll stand in line to inherit three millions; and that restaurant you see over there with the autos around it will be too cheap for me to eat in. Don't believe it, do you?"

"Without the slightest trouble," said Vallance, with a laugh. "I lunched there yesterday. To-night I couldn't buy a five-cent cup of coffee."

"You don't look like one of us. Well, I guess those things happen. I used to be a high-flyer myself—some years ago. What knocked you out of the game?"

"I—oh, I lost my job," said Vallance.

"It's undiluted Hades, this city," went on the other. "One day you're eating from China; the next you are eating in China—a chop-suey joint. I've had more than my share of hard luck. For five years I've been little better than a panhandler. I was raised up to live expensively and do nothing. Say—I don't mind telling you—I've got to talk to somebody, you see, because I'm afraid—I'm afraid. My name's Ide. You wouldn't think that old Paulding, one of the millionaires on Riverside Drive, was my uncle, would you? Well, he is. I lived in his house once, and had all the money I wanted. Say, haven't you got the price of a couple of drinks about you—er—what's your name——"

"Dawson," said Vallance. "No; I'm sorry to say that I'm all in financially."

"I've been living for a week in a coal cellar on Division Street," went on Ide, "with a crook they call 'Blinky' Morris. I didn't have anywhere else to go. While I was out to-day a chap with some papers in his pocket was there, asking for me. I didn't know but what he was a fly cop, so I didn't go around again till after dark. There was a letter there he had left for me. Say—Dawson, it was from a big downtown lawyer, Mead. I've seen his sign on Ann Street. Paulding wants me to play the prodigal nephew—wants me to come back and be his heir again and blow in his money. I'm to call at the lawyer's office at ten to-morrow and step into my old shoes again—heir to three million, Dawson, and $10,000 a year pocket money. And—I'm afraid—I'm afraid."

The vagrant leaped to his feet and raised both trembling arms above his head. He caught his breath and moaned hysterically.

Vallance seized his arm and forced him back to the bench.

"Be quiet!" he commanded with something like disgust in his tones. "One would think you had lost a fortune, instead of being about to acquire one. Of what are you afraid?"

Ide cowered and shivered on the bench. He clung to Vallance's sleeve, and even in the dim glow of the Broadway lights the latest disinherited one could see drops on the other's brow wrung out by some strange terror.

"Why, I'm afraid something will happen to me before morning. I don't know what—something to keep me from coming into that money. I'm afraid a tree will fall on me—I'm afraid a cab will run over me, or a stone drop on me from a housetop, or something. I never was afraid before. I've sat in this park a hundred nights as calm as a graven image without knowing where my breakfast was to come from. But now it's different. I love money, Dawson—I'm happy as a god when it's trickling through my fingers, and people are bowing to me, with the music and the flowers and fine clothes all around. As long as I knew I was out of the game I didn't mind. I was even happy sitting here ragged and hungry, listening to the fountain jump and watching the carriages go up the avenue. But it's in reach of my hand again now—almost—and I can't stand it to wait twelve hours, Dawson—I can't stand it. There are fifty things that could happen to me—I could go blind—I might be attacked with heart disease— the world might come to an end before I could——"

Ide sprang to his feet again, with a shriek. People stirred on the benches and began to look. Vallance took his arm.

"Come and walk," he said, soothingly. "And try to calm yourself. There is no need to become excited or alarmed. Nothing is going to happen to you. One night is like another."

"That's right," said Ide. "Stay with me, Dawson—that's a good fellow. Walk around with me awhile. I never went to pieces like this before, and I've had a good many hard knocks. Do you think you could hustle something in the way of a little lunch, old man? I'm afraid my nerve's too far gone to try any panhandling."

Vallance led his companion up almost deserted Fifth Avenue, and then westward along the Thirties toward Broadway. "Wait here a few minutes," he said, leaving Ide in a quiet and shadowed spot. He entered a familiar hotel, and strolled toward the bar quite in his old assured way.

"There's a poor devil outside, Jimmy," he said to the bartender, "who says he's hungry and looks it. You know what they do when you give them money. Fix up a sandwich or two for him; and I'll see that he doesn't throw it away."

"Certainly, Mr. Vallance," said the bartender. "They ain't all fakes. Don't like to see anybody go hungry."

He folded a liberal supply of the free lunch into a napkin. Vallance went with it and joined his companion. Ide pounced upon the food ravenously. "I haven't had any free lunch as good as this in a year," he said. "Aren't you going to eat any, Dawson?"

"I'm not hungry—thanks," said Vallance.

"We'll go back to the Square," said Ide. "The cops won't bother us there. I'll roll up the rest of this ham and stuff for our breakfast. I won't eat any more; I'm afraid I'll get sick. Suppose I'd die of cramps or something to-night, and never get to touch that money again! It's eleven hours yet till time to see that lawyer. You won't leave me, will you, Dawson? I'm afraid something might happen. You haven't any place to go, have you?"

"No," said Vallance, "nowhere to-night. I'll have a bench with you."

"You take it cool," said Ide, "if you've told it to me straight. I should think a man put on the bum from a good job just in one day would be tearing his hair."

"I believe I've already remarked," said Vallance, laughing, "that I would have thought that a man who was expecting to come into a fortune on the next day would be feeling pretty easy and quiet."

"It's funny business," philosophized Ide, "about the way people take things, anyhow. Here's your bench, Dawson, right next to mine. The light don't shine in your eyes here. Say, Dawson, I'll get the old man to give you a letter to somebody about a job when I get back home. You've helped me a lot to-night. I don't believe I could have gone through the night if I hadn't struck you."

"Thank you," said Vallance. "Do you lie down or sit up on these when you sleep?"

For hours Vallance gazed almost without winking at the stars through the branches of the trees and listened to the sharp slapping of horses' hoofs on the sea of asphalt to the south. His mind was active but his feelings were dormant. Every emotion seemed to have been eradicated. He felt no regrets, no fears, no pain or discomfort. Even when he thought of the girl, it was as of an inhabitant of one of those remote stars at which he gazed. He remembered the absurd antics of his companion and laughed softly, yet without a feeling of mirth. Soon the daily army of milk wagons made of the city a roaring drum to which they marched. Vallance fell asleep on his comfortless bench.

At ten o'clock on the next day the two stood at the door of Lawyer Mead's office in Ann Street.

Ide's nerves fluttered worse than ever when the hour approached; and Vallance could not decide to leave him a possible prey to the dangers he dreaded.

When they entered the office, Lawyer Mead looked at them wonderingly. He and Vallance were old friends. After his greeting, he turned to Ide, who stood with white face and trembling limbs before the expected crisis.

"I sent a second letter to your address last night, Mr. Ide," he said. "I learned this morning that you were not there to receive it. It will inform you that Mr. Paulding has reconsidered his offer to take you back into favor. He has decided not to do so, and desires you to understand that no change will be made in the relations existing between you and him."

Ide's trembling suddenly ceased. The color came back to his face, and he straightened his back. His jaw went forward half an inch, and a gleam came into his eye. He pushed back his battered hat with one hand, and extended the other, with levelled fingers, toward the lawyer. He took a long breath and then laughed sardonically.

"Tell old Paulding he may go to the devil," he said, loudly and clearly, and turned and walked out of the office with a firm and lively step.

Lawyer Mead turned on his heel to Vallance and smiled.

"I am glad you came in," he said, genially. "Your uncle wants you to return home at once. He is reconciled to the situation that led to his hasty action, and desires to say that all will be as——"

"Hey, Adams!" cried Lawyer Mead, breaking his sentence, and calling to his clerk. "Bring a glass of water—Mr. Vallance has fainted."

THE PLUTONIAN FIRE

THERE are a few editor men with whom I am privileged to come in contact. It has not been long since it was their habit to come in contact with me. There is a difference.

They tell me that with a large number of the manuscripts that are submitted to them come advices (in the way of a boost) from the author asseverating that the incidents in the story are true. The destination of such contributions de· pends wholly upon the question of the inclosure of stamps. Some are returned, the rest are thrown on the floor in a corner on top of a pair of gum shoes, an overturned statuette of the Winged Victory, and a pile of old magazines containing a picture of the editor in the act of reading the latest copy of *Le Petit Journal,* right side up—you can tell by the illustrations. It is only a legend that there are waste baskets in editors' offices.

Thus the truth is held in disrepute. But in time truth and science and nature will adapt themselves to art. Things will happen logically, and the villain be discomfited instead of being elected to the board of directors. But in the meantime fiction must not only be divorced from fact, but must pay alimony and be awarded custody of the press dispatches.

This preamble is to warn you off the grade crossing of a true story. Being that, it shall be told simply, with conjunctions substituted for adjectives wherever possible, and whatever evidences of style may appear in it shall be due to the linotype man. It is a story of the literary life in a great city, and it should be of interest to every author within a 20-mile radius of Gosport, Ind., whose desk holds a MS. story beginning thus: "While the cheers following his nomination were still ringing through the old court-house, Harwood broke away from the congratulating handclasps of his henchmen and hurried to Judge Creswell's house to find Ida."

Pettit came up out of Alabama to write fiction. The Southern papers had printed eight of his stories under an editorial caption identifying the author as the son of "the gallant Major Pettingill Pettit, our former County Attorney and hero of the battle of Lookout Mountain."

Pettit was a rugged fellow, with a kind of shame-faced culture, and my good friend. His father kept a general store in a little town called Hosea. Pettit had been raised in the pine-woods and broom-sedge fields adjacent thereto. He had in his gripsack two manuscript novels of the adventures in Picardy of one Gaston Laboulaye, Vicompte de Montrepos, in the year 1329. That's nothing. We all do that. And some day when we make a hit with the little sketch about a newsy and his lame dog, the editor prints the other one for us—or "on us," as the saying is—and then—and then we have to get a big valise and peddle those air-draft gas burners. At $1.25 everybody should have 'em.

I took Pettit to the red-brick house which was to appear in an article entitled "Literary Landmarks of Old New York," some day when we got through with it. He engaged a room there, drawing on the general store for his expenses. I showed New York to him, and he did not mention how much narrower Broadway is than Lee Avenue in Hosea. This seemed a good sign, so I put the final test.

"Suppose you try your hand at a descriptive article," I suggested, "giving your impressions of New York as seen from the Brooklyn Bridge. The fresh point of view, the——"

"Don't be a fool," said Pettit. "Let's go have some beer. On the whole, I rather like the city."

We discovered and enjoyed the only true Bohemia. Every day and night we repaired to one of those palaces of marble and glass and tilework, where goes on a tremendous and sound epic of life. Valhalla itself could not be more glorious and sonorous. The classic marble on which we ate, the great, light-flooded, vitreous front, adorned with snow-white scrolls; the grand Wagnerian din of clanking cups and bowls, the flashing staccato of brandishing cutlery, the piercing recitative of the white-aproned grub-maidens at the morgue-like banquet tables; the recurrent lied-motif of the cash-register—it was gigantic, triumphant welding of art and sound, a deafening, soul-uplifting pageant of heroic and emblematic life. And the beans were only ten cents. We wondered why our fellow-artists cared to dine at sad little tables in their so-called Bohemian restaurants; and we shuddered lest they should seek out our resorts and make them conspicuous with their presence.

Pettit wrote many stories, which the editors returned to him. He wrote love stories, a thing I have always kept free from, holding the belief that the well-known and popular sentiment is not properly a matter for publication, but something to be privately handled by the alienists and florists. But the editors had told him that they wanted love stories, because they said the women read them.

Now, the editors are wrong about that, of course. Women do not read the love stories in the magazines. They read the poker-game stories and the recipes for cucumber lotion. The love stories are read by fat cigar drummers and little ten-year-old girls. I am not criticizing the judgment of editors. They are mostly very fine men, but a man can be but one man, with individual opinions and tastes. I knew two associate editors of a magazine who were wonderfully alike in almost everything. And yet one of them was very fond of Flaubert, while the other preferred gin.

Pettit brought me his returned manuscripts, and we looked them over together to find out why they were not accepted. They seemed to me pretty fair stories, written in a good style, and ended, as they should, at the bottom of the last page.

They were well constructed and the events were marshalled in orderly and logical sequence. But I thought I detected a lack of living substance—it was much as if I gazed at a symmetrical array of presentable clamshells from which the succulent and vital inhabitants had been removed. I intimated that the author might do well to get better acquainted with his theme.

"You sold a story last week," said Pettit, "about a gun fight in an Arizona mining town in which the hero drew his Colt's .45 and shot seven bandits as fast as they came in the door. Now, if a six-shooter could——"

"Oh, well," said I, " that's different. Arizona is a long way from New York. I could have a man stabbed with a lariat or chased by a pair of chaparreras if I wanted to, and it wouldn't be noticed until the usual error-sharp from around McAdams Junction isolates the erratum and writes in to the papers about it. But you are up against another proposition. This thing they call love is as common around New York as it is in Sheboygan during the young onion season. It may be mixed here with a little commercialism—they read Byron, but they look up Bradstreet's, too, while they're among the B's, and Brigham also if they have time—but it's pretty much the same old internal disturbance everywhere. You can fool an editor with a fake picture of a cowboy mounting a pony with his left hand on the saddle horn, but you can't put him up a tree with a love story. So, you've got to fall in love and then write the real thing."

Pettit did. I never knew whether he was taking my advice or whether he fell an accidental victim.

There was a girl he had met at one of these studio contrivances—a glorious, impudent, lucid, open-minded girl with hair the color of Culmbacher, and a good-natured way of despising you. She was a New York girl.

Well (as the narrative style permits us to say infrequently), Pettit went to pieces. All those pains, those lover's doubts, those heart-burnings and tremors of which he had written so unconvincingly were his. Talk about Shylock's pound of flesh! Twenty-five pounds Cupid got from Pettit. Which is the usurer?

One night Pettit came to my room exalted. Pale and haggard but exalted. She had given him a jonquil.

"Old Hoss," said he, with a new smile flickering around his mouth, "I believe I could write that story to-night—the one, you know, that is to win out. I can feel it. I don't know whether it will come out or not, but I can feel it."

I pushed him out of my door. "Go to your room and write it," I ordered. "Else I can see your finish. I told you this must come first. Write it to-night and put it under my door when it is done. Put it under my door to-night when it is finished—don't keep it until to-morrow."

I was reading my bully old pal Montaigne at two o'clock when I heard the sheets rustle under my door. I gathered them up and read the story.

The hissing of geese, the languishing cooing of doves, the braying of donkeys, the chatter of irresponsible sparrows—these were in my mind's ear as I read. "Suffering Sappho!" I exclaimed to myself. "Is this the divine fire that is supposed to ignite genius and make it practical and wage-earning?"

The story was sentimental drivel, full of whimpering soft-heartedness and gushing egoism. All the art that Pettit had acquired was gone. A perusal of its buttery phrases would have made a cynic of a sighing chamber-maid.

In the morning Pettit came to my room. I read him his doom mercilessly. He laughed idiotically.

"All right, Old Hoss," he said, cheerily, "make cigar-lighters of it. What's the difference? I'm going to take her to lunch at Claremont to-day."

There was about a month of it. And then Pettit came to me bearing an invisible mitten, with the fortitude of a dish-rag. He talked of the grave and South America and prussic acid; and I lost an afternoon getting him straight. I took him out and saw that large and curative doses of whiskey were administered to him. I warned you this was a true story—'ware your white ribbons if you follow this tale. For two weeks I fed him whiskey and Omar, and read to him regularly every evening the column in the evening paper that reveals the secrets of female beauty. I recommend the treatment.

After Pettit was cured he wrote more stories. He recovered his old-time facility and did work just short of good enough. Then the curtain rose on the third act.

A little, dark-eyed, silent girl from New Hampshire, who was studying applied design, fell deeply in love with him. She was the intense sort, but externally glacée, such as New England sometimes fools us with. Pettit liked her mildly, and took her about a good deal. She worshipped him, and now and then bored him.

There came a climax when she tried to jump out of a window, and he had to save her by some perfunctory, unmeant wooing. Even I was shaken by the depths of the absorbing affection she showed. Home, friends, traditions, creeds went up like thistle-down in the scale against her love. It was really discomposing.

One night again Pettit sauntered in, yawning. As he had told me before, he said he felt that he could do a great story, and as before I hunted him to his room and saw him open his inkstand. At one o'clock the sheets of paper slid under my door.

I read that story, and I jumped up, late as it was, with a whoop of joy. Old Pettit had done it. Just as though it lay there, red and bleeding, a woman's heart was written into the lines. You couldn't see the joining, but art, exquisite art, and pulsing nature had been combined into a love story that took you by the throat like the quinsy. I broke into Pettit's room and beat him on the back and called him names—names high up in the galaxy of the immortals that we admired. And Pettit yawned and begged to be allowed to sleep.

On the morrow, I dragged him to an editor. The great man read, and rising, gave Pettit his hand. That was a decoration, a wreath of bay, and a guarantee of rent.

And then old Pettit smiled slowly. I call him Gentleman Pettit now to myself. It's a miserable name to give a man, but it sounds better than it looks in print.

"I see," said old Pettit, as he took up his story and began tearing it into small strips. "I see the game now. You can't write with ink, and you can't write with your own heart's blood, but you can write with the heart's blood of someone else. You have to be a cad before you can be an artist. Well, I am for old Alabam and the Major's store. Have you got a light, Old Hoss?"

I went with Pettit to the depot and died hard.

"Shakespeare's sonnets?" I blurted, making a last stand. "How about him?"

"A cad," said Pettit. "They give it to you, and you sell it—love, you know. I'd rather sell ploughs for father."

"But," I protested, "you are reversing the decision of the world's greatest——"

"Good-by, Old Hoss," said Pettit.

"Critics," I continued. "But—say if the Major can use a fairly good salesman and book-keeper down there in the store, let me know, will you?"

NEMESIS AND THE CANDY MAN

"We sail at eight in the morning on the *Celtic*," said Honoria, plucking a loose thread from her lace sleeve.

"I heard so," said young Ives, dropping his hat, and muffing it as he tried to catch it, "and I came around to wish you a pleasant voyage."

"Of course you heard it," said Honoria, coldly sweet, "since we have had no opportunity of informing you ourselves."

Ives looked at her pleadingly, but with little hope.

Outside in the street a high-pitched voice chanted, not unmusically, a commercial gamut of "Cand-ee-ee-ee-s! Nice, fresh cand-ee-ee-ce-ees!"

"It's our old candy man," said Honoria, leaning out of the window and beckoning. "I want some of his motto kisses. There's nothing in the Broadway shops half so good."

The candy man stopped his pushcart in front of the old Madison Avenue home. He had a holiday and festival air unusual to street peddlers. His tie was new and bright red, and a horseshoe pin, almost life-size, glittered speciously from its folds. His brown, thin face was crinkled into a semi-foolish smile. Striped cuffs with dog-head buttons covered the tan on his wrists.

"I do believe he's going to get married," said Honoria, pityingly. "I never saw him taken that way before. And to-day is the first time in months that he has cried his wares, I am sure."

Ives threw a coin to the sidewalk. The candy man knows his customers. He filled a paper bag, climbed the old-fashioned stoop and handed it in.

"I remember——" said Ives.

"Wait," said Honoria.

She took a small portfolio from the drawer of a writing desk and from the portfolio a slip of flimsy paper one-quarter of an inch by two inches in size.

"This," said Honoria, inflexibly, "was wrapped about the first one we opened."

"It was a year ago," apologized Ives, as he held out his hand for it,

"As long as skies above are blue
    To you, my love, I will be true."

This he read from a slip of flimsy paper.

"We were to have sailed a fortnight ago," said Honoria, gossipingly. "It has been such a warm summer. The town is quite deserted. There is nowhere to go. Yet I am told that one or two of the roof gardens are amusing. The singing—and the dancing—on one or two seem to have met with approval."

Ives did not wince. When you are in the ring you are not surprised when your adversary taps you on the ribs.

"I followed the candy man that time," said Ives, irrelevantly, "and gave him five dollars at the corner of Broadway."

He reached for the paper bag in Honoria's lap, took out one of the square, wrapped confections and slowly unrolled it.

"Sara Chillingworth's father," said Honoria, "has given her an automobile."

"Read that," said Ives, handing over the slip that had been wrapped around the square of candy.

"Life teaches us—how to live,
    Love teaches us—to forgive."

Honoria's cheeks turned pink.

"Honoria!" cried Ives, starting up from his chair.

"Miss Clinton," corrected Honoria, rising like Venus from the bead on the surf. "I warned you not to speak that name again."

"Honoria," repeated Ives, "you must hear me. I know I do not deserve your forgiveness, but I must have it. There is a madness that possesses one sometimes for which his better nature is not responsible. I throw everything else but you to the winds. I strike off the chains that have bound me. I renounce the siren that lured me from you. Let the bought verse of that street peddler plead for me. It is you only whom I can love. Let your love forgive, and I swear to you that mine will be true 'as long as skies above are blue.' "

.   .   .   .

On the west side, between Sixth and Seventh avenues, an alley cuts the block in the middle. It perishes in a little court in the centre of the block. The district is theatrical; the inhabitants, the bubbling froth of half a dozen nations. The atmosphere is Bohemian, the language polyglot, the locality precarious.

In the court at the rear of the alley lived the candy man. At seven o'clock he pushed his cart into the narrow entrance, rested it upon the irregular stone slats and sat upon one of the handles to cool himself. There was a great draught of cool wind through the alley.

There was a window above the spot where he always stopped his pushcart. In the cool of the afternoon, Mlle. Adèle, drawing card of the Aërial Roof Garden, sat at the window and took the air. Generally her ponderous mass of dark auburn hair was down, that the breeze might have the felicity of aiding Sidonie, the maid, in drying and airing it. About her shoulders—the point of her that the photographers always made the most of—was loosely draped a heliotrope scarf. Her arms to the elbow were bare—there were no sculptors there to rave over them—but even the stolid bricks in the walls of the alley should not have been so insensate as to disapprove. While she sat thus Félice, another maid, anointed and bathed the small feet that twinkled and so charmed the nightly Aërial audiences.

Gradually Mademoiselle began to notice the candy man stopping to mop his brow and cool himself beneath her window. In the hands of her maids she was deprived for the time of her vocation—the charming and binding to her chariot of man. To lose time was displeasing to Mademoiselle. Here was the candy man—no fit game for her darts, truly—but of the sex upon which she had been born to make war.

After casting upon him looks of unseeing coldness for a dozen times, one afternoon she suddenly thawed and poured down upon him a smile that put to shame the sweets upon his cart.

"Candy man," she said, cooingly, while Sidonie followed her impulsive dive, brushing the heavy auburn hair, "don't you think I am beautiful?"

The candy man laughed harshly, and looked up, with his thin jaw set, while he wiped his forehead with a red-and-blue handkerchief.

"Yer'd make a dandy magazine cover," he said grudgingly. "Beautiful or not is for them that cares. It's not my line. If yer lookin' for bouquets apply elsewhere between nine and twelve. I think we'll have rain."

Truly, fascinating a candy man is like killing rabbits in a deep snow; but the hunter's blood is widely diffused. Mademoiselle tugged a great coil of hair from Sidonie's hands and let it fall out the window.

"Candy man, have you a sweetheart anywhere with hair as long and soft as that? And with an arm so round?" She flexed an arm like Galatea's after the miracle across the window-sill.

The candy man cackled shrilly as he arranged a stock of butter-scotch that had tumbled down.

"Smoke up!" said he, vulgarly. "Nothin' doin' in the complimentary line. I'm too wise to be bamboozled by a switch of hair and a newly massaged arm. Oh, I guess you'll make good in the calcium, all right, with plenty of powder and paint on and the orchestra playing 'Under the Old Apple Tree.' But don't put on your hat and chase downstairs to fly to the Little Church Around the Corner with me. I've been up against peroxide and made up boxes before. Say, all joking aside—don't you think we'll have rain?"

"Candy man," said Mademoiselle, softly, with her lips curving and her chin dimpling, "don't you think I'm pretty?"

The candy man grinned.

"Savin' money, ain't yer?" said he, "by bein' yer own press agent. I smoke, but I haven't seen yer mug on any of the five-cent cigar boxes. It'd take a new brand of woman to get me goin', anyway. I know 'em from sidecombs to shoelaces. Gimmie a good day's sales and steak-and-onions at seven and a pipe and an evenin' paper back there in the court, and I'll not trouble Lillian Russell herself to wink at me, if you please."

Mademoiselle pouted.

"Candy man," she said, softly, and deeply, "yet you shall say that I am beautiful. All men say so and so shall you."

The candy man laughed and pulled out his pipe.

"Well," said he, "I must be goin' in. There is a story in the evening paper that I am readin'. Men are divin' in the seas for a treasure, and pirates are watchin' them from behind a reef. And there ain't a woman on land or water or in the air. Good-evenin'." And he trundled his pushcart down the alley and back to the musty court where he lived.

Incredibly to him who has not learned woman, Mademoiselle sat at the window each day and spread her nets for the ignominious game. Once she kept a grand cavalier waiting in her reception chamber for half an hour while she battered in vain the candy man's tough philosophy. His rough laugh chafed her vanity to its core. Daily he sat on his cart in the breeze of the alley while her hair was being ministered to, and daily the shafts of her beauty rebounded from his dull bosom pointless and ineffectual. Unworthy pique brightened her eyes. Pride-hurt she glowed upon him in a way that would have sent her higher adorers into an egoistic paradise. The candy man's hard eyes looked upon her with a half-concealed derision that urged her to the use of the sharpest arrow in her beauty's quiver.

One afternoon she leaned far over the sill, and she did not challenge and tor-ment him as usual.

"Candy man," said she, "stand up and look into my eyes."

He stood up and looked into her eyes, with his harsh laugh like the sawing of wood. He took out his pipe, fumbled with it, and put it back into his pocket with a trembling hand.

"That will do," said Mademoiselle, with a slow smile. "I must go now to my *masseuse*. Good-evening."

The next evening at seven the candy man came and rested his cart under the window. But was it the candy man? His clothes were a bright new check. His necktie was a flaming red, adorned by a glittering horseshoe pin, almost life-size. His shoes were polished; the tan of his cheeks had paled—his hands had been washed. The window was empty, and he waited under it with his nose upward, like a hound hoping for a bone.

Mademoiselle came, with Sidonie carrying her load of hair. She looked at the candy man and smiled a slow smile that faded away into ennui. Instantly she knew that the game was bagged; and so quickly she wearied of the chase. She began to talk to Sidonie.

"Been a fine day," said the candy man, hollowly. "First time in a month I've felt first-class. Hit it up down old Madison, hollering out like I useter. Think it'll rain to-morrow?"

Mademoiselle laid two round arms on the cushion on the window-sill, and a dimpled chin upon them.

"Candy man," said she, softly, "do you not love me?"

The candy man stood up and leaned against the brick wall.

"Lady," said he, chokingly, "I've got $800 saved up. Did I say you wasn't beautiful? Take it every bit and buy a collar for your dog with it."

A sound as of a hundred silvery bells tinkled in the room of Mademoiselle. The laughter filled the alley and trickled back into the court, as strange a thing to enter there as sunlight itself. Mademoiselle was amused. Sidonie, a wise echo, added a sepulchral but faithful contralto. The laughter of the two seemed at last to penetrate the candy man. He fumbled with his horseshoe pin. At length Mademoiselle, exhausted, turned her flushed, beautiful face to the window.

"Candy man," said she, "go away. When I laugh Sidonie pulls my hair. I can but laugh while you remain there."

"Here is a note for Mademoiselle," said Félice, coming to the window in the room.

"There is no justice," said the candy man, lifting the handle of his cart and moving away.

Three yards he moved, and stopped. Loud shriek after shriek came from the window of Mademoiselle. Quickly he ran back. He heard a body thumping upon the floor and a sound as though heels beat alternately upon it.

"What is it?" he called.

Sidonie's severe head came into the window.

"Mademoiselle is overcome by bad news," she said. "One whom she loved with all her soul has gone—you may have heard of him—he is Monsieur Ives. He sails across the ocean to-morrow. Oh, you men!"

SQUARING THE CIRCLE

AT the hazard of wearying you this tale of vehement emotions must be prefaced by a discourse on geometry.

Nature moves in circles; Art in straight lines. The natural is rounded; the artificial is made up of angles. A man lost in the snow wanders, in spite of himself, in perfect circles; the city man's feet, denaturalized by rectangular streets and floors, carry him ever away from himself.

The round eyes of childhood typify innocence; the narrow line of the flirt's optic proves the invasion of art. The horizontal mouth is the mark of determined cunning; who has not read Nature's most spontaneous lyric in lips rounded for the candid kiss?

Beauty is Nature in perfection; circularity is its chief attribute. Behold the full moon, the enchanting gold ball, the domes of splendid temples, the huckleberry pie, the wedding ring, the circus ring, the ring for the waiter, and the "round" of drinks.

On the other hand, straight lines show that Nature has been deflected. Imagine Venus's girdle transformed into a "straight front!"

When we began to move in straight lines and turn sharp corners our natures begin to change. The consequence is that Nature, being more adaptive than Art, tries to conform to its sterner regulations. The result is often a rather curious product—for instance: A prize chrysanthemum, wood alcohol whiskey, a Republican Missouri, cauliflower *au gratin*, and a New Yorker.

Nature is lost quickest in a big city. The cause is geometrical, not moral. The straight lines of its streets and architecture, the rectangularity of its laws and social customs, the undeviating pavements, the hard, severe, depressing, uncompromising rules of all its ways—even of its recreation and sports—coldly exhibit a sneering defiance of the curved line of Nature.

Wherefore, it may be said that the big city has demonstrated the problem of squaring the circle. And it may be added that this mathematical introduction precedes an account of the fate of a Kentucky feud that was imported to the city that has a habit of making its importations conform to its angles.

The feud began in the Cumberland Mountains between the Folwell and the Harkness families. The first victim of the homespun vendetta was a 'possum dog belonging to Bill Harkness. The Harkness family evened up this dire loss by laying out the chief of the Folwell clan. The Folwells were prompt at repartee. They oiled up their squirrel rifles and made it feasible for Bill Harkness to follow his dog to a land where the 'possums come down when treed without the stroke of an ax.

The feud flourished for forty years. Harknesses were shot at the plough, through their lamp-lit cabin windows, coming from camp-meeting, asleep, in duello, sober and otherwise, singly and in family groups, prepared and unprepared. Folwells had the branches of their family tree lopped off in similar ways, as the traditions of their country prescribed and authorized.

By and by the pruning left but a single member of each family. And then Cal Harkness, probably reasoning that further pursuance of the controversy would give a too decided personal flavor to the feud, suddenly disappeared from the relieved Cumberlands, baulking the avenging hand of Sam, the ultimate opposing Folwell.

A year afterward Sam Folwell learned that his hereditary, unsuppressed enemy was living in New York City. Sam turned over the big iron wash-pot in the yard, scraped off some of the soot, which he mixed with lard and shined his boots with the compound. He put on his store clothes of butternut dyed black, a white shirt and collar, and packed a carpet-sack with Spartan *lingerie*. He took his squirrel rifle from its hooks, but put it back again with a sigh. However ethical and plausible the habit might be in the Cumberlands, perhaps New York would not swallow his pose of hunting squirrels among the skyscrapers along Broadway. An ancient but reliable Colt's revolver that he resurrected from a bureau drawer seemed to proclaim itself the pink of weapons for metropolitan adventure and vengeance. This and a hunting-knife in a leather sheath, Sam packed in the carpet-sack. As he started, muleback, for the lowland railroad station the last Folwell turned in his saddle and looked grimly at the little cluster of white-pine slabs in the clump of cedars that marked the Folwell burying-ground.

Sam Folwell arrived in New York in the night. Still moving and living in the free circles of nature, he did not perceive the formidable, pitiless, restless, fierce angles of the great city waiting in the dark to close about the rotundity of his heart and brain and mould him to the form of its millions of reshaped victims. A cabby picked him out of the whirl, as Sam himself had often picked a nut from a bed of wind-tossed autumn leaves, and whisked him away to a hotel commensurate to his boots and carpet-sack.

On the next morning the last of the Folwells made his sortie into the city that sheltered the last Harkness. The Colt was thrust beneath his coat and secured by a narrow leather belt; the hunting-knife hung between his shoulder-blades, with the haft an inch below his coat collar. He knew this much—that Cal Harkness drove an express wagon somewhere in that town, and that he, Sam Folwell, had come to kill him. And as he stepped upon the sidewalk the red came into his eye and the feud-hate into his heart.

The clamor of the central avenues drew him thitherward. He had half expected to see Cal coming down the street in his shirt-sleeves with a jug and a whip in his hand, just as he would have seen him in Frankfort or Laurel City. But an hour went by and Cal did not appear. Perhaps he was waiting in ambush, to shoot him from a door or a window. Sam kept a sharp eye on doors and windows for a while.

About noon the city tired of playing with its mouse and suddenly squeezed him with its straight lines.

Sam Folwell stood where two great, rectangular arteries of the city cross. He looked four ways, and saw the world hurled from its orbit and reduced by spirit level and tape to an edged and cornered plane. All life moved on tracks, in grooves, according to system, within boundaries, by rote. The root of life was the cube root; the measure of existence was square measure. People streamed by in straight rows; the horrible din and crash stupefied him.

Sam leaned against the sharp corner of a stone building. Those faces passed him by thousands, and none of them were turned toward him. A sudden foolish fear that he had died and was a spirit, and that they could not see him, seized him. And then the city smote him with loneliness.

A fat man dropped out of the stream and stood a few feet distant, waiting for his car. Sam crept to his side and shouted above the tumult into his ear:

"The Rankinses' hogs weighed more'n ourn a whole passel, but the mast in thar neighborhood was a fine chance better than what it was down——"

The fat man moved away unostentatiously, and bought roasted chestnuts to cover his alarm.

Sam felt the need of a drop of mountain dew. Across the street men passed in and out through swinging doors. Brief glimpses could be had of a glistening bar and its bedeckings. The feudist crossed and essayed to enter. Again had Art eliminated the familiar circle. Sam's hand found no door-knob—it slid, in vain, over a rectangular brass plate and polished oak with nothing even so large as a pin's head upon which his fingers might close.

Abashed, reddened, heartbroken, he walked away from the bootless door and sat upon a step. A locust club tickled him in the ribs.

"Take a walk for yourself," said the policeman. "You've been loafing around here long enough."

At the next corner a shrill whistle sounded in Sam's ear. He wheeled around and saw a black-browed villain scowling at him over peanuts heaped on a steaming machine. He started across the street. An immense engine, running without mules, with the voice of a bull and the smell of a smoky lamp, whizzed past, grazing his knee. A cab-driver bumped him with a hub and explained to him that kind words were invented to be used on other occasions. A motorman clanged his bell wildly and, for once in his life, corroborated a cab-driver. A large lady in a changeable silk waist dug an elbow into his back, and a newsy pensively pelted him with banana rinds, murmuring, "I hates to do it—but if anybody seen me let it pass!'"

Cal Harkness, his day's work over and his express wagon stabled, turned the sharp edge of the building that, by the cheek of architects, is modelled upon a safety razor. Out of the mass of hurrying people his eye picked up, three yards away, the surviving bloody and implacable foe of his kith and kin.

He stopped short and wavered for a moment, being unarmed and sharply surprised. But the keen mountaineer's eye of Sam Folwell had picked him out.

There was a sudden spring, a ripple in the stream of passers-by and the sound of Sam's voice crying:

"Howdy, Cal! I'm durned glad to see ye."

And in the angles of Broadway, Fifth Avenue, and Twenty-third Street the Cumberland feudists shook hands.

ROSES, RUSES AND ROMANCE

RAVENEL—Ravenel, the traveller, artist and poet, threw his magazine to the floor. Sammy Brown, broker's clerk, who sat by the window, jumped.

"What is it, Ravvy?" he asked. "The critics been hammering your stock down?"

"Romance is dead," said Ravenel, lightly. When Ravenel spoke lightly he was generally serious. He picked up the magazine and fluttered its leaves.

"Even a Philistine, like you, Sammy," said Ravenel, seriously (a tone that insured him to be speaking lightly), "ought to understand. Now, here is a magazine that once printed Poe and Lowell and Whitman and Bret Harte and Du Maurier and Lanier and—well, that gives you the idea. The current number has this literary feast to set before you: an article on the stokers and coal bunkers of battleships, an exposé of the methods employed in making liverwurst, a continued story of a Standard Preferred International Baking Powder deal in Wall Street, a 'poem' on the bear that the President missed, another 'story' by a young woman who spent a week as a spy making overalls on the East Side, another 'fiction' story that reeks of the 'garage' and certain make of automobile. Of course, the title contains the words 'Cupid' and 'Chauffeur'—an article on naval strategy, illustrated with cuts of the Spanish Armada, and the new Staten Island ferryboats; another story of a political boss who won the love of a Fifth Avenue belle by blackening her eye and refusing to vote for an iniquitous ordinance (it doesn't say whether it was in the Street Cleaning Department or

Congress), and nineteen pages by the editors bragging about the circulation. The whole thing, Sammy, is an obituary on Romance."

Sammy Brown sat comfortably in the leather armchair by the open window. His suit was a vehement brown with visible checks, beautifully matched in shade by the ends of four cigars that his vest pocket poorly concealed. Light tan were his shoes, gray his socks, sky-blue his apparent linen, snowy and high and adamantine his collar, against which a black butterfly had alighted and spread his wings. Sammy's face—least important—was round and pleasant and pinkish, and in his eyes you saw no haven for fleeing Romance.

That window of Ravenel's apartment opened upon an old garden full of ancient trees and shrubbery. The apartment-house towered above one side of it; a high brick wall fended it from the street; opposite Ravenel's window an old, old mansion stood, half-hidden in the shade of the summer foliage. The house was a castle besieged. The city howled and roared and shrieked and beat upon its double doors, and shook white, fluttering checks above the wall, offering terms of surrender. The gray dust settled upon the trees; the siege was pressed hotter, but the drawbridge was not lowered. No further will the language of chivalry serve. Inside lived an old gentleman who loved his home and did not wish to sell it. That is all the romance of the besieged castle.

Three or four times every week came Sammy Brown to Ravenel's apartment. He belonged to the poet's club, for the former Browns had been conspicuous, though Sammy had been vulgarized by Business. He had no tears for departed Romance. The song of the ticker was the one that reached his heart, and when it came to matters equine and batting scores he was something of a pink edition. He loved to sit in the leather armchair by Ravenel's window. And Ravenel didn't mind particularly. Sammy seemed to enjoy his talk; and then the broker's clerk was such a perfect embodiment of modernity and the day's sordid practicality that Ravenel rather liked to use him as a scapegoat.

"I'll tell you what's the matter with you," said Sammy, with the shrewdness that business had taught him. "The magazine has turned down some of your poetry stunts. That's why you are sore at it."

"That would be a good guess in Wall Street or in a campaign for the presidency of a woman's club," said Ravenel, quietly. "Now, there is a poem—if you will allow me to call it that—of my own in this number of the magazine."

"Read it to me," said Sammy, watching a cloud of pipe-smoke he had just blown out the window.

Ravenel was no greater than Achilles. No one is. There is bound to be a spot. The Somebody-or-Other must take hold of us somewhere when she dips us in the Something-or-Other that makes us invulnerable. He read aloud this verse in the magazine:

THE FOUR ROSES

"One rose I twined within your hair—
        (White rose, that spake of worth);
And one you placed upon your breast—
        (Red rose, love's seal of birth).
You plucked another from its stem—
        (Tea rose, that means for aye);
And one you gave—that bore for me
        The thorns of memory."

"That's a crackerjack," said Sammy, admiringly.

"There are five more verses," said Ravenel, patiently sardonic. "One naturally pauses at the end of each. Of course——"

"Oh, let's have the rest, old man," shouted Sammy, contritely, "I didn't mean to cut you off. I'm not much of a poetry expert, you know. I never saw a poem that didn't look like it ought to have terminal facilities at the end of every verse. Reel off the rest of it.'"

Ravenel sighed, and laid the magazine down. "All right," said Sammy, cheerfully, "we'll have it next time. I'll be off now. Got a date at five o'clock."

He took a last look at the shaded green garden and left, whistling in an off key an untuneful air from a roofless farce comedy.

The next afternoon Ravenel, while polishing a ragged line of a new sonnet, reclined by the window overlooking the beseiged garden of the unmercenary baron. Suddenly he sat up, spilling two rhymes and a syllable or two.

Through the trees one window of the old mansion could be seen clearly. In its window, draped in flowing white, leaned the angel of all his dreams of romance and poesy. Young, fresh as a drop of dew, graceful as a spray of clematis, conferring upon the garden hemmed in by the roaring traffic the air of a princess's bower, beautiful as any flower sung by poet—thus Ravenel saw her for the first time. She lingered for a while, and then disappeared within, leaving a few notes of a birdlike ripple of song to reach his entranced ears through the rattle of cabs and the snarling of the electric cars.

Thus, as if to challenge the poet's flaunt at romance and to punish him for his recreancy to the undying spirit of youth and beauty, this vision had dawned upon him with a thrilling and accusive power. And so metabolic was the power that in an instant the atoms of Ravenel's entire world were redistributed. The laden drays that passed the house in which she lived rumbled a deep double-bass to the tune of love. The newsboys' shouts were the notes of singing birds; that garden was the pleasance of the Capulets; the janitor was an ogre; himself a knight, ready with sword, lance or lute.

Thus does Romance show herself amid forests of brick and stone when she gets lost in the city, and there has to be sent out a general alarm to find her again.

At four in the afternoon Ravenel looked out across the garden. In the window of his hopes were set four small vases, each containing a great, full-blown rose—red and white. And, as he gazed, she leaned above them, shaming them with her loveliness and seeming to direct her eyes pensively toward his own window. And then, as though she had caught his respectful but ardent regard, she melted away, leaving the fragrant emblems on the window-sill.

Yes, emblems!—he would be unworthy if he had not understood. She had read his poem, "The Four Roses"; it had reached her heart; and this was its romantic answer. Of course she must know that Ravenel, the poet, lived there across her garden. His picture, too, she must have seen in the magazines. The delicate, tender, modest, flattering message could not be ignored.

Ravenel noticed beside the roses a small flower-pot containing a plant. Without shame he brought his opera-glasses and employed them from the cover of his window-curtain. A nutmeg geranium!

With the true poetic instinct he dragged a book of useless information from his shelves, and tore open the leaves at "The Language of Flowers."

"Geranium, Nutmeg—I expect a meeting." So! Romance never does things by halves. If she comes back to you she brings gifts and her knitting, and will sit in your chimney-corner if you will let her.

And now Ravenel smiled. The lover smiles when he thinks he has won. The woman who loves ceases to smile with victory. He ends a battle; she begins hers. What a pretty idea to set the four roses in her window for him to see! She must have a sweet, poetic soul. And now to contrive the meeting.

A whistling and slamming of doors preluded the coming of Sammy Brown.

Ravenel smiled again. Even Sammy Brown was shone upon by the far-flung rays of the renaissance. Sammy, with his ultra clothes, his horseshoe pin, his plump face, his trite slang, his uncomprehending admiration of Ravenel—the broker's clerk made an excellent foil to the new, bright unseen visitor to the poet's sombre apartment.

Sammy went to his old seat by the window, and looked out over the dusty green foliage in the garden. Then he looked at his watch, and rose hastily.

"By grabs!" he exclaimed. "Twenty after four! I can't stay, old man; I've got a date at 4:30."

"Why did you come, then," asked Ravenel, with sarcastic jocularity, "if you had an engagement at that time? I thought you business men kept better account of your minutes and seconds than that."

Sammy hesitated in the doorway and turned pinker.

"Fact is, Ravvy," he explained, as to a customer whose margin is exhausted, "I didn't know I had it until I came. I'll tell you, old man—there's a dandy girl in that old house next door that I'm dead gone on. I put it straight—we're engaged. The old man says 'nit'—but that don't go. He keeps her pretty close. I can see Edith's window from yours here. She gives me a tip when she's going shopping, and I meet her. It's 4:30 to-day. Maybe I ought to have explained sooner, but I know it's all right with you—so long."

"How do you get your 'tip,' as you call it?" asked Ravenel, losing a little spontaneity from his smile.

"Roses," said Sammy, briefly. "Four of 'em to-day. Means four o'clock at the corner of Broadway and Twenty-third."

"But the geranium?" persisted Ravenel, clutching at the end of flying Romance's trailing robe.

"Means half-past," shouted Sammy from the hall. "See you to-morrow."

THE CITY OF DREADFUL NIGHT

"DURING the recent warmed-over spell," said my friend Carney, driver of express wagon No. 8,606, "a good many opportunities was had of observing human nature through peekaboo waists.

"The Park Commissioner and the Commissioner of Polis and the Forestry Commission gets together and agrees to let the people sleep in the parks until the Weather Bureau gets the thermometer down again to a living basis. So they draws up open-air resolutions and has them O.K'd by the Secretary of Agriculture, Mr. Comstock and the Village Improvement Mosquito Exterminating Society of South Orange, N. J.

"When the proclamation was made opening up to the people by special grant the public parks that belong to 'em, there was a general exodus into Central Park by the communities existing along its borders. In ten minutes after sundown you'd have thought that there was an undress rehearsal of a potato famine in Ireland and a Kishineff massacre. They come by families, gangs, clambake societies, clans, clubs and tribes from all sides to enjoy a cool sleep on the grass. Them that didn't have oil stoves brought along plenty of blankets, so as not to be upset with the cold and discomforts of sleeping outdoors. By building fires of the shade trees and huddling together in the bridle paths, and burrowing under the grass where the ground was soft enough, the likes of 5,000 head of people successfully battled against the night air in Central Park alone.

"Ye know I live in the elegant furnished apartment house called the Beersheba Flats, over against the elevated portion of the New York Central Railroad.

"When the order come to the flats that all hands must turn out and sleep in the park, according to the instructions of the consulting committee of the City Club and the Murphy Draying, Returfing and Sodding Company, there was a look of a couple of fires and an eviction all over the place.

"The tenants began to pack up feather beds, rubber boots, strings of garlic, hot-water bags, portable canoes and scuttles of coal to take along for the sake of comfort. The sidewalk looked like a Russian camp in Oyama's line of march. There was wailing and lamenting up and down stairs from Danny Geoghegan's flat on the top floor to the apartments of Missis Goldsteinupski on the first.

"'For why,' says Danny, coming down and raging in his blue yarn socks to the janitor, 'should I be turned out of me comfortable apartments to lay in the dirty grass like a rabbit? 'Tis like Jerome to stir up trouble wid small matters like this instead of——'

"'Whist!' says Officer Reagan on the sidewalk, rapping with his club. ''Tis not Jerome. 'Tis by order of the Polis Commissioner. Turn out every one of yez and hike yerselves to the park.'

"Now, 'twas a peaceful and happy home that all of us had in them same Beersheba Flats. The O'Dowds and the Steinowitzes and the Callahans and the Cohens and the Spizzinellis and the McManuses and the Spiegelmayers and the Joneses—all the nations of us, we lived like one big family together. And when the hot nights come along we kept a line of childher reaching from the front door to Kelly's on the corner, passing along the cans of beer from one to another without the trouble of running after it. And with no more clothing on than is provided for in the statutes, sitting in all the windies, with a cool growler in every one, and your feet out in the air, and the Rosenstein girls singing on the fire escape of the sixth floor, and Patsy Rourke's flute going in the eighth, and the ladies calling each other synonyms out the windies, and now and then a breeze sailing in over Mister Depew's Central—I tell you the Beersheba Flats was a summer resort that made the Catskills look like a hole in the ground. With his person full of beer and his feet out the windy and his old woman frying pork chops over a charcoal furnace and the childher dancing in cotton slips on the sidewalk around the organ-grinder and the rent paid for a week—what does a man want better on a hot night than that? And then comes this ruling of the polis driving people out o' their comfortable homes to sleep in parks—'twas for all the world like a ukase of them Russians—'twill be heard from again at next election time.

"Well, then, Officer Reagan drives the whole lot of us to the park and turns us in by the nearest gate. 'Tis dark under the trees, and all the childher sets up to howling that they want to go home.

"'Ye'll pass the night in this stretch of woods and scenery,' says Officer Reagan. ''Twill be fine and imprisonment for insoolting the Park Commissioner and the Chief of the Weather Bureau if ye refuse. I'm in charge of thirty acres between here and the Agyptian Monument, and I advise ye to give no trouble. 'Tis sleeping on the grass yez all have been condemned to by the authorities. Yez'll be permitted to leave in the morning, but ye must retoorn be night. Me orders was silent on the subject of bail, but I'll find out if 'tis required and there'll be bondsmen at the gate.'

"There being no lights except along the automobile drives, us 179 tenants of the Beersheba Flats prepared to spend the night as best we could in the raging forest. Them that brought blankets and kindling wood was best off. They got fires started and wrapped the blankets round their heads and laid down, cursing, in the grass. There was nothing to see, nothing to drink, nothing to do. In the dark we had no way of telling friend or foe, except by feeling the noses of 'em.

I brought along me last winter overcoat, me tooth-brush, some quinine pills and the red quilt off the bed in me flat. Three times during the night somebody rolled on me quilt and stuck his knees against the Adam's apple of me. And three times I judged his character by running me hand over his face, and three times I rose up and kicked the intruder down the hill to the gravelly walk below. And then someone with a flavor of Kelly's whiskey snuggled up to me, and I found his nose turned up the right way, and I says: 'Is that you, then Patsey?' and he says, 'It is, Carney. How long do you think it'll last?'

" 'I'm no weather-prophet,' says I, 'but if they bring out a strong anti-Tammany ticket next fall it ought to get us home in time to sleep on a bed once or twice before they line us up at the polls.'

" 'A-playing of my flute in the airshaft,' says Patsey Rourke, 'and a-perspiring in me own windy to the joyful noise of the passing trains and the smell of liver and onions and a-reading of the latest murder in the smoke of the cooking is well enough for me,' says he. 'What is this herding us in grass for, not to mention the crawling things with legs that walk up the trousers of us, and the Jersey snipes that peck at us, masquerading under the name and denomination of mosquitoes. What is it all for, Carney, and the rint going on just the same over at the flats?'

" ' 'Tis the great annual Municipal Free Night Outing Lawn Party,' says I, 'given by the polis, Hetty Green and the Drug Trust. During the heated season they hold a week of it in the principal parks. 'Tis a scheme to reach that portion of the people that's not worth taking up to North Beach for a fish fry.'

" 'I can't sleep on the ground,' says Patsey, 'wid any benefit. I have the hay fever and the rheumatism, and me ear is full of ants.'

"Well, the night goes on, and the ex-tenants of the Flats groans and stumbles around in the dark, trying to find rest and recreation in the forest. The childher is screaming with the coldness, and the janitor makes hot tea for 'em and keeps the fires going with the signboards that point to the Tavern and the Casino. The tenants try to lay down on the grass by families in the dark, but you're lucky if you can sleep next to a man from the same floor or believing in the same religion. Now and then a Murphy, accidental, rolls over on the grass of a Rosenstein, or a Cohen tries to crawl under the O'Grady bush, and then there's a feeling of noses and somebody is rolled down the hill to the driveway and stays there. There is some hair-pulling among the women folks, and everybody spanks the nearest howling kid to him by the sense of feeling only, regardless of its parentage and ownership. 'Tis hard to keep up the social distinctions in the dark that flourish by daylight in the Beersheba Flats. Mrs. Rafferty, that despises the asphalt that a Dago treads on, wakes up in the morning with her feet in the bosom of Antonio Spizzinelli. And Mike O'Dowd, that always threw peddlers downstairs as fast as he came up 'em, has to unwind old Isaacstein's whiskers from around his neck, and wake up the whole gang at daylight. But here and there some few got acquainted and overlooked the discomforts of the elements. There was five engagements to be married announced at the flats the next morning.

"About midnight I gets up and wrings the dew out of my hair, and goes to the side of the driveway and sits down. At one side of the park I could see the lights in the streets and houses; and I was thinking how happy them folks was who could chase the duck and smoke their pipes at their windows, and keep cool and pleasant like nature intended for 'em to.

"Just then an automobile stops by me, and a fine-looking, well-dressed man steps out.

" 'Me man,' says he, 'can you tell me why all these people are lying around on the grass in the park? I thought it was against the rules.'

" ' 'Twas an ordinance,' says I, 'just passed by the Polis Department and ratified by the Turf Cutters' Association, providing that all persons not carrying a license number on their rear axles shall keep in the public parks until further notice. Fortunately, the orders comes this year during a spell of fine weather, and the mortality, except on the borders of the lake and along the automobile drives, will not be any greater than usual.'

"'Who are these people on the side of the hill?' asks the man.

"'Sure,' says I, 'none others than the tenants of the Beersheba Flats—a fine home for any man, especially on hot nights. May daylight come soon!'

"'They come here by night,' says he, 'and breathe in the pure air and the fragrance of the flowers and trees. They do that,' says he, 'coming every night from the burning heat of dwellings of brick and stone.'

"'And wood,' says I. 'And marble and plaster and iron.'

"'The matter will be attended to at once,' says the man, putting up his book.

"'Are ye the Park Commissioner?' I asks.

"'I own the Beersheba Flats,' says he. 'God bless the grass and the trees that give extra benefits to a man's tenants. The rents shall be raised fifteen per cent, to-morrow. Good-night,' says he."

THE EASTER OF THE SOUL

IT is hardy likely that a goddess may die. Then Eastre, the old Saxon goddess of spring, must be laughing in her muslin sleeve at people who believe that Easter, her namesake, exists only along certain strips of Fifth Avenue pavement after church service.

Aye! It belongs to the world. The ptarmigan in Chilkoot Pass discards his winter white feathers for brown; the Patagonian Beau Brummell oils his chignon and clubs him another sweetheart to drag to his skull-strewn flat. And down in Chrystie Street——

Mr. "Tiger" McQuirk arose with a feeling of disquiet that he did not understand. With a practised foot he rolled three of his younger brothers like logs out of his way as they lay sleeping on the floor. Before a foot-square looking glass that hung by the window he stood and shaved himself. If that may seem to you a task too slight to be thus impressively chronicled, I bear with you; you do not know of the areas to be accomplished in traversing the cheek and chin of Mr. McQuirk.

McQuirk, senior, had gone to work long before. The big son of the house was idle. He was a marble-cutter, and the marble-cutters were out on a strike.

"What ails ye?" asked his mother, looking at him curiously; "are ye not feeling well the morning, maybe now?"

"He's thinking along of Annie Maria Doyle," impudently explained younger brother Tim, ten years old.

"Tiger" reached over the hand of a champion and swept the small McQuirk from his chair.

"I feel fine," said he, "beyond a touch of the I-don't-know-what-you-call-its. I feel like there was going to be earthquakes or music or a trifle of chills and fever or maybe a picnic. I don't know how I feel. I feel like knocking the face off a policeman, or else maybe like playing Coney Island straight across the board from pop-corn to the elephant houdahs."

"It's the spring in yer bones," said Mrs. McQuirk. "It's the sap risin'. Time was when I couldn't keep me feet still nor me head cool when the earthworms began to crawl out in the dew of the mornin'. 'Tis a bit of tea will do ye good, made from pipsissewa and gentian bark at the druggist's."

"Back up!" said Mr. McQuirk, impatiently. "There's no spring in sight. There's snow yet on the shed in Donovan's backyard. And yesterday they puts open cars on the Sixth Avenue lines, and the janitors have quit ordering coal. And that means six weeks more of winter, by all the signs that be."

After breakfast Mr. McQuirk spent fifteen minutes before the corrugated mirror, subjugating his hair and arranging his green-and-purple ascot with its amethyst tombstone pin—eloquent of his chosen calling.

Since the strike had been called it was this particular striker's habit to hie himself each morning to the corner saloon of Flaherty Brothers, and there establish himself upon the sidewalk, with one foot resting on the bootblack's stand, observing the panorama of the street until the pace of time brought twelve o'clock and the dinner hour. And Mr. "Tiger" Quirk, with his athletic seventy inches, well trained in sport and battle; his smooth, pale, solid, amiable face—blue where the razor had travelled; his carefully considered clothes and air of capability, was himself a spectacle not displeasing to the eye.

But on this morning Mr. McQuirk did not hasten immediately to his post of leisure and observation. Something unusual that he could not quite grasp was in the air. Something disturbed his thoughts, ruffled his senses, made him at once languid, irritable, elated, dissatisfied and sportive. He was no diagnostician, and he did not know that Lent was breaking up physiologically in his system.

Mrs. McQuirk had spoken of spring. Sceptically "Tiger" looked about him for signs. Few they were. The organ-grinders were at work; but they were always precocious harbingers. It was near enough spring for them to go penny-hunting when the skating ball dropped at the park. In the milliners' windows Easter hats, grave, gay, and jubilant, blossomed. There were green patches among the sidewalk débris of the grocers. On a third-story window-sill the first elbow cushion of the season—old gold stripes on a crimson ground—supported the kimonoed arms of a pensive brunette. The wind blew cold from the East River, but the sparrows were flying to the eaves with straws. A second-hand store, combining foresight with faith, had set out an ice-chest and baseball goods.

And then "Tiger's" eye, discrediting these signs, fell upon one that bore a bud of promise. From a bright, new lithograph the head of Capricornus confronted him, betokening the forward and heady brew.

Mr. McQuirk entered the saloon and called for his glass of bock. He threw his nickel on the bar, raised the glass, set it down without tasting and strolled toward the door.

"What's the matter, Lord Bolinbroke?" inquired the sarcastic bartender; "want a chiny vase or a gold-lined épergne to drink it out of—hey?"

"Say," said Mr. McQuirk, wheeling and shooting out a horizontal hand and a forty-five-degree chin, "you know your place only, when it comes for givin' titles. I've changed me mind about drinkin'—see? You got your money, ain't you? Wait till you get stung before you get the droop to your lip, will you?"

Thus Mr. McQuirk added mutability of desires to the strange humors that had taken possession of him.

Leaving the saloon, he walked away twenty steps and leaned in the open doorway of Lutz, the barber. He and Lutz were friends, masking their sentiments behind abuse and bludgeons of repartee.

"Irish loafer," roared Lutz, "how do you do? So, not yet haf der bolicemans or der catcher of dogs done deir duty!"

"Hello, Dutch," said Mr. McQuirk. "Can't get your mind off of frankfurters, can you?"

"Bah!" exclaimed the German, coming and leaning in the door. "I haf a soul above frankfurters to-day. Dere is springtime in der air. I can feel it coming in ofer der mud of der streets and das ice in der river. Soon will dere be bicnics in der islands, mit kegs of beer under der trees."

"Say," said Mr. McQuirk, setting his hat on one side, "is everybody kiddin' me about gentle Spring? There ain't any more spring in the air than there is in a horsehair sofa in a Second Avenue furnished room. For me the winter underwear yet and the buckwheat cakes."

"You haf no boetry," said Lutz. "True, it is yedt cold, und in der city we haf not many of der signs; but dere are dree kinds of beoble dot should always feel der approach of spring first—dey are boets, lovers, and poor vidows."

Mr. McQuirk went on his way, still possessed by the strange perturbation that he did not understand. Something was lacking to his comfort, and it made him half angry because he did not know what it was.

Two blocks away he came upon a foe, one Conover, whom he was bound in honor to engage in combat.

Mr. McQuirk made the attack with the characteristic suddenness and fierceness that had gained for him the endearing sobriquet of "Tiger." The defence of Mr. Conover was so prompt and admirable that the conflict was protracted until the onlookers unselfishly gave the warning cry of "Cheese it—the cop!" The principals escaped easily by running through the nearest open doors into the communicating backyards at the rear of the houses.

Mr. McQuirk emerged into another street. He stood by a lamp-post for a few minutes engaged in thought and then he turned and plunged into a small notion and news shop. A red-haired young woman, eating gum-drops, came and looked freezingly at him across the ice-bound steppes of the counter.

"Say, lady," he said, "have you got a song book with this in it? Let's see how it leads off—

"When the springtime comes we'll wander in the dale, love,
And whisper of those days of yore——

"I'm having a friend," explained Mr. McQuirk, "laid up with a broken leg, and he sent me after it. He's a devil for songs and poetry when he can't get out to drink."

"We have not," replied the young woman, with unconcealed contempt. "But there is a new song out that begins this way:

"Let us sit together in the old arm-chair,
And while the firelight flickers we'll be comfortable there."

There will be no profit in following Mr. "Tiger" McQuirk through his further vagaries of that day until he comes to stand knocking at the door of Annie Maria Doyle. The goddess Eastre, it seems, had guided his footsteps aright at last.

"Is that you now, Jimmy McQuirk?" she cried, smiling through the opened door (Annie Maria had never accepted the "Tiger"). "Well, whatever!"

"Come out in the hall," said Mr. McQuirk. "I want to ask your opinion of the weather—on the level."

"Are you crazy, sure?" said Annie Maria.

"I am," said the "Tiger." "They've been telling me all day there was spring in the air. Were they liars? Or am I?"

"Dear me!" said Annie Maria—"haven't you noticed it? I can almost smell the violets. And the green grass. Of course, there ain't any yet—it's just a kind of feeling, you know."

"That's what I'm getting at," said Mr. McQuirk. "I've had it. I didn't recognize it at first. I thought maybe it was en-wee, contracted the other day when I stepped above Fourteenth Street. But the katzenjammer I've got don't spell violets. It spells yer own name, Annie Maria, and it's you I want. I go to work next Monday, and I make four dollars a day. Spiel up, old girl—do we make a team?"

"Jimmy," sighed Annie Maria, suddenly disappearing in his overcoat, "don't you see that spring is all over the world right this minute?"

But you yourself remember how that day ended. Beginning with so fine a promise of vernal things, late in the afternoon the air chilled and an inch of snow fell—even so late in March. On Fifth Avenue the ladies drew their winter furs close about them. Only in the florists' windows could be perceived any signs of the morning smile of the coming goddess Eastre.

As six o'clock Herr Lutz began to close his shop. He heard a well-known shout: "Hello, Dutch!"

"Tiger" McQuirk, in his shirt-sleeves, with his hat on the back of his head, stood outside in the whirling snow, puffing at a black cigar.

"Donnerwetter!" shouted Lutz, "der vinter, he has come back again yet!"

"Yer a liar, Dutch," called back Mr. McQuirk, with friendly geniality, "it's spring-time, by the watch."

THE FOOL-KILLER

Down South whenever any one perpetrates some particularly monumental piece of foolishness everybody says: "Send for Jesse Holmes."

Jesse Holmes is the Fool-Killer. Of course he is a myth, like Santa Claus and Jack Frost and General Prosperity and all those concrete conceptions that are supposed to represent an idea that Nature had failed to embody. The wisest of the Southrons cannot tell you whence comes the Fool-Killer's name; but few and happy are the households from the Roanoke to the Rio Grande in which the name of Jesse Holmes has not been pronounced or invoked. Always with a smile, and often with a tear, is he summoned to his official duty. A busy man is Jesse Holmes.

I remember the clear picture of him that hung on the walls of my fancy during my barefoot days when I was dodging his oft-threatened devoirs. To me he was a terrible old man, in gray clothes, with a long, ragged, gray beard, and reddish, fierce eyes. I looked to see him come stumping up the road in a cloud of dust, with a white oak staff in his hand and his shoes tied with leather thongs. I may yet——

But this is a story, not a sequel.

I have taken notice with regret that few stories worth reading have been written that did not contain drink of some sort. Down go the fluids, from Arizona Dick's three fingers of red pizen to the inefficacious Oolong that nerves Lionel Monstresser to repartee in the "Dotty Dialogues." So, in such good company I may introduce an absinthe drip—one absinthe drip, dripped through a silver dripper, orderly, opalescent, cool, green-eyed—deceptive.

Kerner was a fool. Besides that, he was an artist and my good friend. Now, if there is one thing on earth utterly despicable to another, it is an artist in the eyes of an author whose story he has illustrated. Just try it once. Write a story about a mining camp in Idaho. Sell it. Spend the money, and then, six months later, borrow a quarter (or a dime), and buy the magazine containing it. You find a full-page wash drawing of your hero, Black Bill, the cowboy. Somewhere in your story you employed the word "horse." Aha! the artist has grasped the idea. Black Bill has on the regulation trousers of the M. F. H. of the Westchester County Hunt. He carries a parlor rifle, and wears a monocle. In the distance is a section of Forty-second Street during a search for a lost gaspipe, and the Taj Mahal, the famous mausoleum in India.

Enough! I hated Kerner, and one day I met him and we became friends. He was young and gloriously melancholy because his spirits were so high and life had so much in store for him. Yes, he was almost riotously sad. That was his youth. When a man begins to be hilarious in a sorrowful way you can bet a million that he is dyeing his hair. Kerner's hair was plentiful and carefully matted as an artist's thatch should be. He was a cigaretteur, and he audited his dinners with red wine. But, most of all, he was a fool. And, wisely, I envied him, and listened patiently while he knocked Velasquez and Tintoretto. Once he told me that he liked a story of mine that he had come across in an anthology. He described it to me, and I was sorry that Mr. Fitz James O'Brien was dead and could not learn of the eulogy of his work. But mostly Kerner made few breaks and was a consistent fool.

I'd better explain what I mean by that. There was a girl. Now, a girl, as far as I am concerned, is a thing that belongs in a seminary or an album; but I conceded the existence of the animal in order to retain Kerner's friendship. He showed me her picture in a locket—she was a blonde or a brunette—I have forgotten which. She worked in a factory for eight dollars a week. Lest factories quote this wage by way of vindication, I will add that the girl had worked for five years to reach that supreme elevation of renumeration, beginning at $1.50 per week.

Kerner's father was worth a couple of millions. He was willing to stand for art, but he drew the line at the factory girl. So Kerner disinherited his father and walked out to a cheap studio and lived on sausages for breakfast and on Farroni for dinner. Farroni had the artistic soul and a line of credit for painters and poets, nicely adjusted. Sometimes Kerner sold a picture and bought some new tapestry, a ring and a dozen silk cravats, and paid Farroni two dollars on account.

One evening Kerner had me to dinner with himself and the factory girl. They were to be married as soon as Kerner could slosh paint profitably. As for the ex-father's two millions—pouf!

She was a wonder. Small and halfway pretty, and as much at her ease in that cheap café as though she were only in the Palmer House, Chicago, with a souvenir spoon already safely hidden in her shirt waist. She was natural. Two things I noticed about her especially. Her belt buckle was exactly in the middle of her back, and she didn't tell us that a large man with a ruby stick-pin had followed her up all the way from Fourteenth Street. Was Kerner such a fool? I wondered. And then I thought of the quantity of striped cuffs and blue glass beads that $2,000,000 can buy for the heathen, and I said to myself that he was. And then Elise—certainly that was her name—told us, merrily, that the brown spot on her waist was caused by her landlady knocking at the door while she (the girl—confound the English language) was heating an iron over the gas jet, and she hid the iron under the bedclothes until the coast was clear, and there was a piece of chewing gum stuck to it when she began to iron the waist and—well, I wondered how in the world the chewing gum came to be there— don't they ever stop chewing it?

A while after that—don't be impatient, the absinthe drip is coming now—

Kerner and I were dining at Farroni's. A mandolin and a guitar were being attacked; the room was full of smoke in nice, long crinkly layers just like the artists draw the steam from a plum pudding on Christmas posters and a lady in a blue silk and gasolined gauntlets was beginning to hum an air from the Catskills.

"Kerner," said I, "you are a fool."

"Of course," said Kerner, "I wouldn't let her go on working. Not my wife. What's the use to wait? She's willing. I sold that water color of the Palisades yesterday. We could cook on a two-burner gas stove. You know the ragouts I can throw together? Yes, I think we will marry next week."

"Kerner," said I, "you are a fool."

"Have an absinthe drip?" said Kerner, grandly. "To-night you are a guest of Art in paying quantities. I think we will get a flat with a bath."

"I never tried one—I mean an absinthe drip," said I.

The waiter brought it and poured the water slowly over the ice in the dipper. "It looks exactly like the Mississippi River water in the big bend below Natchez," said I, fascinated, gazing at the be-muddled drip.

"There are such flats for eight dollars a week," said Kerner.

"You are a fool," said I, and began to sip the filtration. "What you need," I continued, "is the official attention of one Jesse Holmes."

Kerner, not being a Southerner, did not comprehend, so he sat, sentimental, figuring on his flat in his sordid, artistic way, while I gazed into the green eyes of the sophisticated Spirit of Wormwood.

Presently I noticed causally that a procession of bacchantes limned on the wall immediately below the ceiling had begun to move, traversing the room from right to left in a gay and spectacular pilgrimage. I did not confide my discovery to Kerner. The artistic temperament is too high-strung to view deviations from the natural laws of the art of kalsomining. I sipped my absinthe drip and sawed wormwood.

One absinthe drip is not much—but I said again to Kerner, kindly:

"You are a fool." And then, in the vernacular: "Jesse Holmes for yours."

And then I looked around and saw the Fool-Killer, as he had always appeared to my imagination, sitting at a nearby table, and regarding us with his reddish, fatal, relentless eyes. He was Jesse Holmes from top to toe; he had the long, gray, ragged beard, the gray clothes of ancient cut, the executioner's look, and the dusty shoes of one who had been called from afar. His eyes were turned fixedly upon Kerner. I shuddered to think that I had invoked him from his assiduous southern duties. I thought of flying, and then I kept my seat, reflecting that many men had escaped his ministrations when it seemed that nothing short of an appointment as Ambassador to Spain could save them from him. I had called my brother Kerner a fool and was in danger of hell fire. That was nothing; but I would try to save him from Jesse Holmes.

The Fool-Killer got up from his table and came over to ours. He rested his hands upon it, and turned his burning, vindictive eyes upon Kerner, ignoring me.

"You are a hopeless fool," he said to the artist. "Haven't you had enough of starvation yet? I offer you one more opportunity. Give up this girl and come back to your home. Refuse, and you must take the consequences."

The Fool-Killer's threatening face was within a foot of his victim's; but to my horror, Kerner made not the slightest sign of being aware of his presence.

"We will be married next week," he muttered absent-mindedly. "With my studio furniture and some second-hand stuff we can make out."

"You have decided your own fate," said the Fool-Killer, in a low but terrible voice. "You may consider yourself as one dead. You have had your last chance."

"In the moonlight," went on Kerner, softly, "we will sit under the skylight with our guitar and sing away the false delights of pride and money."

"On your own head be it," hissed the Fool-Killer, and my scalp prickled when I perceived that neither Kerner's eyes nor his ears took the slightest cognizance of Jesse Holmes. And then I knew that for some reason the veil had been lifted for me alone, and that I had been elected to save my friend from destruction at the Fool-Killer's hand. Something of the fear and wonder of it must have showed itself in my face.

"Excuse me," said Kerner, with his wan, amiable smile; "was I talking to myself? I think it is getting to be a habit with me."

The Fool-Killer turned and walked out of Farroni's.

"Wait here for me," said I, rising; "I must speak to that man. Had you no answer for him? Because you are a fool must you die like a mouse under his foot? Could you not utter one squeak in your own defence?"

"You are drunk," said Kerner, heartlessly. "No one addressed me."

"The destroyer of your mind," said I, "stood above you just now and marked you for his victim. You are not blind or deaf."

"I recognize no such person," said Kerner. "I have seen no one but you at this table. Sit down. Hereafter you shall have no more absinthe drips."

"Wait here," said I, furious; "if you don't care for your own life, I will save it for you."

I hurried out and overtook the man in gray halfway down the block. He looked as I had seen him in my fancy a thousand times—truculent, gray and awful. He walked with the white oak staff, and but for the street-sprinkler the dust would have been flying under his tread.

I caught him by the sleeve and steered him to a dark angle of a building. I knew he was a myth, and I did not want a cop to see me conversing with vacancy, for I might land in Bellevue minus my silver matchbox and diamond ring.

"Jesse Holmes," said I, facing him with apparent bravery, "I know you. I have heard of you all my life. I know now what a scourge you have been to your country. Instead of killing fools you have been murdering the youth and genius that are necessary to make a people live and grow great. You are a fool yourself, Holmes; you began killing off the brightest and best of your countrymen three generations ago, when the old and obsolete standards of society and honor and orthodoxy were narrow and bigoted. You proved that when you put your murderous mark upon my friend Kerner—the wisest chap I ever knew in my life."

The Fool-Killer looked at me grimly and closely.

"You're a queer jag," said he curiously. "Oh, yes; I see who you are now. You were sitting with him at the table. Well, if I'm not mistaken, I heard you call him a fool, too."

"I did," said I. "I delight in doing so. It is from envy. By all the standards that you know he is the most egregious and grandiloquent and gorgeous fool in all the world. That's why you want to kill him."

"Would you mind telling me who or what you think I am?" asked the old man.

I laughed boisterously and then stopped suddenly, for I remembered that it would not do to be seen so hilarious in the company of nothing but a brick wall.

"You are Jesse Holmes, the Fool-Killer," I said, solemnly, "and you are going to kill my friend Kerner. I don't know who rang you up, but if you do kill him I'll see that you get pinched for it. That is," I added, despairingly, "if I can get a cop to see you. They have a poor eye for mortals, and I think it would take the whole force to round up a myth murderer."

"Well," said the Fool-Killer, briskly, "I must be going. You had better go home and sleep it off. Good-night."

At this I was moved at a sudden fear for Kerner to a softer and more pleading mood. I leaned against the gray man's sleeve and besought him:

"Good Mr. Fool-Killer, please don't kill little Kerner. Why can't you go back South and kill Congressmen and clay-eaters and let us alone? Why don't you go up on Fifth Avenue and kill millionaires that keep their money locked up and won't let young fools marry because one of 'em lives on the wrong street? Come and have a drink, Jesse. Will you never get on to your job?"

"Do you know this girl that your friend has made himself a fool about?" asked the Fool-Killer.

"I have the honor," said I, "and that's why I called Kerner a fool. He is a fool because he has waited so long before marrying her. He is a fool because he has been waiting in the hopes of getting the consent of some absurd two-million-dollar-fool parent or something of the sort."

"Maybe," said the Fool-Killer—"maybe I—I might have looked at it differently. Would you mind going back to the restaurant and bringing your friend Kerner here?"

"Oh, what's the use, Jesse," I yawned. "He can't see you. He didn't know you were talking to him at the table. You are a fictitious character, you know."

"Maybe he can this time. Will you go fetch him?"

"All right," said I, "but I've a suspicion that you're not strictly sober, Jesse. You seem to be wavering and losing your outlines. Don't vanish before I get back."

I went back to Kerner and said:

"There's a man with an invisible homicidal mania waiting to see you outside. I believe he wants to murder you. Come along. You won't see him, so there's nothing to be frightened about."

Kerner looked anxious.

"Why," said he, "I had no idea one absinthe would do that. You'd better stick to Wurzburger. I'll walk home with you."

I led him to Jesse Holmes's.

"Rudolph," said the Fool-Killer, "I'll give in. Bring her up to the house. Give me your hand, boy."

"Good for you, dad," said Kerner, shaking hands with the old man. "You'll never regret it after you know her."

"So, you did see him when he was talking to you at the table?" I asked Kerner.

"We hadn't spoken to each other in a year," said Kerner. "It's all right now."

I walked away.

"Where are you going?" called Kerner.

"I am going to look for Jesse Holmes," I answered, with dignity and reserve.

TRANSIENTS IN ARCADIA

THERE is a hotel on Broadway that has escaped discovery by the summer-resort promoters. It is deep and wide and cool. Its rooms are finished in dark oak of a low temperature. Home-made breezes and deep-green shrubbery give it the delights without the inconveniences of the Adirondacks. One can mount its broad staircases or glide dreamily upward in its aërial elevators, attended by guides in brass buttons, with a serene joy that Alpine climbers have never attained. There is a chef in its kitchen who will prepare for you brook trout better than the White Mountains ever served, sea food that would turn Old Point Comfort—"by Gad, sah!"—green with envy, and Maine venison that would melt the official heart of the game warden.

A few have found out this oasis in the July desert of Manhattan. During that month you will see the hotel's reduced array of guests scattered luxuriously about in the cool twilight of its lofty dining-room, gazing at one another across the snowy waste of unoccupied tables, silently congratulatory.

Superfluous, watchful, pneumatically moving waiters hover near, supplying every want before it is expressed. The temperature is perpetual April. The ceiling is painted in water colors to counterfeit a summer sky across which delicate clouds drift and do not vanish as those of nature do to our regret.

The pleasing, distant roar of Broadway is transformed in the imagination of the happy guests to the noise of a waterfall filling the woods with its restful sound. At every strange footstep the guests turn an anxious ear, fearful lest their retreat be discovered and invaded by the restless pleasure-seekers who are forever hounding Nature to her deepest lairs.

Thus in the depopulated caravansary the little band of connoisseurs jealously hide themselves during the heated season, enjoying to the uttermost the delights of mountain and seashore that art and skill have gathered and served to them.

In this July came to the hotel one whose card that she sent to the clerk for her name to be registered read "Mme. Héloise D'Arcy Beaumont."

Madame Beaumont was a guest such as the Hotel Lotus loved. She possessed the fine air of the élite, tempered and sweetened by a cordial graciousness that made the hotel employés her slaves. Bell-boys fought for the honor of answering her ring; the clerks, but for the question of ownership, would have deeded to her the hotel and its contents; the other guests regarded her as the final touch of feminine exclusiveness and beauty that rendered the entourage perfect.

This super-excellent guest rarely left the hotel. Her habits were consonant with the customs of the discriminating patrons of the Hotel Lotus. To enjoy that delectable hostelry one must forego the city as though it were leagues away. By night a brief excursion to the nearby roofs is in order; but during the torrid day one remains in the umbrageous fastnesses of the Lotus as a trout hangs poised in the pellucid sanctuaries of his favorite pool.

Though alone in the Hotel Lotus, Madame Beaumont preserved the state of a queen whose loneliness was of position only. She breakfasted at ten, a cool, sweet, leisurely, delicate being who glowed softly in the dimness like a jasmine flower in the dusk.

But at dinner was Madame's glory at its height. She wore a gown as beautiful and immaterial as the mist from an unseen cataract in a mountain gorge. The nomenclature of this gown is beyond the guess of the scribe. Always pale-red roses reposed against its lace-garnished front. It was a gown that the head-waiter viewed with respect and met at the door. You thought of Paris when you saw it, and maybe of mysterious countesses, and certainly of Versailles and rapiers and Mrs. Fiske and rouge-et-noir. There was an untraceable rumor in the Hotel Lotus that Madame was a cosmopolite, and that she was pulling with her slender white hands certain strings between the nations in the favor of Russia. Being a citizeness of the world's smoothest roads it was small wonder that she was quick to recognize in the refined purlieus of the Hotel Lotus the most desirable spot in America for a restful sojourn during the heat of mid-summer.

On the third day of Madame Beaumont's residence in the hotel a young man entered and registered himself as a guest. His clothing—to speak of his points in approved order—was quietly in the mode; his features good and regular; his expression that of a poised and sophisticated man of the world. He informed the clerk that he would remain three or four days, inquired concerning the sailing of European steamships, and sank into the blissful inanition of the nonpareil hotel with the contented air of a traveller in his favorite inn.

The young man—not to question the veracity of the register—was Harold Farrington. He drifted into the exclusive and calm current of life in the Lotus so tactfully and silently that not a ripple alarmed his fellow-seekers after rest. He ate in the Lotus and of its patronym, and was lulled into blissful peace with the other fortunate mariners. In one day he acquired his table and his waiter and the fear lest the panting chasers after repose that kept Broadway warm should pounce upon and destroy this contiguous but covert haven.

After dinner on the next day after the arrival of Harold Farrington Madame Beaumont dropped her handkerchief in passing out. Mr. Farrington recovered and returned it without the effusiveness of a seeker after acquaintance.

Perhaps there was a mystic freemasonry between the discriminating guests of the Lotus. Perhaps they were drawn one to another by the fact of their common good fortune in discovering the acme of summer resorts in a Broadway hotel. Words delicate in courtesy and tentative in departure from formality passed between the two. And, as if in the expedient atmosphere of a real summer resort, an acquaintance grew, flowered and fructified on the spot as does the mystic plant of the conjuror. For a few moments they stood on a balcony upon which the corridor ended, and tossed the feathery ball of conversation.

"One tires of the old resorts," said Madame Beaumont, with a faint but sweet smile. "What is the use to fly to the mountains or the seashore to escape noise and dust when the very people that make both follow us there?"

"Even on the ocean," remarked Farrington sadly, "the Philistines be upon you. The most exclusive steamers are getting to be scarcely more than ferry boats. Heaven help us when the summer resorter discovers that the Lotus is further away from Broadway than Thousand Islands or Mackinac."

"I hope our secret will be safe for a week, anyhow," said Madame, with a sigh and a smile. "I do not know where I would go if they should descend upon the dear Lotus. I know of but one place so delightful in summer, and that is the castle of Count Polinski, in the Ural Mountains."

"I hear that Baden-Baden and Cannes are almost deserted this season," said Farrington. "Year by year the old resorts fall in disrepute. Perhaps many others, like ourselves, are seeking out the quiet nooks that are overlooked by the majority."

"I promise myself three days more of this delicious rest," said Madame Beaumont. "On Monday the *Cedric* sails."

Harold Farrington's eyes proclaimed his regret. "I too must leave on Monday," he said, "but I do not go abroad."

Madame Beaumont shrugged one round shoulder in a foreign gesture.

"One cannot hide here forever, charming though it may be. The château has been in preparation for me longer than a month. Those house parties that one must give—what a nuisance! But I shall never forget my week in the Hotel Lotus."

"Nor shall I," said Farrington in a low voice, "and I shall never *forgive* the *Cedric*."

On Sunday evening, three days afterward, the two sat at a little table on the same balcony. A discreet waiter brought ices and small glasses of claret cup.

Madame Beaumont wore the same beautiful evening gown that she had worn each day at dinner. She seemed thoughtful. Near her hand on the table lay a small chatelaine purse. After she had eaten her ice she opened the purse and took out a one-dollar bill.

"Mr. Farrington," she said, with the smile that had won the Hotel Lotus, "I want to tell you something. I'm going to leave before breakfast in the morning, because I've got to go back to my work. I'm behind the hosiery counter at

Casey's Mammoth Store, and my vacation's up at eight o'clock to-morrow. That paper dollar is the last cent I'll see till I draw my eight dollars salary next Saturday night. You're a real gentleman, and you've been good to me, and I wanted to tell you before I went.

"I've been saving up out of my wages for a year just for this vacation. I wanted to spend one week like a lady if I never do another one. I wanted to get up when I please instead of having to crawl out at seven every morning; and I wanted to live on the best and be waited on and ring bells for things just like rich folks do. Now I've done it, and I've had the happiest time I ever expect to have in my life. I'm going back to my work and my little hall bedroom satisfied for another year. I wanted to tell you about it, Mr. Farrington, because I— I thought you kind of liked me, and I—I liked you. But, oh, I couldn't help deceiving you up till now, for it was all just like a fairy tale to me. So I talked about Europe and the things I've read about in other countries, and made you think I was a great lady.

"This dress I've got on—it's the only one I have that's fit to wear—I bought from O'Dowd & Levinsky on the instalment plan.

"Seventy-five dollars is the price, and it was made to measure. I paid $10 down, and they're to collect $1 a week till it's paid for. That'll be about all I have to say, Mr. Farrington, except that my name is Mamie Siviter instead of Madame Beaumont, and I thank you for your attentions. This dollar will pay the instalment due on the dress to-morrow. I guess I'll go up to my room now."

Harold Farrington listened to the recital of the Lotus's loveliest guest with an impassive countenance. When she had concluded he drew a small book like a checkbook from his coat pocket. He wrote upon a blank form in this with a stub of pencil, tore out the leaf, tossed it over to his companion and took up the paper dollar.

"I've got to go to work, too, in the morning," he said, "and I might as well begin now. There's a receipt for the dollar instalment. I've been a collector for O'Dowd & Levinsky for three years. Funny, ain't it, that you and me both had the same idea about spending our vacation? I've always wanted to put up at a swell hotel, and I saved up out of my twenty per, and did it. Say, Mame, how about a trip to Coney Saturday night on the boat—what?"

The face of the pseudo Madame Héloise D'Arcy Beaumont beamed.

"Oh, you bet I'll go, Mr. Farrington. The store closes at twelve on Saturdays. I guess Coney'll be all right even if we did spend a week with the swells."

Below the balcony he sweltering city growled and buzzed in the July night. Inside the Hotel Lotus the tempered, cool shadows reigned, and the solicitous waiter single-footed near the low windows, ready at a nod to serve Madame and her escort.

At the door of the elevator Farrington took his leave, and Madame Beaumont made her last ascent. But before they reached the noiseless cage he said: "Just forget that 'Harold Farrington,' will you?—McManus is the name—James McManus. Some call me Jimmy."

"Good-night, Jimmy," said Madame.

THE RATHSKELLER AND THE ROSE

MISS POSIE CARRINGTON had earned her success. She began life handicapped by the family name of "Boggs," in the small town known as Cranberry Corners. At the age of eighteen she had acquired the name of "Carrington" and a position in the chorus of a metropolitan burlesque company. Thence upward she had ascended by the legitimate and delectable steps of "broiler," member of the famous "Dickey-bird" octette, in the successful musical comedy, "Fudge and Fellows," leader of the potato-bug dance in "Fol-de-Rol," and at length to the part of the maid "'Tointette" in "The King's Bath-Robe," which captured the critics and gave her her chance. And when we come to consider Miss Carrington she is in the heydey of flattery, fame and fizz; and that astute manager Herr Timothy Goldstein has her signature to iron-clad papers that she will star the coming season in Dyde Rich's new play, "Paresis by Gaslight."

Promptly there came to Herr Timothy a capable twentieth-century young character actor by the name of Highsmith, who besought engagement as "Sol Haytosser," the comic and chief male character part in "Paresis by Gaslight."

"My boy," said Goldstein, "take the part if you can get it. Miss Carrington won't listen to any of my suggestions. She has turned down half a dozen of the best imitators of the rural dub in the city. She declares she won't set a foot on the stage unless 'Haytosser' is the best that can be raked up. She was raised in a village, you know, and when a Broadway orchid sticks a straw in his hair and tries to call himself a clover blossom she's on, all right. I asked her, in a sarcastic vein, if she thought Denman Thompson would make any kind of a show in the part. 'Oh, no,' says she. 'I don't want him or John Drew or Jim Corbett or any of these swell actors that don't know a turnip from a turnstile. I want the real article.' So, my boy, if you want to play 'Sol Haytosser' you will have to convince Miss Carrington. Luck be with you."

Highsmith took the train the next day for Cranberry Corners. He remained in that forsaken and inanimate village three days. He found the Boggs family and corkscrewed their history unto the third and fourth generation. He amassed the facts and the local color of Cranberry Corners. The village had not grown as rapidly as had Miss Carrington. The actor estimated that it had suffered as few actual changes since the departure of its solitary follower of Thespis as had a stage upon which "four years is supposed to have elapsed." He absorbed Cranberry Corners and returned to the city of chameleon changes.

It was in the rathskeller that Highsmith made the hit of his histrionic career. There is no need to name the place; there is but one rathskeller where you could hope to find Miss Posie Carrington after a performance of "The King's Bath-Robe."

There was a jolly small party at one of the tables that drew many eyes. Miss Carrington, petite, marvellous, bubbling, electric, fame-drunken, shall be named first. Herr Goldstein follows, sonorous, curly-haired, heavy, a trifle anxious, as some bear that had caught, somehow, a butterfly in his claws. Next, a man condemned to a newspaper, sad, courted, armed, analyzing for press agent's dross every sentence that was poured over him, eating his à la Newburg in the silence of greatness. To conclude, a youth with parted hair, a name that is ochre to red journals and gold on the back of a supper check. These sat at a table while the musicians played, while waiters moved in the mazy performance of their duties with their backs toward all who desired their service, and all was bizarre and merry because it was nine feet below the level of the sidewalk.

At 11.45 a being entered the rathskeller. The first violin perceptibly flatted a C that should have been natural; the clarionet blew a bubble instead of a grace note; Miss Carrington giggled and the youth with parted hair swallowed an olive seed.

Exquisitely and irreproachably rural was the new entry. A lank, disconcerted, hesitating young man it was, flaxen-haired, gaping of mouth, awkward, stricken to misery by the lights and company. His clothing was butternut, with bright blue tie, showing four inches of bony wrist and white-socked ankle.

He upset a chair, sat in another one, curled a foot around a table leg and cringed at the approach of a waiter.

"You may fetch me a glass of lager beer," he said, in response to the discreet questioning of the servitor.

The eyes of the rathskeller were upon him. He was as fresh as a collard and as ingenuous as a hay rake. He let his eye rove about the place as one who regards, big-eyed, hogs in the potato patch. His gaze rested at length upon Miss Carrington. He rose and went to her table with a lateral, shining smile and a blush of pleased trepidation.

"How're ye, Miss Posie?" he said in accents not to be doubted. "Don't ye remember me—Bill Summers—the Summerses that lived back of the blacksmith shop? I reckon I've growed up some since ye left Cranberry Corners.

"'Liza Perry 'lowed I might see ye in the city while I was here. You know 'Liza married Benny Stanfield, and she says——"

"Ah, say!" interrupted Miss Carrington, brightly, "Lize Perry is never married —what! Oh, the freckles of her!"

"Married in June," grinned the gossip, "and livin' in the old Tatum Place. Ham Riley perfessed religion; old Mrs. Blithers sold her place to Cap'n Spooner; the youngest Waters girl run away with a music teacher; the courthouse burned up last March; your uncle Wiley was elected constable; Matilda Hoskins died from runnin' a needle in her hand, and Tom Beedle is courtin' Sallie Lathrop— they say he don't miss a night but what he's settin' on their porch."

"The wall-eyed thing!" exclaimed Miss Carrington, with asperity. "Why, Tom Beedle once—say, you folks, excuse me a while—this is an old friend of mine— Mr.—what was it? Yes, Mr. Summers—Mr. Goldstein, Mr. Ricketts, Mr.—— Oh, what's yours? 'Johnny' 'll do—come over here and tell me some more."

She swept him to an isolated table in a corner. Herr Goldstein shrugged his fat shoulders and beckoned to the waiter. The newspaper man brightened a little and mentioned absinthe. The youth with parted hair was plunged into melancholy. The guests of the rathskeller laughed, clinked glasses and enjoyed the comedy that Posie Carrington was treating them to after her regular performance. A few cynical ones whispered "press agent" and smiled wisely.

Posie Carrington laid her dimpled and desirable chin upon her hands, and forgot her audience—a faculty that had won her laurels for her.

"I don't seem to recollect any Bill Summers," she sad thoughtfully, gazing straight into the innocent blue eyes of the rustic young man. "But I know the Summerses, all right. I guess there ain't many changes in the old town. You see any of my folks lately?"

And then Highsmith played his trump. The part of "Sol Haytosser" called for pathos as well as comedy. Miss Carrington should see that he could do that as well.

"Miss Posie," said "Bill Summers," "I was up to your folkses house jist two or three days ago. No, there ain't many changes to speak of. The lilac bush by the kitchen window is over a foot higher, and the elm in the front yard died and had to be cut down. And yet it don't seem the same place that it used to be."

"How's ma?" asked Miss Carrington.

"She was settin' by the front door, crocheting a lamp-mat when I saw her last," said "Bill." "She's older'n she was, Miss Posie. But everything in the house looked jest the same. Your ma asked me to set down. 'Don't touch that willow rocker, William,' says she. 'It ain't been moved since Posie left; and that's the apron she was hemmin' layin' over the arm of it, jist as she flung it. I'm in hopes,' she goes on, 'that Posie'll finish runnin' out that hem some day.'"

Miss Carrington beckoned peremptorily to a waiter.

"A pint of extra dry," she ordered, briefly; "and give the check to Goldstein."

"The sun was shinin' in the door," went on the chronicler from Cranberry, "and your ma was settin' right in it. I asked her if she hadn't better move back a little. 'William,' says she, 'when I get sot down and lookin' down the road, I can't bear to move. Never a day,' says she, 'but what I set here every minute that I can spare and watch over them palin's for Posie. She went away down that road in the night, for we seen her little shoe tracks in the dust, and somethin' tells me she'll come back that way ag'in when she's weary of the world and begins to think about her old mother.'

"When I was comin' away," concluded "Bill," "I pulled this off'n the bush by the front steps. I thought maybe I might see you in the city, and I knowed you'd like somethin' from the old home."

He took from his coat pocket a rose—a drooping, yellow, velvet, odorous rose, that hung its head in the foul atmosphere of that tainted rathskeller like a virgin bowing before the hot breath of the lions in a Roman arena.

Miss Carrington's penetrating but musical laugh rose above the orchestra's rendering of "Bluebells."

"Oh, say!" she cried, with glee, "ain't those poky places the limit? I just know that two hours at Cranberry Corners would give me the horrors now. Well, I'm awful glad to have seen you, Mr. Summers. I guess I'll hustle around to the hotel now and get my beauty sleep."

She thrust the yellow rose into the bosom of her wonderful, dainty, silken garments, stood up and nodded imperiously at Herr Goldstein.

Her three companions and "Bill Summers" attended her to her cab. When her flounces and streamers were all safely tucked inside she dazzled them with au revoirs from her shining eyes and teeth.

"Come around to the hotel and see me, Bill, before you leave the city," she called as the glittering cab rolled away.

Highsmith, still in his make-up, went with Herr Goldstein to a café booth.

"Bright idea, eh?" asked the smiling actor. "Ought to land 'Sol Haytosser' for me, don't you think? The little lady never once tumbled."

"I didn't hear your conversation," said Goldstein, "but your make-up and acting was O. K. Here's to your success. You'd better call on Miss Carrington early to-morrow and strike her for the part. I don't see how she can keep from being satisfied with your exhibition of ability."

At 11.45 A. M. on the next day Highsmith, handsome, dressed in the latest mode, confident, with a fuchsia in his buttonhole, sent up his card to Miss Carrington in her select apartment hotel.

He was shown up and received by the actress's French maid.

"I am sorree," said Mlle. Hortense, "but I am to say this to all. It is with great regret. Mees Carrington have cancelled all engagements on the stage and have returned to live in that—how you call that town? Cranberry Cornaire!"

THE CLARION CALL

HALF of this story can be found in the records of the Police Department; the other half belongs behind the business counter of a newspaper office.

One afternoon two weeks after Millionaire Norcross was found in his apartment murdered by a burglar, the murderer, while strolling serenely down Broadway, ran plump against Detective Barney Woods.

"Is that you, Johnny Kernan?" asked Woods, who had been near-sighted in public for five years.

"No less," cried Kernan, heartily. "If it isn't Barney Woods, late and early of old Saint Jo! You'll have to show me! What are you doing East? Do the green-goods circulars get out that far?"

"I've been in New York some years," said Woods. "I'm on the city detective force."

"Well, well!" said Kernan, breathing smiling joy and patting the detective's arm.

"Come into Muller's," said Woods, "and let's hunt a quiet table. I'd like to talk to you awhile."

It lacked a few minutes to the hour of four. The tides of trade were not yet loosed, and they found a quiet corner of the café. Kernan, well dressed, slightly swaggering, self-confident, seated himself opposite the little detective, with his pale, sandy mustache, squinting eyes, and ready-made cheviot suit.

"What business are you in now?" asked Woods. "You know you left Saint Jo a year before I did."

"I'm selling shares in a copper mine," said Kernan. "I may establish an office here. Well, well! and so old Barney is a New York detective. You always had a turn that way. You were on the police in Saint Jo after I left there, weren't you?"

"Six months," said Woods. "And now there's one more question, Johnny. I've followed your record pretty close ever since you did that hotel job in Saratoga, and I never knew you to use your gun before. Why did you kill Norcross?"

Kernan stared for a few moments with concentrated attention at the slice of lemon in his high-ball; and then he looked at the detective with a sudden crooked, brilliant smile.

"How did you guess it, Barney?" he asked, admiringly. "I swear I thought the job was as clean and as smooth as a peeled onion. Did I leave a string hanging out anywhere?"

Woods laid upon the table a small gold pencil intended for a watch-charm.

"It's the one I gave you the last Christmas we were in Saint Jo. I've got your shaving mug yet. I found this under a corner of the rug in Norcross's room. I warn you to be careful what you say. I've got it put on to you, Johnny. We were old friends once, but I must do my duty. You'll have to go to the chair for Norcross."

Kernan laughed.

"My luck stays with me," said he. "Who'd have thought old Barney was on my trail!" He slipped one hand inside his coat. In an instant Woods had a revolver against his side.

"Put it away," said Kernan, wrinkling his nose. "I'm only investigating. Aha! It takes nine tailors to make a man, but one can do a man up. There's a hole in that vest pocket. I took that pencil off my chain and slipped it in there in case of a scrap. Put up your gun, Barney, and I'll tell you why I had to shoot Norcross. The old fool started down the hall after me, popping at the buttons on the back of my coat with a peevish little .22 and I had to stop him. The old lady was a darling. She just lay in bed and saw her $12,000 diamond necklace go without a chirp, while she begged like a panhandler to have back a little thin gold ring with a garnet worth about $3. I guess she married old Norcross for his money, all right. Don't they hang on to the little trinkets from the Man Who Lost Out, though? There were six rings, two brooches and a chatelaine watch. Fifteen thousand would cover the lot."

"I warned you not to talk," said Woods.

"Oh, that's all right," said Kernan. "The stuff is in my suit case at the hotel. And now I'll tell you why I'm talking. Because it's safe. I'm talking to a man I know. You owe me a thousand dollars, Barney Woods, and even if you wanted to arrest me your hand wouldn't make the move."

"I haven't forgotten," said Woods. "You counted out twenty fifties without a word. I'll pay it back some day. That thousand saved me and—well, they were piling my furniture out on the sidewalk when I got back to the house."

"And so," continued Kernan, "you being Barney Woods, born as true as steel, and bound to play a white man's game, can't lift a finger to arrest the man you're indebted to. Oh, I have to study men as well as Yale locks and window fastenings in my business. Now, keep quiet while I ring for the waiter. I've had a thirst for a year or two that worries me a little. If I'm ever caught the lucky sleuth will have to divide honors with the old boy Booze. But I never drink during business hours. After a job I can crook elbows with my old friend Barney with a clear conscience. What are you taking?"

The waiter came with the little decanters and the siphon and left them alone again.

"You've called the turn," said Woods, as he rolled the little gold pencil about with a thoughtful forefinger. "I've got to pass you up. I can't lay a hand on you. If I'd a-paid that money back—but I didn't, and that settles it. It's a bad break I'm making, Johnny, but I can't dodge it. You helped me once, and it calls for the same."

"I knew it," said Kernan, raising his glass, with a flushed smile of self-appreciation. "I can judge men. Here's to Barney, for—'he's a jolly good fellow.'"

"I don't believe," went on Woods quietly, as if he were thinking aloud, "that if accounts had been square between you and me, all the money in all the banks in New York could have bought you out of my hands to-night."

"I know it couldn't," said Kernan. "That's why I knew I was safe with you."

"Most people," continued the detective, "look sideways at my business. They don't class it among the fine arts and the professions. But I've always taken a kind of fool pride in it. And here is where I go 'busted.' I guess I'm a man first and a detective afterward. I've got to let you go, and then I've got to resign from the force. I guess I can drive an express wagon. Your thousand dollars is further off than ever, Johnny."

"Oh, you're welcome to it," said Kernan, with a lordly air. "I'd be willing to call the debt off, but I know you wouldn't take it. It was a lucky day for me when you borrowed it. And now, let's drop the subject. I'm off to the West on a morning train. I know a place out there where I can negotiate the Norcross sparks. Drink up, Barney, and forget your troubles. We'll have a jolly time while the police are knocking their heads together over the case. I've got one of my Sahara thirsts on to-night. But I'm in the hands—the unofficial hands—of my old friend Barney, and I won't even dream of a cop."

And then, as Kernan's ready finger kept the button and the waiter working, his weak point—a tremendous vanity and arrogant egotism, began to show itself. He recounted story after story of his successful plunderings, ingenious plots and infamous transgressions until Woods, with all his familiarity with evil-doers, felt growing within him a cold abhorrence toward the utterly vicious man who had once been his benefactor.

"I'm disposed of, of course," said Woods, at length. "But I advise you to keep under cover for a spell. The newspapers may take up this Norcross affair. There has been an epidemic of burglaries and manslaughter in town this summer."

The word sent Kernan into a high glow of sullen and vindictive rage.

"To h—l with the newspapers," he growled. "What do they spell but brag and blow and boodle in box-car letters? Suppose they do take up a case—what does it amount to? The police are easy enough to fool; but what do the newspapers do? They send a lot of pin-head reporters around to the scene; and they make for the nearest saloon and have beer while they take photos of the bartender's oldest daughter in evening dress to print as the fiancée of the young man in the tenth story, who thought he heard a noise below on the night of the murder. That's about as near as the newspapers ever come to running down Mr. Burglar."

"Well, I don't know," said Woods, reflecting. "Some of the papers have done good work in that line. There's the *Morning Mars*, for instance. It warmed up two or three trails, and got the man after the police had let 'em get cold."

"I'll show you," said Kernan, rising, and expanding his chest. "I'll show you what I think of newspapers in general, and your *Morning Mars* in particular."

Three feet from their table was the telephone booth. Kernan went inside and sat at the instrument, leaving the door open. He found a number in the book, took down the receiver and made his demand upon Central. Woods sat still, looking at the sneering, cold, vigilant face waiting close to the transmitter, and listened to the words that came from the thin, truculent lips curved into a contemptuous smile.

"That the *Morning Mars?* . . . I want to speak to the managing editor. . . . Why, tell him it's someone who wants to talk to him about the Norcross murder.

"You the editor? . . . All right. . . . I am the man who killed old Norcross. . . . Wait! Hold the wire; I'm not the usual crank . . . Oh, there isn't the slightest danger. I've just been discussing it with a detective friend of mine. I killed the old man at 2.30 A. M. two weeks ago to-morrow. . . . Have a drink with you? Now, hadn't you better leave that kind of talk to your funny man? Can't you tell whether a man's guying you or whether you're being offered the biggest scoop your dull dishrag of a paper ever had? . . . Well, that's so; it's a bobtail scoop—but you can hardly expect me to 'phone in my name and address. . . . Why! Oh, because I heard you make a specialty of solving mysterious crimes that stump the police. . . . No, that's not all. I want to tell you that your rotten, lying penny sheet is of no more use in tracking an intelligent murderer or highway man than a blind poodle would be. . . . What? . . . Oh, no, this isn't a rival newspaper office; you're getting it straight. I did the Norcross job, and I've got the jewels in my suit case at—'the name of the hotel could not be learned'—you recognize that phrase, don't you? I thought so. You've used it often enough. Kind of rattles you, doesn't it, to have the mysterious villain call up your great, big, all-powerful organ of right and justice and good government and tell you what a helpless old gas-bag you are? . . . Cut that out; you're not that big a fool—no, you don't think I'm a fraud. I call tell it by your voice. . . . Now, listen, and I'll give you a pointer that will prove it to you. Of course you've had this murder case worked over by your staff of bright young blockheads. Half of the second button on old Mrs. Norcross's nightgown is broken off. I saw it when I took the garnet ring off her finger. I thought it was a ruby. . . . Stop that! It won't work."

Kernan turned to Woods with a diabolic smile.

"I've got him going. He believes me now. He didn't quite cover the transmitter with his hand when he told somebody to call up Central on another 'phone and get our number. I'll give him just one more dig and then we'll make a 'get-away.'

"Hello! . . . Yes. I'm here yet. You didn't think I'd run from such a little subsidized, turncoat rag of a newspaper, did you? . . . Have me inside of forty-eight hours? Say, will you quit being funny? Now, you let grown men alone and attend to your business of hunting up divorce cases and street-car accidents and printing the filth and scandal that you make your living by. Good-by, old boy—sorry I haven't time to call on you. I'd feel perfectly safe in your sanctum asinorum. Tra-la!"

"He's as mad as a cat that's lost a mouse," said Kernan, hanging up the receiver and coming out. "And now, Barney, my boy, we'll go to a show and enjoy ourselves until a reasonable bedtime. Four hours' sleep for me, and then the west-bound."

The two dined in a Broadway restaurant. Kernan was pleased with himself. He spent money like a prince of fiction. And then a weird and gorgeous musical comedy engaged their attention. Afterward there was a late supper in a grill-room, with champagne, and Kernan at the height of his complacency.

Half-past three in the morning found them in a corner of an all-night café, Kernan still boasting in a vapid and rambling way, Woods thinking moodily over the end that had come to his usefulness as an upholder of the law.

But, as he pondered, his eye brightened with a speculative light.

"I wonder if it's possible," he said to himself, "I won-der if it's pos-si-ble!"

And then outside the café the comparative stillness of the early morning was punctured by faint, uncertain cries that seemed mere fireflies of sound, some growing louder, some fainter, waxing and waning amid the rumble of milk wagons and infrequent cars. Shrill cries they were when near—well-known cries that conveyed many meanings to the ears of those of the slumbering millions of the great city who waked to hear them. Cries that bore upon their significant, small volume the weight of a world's woe and laughter and delight and stress. To some, cowering beneath the protection of a night's ephemeral cover, they brought news of the hideous, bright day; to others, wrapped in happy sleep, they announced a morning that would dawn blacker than sable night. To many of the rich they brought a besom to sweep away what had been theirs while the stars shone; to the poor they brought—another day.

All over the city the cries were starting up, keen and sonorous, heralding the chances that the slipping of one cogwheel in the machinery of time had made; apportioning to the sleepers while they lay at the mercy of fate, the vengeance, profit, grief, reward and doom that the new figure in the calendar had brought them. Shrill and yet plaintive were the cries, as if the young voices grieved that so much evil and so little good was in their irresponsible hands. Thus echoed in the streets of the helpless city the transmission of the latest decrees of the gods, the cries of the newsboys—the Clarion Call of the Press.

Woods flipped a dime to the waiter, and said:

"Get me a *Morning Mars*."

When the paper came he glanced at its first page, and then tore a leaf out of his memorandum book and began to write on it with the little gold pencil.

"What's the news?" yawned Kernan.

Woods flipped over to him the piece of writing:

The New York *Morning Mars*:
Please pay to the order of John Kernan the one thousand dollars reward coming to me for his arrest and conviction.

                                        BARNARD WOODS.

"I kind of thought they would do that," said Woods, "when you were jollying 'em so hard. Now, Johnny, you'll come to the police station with me."

EXTRADITED FROM BOHEMIA

FROM near the village of Harmony, at the foot of the Green Mountains, came Miss Medora Martin to New York with her color-box and easel.

Miss Medora resembled the rose which the autumnal frosts had spared the longest of all her sister blossoms. In Harmony, when she started alone to the wicked city to study art, they said she was a mad, reckless, headstrong girl. In New York, when she first took her seat at a West Side boarding-house table, the boarders asked: "Who is the nice-looking old maid?"

Medora took heart, a cheap hall bedroom, and two art lessons a week from Professor Angelini, a retired barber who had studied his profession in a Harlem dancing academy. There was no one to set her right, for here in the big city they do it unto all of us. How many of us are badly shaved daily and taught the two-step imperfectly by ex-pupils of Bastien Le Page and Gérôme? The most pathetic sight in New York—except the manners of the rush-hour crowds—is the dreary march of the hopeless army of Mediocrity. Here Art is no benignant goddess, but a Circe who turns her wooers into mewing Toms and Tabbies who linger about the doorsteps of her abode, unmindful of the flying brickbats and boot-jacks of the critics. Some of us creep back to our native villages to the skim-milk of "I told you so"; but most of us prefer to remain in the cold courtyard of our mistress's temple, snatching the scraps that fall from her divine table d'hôte. But some of us grow weary at last of the fruitless service. And then there are two fates open to us. We can get a job driving a grocer's wagon, or we can get swallowed up in the Vortex of Bohemia. The latter sounds good; but the former really pans out better. For, when the grocer pays us off we can rent a dress suit—and the capitalized system of humor describes it best—Get Bohemia On the Run.

Miss Medora chose the Vortex and thereby furnishes us with our little story.

Professor Angelini praised her sketches excessively. Once, when she had made a neat study of a horse-chestnut tree in the park, he declared she would become a second Rosa Bonheur. Again—a great artist has his moods—he would say cruel and cutting things. For example, Medora had spent an afternoon patiently sketching the statue and the architecture at Columbus Circle. Tossing it aside with a sneer, the professor informed her that Giotto had once drawn a perfect circle with one sweep of his hand.

One day it rained, the weekly remittance from Harmony was overdue, Medora had a headache, the professor had tried to borrow two dollars from her, her art dealer had sent back all her water-colors unsold and—Mr. Binkley asked her out to dinner.

Mr. Binkley was the gay boy of the boarding-house. He was forty-nine, and owned a fish-stall in a downtown market. But after six o'clock he wore an evening suit and whooped things up connected with the beaux arts. The young men said he was an "Indian." He was supposed to be an accomplished habitué of the inner circles of Bohemia. It was no secret that he had once loaned $10 to a young man who had had a drawing printed in *Puck*. Often has one thus obtained his entrée into the charmed circle, while the other obtained both his entrée and roast.

The other boarders enviously regarded Medora as she left at Mr. Binkley's side at nine o'clock. She was as sweet as a cluster of dried autumn grasses in her pale blue—oh—er—that very thin stuff—in her pale blue Comstockized silk waist and box-pleated voile skirt, with a soft pink glow on her thin cheeks and the tiniest bit of rouge powder on her face, with her handkerchief and room key in her brown walrus, pebble-grain hand-bag.

And Mr. Binkley looked imposing and dashing with his red face and gray mustache, and his tight dress coat, that made the back of his neck roll up just like a successful novelist's.

They drove in a cab to the Café Terence, just off the most glittering part of Broadway, which, as everyone knows, is one of the most popular and widely patronized, jealously exclusive Bohemian resorts in the city.

Down between the rows of little tables tripped Medora, of the Green Mountains,

after her escort. Thrice in a lifetime may woman walk upon clouds—once when she trippeth to the altar, once when she first enters Bohemian halls, the last when she marches back across her first garden with the dead hen of her neighbor in her hand.

There was a table set, with three or four about it. A waiter buzzed around it like a bee, and silver and glass shone upon it. And, preliminary to the meal, as the prehistoric granite strata heralded the protozoa, the bread of Gaul, compounded after the formula of the recipe for the eternal hills, was there set forth to the hand and tooth of a long-suffering city, while the gods lay beside their nectar and home-made biscuits and smiled, and the dentists leaped for joy in their gold-leafy dens.

The eye of Binkley fixed a young man at his table with the Bohemian gleam, which is a compound of the look of the Basilisk, the shine of a bubble of Würzburger, the inspiration of genius and the pleading of a panhandler.

The young man sprang to his feet. "Hello, Bink, old boy!" he shouted. "Don't tell me you were going to pass our table. Join us—unless you've another crowd on hand."

"Don't mind, old chap," said Binkley, of the fish-stall. "You know how I like to butt up against the fine arts. Mr. Vandyke—Mr. Madder—er—Miss Martin, one of the elect also in art—er——"

The introduction went around. There were also Miss Elise and Miss 'Toinette. Perhaps they were models, for they chattered of the St. Regis decorations and Henry James—and they did it not badly.

Medora sat in transport. Music—wild, intoxicating music made by troubadours direct from a rear basement room in Elysium—set her thoughts to dancing. Here was a world never before penetrated by her warmest imagination or any of the lines controlled by Harriman. With the Green Mountains' external calm upon her she sat, her soul flaming in her with the fire of Andalusia. The tables were filled with Bohemia. The room was full of the fragrance of flowers —both mille and cauli. Questions and corks popped; laughter and silver rang; champagne flashed in the pail, wit flashed in the pan.

Vandyke ruffled his long, black locks, disarranged his careless tie and leaned over to Madder.

"Say, Maddy," he whispered, feelingly, "sometimes I'm tempted to pay this Philistine his ten dollars and get rid of him."

Madder ruffled his long, sandy locks and disarranged his careless tie.

"Don't think of it, Vandy," he replied. "We are short, and Art is long."

Medora ate strange viands and drank elderberry wine that they poured in her glass. It was just the color of that in the Vermont home. The waiter poured something in another glass that seemed to be boiling, but when she tasted it it was not hot. She had never felt so light-hearted before. She thought lovingly of Green Mountain farm and its fauna. She leaned, smiling, to Miss Elise.

"If I were at home," she said, beamingly, "I could show you the cutest little calf!"

"Nothing for you in the White Lane," said Miss Elise. "Why don't you pad?"

The orchestra played a wailing waltz that Medora had learned from the hand-organs. She followed the air with nodding head in a sweet soprano hum. Madder looked across the table at her, and wondered in what strange waters Binkley had caught her in his seine. She smiled at him, and they raised glasses and drank of the wine that boiled when it was cold.

Binkley had abandoned art and was prating of the unusual spring catch of shad. Miss Elise arranged the palette-and-maul-stick tie pin of Mr. Vandyke. A Philistine at some distant table was maundering volubly either about Jerome or Gérôme. A famous actress was discoursing excitably about monogrammed hosiery. A hose clerk from a department store was loudly proclaiming his opinions of the drama. A writer was abusing Dickens. A magazine editor and a photographer were drinking a dry brand at a reserved table. A 36-25-42 young lady was saying to an eminent sculptor: "Fudge for your Prax Italys! Bring one of your Venus Anno Dominus down to Cohen's and see how quickly she'd be turned down for a cloak model. Back to the quarries with your Greeks and Dagos!"

Thus went Bohemia.

At eleven Mr. Binkley took Medora to the boarding-house and left her, with a society bow, at the foot of the hall stairs. She went up to her room and lit the gas.

And then, as suddenly as the dreadful genie arose in vapor from the copper vase of the fisherman, arose in that room the formidable shape of the New England Conscience. The terrible thing that Medora had done was revealed to her in its full enormity. She had sat in the presence of the ungodly and looked upon the wine both when it was red and effervescent.

At midnight she wrote this letter:

Mr. Beriah Hoskins, Harmony, Vermont.

Dear Sir: Henceforth, consider me as dead to you forever. I have loved you too well to blight your career by bringing into it my guilty and sin-stained life. I have succumbed to the insidious wiles of this wicked world and have been drawn into the vortex of Bohemia. There is scarcely any depth of glittering iniquity that I have not sounded. It is hopeless to combat my decision. There is no rising from the depths to which I have sunk. Endeavor to forget me. I am lost forever in the fair but brutal maze of awful Bohemia. Farewell.

ONCE YOUR MEDORA.

On the next day Medora formed her resolutions. Beelzebub, flung from heaven, was no more cast down. Between her and the apple blossoms of Harmony there was a fixed gulf. Flaming cherubim warded her from the gates of her lost paradise. In one evening, by the aid of Binkley and Mumm, Bohemia had gathered her into its awful midst.

There remained to her but one thing—a life of brilliant but irremediable error. Vermont was a shrine that she never would dare to approach again. But she would not sink—there were great and compelling ones in history upon whom she would model her meteoric career—Camille, Lola Montez, Royal Mary, Zaza —such a name as one of these would that of Medora Martin be to future generations.

For two days Medora kept her room. On the third she opened a magazine at the portrait of the King of Belgium, and laughed sardonically. If that far-famed breaker of women's hearts should cross her path, he would have to bow before her cold and imperious beauty. She would not spare the old or the young. All America—all Europe should do homage to her sinister but compelling charm.

As yet she could not bear to think of the life she had once desired—a peaceful one in the shadow of the Green Mountains with Beriah at her side, and orders for expensive oil paintings coming in by each mail from New York. Her one fatal misstep had shattered that dream.

On the fourth day Medora powdered her face and rouged her lips. Once she had seen Carter in "Zaza." She stood before the mirror in a reckless attitude and cried: "Zut! zut!" She rhymed it with "nut," but with the lawless word Harmony seemed to pass away forever. The Vortex had her. She belonged to Bohemia for evermore. And never would Beriah——

The door opened and Beriah walked in.

" 'Dory," said he, "what's all that chalk and pink stuff on your face, honey?"

Medora extended an arm.

"Too late," she said solemnly. "The die is cast. I belong to another world. Curse me if you will—it is your right. Go, and leave me in the path I have chosen. Bid them all at home never to mention my name again. And sometimes, Beriah, pray for me when I am revelling in the gaudy, but hollow, pleasures of Bohemia."

"Get a towel, 'Dory," said Beriah, "and wipe that paint off your face. I came as soon as I got your letter. Them pictures of yours ain't amounting to anything. I've got tickets for both of us back on the evening train. Hurry and get your things in your trunk."

"Fate was too strong for me, Beriah. Go while I am strong to bear it."

"How do you fold this easel, 'Dory?—now begin to pack, so we have time to eat before train time. The maples is all out in full-grown leaves, 'Dory—you just ought to see 'em!"

"Not this early, Beriah?"

"You ought to see 'em, 'Dory; they're like an ocean of green in the morning sunlight."

"Oh, Beriah!"

On the train she said to him suddenly:

"I wonder why you came when you got my letter."

"Oh, shucks!" said Beriah. "Did you think you could fool me? How could you be run away to that Bohemia country like you said when your letter was postmarked New York as plain as day?"

A PHILISTINE IN BOHEMIA

GEORGE WASHINGTON, with his right arm upraised, sits his iron horse at the lower corner of Union Square, forever signalling the Broadway cars to stop as they round the curve into Fourteenth Street. But the cars buzz on, heedless, as they do at the beck of a private citizen, and the great General must feel, unless his nerves are iron, that rapid transit gloria mundi.

Should the General raise his left hand as he has raised his right it would point to a quarter of the city that forms a haven for the oppressed and suppressed of foreign lands. In the cause of national or personal freedom they have found a refuge here, and the patriot who made it for them sits his steed, overlooking their district, while he listens through his left ear to vaudeville that caricatures the posterity of his protégés. Italy, Poland, the former Spanish possessions and the polyglot tribes of Austria-Hungary have spilled here a thick lather of their effervescent sons. In the eccentric cafés and lodging-houses of the vicinity they hover over their native wines and political secrets. The colony changes with much frequency. Faces disappear from the haunts to be replaced by others. Whither do these uneasy birds flit? For half of the answer observe carefully the suave foreign air and foreign courtesy of the next waiter who serves your table d'hôte. For the other half, perhaps if the barber shops had tongues (and who will dispute it?) they could tell their share.

Titles are as plentiful as finger rings among these transitory exiles. For lack of proper exploitation a stock of title goods large enough to supply the trade of upper Fifth Avenue is here condemned to a mere pushcart traffic. The new-world landlords who entertain these off-shoots of nobility are not dazzled by coronets and crests. They have doughnuts to sell instead of daughters. With them it is a serious matter of trading in flour and sugar instead of pearl powder and bonbons.

These assertions are deemed fitting as an introduction to the tale, which is of plebeians and contains no one with even the ghost of a title.

Katy Dempsey's mother kept a furnished-room house in this oasis of the aliens. The business was not profitable. If the two scraped together enough to meet the landlord's agent on rent day and negotiate for the ingredients of a daily Irish stew they called it success. Often the stew lacked both meat and potatoes. Sometimes it became as bad as consommé with music.

In this mouldy old house Katy waxed plump and pert and wholesome and as beautiful and freckled as a tiger lily. She was the good fairy who was guilty of placing the damp clean towels and cracked pitchers of freshly laundered Croton in the lodgers' rooms.

You are informed (by virtue of the privileges of astronomical discovery) that the star lodger's name was Mr. Brunelli. His wearing a yellow tie and paying his rent promptly distinguished him from the other lodgers. His raiment was splendid, his complexion olive, his mustache fierce, his manners a prince's, his rings and pins as magnificent as those of a travelling dentist.

He had breakfast served in his room, and he ate it in a red dressing gown with green tassels. He left the house at noon and returned at midnight. Those were mysterious hours, but there was nothing mysterious about Mrs. Dempsey's lodgers except the things that were not mysterious. One of Mr. Kipling's poems is addressed to "Ye who hold the unwritten clue to all save all unwritten things." The same "readers" are invited to tackle the foregoing assertion.

Mr. Brunelli, being impressionable and a Latin, fell to conjugating the verb "amare," with Katy in the objective case, though not because of antipathy. She talked it over with her mother.

"Sure, I like him," said Katy. "He's more politeness than twinty candidates for Alderman, and he makes me feel like a queen whin he walks at me side. But what is he, I dinno? I've me suspicions. The marnin'll coom whin he'll throt out the picture av his baronial halls and ax to have the week's rint hung up in the ice chist along wid all the rist of 'em."

" 'Tis thrue," admitted Mrs. Dempsey, "that he seems to be a sort iv a Dago and too coolchured in his spache for a rale gintleman. But ye may be mis-judgin' him. Ye should niver suspect any wan of bein' of noble descint that pays cash and pathronizes the laundry rig'lar."

"He's the same thricks of spakin' and blarneyin' wid his hands," sighed Katy, "as the Frinch nobleman at Mrs. Toole's that ran away wid Mr. Toole's Sunday pants and left the photograph of the Bastile, his grandfather's chat-taw, as security for tin weeks' rint."

Mr. Brunelli continued his calorific wooing. Katy continued to hesitate. One day he asked her out to dine and she felt that a dénouement was in the air. While they are on their way, with Katy in her best muslin, you must take as an entr'acte a brief peep at New York's Bohemia.

'Tonio's restaurant is in Bohemia. The very location of it is secret. If you wish to know where it is ask the first person you meet. He will tell you in a whisper. 'Tonio discountenances custom; he keeps his house-front black and forbidding; he gives you a pretty bad dinner; he locks his door at the dining hour; but he knows spaghetti as the boarding-house knows cold veal; and—he has deposited many dollars in a certain Banco di —— something with many gold vowels in the name on its windows.

To this restaurant Mr. Brunelli conducted Katy. The house was dark and the shades were lowered; but Mr. Brunelli touched an electric button by the basement door, and they were admitted.

Along a long, dark, narrow hallway they went and then through a shining and spotless kitchen that opened directly upon a backyard.

The walls of houses hemmed three sides of the yard; a high board fence, surrounded by cats, the other. A wash of clothes was suspended high upon a line stretched from diagonal corners. Those were property clothes, and were never taken in by 'Tonio. They were there that wits with defective pronunciation might make puns in connection with the ragout.

A dozen and a half little tables set upon the bare ground were crowded with Bohemia-hunters, who flocked there because 'Tonio pretended not to want them and pretended to give them a good dinner. There was a sprinkling of real Bohemians present who came for a change because they were tired of the real Bohemia, and a smart shower of the men who originate the bright sayings of Congressmen and the little nephew of the well-known general passenger agent of the Evansville and Terre Haute Railroad Company.

Here is a bon mot that was manufactured at 'Tonio's:

"A dinner at 'Tonio's," said a Bohemian, "always amounts to twice the price that is asked for it."

Let us assume that an accommodating voice inquires:

"How so?"

"The dinner costs you 40 cents; you give 10 cents to the waiter, and it makes you feel like 30 cents."

Most of the diners were confirmed table d'hôters—gastronomic adventurers, forever seeking the El Dorado of a good claret, and consistently coming to grief in California.

Mr. Brunelli escorted Katy to a little table embowered with shrubbery in tubs, and asked her to excuse him for a while.

Katy sat, enchanted by a scene so brilliant to her. The grand ladies, in splendid dresses and plumes and sparkling rings; the fine gentlemen who laughed so loudly, the cries of "Garsong" and "We, monseer," and "Hello, Mame!" that distinguish Bohemia; the lively chatter, the cigarette smoke, the interchange of bright smiles and eye-glances—all this display and magnificence overpowered the daughter of Mrs. Dempsey and held her motionless.

Mr. Brunelli stepped into the yard and seemed to spread his smile and bow over the entire company. And everywhere there was a great clapping of hands and a few cries of "Bravo!" and "'Tonio! 'Tonio!" whatever those words might mean. Ladies waved their napkins at him, gentlemen almost twisted their necks off, trying to catch his nod.

When the ovation was concluded Mr. Brunelli, with a final bow, stepped nimbly into the kitchen and flung off his coat and waistcoat.

Flaherty, the nimblest "garsong" among the waiters, had been assigned to the special service of Katy. She was a little faint from hunger, for the Irish stew on the Dempsey table had been particularly weak that day. Delicious odors from unknown dishes tantalized her. And Flaherty began to bring to her table course after course of ambrosial food that the gods might have pronounced excellent.

But even in the midst of her Lucullian repast Katy laid down her knife and fork. Her heart sank as lead, and a tear fell upon her filet mignon. Her haunting suspicions of the star lodger rose again, fourfold. Thus courted and admired and smiled upon by that fashionable and gracious assembly, what else could Mr. Brunelli be but one of these dazzling titled patricians, glorious of name but shy of rent money, concerning whom experience had made her wise? With a sense of his ineligibility growing within her there was mingled a torturing conviction that his personality was becoming more pleasing to her day by day. And why had he left her to dine alone?

But here he was coming again, now coatless, his snowy shirt-sleeves rolled high above his Jeffriesonian elbows, a white yachting cap perched upon his jetty curls.

"'Tonio! 'Tonio!" shouted many, and "The spaghetti!" shouted the rest.

Never at 'Tonio's did a waiter dare to serve a dish of spaghetti until 'Tonio came to test it, to prove the sauce and add the needful dash of seasoning that gave it perfection.

From table to table moved 'Tonio, like a prince in his palace, greeting his guests. White, jewelled hands signalled him from every side.

A glass of wine with this one and that, smiles for all, a jest and repartee for any that might challenge—truly few princes could be so agreeable a host! And what artist could ask for further appreciation of his handiwork? Katy did not know that the proudest consummation of a New Yorker's ambition is to shake hands with a spaghetti chef or to receive a nod from a Broadway head-waiter.

At last the company thinned, leaving but a few couples and quartettes lingering over new wine and old stories. And then came Mr. Brunelli to Katy's secluded table, and drew a chair close to hers.

Katy smiled at him dreamily. She was eating the last spoonful of a raspberry roll with Burgundy sauce.

"You have seen!" said Mr. Brunelli, laying one hand upon his collar bone. "I am Antonio Brunelli! Yes; I am the great 'Tonio! You have not suspect that! I loave you, Katy, and you shall marry with me. Is it not so? Call me 'Antonio,' and say that you will be mine."

Katy's head dropped to the shoulder that was now freed from all suspicion of having received the knightly accolade.

"Oh, Andy," she sighed, "this is great! Sure, I'll marry wid ye. But why didn't ye tell me ye was the cook? I was near turnin' ye down for bein' one of thim foreign counts!"

FROM EACH ACCORDING TO HIS ABILITY

VUYNING left his club, cursing it softly, without any particular anger. From ten in the morning until eleven it had bored him immeasurably. Kirk with his fish story, Brooks with his Porto Rico cigars, old Morrison with his anecdote about the widow, Hepburn with his invariable luck at billiards—all these afflictions had been repeated without change of bill or scenery. Besides these morning evils Miss Allison had refused him again on the night before. But that was a chronic trouble. Five times she had laughed at his offer to make her Mrs. Vuyning. He intended to ask her again the next Wednesday evening.

Vuyning walked along Forty-fourth Street to Broadway, and then drifted down the great sluice that washes out the dust of the goldmines of Gotham. He wore a morning suit of light gray, low, dull kid shoes, a plain, finely woven straw hat, and his visible linen was the most delicate possible shade of heliotrope. His necktie was the blue-gray of a November sky, and its knot was plainly the outcome of a lordly carelessness combined with an accurate conception of the most recent dictum of fashion.

Now, to write of a man's haberdashery is a worse thing than to write a historical novel "around" Paul Jones, or to pen a testimonial to a hay-fever cure.

Therefore, let it be known that the description of Vuyning's apparel is germane to the movements of the story, and not to make room for the new fall stock of goods.

Even Broadway that morning was a discord in Vuyning's ears; and in his eyes it paralleled for a few dreamy, dreary minutes a certain howling, scorching, seething, malodorous slice of street that he remembered in Morocco. He saw the struggling mass of dogs, beggars, fakirs, slave-drivers and veiled women in carts without horses, the sun blazing brightly among the bazaars, the piles of rubbish from ruined temples in the street—and then a lady passing, jabbed the ferrule of a parasol in his side and brought him back to Broadway.

Five minutes of his stroll brought him to a certain corner, where a number of silent, pale-faced men are accustomed to stand, immovably, for hours, busy with the file blades of their penknives, with their hat brims on a level with their eyelids. Wall Street speculators, driving home in their carriages, love to point out these men to their visiting friends and tell them of this rather famous lounging-place of the "crooks." On Wall Street the speculators never use the file blades of their knives.

Vuyning was delighted when one of this company stepped forth and addressed him as he was passing. He was hungry for something out of the ordinary, and to be accosted by this smooth-faced, keen-eyed, low-voiced, athletic member of the under world, with his grim yet pleasant smile, had all the taste of an adventure to the convention-weary Vuyning.

"Excuse me, friend," said he. "Could I have a few minutes' talk with you—on the level?"

"Certainly," said Vuyning, with a smile. "But, suppose we step aside to a quieter place. There is a divan—a café over here that will do. Schrumm will give us a private corner."

Schrumm established them under a growing palm, with two seidls between them. Vuyning made a pleasant reference to meteorological conditions, thus forming a hinge upon which might be swung the door leading from the thought repository of the other.

"In the first place," said his companion, with the air of one who presents his credentials, "I want you to understand that I am a crook. Out West I am known as Rowdy the Dude. Pickpocket, supper man, second-story man, yeggman, boxman, all-round burglar, card-sharp and slickest con man west of the Twenty-third Street ferry landing—that's my history. That's to show I'm on the square—with you. My name's Emerson."

"Confound old Kirk with his fish stories," said Vuyning to himself, with silent glee as he went through his pockets for a card. "It's pronounced 'Vining,'" he said, as he tossed it over to the other. "And I'll be as frank with you. I'm just a kind of a loafer, I guess, living on my daddy's money. At the club they call me 'Left-at-the-Post.' I never did a day's work in my life; and I haven't the heart to run over a chicken when I'm motoring. It's a pretty shabby record, altogether."

"There's one thing you can do," said Emerson, admiringly; "you can carry duds. I've watched you several times pass on Broadway. You look the best-dressed man I've seen. And I'll bet you a gold mine I've got $50 worth more gent's furnishings on my frame than you have. That's what I wanted to see you about. I can't do the trick. Take a look at me. What's wrong?"

"Stand up," said Vuyning.

Emerson arose, and slowly revolved.

"You've been 'outfitted,'" declared the clubman. "Some Broadway window-dresser has misused you. That's an expensive suit, though, Emerson."

"A hundred dollars," said Emerson.

"Twenty too much," said Vuyning. "Six months old in cut, one inch too long, and half an inch too much lapel. Your hat is plainly dated one year ago, although there's only a sixteenth of an inch lacking in the brim to tell the story. That English poke in your collar is too short by the distance between Troy and London. A plain gold link cuff-button would take all the shine out of those pearl ones with diamond settings. Those tan shoes would be exactly the articles to work into the heart of a Brooklyn school-ma'am on a two weeks' visit to Lake Ronkonkoma. I think I caught a glimpse of a blue silk sock embroidered with russet lilies of the valley when you—improperly—drew up your trousers as you sat down. There are always plain ones to be had in stores. Have I hurt your feelings, Emerson?"

"Double the ante!" cried the criticized one, greedily. "Give me more of it. There's a way to tote the haberdashery, and I want to get wise to it. Say, you're the right kind of a swell. Anything else to the queer about me?"

"Your tie," said Vuyning, "is tied with absolute precision and correctness."

"Thanks," gratefully—"I spent over half an hour at it before I——"

"Thereby," interrupted Vuyning, "completing your resemblance to a dummy in a Broadway store window."

"Yours truly," said Emerson, sitting down again. "It's bully of you to put me wise. I knew there was something wrong, but I couldn't just put my finger on it. I guess it comes by nature to know how to wear clothes."

"Oh, I suppose," said Vuyning, with a laugh, "that my ancestors picked up the knack while they were peddling clothes from house to house a couple of hundred years ago. I'm told they did that."

"And mine," said Emerson, cheerfully, "were making their visits at night, I guess, and didn't have a chance to catch on to the correct styles."

"I tell you what," said Vuyning, whose ennui had taken wings, "I'll take you to my tailor. He'll eliminate the mark of the beast from your exterior. That is, if you care to go on further in the way of expense."

"Play 'em to the ceiling," said Emerson, with a boyish smile of joy. "I've got a roll as big around as a barrel of black-eyed peas and as loose as the wrapper of a two-for-fiver. I don't mind telling you that I was not touring among the Antipodes when the burglar-proof safe of the Farmers' National Bank of Butterville, Ia., flew open some moonless nights ago to the tune of $16,000."

"Aren't you afraid," asked Vuyning, "that I'll call a cop and hand you over?"

"You tell me," said Emerson, cooly, "why I didn't keep them."

He laid Vuyning's pocketbook and watch—the Vuyning 100-year-old family watch—on the table.

"Man," said Vuyning, revelling, "did you ever hear the tale Kirk tells about the six-pound trout and the old fisherman?"

"Seems not," said Emerson, politely. "I'd like to."

"But you won't," said Vuyning. "I've heard it scores of times. That's why I won't tell you. I was just thinking how much better this is than a club. Now, shall we go to my tailor?"

.   .   .   .

"Boys, and elderly gents," said Vuyning, five days later at his club, standing up against the window where his coterie was gathered, and keeping out the breeze, "a friend of mine from the West will dine at our table this evening."

"Will he ask if we have heard the latest from Denver?" said a member, squirming in his chair.

"Will he mention the new twenty-three-story Masonic Temple, in Quincy, Ill.?" inquired another, dropping his nose-glasses.

"Will he spring one of those Western Mississippi River catfish stories, in which they use yearling calves for bait?" demanded Kirk, fiercely.

"Be comforted," said Vuyning. "He has none of the little vices. He is a burglar and safe-blower, and a pal of mine."

"Oh, Mary Ann!" said they. "Must you always adorn every statement with your alleged humor?"

It came to pass that at eight in the evening a calm, smooth, brilliant, affable man sat at Vuyning's right hand during dinner. And when the ones who pass their lives in city streets spoke of skyscrapers or of the little Czar on his far, frozen throne, or of insignificant fish from inconsequential streams, this big, deep-chested man, faultlessly clothed, and eyed like an Emperor, disposed of their Lilliputian chatter with a wink of his eyelash.

And then he painted for them with hard, broad strokes a marvellous lingual panorama of the West. He stacked snow-topped mountains on the table, freezing the hot dishes of the waiting diners. With a wave of his hand he swept the clubhouse into a pine-crowned gorge, turning the waiters into a grim posse, and each listener into a blood-stained fugitive, climbing with torn fingers upon the ensanguined rocks. He touched the table and spake, and the five panted as they gazed on barren lava beds, and each man took his tongue between his teeth and felt his mouth bake at the tale of a land empty of water and food. As simply as Homer sang, while he dug a tine of his fork leisurely into the tablecloth, he opened a new world to their view, as does one who tells a child of the Looking-Glass Country.

As one of his listeners might have spoken of tea too strong at a Madison Square "afternoon," so he depicted the ravages of "redeye" in a border town when the caballeros of the lariat and "forty-five" reduced ennui to a minimum.

And then, with a sweep of his white, unringed hands, he dismissed Melpomene, and forthwith Diana and Amaryllis footed it before the mind's eyes of the clubmen.

The savannas of the continent spread before them. The wind, humming through a hundred leagues of sage brush and mesquite, closed their ears to the city's staccato noises. He told them of camps, of ranches marooned in a sea of fragrant prairie blossoms, of gallops in the stilly night that Apollo would have forsaken his daytime steeds to enjoy; he read them the great, rough epic of the cattle and the hills that had not been spoiled by the hand of man, the mason. His words were a telescope to the city men, whose eyes had looked upon Youngstown, O., and whose tongues had called it "West."

In fact, Emerson had them "going."

.   .   .   .

The next morning at ten he met Vuyning, by appointment, at a Forty-second Street café.

Emerson was to leave for the West that day. He wore a suit of dark cheviot that looked to have been draped upon him by an ancient Grecian tailor who was a few thousand years ahead of the styles.

"Mr. Vuyning," said he, with the clear, ingenuous smile of the successful "crook," "it's up to me to go the limit for you any time I can do so. You're the real thing; and if I can ever return the favor, you bet your life I'll do it."

"What was that cow-puncher's name?" asked Vuyning, "who used to catch a mustang by the nose and mane, and throw him till he put the bridle on?"

"Bates," said Emerson.

"Thanks," said Vuyning. "I thought it was Yates. Oh, about that toggery business—I'd forgotten that."

"I've been looking for some guy to put me on the right track for years," said Emerson. "You're the goods, duty free, and halfway to the warehouse in a red wagon."

"Bacon, toasted on a green willow switch over red coals, ought to put broiled lobsters out of business," said Vuyning. "And you say a horse at the end of a thirty-foot rope can't pull a ten-inch stake out of wet prairie? Well, good-bye, old man, if you must be off."

At one o'clock Vuyning had luncheon with Miss Allison by previous arrangement.

For thirty minutes he babbled to her, unaccountably, of ranches, horses, cañons, cyclones, round-ups, Rocky Mountains, and beans and bacon. She looked at him with wondering and half-terrified eyes.

"I was going to propose again to-day," said Vuyning, cheerily, "but I won't. I've worried you often enough. You know dad has a ranch in Colorado. What's the good of staying here? Jumping jonquils! but it's great out there. I'm going to start next Tuesday."

"No, you won't," said Miss Allison.

"What?" said Vuyning.

"Not alone," said Miss Allison, dropping a tear upon her salad. "What do you think?"

"Betty!" exclaimed Vuyning, "what do you mean?"

"I'll go too," said Miss Allison, forcibly.

Vuyning filled her glass with Apollinaris.

"Here's to Rowdy the Dude!" he gave—a toast mysterious.

"Don't know him," said Miss Allison; "but if he's your friend, Jimmy—here goes!"

THE MEMENTO

MISS LYNNETTE D'ARMANDE turned her back on Broadway. This was but tit for tat, because Broadway had often done the same thing to Miss D'Armande. Still, the "tats" seemed to have it, for the ex-leading lady of the "Reaping the Whirlwind" company had everything to ask of Broadway, while there was no vice-versa.

So Miss Lynnette D'Armande turned the back of her chair to her window that overlooked Broadway, and sat down to stitch in time the lisle-thread heel of a black silk stocking. The tumult and glitter of the roaring Broadway beneath her window had no charm for her; what she greatly desired was the stifling air of a dressing-room on that fairyland street and the roar of an audience gathered in that capricious quarter. In the meantime, those stockings must not be neglected. Silk does wear out so, but—after all, isn't it just the only goods there is?

The Hotel Thalia looks on Broadway as Marathon looks on the sea. It stands like a gloomy cliff above the whirlpool where the tides of two great thoroughfares clash. Here the player-bands gather at the end of their wanderings to loosen the buskin and dust the sock. Thick in the streets around it are booking-offices, theatres, agents, schools, and the lobster-palaces to which those thorny paths lead.

Wandering through the eccentric halls of the dim and fusty Thalia, you seem to have found yourself in some great ark or caravan about to sail, or fly, or roll away on wheels. About the house lingers a sense of unrest, of expectation, of transientness, even of anxiety and apprehension. The halls are a labyrinth. Without a guide, you wander like a lost soul in a Sam Lloyd puzzle.

Turning any corner, a dressing-sack or a *cul-de-sac* may bring you up short. You meet alarming tragedians stalking in bath-robes in search of rumored bath-rooms. From hundreds of rooms come the buzz of talk, scraps of new and old songs, and the ready laughter of the convened players.

Summer has come; their companies have disbanded, and they take their rest in their favorite caravansary, while they besiege the managers for engagements for the coming season.

At this hour of the afternoon the day's work of tramping the rounds of the agents' offices is over. Past you, as you ramble distractedly through the mossy halls, flit audible visions of houris, with veiled, starry eyes, flying tag-ends of things and a swish of silk, bequeathing to the dull hallways an odor of gaiety and a memory of *frangipanni*. Serious young comedians, with versatile Adam's apples, gather in doorways and talk of Booth. Far-reaching from somewhere comes the smell of ham and red cabbage, and the crash of dishes on the American plan.

The indeterminate hum of life in the Thalia is enlivened by the discreet pop-ping—at reasonable and salubrious intervals—of beer-bottle corks. Thus punc-tuated, life in the genial hostel scans easily—the comma being the favorite mark, semicolons frowned upon, and periods barred.

Miss D'Armande's room was a small one. There was room for her rocker between the dresser and the wash-stand if it were placed longitudinally. On the dresser were its usual accoutrements, plus the ex-leading lady's collected souvenirs of road engagements and photographs of her dearest and best pro-fessional friends.

At one of these photographs she looked twice or thrice as she darned, and smiled friendlily.

"I'd like to know where Lee is just this minute," she said, half-aloud.

If you had been privileged to view the photograph thus flattered, you would have thought at the first glance that you saw the picture of a many-petalled white flower, blown through the air by a storm. But the floral kingdom was not re-sponsible for that swirl of petalous whiteness.

You saw the filmy, brief skirt of Miss Rosalie Ray as she made a complete heels-over-head turn in her wistaria-entwined swing, far out from the stage, high above the heads of the audience. You saw the camera's inadequate repre-sentation of the graceful, strong kick, with which she, at this exciting moment, sent flying, high and far, the yellow silk garter that each evening spun from her agile limb and descended upon the delighted audience below.

You saw, too, amid the black-clothed, mainly masculine patrons of select vaudeville a hundred hands raised with the hope of staying the flight of the brilliant aërial token.

Forty weeks of the best circuits this act had brought Miss Rosalie Ray, for each of two years. She did other things during her twelve minutes—a song and dance, imitations of two or three actors who are but imitations of themselves, and a balancing feat with a step-ladder and feather-duster; but when the blossom-decked swing was let down from the flies, and Miss Rosalie sprang smil-ing into the seat, with the golden circlet conspicuous in the place whence it was soon to slide and become a soaring and coveted guerdon—then it was that the audience rose in its seat as a single man—or presumably so—and indorsed the specialty that made Miss Ray's name a favorite in the booking-offices.

At the end of two years Miss Ray suddenly announced to her dear friend, **Miss**

D'Armande, that she was going to spend the summer at an antediluvian village on the north shore of Long Island, and that the stage would see her no more.

Seventeen minutes after Miss Lynnette D'Armande had expressed her wish to know the whereabouts of her old chum, there were sharp raps at her door.

Doubt not that it was Rosalié Ray. At the shrill command to enter she did so, with something of a tired flutter, and dropped a heavy hand-bag on the floor. Upon my word, it was Rosalie, in a loose, travel-stained automobileless coat, closely tied brown veil with yard-long flying ends, gray walking suit, and tan oxfords with lavender overgaiters.

When she threw off her veil and hat, you saw a pretty enough face, now flushed and disturbed by some unusual emotion, and restless, large eyes with discontent marring their brightness. A heavy pile of dull auburn hair, hastily put up, was escaping in crinkly, waving strands and curling, small locks from the confining combs and pins.

The meeting of the two was not marked by the effusion vocal, gymnastical, osculatory, and catechetical that distinguishes the greetings of their unprofessional sisters in society. There was a brief clinch, two simultaneous labial dabs, and they stood on the same footing of the old days. Very much like the short salutations of soldiers or of travellers in foreign wilds are the welcomes between the strollers at the corners of their criss-cross roads.

"I've got the hall-room two flights up above yours," said Rosalie, "but I came straight to see you before going up. I didn't know you were here till they told me."

"I've been in since the last of April," said Lynnette. "And I'm going on the road with a 'Fatal Inheritance' Company. We open next week in Elizabeth. I thought you'd quit the stage, Lee. Tell me about yourself."

Rosalie settled herself with a skilful wriggle on the top of Miss D'Armande's wardrobe trunk, and leaned her head against the papered wall. From long habit, thus can peripatetic leading ladies and their sisters make themselves as comfortable as though the deepest armchairs embraced them.

"I'm going to tell you, Lynn," she said, with a strangely sardonic and yet carelessly resigned look on her youthful face. "And then to-morrow I'll strike the old Broadway trail again, and wear some more paint off the chairs in the agents' offices. If anybody had told me any time in the last three months up to four o'clock this afternoon that I'd ever listen to that 'Leave-your-name-and-address' rot of the booking bunch again, I'd have given 'em the real Mrs. Fiske laugh. Loan me a handkerchief, Lynn. Gee! but those Long Island trains are fierce. I've got enough soft-coal cinders on my face to go on and play *Topsy* without using the cork. And, speaking of corks—got anything to drink, Lynn?"

Miss D'Armande opened a door of the washstand and took out a bottle.

"There's nearly a pint of Manhattan. There's a cluster of carnations in the drinking glass, but——"

"Oh, pass the bottle. Save the glass for company. Thanks! That hits the spot. The same to you. My first drink in three months!

"Yes, Lynn, I quit the stage at the end of last season. I quit it because I was sick of the life. And especially because my heart and soul were sick of men—of the kind of men we stage people have to be up against. You know what the game is to us—it's a fight against 'em all the way down the line from the manager who wants us to try his new motor-car to the bill-posters who want to call us by our front names.

"And the men we have to meet after the show are the worst of all. The stage-door kind, and the manager's friends who take us to supper and show their diamonds and talk about seeing 'Dan' and 'Dave' and 'Charlie' for us. They're beasts, and I hate 'em.

"I tell you, Lynn, it's the girls like us on the stage that ought to be pitied.

It's girls from good homes that are honestly ambitious and work hard to rise in the profession, but never do get there. You hear a lot of sympathy sloshed around on chorus girls and their fifteen dollars a week. Piffle! There ain't a sorrow in the chorus that a lobster cannot heal.

"If there's any tears to shed, let 'em fall for the actress that gets a salary of from thirty to forty-five dollars a week for taking a leading part in a bum show. She knows she'll never do any better; but she hangs on for years, hoping for the 'chance' that never comes.

"And the fool plays we have to work in! Having another girl roll you around the stage by the hind legs in a 'Wheelbarrow Chorus' in a musical comedy is dignified drama compared with the idiotic things I've had to do in the thirty-centers.

"But what I hated most was the men—the men leering and blathering at you across tables, trying to buy you with Würzburger or Extra Dry, according to their estimate of your price. And the men in the audiences, clapping, yelling, snarling, crowding, writhing, gloating—like a lot of wild beasts, with their eyes fixed on you, ready to eat you up if you come in reach of their claws. Oh, how I hate 'em!

"Well, I'm not telling you much about myself, am I, Lynn?

"I had two hundred dollars saved up, and I cut the stage the first of the summer. I went over on Long Island and found the sweetest little village that ever was, called Soundport, right on the water. I was going to spend the summer there, and study up on elocution, and try to get a class in the fall. There was an old widow lady with a cottage near the beach who sometimes rented a room or two just for company, and she took me in. She had another boarder, too—the Reverend Arthur Lyle.

"Yes, he was the head-liner. You're on, Lynn. I'll tell you all of it in a minute. It's only a one-act play.

"The first time he walked on, Lynn, I felt myself going; the first lines he spoke, he had me. He was different from the men in audiences. He was tall and slim, and you never heard him come in the room, but you *felt* him. He had a face like a picture of a knight—like one of that Round Table bunch—and a voice like a 'cello solo. And his manners!

"Lynn, if you'd take John Drew in his best drawing-room scene and compare the two, you'd have John arrested for disturbing the peace.

"I'll spare you the particulars; but in less than a month Arthur and I were engaged. He preached at a little one-night stand of a Methodist church. There was to be a parsonage the size of a lunch-wagon, and hens and honeysuckles when we were married. Arthur used to preach to me a good deal about Heaven, but he never could get my mind quite off those honeysuckles and hens.

"No; I didn't tell him I'd been on the stage. I hated the business and all that went with it; I'd cut it out forever, and I didn't see any use of stirring things up. I was a good girl, and I didn't have anything to confess, except being an elocutionist, and that was about all the strain my conscience would stand.

"Oh, I tell you, Lynn, I was happy. I sang in the choir and attended the sewing society, and recited that 'Annie Laurie' thing with the whistling stunt in it, 'in a manner bordering upon the professional,' as the weekly village paper reported it. And Arthur and I went rowing, and walking in the woods, and clamming, and that poky little village seemed to me the best place in the world. I'd have been happy to live there always, too, if——

"But one morning old Mrs. Gurley, the widow lady, got gossipy while I was helping her string beans on the back porch, and began to gush information, as folks who rent out their rooms usually do. Mr. Lyle was her idea of a saint on her earth—as he was mine, too. She went over all his virtues and graces, and wound up by telling me that Arthur had had an extremely romantic love-affair, not long before, that had ended unhappily. She didn't seem to be on to the details, but she knew that he had been hit pretty hard. He was paler and thinner, she said, and he had some kind of a remembrance or keepsake of the lady in a little rosewood box that he kept locked in his desk drawer in his study.

" 'Several times,' says she, 'I've seen him gloomerin' over that box of evenings, and he always locks it up right away if anybody comes into the room.'

"Well, you can imagine how long it was before I got Arthur by the wrist and led him down stage and hissed in his ear.

"That same afternoon we were lazying around in a boat among the water-lilies at the edge of the bay.

" 'Arthur,' says I, 'you never told me you'd had another love-affair. But Mrs. Gurley did,' I went on, to let him know I knew. I hate to hear a man lie.

" 'Before you came,' says he, looking me frankly in the eye, 'there was a previous affection—a strong one. Since you know of it, I will be perfectly candid with you.'

" 'I am waiting,' says I.

" 'My dear Ida,' says Arthur—of course I went by my real name, while I was in Soundport—'this former affection was a spiritual one, in fact. Although the lady aroused my deepest sentiments, and was, as I thought, my ideal woman, I never met her, and never spoke to her. It was an ideal love. My love for you, while no less ideal, is different. You wouldn't let that come between us.'

" 'Was she pretty?' I asked.

" 'She was very beautiful,' said Arthur.

" 'Did you see her often?' I asked.

" 'Something like a dozen times,' says he.

" 'Always from a distance?' says I.

" 'Always from quite a distance,' says he.

" 'And you loved her?' I asked.

" 'She seemed my ideal of beauty and grace—and soul,' says Arthur.

" 'And this keepsake that you keep under lock and key, and moon over at times, is that a remembrance from her?'

" 'A memento,' says Arthur, 'that I have treasured.'

" 'Did she send it to you?'

" 'It came from her,' says he.

" 'In a roundabout way?' I asked.

" 'Somewhat roundabout,' says he, 'and yet rather direct.'

" 'Why didn't you ever meet her?' I asked. 'Were your positions in life so different?'

" 'She was far above me,' says Arthur. 'Now, Ida,' he goes on, 'this is all of the past. You're not going to be jealous, are you?'

" 'Jealous!' says I. 'Why, man, what are you talking about? It makes me think ten times as much of you as I did before I knew about it.'

"And it did, Lynn—if you can understand it. That ideal love was a new one on me, but it struck me as being the most beautiful and glorious thing I'd ever heard of. Think of a man loving a woman he'd never even spoken to, and being faithful just to what his mind and heart pictured her! Oh, it sounded great to me. The men I'd always known come at you with either diamonds, knock-out drops, or a raise of salary—and their ideals!—well, we'll say no more.

"Yes, it made me think more of Arthur than I did before. I couldn't be jealous of that far-away divinity that he used to worship, for I was going to have him myself. And I began to look upon him as a saint on earth, just as old lady Gurley did.

"About four o'clock this afternoon a man came to the house for Arthur to go and see somebody that was sick among his church bunch. Old lady Gurley was taking her afternoon snore on the couch, so that left me pretty much alone.

"In passing by Arthur's study I looked in, and saw his bunch of keys hanging in the drawer of his desk, where he'd forgotten 'em. Well, I guess we're all to the Mrs. Bluebeard now and then, ain't we, Lynn? I made up my mind I'd have a look at that memento he kept so secret. Not that I cared what it was—it was just curiosity.

"While I was opening the drawer I imagined one or two things it might be. I thought it might be a dried rosebud she'd dropped down to him from a balcony, or maybe a picture of her he'd cut out of a magazine, she being so high up in the world.

"I opened the drawer, and there was the rosewood casket about the size of a gent's collar box. I found the little key in the bunch that fitted it, and raised the lid.

"I took one look at that memento, and then I went to my room and packed my trunk. I threw a few things into my grip, gave my hair a flirt or two with a side-comb, put on my hat, and went in and gave the old lady's foot a kick. I'd tried awfully hard to use proper and correct language while I was there for Arthur's sake, and I had the habit down pat, but it left me then.

"'Stop sawing gourds,' says I, 'and sit up and take notice. The ghost's about to walk. I'm going away from here, and I owe you eight dollars. The express-man will call for my trunk.'

"I handed her the money.

"'Dear me, Miss Crosby!' says she. 'Is anything wrong? I thought you were pleased here. Dear me, young women are so hard to understand, and so different from what you expect 'em to be.'

"'You're damn right,' says I. 'Some of 'em are. But you can't say that about men. *When you know one man you know 'em all!* That settles the human race question.'

"And then I caught the four-thirty-eight, soft-coal unlimited; and here I am."

"You didn't tell me what was in that box, Lee," said Miss D'Armande, anxiously.

"One of those yellow silk garters that I used to kick off my leg into the audience during that old vaudeville swing act of mine. Is there any of the cocktail left, Lynn?"

THE TRIMMED LAMP

THE TRIMMED LAMP

THE TRIMMED LAMP

O F course there are two sides to the question. Let us look at the other.
We often hear "shop-girls" spoken of. No such persons exist. There
are girls who work in shops. They make their living that way. But
why turn their occupation into an adjective? Let us be fair. We do not refer
to the girls who live on Fifth Avenue as "marriage-girls."

Lou and Nancy were chums. They came to the big city to find work because
there was not enough to eat at their homes to go around. Nancy was nineteen;
Lou was twenty. Both were pretty, active country girls who had no ambition
to go on the stage.

The little cherub that sits up aloft guided them to a cheap and respectable
boarding-house. Both found positions and became wage-earners. They remained
chums. It is at the end of six months that I would beg you to step forward
and be introduced to them. Meddlesome Reader: My Lady Friends, Miss Nancy
and Miss Lou. While you are shaking hands please take notice—cautiously—
of their attire. Yes, cautiously; for they are as quick to resent a stare as a
lady in a fox at the horse show is.

Lou is a piece-work ironer in a hand laundry. She is clothed in a badly
fitting purple dress, and her hat plume is four inches too long; but her ermine
muff and scarf cost $25, and its fellow beasts will be ticketed in the windows
at $7.98 before the season is over. Her cheeks are pink, and her light blue
eyes bright. Contentment radiates from her.

Nancy you would call a shop-girl—because you have the habit. There is
no type; but a perverse generation is always seeking a type; so this is what
the type should be. She has the high-ratted pompadour and the exaggerated
straight-front. Her skirt is shoddy, but has the correct flare. No furs protect
her against the bitter spring air, but she wears her short broadcloth jacket as
jauntily as though it were Persian lamb! On her face and in her eyes, re-
morseless type-seeker, is the typical shop-girl expression. It is a look of silent
but contemptuous revolt against cheated womanhood; of sad prophecy of the
vengeance to come. When she laughs her loudest the look is still there. The
same look can be seen in the eyes of Russian peasants; and those of us left
will see it some day on Gabriel's face when he comes to blow us up. It is
a look that should wither and abash man; but he has been known to smirk at
it and offer flowers—with a string tied to them.

Now lift your hat and come away, while you receive Lou's cheery "See you
again," and the sardonic, sweet smile of Nancy that seems, somehow, to miss
you and go fluttering like a white moth up over the housetops to the stars.

The two waited on the corner for Dan. Dan was Lou's steady company.
Faithful? Well, he was on hand when Mary would have had to hire a dozen
subpœna servers to find her lamb.

"Ain't you cold, Nancy?" said Lou. "Say, what a chump you are for working in that old store for $8 a week! I made $18.50 last week. Of course ironing ain't as swell work as selling lace behind a counter, but it pays. None of us ironers make less than $10. And I don't know that it's any less respectful work, either."

"You can have it," said Nancy, with uplifted nose. "I'll take my eight a week and hall bedroom. I like to be among nice things and swell people. And look what a chance I've got! Why, one of our glove girls married a Pittsburg—steel maker, or blacksmith or something—the other day worth a million dollars. I'll catch a swell myself some time. I ain't bragging on my looks or anything; but I'll take my chances where there's big prizes offered. What show would a girl have in a laundry?"

"Why, that's where I met Dan," said Lou, triumphantly. "He came in for his Sunday shirt and collars and saw me at the first board, ironing. We all try to get to work at the first board. Ella Maginnis was sick that day, and I had her place. He said he noticed my arms first, how round and white they was. I had my sleeves rolled up. Some nice fellows come into laundries. You can tell 'em by their bringing their clothes in suit cases, and turning in the door sharp and sudden."

"How can you wear a waist like that, Lou?" said Nancy, gazing down at the offending article with sweet scorn in her heavy-lidded eyes. "It shows fierce taste."

"This waist?" said Lou, with wide-eyed indignation. "Why, I paid $16 for this waist. It's worth twenty-five. A woman left it to be laundered, and never called for it. The boss sold it to me. It's got yards and yards of hand embroidery on it. Better talk about that ugly, plain thing you've got on."

"This ugly, plain thing," said Nancy, calmly, "was copied from one that Mrs. Van Alstyne Fisher was wearing. The girls say her bill in the store last year was $12,000. I made mine, myself. It cost me $1.50. Ten feet away you couldn't tell it from hers."

"Oh, well," said Lou, good-naturedly, "if you want to starve and put on airs, go ahead. But I'll take my job and good wages; and after hours give me something as fancy and attractive to wear as I am able to buy."

But just then Dan came—a serious young man with a ready-made necktie, who had escaped the city's brand of frivolity—an electrician earning $30 per week who looked upon Lou with the sad eyes of Romeo, and thought her embroidered waist a web in which any fly should delight to be caught.

"My friend, Mr. Owens—shake hands with Miss Danforth," said Lou.

"I'm mighty glad to know you, Miss Danforth," said Dan, with outstretched hand. "I've heard Lou speak of you so often."

"Thanks," said Nancy, touching his fingers with the tips of her cool ones, "I've heard her mention you—a few times."

Lou giggled.

"Did you get that handshake from Mrs. Van Alstyne Fisher, Nance?" she asked.

"If I did, you can feel safe in copying it," said Nancy.

"Oh, I couldn't use it at all. It's too stylish for me. It's intended to set off diamond rings, that high shake is. Wait till I get a few and then I'll try it."

"Learn it first," said Nancy, wisely, "and you'll be more likely to get the rings."

"Now, to settle this argument," said Dan, with his ready, cheerful smile, "let me make a proposition. As I can't take both of you up to Tiffany's and do the right thing, what do you say to a little vaudeville? I've got the tickets. How about looking at stage diamonds since we can't shake hands with the real sparklers?"

The faithful squire took his place close to the curb; Lou next, a little peacocky in her bright and pretty clothes; Nancy on the inside, slender, and soberly clothed as the sparrow, but with the true Van Alstyne Fisher walk—thus they set out for their evening's moderate diversion.

I do not suppose that many look upon a great department store as an educational institution. But the one in which Nancy worked was something like that to her. She was surrounded by beautiful things that breathed of taste and refinement. If you live in an atmosphere of luxury, luxury is yours whether your money pays for it, or another's.

The people she served were mostly women whose dress, manners, and position in the social world were quoted as criterions. From them Nancy began to take toll—the best from each according to her view.

From one she would copy and practise a gesture, from another an eloquent lifting of an eyebrow, from others, a manner of walking, of carrying a purse, of smiling, of greeting a friend, of addressing "inferiors in station." From her best beloved model, Mrs. Van Alstyne Fisher, she made requisition for that excellent thing, a soft, low voice as clear as silver and as perfect in articulation as the notes of a thrush. Suffused in the aura of this high social refinement and good breeding, it was impossible for her to escape a deeper effect of it. As good habits are said to be better than good principles, so, perhaps, good manners are better than good habits. The teachings of your parents may not keep alive your New England conscience; but if you sit on a straight-back chair and repeat the words "prisms and pilgrims" forty times the devil will flee from you. And when Nancy spoke in the Van Alstyne Fisher tones she felt the thrill of *noblesse oblige* to her very bones.

There was another source of learning in the great departmental school. Whenever you see three or four shop-girls gather in a bunch and jingle their wire bracelets as an accompaniment to apparently frivolous conversation, do not think that they are there for the purpose of criticizing the way Ethel does her back hair. The meeting may lack the dignity of the deliberative bodies of man; but it has all the importance of the occasion on which Eve and her first daughter first put their heads together to make Adam understand his proper place in the household. It is Woman's Conference for Common Defense and Exchange of Strategical Theories of Attack and Repulse upon and against the World, which is a Stage, and Man, its Audience who Persists in Throwing Bouquets Thereupon. Woman, the most helpless of the young of any animal—with the fawn's grace but without its fleetness; with the bird's beauty but without its power of flight; with the honey-bee's burden of sweetness but without its—— Oh, let's drop that simile—some of us may have been stung.

During this council of war they pass weapons one to another, and exchange stratagems that each has devised and formulated out of the tactics of life.

"I says to 'im," says Sadie, "ain't you the fresh thing! Who do you suppose I am, to be addressing such a remark to me? And what do you think he says back to me?"

The heads, brown, black, flaxen, red, and yellow bob together; the answer is given; and the parry to the thrust is decided upon, to be used by each thereafter in passages-at-arms with the common enemy, man.

Thus Nancy learned the art of defense; and to women successful defense means victory.

The curriculum of a department store is a wide one. Perhaps no other college could have fitted her as well for her life's ambition—the drawing of a matrimonial prize.

Her station in the store was a favored one. The music room was near enough for her to hear and become familiar with the works of the best composers—at least to acquire the familiarity that passed for appreciation in the social world in which she was vaguely trying to set a tentative and aspiring foot. She absorbed the educating influence of art wares, of costly and dainty fabrics, of adornments that are almost culture to women.

The other girls soon became aware of Nancy's ambition. "Here comes your millionaire, Nancy," they would call to her whenever any man who looked the rôle approached her counter. It got to be a habit of men, who were hanging about while their women folk were shopping, to stroll over to the handkerchief counter and dawdle over the cambric squares. Nancy's imitation high-bred air and genuine dainty beauty was what attracted. Many men thus came to display their graces before her. Some of them may have been millionaires; others were certainly no more than their sedulous apes. Nancy learned to discriminate. There was a window at the end of the handkerchief counter; and she could see the rows of vehicles waiting for the shoppers in the street below. She looked and perceived that automobiles differ as well as do their owners.

Once a fascinating gentleman bought four dozen handkerchiefs, and wooed her across the counter with a King Cophetua air. When he had gone one of the girls said:

"What's wrong, Nance, that you didn't warm up to that fellow? He looks the swell article, all right, to me."

"Him?" said Nancy, with her coolest, sweetest, most impersonal, Van Alstyne Fisher smile; "not for mine. I saw him drive up outside. A 12 H. P. machine and an Irish chauffeur! And you saw what kind of handkerchiefs he bought— silk! And he's got dactylis on him. Give me the real thing or nothing, if you please."

Two of the most "refined" women in the store—a forelady and a cashier— had a few "swell gentlemen friends" with whom they now and then dined. Once they included Nancy in an invitation. The dinner took place in a spectacular café whose tables are engaged for New Year's Eve a year in advance. There were two "gentlemen friends"—one without any hair on his head—high living ungrew it; and we can prove it—the other a young man whose worth and sophistication he impressed upon you in two convincing ways—he swore that all the wine was corked; and he wore diamond cuff buttons. This young man perceived irresistible excellencies in Nancy. His taste ran to shop-girls; and here was one that added the voice and manners of his high social world to the franker charms of her own caste. So, on the following day, he appeared in the store and made her a serious proposal of marriage over a box of hemstitched, grass-bleached Irish linens. Nancy declined. A brown pompadour ten feet away had been using her eyes and ears. When the rejected suitor had gone she heaped carboys of upbraidings and horror upon Nancy's head.

"What a terrible little fool you are! That fellow's a millionaire—he's a nephew of old Van Skittles himself. And he was talking on the level, too. Have you gone crazy, Nance?"

"Have I?" said Nancy. "I didn't take him, did I? He isn't a millionaire so hard that you could notice it, anyhow. His family only allows him $20,000 a year to spend. The bald-headed fellow was guying him about it the other night at supper."

The brown pompadour came nearer and narrowed her eyes.

"Say, what do you want?" she inquired, in a voice hoarse for lack of chewing-gum. "Ain't that enough for you? Do you want to be a Mormon, and marry Rockefeller and Gladstone Dowie and the King of Spain and the whole bunch? Ain't $20,000 a year good enough for you?"

Nancy flushed a little under the level gaze of the black, shallow eyes.

"It wasn't altogether the money, Carrie," she explained. "His friend caught him in a rank lie the other night at dinner. It was about some girl he said he hadn't been to the theater with. Well, I can't stand a liar. Put everything together—I don't like him; and that settles it. When I sell out it's not going to be on any bargain day. I've got to have something that sits up in a chair like a man, anyhow. Yes, I'm looking out for a catch; but it's got to be able to do something more than make a noise like a toy bank."

"The physiopathic ward for yours!" said the brown pompadour, walking away.

These high ideas, if not ideals—Nancy continued to cultivate on $8 per week. She bivouacked on the trail of the great unknown "catch" eating her dry bread and tightening her belt day by day. On her face was the faint, soldierly, sweet, grim smile of the preordained man-hunter. The store was her forest; and many times she raised her rifle at game that seemed broad-antlered and big; but always some deep unerring instinct—perhaps of the huntress, perhaps of the woman— made her hold her fire and take up the trail again.

Lou flourished in the laundry. Out of her $18.50 per week she paid $6 for her room and board. The rest went mainly for clothes. Her opportunities for bettering her taste and manners were few compared with Nancy's. In the steam-ing laundry there was nothing but work, work and her thoughts of the evening pleasures to come. Many costly and showy fabrics passed under her iron; and it may be that her growing fondness for dress was thus transmitted to her through the conducting metal.

When the day's work was over Dan awaited her outside, her faithful shadow in whatever light she stood.

Sometimes he cast an honest and troubled glance at Lou's clothes that in-creased in conspicuity rather than in style; but this was no disloyalty; he deprecated the attention they called to her in the streets.

And Lou was no less faithful to her chum. There was a law that Nancy should go with them on whatsoever outings they might take. Dan bore the extra burden heartily and in good cheer. It might be said that Lou furnished the color, Nancy the tone, and Dan the weight of the distraction-seeking trio. The escort, in his neat but obviously ready-made suit, his ready-made tie and unfail-ing, genial, ready-made wit never startled or clashed. He was of that good kind that you are likely to forget while they are present, but remember distinctly after they are gone.

To Nancy's superior taste the flavor of these ready-made pleasures was some-times a little bitter: but she was young; and youth is a gourmand, when it cannot be a gourmet.

"Dan is always wanting me to marry him right away," Lou told her once. "But why should I? I'm independent. I can do as I please with the money I earn; and he never would agree for me to keep on working afterward. And say, Nance, what do you want to stick to that old store for, and half starve and half dress yourself? I could get you a place in the laundry right now if you'd come. It seems to me that you could afford to be a little less stuck-up if you could make a good deal more money."

"I don't think I'm stuck-up, Lou," said Nancy, "but I'd rather live on half rations and stay where I am. I suppose I've got the habit. It's the chance that I want. I don't expect to be always behind a counter. I'm learning something new every day. I'm right up against refined and rich people all the time— even if I do only wait on them; and I'm not missing any pointers that I see passing around."

"Caught your millionaire yet?" asked Lou with her teasing laugh.

"I haven't selected one yet," answered Nancy. "I've been looking them over."

"Goodness! the idea of picking over 'em! Don't you ever let one get by you, Nance—even if he's a few dollars shy. But of course you're joking—millionaires don't think about working girls like us."

"It might be better for them if they did," said Nancy, with cool wisdom. "Some of us could teach them how to take care of their money."

"If one was to speak to me," laughed Lou, "I know I'd have a duck-fit."

"That's because you don't know any. The only difference between swells and other people is you have to watch 'em closer. Don't you think that red silk lining is just a little bit too bright for that coat, Lou?"

Lou looked at the plain, dull olive jacket of her friend.

"Well, no, I don't—but it may seem so beside that faded-looking thing you've got on."

"This jacket," said Nancy, complacently, "has exactly the cut and fit of one that Mrs. Van Alstyne Fisher was wearing the other day. The material cost me $3.98. I suppose hers cost about $100 more."

"Oh, well," said Lou, lightly, "it don't strike me as millionaire bait. Shouldn't wonder if I catch one before you do, anyway."

Truly it would have taken a philosopher to decide upon the values of the theories held by the two friends. Lou, lacking that certain pride and fastidiousness that keeps stores and desks filled with girls working for the barest living, thumped away gaily with her iron in the noisy and stifling laundry. Her wages supported her even beyond the point of comfort: so that her dress profited until sometimes she cast a sidelong glance of impatience at the neat but inelegant apparel of Dan—Dan the constant, the immutable, the undeviating.

As for Nancy, her case was one of tens of thousands. Silk and jewels and laces and ornaments and the perfume and music of the fine world of good-breeding and taste—these were made for woman; they are her equitable portion. Let her keep near them if they are a part of life to her, and if she will. She is no traitor to herself, as Esau was; for she keeps her birthright and the pottage she earns is often very scant.

In this atmosphere Nancy belonged; and she throve in it and ate her frugal meals and schemed over her cheap dresses with a determined and contented mind. She already knew woman; and she was studying man, the animal, both as to his habits and eligibility. Some day she would bring down the game that she wanted; but she promised herself it would be what seemed to her the biggest and the best, and nothing smaller.

Thus she kept her lamp trimmed and burning to receive the bridegroom when he should come.

But, another lesson she learned, perhaps unconsciously. Her standard of values began to shift and change. Sometimes the dollar-mark grew blurred in her mind's eye, and shaped itself into letters that spelled such words as "truth" and "honor" and now and then just "kindness." Let us make a likeness of one who hunts the moose or elk in some mighty wood. He sees a little dell, mossy and embowered, where a rill trickles, babbling to him of rest and comfort. At these times the spear of Nimrod himself grows blunt.

So, Nancy wondered sometimes if Persian lamb was always quoted at its market value by the hearts that it covered.

One Thursday evening Nancy left the store and turned across Sixth Avenue westward to the laundry. She was expected to go with Lou and Dan to a musical comedy.

Dan was just coming out of the laundry when she arrived. There was a queer, strained look on his face.

"I thought I would drop around to see if they had heard from her," he said.

"Heard from who?" asked Nancy. "Isn't Lou there?"

"I thought you knew," said Dan. "She hasn't been here or at the house where she lived since Monday. She moved all her things from there. She told one of the girls in the laundry she might be going to Europe."

"Hasn't anybody seen her anywhere?" asked Nancy.

Dan looked at her with his jaws set grimly, and a steely gleam in his steady gray eyes.

"They told me in the laundry," he said, harshly, "that they saw her pass yesterday—in an automobile. With one of the millionaires, I suppose, that you and Lou were forever busying your brains about."

For the first time Nancy quailed before a man. She laid her hand that trembled slightly on Dan's sleeve.

"You've no right to say such a thing to me, Dan—as if I had anything to do with it!"

"I didn't mean it that way," said Dan, softening. He fumbled in his vest pocket.

"I've got the tickets for the show to-night," he said, with a gallant show of lightness. "If you——"

Nancy admired pluck whenever she saw it.

"I'll go with you, Dan," she said.

Three months went by before Nancy saw Lou again.

At twilight one evening the shop-girl was hurrying home along the border of a little quiet park. She heard her name called, and wheeled about in time to catch Lou rushing into her arms.

After the first embrace they drew their heads back as serpents do, ready to attack or to charm, with a thousand questions trembling on their swift tongues. And then Nancy noticed that prosperity had descended upon Lou, manifesting itself in costly furs, flashing gems, and creations of the tailor's art.

"You little fool!" cried Lou, loudly and affectionately. "I see you are still working in that store, and as shabby as ever. And how about that big catch you were going to make—nothing doing yet, I suppose?"

And then Lou looked, and saw that something better than prosperity had descended upon Nancy—something that shone brighter than gems in her eyes and redder than a rose in her cheeks, and that danced like electricity anxious to be loosed from the tip of her tongue.

"Yes, I'm still in the store," said Nancy, "but I'm going to leave it next week. I've made my catch—the biggest catch in the world. You won't mind now Lou, will you?—I'm going to be married to Dan—to Dan!—he's my Dan now—why, Lou!"

Around the corner of the park strolled one of those new-crop, smooth-faced young policemen that are making the force more endurable—at least to the eye. He saw a woman with an expensive fur coat and diamond-ringed hands crouching down against the iron fence of the park sobbing turbulently, while a slender, plainly dressed working girl leaned close, trying to console her. But the Gibsonian cop, being of the new order, passed on, pretending not to notice, for he was wise enough to know that these matters are beyond help so far as the power he represents is concerned, though he rap the pavement with his nightstick till the sound goes up to the furthermost stars.

A MADISON SQUARE ARABIAN NIGHT

To Carson Chalmers, in his apartment near the square, Phillips brought the evening mail. Besides the routine correspondence there were two items bearing the same foreign postmark.

One of the incoming parcels contained a photograph of a woman. The other contained an interminable letter, over which Chalmers hung, absorbed, for a long time. The letter was from another woman; and it contained poisoned barbs, sweetly dipped in honey, and feathered with innuendoes concerning the photographed woman.

Chalmers tore this letter into a thousand bits and began to wear out his expensive rug by striding back and forth upon it. Thus an animal from the jungle acts when it is caged, and thus a caged man acts when he is housed in a jungle of doubt.

By and by the restless mood was overcome. The rug was not an enchanted one. For sixteen feet he could travel along it; three thousand miles was beyond its power to aid.

Phillips appeared. He never entered; he invariably appeared, like a well-oiled genie.

"Will you dine here, sir, or out?" he asked.

"Here," said Chalmers, "and in half an hour." He listened glumly to the January blasts making an Æolian trombone of the empty street.

"Wait," he said to the disappearing genie. "As I came home across the end of the square I saw many men standing there in rows. There was one mounted upon something, talking. Why do those man stand in rows, and why are they there?"

"They are homeless men, sir," said Phillips. "The man standing on the box tries to get lodging for them for the night. People come around to listen and give him money. Then he sends as many as the money will pay for to some lodging-house. That is why they stand in rows; they get sent to bed in order as they come."

"By the time dinner is served," said Chalmers, "have one of those men here. He will dine with me."

"W-w-which——" began Phillips, stammering for the first time during his service.

"Choose one at random," said Chalmers. "You might see that he is reasonably sober—and a certain amount of cleanliness will not be held against him. That is all."

It was an unusual thing for Carson Chalmers to play the Caliph. But on that night he felt the inefficacy of conventional antidotes to melancholy. Something wanton and egregious, something high-flavored and Arabian, he must have to lighten his mood.

On the half hour Phillips had finished his duties as slave of the lamp. The waiters from the restaurant below had whisked aloft the delectable dinner. The dining table, laid for two, glowed cheerily in the glow of the pink-shaded candles.

And now Phillips, as though he ushered a cardinal—or held in charge a burglar—wafted in the shivering guest who had been haled from the line of mendicant lodgers.

It is a common thing to call such men wrecks; if the comparison be used here it is the specific one of a derelict come to grief through fire. Even yet some flickering combustion illuminated the drifting hulk. His face and hands had been recently washed—a rite insisted upon by Phillips as a memorial to the slaughtered conventions. In the candle-light he stood, a flaw in the decorous fittings of the apartment. His face was a sickly white, covered almost to the eyes with a stubble the shade of a red Irish setter's coat. Phillips's comb had failed to control the pale brown hair, long matted and conformed to the contour of a constantly worn hat. His eyes were full of hopeless, tricky defiance like that seen in a cur's that is cornered by his tormentors. His shabby coat was buttoned high, but a quarter inch of redeeming collar showed above it. His manner was singularly free from embarrassment when Chalmers rose from his chair across the round dining table.

"If you will oblige me," said the host, "I will be glad to have your company at dinner."

"My name is Plumer," said the highway guest, in harsh and aggressive tones. "If you're like me, you like to know the name of the party you're dining with."

"I was going on to say," continued Chalmers somewhat hastily, "that mine is Chalmers. Will you sit opposite?"

Plumer, of the ruffled plumes, bent his knee for Phillips to slide the chair beneath him. He had an air of having sat at attended boards before. Phillips set out the anchovies and olives.

"Good!" barked Plumer; "going to be in courses, is it? All right, my jovial ruler of Bagdad. I'm your Scheherezade all the way to the toothpicks. You're the first Caliph with a genuine Oriental flavor I've struck since frost. What luck! And I was forty-third in line. I finished counting, just as your welcome emissary arrived to bid me to the feast. I had about as much chance of getting a bed to-night as I have of being the next President. How will you have the sad story of my life, Mr. Al Raschid—a chapter with each course or the whole edition with the cigars and coffee?"

"The situation does not seem a novel one to you," said Chalmers with a smile.

"By the chin whiskers of the prophet—no!" answered the guest. "New York's as full of cheap Haroun al Raschids as Bagdad is of fleas. I've been held up for my story with a loaded meal pointed at my head twenty times. Catch anybody in New York giving you something for nothing! They spell curiosity and charity with the same set of building blocks. Lots of 'em will stake you to a dime and chop-suey; and a few of 'em will play Caliph to the tune of a top sirloin; but every one of 'em will stand over you till they screw your autobiography out of you with foot notes, appendix and unpublished fragments. Oh, I know what to do when I see victuals coming toward me in little old Bagdad-on-the-Subway. I strike the asphalt three times with my forehead and get ready to spiel yarns for my supper. I claim descent from the late Tommy Tucker, who was forced to hand out vocal harmony for his pre-digested wheaterina and spoopju."

"I do not ask your story," said Chalmers. "I tell you frankly that it was a sudden whim that prompted me to send for some stranger to dine with me. I assure you you will not suffer through any curiosity of mine."

"Oh, fudge!" exclaimed the guest, enthusiastically tackling his soup; "I don't mind it a bit. I'm a regular Oriental magazine with a red cover and the leaves cut when the Caliph walks abroad. In fact, we fellows in the bed line have a sort of union rate for things of this sort. Somebody's always stopping and wanting to know what brought us down so low in the world. For a sandwich and a glass of beer I tell 'em that drink did it. For corned beef and cabbage and a cup of coffee I give 'em the hard-hearted-landlord—six-months-in-the-hospital-lost-job story. A sirloin steak and a quarter for a bed gets the Wall Street tragedy of the swept-away fortune and the gradual descent. This is the first spread of this kind I've stumbled against. I haven't got a story to fit it. I'll tell you what, Mr. Chalmers, I'm going to tell you the truth for this, if you'll listen to it. It'll be harder for you to believe than the made-up ones."

An hour later the Arabian guest lay back with a sigh of satisfaction while Phillips brought the coffee and cigars and cleared the table.

"Did you ever hear of Sherrard Plumer?" he asked, with a strange smile.

"I remember the name," said Chalmers. "He was a painter, I think, of a good deal of prominence a few years ago."

"Five years," said the guest. "Then I went down like a chunk of lead. I'm Sherrard Plumer! I sold the last portrait I painted for $2,000. After that I couldn't have found a sitter for a gratis picture."

"What was the trouble?" Chalmers could not resist asking.

"Funny thing," answered Plumer, grimly. "Never quite understood it myself. For a while I swam like a cork. I broke into the swell crowd and got commissions right and left. The newspapers called me a fashionable painter. Then the funny things began to happen. Whenever I finished a picture people would come to see it, and whisper and look queerly at one another.

"I soon found out what the trouble was. I had a knack of bringing out in the face of a portrait the hidden character of the original. I don't know how I did it—I painted what I saw—but I know it did me. Some of my sitters were fearfully enraged and refused their pictures. I painted the portrait of a very beautiful and popular society dame. When it was finished her husband looked at it with a peculiar expression on his face, and the next week he sued for divorce.

"I remember one case of a prominent banker who sat to me. While I had his portrait on exhibition in my studio an acquaintance of his came in to look at it. 'Bless me,' says he, 'does he really look like that?' I told him it was considered a faithful likeness. 'I never noticed that expression about his eyes before,' said he; 'I think I'll drop downtown and change my bank account.' He did drop down, but the bank account was gone and so was Mr. Banker.

"It wasn't long till they put me out of business. People don't want their secret meannesses shown up in a picture. They can smile and twist their own faces and deceive you, but the picture can't. I couldn't get an order for another picture, and I had to give up. I worked as a newspaper artist for a while, and then for a lithographer, but my work with them got me into the same trouble. If I drew from a photograph my drawing showed up characteristics and expressions that you couldn't find in the photo, but I guess they were in the original, all right. The customers raised lively rows, especially the women, and I never could hold a job long. So I began to rest my weary head upon the breast of Old Booze for comfort. And pretty soon I was in the free-bed line and doing oral fiction for hand-outs among the food bazaars. Does the truthful statement weary thee, O Caliph? I can turn on the Wall Street disaster stop if you prefer, but that requires a tear, and I'm afraid I can't hustle one up after that good dinner."

"No, no," said Chalmers, earnestly, "you interest me very much. Did all of your portraits reveal some unpleasant trait, or were there some that did not suffer from the ordeal of your peculiar brush?"

"Some? Yes," said Plumer. "Children generally, a good many women and a sufficient number of men. All people aren't bad, you know. When they were all right the pictures were all right. As I said, I don't explain it, but I'm telling you facts."

On Chalmer's writing-table lay the photograph that he had received that day in the foreign mail. Ten minutes later he had Plumer at work making a sketch from it in pastels. At the end of an hour the artist rose and stretched wearily. "It's done," he yawned. "You'll excuse me for being so long. I got interested in the job. Lordy! but I'm tired. No bed last night, you know. Guess it'll have to be good-night now, O Commander of the Faithful!"

Chalmers went as far as the door with him and slipped some bills into his hand.

"Oh! I'll take 'em," said Plumer. "All that's included in the fall. Thanks. And for the very good dinner. I shall sleep on feathers to-night and dream of Bagdad. I hope it won't turn out to be a dream in the morning. Farewell, most excellent Caliph!"

Again Chalmers paced restlessly upon his rug. But his beat lay as far from the table whereon lay the pastel sketch as the room would permit. Twice, thrice, he tried to approach it, but failed. He could see the dun and gold and brown of the colors, but there was a wall about it built by his fears that kept him at a distance. He sat down and tried to calm himself. He sprang up and rang for Phillips.

"There is a young artist in this building," he said—"a Mr. Reineman—do you know which is his apartment?"

"Top floor, front, sir," said Phillips.

"Go up and ask him to favor me with his presence here for a few minutes."

Reineman came at once. Chalmers introduced himself.

"Mr. Reineman," said he, "there is a little pastel sketch on yonder table. I would be glad if you will give me your opinion of it as to its artistic merits and as a picture."

The young artist advanced to the table and took up the sketch. Chalmers half turned away, leaning upon the back of a chair.

"How—do—you find it?" he asked, slowly.

"As a drawing," said the artist, "I can't praise it enough. It's the work of a master—bold and fine and true. It puzzles me a little; I haven't see any pastel work near as good in years."

"The face, man—the subject—the original—what would you say of that?"

"The face," said Reineman, "is the face of one of God's own angels. May I ask who——"

"My wife!" shouted Chalmers, wheeling and pouncing upon the astonished artist, gripping his hand and pounding his back. "She is traveling in Europe. Take that sketch, boy, and paint the picture of your life from it and leave the price to me."

THE RUBAIYAT OF A SCOTCH HIGHBALL

This document is intended to strike somewhere between a temperance lecture and the "Bartender's Guide." Relative to the latter, drink shall swell the theme and be set forth in abundance. Agreeably to the former, not an elbow shall be crooked.

Bob Babbitt was "off the stuff." Which means—as you will discover by referring to the unabridged dictionary of Bohemia—that he had "cut out the booze," that he was "on the water wagon." The reason for Bob's sudden attitude of hostility toward the "demon rum"—as the white ribboners miscall whiskey (see the "Bartender's Guide"), should be of interest to reformers and saloon-keepers.

There is always hope for a man who, when sober, will not concede or acknowledge that he was ever drunk. But when a man will say (in the apt words of the phrase-distiller), "I had a beautiful skate on last night," you will have to put stuff in his coffee as well as pray for him.

One evening on his way home Babbitt dropped in at the Broadway bar that he liked best. Always there were three or four fellows there from the downtown offices whom he knew. And then there would be highballs and stories, and he would hurry home to dinner a little late but feeling good, and a little sorry for the poor Standard Oil Company. On this evening as he entered he heard some one say: "Babbitt was in last night as full as a boiled owl."

Babbitt walked to the bar, and saw in the mirror that his face was as white as chalk. For the first time he had looked Truth in the eyes. Others had lied to him; he had dissembled with himself. He was a drunkard, and had not known it. What he had fondly imagined was a pleasant exhilaration had been maudlin intoxication. His fancied wit had been drivel, his gay humors nothing but the noisy vagaries of a sot. But, never again!

"A glass of seltzer," he said to the bartender.

A little silence fell upon the group of his cronies, who had been expecting him to join them.

"Going off the stuff, Bob?" one of them asked politely and with more formality than the highballs ever called forth.

"Yes," said Babbitt.

Some one of the group took up the unwashed thread of a story he had been telling; the bartender shoved over a dime and a nickel change from the quarter, ungarnished with his customary smile; and Babbitt walked out.

Now, Babbitt had a home and a wife—but that is another story. And I will tell you that story, which will show you a better habit and a worse story than you could find in the man who invented the phrase.

It began away up in Sullivan County, where so many rivers and so much trouble begins—or begin; how would say that? It was July, and Jessie was a summer boarder at the Mountain Squint Hotel, and Bob, who was just out of college, saw her one day—and they were married in September. That's the tabloid novel—one swallow of water, and it's gone.

But those July days!

Let the exclamation point expound it, for I shall not. For particulars you might read up on "Romeo and Juliet," and Abraham Lincoln's thrilling sonnet about "You can fool some of the people," &c., and Darwin's works.

But one thing I must tell you about. Both of them were made over Omar's Rubaiyat. They knew every verse of the old bluffer by heart—not consecutively, but picking 'em out here and there as you fork the mushrooms in a fifty-cent steak à la Bordelaise. Sullivan County is full of rocks and trees; and Jessie used to sit on them, and—please be good—used to sit on the rocks; and Bob had a way of standing behind her with his hands over her shoulders holding her hands, and his face close to hers, and they would repeat over and over their favorite verses of the old tent-maker. They saw only the poetry and philosophy of the lines then—indeed, they agreed that the Wine was only an image, and that what was meant to be celebrated was some divinity, or maybe Love or Life. However, at that time neither of them had tasted the stuff that goes with a sixty-cent *table d'hôte*.

Where was I? Oh, they married and came to New York. Bob showed his college diploma, and accepted a position filling inkstands in a lawyer's office at $15 a week. At the end of two years he had worked up to $50, and gotten his first taste of Bohemia—the kind that won't stand the borax and formaldehyde tests.

They had two furnished rooms and a little kitchen. To Jess, accustomed to the mild but beautiful savor of a country town, the dreggy Bohemia was sugar and spice. She hung fish seines on the walls of her rooms, and bought a rakish-looking sideboard, and learned to play the banjo. Twice or thrice a week they dined at French or Italian *tables d'hôte* in a cloud of smoke, and brag and un-shorn hair. Jess learned to drink a cocktail in order to get the cherry. At home she smoked a cigarette after dinner. She learned to pronounce Chianti, and leave her olive stones for the waiter to pick up. Once she essayed to say la, la la! in a crowd but got only as far as the second one. They met one or two couples while dining out and became friendly with them. The sideboard was stocked with Scotch and rye and a liqueur. They had their new friends in to dinner and all were laughing at nothing by 1 A. M. Some plastering fell in the room below them, for which Bob had to pay $4.50. Thus they footed it merrily on the ragged frontiers of the country that has no boundary lines or government.

And soon Bob fell in with his cronies and learned to keep his foot on the little rail six inches above the floor for an hour or so every afternoon before he went home. Drink always rubbed him the right way, and he would reach his rooms as jolly as a sandboy. Jessie would meet him at the door, and generally they would dance some insane kind of a rigadoon about the floor by way of greeting. Once when Bob's feet became confused and he tumbled headlong over a foot-stool Jessie laughed so heartily and long that he had to throw all the couch pillows at her to make her hush.

In such wise life was speeding for them on the day when Bob Babbitt first felt the power that the giftie gi'ed him.

But let us get back to our lamb and mint sauce.

When Bob got home that evening he found Jessie in a long apron cutting up a lobster for the Newburg. Usually when Bob came in mellow from his hour at the bar his welcome was hilarious, though somewhat tinctured with Scotch smoke.

By screams and snatches of song and certain audible testimonials of domestic felicity was his advent proclaimed. When she heard his foot on the stairs the old maid in the hall room always stuffed cotton into her ears. At first Jessie had shrunk from the rudeness and flavor of these spiritual greetings, but as the fog of the false Bohemia gradually encompassed her she came to accept them as love's true and proper greeting.

Bob came in without a word, smiled, kissed her neatly but noiselessly, took up a paper and sat down. In the hall room the old maid held her two plugs of cotton poised, filled with anxiety.

Jessie dropped lobster and knife and ran to him with frightened eyes.

"What's the matter, Bob, are you ill?"

"Not at all, dear."

"Then what's the matter with you?"

"Nothing."

Hearken, brethren. When She-who-has-a-right-to-ask interrogates you concerning a change she finds in your mood answer her thus: Tell her that you, in a sudden rage, have murdered your grandmother; tell her that you have robbed orphans and that remorse has stricken you; tell her your fortune is swept away; that you are beset by enemies, by bunions, by any kind of malevolent fate; but do not, if peace and happiness are worth as much as a grain of mustard seed to you—do not answer her "Nothing."

Jessie went back to the lobster in silence. She cast looks of darkest suspicion at Bob. He had never acted that way before.

When dinner was on the table she set out the bottle of Scotch and the glasses. Bob declined. "Tell you the truth, Jess," he said. "I've cut out the drink. Help yourself, of course. If you don't mind I'll try some of the seltzer straight."

"You've stopped drinking?" she said, looking at him steadily and unsmilingly. "What for?"

"It wasn't doing me any good," said Bob. "Don't you approve of the idea?"

Jessie raised her eyebrows and one shoulder slightly.

"Entirely," she said with a sculptured smile. "I could not conscientiously advise any one to drink or smoke, or whistle on Sunday."

The meal was finished almost in silence. Bob tried to make talk, but his efforts lacked the stimulus of previous evenings. He felt miserable, and once or twice his eye wandered toward the bottle, but each time the scathing words of his bibulous friend sounded in his ear, and his mouth set with determination.

Jessie felt the change deeply. The essence of their lives seemed to have departed suddenly. The restless fever, the false gayety, the unnatural excitement of the shoddy Bohemia in which they lived had dropped away in the space of the popping of a cork. She stole curious and forlorn glances at the dejected Bob, who bore the guilty look of at least a wife-beater or a family tyrant.

After dinner the colored maid who came in daily to perform such chores cleared away the things. Jessie, with an unreadable countenance, brought back the bottle of Scotch and the glasses and a bowl of cracked ice and set them on the table.

"May I ask," she said, with some of the ice in her tones, "whether I am to be included in your sudden spasm of goodness? If not, I'll make one for myself. It's rather chilly this evening, for some reason."

"Oh, come now, Jess," said Bob, good-naturedly, "don't be too rough on me. Help yourself, by all means. There's no danger of your overdoing it. But I thought there was with me; and that's why I quit. Have yours, and then let's get out the banjo and try over that new quickstep."

"I've heard," said Jessie in the tones of the oracle, "that drinking alone is a pernicious habit. No, I don't think I feel like playing this evening. If we are going to reform we may as well abandon the evil habit of banjo-playing, too."

She took up a book and sat in her little willow rocker on the other side of the table. Neither of them spoke for half an hour.

And then Bob laid down his paper and got up with a strange, absent look on his face and went behind her chair and reached over her shoulders, taking her hands in his, and laid his face close to hers.

In a moment to Jessie the walls of the seine-hung room vanished, and she saw the Sullivan County hills and rills. Bob felt her hands quiver in his as he began the verse from Old Omar:

> "Come, fill the Cup, and in the Fire of Spring
> The Winter Garment of Repentance fling:
> The Bird of Time has but a little way
> To fly—and Lo! the Bird is on the Wing!"

And then he walked to the table and poured a stiff drink of Scotch into a glass.

But in that moment a mountain breeze had somehow found its way in and blown away the mist of the false Bohemia.

Jessie leaped and with one fierce sweep of her hand sent the bottle and glasses crashing to the floor. The same motion of her arm carried it around Bob's neck, where it met its mate and fastened tight.

"Oh, my God, Bobbie—not that verse—I see now. I wasn't always such a fool, was I? The other one, boy—the one that says: 'Remould it to the Heart's Desire.' Say that one—'to the Heart's Desire.'"

"I know that one," said Bob. "It goes:

> "Ah! Love, could you and I with Him conspire
> To grasp this sorry Scheme of Things entire
> Would not we——"

"Let me finish it," said Jessie.

> "Would not we shatter it to bits—and then
> Remould it nearer to the heart's Desire!

"It's shattered all right," said Bob, crunching some glass under his heel.

In some dungeon below the accurate ear of Mrs. Pickens, the landlady, located the smash.

"It's that wild Mr. Babbitt coming home soused again," she said. "And he's got such a nice little wife, too!"

THE PENDULUM

"EIGHTY-FIRST STREET—let 'em out, please," yelled the shepherd in blue.

A flock of citizen sheep scrambled out and another flock scrambled aboard. Ding-ding! The cattle cars of the Manhattan Elevated rattled away, and John Perkins drifted down the stairway of the station with the released flock.

John walked slowly toward his flat. Slowly, because in the lexicon of his daily life there was no such word as "perhaps." There are no surprises awaiting a man who has been married two years and lives in a flat. As he walked John Perkins prophesied to himself with gloomy and downtrodden cynicism the foregone conclusions of the monotonous day.

Katy would meet him at the door with a kiss flavored with cold cream and butter-scotch. He would remove his coat, sit upon a macadamized lounge and read, in the evening paper, of Russians and Japs slaughtered by the deadly linotype. For dinner there would be pot roast, a salad flavored with a dressing warranted not to crack or injure the leather, stewed rhubarb and the bottle of strawberry marmalade blushing at the certificate of chemical purity on its lable. After dinner Katy would show him the new patch in her crazy quilt that the iceman had cut for her off the end of his four-in-hand. At half-past seven they would spread newspapers over the furniture to catch the pieces of plastering that fell when the fat man in the flat overhead began to take his physical culture exercises. Exactly at eight Hickey & Mooney, of the vaudeville team (unbooked) in the flat across the hall, would yield to the gentle influence of delirium tremens and begin to overturn chairs under the delusion that Hammerstein was pursuing them with a five-hundred-dollar-a-week contract. Then the gent at the window across the air-shaft would get out his flute; the nightly gas leak would steal forth to frolic in the highways; the dumbwaiter would slip off its trolley; the janitor would drive Mrs. Zanowitski's five children once more across the Yalu; the lady with the champagne shoes and the Skye terrier would trip downstairs and paste her Thursday name over her bell and letter-box—and the evening routine of the Frogmore flats would be under way.

John Perkins knew these things would happen. And he knew that at a quarter past eight he would summon his nerve and reach for his hat, and that his wife would deliver this speech in a querulous tone:

"Now, where are you going, I'd like to know, John Perkins?"

"Thought I'd drop up to McCloskey's," he would answer, "and play a game or two of pool with the fellows."

Of late such had been John Perkins's habit. At ten or eleven he would return. Sometimes Katy would be asleep; sometimes waiting up, ready to melt in the crucible of her ire a little more gold plating from the wrought steel chains of matrimony. For these things Cupid will have to answer when he stands at the bar of justice with his victims from the Frogmore flats.

To-night John Perkins encountered a tremendous upheaval of the commonplace when he reached his door. No Katy was there with her affectionate, confectionate kiss. The three rooms seemed in portentous disorder. All about lay her things in confusion. Shoes in the middle of the floor, curling tongs, hair bows, kimonos, powder box, jumbled together on dresser and chairs—this was not Katy's way. With a sinking heart John saw the comb with a curling cloud of her brown hair among its teeth. Some unusual hurry and perturbation must have possessed her, for she always carefully placed these combings in the little blue vase on the mantel to be some day formed into the coveted feminine "rat."

Hanging conspicuously to the gas jet by a string was a folded paper. John seized it. It was a note from his wife running thus:

Dear John:

I just had a telegram saying mother is very sick. I am going to take the 4:30 train. Brother Sam is going to meet me at the depot there. There is cold mutton in the icebox. I hope it isn't her quinzy again. Pay the milkman 50 cents. She had it bad last spring. Don't forget to write to the company about the gas meter, and your good socks are in the top drawer. I will write to-morrow.

Hastily,

Katy.

Never during their two years of matrimony had he and Katy been separated for a night. John read the note over and over in a dumbfounded way. Here was a break in a routine that had never varied, and it left him dazed.

There on the back of a chair hung, pathetically empty and formless, the red wrapper with black dots that she always wore while getting the meals. Her week-day clothes had been tossed here and there in her haste. A little paper bag of her favorite butter-scotch lay with its string yet unwound. A daily paper sprawled on the floor, gaping rectangularly where a railroad time-table had been clipped from it. Everything in the room spoke of a loss, of an essence gone, of its soul and life departed. John Perkins stood among the dead remains with a queer feeling of desolation in his heart.

He began to set the rooms tidy as well as he could. When he touched her clothes a thrill of something like terror went through him. He had never thought what existence would be without Katy. She had become so thoroughly annealed into his life that she was like the air he breathed—necessary but scarcly noticed. Now, without warning, she was gone, vanished, as completely absent as if she had never existed. Of course it would be only for a few days, or at most a week or two, but it seemed to him as if the very hand of death had pointed a finger at his secure and uneventful home.

John dragged the cold mutton from the ice-box, made coffee, and sat down to a lonely meal face to face with the strawberry marmalade's shameless certificate of purity. Bright among withdrawn blessings now appeared to him the ghosts of pot roasts and the salad with tan polish dressing. His home was dismantled. A quinzied mother-in-law had knocked his lares and penates sky-high. After his solitary meal John sat at a front window.

He did not care to smoke. Outside the city roared to him to come join in its dance of folly and pleasure. The night was his. He might go forth unquestioned and thrum the strings of jollity as free as any gay bachelor there. He might carouse and wander and have his fling until dawn if he liked; and there would be no wrathful Katy waiting for him, bearing the chalice that held the dregs of his joy. He might play pool at McCloskey's with his roistering friends until Aurora dimmed the electric bulbs if he chose. The hymeneal strings that had curbed him always when the Frogmore flats had palled upon him were loosened. Katy was gone.

John Perkins was not accustomed to analyzing his emotions. But as he sat in his Katy-bereft 10 x 12 parlor he hit unerringly upon the keynote of his discomfort. He knew now that Katy was necessary to his happiness. His feeling for her, lulled into unconsciousness by the dull round of domesticity, had been sharply stirred by the loss of her presence. Has it not been dinned into us by proverb and sermon and fable that we never prize the music till the sweet-voiced bird has flown—or in other no less florid and true utterances?

"I'm a double-dyed dub," mused John Perkins, "the way I've been treating Katy. Off every night playing pool and bumming with the boys instead of staying home with her. The poor girl here all alone with nothing to amuse her, and me acting that way! John Perkins, you're the worst kind of a shine. I'm going to make it up for the little girl. I'll take her out and let her see some amusement. And I'll cut out the McCloskey gang right from this minute."

Yes, there was the city roaring outside for John Perkins to come dance in the train of Momus. And at McCloskey's the boys were knocking the balls idly into the pockets against the hour for the nightly game. But no primrose way nor clicking cue could woo the remorseful soul of Perkins the bereft. The thing that was his, lightly held and half scorned, had been taken away from him, and he wanted it. Backward to a certain man named Adam, whom the cherubim bounced from the orchard, could Perkins, the remorseful, trace his descent.

Near the right hand of John Perkins stood a chair. On the back of it stood Katy's blue shirtwaist. It still retained something of her contour. Midway of the sleeves were fine, individual wrinkles made by the movements of her arms in working for his comfort and pleasure. A delicate but impelling odor of bluebells came from it. John took it and looked long and soberly at the unresponsive grenadine. Katy had never been unresponsive. Tears:—yes, tears— came into John Perkins's eyes. When she came back things would be different. He would make up for all his neglect. What was life without her?

The door opened. Katy walked in carrying a little hand satchel. John stared at her stupidly.

"My! I'm glad to get back," said Katy. "Ma wasn't sick to amount to anything. Sam was at the depot, and said she just had a little spell, and got all right soon after they telegraphed. So I took the next train back. I'm just dying for a cup of coffee."

Nobody heard the click and rattle of the cogwheels as the third-floor-front of the Frogmore flats buzzed its machinery back into the Order of Things. A band slipped, a spring was touched, the gear was adjusted and the wheels revolve in their old orbit.

John Perkins looked at the clock. It was 8.15. He reached for his hat and walked to the door.

"Now, where are you going, I'd like to know, John Perkins?" asked Katy, in a querulous tone.

"Thought I'd drop up to McCloskey's," said John, "and play a game or two of pool with the fellows."

TWO THANKSGIVING DAY GENTLEMEN

THERE is one day that is ours. There is one day when all we Americans who are not self-made go back to the old home to eat saleratus biscuits and marvel how much nearer to the porch the old pump looks than it used to. Bless the day. President Roosevelt gives it to us. We hear some talk of the Puritans, but don't just remember who they were. Bet we can lick 'em, anyhow, if they try to land again. Plymouth Rocks? Well, that sounds more familiar. Lots of us have had to come down to hens since the Turkey Trust got its work in. But somebody in Washington is leaking out advance information to 'em about these Thanksgiving proclamations.

The big city east of the cranberry bogs has made Thanksgiving Day an institution. The last Thursday in November is the only day in the year on which it recognizes the part of America lying across the ferries. It is the one day that is purely American. Yes, a day of celebration, exclusively American.

And now for the story which is to prove to you that we have traditions on this side of the ocean that are becoming older at a much rapider rate than those of England are—thanks to our git-up and enterprise.

Stuffy Pete took his seat on the third bench to the right as you enter Union Square from the east, at the walk opposite the fountain. Every Thanksgiving Day for nine years he had taken his seat there promptly at 1 o'clock. For every time he had done so things had happened to him—Charles Dickensy things that swelled his waistcoat above his heart, and equally on the other side.

But to-day Stuffy Pete's appearance at the annual trysting place seemed to have been rather the result of habit than of the yearly hunger which, as the philanthropists seem to think, afflicts the poor at such extended intervals.

Certainly Pete was not hungry. He had just come from a feast that had left him of his powers barely those of respiration and locomotion. His eyes were like two pale gooseberries firmly imbedded in a swollen and gravy-smeared mask of putty. His breath came in short wheezes; a senatorial roll of adipose tissue denied a fashionable set to his upturned coat collar. Buttons that had been sewed upon his clothes by kind Salvation fingers a week before flew like pop-corn, strewing the earth around him. Ragged he was, with a split shirt front open to the wishbone; but the November breeze, carrying fine snowflakes, brought him only a grateful coolness. For Stuffy Pete was overcharged with the caloric produced by a super-bountiful dinner, beginning with oysters and ending with plum pudding, and including (it seemed to him) all the roast turkey and baked potatoes and chicken salad and squash pie and ice cream in the world. Wherefore he sat, gorged, and gazed upon the world with after-dinner contempt.

The meal had been an unexpected one. He was passing a red brick mansion near the beginning of Fifth Avenue, in which lived two old ladies of ancient family and a reverence for traditions. They even denied the existence of New York, and believed that Thanksgiving Day was declared solely for Washington Square. One of their traditional habits was to station a servant at the postern gate with orders to admit the first hungry wayfarer that came along after the hour of noon had struck, and banquet him to a finish. Stuffy Pete happened to pass by on his way to the park, and the seneschals gathered him in and upheld the custom of the castle.

After Stuffy Pete had gazed straight before him for ten minutes he was conscious of a desire for a more varied field of vision. With a tremendous effort he moved his head slowly to the left. And then his eyes bulged out fearfully, and his breath ceased, and the rough-shod ends of his short legs wriggled and rustled on the gravel.

For the Old Gentleman was coming across Fourth Avenue toward his bench.

Every Thanksgiving Day for nine years the Old Gentleman had come there and found Stuffy Pete on his bench. That was a thing that the Old Gentleman was trying to make a tradition of. Every Thanksgiving Day for nine years he had found Stuffy there, and had led him to a restaurant and watched him eat a big dinner. They do those things in England unconsciously. But this is a young country, and nine years is not so bad. The Old Gentleman was a stanch American patriot, and considered himself a pioneer in American tradition. In order to become picturesque we must keep on doing one thing for a long time without ever letting it get away from us. Something like collecting the weekly dimes in industrial insurance. Or cleaning the streets.

The Old Gentleman moved, straight and stately, toward the Institution that he was rearing. Truly, the annual feeling of Stuffy Pete was nothing national in its character, such as the Magna Charta or jam for breakfast was in England. But it was a step. It was almost feudal. It showed, at least, that a Custom was not impossible to New Y— ahem!—America.

The Old Gentleman was thin and tall and sixty. He was dressed all in black, and wore the old-fashioned kind of glasses that won't stay on your nose. His hair was whiter and thinner than it had been last year, and he seemed to make more use of his big, knobby cane with the crooked handle.

As his established benefactor came up Stuffy wheezed and shuddered like some woman's over-fat pug when a street dog bristles up at him. He would have flown, but all the skill of Santos-Dumont could not have separated him from his bench. Well had the myrmidons of the two old ladies done their work.

"Good morning," said the Old Gentleman. "I am glad to perceive that the vicissitudes of another year have spared you to move in health about the beautiful world. For that blessing alone this day of thanksgiving is well proclaimed to each of us. If you will come with me, my man, I will provide you with a dinner that should make your physical being accord with the mental."

That is what the Old Gentleman said every time. Every Thanksgiving Day for nine years. The words themselves almost formed an Institution. Nothing could be compared with them except the Declaration of Independence. Always before they had been music in Stuffy's ears. But now he looked up at the Old Gentleman's face with tearful agony in his own. The fine snow almost sizzled when it fell upon his perspiring brow. But the Old Gentleman shivered a little and turned his back to the wind.

Stuffy had always wondered why the Old Gentleman spoke his speech rather sadly. He did not know that it was because he was wishing every time that he had a son to succeed him. A son who would come there after he was gone—a son who would stand proud and strong before some subsequent Stuffy, and say: "In memory of my father." Then it would be an Institution.

But the Old Gentleman had no relatives. He lived in rented rooms in one of the decayed old family brownstone mansions in one of the quiet streets east of the park. In the winter he raised fuchsias in a little conservatory the size of a steamer trunk. In the spring he walked in the Easter parade. In the summer he lived at a farmhouse in the New Jersey hills, and sat in a wicker armchair, speaking of a butterfly, the ornithoptera amphrisius, that he hoped to find some day. In the autumn he fed Stuffy a dinner. These were the Old Gentleman's occupations.

Stuffy Pete looked up at him for a half minute, stewing and helpless in his own self-pity. The Old Gentleman's eyes were bright with the giving-pleasure. His face was getting more lined each year, but his little black necktie was in as jaunty a bow as ever, and his linen was beautiful and white, and his gray mustache was curled gracefully at the ends. And then Stuffy made a noise that sounded like peas bubbling in a pot. Speech was intended; and as the Old Gentleman had heard the sounds nine times before, he rightly construed them into Stuffy's old formula of acceptance.

"Thankee, sir. I'll go with ye, and much obliged. I'm very hungry, sir."

The coma of repletion had not prevented from entering Stuffy's mind the conviction that he was the basis of an Institution. His Thanksgiving appetite was not his own; it belonged by all the sacred rights of established custom, if not by the actual Statute of Limitations, to this kind old gentleman who had preempted it. True, America is free; but in order to establish tradition some one must be a repetend— a repeating decimal. The heroes are not all heroes of steel and gold. See one here that wielded only weapons of iron, badly silvered, and tin.

The Old Gentleman led his annual protégé southward to the restaurant, and to the table where the feast had always occurred. They were recognized.

"Here comes de old guy," said a waiter, "dat blows dat same bum to a meal every Thanksgiving."

The Old Gentleman sat across the table glowing like a smoked pearl at his corner-stone of future ancient Tradition. The waiters heaped the table with holiday food—and Stuffy, with a sigh that was mistaken for hunger's expression, raised knife and fork and carved for himself a crown of imperishable bay.

No more valiant hero ever fought his way through the ranks of an enemy. Turkey, chops, soups, vegetables, pies, disappeared before him as fast as they could be served. Gorged nearly to the uttermost when he entered the restaurant, the smell of food had almost caused him to lose his honor as a gentleman, but he rallied like a true knight. He saw the look of beneficent happiness on the Old Gentleman's face—a happier look than even the fuchsias and the ornithoptera amphrisius had ever brought to it—and he had not the heart to see it wane.

In an hour Stuffy leaned back with a battle won.

"Thankee kindly, sir," he puffed like a leaky steam pipe; "thankee kindly for a hearty meal."

Then he arose heavily with glazed eyes and started toward the kitchen. A waiter turned him about like a top, and pointed him toward the door. The Old Gentleman carefully counted out $1.30 in silver change, leaving three nickels for the waiter.

They parted as they did each year at the door, the Old Gentleman going south, Stuffy north.

Around the first corner Stuffy turned, and stood for one minute. Then he seemed to puff out his rags as an owl puffs out his feathers, and fell to the sidewalk like a sunstricken horse.

When the ambulance came the young surgeon and the driver cursed softly at his weight. There was no smell of whiskey to justify a transfer to the patrol wagon, so Stuffy and his two dinners went to the hospital. There they stretched him on a bed and began to test him for strange diseases, with the hope of getting a chance at some problem with the bare steel.

And lo! an hour later another ambulance brought the Old Gentleman. And they laid him on another bed and spoke of appendicitis, for he looked good for the bill.

But pretty soon one of the young doctors met one of the young nurses whose eyes he liked, and stopped to chat with her about the cases.

"That nice old gentleman over there, now," he said, "you wouldn't think that was a case of almost starvation. Proud old family, I guess. He told me he hadn't eaten a thing for three days."

THE ASSESSOR OF SUCCESS

HASTINGS BEAUCHAMP MORLEY sauntered across Union Square with a pitying look at the hundreds that lolled upon the park benches. They were a motley lot, he thought; the men with stolid, animal, unshaven faces; the women wriggling and self-conscious, twining and untwining their feet that hung four inches above the gravelled walks.

Were I Mr. Carnegie or Mr. Rockefeller I would put a few millions in my inside pocket and make an appointment with all the Park Commissioners (around the corner, if necessary) and arrange for benches in all the parks of the world low enough for women to sit upon, and rest their feet upon the ground. After that I might furnish libraries to towns that would pay for 'em, or build sanitariums for crank professors, and call 'em colleges, if I wanted to.

Women's rights societies have been laboring for many years after equality with man. With what result? When they sit on a bench they must twist their ankles together and uncomfortably swing their highest French heels clear of earthly support. Begin at the bottom, ladies. Get your feet on the ground, and then rise to theories of mental equality.

Hastings Beauchamp Morley was carefully and neatly dressed. That was the result of an instinct due to his birth and breeding. It is denied us to look further into a man's bosom than the starch on his shirt front; so it is left to us only to recount his walks and conversation.

Morley had not a cent in his pockets; but he smiled pityingly at a hundred grimy, unfortunate ones who had no more, and who would have no more when the sun's first rays yellowed the tall paper-cutter building on the west side of the square. But Morley would have enough by then. Sundown had seen his pockets empty before; but sunrise had always seen them lined.

First he went to the house of a clergyman off Madison Avenue and presented a forged letter of introduction that holily purported to issue from a pastorate in Indiana. This netted him $5 when backed up a by a realistic romance of a delayed remittance.

On the sidewalk, twenty steps from the clergyman's door, a pale-faced, fat man huskily enveloped him with a raised red fist and the voice of a bell buoy, demanding payment of an old score.

"Why, Bergman, man," sang Morley, dulcetly, "is this you? I was just on my way up to your place to settle up. That remittance from my aunt arrived only this morning. Wrong address was the trouble. Come up to the corner and I'll square up. Glad to see you. Saves me a walk."

Four drinks placated the emotional Bergman. There was an air about Morley when he was backed by money in hand that would have stayed off a call loan at Rothschilds'. When he was penniless his bluff was pitched half a tone lower, but few were competent to detect the difference in the notes.

"You gum to mine blace and bay me tomorrow, Mr. Morley," said Bergman. "Oxcuse me dat I dun you on der street. But I haf not seen you in dree mont'. Pros't!"

Morley walked away with a crooked smile on his pale, smooth face. The credulous, drink-softened German amused him. He would have to avoid Twenty-ninth Street in the future. He had not been aware that Bergman ever went home by that route.

At the door of a darkened house two squares to the north Morley knocked with a peculiar sequence of raps. The door opened to the length of a six-inch chain, and the pompous, important black face of an African guardian imposed itself in the opening. Morley was admitted.

In a third-story room, in an atmosphere opaque with smoke, he hung for ten minutes above a roulette wheel. Then downstairs he crept, and was out-sped by the important Negro, jingling in his pocket the 40 cents in silver that remained to him of his five-dollar capital. At the corner he lingered, undecided.

Across the street was a drug store, well lighted, sending forth gleams from the German silver and crystal of its soda fountain and glasses. Along came a youngster of five, headed for the dispensary, stepping high with the consequence of a big errand, possibly one to which his advancing age had earned him promotion. In his hand he clutched something tightly, publicly, proudly, conspicuously.

Morley stopped him with his winning smile and soft speech.

"Me?" said the youngster. "I'm doin' to the drug 'tore for Mamma. She dave me a dollar to buy a bottle of med'cin."

"Now, now, now!" said Morley. "Such a big man you are to be doing errands for Mamma. I must go along with my little man to see that the cars don't run over him. And on the way we'll have some chocolates. Or would he rather have lemon drops?"

Morley entered the drug store leading the child by the hand. He presented the prescription that had been wrapped around the money.

On his face was a smile, predatory, parental, politic, profound.

"Aqua pura, one pint," said he to the druggist. "Sodium chloride, ten grains. Fiat solution. And don't try to skin me, because I know all about the number of gallons of H_2O in the Croton reservoir, and I always use the other ingredient on my potatoes."

"Fifteen cents," said the druggist, with a wink, after he had compounded the order. "I see you understand pharmacy. A dollar is the regular price."

"To gulls," said Morley, smilingly.

He settled the wrapped bottle carefully in the child's arms and escorted him to the corner. In his own pocket he dropped the 85 cents accruing to him by virtue of his chemical knowledge.

"Look out for the cars, sonny," he said, cheerfully, to his small victim.

Two street cars suddenly swooped in opposite directions upon the youngster. Morley dashed between them and pinned the infantile messenger by the neck, holding him in safety. Then from the corner of his street he sent him on his way, swindled, happy, and sticky with vile, cheap candy from the Italian's fruit stand.

Morley went to a restaurant and ordered a sirloin and a pint of inexpensive Château Breuille. He laughed noiselessly, but so genuinely that the waiter ventured to premise that good news had come his way.

"Why, no," said Morley, who seldom held conversation with any one. "It is not that. It is something else that amuses me. Do you know what three diversions of people are easiest to over-reach in transactions of all kinds?"

"Sure," said the waiter, calculating the size of the tip promised by the careful knot of Morley's tie; "there's the buyers from the dry goods stores in the South during August, and honeymooners from Staten Island, and——"

"Wrong!" said Morley, chuckling happily. "The answer is just—men, women, and children. The world—well, say New York and as far as summer boarders can swim out from Long Island—is full of greenhorns. Two minutes longer on the broiler would have made this steak fit to be eaten by a gentleman, François."

"If yez t'inks it's on de bum," said the waiter, "Oi'll——"

Morley lifted his hand in protest—slightly martyred protest.

"It will do," he said, magnanimously. "And now, green Chartreuse, frappé and a demitasse."

Morley went out leisurely and stood on a corner where two tradeful arteries of the city cross. With a solitary dime in his pocket, he stood on the curb watching with confident, cynical, smiling eyes the tides of people that flowed past him. Into that stream he must cast his net and draw fish for his further sustenance and need. Good Izaak Walton had not the half of his self-reliance and bait-lore.

A joyful party of four—two women and two men—fell upon him with cries of delight. There was a dinner party on—where had he been for a fortnight past?—what luck to thus run upon him! They surrounded and engulfed him— he must join them—tra la la—and the rest.

One with a white hat plume curving to the shoulder touched his sleeve, and cast at the others a triumphant look that said: "See what I can do with him?" and added her queen's command to the invitations.

"I leave you to imagine," said Morley, pathetically, "how it desolates me to forego the pleasure. But my friend Carruthers, of the New York Yacht Club, is to pick me up here in his motor car at 8."

The white plume tossed, and the quartet danced like midges around an arc light down the frolicsome way.

Morley stood, turning over and over the dime in his pocket and laughing gleefully to himself.

"'Front,'" he chanted under his breath; "'front' does it. It is trumps in the game. How they take it in! Men, women, and children—forgeries, water-and-salt lies—how they all take it in!"

An old man with an ill-fitting suit, a straggling gray beard, and a corpulent umbrella hopped from the conglomeration of cabs and street cars to the sidewalk at Morley's side.

"Stranger," said he, "excuse me for troubling you, but do you know anybody in this here town named Solomon Smothers? He's my son, and I've come down from Ellenville to visit him. Be darned if I know what I done with his street and number."

"I do not, sir," said Morley, half closing his eyes to veil the joy in them. "You had better apply to the police."

"The police!" said the old man. "I ain't done nothin' to call in the police about. I just come down to see Ben. He lives in a five-story house, he writes me. If you know anybody by that name and could——"

"I told you I did not," said Morley, coldly. "I know no one by the name of Smithers, and I advise you to——"

"Smothers not Smithers," interrupted the old man, hopefully. "A heavy-set man, sandy complected, about twenty-nine, two front teeth out, about five foot——"

"Oh, 'Smothers!'" exclaimed Morley. "Sol Smothers? Why, he lives in the next house to me. I thought you said 'Smithers.'"

Morley looked at his watch. You must have a watch. You can do it for a dollar. Better go hungry than forego a gunmetal or the ninety-eight-cent one that the railroads—according to these watchmakers—are run by.

"The Bishop of Long Island," said Morley, "was to meet me here at 8 to dine with me at the Kingfishers' Club. But I can't leave the father of my friend Sol Smothers alone on the street. By St. Swithin, Mr. Smothers, we Wall Street men have to work! Tired is no name for it! I was about to step across to the other corner and have a glass of ginger ale with a dash of sherry when you approached me. You must let me take you to Sol's house, Mr. Smothers. But before we take the car I hope you will join me in——"

An hour later Morley seated himself on the end of a quiet bench in Madison Square, with a twenty-five-cent cigar between his lips and $140 in deeply creased bills in his inside pocket. Content, light-hearted, ironical, keenly philosophic, he watched the moon drifting in and out amidst a maze of flying clouds. An old, ragged man with a low-bowed head sat at the other end of the bench.

Presently the old man stirred and looked at his bench companion. In Morley's appearance he seemed to recognize something superior to the usual nightly occupants of the benches.

"Kind sir," he whined, "if you could spare a dime or even a few pennies to one who——"

Morley cut short his stereotyped appeal by throwing him a dollar.

"God bless you!" said the old man. "I've been trying to find work for——"

"Work!" echoed Morley with his ringing laugh. "You are a fool, my friend. The world is a rock to you, no doubt; but you must be an Aaron and smite it with your rod. Then things better than water will gush out of it for you. That is what the world is for. It gives to me whatever I want from it."

"God has blessed you," said the old man. "It is only work that I have known. And now I can get no more."

"I must go home," said Morley, rising and buttoning his coat. "I stopped here only for a smoke. I hope you may find work."

"May your kindness be rewarded this night," said the old man.

"Oh," said Morley, "you have your wish already. I am satisfied. I think good luck follows me like a dog. I am for yonder bright hotel across the square for the night. And what a moon that is lighting up the city to-night. I think no one enjoys the moonlight and such little things as I do. Well, a good-night to you."

Morley walked to the corner where he would cross to his hotel. He blew slow streams of smoke from his cigar heavenward. A policeman passing saluted to his benign nod. What a fine moon it was.

The clock struck nine as a girl just entering womanhood stopped on the corner waiting for the approaching car. She was hurrying as if homeward from employment or delay. Her eyes were clear and pure, she was dressed in simple white, she looked eagerly for the car and neither to the right nor the left.

Morley knew her. Eight years before he had sat on the same bench with her at school. There had been no sentiment between them—nothing but the friendship of innocent days.

But he turned down the side street to a quiet spot and laid his suddenly burning face against the cool iron of a lamp-post, and said dully:

"God! I wish I could die."

THE BUYER FROM CACTUS CITY

IT is well that hay fever and colds do not obtain in the healthful vicinity of Cactus City, Texas, for the dry goods emporium of Navarro & Platt, situated there, is not to be sneezed at.

Twenty thousand people in Cactus City scatter their silver coin with liberal hands for the things that their hearts desire. The bulk of this semi-precious metal goes to Navarro & Platt. Their huge brick building covers enough ground to graze a dozen head of sheep. You can buy of them a rattlesnake-skin necktie, an automobile, or an eighty-five dollar, latest style, lady's tan coat in twenty different shades. Navarro & Platt first introduced pennies west of the Colorado River. They had been ranchmen with business heads, who saw that the world did not necessarily have to cease its revolutions after free grass went out.

Every Spring, Navarro, senior partner, fifty-five, half-Spanish, cosmopolitan, able, polished, had "gone on" to New York to buy goods. This year he shied at taking up the long trail. He was undoubtedly growing older; and he looked at his watch several times a day before the hour came for his siesta.

"John," he said, to his junior partner, "you shall go on this year to buy the goods."

Platt looked tired.

"I'm told," said he, "that New York is a plumb dead town; but I'll go. I can take a whirl in San Antone for a few days on my way and have some fun."

Two weeks later a man in a Texas full dress suit—black frock coat, broad-brimmed soft white hat, and lay-down collar 3-4 inch high, with black, wrought-iron necktie—entered the wholesale cloak and suit establishment of Zizzbaum & Son, on lower Broadway.

Old Zizzbaum had the eye of an osprey, the memory of an elephant, and a mind that unfolded from him in three movements like the puzzle of the carpenter's rule. He rolled to the front like a brunette polar bear, and shook Platt's hand.

"And how is the good Mr. Navarro in Texas?" he said. "The trip was too long for him this year, so? We welcome Mr. Platt instead."

"A bull's eye," said Platt, "and I'd give forty acres of unirrigated Pecos County land to know how you did it."

"I knew," grinned Zizzbaum, "just as I know that the rainfall in El Paso for the year was 28.5 inches, or an increase of 15 inches, and that therefore Navarro & Platt will buy a $15,000 stock of suits this spring instead of $10,-000, as in a dry year. But that will be to-morrow. There is first a cigar in my private office that will remove from your mouth the taste of the ones you smuggle across the Rio Grande and like—because they are smuggled."

It was late in the afternoon and business for the day had ended. Zizzbaum left Platt with a half-smoked cigar, and came out of the private office to Son, who was arranging his diamond scarfpin before a mirror, ready to leave.

"Abey," he said, "you will have to take Mr. Platt around to-night and show him things. They are customers for ten years. Mr. Navarro and I we played chess every moment of spare time when he came. That is good, but Mr. Platt is a young man and this is his first visit to New York. He should amuse easily."

"All right," said Abey, screwing the guard tightly on his pin. "I'll take him on. After he's seen the Flatiron and the head waiter at the Hotel Astor and heard the phonograph play 'Under the Old Apple Tree' it'll be half-past ten, and Mr. Texas will be ready to roll up in his blanket. I've got a supper engagement at 11:30, but he'll be all to the Mrs. Winslow before then."

The next morning at 10 Platt walked into the store ready to do business. He had a bunch of hyacinths pinned on his lapel. Zizzbaum himself waited on him. Navarro & Platt were good customers, and never failed to take their discount for cash.

"And what did you think of our little town?" asked Zizzbaum, with the fatuous smile of the Manhattanite.

"I shouldn't care to live in it," said the Texan. "Your son and I knocked around quite a little last night. You've got good water, but Cactus City is better lit up."

"We've got a few lights on Broadway, don't you think, Mr. Platt?"

"And a good many shadows," said Platt. "I think I like your horses best. I haven't seen a crowbait since I've been in town."

Zizzbaum led him up stairs to show the samples of suits.

"Ask Miss Asher to come," he said to a clerk.

Miss Asher came, and Platt, of Navarro & Platt, felt for the first time the wonderful bright light of romance and glory descend upon him. He stood still as a granite cliff above the cañon of the Colorado, with his wide-open eyes fixed upon her. She noticed his look and flushed a little, which was contrary to her custom.

Miss Asher was the crack model of Zizzbaum & Son. She was of the blond type known as "medium," and her measurements even went the required 38-25-42 standard a little better. She had been at Zizzbaum's two years, and knew her business. Her eye was bright, but cool; and had she chosen to match her gaze against the optic of the famed basilisk, that fabulous monster's gaze would have wavered and softened first. Incidentally, she knew buyers.

"Now, Mr. Platt," said Zizzbaum, "I want you to see these princess gowns in the light shades. They will be the thing in your climate. This first, if you please, Miss Asher."

Swiftly in and out of the dressing-room the prize model flew, each time wearing a new costume and looking more stunning with every change. She

posed with absolute self-possession before the stricken buyer, who stood, tongue-tied and motionless, while Zizzbaum orated oilily of the styles. On the model's face was her faint, impersonal professional smile that seemed to cover something like weariness or contempt.

When the display was over Platt seemed to hesitate. Zizzbaum was a little anxious, thinking that his customer might be inclined to try elsewhere. But Platt was only looking over in his mind the best building sites in Cactus City, trying to select one on which to build a house for his wife-to-be—who was just then in the dressing-room taking off an evening gown of lavender and tulle.

"Take your time, Mr. Platt," said Zizzbaum. "Think it over to-night. You won't find anybody else meet our prices on goods like these. I'm afraid you're having a dull time in New York, Mr. Platt. A young man like you—of course, you miss the society of the ladies. Wouldn't you like a nice young lady to take out to dinner this evening? Miss Asher, now, is a very nice young lady; she will make it agreeable for you."

"Why, she doesn't know me," said Platt, wonderingly. "She doesn't know anything about me. Would she go? I'm not acquainted with her."

"Would she go?" repeated Zizzbaum, with uplifted eyebrows. "Sure, she would go. I will introduce you. Sure, she would go."

He called Miss Asher loudly.

She came, calm and slightly contemptuous, in her white shirt waist and plain black skirt.

"Mr. Platt would like the pleasure of your company to dinner this evening," said Zizzbaum, walking away.

"Sure," said Miss Asher, looking at the ceiling. "I'd be much pleased. Nine-eleven West Twentieth Street. What time?"

"Say seven o'clock."

"All right, but please don't come ahead of time. I room with a school teacher, and she doesn't allow any gentleman to call in the room. There isn't any parlor, so you'll have to wait in the hall. I'll be ready."

At half-past seven Platt and Miss Asher sat at a table in a Broadway restaurant. She was dressed in a plain, filmy black. Platt didn't know that it was all a part of her day's work.

With the unobtrusive aid of a good waiter he managed to order a respectable dinner, minus the usual Broadway preliminaries.

Miss Asher flashed upon him a dazzling smile.

"Mayn't I have something to drink?" she asked.

"Why, certainly," said Platt. "Anything you want."

"A dry Martini," she said to the waiter.

When it was brought and set before her Platt reached over and took it away.

"What is this?" he asked.

"A cocktail, of course."

"I thought it was some kind of tea you ordered. This is liquor. You can't drink this. What is your first name?"

"To my intimate friends," said Miss Asher, freezingly, "it is 'Helen.'"

"Listen, Helen," said Platt, leaning over the table. "For many years every time the spring flowers blossomed out on the prairies I got to thinking of somebody that I'd never seen or heard of. I knew it was you the minute I saw you yesterday. I'm going back home to-morrow, and you're going with me. I know it, for I saw it in your eyes when you first looked at me. You needn't kick, for you've got to fall into line. Here's a little trick I picked out for you on my way over."

He flicked a two-carat diamond solitaire ring across the table. Miss Asher flipped it back to him with her fork.

"Don't get fresh," she said, severely

"I'm worth a hundred thousand dollars," said Platt. "I'll build you the finest house in west Texas."

"You can't buy me, Mr. Buyer," said Miss Asher, "if you had a hundred million. I didn't think I'd have to call you down. You didn't look like the others to me at first, but I see you're all alike."

"All who?" asked Platt.

"All you buyers. You think because we girls have to go out to dinner with you or lose our jobs that you're privileged to say what you please. Well, forget it. I thought you were different from the others, but I see I was mistaken."

Platt struck his fingers on the table with a gesture of sudden, illuminating satisfaction.

"I've got it!" he exclaimed, almost hilariously—"the Nicholson place, over on the north side. There's a big grove of live oaks and a natural lake. The old house can be pulled down and the new one set further back."

"Put out your pipe," said Miss Asher. "I'm sorry to wake you up, but you fellows might as well get wise, once for all, to where you stand. I'm supposed to go to dinner with you and help jolly you along so you'll trade with old Zizzy, but don't expect to find me in any of the suits you buy."

"Do you mean to tell me," said Platt, "that you go out this way with customers, and they all—they all talk to you like I have?"

"They all make plays," said Miss Asher. "But I must say that you've got 'em beat in one respect. They generally talk diamonds, while you've actually dug one up."

"How long have you been working, Helen?"

"Got my name pat, haven't you? I've been supporting myself for eight years. I was a cash girl and a wrapper and then a shop girl until I was grown, and then I got to be a suit model. Mr. Texas Man, don't you think a little wine would make this dinner a little less dry?"

"You're not going to drink wine any more, dear. It's awful to think how—— I'll come to the store to-morrow and get you. I want you to pick out an automobile before we leave. That's all we need to buy here."

"Oh, cut that out. If you knew how sick I am of hearing such talk."

After the dinner they walked down Broadway and came upon Diana's little wooded park. The trees caught Platt's eye at once, and he must turn along under the winding walk beneath them. The lights shone upon two bright tears in the model's eyes.

"I don't like that," said Platt. "What's the matter?"

"Don't you mind," said Miss Asher. "Well, its because—well, I didn't think you were that kind when I first saw you. But you are all alike. And now will you take me home, or will I have to call a cop?"

Platt took her to the door of her boarding-house. They stood for a minute in the vestibule. She looked at him with such scorn in her eyes that even his heart of oak began to waver. His arm was halfway around her waist, when she struck him a stinging blow on the face with her open hand.

As he stepped back a ring fell from somewhere and bounded on the tiled floor. Platt groped for it and found it.

"Now, take your useless diamond and go, Mr. Buyer," she said.

"This was the other one—the wedding ring," said the Texan, holding the smooth gold band on the palm of his hand.

Miss Asher's eyes blazed upon him in the half darkness.

"Was that what you meant?—did you——"

Somebody opened the door from inside the house.

"Good-night," said Platt. "I'll see you at the store to-morrow."

Miss Asher ran up to her room and shook the school teacher until she sat up in bed ready to scream "Fire!"

"Where is it?" she cried.

"That's what I want to know," said the model. "You've studied geography, Emma, and you ought to know. Where is a town called Cac—Cac—Carac—Caracas City, I think they called it?"

"How dare you wake me up for that?" said the school teacher. "Caracas is in Venezuela, of course."

"What's it like?"

"Why, it's principally earthquakes and Negroes and monkeys and malarial fever and volcanoes."

"I don't care," said Miss Asher, blithely; "I'm going there to-morrow."

THE BADGE OF POLICEMAN O'ROON

It cannot be denied that men and women have looked upon one another for the first time and become instantly enamored. It is a risky process, this love at first sight, before she has seen him in Bradstreet or he has seen her in curl papers. But these things do happen; and one instance must form a theme for this story—though not, thank Heaven, to the overshadowing of more vital and important subjects, such as drink, policemen, horses, and earldoms.

During a certain war a troop calling itself the Gentle Riders rode into history and one or two ambuscades. The Gentle Riders were recruited from the aristocracy of the wild men of the West and the wild men of the aristocracy of the East. In khaki there is little telling them one from another, so they became good friends and comrades all around.

Ellsworth Remsen, whose old Knickerbocker descent atoned for his modest rating at only ten millions, ate his canned beef gayly by the campfires of the Gentle Riders. The war was a great lark to him, so that he scarcely regretted polo and planked shad.

One of the troopers was a well-set-up, affable, cool young man, who called himself O'Roon. To this young man Remsen took an especial liking. The two rode side by side during the famous mooted up-hill charge that was disputed so hotly at the time by the Spaniards and afterward by the Democrats.

After the war Remsen came back to his polo and shad. One day a well-set-up, affable, cool young man disturbed him at his club, and he and O'Roon were soon pounding each other and exchanging opprobrious epithets after the manner of long-lost friends. O'Roon looked seedy and out of luck and perfectly contented. But it seemed that his content was only apparent.

"Get me a job, Remsen," he said. "I've just handed a barber my last shilling."

"No trouble at all," said Remsen. "I know a lot of men who have banks and stores and things downtown. Any particular line you fancy?"

"Yes," said O'Roon, with a look of interest. "I took a walk in your Central Park this morning. "I'd like to be one of those bobbies on horseback. That would be about the ticket. Besides, it's the only thing I could do. I can ride a little and the fresh air suits me. Think you could land that for me?"

Remsen was sure that he could. And in a very short time he did. And they who were not above looking at mounted policemen might have seen a well-set-up, affable, cool young man on a prancing chestnut steed attending to his duties along the driveways of the park.

And now at the extreme risk of wearying old gentlemen who carry leather fob chains, and elderly ladies who—but no! grandmother herself yet thrills at foolish, immortal Romeo—there must be a hint of love at first sight.

It came just as Remsen was strolling into Fifth Avenue from his club a few doors away.

A motor car was creeping along foot by foot, impeded by a freshet of vehicles that filled the street. In the car was a chauffeur and an old gentleman with snowy side whiskers and a Scotch plaid cap which could not be worn while automobiling except by a personage. Not even a wine agent would dare do it. But these two were of no consequence—except, perhaps, for the guiding of the machine and the paying for it. At the old gentleman's side sat a young lady more beautiful than pomegranate blossoms, more exquisite than the first quarter moon viewed at twilight through the tops of oleanders. Remsen saw her and knew his fate. He could have flung himself under the very wheels that conveyed her, but he knew that would be the last means of attracting the attention of those who ride in motor cars. Slowly the auto passed, and, if we place the poets above the autoists, carried the heart of Remsen with it. Here was a large city of millions, and many women who at a certain distance appear to resemble pomegranate blossoms. Yet he hoped to see her again; for each one fancies that his romance has its own tutelary guardian and divinity.

Luckily for Remsen's peace of mind there came a diversion in the guise of a reunion of the Gentle Riders of the city. There were not many of them —perhaps a score—and there was wassail and things to eat, and speeches and the Spaniard was bearded again in recapitulation. And when daylight threatened them the survivors prepared to depart. But some remained upon the battle-field. One of these was Trooper O'Roon, who was not seasoned to potent liquids. His legs declined to fulfil the obligations they had sworn to the police department.

"I'm stewed, Remsen," said O'Roon to his friend. "Why do they build hotels that go round and round like catherine wheels? They'll take away my shield and break me. I can think and talk con-con-consec-sec-secutively, but I s-s-stammer with my feet. I've got to go on duty in three hours. The jig is up, Remsen. The jig is up, I tell you."

"Look at me," said Remsen, who was his smiling self, pointing to his own face; "whom do you see here?"

"Goo' fellow," said O'Roon, dizzily, "Goo' old Remsen."

"Not so," said Remsen. "You see Mounted Policeman O'Roon. Look at your face—no; you can't do that without a glass—but look at mine, and think of yours. How much alike are we? As two French *table d'hôte* dinners. With your badge, on your horse, in your uniform, will I charm nurse-maids and prevent the grass from growing under people's feet in the Park this day. I will have your badge and your honor, besides having the jolliest lark I've been blessed with since we licked Spain."

Promptly on time the counterfeit presentment of Mounted Policeman O'Roon single-footed into the Park on his chestnut steed. In a uniform two men who are unlike will look alike; two who somewhat resemble each other in feature and figure will appear as twin brothers. So Remsen trotted down the bridle paths, enjoying himself hugely, so few real pleasures do ten-millionaires have.

Along the driveway in the early morning spun a victoria drawn by a pair of fiery bays. There was something foreign about the affair, for the Park is rarely used in the morning, except by unimportant people who love to be healthy, poor, and wise. In the vehicle sat an old gentleman with snowy side-whiskers and a Scotch plaid cap which could not be worn while driving except by a personage. At his side sat the lady of Remsen's heart—the lady who looked like pomegranate blossoms and the gibbous moon.

Remsen met them coming. At the instant of their passing her eyes looked into his, and but for the ever coward's heart of a true lover he could have sworn that she flushed a faint pink. He trotted on for twenty yards, and then wheeled his horse at the sound of runaway hoofs. The bays had bolted.

Remsen sent his chestnut after the victoria like a shot. There was work cut out for the impersonator of Policeman O'Roon. The chestnut ranged alongside the off bay thirty seconds after the chase began, rolled nis eye back at Remsen, and said in the only manner open to policeman's horses:

"Well, you duffer, are you going to do your share? You're not O'Roon, but it seems to me if you'd lean to the right you could reach the reins of that foolish slow-running bay—ah! you're all right; O'Roon couldn't have done it more neatly!"

The runaway team was tugged to an inglorious halt by Remsen's tough muscles. The driver released his hands from the wrapped reins, jumped from his seat and stood at the heads of the team. The chestnut, approving his new rider, danced and pranced, reviling equinely the subdued bays. Remsen, lingering, was dimly conscious of a vague, impossible, unnecessary old gentleman in a Scotch cap who talked incessantly about something. And he was acutely conscious of a pair of violet eyes that would have drawn Saint Pyrites from his iron pillar—or whatever the allusion is—and of the lady's smile and look—a little frightened, but a look that, with the ever coward heart of a true lover, he could not yet construe. They were asking his name and bestowing upon him well-bred thanks for his heroic deed, and the Scotch cap was especially babbling and insistent. But the eloquent appeal was in the eyes of the lady.

A little thrill of satisfaction ran through Remsen, because he had a name to give which, without undue pride, was worthy of being spoken in high places, and a small fortune which, with due pride, he could leave at his end without disgrace.

He opened his lips to speak and closed them again.

Who was he? Mounted Policeman O'Roon. The badge and the honor of his comrade were in his hands. If Ellsworth Remsen, ten-millionaire and Knickerbocker, had just rescued pomegranate blossoms and Scotch cap from possible death, where was Policeman O'Roon? Off his beat, exposed, disgraced, discharged. Love had come, but before that there had been something that demanded precedence—the fellowship of men on battlefields fighting an alien foe.

Remsen touched his cap, looked between the chestnut's ears, and took refuge in vernacularity.

"Don't mention it," he said, stolidly. "We policemen are paid to do these things. It's our duty."

And he rode away—rode away cursing *noblesse oblige*, but knowing he could never have done anything else.

At the end of the day Remsen sent the chestnut to his stable and went to O'Roon's room. The policeman was again a well-set-up, affable, cool young man who sat by the window smoking cigars.

"I wish you and the rest of the police force and all badges, horses, brass buttons, and men who can't drink two glasses of *brut* without getting upset were at the devil," said Remsen, feelingly.

O'Roon smiled with evident satisfaction.

"Good old Remsen," he said, affably, "I know all about it. They trailed me down and cornered me here two hours ago. There was a little row at home, you know, and I cut sticks just to show them. I don't believe I told you that my Governor was the Earl of Ardsley. Funny you should bob against them in the Park. If you damaged that horse of mine I'll never forgive you. I'm going to buy him and take him back with me. Oh, yes, and I think my sister—Lady

Angela, you know—wants particularly for you to come up to the hotel with me this evening. Didn't lose my badge, did you, Remsen? I've got to turn that in at Headquarters when I resign."

BRICKDUST ROW

BLINKER was displeased. A man of less culture and poise and wealth would have sworn. But Blinker always remembered that he was a gentleman—a thing that no gentleman should do. So he merely looked bored and sardonic while he rode in a hansom to the centre of disturbance, which was the Broadway office of Lawyer Oldport, who was agent for the Blinker estate.

"I don't see," said Blinker, "why I should be always signing confounded papers. I am packed, and was to have left for the North Woods this morning. Now I must wait until to-morrow morning. I hate night trains. My best razors are, of course, at the bottom of some unidentifiable trunk. It is a plot to drive me to bay rum and a monologuing, thumb-handed barber. Give me a pen that doesn't scratch. I hate pens that scratch."

"Sit down," said double-chinned, gray Lawyer Oldport. "The worst has not been told you. Oh, the hardships of the rich! The papers are not yet ready to sign. They will be laid before you to-morrow at eleven. You will miss another day. Twice shall the barber tweak the helpless nose of a Blinker. Be thankful that your sorrows do not embrace a haircut."

"If," said Blinker, rising, "the act did not involve more signing of papers I would take my business out of your hands at once. Give me a cigar, please."

"If," said Lawyer Oldport, "I had cared to see an old friend's son gulped down at one mouthful by sharks I would have ordered you to take it away long ago. Now, let's quit fooling, Alexander. Besides the grinding task of signing your name some thirty times to-morrow, I must impose upon you the consideration of a matter of business—of business, and I may say humanity or right. I spoke to you about this five years ago, but you would not listen—you were in a hurry for a coaching trip, I think. The subject has come up again. The property——"

"Oh, property!" interrupted Blinker. "Dear Mr. Oldport, I think you mentioned to-morrow. Let's have it all at one dose to-morrow—signatures and property and snappy rubber bands and that smelly sealing-wax and all. Have luncheon with me? Well, I'll try to remember to drop in at eleven to-morrow. Morning."

The Blinker wealth was in lands, tenements, and hereditaments, as the legal phrase goes. Lawyer Oldport had once taken Alexander in his little pulmonary gasoline runabout to see the many buildings and rows of buildings that he owned in the city. For Alexander was sole heir. They had amused Blinker very much. The houses looked so incapable of producing the big sums of money that Lawyer Oldport kept piling up in banks for him to spend.

In the evening Blinker went to one of his clubs, intending to dine. Nobody was there except some old fogies playing whist who spoke to him with grave politeness and glared at him with savage contempt. Everybody was out of town. But here he was kept in like a schoolboy to write his name over and over on pieces of paper. His wounds were deep.

Blinker turned his back on the fogies, and said to the club steward who had come forward with some nonsense about cold fresh salmon roe:

"Symons, I'm going to Coney Island." He said it as one might say: "All's off, I'm going to jump into the river."

The joke pleased Symons. He laughed within a sixteenth of a note of the audibility permitted by the laws governing employees.

"Certainly, sir," he tittered. "Of course, sir, I think I can see you at Coney, Mr. Blinker."

Blinker got a paper and looked up the movements of Sunday steamboats. Then he found a cab at the first corner and drove to a North River pier. He stood in line, as democratic as you or I, and bought a ticket, and was trampled upon and shoved forward until, at last, he found himself on the upper deck of the boat staring brazenly at a girl who sat alone upon a camp stool. But Blinker did not intend to be brazen; the girl was so wonderfully good looking that he forgot for one minute that he was the prince incog, and behaved just as he did in society.

She was looking at him, too, and not severely. A puff of wind threatened Blinker's straw hat. He caught it warily and settled it again. The movement gave the effect of a bow. The girl nodded and smiled, and in another instant he was seated at her side. She was dressed all in white, she was paler than Blinker imagined milkmaids and girls of humble stations to be, but she was as tidy as a cherry blossom, and her steady, supremely frank gray eyes looked out from the intrepid depths of an unshadowed and untroubled soul.

"How dare you raise your hat to me?" she asked, with a smile-redeemed severity.

"I didn't," Blinker said, but he quickly covered the mistake by extending it to "I didn't know how to keep from it after I saw you."

"I do not allow gentlemen to sit by me to whom I have not been introduced," she said with a sudden haughtiness that deceived him. He rose reluctantly, but her clear, teasing laugh brought him down to his chair again.

"I guess you weren't going far," she declared, with beauty's magnificent self-confidence.

"Are you going to Coney Island?" asked Blinker.

"Me?" She turned upon him wide-open eyes full of bantering surprise. "Why, what a question! Can't you see that I'm riding a bicycle in the park?" Her drollery took the form of impertinence.

"And I'm laying bricks on a tall factory chimney," said Blinker. "Mayn't we see Coney together? I'm all alone and I've never been there before."

"It depends," said the girl, "on how nicely you behave. I'll consider your application until we get there."

Blinker took pains to provide against the rejection of his application. He strove to please. To adopt the metaphor of his nonsensical phrase, he laid brick upon brick on the tall chimney of his devoirs until, at length, the structure was stable and complete. The manners of the best society come around finally to simplicity; and as the girl's way was that naturally, they were on a mutual plane of communication from the beginning.

He learned that she was twenty, and her name was Florence; that she trimmed hats in a millinery shop; that she lived in a furnished room with her best chum Ella, who was cashier in a shoe store; and that a glass of milk from the bottle on the window-sill and an egg that boils itself while you twist up your hair makes a breakfast good enough for any one. Florence laughed when she heard "Blinker."

"Well," she said. "It certainly shows that you have imagination. It gives the 'Smiths' a chance for a little rest, anyhow."

They landed at Coney, and were dashed on the crest of a great human wave of mad pleasure-seekers into the walks and avenues of Fairyland gone into vaudeville.

With a curious eye, a critical mind, and a fairly withheld judgment Blinker considered the temples, pagodas and kiosks of popularized delights. Hoi polloi trampled, hustled, and crowded him. Basket parties bumped him; sticky children tumbled, howling, under his feet, candying his clothes. Insolent youths strolling among the booths with hard-won canes under one arm and easily won girls on the other, blew defiant smoke from cheap cigars into his face. The publicity gentlemen with megaphones, each before his own stupendous attraction, roared like Niagara in his ears. Music of all kinds that could be tortured from brass, reed, hide, or string, fought in the air to gain space for its vibrations against its competitors. But what held Blinker in awful fascination was the mob, the multitude, the proletariat shrieking, struggling, hurrying, panting, hurling itself in incontinent frenzy, with unabashed abandon, into the ridiculous sham palaces of trumpery and tinsel pleasures. The vulgarity of it, its brutal overriding of all the tenets of repression and taste that were held by his caste, repelled him strongly.

In the midst of his disgust he turned and looked down at Florence by his side. She was ready with her quick smile and upturned, happy eyes, as bright and clear as the water in trout pools. The eyes were saying that they had the right to be shining and happy, for was their owner not with her (for the present) Man, her Gentleman Friend and holder of the keys to the enchanted city of fun

Blinker did not read her look accurately, but by some miracle he suddenly saw Coney aright.

He no longer saw a mass of vulgarians seeking gross joys. He now looked clearly upon a hundred thousand true idealists. Their offenses were wiped out. Counterfeit and false though the garish joys of these spangled temples were, he perceived that deep under the gilt surface they offered saving and apposite balm and satisfaction to the restless human heart. Here, at least, was the husk of Romance, the empty but shining casque of Chivalry, the breath-catching though safe-guarded dip and flight of Adventure, the magic carpet that transports you to the realms of fairyland, though its journey be through but a few poor yards of space. He no longer saw a rabble, but his brothers seeking the ideal. There was no magic of poesy here or of art; but the glamour of their imagination turned yellow calico into cloth of gold and the megaphone into the silver trumpets of joy's heralds.

Almost humbled, Blinker rolled up the shirt sleeves of his mind and joined the idealists.

"You are the lady doctor," he said to Florence. "How shall we go about doing this jolly conglomeration of fairy tales, incorporated?"

"We will begin there," said the Princess, pointing to a fun pagoda on the edge of the sea, "and we will take them all in, one by one."

They caught the eight o'clock returning boat and sat, filled with pleasant fatigue, against the rail in the bow, listening to the Italians' fiddle and harp. Blinker had thrown off all care. The North Woods seemed to him an uninhabitable wilderness. What a fuss he had made over signing his name—pooh! he could sign it a hundred times. And her name was as pretty as she was— "Florence," he said it to himself a great many times.

As the boat was nearing its pier in the North River a two-funnelled, drab, foreign-looking sea-going steamer was dropping down toward the bay. The boat turned its nose in towards its slip. The steamer veered as if to seek mid-stream, and then yawed, seemed to increase its speed and struck the Coney boat on the side near the stern, cutting into it with a terrifying shock and crash.

While the six hundred passengers on the boat were mostly tumbling about the decks in a shrieking panic the captain was shouting at the steamer that it should not back off and leave the rent exposed for the water to enter. But the steamer tore its way out like a savage sawfish and cleaved its heartless way, full speed ahead.

The boat began to sink at its stern, but moved slowly toward the slip. The passengers were a frantic mob, unpleasant to behold.

Blinker held Florence tightly until the boat had righted itself. She made no sound or sign of fear. He stood on a camp stool, ripped off the slats above his head and pulled down a number of the life preservers. He began to buckle one around Florence. The rotten canvas split and the fraudulent granulated cork came pouring out in a stream. Florence caught a handful of it and laughed gleefully.

"It looks like breakfast food," she said. "Take it off. They're no good."

She unbuckled it and threw it on the deck. She made Blinker sit down and sat by his side and put her hand in his. "What'll you bet we don't reach the pier all right?" she said, and began to hum a song.

And now the captain moved among the passengers and compelled order. The boat would undoubtedly make her slip, he said, and ordered the women and children to the bow, where they could land first. The boat, very low in the water at the stern, tried gallantly to make his promise good.

"Florence," said Blinker, as she held him close by an arm and hand, "I love you."

"That's what they all say," she replied, lightly.

"I am not one of 'they all,'" he persisted. "I never knew any one I could love before. I could pass my life with you and be happy every day. I am rich. I can make things all right for you."

"That's what they all say," said the girl again, weaving the words into her little, reckless song.

"Don't say that again," said Blinker in a tone that made her look at him in frank surprise.

"Why shouldn't I say it?" she asked, calmly. "They all do."

"Who are 'they'?" he asked, jealous for the first time in his existence.

"Why, the fellows I know."

"Do you know so many?"

"Oh, well, I'm not a wall flower," she answered with modest complacency.

"Where do you see these—these men? At your home?"

"Of course not. I meet them just as I did you. Sometimes on the boat, sometimes in the park, sometimes on the street. I'm a pretty good judge of a man. I can tell in a minute if a fellow is one who is likely to get fresh."

"What do you mean by 'fresh'?"

"Who, try to kiss you—me, I mean."

"Do any of them try that?" asked Blinker, clenching his teeth.

"Sure. All men do. You know that."

"Do you allow them?"

"Some. Not many. They won't take you out anywhere unless you do."

She turned her head and looked searchingly at Blinker. Her eyes were as innocent as a child's. There was a puzzled look in them, as though she did not understand him.

"What's wrong about my meeting fellows?" she asked, wonderingly.

"Everything," he answered, almost savagely. "Why don't you entertain your company in the house where you live? Is it necessary to pick up Tom, Dick, and Harry on the streets?"

She kept her absolutely ingenuous eyes upon his.

"If you could see the place where I live you wouldn't ask that. I live in Brickdust Row. They call it that because there's red dust from the bricks crumbling over everything. I've lived there for more than four years. There's no place to receive company. You can't have anybody come to your room. What else is there to do? A girl has got to meet the men, hasn't she?"

"Yes," he said, hoarsely. "A girl has got to meet a—has got to meet the men."

"The first time one spoke to me on the street," she continued, "I ran home and cried all night. But you get used to it. I meet a good many nice fellows at church. I go on rainy days and stand in the vestibule until one comes up with an umbrella. I wish there was a parlor, so I could ask you to call, Mr. Blinker—are you really sure it isn't 'Smith,' now?"

The boat landed safely. Blinker had a confused impression of walking with the girl through quiet crosstown streets until she stopped at a corner and held out her hand.

"I live just one more block over," she said. "Thank you for a very pleasant afternoon."

Blinker muttered something and plunged northward till he found a cab. A big, gray church loomed slowly at his right. Blinker shook his fist at it through the window.

"I gave you a thousand dollars last week," he cried under his breath, "and she meets them in your very doors. There is something wrong; there is something wrong."

At eleven the next day Blinker signed his name thirty times with a new pen provided by Lawyer Oldport.

"Now let me get to the woods," he said, surlily.

"You are not looking well," said Lawyer Oldport. "The trip will do you good. But listen, if you will, to that little matter of business of which I spoke to you yesterday, and also five years ago. There are some buildings, fifteen in number, of which there are new five-year leases to be signed. Your father contemplated a change in the lease provisions, but never made it. He intended that the parlors of these houses should not be sub-let, but that the tenants should be allowed to use them for reception rooms. These houses are in the shopping districts, and are mainly tenanted by young working girls. As it is they are forced to seek companionship outside. This row of red brick——"

Blinker interrupted him with a loud, discordant laugh.

"Brickdust Row for an even hundred," he cried. "And I own it. Have I guessed right?"

"The tenants have some such name for it," said Lawyer Oldport.

Blinker arose and jammed his hat down to his eyes.

"Do what you please with it," he said, harshly. "Remodel it, burn it, raze it to the ground. But, man, it's too late, I tell you. It's too late. It's too late. It's too late."

THE MAKING OF A NEW YORKER

BESIDES many things, Raggles was a poet. He was called a tramp; but that was only an elliptical way of saying that he was a philosopher, an artist, a traveller, a naturalist, and a discoverer. But most of all he was a poet. In all his life he never wrote a line of verse; he lived his poetry. His Odyssey would have been a Limerick, had it been written. But, to linger with the primary proposition, Raggles was a poet.

Raggles's specialty, had he been driven to ink and paper, would have been sonnets to the cities. He studied cities as women study their reflections in mirrors; as children study the glue and sawdust of a dislocated doll; as the men who write about wild animals study the cages in the zoo. A city to Raggles was not merely a pile of bricks and mortar, peopled by a certain number of inhabitants; it was a thing with soul characteristic and distinct; an individual conglomeration of life, with its own peculiar essence, flavor, and feeling. Two thousand miles to the north and south, east and west, Raggles wandered in poetic fervor, taking the cities to his breast. He footed it on dusty roads, or sped magnificently in freight cars, counting time as of no account. And when he had found the heart of a city and listened to its secret confession, he strayed on, restless, to another. Fickle Raggles!—but perhaps he had not met the civic corporation that could engage and hold his critical fancy.

Through the ancient poets we have learned that the cities are feminine. So they were to poet Raggles; and his mind carried a concrete and clear conception of the figure that symbolized and typified each one that he had wooed.

Chicago seemed to swoop down upon him with a breezy suggestion of Mrs. Partington, plumes and patchouli, and to disturb his rest with a soaring and beautiful song of future promise. But Raggles would awake to a sense of shivering cold and a haunting impression of ideals lost in a depressing aura of potato salad and fish.

Thus Chicago affected him. Perhaps there is a vagueness and inaccuracy in the description; but that is Raggles's fault. He should have recorded his sensations in magazine poems.

Pittsburg impressed him as the play of "Othello" performed in the Russian language in a railroad station by Dockstader's minstrels. A royal and generous lady this Pittsburg, though—homely, hearty, with flushed face, washing the dishes in a silk dress and white kid slippers, and bidding Raggles sit before the roaring fireplace and drink champagne with his pigs' feet and fried potatoes.

New Orleans had simply gazed down upon him from a balcony. He could see her pensive, starry eyes and catch the flutter of her fan, and that was all. Only once he came face to face with her. It was at dawn, when she was flushing the red bricks of the banquette with a pail of water. She laughed and hummed a chansonette and filled Raggles's shoes with ice-cold water. Allons!

Boston construed herself to the poetic Raggles in an erratic and singular way. It seemed to him that he had drunk cold tea and that the city was a white, cold cloth that had been bound tightly around his brow to spur him to some unknown but tremendous mental effort. And, after all, he came to shovel snow for a livelihood; and the cloth, becoming wet, tightened its knots and could not be removed.

Indefinite and unintelligible ideas, you will say; but your disapprobation should be tempered with gratitude, for these are poets' fancies—and suppose you had come upon them in verse!

One day Raggles came and laid siege to the heart of the great city of Manhattan. She was the greatest of all; and he wanted to learn her note in the scale; to taste and appraise and classify and solve and label her and arrange her with the other cities that had given him up the secret of their individuality. And here we cease to be Raggles's translator and become his chronicler.

Raggles landed from a ferry-boat one morning and walked into the core of the town with the blasé air of a cosmopolite. He was dressed with care to play the rôle of an "unidentified man." No country, race, class, clique, union, party clan, or bowling association could have claimed him. His clothing, which had been donated to him piece-meal by citizens of different height, but same number of inches around the heart, was not yet as uncomfortable to his figure as those specimens of raiment, self-measured, that are railroaded to you by trans-continental tailors with a suit case, suspenders, silk handkerchief and pearl studs as a bonus. Without money—as a poet should be—but with the ardor of an astronomer discovering a new star in the chorus of the milky way, or a man who has seen ink suddenly flow from his fountain pen, Raggles wandered into the great city.

Late in the afternoon he drew out of the roar and commotion with a look of dumb terror on his countenance. He was defeated, puzzled, discomfited, frightened. Other cities had been to him as long primer to read; as country maidens quickly to fathom; as send-price-of-subscription-with-answer rebuses to solve; as oyster cocktails to swallow; but here was one as cold, glittering, serene, impossible as a four-carat diamond in a window to a lover outside fingering damply in his pocket his ribbon-counter salary.

The greetings of the other cities he had known—their homespun kindliness, their human gamut of rough charity, friendly curses, garrulous curiosity, and easily estimated credulity or indifference. This city of Manhattan gave him no clue; it was walled against him. Like a river of adamant it flowed past him in the streets. Never an eye was turned upon him; no voice spoke to him. His heart yearned for the clap of Pittsburg's sooty hand on his shoulder; for Chicago's menacing but social yawp in his ear; for the pale and eleemosynary stare through the Bostonian eyeglass—even for the precipitate but unmalicious boot-toe of Louisville or St. Louis.

On Broadway Raggles, successful suitor of many cities, stood, bashful, like any country swain. For the first time he experienced the poignant humiliation of being ignored. And when he tried to reduce this brilliant, swiftly changing, ice-cold city to a formula he failed utterly. Poet though he was, it offered him no color similes, no points of comparison, no flaw in its polished facets, no handle by which he could hold it up and view its shape and structure, as he familiarly and often contemptuously had done with other towns. The houses were interminable ramparts loopholed for defense; the people were bright but bloodless spectres passing in sinister and selfish array.

The thing that weighed heaviest on Raggles's soul and clogged his poet's fancy was the spirit of absolute egotism that seemed to saturate the people as toys are saturated with paint. Each one that he considered appeared a monster of abominable and insolent conceit. Humanity was gone from them; they were toddling idols of stone and varnish, worshipping themselves and greedy for though oblivious of worship from their fellow graven images. Frozen, cruel, implacable, impervious, cut to an identical pattern, they hurried on their ways like statues brought by some miracle to motion, while soul and feeling lay unaroused in the reluctant marble.

Gradually Raggles became conscious of certain types. One was an elderly gentleman with a snow-white, short beard, pink, unwrinkled face, and stony, sharp blue eyes, attired in the fashion of a gilded youth, who seemed to personify the city's wealth, ripeness and frigid unconcern. Another type was a woman, tall, beautiful, clear as a steel engraving, goddess-like, calm, clothed like the princesses of old, with eyes as coldly blue as the reflection of sunlight on a glacier. And another was a by-product of this town of marionettes—a broad, swaggering, grim, threateningly sedate fellow, with a jowl as large as a harvested wheat field, the complexion of a baptized infant, and the knuckles of a prize-fighter. This type leaned against cigar signs and viewed the world with frappéd contumely.

A poet is a sensitive creature, and Raggles soon shriveled in the bleak embrace of the undecipherable. The chill, sphinx-like, ironical, illegible, unnatural, ruthless expression of the city left him downcast and bewildered. Had it no heart? Better the woodpile, the scolding of vinegar-faced housewives at back doors, the kindly spleen of bartenders behind provincial free-lunch counters, the amiable truculence of rural constables, the kicks, arrests, and happy-go-lucky chances of the other vulgar, loud, crude cities than this freezing heartlessness.

Raggles summoned his courage and sought alms from the populace. Unheeding, regardless, they passed on without the wink of an eyelash to testify that they were conscious of his existence. And then he said to himself that this fair but pitiless city of Manhattan was without a soul; that its inhabitants were mannikins moved by wires and springs, and that he was alone in a great wilderness.

Raggles started to cross the street. There was a blast, a roar, a hissing and a crash as something struck him and hurled him over and over six yards from where he had been. As he was coming down like the stick of a rocket the earth and all the cities thereof turned to a fractured dream.

Raggles opened his eyes. First an odor made itself known to him—an odor of the earliest spring flowers of Paradise. And then a hand soft as a falling petal touched his brow. Bending over him was the woman clothed like the princess of old, with blue eyes, now soft and humid with human sympathy. Under his head on the pavement were silks and furs. With Raggles's hat in his hand and with his face pinker than ever from a vehement outburst of oratory against reckless driving, stood the elderly gentleman who personified the city's wealth and ripeness. From a near-by café hurried the by-product with the vast jowl and baby complexion, bearing a glass full of crimson fluid that suggested delightful possibilities.

"Drink dis, sport," said the by-product, holding the glass to Raggles's lips.

Hundreds of people huddled around in a moment, their faces wearing the deepest concern. Two flattering and gorgeous policemen got into the circle and pressed back the overplus of Samaritans. An old lady in a black shawl spoke loudly of camphor; a newsboy slipped one of his papers beneath Raggles's elbow, where it lay on the muddy pavement. A brisk young man with a notebook was asking for names.

A bell clanged importantly, and the ambulance cleaned a lane through the crowd. A cool surgeon slipped into the midst of affairs.

"How do you feel, old man?" asked the surgeon, stooping easily to his task. The princess of silks and satins wiped a red drop or two from Raggles's brow with a fragrant cobweb.

"Me?" said Raggles, with a seraphic smile, "I feel fine."

He had found the heart of his new city.

In three days they let him leave his cot for the convalescent ward in the hospital. He had been in there an hour when the attendants heard sounds of conflict. Upon investigation they found that Raggles had assaulted and damaged a brother convalescent—a glowering transient whom a freight train collision had sent in to be patched up.

"What's all this about?" inquired the head nurse.

"He was runnin' down me town," said Raggles.

"What town?" asked the nurse.

"Noo York," said Raggles.

VANITY AND SOME SABLES

WHEN "Kid" Brady was sent to the ropes by Molly McKeever's blue-black eyes he withdrew from the Stovepipe Gang. So much for the power of a colleen's blanderin' tongue and stubborn true-heartedness. If you are a man who read this, may such an influence be sent you before 2 o'clock to-morrow; if you are a woman, may your Pomeranian greet you this morning with a cold nose—a sign of doghealth and your happiness.

The Stovepipe Gang borrowed its name from a sub-district of the city called the "Stovepipe," which is a narrow and natural extension of the familiar district known as "Hell's Kitchen." The "Stovepipe" strip of town runs along Eleventh and Twelfth avenues on the river, and bends a hard and sooty elbow around little, lost, homeless De Witt Clinton park. Consider that a stovepipe is an important factor in any kitchen and the situation is analyzed. The chefs in "Hell's Kitchen" are many, and the "Stovepipe" gang wears the cordon blue.

The members of this unchartered but widely known brotherhood appeared to pass their time on street corners arrayed like the lilies of the conservatory and busy with nail files and penknives. Thus displayed as a guarantee of good faith, they carried on an innocuous conversation in a 200-word vocabulary, to the casual observer as innocent and immaterial as that heard in the clubs seven blocks to the east.

But off exhibition the "Stovepipes" were not mere street corner ornaments addicted to posing and manicuring. Their serious occupation was the separating of citizens from their coin and valuables. Preferably this was done by weird and singular tricks without noise or bloodshed; but whenever the citizen honored by their attentions refused to impoverish himself gracefully, his objections came to be spread finally upon some police station blotter or hospital register.

The police held the "Stovepipe" gang in perpetual suspicion and respect. As the nightingale's liquid note is heard in the deepest shadows, so along the "Stovepipe's" dark and narrow confines the whistle for reserves punctures the dull ear of night. Whenever there was smoke in the "Stovepipe" the tasselled men in blue knew there was a fire in "Hell's Kitchen."

"Kid" Brady promised Molly to be good. "Kid" was the vainest, the strongest, the wariest, and the most successful plotter in the gang. Therefore, the boys were sorry to give him up.

But they witnessed his fall to a virtuous life without protest. For, in the Kitchen it is considered neither unmanly nor improper for a guy to do as his girl advises.

Black her eyes for love's sake, if you will; but it is all-to-the-good business to do a thing when she wants you to do it.

"Turn off the hydrant," said the Kid, one night when Molly, tearful, besought him to amend his ways. "I'm going to cut out the gang. You for mine, and the simple life on the side. I'll tell you, Moll—I'll get work; and in a year we'll get married. I'll do it for you. We'll get a flat and a flute, and a sewing machine and a rubber plant and live as honest as we can."

"Oh, Kid," sighed Molly, wiping the powder off his shoulder with her handkerchief, "I'd rather hear you say that than to own all of New York. And we can be happy on so little!"

The Kid looked down at his speckless cuffs and shining patent leathers with a suspicion of melancholy.

"It'll hurt hardest in the rags department," said he. "I've kind of always liked to rig out swell when I could. You know how I hate cheap things, Moll. This suit set me back sixty-five. Anything in the wearing apparel line has got to be just so, or it's to the misfit parlors for it, for mine. If I work I won't have so much coin to hand over to the little man with the big shears."

"Never mind, Kid. I'll like you just as much in a blue jumper as I would in a red automobile."

Before the Kid had grown large enough to knock out his father he had been compelled to learn the plumber's art. So now back to this honorable and useful profession he returned. But it was as an assistant that he engaged himself; and it is the master plumber and not the assistant, who wears diamonds as large as hailstones and looks contemptuously upon the marble colonnades of Senator Clark's mansion.

Eight months went by as smoothly and surely as though they had "elapsed" on a theatre program. The Kid worked away at his pipes and solder with no symptoms of backsliding. The Stovepipe gang continued its piracy on the high avenues, cracked policeman's heads, held up late travelers, invented new methods of peaceful plundering, copied Fifth Avenue's cut of clothes and neckwear fancies, and comported itself according to its lawless bylaws. But the Kid stood firm and faithful to his Molly, even though the polish was gone from his fingernails and it took him 15 minutes to tie his purple silk ascot so that the worn places would not show.

One evening he brought a mysterious bundle with him to Molly's house.

"Open that, Moll!" he said in his large, quiet way. "It's for you."

Molly's eager fingers tore off the wrappings. She shrieked aloud, and in rushed a sprinkling of little McKeevers, and Ma McKeever, dishwashy, but an undeniable relative of the late Mrs. Eve.

Again Molly shrieked, and something dark and long and sinuous flew and enveloped her neck like an anaconda.

"Russian sables," said the Kid, pridefully, enjoying the sight of Molly's round cheek against the clinging fur. "The real thing. They don't grow anything in Russia too good for you, Moll."

Molly plunged her hands into the muff, over-turned a row of the family infants, and flew to the mirror. Hint for the beauty column. To make bright eyes, rosy cheeks, and a bewitching smile: Recipe—one set Russian sables. Apply.

When they were alone Molly became aware of a small cake of the ice of common sense floating down the full tide of her happiness.

"You're a bird, all right, Kid," she admitted, gratefully. "I never had any furs on before in my life. But ain't Russian sables awful expensive? Seems to me I've heard they were."

"Have I ever chucked any bargain-sale stuff at you, Moll?" asked the Kid, with calm dignity. "Did you ever notice me leaning on the remnant counter or peering in the window of the five-and-ten? Call that scarf $250 and the muff $175 and you won't make any mistake about the price of Russian sables. The swell goods for me. Say, they look fine on you, Moll."

Molly hugged the sables to her bosom in rapture. And then her smile went away little by little, and she looked the Kid straight in the eye sadly and steadily.

He knew what every look of hers meant; and he laughed with a faint flush upon his face.

"Cut it out," he said, with affectionate roughness. "I told you I was done with that. I bought 'em and paid for 'em, all right, with my own money."

"Out of the money you worked for, Kid? Out of $75 a month?"

"Sure. I been saving up."

"Let's see—saved $425 in eight months, Kid?"

"Ah, let up," said the Kid, with some heat. "I had some money when I went to work. Do you think I've been holding 'em up again? I told you I'd quit. They're paid for on the square. Put 'em on and come out for a walk."

Molly calmed her doubts. Sables are soothing. Proud as a queen she went forth in the streets at the Kid's side. In all that region of low-lying streets Russian sables had never been seen before. The word sped, and the doors and windows blossomed with heads eager to see the swell furs Kid Brady had given his girl. All down the street there were "Oh's" and "Ah's" and the reported fabulous sum paid for the sables was passed from lip to lip, increasing as it went. At her right elbow sauntered the Kid with the air of a prince. Work had not diminished his love of pomp and show and his passion for the costly and genuine.

On a corner they saw a group of the Stovepipe Gang loafing, immaculate. They raised their hats to the Kid's girl and went on with their calm, unaccented palaver.

Three blocks behind the admired couple strolled Detective Ransom, of the Central office. Ransom was the only detective on the force who could walk abroad with safety in the Stovepipe district. He was fair dealing and unafraid and went there with the hypothesis that the inhabitants were human. Many liked him, and now and then would tip off to him something that he was looking for.

"What's the excitement down the street?" asked Ransom of a pale youth in a red sweater.

"Dey're out rubberin' at a set of buffalo robes Kid Brady staked his girl to," answered the youth. "Some say he paid $900 for de skins. Dey're swell all right enough."

"I hear Brady has been working at his old trade for nearly a year," said the detective. "He doesn't travel with the gang any more, does he?"

"He's workin', all right," said the red sweater, "but—say, sport, are you trailin' anything in the fur line? A job in a plumbin' shop don't match wid dem skins de Kid's girl's got on."

Ransom overtook the strolling couple on an empty street near the river bank. He touched the Kid's arm from behind.

"Let me see you a moment, Brady," he said, quietly. His eye rested for a second on the long fur scarf thrown stylishly back over Molly's left shoulder. The Kid, with his old-time police-hating frown on his face, stepped a yard or two aside with the detective.

"Did you go to Mrs. Hethcote's on West 7—th Street yesterday to fix a leaky water pipe?" asked Ransom.

"I did," said the Kid. "What of it?"

"The lady's $1,000 set of Russian sables went out of the house about the same time you did. The description fits the ones this lady has on."

"To h—Harlem with you," cried the Kid, angrily. "You know I've cut out that sort of thing, Ransom. I bought them sables yesterday at——"

The Kid stopped short.

"I know you've been working straight lately," said Ransom. "I'll give you every chance. I'll go with you where you say you bought the furs and investigate. The lady can wear 'em along with us and nobody'll be on. That's fair, Brady."

"Come on," agreed the Kid, hotly. And then he stopped suddenly in his tracks and looked with an odd smile at Molly's distressed and anxious face.

"No use," he said, grimly. "They're the Hethcote sables, all right. You'll have to turn 'em over, Moll, but they ain't too good for you if they cost a million."

Molly, with anguish in her face, hung upon the kid's arm.

"Oh, Kiddy, you've broke my heart," she said. "I was so proud of you—and now they'll do you—and where's our happiness gone?"

"Go home," said the Kid, wildly. "Come on, Ransom—take the furs. Let's get away from here. Wait a minute—I've a good mind to—— No, I'll be d— if I can do it—run along, Moll—I'm ready, Ransom."

Around the corner of a lumber-yard came Policeman Kohen on his way to his beat along the river. The detective signed to him for assistance. Kohen joined the group. Ransom explained.

"Sure," said Kohen. "I hear about those saples dat vas stole. You say you have dem here?"

Policeman Kohen took the end of Molly's late scarf in his hands and looked at it closely.

"Once," he said, "I sold furs in Sixth Avenue. Yes, dese are saples. Dey came from Alaska. Dis scarf is vort $12 and dis muff——"

"Biff!" came the palm of the Kid's powerful hand upon the policeman's mouth.

Kohen staggered and rallied. Molly screamed. The detective threw himself upon Brady and with Kohen's aid got the nippers on his wrist.

"The scarf is vort $12 and the muff is vort $9," persisted the policeman. "Vot is dis talk about $1,000 saples?"

The Kid sat upon a pile of lumber and his face turned dark red.

"Correct, Solomonski!" he declared, viciously. "I paid $21.50 for the set. I'd rather have got six months and not have told it. Me, the swell guy that wouldn't look at anything cheap! I'm a plain bluffer. Moll—my salary couldn't spell sables in Russian."

Molly cast herself upon his neck.

"What do I care for all the sables and money in the world," she cried. "It's my Kiddy I want. Oh, you dear, stuck-up, crazy blockhead!"

"You can take dose nippers off," said Kohen to the detective. "Before I leaf de station de report come in dat de lady vind her saples—hanging in her wardrobe. Young man, I excuse you dat punch in my vace—dis von time."

Ransom handed Molly her furs. Her eyes were smiling upon the Kid. She wound the scarf and threw the end over her left shoulder with a duchess's grace.

"A gouple of young vools," said Policeman Kohen to Ransom; "come on away."

THE SOCIAL TRIANGLE

At the stroke of six Ikey Snigglefritz laid down his goose. Ikey was a tailor's apprentice. Are there tailors' apprentices nowadays?

At any rate, Ikey toiled and snipped and basted and pressed and patched and sponged all day in the steamy fetor of a tailor-shop. But when work was done Ikey hitched his wagon to such stars as his firmament let shine.

It was Saturday night, and the boss laid twelve begrimed and begrudged dollars in his hand. Ikey dabbled discreetly in water, donned coat, hat and collar with its frazzled tie, and chalcedony pin, and set forth in pursuit of his ideals.

For each of us, when our day's work is done, must seek our ideal, whether it be love or pinochle or lobster à la Newburg, or the sweet silence of the musty bookshelves.

Behold Ikey as he ambles up the street beneath the roaring "El" between the rows of reeking sweatshops. Pallid, stooping, insignificant, squalid, doomed to exist forever in penury of body and mind, yet, as he swings his cheap cane and projects the noisome inhalations from his cigarette you perceive that he nurtures in his narrow bosom the bacillus of society.

Ikey's legs carried him to and into that famous place of entertainment known as the Café Maginnis—famous because it was the rendezvous of Billy McMahan, the greatest man, the most wonderful man, Ikey thought, that the world had ever produced.

Billy McMahan was the district leader. Upon him the Tiger purred, and his hand held manna to scatter. Now, as Ikey entered, McMahan stood, flushed and triumphant and mighty, the centre of a huzzaing concourse of his lieutenants and constituents. It seems there had been an election; a signal victory had been won; the city had been swept back into line by a resistless besom of ballots.

Ikey slunk along the bar and gazed, breath-quickened, at his idol.

How magnificent was Billy McMahan, with his great, smooth, laughing face;

his gray eye, shrewd as a chicken hawk's; his diamond ring, his voice like a bugle call, his prince's air, his plump and active roll of money, his clarion call to friend and comrade—oh, what a king of men he was! How he obscured his lieutenants, though they themselves loomed large and serious, blue of chin and important of mien, with hands buried deep in the pockets of their short over-coats! But Billy—oh, what small avail are words to paint for you his glory as seen by Ikey Snigglefritz!

The Café Maginnis rang to the note of victory. The white-coated bartenders threw themselves featfully upon bottle, cork and glass. From a score of clear Havanas the air received its paradox of clouds. The leal and the hopeful shook Billy McMahan's hand. And there was born suddenly in the worshipful soul of Ikey Snigglefritz an audacious, thrilling impulse.

He stepped forward into the little cleared space in which majesty moved, and held out his hand.

Billy McMahan grasped it unhesitatingly, shook it and smiled.

Made mad now by the gods who were about to destroy him, Ikey threw away his scabbard and charged upon Olympus.

"Have a drink with me, Billy," he said familiarly, "you and your friends?"

"Don't mind if I do, old man," said the great leader, "just to keep the ball rolling."

The last spark of Ikey's reason fled.

"Wine," he called to the bartender, waving a trembling hand.

The corks of three bottles were drawn; the champagne bubbled in the long row of glasses set upon the bar. Billy McMahan took his and nodded, with his beam-ing smile, at Ikey. The lieutenants and satellites took theirs and growled "Here's to you." Ikey took his nectar in delirium. All drank.

Ikey threw his week's wages in a crumpled roll upon the bar.

"C'rect," said the bartender, smoothing the twelve one-dollar notes. The crowd surged around Billy McMahan again. Some one was telling how Bran-nigan fixed 'em over in the Eleventh. Ikey leaned against the bar a while, and then went out.

He went down Hester street and up Chrystie, and down Delancey to where he lived. And there his women folk, a bibulous mother and three dingy sisters, pounced upon him for his wages. And at his confession they shrieked and ob-jurgated him in the pithy rhetoric of the locality.

But even as they plucked at him and struck him Ikey remained in his ecstatic trance of joy. His head was in the clouds; the star was drawing his wagon. Compared with what he had achieved the loss of wages and the bray of women's tongues were slight affairs.

He had shaken the hand of Billy McMahan.

*　　*　　*　　*　　*　　*　　*　　*　　*　　*　　*　　*

Billy McMahan had a wife, and upon her visiting cards was engraved the name "Mrs. William Darragh McMahan." And there was a certain vexation attendant upon these cards; for, small as they were, there were houses in which they could not be inserted. Billy McMahan was a dictator in politics, a four-walled tower in business, a mogul, dread, loved and obeyed among his own people. He was growing rich; the daily papers had a dozen men on his trail to chronicle his every word of wisdom; he had been honored in caricature holding the Tiger cringing in leash.

But the heart of Billy was sometimes sore within him. There was a race of men from which he stood apart but that he viewed with the eye of Moses looking over into the promised land. He, too, had ideals, even as had Ikey Snigglefritz; and sometimes, hopeless of attaining them, his own solid success was as dust and ashes in his mouth. And Mrs. William Darragh McMahan wore a look of discontent upon her plump but pretty face, and the very rustle of her silks seemed a sigh.

There was a brave and conspicuous assemblage in the dining saloon of a noted hostelry where Fashion loves to display her charms. At one table sat Billy Mc-Mahan and his wife. Mostly silent they were, but the accessories they enjoyed little needed the indorsement of speech. Mrs. McMahan's diamonds were outshone by few in the room. The waiter bore the costliest brands of wine to their table. In evening dress, with an expression of gloom upon his smooth and massive countenance, you would look in vain for a more striking figure than Billy's.

Four tables away sat alone a tall, slender man, about thirty, with thoughtful, melancholy eyes, a Van Dyke beard and peculiarly white, thin hands. He was dining on filet mignon, dry toast and apollinaris. That man was Cortlandt Van Duyckink, a man worth eighty millions, who inherited and held a sacred seat in the exclusive inner circle of society.

Billy McMahan spoke to no one around him, because he knew no one. Van Duyckink kept his eyes on his plate because he knew that every one present was hungry to catch his. He could bestow knighthood and prestige by a nod, and he was chary of creating a too extensive nobility.

And then Billy McMahan conceived and accomplished the most startling and audacious act of his life. He rose deliberately and walked over to Cortlandt Van Duyckink's table and held out his hand.

"Say, Mr. Van Duyckink," he said, "I've heard you was talking about starting some reforms among the poor people down in my district. I'm McMahan, you know. Say, now, if that's straight I'll do all I can to help you. And what I says goes in that neck of the woods, don't it? Oh, says, I rather guess it does."

Van Duyckink's rather somber eyes lighted up. He rose to his lank height and grasped Billy McMahan's hand.

"Thank you, Mr. McMahan," he said, in his deep, serious tones. "I have been thinking of doing some work of that sort. I shall be glad of your assistance. It pleases me to have become acquainted with you."

Billy walked back to his seat. His shoulder was tingling from the accolade bestowed by royalty. A hundred eyes were now turned upon him in envy and new admiration. Mrs. William Darragh McMahan trembled with ecstasy, so that her diamonds smote the eye almost with pain. And now it was apparent that at many tables there were those who suddenly remembered that they enjoyed Mr. McMahan's acquaintance. He saw smiles and bows about him. He became enveloped in the aura of dizzy greatness. His campaign coolness deserted him.

"Wine for that gang!" he commanded the waiter, pointing with his finger. "Wine over there. Wine to those three gents by that green bush. Tell 'em it's on me. D——n it! Wine for everybody!"

The waiter ventured to whisper that it was perhaps inexpedient to carry out the order, in consideration of the dignity of the house and its custom.

"All right," said Billy, "if it's against the rules. I wonder if 'twould do to send my friend Van Duyckink a bottle? No? Well, it'll flow all right at the caffy to-night, just the same. It'll be rubber boots for anybody who comes in there any time up to 2 A. M."

Billy McMahan was happy.

He had shaken the hand of Cortlandt Van Duyckink.

* * * * * * * * * * *

The big pale-gray auto with its shining metal work looked out of place moving slowly among the push carts and trash-heaps on the lower east side. So did Cortlandt Van Duyckink, with his aristocratic face and white, thin hands, as he steered carefully between the groups of ragged, scurrying youngsters in the streets. And so did Miss Constance Schuyler, with her dim, ascetic beauty, seated at his side.

"Oh, Cortlandt," she breathed, "isn't it sad that human beings have to live in such wretchedness and poverty? And you—how noble it is of you to think of them, to give your time and money to improve their condition!"

Van Duyckink turned his solemn eyes upon her.

"It is little," he said, sadly, "that I can do. The question is a large one, and belongs to society. But even individual effort is not thrown away. Look, Constance! On this street I have arranged to build soup kitchens, where no one who is hungry will be turned away. And down this other street are the old buildings that I shall cause to be torn down and there erect others in place of those death-traps of fire and disease."

Down Delancey slowly crept the pale-gray auto. Away from it toddled coveys of wondering, tangle-haired, barefooted, unwashed children. It stopped before a crazy brick structure, foul and awry.

Van Duyckink alighted to examine at a better perspective one of the leaning walls. Down the steps of the building came a young man who seemed to epitomize its degradation, squalor and infelicity—a narrow-chested, pale unsavory young man, puffing at a cigarette.

Obeying a sudden impulse, Van Duyckink stepped out and warmly grasped the hand of what seemed to him a living rebuke.

"I want to know you people," he said, sincerely. "I am going to help you as much as I can. We shall be friends."

As the auto crept carefully away Cortlandt Van Duyckink felt an unaccustomed glow about his heart. He was near to being a happy man.

He had shaken the hand of Ikey Snigglefritz.

THE PURPLE DRESS

WE are to consider the shade known as purple. It is a color justly in repute among the sons and daughters of man. Emperors claim it for their especial dye. Good fellows everywhere seek to bring their noses to the genial hue that follows the commingling of the red and blue. We say of princes that they are born to the purple; and no doubt they are, for the colic tinges their faces with the royal tint equally with the snub-nosed countenance of a woodchopper's brat. All women love it—when it is the fashion.

And now purple is being worn. You notice it on the streets. Of course other colors are quite stylish as well—in fact, I saw a lovely thing the other day in olive-green albatross, with a triple-lapped flounce skirt trimmed with insert squares of silk, and a draped fichu of lace opening over a shirred vest and double puff sleeves with a lace band holding two gathered frills—but you see lots of purple too. Oh, yes, you do; just take a walk down Twenty-third Street any afternoon.

Therefore Maida—the girl with the big brown eyes and cinnamon-colored hair in the Bee-Hive Store—said to Grace—the girl with the rhinestone brooch and peppermint-pepsin flavor to her speech—"I'm going to have a purple dress—a tailor-made purple dress—for Thanksgiving."

"Oh, are you," said Grace, putting away some 7½ gloves into the 6¾ box.

"Well, it's me for red. You see more red on Fifth Avenue. And the men all seem to like it."

"I like purple best," said Maida. "And old Schlegel has promised to make it for $8. It's going to be lovely. I'm going to have a plaited skirt and a blouse coat trimmed with a band of galloon under a white cloth collar with two rows of——"

"Sly boots!" said Grace with an educated wink.

"—soutache braid over a surpliced white vest; and a plaited basque and——"

"Sly boots—sly boots!" repeated Grace.

"—plaited gigot sleeves with a drawn velvet ribbon over an inside cuff. What do you mean by saying that?"

"You think Mr. Ramsay likes purple. I heard him say yesterday he thought some of the dark shades of red were stunning."

"I don't care," said Maida. "I prefer purple, and them that don't like it can just take the other side of the street."

Which suggests the thought that after all, the followers of purple may be subject to slight delusions. Danger is near when a maiden thinks she can wear purple regardless of complexions and opinions; and when emperors think their purple robes will wear forever.

Maida had saved $18 after eight months of economy; and this had bought the goods for the purple dress and paid Schlegel $4 on the making of it. On the day before Thanksgiving she would have just enough to pay the remaining $4. And then for a holiday in a new dress—can earth offer anything more enchanting?

Old Bachman, the proprietor of the Bee-Hive Store, always gave a Thanksgiving dinner to his employees. On every one of the subsequent 364 days, excusing Sundays, he would remind them of the joys of the past banquet and the hopes of the coming ones, thus inciting them to increased enthusiasm in work. The dinner was given in the store on one of the long tables in the middle of the room. They tacked wrapping paper over the front windows; and the turkeys and other good things were brought in the back way from the restaurant on the corner. You will perceive that the Bee-Hive was not a fashionable department store, with escalators and pompadours. It was almost small enough to be called an emporium; and you could actually go in there and get waited on and walk out again. And always at the Thanksgiving dinners Mr. Ramsay——

Oh, bother! I should have mentioned Mr. Ramsay first of all. He is more important than purple or green, or even the red cranberry sauce. Mr. Ramsay was the head clerk; and as far as I am concerned I am for him. He never pinched the girls' arms when he passed them in dark corners of the store; and when he told them stories when business was dull and the girls giggled and said: "Oh, pshaw!" it wasn't G. Bernard they meant at all. Besides being a gentleman, Mr. Ramsay was queer and original in other ways. He was a health crank, and believed that people should never eat anything that was good for them. He was violently opposed to anybody being comfortable, and coming in out of snow storms, or wearing overshoes, or taking medicine, or coddling themselves in any way. Every one of the ten girls in the store had little pork-chop-and-fried-onion dreams every night of becoming Mrs. Ramsay. For, next year old Bachman was going to take him in for a partner. And each one of them knew that if she should catch him she would knock those cranky health notions of his sky high before the wedding cake indigestion was over.

Mr. Ramsay was master of ceremonies at the dinners. Always they had two Italians in to play a violin and harp and had a little dance in the store.

And here were two dresses being conceived to charm Ramsay—one purple and the other red. Of course, the other eight girls were going to have dresses too, but they didn't count. Very likely they'd wear some shirt-waist-and-black-skirt-affairs—nothing as resplendent as purple or red.

Grace had saved her money, too. She was going to buy her dress ready-made. Oh, what's the use of bothering with a tailor—when you've got a figger it's easy to get a fit—the ready-made are intended for a perfect figger—except I have to have 'em all taken in at the waist—the average figger is so large waisted.

The night before Thanksgiving came. Maida hurried home, keen and bright with the thoughts of the blessed morrow. Her thoughts were of purple, but they were white themselves—the joyous enthusiasm of the young for the pleasures that youth must have or wither. She knew purple would become her, and—for the thousandth time she tried to assure herself that it was purple Mr. Ramsay said he liked and not red. She was going home first to get the $4 wrapped in a piece of tissue paper in the bottom drawer of her dresser, and then she was going to pay Schlegel and take the dress home herself.

Grace lived in the same house. She occupied the hall room above Maida's.

At home Maida found clamor and confusion. The landlady's tongue clattering sourly in the halls like a churn dasher dabbing in buttermilk. And then Grace come down to her room crying with eyes as red as any dress.

"She says I've got to get out," said Grace. "The old beast. Because I owe her $4. She's put my trunk in the hall and locked the door. I can't go anywhere else. I haven't got a cent of money."

"You had some yesterday," said Maida.

"I paid it on my dress," said Grace. "I thought she'd wait till next week for the rent."

Sniffle, sniffle, sob, sniffle.

Out came—out it had to come—Maida's $4.

"You blessed darling," cried Grace, now a rainbow instead of sunset. "I'll pay the mean old thing and then I'm going to try on my dress. I think it's heavenly. Come up and look at it. I'll pay the money back, a dollar a week—honest I will."

Thanksgiving.

The dinner was to be at noon. At a quarter to twelve Grace switched into Maida's room. Yes, she looked charming. Red was her color. Maida sat by the window in her old cheviot skirt and blue waist darning a st——. Oh, doing fancy work.

"Why, goodness me! ain't you dressed yet?" shrilled the red one. "How does it fit in the back? Don't you think these velvet tabs look awful swell? Why ain't you dressed, Maida?"

"My dress didn't get finished in time," said Maida. "I'm not going to the dinner."

"That's too bad. Why, I'm awfully sorry, Maida. Why don't you put on anything and come along—it's just the store folks, you know, and they won't mind."

"I was set on my purple," said Maida. "If I can't have it I won't go at all. Don't bother about me. Run along or you'll be late. You look awful nice in red."

At her window Maida sat through the long morning and past the time of the dinner at the store. In her mind she could hear the girls shrieking over a pull-bone, could hear old Bachman's roar over his own deeply-concealed jokes, could see the diamonds of fat Mrs. Bachman, who came to the store only on Thanksgiving days, could see Mr. Ramsay moving about, alert, kindly, looking to the comfort of all.

At four in the afternoon, with an expressionless face and a lifeless air she slowly made her way to Schlegel's shop and told him she could not pay the $4 due on the dress.

"Gott!" cried Schlegel, angrily. "For what do you look so glum? Take him away. He is ready. Pay me some time. Haf I not seen you pass mine shop every day in two years? If I make clothes is it that I do not know how to read beoples because? You will pay me some time when you can. Take him away. He is made goot; and if you look bretty in him all right. So. Pay me when you can."

Maida breathed a millionth part of the thanks in her heart, and hurried away with her dress. As she left the shop a smart dash of rain struck upon her face. She smiled and did not feel it.

Ladies who shop in carriages, you do not understand. Girls whose wardrobes are charged to the old man's account, you cannot begin to comprehend—you could not understand why Maida did not feel the cold dash of the Thanksgiving rain.

At five o'clock she went out upon the street wearing her purple dress. The rain had increased, and it beat down upon her in a steady, wind-blown pour. People were scurrying home and to cars with close-held umbrellas and tight buttoned raincoats. Many of them turned their heads to marvel at this beautiful, serene, happy-eyed girl in the purple dress walking through the storm as though she were strolling in a garden under summer skies.

I say you do not understand it, ladies of the full purse and varied wardrobe. You do not know what it is to live with a perpetual longing for pretty things—to starve eight months in order to bring a purple dress and a holiday together. What difference if it rained, hailed, blew, snowed, cycloned?

Maida had no umbrella nor overshoes. She had her purple dress and she walked abroad. Let the elements do their worst. A starved heart must have one crumb during a year. The rain ran down and dripped from her fingers.

Some one turned a corner and blocked her way. She looked up into Mr. Ramsay's eyes, sparkling with admiration and interest.

"Why, Miss Maida," said he, "you look simply magnificent in your new dress. I was greatly disappointed not to see you at our dinner. And of all the girls I ever knew, you show the greatest sense and intelligence. There is nothing more healthful and invigorating than braving the weather as you are doing. May I walk with you?"

And Maida blushed and sneezed.

THE FOREIGN POLICY OF COMPANY 99

JOHN BYRNES, hose-cart driver of Engine Company No. 99, was afflicted with what his comrades called Japanitis.

Byrnes had a war map spread permanently upon a table in the second story of the engine-house, and he could explain to you at any hour of the day or night the exact positions, conditions and intentions of both the Russian and Japanese armies. He had little clusters of pins stuck in the map which represented the opposing forces, and these he moved about from day to day in conformity with the war news in the daily papers.

Wherever the Japs won a victory John Byrnes would shift his pins, and then he would execute a war dance of delight, and the other firemen would hear him yell: "Go it, you blamed little, sawed-off, huckleberry-eyed, monkey-faced hot tamales! Eat 'em up, you little sleight-o'-hand, bow-legged bull terriers—give 'em another of them Yalu looloos, and you'll eat rice in St. Petersburg. Talk about your Russians—say, wouldn't they give you painsky when it comes to a scrapovitch?"

Not even on the fair island of Nippon was there a more enthusiastic champion of the Mikado's men. Supporters of the Russian cause did well to keep clear of Engine-House No. 99.

Sometimes all thoughts of the Japs left John Byrnes's head. That was when the alarm of fire had sounded and he was strapped in his driver's seat on the swaying cart, guiding Erebus and Joe, the finest team in the whole department— according to the crew of 99.

Of all the codes adopted by man for regulating his actions toward his fellow-mortals, the greatest are these—the code of King Arthur's Knights of the Round Table, the Constitution of the United States and the unwritten rules of the New York Fire Department. The Round Table methods are no longer practicable since the invention of street cars and breach-of-promise suits, and our Constitution is being found more and more unconstitutional every day, so the code of our firemen must be considered in the lead, with the Golden Rule and Jeffries's new punch trying for place and show.

The Constitution says that one man is as good as another; but the Fire Department says he is better. This is a too generous theory, but the law will not allow itself to be construed otherwise. All of which comes perilously near to being a paradox, and commends itself to the attention of the S. P. C. A.

One of the transatlantic liners dumped out at Ellis Island a lump of protozoa which was expected to evolve into an American citizen. A steward kicked him down the gangway, a doctor pounced upon his eyes like a raven, seeking for trachoma or ophthalmia; he was hustled ashore and ejected into the city in the name of Liberty—perhaps, theoretically, thus inoculating against kingocracy with a drop of its own virus. This hypodermic injection of Europeanism wandered happily into the veins of the city with the broad grin of a pleased child. It was not burdened with baggage, cares or ambitions. Its body was lithely built and clothed in a sort of foreign fustian; its face was brightly vacant, with a small, flat nose, and was mostly covered by a thick, ragged, curling beard like the coat of a spaniel. In the pocket of the imported Thing were a few coins—denarii—scudi—kopecks—pfennigs—pilasters—whatever the financial nomenclature of his unknown country may have been.

Prattling to himself, always broadly grinning, pleased by the roar, and movement of the barbarous city into which the steamship cut-rates had shunted him, the alien strayed away from the sea, which he hated, as far as the district covered by Engine Company No. 99. Light as a cork, he was kept bobbing along by the human tide, the crudest atom in all the silt of the stream that emptied into the reservoir of Liberty.

While crossing Third avenue he slowed his steps, enchanted by the thunder of the elevated trains above him and the soothing crash of the wheels on the cobbles. And then there was a new, delightful chord in the uproar—the musical clanging of a gong and a great shining juggernaut belching fire and smoke, that people were hurrying to see.

This beautiful thing, entrancing to the eye, dashed past, and the protoplasmic immigrant stepped into the wake of it with his broad, enraptured, uncomprehending grin. And so stepping, stepped into the path of No. 99's flying hose-cart, with John Byrnes gripping, with arms of steel, the reins over the plunging backs of Erebus and Joe.

The unwritten constitutional code of the fireman has no exceptions or amendments. It is a simple thing—as simple as the rule of three. There was the heedless unit in the right of way; there was the hose-cart, and the iron pillar of the elevated railroad.

John Byrnes swung all his weight and muscle on the left rein. The team and cart swerved that way and crashed like a torpedo into the pillar. The men on the cart went flying like skittles. The driver's strap burst, the pillar rang with the shock, and John Byrnes fell on the car track with a broken shoulder twenty feet away, while Erebus—beautiful, raven-black, best-loved Erebus—lay whickering in his harness with a broken leg.

In consideration for the feelings of Engine Company No. 99 the details will be lightly touched. The company does not like to be reminded of that day. There was a great crowd, and hurry calls were sent in; and while the ambulance gong was clearing the way the men of No. 99 heard the crack of the S. P. C. A. agent's pistol, and turned their heads away, not daring to look toward Erebus again.

When the firemen got back to the engine-house they found that one of them was dragging by the collar the cause of their desolation and grief. They set it in the middle of the floor and gathered grimly about it. Through its whiskers the calamitous object chattered effervescently and waved its hands.

"Sounds like a seidlitz powder," said Mike Dowling, disgustedly, "and it makes me sicker than one. Call that a man!—that hoss was worth a steamer full of such two-legged animals. It's a immigrant—that's what it is."

"Look at the doctor's chalk mark on its coat," said Reilly, the desk man. "It's just landed. It must be a kind of a Dago or a Hun or one of them Finns, I guess. That's the kind of truck that Europe unloads onto us."

"Think of a thing like that getting in the way and laying John up in hospital and spoiling the best fire team in the city," groaned another fireman. "It ought to be taken down to the dock and drowned."

"Somebody go around and get Sloviski," suggested the engine driver, "and let's see what nation is responsible for this conglomeration of hair and head noises."

Sloviski kept a delicatessen store around the corner on Third Avenue, and was reputed to be a linguist.

One of the men fetched him—a fat, cringing man, with a discursive eye and the odors of many kinds of meats upon him.

"Take a whirl at this importation with your jaw-breakers, Sloviski," requested Mike Dowling. "We can't quite figure out whether he's from the Hackensack bottoms or Hongkong-on-the-Ganges."

Sloviski addressed the stranger in several dialects, that ranged in rhythm and cadence from the sounds produced by a tonsillitis gargle to the opening of a can of tomatoes with a pair of scissors. The immigrant replied in accents resembling the uncorking of a bottle of ginger ale.

"I have you his name," reported Sloviski. "You shall not pronounce it. Writing of it in paper is better." They gave him paper, and he wrote, "Demetre Svangvsk."

"Looks like short hand," said the desk man.

"He speaks some language," continued the interpreter, wiping his forehead, "of Austria and mixed with a little Turkish. And, den, he have some Magyar words and a Polish or two, and many like the Roumanian, but not without talk of one tribe in Bessarabia. I do not quite understand."

"Would you call him a Dago or a Polocker, or what?" asked Mike, frowning at the polyglot description.

"He is a"—answered Sloviski—"he is a—I dink he come from—I dink he is a fool," he concluded, impatient at his linguistic failure, "and if you pleases I will go back at mine delicatessen."

"Whatever he is, he's a bird," said Mike Dowling; "and you want to watch him fly."

Taking by the wing the alien fowl that had fluttered into the nest of Liberty, Mike led him to the door of the engine-house and bestowed upon him a kick hearty enough to convey the entire animus of Company 99. Demetre Svangvsk hustled away down the sidewalk, turning once to show his ineradicable grin to the aggrieved firemen.

In three weeks John Byrnes was back at his post from the hospital. With great gusto he proceeded to bring his war map up to date. "My money on the Japs every time," he declared. "Why, look at them Russians—they're nothing but wolves. Wipe 'em out, I say—and the little old jiu-jitsu gang are just the cherry blossoms to do the trick, and don't you forget it!"

The second day after Byrnes's reappearance came Demetre Svangvsk, the un-identified, to the engine-house, with a broader grin than ever. He managed to convey the idea that he wished to congratulate the hose-cart driver on his recovery and to apologize for having caused the accident. This he accomplished by so many extravagant gestures and explosive noises that the company was diverted for half an hour. Then they kicked him out again, and on the next day he came back grinning. How or where he lived no one knew. And then John Byrnes's nine-year-old son, Chris, who brought him convalescent delicacies from home to eat, took a fancy to Svangvsk, and they allowed him to loaf about the door of the engine-house occasionally.

One afternoon the big drab automobile of the Deputy Fire Commissioner buzzed up to the door of No. 99 and the Deputy stepped inside for an informal inspection. Then men kicked Svangvsk out a little harder than usual and proudly escorted the Deputy around 99, in which everything shone like my lady's mirror.

The Deputy respected the sorrow of the company concerning the loss of Erebus, and he had come to promise it another mate for Joe that would do him credit. So they let Joe out of his stall and showed the Deputy how deserving he was of the finest mate that could be in horsedom.

While they were circling around Joe confabbing, Chris climbed into the Deputy's auto and threw the power full on. The men heard a monster puffing and a shriek from the lad, and sprang out too late. The big auto shot away, luckily taking a straight course down the street. The boy knew nothing of its machinery; he sat clutching the cushions and howling. With the power on nothing could have stopped that auto except a brick house, and there was nothing for Chris to gain by such a stoppage.

Demetre Svangvsk was just coming in again with a grin for another kick when Chris played his merry little prank. While the others sprang for the door Demetre sprang for Joe. He glided upon the horse's bare back like a snake and shouted something at him like the crack of a dozen whips. One of the firemen afterward swore that Joe answered him back in the same language. Ten seconds after the auto started the big horse was eating up the asphalt behind it like a strip of macaroni.

Some people two blocks and a half away saw the rescue. They said that the auto was nothing but a drab noise with a black speck in the middle of it for Chris, when a big bay horse with a lizard lying on its back cantered up along-side of it, and the lizard reached over and picked the black speck out of the noise.

Only fifteen minutes after Svangvsk's last kicking at the hands—or rather the feet—of Engine Company No. 99 he rode Joe back through the door with the boy safe, but acutely conscious of the licking he was going to receive.

Svangvsk slipped to the floor, leaned his head against Joe's and made a noise like a clucking hen. Joe nodded and whistled loudly through his nostrils, putting to shame the knowledge of Sloviski, of the delicatessen.

John Byrnes walked up to Svangvsk, who grinned, expecting to be kicked. Byrnes gripped the outlander so strongly by the hand that Demetre grinned any-how, conceiving it to be a new form of punishment.

"The heathen rides like a Cossack," remarked a fireman who had seen a Wild West show—"they're the greatest riders in the world."

The word seemed to electrify Svangvsk. He grinned wider than ever.

"Yas—yas—me Cossack," he spluttered, striking his chest.

"Cossack!" repeated John Byrnes, thoughtfully, "ain't that a kind of a Russian?"

"They're one of the Russian tribes, sure," said the desk man, who read books between fire alarms.

Just then Alderman Foley, who was on his way home and did not know of the runaway, stopped at the door of the engine-house and called to Byrnes.

"Hello there, Jimmy, me boy—how's the war coming along? Japs still got the bear on the trot, have they?"

"Oh, I don't know," said John Byrnes, argumentatively, "them Japs haven't got any walkover. You wait till Kuropatkin gets a good whack at 'em and they won't be knee-high to a puddle-ducksky."

THE LOST BLEND

SINCE the bar has been blessed by the clergy, and cocktails open the dinners of the elect, one may speak of the saloon. Teetotalers need not listen, if they choose; there is always the slot restaurant, where a dime dropped into the cold bouillon aperture will bring forth a dry Martini.

Con Lantry worked on the sober side of the bar in Kenealy's café. You and I stood, one-legged like geese, on the other side and went into voluntary liquidation with our week's wages. Opposite danced Con, clean, temperate, clear-headed, polite, white-jacketed, punctual, trustworthy, young, responsible, and took our money.

The saloon (whether blessed or cursed) stood in one of those little "places" which are parallelograms instead of streets, and inhabited by laundries, decayed Knickerbocker families and Bohemians who have nothing to do with either.

Over the café lived Kenealy and his family. His daughter Katherine had eyes of dark Irish—but why should you be told? Be content with your Geraldine or your Eliza Ann. For Con dreamed of her; and when she called softly at the foot of the back stairs for the pitcher of beer for dinner, his heart went up and down like a milk punch in the shaker. Orderly and fit are the rules of Romance; and if you hurl the last shilling of your fortune upon the bar for whiskey, the bartender shall take it, and marry his boss's daughter, and good will grow out of it.

But not so Con. For in the presence of woman he was tongue-tied and scarlet. He who would quell with his eye the sonorous youth whom the claret punch made loquacious, or smash with lemon squeezer the obstreperous, or hurl gutterward the cantankerous without a wrinkle coming to his white iawn tie, when he stood before a woman he was voiceless, incoherent, stuttering, buried beneath a hot avalanche of bashfulness and misery. What then was he before Katherine? A trembler, with no word to say for himself, a stone without blarney, the dumbest lover that ever babbled of the weather in the presence of his divinity.

There came to Kenealy's two sunburned men, Riley and McQuirk. They had conference with Kenealy; and then they took possession of a back room which they filled with bottles and siphons and jugs and druggist's measuring glasses. All the appurtenances and liquids of a saloon were there, but they dispensed

no drinks. All day long the two sweltered in there, pouring and mixing unknown brews and decoctions from the liquors in their store. Riley had the
education, and he figured on reams of paper, reducing gallons to ounces and
quarts to fluid drams. McQuirk, a morose man with a red eye, dashed each
unsuccessful completed mixture into the waste pipe with curses gentle, husky
and deep. They labored heavily and untiringly to achieve some mysterious solution like two alchemists striving to resolve gold from the elements.

Into this back room one evening when his watch was done sauntered Con. His
professional curiosity had been stirred by these occult bartenders at whose bar
none drank, and who daily drew upon Kenealy's store of liquors to follow their
consuming and fruitless experiments.

Down the back stairs came Katherine with her smile like sunrise on Gweebarra
Bay.

"Good evening, Mr. Lantry," says she. "And what is the news to-day, if you
please?"

"It looks like r-rain," stammered the shy one, backing to the wall.

"It couldn't do better," said Katherine. "I'm thinking there's nothing the
worse off for a little water." In the back room Riley and McQuirk toiled like
bearded witches over their strange compounds. From fifty bottles they drew
liquids carefully measured after Riley's figures, and shook the whole together
in a great glass vessel. Then McQuirk would dash it out, with gloomy profanity,
and they would begin again.

"Sit down," said Riley to Con, "and I'll tell you.

"Last summer me and Tim concludes that an American bar in this nation of Nicaragua would pay. There was a town on the coast where there's nothing to eat
but quinine and nothing to drink but rum. The natives and foreigners lay down
with chills and get up with fevers; and a good mixed drink is nature's remedy
for all such tropical inconveniences.

"So we lays in a fine stock of wet goods in New York, and bar fixtures and
glassware, and we sails for that Santa Palma town on a lime steamer. On the
way me and Tim sees flying fish and play seven-up with the captain and steward,
and already begins to feel like the high-ball kings of the tropics of Capricorn.

"When we gets in five hours of the country that we was going to introduce
to long drinks and short change the captain calls us over to the starboard bin-
nacle and recollects a few things.

"'I forgot to tell you, boys,' says he, 'that Nicaragua slapped an import duty
of 48 per cent. ad valorem on all bottled goods last month. The President took
a bottle of Cincinnati hair tonic by mistake for tabasco sauce, and he's getting
even. Barrelled goods is free.'

"'Sorry you didn't mention it sooner,' says we. And we bought two forty-two
gallon casks from the captain, and opened every bottle we had and dumped the
stuff altogether in the casks. That 48 per cent. would have ruined us; so we
took the chances on making that $1,200 cocktail rather than throw the stuff
away.

"Well, when we landed we tapped one of the barrels. The mixture was something heartrending. It was the color of a plate of Bowery pea soup, and it
tasted like one of those coffee substitutes your aunt makes you take for the heart
trouble you get by picking losers. We gave a nigger four fingers of it to try
it, and he lay under a cocoanut tree three days beating the sand with his heels
and refused to sign a testimonial.

"But the other barrel! Say, bartender, did you ever put on a straw hat with
a yellow band around it and go up in a balloon with a pretty girl with $8,000,000
in your pocket all at the same time? That's what thirty drops of it would
make you feel like. With two fingers of it inside you you would bury your face
in your hands and cry because there wasn't anything more worth while around

for you to lick than little Jim Jeffries. Yes, sir, that stuff in that second barrel was distilled elixir of battle, money and high life. It was the color of gold and as clear as glass, and it shone after dark like the sunshine was still in it. A thousand years from now you'll get a drink like that across the bar.

"Well, we started up business with that one line of drinks, and it was enough. The piebald gentry of that country stuck to it like a hive of bees. If that barrel had lasted that country would have become the greatest on earth. When we opened up of mornings we had a line of generals and colonels and ex-presidents and revolutionists a block long waiting to be served. We started in at 50 cents silver a drink. The last ten gallons went easy at $5 a gulp. It was wonderful stuff. It gave a man courage and ambition and nerve to do anything; at the same time he didn't care whether his money was tainted or fresh from the Ice Trust. When that barrel was half gone Nicaragua had repudiated the National debt, removed the duty on cigarettes and was about to declare war on the United States and England.

"'Twas by accident we discovered this king of drinks, and 'twill be by good luck if we strike it again. For ten months we've been trying. Small lots at a time, we've mixed barrels of all the harmful ingredients known to the profession of drinking. Ye could have stocked ten bars with the whiskies, brandies, cordials, bitters, gins and wines me and Tim have wasted. A glorious drink like that to be denied the world! 'Tis a sorrow and a loss of money. The United States as a nation would welcome a drink of that sort, and pay for it."

All the while McQuirk had been carefully measuring and pouring together small quantities of various spirits, as Riley called them, from his latest pencilled prescription. The completed mixture was of a vile, mottled chocolate color. McQuirk tasted it, and hurled it, with appropriate epithets, into the waste sink.

"'Tis a strange story, even if true," said Con. "I'll be going now along to my supper."

"Take a drink," said Riley. "We've all kinds except the lost blend."

"I never drink," said Con, "anything stronger than water. I am just after meeting Miss Katherine by the stairs. She said a true word, 'There's not anything,' says she, 'but is better off for a little water.'"

When Con had left them Riley almost felled McQuirk by a blow on the back.

"Did ye hear that?" he shouted. "Two fools are we. The six dozen bottles of 'pollinaris we had on the ship—ye opened them yourself—which barrel did ye pour them in—which barrel, ye mudhead?"

"I mind," said McQuirk, slowly, "'twas in the second barrel we opened. I mind the blue piece of paper pasted on the side of it."

"We've got it now," cried Riley. "'Twas that we lacked. 'Tis the water that does the trick. Everything else we had right. Hurry, man, and get two bottles of 'pollinaris from the bar, while I figure out the proportionments with me pencil."

An hour later Con strolled down the sidewalk toward Kenealy's café. Thus faithful employees haunt, during their recreation hours, the vicinity where they labor, drawn by some mysterious attraction.

A police patrol wagon stood at the side door. Three able cops were half carrying, half hustling Riley and McQuirk up its rear steps. The eyes and faces of each bore the bruises and cuts of sanguinary and assiduous conflict. Yet they whooped with strange joy, and directed upon the police the feeble remnants of their pugnacious madness.

"Began fighting each other in the back room," explained Kenealy to Con. "And singing! That was worse. Smashed everything pretty much up. But they're good men. They'll pay for everything. Trying to invent some new kind of cocktail, they was. I'll see they come out all right in the morning."

Con sauntered into the back room to view the battlefield. As he went through the hall Katherine was just coming down the stairs.

"Good evening again, Mr. Lantry," said she. "And is there no news from the weather yet?"

"Still threatens r-rain," said Con, slipping past with red in his smooth, pale cheek.

Riley and McQuirk had indeed waged a great and friendly battle. Broken bottles and glasses were everywhere. The room was full of alcohol fumes; the floor was variegated with spirituous puddles.

On the table stood a 32-ounce glass graduated measure. In the bottom of it were two tablespoonfuls of liquid—a bright golden liquid that seemed to hold the sunshine a prisoner in its auriferous depths.

Con smelled it. He tasted it. He drank it.

As he returned through the hall Katherine was just going up the stairs.

"No news yet, Mr. Lantry?" she asked with her teasing laugh.

Con lifted her clear from the floor and held her there.

"The news is," he said, "that we're to be married."

"Put me down, sir!" she cried indignantly, "or I will—— Oh, Con, oh, wherever did you get the nerve to say it?"

A HARLEM TRAGEDY

HARLEM.

Mrs. Fink had dropped into Mrs. Cassidy's flat one flight below.

"Ain't it a beaut?" said Mrs. Cassidy.

She turned her face proudly for her friend Mrs. Fink to see. One eye was nearly closed, with a great, greenish-purple bruise around it. Her lip was cut and bleeding a little and there were red finger-marks on each side of her neck.

"My husband wouldn't ever think of doing that to me," said Mrs. Fink, concealing her envy.

"I wouldn't have a man," declared Mrs. Cassidy, "that didn't beat me up at least once a week. Shows he thinks something of you. Say! but that last dose Jack gave me wasn't no homeopathic one. I can see stars yet. But he'll be the sweetest man in town for the rest of the week to make up for it. This eye is good for theater tickets and a silk shirt waist at the very least."

"I should hope," said Mrs. Fink, assuming complacency, "that Mr. Fink is too much of a gentleman ever to raise his hand against me."

"Oh, go on, Maggie!" said Mrs. Cassidy, laughing and applying witch hazel, "you're only jealous. Your old man is too frappéd and slow to ever give you a punch. He just sits down and practises physical culture with a newspaper when he comes home—now ain't that the truth?"

"Mr. Fink certainly peruses of the papers when he comes home," acknowledged Mrs. Fink, with a toss of her head; "but he certainly don't ever make no Steve O'Donnell out of me just to amuse himself—that's a sure thing."

Mrs. Cassidy laughed the contented laugh of the guarded and happy matron. With the air of Cornelia exhibiting her jewels, she drew down the collar of her kimono and revealed another treasured bruise, maroon-colored, edged with olive and orange—a bruise now nearly well, but still to memory dear.

Mrs. Fink capitulated. The formal light in her eye softened to envious admiration. She and Mrs. Cassidy had been chums in the downtown paper-box factory before they had married, one year before. Now she and her man occupied the flat above Mame and her man. Therefore she could not put on airs with Mame.

"Don't it hurt when he soaks you?" asked Mrs. Fink, curiously.

"Hurt!"—Mrs. Cassidy gave a soprano scream of delight. "Well, say—did you ever have a brick house fall on you?—well, that's just the way it feels— just like when they're digging you out of the ruins. Jack's got a left that spells two matinées and a new pair of Oxfords—and his right!—well, it takes a trip to Coney and six pairs of openwork silk lisle threads to make that good."

"But what does he beat you for?" inquired Mrs. Fink, with wide-open eyes.

"Silly!" said Mrs. Cassidy, indulgently. "Why, because he's full. It's generally on Saturday nights."

"But what cause do you give him?" persisted the seeker after knowledge.

"Why, didn't I marry him? Jack comes in tanked up; and I'm here, ain't I? Who else has he got a right to beat? I'd just like to catch him once beating anybody else! Sometimes it's because supper ain't ready; and sometimes it's because it is. Jack ain't particular about causes. He just lushes till he remembers he's married, and then he makes for home and does me up. Saturday nights I just move the furniture with sharp corners out of the way, so I won't cut my head when he gets his work in. He's got a left swing that jars you! Sometimes I take the count in the first round; but when I feel like having a good time during the week or want some new rags I come up again for more punishment. That's what I done last night. Jack knows I've been wanting a black silk waist for a month, and I didn't think just one black eye would bring it. Tell you what, Mag, I'll bet you the ice cream he brings it to-night."

Mrs. Fink was thinking deeply.

"My Mart," she said, "never hit me a lick in his life. It's just like you said, Mame; he comes in grouchy and ain't got a word to say. He never takes me out anywhere. He's a chair-warmer at home for fair. He buys me things, but he looks so glum about it that I never appreciate 'em."

Mrs. Cassidy slipped an arm around her chum.

"You poor thing!" she said. "But everybody can't have a husband like Jack. Marriage wouldn't be no failure if they was all like him. These discontented wives you hear about—what they need is a man to come home and kick their slats in once a week, and then make it up in kisses, and chocolate creams. That'd give 'em some interest in life. What I want is a masterful man that slugs you when he's jagged and hugs you when he ain't jagged. Preserve me from the man that ain't got the sand to do neither!"

Mrs. Fink sighed.

The hallways were suddenly filled with sound. The door flew open at the kick of Mr. Cassidy. His arms were occupied with bundles. Mame flew and hung about his neck. Her sound eye sparkled with the love light that shines in the eye of the Maori maid when she recovers consciousness in the hut of the wooer who has stunned and dragged her there.

"Hello, old girl!" shouted Mr. Cassidy. He shed his bundles and lifted her off her feet in a mighty hug. "I got tickets for Barnum & Bailey's, and if you'll bust the string of one of them bundles I guess you'll find that silk waist— why, good evening, Mrs. Fink—I didn't see you at first. How's old Mart coming along?"

"He's very well, Mr. Cassidy—thanks," said Mrs. Fink. "I must be going along up now. Mart'll be home for supper soon. I'll bring you down the pattern you wanted to-morrow, Mame."

Mrs. Fink went up to her flat and had a little cry. It was a meaningless cry, the kind of cry that only a woman knows about, a cry from no particular cause, altogether an absurd cry; the most transient and the most hopeless cry in the repertory of grief. Why had Martin never thrashed her? He was as big and strong as Jack Cassidy. Did he not care for her at all? He never quarrelled; he came home and lounged about silent, glum, idle. He was a fairly good provider, but he ignored the spices of life.

Mrs. Fink's ship of dreams was becalmed. Her captain ranged between plum duff and his hammock. If only he would shiver his timbers or stamp his foot on the quarter-deck now and then! And she had thought to sail so merrily, touching at ports in the Delectable Isles! But now, to vary the figure, she was ready to throw up the sponge, tired out, without a scratch to show for all those tame rounds with her sparring partner. For one moment she almost hated Mame—Mame, with her cuts and bruises, her salve of presents and kisses; her stormy voyage with her fighting, brutal, loving mate.

Mr. Fink came home at 7. He was permeated with the curse of domesticity. Beyond the portals of his cozy home he cared not to roam, to roam. He was the man who had caught the street car, the anaconda that had swallowed its prey, the tree that lay as it had fallen.

"Like the supper, Mart?" asked Mrs. Fink, who had striven over it.

"M-m-m-yep," grunted Mr. Fink.

After supper he gathered his newspapers to read. He sat in his stocking feet.

Arise, some new Dante, and sing me the befitting corner of perdition for the man who sitteth in the house in his stockinged feet. Sisters in Patience who by reason of ties or duty have endured it in silk, yarn, cotton, lisle thread or woollen—does not the new canto belong?

The next day was Labor Day. The occupations of Mr. Cassidy and Mr. Fink ceased for one passage of the sun. Labor, triumphant, would parade and otherwise disport itself.

Mrs. Fink took Mrs. Cassidy's pattern down early. Mame had on her new silk waist. Even her damaged eye managed to emit a holiday gleam. Jack was fruitfully penitent, and there was a hilarious scheme for the day afoot, with parks and picnics and Pilsener in it.

A rising, indignant jealousy seized Mrs. Fink as she returned to her flat above. Oh, happy Mame, with her bruises and her quick-following balm! But was Mame to have a monopoly of happiness? Surely Martin Fink was as good a man as Jack Cassidy. Was his wife to go always unbelabored and uncaressed? A sudden, brilliant breathless idea came to Mrs. Fink. She would show Mame that there were husbands as able to use their fists and perhaps to be as tender afterward as any Jack.

The holiday promised to be a nominal one with the Finks. Mrs. Fink had the stationary washtubs in the kitchen filled with a two-weeks' wash that had been soaking overnight. Mr. Fink sat in his stockinged feet reading a newspaper. Thus Labor Day presaged to speed.

Jealousy surged high in Mrs. Fink's heart and higher still surged an audacious resolve. If her man would not strike her—if he would not so far prove his manhood, his prerogative and his interest in conjugal affairs, he must be prompted to do his duty.

Mr. Fink lit his pipe and peacefully rubbed an ankle with a stockinged toe. He reposed in the state of matrimony like a lump of unblended suet in a pudding. This was his level Elysium—to sit at ease vicariously girdling the world in print amid the wifely splashing of suds and the agreeable smells of breakfast dishes departed and dinner ones to come. Many ideas were far from his mind; but the furthest one was the thought of beating his wife.

Mrs. Fink turned on the hot water and set the washboards in the suds. Up from the flat below came the gay laugh of Mrs. Cassidy. It sounded like a taunt, a flaunting of her own happiness in the face of the unslugged bride above. Now was Mrs. Fink's time.

Suddenly she turned like a fury upon the man reading.

"You lazy loafer!" she cried, "must I work my arms off washing and toiling for the ugly likes of you? Are you a man or are you a kitchen hound?"

Mr. Fink dropped his paper, motionless from surprise. She feared that he would not strike—that the provocation had been insufficient. She leaped at him and struck him fiercely in the face with her clenched hand. In that instant she felt a thrill of love for him such as she had not felt for many a day. Rise up, Martin Fink, and come into your kingdom! Oh, she must feel the weight of his hand now—just to show that he cared—just to show that he cared!

Mr. Fink sprang to his feet—Maggie caught him again on the jaw with a wide swing of her other hand. She closed her eyes in that fearful, blissful moment before his blow should come—she whispered his name to herself—she leaned to the expected shock, hungry for it.

In the flat below Mr. Cassidy, with a shamed and contrite face was powdering Mame's eye in preparation for their junket. From the flat above came the sound of a woman's voice, high-raised, a bumping, a stumbling and a shuffling, a chair overturned—unmistakable sounds of domestic conflict.

"Mart and Mag scrapping?" postulated Mr. Cassidy. "Didn't know they ever indulged. Shall I trot up and see if they need a sponge holder?"

One of Mrs. Cassidy's eyes sparkled like a diamond. The other twinkled at least like paste.

"Oh, oh," she said, softly and without apparent meaning, in the feminine ejaculatory manner. "I wonder if—wonder if! Wait, Jack, till I go up and see."

Up the stairs she sped. As her foot struck the hallway above out from the kitchen door of her flat wildly flounced Mrs. Fink.

"Oh, Maggie," cried Mrs. Cassidy, in a delighted whisper; "did he? Oh, did he?"

Mrs. Fink ran and laid her face upon her chum's shoulder and sobbed hopelessly.

Mrs. Cassidy took Maggie's face between her hands and lifted it gently. Tear-stained it was, flushing and paling, but its velvety, pink-and-white, becomingly freckled surface was unscratched, unbruised, unmarred by the recreant fist of Mr. Fink.

"Tell me, Maggie," pleaded Mame, "or I'll go in there and find out. What was it? Did he hurt you—what did he do?"

Mrs. Fink's face went down again despairingly on the bosom of her friend.

"For God's sake don't open that door, Mame," she sobbed. "And don't ever tell nobody—keep it under your hat. He—he never touched me, and—he's—oh, Gawd—he's washin' the clothes—he's washin' the clothes!"

"THE GUILTY PARTY"

A RED-HAIRED, unshaven, untidy man sat in a rocking chair by a window. He had just lighted a pipe, and was puffing blue clouds with great satisfaction. He had removed his shoes and donned a pair of blue, faded carpet-slippers. With the morbid thirst of the confirmed daily news drinker, he awkwardly folded back the pages of an evening paper, eagerly gulping down the strong, black headlines, to be followed as a chaser by the milder details of the smaller type.

In an adjoining room a woman was cooking supper. Odors from strong bacon and boiling coffee contended against the cut-plug fumes from the vespertine pipe.

Outside was one of those crowded streets of the east side, in which, as twilight falls, Satan sets up his recruiting office. A mighty host of children danced and ran and played in the street. Some in rags, some in clean white and beribboned, some wild and restless as young hawks, some gentle-faced and shrinking, some shrieking rude and sinful words, some listening, awed, but soon, grown familiar, to embrace—here were the children playing in the corridors of the House of Sin. Above the playground forever hovered a great bird. The bird was known to humorists as the stork. But the people of Chrystie Street were better ornithologists. They called it a vulture.

A little girl of twelve came up timidly to the man reading and resting by the window, and said:

"Papa, won't you play a game of checkers with me if you aren't too tired?"

The red-haired, unshaven, untidy man sitting shoeless by the window answered, with a frown.

"Checkers. No, I won't. Can't a man who works hard all day have a little rest when he comes home? Why don't you go out and play with the other kids on the sidewalk?"

The woman who was cooking came to the door.

"John," she said. "I don't like for Lizzie to play in the street. They learn too much there that ain't good for 'em. She's been in the house all day long. It seems that you might give up a little of your time to amuse her when you come home."

"Let her go out and play like the rest of 'em if she wants to be amused," said the red-haired, unshaven, untidy man, "and don't bother me."

.   .   .   .

"You're on," said Kid Mullaly. "Fifty dollars to $25 I take Annie to the dance. Put up."

The Kid's black eyes were snapping with the fire of the baited and challenged. He drew out his "roll" and slapped five tens upon the bar. The three or four young fellows who were thus "taken" more slowly produced their stake. The bartender, ex-officio stakeholder, took the money, laboriously wrapped it, recorded the bet with an inch-long pencil and stuffed the whole into a corner of the cash register.

"And, oh, what'll be done to you'll be a plenty," said a bettor, with anticipatory glee.

"That's my lookout," said the "Kid," sternly. "Fill 'em up all around, Mike."

After the round Burke, the Kid's sponge, sponge-holder, pal, mentor and Grand Vizier, drew him out to the bootblack stand at the saloon corner where all the official and important matters of the Small Hours Social Club were settled. As Tony polished the light tan shoes of the club's President and Secretary for the fifth time that day, Burke spake words of wisdom to his chief.

"Cut that blonde out, Kid," was his advice, "or there'll be trouble. What do you want to throw down that girl of yours for? You'll never find one that'll freeze to you like Liz has. She's worth a hallful of Annies."

"I'm no Annie admirer!" said the Kid, dropping a cigarette ash on his polished toe, and wiping it off on Tony's shoulder. "But I want to teach Liz a lesson. She thinks I belong to her. She's been bragging that I daren't speak to another girl. Liz is all right—in some ways. She's drinking a little too much lately. And she uses language that a lady oughtn't."

"You're engaged, ain't you?" asked Burke.

"Sure. We'll get married next year, maybe."

"I saw you make her drink her first glass of beer," said Burke. "That was two years ago, when she used to come down to the corner of Chrystie bareheaded to meet you after supper. She was a quiet sort of a kid then, and couldn't speak without blushing."

"She's a little spitfire, sometimes, now," said the Kid. "I hate jealousy. That's why I'm going to the dance with Annie. It'll teach her some sense."

"Well, you better look a little out," were Burke's last words. "If Liz was my girl and I was to sneak out to a dance coupled up with an Annie, I'd want a suit of chain armor on under my gladsome rags, all right."

Through the land of the stork-vulture wandered Liz. Her black eyes searched the passing crowds fiercely but vaguely. Now and then she hummed bars of foolish little songs. Between times she set her small, white teeth together, and spake crisp words that the east side has added to language.

Liz's skirt was green silk. Her waist was a large brown-and-pink plaid, well-fitting and not without style. She wore a cluster ring of huge imitation rubies, and a locket that banged her knees at the bottom of a silver chain. Her shoes were run down over twisted high heels, and were strangers to polish. Her hat would scarcely have passed into a flour barrel.

The "Family Entrance" of the Blue Jay Café received her. At a table she sat, and punched the button with the air of milady ringing for her carriage. The waiter came with his large-chinned, low-voiced manner of respectful familiarity. Liz smoothed her silken skirt with a satisfied wriggle. She made the most of it. Here she could order and be waited upon. It was all that her world offered her of the prerogative of woman.

"Whiskey, Tommy," she said as her sisters further uptown murmur, "Champagne, James."

"Sure, Miss Lizzie. What'll the chaser be?"

"Seltzer. And say, Tommy, has the Kid been around to-day?"

"Why, no, Miss Lizzie, I haven't saw him to-day."

Fluently came the "Miss Lizzie," for the Kid was known to be one who required rigid upholdment of the dignity of his fiancée.

"I'm lookin' for 'm," said Liz, after the chaser had sputtered under her nose. "It's got to me that he says he'll take Annie Karlson to the dance. Let him. The pink-eyed white rat! I'm lookin' for 'm. You know me, Tommy. Two years me and the Kid's been engaged. Look at that ring. Five hundred, he said it cost. Let him take her to the dance. What'll I do? I'll cut his heart out. Another whiskey, Tommy."

"I wouldn't listen to no such reports, Miss Lizzie," said the waiter smoothly, from the narrow opening above his chin. "Kid Mullaly's not the guy to throw a lady like you down. Seltzer on the side?"

"Two years," repeated Liz, softening a little to sentiment under the magic of the distiller's art. "I always used to play out on the street of evenin's 'cause there was nothin' doin' for me at home. For a long time I just sat on doorsteps and looked at the lights and the people goin' by. And then the Kid came along one evenin' and sized me up, and I was mashed on the spot for fair. The first drink he made me take, I cried all night at home, and got a lickin' for makin' a noise. And now—say, Tommy, you ever see this Annie Karlson? If it wasn't for peroxide the chloroform limit would have put her out long ago. Oh, I'm lookin' for 'm. You tell the Kid if he comes in. Me? I'll cut his heart out. Leave it to me. Another whiskey, Tommy."

A little unsteadily, but with watchful and brilliant eyes, Liz walked up the avenue. On the doorstep of a brick tenement a curly-haired child sat, puzzling over the convolutions of a tangled string. Liz flopped down beside her, with a crooked, shifting smile on her flushed face. But her eyes had grown clear and artless of a sudden.

"Let me show you how to make a cat's-cradle, kid," she said, tucking her green silk skirt under her rusty shoes.

And while they sat there the lights were being turned on for the dance in the hall of the Small Hours Social Club. It was a bi-monthly dance, a dress affair in which the members took great pride and bestirred themselves huskily to further and adorn.

At 9 o'clock the President, Kid Mullaly, paced upon the floor with a lady on his arm. As the Loreley's was her hair golden. Her "yes" was softened to a "yah," but its quality of assent was patent to the most Milesian ears. She stepped upon her own train and blushed, and—she smiled into the eyes of Kid Mullaly.

And then, as the two stood in the middle of the waxed floor, the thing happened to prevent which many lamps are burning nightly in many studies and libraries.

Out from the circle of spectators in the hall leaped Fate in a green silk skirt, under the *nom de guerre* of "Liz." Her eyes were hard and blacker than jet. She did not scream or waver. Most unwomanly, she cried out one oath—the Kid's own favorite oath—and in his own deep voice; and then while the Small Hours Social Club went frantically to pieces, she made good her boast to Tommy, the waiter—made good as far as the length of her knife blade and the strength of her arm permitted.

And next came the primal instinct of self-preservation—or was it self-annihilation, the instinct that society has grafted on the natural branch?

Liz ran out and down the street swift and true as a woodcock flying through a grove of saplings at dusk.

And then followed the big city's biggest shame, its most ancient and rotten surviving canker, its pollution and disgrace, its blight and perversion, its forever infamy and guilt, fostered, unreproved and cherished, handed down from a long-ago century of the basest barbarity—the Hue and Cry. Nowhere but in the big cities does it survive, and here most of all, where the ultimate perfection of culture, citizenship and alleged superiority joins, bawling, in the chase.

They pursued—a shrieking mob of fathers, mothers, lovers and maidens—howling, yelling, calling, whistling, crying for blood. Well may the wolf in the big city stand outside the door. Well may his heart, the gentler, falter at the siege. Knowing her way, and hungry for her surcease, she darted down the familiar ways until at last her feet struck the dull solidity of the rotting pier. And then it was but a few more panting steps—and good mother East River took Liz to her bosom, smoothed her muddily but quickly, and settled in five minutes the problem that keeps lights burning o' nights in thousands of pastorates and colleges.

.   .   .   .

It's mighty funny what kind of dreams one has sometimes. Poets call them visions, but a vision is only a dream in blank verse. I dreamed the rest of this story.

I thought I was in the next world. I don't know how I got there; I suppose I had been riding on the Ninth Avenue elevated or taking patent medicine or trying to pull Jim Jeffries's nose, or doing some such little injudicious stunt. But, anyhow, there I was, and there was a great crowd of us outside the court-room where the judgments were going on. And every now and then a very beautiful and imposing court-officer angel would come outside the door and call another case.

While I was considering my own worldly sins and wondering whether there would be any use of my trying to prove an alibi by claiming that I lived in New Jersey, the bailiff angel came to the door and sang out:

"Case No. 99,852,743."

Up stepped a plain-clothes man—there were lots of 'em there, dressed exactly like preachers and hustling us spirits around just like cops do on earth—and by the arm he dragged—whom, do you think? Why, Liz!

The court officer took her inside and closed the door. I went up to Mr. Fly-Cop and inquired about the case.

"A very sad one," says he, laying the points of his manicured fingers together. "An utterly incorrigible girl. I am Special Terrestrial Officer the Reverend Jones. The case was assigned to me. The girl murdered her fiancé and committed suicide. She had no defense. My report to the court relates the facts in detail, all of which are substantiated by reliable witnesses. The wages of sin is death. Praise the Lord."

The court officer opened the door and stepped out.

"Poor girl," said Special Terrestrial Officer the Reverend Jones, with a tear in his eye. "It was one of the saddest cases that I ever met with. Of course she was——"

"Discharged," said the court officer. "Come here, Jonesy. First thing you know you'll be switched to the pot-pie squad. How would you like to be on the missionary force in the South Sea Islands—hey? Now, you quit making these false arrests, or you'll be transferred—see? The guilty party you've got to look for in this case is a red-haired, unshaven, untidy man, sitting by the window reading, in his stocking feet, while his children play in the streets. Get a move on you."

Now, wasn't that a silly dream?

ACCORDING TO THEIR LIGHTS

SOMEWHERE in the depths of the big city, where the unquiet dregs are forever being shaken together, young Murray and the Captain had met and become friends. Both were at the lowest ebb possible to their fortunes; both had fallen from at least an intermediate Heaven of respectability and importance, and both were typical products of the monstrous and peculiar social curriculum of their over-weening and bumptious civic alma mater.

The Captain was no longer a captain. One of those sudden moral cataclysms that sometimes sweep the city had hurled him from a high and profitable position in the Police Department, ripping off his badge and buttons and washing into the hands of his lawyers the solid pieces of real estate that his frugality had enabled him to accumulate. The passing of the flood left him low and dry. One month after his dishabilitation a saloon-keeper plucked him by the neck from his free-lunch counter as a tabby plucks a strange kitten from her nest, and cast him asphaltward. This seems low enough. But after that he acquired a pair of cloth-top, button Congress gaiters and wrote complaining letters to the newspapers. And then he fought the attendant at the Municipal Lodging House who tried to give him a bath. When Murray first saw him he was holding the hand of an Italian woman who sold apples and garlic on Essex Street, and quoting the words of a song book ballad.

Murray's fall had been more Luciferian, if less spectacular. All the pretty, tiny little kickshaws of Gotham had once been his. The megaphone man roars out at you to observe the house of his uncle on a grand and revered avenue. But there had been an awful row about something, and the prince had been escorted to the door by the butler, which, in said avenue, is equivalent to the impact of the avuncular shoe. A weak Prince Hal, without inheritance or sword, he drifted downward to meet his humorless Falstaff, and to pick the crusts of the streets with him.

One evening they sat on a bench in a little downtown park. The great bulk of the Captain, which starvation seemed to increase—drawing irony instead of pity to his petitions for aid—was heaped against the arm of the bench in a shapeless mass. His red face, spotted by tufts of vermilion, week-old whiskers and topped by a sagging white straw hat, looked, in the gloom, like one of those structures that you may observe in a dark Third Avenue window, challenging your imagination to say whether it be something recent in the way of ladies' hats or a strawberry shortcake. A tight-drawn belt—last relic of his official spruceness—made a deep furrow in his circumference. The Captain's shoes were buttonless. In a smothered bass he cursed his star of ill-luck.

Murray, at his side, was shrunk into his dingy and ragged suit of blue serge. His hat was pulled low; he sat quiet and a little indistinct, like some ghost that had been dispossessed.

"I'm hungry," growled the Captain—"by the top sirloin of the Bull of Bashan, I'm starving to death. Right now I could eat a Bowery restaurant clear through to the stovepipe in the alley. Can't you think of nothing, Murray? You sit there with your shoulders scrunched up, giving an imitation of Reginald Vanderbilt driving his coach—what good are them airs doing you now? Think of some place we can get something to chew."

"You forget, my dear captain," said Murray, without moving, "that our last attempt at dining was at my suggestion."

"You bet it was," groaned the Captain, "you bet your life it was. Have you got any more like that to make—hey?"

"I admit we failed," sighed Murray. "I was sure Malone would be good for one more free lunch after the way he talked baseball with me the last time I spent a nickel in his establishment."

"I had this hand," said the Captain, extending the unfortunate member—"I had this hand on the drumstick of a turkey and two sardine sandwiches when them waiters grabbed us."

"I was within two inches of the olives," said Murray. "Stuffed olives. I haven't tasted one in a year."

"What'll we do?" grumbled the Captain. "We can't starve."

"Can't we?" said Murray, quietly. "I'm glad to hear that. I was afraid we could."

"You wait here," said the Captain, rising heavily and puffily to his feet. "I'm going to try to make one more turn. You stay here till I come back, Murray. I won't be over half an hour. If I turn the trick I'll come back flush."

He made some elephantine attempts at smartening his appearance. He gave his fiery mustache a heavenward twist; he dragged into sight a pair of black-edged cuffs, deepened the crease in his middle by tightening his belt another hole, and set off, jaunty as a zoo rhinoceros, across the south end of the park.

When he was out of sight Murray also left the park, hurrying swiftly eastward. He stopped at a building whose steps were flanked by two green lights.

"A police captain named Maroney," he said to the desk sergeant, "was dismissed from the force after being tried under charges three years ago. I believe sentence was suspended. Is this man wanted now by the police?"

"Why are ye asking?" inquired the sergeant, with a frown.

"I thought there might be a reward standing," explained Murray, easily. "I know the man well. He seems to be keeping himself pretty shady at present. I could lay my hands on him at any time. If there should be a reward——"

"There's no reward," interrupted the sergeant, shortly. "The man's not wanted. And neither are ye. So, get out. Ye are frindly with um, and ye would be selling um. Out with ye quick, or I'll give ye a start."

Murray gazed at the officer with serene and virtuous dignity.

"I would be simply doing my duty as a citizen and gentleman," he said, severely, "if I could assist the law in laying hold of one of its offenders."

Murray hurried back to the bench in the park. He folded his arms and shrank within his clothes to his ghost-like presentment.

Ten minutes afterward the Captain arrived at the rendezvous, windy and thunderous as a dog-day in Kansas. His collar had been torn away; his straw hat had been twisted and battered; his shirt with ox-blood stripes split to the waist. And from head to knee he was drenched with some vile and ignoble greasy fluid that loudly proclaimed to the nose its component leaven of garlic and kitchen stuff.

"For Heaven's sake, Captain," sniffed Murray, "I doubt that I would have waited for you if I had suspected you were so desperate as to resort to swill barrels. I——"

"Cheese it," said the Captain, harshly. "I'm not hogging it yet. It's all on the outside. I went around on Essex and proposed marriage to that Catrina that's got the fruit shop there. Now, that business could be built up. She's a peach as far as a Dago could be. I thought I had that senoreena mashed sure last week. But look what she done to me! I guess I got too fresh. Well there's another scheme queered."

"You don't mean to say," said Murray, with infinite contempt, "that you would have married that woman to help yourself out of your disgraceful troubles!"

"Me?" said the Captain. "I'd marry the Empress of China for one bowl of chop suey. I'd commit murder for a plate of beef stew. I'd steal a wafer from a waif. I'd be a Mormon for a bowl of chowder."

"I think," said Murray, resting his head on his hands, "that I would play Judas for the price of one drink of whiskey. For thirty pieces of silver I would——"

"Oh, come now!" exclaimed the Captain in dismay. "You wouldn't do that, Murray? I always thought that Kike's squeal on his boss was about the lowest-down play that ever happened. A man that gives his friend away is worse than a pirate."

Through the park stepped a large man scanning the benches where the electric light fell.

"Is that you, Mac?" he said, halting before the derelicts. His diamond stick-pin dazzled. His diamond-studded fob chain assisted. He was big and smooth and well fed. "Yes, I see it's you," he continued. "They told me at Mike's that I might find you over here. Let me see you a few minutes, Mac."

The Captain lifted himself with a grunt of alacrity. If Charlie Finnegan had come down in the bottomless pit to seek him there must be something doing. Charlie guided him by an arm into a patch of shadow.

"You know, Mac," he said, "they're trying Inspector Pickering on graft charges."

"He was my inspector," said the Captain.

"O'Shea wants the job," went on Finnegan. "He must have it. It's for the good of the organization. Pickering must go under. Your testimony will do it. He was your 'man higher up' when you were on the force. His share of the boodle passed through your hands. You must go on the stand and testify against him."

"He was"—began the Captain.

"Wait a minute," said Finnegan. A bundle of yellowish stuff came out of his inside pocket. "Five hundred dollars in it for you. Two-fifty on the spot, and the rest——"

"He was my friend, I say," finished the Captain. "I'll see you and the gang, and the city, and the party in the flames of Hades before I'll take the stand against Dan Pickering. I'm down and out; but I'm no traitor to a man that's been my friend." The Captain's voice rose and boomed like a split trombone. "Get out of this park, Charlie Finnegan, where us thieves and tramps and boozers are your betters; and take your dirty money with you."

Finnegan drifted out by another walk. The Captain returned to his seat.

"I couldn't avoid hearing," said Murray, drearily. "I think you are the biggest fool I ever saw."

"What would you have done?" asked the Captain.

"Nailed Pickering to the cross," said Murray.

"Sonny," said the Captain, huskily and without heat. "You and me are different. New York is divided into two parts—above Forty-second Street, and below Fourteenth. You come from the other part. We both act according to our lights."

An illuminated clock above the trees retailed the information that it lacked the half hour of twelve. Both men rose from the bench and moved away together as if seized by the same idea. They left the park, struck through a narrow cross street, and came into Broadway, at this hour as dark, echoing and depeopled as a byway in Pompeii.

Northward they turned; and a policeman who glanced at their unkempt and slinking figures withheld the attention and suspicion that he would have granted them at any other hour and place. For on every street in that part of the city other unkempt and slinking figures were shuffling and hurrying toward a converging point—a point that is marked by no monument save that groove on the pavement worn by tens of thousands of waiting feet.

At Ninth Street a tall man wearing an opera hat alighted from a Broadway car and turned his face westward. But he saw Murray, pounced upon him and dragged him under a street light. The Captain lumbered slowly to the corner, like a wounded bear, and waited, growling.

"Jerry!" cried the hatted one. "How fortunate! I was to begin a search for you to-morrow. The old gentleman has capitulated. You're to be restored to favor. Congratulate you. Come to the office in the morning and get all the money you want. I've liberal instructions in that respect."

"And the little matrimonial arrangement?" said Murray, with his head turned sidewise.

"Why—er—well, of course, your uncle understands—expects that the engagement between you and Miss Vanderhurst shall be——"

"Good night," said Murray, moving away.

"You madman!" cried the other, catching his arm. "Would you give up two millions on account of——"

"Did you ever see her nose, old man?" asked Murray, solemnly.

"But, listen to reason, Jerry. Miss Vanderhurst is an heiress, and——"

"Did you ever see it?"

"Yes, I admit that her nose isn't——"

"Good night!" said Murray. "My friend is waiting for me. I am quoting him when I authorize you to report that there is 'nothing doing.' Good night."

A wriggling line of waiting men extended from a door in Tenth Street far up Broadway, on the outer edge of the pavement. The Captain and Murray fell in at the tail of the quivering millipede.

"Twenty feet longer than it was last night," said Murray, looking up at his measuring angle of Grace Church.

"Half an hour," growled the Captain, "before we get our punk."

The city clocks began to strike 12; the Bread Line moved forward slowly, its leathern feet sliding on the stones with the sound of a hissing serpent, as they who had lived according to their lights closed up in the rear.

A MIDSUMMER KNIGHT'S DREAM

> *"The knights are dead;*
> *Their swords are rust.*
> *Except a few who have to hust-*
> *Le all the time*
> *To raise the dust."*

DEAR READER: It was summertime. The sun glared down upon the city with pitiless ferocity. It is difficult for the sun to be ferocious and exhibit compunction simultaneously. The heat was—oh, bother thermometers!—who cares for standard measures, anyhow? It was so hot that——

The roof gardens put on so many extra waiters that you could hope to get your gin fizz now—as soon as all the other people got theirs. The hospitals were putting in extra cots for bystanders. For when little woolly dogs loll their tongues out and say "woof, woof!" at the fleas that bite 'em, and nervous old black bombazine ladies screech "Mad dog!" and policemen begin to shoot, somebody is going to get hurt. The man from Pompton, N. J., who always wears an overcoat in July, had turned up in a Broadway hotel drinking hot Scotches and enjoying his annual ray from the calcium. Philanthropists were petitioning the Legislature to pass a bill requiring builders to make tenement fire-escapes more commodious, so that families might die all together of the heat instead of one or two at a time. So many men were telling you about the number of baths they took each day that you wondered how they got along after the real lessee of the apartment came back to town and thanked 'em for taking such good care of it. The young man who called loudly for cold beef and beer in the restaurant, protesting that roast pullet and Burgundy was really to heavy for such weather, blushed when he met your eye, for you had heard him all winter calling, in modest tones, for the same ascetic viands. Soup, pocketbooks, shirt waists, actors and baseball excuses grew thinner. Yes, it was summertime.

A man stood at Thirty-fourth Street waiting for a downtown car. A man of forty, gray-haired, pink-faced, keen, nervous, plainly dressed, with a harassed look around the eyes. He wiped his forehead and laughed loudly when a fat man with an outing look stopped and spoke with him.

"No, siree," he shouted with defiance and scorn. "None of your old mosquito-haunted swamps and skyscraper mountains without elevators for me. When I want to get away from hot weather I know how to do it. New York, sir, is the finest summer resort in the country. Keep in the shade and watch your diet, and don't get too far away from an electric fan. Talk about your Adirondacks and your Catskills! There's more solid comfort in the borough of Manhattan than in all the rest of the country together. No, siree! No tramping up perpendicular cliffs and being waked up at 4 in the morning by a million flies, and eating canned goods straight from the city for me. Little old New York will take a few select summer boarders; comforts and conveniences of home—that's the ad. that I answer every time."

"You need a vacation," said the fat man, looking closely at the other. "You haven't been away from town in years. Better come with me for two weeks, anyhow. The trout in the Beaverkill are jumping at anything now that looks like a fly. Harding writes me that he landed a three-pound brown last week."

"Nonsense!" cried the other man.. "Go ahead, if you like, and boggle around in rubber boots wearing yourself out trying to catch fish. When I want one I go to a cool restaurant and order it. I laugh at you fellows whenever I think of you hustling around in the heat in the country thinking you are having a good time. For me Father Knickerbocker's little improved farm with the big shady lane running through the middle of it."

The fat man sighed over his friend and went his way. The man who thought New York was the greatest summer resort in the country boarded a car and went buzzing down to his office. On the way he threw away his newspaper and looked up at a ragged patch of sky above the housetops.

"Three pounds!" he muttered, absently. "And Harding isn't a liar. I believe, if I could—but it's impossible—they've got to have another month—another month at least."

In his office the upholder of urban midsummer joys dived, head foremost, into the swimming pool of business. Adkins, his clerk, came and added a spray of letters, memoranda and telegrams.

At 5 o'clock in the afternoon the busy man leaned back in his office chair, put his feet on the desk and mused aloud:

"I wonder what kind of bait Harding used."

*　　*　　*　　*　　*　　*　　*　　*　　*　　*　　*　　*

She was all in white that day; and thereby Compton lost a bet to Gaines. Compton had wagered she would wear light blue, for she knew that was his favorite color, and Compton was a millionaire's son, and that almost laid him open to the charge of betting on a sure thing. But white was her choice, and Gaines held up his head with twenty-five's lordly air.

The little summer hotel in the mountains had a lively crowd that year. There were two or three young college men and a couple of artists and a young naval officer on one side. On the other there were enough beauties among the young ladies for the correspondent of a society paper to refer to them as a "bevy." But the moon among the stars was Mary Sewell. Each one of the young men greatly desired to arrange matters so that he could pay her millinery bills, and fix the furnace, and have her do away with the "Sewell" part of her name forever. Those who could stay only a week or two went away hinting at pistols and blighted hearts. But Compton stayed like the mountains themselves, for he could afford it. And Gaines stayed because he was a fighter and wasn't afraid of millionaires' sons, and—well, he adored the country.

"What do you think, Miss Mary?" he said once. "I knew a duffer in New York who claimed to like it in the summer time. Said you could keep cooler there than you could in the woods. Wasn't he an awful silly? I don't think I could breathe on Broadway after the 1st of June."

"Mamma was thinking of going back week after next," said Miss Mary with a lovely frown.

"But when you think of it," said Gaines, "there are lots of jolly places in town in the summer. The roof gardens, you know, and the—er—the roof gardens."

Deepest blue was the lake that day—the day when they had the mock tournament, and the men rode clumsy farm horses around in a glade in the woods and caught curtain rings on the end of a lance. Such fun!

Cool and dry as the finest wine came the breath of the shadowed forest. The valley below was a vision seen through an opal haze. A white mist from hidden falls blurred the green of a hand's breadth of tree tops halfway down the gorge. Youth made merry hand-in-hand with young summer. Nothing on Broadway like that.

The villagers gathered to see the city folks pursue their mad drollery. The woods rang with the laughter of pixies and naiads and sprites. Gaines caught most of the rings. His was the privilege to crown the queen of the tournament. He was the conquering knight—as far as the rings went. On his arm he wore a white scarf. Compton wore light blue. She had declared her preference for blue, but she wore white that day.

Gaines looked about for the queen to crown her. He heard her merry laugh, as if from the clouds. She had slipped away and climbed Chimney Rock, a little granite bluff, and stood there, a white fairy among the laurels, fifty feet above their heads.

Instantly he and Compton accepted the implied challenge. The bluff was easily mounted at the rear, but the front offered small hold to hand or foot. Each man quickly selected his route and began to climb. A crevice, a bush, a slight projection, a vine or tree branch—all of these were aids that counted in the race. It was all foolery—there was no stake; but there was youth in it, cross reader, and light hearts, and something else that Miss Clay writes so charmingly about.

Gaines gave a great tug at the root of a laurel and pulled himself to Miss Mary's feet. On his arm he carried the wreath of roses; and while the villagers and summer boarders screamed and applauded below he placed it on the queen's brow.

"You are a gallant knight," said Miss Mary.

"If I could be your true knight always," began Gaines, but Miss Mary laughed him dumb, for Compton scrambled over the edge of the rock one minute behind time.

What a twilight that was when they drove back to the hotel! The opal of the valley turned slowly to purple, the dark woods framed the lake as a mirror, the tonic air stirred the very soul in one. The first pale stars came out over the mountain tops where yet a faint glow of——

*   *   *   *   *   *   *   *   *   *   *   *

"I beg your pardon, Mr. Gaines," said Adkins.

The man who believed New York to be the finest summer resort in the world opened his eyes and kicked over the mucilage bottle on his desk.

"I—I believe I was asleep," he said.

"It's the heat," said Adkins. "It's something awful in the city these——"

"Nonsense!" said the other. "The city beats the country ten to one in summer. Fools go out tramping in muddy brooks and wear themselves out trying to catch little fish as long as your finger. Stay in town and keep comfortable—that's my idea."

"Some letters just came," said Adkins. "I thought you might like to glance at them before you go."

Let us look over his shoulder and read just a few lines of one of them:

MY DEAR, DEAR HUSBAND: Just received your letter ordering us to stay another month. . . . Rita's cough is almost gone. . . . Johnny has simply gone wild like a little Indian. . . . Will be the making of both children . . . work so hard, and I know that your business can hardly afford to keep us here so long . . . best man that ever . . . you always pretend that you like the city in summer . . . trout fishing that you used to be so fond of . . . and all to keep us well and happy . . . come to you if it were not doing the babies so much good. . . . I stood last evening on Chimney Rock in exactly the same spot where I was when you put the wreath of roses on my head . . . through all the world . . . when you said you would be my true knight . . . fifteen years ago, dear, just think! . . . have always been that to me . . . ever and ever,

MARY.

The man who said he thought New York the finest summer resort in the country dropped into a café on his way home and had a glass of beer under an electric fan.

"Wonder what kind of a fly old Harding used," he said to himself.

THE LAST LEAF

IN a little district west of Washington Square the streets have run crazy and broken themselves into small strips called "places." These "places" make strange angles and curves. One street crosses itself a time or two. An artist once discovered a valuable possibility in this street. Suppose a collector with a bill for paints, paper and canvas should, in traversing this route, suddenly meet himself coming back, without a cent having been paid on account!

So, to quaint old Greenwich Village the art people soon came prowling, hunting for north windows and eighteenth-century gables and Dutch attics and low rents. Then they imported some pewter mugs and a chafing dish or two from Sixth Avenue, and became a "colony."

At the top of a squatty, three-story brick Sue and Johnsy had their studio. "Johnsy" was familiar for Joanna. One was from Maine; the other from California. They had met at the *table d'hôte* of an Eighth Street "Delmonico's," and found their tastes in art, chicory salad and bishop sleeves so congenial that the joint studio resulted.

That was in May. In November a cold, unseen stranger, whom the doctors called Pneumonia, stalked about the colony, touching one here and there with his icy fingers. Over on the east side this ravager strode boldly, smiting his victims by scores, but his feet trod slowly through the maze of the narrow and moss-grown "places."

Mr. Pneumonia was not what you would call a chivalric old gentleman. A mite of a little woman with blood thinned by California zephyrs was hardly fair game for the red-fisted, short-breathed old duffer. But Johnsy he smote; and she lay, scarcely moving, on her painted iron bedstead, looking through the small Dutch window-panes at the blank side of the next brick house.

One morning the busy doctor invited Sue into the hallway with a shaggy, gray eyebrow.

"She has one chance in—let us say, ten," he said, as he shook down the mercury in his clinical thermometer. "And that chance is for her to want to live. This way people have of lining-up on the side of the undertaker makes the entire pharmacopœia look silly. Your little lady has made up her mind that she's not going to get well. Has she anything on her mind?"

"She—she wanted to paint the Bay of Naples some day," said Sue.

"Paint?—bosh! Has she anything on her mind worth thinking about twice—a man, for instance?"

"A man?" said Sue, with a jew's-harp twang in her voice. "Is a man worth—but, no, doctor; there is nothing of the kind." .

"Well, it is the weakness, then," said the doctor. "I will do all that science, so far as it may filter through my efforts, can accomplish. But whenever my patient begins to count the carriages in her funeral procession I subtract 50 per cent. from the curative power of medicines. If you will get her to ask one question about the new winter styles in cloak sleeves I will promise you a one-in-five chance for her, instead of one in ten."

After the doctor had gone Sue went into the workroom and cried a Japanese napkin to a pulp. Then she swaggered into Johnsy's room with her drawing board, whistling ragtime.

Johnsy, lay, scarcely making a ripple under the bedclothes, with her face toward the window. Sue stopped whistling, thinking she was asleep.

She arranged her board and began a pen-and-ink drawing to illustrate a magazine story. Young artists must pave their way to Art by drawing pictures for magazine stories that young authors write to pave their way to Literature.

As Sue was sketching a pair of elegant horseshow riding trousers and a monocle on the figure of the hero, an Idaho cowboy, she heard a low sound, several times repeated. She went quickly to the bedside.

Johnsy's eyes were open wide. She was looking out the window and counting—counting backward.

"Twelve," she said, and a little later "eleven"; and then "ten," and "nine"; and then "eight" and "seven," almost together.

Sue looked solicitously out of the window. What was there to count? There was only a bare, dreary yard to be seen, and the blank side of the brick house twenty feet away. An old, old ivy vine, gnarled and decayed at the roots, climbed half way up the brick wall. The cold breath of autumn had stricken its leaves from the vine until its skeleton branches clung, almost bare, to the crumbling bricks.

"What is it, dear?" asked Sue.

"Six," said Johnsy, in almost a whisper. "They're falling faster now. Three days ago there were almost a hundred. It made my head ache to count them. But now its easy. There goes another one. There are only five left now."

"Five what, dear. Tell your Sudie."

"Leaves. On the ivy vine. When the last one falls I must go, too. I've known that for three days. Didn't the doctor tell you?"

"Oh, I never heard of such nonsense," complained Sue, with magnificent scorn. "What have old ivy leaves to do with your getting well? And you used to love that vine, so, you naughty girl. Don't be a goosey. Why, the doctor told me this morning that your chances for getting well real soon were—let's see exactly what he said—he said the chances were ten to one! Why, that's almost as good a chance as we have in New York when we ride on the street cars or walk past a new building. Try to take some broth now, and let Sudie go back to her drawing, so she can sell the editor man with it, and buy port wine for her sick child, and pork chops for her greedy self."

"You needn't get any more wine," said Johnsy, keeping her eyes fixed out the window. "There goes another. No, I don't want any broth. That leaves just four. I want to see the last one fall before it gets dark. Then I'll go, too."

"Johnsy, dear," said Sue, bending over her, "will you promise me to keep your eyes closed, and not look out the window until I am done working? I must hand those drawings in by to-morrow. I need the light, or I would draw the shade down."

"Couldn't you draw in the other room?" asked Johnsy, coldly.

"I'd rather be here by you," said Sue. "Besides, I don't want you to keep looking at those silly ivy leaves."

"Tell me as soon as you have finished," said Johnsy, closing her eyes, and lying white and still as a fallen statue, "because I want to see the last one fall. I'm tired of waiting. I'm tired of thinking. I went to turn loose my hold on everything, and go sailing down, down, just like one of those poor, tired leaves."

"Try to sleep," said Sue. "I must call Behrman up to be my model for the old hermit miner. I'll not be gone a minute. Don't try to move 'til I come back."

Old Behrman was a painter who lived on the ground floor beneath them. He was past sixty and had a Michael Angelo's Moses beard curling down from the head of a satyr along the body of an imp. Behrman was a failure in art. Forty years he had wielded the brush without getting near enough to touch the hem of his Mistress's robe. He had been always about to paint a master-piece, but had never yet begun it. For several years he had painted nothing except now and then a daub in the line of commerce or advertising. He earned a little by serving as a model to those young artists in the colony who could not pay the price of a professional. He drank gin to excess, and still talked of his coming masterpiece. For the rest he was a fierce little old man, who scoffed terribly at softness in any one, and who regarded himself as especial mastiff-in-waiting to protect the two young artists in the studio above.

Sue found Behrman smelling strongly of juniper berries in his dimly lighted den below. In one corner was a blank canvas on an easel that had been waiting there for twenty-five years to receive the first line of the masterpiece. She told him of Johnsy's fancy, and how she feared she would, indeed, light and fragile as a leaf herself, float away, when her slight hold upon the world grew weaker.

Old Behrman, with his red eyes plainly streaming, shouted his contempt and derision for such idiotic imaginings.

"Vass!" he cried. "Is dere people in de world mit der foolishness to die because leafs dey drop off from a confounded vine? I haf not heard of such a thing. No, I will not bose as a model for your fool hermit-dunderhead. Vy do you allow dot silly pusiness to come in der prain of her? Ach, dot poor leetle Miss Yohnsy."

"She is very ill and weak," said Sue, "and the fever has left her mind morbid and full of strange fancies. Very well, Mr. Behrman, if you do not care to pose for me, you needn't. But I think you are a horrid old—old flibbertigibbet."

"You are just like a woman!" yelled Behrman. "Who said I will not bose? Go on. I come mit you. For half an hour I haf peen trying to say dot I am ready to bose. Gott! dis is not any blace in which one so goot as Miss Yohnsy shall lie sick. Some day I vill baint a masterpiece, and ve shall all go away. Gott! yes."

Johnsy was sleeping when they went upstairs. Sue pulled the shade down to the window-sill, and motioned Behrman into the other room. In there they peered out the window fearfully at the ivy vine. Then they looked at each other for a moment without speaking. A persistent, cold rain was falling, mingled with snow. Behrman, in his old blue shirt, took his seat as the hermit-miner on an upturned kettle for a rock.

When Sue awoke from an hour's sleep the next morning she found Johnsy with dull, wide-open eyes staring at the drawn green shade.

"Pull it up; I want to see," she ordered, in a whisper.

Wearily Sue obeyed.

But, lo! after the beating rain and fierce gusts of wind that had endured through the livelong night, there yet stood out against the brick wall one ivy leaf. It was the last one on the vine. Still dark green near its stem, but with its serrated edges tinted with the yellow of dissolution and decay, it hung bravely from a branch some twenty feet above the ground.

"It is the last one," said Johnsy. "I thought it would surely fall during the night. I heard the wind. It will fall to-day, and I shall die at the same time."

"Dear, dear!" said Sue, leaning her worn face down to the pillow, "think of me, if you won't think of yourself. What would I do?"

But Johnsy did not answer. The lonesomest thing in all the world is a soul when it is making ready to go on its mysterious, far journey. The fancy seemed to possess her more strongly as one by one the ties that bound her to friendship and to earth were loosed.

The day wore away, and even through the twilight they could see the lone ivy leaf clinging to its stem against the wall. And then, with the coming of the night the north wind was again loosed, while the rain still beat against the windows and pattered down from the low Dutch eaves.

When it was light enough Johnsy, the merciless, commanded that the shade be raised.

The ivy leaf was still there.

Johnsy lay for a long time looking at it. And then she called to Sue, who was stirring her chicken broth over the gas stove.

"I've been a bad girl, Sudie," said Johnsy. "Something has made that last leaf stay there to show me how wicked I was. It is a sin to want to die. You may bring me a little broth now, and some milk with a little port in it, and—no; bring me a hand-mirror first, and then pack some pillows about me, and I will sit up and watch you cook."

An hour later she said.

"Sudie, some day I hope to paint the Bay of Naples."

The doctor came in the afternoon, and Sue had an excuse to go into the hallway as he left.

"Even chances," said the doctor, taking Sue's thin, shaking hand in his. "With good nursing you'll win. And now I must see another case I have downstairs. Behrman, his name is—some kind of an artist, I believe. Pneumonia, too. He is an old, weak man, and the attack is acute. There is no hope for him; but he goes to the hospital to-day to be made more comfortable."

The next day the doctor said to Sue: "She's out of danger. You've won. Nutrition and care now—that's all."

And that afternoon Sue came to the bed where Johnsy lay, contentedly knitting a very blue and very useless woollen shoulder scarf, and put one arm around her, pillows and all.

"I have something to tell you, white mouse," she said. "Mr. Behrman died of pneumonia to-day in the hospital. He was ill only two days. The janitor found him on the morning of the first day in his room downstairs helpless with pain. His shoes and clothing were wet through and icy cold. They couldn't imagine where he had been on such a dreadful night. And then they found a lantern, still lighted, and a ladder that had been dragged from its place, and some scattered brushes, and a palette with green and yellow colors mixed on it, and—look out the window, dear, at the last ivy leaf on the wall. Didn't you wonder why it never fluttered or moved when the wind blew? Ah, darling, it's Behrman's masterpiece—he painted it there the night that the last leaf fell."

THE COUNT AND THE WEDDING GUEST

ONE evening when Andy Donovan went to dinner at his Second Avenue boarding-house, Mrs. Scott introduced him to a new boarder, a young lady, Miss Conway. Miss Conway was small and unobtrusive. She wore a plain, snuffy-brown dress, and bestowed her interest, which seemed languid, upon her plate. She lifted her diffident eyelids and shot one perspicuous, judicial glance at Mr. Donovan, politely murmured his name, and returned to her mutton. Mr. Donovan bowed with the grace and beaming smile that were rapidly winning for him social, business and political advancement, and erased the snuffy-brown one from the tablets of his consideration.

Two weeks later Andy was sitting on the front steps enjoying his cigar. There was a soft rustle behind and above him and Andy turned his head—and had his head turned.

Just coming out of the door was Miss Conway. She wore a night-black dress of crêpe de—crêpe de—oh, this thin black goods. Her hat was black, and from it drooped and fluttered an ebon veil, filmy as a spider's web. She stood on the top step and drew on black silk gloves. Not a speck of white or a spot of color about her dress anywhere. Her rich golden hair was drawn, with scarcely a ripple, into a shining, smooth knot low on her neck. Her face was plain rather than pretty, but it was now illuminated and made almost beautiful by her large gray eyes that gazed above the houses across the street into the sky with an expression of the most appealing sadness and melancholy.

Gather the idea, girls—all black, you know, with the preference for crêpe de—oh, crêpe de Chine—that's it. All black, and that sad, faraway look, and the hair shining under the black veil (you have to be a blonde, of course), and try to look as if, although your young life had been blighted just as it was about to give a hop-skip-and-a-jump over the threshold of life, a walk in the park might do you good, and be sure to happen out the door at the right moment, and—oh, it'll fetch 'em every time. But it's fierce, now, how cynical I am, ain't it?—to talk about mourning costumes this way.

Mr. Donovan suddenly reinscribed Miss Conway upon the tablets of his consideration. He threw away the remaining inch and a quarter of his cigar, that would have been good for eight minutes yet, and quickly shifted his center of gravity to his low-cut patent leathers.

"It's a fine, clear evening, Miss Conway," he said; and if the Weather Bureau could have heard the confident emphasis of his tones it would have hoisted the square white signal, and nailed it to the mast.

"To them that has the heart to enjoy it, it is, Mr. Donovan," said Miss Conway, with a sigh.

Mr. Donovan, in his heart, cursed fair weather. Heartless weather! It should hail and blow and snow to be consonant with the mood of Miss Conway.

"I hope none of your relatives—I hope you haven't sustained a loss?" ventured Mr. Donovan.

"Death has claimed," said Miss Conway, hesitating—"not a relative, but one who—but I will not intrude my grief upon you, Mr. Donovan."

"Intrude?" protested Mr. Donovan. "Why, say, Miss Conway, I'd be delighted, that is, I'd be sorry—I mean I'm sure nobody could sympathize with you truer than I would."

Miss Conway smiled a little smile. And oh, it was sadder than her expression in repose.

"'Laugh, and the world laughs with you; weep, and they give you the laugh,' " she quoted. "I have learned that, Mr. Donovan. I have no friends or acquaintances in this city. But you have been kind to me. I appreciate it highly."

He had passed her the pepper twice at the table.

"It's tough to be alone in New York—that's a cinch," said Mr. Donovan. "But, say—whenever this little old town does loosen up and get friendly it goes the limit. Say you took a little stroll in the park, Miss Conway—don't you think it might chase away some of your mullygrubs? And if you'd allow me——"

"Thanks, Mr. Donovan. I'd be pleased to accept of your escort if you think the company of one whose heart is filled with gloom could be anyways agreeable to you."

Through the open gates of the iron-railed, old, downtown park, where the elect once took the air, they strolled, and found a quiet bench.

There is this difference between the grief of youth and that of old age; youth's burden is lightened by as much of it as another shares; old age may give and give, but the sorrow remains the same.

"He was my fiancé," confided Miss Conway, at the end of an hour. "We were going to be married next spring. I don't want you to think that I am stringing you, Mr. Donovan, but he was a real Count. He had an estate and a castle in Italy. Count Fernando Mazzini was his name. I never saw the beat of him for elegance. Papa objected, of course, and once we eloped, but Papa overtook us, and took us back. I thought sure Papa and Fernando would fight a duel. Papa has a livery business—in P'kipsee, you know.

"Finally, Papa came 'round, all right, and said we might be married next spring. Fernando showed him proofs of his title and wealth, and then went over to Italy to get the castle fixed up for us. Papa's very proud and, when Fernando wanted to give me several thousand dollars for my trousseau he called him down something awful. He wouldn't even let me take a ring or any presents from him. And when Fernando sailed I came to the city and got a position as cashier in a candy store.

"Three days ago I got a letter from Italy, forwarded from P'kipsee, saying that Fernando had been killed in a gondola accident.

"That is why I am in mourning. My heart, Mr. Donovan, will remain forever in his grave. I guess I am poor company, Mr. Donovan, but I cannot take any interest in no one. I should not care to keep you from gayety and your friends who can smile and entertain you. Perhaps you would prefer to walk back to the house?"

Now, girls, if you want to observe a young man hustle out after a pick and shovel, just tell him that your heart is in some other fellow's grave. Young men are grave-robbers by nature. Ask any widow. Something must be done to restore that missing organ to weeping angels in *crêpe de Chine*. Dead men certainly get the worst of it from all sides.

"I'm awful sorry," said Mr. Donovan, gently. "No, we won't walk back to the house just yet. And don't say you haven't no friends in this city, Miss Conway. I'm awful sorry, and I want you to believe I'm your friend, and that I'm awful sorry."

"I've got his picture here in my locket," said Miss Conway, after wiping her eyes with her handkerchief. "I never showed it to anybody; but I will to you, Mr. Donovan, because I believe you to be a true friend."

Mr. Donovan gazed long and with much interest at the photograph in the locket that Miss Conway opened for him. The face of Count Mazzini was one to command interest. It was a smooth, intelligent, bright, almost a handsome face —the face of a strong, cheerful man who might well be a leader among his fellows.

"I have a larger one, framed, in my room," said Miss Conway. "When we return I will show you that. They are all I have to remind me of Fernando. But he ever will be present in my heart, that's a sure thing."

A subtle task confronted Mr. Donovan—that of supplanting the unfortunate Count in the heart of Miss Conway. This his admiration for her determined him to do. But the magnitude of the undertaking did not seem to weigh upon his spirits. The sympathetic but cheerful friend was the rôle he essayed; and he played it so successfully that the next half-hour found them conversing pensively across two plates of ice-cream, though yet there was no diminution of the sadness in Miss Conway's large gray eyes.

Before they parted in the hall that evening she ran upstairs and brought down the framed photograph wrapped lovingly in a white silk scarf. Mr. Donovan surveyed it with inscrutable eyes.

"He gave me this the night he left for Italy," said Miss Conway. "I had the one for the locket made from this."

"A fine-looking man," said Mr. Donovan, heartily. "How would it suit you, Miss Conway, to give me the pleasure of your company to Coney next Sunday afternoon?"

A month later they announced their engagement to Mrs. Scott and the other boarders. Miss Conway continued to wear black.

A week after the announcement the two sat on the same bench in the downtown park, while the fluttering leaves of the trees made a dim kinetoscopic picture of them in the moonlight. But Donovan had worn a look of abstracted gloom all day. He was so silent to-night that love's lips could not keep back any longer the questions that love's heart propounded.

"What's the matter, Andy, you are so solemn and grouchy to-night?"

"Nothing, Maggie."

"I know better. Can't I tell? You never acted this way before. What is it?"

"It's nothing much, Maggie?"

"Yes it is; and I want to know. I'll bet it's some other girl you are thinking about. All right. Why don't you go get her if you want her? Take your arm away, if you please."

"I'll tell you then," said Andy, wisely, "but I guess you won't understand it exactly. You've heard of Mike Sullivan, haven't you? 'Big Mike' Sullivan, everybody calls him."

"No, I haven't," said Maggie. "And I don't want to, if he makes you act like this. Who is he?"

"He's the biggest man in New York," said Andy, almost reverently. "He can about do anything he wants to with Tammany or any other old thing in the political line. He's a mile high and as broad as East River. You say anything against Big Mike, and you'll have a million men on your collarbone in about two seconds. Why, he made a visit over to the old country awhile back, and the kings took to their holes like rabbits.

"Well, Big Mike's a friend of mine. I ain't more than deuce-high in the district as far as influence goes, but Mike's as good a friend to a little man, or a poor man as he is to a big one. I met him to-day on the Bowery, and what do you think he does? Comes up and shakes hands. 'Andy,' says he, 'I've been keeping cases on you. You've been putting in some good licks over on your side of the street, and I'm proud of you. What'll you take to drink?' He takes a cigar and I take a highball. I told him I was going to get married in two weeks. 'Andy,' says he, 'send me an invitation, so I'll keep in mind of it, and I'll come to the wedding.' That's what Big Mike says to me; and he always does what he says.

"You don't understand it, Maggie, but I'd have one of my hands cut off to have Big Mike Sullivan at our wedding. It would be the proudest day of my life.

When he goes to a man's wedding, there's a guy being married that's made **for** life. Now, that's why I'm maybe looking sore to-night."

"Why don't you invite him, then, if he's so much to the mustard?" said Maggie, lightly.

"There's a reason why I can't," said Andy, sadly. "There's a reason why he mustn't be there. Don't ask me what it is, for I can't tell you."

"Oh, I don't care," said Maggie. "It's something about politics, of course. But it's no reason why you can't smile at me."

"Maggie," said Andy, presently, "do you think as much of me as you did of your—as you did of the Count Mazzini?"

He waited a long time, but Maggie did not reply. And then, suddenly she leaned against his shoulder and began to cry—to cry and shake with sobs, holding his arm tightly, and wetting the *crêpe de Chine* with tears.

"There, there, there!" soothed Andy, putting aside his own trouble. "And what is it, now?"

"Andy," sobbed Maggie. "I've lied to you, and you'll never marry me, or love me any more. But I feel that I've got to tell. Andy, there never was so much as the little finger of a count. I never had a beau in my life. But all the other girls had; and they talked about 'em; and that seemed to make the fellows like 'em more. And, Andy, I look swell in black—you know I do. So I went out to a photograph store and bought that picture, and had a little one made for my locket, and made up all that story about the Count and about his being killed, so I could wear black. And nobody can love a liar, and you'll shake me, Andy, and I'll die for shame. Oh, there never was anybody I liked but you—and that's all."

But instead of being pushed away, she found Andy's arm folding her closer. She looked up and saw his face cleared and smiling.

"Could you—could you forgive me, Andy?"

"Sure," said Andy. "It's all right about that. Back to the cemetery for the Count. You've straightened everything out, Maggie. I was in hopes you would before the wedding-day. Bully girl!"

"Andy," said Maggie, with a somewhat shy smile, after she had been thoroughly assured of forgiveness, "did you believe all that story about the Count?"

"Well, not to any large extent," said Andy, reaching for his cigar case; "because it's Big Mike Sullivan's picture you've got in that locket of yours."

THE COUNTRY OF ELUSION

THE cunning writer will choose an indefinable subject; for he can then set down his theory of what it is; and next, at length, his conception of what it is not—and lo! his paper is covered. Therefore let us follow the prolix and unmapable trail into that mooted country, Bohemia.

Grainger, sub-editor of *Doc's Magazine*, closed his roll-top desk, put on his hat, walked into the hall, punched the "down" button, and waited for the elevator.

Grainger's day had been trying. The chief had tried to ruin the magazine a dozen times by going against Grainger's ideas for running it. A lady whose grandfather had fought with McClellan had brought a portfolio of poems in person.

Grainger was curator of the Lion's House of the magazine. That day he had "lunched" an Arctic explorer, a short-story writer, and the famous conductor of a slaughter-house exposé. Consequently his mind was in a whirl of icebergs, Maupassant, and trichinosis.

But there was a surcease and a recourse; there was Bohemia. He would seek distraction there; and, let's see—he would call by for Mary Adrian.

Half an hour later he threaded his way like a Brazilian orchid-hunter through the palm forest in the tiled entrance hall of the "Idealia" apartment-house. One day the christeners of apartment-houses and the cognominators of sleeping-cars will meet, and there will be some jealous and sanguinary knifing.

The clerk breathed Grainger's name so languidly into the house telephone that it seemed it must surely drop, from sheer inertia, down to the janitor's regions. But, at length, it soared dilatorily up to Miss Adrian's ear. Certainly, Mr. Grainger was to come up immediately.

A colored maid with an Eliza-crossing-the-ice expression opened the door of the apartment for him. Grainger walked sideways down the narrow hall. A bunch of burnt-umber hair and a sea-green eye appeared in the crack of a door. A long, white, undraped arm came out, barring the way.

"So glad you came, Ricky, instead of any of the others," said the eye. "Light a cigarette and give it to me. Going to take me to dinner? Fine. Go into the front room till I finish dressing. But don't sit in your usual chair. There's pie in it—Meringue. Kappelman threw it at Reeves last evening while he was reciting. Sophy has just come to straighten up. Is it lit? Thanks. There's Scotch on the mantel—oh, no, it isn't—that's chartreuse. Ask Sophy to find you some. I won't be long."

Grainger escaped the meringue. As he waited his spirits sank still lower. The atmosphere of the room was as vapid as a zephyr wandering over a Vesuvian lava-bed. Relics of some feast lay about the room, scattered in places where even a prowling cat would have been surprised to find them. A straggling cluster of deep red roses in a marmalade jar bowed their heads over tobacco ashes and unwashed goblets. A chafing-dish stood on the piano; a leaf of sheet music supported a stack of sandwiches in a chair.

Mary came in, dressed and radiant. Her gown was of that thin, black fabric whose name through the change of a single vowel seems to summon visions ranging between the extremes of man's experience. Spelled with an "é" it belongs to Gallic witchery and diaphanous dreams; with an "a" it drapes lamentation and woe.

That evening they went to the Café André. And, as people would confide to you in a whisper that André's was the only truly Bohemian restaurant in town, it may be well to follow them.

André began his professional career as a waiter in a Bowery ten-cent eating-house. Had you seen him there you would have called him tough—to yourself. Not aloud, for he would have "soaked" you as quickly as he would have soaked his thumb in your coffee. He saved money and started a basement *table d'hôte* in Eight (or Ninth) Street. One afternoon André drank too much absinthe. He announced to his startled family that he was the Grand Llama of Thibet, therefore requiring an empty audience hall in which to be worshiped. He moved all the tables and chairs from the restaurant into the back yard, wrapped a red table-cloth around himself, and sat on a step-ladder for a throne. When the diners began to arrive, Madame in a flurry of despair, laid cloths and ushered them, trembling, outside. Between the tables clothes-lines were stretched, bearing the family wash. A party of Bohemia hunters greeted the artistic innovation with shrieks and acclamations of delight. That week's washing was not taken in for two years. When André came to his senses he had the menu printed on stiffly starched cuffs, and served the ices in little wooden tubs. Next he took down his sign and darkened the front of the house. When you went there to dine you fumbled for an electric button and pressed it. A lookout slid open a panel in the door, looked at you suspiciously, and asked if you were acquainted with Senator Herodotus Q. McMilligan, of the Chickasaw Nation. If you were, you were admitted and allowed to dine. If you were not, you were admitted and allowed to dine. There you have one of the abiding principles of Bohemia. When André had accumulated $20,000 he moved uptown, near Broadway, in the fierce light that beats upon the thrown-down. There we find him and leave him, with customers in pearls and automobile veils, striving to catch his excellently graduated nod of recognition.

There is a large round table in the northeast corner of André's at which six can sit. To this table Grainger and Mary Adrian made their way. Kappelman and Reeves were already there. And Miss Tooker, who designed the May cover for the *Ladies' Notathome Magazine*. And Mrs. Pothunter, who never drank anything but black-and-white highballs, being in mourning for her husband, who—oh, I've forgotten what he did—died, like as not.

Spaghetti-weary reader, wouldst take one penny-in-the-slot peep into the fair land of Bohemia? Then look; and when you think you have seen it you have not. And it is neither thimbleriggery nor astigmatism.

The walls of the Café André were covered with original sketches by the artists who furnished much of the color and sound of the place. Fair woman furnished the theme for the bulk of the drawings. When you say "sirens and siphons" you come near to estimating the alliterative atmosphere of André's.

First, I want you to meet my friend, Miss Adrian. Miss Tooker and Mrs. Pothunter you already know. While she tucks in the fingers of her elbow gloves you shall have her daguerreotype. So faint and uncertain shall the portrait be:

Age, somewhere between twenty-seven and high-neck evening dresses. Camaraderie in large bunches—whatever the fearful word may mean. Habitat—anywhere from Seattle to Tierra del Fuego. Temperament uncharted—she let Reeves squeeze her hand after he recited one of his poems; but she counted the change after sending him out with a dollar to buy some pickled pig's feet. Deportment 75 out of a possible 100. Morals 100.

Mary was one of the princesses of Bohemia. In the first place, it was a royal and a daring thing to have been named Mary. There are twenty Fifines and Héloïses to one Mary in the Country of Elusion.

Now her gloves are tucked in. Miss Tooker has assumed a June poster pose; Mrs. Pothunter has bitten her lips to make the red show; Reeves has several times felt his coat to make sure that his latest poem is in the pocket. (It had been neatly typewritten; but he has copied it on the backs of letters with a pencil.) Kappelman is underhandedly watching the clock. It is ten minutes to nine. When the hour comes it is to remind him of a story. Synopsis: A French girl says to her suitor: "Did you ask my father for my hand at nine o'clock this morning, as you said you would?" "I did not," he replies. "At nine o'clock I was fighting a duel with swords in the Bois de Boulogne." "Coward!" she hisses.

The dinner was ordered. You know how long the Bohemian feast of reason keeps up with the courses. Humor with the oysters; wit with the soup; repartee with the entrée; brag with the roast; knocks for Whistler and Kipling with the salad; songs with the coffee, the slapsticks with the cordials.

Between Miss Adrian's eyebrows was the pucker that shows the intense strain it requires to be at ease in Bohemia. Pat must come each sally, *mot*, and epigram. Every second of deliberation upon a reply costs you a bay leaf. Fine as a hair, a line began to curve from her nostrils to her mouth. To hold her own not a chance must be missed. A sentence addressed to her must be as a piccolo, each word of it a stop, which she must be prepared to seize upon and play. And she must always be quicker than a Micmac Indian to paddle the light canoe of conversation away from the rocks in the rapids that flow from the

Pierian spring. For, plodding reader, the handwriting on the wall in the banquet hall of Bohemia is *"Laisser faire."* The gray ghost that sometimes peeps through the rings of smoke is that of slain old King Convention. Freedom is the tyrant that holds them in slavery.

As the dinner waned, hands reached for the pepper cruet rather than for the shaker of Attic salt. Miss Tooker, with an elbow to business, leaned across the table toward Grainger, upsetting her glass of wine.

"Now, while you are fed and in good humor," she said, "I want to make a suggestion to you about a new cover."

"A good idea," said Grainger, mopping the tablecloth with his napkin. "I'll speak to the waiter about it."

Kappleman, the painter, was the cut-up. As a piece of delicate Athenian wit he got up from his chair and waltzed down the room with a waiter. That dependent, no doubt an honest, pachydermatous, worthy, tax-paying, art-despising biped, released himself from the unequal encounter, carried his professional smile back to the dumb-waiter and dropped it down the shaft to eternal oblivion. Reeves began to make Keats turn in his grave. Mrs. Pothunter told the story of the man who met the widow on the train. Miss Adrian hummed what is still called a *chanson* in the cafés of Bridgeport. Grainger edited each individual effort with his assistant editor's smile, which meant: "Great! but you'll have to send them in through the regular channels. If I were the chief now—but you know how it is."

And soon the head waiter bowed before them, desolated to relate that the closing hour had already become chronologically historical; so out all trooped into the starry midnight, filling the street with gay laughter, to be barked at by hopeful cabmen and enviously eyed by the dull inhabitants of an uninspired world.

Grainger left Mary at the elevator in the trackless palm forest of the Idealia. after he had gone she came down again carrying a small hand-bag, 'phoned for a cab, drove to the Grand Central Station, boarded a 12.55 commuter's train, rode four hours with her burnt-umber head bobbing against the red-plush back of the seat, and landed during a fresh, stinging, glorious sunrise at a deserted station, the size of a peach crate, called Crocusville.

She walked a mile and clicked the latch of a gate. A bare, brown cottage stood twenty yards back; an old man with a pearl-white, Calvinistic face and clothes dyed blacker than a raven in a coal-mine was washing his hands in a tin basin on the front porch.

"How are you, Father?" said Mary timidly.

"I am as well as Providence permits, Mary Ann. You will find your mother in the kitchen."

In the kitchen a cryptic, gray woman kissed her glacially on the forehead, and pointed out the potatoes which were not yet peeled for breakfast. Mary sat in a wooden chair and decorticated spuds, with a thrill in her heart.

For breakfast there were grace, cold bread, potatoes, bacon, and tea.

"You are pursuing the same avocation in the city concerning which you have advised us from time to time by letter, I trust," said her father.

"Yes," said Mary. "I am still reviewing books for the same publication."

After breakfast she helped wash the dishes, and then all three sat in straight-back chairs in the barefloored parlor.

"It is my custom," said the old man, "on the Sabbath day to read aloud from the great work entitled the 'Apology for Authorized and Set Forms of Liturgy,' by the ecclesiastical philosopher and revered theologian, Jeremy Taylor."

"I know it," said Mary blissfully, folding her hands.

For two hours the numbers of the great Jeremy rolled forth like the notes of an oratorio played on the violoncello. Mary sat gloating in the new sensa-

tion of racking physical discomfort that the wooden chair brought her. Perhaps there is no happiness in life so perfect as the martyr's. Jeremy's minor
chords soothed her like the music of tom-tom. "Why, oh why," she said to herself, "does some one not write words to it?"

At eleven they went to church in Crocusville. The back of the pine bench
on which she sat had a penitential forward tilt that would have brought St.
Simeon down, in jealousy, from his pillar. The preacher singled her out, and
thundered upon her vicarious head the damnation of the world. At each side
of her an adamant parent held her rigidly to the bar of judgment. An ant
crawled upon her neck, but she dared not move. She lowered her eyes before the
congregation—a hundred-eyed Cerberus that watched the gates through which
her sins were fast thrusting her. Her soul was filled with a delirious, almost a
fanatic joy. For she was out of the clutch of the tyrant, Freedom. Dogma and
creed pinioned her with beneficent cruelty, as steel braces bind the feet of a
crippled child. She was hedged, adjured, shackled, shored up, strait-jacketed,
silenced, ordered. When they came out the minister stopped to greet them. Mary
could only hang her head and answer "Yes, sir," and "No, sir," to his questions.
When she saw that the other women carried their hymn-books at their waists
with their left hands, she blushed and moved hers there, too, from her right.

She took the three-o'clock train back to the city. At nine she sat at the round
table for dinner in the Café André. Nearly the same crowd was there.

"Where have you been to-day?" asked Mrs. Pothunter. "I 'phoned to you at
twelve."

"I have been away in Bohemia," answered Mary, with a mystic smile.

There! Mary has given it away. She has spoiled my climax. For I was
to have told you that Bohemia is nothing more than the little country in which
you do not live. If you try to obtain citizenship in it, at once the court and
retinue pack the royal archives and treasure and move away beyond the hills.
It is a hillside that you turn your head to peer at from the windows of the
Through Express.

At exactly half past eleven Kappelman, deceived by a new softness and slowness of *riposte* and parry in Mary Adrian, tried to kiss her. Instantly she
slapped his face with such strength and cold fury that he shrank down, sobered,
with the flaming red print of a hand across his leering features. And all sounds
ceased, as when the shadows of great wings come upon a flock of chattering
sparrows. One had broken the paramount law of sham-Bohemia—the law of
"*Laisser faire.*" The shock came not from the blow delivered, but from the
blow received. With the effect of a schoolmaster entering the play-room of his
pupils was that blow administered. Women pulled down their sleeves and laid
prim hands against their ruffled side locks. Men looked at their watches. There
was nothing of the effect of a brawl about it; it was purely the still panic produced by the sound of the ax of the fly cop, Conscience, hammering at the
gambling-house doors of the Heart.

With their punctilious putting on of cloaks, with their exaggerated pretense of
not having seen or heard, with their stammering exchange of unaccustomed formalities, with their false show of a light-hearted exit I must take leave of my
Bohemian party. Mary has robbed me of my climax; and she may go.

But I am not defeated. Somewhere there exists a great vault miles broad and
miles long—more capacious than the champagne caves of France. In that vault
are stored the anti-climaxes that should have been tagged to all the stories that
have been told in the world. I shall cheat that vault of one deposit.

Minnie Brown, with her aunt, came from Crocusville down to the city to see
the sights. And because she had escorted me to fishless trout streams and exhibited to me open-plumbed waterfalls and broken my camera while I Julyed in

her village, I must escort her to the hives containing the synthetic clover honey of town.

Especially did the custom-made Bohemia charm her. The spaghetti wound its tendrils about her heart; the free red wine drowned her belief in the existence of commercialism in the world; she was dazed and enchanted by the rugose wit that can be churned out of California claret.

But one evening I got her away from the smell of halibut and linoleum long enough to read to her the manuscript of this story, which then ended before her entrance into it. I read it to her because I knew that all the printing-presses in the world were running to try to please her and some others. And I asked her about it. "I didn't quite catch the trains," said she. "How long was Mary in Crocusville?"

"Ten hours and five minutes." I replied.

"Well, then the story may do," said Minnie. "But if she had stayed there a week Kappelman would have got his kiss."

THE FERRY OF UNFULFILMENT

At the street corner, as solid as granite in the "rush-hour" tide of humanity, stood the Man from Nome. The Arctic winds and sun had stained him berry-brown. His eye still held the azure glint of the glaciers.

He was as alert as a fox, as tough as a caribou cutlet and as broad-gauged as the aurora borealis. He stood sprayed by a Niagara of sound—the crash of the elevated trains, clanging cars, pounding of rubberless tires and the antiphony of the cab and truck-drivers indulging in scarifying repartee. And so, with his gold dust cashed in to the merry air of a hundred thousand, and with the cakes and ale of one week in Gotham turning bitter on his tongue, the Man from Nome sighed to set foot again in Chilkoot, the exit from the land of street noises and Dead Sea apple pies.

Up Sixth Avenue, with the tripping, scurrying, chattering, bright-eyed, homing tide came the Girl from Sieber-Mason's. The Man from Nome looked and saw, first, that she was supremely beautiful after his own conception of beauty; and next, that she moved with exactly the steady grace of a dog sled on a level crust of snow. His third sensation was an instantaneous conviction that he desired her greatly for his own. Thus quickly do men from Nome make up their minds. Besides, he was going back to the North in a short time and to act quickly was no less necessary.

A thousand girls from the great department store of Sieber-Mason flowed along the side-walk, making navigation dangerous to men whose feminine field of vision for three years has been chiefly limited to Siwash and Chilkat squaws. But the Man from Nome, loyal to her who had resurrected his long-cached heart, plunged into the stream of pulchritude and followed her.

Down Twenty-third Street she glided swiftly, looking to neither side; no more flirtatious than the bronze Diana above the Garden. Her fine brown hair was neatly braided; her neat waist and unwrinkled black skirt were eloquent of the double virtues—taste and economy. Ten yards behind followed the smitten Man from Nome.

Miss Claribel Colby, the Girl from Sieber-Mason's, belonged to that sad company of mariners known as Jersey commuters. She walked into the waiting-room of the ferry, and up the stairs, and by a marvellous swift, little run, caught the ferry-boat that was just going out. The Man from Nome closed up his ten yards in three jumps and gained the deck close beside her.

Miss Colby chose a rather lonely seat on the outside of the upper cabin. The night was not cold, and she desired to be away from the curious eyes and tedious voices of the passengers. Besides, she was extremely weary and drooping from lack of sleep. On the previous night she had graced the annual ball and oyster fry of the West Side Wholesale Fish Dealers' Assistants' Social Club No. 2, thus reducing her usual time of sleep to only three hours.

And the day had been uncommonly troublous. Customers had been inordinately trying; the buyer in her department had scolded her roundly for letting her stock run down; her best friend, Mamie Tuthill, had snubbed her by going to lunch with that Dockery girl.

The Girl from Sieber-Mason's was in that relaxed, softened mood that often comes to the independent feminine wage-earner. It is a mood most propitious for the man who would woo her. Then she has yearnings to be set in some home and heart; to be comforted, and to hide behind some strong arm and rest, rest. But Miss Claribel Colby was also very sleepy.

There came to her side a strong man, browned and dressed carelessly in the best of clothes with his hat in his hand.

"Lady," said the Man from Nome, respectfully, "excuse me for speaking to you, but I—I—saw you on the street, and—and——"

"Oh, gee!" remarked the Girl from Sieber-Mason's, glancing up with the most capable coolness. "Ain't there any way to ever get rid of you mashers? I've tried everything from eating onions to using hatpins. Be on your way, Freddie."

"I'm not one of that kind, lady," said the Man from Nome—"honest, I'm not. As I say, I saw you on the street, and I wanted to know you so bad I couldn't help followin' after you. I was afraid I wouldn't ever see you again in this big town unless I spoke; and that's why I done so."

Miss Colby looked once shrewdly at him in the dim light on the ferry-boat. No; he did not have the perfidious smirk or the brazen swagger of the lady-killer. Sincerity and modesty shone through his boreal tan. It seemed to her that it might be good to hear a little of what he had to say.

"You may sit down," she said, laying her hand over a yawn with ostentatious politeness; "and—mind—don't get fresh or I'll call the steward."

The Man from Nome sat by her side. He admired her greatly. He more than admired her. She had exactly the looks he had tried so long in vain to find in a woman. Could she ever come to like him? Well, that was to be seen. He must do all in his power to stake his claim, anyhow.

"My name's Blayden," said he—"Henry Blayden."

"Are you real sure it ain't Jones?" asked the girl, leaning toward him, with delicious, knowing raillery.

"I'm down from Nome," he went on with anxious seriousness. "I scraped together a pretty good lot of dust up there, and brought it down with me."

"Oh, say!" she rippled, pursuing persiflage with engaging lightness, "then you must be on the White Wings force. I thought I'd seen you somewhere."

"You didn't see me on the street to-day when I saw you."

"I never look at fellows on the street."

"Well, I looked at you; and I never looked at anything before that I thought was half as pretty."

"Shall I keep the change?"

"Yes, I reckon so. I reckon you could keep anything I've got. I reckon I'm what you would call a rough man, but I could be awful good to anybody I liked. I've had a rough time of it up yonder, but I beat the game. Nearly 5,000 ounces of dust was what I cleaned up while I was there."

"Goodness!" exclaimed Miss Colby, obligingly sympathetic. "It must be an awful dirty place, wherever it is."

And then her eyes closed. The voice of the Man from Nome had a monotony in its very earnestness. Besides, what dull talk was this of brooms and sweeping and dust? She leaned her head back against the wall.

"Miss," said the Man from Nome, with deeper earnestness and monotony, "I never saw anybody I liked as well as I do you. I know you can't think that way of me right yet; but can't you give me a chance? Won't you let me know you, and see if I can't make you like me?"

The head of the Girl from Sieber-Mason's slid over gently and rested upon his shoulder. Sweet sleep had won her, and she was dreaming rapturously of the Wholesale Fish Dealer's Assistants' ball.

The gentleman from Nome kept his arms to himself. He did not suspect sleep, and yet he was too wise to attribute the movement to surrender. He was greatly and blissfully thrilled, but he ended by regarding the head upon his shoulder as an encouraging preliminary, merely advanced as a harbinger of his success, and not to be taken advantage of.

One small speck of alloy discounted the gold of his satisfaction. Had he spoken too freely of his wealth? He wanted to be liked for himself.

"I want to say, Miss," he said, "that you can count on me. They know me in the Klondike from Juneau to Circle City and down the whole length of the Yukon. Many a night I've laid in the snow up there where I worked like a slave for three years, and wondered if I'd ever have anybody to like me. I didn't want all that dust just myself. I thought I'd meet just the right one some time, and I done it to-day. Money's a mighty good thing to have, but to have the love of the one you like best is better still. If you was ever to marry a man, Miss, which would you rather he'd have?"

"Cash!"

The word came sharply and loudly from Miss Colby's lips, giving evidence that in her dreams she was now behind her counter in the great department store of Sieber-Mason.

Her head suddenly bobbed over sideways. She awoke, sat straight, and rubbed her eyes. The Man from Nome was gone.

"Gee! I believe I've been asleep," said Miss Colby. "Wonder what became of the White Wings!"

THE TALE OF A TAINTED TENNER

MONEY talks. But you may think that the conversation of a little old ten-dollar bill in New York would be nothing more than a whisper. Oh, very well! Pass up this *sotto voce* autobiography of an X if you like. If you are one of the kind that prefers to listen to John D's checkbook roar at you through a megaphone as it passes by, all right. But don't forget that small change can say a word to the point now and then. The next time you tip your grocer's clerk a silver quarter to give you extra weight of his boss's goods read the four words above the lady's head. How are they for repartee?

I am a ten-dollar Treasury note, series of 1901. You may have seen one in a friend's hand. On my face, in the centre, is a picture of the bison Americanus, miscalled a buffalo by fifty or sixty millions of Americans. The heads of Capt. Lewis and Capt. Clark adorn the ends. On my back is the graceful figure of Liberty or Ceres or Maxine Elliot standing in the centre of the stage on a conservatory plant. My references is—or are—Section 3,588, Revised Statutes. Ten cold, hard dollars—I don't say whether silver, gold, lead or iron—Uncle Sam will hand you over his counter if you want to cash me in.

I beg you will excuse any conversational breaks that I make—thanks, I knew you would—got that sneaking little respect and agreeable feeling toward even an X, haven't you? You see, a tainted bill doesn't have much chance to acquire a correct form of expression. I never knew a really cultured and educated person that could afford to hold a ten-spot any longer than it would take to do an Arthur Duffy to the nearest That's All! sign or delicatessen store.

For a six-year-old, I've had a lively and gorgeous circulation. I guess I've paid as many debts as the man who dies. I've been owned by a good many kinds of people. But a little old ragged, damp, dingy five-dollar silver certificate gave me a jar one day. I was next to it in the fat and bad-smelling purse of a butcher.

"Hey, you Sitting Bull," says I, "don't scrouge so. Anyhow, don't you think it's about time you went in on a customs payment and got reissued? For a series of 1899 you're a sight."

"Oh, don't get crackly just because you're a Buffalo bill," says the fiver. "You'd be limp, too, if you'd been stuffed down in a thick cotton-and-lisle-thread under an elastic all day, and the thermometer not a degree under 85 in the store."

"I never heard of a pocketbook like that," says I. "Who carried you?"

"A shopgirl," says the five-spot.

"What's that?" I had to ask.

"You'll never know till their millennium comes," says the fiver.

Just then a two-dollar bill behind me with a George Washington head, spoke up to the fiver:

"Aw, cut out yer kicks. Ain't lisle thread good enough for yer? If you was under all cotton like I've been to-day, and choked up with factory dust till the lady with the cornucopia on me sneezed half a dozen times, you'd have some reason to complain."

That was the next day after I arrived in New York. I came in a $500 package of tens to a Brooklyn bank from one if its Pennsylvania correspondents—and I haven't made the acquaintance of any of the five and two spot's friends' pocketbooks yet. Silk for mine, every time.

I was lucky money. I kept on the move. Sometimes I changed hands twenty times a day. I saw the inside of every business; I fought for my owner's every pleasure. It seemed that on Saturday nights I never missed being slapped down on a bar. Tens were always slapped down, while ones and twos were slid over to the bartenders folded. I got in the habit of looking for mine, and I managed to soak in a little straight or some spilled Martini or Manhattan whenever I could. Once I got tied up in a great greasy roll of bills in a push-cart peddler's jeans. I thought I never would get in circulation again, for the future department store owner lived on eight cents' worth of dog meat and onions a day. But this peddler got into trouble one day on account of having his cart too near a crossing, and I was rescued. I always will feel grateful to the cop that got me. He changed me at a cigar store near the Bowery that was running a crap game in the back room. So it was the Captain of the precinct, after all, that did me the best turn, when he got his. He blew me for wine the next evening in a Broadway restaurant; and I really felt as glad to get back again as an Astor does when he sees the lights of Charing Cross.

A tainted ten certainly does get action on Broadway. I was alimony once, and got folded in a little dogskin purse among a lot of dimes. They were bragging about the busy times there were in Ossining whenever three girls got hold of one of them during the ice cream season. But it's Slow Moving Vehicles Keep to the Right for the little Bok tips when you think of the way we bison plasters refuse to stick to anything during the rush lobster hour.

The first I ever heard of tainted money was one night when a good thing with a Van to his name threw me over with some other bills to buy a stack of blues.

About midnight a big, easy-going man with a fat face like a monk's and the eye of a janitor with his wages raised took me and a lot of other notes and rolled us into what is termed a "wad" among the money tainters.

"Ticket me for five hundred," said he to the banker, "and look out for everything, Charlie. I'm going out for stroll in the glen before the moonlight fades from the brow of the cliff. If anybody finds the roof in their way there's $60,000 wrapped in a comic supplement in the upper left-hand corner of the safe. Be bold; everywhere be bold, but be not bowled over. 'Night."

I found myself between two $20 gold certificates. One of 'em says to me:

"Well, old shorthorn, you're in luck to-night. You'll see something of life. Old Jack's going to make the Tenderloin look like a hamburg steak."

"Explain," says I. "I'm used to joints, but I don't care for filet mignon with the kind of sauce you serve."

" 'Xcuse me," said the twenty. "Old Jack is the proprietor of this gambling house. He's going on a whiz to-night because he offered $50,000 to a church and it refused to accept it because they said his money was tainted."

"What is a church?" I asked.

"Oh, I forgot," says the twenty, "that I was talking to a tenner. Of course you don't know. You're too much to put into the contribution basket, and not enough to buy anything at a bazaar. A church is—a large building in which penwipers and tidies are sold at $20 each."

I don't care much about chinning with gold certificates. There's a streak of yellow in 'em. All is not gold that quitters.

Old Jack certainly was a gild-edged sport. When it came his time to loosen up he never referred the waiter to an actuary.

By and by it got around that he was smiting the rock in the wilderness; and all along Broadway things with cold noses and hot gullets fell in on our trail. The third Jungle Book was there waiting for somebody to put covers on it. Old Jack's money may have had a taint to it, but all the same he had orders for his Camembert piling up on him every minute. First his friends rallied round him; and then the fellows that his friends knew by sight; and then a few of his enemies buried the hatchet; and finally he was buying souvenirs for so many Neapolitan fisher maidens and butterfly octettes that the head waiters were 'phoning all over town for Julian Mitchell to please come around and get them into some kind of order.

At last we floated into an uptown café that I knew by heart. When the hod-carriers' union in jackets and aprons saw us coming the chief goal kicker called out: "Six—eleven—forty-two—nineteen—twelve" to his men, and they put on nose guards till it was clear whether we meant Port Arthur or Portsmouth. But old Jack wasn't working for the furniture and glass factories that night. He sat down quiet and sang "Ramble" in a half-hearted way. His feelings had been hurt, so the twenty told me, because his offer to the church had been refused.

But the wassail went on; and Brady himself couldn't have hammered the thirst mob into a better imitation of the real penchant for the stuff that you screw out of a bottle with a napkin.

Old Jack paid the twenty above me for a round, leaving me on the outside of his roll. He laid the roll on the table and sent for the proprietor.

"Mike," says he, "here's money that the good people have refused. Will it buy of your wares in the name of the devil? They say it's tainted."

"It will," says Mike, "and I'll put it in the drawer next to the bills that was paid to the parson's daughter for kisses at the church fair to build a new parsonage for the parson's daughter to live in."

At 1 o'clock when the hod-carriers were making ready to close up the front and keep the inside open, a woman slips in the door of the restaurant and comes up to Old Jack's table. You've seen the kind—black shawl, creepy hair, ragged skirt, white face, eyes a cross between Gabriel's and a sick kitten's—the kind of woman that's always on the lookout for an automobile or the mendicancy squad—and she stands there without a word and looks at the money.

Old Jack gets up, peels me off the roll and hands me to her with a bow.

"Madam," says he, just like actors I've heard, "here is a tainted bill. I am a gambler. This bill came to me to-night from a gentleman's son. Where he got it I do not know. If you will do me the favor to accept it, it is yours."

The woman took me with a trembling hand.

"Sir," said she, "I counted thousands of this issue of bills into packages when they were virgin from the presses. I was a clerk in the Treasury Department. There was an official to whom I owed my position. You say they are tainted now. If you only knew—but I won't say any more. Thank you with all my heart, sir—thank you—thank you."

Where do you suppose that woman carried me almost at a run? To a bakery. Away from Old Jack and a sizzling good time to a bakery. And I got changed, and she does a Sheridan-twenty-miles-away with a dozen rolls and a section of jelly cake as big as a turbine water-wheel. Of course I lost sight of her then, for I was snowed up in the bakery, wondering whether I'd get changed at the drug store the next day in an alum deal or paid over to the cement works.

A week afterward I butted up against one of the one-dollar bills the baker had given the woman for change.

"Hallo, E35039669," says I, "weren't you in the change for me in a bakery last Saturday night?"

"Yep," says the solitaire in his free and easy style.

"How did the deal turn out?" I asked.

"She blew E17051431 for milk and round steak," says the one-spot. "She kept me till the rent man came. It was a bum room with a sick kid in it. But you ought to have seen him go for the bread and tincture of formaldehyde. Half-starved, I guess. Then she prayed some. Don't get stuck up, tenner. We one-spots hear ten prayers, where you hear one. She said something about 'who giveth to the poor.' Oh, let's cut out the slum talk. I'm certainly tired of the company that keeps me. I wish I was big enough to move in society with you tainted bills."

"Shut up," says I, "there's no such thing. I know the rest of it. There's a 'lendeth to the Lord' somewhere in it. Now look on my back and read what you see there."

"This note is a legal tender at its face value for all debts public and private."

"This talk about tainted money makes me tired," says I.

ELSIE IN NEW YORK

No, bumptious reader, this story is not a continuation of the Elsie series. But if your Elsie had lived over here in our big city there might have been a chapter in her books not very different from this.

Especially for the vagrant feet of youth are the roads of Manhattan beset "with pitfall and with gin." But the civic guardians of the young have made themselves acquainted with the snares of the wicked and, most of the dangerous paths are patrolled by their agents, who seek to turn straying ones away from the peril that menaces them. And this will tell you how they guided my Elsie safely through all peril to the goal that she was seeking.

Elsie's father had been a cutter for Fox & Otter, cloaks and furs, on lower Broadway. He was an old man, with a slow and limping gait, so a pot-hunter of a newly licensed chauffeur ran him down one day when livelier game was scarce. They took the old man home, where he lay on his bed for a year and then died, leaving $2.50 in cash and a letter from Mr. Otter offering to do anything he could to help his faithful old employee. The old cutter regarded this letter as a valuable legacy to his daughter, and he put it into her hands with pride as the shears of the dread Cleaner and Repairer snipped off his thread of life.

That was the landlord's cue; and forth he came and did his part in the great eviction scene. There was no snowstorm ready for Elsie to steal out into, drawing her little red woollen shawl about her shoulders, but she went out, regardless of the unities. And as for the red shawl—back to Blaney with it! Elsie's fall tan coat was cheap, but it had the style and fit of the best at Fox & Otter's. And her lucky stars had given her good looks, and eyes as blue and innocent as the new shade of note paper, and she had $1 left of the $2.50. And the letter from Mr. Otter. Keep your eye on the letter from Mr. Otter. That is the clue. I desire that everything be made plain as we go. Detective stories are so plentiful now that they do not sell.

And so we find Elsie, thus equipped, starting out in the world to seek her fortune. One trouble about the letter from Mr. Otter was that it did not bear the new address of the firm, which had moved about a month before. But Elsie thought she could find it. She had heard that policemen, when politely addressed, or thumbscrewed by an investigation committee, will give up information and addresses. So she boarded a downtown car at One Hundred and Seventy-seventh Street and rode south to Forty-second, which she thought must surely be the end of the island. There she stood against the wall undecided, for the city's roar and dash was new to her. Up where she lived was rural New York, so far out that the milkmen awaken you in the morning by the squeaking of pumps instead of the rattling of cans.

A kind-faced, sunburned, young man in a soft-brimmed hat went past Elsie into the Grand Central Depot. That was Hank Ross, of the Sunflower Ranch, in Idaho, on his way home from a visit to the East. Hank's heart was heavy, for the Sunflower Ranch was a lonesome place, lacking the presence of a woman. He had hoped to find one during his visit who would congenially share his prosperity and home, but the girls of Gotham had not pleased his fancy. But, as he passed in, he noted, with a jumping of his pulses, the sweet, ingenuous face of Elsie and her pose of doubt and loneliness. With true and honest Western impulse he said to himself that here was his mate. He could love her, he knew; and he would surround her with so much comfort, and cherish her so carefully that she would be happy, and make two sunflowers grow on the ranch where there grew but one before.

Hank turned and went back to her. Backed by his never-before-questioned honesty of purpose, he approached the girl and removed his soft-brimmed hat. Elsie had but time to sum up his handsome frank face with one shy look of modest admiration when a burly cop hurled himself upon the ranchman, seized him by the collar and backed him against the wall. Two blocks away a burglar was coming out of an apartment-house with a bag of silverware on his shoulder; but that is neither here nor there.

"Carry on yez mashin' tricks right before me eyes, will yez?" shouted the cop. "I'll teach yez to speak to ladies on me beat that ye're not acquainted with. Come along."

Elsie turned away with a sigh as the ranchman was dragged away. She had liked the effect of his light blue eyes against his tanned complexion. She walked southward, thinking herself already in the district where her father used to work, and hoping to find some one who could direct her to the firm of Fox & Otter.

But did she want to find Mr. Otter? She had inherited much of the old cutter's independence. How much better it would be if she could find work and support herself without calling on him for aid!

Elsie saw a sign "Employment Agency" and went in. Many girls were sitting against the wall in chairs. Several well-dressed ladies were looking them over. One white-haired, kind-faced old lady in rustling black silk hurried up to Elsie.

"My dear," she said in a sweet, gentle voice, "are you looking for a position? I like your face and appearance so much. I want a young woman who will be half maid and half companion to me. You will have a good home and I will pay you $30 a month."

Before Elsie could stammer forth her gratified acceptance, a young woman with gold glasses on her bony nose and her hands in her jacket pockets seized her arm and drew her aside.

"I am Miss Ticklebaum," said she, "of the Association for the Prevention of Jobs Being Put Up on Working Girls Looking for Jobs. We prevented forty-seven girls from securing positions last week. I am here to protect you. Beware of any one who offers you a job. How do you know that this woman does not want to make you work as a breaker-boy in a coal mine or murder you to get your teeth? If you accept work of any kind without permission of our association you will be arrested by one of our agents."

"But what am I to do?" asked Elsie. "I have no home or money. I must do something. Why am I not allowed to accept this kind lady's offer?"

"I do not know," said Miss Ticklebaum. "That is the affair of our Committee on the Abolishment of Employers. It is my duty simply to see that you do not get work. You will give me your name and address and report to our secretary every Thursday. We have 600 girls on the waiting list who will in time be allowed to accept positions as vacancies occur on our roll of Qualified Employers, which now comprise twenty-seven names. There is prayer, music and lemonade in our chapel the third Sunday of every month."

Elsie hurried away after thanking Miss Ticklebaum for her timely warning and advice. After all, it seemed that she must try to find Mr. Otter.

But after walking a few blocks she saw a sign, "Cashier wanted," in the window of a confectionery store. In she went and applied for the place, after casting a quick glance over her shoulder to assure herself that the job-preventer was not on her trail.

The proprietor of the confectionery was a benevolent old man with a peppermint flavor, who decided, after questioning Elsie pretty closely, that she was the very girl he wanted. Her services were needed at once, so Elsie, with a thankful heart, drew off her tan coat and prepared to mount the cashier's stool.

But before she could do so a gaunt lady wearing steel spectacles and black mittens stood before her, with a long finger pointing, and exclaimed: "Young woman, hesitate!"

Elsie hesitated.

"Do you know," said the black-and-steel lady, "that in accepting this position you may this day cause the loss of a hundred lives in agonizing physical torture and the sending as many souls to perdition?"

"Why, no," said Elsie, in frightened tones. "How could I do that?"

"Rum," said the lady—"the demon rum. Do you know why so many lives are lost when a theatre catches fire? Brandy balls. The demon rum lurking in brandy balls. Our society women while in theatres sit grossly intoxicated from eating these candies filled with brandy. When the fire fiend sweeps down upon them they are unable to escape. The candy stores are the devil's distilleries. If you assist in the distribution of these insidious confections you assist in the destruction of the bodies and souls of your fellow-beings, and in the filling of our jails, asylums and almshouses. Think, girl, ere you touch the money for which brandy balls are sold."

"Dear me," said Elsie, bewildered. "I didn't know there was rum in brandy balls. But I must live by some means. What shall I do?"

"Decline the position," said the lady, "and come with me. I will tell you what to do."

After Elsie had told the confectioner that she had changed her mind about the cashiership she put on her coat and followed the lady to the sidewalk, where awaited an elegant victoria.

"Seek some other work," said the black-and-steel lady, "and assist in crushing the hydra-headed demon rum." And she got into the victoria and drove away.

"I guess that puts it up to Mr. Otter again," said Elsie, ruefully, turning down the street. "And I'm sorry, too, for I'd much rather make my way without help."

Near Fourteenth Street Elsie saw a placard tacked on the side of a doorway that read: "Fifty girls, neat sewers, wanted immediately on theatrical costumes. Good pay."

She was about to enter, when a solemn man, dressed all in black, laid his hand on her arm.

"My dear girl," he said, "I entreat you not to enter that dressing-room of the devil."

"Goodness me!" exclaimed Elsie, with some impatience. "The devil seems to have a cinch on all the business in New York. What's wrong about the place?"

"It is here," said the solemn man, "that the regalia of Satan—in other words, the costumes worn on the stage—are manufactured. The stage is the road to ruin and destruction. Would you imperil your soul by lending the work of your hands to its support? Do you know, my dear girl, what the theatre leads to? Do you know where actors and actresses go after the curtain of the playhouse has fallen upon them for the last time?"

"Sure," said Elsie. "Into vaudeville. But do you think it would be wicked for me to make a little money to live on by sewing? I must get something to do pretty soon."

"The flesh-pots of Egypt," exclaimed the reverend gentleman, uplifting his hands. "I beseech you, my child, to turn away from this place of sin and iniquity."

"But what will I do for a living?" asked Elsie. "I don't care to sew for this musical comedy, if it's as rank as you say it is; but I've got to have a job."

"The Lord will provide," said the solemn man. "There is a free Bible class every Sunday afternoon in the basement of the cigar store next to the church. Peace be with you. Amen. Farewell."

Elsie went on her way. She was soon in the downtown district where factories abound. On a large brick building was a gilt sign, "Posey & Trimmer, Artificial Flowers." Below it was hung a newly stretched canvas bearing the words, "Five hundred girls wanted to learn trade. Good wages from the start. Apply one flight up."

Elsie started toward the the door, near which were gathered in groups some twenty or thirty girls. One big girl with a black straw hat tipped down over her eyes stepped in front of her.

"Say, you'se," said the girl, "are you'se goin' in there after a job?"

"Yes," said Elsie; "I must have work."

"Now don't do it," said the girl. "I'm chairman of our Scab Committee. There's 400 of us girls locked out just because we demanded 50 cents a week raise in wages, and ice water, and for the foreman to shave off his mustache. You're too nice a looking girl to be a scab. Wouldn't you please help us along by trying to find a job somewhere else, or would you'se rather have your face pushed in?"

"I'll try somewhere else," said Elsie.

She walked aimlessly eastward on Broadway, and there her heart leaped to see the sign, "Fox & Otter," stretching entirely across the front of a tall building. It was as though an unseen guide had led her to it through the byways of her fruitless search for work.

She hurried into the store and sent in to Mr. Otter by a clerk her name and the letter he had written her father. She was shown directly into his private office.

Mr. Otter arose from his desk as Elsie entered and took both hands with a hearty smile of welcome. He was a slightly corpulent man of nearly middle age, a little bald, gold spectacled, polite, well dressed, radiating.

"Well, well, and so this is Beatty's little daughter! Your father was one of our most efficient and valued employees. He left nothing? Well, well. I hope we have not forgotten his faithful services. I am sure there is a vacancy now among our models. Oh, it is easy work—nothing easier."

Mr. Otter struck a bell. A long-nose clerk thrust a portion of himself inside the door.

"Send Miss Hawkins in," said Mr. Otter. Miss Hawkins came.

"Miss Hawkins," said Mr. Otter, "bring for Miss Beatty to try on one of those Russian sable coats and—let's see—one of those latest model black tulle hats with white tips."

Elsie stood before the full-length mirror with pink cheeks and quick breath. Her eyes shone like faint stars. She was beautiful. Alas! she was beautiful.

I wish I could stop this story here. Confound it! I will. No; it's got to run it out. I didn't make it up. I'm just repeating it.

I'd like to throw bouquets at the wise cop and the lady who rescues Girls from Jobs, and the prohibitionist who is trying to crush brandy balls, and the sky pilot who objects to costumes for stage people (there are others), and all the thousands of good people who are at work protecting young people from the pitfalls of a great city; and then wind up by pointing out how they were the means of Elsie reaching her father's benefactor and her kind friend and rescuer from poverty. This would make a fine Elsie story of the old sort. I'd like to do this; but there's just a word or two to follow.

While Elsie was admiring herself in the mirror, Mr. Otter went to the telephone booth and called up some number. Don't ask me what it was.

"Oscar," said he, "I want you to reserve the same table for me this evening. . . . What? Why, the one in the Moorish room to the left of the shrubbery. . . . Yes; two. . . . Yes, the usual brand; and the '85 Johannisburger with the roast. If it isn't the right temperature I'll break your neck. . . . No; not her . . . No, indeed . . . A new one—a peacherino, Oscar, a peacherino!"

Tired and tiresome reader, I will conclude, if you please, with a paraphrase of a few words that you will remember were written by him—by him of Gad's Hill, before whom, if you doff not your hat, you shall stand with a covered pumpkin —aye, sir, a pumpkin.

Lost, Your Excellency. Lost, Associations, and Societies. Lost, Right Reverends and Wrong Reverends of every order. Lost, Reformers and Lawmakers, born with heavenly compassion in your hearts, but with the reverence of money in your souls. And lost thus around us every day.

STRICTLY BUSINESS

STRICTLY BUSINESS

STRICTLY BUSINESS

I SUPPOSE you know all about the stage and stage people. You've been touched with and by actors, and you read the newspaper criticisms and the jokes in the weeklies about the Rialto and the chorus girls and the long-haired tragedians. And I suppose that a condensed list of your ideas about the mysterious stageland would boil down to something like this:

Leading ladies have five husbands, paste diamonds, and figures no better than your own (madam) if they weren't padded. Chorus girls are inseparable from peroxide, Panhards, and Pittsburg. All shows walk back to New York on tan oxford and railroad ties. Irreproachable actresses reserve the comic-landlady part for their mothers on Broadway and their step-aunts on the road. Kyrle Bellew's real name is Boyle O'Kelley. The ravings of John McCullough in the phonograph were stolen from the first sale of the Ellen Terry memoirs. Joe Weber is funnier than E. H. Sothern; but Henry Miller is getting older than he was.

All theatrical people on leaving the theatre at night drink champagne and eat lobsters until noon the next day. After all, the moving pictures have got the whole bunch pounded to a pulp.

Now, few of us know the real life of the stage people. If we did, the profession might be more overcrowded than it is. We look askance at the players with an eye full of patronizing superiority—and we go home and practise all sorts of elocution and gestures in front of our looking glasses.

Latterly there has been much talk of the actor people in a new light. It seems to have been divulged that instead of being motoring bacchanalians and diamond-hungry *loreleis* they are businesslike folk, students and ascetics with childer and homes and libraries, owning real estate, and conducting their private affairs in as orderly and unsensational a manner as any of us good citizens who are bound to the chariot wheels of the gas, rent, coal, ice, and wardmen.

Whether the old or the new report of the sock-and-buskiners be the true one is a surmise that has no place here. I offer you merely this little story of two strollers; and for proof of its truth I can show you only the dark patch above the cast-iron handle of the stage-entrance door of Keetor's old vaudeville theatre made there by the petulant push of gloved hands too impatient to finger the clumsy thumb-latch—and where I last saw Cherry whisking through like a swallow into her nest, on time to the minute, as usual, to dress for her act.

The vaudeville team of Hart & Cherry was an inspiration. Bob Hart had been roaming through the Eastern and Western circuits for four years with a mixed-up act comprising a monologue, three lightning changes with songs, a couple of imitations of celebrated imitators, and a buck-and-wing dance that had drawn a glance of approval from the bass-viol player in more than one house—than which no performer ever received more satisfactory evidence of good work.

The greatest treat an actor can have is to witness the pitiful performance

1157

with which all other actors desecrate the stage. In order to give himself this pleasure he will often forsake the sunniest Broadway corner between Thirty-fourth and Forty-fourth to attend a matinée offering by his less gifted brothers. Once during the lifetime of a minstrel joke one comes to scoff and remains to go through with that most difficult exercise of Thespian muscles—the audible contact of the palm of one hand against the palm of the other.

One afternoon, Bob Hart presented his solvent, serious, well-known vaudevillian face at the box-office window of a rival attraction and got his d. h. coupon for an orchestra seat.

A, B, C, and D glowed successively on the announcement spaces and passed into oblivion, each plunging Mr. Hart deeper into gloom. Others of the audience shrieked, squirmed, whistled and applauded; but Bob Hart, "All the Mustard and a Whole Show in Himself," sat with his face as long and his hands as far apart as a boy holding a hank of yarn for his grandmother to wind into a ball.

But when H came on, "The Mustard" suddenly sat up straight. H was the happy alphabetical prognosticator of Winona Cherry, in Character Songs and Impersonations. There were scarcely more than two bits to Cherry; but she delivered the merchandise tied with a pink cord and charged to the old man's account. She first showed you a deliciously dewy and ginghamy country girl with a basket of property daisies who informed you ingenuously that there were other things to be learned at the old log school-house besides cipherin' and nouns, especially "When the Teach-er Kept Me in." Vanishing, with a quick flirt of gingham apron-strings, she reappeared in considerably less than a "trice" as a fluffy "Parisienne"—so near does Art bring the old red mill to the Moulin Rouge. And then——

But you know the rest. And so did Bob Hart; but he saw somebody else. He thought he saw that Cherry was the only professional on the short order stage that he had seen who seemed exactly to fit the part of "Helen Grimes" in the sketch he had written and kept tucked away in the tray of his trunk. Of course Bob Hart, as well as every other normal actor, grocer, newspaper man, professor, curb broker, and farmer, has a play tucked away somewhere. They tuck 'em in trays of trunks, trunks of trees, desks, haymows, pigeonholes, inside pockets, safe-deposit vaults, handboxes, and coal cellars, waiting for Mr. Frohman to call. They belong among the fifty-seven different kinds.

But Bob Hart's sketch was not destined to end in a pickle jar. He called it "Mice Will Play." He had kept it quiet and hidden away ever since he wrote it, waiting to find a partner who fitted his conception of "Helen Grimes." And here was "Helen" herself, with all the innocent abandon, the youth, the sprightliness, and the flawless stage of art that his critical taste demanded.

After the act was over Hart found the manager in the box office, and got Cherry's address. At five the next afternoon he called at the musty old house in the West Forties and sent up his professional card.

By daylight, in a secular shirtwaist and plain voile skirt, with her hair curbed and her Sister of Charity eyes, Winona Cherry might have been playing the part of Prudence Wise, the deacon's daughter, in the great (unwritten) New England drama not yet entitled anything.

"I know your act, Mr. Hart," she said after she had looked over his card carefully. "What did you wish to see me about?"

"I saw you work last night," said Hart. "I've written a sketch that I've been saving up. It's for two; and I think you can do the other part. I thought I'd see you about it."

"Come in the parlor," said Miss Cherry. "I've been wishing for something of the sort. I think I'd like to act instead of doing turns."

Bob Hart drew his cherished "Mice Will Play" from his pocket, and read it to her.

"Read it again, please," said Miss Cherry.

And then she pointed out to him clearly how it could be improved by introducing a messenger instead of a telephone call, and cutting the dialogue just before the climax while they were struggling with the pistol, and by completely changing the lines and business of Helen Grimes at the point where her jealousy overcomes her. Hart yielded to all her strictures without argument. She had at once put her finger on the sketch's weaker points. That was her woman's intuition that he had lacked. At the end of their talk Hart was willing to stake the judgment, experience, and savings of his four years of vaudeville that "Mice Will Play" would blossom into a perennial flower in the garden of the circuits. Miss Cherry was slower to decide. After many puckerings of her smooth young brow and tappings on her small, white teeth with the end of a lead pencil she gave out her dictum.

"Mr. Hart," said she, "I believe your sketch is going to win out. That Grimes part fits me like a shrinkable flannel after its first trip to a handless hand laundry. I can make it stand out like the colonel of the Forty-fourth Regiment at a Little Mothers' Bazaar. And I've seen you work. I know what you can do with the other part. But business is business. How much do you get a week for the stunt you do now?"

"Two hundred," answered Hart.

"I get one hundred for mine," said Cherry. "That's about the natural discount for a woman. But I live on it and put a few simoleons every week under the loose brick in the old kitchen hearth. The stage is all right. I love it; but there's something else I love better—that's a little country home, some day, with Plymouth Rock chickens and six ducks wandering around the yard.

"Now, let me tell you, Mr. Hart, I am STRICTLY BUSINESS. If you want me to play the opposite part in your sketch, I'll do it. And I believe we can make it go. And there's something else I want to say: There's no nonsense in my make-up; I'm *on the level*, and I'm on the stage for what it pays me, just as other girls work in stores and offices. I'm going to save my money to keep me when I'm past doing my stunts. No Old Ladies' Home or Retreat for Imprudent Actresses for me.

"If you want to make this a business partnership, Mr. Hart, with all nonsense cut out of it, I'm in on it. I know something about vaudeville teams in general; but this would have to be one in particular. I want you to know that I'm on the stage for what I can cart away from it every pay-day in a little manila envelope with nicotine stains on it, where the cashier has licked the flap. It's kind of a hobby of mine to want to cravenette myself for plenty of rainy days in the future. I want you to know just how I am. I don't know what an all-night restaurant looks like; I drink only weak tea; I never spoke to a man at a stage entrance in my life and I've got money in five savings banks."

"Miss Cherry," said Bob Hart in his smooth, serious tones, "you're in on your own terms. I've got 'strictly business' pasted in my hat and stenciled on my make-up box. When I dream of nights I always see a five-room bungalow on the north shore of Long Island, with a Jap cooking clam broth and duckling in the kitchen, and me with the title deeds to the place in my pongee coat pocket, swinging in a hammock on the side porch, reading Stanley's 'Explorations into Africa.' And nobody else around. You never was interested in Africa, was you, Miss Cherry?"

"Not any," said Cherry. "What I'm going to do with my money is to bank it. You can get four per cent. on deposits. Even at the salary I've been earning, I've figured out that in ten years I'd have an income of about $50 a month just from the interest alone. Well, I might invest some of the principal in a little business—say, trimming hats or a beauty parlor, and make more."

"Well," said Hart, "you've got the proper idea all right, all right, anyhow.

There are mighty few actors that amount to anything at all who couldn't fix themselves for the wet days to come if they'd save their money instead of blowing it. I'm glad you've got the correct business idea of it, Miss Cherry. I think the same way; and I believe this sketch will more than double what both of us earn now when we get it shaped up."

The subsequent history of "Mice Will Play" is the history of all successful writings for the stage. Hart & Cherry cut it, pieced it, remodeled it, performed surgical operations on the dialogue and business, changed the lines, restored 'em, added more, cut 'em out, renamed it, gave it back the old name, rewrote it, substituted a dagger for the pistol, restored the pistol—put the sketch through all the known processes of condensation and improvement.

They rehearsed it by the old-fashioned boarding-house clock in the rarely used parlor until its warning click at five minutes to the hour would occur every time exactly half a second before the click of the unloaded revolver that Helen Grimes used in rehearsing the thrilling climax of the sketch.

Yes, that was a thriller and a piece of excellent work. In the act a real 32-caliber revolver was used loaded with a real cartridge. Helen Grimes, who is a Western girl of decidedly Buffalo Billish skill and daring, is tempestuously in love with Frank Desmond, the private secretary and confidential prospective son-in-law of her father, "Arapahoe" Grimes, quarter-million-dollar cattle king, owning a ranch that, judging by the scenery, is in either the Bad Lands or Amagansett, L. I. Desmond (in private life Mr. Bob Hart) wears puttees and Meadow Brook Hunt riding trousers, and gives his address as New York, leaving you to wonder why he comes to the Bad Lands or Amagansett (as the case may be) and at the same time to conjecture mildly why a cattleman should want puttees about his ranch with a secretary in 'em.

Well, anyhow, you know as well as I do that we all like that kind of play, whether we admit it or not—something along in between "Bluebeard, Jr.," and "Cymbeline" played in the Russian.

There were only two parts and a half in "Mice Will Play." Hart and Cherry were the two, of course; and the half was a minor part always played by a stage hand, who merely came in once in a Tuxedo coat and a panic to announce that the house was surrounded by Indians, and to turn down the gas fire in the grate by the manager's orders.

There was another girl in the sketch—a Fifth Avenue society swelless—who was visiting the ranch and who had sirened Jack Valentine when he was a wealthy clubman on lower Third Avenue before he lost his money. This girl appeared on the stage only in the photographic state—Jack had her Sarony stuck up on the mantel of the Amagan—of the Bad Lands droring room. Helen was jealous, of course.

And now for the thriller. Old "Arapahoe" Grimes dies of angina pectoris one night—so Helen informs us in a stage-ferryboat whisper over the footlights—while only his secretary was present. And that same day he was known to have had $647,000 in cash in his (ranch) library just received for the sale of a drove of beeves in the East (that accounts for the prices we pay for steak!). The cash disappears at the same time. Jack Valentine was the only person with the ranchman when he made his (alleged) croak.

"Gawd knows I love him; but if he has done this deed—" you sabe, don't you? And then there are some mean things said about the Fifth Avenue girl—who doesn't come on the stage—and can we blame her, with the vaudeville trust holding down prices until one actually must be buttoned in the back by a call boy, maids cost so much?

But, wait. Here's the climax. Helen Grimes, chaparralish as she can be, is goaded beyond imprudence. She convinces herself that Jack Valentine is not only a falsetto, but a financier. To lose at one fell swoop $647,000 and a lover in riding trousers with angles in the sides like the variations on the chart of a typhoid-fever patient is enough to make any perfect lady mad. So, then!

They stand in the (ranch) library, which is furnished with mounted elk heads (didn't the Elks have a fish fry in Amagansett once?), and the dénouement begins. I know of no more interesting time in the run of a play unless it be when the prologue ends.

Helen thinks Jack has taken the money. Who else was there to take it? The box-office manager was at the front on his job; the orchestra hadn't left their seats; and no man could get past "Old Jimmy," the stage door-man, unless he could show a Skye terrier or an automobile as a guarantee of eligibility.

Goaded beyond imprudence (as before said), Helen says to Jack Valentine: "Robber and thief—and worse yet, stealer of trusting hearts, this should be your fate!"

With that out she whips, of course, the trusty 32-caliber.

"But I will be merciful," goes on Helen. "You shall live—that will be your punishment. I will show you how easily I could have sent you to the death that you deserve. There is *her* picture on the mantel. I will send through her more beautiful face the bullet that should have pierced your craven heart."

And she does it. And there's no fake blank cartridges or assistants pulling strings. Helen fires. The bullet—the actual bullet—goes through the face of the photograph—and then strikes the hidden spring of the sliding panel in the wall—and lo! the panel slides, and there is the missing $647,000 in convincing stacks of currency and bags of gold. It's great. You know how it is. Cherry practised for two months at a target on the roof of her boarding house. It took good shooting. In the sketch she had to hit a brass disk only three inches in diameter, covered by wall paper in the panel; and she had to stand in exactly the same spot every night, and the photo had to be in exactly the same spot, and she had to shoot steady and true every time.

Of course old "Arapahoe" had tucked the funds away there in the secret place; and, of course, Jack hadn't taken anything except his salary (which really might have come under the head of "obtaining money under"; but that is neither here nor there); and, of course, the New York girl was really engaged to a concrete house contractor in the Bronx; and, necessarily, Jack and Helen ended in a half-Nelson—and there you are.

After Hart and Cherry had gotten "Mice Will Play" flawless, they had a try-out at a vaudeville house that accommodates. The sketch was a house wrecker. It was one of those rare strokes of talent that inundates a theatre from the roof down. The gallery wept; and the orchestra seats, being dressed for it, swam in tears.

After the show the booking agents signed blank checks and pressed fountain pens upon Hart and Cherry. Five hundred dollars a week was what it panned out.

That night at 11:30 Bob Hart took off his hat and bade Cherry good-night at her boarding-house door.

"Mr. Hart," said she thoughtfully, "come inside just a few minutes. We've got our chance now to make good and to make money. What we want to do is to cut expenses every cent we can and save all we can."

"Right," said Bob. "It's business with me. You've got your scheme for banking yours; and I dream every night of that bungalow with the Jap cook and nobody around to raise trouble. Anything to enlarge the net receipts will engage my attention."

"Come inside just a few minutes," repeated Cherry, deeply thoughtful. "I've got a proposition to make to you that will reduce our expenses a lot and help you to work out your own future and help me to work out mine—and all on business principles."

"Mice Will Play" had a tremendously successful run in New York for ten weeks—rather neat for a vaudeville sketch—and then it started on the circuits. Without following it, it may be said that it was a solid drawing card for two years without a sign of abated popularity.

Sam Packard, manager of one of Keetor's New York houses, said of Hart & Cherry:

"As square and high-toned a little team as ever came over the circuit. It's a pleasure to read their names on the booking list. Quiet, hard workers, no Johnny and Mabel nonsense, on the job to the minute, straight home after their act, and each of 'em as gentlemanlike as a lady. I don't expect to handle any attractions that give me less trouble or more respect for the profession."

And now, after so much cracking of a nut-shell, here is the kernel of the story:

At the end of its second season "Mice Will Play" came back to New York for another run at the roof gardens and summer theatres. There was never any trouble in booking it at the top-notch price. Bob Hart had his bungalow nearly paid for, and Cherry had so many savings deposit bank books that she had begun to buy sectional bookcases on the instalment plan to hold them.

I tell you these things to assure you, even if you can't believe it, that many, very many of the stage people are workers with abiding ambitions—just the same as the man who wants to be president, or the grocery clerk who wants a home in Flatbush, or a lady who is anxious to flop out of the Count-pan into the Prince-fire. And I hope I may be allowed to say, without chipping into the contribution basket, that they often move in a mysterious way their wonders to perform.

But, listen.

At the first performance of "Mice Will Play" in New York at the new Westphalia (no hams alluded to) Theatre, Winona Cherry was nervous. When she fired at the photograph of the Eastern beauty on the mantel, the bullet, instead of penetrating the photo and then striking the disk, went into the lower left side of Bob Hart's neck. Not expecting to get it there, Hart collapsed neatly, while Cherry fainted in a most artistic manner.

The audience, surmising that they viewed a comedy instead of a tragedy in which the principals were married or reconciled, applauded with great enjoyment. The Cool Head, who always graces such occasions, rang the curtain down, and two platoons of scene shifters respectively and more or less respectfully removed Hart & Cherry from the stage. The next turn went on, and all went as merry as an alimony bell.

The stage hands found a young doctor at the stage entrance who was waiting for a patient with a decoction of Am. B'ty roses. The doctor examined Hart carefully and laughed heartily.

"No headlines for you, Old Sport," was his diagnosis. "If it had been two inches to the left it would have undermined the carotid artery as far as the Red Front Drug Store in Flatbush and Back Again. As it is, you just get the property man to bind it up with a flounce torn from any one of the girls' Valenciennes and go home and get it dressed by the parlor-floor practitioner on your block, and you'll be all right. Excuse me; I've got a serious case outside to look after."

After that Bob Hart looked up and felt better. And then to where he lay come Vincente, the Tramp Juggler, great in his line. Vincente, a solemn man from Brattleboro, Vt., named Sam Griggs at home, sent toys and maple sugar home to two small daughters from every town he played. Vincente had moved on the same circuits with Hart & Cherry, and was their peripatetic friend.

"Bob," said Vincente in his serious way, "I'm glad it's no worse. The little lady is wild about you."

"Who?" asked Hart.

"Cherry," said the juggler. "We didn't know how bad you were hurt; and we kept her away. It's taking the manager and three girls to hold her."

"It was an accident, of course," said Hart. "Cherry's all right. She wasn't feeling in good trim or she couldn't have done it. There's no hard feelings. She's strictly business. The doctor says I'll be on the job again in three days. Don't let her worry."

"Man," said Sam Griggs severely, puckering his old, smooth, lined face, "are you a chess automaton or a human pincushion? Cherry's crying her heart out for you—calling 'Bob, Bob,' every second, with them holding her hands and keeping her from coming to you."

"What's the matter with her?" asked Hart, with wide-open eyes. "The sketch'll go on again in three days. I'm not hurt bad, the doctor says. She won't lose out half a week's salary. I know it was an accident. What's the matter with her?"

"You seem to be blind, or a sort of a fool," said Vincente. "The girl loves you and is almost mad about your hurt. What's the matter with *you?* Is she nothing to you? I wish you could hear her call you."

"Loves me?" asked Bob Hart, rising from the stack of scenery on which he lay. "Cherry loves me? Why, it's impossible."

"I wish you could see her and hear her," said Griggs.

"But, man," said Bob Hart, sitting up, "it's impossible. It's impossible, I tell you. I never dreamed of such a thing."

"No human being," said the Tramp Juggler, "could mistake it. She's wild for love of you. How have you been so blind?"

"But, my God," said Bob Hart, rising to his feet, "*it's too late*. It's too late, I tell you, Sam; *it's too late*. It can't be. You must be wrong. It's *impossible*. There's some mistake."

"She's crying for you," said the Tramp Juggler. "For love of you she's fighting three, and calling your name so loud they don't dare to raise the curtain. Wake up, man."

"For love of me?" said Bob Hart with staring eyes. "Don't I tell you it's too late? It's too late, man. Why, *Cherry and I have been married two years!*"

THE GOLD THAT GLITTERED

A STORY with a moral appended is like the bill of a mosquito. It bores you, and then injects a stinging drop to irritate your conscience. Therefore let us have the moral first and be done with it. All is not gold that glitters, but it is a wise child that keeps the stopper in his bottle of testing acid.

Where Broadway skirts the corner of the square presided over by George the Veracious is the Little Rialto. Here stands the actors of that quarter, and this is their shibboleth: "'Nit,' says I to Frohman, 'you can't touch me for a kopeck less than two-fifty per,' and out I walks."

Westward and southward from the Thespian glare are one or two streets where a Spanish-American colony has huddled for a little tropical warmth in the nipping North. The centre of life in this precinct is "El Refugio," a café and restaurant that caters to the volatile exiles from the South. Up from Chili, Bolivia, Colombia, the rolling republics of Central America and the ireful islands of the Western Indies flit the cloaked and sombreroed señores, who are scattered like burning lava by the political eruptions of their several countries. Hither they come to lay counterplots, to bide their time, to solicit funds, to enlist filibusterers, to smuggle out arms and ammunitions, to play the game at long taw. In El Refugio they find the atmosphere in which they thrive.

In the restaurant of El Refugio are served compounds delightful to the palate of the man from Capricorn or Cancer. Altruism must halt the story thus long. Oh, diner, weary of the culinary subterfuges of the Gallic chef, hie thee to El Refugio! There only will you find a fish—bluefish, shad, or pompano from the Gulf—baked after the Spanish method. Tomatoes give it color, individuality, and soul; chili colorado bestows upon it zest, originality, and fervor; unknown herbs furnish piquancy and mystery, and—but its crowning glory deserves a new sentence. Around it, above it, beneath it, in its vicinity—but never in it— hovers an ethereal aura, an effluvium so rarefied and delicate that only the Society for Physical Research could note its origin. Do not say that garlic is in the fish at El Refugio. It is not otherwise than as if the spirit of Garlic, flitting past, has wafted one kiss that lingers in the parsley-crowned dish as haunting as those kisses in life, "by hopeless fancy feigned on lips that are for others." And then, when Conchito, the waiter, brings you a plate of brown frijoles and a carafe of wine that has never stood still between Oporto and El Refugio—ah, Dios!

One day a Hamburg-American liner deposited upon Pier No. 55 Gen. Perrico Zimenes Villablanca Falcon, a passenger from Cartagena. The General was between a claybank and a bay in complexion, had a 42-inch waist and stood 5 feet 4 with his Du Barry heels. He had the mustache of a shooting-gallery proprietor, he wore the full dress of a Texas congressman, and had the important aspect of an uninstructed delegate.

Gen. Falcon had enough English under his hat to enable him to inquire his way to the street in which El Refugio stood. When he reached that neighborhood he saw a sign before a respectable red-brick house that read, "Hotel Español." In the window was a card in Spanish, "Aqui se habla Español." The General entered, sure of a congenial port.

In the cozy office was Mrs. O'Brien, the proprietress. She had blonde—oh, unimpeachably blonde hair. For the rest she was amiability, and ran largely to inches around. Gen. Falcon brushed the floor with his broad-brimmed hat, and emitted a quantity of Spanish, the syllables sounding like firecrackers gently popping their way down the string of a bunch.

"Spanish or Dago?" asked Mrs. O'Brien, pleasantly.

"I am a Colombian, madam," said the General proudly. "I speak the Spanish. The advisement in your window say the Spanish he is spoken here. How is that?"

"Well, you've been speaking it, ain't you?" said the madam. "I'm sure I can't."

At the Hotel Español General Falcon engaged rooms and established himself. At dusk he sauntered out upon the streets to view the wonders of this roaring city of the North. As he walked he thought of the wonderful golden hair of Mme. O'Brien. "It is here," said the General to himself, no doubt in his own language, "that one shall find the most beautiful señoras in the world. I have not in my Colombia viewed among our beauties one so fair. It is not for the General Falcon to think of beauty. It is my country that claims my devotion."

At the corner of Broadway and the Little Rialto the General became involved. The street cars bewildered him, and the fender of one upset him against a pushcart laden with oranges. A cab driver missed him an inch with a hub, and poured barbarous execrations upon his head. He scrambled to the sidewalk and skipped again in terror when the whistle of a peanut-roaster puffed a hot scream into his ear. "Válgame Dios! What devil's city is this?"

As the General fluttered out of the streamers of passers like a wounded snipe he was marked simultaneously as game by two hunters. One was "Bully" McGuire, whose system of sport required the use of a strong arm and the misuse of an eight-inch piece of lead pipe. The other Nimrod of the asphalt was "Spider" Kelley, a sportsman with more refined methods.

In pouncing upon their self-evident prey, Mr. Kelley was a shade the quicker. His elbow fended accurately the onslaught of Mr. McGuire.

"G'wan!" he commanded harshly. "I saw it first." McGuire slunk away, awed by superior intelligence.

"Pardon me," said Mr. Kelley, to the General, "but you got balled up in the shuffle, didn't you? Let me assist you." He picked up the General's hat and brushed the dust from it.

The ways of Mr. Kelley could not but succeed. The General, bewildered and dismayed by the resounding streets, welcomed his deliverer as a caballero with a most disinterested heart.

"I have a desire," said the General, "to return to the hotel of O'Brien, in which I am stop. Caramba! señor, there is a loudness and rapidness of going and coming in the city of this Nueva York."

Mr. Kelley's politeness would not suffer the distinguished Colombian to brave the dangers of the return unaccompanied. At the door of the Hotel Español they paused. A little lower down on the opposite side of the street shone the modest illuminated sign of El Refugio. Mr. Kelley, to whom few streets were unfamiliar, knew the place exteriorly as a "Dago joint." All foreigners Mr. Kelley classed under the two heads of "Dagoes" and Frenchmen. He proposed to the General that they repair thither and substantiate their acquaintance with a liquid foundation.

An hour later found General Falcon and Mr. Kelley seated at a table in the conspirator's corner of El Refugio. Bottles and glasses were between them. For the tenth time the General confided the secret of his mission to the Estados Unidos. He was here, he declared, to purchase arms—2,000 stands of Winchester rifles—for the Colombian revolutionists. He had drafts in his pocket drawn by the Cartagena Bank on its New York correspondent for $25,000. At other tables other revolutionists were shouting their political secrets to their fellow-plotters; but none was as loud as the General. He pounded the table; he hallooed for some wine; he roared to his friend that his errand was a secret one, and not to be hinted at to a living soul. Mr. Kelley himself was stirred to sympathetic enthusiasm. He grasped the General's hand across the table.

"Monseer," he said, earnestly, "I don't know where this country of yours is, but I'm for it. I guess it must be a branch of the United States, though, for the poetry guys and the schoolmarms call us Columbia, too, sometimes. It's a lucky thing for you that you butted into me to-night. I'm the only man in New York that can get this gun deal through for you. The Secretary of War of the United States is me best friend. He's in the city now, and I'll see him for you to-morrow. In the meantime, monseer, you keep them drafts tight in your inside pocket. I'll call for you to-morrow, and take you to see him. Say! that ain't the District of Columbia you're talking about, is it?" concluded Mr. Kelley, with a sudden qualm. "You can't capture that with no 2,000 guns—it's been tried with more."

"No, no, no!" exclaimed the General. "It is the Republic of Colombia—it is a g-r-reat republic on the top side of America of the South. Yes. Yes."

"All right," said Mr. Kelley, reassured. "Now suppose we trek along home and go by-by. I'll write to the Secretary to-night and make a date with him

It's a ticklish job to get guns out of New York. McClusky himself can't do it."

They parted at the door of the Hotel Español. The General rolled his eyes at the moon and sighed.

"It is a great country, your Nueva York," he said. "Truly the cars in the streets devastate one, and the engine that cooks the nuts terribly makes a squeak in the ear. But, ah, Señor Kelley—the señoras with hair of much goldness, and admirable fatness—they are magnificas! Muy magnificas!"

Kelley went to the nearest telephone booth and called up McCrary's café, far up on Broadway. He asked for Jimmy Dunn.

"Is that Jimmy Dunn?" asked Kelley.

"Yes," came the answer.

"You're a liar," sang back Kelley, joyfully. "You're the Secretary of War. Wait there till I come up. I've got the finest thing down here in the way of a fish you ever baited for. It's a Colorado-maduro, with a gold band around it and free coupons enough to buy a red hall lamp and a statuette of Psyche rubbering in the brook. I'll be up on the next car."

Jimmy Dunn was an A. M. of Crookdom. He was an artist in the confidence line. He never saw a bludgeon in his life; and he scorned knockout drops. In fact, he would have set nothing before an intended victim but the purest of drinks, if it had been possible to procure such a thing in New York. It was the ambition of "Spider" Kelley to elevate himself into Jimmy's class.

These two gentlemen held a conference that night at McCrary's. Kelley explained.

"He's as easy as a gum shoe. He's from the Island of Colombia, where there's a strike, or a feud, or something going on, and they've sent him up here to buy 2,000 Winchesters to arbitrate the thing with. He showed me two drafts for $10,000 each, and one for $5,000 on a bank here. 'S truth, Jimmy, I felt real mad with him because he didn't have it in thousand-dollar bills, and hand it to me on a silver waiter. Now, we've got to wait till he goes to the bank and gets the money for us."

They talked it over for two hours, and then Dunn said: "Bring him to No.— Broadway, at four o'clock to-morrow afternoon."

In due time Kelley called at the Hotel Español for the General. He found that wily warrior engaged in delectable conversation with Mrs. O'Brien.

"The Secretary of War is waitin' for us," said Kelley.

The General tore himself away with an effort.

"Ay, señor," he said, with a sigh, "duty makes a call. But, senor, the señoras of your Estados Unidos—how beauties! For exemplification, take you la Madame O'Brien—que magnifica! She is one goddess—one Juno—what you call one ox-eyed Juno."

Now Mr. Kelley was a wit; and better men have been shriveled by the fire of their own imagination.

"Sure!" he said with a grin; "but you mean a peroxide Juno, don't you?"

Mrs. O'Brien heard, and lifted an auriferous head. Her business like eye rested for an instant upon the disappearing form of Mr. Kelley. Except in street cars one should never be unnecessarily rude to a lady.

When the gallant Colombian and his escort arrived at the Broadway address, they were held in an anteroom for half an hour, and then admitted into a well-equipped office where a distinguished looking man, with a smooth face, wrote at a desk. General Falcon was presented to the Secretary of War of the United States, and his mission made known by his old friend, Mr. Kelley.

"Ah—Colombia!" said the Secretary, significantly, when he was made to understand; "I'm afraid there will be a little difficulty in that case. The President and I differ in our sympathies there. He prefers the established government, while I——" The Secretary gave the General a mysterious but encouraging smile.

"You, of course, know, General Falcon, that since the Tammany war, an act of Congress has been passed requiring all manufactured arms and ammunition exported from this country to pass through the War Department. Now, if I can do anything for you I will be glad to do so to oblige my old friend Mr. Kelley. But it must be in absolute secrecy, as the President, as I have said, does not regard favorably the efforts of your revolutionary party in Colombia. I will have my orderly bring a list of the available arms now in the warehouse."

The Secretary struck a bell, and an orderly with the letters A. D. T. on his cap stepped promptly into the room.

"Bring me Schedule B of the small arms inventory," said the Secretary.

The orderly quickly returned with a printed paper. The Secretary studied it closely.

"I find," he said, "that in Warehouse 9, of Government stores, there is a shipment of 2,000 stands of Winchester rifles that were ordered by the Sultan of Morocco, who forgot to send the cash with his order. Our rule is that legal-tender money must be paid down at the time of purchase. My dear Kelley, your friend, General Falcon, shall have this lot of arms, if he desires it, at the manufacturer's price. And you will forgive me, I am sure, if I curtail our interview. I am expecting the Japanese Minister and Charles Murphy every moment!"

As one result of this interview, the General was deeply grateful to his esteemed friend, Mr. Kelley. As another, the nimble Secretary of War was extremely busy during the next two days buying empty rifle cases and filling them with bricks, which were then stored in a warehouse rented for that purpose. As still another, when the General returned to the Hotel Español, Mrs. O'Brien went up to him, plucked a thread from his lapel, and said:

"Say, señor, I don't want to 'butt in,' but what does that monkey-faced, cat-eyed, rubber-necked tin horn tough want with you?"

"Sangre de mi vida!" exclaimed the General. "Impossible it is that you speak of my good friend, Señor Kelley."

"Come into the summer garden," said Mrs. O'Brien. "I want to have a talk with you."

Let us suppose that an hour has elapsed.

"And you say," said the General, "that for the sum of $18,000 can be purchased the furnishment of the house and the lease of one year with this garden so lovely—so resembling unto the patios of my cara Colombia?"

"And dirt cheap at that," sighed the lady.

"Ah, Dios!" breathed General Falcon. "What to me is war and politics? This spot is one paradise. My country it have other brave heroes to continue the fighting. What to me should be glory and the shooting of mans? Ah! no. It is here I have found one angel. Let us buy the Hotel Español and you shall be mine, and the money shall not be waste on guns."

Mrs. O'Brien rested her blond pompadour against the shoulder of the Colombian patriot.

"Oh, señor," she sighed, happily, "ain't you terrible!"

Two days later was the time appointed for the delivery of the arms to the General. The boxes of supposed rifles were stacked in the rented warehouse, and the Secretary of War sat upon them, waiting for his friend Kelley to fetch the victim.

Mr. Kelley hurried, at the hour, to the Hotel Español. He found the General behind the desk adding up accounts.

"I have decide," said the General, "to buy not guns. I have to-day buy the insides of this hotel, and there shall be marrying of the General Perrico Ximenes Villablanca Falcon with la Madame O'Brien."

Mr. Kelly almost strangled.

"Say, you old bald-headed bottle of shoe polish," he spluttered, "you're a swindler—that's what you are! You've bought a boarding house with money belonging to your infernal country, wherever it is."

"Ah," said the General, footing up a column, "that is what you call politics. War and revolution they are not nice. Yes. It is not best that one shall always follow Minerva. No. It is of quite desirable to keep hotels and be with that Juno—that ox-eyed Juno. Ah! what hair of the gold it is that she have!"

Mr. Kelley choked again.

"Ah, Señor Kelley!" said the General, feelingly and finally, "is it that you have never eaten of the corned beef hash that Madame O'Brien she make?"

BABES IN THE JUNGLE

MONTAGUE SILVER, the finest street man and art grafter in the West, says to me once in Little Rock: "If you ever lose your mind, Billy, and get too old to do honest swindling among grown men, go to New York. In the West a sucker is born every minute; but in New York they appear in chunks of roe—you can't count 'em!"

Two years afterwards I found that I couldn't remember the names of the Russian admirals, and I noticed some gray hairs over my left ear; so I knew the time had arrived for me to take Silver's advice.

I struck New York about noon one day, and took a walk up Broadway. And I run against Silver himself, all encompassed up in a spacious kind of haberdashery, leaning against a hotel and rubbing the half-moons on his nails with a silk handkerchief.

"Paresis or superannuated?" I asks him.

"Hello, Billy," says Silver; "I'm glad to see you. Yes, it seemed to me that the West was accumulating a little too much wiseness. I've been saving New York for dessert. I know it's a low-down trick to take things from these people. They only know this and that and pass to and fro and think ever and anon. I'd hate for my mother to know I was skinning these weak-minded ones. She raised me better."

"Is there a crush already in the waiting rooms of the old doctor that does skin grafting?" I asks.

"Well, no," says Silver; "you needn't back Epidermis to win to-day. I've only been here a month. But I'm ready to begin; and the members of Willie Manhattan's Sunday School class, each of whom has volunteered to contribute a portion of cuticle toward this rehabilitation, may as well send their photos to the *Evening Daily.*

"I've been studying the town," says Silver, "and reading the papers every day, and I know it as well as the cat in the City Hall knows an O'Sullivan. People here lie down on the floor and scream and kick when you are the least bit slow about taking money from them. Come up in my room and I'll tell you. We'll work the town together, Billy, for the sake of old times."

Silver takes me up in a hotel. He has a quantity of irrelevant objects lying about.

"'There's more ways of getting money from these metropolitan hayseeds," says Silver, "than there is of cooking rice in Charleston, S. C. They'll bite at anything. The brains of most of 'em commute. The wiser they are in intelligence the less perception of cognizance they have. Why, didn't a man the other day sell J. P. Morgan an oil portrait of Rockefeller, Jr., for Andrea del Sarto's celebrated painting of the young Saint John!

"You see that bundle of printed stuff in the corner, Billy? That's gold mining stock. I started out one day to sell that, but I quit it in two hours. Why? Got arrested for blocking the street. People fought to buy it. I sold the policeman a block of it on the way to the station-house, and then I took it off the market. I don't want people to give me their money. I want some little consideration connected with the transaction to keep my pride from being hurt. I want 'em to guess the missing letter in Chic—go, or draw to a pair of nines before they pay me a cent of money.

"Now there's another little scheme that worked so easy I had to quit it. You see that bottle of blue ink on the table? I tattooed an anchor on the back of my hand and went to a bank and told 'em I was Admiral Dewey's nephew. They offered to cash my draft on him for a thousand, but I didn't know my uncle's first name. It shows, though, what an easy town it is. As for burglars, they won't go in a house now unless there's a hot supper ready and a few college students to wait on 'em. They're slugging citizens all over the upper part of the city and I guess, taking the town from end to end, it's a plain case of assault and Battery."

"Monty," says I, when Silver had slacked up, "you may have Manhattan correctly discriminated in your perorative, but I doubt it. I've only been in town two hours, but it don't dawn upon me that it's ours with a cherry in it. There ain't enough rus in urbe about it to suit me. I'd be a good deal much better satisfied if the citizens had a straw or more in their hair, and run more to velveteen vests and buckeye watch charms. They don't look easy to me."

"You've got it, Billy," says Silver. "All emigrants have it. New York's bigger than Little Rock or Europe, and it frightens a foreigner. You'll be all right. I tell you I feel like slapping the people here because they don't send me all their money in laundry baskets, with germicide sprinkled over it. I hate to go down on the street to get it. Who wears the diamonds in this town? Why, Winnie, the Wiretapper's wife, and Bella, the Buncosteerer's bride. New Yorkers can be worked easier than a blue rose on a tidy. The only thing that bothers me is I know I'll break the cigars in my vest pocket when I get my clothes all full of twenties."

"I hope you are right, Monty," says I; "but I wish all the same I had been satisfied with a small business in Little Rock. The crop of farmers is never so short out there but what you can get a few of 'em to sign a petition for a new post office that you can discount for $200 at the county bank. The people here appear to possess instincts of self-preservation and illiberality. I fear me that we are not cultivated enough to tackle this game."

"Don't worry," says Silver. "I've got this Jayville-near-Tarrytown correctly estimated as sure as North River is the Hudson and East river ain't a river. Why, there are people living in four blocks of Broadway who never saw any kind of a building except a skyscraper in their lives! A good, live hustling Western man ought to get conspicuous enough here inside of three months to incur either Jerome's clemency or Lawson's displeasure."

"Hyperbole aside," says I, "do you know of any immediate system of buncoing the community out of a dollar or two except by applying to the Salvation Army or having a fit on Miss Helen Gould's doorsteps?"

"Dozens of 'em," says Silver. "How much capital have you got, Billy?"

"A thousand," I told him.

"I've got $1,200," says he. "We'll pool and do a big business. There's so many ways we can make a million that I don't know how to begin."

The next morning Silver meets me at the hotel and he is all sonorous and stirred with a kind of silent joy.

"We're to meet J. P. Morgan this afternoon," says he. "A man I know in the hotel wants to introduce us. He's a friend of his. He says he likes to meet people from the West."

"That sounds nice and plausible," says I. "I'd like to know Mr. Morgan."

"It won't hurt us a bit," says Silver, "to get acquainted with a few finance kings. I kind of like the social way New York has with strangers."

The man Silver knew was named Klein. At three o'clock Klein brought his Wall Street friend to see us in Silver's room. "Mr. Morgan" looked some like his pictures, and he had a Turkish towel wrapped around his left foot, and he walked with a cane.

"Mr. Silver and Mr. Pescud," says Klein. "It sounds superfluous," says he, "to mention the name of the greatest financial——"

"Cut it out, Klein," says Mr. Morgan. "I'm glad to know you gents; I take great interest in the West. Klein tells me you're from Little Rock. I think I've a railroad or two out there somewhere. If either of you guys would like to deal a hand or two of stud poker I——"

"Now, Pierpont," cuts in Klein, "you forget!"

"Excuse me, gents!" says Morgan; "since I've had the gout so bad I sometimes play a social game of cards at my house. Neither of you never knew One-eyed Peters, did you, while you was around Little Rock? He lived in Seattle, New Mexico."

Before we could answer, Mr. Morgan hammered on the floor with his cane and begins to walk up and down, swearing in a loud tone of voice.

"They have been pounding your stocks to-day on the Street, Pierpont?" asks Klein, smiling.

"Stocks! No!" roars Mr. Morgan. "It's that picture I sent an agent to Europe to buy. I just thought about it. He cabled me to-day that it ain't to be found in all Italy. I'd pay $50,000 to-morrow for that picture—yes, $75,-000. I give the agent a la carte in purchasing it. I cannot understand why the art galleries will allow a De Vinchy to——"

"Why, Mr. Morgan," says Klein; "I thought you owned all of the De Vinchy paintings."

"What is the picture like, Mr. Morgan?" asks Silver. "It must be as big as the side of the Flatiron Building."

"I'm afraid your art education is on the bum, Mr. Silver," says Morgan. "The picture is 27 inches by 42; and it is called 'Love's Idle Hour.' It represents a number of cloak models doing the two-step on the bank of a purple river. The cablegram said it might have been brought to this country. My collection will never be complete without that picture. Well, so long, gents; us financiers must keep early hours."

Mr. Morgan and Klein went away together in a cab. Me and Silver talked about how simple and unsuspecting great people was; and Silver said what a shame it would be to try to rob a man like Mr. Morgan; and I said I thought it would be rather imprudent, myself. Klein proposes a stroll after dinner; and me and him and Silver walks down toward Seventh Avenue to see the sights. Klein sees a pair of cuff links that instigate his admiration in a pawnshop window, and we all go in while he buys 'em.

After we got back to the hotel and Klein had gone, Silver jumps at me and waves his hands.

"Did you see it?" says he. "Did you see it, Billy?"

"What?" I asks.

"Why, that picture that Morgan wants. It's hanging in the pawnshop, behind the desk. I didn't say anything because Klein was there. It's the article sure as you live. The girls are as natural as paint can make them, all measuring 36 and 25 and 42 skirts, if they had any skirts, and they're doing a buck-and-wing on the bank of a river with the blues. What did Mr. Morgan say he'd give for it? Oh, don't make me tell you. They can't know what it is in that pawnshop."

When the pawnshop opened the next morning me and Silver was standing there as anxious as if we wanted to soak our Sunday suit to buy a drink. We sauntered inside, and began to look at watch-chains.

"That's a violent specimen of a chromo you've got up there," remarked Silver, casual, to the pawnbroker. "But I kind of enthuse over the girl with the shoulder-blades and red bunting. Would an offer of $2.25 for it cause you to knock over any fragile articles of your stock in hurrying it off the nail?"

The pawnbroker smiles and goes on showing us plate watch-chains.

"That picture," says he, "was pledged a year ago by an Italian gentleman. I loaned him $500 on it. It is called 'Love's Idle Hour,' and it is by Leonardo de Vinchy. Two days ago the legal time expired, and it became an unredeemed pledge. Here is a style of chain that is worn a great deal now."

At the end of half an hour me and Silver paid the pawnbroker $2,000 and walked out with the picture. Silver got into a cab with it and started for Morgan's office. I goes to the hotel and waits for him. In two hours Silver comes back.

"Did you see Mr. Morgan?" I asks. "How much did he pay you for it?"

Silver sits down and fools with a tassel on the table cover.

"I never exactly saw Mr. Morgan," he says, "because Mr. Morgan's been in Europe for a month. But what's worrying me, Billy, is this: The department stores have all got that same picture on sale, framed, for $3.48. And they charge $3.50 for the frame alone—that's what I can't understand."

THE DAY RESURGENT

I CAN see the artist bite the end of his pencil and frown when it comes to drawing his Easter picture; for his legitimate pictorial conceptions of figures pertinent to the festival are but four in number.

First comes Easter, pagan goddess of spring. Here his fancy may have free play. A beautiful maiden with decorative hair and the proper number of toes will fill the bill. Miss Clarice St. Vavasour, the well-known model, will pose for it in the "Lethergogallagher," or whatever it was that Trilby called it.

Second—the melancholy lady with upturned eyes in a framework of lilies. This is magazine-covery, but reliable.

Third—Miss Manhattan in Fifth Avenue Easter Sunday parade.

Fourth—Maggie Murphy with a new red feather in her old straw hat, happy and self-conscious, in the Grand Street turnout.

Of course, the rabbits do not count. Nor the Easter eggs, since the higher criticism has hard-boiled them.

The limited field of its pictorial possibilities proves that Easter, of all our festival days, is the most vague and shifting in our conception. It belongs to all religions, although the pagans invented it. Going back still further to the first spring, we can see Eve choosing with pride a new green leaf from the tree *ficus carica.*

Now, the object of this critical and learned preamble is to set forth the theorem that Easter is neither a date, a season, a festival, a holiday, nor an occasion. What it is you shall find out if you follow in the footsteps of Danny McCree.

Easter Sunday dawned as it should, bright and early, in its place on the calendar between Saturday and Monday. At 5:24 the sun rose, and at 10:30 Danny followed its example. He went into the kitchen and washed his face at the sink. His mother was frying bacon. She looked at his hard, smooth, knowing countenance as he juggled with the round cake of soap, and thought of his father when she first saw him stopping a hot grounder between second and third twenty-two years before on a vacant lot in Harlem, where the La Paloma apartment house now stands. In the front room of the flat Danny's father sat by an open window smoking his pipe, with his dishevelled gray hair tossed about by the breeze. He still clung to his pipe, although his sight had been taken from him two years before by a precocious blast of giant powder that went off without permission. Very few blind men care for smoking, for the reason that they cannot see the smoke. Now, could you enjoy having the news read to you from an evening paper unless you could see the color of the headlines?

" 'Tis Easter Day," said Mrs. McCree.

"Scramble mine," said Danny.

After breakfast he dressed himself in the Sabbath morning costume of the Canal Street importing house dray chauffeur—frock coat, striped trousers, patent leathers, gilded trace chain across front of vest, and wing collar, rolled-brim derby and butterfly bow from Schonstein's (between Fourteenth Street and Tony's fruit stand) Saturday night sale.

"You'll be goin' out this day, of course, Danny," said old man McCree, a little wistfully. " 'Tis a kind of holiday, they say. Well, it's fine spring weather. I can feel it in the air."

"Why should I not be going out?" demanded Danny in his grumpiest chest tones. "Should I stay in? Am I as good as a horse? One day of rest my team has a week. Who earns the money for the rent and the breakfast you've just eat, I'd like to know? Answer me that!"

"All right, lad," said the old man. "I'm not complainin'. While me two eyes was good there was nothin' better to my mind than a Sunday out. There's a smell of turf and burnin' brush comin' in the windy. I have me tobaccy. A good fine day and rist to ye, lad. Times I wished your mother had larned to read, so I might hear the rest about the hippopotamus—but let that be."

"Now, what is this foolishness he talks of hippopotamuses?" asked Danny of his mother, as he passed through the kitchen. "Have you been taking him to the Zoo? And for what?"

"I have not," said Mrs. McCree. "He sets by the windy all day. 'Tis little recreation a blind man among the poor gets at all. I'm thinkin' they wander in their minds at times. One day he talks of grease without stoppin' for the most of an hour. I looks to see if there's lard burnin' in the fryin' pan. There is not. He says I do not understand. 'Tis weary days, Sundays, and holidays and all, for a blind man, Danny. There was no better nor stronger than him when he had his two eyes. 'Tis a fine day, son. Injoy yerself ag'inst the morning. There will be cold supper at six."

"Have you heard any talk of a hippopotamus?" asked Danny of Mike, the janitor, as he went out of the door downstairs.

"I have not," said Mike, pulling his shirtsleeves higher. "But 'tis the only subject in the animal, natural and illegal lists of outrages that I've not been complained to about these two days. See the landlord. Or else move out if ye like. Have ye hippopotamuses in the lease? No, then?"

"It was the old man who spoke of it," said Danny. "Likely there's nothing in it."

Danny walked up the street to the Avenue and then struck northward into the heart of the district where Easter—modern Easter, in new, bright raiment—leads the pascal march. Out of towering brown churches came the blithe music of anthems from the living flowers—so it seemed when your eye looked upon the Easter girl.

Gentlemen, frock-coated, silk-hatted, gardeniaed, sustained the background of the tradition. Children carried lilies in their hands. The windows of the brownstone mansions were packed with the most opulent creations of Flora, the sister of the Lady of the Lilies.

Around a corner, white-gloved, pink-gilled, and tightly buttoned, walked Corrigan, the cop, shield to the curb. Danny knew him.

"Why, Corrigan," he asked, "is Easter? I know it comes the first time you're full after the moon rises on the seventeenth of March—but why? Is it a proper and religious ceremony, or does the Government appoint it out of politics?"

" 'Tis an annual celebration," said Corrigan, with the judicial air of the Third Deputy Police Commissioner, "peculiar to New York. It extends up to Harlem. Sometimes they has the reserves out at One Hundred and Twenty-fifth Street. In my opinion 'tis not political."

"Thanks," said Danny. "And say—did you ever hear a man complain of hippopotamuses? When not specially in drink, I mean."

"Nothing larger than sea turtles," said Corrigan, reflecting, "and there was wood alcohol in that."

Danny wandered. The double, heavy incumbency of enjoying simultaneously a Sunday and a festival day was his.

The sorrows of the hand-toiler fit him easily. They are worn so often that they hang with the picturesque lines of the best tailor-made garments. That is why well-fed artists of pencil and pen find in the griefs of the common people their most striking models. But when the Philistine would disport himself, the grimness of Melpomene, herself, attends upon his capers. Therefore, Danny set his jaw hard at Easter, and took his pleasure sadly.

The family entrance of Dugan's café was feasible; so Danny yielded to the vernal season as far as a glass of bock. Seated in a dark, linoleumed, humid back room, his heart and mind still groped after the mysterious meaning of the springtime jubilee.

"Say, Tim," he said to the waiter, "why do they have Easter?"

"Skiddoo!" said Tim, closing a sophisticated eye. "Is that a new one? All right. Tony Pastor's for you last night, I guess. I give it up. What's the answer—two apples or a yard and a half?"

From Dugan's Danny turned back eastward. The April sun seemed to stir in him a vague feeling that he could not construe. He made a wrong diagnosis and decided that it was Katy Conlon.

A block from her house on Avenue A he met her going to church. They pumped hands on the corner.

"Gee! but you look dumpish and dressed up," said Katy. "What's wrong? Come away with me to church and be cheerful."

"What's doing at church?" asked Danny.

"Why, it's Easter Sunday. Silly! I waited till after eleven expectin' you might come around to go."

"What does this Easter stand for, Katy?" asked Danny gloomily. "Nobody seems to know."

"Nobody as blind as you," said Katy with spirit. "You haven't even looked at my new hat. And skirt. Why, it's when all the girls put on new spring clothes. Silly! Are you coming to church with me?"

"I will," said Danny. "If this Easter is pulled off there, they ought to be able to give some excuse for it. Not that the hat ain't a beauty. The green roses are great."

At church the preacher did some expounding with no pounding. He spoke rapidly, for he was in a hurry to get home to his early Sabbath dinner; but he knew his business. There was one word that controlled his theme—resurrection. Not a new creation; but a new life arising out of the old. The congregation had heard it often before. But there was a wonderful hat, a combination of sweet peas and lavender, in the sixth pew from the pulpit. It attracted much attention.

After church Danny lingered on a corner while Katy waited, with pique in her sky-blue eyes.

"Are you coming along to the house?" she asked. "But don't mind me. I'll get there all right. You seem to be studyin' a lot about something. All right. Will I see you at any time specially, Mr. McCree?"

"I'll be around Wednesday night as usual," said Danny, turning and crossing the street.

Katy walked away with the green roses dangling indignantly. Danny stopped two blocks away. He stood still with his hands in his pockets, at the curb on the corner. His face was that of a graven image. Deep in his soul something stirred so small, so fine, so keen and leavening that his hard fibres did not recognize it. It was something more tender than the April day, more subtle than the call of the senses, purer and deeper-rooted than the love of woman—for had he not turned away from green roses and eyes that had kept him chained for a year? And Danny did not know what it was. The preacher, who was in a hurry to go to his dinner, had told him, but Danny had had no libretto with which to follow the drowsy intonation. But the preacher spoke the truth.

Suddenly Danny slapped his leg and gave forth a hoarse yell of delight.

"Hippopotamus!" he shouted to an elevated road pillar. "Well, how is that for a bum guess? Why, blast my skylights! I know what he was driving at now.

"Hippopotamus! Wouldn't that send you to the Bronx! It's been a year since he heard it; and he didn't miss it so very far. We quit at 469 B. C. and this comes next. Well, a wooden man wouldn't have guessed what he was trying to get out of him."

Danny caught a crosstown car and went up to the rear flat that his labor supported.

Old man McCree was still sitting by the window. His extinct pipe lay on the sill.

"Will that be you, lad?" he asked.

Danny flared into the rage of a strong man who is surprised at the outset of committing a good deed.

"Who pays the rent and buys the food that is eaten in this house?" he snapped, viciously. "Have I no right to come in?"

"Ye're a faithful lad," said old man McCree, with a sigh. "Is it evening yet?"

Danny reached up on a shelf and took down a thick book labeled in gilt letters, "The History of Greece." Dust was on it half an inch thick. He laid it on the table and found a place in it marked by a strip of paper. And then he gave a short roar at the top of his voice, and said:

"Was it the hippopotamus you wanted to be read to about then?"

"Did I hear ye open the book?" said old man McCree. "Many and weary be the months since my lad has read it to me. I dinno; but I took a great likings to them Greeks. Ye left off at a place. 'Tis a fine day outside, lad. Be out and take rest from your work. I have gotten used to me chair by the windy and me pipe."

"Pel-Peloponnesus was the place where we left off, and not hippopotamus," said Danny. "The war began there. It kept something doing for thirty years. The headlines say that a guy named Philip of Macedon, in 338 B. C., got to be boss of Greece by getting the decision at the battle of Cher-Cheronœa. I'll read it."

With his hand to his ear, rapt in the Peloponnesian War, old man McCree sat for an hour, listening.

Then he got up and felt his way to the door of the kitchen. Mrs. McCree was slicing cold meat. She looked up. Tears were running from old man McCree's eyes.

"Do ye hear our lad readin' to me?" he said. "There is none finer in the land. My two eyes have come back to me again."

After supper he said to Danny: "'Tis a happy day, this Easter. And now ye will be off to see Katy in the evening. Well enough."

"Who pays the rent and buys the food that is eaten in this house?" said Danny, angrily. "Have I no right to stay in it? After supper there is yet to come the reading of the battle of Corinth, 146 B. C., when the kingdom, as they say, became an in-integral portion of the Roman Empire. Am I nothing in this house?"

THE FIFTH WHEEL

THE ranks of the Bed Line moved closer together; for it was cold, cold. They were alluvial deposit of the stream of life lodged in the delta of Fifth Avenue and Broadway. The Bed Liners stamped their freezing feet, looked at the empty benches in Madison Square whence Jack Frost had evicted them, and muttered to one another in a confusion of tongues. The Flatiron Building with its impious cloud-piercing architecture looming mistily above them on the opposite delta, might well have stood for the tower of Babel, whence these polyglot idlers had been called by the winged walking delegate of the Lord.

Standing on a pine box a head higher than his flock of goats, the Preacher exhorted whatever transient and shifting audience the north wind doled out to him. It was a slave market. Fifteen cents bought you a man. You deeded him to Morpheus; and the recording angel gave you credit.

The Preacher was incredibly earnest and unwearied. He had looked over the list of things one may do for one's fellow man, and had assumed for himself the task of putting to bed all who might apply at his soap box on the nights of Wednesday and Sunday. That left but five nights for other philanthropists to handle; and had they done their part as well, this wicked city might have become a vast Arcadian dormitory where all might snooze and snore the happy hours away, letting problem plays and the rent man and business go to the deuce.

The hour of eight was but a little while past; sightseers in a small, dark mass of pay ore were gathered in the shadow of General Worth's monument. Now and then, shyly, ostentatiously, carelessly, or with conscientious exactness one would step forward and bestow upon the Preacher small bills or silver. Then a lieutenant of Scandinavian coloring and enthusiasm would march away to a lodging house with a squad of the redeemed. All the while the Preacher exhorted the crowd in terms beautifully devoid of eloquence—splendid with the deadly, accusive monotony of truth. Before the picture of the Bed Liners fades you must hear one phrase of the Preacher's—the one that formed his theme that night. It is worthy of being stenciled on all the white ribbons in the world.

"No man ever learned to be a drunkard on five-cent whiskey."

Think of it, tippler. It covers the ground from the sprouting rye to the Potter's Field.

A clean-profiled, erect young man in the rear rank of the bedless emulated the terrapin, drawing his head far down into the shell of his coat collar. It was a well-cut tweed coat; and the trousers still showed signs of having flattened themselves beneath the compelling goose. But, conscientiously, I must warn the milliner's apprentice who reads this, expecting a Reginald Montressor in straits, to peruse no further. The young man was no other than Thomas McQuade, ex-coachman, discharged for drunkenness one month before, and now reduced to the grimy ranks of the one-night bed seekers.

If you live in smaller New York you must know the Van Smuythe family carriage, drawn by the two 1,500-pound, 100 to 1-shot bays. The carriage is shaped like a bath-tub. In each end of it reclines an old lady Van Smuythe holding a black sunshade the size of a New Year's Eve feather tickler. Before his downfall Thomas McQuade drove the Van Smuythe bays and was himself driven by Annie, the Van Smuythe lady's maid. But it is one of the saddest things about romance that a tight shoe or an empty commissary or an aching tooth will make a temporary heretic of any Cupid-worshipper. And Thomas's physical troubles were not few. Therefore, his soul was less vexed with thoughts of his lost lady's maid than it was by the fancied presence of certain non-existent things that his racked nerves almost convinced him were flying, dancing, crawling, and wriggling on the asphalt and in the air above and around the dismal campus of the Bed Line army. Nearly four weeks of straight whisky and a diet limited to crackers, bologna, and pickles often guarantees a psycho-zoological sequel. Thus desperate, freezing, angry, beset by phantoms as he was, he felt the need of human sympathy and intercourse.

The Bed Liner standing at his right was a young man of about his own age, shabby but neat.

"What's the diagnosis of your case, Freddy?" asked Thomas, with the freemasonic familiarity of the damned—"Booze? That's mine. You don't look like a pan-handler. Neither am I. A month ago I was pushing the lines over the backs of the finest team of Percheron buffaloes that ever made their mile down Fifth Avenue in 2.85. And look at me now! Say; how do you come to be at this bed bargain-counter rummage sale?"

The other young man seemed to welcome the advances of the airy ex-coachman.

"No," said he, "mine isn't exactly a case of drink. Unless we allow that Cupid is a bartender. I married unwisely, according to the opinion of my unforgiving relatives. I've been out of work for a year because I don't know how to work; and I've been sick in Bellevue and other hospitals for four months. My wife and kid had to go back to her mother. I was turned out of the hospital yesterday. And I haven't a cent. That's my tale of woe."

"Tough luck," said Thomas. "A man alone can pull through all right. But I hate to see the woman and kids get the worst of it."

Just then there hummed up Fifth Avenue a motor car so splendid, so red, so smoothly running, so craftily demolishing the speed regulations that it drew the attention even of the listless Bed Liners. Suspended and pinioned on its left side was an extra tire.

When opposite the unfortunate company the fastenings of this tire became loosed. It fell to the asphalt, bounded and rolled rapidly in the wake of the flying car.

Thomas McQuade scenting an opportunity, darted from his place among the Preacher's goats. In thirty seconds he had caught the rolling tire, swung it over his shoulder, and was trotting smartly after the car. On both sides of the avenue people were shouting, whistling, and waving canes at the red car, pointing to the enterprising Thomas coming up with the lost tire.

One dollar, Thomas had estimated, was the smallest guerdon that so grand an automobilist could offer for the service he had rendered, and save his pride.

Two blocks away the car had stopped. There was a little, brown, muffled chauffeur driving, and an imposing gentleman wearing a magnificent sealskin coat and a silk hat on a rear seat.

Thomas proffered the captured tire with his best ex-coachman manner and a look in the brighter of his reddened eyes that was meant to be suggestive to the extent of a silver coin or two and receptive up to higher denominations.

But the look was not so construed. The sealskinned gentleman received the tire, placed it inside the car, gazed intently at the ex-coachman, and muttered to himself inscrutable words.

"Strange—strange!" said he. "Once or twice even I, myself, have fancied that the Chaldean Chiroscope has availed. Could it be possible?"

Then he addressed less mysterious words to the waiting and hopeful Thomas.

"Sir, I thank you for your kind rescue of my tire. And I would ask you, if I may, a question. Do you know the family of Van Smuythes living in Washington Square North?"

"Oughtn't I to?" replied Thomas. "I lived there. Wish I did yet."

The sealskinned gentleman opened a door of the car.

"Step in, please," he said. "You have been expected."

Thomas McQuade obeyed with surprise but without hesitation. A seat in a motor car seemed better than standing room in the Bed Line. But after the lap-robe had been tucked about him and the auto had sped on its course, the peculiarity of the invitation lingered in his mind.

"Maybe the guy hasn't got any change," was his diagnosis. "Lots of these swell rounders don't lug about any ready money. Guess he'll dump me out when he gets to some joint where he can get cash on his mug. Anyhow, it's a cinch that I've got that open-air bed convention beat to a finish."

Submerged in his greatcoat, the mysterious automobilist seemed, himself, to marvel at the surprises of life. "Wonderful! amazing! strange!" he repeated to himself constantly.

When the car had well entered the crosstown Seventies it swung eastward a half block and stopped before a row of high-stooped, brownstone-front houses.

"Be kind enough to enter my house with me," said the sealskinned gentleman when they had alighted. "He's going to dig up, sure," reflected Thomas, following him inside.

There was a dim light in the hall. His host conducted him through a door to the left, closing it after him and leaving them in absolute darkness. Suddenly a luminous globe, strangely decorated, shone faintly in the centre of an immense room that seemed to Thomas more splendidly appointed than any he had ever seen on the stage or read of in fairy stories.

The walls were hidden by gorgeous red hangings embroidered with fantastic gold figures. At the rear end of the room were draped portières of dull gold spangled with silver crescents and stars. The furniture was of the costliest and rarest styles. The ex-coachman's feet sank into rugs as fleecy and deep as snow-drifts. There were three or four oddly shaped stands or tables covered with black velvet drapery.

Thomas McQuade took in the splendors of this palatial apartment with one eye.

With the other he looked for his imposing conductor—to find that he had disappeared.

"B'gee!" muttered Thomas, "this listens like a spook shop. Shouldn't wonder if it ain't one of these Moravian Nights' adventures that you read about. Wonder what became of the furry guy."

Suddenly a stuffed owl that stood on an ebony perch near the illuminated globe slowly raised his wings and emitted from his eyes a brilliant electric glow.

With a fright-born imprecation, Thomas seized a bronze statuette of Hebe from a cabinet near by and hurled it with all his might at the terrifying and impossible fowl. The owl and his perch went over with a crash. With the sound there was a click, and the room was flooded with light from a dozen frosted globes along the walls and ceiling. The gold portières parted and closed, and the mysterious automobilist entered the room. He was tall and wore evening dress of perfect cut and accurate taste. A Vandyke beard of glossy, golden brown, rather long and wavy hair, smoothly parted, and large, magnetic, orientally occult eyes gave him a most impressive and striking appearance. If you can conceive a Russian Grand Duke in a Rajah's throne-room advancing to greet a visiting Emperor, you will gather something of the majesty of his manner. But Thomas McQuade was too near his *d t's* to be mindful of his *p's* and *q's*. When he viewed this silken, polished, and somewhat terrifying host he thought vaguely of dentists.

"Say, doc," said he resentfully, "that's a hot bird you keep on tap. I hope I didn't break anything. But I've nearly got the williwalloos, and when he threw them 32-candle-power lamps of his on me, I took a snapshot at him with that little brass Flatiron Girl that stood on the sideboard."

"That is merely a mechanical toy," said the gentleman with a wave of his hand. "May I ask you to be seated while I explain why I brought you to my house? Perhaps you would not understand nor be in sympathy with the psychological prompting that caused me to do so. So I will come to the point at once by venturing to refer to your admission that you know the Van Smuythe family, of Washington Square North."

"Any silver missing?" asked Thomas tartly. "Any joolry displaced? Of course I know 'em. Any of the old ladies' sunshades disappeared? Well, I know 'em. And then what?"

The Grand Duke rubbed his white hands together softly.

"Wonderful!" he murmured. "Wonderful! Shall I come to believe in the Chaldean Chiroscope myself? Let me assure you," he continued, "that there is nothing for you to fear. Instead, I think I can promise you that very good fortune awaits you. We will see."

"Do they want me back?" asked Thomas, with something of his old professional pride in his voice. "I'll promise to cut out the booze and do the right thing if they'll try me again. But how did you get wise, doc? B'gee, it's the swellest employment agency I was ever in, with its flashlight owls and so forth."

With an indulgent smile the gracious host begged to be excused for two minutes. He went out to the sidewalk and gave an order to the chauffeur, who still waited with the car. Returning to the mysterious apartment, he sat by his guest and began to entertain him so well by his witty and genial converse that the poor Bed Liner almost forgot the cold streets from which he had been so recently and so singularly rescued. A servant brought some tender cold fowl and tea biscuits and a glass of miraculous wine; and Thomas felt the glamor of Arabia envelop him. Thus half an hour sped quickly; and then the honk of the returned motor car at the door suddenly drew the Grand Duke to his feet, with another soft petition for a brief absence.

Two women, well muffled against the cold, were admitted at the front door and suavely conducted by the master of the house down the hall through another door to the left and into a smaller room, which was screened and segregated from the larger front room by heavy double portières. Here the furnishings were even more elegant and exquisitely tasteful than in the other. On a gold-inlaid rosewood table were scattered sheets of white paper and a queer, triangular instrument or toy, apparently of gold, standing on little wheels.

The taller woman threw back her black veil and loosened her cloak. She was fifty, with a wrinkled and sad face. The other, young and plump, took a chair a little distance away and to the rear as a servant or an attendant might have done.

"You sent for me, Professor Cherubusco," said the elder woman, wearily. "I hope you have something more definite than usual to say. I've about lost the little faith I had in your art. I would not have responded to your call this evening if my sister had not insisted upon it."

"Madame," said the professor, with his princeliest smile, "the true Art cannot fail. To find the true psychic and potential branch sometimes requires time. We have not succeeded, I admit, with the cards, the crystal, the stars, the magic formulæ of Zarazin, nor the Oracle of Po. But we have at last discovered the true psychic route. The Chaldean Chiroscope has been successful in our search."

The professor's voice had a ring that seemed to proclaim his belief in his own words. The elderly lady looked at him with a little more interest.

"Why, there was no sense in those words that it wrote with my hands on it," she said. "What do you mean?"

"The words were these," said Professor Cherubusco, rising to his full magnificent height. " 'By the fifth wheel of the chariot he shall come.' "

"I haven't seen many chariots," said the lady, "but I never saw one with five wheels."

"Progress," said the professor—"progress in science and mechanics has accomplished it—though, to be exact, we may speak of it only as an extra tire. Progress in occult art has advanced in proportion. Madame, I repeat that the Chaldean Chiroscope has succeeded. I can not only answer the question that you have propounded, but I can produce before your eyes the proof thereof."

And now the lady was disturbed both in her disbelief and in her poise.

"O professor!" she cried, anxiously—"When?—where? Has he been found? Do not keep me in suspense."

"I beg you will excuse me for a very few minutes," said Professor Cherubusco, "and I think I can demonstrate to you the efficacy of the true Art."

Thomas was contentedly munching the last crumbs of the bread and fowl when the enchanter appeared suddenly at his side.

"Are you willing to return to your old home if you are assured of a welcome and restoration to favor?" he asked, with his courteous, royal smile.

"Do I look bughouse?" answered Thomas. "Enough of the footback life for me. But will they have me again? The old lady is as fixed in her ways as a nut on a new axle."

"My dear young man," said the other, "she has been searching for you everywhere."

"Great!" said Thomas. "I'm on the job. That team of dropsical dromedaries they call horses is a handicap for a first-class coachman like myself; but I'll take the job back, sure, doc. They're good people to be with."

And now a change came o'er the suave countenance of the Caliph of Bagdad. He looked keenly and suspiciously at the ex-coachman.

"May I asked what your name is?" he said shortly.

"You've been looking for me," said Thomas, "and don't know my name? You're a funny kind of sleuth. You must be one of the Central Office gumshoers. I'm Thomas McQuade, of course; and I've been chauffeur of the Van Smuythe elephant team for a year. They fired me a month ago for—well, doc, you saw what I did to your old owl. I went broke on booze, and when I saw the tire drop off your whiz wagon I was standing in that squad of hoboes at the Worth monument waiting for a free bed. Now, what's the prize for the best answer to all this?"

To his intense surprise Thomas felt himself lifted by the collar and dragged, without a word of explanation, to the front door. This was opened, and he was kicked forcibly down the steps with one heavy, disillusionizing, humiliating impact of the stupendous Arabian's shoe.

As soon as the ex-coachman had recovered his feet and his wits he hastened as fast as he could eastward toward Broadway.

"Crazy guy," was his estimate of the mysterious automobilist. "Just wanted to have some fun kiddin', I guess. He might have dug up a dollar, anyhow. Now I've got to hurry up and get back to that gang of bum bed hunters before they all get preached to sleep."

When Thomas reached the end of his two-mile walk he found the ranks of the homeless reduced to a squad of perhaps eight or ten. He took the proper place of a newcomer at the left end of the rear rank. In the file in front of him was the young man who had spoken to him of hospitals and something of a wife and child.

"Sorry to see you back again," said the young man, turning to speak to him. "I hoped you had struck something better than this."

"Me?" said Thomas. "Oh, I just took a run around the block to keep warm! I see the public ain't lending to the Lord very fast to-night."

"In this kind of weather," said the young man, "charity avails itself of the proverb, and both begins and ends at home."

And now the Preacher and his vehement lieutenant struck up a last hymn of petition to Providence and man. Those of the Bed Liners whose windpipes still registered above 32 degrees hopelessly and tunelessly joined in.

In the middle of the second verse Thomas saw a sturdy girl with wind-tossed drapery battling against the breeze and coming straight toward him from the opposite sidewalk. "Annie!" he yelled, and ran toward her.

"You fool, you fool!" she cried, weeping and laughing, and hanging upon his neck, "why did you do it?"

"The Stuff," explained Thomas briefly. "You know. But subsequently nit. Not a drop." He led her to the curb. "How did you happen to see me?"

"I came to find you," said Annie, holding tight to his sleeve. "Oh, you big fool! Professor Cherubusco told us that we might find you here."

"Professor Ch—— Don't know the guy. What saloon does he work in?"

"He's a clearvoyant, Thomas; the greatest in the world. He found you with the Chaldean telescope, he said."

"He's a liar," said Thomas. "I never had it. He never saw me have anybody's telescope."

"And he said you came in a chariot with five wheels or something."

"Annie," said Thomas solicitously, "you're giving me the wheels now. If I had a chariot I'd have gone to bed in it long ago. And without any singing and preaching for a nightcap, either."

"Listen, you big fool. The Missis says she'll take you back. I begged her to. But you must behave. And you can go up to the house to-night; and your old room over the stable is ready."

"Great!" said Thomas earnestly. "You are It, Annie. But when did these stunts happen?"

"To-night at Professor Cherubusco's. He sent his automobile for the Missis, and she took me along. I've been there with her before."

"What's the professor's line?"

"He's a clearvoyant and a witch. The Missis consults him. He knows everything. But he hasn't done the Missis any good yet, though she's paid him hundreds of dollars. But he told us that the stars told him we could find you here."

"What's the old lady want this cherry-buster to do?"

"That's a family secret," said Annie. "And now you've asked enough questions. Come on home, you big fool."

They had moved but a little way up the street when Thomas stopped.

"Got any dough with you, Annie?" he asked.

Annie looked at him sharply.

"Oh, I know what that look means," said Thomas. "You're wrong. Not another drop. But there's a guy that was standing next to me in the bed line over there that's in a bad shape. He's the right kind, and he's got wives or kids or something, and he's on the sick list. No booze. If you could dig up half a dollar for him so he could get a decent bed I'd like it."

Annie's fingers began to wiggle in her purse.

"Sure, I've got money," said she. "Lots of it. Twelve dolars." And then she added, with woman's ineradicable suspicion of vicarious benevolence: "Bring him here and let me see him first."

Thomas went on his mission. The wan Bed Liner came readily enough. As the two drew near, Annie looked up from her purse and screamd:

"Mr. Walter—— Oh—Mr. Walter!"

"Is that you, Annie?" said the young man weakly.

"Oh, Mr. Walter!—and the Missis hunting high and low for you!"

"Does mother want to see me?" he asked, with a flush coming out on his pale cheek.

"She's been hunting for you high and low. Sure, she wants to see you. She wants you to come home. She's tried police and morgues and lawyers and advertising and detectives and rewards and everything. And then she took up clearvoyants. You'll go right home, won't you, Mr. Walter?"

"Gladly, if she wants me," said the young man. "Three years is a long time. I suppose I'll have to walk up, though, unless the street cars are giving free rides. I used to walk and beat that old plug team of bays we used to drive to the carriage. Have they got them yet?"

"They have," said Thomas, feelingly. "And they'll have 'em ten years from now. The life of the royal elephantibus truckhorseibus is one hundred and forty-nine years. I'm the coachman. Just got my reappointment five minutes ago. Let's all ride up in a surface car—that is—er—if Annie will pay the fares."

On the Broadway car Annie handed each one of the prodigals a nickel to pay the conductor.

"Seems to me you are mighty reckless the way you throw large sums of money around," said Thomas, sarcastically.

"In that purse," said Annie, decidedly, "is exactly $11.85. I shall take every cent of it to-morrow and give it to Professor Cherubusco, the greatest man in the world."

"Well," said Thomas, "I guess he must be a pretty fly guy to pipe off things the way he does. I'm glad his spooks told him where you could find me. If you'll give me his address, some day I'll go up there, myself, and shake his hand."

Presently Thomas moved tentatively in his seat, and thoughtfully felt an abrasion or two on his knees and elbows.

"Say, Annie," said he, confidentially, "maybe it's one of the last dreams of the booze, but I've a kind of a recollection of riding in an automobile with a swell guy that took me to a house full of eagles and arc lights. He fed me on biscuits and hot air, and then kicked me down the front steps. If it was the *d t's*, why am I so sore?"

"Shut up, you fool," said Annie.

"If I could find that funny guy's house," said Thomas, in conclusion, "I'd go up there some day and punch his nose for him."

THE POET AND THE PEASANT

THE other day a poet friend of mine, who has lived in close communion with nature all his life, wrote a poem and took it to an editor.

It was a living pastoral, full of the genuine breath of the fields, the song of birds, and the pleasant chatter of trickling streams.

When the poet called again to see about it, with hopes of a beefsteak dinner in his heart, it was handed back to him with the comment:

"Too artificial."

Several of us met over spaghetti and Duchess County chianti, and swallowed indignation with slippery forkfuls.

And there we dug a pit for the editor. With us was Conant, a well-arrived writer of fiction—a man who had trod on asphalt all his life, and who had never looked upon bucolic scenes except with sensations of disgust from the windows of express trains.

Conant wrote a poem and called it "The Doe and the Brook." It was a fine specimen of the kind of work you would expect from a poet who had strayed with Amaryllis only as far as the florist's windows, and whose sole ornithological discussion had been carried on with a waiter. Conant signed this poem, and we sent it to the same editor.

But this has very little to do with the story.

Just as the editor was reading the first line of the poem, on the next morning, a being stumbled off the West Shore ferryboat, and loped slowly up Forty-second Street.

The invader was a young man with light blue eyes, a hanging lip, and hair the exact color of the little orphan's (afterward discovered to be the earl's daughter) in one of Mr. Blaney's plays. His trousers were corduroy, his coat short-sleeved, with buttons in the middle of his back. One bootleg was outside the corduroys. You looked expectantly, though in vain, at his straw hat for ear holes, its shape inaugurating the suspicion that it had been ravaged from a former equine possessor. In his hand was a valise—description of it is an impossible task; a Boston man would not have carried his lunch and law books to his office in it. And above one ear, in his hair, was a wisp of hay—the rustic's letter of credit, his badge of innocence, the last clinging touch of the Garden of Eden lingering to shame the gold-brick men.

Knowingly, smilingly, the city crowds passed him by. They saw the raw stranger stand in the gutter and stretch his neck at the tall buildings. At this they ceased to smile, and even to look at him. It had been done so often. A few glanced at the antique valise to see what Coney "attraction" or brand of chewing gum he might be thus dinning into his memory. But for the most part he was ignored. Even the newsboys looked bored when he scampered like a circus clown out of the way of cabs and street cars.

At Eighth Avenue stood "Bunco Harry," with his dyed mustache and shiny, good-natured eyes. Harry was too good an artist not to be pained at the sight of an actor overdoing his part. He edged up to the countryman, who had stopped to open his mouth at a jewelry store window, and shook his head.

"Too thick, pal," he said, critically—"too thick by a couple of inches. I don't know what your lay is; but you've got the properties on too thick. That hay, now—why, they don't even allow that on Proctor's circuit any more."

"I don't understand you, mister," said the green one. "I'm not lookin' for any circus. I've just run down from Ulster County to look at the town, bein' that the hayin's over with. Gosh! but it's a whopper. I thought Poughkeepsie was some pumpkins; but this here town is five times as big."

"Oh, well," said "Bunco Harry," raising his eyebrows, "I didn't mean to butt in. You don't have to tell. I thought you ought to tone down a little, so I tried to put you wise. Wish you success at your graft, whatever it is. Come and have a drink, anyhow."

"I wouldn't mind having a glass of lager beer," acknowledged the other.

They went to a café frequented by men with smooth faces and shifty eyes, and sat at their drinks.

"I'm glad I come across you, mister," said Haylocks. "How'd you like to play a game or two of seven-up? I've got the keerds."

He fished them out of Noah's valise—a rare, inimitable deck, greasy with bacon suppers and grimy with the soil of cornfields.

"Bunco Harry," laughed loud and briefly.

"Not for me, sport," he said, firmly. "I don't go against that make-up of yours for a cent. But I still say you've overdone it. The Reubs haven't dressed like that since '79. I doubt if you could work Brooklyn for a key-winding watch with that layout."

"Oh, you needn't think I ain't got the money," boasted Haylocks. He drew forth a tightly rolled mass of bills as large as a teacup, and laid it on the table.

"Got that for my share of grandmother's farm," he announced. "There's $950 in that roll. Thought I'd come to the city and look around for a likely business to go into."

"Bunco Harry" took up the roll of money and looked at it with almost respect in his smiling eyes.

"I've seen worse," he said, critically. "But you'll never do it in them clothes. You want to get light tan shoes and a black suit and a straw hat with a colored band, and talk a good deal about Pittsburg and freight differentials, and drink sherry for breakfast in order to work off phony stuff like that."

"What's his line?" asked two or three shifty-eyed men of "Bunco Harry" after Haylocks had gathered up his impugned money and departed.

"The queer, I guess," said Harry. "Or else he's one of Jerome's men. Or some guy with a new graft. He's too much hayseed. Maybe that his—I wonder now— oh, no, it couldn't have been real money."

Haylocks wandered on. Thirst probably assailed him again, for he dived into a dark groggery on a side street and bought beer. Several sinister fellows hung upon one end of the bar. At first sight of him their eyes brightened; but when his insistent and exaggerated rusticity became apparent their expressions changed to wary suspicion.

Haylocks swung his valise across the bar.

"Keep that a while for me, mister," he said, chewing at the end of a virulent clay-bank cigar.

"I'll be back after I knock around a spell. And keep your eye on it, for there's $950 inside of it, though maybe you wouldn't think so to look at me."

Somewhere outside a phonograph struck up a band piece, and Haylocks was off for it, his coat-tail buttons flopping in the middle of his back.

"Divvy, Mike," said the men hanging upon the bar, winking openly at one another.

"Honest, now," said the bartender, kicking the valise to one side. "You don't think I'd fall to that, do you? Anybody can see he ain't no jay. One of McAdoo's come-on squad, I guess. He's a shine if he made himself up. There ain't no parts of the country now where they dress like that since they run rural free delivery to Providence, Rhode Island. If he's got nine-fifty in that valise it's a ninety-eight cent Waterbury that's stopped at ten minutes to ten."

When Haylocks had exhausted the resources of Mr. Edison to amuse he returned for his valise. And then down Broadway he gallivanted, culling the sights with his eager blue eyes. But still and evermore Broadway rejected him with curt glances and sardonic smiles. He was the oldest of the "gags" that the city must endure. He was so flagrantly impossible, so ultra rustic, so exaggerated beyond the most freakish products of the barnyards, the hayfield, and the vaudeville stage, that he excited only weariness and suspicion. And the wisp of hay in his hair was so genuine, so fresh and redolent of the meadows, so clamorously rural that even a shell-game man would have put up his peas and folded his table at the sight of it.

Haylocks seated himself upon a flight of stone steps and once more exhumed his roll of yellow-backs from the valise. The outer one, a twenty, he shucked off and beckoned to a newsboy.

"Son," said he, "run somewhere and get this changed for me. I'm mighty nigh out of chicken feed. I guess you'll get a nickel if you'll hurry up."

A hurt look appeared through the dirt on the newsy's face.

"Aw, watchert'ink! G'wan and get yer funny bill changed yerself. Dey ain't no farm clothes yer got on. G'wan wit yer stage money."

On a corner lounged a keen-eyed steerer for a gambling-house. He saw Haylocks, and his expression suddenly grew cold and virtuous.

"Mister," said the rural one. "I've heard of places in this here town where a fellow could have a good game of old sledge or peg a card at keno. I got $950 in this valise, and I come down from old Ulster to see the sights. Know where a fellow could get action on about $9 or $10? I'm goin' to have some sport, and then maybe I'll buy out a business of some kind."

The steerer looked pained, and investigated a white speck on his left forefinger nail.

"Cheese it, old man," he murmured, reproachfully. "The Central Office must be bughouse to send you out looking like such a gillie. You couldn't get within two blocks of a sidewalk crap game in them Tony Pastor props. The recent Mr. Scotty from Death Valley has got you beat a crosstown block in the way of Elizabethan scenery and mechanical accessories. Let it be skiddoo for yours. Nay, I know of no gilded halls where one may get a patrol wagon on the ace."

Rebuffed again by the great city that is so swift to detect artificialities, Haylocks sat upon the curb and presented his thoughts to hold a conference.

"It's my clothes," said he; "durned if it ain't. They think I'm a hayseed and won't have nothin' to do with me. Nobody never made fun of this hat in Ulster County. I guess if you want folks to notice you in New York you must dress up like they do."

So Haylocks went shopping in the bazaars where men spake through their noses and rubbed their hands and ran the tape line ecstatically over the bulge in his inside pocket where reposed a red nubbin of corn with an even number of rows And messengers bearing parcels and boxes streamed to his hotel on Broadway within the lights of Long Acre.

At 9 o'clock in the evening one descended to the sidewalk whom Ulster County would have foresworn. Bright tan were his shoes; his hat the latest block. His light gray trousers were deeply creased; a gay blue silk handkerchief flapped from the breast pocket of his elegant English walking coat. His collar might have graced a laundry window; his blond hair was trimmed close; the wisp of hay was gone.

For an instant he stood, resplendent, with the leisurely air of a boulevardier concocting in his mind the route for his evening pleasures. And then he turned down the gay, bright street with the easy and graceful tread of a millionaire.

But in the instant that he had paused the wisest and keenest eyes in the city had enveloped him in their field of vision. A stout man with gray eyes picked two of his friends with a lift of his eyebrows from the row of loungers in front of the hotel.

"The juiciest jay I've seen in six months," said the man with gray eyes. "Come along."

It was half-past eleven when a man galloped into the West Forty-seventh Street Police Station with the story of his wrongs.

"Nine hundred and fifty dollars," he gasped, "all my share of grandmother's farm."

The desk sergeant wrung from him the name Jabez Bulltongue, of Locust Valley farm, Ulster County, and then began to take descriptions of the strong-arm gentlemen.

When Conant went to see the editor about the fate of his poem, he was received over the head of the office boy into the inner office that is decorated with the statuettes by Rodin and J. G. Brown.

"When I read the first line of 'The Doe and the Brook,'" said the editor, "I knew it to be the work of one whose life has been heart to heart with Nature. The finished art of the line did not blind me to that fact. To use a somewhat homely comparison, it was as if a wild, free child of the woods and fields were to don the garb of fashion and walk down Broadway. Beneath the apparel the man would show."

"Thanks," said Conant. "I suppose the check will be round on Thursday, as usual."

The morals of this story have somehow gotten mixed. You can take your choice of "Stay on the Farm" or "Don't Write Poetry."

THE ROBE OF PEACE

MYSTERIES follow one another so closely in a great city that the reading public and the friends of Johnny Bellchambers have ceased to marvel at his sudden and unexplained disappearance nearly a year ago. This particular mystery has now been cleared up, but the solution is so strange and incredible to the mind of the average man that only a select few who were in close touch with Bellchambers will give it full credence.

Johnny Bellchambers, as is well known, belonged to the intrinsically inner circle of the *élite*. Without any of the ostentation of the fashionable ones who endeavor to attract notice by eccentric display of wealth and show he still was *au fait* in everything that gave deserved lustre to his high position in the ranks of society.

Especially did he shine in the matter of dress. In this he was the despair of imitators. Always correct, exquisitely groomed, and possessed of an unlimited wardrobe, he was conceded to be the best-dressed man in New York, and, therefore, in America. There was not a tailor in Gotham who would not have deemed it a precious boon to have been granted the privilege of making Bellchambers' clothes without a cent of pay. As he wore them, they would have been a priceless advertisement. Trousers were his especial passion. Here nothing but perfection would he notice. He would have worn a patch as quickly as he would have overlooked a wrinkle. He kept a man in his apartments always busy pressing his ample supply. His friends said that three hours was the limit of time that he would wear these garments without exchanging.

Bellchambers disappeared very suddenly. For three days his absence brought no alarm to his friends, and then they began to operate the usual methods of inquiry. All of them failed. He had left absolutely no trace behind. Then the search for a motive was instituted, but none was found. He had no enemies, he had no debts, there was no woman. There were several thousand dollars in his bank to his credit. He had never showed any tendency toward mental eccentricity; in fact, he was of a particularly calm and well-balanced temperament. Every means of tracing the vanished man was made use of, but without avail. It was one of those cases—more numerous in late years—where men seem to have gone out like the flame of a candle, leaving not even a trail of smoke as a witness.

In May, Tom Eyres and Lancelot Gilliam, two of Bellchambers' old friends, went for a little run on the other side. While pottering around in Italy and Switzerland, they happened, one day, to hear of a monastery in the Swiss Alps that promised something outside of the ordinary tourist-beguiling attractions. The monastery was almost inaccessible to the average sight-seer, being on an extremely rugged and precipitous spur of the mountains. The attractions it possessed but did not advertise were, first, an exclusive and divine cordial made by the monks that was said to far surpass benedictine and chartreuse. Next a huge brass bell so purely and accurately cast that it had not ceased sounding since it was first rung three hundred years ago. Finally, it was asserted that no Englishman had ever set foot within its walls. Eyres and Gilliam decided that these three reports called for investigation.

It took them two days with the aid of two guides to reach the monastery of St. Gondrau. It stood upon a frozen, wind-swept crag with the snow piled about it in treacherous, drifting masses. They were hospitably received by the brothers whose duty it was to entertain the infrequent guest. They drank of the precious cordial, finding it rarely potent and reviving. They listened to the great, ever-echoing bell and learned that they were pioneer travelers, in those gray stone walls, over the Englishman whose restless feet have trodden nearly every corner of the earth.

At three o'clock on the afternoon they arrived, the two young Gothamites stood with good Brother Cristofer in the great, cold hallway of the monastery to watch the monks march past on their way to the refectory. They came slowly, pacing by twos, with their heads bowed, treading noiselessly with sandaled feet upon the rough stone flags. As the procession slowly filed past, Eyres suddenly gripped Gilliam by the arm. "Look," he whispered, eagerly, "at the one just opposite you now—the one on this side, with his hand at his waist—if that isn't Johnny Bellchambers then I never saw him!"

Gilliam saw and recognized the lost glass of fashion.

"What the deuce," said he, wonderingly, "is old Bell doing here? Tommy, it surely can't be he! Never heard of Bell having a turn for the religious. Fact is, I've heard him say things when a four-in-hand didn't seem to tie up just right that would bring him up for court-martial before any church."

"It's Bell, without a doubt," said Eyres, firmly, "or I'm pretty badly in need of an oculist. But think of Johnny Bellchambers, the Royal High Chancellor of swell togs and the Mahatma of pink teas, up here in cold storage doing penance in a snuff-colored bathrobe! I can't get it straight in my mind. Let's ask the jolly old boy that's doing the honors."

Brother Cristofer was appealed to for information. By that time the monks had passed into the refectory. He could not tell to which one they referred. Bell-chambers? Ah, the brothers of St. Gondrau abandoned their worldly names when they took the vows. Did the gentlemen wish to speak with one of the brothers? If they would come to the refectory and indicate the one they wished to see, the reverend abbot in authority would, doubtless, permit it.

Eyres and Gilliam went into the dining hall and pointed out to Brother Cristofer the man they had seen. Yes, it was Johnny Bellchambers. They saw his face plainly now, as he sat among the dingy brothers, never looking up, eating broth from a coarse, brown bowl.

Permission to speak to one of the brothers was granted to the two travelers by the abbot, and they waited in a reception room for him to come. When he did come, treading softly in his sandals, both Eyres and Gilliam looked at him in perplexity and astonishment. It was Johnny Bellchambers, but he had a dif-ferent look. Upon his smooth-shaven face was an expression of ineffable peace, of rapturous attainment, of perfect and complete happiness. His form was proudly erect, his eyes shone with a serene and gracious light. He was as neat and well-groomed as in the old New York days, but how differently was he clad! Now he seemed clothed in but a single garment—a long robe of rough brown cloth, gathered by a cord at the waist, and falling in straight, loose folds nearly to his feet. He shook hands with his visitors with his old ease and grace of manner. If there was any embarrassment in that meeting it was not manifested by Johnny Bellchambers. The room had no seats; they stood to converse.

"Glad to see you, old man," said Eyres, somewhat awkwardly. "Wasn't ex-pecting to find you up here. Not a bad idea, though, after all. Society's an aw-ful sham. Must be a relief to shake the giddy whirl and retire to—er—con-templation and—er—prayer and hymns, and those things."

"Oh, cut that, Tommy," said Bellchambers, cheerfully. "Don't be afraid that I'll pass around the plate. I go through these thing-um-bobs with the rest of these old boys because they are the rules. I'm Brother Ambrose here, you know. I've given just ten minutes to talk to you fellows. That's rather a new design in waistcoats you have on, isn't it, Gilliam? Are they wearing those things on Broadway now?"

'It's the same old Johnny," said Gilliam, joyfully. "What the devil—I mean why—— Oh, confound it! what did you do it for, old man?"

"Peel the bathrobe," pleaded Eyres, almost tearfully, "and go back with us. The old crowd'll go wild to see you. This isn't in your line, Bell. I know half a dozen girls that wore the willow on the quiet when you shook us in that un-accountable way. Hand in your resignation, or get a dispensation, or whatever you have to do to get a release from this ice factory. You'll get catarrh here, Johnny—and—— My God! you haven't any socks on!"

Bellchambers looked down at his sandaled feet and smiled.

"You fellows don't understand," he said, soothingly. "It's nice of you to want me to go back, but the old life will never know me again. I have reached here the goal of all my ambitions. I am entirely happy and contented. Here I shall remain for the remainder of my days. You see this robe that I wear?" Bell-chambers caressingly touched the straight-hanging garment: "At last I have found something that will not bag at the knees. I have attained——"

At that moment the deep boom of the great brass bell reverberated through the monastery. It must have been a summons to immediate devotions, for Brother Ambrose bowed his head, turned and left the chamber without another word. A slight wave of his hand as he passed through the stone doorway seemed to say a farewell to his old friends. They left the monastery without seeing him again.

And this is the story that Tommy Eyres and Lancelot Gilliam brought back with them from their latest European tour.

THE GIRL AND THE GRAFT

THE other day I ran across my old friend Ferguson Pogue. Pogue is a conscientious grafter of the highest type. His headquarters is the Western Hemisphere, and his line of business is anything from speculating in town lots on the Great Staked Plains to selling wooden toys in Connecticut, made by hydraulic pressure from nutmegs ground to a pulp.

Now and then when Pogue has made a good haul he comes to New York for a rest. He says the jug of wine and loaf of bread and Thou in the wilderness business is about as much rest and pleasure to him as sliding down the bumps at Coney would be to President Taft. "Give me," says Pogue, "a big city for my vacation. Especially New York. I'm not much fond of New Yorkers, and Manhattan is about the only place on the globe where I don't find any."

While in the metropolis Pogue can always be found at one of two places. One is a little second-hand bookshop on Fourth Avenue, where he reads books about his hobbies, Mahometanism and taxidermy. I found him at the other—his hall bedroom in Eighteenth Street—where he sat in his stocking feet trying to pluck "The Banks of the Wabash" out of a small zither. Four years he has practised this tune without arriving near enough to cast the longest trout line to the water's edge. On the dresser lay a blued-steel Colt's forty-five and a tight roll of tens and twenties large enough around to belong to the spring rattlesnake-story class. A chambermaid with a room-cleaning air fluttered near by in the hall, unable to enter or to flee, scandalized by the stocking feet, aghast at the Colt's, yet powerless, with her metropolitan instincts, to remove herself beyond the magic influence of the yellow-hued roll.

I sat on his trunk while Ferguson Pogue talked. No one could be franker or more candid in his conversation. Beside his expression the cry of Henry James for lacteal nourishment at the age of one month would have seemed like a Chaldean cryptogram. He told me stories of his profession with pride, for he considered it an art. And I was curious enough to ask him whether he had known any women who followed it.

"Ladies?" said Pogue, with Western chivalry. "Well, not to any great extent. They don't amount to much in special lines of graft, because they're all so busy in general lines. What? Why, they have to. Who's got the money in the world? The men. Did you ever know a man to give a woman a dollar without any consideration? A man will shell out his dust to another man free and easy and gratis. But if he drops a penny in one of the machines run by the Madam Eve's Daughters' Amalgamated Association and the pineapple chewing gum don't fall out when he pulls the lever you can hear him kick to the superintendent four blocks away. Man is the hardest proposition a woman has to go up against. He's a low-grade one, and she has to work overtime to make him pay. Two times out of five she's salted. She can't put in crushers and costly machinery. He'd notice 'em and be onto the game. They have to pan out what they get, and it hurts their tender hands. Some of 'em are natural sluice troughs and can carry out $1,000 to the ton. The dry-eyed ones have to depend on signed letters, false hair, sympathy, the kangaroo walk, cowhide whips, ability to cook, sentimental juries, conversational powers, silk underskirts, ancestry, rouge, anonymous letters, violet sachet powders, witnesses, revolvers, pneumatic forms, carbolic acid, moonlight, cold cream and the evening newspapers."

"You are outrageous, Ferg," I said. "Surely there is none of this 'graft,' as you call it, in a perfect and harmonious matrimonial union!"

"Well," said Pogue, "nothing that would justify you every time in calling up Police Headquarters and ordering out the reserves and a vaudeville manager on a dead run. But it's this way: Suppose you're a Fifth Avenue millionaire, soaring high, on the right side of copper and cappers.

"You come home at night and bring a $9,000,000 diamond brooch to the lady who's staked you for a claim. You hand it over. She says, 'Oh, George!' and looks to see if it's backed. She comes up and kisses you. You've waited for it. You get it. All right. It's graft.

"But I'm telling you about Artemisia Blye. She was from Kansas and she suggested corn in all of its phases. Her hair was as yellow as the silk; her form was as tall and graceful as a stalk in the low grounds during a wet summer; her eyes were as big and startling as bunions, and green was her favorite color.

"On my last trip into the cool recesses of your sequestered city I met a human named Vaucross. He was worth—that is, he had a million. He told me he was in business on the street. 'A sidewalk merchant?' says I, sarcastic. 'Exactly,' says he. 'Senior partner of a paving concern.'

"I kind of took to him. For this reason, I met him on Broadway one night when I was out of heart, luck, tobacco, and place. He was all silk hat, diamonds, and front. He was all front. If you had gone behind him you would have only looked yourself in the face. I looked like a cross between County Tolstoy and a June lobster. I was out of luck. I had—but let me lay my eyes on that dealer again.

"Vaucross stopped and talked to me a few minutes and then he took me to a high-toned restaurant to eat dinner. There was music, and then some Beethoven, and Bordelaise sauce, and cussing in French and frangipani, and some hauteur and cigarettes. When I am flush I know them places.

"I declare, I must have looked as bad as a magazine artist sitting there without any money and my hair all rumpled like I was booked to read a chapter from 'Elsie's School Days' at a Brooklyn Bohemian smoker. But Vaucross treated me like a bear hunter's guide. He wasn't afraid of hurting the waiter's feelings.

"'Mr. Pogue,' he explains to me, 'I am using you.'

"'Go on,' says I; 'I hope you don't wake up.'

"And then he tells me, you know, the kind of man he was. He was a New Yorker. His whole ambition was to be noticed. He wanted to be conspicuous. He wanted people to point him out and bow to him, and tell others who he was. He said it had been the desire of his life always. He didn't have but a million, so he couldn't attract attention by spending money. He said he tried to get into public notice one time by planting a little public square on the east side with garlic for free use of the poor; but Carnegie heard of it, and covered it over at once with a library in the Gaelic language. Three times he had jumped in the way of automobiles; but the only result was five broken ribs and a notice in the papers that an unknown man, five feet ten, with four amalgam-filled teeth, supposed to be the last of the famous Red Leary gang, had been run over.

"'Ever try the reporters?' I asked him.

"'Last month,' says Mr. Vaucross, 'my expenditure for lunches to reporters was $124.80.'

"'Get anything out of that?' I asks.

"'That reminds me,' says he; 'add $8.50 for pepsin. Yes, I got indigestion.'

"'How am I supposed to push along your scramble for prominence?' I inquires. 'Contrast?'

"'Something of that sort to-night,' says Vaucross. 'It grieves me; but I am forced to resort to eccentricity.' And here he drops his napkin in his soup and rises up and bows to a gent who is devastating a potato under a palm across the room.

"'The Police Commissioner,' says my climber, gratified. 'Friend,' says I, in a hurry, 'have ambitions but don't kick a rung out of your ladder. When you use me as a stepping stone to salute the police you spoil my appetite on the grounds that I may be degraded and incriminated. Be thoughtful.'

"At the Quaker City squab en casserole the idea about Artemisia Blye comes to me.

"'Suppose I can manage to get you in the papers,' says I—'a column or two every day in all of 'em and your picture in most of 'em for a week. How much would it be worth to you?'

"'Ten thousand dollars,' says Vaucross, warm in a minute. 'But no murder,' says he; 'and I won't wear pink pants at a cotillon.'

"'I wouldn't ask you to,' says I. 'This is honorable, stylish, and uneffeminate. Tell the waiter to bring a demi tasse and some other beans, and I will disclose to you the opus moderandi.'

"We closed the deal an hour later in the rococo rouge en noise room. I telegraphed that night to Miss Artemisia in Salina. She took a couple of photographs and an autograph letter to an elder in the Fourth Presbyterian Church in the morning, and got some transportation and $80. She stopped in Topeka long enough to trade a flashlight interior and a valentine to the vice-president of a trust company for a mileage book and a package of five-dollar notes with $250 scrawled on the band.

"The fifth evening after she got my wire she was waiting, all décolletée and dressed up, for me and Vaucross to take her to dinner in one of these New York feminine apartment houses where a man can't get in unless he plays bezique and smokes depilatory powder cigarettes.

"'She's a stunner,' says Vaucross when he saw her. 'They'll give her a two-column cut sure.'

"This was the scheme the three of us concocted. It was business straight through. Vaucross was to rush Miss Blye with all the style and display and emotion he could for a month. Of course, that amounted to nothing as far as his ambitions were concerned. The sight of a man in a white tie and patent leather pumps pouring greenbacks through the large end of a cornucopia to purchase nutriment and heartsease for tall, willowy blondes in New York is as common a sight as blue turtles in delirium tremens. But he was to write her love letters—the worst kind of love letters, such as your wife publishes after you are dead—every day. At the end of the month he was to drop her, and she would brings suit for $100,000 for breach of promise.

"Miss Artemisia was to get $10,000. If she won the suit that was all; and if she lost she was to get it anyhow. There was a signed contract to that effect.

"Sometimes they had me out with 'em, but not often. I couldn't keep up to their style. She used to pull out his notes and criticize them like bills of lading.

"'Say, you!' she'd say. 'What do you call this—Letter to a Hardware Merchant from His Nephew on Learning that His Aunt Has Nettlerash? You Eastern duffers know as much about writing love letters as a Kansas grasshopper does about tugboats. "My dear Miss Blye!"—wouldn't that put pink icing and a little red sugar bird on your bridal cake? How long do you expect to hold an audience in a court-room with that kind of stuff? You want to get down to business, and call me "Tweedlums Babe" and "Honeysuckle," and sign yourself "Mamma's Own Big Bad Puggy Wuggy Boy" if you want any limelight to concentrate upon your sparse gray hairs. Get snappy.'

"After that Vaucross dipped his pen in the indelible tabasco. His notes read like something or other in the original. I could see a jury sitting up, and women tearing one another's hats to hear 'em read. And I could see piling up for Mr. Vaucross as much notoriousness as Archbishop Cranmer or the Brooklyn Bridge or cheese-on-salad ever enjoyed. He seemed mighty pleased at the prospects.

"They agreed on a night; and I stood on Fifth Avenue outside a solemn restaurant and watched 'em. A process-server walked in and handed Vaucross the papers at his table. Everybody looked at 'em; and he looked as proud as Cicero. I went back to my room and lit a five-cent cigar, for I knew the $10,-000 was as good as ours.

"About two hours later somebody knocked at my door. There stood Vaucross and Miss Artemisia, and she was clinging—yes, sir, clinging—to his arm. And they tells me they'd been out and got married. And they articulated some trivial cadences about love and such. And they laid down a bundle on the table and said 'Good-night' and left.

"And that's why I say," concluded Ferguson Pogue, "that a woman is too busy occupied with her natural vocation and instinct of graft such as is given her for self-preservation and amusement to make any great success in special lines."

"What was in the bundle that they left?" I asked, with my usual curiosity.

"Why,' said Ferguson, "there was a scalper's railroad ticket as far as Kansas City and two pairs of Mr. Vaucross's old pants."

THE CALL OF THE TAME

When the inauguration was accomplished—the proceedings were made smooth by the presence of the Rough Riders—it is well known that a herd of those competent and loyal ex-warriors paid a visit to the big city. The newspaper reporters dug out of their trunks the old broad-brimmed hats and leather belts that they wear to North Beach fish fries, and mixed with the visitors. No damage was done beyond the employment of the wonderful plural "tenderfeet" in each of the scribe's stories. The Westerners mildly contemplated the skyscrapers as high as the third story, yawned at Broadway, hunched down in the big chairs in hotel corridors, and altogether looked as bored and dejected as a member of Ye Ancient and Honorable Artillery separated during a sham battle from his valet.

Out of this sightseeing delegation of good King Teddy's Gentlemen of the Royal Bear-hounds dropped one Greenbrier Nye, of Pin Feather, Ariz.

The daily cyclone of Sixth Avenue's rush hour swept him away from the company of his pardners true. The dust from a thousand rustling skirts filled his eyes. The mighty roar of trains rushing across the sky deafened him. The lightning-flash of twice ten hundred beaming eyes confused his vision.

The storm was so sudden and tremendous that Greenbrier's first impulse was to lie down and grab a root. And then he remembered that the disturbance was human, and not elemental; and he backed out of it with a grin into a doorway.

The reporters had written that but for the wide-brimmed hats the West was not visible upon these gauchos of the North. Heaven sharpen their eyes! The suit of black diagonal, wrinkled in impossible places; the bright blue four-in-hand, factory tied; the low, turned-down collar, pattern of the days of Seymour and Blair, white glazed as the letters on the window of the open-day-and-night-except-Sunday restaurants; the out-curve at the knees from the straddle grip; the peculiar spread of the half-closed right thumb and fingers from the stiff hold upon the circling lasso; the deeply absorbed weather tan that the hottest sun of Cape May can never equal; the seldom-winking blue eyes that unconsciously divided the rushing crowds into fours, as though they were being counted out of a corral;

the segregated loneliness and solemnity of expression, as of an emperor or of one whose horizons have not intruded upon him nearer than a day's ride—these brands of the West were set upon Greenbrier Nye. Oh, yes; he wore a broad-brimmed hat, gentle reader—just like those the Madison Square Post Office mail carriers wear when they go up to Bronx Park on Sunday afternoons.

Suddenly Greenbrier Nye jumped into the drifting herd of metropolitan cattle, seized upon a man, dragged him out of the stream and gave him a buffet upon his collar-bone that sent him reeling against a wall.

The victim recovered his hat, with the angry look of a New Yorker who has suffered an outrage and intends to write to the Trib. about it. But he looked at his assailant, and knew that the blow was in consideration of love and affection after the manner of the West, which greets its friends with contumely and uproar and pounding fists, and receives its enemies in decorum and order, such as the judicious placing of the welcoming bullet demands.

"God in the mountains!" cried Greenbrier, holding fast to the foreleg of his cull. "Can this be Longhorn Merritt?"

The other man was—oh, look on Broadway any day for the pattern—business man—latest rolled-brim derby—good barber, business, digestion, and tailor.

"Greenbrier Nye!" he exclaimed, grasping the hand that had smitten him. "My dear fellow! So glad to see you! How did you come to—oh, to be sure—the inaugural ceremonies—I remember you joined the Rough Riders. You must come and have luncheon with me, of course."

Greenbrier pinned him sadly but firmly to the wall with a hand the size, shape, and color of a McClellan saddle.

"Longy," he said, in a melancholy voice that disturbed traffic, "what have they been doing to you? You act just like a citizen. They done made you into an inmate of the city directory. You never made no such Johnny Branch execration of yourself as that out on the Gila. 'Come and have lunching with me!' You never defined grub by any such terms of reproach in them days."

"I've been living in New York seven years," said Merritt. "It's been eight since we punched cows together in Old Man Garcia's outfit. Well, let's go to a café, anyhow. It sounds good to hear it called 'grub' again."

They picked their way through the crowd to a hotel, and drifted, as by a natural law, to the bar.

"Speak up," invited Greenbrier.

"A dry Martini," said Merritt.

"Oh, Lord!" cried Greenbrier; "and yet me and you once saw the same pink Gila monsters crawling up on the walls of the same hotel in Cañon Diablo! A dry—but let that pass. Whiskey straight—and they're on you."

Merritt smiled, and paid.

They lunched in a small extension of the dining room that connected with the café. Merritt dexterously diverted his friend's choice, that hovered over ham and eggs, to a purée of celery, a salmon cutlet, a partridge pie, and a desirable salad.

"On the day," said Greenbrier, grieved and thunderous, "when I can't hold but one drink before eating when I meet a friend I ain't seen in eight years at a 2 by 4 table in a thirty-cent town at 1 o'clock on the third day of the week, I want nine broncos to kick me forty times over a 640-acre section of land. Get them statistics?"

"Right, old man," laughed Merritt. "Waiter, bring an absinthe frappé and—what's yours, Greenbrier?"

"Whiskey straight," mourned Nye. "Out of the neck of a bottle you used to take it, Longy—straight out of the neck of a bottle on a galloping pony—Arizona redeye, not this ab—oh, what's the use? They're on you."

Merritt slipped the wine card under his glass.

"All right. I suppose you think I'm spoiled by the city. I'm as good a Westerner as you are, Greenbrier; but, somehow, I can't make up my mind to go back out there. New York is comfortable—comfortable. I make a good living, and I live it. No more wet blankets and riding herd in snowstorms, and bacon and cold coffee, and blowouts once in six months for me. I reckon I'll hang out here in the future. We'll take in the theatre to-night, Greenbrier, and after that we'll dine at——"

"I'll tell you what you are, Merritt," said Greenbrier, laying one elbow in his salad and the other in his butter. "You are a concentrated, effete, unconditional, short-sleeved, gotch-eared Miss Sally Walker. God made you perpendicular and suitable to ride straddle and use cuss words in the original. Wherefore you have suffered His handiwork to elapse by removing yourself to New York and putting on little shoes tied with strings, and making faces when you talk. I've seen you rope and tie a steer in 49½. If you was to see one now you'd write to the Police Commissioner about it. And these flapdoodle drinks that you inoculate your system with—these little essences of cowslip with acorns in 'em, and paregoric flip—they ain't anyways in assent with the cordiality of manhood. I hate to see you this way."

"Well, Greenbrier," said Merritt, with apology in his tone, "in a way you are right. Sometimes I do feel like I was being raised on the bottle. But, I tell you, New York is comfortable—comfortable. There's something about it—the sights and the crowds, and the way it changes every day, and the very air of it that seems to tie a one-mile-long stake rope around a man's neck, with the other end fastened somewhere about Thirty-fourth Street. I don't know what it is."

"God knows," said Greenbrier, sadly, "and I know. The East has gobbled you up. You was venison, and now you're veal. You put me in mind of a japonica in a window. You've been signed, sealed, and diskivered. Requiescat in hoc signo. You make me thirsty."

"A green chartreuse here," said Merritt to the waiter.

"Whiskey straight," sighed Greenbrier, "and they're on you, you renegade of the round-ups."

"Guilty, with an application for mercy," said Merritt. "You don't know how it is, Greenbrier. It's so comfortable here that——"

"Please loan me your smelling salts," pleaded Greenbrier. "If I hadn't seen you once bluff three bluffers from Mazatzal City with an empty gun in Phœnix——"

Greenbrier's voice died away in pure grief.

"Cigars!" he called harshly to the waiter, to hide his emotion.

"A pack of Turkish cigarettes for mine," said Merritt.

"They're on you," chanted Greenbrier, struggling to conceal his contempt.

At seven they dined in the Where-to-Dine-Well column.

That evening a galaxy had assembled there. Bright shone the lights o'er fair women and br—— Let it go, anyhow—brave men. The orchestra played charmingly. Hardly had a tip from a diner been placed in its hands by a waiter when it would burst forth into soniferousness. The more beer you contributed to it the more Meyerbeer it gave you. Which is reciprocity.

Merritt put forth exertions on the dinner. Greenbrier was his old friend, and he liked him. He persuaded him to drink a cocktail.

"I take the horehound tea," said Greenbrier, "for old times' sake. But I'd prefer whiskey straight. They're on you."

"Right!" said Merritt. "Now, run your eye down that bill of fare and see if it seems to hitch on any of the items."

"Lay me on my lava bed!" said Greenbrier, with bulging eyes. "All these specimens of nutriment in the grub wagon! What's this? Horse with the heaves? I pass. But look along! Here's truck for twenty round-ups all spelled out in different sections. Wait till I see."

The viands ordered, Merritt turned to the wine list.

"This medoc isn't bad," he suggested.

"You're the doc," said Greenbrier. "I'd rather have whiskey straight. It's on you."

Greenbrier looked around the room. The waiter brought things and took dishes away. He was observing. He saw a New York restaurant crowd enjoying itself.

"How was the range when you left the Gila?" asked Merritt.

"Fine," said Greenbrier. "You see that lady in the red speckled silk at that table? Well, she could warm over her beans at my campfire. Yes, the range was good. She looks as nice as a white mustang I see once on Black River."

When the coffee came, Greenbrier put one foot on the seat of the chair next to him.

"You said it was a comfortable town, Longy," he said, meditatively. "Yes, it's a comfortable town. It's different from the plains in a blue norther. What did you call that mess in the crock with the handle, Longy? Oh, yes, squabs in a cash roll. They're worth the roll. That white mustang had just such a way of turning his head and shaking his mane—look at her, Longy. If I thought I could sell out my ranch at a fair price, I believe I'd——

"Gyar—song!" he suddenly cried, in a voice that paralyzed every knife and fork in the restaurant.

The waiter dived toward the table.

"Two more of them cocktail drinks," ordered Greenbrier.

Merritt looked at him and smiled significantly.

"They're on me," said Greenbrier, blowing a puff of smoke to the ceiling.

THE UNKNOWN QUANTITY

The poet Longfellow—or was it Confucius, the inventor of wisdom?—remarked:

> "Life is real, life is earnest;
> And things are not what they seem."

As mathematics are—or is: thanks, old subscriber!—the only just rule by which questions of life can be measured, let us, by all means, adjust our theme to the straight edge and the balanced column of the great goddess Two-and-Two-Makes-Four. Figures—unassailable sums in addition—shall be set over against whatever opposing element there may be.

A mathematician, after scanning the above two lines of poetry, would say: "Ahem! young gentlemen, if we assume that X plus—that is, that life is real—then things (all of which life includes) are real. Anything that is real is what it seems. Then if we consider the proposition that 'things are not what they seem,' why——"

But this is heresy, and not poesy. We woo the sweet nymph Algebra; we would conduct you into the presence of the elusive, seductive, pursued, satisfying, mysterious X.

Not long before the beginning of this century, Septimus Kinsolving, an old New

Yorker, invented an idea. He originated the discovery that bread is made from flour and not from wheat futures. Perceiving that the flour crop was short, and that the Stock Exchange was having no perceptible effect on the growing wheat, Mr. Kinsolving cornered the flour market.

The result was that when you or my landlady (before the war she never had to turn her hand to anything; Southerners accommodated) bought a five-cent loaf of bread you laid down an additional two cents, which went to Mr. Kinsolving as a testimonial to his perspicacity.

A second result was that Mr. Kinsolving quit the game with $2,000,000 prof—er—rake-off.

Mr. Kinsolving's son Dan was at college when the mathematical experiment in breadstuffs was made. Dan came home during vacation, and found the old gentleman in a red dressing-gown reading "Little Dorrit" on the porch of his estimable red brick mansion in Washington Square. He had retired from business with enough extra two-cent pieces from bread buyers to reach, if laid side by side, fifteen times around the earth and lap as far as the public debt of Paraguay.

Dan shook hands with his father, and hurried over to Greenwich Village to see his old high-school friend, Kenwitz. Dan had always admired Kenwitz. Kenwitz was pale, curly-haired, intense, serious, mathematical, studious, altruistic, socialistic, and the natural foe of oligarchies. Kenwitz had foregone college, and was learning watch-making in his father's jewelry store. Dan was smiling, jovial, easy-tempered and tolerant alike of kings and rag-pickers. The two foregathered joyously, being opposites. And then Dan went back to college, and Kenwitz to his mainsprings—and to his private library in the rear of the jewelry shop.

Four years later Dan came back to Washington Square with the accumulations of B.A. and two years of Europe thick upon him. He took a filial look at Septimus Kinsolving's elaborate tombstone in Greenwood, and a tedious excursion through typewritten documents with the family lawyer; and then, feeling himself a lonely and hopeless millionaire, hurried down to the old jewelry store across Sixth Avenue.

Kenwitz unscrewed a magnifying glass from his eye, routed out his parent from a dingy rear room, and abandoned the interior of watches for outdoors. He went with Dan, and they sat on a bench in Washington Square. Dan had not changed much; he was stalwart, and had a dignity that was inclined to relax into a grin. Kenwitz was more serious, more intense, more learned, philosophical, and socialistic.

"I know about it now," said Dan, finally. "I pumped it out of the eminent legal lights that turned over to me poor old dad's collection of bonds and boodle. It amounts to $2,000,000, Ken. And I am told that he squeezed it out of the chaps that pay their pennies for loaves of bread at the little bakeries around the corner. You've studied economics Ken, and you know all about monopolies, and the masses, and octopuses, and the rights of laboring people. I never thought about those things before. Football and trying to be white to my fellow-man were about the extent of my college curriculum.

"But since I came back and found out how Dad made his money I've been thinking. I'd like awfully well to pay back those chaps who had to give too much money for bread. I know it would buck the line of my income for a good many yards; but I'd like to make it square with 'em. Is there any way it can be done, old Ways and Means?"

Kenwitz's big black eyes glowed fierily. His thin, intellectual face took on almost a sardonic cast. He caught Dan's arm with the grip of a friend and a judge.

"You can't do it!" he said, emphatically. "One of the chief punishments of you men of ill-gotten wealth is that when you do repent you find that you have lost the power to make reparation or restitution. I admire your good intentions,

Dan, but you can't do anything. Those people were robbed of their precious pennies. It's too late to remedy the evil. You can't pay them back."

"Of course," said Dan, lighting his pipe, "we couldn't hunt up every one of the duffers and hand 'em back the right change. There's an awful lot of 'em buying bread all the time. Funny taste they have—I never cared for bread especially, except for a toasted cracker with the Roquefort. But we might find a few of 'em and chuck some of Dad's cash back where it came from. I'd feel better if I could. It seems tough for people to be held up for a soggy thing like bread. One wouldn't mind standing a rise in broiled lobsters or deviled crabs. Get to work and think, Ken. I want to pay back all of that money I can."

"There are plenty of charities," said Kenwitz, mechanically.

"Easy enough," said Dan, in a cloud of smoke. "I suppose I could give the city a park, or endow an asparagus bed in a hospital. But I don't want Paul to get away with the proceeds of the gold brick we sold Peter. It's the bread shorts I want to cover, Ken."

The thin fingers of Kenwitz moved rapidly.

"Do you know how much money it would take to pay back the losses of consumers during that corner in flour?" he asked.

"I do not," said Dan, stoutly. "My lawyer tells me that I have two millions."

"If you had a hundred millions," said Kenwitz, vehemently, "you couldn't repair a thousandth part of the damage that has been done. You cannot conceive of the accumulated evils produced by misapplied wealth. Each penny that was wrung from the lean purses of the poor reacted a thousandfold to their harm. You do not understand. You do not see how hopeless is your desire to make restitution. Not in a single instance can it be done."

"Back up, philosopher!" said Dan. "The penny has no sorrow that the dollar cannot heal."

"Not in one instance," repeated Kenwitz. "I will give you one, and let us see. Thomas Boyne had a little bakery over there in Varick Street. He sold bread to the poorest people. When the price of flour went up he had had to raise the price of bread. His customers were too poor to pay it, Boyne's business failed, and he lost his $1,000 capital—all he had in the world."

Dan Kinsolving struck the park bench a mighty blow with his fist.

"I accept the instance," he cried. "Take me to Boyne. I will repay his thousand dollars and buy him a new bakery."

"Write your check," said Kenwitz, without moving, "and then begin to write checks in payment of the train of consequences. Draw the next one for $50,-000. Boyne went insane after his failure and set fire to the building from which he was about to be evicted. The loss amounted to that much. Boyne died in an asylum."

"Stick to the instance," said Dan. "I haven't noticed any insurance companies on my charity list."

"Draw your next check for $100,000," went on Kenwitz. "Boyne's son fell into bad ways after the bakery closed, and was accused of murder. He was acquitted last week after a three-years' legal battle, and the state draws upon taxpayers for that much expense."

"Back to the bakery!" exclaimed Dan, impatiently. "The Government doesn't need to stand in the bread line."

"The last item of the instance is—come and I will show you," said Kenwitz, rising.

The socialistic watchmaker was happy. He was a millionaire-baiter by nature and a pessimist by trade. Kenwitz would assure you in one breath that money was but evil and corruption, and that your brand-new watch needed cleaning and a new ratchet-wheel.

He conducted Kinsolving southward out of the square and into ragged, poverty-haunted Varick Street. Up the narrow stairway of a squalid brick tenement he led the penitent offspring of the Octopus. He knocked on a door, and a clear voice called to them to enter.

In that almost bare room a young woman sat sewing at a machine. She nodded to Kenwitz as to a familiar acquaintance. One little stream of sunlight through the dingy window burnished her heavy hair to the color of an ancient Tuscan's shield. She flashed a rippling smile at Kenwitz and a look of somewhat flustered inquiry.

Kinsolving stood regarding her clear and pathetic beauty in heart-throbbing silence. Thus they came into the presence of the last item of the Instance.

"How many this week, Miss Mary?" asked the watchmaker. A mountain of coarse gray shirts lay upon the floor.

"Nearly thirty dozen," said the young woman, cheerfully. "I've made almost $4. I'm improving, Mr. Kenwitz. I hardly know what to do with so much money." Her eyes turned, brightly soft, in the direction of Dan. A little pink spot came out on her round, pale cheek.

Kenwitz chuckled like a diabolic raven.

"Miss Boyne," he said, "let me present Mr. Kinsolving, the son of the man who put bread up five years ago. He thinks he would like to do something to aid those who were inconvenienced by that act."

The smile left the young woman's face. She rose and pointed her forefinger toward the door. This time she looked Kinsolving straight in the eye, but it was not a look that gave delight.

The two men went down into Varick Street. Kenwitz, letting all his pessimism and rancor and hatred of the Octopus come to the surface, gibed at the moneyed side of his friend in an acrid torrent of words. Dan appeared to be listening, and then turned to Kenwitz and shook hands with him warmly.

"I'm obliged to you, Ken, old man," he said, vaguely—"a thousand times obliged."

"Mein Gott! you are crazy!" cried the watchmaker, dropping his spectacles for the first time in years.

Two months afterward Kenwitz went into a large bakery on lower Broadway with a pair of gold-rimmed eye-glasses that he had mended for the proprietor.

A lady was giving an order to a clerk as Kenwitz passed her.

"These loaves are ten cents," said the clerk.

"I always get them at eight cents uptown," said the lady. "You need not fill the order. I will drive by there on my way home."

The voice was familiar. The watchmaker paused.

"Mr. Kenwitz!" cried the lady, heartily. "How do you do?"

Kenwitz was trying to train his socialistic and economic comprehension on her wonderful fur boa and the carriage waiting outside.

"Why, Miss Boyne!" he began.

"Mrs. Kinsolving," she corrected. "Dan and I were married a month ago."

THE THING'S THE PLAY

BEING acquainted with a newspaper reporter who had a couple of free passes, I got to see the performance a few nights ago at one of the popular vaudeville houses.

One of the numbers was a violin solo by a striking-looking man not much past forty, but with very gray thick hair. Not being afflicted with a taste for music, I let the system of noises drift past my ears while I regarded the man.

"There was a story about that chap a month or two ago," said the reporter. "They gave me the assignment. It was to run a column and was to be on the extremely light and joking order. The old man seems to like the funny touch I give to local happenings. Oh, yes, I'm working on a farce comedy now. Well, I went down to the house and got all the details; but I certainly fell down on that job. I went back and turned in a comic write-up of an east side funeral instead. Why? Oh, I couldn't seem to get hold of it with my funny hooks, somehow. Maybe you could make a one-act tragedy out of it for a curtain-raiser. I'll give you the details."

After the performance my friend, the reporter, recited to me the facts over the Würzburger.

"I see no reason," said I, when he had concluded, "why that shouldn't make a rattling good funny story. Those three people couldn't have acted in a more absurd and preposterous manner if they had been real actors in a real theatre. I'm really afraid that all the stage is a world, anyhow, and all the players merely men and woman. 'The thing's the play,' is the way I quote Mr. Shakespeare."

"Try it," said the reporter.

"I will," said I; and I did, to show him how he could have made a humorous column of it for his paper.

There stands a house near Abingdon Square. On the ground floor there has been for twenty-five years a little store where toys and notions and stationery are sold.

One night twenty years ago there was a wedding in the rooms above the store. The Widow Mayo owned the house and store. Her daughter Helen was married to Frank Barry. John Delaney was best man. Helen was eighteen, and her picture had been printed in a morning paper next to the headlines of a "Wholesale Female Murderess" story from Butte, Mont. But after your eye and intelligence had rejected the connection, you seized your magnifying glass and read beneath the portrait her description as one of a series of Prominent Beauties and Belles of the lower west side.

Frank Barry and John Delaney were "prominent" young beaux of the same side, and bosom friends, whom you expected to turn upon each other every time the curtain went up. One who pays his money for orchestra seats and fiction expects this. That is the first funny idea that has turned up in the story yet. Both had made a great race for Helen's hand. When Frank won, John shook his hand and congratulated him—honestly, he did.

After the ceremony Helen ran upstairs to put on her hat. She was getting married in a traveling dress. She and Frank were going to Old Point Comfort for a week. Downstairs the usual horde of gibbering cave-dwellers were waiting with their hands full of old Congress gaiters and paper bags of hominy.

Then there was a rattle of the fire-escape, and into her room jumps the mad and infatuated John Delaney, with a damp curl drooping upon his forehead, and made violent and reprehensible love to his lost one, entreating her to flee or fly with him to the Riviera, or the Bronx, or any old place where there are Italian skies and *dolce far niente*.

It would have carried Blaney off his feet to see Helen repulse him. With blazing and scornful eyes she fairly withered him by demanding whatever he meant by speaking to respectable people that way.

In a few moments she had him going. The manliness that had possessed him departed. He bowed low, and said something about "irresistible impulse" and "forever carry in his heart the memory of"—and she suggested that he catch the first fire-escape going down.

"I will away," said John Delaney, "to the furthermost parts of the earth. I cannot remain near you and know that you are another's. I will to Africa, and there amid other scenes strive to for——"

"For goodness sake, get out," said Helen. "Somebody might come in."

He knelt upon one knee, and she extended him one white hand that he might give it a farewell kiss.

Girls, was this choice boon of the great little god Cupid ever vouchsafed you—to have the fellow you want hard and fast, and have the one you don't want come with a damp curl on his forehead and kneel to you and babble of Africa and love which, in spite of everything, shall forever bloom, an amaranth, in his heart? To know your power, and to feel the sweet security of your own happy state; to send the unlucky one, broken-hearted, to foreign climes, while you congratulate yourself as he presses his last kiss upon your knuckles, that your nails are well manicured—say, girls, it's galluptious—don't ever let it get by you.

And then, of course—how did you guess?—the door opened and in stalked the bridegroom, jealous of slow-tying bonnet strings.

The farewell kiss was imprinted upon Helen's hand, and out of the window and down the fire-escape sprang John Delaney, Africa bound.

A little slow music, if you please—faint violin, just a breath in the clarinet and a touch of the 'cello. Imagine the scene. Frank, white-hot, with the cry of a man wounded to death bursting from him. Helen, rushing and clinging to him, trying to explain. He catches her wrists and tears them from his shoulders—once, twice, thrice he sways her this way and that—the stage manager will show you how—and throws her from him to the floor a huddled, crushed, moaning thing. Never, he cries, will he look upon her face again, and rushes from the house through the staring groups of astonished guests.

And now, because it is the Thing instead of the Play, the audience must stroll out into the real lobby of the world and marry, die, grow gray, rich, poor, happy, or sad during the intermission of twenty years which must precede the rising of the curtain again.

Mrs. Barry inherited the shop and the house. At thirty-eight she could have bested many an eighteen-year-old at a beauty show on points and general results. Only a few people remembered her wedding comedy, but she made of it no secret. She did not pack it in lavender or moth balls, nor did she sell it to a magazine.

One day a middle-aged, money-making lawyer who bought his legal cap and ink of her, asked her across the counter to marry him.

"I'm really much obliged to you," said Helen, cheerfully, "but I married another man twenty years ago. He was more a goose than a man, but I think I love him yet. I have never seen him since about half an hour after the ceremony. Was it copying ink that you wanted or just writing fluid?"

The lawyer bowed over the counter with oldtime grace and left a respectful kiss on the back of her hand. Helen sighed. Parting salutes, however romantic, may be overdone. Here she was at thirty-eight, beautiful and admired; and all that she seemed to have got from her lovers were reproaches and adieus. Worse still, in the last one she had lost a customer, too.

Business languished, and she hung out a Room to Let card. Two large rooms on the third floor were prepared for desirable tenants. Roomers came, and went regretfully, for the house of Mrs. Barry was the abode of neatness, comfort, and taste.

One day came Ramonti, the violinist, and engaged the front room above. The discord and clatter uptown offended his nice ear; so a friend had sent him to this oasis in the desert of noise.

Ramonti, with his still youthful face, his dark eyebrows, his short, pointed, foreign, brown beard, his distinguished head of gray hair, and his artist's temperament—revealed in his light, gay, and sympathetic manner—was a welcome tenant in the old house near Abingdon Square.

Helen lived on the floor above the store. The architecture of it was singular and quaint. The hall was large and almost square. Up one side of it and then across the end of it ascended an open stairway to the floor above. This hall space she had furnished as a sitting room and office combined. There she kept her desk and wrote her business letters; and there she sat of evenings by a warm fire and a bright red light and sewed or read. Ramonti found the atmosphere so agreeable that he spent much time there, describing to Mrs. Barry the wonders of Paris, where he had studied with a particularly notorious and noisy fiddler.

Next comes lodger No. 2, a handsome, melancholy man in the early 40's, with a brown, mysterious beard, and strangely pleading, haunting eyes. He, too, found the society of Helen a desirable thing. With the eyes of Romeo and Othello's tongue, he charmed her with tales of distant climes and wooed her by respectful innuendo.

From the first Helen felt a marvelous and compelling thrill in the presence of this man. His voice somehow took her swiftly back to the days of her youth's romance. This feeling grew, and she gave way to it, and it led her to an instinctive belief that he had been a factor in that romance. And then with a woman's reasoning (oh, yes, they do, sometimes) she leaped over common syllogisms and theory, and logic, and was sure that her husband had come back to her. For she saw in his eyes love, which no woman can mistake, and a thousand tons of regret and remorse, which aroused pity which is perilously near to love requited, which is the *sine qua non* in the house that Jack built.

But she made no sign. A husband who steps around the corner for twenty years and then drops in again should not expect to find his slippers laid out too conveniently near nor a match ready lighted for his cigar. There must be expiation, explanation, and possibly execration. A little purgatory, and then, maybe, if he were properly humble, he might be trusted with a harp and crown. And so she made no sign that she knew or suspected.

And my friend, the reporter, could see nothing funny in this! Sent out on an assignment to write up a roaring, hilarious, brilliant joshing story of—but I will not knock a brother—let us go on with the story.

One evening Ramonti stopped in Helen's hall-office-reception-room and told his love with the tenderness and ardor of the enraptured artist. His words were a bright flame of the divine fire that glows in the heart of a man who is a dreamer and a doer combined.

"But before you give me an answer," he went on, before she could accuse him of suddenness, "I must tell you that 'Ramonti' is the only name I have to offer you. My manager gave me that. I do not know who I am or where I came from. My first recollection is of opening my eyes in a hospital. I was a young man, and I had been there for weeks. My life before that is a blank to me. They told me that I was found lying in the street with a wound on my head and was brought there in an ambulance. They thought I must have fallen and struck my head upon the stones. There was nothing to show who I was. I have never been able to remember. After I was discharged from the hospital, I took up the violin. I have had success. Mrs. Barry—I do not know your name except that —I love you; the first time I saw you I realized that you were the one woman in the world for me—and"—oh, a lot of stuff like that.

Helen felt young again. First a wave of pride and a sweet little thrill of vanity went all over her; and then she looked Ramonti in the eyes, and a tremendous throb went through her heart. She hadn't expected that throb. It took her by surprise. The musician had become a big factor in her life, and she hadn't been aware of it.

"Mr. Ramonti," she said sorrowfully (this was not on the stage, remember; it was in the old home near Abingdon Square), "I'm awfully sorry, but I'm a married woman."

And then she told him the sad story of her life, as a heroine must do, sooner or later, either to a theatrical manager or to a reporter.

Ramonti took her hand, bowed low and kissed it, and went up to his room.

Helen sat down and looked mournfully at her hand. Well she might. Three suitors had kissed it, mounted their red roan steeds and ridden away.

In an hour entered the mysterious stranger with the haunting eyes. Helen was in the willow rocker, knitting a useless thing in cotton-wool. He ricocheted from the stairs and stopped for a chat. Sitting across the table from her, he also poured out his narrative of love. And then he said: "Helen, do you not remember me? I think I have seen it in your eyes. Can you forgive the past and remember the love that has lasted for twenty years? I wronged you deeply —I was afraid to come back to you—but my love overpowered my reason. Can you, will you, forgive me?"

Helen stood up. The mysterious stranger held one of her hands in a strong and trembling clasp.

There she stood, and I pity the stage that it has not acquired a scene like that and her emotions to portray.

For she stood with a divided heart. The fresh, unforgettable, virginal love for her bridegroom was hers; the treasured, sacred, honored memory of her first choice filled half her soul. She leaned to that pure feeling. Honor and faith and sweet, abiding romance bound her to it. But the other half of her heart and soul was filled with something else—a later, fuller, nearer influence. And so the old fought against the new.

And while she hesitated, from the room above came the soft, racking, petitionary music of a violin. The hag, music, bewitches some of the noblest. The daws may peck upon one's sleeve without injury but whoever wears his heart upon his tympanum gets it not far from the neck.

The music and the musician called her, and at her side honor and the old love held her back.

"Forgive me," he pleaded.

"Twenty years is a long time to remain away from the one you say you love," she declared, with a purgatorial touch.

"How could I tell?" he begged. "I will conceal nothing from you. That night when he left I followed him. I was mad with jealousy. On a dark street I struck him down. He did not rise. I examined him. His head had struck a stone. I did not intend to kill him. I was mad with love and jealousy. I hid near by and saw an ambulance take him away. Although you married him, Helen——"

"*Who Are You?*" cried the woman, with wide-open eyes, snatching her hand away.

"Don't you remember me, Helen—the one who has always loved you the best? I am John Delaney. If you can forgive——"

But she was gone, leaping, stumbling, hurrying, flying up the stairs toward the music and him who had forgotten, but who had known her for his in each of his two existences, and as she climbed up she sobbed, cried, and sang: "Frank! Frank! Frank!"

Three mortals thus juggling with years as though they were billiard balls, and my friend, the reporter, couldn't see anything funny in it!

A RAMBLE IN APHASIA

My wife and I parted on that morning in precisely our usual manner. She left her second cup of tea to follow me to the front door. There she plucked from my lapel the invisible strand of lint (the universal act of woman to proclaim ownership) and bade me take care of my cold. I had no cold. Next came her kiss of parting—the level kiss of domesticity flavored with Young Hyson. There was no fear of the extemporaneous, of variety spicing her infinite custom. With the deft touch of long malpractice, she dabbed awry my well-set scarf pin; and then, as I closed the door, I heard her morning slippers pattering back to her cooling tea.

When I set out I had no thought or premonition of what was to occur. The attack came suddenly.

For many weeks I had been toiling, almost night and day, at a famous railroad law case that I won triumphantly but a few days previously. In fact, I had been digging away at the law almost without cessation for many years. Once or twice good Doctor Volney, my friend and physician, had warned me.

"If you don't slacken up, Bellford," he said, "you'll go suddenly to pieces. Either your nerves or your brain will give way. Tell me, does a week pass in which you do not read in the papers of a case of aphasia—of some man lost, wandering nameless, with his past and his identity blotted out—and all from that little brain clot made by overwork or worry?"

"I always thought," said I, "that the clot in those instances was really to be found on the brains of the newspaper reporters."

Doctor Volney shook his head.

"The disease exists," he said. "You need a change or a rest. Court-room, office, and home—there is the only route you travel. For recreation you—read law books. Better take warning in time."

"On Thursday nights," I said, defensively, "my wife and I play cribbage. On Sundays she reads to me the weekly letter from her mother. That law books are not a recreation remains yet to be established."

That morning as I walked I was thinking of Doctor Volney's words. I was feeling as well as I usually did—possibly in better spirits than usual.

I woke with stiff and cramped muscles from having slept long on the incommodious seat of a day coach. I leaned my head against the seat and tried to think. After a long time I said to myself: "I must have a name of some sort." I searched my pockets. Not a card; not a letter; not a paper or monogram could I find. But I found in my coat pocket nearly $3,000 in bills of large denomination. "I must be some one, of course," I repeated to myself, and began to consider.

The car was well crowded with men, among whom, I told myself, there must have been some common interest, for they intermingled freely, and seemed in the best good humor and spirits. One of them—a stout, spectacled gentleman enveloped in a decided odor of cinnamon and aloes—took the vacant half of my seat with a friendly nod, and unfolded a newspaper. In the intervals between his periods of reading, we conversed, as travelers will, on current affairs. I found myself able to sustain the conversation on such subjects with credit, at least to my memory. By and by my companion said:

"You are one of us, of course. Fine lot of men the West sends in this time. I'm glad they held the convention in New York; I've never been East before. My name's R. P. Bolder—Bolder & Son, of Hickory Grove, Missouri."

Though unprepared, I rose to the emergency, as men will when put to it.

Now must I hold a christening, and be at once babe, parson, and parent. My senses came to the rescue of my slower brain. The insistent odor of drugs from my companion supplied one idea; a glance at his newspaper, where my eye met a conspicuous advertisement, assisted me further.

"My name," said I, glibly, "is Edward Pinkhammer. I am a druggist, and my home is in Cornopolis, Kansas."

"I knew you were a druggist," said my fellow traveler, affably. "I saw the callous spot on your right forefinger where the handle of the pestle rubs. Of course, you are a delegate to our National Convention."

"Are all these men druggists?" I asked, wonderingly.

"They are. This car came through from the West. And they're your old-time druggists, too—none of your patent tablet-and-granule pharmashootists that use slot machines instead of a prescription desk. We percolate our own paregoric and roll our own pills, and we ain't above handling a few garden seeds in the spring, and carrying a side line of confectionery and shoes. I tell you, Hampinker, I've got an idea to spring on this convention—new ideas is what they want. Now, you know the shelf bottles of tartar emetic and Rochelle salt Ant. et. Pot. Tart. and Sod. et. Pot. Tart.—one's poison, you know, and the other's harmless. It's easy to mistake one label for the other. Where do druggists mostly keep 'em? Why, as far apart as possible, on different shelves. That's wrong. I say keep 'em side by side, so when you want one you can always compare it with the other and avoid mistakes. Do you catch the idea?"

"It seems to me a very good one," I said.

"All right! When I spring it on the convention you back it up. We'll make some of these Eastern orange-phosphate-and-massage-cream professors that think they're the only lozenges in the market look like hypodermic tablets."

"If I can be of any aid," I said, warming, "the two bottles of—er——"

"Tartrate of antimony and potash, and tartrate of soda and potash."

"Shall henceforth sit side by side," I concluded, firmly.

"Now, there's another thing," said Mr. Bolder. "For an excipient in manipulating a pill mass which do you prefer—the magnesia carbonate or the pulverized glycerrhiza radix?"

"The—er—magnesia," I said. It was easier to say than the other word.

Mr. Bolder glanced at me distrustfully through his spectacles.

"Give me the glycerrhiza," said he. "Magnesia cakes."

"Here's another one of these fake aphasia cases," he said, presently, handing me his newspaper, and laying his finger upon an article. "I don't believe in 'em. I put nine out of ten of 'em down as frauds. A man gets sick of his business and his folks and wants to have a good time. He skips out somewhere, and when they find him he pretends to have lost his memory—don't know his own name, and won't even recognize the strawberry mark on his wife's left shoulder. Aphasia! Tut! Why can't they stay at home and forget?"

I took the paper and read, after the pungent headlines, the following:

DENVER, June 12.—Elwyn C. Bellford, a prominent lawyer, is mysteriously missing from his home since three days ago, and all efforts to locate him have been in vain. Mr. Bellford is a well-known citizen of the highest standing, and has enjoyed a large and lucrative law practice. He is married and owns a fine home and the most extensive private library in the State. On the day of his disappearance, he drew quite a large sum of money from his bank. No one can be found who saw him after he left the bank. Mr. Bellford was a man of singularly quiet and domestic tastes, and seemed to find his happiness in his home and profession. If any clue at all exists to his strange disappearance, it may be found in the fact that for some months he has been deeply absorbed in an important law case in connection with the Q. Y. and Z. Railroad Company. It is feared that overwork may have affected his mind. Every effort is being made to discover the where-abouts of the missing man.

"It seems to me you are not altogether uncynical, Mr. Bolder," I said, after I had read the despatch. "This has the sound, to me, of a genuine case. Why should this man, prosperous, happily married, and respected, choose suddenly to abandon everything? I know that these lapses of memory do occur, and that men do find themselves adrift without a name, a history, or a home."

"Oh, gammon and jalap!" said Mr. Bolder. "It's larks they're after. There's too much education nowadays. Men know about aphasia, and they use it for an excuse. The women are wise, too.. When it's all over they look you in the eye, as scientific as you please, and say: 'He hypnotized me.'"

Thus Mr. Bolder diverted, but did not aid me with his comments and philosophy.

We arrived in New York about ten at night. I rode in a cab to a hotel, and I wrote my name "Edward Pinkhammer" in the register. As I did so I felt pervade me a splendid, wild, intoxicating buoyancy—a sense of unlimited freedom, of newly attained possibilities. I was just born into the world. The old fetters—whatever they had been—were stricken from my hands and feet. The future lay before me a clear road such as an infant enters, and I could set out upon it equipped with a man's learning and experience.

I thought the hotel clerk looked at me five seconds too long. I had no baggage.

"The Druggists' Convention," I said. "My trunk has somehow failed to arrive." I drew out a roll of money.

"Ah!" said he, showing an auriferous tooth, "we have quite a number of the Western delegates stopping here." He struck a bell for the boy.

I endeavored to give color to my rôle.

"There is an important movement on foot among us Westerners," I said, "in regard to a recommendation to the convention that the bottles containing the tartrate of antimony and potash, and the tartrate of sodium and potash be kept in a contiguous position on the shelf."

"Gentleman to three-fourteen," said the clerk, hastily. I was whisked away to my room.

The next day I bought a trunk and clothing, and began to live the life of Edward Pinkhammer. I did not tax my brain with endeavors to solve problems of the past.

It was a piquant and sparkling cup that the great island city held up to my lips. I drank of it gratefully. The keys of Manhattan belong to him who is able to bear them. You must be either the city's guest or its victim.

The following few days were as gold and silver. Edward Pinkhammer, yet counting back to his birth by hours only, knew the rare joy of having come upon so diverting a world full-fledged and unrestrained. I sat entranced on the magic carpets provided in theatres and roof-gardens, that transported one into strange and delightful lands full of frolicsome music, pretty girls, and grotesque, drolly extravagant parodies upon human kind. I went here and there at my own dear will, bound by no limits of space, time, or comportment. I dined in weird cabarets, at weirder *tables d'hôte* to the sound of Hungarian music and the wild shouts of mercurial artists and sculptors. Or, again, where the night life quivers in the electric glare like a kinetoscopic picture, and the millinery of the world, and its jewels, and the ones whom they adorn, and the men who make all three possible are met for good cheer and the spectacular effect. And among all these scenes that I have mentioned I learned one thing that I never knew before. And that is that the key to liberty is not in the hands of License, but Convention holds it. Comity has a toll-gate at which you must pay, or you may not enter the land of Freedom. In all the glitter, the seeming disorder, the parade, the abandon, I saw this law, unobtrusive, yet like iron, prevail. Therefore, in Manhattan you must obey these unwritten laws, and then you will be freest of the free. If you decline to be bound by them, you put on shackles.

Sometimes, as my mood urged me, I would seek the stately, softly murmuring palm rooms, redolent with high-born life and delicate restraint, in which to dine. Again I would go down to the waterways in steamers packed with vociferous, bedecked, unchecked love-making clerks and shop-girls to their crude pleasures on the island shores. And there was always Broadway—glistening, opulent, wily, varying, desirable Broadway—growing upon one like an opium habit.

One afternoon as I entered my hotel a stout man with a big nose and a black mustache blocked my way in the corridor. When I would have passed around him, he greeted me with offensive familiarity.

"Hallo, Bellford!" he cried, loudly. "What the deuce are you doing in New York? Didn't know anything could drag you away from that old book den of yours. Is Mrs. B. along or is this a little business run alone, eh?"

"You have made a mistake, sir," I said, coldly, releasing my hand from his grasp. "My name is Pinkhammer. You will excuse me."

The man dropped to one side, apparently astonished. As I walked to the clerk's desk I heard him call to a bell boy and say something about telegraph blanks.

"You will give me my bill," I said to the clerk, "and have my baggage brought down in half an hour. I do not care to remain where I am annoyed by confidence men."

I moved that afternoon to another hotel, a sedate, old-fashioned one on lower Fifth Avenue.

There was a restaurant a little way off Broadway where one could be served almost *al fresco* in a tropic array of screening flora. Quiet and luxury and a perfect service made it an ideal place in which to take luncheon or refreshment. One afternoon I was there picking my way to a table among the ferns when I felt my sleeve caught.

"Mr. Bellford!" exclaimed an amazingly sweet voice.

I turned quickly to see a lady seated alone—a lady of about thirty, with exceedingly handsome eyes, who looked at me as though I had been her very dear friend.

"You were about to pass me," she said, accusingly. "Don't tell me you did not know me. Why should we not shake hands—at least once in fifteen years?"

I shook hands with her at once. I took a chair opposite her at the table. I summoned with my eyebrows a hovering waiter. The lady was philandering with an orange ice. I ordered a *crême de menthe*. Her hair was reddish bronze. You could not look at it, because you could not look away from her eyes. But you were conscious of it as you are conscious of sunset while you look into the profundities of a wood at twilight.

"Are you sure you know me?" I asked.

"No," she said, smiling, "I was never sure of that."

"What would you think," I said, a little anxiously, "if I were to tell you that my name is Edward Pinkhammer from Cornopolis, Kansas?"

"What would I think?" she repeated with a merry glance. "Why, that you had not brought Mrs. Bellford to New York with you, of course. I do wish you had. I would have liked to see Marian." Her voice lowered slightly—"You haven't changed much, Elwyn."

I felt her wonderful eyes searching mine and my face more closely.

"Yes, you have," she amended, and there was a soft, exultant note in her latest tones; "I see it now. You haven't forgotten. You haven't forgotten for a year or a day or an hour. I told you you never could."

I poked my straw anxiously in the *crême de menthe*.

"I'm sure I beg your pardon," I said, a little uneasy at her gaze. "But that is just the trouble. I have forgotten. I've forgotten everything."

She flouted my denial. She laughed deliciously at something she seemed to see in my face.

"I've heard of you at times," she went on. "You're quite a big lawyer out West—Denver, isn't it, or Los Angeles? Marian must be very proud of you. You knew, I suppose, that I married six months after you did. You may have seen it in the papers. The flowers alone cost two thousand dollars."

She had mentioned fifteen years. Fifteen years is a long time.

"Would it be too late," I asked, somewhat timorously, "to offer you congratulations?"

"Not if you dare do it," she answered, with such fine intrepidity that I was silent, and began to crease patterns on the cloth with my thumb nail.

"Tell me one thing," she said, leaning toward me rather eagerly—"a thing I have wanted to know for many years—just from a woman's curiosity, of course—have you ever dared since that night to touch, smell, or look at white roses—at white roses wet with rain and dew?"

I took a sip of *crême de menthe*.

"It would be useless, I suppose," I said, with a sigh, "for me to repeat that I have no recollection at all about these things. My memory is completely at fault. I need not say how much I regret it."

The lady rested her arms upon the table, and again her eyes disdained my words and went traveling by their own route direct to my soul. She laughed softly, with a strange quality in the sound—it was a laugh of happiness—yes, and of content—and of misery. I tried to look away from her.

"You lie, Elwyn Bellford," she breathed, blissfully. "Oh, I know you lie!"

I gazed dully into the ferns.

"My name is Edward Pinkhammer," I said. "I came with the delegates to the Druggists' National Convention. There is a movement on foot for arranging a new position for the bottles of tartrate of antimony and tartrate of potash, in which, very likely, you would take little interest."

A shining landau stopped before the entrance. The lady rose. I took her hand, and bowed.

"I am deeply sorry," I said to her, "that I cannot remember. I could explain, but fear you would not understand. You will not concede Pinkhammer; and I really cannot at all conceive of the—the roses and other things."

"Good-bye, Mr. Bellford," she said, with her happy, sorrowful smile, as she stepped into her carriage.

I attended the theatre that night. When I returned to my hotel, a quiet man in dark clothes, who seemed interested in rubbing his finger nails with a silk handkerchief, appeared, magically, at my side.

"Mr. Pinkhammer," he said, casually, giving the bulk of his attention to his forefinger, "may I request you to step aside with me for a little conversation? There is a room here."

"Certainly," I answered.

He conducted me into a small, private parlor. A lady and a gentleman were there. The lady, I surmised, would have been unusually good-looking had her features not been clouded by an expression of keen worry and fatigue. She was of a style of figure and possessed coloring and features that were agreeable to my fancy. She was in a traveling dress; she fixed upon me an earnest look of extreme anxiety, and pressed an unsteady hand to her bosom. I think she would have started forward, but the gentleman arrested her movement with an authoritative motion of his hand. He then came, himself, to meet me. He was a man of forty, a little gray about the temples, and with a strong, thoughtful face.

"Bellford, old man," he said, cordially, "I'm glad to see you again. Of course we know everything is all right. I warned you, you know, that you were over-doing it. Now, you'll go back with us, and be yourself again in no time."

I smiled ironically.

"I have been 'Bellforded' so often," I said, "that it has lost its edge. Still, in the end, it may grow wearisome. Would you be willing at all to entertain the hypothesis that my name is Edward Pinkhammer, and that I never saw you before in my life?"

Before the man could reply a wailing cry came from the woman. She sprang past his detaining arm. "Elwyn!" she sobbed, and cast herself upon me, and clung tight. "Elwyn," she cried again, "don't break my heart. I am your wife— call my name once—just once. I could see you dead rather than this way."

I unwound her arms respectfully, but firmly.

"Madame," I said, severely, "pardon me if I suggest that you accept a re-semblance too precipitately. It is a pity," I went on, with an amused laugh, as the thought occurred to me, "that this Bellford and I could not be kept side by side upon the same shelf like tartrates of sodium and antimony for purposes of identification. In order to understand this allusion," I concluded airily, "it may be necessary for you to keep an eye on the proceedings of the Druggists' National Convention."

The lady turned to her companion, and grasped his arm.

"What is it, Doctor Volney? Oh, what is it?" she moaned.

He led her to the door.

"Go to your room for a while," I heard him say. "I will remain and talk with him. His mind? No, I think not—only a portion of the brain. Yes, I am sure he will recover. Go to your room and leave me with him."

The lady disappeared. The man in dark clothes also went outside, still mani-curing himself in a thoughtful way. I think he waited in the hall.

"I would like to talk with you a while, Mr. Pinkhammer, if I may," said the gentleman who remained.

"Very well, if you care to," I replied, "and will excuse me if I take it com-fortably; I am rather tired." I stretched myself upon a couch by a window and lit a cigar. He drew a chair near by.

"Let us speak to the point," he said, soothingly. "Your name is not Pink-hammer."

"I know that as well as you do," I said coolly. "But a man must have a name of some sort. I can assure you that I do not extravagantly admire the name of Pinkhammer. But when one christens one's self suddenly, the fine names do not seem to suggest themselves. But, suppose it had been Scheringhausen or Scroggins! I think I did very well with Pinkhammer."

"Your name," said the other man, seriously, "is Elwyn C. Bellford. You are one of the first lawyers in Denver. You are suffering from an attack of aphasia, which has caused you to forget your identity. The cause of it was over-application to your profession, and perhaps a life too bare of natural recreation and pleasures. The lady who has just left the room is your wife."

"She is what I would call a fine-looking woman," I said, after a judicial pause. "I particularly admire the shade of brown in her hair."

"She is a wife to be proud of. Since your disappearance, nearly two weeks ago, she has scarcely closed her eyes. We learned that you were in New York through a telegram sent by Isidore Newman, a traveling man from Denver. He said that he had met you in a hotel here, and that you did not recognize him."

"I think I remember the occasion," I said. "The fellow called me 'Bellford,' if I am not mistaken. But don't you think it about time, now, for you to introduce yourself?"

"I am Robert Volney—Doctor Volney. I have been your close friend for twenty years, and your physician for fifteen. I came with Mrs. Bellford to trace you as soon as we got the telegram. Try, Elwyn, old man—try to remember!"

"What's the use to try?" I asked, with a little frown. "You say you are a physician. Is aphasia curable? When a man loses his memory does it return slowly, or suddenly?"

"Sometimes gradually and imperfectly; sometimes as suddenly as it went."

"Will you undertake the treatment of my case, Doctor Volney?" I asked.

"Old friend," said he, "I'll do everything in my power, and will have done everything that science can do to cure you."

"Very well," said I. "Then you will consider that I am your patient. Everything is in confidence now—professional confidence."

"Of course," said Doctor Volney.

I got up from the couch. Some one had set a vase of white roses on the centre table—a cluster of white roses, freshly sprinkled and fragrant. I threw them far out of the window, and then I laid myself upon the couch again.

"It will be best, Bobby," I said, "to have this cure happen suddenly. I'm rather tired of it all, anyway. You may go now and bring Marian in. But, oh, Doc," I said, with a sigh, as I kicked him on the shin—"good old Doc—it was glorious!"

A MUNICIPAL REPORT

The cities are full of pride,
Challenging each to each—
This from her mountainside,
That from her burthened beach.

R. KIPLING.

Fancy a novel about Chicago or Buffalo, let us say, of Nashville, Tennessee! There are just three big cities in the United States that are "story cities"—New York, of course, New Orleans, and, best of the lot, San Francisco.—FRANK NORRIS.

EAST is East, and West is San Francisco, according to Californians. Californians are a race of people; they are not merely inhabitants of a State. They are the Southerners of the West. Now, Chicagoans are no less loyal to their city; but when you ask them why, they stammer and speak of lake fish and the new Odd Fellows Building. But Californians go into detail.

Of course they have, in the climate, an argument that is good for half an hour while you are thinking of your coal bills and heavy underwear. But as soon as they come to mistake your silence for conviction, madness comes upon them, and they picture the city of the Golden Gate as the Bagdad of the New World. So far, as a matter of opinion, no refutation is necessary. But dear cousins all (from Adam and Eve descended), it is a rash one who will lay his finger on the map and say: "In this town there can be no romance—what could happen here?" Yes, it is a bold and a rash deed to challenge in one sentence history, romance, and Rand and McNally.

NASHVILLE.—A city, port of delivery, and the capital of the State of Tennessee, is on the Cumberland River and on the N. C. & St. L. and the L. & N. railroads. This city is regarded as the most important educational centre in the South.

I stepped off the train at 8 P. M. Having searched thesaurus in vain for adjectives, I must, as a substitution, hie me to comparison in the form of a recipe.

Take of London fog 30 parts; malaria 10 parts; gas leaks 20 parts; dewdrops gathered in a brick yard at sunrise, 25 parts; odor of honeysuckle 15 parts. Mix.

The mixture will give you an approximate conception of a Nashville drizzle. It is not so fragrant as a moth-ball nor as thick as pea-soup; but 'tis enough— 'twill serve.

I went to a hotel in a tumbril. It required strong self-suppression for me to keep from climbing to the top of it and giving an imitation of Sidney Carton. The vehicle was drawn by beasts of a bygone era and driven by something dark and emancipated.

I was sleepy and tired, so when I got to the hotel I hurriedly paid it the fifty cents it demanded (with approximate lagniappe, I assure you). I knew its habits; and I did not want to hear it prate about its old "marster" or anything that happened "befo' de wah."

The hotel was one of the kind described as "renovated." That means $20,000 worth of new marble pillars, tiling, electric lights and brass cuspidors in the lobby, and a new L. & N. time table and a lithograph of Lookout Mountain in each one of the great rooms above. The management was without reproach, the attention full of exquisite Southern courtesy, the service as slow as the progress of a snail and as good-humored as Rip Van Winkle. The food was worth traveling a thousand miles for. There is no other hotel in the world where you can get such chicken livers *en brochette.*

At dinner I asked a Negro waiter if there was anything doing in town. He pondered gravely for a minute, and then replied: "Well, boss, I don't really reckon there's anything at all doin' after sundown."

Sundown had been accomplished; it had been drowned in the drizzle long before. So that spectacle was denied me. But I went forth upon the streets in the drizzle to see what might be there.

It is built on undulating grounds; and the streets are lighted by electricity at a cost of $32,470 per annum.

As I left the hotel there was a race riot. Down upon me charged a company of freedmen, or Arabs, or Zulus, armed with—no, I saw with relief that they were not rifles, but whips. And I saw dimly a caravan of black, clumsy vehicles; and at the reassuring shouts, "Kyar you anywhere in the town, boss, fuh fifty cents," I reasoned that I was merely a "fare" instead of a victim.

I walked through long streets, all leading uphill. I wondered how those streets ever came down again. Perhaps they didn't until they were "graded." On a few of the "main streets" I saw lights in stores here and there; saw street cars go by conveying worthy burghers hither and yon; saw people pass engaged in the art of conversation, and heard a burst of semi-lively laughter issuing from a soda-water and ice-cream parlor. The streets other than "main" seemed to have enticed upon their borders houses consecrated to peace and domesticity. In many of them lights shone behind discreetly drawn window shades, in a few pianos tinkled orderly and irreproachable music. There was, indeed, little "doing." I wished I had come before sundown. So I returned to my hotel.

In November, 1864, the Confederate General Hood advanced against Nashville, where he shut up a National force under General Thomas. The latter then sallied forth and defeated the Confederates in a terrible conflict.

All my life I have heard of, admired, and witnessed the fine markmanship of the

South in its peaceful conflicts in the tobacco-chewing regions. But in my hotel
a surprise awaited me. There were twelve bright, new, imposing, capacious
brass cuspidors in the great lobby, tall enough to be called urns and so wide-
mouthed that the crack pitcher of a lady baseball team should have been able
to throw a ball into one of them at five paces distant. But, although a terrible
battle had raged and was still raging, the enemy had not suffered. Bright,
new, imposing, capacious, untouched, they stood. But, shades of Jefferson Brick!
the tile floor—the beautiful tile floor! I could not avoid thinking of the battle
of Nashville, and trying to draw, as is my foolish habit, some deductions about
hereditary marksmanship.

Here I first saw Major (by misplaced courtesy) Wentworth Caswell. I knew
him for a type the moment my eyes suffered from the sight of him. A rat has
no geographical habitat. My old friend, A. Tennyson, said, as he so well said
almost everything:

> Prophet, curse me the blabbing lip,
> And curse me the British vermin, the rat.

Let us regard the word "British" as interchangeable *ad lib.* A rat is a rat.
This man was hunting about the hotel lobby like a starved dog that had forgotten where he had buried a bone. He had a face of great acreage, red, pulpy,
and with a kind of sleepy massiveness like that of Buddha. He possessed one
single virtue—he was very smoothly shaven. The mark of the beast is not
indelible upon a man until he goes about with a stubble. I think that if he had
not used his razor that day I would have repulsed his advances, and the criminal
calendar of the world would have been spared the addition of one murder.

I happened to be standing within five feet of a cuspidor when Major Caswell
opened fire upon it. I had been observant enough to perceive that the attacking
force was using Gatlings instead of squirrel rifles, so I sidestepped so promptly
that the major seized the opportunity to apologize to a noncombatant. He had
the blabbing lip. In four minutes he had become my friend and had dragged
me to the bar.

I desire to interpolate here that I am a Southerner. But I am not one by
profession or trade. I eschew the string tie, the slouch hat, the Prince Albert,
the number of bales of cotton destroyed by Sherman, and plug chewing. When the
orchestra plays "Dixie" I do not cheer. I slide a little lower on the leather-
cornered seat and, well, order another Würzburger and wish that Longstreet had
—but what's the use?

Major Caswell banged the bar with his fist, and the first gun at Fort Sumter re-
echoed. When he fired the last one at Appomattox I began to hope. But then
he began on family trees, and demonstrated that Adam was only a third cousin
of a collateral branch of the Caswell family. Genealogy disposed of, he took
up, to my distaste, his private family matters. He spoke of his wife, traced her
descent back to Eve, and profanely denied any possible rumor that she may have
had relations in the land of Nod.

By this time I began to suspect that he was trying to obscure by noise the fact
that he had ordered the drinks, on the chance that I would be bewildered into
paying for them. But when they were down he crashed a silver dollar loudly
upon the bar. Then, of course, another serving was obligatory. And when I had
paid for that I took leave of him brusquely; for I wanted no more of him. But
before I had obtained my release he had prated loudly of an income that his
wife received, and showed a handful of silver money.

When I got my key at the desk the clerk said to me courteously: "If that
man Caswell has annoyed you, and if you would like to make a complaint, we
will have him ejected. He is a nuisance, a loafer, and without any known means

of support, although he seems to have some money most the time. But we don't seem to be able to hit upon any means of throwing him out legally."

"Why, no," said I, after some reflection; "I don't see my way clear to making a complaint. But I would like to place myself on record as asserting that I do not care for his company. Your town," I continued, "seems to be a quiet one. What manner of entertainment, adventure, or excitement have you to offer to the stranger within your gates?"

"Well, sir," said the clerk, "there will be a show here next Thursday. It is— I'll look it up and have the announcement sent up to your room with the ice water. Good-night."

After I went up to my room I looked out the window. It was only about ten o'clock, but I looked upon a silent town. The drizzle continued, spangled with dim lights, as far apart as currants in a cake sold at the Ladies' Exchange.

"A quiet place," I said to myself, as my first shoe struck the ceiling of the occupant of the room beneath mine. "Nothing of the life here that gives color and good variety to the cities in the East and West. Just a good, ordinary, humdrum, business town."

Nashville occupies a foremost place among the manufacturing centres of the country. It is the fifth boot and shoe market in the United States, the largest candy and cracker manufacturing city in the South, and does an enormous wholesale drygoods, grocery, and drug business.

I must tell you how I came to be in Nashville, and I assure you the digression brings as much tedium to me as it does to you. I was traveling elsewhere on my own business, but I had a commission from a Northern literary magazine to stop over there and establish a personal connection between the publication and one of its contributors, Azalea Adair.

Adair (there was no clue to the personality except the handwriting) had sent in some essays (lost art!) and poems that had made the editors swear approvingly over their one o'clock luncheon. So they had commissioned me to round up said Adair and corner by contract his or her output at two cents a word before some other publisher offered her ten or twenty.

At nine o'clock the next morning, after my chicken livers *en brochette* (try them if you can find that hotel), I strayed out into the drizzle, which was still on for an unlimited run. At the first corner I came upon Uncle Cæsar. He was a stalwart Negro, older than the pyramids, with gray wool and a face that reminded me of Brutus, and a second afterwards of the late King Cettiwayo. He wore the most remarkable coat that I ever had seen or expect to see. It reached to his ankles and had once been a Confederate gray in colors. But rain and sun and age had so variegated it that Joseph's coat, beside it, would have faded to a pale monochrome. I must linger with that coat, for it has to do with the story— the story that is so long in coming, because you can hardly expect anything to happen in Nashville.

Once it must have been the military coat of an officer. The cape of it had vanished, but all adown its front it had been frogged and tasseled magnificently. But now the frogs and tassels were gone. In their stead had been patiently stitched (I surmised by some surviving "black mammy") new frogs made of cunningly twisted common hempen twine. This twine was frayed and disheveled. It must have been added to the coat as a substitute for vanished splendors, with tasteless but painstaking devotion, for it followed faithfully the curves of the long-missing frogs. And, to complete the comedy and pathos of the garment, all its buttons were gone save one. The second button from the top alone remained. The coat was fastened by other twine strings tied through the buttonholes and other holes rudely pierced in the opposite side. There was never such a weird garment so fantastically bedecked and of so many mottled hues. The lone button was the size of a half-dollar, made of yellow horn and sewed on with coarse twine.

This Negro stood by a carriage so old that Ham himself might have started a hack line with it after he left the ark with the two animals hitched to it. As I approached he threw open the door, drew out a feather duster, waved it without using it, and said in deep, rumbling tones:

"Step right in, suh; ain't a speck of dust in it—jus' got back from a funeral, suh."

I inferred that on such gala occasions carriages were given an extra cleaning. I looked up and down the street and perceived that there was little choice among the vehicles for hire that lined the curb. I looked in my memorandum book for the address of Azalea Adair.

"I want to go to 861 Jessamine Street," I said, and was about to step into the hack. But for an instant the thick, long, gorilla-like arm of the Negro barred me. On his massive and saturnine face a look of sudden suspicion and enmity flashed for a moment. Then, with quickly returning conviction, he asked, blandishingly: "What are you gwine there for, boss?"

"What is that to you?" I asked, a little sharply.

"Nothin', suh, jus' nothin'. Only it's a lonesome kind of part of town and few folks ever has business out there. Step right in. The seats is clean—jes' got back from a funeral, suh."

A mile and a half it must have been to our journey's end. I could hear nothing but the fearful rattle of the ancient hack over the uneven brick paving; I could smell nothing but the drizzle, now further flavored with coal smoke and something like a mixture of tar and oleander blossoms. All I could see through the streaming windows were two rows of dim houses.

The city has an area of 10 square miles; 181 miles of streets, of which 137 miles are paved; a system of waterworks that cost $2,000,000, with 77 miles of mains.

Eight-sixty-one Jessamine Street was a decayed mansion. Thirty yards back from the street it stood, outmerged in a splendid grove of trees and untrimmed shrubbery. A row of box bushes overflowed and almost hid the paling fence from sight; the gate was kept closed by a rope noose that encircled the gate post and the first paling of the gate. But when you got inside you saw that 861 was a shell, a shadow, a ghost of former grandeur and excellence. But in the story, I have not yet got inside.

When the hack had ceased from rattling and the weary quadrupeds came to a rest I handed my jehu his fifty cents with an additional quarter, feeling a glow of conscious generosity as I did so. He refused it.

"It's two dollars, suh," he said.

"How's that?" I asked. "I plainly heard you call out at the hotel. 'Fifty cents to any part of the town.'"

"It's two dollars, suh," he repeated obstinately. "It's a long ways from the hotel."

"It is within the city limits and well within them," I argued. "Don't think that you have picked up a greenhorn Yankee. Do you see those hills over there?" I went on, pointing toward the east (I could not see them, myself, for the drizzle); "well, I was born and raised on their other side. You old fool nigger, can't you tell people from other people when you see 'em?"

The grim face of King Cettiwayo softened. "Is you from the South, suh? I reckon it was them shoes of yourn fooled me. They is somethin' sharp in the toes for a Southern gen'l'man to wear."

"Then the charge is fifty cents, I suppose?" said I, inexorably.

His former expression, a mingling of cupidity and hostility, returned, remained ten seconds, and vanished.

"Boss," he said, "fifty cents is right; but I *needs* two dollars, suh; I'm *obleeged* to have two dollars. I ain't *demandin'* it now, suh; after I knows whar you's from; I'm jus sayin' that I *has* to have two dollars to-night and business is mighty po'."

Peace and confidence settled upon his heavy features. He had been luckier than he had hoped. Instead of having picked up a greenhorn, ignorant of rates, he had come upon an inheritance.

"You confounded old rascal," I said, reaching down to my pocket, "you ought to be turned over to the police."

For the first time I saw him smile. He knew; *he knew;* HE KNEW.

I gave him two one-dollar bills. As I handed them over I noticed that one of them had seen parlous times. Its upper right-hand corner was missing, and it had been torn through in the middle, but joined again. A strip of blue tissue paper, pasted over the split, preserved its negotiability.

Enough of the African bandit for the present: I left him happy, lifted the rope, and opened the creaky gate.

The house, as I said, was a shell. A paint brush had not touched it in twenty years. I could not see why a strong wind should not have bowled it over like a house of cards until I looked again at the trees that hugged it close—the trees that saw the battle of Nashville and still drew their protecting branches around it against storm and enemy and cold.

Azalea Adair, fifty years old, white-haired, a descendant of the cavaliers, as thin and frail as the house she lived in, robed in the cheapest and cleanest dress I ever saw, with an air as simple as a queen's, received me.

The reception room seemed a mile square, because there was nothing in it except some rows of books, on unpainted white-pine bookshelves, a cracked marble-topped table, a rag rug, a hairless horsehair sofa, and two or three chairs. Yes, there was a picture on the wall, a colored crayon drawing of a cluster of pansies. I looked around for the portrait of Andrew Jackson and the pinecone hanging basket but they were not there.

Azalea Adair and I had conversation, a little of which will be repeated to you. She was a product of the old South, gently nurtured in the sheltered life. Her learning was not broad, but was deep and of splendid originality in its somewhat narrow scope. She had been educated at home, and her knowledge of the world was derived from inference and by inspiration. Of such is the precious, small group of essayists made. While she talked to me I kept brushing my fingers, trying, unconsciously, to rid them guiltily of the absent dust from the half-calf backs of Lamb, Chaucer, Hazlitt, Marcus Aurelius, Montaigne, and Hood. She was exquisite, she was a valuable discovery. Nearly everybody nowadays knows too much—oh, so much too much—of real life.

I could perceive clearly that Azalea Adair was very poor. A house and a dress she had, not much else, I fancied. So, divided between my duty to the magazine and my loyalty to the poets and essayists who fought Thomas in the valley of the Cumberland, I listened to her voice which was like a harpsichord's, and found that I could not speak of contracts. In the presence of the nine Muses and the three Graces one hesitated to lower the topic to two cents. There would have to be another colloquy after I had regained my commercialism. But I spoke of my mission, and three o'clock of the next afternoon was set for the discussion of the business proposition.

"Your town," I said, as I began to make ready to depart (which is the time for smooth generalities) "seems to be a quiet, sedate place. A home town, I should say, where few things out of the ordinary ever happen."

It carries on an extensive trade in stoves and hollow ware with the West and South, and its flouring mills have a daily capacity of more than 2,000 barrels.

Azalea Adair seemed to reflect.

"I have never thought of it that way," she said, with a kind of sincere intensity that seemed to belong to her. "Isn't it in the still, quiet places that things do happen? I fancy that when God began to create the earth on the first Monday morning one could have leaned out one's window and heard the drops of mud splashing from His trowel as He built up the everlasting hills. What did the noisest project in the world—I mean the building of the tower of Babel—result in finally? A page and a half of Esperanto in the *North American Review*."

"Of course," said I, platitudinously, "human nature is the same everywhere; but there is more color—er—more drama and movement and—er—romance in some cities than in others."

"On the surface," said Azalea Adair. "I have traveled many times around the world in a golden airship wafted on two wings—print and dreams. I have seen (on one of my imaginary tours) the Sultan of Turkey bowstring with his own hands one of his wives who had uncovered her face in public. I have seen a man in Nashville tear up his theatre tickets because his wife was going out with her face covered—with rice powder. In San Francisco's Chinatown I saw the slave girl Sing Yee dipped slowly, inch by inch, in boiling almond oil to make her swear she would never see her American lover again. She gave in when the boiling oil had reached three inches above her knee. At a euchre party in East Nashville the other night I saw Kitty Morgan cut dead by seven of her schoolmates and lifelong friends because she had married a house painter. The boiling oil was sizzling as high as her heart; but I wish you could have seen the fine little smile that she carried from table to table. Oh, yes, it is a humdrum town. Just a few miles of red brick houses and mud and stores and lumber yards."

Some one had knocked hollowly at the back of the house. Azalea Adair breathed a soft apology and went to investigate the sound. She came back in three minutes with brightened eyes, a faint flush on her cheeks, and ten years lifted from her shoulders.

"You must have a cup of tea before you go," she said, "and a sugar cake."

She reached and shook a little iron bell. In shuffled a small Negro girl about twelve, barefoot, not very tidy, glowering at me with thumb in mouth and bulging eyes.

Azalea Adair opened a tiny, worn purse and drew out a dollar bill, a dollar bill with the upper right-hand corner missing, torn in two pieces and pasted together again with a strip of blue tissue paper. It was one of those bills I had given the piratical Negro—there was no doubt of it.

"Go up to Mr. Baker's store on the corner, Impy," she said, handing the girl the dollar bill, "and get a quarter of a pound of tea—the kind he always sends me—and ten cents' worth of sugar cakes. Now, hurry. The supply of tea in the house happens to be exhausted," she explained to me.

Impy left by the back way. Before the scrape of her hard, bare feet had died away on the back porch, a wild shriek—I was sure it was hers—filled the hollow house. Then the deep, gruff tones of an angry man's voice mingled with the girl's further squeals and unintelligible words.

Azalea Adair rose without surprise or emotion and disappeared. For two minutes I heard the hoarse rumble of the man's voice; then something like an oath and a slight scuffle, and she returned calmly to her chair.

"This is a roomy house," she said, "and I have a tenant for part of it. I am sorry to have to rescind my invitation to tea. It is impossible to get the kind I always use at the store. Perhaps to-morrow Mr. Baker will be able to supply me."

I was sure that Impy had not had time to leave the house. I inquired concerning street-car lines and took my leave. After I was well on my way I remembered that I had not learned Azalea Adair's name. But to-morrow would do.

That same day I started in on the course of iniquity that this uneventful city forced upon me. I was in the town only two days, but in that time I managed to lie shamelessly by telegraph, and to be an accomplice—after the fact, if that is the correct legal term—to a murder.

As I rounded the corner nearest my hotel the Afrite coachman of the polychromatic, nonpareil coat seized me, swung open the dungeony door of his peripatetic sarcophagus, flirted his feather duster and began his ritual: "Step right in, boss. Carriage is clean—jus' got back from a funeral. Fifty cents to any——"

And then he knew me and grinned broadly. "'Scuse me, boss; you is de gen'l'man what rid out with me dis mawnin'. Thank you kindly, suh."

"I am going out to 861 again to-morrow afternoon at three," said I, "and if you will be here, I'll let you drive me. So you know Miss Adair?" I concluded, thinking of my dollar bill.

"I belonged to her father, Judge Adair, suh," he replied.

"I judge that she is pretty poor," I said, "She hasn't much money to speak of, has she?"

For an instant I looked again at the fierce countenance of King Cettiwayo, and then he changed back to an extortionate old Negro hack driver.

"She ain't gwine to starve, suh," he said, slowly. "She has reso'ces, suh; she has reso'ces."

"I shall pay you fifty cents for the trip," said I.

"Dat is puffeckly correct, suh," he answered, humbly. "I jus' *had* to have dat two dollars dis mawnin', boss."

I went to the hotel and lied by electricity. I wired the magazine: "A. Adair holds out for eight cents a word."

The answer that came back was: "Give it to her quick, you duffer."

Just before dinner "Major" Wentworth Caswell bore down upon me with the greetings of a long-lost friend. I have seen few men whom I have so instantaneously hated, and of whom it was so difficult to be rid. I was standing at the bar when he invaded me; therefore I could not wave the white ribbon in his face. I would have paid gladly for the drinks, hoping thereby, to escape another; but he was one of those despicable, roaring, advertising bibbers who must have brass bands and fireworks attend upon every cent that they waste in their follies.

With an air of producing millions he drew two one-dollar bills from a pocket and dashed one of them upon the bar. I looked once more at the dollar bill with the upper right-hand corner missing, torn through the middle, and patched with a strip of blue tissue paper. It was my dollar bill again. It could have been no other.

I went up to my room. The drizzle and the monotony of a dreary, eventless Southern town had made me tired and listless. I remember that just before I went to bed I mentally disposed of the mysterious dollar bill (which might have formed the clue to a tremendously fine detective story of San Francisco) by saying to myself sleepily: "Seems as if a lot of people here own stock in the Hack-Driver's Trust. Pays dividends promptly, too. Wonder if——" Then I fell asleep.

King Cettiwayo was at his post the next day, and rattled my bones over the stones out to 861. He was to wait and rattle me back again when I was ready.

Azalea Adair looked paler and cleaner and frailer than she had looked on the day before. After she had signed the contract at eight cents per word she grew still paler and began to slip out of her chair. Without much trouble I managed to get her up on the antediluvian horsehair sofa and then I ran out to the sidewalk and yelled to the coffee-colored Pirate to bring a doctor. With a wisdom that I had not suspected in him, he abandoned his team and struck off up the street afoot, realizing the value of speed. In ten minutes he returned with a grave, gray-haired, and capable man of medicine. In a few words (worth much less than eight cents each) I explained to him my presence in the hollow house of mystery. He bowed with stately understanding, and turned to the old Negro.

"Uncle Cæsar," he said, calmly, "run up to my house and ask Miss Lucy to give you a cream pitcher full of fresh milk and half a tumbler of port wine. And hurry back. Don't drive—run. I want you to get back sometime this week."

It occurred to me that Dr. Merriman also felt a distrust as to the speeding powers of the land-pirate's steeds. After Uncle Cæsar was gone, lumberingly, but swiftly, up the street, the doctor looked me over with great politeness and as much careful calculation until he had decided that I might do.

"It is only a case of insufficient nutrition," he said. "In other words, the result of poverty, pride, and starvation. Mrs. Caswell has many devoted friends who would be glad to aid her, but she will accept nothing except from that old Negro, Uncle Cæsar, who was once owned by her family."

"Mrs. Caswell!" said I, in surprise. And then I looked at the contract and saw that she had signed it "Azalea Adair Caswell."

"I thought she was Miss Adair," I said.

"Married to a drunken, worthless loafer, sir," said the doctor. "It is said that he robs her even of the small sums that her old servant contributes toward her support."

When the milk and wine had been brought the doctor soon revived Azalea Adair. She sat up and talked of the beauty of the autumn leaves that were then in season and their height of color. She referred lightly to her fainting seizure as the outcome of an old palpitation of the heart. Impy fanned her as she lay on the sofa. The doctor was due elsewhere, and I followed him to the door. I told him that it was within my power and intentions to make a reasonable advance of money to Azalea Adair on future contributions to the magazine, and he seemed pleased.

"By the way," he said, "perhaps you would like to know that you have had royalty for a coachman. Old Cæsar's grandfather was a king in Congo. Cæsar himself has royal ways, as you may have observed."

As the doctor was moving off I heard Uncle Cæsar's voice inside: "Did he git bofe of dem two dollars from you, Mis' Zalea?"

"Yes, Cæsar," I heard Azalea Adair answer, weakly. And then I went in and concluded business negotiations with our contributor. I assumed the responsibility of advancing fifty dollars, putting it as a necessary formality in binding our bargain. And then Uncle Cæsar drove me back to the hotel.

Here ends all of the story as far as I can testify as a witness. The rest must be only bare statements of facts.

At about six o'clock I went out for a stroll. Uncle Cæsar was at his corner. He threw open the door of his carriage, flourished his duster, and began his depressing formula: "Step right in, suh. Fifty cents to anywhere in the city—hack's puffickly clean, suh—jus' got back from a funeral——"

And then he recognized me. I think his eyesight was getting bad. His coat had taken on a few more faded shades of color, the twine strings were more frayed and ragged, the last remaining button—the button of yellow horn—was gone. A motley descendant of kings was Uncle Cæsar!

About two hours later I saw an excited crowd besieging the front of the drug store. In a desert where nothing happens this was manna; so I wedged my way inside. On an extemporized couch of empty boxes and chairs was stretched the mortal corporeality of Major Wentworth Caswell. A doctor was testing him for the mortal ingredient. His decision was that it was conspicuous by its absence.

The erstwhile Major had been found dead on a dark street and brought by curious and ennuied citizens to the drug store. The late human being had been engaged in terrific battle—the details showed that. Loafer and reprobate though he had been, he had been also a warrior. But he had lost. His hands were yet clinched so tightly that his fingers would not be opened. The gentle citizens who had known him stood about and searched their vocabularies to find some good words, if it were possible, to speak of him. One kind-looking man said, after much thought: "When 'Cas' was about fo'teen he was one of the best spellers in the school."

While I stood there the fingers of the right hand of "the man that was," which hung down the side of a white pine box, relaxed, and dropped something at my feet. I covered it with one foot quietly, and a little later on I picked it up and pocketed it. I reasoned that in his last struggle his hand must have seized that object unwittingly and held it in a death grip.

At the hotel that night the main topic of conversation, with the possible exceptions of politics and prohibition, was the demise of Major Caswell. I heard one man say to a group of listeners:

"In my opinion, gentlemen, Caswell was murdered by some of these no-account niggars for his money. He had fifty dollars this afternoon which he showed to several gentlemen in the hotel. When he was found the money was not on his person."

I left the city the next morning at nine, and as the train was crossing the bridge over the Cumberland River I took out of my pocket a yellow horn overcoat button the size of a fifty-cent piece, with frayed ends of coarse twine hanging from it, and cast it out of the window into the slow, muddy waters below.

I wonder what's doing in Buffalo!

PSYCHE AND THE PSKYSCRAPER

IF you are a philosopher you can do this thing: you can go to the top of a high building, look down upon your fellow men 300 feet below, and despise them as insects. Like the irresponsible black waterbugs on summer ponds, they crawl and circle and hustle about idiotically without aim or purpose. They do not even move with the admirable intelligence of ants, for ants always know when they are going home. The ant is of a lowly station, but he will often reach home and get his slippers on while you are left at your elevated station.

Man, then, to the housetopped philosopher, appears to be but a creeping, contemptible beetle. Brokers, poets, millionaires, bootblacks, beauties, hod-carriers, and politicians become little black specks dodging bigger black specks in streets no wider than your thumb.

From this high view the city itself becomes degraded to an unintelligible mass of distorted buildings and impossible perspectives; the revered ocean is a duck pond; the earth itself a lost golf ball. All the minutiæ of life are gone. The philosopher gazes into the infinite heavens above him, and allows his soul to expand in the influence of his new view. He feels that he is the heir to Eternity and the child of Time. Space, too, should be his by the right of his immortal heritage, and he thrills at the thought that some day his kind shall traverse those mysterious aerial roads between planet and planet. The tiny world beneath his feet upon which this towering structure of steel rests as a speck of dust upon a Himalayan mountain—it is but one of a countless number of such whirling atoms. What are the ambitions, the achievements, the paltry conquests and loves of those restless black insects below compared with the serene and awful immensity of the universe that lies above and around their insignificant city?

It is guaranteed that the philosopher will have these thoughts. They have been expressly compiled from the philosophies of the world and set down with the proper interrogation point at the end of them to represent the invariable musings of deep thinkers on high places. And when the philosopher takes the elevator down his mind is broader, his heart is at peace, and his conception of the cosmogony of creation is as wide as the buckle of Orien's summer belt.

But if your name happened to be Daisy, and you worked in an Eighth Avenue candy store and lived in a little cold hall bedroom, five feet by eight, and earned $6 per week, and ate ten-cent lunches and were nineteen years old, and got up at 6.30 and worked till 9, and never had studied philosophy, maybe things wouldn't look that way to you from the top of a skyscraper.

Two sighed for the hand of Daisy, the unphilosophical. One was Joe, who kept the smallest store in New York. It was about the size of a tool-box of the D. P. W., and was stuck like a swallow's nest against a corner of a down-town sky-scraper. Its stock consisted of fruit, candies, newspapers, song books, cigarettes, and lemonade in season. When stern winter shook his congealed locks and Joe had to move himself and the fruit inside, there was exactly room in the store for the proprietor, his wares, a stove the size of a vinegar cruet, and one customer.

Joe was not of the nation that keeps us forever in a furore with fugues and fruit. He was a capable American youth who was laying by money, and wanted Daisy to help him spend it. Three times he had asked her.

"I got money saved up, Daisy," was his love song; "and you know how bad I want you. That store of mine ain't very big, but——"

"Oh, ain't it?" would be the antiphony of the unphilosophical one. "Why, I heard Wanamaker's was trying to get you to sublet part of your floor space to them for next year."

Daisy passed Joe's corner every morning and evening.

"Hello, Two-by-Four!" was her usual greeting. "Seems to me your store looks emptier. You must have sold a package of chewing gum."

"Ain't much room in here, sure," Joe would answer, with his slow grin, "except for you, Daise. Me and the store are waitin' for you whenever you'll take us. Don't you think you might before long?"

"Store!"—a fine scorn was expressed by Daisy's uptilted nose—"sardine box! Waitin' for me, you say? Gee! you'd have to throw out about a hundred pounds of candy before I could get inside of it, Joe."

"I wouldn't mind an even swap like that," said Joe, complimentary.

Daisy's existence was limited in every way. She had to walk sideways between the counter and the shelves in the candy store. In her own hall bedroom coziness had been carried close to cohesiveness. The walls were so near to one another that the paper on them made a perfect Babel of noise. She could light the gas with one hand and close the door with the other without taking her eyes off the reflection of her brown pompadour in the mirror. She had Joe's picture in a gilt frame on the dresser and sometimes—but her next thought would always be of Joe's funny little store tacked like a soap box to the corner of that great building, and away would go her sentiment in a breeze of laughter.

Daisy's other suitor followed Joe by several months. He came to board in the house where she lived. His name was Dabster, and he was a philosopher. Though young, attainments stood out upon him like continental labels on a Passaic (N. J.) suit-case. Knowledge he had kidnapped from cyclopedias and handbooks of useful information; but as for wisdom, when she passed he was left sniffing in the road without so much as the number of her motor car. He could and would tell you the proportions of water and muscle-making properties of peas and veal, the shortest verse in the Bible, the number of pounds of shingle nails required to fasten 256 shingles laid four inches to the weather, the population of Kanakee, Ill., the theories of Spinoza, the name of Mr. H. McKay Twombly's second hall footman, the length of the Hoosac Tunnel, the best time to set a hen, the salary of the railway post-office messenger between Driftwood and Red Bank Furnace, Pa., and the number of bones in the foreleg of a cat.

This weight of learning was no handicap to Dabster. His statistics were the sprigs of parsley with which he garnished the feast of small talk that he would set before you if he conceived that to be your taste. And again he used them as breastworks in foraging at the boarding-house. Firing at you a volley of figures concerning the weight of a lineal foot of bar-iron 5 x 2¾ inches, and the average annual rainfall at Fort Snelling, Minn., he would transfix with his fork the best piece of chicken on the dish while you were trying to rally sufficiently to ask him weakly why does a hen cross the road.

Thus, brightly armed, and further equipped with a measure of good looks, of a hair-oily, shopping-district-at-three-in-the-afternoon kind, it seems that Joe, of the Lilliputian emporium, had a rival worthy of his steel. But Joe carried no steel. There wouldn't have been room in his store to draw it if he had.

One Saturday afternoon, about four o'clock, Daisy and Mr. Dabster stopped before Joe's booth. Dabster wore a silk hat, and—well, Daisy was a woman, and that hat has no chance to get back in its box until Joe had seen it. A stick of pineapple chewing gum was the ostensible object of the call. Joe supplied it through the open side of his store. He did not pale or falter at sight of the hat.

"Mr. Dabsters's going to take me on top of the building to observe the view," said Daisy, after she had introduced her admirers. "I never was on a skyscraper. I guess it must be awful nice and funny up there."

"H'm!" said Joe.

"The panorama," said Mr. Dabster, "exposed to the gaze from the top of a lofty building is not only sublime, but instructive. Miss Daisy has a decided pleasure in store for her."

"It's windy up there, too, as well as here," said Joe. "Are you dressed warm enough, Daise?"

"Sure thing! I'm all lined," said Daisy, smiling shyly at his clouded brow. "You look just like a mummy in a case, Joe. Ain't you just put in an invoice of a pint of peanuts or another apple? Your stock looks awful over-stocked."

Daisy giggled at her favorite joke; and Joe had to smile with her.

"Your quarters are somewhat limited, Mr.—er—er," remarked Dabster, "in comparison with the size of this building. I understand the area of its side to be about 340 by 100 feet. That would make you occupy a proportionate space as if half of Beloochistan were placed upon a territory as large as the United States east of the Rocky Mountains, with the province of Ontario and Belgium added."

"Is that so, sport?" said Joe, genially. "You are Weisenheimer on figures, all right. How many square pounds of baled hay do you think a jackass could eat if he stopped brayin' long enough to keep still a minute and five eighths?"

A few minutes later Daisy and Mr. Dabster stepped from an elevator to the top floor of the skyscraper. Then up a short, steep stairway and out upon the roof. Dabster led her to the parapet so she could look down at the black dots moving in the street below.

"What are they?" she asked, trembling. She had never been on a height like this before.

And then Dabster must needs play the philosopher on the tower, and conduct her soul forth to meet the immensity of space.

"Bipeds," he said, solemnly. "See what they become even at the small elevation of 340 feet—mere crawling insects going to and fro at random."

"Oh, they ain't anything of the kind," exclaimed Daisy, suddenly—"they're folks! I saw an automobile. Oh, gee! are we that high up?"

"Walk over this way," said Dabster.

He showed her the great city lying like an orderly array of toys far below, starred here and there, early as it was, by the first beacon lights of the winter afternoon. And then the bay and sea to the south and east vanishing mysteriously into the sky.

"I don't like it," declared Daisy, with troubled blue eyes. "Say we go down."

But the philosopher was not to be denied his opportunity. He would let her behold the grandeur of his mind, the half-nelson he had on the infinite, and the memory he had for statistics. And then she would never more be content to buy chewing gum at the smallest store in New York. And so he began to prate of the smallness of human affairs, and how that even so slight a removal from earth made man and his works look like one tenth part of a dollar thrice computed. And that one should consider the sidereal system and the maxims of Epictetus and be comforted.

"You don't carry me with you," said Daisy. "Say, I think it's awful to be up so high that folks look like fleas. One of them we saw might have been Joe. Why, Jimmy! we might as well be in New Jersey! Say, I'm afraid up here!"

The philosopher smiled fatuously.

"The earth," said he, "is itself only as a grain of wheat in space. Look up there."

Daisy gazed upward apprehensively. The short day was spent and the stars were coming out above.

"Yonder star," said Dabster, "is Venus, the evening star. She is 66,000,000 miles from the sun."

"Fudge!" said Daisy, with a brief flash of spirit, "where do you think I come from—Brooklyn? Susie Price, in our store—her brother sent her a ticket to go to San Francisco—that's only three thousand miles."

The philosopher smiled indulgently.

"Our world," he said, "is 91,000,000 miles from the sun. There are eighteen stars of the first magnitude that are 211,000 times farther from us than the sun is. If one of them should be extinguished it would be three years before we would see its light go out. There are six thousand stars of the sixth magnitude. It takes thirty-six years for the light of one of them to reach the earth. With an eighteen-foot telescope we can see 43,000,000 stars, including those of the thirteenth magnitude, whose light takes 2,700 years to reach us. Each of these stars——"

"You're lyin'," cried Daisy, angrily. "You're tryin' to scare me. And you have; I want to go down!"

She stamped her foot.

"Arcturus——" began the philosopher, soothingly, but he was interrupted by a demonstration out of the vastness of the nature that he was endeavoring to portray with his memory instead of his heart. For to the heart-expounder of nature, the stars were set in the firmament expressly to give soft light to lovers wandering happily beneath them; and if you stand tiptoe some September night with your sweetheart on your arm you can almost touch them with your hand. Three years for their light to reach us, indeed!

Out of the west leaped a meteor, lighting the roof of the skyscraper almost to midday. Its fiery parabola was limned against the sky toward the east. It hissed as it went, and Daisy screamed.

"Take me down," she cried, vehemently, "you—you mental arithmetic!"

Dabster got her to the elevator, and inside of it. She was wild-eyed, and she shuddered when the express made its debilitating drop.

Outside the revolving door of the skyscraper the philosopher lost her. She vanished; and he stood, bewildered without figures or statistics to aid him.

Joe had a lull in trade, and by squirming among his stock succeeded in lighting a cigarette and getting one cold foot against the attenuated stove.

The door was burst open, and Daisy, laughing, crying, scattering fruit and candies, tumbled into his arms.

"Oh, Joe, I've been up on the skyscraper. Ain't it cozy and warm and homelike in here! I'm ready for you, Joe, whenever you want me."

A BIRD OF BAGDAD

WITHOUT doubt much of the spirit and genius of the Caliph Harun Al Rashid descended to the Margrave August Michael von Paulsen Quigg.

Quigg's restaurant is in Fourth Avenue—that street that the city seems to have forgotten in its growth. Fourth Avenue—born and bred in the Bowery—staggers northward full of good resolutions.

Where it crosses Fourteenth Street it struts for a brief moment proudly in the glare of the museums and cheap theatres. It may yet become a fit mate for its high-born sister boulevard to the west, or its roaring, polyglot, broad-waisted cousin to the east. It passes Union Square; and here the hoofs of the dray horses seem to thunder in unison, recalling the tread of marching hosts—Hooray! But now comes the silent and terrible mountains—buildings square as forts, high as the clouds, shutting out the sky, where thousands of slaves bend over desks all day. On the ground floors are only little fruit shops and laundries and book shops, where you see copies of "Littell's Living Age" and G. W. M. Reynold's novels in the windows. And next—poor Fourth Avenue!—the street glides into mediæval solitude. On each side are the shops devoted to "Antiques."

Let us say it is night. Men in rusty armor stand in the windows and menace the hurrying cars with raised iron gauntlets. Hauberks and helms, blunderbusses, Cromwellian breastplates, matchlocks, creeses, and the swords and daggers of an army of dead-and-gone gallants gleam dully in the ghostly light. Here and there from a corner saloon (lit with Jack-o'-lanterns or phosphorus) stagger forth shuddering, homebound citizens, nerved by the tankards within to their fearsome journey adown that eldritch avenue lined with the blood-stained weapons of the fighting dead. What street could live inclosed by these mortuary relics, and trod by these spectral citizens in whose sunken hearts scarce one good whoop or tra-la-la remained?

Not Fourth Avenue. Not after the tinsel but enlivening glories of the Little Rialto—not after the echoing drum-beats of Union Square. There need be no tears, ladies and gentlemen; 'tis but the suicide of a street. With a shriek and a crash Fourth Avenue dives headlong into the tunnel at Thirty-fourth and is never seen again.

Near the sad scene of the thoroughfare's dissolution stood the modest restaurant of Quigg. It stands there yet if you care to view its crumbling red-brick front, its show window heaped with oranges, tomatoes, layer cakes, pies, canned asparagus—its papier-mâche lobster and two Maltese kittens asleep on a bunch of lettuce—if you care to sit at one of the little tables upon whose cloth has been traced in the yellowest of coffee stains the trail of the Japanese advance—to sit there with one eye on your umbrella and the other upon the bogus bottle from which you drop the counterfeit sauce foisted upon us by the cursed charlatan who assumes to be our dear old lord and friend, the "Nobleman in India."

Quigg's title came through his mother. One of her ancestors was a Margravine of Saxony. His father was a Tammany brave. On account of the dilution of his heredity he found that he could neither become a reigning potentate nor get a job in the City Hall. So he opened a restaurant. He was a man full of thought and reading. The business gave him a living, though he gave it little attention. One side of his house bequeathed to him a poetic and romantic nature. The other gave him the restless spirit that made him seek adventure. By day he was Quigg, the restaurateur. By night he was the Margrave—the Caliph—the Prince of Bohemia—going about the city in search of the odd, the mysterious, the inexplicable, the recondite.

One night at 9, at which hour the restaurant closed, Quigg set forth upon his quest. There was a mingling of the foreign, the military, and the artistic in his appearance as he buttoned his coat high up under his short-trimmed brown and gray beard and turned westward toward the more central life conduits of the city. In his pocket he had stored an assortment of cards, written upon, without which he never stirred out of doors. Each of those cards was good at his own restaurant for its face value. Some called simply for a bowl of soup or sandwiches and coffee; others entitled their bearers to one, two, three, or more days of full meals; a few were for single regular meals; a very few were, in effect, meal tickets good for a week.

Of riches and power Margrave Quigg had none; but he had a Caliph's heart—it may be forgiven him if his head fell short of the measure of Harun Al Rashid's. Perhaps some of the gold pieces in Bagdad had put less warmth and hope into the complainants among the bazaars than had Quigg's beef stew among the fishermen and one-eyed calenders of Manhattan.

Continuing his progress in search of romance to divert him, or of distress that he might aid, Quigg became aware of a fast-gathering crowd that whooped and fought and eddied at a corner of Broadway and the crosstown street that he was traversing. Hurrying to the spot he beheld a young man of an exceedingly melancholy and preoccupied demeanor engaged in the pastime of casting silver money from his pockets in the middle of the street. With each motion of the generous one's hand the crowd huddled upon the falling largesse with yells of joy. Traffic was suspended. A policeman in the centre of the mob stooped often to the ground as he urged the blockaders to move on.

The Margrave saw at a glance that here was food for his hunger after knowledge concerning abnormal workings of the human heart. He made his way swiftly to the young man's side and took his arm. "Come with me at once," he said, in a low but commanding voice that his waiters had learned to fear.

"Pinched," remarked the young man, looking up at him with expressionless eyes. "Pinched by a painless dentist. Take me away, flatty, and give me gas. Some lay eggs and some lay none. When is a hen?"

Still deeply seized by some inward grief, but tractable, he allowed Quigg to lead him away and down the street to a little park.

There, seated on a bench, he upon whom a corner of the great Caliph's mantle had descended, spake with kindness and discretion, seeking to know what evil had come upon the other, disturbing his soul and driving him to such ill-considered and ruinous waste of his substance and stores.

"I was doing the Monte Cristo act as adapted by Pompton, N. J., wasn't I?" asked the young man.

"You were throwing small coins into the street for the people to scramble after," said the Margrave.

"That's it. You buy all the beer you can hold, and then you throw chicken feed to—— Oh, curse that word chicken, and hens, feathers, roosters, eggs, and everything connected with it!"

"Young sir," said the Margrave, kindly, but with dignity, "though I do not ask your confidence, I invite it. I know the world and I know humanity. Man is my study, though I do not eye him as the scientist eyes a beetle or as the philanthropist gazes at the objects of his bounty—through a veil of theory and ignorance. It is my pleasure and distraction to interest myself in the peculiar and complicated misfortunes that life in a great city visits upon my fellow men. You may be familiar with the history of that glorious and immortal ruler, the Caliph Harun Al Rashid, whose wise and beneficent excursions among his people in the city of Bagdad secured him the privilege of relieving so much of their distress. In my humble way I walk in his footsteps. I seek for romance and adventure in city streets—not in ruined castles or in crumbling palaces. To me the greatest marvels of magic are those that take place in men's hearts when acted upon by the furious and diverse forces of a crowded population. In your strange behavior this evening I fancy a story lurks. I read in your act something deeper than the wanton wastefulness of a spendthrift. I observe in your countenance the certain traces of consuming grief or despair. I repeat—I invite your confidence. I am not without some powers to alleviate and advise. Will you not trust me?"

"Gee, how you talk!" exclaimed the young man, a gleam of admiration supplanting for a moment the dull sadness of his eyes. "You've got the Astor Library skinned to a synopsis of preceding chapters. I mind that old Turk you speak of. I read 'The Arabian Nights' when I was a kid. He was a kind of Bill Devery and Charlie Schwab rolled into one. But, say, you might wave enchanted dishrags and make copper bottles smoke up coon giants all night without ever touching me. My case won't yield to that kind of treatment."

"If I could hear your story," said the Margrave, with his lofty, serious smile.

"I'll spiel it in about nine words," said the young man, with a deep sigh, "but I don't think you can help me any. Unless you're a peach at guessing it's back to the Bosphorus for you on your magic linoleum."

THE STORY OF THE YOUNG MAN AND THE HARNESS MAKER'S RIDDLE

"I work in Hildebrant's saddle and harness shop down in Grant Street. I've worked there five years. I get $18 a week. That's enough to marry on, ain't it? Well, I'm not going to get married. Old Hildebrant is one of these funny Dutchmen—you know the kind—always getting off bum jokes. He's got about a million riddles and things that he faked from Rogers Brothers' great-grandfather. Bill Watson works there, too. Me and Bill have to stand for them chestnuts day after day. Why do we do it? Well, jobs ain't to be picked off every Anheuser bush—— And then there's Laura.

"What? The old man's daughter. Comes in the shop every day. About nineteen, and the picture of the blonde that sits on the palisades of the Rhine and charms the clam-diggers into the surf. Hair the color of straw matting, and eyes as black and shiny as the best harness blacking—think of that!

"Me? Well, it's either me or Bill Watson. She treats us both equal. Bill is all to the psychopathic about her; and me?—well, you saw me plating the road-bed of the Great Maroon Way with silver to-night. That was on account of Laura. I was spifflicated, Your Highness, and I wot not of what I wouldst.

"How? Why, old Hildebrant says to me and Bill this afternoon: 'Boys, one riddle have I for you gehabt haben. A young man who cannot riddles antworten, he is not so good by business for ein family to provide—is not that—hein?' And he hands us a riddle—conundrum, some calls it—and he chuckles interiorly and gives both of us till to-morrow morning to work out the answer to it. And he says whichever of us guesses the repartee end of it goes to his house o' Wednesday night to his daughter's birthday party. And it means Laura for whichever of us goes, for she's naturally aching for a husband, and it's either me or Bill Watson, for old Hildebrant likes us both, and wants her to marry somebody that'll carry on the business after he's stitched his last pair of traces.

"The riddle? Why, it was this: 'What kind of a hen lays the longest?' Think of that! What kind of a hen lays the longest? Ain't it like a Dutchman to risk a man's happiness on a fool proposition like that? Now, what's the use? What I don't know about hens would fill several incubators. You say you're giving imitations of the old Arab guy that gave away—libraries in Bagdad. Well, now, can you whistle up a fairy that'll solve this hen query, or not?"

When the young man ceased the Margrave arose and paced to and fro by the park bench for several minutes. Finally he sat again, and said, in grave and impressive tones:

"I must confess, sir, that during the eight years that I have spent in search of adventure and in relieving distress I have never encountered a more interesting or a more perplexing case. I fear that I have overlooked hens in my researches and observations. As to their habits, their time and manner of laying, their many varieties and cross-breedings, their span of life, their——"

"Oh, don't make an Ibsen drama of it!" interrupted the young man, flippantly. "Riddles—especially old Hildebrant's riddles—don't have to be worked out seriously. They are light themes such as Sim Ford and Harry Thurston Peck like to handle. But, somehow, I can't strike just the answer. Bill Watson may, and he may not. To-morrow will tell. Well, Your Majesty, I'm glad anyhow that you butted in and whiled the time away. I guess Mr. Al Rashid himself would have bounced back if one of his constituents had conducted him up against this riddle. I'll say good-night. Peace fo' yours, and what-you-may-call-its of Allah."

The Margrave, with a gloomy air, held out his hand.

"I cannot express my regret," he said, sadly. "Never before have I found myself unable to assist in some way. 'What kind of a hen lays the longest?' It is a baffling problem. There is a hen, I believe, called the Plymouth Rock that——"

"Cut it out," said the young man. "The Caliph trade is a mighty serious one. I don't suppose you'd even see anything funny in a preacher's defense of John D. Rockefeller. Well, good-night, Your Nibs."

From habit the Margrave began to fumble in his pockets. He drew forth a card and handed it to the young man.

"Do me the favor to accept this, anyhow," he said. "The time might come when it might be of use to you."

"Thanks!" said the young man, pocketing it carelessly. "My name is Simmons."

.   .   .   .

Shame to him who would hint that the reader's interest shall altogether pursue the Margrave August Michael von Paulsen Quigg. I am indeed astray if my hand fail in keeping the way where my peruser's heart would follow. Then let us, on the morrow, peep quickly in at the door of Hildebrant, harness maker.

Hildebrant's 200 pounds reposed on a bench, silver buckling a raw leather martingale.

Bill Watson came in first.

"Vell," said Hildebrant, shaking all over with the vile conceit of the joke-maker, "haf you guessed him? 'Vat kind of a hen lays der longest?'"

"Er—why, I think so," said Bill, rubbing a servile chin. "I think so, Mr. Hildebrant—the one that lives the longest—— Is that right?"

"Nein!" said Hildebrant, shaking his head, violently. "You haf not guessed der answer."

Bill passed on and donned a bed-tick apron and bachelorhood.

In came the young man of the Arabian Night's fiasco—pale, melancholy, hopeless.

"Vell," said Hildebrant, "haf you guessed him? 'Vat kind of a hen lays der longest?'"

Simmons regarded him with dull savagery in his eye. Should he curse this mountain of pernicious humor—curse him and die? Why should—— But there was Laura.

Dogged, speechless, he thrust his hands into his coat pockets and stood. His hand encountered the strange touch of the Margrave's card. He drew it out and looked at it, as men about to be hanged look at a crawling fly. There was written on it in Quigg's bold, round hand:

"Good for one roast chicken to bearer."

Simmons looked up with a flashing eye.

"A dead one!" said he.

"Goot!" roared Hildebrant, rocking the table with giant glee. "Dot is right! You gome at mine house at 8 o'clock to der party."

COMPLIMENTS OF THE SEASON

There are no more Christmas stories to write. Fiction is exhausted; and newspaper items, the next best, are manufactured by clever young journalists who have married early and have an engagingly pessimistic view of life. Therefore, for seasonable diversion, we are reduced to two very questionable sources—facts and philosophy. We will begin with—whichever you choose to call it.

Children are pestilential little animals with which we have to cope under a bewildering variety of conditions. Especially when childish sorrows overwhelm them are we put to our wits' ends. We exhaust our paltry store of consolation; and then beat them, sobbing, to sleep. Then we grovel in the dust of a million years, and ask God why. Thus we call out of the rat-trap. As for the children, no one understands them except old maids, hunchbacks, and shepherd dogs.

Now comes the facts in the case of the Rag-Doll, the Tatterdemalion, and the Twenty-fifth of December.

On the tenth of that month the Child of the Millionaire lost her rag-doll. There were many servants in the Millionaire's palace on the Hudson, and these ransacked the house and grounds, but without finding the lost treasure. The Child was a girl of five, and one of those perverse little beasts that often wound the sensibilities of wealthy parents by fixing their affections upon some vulgar, inexpensive toy instead of upon diamond-studded automobiles and pony phaetons. The Child grieved sorely and truly, a thing inexplicable to the Millionaire, to whom the rag-doll market was about as interesting as Bay State Gas; and to the Lady, the Child's mother, who was all form—that is, nearly all, as you shall see.

The Child cried inconsolably, and grew hollow-eyed, knock-kneed, spindling, and cory-kilverty in many other respects. The Millionaire smiled and tapped his coffers confidently. The pick of the output of the French and German toymakers was rushed by special delivery to the mansion; but Rachel refused to be comforted. She was weeping for her rag child, and was for a high protective tariff against all foreign foolishness. Then doctors with the finest bedside manners and stop-watches were called in. One by one they chattered futilely about peptomanganate of iron and sea voyages and hypophosphites until their stop-watches showed that Bill Rendered was under the wire for show or place. Then, as men, they advised that the rag-doll be found as soon as possible and restored to its mourning parent. The Child sniffed at therapeutics, chewed a thumb, and wailed for her Betsy. And all this time cablegrams were coming from Santa Claus saying that he would soon be here and enjoining us to show a true Christian spirit and let up on the poolrooms and tontine policies and platoon systems long enough to give him a welcome. Everywhere the spirit of Christmas was diffusing itself. The banks were refusing loans, the pawn-brokers had doubled their gang of helpers, people bumped your shins on the streets with red sleds, Thomas and Jeremiah bubbled before you on the bars while you waited on one foot, hollywreaths of hospitality were hung in windows of the stores, they who had 'em were getting out their furs. You hardly knew which was the best bet in balls—three, high, moth, or snow. It was no time at which to lose the rag-doll of your heart.

If Doctor Watson's investigating friend had been called in to solve this mysterious disappearance he might have observed on the Millionaire's wall a copy of "The Vampire." That would have quickly suggested, by induction, "A rag and a bone and a hank of hair." "Flip," a Scotch terrier, next to the rag-doll in the Child's heart, frisked through the halls. The hank of hair! Aha! X, the unfound quantity, represented the rag-doll. But, the bone? Well, when dogs find bones they—— Done! it were an easy and a fruitful task to examine Flip's forefeet. Look, Watson! Earth—dried earth between the toes. Of course, the dog—but Sherlock was not there. Therefore it devolves. But topography and architecture must intervene.

The Millionaire's palace occupied a lordly space. In front of it was a lawn close-mowed as a South Ireland man's face two days after a shave. At one side of it, and fronting on another street, was a pleasaunce trimmed to a leaf, and the garage and stables. The Scotch pup had ravished the rag-doll from the nursery, dragged it to a corner of the lawn, dug a hole, and buried it after the manner of careless undertakers. There you have the mystery solved, and no checks to write for the hypodermical wizard or fi'-pun notes to toss to the sergeant. Then let's get down to the heart of the thing, tiresome readers—the Christmas heart of the thing.

Fuzzy was drunk—not riotously or helplessly or loquaciously, as you or I might get, but decently, appropriately, and inoffensively, as becomes a gentleman down on his luck.

Fuzzy was a soldier of misfortune. The road, the haystack, the park bench, the kitchen door, the bitter round of eleemosynary beds-with-shower-bath-attachment, the petty pickings and ignobly garnered largesse of great cities—these formed the chapters of his history.

Fuzzy walked toward the river, down the street that bounded one side of the Millionaire's house and grounds. He saw a leg of Betsy, the lost rag-doll, protruding, like the clue to a Lilliputian murder mystery, from its untimely grave in a corner of the fence. He dragged forth the maltreated infant, tucked it under his arm, and went on his way crooning a road song of his brethren that no doll that has been brought up to the sheltered life should hear. Well for Betsy that she had no ears. And well that she had no eyes save unseeing circles of black; for the faces of Fuzzy and the Scotch terrier were those of brothers, and the heart of no rag-doll could withstand twice to become the prey of such fearsome monsters.

Though you may never knew it Grogan's saloon stands near the river and near the foot of the street down which Fuzzy traveled. In Grogan's, Christmas cheer was already rampant.

Fuzzy entered with his doll. He fancied that as a mummer at the feast of Saturn he might earn a few drops from the wassail cup.

He set Betsy on the bar and addressed her loudly and humorously, seasoning his speech with exaggerated compliments and endearments as one entertaining his lady friend. The loafers and bibbers around caught the farce of it, and roared. The bartender gave Fuzzy a drink. Oh, many of us carry rag-dolls.

"One for the lady?" suggested Fuzzy, impudently, and tucked another contribution to Art beneath his waistcoat.

He began to see possibilities in Betsy. His first-night had been a success. Visions of a vaudeville circuit about town dawned upon him.

In a group near the stove sat "Pigeon" McCarthy, Black Riley, and "One-ear" Mike, well and unfavorably known in the tough shoe-string district that blackened the left bank of the river. They passed a newspaper back and forth among themselves. The item that each solid and blunt forefinger pointed out was an advertisement headed "One Hundred Dollars Reward." To earn it one must return the rag-doll lost, strayed, or stolen from the Millionaire's mansion. It seemed that grief still ravaged, unchecked, in the bosom of the too faithful Child. Flip, the terrier, capered and shook his absurd whisker before her, powerless to distract. She wailed for her Betsy in the faces of walking, talking, mamaing, and eye-closing French Mabelles and Violettes. The advertisement was a last resort.

Black Riley came from behind the stove and approached Fuzzy in his one-sided parabolic way.

The Christmas mummer, flushed with success, had tucked Betsy under his arm, and was about to depart to the filling of impromptu dates elsewhere.

"Say, 'Bo," said Black Riley to him, "where did you cop out dat doll?"

"This doll?" asked Fuzzy, touching Betsy with his forefinger to be sure that she was the one referred to. "Why, this doll was presented to me by the Emperor of Beloochistan. I have seven hundred others in my country home in Newport. This doll——"

"Cheese the funny business," said Riley. "You swiped it or picked it up at de house on de hill where—but never mind dat. You want to take fifty cents for de rags, and take it quick. Me brother's kid at home might be wantin' to play wid it. Hey—what?"

He produced the coin.

Fuzzy laughed a gurgling, insolent, alcoholic laugh in his face. Go to the office of Sarah Bernhardt's manager and propose to him that she be released from a night's performance to entertain the Tackytown Lyceum and Literary Coterie. You will hear the duplicate of Fuzzy's laugh.

Black Riley gauged Fuzzy quickly with his blueberry eye as a wrestler does. His hand was itching to play the Roman and wrest the rag Sabine from the extemporaneous merry-andrew who was entertaining an angel unaware. But he refrained. Fuzzy was fat and solid and big. Three inches of well-nourished corporeity, defended from the winter winds by dingy linen, intervened between his vest and trousers. Countless small, circular wrinkles running around his coat-sleeves and knees guaranteed the quality of his bone and muscle. His small, blue eyes, bathed in the moisture of altruism and wooziness, looked upon you kindly, yet without abashment. He was whiskerly, whiskyly, fleshily formidable. So, Black Riley temporized.

"Wot'll you take for it, den?" he asked.

"Money," said Fuzzy, with husky firmness, "cannot buy her."

He was intoxicated with the artist's first sweet cup of attainment. To set a faded-blue, earth-stained rag-doll on a bar, to hold mimic converse with it, and to find his heart leaping with the sense of plaudits earned and his throat scorching with free libations poured in his honor—could base coin buy him from such achievements? You will perceive that Fuzzy had the temperament.

Fuzzy walked out with the gait of a trained sea-lion in search of other cafés to conquer.

Though the dusk of twilight was hardly yet apparent, lights were beginning to spangle the city like pop-corn bursting in a deep skillet. Christmas Eve, impatiently expected, was peeping over the brink of the hour. Millions had prepared for its celebration. Towns would be painted red. You, yourself, have heard the horns and dodged the capers of the Saturnalians.

"Pigeon" McCarthy, Black Riley, and "One-ear" Mike held a hasty converse outside Grogan's. They were narrow-chested, pallid striplings, not fighters in the open, but more dangerous in their ways of warfare than the most terrible of Turks. Fuzzy, in a pitched battle, could have eaten the three of them. In a go-as-you-please encounter he was already doomed.

They overtook him just as he and Betsy were entering Costigan's Casino. They deflected him, and shoved the newspaper under his nose. Fuzzy could read—and more.

"Boys," said he, "you are certainly damn true friends. Give me a week to think it over."

The soul of the real artist is quenched with difficulty.

The boys carefully pointed out to him that advertisements were soulless, and that the deficiencies of the day might not be supplied by the morrow.

"A cool hundred," said Fuzzy, thoughtfully and mushily.

"Boys," said he, "you are true friends. I'll go up and claim the reward. The show business is not what it used to be."

Night was falling more surely. The three tagged at his sides to the foot of the rise on which stood the Millionaire's house. There Fuzzy turned upon them acrimoniously.

"You are a pack of putty-faced beagle-hounds," he roared. "Go away."

They went away—a little way.

In "Pigeon" McCarthy's pocket was a section of one-inch gas-pipe eight inches long. In one end of it and in the middle of it was a lead plug. One-half of it was packed tight with solder. Black Riley carried a slung-shot, being a conventional thug. "One-ear" Mike relied upon a pair of brass knucks—an heirloom in the family.

"Why fetch and carry," said Black Riley, "when some one will do it for ye? Let him bring it out to us. Hey—what?"

"We can chuck him in the river," said "Pigeon" McCarthy, "with a stone tied to his feet."

"Youse guys make me tired," said "One-ear" Mike sadly. "Ain't progress ever appealed to none of yez? Sprinkle a little gasoline on 'im, and drop 'im on the Drive—well?"

Fuzzy entered the Millionaire's gate and zigzagged toward the softly glowing entrance of the mansion. The three goblins came up to the gate and lingered—one on each side of it, one beyond the roadway. They fingered their cold metal and leather, confident.

Fuzzy rang the door-bell, smiling foolishly and dreamily. An atavistic instinct prompted him to reach for the button of his right glove. But he wore no gloves; so his left hand dropped, embarrassed.

The particular menial whose duty it was to open doors to silks and laces shied at first sight of Fuzzy. But a second glance took in his passport, his card of admission, his surety of welcome—the lost rag-doll of the daughter of the house dangling under his arm.

Fuzzy was admitted into a great hall, dim with the glow from unseen lights. The hireling went away and returned with a maid and the Child. The doll was restored to the mourning one. She clasped her lost darling to her breast; and then, with the inordinate selfishness and candor of childhood, stamped her foot and whined hatred and fear of the odious being who had rescued her from the depths of sorrow and despair. Fuzzy wriggled himself into an ingratiatory attitude and essayed the idiotic smile and blattering small talk that is supposed to charm the budding intellect of the young. The Child bawled, and was dragged away, hugging her Betsy close.

There came the Secretary, pale, poised, polished, gliding in pumps, and worshipping pomp and ceremony. He counted out into Fuzzy's hand ten ten-dollar bills; then dropped his eye upon the door, transferred it to James, its custodian, indicated the obnoxious earner of the reward with the other, and allowed his pumps to waft him away to secretarial regions.

James gathered Fuzzy with his own commanding optic and swept him as far as the front door.

When the money touched Fuzzy's dingy palm his first instinct was to take to his heels; but a second thought restrained him from that blunder of etiquette. It was his; it had been given him. It—and, oh, what an elysium it opened to the gaze of his mind's eye! He had tumbled to the foot of the ladder; he was hungry, homeless, friendless, ragged, cold, drifting; and he held in his hand the key to a paradise of the mud-honey that he craved. The fairy doll had waved a wand with her rag-stuffed hand; and now wherever he might go the enchanted palaces with shining foot-rests and magic red fluids in gleaming glassware would be open to him.

He followed James to the door.

He paused there as the flunky drew open the great mahogany portal for him to pass into the vestibule.

Beyond the wrought-iron gates in the dark highway Black Riley and his two pals casually strolled, fingering under their coats the inevitably fatal weapons that were to make the reward of the rag-doll theirs.

Fuzzy stopped at the Millionaire's door and bethought himself. Like little sprigs of mistletoe on a dead tree, certain living green thoughts and memories began to decorate his confused mind. He was quite drunk, mind you, and the present was beginning to fade. Those wreaths and festoons of holly with their scarlet berries making the great hall gay—where had he seen such things before? Somewhere he had known polished floors and odors of fresh flowers in winter, and—some one was singing a song in the house that he thought he had heard before. Some one singing and playing a harp. Of course, it was Christmas—Fuzzy thought he must have been pretty drunk to have overlooked that.

And then he went out of the present, and there came back to him out of some impossible, vanished, and irrevocable past a little, pure-white, transient, forgotten ghost—the spirit of *noblesse oblige*. Upon a gentleman certain things devolve.

James opened the outer door. A stream of light went down the graveled walk to the iron gate. Black Riley, McCarthy, and "One-ear" Mike saw, and carelessly drew their sinister cordon closer about the gate.

With a more imperious gesture than James's master had ever used or could ever use, Fuzzy compelled the menial to close the door. Upon a gentleman certain things devolve. Especially at the Christmas season.

"It is cust—customary," he said to James, the flustered, "when a gentleman calls on Christmas Eve to pass the compliments of the season with the lady of the house. You und'stand? I shall not move shtep till I pass compl'ments season with lady the house. Und'stand?"

There was an argument. James lost. Fuzzy raised his voice and sent it through the house unpleasantly. I did not say he was a gentleman. He was simply a tramp being visited by a ghost.

A sterling silver bell rang. James went back to answer it, leaving Fuzzy in the hall. James explained somewhere to some one.

Then he came and conducted Fuzzy to the library.

The Lady entered a moment later. She was more beautiful and holy than any picture that Fuzzy had seen. She smiled, and said something about a doll. Fuzzy didn't understand that; he remembered nothing about a doll.

A footman brought in two small glasses of sparkling wine on a stamped sterling-silver waiter. The Lady took one. The other was handed to Fuzzy.

As his fingers closed on the slender glass stem his disabilities dropped from him for one brief moment. He straightened himself; and Time, so disobliging to most of us, turned backward to accommodate Fuzzy.

Forgotten Christmas ghosts whiter than the false beards of the most opulent Kris Kringle were rising in the fumes of Grogan's whisky. What had the Millionaire's mansion to do with a long wainscoted Virginia hall, where the riders were grouped around a silver punch-bowl drinking the ancient toast of the House? And why should the patter of the cab horses' hoofs on the frozen street be in any wise related to the sound of the saddled hunters stamping under the shelter of the west veranda? And what had Fuzzy to do with any of it?

The Lady, looking at him over her glass, let her condescending smile fade away like a false dawn. Her eyes turned serious. She saw something beneath the rags and Scotch terrier whiskers that she did not understand. But it did not matter.

Fuzzy lifted his glass and smiled vacantly.

"P-pardon, lady," he said, "but couldn't leave without exchangin' comp'ments sheason with lady th' house. 'Gainst princ'ples gen'leman do sho.'"

And then he began the ancient salutation that was a tradition in the House when men wore lace ruffles and powder.

"The blessings of another year——"

Fuzzy's memory failed him. The Lady prompted:

"—Be upon this hearth."

"—The guest——" stammered Fuzzy.

"—And upon her who——" continued the Lady, with a leading smile.

"Oh, cut it out," said Fuzzy, ill-manneredly. "I can't remember. Drink hearty."

Fuzzy has shot his arrow. They drank. The Lady smiled again the smile of her caste. James enveloped Fuzzy and re-conducted him toward the front door. The harp music still softly drifted through the house.

Outside, Black Riley breathed on his cold hands and hugged the gate.

"I wonder," said the Lady to herself, musing, "who—but there were so many who came. I wonder whether memory is a curse or a blessing to them after they have fallen so low."

Fuzzy and his escort were nearly at the door. The Lady called: "James!"

James stalked back obsequiously, leaving Fuzzy waiting unsteadily, with his brief spark of the divine fire gone.

Outside, Black Riley stamped his cold feet and got a firmer grip on his section of gas-pipe.

"You will conduct this gentleman," said the Lady, "downstairs. Then tell Louis to get out the Mercedes and take him to whatever place he wishes to go."

A NIGHT IN NEW ARABIA

THE great city of Bagdad-on-the-Subway is caliph-ridden. Its palaces, bazaars, khans, and byways are thronged with Al Rashids in divers disguises, seeking diversion and victims for their unbridled generosity. You can scarcely find a poor beggar whom they are willing to let enjoy the spoils unsuccored, nor a wrecked unfortunate upon whom they will not reshower the means of fresh misfortune. You will hardly find anywhere a hungry one who has not had the opportunity to tighten his belt in gift libraries, nor a poor pundit who has not blushed at the holiday basket of celery-crowned turkey forced resoundingly through his door by the eleemosynary press.

So then, fearfully through the Harun-haunted streets creep the one-eyed calenders, the Little Hunchback and the Barber's Sixth Brother, hoping to escape the ministrations of the roving horde of caliphoid sultans.

Entertainment for many Arabian nights might be had from the histories of those who have escaped the largesse of the army of Commanders of the Faithful. Until dawn you might sit on the enchanted rug and listen to such stories as are told of the powerful genie Roc-Ef-El-Er who sent the Forty Thieves to soak up the oil plant of Ali Baba; of the good Caliph Kar-Neg-Ghe, who gave away palaces; of the Seven Voyages of Sailbad, the Sinner, who frequented wooden excursion steamers among the islands; of the Fisherman and the Bottle; of the Barmecides' Boarding house; of Aladdin's rise to wealth by means of his Wonderful Gas-meter.

But now, there being ten sultans to one Sheherazade, she is held too valuable to be in fear of the bowstring. In consequence the art of narrative languishes. And, as the lesser caliphs are hunting the happy poor and the resigned unfortunate from cover to cover in order to heap upon them strange mercies and mysterious benefits, too often comes the report from Arabian headquarters that the captive refused "to talk."

This reticence, then, in the actors who perform the sad comedies of their philanthropy-scourged world, must, in a degree, account for the shortcomings of this painfully gleaned tale, which shall be called

THE STORY OF THE CALIPH WHO ALLEVIATED HIS CONSCIENCE

Old Jacob Spraggins mixed for himself some Scotch and lithia water at his $1,200 oak sideboard. Inspiration must have resulted from its imbibition, for immediately afterward he struck the quartered oak soundly with his fist and shouted to the empty dining room:

"By the coke ovens of hell, it must be that ten thousand dollars! If I can get that squared, it'll do the trick."

Thus, by the commonest artifice of the trade, having gained your interest, the action of the story will now be suspended, leaving you grumpily to consider a sort of doll biography beginning fifteen years before.

When old Jacob was young Jacob he was a breaker boy in a Pennsylvania coal mine. I don't know what a breaker boy is; but his occupation seems to be standing by a coal dump with a wan look and a dinner-pail to have his picture taken for magazine articles. Anyhow, Jacob was one. But, instead of dying of overwork at nine, and leaving his helpless parents and brothers at the mercy of the union strikers' reserve fund, he hitched up his galluses, put a dollar or two in a side proposition now and then, and at forty-five was worth $20,000,000.

There now! it's over. Hardly had time to yawn, did you? I've seen biographies that—— But let us dissemble.

I want you to consider Jacob Spraggins, Esq., after he had arrived at the seventh stage of his career. The stages meant are, first, humble origin; second, deserved promotion; third, stockholder; fourth, capitalist; fifth, trust magnate; sixth, rich malefactor; seventh, caliph; eight, x. The eighth stage shall be left to the higher mathematics.

At fifty-five Jacob retired from active business. The income of a czar was still rolling in on him from coal, iron, real estate, oil, railroads, manufactories, and corporations, but none of it touched Jacob's hands in a raw state. It was a sterilized increment, carefully cleaned and dusted and fumigated until it arrived at its ultimate stage of untainted, spotless checks in the white fingers of his private secretary. Jacob built a three-million-dollar palace on a corner lot fronting on Nabob Avenue, city of New Bagdad, and began to feel the mantle of the late H. A. Rashid descending upon him. Eventually Jacob slipped the mantle under his collar, tied it in a neat four-in-hand, and became a licensed harrier of our Mesopotamian proletariat.

When a man's income becomes so large that the butcher actually sends him the kind of steak he orders he begins to think about his soul's salvation. Now, the various stages or classes of rich men must not be forgotten. The capitalist can tell you to a dollar the amount of his wealth. The trust magnate "estimates" it. The rich malefactor hands you a cigar and denies that he has bought the P. D. & Q. The caliph merely smiles and talks about Hammerstein and the musical lasses. There is a record of tremendous altercation at breakfast in a "Where-to-Dine-Well" tavern between a magnate and his wife, the rift within the loot being that the wife calculated their fortune at a figure $3,000,000 higher than did her future divorcé. Oh, well, I, myself, heard a similar quarrel between a man and his wife because he found fifty cents less in his pockets than he thought he had. After all, we are all human —Count Tolstoi, R. Fitzsimmons, Peter Pan, and the rest of us.

Don't lose heart because the story seems to be degenerating into a sort of moral essay for intellectual readers.

There will be dialogue and stage business pretty soon.

When Jacob first began to compare the eyes of the needle with the camels in the zoo he decided upon organized charity. He had his secretary send a check for one million to the Universal Benevolent Association of the globe.

You may have looked down through a grating in front of a decayed warehouse for a nickel that you had dropped through. But that is neither here nor there. The Association acknowledged receipt of his favor of the 24th ult. with enclosure as stated. Separated by a double line, but still mighty close to the matter under the caption of "Oddities of the Day's News" in an evening paper, Jacob Spraggins read that one "Jasper Spargyous" had "donated $100,000 to the U. B. A. of G." A camel may have a stomach for each day in the week; but I dare not venture to accord him whiskers, for fear of the Great Displeasure at Washington; but if he have whiskers, surely not one of them will seem to have been inserted in the eye of a needle by that effort of that rich man to enter the K. of H. The right is reserved to reject any and all bids; signed, S. Peter, secretary and gatekeeper.

Next, Jacob selected the best endowed college he could scare up and presented it with a $200,000 laboratory. The college did not maintain a scientific course, but it accepted the money and built an elaborate lavatory instead, which was no diversion of funds so far as Jacob ever discovered.

The faculty met and invited Jacob to come over and take his A B C degree. Before sending the invitation they smiled, cut out the C, added the proper punctuation marks, and all was well.

While walking on the campus before being capped and gowned, Jacob saw two professors strolling near by. Their voices, long adapted to indoor acoustics, undesignedly reached his ear.

"There goes the latest *chevalier d'industrie*," said one of them, "to buy a sleeping powder from us. He gets his degree to-morrow."

"*In foro conscientiœ*," said the other. "Let's 'eave 'arf a brick at 'im."

Jacob ignored the Latin, but the brick pleasantry was not too hard for him. There was no mandragora in the honorary draught of learning that he had bought. That was before the passage of the Pure Food and Drugs Act.

Jacob wearied of philanthropy on a large scale.

"If I could see folks made happier," he said to himself—"If I could see 'em myself and hear 'em express their gratitude for what I done for 'em it would make me feel better. This donatin' funds to institutions and societies is about as satisfactory as dropping money into a broken slot machine."

So Jacob followed his nose, which led him through unswept streets to the homes of the poorest.

"The very thing!" said Jacob. "I will charter two river steamboats, pack them full of these unfortunate children and—say ten thousand dolls and drums and a thousand freezers of ice cream, and give them a delightful outing up the Sound. The sea breezes on that trip ought to blow the taint off some of this money that keeps coming in faster than I can work it off my mind."

Jacob must have leaked some of his benevolent intentions, for an immense person with a bald face and a mouth that looked as if it ought to have a "Drop Letters Here" sign over it hooked a finger around him and set him in a space between a barber's pole and a stack of ash cans. Words came out of the post-office slit—smooth, husky words with gloves on 'em, but sounding as if they might turn to bare knuckles any moment.

"Say, Sport, do you know where you are at? Well, dis is Mike O'Grady's district you're buttin' into—see? Mike's got de stomach-ache privilege for every kid in dis neighborhood—see? And if dere's any picnics or red balloons to be dealt out here, Mike's money pays for 'em—see? Don't you butt in, or something'll be handed to you. Youse d—— settlers and reformers with your social ologies and your millionaire detectives have got dis district in a hell of a fix, anyhow. With your college students and professors rough-housing de sodawater stands and dem rubber-neck coaches fillin' de streets, de folks down here are 'fraid to go out of de houses. Now, you leave 'em to Mike. Dey belongs to him, and he knows how to handle 'em. Keep on your own side of de town. Are you some wiser now, uncle, or do you want to scrap wit' Mike O'Grady for de Santa Claus belt in dis district?"

Clearly, that spot in the moral vineyard was preëmpted. So Caliph Spraggins menaced no more the people in the bazaars of the East Side. To keep down his growing surplus he doubled his donations to organized charity, presented the Y. M. C. A. of his native town with a $10,000 collection of butterflies, and sent a check to the famine sufferers in China big enough to buy new emerald eyes and diamond-filled teeth for all their gods. But none of these charitable acts seemed to bring peace to the caliph's heart. He tried to get a personal note into his benefactions by tipping bellboys and waiters $10 and $20 bills. He got well snickered at and derided for that by the minions who accept with respect gratuities commensurate to the service performed. He sought out an ambitious and talented but poor young woman, and bought for her the star part in a new comedy. He might have gotten rid of $50,000 more of his cumbersome money in this philanthropy if he had not neglected to write letters to her. But she lost the suit for lack of evidence, while his capital still kept piling up, and his *optikos needleorum camelibus*—or rich man's disease—was unrelieved.

In Caliph Spraggins's $3,000,000 home lived his sister Henrietta, who used to cook for the coal miners in a twenty-five-cent eating house in Coketown, Pa., and who now would have offered John Mitchell only two fingers of her hand to shake. And his daughter Celia, nineteen, back from boarding-school and from being polished off by private instructors in the restaurant languages and those études and things.

Celia is the heroine. Lest the artist's delineation of her charms on this very page humbug your fancy, take from me her authorized description. She was a nice-looking, awkward, loud, rather bashful, brown-haired girl, with a sallow complexion, bright eyes, and a perpetual smile. She had a wholesome, Spraggins-inherited love for plain food, loose clothing, and the society of the lower classes. She had too much health and youth to feel the burden of wealth. She had a wide mouth that kept the peppermint-pepsin tablets rattling like hail from the slot-machine wherever she went, and she could whistle hornpipes. Keep this picture in mind; and let the artist do his worst.

Celia looked out of her window one day and gave her heart to the grocer's young man. The receiver thereof was at that moment engaged in conceding immortality to his horse and calling down upon him the ultimate fate of the wicked; so he did not notice the transfer. A horse should stand still when you are lifting a crate of strictly new-laid eggs out of the wagon.

Young lady reader, you would have liked that grocer's young man yourself. But you wouldn't have given him your heart, because you are saving it for a riding-master, or a shoe-manufacturer with a torpid liver, or something quiet but rich in gray tweeds at Palm Beach. Oh, I know about it. So I am glad the grocer's young man was for Celia, and not for you.

The grocer's young man was slim and straight and as confident and easy in his movements as the man in the back of the magazines who wears the new frictionless roller suspenders. He wore a gray bicycle cap on the back of his head, and his hair was straw-colored and curly, and his sunburned face looked like one that smiled a good deal when he was not preaching the doctrine of everlasting punishment to delivery-wagon horses. He slung imported A1 fancy groceries about as though they were only the stuff he delivered at boarding-houses; and when he picked up his whip, your mind instantly recalled Mr. Tackett and his air with the buttonless foils.

Tradesmen delivered their goods at a side gate at the rear of the house. The grocer's wagon came about ten in the morning. For three days Celia watched the driver when he came, finding something new each time to admire in the lofty and almost contemptuous way he had of tossing around the choicest gifts of Pomona, Ceres, and the canning factories. Then she consulted Annette.

To be explicit, Annette McCorkle, the second housemaid who deserves a paragraph herself. Annette Fletcherized large numbers of romantic novels which she obtained at a free public library branch (donated by one of the biggest caliphs in the business). She was Celia's sidekicker and chum, though Aunt Henrietta didn't know it, you may hazard a bean or two.

"Oh, canary-bird seed!" exclaimed Annette. "Ain't it a corkin' situation? You a heiress, and fallin' in love with him on sight! He's a sweet boy, too, and above his business. But he ain't suspectible like the common run of grocer's assistants. He never pays no attention to me."

"He will to me," said Celia.

"Riches——" began Annette, unsheathing the not unjustifiable feminine sting.

"Oh, you're not so beautiful," said Celia, with her wide, disarming smile. "Neither am I; but he shan't know that there's any money mixed up with my looks, such as they are. That's fair. Now, I want you to lend me one of your caps and an apron, Annette."

"Oh, marshmallows!" cried Annette. "I see. Ain't it lovely? It's just like 'Lurline, the Left-Handed; or, A Buttonhole Maker's Wrongs.' I'll bet he'll turn out to be a count."

There was a long hallway (or "passageway," as they call it in the land of the Colonels) with one side latticed, running along the rear of the house. The grocer's young man went through this to deliver his goods. One morning he passed a girl in there with shining eyes, sallow complexion, and wide, smiling mouth, wearing a maid's cap and apron. But as he was cumbered with a basket of Early Drumhead lettuce and Trophy tomatoes and three bunches of asparagus and six bottles of the most expensive Queen olives, he saw no more than that she was one of the maids.

But on his way out he came up behind her, and she was whistling "Fisher's Hornpipe" so loudly and clearly that all the piccolos in the world should have disjoined themselves and crept into their cases for shame.

The grocer's young man stopped and pushed back his cap until it hung on his collar button behind.

"That's out o' sight, Kid," said he.

"My name is Celia, if you please," said the whistler, dazzling him with a three-inch smile.

"That's all right. I'm Thomas McCleod. What part of the house do you work in?"

"I'm the—the second parlor maid."

"Do you know the 'Falling Waters'?"

"No," said Celia, "we don't know anybody. We got rich too quick—that is, Mr. Spraggins did."

"I'll make you acquainted," said Thomas McCleod. "It's a strathspey—a first cousin to a hornpipe."

If Celia's whistling put the piccolos out of commission, Thomas McCleod's surely made the biggest flutes hunt their holes. He could actually whistle *bass*.

When he stopped Celia was ready to jump into his delivery wagon and ride with him clear to the end of the pier and on to the ferry-boat of the Charon line.

"I'll be around to-morrow at 10:15," said Thomas, "with some spinach and a case of carbonic."

"I'll practice that what-you-may-call-it," said Celia. "I can whistle a fine second."

The processes of courtship are personal, and do not belong to general literature. They should be chronicled in detail only in advertisements of iron tonics and in the secret by-laws of the Woman's Auxiliary of the Ancient Order of the Rat

Trap. But genteel writing may contain a description of certain stages of its progress without intruding upon the province of the X-ray or of park policemen.

A day came when Thomas McCleod and Celia lingered at the end of the latticed "passage."

"Sixteen a week isn't much," said Thomas, letting his cap rest on his shoulder blades.

Celia looked through the lattice-work and whistled a dead march. Shopping with Aunt Henrietta the day before, she had paid that much for a dozen handkerchiefs.

"Maybe I'll get a raise next month," said Thomas. "I'll be around to-morrow at the same time with a bag of flour and the laundry soap."

"All right," said Celia. "Annette's married cousin pays only $20 a month for a flat in the Bronx."

Never for a moment did she count on the Spraggins money. She knew Aunt Henrietta's invincible pride of caste and pa's mightiness as a Colossus of cash, and she understood that if she chose Thomas she and her grocer's young man might go whistle for their living.

Another day came, Thomas violating the dignity of Nabob Avenue with "The Devil's Dream," whistled keenly between his teeth.

"Raised to eighteen a week yesterday," he said. "Been pricing flats around Morningside. You want to start untying those apron strings and unpinning that cap, old girl."

"Oh, Tommy!" said Celia, with her broadest smile. "Won't that be enough? I got Betty to show me how to make a cottage pudding. I guess we could call it a flat pudding if we wanted to."

"And tell no lie," said Thomas.

"And I can sweep and polish and dust—of course, a parlor maid learns that. And we could whistle duets of evenings."

"The old man said he'd raise me to twenty at Christmas if Bryan couldn't think of any harder name to call a Republican than a 'postponer,'" said the grocer's young man.

"I can sew," said Celia; "and I know that you must make the gas company's man show his badge when he comes to look at the meter; and I know how to put up quince jam and window curtains."

"Bully! you're all right, Cele. Yes, I believe we can pull it off on eighteen."

As he was jumping into the wagon the second parlor maid braved discovery by running swiftly to the gate.

"And, oh, Tommy, I forgot," she called, softly, "I believe I could make your neckties."

"Forget it," said Thomas, decisively.

"And another thing," she continued. "Sliced cucumbers at night will drive away cockroaches."

"And sleep, too, you bet," said Mr. McCleod. "Yes, I believe if I have a delivery to make on the West Side this afternoon I'll look in at a furniture store I know over there."

It was just as the wagon dashed away that old Jacob Spraggins struck the sideboard with his fist and made the mysterious remark about ten thousand dollars that you perhaps remember. Which justifies the reflection that some stories, as well as life, and puppies thrown into wells, move around in circles. Painfully but briefly we must shed light on Jacob's words.

The foundation of his fortune was made when he was twenty. A poor coal-digger (ever hear of a rich one?) had saved a dollar or two and bought a small tract of land on a hillside on which he tried to raise corn. Not a nubbin. Jacob, whose nose was a divining-rod, told him there was a vein of coal beneath. He bought the land from the miner for $125 and sold it a month afterward for $10,000. Luckily the miner had enough left of his sale money to drink himself into a black coat opening in the back, as soon as he heard the news.

And so, forty years afterward, we find Jacob illuminated with the sudden thought that if he could make restitution of this sum of money to the heirs or assigns of the unlucky miner, respite and Nepenthe might be his.

And now must come swift action, for we have here some four thousand words and not a tear shed and never a pistol, joke, safe, nor bottle cracked.

Old Jacob hired a dozen private detectives to find the heirs, if any existed, of the old miner, Hugh McLeod.

Get the point? Of course I know as well as you do that Thomas is going to be the heir. I might have concealed the name; but why always hold back your mystery till the end? I say, let it come near the middle so people can stop reading there if they want to.

After the detectives had trailed false clues about three thousand dollars— I mean miles—they cornered Thomas at the grocery and got his confession that Hugh McLeod had been his grandfather, and that there were no other heirs. They arranged a meeting for him and old Jacob one morning in one of their offices.

Jacob liked the young man very much. He liked the way he looked straight at him when he talked, and the way he threw his bicycle cap over the top of a rose-colored vase on the centre-table.

There was a slight flaw in Jacob's system of restitution. He did not consider that the act, to be perfect, should include confession. So he represented himself to be the agent of the purchaser of the land who had sent him to refund the sale price for the ease of his conscience.

"Well, sir," said Thomas, "this sounds to me like an illustrated post-card from South Boston with 'We're having a good time here' written on it. I don't know the game. Is this ten thousand dollars money, or do I have to save so many coupons to get it?"

Old Jacob counted out to him twenty five-hundred-dollar bills.

That was better, he thought, than a check. Thomas put them thoughtfully into his pocket.

"Grandfather's best thanks," he said, "to the party who sends it."

Jacob talked on, asking him about his work, how he spent his leisure time, and what his ambitions were. The more he saw and heard of Thomas, the better he liked him. He had not met many young men in Bagdad so frank and wholesome.

"I would like to have you visit my house," he said. "I might help you in investing or laying out your money. I am a very wealthy man. I have a daughter about grown, and I would like for you to know her. There are not many young men I would care to have call on her."

"I'm obliged," said Thomas. "I'm not much at making calls. It's generally the side entrance for mine. And, besides, I'm engaged to a girl that has the Delaware peach crop killed in the blossom. She's a parlor maid in a house where I deliver goods. She won't be working there much longer, though. Say, don't forget to give your friend my grandfather's best regards. You'll excuse me now; my wagon's outside with a lot of green stuff that's got to be delivered. See you again, sir."

At eleven Thomas delivered some bunches of parsley and lettuce at the Spraggins mansion. Thomas was only twenty-two; so, as he came back, he took out the handful of five-hundred-dollar bills and waved them carelessly. Annette took a pair of eyes as big as creamed onions to the cook.

"I told you he was a count," she said, after relating. "He never would carry on with me."

"But you say he showed money," said the cook.

"Hundreds of thousands," said Annette. "Carried around loose in his pockets. And he never would look at me."

"It was paid to me to-day," Thomas was explaining to Celia outside. "It came from my grandfather's estate. Say, Cele, what's the use of waiting now? I'm going to quit the job to-night. Why can't we get married next week?"

"Tommy," said Celia, "I'm no parlor maid. I've been fooling you. I'm Miss Spraggins—Celia Spraggins. The newspapers say I'll be worth forty million dollars some day."

Thomas pulled his cap down straight on his head for the first time since we have known him.

"I suppose then," said he, "I suppose then you'll not be marrying me next week. But you *can* whistle."

"No," said Celia, "I'll not be marrying you next week. My father would never let me marry a grocer's clerk. But I'll marry you to-night, Tommy, if you say so."

Old Jacob Spraggins came home at 9:30 P. M., in his motor car. The make of it you will have to surmise sorrowfully; I am giving you unsubsidized fiction; had it been a street car I could have told you its voltage and the number of flat wheels it had. Jacob called for his daughter; he had bought a ruby necklace for her, and wanted to hear her say what a kind, thoughtful, dear old dad he was.

There was a brief search in the house for her, and then came Annette, glowing with the pure flame of truth and loyalty well mixed with envy and histrionics.

"Oh, sir," said she, wondering if she should kneel, "Miss Celia's just this minute running away out of the side gate with a young man to be married. I couldn't stop her, sir. They went in a cab."

"What young man?" roared old Jacob.

"A millionaire, if you please, sir—a rich nobleman in disguise. He carries his money with him, and the red peppers and the onions was only to blind us, sir. He never did seem to take to me."

Jacob rushed out in time to catch his car. The chauffeur had been delayed by trying to light a cigarette in the wind.

"Here, Gaston, or Mike, or whatever you call yourself, scoot around the corner quicker than blazes and see if you can see a cab. If you do, run it down."

There was a cab in sight a block away. Gaston, or Mike, with his eyes half shut and his mind on his cigarette, picked up the trail, neatly crowded the cab to the curb, and pocketed it.

"What t'ell you doin'?" yelled the cabman.

"Pa!" shrieked Celia.

"Grandfather's remorseful friend's agent!" said Thomas. "Wonder what's on his conscience now."

"A thousand thunders!" said Gaston, or Mike. "I have no other match."

"Young man," said old Jacob, severely, "how about that parlor maid you were engaged to?"

A couple of years afterward old Jacob went into the office of his private secretary.

"The Amalgamated Missionary Society solicits a contribution of $30,000 toward the conversion of the Koreans," said the secretary.

"Pass 'em up," said Jacob.

"The University of Plumville writes that its yearly endowment fund of $50,000 that you bestowed upon it is past due."

"Tell 'em it's been cut out."

"The Scientific Society of Clam Cove, Long Island, asks for $10,000 to buy alcohol to preserve specimens."

"Waste basket."

"The Society for Providing Healthful Recreation for Working Girls wants $20,000 from you to lay out a golf course."

"Tell 'em to see an undertaker.

"Cut 'em all out," went on Jacob. "I've quit being a good thing. I need every dollar I can scrape or save. I want you to write to the directors of every company that I'm interested in and recommend a 10 per cent. cut in salaries. And say—I noticed half a cake of soap lying in a corner of the hall as I came in. I want you to speak to the scrubwoman about waste. I've got no money to throw away. And say—we've got vinegar pretty well in hand, haven't we?"

"The Globe Spice & Seasons Company," said the secretary, "controls the market at present."

"Raise vinegar two cents a gallon. Notify all our branches."

Suddenly Jacob Spraggins's plump red face relaxed into a pulpy grin. He walked over to the secretary's desk and showed a small red mark on his thick forefinger.

"Bit it," he said, "darned if he didn't, and he ain't had the tooth three weeks —Jaky McLeod, my Celia's kid. He'll be worth a hundred millions by the time he's twenty-one if I can pile it up for him."

As he was leaving, old Jacob turned at the door, and said:

"Better make that vinegar raise three cents instead of two. I'll be back in an hour and sign the letters."

The true history of the Caliph Harun Al Rashid relates that toward the end of his reign he wearied of philanthropy, and caused to be beheaded all his former favorites and companions of his "Arabian Nights" rambles. Happy are we in these days of enlightenment when the only death warrant the caliphs can serve on us is in the form of a tradesman's bill.

THE GIRL AND THE HABIT

HABIT—a tendency or aptitude acquired by custom or frequent repetition.

THE critics have assailed every source of inspiration save one. To that one we are driven for our moral theme. When we levied upon the masters of old they gleefully dug up the parallels to our columns. When we strove to set forth real life they reproached us for trying to imitate Henry George, George Washington Irving, Washington Irving, and Irving Bacheller. We wrote of the West and the East, and they accused us of both Jesse and Henry James. We wrote from our heart—and they said something about a disordered liver. We took a text from Matthew or—er—yes, Deuteronomy, but the preachers were hammering away at the inspiration idea before we could get into type. So, driven to the wall, we go for our subject-matter to the reliable, old, moral, unassailable vade mecum—the unabridged dictionary.

Miss Merriam was cashier at Hinkle's. Hinkle's is one of the big downtown restaurants. It is in what the papers call the "financial district." Each day from 12 o'clock to 2 Hinkle's was full of hungry customers—messenger boys, stenographers, brokers, owners of mining stock, promoters, inventors with patents pending—and also people with money.

The cashiership at Hinkle's was no sinecure. Hinkle egged and toasted and griddle-caked and coffeed a good many customers; and he lunched (as good a word as "dined") many more. It might be said that Hinkle's breakfast crowd was a contingent, but his luncheon patronage amounted to a horde.

Miss Merriam sat at a stool at her desk inclosed on three sides by a strong, high fencing of woven brass wire. Through an arched opening at the bottom you thrust your waiter's check and the money, while your heart went pit-a-pat.

For Miss Merriam was lovely and capable. She could take 45 cents out of a $2 bill and refuse an offer of marriage before you could—— Next!—lost your chance—please don't shove. She could keep cool and collected while she collected your check, give you the correct change, win your heart, indicate the toothpick stand, and rate you to a quarter of a cent better than Bradstreet could to a thousand in less time than it takes to pepper an egg with one of Hinkle's casters.

There is an old and dignified allusion to the "fierce light that beats upon a throne." The light that beats upon the young lady cashier's cage is also something fierce. The other fellow is responsible for the slang.

Every male patron of Hinkle's from the A. D. T. boys up to the curbstone brokers, adored Miss Merriam. When they paid their checks they wooed her with every wile known to Cupid's art. Between the meshes of the brass railing went smiles, winks, compliments, tender vows, invitations to dinner, sighs, languishing looks, and merry banter that was wafted pointedly back by the gifted Miss Merriam.

There is no coign of vantage more effective than the position of young lady cashier. She sits there, easily queen of the court of commerce; she is duchess of dollars and devoirs, countess of compliments and coin, leading lady of love and luncheon. You take from her a smile and a Canadian dime, and you go your way uncomplaining. You count the cheery word or two that she tosses you as misers count their treasures; and you pocket the change for a five uncomputed. Perhaps the brass-bound inaccessibility multiplies her charms—anyhow, she is a shirt-waisted angel, immaculate, trim, manicured, seductive, bright-eyed, ready, alert—Psyche, Circe, and Ate in one, separating you from your circulating medium after your sirloin medium.

The young men who broke bread at Hinkle's never settled with the cashier without an exchange of badinage and open compliment. Many of them went to greater lengths and dropped promissory hints of theatre tickets and chocolates. The older men spoke plainly of orange blossoms, generally withering the tentative petals by after-allusions to Harlem flats. One broker, who had been squeezed by copper, proposed to Miss Merriam more regularly than he ate.

During a brisk luncheon hour Miss Merriam's conversation, while she took money for checks, would run something like this:

"Good morning, Mr. Haskins—sir?—it's natural, thank you—don't be quite so fresh . . . Hello, Johnny—ten, fifteen, twenty—chase along now or they'll take the letters off your cap . . . Beg pardon—count it again, please—Oh, don't mention it . . . Vaudeville?—thanks; not on your moving picture—I was to see Carter in Hedda Gabler on Wednesday night with Mr. Simmons . . . 'Scuse me, I thought that was a quarter . . . Twenty-five and seventy-five's a dollar —got that ham-and-cabbage habit yet. I see, Billy . . . Who are you addressing? —say—you'll get all that's coming to you in a minute . . . Oh, fudge! Mr. Bassett—you're always fooling—no—? Well, maybe I'll marry you some day —three, four, and sixty-five is five . . . Kindly keep them remarks to yourself, if you please . . . Ten cents?—'scuse me; the check calls for seventy—well, maybe it is a one instead of a seven . . . Oh, do you like it that way, Mr. Saunders?—some prefer a pomp; but they say this Cleo de Merody does suit refined features . . . and ten is fifty . . . Hike along there, buddy; don't take this for a Coney Island ticket booth . . . Huh?—why, Macy's—don't it fit nice? Oh, no, it isn't too cool—these light-weight fabrics is all the go this season . . . Come again, please—that's the third time you've tried to—what?—forget it—that lead quarter is an old friend of mine . . . Sixty-five—must have had your salary raised, Mr. Wilson . . . I seen you on Sixth Avenue Tuesday afternoon, Mr. De Forest—swell?—oh, my!—who is she? . . . What's the matter with it?—why, it ain't money—what?—Columbian half?—well, this ain't South America . . . Yes, I like the mixed best—Friday?—awfully sorry, but I take my jiu-jitsu lesson on Friday—Thursday, then . . . Thanks—that's sixteen times I've been told that this morning—I guess I must be beautiful . . . Cut that out, please—who do you think I am? . . . Why, Mr. Westbrook—do you really think so?—the idea!—one—eighty and twenty's a dollar—thank you ever so much; but I don't ever go automobile riding with gentlemen—your aunt?—well, that's different—perhaps . . . Please don't get fresh—your check was fifteen cents, I believe—kindly step aside and let . . . Hello, Ben—coming around Thursday evening?—there's a gentleman going to send around a box of chocolates, and . . . forty and sixty is a dollar, and one is two . . ."

About the middle of one afternoon the dizzy goddess Vertigo—whose other name is Fortune—suddenly smote an old, wealthy, and eccentric banker while he was walking past Hinkle's, on his way to a street car. A wealthy and eccentric banker who rides in street cars is—move up, please; there are others.

A Samaritan, a Pharisee, a man and a policeman who were first on the spot lifted Banker McRamsey and carried him into Hinkle's restaurant. When the aged but indestructible banker opened his eyes he saw a beautiful vision bending over him with a pitiful, tender smile, bathing his forehead with beef tea and chafing his hands with something frappé out of a chafing-dish. Mr. McRamsey sighed, lost a vest button, gazed with deep gratitude upon his fair preserveress, and then recovered consciousness.

To the Seaside Library all who are anticipating a romance! Banker McRamsey had an aged and respected wife, and his sentiments toward Miss Merriam were fatherly. He talked to her for half an hour with interest—not the kind that went with his talks during business hours. The next day he brought Mrs. McRamsey down to see her. The old couple were childless—they had only a married daughter living in Brooklyn.

To make a short story shorter, the beautiful cashier won the hearts of the good old couple. They came to Hinkle's again and again; they invited her to their old-fashioned but splendid home in one of the East Seventies. Miss Merriam's winning loveliness, her sweet frankness and impulsive heart took them by storm. They said a hundred times that Miss Merriam reminded them so much of their lost daughter. The Brooklyn matron, née Ramsey, had the figure of Buddha and a face like the ideal of an art photographer. Miss Merriam was a combination of curves, smiles, rose leaves, pearls, satin, and hair-tonic posters. Enough of the fatuity of parents.

A month after the worthy couple became acquainted with Miss Merriam, she stood before Hinkle one afternoon and resigned her cashiership.

"They're going to adopt me," she told the bereft restaurateur. "They're funny old people, but regular dears. And the swell home they have got! Say, Hinkle, there isn't any use of talking—I'm on the à la carte to wear brown duds and goggles in a whiz wagon, or marry a duke at least. Still, I somehow hate to break out of the old cage. I've been cashiering so long I feel funny doing anything else. I'll miss joshing the fellows awfully when they line up to pay for the buckwheats and. But I can't let this chance slide. And they're awfully good, Hinkle; I know I'll have a swell time. You owe me nine-sixty-two and a half for the week. Cut out the half if it hurts you, Hinkle."

And they did. Miss Merriam became Miss Rosa McRamsey. And she graced the transition. Beauty is only skin-deep, but the nerves lie very near to the skin. Nerve—but just here will you oblige by perusing again the quotation with which this story begins?

The McRamsey's poured out money like domestic champagne to polish their adopted one. Milliners, dancing masters, and private tutors got it. Miss—er —McRamsey was grateful, loving, and tried to forget Hinkle's. To give ample credit to the adaptability of the American girl, Hinkle's did fade from her memory and speech most of the time.

Not every one will remember when the Earl of Hitesbury came to East Seventy——Street, America. He was only a fair-to-medium earl, without debts, and he created little excitement. But you will surely remember the evening when the Daughters of Benevolence held their bazaar in the W——f-A——a Hotel. For you were there, and you wrote a note to Fannie on the hotel paper, and mailed it, just to show her that—you did not? Very well; that was the evening the baby was sick, of course.

At the Bazaar the McRamseys were prominent. Miss Mer—er—McRamsey was exquisitely beautiful. The Earl of Hitesbury had been very attentive to her since he dropped in to have a look at America. At the charity bazaar the affair was supposed to be going to be pulled off to a finish. An earl is as good as a duke. Better. His standing may be lower, but his outstanding accounts are also lower.

Our ex-young-lady-cashier was assigned to a booth. She was expected to sell worthless articles to nobs and snobs at exorbitant prices. The proceeds of the bazaar were to be used for giving to the poor children of the slums a Christmas din—— Say! did you ever wonder where they get the other 364?

Miss McRamsey—beautiful, palpitating, excited, charming, radiant—fluttered about in her booth. An imitation brass network, with a little arched opening, fenced her in.

Along came the Earl, assured, delicate, accurate, admiring—admiring greatly, and faced the open wicket.

"You look chawming, you know—'pon my word you do—my deah," he said, beguilingly.

Miss McRamsey whirled around.

"Cut that joshing out," she said, cooly and briskly. "Who do you think you are talking to? Your check, please. Oh, Lordy!——"

Patrons of the bazaar became aware of a commotion and pressed around a certain booth. The Earl of Hitesbury stood near by pulling a pale blond and puzzled whisker.

"Miss McRamsey has fainted," some one explained.

PROOF OF THE PUDDING

Spring winked a vitreous optic at Editor Westbrook of the *Minerva Magazine*, and deflected him from his course. He had lunched in his favorite corner of a Broadway hotel, and was returning to his office when his feet became entangled in the lure of the vernal coquette. Which is by way of saying that he turned eastward in Twenty-sixth Street, safely forded the spring freshet of vehicles in Fifth Avenue, and meandered along the walks of budding Madison Square.

The lenient air and the settings of the little park almost formed a pastoral;

the color motif was green—the presiding shade at the creation of man and vegetation.

The callow grass between the walks was the color of verdigris, a poisonous green, reminiscent of the horde of derelict humans that had breathed upon the soil during the summer and autumn. The bursting tree buds looked strangely familiar to those who had botanized among the garnishings of the fish course of a forty-cent dinner. The sky above was of that pale aquamarine tint that hall-room poets rhyme with "true" and "Sue" and "coo." The one natural and frank color visible was the ostensible green of the newly painted benches—a shade between the color of a pickled cucumber and that of a last year's fast-black cravenette raincoat. But, to the city-bred eye of Editor Westbrook, the landscape appeared a masterpiece.

And now, whether you are of those who rush in, or of the gentle concourse that fears to tread, you must follow in a brief invasion of the editor's mind.

Editor Westbrook's spirit was contented and serene. The April number of the *Minerva* had sold its entire edition before the tenth day of the month—a newsdealer in Keokuk had written that he could have sold fifty copies more if he had had 'em. The owners of the magazine had raised his (the editor's) salary; he had just installed in his home a jewel of a recently imported cook who was afraid of policemen; and the morning papers had published in full a speech he had made at a publishers' banquet. Also there were echoing in his mind the jubilant notes of a splendid song that his charming young wife had sung to him before he left his up-town apartment that morning. She was taking enthusiastic interest in her music of late, practising early and diligently. When he had complimented her on the improvement in her voice she had fairly hugged him for joy at his praise. He felt, too, the benign, tonic medicament of the trained nurse, Spring, tripping softly adown the wards of the convalescent city.

While Editor Westbrook was sauntering between the rows of park benches (already filling with vagrants and the guardians of lawless childhood) he felt his sleeve grasped and held. Suspecting that he was about to be panhandled, he turned a cold and unprofitable face, and saw that his captor was—Dawe—Shackleford Dawe, dingy, almost ragged, the genteel scarcely visible in him through the deeper lines of the shabby.

While the editor is pulling himself out of his surprise a flashlight biography of Dawe is offered.

He was a fiction writer and one of Westbrook's old acquaintances. At one time they might have called each other old friends. Dawe had some money in those days, and lived in a decent apartment house near Westbrook's. The two families often went to theatres and dinners together. Mrs. Dawe and Mrs. Westbrook became "dearest" friends. Then one day a little tentacle of the octopus, just to amuse itself, ingurgitated Dawe's capital, and he moved to the Gramercy Park neighborhood where one, for a few groats per week, may sit upon one's trunk under eight-branched chandeliers and opposite Carrara marble mantels and watch the mice play upon the floor. Dawe thought to live by writing fiction. Now and then he sold a story. He submitted many to Westbrook. The *Minerva* printed one or two of them; the rest were returned. Westbrook sent a careful and conscientious personal letter with each rejected manuscript, pointing out in detail his reasons for considering it unavailable. Editor Westbrook had his own clear conception of what constituted good fiction. So had Dawe. Mrs. Dawe was mainly concerned about the constituents of the scanty dishes of food that she managed to scrape together. One day Dawe had been spouting to her about the excellencies of certain French writers. At dinner they sat down to a dish that a hungry schoolboy could have encompassed at a gulp. Dawe commented.

"It's Maupassant hash," said Mrs. Dawe. "It may not be art, but I do wish you would do a five-course Marion Crawford serial with an Ella Wheeler Wilcox sonnet for dessert. I'm hungry."

As far as this from success was Shackleford Dawe when he plucked Editor Westbrook's sleeve in Madison Square. That was the first time the editor had seen Dawe in several months.

"Why, Shack, is this you?" said Westbrook, somewhat awkwardly, for the form of his phrase seemed to touch upon the other's changed appearance.

"Sit down for a minute," said Dawe, tugging at his sleeve. "This is my office. I can't come to yours, looking as I do. Oh, sit down—you won't be disgraced. Those half-plucked birds on the other benches will take you for a swell porch-climber. They won't know you are only an editor."

"Smoke, Shack?" said Editor Westbrook, sinking cautiously upon the virulent green bench. He always yielded gracefully when he did yield.

Dawe snapped at the cigar as a kingfisher darts at a sunperch, or a girl pecks at a chocolate cream.

"I have just——" began the editor.

"Oh, I know; don't finish," said Dawe. "Give me a match. You have just ten minutes to spare. How did you manage to get past my office-boy and invade my sanctum? There he goes now, throwing his club at a dog that couldn't read the 'Keep off the Grass' signs."

"How goes the writing?" asked the editor.

"Look at me," said Dawe, "for your answer. Now don't put on that embarrassed, friendly-but-honest look and ask me why I don't get a job as a wine agent or a cab driver. I'm in the fight to a finish. I know I can write good fiction and I'll force you fellows to admit it yet. I'll make you change the spelling of 'regrets' to 'c-h-e-q-u-e' before I'm done with you."

Editor Westbrook gazed through his noseglasses with a sweetly sorrowful, omniscient, sympathetic, skeptical expression—the copyrighted expression of the editor beleaguered by the unavailable contributor.

"Have you read the last story I sent you—'The Alarum of the Soul'?" asked Dawe.

"Carefully. I hesitated over that story, Shack, really I did. It had some good points. I was writing you a letter to send with it when it goes back to you. I regret——"

"Never mind the regrets," said Dawe, grimly.

"There's neither salve nor sting in 'em any more. What I want to know is *why*. Come, now; out with the good points first."

"The story," said Westbrook, deliberately, after a suppressed sigh, "is written around an almost original plot. Characterization—the best you have done. Construction—almost as good, except for a few weak joints which might be strengthened by a few changes and touches. It was a good story, except——"

"I can write English, can't I?" interrupted Dawe.

"I have always told you," said the editor, "that you had a style."

"Then the trouble is the——"

"Same old thing," said Editor Westbrook. "You work up to your climax like an artist. And then you turn yourself into a photographer. I don't know what form of obstinate madness possesses you, Shack, but that is what you do with everything that you write. No, I will retract the comparison with the photographer. Now and then photography, in spite of its impossible perspective, manages to record a fleeting glimpse of truth. But you spoil every dénouement by those flat, drab, obliterating strokes of your brush that I have so often complained of. If you would rise to the literary pinnacle of your dramatic scenes, and paint them in the high colors that art requires, the postman would leave fewer bulky, self-addressed envelopes at your door."

"Oh, fiddles and footlights!" cried Dawe, derisively. "You've got that old sawmill drama king in your brain yet. When the man with the black mustache kidnaps golden-haired Bessie you are bound to have the mother kneel and raise her hands in the spotlight and say: 'May high heaven witness that I will rest neither night nor day till the heartless villain that has stolen me child feels the weight of a mother's vengeance!'"

Editor Westbrook conceded a smile of impervious complacency.

"I think," said he, "that in real life the woman would express herself in those words or in very similar ones."

"Not in a six hundred nights' run anywhere but on the stage," said Dawe, hotly. "I'll tell you what she'd say in real life. She'd say: 'What! Bessie led away by a strange man? Good Lord! It's one trouble after another! Get my other hat, I must hurry around to the police-station. Why wasn't somebody looking after her, I'd like to know? For God's sake, get out of my way or I'll never get ready. Not that hat—the brown one with the velvet bows. Bessie must have been crazy; she's usually shy of strangers. Is that too much powder? Lordy! How I'm upset!'

"That's the way she'd talk," continued Dawe. "People in real life don't fly into heroics and blank verse at emotional crises. They simply can't do it. If they talk at all on such occasions they draw from the same vocabulary that they use every day, and muddle up their words and ideas a little more, that's all."

"Shack," said Editor Westbrook, impressively, "did you ever pick up the mangled and lifeless form of a child from under the fender of a street car, and carry it in your arms and lay it down before the distracted mother? Did you ever do that and listen to the words of grief and despair as they flowed spontaneously from her lips?"

"I never did," said Dawe. "Did you?"

"Well, no," said Editor Westbrook, with a slight frown. "But I can well imagine what she would say."

"So can I," said Dawe.

And now the fitting time had come for Editor Westbrook to play the oracle and silence his opinionated contributor. It was not for an unarrived fictionist to dictate words to be uttered by the heroes and heroines of the *Minerva Magazine*, contrary to the theories of the editor thereof.

"My dear Shack," said he, "if I know anything of life I know that every sudden, deep, and tragic emotion in the human heart calls forth an opposite, concordant, conformable, and proportionate expression of feeling. How much of this inevitable accord between expression and feeling should be attributed to nature, and how much to the influence of art, it would be difficult to say. The sublimely terrible roar of the lioness that has been deprived of her cubs is dramatically as far above her customary whine and purr as the kingly and transcendent utterances of Lear are above the level of his senile vaporings. But it is also true that all men and women have what may be called a subconscious dramatic sense that is awakened by a sufficiently deep and powerful emotion—a sense unconsciously acquired from literature and the stage that prompts them to express those emotions in language befitting their importance and histrionic value."

"And in the name of the seven sacred saddle-blankets of Sagittarius, where did the stage and literature get the stunt?" asked Dawe.

"From life," answered the editor, triumphantly.

The story writer rose from the bench and gesticulated eloquently but dumbly. He was beggared for words with which to formulate adequately his dissent.

On a bench near by a frowzy loafer opened his red eyes and perceived that his moral support was due a downtrodden brother.

"Punch him one, Jack," he called hoarsely to Dawe.

"W'at's ⬤ come makin' a noise like a penny arcade for amongst gen'lemen that comes in the Square to set and think?"

Editor Westbrook looked at his watch with an affected show of leisure.

"Tell me," asked Dawe, with truculent anxiety, "what especial faults in 'The Alarum of the Soul' caused you to throw it down?"

"When Gabriel Murray," said Westbrook, "goes to his telephone and is told that his fiancée has been shot by a burglar, he says—I do not recall the exact words, but——"

"I do," said Dawe. "He says: 'Damn Central; she always cuts me off.' (And then to his friend) 'Say, Tommy, does a thirty-two bullet make a big hole? It's kind of hard luck, ain't it? Could you get me a drink from the sideboard, Tommy? No; straight; nothing on the side.'"

"And again," continued the editor, without pausing for argument, "when Berenice opens the letter from her husband informing her that he has fled with the manicure girl, her words are—let me see——"

"She says," interposed the author: "'Well, what do you think of that!'"

"Absurdly inappropriate words," said Westbrook, "presenting an anti-climax—plunging the story into hopeless bathos. Worse yet; they mirror life falsely. No human being ever uttered banal colloquialisms when confronted by sudden tragedy."

"Wrong," said Dawe, closing his unshaven jaws doggedly. "I say no man or woman ever spouts 'high-falutin' talk when they go up against a real climax. They talk naturally and a little worse."

The editor rose from the bench with his air of indulgence and inside information.

"Say, Westbrook," said Dawe, pinning him by the lapel, "would you have accepted 'The Alarum of the Soul' if you had believed that the actions and words of the characters were true to life in the parts of the story that we discussed?"

"It is very likely that I would, if I believed that way," said the editor. "But I have explained to you that I do not."

"If I could prove to you that I am right?"

"I'm sorry, Shack, but I'm afraid I haven't time to argue any further just now."

"I don't want to argue," said Dawe. "I want to demonstrate to you from life itself that my view is the correct one."

"How could you do that?" asked Westbrook, in a surprised tone.

"Listen," said the writer, seriously. "I have thought of a way. It is important to me that my theory of true-to-life fiction be recognized as correct by the magazines. I've fought for it for three years, and I'm down to my last dollar, with two months' rent due."

"I have applied the opposite of your theory," said the editor, "in selecting the fiction for the *Minerva Magazine*. The circulation has gone up from ninety thousand to——"

"Four hundred thousand," said Dawe. "Whereas it should have been boosted to a million."

"You said something to me just now about demonstrating your pet theory."

"I will. If you'll give me about half an hour of your time I'll prove to you that I am right. I'll prove it by Louise."

"Your wife!" exclaimed Westbrook. "How?"

"Well, not exactly by her, but *with* her," said Dawe. "Now, you know how devoted and loving Louise has always been. She thinks I'm the only genuine preparation on the market that bears the old doctor's signature. She's been fonder and more faithful than ever, since I've been cast for the neglected genius part."

"Indeed, she is a charming and admirable life companion," agreed the editor. "I remember what inseparable friends she and Mrs. Westbrook once were. We are both lucky chaps, Shack, to have such wives. You must bring Mrs. Dawe up some evening soon, and we'll have one of those informal chafing-dish suppers that we used to enjoy so much."

"Later," said Dawe. "When I get another shirt. And now I'll tell you my scheme. When I was about to leave home after breakfast—if you can call tea and oatmeal breakfast—Louise told me she was going to visit her aunt in Eighty-ninth Street. She said she would return home at three o'clock. She is always on time to a minute. It is now——"

Dawe glanced toward the editor's watch pocket.

"Twenty-seven minutes to three," said Westbrook, scanning his time-piece.

"We have just enough time," said Dawe. "We will go to my flat at once. I will write a note, address it to her and leave it on the table where she will see it as she enters the door. You and I will be in the dining room concealed by the portières. In that note I'll say that I have fled from her forever with an affinity who understands the needs of my artistic soul as she never did. When she reads it we will observe her actions and hear her words. Then we will know which theory is the correct one—yours or mine."

"Oh, never!" exclaimed the editor, shaking his head. "That would be inexcusably cruel.. I could not consent to have Mrs. Dawe's feelings played upon in such a manner."

"Brace up," said the writer, "I guess I think as much of her as you do. It's for her benefit as well as mine. I've got to get a market for my stories in some way. It won't hurt Louise. She's healthy and sound. Her heart goes as strong as a ninety-eight-cent watch. It'll last for only a minute, and then I'll step out and explain to her. You really owe it to me to give me the chance, Westbrook."

Editor Westbrook at length yielded, though but half willingly. And in the half of him that consented lurked the vivisectionist that is in all of us. Let him who has not used the scalpel rise and stand in his place. Pity 'tis that there are not enough rabbits and guinea-pigs to go around.

The two experimenters in Art left the Square and hurried eastward and then to the south until they arrived in the Gramercy neighborhood. Within its high iron railings the little park had put on its smart coat of vernal green, and was admiring itself in its fountain mirror. Outside the railings the hollow square of crumbling houses, shells of a bygone gentry, leaned as if in ghostly gossip over the forgotten doings of the vanished quality. *Sic transit gloria urbis.*

A block or two north of the Park, Dawe steered the editor again eastward, then, after covering a short distance, into a lofty but narrow flathouse burdened with a floridly over-decorated façade. To the fifth story they toiled, and Dawe, panting, pushed his latch-key into the door of one of the front flats.

When the door opened Editor Westbrook saw, with feelings of pity, how meanly and meagrely the rooms were furnished.

"Get a chair, if you can find one," said Dawe, "while I hunt up pen and ink. Hello, what's this? Here's a note from Louise. She must have left it there when she went out this morning."

He picked up an envelope that lay on the centre-table and tore it open. He began to read the letter that he drew out of it; and once having begun it aloud he so read it through to the end. These are the words that Editor Westbrook heard:

"DEAR SHACKLEFORD:

"By the time you get this I will be about a hundred miles away and still a-going. I've got a place in the chorus of the Occidental Opera Co., and we start on the road to-day at twelve o'clock. I didn't want to starve to death, and so I decided to make my own living. I'm not coming back. Mrs. Westbrook is going with me. She said she was tired of living with a combination phonograph, iceberg, and dictionary, and she's not coming back, either. We've been practising the songs and dances for two months on the quiet. I hope you will be successful, and get along all right! Good-bye.

　　　　　　　　　　　　　　　　　　　　　　　　　　　"LOUISE."

Dawe dropped the letter, covered his face with his trembling hands, and cried out in a deep, vibrating voice:

"*My God, why hast thou given me this cup to drink? Since she is false, then let Thy Heaven's fairest gifts, faith and love, become the jesting by-words of traitors and fiends!*"

Editor Westbrook's glasses fell to the floor. The fingers of one hand fumbled with a button on his coat as he blurted between his pale lips:

"*Say, Shack, ain't that a hell of a note? Wouldn't that knock you off your perch, Shack? Ain't it hell, now, Shack—ain't it?*"

PAST ONE AT ROONEY'S

ONLY on the lower East Side of New York do the houses of Capulet and Montagu survive. There they do not fight by the book of arithmetic. If you but bite your thumb at an upholder of your opposing house you have work cut out for your steel. On Broadway you may drag your man along a dozen blocks by his nose, and he will only bawl for the watch; but in the domain of the East Side Tybalts and Mercutios you must observe the niceties of deportment to the wink of an eyelash and to an inch of elbow room at the bar when its patrons include foes of your house and kin.

So, when Eddie McManus, known to the Capulets as Cork McManus, drifted into Dutch Mike's for a stein of beer, and came upon a bunch of Montagus making merry with the suds, he began to observe the strictest parliamentary rules. Courtesy forbade his leaving the saloon with his thirst unslaked; caution steered him to a place at the bar where the mirror supplied the cognizance of the enemy's movements that his indifferent gaze seemed to disdain; experience whispered to him that the finger of trouble would be busy among the chattering steins at Dutch Mike's that night. Close by his side drew Brick Cleary, his Mercutio, companion of his perambulations. Thus they stood, four of the Mulberry Hill Gang and two of the Dry Dock Gang, minding their P's and Q's so solicitously that Dutch Mike kept one eye on his customers and the other on an open space beneath his bar in which it was his custom to seek safety whenever the ominous politeness of the rival associations congealed into the shapes of bullets and old steel.

But we have not to do with the wars of the Mulberry Hills and the Dry Docks. We must to Rooney's where, on the most blighted dead branch of the tree of life, a little pale orchid shall bloom.

Overstained etiquette at last gave way. It is not known who first overstepped the bounds of punctilio; but the consequences were immediate. Buck Malone, of the Mulberry Hills, with a Dewey-like swiftness, got an eight-inch gun swung round from his hurricane deck. But McManus's simile must be the torpedo. He glided in under the guns and slipped a scant three inches of knife blade between the ribs of the Mulberry Hills cruiser. Meanwhile Brick Cleary, a devotee to strategy, had skimmed across the lunch counter and thrown the switch of the electrics, leaving the combat to be waged by the l'ght of gunfire alone. Dutch Mike crawled from his haven and ran into the street crying for the watch instead of for a Shakespeare to immortalize the Cimmerian shindy.

The cop came and found a prostrate, bleeding Montagu supported by three distrait and reticent followers of the House. Faithful to the ethics of the gangs, no one knew whence the hurt came. There was no Capulet to be seen. "Raus mit der interrogatories," said Buck Malone to the officer. "Sure I know who done it. I always manages to get a bird's eye view of any guy that comes up an' makes a show case for a hardware store out of me. No. I'm not telling his name. I'll settle with um meself. Wow—ouch! Easy, boys! Yes, I'll attend to his case meself. I'm not making any complaint."

At midnight McManus strolled around a pile of lumber near an East Side dock, and lingered in the vicinity of a certain water plug. Brick Cleary drifted casually to the trysting place ten minutes later. "He'll maybe not croak," said Brick; "and he won't tell, of course. But Dutch Mike did. He told the police he was tired of having his place shot up. It's unhandy just now, because Tim Corrigan's in Europe for a week's end with Kings. He'll be back on the *Kaiser Williams* next Friday. You'll have to duck out of sight till then. Tim'll fix it up all right for us when he comes back."

This goes to explain why Cork McManus went into Rooney's one night and there looked upon the bright, strange face of Romance for the first time in his precarious career.

Until Tim Corrigan should return from his jaunt among Kings and Princes and hold up his big white finger in private offices, it was unsafe for Cork in any of the old haunts of his gang. So he lay, perdu, in the high rear room of a Capulet, reading pink sporting sheets and cursing the slow paddle wheels of the *Kaiser Wilhelm.*

It was on Thursday evening that Cork's seclusion became intolerable to him. Never a hart panted for water fountain as he did for the cool touch of a drifting stein, for the firm security of a foot-rail in the hollow of his shoe, and the quiet, hearty challenges of friendship and repartee along and across the shining bars. But he must avoid the district where he was known. The cops were looking for him everywhere, for news was scarce, and the newspapers were harping again on the failure of the police to suppress the gangs. If they got him before Corrigan came back, the big white finger could not be uplifted; it would be too late then. But Corrigan would be home the next day, so he felt sure there would be small danger in a little excursion that night among the crass pleasures that represented life to him.

At half-past twelve McManus stood in a darkish cross-town street looking up at the name "Rooney's," picked out by incandescent lights against a signboard over a second-story window. He had heard of the place as a tough "hangout"; with its frequenters and its locality he was unfamiliar. Guided by certain unerring indications common to all such resorts, he ascended the stairs and entered the large room over the café.

Here were some twenty or thirty tables, at this time about half-filled with Rooney's guests. Waiters served drinks. At one end a human pianola with drugged eyes hammered the keys with automatic and furious unprecision. At merciful intervals a waiter would roar or squeak a song—songs full of "Mr.

Johnsons" and "babes" and "coons"—historical word guaranties of the genuineness of African melodies composed by red waistcoated young gentlemen, natives of the cotton fields and rice swamps of West Twenty-eighth Street.

For one brief moment you must admire Rooney with me as he receives, seats, manipulates, and chaffs his guests. He is twenty-nine. He has Wellington's nose, Dante's chin, the cheek-bones of an Iroquois, the smile of Talleyrand, Corbett's foot work, and the poise of an eleven-year-old East Side Central Park Queen of the May. He is assisted by a lieutenant known as Frank, a pudgy, easy chap, swell-dressed, who goes among the tables seeing that dull care does not intrude. Now, what is there about Rooney's to inspire all this pother? It is more than respectable by daylight; stout ladies with children and mittens and bundles and unpedigreed dogs drop up of afternoons for a stein and a chat. Even by gaslight the diversions are melancholy i' the mouth—drink and rag-time, and an occasional surprise when the waiter swabs the suds from under your sticky glass. There is an answer. Transmigration! The soul of Sir Walter Raleigh has traveled from beneath his slashed doublet to a kindred home under Rooney's visible plaid waistcoat. Rooney's is twenty years ahead of the times. Rooney has removed the embargo. Rooney has spread his cloak upon the soggy crossing of public opinion, and any Elizabeth who treads upon it is as much a queen as another. Attend to the revelation of the secret. In Rooney's ladies may smoke!

McManus sat down at a vacant table. He paid for a glass of beer that he ordered, tilted his narrow-brimmed derby to the back of his brick-dust head, twined his feet among the rungs of his chair, and heaved a sigh of contentment from the breathing spaces of his innermost soul; for this mud honey was clarified sweetness to his taste. The sham gaiety, the hectic glow of counterfeit hospitality, the self-conscious, joyless laughter, the wine-born warmth, the loud music retrieving the hour from frequent whiles of awful and corroding silence, the presence of well-clothed and frank-eyed beneficiaries of Rooney's removal of the restrictions laid upon the weed, the familiar blended odors of soaked lemon peel, flat beer, and *peau d'Espagne*—all these were manna to Cork McManus, hungry for his week in the desert of the Capulet's high rear room.

A girl, alone, entered Rooney's, glanced around with leisurely swiftness, and sat opposite McManus at his table. Her eyes rested upon him for two seconds in the look with which woman reconnoitres all men whom she for the first time confronts. In that space of time she will decide upon one of two things—either to scream for the police, or that she may marry him later on.

Her brief inspection concluded, the girl laid on the table a worn red morocco shopping bag with the inevitable top-gallant sail of frayed lace handkerchief flying from a corner of it. After she had ordered a small beer from the immediate waiter she took from her bag a box of cigarettes and lighted one with slightly exaggerated ease of manner. Then she looked again in the eyes of Cork McManus and smiled.

Instantly the doom of each was sealed.

The unqualified desire of a man to buy clothes and build fires for a woman for a whole lifetime at first sight of her is not uncommon among that humble portion of humanity that does not care for Bradstreet or coats-of-arms or Shaw's plays. Love at first sight has occurred a time or two in high life; but, as a rule, the extempore mania is to be found among unsophisticated creatures such as the dove, the blue-tailed dingbat, and the ten-dollar-a-week clerk. Poets, subscribers to all fiction magazines, and schatchens, take notice.

With the exchange of the mysterious magnetic current came to each of them the instant desire to lie, pretend, dazzle, and deceive, which is the worst thing about the hypocritical disorder known as love.

"Have another beer?" suggested Cork. In his circle the phrase was considered to be a card, accompanied by a letter of introduction and references.

"No, thanks," said the girl, raising her eyebrows and choosing her conventional words carefully. "I—merely dropped in for—a slight refreshment." The cigarette between her fingers seemed to require explanation. "My aunt is a Russian lady," she concluded, "and we often had a post perannual cigarette after dinner at home."

"Cheese it!" said Cork, whom society airs oppressed. "Your fingers are as yellow as mine."

"Say," said the girl, blazing upon him with low-voiced indignation, "what do you think I am? Say, who do you think you are talking to? What?"

She was pretty to look at. Her eyes were big, brown, intrepid, and bright. Under her flat sailor hat, planted jauntily on one side, her crinkly, tawny hair parted and was drawn back, low and massy, in a thick, pendent knot behind. The roundness of girlhood still lingered in her chin and neck, but her cheeks and fingers were thinning slightly. She looked upon the world with defiance, suspicion, and sullen wonder. Her smart short tan coat was soiled and expensive. Two inches below her black dress dropped the lowest flounce of a heliotrope silk underskirt.

"Beg your pardon," said Cork, looking at her admiringly. "I didn't mean anything. Sure, it's no harm to smoke, Maudy."

"Rooney's," said the girl, softened at once by his amends, "is the only place I know where a lady can smoke. Maybe it ain't a nice habit, but aunty let us at home. And my name ain't Maudy, if you please; it's Ruby Delamere."

"That's a swell handle," said Cork, approvingly. "Mine's McManus—Cor—er—Eddie McManus."

"Oh, you can't help that," laughed Ruby. "Don't apologize."

Cork looked seriously at the big clock on Rooney's wall. The girl's ubiquitous eyes took in the movement.

"I know it's late," she said, reaching for her bag; "but you know how you want a smoke when you want one. Ain't Rooney's all right? I never saw anything wrong here. This is twice I've been in. I work in a bookbindery on Third Avenue. A lot of us girls have been working overtime three nights a week. They won't let you smoke there, of course. I just dropped in here on my way home for a puff. Ain't it all right in here? If it ain't, I won't come any more."

"It's a little bit late for you to be out alone anywhere," said Cork. "I'm not wise to this particular joint; but anyhow you don't want to have your picture taken in it for a present to your Sunday School teacher. Have one more beer, and then say I take you home."

"But I don't know you," said the girl, with fine scrupulosity. "I don't accept the company of gentlemen I ain't acquainted with. My aunt never would allow that."

"Why," said Cork McManus, pulling his ear, "I'm the latest thing in suitings with side vents and bell skirt when it comes to escortin' a lady. You bet you'll find me all right, Ruby. And I'll give you a tip as to who I am. My governor is one of the hottest cross-buns of the Wall Street push. Morgan's cab horse casts a shoe every time the old man sticks his head out of the window. Me! Well, I'm in trainin' down the Street. The old man's goin' to put a seat on the Stock Exchange in my stockin' my next birthday. But it sounds like a lemon to me. What I like is golf and yachtin' and—er—well, say a corkin' fast ten-round bout between welter-weights with walkin' gloves."

"I guess you can walk to the door with me," said the girl, hesitatingly, but with a certain pleased flutter. "Still I never heard anything extra good about Wall Street brokers, or sports who go to prize fights, either. Ain't you got any other recommendations?"

"I think you're the swellest looker I've had my lamps on in little old New York," said Cork, impressively.

"That'll be about enough of that, now. Ain't you the kidder!" She modified her chiding words by a deep, long, beaming, smile-embellished look at her cavalier. "We'll drink our beer before we go, ha?"

A waiter sang. The tobacco smoke grew denser, drifting and rising in spirals, waves, tilted layers, cumulus clouds, cataracts, and suspended fogs like some fifth element created from the ribs of the ancient four. Laughter and chat grew louder, stimulated by Rooney's liquids and Rooney's gallant hospitality to Lady Nicotine.

One o'clock struck. Downstairs there was a sound of closing and locking doors. Frank pulled down the green shades of the front windows carefully. Rooney went below in the dark hall and stood at the front door, his cigarette cached in the hollow of his hand. Thenceforth whoever might seek admittance must present a countenance familiar to Rooney's hawk's eye—the countenance of a true sport.

Cork McManus and the bookbindery girl conversed absorbedly, with their elbows on the table. Their glasses of beer were pushed to one side, scarcely touched, with the foam on them sunken to a thin white scum. Since the stroke of one the stale pleasures of Rooney's had become renovated and spiced; not by any addition to the list of distractions, but because from that moment the sweets became stolen ones. The flattest glass of beer acquired the tang of illegality; the mildest claret punch struck a knockout blow at law and order; the harmless and genial company became outlaws, defying authority and rule. For after the stroke of one in such places as Rooney's, where neither bed nor board is to be had, drink may not be set before the thirsty of the city of the four million. It is the law.

"Say," said Cork McManus, almost covering the table with his eloquent chest and elbows, "was that dead straight about you workin' in the bookbindery and livin' at home—and just happenin' in here—and—and all that spiel you gave me?"

"Sure it was," answered the girl with spirit. "Why, what do you think? Do you suppose I'd lie to you? Go down to the shop and ask 'em. I handed it to you on the level."

"On the dead level?" said Cork. "That's the way I want it; because——"

"Because what?"

"I throw up my hands," said Cork. "You've got me goin'. You're the girl I've been lookin' for. Will you keep company with me, Ruby?"

"Would you like me to—Eddie?"

"Surest thing. But I want a straight story about—about yourself, you know. When a fellow has a steady girl—she's got to be all right, you know. She's got to be straight goods."

"You'll find I'll be straight goods, Eddie."

"Of course you will. I believe what you told me. But you can't blame me for wantin' to find out. You don't see many girls smokin' cigarettes in places like Rooney's after midnight that are like you."

The girl flushed a little and lowered her eyes. "I see that now," she said, meekly. "I didn't know how bad it looked. But I won't do it any more. And I'll go straight home every night and stay there. And I'll give up cigarettes if you say so, Eddie—I'll cut 'em out from this minute on."

Cork's air became judicial, proprietary, condemnatory, yet sympathetic. "A lady can smoke," he decided, slowly, "at times and places. Why? Because it's bein' a lady that helps her to pull it off."

"I'm going to quit. There's nothing to it," said the girl. She flicked the stub of her cigarette to the floor.

"At times and places," repeated Cork. "When I call round for you of evenin's we'll hunt out a dark bench in Stuyvesant Square and have a puff or two. But no more Rooney's at one o'clock—see?"

"Eddie, do you really like me?" The girl searched his hard but frank features eagerly with anxious eyes.

"On the dead level."

"When are you coming to see me—where I live?"

"Thursday—day after to-morrow evenin'. That suit you?"

"Fine. I'll be ready for you. Come about seven. Walk to the door with me to-night and I'll show you where I live. Don't forget, now. And don't you go to see any other girls before then, mister! I bet you will, though."

"On the dead level," said Cork, "you make 'em all look like rag-dolls to me. Honest, you do. I know when I'm suited. On the dead level, I do."

Against the front door downstairs repeated heavy blows were delivered. The loud crashes resounded in the room above. Only a triphammer or a policeman's foot could have been the author of those sounds. Rooney jumped like a bull-frog to a corner of the room, turned off the electric lights, and hurried swiftly below.

The room was left utterly dark except for the winking red glow of cigars and cigarettes. A second volley of crashes came up from the assaulted door. A little, rustling, murmuring panic moved among the besieged guests. Frank, cool, smooth, reassuring, could be seen in the rosy glow of the burning tobacco, going from table to table.

"All keep still!" was his caution. "Don't talk or make any noise! Everything will be all right. Now, don't feel the slightest alarm. We'll take care of you all."

Ruby felt across the table until Cork's firm hand closed upon hers. "Are you afraid, Eddie?" she whispered. "Are you afraid you'll get a free ride?"

"Nothin' doin' in the teeth-chatterin' line," said Cork. "I guess Rooney's been slow with his envelope. Don't your worry, girly; I'll look out for you all right."

Yet Mr. McManus's ease was only skin- and muscle-deep. With the police looking everywhere for Buck Malone's assailant, and with Corrigan still on the ocean wave, he felt that to be caught in a police raid would mean an ended career for him. And just when he had met Ruby, too! He wished he had remained in the high rear room of the true Capulet reading the pink extras.

Rooney seemed to have opened the front door below and engaged the police in conference in the dark hall. The wordless low growl of their voices came up the stairway. Frank made a wireless news station of himself at the upper door. Suddenly he closed the door, hurried to the extreme rear of the room and lighted a dim gas jet.

"This way, everybody!" he called, sharply. "In a hurry; but no noise, please!"

The guests crowded in confusion to the rear. Rooney's lieutenant swung open a panel in the wall, overlooking the back yard, revealing a ladder already placed for the escape.

"Down and out, everybody!" he commanded. "Ladies first! Less talking, please! Don't crowd! There's no danger."

Among the last, Cork and Ruby waited their turn at the open panel. Suddenly she swept him aside and clung to his arm fiercely.

"Before we go out," she whispered in his ear—"before anything happens, tell me again, Eddie, do you l— do you really like me?"

"On the dead level," said Cork, holding her close with one arm, "when it comes to you, I'm all in."

When they turned they found they were lost and in darkness. The last of the fleeing customers had descended. Halfway across the yard they bore the ladder, stumbling, giggling, hurrying to place it against an adjoining low building over the roof of which lay their only route to safety.

"We may as well sit down," said Cork, grimly. "Maybe Rooney will stand the cops off, anyhow."

They sat at a table; and their hands came together again.

A number of men then entered the dark room, feeling their way about. One of them, Rooney himself, found the switch and turned on the electric light. The other man was a cop of the old régime—a big cop, a thick cop, a fuming, abrupt cop—not a pretty cop. He went up to the pair at the table and sneered familiarly at the girl.

"What are youse doin' in here?" he asked.

"Dropped in for a smoke," said Cork, mildly.

"Had any drinks?"

"Not later than one o'clock."

"Get out—quick!" ordered the cop. Then, "Sit down!" he countermanded. He took off Cork's hat roughly and scrutinized him shrewdly. "Your name's McManus."

"Bad guess," said Cork. "It's Peterson."

"Cork McManus, or something like that," said the cop. "You put a knife into a man in Dutch Mike's saloon a week ago."

"Aw, forget it!" said Cork, who perceived a shade of doubt in the officer's tones. "You've got my mug mixed with somebody else's."

"Have I? Well, you'll come to the station with me, anyhow, and be looked over. The description fits you all right." The cop twisted his fingers under Cork's collar. "Come on!" he ordered roughly.

Cork glanced at Ruby. She was pale, and her thin nostrils quivered. Her quick eye danced from one man's face to the other as they spoke or moved. What hard luck! Cork was thinking—Corrigan on the briny; and Ruby met and lost almost within an hour! Somebody at the police station would recognize him, without a doubt. Hard luck!

But suddenly the girl sprang up and hurled herself with both arms extended against the cop. His hold on Cork's collar was loosened and he stumbled back two or three paces.

"Don't go so fast, Maguire!" she cried in shrill fury. "Keep your hands off my man! You know me, and you know I'm givin' you good advice. Don't you touch him again! He's not the guy you are lookin' for—I'll stand for that."

"See here, Fanny," said the Cop, red and angry, "I'll take you, too, if you don't look out! How do you know this ain't the man I want? What are you doing in here with him?"

"How do I know?" said the girl, flaming red and white by turns. "Because I've known him a year. He's mine. Oughtn't I to know? And what am I doin' here with him? That's easy."

She stooped low and reached down somewhere into a swirl of flirted draperies, heliotrope and black. An elastic snapped, she threw on the table toward Cork a folded wad of bills. The money slowly straightened itself with little leisurely jerks.

"Take that, Jimmy, and let's go," said the girl. "I'm declarin' the usual dividends, Maguire," she said to the officer. "You had your usual five-dollar graft at the usual corner at ten."

"A lie!" said the cop, turning purple. "You go on my beat again and I'll arrest you every time I see you."

"No, you won't," said the girl. "And I'll tell you why. Witnesses saw me give you the money to-night, and last week, too. I've been getting fixed for you."

Cork put the wad of money carefully into his pocket and said: "Come on, Fanny; let's have some chop suey before we go home."

"Clear out, quick, both of you, or I'll——"

The cop's bluster trailed away into inconsequentiality.

At the corner of the street the two halted. Cork handed back the money without a word. The girl took it and slipped it slowly into her hand-bag. Her expression was the same she had worn when she entered Rooney's that night— she looked upon the world with defiance, suspicion, and sullen wonder.

"I guess I might as well say good-by here," she said, dully. "You won't want to see me again, of course. Will you—shake hands—Mr. McManus?"

"I mightn't have got wise if you hadn't give the snap away," said Cork. "Why did you do it?"

"You'd have been pinched if I hadn't. That's why. Ain't that reason enough?" Then she began to cry. "Honest, Eddie, I was goin' to be the best girl in the world. I hated to be what I am; I hated men; I was ready almost to die when I saw you. And you seemed different from everybody else. And when I found you liked me, too, why, I thought I'd make you believe I was good, and I was goin' to be good. When you asked to come to my house and see me, why, I'd have died rather than do anything wrong after that. But what's the use of talking about it? I'll say good-by, if you will, Mr. McManus."

Cork was pulling at his ear. "I knifed Malone," said he. "I was the one the cop wanted."

"Oh, that's all right," said the girl, listlessly. "It didn't make any difference about that."

"That was all hot air about Wall Street. I don't do nothin' but hang out with a tough gang on the East Side."

"That was all right, too," repeated the girl. "It didn't make any difference."

Cork straightened himself, and pulled his hat down low. "I could get a job at O'Brien's," he said aloud, but to himself.

"Good-by," said the girl.

"Come on," said Cork, taking her arm. "I know a place."

Two blocks away he turned with her up the steps of a red brick house facing a little park.

"What house is this?" she asked, drawing back. "Why are you going in there?"

A street lamp shone brightly in front. There was a brass nameplate at one side of the closed front doors. Cork drew her firmly up the steps. "Read that," said he.

She looked at the name on the plate, and gave a cry between a moan and a scream. "No, no, no, Eddie! Oh, my God, no! I won't let you do that— not now! Let me go! You shan't do that! You can't—you mus'n't! Not after you know! No, no! Come away quick! Oh, my God! Please, Eddie, come!"

Half fainting, she reeled, and was caught in the bend of his arm. Cork's right hand felt for the electric button and pressed it long.

Another cop—how quickly they scent trouble when trouble is on the wing! —came along, saw them, and ran up the steps. "Here! What are you doing with that girl?" he called, gruffly.

"She'll be all right in a minute," said Cork. "It's a straight deal."

"Reverend Jeremiah Jones," read the cop from the door-plate with true detective cunning.

"Correct," said Cork. "On the dead level, we're goin' to get married."

THE VENTURERS

LET the story wreck itself on the spreading rails of the *Non Sequitur* Limited, if it will; first you must take your seat in the observation car *"Raison d'être"* for one moment. It is for no longer than to consider a brief essay on the subject— let us call it: "What's Around the Corner."

Omne mundus in duas partes divisum est—men who wear rubbers and pay poll-taxes, and men who discover new continents. There are no more continents to discover; but by the time overshoes are out of date and the poll has developed into an income tax, the other half will be paralleling the canals of Mars with radium railways.

Fortune, Chance, and Adventure are given as synonyms in the dictionaries. To the knowing each has a different meaning. Fortune is a prize to be won. Adventure is the road to it. Chance is what may lurk in the shadows at the roadside. The face of Fortune is radiant and alluring; that of Adventure flushed and heroic. The face of Chance is the beautiful countenance—perfect because vague and dream-born—that we see in our tea-cups at breakfast while we growl over our chops and toast.

The VENTURER is one who keeps his eye on the hedgerows and wayside groves and meadows while he travels the road to Fortune. That is the difference between him and the Adventurer. Eating the forbidden fruit was the best record ever made by a Venturer. Trying to prove that it happened is the highest work of the Adventuresome. To be either is disturbing to the cosmogony of creation. So, as bracket-sawed and city-directoried citizens, let us light our pipes, chide the children and the cat, arrange ourselves in the willow rocker under the flickering gas jet at the coolest window and scan this little tale of two modern followers of Chance.

"Did you ever hear that story about the man from the West?" asked Billinger, in the little dark-oak room to your left as you penetrate the interior of the Powhatan Club.

"Doubtless," said John Reginald Forster, rising and leaving the room.

Forster got his straw hat (straws will be in and maybe out again long before this is printed) from the check-room boy, and walked out of the air (as Hamlet says). Billinger was used to having his stories insulted and would not mind. Forster was in his favorite mood and wanted to go away from anywhere. A man, in order to get on good terms with himself, must have his opinions corroborated and his moods matched by some one else. (I had written that "somebody"; but an A. D. T. boy who once took a telegram from me pointed out that I could save money by using the compound word. This is a vice versa case.)

Forster's favorite mood was that of greatly desiring to be a follower of Chance. He was a Venturer by nature, but convention, birth, tradition, and the narrowing influences of the tribe of Manhattan had denied him full privilege. He had trodden all the main-traveled thoroughfares and many of the side roads that are supposed to relieve the tedium of life. But none had sufficed. The reason was that he knew what was to be found at the end of every street. He knew from experience and logic almost precisely to what end each digression from routine must lead. He found a depressing monotony in all the variations that the music of his sphere had grafted upon the tune of life. He had not learned that, although the world was made round, the circle has been squared, and that its true interest is to be found in "What's Around the Corner."

Forster walked abroad aimlessly from the Powhatan, trying not to tax either his judgment or his desire as to what streets he traveled. He would have been glad to lose his way if it were possible; but he had no hope of that. Adventure and Fortune move at your beck and call in the Greater City; but Chance is oriental. She is a veiled lady in a sedan chair, protected by a special traffic squad of dragomans. Crosstown, uptown, and downtown you may move without seeing her.

At the end of an hour's stroll, Forster stood on a corner of a broad, smooth avenue, looking disconsolately across it at a picturesque old hotel softly but brilliantly lit. Disconsolately, because he knew that he must dine; and dining in that hotel was no venture. It was one of his favorite caravansaries, and so silent and swift would be the service and so delicately choice the food, that he regretted the hunger that must be appeased by the "dead perfection" of the place's cuisine. Even the music there seemed to be always playing *da capo*.

Fancy came to him that he would dine at some cheap, even dubious, restaurant lower down in the city, where the erratic chefs from all countries of the world spread their national cookery for the omnivorous American. Something might happen there out of the routine—he might come upon a subject without a predicate, a road without an end, a question without an answer, a cause without an effect, a gulf stream in life's salt ocean. He had not dressed for evening; he wore a dark business suit that would not be questioned even where the waiters served the spaghetti in their shirt sleeves.

So John Reginald Forster began to search his clothes for money; because the more cheaply you dine, the more surely must you pay. All of the thirteen pockets, large and small, of his business suit he explored carefully and found not a penny. His bank book showed a balance of five figures to his credit in the Old Ironsides Trust Company, but——

Forster became aware of a man near by at his left hand who was really regarding him with some amusement. He looked like any business man of thirty or so, neatly dressed and standing in the attitude of one waiting for a street car. But there was no car line on that avenue. So his proximity and unconcealed curiosity seemed to Forster to partake of the nature of a personal intrusion. But, as he was a consistent seeker after "What's Around the Corner," instead of manifesting resentment he only turned a half-embarrassed smile upon the other's grin of amusement.

"All in?" asked the intruder, drawing nearer.

"Seems so," said Forster. "Now, I thought there was a dollar in——"

"Oh, I know," said the other man, with a laugh. "But there wasn't. I've just been through the same process myself, as I was around the corner. I found in an upper vest pocket—I don't know how they got there—exactly two pennies. You know what kind of a dinner exactly two pennies will buy!"

"You haven't dined, then?" asked Forster.

"I have not. But I would like to. Now, I'll make you a proposition. You look like a man who would take up one. Your clothes look neat and respectable. Excuse personalities. I think mine will pass the scrutiny of a head waiter, also. Suppose we go over to that hotel and dine together. We will choose from the menu like millionaires—or, if you prefer, like gentlemen in moderate circumstances dining extravagantly for once. When we have finished we will match with my two pennies to see which of us will stand the brunt of the house's displeasure and vengeance. My name is Ives. I think we have lived in the same station of life—before our money took wings."

"You're on," said Forster, joyfully.

Here was a venture at least within the borders of the mysterious country of Chance—anyhow, it promised something better than the stale infestivity of a table d'hôte.

The two were soon seated at a corner table in the hotel dining room. Ives chucked one of his pennies across the table to Forster.

"Match for which of us gives the order," he said.

Forster lost.

Ives laughed and began to name liquids and viands to the waiter with the absorbed but calm deliberation of one who was to the menu born. Forster, listening, gave his admiring approval of the order.

"I am a man," said Ives, during the oysters, "who has made a lifetime search after the to-be-continued-in-our-next. I am not like the ordinary adventurer who strikes for a coveted prize. Nor yet am I like a gambler who knows he is either to win or lose a certain set stake. What I want is to encounter an adventure to which I can predict no conclusion. It is the breath of existence to me to dare Fate in its blindest manifestations. The world has come to run so much by rote and gravitation that you can enter upon hardly any foot-path of chance in which you do not find signboards informing you of what you may expect at its end. I am like the clerk in the Circumlocution Office who always complained bitterly when any one came in to ask information. 'He wanted to *know!*' was the kick he made to his fellow-clerks. Well, I don't want to know, I don't want to reason, I don't want to guess—I want to bet my hand without seeing it."

"I understand," said Forster, delightedly. "I've often wanted the way I feel put into words. You've done it. I want to take chances on what's coming. Suppose we have a bottle of Moselle with the next course."

"Agreed," said Ives. "I'm glad you catch my idea. It will increase the animosity of the house toward the loser. If it does not weary you, we will pursue the theme. Only a few times have I met a true venturer—one who does not ask a schedule and map from Fate when he begins a journey. But, as the world becomes more civilized and wiser, the more difficult it is to come upon an adventure the end of which you cannot foresee. In the Elizabethan days you could assault the watch, wring knockers from doors, and have a jolly set-to with the blades in any convenient angle of a wall and 'get away with it.' Nowadays, if you speak disrespectfully to a policeman, all that is left to the most romantic fancy is to conjecture in what particular police station he will land you."

"I know—I know," said Forster, nodding approval.

"I returned to New York to-day," continued Ives, "from a three years' ramble around the globe. Things are not much better abroad than they are at home. The whole world seems to be overrun by conclusions. The only thing that interests me greatly is a premise. I've tried shooting big game in Africa. I know what an express rifle will do at so many yards; and when an elephant or a rhinoceros falls to the bullet, I enjoy it about as much as I did when I was kept in after school to do a sum in long division on the blackboard."

"I know—I know," said Forster.

"There might be something in aeroplanes," went on Ives, reflectively. "I've tried ballooning; but it seems to be merely a cut-and-dried affair of wind and ballast."

"Women," suggested Forster, with a smile.

"Three months ago," said Ives, "I was pottering around in one of the bazaars in Constantinople. I noticed a lady, veiled, of course, but with a pair of especially fine eyes visible, who was examining some amber and pearl ornaments at one of the booths. With her was an attendant—a big Nubian, as black as coal. After a while the attendant drew nearer to me by degrees and slipped a scrap of paper into my hand. I looked at it when I got a chance. On it was scrawled hastily in pencil: 'The arched gate of the Nightingale Garden at nine to-night.' Does that appear to you to be an interesting premise, Mr. Forster?"

"Go on," said Forster eagerly.

"I made inquiries and learned that the Nightingale Garden was the property of an old Turk—a grand vizier, or something of the sort. Of course I prospected for the arched gate and was there at nine. The same Nubian attendant opened the gate promptly on time, and I went inside and sat on a bench by a perfumed fountain with the veiled lady. We had quite an extended chat. She was Myrtle Thompson, a lady journalist, who was writing up the Turkish harems for a Chicago newspaper. She said she noticed the New York cut of my clothes in the bazaar and wondered if I couldn't work something into the metropolitan papers about it."

"I see," said Forster. "I see."

"I've canoed through Canada," said Ives, "down many rapids and over many falls. But I didn't seem to get what I wanted out of it because I knew there were only two possible outcomes—I would either go to the bottom or arrive at the sea level. I've played all games at cards; but the mathematicians have spoiled that sport by computing the percentages. I've made acquaintances on trains, I've answered advertisements, I've rung strange door-bells, I've taken every chance that presented itself; but there has always been the conventional ending— the logical conclusion to the premise."

"I know," repeated Forster. "I've felt it all. But I've had few chances to take my chance at chances. Is there any life so devoid of impossibilities as life in this city? There seems to be a myriad of opportunities for testing the undeterminable; but not one in a thousand fails to land you where you expected it to stop. I wish the subways and street cars disappointed one as seldom."

"The sun has risen," said Ives, "on the Arabian nights. There are no more caliphs. The fisherman's vase is turned to a vacuum bottle, warranted to keep any genie boiling or frozen for forty-eight hours. Life moves by rote. Science has killed adventure. There are no more opportunities such as Columbus and the man who ate the first oyster had. The only certain thing is that there is nothing uncertain."

"Well," said Forster, "my experience has been the limited one of a city man. I haven't seen the world as you have; but it seems that we view it with the same opinion. But, I tell you I am grateful for even this little venture of ours into the borders of the haphazard. There may be at least one breathless moment when the bill for the dinner is presented. Perhaps, after all, the pilgrims who traveled without scrip or purse found a keener taste to life than did the knights of the Round Table who rode abroad with a retinue and King Arthur's certified checks in the lining of their helmets. And now, if you've finished your coffee, suppose we match one of your insufficient coins for the impending blow of Fate. What have I up?"

"Heads," called Ives.

"Heads it is," said Forster, lifting his hand. "I lose. We forgot to agree upon a plan for the winner to escape. I suggest that when the waiter comes you make a remark about telephoning to a friend. I will hold the fort and the dinner check long enough for you to get your hat and be off. I thank you for an evening out of the ordinary, Mr. Ives, and wish we might have others."

"If my memory is not at fault," said Ives, laughing, "the nearest police station is in MacDougal Street. I have enjoyed the dinner, too, let me assure you."

Forster crooked his finger for the waiter. Victor, with a locomotive effort that seemed to owe more to pneumatics than to pedestrianism, glided to the table and laid the card, face downward, by the loser's cup. Forster took it up and added the figures with deliberate care. Ives leaned back comfortably in his chair.

"Excuse me," said Forster; "but I thought you were going to ring up Grimes about that theatre party for Thursday night. Had you forgotten about it?"

"Oh," said Ives, settling himself more comfortably, "I can do that later on. Get me a glass of water, waiter."

"Want to be in at the death, do you?" asked Forster.

"I hope you don't object," said Ives, pleadingly. "Never in my life have I seen a gentleman arrested in a public restaurant for swindling it out of a dinner."

"All right," said Forster, calmly. "You are entitled to see a Christian die in the arena as your *pousse-café*."

Victor came with the glass of water and remained, with the disengaged air of an inexorable collector.

Forster hesitated for fifteen seconds, and then took a pencil from his pocket and scribbled his name on the dinner check. The waiter bowed and took it away.

"The fact is," said Forster, with a little embarrassed laugh, "I doubt whether I'm what they call a 'game sport,' which means the same as a 'soldier of Fortune.' I'll have to make confession. I've been dining at this hotel two or three times a week for more than a year. I always sign my checks." And then, with a note of appreciation in his voice: "It was first-rate of you to stay to see me through with it when you knew I had no money, and that you might be scooped in, too."

"I guess I'll confess, too," said Ives, with a grin. "I own the hotel. I don't run it, of course, but I always keep a suite on the third floor for my use when I happen to stray into town."

He called a waiter and said: "Is Mr. Gilmore still behind the desk? All right. Tell him that Mr. Ives is here, and ask him to have my rooms made ready and aired."

"Another venture cut short by the inevitable," said Forster. "Is there a conundrum without an answer in the next number? But let's hold to our subject just for a minute or two, if you will. It isn't often that I meet a man who understands the flaws I pick in existence. I am engaged to be married a month from to-day."

"I reserve comment," said Ives.

"Right; I am going to add to the assertion. I am devotedly fond of the lady; but I can't decide whether to show up at the church or make a sneak for Alaska. It's the same idea, you know, that we were discussing—it does for a fellow as far as possibilities are concerned. Everybody knows the routine—you get a kiss flavored with Ceylon tea after breakfast; you go to the office; you come back home and dress for dinner—theatre twice a week—bills—moping around most evenings trying to make conversation—a little quarrel occasionally—maybe sometimes a big one, and a separation—or else a settling down into a middle-aged contentment, which is worst of all."

"I know," said Ives, nodding wisely.

"It's the dead certainty of the thing," went on Forster, "that keeps me in doubt. There'll nevermore be anything around the corner."

"Nothing after the 'Little Church,'" said Ives. "I know."

"Understand," said Forster, "that I am in no doubt as to my feelings toward the lady. I may say that I love her truly and deeply. But there is something in the current that runs through my veins that cries out against any form of the calculable. I do not know what I want; but I know that I want it. I'm talking like an idiot, I suppose, but I'm sure of what I mean."

"I understand you," said Ives, with a slow smile. "Well I think I will be going up to my rooms now. If you would dine with me here one evening soon, Mr. Forster, I'd be glad."

"Thursday?" suggested Forster.

"At seven, if it's convenient," answered Ives.

"Seven goes," assented Forster.

At half-past eight Ives got into a cab and was driven to a number in one of the correct West Seventies. His card admitted him to the reception room of an old-fashioned house into which the spirits of Fortune, Chance, and Adventure had never dared to enter. On the walls were the Whistler etchings, the steel engravings by Oh-what's his-name?, the still-life paintings of the grapes and garden truck with the watermelon seeds spilled on the table as natural as life, and the Greuze head. It was a household. There were even brass andirons. On a table was an album, half-morocco, with oxidized-silver protections on the corners of the lids. A clock on the mantel ticked loudly, with a warning click at five minutes to nine. Ives looked at it curiously, remembering a time-piece in his grandmother's home that gave such a warning.

And then down the stairs into the room came Mary Marsden. She was twenty-four, and I leave her to your imagination. But I must say this much—youth and health and simplicity and courage and greenish-violet eyes are beautiful, and she had all these. She gave Ives her hand with the sweet cordiality of an old friendship.

"You can't think what a pleasure it is," she said, "to have you drop in once every three years or so."

For half an hour they talked. I confess that I cannot repeat the conversation. You will find it in books in the circulating library. When that part of it was over, Mary said:

"And did you find what you wanted while you were abroad?"

"What I wanted?" said Ives.

"Yes. You know you were always queer. Even as a boy you wouldn't play marbles or baseball or any games with rules. You wanted to dive in water where you didn't know whether it was ten inches or ten feet deep. And when you grew up you were just the same. We've often talked about your peculiar ways."

"I suppose I am an incorrigible," said Ives. "I am opposed to the doctrine of predestination, to the rule of three, gravitation, taxes, and everything of the kind. Life has always seemed to me something like a serial story would be if they printed above each instalment a synopsis of *succeeding* chapters."

Mary laughed merrily.

"Bob Ames told us once," she said, "of a funny thing you did. It was when you and he were on a train in the South, and you got off at a town where you hadn't intended to stop just because the brakeman hung up a sign in the end of the car with the name of the next station on it."

"I remember," said Ives. "That 'next station' has been the thing I've always tried to get away from."

"I know it," said Mary. "And you've been very foolish. I hope you didn't find what you wanted not to find, or get off at the station where there wasn't any, or whatever it was you expected wouldn't happen to you during the three years you've been away."

"There was something I wanted before I went away," said Ives.

Mary looked in his eyes clearly, with a slight but perfectly sweet smile.

"There was," she said. "You wanted me. And you could have had me as you very well know."

Without replying, Ives let his gaze wander slowly about the room. There had been no change in it since last he had been in it, three years before. He vividly recalled the thoughts that had been in his mind then. The contents of that room were as fixed, in their way, as the everlasting hills. No change would ever come there except the inevitable ones wrought by time and decay. That silver-mounted album would occupy that corner of that table, those pictures would hang on the walls, those chairs be found in their same places every morn and noon and night while the household hung together. The brass andirons were monuments to order and stability. Here and there were relics of a hundred years ago which were still living mementos and would be for many years to come. One going from and coming back to that house would never need to forecast or doubt. He would find what he left, and leave what he found. The veiled lady, Chance, would never lift her hand to the knocker on the outer door.

And before him sat the lady who belonged in the room. Cool and sweet and unchangeable she was. She offered no surprises. If one should pass his life with her, though she might grow white-haired and wrinkled, he would never perceive the change. Three years he had been away from her, and she was still waiting for him as established and constant as the house itself. He was sure that she had once cared for him. It was the knowledge that she would always do so that had driven him away. Thus his thoughts ran.

"I am going to be married soon," said Mary.

On the next Thursday afternoon Forster came hurriedly to Ives's hotel.

"Old man," said he, "we'll have to put that dinner off for a year or so; I'm going abroad. The steamer sails at four. That was a great talk we had the other night, and it decided me. I'm going to knock around the world and get rid of that incubus that has been weighing on both you and me—the terrible dread of knowing what's going to happen. I've done one thing that hurts my conscience a little; but I know it's best for both of us. I've written to the lady to whom I was engaged and explained everything—told her plainly why I was leaving—that the monotony of matrimony would never do for me. Don't you think I was right?"

"It is not for me to say," answered Ives. "Go ahead and shoot elephants if you think it will bring the element of chance into your life. We've got to decide these things for ourselves. But I tell you one thing, Forster, I've found the way. I've found out the biggest hazard in the world—a game of chance that never is concluded, a venture that may end in the highest heaven or the blackest pit. It will keep a man on edge until the clods fall on his coffin, because he will never know—not until his last day, and not then will he know. It is a voyage without a rudder or compass, and you must be captain and crew and keep watch, every day and night, yourself, with no one to relieve you. I have found the VENTURE. Don't bother yourself about leaving Mary Marsden, Forster. I married her yesterday at noon."

THE DUEL

THE gods, lying beside their nectar on 'Lympus and peeping over the edge of the cliff, perceive a difference in cities. Although it would seem that to their vision towns must appear as large or small ant-hills without special characteristics, yet it is not so. Studying the habits of ants from so great a height should be but a mild diversion when coupled with the soft drink that mythology tells us is their only solace. But doubtless they have amused themselves by the comparison of villages and towns; and it will be no news to them (nor, perhaps, to many mortals), that in one particularity New York stands unique among the cities of the world. This shall be the theme of a little story addressed to the man who sits smoking with his Sabbath-slippered feet on another chair, and to the woman who snatches the paper for a moment while boiling greens or a narcotized baby leaves her free. With these I love to sit upon the ground and tell sad stories of the death of kings.

New York City is inhabited by 4,000,000 mysterious strangers; thus beating Bird Centre by three millions and half a dozen nine's. They came here in various ways and for many reasons—Hendrik Hudson, the art schools, green goods, the stork, the annual dress-makers' convention, the Pennsylvania Railroad, love of money, the stage, cheap excursion rates, brains, personal column ads., heavy walking shoes, ambition, freight trains—all these have had a hand in making up the population.

But every man Jack when he first sets foot on the stones of Manhattan has got to fight. He has got to fight at once until either he or his adversary wins. There is no resting between rounds, for there are no rounds. It is slugging from the first. It is a fight to a finish.

Your opponent is the City. You must do battle with it from the time the ferry-boat lands you on the island until either it is yours or it has conquered you. It is the same whether you have a million in your pocket or only the price of a week's lodging.

The battle is to decide whether you shall become a New Yorker or turn the rankest outlander and Philistine. You must be one or the other. You cannot remain neutral. You must be for or against—lover or enemy—bosom friend or outcast. And, oh, the city is a general in the ring. Not only by blows does it seek to subdue you. It woos you to its heart with the subtlety of a siren. It is a combination of Delilah, green Chartreuse, Beethoven, chloral, and John L. in his best days.

In other cities you may wander and abide as a stranger man as long as you please. You may live in Chicago until your hair whitens, and be a citizen and still prate of beans if Boston mothered you, and without rebuke. You may become a civic pillar in any other town but Knickerbocker's, and all the time publicly sneering at its buildings, comparing them with the architecture of Colonel Telfair's residence in Jackson, Miss., whence you hail, and you will not be set upon. But in New York you must be either a New Yorker or an invader of a modern Troy, concealed in the wooden horse of your conceited provincialism. And this dreary preamble is only to introduce to you the unimportant figures of William and Jack.

They came out of the West together, where they had been friends. They came to dig their fortunes out of the big city.

Father Knickerbocker met them at the ferry, giving one a right-hander on the nose and the other an uppercut with his left, just to let them know that the fight was on.

William was for business; Jack was for Art. Both were young and ambitious; so they countered and clinched. I think they were from Nebraska or possibly Missouri or Minnesota. Anyhow, they were out for success and scraps and scads, and they tackled the city like two Lochinvars with brass knucks and a pull at the City Hall.

Four years afterward William and Jack met at luncheon. The business man blew in like a March wind, hurled his silk hat at a waiter, dropped into a chair that was pushed under him, seized the bill of fare, and had ordered as far as cheese before the artist had time to do more than nod. After the nod a humorous smile came into his eyes.

"Billy," he said, "you're done for. The city has gobbled you up. It has taken you and cut you to its pattern and stamped you with its brand. You are so nearly like ten thousand men I have seen to-day that you couldn't be picked out from them if it weren't for your laundry marks."

"Camembert," finished William. "What's that? Oh, you've still got your hammer out for New York, have you? Well, little old Noisyville-on-the-Subway is good enough for me. It's giving me mine. And, say, I used to think the West was the whole round world—only slightly flattened at the poles whenever

Bryan ran. I used to yell myself hoarse about the free expanse and hang my hat on the horizon, and say cutting things in the grocery to little soap drummers from the East. But I'd never seen New York then, Jack. Me for it from the rathskellers up. Sixth Avenue is the West to me now. Have you heard this fellow Crusoe sing? The desert isle for him, I say, but my wife made me go. Give me May Irwin or E. S. Willard any time."

"Poor Billy," said the artist, delicately fingering a cigarette. "You remember, when we were on our way to the East how we talked about this great, wonderful city, and how we meant to conquer it and never let it get the best of us? We were going to be just the same fellows we had always been, and never let it master us. It has downed you, old man. You have changed from a maverick into a butterick."

"Don't see exactly what you are driving at," said William. "I don't wear an alpaca coat with blue trousers and a seersucker vest on dress occasions, like I used to do at home. You talk about being cut to a pattern—well, ain't the pattern all right? When you're in Rome you've got to do as the Dagoes do. This town seems to me to have other alleged metropolises skinned to flag stations. According to the railroad schedule I've got in my mind, Chicago and Saint Jo and Paris, France, are asterisk stops—which means you wave a red flag and get on every other Tuesday. I like this little suburb of Tarrytown-on-the-Hudson. There's something or somebody doing all the time. I'm clearing $8,000 a year selling automatic pumps, and I'm living like kings-up. Why, yesterday, I was introduced to John W. Gates. I took an auto ride with a wine agent's sister. I saw two men run over by a street car, and I seen Edna May play in the evening. Talk about the West, why, the other night I woke everybody up in the hotel hollering. I dreamed I was walking on a board sidewalk in Oshkosh. What have you got against this town, Jack? There's only one thing in it that I don't care for, and that's a ferryboat."

The artist gazed dreamily at the cartridge paper on the wall. "This town," said he, "is a leech. It drains the blood of the country. Whoever comes to it accepts a challenge to a duel. Abandoning the figure of the leech, it is a juggernaut, a Moloch, a monster to which the innocence, the genius, and the beauty of the land must pay tribute. Hand to hand every newcomer must struggle with the leviathan. You've lost, Billy. It shall never conquer me. I hate it as one hates sin or pestilence or—the color work in a ten-cent magazine. I despise its very vastness and power. It has the poorest millionaires, the littlest great men, the haughtiest beggars, the plainest beauties, the lowest skyscrapers, the dolefulest pleasures of any town I ever saw. It has caught you, old man, but I will never run beside its chariot wheels. It glosses itself as the Chinaman glosses his collars. Give me the domestic finish. I could stand a town ruled by wealth or one ruled by an aristocracy; but this is one controlled by its lowest ingredients. Claiming culture, it is the crudest; asseverating its pre-eminence, it is the basest; denying all outside values and virtue, it is the narrowest. Give me the pure air and the open heart of the West country. I would go back there tomorrow if I could."

"Don't you like this *filet mignon?*" said William. "Shucks, now, what's the use to knock the town! It's the greatest ever. I couldn't sell one automatic pump between Harrisburg and Tommy O'Keefe's saloon, in Sacramento, where I sell twenty here. And have you seen Sara Bernhardt in 'Andrew Mack' yet?"

"The town's got you, Billy," said Jack.

"All right," said William. "I'm going to buy a cottage on Lake Ronkonkoma next summer."

At midnight Jack raised his window and sat close to it. He caught his breath at what he saw, though he had seen and felt it a hundred times.

Far below and around lay the city like a ragged purple dream. The irregular houses were like the broken exteriors of cliffs lining deep gulches and winding streams. Some were mountainous; some lay in long, monotonous rows like the basalt precipices hanging over desert cañons. Such was the background of the wonderful, cruel, enchanting, bewildering, fatal, great city. But into this background were cut myriads of brilliant parallelograms and circles and squares through which glowed many colored lights. And out of the violet and purple depths ascended like the city's soul sounds and odors and thrills that make up the civic body. There arose the breath of gaiety unrestrained, of love, of hate, of all the passions that man can know. There below him lay all things, good or bad, that can be brought from the four corners of the earth to instruct, please, thrill, enrich, despoil, elevate, cast down, nurture, or kill. Thus the flavor of it came to him and went into his blood.

There was a knock on his door. A telegram had come for him. It came from the West, and these were its words:

Come back home and the answer will be yes.

DOLLY.

He kept the boy waiting ten minutes, and then wrote the reply: "Impossible to leave here at present." Then he sat at the window again and let the city put its cup of mandragora to his lips again.

After all, it isn't a story; but I wanted to know which one of the heroes won the battle against the city. So I went to a very learned friend and laid the case before him. What he said was: "Please don't bother me, I have Christmas presents to buy."

So there it rests; and you will have to decide for yourself.

"WHAT YOU WANT"

NIGHT had fallen on that great and beautiful city known as Bagdad-on-the-Subway. And with the night came the enchanted glamour that belongs not to Arabia alone. In different masquerade the streets, bazaars, and walled houses of the occidental city of romance were filled with the same kind of folk that so much interested our interesting old friend, the late Mr. H. A. Rashid. They wore clothes eleven hundred years nearer to the latest styles than H. A. saw in the old Bagdad; but they were about the same people underneath. With the eye of faith, you could have seen the Little Hunchback, Sinbad the Sailor, Fitbad the Tailor, the Beautiful Persian, the one-eyed Calenders, Ali Baba and Forty Robbers on every block, and the Barber and his Six Brothers, and all the old Arabian gang easily.

But let us revenue to our lamb chops.

Old Tom Crowley was a caliph. He had $42,000,000 in preferred stocks and bonds with solid gold edges. In these times, to be called a caliph, you must have money. The old-style caliph business as conducted by Mr. Rashid is not safe. If you hold up a person nowadays in a bazaar or a Turkish bath or a side street, and inquire into his private and personal affairs, the police court'll get you.

Old Tom was tired of clubs, theatres, dinners, friends, music, money, and everything. That's what makes a caliph—you must get to despise everything that money can buy, and then go out and try to want something that you can't pay for.

"I'll take a little trot around town all by myself," thought old Tom, "and try if I can stir up anything new. Let's see—it seems I've read about a king or a Cardiff giant or something in old times who used to go about with false whiskers on, making Persian dates with folks he hadn't been introduced to. That don't listen like a bad idea. I certainly have got a case of humdrumness and fatigue on for the ones I do know. That old Cardiff used to pick up cases of trouble as he ran upon 'em and give 'em gold—sequins, I think it was—and make 'em marry or got 'em good government jobs. Now, I'd like something of that sort. My money is as good as his was even if the magazines do ask me every month where I got it. Yes, I guess I'll do a little Cardiff business to-night, and see how it goes."

Plainly dressed, old Tom Crowley left his Madison Avenue palace, and walked westward and then south. As he stepped to the sidewalk, Fate, who holds the ends of the strings in the central offices of all the enchanted cities, pulled a thread, and a young man twenty blocks away looked at a wall clock, and then put on his coat.

James Turner worked in one of those little hat-cleaning establishments on Sixth Avenue in which a fire alarm rings when you push the door open, and where they clean your hat while you wait—two days. James stood all day at an electric machine that turned hats around faster than the best brands of champagne ever could have done. Overlooking your mild impertinence in feeling a curiosity about the personal appearance of a stranger, I will give you a modified description of him. Weight, 118; complexion, hair and brain, light; height, five feet six; age, about twenty-three; dressed in a $10 suit of greenish-blue serge; pockets containing two keys and sixty-three cents in change.

But do not misconjecture because this description sounds like a General Alarm that James was either lost or a dead one.

Allons!

James stood all day at his work. His feet were tender and extremely susceptible to impositions being put upon or below them. All day long they burned and smarted, causing him much suffering and inconvenience. But he was earning twelve dollars per week, which he needed to support his feet whether his feet would support him or not.

James Turner had his own conception of what happiness was, just as you and I have ours. Your delight is to gad about the world in yachts and motor-cars and to hurl ducats at wild fowl. Mine is to smoke a pipe at evenfall and watch a badger, a rattlesnake, and an owl go into their common prairie home one by one.

James Turner's idea of bliss was different; but it was his. He would go directly to his boarding-house when his day's work was done. After his supper of small steak, Bessemer potatoes, stooed (not stewed) apples and infusion of chicory, he would ascend to his fifth-floor-back hall room. Then he would take off his shoes and socks, place the soles of his burning feet against the cold bars of his iron bed, and read Clark Russell's sea yarns. The delicious relief of the cool metal applied to his smarting soles was his nightly joy. His favorite novels never palled upon him; the sea and the adventures of its navigators were his sole intellectual passion. No millionaire was ever happier than James Turner taking his ease.

When James left the hat-cleaning shop he walked three blocks out of his way home to look over the goods of a second-hand bookstall. On the sidewalk stands he had more than once picked up a paper-covered volume of Clark Russell at half price.

While he was bending with a scholarly stoop over the marked-down miscellany of cast-off literature, old Tom the caliph sauntered by. His discerning eye, made keen by twenty years' experience in the manufacture of laundry soap (save the wrappers!), recognized instantly the poor and discerning scholar, a worthy object of his caliphanous mood. He descended the two shallow stone steps that led from the sidewalk, and addressed without hesitation the object of his designed munificence. His first words were no worse than salutatory and tentative.

James Turner looked up coldly with "Sartor Resartus" in one hand and "A Mad Marriage" in the other.

"Beat it," said he. "I don't want to buy any coat hangers or town lots in Hankipoo, New Jersey. Run along, now, and play with your Teddy bear."

"Young man," said the caliph, ignoring the flippancy of the hat cleaner, "I observe that you are of a studious disposition. Learning is one of the finest things in the world. I never had any of it worth mentioning, but I admire to see it in others. I come from the West, where we imagine nothing but facts. Maybe I couldn't understand the poetry and allusions in them books you are picking over, but I like to see somebody else seem to know what they mean. Now, I'd like to make you a proposition. I'm worth about $40,000,000, and I'm getting richer every day. I made the height of it manufacturing Aunt Patty's Silver Soap. I invented the art of making it. I experimented for three years before I got just the right quantity of chloride of sodium solution and caustic potash mixture to curdle properly. And after I had taken some $9,000,000 out of the soap business I made the rest in corn and wheat futures. Now, you seem to have the literary and scholarly turn of character; and I'll tell you what I'll do. I'll pay for your education at the finest college in the world. I'll pay the expense of your rummaging over Europe and the art galleries, and finally set you up in a good business. You needn't make it soap if you have any objections. I see by your clothes and frazzled necktie that you are mighty poor; and you can't afford to turn down the offer. Well, when do you want to begin?"

The hat cleaner turned upon old Tom the eye of the Big City, which is an eye expressive of cold and justifiable suspicion, of judgment suspended as high as Haman was hung, of self-preservation, of challenge, curiosity, defiance, cynicism, and, strange as you may think it, of a childlike yearning for friendliness and fellowship that must be hidden when one walks among the "stranger bands." For in New Bagdad one, in order to survive, must suspect whosoever sits, dwells, drinks, rides, walks, or sleeps in the adjacent chair, house, booth, seat, path, or room.

"Say, Mike," said James Turner, "what's your line, anyway—shoe laces? I'm not buying anything. You better put an egg in your shoe and beat it before incidents occur to you. You can't work off any fountain pens, gold spectacles you found on the street, or trust company certificate house clearings on me. Say, do I look like I'd climbed down one of them missing fire escapes at Helicon Hall? What's vitiating you, anyhow?"

"Son," said the caliph, in his most Harunish tones, "as I said, I'm worth $40,000,000. I don't want to have it all put in my coffin when I die. I want to do some good with it. I seen you handling over these here volumes of literature, and I thought I'd keep you. I've give the missionary societies $2,000,000, but what did I get out of it? Nothing but a receipt from the secretary. Now, you are just the kind of young man I'd like to take up and see what money could make of him."

Volumes of Clark Russell were hard to find that evening at the Old Book Shop. And James Turner's smarting and aching feet did not tend to improve his temper. Humble hat cleaner though he was, he had a spirit equal to any caliph's.

"Say, you old faker," he said, angrily, "be on your way. I don't know what your game is, unless you want change for a bogus $40,000,000 bill. Well, I don't carry that much around with me. But I do carry a pretty fair left-handed punch that you'll get if you don't move on."

"You are a blamed impudent little gutter pup," said the caliph.

Then James delivered his self-praised punch; old Tom seized him by the collar and kicked him thrice; the hat cleaner rallied and clinched; two bookstands were overturned, and the books sent flying. A cop came up, took an arm of each, and marched them to the nearest station house. "Fighting and disorderly conduct," said the cop to the sergeant.

"Three hundred dollars bail," said the sergeant at once, asseveratingly and inquiringly.

"Sixty-three cents," said James Turner with a harsh laugh.

The caliph searched his pockets and collected small bills and change amounting to four dollars.

"I am worth," he said, "$40,000,000, but——"

"Lock 'em up," ordered the sergeant.

In his cell, James Turner laid himself on his cot, ruminating. "Maybe he's got the money, and maybe he ain't. But if he has or he ain't, what does he want to go 'round butting into other folks's business for? When a man knows what he wants, and can get it, it's the same as $40,000,000 to him."

Then an idea came to him that brought a pleased look to his face.

He removed his socks, drew his cot close to the door, stretched himself out luxuriously, and placed his tortured feet against the cold bars of the cell door. Something hard and bulky under the blankets of his cot gave one shoulder discomfort. He reached under, and drew out a paper-covered volume by Clark Russell called "A Sailor's Sweetheart." He gave a great sigh of contentment.

Presently to his cell came the doorman and said:

"Say, kid, that old gazabo that was pinched with you for scrapping seems to have been the goods, after all. He 'phoned to his friends, and he's out at the desk now with a roll of yellowbacks as big as a Pullman car pillow. He wants to bail you, and for you to come out and see him."

"Tell him I ain't in," said James Turner.

WAIFS AND STRAYS
PART 1
TWELVE STORIES

WAIFS AND STRAYS

PART I

TWELVE STORIES

THE RED ROSES OF TONIA

A TRESTLE burned down on the International Railroad. The south-bound from San Antonio was cut off for the next forty-eight hours. On that train was Tonia Weaver's Easter hat.

Espirition, the Mexican, who had been sent forty miles in a buckboard from the Espinosa Ranch to fetch it, returned with a shrugging shoulder and hands empty except for a cigarette. At the small station, Nopal, he had learned of the delayed train and, having no commands to wait, turned his ponies toward the ranch again.

Now, if one supposes that Easter, the Goddess of Spring, cares any more for the after-church parade on Fifth Avenue than she does for her loyal outfit of subjects that assemble at the meeting-house at Cactus, Tex., a mistake has been made. The wives and daughters of the ranchmen of the Frio country put forth Easter blossoms of new hats and gowns as faithfully as is done anywhere, and the Southwest is, for one day, a mingling of prickly pear, Paris, and paradise. And now it was Good Friday, and Tonia Weaver's Easter hat blushed unseen in the desert air of an impotent express car, beyond the burned trestle. On Saturday noon the Rogers girls, from the Shoestring Ranch, and Ella Reeves, from the Anchor-O, and Mrs. Bennet and Ida, from Green Valley, would convene at the Espinosa and pick up Tonia. With their Easter hats and frocks carefully wrapped and bundled against the dust, the fair aggregation would then merrily jog the ten miles to Cactus, where on the morrow they would array themselves, subjugate man, do homage to Easter, and cause jealous agitation among the lilies of the field.

Tonia sat on the steps of the Espinosa ranch house flicking gloomily with a quirt at a tuft of curly mesquite. She displayed a frown and a contumelious lip, and endeavored to radiate an aura of disagreeableness and tragedy.

"I hate railroads," she announced positively. "And men. Men pretend to run them. Can you give any excuse why a trestle should burn? Ida Bennett's hat is to be trimmed with violets. I shall not go one step toward Cactus without a new hat. If I were a man I would get one."

Two men listened uneasily to this disparagement of their kind. One was Wells Pearson, foreman of the Mucho Calor cattle ranch. The other was Thompson Burrows, the prosperous sheepman from the Quintana Valley. Both thought Tonia Weaver adorable, especially when she railed at railroads and menaced men. Either would have given up his epidermis to make for her an Easter hat more

1271

cheerfully than the ostrich gives up his tip or the aigrette lays down its life. Neither possessed the ingenuity to conceive a means of supplying the sad deficiency against the coming Sabbath. Pearson's deep brown face and sunburned light hair gave him the appearance of a schoolboy seized by one of youth's profound and insolvable melancholies. Tonia's plight grieved him through and through. Thompson Burrows was the more skilled and pliable. He hailed from somewhere in the East originally; and he wore neckties and shoes, and was not made dumb by woman's presence.

"The big water-hole on Sandy Creek," said Pearson, scarcely hoping to make a hit, "was filled up by that last rain."

"Oh! Was it?" said Tonia sharply. "Thank you for the information. I suppose a new hat is nothing to you, Mr. Pearson. I suppose you think a woman ought to wear an old Stetson five years without a change, as you do. If your old water-hole could have put out the fire on that trestle you might have some reason to talk about it."

"I am deeply sorry," said Burrows, warned by Pearson's fate, "that you failed to receive your hat, Miss Weaver—deeply sorry, indeed. If there was anything I could do——"

"Don't bother," interrupted Tonia, with sweet sarcasm. "If there was anything you could do, you'd be doing it, of course. There isn't."

Tonia paused. A sudden sparkle of hope had come into her eye. Her frown smoothed away. She had an inspiration.

"There's a store over at Lone Elm Crossing on the Nueces," she said, "that keeps hats. Eva Rogers got hers there. She said it was the latest style. They might have some left. But it's twenty-eight miles to Lone Elm."

The spurs of two men who hastily arose jingled; and Tonia almost smiled. The Knights, then, were not all turned to dust; nor were their rowels rust.

"Of course," said Tonia, looking thoughtfully at a white gulf cloud sailing across the cerulean dome, "nobody could ride to Lone Elm and back by the time the girls call by for me to-morrow. So, I reckon I'll have to stay at home this Easter Sunday."

And then she smiled.

"Well, Miss Tonia," said Pearson, reaching for his hat, as guileful as a sleeping babe. "I reckon I'll be trotting along back to Mucho Calor. There's some cutting out to be done on Dry Branch first thing in the morning; and me and Road Runner has got to be on hand. It's too bad your hat got sidetracked. Maybe they'll get that trestle mended yet in time for Easter."

"I must be riding, too, Miss Tonia," announced Burrows, looking at his watch. "I declare, it's nearly five o'clock! I must be out at my lambing camp in time to help pen those crazy ewes."

Tonia's suitors seemed to have been smitten with a need for haste. They bade her a ceremonious farewell, and then shook each other's hands with the elaborate and solemn courtesy of the Southwesterner.

"Hope I'll see you again soon, Mr. Pearson," said Burrows.

"Same here," said the cowman, with the serious face of one whose friend goes upon a whaling voyage. "Be gratified to see you ride over to Mucho Calor any time you strike that section of the range."

Pearson mounted Road Runner, the soundest cow-pony on the Frio, and let him pitch for a minute, as he always did on being mounted, even at the end of a hard day's travel.

"What kind of a hat was that, Miss Tonia," he called, "that you ordered from San Antone? I can't help but be sorry about that hat."

"A straw," said Tonia; "the latest shape, of course; trimmed with red roses. That's what I like—red roses."

"There's no color more becoming to your complexion and hair," said Burrows, admiringly.

"It's what I like," said Tonia. "And of all the flowers, give me red roses. Keep all the pinks and blues for yourself. But what's the use, when trestles burn and leave you without anything? It'll be a dry old Easter for me!"

Pearson took off his hat and drove Road Runner at a gallop into the chaparral east of the Espinosa ranch house.

As his stirrups rattled against the brush Burrows's long-legged sorrel struck out down the narrow stretch of open prairie to the southwest.

Tonia hung up her quirt and went into the sitting-room.

"I'm mighty sorry, daughter, that you didn't get your hat," said her mother.

"Oh, don't worry, mother," said Tonia coolly. "I'll have a new hat, all right, in time to-morrow."

When Burrows reached the end of the strip of prairie he pulled his sorrel to the right and let him pick his way daintily across a sacuista flat through which ran the ragged, dry bed of an arroyo. Then up a gravelly hill, matted with bush, the horse scrambled, and at length emerged, with a snort of satisfaction, into a stretch of high, level prairie, grassy and dotted with the lighter green of mesquites in their fresh spring foliage. Always to the right Burrows bore, until in a little while he struck the old Indian trail that followed the Nueces southward, and that passed, twenty-eight miles to the southeast, through Lone Elm.

Here Burrows urged the sorrel into a steady lope. As he settled himself in the saddle for a long ride he heard the drumming of hoofs, the hollow "thwack" of chaparral against wooden stirrups, the whoop of a Comanche; and Wells Pearson burst out of the brush at the right of the trail like a precocious yellow chick from a dark green Easter egg.

Except in the presence of awing femininity melancholy found no place in Pearson's bosom. In Tonia's presence his voice was as soft as a summer bull-frog's in his reedy nest. Now, at his gleesome yawp, rabbits, a mile away, ducked their ears, and sensitive plants closed their fearful fronds.

"Moved your lambing camp pretty far from the ranch, haven't you, neighbor?" asked Pearson, as Road Runner fell in at the sorrel's side.

"Twenty-eight miles," said Burrows, looking a little grim. Pearson's laugh woke an owl one hour too early in his water-elm on the river bank, half a mile away.

"All right for you, sheepman. I like an open game, myself. We're two locoed he-milliners hat-hunting in the wilderness. I notify you, Burr, to mind your corrals. We've got an even start; and the one that gets the headgear will stand some higher at the Espinosa."

"You've got a good pony," said Burrows, eyeing Road Runner's barrel-like body and tapering legs that moved as regularly as the pistonrod of an engine. "It's a race, of course; but you're too much of a horseman to whoop it up this soon. Say we travel together till we get to the home stretch."

"I'm your company," agreed Pearson, "and I admire your sense. If there's hats at Lone Elm, one of 'em shall set on Miss Tonia's brow to-morrow, and you won't be at the crowning. I ain't bragging, Burr, but that sorrel of yours is weak in the fore-legs."

"My horse against yours," offered Burrows, "that Miss Tonia wears the hat I take her to Cactus to-morrow."

"I'll take you up," shouted Pearson. "But oh, it's just like horse-stealing for me! I can use that sorrel for a lady's animal when—when somebody comes over to Mucho Calor, and——"

Burrows's dark face glowered so suddenly that the cowman broke off his sentence. But Pearson could never feel any pressure for long.

"What's all this Easter business about, Burr?" he asked, cheerfully. "Why do the women folks have to have new hats by the almanac or bust all cinches trying to get 'em?"

"It's a seasonable statute out of the testaments," explained Burrows. "It's ordered by the Pope or somebody. And it has something to do with the Zodiac. I don't know exactly, but I think it was invented by the Egyptians."

"It's an all-right jubilee if the heathens did put their brand on it," said Pearson; "or else Tonia wouldn't have anything to do with it. And they pull it off at church, too. Suppose there ain't but one hat in the Lone Elm store, Burr!"

"Then," said Burrows, darkly, "the best man of us'll take it back to the Espinosa."

"Oh, man!" cried Pearson, throwing his hat high and catching it again, "there's nothing like you come off the sheep ranges before. You talk good and collateral to the occasion. And if there's more than one?"

"Then," said Burrows, "we'll pick our choice and one of us'll get back first with his and the other won't."

"There never was two souls," proclaimed Pearson to the stars, "that beat more like one heart than yourn and mine. Me and you might be riding on a unicorn and thinking out of the same piece of mind."

At a little past midnight the riders loped into Lone Elm. The half a hundred houses of the big village were dark. On its only street the big wooden store stood barred and shuttered.

In a few moments the horses were fastened and Pearson was pounding cheerfully on the door of old Sutton, the storekeeper.

The barrel of a Winchester came through a cranny of a solid window shutter, followed by a short inquiry.

"Wells Pearson, of the Mucho Calor, and Burrows, of Green Valley," was the response. "We want to buy some goods in the store. Sorry to wake you up, but we must have 'em. Come out, Uncle Tommy, and get a move on you."

Uncle Tommy was slow, but at length they got him behind his counter with a kerosene lamp lit, and told him of their dire need.

"Easter hats?" said Uncle Tommy, sleepily. "Why, yes, I believe I have got just a couple left. I only ordered a dozen this spring. I'll show 'em to you."

Now, Uncle Tommy Sutton was a merchant, half asleep or awake. In dusty pasteboard boxes under the counter he had two left-over spring hats. But, alas! for his commercial probity on that early Saturday morn—they were hats of two springs ago, and a woman's eye would have detected the fraud at half a glance. But to the unintelligent gaze of the cowpuncher and the sheepman they seemed fresh from the mint of contemporaneous April.

The hats were of a variety once known as "cart-wheels." They were of stiff straw, colored red, and flat brimmed. Both were exactly alike, and trimmed lavishly around their crowns with full blown, immaculate, artificial white roses.

"That all you got, Uncle Tommy?" said Pearson. "All right. Not much choice here, Burr. Take your pick."

"They're the latest styles," lied Uncle Tommy. "You'd see 'em on Fifth Avenue, if you was in New York."

Uncle Tommy wrapped and tied each hat in two yards of dark calico for a protection. One Pearson tied carefully to his calfskin saddle-thongs; and the other became part of Road Runner's burden. They shouted thanks and farewells to Uncle Tommy, and cantered back into the night on the home stretch.

The horsemen jockeyed with all their skill. They rode more slowly on their way back. The few words they spoke were not unfriendly. Burrows had a

Winchester under his left leg slung over his saddle horn. Pearson had a six-shooter belted around him. Thus men rode in the Frio country.

At half-past seven in the morning they rode to the top of a hill and saw the Espinosa Ranch, a white spot under a dark patch of live-oaks, five miles away.

The sight roused Pearson from his drooping pose in the saddle. He knew what Road Runner could do. The sorrel was lathered, and stumbling frequently; Road Runner was pegging away like a donkey engine.

Pearson turned toward the sheepman and laughed. "Good-bye, Burr," he cried, with a wave of his hand. "It's a race now. We're on the home stretch."

He pressed Road Runner with his knees and leaned toward the Espinosa. Road Runner struck into a gallop, with tossing head and snorting nostrils, as if he were fresh from a month in pasture.

Pearson rode twenty yards and heard the unmistakable sound of a Winchester lever throwing a cartridge into the barrel. He dropped flat along his horse's back before the crack of the rifle reached his ears.

It is possible that Burrows intended only to disable the horse—he was a good enough shot to do that without endangering his rider. But as Pearson stooped the ball went through his shoulder and then through Road Runner's neck. The horse fell and the cowman pitched over his head into the hard road, and neither of them tried to move.

Burrows rode on without stopping.

In two hours Pearson opened his eyes and took inventory. He managed to get to his feet and staggered back to where Road Runner was lying.

Road Runner was lying there, but he appeared to be comfortable. Pearson examined him and found that the bullet had "creased" him. He had been knocked out temporarily, but not seriously hurt. But he was tired, and he lay there on Miss Tonia's hat and ate leaves from a mesquite branch that obligingly hung over the road.

Pearson made the horse get up. The Easter hat, loosed from the saddle-thongs, lay there in its calico wrappings, a shapeless thing from its sojourn beneath the solid carcass of Road Runner. Then Pearson fainted and fell head-long upon the poor hat again, crumpling it under his wounded shoulders.

It is hard to kill a cowpuncher. In half an hour he revived—long enough for a woman to have fainted twice and tried ice-cream for a restorer. He got up carefully and found Road Runner who was busy with the near-by grass. He tied the unfortunate hat to the saddle again, and managed to get himself there, too, after many failures.

At noon a gay and fluttering company waited in front of the Espinosa Ranch. The Rogers girls were there in their new buckboard, and the Anchor-O outfit, and the Green Valley folks—mostly women. And each and every one wore her new Easter hat, even upon the lonely prairies, for they greatly desired to shine forth and do honor to the coming festival.

At the gate stood Tonia, with undisguised tears upon her cheeks. In her hand she held Burrow's Lone Elm hat, and it was at its white roses, hated by her, that she wept. For her friends were telling her, with the ecstatic joy of true friends, that cart-wheels could not be worn, being three seasons passed into oblivion.

"Put on your old hat and come, Tonia," they urged.

"For Easter Sunday?" she answered. "I'll die first." And wept again.

The hats of the fortunate ones were curved and twisted into the style of spring's latest proclamation.

A strange being rode out of the brush among them, and there sat his horse languidly. He was stained and disfigured with the green of the grass and the limestone of rocky roads.

"Hallo, Pearson," said Daddy Weaver. "Look like you've been breaking a mustang. What's that you've got tied to your saddle—a pig in a poke?"

"Oh, come on, Tonia, if you're going," said Betty Rogers. "We mustn't wait any longer. We've saved a seat in the buckboard for you. Never mind the hat. That lovely muslin you've got on looks sweet enough with any old hat."

Pearson was slowly untying the queer thing on his saddle. Tonia looked at him with a sudden hope. Pearson was a man who created hope. He got the thing loose and handed it to her. Her quick fingers tore at the strings.

"Best I could do," said Pearson slowly. "What Road Runner and me done to it will be about all it needs."

"Oh, oh! it's just the right shape," shrieked Tonia. "And red roses! Wait till I try it on!"

She flew in to the glass, and out again, beaming, radiating, blossomed.

"Oh, don't red become her?" chanted the girls in recitative. "Hurry up, Tonia!"

Tonia stopped for a moment by the side of Road Runner.

"Thank you, thank you, Wells," she said, happily. "It's just what I wanted. Won't you come over to Cactus to-morrow and go to church with me?"

"If I can," said Pearson. He was looking curiously at her hat, and then he grinned weakly.

Tonia flew into the buckboard like a bird. The vehicles sped away for Cactus.

"What have you been doing, Pearson?" asked Daddy Weaver. "You ain't looking so well as common."

"Me?" said Pearson. "I've been painting flowers. Them roses was white when I left Lone Elm. Help me down, Daddy Weaver, for I haven't got any more paint to spare."

ROUND THE CIRCLE [1]

"Find yo' shirt all right, Sam?" asked Mrs. Webber, from her chair under the live-oak, where she was comfortably seated with a paper-back volumn for company.

"It balances perfeckly, Marthy," answered Sam, with a suspicious pleasantness in his tone. "At first I was about ter be a little reckless and kick 'cause ther buttons was all off, but since I diskiver that the button holes is all busted out, why, I wouldn't go so fur as to say the buttons is any loss to speak of."

"Oh, well," said his wife, carelessly, "put on your necktie—that'll keep it together."

Sam Webber's sheep ranch was situated in the loneliest part of the country between the Nueces and the Frio. The ranch house—a two-room box structure—was on the rise of a gently swelling hill in the midst of a wilderness of high chaparral. In front of it was a small clearing where stood the sheep pens, shearing shed, and wool house. Only a few feet back of it began the thorny jungle.

Sam was going to ride over to the Chapman ranch to see about buying some more improved merino rams. At length he came out, ready for his ride. This being a business trip of some importance, and the Chapman ranch being almost a small town in population and size, Sam had decided to "dress up" accordingly.

[1] This story is especially interesting as an early treatment (1902) of the theme afterward developed with a surer hand in The Pendulum.

The result was that he had transformed himself from a graceful, picturesque frontiersman into something much less pleasing to the sight. The tight white collar awkwardly constricted his muscular, mahogany-colored neck. The buttonless shirt bulged in stiff waves beneath his unbuttoned vest. The suit of "readymade" effectually concealed the fine lines of his straight, athletic figure. His berry-brown face was set to the melancholy dignity befitting a prisoner of state. He gave Randy, his three-year-old son, a pat on the head, and hurried out to where Mexico, his favorite saddle horse, was standing.

Marthy, leisurely rocking in her chair, fixed her place in the book with her finger, and turned her head, smiling mischievously as she noted the havoc Sam had wrought with his appearance in trying to "fix up."

"Well, ef I must say it, Sam," she drawled, "you look jest like one of them hayseeds in the picture papers, 'stead of a free and independent sheepman of the State o' Texas."

Sam climbed awkwardly into the saddle.

"You're the one ought to be 'shamed to say so," he replied hotly. " 'Stead of 'tendin' to a man's clothes you're al'ays settin' around a-readin' them billy-by-dam yaller-back novils."

"Oh, shet up and ride along," said Mrs. Webber, with a little jerk at the handles of her chair; "you al'ays fussin' 'bout my readin'. I do a-plenty; and I'll read when I wanter. I live in the bresh here like a varmint, never seein' nor hearin' nothin', and what other 'musement kin I have? Not in listenin' to you talk, for it's complain, complain, one day after another. Oh, go on, Sam, and leave me in peace."

Sam gave his pony a squeeze with his knees and "shoved" down the wagon trail that connected his ranch with the old, open Government road. It was eight o'clock, and already beginning to be very warm. He should have started three hours earlier. Chapman ranch was only eighteen miles away, but there was a road for only three miles of the distance. He had ridden over there once with one of the Half-Moon cowpunchers, and he had the direction well-defined in his mind.

Sam turned off the old Government road at the split mesquite, and struck down the arroyo of the Quintanilla. Here was a narrow stretch of smiling valley, upholstered with a rich mat of green, curly mesquite grass; and Mexico consumed those few miles quickly with his long, easy lope. Again, upon reaching Wild Duck Waterhole, must he abandon well-defined ways. He turned now to his right up a little hill, pebble-covered, upon which grew only the tenacious and thorny prickly pear and chaparral. At the summit of this he paused to take his last general view of the landscape for, from now on, he must wind through brakes and thickets of chaparral, pear, and mesquite, for the most part seeing scarcely farther than twenty yards in any direction, choosing his way by the prairie-dweller's instinct, guided only by an occasional glimpse of a far distant hilltop, a peculiarly shaped knot of trees, or the position of the sun.

Sam rode down the sloping hill and plunged into the great pear flat that lies between the Quintanilla and the Piedra.

In about two hours he discovered that he was lost. Then came the usual confusion of mind and the hurry to get somewhere. Mexico was anxious to redeem the situation, twisting with alacrity along the tortuous labyrinths of the jungle. At the moment his master's sureness of the route had failed his horse had divined the fact. There were no hills now that they could climb to obtain a view of the country. They came upon a few, but so dense and interlaced was the brush that scarcely could a rabbit penetrate the mass. They were in the great, lonely thicket of the Frio bottoms.

It was a mere nothing for a cattleman or a sheepman to be lost for a day or a night. The thing often happened. It was merely a matter of missing a meal or two and sleeping comfortably on your saddle blankets on a soft mattress of mesquite grass. But in Sam's case it was different. He had never been away from his ranch at night. Marthy was afraid of the country—afraid of Mexicans, of snakes, of panthers, even of sheep. So he had never left her alone.

It must have been about four in the afternoon when Sam's conscience awoke. He was limp and drenched, rather from anxiety than the heat or fatigue. Until now he had been hoping to strike the trail that led to the Frio crossing and the Chapman ranch. He must have crossed it at some dim part of it and ridden beyond. If so he was now something like fifty miles from home. If he could strike a ranch—a camp—any place where he could get a fresh horse and inquire the road, he would ride all night to get back to Marthy and the kid.

So, I have hinted, Sam was seized by remorse. There was a big lump in his throat as he thought of the cross words he had spoken to his wife. Surely it was hard enough for her to live in that horrible country without having to bear the burden of his abuse. He cursed himself grimly, and felt a sudden flush of shame that over-glowed the summer heat as he remembered the many times he had flouted and railed at her because she had a liking for reading fiction.

"Ther only so'ce ov amusement ther po' gal's got," said Sam aloud, with a sob, which unaccustomed sound caused Mexico to shy a bit. "A-livin' with a sore-headed kiote like me—a low-down skunk that ought to be licked to death with a saddle cinch—a-cookin' and a-washin' and a-livin' on mutton and beans and me abusin' her fur takin' a squint or two in a little book!"

He thought of Marthy as she had been when he first met her in Dogtown—smart, pretty, and saucy—before the sun had turned the roses in her cheeks brown and the silence of the chaparral had tamed her ambitions.

"Ef I ever speaks another hard word to ther little gal," muttered Sam, "or fails in the love and affection that's comin' to her in the deal, I hopes a wild-cat'll t'ar me to pieces."

He knew what he would do. He would write to Garcia & Jones, his San Antonio merchants where he bought his supplies and sold his wool, and have them send down a big box of novels and reading matter for Marthy. Things were going to be different. He wondered whether a little piano could be placed in one of the rooms of the ranch house without the family having to move out of doors.

In nowise calculated to allay his self-reproach was the thought that Marthy and Randy would have to pass the night alone. In spite of their bickerings, when night came Marthy was wont to dismiss her fears of the country, and rest her head upon Sam's strong arm with a sigh of peaceful content and dependence. And were her fears so groundless? Sam thought of roving, marauding Mexicans, of stealthy cougars that sometimes invaded the ranches, of rattlesnakes, centipedes, and a dozen possible dangers. Marthy would be frantic with fear. Randy would cry, and call for "dada" to come.

Still the interminable succession of stretches of brush, cactus, and mesquite. Hollow after hollow, slope after slope—all exactly alike—all familiar by constant repetition, and yet all strange and new. If he could only arrive *somewhere*.

The straight line is Art. Nature moves in circles. A straightforward man is more an artificial product than a diplomatist is. Men lost in the snow travel in exact circles until they sink, exhausted, as their footprints have attested. Also, travellers in philosophy and other mental processes frequently wind up at their starting-point.

It was when Sam Webber was fullest of contrition and good resolves that Mexico, with a heavy sigh, subsided from his regular, brisk trot into a slow, complacent walk. They were winding up an easy slope covered with brush ten or twelve feet high.

"I say now, Mex," demurred Sam, "this here won't do. I know you're plumb tired out, but we got ter git along. Oh, Lordy, ain't there no mo' houses in the world!" He gave Mexico a smart kick with his heels.

Mexico gave a protesting grunt as if to say: "What's the use of that, now we're so near?" He quickened his gait into a languid trot. Rounding a great clump of black chaparral he stopped short. Sam dropped the bridle reins and sat, looking into the back door of his own house, not ten yards away.

Marthy, serene and comfortable, sat in her rocking-chair before the door in the shade of the house, with her feet resting luxuriously upon the steps. Randy, who was playing with a pair of spurs on the ground, looked up for a moment at his father and went on spinning the rowels and singing a little song. Marthy turned her head lazily against the back of the chair and considered the arrivals with emotionless eyes. She held a book in her lap with her finger holding the place.

Sam shook himself queerly, like a man coming out of a dream, and slowly dismounted. He moistened his dry lips.

"I see you are still a-settin'," he said, "a-readin' of them billy-by-dam yaller-back novils."

Sam had traveled round the circle and was himself again.

THE RUBBER PLANT'S STORY

We rubber plants form the connecting link between the vegetable kingdom and the decorations of a Waldorf-Astoria scene in a Third Avenue theatre. I haven't looked up our family tree, but I believe we were raised by grafting a gum over-shoe on to a 30-cent table d'hôte stalk of asparagus. You take a white bulldog with a Bourke Cockran air of independence about him and a rubber plant and there you have the fauna and flora of a flat. What the shamrock is to Ireland the rubber plant is to the dweller in flats and furnished rooms. We get moved from one place to another so quickly that the only way we can get our picture taken is with a kinetoscope. We are the vagrant vine and the flitting fig tree. You know the proverb: "Where the rubber plant sits in the window the moving van draws up to the door."

We are the city equivalent to the woodbine and the honeysuckle. No other vegetable except the Pittsburg stogie can withstand as much handling as we can. When the family to which we belong moves into a flat they set us in the front window and we become lares and penates, fly-paper and the peripatetic emblem of "Home Sweet Home." We aren't as green as we look. I guess we are about what you would call the soubrettes of the conservatory. You try sitting in the front window of a $40 flat in Manhattan and looking out into the street all day, and back into the flat at night, and see whether you get wise or not—hey? Talk about the tree of knowledge of good and evil in the garden of Eden—say! suppose there had been a rubber plant there when Eve—but I was going to tell you a story.

The first thing I can remember I had only three leaves and belonged to a member of the pony ballet. I was kept in a sunny window, and was generally watered with seltzer and lemon. I had plenty of fun in those days. I got cross-eyed trying to watch the numbers of the automobiles in the street and the dates on the labels inside at the same time.

Well, then the angel that was molting for the musical comedy lost his last feather and the company broke up. The ponies trotted away and I was left in the window ownerless. The janitor gave me to a refined comedy team on the eighth floor, and in six weeks I had been set in the window of five different flats. I took on experience and put out two more leaves.

Miss Carruthers, of the refined comedy team—did you ever see her cross both feet back of her neck?—gave me to a friend of hers who had made an unfortunate marriage with a man in a store. Consequently I was placed in the window of a furnished room, rent in advance, water two flights up, gas extra after ten o'clock at night. Two of my leaves withered off here. Also, I was moved from one room to another so many times that I got to liking the odor of the pipes the express-men smoked.

I don't think I ever had so dull a time as I did with this lady. There was never anything amusing going on inside—she was devoted to her husband, and, besides leaning out the window and flirting with the iceman, she never did a thing toward breaking the monotony.

When the couple broke up they left me with the rest of their goods at a second-hand store. I was put out in front for sale along with the jobbiest lot you ever heard of being lumped into one bargain. Think of this little cornucopia of wonders, all for $1.89: Henry James's works, six talking machine records, one pair of tennis shoes, two bottles of horse radish, and a rubber plant—that was me!

One afternoon a girl came along and stopped to look at me. She had dark hair and eyes, and she looked slim, and sad around the mouth.

"Oh, oh!" she says to herself. "I never thought to see one up here."

She pulls out a little purse about as thick as one of my leaves and fingers over some small silver in it. Old Koen, always on the lookout, is ready, rubbing his hands. This girl proceeds to turn down Mr. James and the other commodities. Rubber plants or nothing is the burden of her song. And at last Koen and she come together at 39 cents, and away she goes with me in her arms.

She was a nice girl, but not my style. Too quiet and sober looking. Thinks I to myself: "I'll just about land on the fire-escape of a tenement, six stories up. And I'll spend the next six months looking at clothes on the line."

But she carried me to a nice little room only three flights up in quite a decent street. And she put me in the window, of course. And then she went to work and cooked dinner for herself. And what do you suppose she had? Bread and tea and a little dab of jam! Nothing else. Not a single lobster, nor so much as one bottle of champagne. The Carruthers comedy team had both every evening, except now and then when they took a notion for pig's knuckle and kraut.

After she had finished her dinner my new owner came to the window and leaned down close to my leaves and cried softly to herself for a while. It made me feel funny. I never knew anybody to cry that way over a rubber plant before. Of course, I've seen a few of 'em turn on the tears for what they could get out of it, but she seemed to be crying just for the pure enjoyment of it. She touched my leaves like she loved 'em, and she bent down her head and kissed each one of 'em. I guess I'm about the toughest specimen of a peripatetic orchid on earth, but I tell you it made me feel sort of queer. Home never was like that to me before. Generally I used to get chewed by poodles and have shirt-waists hung on me to dry, and get watered with coffee grounds and peroxide of hydrogen.

This girl had a piano in the room, and she used to disturb it with both hands while she made noises with her mouth for hours at a time. I suppose she was practising vocal music.

One day she seemed very much excited and kept looking at the clock. At eleven somebody knocked and she let in a stout, dark man with towsled black hair. He sat down at once at the piano and played while she sang for him.

When she finished she laid one hand on her bosom and looked at him. He shook his head, and she leaned against the piano.

"Two years already," she said, speaking slowly—"do you think in two more —or even longer?"

The man shook his head again. "You waste your time," he said, roughly I thought. "The voice is not there." And then he looked at her in a peculiar way. "But the voice is not everything," he went on. "You have looks. I can place you, as I told you if——"

The girl pointed to the door without saying anything, and the dark man left the room. And then she came over and cried around me again. It's a good thing I had enough rubber in me to be water-proof.

About that time somebody else knocked at the door. "Thank goodness," I said to myself. "Here's a chance to get the water-works turned off. I hope it's somebody that's game enough to stand a bird and a bottle to liven things up a little." Tell you the truth, this little girl made me tired. A rubber plant likes to see a little sport now and then. I don't suppose there's another green thing in New York that sees as much of gay life unless it's the chartreuse or the sprigs of parsley around the dish.

When the girl opens the door in steps a young chap in a traveling cap and picks her up in his arms, and she sings out "Oh, Dick!" and stays there long enough to—well, you've been a rubber plant too, sometimes, I suppose.

"Good thing!" says I to myself. "This is livelier than scales and weeping. Now there'll be something doing."

"You've got to go back with me," says the young man. "I've come two thousand miles for you. Aren't you tired of it yet, Bess? You've kept all of us waiting so long. Haven't you found out yet what is best?"

"The bubble burst only to-day," says the girl. "Come here, Dick, and see what I found the other day on the sidewalk for sale." She brings him by the hand and exhibits yours truly. "How one ever got away up here who can tell? I bought it with almost the last money I had."

He looked at me, but he couldn't keep his eyes off her for more than a second. "Do you remember the night, Bess," he said, "when we stood under one of those on the bank of the bayou and what you told me then?"

"Geewillikins!" I said to myself. "Both of them stand under a rubber plant! Seems to me they are stretching matters somewhat!"

"Do I not," says she, looking up at him and sneaking close to his vest, "and now I say it again, and it is to last forever. Look, Dick, at its leaves, how wet they are. Those are my tears, and it was thinking of you that made them fall."

"The dear old magnolias!" says the young man, pinching one of my leaves. "I love them all."

Magnolia! Well, wouldn't that—say! those innocents thought I was a magnolia! What the—well, wasn't that tough on a genuine little old New York rubber plant?

OUT OF NAZARETH

Okochee, in Georgia, had a boom, and J. Pinkney Bloom came out of it with a "wad." Okochee came out of it with a half-million-dollar debt, a two and a half per cent. city property tax, and a city council that showed a propensity for traveling the back streets of the town. These things came about through a fatal resemblance of the river Cooloosa to the Hudson, as set forth and expounded by a Northern tourist. Okochee felt that New York should not be allowed to consider itself the only alligator in the swamp, so to speak. And then that harmless, but persistent, individual so numerous in the South—the man who is always clamoring for more cotton mills, and is ready to take a dollar's worth of stock, provided he can borrow the dollar—that man added his deadly work to the tourist's innocent praise, and Okochee fell.

The Cooloosa River winds through a range of small mountains, passes Okochee, and then blends its waters trippingly, as fall the mellifluous Indian syllables, with the Chattahoochee.

Okochee rose, as it were, from its sunny seat on the post-office stoop, hitched up its suspender, and threw a granite dam two hundred and forty feet long and sixty feet high across the Cooloosa one mile above the town. Thereupon, a dimpling, sparkling lake backed up twenty miles among the little mountains. Thus in the great game of municipal rivalry did Okochee match that famous drawing card, the Hudson. It was conceded that nowhere could the Palisades be judged superior in the way of scenery and grandeur. Following the picture card was played the ace of commercial importance. Fourteen thousand horsepower would this dam furnish. Cotton mills, factories, and manufacturing plants would rise up as the green corn after a shower. The spindle and the flywheel and turbine would sing the shrewd glory of Okochee. Along the picturesque heights above the lake would rise in beauty the costly villas and the splendid summer residences of capital. The naphtha launch of the millionaire would spit among the romantic coves; the verdured hills would take formal shapes of terrace, lawn, and park. Money would be spent like water in Okochee, and water would be turned into money.

The fate of the good town is quickly told. Capital decided not to invest. Of all the great things promised, the scenery alone came to fulfilment. The wooded peaks, the impressive promontories of solemn granite, the beautiful green slants of bank and ravine did all they could to reconcile Okochee to the delinquency of miserly gold. The sunsets gilded the dreamy draws and coves with a minting that should charm away heart-burning. Okochee, true to the instinct of its blood and clime, was lulled by the spell. It climbed out of the arena, loosed its suspender, sat down again on the post-office stoop, and took a chew. It consoled itself by drawling sarcasms at the city council which was not to blame, causing the fathers, as has been said, to seek back streets and figure perspiringly on the sinking fund and the appropriation for interest due.

The youth of Okochee—they who were to carry into the rosy future the burden of the debt—accepted failure with youth's uncalculating joy. For, here was sport, aquatic and nautical, added to the meagre round of life's pleasures. In yachting caps and flowing neckties they pervaded the lake to its limits. Girls wore silk waists embroidered with anchors in blue and pink. The trousers of the young men widened at the bottom, and their hands were proudly calloused by the oft-plied oar. Fishermen were under the spell of a deep and tolerant joy. Sailboats and rowboats furrowed the lenient waves, popcorn and ice-cream booths sprang up about the little wooden pier. Two small excursion steamboats were built, and plied the delectable waters. Okochee philosophically gave up the hope of eating turtle soup with a gold spoon, and settled back, not ill content, to its regular diet of lotus and fried hominy. And out of this slow wreck of great expectations rose up J. Pinkney Bloom with his "wad" and his prosperous, cheery smile.

Needless to say J. Pinkney was no product of Georgia soil. He came out of that flushed and capable region known as the "North." He called himself a "promoter"; his enemies had spoken of him as a "grafter"; Okochee took a middle course, and held him to be no better nor no worse than a "Yank."

Far up the lake—eighteen miles above the town—the eye of this cheerful camp-follower of booms had spied out a graft. He purchased there a precipitous tract of five hundred acres at forty-five cents per acre; and this he laid out and subdivided as the city of Skyland—the Queen City of the Switzerland of the South. Streets and avenues were surveyed; parks designed; corners of central squares reserved for the "proposed" opera house, board of trade, lyceum, market, public schools, and "Exposition Hall." The price of lots ranged from five to five hundred dollars. Positively, no lot would be priced higher than five hundred dollars.

While the boom was growing in Okochee, J. Pinkney's circulars, maps, and prospectuses were flying through the mails to every part of the country. Investors sent in their money by post, and the Skyland Real Estate Company (J. Pinkney Bloom) returned to each a deed, duly placed on record, to the best lot, at the price, on hand that day. All this time the catamount screeched upon the reserved lot of the Skyland Board of Trade, the opossum swung by his tail over the site of the exposition hall, and the owl hooted a melancholy recitative to his audience of young squirrels in opera house square. Later, when the money was coming in fast, J. Pinkney caused to be erected in the coming city half a dozen cheap box houses, and persuaded a contingent of indigent natives to occupy them, thereby assuming the rôle of "population" in subsequent prospectuses, which became, accordingly, more seductive and remunerative.

So, when the dream faded and Okochee dropped back to digging bait and nursing its two and a half per cent. tax, J. Pinkney Bloom (unloving of checks and drafts and the cold interrogatories of bankers) strapped about his fifty-two-inch waist a soft leather belt containing eight thousand dollars in big bills, and said that all was very good.

One last trip he was making to Skyland before departing to other salad fields. Skyland was a regular post-office, and the steamboat, *Dixie Belle*, under contract, delivered the mail bag (generally empty) twice a week. There was a little business there to be settled—the postmaster was to be paid off for his light but lonely services, and the "inhabitants" had to be furnished with another month's homely rations, as per agreement. And then Skyland would know J. Pinkney Bloom no more. The owners of these precipitous, barren, useless lots might come and view the scene of their invested credulity, or they might leave them to their fit tenants, the wild hog and the browsing deer. The work of the Skyland Real Estate Company was finished.

The little steamboat *Dixie Belle* was about to shove off on her regular up-the-lake trip, when a rickety hired carriage rattled up to the pier, and a tall, elderly gentleman, in black, stepped out, signaling courteously but vivaciously for the boat to wait. Time was of the least importance in the schedule of the *Dixie Belle;* Captain MacFarland gave the order, and the boat received its ultimate two passengers. For, upon the arm of the tall, elderly gentleman, as he crossed the gangway, was a little elderly lady, with a gray curl depending quaintly forward of her left ear.

Captain MacFarland was at the wheel; therefore it seemed to J. Pinkney Bloom, who was the only other passenger, that it should be his to play the part of host to the boat's new guests, who were, doubtless, on a scenery-viewing expedition. He stepped forward, with that translucent, child-candid smile upon his fresh, pink countenance, with that air of unaffected sincerity that was redeemed from bluffness only by its exquisite calculation, with that promptitude and masterly decision of manner that so well suited his calling—with all his stock in trade well to the front, he stepped forward to receive Colonel and Mrs. Peyton Blaylock. With the grace of a grand marshal or a wedding usher, he escorted the two passengers to a side of the upper deck, from which the scenery was supposed to present itself to the observer in increased quantity and quality.

There, in comfortable steamer chairs, they sat and began to piece together the random lines that were to form an intelligent paragraph in the big history of little events.

"Our home, sir," said Colonel Blaylock, removing his wide-brimmed, rather shapeless black felt hat, "is in Holly Springs—Holly Springs, Georgia. I am very proud to make your acquaintance, Mr. Bloom. Mrs. Blaycock and myself have just arrived in Okochee this morning, sir, on business—business of importance in connection with the recent rapid march of progress in this section of our state."

The Colonel smoothed back, with a sweeping gesture, his long, smooth, gray locks. His dark eyes, still fiery under the heavy black brows, seemed inappropriate to the face of a business man. He looked rather to be an old courtier handed down from the reign of Charles, and re-attired in a modern suit of fine, but raveling and seam-worn, broadcloth.

"Yes, sir," said Mr. Bloom, in his heartiest prospectus voice, "things have been whizzing around Okochee. Biggest industrial revival and waking up to natural resources Georgia ever had. Did you happen to squeeze in on the ground floor in any of the gilt-edged grafts, Colonel?"

"Well, sir," said the Colonel, hesitating in courteous doubt, "if I understand your question, I may say that I took the opportunity to make an investment that I believe will prove quite advantageous—yes, sir, I believe it will result in both pecuniary profit and agreeable occupation."

"Colonel Blaylock," said the little elderly lady, shaking her gray curl and smiling indulgent explanation at J. Pinkney Bloom, "is so devoted to business. He has such a talent for financiering and markets and investments and those kind of things. I think myself extremely fortunate in having secured him for a partner on life's journey—I am so unversed in those formidable but very useful branches of learning."

Colonel Blaylock rose and made a bow—a bow that belonged with silk stockings and lace ruffles and velvet.

"Practical affairs," he said, with a wave of his hand toward the promoter, "are, if I may use the comparison, the garden walks upon which we tread through life, viewing upon either side of us the flowers which brighten that journey. It is my pleasure to be able to lay out a walk or two. Mrs. Blaylock, sir, is one of those fortunate higher spirits whose mission it is to make the flowers grow. Perhaps, Mr. Bloom, you have perused the lines of Lorella, the Southern poetess. That is the name above which Mrs. Blaylock has contributed to the press of the South for many years."

"Unfortunately," said Mr. Bloom, with a sense of the loss clearly written upon his frank face, "I'm like the Colonel—in the walk-making business myself—and I haven't had time to even take a sniff at the flowers. Poetry is a line I never dealt in. It must be nice, though—quite nice."

"It is the region," smiled Mrs. Blaylock, "in which my soul dwells. My shawl, Peyton, if you please—the breeze comes a little chilly from yon verdured hills."

The Colonel drew from the tail pocket of his coat a small shawl of knitted silk and laid it solicitously about the shoulders of the lady. Mrs. Blaylock sighed contentedly, and turned her expressive eyes—still as clear and unworldly as a child's—upon the steep slopes that were slowly slipping past. Very fair and stately they looked in the clear morning air. They seemed to speak in familiar terms to the responsive spirit of Lorella. "My native hills!" she murmured, dreamily. "See how the foliage drinks the sunlight from the hollows and dells."

"Mrs. Blaylock's maiden days," said the Colonel, interpreting her mood to J. Pinkney Bloom, "were spent among the mountains of northern Georgia. Mountain air and mountain scenery recall to her those days. Holly Springs, where we

have lived for twenty years, is low and flat. I fear that she may have suffered
in health and spirits by so long a residence there. That is one potent reason for
the change we are making. My dear, can you not recall those lines you wrote—
entitled, I think, 'The Georgia Hills'—the poem that was so extensively copied
by the Southern press and praised so highly by the Atlanta critics?"

Mrs. Blaylock turned a glance of speaking tenderness upon the Colonel, fingered
for a moment the silvery curl that drooped upon her bosom, then looked again
toward the mountains. Without preliminary or affectation or demurral she began, in rather thrilling and more deeply pitched tones to recite these lines:

> "The Georgia hills, the Georgia hills!—
> Oh, heart, why dost thou pine?
> Are not these sheltered lowlands fair
> With mead and bloom and vine?
> Ah! as the slow-paced river here
> Broods on its natal rills
> My spirit drifts, in longing sweet,
> Back to the Georgia hills.

> "And through the close-drawn, curtained night
> I steal on sleep's slow wings
> Back to my heart's ease—slopes of pine—
> Where end my wanderings.
> Oh, heaven seems nearer from their tops—
> And farther earthly ills—
> Even in dreams, if I may but
> Dream of my Georgia hills.

> The grass upon their orchard sides
> Is a fine couch to me;
> The common note of each small bird
> Passes all minstrelsy.
> It would not seem so dread a thing
> If, when the Reaper wills,
> He might come there and take my hand
> Up in the Georgia hills."

"That's great stuff, ma'am," said J. Pinkney Bloom, enthusiastically, when the
poetess had concluded. "I wish I had looked up poetry more than I have. I
was raised in the pine hills myself."

"The mountains ever call to their children," murmured Mrs. Blaylock. "I
feel that life will take on the rosy hue of hope again in among these beautiful
hills. Peyton—a little taste of the currant wine, if you will be so good. The
journey, though delightful in the extreme, slightly fatigues me."

Colonel Blaylock again visited the depths of his prolific coat, and produced a
tightly corked, rough, black bottle. Mr. Bloom was on his feet in an instant.
"Let me bring a glass, ma'am. You come along, Colonel—there's a little table we
can bring, too. Maybe we can scare up some fruit or a cup of tea on board. I'll
ask Mac."

Mrs. Blaylock reclined at ease. Few royal ladies have held their royal
prerogative with the serene grace of the petted Southern woman. The Colonel,
with an air as gallant and assiduous as in the days of his courtship, and J.
Pinkney Bloom, with a ponderous agility half professional and half directed by
some resurrected, unnamed, long-forgotten sentiment, formed a diversified but

attentive court. The currant wine—wine home made from the Holly Springs fruit—went round; and then J. Pinkney began to hear something of Holly Springs life.

It seemed (from the conversation of the Blaylocks) that the Springs was decadent. A third of the population had moved away. Business—and the Colonel was an authority on business—had dwindled to nothing. After carefully studying the field of opportunities open to capital he had sold his little property there for eight hundred dollars and invested it in one of the enterprises opened up by the book in Okochee.

"Might I inquire, sir," said Mr. Bloom, "in what particular line of business you inserted your coin? I know that town as well as I know the regulations for illegal use of the mails. I might give you a hunch as to whether you can make the game go or not."

J. Pinkney, somehow, had a kindly feeling toward these unsophisticated representatives of by-gone days. They were so simple, impractical, and unsuspecting. He was glad that he happened not to have a gold brick or a block of that western Bad Boy Silver Mine stock along with him. He would have disliked to unload on people he liked so well as he did these; but there are some temptations too enticing to be resisted.

"No, sir," said Colonel Blaylock, pausing to arrange the queen's wrap. "I did not invest in Okochee. I have made an exhaustive study of business conditions, and I regard old settled towns as unfavorable fields in which to place capital that is limited in amount. Some months ago, through the kindness of a friend, there came into my hands a map and description of this new town of Skyland that has been built upon the lake. The description was so pleasing, the future of the town set forth in such convincing arguments, and its increasing prosperity portrayed in such an attractive style that I decided to take advantage of the opportunity it offered. I carefully selected a lot in the centre of the business district, although its price was the highest in the schedule—five hundred dollars—and made the purchase at once."

"Are you the man—I mean, did you pay five hundred dollars for a lot in Skyland?" asked J. Pinkney Bloom.

"I did, sir," answered the Colonel, with the air of a modest millionaire explaining his success; "a lot most excellently situated on the same square with the opera house, and only two squares from the board of trade. I consider the purchase a most fortuitous one. It is my intention to erect a small building upon it at once, and open a modest book and stationery store. During past years I have met with many pecuniary reverses, and I now find it necessary to engage in some commercial occupation that will furnish me with a livelihood. The book and stationery business, though an humble one, seems to me not inapt nor altogether uncongenial. I am a graduate of the University of Virginia; and Mrs. Blaylock's really wonderful acquaintance with belles-lettres and poetic literature should go far toward insuring success. Of course, Mrs. Blaylock would not personally serve behind the counter. With the nearly three hundred dollars I have remaining I can manage the building of a house, by giving a lien on the lot. I have an old friend in Atlanta who is a partner in a large book store, and he has agreed to furnish me with a stock of goods on credit, on extremely easy terms. I am pleased to hope, sir, that Mrs. Blaylock's health and happiness will be increased by the change of locality. Already I fancy I can perceive the return of those roses that were once the hope and despair of Georgia cavaliers."

Again followed that wonderful bow, as the Colonel lightly touched the pale cheek of the poetess. Mrs. Blaylock, blushing like a girl, shook her curl and gave the Colonel an arch, reproving tap. Secret of eternal youth—where art thou? Every second the answer comes—"Here, here, here." Listen to thine own heartbeats, O weary seeker after external miracles.

Those years," said Mrs. Blaylock, "in Holly Springs were long, long, long. But now is the promised land in sight. Skyland!—a lovely name."

"Doubtless," said the Colonel, "we shall be able to secure comfortable accommodations at some modest hotel at reasonable rates. Our trunks are in Okochee, to be forwarded when we shall have made permanent arrangements."

J. Pinkney Bloom excused himself, went forward, and stood by the captain at the wheel.

"Mac," said he, "do you remember my telling you once that I sold one of those five-hundred-dollar lots in Skyland?"

"Seems I do," grinned Captain MacFarland.

"I'm not a coward, as a general rule," went on the promoter, "but I always said that if I ever met the sucker that bought that lot I'd run like a turkey. Now, you see that old babe-in-the-wood over there? Well, he's the boy that drew the prize. That was the only five-hundred-dollar lot that went. The rest ranged from ten dollars to two hundred. His wife writes poetry. She's invented one about the high grounds of Georgia, that's way up in G. They're going to Skyland to open a book store."

"Well," said MacFarland, with another grin, "it's a good thing you are along, J. P.; you can show 'em around town until they begin to feel at home."

"He's got three hundred dollars left to build a house and store with," went on J. Pinkney, as if he were talking to himself. "And he thinks there's an opera house up there."

Captain MacFarland released the wheel long enough to give his leg a roguish slap.

"You old fat rascal!" he chuckled, with a wink.

"Mac, you're a fool," said J. Pinkney Bloom, coldly. He went back and joined the Blaylocks, where he sat, less talkative, with that straight furrow between his brows that always stood as a signal of schemes being shaped within.

"There's a good many swindles connected with these booms," he said presently. "What if this Skyland should turn out to be one—that is, suppose business should be sort of dull there, and no special sale for books?"

"My dear sir," said Colonel Blaylock, resting his hand upon the back of his wife's chair, "three times I have been reduced to almost penury by the duplicity of others, but I have not yet lost faith in humanity. If I have been deceived again, still we may glean health and content, if not worldly profit. I am aware that there are dishonest schemers in the world who set traps for the unwary, but even they are not altogether bad. My dear, can you recall those verses entitled, 'He Giveth the Increase,' that you composed for the choir of our church in Holly Springs?"

"That was four years ago," said Mrs. Blaylock; "perhaps I can repeat a verse or two.

"The lily springs from the rotting mould;
　　Pearls from the deep sea slime;
　Good will come out of Nazareth
　　All in God's own time.

"To the hardest heart the softening grace
　　Cometh, at last, to bless;
　Guiding it right to help and cheer
　　And succor in distress.

"I cannot remember the rest. The lines were not ambitious. They were written to the music composed by a dear friend."

"It's a fine rhyme, just the same," declared Mr. Bloom. "It seems to ring the bell, all right. I guess I gather the sense of it. It means that the rankest kind of a phony will give you the best end of it once in a while."

Mr. Bloom strayed thoughtfully back to the captain, and stood meditating.

"Ought to be in sight of the spires and gilded domes of Skyland now in a few minutes," chirruped MacFarland, shaking with enjoyment.

"Go to the devil," said Mr. Bloom, still pensive.

And now, upon the left bank, they caught a glimpse of a white village, high up on the hills, smothered among green trees. That was Cold Branch—no boom town, but the slow growth of many years. Cold Branch lay on the edge of the grape and corn lands. The big country road ran just back of the heights. Cold Branch had nothing in common with the frisky ambition of Okochee with its impertinent lake.

"Mac," said J. Pinkney suddenly, "I want you to stop at Cold Branch. There's a landing there that they made to use sometimes when the river was up."

"Can't," said the captain, grinning more broadly. "I've got the United States mails on board. Right to-day this boat's in the government service. Do you want to have the poor old captain keelhauled by Uncle Sam? And the great city of Skyland, all disconsolate, waiting for its mail? I'm ashamed of your extravagance, J. P."

"Mac," almost whispered J. Pinkney, in his danger-line voice, "I looked into the engine room of the *Dixie Belle* a while ago. Don't you know of somebody that needs a new boiler? Cement and black Japan can't hide flaws from me. And then, those shares of building and loan that you traded for repairs—they were all yours, of course. I hate to mention these things, but——"

"Oh, come now, J. P.," said the captain. "You know I was just fooling. I'll put you off at Cold Branch, if you say so."

"The other passengers get off there, too," said Mr. Bloom.

Further conversation was held, and in ten minutes the *Dixie Belle* turned her nose toward a little, cranky wooden pier on the left bank, and the captain, relinquishing the wheel to a roustabout, came to the passenger deck and made the remarkable announcement: "All out for Skyland."

The Blaylocks and J. Pinkney Bloom disembarked, and the *Dixie Belle* proceeded on her way up the lake. Guided by the indefatigable promoter, they slowly climbed the steep hillside, pausing often to rest and admire the view. Finally they entered the village of Cold Branch. Warmly both the Colonel and his wife praised it for its homelike and peaceful beauty. Mr. Bloom conducted them to a two-story building on a shady street that bore the legend, "Pine-top Inn." Here he took his leave, receiving the cordial thanks of the two for his attentions, the Colonel remarking that he thought they would spend the remainder of the day in rest, and take a look at his purchase on the morrow.

J. Pinkney Bloom walked down Cold Branch's main street. He did not know this town, but he knew towns, and his feet did not falter. Presently he saw a sign over a door: "Frank E. Cooly, Attorney-at-Law and Notary Public." A young man was Mr. Cooly, and awaiting business.

"Get your hat, son," said Mr. Bloom, in his breezy way, "and a blank deed, and come along. It's a job for you."

"Now," he continued, when Mr. Cooly had responded with alacrity, "is there a bookstore in town?"

"One," said the lawyer. "Henry Williams's."

"Get there," said Mr. Bloom. "We're going to buy it."

Henry Williams was behind his counter. His store was a small one, containing a mixture of books, stationery, and fancy rubbish. Adjoining it was Henry's home—a decent cottage, vine-embowered and cosy. Henry was lank and soporific, and not inclined to rush his business.

"I want to buy your house and store," said Mr. Bloom. "I haven't got time to dicker—name your price."

"It's worth eight hundred," said Henry, too much dazed to ask more than its value.

"Shut that door," said Mr. Bloom to the lawyer. Then he tore off his coat and vest, and began to unbutton his shirt.

"Wanter fight about it, do yer?" said Henry Williams, jumping up and cracking his heels together twice. "All right, hunky—sail in and cut yer capers."

"Keep your clothes on," said Mr. Bloom. "I'm only going down to the bank."

He drew eight one-hundred-dollar bills from his money belt and planked them down on the counter. Mr. Cooly showed signs of future promise, for he already had the deed spread out, and was reaching across the counter for the ink bottle. Never before or since was such quick action had in Cold Branch.

"Your name, please?" asked the lawyer.

"Make it out to Peyton Blaylock," said Mr. Bloom. "God knows how to spell it."

Within thirty minutes Henry Williams was out of business, and Mr. Bloom stood on the brick sidewalk with Mr. Cooly, who held in his hand the signed and attested deed.

"You'll find the party at the Pinetop Inn," said J. Pinkney Bloom. "Get it recorded, and take it down and give it to him. He'll ask you a hell's mint of questions; so here's ten dollars for the trouble you'll have in not being able to answer 'em. Never run much to poetry, did you, young man?"

"Well," said the really talented Cooly, who even yet retained his right mind, "now and then."

"Dig into it," said Mr. Bloom, "it'll pay you. Never heard a poem, now, that run something like this, did you?—

> "A good thing out of Nazareth
> Comes up sometimes, I guess,
> On hand, all right, to help and cheer
> A sucker in distress."

"I believe not," said Mr. Cooly.

"It's a hymn," said J. Pinkney Bloom. "Now, show me the way to a livery stable, son, for I'm going to hit the dirt road back to Okochee."

CONFESSIONS OF A HUMORIST

THERE was a painless stage of incubation that lasted twenty-five years, and then it broke out on me, and people said I was It.

But they called it humor instead of measles.

The employees in the store bought a silver inkstand for the senior partner on his fiftieth birthday. We crowded into his private office to present it.

I had been selected for spokesman, and I made a little speech that I had been preparing for a week.

It made a hit. It was full of puns and epigrams and funny twists that brought down the house—which was a very solid one in the wholesale hardware line.

Old Marlowe himself actually grinned, and the employees took their cue and roared.

My reputation as a humorist dates from half-past nine o'clock on that morning. For weeks afterward my fellow clerks fanned the flame of my self-esteem. One by one they came to me, saying what an awfully clever speech that was, old man, and carefully explained to me the point of each one of my jokes.

Gradually I found that I was expected to keep it up. Others might speak sanely on business matters and the day's topics, but from me something gamesome and airy was required.

I was expected to crack jokes about the crockery and lighten up the granite ware with persiflage. I was second bookkeeper, and if I failed to show up a balance sheet without something comic about the footings or could find no cause for laughter in an invoice of plows, the other clerks were disappointed.

By degrees my fame spread, and I became a local "character." Our town was small enough to make this possible. The daily newspaper quoted me. At social gatherings I was indispensable.

I believe I did possess considerable wit and a facility for quick and spontaneous repartee. This gift I cultivated and improved by practice. And the nature of it was kindly and genial, not running to sarcasm or offending others. People began to smile when they saw me coming, and by the time we had met I generally had the word ready to broaden the smile into a laugh.

I had married early. We had a charming boy of three and a girl of five. Naturally, we lived in a vine-covered cottage, and were happy. My salary as bookkeeper in the hardware concern kept at a distance those ills attendant upon superfluous wealth.

At sundry times I had written out a few jokes and conceits that I considered peculiarly happy, and had sent them to certain periodicals that print such things. All of them had been instantly accepted. Several of the editors had written to request further contributions.

One day I received a letter from the editor of a famous weekly publication. He suggested that I submit to him a humorous composition to fill a column of space; hinting that he would make it a regular feature of each issue if the work proved satisfactory. I did so, and at the end of two weeks he offered to make a contract with me for a year at a figure that was considerably higher than the amount paid me by the hardware firm.

I was filled with delight. My wife already crowned me in her mind with the imperishable evergreens of literary success. We had lobster croquettes and a bottle of blackberry wine for supper that night. Here was the chance to liberate myself from drudgery. I talked over the matter very seriously with Louisa. We agreed that I must resign my place at the store and devote myself to humor.

I resigned. My fellow clerks gave me a farewell banquet. The speech I made there coruscated. It was printed in full by the *Gazette*. The next morning I awoke and looked at the clock.

"Late, by George!" I exclaimed, and grabbed for my clothes. Louisa reminded me that I was no longer a slave to hardware and contractors' supplies. I was now a professional humorist.

After breakfast she proudly led me to the little room off the kitchen. Dear girl! There was my table and chair, writing pad, ink, and pipe tray. And all the author's trappings—the celery stand full of fresh roses and honeysuckle, last year's calendar on the wall, the dictionary, and a little bag of chocolates to nibble between inspirations. Dear girl!

I sat me to work. The wall paper is patterned with arabesques or odalisks or—perhaps—it is trapezoids. Upon one of the figures I fixed my eyes. I bethought me of humor.

A voice startled me—Louisa's voice.

"If you aren't too busy, dear," it said, "come to dinner."

I looked at my watch. Yes, five hours had been gathered in by the grim scythe-man. I went to dinner.

"You mustn't work too hard at first," said Louisa. "Goethe—or was it Napoleon?—said five hours a day is enough for mental labor. Couldn't you take me and the children to the woods this afternoon?"

"I *am* a little tired," I admitted. So we went to the woods.

But I soon got the swing of it. Within a month I was turning out copy as regular as shipments of hardware.

And I had success. My column in the weekly made some stir, and I was referred to in a gossipy way by the critics as something fresh in the line of humorists. I augmented my income considerably by contributing to other publications.

I picked up the tricks of the trade. I could take a funny idea and make a two-line joke of it, earning a dollar. With false whiskers on, it would serve up cold as a quatrain, doubling its producing value. By turning the skirt and adding a ruffle of rhyme you would hardly recognize it as *vers de société* with neatly shod feet and a fashion-plate illustration.

I began to save up money, and we had new carpets, and a parlor organ. My townspeople began to look upon me as a citizen of some consequence instead of the merry trifler I had been when I clerked in the hardware store.

After five or six months the spontaniety seemed to depart from my humor. Quips and droll sayings no longer fell carelessly from my lips. I was sometimes hard run for material. I found myself listening to catch available ideas from the conversation of my friends. Sometimes I chewed my pencil and gazed at the wall paper for hours trying to build up some gay little bubble of unstudied fun.

And then I became a harpy, a Moloch, a Jonah, a vampire, to my acquaintances. Anxious, haggard, greedy, I stood among them like a veritable killjoy. Let a bright saying, a witty comparison, a piquant phrase fall from their lips and I was after it like a hound springing upon a bone. I dared not trust my memory; but, turning aside guiltily and meanly, I would make a note of it in my ever-present memorandum book or upon my cuff for my own future use.

My friends regarded me in sorrow and wonder. I was not the same man. Where once I had furnished them entertainment and jollity, I now preyed upon them. No jests from me ever bid for their smiles now. They were too precious. I could not afford to dispense gratuitously the means of my livelihood.

I was a lugubrious fox praising the singing of my friends, the crows, that they might drop from their beaks the morsels of wit that I coveted.

Nearly every one began to avoid me. I even forgot how to smile, not even paying that much for the sayings I appropriated.

No persons, places, times, or subjects were exempt from my plundering in search of material. . Even in church my demoralized fancy went hunting among the solemn aisles and pillars for spoil.

Did the minister give out the long-meter doxology, at once I began: "Dox-ology—sockdology—sockdolager—meter—meet her."

The sermon ran through my mental sieve, its precepts filtering unheeded, could I but glean a suggestion of a pun or a *bon mot*. The solemnest anthems of the choir were but an accompaniment to my thoughts as I conceived new changes to ring upon the ancient comicalities concerning the jealousies of soprano, tenor, and basso.

My own home became a hunting ground. My wife is a singularly feminine creature, candid, sympathetic, and impulsive. Once her conversation was my delight, and her ideas a source of unfailing pleasure. Now I worked her. She was a gold mine of those amusing but lovable inconsistencies that distinguish the female mind.

I began to market those pearls of unwisdom and humor that should have enriched only the sacred precincts of home. With devilish cunning I encouraged her to talk. Unsuspecting, she laid her heart bare. Upon the cold, conspicuous, common, printed page I offered it to the public gaze.

A literary Judas, I kissed her and betrayed her. For pieces of silver I dressed her sweet confidences in the pantalettes and frills of folly and made them dance in the market place.

Dear Louisa! Of nights I have bent over her cruel as a wolf above a tender lamb, hearkening even to her soft words murmured in sleep, hoping to catch an idea for my next day's grind. There is worse to come.

God help me! Next my fangs were buried deep in the neck of the fugitive sayings of my little children.

Guy and Viola were two bright fountains of childish, quaint thoughts and speeches. I found a ready sale for this kind of humor, and was furnishing a regular department in a magazine with "Funny Fancies of Childhood." I began to stalk them as an Indian stalks the antelope. I would hide behind sofas and doors, or crawl on my hands and knees among the bushes in the yard to eavesdrop while they were at play. I had all the qualities of a harpy except remorse.

Once, when I was barren of ideas, and my copy must leave in the next mail, I covered myself in a pile of autumn leaves in the yard, where I knew they intended to come to play. I cannot bring myself to believe that Guy was aware of my hiding place, but even if he was, I would be loath to blame him for his setting fire to the leaves, causing the destruction of my new suit of clothes, and nearly cremating a parent.

Soon my own children began to shun me as a pest. Often, when I was creeping upon them like a melancholy ghoul, I would hear them say to each other: "Here comes papa," and they would gather their toys and scurry away to some safer hiding place. Miserable wretch that I was!

And yet I was doing well financially. Before the first year had passed I had saved a thousand dollars, and we had lived in comfort.

But at what a cost! I am not quite clear as to what a pariah is, but I was everything that it sounds like. I had no friends, no amusements, no enjoyment of life. The happiness of my family had been sacrificed. I was a bee, sucking sordid honey from life's fairest flowers, dreaded and shunned on account of my sting.

One day a man spoke to me, with a pleasant and friendly smile. Not in months had the thing happened. I was passing the undertaking establishment of Peter Heffelbower. Peter stood in the door and saluted me. I stopped, strangely wrung in my heart by his greeting. He asked me inside.

The day was chill and rainy. We went into the back room, where a fire burned in a little stove. A customer came, and Peter left me alone for a while. Presently I felt a new feeling stealing over me—a sense of beautiful calm and content, I looked around the place. There were rows of shining rosewood caskets, black palls, trestles, hearse plumes, mourning streamers, and all the paraphernalia of the solemn trade. Here was peace, order, silence, the abode of grave and dignified reflections. Here, on the brink of life, was a little niche pervaded by the spirit of eternal rest.

When I entered it, the follies of the world abandoned me at the door. I felt no inclination to wrest a humorous idea from those sombre and stately trappings. My mind seemed to stretch itself to grateful repose upon a couch draped with gentle thoughts.

A quarter of an hour ago I was an abandoned humorist. Now I was a philosopher, full of serenity and ease. I had found a *refuge* from humor, from the hot chase of the shy quip, from the degrading pursuit of the panting joke, from the restless reach after the nimble repartee.

I had not known Heffelbower well. When he came back, I let him talk, fearful that he might prove to be a jarring note in the sweet, dirgelike harmony of his establishment.

But, no. He chimed truly. I gave a long sigh of happiness. Never have I known a man's talk to be as magnificently dull as Peter's was. Compared with it the Dead Sea is a geyser. Never a sparkle or a glimmer of wit marred his words. Commonplaces as trite and as plentiful as blackberries flowed from his lips no more stirring in quality than a last week's tape running from a ticker. Quaking a little, I tried upon him one of my best pointed jokes. It fell back ineffectual, with the point broken. I loved that man from then on.

Two or three evenings each week I would steal down to Heffelbower's and revel in his back room. That was my only joy. I began to rise early and hurry through my work, that I might spend more time in my haven. In no other place could I throw off my habit of extracting humorous ideas from my surroundings. Peter's talk left me no opening had I besieged it ever so hard.

Under this influence I began to improve in spirits. It was the recreation from one's labor which every man needs. I surprised one or two of my former friends by throwing them a smile and a cheery word as I passed them on the streets. Several times I dumfounded my family by relaxing long enough to make a jocose remark in their presence.

I had so long been ridden by the incubus of humor that I seized my hours of holiday with a schoolboy's zest.

My work began to suffer. It was not the pain and burden to me that it had been. I often whistled at my desk, and wrote with far more fluency than before. I accomplished my tasks impatiently, as anxious to be off to my helpful retreat as a drunkard is to get to his tavern.

My wife had some anxious hours in conjecturing where I spent my afternoons. I thought it best not to tell her; women do not understand these things. Poor girl!—she had one shock out of it.

One day I brought home a silver coffin handle for a paper weight and a fine, fluffy hearse plume to dust my papers with.

I loved to see them on my desk, and think of the beloved back room down at Heffelbower's. But Louisa found them, and she shrieked with horror. I had to console her with some lame excuse for having them, but I saw in her eyes that the prejudice was not removed. I had to remove the articles, though, at double-quick time.

One day Peter Heffelbower laid before me a temptation that swept me off my feet. In his sensible, uninspired way he showd me his books, and explained that his profits and his business were increasing rapidly. He had thought of taking in a partner with some cash. He would rather have me than any one he knew. When I left his place that afternoon Peter had my check for the thousand dollars I had in the bank, and I was a partner in his undertaking business.

I went home with feelings of delirious joy, mingled with a certain amount of doubt. I was dreading to tell my wife about it. But I walked on air. To give up the writing of humorous stuff, once more to enjoy the apples of life, instead of squeezing them to a pulp for a few drops of hard cider to make the public feel funny—what a boon that would be!

At the supper table Louisa handed me some letters that had come during my absence. Several of them contained rejected manuscript. Ever since I first began going to Heffelbower's my stuff had been coming back with alarming frequency. Lately I had been dashing off my jokes and articles with the greatest fluency. Previously I had labored like a bricklayer, slowly and with agony.

Presently I opened a letter from the editor of the weekly with which I had a regular contract. The checks for that weekly article were still our main dependence. The letter ran thus:

DEAR SIR:

As you are aware, our contract for the year expires with the present month. While regretting the necessity for so doing, we must say that we do not care to renew same for the coming year. We were quite pleased with your style of humor, which seems to have delighted quite a large proportion of our readers. But for the past two months we have noticed a decided falling off in its quality.

Your earlier work showed a spontaneous, easy, natural flow of fun and wit. Of late it is labored, studied, and unconvincing, giving painful evidence of hard toil and drudging mechanism.

Again regretting that we do not consider your contributions available any longer, we are, yours sincerely,

THE EDITOR.

I handed this letter to my wife. After she had read it her face grew extremely long, and there were tears in her eyes.

"The mean old thing!" she exclaimed indignantly. "I'm sure your pieces are just as good as they ever were. And it doesn't take you half as long to write them as it did." And then, I suppose, Louisa thought of the checks that would cease coming. "Oh, John," she wailed, "what will you do now?"

For an answer I got up and began to do a polka step around the supper table. I am sure Louisa thought the trouble had driven me mad; and I think the children hoped it had, for they tore after me, yelling with glee and emulating my steps. I was now something like their old playmate of yore.

"The theatre for us to-night!" I shouted; "nothing less. And a late, wild, disreputable supper for all of us at the Palace Restaurant. Lumpty-diddle-de-dee-de-dum!"

And then I explained my glee by declaring that I was now a partner in a prosperous undertaking establishment, and that written jokes might go hide their heads in sackcloth and ashes for all me.

With the editor's letter in her hand to justify the deed I had done, my wife could advance no objections save a few mild ones based on the feminine inability to appreciate a good thing such as the little back room of Peter Heffel—no, of Heffelbower & Co's. undertaking establishment.

In conclusion, I will say that to-day you will find no man in our town as well liked, as jovial, and full of merry sayings as I. My jokes are again noised about and quoted; once more I take pleasure in my wife's confidential chatter without a mercenary thought, while Guy and Viola play at my feet distributing gems of childish humor without fear of the ghastly tormentor who used to dog their steps, notebook in hand.

Our business has prospered finely. I keep the books and look after the shop, while Peter attends to outside matters. He says that my levity and high spirits would simply turn any funeral into a regular Irish wake.

THE SPARROWS IN MADISON SQUARE

THE young man in straitened circumstances who comes to New York City to enter literature has but one thing to do, provided he has studied carefully his field in advance. He must go straight to Madison Square, write an article about the sparrows there, and sell it to the *Sun* for $15.

I cannot recall either a novel or a story dealing with the popular theme of the young writer from the provinces who comes to the metropolis to win fame and fortune with his pen in which the hero does not get his start that way. It does seem strange that some author, in casting about for startlingly original plots, has not hit upon the idea of having his hero write about the bluebirds in Union Square and sell it to the *Herald*. But a search through the files of metropolitan fiction counts up overwhelmingly for the sparrows and the old Garden Square, and the *Sun* always writes the check.

Of course it is easy to understand why this first city venture of the budding author is always successful. He is primed by necessity to a superlative effort; mid the iron and stone and marble of the roaring city he has found this spot of singing birds and green grass and trees; every tender sentiment in his nature is battling with the sweet pain of homesickness; his genius is aroused as it never may be again; the birds chirp, the tree branches sway, the noise of wheels is forgotten; he writes with his soul in his pen—and he sells it to the *Sun* for $15.

I had read of this custom during many years before I came to New York. When my friends were using their strongest arguments to dissuade me from coming, I only smiled serenely. They did not know of that sparrow graft I had up my sleeve.

When I arrived in New York, and the car took me straight from the ferry up Twenty-third Street to Madison Square, I could hear that $15 check rustling in my inside pocket.

I obtained lodging at an unhyphenated hostelry, and the next morning I was on a bench in Madison Square almost by the time the sparrows were awake. Their melodious chirping, the benignant spring foliage of the noble trees and the clean, fragrant grass reminded me so potently of the old farm I had left that tears almost came into my eyes.

Then, all in a moment, I felt my inspiration. The brave, piercing notes of those cheerful small birds formed a keynote to a wonderful, light, fanciful song of hope and joy and altruism. Like myself, they were creatures with hearts pitched to the tune of woods and fields; as I was, so were they captives by circumstance in the discordant, dull city—yet with how much grace and glee they bore the restraint!

And then the early morning people began to pass through the square to their work—sullen people, with sidelong glances and glum faces, hurrying, hurrying, hurrying. And I got my theme cut out clear from the bird notes, and wrought it into a lesson, and a poem, and a carnival dance, and a lullaby; and then translated it all into prose and began to write.

For two hours my pencil traveled over my pad with scarcely a rest. Then I went to the little room I had rented for two days, and there I cut it to half, and then mailed it, white-hot, to the *Sun*.

The next morning I was up by daylight and spent two cents of my capital for a paper. If the word "sparrow" was in it I was unable to find it.

I took it up to my room and spread it out on the bed and went over it, column by column. Something was wrong.

Three hours afterward the postman brought me a large envelope containing my MS. and a piece of inexpensive paper, about 3 inches by 4—I suppose some of you have seen them—upon which was written in violet ink, "With the *Sun's* thanks."

I went over to the square and sat upon a bench. No; I did not think it necessary to eat any breakfast that morning. The confounded pests of sparrows were making the square hideous with their idiotic "cheep, cheep." I never saw birds so persistently noisy, impudent, and disagreeable in all my life.

By this time, according to all traditions, I should have been standing in the office of the editor of the *Sun*. That personage—a tall, grave, white-haired man—would strike a silver bell as he grasped my hand and wiped a suspicious moisture from his glasses.

"Mr. McChesney," he would be saying when a subordinate appeared, "this is Mr. Henry, the young man who sent in that exquisite gem about the sparrows in Madison Square. You may give him a desk at once. Your salary, sir, will be $80 a week, to begin with."

This was what I had been led to expect by all writers who have evolved romances of literary New York.

Something was decidedly wrong with tradition. I could not assume the blame; so I fixed it upon the sparrows. I began to hate them with intensity and heat.

At that moment an individual wearing an excess of whiskers, two hats, and a pestilential air slid into the seat beside me.

"Say, Willie," he muttered cajolingly, "could you cough up a dime out of your coffers for a cup of coffee this morning?"

"I'm lung-weary, my friend," said I. "The best I can do is three cents."

"And you look like a gentleman, too," said he. "What brung you down—booze?"

"Birds," I said fiercely. "The brown-throated songsters carolling songs of hope and cheer to weary man toiling amid the city's dust and din. The little feathered couriers from the meadows and woods chirping sweetly to us of blue skies and flowering fields. The confounded little squint-eyed nuisances yawping like a flock of steam pianos, and stuffing themselves like aldermen with grass seeds and bugs, while a man sits on a bench and goes without his breakfast. Yes, sir, birds! look at them!"

As I spoke I picked up a dead tree branch that lay by the bench, and hurled it with all my force into a close congregation of the sparrows on the grass. The flock flew to the trees with a babel of shrill cries; but two of them remained prostrate upon the turf.

In a moment my unsavory friend had leaped over the row of benches and secured the fluttering victims, which he thrust hurriedly into his pockets. Then he beckoned me with a dirty forefinger.

"Come on, cully," he said hoarsely. "You're in on the feed."

Weakly I followed my dingy acquaintance. He led me away from the park down a side street and through a crack in a fence into a vacant lot where some excavating had been going on. Behind a pile of old stones and lumber he paused, and took out his birds.

"I got matches," said he. "You got any paper to start a fire with?"

I drew forth my manuscript story of the sparrows, and offered it for burnt sacrifice. There were old planks, splinters, and chips for our fire. My frowsy friend produced from some interior of his frayed clothing half a loaf of bread, pepper, and salt.

In ten minutes each of us was holding a sparrow spitted upon a stick over the leaping flames.

"Say," said my fellow bivouacker, "this ain't so bad when a fellow's hungry. It reminds me of when I struck New York first—about fifteen years ago. I come in from the West to see if I could get a job on a newspaper. I hit the Madison Square Park the first mornin' after, and was sitting around on the benches. I noticed the sparrows chirpin', and the grass and trees so nice and green that I thought I was back in the country again. Then I got some papers out of my pocket, and——"

"I know," I interrupted. "You sent it to the *Sun* and got $15."

"Say," said my friend, suspiciously, "you seem to know a good deal. Where was you? I went to sleep on the bench there, in the sun, and somebody touched me for every cent I had—$15."

HEARTS AND HANDS

AT Denver there was an influx of passengers into the coaches on the eastbound B. & M. express. In one coach there sat a very pretty young woman dressed in elegant taste and surrounded by all the luxurious comforts of an experienced traveler. Among the newcomers were two young men, one of handsome presence with a bold, frank countenance and manner; the other a ruffled, glum-faced person, heavily built and roughly dressed. The two were handcuffed together.

As they passed down the aisle of the coach the only vacant seat offered was a reversed one facing the attractive young woman. Here the linked couple seated themselves. The young woman's glance fell upon them with a distant, swift disinterest; then with a lovely smile brightening her countenance and a tender pink tingeing her rounded cheeks, she held out a little gray-gloved hand. When she spoke her voice, full, sweet, and deliberate, proclaimed that its owner was accustomed to speak and be heard.

"Well, Mr. Easton, if you *will* make me speak first, I suppose I must. Don't you ever recognize old friends when you meet them in the West?"

The younger man roused himself sharply at the sound of her voice, seemed to struggle with a slight embarrassment which he threw off instantly, and then clasped her fingers with his left hand.

"It's Miss Fairchild," he said, with a smile. "I'll ask you to excuse the other hand; it's otherwise engaged just at present."

He slightly raised his right hand, bound at the wrist by the shining "bracelet" to the left one of his companion. The glad look in the girl's eyes slowly changed to a bewildered horror. The glow faded from her cheeks. Her lips parted in a vague, relaxing distress. Easton, with a little laugh, as if amused, was about to speak again when the other forestalled him. The glum-faced man had been watching the girl's countenance with veiled glances from his keen, shrewd eyes.

"You'll excuse me for speaking, miss, but, I see you're acquainted with the marshall here. If you'll ask him to speak a word for me when we get to the pen he'll do it, and it'll make things easier for me there. He's taking me to Leavenworth prison. It's seven years for counterfeiting."

"Oh!" said the girl, with a deep breath and returning color. "So that is what you are doing out here? A marshal!"

"My dear Miss Fairchild," said Easton, calmly, "I had to do something. Money has a way of taking wings unto itself, and you know it takes money to keep step with our crowd in Washington. I saw this opening in the West, and—well, a marshalship isn't quite as high a position as that of ambassador, but——"

"The ambassador," said the girl, warmly, "doesn't call any more. He needn't ever have done so. You ought to know that. And so now you are one of these dashing Western heroes, and you ride and shoot and go into all kinds of dangers. That's different from the Washington life. You have been missed from the old crowd."

The girl's eyes, fascinated, went back, widening a little, to rest upon the glittering handcuffs.

"Don't you worry about them, miss," said the other man. "All marshals handcuff themselves to their prisoners to keep them from getting away. Mr. Easton knows his business."

"Will we see you again soon in Washington?" asked the girl.

"Not soon, I think," said Easton. "My butterfly days are over, I fear."

"I love the West," said the girl, irrelevantly. Her eyes were shining softly.

She looked away out the car window. She began to speak truly and simply, without the gloss of style and manner: "Mamma and I spent the summer in Denver. She went home a week ago because father was slightly ill. I could live and be happy in the West. I think the air here agrees with me. Money isn't everything. But people always misunderstand things and remain stupid——"

"Say, Mr. Marshal," growled the glum-faced man. "This isn't quite fair. I'm needin' a drink, and haven't had a smoke all day. Haven't you talked long enough? Take me in the smoker now, won't you? I'm half dead for a pipe."

The bound travelers rose to their feet, Easton with the same slow smile on his face.

"I can't deny a petition for tobacco," he said, lightly. "It's the one friend of the unfortunate. Good-bye, Miss Fairchild. Duty calls, you know." He held out his hand for a farewell.

"It's too bad you are not going East," she said, reclothing herself with manner and style. "But you must go on to Leavenworth, I suppose?"

"Yes," said Easton, "I must go on to Leavenworth."

The two men sidled down the aisle into the smoker.

The two passengers in a seat near by had heard most of the conversation. Said one of them: "That marshal's a good sort of chap. Some of these Western fellows are all right."

"Pretty young to hold an office like that, isn't he?" asked the other.

"Young!" exclaimed the first speaker, "why—— Oh! didn't you catch on? Say—did you ever know an officer to handcuff a prisoner to his *right* hand?"

THE CACTUS

The most notable thing about Time is that it is so purely relative. A large amount of reminiscence is, by common consent, conceded to the drowning man; and it is not past belief that one may review an entire courtship while removing one's gloves.

That is what Trysdale was doing, standing by a table in his bachelor apartments. On the table stood a singular-looking green plant in a red earthen jar. The plant was one of the species of cacti, and was provided with long, tentacular leaves that perpetually swayed with the slightest breeze with a peculiar beckoning motion.

Trysdale's friend, the brother of the bride, stood at a sideboard complaining at being allowed to drink alone. Both men were in evening dress. White favors like stars upon their coats shone through the gloom of the apartment.

As he slowly unbuttoned his gloves, there passed through Trysdale's mind a swift, scarifying retrospect of the last few hours. It seemed that in his nostrils was still the scent of the flowers that had been banked in odorous masses about the church, and in his ears the lowpitched hum of a thousand well-bred voices, the rustle of crisp garments, and, most insistently recurring, the drawling words of the minister irrevocably binding her to another.

From this last hopeless point of view he still strove, as if it had become a habit of his mind, to reach some conjecture as to why and how he had lost her. Shaken rudely by the uncompromising fact, he had suddenly found himself confronted by a thing he had never before faced—his own innermost, unmitigated, and unbedecked self. He saw all the garbs of pretence and egoism that he had worn now turn to rags of folly. He shuddered at the thought that to others, before now, the garments of his soul must have appeared sorry and threadbare. Vanity and conceit? These were the joints in his armor. And how free from either she had always been——— But why———

As she had slowly moved up the aisle toward the altar he had felt an unworthy, sullen exultation that had served to support him. He had told himself that her paleness was from thoughts of another than the man to whom she was about to give herself. But even that poor consolation had been wrenched from him. For, when he saw that swift, limpid, upward look that she gave the man when he took her hand, he knew himself to be forgotten. Once that same look had been raised to him, and he had gauged its meaning. Indeed, his conceit had crumbled; its last prop was gone. Why had it ended thus? There had been no quarrel between them, nothing———

For the thousandth time he remarshalled in his mind the events of those last few days before the tide had so suddenly turned.

She had always insisted upon placing him upon a pedestal, and he had accepted her homage with royal grandeur. It had been a very sweet incense that she had burned before him; so modest (he told himself); so childlike and worshipful, and (he would once have sworn) so sincere. She had invested him with an almost supernatural number of high attributes and excellencies and talents, and he had absorbed the oblation as a desert drinks the rain that can coax from it no promise of blossom or fruit.

As Trysdale grimly wrenched apart the seam of his last glove, the crowning instance of his fatuous and tardily mourned egoism came vividly back to him.

The scene was the night when he had asked her to come up on his pedestal with him and share his greatness. He could not, now, for the pain of it, allow his mind to dwell upon the memory of her convincing beauty that night—the careless wave of her hair, the tenderness and virginal charm of her looks and words. But they had been enough, and they had brought him to speak. During their conversation she had said:

"And Captain Carruthers tells me that you speak the Spanish language like a native. Why have you hidden this accomplishment from me? Is there anything you do not know?"

Now, Carruthers was an idiot. No doubt he (Trysdale) had been guilty (he sometimes did such things) of airing at the club some old, canting Castilian proverb dug from the hotchpotch at the back of dictionaries. Carruthers, who was one of his incontinent admirers, was the very man to have magnified this exhibition of doubtful erudition.

But, alas! the incense of her admiration had been so sweet and flattering. He allowed the imputation to pass without denial. Without protest, he allowed her to twine about his brow this spurious bay of Spanish scholarship. He let it grace his conquering head, and, among its soft convolutions, he did not feel the prick of the thorn that was to pierce him later.

How glad, how shy, how tremulous she was! How she fluttered like a snared bird when he laid his mightiness at her feet! He could have sworn, and he could swear now, that unmistakable consent was in her eyes, but, coyly, she would give him no direct answer. "I will send you my answer to-morrow," she said; and he, the indulgent, confident victor, smilingly granted the delay.

The next day he waited, impatient, in his rooms for the word. At noon her groom came to the door and left the strange cactus in the red earthen jar. There was no note, no message, merely a tag upon the plant bearing a barbarous foreign or botanical name. He waited until night, but her answer did not come. His large pride and hurt vanity kept him from seeking her. Two evenings later they met at a dinner. Their greetings were conventional, but she looked at him, breathless, wondering, eager. He was courteous, adamant, waiting her explanation. With womanly swiftness she took her cue from his manner, and turned to snow and ice. Thus, and wider from this on, they had drifted apart. Where was his fault? Who had been to blame? Humbled now, he sought the answer amid the ruins of his self-conceit. If——

The voice of the other man in the room, querulously intruding upon his thoughts, aroused him.

"I say, Trysdale, what the deuce is the matter with you? You look unhappy as if you yourself had been married instead of having acted merely as an accomplice. Look at me, another accessory, come two thousand miles on a garlicky, cockroachy banana steamer all the way from South America to connive at the sacrifice—please to observe how lightly my guilt rests upon my shoulders. Only little sister I had, too, and now she's gone. Come now! take something to ease your conscience."

"I don't drink just now, thanks," said Trysdale.

"Your brandy," resumed the other, coming over and joining him, "is abominable. Run down to see me some time at Punta Redonda, and try some of our stuff that old Garcia smuggles in. It's worth the trip. Hallo! here's an old acquaintance. Wherever did you rake up this cactus, Trysdale?"

"A present," said Trysdale, "from a friend. Know the species?"

"Very well. It's a tropical concern. See hundreds of 'em around Punta every day. Here's the name on this tag tied to it. Know any Spanish, Trysdale?"

"No," said Trysdale, with the bitter wraith of a smile—"Is it Spanish?"

"Yes. The natives imagine the leaves are reaching out and beckoning to you. They call it by this name—*Ventomarme*. Name means in English, 'Come and take me.'"

THE DETECTIVE DETECTOR

I was walking in Central Park with Avery Knight, the great New York burglar, highwayman, and murderer.

"But, my dear Knight," said I, "it sounds incredible. You have undoubtedly performed some of the most wonderful feats in your profession known to modern crime. You have committed some marvellous deeds under the very noses of the police—you have boldly entered the homes of millionaires and held them up with an empty gun while you made free with their silver and jewels; you have sandbagged citizens in the glare of Broadway's electric lights; you have killed and robbed with superb openness and absolute impunity—but when you boast that within forty-eight hours after committing a murder you can run down and actually bring me face to face with the detective assigned to apprehend you, I must beg leave to express my doubts—remember, you are in New York."

Avery Knight smiled indulgently.

"You pique my professional pride, doctor," he said in a nettled tone. "I will convince you."

About twelve yards in advance of us a prosperous-looking citizen was rounding a clump of bushes where the walk curved. Knight suddenly drew a revolver and shot the man in the back. His victim fell and lay without moving.

The great murderer went up to him leisurely and took from his clothes his money, watch, and a valuable ring and cravat pin. He then rejoined me smiling calmly, and we continued our walk.

Ten steps and we met a policeman running toward the spot where the shot had been fired. Avery Knight stopped him.

"I have just killed a man," he announced, seriously, "and robbed him of his possessions."

"G'wan," said the policeman, angrily, "or I'll run yez in! Want yer name in the papers, don't yez? I never knew the cranks to come around so quick after a shootin' before. Out of th' park, now, for yours, or I'll fan yez."

"What you have done," I said, argumentatively, as Knight and I walked on, "was easy. But when you come to the task of hunting down the detective that they send upon your trail you will find that you have undertaken a difficult feat."

"Perhaps so," said Knight, lightly. "I will admit that my success depends in a degree upon the sort of man they start after me. If it should be an ordinary plain-clothes man I might fail to gain a sight of him. If they honor me by giving the case to some one of their celebrated sleuths I do not fear to match my cunning and powers of induction against his."

On the next afternoon Knight entered my office with a satisfied look on his keen countenance.

"How goes the mysterious murder?" I asked.

"As usual," said Knight, smilingly. "I have put in the morning at the police station and at the inquest. It seems that a card case of mine containing cards with my name and address was found near the body. They have three witnesses who saw the shooting and gave a description of me. The case has been placed in the hands of Shamrock Jolnes, the famous detective. He left Headquarters at 11:30 on the assignment. I waited at my address until two, thinking he might call there."

I laughed, tauntingly.

"You will never see Jolnes," I continued, "until this murder has been forgotten, two or three weeks from now. I had a better opinion of your shrewdness, Knight. During the three hours and a half that you waited he has got out of your ken. He is after you on true induction theories now, and no wrongdoer has yet been known to come upon him while thus engaged. I advise you to give it up."

"Doctor," said Knight, with a sudden glint in his keen gray eye and a squaring of his chin, "in spite of the record your city holds of something like a dozen homicides without a subsequent meeting of the perpetrator and the sleuth in charge of the case, I will undertake to break that record. To-morrow I will take you to Shamrock Jolnes—I will unmask him before you and prove to you that it is not an impossibility for an officer of the law and a manslayer to stand face to face in your city."

"Do it," said I, "and you'll have the sincere thanks of the Police Department."

On the next day Knight called for me in a cab.

"I've been on one or two false scents, doctor," he admitted. "I know something of detectives' methods, and I followed out a few of them, expecting to find Jolnes at the other end. The pistol being a .45-caliber, I thought surely I would find him at work on the clue in Forty-fifth Street. Then, again, I looked for the detective at the Columbia University, as the man's being shot in the back naturally suggested hazing. But I could not find a trace of him."

"—Nor will you," I said, emphatically.

"Not by ordinary methods," said Knight. "I might walk up and down Broadway for a month without success. But you have aroused my pride, doctor; and if I fail to show you Shamrock Jolnes this day, I promise you I will never kill or rob in your city again."

"Nonsense, man," I replied. "When our burglars walk into our houses and politely demand thousands of dollars' worth of jewels, and then dine and bang the piano an hour or two before leaving, how do you, a mere murderer, expect to come in contact with the detective that is looking for you?"

Avery Knight sat lost in thought for a while. At length he looked up brightly.

"Doc," said he, "I have it. Put on your hat, and come with me. In half an hour I guarantee that you shall stand in the presence of Shamrock Jolnes."

I entered a cab with Avery Knight. I did not hear his instructions to the driver, but the vehicle set out at a smart pace up Broadway, turning presently into Fifth Avenue, and proceeding northward again. It was with a rapidly beating heart that I accompanied this wonderful and gifted assassin, whose analytical genius and superb self-confidence had prompted him to make me the tremendous promise of bringing me into the presence of a murderer and the New York detective in pursuit of him simultaneously. Even yet I could not believe it possible.

"Are you sure that you are not being led into some trap?" I asked. "Suppose that your clue, whatever it is, should bring us only into the presence of the Commissioner of Police and a couple of dozen cops!"

"My dear doctor," said Knight, a little stiffly. "I would remind you that I am no gambler."

"I beg your pardon," said I. "But I do not think you will find Jolnes."

The cab stopped before one of the handsomest residences on the avenue. Walking up and down in front of the house was a man with long red whiskers, with a detective's badge showing on the lapel of his coat. Now and then the man would remove his whiskers to wipe his face, and then I would recognize at once the well-known features of the great New York detective. Jolnes was keeping a sharp watch upon the doors and windows of the house.

"Well, doctor," said Knight, unable to repress a note of triumph in his voice, "have you seen?"

"It is wonderful—wonderful!" I could not help exclaiming as our cab started on its return trip. "But how did you do it? By what process of induction——"

"My dear doctor," interrupted the great murderer, "the inductive theory is what the detectives use. My process is more modern. I call it the saltatorial theory. Without bothering with the tedious mental phenomena necessary to the solution of a mystery from slight clues, I jump at once to a conclusion. I will explain to you the method I employed in this case.

"In the first place, I argued that as the crime was committed in New York City in broad daylight, in a public place and under peculiarly atrocious circumstances, and that as the most skilful sleuth available was let loose upon the case, the perpetrator would never be discovered. Do you not think my postulation justified by precedent?"

"Perhaps so," I replied, doggedly. "But if Big Bill Dev——"

"Stop that," interrupted Knight, with a smile, "I've heard that several times. It's too late now. I will proceed.

"If homicides in New York went undiscovered, I reasoned, although the best detective talent was employed to ferret them out, it must be true that the detectives went about their work in the wrong way. And not only in the wrong way, but exactly opposite from the right way. That was my clue.

"I slew the man in Central Park. Now, let me describe myself to you.

"I am tall, with a black beard, and I hate publicity. I have no money to speak of; I do not like oatmeal, and it is the one ambition of my life to die rich. I am of a cold and heartless disposition. I do not care for my fellowmen and I never give a cent to beggars or charity.

"Now, my dear doctor, that is the true description of myself, the man whom that shrewd detective was to hunt down. You who are familiar with the history of crime in New York of late should be able to foretell the result. When I promised you to exhibit to your incredulous gaze the sleuth who was set upon me, you laughed at me because you said that detectives and murderers never met in New York. I have demonstrated to you that the theory is possible."

"But how did you do it?" I asked again.

"It was very simple," replied the distinguished murderer. "I assumed that the detective would go exactly opposite to the clues he had. I have given you a description of myself. Therefore, he must necessarily set to work and trail a short man with a white beard who likes to be in the papers, who is very wealthy, is fond of oatmeal, wants to die poor, and is of an extremely generous and philanthropic disposition. When thus far is reached the mind hesitates no longer. I conveyed you at once to the spot where Shamrock Jolnes was piping off Andrew Carnegie's residence."

"Knight," said I, "you're a wonder. If there was no danger of your reforming, what a rounds man you'd make for the Nineteenth Precinct!"

THE DOG AND THE PLAYLET [1]

USUALLY it is a cold day in July when you can stroll up Broadway in that month and get a story out of the drama. I found one a few breathless, parboiling days ago, and it seems to decide a serious question in art.

There was not a soul left in the city except Hollis and me—and two or three million sunworshippers who remained at desks and counters. The elect had fled to seashore, lake, and mountain, and had already begun to draw for additional funds. Every evening Hollis and I prowled about the deserted town searching for coolness in empty cafés, dining-rooms, and roofgardens. We knew to the tenth part of a revolution the speed of every electric fan in Gotham, and we followed the swiftest as they varied. Hollis's fiancée, Miss Loris Sherman, had been in the Adirondacks, at Lower Saranac Lake, for a month. In another week he would join her party there. In the meantime, he cursed the city cheerfully and optimistically, and sought my society because I suffered him to show me her photograph during the black coffee every time we dined together.

My revenge was to read to him my one-act play.

It was one insufferable evening when the overplus of the day's heat was being hurled quiveringly back to the heavens by every surcharged brick and stone and inch of iron in the panting town. But with the cunning of the two-legged beasts we had found an oasis where the hoofs of Apollo's steed had not been allowed to strike. Our seats were on an ocean of cool, polished oak; the white linen of fifty deserted tables flapped like seagulls in the artificial breeze; a mile away a waiter lingered for a heliographic signal—we might have roared songs there or fought a duel without molestation.

Out came Miss Loris's photo with the coffee, and I once more praised the elegant poise of the neck, the extremely low-coiled mass of heavy hair, and the eyes that followed one, like those in an oil painting.

"She's the greatest ever," said Hollis, with enthusiasm. "Good as Great Northern Preferred, and a disposition built like a watch. One week more and

1 This story has been rewritten and published in "Strictly Business" under the title, The Proof of the Pudding.

I'll be happy Johnny-on-the-spot. Old Tom Tolliver, my best college chum, went up there two weeks ago. He writes me that Loris doesn't talk about anything but me. Oh, I guess Rip Van Winkle didn't have all the good luck!"

"Yes, yes," said I, hurriedly, pulling out my typewritten play. "She's no doubt a charming girl. Now, here's that little curtain-raiser you promised to listen to."

"Ever been tried on the stage?" asked Hollis.

"Not exactly," I answered. "I read half of it the other day to a fellow whose brother knows Robert Edeson; but he had to catch a train before I finished."

"Go on," said Hollis, sliding back in his chair like a good fellow. "I'm no stage carpenter, but I'll tell you what I think of it from a first-row balcony standpoint. I'm a theatre bug during the season, and I can size up a fake play almost as quick as the gallery can. Flag the waiter once more, and then go ahead as hard as you like with it. I'll be the dog."

I read my little play lovingly, and, I fear, not without some elocution. There was one scene in it that I believed in greatly. The comedy swiftly rises into thrilling and unexpectedly developed drama. Capt. Marchmont suddenly becomes cognizant that his wife is an unscrupulous adventuress, who has deceived him from the day of their first meeting. The rapid and mortal duel between them from that moment—she with her magnificent lies and siren charm, winding about him like a serpent, trying to recover her lost ground; he with his man's agony and scorn and lost faith, trying to tear her from his heart. That scene I always thought was a crackerjack. When Capt. Marchmont discovers her duplicity by reading on a blotter in a mirror the impression of a note that she has written to the Count, he raises his hand to heaven and exclaims: "O God, who created woman while Adam slept, and gave her to him for a companion, take back Thy gift and return instead the sleep, though it last forever!"

"Rot!" said Hollis, rudely, when I had given those lines with proper emphasis.

"I beg your pardon!" I said as sweetly as I could.

"Come now," went on Hollis, "don't be an idiot. You know very well that nobody spouts any stuff like that these days. That sketch went along all right until you rang in the skyrockets. Cut out that right-arm exercise and the Adam and Eve stunt, and make your captain talk as you or I or Bill Jones would."

"I'll admit," said I, earnestly (for my theory was being touched upon), "that on all ordinary occasions all of us use commonplace language to convey our thoughts. You will remember that up to the moment when the captain makes his terrible discovery all the characters on the stage talk pretty much as they would in real life. But I believe that I am right in allowing him lines suitable to the strong and tragic situation into which he falls."

"Tragic, my eye!" said my friend, irreverently. "In Shakespeare's day he might have sputtered out some high-cockalorum nonsense of that sort, because in those days they ordered ham and eggs in blank verse and discharged the cook with an epic. But not for B'way in the summer of 1905!"

"It is my opinion," said I, "that great human emotions shake up our vocabulary and leave the words best suited to express them on top. A sudden violent grief or loss or disappointment will bring expressions out of an ordinary man as strong and solemn and dramatic as those used in fiction or on the stage to portray those emotions."

"That's where you fellows are wrong," said Hollis. "Plain, every-day talk is what goes. Your captain would very likely have kicked the cat, lit a cigar, stirred up a highball, and telephoned for a lawyer, instead of getting off those Robert Mantell pyrotechnics."

"Possibly, a little later," I continued. "But just at the time—just as the blow is delivered, if something Scriptural or theatrical and deep-tongued isn't wrung from a man in spite of his modern and practical way of speaking, then I'm wrong."

"Of course," said Hollis, kindly, "you've got to whoop her up some degrees for the stage. The audience expects it. When the villain kidnaps little Effie you have to make her mother claw some chunks out of the atmosphere, and scream: 'Me chee-ild, me chee-ild!' What she would actually do would be to call up the police by 'phone, ring for some strong tea, and get the little darling's photo out, ready for the reporters. When you get your villain in a corner—a stage corner—it's all right for him to clap his hand to his forehead and hiss: 'All is lost!' Off the stage he would remark: 'This is a conspiracy against me—I refer you to my lawyers.'"

"I get no consolation," said I, gloomily, "from your concession of an accentuated stage treatment. In my play I fondly hoped that I was following life. If people in real life meet great crises in a commonplace way, they should do the same on the stage."

And then we drifted, like two trout, out of our cool pool in the great hotel and began to nibble languidly at the gay flies in the swift current of Broadway. And our question of dramatic art was unsettled.

We nibbled at the flies, and avoided the hooks, as wise trout do; but soon the weariness of Manhattan in summer overcame us. Nine stories up, facing the south, was Hollis's apartment, and we soon stepped into an elevator bound for that cooler haven.

I was familiar in those quarters, and quickly my play was forgotten, and I stood at a sideboard mixing things, with cracked ice and glasses all about me. A breeze from the bay came in the windows not altogether blighted by the asphalt furnace over which it had passed. Hollis, whistling softly, turned over a late-arrived letter or two on his table, and drew around the coolest wicker armchairs.

I was just measuring the Vermouth carefully when I heard a sound. Some man's voice groaned hoarsely: "False, oh, God!—false, and Love is a lie and friendship but the byword of devils!"

I looked around quickly. Hollis lay across the table with his head down upon his outstretched arms. And then he looked up at me and laughed in his ordinary manner.

I knew him—he was poking fun at me about my theory. And it did seem so unnatural, those swelling words during our quiet gossip, that I half began to believe I had been mistaken—that my theory was wrong.

Hollis raised himself slowly from the table.

"You were right about that theatrical business, old man," he said, quietly, as he tossed a note to me.

I read it.

Loris had run away with Tom Tolliver.

A LITTLE TALK ABOUT MOBS

"I SEE," remarked the tall gentleman in the frock coat and black slouch hat, "that another street car motorman in your city has narrowly escaped lynching at the hands of an infuriated mob by lighting a cigar and walking a couple of blocks down the street."

"Do you think they would have lynched him?" asked the New Yorker, in the next seat of the ferry station, who was also waiting for the boat.

"Not until after the election," said the tall man, cutting a corner off his plug of tobacco. "I've been in your city long enough to know something about your mobs. The motorman's mob is about the least dangerous of them all, except the National Guard and the Dressmakers' Convention.

"You see, when little Willie Goldstein is sent by his mother for pigs' knuckles, with a nickel tightly grasped in his chubby fist, he always crosses the street car track safely twenty feet ahead of the car; and then suddenly turns back to ask his mother whether it was pale ale or a spool of 80 white cotton that she wanted. The motorman yells and throws himself on the brakes like a football player. There is a horrible grinding and then a ripping sound, and a piercing shriek, and Willie is sitting, with part of his trousers torn away by the fender, screaming for his lost nickel.

"In ten seconds the car is surrounded by 600 infuriated citizens, crying, 'Lynch the motorman! Lynch the motorman!' at the top of their voices. Some of them run to the nearest cigar store to get a rope; but they find the last one has just been cut up and labelled. Hundreds of the excited mob press close to the cowering motorman, whose hand is observed to tremble perceptibly as he transfers a stick of pepsin gum from his pocket to his mouth.

"When the bloodthirsty mob of maddened citizens has closed in on the motorman, some bringing camp stools and sitting quite close to him, and all shouting, 'Lynch him!' Policeman Fogarty forces his way through them to the side of their prospective victim.

"'Hello, Mike,' says the motorman in a low voice, 'nice day. Shall I sneak off a block or so, or would you like to rescue me?'

"'Well, Jerry, if you don't mind,' says the policeman, 'I'd like to disperse the infuriated mob singlehanded. I haven't defeated a lynching mob since last Tuesday; and that was a small one of only 300, that wanted to string up a Dago boy for selling wormy pears. It would boost me some down at the station.'

"'All right, Mike,' says the motorman, 'anything to oblige. I'll turn pale and tremble.'

"And he does so; and Policeman Fogarty draws his club and says, 'G'wan wid yez!' and in eight seconds the desperate mob has scattered and gone about its business, except about a hundred who remain to search for Willie's nickel."

"I never heard of a mob in our city doing violence to a motorman because of an accident," said the New Yorker.

"You are not liable to," said the tall man. "They know the motorman's all right, and that he wouldn't even run over a stray dog if he could help it. And they know that not a man among 'em would tie the knot to hang even a Thomas cat that had been tried and condemned and sentenced according to law."

"Then why do they become infuriated and make threats of lynching?" asked the New Yorker.

"To assure the motorman," answered the tall man, "that he is safe. If they really wanted to do him up they would go into the houses and drop bricks on him from the third-story windows."

"New Yorkers are not cowards," said the other man, a little stiffly.

"Not one at a time," agreed the tall man, promptly. "You've got a fine lot of single-handed scrappers in your town. I'd rather fight three of you than one; and I'd go up against all the Gas Trust's victims in a bunch before I'd pass two citizens on a dark corner, with my watch chain showing. When you get rounded up in a bunch you lose your nerve. Get you in crowds and you're easy. Ask the 'L' road guards and George B. Cortelyou and the tintype booths at Coney Island. Divided you stand, united you fall. *E pluribus nihil.* Whenever one of your mobs surrounds a man and begins to holler, 'Lynch him!' he says to himself,

'Oh, dear, I suppose I must look pale to please the boys, but I will, forsooth, let my life insurance premium lapse to-morrow. This is a sure tip for me to play Methuselah straight across the board in the next handicap.'

"I can imagine the tortured feelings of a prisoner in the hands of New York policemen when an infuriated mob demands that he be turned over to them for lynching. 'For God's sake, officers,' cries the distracted wretch, 'have ye hearts of stone, that ye will not let them wrest me from ye?'

" 'Sorry, Jimmy,' says one of the policemen, 'but it won't do. There's three of us—me and Darrel and the plain-clothes man; and there's only sivin thousand of the mob. How'd we explain it at the office if they took ye? Jist chase the infuriated aggregation around the corner, Darrel, and we'll be movin' along to the station.' "

"Some of our gatherings of excited citizens have not been so harmless," said the New Yorker, with a faint note of civic pride.

"I'll admit that," said the tall man. "A cousin of mine who was on a visit here once had an arm broken and lost an ear in one of them."

"That must have been during the Cooper Union riots," remarked the New Yorker.

"Not the Cooper Union," explained the tall man—"but it was a union riot—at the Vanastor wedding."

"You seem to be in favor of lynch law," said the New Yorker, severely.

"No, sir, I am not. No intelligent man is. But, sir, there are certain cases when people rise in their just majesty and take a righteous vengeance for crimes that the law is slow in punishing. I am an advocate of law and order, but I will say to you that less than six months ago I myself assisted at the lynching of one of that race that is creating a wide chasm between your section of country and mine, sir."

"It is a deplorable condition," said the New Yorker, "that exists in the South, but——"

"I am from Indiana, sir," said the tall man, taking another chew; "and I don't think you will condemn my course when I tell you that the colored man in question had stolen $9.60 in cash, sir, from my own brother."

THE SNOW MAN

EDITORIAL NOTE.—*Before the fatal illness of William Sydney Porter (known through his literary work as "O. Henry") this American master of short-story writing had begun for Hampton's Magazine the story printed below. Illness crept upon him rapidly and he was compelled to give up writing about at the point where the girl enters the story.*

When he realized that he could do no more (it was his lifelong habit to write with a pencil, never dictating to a stenographer), O. Henry told in detail the remainder of The Snow Man to Harris Merton Lyon, whom he had often spoken of as one of the most effective short-story writers of the present time. Mr. Porter had delineated all of the characters, leaving only the rounding out of the plot in the final pages to Mr. Lyon.

HOUSED and windowpaned from it, the greatest wonder to little children is the snow. To men, it is something like a crucible in which their world melts into a white star ten million miles away. The man who can stand the test is a Snow

Man; and this is his reading by Fahrenheit, Réaumur, or Moses's carven tablets of stone.

Night had fluttered a sable pinion above the cañon of Big Lost River, and I urged my horse toward the Bay Horse Ranch because the snow was deepening. The flakes were as large as an hour's circular tatting by Miss Wilkins's ablest spinster, betokening a heavy snowfall and less entertainment and more adventure than the completion of the tatting could promise. I knew Ross Curtis of the Bay Horse, and that I would be welcome as a snow-bound pilgrim, both for hospitality's sake and because Ross had few chances to confide in living creatures who did not neigh, bellow, bleat, yelp, or howl during his discourse.

The ranch house was just within the jaws of the cañon where its builder may have fatuously fancied that the timbered and rocky walls on both sides would have protected it from the wintry Colorado winds; but I feared the drift. Even now through the endless, bottomless rift in the hills—the speaking tube of the four winds—came roaring the voice of the proprietor to the little room on the top floor.

At my "hello," a ranch hand came from an outer building and received my thankful horse. In another minute, Ross and I sat by a stove in the dining-room of the four-room ranch house, while the big, simple welcome of the household lay at my disposal. Fanned by the whizzing norther, the fine, dry snow was sifted and bolted through the cracks and knotholes of the logs. The cook room, without a separating door, appended.

In there I could see a short, sturdy, leisurely and weather-beaten man moving with professional sureness about his red-hot stove. His face was stolid and unreadable—something like that of a great thinker, or of one who had no thoughts to conceal. I thought his eye seemed unwarrantably superior to the elements and to the man, but quickly attributed that to the characteristic self-importance of a petty chef. "Camp cook" was the niche that I gave him in the Hall of Types; and he fitted it as an apple fits a dumpling.

Cold it was in spite of the glowing stove; and Ross and I sat and talked, shuddering frequently, half from nerves and half from the freezing draughts. So he brought the bottle and the cook brought boiling water, and we made prodigious hot toddies against the attacks of Boreas. We clinked glasses often. They sounded like icicles dropping from the eaves, or like the tinkle of a thousand prisms on a Louis XIV chandelier that I once heard at a boarders' dance in the parlor of a ten-a-week boarding-house in Gramercy Square. *Sic transit.*

Silence in the terrible beauty of the snow and of the Sphinx and of the stars; but they who believe that all things, from a without-wine table d'hôte to the crucifixion, may be interpreted through music, might have found a nocturne or a symphony to express the isolation of that blotted-out world. The clink of glass and bottle, the æolian chorus of the wind in the house crannies, its deeper trombone through the cañon below, and the Wagnerian crash of the cook's pots and pans, united in a fit, discordant melody, I thought. No less welcome an accompaniment was the sizzling of broiling ham and venison cutlets, indorsed by the solvent fumes of true Java, bringing rich promises of comfort to our yearning souls.

The cook brought the smoking supper to the table. He nodded to me democratically as he cast the heavy plates around as though he were pitching quoits or hurling the discus. I looked at him with some appraisement and curiosity and much conciliation. There was no prophet to tell us when that drifting evil outside might cease to fall; and it is well, when snow-bound, to stand somewhere within the radius of the cook's favorable consideration. But I could read neither favor nor disapproval in the face and manner of our pot-wrestler.

He was about five feet nine inches, and two hundred pounds of commonplace, bull-necked, pink-faced, callous calm. He wore brown duck trousers too tight and too short, and a blue flannel shirt with sleeves rolled above his elbows. There was a sort of grim, steady scowl on his features that looked to me as though he had fixed it there purposely as a protection against the weakness of an inherent amiability that, he fancied, were better concealed. And then I let supper usurp his brief occupancy of my thoughts.

"Draw up, George," said Ross. "Let's all eat while the grub's hot."

"You fellows go on and chew," answered the cook. "I ate mine in the kitchen before sun-down."

"Think it'll be a big snow, George?" asked the ranchman.

George had turned to reënter the cook room. He moved slowly around and, looking at his face, it seemed to me that he was turning over the wisdom and knowledge of centuries in his head.

"It might," was his delayed reply.

At the door of the kitchen he stopped and looked back at us. Both Ross and I held our knives and forks poised and gave him our regard. Some men have the power of drawing the attention of others without speaking a word. Their attitude is more effective than a shout.

"And again it mightn't," said George, and went back to his stove.

After we had eaten, he came in and gathered the emptied dishes. He stood for a moment, while his spurious frown deepened.

"It might stop any minute," he said, "or it might keep up for days."

At the farther end of the cook room I saw George pour hot water into his dishpan, light his pipe, and put the tableware through its required lavation. He then carefully unwrapped from a piece of old saddle blanket a paper-back book, and settled himself to read by his dim oil lamp.

And then the ranchman threw tobacco on the cleared table and set forth again the bottles and glasses; and I saw that I stood in a deep channel through which the long dammed flood of his discourse would soon be booming. But I was half content, comparing my fate with that of the late Thomas Tucker, who had to sing for his supper, thus doubling the burdens of both himself and his host.

"Snow is a hell of a thing," said Ross, by way of a foreword. "It ain't, somehow, it seems to me, salubrious. I can stand water and mud and two inches below zero and a hundred and ten in the shade and medium-sized cyclones, but this here fuzzy white stuff naturally gets me all locoed. I reckon the reason it rattles you is because it changes the look of things so much. It's like you had a wife and left her in the morning with the same old blue cotton wrapper on, and rides in of a night and runs across her all outfitted in a white silk evening frock, waving an ostrich-feather fan, and monkeying with a posy of lily flowers. Wouldn't it make you look for your pocket compass? You'd be liable to kiss her before you collected your presence of mind."

By and by, the flood of Ross's talk was drawn up into the clouds (so it pleased me to fancy) and there condensed into the finer snowflakes of thought; and we sat silent about the stove, as good friends and bitter enemies will do. I thought of Ross's preamble about the mysterious influence upon man exerted by that ermine-lined monster that now covered our little world, and knew he was right.

Of all the curious knickknacks, mysteries, puzzles, Indian gifts, rat-traps, and well-disguised blessings that the gods chuck down to us from the Olympian peaks, the most disquieting and evil-bringing is the snow. By scientific analysis it is absolute beauty and purity—so, at the beginning we look doubtfully at chemistry.

It falls upon the world, and lo! we live in another. It hides in a night the old scars and familiar places with which we have grown heart-sick or enamored. So, as quietly as we can, we hustle on our embroidered robes and hie us on Prince Camaralzaman's horse or in the reindeer sleigh into the white country where the seven colors converge. This is when our fancy can overcome the bane of it.

But in certain spots of the earth comes the snow-madness, made known by people turned wild and distracted by the bewildering veil that has obscured the only world they know. In the cities, the white fairy who sets the brains of her dupes whirling by a wave of her wand is cast for the comedy rôle. Her diamond shoe buckles glitter like frost; with a pirouette she invites the spotless carnival.

But in the waste places the snow is sardonic. Sponging out the world of the outliers, it gives no foothold on another sphere in return. It makes of the earth a firmament under foot; it leaves us clawing and stumbling in space in an inimical fifth element whose evil outdoes its strangeness and beauty. There Nature, low comedienne, plays her tricks on man. Though she has put him forth as her highest product, it appears that she has fashioned him with what seems almost incredible carelessness and indexterity. One-sided and with-out balance, with his two halves unequally fashioned and joined, must he ever jog his eccentric way. The snow falls, the darkness caps it, and the ridiculous man-biped strays in accurate circles until he succumbs in the ruins of his defective architecture.

In the throat of the thirsty the snow is vitriol. In appearance as plausible as the breakfast food of the angels, it is as hot in the mouth as ginger, in-creasing the pangs of the water-famished. It is a derivative from water, air, and some cold, uncanny fire from which the caloric has been extracted. Good has been said of it; even the poets, crazed by its spell and shivering in their attics under its touch, have indited permanent melodies commemorative of its beauty.

Still, to the saddest overcoated optimist it is a plague—a corroding plague that Pharaoh successfully side-stepped. It beneficently covers the wheat fields, swelling the crop—and the Flour Trust gets us by the throat like a sudden quinsy. It spreads the tail of its white kirtle over the red seams of the rugged north—and the Alaskan short story is born. Etiolated perfidy, it shelters the mountain traveler burrowing from the icy air—and, melting to-morrow, drowns his brother in the valley below.

At its worst it is lock and key and crucible, and the wand of Circe. When it corrals man in lonely ranches, mountain cabins, and forest huts, the snow makes apes and tigers of the hardiest. It turns the bosoms of weaker ones to glass, their tongues to infants' rattles, their hearts to lawlessness and spleen. It is not all from the isolation; the snow is not merely a blockader; it is a Chemical Test. It is a good man who can show a reaction that is not chiefly composed of a drachm or two of potash and magnesia, with traces of Adam, Ananias, Nebuchadnezzar, and the fretful porcupine.

This is no story, you say; well, let it begin.

There was a knock at the door (is the opening not full of context and reminiscence oh, best buyers of best sellers?).

We drew the latch, and in stumbled Étienne Girod (as he afterward named himself). But just then he was no more than a worm struggling for life, enveloped in a killing white chrysalis.

We dug down through snow, overcoats, mufflers, and waterproofs, and dragged forth a living thing with a Van Dyck beard and marvellous diamond rings. We put it through the approved curriculum of snow-rubbing, hot milk, and teaspoonful doses of whiskey, working him up to a graduating class entitled to a diploma of three fingers of rye in half a glassful of hot water. One of the ranch boys had already come from the quarters at Ross's bugle-like yell and kicked the stranger's staggering pony to some sheltered corral where beasts were entertained.

Let a paragraphic biography of Girod intervene.

Étienne was an opera singer originally, we gathered; but adversity and the snow had made him *non compos vocis.* The adversity consisted of the stranded San Salvador Opera Company, a period of hotel second-story work, and then a career as a professional palmist, jumping from town to town. For, like other professional palmists, every time he worked the Heart Line too strongly he immediately moved along the Line of Least Resistance. Though Étienne did not confide this to us, we surmised that he had moved out into the dusk about twenty minutes ahead of a constable, and had thus encountered the snow. In his most sacred blue language he dilated upon the subject of snow; for Étienne was Paris-born and loved the snow with the same passion that an orchid does.

"Mee-ser-rhable!" commented Étienne, and took another three fingers.

"Complete, cast-iron, pussy-footed, blank . . . blank!" said Ross, and followed suit.

"Rotten," said I.

The cook said nothing. He stood in the door weighing our outburst; and insistently from behind that frozen visage I got two messages (*via* the M. A. M. wireless). One was that George considered our vituperation against the snow childish; the other was that George did not love Dagoes. Inasmuch as Étienne was a Frenchman, I concluded I had the message wrong. So I queried the other: "Bright eyes, you don't really mean Dagoes, do you?" and over the wireless came three deathly, psychic taps: "Yes." Then I reflected that to George all foreigners were probably "Dagoes." I had once known another camp cook who had thought Mons., Sig., and Millie (Trans-Mississippi for Mlle.) were Italian given names; this cook used to marvel therefore at the paucity of Neo-Roman precognomens, and therefore why not——

I have said that snow is a test of men. For one day, two days, Étienne stood at the window, Fletcherizing his finger nails and shrieking and moaning at the monotony. To me, Étienne was just about as unbearable as the snow; and so, seeking relief, I went out on the second day to look at my horse, slipped on a stone, broke my collarbone, and thereafter underwent not the snow test, but the test of flat-on-the-back. A test that comes once too often for any man to stand.

However, I bore up cheerfully. I was now merely a spectator, and from my couch in the big room I could lie and watch the human interplay with that detached, impassive, impersonal feeling which French writers tell us is so valuable to the littérateur, and American writers to the faro-dealer.

"I shall go crazy in this abominable, mee-ser-rhable place!" was Étienne's constant prediction.

"Never knew Mark Twain to bore me before," said Ross, over and over. He sat by the other window, hour after hour, a box of Pittsburg stogies of the length, strength, and odor of a Pittsburg graft scandal deposited on one side of him, and "Roughing It," "The Jumping Frog," and "Life on the Mississippi" on the other. For every chapter he lit a new stogy, puffing furiously. This, in time, gave him a recurrent premonition of cramps, gastritis, smoker's colic, or whatever it is they have in Pittsburg after a too deep indulgence in graft scandals. To fend off the colic, Ross resorted time and again to Old Doctor Still's Amber-Colored U. S. A. Colic Cure. Result, after forty-eight hours—nerves.

"Positive fact I never knew Mark Twain to make me tired before. Positive fact." Ross slammed "Roughing It" on the floor. "When you're snowbound this-away you want tragedy, I guess. Humor just seems to bring out all your cussedness. You read a man's poor, pitiful attempts to be funny and it makes you so nervous you want to tear the book up, get out your bandana, and have a good, long cry."

At the other end of the room, the Frenchman took his finger nails out of his mouth long enough to exclaim: "Humor! Humor at such a time as thees! My God, I shall go crazy in thees abominable——"

"Supper," announced George.

These meals were not the meals of Rabelais who said, "the great God makes the planets and we make the platters neat." By that time, the ranch-house meals were not affairs of gusto; they were mental distraction, not bodily provender. What they were to be later shall never be forgotten by Ross or me or Étienne.

After supper, the stogies and finger nails began again. My shoulder ached wretchedly, and with half-closed eyes I tried to forget it by watching the deft movements of the stolid cook.

Suddenly I saw him cock his ear, like a dog. Then, with a swift step, he moved to the door, threw it open, and stood there.

The rest of us had heard nothing.

"What is it, George?" asked Ross.

The cook reached out his hand into the darkness alongside the jamb. With careful precision he prodded something. Then he made one careful step into the snow. His back muscles bulged a little under the arms as he stooped and lightly lifted a burden. Another step inside the door, which he shut methodically behind him, and he dumped the burden at a safe distance from the fire.

He stood up and fixed us with a solemn eye. None of us moved under that Orphic suspense until,

"A woman," remarked George.

Miss Willie Adams was her name. Vocation, school-teacher. Present avocation, getting lost in the snow. Age, yum-yum (the Persian for twenty). Take to the woods if you would describe Miss Adams. A willow for grace; a hickory for fibre; a birch for the clear whiteness of her skin; for eyes, the blue sky seen through treetops; the silk in cocoons for her hair; her voice, the murmur of the evening June wind in the leaves; her mouth, the berries of the wintergreen; fingers as light as ferns; her toe as small as a deer track. General impression upon the dazed beholder—you could not see the forest for the trees.

Psychology, with a capital P and the foot of a lynx, at this juncture stalks into the ranch house. Three men, a cook, a pretty young woman—all snowbound. Count me out of it, as I did not count, anyway. I never did, with women. Count the cook out, if you like. But note the effect upon Ross and Étienne Girod.

Ross dumped Mark Twain in a trunk and locked the trunk. Also, he discarded the Pittsburg scandals. Also, he shaved off a three days' beard.

Étienne, being French, began on the beard first. He pomaded it, from a little tube of grease Hongroise in his vest pocket. He combed it with a little aluminum comb from the same vest pocket. He trimmed it with manicure scissors from the same vest pocket. His light and Gallic spirits underwent a sudden, miraculous change. He hummed a blithe San Salvador Opera Company tune; he grinned, smirked, bowed, pirouetted, twiddled, twaddled, twisted, and tooralooed. Gayly, the notorious troubadour, could not have equalled Étienne.

Ross's method of advance was brusque, domineering. "Little woman," he said, "you're welcome here!"—and with what he thought subtle double meaning—"welcome to stay here as long as you like, snow or no snow."

Miss Adams thanked him a little wildly, some of the wintergreen berries creeping into the birch bark. She looked around hurriedly as if seeking escape. But there was none, save the kitchen and the room allotted her. She made an excuse and disappeared into her own room.

Later I, feigning sleep, heard the following:

"Mees Adams, I was almos' to perish-die-of monotony w'en your fair and beautiful face appear in thees mee-ser-rhable house." I opened my starboard eye. The beard was being curled furiously around a finger, the Svengali eye was rolling, the chair was being hunched closer to the school-teacher's. "I am French—you see—temperamental—nervous! I cannot endure thees dull hours in thees ranch house; but—a woman comes! Ah!" The shoulders gave nine 'rahs and a tiger. "What a difference! All is light and gay; ever'ting smile w'en you smile. You have 'eart, beauty, grace. My 'eart comes back to me w'en I feel your 'eart. So!" He laid his hand upon his vest pocket. From this vantage point he suddenly snatched at the school-teacher's own hand. "Ah! Mees Adams, if I could only tell you how I ad——"

"Dinner," remarked George. He was standing just behind the Frenchman's ear. His eyes looked straight into the school-teacher's eyes. After thirty seconds of survey, his lips moved, deep in the flinty, frozen maelstrom of his face: "Dinner," he concluded, "will be ready in two minutes."

Miss Adams jumped to her feet, relieved. "I must get ready for dinner," she said brightly, and went into her room.

Ross came in fifteen minutes late. After the dishes had been cleaned away, I waited until a propitious time when the room was temporarily ours alone, and told him what had happened.

He became so excited that he lit a stogy without thinking. "Yeller-hided, unwashed, palm-readin' skunk," he said under his breath. "I'll shoot him full o' holes if he don't watch out—talkin' that way to my wife!"

I gave a jump that set my collarbone back another week. "Your wife!" I gasped.

"Well, I mean to make her that," he announced.

The air in the ranch house the rest of that day was tense with pent-up emotions, oh, best buyers of best sellers.

Ross watched Miss Adams as a hawk does a hen; he watched Étienne as a hawk does a scarecrow. Étienne watched Miss Adams as a weasel does a henhouse. He paid no attention to Ross.

The condition of Miss Adams, in the rôle of sought-after, was feverish. Lately escaped from the agony and long torture of the white cold, where for hours Nature had kept the little school-teacher's vision locked in and turned upon herself, nobody knows through what profound feminine introspections she had gone. Now, suddenly cast among men, instead of finding relief and security, she beheld herself plunged anew into other discomforts. Even in her own room she could hear the loud voices of her imposed suitors. "I'll blow you full o' holes!" shouted Ross. "Witnesses," shrieked Étienne, waving his hand at the cook and me. She could not have known the previous harassed condition of the men, fretting under indoor conditions. All she knew was, that where she had expected the frank freemasonry of the West, she found the subtle tangle of two men's minds, bent upon exacting whatever romance there might be in her situation.

She tried to dodge Ross and the Frenchman by spells of nursing me. They also came over to help nurse. This combination aroused such a natural state of invalid cussedness on my part that they were all forced to retire. Once she did manage to whisper: "I am so worried here. I don't know what to do."

To which I replied, gently, hitching up my shoulder, that I was a hunch-savant and that the Eighth House under this sign, the Moon being in Virgo, showed that everything would turn out all right.

But twenty minutes later I saw Étienne reading her palm and felt that perhaps I might have to recast her horoscope, and try for a dark man coming with a bundle.

Toward sunset, Étienne left the house for a few moments and Ross, who had been sitting taciturn and morose, having unlocked Mark Twain, made an-other dash. It was typical Ross talk.

He stood in front of her and looked down majestically at that cool and per-fect spot where Miss Adams' forehead met the neat part in her fragrant hair. First, however, he cast a desperate glance at me. I was in a profound slumber.

"Little woman," he began, "it's certainly tough for a man like me to see you bothered this way. You"—gulp—"you have been alone in this world too long. You need a protector. I might say that at a time like this you need a protector the worst kind—a protector who would take a three-ring delight in smashing the saffron-colored kisser off of any yeller-skinned skunk that made himself obnoxious to you. Hem. Hem. I am a lonely man, Miss Adams. I have so far had to carry on my life without the"—gulp—"sweet radiance"—gulp—"of a woman around the house. I feel especially doggoned lonely at a time like this, when I am pretty near locoed from havin' to stall indoors, and hence it was with delight I welcomed your first appearance in this here shack. Since then I have been packed jam full of more different kinds of feelings, ornery, mean, dizzy, and superb, than has fallen my way in years." Miss Adams made a useless movement toward escape. The Ross chin stuck firm. "I don't want to annoy you, Miss Adams, but, by heck, if it comes to that you'll have to be annoyed. And I'll have to have my say. This palm-ticklin' slob of a Frenchman ought to be kicked off the place and if you'll say the word, off he goes. But I don't want to do the wrong thing. You've got to show a preference. I'm gettin' around to the point, Miss—Miss Willie, in my own brick fashion. I've stood about all I can stand these last two days and somethin's got to happen. The suspense hereabouts is enough to hang a sheepherder. Miss Willie"—he lassooed her hand by main force—"just say the word. You need somebody to take your part all your life long. Will you mar——"

"Supper," remarked George, tersely, from the kitchen door.

Miss Adams hurried away.

Ross turned angrily. "You——"

"I have been revolving it in my head," said George.

He brought the coffee pot forward heavily. Then bravely the big platter of pork and beans. Then somberly the potatoes. Then profoundly the biscuits. "I have been revolving it in my mind. There ain't no use waitin' any longer for Swengalley. Might as well eat now."

From my excellent vantage-point on the couch I watched the progress of that meal. Ross, muddled, glowering, disappointed; Étienne, eternally blandish-ing, attentive, ogling; Miss Adams, nervous, picking at her food, hesitant about answering questions, almost hysterical; now and then the solid, flitting shadow of the cook, passing behind their backs like a Dreadnaught in a fog.

I used to own a clock which gurgled in its throat three minutes before it struck the hour. I know, therefore, the slow freight of Anticipation. For I have awakened at three in the morning, heard the clock gurgle, and waited those three minutes for the three strokes I knew were to come. *Alors.* In

Ross's ranch house that night the slow freight of Climax whistled in the distance.

Étienne began it after supper. Miss Adams had suddenly displayed a lively interest in the kitchen layout and I could see her in there, chatting brightly at George—not with him—the while he ducked his head and rattled his pans.

"My fren'," said Étienne, exhaling a large cloud from his cigarette and patting Ross lightly on the shoulder with a bediamonded hand which hung limp from a yard or more of bony arm, "I see I mus' be frank with you. Firs', because we are rivals; second, because you take these matters so serious. I—I am Frenchman. I love the women"—he threw back his curls, bared his yellow teeth, and blew an unsavory kiss toward the kitchen. "It is, I suppose, a trait of my nation. All Frenchmen love the women—pretty women. Now, look: Here I am!" He spread out his arms. "Cold outside! I detes' the col-l-l'! Snow! I abominate the mees-ser-rhable snow! Two men! This"—pointing to me—"an' this!" Pointing to Ross. "I am distracted! For two whole days I stan' at the window an' tear my 'air! I am nervous, upset, pr-r-ro-foun'ly distress inside my 'ead! An' suddenly—be'old! A woman, a nice, pretty, charming, innocen' young woman! I, naturally, rejoice. I become myself again—gay, light-'earted, 'appy. I address myself to mademoiselle; it passes the time. That, m'sieu', is wot the women are for—pass the time! Entertainment—like the music, like the wine!

"They appeal to the mood, the caprice, the temperamen'. To play with thees woman, follow her through her humor, pursue her—ah! that is the mos' delightful way to sen' the hours about their business."

Ross banged the table. "Shut up, you miserable yeller pup!" he roared. "I object to your pursuin' anything or anybody in my house. Now, you listen to me, you——" He picked up the box of stogies and used it on the table as an emphasizer. The noise of it awoke the attention of the girl in the kitchen. Unheeded, she crept into the room. "I don't know anything about your French ways of lovemakin' an' I don't care. In my section of the country, it's the best man wins. And I'm the best man here, and don't you forget it! This girl's goin' to be mine. There ain't going to be any playing, or philandering, or palm reading about it. I've made up my mind I'll have this girl, and that settles it. My word is the law in this neck o' the woods. She's mine, and as soon as she says she's mine, you pull out." The box made one final, tremendous punctuation point.

Étienne's bravado was unruffled. "Ah! that is no way to win a woman," he smiled, easily. "I make prophecy you. will never win 'er that way. No. Not thees woman. She mus' be played along an' then keessed, this charming, delicious little creature. One kees! An' then you 'ave her." Again he displayed his unpleasant teeth. "I make you a bet I will kees her——"

As a cheerful chronicler of deeds done well, it joys me to relate that the hand which fell upon Étienne's amorous lips was not his own. There was one sudden sound, as of a mule kicking a lath fence, and then—through the swinging doors of oblivion for Étienne.

I had seen this blow delivered. It was an aloof, unstudied, almost absent-minded affair. I had thought the cook was rehearsing the proper method of turning a flapjack.

Silently, lost in thought, he stood there scratching his head. Then he began rolling down his sleeves.

"You'd better get your things on, Miss, and we'll get out of here," he decided. "Wrap up warm."

I heard her heave a little sigh of relief as she went to get her cloak, sweater, and hat.

Ross jumped to his feet, and said: "George, what are you goin' to do?"

George, who had been headed in my direction, slowly swivelled around and faced his employer. "Bein' a camp cook, I ain't over-burdened with hosses," George enlightened us. "Therefore, I am going to try to borrow this feller's here."

For the first time in four days my soul gave a genuine cheer. "If it's for Lochinvar purposes, go as far as you like," I said, grandly.

The cook studied me a moment, as if trying to find an insult in my words. "No," he replied. "It's for mine and the young lady's purposes, and we'll go only three miles—to Hicksville. Now let me tell you somethin', Ross." Suddenly I was confronted with the cook's chunky back and I heard a low, curt, carrying voice shoot through the room at my host. George had wheeled just as Ross started to speak. "You're nutty. That's what's the matter with you. You can't stand the snow. You're gettin' nervouser, and nuttier every day. That and this Dago"—he jerked a thumb at the half-dead Frenchman in the corner—"has got you to the point where I thought I better horn in. I got to revolvin' it around in my mind and I seen if somethin' wasn't done, and done soon, there'd be murder around here and maybe"—his head gave an imperceptible list toward the girl's room—"worse."

He stopped, but he held up a stubby finger to keep any one else from speaking. Then he plowed slowly through the drift of his ideas. "About this here woman. I know you, Ross, and I know what you reely think about women. If she hadn't happened in here durin' this here snow, you'd never have given two thoughts to the whole woman question. Likewise, when the storm clears, and you and the boys go hustlin' out, this here whole business 'll clear out of your head and you won't think of a skirt again until Kingdom Come. Just because o' this snow here, don't forget you're livin' in the selfsame world you was in four days ago. And you're the same man, too. Now, what's the use o' gettin' all snarled up over four days of stickin' in the house? That there's what I been revolvin' in my mind and this here's the decision I've come to."

He plodded to the door and shouted to one of the ranch hands to saddle my horse.

Ross lit a stogy and stood thoughtful in the middle of the room. Then he began: "I've a durn good notion, George, to knock your confounded head off and throw you into that snowbank, if——"

"You're wrong, mister. That ain't a durned good notion you've got. It's durned bad. Look here!" He pointed steadily out of doors until we were both forced to follow his finger. 'You're in here for more'n a week yet." After allowing this fact to sink in, he barked out at Ross: "Can *you* cook?" Then at me: "Can *you* cook?" Then he looked at the wreck of Étienne and sniffed. There was an embarrassing silence as Ross and I thought solemnly of a foodless week.

"If you just use hoss sense," concluded George, "and don't go for to hurt my feelin's, all I want to do is to take this young gal down to Hicksville; and then I'll head back here and cook fer you."

The horse and Miss Adams arrived simultaneously, both of them very serious and quiet. The horse because he knew what he had before him in that weather; the girl because of what she had left behind.

Then all at once I awoke to a realization of what the cook was doing. "My God, man!" I cried, "aren't you afraid to go out in that snow?"

Behind my back I heard Ross mutter, "Not him."

George lifted the girl daintily up behind the saddle, drew on his gloves, put his foot in the stirrup, and turned to inspect me leisurely.

As I passed slowly in his review, I saw in my mind's eye the algebraic equation of Snow, the equals sign, and the answer in the man before me.

"Snow is my last name," said George. He swung into the saddle and they started cautiously out into the darkening swirl of fresh new currency just issuing from the Snowdrop Mint. The girl, to keep her place, clung happily to the sturdy figure of the camp cook.

I brought three things away from Ross Curtis's ranch house—yea, four. One was the appreciation of snow, which I have so humbly tried here to render; (2) was a collarbone, of which I am extra careful; (3) was a memory of what it is to eat very extremely terribly bad food for a week; and (4) was the cause of (3) a little note delivered at the end of the week and hand-painted in blue pencil on a sheet of meat paper.

"I cannot come back there to that there job. Mrs. Snow say no, George. I been revolvin' it in my mind; considerin' circumstances she's right."

PART II
CRITICAL AND BIOGRAPHICAL COMMENT

PART II

CRITICAL AND BIOGRAPHICAL COMMENT

PART II

CRITICAL AND BIOGRAPHICAL COMMENT

LITTLE PICTURES OF O. HENRY

By Arthur W. Page

PART I—BORN AND RAISED IN NO'TH CA'LINA

IN Greensboro, North Carolina, at the time of Will Porter's youth there were four classes of people: decent white folks, mean white folks, decent "niggers," and mean "niggers." Will Porter and his people belonged to the first class. During the time that he was growing up there were about twenty-five hundred people in Greensboro. It was a simple, democratic little place with rather more intellectual ambitions than most places of its size, but without the hum of modern industry which the cotton mills have latterly brought to it or the great swarm of eager students that now flock to the State Normal School.

In this quiet and pleasant community William Sydney Porter grew up. Algernon Sidney Porter, his father, was a doctor of skill and distinction, who in late life practised his profession little but worked upon many inventions. His mother is said to have written poetry and her father was at one time editor of the Greensboro *Patriot*. A President, a planter, a banker, a blacksmith, a short-story writer or a sailor might any of them have such forbears as these.

If any dependence can be laid upon early "influences" that affect an author's work, in O. Henry's case we must certainly consider Aunt "Henry" Porter. She attended to his bringing up at home and he attended her instruction at school. His mother died when Will Porter was very young, and his aunt, Miss Evelina Porter, ran the Porter household as well as the school next door, and a most remarkable school it was.

Porter's desk-mate in that school, Tom Tate, not long ago wrote the following account, for his niece to read:

"Miss Porter was a maiden lady and conducted a private school on West Market Street, in Greensboro, adjoining the Porter residence. Will was educated there, and this was his whole school education (with the exception of a term or two at graded school). There was a great deal more learned in this little one-story, one-roomed school house than the three R's. It was the custom of 'Miss Lina,' as every one called her, during the recess hour to read aloud to those of her scholars who cared to hear her, and there was always a little group around her chair, listening. She selected good books, and a great many of her old scholars showed the impress of these little readings in after life. On Friday night there was a gathering of the scholars at her home, and those were good times, too. They ate roasted chestnuts, popped corn, or barbecued quail and rabbits before the big open wood fire in her room. There was always a book to read or a story to be told. Then there was a game of story-telling; one of the gathering would start the story and each one of the others was called on in turn to add his quota until the end. Miss Lina's and Will's were always interesting. In the summer time there were picnics and fishing expeditions; in the autumn chinquapin and hickory gatherings; and in the spring wild-flower hunts, all personally conducted by Miss Lina.

"During these days Will showed decided artistic talent, and it was predicted that he would follow in the footsteps of his kinsman, Tom Worth, the cartoonist, but the literary instinct was there, too, and the quaint dry humor and the keen insight into the peculiarities of human nature.

"The boys of the school were divided in two clubs, the Brickbats and the Union Jacks. The members of the Union Jacks were Percy Gray, Will Porter, Jim Doak, and Tom Tate, three of whom died before reaching middle age. Tom Tate is the sole survivor of this little party of four.

"This club had headquarters in an outbuilding on the grounds of the old Edgeworth Female College, which some years previously had been 'destroyed by fire. In this house they kept their arms and accoutrements, consisting of wooden battle-axes, shields, and old cavalry sabers, and on Friday nights it was their custom to sally forth armed and equipped in search of adventure, like knights of old from their castle, carefully avoiding the dark nooks where the moonlight did not fall. Will was the leading spirit in these daring pursuits, and many was the hair-raising adventure these ten-year-old heroes encountered, and the shields and battle-axes were oft-times thrown aside so as not to impede the free action of the nether limbs when safety lay only in flight. Ghosts were of common occurrence in those days, or rather nights, and arms were useless to cope with the supernatural; it took good sturdy legs.

"In the summer an occasional banquet was spread on the moss and grass under the spreading branches of the old oaks that surrounded the club house. On one such festal gathering ginger cakes and lemonade constituted the refreshments. The lemonade was made in a tub furnished by Percy Gray, and during the after-dinner talks one of the Sir Knights imprudently asked if the tub was a new one, and Percy replied in an injured tone: 'Why, of course it is; papa has only bathed in it three times.' To use an old quotation, 'Ah! then and there was hurrying to and fro and blanching of red lips and so forth.' . . .

"After the short school-days Porter found employment as prescription clerk in the drugstore of his uncle, Clarke Porter, and it was there that his genius as an artist and writer budded forth and gave the first promise of the work of after years. The old Porter drugstore was the social club of the town in those days. A game of chess went on in the back room always, and around the old stove behind the prescription counter the judge, the colonel, the doctor, and other local celebrities gathered and discussed affairs of state, the fate of nations, and other things, and incidentally helped themselves to liberal portions of Clarke's Vini Gallaci or smoked his cigars without money and without price. There were some rare characters who gathered around that old stove, some queer personalities, and Porter caught them and transferred them to paper by both pen and pencil in an illustrated comedy satire that was his first public literary and artistic effort.

"When this was read and shown around the stove the picture was so true to life and caught the peculiarities of the *dramatis personæ* so aptly that it was some time before the young playwright was on speaking terms with some of his old friends. 'Alias Jimmy Valentine's' hit [1] is history now, but I doubt if at any time there was a more genuine tribute to Porter's ability than from the audience around the old stove, behind the prescription counter nearly thirty years ago.

[1] This play is the dramatized version of A Retrieved Reformation. (See "Roads of Destiny.")

"In those days Sunday was a day of rest, and Porter with a friend would spend the long afternoons out on some sunny hillside sheltered from the wind by the thick brown broom sedge, lying on their backs gazing up into the blue sky dreaming, planning, talking, or turning to their books, reading. He was an ardent lover of God's great out-of-doors, a dreamer, a thinker, and a constant reader. He was such a man—true-hearted and steadfast to those he cared for, as gentle and sensitive as a woman, retiring to a fault, pure, clean, and honorable."

In these characteristics Will Porter followed in his father's footsteps. It was a saying in Greensboro that if there were cushioned seats in Heaven old Dr. Porter would have one, because of his charity and goodness to the poor. And there was an active sympathy between the old man and his son. The old gentleman on cold stormy nights when his boy was late getting home from the drugstore always had a roaring wood fire for him, and a pot of coffee and potatoes and eggs warming in the fire for his midnight supper.

This timid, quiet lad, who would slip around to the back door of "Miss Lina's," if there was company in the front of the house, held a little court of his own at the drugstore. He was the delight and pride of men two and three times his age. They still talk of the pictures he drew, the quiet pranks he played; but their greatest pride in him, as indicated above, is as a playwright. If you find one of that group now, and speak of O. Henry he will ask: "Did you ever hear of the play Will wrote when he was sixteen?" and then he will launch into laughing description of the little play written thirty-five years ago.

His pencil was busy most of the time, if not with writing, with drawing. He was a famous cartoonist. There are several versions of the story about him and an important customer at his uncle's store. Young Porter did not remember the customer's name, but when the man asked him to charge some articles he did not wish to admit his ignorance. So he put down the items and drew a picture of the customer. His uncle had no difficulty in recognizing the likeness. Perhaps one of the other versions of this story is the true one, but as they all unite upon the fact that he made a likeness that was accurate enough for his uncle to base his accounts upon, we may be certain that during his drugstore-club days young Porter was an adept at pencil mimicry as well as personal playwright. It is as certain, too, that he dearly loved practical jokes. According to Mr. Charles Benbow, of Greensboro, "there was an old darkey by the name of Pink Lindsay who swept out the drugstore, made fires, and so forth. He was very fond of whiskey, and it took great care on the part of Will Porter and Ed. Michaux, clerks, to keep Pink away from the whiskey used in prescriptions. They had a barrel of whiskey in the cellar and used a rubber tube to syphon the whiskey out of the barrel into a big bottle which was kept at the prescription counter. Notwithstanding the fact that the rubber tube was kept under lock and key old Pink or somebody was getting the whiskey. One day Will was in the cellar having Pink clean up the rubbish, and while sweeping down cobwebs he discovered two long straws hid on the wall of earth near the whiskey barrel. He said nothing. When Pink was out he examined the barrel and discovered a small hole bored into the top near the end of the cask. Immediately he divined how and where the whiskey went. He quietly took the straws upstairs and filled them with capsicum. He put them back exactly where he had found them. In those days we did not need pure food laws—capsicum was red pepper genuine. Pink was kept out of the cellar all day. The next morning being a cold one, Pink was both dry and cold. When Will sent him down cellar he was more than ready to comply. The cellar door opened out on the sidewalk and was one of those folding doors that when closed down act as a part of the sidewalk. It is usually closed as one goes down cellar. This time Pink happened to leave it open, and it was well for him. A few minutes elapsed and he let out a howl that would have done credit to a Comanche Indian. Yelling that he was poisoned, he made a bee line for the pump out in the street. Will pumped water for him until he could talk, and then he pumped the truth out of Pink about the straws. He was 'pizened,' and he was afire, and he promised never to use the straws again. All the while Will was as sober as a judge. He never smiled, and Pink did not suspect him."

In 1882 Dr. and Mrs. J. K. Hall went to Texas to visit their sons, Richard and Lee Hall, of Texas-ranger fame, and Will Porter was sent with them, because it was thought that the close confinement in the drugstore was undermining his health. He never again lived in Greensboro, but Greensboro was never altogether out of his mind. Many years later, when he was living in New York, he wrote this account of himself—an account which gives an inkling of the whimsical charm of the man and his fondness for the old life in the old land of his birth.

"I take my pen in hand to say that I am from the South and have been a stranger in New York for four years. I am sometimes full of sunshine and at other times about as cross and disagreeable as you ever see 'em. But I know a restaurant where you can get real Corn Bread, clean, respectable, cozy, and draw the line at two things. I will not go to Coney Island and will not take walks on Sunday afternoons.

"It's a hard task to tell about one's self, for if you say too much you get turned down for an egotist, and if you don't say enough the man with the black mustache and side-bar buggy gets ahead of you.

"Now for something very personal and thrilling. It's about me."

(*The following paragraph was cut from a newspaper and pasted on the letter.*)

"'He is a true soldier of fortune. He is still a very young man, but he has lived a varied life. He has been a cowboy, sheepherder, merchant, salesman, miner, and a great many other nameless things in the course of a number of very full years spent doing our West, South-west, Mexico, South and Central America. He went about with a keen eye and supplemented it with a ready notebook, into which he jotted down his impressions and things that happened his way.'

"There are a few misstatements in the excerpt. I am not a 'very young man.' Wish I was. I have never been a cowboy, sheepherder, merchant, salesman, or miner. But I lived 'on the ground' with cowboys for two years. I never carried a notebook in my life. But here I plead guilty."

(*Here follows another newspaper clipping.*)

"'He carried an abundant good fellowship and humor with him and saw the bright and amusing side of things.'

"Don't forget that I am the only original dispenser of sunshine.

"You may notice that I suppress my pen name in the quotations. I do that because I have been trying to keep my personality separate from my *nom de guerre* except from my intimate friends and publishers.

"I was born and raised in 'No'th Ca'lina' and at eighteen went to Texas and ran wild on the prairies. Wild yet, but not so wild. Can't get to loving New Yorkers. Live all alone in a great big two rooms on quiet old Irving Place three doors from Wash. Irving's old home. Kind of lonesome. Was thinking lately (since the April moon commenced to shine) how I'd like to be down South, where I could happen over to Miss Ethel's or Miss Sallie's and sit on the porch—not on a chair—on the edge of the porch, and lay my straw hat on the steps and lay my head back against the honeysuckle on the post—and just talk. And Miss Ethel would go in directly (they say presently up here) and bring out the guitar. She would complain that the E string was broken, but no one would believe her, and pretty soon all of us would be singing the 'Swanee River' and 'In the Evening by the Moonlight' and—oh, gol darn it, what's the use of wishing.''

PART II—TEXAN DAYS

Will Porter found a new kind of life in Texas—a life that filled his mind with that rich variety of types and adventures which later was translated into his stories. Here he got—from observation, and not from experience, as has often been said, for he was never a cowboy—the originals of his Western characters and Western scenes. He looked on at the more picturesque life about him rather than shared in it; though through his warm sympathy and his vivid imagination he entered into its spirit as completely as any one who had fully lived its varied parts.

It was while he was living on the Hall ranch, to which he had gone in search of health, that he wrote—and at once destroyed—his first stories of Western life. And it was there, too, that he drew the now famous series of illustrations for a book that never was printed. The author of that book, "Uncle Joe" Dixon, was a prospector in the bonanza mining days in Colorado. Now he is a newspaper editor in Florida; and he has lately told, for the survivors of Will Porter's friends of that period, the story of the origin of these drawings. His narrative illustrates anew the remarkable impression that Will Porter's quaint and whimsical personality, even in his boyhood, made upon those who knew him.

Other friends, who knew him more intimately than "Uncle Joe" Dixon, saw other sides of Will Porter's character. With them his boyish love of fun and of good-natured and sometimes daredevil mischief came again to the surface, as well as those refinements of feeling and manner that were his heritage as one of the "decent white folks" of Greensboro. And with them, too, came out the ironical fate that pursued him most of his life—to be a dreamer and yet to be harnessed to tasks that brought his head from the clouds to the commonplaces of the store and the street. Perhaps it was this very bending of a sky-seeking imagination to the dusty comedy of every day that brought him later to see life as he pictured it in "The Four Million," with its mingling of Caliph Haroun-al-Raschid's romance with the adventures of shop girls and restaurant-keepers. At any rate, even the Texas of the drug-clerk days and of the bank-clerk period appealed to his sense of the humorous and romantic and grotesque. Here is what one intimate of those days recalls of his character and exploits:

"Will Porter, shortly after coming to Texas, became a member of the Hill City Quartette, of Austin, composed of C. E. Hillyer, R. H. Edmundson, Howard Long, and himself. Porter was the littlest man in the crowd, and, of course, basso profundo. He was about five feet six inches tall, weighed about one hundred and thirty pounds, had coal-black hair, gray eyes, and a long, carefully twisted moustache; looked as though he might be a combination between the French and the Spanish, and I think he once told me that the blood of the Huguenot flowed in his veins. He was one of the most accomplished gentlemen I ever knew. His voice was soft and musical, with just enough rattle in it to rid it of all touch of effeminacy. He had a keen sense of humor, and there were two distinct methods of address which were characteristic with him—his business address and his friendly address. As a business man, his face was calm, almost expressionless; his demeanor was steady, even calculated. He always worked for a high class of employers, was never wanting for a position, and was prompt, accurate, talented, and very efficient; but the minute he was out of business—that was all gone. He always approached a friend with a merry twinkle in his eye and an expression which said: 'Come on, boys, we are going to have a lot of fun,' and we usually did.

"The story of The Green Door [1] in its spirit and in its fact was just such a thing as might happen with him any night. It is but justice, in order to give balance to this unique character, to say that he made no religious professions; he never talked infidelity nor scepticism; he had such a reverence for other people's views that he never entered into religious discussions; and personally he seemed rather indifferent to the subject, though in no wise opposed to it. He rarely ever missed church, and the Hill City Quartette were nearly always to be found in either the Baptist or the St. David's Episcopal Church choirs, though he usually attended church on Sunday evenings at the Presbyterian Church and sang in their choir.

"He got interested in society and lost all taste for the drug business. Being a fine penman, a good accountant, well educated, and with good address, it was an easy matter for him to make a living without working every day and Sunday, too, and most of the evenings besides. The fact of the matter is, while W. S. P. would not have admitted it for the world, I think he really wanted a little more time for love-making. So during the time of our association, he went to work at eight in the morning and quit at four. He always had sufficient money for what he needed; if he had any more, no one knew it. He was very fond of going fishing, but he let you do the fishing after he went. He loved to go hunting, but he let you kill the birds, and somehow I always thought that on these trips he got something out of the occasion that he enjoyed all by himself; they were not occasions which invited the introduction of sentiment, yet I believe his enjoyment of them was purely sentimental. He loved the mountains and the plains; he loved to hear the birds sing and the brooks babble, and all those things, but he did not talk to the boys about it.

"He was accomplished in all the arts of a society man; had a good bass voice and sang well; was a good dancer and skater; played an interesting game of cards, and was preëminently an entertainer. There were no wall flowers to Porter, and the girl who went with him never lacked for attention.

"The Hill City Quartette formed the centre of the Social Circle in which W. S. P. was the central figure during the period of this writing.

"If W. S. P. at this time had any ambitions as a writer, he never mentioned it to me. I do not recall that he was fond of reading. One day I quoted some lines to him from a poem by John Alexander Smith. He made inquiry about the author, borrowed the book, and committed to memory a great many passages from it, but I do not recall ever having known him to read any other book. I asked him one day why he never read fiction. His reply was: 'That it was all tame compared with the romance in his own life,'—which was really true.

"Mr. Porter was very careful in the use and selection of language. He rarely used slang, and his style in ordinary conversation was very much purer and more perfect than it is in his writings. This can be accounted for in the fact that he was an unusually polished gentleman, but writing in the first person, the character which he selects to represent himself appears to be along a much lower and commoner line than he himself actually lived; but, on the other hand, the stories that he writes and the quaint way he has of putting things were largely characteristic of his personal daily life, and the peculiar

1 See "The Four Million."

turn that he gives to his stories—in which he leads you to think along logical lines until you think you have anticipated his conclusion, then suddenly brings the story to a reasonable but wholly unexpected conclusion—was even in this early day an element in his common conversation.

"In the great railroad strike at Fort Worth, Texas, the Governor called out the State Militia, and the company to which we belonged was sent, but as we were permitted a choice in the matter, Porter and I chose not to go. In a little while a girl he was in love with went to Waco on a visit. Porter moped around disconsolate for a few days, and suddenly said to me: 'I believe I'll take a visit at the Government's expense.' With him to think was to act. A telegram was sent to Fort Worth: 'Capt. Blank, Fort Worth, Texas. Squad of volunteers Company Blank, under my command, tender you their services if needed. Reply.' 'Come next train,' Captain Blank commanded. Upon reaching the depot no orders for transportation of squad had been received. Porter actually held up the train until he could telegraph and get transportation for his little squad, because the girl had been notified that he would be in Waco on a certain train. She afterward said that when the train pulled into Waco he was sitting on the engine pilot with a gun across his lap and a distant glance at her was all that he got, but he had had his adventure and was fully repaid.

"This adventure is only one of thousands of such incidents that commonly occurred in his life. He lived in an atmosphere of adventure that was the product of his own imagination. He was an inveterate story-teller, seemingly purely from the pleasure of it, but he never told a vulgar joke, and as much as he loved humor he would not sacrifice decency for its sake, and his stories about women were always refined.

"He told a great many stories in the first person. We were often puzzled to know whether they were real or imaginary, and when we made inquiry his stock reply was: 'Never question the validity of a joke.'

"One night at the Lampasas Military Encampment of Texas Volunteer Guards, the Quartette, with others, had leave of absence to attend the big ball at the Park Hotel, with orders to report at 12:00 sharp. Somehow, with girls and gaiety and music and balmy Southern breezes and cooing voices, time flies, and before any of us had thought to look at a watch it was five minutes past twelve and we were in trouble. We had all gathered near the doorway looking toward Camp when we saw the Corporal of the guard approaching the building to arrest us. Of course, what follows could never have happened in a camp of tried veterans, but Porter knew the human animal as few people do. He got a friend with an unlimited leave of absence to meet the Corporal's squad at another door and suggest to them that they should not carry the guns in among the ladies. So the squad stacked their guns on the outside and went into the other door to arrest us. Up to this point Porter had worked the thing without taking us into his confidence. As soon as the guns were stacked he beckoned to us to follow and we did not stop for explanation. We knew where Porter led there would be adventure, if not success. He took command; we unstacked the arms of the corporal's squad; all our boys who did not carry guns were marched as under arrest. Now none of us knew the countersign, and our success in getting by the sentry was a matter of pure grit. As we approached the sentry we were crossing a narrow plank bridge in single file, at the end of which the sentry threw up his gun and Porter marched us right straight up to that gun until the front man was marking time with the point of the gun right against his stomach. Porter just said to the sentry, 'Squad under arrest. Stand aside!' The whole thing was done with such courage, decision, and audacity, that the sentry never noticed that we had not given the countersign, but stepped aside and let us pass. A few yards into the camp we stacked our guns, and sneaked into our tents. When the real corporal and squad came back to camp and told his story the sentry refused to accept it and had the whole squad placed in the guardhouse for the night. When the boys began to whisper the joke to their comrades in their tents, the disturbance became so great that the Corporal's Guard came down to ascertain the cause of the disturbance, but on looking into the tent found only tired soldier boys snoring as though they had been drugged. There was quite a time at the court-martial next morning, at which the Corporal and his body were given extra duty for their inglorious behavior on the previous night, but no one ever knew our connection with the story."

But the lure of the pen was getting too strong for Will Porter to resist. Life as a teller in the First National Bank of Austin was too routine not to be relieved by some outlet for his love of fun and for his creative literary instinct. An opportunity opened to buy a printing outfit, and he seized it and used it for a year to issue the *Rolling Stone*, a weekly paper that suggested even then his later method as a humorist and as a photographic portrayer of odd types of humanity. Dr. D. Daniels—"Dixie" he was to Will Porter—now a dentist in Galveston, Texas, was his partner in this enterprise, and his story of that year of fun gives also a picture of Will Porter's habit of studying human nature at first hand—a habit that later carried him into many quaint byways of New York and into many even more quaint and revealing byways of the human heart. Here is Dr. Daniels's story:

"It was in the spring of 1894 that I floated into Austin," said Daniels, "and I got a place in the State printing office. I had been working there for a short time when I heard that a man named Porter had bought out the old *Iconoclast* plant—known everywhere as Brann's *Iconoclast*—and was looking for a printer to go into the game with him. I went around to see him, and that was the first time I met O. Henry. Porter had been a clerk in the Texas Land Office, and a teller in the First National Bank in Austin, and when W. C. Brann went to Waco decided to buy out his plant and run a weekly humorous paper.

"I talked things over with him, the proposition looked good, and we formed a partnership then and there. We christened the paper the *Rolling Stone* after a few discussions, and in smaller type across the full-page head we printed 'Out for the moss.' Which is exactly what we were out for. Our idea was to run this weekly with a lot of current events treated in humorous fashion, and also to run short sketches, drawings, and verse. I had been doing a lot of chalk-plate work and the specimens I showed seemed to make a hit with Porter. Those chalk-plates were the way practically all of our cuts were printed.

"Porter was one of the most versatile men I had ever met. He was a fine singer, could write remarkably clever stuff under all circumstances, and was a good hand at sketching. And he was the best mimic I ever saw in my life. He was one of the genuine democrats that you hear about more often than you meet. Night after night, after we would shut up shop, he would call to me to come along and 'go bumming.' That was his favorite expression for the night-time prowling in which we indulged. We would wander through streets and alleys, meeting with some of the worst specimens of down-and-outers it has ever been my privilege to see at close range. I've seen the most ragged specimen of a bum hold up Porter, who would always do anything he could for the man. His one great failing was his inability to say 'No' to a man.

"He never cared for the so-called 'higher classes' but watched the people on the streets and in the shops and cafés, getting his ideas from them night after night. I think that it was in this way he was able to picture the average man with such marvellous fidelity.

"Well, as I started to say, we moved into the old *Iconoclast* plant, got out a few issues, and moved into the Brueggerhoff Building. The *Rolling Stone* met with unusual success at the start, and we had in our files letters from men like Bill Nye and John Kendrick Bangs praising us for the quality of the sheet. We were doing nicely, getting the paper out every Saturday—approximately—and blowing the gross receipts every night. Then we began to strike snags. One of our features was a series of cuts with humorous underlines of verse. One of the cuts was the rear view of a fat German professor leading an orchestra, beating the air wildly with his baton. Underneath the cut Porter had written the following verse:

> With his baton the professor beats the bars,
> 'Tis also said he beats them when he treats.
> But it made that German gentleman see stars
> When the bouncer got the cue to bar the beats.

"For some reason or other that issue alienated every German in Austin from the *Rolling Stone*, and cost us more than we were able to figure out in subscriptions and advertisements.

"Another mistake Porter made was when he let himself be dragged into a San Antonio political fight—the O'Brien-Callighan mayoralty campaign. He was pulled into this largely through a broken-down English writer, whose name, as I remember, was Henry Rider Taylor. How Taylor had any influence over him I never was able to make out, for he used constantly to make fun of him. 'Here comes that man Taylor,' he'd say. 'Got a diamond on him as big as a two-bit piece and shinin' like granulated sugar.' But he went into the political scrap just the same, and it cost him more than it was worth.

"We got out one feature of the paper that used to meet with pretty general approval. It was a page gotten up in imitation of a backwoods country paper, and we christened it *The Plunkville Patriot*. That idea has been carried out since then in a dozen different forms, like *The Hogwallow Kentuckian*, and *The Bingville Bugle*, to give two of the prominent examples. Porter and I used to work on this part of the paper nights and Sundays. I would set the type for it, as there was a system to all of the typographical errors that we made, and I couldn't trust any one else to set it up as we wanted it.

"Porter used to think up some right amusing features for this part of the paper. I remember that about when we had on hand a lot of cuts of Gilmore, of Gilmore's Band, which played at the dedication of the State capitol at Austin. We would run these cuts of Gilmore for any one, from Li Hung Chang to Governor Hogg.

"The Populist Party was coming in for all sorts of publicity at this time, and the famous 'Sockless' Simpson, of Kansas, was running for Congress. Porter worked out a series of 'Tictocq, the Great French Detective,' in burlesque of 'Lecoq,' and in one story, I remember, had a deep-laid conspiracy to locate a pair of socks in Simpson's luggage, thus discrediting him with his political following.

"The paper ran along for something over a year, and then was discontinued. Following the political trouble and the other troubles in which Porter became involved, he left the State. Some time was spent in Houston; the next stop was New Orleans; then he jumped to South America, and only returned to Texas for a short period before leaving the State forever. His experiences on a West Texas ranch, in Texas cities and in South America, however, gave him a thorough insight into the average run of people whom he pictured so vividly in his later work. He was a greater man than any of us knew when we were with him in the old days."

Part III—The New York Days—*Richard Duffy's narrative*

His coming to New York, with the resolution "to write for bread," as he said once in a mood of acrid humor, was dramatic, as is a whisper compared to a subdued tumult of voices. I believe I am correct in saying that outside his immediate family few were aware that O. Henry was entering this "nineday town" except Gilman Hall, my associate on *Ainslee's Magazine*, the publishers, Messrs. Street and Smith, and myself. For some time we had been buying stories from him, written in his perfect Spencerian copperplate hand that was to become familiar to so many editors. Only then he wrote always with a pen on white paper, whereas once he was established in New York he used a lead pencil sharpened to a needle's point on one of the yellow pads that were always to be seen on his table. The stories he published at this period were laid either in the Southwest or in Central America, and those of the latter countries form the bulk of his first issued volume, "Cabbages and Kings." It was because we were sure of him as a writer that our publishers willingly advanced the check that brought him to New York and assured him a short breathing spell to look round and settle. Also, it was because O. Henry wanted to come. You could always make him do anything he wanted to do, as he had a way of saying, if you were coaxing him into an invitation he had no intention of pursuing into effect.

It was getting late on a fine spring afternoon down at Duane and William streets when he came to meet us. From the outer gate the boy presented a card bearing the name William Sydney Porter. I don't remember just when we found out that "O. Henry" was merely a pen name; but think it was during the correspondence arranging that he come to New York. I do remember, however, that when we were preparing our yearly prospectus, we had written to him, asking that he tell us what the initial O. stood for, as we wished to use his photograph and preferred to have his name in full. It was the custom and would make his name stick faster in the minds of readers. With a courteous flourish of appreciation at the honor we were offering him in making him known to the world, he sent us 'Oliver,' and so he appeared as Oliver Henry in the first publishers' announcement in which his stories were heralded. Later he confided to us, smiling, what a lot of fun he had had in picking out a first name of sufficient advertising effectiveness that began with O.

As happens in these matters, whatever mind picture Gilman Hall or I had formed of him from his letters, his handwriting, his stories, vanished before the impression of the actual man. He wore a dark suit of clothes, I recall, and a four-in-hand tie of bright color. He carried a black derby, high-crowned, and walked with a springy, noiseless step. To meet him for the first time you felt his most notable quality to be reticence, not a reticence of social timidity, but a reticence of deliberateness. If you also were observing, you would soon understand that his reticence proceeded from the fact that civilly yet masterfully he was taking in every item of the "you" being presented to him to the accompaniment of convention's phrases and ideas, together with the "you" behind this presentation. It was because he was able thus to assemble and sift all the multifarious elements of a personality with sleight-of-hand swiftness that you find him characterizing a person or a neighborhood in a sentence or two; and once I heard him characterize a list of editors he knew each in a phrase.

On his first afternoon in New York we took him on our usual walk uptown from Duane Street to about Madison Square. That was a long walk for O. Henry, as any one who knew him may witness. Another long one was when he walked about a mile over a fairly high hill with me on a zigzag path through autumn woods. I showed him plains below us and hills stretching away so far and blue they looked like the illimitable sea from the deck of an ocean liner. But it was not until we approached the station from which we were to take the train back to New York that he showed the least sign of animation. "What's the matter, Bill?" I asked, "I thought you'd like to see some real country." His answer was: "Kunn'l, how kin you expeck me to appreciate the glories of nature when you walk me over a mounting like that an' I got new shoes on?" Then he stood on one foot and on the other, caressing each aching member for a second or two, and smiled with bashful knowingness so like him.

It was one of his whimsical amusements, I must say here, to speak in a kind of country style of English, as though the English language were an instrument he handled with hesitant unfamiliarity. Thus it happened that a woman who had written to him about his stories and asked if her "lady friend" and she might meet him, informed him afterward: "You mortified me nearly to death, you talked so ungrammatical!"

We never knew just where he stopped the first night in New York, beyond his statement that it was at a hotel not far from the ferry in a neighborhood of so much noise that he had not been able to sleep. I suppose we were voluminous with suggestions as to where he might care to live, because we felt we had some knowledge of the subject of board and lodging, and because he was the kind of man you'd give your best hat to on short acquaintance, if he needed a hat—but also he was the kind of man who would get a hat for himself. Within about twenty-four hours he called at the office again to say that he had taken a large room in a French table d'hôte hotel in Twenty-fourth Street, between Broadway and Sixth Avenue. Moreover, he brought us a story. In those days he was very prolific. He wrote not only stories, but occasional skits and light verse. In a single number of *Ainslee's*, as I remember, we had three short stories of his, one of which was signed "O. Henry" and the other two with pseudonyms. Of the latter, While the Auto Waits,[1] was picked out by several newspapers outside New York as an unusually clever short story. But as O. Henry naturally he appeared most frequently, as frequently as monthly publication allows, for to my best recollection of the many stories we saw of his there were only three about which we said to him we would rather have another instead.

Still he lived in West Twenty-fourth Street, although the place had no particular fascination for him. We used to see him every other day or so, at luncheon, at dinner, or in the evening. Various magazine editors began to look up O. Henry, which was a job somewhat akin to tracing a lost person. While his work was coming under general notice rapidly, he made no effort to push himself into general acquaintance; and all who knew him when he was actually somewhat of a celebrity should be able to say that it was about as easy to induce him to "go anywhere" to meet somebody, as it is to have a child take medicine. He was persuaded once to be the guest of a member of the Periodical Publishers' Association on a sail up the Hudson; but when the boat made a stop at Poughkeepsie, O. Henry slipped ashore and took the first train back to New York. Yet he was not unsociable, but a man that liked a few friends round him and who dreaded and avoided a so-called "party" as he did a crowd in the subway.

---

1 See "Voice of the City."

It was at his Twenty-fourth Street room that Robert H. Davis, then of the staff of the New York *World*, ran him to cover, as it were, and concluded a contract with him to furnish one story a week for a year at a fixed salary. It was a gigantic task to face, and I have heard of no other writer who put the same quality of effort and material in his work able to produce one story every seven days for fifty-two successive weeks. The contract was renewed, I believe, and all during this time O. Henry was selling stories to magazines as well. His total of stories amounts to two hundred and fifty-one, and when it is considered that they were written in about eight years, one may give him a good mark for industry, especially as he made no professional vaunt about "loving his work." Once, when dispirited, he said that almost any other way of earning a living was less of a toil than writing. The mood is common to writers, but not so common as to happen to a man who practically had editors or agents of editors sitting on his doorstep requesting copy.

When he undertook his contract with the *World* he moved to have more room and more comfortable surroundings for the new job. But he did not move far, no farther than across Madison Square, in East Twenty-fourth Street, to a house near Fourth Avenue. Across the street stands the Metropolitan Building, although it was not so vast then. He had a bedroom and sitting-room at the rear of the parlor floor with a window that looked out on a typical New York yard, boasting one ailanthus tree frowned upon by time-stained extension walls of other houses. More and more men began to seek him out, and he was glad to see them, for a good deal of loneliness enters into the life of a man that writes fiction during the better part of the day, and when his work is over feels he must move about somewhere to gather new material. Here it was that he received a visit one day from a stranger, who announced that he was a business man, but had decided to change his line. He meant to write stories, and having read several of O. Henry's, he was convinced that that kind of story would be the best paying proposition. O. Henry liked the man off-hand, but he could not help being amused at his attitude toward a "literary career." I asked what advice he gave the visitor, and he answered: "I told him to go ahead!" The sequel no doubt O. Henry thoroughly enjoyed, for within a few years the stranger had become a best-seller, and continues such.

O. Henry remained only for a few months in these lodgings, having among a dozen reasons for moving the fact that he had more money.

I follow his movings with his trunks, his bags, his books, a few, but books he read, and his pictures, likewise a few, that were original drawings presented to him, or some familiar printed picture that had caught his fancy, because in his movings you trace his life in New York. His next abiding-place was at 55 Irving Place, as he has said in a letter, "a few doors from old Wash. Irving's house." Here he had almost the entire parlor floor with a window large as a store front, opening only at the sides in long panels. At either one of these panels he would sit for hours watching the world go by along the street, not gazing idly, but noting men and women with penetrating eyes, making guesses at what they did for a living, and what fun they got out of it when they had earned it.

He was a man you could sit with a long while and feel no necessity for talking; but every so often a passerby would evoke a remark from him that converted an iota of humanity into the embryo of a story. Although he spoke hardly ever to any one in the house except the people who managed it, he had the lodgers all ticketed in his mind. He was friendly but distant with persons of the neighborhood he was bound to meet regularly, because he lived so long there, and I have often thought he must have persisted as a mysterious man to them simply because he was so far from being communicative.

From Irving Place he went back across the Square to live in a house next to the rectory of Trinity Chapel in West Twenty-fifth Street. But now he moved because the landlady and several lodgers were moving to the same house. From here his next change was to the Caledonia, in West Twenty-sixth Street, whence, as everybody knows, he made his last move to the Polyclinic Hospital, where he died.

PART IV—AS HE SHOWED HIMSELF IN HIS LETTERS

Collections of material about an author are not respecters of chronology, and in the material concerning O. Henry, assembled chiefly by the energy of the late Harry Peyton Steger, are many curious contrasts—little printed rejection slips from Sunday newspapers of an early date keeping company with long and appreciative letters of later date from magazine editors, and clippings from the London *Spectator* comparing O. Henry with Stevenson.

There are letters of O. Henry's telling of his first experiences with "the editor fellers" and recent book reports which show that the public has bought seven hundred and fifty thousand copies of his books in twelve months, and that two of his stories have been put on the stage and many of them dramatized for the "movies."

But in all the material, reports, biographical sketches, and so forth, the most revealing things are his own letters. Almost always they are filled with quaint conceits, usually with a kind of cartoon humor and sometimes with puns. They show little scholarship but much humanity. They are the kind of letters that give the most pleasure to an average person.

In the last years of his life Sydney Porter was never well and he constantly referred to his ill health in his letters, but always with good humor and good cheer.

For instance, he wrote in a letter to his publishers:

MY DEAR LANIER:

In a short time, say two weeks at the outside, I'll turn in enough of the book for the purposes you require, as per your recent letter.

I've been pretty well handicapped for a couple of months and am in the hands of a fine tyrant of a doctor, who makes me come to see him every other day, and who has forbidden me to leave the city until he is through with me, and then only under his own auspices and direction. It seems that the goddess Hygiene and I have been strangers for years; and now Science must step in and repair the damage. My doctor is a miracle worker and promises that in a few weeks he will double my capacity, which sounds very good both for me and for him, when the payment of the bill is considered.

Later he wrote Mr. Steger from Asheville:

DEAR COLONEL STEGER:

I'd have answered your letter, but I've been under the weather with a slight relapse. But on the whole I'm improving vastly. I've a doctor who says I've absolutely no physical trouble except neurasthenia, and that outdoor exercise and air will fix me as good as new. As for the diagnoses of the New York doctors—they are absolutely without foundation. I am twenty pounds lighter and can climb mountains like a goat.

Some time previous to this he wrote in a similar vein to a New York editor:

MY DEAR COLONEL:

I've been intending to write you a long time, but the fact is, I haven't written a line of MS. and scarcely a letter since I've been down here. I've been putting in all my time trying to get back in good shape again. The simple life has been the thing I needed, and by or before Christmas I expect to be at work again in better condition than ever. It is lonesome down here as Broadway when you are broke, but I shall try to stick it out a couple of weeks or so longer.

Tell *Hampton's* not to get discouraged about their story. It'll come pretty soon, and be all the better for the wait. As I said, I haven't sent out a line since I've been here—haven't earned a cent; just lived on nerve and persimmons.

Hope you'll get your project through all right, and make a million. With the same old fraternal and nocturnal regards, I remain,

Yours as usual,

S. P.

His ill health kept him from writing either much or regularly, and consequently he was often temporarily out of money in spite of the fact that his stories were in great demand. To the same editor to whom he wrote of his health at another time, he sent this typical letter concerning finances:

The Caledonia.

MY DEAR COLONEL GRIFFITH:

If you've got $100 right in your desk drawer you can have my next story, which will be ready next Tuesday at the latest. That will pay half. The other half on delivery.

I'm always wanting money, and I have to have a century this morning.

I just wanted to give you a chance at the story *at summer rates*, if you want it.

Please give the bearer a positive answer, as I'll have to know at once so as to place it elsewhere this forenoon.

Your very truly,

SYDNEY PORTER.

P.S.—Story guaranteed satisfactory or another supplied.

This letter was written when his stories were in great demand, when he could sell many more than he could write, and sell them at higher prices than this letter indicates. Not ten years before that, however, he was unknown to the magazine field of literature.

About the time that he succeeded in selling his first stories to *Everybody's* he began a correspondence with an old friend, A. J. Jennings, ex-train robber, lawyer, author, and reformer, which contains the history of the now famous story Holding Up a Train.[1] The first letter was as follows:

DEAR JENNINGS:

I have intended to write you and Billy every week since I left, but kept postponing it because I expect to move on to Washington (sounds like Stonewall Jackson talk, doesn't it?) almost any time. I am very comfortably situated here, but expect to leave in a couple of weeks anyhow.

[1] See "Sixes and Sevens."

I have been doing quite a deal of business with the editors since I got down to work, and have made more than I could at any other business.

.   .   .   .

Special regards to "Tex." Love to Hans and Fritz.   Sincerely yours,
                                                                S. P.

This letter suggested the idea which was later worked out between them, Jennings supplying the data and Porter putting on the finishing touches. In a second letter [included in the Letters already published in "Rolling Stones"] O. Henry explained how the article ought to be written. A part of this letter might well be in every beginner's scrapbook, for there was never better advice about writing: "Begin abruptly without any philosophizing" is part of his doctrine. I know of one magazine office where they take out the first paragraph of at least a third of the articles that are accepted for the simple reason that they do not add anything to the story. These first paragraphs bear the same relation to progress in the story as cranking an automobile does to progress on the road. They are merely to get the engine running.

"Describe the facts and details—information is what we want—the main idea is to be natural, direct, and concise." It would be hard to get better advice than this.

In the spirit of these later letters and in their style there is little to distinguish them from the epistles he sent back to North Carolina when he first went to Texas, except the difference in length. This letter to Mrs. Hall, the mother of the men on whose ranch Porter lived, is a fair sample of these early writings.

La Salle Co., Texas.

DEAR MRS. HALL:

Your welcome letter, which I received a good while ago, was much appreciated, and I thought I would answer it in the hopes of getting another from you. I am very short of news, so if you find anything in this letter rather incredible, get Dr. Beall to discount it for you to the proper size. He always questions my veracity since I came out here. Why didn't he do it when I was at home? Dick has got his new house done, and it looks very comfortable and magnificent. It has a tobacco-barn-like grandeur about it that always strikes a stranger with awe, and during a strong north wind the safest place about it is outside at the northern end.

A colored lady is now slinging hash in the kitchen and has such an air of command and condescension about her that the pots and kettles all get out of her way with a rush. I think she is a countess or a dukess in disguise. Catulla has grown wonderfully since you left; thirty or forty new houses have gone up and thirty or forty barrels of whiskey gone down. The bar-keeper is going to Europe on a tour next summer and is thinking of buying Mexico for his little boy to play with. They are getting along finely with the pasture; there are sixty or seventy men at work on the fence and have been having good weather for working. Ed. Brockman is there in charge of the commissary tent, and issues provisions to the contractors. I saw him last week, and he seemed very well.

Lee came up and asked me to go down to the camps and take Brockman's place for a week or so while he went to San Antonio. Well, I went down some six or seven miles from the ranch. On arriving I counted at the commissary tent nine niggers, sixteen Mexicans, seven hounds, twenty-one six-shooters, four desperadoes, three shotguns, and a barrel of molasses. Inside there were a good many sacks of corn, flour, meal, sugar, beans, coffee, and potatoes, a big box of bacon, some boots, shoes, clothes, saddles, rifles, tobacco, and some more hounds.

The work was to issue the stores to the contractors as they sent for them, and was light and easy to do. Out at the rear of the tent they had started a grave-yard of men who had either kicked one of the hounds or prophesied a norther. When night came, the gentleman whose good fortune it was to be dispensing the stores gathered up his saddle-blankets, four old corn sacks, an oil coat and a sheep skin, made all the room he could in the tent by shifting and arranging the bacon, meal, etc., gave a sad look at the dogs that immediately filled the vacuum, and went and slept outdoors. The few days I was there I was treated more as a guest than one doomed to labor. Had an offer to gamble from the nigger cook, and was allowed as an especial favor to drive up the nice, pretty horses and give them some corn. And the kind of accommodating old tramps and cowboys that constitute the outfit would drop in and board, and sleep and smoke, and cuss and gamble, and lie and brag, and do everything in their power to make the time pass pleasantly and profitably—to themselves. I enjoyed the thing very much, and one evening when I saw Brockman roll up to the camp, I was very sorry, and went off very early next morning in order to escape the heartbreaking sorrow of parting and leave-taking with the layout.

Now, if you think this fine letter worth a reply, write me a long letter and tell me what I would like to know, and I will rise up and call you a friend in need, and send you a fine cameria obscuria view of this ranch and itemized account of its operations and manifold charms. Tell Dr. Beall not to send me any cake, it would make some postmaster on the road ill if he should eat too much, and I am a friend to all humanity. I am writing by a very poor light, which must excuse bad spelling and uninteresting remarks.

I remain,

Very respectfully yours,
W. S. PORTER.

Everybody well.

More interesting, however, than these early Texas letters in showing the spirit of the man are the letters that he wrote from time to time to his daughter, Margaret, especially those written when she was a little girl. In them he speaks quite often of Uncle Remus, which they evidently read together, and they are all filled with the quaint conceits that enliven the two following:

MY DEAR MARGARET:

I ought to have answered your last letter sooner, but I haven't had a chance. It's getting mighty cool now. It won't be long before persimmons are ripe in Tennessee. I don't think you ever ate any persimmons, did you? I think persimmons pudden (not pudding) is better than cantalope or watermelon either. If you stay until they get ripe you must get somebody to make you one.

If it snows while you are there, you must try some fried snowballs, too. They are mighty good with Jack Frost gravy.

You must see how big and fat you can get before you go back to Austin.

When I come home I want to find you big and strong enough to pull me all about town on a sled when we have a snow storm. Won't that be nice? I just thought I'd write this little letter in a hurry so the postman would get it, and when I'm in a hurry I never can think of anything to write about. You and Mummy must have a good time, and keep a good lookout and don't let tramps or yellowjackets catch you. I'll try to write something better next time. Write soon.

Your loving
PAPA.

February 14, 1900.

DEAR MARGARET:

It has been quite a long time since I heard from you. I got a letter from you in the last century, and a letter once every hundred years is not very often. I have been waiting from day to day, putting off writing to you, as I have been expecting to have something to send you, but it hasn't come yet, and I thought I would write anyhow.

I hope your watch runs all right. When you write again be sure and look at it and tell me what time it is, so I won't have to get up and look at the clock.

With much love,
PAPA.

As the last of these little sidelights on his character and humor which these letters convey it is fitting to give two showing a peculiarly strong trait—his modesty. He did not seek publicity for himself and he had a lower opinion of his work as work that would last than almost any one else. He wrote in all sincerity to his publishers after the Christmas of 1908:

January 1, 1909.

MY DEAR MR. LANIER:

I want to say how very much I admire and appreciate the splendid edition of my poor stories that you all put in my stocking for Christmas. Unworthy though they were for such a dress, they take on from it such an added importance that I am sure they will stimulate me to do something worthy of such a binding.

I would say by all means don't let the Lipton Pub. Co. escape. Wine 'em or chase 'em in an auto and sell 'em all the "Pancakes" they can eat. Any little drippings of Maple Syrup will come in handy after the havoc of Christmas. I'll leave things of this sort freely to your judgment.

A Happy New Year to yourself and the House.

Very truly yours,
SYDNEY PORTER.

To an admirer who asked for his picture for publication he jocularly refused a request which to most authors is merely a business opportunity. It is a characteristic letter. It was not until very shortly before his death that through much persuasion Sydney Porter finally allowed himself, his picture, and O. Henry to be identified together.

MY DEAR MR. HANNIGAN:

Your letter through McClures' received. Your brief submitted (in re photo) is so flattering that I almost regret being a modest man. I have had none taken for several years except one, which was secured against my wishes and printed by a magazine. I haven't even one in my own possession. I don't believe in inflicting one's picture on the public unless one has done something to justify it—and I never take Peruna.

Sorry! you'd get one if I had it.

That lunch proposition sounds all right—may be in Boston some time and need it.

With regards,
Yours truly,
O. HENRY.

THE KNIGHT IN DISGUISE [1]

CONCERNING O. HENRY

(SYDNEY PORTER)

By Nicholas Vachel Lindsay

Is this Sir Philip Sidney, this loud clown,
The darling of the glad and gaping town?
This is that dubious hero of the press
Whose slangy tongue and insolent address
Were spiced to rouse on Sunday afternoon
The man with yellow journals round him strewn.
We laughed and dozed, then roused and read again
And vowed O. Henry funniest of men.
He always worked a triple-hinged surprise
To end the scene and make one rub his eyes.

He comes with vaudeville, with stare and leer.
He comes with megaphone and specious cheer.
His troup, too fat or short or long or lean,
Step from the pages of the magazine
With slapstick or sombrero or with cane:
The rube, the cowboy, or the masher vain.
They overact each part. But at the height
Of banter and of canter, and delight
The masks fall off for one queer instant there
And show real faces; faces full of care
And desperate longing; love that's hot or cold;
And subtle thoughts, and countenances bold.
The masks go back. 'Tis one more joke. Laugh on!
The goodly grown-up company is gone.

No doubt, had he occasion to address
The brilliant court of purple-clad Queen Bess,
He would have wrought for them the best he knew
And led more loftily his actor-crew.
How coolly he misquoted. 'Twas his art—
Slave-scholar, who misquoted—from the heart.
So when we slapped his back with friendly roar
Esop awaited him without the door,—
Esop the Greek, who made dull masters laugh
With little tales of *fox* and *dog* and *calf*.

And be it said amid his pranks so odd
With something nigh to chivalry he trod—
The fragile drear and driven would defend—
The little shop-girls' knight unto the end.

[1] This poem is reprinted with one or two slight changes which we make at the author's request, from "General Wil'iam Booth Enters into Heaven, and Other Poems," by Nicholas Vachel Lindsay, published in 1916 by the Macmillan Company.

Yea, he had passed, ere we could understand
The blade of Sidney glimmered in his hand.
Yea, ere we knew, Sir Philip's sword was drawn
With valiant cut and thrust, and he was gone.

THE AMAZING GENIUS OF O. HENRY [1]

By Stephen Leacock

To British readers of this book the above heading may look like the title of a comic story of Irish life with the apostrophe gone wrong. It is, alas! only too likely that many, perhaps the majority, of British readers have never heard of O. Henry. It is quite possible also that they are not ashamed of themselves on that account. Such readers would, in truly British fashion, merely classify O. Henry as one of the people that "one has never heard of." If there was any disparagement implied, it would be, as O. Henry himself would have remarked, "on him." And yet there have been sold in the United States, so it is claimed, one million copies of his books.

The point is one which illustrates some of the difficulties which beset the circulation of literature, though written in a common tongue, to and fro across the Atlantic. The British and the American public has each its own preconceived ideas about what it proposes to like. The British reader turns with distaste from anything which bears to him the taint of literary vulgarity or cheapness; he instinctively loves anything which seems to have the stamp of scholarship and revels in a classical allusion even when he doesn't understand it.

This state of mind has its qualities and its defects. Undoubtedly it makes for the preservation of a standard and a proper appreciation of the literature of the past. It helps to keep the fool in his place, imitating, like a watchful monkey, the admirations of better men. But on its defective side it sins against the light of intellectual honesty.

The attitude of the American reading public is turned the other way. I am not speaking here of the small minority which reads Walter Pater in a soft leather cover, listens to lectures on Bergsonian illusionism and prefers a drama league to a bridge club. I refer to the great mass of the American people, such as live in frame dwellings in the country, or exist in city boarding-houses, ride in the subway, attend a ten-twenty-thirty vaudeville show in preference to an Ibsen drama, and read a one-cent newspaper because it is intellectually easier than a two. This is the real public. It is not, of course, ignorant in the balder sense. A large part of it is, technically, highly educated and absorbs the great mass of the fifty thousand college degrees granted in America each year. But it has an instinctive horror of "learning," such as a cat feels toward running water. It has invented for itself the ominous word "highbrow" as a sign of warning placed over things to be avoided. This word to the American mind conveys much the same "taboo" as haunts the tomb of a Polynesian warrior, or the sacred horror that enveloped in ancient days the dark pine grove of a sylvan deity.

For the ordinary American this word "highbrow" has been pieced together out of recollections of a college professor in a black tail coat and straw hat destroying the peace of an Adirondack boarding-house: out of the unforgotten dullness

[1] From "Essays and Literary Studies," 1916, John Lane Co.

of a Chautauqua lecture course, or the expiring agonies of a Browning Society. To such a mind the word "highbrow" sweeps a wide and comprehensive area with the red flag of warning. It covers, for example, the whole of history, or, at least, the part of it antecedent to the two last presidential elections. All foreign literature and all references to it are "highbrow." Shakespeare, except as revived at twenty-five cents a seat with proper alterations in the text, is "highbrow." The works of Milton, the theory of evolution, and, in fact, all science other than Christian science, is "highbrow." A man may only read and discuss such things at his peril. If he does so, he falls forthwith into the class of the Chautauqua lecturer and the vacation professor; he loses all claim to mingle in the main stream of life by taking a hand at ten-cent poker, or giving his views on the outcome of the 1916 elections.

All this, however, by way of preliminary discussion suggested by the strange obscurity of O. Henry in Great Britain, and the wide and increasing popularity of his books in America. O. Henry is, more than any author who ever wrote in the United States, an American writer. As such his work may well appear to a British reader strange and unusual, and, at a casual glance, not attractive. It looks at first sight as if written in American slang, as if it were the careless, unrevised production of a journalist. But this is only the impression of an open page, or at best, a judgment formed by a reader who has had the ill-fortune to light upon the less valuable part of O. Henry's output. Let it be remembered that he wrote over two hundred stories. Even in Kentucky, where it is claimed that all whiskey is good whiskey, it is admitted that some whiskey is not so good as the rest. So it may be allowed to the most infatuated admirer of O. Henry, to admit that some of his stories are not as good as the others. Yet even that admission would be reluctant.

But let us recommence in more orthodox fashion.

O. Henry—as he signed himself—was born in 1867, most probably at Greensboro, North Carolina. For the first thirty or thirty-five years of his life, few knew or cared where he was born, or whither he was going. Now that he has been dead five years he shares already with Homer the honor of a disputed birthplace.

His real name was William Sydney Porter. His *nom de plume*, O. Henry—hopelessly tame and colorless from a literary point of view—seems to have been adopted in a whimsical moment, with no great thought as to its aptness. It is amazing that he should have selected so poor a pen name. Those who can remember their first shock of pleased surprise on hearing that Rudyard Kipling's name was really Rudyard Kipling, will feel something like pain in learning that any writer could deliberately christen himself "O. Henry."

The circumstance is all the more peculiar inasmuch as O. Henry's works abound in ingenious nomenclature. The names that he claps on his Central American adventurers are things of joy to the artistic eye—General Perrico Ximenes Villablanca Falcon! Ramon Angel de las Cruzes y Miraflores, president of the republic of Anchuria! Don Señor el Coronel Encarnación Rios! The very spirit of romance and revolution breathes through them! Or what more beautiful for a Nevada town than Topaz City? What name more appropriate for a commuter's suburb than Floralhurst? And these are only examples among thousands. In all the two hundred stories that O. Henry wrote, there is hardly a single name that is inappropriate or without a proper literary suggestiveness, except the name that he signed to them.

While still a boy, O. Henry (there is no use in calling him anything else) went to Texas, where he worked for three years on a ranch. He drifted into the city of Houston and got employment on a newspaper. A year later he bought a newspaper of his own in Austin, Texas, for the sum of two hundred and fifty dollars. He rechristened it the *Rolling Stone*, wrote it, and even illustrated it, himself. But the paper was too well named. Its editor himself rolled away from it, and from the shores of Texas the wandering restlessness that was characteristic of him wafted him down the great Gulf to the enchanted land of Central America. Here he "knocked around," as he himself has put it, "mostly among refugees and consuls." Here, too, was laid the foundation of much of his most characteristic work—his "Cabbages and Kings," and such stories as Phœbe and The Fourth in Salvador.

Latin America fascinated O. Henry. The languor of the tropics; the sunlit seas with their open bays and broad sanded beaches, with green palms nodding on the slopes above—white-painted steamers lazily at anchor—quaint Spanish towns, with adobe houses and wide squares, sunk in their noon-day sleep—beautiful Señoritas, drowsing away the afternoon in hammocks; the tinkling of the mule bells on the mountain track above the town—the cries of unknown birds issuing from the dense green of the unbroken jungle—and at night, in the soft darkness, the low murmur of the guitar, soft thrumming with the voice of love—these are the sights and sounds of O. Henry's Central America. Here live and move his tattered revolutionists, his gaudy generals of the mimic army of the existing republic; hither ply his white-painted steamers of the fruit trade; here the American consul, with a shadowed past and $600 a year, drinks away the remembrance of his northern energy and his college education in the land of forgetfulness. Hither the absconding banker from the States is dropped from the passing steamer, clutching tight in his shaking hand his valise of stolen dollars; him the disguised detective, lounging beside the little drinking shop, watches with a furtive eye. And here in this land of enchantment the broken lives, the wasted hopes, the ambition that was never reached, the frailty that was never conquered, are somehow pieced together and illuminated into what they might have been— and even the reckless crime and the open sin, viewed in the softened haze of such an atmosphere, are half forgiven.

Whether this is the "real Central America" or not is of no consequence. It probably is not. The "real Central America" may best be left to the up-to-date specialist, the energetic newspaper expert, or the traveling lady correspondent— to all such persons, in fact, as are capable of writing "Six Weeks in Nicaragua," or "Costa Rica as I Saw It." Most likely the Central America of O. Henry is as gloriously unreal as the London of Charles Dickens, or the Salem of Nathaniel Hawthorne, or any other beautiful picture of the higher truth of life that can be shattered into splinters in the distorting of cold fact.

From Central America O. Henry rolled, drifted or floated—there was no method in his life—back to Texas again. Here he worked for two weeks in a drugstore. This brief experience supplied him all the rest of his life with local color and technical material for his stories.[1] So well has he used it that the obstinate legend still runs that O. Henry was a druggist. A strict examination of his work would show that he knew the names of about seventeen drugs and was able to describe the rolling of pills with the life-like accuracy of one who has rolled them. But it was characteristic of his instinct for literary values that even on this slender basis O. Henry was able to make his characters "take down from shelves" such mysterious things as *Sod. et Pot. Tart.* or discuss whether magnesia carbonate or pulverized glycerine is the best excipient, and in moments of high tragedy poison themselves with "tincture of aconite."

Whether these terms are correctly used or not I do not know. Nor can I conceive that it matters. O. Henry was a literary artist first, last, and always. It was the effect and the feeling that he wanted. For technical accuracy he

---

[1] As a matter of fact, he did serve as a drug clerk for a considerable period of time, when a very young man, in his uncle's drugstore in Greensboro.—ED.

cared not one whit. There is a certain kind of author who thinks to make literature by introducing, let us say, a plumber using seven different kinds of tap-washers with seven different names; and there is a certain type of reader who is thereby conscious of seven different kinds of ignorance and is fascinated forthwith. From pedantry of this sort O. Henry is entirely free. Even literal accuracy is nothing to him so long as he gets his effect. Thus he commences one of his stories with the brazen statement: "In Texas you may journey for a thousand miles in a straight line." You can't, of course; and O. Henry knew it. It is only his way of saying that Texas is a very big place. So with his tincture of aconite. It may be poisonous or it may not be. But it sounds poisonous and that is enough for O. Henry. This is true art.

After his brief drugstore experience O. Henry moved to New Orleans. Even in his Texan and Central American days he seems to have scribbled stories. In New Orleans he set to work deliberately as a writer. Much of his best work was poured forth with prodigality of genius into the columns of the daily press without thought of fame. The money that he received, so it is said, was but a pittance. Stories that would sell to-day—were O. Henry alive and writing them now—for a thousand dollars, went for next to nothing. Throughout his life money meant little or nothing to him. If he had it, he spent it, loaned it; or gave it away. When he had it not he bargained with an editor for the payment in advance of a story which he meant to write, and of which he exhibited the title or a few sentences as a sample, and which he wrote, faithfully enough, "when he got round to it." The story runs of how one night a beggar on the street asked O. Henry for money. He drew forth a coin from his pocket in the darkness and handed it to the man. A few moments later the beggar looked at the coin under a street lamp, and, being even such a beggar as O. Henry loved to write about, he came running back with the words, "Say, you made a mistake, this is a twenty-dollar gold piece." "I know it is," said O. Henry, "but it's all I have." The story may not be true. But at least it ought to be.

From New Orleans O. Henry moved to New York and became, for the rest of his life, a unit among the "four million" dwellers in flats and apartment houses and sandstone palaces who live within the roar of the elevated railway, and from whom the pale light of the moon and the small effects of the planetary system are overwhelmed in the glare of the Great White Way. Here O. Henry's finest work was done—inimitable, unsurpassable stories that make up the volumes entitled "The Four Million," "The Trimmed Lamp," and "The Voice of the City."

Marvellous indeed they are. Written offhand with the bold carelessness of the pen that only genius dare use, but revealing behind them such a glow of the imagination and such a depth of understanding of the human heart as only genius can make manifest.

What O. Henry did for Central America he does again for New York. It is transformed by the magic of his imagination. He waves a wand over it and it becomes a city of mystery and romance. It is no longer the roaring, surging metropolis that we thought we knew, with its clattering elevated, its unending crowds, and on every side the repellent selfishness of the rich, the grim struggle of the poor, and the listless despair of the outcast. It has become, as O. Henry loves to call it, Bagdad upon the Subway. The glare has gone. There is a soft light suffusing the city. Its corner drugstores turn to enchanted bazaars. From the open doors of its restaurants and palm rooms there issues such a melody of softened music that we feel we have but to cross the threshold and there is Bagdad waiting for us beyond. A transformed waiter hands us to a chair at a little table—Arabian, I will swear it—beside an enchanted rubber tree. There is red wine such as Omar Khayyam drank, here on Sixth Avenue. At the tables about us are a strange and interesting crew—dervishes in the disguise of American business men, caliphs masquerading as tourists, bedouins from Syria, and fierce fantassins from the desert turned into western visitors from Texas, and among them—can we believe our eyes—houris from the inner harems of Ispahan and Candahar, whom we mistook but yesterday for the ladies of a Shubert chorus! As we pass out we pay our money to an enchanted cashier with golden hair—sitting behind glass—under the spell of some magician without a doubt, and then taking O. Henry's hand we wander forth among the everchanging scenes of night adventure, the mingled tragedy and humor of The Four Million that his pen alone can depict. Nor did ever Haroun-al-Raschid and his viziers, wandering at will in the narrow streets of their Arabian city, meet such varied adventure as lies before us, strolling hand in hand with O. Henry in the new Bagdad that he reveals.

But let us turn to the stories themselves. O. Henry wrote in all two hundred short stories of an average of about fifteen pages each. This was the form in which his literary activity shaped itself by instinct. A novel he never wrote, a play he often meditated but never achieved. One of his books—"Cabbages and Kings"—can make a certain claim to be continuous. But even this is rather a collection of little stories than a single piece of fiction. But it is an error of the grossest kind to say that O. Henry's work is not sustained. In reality his canvas is vast. His New York stories, like those of Central America or of the West, form one great picture as gloriously comprehensive in its scope as the lengthiest novels of a Dickens or the canvas of a Da Vinci. It is only the method that is different, not the result.

It is hard indeed to illustrate O. Henry's genius by the quotation of single phrases and sentences. The humor that is in his work lies too deep for that. His is not the comic wit that explodes the reader into a huge guffaw of laughter and vanishes. His humor is of that deep quality that smiles at life itself and mingles our amusement with our tears.

Still harder is it to try to show the amazing genius of O. Henry as a "plot maker," as a designer of incident. No one better than he can hold the reader in suspense. Nay, more than that, the reader scarcely knows that he is "suspended," until at the very close of the story O. Henry, so to speak, turns on the lights and the whole tale is revealed as an entirety. But to do justice to a plot in a few paragraphs is almost impossible. Let the reader consider to what a few poor shreds even the best of our novels or plays is reduced, when we try to set forth the basis of it in the condensed phrase of a text-book of literature, or diminish it to the language of the "scenario" of a moving picture. Let us take an example.

We will transcribe our immortal "Hamlet" as faithfully as we can into a few words with an eye to explain the plot and nothing else. It will run about as follows:

"Hamlet's uncle kills his father and marries his mother, and Hamlet is so disturbed about this that he is either mad or pretends to be mad. In this condition he drives his sweetheart insane and she drowns, or practically drowns, herself. Hamlet then kills his uncle's chief adviser behind an arras either in mistake for a rat, or not. Hamlet then gives poison to his uncle and his mother, stabs Laertes and kills himself. There is much discussion among the critics as to whether his actions justify us in calling him insane."

There! The example is, perhaps, not altogether convincing. It does not seem somehow, faithful though it is, to do Shakespeare justice. But let it at least illustrate the point under discussion. The mere bones of a plot are nothing. We could scarcely form a judgment on female beauty by studying the skeletons of a museum of anatomy.

But with this distinct understanding, let me try to present the outline of a typical O. Henry story. I select it from the volume entitled "The Gentle Grafter," a book that is mainly concerned with the wiles of Jeff Peters and his partners and associates. Mr. Peters, who acts as the narrator of most of the stories, typifies the perennial fakir and itinerant grafter of the Western States— ready to turn his hand to anything from selling patent medicines under a naptha lamp on the street corner of a Western town to peddling bargain Bibles from farm to farm—anything, in short, that does not involve work and carries with it the peculiar excitement of trying to keep out of the State penitentiary. All the world loves a grafter—at least a genial and ingenious grafter—a Robin Hood who plunders an abbot to feed a beggar, an Alfred Jingle, a Scapin, a Raffles, or any of the multifarious characters of the world's literature who reveal the fact that much that is best in humanity may flourish even on the shadowy side of technical iniquity. Of this glorious company is Mr. Jefferson Peters. But let us take him as he is revealed in "Jeff Peters as a Personal Magnet" and let us allow him to introduce himself and his business.

"I struck Fisher Hill," Mr. Peters relates, "in a buckskin suit, moccasins, long hair, and a thirty-carat diamond ring that I got from an actor in Texarkana. I don't know what he ever did with the pocket-knife I swapped him for it.

"I was Dr. Waugh-hoo, the celebrated Indian medicine man. I carried only one best bet just then, and that was Resurrection Bitters. It was made of life-giving plants and herbs accidentally discovered by Ta-qua-la, the beautiful wife of the chief of the Choc-taw Nation, while gathering truck to garnish a platter of boiled dog for an annual corn dance. . . ." In the capacity of Dr. Waugh-hoo, Mr. Peters "struck Fisher Hill." He went to a druggist and got credit for half a gross of eight-ounce bottles and corks, and with the help of the running water from the tap in the hotel room, he spent a long evening manufacturing Resurrection Bitters. The next evening the sales began. The bitters at fifty cents a bottle "started off like sweetbreads on toast at a vegetarian dinner." Then there intervenes a constable with a German silver badge. "Have you got a city license?" he asks, and Mr. Peters's medicinal activity comes to a full stop. The threat of prosecution under the law for practising medicine without a license puts Mr. Peters for the moment out of business.

He returns sadly to his hotel, pondering on his next move. Here by good fortune he meets a former acquaintance, a certain Andy Tucker, who has just finished a tour in the Southern States, working the Great Cupid Combination Package on the chivalrous and unsuspecting South.

"Andy," says Jeff, in speaking of his friend's credentials, "was a good street man: and he was more than that—he respected his profession and was satisfied with 300 per cent. profit. He had plenty of offers to go into the illegitimate drug and garden seed business, but he was never to be tempted off the straight path."

Andy and Jeff took counsel together in long debate on the porch of the hotel. And here, apparently, a piece of good luck came to Jeff's help. The very next morning a messenger brings word that the Mayor of the town is suddenly taken ill. The only doctor of the place is twenty miles away. Jeff Peters is summoned to the Mayor's bedside. . . . "This Mayor Banks," Jeff relates, "was in bed all but his whiskers and feet. He was making internal noises that would have had everybody in San Francisco hiking for the parks. A young man was standing by the bedside holding a cup of water. . . ." Mr. Peters, called to the patient's side, is very cautious. He draws attention to the fact that he is not a qualified practitioner, is not "a regular disciple of S. Q. Lapius."

The Mayor groans in pain. The young man at the bedside, introduced as Mr. Biddle, the Mayor's nephew, urges Mr. Peters—or Doctor Waugh-hoo—in the name of common humanity to attempt a cure.

Finally Jeff Peters promises to treat the Mayor by "scientific demonstration." He proposes, he says, to make use of the "great doctrine of psychic financiering— of the enlightening school of long-distance subconscious treatment of fallacies and meningitis—of that wonderful indoor sport known as personal magnetism." But he warns the Mayor that the treatment is difficult. It uses up great quantities of soul strength. It comes high. It cannot be attempted under two hundred and fifty dollars.

The Mayor groans. But he yields. The treatment begins.

"You ain't sick," says Dr. Waugh-hoo, looking the patient right in the eye. "You ain't got any pain. The right lobe of your perihelion is subsided."

The result is surprising. The Mayor's system seems to respond at once. "I do feel some better, Doc," he says, "darned if I don't."

Mr. Peters assumes a triumphant air. He promises to return next day for a second and final treatment.

"I'll come back," he says to the young man, "at eleven. You may give him eight drops of turpentine and three pounds of steak. Good-morning."

Next day the final treatment is given. The Mayor is completely restored. Two hundred and fifty dollars, all in cash, is handed to "Dr. Waugh-hoo." The young man asks for a receipt. It is no sooner written out by Jeff Peters, than:

" 'Now do your duty, officer,' says the Mayor, grinning much unlike a sick man.

"Mr. Biddle lays his hand on my arm.

" 'You're under arrest, Dr. Waugh-hoo, alias Peters,' says he, 'for practising medicine without authority under the State law.'

" 'Who are you?' I asks.

" 'I'll tell you who he is,' says Mr. Mayor, sitting up in bed. 'He's a detective employed by the State Medical Society. He's been following you over five counties. He came to me yesterday and we fixed up this scheme to catch you. I guess you won't do any more doctoring around these parts, Mr. Fakir. What was it you said I had, Doc?' the Mayor laughs, 'compound—well, it wasn't softening of the brain, I guess, anyway.' "

Ingenious, isn't it? One hadn't suspected. But let the reader kindly note the conclusion of the story as it follows, handled with the lightning rapidity of a conjuring trick.

" 'Come on, officer,' says I, dignified. 'I may as well make the best of it.' And then I turns to old Banks and rattles my chains.

" 'Mr. Mayor,' says I, 'the time will come soon when you'll believe that personal magnetism is a success. And you'll be sure that it succeeded in this case, too.'

"And I guess it did.

"When we got nearly to the gate, I says: 'We might meet somebody now, Andy. I reckon you better take 'em off, and——' Hey? Why, of course it was Andy Tucker. That was his scheme; and that's how we got the capital to go into business together."

Now let us set beside this a story of a different type, The Furnished Room, which appears in the volume called "The Four Million." It shows O. Henry at his best as a master of that supreme pathos that springs, with but little adventitious aid of time or circumstance, from the fundamental things of life itself. In the sheer art of narration there is nothing done by Maupassant that surpasses The Furnished Room. The story runs—so far as one dare attempt to reproduce it without quoting it all word for word—after this fashion.

The scene is laid in New York in the lost district of the lower West Side, where the wandering feet of actors and one-week transients seek furnished rooms in dilapidated houses of fallen grandeur.

One evening after dark a young man prowled among these crumbling red mansions, ringing their bells. At the twelfth he rested his lean hand-baggage upon the step and wiped the dust from his hatband and forehead. The bell sounded faint and far away in some remote hollow depths. . . . "I have the third-floor-back vacant since a week back," says the landlady. . . . "It's a nice room. It ain't often vacant. I had some most elegant people in it last summer—no trouble at all and paid in advance to the minute. The water's at the end of the hall. Sprowls and Mooney kept it three months. They done a vaudeville sketch. Miss B'retta Sprowls, you may have heard of her—Oh, that was just the stage name—right there over the dresser is where the marriage certificate hung, framed. The gas is here and you see there's plenty of closet room. It's a room every one likes. It never stays idle long——"

The young man takes the room, paying a week in advance. Then he asks:

"A young girl—Miss Vashner—Miss Eloise Vashner—do you remember such a one among your lodgers? She would be singing on the stage most likely."

The landlady shakes her head. They comes and goes, she tells him, she doesn't call that one to mind.

It is the same answer that he has been receiving, up and down, in the crumbling houses of the lost district, through weeks and months of wandering. No, always no. Five months of ceaseless interrogation and the inevitable negative. So much time spent by day in questioning managers, agents, schools, and choruses, by night among the audiences of theatres from all-star casts down to music halls so low that he dreaded to find what he most hoped for. . . . The young man, left in his sordid room of the third-floor-back, among its decayed furniture, its ragged brocade upholstery, sinks into a chair. The dead weight of despair is on him. . . . Then, suddenly, as he rested there, the room was filled with the strong, sweet odor of mignonette—the flower that she had always loved, the perfume that she had always worn. It is as if her very presence was beside him in the empty room. He rises. He cries aloud, "What, dear?" as if she had called to him. She has been there in the room. He knows it. He feels it. Then eager, tremulous with hope, he searches the room, tears open the crazy chest of drawers, fumbles upon the shelves, for some sign of her. Nothing and still nothing—a crumpled playbill, a half-smoked cigar, the dreary and ignoble small records of many a peripatetic tenant, but of the woman that he seeks, nothing. Yet still that haunting perfume that seems to speak her presence at his very side.

The young man dashes trembling from the room. Again he questions the landlady—was there not, before him in the room, a young lady? Surely there must have been—fair, of medium height, and with reddish gold hair? Surely there was?

But the landlady, as if obdurate, shakes her head. "I can tell you again," she says, "'twas Sprowls and Mooney, as I said. Miss B'retta Sprowls, it was, in the theatres, but Missis Mooney she was. The marriage certificate hung, framed, on a nail over——"

. . . The young man returns to his room. It is all over. His search in vain. The ebbing of his last hope has drained his faith. . . . For a time he sat staring at the yellow, singing gaslight. Then he rose. He walked to the bed and began to tear the sheets into strips. With the blade of his knife he drove them tightly into every crevice around windows and door. When all was snug and taut he turned out the light, turned the gas full on again, and laid himself gratefully upon the bed.

And now let the reader note the ending paragraphs of the story, so told that not one word of it must be altered or abridged from the form in which O. Henry framed it.

It was Mrs. McCool's night to go with the can for beer. So she fetched it and sat with Mrs. Purdy (the landlady) in one of those subterranean retreats where housekeepers foregather and the worm dieth seldom.

"I rented out my third-floor-back this evening," said Mrs. Purdy, across a fine circle of foam. "A young man took it. He went up to bed two hours ago."

"Now, did ye, Mrs. Purdy, ma'am!" said Mrs. McCool with intense admiration. "You do be a wonder for rentin' rooms of that kind. And did ye tell him, then?" she concluded in a husky whisper laden with mystery.

"Rooms," said Mrs. Purdy, in her furriest tones, "are furnished for to rent. I did not tell him, Mrs. McCool."

"'Tis right ye are, ma'am; 'tis by renting rooms we kape alive. Ye have the rale sense for business, ma'am. There be many people will rayjict the rentin' of a room if they be tould a suicide has been after dyin' in the bed of it."

"As you say, we has our living to be making," remarked Mrs. Purdy.

"Yis, ma'am; 'tis true. 'Tis just one wake ago this day I helped ye lay out the third floor back. A pretty slip of a colleen she was to be killin' herself wid the gas—a swate little face she had, Mrs. Purdy, ma'am."

"She'd a-been called handsome, as you say," said Mrs. Purdy, assenting but critical, "but for that mole she had a-growin' by her left eyebrow. Do fill up your glass again, Mrs. McCool."

Beyond these two stories I do not care to go. But if the reader is not satisfied let him procure for himself the story called A Municipal Report in the volume "Strictly Business." After he has read it he will either pronounce O. Henry one of the greatest masters of modern fiction or else—well, or else he is a jackass. Let us put it that way.

O. Henry lived some nine years in New York but little known to the public at large. Toward the end there came to him success, a competence, and something that might be called celebrity if not fame. But it was marvellous how his light remained hid. The time came when the best-known magazines eagerly sought his work. He could have commanded his own price. But the notoriety of noisy success, the personal triumph of literary conspicuousness he neither achieved nor envied. A certain cruel experience of his earlier days—tragic, unmerited, and not here to be recorded—had left him shy of mankind at large and, in the personal sense, anxious only for obscurity. Even when the American public in tens and hundreds of thousands read his matchless stories, they read them, so to speak, in isolated fashion, as personal discoveries, unaware for years of the collective greatness of O. Henry's work viewed as a total. The few who were privileged to know him seem to have valued him beyond all others and to have found him even greater than his work. And then, in mid-career as it seemed, there was laid upon him the hand of a wasting and mortal disease, which brought him slowly to his end, his courage and his gentle kindness unbroken to the last. "I shall die," he said one winter with one of the quoted phrases that fell so aptly from his lips, "in the good old summer time." And "in the good old summer time" with a smile and a jest upon his lips he died. "Don't turn down the light," he is reported to have said to those beside his bed, and then, as the words of a popular song flickered across his mind, he added, "I'm afraid to go home in the dark."

That was in the summer of 1910. Since his death, his fame in America has grown greater and greater with every year. The laurel wreath that should have crowned his brow is exchanged for the garland laid upon his grave. And the time is coming, let us hope, when the whole English-speaking world will recognize in O. Henry one of the great masters of modern literature.

O. HENRY: AN ENGLISH VIEW

By A. St. John Adcock

USUALLY, when we write of how the critics and the public of an earlier generation were slow to recognize the genius of Meredith or Mark Rutherford, we do it with an air of severe self-righteousness which covers an implication that we in our more enlightened age are not likely to repeat such blunders, that the general taste and critical acumen of our time may safely be relied upon to assess contemporary authors at their true value and put them, with unerring promptitude, into their proper places. The fact is, of course, that even our modern literary judgments are not infallible, and that we are really in no position at all to throw stones at our forefathers. It were sufficient for us if we devoted our energies to getting the beam out of our own eye and left the dead past to buy its dead mistakes.

Take the very modern instance of O. Henry. Thousands of us are reading his stories at present and realizing with astonishment that he was a great literary artist—with astonishment because, though we are only just arriving at this knowledge of him, we learn that he commenced to write before the end of the last century, and has been five years dead. Even in America, where he belonged, recognition came to him slowly; it was only toward the close of his life that he began to be counted as anything more than a popular magazine author; but now, in the States, they have sold more than a million copies of his books. His publishers announce in their advertisements that "up goes the sale of O. Henry, higher and higher every day," that he has "beaten the world record for the sale of short stories"; and the critics compete with each other in comparing him to Poe and Bret Harte, to Mark Twain and Dickens, to de Maupassant and Kipling. We cannot put ourselves right by saying that he was an American, for in the last few years at least two attempts have been made to introduce him to English readers, and both of them failed. Then a little while ago Mr. Eveleigh Nash embarked on a third attempt and commenced the publication of a uniform edition of the works of O. Henry in twelve three-and-sixpenny volumes. They hung fire a little at first, I believe, but by degrees made headway, and before the series was completed it had achieved a large and increasing success. This was recently followed by an announcement of the issue of the twelve volumes in a shilling edition by Messrs. Hodder & Stoughton; the first six have appeared, and the remainder are to be published before the end of the year, and as the publishers estimate that by then, at the present rate of sale, at least half a million copies will have been sold, one may take it that, at long last, O. Henry is triumphantly entering into his kingdom.

In a brilliant appreciation of The Amazing Genius of O. Henry,[1] in his new book, "Essays and Literary Studies" (John Lane), Professor Stephen Leacock

---

[1] Reprinted in this volume, pp. 1339–1345.

speaks of the wide and increasing popularity of O. Henry in America, and of his "strange obscurity" in Great Britain. He thinks it "only too likely that many, perhaps the majority, of British readers have never heard of O. Henry." That was certainly true when it was written, but in the last six months our long-suffering public has risen above the reproach. Professor Leacock tries to suggest a reason for our indifference. "The British reader turns with distaste," he says, "from anything which bears to him the taint of literary vulgarity or cheapness; he instinctively loves anything which seems to have the stamp of scholarship, and revels in a classical allusion even when he doesn't understand it." But for the sting in its tail and the passage that succeeds it, I should suspect this sentence of irony, for the British reader received at once and with open arms the joyous extravagances of Max Adeler (who, by the way, should not have been entirely ignored in Professor Leacock's essay on "American Humor"), and there is nothing in "Elbow Room" or "Out of the Hurly-Burly" that is funnier or more quaintly humorous than some of Henry's stories. But O. Henry can move you to tears as well as laughter—you have not finished with him when you have called him a humorist. He has all the gifts of the supreme teller of tales, is master of tragedy as well as of burlesque, of comedy and of romance, of the domestic and the mystery-tale of common life, and has a delicate skill in stories of the super-natural. Through every change of his theme runs a broad, genial understanding of all sorts of humanity, and his familiar, sometimes casually conversational style conceals a finished narrative art that amply justifies Professor Leacock in naming him "one of the great masters of modern literature." He is not, then, of that cheap type of author from whom, as the Professor says, the British reader "turns with distaste." He has not been received among us sooner simply because, to repeat Mr. Leacock's statement, "the majority of British readers have never heard of O. Henry," and obviously until they have heard of him it is impossible that they should read him. Therefore, the blame for our not sooner appreciating him rests, not on our general public, but on our critics and publishers. If he had been adequately published, and adequately reviewed over here before, British readers must have heard of him, and their complete vindication lies in the fact that now, when at length he has been adequately published and reviewed and so brought to their notice, they are reading his books as fast as they can lay hands on them. . . .

The life he lived was the life that was best for him. Every phase of it had its share in making him the prose troubadour that he became. Half his books are filled with stories that are shaped and colored by his roamings, and the other half with stories that he gathered in the busy ways and, particularly, in the byways of—"Little Old New York." For the scenes, incidents, and characters of his tales he did not need to travel far outside the range of his own experiences, and it is probably this that helps to give them the carelessly intimate air of reality that is part of their strength. He touches in his descriptions lightly and swiftly, yet whether he is telling of the old-world quaintness of North Carolina, the rough lawlessness of Texas, the strange glamour of New Orleans, the slumberous, bizarre charm of obscure South American coast towns, or the noise and bustle and squalor and up-to-date magnificence of New York, his stories are steeped in color and atmosphere. You come to think of his men and women less as characters he has drawn than as people he has known, he writes of them with such familiar acquaintance, and makes them so vividly actual to you. He is as sure and as cunning in the presentment of his exquisite señoritas, his faded, dignified Spanish grandees and planters and traders and picturesque rather comic-opera Presidents of small South American republics, as in drawing his wonderful gallery of Bowery boys, financiers, clerks, shop-girls, workers, and New York aristocrats. You scarcely realize them as creations, they seem to walk into his pages without effort. His women are, at least, as varied in type and as intensely human as his men: he wins your sympathy for Isabel Guilbert,[1] who was "Eve after the fall but before the bitterness of it was felt," who "wore life as a rose in her bosom," and who, according to Keogh, could "look at a man once, and he'll turn monkey and climb trees to pick cocoanuts for her," no less than he wins it for Norah, the self-sacrificing little sewing-girl, of Blind Man's Holiday,[2] or the practical, loyally passionate wife, Santa Yeager, of Hearts and Crosses,[3] or the delightful Mrs. Cassidy who accepts the blows of her drunken husband as proof of his love ("Who else has got a right to be beat? I'd just like to catch him once beating anybody else!") in a A Harlem Tragedy,[4] which would be grotesquely farcical if it were not for its droll air of truth and the curious sense of pathos that underlies it. . . .

I am not going to attempt to say which is the best of his tales; they vary so widely in subject and manner that it is impossible to compare them. There were moods in which he saw New York in all its solid, material, commonplace realism, and moods in which it became to him "Bagdad-on-the-Subway," and was full of romance, as Soho is in Stevenson's "New Arabian Nights." His Wild West stories are a subtle blend of humor, pathos, and picturesqueness; some of his town and country stories delight you by their homely naturalness, others are alive with sensation and excitement, others again are pure fantasy or things for nothing but laughter. Then there are such as "Roads of Destiny," which, with a strange dream-like quality, a haunting, imaginative suggestiveness, unfolds three stories of the same man—as one might see them in prevision—showing that whichever way of life he had chosen he would have been brought to the same appointed end. The eerie touch of other-world influences is upon you in this, as it is in The Door of Unrest,[5] an uncanny, queerly humorous legend of the Wandering Jew in a modern American city; and as it is in The Furnished Room,[6] which Professor Leacock justly singles out as one of the finest of O. Henry's works. "It shows O. Henry at his best," he says, "as a master of that supreme pathos that springs, with but little adventitious aid of time or circumstance, from the fundamental things of life itself. In the sheer art of narration there is nothing done by Maupassant that surpasses The Furnished Room." It could only be misrepresented in a summary, for though O. Henry always has a good story to tell, its effectiveness is always heightened immeasurably by his manner of telling it.

It is in sheer art of narration, and in the breadth and depth of his knowledge of humanity and his sympathy with it that he chiefly excels. He was too big a man to be nothing but an artist, and the bigger artist for that reason. He has none of the conscious stylist's elaborate little tricks with words, for he is a master of language and not its slave. He is as happily colloquial as Kipling was in his early tales, but his style is as individual, as naturally his own, as a man's voice may be. He seems to go as he pleases, writing apparently just whatever words happen to be in the ink, yet all the while he is getting hold of his reader's interest, subtly shaping his narrative with the storyteller's unerring instinct, generally allowing you no glimpse of its culminating point until you are right on it. "The art of narrative," said Keogh, in "Cabbages and Kings," "consists in concealing from your audience everything it wants to know until after you expose your favorite opinions on topics foreign to the subject. A good story is like a bitter pill with the sugar coating inside of it"; and this art O. Henry practices with a skill that is invariably admirable and at times startling. More than once he leads you deftly on till you arrive at what would seem an ingenious

1 See "Cabbages and Kings."
2 See "Whirligigs."
3 See "Heart of the West."
4 See "The Trimmed Lamp."
5 See "Sixes and Sevens."
6 See "The Four Million."

ending, then in a sudden paragraph he will give the whole thing a quick turn and land you in a still more ingenious climax that leaves victory in the hands of the character who had seemed to have lost.

"Cabbages and Kings," a series of stories held together by a central thread of interest, is the nearest O. Henry came to writing a novel. Toward the end of his career his publishers urged him to write one and among his papers after his death was found an unfinished reply to them setting out something of his idea of the novel he would like to attempt. It was to be the story of an individual, not of a type—"the *true* record of a man's thoughts, his descriptions of his mischances and adventures, his *true* opinions of life as he has seen it, and his *absolutely honest* deductions, comments, and views upon the different phases of life he passes through." It was not to be autobiography: "most autobiographies are insincere from beginning to end. About the only chance for the truth to be told is in fiction."

But this novel remains without a title in the list of unwritten books. Whether, if it had been written, it would have proved him as great an artist on the larger canvas as he is on the smaller, is a vain speculation and a matter of no moment. What matters is that in these twelve volumes of his he has done enough to add much and permanently to the world's sources of pleasure, and enough to give him an assured place among the masters of modern fiction.

THE MISADVENTURES IN MUSICAL COMEDY
OF O. HENRY AND FRANKLIN P. ADAMS [1]

A CHICAGO manager started the trouble. He wrote as follows to Mr. Adams:

I am very anxious to secure a piece on the lines of "The Time, the Place, and the Girl." I say that for the reason that I have a star who is really a sensation, and we want to get him a piece that will suit him. It must be a modern character as he is a nice-looking fellow and I believe in a man continuing in a character in which he has achieved success. He is quite a fast talker, natty, dances very well, and sings excellently and is in every way very clever. We will have an opportunity to do a piece here by April and my ambition now is to get a play for him.

O. Henry has written a story for *Collier's* that fits Y—— to the ground. How would you like to coöperate with him?

The foregoing letter was received February 10, 1909. Mr. Adams welcomed the opportunity it presented, and took kindly to the idea of collaborating with O. Henry.

He says: "I called on O. Henry and we discussed it at length. His other pseudonym was Barkis. We agreed to collaborate, both of us to work on the dialogue and both on the lyrics. And as it happened it was almost a complete collaboration. Hardly an independent line was written. . . .

[1] Adapted from "Lo, the Poor Musical Comedy," by Franklin P. Adams, published in *The Success Magazine*, October, 1910.

"We were interested in the piece and anxious to please the manager who had gone out of his way to get us. . . . O. Henry and I would convene nearly every afternoon and talk the thing over, outlining scenes, making notes of lines of dialogue, tentative ideas for lyrics, etc. . . . We enjoyed working at this time. It was fun blocking out the plans and O. Henry was simply shedding whimsical ideas for lines and situations."

The plot concerned an anthropological expedition to Yucatan to inquire into the theory that the American Indian was descended from the ancient Aztecs. O. Henry called this *aztechnology* and "The Enthusiaztecs" was at first suggested for the title; but the manager would have none of it—was pleased to say that it sounded like the title of an amateur performance given by the Lincoln Memorial High School, and even went so far as to accuse the librettists of offences smacking not a little of the crime of highbrowism.

However, "The title inspiration soon came," says Mr. Adams. "It was O. Henry's and I am still of the opinion that it was an excellent title—'Lo.' As originally written the comedy emphasized the reversion to type of the Indian, and tried to show, as Pope suggested, after

> Lo, the poor Indian! whose untutored mind
> Sees God in clouds, or hears him in the wind. . . .

that

> To be, contents his natural desire.
> He asks no angel's wing, no seraph's fire.

The manager accepted this title with enthusiasm, for "You can advertise it easy and it looks good in type."

They had supposed that in the construction of a musical comedy the librettist first wrote some verses and the composer then evolved a melody to fit them. "But," Mr. Adams states, "most of our songs were constructed to fit tunes the composer had already written. I am not saying that this method is absolutely wrong, but it is infinitely harder work for the lyricist. Take an unfamiliar melody—often irregular as to meter—and try to fit intelligible, singable, rhythmical words to it. No wonder that after a month or two of it the barber tells you that it's getting pretty thin on top."

Difficulties and disagreements with the manager now came thick and fast: "'Two and two,' says the manager, profoundly and confidentially, 'are five.' 'But'—you begin. 'You're inexperienced,' says the manager, 'and you don't know; *believe me*. I've been in this business twenty-seven years. We need comedy here. Laughs is what we want, all the time.'"

The infallible manager became convinced of the hopelessness of their ignorance of practical theatrical exigencies. "The second act was bad, the first scene was an interior," etc., etc. He engaged another man to rewrite the book. This was done. The manager approved the new man's outline. But his dialogue was rejected wholly, and the original collaborators had more rewriting to do. O. Henry never worked harder or more conscientiously on anything in his life. He lost weight. He worried. Day and night they worked on the comedy. Again they sent on the completed script, this being the third or fourth "rewrite." As they mailed it, O. Henry recited in a singular minor key:

> "Dramatization is vexation;
> Revision is as bad;
> This comedy perplexes me
> And managers drive me mad!"

Followed more dissatisfaction on the manager's part, and several harassing trips to Chicago.

But, finally, "Lo" was produced. Mr. Adams tells the tale: "The first performance was given in Aurora, Illinois, on August 25, 1909. With two exceptions —any members of the company who chance to read this will wonder who the second one I have in mind is—the acting was mediocre. But it 'went' well and the unbiased Auroran seemed to like it. I rather enjoyed it myself. There was no Night of Triumph, however. After the performance the manager met me on the street. 'Come to my room before you go to bed,' he said. 'Got to fix up that second act. It's rotten. . . .' So I did some more rewriting, which I think was never even tried out. I never heard of it, at any rate.

"After performances in Waukegan, Illinois, and Janesville, Wisconsin, 'Lo' opened in Milwaukee for a week's engagement. It seemed to please; the newspapers 'treated us lovely,' as the management had it.

"But at the age of fourteen weeks it breathed its last, on December 5th, in St. Joseph, Missouri. Its parents, bearing up nobly, learned the sad news through a stray newspaper paragraph. . . .

"That is the plain, unjapalacked story. I'm not recriminating. Taking one consideration with another, however, the librettist's lot is not a snappy one."

What Mr. Adams calls "Lo, the Poor Musical Comedy," is dead and gone, and no man knoweth the place of its sepulture. But most of the lyrics have survived.

Mr. Adams tells us that his collaboration with O. Henry was unusually thoroughgoing—hardly an independent line was written. But "Snap Shots" was all O. Henry's.

SNAP SHOTS

Watch out, lovers, when you promenade;
When you kiss and coo, in the deep moon shade.
When you're close together in the grape-vine swing,
When you are a-courting or philandering.
Mabel, Maud and Ann, Nellie, May and Fan,
Keep your eyes open for the Snap Shot Man!

Snap! Shots! Hear the shutter close!
What a world of roguishness the little snapper shows!
Click! Click! Caught you unaware—
Snap Shot Man'll get you if you don't take care!

Watch out, you, Sir, when your wife's away,
When you take your "cousin" to see the play,
With best aisle seats and in the bass drum row,
And holding her hand when all the lights are low.
Billy, Bob and Dan, Smith and Harrigan,
Keep your eyes open for the Snap Shot Man!

Snap! Shot! Hear the snapper snap!
Got you just as safe as any squirrel in a trap.
Click! Click! Got you just as slick—
Cam'ra man'll snap you if you don't be quick!

When you're swimming in your bathing suit,
And Hubby's in town, slaving like a brute,
And handsome young stranger, "Teach you how to swim?"
It's not my affair, it's up to you and him.
But, Adele and Pearl, in the water's swirl,
Keep your eyes open for the Snap Shot Girl.

Snap! Shots! Just a button pressed—
Only seems a trifle, but the courts'll do the rest.
Click! Click! Caught you P. Q. D.
Snap Shot Girl'll get you if you trifle in the sea.

"In Yucatan," of course owes its inspiration to O. Henry's sojourn in the exiles' haven, Honduras. But its lyrical tone is so strong, the farcical so nearly absent, that one guesses it to be mainly from the pen of Mr. Adams.

IN YUCATAN

In a *dolce far niente*
Mood amid the fruits and flowers,
Ladies in a land of plenty
Idly watch the ebbing hours;
In this paradise Utopian
Time and tide are cornucopian;
So we say "*Festina lente*,"
All the sands of time are ours.

In Yucatan, in Yucatan,
Land of eternal lotus chewing,
In Yucatan, in Yucatan,
Where sunny skies are blue as bluing,
In Yucatan, in Yucatan,
Oh, land of honeyed "Nothing Doing,"
Land of lyric, love, and leisure,
Place of poetry and pleasure,
Fairy-land of "Nothing Doing"—
Yucatan—in Yucatan.

Banish we the thoughts of sorrow
In this country of the blest;
Brood we not on a to-morrow,
Life is only brief at best.
In this land of summer season,
Reck we not of rhyme or reason,
As we puff the mild cigarro,
Singing "Life's a merry jest."

In Yucatan, in Yucatan,
Land of eternal lotus chewing,
In Yucatan, in Yucatan,
Where sunny skies are blue as bluing,

In Yucatan, in Yucatan,
Oh, land of honeyed "Nothing Doing,"
Land of lyric, love, and leisure,
Place of poetry and pleasure,
Fairy-land of "Nothing Doing"—
Yucatan—in Yucatan.

The following group of five songs was probably written soon after the collaborators had received a managerial lecture on the practical requirements of the theatre. They breathe the spirit of stagy sophistication as to "what they want," and "how to get it over."

LET US SING

There is nothing new, my lady, in the lexicon of love;
It is all as old as time.
They were vowing by the moon and to the twinkling stars above,
When they handed Eve the line.
There is nothing new to tell you, there is nothing to sing.
There is nothing new to say;
So you'll have to be contented with the ordinary thing,
In the ordinary way.

Let us sing in the manner traditional,
For we must have a lovers' duet,
With a silly refrain repetitional,
In a chorus you cannot forget.
They'll applaud from Topeka to Gloversville,
At the mention of "Love" or a "Kiss";
Oh, you bet we are lovers from Loversville
And we love in a lyric like this:—

LOVE IS ALL THAT MATTERS

An audience is generally clamorous,
For something in the nature of a waltz;
Be it ne'er so senseless,
Wherefore-less and whence-less,
Be its logic ne'er so full of faults,
Just let the theme and melody be amorous,
And let the honeyed sentiment be plain;
If the music's tuneful,
If the words are spoon-ful,
Love is all you need in a refrain.

For love is all that matters
In a waltz refrain—
A lilt that softly patters
Like a summer rain;

A theme that's worn to tatters;
And an ancient strain.
Yet love is all that matters
In a waltz refrain.

Now I might sing a sing of high society,
And I might sing about a lot of things;
I might spend the time on
Warbling you a rhyme on
Anything from cabbages to kings.
But though I have an infinite variety
Of themes that I might sing about to you,
There is only one thing,
Though an overdone thing,
Love, the olden theme that's always new.

For love is all that matters
In a waltz refrain—
A lilt that softly patters
Like a summer rain;
A theme that's worn to tatters;
And an ancient strain.
Yet love is all that matters
In a waltz refrain.

Let who will construct a nation's laws if I may write its songs,
As the poet used to say;
Though it's absolutely simple if you figure what belongs
To the usual National lay.
Take the songs of Andalusia as presented on the stage
By a dashing young brunette,
Who can stamp her feet in anger and can snap her eyes in rage,
And can smoke a cigarette.

Let us sing in a manner Castilian
To the twang of the gladsome guitar,
With a color scheme black and vermilion,
And the music staccato bizarre;
Let us sing all that sad señorita stuff
To a dance that is mildly insane;
Let us steal all that old Carmencita stuff,
That's the way of the lovers in Spain:—

CARAMBA

Spanish Burlesque Song

Caramba di Sar-sa-pa-ril-li-o,
Cinchona, Peruna, Mon-doo;
Bologna, Cologna, Vanillio,
Northwestern and eke "C. B. Q."

Oh, Chilli con carne and Piccolo—
Mazeppa di Buffalo Bill—
So hurry and drop in your nickle-o,
Caramba di Sar-sa-pa-rill!

Backward, turn a little backward, Father Tempus in thy **flight,**
To the days of long ago;
When Variety was funny and a "team" was a delight
In a biff-bang slap-stick show.
If you'll give us your attention for a moment we will **try**
Quite a job of comedy,
For a couple of comedians you see in she and I,
As you can quite plainly see.

Let us sing in a way vaudevillian,
In the way of the "ten-twenty-thirt"
When the "Varnishes" (Eddie and Lillian)
Made you laugh till you honestly hurt.
Let us hand out a sad little "mother" **song,**
In a way that is truly refined;
Let us follow it up with another song,
Of the best song-and-danciest kind:—

NEVER FORGET YOUR PARENTS

A young man once was sitting
Within a swell café,
The music it did play so sweet,
The people were so gay.
But he alone was silent,
A tear was in his eye,
A waitress she stepped up to **him,**
And asked him gently why.
He turned to her in sorrow,
And at first he spoke no word;
But soon he spoke unto her,
For she was an honest girl.
He rose up from that table,
In that elegant café,
And in a voice replete with **tears,**
To her, he then did say:

"Never forget your father,
Think all he done for you,
Do not desert your mother **dear,**
So loving, kind, and true.
Think of all they have gave you—
Do not cast it away—
For if it had not been for them
We would not be here to-day."

WHILE STROLLING THRO' THE FOREST

While strolling thro' the forest
Upon a summer's day,
I chanced to see, and she smiled at me,
A lady, and her name was May.
Oh my! Wasn't she a beaut!
Root-ti-toot, ti-toot-ti-toot-ti-toot!
She's the neatest, she's the sweetest,
She's also the completest.
She's the lady who I dearly love,
And—ah—this is—ah—what she said:

We have tried for to amuse you
With our remarks so bright,
And now that we have finished,
We're going to say good-night.
We are chatty, we are happy,
And we think the same of you,
And with your kind permission
We're going to say "Adoo."

"Dear Yankee Maid," one guesses, was intended to suit the requirements of the manager's protégé, the nice-looking fellow who danced well and sang excellently; and "You May Always Be My Sweetheart" was a duet to be sung probably by this paragon and the leading lady.

DEAR YANKEE MAID

There's a lilt that is tuneful and fetchin'!
When you sing of an Irish colleen;
And the lyrical praise of a Gretchen
Is a theme that is fit for a queen:
The bewitching young lady of Paris—
She may hold many fast in her thrall—
But this song (which is published by Harris)
Is to tell of the best of them all.

O Yankee maid! My Yankee maid!
You are the one best bet.
You are the goods, with duty prepaid.
You are the finest yet.
I am for you, brown eyes or blue,
Tresses of gold or jet.
I serenade you, Yankee maid;
You are the one best bet.

Of the maiden seductive and Spanish,
There is many a song has been sung.
And the ladies Norwegian and Danish

Were a theme when Columbus was young:
Oh, the ladies of England are pretty;
There are those who declare for the Jap.
But the best is the girl of this ditty,
Yankee maids are the best on the map.

O Yankee maid!   My Yankee maid!
You are the one best bet.
You are the goods, with duty prepaid.
You are the finest yet.
I am for you, brown eyes or blue,
Tresses of gold or jet.
I serenade you, Yankee maid;
You are the one best bet.

YOU MAY ALWAYS BE MY SWEETHEART

(If You Care to Be)

A maid of simple station, I, unlearned in lovers' lore,
  Sweetly shy;
The art of osculation I had never tried before,
  Which is why
Your recent demonstration of that proud and manly art—
  Is it plain?—
Has caused a queer sensation in the region of my heart,
  And this refrain:

I've never had a sweetheart, for I've been fancy free.
My heart's been locked to lovers, and there's no key.
But if you should continue to be so kind to me,
You may always be my sweetheart if you care to be.

Dear Madam: Contents noted in your favor of this date;
  I remain
As ever, Yours Devotedly—P. S., I beg to state
  And explain
Your recent proposition has a sweet and pleasant sound
  To my ears,
'Twill be my fond ambition just to have you stick around
  A million years.
I've never had a sweetheart, for I've been fancy free.
My heart's been locked to lovers, and there's no key.
But if you should continue to be so kind to me,
I will always be your sweetheart if you'll let me be.

The "Statue Song" was written as a substitute for one the composer was guilty
of, to fit a tune which was described as "a lutherburbank of 'Anitra's Dance' in
the Peer Gynt suite and Moskowski's 'Spanish Dance.' "

STATUE SONG

Idol of my race I sing,
Humbly kneeling at thy shrine.
Take the sacrifice I bring;
All that I possess is thine:

Humbly kneeling at thy shrine,
Let me chant my idol song,
All that I possess is thine,
I have loved thee overlong.

Let me chant my idol song,
Take the sacrifice I bring.
I have loved thee overlong.
Idol of my race I sing.

Beloved let me lay these at thy feet—
These flowers of forgetfulness so sweet.
Forsake thou thoughts of other days and pride,
And come thou back with me, thine Indian bride,
Untamed and free.
Return to me
Thine own predestined bride.

"Little Old Main Street" is a protest and natural reaction from the wave of Broadway and Little-Old-New-York songs which for so long inundated long-suffering Oshkosh and Kalamazoo.

LITTLE OLD MAIN STREET

Singers may boast about Broadway,
And they most gen'rally do:
Spring all that flowery fluff on the Bowery—
Take it. I'll stake it to you;
Call me a yap if you care to,
Say I'm a rube or a shine,
But give me the street that has got 'em all beat—
Little old Main Street for mine.

Little old Main Street for mine!
Take a look at the lovers in line—
Three village charmers and twenty-eight farmers,
All meeting the six-twenty-nine—
Little old Main Street for mine,
When you're back with the pigs and the kine,
Broadway and such for Your Uncle? Not much
For it's little old Main Street for mine.

> Sing if you must of your State Street,
> Sing of the Bois and the Strand,
> And if you have a new song of the Avenue,
> Sing it to beat the old band!
> Sing of the streets of the city,
> Not for Yours Truly—"Uh, Uh!"
> But give me the street of the village élite;
> Little old Main Street for *muh!*
>
> Little old Main Street for mine,
> And right down by the Post Office sign
> Hear 'em say, "Well, what a long rainy spell!
> But it looks like to-morrow'll be fine."
> Little old Main Street for mine,
> Where it's dead at a quarter past nine
> See the folks flock past the Opry-House block,
> Oh, it's little old Main Street for mine.

"It's the Little Things that Count," even in the success of a musical comedy. A few trifles like the following would have gone far toward making a Broadway success.

IT'S THE LITTLE THINGS THAT COUNT

Girl— Little drops of water, little grains of sand,
   Make the mighty ocean and the pleasant land.
Boy— Little drops of seltzer, little drops of rye,
   Make the pleasant highball, when a man is dry.
Both—It's the little things that count, ev'rywhere you go;
   Trifles make a large amount. Don't you find it so?
Girl— Little deeds of kindness, little words of love,
   Make our life an Eden, like the heaven above.
Boy— Little drops of promise, made to little wives,
   Make us little fibbers all our little lives.
Both—It's the little things that count, ev'rywhere you go;
   Trifles make a large amount. Don't you find it so?

O. HENRY IN HIS OWN BAGDAD

By George Jean Nathan

In the summer of 1908 William Sydney Porter and Robert Hobart Davis, alias "O. Henry" and "Bob" Davis respectively—and likewise respectively one of the greatest of American short-story writers and one of the greatest rejectors of all species of stories—were discussing the merits and demerits of New York City during the tropical, asphalt-smelly season. "Let's get out of it for a few days," suggested Davis. "I'll take you to a wonderful place down on Long Island, where the fishing is immense and the fish correspondingly large."

"Well," said Henry, "New York is a bit warm and I'll just take you up."

They started. They arrived. Fishing tackle was put in order; collars and coats were cast aside; Henry expressed admiration at the ability of the masculine natives to expectorate tobacco juice "as far as the eye could see"; Davis lit a cigar; and the expedition was off. It was a mile walk. "We won't ride, because the exercise will do us good," suggested Davis. Henry assented. The day was gray-blue and sizzling. They had not gone more than three city blocks when Henry was already drenched with perspiration. But he kept on manfully. A little way farther on, however, Davis noticed that his companion was desperately endeavoring to find something in his trousers' pockets. "What are you looking for?" he asked. "I am looking for my return ticket to New York," replied Henry, positively, "and let me tell you that as soon as I find it, I'm going to take a 'hitch' on a wagon and go back—fast! I know it's blamed hot in town, but there are just as good fish left on the menu as there are in the sea."

"Bagdad," as O. Henry referred to New York in his modern Arabian Nights, was, in his own words to a close friend, "the cosy haven for everybody, including amateur fishermen and other disappointed persons." O. Henry loved the metropolis, and its intense heat or cold made little change in his affection for it. "If you like the city so well, then," he was once asked, "why do you live in Asheville so much of the time?" "Because," he answered, "New York gets into my veins so strongly that I have to go away from it when I want to work. For the same reason, I venture, that a man who is deeply in love with a woman can't think of anything but that woman when he is anywhere near her."

During his frequent visits in his own sky-scraper-filled Bagdad, this literary Haroun-al-Raschid prowled about in curious corners, brushed up against curious individuals, and ferreted out curious secrets, curious heart mysteries, and curious little lights on the human machine—all of which subsequently found their way into his stories. Some of his adventures while Haroun-al-Raschiding must, therefore, possess interest for the vast reading throng that has smiled and felt a tear while turning his pages. It was during one of his prowling tours several years ago that O. Henry, with H. H. McClure, who suggested the writing of the modern Arabian Nights tales to the short-story king, was seated in a Broadway restaurant at luncheon. "What are you going to do to-night?" asked McClure. "I'm going to persuade a 'hobo' to give me three hundred dollars," answered the writer. "On a bet?" asked McClure. "Not at all," replied O. Henry "that's the price of a story and I'm going to rub up against some tramps down on the Bowery until one of them suggests the plot to me." That night O. Henry did travel downtown and started on a Haroun-al-Raschid expedition in the vicinity of the famous bread-line. His genial, well-fleshed personality always stood him in good stead, and no matter how tough the community he chanced to enter, unpleasantness of any sort was a rare occurrence. When he talked with a "hobo" he was a "hobo." When he talked with a railroad president he was a railroad president. O. Henry was a chameleon of conversation and of what is known colloquially as "front." He always took on the air—it seemed—of the person to whom he was talking. One of his friends has said of him that there was no better "mixer" in the world—and the truth of the statement is borne out by a survey of the intimate and varied insight revealed in his diverse writings. On the night in question O. Henry moved around among the Bowery derelicts until he finally got into touch with a typical "bum." They strolled down the street a way together and asked a passer-by for the time. "Almost midnight," said the latter. "Gee," remarked Henry to his tattered companion. "I feel like a cup o' coffee. Come on, I've got a quarter and we'll blow some of it in this place." They entered the dingy eating-house, sat up to the counter and each ordered a

cup of coffee and a ham sandwich. Although the two men had now been together for some time, the short-story writer had detected the gleam of nothing
definite in the tramp that promised to provide the "copy" he was seeking. But
he felt sure he had picked his man right and he felt equally sure that the fellow
sooner or later would unconsciously suggest to him something or other by which
he would profit. O. Henry rarely "led" the conversation. He preferred to let it
come naturally. He said nothing to his companion, who was busily concerning
himself with the food before him. When they had finished and had reached the
street, Henry suggested that they walk leisurely up the Bowery and see if there
was anything to be seen. They wandered around aimlessly for fully an hour and
a half and then Henry said he felt like having another cup of coffee. The two
men went into another eating-place and ordered two cups of coffee—at two cents
a cup. Then they walked around some more, but still Henry had succeeded in
getting no idea from his bedraggled companion. Finally, tired out, he told the
latter he was going to leave him. He reached out his hand to "shake" with the
tramp and, as their hands met, Henry suddenly surprised the "hobo" by laughing.
"What's up, cull?" asked the latter. "Oh, nothin'," replied Henry, "I just thought
of something." This was true, as he afterward confessed, the "something" in
point having been an odd twist for a new story. But the oddest twist to this
particular Haroun-al-Raschid anecdote—and a typical O. Henry twist it is—is
the fact that the idea O. Henry suddenly got for his story had absolutely nothing
to do with the Bowery, with tramps, with two-cent coffee, or anything even
remotely related thereto. "Well, then," remarked a friend to whom he had narrated the incident, "what good did the Bowery sojourn do you? You didn't get
your three-hundred-dollar idea from a tramp after all, did you?"

"Indeed, I did," replied O. Henry. "That is, in a way. The tramp didn't give
me the idea, to be sure, but he did not drive it out of my head—which is just
as important. If I had not gone down on the Bowery and had chosen an uptown
friend for a companion instead of that tramp, my more cultured companion would
not have allowed me a moment's conversational respite in which my mind could
have worked, and, as a consequence, the idea would never have come to me. So,
you see, the Bowery 'hobo' served a lot of good, after all."

Strolling through Madison Square one night after the theatre, O. Henry came
upon a young girl crying as if her heart were surely cracking, if not already
broken. The man with Henry, his pity and sympathy aroused, walked over to
the girl, touched her on the shoulder, and inquired into the cause of her grief.
It developed that the girl had come to the city from a town in central New
Jersey, had lost her way, and was without money, friends, or a place to sleep.
Deeply touched, the man with the short-story writer gave the girl a couple of
dollars, put her in charge of a policeman, whose latent sympathy he managed to
arouse with a one-dollar bill, and, satisfied with his act of charity, locked arms
with Henry and continued on through the dark square toward Twenty-third
Street. "Why didn't you speak to her?" he asked Henry. "I'll bet there was a
corking story in that girl that you could have dragged out." O. Henry smiled.
"Old man," he said, "there never is a story where there seems to be one. That's
one rule I always work on—it saves time, and let me see—two plus one—yes,
three dollars!"

O. Henry's metropolitan sales- and shop-girl types are known to his readers.
"Do you ever go into the department stores to study them?" some one once asked
the writer. "Indeed, not," answered the latter. "It is not the sales-girl in the
department store who is worth studying, it is the sales-girl out of it. You can't
get romance over a counter."

With two friends O. Henry was walking down Broadway one evening in
December—Broadway, the sack of New York "life," the big paper Bagdad out of
which O. Henry drew many of his characters. Near Herald Square the men were

approached by a rather well-dressed young man who, in a calm, gentle voice, told his "hard luck story" and begged for the "loan" of a quarter. One of the men handed over the twenty-five cents to the stranger and the latter disappeared quickly 'round the corner into Thirty-sixth Street. "Seemed like an honest, worthy chap," remarked the man who had parted with the quarter. "Yes," added O. Henry, quietly, "he seemed like an honest, worthy chap to me, too—last night."

While walking down Broadway on another occasion, O. Henry accidentally bumped against a man who was not looking in the direction he was walking. "I beg your pardon," said Henry, "but really you ought to look where you are going." "If I did in this town, I probably wouldn't go," replied the man with a sarcastic smile. "Ah," said O. Henry, quickly, "and how are all the folks in Chicago?"

When O. Henry collaborated with F. P. Adams in writing the libretto for the musical comedy, "Lo," a friend said to him: "Adams says he got the idea for his share of the play from a check for advance royalties. Where did you get the idea for your share?" "From the *hope* for a check for advance royalties," he answered.

While "Harouning" along the river front one night, O. Henry happened upon a couple of sailors, one of whom was much the worse for liquor. "I see your friend is intoxicated," he remarked to the sober sailor. "You don't say!" exclaimed the latter in mock astonishment. And the short-story king appreciated the answer at his expense as much as did those to whom he subsequently repeated it. O. Henry never missed a favorable opportunity to have a chat with an amiable policeman. "Policeman know so many odd things and so few necessary ones," he would remark. While talking with one of the blue-coats in Hell's Kitchen one night, years ago, Henry said that they were suddenly startled—at least, that he was—by two loud revolver shots. "Some one's been killed!" he exclaimed. "No, don't worry," returned the "cop," coolly, "only injured. It takes at least three bullets to kill any one in this part of town."

O. HENRY—APOTHECARY [1]

By Christopher Morley

WHERE once he measured camphor, glycerine,
    Cloves, aloes, potash, peppermint in bars,
And all the oils and essences so keen
    That druggists keep in rows of stoppered jars—
Now, blender of strange drugs more volatile,
    The master pharmicist of joy and pain
Dispenses sadness tinctured with a smile
    And laughter that dissolves in tears again.

O brave apothecary! You who knew
    What dark and acid doses life prefers,
And yet with smiling face resolved to brew
    These sparkling potions for your customers—
Glowing with globes of red and purple glass
    Your window gladdens travelers who pass.

[1] From a volume of Mr. Morley's poems published by the George H. Doran Company.

O. HENRY [1]

By William Lyon Phelps

IN North Carolina they have just erected a memorial to "O. Henry." He was a profoundly sincere artist, as is shown, not only in his finished work but in his private correspondence. His worst defect was a fear and hatred of conventionality; he had such mortal terror of stock phrases that, as some one has said, he wrote no English at all—he wrote the dot, dash, telegraphic style. Yet leaving aside all his perversities and his whimsicalities, and the poorer part of his work where the desire to be original is more manifest than any valuable result of it, there remain a sufficient number of transcripts from life and interpretations of it to give him abiding fame. There is a humorous tenderness in The Whirligig of Life,[2] and profound ethical passion in A Blackjack Bargainer.[3] A highly intelligent though unfavorable criticism of Porter that came to me in a private letter —I wish it might be printed—condemns him for the vagaries of his plots— which remind my correspondent of the quite serious criticism he read in a Philadelphia newspaper, which spoke of "the interesting but hardy credible adventures of Ulysses." Now hyperbole is a great American failing; and Porter was so out and out American that this disease of art raised blotches on his work. Yet his best emphasis is placed where it belongs.

No writer of distinction has, I think, been more closely identified with the short story in English than O. Henry. Irving, Poe, Hawthorne, Bret Harte, Stevenson, Kipling attained fame in other fields; but although Porter had his mind fully made up to launch what he hoped would be the great American novel, the veto of death intervened, and the many volumes of his "complete works" are made up of brevities. The essential truthfulness of his art is what gave his work immediate recognition and accounts for his rise from journalism to literature. There is poignancy in his pathos; desolation in his tragedy; and his extraordinary humor is full of those sudden surprises that give us delight. Uncritical readers have never been so deeply impressed with O. Henry as have the professional jaded critics, weary of the old trick a thousand times repeated, who found in his writings a freshness and originality amounting to genius.

ABOUT NEW YORK WITH O. HENRY

By Arthur Bartlett Maurice

I

THE HEART OF O. HENRY-LAND

IRVING PLACE, beginning at Fourteenth Street, runs north for six blocks to perish against the iron palings that line the southerly side of Gramercy Park. Halfway up, on the west side of the thoroughfare, between Seventeenth and Eighteenth streets, there is a dingy, four-story, brownstone house. The shutters

---

[1] From "The Advance of the English Novel," by William Lyon Phelps; Dodd, Mead, & Co., 1916.
[2] See "Whirligigs."

are up. The casements of the upper stories frame vacancy. That vacancy stares down at the passer-by with a kind of hurt blindness. It is as if the structure itself was conscious of an imminent demise, of a swiftly coming demolition. For next year, next month, next week, to-morrow, perhaps, the old ramshackle edifice will be gone, with a towering skyscraper springing up on the site. The number of the building is 55. There, in the front room on the second floor, William Sydney Porter lived in the days when he was learning to read the heart of the Big City of Razzle-Dazzle. And as he was constitutionally opposed to anything that involved arduous physical exercise, the quintessence of O. Henry-Land lies within a circle of half a mile radius, with No. 55 as the centre.

Within that circle may be found the hotels of the Spanish-American New York stories, Chubbs' Third Avenue Restaurant, the Old Munich of the Halberdier of the Little Rheinschloss,[1] the particular saloon which served as the background for The Lost Blend [2]—as a matter of fact that saloon is directly across the street from No. 55 and behind the bar there presides a white-aproned, genial cocktail mixer who will answer to the name of "Con" just as in the story—the four sides of Gramercy Park which are so conspicuous in the tales of aristocratic flavor, the bench—which could be confused with no other bench in the world—which Stuffy Pete, one of Two Thanksgiving-day Gentlemen,[2] regarded in the light of personal property, and those other benches in the other square, a few blocks to the north, where prepossessing young women, inspired by Robert Louis Stevenson's "New Arabian Nights," were moved to romantic narrative, where disconsolate caliphs, shorn of their power, sat brooding over the judgments of Allah, where fifth wheels rolled along asphalted pavements and djinns came obedient to the rubbing of the lamp.

To Mr. Robert Rudd Whiting, with whom he had been associated in the early days when he first began to contribute to the columns of *Ainslee's Magazine*, Sydney Porter once extended a luncheon invitation. It was to be a Spanish-American luncheon in the course of which O. Henry was to introduce his guests to certain flavors and dishes that he himself had learned to like or at least to endure in the days of his exile in the Land of the Lotus Eaters. The two men were crossing Union Square. "Come with me," said Porter, "I will show you the real place. Over at M——'s [he mentioned a restaurant in a street to the south] you may find the Señors, the Captains, the Majors, the Colonels. But if you would sit with the Generalissimos, the Imperators, the truly exalted who hail from Central and South American countries, accept my guiding hand." So from the Square they turned in Fifteenth Street and found, on the south side, some seventy-five yards east of Fourth Avenue, the Hotel America, with its clientèle of gesticulating Latins, who, if not planning revolution, had all the outward appearance of arch-conspirators. It was the atmosphere that went to the making of The Gold that Glittered,[3] which, if the reader remembers, began at the very spot at which the invitation had been extended "where Broadway skirts the corner of the Square presided over by George the Veracious."

The Halberdier of the Little Rheinschloss [4] dealt with a restaurant which O. Henry designated as Old Munich. Long ago, the story-teller told us, it was the resort of interesting Bohemians, but now "only artists and musicians and literary folk frequent it." For many years, so the tale runs, the customers of Old Munich have accepted the place as a faithful copy from the ancient German town. The big hall, with its smoky rafters, rows of imported steins, portrait of Goethe, and verses printed on the walls—translated into German from the original of the Cincinnati Poets—seemed atmospherically correct when viewed through the

1 See "Roads of Destiny."
2 See "The Trimmed Lamp."
3 See "Strictly Business."
4 See "Roads of Destiny."

bottom of a glass. Then the proprietors rented the room above, called it the Little Rheinschloss, and built in a stairway. Up there was an imitation stone parapet, ivy-covered, and the walls painted to represent depth and distance, with the Rhine winding at the base of the vineyarded slopes and the Castle of Ehrenbreitstein looming directly opposite the entrance. To Old Munich came the young man with the wrecked good clothes and the hungry look, to assume the armor of the ancient halberdier and, on a certain momentous evening, to be confiscated by the aristocrats to serve menially at the banquet-board.

As the tale had always been an especial favorite, the present writer had ventured into many parts of the city in his search for the background that would best fit the O. Henry description. For a time the hunt seemed vain. But one day he spoke to Mr. Gilman Hall on the subject. The latter laughed. "Do I know the real Old Munich? Very well, indeed. Often I dined there with Porter. No wonder you have not found it. You have been looking too far to the north, to the south, to the west. Don't you realize that Porter would never have walked that far if he could have helped it? The only time I ever persuaded him afoot as far as Seventy-second Street and Riverside Drive, he stopped, and, with an injured air, asked if we had not yet passed Peekskill. We are just before his old home, No. 55. Why not try round the corner?" So fifty feet to the south, and a short block to the east, in the restaurant and beer-hall known to some as Allaire's and to others as Scheffel Hall, the setting of the tale was found. There was a natural free-hand swing to certain parts of the O. Henry descriptions, but even without the corroboration of those who knew personally of Porter's associations with the place, one glance at the long raftered room is enough to stamp it as the place where the waiter known simply as No. 18 witnessed the comedy of the hot soup tureen and the blistered hands, and William Deering finished the three months of earning his own living without once being discharged for incompetence.

II

THE O. HENRY APPEAL

Three or four years ago, in the columns of a literary magazine of which he was then the editor, the present writer invited the expression of various opinions with the idea of finding out which of the stories of O. Henry had had the widest appeal. To the person whom he then designated as The Thousandth Reader he presented ten volumes of the short stories. She was being introduced for the first time to the work of O. Henry, and for a month, day after day, she gave herself over to the two hundred and fifty odd tales of the modern Scheherazade. When she had finished the last story he asked her to jot down the names of the ten that had most appealed to her, in the order of their appeal. Her choice was in many ways so surprising that it suggested the symposium. This was the list of The Thousandth Reader:

1. A Municipal Report.
2. The Pendulum.
3. A Blackjack Bargainer.
4. A Retrieved Reformation.
5. The Furnished Room.
6. The Hypotheses of Failure.
7. Roads of Destiny.

8. Next to Reading Matter.
9. The Enchanted Profile.
10. Two Renegades.

To that list the present writer decided to add nine others. First were three from men who were themselves spinners of tales, Booth Tarkington, Owen Johnson, and George Barr McCutcheon.

Mr. Tarkington, commenting upon his list, said: "The ten are not his best stories. I don't know which his 'best' are, of course. These ten are what you asked for—the ten I have enjoyed most. There is one I wanted to include. The boy who went to war after the girl flouted him and came back the town hero and said to her (she was married then): 'Oh, I don't know—maybe I could if I tried!' but I couldn't remember the title and couldn't find it." (The title of the story Mr. Tarkington had in mind was The Moment of Victory in "Options.")

Mr. Tarkington's list:

1. The Ransom of Red Chief.
2. The Harbinger.
3. The Passing of Black Eagle.
4. Squaring the Circle.
5. Past One at Rooney's.
6. The Handbook of Hymen.
7. Strictly Business.
8. The Clarion Call.
9. Jeff Peters as a Personal Magnet.
10. The Memento.

The following titles represented the choice of Mr. Owen Johnson:

1. An Unfinished Story.
2. A Municipal Report.
3. The Rose of Dixie.
4. A Lickpenny Lover.
5. According to Their Lights.
6. Mammon and the Archer.
7. The Defeat of the City.
8. The Girl and the Graft.
9. The Shamrock and the Palm.
10. The Pendulum.

Mr. George Barr McCutcheon's list:

1. The Tale of a Tainted Tenner.
2. Let Me Feel Your Pulse.
3. A Fog in Santone.
4. The Lost Blend.
5. The Duplicity of Hargraves.
6. The Marquis and Miss Sally.
7. The Gift of the Magi.
8. A Cosmopolite in a Café.

9. According to Their Lights.
10. The Making of a New Yorker.

Fifth in order, but naturally first in sentimental interest, was the list indicating the feelings of The One Who Knew Him Best—Mrs. William Sydney Porter. It was in a very beautiful letter that Mrs. Porter told of her preferences. To her the stories *were* Mr. Porter. She found it hard to name them in a list in order. But immediately one story came to her mind. That was A Municipal Report.[1]

"After all," she wrote, "I am not sure that it is the story—good as it is—for O. Henry's own face lifts from a Nashville 'roast' that was given that story and I hear his puzzled, 'Why did it offend? Do you see anything in it that should offend?' The Fifth Wheel [1]—and we stand together on Madison Square in the deep snow, or the biting wind, looking at the line waiting for beds. When we turn away, ten men have found shelter. The recording angel must have seen us there some of the snowy nights of 1908. He must have known that when we turned homeward there were times when O. Henry had not a dollar fifty left in his pocket." One story in Mrs. Porter's list likely to surprise readers is Madame Bo-Peep of the Ranches.[2] But Mrs. Porter said that that story figured largely in her own life. In the spring of 1905 her mother came home from Greensboro and said to her: "Your old friend Will Porter is a writer. He lives in New York and writes under the name of O. Henry." "O. Henry! In my desk lay Madame Bo-Peep and I loved her. I wrote O. Henry a note. 'If you are not Will Porter don't bother to answer,' I said. He bothered to answer. The letter came as fast as Uncle Sam could bring it. 'Some day when you are not real busy,' he wrote, 'won't you sit down at your desk where you keep those antiquated stories and write to me? I'd be so pleased to hear something about what the years have done for you, and what you think about when the tree frogs begin to holler in the evening.' Thus after many years a boy and girl friendship was renewed. Last in my list, but first in my heart, is Adventures in Neurasthenia, the new title, Let Me Feel Your Pulse,[3] the publishers gave. It brings back the little office in Asheville, the pad, empty except for the title and the words: 'So I went to the doctor.' So often at the last the pad was empty. The sharp pencil points in their waiting seemed to me to mock the empty pencil, the weary brain. The picture is too vivid." This was Mrs. Porter's list:

1. A Municipal Report.
2. The Fifth Wheel.
3. A Lickpenny Lover.
4. A Doubledyed Deceiver.
5. Brickdust Row.
6. The Trimmed Lamp.
7. The Brief Début of Tildy.
8. An Unfinished Story.
9. Madame Bo-Peep of the Ranches.
10. Let Me Feel Your Pulse.

The sixth list was from a man (incidentally he was one of O. Henry's closest friends in the New York years) who has read, accepted, and rejected more short stories than any other man in the world. That man was Mr. Robert H. Davis,

1 See "Strictly Business."
2 See "Whirligigs."
3 See "Sixes and Sevens."

and among the accepted stories were many of the stories of O. Henry. Prefacing his selection, Mr. Davis expressed the opinion that The Last Leaf [1] would become more impressive as he grew older, where as at the time of writing A Tempered Wind [2] and An Unfinished Story [3] entertained him greatly. There were times when he laughed inordinately at The Handbook of Hymen [4] and Hostages to Momus.[5] "It is rather remarkable," wrote Mr. Davis, "that a man of his temperament could do so many good stories under the high pressure of necessity. He was buoyant and lazy in prosperity, depressed and productive in adversity. How few of the millions who read him know what it cost O. Henry to make them laugh!" These were the ten tales that had been caught in the meshes of Mr. Davis's memory:

1. A Tempered Wind.
2. The Last Leaf.
3. An Unfinished Story.
4. Hostages to Momus.
5. The Trimmed Lamp.
6. Friend Telemachus.
7. The Handbook of Hymen.
8. The Moment of Victory.
9. The Ethics of Pig.
10. A Technical Error.

The following list made by Mr. Arthur W. Page represents, in a measure, the opinion of Mr. Porter's publishers:

1. The Rose of Dixie.
2. The Gift of the Magi.
3. The Cop and the Anthem.
4. Let Me Feel Your Pulse.
5. An Unfinished Story.
6. A Municipal Report.
7. The Guardian of the Accolade.
8. Witches' Loaves.
9. Hearts and Crosses.
10. The Fifth Wheel.

Many persons have come forward claiming to have discovered O. Henry. Some of these claims have come from sources that would have moved Sydney Porter himself to mingled delight and astonishment. But the man who was responsible for O. Henry's going to New York, who persuaded the publisher of a magazine to forward the money that made the journey possible, Was Mr. Gilman Hall. So among all claimants Mr. Hall has the best title to recognition as O. Henry's discoverer. Mr. Hall's list:

1. An Unfinished Story.
2. A Municipal Report.
3. Roads of Destiny.
4. The Buyer from Cactus City.

1 See "The Trimmed Lamp."
2 See "The Four Million."
3 See "Heart of the West."
4 See "The Gentle Grafter."
5 See "The Gentle Grafter."

5. The Furnished Room.
6. The Passing of Black Eagle.
7. The Gift of the Magi.
8. From the Cabby's Seat.
9. Brickdust Row.
10. A Retrieved Reformation.

To the opinions of writers of stories and buyers of stories it was thought wise to add the point of view of those whose business it is to sell stories. Three literary agents were consulted. This is a composite list representing their opinions:

1. A Harlem Tragedy.
2. Mammon and the Archer.
3. A Lickpenny Lover.
4. The Furnished Room.
5. The Marry Month of May.
6. The Gift of the Magi.
7. The Enchanted Profile.
8. An Unfinished Story.
9. The Last Leaf.
10. The Thing's the Play.

In conclusion the present writer insisted on presenting a list indicating his own favorites. It was as follows:

1. The Defeat of the City.
2. Mammon and the Archer.
3. The Furnished Room.
4. The Shamrock and the Palm.
5. The Halberdier of the Rheinschloss.
6. The Lost Blend.
7. A Lickpenny Lover.
8. A Municipal Report.
9. Two Renegades.
10. Thimble, Thimble.

Curious, indeed, is the story told by these lists. It illustrates strikingly the wide range of O. Henry's appeal. Ten lists of ten tales apiece, and sixty-two different titles, most of them appearing on but one list. A few favorites there are: A Municipal Report [1] (the narrative which probably shows its author at the highwater mark of his powers) with six mentions; An Unfinished Story [2] with seven mentions; A Lickpenny Lover, [2] the Gift of the Magi, [2] and The Furnished Room, [3] with four mentions; and Mammon and the Archer [3] and Let Me Feel Your Pulse [4] with three mentions. On the basis of these lists the New York stories have had the greatest appeal. Some of the individual selections were significant. For example, Mr. Tarkington picked as his first choice The Ransom of Red Chief, [5] a tale to be found in no other list. Perhaps that was only the expression of the mood of a moment, the liking of a man who dur-

1 See "Strictly Business."
2 See "The Four Million."
3 See "The Voice of the City."
4 See "Sixes and Sevens."
5 See "Whirligigs."

ing the previous two or three years had invented Hedrick Madison and Penrod Schofield for a delightfully diabolical boy.

III

THE "EAST SIDE" OF O. HENRY

In his nightly wanderings through his City of Bagdad, the good Haroun-al-Raschid in his golden prime did not confine himself to those thoroughfares that were analogous to London's Park Lane, Paris's Avenue Bois de Boulogne, or New York's Riverside Drive. On the contrary, he preferred to seek out the purlieus, and to listen wisely in the humble shop of "Fitbad the Tailor." Likewise the Haroun-al-Raschid of the modern Bagdad-on-the-Subway. The Editorman, or more likely two or three of him, would be waiting for the promised (and in many cases already paid for) story, so Sydney Porter would say good-bye to the companions with whom he was sitting in a Broadway restaurant, proceed downtown, and stroll along the Bowery or adjacent streets until he fell in with the particular tramp who seemed most promising as copy. Sometimes he found the story and sometimes he did not. Often, when the idea came, it had absolutely nothing to do with the Bowery, or with tramps, or with two-cent coffee, or with anything remotely related thereto. But to Sydney Porter that was no reason for withholding the credit he considered due to the tramp. "He did not give me the idea," he once said in explanation, "but he did not drive it out of my head—which is just as important."

Whether the particular tramp of an evening's ramble meant the inked pages of a tale of Texas, or Central America, or New Orleans, O. Henry's wanderings about the East Side are reflected in some twenty or thirty stories with very definite backgrounds. The care with which Porter sought his local color is indicated in The Sleuths,[1] in which a man from the Middle West goes to New York to find his sister. At her address he learns that she has moved away a month before, leaving no clue, and to help in the search he enlists the services of the famous detectives, Mullins & Shamrock Jolnes. The science of deduction leads to No. 12 Avenue C, which is described as an "old-fashioned brownstone house in a prosperous and respectable neighborhood." Now, if any neighborhood in New York City is not prosperous and respectable, it is that about Avenue C and Second Street. The Mulberry Bend of other years was hardly more unkempt. O. Henry had sensed its offensiveness through his eyes and his nostrils. The selection of the No. 12 was not mere chance. He knew that there was no such number: that on the southeast corner was a saloon bearing the number 10, and on the northeast corner the pharmacy was designated as No. 14. Just as there is no No. 13 Washington Square, there is no No. 12 Avenue C. Also there is no No. 162 Chilton Street, where the missing sister was eventually found, for the reason that in the Borough of Manhattan there is no Chilton Street at all.

Somewhere on the East Side is the famous Café Maginnis, where Ikey Snigglefritz, in the proudest, maddest moment of his life shook the hand of the great Billy McMahon. An indication as to the Café Maginnis's exact whereabouts is given in the information that Ikey leaving it, "went down Hester Street, and up Chrystie and down Delancey" to where he lived. Ikey's home was in a crazy brick structure, "foul and awry," and there Cortlandt Van Duykinck found him and shook his hand, thereby completing the social triangle.

[1] See "Sixes and Sevens."

There somewhere was the saloon of Dutch Mike where the Mulberry Hill gang and the Dry Dock gang met in the Homeric conflict the outcome of which sent Cork McManus to strange lands west of the Bowery and the adventures narrated in Past One at Rooney's. There may be found the Second Avenue boarding-house where Miss Conway showed Andy Donovan the locket containing the portrait of her purely imaginary lover (The Count and the Wedding Guest) [1]. Between the Bowery and First Avenue, where the distance between the two streets is the shortest, was the Blue Light Drug Store, where Ikey Schoenstein [2] concocted the love philtre that was to work the downfall of his rival, Chunk Macgowan. In Orchard Street were the rooms of the Give and Take Athletic Association where, as told in The Coming Out of Maggie,[3] Tony Spinelli played Prince Charming at the ball of the Clover Leaf Social Club under the pseudonym of Terry O'Sullivan; and farther up on the East Side, over against the elevated portion of the railroad, were the Beersheba Flats, from which the variegated tenants were driven forth by official edict to the grass of the park, and The City of Dreadful Night.[4]

IV

"HE SAW NO LONGER A RABBLE, BUT HIS BROTHERS SEEKING THE IDEAL"

To look at the matter in its chronological aspect, the first appearance of New York in the romance of O. Henry was probably in the last part of "Cabbages and Kings." There is a picture of two men sitting on a stringer of a North River pier while a steamer from the tropics is unloading bananas and oranges. One of the men is O'Day, formerly of the Columbia Detective Agency. In a moment of confidence he tells his companion of the mistake which has brought him to his unenviable condition, and incidentally clears up for the reader the rather ugly mystery that throughout the book obscured the marriage of Frank Goodwin and the lady known in Coralio as Isabel Guilbert. To begin in another way, that is at the gateway of the city and of the new world, in the story The Lady Higher Up,[5] O. Henry pictures a dialogue between Mrs. Liberty, on her pedestal in the bay, and Miss Diana at the top of the tower of Madison Square Garden. Even the thick brogue which Mrs. Liberty has acquired cannot hide her envy of the other lady. In the matron's opinion Miss Diana has the best job for a statue in the whole town, with the Cat Show, and the Horse Show, and the military tournaments where the privates "look grand as generals, and the generals try to look grand as floorwalkers," and the Sportsman's Show, and above all, the French Ball "where the original Cohens and the Robert Emmet-Sangerbund Society dance the Highland Fling one with another."

But even before his first glimpse at Mrs. Liberty the visitor from a foreign shore has a sight of O. Henry's New York, as, from the deck of the transatlantic liner, the great wheels and towers of Coney Island are pointed out to him. Among these wheels and towers Alexander Blinker, the owner of Brick Dust Row,[6] walked with Florence, his chance acquaintance of the boat, learned a

1 See "Strictly Business."
2 See "The Trimmed Lamp."
3 See "The Four Million."
4 See "The Voice of the City."
5 See "Sixes and Sevens."
6 See "The Trimmed Lamp."

lesson, and saw a light. No more was the jostling crowd a mass of vulgarians seeking gross joys. Counterfeit and false though the garish pleasures of the spangled temples were, he perceived that deep under the gilt surface they offered saving and apposite balm and satisfaction to the restless human heart. Here, at least, was the husk of Romance, the empty but shining casque of Chivalry, the breath-catching though safeguarded dip and flight of Adventure. He saw no longer a rabble, but his brothers seeking the ideal. Again here, in the enchanted chicken coop of Madame Zozo, there was reading of Tobin's Palm,[1] and prophecies of a dark man and a light woman, of trouble and financial loss, of a voyage by water, and of a meeting with a man with a crooked nose. In The Greater Coney [2] Dennis Carnahan expatiated ironically on the new city which has risen, Phœnix-like, out of the ashes of the old, and the wiping-out process, which, to his way of thinking, consisted of raising the price of admission from ten to twenty-five cents, and having a blonde named Maudie to take tickets instead of Micky, the Bowery Bite. The Babylonian towers and the Hindoo roof gardens blazing with lights, the camels moving with undulating walk, and the tawdry gondolas of artificial Venetian streets. These were what Mazie knew—Mazie of A Lickpenny Lover.[3] These things her little soul of a shop-girl saw when the millionaire painter-traveler, Irving Carter, whose heart she had so strangely won, proposed to her and drew his eloquent picture of a honeymoon in lands beyond the seas. These and no more. The next day her chum in the store asks about her "swell friend." "Him," is the retort. "Oh, he's a cheap skate. He ain't in it no more. What do you suppose that guy wanted me to do? He wanted me to marry him and go to Coney Island for a wedding trip."

A Lickpenny Lover is just one of the stories in which the specified location is not merely a scene of the tale, but partly an explanation of it. For example, the next time that the reader of these notes happens to be at that point of New York City where Sixth Avenue, Broadway, and Thirty-fourth Street meet, let him recall Mammon and the Archer.[4] In that story O. Henry is at his O. Henriest. Listen. The last opportunity that the hero of the story, Richard Rockwell, was to have to see Miss Lantry before her departure the next day for a two years' absence in Europe, was to be in the hansom cab in which he was to take her from the Grand Central Station to a box party at Wallack's Theatre. His father, the old soap manufacturer, cheered him with expression of rough optimism and offered to back him with his money. His aunt gave him as an amulet his mother's wedding ring in wishing him Godspeed and success. Robert took the ring and started out on knightly quest. As the cab approached the crossing indicated the ring dropped tinkling to the pavement. In the few minutes' resulting delay the traffic assumed a tangled condition which held hero and heroine prisoners for hours, and late that night the boy's aunt went to the father with the news that the young people were engaged, and a warning that he should never boast of the power of money again, as the little gold band, an emblem of love and loyalty, had done what mere wealth could not accomplish. The story should have ended there, but with the characteristic touch, O. Henry introduced into the soap manufacturer's office the next morning a man who wore a red necktie and who answered to the name of Kelly. "Well," says the millionaire, "it was a pretty good bilin' of soap and how much do I owe you?" To which Kelly makes the reply that he has had five thousand dollars on account, that he had got the express wagons and cabs mostly for five dollars, but that the truckmen and motormen cost him ten dollars apiece, and

1 See "The Four Million."
2 See "Sixes and Sevens."
3 See "The Voice of the City."
4 See "The Four Million."

the policemen twenty-five and fifty, "but," he adds enthusiastically, "when I got through I had a stage setting that would have made David Belasco envious. Why, a snake couldn't have got across Thirty-fourth Street."

V

SQUARES AND AVENUES

It is not likely that the Fourth Avenue of to-day would have had much to appeal to O. Henry's imagination. As it was half a dozen years ago it was one of his favorite thoroughfares, and reached its apotheosis in A Bird of Bagdad.[1] There O. Henry pictures it as a street that the city seemed to have forgotten in its growth, a street, born and bred in the Bowery, staggering northward full of good resolutions. At Fourteenth Street "it struts for a brief moment proudly in the glare of the museums and cheap theatres. It may yet become a fit mate for its highborn sister boulevard to the west, or its roaring, polyglot, broad-waisted cousin to the east." Then it passes what O. Henry in The Gold That Glittered[1] called "the square presided over by George the Veracious," and comes to the silent and terrible mountains, buildings square as forts, high as the clouds, shutting out the sky, where thousands of slaves bend over desks all day. Next it glides into a mediæval solitude. On each side are the shops devoted to antiques. "Men in rusting armor stand in the windows and menace the hurrying cars with raised, rusty iron bumpers, hauberks, and helms, blunder-buses, Cromwellian breastplates, matchlocks, creeses, and the swords and daggers of an army of dead and gone gallants gleam dully in the ghostly light." This mediæval solitude forbodes an early demise. What street could live inclosed by these mortuary relics and trod by these spectral citizens? "Not Fourth Avenue. Not after the tinsel but enlivening glory of the Little Rialto—not after the echoing drum beats of Union Square. There need be no tears, ladies and gentlemen. 'Tis but the suicide of a street. With a shriek and a crash Fourth Avenue dives headlong into the tunnel at Thirty-fourth Street and is never seen again."

Three of the city squares, Madison Square, Union Square, and Gramercy Park play conspicuous parts in O. Henry's stories. His tales are full of human derelicts and where is there a more natural background for such than the public benches of these parks? He shows you the Bed Liners stamping their freezing feet, and the preacher standing on a pine box exhorting his transient and shifting audience. In this Bed Line were Walter Smuythe and the discharged coachman, Thomas McQuade, the night that the red motor car, humming up Fifth Avenue, lost its extra tire as narrated in The Fifth Wheel.[1] It was on a bench of the Square that the millionaire Pilkins found the penniless young eloping couple, Marcus Clayton of Roanoke County, Virginia, and Eva Bedford of Bedford County, of the same State. It was perhaps on the same bench that Soapy sat meditating just what violation of the law would insure his deportation to the hospitable purlieus of Blackwell's Island, which was his Palm Beach and Riviera for the winter months. It was near by at least that Prince Michael, of the Electorate of Valle Luna, known otherwise as Dopey Mike, looked up at the clock in the Metropolitan Tower and gave sage advice and consolation to the young man who was waiting to learn his fate as told in The Caliph,

1 See "Strictly Business."

Cupid and the Clock.[1] While the auto with the white body and the red running gear was waiting near the corner of Twenty-sixth Street and Fifth Avenue,
Parkenstacker made the acquaintance of the girl in gray and listened to the
strange story born in the pages of Robert Louis Stevenson's "New Arabian
Nights." Over on the sidewalk just in front of the Flatiron Building Sam
Folwell and Cal Harkness, the Cumberland feudists, shook hands in Squaring
the Circle.[2]

In following the trail of O. Henry's men and women through Madison Square
you have the choice of many benches. This is not the case when Union Square
is introduced in the story of Two Thanksgiving Day Gentlemen.[3] The writer
tells you that when Stuffy Pete went to the Square to await the coming of the
tall thin old gentleman dressed in black and wearing the old-fashioned kind of
glasses that won't stay on the nose—the old gentleman who had been Stuffy's
host every Thanksgiving Day for nine years—he "took his seat on the third
bench to the right as you enter Union Square from the east, at the walk opposite
the fountain." Across Union Square Hastings Beauchamp Morely sauntered
with a pitying look at the hundreds that lolled upon the park benches in The
Assessor of Success.[4] One evening in the Square Murray and the dismissed
police captain Marony were sitting side by side trying to think of schemes to
repair their fallen fortunes. When opportunity came both acted According to
Their Lights.[5] The captain was reduced to the point where, to use his own
words, he would "marry the Empress of China for one bowl of chop suey,
commit murder for a plate of beef stew, steal a wafer from a waif, or be a
Mormon for a bowl of chowder." But his code of honor he still retained.
He would not "squeal." It is to the other extreme of society that O. Henry
takes us when he deals with Gramercy Park. All about that private square
with its locked gates are the severe mansions of his aristocrats. There dwelt
Alicia Van Der Pool before she married Robert Walmesley in The Defeat of the
City.[6] A house facing the west side of the park was unquestionably the home
of the Von der Ruyslings. That illustrious family had dwelt there for many
years. In fact, in a spirit of obvious awe, O. Henry imparted the information
that the Von der Ruyslings had received the first key ever made to Gramercy
Park. In the Marry Month of May[7] we learn that near the Park old Mr.
Coulson had a house, the gout, half a million dollars, a daughter and a
housekeeper. It was the daughter who thought to chill her father's springtime
ardor by the introduction of a thousand pounds of ice into the basement. It
was the housekeeper that thwarted the scheme, with the result that the old
millionaire uttered his deferred proposal while Miss Van Meeker Constantia
Coulson ran away with the iceman.

VI

GREENWICH VILLAGE

Of all men Sydney Porter was one of the most difficult of approach. To his
last day he was shy and almost suspicious of the stranger who was not the

---

1 See "The Four Million."
2 See "The Voice of the City."
3 See "The Trimmed Lamp."
4 See "The Trimmed Lamp."
5 See "The Trimmed Lamp."
6 See "The Voice of the City."
7 See "Whirligigs."

casual stranger, that is, the acquaintance scraped in a mood on a bench in Madison Square, or Sheridan Park, or at some corner of "that thoroughfare which parallels and parodies Broadway." There was a little circle of his intimates consisting of such men as Richard Duffy, Gilman Hall, Robert H. Davis, H. Peyton Steger, Robert Rudd Whiting and a few more, to whom he was accessible at any hour of the night or day. But these men knew that it was out of the question to arrange formally a meeting between O. Henry and some one who wanted to konw him; knew that at the first hint the quarry would take fright and disappear. So the encounter had to have every appearance of mere chance. Into Porter's rooms on Irving Place or in the Caledonia, where he lived later, the friend would drop, apparently for a word or two of business. With him there would be a stranger, whom the friend had chanced to pick up on the way. Nine times out of ten the friend would not introduce the other two. But after a few minutes' talk and response to a prearranged signal, the stranger would remark that he had stumbled on a joint near the Bowery, or on upper Broadway, where there was a cocktail mixer who had tended bar in forty-seven cities of the United States. Before the words were out of his mouth Porter had reached for his hat. The friend was forgotten, and arm in arm story-spinner and stranger sallied forth into the night.

The bait thrown out was not always a cocktail mixer and his experiences. "The most picturesque bit of rear tenement that remains in New York." "That was the hint that I used when the nod came," one man who had found O. Henry in the manner suggested told the writer, "and in three minutes we were in the street. I led him down Irving Place to Fourteenth, to Sixth Avenue, past the Jefferson Market Police Court, into Greenwich Village, past Sheridan Park, and down Grove Street to the very end. There, between the front houses, Nos. 10 and 12 there is an opening. Beyond the opening is a triangle, in the middle of which is a tall telegraph pole, and at the back there are three old brick houses, the front windows of which look out diagonally at a wall against which leaves are growing. 'There is a story there,' said Porter, 'a story that suggests an episode in Murger's *Vie de Bohème*, where the grisette at night waters the flowers to keep them alive. The lifetime of the flowers, you remember, was to be the lifetime of that transient love.' He wrote that story, I am sure, in The Last Leaf,[1] and when I see that bare, dreary yard, and the blank wall of the house twenty feet away, and the old ivy vine, I recall the pathetic tale of Sue and Joanna and the masterpiece that old Behrman painted at the cost of his life."

This Greenwich Village section of the city always appealed strongly to O. Henry's imagination. He liked to picture the odd zigzagging of the streets and to people them with the artists of his creation. Somewhere down in Greenwich Village was the "Vallambrosa" where the self-reliant Hetty lived and furnished the beef for the making of the Irish stew as related in The Third Ingredient.[2] There, too—in the red brick district, was The Furnished Room,[3] with its suggestion of mignonette. A few blocks away to the south and west is Abingdon Square. In The Thing's the Play,[4] we are told "there stands a house near Abingdon Square. On the ground floor there has been for twenty-five years a little store where toys and notions and stationery are sold." There Mrs. Frank Barry, deserted on her wedding night on account of a strange misunderstanding, lived out her life awaiting the return of her husband.

Fifth Avenue or First, Riverside Drive or Division Street, Broadway or the Bowery, Corlears Hook Park or Gramercy; no matter what the locality or the

1 See "The Trimmed Lamp."
2 See "Options."
3 See "The Four Million."
4 See "Strict'y Business."

social scale of its denizens, it is always Bagdad. And with the night comes the glamour that belongs not to Arabia alone. In different masquerade the streets, bazaars, and walled houses of the Occidental city of romance are filled with the same kind of people that interested Haroun-al-Raschid in his golden prime. Clothes may be different, but underneath men and women are unchanged. With the eye of faith the traveler can see the Little Hunchback, Sinbad the Sailor, Fitbad the Tailor, the Beautiful Persian, the one-eyed Calenders, the Barber and his Six Brothers, and Ali Baba and Forty Robbers on every block.

Many have been the men and the women who have invaded New York as a literary field. But so far there has been but one conqueror of Alexander-like ambitions. And as became a conqueror, he was constantly rechristening the city to suit his own whimsical humor. At one moment it was his "Little Old Bagdad-on-the-Subway"; at another, the "City of Too Many Caliphs"; at another, "Noisyville-on-the-Hudson"; or "The Big Town of Razzle-Dazzle"; or, "Wolfville-on-the-Subway"; or, "The City of Chameleon Changes." Yet Porter discovered New York comparatively late in life; lived in it but the few brief last years. The story has often been told of how, a few minutes before the end came, he whispered to those about him: "Pull up the shades. I don't want to go home in the dark." I like to believe that he did not want to go home without one last glimpse of the town that he had learned to love so well; one last glimpse of his "Little Old Bagdad-on-the-Subway"; his "City of Too Many Caliphs."

O. HENRY AND NEW ORLEANS

By Caroline Francis Richardson

A SETTING that appealed strongly both to O. Henry's story-instinct and to his sympathy was downtown New Orleans. Like many other writers he found inspiration in the narrow, dingy, shadowy Quarter whose buildings and street names and traditions tell of many things that to-day are lost: riches and lives and causes. But O. Henry used his "copy" differently from other story-tellers who have found suggestion in New Orleans. In the O. Henry tales no plot hinges on a mixture of blood; no hero or heroine is engulfed by flood or devoured by plague; no person speaks an unintelligible dialect. There is no use of Mardi Gras, All Saints' Day, or *quatorze juillet*. And this handling of material is quite characteristic of the author. In all his stories, wherever placed, he makes use of every detail that will add reality to a character or an occurrence. But he does not introduce localities and localisms merely for their intrinsic interest.

As a setting New Orleans can claim but a scant share in the lives of some of O. Henry's knights of high adventure. This is the case with a certain grafter and his partner, Caligula, who of their stay could remember only some drinks "invented by the creoles during the period of Louey Cans, in which they are still served at the side doors"; and an attempt "to make the French Quarter pay up the back trading stamps due on the Louisiana Purchase." It is in that story, Hostages to Momus,[1] that the Grafter explains the component parts of a perfect

1 See "The Gentle Grafter."

breakfast: "There'll never be a perfect breakfast eaten until some man grows arms long enough to stretch down to New Orleans for his coffee and over to Norfolk for his rolls, and reaches up to Vermont and digs a slice of butter out of a spring-house, and then turns over a beehive close to a clover patch out in Indiana for the rest. Then he'd come pretty close to making a meal that the gods eat on Mount Olympus."

Many of these birds of passage merely arrive and depart by way of fruit steamers coming from or going to an explosion in Central America. In that case, the city sees them only while they pick their way over a banana-strewn wharf, dodging the long line of men who pass the green bunches in a swaying chain from the hold of the ship to the freight cars near by. It was by pretending to be a part of such a line that the too sympathetic, too easily won Clancy and the escaping revolutionist, General de Vega, landed undetected from the ship in which they had traveled as stowaways (The Shamrock and the Palm [1]). In Lafayette Square Clancy consummated his dark scheme. With the connivance of a policeman, a fellow Irishman, the General was arrested as a vagrant and sentenced to sixty days' hard labor. The General, be it remembered, had lured Clancy to Guatemala as a revolutionist, but had forced him to assist for sixty days in building a railroad. And now—"Havin' no money, they set him (The General) to work his fine out with a gang from the parish prison clearing Ursulines Street. Around the corner was a saloon decorated genially with electric fans and cool merchandise. I made that me headquarters, and every fifteen minutes I'd walk around and take a look at the little man filibustering with a rake and shovel. . . . Carrambos. Erin go bragh!"

In Phœbe [2] a less triumphant Irishman is shown us: "Bad-luck Kearney." His untoward adventures reach us through Captain Patricio Maloné, "a Hiberno-Iberian creole," who tells the story while sitting over cognac in a "little red-tiled café near Congo Square." From his first sight of Kearney falling into a cellar on Tchoupitoulas Street, the Captain should have taken warning. But though Kearney conscientiously declares his handicap, even leading his new friend out into the middle of the great width of Canal Street in order to point out the sinister Saturn and the evil satellite, Phœbe, under which he, Kearney, was born, Captain Maloné refuses to yield to superstition. Later, however, circumstances oblige him to admit the power of the stars, and for the good of the cause, they part. The Captain's conversion is confirmed by his meeting with Kearney a year afterward. On this final occasion Captain Maloné, walking near Poydras Market, is brushed aside by "an immensely stout, pink-faced lady in black satin." . . . "Behind her trailed a little man laden to the gunwale with bundles and bags of goods and vegetables." And the little man calls conciliatingly, "I'm coming, Phœbe!"

Very rarely do historic buildings slip into these stories, so it is only as a measure of distance that the old Bourbon Street opera house is used. In A Matter of Mean Elevation,[3] the reader learns that "The Carabobo Indians are easily the most enthusiastic lovers of music between the equator and the French Opera House in New Orleans." In Blind Man's Holiday,[3] too, there are buildings we might see on a post card: "the Rue Chartres perishes in the old Place d'Armes. The ancient Cabildo, where Spanish justice fell like hail, faces it, and the Cathedral, another provincial ghost, overlooks it. Its centre is a little iron-railed park. . . . Pedestalled high above it, the general sits his cavorting steed."

In the same story O. Henry makes another departure and yields to the sentiment

1 See "Cabbages and Kings."
2 See "Roads of Destiny."
3 See "Whirligigs."

of French Town: "The Rue Chartres, in New Orleans, is a street of ghosts. It lies in the quarter where the Frenchman in his prime set up translated pride and glory; where, also, the arrogant don had swaggered, and dreamed of gold grants and ladies' gloves. Every flagstone has its grooves worn by footsteps going royally to the wooing and the fighting. Every house has a princely heartbreak; each doorway its untold tale of gallant promise and slow decay. By night the Rue Chartres is now but a murky fissure, from which the groping wayfarer sees, flung up against the sky, the tangled filigree of Moorish balconies. The old houses of monsieur stand yet, indomitable against the century, but their essence is gone. The street is one of ghosts to whosoever can see them." And in this story is O. Henry's one use of a New Orleans festival: it is on Carnival costumes that Norah Greenway works every and all night—Norah Greenway, the girl who fabricates a past so that her lover, a self-confessed sinner, may have the courage to ask her to marry him.

O. Henry's philosophers of Fortune usually shun hotels. An emphasized instance is that of William Trotter (Helping the Other Fellow [1]) who comes to New Orleans after a long stay in Aguas Frescas. His brother has offered him a position at a salary of five thousand a year, and expects to meet him at the St. Charles Hotel where they will discuss details. "When I arrived at the Crescent City, I hurried away—far away from St. Charles to a dim *chambre garnie* in Bienville Street. And there, looking down from my attic window from time to time at the old absinthe house across the street, I wrote this story to buy my bread and butter."

And it was in "one of those rare old hostelries in Royal Street" that Monsieur Morin lodged—the Monsieur Morin who is so important though unseen a figure in "Cherchez la Femme." [2] The search for the lady is the self-assumed responsibility of two reporters: Robbins, of the *Picayune*, and Dumars, of *L'Abeille*, "the old French newspaper that has buzzed for nearly a century." In a café in Dumaine Street they argue and conjecture as to M. Morin's disposition of Madame Thibault's twenty thousand dollars, of which he had had the care. The money is finally found in the shape of government bonds carefully pasted by Madame Thibault herself over the unsightly cracks in the wall of one of her rear rooms.

Another native protagonist, in The Renaissance of Charleroi,[3] is Grandemont Charles, "a little creole gentleman, aged thirty-four, with a bald spot on the top of his head and the manners of a prince. By day he was a clerk in a cotton broker's office in one of those cold, rancid mountains of oozy brick, down near the levee. By night, in the old French Quarter, he was again the last male descendant of the Charles family." And in this last character he determines to spend his painfully saved hoard of six hundred dollars in a renaissance of past glories. He secures the use of the old plantation house, Charleroi; he fills it with appropriate furniture, rented from the antique shops in Royal and Chartres streets; he orders wines and food from famous places—and for an evening, Charleroi lives again. That no one of his invited guests appears, that an uninvited guest does appear, whose presence means more to Grandemont than even the glorious past—all this makes it an O. Henry story.

A plantation below the city is the setting for a climax in Whistling Dick's Christmas Stocking.[3] By means of a freight-car Dick arrives in the "big, almsgiving, long-suffering city of the South, the cold weather paradise of tramps." After a cautious survey that includes the levee "pimpled with dark bulks of merchandise," the long line of Algiers across the river, the tugs, the ferries, and the Italian luggers, Dick climbs warily down and starts, whistling, toward

1 See "Rolling Stones."
2 See "Roads of Destiny."
3 See "Roads of Destiny."

Lafayette Square to meet a pal. But a friendly policeman warns Dick of a new and inhospitable city ordinance, and he departs hastily for the open road. A stall keeper in the French Market gives him breakfast, and he is almost happy until Chalmette, with its "vast and bewildering industry," frightens him and drives him along a country road hemmed in on one side by the high green levee and on the other by a mysterious, frog-haunted, mosquito-infested marsh. The incident of a tramp saving a family from burglary and fire, because of a kindly word from a young girl, is not new; and the plantation house and household are typical and trite. But Whistling Dick is real. It is entirely logical that after his glorious evening as honored guest, and his comfortable night on the floor of his well-furnished room, he should, on looking out of the window at the dawn of Christmas Day, feel a distinct shock. He sees and hears the evidences of the labor that a monster sugar crop has forced upon a part even of the world holiday. "Here was a poem; an epic—nay, a tragedy—with work, the curse of the world, for its theme." A few moments later Whistling Dick, carefree and happy, strolls along the top of the levee, away from his grateful hosts, away into the new day and the untrammelled life.

"A YANKEE MAUPASSANT"

A SUMMARY OF THE CRITICISM OF TEN YEARS AGO

EVERY reader of current American newspapers and magazines is familiar with the name "O. Henry." It is a pen name, concealing the identity of Mr. Sydney Porter, the author of sundry books of short stories. For some time now his reputation has been steadily growing. Throughout the country are people of all sorts and conditions who agree enthusiastically on one point—that no one else can write short stories like O. Henry's. The critics were at first slow to accept his work. The suggestion that he was "a Yankee Maupassant," [1] came from his publishers, and did not, for a while, impress the writing fraternity. But now the tables are completely turned. We find William Marion Reedy, of the St. Louis *Mirror*, affirming that, to his thinking, Mr. Porter deserves the very flattering designation conferred upon him; and Henry James Forman, of the editorial staff of the *North American Review*, declares: "He writes with the skill of a Maupassant, and a humor Maupassant never dreamed of." The *Bookman* says, editorially:

"While we are inclined to be conservative in the matter of estimating a contemporary writer, and find exceedingly exasperating these impulsive and extravagant recognitions of 'new Stevensons' and 'new Kiplings,' and 'new de Maupassants' and 'American Dickenses,' the time is past for any restraint in the frank appreciation of the work of the author who signs himself 'O. Henry.' The man is in many respects an extraordinary workman and a consummate artist."

[1] This appellation is an unconscious tribute to the broad Americanism of a man who lived most of his life in North Carolina and Texas.

The distinguishing characteristics of O. Henry's work are his journalistic style and his democratic instinct. The two combine, as Francis Hackett, the literary editor of the Chicago *Evening Post*, points out, in what is distinctly "an original revelation of life." Mr. Hackett says:

"O. Henry writes with a glitter that is characteristic half of the New York *Sun*, half of the *Smart Set*. . . . His scope is restricted. His manner is not discursive. He gets sensational contrasts and assertive coloring into each short story. Allowing for this, he gives us a humorous yet profound understanding of a phrase that has not yet been treated before in American art, gives us intimacy with an order of metropolitan characters and circumstances not likely to be better focussed or illumined in our generation.

"O Henry accepts, with a mixture of irony, wit, and sympathy, the distressing fact that a human being can be a clerk, the remarkable fact that a clerk can be a human being. He knows the clerk, knows him in his works and pomps. But there is a peculiarity in O. Henry's attitude toward the clerk. . . . Most literary men are intrenched in culture, obfuscated by it. They take the uncultured morosely or pityingly or mordantly. They discuss those who are not 'élite' as a physician would discuss a case—scientifically, often humanly, interested, but always with a strong sense of the case's defects and deficiencies.

"To O. Henry, on the contrary, the clerk is neither abnormal nor subnormal. He writes of him without patronizing him. He realizes the essential and stupendous truth that to himself the clerk is not pitiable. He takes into account, in other words, the adjustments that every man makes to constitute himself the apex of this sphere—for, after all, there are 800,000,000 apices on this sphere, if we dare to assume that fowl and fishes are not also self-conscious and self-centred.

"When one says 'clerk' one means $15-a-week humanity. O. Henry has specialized in this humanity with loving care, with a Kiplingesque attention to detail. But his is far from the humorless method of Gissing and Merrick, who were no more happy in a boarding-house than Thoreau would have been in the Waldorf-Astoria. O. Henry never forgets the inherent, the unconscious humor in the paradoxes and contrasts of mixed civilization, the crudities of which serve only to exasperate the misplaced and morbid. He is no moral paradoxist, like Shaw, no soured idealist, like Zola, no disgruntled esthete, like Gissing. It is the comedy of the paradoxes and contrasts that he searches and displays—a comedy in which he miraculously keeps the balance, often by the adventitious aid of irony and satire, not sacrificing the clerk to the man of culture, nor, on the other hand, losing perspective in magnifying the clerk."

But O. Henry does not confine himself to the clerk. As Mr. Hackett tells us:

"In one sense Broadway is the spinal column of his art, and the nerve branches cover all Manhattan. He knows the side streets where Mamie boards. He knows Harlem. He knows the narrow-chested flat. He knows the Bowery, Irish and Yiddish. He knows the Tenderloin, cop, panhandler, man about town, sport, bartender, and waiter. He knows Shanley's and Childs's, the lemon-odored buffet and the French table d'hôte. He knows the sham Bohemia, the real Bohemia. And his stories are starred with little vignettes of the town, paragraphs of unostentatious art that let us see Madison Square, or the White Way, or the Park (over and over again the Park), or the side street in springtime—all clear as the vision in the crystal.

"O. Henry's triumphs are often triumphs of fancy. He has the sense of the marvellous which belongs to tellers of the short story since the nights of Arabia. And O. Henry can discover in Manhattan the wonder of fable and adventure, the eternal symbols of imagination, the beauty of the jewel in the toad."

To this should be added the tribute of William Marion Reedy:

"As a depicter of the life of New York's four million—club men, fighters, thieves, policemen, touts, shop-girls, lady cashiers, hoboes, actors, stenographers, and what not—O. Henry has no equal for keen insight into the beauties and meanness of character or motive. Mordant though he be at times his heart is with innocence and right, but he sees the fun that underlies sophistication and selfishness. Not only does he see life, but he sees its problems and in a certain shy-sly way suggests his solutions therefor. His gifts of description are of a surprising variety in method. His pictures, mostly small, intimate greater scopes and deeper vistas. Afraid of pathos, his very promptness to avoid it upon its slightest hint of imminence gives poignancy to the note he thus strikes as by suggestion. He loves the picaroon and the vagabond, and dowers them with vocabularies rich and strange and fanciful. . . . He always has a story. The style or the mood may lure you away from it momentarily, but the tale always asserts its primacy, and its end comes always in just the whimsical way you didn't expect. O. Henry is inexhaustible in quip, in imagery, in quick, sharp, spontaneous invention. In his apparent carelessness we suspect a carefulness, but this is just wherein he is sib to the French short-story writers, chief among them de Maupassant. Della Cruscan critics may disapprove of him for his slang, but until you know his slang, you never know what a powerful vehicle slang can be in the hands of one who can mate it with the echoes from and essences of true literary expression. It is not the slang of George Ade, or Henry M. Blossom, or George V. Hobart. Henry's slang has some of the savor that we find in the archaic vocabulary invented for himself by Chatterton. Its content transcends the capacity of the mere argot of the street. In the American short story to-day O. Henry has demonstrated himself a delightful master, one absolutely unapproachable in swift visualization and penetrative interpretation of life, as any and all of the books now to his credit will show to any one capable of understanding."

O. HENRY'S SHORT STORIES

By Henry James Forman

MR. SYDNEY PORTER, the gentleman who, in the language of some of his characters, is "denounced" by the euphonious pen name of O. Henry, has breathed new life into the short story. Gifted as he is with a flashing wit, abundant humor, and quick observation, no subject has terrors for him. If it be too much to say, in the old phrase, that nothing human is alien to him, at least the larger part of humanity is his domain. The very title of one of his books, "The Four Million," is a protest against those who believe that New York contains only four hundred people worth while. O. Henry backs the census-taker against the social arbiter. The rich and the fashionable are, in his tales, conceived much in the spirit of similar characters in melodrama, except that the ingredient of humor is put in to mitigate them. Indeed, they figure but seldom. But the poor and the lowly, the homeless lodger of the city park, the vagabond of the "bread line," the waitress, the shop and factory girl, the ward politician, the city policeman, the whole "ruck and rabble" of life, so meaningless to the comfortable, unobservant bourgeois, are set forth always with keen knowledge, with a laughing humour, and not infrequently with a tender, smiling pathos. As this panorama of the undenoted faces of the great city passes before the reader, he becomes his own Caliph Haroun-al-Raschid, and New York, a teeming Bagdad, full of romance and mystery.

The facility, the light touch of O. Henry, his mastery of the vernacular, his insight into the life of the disinherited, make it needless for him to resort to such inventions as Stevenson's learned Arabian, imaginary author of the "New Arabian Nights." The piquant and picturesque phrasing, the dash of slang, the genial and winning fancy seem to carry off the most fantastic situations. The Touchstone, the jester, the merry-maker has always enjoyed a certain license if he had but the wit not to abuse it. O. Henry's fun is never of the slap-stick variety and his pathos never bathos. We are shaken with sad laughter at the many and divers attempts of the park-bench vagabond, Soapy,[1] to be arrested and sent to the workhouse for the winter months. He eats a meal and does not pay, he steals an umbrella, he accosts unescorted women, but all to no purpose. The police seem to regard him "as a king who could do no wrong." But as he passes by a church the organ music of an anthem vividly recalls his boyhood, stirs the tramp to his depths, and he resolves to turn over a new leaf. He will seek work and be a man. Then the policeman lays a hand upon him, hales him before a magistrate as a vagrant, and the city's swirling machinery of the law sends Soapy to "the Island" after all. And the author smiles with tender compassion over this poor shuttlecock of fate.

With no less humorous kindness does he deal with 'Tildy, "the unwooed drudge," the plain little waitress in an Eighth Avenue chop-house.[2] All the hurrying *clientèle* of that eating-house admired Aileen, who "was tall, beautiful, lively, gracious, and learned in persiflage." But no one had a word for 'Tildy of the freckles and the hay-colored hair, until one day a tipsy laundry clerk put his arm round 'Tildy's waist and kissed her. For a brief space that transformed her life. 'Tildy the unnoticed began to bind ribbons in her hair, to prink and to preen after the fashion of daughters of Eve. "A gentleman insulted me to-day," she modestly informed all her customers. "He put his arm around my waist and kissed me." And as the diners turned upon her the stream of badinage hitherto directed at Aileen alone, 'Tildy's heart swelled in her bosom, "for she saw at last the towers of Romance rise above the horizon of the gray plain in which she had for so long traveled." 'Tildy had a thrilling sensation of fear lest Seeders, the laundry clerk, in a mood of jealous love-madness, rush in and shoot her with a pistol. This she deplored, for no one had shot Aileen for love, and she did not wish to overshadow her friend. When Seeders does come in it is only to apologize, with the plea that he was tipsy. 'Tildy's towers of romance crumble to earth. The glory fades suddenly, for it was not love at all that actuated Seeders. But Aileen the staunch-hearted comforts 'Tildy in her sorrow, for if Seeders "were any kind of a gentleman," she tells her, "he wouldn't of apologized."

"The Trimmed Lamp" is of a piece with "The Four Million," filled with the tragi-comedy of life much as it appeared to Dickens and to François Villon. In "Heart of the West" the author exploits a vein many have attempted in a short story as well as in the novel—the so-called "wild West." But no one, it is safe to say, has brought so much fun and humor to the Western story. Cattle-king, cowboy, miner, the plains and the chaparral—material of the "dime novel," but all treated with the skill of a Maupassant, and a humor Maupassant never dreamed of. The merest sketch of them has a certain substance to it. Yet it is idle

1 The Cop and the Anthem, in "The Four Million."
2 The Brief Début of 'Tildy, in "The Four Million."

to compare O. Henry with anybody. No talent could be more original or more delightful. The combination of technical excellence with whimsical, sparkling wit, abundant humor, and a fertile invention is so rare that the reader is content without comparisons.

INDEX

O. HENRY INDEX

A

B

C